Pr

'A blistering piece of crime writing'
Sunday Times

'Confirms [Galbraith's] exceptional ability as a storyteller'
Daily Mail

'Ambitious, sophisticated and stylish'
The Times

'Hugely absorbing . . . the best Strike novel yet'
Sunday Mirror

'Thoroughly enjoyable with some brilliant plot developments'
Mail on Sunday

'Strike remains a compelling hero'
Daily Telegraph

'Come for the twists and turns and stay for the beautifully drawn central relationship'
Independent

'Highly inventive storytelling'
Guardian

'[An] obsessive reading experience'
Observer

'Outrageously entertaining'
Financial Times

'Dark but gripping'
Glamour

By Robert Galbraith

The Cuckoo's Calling

The Silkworm

Career of Evil

Lethal White

Troubled Blood

LETHAL WHITE

ROBERT GALBRAITH

sphere

SPHERE

First published in Great Britain in 2018 by Sphere
Paperback edition published in 2019 by Sphere

11

A CIP catalogue record for this book
is available from the British Library.

ISBN 978-0-7515-7287-2

Typeset in Bembo by M Rules
Printed and bound in Great Britain by
Clays Ltd, Elcograf S.p.A.

Papers used by Sphere are from well-managed forests
and other responsible sources.

Sphere
An imprint of
Little, Brown Book Group
Carmelite House
50 Victoria Embankment
London EC4Y 0DZ

An Hachette UK Company
www.hachette.co.uk

www.littlebrown.co.uk

To Di and Roger,

and in memory

of the lovely white Spike

PROLOGUE

Happiness, dear Rebecca, means first and foremost the calm, joyous sense of innocence.

Henrik Ibsen, *Rosmersholm*

If only the swans would swim side by side on the dark green lake, this picture might turn out to be the crowning achievement of the wedding photographer's career.

He was loath to change the couple's position, because the soft light beneath the canopy of trees was turning the bride, with her loose red-gold curls, into a pre-Raphaelite angel and emphasising the chiselled cheekbones of her husband. He couldn't remember when he had last been commissioned to photograph so handsome a couple. There was no need for tactful tricks with the new Mr and Mrs Matthew Cunliffe, no need to angle the lady so that rolls of back fat were hidden (she was, if anything, fractionally too slender, but that would photograph well), no need to suggest the groom 'try one with your mouth closed', because Mr Cunliffe's teeth were straight and white. The only thing that needed concealing, and it could be retouched out of the final pictures, was the ugly scar running down the bride's forearm: purple and livid, with the puncture marks of stitches still visible.

She had been wearing a rubber and stockinette brace when the photographer arrived at her parents' house that morning. It had given him quite a start when she had removed it for the photographs. He had even wondered whether she had made a botched attempt to kill herself before the wedding, because he had seen it all. You did, after twenty years in the game.

'I was assaulted,' Mrs Cunliffe – or Robin Ellacott, as she had been two hours ago – had said. The photographer was a squeamish man. He had fought off the mental image of steel slicing into that soft, pale flesh. Thankfully, the ugly mark was now hidden in the shadow cast by Mrs Cunliffe's bouquet of creamy roses.

The swans, the damned swans. If both would clear out of the background it wouldn't matter, but one of them was repeatedly diving, its fluffy pyramid of a backside jutting out of the middle of the lake like a feathered iceberg, its contortions ruffling the surface of the water so that its digital removal would be far more complicated than young Mr Cunliffe, who had already suggested this remedy, realised. The swan's mate, meanwhile, continued to lurk over by the bank: graceful, serene and determinedly out of shot.

'Have you got it?' asked the bride, her impatience palpable.

'You look gorgeous, flower,' said the groom's father, Geoffrey, from behind the photographer. He sounded tipsy already. The couple's parents, best man and bridesmaids were all watching from the shade of nearby trees. The smallest bridesmaid, a toddler, had had to be restrained from throwing pebbles into the lake, and was now whining to her mother, who talked to her in a constant, irritating whisper.

'Have you got it?' Robin asked again, ignoring her father-in-law.

'Almost,' lied the photographer. 'Turn in to him a little bit more, please, Robin. That's it. Nice big smiles. Big smiles, now!'

There was a tension about the couple that could not be wholly attributed to the difficulty of getting the shot. The photographer didn't care. He wasn't a marriage counsellor. He had known couples to start screaming at each other while he read his light meter. One bride had stormed out of her own reception. He still kept, for the amusement of friends, the blurred shot from 1998 that showed a groom head-butting his best man.

Good-looking as they were, he didn't fancy the Cunliffes' chances. That long scar down the bride's arm had put him off her from the start. He found the whole thing ominous and distasteful.

'Let's leave it,' said the groom suddenly, releasing Robin. 'We've got enough, haven't we?'

'Wait, wait, the other one's coming now!' said the photographer crossly.

The moment Matthew had released Robin, the swan by the far shore had begun to paddle its way across the dark green water towards its mate.

'You'd think the buggers were doing it on purpose, eh, Linda?' said Geoffrey with a fat chuckle to the bride's mother. 'Bloody things.'

'It doesn't matter,' said Robin, pulling her long skirt up clear of her shoes, the heels of which were a little too low. 'I'm sure we've got something.'

She strode out of the copse of trees into the blazing sunlight and off across the lawn towards the seventeenth-century castle, where most of the wedding guests were already milling, drinking champagne as they admired the view of the hotel grounds.

'I think her arm's hurting her,' the bride's mother told the groom's father.

Bollocks it is, thought the photographer with a certain cold pleasure. *They rowed in the car.*

The couple had looked happy enough beneath the shower of confetti in which they had departed the church, but on arrival at the country house hotel they had worn the rigid expressions of those barely repressing their rage.

'She'll be all right. Just needs a drink,' said Geoffrey comfortably. 'Go keep her company, Matt.'

Matthew had already set off after his bride, gaining on her easily as she navigated the lawn in her stilettos. The rest of the party followed, the bridesmaids' mint-green chiffon dresses rippling in the hot breeze.

'Robin, we need to talk.'

'Go on, then.'

'Wait a minute, can't you?'

'If I wait, we'll have the family on us.'

Matthew glanced behind him. She was right.

'Robin—'

'*Don't touch my arm!*'

Her wound was throbbing in the heat. Robin wanted to find the holdall containing the sturdy rubber protective brace, but it would be somewhere out of reach in the bridal suite, wherever that was.

The crowd of guests standing in the shadow of the hotel was coming into clearer view. The women were easy to tell apart, because of their hats. Matthew's Aunt Sue wore an electric blue wagon wheel, Robin's sister-in-law, Jenny, a startling confection of yellow feathers. The male guests blurred into conformity in their dark suits. It was impossible to see from this distance whether Cormoran Strike was among them.

'Just stop, will you?' said Matthew, because they had fast outstripped the family, who were matching their pace to his toddler niece.

Robin paused.

'I was shocked to see him, that's all,' said Matthew carefully.

'I suppose you think I was expecting him to burst in halfway through the service and knock over the flowers?' asked Robin.

Matthew could have borne this response if not for the smile she was trying to suppress. He had not forgotten the joy in her face when her ex-boss had crashed into their wedding ceremony. He wondered whether he would ever be able to forgive the fact that she had said 'I do' with her eyes fastened upon the big, ugly, shambolic figure of Cormoran Strike, rather than her new husband. The entire congregation must have seen how she had beamed at him.

Their families were gaining on them again. Matthew took Robin's upper arm gently, his fingers inches above the knife wound, and walked her on. She came willingly, but he suspected that this was because she hoped she was moving closer to Strike.

'I said in the car, if you want to go back to work for him—'

'—I'm an "effing idiot",' said Robin.

The men grouped on the terrace were becoming distinguishable now, but Robin could not see Strike anywhere. He was a big man. She ought to have been able to make him out even among her brothers and uncles, who were all over six foot. Her spirits, which had soared when Strike had appeared, tumbled earthwards like rain-soaked fledglings. He must have left after the service rather than boarding a minibus to the hotel. His brief appearance had signified a gesture of goodwill, but nothing more. He had not come to rehire her, merely to congratulate her on a new life.

'Look,' said Matthew, more warmly. She knew that he, too, had scanned the crowd, found it Strike-less and drawn the same conclusion. 'All I was trying to say in the car was:

it's up to you what you do, Robin. If he wanted – if he wants you back – I was just worried, for Christ's sake. Working for him wasn't exactly safe, was it?'

'No,' said Robin, with her knife wound throbbing. 'It wasn't safe.'

She turned back towards her parents and the rest of the family group, waiting for them to catch up. The sweet, ticklish smell of hot grass filled her nostrils as the sun beat down on her uncovered shoulders.

'Do you want to go to Auntie Robin?' said Matthew's sister.

Toddler Grace obligingly seized Robin's injured arm and swung on it, eliciting a yelp of pain.

'Oh, I'm so sorry, Robin – Gracie, let go—'

'Champagne!' shouted Geoffrey. He put his arm around Robin's shoulders and steered her on towards the expectant crowd.

The gents' bathroom was, as Strike would have expected of this upmarket country hotel, odour-free and spotless. He wished he could have brought a pint into the cool, quiet toilet cubicle, but that might have reinforced the impression that he was some disreputable alcoholic who had been bailed from jail to attend the wedding. Reception staff had met his assurances that he was part of the Cunliffe-Ellacott wedding party with barely veiled scepticism as it was.

Even in an uninjured state Strike tended to intimidate, given that he was large, dark, naturally surly-looking and sported a boxer's profile. Today he might have just climbed out of the ring. His nose was broken, purple and swollen to twice its usual size, both eyes were bruised and puffy, and one ear was inflamed and sticky with fresh black stitches. At least the knife wound across the palm of his hand was concealed by bandages, although his best suit was crumpled and stained from a wine spill on the last occasion he had worn it. The best you could say for his appearance was that he had managed to grab matching shoes before heading for Yorkshire.

He yawned, closed his aching eyes and rested his head momentarily against the cold partition wall. He was so tired he might easily fall asleep here, sitting on the toilet. He needed to find Robin, though, and ask her – beg her, if necessary – to forgive him for sacking her and come back to work. He had thought he read delight in her face when their eyes met in church. She had certainly beamed at him as she walked past on Matthew's arm on the way out, so he had hurried back through the graveyard to ask his friend Shanker, who was now asleep in the car park in the Mercedes he had borrowed for the journey, to follow the minibuses to the reception.

Strike had no desire to stay for a meal and speeches: he had not RSVPed the invitation he had received before sacking Robin. All he wanted was a few minutes to talk to her, but so far this had proved impossible. He had forgotten what weddings were like. As he sought Robin on the crowded terrace he had found himself the uncomfortable focus of a hundred pairs of curious eyes. Turning down champagne, which he disliked, he had retreated into the bar in search of a pint. A dark-haired young man who had a look of Robin about the mouth and forehead had followed, a gaggle of other young people trailing in his wake, all of them wearing similar expressions of barely suppressed excitement.

'You're Strike, aye?' said the young man.

The detective agreed to it.

'Martin Ellacott,' said the other. 'Robin's brother.'

'How d'you do?' said Strike, raising his bandaged hand to show that he could not shake without pain. 'Where is she, d'you know?'

'Having photos done,' said Martin. He pointed at the

iPhone clutched in his other hand. 'You're on the news. You caught the Shacklewell Ripper.'

'Oh,' said Strike. 'Yeah.'

In spite of the fresh knife wounds on his palm and ear, he felt as though the violent events of twelve hours previously had happened long ago. The contrast between the sordid hideout where he had cornered the killer and this four-star hotel was so jarring that they seemed separate realities.

A woman whose turquoise fascinator was trembling in her white-blonde hair now arrived in the bar. She, too, was holding a phone, her eyes moving rapidly upwards and downwards, checking the living Strike against what he was sure was a picture of him on her screen.

'Sorry, need a pee,' Strike had told Martin, edging away before anybody else could approach him. After talking his way past the suspicious reception staff, he had taken refuge in the bathroom.

Yawning again, he checked his watch. Robin must, surely, have finished having pictures taken by now. With a grimace of pain, because the painkillers they had given him at the hospital had long since worn off, Strike got up, unbolted the door and headed back out among the gawping strangers.

A string quartet had been set up at the end of the empty dining room. They started to play while the wedding group organised themselves into a receiving line that Robin assumed she must have agreed to at some point during the wedding preparations. She had abnegated so much responsibility for the day's arrangements that she kept receiving little surprises like this. She had forgotten, for instance, that they had agreed to have photographs taken at the hotel rather than the church. If only they had not sped away in the Daimler immediately after the service, she might have had a chance to speak to Strike and to ask him – beg him, if necessary – to take her back. But he had left without talking to her, leaving her wondering whether she had the courage, or the humility, to call him after this and plead for her job.

The room seemed dark after the brilliance of the sunlit gardens. It was wood-panelled, with brocade curtains and gilt-framed oil paintings. Scent from the flower arrangements lay heavy in the air, and glass and silverware gleamed on snow-white tablecloths. The string quartet, which had sounded loud in the echoing wooden box of a room, was soon drowned out by the sound of guests clambering up the stairs outside, crowding onto the landing, talking and laughing, already full of champagne and beer.

'Here we go, then!' roared Geoffrey, who seemed to be enjoying the day more than anybody else. 'Bring 'em on!'

If Matthew's mother had been alive, Robin doubted that Geoffrey would have felt able to give his ebullience full expression. The late Mrs Cunliffe had been full of cool sidestares and nudges, constantly checking any signs of unbridled emotion. Mrs Cunliffe's sister, Sue, was one of the first down the receiving line, bringing a fine frost with her, for she had wanted to sit at the top table and been denied that privilege.

'How are you, Robin?' she asked, pecking the air near Robin's ear. Miserable, disappointed and guilty that she was not feeling happy, Robin suddenly sensed how much this woman, her new aunt-in-law, disliked her. 'Lovely dress,' said Aunt Sue, but her eyes were already on handsome Matthew.

'I wish your mother—' she began, then, with a gasp, she buried her face in the handkerchief that she held ready in her hand.

More friends and relatives shuffled inside, beaming, kissing, shaking hands. Geoffrey kept holding up the line, bestowing bear hugs on everybody who did not actively resist.

'He came, then,' said Robin's favourite cousin, Katie. She would have been a bridesmaid had she not been hugely pregnant. Today was her due date. Robin marvelled that she could still walk. Her belly was watermelon-hard as she leaned in for a kiss.

'Who came?' asked Robin, as Katie sidestepped to hug Matthew.

'Your boss. Strike. Martin was just haranguing him down in the—'

'You're over there, I think, Katie,' said Matthew, pointing her towards a table in the middle of the room. 'You'll want to get off your feet, must be difficult in the heat, I guess?'

Robin barely registered the passage of several more guests down the line. She responded to their good wishes at random, her eyes constantly drawn to the doorway through which they were all filing. Had Katie meant that Strike was here at the hotel, after all? Had he followed her from the church? Was he about to appear? Where had he been hiding? She had searched everywhere – on the terrace, in the hallway, in the bar. Hope surged only to fail again. Perhaps Martin, famous for his lack of tact, had driven him away? Then she reminded herself that Strike was not such a feeble creature as that and hope bubbled up once more, and while her inner self performed these peregrinations of expectation and dread, it was impossible to simulate the more conventional wedding day emotions whose absence, she knew, Matthew felt and resented.

'Martin!' Robin said joyfully, as her younger brother appeared, already three pints to the bad, accompanied by his mates.

'S'pose you already knew?' said Martin, taking it for granted that she must. He was holding his mobile in his hand. He had slept at a friend's house the previous evening, so that his bedroom could be given to relatives from Down South.

'Knew what?'

'That he caught the Ripper last night.'

Martin held up the screen to show her the news story. She gasped at the sight of the Ripper's identity. The knife wound that man had inflicted was throbbing on her forearm.

'Is he still here?' asked Robin, throwing pretence to the wind. 'Strike? Did he say he was staying, Mart?'

'For Christ's sake,' muttered Matthew.

'Sorry,' said Martin, registering Matthew's irritation. 'Holding up the queue.'

He slouched off. Robin turned to look at Matthew and saw, as though in thermal image, the guilt glowing through him.

'You knew,' she said, shaking hands absently with a great aunt who had leaned in, expecting to be kissed.

'Knew what?' he snapped.

'That Strike had caught—'

But her attention was now demanded by Matthew's old university friend and workmate, Tom, and his fiancée, Sarah. She barely heard a word that Tom said, because she was constantly watching the door, where she hoped to see Strike.

'You knew,' Robin repeated, once Tom and Sarah had walked away. There was another hiatus. Geoffrey had met a cousin from Canada. 'Didn't you?'

'I heard the tail end of it on the news this morning,' muttered Matthew. His expression hardened as he looked over Robin's head towards the doorway. 'Well, here he is. You've got your wish.'

Robin turned. Strike had just ducked into the room, one eye grey and purple above his heavy stubble, one ear swollen and stitched. He raised a bandaged hand when their eyes met and attempted a rueful smile, which ended in a wince.

'Robin,' said Matthew. 'Listen, I need—'

'In a minute,' she said, with a joyfulness that had been conspicuously absent all day.

'Before you talk to him, I need to tell—'

'Matt, please, can't it wait?'

Nobody in the family wanted to detain Strike, whose injury meant that he could not shake hands. He held the bandaged one in front of him and shuffled sideways down the line. Geoffrey glared at him and even Robin's mother, who had liked him on their only previous encounter, was unable to muster a smile as he greeted her by name. Every guest in the dining room seemed to be watching.

'You didn't have to be so dramatic,' Robin said, smiling up into his swollen face when at last he was standing in front of her. He grinned back, painful though it was: the two-hundred-mile journey he had undertaken so recklessly had been worth it, after all, to see her smile at him like that. 'Bursting into church. You could have just called.'

'Yeah, sorry about knocking over the flowers,' said Strike, including the sullen Matthew in his apology. 'I did call, but—'

'I haven't had my phone on this morning,' said Robin, aware that she was holding up the queue, but past caring. 'Go round us,' she said gaily to Matthew's boss, a tall red-headed woman.

'No, I called – two days ago, was it?' said Strike.

'What?' said Robin, while Matthew had a stilted conversation with Jemima.

'A couple of times,' said Strike. 'I left a message.'

'I didn't get any calls,' said Robin, 'or a message.'

The chattering, chinking, tinkling sounds of a hundred guests and the gentle melody of the string quartet seemed suddenly muffled, as though a thick bubble of shock had pressed in upon her.

'When did – what did you – two days ago?'

Since arriving at her parents' house she had been occupied non-stop with tedious wedding chores, yet she had still managed to check her phone frequently and surreptitiously, hoping that Strike had called or texted. Alone in bed at one that morning she had checked her entire call history in the vain hope that she would find a missed communication, but had found the history deleted. Having barely slept in the last couple of weeks, she had concluded that she had made an exhausted blunder, pressed the wrong button, erased it accidentally . . .

'I don't want to stay,' Strike mumbled. 'I just wanted to say I'm sorry, and ask you to come—'

'You've got to stay,' she said, reaching out and seizing his arm as though he might escape.

Her heart was thudding so fast that she felt breathless. She knew that she had lost colour as the buzzing room seemed to wobble around her.

'Please stay,' she said, still holding tight to his arm, ignoring Matthew as he bristled beside her. 'I need – I want to talk to you. Mum?' she called.

Linda stepped out of the receiving line. She seemed to have been waiting for the summons, and she didn't look happy.

'Please could you add Cormoran to a table?' said Robin. 'Maybe put him with Stephen and Jenny?'

Unsmiling, Linda led Strike away. There were a few last guests waiting to offer their congratulations. Robin could no longer muster smiles and small talk.

'Why didn't I get Cormoran's calls?' she asked Matthew, as an elderly man shuffled away towards the tables, neither welcomed nor greeted.

'I've been trying to tell you—'

'Why didn't I get the calls, Matthew?'

'Robin, can we talk about this later?'

The truth burst upon her so suddenly that she gasped.

'*You* deleted my call history,' she said, her mind leaping

rapidly from deduction to deduction. 'You asked for my passcode number when I came back from the bathroom at the service station.' The last two guests took one look at the bride and groom's expressions and hurried past without demanding their greeting. 'You took my phone away. You said it was about the honeymoon. Did you listen to his message?'

'Yes,' said Matthew. 'I deleted it.'

The silence that seemed to have pressed in on her had become a high-pitched whine. She felt light-headed. Here she stood in the big white lace dress she didn't like, the dress she had had altered because the wedding had been delayed once, pinned to the spot by ceremonial obligations. On the periphery of her vision, a hundred blurred faces swayed. The guests were hungry and expectant.

Her eyes found Strike, who was standing with his back to her, waiting beside Linda while an extra place was laid at her elder brother Stephen's table. Robin imagined striding over to him and saying: 'Let's get out of here.' What would he say if she did?

Her parents had spent thousands on the day. The packed room was waiting for the bride and groom to take their seats at the top table. Paler than her wedding dress, Robin followed her new husband to their seats as the room burst into applause.

The finicky waiter seemed determined to prolong Strike's discomfort. He had no choice but to stand in full view of every table while he waited for his extra place to be laid. Linda, who was almost a foot shorter than the detective, remained at Strike's elbow while the youth made imperceptible adjustments to the dessert fork and turned the plate so that the design aligned with its neighbours'. The little Strike could see of Linda's face below the silvery hat looked angry.

'Thanks very much,' he said at long last, as the waiter stepped out of the way, but as he took hold of the back of his chair, Linda laid a light hand on his sleeve. Her gentle touch might as well have been a shackle, accompanied as it was by an aura of outraged motherhood and offended hospitality. She greatly resembled her daughter. Linda's fading hair was red-gold, too, the clear grey-blue of her eyes enhanced by her silvery hat.

'Why are you here?' she asked through clenched teeth, while waiters bustled around them, delivering starters. At least the arrival of food had distracted the other guests. Conversation broke out as people's attention turned to their long-awaited meal.

'To ask Robin to come back to work with me.'

'You sacked her. It broke her heart.'

There was much he could have said to that, but he chose not to say it out of respect for what Linda must have suffered when she had seen that eight-inch knife wound.

'Three times she's been attacked, working for you,' said Linda, her colour rising. 'Three times.'

Strike could, with truth, have told Linda that he accepted liability only for the first of those attacks. The second had happened after Robin disregarded his explicit instructions and the third as a consequence of her not only disobeying him, but endangering a murder investigation and his entire business.

'She hasn't been sleeping. I've heard her at night . . . '

Linda's eyes were over-bright. She let go of him, but whispered, 'You haven't got a daughter. You can't understand what we've been through.'

Before Strike could muster his exhausted faculties, she had marched away to the top table. He caught Robin's eye over her untouched starter. She pulled an anguished expression, as though afraid that he might walk out. He raised his eyebrows slightly and dropped, at last, into his seat.

A large shape to his left shifted ominously. Strike turned to see more eyes like Robin's, set over a pugnacious jaw and surmounted by bristling brows.

'You must be Stephen,' said Strike.

Robin's elder brother grunted, still glaring. They were both large men; packed together, Stephen's elbow grazed Strike's as he reached for his pint. The rest of the table was staring at Strike. He raised his right hand in a kind of half-hearted salute, remembered that it was bandaged only when he saw it, and felt that he was drawing even more attention to himself.

'Hi, I'm Jenny, Stephen's wife,' said the broad-shouldered brunette on Stephen's other side. 'You look as though you could use this.'

She passed an untouched pint across Stephen's plate. Strike was so grateful he could have kissed her. In deference to Stephen's scowl, he confined himself to a heartfelt 'thanks' and downed half of it in one go. Out of the corner of his eye he saw Jenny mutter something in Stephen's ear. The latter watched Strike set the pint glass down again, cleared his throat and said gruffly:

'Congratulations in order, I s'pose.'

'Why?' said Strike blankly.

Stephen's expression became a degree less fierce.

'You caught that killer.'

'Oh yeah,' said Strike, picking up his fork in his left hand and stabbing the salmon starter. Only after he had swallowed it in its entirety and noticed Jenny laughing did he realise he ought to have treated it with more respect. 'Sorry,' he muttered. 'Very hungry.'

Stephen was now contemplating him with a glimmer of approval.

'No point in it, is there?' he said, looking down at his own mousse. 'Mostly air.'

'Cormoran,' said Jenny, 'would you mind just waving at Jonathan? Robin's other brother – over there.'

Strike looked in the direction indicated. A slender youth with the same colouring as Robin waved enthusiastically from the next table. Strike gave a brief, sheepish salute.

'Want her back, then, do you?' Stephen fired at him.

'Yeah,' said Strike. 'I do.'

He half-expected an angry response, but instead Stephen heaved a long sigh.

'S'pose I've got to be glad. Never seen her happier than when she was working for you. I took the piss out of her when we were kids for saying she wanted to be a policewoman,' he added. 'Wish I hadn't,' he said, accepting a fresh pint from the waiter and managing to down an impressive amount before continuing. 'We were dicks to her, looking back, and then she . . . well, she stands up for herself a bit better these days.'

Stephen's gaze wandered to the top table and Strike, who had his back to it, felt justified in stealing a look at Robin, too. She was silent, neither eating nor looking at Matthew.

'Not now, mate,' he heard Stephen say and turned to see his neighbour holding out a long thick arm to form a barrier between Strike and one of Martin's friends, who was on his feet and already bending low to ask Strike a question. The friend retreated, abashed.

'Cheers,' said Strike, finishing Jenny's pint.

'Get used to it,' said Stephen, demolishing his own mousse in a mouthful. 'You caught the Shacklewell Ripper. You're going to be famous, mate.'

*

People talked of things passing in a blur after a shock, but it was not like that for Robin. The room around her remained only too visible, every detail distinct: the brilliant squares of light that fell through the curtained windows, the enamel brightness of the azure sky beyond the glass, the damask tablecloths obscured by elbows and disarranged glasses, the gradually flushing cheeks of the scoffing and quaffing guests, Aunt Sue's patrician profile unsoftened by her neighbours' chat, Jenny's silly yellow hat quivering as she joked with Strike. She saw Strike. Her eyes returned so often to his back that she could have sketched with perfect accuracy the creases in his suit jacket, the dense dark curls of the back of his head, the difference in the thickness of his ears due to the knife injury to the left.

No, the shock of what she had discovered in the receiving line had not rendered her surroundings blurred. It had instead affected her perception of both sound and time. At one point, she knew that Matthew had urged her to eat, but it did not register with her until after her full plate had been removed by a solicitous waiter, because everything said to her had to permeate the thick walls that had closed in on her in the aftermath of Matthew's admission of perfidy. Within the invisible cell that separated her entirely from everyone else in the room, adrenaline thundered through her, urging her again and again to stand up and walk out.

If Strike had not arrived today, she might never have known that he wanted her back, and that she might be spared the shame, the anger, the humiliation, the hurt with which she had been racked since that awful night when he had sacked her. Matthew had sought to deny her the thing that might save her, the thing for which she had cried in the small hours of the night when everybody else was asleep: the restoration of her self-respect, of the job that had meant everything to her, of the friendship she had not known was one of the prizes of her life until it was torn away from her. Matthew had lied and kept lying. He had smiled and laughed as she dragged herself through the days before the wedding trying to pretend that she was happy that she had lost a life she had loved. Had she fooled him? Did he believe that she was truly glad her life with Strike was over? If he did, she had married a man who did not know her at all, and if he didn't . . .

The puddings were cleared away and Robin had to fake a smile for the concerned waiter who this time asked whether he could bring her something else, as this was the third course that she had left uneaten.

'I don't suppose you've got a loaded gun?' Robin asked him.

Fooled by her serious manner, he smiled, then looked confused.

'It doesn't matter,' she said. 'Never mind.'

'For Christ's sake, Robin,' Matthew said, and she knew, with a throb of fury and pleasure, that he was panicking, scared of what she would do, scared of what was going to happen next.

Coffee was arriving in sleek silver pots. Robin watched the waiters pouring, saw the little trays of petits fours placed upon the tables. She saw Sarah Shadlock in a tight turquoise sleeveless dress, hurrying across the room to the bathroom ahead of the speeches, watched heavily pregnant Katie following her in her flat shoes, swollen and tired, her enormous belly to the fore, and, again, Robin's eyes returned to Strike's back. He was scoffing petits fours and talking to Stephen. She was glad she had put him beside Stephen. She had always thought they would get on.

Then came the call for quiet, followed by rustling, fidgeting and a mass scraping of chairs as all those who had their backs to the top table dragged themselves around to watch the speakers. Robin's eyes met Strike's. She could not read his expression. He didn't look away from her until her father stood up, straightened his glasses and began to speak.

Strike was longing to lie down or, failing that, to get back into the car with Shanker, where he could at least recline the seat. He had had barely two hours' slumber in the past forty-eight, and a mixture of heavy-duty painkillers and what was now four pints was rendering him so sleepy that he kept dozing off against the hand supporting his head, jerking back awake as his temple slid off his knuckles.

He had never asked Robin what either of her parents did for a living. If Michael Ellacott alluded to his profession at any point during his speech, Strike missed it. He was a mild-looking man, almost professorial, with his horn-rimmed glasses. The children had all got his height, but only Martin had inherited his dark hair and hazel eyes.

The speech had been written, or perhaps rewritten, when Robin was jobless. Michael dwelled with patent love and appreciation on Robin's personal qualities, on her intelligence, her resilience, her generosity and her kindness. He had to stop and clear his throat when he started to speak of his pride in his only daughter, but there was a blank where her achievements ought to have been, an empty space for what she had actually done, or lived through. Of course, some of the things that Robin had survived were unfit to be spoken in this giant humidor of a room, or heard by these feathered and buttonholed guests, but the fact of her survival was, for Strike, the highest proof of those qualities and to him it seemed, sleep-befuddled though he was, that an acknowledgement ought to have been made.

Nobody else seemed to think so. He even detected a faint

relief in the crowd as Michael drew to a conclusion without alluding to knives or scars, gorilla masks or balaclavas.

The time had come for the bridegroom to speak. Matthew got to his feet amid enthusiastic applause, but Robin's hands remained in her lap as she stared at the window opposite, where the sun now hung low in the cloudless sky, casting long dark shadows over the lawn.

Somewhere in the room, a bee was buzzing. Far less concerned about offending Matthew than he had been about Michael, Strike adjusted his position in his chair, folding his arms and closing his eyes. For a minute or so, he listened as Matthew told how he and Robin had known each other since childhood, but only in their sixth form had he noticed how very good-looking the little girl who had once beaten him in the egg-and-spoon race had become . . .

'Cormoran!'

He jerked awake suddenly and, judging by the wet patch on his chest, knew that he had been drooling. Blearily he looked around at Stephen, who had elbowed him.

'You were snoring,' Stephen muttered.

Before he could reply the room broke into applause again. Matthew was sitting down, unsmiling.

Surely it had to be nearly over . . . but no, Matthew's best man was getting to his feet. Now that he was awake again, Strike had become aware just how full his bladder was. He hoped to Christ this bloke would speak fast.

'Matt and I first met on the rugby pitch,' he said and a table towards the rear of the room broke into drunken cheers.

'Upstairs,' said Robin. 'Now.'

They were the first words she had spoken to her husband since they had sat down at the top table. The applause for the best man's speech had barely died away. Strike was standing, but she could tell that he was only heading for the bathroom because she saw him stop a waiter and ask directions. In any case, she knew, now, that he wanted her back, and was convinced that he would stay long enough to hear her agreement. The look they had exchanged during the starters had told her as much.

'They'll be bringing in the band in half an hour,' said Matthew. 'We're s'posed to—'

But Robin walked off towards the door, taking with her the invisible isolation cell that had kept her cold and tearless through her father's speech, through Matthew's nervous utterings, through the tedium of the familiar old anecdotes from the rugby club regurgitated by the best man. She had the vague impression that her mother tried to waylay her as she ploughed through the guests, but paid no attention. She had sat obediently through the meal and the speeches. The universe owed her an interlude of privacy and freedom.

Up the staircase she marched, her skirt held out of the way of her cheap shoes, and off along a plush carpeted corridor, unsure where she was going, with Matthew's footsteps hurrying behind her.

'Excuse me,' she said to a waistcoated teenager who was wheeling a linen basket out of a cupboard, 'where's the bridal suite?'

He looked from her to Matthew and smirked, actually smirked.

'Don't be a jerk,' said Robin coldly.

'Robin!' said Matthew, as the teenager blushed.

'That way,' said the youth hoarsely, pointing.

Robin marched on. Matthew, she knew, had the key. He had stayed at the hotel with his best man the previous evening, though not in the bridal suite.

When Matthew opened the door, she strode inside,

registering the rose petals on the bed, the champagne standing in its cooler, the large envelope inscribed to Mr and Mrs Cunliffe. With relief, she saw the holdall that she had intended to take as hand luggage to their mystery honeymoon. Unzipping it, she thrust her uninjured arm inside and found the brace that she had removed for the photographs. When she had pulled it back over her aching forearm, with its barely healed wound, she wrenched the new wedding ring off her finger and slammed it down on the bedside table beside the champagne bucket.

'What are you doing?' said Matthew, sounding both scared and aggressive. 'What – you want to call it off? You don't want to be married?'

Robin stared at him. She had expected to feel release once they were alone and she could speak freely, but the enormity of what he had done mocked her attempts to express it. She read his fear of her silence in his darting eyes, his squared shoulders. Whether he was aware of it or not, he had placed himself precisely between her and the door.

'All right,' he said loudly, 'I know I should've—'

'You knew what that job meant to me. You knew.'

'I didn't want you to go back, all right?' Matthew shouted. 'You got attacked and stabbed, Robin!'

'That was my own fault!'

'He fucking sacked you!'

'Because I did something he'd told me not to do—'

'*I knew you'd fucking defend him!*' Matthew bellowed, all control gone. 'I knew if you spoke to him you'd go scurrying back like some fucking lapdog!'

'You don't get to make those decisions for me!' she yelled. 'Nobody's got the right to intercept my fucking calls and delete my messages, Matthew!'

Restraint and pretence were gone. They heard each

other only by accident, in brief pauses for breath, each of them howling their resentment and pain across the room like flaming spears that burned into dust before touching their target. Robin gesticulated wildly, then screeched with pain as her arm protested sharply, and Matthew pointed with self-righteous rage at the scar she would carry for ever because of her reckless stupidity in working with Strike. Nothing was achieved, nothing was excused, nothing was apologised for: the arguments that had defaced their last twelve months had all led to this conflagration, the border skirmishes that presage war. Beyond the window, afternoon dissolved rapidly into evening. Robin's head throbbed, her stomach churned, her sense of being stifled threatened to overcome her.

'You hated me working those hours – you didn't give a damn that I was happy in my job for the first time in my life, so you *lied*! You knew what it meant to me, and you *lied*! How could you delete my call history, how could you delete my voicemail—?'

She sat down suddenly in a deep, fringed chair, her head in her hands, dizzy with the force of her anger and shock on an empty stomach.

Somewhere, distantly in the carpeted hush of the hotel corridors, a door closed, a woman giggled.

'Robin,' said Matthew hoarsely.

She heard him approaching her, but she put out a hand, holding him away.

'Don't touch me.'

'Robin, I shouldn't have done it, I know that. I didn't want you hurt again.'

She barely heard him. Her anger was not only for Matthew, but also for Strike. He should have called back. He should have tried and kept trying. *If he had, I might not be here now.*

The thought scared her.

If I'd known Strike wanted me back, would I have married Matthew?

She heard the rustle of Matthew's jacket and guessed that he was checking his watch. Perhaps the guests waiting downstairs would think that they had disappeared to consummate the marriage. She could imagine Geoffrey making ribald jokes in their absence. The band must have been in place for an hour. Again she remembered how much this was all costing her parents. Again, she remembered that they had lost deposits on the wedding that had been postponed.

'All right,' she said, in a colourless voice. 'Let's go back down and dance.'

She stood up, automatically smoothing her skirt. Matthew looked suspicious.

'You're sure?'

'We've got to get through today,' she said. 'People have come a long way. Mum and Dad have paid a lot of money.'

Hoisting her skirt up again, she set off for the suite door.

'Robin!'

She turned back, expecting him to say 'I love you', expecting him to smile, to beg, to urge a truer reconciliation.

'You'd better wear this,' he said, holding out the wedding ring she had removed, his expression as cold as hers.

Strike had not been able to think of a better course of action, given that he intended to stay until he had spoken to Robin again, than continuing to drink. He had removed himself from Stephen and Jenny's willing protection, feeling that they ought to be free to enjoy the company of friends and family, and fallen back on the methods by which he usually repelled strangers' curiosity: his own intimidating size and habitually surly expression. For a while he lurked at the end of the bar, nursing a pint on his own, and then repaired to the terrace, where he had stood apart from the other smokers and contemplated the dappled evening, breathing in the sweet meadow smell beneath a coral sky. Even Martin and his friends, now full of drink themselves and smoking in a circle like teenagers, failed to muster sufficient nerve to badger him.

After a while, the guests were skilfully rounded up and ushered *en masse* back into the wood-panelled room, which had been transformed in their absence into a dance floor. Half the tables had been removed, the others shifted to the sides. A band stood ready behind amplifiers, but the bride and groom remained absent. A man whom Strike understood to be Matthew's father, sweaty, rotund and red-faced, had already made several jokes about what they might be getting up to when Strike found himself addressed by a woman in a tight turquoise dress whose feathery hair adornment tickled his nose as she closed in for a handshake.

'It's Cormoran Strike, isn't it?' she said. 'What an honour! Sarah Shadlock.'

Strike knew all about Sarah Shadlock. She had slept with Matthew at university, while he was in a long-distance relationship with Robin. Once again, Strike indicated his bandage to show why he could not shake her hand.

'Oh, you poor thing!'

A drunk, balding man who was probably younger than he looked loomed up behind Sarah.

'Tom Turvey,' he said, fixing Strike with unfocused eyes. 'Bloody good job. Well done, mate. *Bloody good job*.'

'We've wanted to meet you for ages,' said Sarah. 'We're old friends of Matt and Robin's.'

'Shacklewell Rip – Ripper,' said Tom, on a slight hiccough. 'Bloody good job.'

'*Look* at you, you poor thing,' said Sarah again, touching Strike on the bicep as she smiled up into his bruised face. '*He* didn't do that to you, did he?'

'Ev'ryone wants to know,' said Tom, grinning blearily. 'Can hardly contain their bloody selves. You should've made a speech instead of Henry.'

'Ha ha,' said Sarah. 'Last thing you'd want to do, I expect. You must have come here straight from catching – well, I don't know – *did* you?'

'Sorry,' said Strike, unsmiling, 'police have asked me not to talk about it.'

'Ladies and gentlemen,' said the harried MC, who had been caught unawares by Matthew and Robin's unobtrusive entrance into the room, 'please welcome Mr and Mrs Cunliffe!'

As the newlyweds moved unsmilingly into the middle of the dance floor, everybody but Strike began to applaud. The lead singer of the band took the microphone from the MC.

'This is a song from their past that means a lot to Matthew and Robin,' the singer announced, as Matthew slid his hand around Robin's waist and grasped her other hand.

The wedding photographer moved out of the shadows and began clicking away again, frowning a little at the reappearance of the ugly rubber brace on the bride's arm.

The first acoustic bars of 'Wherever You Will Go' by The Calling struck up. Robin and Matthew began to revolve on the spot, their faces averted from each other.

So lately, been wondering,
Who will be there to take my place
When I'm gone, you'll need love
To light the shadows on your face . . .

Strange choice for an 'our song', Strike thought . . . but as he watched he saw Matthew move closer to Robin, saw his hand tighten on her narrow waist as he bent his handsome face to whisper something in her ear.

A jolt somewhere around the solar plexus pierced the fug of exhaustion, relief and alcohol that had cushioned Strike all day long from the reality of what this wedding meant. Now, as Strike watched the newlyweds turn on the dance floor, Robin in her long white dress, with a circlet of roses in her hair, Matthew in his dark suit, his face close to his bride's cheek, Strike was forced to recognise how long, and how deeply, he had hoped that Robin would not marry. He had wanted her free, free to be what they had been together. Free, so that if circumstances changed . . . so the possibility was there . . . free, so that one day, they might find out what else they could be to each other.

Fuck this.

If she wanted to talk, she would have to call him. Setting down his empty glass on a windowsill, he turned and made his way through the other guests, who shuffled aside to let him pass, so dark was his expression.

As she turned, staring into space, Robin saw Strike leaving. The door opened. He was gone.

'Let go of me.'

'What?'

She pulled free, hoisted up her dress once more for freedom of movement, then half-walked, half-ran off the dance floor, almost careering into her father and Aunt Sue, who were waltzing sedately nearby. Matthew was left standing alone in the middle of the room as Robin fought her way through the startled onlookers towards the door that had just swung shut.

'Cormoran!'

He was already halfway down the stairs, but on hearing his name he turned back. He liked her hair in its long loose waves beneath the crown of Yorkshire roses.

'Congratulations.'

She walked down another couple of steps, fighting the lump in her throat.

'You really want me back?'

He forced a smile.

'I've just driven for bloody hours with Shanker in what I strongly suspect is a stolen car. Of course I want you back.'

She laughed, though tears sprang to her eyes.

'Shanker's here? You should have brought him in!'

'Shanker? In here? He'd have been through everyone's pockets then nicked the reception till.'

She laughed some more, but tears spilled out of her brimming eyes and bounced down her cheek.

'Where are you going to sleep?'

'In the car, while Shanker drives me home. He's going to charge me a fortune for this. Doesn't matter,' he added gruffly, as she opened her mouth. 'Worth it if you're coming back. More than worth it.'

'I want a contract this time,' said Robin, the severity of her tone belied by the expression of her eyes. 'A proper one.'

'You've got it.'

'OK, then. Well, I'll see you . . .'

When would she see him? She was supposed to be on honeymoon for two weeks.

'Let me know,' said Strike.

He turned and began to descend the stairs again.

'Cormoran!'

'What?'

She walked towards him until she stood on the step above. Their eyes were on a level now.

'I want to hear all about how you caught him and everything.'

He smiled.

'It'll keep. Couldn't have done it without you, though.'

Neither of them could tell who had made the first move, or whether they acted in unison. They were holding each other tightly before they knew what had happened, Robin's chin on Strike's shoulder, his face in her hair. He smelled of sweat, beer and surgical spirits, she, of roses and the faint perfume that he had missed when she was no longer in the office. The feel of her was both new and familiar, as though he had held her a long time ago, as though he had missed it without knowing it for years. Through the closed door upstairs the band played on:

I'll go wherever you will go
If I could make you mine . . .

As suddenly as they had reached for each other, they broke apart. Tears were rolling down Robin's face. For one moment of madness, Strike yearned to say, 'Come with me', but there are words that can never be unsaid or forgotten, and those, he knew, were some of them.

'Let me know,' he repeated. He tried to smile, but it hurt his face. With a wave of his bandaged hand, he continued down the stairs without looking back.

She watched him go, wiping the hot tears frantically from her face. If he had said 'come with me', she knew she would have gone: but then what? Gulping, wiping her nose on the back of her hand, Robin turned, hoisted up her skirts again, and climbed slowly back towards her husband.

ONE YEAR LATER

1

I hear that he means to enlarge . . . that he is looking for a competent assistant.

Henrik Ibsen, *Rosmersholm*

Such is the universal desire for fame that those who achieve it accidentally or unwillingly will wait in vain for pity.

For many weeks after the capture of the Shacklewell Ripper, Strike had feared that his greatest detective triumph might have dealt his career a fatal blow. The smatterings of publicity his agency had hitherto attracted seemed now like the two submersions of the drowning man before his final descent to the depths. The business for which he had sacrificed so much, and worked so hard, relied largely on his ability to pass unrecognised in the streets of London, but with the capture of a serial killer he had become lodged in the public imagination, a sensational oddity, a jokey aside on quiz shows, an object of curiosity all the more fascinating because he refused to satisfy it.

Having wrung every last drop of interest out of Strike's ingenuity in catching the Ripper, the papers had exhumed Strike's family history. They called it 'colourful', though to him it was a lumpen internal mass that he had carried with him all his life and preferred not to probe: the rock star father, the dead groupie mother, the army career that ended with the loss of half his right leg. Grinning journalists bearing chequebooks had descended on the only sibling with whom he had shared a childhood, his half-sister, Lucy. Army acquaintances had given off-the-cuff remarks that, shorn of what Strike knew was rough humour, assumed the appearance of envy and disparagement. The father whom Strike had only met twice, and whose surname he did not use, released a statement through a publicist, implying a non-existent, amicable relationship that was proceeding far from prying eyes. The aftershocks of the Ripper's capture had reverberated through Strike's life for a year, and he was not sure they were spent yet.

Of course, there was an upside to becoming the best-known private detective in London. New clients had swarmed to Strike in the aftermath of the trial, so that it had become physically impossible for him and Robin to cover all the jobs themselves. Given that it was advisable for Strike to keep a low profile for a while, he had remained largely office-bound for several months while subcontracted employees – mostly ex-police and military, many from the world of private security – took on the bulk of the work, Strike covering nights and paperwork. After a year of working on as many jobs as the enlarged agency could handle, Strike had managed to give Robin an overdue pay rise, settle the last of his outstanding debts and buy a thirteen-year-old BMW 3 series.

Lucy and his friends assumed that the presence of the car and additional employees meant that Strike had at last achieved a state of prosperous security. In fact, once he had paid the exorbitant costs of garaging the car in central London and met payroll, Strike was left with almost nothing to spend on himself and continued to live in two rooms over the office, cooking on a single-ringed hob.

The administrative demands freelance contractors made and the patchy quality of the men and women available to the agency were a constant headache. Strike had found only one man whom he had kept on semi-permanently: Andy Hutchins, a thin, saturnine ex-policeman ten years older than his new boss, who had come highly recommended by Strike's friend in the Met, Detective Inspector Eric Wardle. Hutchins had taken early retirement when he had been struck by a sudden bout of near-paralysis of his left leg, followed by a diagnosis of multiple sclerosis. When he had applied for contract work, Hutchins had warned Strike that he might not always be fit; it was, he explained, an unpredictable disease, but he had not relapsed in three years. He followed a special low-fat diet that to Strike sounded positively punitive: no red meat, no cheese, no chocolate, nothing deep-fried. Methodical and patient, Andy could be trusted to get the job done without constant supervision, which was more than could be said for any of Strike's other hires apart from Robin. It seemed incredible to him, still, that she had walked into his life as a temporary secretary to become his partner and outstanding colleague.

Whether they were still friends, though, was another question.

Two days after Robin and Matthew's wedding, when the press had driven him out of his flat, while it was still impossible to turn on the TV without hearing his own name, Strike had sought refuge, in spite of invitations from friends and his sister, in a Travelodge near Monument station. There he had attained the solitude and privacy he craved; there he had been free to sleep for hours undisturbed; and there he had downed nine cans of lager and become increasingly desirous of speaking to Robin with each empty can that he threw, with diminishing accuracy, across the room into the bin.

They had had no contact since their hug on the stairs, to which Strike's thoughts had turned repeatedly in the ensuing days. He was sure that Robin would be going through a hellish time, holed up in Masham while deciding whether to pursue a divorce or an annulment, arranging the sale of their flat while dealing with both press and family fallout. What exactly he was going to say when he reached her, Strike did not know. He only knew that he wanted to hear her voice. It was at this point, drunkenly searching his kit bag, that he discovered that in his sleep-deprived haste to leave his flat, he had not packed a recharging lead for his mobile, which was out of battery. Undeterred, he had dialled directory enquiries and succeeded, after many requests to repeat himself more clearly, in getting connected to Robin's parents' house.

Her father had answered.

'Hi, c'n'I speak t'Robinplease?'

'To Robin? I'm afraid she's on her honeymoon.'

For a muzzy moment or two, Strike had not quite comprehended what he had been told.

'Hello?' Michael Ellacott had said, and then, angrily, 'I suppose this is another journalist. My daughter's abroad and I would like you to stop calling my house.'

Strike had hung up, then continued to drink until he passed out.

His anger and disappointment had lingered for days and were in no way abated by his awareness that many would say that he had no claims upon his employee's private life. Robin wasn't the woman he had thought her if she could have got meekly on a plane with the man he mentally referred to as 'that twat'. Nevertheless, something close to depression weighed upon him while he sat in his Travelodge with his brand-new recharging lead and more lager, waiting for his name to disappear from the news.

Consciously seeking to distract himself from thoughts of Robin, he had ended his self-imposed isolation by accepting an invitation that he would usually have avoided: dinner with Detective Inspector Eric Wardle, Wardle's wife April and their friend Coco. Strike knew perfectly well that he was being set up. Coco had previously tried to find out through Wardle whether Strike was single.

She was a small, lithe, very pretty girl with tomato-red hair, a tattoo artist by trade and a part-time burlesque dancer. He ought to have read the danger signs. She was giggly and slightly hysterical even before they started drinking. Strike had taken her to bed in the Travelodge in the same way he had drunk nine cans of Tennent's.

Coco had taken some shaking loose in the weeks that followed. Strike did not feel good about it, but one advantage of being on the run from the press was that one-night stands found it far harder to track you down.

One year on, Strike had no idea why Robin had chosen to remain with Matthew. He supposed her feelings for her husband ran so deep that she was blind to what he really was. He was in a new relationship himself, now. It had lasted ten months, the longest since he had split up with Charlotte, who had been the only woman whom he had ever contemplated marrying.

The emotional distance between the detective partners had become a simple fact of daily existence. Strike could not fault Robin's work. She did everything she was told promptly, meticulously and with initiative and ingenuity. Nevertheless, he had noticed a pinched look that had never been there before. He thought her slightly jumpier than usual and, once or twice while parcelling out work between his partner and subcontractors, he had caught an uncharacteristic blank, unfocused expression that troubled him. He knew some of the signs of post-traumatic stress disorder and she had now survived two near-fatal attacks. In the immediate aftermath of losing half his leg in Afghanistan, he, too, had experienced dissociation, finding himself suddenly and abruptly removed from his present surroundings to those few seconds of acute foreboding and terror that had preceded the disintegration of the Viking in which he had been sitting, and of his body and military career. He had been left with a deep dislike of being driven by anybody else and, to this day, with dreams of blood and agony that sometimes woke him, bathed in sweat.

However, when he had attempted to discuss Robin's mental health in the calm, responsible tones of her employer, she had cut him off with a finality and a resentment that he suspected could be traced to the sacking. Thereafter, he had noticed her volunteering for trickier, after-dark assignments and it had been something of a headache to arrange work so that he did not appear to be trying, as in fact he was, to keep her on the safest, most mundane jobs.

They were polite, pleasant and formal with each other, talking about their private lives in the broadest brushstrokes, and then only when necessary. Robin and Matthew had just moved house and Strike had insisted that she take a full week off to do it. Robin had been resistant, but Strike had overruled her. She had taken very little leave all year, he reminded her, in a tone that brooked no argument.

On Monday, the latest of Strike's unsatisfactory subcontractors, a cocky ex-Red Cap Strike had not known while in the service, had driven his moped into the rear of a taxi he was supposed to be tailing. Strike had enjoyed sacking him. It had given him somebody on whom to vent his anger, because his landlord had also chosen this week to inform Strike that, along with nearly every other owner of office space in Denmark Street, he had sold out to a developer. The threat of losing both office and home now loomed over the detective.

To set the seal on a particularly shitty few days, the temp he had hired to cover basic paperwork and answer the phone in Robin's absence was as irritating a woman as Strike had ever met. Denise talked nonstop in a whiny, nasal voice that carried even through the closed door of his inner office. Strike had latterly resorted to listening to music on headphones, with the result that she had had to bang on the door repeatedly and shout before he heard her.

'What?'

'I've just found this,' said Denise, brandishing a scribbled note in front of him. 'It says "clinic" . . . there's a word beginning with "V" in front . . . the appointment's for half an hour's time – should I have reminded you?'

Strike saw Robin's handwriting. The first word was indeed illegible.

'No,' he said. 'Just throw it away.'

Mildly hopeful that Robin was quietly seeking professional help for any mental problems she might be suffering, Strike replaced his earphones and returned to the report he was reading, but found it hard to concentrate. He therefore decided to leave early for the interview he had scheduled with a possible new subcontractor. Mainly to get away from Denise, he was meeting the man in his favourite pub.

Strike had had to avoid the Tottenham for months in the aftermath of his capture of the Shacklewell Ripper, because journalists had lain in wait for him here, word having got out that he was a regular. Even today, he glanced around suspiciously before deciding that it was safe to advance on the bar, order his usual pint of Doom Bar and retire to a corner table.

Partly because he had made an effort to give up the chips that were a staple of his diet, partly because of his workload, Strike was thinner now than he had been a year ago. The weight loss had relieved pressure on his amputated leg, so that both the effort and the relief of sitting were less noticeable. Strike took a swig of his pint, stretching his knee from force of habit and enjoying the relative ease of movement, then opened the cardboard file he had brought with him.

The notes within had been made by the idiot who had crashed his moped into the back of the taxi, and they were barely adequate. Strike couldn't afford to lose this client, but he and Hutchins were struggling to cover workload as it was. He urgently needed a new hire, and yet he wasn't entirely sure that the interview he was about to conduct was wise. He had not consulted Robin before making the bold decision to hunt down a man he had not seen for five years, and even as the door of the Tottenham opened to admit Sam Barclay, who was punctual to the minute, Strike was wondering whether he was about to make an almighty mistake.

He would have known the Glaswegian almost anywhere as an ex-squaddie, with his T-shirt under his thin V-neck jumper, his close-cropped hair, his tight jeans and over-white trainers. As Strike stood up and held out his hand, Barclay, who appeared to have recognised him with similar ease, grinned and said:

'Already drinking, aye?'

'Want one?' asked Strike.

While waiting for Barclay's pint, he watched the ex-Rifleman in the mirror behind the bar. Barclay was only a little over thirty, but his hair was prematurely greying. He was otherwise exactly as Strike remembered. Heavy browed, with large round blue eyes and a strong jaw, he had the slightly beaky appearance of an affable owl. Strike had liked Barclay even while working to court-martial him.

'Still smoking?' Strike asked, once he'd handed over the beer and sat down.

'Vapin' now,' said Barclay. 'We've had a baby.'

'Congratulations,' said Strike. 'On a health kick, then?'

'Aye, somethin' like that.'

'Dealing?'

'I wasnae dealin',' said Barclay hotly, 'as you fuckin' well know. Recreational use only, pal.'

'Where are you buying it now, then?'

'Online,' said Barclay, sipping his pint. 'Easy. First time I did it, I thought, this cannae fuckin' work, can it? But then I thought, "Och, well, it's an adventure." They send it to you disguised in fag packets and that. Choose off a whole menu. Internet's a great thing.'

He laughed and said, 'So whut's this all about? Wasnae expectin' to hear from *you* any time soon.'

Strike hesitated.

'I was thinking of offering you a job.'

There was a beat as Barclay stared at him, then he threw back his head and roared with laughter.

'Fuck,' he said. 'Why didn't ye say that straight off, like?'

'Why d'you think?'

'I'm no vapin' every night,' said Barclay earnestly. 'I'm no, seriously. The wife doesnae like it.'

Strike kept his hand closed on the file, thinking.

He had been working a drugs case in Germany when he had run across Barclay. Drugs were bought and sold within the British army as in every other part of society, but the Special Investigation Branch had been called in to investigate what appeared to be a rather more professional operation than most. Barclay had been fingered as a key player and the discovery of a kilo brick of prime Moroccan hash among his effects had certainly justified an interview.

Barclay insisted that he had been stitched up and Strike, who was sitting in on his interrogation, was inclined to agree, not least because the Rifleman seemed far too intelligent not to have found a better hiding place for his hashish than the bottom of an army kit bag. On the other hand, there was ample evidence that Barclay had been using regularly, and there was more than one witness to the fact that his behaviour was becoming erratic. Strike felt that Barclay had been lined up as a convenient scapegoat, and decided to undertake a little side excavation on his own.

This threw up interesting information relating to building materials and engineering supplies that were being reordered at a thoroughly implausible rate. While it was not the first time that Strike had uncovered this kind of corruption, it so happened that the two officers in charge of these mysteriously vanishing and highly resaleable commodities were the very men so keen to secure Barclay's court martial.

Barclay was startled, during a one-to-one interview with Strike, to find the SIB sergeant suddenly interested, not in hashish, but in anomalies relating to building contracts. At first wary, and sure he would not be believed given the situation in which he found himself, Barclay finally admitted to Strike that he had not only noticed what others had failed to see, or chosen not to enquire into, but begun to tabulate and document exactly how much these officers were stealing. Unfortunately for Barclay, the officers in question had got wind of the fact that he was a little too interested in their activities, and it was shortly after this that a kilo of hashish had turned up in Barclay's effects.

When Barclay showed Strike the record he had been keeping (the notebook had been hidden a good deal more skilfully than the hashish), Strike had been impressed by the method and initiative it displayed, given that Barclay had never been trained in investigative technique. Asked why he had undertaken the investigation for which nobody was paying, and which had landed him in so much trouble, Barclay had shrugged his broad shoulders and said 'no right, is it? That's the army they're robbin'. Taxpayers' money they're fuckin' pocketin'.'

Strike had put in many more hours on the case than his colleagues felt was merited, but finally, with Strike's additional investigations into the matter to add weight, the dossier on his superiors' activities that Barclay had compiled led to their conviction. The SIB took credit for it, of course, but Strike had made sure that accusations against Barclay were quietly laid to rest.

'When ye say "work",' Barclay wondered aloud now, as the pub hummed and tinkled around them, 'ye mean detective stuff?'

Strike could see that the idea appealed.

'Yeah,' said Strike. 'What have you been doing since I last saw you?'

The answer was depressing, though not unexpected. Barclay had found it hard to get or keep a regular job in the first couple of years out of the army and had been doing a bit of painting and decorating for his brother-in-law's company.

'The wife's bringin' in most o' the money,' he said. 'She's got a good job.'

'OK,' said Strike, 'I reckon I can give you a couple of days a week for starters. You'll bill me as a freelancer. If it doesn't work out, either of us can walk away at any time. Sound fair?'

'Aye,' said Barclay, 'aye, fair enough. What are you paying, like?'

They discussed money for five minutes. Strike explained how his other employees set themselves up as private contractors and how receipts and other professional expenses should be brought into the office for reimbursement. Finally he opened the file and slid it around to show Barclay the contents.

'I need this guy followed,' he said, pointing out a photograph of a chubby youth with thick curly hair. 'Pictures of whoever he's with and what he's up to.'

'Aye, all right,' said Barclay, getting out his mobile and taking pictures of the target's photograph and address.

'He's being watched today by my other guy,' said Strike, 'but I need you outside his flat from six o'clock tomorrow morning.'

He was pleased to note that Barclay did not query the early start.

'Whut happened to that lassie, though?' Barclay enquired as he put his phone back into his pocket. 'The one who was in the papers with ye?'

'Robin?' said Strike. 'She's on holiday. Back next week.'

They parted with a handshake, Strike enjoying a moment's fleeting optimism before remembering that he would now have to return to the office, which meant proximity to Denise, with her parrot-like chatter, her habit of talking with her mouth full and her inability to remember that he detested pale, milky tea.

He had to pick his way through the ever-present roadworks at the top of Tottenham Court Road to get back to his office. Waiting until he was past the noisiest stretch, he called Robin to tell her that he had hired Barclay, but his call went straight to voicemail. Remembering that she was supposed to be at the mysterious clinic right now, he cut the call without leaving a message.

Walking on, a sudden thought occurred to him. He had assumed that the clinic related to Robin's mental health, but what if—?

The phone in his hand rang: the office number.

'Hello?'

'Mr Strike?' said Denise's terrified squawk in his ear. 'Mr Strike, could you come back quickly, please? Please – there's a gentleman – he wants to see you very urgently—'

Behind her, Strike heard a loud bang and a man shouting.

'Please come back as soon as you can!' screamed Denise.

'On my way!' Strike shouted and he broke into an ungainly run.

2

. . . he doesn't look the sort of man one ought to allow in here.

Henrik Ibsen, *Rosmersholm*

Panting, his right knee aching, Strike used the handrail to pull himself up the last few steps of the metal staircase leading to his office. Two raised voices were reverberating through the glass door, one male, the other shrill, frightened and female. When Strike burst into the room, Denise, who was backed against the wall, gasped, 'Oh, thank God!'

Strike judged the man in the middle of the room to be in his mid-twenties. Dark hair fell in straggly wisps around a thin and dirty face that was dominated by burning, sunken eyes. His T-shirt, jeans and hoodie were all torn and filthy, the sole of one of his trainers peeling away from the leather. An unwashed animal stench hit the detective's nostrils.

That the stranger was mentally ill could be in no doubt. Every ten seconds or so, in what seemed to be an uncontrollable tic, he touched first the end of his nose, which had grown red with repeated tapping, then, with a faint hollow thud, the middle of his thin sternum, then let his hand drop to his side. Almost immediately, his hand would fly to the tip of his nose again. It was as though he had forgotten how to cross himself, or had simplified the action for speed's sake. Nose, chest, hand at his side; nose, chest, hand at his side; the mechanical movement was distressing to watch, and the more so as he seemed barely conscious that he was doing it. He was one of those ill and desperate people you saw in the capital who were always somebody else's problem, like the traveller on the Tube everybody tried to avoid making eye contact with and the ranting woman on the street corner whom people crossed the street to avoid, fragments of shattered humanity who were too common to trouble the imagination for long.

'You him?' said the burning-eyed man, as his hand touched nose and chest again. 'You Strike? You the detective?'

With the hand that was not constantly flying from nose to chest, he suddenly tugged at his flies. Denise whimpered, as if scared he might suddenly expose himself, and, indeed, it seemed entirely possible.

'I'm Strike, yeah,' said the detective, moving around to place himself between the stranger and the temp. 'You OK, Denise?'

'Yes,' she whispered, still backed against the wall.

'I seen a kid killed,' said the stranger. 'Strangled.'

'OK,' said Strike, matter-of-factly. 'Why don't we go in here?'

He gestured to him that he should proceed into the inner office.

'I need a piss!' said the man, tugging at his zip.

'This way, then.'

Strike showed him the door to the toilet just outside the office. When the door had banged shut behind him, Strike returned quietly to Denise.

'What happened?'

'He wanted to see you, I said you weren't here and he got angry and started punching things!'

'Call the police,' said Strike quietly. 'Tell them we've got a very ill man here. Possibly psychotic. Wait until I've got him into my office, though.'

The bathroom door banged open. The stranger's flies were gaping. He did not seem to be wearing underpants. Denise whimpered again as he frantically touched nose and chest, nose and chest, unaware of the large patch of dark pubic hair he was exposing.

'This way,' said Strike pleasantly. The man shuffled through the inner door, the stench of him doubly potent after a brief respite.

On being invited to sit down, the stranger perched himself on the edge of the client's chair.

'What's your name?' Strike asked, sitting down on the other side of the desk.

'Billy,' said the man, his hand flying from nose to chest three times in quick succession. The third time his hand fell, he grabbed it with his other hand and held it tightly.

'And you saw a child strangled, Billy?' said Strike, as in the next room Denise gabbled:

'Police, quickly!'

'What did she say?' asked Billy, his sunken eyes huge in his face as he glanced nervously towards the outer office, one hand clasping the other in his effort to suppress his tic.

'That's nothing,' said Strike easily. 'I've got a few different cases on. Tell me about this child.'

Strike reached for a pad and paper, all his movements slow and cautious, as though Billy were a wild bird that might take fright.

'He strangled it, up by the horse.'

Denise was now gabbling loudly into the phone beyond the flimsy partition wall.

'When was this?' asked Strike, still writing.

'Ages . . . I was a kid. Little girl it was, but after they said it was a little boy. Jimmy was there, he says I never saw it, but I did. I saw him do it. Strangled. I saw it.'

'And this was up by the horse, was it?'

'Right up by the horse. That's not where they buried her, though. Him. That was down in the dell, by our dad's. I seen them doing it, I can show you the place. She wouldn't let me dig, but she'd let you.'

'And Jimmy did it, did he?'

'Jimmy never strangled nobody!' said Billy angrily. 'He saw it with me. He says it didn't happen but he's lying, he was there. He's frightened, see.'

'I see,' lied Strike, continuing to take notes. 'Well, I'll need your address if I'm going to investigate.'

He half-expected resistance, but Billy reached eagerly for the proffered pad and pen. A further gust of body odour reached Strike. Billy began to write, but suddenly seemed to think better of it.

'You won't come to Jimmy's place, though? He'll fucking tan me. You can't come to Jimmy's.'

'No, no,' said Strike soothingly. 'I just need your address for my records.'

Through the door came Denise's grating voice.

'I need someone here quicker than that, he's very disturbed!'

'What's she saying?' asked Billy.

To Strike's chagrin, Billy suddenly ripped the top sheet from the pad, crumpled it, then began to touch nose and chest again with his fist enclosing the paper.

'Don't worry about Denise,' said Strike, 'she's dealing with another client. Can I get you a drink, Billy?'

'Drink of what?'

'Tea? Or coffee?'

'Why?' asked Billy. The offer seemed to have made him even more suspicious. 'Why do you want me to drink something?'

'Only if you fancy it. Doesn't matter if you don't.'

'I don't need medicine!'

'I haven't got any medicine to give you,' said Strike.

'I'm not mental! He strangled the kid and they buried it, down in the dell by our dad's house. Wrapped in a blanket it was. Pink blanket. It wasn't my fault. I was only a kid. I didn't want to be there. I was just a little kid.'

'How many years ago, do you know?'

'Ages . . . years . . . can't get it out of my head,' said Billy, his eyes burning in his thin face as the fist enclosing the piece of paper fluttered up and down, touching nose, touching chest. 'They buried her in a pink blanket, down in the dell by my dad's house. But afterwards they said it was a boy.'

'Where's your dad's house, Billy?'

'She won't let me back now. *You* could dig, though. *You* could go. Strangled her, they did,' said Billy, fixing Strike with his haunted eyes. 'But Jimmy said it was a boy. Strangled, up by the—'

There was a knock on the door. Before Strike could tell her not to enter, Denise had poked her head inside, much braver now that Strike was here, full of her own importance.

'They're coming,' she said, with a look of exaggerated meaning that would have spooked a man far less jumpy than Billy. 'On their way now.'

'Who's coming?' demanded Billy, jumping up. 'Who's on their way?'

Denise whipped her head out of the room and closed the

door. There was a soft thud against the wood, and Strike knew that she was leaning against it, trying to hold Billy in.

'She's just talking about a delivery I'm expecting,' Strike said soothingly, getting to his feet. 'Go on about the—'

'What have you done?' yelped Billy, backing away towards the door while he repeatedly touched nose and chest. 'Who's coming?'

'Nobody's coming,' said Strike, but Billy was already trying to push the door open. Meeting resistance, he flung himself hard against it. There was a shriek from outside as Denise was thrown aside. Before Strike could get out from around the desk, Billy had sprinted through the outer door. They heard him jumping down the metal stairs three at a time and Strike, infuriated, knowing that he had no hope of catching a younger and, on the evidence, fitter man, turned and ran back into his office. Throwing up the sash window, he leaned outside just in time to see Billy whipping around the corner of the street out of sight.

'*Bollocks!*'

A man heading inside the guitar shop opposite stared around in some perplexity for the source of the noise.

Strike withdrew his head and turned to glare at Denise, who was dusting herself down in the doorway to his office. Incredibly, she looked pleased with herself.

'I tried to hold him in,' she said proudly.

'Yeah,' said Strike, exercising considerable self-restraint. 'I saw.'

'The police are on their way.'

'Fantastic.'

'Would you like a cup of tea?'

'No,' he said through gritted teeth.

'Then I think I'll go and freshen up the bathroom,' she said, adding in a whisper, 'I don't think he used the flush.'

3

I fought out that fight alone and in the completest secrecy.

Henrik Ibsen, *Rosmersholm*

As she walked along the unfamiliar Deptford street, Robin was raised to temporary light-heartedness, then wondered when she had last felt this way and knew that it had been over a year. Energised and uplifted by the afternoon sunshine, the colourful shopfronts and general bustle and noise, she was currently celebrating the fact that she never need see the inside of the Villiers Trust Clinic again.

Her therapist had been unhappy that she was terminating treatment.

'We recommend a full course,' she had said.

'I know,' Robin replied, 'but, well, I'm sorry, I think this has done me as much good as it's going to.'

The therapist's smile had been chilly.

'The CBT's been great,' Robin had said. 'It's really helped with the anxiety, I'm going to keep that up . . . '

She had taken a deep breath, eyes fixed on the woman's low-heeled Mary Janes, then forced herself to look her in the eye.

' . . . but I'm not finding this part helpful.'

Another silence had ensued. After five sessions, Robin was used to them. In normal conversation, it would be considered rude or passive aggressive to leave these long pauses and simply watch the other person, waiting for them to speak, but in psychodynamic therapy, she had learned, it was standard.

Robin's doctor had given her a referral for free treatment on the NHS, but the waiting list had been so long that she had decided, with Matthew's tight-lipped support, to pay for treatment. Matthew, she knew, was barely refraining from saying that the ideal solution would be to give up the job that had landed her with PTSD and which in his view paid far too poorly considering the dangers to which she had been exposed.

'You see,' Robin had continued with the speech she had prepared, 'my life is pretty much wall to wall with people who think they know what's best for me.'

'Well, yes,' said the therapist, in a manner that Robin felt would have been considered condescending beyond the clinic walls, 'we've discussed—'

'—and . . . '

Robin was by nature conciliatory and polite. On the other hand, she had been urged repeatedly by the therapist to speak the unvarnished truth in this dingy little room with the spider plant in its dull green pot and the man-sized tissues on the low pine table.

' . . . and to be honest,' she said, 'you feel like just another one of them.'

Another pause.

'Well,' said the therapist, with a little laugh, 'I'm here to help you reach your own conclusions about—'

'Yes, but you do it by – by *pushing* me all the time,' said Robin. 'It's combative. You challenge everything I say.'

Robin closed her eyes, as a great wave of weariness swept over her. Her muscles ached. She had spent all week putting together flat-pack furniture, heaving around boxes of books and hanging pictures.

'I come out of here,' said Robin, opening her eyes again, 'feeling wrung out. I go home to my husband, and he does it, too. He leaves big sulky silences and challenges me on the smallest things. Then I phone my mother, and it's more of the same. The only person who isn't *at me* all the time to sort myself out is—'

She pulled up short, then said:

'—is my work partner.'

'Mr Strike,' said the therapist sweetly.

It had been a matter of contention between Robin and the therapist that she had refused to discuss her relationship with Strike, other than to confirm that he was unaware of how much the Shacklewell Ripper case had affected her. Their personal relationship, she had stated firmly, was irrelevant to her present issues. The therapist had raised him in every session since, but Robin had consistently refused to engage on the subject.

'Yes,' said Robin. 'Him.'

'By your own admission you haven't told him the full extent of your anxiety.'

'So,' said Robin, ignoring the last comment, 'I really only came today to tell you I'm leaving. As I say, I've found the CBT really useful and I'm going to keep using the exercises.'

The therapist had seemed outraged that Robin wasn't even prepared to stay for the full hour, but Robin had paid for the entire session and therefore felt free to walk out, giving her what felt like a bonus hour in the day. She felt justified in not hurrying home to do more unpacking, but to buy herself a Cornetto and enjoy it as she wandered through the sun-drenched streets of her new area.

Chasing her own cheerfulness like a butterfly, because she was afraid it might escape, she turned up a quieter street, forcing herself to concentrate, to take in the unfamiliar scene. She was, after all, delighted to have left behind the old flat in West Ealing, with its many bad memories. It had become clear during his trial that the Shacklewell Ripper had been tailing and watching Robin for far longer than she had ever suspected. The police had even told her that they thought he had hung around Hastings Road, lurking behind parked cars, yards from her front door.

Desperate though she had been to move, it had taken her and Matthew eleven months to find a new place. The main problem was that Matthew had been determined to 'take a step up the property ladder', now that he had a better-paid new job and a legacy from his late mother. Robin's parents, too, had expressed a willingness to help them, given the awful associations of the old flat, but London was excruciatingly expensive. Three times had Matthew set his heart on flats that were, realistically, well out of their price range. Three times had they failed to buy what Robin could have told him would sell for thousands more than they could offer.

'It's ridiculous!' he kept saying, 'it isn't worth that!'

'It's worth whatever people are prepared to pay,' Robin had said, frustrated that an accountant didn't understand the operation of market forces. She had been ready to move anywhere, even a single room, to escape the shadow of the killer who continued to haunt her dreams.

On the point of doubling back towards the main road, her eye was caught by the opening in a brick wall, which was flanked by gateposts topped with the strangest finials she had ever seen.

A pair of gigantic, crumbling stone skulls sat on top of carved bones on gateposts, beyond which a tall square tower rose. The finials would have looked at home, Robin thought, moving closer to examine the empty black eye sockets, garnishing the front of a pirate's mansion in some fantasy film. Peering through the opening, Robin saw a church and mossy tombs lying amid an empty rose garden in full bloom.

She finished her ice cream while wandering around St Nicholas's, a strange amalgam of an old red-brick school grafted onto the rough stone tower. Finally she sat down on a wooden bench that had grown almost uncomfortably hot in the sun, stretched her aching back, drank in the delicious scent of warm roses and was suddenly transported, entirely against her will, back to the hotel suite in Yorkshire, almost a year ago, where a blood-red bouquet of roses had witnessed the aftermath of her abandonment of Matthew on the dance floor at her wedding reception.

Matthew, his father, his Aunt Sue, Robin's parents and brother Stephen had all converged on the bridal suite where Robin had retreated to escape Matthew's fury. She had been changing out of her wedding dress when they had burst in, one after another, all demanding to know what was going on.

A cacophony had ensued. Stephen, first to grasp what Matthew had done in deleting Strike's calls, started to shout at him. Geoffrey was drunkenly demanding to know why Strike had been allowed to stay for dinner given he hadn't RSVPed. Matthew was bellowing at all of them to butt out, that this was between him and Robin, while Aunt Sue said over and over, 'I've never seen a bride walk out of her first dance. *Never!* I've *never* seen a bride walk out of her first dance.'

Then Linda had finally grasped what Matthew had done, and began telling him off, too. Geoffrey had leapt to his son's defence, demanding to know why Linda wanted her daughter to go back to a man who allowed her to get stabbed. Martin had arrived, extremely drunk, and had taken a swing at Matthew for reasons that nobody had ever explained satisfactorily, and Robin had retreated to the bathroom where, incredibly, given that she had barely eaten all day, she had thrown up.

Five minutes later, she had been forced to let Matthew in because his nose was bleeding and there, with their families still shouting at each other in the next door bedroom, Matthew had asked her, a wodge of toilet roll pressed to his nostrils, to come with him to the Maldives, not as a honeymoon, not any more, but to sort things out in private, 'away,' as he put it thickly, gesturing towards the source of the yelling, 'from *this*. And there'll be press,' he added, accusingly. 'They'll be after you, for the Ripper business.'

He was cold-eyed over the bloody toilet paper, furious with her for humiliating him on the dance floor, livid with Martin for hitting him. There was nothing romantic in his invitation to board the plane. He was proposing a summit, a chance for calm discussion. If, after serious consideration, they came to the conclusion that the marriage was a mistake, they would come home at the end of the fortnight, make a joint announcement, and go their separate ways.

And at that moment, the wretched Robin, arm throbbing, shaken to the core by the feelings that had risen inside when she had felt Strike's arms around her, knowing that the press might even now be trying to track her down, had seen Matthew, if not as an ally, at least as an escape. The idea of getting on a plane, of flying out of reach of the tsunami of curiosity, gossip, anger, solicitude and unsought advice that she knew would engulf her as long as she remained in Yorkshire, was deeply appealing.

So they had left, barely speaking during the flight. What Matthew had been thinking through those long hours, she had never enquired. She knew only that she had thought about Strike. Over and again, she had returned to the memory of their embrace as she watched the clouds slide past the window.

Am I in love with him? she had asked herself repeatedly, but without reaching any firm conclusion.

Her deliberations on the subject had lasted days, an inner torment she could not reveal to Matthew as they walked on white beaches, discussing the tensions and resentments that lay between the two of them. Matthew slept on the living-room sofa at night, Robin in the net-draped double bed upstairs. Sometimes they argued, at other times they retreated into hurt and furious silences. Matthew was keeping tabs on Robin's phone, wanting to know where it was, constantly picking it up and checking it, and she knew that he was looking for messages or calls from her boss.

What made things worse was that there were none. Apparently Strike wasn't interested in talking to her. The hug on the stairs, to which her thoughts kept scampering back like a dog to a blissfully pungent lamppost, seemed to have meant far less to him than it had to her.

Night after night, Robin walked by herself on the beach, listening to the sea's deep breathing, her injured arm sweating beneath its rubber protective brace, her phone left at the villa so that Matthew had no excuse to tail her and find out whether she was talking secretly to Strike.

But on the seventh night, with Matthew back at the villa, she had decided to call Strike. Almost without acknowledging it to herself, she had formulated a plan. There was a landline at the bar and she knew the office number off by heart. It would be diverted to Strike's mobile automatically.

What she was going to say when she reached him, she didn't know, but she was sure that if she heard him speak, the truth about her feelings would be revealed to her. As the phone rang in distant London, Robin's mouth had become dry.

The phone was answered, but nobody spoke for a few seconds. Robin listened to the sounds of movement, then heard a giggle, and then at last somebody spoke.

'Hello? This is Cormy-Warmy—'

As the woman broke into loud, raucous laughter, Robin heard Strike somewhere in the background, half-amused, half-annoyed and certainly drunk:

'Gimme that! Seriously, give it—'

Robin had slammed the receiver back onto its rest. Sweat had broken out on her face and chest: she felt ashamed, foolish, humiliated. He was with another woman. The laughter had been unmistakably intimate. The unknown girl had been teasing him, answering his mobile, calling him (how revolting) 'Cormy'.

She would deny phoning him, she resolved, if ever Strike asked her about the dropped call. She would lie through her teeth, pretend not to know what he was talking about . . .

The sound of the woman on the phone had affected her like a hard slap. If Strike could have taken somebody to bed so soon after their hug – and she would have staked her life on the fact that the girl, whoever she was, had either just slept with Strike, or was about to – then he wasn't sitting in London torturing himself about his true feelings for Robin Ellacott.

The salt on her lips made her thirsty as she trudged through the night, wearing a deep groove in the soft white sand as the waves broke endlessly beside her. Wasn't it possible, she asked herself, when she was cried out at last, that she was confusing gratitude and friendship with something deeper? That she had mistaken her love of detection for love of the man who had given her the job? She admired Strike, of course, and was immensely fond of him. They had passed through many intense experiences together, so that it was natural to feel close to him, but was that love?

Alone in the balmy, mosquito-buzzing night, while the waves sighed on the shore and she cradled her aching arm, Robin reminded herself bleakly that she had had very little experience with men for a woman approaching her twenty-eighth birthday. Matthew was all she had ever known, her only sexual partner, a place of safety to her for ten long years now. If she *had* developed a crush on Strike – she employed the old-fashioned word her mother might have used – mightn't it also be the natural side effect of the lack of variety and experimentation most women of her age had enjoyed? For so long faithful to Matthew, hadn't she been bound to look up one day and remember that there were other lives, other choices? Hadn't she been long overdue to notice that Matthew was not the only man in the world? Strike, she told herself, was simply the one with whom she had been spending the most time, so naturally it had been he onto whom she projected her wondering, her curiosity, her dissatisfaction with Matthew.

Having, as she told herself, talked sense into that part of her that kept yearning for Strike, she reached a hard decision on the eighth evening of her honeymoon. She wanted to go home early and announce their separation to their families. She must tell Matthew that it had nothing to do with anybody else, but after agonising and serious reflection, she did not believe they were well suited enough to continue in the marriage.

She could still remember her feeling of mingled panic and dread as she had pushed open the cabin door, braced for a fight that had never materialised. Matthew had been sitting slumped on the sofa and when he saw her, he mumbled, 'Mum?'

His face, arms and legs had been shining with sweat. As she moved towards him, she saw an ugly black tracing of veins up the inside of his left arm, as though somebody had filled them with ink.

'Matt?'

Hearing her, he had realised that she was not his dead mother.

'Don't . . . feel well, Rob . . . '

She had dashed for the phone, called the hotel, asked for a doctor. By the time he arrived, Matthew was drifting in and out of delirium. They had found the scratch on the back of his hand and, worried, concluded that he might have cellulitis, which Robin could tell, from the faces of the worried doctor and nurse, was serious. Matthew kept seeing figures moving in the shadowy corners of the cabin, people who weren't there.

'Who's that?' he kept asking Robin. 'Who's that over there?'

'There's nobody else here, Matt.'

Now she was holding his hand while the nurse and doctor discussed hospitalisation.

'Don't leave me, Rob.'

'I'm not going to leave you.'

She had meant that she was going nowhere just now, not that she would stay for ever, but Matthew had begun to cry.

'Oh, thank God. I thought you were going to walk . . . I love you, Rob. I know I fucked up, but I love you . . . '

The doctor gave Matthew oral antibiotics and went to make telephone calls. Delirious, Matthew clung to his wife, thanking her. Sometimes he drifted into a state where, again, he thought he saw shadows moving in the empty corners of the room, and twice more he muttered about his dead mother. Alone in the velvety blackness of the tropical night, Robin listened to winged insects colliding with the screens at the windows, alternately comforting and watching over the man she had loved since she was seventeen.

It hadn't been cellulitis. The infection had responded, over the next twenty-four hours, to antibiotics. As he recovered from the sudden, violent illness, Matthew watched her constantly, weak and vulnerable as she had never seen him, afraid, she knew, that her promise to stay had been temporary.

'We can't throw it all away, can we?' he had asked her hoarsely from the bed where the doctor had insisted he stay. 'All these years?'

She had let him talk about the good times, the shared times, and she had reminded herself about the giggling girl who had called Strike 'Cormy'. She envisioned going home and asking for an annulment, because the marriage had still not been consummated. She remembered the money her parents had spent on the wedding day she had hated.

Bees buzzed in the churchyard roses around her as Robin wondered, for the thousandth time, where she would be right now if Matthew hadn't scratched himself on coral. Most of her now-terminated therapy sessions had been full of her need to talk about the doubts that had plagued her ever since she had agreed to remain married.

In the months that had followed, and especially when she and Matthew were getting on reasonably well, it seemed to her that it had been right to give the marriage a fair trial, but she never forgot to think of it in terms of a trial, and this in itself sometimes led her, sleepless at night, to castigate herself for the pusillanimous failure to pull herself free once Matthew had recovered.

She had never explained to Strike what had happened, why she had agreed to try and keep the marriage afloat. Perhaps that was why their friendship had grown so cold and distant. When she had returned from her honeymoon, it was to find Strike changed towards her – and perhaps, she acknowledged, she had changed towards him, too, because of what she had heard on the line when she had called, in desperation, from the Maldives bar.

'Sticking with it, then, are you?' he had said roughly, after a glance at her ring finger.

His tone had nettled her, as had the fact that he had never asked why she was trying, never asked about her home life from that point onwards, never so much as hinted that he remembered the hug on the stairs.

Whether because Strike had arranged matters that way or not, they had not worked a case together since that of the Shacklewell Ripper. Imitating her senior partner, Robin had retreated into a cool professionalism.

But sometimes she was afraid that he no longer valued her as he once had, now that she had proven herself so conventional and cowardly. There had been an awkward conversation a few months ago in which he had suggested that she take time off, asked whether she felt she was fully recovered after the knife attack. Taking this as a slight upon her bravery, afraid that she would again find herself sidelined, losing the only part of her life that she currently found fulfilling, she had insisted that she was perfectly well and redoubled her professional efforts.

The muted mobile in her bag vibrated. Robin slipped her hand inside and looked to see who was calling. Strike. She also noticed that he had called earlier, while she was saying a joyful goodbye to the Villiers Trust Clinic.

'Hi,' she said. 'I missed you earlier, sorry.'

'Not a problem. Move gone all right?'

'Fine,' she said.

'Just wanted to let you know, I've hired us a new subcontractor. Name of Sam Barclay.'

'Great,' said Robin, watching a fly shimmering on a fat, blush-pink rose. 'What's his background?'

'Army,' said Strike.

'Military police?'

'Er – not exactly.'

As he told her the story of Sam Barclay, Robin found herself grinning.

'So you've hired a dope-smoking painter and decorator?'

'Vaping, dope *vaping*,' Strike corrected her, and Robin could tell that he was grinning, too. 'He's on a health kick. New baby.'

'Well, he sounds . . . interesting.'

She waited, but Strike did not speak.

'I'll see you Saturday night, then,' she said.

Robin had felt obliged to invite Strike to her and Matthew's house-warming party, because she had given their most regular and reliable subcontractor, Andy Hutchins, an invitation, and felt it would be odd to leave out Strike. She had been surprised when he had accepted.

'Yeah, see you then.'

'Is Lorelei coming?' Robin asked, striving for casualness, but not sure she had succeeded.

Back in central London, Strike thought he detected a sardonic note in the question, as though challenging him to admit that his girlfriend had a ludicrous moniker. He would once have pulled her up on it, asked what her problem was with the name 'Lorelei', enjoyed sparring with her, but this was dangerous territory.

'Yeah, she's coming. The invitation was to both—'

'Yes, of course it was,' said Robin hastily. 'All right, I'll see you—'

'Hang on,' said Strike.

He was alone in the office, because he had sent Denise home early. The temp had not wanted to leave: she was paid by the hour, after all, and only after Strike had assured her that he would pay for a full day had she gathered up all her possessions, talking nonstop all the while.

'Funny thing happened this afternoon,' said Strike.

Robin listened intently, without interrupting, to Strike's vivid account of the brief visit of Billy. By the end of it, she had forgotten to worry about Strike's coolness. Indeed, he now sounded like the Strike of a year ago.

'He was definitely mentally ill,' said Strike, his eyes on the clear sky beyond the window. 'Possibly psychotic.'

'Yeah, but—'

'I know,' said Strike. He picked up the pad from which Billy had ripped his half-written address and turned it absently in his free hand. 'Is he mentally ill, *so* he thinks he saw a kid strangled? Or is he mentally ill *and* he saw a kid strangled?'

Neither spoke for a while, during which time both turned over Billy's story in their minds, knowing that the other was doing the same. This brief, companionable spell of reflection ended abruptly when a cocker spaniel, which Robin had not noticed as it came snuffling through the roses, laid its cold nose without warning on her bare knee and she shrieked.

'What the fuck?'

'Nothing – a dog—'

'Where are you?'

'In a graveyard.'

'What? Why?'

'Just exploring the area. I'd better go,' she said, getting to her feet. 'There's another flat-pack waiting for me at home.'

'Right you are,' said Strike, with a return to his usual briskness. 'See you Saturday.'

'I'm so sorry,' said the cocker spaniel's elderly owner, as Robin slid her mobile back into her bag. 'Are you frightened of dogs?'

'Not at all,' said Robin, smiling and patting the dog's soft golden head. 'He surprised me, that's all.'

As she headed back past the giant skulls towards her new home, Robin thought about Billy, whom Strike had described with such vividness that Robin felt as though she had met him, too.

So deeply absorbed in her thoughts was she, that for the first time all week, Robin forgot to glance up at the White Swan pub as she passed it. High above the street, on the corner of the building, was a single carved swan, which reminded Robin, every time she passed it, of her calamitous wedding day.

4

But what do you propose to do in the town, then?

Henrik Ibsen, *Rosmersholm*

Six and a half miles away, Strike set his mobile down on his desk and lit a cigarette. Robin's interest in his story had been soothing after the interview he had endured half an hour after Billy had fled. The two policemen who had answered Denise's call had seemed to relish their opportunity to make the famous Cormoran Strike admit his fallibility, taking their time as they ascertained that he had succeeded in finding out neither full name nor address of the probably psychotic Billy.

The late afternoon sun hit the notebook on his desk at an angle, revealing faint indentations. Strike dropped his cigarette into an ashtray he had stolen long ago from a German bar, picked up the notepad and tilted it this way and that, trying to make out the letters formed by the impressions, then reached for a pencil and lightly shaded over them. Untidy capital letters were soon revealed, clearly spelling the words 'Charlemont Road'. Billy had pressed less hard on the house or flat number than the street name. One of the faint indents looked like either a 5 or an incomplete 8, but the spacing suggested more than one figure, or possibly a letter.

Strike's incurable predilection for getting to the root of puzzling incidents tended to inconvenience him quite as much as other people. Hungry and tired though he was, and despite the fact that he had sent his temp away so he could shut up the office, he tore the paper carrying the revealed street name off the pad and headed into the outer room, where he switched the computer back on.

There were several Charlemont Roads in the UK, but on the assumption that Billy was unlikely to have the means to travel very far, he suspected that the one in East Ham had to be the right one. Online records showed two Williams living there, but both were over sixty. Remembering that Billy had been scared that Strike might turn up at 'Jimmy's place', he had searched for Jimmy and then James, which turned up the details of James Farraday, 49.

Strike made a note of Farraday's address beneath Billy's indented scribbles, though not at all confident that Farraday was the man he sought. For one thing, his house number contained no fives or eights and, for another, Billy's extreme unkemptness suggested that whomever he lived with must take a fairly relaxed attitude to his personal hygiene. Farraday lived with a wife and what appeared to be two daughters.

Strike turned off the computer, but continued to stare abstractedly at the dark screen, thinking about Billy's story. It was the detail of the pink blanket that kept nagging at him. It seemed such a specific, unglamorous detail for a psychotic delusion.

Remembering that he needed to be up early in the morning for a paying job, he pulled himself to his feet. Before leaving the office, he inserted the piece of paper bearing both the impressions of Billy's handwriting and Farraday's address into his wallet.

*

London, which had recently been at the epicentre of the Queen's Diamond Jubilee celebrations, was preparing to host the Olympics. Union Jacks and the London 2012 logo were everywhere – on signs, banners, bunting, keyrings, mugs and umbrellas – while jumbles of Olympic merchandise cluttered virtually every shop window. In Strike's opinion, the logo resembled shards of fluorescent glass randomly thrown together and he was equally unenamoured of the official mascots, which looked to him like a pair of cycloptic molars.

There was a tinge of excitement and nervousness about the capital, born, no doubt, of the perennially British dread that the nation might make a fool of itself. Complaints about non-availability of Olympics tickets were a dominant theme in conversation, unsuccessful applicants decrying the lottery that was supposed to have given everybody a fair and equal chance of watching events live. Strike, who had hoped to see some boxing, had not managed to get tickets, but laughed out loud at his old school friend Nick's offer to take his place at the dressage, which Nick's wife Ilsa was overjoyed to have bagged.

Harley Street, where Strike was due to spend Friday running surveillance on a cosmetic surgeon, remained untouched by Olympic fever. The grand Victorian façades presented their usual implacable faces to the world, unsullied by garish logos or flags.

Strike, who was wearing his best Italian suit for the job, took up a position near the doorway of a building opposite and pretended to be talking on his mobile, actually keeping watch over the entrance of the expensive consulting rooms of two partners, one of whom was Strike's client.

'Dodgy Doc', as Strike had nicknamed his quarry, was taking his time living up to his name. Possibly he had been scared out of his unethical behaviour by his partner, who had confronted him after realising that Dodgy had recently performed two breast augmentations that had not been run through the business's books. Suspecting the worst, the senior partner had come to Strike for help.

'His justification was feeble, full of holes. He is,' said the white-haired surgeon, stiff-lipped but full of foreboding, 'and always has been a . . . ah . . . womaniser. I checked his internet history before confronting him and found a website where young women solicit cash contributions for their cosmetic enhancements, in return for explicit pictures. I fear . . . I hardly know what . . . but it might be that he has made an arrangement with these women that is not . . . monetary. Two of the younger women had been asked to call a number I did not recognise, but which suggested surgery might be arranged free in return for an "exclusive arrangement".'

Strike had not so far witnessed Dodgy meeting any women outside his regular hours. He spent Mondays and Fridays in his Harley Street consulting rooms and the mid-week at the private hospital where he operated. Whenever Strike had tailed him outside his places of work, he had merely taken short walks to purchase chocolate, to which he seemed addicted. Every night, he drove his Bentley home to his wife and children in Gerrards Cross, tailed by Strike in his old blue BMW.

Tonight, both surgeons would be attending a Royal College of Surgeons dinner with their wives, so Strike had left his BMW in its expensive garage. The hours rolled by in tedium, Strike mostly concerned with shifting the weight off his prosthesis at regular intervals as he leaned up against railings, parking meters and doorways. A steady trickle of clients pressed the bell at Dodgy's door and were admitted, one by one. All were female and most were sleek and well-groomed. At five o'clock, Strike's mobile vibrated in his breast pocket and he saw a text from his client.

Safe to clock off, about to leave with him for the Dorchester.

Perversely, Strike hung around, watching as the partners left the building some fifteen minutes later. His client was tall and white-haired; Dodgy, a sleek, dapper olive-skinned man with shiny black hair, who wore three-piece suits. Strike watched them get into a taxi and leave, then yawned, stretched and contemplated heading home, possibly with a takeaway.

Almost against his will, he pulled out his wallet and extracted the piece of crumpled paper on which he had managed to reveal Billy's street name.

All day, at the back of his mind, he had thought he might go and seek out Billy in Charlemont Road if Dodgy Doc left work early, but he was tired and his leg sore. If Lorelei knew that he had the evening off, she would expect Strike to call. On the other hand, they were going to Robin's housewarming together tomorrow night and if he spent tonight at Lorelei's, it would be hard to extricate himself tomorrow, after the party. He never spent two nights in a row at Lorelei's flat, even when the opportunity had occurred. He liked to set limits on her rights to his time.

As though hoping to be dissuaded by the weather, he glanced up at the clear June sky and sighed. The evening was clear and perfect, the agency so busy that he did not know when he would next have a few hours to spare. If he wanted to visit Charlemont Road, it would have to be tonight.

5

I can quite understand your having a horror of public meetings and . . . of the rabble that frequents them.

Henrik Ibsen, *Rosmersholm*

His journey coinciding with rush hour, it took Strike over an hour to travel from Harley Street to East Ham. By the time he had located Charlemont Road his stump was aching and the sight of the long residential street made him regret that he was not the kind of man who could simply write off Billy as a mental case.

The terraced houses had a motley appearance: some were bare brick, others painted or pebble-dashed. Union Jacks hung at windows: further evidence of Olympic fever or relics of the Royal Jubilee. The small plots in front of the houses had been made into pocket gardens or dumps for debris, according to preference. Halfway along the road lay a dirty old mattress, abandoned to whoever wanted to deal with it.

His first glimpse of James Farraday's residence did not encourage Strike to hope that he had reached journey's end, because it was one of the best-maintained houses in the street. A tiny porch with coloured glass had been added around the front door, ruched net curtains hung at each window and the brass letterbox gleamed in the sunshine. Strike pressed the plastic doorbell and waited.

After a short wait, a harried woman opened the door, releasing a silver tabby, which appeared to have been waiting, coiled behind the door, for the first chance to escape. The woman's cross expression sat awkwardly above an apron printed with a 'Love Is . . . ' cartoon. A strong odour of cooking meat wafted out of the house.

'Hi,' said Strike, salivating at the smell. 'Don't know whether you can help me. I'm trying to find Billy.'

'You've got the wrong address. There's no Billy here.'

She made to close the door.

'He said he was staying with Jimmy,' said Strike, as the gap narrowed.

'There's no Jimmy here, either.'

'Sorry, I thought somebody called James—'

'Nobody calls him Jimmy. You've got the wrong house.'

She closed the door.

Strike and the silver tabby eyed each other; in the cat's case, superciliously, before it sat down on the mat and began to groom itself with an air of dismissing Strike from its thoughts.

Strike returned to the pavement, where he lit a cigarette and looked up and down the street. By his estimate there were two hundred houses on Charlemont Road. How long would it take to knock on every household's door? More time than he had this evening, was the unfortunate answer, and more time than he was likely to have any time soon. He walked on, frustrated and increasingly sore, glancing in through windows and scrutinising passers-by for a resemblance to the man he had met the previous day. Twice, he asked people entering or leaving their houses whether they knew 'Jimmy and Billy', whose address he claimed to have lost. Both said no.

Strike trudged on, trying not to limp.

At last he reached a section of houses that had been bought up and converted into flats. Pairs of front doors stood crammed side by side and the front plots had been concreted over.

Strike slowed down. A torn sheet of A4 had been pinned to one of the shabbiest doors, from which the white paint was peeling. A faint but familiar prickle of interest that he would never have dignified with the name 'hunch' led Strike to the door.

The scribbled message read:

7.30 Meeting moved from pub to Well Community Centre in Vicarage Lane – end of street turn left
Jimmy Knight

Strike lifted the sheet of paper with a finger, saw a house number ending in 5, let the note fall again and moved to peer through the dusty downstairs window.

An old bed sheet had been pinned up to block out sunlight, but a corner had fallen down. Tall enough to squint through the uncovered portion of glass, Strike saw a slice of empty room containing an open sofa bed with a stained duvet on it, a pile of clothes in the corner and a portable TV standing on a cardboard box. The carpet was obscured by a multitude of empty beer cans and overflowing ashtrays. This seemed promising. He returned to the peeling front door, raised a large fist and knocked.

Nobody answered, nor did he hear any sign of movement within.

Strike checked the note on the door again, then set off. Turning left into Vicarage Lane, he saw the community centre right in front of him, 'The Well' spelled out boldly in shining Perspex letters.

An elderly man wearing a Mao cap and a wispy, greying

beard was standing just outside the glass doors with a pile of leaflets in his hand. As Strike approached, the man, whose T-shirt bore the washed-out face of Che Guevara, eyed him askance. Though tieless, Strike's Italian suit struck an inappropriately formal note. When it became clear that the community centre was Strike's destination, the leaflet-holder shuffled sideways to bar the entrance.

'I know I'm late,' said Strike, with well-feigned annoyance, 'but I've only just found out the bloody venue's been changed.'

His assurance and his size both seemed to disconcert the man in the Mao cap, who nevertheless appeared to feel that instant capitulation to a man in a suit would be unworthy of him.

'Who are you representing?'

Strike had already taken a swift inventory of the capitalised words visible on the leaflets clutched against the other man's chest: DISSENT – DISOBEDIENCE – DISRUPTION and, rather incongruously, ALLOTMENTS. There was also a crude cartoon of five obese businessmen blowing cigar smoke to form the Olympic rings.

'My dad,' Strike said. 'He's worried they're going to concrete over his allotment.'

'Ah,' said the bearded man. He moved aside. Strike tugged a leaflet out of his hand and entered the community centre.

There was nobody in sight except for a grey-haired woman of West Indian origin, who was peering through an inner door that she had opened an inch. Strike could just hear a female voice in the room beyond. Her words were hard to distinguish, but her cadences suggested a tirade. Becoming aware that somebody was standing immediately behind her, the woman turned. The sight of Strike's suit seemed to affect her in opposite fashion to the bearded man at the door.

'Are you from the Olympics?' she whispered.

'No,' said Strike. 'Just interested.'

She eased the door open to admit him.

Around forty people were sitting on plastic chairs. Strike took the nearest vacant seat and scanned the backs of the heads in front of him for the matted, shoulder-length hair of Billy.

A table for speakers had been set up at the front. A young woman was currently pacing up and down in front of it as she addressed the audience. Her hair was dyed the same bright red shade as Coco's, Strike's hard-to-shake one-night stand, and she was speaking in a series of unfinished sentences, occasionally losing herself in secondary clauses and forgetting to drop her 'h's. Strike had the impression that she had been talking for a long time.

'. . . think of the squatters and artists who're all being – 'cause this is a proper community, right, and then in they come wiv like clipboards and it's, like, get out if you know what's good for you, thin end of the, innit, oppressive laws, it's the Trojan 'orse – it's a coordinated campaign of, like . . .'

Half the audience looked like students. Among the older members, Strike saw men and women who he marked down as committed protestors, some wearing T-shirts with leftist slogans like his friend on the door. Here and there he saw unlikely figures who he guessed were ordinary members of the community who had not taken kindly to the Olympics' arrival in East London: arty types who had perhaps been squatting, and an elderly couple, who were currently whispering to each other and who Strike thought might be genuinely worried about their allotment. Watching them resume the attitudes of meek endurance appropriate to those sitting in church, Strike guessed that they had agreed that they could not easily leave without drawing too much attention to themselves. A much-pierced boy covered in anarchist tattoos audibly picked his teeth.

Behind the girl who was speaking sat three others: an older woman and two men, who were talking quietly to each other. One of them was at least sixty, barrel-chested and lantern-jawed, with the pugnacious air of a man who had served his time on picket lines and in successful show-downs with recalcitrant management. Something about the dark, deep-set eyes of the other made Strike scan the leaflet in his hand, seeking confirmation of an immediate suspicion.

COMMUNITY OLYMPIC RESISTANCE (CORE)

15 June 2012

7.30pm White Horse Pub East Ham E6 6EJ

Speakers:

Lilian Sweeting	**Wilderness Preservation, E. London**
Walter Frett	**Workers' Alliance/CORE activist**
Flick Purdue	**Anti-poverty campaigner/CORE activist**
Jimmy Knight	**Real Socialist Party/CORE organizer**

Heavy stubble and a general air of scruffiness notwithstanding, the man with the sunken eyes was nowhere near as filthy as Billy and his hair had certainly been cut within the last couple of months. He appeared to be in his mid-thirties, and while squarer of face and more muscular, he had the same dark hair and pale skin as Strike's visitor. On the available evidence, Strike would have put a sizeable bet on Jimmy Knight being Billy's older brother.

Jimmy finished his muttered conversation with his Workers' Alliance colleague, then leaned back in his seat, thick arms folded, wearing an expression of abstraction that showed he was not listening to the young woman any more than her increasingly fidgety audience.

Strike now became aware that he was under observation from a nondescript man sitting in the row in front of him. When Strike met the man's pale blue gaze, he redirected his attention hastily towards Flick, who was still talking. Taking note of the blue-eyed man's clean jeans, plain T-shirt and the short, neat hair, Strike thought that he would have done better to have forgone the morning's close shave, but perhaps, for a ramshackle operation like CORE, the Met had not considered it worthwhile to send their best. The presence of a plainclothes officer was to be expected, of course. Any group currently planning to disrupt or resist the arrangements for the Olympics was likely to be under surveillance.

A short distance from the plainclothes policeman sat a professional-looking young Asian man in shirtsleeves. Tall and thin, he was watching the speaker fixedly, chewing the fingernails of his left hand. As Strike watched, the man gave a little start and took his finger away from his mouth. He had made it bleed.

'All right,' said a man loudly. The audience, recognising a voice of authority, sat a little straighter. 'Thanks very much, Flick.'

Jimmy Knight got to his feet, leading the unenthusiastic applause for Flick, who walked back around the table and sat down in the empty chair between the two men.

In his well-worn jeans and unironed T-shirt, Jimmy Knight reminded Strike of the men his dead mother had taken as lovers. He might have been the bass player in a grime band or a good-looking roadie, with his muscled arms and tattoos. Strike noticed that the back of the nondescript blue-eyed man had tensed. He had been waiting for Jimmy.

'Evening, everyone, and thanks very much for coming.'

His personality filled the room like the first bar of a hit song. Strike knew him from those few words as the kind of man who, in the army, was either outstandingly useful or an insubordinate bastard. Jimmy's accent, like Flick's, revealed an uncertain provenance. Strike thought that Cockney might have been grafted, in his case more successfully, onto a faint, rural burr.

'So, the Olympic threshing machine's moved into East London!'

His burning eyes swept the newly attentive crowd.

'Flattening houses, knocking cyclists to their deaths, churning up land that belongs to all of us. Or it did.

'You've heard from Lilian what they're doing to animal and insect habitats. I'm here to talk about the encroachment on human communities. They're concreting over our common land, and for what? Are they putting up the social housing or the hospitals we need? Of course not! No, we're getting stadiums costing billions, showcases for the capitalist system, ladies and gentlemen. We're being asked to celebrate elitism while, beyond the barriers, ordinary people's freedoms are encroached, eroded, removed.

'They tell us we should be celebrating the Olympics, all the glossy press releases the right-wing media gobbles up and regurgitates. Fetishise the flag, whip up the middle classes into a frenzy of jingoism! Come worship our glorious medallists – a shiny gold for everyone who passes over a big enough bribe with a pot of someone else's piss!'

There was a murmur of agreement. A few people clapped.

'We're supposed to get excited about the public schoolboys and girls who got to practise sports while the rest of us were having our playing fields sold off for cash! Sycophancy should be our national Olympic sport! We deify people who've had millions invested in them because they can ride a bike, when they've sold themselves as fig leaves for all the planet-raping, tax-dodging bastards who are queuing up to get their names on the barriers – barriers shutting working people off their own land!'

The applause, in which Strike, the old couple beside him and the Asian man did not join, was as much for the performance as the words. Jimmy's slightly thuggish but handsome face was alive with righteous anger.

'See this?' he said, sweeping from the table behind him a piece of paper with the jagged '2012' that Strike disliked so much. 'Welcome to the Olympics, my friends, a fascist's wet dream. See the logo? D'you see it? It's a broken swastika!'

The crowd laughed and applauded some more, masking the loud rumble of Strike's stomach. He wondered whether there might be a takeaway nearby. He had even started to calculate whether he might have time to leave, buy food and return, when the grey-haired West Indian woman whom he had seen earlier opened the door to the hall and propped it open. Her expression clearly indicated that CORE had now outstayed its welcome.

Jimmy, however, was still in full flow.

'This so-called celebration of the Olympic spirit, of fair play and amateurism is normalising repression and authoritarianism! Wake up: London's being militarised! The British state, which has honed the tactics of colonisation and invasion for centuries, has seized on the Olympics as the perfect excuse to deploy police, army, helicopters and guns against ordinary citizens! One thousand extra CCTV cameras – extra laws hurried through – and you think they'll be repealed when this carnival of capitalism moves on?

'Join us!' shouted Jimmy, as the community centre worker edged along the wall towards the front of the hall, nervous but determined. 'CORE is part of a broader global justice movement that meets repression with resistance! We're making common cause with all leftist, anti-oppressive movements across the capital! We're going to be staging lawful demonstrations and using every tool of peaceful protest still permitted to us in what is rapidly becoming an occupied city!'

More applause followed, though the elderly couple beside Strike seemed thoroughly miserable.

'All right, all right, I know,' added Jimmy to the community centre worker, who had now reached the front of the audience and was gesturing timidly. 'They want us out,' Jimmy told the crowd, smirking and shaking his head. 'Of course they do. Of course.'

A few people hissed at the community centre worker.

'Anyone who wants to hear more,' said Jimmy, 'we'll be in the pub down the road. Address on your leaflets!'

Most of the crowd applauded. The plainclothes policeman got to his feet. The elderly couple was already scuttling towards the door.

6

I . . . have the reputation of being a wicked fanatic, I am told.

Henrik Ibsen, *Rosmersholm*

Chairs clattered, bags were hoisted onto shoulders. The bulk of the audience began to head for the doors at the back, but some appeared reluctant to leave. Strike took a few steps towards Jimmy, hoping to talk to him, but was outpaced by the young Asian man, who was striding jerkily towards the activist with an air of nervous determination. Jimmy exchanged a few more words with the man from the Workers' Alliance, then noticed the newcomer, bade Walter goodbye and moved forward with every appearance of goodwill to speak to what he clearly assumed was a convert.

As soon as the Asian man began to speak, however, Jimmy's expression clouded. As they talked in low voices in the middle of the rapidly emptying room, Flick and a cluster of young people loitered nearby, waiting for Jimmy. They seemed to consider themselves above manual labour. The community centre worker cleared away chairs alone.

'Let me do that,' Strike offered, taking three from her and

ignoring the sharp twinge in his knee as he hoisted them onto a tall stack.

'Thanks very much,' she panted. 'I don't think we'll be letting this lot—'

She allowed Walter and a few others to pass before continuing. None of them thanked her.

'—use the centre again,' she finished resentfully. 'I didn't realise what they were all about. Their leaflet's on about civil disobedience and I don't know what else.'

'Pro-Olympics, are you?' Strike asked, placing a chair onto a pile.

'My granddaughter's in a running club,' she said. 'We got tickets. She can't wait.'

Jimmy was still locked in conversation with the young Asian man. A minor argument seemed to have developed. Jimmy seemed tense, his eyes shifting constantly around the room, either seeking an escape or checking that nobody else was within earshot. The hall was emptying. The two men began to move towards the exit. Strike strained his ears to hear what they were saying to each other, but the clumping footsteps of Jimmy's acolytes on the wooden floor obliterated all but a few words.

'. . . for years, mate, all right?' Jimmy was saying angrily. 'So do whatever the fuck you want, you're the one who volunteered yourself . . .'

They passed out of earshot. Strike helped the community centre volunteer stack the last of the chairs and, as she turned off the light, asked for directions to the White Horse.

Five minutes later, and in spite of his recent resolution to eat more healthily, Strike bought a bag of chips at a takeaway and proceeded along White Horse Road, at the end of which he had been told he would find the eponymous pub.

As he ate, Strike pondered the best way to open conversation with Jimmy Knight. As the reaction of the elderly Che Guevara fan on the door had shown, Strike's current attire did not tend to foster trust with anti-capitalist protestors. Jimmy had the air of an experienced hard-left activist and was probably anticipating official interest in his activities in the highly charged atmosphere preceding the opening of the Games. Indeed, Strike could see the nondescript, blue-eyed man walking behind Jimmy, hands in his jean pockets. Strike's first job would be to reassure Jimmy that he was not there to investigate CORE.

The White Horse turned out to be an ugly prefabricated building, which stood on a busy junction facing a large park. A white war memorial with neatly ranged poppy wreaths at its base rose like an eternal reproach to the outside drinking area opposite, where old cigarette butts lay thickly on cracked concrete riven with weeds. Drinkers were milling around the front of the pub, all smoking. Strike spotted Jimmy, Flick and several others standing in a group in front of a window that was decorated with an enormous West Ham banner. The tall young Asian man was nowhere to be seen, but the plainclothes policeman loitered alone on the periphery of their group.

Strike went inside to fetch a pint. The décor inside the pub consisted mostly of Cross of St George flags and more West Ham paraphernalia. Having bought a pint of John Smith's, Strike returned to the forecourt, lit a fresh cigarette and advanced on the group around Jimmy. He was at Flick's shoulder before they realised that the large stranger in a suit wanted something from them. All talk ceased as suspicion flared on every face.

'Hi,' said Strike, 'my name's Cormoran Strike. Any chance of a quick word, Jimmy? It's about Billy.'

'Billy?' repeated Jimmy sharply. 'Why?'

'I met him yesterday. I'm a private detect—'

'Chizzle's sent him!' gasped Flick, turning, frightened, to Jimmy.

''K'up!' he growled.

While the rest of the group surveyed Strike with a mixture of curiosity and hostility, Jimmy beckoned to Strike to follow him to the edge of the crowd. To Strike's surprise, Flick tagged along. Men with buzz cuts and West Ham tops nodded at the activist as he passed. Jimmy came to a halt beside two old white bollards topped by horse heads, checked that nobody else was within earshot, then addressed Strike.

'What did you say your name was again?'

'Cormoran, Cormoran Strike. Is Billy your brother?'

'Younger brother, yeah,' said Jimmy. 'Did you say he came to see you?'

'Yep. Yesterday afternoon.'

'You're a private—?'

'Detective. Yes.'

Strike saw dawning recognition in Flick's eyes. She had a plump, pale face that would have been innocent without the savage eyeliner and the uncombed tomato-red hair. She turned quickly to Jimmy again.

'Jimmy, he's—'

'Shacklewell Ripper?' asked Jimmy, eyeing Strike over his lighter as he lit another cigarette. 'Lula Landry?'

'That's me,' said Strike.

Out of the corner of Strike's eye, he noticed Flick's eyes travelling down his body to his lower legs. Her mouth twisted in seeming contempt.

'Billy came to see you?' repeated Jimmy. 'Why?'

'He told me he'd witnessed a kid being strangled,' said Strike.

Jimmy blew out smoke in angry gusts.

'Yeah. He's fucked in the head. Schizoid affective disorder.'

'He seemed ill,' agreed Strike.

'Is that all he told you? That he saw a kid being strangled?'

'Seemed enough to be getting on with,' said Strike.

Jimmy's lips curved in a humourless smile.

'You didn't believe him, did you?'

'No,' said Strike truthfully, 'but I don't think he should be roaming the streets in that condition. He needs help.'

'I don't think he's any worse than usual, do you?' Jimmy asked Flick, with a somewhat artificial air of dispassionate enquiry.

'No,' she said, turning to address Strike with barely concealed animosity. 'He has ups and downs. He's all right if he takes his meds.'

Her accent had become markedly more middle-class away from the rest of their friends. Strike noticed that she had painted eyeliner over a clump of sleep in the corner of one eye. Strike, who had spent large portions of his childhood living in squalor, found a disregard for hygiene hard to like, except in those people so unhappy or ill that cleanliness became an irrelevance.

'Ex-army, aren't you?' she asked, but Jimmy spoke over her.

'How did Billy know how to find you?'

'Directory enquiries?' suggested Strike. 'I don't live in a bat cave.'

'Billy doesn't know how to use directory enquiries.'

'He managed to find my office OK.'

'There's no dead kid,' Jimmy said abruptly. 'It's all in his head. He goes on about it when he's having an episode. Didn't you see his tic?'

Jimmy imitated, with brutal accuracy, the compulsive nose to chest movement of a twitching hand. Flick laughed.

'Yeah, I saw that,' said Strike, unsmiling. 'You don't know where he is, then?'

'Haven't seen him since yesterday morning. What do you want him for?'

'Like I say, he didn't seem in any fit state to be wandering around on his own.'

'Very public spirited of you,' said Jimmy. 'Rich and famous detective worrying about our Bill.'

Strike said nothing.

'Army,' Flick repeated, 'weren't you?'

'I was,' said Strike, looking down at her. 'How's that relevant?'

'Just saying.' She had flushed a little in her righteous anger. 'Haven't always been this worried about people getting hurt, have you?'

Strike, who was familiar with people who shared Flick's views, said nothing. She would probably believe him if he told her he had joined the forces in the hope of bayoneting children.

Jimmy, who also seemed disinclined to hear more of Flick's opinions on the military, said:

'Billy'll be fine. He crashes at ours sometimes, then goes off. Does it all the time.'

'Where does he stay when he's not with you?'

'Friends,' said Jimmy, shrugging. 'I don't know all their names.' Then, contradicting himself, 'I'll ring around tonight, make sure he's OK.'

'Right you are,' said Strike, downing his pint and handing the empty to a tattooed bar worker, who was marching through the forecourt, grabbing glasses from all who had finished with them. Strike took a last drag on his cigarette, dropped it to join the thousands of its brethren on the cracked forecourt, ground it out beneath his prosthetic foot, then pulled out his wallet.

'Do me a favour,' he said to Jimmy, taking out a card and handing it over, 'and contact me when Billy turns up, will you? I'd like to know he's safe.'

Flick gave a derisive snort, but Jimmy seemed caught off guard.

'Yeah, all right. Yeah, I will.'

'D'you know which bus would get me back to Denmark Street quickest?' Strike asked them. He could not face another long walk to the Tube. Buses were rolling past the pub with inviting frequency. Jimmy, who seemed to know the area well, directed Strike to the appropriate stop.

'Thanks very much.' As he put his wallet back inside his jacket, Strike said casually, 'Billy told me you were there when the child was strangled, Jimmy.'

Flick's rapid turn of the head towards Jimmy was the giveaway. The latter was better prepared. His nostrils flared, but otherwise he did a creditable job of pretending not to be alarmed.

'Yeah, he's got the whole sick scene worked out in his poor fucked head,' he said. 'Some days he thinks our dead mum might've been there, too. Pope next, I expect.'

'Sad,' said Strike. 'Hope you manage to track him down.'

He raised a hand in farewell and left them standing on the forecourt. Hungry in spite of the chips, his stump now throbbing, he was limping by the time he reached the bus stop.

After a fifteen-minute wait, the bus arrived. Two drunk youths a few seats in front of Strike got into a long, repetitive argument about the merits of West Ham's new signing, Jussi Jääskeläinen, whose name neither of them could pronounce. Strike stared unseeingly out of the grimy window, leg sore, desperate for his bed, but unable to relax.

Irksome though it was to admit it, the trip to Charlemont

Road had not rid him of the tiny niggling doubt about Billy's story. The memory of Flick's sudden, frightened peek at Jimmy, and above all her blurted exclamation 'Chizzle's sent him!' had turned that niggling doubt into a significant and possibly permanent impediment to the detective's peace of mind.

7

Do you think you will remain here? Permanently, I mean?

Henrik Ibsen, *Rosmersholm*

Robin would have been happy to spend the weekend relaxing after her long week unpacking and putting together furniture, but Matthew was looking forward to the house-warming party, to which he had invited a large number of colleagues. His pride was piqued by the interesting, romantic history of the street, which had been built for shipwrights and sea captains back when Deptford had been a shipbuilding centre. Matthew might not yet have arrived in the postcode of his dreams, but a short cobbled street full of pretty old houses was, as he had wanted, a 'step up', even if he and Robin were only renting the neat brick box with its sash windows and the mouldings of cherubs over the front door.

Matthew had objected when Robin first suggested renting again, but she had overridden him, saying that she could not stand another year in Hastings Road while further purchases of overpriced houses fell through. Between the legacy and Matthew's new job, they were just able to make rent on the smart little three-bedroomed house, leaving the money they had received from the sale of their Hastings Road flat untouched in the bank.

Their landlord, a publisher who was off to New York to work at head office, had been delighted with his new tenants. A gay man in his forties, he admired Matthew's clean-cut looks and made a point of handing over the keys personally on their moving day.

'I agree with Jane Austen on the ideal tenant,' he told Matthew, standing in the cobbled street. '"A married man, and without children; the very state to be wished for." A house is never well cared for without a lady! Or do you two share the hoovering?'

'Of course,' Matthew had said, smiling. Robin, who was carrying a box of plants over the threshold behind the two men, had bitten back a caustic retort.

She had a suspicion that Matthew was not disclosing to friends and workmates that they were tenants rather than owners. She deplored her own increasing tendency to watch Matthew for shabby or duplicitous behaviour, even in small matters, and imposed private penances on herself for thinking the worst of him all the time. It was in this spirit of self-castigation that she had agreed to the party, bought alcohol and plastic tumblers, made food and set everything up in the kitchen. Matthew had rearranged the furniture and, over several evenings, organised a playlist now blaring out of his iPod in its dock. The first few bars of 'Cutt Off' by Kasabian started as Robin hurried upstairs to change.

Robin's hair was in foam rollers, because she had decided to wear it as she had on their wedding day. Running out of time before guests were due, she pulled out the rollers one-handed as she yanked open the wardrobe door. She had a new dress, a form-fitting pale grey affair, but she was afraid that it drained her of colour. She hesitated, then took out the emerald-green Roberto Cavalli that she had never worn in public. It was the most expensive item of clothing she owned, and the most beautiful: the 'leaving' present that Strike had bought her after she had gone to him as a temp and helped him catch their first killer. The expression on Matthew's face when she had excitedly shown him the gift had prevented her ever wearing it.

For some reason her mind drifted to Strike's girlfriend, Lorelei, as she held the dress up against herself. Lorelei, who always wore jewel-bright colours, affected the style of a 1940s pin-up. As tall as Robin, she had glossy brunette hair that she wore over one eye like Veronica Lake. Robin knew that Lorelei was thirty-three, and that she co-owned and ran a vintage and theatrical clothing store on Chalk Farm Road. Strike had let slip this information one day and Robin, making a mental note of the name, had gone home and looked it up online. The shop appeared to be glamorous and successful.

'It's a quarter to,' said Matthew, hurrying into the bedroom, stripping off his T-shirt as he came. 'I might shower quickly.'

He caught sight of her, holding the green dress against herself.

'I thought you were wearing the grey one?'

Their eyes met in the mirror. Bare-chested, tanned and handsome, Matthew's features were so symmetrical that his reflection was almost identical to his real appearance.

'I think it makes me look pale,' said Robin.

'I prefer the grey one,' he said. 'I like you pale.'

She forced a smile.

'All right,' she said. 'I'll wear the grey.'

Once changed, she ran fingers through her curls to loosen them, pulled on a pair of strappy silver sandals and hurried back downstairs. She had barely reached the hall when the doorbell rang.

If she had been asked to guess who would arrive first, she would have said Sarah Shadlock and Tom Turvey, who had recently got engaged. It would be like Sarah to try and catch Robin on the hop, to make sure she had an opportunity to nose around the house before anybody else, and to stake out a spot where she could look over all the arrivals. Sure enough, when Robin opened up, there stood Sarah in shocking pink, a big bunch of flowers in her arms, Tom carrying beer and wine.

'Oh, it's *gorgeous*, Robin,' crooned Sarah, the moment she got over the doorstep, staring around the hall. She hugged Robin absent-mindedly, her eyes on the stairs as Matthew descended, doing up his shirt. '*Lovely*. These are for you.'

Robin found herself encumbered by an armful of stargazer lilies.

'Thanks,' she said. 'I'll just go and put them in water.'

They didn't have a vase big enough for the flowers, but Robin could hardly leave them in the sink. She could hear Sarah's laugh from the kitchen, even over Coldplay and Rihanna, who were now belting out 'Princess of China' from Matthew's iPod. Robin dragged a bucket out of the cupboard and began to fill it, splattering herself with water in the process.

The idea had once been mooted, she remembered, that Matthew would refrain from taking Sarah out for lunches during their office lunch hours. There had even been talk of stopping socialising with her, after Robin had found out that Matthew had been cheating with Sarah in their early twenties. However, Tom had helped Matthew get the higher-paid position he now enjoyed at Tom's firm, and now that Sarah was the proud owner of a large solitaire diamond, Matthew did not seem to think that there should be the slightest awkwardness attached to social events including the future Mr and Mrs Turvey.

Robin could hear the three of them moving around upstairs. Matthew was giving a tour of the bedrooms. She heaved the lily-filled bucket out of the sink and shoved it into a corner beside the kettle, wondering whether it was mean-spirited to suspect that Sarah had brought flowers just to get Robin out of the way for a bit. Sarah had never lost the flirtatious manner towards Matthew she had had since their shared years at university.

Robin poured herself a glass of wine and emerged from the kitchen as Matthew led Tom and Sarah into the sitting room.

'. . . and Lord Nelson and Lady Hamilton are supposed to have stayed in number 19, but it was called Union Street then,' he said. 'Right, who wants a drink? It's all set up in the kitchen.'

'Gorgeous place, Robin,' said Sarah. 'Houses like this don't come up that often. You must've got really lucky.'

'We're only renting,' said Robin.

'Really?' said Sarah beadily, and Robin knew that Sarah was drawing her own conclusions, not about the housing market, but about Robin and Matthew's marriage.

'Nice earrings,' said Robin, keen to change the subject.

'Aren't they?' said Sarah, pulling back her hair to give Robin a better view. 'Tom's birthday present.'

The doorbell rang again. Robin went to answer it, hoping that it would be one of the few people she had invited. She had no hope of Strike, of course. He was bound to be late, as he had been to every other personal event to which she had invited him.

'Oh, thank God,' said Robin, surprised at her own relief when she saw Vanessa Ekwensi.

Vanessa was a police officer: tall, black, with almond-shaped eyes, a model's figure and a self-possession Robin envied. She had come to the party alone. Her boyfriend, who worked in Forensic Services at the Met, had a prior commitment. Robin was disappointed: she had looked forward to meeting him.

'You all right?' Vanessa asked as she entered. She was carrying a bottle of red wine and wearing a deep purple slip dress. Robin thought again of the emerald-green Cavalli upstairs and wished she had worn it.

'I'm fine,' she said. 'Come through to the back, you can smoke there.'

She led Vanessa through the sitting room, past Sarah and Matthew, who were now mocking Tom's baldness to his face.

The rear wall of the small courtyard garden was covered in ivy. Well-maintained shrubs stood in terracotta tubs. Robin, who did not smoke, had put ashtrays and a few fold-up chairs out there, and dotted tea candles around. Matthew had asked her with an edge in his voice why she was taking so much trouble over the smokers. She had known perfectly well why he was saying it and pretended not to.

'I thought Jemima smoked?' she asked, with a feigned air of confusion. Jemima was Matthew's boss.

'Oh,' he said, caught off balance. 'Yeah – yeah, but only socially.'

'Well, I'm pretty sure this is a social occasion, Matt,' said Robin sweetly.

She fetched Vanessa a drink and came back to find her lighting up, her lovely eyes fixed on Sarah Shadlock, who was still mocking Tom's hairline, with Matthew her hearty accomplice.

'That's her, is it?' Vanessa asked.

'That's her,' said Robin.

She appreciated the small show of moral support. Robin and Vanessa had been friends for months before Robin had confided the history of her relationship with Matthew. Before that they had talked police work, politics and clothes on evenings that took them to the cinema, or to cheap restaurants. Robin found Vanessa better company than any other woman she knew. Matthew, who had met her twice, told Robin he found her 'cold', but said he could not explain why.

Vanessa had had a succession of partners; she had been engaged once, but broken it off when he had cheated. Robin sometimes wondered whether Vanessa found her laughably inexperienced: the woman who'd married her boyfriend from school.

A few moments later, a dozen people, colleagues of Matthew's with their partners, who had obviously been to the pub first, streamed into the sitting room. Robin watched Matthew greeting them and showing them where the drinks were. He had adopted the loud, bantering tone that she had heard him using on work nights out. It irritated her.

The party quickly became crowded. Robin effected introductions, showed people where to find drink, set out more plastic cups and handed a couple of plates of food around because the kitchen was becoming packed. Only when Andy Hutchins and his wife arrived did she feel she could relax for a moment and spend some more time with her own guests.

'I made you some special food,' Robin told Andy, after she had shown him and Louise out into the courtyard. 'This is Vanessa. She's Met. Vanessa, Andy and Louise – stay there, Andy, I'll get it, it's dairy-free.'

Tom was standing against the fridge when she got to the kitchen.

'Sorry, Tom, need to get in—'

He blinked at her, then moved aside. He was already drunk, she thought, and it was barely nine o'clock. Robin could hear Sarah's braying laugh from the middle of the crowd outside.

'Lemmelp,' said Tom, holding the fridge door that threatened to close on Robin as she bent down to the lower shelf to get the tray of dairy-free, non-fried food she had saved for Andy. 'God, you've got a nice arse, Robin.'

She straightened up without comment. In spite of the drunken grin, she could feel the unhappiness flowing from behind it, like a cool draught. Matthew had told her how self-conscious Tom was about his hairline, that he was even considering a transplant.

'That's a nice shirt,' said Robin.

'Wha' this? You like it? She bought it for me. Matt's got one like it, hasn't he?'

'Er – I'm not sure,' said Robin.

'You're not sure,' repeated Tom, with a short, nasty laugh. 'So much f' surveillance training. You wanna pay more attention at home, Rob.'

Robin contemplated him for a moment in equal amounts of pity and anger, then, deciding that he was too drunk to argue with, she left, carrying Andy's food.

The first thing she saw as people cleared out of the way to let her back into the courtyard was that Strike had arrived. He had his back to her and was talking to Andy. Lorelei was beside him, wearing a scarlet silk dress, the gleaming fall of dark hair down her back like an advertisement for expensive shampoo. Somehow, Sarah had inveigled her way into the group in Robin's brief absence. When Vanessa caught Robin's eye, the corner of her mouth twitched.

'Hi,' said Robin, setting the platter of food down on the wrought iron table beside Andy.

'Robin, hi!' said Lorelei. 'It's such a pretty street!'

'Yes, isn't it?' said Robin, as Lorelei kissed the air behind Robin's ear.

Strike bent down, too. His stubble grazed Robin's face, but his lips did not touch skin. He was already opening one of the six-pack of Doom Bar he had brought with him.

Robin had mentally rehearsed things to say to Strike once he was in her new house: calm, casual things that made it sound as though she had no regrets, as though there were some wonderful counterweight that he couldn't appreciate that tipped the scales in Matthew's favour. She also wanted to question him about the strange matter of Billy and the strangled child. However, Sarah was currently holding forth on the subject of the auction house, Christie's, where she worked, and the whole group was listening to her.

'Yeah, we've got "The Lock" coming up at auction on the third,' she said. 'Constable,' she added kindly, for the benefit of anyone who did not know art as well as she did. 'We're expecting it to make over twenty.'

'Thousand?' asked Andy.

'Million,' said Sarah, with a patronising little snort of laughter.

Matthew laughed behind Robin and she moved automatically to let him join the circle. His expression was rapt, Robin noticed, as so often when large sums of money were under discussion. Perhaps, she thought, this is what he and Sarah talk about when they have lunch: money.

'"Gimcrack" went for over twenty-two last year. Stubbs. Third most valuable Old Master ever sold.'

Out of the corner of her eye, Robin saw Lorelei's scarlet-tipped hand slide into Strike's, which had been marked across the palm with the very same knife that had forever scarred Robin's arm.

'Anyway, boring, boring, boring!' said Sarah insincerely. 'Enough work chat! Anyone got Olympics tickets? Tom – my fiancé – he's furious. We got *ping pong*.' She pulled a droll face. 'How have you lot got on?'

Robin saw Strike and Lorelei exchange a fleeting look, and knew that they were mutually consoling each other for having to endure the tedium of the Olympics ticket conversation. Suddenly wishing that they hadn't come, Robin backed out of the group.

An hour later, Strike was in the sitting room, discussing the England football team's chances in the European Championships with one of Matthew's friends from work while Lorelei danced. Robin, with whom he had not exchanged a word since they had met outside, crossed the room with a plate of food, paused to talk to a redheaded woman, then continued to offer the plate around. The way she had done her hair reminded Strike of her wedding day.

The suspicions provoked by her visit to that unknown clinic uppermost in his mind, he appraised her figure in the clinging grey dress. She certainly didn't appear to be pregnant, and the fact that she was drinking wine seemed a further counter-indication, but they might only just have begun the process of IVF.

Directly opposite Strike, visible through the dancing bodies, stood DI Vanessa Ekwensi, whom Strike had been surprised to find at the party. She was leaning up against the wall, talking to a tall blond man who seemed, by his over-attentive attitude, to have temporarily forgotten that he was wearing a wedding ring. Vanessa glanced across the room at Strike and by a wry look signalled that she would not mind him breaking up the tête-à-tête. The football conversation was not so fascinating that he would be disappointed to leave it, and at the next convenient pause he circumnavigated the dancers to talk to Vanessa.

'Evening.'

'Hi,' she said, accepting his peck on the cheek with the elegance that characterised all her gestures. 'Cormoran, this is Owen – sorry, I didn't catch your surname?'

It didn't take long for Owen to lose hope of whatever he had wanted from Vanessa, whether the mere pleasure of flirting with a good-looking woman, or her phone number.

'Didn't realise you and Robin were this friendly,' said Strike, as Owen walked away.

'Yeah, we've been hanging out,' said Vanessa. 'I wrote her a note after I heard you sacked her.'

'Oh,' said Strike, swigging Doom Bar. 'Right.'

'She rang to thank me and we ended up going for a drink.'

Robin had never mentioned this to Strike, but then, as Strike knew perfectly well, he had been at pains to discourage anything but work talk since she had come back from her honeymoon.

'Nice house,' he commented, trying not to compare the tastefully decorated room with his combined kitchen and sitting room in the attic over the office. Matthew must be earning very good money to have afforded this, he thought. Robin's pay rise certainly couldn't have done it.

'Yeah, it is,' said Vanessa. 'They're renting.'

Strike watched Lorelei dance for a few moments while he pondered this interesting piece of information. An arch something in Vanessa's tone told him that she, too, read this as a choice not entirely related to the housing market.

'Blame sea-borne bacteria,' said Vanessa.

'Sorry?' said Strike, thoroughly confused.

She threw him a sharp look, then shook her head, laughing.

'Nothing. Forget it.'

'Yeah, we didn't do too badly,' Strike heard Matthew telling the redheaded woman in a lull in the music. 'Got tickets for the boxing.'

Of course you fucking did, thought Strike irritably, feeling in his pocket for more cigarettes.

'Enjoy yourself?' asked Lorelei in the taxi, at one in the morning.

'Not particularly,' said Strike, who was watching the headlights of oncoming cars.

He had had the impression that Robin had been avoiding him. After the relative warmth of their conversation on Thursday, he had expected – what? A conversation, a laugh? He had been curious to know how the marriage was progressing, but was not much the wiser. She and Matthew seemed amicable enough together, but the fact that they were renting was intriguing. Did it suggest, even subconsciously, a lack of investment in a joint future? An easier arrangement to untangle? And then there was Robin's friendship with Vanessa Ekwensi, which Strike saw as another stake in the life she led independently of Matthew.

Blame sea-borne bacteria.

What the hell did that mean? Was it connected to the mysterious clinic? Was Robin ill?

After a few minutes' silence it suddenly occurred to Strike that he ought to ask Lorelei how her evening had been.

'I've had better,' sighed Lorelei. 'I'm afraid your Robin's got a lot of boring friends.'

'Yeah,' said Strike. 'I think that's mainly her husband. He's an accountant. And a bit of a tit,' he added, enjoying saying it.

The taxi bowled on through the night, Strike remembering how Robin's figure had looked in the grey dress.

'Sorry?' he said suddenly, because he had the impression that Lorelei had spoken to him.

'I said, "What are you thinking about?"'

'Nothing,' lied Strike, and because it was preferable to talking, he slid an arm around her, pulled her close and kissed her.

8

. . . my word! Mortensgaard has risen in the world.
There are lots of people who run after him now.

Henrik Ibsen, *Rosmersholm*

Robin texted Strike on Sunday evening to ask what he wanted her to do on Monday, because she had handed over all her jobs before taking a week's leave. His terse response had been 'come to office', which she duly entered at a quarter to nine the following day, glad, no matter how matters stood between her and her partner, to be back in the shabby old rooms.

The door to Strike's inner office was standing open when she arrived. He was sitting behind his desk, listening to someone on his mobile. Sunlight fell in treacle-gold pools across the worn carpet. The soft mumble of traffic was soon obliterated by the rattle of the old kettle and, five minutes after her arrival, Robin set a mug of steaming dark brown Typhoo in front of Strike, who gave her a thumbs up and a silent 'thanks'. She returned to her desk, where a light was flashing on the phone to indicate a recorded message. She dialled their answering service and listened while a cool female voice informed her that the call had been made ten minutes before Robin had arrived and, presumably, while Strike was either upstairs, or busy with the other call.

A cracked whisper hissed in Robin's ear.

'I'm sorry I ran out on you, Mr Strike, I'm sorry. I can't come back, though. He's keeping me here, I can't get out, he's wired the doors . . .'

The end of the sentence was lost in sobs. Worried, Robin tried to attract Strike's attention, but he had turned in his swivel chair to look out of the window, still listening to his mobile. Random words reached Robin through the pitiable sounds of distress on the phone.

' . . . can't get out . . . I'm all alone . . . '

'Yeah, OK,' Strike was saying in his office. 'Wednesday, then, OK? Great. Have a good one.'

' . . . *please help me, Mr Strike!*' wailed the voice in Robin's ear.

She smacked the button to switch to speakerphone and at once the tortured voice filled the office.

'The doors will explode if I try and escape Mr Strike, please help me, please come and get me, I shouldn't have come, I told him I know about the little kid and it's bigger, much bigger, I thought I could trust him—'

Strike spun in his desk chair, got up and came striding through to the outer office. There was a clunk as though the receiver had been dropped. The sobbing continued at a distance, as though the distraught speaker was stumbling away from the phone.

'That's him again,' said Strike. 'Billy, Billy Knight.'

The sobbing and gasping grew louder again and Billy said in a frantic whisper, his lips evidently pressed against the mouthpiece:

'There's someone at the door. Help me. Help me, Mr Strike.'

The call was cut.

'Get the number,' said Strike. Robin reached for the receiver to dial 1471, but before she could do so, the phone rang again. She snatched it up, her eyes on Strike's.

'Cormoran Strike's office.'

'Ah . . . yes, good morning,' said a deep, patrician voice.

Robin grimaced at Strike and shook her head.

'Shit,' he muttered, and moved back into his office to get his tea.

'I'd like to speak to Mr Strike, please.'

'I'm afraid he's on another call right now,' lied Robin.

Their standard practice for a year had been to phone the client back. It weeded out journalists and cranks.

'I'll hold,' said the caller, who sounded captious, unused to not getting his way.

'He'll be a while, I'm afraid. Could I take a number and get him to call you back?'

'Well, it needs to be within the next ten minutes, because I'm about to go into a meeting. Tell him I want to discuss a job I'd like him to do for me.'

'I'm afraid I can't guarantee that Mr Strike will be able to undertake the job in person,' said Robin, which was also the standard response to deflect press. 'Our agency's quite booked up at the moment.'

She pulled pen and paper towards her.

'What kind of job are you—?'

'It has to be Mr Strike,' said the voice firmly. 'Make that clear to him. It has to be Mr Strike himself. My name's Chizzle.'

'How are you spelling that?' asked Robin, wondering whether she had heard correctly.

'C – H – I – S – W – E – L – L. Jasper Chiswell. Ask him to call me on the following number.'

Robin copied down the digits Chiswell gave her and bade him good morning. As she set down the receiver, Strike sat down on the fake leather sofa they kept in the outer room for clients. It had a disobliging habit of making unexpected farting noises when you shifted position.

'A man called Jasper Chizzle, spelled "Chiswell", wants you to take on a job for him. He says it's got to be you, nobody else.' Robin screwed up her forehead in perplexity. 'I know the name, don't I?'

'Yeah,' said Strike. 'He's Minister for Culture.'

'Oh my God,' said Robin, realisation dawning. '*Of course!* The big man with the weird hair!'

'That's him.'

A clutch of vague memories and associations assailed Robin. She seemed to remember an old affair, resignation in disgrace, rehabilitation and, somewhat more recently, a fresh scandal, another nasty news story . . .

'Didn't his son get sent to jail for manslaughter not that long ago?' she said. 'That was Chiswell, wasn't it? His son was stoned and driving and he killed a young mother?'

Strike recalled his attention, it seemed, from a distance. He was wearing a peculiar expression.

'Yeah, that rings a bell,' said Strike.

'What's the matter?'

'A few things, actually,' said Strike, running a hand over his stubbly chin. 'For starters: I tracked down Billy's brother on Friday.'

'How?'

'Long story,' said Strike, 'but turns out Jimmy's part of a group that's protesting against the Olympics. "CORE", they call themselves. Anyway, he was with a girl, and the first thing she said when I told them I was a private detective was: "Chiswell's sent him."'

Strike pondered this point while drinking his perfectly brewed tea.

'But Chiswell wouldn't need me to keep an eye on CORE,' he went on, thinking aloud. 'There was already a plainclothes guy there.'

Though keen to hear what other things troubled Strike about Chiswell's call, Robin did not prompt him, but sat in silence, allowing him to mull the new development. It was precisely this kind of tact that Strike had missed when she was out of the office.

'And get this,' he went on at last, as though there had been no interruption. 'The son who went to jail for manslaughter isn't – or wasn't – Chiswell's only boy. His eldest was called Freddie and he died in Iraq. Yeah. Major Freddie Chiswell, Queen's Royal Hussars. Killed in an attack on a convoy in Basra. I investigated his death in action while I was still SIB.'

'So you *know* Chiswell?'

'No, never met him. You don't meet families, usually . . . I knew Chiswell's daughter years ago, as well. Only slightly, but I met her a few times. She was an old school friend of Charlotte's.'

Robin experienced a tiny frisson at the mention of Charlotte. She had a great curiosity, which she successfully concealed, about Charlotte, the woman Strike had been involved with on and off for sixteen years, whom he had been supposed to marry before the relationship ended messily and, apparently, permanently.

'Pity we couldn't get Billy's number,' said Strike, running a large, hairy-backed hand over his jaw again.

'I'll make sure I get it if he calls again,' Robin assured him. 'Are you going to ring Chiswell back? He said he was about to go into a meeting.'

'I'm keen to find out what he wants, but the question is whether we've got room for another client,' said Strike. 'Let's think . . .'

He put his hands behind his head, frowning up at the ceiling, on which many fine cracks were exposed by the sunlight. *Screw that now* . . . the office would soon be a developer's problem, after all . . .

'I've got Andy and Barclay watching the Webster kid. Barclay's doing well, by the way. I've had three solid days' surveillance out of him, pictures, the lot.

'Then there's old Dodgy Doc. He still hasn't done anything newsworthy.'

'Shame,' said Robin, then she caught herself. 'No, I don't mean that, I mean good.' She rubbed her eyes. 'This job,' she sighed. 'It messes with your ethics. Who's watching Dodgy today?'

'I was going to ask you to do it,' said Strike, 'but the client called yesterday afternoon. He'd forgotten to tell me Dodgy's at a symposium in Paris.'

Eyes still on the ceiling, brow furrowed in thought, Strike said:

'We've got two days at that tech conference starting tomorrow. Which do you want to do, Harley Street or a conference centre out in Epping Forest? We can swap over if you want. D'you want to spend tomorrow watching Dodgy, or with hundreds of stinking geeks in superhero T-shirts?'

'Not all tech people smell,' Robin reprimanded him. 'Your mate Spanner doesn't.'

'You don't want to judge Spanner by the amount of deodorant he puts on to come here,' said Strike.

Spanner, who had overhauled their computer and telephone system when the business had received its dramatic boost in business, was the younger brother of Strike's old friend Nick. He fancied Robin, as she and Strike were equally aware.

Strike mulled over options, rubbing his chin again.

'I'll call Chiswell back and find out what he's after,' he said at last. 'You never know, it might be a bigger job than that lawyer whose wife's sleeping around. He's next on the waiting list, right?'

'Him, or that American woman who's married to the Ferrari dealer. They're both waiting.'

Strike sighed. Infidelity formed the bulk of their workload.

'I hope Chiswell's wife isn't cheating. I fancy a change.'

The sofa made its usual flatulent noises as Strike quit it. As he strode back to the inner office, Robin called after him:

'Are you happy for me to finish up this paperwork, then?'

'If you don't mind,' said Strike, closing the door behind him.

Robin turned back to her computer feeling quite cheerful. A busker had just started singing 'No Woman, No Cry' in Denmark Street and for a while there, while they talked about Billy Knight and the Chiswells, she had felt as though they were the Strike and Robin of a year ago, before he had sacked her, before she had married Matthew.

Meanwhile, in the inner office, Strike's call to Jasper Chiswell had been answered almost instantly.

'Chiswell,' he barked.

'Cormoran Strike here,' said the detective. 'You spoke to my partner a short while ago.'

'Ah, yes,' said the Minister for Culture, who sounded as though he were in the back of a car. 'I've got a job for you. Nothing I want to discuss over the phone. I'm busy today and this evening, unfortunately, but tomorrow would suit.'

'*Ob-observing the hypocrites* . . . ' sang the busker down in the street.

'Sorry, no chance tomorrow,' said Strike, watching motes of dust fall through the bright sunlight. 'No chance until Friday, actually. Can you give me an idea what kind of job we're talking about, Minister?'

Chiswell's response was both tense and angry.

'I can't discuss it over the phone. I'll make it worth your while to meet me, if that's what you want.'

'It isn't a question of money, it's time. I'm solidly booked until Friday.'

'Oh, for Christ's sake—'

Chiswell suddenly removed his phone from his mouth and Strike heard him talking furiously to somebody else.

'—*left* here, you moron! *Lef* – for fuck's sake! No, I'll walk. I'll bloody walk, open the door!'

In the background, Strike heard a nervous man say:

'I'm sorry, Minister, it was No Entry—'

'Never mind that! Open this – *open this bloody door*!'

Strike waited, eyebrows raised. He heard a car door slam, rapid footsteps and then Jasper Chiswell spoke again, his mouth close to the receiver.

'The job's urgent!' he hissed.

'If it can't wait until Friday, you'll have to find someone else, I'm afraid.'

'*My feet is my only carriage*,' sang the busker.

Chiswell said nothing for a few seconds; then, finally:

'It's got to be you. I'll explain when we meet, but – all right, if it *has* to be Friday, meet me at Pratt's Club. Park Place. Come at twelve, I'll give you lunch.'

'All right,' Strike agreed, now thoroughly intrigued. 'See you at Pratt's.'

He hung up and returned to the office where Robin was opening and sorting mail. When he told her the upshot of the conversation, she Googled Pratt's for him.

'I didn't think places like this still existed,' she said in disbelief, after a minute's reading off the monitor.

'Places like what?'

'It's a gentlemen's club ... very Tory ... no women allowed, except as guests of club members at lunchtime ... and "to avoid confusion",' Robin read from the Wikipedia page, '"all male staff members are called George".'

'What if they hire a woman?'

'Apparently they did in the eighties,' said Robin, her expression midway between amusement and disapproval. 'They called her Georgina.'

9

It is best for you not to know. Best for us both.

Henrik Ibsen, *Rosmersholm*

At half past eleven the following Friday, a suited and freshly shaven Strike emerged from Green Park Tube station and proceeded along Piccadilly. Double-deckers rolled past the windows of luxury shops, which were capitalising on Olympics fever to push an eclectic mix of goods: gold-wrapped chocolate medals, Union Jack brogues, antique sporting posters and, over and again, the jagged logo that Jimmy Knight had compared to a broken swastika.

Strike had allowed a generous margin of time to reach Pratt's, because his leg was again aching after two days in which he had rarely been able to take the weight off his prosthesis. He had hoped that the tech conference in Epping Forest, where he had spent the previous day, might have offered intervals of rest, but he had been disappointed. His target, the recently fired partner of a start-up, was suspected of trying to sell key features of their new app to competitors. For hours, Strike had tailed the young man from booth to booth, documenting all his movements and his interactions, hoping at some point that he would tire and sit. However, between the coffee bar where customers stood at high tables, and the sandwich bar where everyone stood and ate sushi with their fingers out of plastic boxes, the target had spent eight hours walking or standing. Coming after long hours of lurking in Harley Street the day before, it was hardly surprising that the removal of his prosthesis the previous evening had been an uncomfortable affair, the gel pad that separated stump from artificial shin difficult to prise off. As Strike passed the cool off-white arches of the Ritz, he hoped Pratt's contained at least one comfortable chair of generous proportions.

He turned right into St James's Street, which led him in a gentle slope straight down to the sixteenth-century St James's Palace. This was not an area of London that Strike usually visited on his own account, given that he had neither the means nor the inclination to buy from gentlemen's outfitters, long-established gun shops or centuries-old wine dealers. As he drew nearer to Park Place, though, he was visited by a personal memory. He had walked this street more than ten years previously, with Charlotte.

They had walked up the slope, not down it, heading for a lunch date with her father, who was now dead. Strike had been on leave from the army and they had recently resumed what was, to everyone who knew them, an incomprehensible and obviously doomed affair. On neither side of their relationship had there ever been a single supporter. His friends and family had viewed Charlotte with everything from mistrust to loathing, while hers had always considered Strike, the illegitimate son of an infamous rock star, as one more manifestation of Charlotte's need to shock and rebel. Strike's military career had been nothing to her family, or rather, it had been just another sign of his plebeian unfitness to aspire to the well-bred beauty's hand, because gentlemen of Charlotte's class did not enter the Military Police, but Cavalry or Guards regiments.

She had clutched his hand very tightly as they entered an Italian restaurant somewhere nearby. Its precise location escaped Strike now. All he remembered was the expression of rage and disapproval on Sir Anthony Campbell's face as they had approached the table. Strike had known before a word was spoken that Charlotte had not told her father that she and Strike had resumed their affair, or that she would be bringing him with her. It had been a thoroughly Charlottian omission, prompting the usual Charlottian scene. Strike had long since come to believe that she engineered situations out of an apparently insatiable need for conflict. Prone to outbursts of lacerating honesty amid her general mythomania, she had told Strike towards the end of their relationship, that at least, while fighting, she knew she was alive.

As Strike drew level with Park Place, a line of cream-painted townhouses leading off St James's Street, he noted that the sudden memory of Charlotte clinging to his hand no longer hurt, and felt like an alcoholic who, for the first time, catches a whiff of beer without breaking into a sweat or having to grapple with his desperate craving. *Perhaps this is it,* he thought, as he approached the black door of Pratt's, with its wrought iron balustrade above. Perhaps, two years after she had told him the unforgivable lie and he had left for good, he was healed, clear of what he sometimes, even though not superstitious, saw as a kind of Bermuda triangle, a danger zone in which he feared being pulled back under, dragged to the depths of anguish and pain by the mysterious allure Charlotte had held for him.

With a faint sense of celebration, Strike knocked on the door of Pratt's.

A petite, motherly woman opened up. Her prominent bust and alert, bright-eyed mien put him in mind of a robin or a wren. When she spoke, he caught a trace of the West Country.

'You'll be Mr Strike. The minister's not here yet. Come along in.'

He followed her across the threshold into a hall through which could be glimpsed an enormous billiard table. Rich crimsons, greens and dark wood predominated. The stewardess, who he assumed was Georgina, led him down a set of steep stairs, which Strike took carefully, maintaining a firm grip on the banister.

The stairs led to a cosy basement. The ceiling had sunk so low that it appeared partially supported by a large dresser on which sundry porcelain platters were displayed, the topmost ones half embedded into the plaster.

'We aren't very big,' she said, stating the obvious. 'Six hundred members, but we can only serve fourteen a meal at a time. Would you like a drink, Mr Strike?'

He declined, but accepted an invitation to sit down in one of the leather chairs grouped around an aged cribbage board.

The small space was divided by an archway into sitting and dining areas. Two places had been set at the long table in the other half of the room, beneath small, shuttered windows. The only other person in the basement apart from himself and Georgina was a white-coated chef working in a minuscule kitchen a mere yard from where Strike sat. The chef bade Strike welcome in a French accent, then continued carving cold roast beef.

Here was the very antithesis of the smart restaurants where Strike tailed errant husbands and wives, where the lighting was chosen to complement glass and granite, and sharp-tongued restaurant critics sat like stylish vultures on uncomfortable modern chairs. Pratt's was dimly lit. Brass picture lights dotted walls papered in dark red, which was largely obscured by stuffed fish in glass cases, hunting prints and political cartoons. In a blue and white tiled niche along one side of the room sat an ancient iron stove. The china plates, the threadbare carpet, the table bearing its homely load of ketchup and mustard all contributed to an ambience of cosy informality, as though a bunch of aristocratic boys had dragged all the things they liked about the grown-up world – its games, its drink and its trophies – down into the basement where Nanny would dole out smiles, comfort and praise.

Twelve o'clock arrived, but Chiswell did not. 'Georgina', however, was friendly and informative about the club. She and her husband, the chef, lived on the premises. Strike could not help but reflect that this must be some of the most expensive real estate in London. To maintain the little club, which, Georgina told him, had been established in 1857, was costing somebody a lot of money.

'The Duke of Devonshire owns it, yes,' said Georgina brightly. 'Have you seen our betting book?'

Strike turned the pages of the heavy, leather-bound tome, where long ago wagers had been recorded. In a gigantic scrawl dating back to the seventies, he read: 'Mrs Thatcher to form the next government. Bet: one lobster dinner, the lobster to be larger than a man's erect cock.'

He was grinning over this when a bell rang overhead.

'That'll be the minister,' said Georgina, bustling away upstairs.

Strike replaced the betting book on its shelf and returned to his seat. From overhead came heavy footsteps and then, descending the stairs, the same irascible, impatient voice he had heard on Monday.

'—no, Kinvara, I can't. I've just told you why, I've got a lunch meeting . . . no, you can't . . . Five o'clock, then, yes . . . yes . . . *yes!* . . . Goodbye!'

A pair of large, black-shod feet descended the stairs until Jasper Chiswell emerged into the basement, peering around with a truculent air. Strike rose from his armchair.

'Ah,' said Chiswell, scrutinising Strike from beneath his heavy eyebrows. 'You're here.'

Jasper Chiswell wore his sixty-eight years reasonably well. A big, broad man, though round-shouldered, he still had a full head of grey hair which, implausible though it seemed, was his own. This hair made Chiswell an easy target for cartoonists, because it was coarse, straight and rather long, standing out from his head in a manner that suggested a wig or, so the unkind suggested, a chimney brush. To the hair was added a large red face, small eyes and a protuberant lower lip, which gave him the air of an overgrown baby perpetually on the verge of a tantrum.

'M'wife,' he told Strike, brandishing the mobile still in his hand. 'Come up to town without warning. Sulking. Thinks I can drop everything.'

Chiswell stretched out a large, sweaty hand, which Strike shook, then eased off the heavy overcoat he was wearing despite the heat of the day. As he did so, Strike noticed the pin on his frayed regimental tie. The uninitiated might think it a rocking horse, but Strike recognised it at once as the White Horse of Hanover.

'Queen's Own Hussars,' said Strike, nodding at it as both men sat down.

'Yerse,' said Chiswell. 'Georgina, I'll have some of that sherry you gave me when I was in with Alastair. You?' he barked at Strike.

'No thanks.'

Though nowhere near as dirty as Billy Knight, Chiswell did not smell very fresh.

'Yerse, Queen's Own Hussars. Aden and Singapore. Happy days.'

He didn't seem happy at the moment. His ruddy skin had an odd, plaque-like appearance close up. Dandruff lay thick in the roots of his coarse hair and large patches of sweat spread around the underarms of his blue shirt. The minister bore the unmistakable appearance, not unusual in Strike's clients, of a man under intense strain, and when his sherry arrived, he swallowed most of it in a single gulp.

'Shall we move through?' he suggested, and without waiting for an answer he barked, 'We'll eat straight away, Georgina.'

Once they were seated at the table, which had a stiff, snowy-white tablecloth like those at Robin's wedding, Georgina brought them thick slices of cold roast beef and boiled potatoes. It was English nursery food, plain and unfussy, and none the worse for it. Only when the stewardess had left them in peace, in the dim dining room full of oil paintings and more dead fish, did Chiswell speak again.

'You were at Jimmy Knight's meeting,' he said, without preamble. 'A plainclothes officer there recognised you.'

Strike nodded. Chiswell shoved a boiled potato in his mouth, masticated angrily, and swallowed before saying:

'I don't know who's paying you to get dirt on Jimmy Knight, or what you may already have on him, but whoever it is and whatever you've got, I'm prepared to pay double for the information.'

'I haven't got anything on Jimmy Knight, I'm afraid,' said Strike. 'Nobody was paying me to be at the meeting.'

Chiswell looked stunned.

'But then, why were you there?' he demanded. 'You're not telling me *you* intend to protest against the Olympics?'

So plosive was the 'p' of 'protest' that a small piece of potato flew out of his mouth across the table.

'No,' said Strike. 'I was trying to find somebody I thought might be at the meeting. They weren't.'

Chiswell attacked his beef again as though it had personally wronged him. For a while, the only sounds were those of their knives and forks scraping the china. Chiswell speared the last of his boiled potatoes, put it whole into his mouth, let his knife and fork fall with a clatter onto his plate and said:

'I'd been thinking of hiring a detective before I heard you were watching Knight.'

Strike said nothing. Chiswell eyed him suspiciously.

'You have the reputation of being very good.'

'Kind of you to say so,' said Strike.

Chiswell continued to glare at Strike with a kind of furious desperation, as though wondering whether he dared hope that the detective would not prove yet another disappointment in a life beset with them.

'I'm being blackmailed, Mr Strike,' he said abruptly. 'Blackmailed by a pair of men who have come together in a temporary, though probably unstable, alliance. One of them is Jimmy Knight.'

'I see,' said Strike.

He, too, put his knife and fork together. Georgina appeared to know by some psychic process that Strike and Chiswell had eaten their fill of the main course. She arrived to clear away, reappearing with a treacle tart. Only once she had retired to the kitchen, and both men had helped themselves to large slices of pudding, did Chiswell resume his story.

'There's no need for sordid details,' he said, with an air of finality. 'All you need to know is that Jimmy Knight is aware that I did something that I would not wish to see shared with the gentlemen of the fourth estate.'

Strike said nothing, but Chiswell seemed to think his silence had an accusatory flavour, because he added sharply:

'No crime was committed. Some might not like it, but it wasn't illegal at the – but that's by the by,' said Chiswell, and took a large gulp of water. 'Knight came to me a couple of months ago and asked for forty thousand pounds in hush money. I refused to pay. He threatened me with exposure, but as he didn't appear to have any proof of his claim, I dared hope he would be unable to follow through on the threat.

'No press story resulted, so I concluded that I was right in thinking he had no proof. He returned a few weeks later and asked for half the former sum. Again, I refused.

'It was then, thinking to increase the pressure on me, I assume, that he approached Geraint Winn.'

'I'm sorry, I don't know who—?'

'Della Winn's husband.'

'Della Winn, the Minister for Sport?' said Strike, startled.

'Yes, of course Della-Winn-the-Minister-for-Sport,' snapped Chiswell.

The Right Honourable Della Winn, as Strike knew well, was a Welshwoman in her early sixties who had been blind since birth. No matter their party affiliation, people tended to admire the Liberal Democrat, who had been a human rights lawyer before standing for Parliament. Usually photographed with her guide dog, a pale yellow Labrador, she had been much in evidence in the press of late, her current bailiwick being the Paralympics. She had visited Selly Oak while Strike had been in the hospital, readjusting to the loss of his leg in Afghanistan. He had been left with a favourable impression of her intelligence and her empathy. Of her husband, Strike knew nothing.

'I don't know whether Della knows what Geraint's up to,' said Chiswell, spearing a piece of treacle tart and continuing to speak while he chewed it. 'Probably, but keeping her nose clean. Plausible deniability. Can't have the sainted Della involved in blackmail, can we?'

'Her husband's asked you for money?' asked Strike, incredulous.

'Oh no, no. Geraint wants to force me from office.'

'Any particular reason why?' said Strike.

'There's an enmity between us dating back many years, rooted in a wholly baseless – but that's irrelevant,' said Chiswell, with an angry shake of the head. 'Geraint approached me, "hoping it isn't true", and "offering me a chance to explain". He's a nasty, twisted little man who's spent his life holding his wife's handbag and answering her telephone calls. Naturally he's relishing the idea of wielding some actual power.'

Chiswell took a swig of sherry.

'So, as you can see, I'm in something of a cleft stick, Mr Strike. Even if I were minded to pay off Jimmy Knight, I still have to contend with a man who wants my disgrace, and who may well be able to lay hands on proof.'

'How could Winn get proof?'

Chiswell took another large mouthful of treacle tart and glanced over his shoulder to check that Georgina remained safely in the kitchen.

'I've heard,' he muttered, and a fine mist of pastry flew from the slack lips, 'that there may be photographs.'

'Photographs?' repeated Strike.

'Winn can't *have* them, of course. If he had, it would all be over. But he might be able to find a way of getting hold of them. Yerse.'

He shoved the last piece of tart into his mouth, then said:

'Of course, there's a chance the photographs don't incriminate me. There are no distinguishing marks, so far as I'm aware.'

Strike's imagination frankly boggled. He yearned to ask, 'Distinguishing marks on what, Minister?' but refrained.

'It all happened six years ago,' continued Chiswell. 'I've been over and over the damn thing in my head. There were others involved who might have talked, but I doubt it, I doubt it very much. Too much to lose. No, it's all going to come down to what Knight and Winn can dig up. I strongly suspect that if he gets hold of the photographs, Winn will go straight to the press. I don't think that would be Knight's first choice. He simply wants money.

'So here I am, Mr Strike, *a fronte praecipitium, a tergo lupi*. I've lived with this hanging over me for weeks now. It hasn't been enjoyable.'

He peered at Strike through his tiny eyes, and the detective was irresistibly put in mind of a mole, blinking up at a hovering spade that waited to crush it.

'When I heard you were at that meeting I assumed you were investigating Knight and had some dirt on him. I've come to the conclusion that the only way out of this diabolical situation is to find something that I can use against each of them, before they get their hands on those photographs. Fight fire with fire.'

'Blackmail with blackmail?' said Strike.

'I don't want anything from them except to leave me the hell alone,' snapped Chiswell. 'Bargaining chips, that's all I want. I acted within the law,' he said firmly, 'and in accordance with my conscience.'

Chiswell was not a particularly likeable man, but Strike could well imagine that the ongoing suspense of waiting for public exposure would be torture, especially to a man who had already endured his fair share of scandals. Strike's scant research on his prospective client the previous evening had unearthed gleeful accounts of the affair that had ended his first marriage, of the fact that his second wife had spent a week in a clinic for 'nervous exhaustion' and of the grisly drug-induced car crash in which his younger son had killed a young mother.

'This is a very big job, Mr Chiswell,' said Strike. 'It'll take two or three people to thoroughly investigate Knight and Winn, especially if there's time pressure.'

'I don't care what it costs,' said Chiswell. 'I don't care if you have to put your whole agency on it.

'I refuse to believe there isn't anything dodgy about Winn, sneaking little toad that he is. There's something funny about them as a couple. She, the blind angel of light,' Chiswell's lip curled, 'and he, her potbellied henchman, always scheming and backstabbing and grubbing up every freebie he can get. There must be something there. Must be.

'As for Knight, Commie rabble rouser, there's bound to be something the police haven't yet caught up with. He was always a tearaway, a thoroughly nasty piece of work.'

'You knew Jimmy Knight before he started trying to blackmail you?' asked Strike.

'Oh, yes,' said Chiswell. 'The Knights are from my constituency. The father was an odd-job man who did a certain amount of work for our family. I never knew the mother. I believe she died before the three of them moved into Steda Cottage.'

'I see,' said Strike.

He was recalling Billy's anguished words, '*I seen a child strangled and nobody believes me*', the nervous movement from nose to chest as he made his slipshod half-cross, and the prosaic, precise detail of the pink blanket in which the dead child had been buried.

'There's something I think I should tell you before we discuss terms, Mr Chiswell,' said Strike. 'I was at the CORE meeting because I was trying to find Knight's younger brother. His name's Billy.'

The crease between Chiswell's myopic eyes deepened a fraction.

'Yerse, I remember that there were two of them, but Jimmy was the elder by a considerable amount – a decade or more, I would guess. I haven't seen – Billy, is it? – in many years.'

'Well, he's seriously mentally ill,' said Strike. 'He came to me last Monday with a peculiar story, then bolted.'

Chiswell waited, and Strike was sure he detected tension.

'Billy claims,' said Strike, 'that he witnessed the strangling of a small child when he was very young.'

Chiswell did not recoil, horrified; he did not bluster or storm. He did not demand whether he was being accused, or ask what on earth that had to do with him. He responded with none of the flamboyant defences of the guilty man, and yet Strike could have sworn that to Chiswell, this was not a new story.

'And who does he claim strangled the child?' he asked, fingering the stem of his wine glass.

'He didn't tell me – or wouldn't.'

'You think this is what Knight is blackmailing me over? Infanticide?' asked Chiswell roughly.

'I thought you ought to know why I went looking for Jimmy,' said Strike.

'I have no deaths on my conscience,' said Jasper Chiswell forcefully. He swallowed the last of his water. 'One cannot,' he added, replacing the empty glass on the table, 'be held accountable for unintended consequences.'

10

I have believed that we two together would be equal to it.

Henrik Ibsen, *Rosmersholm*

The detective and the minister emerged from 14 Park Place an hour later and walked the few yards that took them back to St James's Street. Chiswell had become less curmudgeonly and gnomic over coffee, relieved, Strike suspected, to have put in train some action that might lift from him what had clearly become an almost intolerable burden of dread and suspense. They had agreed terms and Strike was pleased with the deal, because this promised to be a better-paid and more challenging job than the agency had been given in a while.

'Well, thank you, Mr Strike,' said Chiswell, staring off down St James's as they both paused on the corner. 'I must leave you here. I have an appointment with my son.'

Yet he did not move.

'You investigated Freddie's death,' he said abruptly, glancing at Strike out of the corner of his eyes.

Strike had not expected Chiswell to raise the subject, and especially not here, as an afterthought, after the intensity of their basement discussion.

'Yes,' he replied. 'I'm sorry.'

Chiswell's eyes remained fixed on a distant art gallery.

'I remembered your name on the report,' said Chiswell. 'It's an unusual one.'

He swallowed, still squinting at the gallery. He seemed strangely unwilling to depart for his appointment.

'Wonderful boy, Freddie,' he said. 'Wonderful. Went into my old regiment – well, as good as. Queen's Own Hussars amalgamated with the Queen's Royal Irish back in ninety-three, as you'll know. So it was the Queen's Royal Hussars he joined.

'Full of promise. Full of life. But of course, you never knew him.'

'No,' said Strike.

Some polite comment seemed necessary.

'He was your eldest, wasn't he?'

'Of four,' said Chiswell, nodding. 'Two girls,' and by his inflection he waved them away, mere females, chaff to wheat, 'and this other boy,' he added darkly. 'He went to jail. Perhaps you saw the newspapers?'

'No,' lied Strike, because he knew what it felt like to have your personal details strewn across the newspapers. It was kindest, if at all credible, to pretend you hadn't read it all, politest to let people tell their own story.

'Been trouble all his life, Raff,' said Chiswell. 'I got him a job in there.'

He pointed a thick finger at the distant gallery window.

'Dropped out of his History of Art degree,' said Chiswell. 'Friend of mine owns the place, agreed to take him on. M'wife thinks he's a lost cause. He killed a young mother in a car. He was high.'

Strike said nothing.

'Well, goodbye,' said Chiswell, appearing to come out of

a melancholy trance. He offered his sweaty hand once more, which Strike shook, then strode away, bundled up in the thick coat that was so inappropriate on this fine June day.

Strike proceeded up St James's Street in the opposite direction, pulling out his mobile as he went. Robin picked up on the third ring.

'Need to meet you,' said Strike without preamble. 'We've got a new job, a big one.'

'Damn!' she said. 'I'm in Harley Street. I didn't want to bother you, knowing you were with Chiswell, but Andy's wife broke her wrist falling off a stepladder. I said I'd cover Dodgy while Andy takes her to hospital.'

'Shit. Where's Barclay?'

'Still on Webster.'

'Is Dodgy in his consulting room?'

'Yes.'

'We'll risk it,' said Strike. 'He usually goes straight home on Fridays. This is urgent. I need to tell you about it face to face. Can you meet me in the Red Lion in Duke of York Street?'

Having refused all alcohol during his meal with Chiswell, Strike fancied a pint rather than returning to the office. If he had stuck out in his suit at the White Horse in East Ham, he was perfectly dressed for Mayfair, and two minutes later he entered the Red Lion in Duke of York Street, a snug Victorian pub whose brass fittings and etched glass reminded him of the Tottenham. Taking a pint of London Pride off to a corner table, he looked up Della Winn and her husband on his phone and began reading an article about the forthcoming Paralympics, in which Della was extensively quoted.

'Hi,' said Robin, twenty-five minutes later, dropping her bag onto the seat opposite him.

'Want a drink?' he asked.

'I'll get it,' said Robin. 'Well?' she said, rejoining him a couple of minutes later, holding an orange juice. Strike smiled at her barely contained impatience. 'What was it all about? What did Chiswell want?'

The pub, which comprised only a horseshoe space around a single bar, was already tightly packed with smartly dressed men and women, who had started their weekend early or, like Strike and Robin, were finishing work over a drink. Lowering his voice, Strike told her what had passed between him and Chiswell.

'Oh,' said Robin blankly, when at last Strike had finished filling her in. 'So we're . . . we're going to try and get dirt on Della Winn?'

'On her husband,' Strike corrected her, 'and Chiswell prefers the phrase "bargaining chips".'

Robin said nothing, but sipped her orange juice.

'Blackmail's illegal, Robin,' said Strike, correctly reading her uneasy expression. 'Knight's trying to screw forty grand out of Chiswell and Winn wants to force him out of his job.'

'So he's going to blackmail them back and we're going to help him do it?'

'We get dirt on people every day,' said Strike roughly. 'It's a bit late to start getting a conscience about it.'

He took a long pull on his pint, annoyed not only by her attitude, but by the fact that he had let his resentment show. She lived with her husband in a desirable sash-windowed house in Albury Street, while he remained in two draughty rooms, from which he might soon be ejected by the redevelopment of the street. The agency had never before been offered a job that gave three people full employment, possibly for months. Strike was not about to apologise for being keen to take it. He was tired, after years of graft, of being plunged back into the red whenever the agency hit a lean patch. He had ambitions for his business that couldn't be achieved without building up a far healthier bank balance. Nevertheless, he felt compelled to defend his position.

'We're like lawyers, Robin. We're on the client's side.'

'You turned down that investment banker the other day, who wanted to find out where his wife—'

'—because it was bloody obvious he'd do her harm if he found her.'

'Well,' said Robin, a challenging look in her eye, 'what if the thing they've found out about Chiswell—'

But before she could finish her sentence, a tall man in deep conversation with a colleague walked straight into Robin's chair, flinging her forward into the table and knocking over her orange juice.

'Oi!' barked Strike, as Robin tried to wipe the juice off her sopping dress. 'Fancy apologising?'

'Oh dear,' said the man in a drawl, eyeing the juice-soaked Robin as several people turned to stare. 'Did I do that?'

'Yes, you bloody did,' said Strike, heaving himself up and moving around the table. 'And that's not an apology!'

'Cormoran!' said Robin warningly.

'Well, I'm sorry,' said the man, as though making an enormous concession, but taking in Strike's size, his regret seemed to become more sincere. 'Seriously, I do apol—'

'Bugger off,' snarled Strike. 'Swap seats,' he said to Robin. 'Then if some other clumsy tosser walks by they'll get me, not you.'

Half-embarrassed, half-touched, she picked up her handbag, which was also soaked, and did as he had requested. Strike returned to the table clutching a fistful of paper napkins, which he handed to her.

'Thanks.'

It was difficult to maintain a combative stance given that

he was voluntarily sitting in a chair covered in orange juice to spare her. Still dabbing off the juice, Robin leaned in and said quietly:

'You know what I'm worried about. The thing Billy said.'

The thin cotton dress was sticking to her everywhere: Strike kept his gaze resolutely on her eyes.

'I asked Chiswell about that.'

'Did you?'

'Of course I did. What else was I going to think, when he said he was being blackmailed by Billy's brother?'

'And what did he say?'

'He said he had no deaths on his hands, but "one cannot be held accountable for unintended consequences".'

'What on earth does *that* mean?'

'I asked. He gave me the hypothetical example of a man dropping a mint, on which a small child later choked to death.'

'*What?*'

'Your guess is as good as mine. Billy hasn't called back, I suppose?'

Robin shook her head.

'Look, the overwhelming probability is Billy's delusional,' said Strike. 'When I told Chiswell what Billy had said, I didn't get any sense of guilt or fear . . .'

As he said it, he remembered the shadow that had passed over Chiswell's face, and the impression he had received that the story was not, to Chiswell, entirely new.

'So what are they blackmailing Chiswell about?' asked Robin.

'Search me,' said Strike. 'He said it happened six years ago, which doesn't fit with Billy's story, because he wouldn't have been a little kid six years ago. Chiswell said some people would think what he did was immoral, but it wasn't illegal.

He seemed to be suggesting that it wasn't against the law when he did it, but is now.'

Strike suppressed a yawn. Beer and the heat of the afternoon were making him drowsy. He was due at Lorelei's later.

'So you trust him?' Robin asked.

'Do I trust Chiswell?' Strike wondered aloud, his eyes on the extravagantly engraved mirror behind Robin. 'If I had to bet on it, I'd say he was being truthful with me today because he's desperate. Do I think he's generally trustworthy? Probably no more than anyone else.'

'You didn't *like* him, did you?' asked Robin, incredulously. 'I've been reading about him.'

'And?'

'Pro-hanging, anti-immigration, voted against increasing maternity leave—'

She didn't notice Strike's involuntary glance down her figure as she continued:

'—banged on about family values, then left his wife for a journalist—'

'All right, I wouldn't choose him for a drinking buddy, but there's something slightly pitiable about him. He's lost one son, the other one's just killed a woman—'

'Well, yes, there you are,' said Robin. 'He advocates locking up petty criminals and throwing away the key, then his son runs over someone's mother and he pulls out all the stops to get him a short sen—'

She broke off suddenly as a loud female voice said: 'Robin! How lovely!'

Sarah Shadlock had entered the pub with two men.

'Oh God,' muttered Robin, before she could help herself, then, more loudly, 'Sarah, hi!'

She would have given much to avoid this encounter. Sarah would be delighted to tell Matthew that she had found Robin and Strike having a tête-à-tête in a Mayfair pub, when she herself had told Matthew by phone only an hour ago that she was alone in Harley Street.

Sarah insisted on wiggling around the table to embrace Robin, something the latter was sure she would not have done had she not been with men.

'Darling, what's happened to you? You're all sticky!'

She was just a little posher here, in Mayfair, than anywhere else Robin had met her, and several degrees warmer to Robin.

'Nothing,' muttered Robin. 'Spilled orange juice, that's all.'

'Cormoran!' said Sarah blithely, swooping in for a kiss on his cheek. Strike, Robin was pleased to note, sat impassive and did not respond. 'Bit of R and R?' said Sarah, embracing them both in her knowing smile.

'Work,' said Strike bluntly.

Receiving no encouragement to stay, Sarah moved along the bar, taking her colleagues with her.

'I forgot Christie's is round the corner,' muttered Robin.

Strike checked his watch. He didn't want to have to wear his suit to Lorelei's, and indeed, it was now stained with orange juice from having taken Robin's seat.

'We need to talk about how we're going to do this job, because it starts tomorrow.'

'OK,' said Robin with some trepidation, because it had been a long time since she had worked a weekend. Matthew had got used to her coming home.

'It's all right,' said Strike, apparently reading her mind, 'I won't need you till Monday.

'The job's going to take three people at a minimum. I reckon we've already got enough on Webster to keep the client happy, so we'll put Andy full time on Dodgy Doc, let the two waiting-list clients know we're not going to be able to do them this month and Barclay can come in with us on the Chiswell case.

'On Monday, you're going into the House of Commons.'

'I'm what?' said Robin, startled.

'You're going to go in as Chiswell's goddaughter, who's interested in a career in Parliament, and get started on Geraint, who runs Della's constituency office at the other end of the corridor to Chiswell's. Chat him up . . .'

He took a swig of beer, frowning at her over the top of the glass.

'What?' said Robin, unsure what was coming.

'How d'you feel,' said Strike, so quietly that she had to lean in to hear him, 'about breaking the law?'

'Well, I tend to be opposed to it,' said Robin, unsure whether to be amused or worried. 'That's sort of why I wanted to do investigative work.'

'And if the law's a bit of a grey area, and we can't get the information any other way? Bearing in mind that Winn's definitely breaking the law, trying to blackmail a Minister of the Crown out of his job?'

'Are you talking about bugging Winn's office?'

'Right in one,' said Strike. Correctly reading her dubious expression, he went on. 'Listen, by Chiswell's account, Winn's a slapdash loudmouth, which is why he's stuck in the constituency office and kept well away from his wife's work at the Department for Sport. Apparently he leaves his office door open most of the time, shouts about constituents' confidential affairs and leaves private papers lying around in the communal kitchen. There's a good chance you'll be able to inveigle indiscretions out of him without needing the bug, but I don't think we can count on it.'

Robin swilled the last of her orange juice in her glass, deliberating, then said:

'All right, I'll do it.'

'Sure?' said Strike. 'OK, well you won't be able to take

devices in, because you'll have to go through a metal detector. I've said I'm going to get a handful to Chiswell tomorrow. He'll pass them to you once you're inside.

'You'll need a cover name. Text it to me when you've thought of one so I can let Chiswell know. You could use "Venetia Hall" again, actually. Chiswell's the kind of bloke who'd have a goddaughter called Venetia.'

'Venetia' was Robin's middle name, but Robin was too full of apprehension and excitement to care that Strike, from his smirk, continued to find it amusing.

'You're going to have to work a disguise as well,' said Strike. 'Nothing major, but Chiswell remembered what you look like from the Ripper coverage, so we've got to assume Winn might, too.'

'It'll be too hot for a wig,' she said. 'I might try coloured contact lenses. I could go and buy some now. Maybe some plain-lensed glasses on top.' A smile she could not suppress surfaced again. 'The House of Commons!' she repeated excitedly.

Robin's excited grin faded as Sarah Shadlock's white-blonde head intruded on the periphery of her vision, on the other side of the bar. Sarah had just repositioned herself to keep Robin and Strike in her sights.

'Let's go,' Robin said to Strike.

As they walked back towards the Tube, Strike explained that Barclay would be tailing Jimmy Knight.

'I can't do it,' said Strike regretfully. 'I've blown my cover with him and his CORE mates.'

'So what will you be up to?'

'Plug gaps, follow up leads, cover nights if we need them,' said Strike.

'Poor Lorelei,' said Robin.

It had slipped out before she could stop herself. Increasingly heavy traffic was rolling past, and when Strike did not answer, Robin hoped that he hadn't heard her.

'Did Chiswell mention his son who died in Iraq?' she asked, rather like a person hastily coughing to hide a laugh that has already escaped them.

'Yeah,' said Strike. 'Freddie was clearly his favourite child, which doesn't say much for his judgement.'

'What d'you mean?'

'Freddie Chiswell was a prize shit. I investigated a lot of Killed in Actions, and I never had so many people ask me whether the dead officer had been shot in the back by his own men.'

Robin looked shocked.

'*De mortuis nil nisi bonum?*' asked Strike.

Robin had learned quite a lot of Latin, working with Strike.

'Well,' she said quietly, for the first time finding some pity in her heart for Jasper Chiswell, 'you can't expect his father to speak ill of him.'

They parted at the top of the street, Robin to shop for coloured contact lenses, Strike heading for the Tube.

He felt unusually cheerful after the conversation with Robin: as they contemplated this challenging job, the familiar contours of their friendship had suddenly resurfaced. He had liked her excitement at the prospect of entering the House of Commons; liked being the one who had offered the chance. He had even enjoyed the way she stress-tested his assumptions about Chiswell's story.

On the point of entering the station, Strike turned suddenly aside, infuriating the irate businessman who had been walking six inches in his wake. Tutting furiously, the man barely avoided a collision and strode off huffily into the Underground while the indifferent Strike leaned up against the sun-soaked wall, enjoying the sensation of heat permeating his suit jacket as he phoned Detective Inspector Eric Wardle.

Strike had told Robin the truth. He didn't believe that Chiswell had ever strangled a child, yet there had been something undeniably odd about his reaction to Billy's story. Thanks to the minister's revelation that the Knight family had lived in proximity to his family home, Strike now knew that Billy had been a 'little kid' in Oxfordshire. The first logical step in assuaging his continued unease about that pink blanket was to find out whether any children in the area had disappeared a couple of decades ago, and never been found.

11

. . . let us stifle all memories in our sense of freedom, in joy, in passion.

Henrik Ibsen, *Rosmersholm*

Lorelei Bevan lived in an eclectically furnished flat over her thriving vintage clothes store in Camden. Strike arrived that night at half past seven, a bottle of Pinot Noir in one hand and his mobile clamped to his ear with the other. Lorelei opened the door, smiled good-naturedly at the familiar sight of him on the phone, kissed him on the mouth, relieved him of his wine and returned to the kitchen, from which a welcome smell of Pad Thai was issuing.

'. . . or try and get into CORE itself,' Strike told Barclay, closing the door behind him and proceeding to Lorelei's sitting room, which was dominated by a large print of Warhol's Elizabeth Taylors. 'I'll send you everything I've got on Jimmy. He's involved with a couple of different groups. No idea whether he's working. His local's the White Horse in East Ham. Think he's a Hammers fan.'

'Could be worse,' said Barclay, who was speaking quietly, as he had just got the teething baby to sleep. 'Could be Chelsea.'

'You'll have to admit to being ex-army,' said Strike, sinking into an armchair and hoisting his leg up onto a conveniently positioned square pouffe. 'You look like a squaddie.'

'Nae problem,' said Barclay. 'I'll be the poor wee laddie who didnae know whut he was gettin' himself intae. Hard lefties love that shit. Let 'em patronise me.'

Grinning, Strike took out his cigarettes. For all his initial doubts, he was starting to think that Barclay might have been a good hire.

'All right, hang fire till you hear from me again. Should be sometime Sunday.'

As Strike rang off, Lorelei appeared with a glass of red for him.

'Want some help in the kitchen?' Strike asked, though without moving.

'No, stay there. I won't be long,' she replied, smiling. He liked her fifties-style apron.

As she returned to the kitchen, he lit up. Although Lorelei did not smoke, she had no objection to Strike's Benson & Hedges as long as he used the kitsch ashtray, decorated with cavorting poodles, that she had provided for the purpose.

Smoking, he admitted to himself that he envied Barclay infiltrating Knight and his band of hard-left colleagues. It was the kind of job Strike had relished in the Military Police. He remembered the four soldiers in Germany who had become enamoured of a local far-right group. Strike had managed to persuade them that he shared their belief in a white ethno-nationalist super-state, infiltrated a meeting and secured four arrests and prosecutions that had given him particular satisfaction.

Turning on the TV, he watched Channel 4 News for a while, drinking his wine, smoking in pleasurable anticipation of Pad Thai and other sensual delights, and for once enjoying what so many of his fellow workers took for granted, but which he had rarely experienced: the relief and release of a Friday night.

Strike and Lorelei had met at Eric Wardle's birthday party. It had been an awkward evening in some ways, because Strike had seen Coco there for the first time since telling her by phone that he had no interest in another date. Coco had got very drunk; at one in the morning, while he was sitting on a sofa deep in conversation with Lorelei, she had marched across the room, thrown a glass of wine over both of them and stormed off into the night. Strike had not been aware that Coco and Lorelei were old friends until the morning after he woke up in Lorelei's bed. He considered that this was really more Lorelei's problem than his. She seemed to think the exchange, for Coco wanted nothing more to do with her, more than fair.

'How d'you do it?' Wardle had asked, the next time they met, genuinely puzzled. 'Blimey, I'd like to know your—'

Strike raised his heavy eyebrows and Wardle appeared to gag on what had come perilously close to a compliment.

'There's no secret,' said Strike. 'Some women just like fat one-legged pube-headed men with broken noses.'

'Well, it's a sad indictment of our mental health services that they're loose on the streets,' Wardle had said, and Strike had laughed.

Lorelei was her real name, taken not from the mythical siren of the Rhine, but from Marilyn Monroe's character in *Gentlemen Prefer Blondes*, her mother's favourite film. Men's eyes swivelled when she passed them in the street, but she evoked neither the profound longing nor the searing pain that Charlotte had caused Strike. Whether this was because Charlotte had stunted his capacity to feel so intensely, or because Lorelei lacked some essential magic, he did not know. Neither Strike nor Lorelei had said 'I love you'. In Strike's case this was because, desirable and amusing though he found her, he could not have said it honestly. It was convenient to him to assume that Lorelei felt the same way.

She had recently ended a five-year-long live-in relationship when, after several lingering looks across Wardle's dark sitting room, he had strolled across to talk to her. He had wanted to believe her when she had told him how glorious it was to have her flat to herself and her freedom restored, yet lately he had felt tiny spots of displeasure when he had told her he had to work weekends, like the first heavy drops of rain that presage a storm. She denied it when challenged: *no, no, of course not, if you've got to work . . .*

But Strike had set out his uncompromising terms at the outset of the relationship: his work was unpredictable and his finances poor. Hers was the only bed he intended to visit, but if she sought predictability or permanence, he was not the man for her. She had appeared content with the deal, and if, over the course of ten months, she had grown less so, Strike was ready to call things off with no hard feelings. Perhaps she sensed this, because she had forced no argument. This pleased him, and not merely because he could do without the aggravation. He liked Lorelei, enjoyed sleeping with her and found it desirable – for a reason he did not bother to dwell on, being perfectly aware what it was – to be in a relationship just now.

The Pad Thai was excellent, their conversation light and amusing. Strike told Lorelei nothing about his new case, except that he hoped it would be both lucrative and interesting. After doing the dishes together, they repaired to the bedroom, with its candy-pink walls and its curtains printed with cartoonish cowgirls and ponies.

Lorelei liked to dress up. To bed that night, she wore

stockings and a black corset. She had the talent, by no means usual, of staging an erotic scene without tipping into parody. Perhaps, with his one leg and his broken nose, Strike ought to have felt ludicrous in this boudoir, which was all frivolity and prettiness, but she played Aphrodite to his Hephaestus so adeptly that thoughts of Robin and Matthew were sometimes driven entirely from his mind.

There was, after all, little pleasure to compare with that given by a woman who really wanted you, he thought next day at lunchtime, as they sat side by side at a pavement café, reading separate papers, Strike smoking, Lorelei's perfectly painted nails trailing absently along the back of his hand. So why had he already told her that he needed to work this afternoon? It was true that he needed to drop off the listening devices at Chiswell's Belgravia flat, but he could easily have spent another night with her, returned to the bedroom, the stockings and the basque. The prospect was certainly tempting.

Yet something implacable inside him refused to give in. Two nights in a row would break the pattern; from there, it would be a short slide into true intimacy. In the depths of himself Strike could not imagine a future in which he lived with a woman, married or fathered children. He had planned some of those things with Charlotte, in the days when he had been readjusting to life minus half his leg. An IED on a dusty road in Afghanistan had blasted Strike out of his chosen life into an entirely new body and a new reality. Sometimes he saw his proposal to Charlotte as the most extreme manifestation of his temporary disorientation in the aftermath of his amputation. He had needed to relearn how to walk, and, almost as hard, to live a life outside the military. From a distance of two years, he saw himself trying to hold tight to some part of his past as everything else slipped away. The allegiance he had given the army, he had transferred to a future with Charlotte.

'Good move,' his old friend Dave Polworth had said without missing a beat, when Strike told him of the engagement. 'Shame to waste all that combat training. Slightly increased risk of getting killed, though, mate.'

Had he ever really thought the wedding would happen? Had he truly imagined Charlotte settling for the life he could give her? After everything they had been through, had he believed that they could achieve redemption together, each of them damaged in their own untidy, personal and peculiar ways? It seemed to Strike sitting in the sunshine with Lorelei that for a few months he had both believed it wholeheartedly and known that it was impossible, never planning more than a few weeks ahead, holding Charlotte at night as though she were the last human on earth, as though only Armageddon could separate them.

'Want another coffee?' murmured Lorelei.

'I'd better make a move,' said Strike.

'When will I see you?' she asked, as Strike paid the waiter.

'Told you, I've got this big new job on,' he said. 'Timings are going to be a bit unpredictable for a while. I'll call you tomorrow. We'll go out as soon as I can get a clear evening.'

'All right,' she said, smiling, and added softly, 'Kiss me.'

He did so. She pressed her full lips against his, irresistibly recalling certain highlights of the early morning. They broke apart. Strike grinned, bade her goodbye and left her sitting in the sun with her newspaper.

The Minister for Culture did not invite Strike inside when he opened the door of his house in Ebury Street. Chiswell seemed keen, in fact, for the detective to leave as quickly as possible. After taking the box of listening devices, he muttered, 'Good, right, I'll make sure she gets them,' and was on the point of closing the door when he suddenly called after Strike, 'what's her name?'

'Venetia Hall,' said Strike.

Chiswell shut the door, and Strike turned his tired footsteps back along the street of quiet golden townhouses, towards the Tube and Denmark Street.

His office seemed stark and gloomy after Lorelei's flat. Strike threw open the windows to let in the noise of Denmark Street down below, where music lovers continued to visit the instrument stores and old record shops that Strike feared were doomed by the forthcoming redevelopment. The sound of engines and horns, of conversation and footsteps, of guitar riffs played by would-be purchasers and the distant bongos of another busker were pleasant to Strike as he settled to work, knowing that he had hours ahead in the computer chair if he were to wrest the bare bones of his targets' lives from the internet.

If you knew where to search and had time and expertise, the outline of many existences could be unearthed in cyberspace: ghostly exoskeletons, sometimes partial, sometimes unnervingly complete, of the lives led by their flesh and blood counterparts. Strike had learned many tricks and secrets, become adept ferreting in even the darkest corners of the internet, but often the most innocent social media sites held untold wealth, a minor amount of cross-referencing all that was necessary to compile detailed private histories that their careless owners had never meant to share with the world.

Strike first consulted Google Maps to examine the place where Jimmy and Billy had grown up. Steda Cottage was evidently too small and insignificant to be named, but Chiswell House was clearly marked, a short way outside the village of Woolstone. Strike spent five minutes fruitlessly scanning the patches of woodland around Chiswell House, noticing a couple of tiny squares that might be estate cottages – *they buried it down in the dell by my dad's house* – before resuming his investigation of the older, saner brother.

CORE had a website where Strike found, sandwiched between lengthy polemics about celebration capitalism and neo-liberalism, a useful schedule of protests at which Jimmy was planning to demonstrate or speak, which the detective printed out and added to his file. He then followed a link to the Real Socialist Party website, which was an even busier and more cluttered affair than that of CORE. Here he found another lengthy article by Jimmy, arguing for the dissolution of the 'apartheid state' of Israel and the defeat of the 'Zionist lobby' which had a stranglehold on the Western capitalist establishment. Strike noted that Jasper Chiswell was among the 'Western Political Elite' listed at the bottom of this article as a 'publicly declared Zionist'.

Jimmy's girlfriend, Flick, appeared in a couple of photographs on the Real Socialist website, sporting black hair as she marched against Trident and blonde shaded to pink as she cheered Jimmy, who was speaking on an open-air stage at a Real Socialist Party rally. Following a link to Flick's Twitter handle, he perused her timeline, which was a strange mixture of the cloying and the vituperative. 'I hope you get fucking arse cancer, you Tory cunt' sat directly above a video clip of a kitten sneezing so hard that it fell out of its basket.

As far as Strike could tell, neither Jimmy nor Flick owned or ever had owned property, something that he had in common with both of them. He could find no indication online of how they were supporting themselves, unless writing for far-left websites paid better than he had imagined. Jimmy was renting the miserable flat in Charlemont Road from a man called Kasturi Kumar, and while Flick made casual mention on social media of living in Hackney, he could not find an address for her anywhere online.

Digging deeper into online records, Strike discovered a James Knight of the correct age who seemed to have cohabited for five years with a woman called Dawn Clancy, and upon delving into Dawn's highly informative, emoji-strewn Facebook page, Strike discovered that they had been married. Dawn was a hairdresser who had run a successful business in London before returning to her native Manchester. Thirteen years older than Jimmy, she seemed to have neither children nor any present-day contact with her ex-husband. However, a comment she had made to a jilted girlfriend's 'all men are trash' post, caught Strike's eye: 'Yeah, he's a shit, but at least he hasn't sued you! I win (again)!'

Intrigued, Strike turned his attention to court records and, after a little digging, found several useful nuggets of information. Jimmy had been charged with affray twice, once on an anti-capitalism march, once at an anti-Trident protest, but this, Strike had expected. What was far more interesting was to find Jimmy on a list of vexatious litigants on the website of HM Courts and Tribunals Service. Due to a longstanding habit of beginning frivolous legal actions, Knight was now 'forbidden from starting civil cases in courts without permission'.

Jimmy had certainly had a good run for his, or the state's, money. Over the past decade he had brought civil actions against sundry individuals and organisations. The law had taken his side only once, when, in 2007, he had won compensation from Zanet Industries, who were found not to have followed due process when dismissing him.

Jimmy had represented himself in court against Zanet and, presumably elated by his win, had gone on to represent himself in suing several others, among them a garage owner, two neighbours, a journalist he alleged had defamed him, two officers in the Metropolitan Police he claimed had assaulted him, two more employers and, finally, his ex-wife, who he said had harassed him and caused him loss of earnings.

In Strike's experience, those who disdained the use of representation in court were either unbalanced or so arrogant that it came to the same thing. Jimmy's litigious history suggested that he was greedy and unprincipled, sharp without being wise. It was always useful to have a handle on a man's vulnerabilities when trying to ferret out his secrets. Strike added the names of all the people Jimmy had tried to sue, plus the current address of his ex-wife, to the file beside him.

At close to midnight Strike retired to his flat for some much-needed sleep, rose early on Sunday, and transferred his attention to Geraint Winn, remaining hunched at the computer until the light began to fade again, by which time a new cardboard file labelled CHISWELL sat beside him, fat with miscellaneous but crosschecked information on Chiswell's two blackmailers.

Stretching and yawning, he became suddenly aware of the noises reaching him through the open windows. The music shops had closed at last, the bongos had ceased, but traffic continued to swish and rumble along Charing Cross Road. Strike heaved himself up, supporting himself on the desk because his remaining ankle was numb after hours in the computer chair, and stooped to look through the inner office window at a tangerine sky spread beyond the rooftops.

It was Sunday evening and in less than two hours England would be playing Italy at the quarter-finals of the European Football Championships in Kiev. The small portable TV that was all his flat upstairs could comfortably accommodate might not be the ideal medium on which to watch such an important game, but he could not justify a night in a pub given that he had an early start on Monday, covering Dodgy Doc again, a prospect that gave him little pleasure.

He checked his watch. He had time to get a Chinese takeaway before the match, but he still needed to call both Barclay and Robin with instructions for the next few days. As he was on the point of picking up the phone, a musical alert told him that he had received an email.

The subject line read: 'Missing Kids in Oxfordshire'. Strike laid his mobile and keys back on the desk and clicked it open.

> Strike –
> This is best I can do on a quick search. Obviously without exact time frame it's difficult. 2 missing child cases in Oxfordshire/Wiltshire from the early/mid 90s unresolved as far as I can tell. Suki Lewis, 12, went missing from care October 1992. Also Immamu Ibrahim, 5-year-old, disappeared 1996. Father disappeared at the same time, is believed to be in Algeria. Without further information, not much to be done.
> Best, E

12

The atmosphere we breathe is heavy with storms.

Henrik Ibsen, *Rosmersholm*

The sunset cast a ruddy glow across the duvet behind Robin as she sat at the dressing table in her and Matthew's spacious new bedroom. Next-door's barbecue was now smoking the air that had earlier been fragrant with honeysuckle. She had just left Matthew downstairs, lying on the sofa watching the warm-up to the England–Italy game, a cold bottle of Peroni in his hand.

Opening the dressing table drawer, she took out a pair of coloured contact lenses she had concealed there. After trial and error the previous day, she had decided the hazel ones appeared most natural with her strawberry-blonde hair. Gingerly, she extracted first one, then the other, placing them over her watering blue-grey irises. It was essential that she get used to wearing them. Ideally she would have had them in all weekend, but Matthew's reaction when he had seen her in them had dissuaded her.

'Your eyes!' he had said, after staring at her, perplexed, for a few seconds. 'Bloody hell, that looks horrible, take them out!'

As Saturday had already been ruined by one of their tense disagreements about her job, she had chosen not to wear the lenses all weekend, because they would serve as a constant reminder to Matthew about what she was up to the following week. He seemed to think that working undercover in the House of Commons was tantamount to treason, and her refusal to tell him who either her client or her targets were had further aggravated him.

Robin kept telling herself that Matthew was worried about her safety and that he could hardly be blamed for it. It had become a mental exercise she performed like a penance: *you can't blame him for being concerned, you nearly got killed last year, he wants you to be safe.* However, the fact that she had gone for a drink with Strike on Friday seemed to be worrying Matthew far more than any potential killer.

'Don't you think you're being bloody hypocritical?' he said.

Whenever he was angry, the skin around his nose and upper lip became taut. Robin had noticed it years ago, but lately it gave her a sensation close to revulsion. She had never mentioned this to her therapist. It had felt too nasty, too visceral.

'How am I hypocritical?'

'Going for cosy little drinks with him—'

'Matt, I work with—'

'—then complaining when I have lunch with Sarah.'

'Have lunch with her!' said Robin, her pulse quickening in anger. 'Do it! As a matter of fact, I met her in the Red Lion, out with some men from work. Do you want to call Tom and tell him his fiancée's drinking with colleagues? Or am I the only one who's not allowed to do it?'

The skin around his nose and mouth looked like a muzzle as it tightened, Robin thought: a pale muzzle on a snarling dog.

'Would you have told me you'd gone for a drink with him if Sarah hadn't seen you?'

'Yes,' said Robin, her temper snapping, 'and I'd've known you'd be a dick about it, too.'

The tense aftermath of this argument, by no means their most serious of the last month, had lingered all through Sunday. Only in the last couple of hours, with the prospect of the England game to cheer him, had Matthew become amiable again. Robin had even volunteered to fetch him a Peroni from the kitchen and kissed him on the forehead before leaving him, with a sense of liberation, for her coloured contact lenses and her preparations for the following day.

Her eyes felt gradually less uncomfortable with repeated blinking. Robin moved across to the bed, where her laptop lay. Pulling it towards her, she saw that an email from Strike had just arrived.

Robin,
Bit of research on the Winns attached. I'll call you shortly for quick brief before tomorrow.
CS

Robin was annoyed. Strike was supposed to be 'plugging gaps' and working nights. Did he think she had done no research of her own over the weekend? Nevertheless, she clicked on the first of several attachments, a document summarising the fruits of Strike's online labour.

Geraint Winn

Geraint Ifon Winn, d.o.b. 15th July 1950. Born Cardiff. Father a miner. Grammar school educated, met Della at University of Cardiff. Was 'property consultant' prior to acting as her election agent and running her Parliamentary office post-election. No details of former career available online. No company ever registered in his name. Lives with Della, Southwark Park Road, Bermondsey.

Strike had managed to dig up a couple of poor-quality pictures of Geraint with his well-known wife, both of which Robin had already found and saved to her laptop. She knew how hard Strike had had to work to find an image of Geraint, because it had taken her a long time the previous night, while Matthew slept, to find them. Press photographers did not seem to feel he added much to pictures. A thin, balding man who wore heavy-framed glasses, he had a lipless mouth, a weak chin and a pronounced overbite, which taken together put Robin in mind of an overweight gecko.

Strike had also attached information on the Minister for Sport.

Della Winn

D.o.b. 8th August 1947. Née Jones. Born and raised Vale of Glamorgan, Wales. Both parents teachers. Blind from birth due to bilateral microphthalmia. Attended St Enodoch Royal School for the Blind from age 5 – 18. Won multiple swimming awards as teenager. (See attached articles for further details, also of The Playing Field charity).

Even though Robin had read as much as she could about Della over the weekend, she ploughed diligently through both articles. They told her little that she did not already know. Della had worked for a prominent human rights charity before successfully standing for election in the Welsh constituency in which she had been born. She was a long-time advocate for the benefit of sports in deprived areas, a champion of disabled athletes and a supporter for projects that used sport to rehabilitate injured veterans. The founding of her charity, the Level Playing Field, to support young athletes and sportspeople facing challenges, whether of poverty or physical impairment, had received a fair amount of press coverage. Many high-profile sportspeople had given their time to fundraisers.

The articles that Strike had attached both mentioned something that Robin already knew from her own research: the Winns, like the Chiswells, had lost a child. Della and Geraint's daughter and only offspring had killed herself at the age of sixteen, a year before Della had stood for Parliament. The tragedy was mentioned in every profile Robin had read on Della Winn, even those lauding her substantial achievements. Her maiden speech in Parliament had supported a proposed bullying hotline, but she had never otherwise discussed her child's suicide.

Robin's mobile rang. After checking that the bedroom door was closed, Robin answered.

'That was quick,' said Strike thickly, through a mouthful of Singapore noodles. 'Sorry – took me by surprise – just got a takeaway.'

'I've read your email,' said Robin. She heard a metallic snap and was sure he was opening a can of beer. 'Very useful, thanks.'

'Got your disguise sorted?' Strike asked.

'Yes,' said Robin, turning to examine herself at the mirror. It was strange how much a change of eye colour transformed your face. She was planning to wear a pair of clear-lensed glasses over her hazel eyes.

'And you know enough about Chiswell to pretend to be his goddaughter?'

'Of course,' said Robin.

'Go on then,' said Strike, 'impress me.'

'Born 1944,' Robin said at once, without reading her notes. 'Studied Classics at Merton College, Oxford, then joined Queen's Own Hussars, saw active service in Aden and Singapore.

'First wife, Lady Patricia Fleetwood, three children: Sophia, Isabella and Freddie. Sophia's married and lives in Northumberland, Isabella runs Chiswell's Parliamentary office—'

'Does she?' said Strike, sounding vaguely surprised, and Robin was pleased to know that she had discovered something he had not.

'Is she the daughter you knew?' she asked, remembering what Strike had said in the office.

'Wouldn't go as far as "knew". I met her a couple of times with Charlotte. Everyone called her "Izzy Chizzy". One of those upper-class nicknames.'

'Lady Patricia divorced Chiswell after he got a political journalist pregnant—'

'—which resulted in the disappointing son at the art gallery.'

'Exactly—'

Robin moved the mouse around to bring up a saved picture, this time of a dark and rather beautiful young man in a charcoal suit, heading up courtroom steps accompanied by a stylish, black-haired woman in sunglasses whom he closely resembled, though she looked hardly old enough to be his mother.

'—but Chiswell and the journalist split up not long after Raphael was born,' said Robin.

'The family calls him "Raff",' said Strike, 'and the second

wife doesn't like him, thinks Chiswell should have disowned him after the car crash.'

Robin made a further note.

'Great, thanks. Chiswell's current wife, Kinvara, was unwell last year,' Robin continued, bringing up a picture of Kinvara, a curvaceous redhead in a slinky black dress and heavy diamond necklace. She was some thirty years younger than Chiswell and pouting at the camera. Had she not known, Robin would have guessed them father and daughter rather than a married couple.

'With nervous exhaustion,' said Strike, beating her to it. 'Yeah. Drink or drugs, d'you reckon?'

Robin heard a clang and surmised that Strike had just dropped an empty Tennent's can in the office bin. He was alone, then. Lorelei never stayed in the tiny flat upstairs.

'Who knows?' said Robin, her eyes still on Kinvara Chiswell.

'One last thing,' said Strike. 'Just in. A couple of kids went missing in Oxfordshire around the right time to tally with Billy's story.'

There was a brief pause.

'You still there?' asked Strike.

'Yes ... I thought you don't believe Chiswell strangled a child?'

'I don't,' said Strike. 'The timescale doesn't fit, and if Jimmy knew a Tory minister had strangled a kid, he wouldn't have waited twenty years to try and monetise it. But I'd still like to know whether Billy's imagining that he saw someone throttled. I'm going to do a bit of digging on the names Wardle's given me and if either seem credible I might ask you to sound Izzy out. She might remember something about a kid disappearing in the vicinity of Chiswell House.'

Robin said nothing.

'Like I said in the pub, Billy's very ill. It's probably

nothing,' said Strike, with a trace of defensiveness. As he and Robin were both well aware, he had previously jettisoned paid cases and rich clients to pursue mysteries that others might have let lie. 'I just—'

'—can't rest easy until you've looked into it,' said Robin. 'All right. I understand.'

Unseen by her, Strike grinned and rubbed his tired eyes.

'Well, best of luck tomorrow,' he said. 'I'll be on my mobile if you need me.'

'What are you going to be up to?'

'Paperwork. Jimmy Knight's ex doesn't work Mondays. I'm off to Manchester to find her on Tuesday.'

Robin experienced a sudden wave of nostalgia for the previous year, when she and Strike had undertaken a road trip together to interrogate women left behind in the wake of dangerous men. She wondered whether he had thought about it while he planned this journey.

'Watching England–Italy?' she asked.

'Yeah,' said Strike. 'There's nothing else, is there?'

'No,' said Robin hurriedly. She had not meant to sound as though she wanted to detain him. 'Speak soon, then.'

She cut the call on his farewell and tossed the mobile aside onto the bed.

13

I am not going to let myself be beaten to the ground by the dread of what may happen.

Henrik Ibsen, *Rosmersholm*

The following morning, Robin woke, gasping, her fingers at her own throat, trying to loosen a non-existent hold. She was already at the bedroom door when Matthew woke, confused.

'It's nothing, I'm fine,' she muttered, before he could articulate a question, groping to find the handle that would let her out of the bedroom.

The surprise was that it hadn't happened more often since she had heard the story of the strangled child. Robin knew exactly how it felt to have fingers close tightly around your neck, to feel your brain flood with darkness, to know that you were seconds from being blotted out of existence. She had been driven into therapy by sharp-edged fragments of recollection that were unlike normal memories and which had the power to drag her suddenly out of her body and plunge her back into a past where she could smell the strangler's nicotine-stained fingers, and feel the stabber's soft, sweatshirted belly against her back.

She locked the bathroom door and sat down on the floor

in the loose T-shirt she had worn to bed, focusing on her breathing, on the feel of the cool tiles beneath her bare legs, observing, as she had been taught, the rapid beating of her heart, the adrenaline jolting through her veins, not fighting her panic, but watching it. After a while, she consciously noticed the faint smell of the lavender body wash she had used last night, and heard the distant passing of an aeroplane.

You're safe. Just a dream. Just a dream.

Through two closed doors, she heard Matthew's alarm go off. A few minutes later, he knocked on the door.

'You all right?'

'Fine,' Robin called back, over the running tap.

She opened the door.

'Everything OK?' he asked, watching her closely.

'Just needed a pee,' said Robin brightly, heading back to the bedroom for her coloured contact lenses.

Before starting work with Strike, Robin had signed on with an agency called Temporary Solutions. The offices to which they had sent her were jumbled in her memory now, so that only anomalies, eccentrics and oddities remained. She remembered the alcoholic boss whose dictated letters she had reworded out of kindness, the desk drawer she had opened to find a complete set of dentures and a pair of stained underpants, the hopeful young man who had nicknamed her 'Bobbie' and tried, ineptly, to flirt over their back-to-back monitors, the woman who had plastered the interior of her cubicle workspace with pictures of the actor Ian McShane and the girl who had broken up with her boyfriend on the telephone in the middle of the open-plan office, indifferent to the prurient hush falling over the rest of the room. Robin doubted whether any of the people with whom she had come into glancing contact remembered her any better than she remembered them, even the timid romancer who had called her 'Bobbie'.

However, from the moment that she arrived at the Palace of Westminster, she knew that what happened here would live in her memory for ever. She felt a ripple of pleasure simply to leave the tourists behind and pass through the gate where the policeman stood guard. As she approached the palace, with its intricate gold mouldings starkly shadowed in the early morning sun, the famous clock tower silhouetted against the sky, her nerves and her excitement mounted.

Strike had told her which side door to use. It led into a long, dimly lit stone hall, but first she must pass through a metal detector and X-ray machine of the kind used at airports. As she took off her shoulder bag to be scanned, Robin noticed a tall, slightly dishevelled natural blonde in her thirties waiting a short distance away, holding a small package wrapped in brown paper. The woman watched as Robin stood for an automated picture that would appear on a paper day pass, to be worn on a lanyard around her neck, and when the security man waved Robin on, stepped forwards.

'Venetia?'

'Yes,' said Robin.

'Izzy,' said the other, smiling and holding out a hand. She was wearing a loose blouse with a splashy pattern of oversize flowers on it, and wide-legged trousers. 'This is from Papa.' She pressed the package she was holding into Robin's hands. 'I'm *rilly* sorry, we've got to dash – so glad you got here on time—'

She set off at a brisk walk, and Robin hastened to follow.

'—I'm in the middle of printing off a bunch of papers to take over to Papa at DCMS – I'm *snowed under* just now. Papa being Minister for Culture, with the Olympics coming, it's just crazy—'

She led Robin at a near jog through the hall, which had stained-glass windows at the far end, and off along labyrinthine corridors, talking all the while in a confident, upper-class accent, leaving Robin impressed by her lungpower.

'Yah, I'm leaving at the summer recess – setting up a decorating company with my friend Jacks – I've been here for five years – Papa's not happy – he needs somebody *rilly* good and the only applicant he liked turned us down.'

She talked over her shoulder at Robin, who was hurrying to keep up.

'I don't s'pose you know any *fabulous* PAs?'

'I'm afraid not,' said Robin, who had retained no friends from her temping career.

'Nearly there,' said Izzy, who had led Robin through a bewildering number of narrow corridors, all carpeted in the same forest green as the leather seats Robin had seen in the Commons on TV. At last they reached a side-passage off which led several heavy wooden doors, arched in the gothic style.

'That,' said Izzy in a stage whisper, pointing as they passed the first door on the right, 'is Winn's. This,' she said, marching to the last door on the left, 'is ours.'

She stood aside to let Robin pass into the room first.

The office was cramped and cluttered. The arched stone windows were hung with net curtains, beyond which lay the terrace bar, where shadowy figures moved against the dazzling brightness of the Thames. There were two desks, a multitude of bookshelves and a sagging green armchair. Green drapes hung at the overflowing bookshelves that covered one wall, only partially concealing the untidy stacks of files stacked there. On top of a filing cabinet stood a TV monitor, showing the currently empty interior of the Commons, its green benches deserted. A kettle sat beside mismatched mugs on a low shelf and had stained the wallpaper above it. The desktop printer whirred wheezily in a corner. Some of the papers it was disgorging had slid onto the threadbare carpet.

'Oh, shit,' said Izzy, dashing over and scooping them up, while Robin closed the door behind her. As she tapped the fallen papers back into a neat stack on her desk, Izzy said:

'I'm *thrilled* Papa's brought you in. He's been under *so much* strain, which he really doesn't need with everything we've got on now, but you and Strike will sort it out, won't you? Winn's a horrible little man,' said Izzy, reaching for a leather folder. '*Inadequate*, you know. How long have you worked with Strike?'

'A couple of years,' said Robin, as she undid the package Izzy had given her.

'I've met him, did he tell you? Yah – I was at school with his ex, Charlie Campbell. Gorgeous but trouble, Charlie. D'you know her?'

'No,' said Robin. A long-ago near-collision outside Strike's office had been her only contact with Charlotte.

'I always quite fancied Strike,' said Izzy.

Robin glanced around, surprised, but Izzy was matter-of-factly inserting papers into the folder.

'Yah, people couldn't see it, but *I* could. He was so butch and so . . . well . . . unapologetic.'

'Unapologetic?' Robin repeated.

'Yah. He never took any crap from anyone. Didn't give a toss that people thought he wasn't, you know—'

'Good enough for her?'

As soon as the words escaped her, Robin felt embarrassed. She had felt suddenly strangely protective of Strike. It was absurd, of course: if anybody could look after themselves, it was he.

'S'pose so,' said Izzy, still waiting for her papers to print. 'It's been ghastly for Papa, these past couple of months. And it isn't as though what he did was wrong!' she said fiercely. 'One minute it's legal, the next it isn't. That's not Papa's fault.'

'What wasn't legal?' asked Robin innocently.

'Sorry,' Izzy replied, pleasantly but firmly. 'Papa says, the fewer people know, the better.'

She peeked through the net curtains at the sky. 'I won't need a jacket, will I? No . . . sorry to dash, but Papa needs these and he's off to meet Olympic sponsors at ten. Good luck.'

And in a rush of flowered fabric and tousled hair, she was gone, leaving Robin curious but strangely reassured. If Izzy could take this robust view of her father's misdemeanour, it surely could not be anything dreadful – always assuming, of course, that Chiswell had told his daughter the truth.

Robin ripped the last piece of wrapping from the small parcel Izzy had given her. It contained, as she had known it would, the half-dozen listening devices that Strike had given to Jasper Chiswell over the weekend. As a Minister of the Crown, Chiswell was not required to pass through the security scanner every morning, as Robin was. She examined the bugs carefully. They had the appearance of normal plastic power points, and were designed to be fitted over genuine plug sockets, allowing the latter to function as normal. They would begin to record only when somebody spoke in their vicinity. She could hear her own heartbeat in the silence left by Izzy's departure. The difficulty of her task was only just beginning to sink in.

She took off her coat, hung it up, then removed from her shoulder bag a large box of Tampax, which she had brought for the purpose of concealing the listening devices she wasn't using. After hiding all but one of the bugs inside it, she placed the box in the bottom drawer of her desk. Next, she searched the cluttered shelves until she found an empty box file, in which she hid the remaining device beneath a handful of letters with typos that she took out of a pile labelled 'for shredding'. Thus armed, Robin took a deep breath and left the room.

Winn's door had opened since she had arrived. As Robin walked past, she saw a tall young Asian man wearing thick-lensed glasses and carrying a kettle.

'Hi!' said Robin at once, imitating Izzy's bold, cheery approach. 'I'm Venetia Hall, we're neighbours! Who are you?'

'Aamir,' muttered the other, in a working-class London accent. 'Mallik.'

'Do you work for Della Winn?' asked Robin.

'Yeah.'

'Oh, she's *so* inspirational,' gushed Robin. 'One of my heroines, actually.'

Aamir did not reply, but radiated a desire to be left alone. Robin felt like a terrier trying to harass a racehorse.

'Have you worked here long?'

'Six months.'

'Are you going to the café?'

'No,' said Aamir, as though she had propositioned him, and he turned sharply away towards the bathroom.

Robin walked on, holding her box file, wondering whether she had imagined animosity rather than shyness in the young man's demeanour. It would have been helpful to make a friend in Winn's office. Having to pretend to be an Izzy-esque goddaughter of Jasper Chiswell was hampering her. She couldn't help but feel that Robin Ellacott from Yorkshire might have befriended Aamir more easily.

Having set off with fake purpose, she decided to explore for a while before returning to Izzy's office.

Chiswell's and Winn's offices were in the Palace of Westminster itself, which, with its vaulted ceilings, libraries, tearooms and air of comfortable grandeur, might have been an old university college.

A half-covered passageway, watched over by large stone statues of a unicorn and lion, led to an escalator to Portcullis House. This was a modern crystal palace, with a folded glass roof, triangular panes held in place by thick black struts. Beneath was a wide, open-plan area including a café, where MPs and civil servants mingled. Flanked by full-grown trees, large water features consisting of long blocks of covered-in shallow pools became dazzling strips of quicksilver in the June sunshine.

There was a shiver of ambition in the thrumming air, and the sense of being part of a vital world. Beneath the ceiling of artfully fragmented glass, Robin passed political journalists perched on leather benches, all of whom were checking or talking on their mobiles, typing onto laptops or intercepting politicians for comment. Robin wondered whether she might have enjoyed working here if she had never been sent to Strike.

Her explorations ended in the third, dingiest and least interesting of the buildings that housed MPs' offices, which resembled nothing so much as a three-star hotel, with worn carpets and cream walls and row upon row of identical doors. Robin doubled back, still clutching her file, and passed Winn's door again fifty minutes after she had last seen it. Quickly checking that the corridor was deserted, she pressed her ear against the thick oak and thought she heard movement within.

'How's it going?' asked Izzy, when Robin re-entered her office a couple of minutes later.

'I haven't seen Winn yet.'

'He might be over at DCMS. He goes to see Della on any excuse,' said Izzy. 'Fancy a coffee?'

But before she could leave her desk, her telephone rang.

While Izzy fielded a call from an irate constituent who had been unable to secure tickets for the Olympic diving – 'yes, I like Tom Daley, too,' she said, rolling her eyes at Robin, 'but it's a *lottery*, madam' – Robin spooned out instant coffee and poured UHT milk, wondering how many times she had done this in offices she hated, and feeling suddenly extraordinarily grateful that she had escaped that life for ever.

'Hung up,' said Izzy indifferently, setting down the receiver. 'What were we talking about? Oh, Geraint, yah. He's furious Della didn't make him a SPAD.'

'What's a SPAD?' Robin asked, setting Izzy's coffee down and taking a seat at the other desk.

'Special Advisor. They're like temporary civil servants. Lots more prestige, but you don't hand the posts out to family, it's not done. Anyway, Geraint's hopeless, she wouldn't want him even if it were possible.'

'I just met the man who works with Winn,' said Robin. 'Aamir. He wasn't too friendly.'

'Oh, he's odd,' said Izzy, dismissively. 'Barely civil to me. It's probably because Geraint and Della hate Papa. I've never really got to the bottom of why, but they seem to hate all of us – oh, that reminds me: Papa texted a minute ago. My brother Raff's going to be coming in later this week, to help out in here. Maybe,' Izzy added, though she did not sound particularly hopeful, 'if Raff's any good, he might be able to take over from me. But Raff doesn't know anything about the blackmail or who you really are, so don't say anything, will you? Papa's got about fourteen godchildren. Raff'll never know the difference.'

Izzy sipped her coffee again, then, suddenly subdued, she said:

'I suppose you know about Raff. It was all over the papers. That poor woman . . . it was awful. She had a four-year-old daughter . . .'

'I did see something,' said Robin, noncommittally.

'I was the only one in the family who visited him in jail,' said Izzy. 'Everyone was so disgusted by what he'd done. Kinvara – Papa's wife – said he should have got life, but she's got no idea,' she continued, 'how *ghastly* it was in there . . . people don't realise what prison's like . . . I mean, I *know* he did a terrible thing, but . . .'

Her words trailed away. Robin wondered, perhaps ungenerously, whether Izzy was suggesting that jail was no place for a young man as refined as her half-brother. Doubtless it *had* been a horrible experience, Robin thought, but after all, he had taken drugs, climbed into a car and mown down a young mother.

'I thought he was working in an art gallery?' Robin asked.

'He's gone and messed up at Drummond's,' sighed Izzy. 'Papa's really taking him in to keep an eye on him.'

Public money paid for these salaries, Robin thought, remembering again the unusually short prison sentence the son of the minister had served for that drug-induced fatal accident.

'How did he mess up at the gallery?'

To her great surprise, Izzy's doleful expression vanished in a sudden spurt of laughter.

'Oh, God, I'm sorry, I shouldn't laugh. He shagged the other sales assistant in the loo,' she said, quaking with giggles. 'I know it isn't funny really – but he'd just got out of jail, and Raff's lovely looking and he's always pulled anyone he wants. They shoved him into a suit and put him in close proximity with some pretty little blonde art graduate, what did they think was going to happen? But as you can imagine, the gallery owner wasn't too chuffed. He heard them going at it and put Raff on a final warning. Then Raff and the girl went and did it again, so Papa had a total fit and says he's coming here instead.'

Robin didn't feel particularly amused, but Izzy appeared not to notice, lost in her own thoughts.

'You never know, it could be the making of them, Papa and Raff,' she said hopefully, then checked her watch.

'Better return some calls,' she sighed, setting down her coffee mug, but as she reached for her phone she froze, fingers on the receiver as a sing-song male voice rang out in the corridor beyond the closed door.

'That's him! Winn!'

'Well, here I go,' said Robin, snatching up her box file again.

'Good luck!' whispered Izzy.

Emerging into the corridor, Robin saw Winn standing in the doorway of his office, apparently talking to Aamir, who was inside. Winn was holding a folder with orange lettering on it saying 'The Level Playing Field'. At the sound of Robin's footsteps, he turned to face her.

'Well, hello there,' he said with a Cardiff lilt, stepping back into the corridor.

His gaze dribbled down Robin's neck, fell onto her breasts, then up again to her mouth and her eyes. Robin knew him from that single look. She had met plenty of them in offices, the type who watched you in a way that made you feel clumsy and self-conscious, who would place a hand in the small of the back as they sidled behind you or ushered you through doors, who peered over your shoulder on the excuse of reading your monitor and made chancy little comments on your clothes that progressed to comments on your figure during after-work drinks. They cried 'joke!' if you got angry, and became aggressive in the face of complaints.

'Where d'you fit in, then?' asked Geraint, making the question sound salacious.

'I'm interning for Uncle Jasper,' said Robin, smiling brightly.

'*Uncle* Jasper?'

'Jasper Chiswell, yes,' said Robin, pronouncing the name, as the Chiswells did themselves, 'Chizzle'. 'He's my godfather. Venetia Hall,' said Robin, holding out her hand.

Everything about Winn seemed faintly amphibian, down to his damp palm. He was less like a gecko in the flesh, she thought, and more like a frog, with a pronounced potbelly and spindly arms and legs, his thinning hair rather greasy.

'And how did it come about that you're Jasper's goddaughter?'

'Oh, Uncle Jasper and Daddy are old friends,' said Robin, who had a full backstory prepared.

'Army?'

'Land management,' said Robin, sticking to her prearranged story.

'Ah,' said Geraint; then, 'Lovely hair. Is it natural?'

'Yes,' said Robin.

His eyes slid down her body again. It cost Robin an effort to keep smiling at him. At last, gushing and giggling until her cheek muscles ached, agreeing that she would indeed give him a shout should she need any assistance, Robin walked on down the corridor. She could feel him watching her until she turned out of sight.

Just as Strike had felt after discovering Jimmy Knight's litigious habits, Robin was sure that she had just gained a valuable insight into Winn's weakness. In her experience, men like Geraint were astoundingly prone to believe that their scattergun sexual advances were appreciated and even reciprocated. She had spent no inconsiderable part of her temping career trying to rebuff and avoid such men, all of whom saw lubricious invitations in the merest pleasantry, and for whom youth and inexperience were an irresistible temptation.

How far, she asked herself, was she prepared to go in her quest to find out things to Winn's discredit? Walking with sham purpose through endless corridors to support her pretence of having papers to deliver, Robin pictured herself leaning over his desk while the inconvenient Aamir was elsewhere, breasts at eye-level, asking for help and advice, giggling at smutty jokes.

Then, with a sudden, dreadful lurch of imagination she saw, clearly, Winn's lunge, saw the sweaty face swooping for her, its lipless mouth agape, felt hands gripping her arms, pinning them to her sides, felt the pot-belly press itself into her, squashing her backwards into a filing cabinet . . .

The endless green of carpet and chairs, the dark wood arches and the square panels seemed to blur and contract as Winn's imagined pass became an attack. She pushed through the door ahead as though she could physically force herself past her panic . . .

Breathe. Breathe. Breathe.

'Bit overwhelming the first time you see it, eh?'

The man sounded kindly and not very young.

'Yes,' said Robin, barely knowing what she said. *Breathe.*

'Temporary, eh?' And then, 'You all right, dear?'

'Asthma,' said Robin.

She had used the excuse before. It gave her an excuse to stop, to breathe deeply, to re-anchor herself to reality.

'Got an inhaler?' asked the elderly steward in concern.

He wore a frock coat, white tie and tails and an ornate badge of office. In his unexpected grandeur, Robin thought wildly of the white rabbit, popping up in the middle of madness.

'I left it in my office. I'll be fine. Just need a second . . . '

She had blundered into a blaze of gold and colour that was increasing her feeling of oppression. The Members' Lobby, that familiar, ornate, Victorian-gothic chamber she had seen on television, stood right outside the Commons, and on the periphery of her vision loomed four gigantic bronze statues of previous prime ministers – Thatcher, Attlee, Lloyd George and Churchill – while busts of all the others lined the walls. They appeared to Robin like severed heads and the gilding, with its intricate tracery and richly coloured embellishments, danced around her, jeering at her inability to cope with its ornate beauty.

She heard the scraping of a chair's legs. The steward had brought her a seat and was asking a colleague to fetch a glass of water.

'Thank you . . . thank you . . . ' said Robin numbly, feeling inadequate, ashamed and embarrassed. Strike must never know about this. He would send her home, tell her she wasn't fit to do the job. Nor must she tell Matthew, who treated these episodes as shameful, inevitable consequences of her stupidity in continuing surveillance work.

The steward talked to her kindly while she recovered and within a few minutes she was able to respond appropriately to his well-intentioned patter. While her breathing returned to normal, he told her the tale of how Edward Heath's bust had begun to turn green on the arrival of the full-sized Thatcher statue beside him, and how it had had to be treated to turn it back to its dark brown bronze.

Robin laughed politely, got to her feet and handed him the empty glass with renewed thanks.

What treatment would it take, she wondered as she set off again, to return her to what she had once been?

14

. . . how happy I should feel if I could succeed in bringing a little light into all this murky ugliness.

Henrik Ibsen, *Rosmersholm*

Strike rose early on Tuesday morning. After showering, putting on his prosthesis and dressing, he filled a thermos with dark brown tea, took the sandwiches he had made the previous evening out of the fridge, stowed them in a carrier bag along with two packets of Club biscuits, chewing gum and a few bags of salt and vinegar crisps, then headed out into the sunrise and off to the garage where he kept his BMW. He had an appointment for a haircut at half past twelve, with Jimmy Knight's ex-wife, in Manchester.

Once settled in the car, his bag of provisions within easy reach, Strike pulled on the trainers he kept in the car, which gave his fake foot better purchase on the brake. He then took out his mobile and began to compose a text to Robin.

Starting with the names that Wardle had given him, Strike had spent much of Monday researching, as best as he could, the two children the policemen had told him had vanished from the Oxfordshire area twenty years previously. Wardle had misspelled the boy's first name, which had cost Strike time, but Strike had finally dug out archived press reports about Imamu Ibrahim, in which Imamu's mother had asserted that her estranged husband had kidnapped the boy and taken him to Algeria. Strike had finally dredged up two lines about Imamu and his mother on the website of an organisation that worked to resolve international custody issues. From this, Strike had to conclude that Imamu had been found alive and well with his father.

The fate of Suki Lewis, the twelve-year-old runaway from a care home, was more mysterious. Strike had finally discovered an image of her, buried in an old news story. Suki had vanished from her residential care home in Swindon in 1992 and Strike could find no other mention of her since. Her blurry picture showed a rather toothy, undersized child, fine-featured, with short dark hair.

Little girl it was, but after they said it was a little boy.

So a vulnerable, androgynous child might have disappeared off the face of the earth around the same time, and in the approximate area, that Billy Knight claimed to have witnessed the strangling of a boy-girl.

In the car, he composed a text to Robin.

If you can make it sound natural, ask Izzy if she remembers anything about a 12-year-old called Suki Lewis. She ran away 20 years ago from a care home near their family house.

The dirt on his windscreen shimmered and blurred in the rising sun as he left London. Driving was no longer the pleasure it had once been. Strike could not afford a specially adapted vehicle, and even though it was an automatic, the operation of the BMW's pedals remained challenging with his prosthesis. In challenging conditions, he sometimes reverted to operating brake and accelerator with his left foot.

When he finally joined the M6, Strike hoped to settle in at sixty miles an hour, but some arsehole in a Vauxhall Corsa decided to tailgate him.

'Fucking overtake,' growled Strike. He was not minded to alter his own speed, having settled in comfortably without needing to use his false foot more than was necessary, and for a while he glowered into his rear view mirror until the Vauxhall driver got the hint and took himself off.

Relaxing to the degree that was ever possible behind the wheel these days, Strike wound down the window to admit the fine, fresh summer's day and allowed his thoughts to return to Billy and the missing Suki Lewis.

She wouldn't let me dig, he had said in the office, compulsively tapping his nose and his chest, *but she'd let you.*

Who, Strike wondered, was 'she'? Perhaps the new owner of Steda Cottage? They might well object to Billy asking to dig up flowerbeds in search of bodies.

After feeling around with his left hand inside his provisions bag, extracting and ripping open a bag of crisps with his teeth, Strike reminded himself for the umpteenth time that Billy's whole story might be a chimera. Suki Lewis could be anywhere. Not every lost child was dead. Perhaps Suki, too, had been stolen away by an errant parent. Twenty years previously, in the infancy of the internet, imperfect communication between regional police forces could be exploited by those wishing to reinvent themselves or others. And even if Suki was no longer alive, there was nothing to suggest that she had been strangled, let alone that Billy Knight had witnessed it. Most people would surely conclude that this was a case of much smoke, but no fire.

Chewing crisps by the handful, Strike reflected that

whenever it came to a question of what 'most people' would think, he usually envisaged his half-sister Lucy, the only one of his eight half-siblings with whom he had shared his chaotic and peripatetic childhood. To him, Lucy represented the acme of all that was conventional and unimaginative, even though they had both grown up on intimate terms with the macabre, the dangerous and the frightening.

Before Lucy had gone to live permanently with their aunt and uncle in Cornwall, at the age of fourteen, their mother had hauled her and Strike from squat to commune to rented flat to friend's floor, rarely remaining in the same place more than six months, exposing her children to a parade of eccentric, damaged and addicted human beings along the way. Right hand on the wheel, left hand now groping around for biscuits, Strike recalled some of the nightmarish spectacles that he and Lucy had witnessed as children: the psychotic youth fighting an invisible devil in a basement flat in Shoreditch, the teenager literally being whipped at a quasi-mystical commune in Norfolk (still, for Strike's money, the worst place that Leda had ever taken them) and Shayla, one of the most fragile of Leda's friends and a part-time prostitute, sobbing about the brain damage inflicted on her toddler son by a violent boyfriend.

That unpredictable and sometimes terrifying childhood had left Lucy with a craving for stability and conformity. Married to a quantity surveyor whom Strike disliked, with three sons he barely knew, she would probably dismiss Billy's story of the strangled boy-girl as the product of a broken mind, sweeping it swiftly away into the corner with all the other things she could not bear to think about. Lucy needed to pretend that violence and strangeness had vanished into a past as dead as their mother; that with Leda gone, life was unshakeably secure.

Strike understood. Profoundly different though they were, often though she exasperated him, he loved Lucy. Nevertheless, he could not help comparing her with Robin as he bowled towards Manchester. Robin had grown up in what seemed to Strike the very epitome of middle-class stability, but she was courageous in a way that Lucy was not. Both women had been touched by violence and sadism. Lucy had reacted by burying herself where she hoped it would never reach her again; Robin, by facing it almost daily, investigating and resolving other crimes and traumas, driven to do so by the same impulse to actively disentangle complications and disinter truths that Strike recognised in himself.

As the sun climbed higher, still dappling the grubby windscreen, he experienced a powerful regret that she wasn't here with him now. She was the best person he had ever met to run a theory past. She'd unscrew the thermos for him and pour him tea. *We'd have a laugh.*

They had slipped back into their old bantering ways a couple of times lately, since Billy had entered the office with a story troubling enough to break down the reserve that had, over a year, hardened into a permanent impediment to their friendship . . . *or whatever it was*, thought Strike, and for a moment or two he felt her again in his arms on the stairs, breathed in the scent of white roses and of the perfume that hung around the office when Robin was at her desk . . .

With a kind of mental grimace, he reached for another cigarette, lit up and forced his mind towards Manchester, and the line of questioning he intended to take with Dawn Clancy, who, for five years, had been Mrs Jimmy Knight.

15

Yes, she is a queer one, she is. She has always been very much on the high horse . . .

Henrik Ibsen, *Rosmersholm*

While Strike was speeding northwards, Robin was summoned without explanation to a personal meeting with the Minister for Culture himself.

Walking in the sunshine towards the Department for Culture, Media and Sport, which stood in a large white Edwardian building a few minutes away from the Palace of Westminster, Robin found herself almost wishing that she were one of the tourists cluttering the pavement, because Chiswell had sounded bad tempered on the phone.

Robin would have given a great deal to have something useful to tell the minister about his blackmailer, but as she had only been on the job a day and a half, all she could say with any certainty was that her first impressions of Geraint Winn had now been confirmed: he was lazy, lecherous, self-important and indiscreet. The door of his office stood open more often than not, and his sing-song voice rang down the corridor as he talked with injudicious levity about his constituents' petty concerns, name-dropped celebrities and senior politicians and generally sought to give the impression of a man for whom running a mere constituency office was an unimportant sideshow.

He hailed Robin jovially from his desk whenever she passed his open door, showing a pronounced eagerness for further contact. However, whether by chance or design, Aamir Mallik kept thwarting Robin's attempts to turn these greetings into conversations, either interrupting with questions for Winn or, as he had done just an hour previously, simply closing the door in Robin's face.

The exterior of the great block that housed the DCMS, with its stone swags, its columns and its neoclassical façade, was not reassuring. The interior had been modernised and hung with contemporary art, including an abstract glass sculpture that hung from the cupola over the central staircase, up which Robin was led by an efficient-seeming young woman. Believing her to be the minister's goddaughter, her companion was at pains to show her points of interest.

'The Churchill Room,' she said, pointing left as they turned right. 'That's the balcony he gave his speech from, on VE Day. The minister's just along here . . .'

She led Robin down a wide, curving corridor that doubled as an open-plan workspace. Smart young people sat at an array of desks in front of lengthy windows to the right, which looked out onto a quadrangle, which, in size and scale, bore the appearance of a colosseum, with its high white windowed walls. It was all very different from the cramped office where Izzy made their instant coffee from a kettle. Indeed, a large, expensive machine complete with pods sat on one desk for that purpose.

The offices to the left were separated from this curving space by glass walls and doors. Robin spotted the Minister for Culture from a distance, sitting at his desk beneath a contemporary painting of the Queen, talking on the telephone. He indicated by a brusque gesture that her escort should show Robin inside the office and continued talking on the telephone as Robin waited, somewhat awkwardly, for him to finish his call. A woman's voice was issuing from the earpiece, high-pitched and to Robin, even eight feet away, hysterical.

'I've got to go, Kinvara!' barked Chiswell into the mouthpiece. 'Yes . . . we'll talk about this later. *I've got to go.*'

Setting down the receiver harder than was necessary, he pointed Robin to a chair opposite him. His coarse, straight grey hair stood out around his head in a wiry halo, his fat lower lip giving him an air of angry petulance.

'The newspapers are sniffing around,' he growled. 'That was m'wife. The *Sun* rang her this morning, asking whether the rumours are true. She said "what rumours?" but the fella didn't specify. Fishing, obviously. Trying to surprise something out of her.'

He frowned at Robin, whose appearance he seemed to find wanting.

'How old are you?'

'Twenty-seven,' she said.

'You look younger.'

It didn't sound like a compliment.

'Managed to plant the surveillance device yet?'

'I'm afraid not,' said Robin.

'Where's Strike?'

'In Manchester, interviewing Jimmy Knight's ex-wife,' said Robin.

Chiswell made the angry, subterranean noise usually rendered as 'harrumph', then got to his feet. Robin jumped up, too.

'Well, you'd better get back and get on with it,' said Chiswell. 'The National Health Service,' he added, with no change of tone, as he headed towards the door. 'People are going to think we're bloody mad.'

'Sorry?' said Robin, entirely thrown.

Chiswell pulled open the glass door and indicated that Robin should pass through it ahead of him, out into the open-plan area where all the smart young people sat working beside their sleek coffee machine.

'Olympics opening ceremony,' he explained, following her. 'Lefty bloody crap. We won two bloody world wars, but we're not supposed to celebrate that.'

'Nonsense, Jasper,' said a deep, melodious Welsh voice close at hand. 'We celebrate military victories all the time. This is a different kind of celebration.'

Della Winn, the Minister for Sport, was standing just outside Chiswell's door, holding the leash of her near-white Labrador. A woman of stately appearance, with grey hair swept back off a broad forehead, she wore sunglasses so dark that Robin could make out nothing behind them. Her blindness, Robin knew from her research, had been due to a rare condition in which neither eyeball had grown *in utero*. She sometimes wore prosthetic eyes, especially when she was to be photographed. Della was sporting a quantity of heavy, tactile jewellery in gold, with a large necklace of intaglios, and dressed from head to foot in sky blue. Robin had read in one of Strike's printed profiles of the politician that Geraint laid out Della's clothes for her every morning and that it was simplest for him, not having a great feel for fashion, to select things in the same colour. Robin had found this rather touching when she read it.

Chiswell did not appear to relish the sudden appearance of his colleague and indeed, given that her husband was blackmailing him, Robin supposed that this was hardly surprising. Della, on the other hand, gave no sign of embarrassment.

'I thought we might share the car over to Greenwich,' she said to Chiswell, while the pale Labrador snuffled gently at the hem of Robin's skirt. 'Give us a chance to go over the plans for the twelfth. What are you doing, Gwynn?' she added, feeling the Labrador's head tugging.

'She's sniffing me,' said Robin nervously, patting the Labrador.

'This is my goddaughter, ah . . . '

'Venetia,' said Robin, as Chiswell was evidently struggling to remember her name.

'How do you do?' said Della, holding out her hand. 'Visiting Jasper?'

'No, I'm interning in the constituency office,' said Robin, shaking the warm, be-ringed hand, as Chiswell walked away to examine the document held by a hovering young man in a suit.

'Venetia,' repeated Della, her face still turned towards Robin. A faint frown appeared on the handsome face, half-masked behind the impenetrable black glasses. 'What's your surname?'

'Hall,' said Robin.

She felt a ridiculous flutter of panic, as though Della were about to unmask her. Still poring over the document he had been shown, Chiswell moved away, leaving Robin, or so it felt, entirely at Della's mercy.

'You're the fencer,' said Della.

'Sorry?' said Robin, totally confused again, her mind on posts and rails. Some of the young people around the space-age coffee machine had turned around to listen, expressions of polite interest on their faces.

'Yes,' said Della. 'Yes, I remember you. You were on the English team with Freddie.'

Her friendly expression had hardened. Chiswell was now

leaning over a desk while he struck through phrases on the document.

'No, I never fenced,' said Robin, thoroughly out of her depth. She had realised at the mention of the word 'team' that swords were under discussion, rather than fields and livestock.

'You certainly did,' said Della flatly. 'I remember you. Jasper's goddaughter, on the team with Freddie.'

It was a slightly unnerving display of arrogance, of complete self-belief. Robin felt inadequate to the job of continuing to protest, because there were now several listeners. Instead, she merely said, 'Well, nice to have met you,' and walked away.

'*Again*, you mean,' said Della sharply, but Robin made no reply.

16

. . . a man with as dirty a record as his! . . . This is the sort of man that poses as a leader of the people! And successfully, too!

Henrik Ibsen, *Rosmersholm*

After four and a half hours in the driving seat, Strike's exit from the BMW in Manchester was far from graceful. He stood for a while in Burton Road, a broad, pleasant street with its mixture of shops and houses, leaning on the car, stretching his back and leg, grateful that he had managed to find a parking space only a short way from 'Stylz'. The bright pink shopfront stood out between a café and a Tesco Express, pictures of moody models with unnaturally tinted hair in the window.

With its black and white tiled floor and pink walls that reminded Strike of Lorelei's bedroom, the interior of the small shop was determinedly trendy, but it did not appear to cater to a particularly youthful or adventurous clientele. There were currently only two clients, one of whom was a large woman of at least sixty, who was reading *Good Housekeeping* in front of a mirror, her hair a mass of foil. Strike made a bet with himself as he entered that Dawn would prove to be the slim peroxide blonde with her back to him, chatting animatedly to an elderly lady whose blue hair she was perming.

'I've got an appointment with Dawn,' Strike told the young receptionist, who looked slightly startled to see anything so large and male in this fug of perfumed ammonia. The peroxided blonde turned at the sound of her name. She had the leathery, age-spotted skin of a committed sunbed user.

'With you in a moment, cock,' she said, smiling. He settled to wait on a bench in the window.

Five minutes later, she was leading him to an upholstered pink chair at the back of the shop.

'What are you after, then?' she asked him, inviting him with a gesture to sit down.

'I'm not here for a haircut,' said Strike, still standing. 'I'll happily pay for one, I don't want to waste your time, but,' he pulled a card and his driver's licence from his pocket, 'my name's Cormoran Strike. I'm a private detective and I was hoping to talk to you about your ex-husband, Jimmy Knight.'

She looked stunned, as well she might, but then fascinated.

'Strike?' she repeated, gaping. 'You aren't him that caught that Ripper guy?'

'That's me.'

'Jesus, what's Jimmy done?'

'Nothing much,' said Strike easily. 'I'm just after background.'

She didn't believe him, of course. Her face, he suspected, was full of filler, her forehead suspiciously smooth and shiny above the carefully pencilled eyebrows. Only her stringy neck betrayed her age.

'That's over. It was over ages ago. I never talk about Jimmy. Least said, soonest mended, don't they say?'

But he could feel the curiosity and excitement radiating

from her like heat. Radio 2 jangled in the background. She glanced towards the two women sitting at the mirrors.

'Sian!' she said loudly, and the receptionist jumped and turned. 'Take out her foils and keep an eye on the perm for me, love.' She hesitated, still holding Strike's card. 'I'm not sure I should,' she said, wanting to be talked into it.

'It's only background,' he said. 'No strings.'

Five minutes later she was handing him a milky coffee in a tiny staffroom at the rear of the shop, talking merrily, a little haggard in the fluorescent overhead light, but still good-looking enough to explain why Jimmy had first shown interest in a woman thirteen years his senior.

'. . . yeah, a demonstration against nuclear weapons. I went with this friend of mine, Wendy, she was big into all that. Vegetarian,' she added, nudging the door into the shop closed with her foot and taking out a pack of Silk Cut. 'You know the type.'

'Got my own,' said Strike, when she offered the pack. He lit her cigarette for her, then one of his Benson & Hedges. They blew out simultaneous streams of smoke. She crossed her legs towards him and rattled on.

'. . . yeah, so Jimmy gave a speech. Weapons and how much we could save, give to the NHS and everything, what was the point . . . he talks well, you know,' said Dawn.

'He does,' agreed Strike, 'I've heard him.'

'Yeah, and I fell for it, hook, line and sinker. Thought he was some kind of Robin Hood.'

Strike heard the joke coming before she made it. He knew it was not the first time.

'*Robbing* Hood, more like,' she said.

She was already divorced when she had met Jimmy. Her first husband had left her for another girl at the London salon they had owned together. Dawn had done well out of the divorce, managing to retain the business. Jimmy had seemed a romantic figure after her wide-boy first husband and, on the rebound, she had fallen for him hard.

'But there were always girls,' she said. 'Lefties, you know. Some of them were really young. He was like a pop star to them or something. I only found out how many of them there were later, after he'd set up cards on all my accounts.'

Dawn told Strike at length how Jimmy had persuaded her to bankroll a lawsuit against his ex-employer, Zanet Industries, who had failed to follow due process in firing him.

'Very keen on his rights, Jimmy. He's not stupid, though, you know. Ten grand payout he got from Zanet. I never saw a penny of it. He pissed it all away, trying to sue other people. He tried to take me to court, after we split up. Loss of earnings, don't make me laugh. I'd kept him for five years and he claimed he'd been working with me, building up the business for no pay and left with occupational asthma from the chemicals – so much shit, he talked – they chucked it out of court, thank God. And then he tried to get me on a harassment charge. Said I'd keyed his car.'

She ground out her cigarette and reached for another one.

'I had, too,' she said, with a sudden, wicked smile. 'You know he's been put on a list, now? Can't sue anyone without permission.'

'I did know, yeah,' said Strike. 'Was he ever involved in any criminal activity while you were together, Dawn?'

She lit up again, watching Strike over her fingers, still hoping to hear what Jimmy was supposed to have done to have Strike after him. Finally she said:

'I'm not sure he was too careful about checking all the girls he was playing around with were sixteen. I heard, after, one of them . . . but we'd split up by then. It wasn't my problem any more,' said Dawn, as Strike made a note.

'And I wouldn't trust him if it was anything to do with Jews. He doesn't like them. Israel's the root of all evil, according to Jimmy. Zionism: I got sick of the bloody sound of the word. You'd think they'd suffered enough,' said Dawn vaguely. 'Yeah, his manager at Zanet was Jewish and they hated each other.'

'What was his name?'

'What was it?' Dawn drew heavily on her cigarette, frowning. 'Paul something . . . Lobstein, that's it. Paul Lobstein. He's probably still at Zanet.'

'D'you still have any contact with Jimmy, or any of his family?'

'Christ, no. Good riddance. The only one of his family I ever met was little Billy, his brother.'

She softened a little as she said the name.

'He wasn't right. He stayed with us for a bit at one point. He was a sweetheart, really, but not right. Jimmy said it was their father. Violent alkie. Raised them on his own and knocked the shit out of them, from what the boys said, used the belt and everything. Jimmy got away to London, and poor little Billy was left alone with him. No surprise he was how he was.'

'What d'you mean?'

'He 'ad a – a tic, do they call it?'

She mimicked with perfect accuracy the nose to chest tapping Strike had witnessed in his office.

'He was put on drugs, I know that. Then he left us, went to share a flat with some other lads for a bit. I never saw him again after Jimmy and I split. He was a sweet boy, yeah, but he annoyed Jimmy.'

'In what way?' Strike asked.

'Jimmy didn't like him talking about their childhood. I dunno, I think Jimmy felt guilty he'd left Billy in the house alone. There was something funny about that whole business . . . '

Strike could tell she hadn't thought about these things for a while.

'Funny?' he prompted.

'A couple of times, when he'd had a few, Jimmy went on about how his dad would burn for how he made his living.'

'I thought he was an odd-job man?'

'Was he? They told me he was a joiner. He worked for that politician's family, what's his name? The one with the hair.'

She mimed stiff bristles coming out of her head.

'Jasper Chiswell?' Strike suggested, pronouncing the name the way it was spelled.

'Him, yeah. Old Mr Knight had a rent-free cottage in the family grounds. The boys grew up there.'

'And he said his father would go to hell for what he did for a living?' repeated Strike.

'Yeah. It's probably just because he was working for Tories. It was all about politics with Jimmy. I don't get it,' said Dawn restlessly. 'You've got to live. Imagine me asking my clients how they vote before I'll—

'Bloody hell,' she gasped suddenly, grinding out her cigarette and jumping to her feet, 'Sian had better've taken out Mrs Horridge's rollers or she'll be bald.'

17

I see he is altogether incorrigible.

Henrik Ibsen, *Rosmersholm*

Watching for an opportunity to plant the bug in Winn's office, Robin spent most of the afternoon hanging around the quiet corridor on which both his and Izzy's offices lay, but her efforts were fruitless. Even though Winn had left for a lunchtime meeting, Aamir remained inside. Robin paced up and down, box file in her arms, waiting for the moment when Aamir might go to the bathroom and returning to Izzy's office whenever any passer-by tried to engage her in conversation.

Finally, at ten past four, her luck changed. Geraint Winn swaggered around the corner, rather tipsy after what seemed to have been a prolonged lunch, and in sharp contrast to his wife, he seemed delighted to meet her as she set off towards him.

'There she is!' he said, over-loudly. 'I wanted a word with you! Come in here, come in!'

He pushed open the door of his office. Puzzled, but only too eager to see the interior of the room she was hoping to bug, Robin followed him.

Aamir was working in shirtsleeves at his desk, which formed a tiny oasis of order in the general clutter. Stacks of folders lay around Winn's desk. Robin noticed the orange logo of the Level Playing Field on a pile of letters in front of him. There was a power point directly under Geraint's desk that would be an ideal position for the listening device.

'Have you two met?' Geraint asked jovially. 'Venetia, Aamir.'

He sat down and invited Robin to take the armchair on which a sliding pile of card folders lay.

'Did Redgrave call back?' Winn asked Aamir, struggling out of his suit jacket.

'Who?' said the latter.

'Sir Steve Redgrave!' said Winn, with the suspicion of an eye roll in Robin's direction. She felt embarrassed for him, especially as Aamir's muttered 'no' was cold.

'Level Playing Field,' Winn told Robin.

He had managed to get his jacket off. With an attempted flourish, he threw it onto the back of his chair. It slid limply onto the floor, but Geraint appeared not to notice, and instead tapped the orange logo on the topmost letter in front of him. 'Our cha—' he belched. 'Pardon me – our charity. Disadvantaged and disabled athletes, you know. Lots of high profile supporters. Sir Steve keen to—' he belched again, '—pardon – help. Well, now. I wanted to apologise. For my poor wife.'

He seemed to be enjoying himself hugely. Out of the corner of her eye, Robin saw Aamir fling Geraint a sharp look, like the flash of a claw, swiftly retracted.

'I don't understand,' said Robin.

'Gets names wrong. Does it all the time. If I didn't keep an eye on her, we'd have all sorts going on, wrong letters going out to the wrong people ... she thought you were someone else. I had her on the phone over lunch, insisting you were somebody our daughter ran across years ago. Verity Pulham. 'Nother of your godfather's godchildren. Told her straight away it wasn't you, said I'd pass on her apologies. Silly girl, she is. Very stubborn when she thinks she's right, but,' he rolled his eyes again and tapped his forehead, the long-suffering husband of an infuriating wife, 'I managed to penetrate in the end.'

'Well,' said Robin carefully, 'I'm glad she knows she was mistaken, because she didn't seem to like Verity very much.'

'Truth to tell, Verity *was* a little bitch,' said Winn, still beaming. Robin could tell he enjoyed using the word. 'Nasty to our daughter, you see.'

'Oh dear,' said Robin, with a thud of dread beneath her ribs as she remembered that Rhiannon Winn had killed herself. 'I'm sorry. How awful.'

'You know,' said Winn, sitting down and tipping back his chair against the wall, hands behind his head, 'you seem far too sweet a girl to be associated with the Chiswell family.' He was definitely a little drunk. Robin could smell faint wine dregs on his breath and Aamir threw him another of those sharp, scathing looks. 'What were you doing before this, Venetia?'

'PR,' said Robin, 'but I'd like to do something more worthwhile. Politics, or maybe a charity. I was reading about the Level Playing Field,' she said truthfully. 'It seems wonderful. You do a lot with veterans, too, don't you? I saw an interview with Terry Byrne yesterday. The Paralympian cyclist?'

Her attention had been caught by the fact that Byrne had the same below the knee amputation as Strike.

'You'll have a personal interest in veterans, of course,' said Winn.

Robin's stomach swooped and fell again.

'Sorry?'

'Freddie Chiswell?' Winn prompted.

'Oh, yes, of course,' said Robin. 'Although I didn't know Freddie very well. He was a bit older than me. Obviously, it was dreadful when he – when he was killed.'

'Oh, yes, awful,' said Winn, though he sounded indifferent. 'Della was very much against the Iraq war. Very much against it. Your Uncle Jasper was all for it, mind you.'

For a moment, the air seemed to thrum with Winn's unexpressed implication that Chiswell had been well served for his enthusiasm.

'Well, I don't know about that,' said Robin carefully. 'Uncle Jasper thought military action justified on the evidence we had at the time. Anyway,' she said bravely, 'nobody can accuse him of acting out of self-interest, can they, when his son had to go and fight?'

'Ah, if you're going to take that line, who can argue?' said Winn. He raised his hands in mock surrender, his chair slipped a little on the wall and for a few seconds he struggled to maintain balance, seizing the desk and pulling himself and the chair upright again. With a substantial effort, Robin managed not to laugh.

'Geraint,' said Aamir, 'we need those letters signed if we're going to get them off by five.'

''S'only half four,' said Winn, checking his watch. 'Yes, Rhiannon was on the British junior fencing team.'

'How marvellous,' said Robin.

'Sporty, like her mother. Fencing for the Welsh juniors at fourteen. I used to drive her all over the place for tournaments. Hours on the road together! She made the British juniors at sixteen.

'But the English lot were very stand-offish to her,' said Winn, with a glimmer of Celtic resentment. 'She wasn't at one of your big public schools, you see. It was all about connections with them. Verity Pulham, she didn't have the ability, not really. As a matter of fact, it was only when Verity broke her ankle that Rhiannon, who was a far better fencer, got on the British team at all.'

'I see,' said Robin, trying to balance sympathy with a feigned allegiance to the Chiswells. Surely this could not be the grievance that Winn had against the family? Yet Geraint's fanatic tone spoke of longstanding resentment. 'Well, these things should come down to ability, of course.'

'That's right,' said Winn. 'They should. Look at this, now . . .'

He fumbled for his wallet and pulled from it an old photograph. Robin held out her hand, but Geraint, keeping a firm hold on the picture, got up clumsily, stumbled over a stack of books lying beside his chair, walked around the desk, came so close that Robin could feel his breath on her neck, and showed her the image of his daughter.

Dressed in fencing garb, Rhiannon Winn stood beaming and holding up the gold medal around her neck. She was pale and small-featured, and Robin could see very little of either parent in her face, although perhaps there was a hint of Della in the broad, intelligent brow. But with Geraint's loud breathing in her ear, trying to stop herself leaning away from him, Robin had a sudden vision of Geraint Winn striding, with his wide, lipless grin, through a large hall of sweaty teenage girls. Was it shameful to wonder whether it had been parental devotion that had spurred him to chauffeur his daughter all over the country?

'What have you done to yourself, eh?' Geraint asked, his hot breath in her ear. Leaning in, he touched the purple knife scar on her bare forearm.

Unable to prevent herself, Robin snatched her arm away.

The nerves around the scar had not yet fully healed: she hated anyone touching it.

'I fell through a glass door when I was nine,' she said, but the confidential, confiding atmosphere had been dispersed like cigarette smoke.

Aamir hovered on the edge of her vision, rigid and silent at his desk. Geraint's smile had become forced. She had worked too long in offices not to know that a subtle transfer of power had just taken place within the room. Now she stood armed with his little drunken inappropriateness and Geraint was resentful and a little worried. She wished that she had not pulled away from him.

'I wonder, Mr Winn,' she said breathily, 'whether you'd mind giving me some advice about the charitable world? I just can't make up my mind, politics – charity – and I don't know anyone else who's done both.'

'Oh,' said Geraint, blinking behind his thick glasses. 'Oh, well . . . yes, I daresay I could . . .'

'Geraint,' said Aamir again, 'we really do need to get those letters—'

'Yes, all right, all right,' said Geraint loudly. 'We'll talk later,' he said to Robin, with a wink.

'Wonderful,' she said, with a smile.

As Robin walked out she threw Aamir a small smile, which he didn't return.

18

So matters have got as far as that already, have they!

Henrik Ibsen, *Rosmersholm*

After nearly nine hours at the wheel, Strike's neck, back and legs were stiff and sore and his bag of provisions long since empty. The first star was glimmering out of the pale, inky wash above when his mobile rang. It was the usual time for his sister, Lucy, to call 'for a chat'; he ignored three out of four of her calls, because, much as he loved her, he could muster no interest in her sons' schooling, the PTA's squabbles or the intricacies of her husband's career as a quantity surveyor. Seeing that it was Barclay on the line, however, he turned into a rough and ready lay-by, really the turnoff to a field, cut the engine and answered.

''M in,' said Barclay laconically. 'Wi' Jimmy.'

'Already?' said Strike, seriously impressed. 'How?'

'Pub,' said Barclay. 'Interrupted him. He was talkin' a load o' pish about Scottish independence. The grea' thing about English lefties,' he continued, 'is they love hearin' how shit England is. Havenae hadtae buy a pint all afternoon.'

'Bloody hell, Barclay,' said Strike, lighting himself another cigarette on top of the twenty he had already had that day, 'that was good work.'

'That was just fer starters,' said Barclay. 'You shoulda heard them when I told them how I've seen the error of the army's imperialist ways. Fuck me, they're gullible. I'm off tae a CORE meetin' the morrow.'

'How's Knight supporting himself? Any idea?'

'He told me he's a journalist on a couple o' lefty websites and he sells CORE T-shirts and a bit o' dope. Mind, his shit's worthless. We went back tae his place, after the pub. Ye'd be better off smokin' fuckin' Oxo cubes. I've said I'll get him better. We can run that through office expenses, aye?'

'I'll put it under "sundries",' said Strike. 'All right, keep me posted.'

Barclay rang off. Deciding to take the opportunity to stretch his legs, Strike got out of the car, still smoking, leaned on the five-bar gate facing a wide, dark field, and rang Robin.

'It's Vanessa,' Robin lied, when she saw Strike's number come up on her phone.

She and Matthew had just eaten a takeaway curry off their knees while watching the news. He had arrived home late and tired; she didn't need another argument.

Picking up the mobile, she headed out through the French doors onto the patio that had served as the smoking area for the party. After making sure that the doors were completely closed, she answered.

'Hi. Everything OK?'

'Fine. All right to talk for a moment?'

'Yes,' said Robin, leaning against the garden wall, and watching a moth banging fruitlessly against the bright glass, trying to enter the house. 'How did it go with Dawn Clancy?'

'Nothing useable,' said Strike. 'I thought I might have a lead, some Jewish ex-boss Jimmy had a vendetta against, but I rang the company and the poor bloke died of a stroke last

September. Then I got a call from Chiswell just after I left her. He says the *Sun*'s sniffing around.'

'Yes,' said Robin. 'They called his wife.'

'We could've done without that,' said Strike, with what Robin felt was considerable understatement. 'I wonder who's tipped off the papers?'

'I'd bet on Winn,' said Robin, remembering the way that Geraint had talked that afternoon, the name-dropping, the self-importance. 'He's just the type to hint to a journalist that there's a story on Chiswell, even if he hasn't got proof of it yet. Seriously,' she said again, with no real hope of an answer, 'what d'you think Chiswell did?'

'Be nice to know, but it doesn't really matter,' said Strike, who sounded tired. 'We aren't being paid to get the goods on *him*. Speaking of which—'

'I haven't been able to plant the bug yet,' said Robin, anticipating the question. 'I hung around as late as possible, but Aamir locked the door after they both left.'

Strike sighed.

'Well, don't get overeager and balls it up,' he said, 'but we're up against it if the *Sun*'s involved. Anything you can do. Get in early or something.'

'I will, I'll try,' said Robin. 'I did get something odd about the Winns today, though,' and she told him about the confusion Della had made between herself and one of Chiswell's real goddaughters, and the story of Rhiannon on the fencing team. Strike seemed only distantly interested.

'Doubt that explains the Winns wanting Chiswell out of office. Anyway—'

'—means before motive,' she said, quoting Strike's own, oft-repeated words.

'Exactly. Listen, can you meet me after work tomorrow, and we'll have a proper debrief?'

'All right,' said Robin.

'Barclay's doing good work, though,' said Strike, as though the thought of it cheered him up. 'He's already well in with Jimmy.'

'Oh,' said Robin. 'Good.'

After telling her that he would text the name of a convenient pub, Strike rang off, leaving Robin alone and pensive in the quiet dark of the yard, while stars grew pin-bright overhead.

Barclay's doing good work, though.

As opposed to Robin, who had found out nothing but an irrelevancy about Rhiannon Winn.

The moth was still fluttering desperately against the sliding doors, frantic to get at the light.

Idiot, Robin thought. *It's better out here.*

The ease with which the lie about Vanessa being on the phone had slid out of her mouth ought, she reflected, to have made her feel guilty, but she was merely glad that she had got away with it. As she watched the moth continuing to bang its wings hopelessly against the brilliant glass, Robin remembered what her therapist had said to her during one of the sessions when Robin had dwelled at length on her need to discern where the real Matthew ended and her illusions about him began.

'People change in ten years,' the therapist had responded. 'Why does it have to be a question of you being mistaken in Matthew? Perhaps it's simply that you've both changed?'

The following Monday would mark their first wedding anniversary. At Matthew's suggestion, they were going to spend next weekend at a fancy hotel near Oxford. In a funny kind of way, Robin was looking forward to it, because she and Matthew seemed to get along better these days with a change of scene. Being surrounded by strangers nudged them out of their tendency to bicker. She had told him the story of Ted Heath's bust turning green, along with several other (to her) interesting facts about the House of Commons. He had maintained a bored expression through all of them, determined to signal his disapproval of the whole venture.

Reaching a decision, she opened the French window and the moth fluttered merrily inside.

'What did Vanessa want?' asked Matthew, his eyes on the news as Robin sat down again. Sarah Shadlock's stargazer lilies were sitting on a table beside her, still in bloom ten days after they had arrived in the house, and Robin could smell their heady scent even over the curry.

'I picked up her sunglasses by mistake last time we went out,' said Robin, feigning exasperation. 'She wants them back, they're Chanel. I said I'll meet her before work.'

'Chanel, eh?' said Matthew, with a smile that Robin found patronising. She knew that he thought he had discovered a weakness in Vanessa, but perhaps he liked her better to think that she valued designer labels and wanted to make sure she got them back.

'I'll have to leave at six,' said Robin.

'Six?' he said, annoyed. 'Christ, I'm knackered, I don't want to wake up at—'

'I was going to suggest I sleep in the spare room,' Robin said.

'Oh,' said Matthew, mollified. 'Yeah, OK. Thanks.'

19

I do not do it willingly – but, enfin – when needs must –

Henrik Ibsen, *Rosmersholm*

Robin left the house at a quarter to six the next morning. The sky was a faint blush pink and the morning already warm, justifying her lack of jacket. Her eyes flickered towards the single carved swan as she passed their local pub, but she forced her thoughts back onto the day ahead and not the man she had left behind.

On arrival in Izzy's corridor an hour later, Robin saw that Geraint's office door was already open. A swift peek inside showed her an empty room, but Aamir's jacket hanging on the back of his chair.

Running to Izzy's office, Robin unlocked it, dashed to her desk, pulled one of the listening devices from the box of Tampax, scooped up a pile of out-of-date agendas as an alibi, then ran back out into the corridor.

As she approached Geraint's office, she slid off the gold bangle that she had worn for this purpose, and threw it lightly so that it rolled into Geraint's office.

'Oh damn,' she said out loud.

Nobody responded from inside the office. Robin knocked

on the open door, said 'hello?' and put her head inside. The room was still empty.

Robin dashed across the room to the double power point just above the skirting board beside Geraint's desk. Kneeling, she took the listening device out of her bag, unplugged the fan on his desk, pressed the device into place over the dual socket, reinserted the fan's plug, checked that it worked, then, panting as though she had just sprinted a hundred yards, looked around for her bangle.

'What are you doing?'

Aamir was standing in the doorway in his shirtsleeves, a fresh tea in his hand.

'I did knock,' Robin said, sure that she was bright pink. 'I dropped my bangle and it rolled – oh, there it is.'

It was lying just beneath Aamir's computer chair. Robin scrambled to pick it up.

'It's my mother's,' she lied. 'I wouldn't be popular if that went missing.'

She slid the bangle back over her wrist, picked up the papers she had left on Geraint's desk, smiled as casually as she could manage, then walked out of the office past Aamir, whose eyes, she saw out of the corner of her own, were narrowed in suspicion.

Jubilant, Robin re-entered Izzy's office. At least she would have some good news for Strike when they met in the pub that evening. Barclay was no longer the only one doing good work. So absorbed was she in her thoughts that Robin didn't realise that there was somebody else in the room until a man said, right behind her: 'Who are you?'

The present dissolved. Both of her attackers had lunged at her from behind. With a scream, Robin spun around, ready to fight for her life: the papers flew into the air and her handbag slipped off her shoulder, fell to the floor and burst open, scattering its contents everywhere.

'Sorry!' said the man. 'Christ, I'm sorry!'

But Robin was finding it hard to draw breath. There was a thundering in her ears and sweat had broken out all over her body. She bent down to scoop everything back up, trembling so much that she kept dropping things.

Not now. Not now.

He was talking to her, but she couldn't understand a word. The world was fragmenting again, full of terror and danger, and he was a blur as he handed her eyeliner and a bottle of drops to moisten her contact lenses.

'Oh,' Robin gasped at random. 'Great. Excuse me. Bathroom.'

She stumbled to the door. Two people were coming towards her down the corridor, their voices fuzzy and indistinct as they greeted her. Hardly knowing what she responded, she half-ran past them towards the Ladies.

A woman from the Secretary for Health's office greeted her from the sink where she was applying lipstick. Robin blundered blindly past, locking the cubicle door with fumbling fingers.

It was no use trying to suppress the panic: that only made it fight back, trying to bend her to its will. She must ride it out, as though the fear was a bolting horse, easing it onto a more manageable course. So she stood motionless, palms pressed against the partition walls, speaking to herself inside her head as though she were an animal handler, and her body, in its irrational terror, a frantic prey creature.

You're safe, you're safe, you're safe . . .

Slowly, the panic began to ebb, though her heart was still leaping erratically. At last, Robin removed her numb hands from the walls of the cubicle and opened her eyes, blinking in the harsh lights. The bathroom was quiet.

Robin peered out of the cubicle. The woman had left. There was nobody there except her own pale reflection in the mirror. After splashing cold water on her face and patting it dry with paper towels, she readjusted her clear-lensed glasses and left the bathroom.

An argument seemed to be in progress in the office she had just left. Taking a deep breath, she re-entered the room.

Jasper Chiswell turned to glare at her, his wiry mass of grey hair sticking out around his pink face. Izzy was standing behind her desk. The stranger was still there. In her shaken state, Robin would have preferred not to be the focus of three pairs of curious eyes.

'What just happened?' Chiswell demanded of Robin.

'Nothing,' said Robin, feeling cold sweat erupting again under her dress.

'You ran out of the room. Did he—' Chiswell pointed at the dark man, '—do something to you? Make a pass?'

'Wha—? No! I didn't realise he was in here, that's all – he spoke and I jumped. And,' she could feel herself blushing harder than ever, 'then I needed the loo.'

Chiswell rounded on the dark man.

'So why are you here so early, eh?'

Now, at last, Robin realised that this was Raphael. She had known from the pictures she had found online that this half-Italian was an exotic in a family that was otherwise uniformly blond and very English in appearance, but had been wholly unprepared for how handsome he was in the flesh. His charcoal-grey suit, white shirt and a conventional dark blue spotted tie were worn with an air that none of the other men along the corridor could muster. So dark-skinned as to appear swarthy, he had high cheekbones, almost black eyes, dark hair worn long and floppy, and a wide mouth that, unlike his father's, had a full upper lip that added vulnerability to his face.

'I thought you liked punctuality, Dad,' he said, raising his arms and letting them fall in a slightly hopeless gesture.

His father turned to Izzy. 'Give him something to do.'

Chiswell marched out. Mortified, Robin headed for her desk. Nobody spoke until Chiswell's footsteps had died away, then Izzy spoke.

'He's under all kinds of stress just now, Raff, babes. It isn't you. He's honestly going berserk about the smallest things.'

'I'm so sorry,' Robin forced herself to say to Raphael. 'I completely overreacted.'

'No problem,' he replied, in the kind of accent that is routinely described as 'public school'. 'For the record, I'm not, in fact, a sex offender.'

Robin laughed nervously.

'You're the goddaughter I didn't know about? Nobody tells me anything. Venetia, yeah? I'm Raff.'

'Um – yes – hi.'

They shook hands and Robin retook her seat, busying herself with some pointless paper shuffling. She could feel her colour fluctuating.

'It's just crazy at the moment,' Izzy said, and Robin knew that she was trying, for not entirely unselfish reasons, to persuade Raphael that their father wasn't as bad to work with as he might appear. 'We're understaffed, we've got the Olympics coming up, TTS is constantly going off on Papa—'

'*What's* going off on him?' asked Raphael, dropping down into the sagging armchair, loosening his tie and crossing his long legs.

'TTS,' Izzy repeated. 'Lean over and put on the kettle while you're there, Raff, I'm dying for a coffee. TTS. It stands for Tinky the Second. It's what Fizz and I call Kinvara.'

The many nicknames of the Chiswell family had been explained to Robin during her office interludes with Izzy. Izzy's older sister Sophia was 'Fizzy', while Sophia's three children rejoiced in the pet names of 'Pringle', 'Flopsy' and 'Pong'.

'Why "Tinky the Second"?' asked Raff, unscrewing a jar of instant coffee with long fingers. Robin was still very aware of all his movements, though keeping her eyes on her supposed work. 'What was Tinky the First?'

'Oh, come on, Raff, you must have heard about Tinky,' said Izzy. 'That ghastly Australian nurse Grampy married last time round, when he was getting senile. He blew most of the money on her. He was the second silly old codger she'd married. Grampy bought her a dud racehorse and loads of horrible jewellery. Papa nearly had to go to court to get her out of the house when Grampy died. She dropped dead of breast cancer before it got really expensive, thank God.'

Startled by this sudden callousness, Robin looked up.

'How d'you take it, Venetia?' Raphael asked as he spooned coffee into mugs.

'White, no sugar, please,' said Robin. She thought it best if she maintained a low profile for a while, after her recent incursion into Winn's office.

'TTS married Papa for his dosh,' Izzy ploughed on, '*and* she's horse-mad like Tinky. You know she's got nine now? Nine!'

'Nine what?' said Raphael.

'Horses, Raff!' said Izzy impatiently. 'Bloody uncontrollable, bad-mannered, hot-blooded horses that she mollycoddles and keeps as child substitutes and spends all the money on! *God*, I wish Papa would leave her,' said Izzy. 'Pass the biscuit tin, babes.'

He did so. Robin, who could feel him looking at her, maintained the pretence of absorption in her work.

The telephone rang.

'Jasper Chiswell's office,' said Izzy, trying to prise off the lid of the biscuit tin one-handed, the receiver under her chin. 'Oh,' she said, suddenly cool. 'Hello, Kinvara. You've just missed Papa . . .'

Grinning at his half-sister's expression, Raphael took the biscuits from her, opened them and offered the tin to Robin, who shook her head. A torrent of indistinguishable words was pouring from Izzy's earpiece.

'No . . . no, he's gone . . . he only came over to say hello to Raff . . .'

The voice at the end of the phone seemed to become more strident.

'Back at DCMS, he's got a meeting at ten,' said Izzy. 'I can't – well, because he's very busy, you know, the Olymp – yes . . . goodbye.'

Izzy slammed the receiver down and struggled out of her jacket.

'She should take another *rest cure.* The last one doesn't seem to have done her much good.'

'Izzy doesn't believe in mental illness,' Raphael told Robin.

He was contemplating her, still slightly curious and, she guessed, trying to draw her out.

'Of course I believe in mental illness, Raff!' said Izzy, apparently stung. 'Of course I do! I was sorry for her when it happened – I *was*, Raff – Kinvara had a stillbirth two years ago,' Izzy explained, 'and *of course* that's sad, *of course* it is, and it was quite understandable that she was a bit, you know, afterwards, but – no, I'm sorry,' she said crossly, addressing Raphael, 'but she uses it. She *does*, Raff. She thinks it entitles her to everything she wants and – well, she'd have been a dreadful mother, anyway,' said Izzy defiantly. 'She can't stand not being the centre of attention. When she's not getting enough she starts her little girl act – *don't leave me alone,*

Jasper, I get scared when you're not here at night. Telling stupid lies . . . funny phone calls to the house, men hiding in the flowerbeds, fiddling with the horses.'

'*What?*' said Raphael, half-laughing, but Izzy cut him short.

'Oh, Christ, look, Papa's left his briefing papers.'

She hurried out from behind her desk, snatched a leather folder off the top of the radiator and called over her shoulder, 'Raff, you can listen to the phone messages and transcribe them for me while I'm gone, OK?'

The heavy wooden door thudded shut behind her, leaving Robin and Raphael alone. If she had been hyperaware of Raphael before Izzy had gone, now he seemed to Robin to fill the entire room, his olive dark eyes on her.

He took Ecstasy and ran his car into a mother of a four-year-old. He barely served a third of his sentence and now his father's put him on the taxpayers' payroll.

'How do I do this, then?' asked Raphael, moving behind Izzy's desk.

'Just press play, I expect,' Robin muttered, sipping her coffee and pretending to make notes on a pad.

Canned messages began to issue from the answering machine, drowning out the faint hum of conversation from the terrace beyond the net-curtained window.

A man named Rupert asked Izzy to call him back about 'the AGM'.

A constituent called Mrs Ricketts spoke for two solid minutes about traffic along the Banbury road.

An irate woman said crossly that she ought to have expected an answering machine and that MPs ought to be answering to the public personally, then spoke until cut off by the machine about her neighbours' failure to lop overhanging branches from a tree, in spite of repeated requests from the council.

Then a man's growl, almost theatrically menacing, filled the quiet office:

'*They say they piss themselves as they die, Chiswell, is that true? Forty grand, or I'll find out how much the papers will pay.*'

20

We two have worked our way forward in complete companionship.

Henrik Ibsen, *Rosmersholm*

Strike had selected the Two Chairmen for his Wednesday evening catch-up with Robin because of its proximity to the Palace of Westminster. The pub was tucked away on a junction of centuries-old back streets – Old Queen Street, Cockpit Steps – amid a motley collection of quaint, sedate buildings that stood at oblique angles to each other. Only as he limped across the road and saw the hanging metal sign over the front door did Strike realise that the 'two chairmen' for whom the pub was named were not, as he had assumed, joint managers of a board, but lowly servants carrying the heavy load of a sedan chair. Tired and sore as Strike was, the image seemed appropriate, although the occupant of the sedan chair in the pub sign was a refined lady in white, not a large, curmudgeonly minister with wiry hair and a short temper.

The bar was crowded with after-work drinkers and Strike had a sudden apprehension that he might not get a seat inside, an unwelcome prospect, because leg, back and neck were tight and sore after yesterday's long drive and the hours he had spent in Harley Street today, watching Dodgy Doc.

Strike had just bought a pint of London Pride when the table by the window became free. With a turn of speed born of necessity, he nabbed the high bench with its back to the street before the nearest group of suited men and women could annexe it. There was no question of anybody challenging his right to sole occupancy of a table made for four. Strike was large enough, and surly enough in appearance to make even this group of civil servants doubt their ability to negotiate a compromise.

The wooden-floored bar was what Strike mentally categorised as 'upmarket utilitarian'. A faded mural on the back wall depicted bewigged eighteenth-century men gossiping together, but otherwise all was pared-back wood and monochrome prints. He peered out of the window to see whether Robin was within sight, but as there was no sign of her he drank his beer, read the day's news on his phone and tried to ignore the menu lying on the table in front of him, which was taunting him with a picture of battered fish.

Robin, who had been due to arrive at six, was still absent at half past. Unable to resist the picture on the menu any longer, Strike ordered himself cod and chips and a second pint, and read a long article in *The Times* about the upcoming Olympics opening ceremony, which was really a long list of the ways in which the journalist feared it might misrepresent and humiliate the nation.

By a quarter to seven, Strike was starting to worry about Robin. He had just decided to call her when she came hurrying in through the door, flushed, wearing glasses that Strike knew she did not need and with an expression that he recognised as the barely contained excitement of one who has something worthwhile to impart.

'Hazel eyes,' he noted, as she sat down opposite him. 'Good one. Changes your whole look. What've you got?'

'How do you know I've—? Well, loads, actually,' she said, deciding it was not worthwhile toying with him. 'I nearly called you earlier but there have been people around all day, and I had a close shave this morning placing the listening device.'

'You did it? Bloody well done!'

'Thanks. I really want a drink, hang on.'

She came back with a glass of red wine and launched immediately into an account of the message that Raphael had found on the answering machine that morning.

'I had no chance of getting the caller's number, because there were four messages after it. The phone system's antiquated.'

Frowning, Strike asked: 'How did the caller pronounce "Chiswell", can you remember?'

'They said it right. *Chizzle.*'

'Fits with Jimmy,' said Strike. 'What happened after the call?'

'Raff told Izzy about it when she got back to the office,' said Robin, and Strike thought he detected a touch of self-consciousness as she said the name 'Raff'. 'He didn't understand what he was passing on, obviously. Izzy called her dad straight away and he went berserk. We could hear him shouting on the end of the line, though not much of what he was actually saying.'

Strike stroked his chin, thinking.

'What did the anonymous caller sound like?'

'London accent,' Robin said. 'Threatening.'

'"They piss themselves as they die",' repeated Strike in an undertone.

There was something that Robin wanted to say, but a brutal personal memory made it hard for her to articulate.

'Strangling victims—'

'Yeah,' said Strike, cutting her off. 'I know.'

Both of them drank.

'Well, assuming the call was Jimmy,' Robin went on, 'he's phoned the department twice today.'

She opened her handbag and showed Strike the listening device hidden inside it.

'You retrieved it?' he asked, staggered.

'And replaced it with another one,' said Robin, unable to suppress a triumphant smile. 'That's why I'm late. I took a chance. Aamir, who works with Winn, left and Geraint came into our office while I was packing up, to chat me up.'

'He did, did he?' asked Strike, amused.

'I'm glad you find it funny,' said Robin coolly. 'He isn't a nice man.'

'Sorry,' said Strike. 'In what way is he not a nice man?'

'Just take it from me,' said Robin. 'I've met plenty of them in offices. He's a pervert, but with creepy add-ons. He was just telling me,' she said, and her indignation showed in the rising tide of pink in her face, 'that I remind him of his dead daughter. Then he touched my hair.'

'Touched your hair?' repeated Strike, unamused.

'Picked a bit of it off my shoulder and ran it through his fingers,' said Robin. 'Then I think he saw what I thought of him and tried to pass it off as fatherly. Anyway, I said I needed the loo but asked him to stay put so we could keep chatting about charities. I nipped down the corridor and swapped the devices.'

'That was bloody good going, Robin.'

'I listened to it on the way here,' said Robin, pulling headphones out of her pocket, 'and—'

Robin handed Strike the headphones.

'—I've cued up the interesting bit.'

Strike obediently inserted the earbuds and Robin switched on the tape in her handbag.

'. . . at three thirty, Aamir.'

The Welsh male voice was interrupted by the sound of a mobile phone ringing. Feet scuffled near the power point, the ring ceased and Geraint said:

'Oh, hello Jimmy . . . half a mo' – Aamir, close that door.'

More scuffling, footsteps.

'Jimmy, yes . . . ?'

There followed a long stretch in which Geraint seemed to be attempting to stem the flow of a mounting tirade.

'Whoa – now, wai . . . Jimmy, lis . . . Jimmy, listen – *listen!* I know you've lost out, Jimmy, I understand how bitter you – *Jimmy, please!* We understand your feelings – that's unfair, Jimmy, neither Della nor I grew up wealth – my father was a coalminer, Jimmy! Now listen, please! *We're close to getting the pictures!*'

There followed a spell in which Strike thought he heard, very faintly, the rise and fall of Jimmy Knight's fluent speech at the end of the telephone.

'I take your point,' said Geraint finally, 'but I urge you to do nothing rash, Jimmy. He isn't going to give you – Jimmy, listen! He isn't going to give you your money, he's made that perfectly clear. It's the newspapers now or nothing, so . . . proof, Jimmy! Proof!'

Another, shorter period of unintelligible gabbling followed.

'I've just told you, haven't I? Yes . . . no, but the Foreign Office . . . well, hardly . . . no, Aamir has a contact . . . yes . . . yes . . . all right then . . . I will, Jimmy. Good – yes, all right. Yes. Goodbye.'

The clunk of a mobile being set down was followed by Geraint's voice.

'Stupid prick,' he said.

There were more footsteps. Strike glanced at Robin, who by a rolling gesture of the hand indicated that he should keep listening. After perhaps thirty seconds, Aamir spoke, diffident and strained.

'Geraint, Christopher didn't promise anything about the pictures.'

Even on the tinny little tape, with the nearby shufflings of paper at Geraint's desk, the silence sounded charged.

'Geraint, did you h—?'

'Yes, I heard!' snapped Winn. 'Good God, boy, a first from the LSE and you can't think of a way to persuade that bastard to give you pictures? I'm not asking you to take them out of the department, just to get copies. That shouldn't be beyond the wit of man.'

'I don't want more trouble,' muttered Aamir.

'Well, I should have thought,' said Geraint, 'after everything Della in particular has done for you . . . '

'And I'm grateful,' said Aamir swiftly. 'You know I am . . . all right, I'll – I'll try.'

For the next minute there were no sounds but scuffing footsteps and papers, followed by a mechanical click. The device automatically switched off after a minute of no talking, activated again when somebody spoke. The next voice was that of a different man asking whether Della would be attending 'the sub-committee' this afternoon.

Strike removed the earbuds.

'Did you catch it all?' Robin asked.

'I think so,' said Strike.

She leaned back, watching Strike expectantly.

'The Foreign Office?' he repeated quietly. 'What the hell can he have done that means the *Foreign Office* has got pictures?'

'I thought we weren't supposed to be interested in what he did?' said Robin, eyebrows raised.

'I never said I wasn't interested. Just that I'm not being paid to find out.'

Strike's fish and chips arrived. He thanked the barmaid and proceeded to add a generous amount of ketchup to his plate.

'Izzy was completely matter of fact about whatever it is,' said Robin, thinking back. 'She couldn't possibly have spoken about it the way she did if he'd – you know – murdered anybody.'

She deliberately avoided the word 'strangled'. Three panic attacks in three days were quite sufficient.

'Got to say,' said Strike, now chewing chips, 'that anonymous call makes you – unless,' he said, struck by a thought, 'Jimmy's had the bright idea of trying to drag Chiswell into the Billy business on top of whatever else he's genuinely done. A child-killing doesn't have to be true to make trouble for a government minister who's already got the press on his tail. You know the internet. Plenty of people out there think being a Tory is tantamount to being a child killer. This might be Jimmy's idea of adding pressure.'

Strike stabbed a few chips moodily with his fork.

'I'd be glad to know where Billy is, if we had somebody free to look for him. Barclay hasn't seen any sign of him and says Jimmy hasn't mentioned having a brother.'

'Billy said he was being held captive,' Robin said tentatively.

'Don't think we can set much store on anything Billy's saying right now, to be honest. I knew a guy in the Shiners who had a psychotic episode on exercises. Thought he had cockroaches living under his skin.'

'In the—?'

'Shiners. Fusiliers. Want a chip?'

'I'd better not,' sighed Robin, though she was hungry. Matthew, whom she had warned by text that she would be late, had told her he would wait for her to get home, so they could eat dinner together. 'Listen, I haven't told you everything.'

'Suki Lewis?' asked Strike, hopefully.

'I haven't been able to work her into the conversation yet. No, it's that Chiswell's wife claims men have been lurking in the flowerbeds and fiddling with her horses.'

'Men?' Strike repeated. 'In the plural?'

'That's what Izzy said – but she also says Kinvara's hysterical and attention-seeking.'

'Getting to be a bit of a theme, that, isn't it? People who're supposed to be too crazy to know what they've seen.'

'D'you think that could have been Jimmy, as well? In the garden?'

Strike thought it over as he chewed.

'I can't see what he's got to gain from lurking in the garden or fiddling with horses, unless he's at the point where he just wants to frighten Chiswell. I'll check with Barclay and see whether Jimmy's got a car or mentioned going to Oxfordshire. Did Kinvara call the police?'

'Raff asked that, when Izzy got back,' said Robin, and once again, Strike thought he detected a trace of self-consciousness as she spoke the man's name. 'Kinvara claims the dogs barked, she saw the shadow of a man in the garden, but he ran away. She says there were footprints in the horses' field next morning and that one of them had been cut with a knife.'

'Did she call a vet?'

'I don't know. It's harder to ask questions with Raff in the office. I don't want to look too nosy, because he doesn't know who I am.'

Strike pushed his plate away from him and felt for his cigarettes.

'Photos,' he mused, returning to the central point. 'Photos at the Foreign Office. What the hell can they show that would incriminate Chiswell? He's never worked at the Foreign Office, has he?'

'No,' said Robin. 'The highest post he's ever held is Minister for Trade. He had to resign from there because of the affair with Raff's mother.'

The wooden clock over the fireplace was telling her it was time to leave. She didn't move.

'You're liking Raff, then?' Strike said suddenly, catching her off guard.

'What?'

Robin was scared that she had blushed.

'What do you mean, I'm "liking" him?'

'Just an impression I got,' said Strike. 'You disapproved of him before you met him.'

'D'you want me to be antagonistic towards him, when I'm supposed to be his father's goddaughter?' demanded Robin.

'No, of course not,' said Strike, though Robin had the sense that he was laughing at her, and resented it.

'I'd better get going,' she said, sweeping the headphones off the table and back into her bag. 'I told Matt I'd be home for dinner.'

She got up, bade Strike goodbye and left the pub.

Strike watched her go, dimly sorry that he had commented on her manner when mentioning Raphael Chiswell. After a few minutes' solitary beer consumption, he paid for his food and ambled out onto the pavement, where he lit a cigarette and called the Minister for Culture, who answered on the second ring.

'Wait there,' said Chiswell. Strike could hear a murmuring crowd behind him. 'Crowded room.'

The clunk of a door closing and the noise of the crowd was muted.

''M at a dinner,' said Chiswell. 'Anything for me?'

'It isn't good news, I'm afraid,' said Strike, walking away from the pub, up Queen Anne Street, between white painted buildings that gleamed in the dusk. 'My partner succeeded in planting the listening device in Mr Winn's office this morning. We've got a recording of him talking to Jimmy Knight. Winn's assistant – Aamir, is it? – is trying to get copies of those photographs you told me about. At the Foreign Office.'

The ensuing silence lasted so long that Strike wondered whether they had been cut off.

'Minist—?'

'I'm here!' snarled Chiswell. 'That boy Mallik, is it? Dirty little bastard. *Dirty little bastard.* He's already lost one job – let him try, that's all. Let him try! Does he think I won't – I know things about Aamir Mallik,' he said. 'Oh yes.'

Strike waited, in some surprise, for elucidation of these remarks, but none were forthcoming. Chiswell merely breathed heavily into the telephone. Soft, muffled thuds told Strike that Chiswell was pacing up and down on carpet.

'Is that all you had to say to me?' demanded the MP at last.

'There was one other thing,' said Strike. 'My partner says your wife's seen a man or men trespassing on your property at night.'

'Oh,' said Chiswell, 'yerse.' He did not sound particularly concerned. 'My wife keeps horses and she takes their security very seriously.'

'You don't think this has any connection with—?'

'Not in the slightest, not in the slightest. Kinvara's sometimes – well, to be candid,' said Chiswell, 'she can be bloody hysterical. Keeps a bunch of horses, always fretting they're going to be stolen. I don't want you wasting time chasing shadows through the undergrowth in Oxfordshire. My problems are in London. Is that everything?'

Strike said that it was and, after a curt farewell, Chiswell hung up, leaving Strike to limp towards St James's Park station.

Settled in a corner seat of the Tube ten minutes later, Strike folded his arms, stretched out his legs and stared unseeingly at the window opposite.

The nature of this investigation was highly unusual. He had never before had a blackmail case where the client was so unforthcoming about his offence – but then, Strike reasoned with himself, he had never had a government minister as a client before. Equally, it was not every day that a possibly psychotic young man burst into Strike's office and insisted that he had witnessed a child murder, though Strike had certainly received his fair share of unusual and unbalanced communications since hitting the newspapers: what he had once called, over Robin's occasional protests, 'the nutter drawer', now filled half a filing cabinet.

It was the precise relationship between the strangled child and Chiswell's case of blackmail that was preoccupying Strike, even though, on the face of it, the connection was obvious: it lay in the fact of Jimmy and Billy's brotherhood. Now somebody (and Strike thought it overwhelmingly likely to be Jimmy, judging from Robin's account of the call) seemed to have decided to tie Billy's story to Chiswell, even though the blackmailable offence that had brought Chiswell to Strike could not possibly have been infanticide, or Geraint Winn would have gone to the police. Like a tongue probing a pair of ulcers, Strike's thoughts kept returning fruitlessly to the Knight brothers: Jimmy, charismatic, articulate, thuggishly good-looking, a chancer and a hothead, and Billy, haunted, filthy, unquestionably ill, bedevilled by a memory no less dreadful for the fact that it might be false.

They piss themselves as they die.

Who did? Again, Strike seemed to hear Billy Knight.

They buried her in a pink blanket, down in the dell by my dad's house. But afterwards they said it was a boy . . .

He had just been specifically instructed by his client to restrict his investigations to London, not Oxfordshire.

As he checked the name of the station at which they had just arrived, Strike remembered Robin's self-consciousness when talking about Raphael Chiswell. Yawning, he took out his mobile again and succeeded in Googling the youngest of his client's offspring, of whom there were many pictures going up the courtroom steps to his trial for manslaughter.

As he scrolled through multiple pictures of Raphael, Strike felt a rising antipathy towards the handsome young man in his dark suit. Setting aside the fact that Chiswell's son resembled an Italian model more than anything British, the images caused a latent resentment, rooted in class and personal injuries, to glow a little redder inside Strike's chest. Raphael was of the same type as Jago Ross, the man whom Charlotte had married after splitting with Strike: upper class, expensively clothed and educated, their peccadillos treated more leniently for being able to afford the best lawyers, for resembling the sons of the judges deciding their fates.

The train set off again and Strike, losing his connection, stuffed his phone back into his pocket, folded his arms and resumed his blank stare at the dark window, trying to deny an uncomfortable idea headspace, but it nosed up against him like a dog demanding food, impossible to ignore.

He now realised that he had never imagined Robin being interested in any man other than Matthew, except, of course, for that moment when he himself had held her on the stairs at her wedding, when, briefly . . .

Angry with himself, he kicked the unhelpful thought aside, and forced his wandering mind back onto the curious case of a government minister, slashed horses and a body buried in a pink blanket, down in a dell.

21

. . . certain games are going on behind your back in this house.

Henrik Ibsen, *Rosmersholm*

'Why are you so busy and I've got bugger all to do?' Raphael asked Robin, late on Friday morning.

She had just returned from tailing Geraint to Portcullis House. Observing him from a distance, she had seen how the polite smiles of the many young women he greeted turned to expressions of dislike as he passed. Geraint had disappeared into a meeting room on the first floor, so Robin had returned to Izzy's office. Approaching Geraint's room she had hoped she might be able to slip inside and retrieve the second listening device, but through the open door she saw Aamir working at his computer.

'Raff, I'll give you something to do in a moment, babes,' muttered a fraught Izzy, who was hammering at her keyboard. 'I've got to finish this, it's for the local party chairwoman. Papa's coming to sign it in five minutes.'

She threw a harried glance at her brother, who was sprawled in the armchair, his long legs spread out in front of him, shirtsleeves rolled up, tie loosened, playing with the paper visitor's pass that hung around his neck.

'Why don't you go and get yourself a coffee on the terrace?' Izzy suggested. Robin knew she wanted him out of the way when Chiswell turned up.

'Want to come for a coffee, Venetia?' asked Raphael.

'Can't,' said Robin. 'Busy.'

The fan on Izzy's desk swept Robin's way and she enjoyed a few seconds of cool breeze. The net-curtained window gave but a misty impression of the glorious June day. Truncated parliamentarians appeared as glowing wraiths on the terrace beyond the glass. It was stuffy inside the cluttered office. Robin was wearing a cotton dress, her hair in a ponytail, but still she occasionally blotted her upper lip with the back of her hand as she pretended to be working.

Having Raphael in the office was, as she had told Strike, a disadvantage. There had been no need to come up with excuses for lurking in the corridor when she had been alone with Izzy. What was more, Raphael watched her a lot, in an entirely different way to Geraint's lewd up-and-down looks. She didn't approve of Raphael, but every now and then she found herself coming perilously close to feeling sorry for him. He seemed nervy around his father, and then – well, *anybody* would think him handsome. That was the main reason she avoided looking at him: it was best not to, if you wanted to preserve any objectivity.

He kept trying to foster a closer relationship with her, which she was attempting to discourage. Only the previous day he had interrupted her as she hovered outside Geraint and Aamir's door, listening with all her might to a conversation that Aamir was having on the phone about an 'inquiry'. From the scant details that Robin had so far heard, she was convinced that the Level Playing Field was under discussion.

'But this isn't a *statutory* inquiry?' Aamir was asking, sounding worried. 'It isn't official? I thought this was just a routine . . . but Mr Winn understood that his letter to the fundraising regulator had answered all their concerns.'

Robin could not pass up the opportunity to listen, but knew her situation to be perilous. What she had not expected was to be surprised by Raphael rather than Winn.

'What are you doing, skulking there?' he had asked, laughing.

Robin walked hastily away, but she heard Aamir's door slam behind her and suspected that he, at least, would make sure that it was closed in future.

'Are you always this jumpy, or is it just me?' Raphael had asked, hurrying after her. 'Come for a coffee, come on, I'm so bloody bored.'

Robin had declined brusquely, but even as she pretended to be busy again, she had to admit that part of her – a tiny part – was flattered by his attentions.

There was a knock on the door and, to Robin's surprise, Aamir Mallik entered the room, holding a list of names. Nervous but determined, he addressed Izzy.

'Yeah, uh, hi. Geraint would like to add the Level Playing Field trustees to the Paralympian reception on the twelfth of July,' he said.

'I've got nothing to do with that reception,' snapped Izzy. 'DCMS are organising it, not me. *Why*,' she erupted, wiping her sweaty fringe off her forehead, 'does everyone come to *me*?'

'Geraint needs them to come,' said Aamir. The list of names quivered in his hand.

Robin wondered whether she dared creep into Aamir's empty office right now and swap the listening devices. She got to her feet quietly, trying not to draw attention to herself.

'Why doesn't he ask Della?' asked Izzy.

'Della's busy. It's only eight people,' said Aamir. 'He really needs—'

'"*Hear the word of Lachesis, the daughter of Necessity!*"'

The Minister for Culture's booming tones preceded him into the room. Chiswell stood in the doorway, wearing a crumpled suit and blocking Robin's exit. She sat down quietly again. Aamir, or so it seemed to Robin, braced himself.

'Know who Lachesis was, Mr Mallik?' asked Chiswell.

'Can't say I do,' said Aamir.

'No? Didn't study the Greeks in your Harringay Comprehensive? You seem to have time on your hands, Raff. Teach Mr Mallik about Lachesis.'

'I don't know, either,' said Raphael, peering up at his father through his thick, dark lashes.

'Playing stupid, eh? Lachesis,' said Chiswell, 'was one of the Fates. She measured out each man's allotted lifespan. Knew when everyone's number would be up. Not a fan of Plato, Mr Mallik? Catullus more up your street, I expect. He produced some fine poetry about men of your habits. *Pedicabo ego vos et irrumabo, Aureli pathice et cinaede Furi*, eh? Poem 16, look it up, you'll enjoy it.'

Raphael and Izzy were both staring at their father. Aamir stood for a few seconds as though he had forgotten what he had come for, then stalked out of the room.

'A little Classics education for everyone,' said Chiswell, turning to watch him go with what appeared to be malicious satisfaction. 'We are never too old to learn, eh, Raff?'

Robin's mobile vibrated on her desk. Strike had texted. They had agreed not to contact each other during working hours unless it was urgent. She slid the phone into her bag.

'Where's my signing pile?' Chiswell asked Izzy. 'Have you finished that letter for Brenda Bloody Bailey?'

'Printing it now,' said Izzy.

While Chiswell scribbled his signature on a stack of letters, breathing like a bulldog in the otherwise quiet room, Robin muttered something about needing to get going, and hurried out into the corridor.

Wanting to read Strike's text without fear of interruption, she followed a wooden sign to the crypt, hastened down the narrow stone staircase indicated and found, at the bottom, a deserted chapel.

The crypt was decorated like a medieval jewel casket, every inch of gold wall embellished with motifs and symbols, heraldic and religious. There were jewel-bright saints' pictures above the altar and the sky-blue organ pipes were wrapped in gold ribbon and scarlet *fleurs-de-lys*. Robin hurried into a red velvet pew and opened Strike's text.

Need a favour. Barclay's done a 10-day stretch on Jimmy Knight, but he's just found out his wife's got to work over the weekend & he can't get anyone else to look after the baby. Andy leaves for a week in Alicante with the family tonight. I can't tail Jimmy, he knows me. CORE are joining an anti-missile march tomorrow. Starts at 2, in Bow. Can you do it?

Robin contemplated the message for several seconds, then let out a groan that echoed around the crypt.

It was the first time in over a year that Strike had asked her to work extra hours at such short notice, but this was her anniversary weekend. The pricey hotel was booked, the bags packed and ready in the car. She was supposed to be meeting Matthew after work in a couple of hours. They were to drive straight to Le Manoir aux Quat'Saisons. Matthew would be furious if she said she couldn't go.

In the gilded hush of the crypt, the words Strike had said to her when he had agreed to give her detective training came back to her.

I need someone who can work long hours, weekends . . . you've got a lot of aptitude for the job, but you're getting married to someone who hates you doing it . . .

And she had told him that it didn't matter what Matthew thought, that it was up to her what she did.

Where did her allegiance lie now? She had said that she would stay in the marriage, promised to give it a chance. Strike had had many hours of unpaid overtime out of her. He could not claim that she was workshy.

Slowly, deleting words, replacing them, overthinking every syllable, she typed out a response.

I'm really sorry, but it's my anniversary weekend. We've got a hotel booked, leaving this evening.

She wanted to write more, but what was there to say? 'My marriage isn't going well, so it's important I celebrate it'? 'I'd much rather disguise myself as a protestor and stalk Jimmy Knight'? She pressed 'send'.

Sitting waiting for his response, feeling as though she were about to get the results of medical tests, Robin's eyes followed the course of twisting vines that covered the ceiling. Strange faces peered down at her out of the moulding, like the wild Green Man of myth. Heraldic and pagan imagery mingled with angels and crosses. It was more than a place of God, this chapel. It harked back to an age of superstition, magic and feudal power.

The minutes slid by and still Strike hadn't answered. Robin got up and walked around the chapel. At the very back she found a cupboard. Opening it, she saw a plaque to suffragette Emily Davison. Apparently, she had slept there overnight so that she could give her place of residence as the House of Commons on the census of 1911, seven years before women were given the vote. Emily Davison, she could not help but feel, would not have approved of Robin's choice to place a failing marriage above freedom to work.

Robin's mobile buzzed again. She looked down, afraid of what she was going to read. Strike had answered with two letters:

OK

A lead weight seemed to slide from her chest to her stomach. Strike, as she was well aware, was still living in the glorified bedsit over the office and working through weekends. The only unmarried person at the agency, the boundary between his professional and private lives was, if not precisely non-existent, then flexible and porous, whereas hers, Barclay's and Hutchins' were not. And the worst of it was that Robin could think of no way of telling Strike that she was sorry, that she understood, that she wished things were different, without reminding both of them of that hug on the stairs at her wedding, now so long unmentioned that she wondered whether he even remembered it.

Feeling utterly miserable, she retraced her steps out of the crypt, still holding the papers she had been pretending to deliver.

Raphael was alone in the office when she returned, sitting at Izzy's PC and typing at a third of her speed.

'Izzy's gone with Dad to do something so tedious it just bounced off my brain,' he said. 'They'll be back in a bit.'

Robin forced a smile, returned to her desk, her mind on Strike.

'Bit weird, that poem, wasn't it?' Raphael asked.

'What? Oh – oh, that Latin thing? Yes,' said Robin. 'It was, a bit.'

'It was like he'd memorised it to use on Mallik. Nobody's got that at their fingertips.'

Reflecting that Strike seemed to know other strange bits of Latin off by heart, too, Robin said, 'No, you wouldn't think so.'

'Has he got it in for that Mallik, or something?'

'I really don't know,' lied Robin.

Running out of ways to occupy her time at the desk, she shuffled papers again.

'How long are you staying, Venetia?'

'I'm not sure. Until Parliament goes into recess, probably.'

'You seriously want to work here? Permanently?'

'Yes,' she said. 'I think it's interesting.'

'What were you doing before this?'

'PR,' said Robin. 'It was quite fun, but I fancied a change.'

'Hoping to bag an MP?' he said, with a faint smile.

'I can't say I've seen anyone round here I'd like to marry,' said Robin.

'Hurtful,' said Raphael, with a mock sigh.

Afraid that she had blushed, Robin tried to cover up by bending down to open a drawer and taking a few objects out at random.

'So, is Venetia Hall seeing anyone?' he persisted, as she straightened up.

'Yes,' she said. 'His name's Tim. We've been together a year now.'

'Yeah? What does Tim do?'

'He works at Christie's,' said Robin.

She had got the idea from the men she had seen with Sarah Shadlock in the Red Lion: immaculate, suited public-school types of the kind she imagined Chiswell's goddaughter would know.

'What about you?' she asked. 'Izzy said something—'

'At the gallery?' said Raphael, cutting her off. 'That was nothing. She was too young for me. Her parents have sent her to Florence now, anyway.'

He had swung his chair around to face her, his expression grave and searching, contemplating her as though he wanted to know something that common conversation would not yield. Robin broke their mutual gaze. Holding a look that intense was not compatible with being the contented girlfriend of the imaginary Tim.

'D'you believe in redemption?'

The question caught Robin totally by surprise. It had a kind of gravity and beauty, like the gleaming jewel of the chapel at the foot of a winding stair.

'I . . . yes, I do,' she said.

He had picked up a pencil from Izzy's desk. His long fingers turned it over and over as he watched her intently. He seemed to be sizing her up.

'You know what I did? In the car?'

'Yes,' she answered.

The silence that unspooled between them seemed to Robin to be peopled with flashing lights and shadowy figures. She could imagine Raphael bloody at the steering wheel, and the broken figure of the young mother on the road, and the police cars and the incident tape and the gawpers in passing cars. He was watching her intently, hoping, she thought, for some kind of benison, as though her forgiveness mattered. And sometimes, she knew, the kindness of a stranger, or even a casual acquaintance, could be transformative, something to cling to while those closest to you dragged you under in their efforts to help. She thought of the elderly steward in the Members' Lobby, uncomprehending but immensely consoling, his hoarse, kindly words a thread to hold on to, which would lead her back to sanity.

The door opened again. Both Robin and Raphael jumped as a curvy redhead entered the room, a visitor's pass hanging around her neck on a lanyard. Robin recognised her at once from online photographs as Jasper Chiswell's wife, Kinvara.

'Hello,' said Robin, because Kinvara was merely staring blankly at Raphael, who had swung hastily back to his computer and begun typing again.

'You must be Venetia,' said Kinvara, switching her clear golden gaze onto Robin. She had a high-pitched, girlish voice. Her eyes were catlike in a slightly puffy face. 'Aren't you pretty? Nobody told me you were so pretty.'

Robin had no idea how to respond to this. Kinvara dropped down into the sagging chair where Raff usually sat, took off the designer sunglasses holding her long red hair off her face and shook it loose. Her bare arms and legs were heavily freckled. The top buttons of her sleeveless green shirt-dress were straining across her heavy bust.

'*Whose* daughter are you?' asked Kinvara with a trace of petulance. 'Jasper didn't tell me. He doesn't tell me anything he doesn't *have* to tell me, actually. I'm used to it. He just said you're a goddaughter.'

Nobody had warned Robin that Kinvara did not know who she really was. Perhaps Izzy and Chiswell had not expected them to come face to face.

'I'm Jonathan Hall's daughter,' said Robin nervously. She had come up with a rudimentary background for Venetia-the-goddaughter, but had never expected to have to elaborate for the benefit of Chiswell's own wife, who presumably knew all Chiswell's friends and acquaintances.

'Who's he?' asked Kinvara. 'I should probably know, Jasper'll be cross I haven't paid attention—'

'He's in land management up in—'

'Oh, was it the Northumberland property?' interrupted

Kinvara, whose interest had not seemed particularly profound. 'That was before my time.'

Thank God, thought Robin.

Kinvara crossed her legs and folded her arms across her large chest. Her foot bounced up and down. She shot Raphael a hard, almost spiteful look.

'Aren't you going to say hello, Raphael?'

'Hello,' he said.

'Jasper told me to meet him here, but if you'd rather I waited in the corridor I can,' Kinvara said in her high, tight voice.

'Of course not,' muttered Raphael, frowning determinedly at his monitor.

'Well, I wouldn't want to interrupt anything,' said Kinvara, turning from Raphael to Robin. The story of the blonde in the art gallery bathroom swam back into Robin's mind. For a second time she pretended to be searching for something in a drawer and it was with relief that she heard the sounds of Chiswell and Izzy coming along the corridor.

'... and by ten o'clock, no later, or I won't have time to read the whole bloody thing. And tell Haines *he'll* have to talk to the BBC, I haven't got time for a bunch of idiots talking about inclu – Kinvara.'

Chiswell stopped dead in the office door and said, without any trace of affection, 'I told you to meet me at DCMS, not here.'

'And it's lovely to see you, too, Jasper, after three days apart,' said Kinvara, getting to her feet and smoothing her crumpled dress.

'Hi, Kinvara,' said Izzy.

'I forgot you said DCMS,' Kinvara told Chiswell, ignoring her stepdaughter. 'I've been trying to call you all morning—'

'I told you,' growled Chiswell, 'I'd be in meetings till one, and if it's about those bloody stud fees again—'

'No, it isn't about the stud fees, Jasper, *actually*, and I'd have preferred to tell you in private, but if you want me to say it in front of your children, I will!'

'Oh, for heaven's sake,' Chiswell blustered. 'Come away, then, come on, we'll find a private room—'

'There was a man last night,' said Kinvara, 'who – *don't look at me like that, Isabella!*'

Izzy's expression was indeed conveying naked scepticism. She raised her eyebrows and walked into the room, acting as though Kinvara had become invisible to her.

'I said you can tell me in a private room!' snarled Chiswell, but Kinvara refused to be deflected.

'I saw a man in the woods by the house last night, Jasper!' she said, in a loud, high-pitched voice that Robin knew would be echoing all the way along the narrow corridor. 'I'm *not* imagining things – there was a man with a spade in the woods, I saw him, and he ran when the dogs chased him! You keep telling me not to make a fuss, but I'm alone in that house at night and if *you're* not going to do anything about this, Jasper, *I'm* going to call the police!'

22

. . . don't you feel called upon to undertake it, for the sake of the good cause?

Henrik Ibsen, *Rosmersholm*

Strike was in a thoroughly bad temper.

Why the fuck, he asked himself, as he limped towards Mile End Park the following morning, was *he*, the senior partner and founder of the firm, having to stake out a protest march on a hot Saturday morning, when he had three employees and a knackered leg? Because, he answered himself, *he* didn't have a baby who needed watching, or a wife who'd booked plane tickets or broken her wrist, or a fucking anniversary weekend planned. *He* wasn't married, so it was his downtime that had to be sacrificed, *his* weekend that became just two more working days.

Everything that Robin feared Strike to be thinking about her, he was, in fact, thinking: of her house on cobbled Albury Street versus his draughty two rooms in a converted attic, of the rights and status conferred by the little gold ring on her finger, set against Lorelei's disappointment when he had explained that lunch and possibly dinner would now be impossible, of Robin's promises of equal responsibility when he had taken her on as a partner, contrasted with the reality of her rushing home to her husband.

Yes, Robin had worked many hours of unpaid overtime in her two years at the agency. Yes, he knew that she had gone way beyond the call of duty for him. Yes, he was, in theory, fucking grateful to her. The fact remained that today, while he was limping along the street towards hours of probably fruitless surveillance, she and her arsehole of a husband were speeding off to a country hotel weekend, a thought that made his sore leg and back no easier to bear.

Unshaven, clad in an old pair of jeans, a frayed, washed-out hoodie and ancient trainers, with a carrier bag swinging from his hand, Strike entered the park. He could see the massing protestors in the distance. The risk of Jimmy recognising him had almost decided Strike to let the march go unwatched, but the most recent text from Robin (which he had, out of sheer bad temper, left unanswered) had changed his mind.

> **Kinvara Chiswell came into the office. She claims she saw a man with a spade in the woods near their house last night. From what she said, Chiswell's been telling her not to call the police about these intruders, but she says she's going to do it unless he does something about them. Kinvara didn't know Chiswell's called us in, btw, she thought I really was Venetia Hall. Also, there's a chance the charity commission's investigating the Level Playing Field. I'm trying to get more details.**

This communication had served only to aggravate Strike. Nothing short of a concrete piece of evidence against Geraint Winn would have satisfied him right now, with the *Sun* on Chiswell's case and their client so tetchy and stressed.

According to Barclay, Jimmy Knight owned a ten-year-old

Suzuki Alto, but it had failed its MOT and was currently off the road. Barclay could not absolutely guarantee that Jimmy wasn't sneaking out under cover of darkness to trespass in Chiswell's gardens and woods seventy miles away, but Strike thought it unlikely.

On the other hand, he thought it just possible that Jimmy might have sent a proxy to intimidate Chiswell's wife. He probably still had friends or acquaintances in the area where he grew up. An even more disturbing idea was that Billy had escaped from the prison, real or imaginary, in which he had told Strike he was being held, and decided to dig for proof that the child lay in a pink blanket by his father's old cottage or, gripped by who knew what paranoid fantasy, to slash one of Kinvara's horses.

Worried by these inexplicable features of the case, by the interest the *Sun* was taking in the minister, and aware that the agency was no closer to securing a 'bargaining chip' against either of Chiswell's blackmailers than on the day that Strike had accepted the minister as a client, he felt he had little choice but to leave no stone unturned. In spite of his tiredness, his aching muscles and his strong suspicion that the protest march would yield nothing useful, he had dragged himself out of bed on Saturday morning, strapped his prosthesis back onto a stump that was already slightly puffy and, unable to think of much he'd like to do less than walk for two hours, set off for Mile End Park.

Once close enough to the crowd of protestors to make out individuals, Strike pulled from the carrier bag swinging from his hand a plastic Guy Fawkes mask, white with curling eyebrows and moustache and now mainly associated with the hacking organisation Anonymous, and put it on. Balling up the carrier bag, he shoved it into a handy bin, then hobbled on towards the cluster of placards and banners: 'No missiles on homes!' 'No snipers on streets!' 'Don't play games with our lives!' and several 'He's got to go!' posters featuring the prime minister's face. Strike's fake foot always found grass one of the most difficult surfaces to navigate. He was sweating by the time he finally spotted the orange CORE banners, with their logo of broken Olympic rings.

There were about a dozen of them. Lurking behind a group of chattering youths, Strike readjusted the slipping plastic mask, which had not been constructed for a man whose nose had been broken, and spotted Jimmy Knight, who was talking to two young women, both of whom had just thrown back their heads, laughing delightedly at something Knight had said. Clamping the mask to his face to make sure the slits aligned with his eyes, Strike scanned the rest of the CORE members and concluded that the absence of tomato-red hair was not because Flick had dyed it another colour, but because she wasn't there.

Stewards now started herding the crowd into something resembling a line. Strike moved into the mass of protestors, a silent, lumbering figure, acting a little obtusely so that the youthful organisers, intimidated by his size, treated him like a rock around which the current must be channelled as he took up a position right behind CORE. A skinny boy who was also wearing an Anonymous mask gave Strike a double thumbs up as he was shunted towards the rear of the line. Strike returned it.

Now smoking a roll-up, Jimmy continued to joke with the two young girls beside him, who were vying for his attention. The darker of the two, who was particularly attractive, was holding a double-sided banner carrying a highly detailed painting of David Cameron as Hitler overlooking the 1936 Olympic Stadium. It was quite an impressive piece of art, and Strike had time to admire it as the procession finally set off at a steady pace, flanked by police and stewards in high visibility jackets, moving gradually out of the park and onto the long, straight Roman Road.

The smooth tarmac was slightly easier on Strike's prosthesis, but his stump was still throbbing. After a few minutes a chant was got up: 'Missiles OUT! Missiles OUT!'

A couple of press photographers were walking backwards in the road ahead, taking pictures of the front of the march.

'Hey, Libby,' said Jimmy, to the girl with the hand-painted Hitler banner. 'Wanna get on my shoulders?'

Strike noted her friend's poorly concealed envy as Jimmy crouched down so that Libby could straddle his neck and be lifted up above the crowd, her banner raised high enough for the photographers in front to see.

'Show 'em your tits, we'll be front page!' Jimmy called up to her.

'Jimmy!' she squealed, in mock outrage. Her friend's smile was forced. The cameras clicked, and Strike, grimacing with pain behind the plastic mask, tried not to limp too obviously.

'Guy with the biggest camera was focused on you the whole time,' said Jimmy, when he finally lowered the girl back to the ground.

'Fuck, if I'm in the papers my mum'll go apeshit,' said the girl excitedly, and she fell into step on Jimmy's other side, taking any opportunity to nudge or slap him as he teased her about being scared of what her parents would say. She was, Strike judged, at least fifteen years younger than he was.

'Enjoying yourself, Jimmy?'

The mask restricted Strike's peripheral vision, so that it was only when the uncombed, tomato-red hair appeared immediately in front of him that Strike realised Flick had joined the march. Her sudden appearance had taken Jimmy by surprise, too.

'There you are!' he said, with a feeble show of pleasure.

Flick glared at the girl called Libby, who sped up, intimidated. Jimmy tried to put his arm around Flick, but she shrugged it off.

'Oi,' he said, feigning innocent indignation. 'What's up?'

'Three fucking guesses,' snarled Flick.

Strike could tell that Jimmy was debating which tack to take with her. His thuggishly handsome face showed irritation but also, Strike thought, a certain wariness. For a second time, he tried to put his arm around her. This time, she slapped it away.

'Oi,' he said again, this time aggressively. 'The fuck was that for?'

'I'm off doing your dirty work and you're fucking around with *her?* What kind of fucking idiot do you think I am, Jimmy?'

'Missiles OUT!' bellowed a steward with a megaphone, and the crowd took up the chant once more. The cries made by the Mohicaned woman beside Strike were as shrill and raucous as a peacock's. The one bonus of the renewed shouting was that it left Strike at liberty to grunt with pain every time he set his prosthetic foot on the road, which was a kind of release and made the plastic mask reverberate in a ticklish fashion against his sweating face. Squinting through the eyeholes he watched Jimmy and Flick argue, but he couldn't hear a word over the din of the crowd. Only when the chant subsided at last could he make out a little of what they were saying to each other.

'I'm fucking sick of this,' Jimmy was saying. '*I'm* not the one who picks up students in bars when—'

'You'd ditched me!' said Flick, in a kind of whispered scream. 'You'd fucking ditched me! You told me you didn't want anything exclusive—'

'Heat of the moment, wasn't it?' said Jimmy roughly. 'I was stressed. Billy was doing my fucking head in. I didn't expect you to go straight to a bar and pick up some fucking—'

'You told me you were sick of—'

'Fuck's sake, I lost my temper and said a bunch of shit I didn't mean. If I went and shagged another woman every time you give me grief—'

'Yeah, well I sometimes think the only reason you even keep me around is Chis—'

'*Keep your fucking voice down!*'

'—and today, you think it was fun at that creep's house—'

'I said I was grateful, fuck's sake, we discussed this, didn't we? I had to get those leaflets printed or I'd've come with you—'

'*And* I do that cleaning,' she said, with a sudden sob, 'and it's disgusting and then today you send me – it was horrible, Jimmy, he should be in hospital, he's in a right state—'

Jimmy glanced around. Coming briefly within Jimmy's eye-line, Strike attempted to walk naturally, though every time he asked his stump to bear his full weight, he felt as though he was pressing it down on a thousand fire ants.

'We'll get him to hospital after,' said Jimmy. 'We will, but he'll screw it all up if we let him loose now, you know what he's like . . . once Winn's got those photos . . . hey,' said Jimmy gently, putting his arm around her for a third time. 'Listen. I'm so fucking grateful to you.'

'Yeah,' choked Flick, wiping her nose on the back of her hand, 'because of the money. Because you wouldn't even know what Chiswell had done if—'

Jimmy pulled her roughly towards him and kissed her. For a second she resisted, then opened her mouth. The kiss went on and on as they walked. Strike could see their tongues working in each other's mouths. They staggered slightly as they walked, locked together, while other CORE members grinned, and the girl whom Jimmy had lifted into the air looked crestfallen.

'Jimmy,' murmured Flick at last, when the kiss had ended, but his arm was still around her. She was doe-eyed with lust now, and soft-spoken. 'I think you should come and talk to him, seriously. He keeps talking about that bloody detective.'

'What?' said Jimmy, though Strike could tell he'd heard.

'Strike. That bastard soldier with the one leg. Billy's fixated on him. Thinks he's going to rescue him.'

The end point of the march came into sight at last: Bow Quarter in Fairfield Road, where the square brick tower of an old match factory, proposed site of some of the planned missiles, punctured the skyline.

'"Rescue him"?' repeated Jimmy scornfully. 'Fuck's sake. It's not like he's being fucking tortured.'

The marchers were breaking ranks now, dissolving back into a formless crowd that milled around a dark green pond in front of the proposed missile site. Strike would have given much to sit down on a bench or lean up against a tree, as many of the protestors were doing, so as to take the weight off his stump. Both the end, where skin that was never meant to bear his weight was irritated and inflamed, and the tendons in his knee were begging for ice and rest. Instead, he limped on after Jimmy and Flick as they walked around the edge of the crowd, away from their CORE colleagues.

'He wanted to see you and I told him you were busy,' he heard Flick say, 'and he cried. It was horrible, Jimmy.'

Pretending to be watching the young black man with a microphone, who was ascending a stage at the front of the crowd, Strike edged closer to Jimmy and Flick.

'I'll look after Billy when I get the money,' Jimmy was telling Flick. He seemed guilty and conflicted now.

'Obviously I'll look after him . . . and you. I won't forget what you've done.'

She liked hearing that. Out of the corner of his eye, Strike saw her grubby face flush with excitement. Jimmy took a pack of tobacco and some Rizlas from his jeans pocket and began to roll himself another cigarette.

'Still talking about that fucking detective, is he?'

'Yeah.'

Jimmy lit up and smoked in silence for a while, his eyes roving abstractedly over the crowd.

'Tell you what,' he said suddenly, 'I'll go see him now. Calm him down a bit. We just need him to stay put a bit longer. Coming?'

He held out his hand and Flick took it, smiling. They walked away.

Strike let them get a short head start, then stripped off the mask and the old grey hoodie, replaced the former with the sunglasses he had pocketed for this eventuality and set off after them, dumping the mask and hoodie on top of their banners.

The pace Jimmy now set was completely different to the leisurely march. Every few strides, Flick had to jog to keep up, and Strike was soon gritting his teeth as the nerve endings at the inflamed skin at the end of his stump rubbed against the prosthesis, his overworked thigh muscles groaning in protest.

He was perspiring hard, his gait becoming more and more unnatural. Passers-by were starting to stare. He could feel their curiosity and pity as he dragged his prosthetic leg along. He knew he should have been doing his bloody physio exercises, that he ought to have kept to the no chips rule, that in an ideal world he'd have taken the day off today, and rested up, the prosthesis off, an ice pack on his stump. On he limped, refusing to listen to the body pleading with him to stop, the distance between himself, Jimmy and Flick growing ever wider, the compensating movement of his upper body and arms becoming grotesque. He could only pray that neither Jimmy nor Flick would turn and look behind them, because there was no way Strike could remain incognito if they saw him hobbling along like this. They were already disappearing into the neat little brick box that was Bow station, while Strike was panting and swearing on the opposite side of the road.

As he stepped off the kerb, an excruciating pain shot through the back of his right thigh, as though a knife had sliced through the muscle. The leg buckled and he fell, his outstretched hand skidding along asphalt, hitting hip, shoulder and head on the open road. Somewhere in the vicinity a woman yelped in shock. Onlookers would think he was drunk. It had happened before when he had fallen. Humiliated, furious, groaning in agony, Strike crawled back onto the pavement, dragging his right leg out of the way of oncoming traffic. A young woman approached nervously to see whether he needed help, he barked at her, then felt guilty.

'Sorry,' he croaked, but she was gone, hurrying away with two friends.

He dragged himself to the railings bordering the pavement and sat there, back against metal, sweating and bleeding. He doubted whether he would be able to stand again without assistance. Running his hands over the back of his stump, he felt an egg-shaped swelling and, with a groan, guessed that he had torn a hamstring. The pain was so sharp that it was making him feel sick.

He tugged his mobile out of his pocket. The screen was cracked where he had fallen on it.

'Fuck. It. All,' he muttered, closing his eyes and leaning his head back against the cold metal.

He sat motionless for several minutes, dismissed as a tramp or a drunk by the people navigating around him, while he silently assessed his limited options. At last, with a sense of being utterly cornered, he opened his eyes, wiped his face with his forearm, and punched in Lorelei's number.

23

. . . ailing and languishing in the gloom of such a marriage . . .

Henrik Ibsen, *Rosmersholm*

In retrospect, Robin knew that her anniversary weekend had been doomed before it had even begun, down in the House of Commons crypt where she had turned down Strike's request to tail Jimmy.

Trying to throw off her sense of guilt, she had confided Strike's request to Matthew when he picked her up after work. Already tense due to the demands of navigating the Friday night traffic in the Land Rover, which he disliked, Matthew went on the offensive, demanding to know why she felt bad after all the slave labour Strike had had out of her over the past two years and proceeding to badmouth Strike so viciously that Robin had felt compelled to defend him. They were still arguing about her job an hour later, when Matthew suddenly noticed that there was neither wedding nor engagement ring on Robin's gesticulating left hand. She never wore these when playing the unmarried Venetia Hall, and had entirely forgotten that she would not be able to retrieve them from Albury Street before leaving for the hotel.

'It's our bloody anniversary and you can't even remember to put your rings back on?' Matthew had shouted.

They drew up outside the soft golden brick hotel an hour and a half later. A beaming man in uniform opened the door for Robin. Her 'thank you' was almost inaudible due to the hard, angry lump in her throat.

They barely spoke over their Michelin-starred dinner. Robin, who might as well have been eating polystyrene and dust, looked around at the surrounding tables. She and Matthew were by far the youngest couple there, and she wondered whether any of these husbands and wives had been through this kind of trough in their marriages, and survived it.

They slept back to back that night.

Robin woke on Saturday in the awareness that every moment in the hotel, every step through the beautifully cultivated grounds, with the lavender walk, the Japanese garden, the orchard and organic vegetable beds, was costing them a small fortune. Perhaps Matthew was thinking the same, because he became conciliatory over breakfast. Nevertheless, their conversation felt perilous, straying regularly into dangerous territory from which they retreated precipitately. A tension headache began pounding behind Robin's temple, but she did not want to ask hotel staff for painkillers, because any sign of dissatisfaction might lead to another argument. Robin wondered what it would be like to have a wedding day and honeymoon about which it was safe to reminisce. They eventually settled on talking about Matthew's job as they strolled the grounds.

There was to be a charity cricket match between his firm and another the following Saturday. Matthew, who was as good at cricket as he had been at rugby, was greatly looking forward to the game. Robin listened to his boasts about his own prowess and jokes about Tom's inadequate bowling, laughed at the appropriate moments and made sounds of agreement, and all the time a chilled and miserable part of her was wondering what was happening right now in Bow, whether Strike had gone on the march, whether he was getting anything useful on Jimmy and wondering how she, Robin, had ended up with the pompous, self-involved man beside her, who reminded her of a handsome boy she had once loved.

For the first time ever, Robin had sex with Matthew that night purely because she could not face the row that would ensue if she refused. It was their anniversary, so they had to have sex, like a notary's stamp on the weekend, and about as pleasurable. Tears stung her eyes as Matthew climaxed, and that cold, unhappy self buried deep in her compliant body wondered why he could not feel her unhappiness even though she was trying so hard to dissemble, and how he could possibly imagine that the marriage was a success.

She put her arm over her wet eyes in the darkness after he had rolled off her and said all the things you were supposed to say. For the first time, when she said 'I love you, too', she knew, beyond doubt, that she was lying.

Very carefully, once Matthew was asleep, Robin reached out in the darkness for the phone that lay on her bedside table, and checked her texts. There was nothing from Strike. She Googled pictures of the march in Bow and thought she recognised, in the middle of the crowd, a tall man with familiar curly hair, who was wearing a Guy Fawkes mask. Robin turned her mobile face down on the bedside table to shut out its light, and closed her eyes.

24

. . . her ungovernable, wild fits of passion – which she expected me to reciprocate . . .

Henrik Ibsen, *Rosmersholm*

Strike returned to his two attic rooms in Denmark Street six days later, early on Friday morning. Leaning on crutches, his prosthesis in a holdall over his shoulder and his right trouser leg pinned up, his expression tended to repel the sidelong glances of sympathy that passers-by gave him as he swung along the short street to number twenty-four.

He hadn't seen a doctor. Lorelei had called her local practice once she and the lavishly tipped cabbie had succeeded in supporting Strike upstairs to her flat, but the GP had asked Strike to come into his surgery for an examination.

'What d'you want me to do, hop there? It's my hamstring, I can feel it,' he had snapped down the phone. 'I know the drill: rest, ice, all that bollocks. I've done it before.'

He had been forced to break his no-consecutive-overnights-at-a-woman's rule, spending four full days and five nights at Lorelei's. He now regretted it, but what choice had he had? He had been caught, as Chiswell would have put it, *a fronte praecipitium, a tergo lupi*. He and Lorelei had been supposed to have dinner on Saturday night. Having chosen to tell her the truth rather than make an excuse not to meet, he had been forced to let her help. Now he wished that he had phoned his old friends Nick and Ilsa, or even Shanker, but it was too late. The damage was done.

The knowledge that he was being unfair and ungrateful was hardly calculated to improve Strike's mood as he dragged himself and his holdall up the stairs. In spite of the fact that parts of the sojourn at Lorelei's flat had been thoroughly enjoyable, all had been ruined by what had happened the previous evening, and it was entirely his own fault. He had let it happen, the thing that he had tried to guard against ever since leaving Charlotte, let it happen because he'd dropped his guard, and accepted mugs of tea, home-cooked meals and gentle affection, until finally, last night in the darkness, she had whispered onto his bare chest, 'I love you'.

Grimacing again with the effort of balancing on his crutches as he unlocked his front door, Strike almost fell into his flat. Slamming the door behind him, he dropped the holdall, crossed to the small chair at the Formica table in his kitchen-cum-living room, fell into it and cast his crutches aside. It was a relief to be home and alone, however difficult it was to manage with his leg in this state. He ought to have returned sooner, of course, but being in no condition to tail anyone and in considerable discomfort, it had been easier to remain in a comfortable armchair, his stump resting on a large square pouffe, texting Robin and Barclay instructions while Lorelei fetched him food and drink.

Strike lit a cigarette and thought back over all the women there had been since he'd left Charlotte. First, Ciara Porter, a gorgeous one-night stand, with no regrets on either side. A few weeks after he had hit the press for solving the Landry case, Ciara had called him. He had become elevated in the model's mind from casual shag to possible boyfriend material by his newsworthiness, but he had turned down further meetings with her. Girlfriends who wanted to be photographed with him were no good to him in his line of work.

Next had come Nina, who had worked for a publisher, and whom he had used to get information on a case. He had liked her, but insufficiently, as he looked back on it, to treat her with common consideration. He had hurt Nina's feelings. He wasn't proud of it, but it hardly kept him up at night.

Elin had been different, beautiful and, best of all, convenient, which was why he'd hung around. She had been in the process of divorcing a wealthy man and her need for discretion and compartmentalisation had been at least as great as his own. They had managed a few months together before he'd spilled wine all over her, and walked out of the restaurant where they were having dinner. He had called her afterwards to apologise and she had dumped him before he finished the sentence. Given that he had left her humiliated in Le Gavroche with a hefty dry-cleaning bill, he felt that it would have been in poor taste to respond with 'that's what I was going to say next'.

After Elin there had been Coco, on whom he preferred not to dwell, and now there was Lorelei. He liked her better than any of the others, which was why he was sorry that it had been she who said 'I love you'.

Strike had made a vow to himself two years previously, and he made very few vows, because he trusted himself to keep them. Having never said 'I love you' to any woman but Charlotte, he would not say it to another unless he knew, beyond reasonable doubt, that he wanted to stay with that woman and make a life with her. It would make a mockery of what he'd been through with Charlotte if he said it under circumstances any less serious. Only love could have justified the havoc they had lived together, or the many times he had resumed the relationship, even while he knew in his soul that it couldn't work. Love, to Strike, was pain and grief sought, accepted, endured. It was not in Lorelei's bedroom, with the cowgirls on the curtains.

And so he had said nothing after her whispered declaration, and then, when she'd asked whether he'd heard her, he'd said, 'Yeah, I did.'

Strike reached for his cigarettes. *Yeah, I did.* Well, that had been honest, as far as it went. There was nothing wrong with his hearing. After that, there'd been a fairly lengthy silence, then Lorelei had got out of bed and gone to the bathroom and stayed there for thirty minutes. Strike assumed that she'd gone there to cry, though she'd been kind enough to do it quietly, so that he couldn't hear her. He had lain in bed, wondering what he could say to her that was both kind and truthful, but he knew that nothing short of 'I love you, too' would be acceptable, and the fact was that he didn't love her, and he wasn't going to lie.

When she came back to bed, he had reached out for her in the bed. She'd let him stroke her shoulder for a while, then told him she was tired and needed some sleep.

What was I supposed to fucking do? he demanded of an imaginary female inquisitor who strongly resembled his sister, Lucy.

You could try not accepting tea and blow jobs, came the snide response, to which Strike, with his stump throbbing, answered, *fuck you.*

His mobile rang. He had sellotaped up the shattered screen, and through this distorted carapace he saw an unknown number.

'Strike.'

'Hi, Strike, Culpepper here.'

Dominic Culpepper, who had worked for the *News of the World* until its closure, had previously put work Strike's way. Relations between them, never personally warm, had become slightly antagonistic when Strike had refused Culpepper the inside story on his two most recent murder cases. Now working for the *Sun*, Culpepper had been one of those journalists who had most enthusiastically raked over Strike's personal life in the aftermath of the Shacklewell Ripper arrest.

'Wondered if you were free to do a job for us,' said Culpepper.

You've got a fucking nerve.

'What kind of thing're you after?'

'Digging up dirt on a government minister.'

'Which one?'

'You'll know if you take the job.'

'I'm pretty stretched just now. What kind of dirt are we talking?'

'That's what we need you to find out.'

'How do you know there's dirt there?'

'A well-placed source,' said Culpepper.

'Why do you need me if there's a well-placed source?'

'He's not ready to talk. He just hinted that there are beans to be spilled. Lots of them.'

'Sorry, can't do it, Culpepper,' said Strike. 'I'm booked solid.'

'Sure? We're paying good money, Strike.'

'I'm not doing too badly these days,' said the detective, lighting a second cigarette from the tip of his first.

'No, I'll bet you aren't, you jammy bastard,' said Culpepper. 'All right, it'll have to be Patterson. D'you know him?'

'The ex-Met guy? Run across him a couple of times,' said Strike.

The call finished with mutually insincere good wishes, leaving Strike with an increased feeling of foreboding. He Googled Culpepper's name and found his byline on a story about the Level Playing Field from two weeks previously.

Of course, it was possible that more than one government minister was currently in danger of being exposed by the *Sun* for an offence against public taste or morals, but the fact that Culpepper had recently been in close proximity with the Winns strongly suggested Robin had been right in suspecting Geraint of tipping off the *Sun*, and that it was Chiswell whom Patterson would shortly be investigating.

Strike wondered whether Culpepper knew that he, Strike, was already working for Chiswell, whether his call had been designed to startle information out of the detective, but it seemed unlikely. The newspaperman would have been very stupid to tell Strike whom he was about to hire, if he was aware that Strike was already in the minister's pay.

Strike knew of Mitch Patterson by reputation: they had twice been hired by different halves of divorcing couples in the last year. Previously a senior officer in the Metropolitan Police who had 'taken early retirement', Patterson was prematurely silver-haired and had the face of an angry pug. Though personally unpleasant, or so Eric Wardle had told Strike, Patterson was a man who 'got results'.

'Course, he won't be able to kick the shit out of people in his new career,' Wardle had commented, 'so that's one useful tool in his arsenal gone.'

Strike didn't much relish the thought that Patterson would shortly be on the case. Picking up his mobile again, he noted that neither Robin nor Barclay had called in an update within the last twelve hours. Only the previous day, he had had to reassure Chiswell, who had called to express his doubts about Robin, given her lack of results thus far.

Frustrated by his employees and his own incapacity, Strike texted Robin and Barclay the same message:

Sun just tried to hire me to investigate Chiswell. Call with update asap. Need useable info NOW.

Pulling his crutches back towards him, he got up to examine the contents of his fridge and kitchen cupboards, discovering that he would be eating nothing but tinned soup for the next four meals unless he made a trip to the supermarket. After pouring spoiled milk down the sink, he made himself a mug of black tea and returned to the Formica table, where he lit a third cigarette and contemplated, without pleasure, the prospect of doing his hamstring stretches.

His phone rang again. Seeing that it was Lucy, he let it go to voicemail. The last thing he needed right now was updates on the school board's last meeting.

A few minutes after that, when Strike was in the bathroom, she called back. He had hopped back into the kitchen with his trousers at half-mast, in the hope that it was either Robin or Barclay. When he saw his sister's number for a second time, he merely swore loudly and returned to the bathroom.

The third call told him that she was not about to give up. Slamming down the can of soup he had been opening, Strike swept up the mobile.

'Lucy, I'm busy, what is it?' he said testily.

'It's Barclay.'

'Ah, about time. Any news?'

'A bit on Jimmy's bird, if that helps. Flick.'

'It all helps,' said Strike. 'Why didn't you let me know earlier?'

'Only found out ten minutes ago,' said Barclay, unfazed.

'I've just heard her tellin' Jimmy in the kitchen. She's been bumpin' money from her work.'

'What work?'

'Didnae tell me. Trouble is, Jimmy's no that keen on her, from whut I've seen. I'm no sure he'd care if she got nicked.'

A distracting beeping sounded in Strike's ear. Another caller was trying to get him. Glancing at the phone, he saw that it was Lucy again.

'Tell ye somethin' else I got out o' him, though,' said Barclay. 'Last night, when he was stoned. He said he knew a government minister who had blood on his hands.'

Beep. Beep. Beep.

'Strike? Ye there?'

'Yeah, I'm here.'

Strike had never told Barclay about Billy's story.

'What exactly did he say, Barclay?'

'He was ramblin' on about the government, the Tories, whut a bunch o' bastards they are. Then, out o' nowhere, he says "and fuckin' killers". I says, what d'ye mean? An' he says, "I know one who's got blood on his fuckin' hands. Kids."'

Beep. Beep. Beep.

'Mind you, they're a bunch o' bampots, CORE. He might be talkin' about benefit cuts. That's as good as murder to this lot. Not that I think too much of Chiswell's politics meself, Strike.'

'Seen any sign of Billy? Jimmy's brother?'

'Nothin'. Naebody's mentioned him, neither.'

Beep. Beep. Beep.

'And no sign of Jimmy nipping off to Oxfordshire?'

'Not on my watch.'

Beep. Beep. Beep.

'All right,' said Strike. 'Keep digging. Let me know if you get anything.'

He rang off, jabbed at his phone's screen and brought up Lucy's call, instead.

'Lucy, hi,' he said impatiently. 'Bit busy now, can I—?'

But as she began to talk, his expression became blank. Before she had finished gasping out the reason for her call, he had grabbed his door keys and was scrabbling for his crutches.

25

We shall try if we cannot make you powerless to do any harm.

Henrik Ibsen, *Rosmersholm*

Strike's text requesting an update reached Robin at ten to nine, as she arrived in the corridor where Izzy and Winn's offices lay. So keen was she to see what he had to say that she stopped dead in the middle of the deserted passage to read it.

'Oh shit,' she murmured, reading that the *Sun* was becoming ever more interested in Chiswell. Leaning up against the wall of the corridor with its curved stone jambs, every oak door shut, she braced herself to call Strike back.

They had not spoken since she had refused to tail Jimmy. When she had phoned him on Monday to apologise directly, Lorelei had answered.

'Oh, hi, Robin, it's me!'

One of the awful things about Lorelei was that she was likeable. For reasons Robin preferred not to explore, she would have much preferred Lorelei to be unpleasant.

'He's in the shower, sorry! He's been here all weekend, he did his knee in following somebody. He won't tell me the details, but I suppose you know! He had to call me from the street, it was dreadful, he couldn't stand up. I got a cabbie to take me there and paid him to help me get Corm upstairs. He can't wear the prosthesis, he's on crutches . . . '

'Just tell him I was checking in,' said Robin, her stomach like ice. 'Nothing important.'

Robin had replayed the conversation several times in her head since. There had been an unmistakably proprietorial note in Lorelei's voice as she talked about Strike. It had been Lorelei whom he had called when he was in trouble (*well, of course it was. What was he going to do, call you in Oxfordshire?*), Lorelei in whose flat he had spent the rest of the weekend (*they're dating, where else was he going to go?*), Lorelei who was looking after him, consoling him and, perhaps, uniting with him in abuse of Robin, without whom this injury might not have happened.

And now she had to call Strike and tell him that, five days on, she had no useful information. Winn's office, which had been so conveniently accessible when she had started work two weeks ago, was now carefully locked up whenever Geraint and Aamir had to leave it. Robin was sure that this was Aamir's doing, that he had become suspicious of her after the incidents of the dropped bangle, and of Raphael calling loud attention to her eavesdropping on Aamir's phone call.

'Post.'

Robin whirled around to see the cart trundling towards her, pushed by a genial grey-haired man.

'I'll take anything for Chiswell and Winn. We're having a meeting,' Robin heard herself say. The postman handed over a stack of letters, along with a box with a clear cellophane window, through which Robin saw a life-size and very realistic plastic foetus. The legend across the top read: *It Is Legal To Murder Me.*

'Oh God, that's horrible,' said Robin.

The postman chortled.

'That's nothing compared to some of what they get,' he said comfortably. 'Remember the white powder that was on the news? Anthrax, they claimed. Proper hoo-hah, that was. Oh, and I delivered a turd in a box once. Couldn't smell it through all the wrapping. The baby's for Winn, not Chiswell. She's the pro-choice one. Enjoying it here, are you?' he said, showing a disposition for chat.

'Loving it,' Robin said, whose attention had been caught by one of the envelopes she had so rashly taken. 'Excuse me.'

Turning her back on Izzy's office, she hurried past the postman, and five minutes later emerged onto the Terrace Café, which sat on the bank of the Thames. It was separated from the river by a low stone wall, which was punctuated with black iron lamps. To the left and right stood Westminster and Lambeth bridges respectively, the former painted the green of the seats in the House of Commons, the latter, scarlet like those in the House of Lords. On the opposite bank rose the white façade of County Hall, while between palace and hall rolled the broad Thames, its oily surface lucent grey over muddy depths.

Sitting down out of earshot of the few early morning coffee drinkers, Robin turned her attention to one of the letters addressed to Geraint Winn that she had so recklessly taken from the postman. The sender's name and address had been carefully inscribed on the reverse of the envelope in a shaky cursive: Sir Kevin Rodgers, 16 The Elms, Fleetwood, Kent and she happened to know, due to her extensive background reading on the Winns' charity, that the elderly Sir Kevin, who had won a silver at the hurdles in the 1956 Olympics, was one of the Level Playing Field's trustees.

What things, Robin asked herself, did people feel the need

to put in writing these days, when phone calls and emails were so much easier and faster?

Using her mobile, she found a number for Sir Kevin and Lady Rodgers at the correct address. They were old enough, she thought, to still use a landline. Taking a fortifying gulp of coffee, she texted Strike back:

Following a lead, will call asap.

She then turned off caller ID on her mobile, took out a pen and the notebook in which she had written Sir Kevin's number and punched in the digits.

An elderly woman answered within three rings. Robin affected what she was afraid was a poor Welsh accent.

'Could I speak to Sir Kevin, please?'

'Is that Della?'

'Is Sir Kevin there?' asked Robin again, a little louder. She had been hoping to avoid actually claiming to be a government minister.

'Kevin!' called the woman. 'Kevin! It's Della!'

There was a noise of shuffling that made Robin think of tartan bedroom slippers.

'Hello?'

'Kevin, Geraint's just got your letter,' said Robin, wincing as her accent wobbled somewhere between Cardiff and Lahore.

'Sorry, Della, what?' said the man feebly.

He seemed to be deaf, which was both help and hindrance. Robin spoke more loudly, enunciating as clearly as she could. Sir Kevin grasped what she was saying on her third attempt.

'I told Geraint I'd have to resign unless he took urgent steps,' he said miserably. 'You're an old friend, Della, and it was – it is – a worthy cause, but I have to think of my own position. I did warn him.'

'But why, Kevin?' said Robin, picking up her pen.

'Hasn't he shown you my letter?'

'No,' said Robin truthfully, pen poised.

'Oh dear,' said Sir Kevin weakly. 'Well, for one thing . . . twenty-five thousand pounds unaccounted for is a serious matter.'

'What else?' asked Robin, making rapid notes.

'What's that?'

'You said "for one thing". What else are you worried about?'

Robin could hear the woman who'd answered the phone talking in the background. Her voice sounded irate.

'Della, I'd rather not go into it all on the phone,' said Sir Kevin, sounding embarrassed.

'Well, this is disappointing,' said Robin, with what she hoped was a touch of Della's mellifluous grandeur. 'I hoped you'd at least tell me why, Kevin.'

'Well, there's the Mo Farah business—'

'Mo Farah?' repeated Robin, in unaffected surprise.

'What was that?'

'*Mo – Farah?*'

'You didn't know?' said Sir Kevin. 'Oh dear. Oh dear . . . '

Robin heard footsteps and then the woman came back on the line, first muffled, then clear.

'Let me speak to her – Kevin, let go – look, Della, Kevin's very upset about all this. He suspected you didn't know what's been going on and, well, here we are, he was right. Nobody ever wants to worry you, Della,' she said, sounding as though she thought this a mistaken protectiveness, 'but the fact of the matter is – no, she's got to know, Kevin – Geraint's been promising people things he can't deliver. Disabled children and their families have been told they're getting visits from David Beckham and Mo Farah and I don't know who else. It's all going to come out, Della, now the Charity Commission's involved, and I'm not having Kevin's name dragged through the mud. He's a conscientious man and he's done his best. He's been urging Geraint to sort out the accounts for months now, and then there's what Elspeth . . . no, Kevin, I'm *not*, I'm just telling her . . . well, it could get very nasty, Della. It might yet come to the police as well as the press, and I'm sorry, but I'm thinking of Kevin's health.'

'What's Elspeth's story?' said Robin, still writing fast.

Sir Kevin said something plaintive in the background.

'I'm not going into that on the phone,' said Lady Rodgers repressively. 'You'll have to ask Elspeth.'

There was more shuffling and Sir Kevin took the receiver again. He sounded almost tearful.

'Della, you know how much I admire you. I wish it could have been otherwise.'

'Yes,' said Robin, 'well, I'll have to call Elspeth, then.'

'What was that?'

'I'll – call – Elspeth.'

'Oh dear,' said Sir Kevin. 'But you know, there might be nothing in it.'

Robin wondered whether she dared ask for Elspeth's number, but decided not. Della would surely have it.

'I wish you'd tell me what Elspeth's story is,' she said, her pen poised over her notebook.

'I don't like to,' said Sir Kevin wheezily. 'The damage these kinds of rumours do to a man's reputation—'

Lady Rodgers came back on the line.

'That's all we've got to say. This whole business has been very hard on Kevin, very stressful. I'm sorry, but that's our final word on the matter, Della. Goodbye.'

Robin set her mobile down on the table beside her and

checked that nobody was looking her way. She picked up her mobile again and scrolled down the list of The Level Playing Field's trustees. One of them was called Dr Elspeth Curtis-Lacey, but her personal number was not listed on the charity's website and appeared, from a search of directory enquiries, to be unlisted.

Robin phoned Strike. The call went straight to voicemail. She waited a couple of minutes and tried again, with the same result. After her third failed attempt to reach him, she texted:

Got some stuff on GW. Call me.

The dank shadow that had lain on the terrace when she had first arrived was moving incrementally backwards. The warm sun slid over Robin's table as she eked out her coffee, waiting for Strike to call back. At last her phone vibrated to show that she had a text: heart leaping, she picked it up, but it was only Matthew.

Fancy a drink with Tom and Sarah tonight after work?

Robin contemplated the message with a mixture of lassitude and dread. Tomorrow was the charity cricket match about which Matthew was so excited. After-work drinks with Tom and Sarah would doubtless mean plenty of banter on the subject. She could already picture the four of them at the bar: Sarah, with her perennially flirtatious attitude towards Matthew, Tom fending off Matthew's jokes about his lousy bowling with increasingly clumsy, angry ripostes, and Robin, as was increasingly the case these days, pretending to be amused and interested, because that was the cost of not being harangued by Matthew for seeming bored, or feeling superior to her company or (as happened during their worst rows) wishing that she were drinking with Strike instead. At least, she consoled herself, it couldn't be a late or drunken night, because Matthew, who took all sporting fixtures seriously, would want a decent sleep before the match. So she texted back:

OK, where?

and continued to wait for Strike to ring her.

After forty minutes, Robin began to wonder whether Strike was somewhere he couldn't call, which left open the question of whether she ought to inform Chiswell of what she had just found out. Would Strike consider that a liberty, or would he be more annoyed if she failed to give Chiswell his bargaining chip, given the time pressure?

After debating the matter inwardly for a while longer, she called Izzy, the upper half of whose office window she could see from where she sat.

'Izzy, it's me. Venetia. I'm calling because I can't say this in front of Raphael. I think I've got some information on Winn for your father—'

'Oh, fabulous!' said Izzy loudly, and Robin heard Raphael in the background saying, 'Is that Venetia? Where is she?' and the clicking of computer keys.

'Checking the diary, Venetia . . . He'll be at DCMS until eleven, but then he's in meetings all afternoon. Do you want me to call him? He could probably see you straight away if you hurry.'

So Robin replaced her mobile, notebook and pen in her bag, gulped down the last of her coffee and hurried off to the Department for Culture, Media and Sport.

Chiswell was pacing up and down his office, speaking on the phone, when Robin arrived outside the glass partition. He beckoned her inside, pointed to a low leather sofa at a short distance from his desk, and continued to talk to somebody who appeared to have displeased him.

'It was a gift,' he was saying distinctly into the receiver, 'from my eldest son. Twenty-four-carat gold, inscribed *Nec Aspera Terrent*. Bloody hell's bells!' he roared suddenly, and Robin saw the heads of the bright young people just outside the office turning towards Chiswell. 'It's Latin! Pass me to somebody who can speak *English*! *Jasper Chiswell.* I'm the *Minister for Culture.* I've given you the date . . . no, you can't . . . I haven't got all bloody day—'

Robin gathered, from the side of the conversation that she could hear, that Chiswell had lost a money clip of sentimental value, which he thought he might have left at a hotel where he and Kinvara had spent the night of her birthday. As far as she could hear, the hotel staff had not only failed to find the clip, they were showing insufficient deference to Chiswell for having deigned to stay at one of their hotels.

'I want somebody to call me back. Bloody useless,' muttered Chiswell, hanging up and peering at Robin as though he had forgotten who she was. Still breathing heavily, he dropped down on the sofa opposite her. 'I've got ten minutes, so this had better be worthwhile.'

'I've got some information on Mr Winn,' said Robin, taking out her notebook. Without waiting for his response, she gave him a succinct summary of the information she had gleaned from Sir Kevin.

' . . . and,' she concluded, barely a minute and a half later, 'there may be further impropriety on Mr Winn's part, but that information is allegedly held by Dr Elspeth Curtis-Lacey, whose number is unlisted. It shouldn't take us long to find a way of contacting her, but I thought,' Robin said apprehensively, because Chiswell's tiny eyes were screwed up in what might have been displeasure, 'I should bring you this immediately.'

For a few seconds he simply stared at her, his expression petulant as ever, but then he slapped his thigh in what was clearly pleasure.

'Well, well, well,' he said. 'He told me you were his best. Yerse. Said so.'

Pulling a crumpled handkerchief out of his pocket he wiped his face, which had become sweaty during his phone call with the unfortunate hotel.

'Well, well, well,' he said again, 'this is turning out to be a rather good day. One by one, they trip themselves up . . . so Winn's a thief and a liar and maybe more?'

'Well,' said Robin cautiously, 'he can't account for the twenty-five thousand pounds, and he's certainly promised things he can't deliver . . .'

'Dr Elspeth Curtis-Lacey,' said Chiswell, following his own train of thought. 'Name's familiar . . .'

'She used to be a Liberal Democrat councillor from Northumberland,' said Robin, who had just read this on the Level Playing Field's website.

'Child abuse,' said Chiswell suddenly. 'That's how I know her. Child abuse. She was on some committee. She's a bloody crank about it, sees it everywhere. Course, it's full of cranks, the Lib Dems. It's where they congregate. Stuffed to the gunnels with oddballs.'

He stood up, leaving a smattering of dandruff behind him on the black leather, and paced up and down, frowning.

'All this charity stuff's bound to come out sooner or later,' he said, echoing Sir Kevin's wife. 'But, my Christ, they wouldn't want it to break right now, not with Della up to her neck in the Paralympics. Winn's going to panic when he finds out I know. Yerse. I think this might well neutralise him . . . in the short term, anyway. If he's been fiddling with children, though—'

'There's no proof of that,' said Robin.

'—that would stymie him for good,' said Chiswell, pacing again. 'Well, well, well. This explains why Winn wanted to bring his trustees to our Paralympian reception next Thursday, doesn't it? He's clearly trying to keep them sweet, stop anyone else deserting the sinking ship. Prince Harry's going to be there. These charity people love a royal. Only reason half of them are in it.'

He scratched his thick mop of grey hair, revealing large patches of underarm sweat.

'Here's what we'll do,' he said. 'We'll add his trustees to the guest list and you can come too. Then you can corner this Curtis-Lacey, find out what she's got. All right? Night of the twelfth?'

'Yes,' said Robin, making a note, 'Fine.'

'In the meantime, I'll let Winn know I know he's had his fingers in the till.'

Robin was almost at the door when Chiswell said abruptly:

'You don't want a PA's job, I suppose?'

'Sorry?'

'Take over from Izzy? What does that detective pay you? I could probably match it. I need somebody with brains and a bit of backbone.'

'I'm . . . happy where I am,' said Robin.

Chiswell grunted.

'Hmm. Well, perhaps it's better this way. I might well have a bit more work for you, once we've got rid of Winn and Knight. Off you go, then.'

He turned his back to her, his hand already on the phone.

Out in the sunshine, Robin took out her mobile again. Strike still hadn't called, but Matthew had texted the name of a pub in Mayfair, conveniently close to Sarah's work. Nevertheless, Robin was now able to contemplate the evening with slightly more cheerfulness than she had felt prior to her meeting with Chiswell. She even started humming Bob Marley as she walked back towards the Houses of Parliament.

He told me you were his best. Yerse. Said so.

26

I am not so entirely alone, even now. There are two of us to bear the solitude together here.

Henrik Ibsen, *Rosmersholm*

It was four in the morning, the hopeless hour when shivering insomniacs inhabit a world of hollow shadow, and existence seems frail and strange. Strike, who had fallen into a doze, woke abruptly in the hospital chair. For a second, all he felt was his aching body and the hunger that tore at his stomach. Then he saw his nine-year-old nephew, Jack, who lay motionless in the bed beside him, jelly pads over his eyes, a tube running down his throat, lines coming out of neck and wrist. A bag of urine hung from the side of the bed, while three separate drips fed their contents into a body that appeared tiny and vulnerable amid the softly humming machines, in the hushed, cavernous space of the intensive care ward.

He could hear the padding of a nurse's soft shoes somewhere beyond the curtain surrounding Jack's bed. They hadn't wanted Strike to spend the night in the chair, but he had dug in and his celebrity, minor though it was, combined with his disability, had worked in his favour. His crutches stood propped against the bedside cabinet. The ward was overwarm, as hospitals always were. Strike had spent many weeks in a series of iron beds after his leg had been blown off. The smell transported him back to a time of pain and brutal readjustment, when he had been forced to recalibrate his life against a backdrop of endless obstacles, indignities and privations.

The curtain rustled and a nurse entered the cubicle, stolid and practical in her overalls. Seeing that he was awake, she gave Strike a brief, professional smile, then took the clipboard off the end of Jack's bed and went to take readings from the screens monitoring his blood pressure and oxygen levels. When she had finished, she whispered, 'Fancy a cup of tea?'

'Is he doing all right?' Strike asked, not bothering to disguise the plea in his voice. 'How's everything looking?'

'He's stable. No need to worry. This is what we expect at this stage. Tea?'

'Yeah, that'd be great. Thanks very much.'

He realised that his bladder was full once the curtain had closed behind the nurse. Wishing he'd thought to ask her to pass his crutches, Strike hoisted himself up, holding the arm of the chair to steady himself, hopped to the wall and grabbed them, then swung out from behind the curtain and off towards the brightly lit rectangle at the far end of the dark ward.

Having relieved himself at a urinal beneath a blue light that was supposed to thwart junkies' ability to locate veins, he headed into the waiting room close to the ward where, late yesterday afternoon, he had sat waiting for Jack to come out of emergency surgery. The father of one of Jack's school friends, with whom Jack was meant to be staying the night when his appendix burst, had kept him company. The man had been determined not to leave Strike alone until they had 'seen the little chap out of the woods', and had talked nervously all the time Jack had been in surgery, saying things like 'they bounce at that age', 'he's a tough little bugger', 'lucky we only live five minutes from school' and, over and over again, 'Greg and Lucy'll be going frantic'. Strike had said nothing, barely listening, holding himself ready for the worst news, texting Lucy every thirty minutes with an update.

Not yet out of surgery.

No news yet.

At last the surgeon had come to tell them that Jack, who had had to be resuscitated on arrival at hospital, had made it through surgery, that he had had 'a nasty case of sepsis' and that he would shortly be arriving in intensive care.

'I'll bring his mates in to see him,' said Lucy and Greg's pal excitedly. 'Cheer him up – Pokémon cards—'

'He won't be ready for that,' said the surgeon repressively. 'He'll be under heavy sedation and on a ventilator for at least the next twenty-four hours. Are you the next of kin?'

'No, that's me,' croaked Strike, speaking at last, his mouth dry. 'I'm his uncle. His parents are in Rome for their wedding anniversary. They're trying to get a flight back right now.'

'Ah, I see. Well, he's not quite out of the woods yet, but the surgery was successful. We've cleaned out his abdomen and put a drain in. They'll be bringing him down shortly.'

'Told you,' said Lucy and Greg's friend, beaming at Strike with tears in his eyes, 'told you they bounce!'

'Yeah,' said Strike, 'I'd better let Lucy know.'

But in a calamity of errors, Jack's panic-stricken parents had arrived at the airport, only to realise that Lucy had somehow lost her passport between hotel room and departure gate. In fruitless desperation they retraced their steps, trying to explain their dilemma to everyone from hotel staff, police and the British embassy, with the upshot that they had missed the last flight of the night.

At ten past four in the morning, the waiting room was mercifully deserted. Strike turned on the mobile he had kept switched off while on the ward and saw a dozen missed calls from Robin and one from Lorelei. Ignoring them, he texted Lucy who, he knew, would be awake in the Rome hotel to which, shortly past midnight, her passport had been delivered by the taxi driver who had found it. Lucy had implored Strike to send a picture of Jack when he got out of surgery. Strike had pretended that the picture wouldn't load. After the stress of the day, Lucy didn't need to see her son ventilated, his eyes covered in pads, his body swamped by the baggy hospital gown.

All looking good, he typed. **Still sedated but nurse confident.**

He pressed send and waited. As he had expected, she responded within two minutes.

You must be exhausted. Have they given you a bed at the hospital?

No, I'm sitting next to him, Strike responded. **I'll stay here until you get back. Try and get some sleep and don't worry x.**

Strike switched off his mobile, dragged himself back onto his one foot, reorganised his crutches and returned to the ward.

The tea was waiting for him, as pale and milky as anything Denise had made, but after emptying two sachets of sugar into it, he drank it in a couple of gulps, eyes moving between Jack and the machines both supporting and monitoring him. He had never before examined the boy so closely. Indeed, he had never had much to do with him, in spite of the pictures he drew for Strike, which Lucy passed on.

'He hero-worships you,' Lucy had told Strike several times. 'He wants to be a soldier.'

But Strike avoided family get-togethers, partly because he disliked Jack's father, Greg, and partly because Lucy's desire to cajole her brother into some more conventional mode of existence was enervating even without the presence of her sons, the eldest of whom Strike found especially like his father. Strike had no desire to have children and while he was prepared to concede that some of them were likeable – was prepared to admit, in fact, that he had conceived a certain detached fondness for Jack, on the back of Lucy's tales of his ambition to join the Red Caps – he had steadfastly resisted birthday parties and Christmas get-togethers at which he might have forged a closer connection.

But now, as dawn crept through the thin curtains blocking Jack's bed from the rest of the ward, Strike saw for the first time the boy's resemblance to his grandmother, Strike's own mother, Leda. He had the same very dark hair, pale skin and finely drawn mouth. He would, in fact, have made a beautiful girl, but Leda's son knew what puberty was about to do to the boy's jaw and neck . . . if he lived.

Course he's going to bloody live. The nurse said—

He's in intensive fucking care. They don't put you in here for hiccoughs.

He's tough. Wants to join the military. He'll be OK.

He'd fucking better be. I never even sent him a text to say thank you for his pictures.

It took Strike a while to drop back into an uneasy doze.

He was woken by early morning sunshine penetrating his eyelids. Squinting against the light, he heard footsteps squeaking on the floor. Next came a loud rattle as the curtain was pulled back, opening Jack's bed to the ward again and revealing more motionless figures, lying in beds all around them. A new nurse stood beaming at him, younger, with a long dark ponytail.

'Hi!' she said brightly, taking Jack's clipboard. 'It's not often we get anyone famous in here! I know all about you, I read everything about how you caught that serial—'

'This is my nephew, Jack,' he said coldly. The idea of discussing the Shacklewell Ripper now was repugnant to him. The nurse's smile faltered.

'Would you mind waiting outside the curtain? We need to take bloods, change his drips and his catheter.'

Strike dragged himself back onto his crutches and made his way laboriously out of the ward again, trying not to focus on any of the other inert figures wired to their own buzzing machines.

The canteen was already half-full when he got there. Unshaven and heavy-eyed, he had slid his tray all the way to the till and paid before he realised he could not carry it and manage his crutches. A young girl clearing tables spotted his predicament and came to help.

'Cheers,' said Strike gruffly, when she had placed the tray on a table beside a window.

'No probs,' said the girl. 'Leave it there after, I'll get it.'

The small kindness made Strike feel disproportionately emotional. Ignoring the fry-up he had just bought, he took out his phone and texted Lucy again.

All fine, nurse changing his drip, will be back with him shortly. X

As he had half-expected, his phone rang as soon as he had cut into his fried egg.

'We've got a flight,' Lucy told him without preamble, 'but it's not until eleven.'

'No problem,' he told her. 'I'm not going anywhere.'

'Is he awake yet?'

'No, still sedated.'

'He'll be so chuffed to see you, if he wakes up before – before—'

She burst into tears. Strike could hear her still trying to talk through her sobs.

' . . . just want to get home . . . want to see him . . . '

For the first time in Strike's life, he was glad to hear Greg, who now took the phone from his wife.

'We're bloody grateful, Corm. This is our first weekend away together in five years, can you believe it?'

'Sod's law.'

'Yeah. He said his belly was sore, but I thought he was at it. Thought he didn't want us to go away. I feel a right bastard now, I can tell you.'

'Don't worry,' said Strike, and again, 'I'm going nowhere.'

After a few more exchanges and a tearful farewell from Lucy, Strike was left to his full English. He ate methodically and without pleasure amid the clatter and jangle of the canteen, surrounded by other miserable and anxious people tucking into fatty, sugar-laden food.

As he was finishing the last of his bacon, a text from Robin arrived.

I've been trying to call with an update on Winn. Let me know when it's convenient to talk.

The Chiswell case seemed a remote thing to Strike just now, but as he read her text he suddenly had a simultaneous craving for nicotine and to hear Robin's voice. Abandoning his tray with thanks to the kind girl who had helped him to his table, he set off again on his crutches.

A cluster of smokers stood around the entrance to the hospital, hunch-shouldered like hyenas in the clean morning air. Strike lit up, inhaled deeply, and called Robin back.

'Hi,' he said, when she answered. 'Sorry I haven't been in touch, I've been at a hospital—'

'What's happened? Are you OK?'

'Yeah, I'm fine. It's my nephew, Jack. His appendix burst yesterday and he – he's got—'

To Strike's mortification, his voice cracked. As he fought to conquer himself, he wondered how long it had been since he had cried. Perhaps not since the tears of pain and rage he had shed in the hospital in Germany to which he had been airlifted away from the patch of bloody ground where the IED had ripped off his leg.

'Fuck,' he muttered at last, the only syllable he seemed able to manage.

'Cormoran, what's happened?'

'He's – they've got him in intensive care,' said Strike, his face crumpled up in the effort to hold himself together, to speak normally. 'His mum – Lucy and Greg are stuck in Rome, so they asked me—'

'Who's with you? Is Lorelei there?'

'Christ, no.'

Lorelei saying 'I love you' seemed weeks in the past, though it was only two nights ago.

'What are the doctors saying?'

'They think he'll be OK, but, you know, he's – he's in intensive care. Shit,' croaked Strike, wiping his eyes, 'sorry. It's been a rough night.'

'Which hospital is it?'

He told her. Rather abruptly, she said goodbye and rang

off. Strike was left to finish his cigarette, intermittently wiping his face and nose on the sleeve of his shirt.

The quiet ward was bright with sun when he returned. He propped his crutches against the wall, sat down again at Jack's bedside with the day-old newspaper he had just pilfered from the waiting room and read an article about how Arsenal might soon be losing Robin van Persie to Manchester United.

An hour later, the surgeon and the anaesthetist in charge of the ward arrived at the foot of Jack's bed to inspect him, while Strike listened uneasily to their muttered conversation.

' . . . haven't managed to get his oxygen levels below fifty per cent . . . persistent pyrexia . . . urine outputs have tailed off in the last four hours . . . '

' . . . another chest X-ray, check there's nothing going on in the lungs . . . '

Frustrated, Strike waited for somebody to throw him digestible information. At last the surgeon turned to speak to him.

'We'll be keeping him sedated just now. He's not ready to come off the oxygen and we need to get his fluid balance right.'

'What does that mean? Is he worse?'

'No, it often goes like this. He had a very nasty infection. We had to wash out the peritoneum pretty thoroughly. I'd just like to X-ray the chest as a precaution, make sure we haven't punctured anything resuscitating him. I'll pop in to see him again later.'

They walked away to a heavily bandaged teenager covered in even more tubes and lines than Jack, leaving Strike anxious and destabilised in their wake. Through the hours of the night Strike had come to see the machines as essentially friendly, assisting his nephew to recovery. Now they seemed implacable judges holding up numbers indicating that Jack was failing.

'Fuck,' Strike muttered again, shifting the chair nearer to the bed. 'Jack . . . your mum and dad . . .' He could feel a traitorous prickle behind the eyelids. Two nurses were walking past. ' . . . shit . . .'

With an almighty effort he controlled himself and cleared his throat.

' . . . sorry, Jack, your mum wouldn't like me swearing in your ear . . . it's Uncle Cormoran here, by the way, if you didn't . . . anyway, Mum and Dad are on their way back, OK? And I'll be with you until they—'

He stopped mid-sentence. Robin was framed in the distant doorway of the ward. He watched her asking directions from a ward sister, and then she came walking towards him, wearing jeans and a T-shirt, her eyes their usual blue-grey and her hair loose, and holding two polystyrene cups.

Seeing Strike's unguarded expression of happiness and gratitude, Robin felt amply repaid for the bruising argument with Matthew, the two changes of bus and the taxi it had taken to get here. Then the slight prone figure beside Strike came into view.

'Oh no,' she said softly, coming to a halt at the foot of the bed.

'Robin, you didn't have to—'

'I know I didn't,' said Robin. She pulled a chair up beside Strike's. 'But I wouldn't want to have to deal with this alone. Be careful, it's hot,' she added, passing him a tea.

He took the cup from her, set it down on the bedside cabinet, then reached out and gripped her hand painfully tightly. He had released her before she could squeeze back. Then both sat staring at Jack for a few seconds, until Robin, her fingers throbbing, asked:

'What's the latest?'

'He still needs the oxygen and he's not peeing enough,' said Strike. 'I don't know what that means. I'd rather have a score out of ten or – I don't fucking know. Oh, and they want to X-ray his chest in case they punctured his lungs putting that tube in.'

'When was the operation?'

'Yesterday afternoon. He collapsed doing cross-country at school. Some friend of Greg and Lucy's who lives right by the school came with him in the ambulance and I met them here.'

Neither spoke for a while, their eyes on Jack.

Then Strike said, 'I've been a bloody terrible uncle. I don't know any of their birthdays. I couldn't have told you how old he was. The dad of his mate's who brought him in knew more than me. Jack wants to be a soldier, Luce says he talks about me and he draws me pictures and I never even bloody thank him.'

'Well,' said Robin, pretending not to see that Strike was dabbing roughly at his eyes with his sleeve, 'you're here for him right now when he needs you and you've got plenty of time to make it up to him.'

'Yeah,' said Strike, blinking rapidly. 'You know what I'll do if he—? I'll take him to the Imperial War Museum. Day trip.'

'Good idea,' said Robin kindly.

'Have you ever been?'

'No,' said Robin.

'Good museum.'

Two nurses, one male, one the woman whom Strike had earlier snubbed, now approached.

'We need to X-ray him,' said the girl, addressing Robin rather than Strike. 'Would you mind waiting outside the ward?'

'How long will you be?' asked Strike.

'Half an hour. Forty minutes-ish.'

So Robin fetched Strike's crutches and they went to the canteen.

'This is really good of you, Robin,' Strike said over two more pallid teas and some ginger biscuits, 'but if you've got things to do—'

'I'll stay until Greg and Lucy come,' said Robin. 'It'll be awful for them, being so far away. Matt's twenty-seven and his dad was still worried sick when Matt was so ill in the Maldives.'

'Was he?'

'Yeah, you know, when he – oh, of course. I never told you, did I?'

'Told me what?'

'He got a nasty infection on our honeymoon. Scratched himself on some coral. They were talking about airlifting him off to hospital at one point, but it was OK. Wasn't as bad as they first thought.'

As she said it, she remembered pushing open the wooden door still hot from the daylong sun, her throat constricted with fear as she prepared to tell Matthew she wanted an annulment, little knowing what she was about to face.

'You know, Matt's mum died not that long ago, so Geoffrey was really scared about Matt . . . but it was all OK,' Robin repeated, taking a sip of her tepid tea, her eyes on the woman behind the counter, who was ladling baked beans onto a skinny teenager's plate.

Strike watched her. He had sensed omissions in her story. *Blame sea-borne bacteria.*

'Must've been scary,' he said.

'Well, it wasn't fun,' said Robin, examining her short, clean fingernails, then checking her watch. 'If you want a cigarette we should go now, he'll be back soon.'

One of the smokers they joined outside was wearing pyjamas. He had brought his drip with him, and held it tightly like a shepherd's crook to keep himself steady. Strike lit up and exhaled towards a clear blue sky.

'I haven't asked about your anniversary weekend.'

'I'm sorry I couldn't work,' said Robin quickly. 'It had been booked and—'

'That's not why I was asking.'

She hesitated.

'It wasn't great, to be honest.'

'Ah, well. Sometimes when there's pressure to have a good time—'

'Yes, exactly,' said Robin.

After another short pause she asked:

'Lorelei's working today, I suppose?'

'Probably,' said Strike. 'What is this, Saturday? Yeah, I suppose so.'

They stood in silence while Strike's cigarette shrank, millimetre by millimetre, watching visitors and arriving ambulances. There was no awkwardness between them, but the air seemed charged, somehow, with things wondered and unspoken. Finally Strike pressed out the stub of his cigarette in a large open ashtray that most smokers had ignored and checked his phone.

'They boarded twenty minutes ago,' he said, reading Lucy's last text. 'They should be here by three.'

'What happened to your mobile?' asked Robin, looking at the heavily sellotaped screen.

'Fell on it,' said Strike. 'I'll get a new one when Chiswell pays us.'

They passed the X-ray machine being rolled out of the ward as they walked back inside.

'Chest looks fine!' said the radiographer pushing it.

They sat by Jack's side talking quietly for another hour, until Robin went to buy more tea and chocolate bars from nearby vending machines, which they consumed in the waiting room while Robin filled Strike in about everything she had discovered about Winn's charity.

'You've outdone yourself,' said Strike, halfway down his second Mars bar. 'That was excellent work, Robin.'

'You don't mind that I told Chiswell?'

'No, you had to. We're up against it time-wise with Mitch Patterson sniffing round. Has this Curtis-Lacey woman accepted the invitation to the reception?'

'I'll find out on Monday. What about Barclay? How's he getting on with Jimmy Knight?'

'Still nothing we can use,' Strike sighed, running a hand over the stubble that was rapidly becoming a beard, 'but I'm hopeful. He's good, Barclay. He's like you. Got an instinct for this stuff.'

A family shuffled into the waiting room, the father sniffing and the mother sobbing. The son, who looked barely older than six, stared at Strike's missing leg as though it was merely one more horrible detail in the nightmarish world he had suddenly entered. Strike and Robin glanced at each other and left, Robin carrying Strike's tea as he swung along on his crutches.

Once settled beside Jack again, Strike asked, 'How did Chiswell react when you told him everything you'd got on Winn?'

'He was delighted. As a matter of fact, he offered me a job.'

'I'm always surprised that doesn't happen more often,' said Strike, unperturbed.

Just then, the anaesthetist and surgeon converged at the foot of Jack's bed again.

'Well, things are looking up,' said the anaesthetist. 'His

X-ray's clear and his temperature's coming down. That's the thing with children,' he said, smiling at Robin. 'They travel fast in both directions. We're going to see how he manages with a little less oxygen, but I think we're getting on top of things.'

'Oh, thank God,' said Robin.

'He's going to live?' said Strike.

'Oh yes, I think so,' said the surgeon, with a touch of patronage. 'We know what we're doing in here, you know.'

'Gotta let Lucy know,' muttered Strike, trying and failing to get up, feeling weaker at good news than he'd felt at bad. Robin fetched his crutches and helped him into a standing position. As she watched him swinging towards the waiting room, she sat back down, exhaled loudly and put her face briefly into her hands.

'Always worst for the mothers,' said the anaesthetist kindly.

She didn't bother to correct him.

Strike was away for twenty minutes. When he returned, he said:

'They've just landed. I've warned her how he looks, so they're prepared. They should be here in about an hour.'

'Great,' said Robin.

'You can head off, Robin. I didn't mean to balls up your Saturday.'

'Oh,' said Robin, feeling oddly deflated. 'OK.'

She stood up, took her jacket off the back of the chair and collected her bag.

'If you're sure?'

'Yeah, yeah, I'll probably try and get a kip in now we know he's going to be all right. I'll walk you out.'

'There's no need—'

'I want to. I can have another smoke.'

But when they reached the exit, Strike walked on with

her, away from the huddled smokers, past the ambulances and the car park that seemed to stretch for miles, roofs glimmering like the backs of marine creatures, surfacing through a dusty haze.

'How did you get here?' he asked, once they were away from the crowds, beside a patch of lawn surrounded by stocks whose scent mingled with the smell of hot tarmac.

'Bus, then cab.'

'Let me give you the cab fare—'

'Don't be ridiculous. Seriously, no.'

'Well . . . thanks, Robin. It made all the difference.'

She smiled up at him.

''S'what friends are for.'

Awkwardly, leaning on his crutches, he bent towards her. The hug was brief and she broke away first, afraid that he was going to overbalance. The kiss that he had meant to plant on her cheek landed on her mouth as she turned her face towards him.

'Sorry,' he muttered.

'Don't be silly,' she said again, blushing.

'Well, I'd better get back.'

'Yes, of course.'

He turned away.

'Let me know how he is,' she called after him, and he raised one hand in acknowledgement.

Robin walked away without looking back. She could still feel the shape of his mouth on hers, her skin tingling where his stubble had scratched her, but she did not rub the sensation away.

Strike had forgotten that he had meant to have another cigarette. Whether because he was now confident that he would be able to take his nephew to the Imperial War Museum, or for some other reason, his exhaustion was now stippled with a crazy light-heartedness, as though he had just taken a shot of spirits. The dirt and heat of a London afternoon, with the smell of stocks in the air, seemed suddenly full of beauty.

It was a glorious thing, to be given hope, when all had seemed lost.

27

They cling to their dead a long time at Rosmersholm.

Henrik Ibsen, *Rosmersholm*

By the time Robin found her way back across London to the unfamiliar cricket ground, it was five in the afternoon and Matthew's charity match was over. She found him back in his street clothes in the bar, fuming and barely speaking to her. Matthew's side had lost. The other team was crowing.

Facing an evening of being ignored by her husband, and having no friends among his colleagues, Robin decided against going on to the restaurant with the two teams and their partners, and made her way home alone.

The following morning, she found Matthew fully dressed on the sofa, snoring drunkenly. They argued when he woke up, a row that lasted hours and resolved nothing. Matthew wanted to know why it was Robin's job to hurry off and hold Strike's hand, given that he had a girlfriend. Robin maintained that you were a lousy person if you left a friend alone to cope with a possibly dying child.

The row escalated, attaining levels of spite that had never yet been reached in a year of marital bickering. Robin lost her temper, and asked whether she was not owed time off for good behaviour, after a decade spent watching Matthew strut around various sports fields. He was genuinely stung.

'Well, if you don't enjoy it, you should have said!'

'Never occurred to you I might not, did it? Because I'm supposed to see all your victories as mine, aren't I, Matt? Whereas *my* achievements—'

'Sorry, remind me what they are again?' Matthew said, a low blow he had never thrown at her before. 'Or are we counting *his* achievements as yours?'

Three days passed, and they had not forgiven each other. Robin had slept in the spare room every night since their row, rising early each morning so she could leave the house before Matthew was out of the shower. She felt a constant ache behind the eyes, an unhappiness which was easier to ignore while at work, but which settled back over her like a patch of low pressure once she turned her footsteps homewards each night. Matthew's silent anger pressed against the walls of their house, which, while twice the size of any space they had shared before, seemed darker and more cramped.

He was her husband. She had promised to try. Tired, angry, guilty and miserable, Robin felt as though she were waiting for something definitive to happen, something that would release them both with honour, without more filthy rows, with reasonableness. Over and again, her thoughts returned to the wedding day, when she had discovered that Matthew had deleted Strike's messages. With her whole heart, she regretted not leaving then, before he could scratch himself on coral, before she could be trapped, as she now saw it, by cowardice disguised as compassion.

As Robin approached the House of Commons on Wednesday morning, not yet focused on the day ahead, but pondering her marital problems, a large man in an overcoat peeled away from the railings where he had been mingling with the first tourists of the day and walked towards her. He was tall and broad-shouldered, with thick silver hair and a squashed, deeply pitted and lined face. Robin did not realise that she was his object until he halted right in front of her, large feet placed firmly at right angles, blocking her onward progress.

'Venetia? Can I have a quick word, love?'

She took a panicked half-step backwards, looking up into the hard, flat face, peppered with wide pores. He had to be press. Did he recognise her? The hazel contact lenses were a little more discernible at close quarters, even through her plain-lensed glasses.

'Just started working for Jasper Chiswell, haven't you, love? I was wondering how that came about. How much is he paying you? Known him long?'

'No comment,' said Robin, trying to sidestep him. He moved with her. Fighting the rising feeling of panic, Robin said firmly, 'Get out of my way. I need to get to work.'

A couple of tall Scandinavian youths with rucksacks were watching the encounter with clear concern.

'I'm only giving you a chance to tell your side of the story, darling,' said her accoster, quietly. 'Think about it. Might be your only chance.'

He moved aside. Robin knocked into her would-be rescuers as she pushed past them. *Shit, shit, shit* . . . who was he?

Once safely past the security scanner, she moved aside in the echoing stone hall where workers were striding past her and called Strike. He didn't pick up.

'Call me, please, urgently,' she muttered to his voicemail.

Rather than heading for Izzy's office, or the wide echoing space of Portcullis House, she took refuge in one of the smaller tearooms, which without its counter and till would have resembled a dons' common room, panelled in dark wood and carpeted in the ubiquitous forest green. A heavy oak screen divided the room, MPs sitting at the far end, away from the lesser employees. She bought a cup of coffee, took a table beside the window, hung her coat on the back of her chair and waited for Strike to call her. The quiet, sedate space did little to calm Robin's nerves.

It was nearly three-quarters of an hour before Strike phoned.

'Sorry, missed you, I was on the Tube,' he said, panting. 'Then Chiswell called. He's only just rung off. We've got trouble.'

'Oh God, what now?' said Robin, setting her coffee down as her stomach contracted in panic.

'The *Sun* think you're the story.'

And at once, Robin knew whom she had just met outside the Houses of Parliament: Mitch Patterson, the private detective the newspaper had hired.

'They've been digging for anything new in Chiswell's life, and there you are, good-looking new woman in his office, of course they're going to check you out. Chiswell's first marriage split up because he had an affair at work. Thing is, it isn't going to take them long to find out you aren't really his goddaughter. *Ouch* – fuck—'

'What's the matter?'

'First day back on two legs and Dodgy Doc's finally decided to go and meet a girl on the sly. Chelsea Physic Garden, Tube to Sloane Square and a bugger of a walk. Anyway,' he panted, 'what's *your* bad news?'

'It's more of the same,' said Robin. 'Mitch Patterson just accosted me outside Parliament.'

'Shit. D'you think he recognised you?'

'He didn't seem to, but I don't know. I should clear out, shouldn't I?' said Robin, contemplating the cream ceiling, which was stuccoed in a pattern of overlapping circles. 'We could put someone else in here. Andy, or Barclay?'

'Not yet,' said Strike. 'If you walk out the moment you meet Mitch Patterson, it'll look like you're the story for sure. Anyway, Chiswell wants you to go to this reception tomorrow night, to try and get the rest of the dirt on Winn from that other trustee – what was her name, Elspeth? *Bollocks* – sorry – having trouble here, it's a bloody woodchip path. Dodgy's taking the girl for a walk into the undergrowth. She looks about seventeen.'

'Don't you need your phone, to take photographs?'

'I'm wearing those glasses with the inbuilt camera . . . oh, here we go,' he added quietly. 'Dodgy's copping a feel in some bushes.'

Robin waited. She could hear a very faint clicking.

'And here come some genuine horticulturalists,' Strike muttered. 'That's driven them back out into the open . . .

'Listen,' he continued, 'meet me at the office tomorrow after work, before you go to that reception. We'll take stock of everything we've got so far and make a decision on what to do next. Try your best to get the second listening device back, but don't replace it, just in case we need to take you out of there.'

'All right,' said Robin, full of foreboding, 'but it's going to be difficult. I'm sure Aamir is suspic— Cormoran, I'm going to have to go.'

Izzy and Raphael had just walked into the tearoom. Raphael had his arm around his half-sister, who, Robin saw at once, was distressed to the point of tears. He saw Robin, who hastily hung up on Strike, made a grimace indicating that Izzy was in a bad way, then muttered something to his sister, who nodded and headed towards Robin's table, leaving Raphael to buy drinks.

'Izzy!' said Robin, pulling out a chair for her. 'Are you all right?'

As Izzy sat down, tears leaked out of her eyes. Robin passed her a paper napkin.

'Thanks, Venetia,' she said huskily. 'I'm so sorry. Making a fuss. Silly.'

She took a deep shuddering breath and sat upright, with the posture of a girl who had been told for years to sit up straight and pull herself together.

'Just silly,' she repeated, tears welling again.

'Dad's just been a total bastard to her,' said Raphael, arriving with a tray.

'Don't say that, Raff,' hiccoughed Izzy, another tear trickling down her nose. 'I know he didn't mean it. He was upset when I arrived and then I made it worse. Did you know he's lost Freddie's gold money clip?'

'No,' said Raphael, without much interest.

'He thinks he left it at some hotel on Kinvara's birthday. They'd just called him back when I arrived. They haven't got it. You know what Papa's like about Freddie, even now.'

An odd look passed over Raphael's face, as though he had been struck by an unpleasant thought.

'And then,' said Izzy, shakily, 'I'd misdated a letter and he flew off the handle . . .'

Izzy twisted the damp napkin between her hands.

'Five years,' she burst out. 'Five years I've worked for him, and I can count on one hand how many times he's thanked me for anything. When I told him I was thinking of leaving he said "not till after the Olympics",' her voice quavered, '"because I don't want to have to break in someone new before then".'

Raphael swore under his breath.

'Oh, but he's not that bad, really,' said Izzy quickly, in

an almost comical *volte-face*. Robin knew that she had just remembered her hope that Raphael would take over her job. 'I'm just upset, making it sound worse than it—'

Her mobile rang. She read the caller's name and let out a moan.

'Not TTS, not now, I can't. Raff, you speak to her.'

She held out the mobile to him, but Raphael recoiled as though asked to hold a tarantula.

'Please, Raff – *please* . . .'

With extreme reluctance, Raphael took the phone.

'Hi, Kinvara. Raff here, Izzy's out of the office. No . . . Venetia's not here . . . no . . . I'm at the office, obviously, I just picked up Izzy's phone . . . He's just gone to the Olympic Park. No . . . no, I'm not . . . I don't know where Venetia is, all I know is, she's not here . . . yes . . . yes . . . OK . . . bye, then—' He raised his eyebrows. 'Hung up.'

He pushed the phone back across the table to Izzy, who asked:

'Why's she so interested in where Venetia is?'

'Three guesses,' said Raphael, amused. Catching his drift, Robin looked out of the window, feeling the colour rising in her face. She wondered whether Mitch Patterson had called Kinvara, and planted this idea in her head.

'Oh, come orf it,' said Izzy. 'She thinks Papa's . . . ? Venetia's young enough to be his daughter!'

'In case you haven't noticed, so's his wife,' said Raphael, 'and you know what she's like. The further down the tubes their marriage goes, the more jealous she gets. Dad's not picking up his phone to her, so she's drawing paranoid conclusions.'

'Papa doesn't pick up because she drives him crazy,' said Izzy, her resentment towards her father suddenly submerged by dislike for her stepmother. 'For the last two years she's refused to budge from home or leave her bloody horses. Suddenly the Olympics are nearly here and London's full of celebrities and all she wants to do is come up to town, dressed up to the nines and play the minister's wife.'

She took another deep breath, blotted her face again, then stood up.

'I'd better get back, we're so busy. Thanks, Raff,' she said, cuffing him lightly on the shoulder.

She walked away. Raphael watched her go, then turned back to Robin.

'Izzy was the only one who bothered to visit me when I was inside, you know.'

'Yes,' said Robin. 'She said.'

'And when I used to have to go to bloody Chiswell House as a kid, she was the only one who'd talk to me. I was the little bastard who'd broken up their family, so they all hated my guts, but Izzy used to let me help her groom her pony.'

He swilled the coffee in his cup, looking sullen.

'I suppose you were in love with swashbuckling Freddie, were you, like all the other girls? He hated me. Used to call me "Raphaela" and pretend Dad had told the family I was another girl.'

'How horrible,' said Robin and Raphael's scowl turned into a reluctant smile.

'You're so sweet.'

He seemed to be debating with himself whether or not to say something. Suddenly he asked:

'Ever meet Jack o'Kent when you were visiting?'

'Who?'

'Old boy who used to work for Dad. Lived in the grounds of Chiswell House. Scared the hell out of me when I was a kid. He had a kind of sunken face and mad eyes and he used to loom out of nowhere when I was in the gardens. He never said a word except to swear at me if I got in his way.'

'I . . . vaguely remember someone like that,' lied Robin.

'Jack o'Kent was Dad's nickname for him. Who *was* Jack o'Kent? Didn't he have something to do with the devil? Anyway, I used to have literal nightmares about the old boy. One time he caught me trying to get into a barn and gave me hell. He put his face up close to mine and said words to the effect of, I wouldn't like what I saw in there, or it was dangerous for little boys, or . . . I can't remember exactly. I was only a kid.'

'That sounds scary,' Robin agreed, her interest awakened now. 'What was he doing in there, did you ever find out?'

'Probably just storing farm machinery,' said Raphael, 'but he made it sound like he was conducting Satanic rituals.

'He was a good carpenter, mind you. He made Freddie's coffin. An English oak had come down . . . Dad wanted Freddie buried in wood from the estate . . . '

Again, he seemed to be wondering whether he ought to say what was on his mind. He scrutinised her through his dark lashes and finally said:

'Does Dad seem . . . well, normal to you at the moment?'

'What d'you mean?'

'You don't think he's acting a bit strangely? Why's he bawling Izzy out for nothing?'

'Pressure of work?' suggested Robin.

'Yeah . . . maybe,' said Raphael. Then, frowning, he said, 'He phoned me the other night, which is strange in itself, because he can't normally stand the sight of me. Just to talk, he said, and that's never happened before. Mind you, he'd had a few too many, I could tell as soon as he spoke.

'Anyway, he started rambling on about Jack o'Kent. I couldn't make out what he was going on about. He mentioned Freddie dying, and Kinvara's baby dying and then,' Raphael leaned in closer. Robin felt his knees touch hers under the table, 'remember that phone call we got, my first day here? That bloody creepy message about people pissing themselves as they die?'

'Yes,' said Robin.

'He said, "It's all punishment. That was Jack o'Kent calling. He's coming for me."'

Robin stared at him.

'But whoever it was on the phone,' said Raphael, 'it can't have been Jack o'Kent. He died years ago.'

Robin said nothing. She had suddenly remembered Matthew's delirium, the depth of that subtropical night, when he had thought she was his dead mother. Raphael's knees seemed to press harder into hers. She moved her chair back slightly.

'I was awake half the night wondering whether he's cracking up. We can't afford to have Dad go bonkers as well, can we? We've already got Kinvara hallucinating horse slashers and gravediggers—'

'Gravediggers?' repeated Robin sharply.

'Did I say gravediggers?' said Raphael restlessly. 'Well, you know what I mean. Men with spades in the woods.'

'You think she's imagining them?' asked Robin.

'No idea. Izzy and the rest of them think she is, but then they've treated her like a hysteric ever since she lost that kid. She had to go through labour even though they knew it had died, did you know that? She wasn't right afterwards, but when you're a Chiswell you're supposed to suck that sort of thing up. Put on a hat and go open a fête or something.'

He seemed to read Robin's thoughts in her face, because he said:

'Did you expect me to hate her, just because the others

do? She's a pain in the arse, and she thinks I'm a total waste of space, but I don't spend my life mentally subtracting everything she spends on her horses from my niece and nephews' inheritance. She's not a gold-digger, whatever Izzy and *Fizzy* think,' he said, laying arch emphasis on his other sister's nickname. 'They thought my mother was a gold-digger, too. It's the only motivation they understand. I'm not supposed to know they've got cosy Chiswell family nicknames for me and my mother, as well . . . ' His dark skin flushed. 'Unlikely as it might seem, Kinvara genuinely fell for Dad, I could tell. She could have done a damn sight better if it was money she was after. He's skint.'

Robin, whose definition of 'skint' did not comprise owning a large house in Oxfordshire, nine horses, a mews flat in London or the heavy diamond necklace she had seen around Kinvara's neck in photographs, maintained an impassive expression.

'Have you been to Chiswell House lately?'

'Not lately,' said Robin.

'It's falling apart. Everything's moth-eaten and miserable.'

'The one time I really remember being at Chiswell House, the grown-ups were talking about a little girl who'd disappeared.'

'Really?' said Raphael, surprised.

'Yes, I can't remember her name. I was young myself. Susan? Suki? Something like that.'

'Doesn't ring any bells,' said Raphael. His knees brushed hers again. 'Tell me, does everyone confide their dark family secrets to you after five minutes of knowing you, or is it just me?'

'Tim always says I look sympathetic,' said Robin. 'Perhaps I should forget politics and go into counselling.'

'Yeah, maybe you should,' he said, looking into her eyes.

'That isn't a very strong prescription. Why bother with glasses? Why not just wear contacts?'

'Oh, I . . . find these more comfortable,' said Robin, pushing the glasses back up her nose and gathering her things. 'You know, I really ought to get going.'

Raphael leaned back in his chair with a rueful smile.

'Message received . . . he's a lucky man, your Tim. Tell him so, from me.'

Robin gave a half-laugh and stood up, catching herself on the corner of the table as she did so. Self-conscious and slightly flustered, she walked out of the tearoom.

Making her way back to Izzy's office, she mulled over the Minister for Culture's behaviour. Explosions of bad temper and paranoid ramblings were not, she thought, surprising in a man currently at the mercy of two blackmailers, but Chiswell's suggestion that a dead man had telephoned him was undeniably odd. He had not struck her on either of their two encounters as the kind of man who would believe in either ghosts or divine retribution, but then, Robin reflected, drink brought out strange things in people . . . and suddenly, she remembered Matthew's snarling face as he had shouted across the sitting room on Sunday.

She was almost level with Winn's office door when she registered the fact that it was standing ajar again. Robin peered into the room beyond. It seemed to be empty. She knocked twice. Nobody answered.

It took her less than five seconds to reach the power socket beneath Geraint's desk. Unplugging the fan, she prised the recording device loose and had just opened her handbag when Aamir's voice said:

'What the hell do you think you're doing?'

Robin gasped, attempted to stand up, hit her head hard on the desk and yelped in pain. Aamir had just unfolded himself from an armchair angled away from the door, was taking headphones from his ears. He seemed to have been taking a few minutes for himself, while listening to an iPod.

'I knocked!' Robin said, her eyes watering as she rubbed the top of her head. The recording device was still in her hand and she hid it behind her back. 'I didn't think anyone was in here!'

'What,' he repeated, advancing on her, 'are you *doing?*'

Before she could answer, the door was pushed fully open. Geraint walked in.

There was no lipless grin this morning, no air of bustling self-importance, no ribald comment at finding Robin on the floor of his office. Winn seemed somehow smaller than usual, with purplish shadows beneath the lens-shrunken eyes. In perplexity he turned from Robin to Aamir, and as Aamir began to tell him that Robin had just walked in uninvited, the latter managed to stuff the recording device into her handbag.

'I'm so sorry,' she said, getting to her feet, sweating profusely. Panic lapped at the edges of her thought, but then an idea bobbed up like a life raft. 'I really am. I was going to leave a note. I was only going to borrow it.'

As the two men frowned at her, she gestured to the unplugged fan.

'Ours is broken. Our room's like an oven. I didn't think you'd mind,' she said, appealing to Geraint. 'I was just going to borrow it for thirty minutes.' She smiled piteously. 'Honestly, I felt faint earlier.'

She plucked the front of her shirt away from her skin, which was indeed clammy. His gaze fell to her chest and the usual lecherous grin resurfaced.

'Though I shouldn't say so, overheating rather suits you,' said Winn, with the ghost of a smirk, and Robin forced a giggle.

'Well, well, we can spare it for thirty minutes, can't we?' he said, turning to Aamir. The latter said nothing, but stood ramrod straight, staring at Robin with undisguised suspicion. Geraint lifted the fan carefully off the desk and passed it to Robin. As she turned to go, he patted her lightly on the lower back.

'Enjoy.'

'Oh, I will,' she said, her flesh crawling. 'Thank you so much, Mr Winn.'

28

Do I take it to heart, to find myself so hampered and thwarted in my life's work?

Henrik Ibsen, *Rosmersholm*

The long hike to and around Chelsea Physic Garden the previous day had not benefited Strike's hamstring injury. As his stomach was playing up from a constant diet of Ibuprofen, he had eschewed painkillers for the past twenty-four hours, with the result that he was in what his doctors liked to describe as 'some discomfort' as he sat with his one and a half legs up on the office sofa on Thursday afternoon, his prosthesis leaning against the wall nearby while he reviewed the Chiswell file.

Silhouetted like a headless watchman against the window of his inner office was Strike's best suit, plus a shirt and tie, which hung from the curtain rail, shoes and clean socks sitting below the limp trouser legs. He was going out to dinner with Lorelei tonight and had organised himself so that he need not climb the stairs to his attic flat again before bed.

Lorelei had been typically understanding about his lack of communication during Jack's hospitalisation, saying with only the slightest edge to her voice that it must have been a horrible thing to go through on his own. Strike had too much sense to tell her that Robin had been there, too. Lorelei had then requested, sweetly and without rancour, dinner, 'to talk a few things through'.

They had been dating for just over ten months and she had just nursed him through five days of incapacity. Strike felt that it was neither fair, nor decent, to ask her to say what she had to say over the phone. Like the hanging suit, the prospect of having to find an answer to the inevitable question 'where do you see this relationship going?' loomed ominously on the periphery of Strike's consciousness.

Dominating his thoughts, however, was what he saw as the perilous state of the Chiswell case, for which he had so far seen not a penny in payment, but which was costing him a significant outlay in salaries and expenses. Robin might have succeeded in neutralising the immediate threat of Geraint Winn, but after a promising start Barclay had nothing whatsoever to use against Chiswell's first blackmailer, and Strike foresaw disastrous consequences should the *Sun* newspaper find its way to Jimmy Knight. Balked of the mysterious photographs at the Foreign Office that Winn had promised him, and notwithstanding Chiswell's assertion that Jimmy would not want the story in the press, Strike thought an angry and frustrated Jimmy was overwhelmingly likely to try and profit from a chance that seemed to be slipping through his fingers. His history of litigation told its own story: Jimmy was a man prone to cutting off his own nose to spite his face.

To compound Strike's bad mood, after several straight days and nights hanging out with Jimmy and his mates, Barclay had told Strike that unless he went home soon, his wife would be initiating divorce proceedings. Strike, who owed Barclay expenses, had told him to come into the office for a cheque, after which he could take a couple of days off.

To his extreme annoyance, the normally reliable Hutchins had then cavilled at having to take over the tailing of Jimmy Knight at short notice, rather than hanging around Harley Street, where Dodgy Doc was once again consulting patients.

'What's the problem?' Strike had asked roughly, his stump throbbing. Much as he liked Hutchins, he had not forgotten that the ex-policeman had recently taken time off for a family holiday and to drive his wife to hospital when she broke her wrist. 'I'm asking you to switch targets, that's all. I can't follow Knight, he knows me.'

'Yeah, all right, I'll do it.'

'Decent of you,' Strike had said, angrily. 'Thanks.'

The sound of Robin and Barclay climbing the metal stairs to the office at half past five made a welcome distraction from Strike's increasingly dark mood.

'Hi,' said Robin, walking into the office with a holdall over her shoulder. Answering Strike's questioning look, she explained, 'Outfit for the Paralympic reception. I'll change in the loo, I won't have time to go home.'

Barclay followed Robin into the room and closed the door.

'We met downstairs,' he told Strike cheerfully. 'Firs' time.'

'Sam was just telling me how much dope he's had to smoke to keep in with Jimmy,' said Robin, laughing.

'I've no been inhalin',' said Barclay, deadpan. 'That'd be remiss, on a job.'

The fact that the pair of them seemed to have hit it off was perversely annoying to Strike, who was now making heavy weather of hoisting himself off the fake leather cushions, which made their usual farting noises.

'It's the sofa,' he snapped at Barclay, who had looked around, grinning. 'I'll get your money.'

'Stay there, I'll do it,' Robin said, setting down her holdall and reaching for the chequebook in the lower drawer of the desk, which she handed to Strike, with a pen. 'Want some tea, Cormoran? Sam?'

'Aye, go on, then,' said Barclay.

'You're both bloody cheerful,' said Strike sourly, writing Barclay his cheque, 'considering we're about to lose the job that's keeping us all in employment. Unless either of you have got information I don't know about, of course.'

'Only excitin' thing tae happen in Knightville this week was Flick havin' a big bust up wi' one o' her flatmates,' said Barclay. 'Lassie called Laura. She reckoned Jimmy had stolen a credit card out o' her handbag.'

'Had he?' asked Strike sharply.

'I'd say it was more likely to be Flick herself. Told ye she was boastin' about helpin' herself to cash from her work, didn't I?'

'Yeah, you did.'

'It all kicked off in the pub. The girl, Laura, was scunnered. She and Flick got intae a row about who was more middle class.'

In spite of the pain he was in, and his grumpy mood, Strike grinned.

'Aye, it got nasty. Ponies and foreign holidays dragged in. Then this Laura said she reckoned Jimmy nicked her new credit card off her, months back. Jimmy got aggressive, said that was slander—'

'Shame he's banned, or he could've sued her,' said Strike, ripping out the cheque.

'—and Laura ran off intae the night, bawlin'. She's left the flat.'

'Got a surname for her?'

'I'll try and find out.'

'What's Flick's background, Barclay?' asked Strike as Barclay put his cheque into his wallet.

'Well, she told me she dropped out o' uni,' said Barclay. 'Failed her first-year exams and gave up.'

'Some of the best people drop out,' said Robin, carrying two mugs of tea over. She and Strike had both left their degree courses without a qualification.

'Cheers,' said Barclay, accepting a mug from Robin. 'Her parents are divorced,' he went on, 'and she's no speaking tae either of them. They don't like Jimmy. Cannae blame them. If my daughter ever hooks up wi' a bawbag like Knight, I'll know what tae do about it. When she's not around, he tells the lads what he gets up to wi' young girls. They all think they're shaggin' a great revolutionary, doin' it for the cause. Flick doesnae know the half o' what he's up tae.'

'Any of them underage? His wife suggested he's got form there. That'd be a bargaining chip.'

'All over sixteen so far's I know.'

'Pity,' said Strike. He caught Robin's eye, as she returned to them holding her own tea. 'You know what I mean.' He turned to Barclay again. 'From what I heard on that march, she's not so monogamous herself.'

'Aye, one o' her pals made a gag about an Indian waiter.'

'A waiter? I heard a student.'

'No reason it couldn'ta been both,' said Barclay. 'I'd say she's a—'

But catching Robin's eye, Barclay decided against saying the word, and instead drank his tea.

'Anything new your end?' Strike asked Robin.

'Yes. I got the second listening device back.'

'You're kidding,' said Strike, sitting up straighter.

'I've only just finished transcribing it all, there was hours of stuff on there. Most of it's useless, but . . . '

She set down her tea, unzipped the holdall and took out the recording device.

'... there's one strange bit. Listen to this.'

Barclay sat down on the arm of the sofa. Robin straightened up in her desk chair and flicked the switch on the device.

Geraint's lilting accent filled the office.

'... keep them sweet, make sure I introduce Elspeth to Prince Harry,' said Geraint. 'Right, that's me off, I'll see you tomorrow.'

'G'night,' said Aamir.

Robin shook her head at Strike and Barclay and mouthed, 'Wait.'

They heard the door close. After the usual thirty-second silence, there was a click, where the tape had stopped then restarted. A deep, Welsh female voice spoke.

'Are you there, sweetheart?'

Strike raised his eyebrows. Barclay stopped chewing.

'Yes,' said Aamir, in his flat London accent.

'Come and give me a kiss,' said Della.

Barclay made a small choking noise into his tea. The sound of lips smacking emanated from the bug. Feet shuffled. A chair was moved. There was a faint, rhythmic thudding.

'What's that?' muttered Strike.

'The guide dog's tail wagging,' said Robin.

'Let me hold your hand,' said Della. 'Geraint won't be back, don't worry, I've sent him out to Chiswick. There. Thank you. Now, I needed a little private word with you. The thing is, darling, your neighbours have complained. They say they've been hearing funny noises through the walls.'

'Like what?' He sounded apprehensive.

'Well, they thought they *might* be animal,' said Della. 'A dog whining or whimpering. You haven't—?'

'Of course I haven't,' said Aamir. 'It must've been the telly. Why would I get a dog? I'm at work all day.'

'I thought it would be like you to bring home some poor little stray,' she said. 'Your soft heart . . . '

'Well, I haven't,' said Aamir. He sounded tense. 'You don't have to take my word for it. You can go and check if you want, you've got a key.'

'Darling, don't be like that,' said Della. 'I wouldn't dream of letting myself in without your permission. I don't snoop.'

'You're within your rights,' he said, and Strike thought he sounded bitter. 'It's your house.'

'You're upset. I knew you would be. I had to mention it, because if Geraint picks up the phone to them next time – it was the purest good luck the neighbour caught me—'

'I'll make sure and keep the volume down from now on,' said Aamir. 'OK? I'll be careful.'

'You understand, my love, that as far as I'm concerned, you're free to do whatever—'

'Look, I've been thinking,' Aamir interrupted. 'I really think I should be paying you some rent. What if—'

'We've been over this. Don't be silly, I don't want your money.'

'But—'

'Apart from everything else,' she said, 'you couldn't afford it. A three-bedroomed house, on your own?'

'But—'

'We've been through this. You seemed happy when you first moved in . . . I thought you liked it—'

'Obviously, I like it. It was very generous of you,' he said stiffly.

'Generous . . . it's not a question of generosity, for heaven's sake . . . Now, listen: how would you like to come and have a curry? I've got a late vote and I was going to nip over to the Kennington Tandoori. My treat.'

'Sorry, I can't,' said Aamir. He sounded stressed. 'I've got to get home.'

'Oh,' said Della, with a great deal less warmth. 'Oh . . . that's disappointing. What a pity.'

'I'm sorry,' he said again. 'I said I'd meet a friend. University friend.'

'Ah. I see. Well, next time, I'll make sure to call ahead. Find a slot in your diary.'

'Della, I—'

'Don't be silly, I'm only teasing. You can walk out with me, at least?'

'Yes. Yes, of course.'

There was more scuffling, then the sound of the door opening. Robin turned off the tape.

'They're *shaggin'*?' said Barclay loudly.

'Not necessarily,' said Robin. 'The kiss might've been on the cheek.'

'"Let me hold your hand"?' repeated Barclay. 'Since when's that normal office procedure?'

'How old's this Aamir bloke?' asked Strike.

'I'd guess mid-twenties,' said Robin.

'And she's, what . . . ?'

'Mid-sixties,' said Robin.

'And she's provided him with a house. He's not related to her, is he?'

'There's no family connection as far as I'm aware,' said Robin. 'But Jasper Chiswell knows something personal about him. He quoted a Latin poem at Aamir when they met in our office.'

'You didn't tell me that.'

'Sorry,' said Robin, remembering that this had happened shortly before she had refused to tail Jimmy on the march. 'I forgot. Yes, Chiswell quoted something Latin, then mentioned "a man of your habits".'

'What was the poem?'

'I don't know, I never did Latin.'

She checked her watch.

'I'd better get changed, I'm supposed to be at DCMS in forty minutes.'

'Aye, that's me off as well, Strike,' said Barclay.

'Two days, Barclay,' Strike said, as the other headed to the door, 'then you're back on Knight.'

'Nae bother,' said Barclay, 'I'll be wantin' a break from the wean by then.'

'I like him,' said Robin, as Barclay's footsteps died away down the metal stairs.

'Yeah,' grunted Strike, as he reached for his prosthesis. 'He's all right.'

He and Lorelei were meeting early, at his request. It was time to begin the onerous process of making himself presentable. Robin retired to the cramped toilet on the landing to change, and Strike, having put his prosthesis back on, withdrew to the inner office.

He had got as far as pulling on his suit trousers when his mobile rang. Half-hoping that it was Lorelei to say that she could not make dinner, he picked up the cracked phone and saw, with an inexplicable sense of foreboding, that it was Hutchins.

'Strike?'

'What's wrong?'

'Strike . . . I've fucked up.'

Hutchins sounded weak.

'What's happened?'

'Knight's with some mates. I followed them into a pub. They're planning something. He's got a placard with Chiswell's face on it—'

'And?' said Strike loudly.

'Strike, I'm sorry . . . my balance has gone . . . I've lost them.'

'You stupid fucker!' roared Strike, losing his temper completely. 'Why didn't you tell me you were ill?'

'I've had a lot of time off lately ... knew you were stretched ...'

Strike switched Hutchins to speakerphone, laid his mobile onto his desk, took his shirt off the hanger and began to dress as fast as possible.

'Mate, I'm so sorry ... I'm having trouble walking ...'

'I know the fucking feeling!'

Fuming, Strike stabbed off the call.

'Cormoran?' Robin called through the door. 'Everything OK?'

'No, it's fucking not!'

He opened the office door.

In one part of his brain, he registered that Robin was wearing the green dress he had bought her two years ago, as a thank you for helping him catch their first killer. She looked stunning.

'Knight's got a placard with Chiswell's face on it. He's planning something with a bunch of mates. I *knew* it, I fucking *knew* this would happen now Winn's bailed on him ... I'll bet you anything he's heading for your reception. Shit,' said Strike, realising he didn't have shoes on and doubling back. 'And Hutchins has lost them,' he shouted over his shoulder. 'The stupid tit didn't tell me he's ill.'

'Maybe you can get Barclay back?' suggested Robin.

'He'll be on the Tube by now. I'm going to have to fucking do it, aren't I?' said Strike. He dropped back into the sofa and slid his feet into his shoes. 'There are going to be press all round that place tonight if Harry's going to be there. All it needs is for a journo to twig what Jimmy's stupid fucking sign means, and Chiswell's out of a job and so're we.' He heaved himself back to his feet. 'Where is this thing, tonight?'

'Lancaster House,' said Robin. 'Stable Yard.'

'Right,' said Strike, heading for the door. 'Stand by. You might have to bail me out. There's a good chance I'm going to have to punch him.'

29

It became impossible for me to remain an idle spectator any longer.

Henrik Ibsen, *Rosmersholm*

The taxi that Strike had picked up in Charing Cross Road turned into St James's Street twenty minutes later, while he was still talking to the Minister for Culture on his mobile.

'A placard? What's on it?'

'Your face,' said Strike. 'That's all I know.'

'And he's heading for the reception? Well, this is bloody it, isn't it?' shouted Chiswell, so loudly that Strike winced and removed the phone from his ear. 'If the press see this, it's all over! You were supposed to stop something like this bloody happening!'

'And I'm going to try,' said Strike, 'but in your shoes I'd want to be forewarned. I'd advise—'

'I don't pay you for advice!'

'I'll do whatever I can,' promised Strike, but Chiswell had already hung up.

'I'm not going to be able to go any further, mate,' said the taxi-driver, addressing Strike in the rear-view mirror from which dangled a swinging mobile, outlined in tufts of multi-coloured cotton and embossed with a golden Ganesh. The end of St James's Street had been blocked off. A swelling crowd of royal watchers and Olympics fans, many clutching small Union Jacks, was congregating behind portable barriers, waiting for the arrival of Paralympians and Prince Harry.

'OK, I'll get out here,' said Strike, fumbling for his wallet.

He was once again facing the crenellated frontage of St James's Palace, its gilded, diamond-shaped clock gleaming in the early evening sun. Strike limped down the slope again towards the crowd, passing the side street where Pratt's stood, while smartly dressed passers-by, workers and customers of galleries and wine merchants moved aside courteously as his uneven gait became progressively more pronounced.

'*Fuck, fuck, fuck*,' he muttered, pain shooting up into his groin every time he put his weight onto the prosthesis as he drew closer to the assembled sports fans and royal watchers. He could see no placards or banners of a political nature, but as he joined the back of the crowd and looked down Cleveland Row, he spotted a press pen and ranks of photographers, which stood waiting for the prince and famous athletes. It was only when a car slid past, containing a glossy-haired brunette Strike vaguely recognised from the television, that he remembered he had not called Lorelei to tell her he would be late to dinner. He hastily dialled her number.

'Hi, Corm.'

She sounded apprehensive. He guessed that she thought he was going to cancel.

'Hi,' he said, his eyes still darting around for some sign of Jimmy. 'I'm really sorry, but something's come up. I might be late.'

'Oh, that's fine,' she said, and he could tell that she was

relieved that he was still intending to come. 'Shall I try and change the booking?'

'Yeah – maybe make it eight instead of seven?'

Turning for the third time to scan Pall Mall behind him, Strike spotted Flick's tomato-red hair. Eight CORE members were heading for the crowd, including a stringy, blond-dreadlocked youth and a short, thickset man who resembled a bouncer. Flick was the only woman. All bar Jimmy were holding placards with the broken Olympic rings on them, and slogans such as 'Fair Play Is Fair Pay' and 'Homes Not Bombs'. Jimmy was holding his own placard upside down, the picture on it turned inwards, parallel with his leg.

'Lorelei, I've got to go. Speak later.'

Uniformed police were walking around the perimeter fencing keeping the crowds back, walkie-talkies in hand, eyes roving constantly over the cheerful spectators. They, too, had spotted CORE, who were trying to reach a spot opposite the press pen.

Gritting his teeth, Strike began to forge a path through the pressing crowd, eyes on Jimmy.

30

There is no denying it would have been more fortunate if we had succeeded in checking the stream at an earlier point.

Henrik Ibsen, *Rosmersholm*

Slightly self-conscious in her clinging green dress and heels, Robin attracted a considerable number of appreciative glances from male passers-by as she climbed out of her taxi at the entrance to the Department for Culture, Media and Sport. As she reached the doorway, she saw approaching from fifty yards away Izzy, who was wearing bright orange, and Kinvara, in what appeared to be the slinky black dress and heavy diamond necklace that she had worn in the photograph that Robin had seen of her online.

Acutely anxious about what was happening with Jimmy and Strike, Robin nevertheless registered that Kinvara appeared to be upset. Izzy rolled her eyes at Robin as they approached. Kinvara gave Robin a pointed up-and-down look that suggested she found the green dress inappropriate, if not indecent.

'We were supposed,' said a booming male voice in Robin's near vicinity, 'to be meeting *here*.'

Jasper Chiswell had just emerged from the building, carrying three engraved invitations, one of which he held out to Robin.

'Yes, I know that now, Jasper, thank you,' said Kinvara, puffing slightly as she approached. 'Very sorry for getting it wrong again. Nobody bothered to check I knew what the arrangements were.'

Passers-by stared at Chiswell, finding him vaguely familiar with his chimney-brush hair. Robin saw a suited man nudge his companion and point. A sleek black Mercedes drew up at the kerb. The chauffeur got out; Kinvara walked around the back of the car to sit behind him. Izzy wriggled over into the middle of the back seat, leaving Robin to take the back seat directly behind Chiswell.

The car pulled away from the kerb, the atmosphere inside unpleasant. Robin turned her head to watch the after-work drinkers and evening shoppers, wondering whether Strike had found Knight yet, scared of what might happen when he did, and wishing she could spirit the car directly to Lancaster House.

'You haven't invited Raphael, then?' Kinvara shot at the back of her husband's head.

'No,' said Chiswell. 'He angled for an invitation, but that will be because he's smitten with Venetia.'

Robin felt her face flood with colour.

'Venetia seems to have quite the fan base,' said Kinvara tersely.

'Going to have a little chat with Raphael tomorrow,' said Chiswell. 'I'm seeing him rather differently these days, I don't mind telling you.'

Out of the corner of her eye, Robin saw Kinvara's hands twist around the chain on her ugly evening bag, which sported a horse's head picked out in crystals. A tense silence settled over the car's interior as it purred on through the warm city.

31

. . . the result was, that he got a thrashing . . .

Henrik Ibsen, *Rosmersholm*

Adrenaline made it easier for Strike to block out the mounting pain in his leg. He was closing on Jimmy and his companions, who were being thwarted in their desire to show themselves clearly to the press, because the excitable crowd had pressed forwards as the first official cars began to glide past, hoping to spot some celebrities. Late to the party, CORE now found themselves faced by an impenetrable mass.

Mercedes and Bentleys swished past, affording the crowd glimpses of the famous and the not-so-famous. A comedian got a loud cheer as he waved. A few flashes went off.

Clearly deciding that he could not hope for a more prominent spot, Jimmy began to drag his homemade banner out of the tangle of legs around him, preparatory to hoisting it aloft.

A woman ahead of Strike gave a shriek of indignation as he pushed her out of the way. In three strides, Strike had closed his large left hand around Jimmy's right wrist, preventing him from raising the placard above waist height, forcing it back towards the ground. Strike had time to see the recognition in his eyes before Jimmy's fist came hurtling at his throat. A second woman saw the punch coming and screamed.

Strike dodged it and brought his left foot down hard on the placard, splintering the pole, but his amputated leg was not equal to bearing all his weight, especially as Jimmy's second punch connected. As Strike crumpled, he hit Jimmy in the balls. Knight gave a soft scream of pain, doubled up, hit the falling Strike and both of them toppled over, knocking bystanders sideways, all of whom shouted their indignation. As Strike hit the pavement, one of Jimmy's companions aimed a kick at his head. Strike caught his foot and twisted it. Through the mounting furore, he heard a third woman shriek:

'They're attacking that man!'

Strike was too intent on seizing hold of Jimmy's mangled cardboard banner to care whether he was being cast as victim or aggressor. Tugging on the banner, which like himself was being trampled underfoot, he succeeded in ripping it. One of the pieces attached to the spike heel of a panicking woman trying to get out of the way of the fight, and was carried away.

Fingers closed around his neck from behind. He aimed an elbow at Jimmy's face and his hold loosened, but then somebody kicked Strike in the stomach and another blow hit him on the back of the head. Red spots popped in front of his eyes.

More shouting, a whistle, and the crowd was suddenly thinning around them. Strike could taste blood, but, from what he could see, the splintered and torn remnants of Jimmy's placard had been scattered by the mêlée. Jimmy's hands were again scrabbling at Strike's neck, but then Jimmy was pulled away, swearing fluently at the top of his voice. The winded Strike was seized and dragged to his feet as well. He put up no resistance. He doubted he could have stood of his own accord.

32

. . . and now we can go in to supper. Will you come in, Mr. Kroll?

Henrik Ibsen, *Rosmersholm*

Chiswell's Mercedes turned the corner of St James's Street onto Pall Mall and set off along Cleveland Row.

'What's going on?' growled Chiswell, as the car slowed, then stopped.

The shouting ahead was not of the excited, enthusiastic kind that royalty or celebrities might expect. Several uniformed officers were converging on the crowd on the left-hand side of the street which was jostling and pushing as it tried to move away from what appeared to be a confrontation between police and protestors. Two dishevelled men in jeans and T-shirts emerged from the fray, both held in arm-locks by uniformed officers: Jimmy Knight, and a youth with limp blond dreadlocks.

Then Robin bit back a cry of dismay as a hobbling, bloody Strike appeared, also being led along by police. Behind them, an altercation in the crowd had not subsided, but was growing. A barrier swayed.

'Pull up, PULL UP!' bellowed Chiswell at the driver, who had just begun to accelerate again. Chiswell wound down his window. 'Door open – Venetia, open your door! – that man!' Chiswell roared at a nearby policeman, who turned, startled, to see the Minister for Culture shouting at him and pointing at Strike. 'He's my guest – that man – bloody well let him go!'

Confronted by an official car, a government minister, the steely, patrician voice, the brandishing of a thick embossed invitation, the policeman did as he was told. Most people's attention was focused on the increasingly violent brawl between police and CORE, and the consequent trampling and pushing of the crowd trying to get away from it. A couple of cameramen had broken away from the press pen up ahead, and were running towards the fracas.

'Izzy, move up – get in, GET IN!' Chiswell snarled at Strike through the window.

Robin squeezed backwards, half-sitting in Izzy's lap to accommodate Strike as he clambered into the back seat. The door slammed. The car rolled on.

'Who are you?' squealed the frightened Kinvara, who was now pinned against the opposite door by Izzy. 'What's going on?'

'He's a private detective,' growled Chiswell. His decision to bring Strike into the car seemed born of panic. Twisting around in his seat to glare at Strike, he said, 'How does it help me if you get bloody arrested?'

'They weren't arresting me,' said Strike, dabbing his nose with the back of his hand. 'They wanted to take a statement. Knight attacked me when I went for his placard. Cheers,' he added, as, with difficulty given how tightly compressed they all were, Robin passed him a box of tissues that had been lying on the ledge behind the rear seat. He pressed one to his nose. 'I got rid of the placard,' Strike added, through the blood-stained tissue, but nobody congratulated him.

'Jasper,' said Kinvara, 'what's going—?'

'Shut up,' snapped Chiswell, without looking at her. 'I can't let you out in front of all these people,' he told Strike angrily, as though the latter had suggested it. 'There are more photographers . . . You'll have to come in with us. I'll fix it.'

The car was now proceeding towards a barrier where police and security were checking ID and invitations.

'Nobody say anything,' Chiswell instructed. '*Shut up*,' he added pre-emptively to Kinvara, who had opened her mouth.

A Bentley up ahead was admitted and the Mercedes rolled forwards.

In pain, because she was bearing a good proportion of Strike's weight across her left hip and leg, Robin heard screeching from behind the car. Turning, she saw a young woman running after the car, a female police officer chasing her. The girl had wild tomato-red hair, a T-shirt with a logo of broken Olympic rings on it, and she screamed after Chiswell's car:

'He put the fucking horse on them, Chiswell! He put the horse on them, you cheating, thieving bastard, you *murderer*—'

'I have a guest here who didn't get his invitation,' Chiswell was shouting through his wound-down window to the armed policeman at the barrier. 'Cormoran Strike, the amputee. He's been in the papers. There was a balls-up at my department, his invitation didn't go. The prince,' he said, with breathtaking chutzpah, 'asked to meet him specifically!'

Strike and Robin were watching what was happening behind the car. Two policemen had seized the struggling Flick and were escorting her away. A few more cameras flashed. Caving under the weight of ministerial pressure, the armed policeman requested ID of Strike. Strike, who always carried a couple of forms of identification, though not necessarily in his own name, passed over his genuine driving licence. A queue of stationary cars grew longer behind them. The prince was due in fifteen minutes' time. Finally, the policeman waved them through.

'Shouldn't have done that,' said Strike in an undertone to Robin. 'Shouldn't have let me in. Bloody lax.'

The Mercedes swung around the inner courtyard and arrived, finally, at the foot of a shallow flight of red-carpeted steps, in front of an enormous, honey-coloured building that resembled a stately home. Wheelchair ramps had been set either side of the carpet, and a celebrated wheelchair basketball player was already manoeuvring his way up one.

Strike pushed open the door, clambered out of the car, then turned and reached back inside to assist Robin. She accepted the offer of help. Her left leg was almost completely numb from where he'd sat on her.

'Nice to see you again, Corm,' said Izzy, beaming, as she got out behind Robin.

'Hi, Izzy,' said Strike.

Now burdened with Strike whether he wanted him or not, Chiswell hurried up the steps to explain to one of the liveried men standing outside the front door that Strike must be admitted without his invitation. They heard a recurrence of the word 'amputee'. All around them, more cars were releasing their smartly dressed passengers.

'What's all this about?' Kinvara said, who had marched around the rear of the Mercedes to address Strike. 'What's going on? What does my husband need a private detective for?'

'*Will you be quiet, you stupid, stupid bitch?*'

Stressed and disturbed though Chiswell undoubtedly was, his naked hostility shocked Robin. *He hates her*, she thought. *He genuinely hates her.*

'You two,' said the minister, pointing at his wife and daughter, 'get inside.

'Give me one good reason I should keep paying you,' he

added, turning on Strike as still more people spilled past them.

'You realise,' said Chiswell, and in his necessarily quiet fury, spit flew from his mouth onto Strike's tie, 'I've just been called a bloody murderer in front of twenty people, including press?'

'They'll think she's a crank,' said Strike.

If the suggestion brought Chiswell any comfort, it didn't show.

'I want to see you tomorrow morning at ten o'clock,' he told Strike. 'Not at my office. Come to the flat in Ebury Street.' He turned away, then, as an afterthought, turned back. 'You too,' he barked at Robin.

Side by side, they watched him lumbering up the steps.

'We're about to get sacked, aren't we?' whispered Robin.

'I'd say it's odds on,' said Strike, who, now that he was on his feet, was in considerable pain.

'Cormoran, what was on the placard?' said Robin.

Strike allowed a woman in peach chiffon to pass, then said quietly:

'Picture of Chiswell hanging from a gallows and, beneath him, a bunch of dead children. One odd thing, though.'

'What?'

'All the kids were black.'

Still dabbing at his nose, Strike reached inside his pocket for a cigarette, then remembered where he was and let his hand fall back to his side.

'Listen, if that Elspeth woman's in here, you might as well try and find out what else she knows about Winn. It'll help justify our final invoice.'

'OK,' said Robin. 'The back of your head's bleeding, by the way.'

Strike dabbed at it ineffectually with the tissues he had pocketed and began to limp up the steps beside Robin.

'We shouldn't be seen together any more tonight,' he told

her, as they passed over the threshold into a blaze of ochre, scarlet and gold. 'There was a café in Ebury Street, not far from Chiswell's house. I'll meet you there at nine o'clock tomorrow, and we can face the firing squad together. Go on, you go ahead.'

But as she moved away from him, towards the grand staircase, he called after her:

'Nice dress, by the way.'

33

I believe you could bewitch any one – if you set yourself to do it.

Henrik Ibsen, *Rosmersholm*

The grand hallway of the mansion constituted a vast empty block of space. A red-and-gold-carpeted central staircase led to an upper balcony that split left and right. The walls, which appeared to be of marble, were ochre, dull green and rose. Sundry Paralympians were being shown to a lift on the left of the entrance, but the limping Strike made his way laboriously to the stairs and heaved himself upwards by liberal use of the banister. The sky visible through a huge and ornate skylight, supported by columns, was fading through technicolour variations that intensified the colours of the massive Venetian paintings of classical subjects hanging on every wall.

Doing his best to walk naturally, because he was afraid he might be mistaken for some veteran Paralympian and perhaps asked to expound on past triumphs, Strike followed the crowd up the right staircase, around the balcony and into a small anteroom overlooking the courtyard where the official cars were parked. From here, the guests were ushered left into a long and spacious picture gallery, where the carpet was apple green and decorated with a rosette pattern. Tall windows stood at either end of the room and almost every inch of white wall was covered in paintings.

'Drink, sir?' said a waiter just inside the doorway.

'Is it champagne?' asked Strike.

'English sparkling wine, sir,' said the waiter.

Strike helped himself, though without enthusiasm, and continued through the crowd, passing Chiswell and Kinvara, who were listening (or, Strike thought, pretending to listen) to a wheelchair-bound athlete. Kinvara shot Strike a swift, suspicious side glance as he passed, aiming for the far wall where he hoped to find either a chair, or something on which he could conveniently lean. Unfortunately, the gallery walls were so densely packed with pictures that leaning was impossible, nor were there any seats, so Strike came to rest beside an enormous painting by Count d'Orsay of Queen Victoria riding a dapple-grey horse. While he sipped his sparkling wine, he tried discreetly to staunch the blood still leaking from his nose, and wipe the worst of the dirt off his suit trousers.

Waiters were circulating, carrying trays of canapés. Strike managed to grab a couple of miniature crab cakes as they passed, then fell to examining his surroundings, noting another spectacular skylight, this one supported by a number of gilded palm trees.

The room had a peculiar energy. The prince's arrival was imminent and the guests' gaiety came and went in nervous spurts, with increasingly frequent glances at the doors. From his vantage point beside Queen Victoria, Strike spotted a stately figure in a primrose-yellow dress standing almost directly opposite him, close beside an ornate black and gold fireplace. One hand was keeping a gentle hold on the harness of a pale yellow Labrador, who sat panting gently at her feet in the overcrowded room. Strike had not immediately recognised Della, because she was not wearing sunglasses, but prosthetic eyes. Her slightly sunken, opaque, china-blue gaze gave her an odd innocence. Geraint stood a short distance from his wife, gabbling at a thin, mousy woman whose eyes darted around, searching for a rescuer.

A sudden hush fell near the doors through which Strike had entered. Strike saw the top of a ginger head and a flurry of suits. Self-consciousness spread through the packed room like a petrifying breeze. Strike watched the top of the ginger head move away, towards the far right side of the room. Still sipping his English wine and wondering which of the women in the room was the trustee with dirt on Geraint Winn, his attention was suddenly caught by a tall woman nearby with her back to him.

Her long dark hair was twisted up into a messy bun and, unlike every other woman present, her outfit gave no suggestion of party best. The straight black knee-length dress was plain to the point of severity, and though barelegged she wore a pair of spike-heeled, open-toed ankle boots. For a sliver of a second Strike thought he must be mistaken, but then she moved and he knew for sure that it was her. Before he could move away from her vicinity, she turned around and looked straight into his eyes.

Colour flooded her face, which as he knew was normally cameo pale. She was heavily pregnant. Her condition had not touched her anywhere but the swollen belly. She was as fine-boned as ever in face and limbs. Less adorned than any other woman in the room, she was easily the most beautiful. For a few seconds they contemplated each other, then she took a few tentative steps forwards, the colour ebbing from her cheeks as fast as it had come.

'Corm?'

'Hello, Charlotte.'

If she thought of kissing him, his stony face deterred her.

'What on earth are you doing here?'

'Invited,' lied Strike. 'Celebrity amputee. You?'

She seemed dazed.

'Jago's niece is a Paralympian. She's . . . '

Charlotte looked around, apparently trying to spot the niece, and took a sip of water. Her hand was shaking. A few drops spilled from the glass. He saw them break like glass beads on her swollen belly.

' . . . well, she's here somewhere,' she said, with a nervous laugh. 'She's got cerebral palsy and she's remarkable, actually, an incredible rider. Her father's in Hong Kong, so her mum invited me, instead.'

His silence was unnerving her. She rattled on:

'Jago's family like to make me go out and do things, only my sister-in-law's cross because I got the dates mixed up. I thought tonight was dinner at the Shard and this thing was Friday, tomorrow, I mean, so I'm not dressed properly for royalty, but I was late and I didn't have time to change.'

She gestured hopelessly at her plain black dress and her spike-heeled boots.

'Jago not here?'

Her gold-flecked green eyes flickered slightly.

'No, he's in the States.'

Her focus moved to his upper lip.

'Have you been in a fight?'

'No,' he said, dabbing at his nose with the back of his hand again. He straightened up, lowering his weight carefully back onto his prosthesis, ready to walk away. 'Well, nice to—'

'Corm, don't go,' she said, reaching out. Her fingers did not quite make contact with his sleeve; she let her hand fall back by her side. 'Don't, not yet, I – you've done such incredible things. I read about them all in the papers.'

The last time they had seen each other he had been bleeding, too, because of the flying ashtray that had caught him in the face as he left her. He remembered the text, 'It was yours', sent on the eve of her wedding to Ross, referring to another baby she had claimed to be bearing, which had vanished before he ever saw proof of its existence. He remembered, too, the picture she had sent to his office of herself, minutes after saying 'I do' to Jago Ross, beautiful and stricken, like a sacrificial victim.

'Congratulations,' he said, keeping his eyes on her face.

'I'm huge because it's twins.'

She did not, as he had seen other pregnant women do, touch her belly as she talked about the babies, but looked down as though slightly surprised to see her changed shape. She had never wanted children when they had been together. It was one of the things they had had in common. The baby that she had claimed was his had been an unwelcome surprise to both of them.

In Strike's imagination, Jago Ross's progeny were curled under the black dress like a pair of white whelps, not entirely human, emissaries of their father, who resembled a dissolute arctic fox. He was glad they were there, if such a joyless emotion could be called gladness. All impediments, all deterrents, were welcome, because it now became apparent to him that the gravitational pull Charlotte had so long exerted over him, even after hundreds of fights and scenes and a thousand lies, was not yet spent. As ever, he had the sense that behind the green and gold-flecked eyes, she knew exactly what he was thinking.

'They aren't due for ages. I had a scan, it's a boy and a girl. Jago's pleased about the boy. Are you here with anyone?'

'No.'

As he said it, he caught a flash of green over Charlotte's shoulder. Robin, who was now talking brightly to the mousy woman in purple brocade who had finally escaped Geraint.

'Pretty,' said Charlotte, who had looked to see what had caught his attention. She had always had a preternatural ability to detect the slightest flicker of interest towards other women. 'No, wait,' she said slowly, 'isn't that the girl who works with you? She was in all the papers – what's her name, Rob—?'

'No,' said Strike, 'that's not her.'

He wasn't remotely surprised that Charlotte knew Robin's name, or that she had recognised her, even with the hazel contact lenses. He had known Charlotte would keep tabs on him.

'You've always liked girls with that colouring, haven't you?' said Charlotte with a kind of synthetic gaiety. 'That little American you started dating after you pretended we'd broken up in Germany had the same kind of—'

There was a kind of hushed scream in their vicinity.

'Ohmigod, *Charlie!*'

Izzy Chiswell was bearing down upon them, beaming, her pink face clashing with her orange dress. She was, Strike suspected, not on her first glass of wine.

'Hello, Izz,' said Charlotte, forcing a smile. Strike could almost feel the effort it cost her to tug herself free of that tangle of ancient grudges and wounds in which their relationship had gradually strangled to death.

Again, he prepared to walk away, but the crowd parted and Prince Harry was suddenly revealed in all his hyperreal familiarity, some ten feet away from where Strike and the two women stood, so that moving away from the area would be done under the scrutiny of half the room. Trapped, Strike startled a passing waiter by reaching out a long arm and snatching another glass of wine from his tray. For a few seconds, both Charlotte and Izzy watched the prince. Then, when it became apparent that he was not about to approach them any time soon, they turned back to each other.

'Showing already!' Izzy said, admiring Charlotte's belly. 'Have you had a scan? D'you know what it is?'

'Twins,' said Charlotte, without enthusiasm. She indicated Strike, 'You remember—?'

'Corm, yah, of course, we brought him here!' said Izzy, beaming and clearly unconscious of any indiscretion.

Charlotte turned from her old schoolfriend to her ex, and Strike could feel her sniffing the air for the reason that Strike and Izzy would have travelled together. She shifted very slightly, apparently allowing Izzy into the conversation, but boxing Strike in so that he couldn't walk away without asking one of them to get out of his way. 'Oh, wait, of course. You investigated Freddie's death in action, didn't you?' she said. 'I remember you telling me about it. Poor Freddie.'

Izzy acknowledged this tribute to her brother with a slight tip of her glass, then peeked back over her shoulder at Prince Harry.

'He gets sexier every passing day, doesn't he?' she whispered.

'Ginger pubes, though, darling,' said Charlotte, deadpan.

Against his will, Strike grinned. Izzy snorted with laughter.

'Speaking of which,' said Charlotte (she never acknowledged that she had been funny), 'isn't that Kinvara Hanratty over there?'

'My ghastly stepmother? Yes,' said Izzy. 'D'you know her?'

'My sister sold her a horse.'

During the sixteen years of Strike's on-off relationship with Charlotte, he had been privy to countless conversations like this. People of Charlotte's class all seemed to know each other. Even if they had never met, they knew siblings or cousins or friends or classmates, or else their parents knew somebody else's parents: all were connected, forming a kind of web that constituted a hostile habitat for outsiders. Rarely did these web-dwellers leave to seek companionship or love among the rest of society. Charlotte had been unique in her circle in choosing somebody as unclassifiable as Strike, whose invisible appeal and low status had, he knew, been subjects of perennial, horrified debate among most of her friends and family.

'Well, I hope it wasn't a horse Amelia liked,' Izzy said, 'because Kinvara will ruin it. Awful hands and a horrible seat, but she thinks she's Charlotte Dujardin. D'you ride, Cormoran?' Izzy asked.

'No,' said Strike.

'He doesn't trust horses,' said Charlotte, smiling at him.

But he did not respond. He had no desire to touch upon old jokes or shared memories.

'Kinvara's livid, look at her,' said Izzy, with some satisfaction. 'Papa's just dropped a heavy hint he's going to try and talk my brother Raff into taking over from me, which is *fabulous*, and what I hoped would happen. Papa used to let Kinvara boss him around about Raff, but he's putting his foot down these days.'

'I think I've met Raphael,' said Charlotte. 'Wasn't he working at Henry Drummond's art gallery a couple of months ago?'

Strike checked his watch and then back around the room. The prince was moving away from their part of the room and Robin was nowhere to be seen. With any luck, she had followed the trustee who had dirt on Winn into the bathroom and was eliciting confidences over the sink.

'Oh Lord,' said Izzy. 'Look out. Geraint Bloody – hello, Geraint!'

Geraint's object, it soon became clear, was Charlotte.

'Hello, hello,' he said, peering at her through heavily smudged glasses, his lipless smile a leer. 'You've just been pointed out to me by your niece. What an extraordinary young woman she is, quite extraordinary. Our charity's involved in supporting the equestrian team. Geraint Winn,' he said, holding out a hand, 'The Level Playing Field.'

'Oh,' said Charlotte. 'Hello.'

Strike had watched her repel lecherous men for years. Having acknowledged his presence, she stared coldly at Geraint, as though quite puzzled to know why he was still in her vicinity.

Strike's mobile vibrated in his pocket. Reaching for it, he saw an unknown number. This was his excuse to leave.

'Need to get going, sorry. 'Scuse me, Izzy.'

'Oh, that's a shame,' Izzy said, pouting. 'I wanted to ask you all about the Shacklewell Ripper!'

Strike saw Geraint's eyes widen. Inwardly cursing her, he said, 'Night. Bye,' he added to Charlotte.

Limping away as fast as he could manage, he accepted the call, but by the time he had raised it to his ear, the caller had gone.

'Corm.'

Somebody lightly touched his arm. He turned. Charlotte had followed him.

'I'm leaving, too.'

'What about your niece?'

'She's met Harry, she'll be thrilled. She doesn't actually like me that much. None of them do. What happened to your mobile?'

'I fell on it.'

He walked on, but, long-legged as she was, she caught up with him.

'I don't think I'm going your way, Charlotte.'

'Well, unless you're tunnelling out, we have to walk two hundred yards together.'

He limped on without answering. To his left, he caught another flash of green. As they reached the grand staircase in the hall, Charlotte reached out and lightly grasped his arm, wobbly in the heels that were so unsuitable for a pregnant woman. He resisted the urge to shake her loose.

His mobile rang again. The same unknown number had appeared on the screen. Charlotte drew up beside him, watching his face as he answered it.

The moment the mobile touched his ear he heard a desperate, haunting scream.

'*They're going to kill me, Mr Strike, help me, help me, please help me . . .*'

34

But who could really foresee what was coming? I am sure I could not.

Henrik Ibsen, *Rosmersholm*

The hazy, clear-skied promise of another summer's day hadn't yet translated itself into actual warmth when Robin arrived next morning at the café closest to Chiswell's house. She could have chosen one of the circular tables outside on the pavement, but instead she huddled down in a corner of the café where she was to meet Strike, hands clasped around her latte for comfort, her reflection in the espresso machine pale and heavy-eyed.

Somehow, she had known that Strike would not be here when she arrived. Her mood was simultaneously depressed and nervy. She would rather not have been alone with her thoughts, but here she was, with only the hiss of the coffeemaker for company, chilly in spite of the jacket she had grabbed on the way out of the house and full of anxiety about the imminent confrontation with Chiswell, who might quibble his bill, after the catastrophe of Strike's fight with Jimmy Knight.

But that wasn't all that was worrying Robin. She had

woken that morning from a confused dream in which the dark, spike-booted figure of Charlotte Ross figured. Robin had recognised Charlotte immediately when she spotted her at the reception. She had tried not to watch the once-engaged couple as they'd talked, angry with herself for being so sharply interested in what was passing between them, yet, even as she had moved from group to group, shamelessly insinuating herself into conversations in the hope of finding the elusive Elspeth Curtis-Lacey, her eyes had sought out Strike and Charlotte, and when they left the reception together she had experienced a nasty sensation in her stomach, akin to the drop of an elevator.

She had arrived home unable to think of anything else, which had made her feel guilty when Matthew emerged from the kitchen, eating a sandwich. She had the impression that he had not been home long. He subjected the green dress to an up-and-down look very like the one Kinvara had given her. She made to walk past him upstairs, but he had moved to block her.

'Robin, come on. Please. Let's talk.'

So they had gone into the sitting room and talked. Tired of conflict, she had apologised for hurting Matthew's feelings by missing the cricket match, and for forgetting her wedding ring on their anniversary weekend. Matthew in turn had expressed regret for the things he had said during Sunday's row, and especially for the remark about her lack of achievements.

Robin felt as though they were moving chess pieces on a board that was vibrating in the preliminary tremors of an earthquake. *It's too late. You know, surely, that none of this matters any more?*

But when the talk was finished, Matthew said, 'So we're OK?'

'Yes,' she replied. 'We're fine.'

He had stood up, held out a hand and helped her up from her chair. She had forced a smile and then he had kissed her, hard, on the mouth, and begun to tug at the green dress. She heard the fabric around the zip tear and when she began to protest, he clamped his mouth on hers again.

She knew that she could stop him, she knew that he was waiting for her to stop him, that she was being tested in an ugly, underhand way, that he would deny what he was really doing, that he would claim to be the victim. She hated him for doing it this way, and part of her wanted to be the kind of woman who could have disengaged from her own revulsion and from her own reluctant flesh, but she had fought too long and too hard to regain possession of her own body to barter it in this way.

'No,' she said, pushing him away. 'I don't want to.'

He released her at once, as she had known he would, with an expression compounded of anger and triumph. Suddenly, she knew that she had not fooled him when they had had sex on their anniversary weekend, and paradoxically that made her feel tender towards him.

'I'm sorry,' she said. 'I'm tired.'

'Yeah,' said Matthew. 'So am I.'

And he had walked out of the room, leaving Robin with a chill down her back where the green dress had torn.

Where the hell was Strike? It was five past nine and she wanted company. She also wanted to know what had happened after he left the reception with Charlotte. Anything would be preferable to sitting here, thinking about Matthew.

As though the thought had summoned him, her phone rang.

'Sorry,' he said, before she could speak. 'Suspicious package at bloody Green Park. I've been stuck on the Tube for twenty minutes and I've only just got reception. I'll be there as quick as I can, but you might have to start without me.'

'Oh, God,' said Robin, closing her tired eyes.

'Sorry,' Strike repeated, 'I'm on my way. Got something to tell you, actually. Funny thing happened last night – oh, hang on, we're moving. See you shortly.'

He hung up, leaving Robin with the prospect of having to deal alone with the first effusions of Jasper Chiswell's anger, and still grappling formless feelings of dread and misery that swirled around a dark, graceful woman who was sixteen years' worth of knowledge and memories ahead of her when it came to Cormoran Strike, which, Robin told herself, *shouldn't matter, for God's sake, haven't you got enough problems without worrying about Strike's love life, it's nothing whatsoever to do with you . . .*

She felt a sudden guilty prickle around her lips, where Strike's missed kiss had landed outside the hospital. As though she could wash it away, she downed the dregs of her coffee, got up and left the café for the broad, straight street, which comprised two symmetrical lines of identical nineteenth-century houses.

She walked briskly, not because she was in any hurry to bear the brunt of Chiswell's anger and disappointment, but because activity helped dispel her uncomfortable thoughts.

Arriving outside Chiswell's house precisely on time, she lingered for a few hopeful seconds beside the glossy black front door, just in case Strike were to appear at the last moment. He didn't. Robin therefore steadied herself, walked up the three clean white steps from the pavement and knocked on the front door, which was on the latch and opened a few inches. A man's muffled voice shouted something that might have been 'come in'.

Robin passed into a small, dingy hall dominated by

vertiginous stairs. The olive-green wallpaper was drab and peeling in places. Leaving the front door as she had found it, she called out:

'Minister?'

He didn't answer. Robin knocked gently on the door to the right, and opened it.

Time froze. The scene seemed to fold in upon her, crashing through her retinas into a mind unprepared for it, and shock kept her standing in the doorway, her hand still on the handle and her mouth slightly open, trying to comprehend what she was seeing.

A man was sitting in a Queen Anne chair, his legs splayed, his arms dangling, and he seemed to have a shiny grey turnip for a head, in which a carved mouth gaped, but no eyes.

Then Robin's struggling comprehension grasped the fact that it was not a turnip, but a human head shrink-wrapped in a clear plastic bag, into which a tube ran from a large canister. The man looked as though he had suffocated. His left foot lay sideways on the rug, revealing a small hole in the sole, his thick fingers dangled, almost touching the carpet, and there was a stain at his groin where his bladder had emptied.

And next she understood that it was Chiswell himself who sat in the chair, and that his thick mass of grey hair was pressed flat against his face in the vacuum created by the bag, and that the gaping mouth had sucked the plastic into itself, which was why it gaped so darkly.

35

. . . the White Horse! In broad daylight!

Henrik Ibsen, *Rosmersholm*

Somewhere in the distance, outside the house, a man shouted. He sounded like a workman, and in some part of her brain Robin knew that that was who she had heard when she was expecting to hear 'come in'. Nobody had invited her into the house. The door had simply been left ajar.

Now, when it might have been expected, she didn't panic. There was no threat here, however horrifying the sight of that awful dummy, with the turnip head and the tube, this poor lifeless figure could not hurt her. Knowing that she must check that life was extinct, Robin approached Chiswell and gently touched his shoulder. It was easier, not being able to see his eyes, because of the coarse hair that obscured them like a horse's forelock. The flesh felt hard beneath his striped shirt and cooler than she had expected.

But then she imagined the gaping mouth speaking, and took several quick steps backwards, until her foot landed with a crunch on something hard on the carpet and she slipped. She had cracked a pale blue plastic tube of pills lying on the carpet. She recognised them as the sort of homeopathic tablets sold in her local chemist.

Taking out her mobile, she called 999 and asked for the police. After explaining that she had found a body and giving the address, she was told that someone would be with her shortly.

Trying not to focus on Chiswell, she took in the frayed curtains, which were of an indeterminate dun colour, trimmed with sad little bobbles, the antiquated TV in its faux wood cladding, the patch of darker wallpaper over the mantelpiece where a painting had once hung, and the silver-framed photographs. But the shrink-wrapped head, the rubber piping and the cold glint of the canister seemed to turn all of this everyday normality into pasteboard. The nightmare alone was real.

So Robin turned her mobile onto its camera function and began to take photographs. Putting a lens between herself and the scene mitigated the horror. Slowly and methodically, she documented the scene.

A glass sat on the coffee table in front of the body, with a few millimetres of what looked like orange juice in it. Scattered books and papers lay beside it. There was a piece of thick cream writing paper headed with a red Tudor rose, like a drop of blood, and the printed address of the house in which Robin stood. Somebody had written in a rounded, girlish hand.

> *Tonight was the final straw. How stupid do you think I am, putting that girl in your office right under my nose? I hope you realise how ridiculous you look, how much people are laughing at you, chasing a girl who's younger than your daughters.*

I've had enough. Make a fool of yourself, I don't care any more, it's over.

I've gone back to Woolstone. Once I've made arrangements for the horses, I'll clear out for good. Your bloody horrible children will be happy, but will you, Jasper? I doubt it, but it's too late.

K

As Robin bent to take a picture of the note, she heard the front door snap shut, and with a gasp, she spun around. Strike was standing on the threshold, large, unshaven, still in the suit he had worn to the reception. He was staring at the figure in the chair.

'The police are on their way,' said Robin. 'I just called them.'

Strike moved carefully into the room.

'Holy shit.'

He spotted the cracked tube of pills on the floor, stepped over them, and scrutinised the tubing and the plastic-covered face.

'Raff said he was behaving strangely,' said Robin, 'but I don't think he ever dreamed . . . '

Strike said nothing. He was still examining the body.

'Was that there yesterday evening?'

'What?'

'That,' said Strike, pointing.

There was a semi-circular mark on the back of Chiswell's hand, dark red against the coarse, pallid skin.

'I can't remember,' said Robin.

The full shock of what had happened was starting to hit her and she was finding it hard to arrange her thoughts, which floated, unmoored and disconnected, through her head: Chiswell barking through the car window to persuade the police to let Strike into last night's reception, Chiswell calling Kinvara a stupid bitch, Chiswell demanding that they meet him here this morning. It was unreasonable to expect her to remember the backs of his hands.

'Hmm,' said Strike. He glanced at the mobile in Robin's hand. 'Have you taken pictures of everything?'

She nodded.

'All of this?' he asked, waving a hand over the table. 'That?' he added, pointing at the cracked pills on the carpet.

'Yes. That was my fault. I trod on them.'

'How did you get in?'

'The door was open. I thought he'd left it on the latch for us,' said Robin. 'A workman shouted in the street and I thought it was Chiswell saying "come in". I was expecting—'

'Stay here,' said Strike.

He left the room. She heard him climbing the stairs and then his heavy footsteps on the ceiling above, but she knew that there was nobody there. She could feel the house's essential lifelessness, its flimsy cardboard unreality, and, sure enough, Strike returned less than five minutes later, shaking his head.

'Nobody.'

He walked past her through a door that led off the sitting room and, hearing his footsteps hit tile, Robin knew that it was the kitchen.

'Completely empty,' Strike said, re-emerging.

'What happened last night?' Robin asked. 'You said something funny happened.'

She wanted to discuss a subject other than the awful form that dominated the room in its grotesque lifelessness.

'Billy called me. He said people were trying to kill him – chasing him. He claimed to be in a phone box in Trafalgar Square. I went to try and find him, but he wasn't there.'

'Oh,' said Robin.

So he hadn't been with Charlotte. Even in this extremity, Robin registered the fact, and was glad.

'The hell?' said Strike quietly, looking past her into a corner of the room.

A buckled sword was leaning against the wall in a dark corner. It looked as though it had been forced or stood on and deliberately bent. Strike walked carefully around the body to examine it, but then they heard the police car pulling up outside the house and he straightened up.

'We'll tell them everything, obviously,' said Strike.

'Yes,' said Robin.

'Except the surveillance devices. Shit – they'll find them in your office—'

'They won't,' said Robin. 'I took them home yesterday, in case we decided I needed to clear out because of the *Sun*.'

Before Strike could express admiration for this clear-eyed foresight, somebody rapped hard on the front door.

'Well, it's been nice while it's lasted, hasn't it?' Strike said, with a grim smile, as he moved towards the hall. 'Being out of the papers?'

PART TWO

36

What has happened can be hushed up – or at any rate can be explained away . . .

Henrik Ibsen, *Rosmersholm*

The Chiswell case maintained its singular character even when their client was no more.

As the usual cumbersome procedures and formalities enveloped the corpse, Strike and Robin were escorted from Ebury Street to Scotland Yard, where they were separately interviewed. Strike knew that a tornado of speculation must be whirling through the newsrooms of London at the death of a government minister, and sure enough, by the time they emerged from Scotland Yard six hours later, the colourful details of Chiswell's private life were being broadcast across TV and radio, while opening the internet browsers on their phones revealed brief news items from news sites, as a tangle of baroque theories spread across blogs and social media, in which a multitude of cartoonish Chiswells died at the hand of myriad nebulous foes. As he rode in a taxi back to Denmark Street, Strike read how Chiswell the corrupt capitalist had been murdered by the Russian mafia after failing to pay back interest on some seedy, illegal transaction, while Chiswell the defender of solid English values had surely been dispatched by vengeful Islamists after his attempts to resist the rise of sharia law.

Strike returned to his attic flat only to collect his belongings, and decamped to the house of his old friends Nick and Ilsa, respectively a gastroenterologist and a lawyer. Robin, who at Strike's insistence had taken a taxi directly home to Albury Street, was given a peremptory hug by Matthew, whose tissue-thin pretence of sympathy was worse, Robin felt, than outright fury.

When he heard that Robin had been summoned back to Scotland Yard for further interrogation the next day, Matthew's self-control crumbled.

'Anyone could have seen this coming!'

'Funny, it seemed to take most people by surprise,' Robin said. She had just ignored her mother's fourth call of the morning.

'I don't mean Chiswell killing himself—'

'—it's pronounced "Chizzle"—'

'—I mean you getting yourself into trouble for sneaking around the Houses of Parliament!'

'Don't worry, Matt. I'll make sure the police know you were against it. Wouldn't want your promotion prospects compromised.'

But she wasn't sure that her second interviewer was a policeman. The softly spoken man in a dark grey suit didn't reveal whom he worked for. Robin found this gentleman far more intimidating than yesterday's police, even though they had, at times, been forceful to the point of aggression. Robin told her new interviewer everything she had seen and heard in the Commons, omitting only the strange conversation between Della Winn and Aamir Mallik, which had been captured on the second listening device. As the interaction had taken place behind a closed door after normal working hours, she could only have heard it by using surveillance equipment. Robin assuaged her conscience by telling herself that this conversation could not possibly have anything to do with Chiswell's death, but squirming feelings of guilt and terror pursued her as she left the building for the second time. So consumed was she by what she hoped was paranoia by this brush with the security services, that she called Strike from a payphone near the Tube, instead of using her mobile.

'I've just had another interview. I'm pretty sure it was MI5.'

'Bound to happen,' said Strike, and she took solace from his matter-of-fact tone. 'They've got to check you out, make sure you are who you claim to be. Isn't there anywhere you can go, other than home? I can't believe the press aren't onto us yet, but it must be imminent.'

'I could go back to Masham, I suppose,' Robin said, 'but they're bound to try there if they want to find me. That's where they came after the Ripper stuff.'

Unlike Strike, she had no friends of her own into whose anonymous homes she felt she could vanish. All her friends were Matthew's, too, and she had no doubt that, like her husband, they would be scared of harbouring anybody who was of interest to the security services. At a loss as to what to do, she went back to Albury Street.

Yet the press didn't come for her, even though the newspapers were hardly holding back on the subject of Chiswell. The *Mail* had already run a double-page spread on the various tribulations and scandals that had plagued Jasper Chiswell's life. '*Once mentioned as a possible prime minister*', '*sexy Italian Ornella Serafin, with whom he had the affair that broke up his first marriage*', '*voluptuous Kinvara Hanratty, who was thirty years his junior*', '*Lieutenant Freddie Chiswell, eldest son, died in the Iraq war his father had staunchly supported*', '*youngest child Raphael, whose drug-filled joy ride ended in the death of a young mother*'.

Broadsheets contained tributes from friends and colleagues: '*a fine mind, a supremely able minister, one of Thatcher's bright young men*', '*but for a somewhat tumultuous private life, there were no heights he might not have reached*', '*the public persona was irascible, even abrasive, but the Jasper Chiswell I knew at Harrow was a witty and intelligent boy*'.

Five days of lurid press coverage passed, yet still, the press's mysterious restraint on the subject of Strike and Robin's involvement held, and still, nobody had printed a word about blackmail.

On the Friday morning following the discovery of Chiswell's body, Strike was sitting quietly at Nick and Ilsa's kitchen table, sunlight pouring through the window behind him.

His host and hostess were at work. Nick and Ilsa, who had been trying for some years to have a baby, had recently adopted a pair of kittens whom Nick had insisted on calling Ossie and Ricky, after the two Spurs players he had revered in his teens. The cats, who had only recently consented to sit on the knees of their adoptive parents, had not appreciated the arrival of the large and unfamiliar Strike. Finding themselves alone with him, they had sought refuge on top of a kitchen wall cabinet. He was currently conscious of the scrutiny of four pale green eyes, which followed his every movement from on high.

Not that he was currently moving a great deal. Indeed, for much of the past half an hour he had been almost motionless, as he pored over the photographs that Robin had taken in Ebury Street, which he had printed out in Nick's study for convenience. Finally, causing Ricky to jump up in a flurry of upended fur, Strike isolated nine of the photographs and put the rest in a pile. While Strike scrutinised his selected images, Ricky settled back down, the tip of a black tail swaying as he awaited the detective's next move.

The first photograph that Strike had selected showed a close-up of the small, semi-circular puncture mark on Chiswell's left hand.

The second and third pictures showed different angles of the glass that had sat on the coffee table in front of Chiswell. A powdery residue was visible on the sides, above an inch of orange juice.

The fourth, fifth and sixth photographs Strike laid together side by side. Each showed a slightly different angle of the body, with slices of the surrounding room caught within its frame. Once again, Strike studied the ghostly outline of the buckled sword in the corner, the dark patch over the mantelpiece where a picture had previously hung and, beneath this, barely noticeable against the dark wallpaper, a pair of brass hooks spaced nearly a yard apart.

The seventh and eighth photographs, when placed side by side, showed the entirety of the coffee table. Kinvara's farewell letter sat on top of a number of papers and books, of which only a sliver of one letter was visible, signed by 'Brenda Bailey'. Of the books, Strike could see nothing but a partial title on an old cloth edition – 'CATUL' – and the lower part of a Penguin paperback. Also in shot was the upturned corner of the threadbare rug beneath the table.

The ninth and final picture, which Strike had enlarged from yet another shot of the body, showed Chiswell's gaping trouser pocket, in which something shiny and golden had been caught in the flash of Robin's camera. While he was still contemplating this gleaming object, Strike's mobile rang. It was his hostess, Ilsa.

'Hi,' he said, standing up and grabbing the packet of

Benson & Hedges and lighter that lay on the side behind him. With an eruption of claws on wood, Ossie and Ricky streaked along the top of the kitchen cabinets, in case Strike was about to start throwing things at them. Checking to see that they were too far away to make a break for the garden, Strike let himself outside and swiftly closed the back door. 'Any news?'

'Yes. Looks like you were right.'

Strike sat down on a wrought iron garden chair and lit up.

'Go on.'

'I've just had coffee with my contact. He can't speak freely, given the nature of what we're talking about, but I put your theory to him and he said "That sounds *very* plausible." Then I said, "Fellow politician?" and he said that sounded very likely, too, and I said I supposed that in that situation, the press would appeal, and he said, yes, he thought so, too.'

Strike exhaled.

'I owe you, Ilsa, thanks. The good news is, I'll be able to get out of your hair.'

'Corm, we don't mind you staying, you know that.'

'The cats don't like me.'

'Nick says they can tell you're a Gooner.'

'The comedy circuit lost a shining light when your husband decided on Medicine. Dinner's on me tonight and I'll clear out afterwards.'

Strike then rang Robin. She picked up on the second ring.

'Everything OK?'

'I've found out why the press aren't all over us. Della's taken out a super-injunction. The papers aren't allowed to report that Chiswell hired us, in case it breaks the blackmail story. Ilsa's just met her High Court contact and he confirmed it.'

There was a pause, while Robin digested this information.

'So Della convinced a judge that Chiswell made up the blackmail?'

'Exactly, that he was using us to dig dirt on enemies. I'm not surprised the judge swallowed it. The whole world thinks Della's whiter than white.'

'But Izzy knew why I was there,' protested Robin. 'The family will have confirmed that he was being blackmailed.'

Strike tapped ash absent-mindedly into Ilsa's pot of rosemary.

'Will they? Or will they want it all hushed up, now he's dead?'

He took her silence as reluctant agreement.

'The press will appeal the injunction, won't they?'

'They're already trying, according to Ilsa. If I were a tabloid editor, I'd be having us watched, so I think we'd better be careful. I'm going back to the office tonight, but I think you should stay home.'

'For how long?' said Robin.

He heard the strain in her voice and wondered whether it was entirely due to the stress of the case.

'We'll play it by ear. Robin, they know you were the one inside the Houses of Parliament. You became the story while he was alive and you're sure as hell the story now they know who you really are, and he's dead.'

She said nothing.

'How're you getting on with the accounts?' he asked.

She had insisted on being given this job, little though either of them enjoyed it.

'They'd look a lot healthier if Chiswell had paid his bill.'

'I'll try and tap the family,' said Strike, rubbing his eyes, 'but it feels tasteless asking for money before the funeral.'

'I've been looking through the photos again,' said Robin. In daily contact since finding the body, every one of their conversations wound its way back to the pictures of Chiswell's corpse and the room in which they had found him.

'Me too. Notice anything new?'

'Yes, two little brass hooks on the wall. I think the sword was usually—'

'—displayed beneath the missing painting?'

'Exactly. D'you think it was Chiswell's, from the army?'

'Very possibly. Or some ancestor's.'

'I wonder why it was taken down? And how it got bent?'

'You think Chiswell grabbed it off the wall to try and defend himself against his murderer?'

'That's the first time,' said Robin quietly, 'you've said it. "Murderer".'

A wasp swooped low over Strike but, repelled by his cigarette smoke, buzzed away again.

'I was joking.'

'Were you?'

Strike stretched out his legs in front of him, contemplating his feet. Stuck in the house, which was warm, he had not bothered with shoes and socks. His bare foot, which rarely saw sunlight, was pale and hairy. The prosthetic foot, a single piece of carbon fibre with no individual toes, had a dull gleam in the sunshine.

'There are odd features,' Strike said, as he waggled his remaining toes, 'but it's been a week and no arrest. The police will have noticed everything we did.'

'Hasn't Wardle heard anything? Vanessa's dad's ill. She's on compassionate leave, or I'd've asked her.'

'Wardle's deep in anti-terrorist stuff for the Olympics. Considerately spared the time to call my voicemail and piss himself laughing at my client dying on me, though.'

'Cormoran, did you notice the name on those homeopathic pills I trod on?'

'No,' said Strike. This wasn't one of the photographs he had isolated. 'What was it?'

'Lachesis. I saw it when I enlarged the picture.'

'Why's that significant?'

'When Chiswell came into our office and quoted that Latin poem at Aamir, and said something about a man of your habits, he mentioned Lachesis. He said she was—'

'One of the Fates.'

'—exactly. The one who "knew when everyone's number was up".'

Strike smoked in silence for a few seconds.

'Sounds like a threat.'

'I know.'

'You definitely can't remember which poem it was? Author, perhaps?'

'I've been trying, but no – wait—' said Robin suddenly. 'He gave it a number.'

'Catullus,' said Strike, sitting up straighter on the iron garden chair.

'How d'you know?'

'Because Catullus's poems are numbered, not titled, there was an old copy on Chiswell's coffee table. Catullus described plenty of interesting habits: incest, sodomy, child rape . . . he might've missed out bestiality. There's a famous one about a sparrow, but nobody buggers it.'

'Funny coincidence, isn't it?' said Robin, ignoring the witticism.

'Maybe Chiswell was prescribed the pills and that put him in mind of the Fate?'

'Did he seem to you like the kind of man who'd trust homeopathy?'

'No,' admitted Strike, 'but if you're suggesting the killer dropped a tube of lachesis as an artistic flourish—'

He heard a distant trill of bells.

'There's someone at the door,' said Robin, 'I'd better—'

'Check who it is, before you answer,' said Strike. He had had a sudden presentiment.

Her footsteps were muffled by what he knew was carpet.

'Oh, God.'

'Who is it?'

'Mitch Patterson.'

'Has he seen you?'

'No, I'm upstairs.'

'Then don't answer.'

'I won't.'

But her breathing had become noisy and ragged.

'You all right?'

'Fine,' she said, her voice constricted.

'What's he—?'

'I'm going to go. I'll call you later.'

The line went dead.

Strike lowered the mobile. Feeling a sudden heat in the fingers of the hand not holding his phone, he realised his cigarette had burned to the filter. Stubbing it out on the hot paving stone, he flicked it over the wall into the garden of a neighbour whom Nick and Ilsa disliked, and immediately lit another, thinking about Robin.

He was concerned about her. It was to be expected, of course, that she was experiencing anxiety and stress after finding a body and being interviewed by the security services, but he had noticed lapses in concentration over the phone, where she asked him the same thing two or three times. There was also what he considered her unhealthy eagerness to get back to the office, or out on the street.

Convinced that she ought to be taking some time out, Strike hadn't told Robin about a line of investigation he was currently pursuing, because he was sure she would insist on being allowed to help.

The fact was that, for Strike, the Chiswell case had begun, not with the dead man's story of blackmail, but with Billy Knight's tale of a strangled child wrapped in a pink blanket in the ground. Ever since Billy's last plea for help, Strike had been phoning the telephone number from which it had been made. Finally, on the previous morning, he had got an answer from a curious passer-by, who had confirmed the phone box's position on the edge of Trafalgar Square.

Strike. That bastard soldier with the one leg. Billy's fixated on him. Thinks he's going to rescue him.

Surely there was a chance, however tiny, that Billy might gravitate back to the place where he had last sought help? Strike had spent a few hours wandering Trafalgar Square on the previous afternoon, knowing how remote was the possibility that Billy would show up, yet feeling compelled to do something, however pointless.

Strike's other decision, which was even harder to justify, because it cost money the agency could currently ill afford, was to keep Barclay embedded with Jimmy and Flick.

'It's your money,' the Glaswegian said, when the detective gave him this instruction, 'but what'm I looking for?'

'Billy,' said Strike, 'and in the absence of Billy, anything strange.'

Of course, the next lot of accounts would show Robin exactly what Barclay was up to.

Strike had a sudden feeling that he was being watched. Ossie, the bolder of Nick and Ilsa's kittens, was sitting at the kitchen window, beside the kitchen taps, staring through the window with eyes of pale jade. His gaze felt judgmental.

37

I shall never conquer this completely. There will always be a doubt confronting me – a question.

Henrik Ibsen, *Rosmersholm*

Wary of breaching the conditions of the super-injunction, photographers stayed away from Chiswell's funeral in Woolstone. News organisations restricted themselves to brief, factual announcements that the service had taken place. Strike, who had considered sending flowers, had decided against it on the basis that the gesture might be taken as a tasteless reminder that his bill remained unpaid. Meanwhile the inquest into Chiswell's death was opened and adjourned, pending further investigations.

And then, quite suddenly, nobody was very interested in Jasper Chiswell. It was as though the corpse that had been borne aloft for a week upon a swell of newsprint, gossip and rumour, now sank beneath stories of sportsmen and women, of Olympic preparations and predictions, the country in the grip of an almost universal preoccupation, for whether they approved or disapproved of the event, it was impossible to ignore or avoid.

Robin was still phoning Strike daily, pressuring him to let

her come back to work, but Strike continued to refuse. Not only had Mitch Patterson twice more appeared in her street, but an unfamiliar young busker had spent the whole week playing on the pavement opposite Strike's office, missing chord changes every time he saw the detective and regularly breaking off halfway through songs to answer his mobile. The press, it seemed, had not forgotten that the Olympics would eventually end, and that there was still a juicy story to be run on the reason Jasper Chiswell had hired private detectives.

None of Strike's police contacts knew anything about the progress of their colleagues' investigation into the case. Usually able to fall asleep under even the most unpropitious conditions, Strike found himself unusually restless and wakeful by night, listening to the increased noise from the London now heaving with Olympics visitors. The last time he had endured such a long stretch of sleeplessness had been his first week of consciousness after his leg had been borne off by the IED in Afghanistan. Then he had been kept awake by a tormenting itch impossible to scratch, because he felt it on his missing foot.

Strike hadn't seen Lorelei since the night of the Paralympic reception. After leaving Charlotte in the street, he had set off for Trafalgar Square to try and locate Billy, with the result that he had been even later to dinner with Lorelei than he had expected. Tired, sore, frustrated at his failure to find Billy and jarred by the unexpected meeting with his ex, he had arrived at the curry house in the expectation, and perhaps the hope, that Lorelei would have already left.

However, she had not only been waiting patiently at the table, she had immediately wrong-footed him with what he mentally characterised as a strategic retreat. Far from forcing a discussion about the future of their relationship, she had apologised for what she claimed to have been a foolish and precipitate declaration of love in bed, which she knew had embarrassed him and which she sincerely regretted.

Strike, who had drunk most of a pint on sitting down, bolstering himself, as he had imagined, for the unpleasant task of explaining that he did not want their relationship to become either more serious or permanent, was stymied. Her claim that she had said 'I love you' as a kind of *cri de joie* rendered his prepared speech useless, and given that she had looked very lovely in the lamp-lit restaurant, it had been easier and pleasanter to accept her explanation at face value rather than force a rupture that, clearly, neither of them wanted. They had texted and spoken a few times during the subsequent week apart, though nowhere near as often as he had talked to Robin. Lorelei had been perfectly understanding about his need to keep a low profile for a while once he explained that his late client had been the government minister who had suffocated in a plastic bag.

Lorelei had even been unfazed when he refused her invitation to watch the opening ceremony of the Olympics with her, because he'd already agreed to spend the evening at Lucy and Greg's. Strike's sister was as yet unwilling to let Jack out of her sight, and had therefore declined Strike's offer to take him to the Imperial War Museum over the weekend, offering dinner instead. When he explained to Lorelei how matters stood, Strike could tell that she was hoping that he would ask her to come with him to meet some of his family for the first time. He said, truthfully, that his motive for going alone was to spend time with the nephew whom he felt he had neglected, and Lorelei accepted this explanation good-naturedly, merely asking whether he was free the following night.

As the taxi bore him from Bromley South station towards Lucy and Greg's, Strike found himself mulling the situation with Lorelei, because Lucy usually demanded a bulletin on his love life. This was one of the reasons he avoided these kinds of get-togethers. It troubled Lucy that her brother was still, at the age of nearly thirty-eight, unmarried. She had gone so far, on one embarrassing occasion, as to invite to dinner a woman whom she imagined he might fancy, which had taught him only that his sister grossly misjudged his taste and needs.

As the taxi bore him deeper and deeper into middle-class suburbia, Strike found himself face to face with the uncomfortable truth, which was that Lorelei's willingness to accept the casualness of their current arrangement did not stem from a shared sense of disengagement, but from a desperation to keep him on almost any terms.

Staring out of the window at the roomy houses with double garages and neat lawns, his thoughts drifted to Robin, who called him daily when her husband was out, and then to Charlotte, holding lightly to his arm as she walked down the Lancaster House staircase in her spike-heeled boots. It had been convenient and pleasurable to have Lorelei in his life these past ten and a half months, affectionately undemanding, erotically gifted and pretending not to be in love with him. He could let the relationship continue, tell himself that he was, in that meaningless phrase, 'seeing how things went', or he could face the fact that he had merely postponed what must be done, and the longer he let things drift, the more mess and pain would result.

These reflections were hardly calculated to cheer him up, and as the taxi drew up outside his sister's house, with the magnolia tree in the front garden, and the net curtain twitching excitedly, he felt an irrational resentment towards his sister, as though all of it was her fault.

Jack opened the front door before Strike could even knock. Given his state the last time Strike had seen him, Jack looked remarkably well, and the detective was torn between pleasure at his recovery, and annoyance that he hadn't been allowed to take his nephew out, rather than making the long and inconvenient journey to Bromley.

However, Jack's delight in Strike's arrival, his eager questions about everything Strike remembered about their time together in hospital, because he himself had been glamorously unconscious, were touching, as was the fact that Jack insisted upon sitting next to his uncle at dinner, and monopolised his attention throughout. It was clear that Jack felt that they had become more closely bonded for each having passed through the tribulation of emergency surgery. He demanded so many details of Strike's amputation that Greg put down his knife and fork and pushed away his plate with a nauseated expression. Strike had previously formed the impression that Jack, the middle son, was Greg's least favourite. He took a slightly malicious pleasure in satisfying Jack's curiosity, especially as he knew that Greg, who would usually have shut the conversation down, was exercising unusual restraint given Jack's convalescent state. Unconscious of all undercurrents, Lucy beamed throughout, her eyes barely leaving Strike and Jack. She asked Strike nothing about his private life. All she seemed to ask was that he would be kind and patient with her son.

Uncle and nephew left the dinner table on excellent terms, Jack choosing a seat next to Strike on the sofa to watch the Olympics opening ceremony and chattering nonstop while they waited for the live broadcast to start, expressing the hope, among other things, that there would be guns, cannons and soldiers.

This innocent remark reminded Strike of Jasper Chiswell

and his annoyance, reported by Robin, that Britain's military prowess was not to be celebrated on this largest of national stages. This made Strike wonder whether Jimmy Knight was sitting in front of a TV somewhere, readying himself to sneer at what he had castigated as a carnival of capitalism.

Greg handed Strike a bottle of Heineken.

'Here we go!' said Lucy excitedly.

The live broadcast began with a countdown. A few seconds in, a numbered balloon failed to burst. *Let it not be shit*, thought Strike, suddenly forgetting everything else in an upsurge of patriotic paranoia.

But the opening ceremony had been so very much the reverse of shit that Strike stayed to watch the whole thing, voluntarily missing his last train, accepting the offer of the sofa bed and breakfasting on Saturday morning with the family.

'Agency doing well, is it?' Greg asked him over the fry-up Lucy had cooked.

'Not bad,' said Strike.

He generally avoided discussing his business with Greg, who seemed to have been wrong-footed by Strike's success. His brother-in-law had always given the impression of being irritated by Strike's distinguished military career. As he fielded Greg's questions about the structure of the business, the rights and responsibilities of his freelance hires, Robin's special status as salaried partner and the potential for expansion, Strike detected, not for the first time, Greg's barely disguised hope that there might be something Strike had forgotten or overlooked, too much the soldier to easily navigate the civilian business world.

'What's the ultimate aim, though?' he asked, while Jack sat patiently at Strike's side, clearly hoping to talk more about the military. 'I suppose you'll be looking to build up the business so that you don't need to be out on the street? Direct them all from the office?'

'No,' said Strike. 'If I'd wanted a desk job I'd've stayed in the army. The aim is to build up enough reliable employees that we can sustain a steady workload, and make some decent money. Short term, I want to build up enough money in the bank to see us through the lean times.'

'Seems under-ambitious,' said Greg. 'With the free advertising you got after the Ripper case—'

'We're not talking about that case now,' said Lucy sharply, from beside the frying pan, and with a glance at his son Greg fell silent, permitting Jack to re-enter the conversation with a question about assault courses.

Lucy, who had loved every moment of her brother's visit, glowed with pleasure as she hugged him goodbye after breakfast.

'Let me know when I can take Jack out,' said Strike, while his nephew beamed up at him.

'I will, and thanks so much, Stick. I'll never forget what you—'

'I didn't do anything,' Strike said, thumping her gently on the back. 'He did it himself. He's tough, aren't you, Jack? Thanks for a nice evening, Luce.'

Strike considered that he had got out just in time. Finishing his cigarette outside the station, with ten minutes to kill before the next train to central London, he reflected that Greg had reverted over breakfast to that combination of chirpiness and heartiness with which he usually treated his brother-in-law, while Lucy's enquiries after Robin as he put on his coat had shown signs of becoming a wide-ranging enquiry into his relationships with women in general. His thoughts had just returned dispiritedly towards Lorelei when his mobile rang.

'Hello?'

'Is this Cormoran?' said an upper-class female voice he did not immediately recognise.

'Yes. Who's this?'

'Izzy Chiswell,' she said, sounding as though she had a head cold.

'Izzy!' repeated Strike, surprised. 'Er . . . how are you?'

'Oh, bearing up. We, ah, got your invoice.'

'Right,' said Strike, wondering whether she was about to dispute the total, which was large.

'I'd be very happy to give you payment immediately, if you could . . . I wonder whether you could possibly come and see me? Today, if that's convenient? How are you fixed?'

Strike checked his watch. For the first time in weeks he had nothing to do except make his way to Lorelei's later for dinner, and the prospect of collecting a large cheque was certainly welcome.

'Yeah, that should be fine,' he said. 'Where are you, Izzy?'

She gave him her address in Chelsea.

'I'll be about an hour.'

'Perfect,' she said, sounding relieved. 'I'll see you then.'

38

Oh, this killing doubt!

Henrik Ibsen, *Rosmersholm*

It was almost midday when Strike arrived at Izzy's mews house in Upper Cheyne Row in Chelsea, a quietly expensive stretch of houses which, unlike those of Ebury Street, were tastefully mismatched. Izzy's was small and painted white, with a carriage lamp beside the front door, and when Strike rang the doorbell she answered within a few seconds.

In her loose black trousers and a black sweater too warm for such a sunny day, Izzy reminded Strike of the first time he had met her father, who had been sporting an overcoat in June. A sapphire cross hung around her neck. Strike thought that she had gone as far into official mourning as modern-day dress and sensibilities would permit.

'Come in, come in,' she said nervously, not making eye contact, and standing back, waved him into an airy open-plan sitting and kitchen area, with white walls, brightly patterned sofas and an Art Nouveau fireplace with sinuous, moulded female figures supporting the mantelpiece. The long rear windows looked out onto a small, private courtyard, where expensive wrought iron furniture sat among carefully tended topiary.

'Sit down,' said Izzy, waving him towards one of the colourful sofas. 'Tea? Coffee?'

'Tea would be great, thanks.'

Strike sat down, unobtrusively extracted a number of uncomfortable, beaded cushions from beneath him, and took stock of the room. In spite of the cheery modern fabrics, a more traditional English taste predominated. Two hunting prints stood over a table laden with silver-framed photographs, including a large black and white study of Izzy's parents on their wedding day, Jasper Chiswell dressed in the uniform of the Queen's Own Hussars, Lady Patricia toothy and blonde in a cloud of tulle. Over the mantelpiece hung a large watercolour of three blond toddlers, which Strike assumed represented Izzy and her two older siblings, dead Freddie and the unknown Fizzy.

Izzy clattered around, dropping teaspoons and opening and closing cupboards without finding what she was looking for. At last, turning down Strike's offer of help, she carried a tray bearing a teapot, bone china mugs and biscuits the short distance between kitchenette and coffee table, and set it down.

'Did you watch the opening ceremony?' she asked politely, busy with teapot and strainer.

'I did, yeah,' said Strike. 'Great, wasn't it?'

'Well, I liked the first part,' said Izzy, 'all the industrial revolution bit, but I thought it went, well, a bit PC after that. I'm not sure foreigners will really get why we were talking about the National Health Service, and I must say, I could have done without all the rap music. Help yourself to milk and sugar.'

'Thanks.'

There was a brief silence, broken only by the tinkling of silver and china; that plush kind of silence achievable in London only by people with plenty of money. Even in winter, Strike's attic flat was never completely quiet: music, footsteps and voices filled the Soho street below, and when pedestrians forsook the area, traffic rumbled through the night, while the slightest breath of wind rattled his insecure windows.

'Oh, your cheque,' gasped Izzy, jumping up again to fetch an envelope on the kitchen side. 'Here.'

'Thanks very much,' said Strike, taking it from her.

Izzy sat down again, took a biscuit, changed her mind about eating it and put it on her plate instead. Strike sipped tea that he suspected was of the finest quality, but which, to him, tasted unpleasantly of dried flowers.

'Um,' said Izzy at last, 'it's quite hard to know where to begin.'

She examined her fingers, which were unmanicured.

'I'm scared you'll think I'm bonkers,' she muttered, glancing up at him through her fair lashes.

'I doubt that,' said Strike, putting down his tea and adopting what he hoped was an encouraging expression.

'Have you heard what they found in Papa's orange juice?'

'No,' said Strike.

'Amitriptyline tablets, ground up into powder. I don't know whether you – they're anti-depressants. The police say it's quite an efficient, painless suicide method. Sort of belt and – belt and braces, the pills and the – the bag.'

She took a sloppy gulp of tea.

'They were quite kind, really, the police. Well, they have training, don't they? They told us, if the helium's concentrated enough, one breath and you're . . . you're asleep.'

She pursed her lips together.

'The thing is,' she said loudly, in a sudden rush of words, 'I absolutely *know* that Papa would never have killed himself, because it was something he detested, he always said it was the coward's way out, awful for the family and everybody left behind.

'And it was strange: there was no packaging for the amitriptyline anywhere in the house. No empty boxes, no blister packs, nothing. Of course, a box would have Kinvara's name on it. Kinvara's the one who's prescribed amitriptyline. She's been taking them for over a year.'

Izzy glanced at Strike to see what effect her words had had. When he said nothing, she plunged on.

'Papa and Kinvara rowed the night before, at the reception, right before I came over to talk to you and Charlie. Papa had just told us he'd asked Raff to come over to the Ebury Street house next morning. Kinvara was furious. She asked why and Papa wouldn't tell her, he just smiled, and that infuriated her.'

'Why would—?'

'Because she hates all of us,' said Izzy, correctly anticipating Strike's question. Her hands were clutched together, the knuckles white. 'She's always hated anything and anyone that competed with her for Papa's attention or his affection, and she *particularly* hates Raff, because he looks just like his mother, and Kinvara's always been insecure about Ornella, because she's still very glamorous, but Kinvara doesn't like that Raff's a boy, either. She's always been frightened he'd replace Freddie, and maybe get put back in the will. Kinvara married Papa for his money. She never loved him.'

'When you say "put back"—'

'Papa wrote Raff out of his will when Raff ran – when he did the thing – in the car. Kinvara was behind that, of course, she was egging Papa on to have nothing more to do with Raff at all – anyway, Papa told us at Lancaster House he'd invited Raff around next day and Kinvara went quiet, and a couple of minutes later she suddenly announced that she was leaving and walked out. She claims she went back to Ebury Street, wrote Papa a farewell note – but you were there. Maybe you saw it?'

'Yes,' said Strike. 'I did.'

'Yes, so, she claims she wrote that note, packed her bag, then caught the train back to Woolstone.

'The way the police were questioning us, they seemed to think Kinvara leaving him would have made Papa kill himself, but that's just too ridiculous for words! Their marriage had been in trouble for ages. I think he'd been able to see through her for months and months before then. She's been telling crazy fibs and doing all kinds of melodramatic things to try and keep Papa's interest. I promise you, if Papa had believed she was about to leave him, he'd have been relieved, not suicidal, but of course, he wouldn't have taken that note seriously, he'd have known perfectly well it was more play-acting. Kinvara's got nine horses and no income. She'll have to be dragged out of Chiswell House, just like Tinky the First – my Grandpa's third wife,' Izzy explained. 'The Chiswell men seem to have a thing for women with big boobs and horses.'

Flushed beneath her freckles, Izzy drew breath, and said:

'I think Kinvara killed Papa. I can't get it out of my head, can't focus, can't think about anything else. She was convinced there was something going on between Papa and Venetia – she was suspicious from the first moment she saw Venetia, and then the *Sun* snooping around convinced her she was right to be worried – and she probably thought Papa reinstating Raff proved that he was getting ready for a new era, and I think she ground up her anti-depressants and put them in his orange juice when he wasn't looking – he always had a glass of juice first thing, that was his routine – then, when he became sleepy and couldn't fight her off, she put the bag over his head and *then*, after she'd killed him, she wrote that note to try and make it look as though she was the one who was going to divorce *him* and I think she sneaked out of the house after she'd done it, went home to Woolstone and pretended she'd been there when Papa died.'

Running out of breath, Izzy felt for the cross around her neck and played with it nervously, watching for Strike's reaction, her expression both nervous and defiant.

Strike, who had dealt with several military suicides, knew that survivors were nearly always left with a particularly noxious form of grief, a poisoned wound that festered even beyond that of those whose relatives had been dispatched by enemy bullets. He might have his own doubts about the way in which Chiswell had met his end, but he was not about to share them with the disorientated, grief-stricken woman beside him. What struck him chiefly about Izzy's diatribe was the hatred she appeared to feel for her stepmother. It was no trivial charge that she laid against Kinvara, and Strike wondered what it was that convinced Izzy that the rather childish, sulky woman with whom he had shared five minutes in a car could be capable of planning what amounted to a methodical execution.

'The police,' he said at last, 'will have looked into Kinvara's movements, Izzy. In a case like this, the spouse is usually the first one to be investigated.'

'But they're accepting her story,' said Izzy feverishly. 'I can tell they are.'

Then it's true, thought Strike. He had too high an opinion of the Met to imagine that they would be slapdash in confirming the movements of the wife who had had easy access to the murder scene, and who had been prescribed the drugs that had been found in the body.

'Who else knew Papa always drank orange juice in the

mornings? Who else had access to amitriptyline and the helium—?'

'Does she admit to buying the helium?' Strike asked.

'No,' said Izzy, 'but she wouldn't, would she? She just sits there doing her hysterical little girl act.' Izzy affected a higher-pitched voice. '"I don't know how it got into the house! Why are you all pestering me, leave me alone, I've been widowed!"

'I told the police, she attacked Papa with a hammer, over a year ago.'

Strike froze in the act of raising his unappetising tea to his lips.

'What?'

'She attacked Papa with a hammer,' said Izzy, her pale blue eyes boring into Strike, willing him to understand. 'They had a massive row, because – well, it doesn't matter why, but they were out in the stables – this was at home, at Chiswell House, obviously – and Kinvara grabbed the hammer off the top of a toolbox and smashed Papa over the head with it. She was bloody lucky she didn't kill him *then*. It left him with olfactory dysfunction. He couldn't smell and taste as well afterwards, and he got cross at the smallest things, but he insisted on hushing it all up. He bundled her off into some residential centre and told everyone she was ill, "nervous exhaustion".

'But the stable girl witnessed the whole thing and told us what had really happened. She had to call the local GP because Papa was bleeding so badly. It would have been all over the papers if Papa hadn't got Kinvara admitted to a psychiatric ward and warned the papers off.'

Izzy picked up her tea, but her hand was now shaking so badly that she was forced to put it back down again.

'She isn't what men think she is,' said Izzy vehemently.

'They all buy the little girl nonsense, even Raff. "She *did* lose a baby, Izzy . . ." But if he heard a *quarter* of what Kinvara says about him behind his back, he'd soon change his tune.

'And what about the open front door?' Izzy said, jumping subject. 'You know all about that, it's how you and Venetia got in, isn't it? That door's never closed properly unless you slam it. Papa knew that. He'd have made sure he closed it properly if he'd been in the house alone, wouldn't he? But if Kinvara was sneaking out early in the morning without wanting to be heard, she'd have had to pull it to and leave it, wouldn't she?

'She isn't very bright, you know. She'd have tidied away all the amitriptyline packaging, thinking it would incriminate her if she left it. I know the police think the absence of packaging is odd, but I can tell they're all leaning towards suicide and that's why I wanted to speak to you, Cormoran,' Izzy finished, edging a little forward in her armchair. 'I want to hire you. I want you to investigate Papa's death.'

Strike had known the request was coming almost from the moment the tea had arrived. The prospect of being paid to investigate what was, in any case, preoccupying Strike to the point of obsession, was naturally inviting. However, clients who sought nothing but confirmation of their own theories were always troublesome. He could not accept the case on Izzy's terms, but compassion for her grief led him to seek a gentler mode of refusal.

'The police won't want me under their feet, Izzy.'

'They don't have to know it's Papa's death you're investigating,' said Izzy eagerly. 'We could pretend we want you to investigate all those stupid trespasses into the garden that Kinvara claims have been going on. It would serve her bloody well right if we took her seriously now.'

'Do the rest of the family know you're meeting me?'

'Oh, yes,' said Izzy eagerly. 'Fizzy's all for it.'

'Is she? Does she suspect Kinvara, too?'

'Well, no,' said Izzy, sounding faintly frustrated, 'but she agrees a hundred per cent that Papa couldn't have killed himself.'

'Who does she think did it, if not Kinvara?'

'Well,' said Izzy, who seemed uneasy at this line of questioning, 'actually, Fizz has got this crazy idea that Jimmy Knight was involved somehow, but obviously, that's ridiculous. Jimmy was in custody when Papa died, wasn't he? You and I saw him being led away by the police the evening before, but Fizz doesn't want to hear that, she's *fixated* on Jimmy! I've said to her, "how did Jimmy Knight know where the amitriptyline and the helium were?" but she won't listen, she keeps going on about how Knight was after revenge—'

'Revenge for what?'

'What?' said Izzy restlessly, though Strike knew she had heard him. 'Oh – that doesn't matter now. That's all over.'

Snatching up the teapot, Izzy marched away into the kitchen area, where she added more hot water from the kettle.

'Fizz is irrational about Jimmy,' she said, returning with her teapot refilled and setting it down with a bang on the table. 'She's never been able to stand him since we were teenagers.'

She poured herself a second cup of tea, her colour heightened. When Strike said nothing, she repeated nervously:

'The blackmail business can't have anything to do with Papa dying. That's all over.'

'You didn't tell the police about it, did you?' asked Strike quietly.

There was a pause. Izzy turned steadily pinker. She sipped her tea, then said:

'No.'

Then she said, in a rush, 'I'm sorry, I can imagine how you and Venetia feel about that, but we're more concerned about Papa's legacy now. We can't face it all getting into the press, Cormoran. The only way the blackmail can have any bearing on his death is if it drove him to suicide, and I just don't believe he'd have killed himself over that, or anything else.'

'Della must have found it easy to get her super-injunction,' said Strike, 'if Chiswell's own family were backing her up, saying nobody was blackmailing him.'

'We care more about how Papa's remembered. The blackmail . . . that's all over and done with.'

'But Fizzy still thinks Jimmy might've had something to do with your father's death.'

'That's not – that would be a separate matter, from what he was blackmailing about,' said Izzy incoherently. 'Jimmy had a grudge . . . it's hard to explain . . . Fizz is just silly about Jimmy.'

'How does the rest of the family feel about bringing me in again?'

'Well . . . Raff isn't awfully keen, but it's nothing to do with him. I'd be paying you.'

'Why isn't he keen?'

'Because,' said Izzy, 'well, because the police questioned Raff more than any of the rest of us, because – look, Raff doesn't matter,' she repeated. 'I'll be the client, I'm the one who wants you. Just break Kinvara's alibis, I know you can do it.'

'I'm afraid,' said Strike, 'I can't take the job on those terms, Izzy.'

'Why not?'

'The client doesn't get to tell me what I can and can't investigate. Unless you want the whole truth, I'm not your man.'

'You *are*, I know you're the best, that's why Papa hired you, and that's why I want you.'

'Then you'll need to answer questions when I ask them, instead of telling me what does and doesn't matter.'

She glared at him over the rim of her teacup, then, to his surprise, gave a brittle laugh.

'I don't know why I'm surprised. I knew you were like this. Remember when you argued with Jamie Maugham in Nam Long Le Shaker? Oh, you must remember. You wouldn't back down – the whole table was at you at one point – what was the argument about, d'you—?'

'The death penalty,' said Strike, caught off guard. 'Yeah. I remember.'

For the space of a blink, he seemed to see, not Izzy's clean, bright sitting room, with its relics of a wealthy English past, but the louche, dimly lit interior of a Vietnamese restaurant in Chelsea where, twelve years previously, he and one of Charlotte's friends had got into an argument over dinner. Jamie Maugham's face was smoothly porcine in his memory. He had wanted to show up the oik whom Charlotte had insisted on bringing to dinner instead of Jamie's old friend, Jago Ross.

' . . . and Jamie got rilly, rilly angry with you,' Izzy said. 'He's quite a successful QC now, you know.'

'Must've learned to keep his temper in an argument, then,' said Strike, and Izzy gave another little giggle. 'Izzy,' he said, returning to the main issue, 'if you mean what you say—'

'—I do—'

'—then you'll answer my questions,' said Strike, drawing a notebook out of his pocket.

Irresolute, she watched him take out a pen.

'I'm discreet,' said Strike. 'In the past couple of years, I've been told the secrets of a hundred families and not shared one of them. Nothing irrelevant to your father's death will ever be mentioned again outside my agency. But if you don't trust me—'

'I do,' said Izzy desperately, and to his slight surprise, she leaned forward and touched him on the knee. 'I do, Cormoran, honestly, but it's . . . it's hard . . . talking about Papa . . .'

'I understand that,' he said, readying his pen. 'So let's start with why the police questioned Raphael so much more than the rest of you.'

He could tell that she didn't want to answer, but after a moment's hesitation she said:

'Well, I think it was partly because Papa phoned Raff early on the morning he died. It was the last call he made.'

'What did he say?'

'Nothing that mattered. It can't have had anything to do with Papa dying. But,' she rushed on, as though wanting to extinguish any impression her last words might have made, 'I think the *main* reason Raff isn't keen on me hiring you is that he rather fell for your Venetia while she was in the office and now, well, obviously, he feels a bit of an idiot that he poured his heart out to her.'

'Fell for her, did he?' said Strike.

'Yes, so it's hardly surprising he feels everyone's made a fool of him.'

'The fact remains—'

'I know what you're going to say, but—'

'—if you want me to investigate, it'll be me who decides what matters, Izzy. Not you. So I want to know,' he ticked off all the times she had said that information 'didn't matter' on his fingers as he named them, 'what your father called Raphael about the morning he died, what your father and Kinvara were rowing about when she hit him around the head with a hammer – and what your father was being blackmailed about.'

The sapphire cross winked darkly as Izzy's chest rose and fell. When at last she spoke, it was jerkily.

'It's not up to me to tell you about what Papa and Raff said to each other, the last t-time they spoke. That's for Raff to say.'

'Because it's private?'

'Yes,' she said, very pink in the face. He wondered whether she was telling the truth.

'You said your father had asked Raphael over to the house in Ebury Street the day he died. Was he rearranging the time? Cancelling?'

'Cancelling. Look, you'll have to ask Raff,' she reiterated.

'All right,' said Strike, making a note. 'What caused your stepmother to hit your father around the head with a hammer?'

Izzy's eyes filled with tears. Then, with a sob, she pulled a handkerchief out of her sleeve and pressed it to her face:

'I d-didn't want to tell you that b-because I d-didn't want you to think badly of Papa now he's . . . now he's . . . you see, he d-did something that . . .'

Her broad shoulders shook as she emitted unromantic snorts. Strike, who found this frank and noisy anguish more touching than he would have found delicate eye dabbing, sat in impotent sympathy while she tried to gasp out her apologies.

'I'm – I'm s—'

'Don't be silly,' he said gruffly. 'Of course you're upset.'

But she seemed deeply ashamed of this loss of control, and her hiccoughing return to calm was punctuated with further flustered 'sorrys'. At last, she wiped her face dry as roughly as though cleaning a window, said one final 'I'm so sorry', straightened her spine and said with a forcefulness Strike rather admired, given the circumstances:

'If you take the case . . . once we've signed on the dotted line . . . I'll tell you what Papa did that made Kinvara hit him.'

'I assume,' said Strike, 'the same goes for the reason that Winn and Knight were blackmailing your father?'

'Look,' she said, tears welling again, 'don't you see, it's Papa's memory, his legacy, now. I don't want those things to be the thing people remember about him – please help us, Corm. *Please.* I know it wasn't suicide, I *know* it wasn't . . .'

He let his silence do the work for him. At last, her expression piteous, she said with a catch in her voice:

'All right. I'll tell you all about the blackmail, but only if Fizz and Torks agree.'

'Who's Torks?' enquired Strike.

'Torquil. Fizzy's husband. We swore we wouldn't ever tell anyone, but I'll t-talk to them and if they agree, I'll t-tell you everything.'

'Doesn't Raphael get consulted?'

'He never knew anything about the blackmail business. He was in jail when Jimmy first came to see Papa and anyway, he didn't grow up with us, so he couldn't – Raff never knew.'

'And what about Kinvara?' asked Strike. 'Did she know?'

'Oh, yes,' said Izzy, and a look of malice hardened her usually friendly features, 'but she *definitely* won't want us to tell you. Oh, not to protect Papa,' she said, correctly reading Strike's expression, 'to protect herself. Kinvara benefited, you see. She didn't mind what Papa was up to, so long as she reaped the rewards.'

39

. . . naturally I talk as little about it as possible; it is better to be silent about such things.

Henrik Ibsen, *Rosmersholm*

Robin was having a bad Saturday, following an even worse night.

She had woken with a yelp at 4 a.m., with the sensation of being still tangled in the nightmare in which she had been carrying a whole bag full of listening devices through darkened streets, knowing that men in masks were following her. The old knife wound on her arm had been gaping open and it was the trail of her spurting blood that her pursuers were following, and she knew she would never make it to the place where Strike was waiting for the bag of bugs . . .

'What?' Matthew had said groggily, half asleep.

'Nothing,' Robin had replied, before lying sleepless until seven, when she felt entitled to get up.

A scruffy young blond man had been lurking in Albury Street for the past two days. He barely bothered to conceal the fact that he was keeping their house under observation. Robin had discussed him with Strike, who was sure that he was a journalist rather than a private detective, probably a junior one, dispatched to keep tabs on her because Mitch Patterson's hourly rate had become an unjustifiable expense.

She and Matthew had moved to Albury Street to escape the place where the Shacklewell Ripper had lurked. It was supposed to be a place of safety, yet it, too, had become contaminated by contact with unnatural death. Mid-morning, Robin had taken refuge in the bathroom before Matthew could realise she was hyperventilating again. Sitting on the bathroom floor, she had recourse to the technique she had learned in therapy, cognitive restructuring, which sought to identify the automatic thoughts of pursuit, pain and danger that sprang into her mind given certain triggers. *He's just some idiot who works for the* Sun. *He wants a story, that's all. You're safe. He can't get at you. You're completely safe.*

When Robin emerged from the bathroom and went downstairs, she found her husband slamming kitchen doors and drawers as he threw together a sandwich. He did not offer to make one for her.

'What are we supposed to tell Tom and Sarah, with that bastard staring through the windows?'

'Why would we tell Tom and Sarah anything?' asked Robin blankly.

'We're going to theirs for dinner tonight!'

'Oh, no,' groaned Robin. 'I mean, yes. Sorry. I forgot.'

'Well, what if the bloody journalist follows us?'

'We ignore him,' said Robin. 'What else can we do?'

She heard her mobile ringing upstairs and, glad of the excuse to get out of Matthew's vicinity, went to answer it.

'Hi,' said Strike. 'Good news. Izzy's hired us to look into Chiswell's death. Well,' he corrected himself, 'what she actually wants is for us to prove Kinvara did it, but I managed to broaden the remit.'

'That's fantastic!' whispered Robin, carefully closing the bedroom door and sitting down on the bed.

'I thought you'd be pleased,' said Strike. 'Now, what we need for starters is a line on the police investigation, especially forensics. I've just tried Wardle, but he's been warned not to talk to us. They seem to have guessed I'd still be sniffing around. Then I tried Anstis, but nothing doing, he's full time on the Olympics and doesn't know anyone on the case. So I was going to ask, is Vanessa back off compassionate leave?'

'Yes!' said Robin, suddenly excited. It was the first time she had had the useful contact, rather than Strike. 'But even better than Vanessa – she's dating a guy in forensics, Oliver, I've never met him, but—'

'If Oliver would agree to talk to us,' said Strike, 'that would be fantastic. Tell you what, I'll call Shanker, see whether he'll sell me something we can offer in exchange. Call you back.'

He hung up. Though hungry, Robin did not go back downstairs, but stretched out on the smart mahogany bed, which had been a wedding gift from Matthew's father. It was so cumbersome and heavy that it had taken the full complement of removal men, sweating and swearing under their breath, to haul it up the stairs in pieces and reassemble it in the bedroom. Robin's dressing table, on the other hand, was old and cheap. Light as an orange crate without its drawers in, it had required only one man to pick it up and place it between the bedroom windows.

Ten minutes later, her mobile rang again.

'That was quick.'

'Yeah, we're in luck. Shanker's having a rest day. Our interests happen to coincide. There's somebody he wouldn't mind the police picking off. Tell Vanessa we're offering information on Ian Nash.'

'Ian Nash?' repeated Robin, sitting up to grab pen and paper and make a note of the name. 'Who exactly—?'

'Gangster. Vanessa will know who he is,' said Strike.

'How much did it cost?' asked Robin. The personal bond between Strike and Shanker, profound in its way, never interfered with Shanker's rules of business.

'Half the first week's fee,' said Strike, 'but it'll be money well spent if Oliver comes across with the goods. How're you?'

'What?' said Robin, disconcerted. 'I'm fine. Why d'you ask?'

'Don't suppose it's ever occurred to you that I've got a duty of care, as your employer?'

'We're partners.'

'You're a salaried partner. You could sue for poor working conditions.'

'Don't you think,' said Robin, examining the forearm where the eight-inch purple scar still stood out, livid, against her pale skin, 'I'd've already done that, if I was going to? But if you're offering to sort out the loo on the landing—'

'I'm just saying,' persisted Strike, 'it'd be natural if you'd had a bit of a reaction. Finding a body isn't many people's idea of fun.'

'I'm absolutely fine,' lied Robin.

I have to be fine, she thought, after they had bidden each other goodbye. *I'm not losing everything, all over again.*

40

Your starting-point is so very widely removed from his, you see.

Henrik Ibsen, *Rosmersholm*

At six o'clock on Wednesday morning, Robin, who had again slept in the spare room, got up and dressed herself in jeans, T-shirt, sweatshirt and trainers. Her backpack contained a dark wig that she had bought online and which had been delivered the previous morning, under the very nose of the skulking journalist. She crept quietly downstairs, so as not to wake Matthew, with whom she had not discussed her plan. She knew perfectly well that he would disapprove.

There was a precarious peace between them, even though dinner on Saturday night with Tom and Sarah had been an awful affair: in fact, precisely because dinner had been so dreadful. It had started inauspiciously because the journalist had indeed followed them up the street. They had succeeded in shaking him off, largely due to Robin's counter-surveillance training, which had led them to dodge unseen out of a crowded Tube compartment just before the doors closed, leaving Matthew aggravated by what he considered undignified, childish tricks. But even Matthew could not lay the blame for the rest of the evening at Robin's door.

What had begun as light-hearted analysis over dinner of their failure to win the charity cricket match had turned suddenly nasty and aggressive. Tom had suddenly lashed out drunkenly at Matthew, telling him he was not half as good as he thought he was, that his arrogance had grated on the rest of the team, that, indeed, he was not popular in the office, that he put people's backs up, rubbed them the wrong way. Rocked by the sudden attack, Matthew had tried to ask what he had done wrong at work, but Tom, so drunk that Robin thought he must have started on the wine long before their arrival, had taken Matthew's hurt incredulity as provocation.

'Don't play the fucking innocent with me!' he had shouted. 'I'm not going to stand for it any more! Belittling me and fucking needling me—'

'Was I?' Matthew asked Robin, shaken, as they walked back towards the Tube in the darkness.

'No,' said Robin, honestly. 'You didn't say anything nasty to him at all.'

She added 'tonight' only in her head. It was a relief to be taking a hurt and bewildered Matthew home, rather than the man she usually lived with, and her sympathy and support had won her a couple of days' ceasefire at home. Robin was not about to jeopardise their truce by telling Matthew what she was planning this morning to throw the still-lurking journalist off her trail. She couldn't afford to be followed to a meeting with a forensic pathologist, especially as Oliver, according to Vanessa, had needed a great deal of persuasion to meet Strike and Robin in the first place.

Letting herself quietly out of the French windows into the courtyard behind the house, Robin used one of the garden chairs to clamber onto the top of the wall that divided their garden from that of the house directly behind them, of which the curtains were, mercifully, closed. With a muffled, earthy thud, she slid off the wall onto the neighbours' lawn.

The next part of her escape was a little trickier. She had first to drag a heavy ornamental bench in their neighbour's garden several feet, until it stood plumb with the fence, then, balancing on the back of it, she climbed over the top of the creosoted panel, which swayed precariously as she dropped down into a flowerbed on the other side, where she staggered and fell. Scrambling up again, she hurried across the new lawn to the opposite fence, in which there was a door to the car park on the other side.

To Robin's relief, the bolt opened easily. As she pulled the garden gate closed behind her, she thought ruefully of the footprints she had just left across the dewy lawns. If the neighbours woke early, it would be only too easy to discover whence had come the intruder who had invaded their gardens, shifted their garden furniture and squashed their begonias. Chiswell's killer, if killer there was, had been far more adept at covering their tracks.

Crouching down behind a parked Skoda in the deserted car park that served the garage-less street, Robin used the wing mirror to adjust the dark wig she had taken out of her backpack, then walked off briskly along the street that ran parallel with Albury Street, until she turned right into Deptford High Street.

Other than a couple of vans making early morning deliveries and the proprietor of a newsagent raising the metal security roller door from his shop front, there was hardly anybody around. Glancing over her shoulder, Robin felt a sudden rush, not of panic, but of elation: nobody was following her. Even so, she didn't remove her wig until she was safely on the Tube, giving the young man who had been eyeing her covertly over his Kindle something of a surprise.

Strike had chosen the Corner Café on Lambeth Road for its proximity to the forensics laboratory where Oliver Bargate worked. When Robin arrived, she found Strike standing outside, smoking. His gaze fell to the muddy knees of her jeans.

'Rough landing in a flowerbed,' she explained, as she came within earshot. 'That journalist is still hanging around.'

'Matthew give you a leg up?'

'No, I used garden furniture.'

Strike ground out his cigarette on the wall beside him and followed her into the café, which smelled pleasantly of frying food. In Strike's opinion, Robin looked paler and thinner than usual, but her manner was cheerful as she ordered coffee and two bacon rolls.

'One,' Strike corrected her. 'One,' he repeated regretfully to the man behind the counter. 'Trying to lose weight,' he told Robin, as they took a recently vacated table. 'Better for my leg.'

'Ah,' said Robin. 'Right.'

As he swept the crumbs from the table with his sleeve, Strike reflected, not for the first time, that Robin was the only woman he had ever met who had shown no interest in improving him. He knew that he could have changed his mind now and ordered five bacon rolls, and she would simply have grinned and handed them over. This thought made him feel particularly affectionate towards her as she joined him at the table in her muddy jeans.

'Everything OK?' he asked, salivating as he watched her put ketchup on her roll.

'Yes,' lied Robin, 'all good. How *is* your leg?'

'Better than it was. What does this bloke we're meeting look like?'

'Tall, black, glasses,' said Robin thickly, through a mouthful of bread and bacon. Her early morning activity had made her hungrier than she had been in days.

'Vanessa back on Olympics duty?'

'Yeah,' said Robin. 'She's badgered Oliver into meeting us. I don't think he was that keen, but she's after promotion.'

'Dirt on Ian Nash will definitely help,' said Strike. 'From what Shanker told me, the Met's been trying—'

'I think this is him,' whispered Robin.

Strike turned to see a lanky, worried-looking black man in rimless glasses standing in the doorway. He was holding a briefcase. Strike raised a hand in greeting and Robin slid her sandwich and coffee over to the next seat, to allow Oliver to sit opposite Strike.

Robin was not sure what she had expected: he was handsome, with his high-rise hairstyle and pristine white shirt, but seemed suspicious and disapproving, neither of which trait she associated with Vanessa. Nevertheless, he shook the hand Strike proffered and, turning to Robin, said:

'You're Robin? We've always missed each other.'

'Yes,' said Robin, shaking hands, too. Oliver's spotless appearance was making her feel self-conscious about her dishevelled hair and muddy jeans. 'Nice to meet you, at last. It's counter service, shall I get you a tea or coffee?'

'Er – coffee, yeah, that'd be good,' said Oliver. 'Thanks.'

As Robin went to the counter, Oliver turned back to Strike.

'Vanessa says you've got some information for her.'

'Might have,' said Strike. 'It all depends on what you've got for us, Oliver.'

'I'd like to know exactly what you're offering before we take this any further.'

Strike drew an envelope out of his jacket pocket and held it up.

'A car registration number and a hand-drawn map.'

Apparently this meant something to Oliver.

'Can I ask where you got this?'

'You can ask,' said Strike cheerfully, 'but that information's not included in the deal. Eric Wardle will tell you my contact's got a record of hundred per cent reliability, though.'

A group of workmen entered the café, talking loudly.

'This'll all be off the record,' said Strike quietly. 'No one'll ever know you talked to us.'

Oliver sighed, then bent down, opened his briefcase and extracted a large notebook. As Robin returned with a mug of coffee for Oliver and sat back down at the table, Strike readied himself to make notes.

'I've spoken to one of the guys on the team who did forensics,' Oliver said, glancing at the workmen who were now bantering loudly at the next table, 'and Vanessa's had a word with someone who knows where the wider investigation's going.' He addressed Robin. 'They don't know Vanessa is friendly with you. If it gets out that we helped—'

'They won't hear it from us,' Robin assured him.

Frowning slightly, Oliver opened his notebook and consulted the details he had jotted there in a small but legible hand.

'Well, forensics are fairly clear-cut. I don't know how much technical detail you want—'

'Minimal,' said Strike. 'Give us the highlights.'

'Chiswell had ingested around 500mg of amitriptyline, dissolved in orange juice, on an empty stomach.'

'That's a sizeable dose, isn't it?' asked Strike.

'It could have been fatal on its own, even without the helium, but it wouldn't have been as quick. On the other hand, he had heart disease, which would have made him more susceptible. Amitriptyline causes dysrhythmia and cardiac arrest in overdose.'

'Popular suicide method?'

'Yeah,' said Oliver, 'but it's not always as painless as people hope. Most of it was still in his stomach. Very small traces in the duodenum. Suffocation is what actually killed him, on analysis of the lung and brain tissue. Presumably the amitriptyline was a back-up.'

'Prints on the glass and the orange juice carton?'

Oliver turned a page in his notebook.

'The glass only had Chiswell's prints on it. They found the carton in the bin, empty, also with Chiswell's prints on, and others. Nothing suspicious. Just as you'd expect if it had been handled during purchase. Juice inside tested negative for drugs. The drugs went directly into the glass.'

'The helium canister?'

'That had Chiswell's prints on it, and some others. Nothing suspicious. Same as the juice carton, like it had been handled during purchase.'

'Does amitriptyline have a taste?' asked Robin.

'Yeah, it's bitter,' said Oliver.

'Olfactory dysfunction,' Strike reminded Robin. 'After the head injury. He might not have tasted it.'

'Would it have made him groggy?' Robin asked Oliver.

'Probably, especially if he wasn't used to taking it, but people can have unexpected reactions. He might've become agitated.'

'Any sign of how or where the pills were crushed up?' asked Strike.

'In the kitchen. There were traces of powder found on the pestle and mortar there.'

'Prints?'

'His.'

'D'you know whether they tested the homeopathic pills?' asked Robin.

'The what?' said Oliver.

'There was a tube of homeopathic pills on the floor. I trod on them,' Robin explained. 'Lachesis.'

'I don't know anything about them,' said Oliver, and Robin felt a little foolish for mentioning them.

'There was a mark on the back of his left hand.'

'Yes,' said Oliver, turning back to his notes. 'Abrasions to face and a small mark on the hand.'

'On the face, too?' said Robin, freezing with her sandwich in her hand.

'Yes,' said Oliver.

'Any explanation?' asked Strike.

'You're wondering whether the bag was forced over his head,' said Oliver; it was a statement, not a question. 'So did MI5. They know he didn't make the marks himself. Nothing under his own nails. On the other hand, there was no bruising to the body to show force, nothing disarranged in the room, no signs of a struggle—'

'Other than the bent sword,' said Strike.

'I keep forgetting you were there,' said Oliver. 'You know all this.'

'Marks on the sword?'

'It had been cleaned recently, but Chiswell's prints were on the handle.'

'What time of death are we looking at?'

'Between 6 and 7 a.m.,' said Oliver.

'But he was fully dressed,' mused Robin.

'From what I've heard about him, he was quite literally the kind of bloke who wouldn't have been caught dead in pyjamas,' said Oliver drily.

'Met's inclining to suicide, then?' asked Strike.

'Off the record, I think an open verdict is quite likely. There are a few discrepancies that need explaining. You know about the open front door, of course. It's warped. It won't close unless you shut it with force, but it sometimes jumps back open again if you slam it too hard. So it could have been accidental, the fact that it was open. Chiswell might not have realised he'd left it ajar, but equally, a killer might not have known the trick to closing it.'

'You don't happen to know how many keys to the door there were?' asked Strike.

'No,' said Oliver. 'As I'm sure you'll appreciate, Van and I had to sound only casually interested, asking all these questions.'

'He's a dead government minister,' said Strike. 'Surely you didn't have to sound too casual?'

'I know one thing,' said Oliver. 'He had plenty of reasons to kill himself.'

'Such as?' enquired Strike, pen poised over his notebook.

'His wife was leaving him—'

'Allegedly,' said Strike, writing.

'—they'd lost a baby, his eldest son died in Iraq, the family say he was acting strangely, drinking heavily and so on, and he had serious money problems.'

'Yeah?' said Strike. 'Like what?'

'He was almost wiped out in the 2008 crash,' said Oliver. 'And then there was . . . well, that business you two were investigating.'

'D'you know where the blackmailers were, at the time of—?'

Oliver made a swift, convulsive movement that nearly knocked over his coffee. Leaning towards Strike he hissed:

'There's a super-injunction out, in case you haven't—'

'Yeah, we've heard,' said Strike.

'Well, I happen to like my job.'

'OK,' said Strike, unperturbed, but lowering his voice. 'I'll rephrase my question. Have they looked into the movements of Geraint Winn and Jimmy—?'

'Yes,' said Oliver curtly, 'and both have alibis.'

'What are they?'

'The former was in Bermondsey with—'

'Not Della?' blurted Robin, before she could stop herself. The idea of his blind wife being Geraint's alibi had struck her, somehow, as indecent. She had formed the impression, whether naively or not, that Della stood apart from Geraint's criminal activity.

'No,' said Oliver tersely, 'and do we have to use names?'

'Who, then?' asked Strike.

'Some employee. He claims he was with the employee and the bloke confirmed it.'

'Were there other witnesses?'

'I don't know,' said Oliver, with a trace of frustration. 'I assume so. They're happy with the alibi.'

'What about Ji – the other man?'

'He was in East Ham with his girlfriend.'

'Was he?' said Strike, making a note of it. 'I saw him being marched off to a police van, the night before Chiswell died.'

'He was let off with a caution. But,' Oliver said quietly, 'blackmailers don't generally kill their victims, do they?'

'Not if they're getting money out of them,' said Strike, still writing. 'But Knight wasn't.'

Oliver looked at his watch.

'Couple more things,' said Strike equably, his elbow still planted on the envelope containing Ian Nash's details. 'Does Vanessa know anything about a phone call to his son that Chiswell made on the morning of his death?'

'Yeah, she said something about that,' said Oliver, flicking backwards and forwards through his notebook to find the information. 'Yeah, he made two calls just after 6 a.m. First to his wife, then to his son.'

Strike and Robin looked at each other again.

'We knew about the call to Raphael. He called his wife as well?'

'Yeah, he called her first.'

Oliver seemed to read their reaction correctly, because he said:

'The wife's totally in the clear. She was the first person they investigated, once they were satisfied it wasn't politically motivated, obviously.

'A neighbour saw her go into the house on Ebury Street the evening before and come out shortly afterwards with a bag, two hours before her husband came back. A taxi driver picked her up halfway down the street and took her to Paddington. She was caught on camera on the train back to wherever she lives – is it Oxfordshire? – and apparently there was someone at the house when she got home, who can vouch for the fact that she arrived there before midnight and never left again until the police came round to tell her Chiswell was dead. Multiple witnesses to her whole journey.'

'Who was at the house with her?'

'That, I don't know.' Oliver's eyes moved to the envelope still lying beneath Strike's elbow. 'And that really is everything I've got.'

Strike had asked everything he had wanted to know, and had gained a couple of bits of information he had not expected, including the abrasions to Chiswell's face, his poor finances and the phone call to Kinvara in the early morning.

'You've been a big help,' he told Oliver, sliding the envelope across the table. 'Much appreciated.'

Oliver appeared relieved that the encounter was over. He

stood up and, with one more hasty handshake and a nod to Robin, departed the café. Once Oliver had stridden out of sight, Robin sat back in her chair and sighed.

'What's that glum expression for?' asked Strike, draining his mug of tea.

'This is going to be the shortest job on record. Izzy wants us to prove it was Kinvara.'

'She wants the truth about her father's death,' said Strike, but he grinned at Robin's sceptical expression, 'and, yeah, she's hoping it was Kinvara. Well, we'll have to see whether we can break all those alibis, won't we? I'm going to Woolstone on Saturday. Izzy's invited me over to Chiswell House, so I can meet her sister. Are you in? I'd rather not drive, the state my leg's in at the moment.'

'Yes, of course,' said Robin immediately.

The idea of getting out of London with Strike, even for a day, was so appealing that she did not bother to consider whether she and Matthew had plans, but surely, in the glow of their unexpected rapprochement, he would raise no difficulties. After all, she had not worked for a week and a half. 'We can take the Land Rover. It'll be better on country roads than your BMW.'

'You might need diversionary tactics if that hack's still watching you,' said Strike.

'I think I could probably throw them off more easily in a car than on foot.'

'Yeah, you probably could,' said Strike.

Robin was in possession of an advanced driving qualification. Though he had never told her so, Robin was the only person by whom he would willingly be driven.

'What time are we supposed to be at Chiswell House?'

'Eleven,' said Strike, 'but plan to be away for the whole day. I fancy taking a look at the Knights' old place while we're there.' He hesitated. 'I can't remember whether I told you . . . I kept Barclay undercover with Jimmy and Flick.'

He was braced for annoyance that he had not discussed it with her, resentment that Barclay had been working when she wasn't, or, perhaps most justifiably, a demand to know what he was playing at, given the state of the agency's finances, but she simply said, with more amusement than rancour:

'You know you didn't tell me. Why did you keep him there?'

'Because I've got a gut feeling there's a lot more to the Knight brothers than meets the eye.'

'You always tell me to mistrust gut feelings.'

'Never claimed not to be a hypocrite, though. And brace yourself,' Strike added, as they got up from the table, 'Raphael's not happy with you.'

'Why not?'

'Izzy says he fell for you. Quite upset you turned out to be an undercover detective.'

'Oh,' said Robin. A faint pink blush spread over her face. 'Well, I'm sure he'll bounce back fast enough. He's that type.'

41

I was thinking of what brought us together from the first,
what links us so closely to one another . . .

Henrik Ibsen, *Rosmersholm*

Strike had spent many hours of his life trying to guess what he had done to cause the sullen silence of a woman in his vicinity. The best that could be said for the prolonged sulk in which Lorelei spent most of Friday evening was that he knew exactly how he had offended her, and was even prepared to concede that her displeasure was, to some extent, justified.

Within five minutes of his arrival at her flat in Camden, Izzy had called his mobile, partly to tell him about a letter that she had received from Geraint Winn, but mainly, he knew, to talk. She was not the first of his clients to assume that they had purchased, along with detective services, a mixture of father-confessor and therapist. Izzy gave every sign that she was settling in to spend her entire Friday evening talking to Strike, and the flirtatiousness that had been apparent in the knee touching of their last encounter was even more pronounced by phone.

A tendency to size Strike up as a potential lover was not uncommon in the sometimes fragile and lonely women he dealt with in his professional life. He had never slept with a client, in spite of occasional temptation. The agency meant too much to him, but even had Izzy held attraction for him, he would have been careful to keep his manner on the antiseptic side of professional, because she would be forever tainted in his mind by association with Charlotte.

In spite of his genuine desire to cut the call short – Lorelei had cooked, and was looking particularly lovely in a silky sapphire blue dress that resembled nightwear – Izzy had displayed the persistent adhesiveness of a teasel. It took Strike nearly three-quarters of an hour to disentangle himself from his client, who laughed long and loudly at even his mildest jokes, so that Lorelei could hardly fail to know that it was a woman who was at the end of the line. Hardly had he got rid of Izzy and begun to explain to Lorelei that she was a grief-stricken client, than Barclay had called with an update on Jimmy Knight. The mere fact that he had taken the second call, considerably briefer though it was, had, in Lorelei's eyes, compounded his original offence.

This was the first time he and Lorelei had met since she had retracted her declaration of love. Her wounded and affronted demeanour over dinner confirmed him in the unwilling belief that, far from wanting their no-strings arrangement to continue, she had clung to the hope that if she stopped pressuring him, he would be free to reach the realisation that he was, in fact, deeply in love with her. Talking on the phone for the best part of an hour, while dinner slowly shrivelled in the oven, had dashed her hopes of a perfect evening, and the reset of their relationship.

Had Lorelei only accepted his sincere apology, he might have felt like sex. However, by half-past two in the morning, at which time she finally burst into tears of mingled self-recrimination and self-justification, he was too tired and bad-tempered to accept physical overtures which would, he feared, assume an importance in her mind that he did not want to give them.

This has to end, he thought, as he rose, hollow-eyed and dark-jawed, at six o'clock, moving as quietly as possible in the hope that she would not wake before he made his way out of her flat. Forgoing breakfast, because Lorelei had replaced the kitchen door with an amusingly retro bead curtain that rattled loudly, Strike made it all the way to the top of the stairs to the street before Lorelei emerged from the dark bedroom, sleep tousled, sad and desirable in a short kimono.

'Weren't you even going to say goodbye?'

Don't cry. Please don't fucking cry.

'You looked very peaceful. I've got to go, Robin's picking me up at—'

'Ah,' said Lorelei. 'No, you wouldn't want to keep Robin hanging around.'

'I'll call you,' said Strike.

He thought he caught a sob as he reached the front door, but by making a noisy business of opening it, he could credibly claim not to have heard.

Having left in plenty of time, Strike made a detour to a handy McDonald's for an Egg McMuffin and a large coffee, which he consumed at an unwiped table, surrounded by other early Saturday risers. A young man with a boil on the back of his neck was reading the *Independent* right ahead of Strike, who read the words '*Sports Minister in Marriage Split*' over the youth's shoulder before he turned a page.

Drawing out his phone, Strike Googled 'Winn marriage'. The news stories popped up immediately: '*Minister for Sport Splits from Husband: Separation "Amicable"*', '*Della Winn Calls Time on Marriage*', '*Blind Paralympics Minister to Divorce*'.

The stories from major newspapers were all factual and on the short side, a few padded out with details of Della's impressive career within politics and outside. The press's lawyers would, of course, be particularly careful around the Winns just now, with their super-injunction still in place. Strike finished his McMuffin in two bites, jammed an unlit cigarette in his mouth and limped out of the restaurant. Out on the pavement he lit up, then brought up the website of a well-known and scurrilous political blogger on his phone.

The brief paragraph had been written only a few hours previously.

> Which creepy Westminster couple known to share a predilection for youthful employees are rumoured to be splitting at last? He is about to lose access to the nubile political wannabes on whom he has preyed so long, but she has already found a handsome young 'helper' to ease the pain of separation.

Less than forty minutes later, Strike emerged from Barons Court Tube station to lean up against the pillar-box in front of the entrance. Cutting a solitary figure beneath the Art Nouveau lettering and open segmented pediment of the grand station behind him, he took out his phone again and continued to read about the Winns' separation. They had been married over thirty years. The only couple he knew who had been together that long were the aunt and uncle back in Cornwall, who had served as surrogate parents to Strike and his sister during those regular intervals when his mother had been unwilling or unable to care for them.

A familiar roar and rattle made Strike look up. The ancient Land Rover that Robin had taken off her parents' hands was trundling towards him. The sight of Robin's bright gold head behind the wheel caught the tired and faintly depressed Strike off-guard. He experienced a wave of unexpected happiness.

'Morning,' said Robin, thinking that Strike looked terrible as he opened the door and shoved in a holdall. 'Oh, sod off,' she added, as a driver behind her slammed on his horn, aggravated by the time Strike was taking to get inside.

'Sorry . . . leg's giving me trouble. Dressed in a hurry.'

'No problem – *and you!*' Robin shouted at the driver now overtaking them, who was gesticulating and mouthing obscenities at her.

Finally dropping down into the passenger seat, Strike slammed the door and Robin pulled away from the kerb.

'Any trouble getting away?' he asked.

'What d'you—?'

'The journalist.'

'Oh,' she said. 'No – he's gone. Given up.'

Strike wondered just how difficult Matthew had been about Robin giving up a Saturday for work.

'Heard about the Winns?' he asked her.

'No, what's happened?'

'They've split up.'

'*No!*'

'Yep. In all the papers. Listen to this . . . '

He read aloud the blind item on the political website.

'God,' said Robin quietly.

'I had a couple of interesting calls last night,' Strike said, as they sped towards the M4.

'Who from?'

'One from Izzy, the other from Barclay. Izzy got a letter from Geraint yesterday,' said Strike.

'Really?' said Robin.

'Yeah. It was sent to Chiswell House a few days back, not her London flat, so she only opened it when she went back to Woolstone. I got her to scan and email it to me. Want to hear?'

'Go on,' said Robin.

'"My very dear Isabella—"'

'Ugh,' said Robin, with a small shudder.

'"As I hope you will understand",' read Strike, '"Della and I did not feel it appropriate to contact you in the immediate, shocking aftermath of your father's death. We do so now in a spirit of friendliness and compassion".'

'If you need to point that out . . . '

'"Della and I may have had political and personal differences with Jasper, but I hope we never forgot that he was a family man, and we are aware that your personal loss will be severe. You ran his office with courtesy and efficiency and our little corridor will be the poorer for your absence".'

'He always cut Izzy dead!' said Robin.

'Exactly what Izzy said on the phone last night,' replied Strike. 'Stand by, you're about to get a mention.

'"I cannot believe that you had anything to do with the almost certainly illegal activities of the young woman calling herself 'Venetia'. We feel it only fair to inform you that we are currently investigating the possibility that she may have accessed confidential data on the multiple occasions she entered this office without consent."'

'I never looked at anything except the plug socket,' said Robin, 'and I didn't access the office on "multiple occasions". Three. That's "a few", at most.'

'"As you know, the tragedy of suicide has touched our own family. We know that this will be an extremely difficult and painful time for you. Our families certainly seem fated to bump into each other in their darkest hours.

'"Sending our very best wishes, our thoughts are with all of you", etc, etc.'

Strike closed the letter on his phone.

'That's not a letter of condolence,' said Robin.

'Nope, it's a threat. If the Chiswells blab about anything you found out about Geraint or the charity, he'll go after them, hard, using you.'

She turned onto the motorway.

'When did you say that letter was sent?'

'Five, six days ago,' said Strike, checking.

'It doesn't sound as though he knew his marriage was over then, does it? All that "our corridor will be poorer for your absence" guff. He's lost his job if he's split with Della, surely?'

'You'd think so,' agreed Strike. 'How handsome would you say Aamir Mallik is?'

'What?' said Robin, startled. 'Oh . . . the "young helper"? Well, he's OK looking, but not model material.'

'It must be him. How many other young men's hands is she holding and calling darling?'

'I can't imagine him as her lover,' said Robin.

'"A man of your habits",' quoted Strike. 'Pity you can't remember what number that poem was.'

'Is there one about sleeping with an older woman?'

'The best-known ones are on that very subject,' said Strike. 'Catullus was in love with an older woman.'

'Aamir isn't in love,' said Robin. 'You heard the tape.'

'He didn't sound smitten, I grant you. I wouldn't mind knowing what causes the animal noises he makes at night, though. The ones the neighbours complain about.'

His leg was throbbing. Reaching down to feel the join between prosthesis and stump, he knew that part of the problem was having put on the former hurriedly, in the dark.

'D'you mind if I readjust—?'

'Carry on,' said Robin.

Strike rolled up his trouser leg and proceeded to remove

the prosthesis. Ever since he had been forced to take two weeks off wearing it, the skin at the end of his stump had shown a tendency to object to renewed friction. Retrieving E45 cream from his holdall, he applied it liberally to the reddened skin.

'Should've done this earlier,' he said apologetically.

Deducing from the presence of Strike's holdall that he had come from Lorelei's, Robin found herself wondering whether he had been too pleasurably occupied to worry about his leg. She and Matthew had not had sex since their anniversary weekend.

'I'll leave it off for a bit,' said Strike, heaving both prosthesis and holdall into the back of the Land Rover, which he now saw was empty but for a tartan flask and two plastic cups. This was a disappointment. There had always been a carrier bag full of food on the previous occasions they had ventured out of London by car.

'No biscuits?'

'I thought you were trying to lose weight?'

'Nothing eaten on a car journey counts, any competent dietician will tell you that.'

Robin grinned.

'"Calories Are Bollocks: the Cormoran Strike Diet".'

'"Hunger Strike: Car Journeys I Have Starved On".'

'Well, you should've had breakfast,' said Robin, and to her own annoyance, she wondered for the second time whether he had been otherwise engaged.

'I did have breakfast. Now I want a biscuit.'

'We can stop somewhere if you're hungry,' said Robin. 'We should have plenty of time.'

As Robin accelerated smoothly to overtake a couple of dawdling cars, Strike was aware of an ease and restfulness that could not be entirely ascribed to the relief of removing his prosthesis, nor even of having escaped Lorelei's flat, with its kitschy décor and its heartsore occupant. The very fact that he had removed his leg while Robin drove, and was not sitting with all muscles clenched, was highly unusual. Not only had he had to work hard to overcome anxiety at being driven by other people in the aftermath of the explosion that had blown off his leg, he had a secret but deep-rooted aversion to women drivers, a prejudice he ascribed largely to early, nerve-wracking experiences with all his female relatives. Yet it was not merely a prosaic appreciation of her competence that had caused that sudden lifting of the heart when he had seen her driving towards him this morning. Now, watching the road, he experienced a spasm of memory, sharp with both pleasure and pain; his nostrils seemed to be full again with the smell of white roses, as he held her on the stairs at her wedding and he felt her mouth beneath his in the hot fug of a hospital car park.

'Could you pass me my sunglasses?' asked Robin. 'In my bag there.'

He handed them over.

'Want a tea?'

'I'll wait,' said Robin, 'you carry on.'

He reached into the back for the thermos and poured himself a plastic cup full. The tea was exactly as he liked it.

'I asked Izzy about Chiswell's will last night,' Strike told Robin.

'Did he leave a lot?' asked Robin, remembering the shabby interior of the house in Ebury Street.

'Much less than you might've thought,' said Strike, taking out the notebook in which he had jotted everything Izzy had told him. 'Oliver was right. The Chiswells are on their uppers – in a relative sense, obviously,' he added.

'Apparently Chiswell's father spent most of the capital on

women and horses. Chiswell had a very messy divorce from Lady Patricia. Her family was wealthy and could afford better lawyers. Izzy and her sister are all right for cash through their mother's family. There's a trust fund, which explains Izzy's smart flat in Chelsea.

'Raphael's mother walked away with hefty child support, which seems to have nearly cleaned Chiswell out. After that, he plunged the little he had left into some risky equities advised by his stockbroker son-in-law. "Torks" feels pretty bad about that, apparently. Izzy would rather we didn't mention it today. The 2008 crash virtually wiped Chiswell out.

'He tried to do some planning against death duties. Shortly after he lost most of his cash, some valuable family heirlooms and Chiswell House itself were made over to the eldest grandson—'

'Pringle,' said Robin.

'What?'

'Pringle. That's what they call the eldest grandson. Fizzy's got three children,' Robin explained, 'Izzy was always banging on about them: Pringle, Flopsy and Pong.'

'Jesus Christ,' muttered Strike. 'It's like interviewing the Teletubbies.'

Robin laughed.

'—and otherwise, Chiswell seems to have been hoping he could put himself right by selling off land around Chiswell House and objects of less sentimental value. The house in Ebury Street's been remortgaged.'

'So Kinvara and all her horses are living in her step-grandson's house?' said Robin, changing up a gear to overtake a lorry.

'Yeah, Chiswell left a letter of wishes with his will, asking that Kinvara has the right to remain in the house lifelong, or until she remarries. How old's this Pringle?'

'About ten, I think.'

'Well, it'll be interesting to see whether the family honour Chiswell's request given that one of them thinks Kinvara killed him. Mind you, it's a moot point whether she'll have enough money to keep the place running, from what Izzy told me last night. Izzy and her sister were each left fifty grand, and the grandchildren get ten grand apiece, and there's hardly enough cash to honour those bequests. That leaves Kinvara with what's left from the house in Ebury Street once it's sold off and all other personal effects, minus the valuable stuff that was already put into the grandson's name. Basically, he's leaving her with the junk that wasn't worth selling and any personal gifts he gave her during the marriage.'

'And Raphael gets nothing?'

'I wouldn't feel too sorry for him. According to Izzy, his glamorous mother's made a career out of asset-stripping wealthy men. He's in line to inherit a flat in Chelsea from her.

'So all in all, it's hard to make a case for Chiswell being killed for his money,' said Strike. 'What *is* the other sister's bloody name? I'm not calling her Fizzy.'

'Sophia,' said Robin, amused.

'Right, well, we can rule her out. I've checked, she was taking a Riding for the Disabled lesson in Northumberland on the morning he died. Raphael had nothing to gain from his father's death, and Izzy thinks he knew it, although we'll need to check that. Izzy herself got what she called "a bit squiffy" at Lancaster House and felt a bit fragile the following day. Her neighbour can vouch for the fact that she was having tea in the shared courtyard behind their flats at the time of death. She told me that quite naturally last night.'

'Which leaves Kinvara,' said Robin.

'Right. Now, if Chiswell didn't trust her with the information that he'd called in a private detective, he might not have been honest about the state of the family finances, either. It's possible she thought she was going to get a lot more than she has, but—'

'—she's got the best alibi in the family,' said Robin.

'Exactly,' said Strike.

They had now left behind the clearly man-made border shrubs and bushes that had lined the motorway as it passed Windsor and Maidenhead. There were real old trees left and right now, trees that had predated the road, and which would have seen their fellows felled to make way for it.

'Barclay's call was interesting,' Strike went on, turning a couple of pages in his notebook. 'Knight's been in a nasty mood ever since Chiswell died, though he hasn't told Barclay why. On Wednesday night he was goading Flick, apparently, said he agreed with her ex-flatmate that Flick had bourgeois instincts – d'you mind if I smoke? I'll wind down the window.'

The breeze was bracing, though it made his tired eyes water. Holding his burning cigarette out of the car between drags, he went on:

'So Flick got really angry, said she'd been doing "that shitty job for you" and then said it wasn't her fault they hadn't got forty grand, at which Jimmy went, to quote Barclay, "apeshit". Flick stormed out and on Thursday morning, Jimmy texted Barclay and told him he was going back to where he grew up, to visit his brother.'

'Billy's in Woolstone?' said Robin, startled. She realised that she had come to think of the younger Knight brother as an almost mythical person.

'Jimmy might've been using him as a cover story. Who knows where he's really got to . . . Anyway, Jimmy and Flick reappeared last night in the pub, all smiles. Barclay says they'd obviously made up over the phone and in the two days he was away, she's managed to find herself a nice non-bourgeois job.'

'That was good going,' said Robin.

'How d'you feel about shop work?'

'I did a bit in my teens,' said Robin. 'Why?'

'Flick's got herself a few hours part time in a jewellery shop in Camden. She told Barclay it's run by some mad Wiccan woman. It's minimum wage and the boss sounds barking mad, so they're having trouble finding anyone else.'

'Don't you think they might recognise me?'

'The Knight lot have never seen you in person,' said Strike. 'If you did something drastic with your hair, broke out the coloured contact lenses again . . . I've got a feeling,' he said, drawing deeply on his cigarette, 'that Flick's hiding a lot. How did she know what Chiswell's blackmailable offence was? She was the one who told Jimmy, don't forget, which is strange.'

'Wait,' said Robin. 'What?'

'Yeah, she said, when I was following them on the march,' said Strike. 'Didn't I tell you?'

'No,' said Robin.

As she said it, Strike remembered that he had spent the week after the march at Lorelei's with his leg up, when he had still been so angry at Robin for refusing to work that he had barely spoken to her. Then they had met at the hospital, and he had been far too distracted and worried to pass on information in his usual methodical fashion.

'Sorry,' he said. 'It was that week after . . .'

'Yes,' she said, cutting him off. She, too, preferred not to think about the weekend of the march. 'So what exactly did she say?'

'That he wouldn't know what Chiswell had done, but for her.'

'That's weird,' said Robin, 'seeing as he's the one who grew up right beside them.'

'But the thing they were blackmailing him about only happened six years ago, after Jimmy had left home,' Strike reminded her. 'If you ask me, Jimmy's been keeping Flick around because she knows too much. He might be scared of ending it, in case she starts talking.

'If you can't get anything useful out of her, you can pretend selling earrings isn't for you and leave, but the state their relationship's in, I think Flick might be in the mood to confide in a friendly stranger. Don't forget,' he said, throwing the end of his cigarette out of the window and winding it back up, 'she's also Jimmy's alibi for the time of death.'

Excited about the prospect of going back undercover, Robin said:

'I hadn't forgotten.'

She wondered how Matthew would react if she shaved the sides of her head, or dyed her hair blue. He had not put up much of a show of resentment at her spending Saturday with Strike. Her long days of effective house arrest, and her sympathy about the argument with Tom, seemed to have bought her credit.

Shortly after half past ten, they turned off the motorway onto a country road that wound down into the valley where the tiny village of Woolstone lay nestled. Robin parked beside a hedgerow full of Traveller's Joy, so that Strike could reattach his prosthesis. Replacing her sunglasses in her handbag, Robin noticed two texts from Matthew. They had arrived two hours earlier, but the alert of her mobile must have been drowned out by the racket of the Land Rover.

The first read:

All day. What about Tom?

The second, which had been sent ten minutes later, said:

Ignore last, was meant for work.

Robin was rereading these when Strike said:

'Shit.'

He had already reattached his prosthesis, and was staring through his window at something she could not see.

'What?'

'Look at that.'

Strike pointed back up the hill down which they had just driven. Robin ducked her head so that she could see what had caught his attention.

A gigantic prehistoric white chalk figure had been cut into the hillside. To Robin, it resembled a stylised leopard, but the realisation of what it was supposed to be had already hit her when Strike said:

'"Up by the horse. He strangled the kid, up by the horse."'

42

In a family there is always something or other going awry . . .

Henrik Ibsen, *Rosmersholm*

A flaking wooden sign marked the turning to Chiswell House. The drive, which was overgrown and full of pot-holes, was bordered on the left by a dense patch of woodland and on the right, by a long field that had been separated into paddocks by electric fences, and contained a number of horses. As the Land Rover lurched and rumbled towards the out-of-sight house, two of the largest horses, spooked by the noisy and unfamiliar car, took off. A chain reaction then occurred, as most of their companions began to canter around, too, the original pair kicking out at each other as they went.

'Wow,' said Robin, watching the horses as the Land Rover swayed over the uneven ground. 'She's got stallions in together.'

'That's bad, is it?' asked Strike, as a hairy creature the colour of jet lashed out with teeth and back legs at an equally large animal he would have categorised as brown, though doubtless the coat colour had some rarefied equine name.

'It's not usually done,' said Robin, wincing as the black stallion's rear legs made contact with its companion's flank.

They turned a corner and saw a plain-faced neo-classical house of dirty yellow stone. The gravelled forecourt, like the drive, had several potholes and was strewn with weeds, the windows were grubby and a large tub of horse feed sat incongruously beside the front door. Three cars were already sitting there: a red Audi Q3, a racing green Range Rover and an old and muddy Grand Vitara. To the right of the house lay a stable block and to the left, a wide croquet lawn that had long since been given over to the daisies. More dense woodland lay beyond.

As Robin braked, an overweight black Labrador and a rough-coated terrier came shooting out of the front door, both barking. The Labrador seemed keen to make friends but the Norfolk terrier, which had a face like a malevolent monkey, barked and growled until a fair-haired man, dressed in stripy shirt and mustard-coloured corduroy trousers, appeared at the doorway and bellowed:

'SHUT UP, RATTENBURY!'

Cowed, the dog subsided into low growls, all directed at Strike.

'Torquil D'Amery,' drawled the fair-haired man, approaching Strike with his hand outstretched. There were deep pockets beneath his pale blue eyes and his shiny pink face looked as though it never needed a razor. 'Ignore the dog, he's a bloody menace.'

'Cormoran Strike. This is—'

Robin had just held out her hand when Kinvara erupted out of the house, wearing old jodhpurs and a washed-out T-shirt, her loose red hair falling everywhere.

'For God's *sake* . . . don't you know *anything* about horses?' she shrieked at Strike and Robin. 'Why did you come up the drive so fast?'

'You should wear a hard hat if you're going in there, Kinvara!' Torquil called at her retreating figure, but she stormed away giving no sign that she had heard him. 'Not your fault,' he assured Strike and Robin, rolling his eyes. 'Got to take the drive at speed or you'll get stuck in one of the bloody holes, ha ha. Come on in – ah, here's Izzy.'

Izzy emerged from the house, wearing a navy shirtdress, the sapphire cross still around her neck. To Robin's slight surprise, she embraced Strike as though he was an old friend come to offer condolences.

'Hi, Izzy,' he said, taking half a step backwards to extricate himself from the embrace. 'You know Robin, obviously.'

'Oh, yah, got to get used to calling you "Robin" now,' said Izzy, smiling and kissing Robin on both cheeks. 'Sorry if I slip up and call you Venetia – I'm bound to, that's how I still think of you.

'Did you hear about the Winns?' she asked, in almost the same breath.

They nodded.

'Horrible, *horrible* little man,' said Izzy. 'I'm delighted Della's given him the push.

'Anyway, come along in . . . where's Kinvara?' she asked her brother-in-law as she led them into the house, which seemed gloomy after the brightness outside.

'Bloody horses are upset again,' said Torquil, over the renewed barking of the Norfolk terrier. 'No, fuck off, Rattenbury, you're staying outside.'

He banged the front door closed on the terrier, which began to whine and scratch at it instead. The Labrador padded quietly in Izzy's wake as she led them through a dingy hallway with wide stone stairs, into a drawing room on the right.

Long windows faced out over the croquet lawn and the

woods. As they entered, three white-blond children raced through the overgrown grass outside with raucous cries, then passed out of sight. There was nothing of modernity about them. In their dress and their hairstyles they might have walked straight out of the 1940s.

'They're Torquil and Fizzy's,' said Izzy fondly.

'Guilty as charged,' said Torquil, proudly. 'M'wife's upstairs, I'll go and get her.'

As Robin turned away from the window she caught a whiff of a strong, heady scent that gave her an unaccountable feeling of tension until she spotted the vase of stargazer lilies standing on a table behind a sofa. They matched the faded curtains, once scarlet and now a washed-out pale rose, and the frayed fabric on the walls, where two patches of darker crimson showed that pictures had been removed. Everything was threadbare and worn. Over the mantelpiece hung one of the few remaining paintings, which showed a stabled horse with a splashy brown and white coat, its nose touching a starkly white foal curled in the straw.

Beneath this painting, and standing so quietly that they had not immediately noticed him, was Raphael. With his back to the empty grate, hands in the pockets of his jeans, he appeared more Italian than ever in this very English room, with its faded tapestry cushions, its gardening books piled in a heap on a small table and its chipped Chinoiserie lamps.

'Hi, Raff,' said Robin.

'Hello, Robin,' he said, unsmiling.

'This is Cormoran Strike, Raff,' said Izzy. Raphael didn't move, so Strike walked over to him to shake hands, which Raphael did reluctantly, returning his hand to his jeans immediately afterwards.

'Yah, so, Fizz and I were just talking about Winn,' said Izzy, who seemed greatly preoccupied with the news of the

Winns' split. 'We just hope to God he's going to keep his mouth shut, because now Papa's gorn, he can say whatever he likes about him and get away with it, can't he?'

'You've got the goods on Winn, if he tries,' Strike reminded her.

She cast him a look of glowing gratitude.

'You're right, of course, and we wouldn't have that if it weren't for you . . . and Venetia – Robin, I mean,' she added, as an afterthought.

'Torks, I'm downstairs!' bellowed a woman from just outside the room, and a woman who was unmistakably Izzy's sister backed into the room carrying a laden tray. She was older, heavily freckled and weather-beaten, her blonde hair streaked with silver, and she wore a striped shirt very like her husband's, though she had twinned hers with pearls. 'TORKS!' she bellowed at the ceiling, making Robin jump. 'I'M DOWN HERE!'

She set the tray with a clatter on the needlepoint ottoman that stood in front of Raff and the fireplace.

'Hi, I'm Fizzy. Where's Kinvara gorn?'

'Faffing around with the horses,' said Izzy, edging around the sofa and sitting down. 'Excuse not to be here, I expect. Grab a pew, you two.'

Strike and Robin took two sagging armchairs that stood side by side, at right angles to the sofa. The springs beneath them seemed to have worn out decades ago. Robin felt Raphael's eyes on her.

'Izz tells me you know Charlie Campbell,' Fizzy said to Strike, pouring everybody tea.

'That's right,' said Strike.

'Lucky man,' said Torquil, who had just re-entered the room.

Strike gave no sign he had heard this.

'Did you ever meet Jonty Peters?' Fizzy continued.

'Friend of the Campbells? He had something to do with the police ... no, Badger, these aren't for you ... Torks, what did Jonty Peters do?'

'Magistrate,' said Torquil promptly.

'Yah, of course,' said Fizzy, 'magistrate. Did you ever meet Jonty, Cormoran?'

'No,' said Strike, 'afraid not.'

'He was married to what's-her-name, lovely gel, Annabel. Did masses for Save the Children, got her CBE last year, so well-deserved. Oh, but if you knew the Campbells, you must have met Rory Moncrieff?'

'Don't think so,' said Strike patiently, wondering what Fizzy would have said if he'd told her that the Campbells had kept him as far from their friends and family as was possible. Perhaps she was equal even to that: *oh, but then, you must have run across Basil Plumley? They loathed him, yah, violent alcoholic, but his wife did climb Kilimanjaro for Dogs Trust ...*

Torquil pushed the fat Labrador away from the biscuits and it ambled away into a corner, where it flopped down for a doze. Fizzy sat down between her husband and Izzy on the sofa.

'I don't know whether Kinvara's intending to come back,' said Izzy. 'We might as well get started.'

Strike asked whether the family had heard any more about the progress of the police investigation. There was a tiny pause, during which the distant shrieks of children echoed across the overgrown lawn.

'We don't know much more than I've already told you,' said Izzy, 'though I think we all get the sense – don't we?' she appealed to the other family members, 'that the police think it's suicide. On the other hand, they clearly feel they have to investigate thoroughly—'

'That's because of who he was, Izz,' Torquil interrupted.

'Minister of the Crown, obviously they're going to look into it more deeply than they would for the bloke in the street. You should know, Cormoran,' he said portentously, adjusting his substantial weight on the sofa, 'sorry, gels, but I'm going to say it – personally, I think it *was* suicide.

'I understand, of course I do, that that's a hard thought to bear, and don't think I'm not happy you've been brought in!' he assured Strike. 'If it puts the gels' minds at rest, that's all to the good. But the, ah, male contingent of the family – eh, Raff? – think there's nothing more to it than, well, m'father-in-law felt he couldn't go on. Happens. Not in his right mind, clearly. Eh, Raff?' repeated Torquil.

Raphael did not seem to relish the implicit order. Ignoring his brother-in-law, he addressed Strike directly.

'My father was acting strangely in the last couple of weeks. I didn't understand why, at the time. Nobody had told me he was being blackm—'

'We're not going into that,' said Torquil quickly. 'We agreed. Family decision.'

Izzy said anxiously:

'Cormoran, I know you wanted to know what Papa was being blackmailed about—'

'Jasper broke no law,' said Torquil firmly, 'and that's the end of it. I'm sure you're discreet,' he said to Strike, 'but these things get out, they always do. We don't want the papers crawling all over us again. We're agreed, aren't we?' he demanded of his wife.

'I suppose so,' said Fizzy, who seemed conflicted. 'No, of course we don't want it all over the papers, but Jimmy Knight had good reason to wish Papa harm, Torks, and I think it's important Cormoran knows that, at least. You know he was *here*, in Woolstone, this week?'

'No,' said Torquil, 'I didn't.'

'Yah, Mrs Ankill saw him,' said Fizzy. 'He asked her whether she'd seen his brother.'

'Poor little Billy,' said Izzy vaguely. 'He wasn't right. Well, you wouldn't be, would you, if you were brought up by Jack o'Kent? Papa was out with the dogs one night years ago,' she told Strike and Robin, 'and he saw Jack *kicking* Billy, literally *kicking* him, all around their garden. The boy was naked. When he saw Papa, Jack o'Kent stopped, of course.'

The idea that this incident should have been reported to either police or social workers seemed not to have occurred to Izzy, or indeed her father. It was as though Jack o'Kent and his son were wild creatures in the wood, behaving, regrettably, as such animals naturally behaved.

'I think the less said about Jack o'Kent,' said Torquil, 'the better. And you say Jimmy had reason to wish your father harm, Fizz, but what he really wanted was money, and killing your father certainly wasn't going—'

'He was angry with Papa, though,' said Fizzy determinedly. 'Maybe, when he realised Papa wasn't going to pay up, he saw red. He was a holy terror when he was a teenager,' she told Strike. 'Got into far-left politics early. He used to be down in the local pub with the Butcher brothers, telling everybody that Tories should be hung, drawn and quartered, trying to sell people the *Socialist Worker* . . .'

Fizzy glanced sideways at her younger sister, who rather determinedly, Strike thought, ignored her.

'He was trouble, always trouble,' Fizzy said. 'The girls liked him, but—'

The drawing room door opened and, to the rest of the family's evident surprise, Kinvara strode in, flushed and agitated. After a little difficulty extricating himself from his sagging armchair, Strike succeeded in standing up and held out a hand.

'Cormoran Strike. How do you do?'

Kinvara looked as though she would have liked to ignore his friendly overture, but shook the offered hand with bad grace. Torquil pulled up another chair beside the ottoman, and Fizzy poured an extra cup of tea.

'Horses all right, Kinvara?' Torquil asked heartily.

'Well, Mystic's taken another chunk out of Romano,' she said with a nasty glance at Robin, 'so I've had to call the vet again. He gets upset every time somebody comes up the drive too fast, otherwise he's absolutely fine.'

'I don't know why you've put the stallions in together, Kinvara,' said Fizzy.

'It's a myth that they don't get along,' Kinvara snapped back. 'Bachelor herds are perfectly common in the wild. There was a study in Switzerland that proved they can coexist peacefully once they've established the hierarchy among themselves.'

She spoke in dogmatic, almost fanatic, tones.

'We were just telling Cormoran about Jimmy Knight,' Fizzy told Kinvara.

'I thought you didn't want to go into—?'

'Not the blackmail,' said Torquil hastily, 'but what a horror he was when he was younger.'

'Oh,' said Kinvara, 'I see.'

'Your stepdaughter's worried that he may have had something to do with your husband's death,' said Strike, watching her for a reaction.

'I know,' said Kinvara, with apparent indifference, her eyes following Raphael, who had just walked away from the grate to fetch a pack of Marlboro Lights that lay beside a table lamp. 'I never knew Jimmy Knight. The first time I ever laid eyes on him was when he turned up at the house a year ago to speak to Jasper. There's an ashtray beneath that magazine, Raphael.'

Her stepson lit his cigarette and returned, carrying the ashtray, which he placed on a table beside Robin, before resuming his position in front of the empty fireplace.

'That was the start of it,' Kinvara continued. 'The blackmail. Jasper wasn't actually there that night, so Jimmy talked to me. Jasper was furious when he came home and I told him.'

Strike waited. He suspected that he wasn't the only one in the room who thought Kinvara might break the family vow of *omerta* and blurt out what Jimmy had come to say. She refrained, however, so Strike drew out his notebook.

'Would you mind if I run through a few routine questions? I doubt there'll be anything you haven't already been asked by the police. Just a couple of points I'd like clarified, if you don't mind.

'How many keys are there, to the house in Ebury Street?'

'Three, as far as *I'm* aware,' said Kinvara. The emphasis suggested that the rest of the family might have been hiding keys from her.

'And who had them?' asked Strike.

'Well, Jasper had his own,' she said, 'and I had one and there was a spare that Jasper had given to the cleaning woman.'

'What's her name?'

'I've no idea. Jasper let her go a couple of weeks before he – he died.'

'Why did he sack her?' asked Strike.

'Well, if you must know, we got rid of her because we were tightening our belts.'

'Had she come from an agency?'

'Oh no. Jasper was old-fashioned. He put up a card in a local shop and she applied. I think she was Romanian or Polish or something.'

'Have you got her details?'

'No. Jasper hired and fired her. I never even met her.'

'What happened to her key?'

'It *was* in the kitchen drawer at Ebury Street, but after he died we found out that Jasper had removed it and locked it up in his desk at work,' said Kinvara. 'It was handed back by the ministry, with all his other personal effects.'

'That seems odd,' Strike said. 'Anyone know why he'd have done that?'

The rest of the family looked blank, but Kinvara said:

'He was always security conscious and he'd been paranoid lately – except when it came to the horses, of course. All the keys to Ebury Street are a special kind. Restricted. Impossible to copy.'

'Tricky to copy,' said Strike, making a note, 'but not impossible, if you know the right people. Where were the other two keys at the time of death?'

'Jasper's was in his jacket pocket and mine was here, in my handbag,' said Kinvara.

'The canister of helium,' said Strike, moving on. 'Does anybody know when it was purchased?'

Total silence greeted these words.

'Was there ever a party,' Strike asked, 'perhaps for one of the children—?'

'Never,' said Fizzy. 'Ebury Street was the place Papa used for work. He never hosted a party there that I can remember.'

'You, Mrs Chiswell,' Strike asked Kinvara. 'Can you remember any occasion—?'

'No,' she said, cutting across him. 'I've already told the police this. Jasper must have bought it himself, there's no other explanation.'

'Has a receipt been found? A credit card bill?'

'He probably paid cash,' said Torquil helpfully.

'Another thing I'd like to clear up,' Strike said, working

down the list he had made himself, 'is this business of the phone calls the minister made on the morning of his death. Apparently he called you, Mrs Chiswell, and then you, Raphael.'

Raphael nodded. Kinvara said:

'He wanted to know whether I meant it when I said I was leaving and I said yes, I did. It wasn't a long conversation. I didn't know – I didn't know who your assistant really was. She appeared out of nowhere and Jasper was odd in his manner when I asked about her and I – I was very upset. I thought there was something going on.'

'Were you surprised that your husband waited until the morning to call you about the note you'd left?' asked Strike.

'He told me he hadn't spotted it when he came in.'

'Where had you left it?'

'On his bedside table. He was probably drunk when he got back. He's been – he *was* – drinking heavily. Ever since the blackmail business started.'

The Norfolk terrier that had been shut out of the house suddenly popped up at one of the long windows and began barking at them again.

'Bloody dog,' said Torquil.

'He misses Jasper,' said Kinvara. 'He was Jasper's d-dog—'

She stood up abruptly and walked away to snatch some tissues from a box sitting on top of the gardening books. Everybody looked uncomfortable. The terrier barked on and on. The sleeping Labrador woke and let out a single deep bark in return, before one of the tow-headed children reappeared on the lawn, shouting for the Norfolk terrier to come and play ball. It bounded off again.

'Good boy, Pringle!' shouted Torquil.

In the absence of barking, Kinvara's small gulps and the sounds of the Labrador flopping down to sleep again filled the room. Izzy, Fizzy and Torquil exchanged awkward glances, while Raphael stared rather stonily ahead. Little though she liked Kinvara, Robin found the family's inaction unfeeling.

'Where did that picture come from?' asked Torquil, with an artificial air of interest, squinting at the equine painting over Raphael's head. 'New, isn't it?'

'That was one of Tinky's,' said Fizzy, squinting up at it. 'She brought a bunch of horsey junk over from Ireland with her.'

'See that foal?' said Torquil, staring critically at the picture. 'You know what it looks like? Lethal white syndrome. Heard of it?' he asked his wife and sister-in-law. '*You'll* know all about that, Kinvara,' he said, clearly under the impression that he was graciously offering a way back into polite conversation. 'Pure white foal, seems healthy when it's born, but defective bowel. Can't pass faeces. M'father bred horses,' he explained to Strike. 'They can't survive, lethal whites. The tragedy is that they're born alive, so the mare feeds them, gets attached and then—'

'Torks,' said Fizzy tensely, but it was too late. Kinvara blundered out of the room. The door slammed.

'What?' said Torquil, surprised. 'What have I—?'

'*Baby*,' whispered Fizzy.

'Oh, Lord,' he said, 'I clean forgot.'

He got to his feet, hitched up his mustard corduroys, embarrassed and defensive.

'Oh, come on,' he said, to the room at large. 'I couldn't expect her to take it that way. Horses in a bloody painting!'

'You know what she's like,' said Fizzy, 'about *anything* connected with birth. Sorry,' she said to Strike and Robin. 'She had a baby that didn't survive, you see. Very sensitive on the subject.'

Torquil approached the painting and squinted over Raphael's head at words etched on a small plaque set into the frame.

'"Mare Mourning",' he read. 'There you are, you see,' he said, with an air of triumph. 'Foal *is* dead.'

'Kinvara likes it,' said Raphael unexpectedly, 'because the mare reminds her of Lady.'

'Who?' said Torquil.

'The mare that got laminitis.'

'What's laminitis?' asked Strike.

'A disease of the hoof,' Robin told him.

'Oh, do you ride?' asked Fizzy keenly.

'I used to.'

'Laminitis is serious,' Fizzy told Strike. 'It can cripple them. They need a lot of care, and sometimes nothing can be done, so it's kindest—'

'My stepmother had been nursing this mare for weeks,' Raphael told Strike, 'getting up in the middle of the night and so on. My father waited—'

'Raff, this really hasn't got anything to do with anything,' said Izzy.

'—waited,' continued Raphael doggedly, 'until Kinvara went out one day, called in the vet without telling her and had the horse put down.'

'Lady was suffering,' said Izzy. 'Papa told me what a state she was in. It was pure selfishness, keeping her alive.'

'Yeah, well,' said Raphael, his eyes on the lawn beyond the windows, 'if I'd gone out and come back to the corpse of an animal I loved, I might've reached for the nearest blunt instrument as well.'

'Raff,' said Izzy, 'please!'

'You're the one who wanted this, Izzy,' he said, with grim satisfaction. 'D'you really think Mr Strike and his glamorous assistant aren't going to find Tegan and talk to her? They'll soon know what a shit Dad could—'

'Raff!' said Fizzy sharply.

'Steady on, old chap,' said Torquil, something that Robin had never thought to hear outside a book. 'This whole thing's been bloody upsetting, but there's no need for that.'

Ignoring all of them, Raphael turned back to Strike.

'I suppose your next question was going to be, what did my father say to *me*, when he called me that morning?'

'That's right,' said Strike.

'He ordered me down here,' said Raphael.

'Here?' repeated Strike. 'Woolstone?'

'*Here*,' said Raphael. 'This house. He told me he thought Kinvara was going to do something stupid. He sounded woolly. A bit odd. Like he had a heavy hangover.'

'What did you understand by "something stupid"?' asked Strike, his pen poised over his pad.

'Well, she's got form at threatening to top herself,' said Raff, 'so that, I suppose. Or he might've been afraid she was going to torch what little he had left.' He gestured around the shabby room. 'As you can see, that wasn't much.'

'Did he tell you she was leaving him?'

'I got the impression that things were bad between them, but I can't remember his exact words. He wasn't very coherent.'

'Did you do as he asked?' asked Strike.

'Yep,' said Raphael. 'Got in my car like an obedient son, drove all the way here and found Kinvara alive and well in the kitchen, raging about Venetia – Robin, I mean,' he corrected himself. 'As you may have gathered, Kinvara thought Dad was fucking her.'

'Raff!' said Fizzy, sounding outraged.

'There's no need,' said Torquil, 'for that kind of language.'

Everybody was carefully avoiding catching Robin's eye. She knew she had turned red.

'Seems odd, doesn't it?' Strike asked. 'Your father asking you to come all the way down to Oxfordshire, when there were people far closer he could have asked to keep an eye on his wife? Didn't I hear that there was someone here overnight?'

Izzy piped up before Raphael could answer.

'Tegan *was* here that night – the stable girl – because Kinvara won't leave the horses without a sitter,' she said, and then, correctly anticipating Strike's next question, 'I'm afraid nobody's got any contact details for her, because Kinvara had a row with her right after Papa died, and Tegan walked out. I don't actually know where she's working now. Don't forget, though,' said Izzy, leaning forwards and addressing Strike earnestly, 'Tegan was probably fast asleep when Kinvara claims she came back here. This is a big house. Kinvara could have claimed to have come back any time and Tegan might not have known.'

'If Kinvara was there with him in Ebury Street, why would he tell me to come and find her here?' Raphael asked, exasperated. 'And how do you explain how she got here ahead of me?'

Izzy looked as though she would like to make a good retort to this, but appeared unable to think of one. Strike knew now why Izzy had said that the content of Chiswell's phone call to his son 'didn't matter': it further undermined the case for Kinvara as murderer.

'What's Tegan's surname?' he asked.

'Butcher,' said Izzy.

'Any relation to the Butcher brothers Jimmy Knight used to hang around with?' Strike asked.

Robin thought the three on the sofa seemed to be avoiding each other's eyes. Fizzy then answered.

'Yes, as a matter of fact, but—'

'I suppose I could try and contact the family, see whether they'll give me Tegan's number,' said Izzy. 'Yes, I'll do that, Cormoran, and let you know how I get on.'

Strike turned back to Raphael.

'So, did you set off immediately after your father asked you to go to Kinvara?'

'No, I ate something, first, and showered,' said Raphael. 'I wasn't exactly looking forward to dealing with her. She and I aren't each other's favourite people. I got here around nine.'

'How long did you stay?'

'Well, in the end, I was here for hours,' said Raphael quietly. 'A couple of police arrived to break the news that Dad was dead. I could hardly walk out after that, could I? Kinvara nearly coll—'

The door reopened and Kinvara walked back in, returned to her hard-backed chair, her face set, tissues clutched in her hand.

'I've only got five minutes,' she said. 'The vet's just called, he's in the area, so he'll pop in to see Romano. I can't stay.'

'Could I ask something?' Robin asked Strike. 'I know it might be nothing at all,' she said, to the room at large, 'but there was a small blue tube of homeopathic pills on the floor beside the minister when I found him. Homeopathy didn't seem to be the kind of thing he'd—'

'What kind of pills?' asked Kinvara sharply, to Robin's surprise.

'Lachesis,' said Robin.

'In a small blue tube?'

'Yes. Were they yours?'

'Yes, they were!'

'You left them in Ebury Street?' asked Strike.

'No, I lost them weeks ago . . . but I never had them *there*,' she said, frowning, more to herself than to the room. 'I bought them in London, because the pharmacy in Woolstone didn't have any.'

She frowned, clearly reconstructing events in her mind.

'I remember, I tasted a couple outside the chemists, because I wanted to know whether he'd notice them in his feed—'

'Sorry, what?' asked Robin, unsure she had heard correctly.

'Mystic's feed,' said Kinvara. 'I was going to give them to Mystic.'

'You were going to give homeopathic tablets to a *horse*?' said Torquil, inviting everyone else to agree that this was funny.

'Jasper thought it was a ludicrous idea, too,' said Kinvara vaguely, still lost in recollection. 'Yes, I opened them up right after I'd paid for them, took a couple, and,' she mimed the action, 'put the tube in my jacket pocket, but when I got home, they weren't there any more. I thought I must have dropped them somehow . . . '

Then she gave a little gasp and turned red. She seemed to be boggling at some inner, private realisation. Then, realising that everybody was still watching her, she said:

'I travelled home from London with Jasper that day. We met at the station, got the train together . . . he took them out of my pocket! He stole them, so I couldn't give them to Mystic!'

'Kinvara, don't be so utterly ridiculous!' said Fizzy, with a short laugh.

Raphael suddenly ground out his cigarette in the china ashtray at Robin's elbow. He seemed to be refraining from comment with difficulty.

'Did you buy more?' Robin asked Kinvara.

'Yes,' said Kinvara, who seemed almost disorientated with shock, though Robin thought her conclusion as to what had happened to her pills very strange. 'They were in a different bottle, though. That blue tube, that's the one I bought first.'

'Isn't homeopathy just placebo effect?' Torquil enquired of the room at large. 'How could a *horse*—?'

'Torks,' muttered Fizzy, through gritted teeth. 'Shut up.'

'Why would your husband have stolen a tube of homeopathic pills from you?' asked Strike curiously. 'It seems—'

'Pointlessly spiteful?' asked Raphael, arms folded beneath the picture of the dead foal. 'Because you're so convinced you're right, and the other person's wrong, that it's OK to stop them doing something harmless?'

'Raff,' said Izzy at once, 'I know you're upset—'

'I'm not upset, Izz,' said Raphael. 'Very liberating, really, going back through all the shitty things Dad did while he was alive—'

'That's enough, boy!' said Torquil.

'Don't call me "boy",' said Raphael, shaking another cigarette out of his packet. 'All right? Don't fucking call me "boy".'

'You'll have to excuse Raff,' Torquil told Strike loudly, 'he's upset with m'late father-in-law because of the will.'

'I already knew I'd been written out of the will!' snapped Raphael, pointing at Kinvara. '*She* saw to that!'

'Your father didn't need any persuasion from me, I promise you!' said Kinvara, scarlet in the face now. 'Anyway, you've got plenty of money, your mother spoils you rotten.' She turned to Robin. 'His mother left Jasper for a diamond merchant, after taking Jasper for everything she could lay her hands on—'

'Could I ask another couple of questions?' said Strike loudly, before a plainly fuming Raphael could speak.

'The vet will be here for Romano in a minute,' said Kinvara. 'I need to get back to the stable.'

'Just a couple, and I'm done,' Strike assured her. 'Did you ever miss any amitriptyline pills? I think you were prescribed them, weren't you?'

'The police asked me this. I might have lost some,' said Kinvara, with irritating vagueness, 'but I can't be sure. There was a box I thought I'd lost and then I found it again and it didn't have as many pills in as I remembered, and I know I meant to leave a pack at Ebury Street in case I ever forgot when I was coming up to London, but when the police asked me I couldn't remember whether I'd actually done it or not.'

'So you couldn't swear to it that you had pills missing?'

'No,' said Kinvara. 'Jasper might have stolen some, but I can't swear to it.'

'Have you had any more intruders in your garden since your husband died?' asked Strike.

'No,' said Kinvara. 'Nothing.'

'I heard that a friend of your husband's tried to call him early the morning that he died, but couldn't get through. D'you happen to know who the friend was?'

'Oh . . . yes. It was Henry Drummond,' said Kinvara.

'And who's—?'

'He's an art dealer, very old friend of Papa's,' interrupted Izzy. 'Raphael worked for him for a little while – didn't you, Raff? – until he came to help Papa at the House of Commons.'

'I can't see what Henry's got to do with anything,' said Torquil, with an angry little laugh.

'Well, I think that's everything,' said Strike, ignoring this comment as he closed his notebook, 'except that I'd be glad to know whether you think your husband's death was suicide, Mrs Chiswell.'

The hand grasping the tissue contracted tightly.

'Nobody's interested in what I think,' she said.

'I assure you, I am,' said Strike.

Kinvara's eyes flickered from Raphael, who was scowling at the lawn outside, to Torquil.

'Well, if you want my opinion, Jasper did a very stupid thing, right before he—'

'Kinvara,' said Torquil sharply, 'you'd be best advised—'

'I'm not interested in your advice!' said Kinvara, turning on him suddenly, eyes narrowed. 'After all, it's your advice that brought this family to financial ruin!'

Fizzy shot her husband a look across Izzy, warning him against retorting. Kinvara turned back to Strike.

'My husband provoked somebody, somebody I warned him he shouldn't upset, shortly before he died—'

'You mean Geraint Winn?' asked Strike.

'No,' said Kinvara, 'but you're close. Torquil doesn't want me to say anything about it, because it involves his good friend Christopher—'

'Bloody hell!' exploded Torquil. He got to his feet, again hitching up his mustard corduroys, and looking incensed. 'My God, are we dragging total outsiders into this fantasy, now? What the bloody hell has Christopher got to do with anything? M'father-in-law killed himself!' he told Strike loudly, before rounding on his wife and sister-in-law. 'I've tolerated this nonsense because you gels want peace of mind, but frankly, if this is where it's going to lead—'

Izzy and Fizzy set up an outcry, both trying to placate him and justify themselves, and in the midst of this mêlée, Kinvara got to her feet, tossed back her long red hair and walked towards the door, leaving Robin with the strong impression that she had lobbed this grenade into the conversation deliberately. At the door she paused, and the others' heads turned, as though she had called to them. In her high, clear, childish voice, Kinvara said:

'You all come back here and treat this house as though you're the real owners and I'm a guest, but Jasper said I could live here as long as I'm alive. Now I need to see the vet and when I get back, I'd like you all to have gone home. You aren't welcome here any more.'

43

. . . I am afraid it will not be long before we hear something of the family ghost.

Henrik Ibsen, *Rosmersholm*

Robin asked whether she might use the bathroom before they departed from Chiswell House and was shown across the hall by Fizzy, who was still fuming at Kinvara.

'How dare she,' said Fizzy, as they crossed the hall. '*How dare she?* This is Pringle's house, not hers.' And, in the next breath, '*Please* don't pay any attention to what she said about Christopher, she's simply trying to get a rise out of Torks, it was a disgusting thing to do, he's simply *livid*.'

'Who *is* Christopher?' Robin asked.

'Well – I don't know whether I should say,' replied Fizzy. 'But I suppose, if you – of course, he can't have anything to do with it. It's just Kinvara's spite. She's talking about Sir Christopher Barrowclough-Burns. Old friend of Torks' family. Christopher's a senior civil servant and he was that boy Mallik's mentor at the Foreign Office.'

The lavatory was chilly and antiquated. As she bolted the door, Robin heard Fizzy striding back to the drawing room, doubtless to placate the angry Torquil. She looked around:

the chipped, painted stone walls were bare except for many small dark holes in which the occasional nail still stuck out. Robin presumed Kinvara was responsible for the removal of a large number of Perspex frames from the wall, which now stood stacked on the floor facing the toilet. They contained a jumble of family photographs in messy collages.

After drying her hands on a damp towel that smelled of dog, Robin crouched down to flick through these frames. Izzy and Fizzy had been almost indistinguishable as children, making it impossible to tell which of them was cartwheeling on the croquet lawn, or jumping a pony at a local gymkhana, dancing in front of a Christmas tree in the hall or embracing the young Jasper Chiswell at a shooting picnic, the men all in tweeds and Barbours.

Freddie, however, was immediately recognisable, because unlike his sisters he had inherited his father's protuberant lower lip. As white-blond in youth as his niece and nephews, he featured frequently, beaming for the camera as a toddler, stony-faced as a child in a new prep school uniform, muddy and triumphant in rugby kit.

Robin paused to examine a group shot of teenagers, all dressed head to toe in white fencing jackets, Union Jacks ran down the sides of everyone's breeches. She recognised Freddie, who was standing in the middle of the group, holding a large silver cup. At the far end of the group was a miserable-looking girl whom Robin recognised immediately as Rhiannon Winn, older and thinner than she had been in the photograph her father had shown Robin, her slightly cringing air at odds with the proud smiles on every other face.

Continuing to search the boards, Robin stopped at the last one to examine the faded photograph of a large party.

It had been taken in a marquee, from what seemed to be a

stage. Many bright blue helium balloons in the shape of the number eighteen danced over the crowd's heads. A hundred or so teenagers had clearly been bidden to face the camera. Robin scanned the scene carefully and found Freddie easily enough, surrounded by a large group of both boys and girls whose arms were slung around each other's shoulders, beaming and, in some cases, braying with laughter. After nearly a minute, Robin spotted the face she had instinctively sought: Rhiannon Winn, thin, pale and unsmiling beside the drinks table. Close behind her, half-hidden in shadow, were a couple of boys who were not in black tie, but jeans and T-shirts. One in particular was darkly handsome and long-haired, his T-shirt bearing a picture of The Clash.

Robin got out her mobile and took a picture of both the fencing team and the eighteenth birthday party photographs, then carefully replaced the stack of Perspex boards as she had found them, and left the bathroom.

She thought for a second that the silent hall was deserted. Then she saw that Raphael was leaning up against a hall table, his arms folded.

'Well, goodbye,' said Robin, starting to walk towards the front door.

'Hang on a minute.'

As she paused, he pushed himself off the table and approached her.

'I've been quite angry with you, you know.'

'I can understand why,' said Robin quietly, 'but I was doing what your father hired me to do.'

He moved closer, coming to a halt beneath an old glass lantern hanging from the ceiling. Half the light bulbs were missing.

'I'd say you're bloody good at it, aren't you? Getting people to trust you?'

'That's the job,' said Robin.

'You're married,' he said, eyes on her left hand.

'Yes,' she said.

'To Tim?'

'No . . . there isn't any Tim.'

'You're not married to *him*?' said Raphael quickly, pointing outside.

'No. We just work together.'

'And that's your real accent,' said Raphael. 'Yorkshire.'

'Yes,' she said. 'This is it.'

She thought he was going to say something insulting. The olive dark eyes moved over her face, then he shook his head slightly.

'I quite like the voice, but I preferred "Venetia". Made me think of masked orgies.'

He turned and walked away, leaving Robin to hurry back out into the sunshine to rejoin Strike, who she presumed would be waiting impatiently in the Land Rover.

She was wrong. He was still standing beside the car's bonnet, while Izzy, who was standing very close to him, talked rapidly in an undertone. When she heard Robin's feet on the gravel behind her, Izzy took a step backwards with what, to Robin, seemed a slightly guilty, embarrassed air.

'Lovely to see you again,' Izzy said, kissing Robin on both cheeks, as though this had been a simple social call. 'And you'll ring me, won't you?' she said to Strike.

'Yep, I'll keep you updated,' he said, moving around to the passenger seat.

Neither Strike nor Robin spoke as she turned the car around. Izzy waved them off, a slightly pathetic figure in her loose shirt dress. Strike raised a hand to her as they took the bend in the drive that hid her from their sight.

Trying not to upset the skittish stallions, Robin drove at a snail's pace. Glancing left, Strike saw that the injured horse had been removed from the field, but in spite of Robin's best intentions, as the noisy old car lurched past its field, the black stallion took off again.

'Who d'you reckon,' said Strike, watching the horse plunge and buck, 'first took a look at something like that and thought, "I should get on its back"?'

'There's an old saying,' said Robin, trying to steer around the worst of the potholes, '"the horse is your mirror". People say dogs resemble their owners, but I think it's truer of horses.'

'Making Kinvara highly strung and prone to lash out on slight provocation? Sounds about right. Turn right here. I want to get a look at Steda Cottage.'

A bare two minutes later, he said:

'Here. Go up here.'

The track to Steda Cottage was so overgrown that Robin had missed it entirely the first time they had passed it. It led deep into the woodland that lay hard up against the gardens of Chiswell House, but unfortunately, the Land Rover was only able to proceed for ten yards before the track became impassable by car. Robin cut the engine, privately worried about how Strike was going to manage a barely discernible path of earth and fallen leaves, overgrown with brambles and nettles, but as he was already getting out, she followed suit, slamming the driver's door behind her.

The ground was slippery, the tree canopy so dense that the track was in deep shade, dank and moist. A pungent, green, bitter smell filled their nostrils, and the air was alive with the rustle of birds and small creatures whose habitat was being rudely invaded.

'So,' said Strike, as they struggled through the bushes and weeds. 'Christopher Barrowclough-Burns. That's a new name.'

'No, it isn't,' said Robin.

Strike looked sideways at her, grinning, and immediately tripped on a root, remaining upright at some cost to his sore knee.

'*Shit* . . . I wondered whether you remembered.'

'"Christopher didn't promise anything about the pictures",' quoted Robin promptly. 'He's a civil servant who mentored Aamir Mallik at the Foreign Office. Fizzy just told me.'

'We're back to "a man of your habits", aren't we?'

Neither spoke for a short spell as they concentrated on a particularly treacherous stretch of path where whip-like branches clung willingly to fabric and skin. Robin's skin was a pale, dappled green in the sun filtered by the ceiling of leaves above them.

'See any more of Raphael, after I went outside?'

'Er – yes, actually,' said Robin, feeling slightly self-conscious. 'He came out of the sitting room as I was coming out of the loo.'

'Didn't think he'd pass up another chance of talking to you,' said Strike.

'It wasn't like that,' Robin said untruthfully, remembering the remark about masked orgies. 'Izzy whispering anything interesting, back there?' she asked.

Amused by the reciprocal jab, Strike took his eyes off the path, thereby failing to spot a muddy stump. He tripped for a second time, this time saving himself from a painful fall by grabbing a tree covered in a prickly climbing plant.

'*Fuck*—'

'Are you—?'

'I'm fine,' he said, angry with himself, examining the palm that was now full of thorns and starting to pull them out with his teeth. He heard a loud snap of wood behind him and turned to see Robin holding out a fallen branch, which she had broken to make a rough walking stick.

'Use this.'

'I don't—' he began, but catching sight of her stern expression, he gave in. 'Thanks.'

They set off again, Strike finding the stick more useful than he wanted to admit.

'Izzy was just trying to convince me that Kinvara could have sneaked back to Oxfordshire, after bumping off Chiswell between six and seven in the morning. I don't know whether she realises there are multiple witnesses to every stage of Kinvara's journey from Ebury Street. The police probably haven't gone into detail with the family yet, but I think, once the penny drops that Kinvara can't have done it in person, Izzy'll start suggesting she hired a hitman. What did you make of Raphael's various outbursts?'

'Well,' said Robin, navigating around a patch of nettles, 'I can't blame him, getting annoyed with Torquil.'

'No,' agreed Strike, 'I think old Torks would grate on me, too.'

'Raphael seems really angry with his father, doesn't he? He didn't *have* to tell us about Chiswell putting that mare down. I thought he was almost going out of his way to paint his father as . . . well . . . '

'A bit of a shit,' agreed Strike. 'He thought Chiswell had stolen those pills of Kinvara's out of malice, too. That whole episode was bloody strange, actually. What made you so interested in those pills?'

'They seemed so out of place for Chiswell.'

'Well, it was a good call. Nobody else seems to have asked questions about them. So what does the psychologist make of Raphael denigrating his dead father?'

Robin shook her head, smiling, as she usually did when Strike referred to her in this way. She had dropped out of her psychology course at university, as he well knew.

'I'm serious,' said Strike, grimacing as his false foot skidded on fallen leaves and he saved himself, this time with the aid of Robin's stick. '*Bollocks* . . . go on. What d'you make of him putting the boot into Chiswell?'

'Well, I think he's hurt and furious,' said Robin, weighing her words. 'He and his father were getting on better than they ever had, from what he told me when I was at the House of Commons, but now Chiswell's dead, Raphael's never going to be able to get properly back on good terms with him, is he? He's left with the fact he was written out of the will and no idea of how Chiswell really felt about him. Chiswell was quite inconsistent with Raphael. When he was drunk and depressed, he seemed to lean on him, but otherwise he was pretty rude to him. Although I can't honestly say I saw Chiswell ever being nice to anybody, except maybe—'

She stopped short.

'Go on,' said Strike.

'Well, actually,' said Robin, 'I was going to say he was quite nice to me, the day I found out all about the Level Playing Field.'

'This was when he offered you a job?'

'Yes, and he said he might have a bit more work for me, once I'd got rid of Winn and Knight.'

'Did he?' said Strike, curiously. 'You never told me that.'

'Didn't I? No, I don't suppose I did.'

And like Strike, she remembered the week that he had been laid up at Lorelei's, followed by the hours at the hospital with Jack.

'I went over to his office, as I told you, and he was on the phone to some hotel about a money clip he'd lost. It was Freddie's. After Chiswell got off the phone, I told him about the Level Playing Field and he was happier than I ever saw him. "One by one, they trip themselves up",' he said.

'Interesting,' panted Strike, whose leg was now killing him. 'So you think Raphael's smarting about the will, do you?'

Robin, who thought she caught a sardonic note in Strike's voice, said:

'It isn't just money—'

'People always say that,' he grunted. 'It *is* the money, and it isn't. Because what *is* money? Freedom, security, pleasure, a fresh chance . . . I think there's more to be got out of Raphael,' said Strike, 'and I think you're going to have to be the one to do it.'

'What else can he tell us?'

'I'd like a bit more clarity on that phone call Chiswell made to him, right before that bag went over his head,' panted Strike, who was now in considerable pain. 'It doesn't make much sense to me, because even if Chiswell knew he was about to kill himself, there were people far better placed to keep Kinvara company than a stepson she didn't like who was miles away in London.

'Trouble is, the call makes even less sense if it was murder. There's something,' said Strike, 'we aren't being t – ah. Thank Christ.'

Steda Cottage had just come into view in a clearing ahead of them. The garden, which was surrounded by a broken-down fence, was now almost as overgrown as its surroundings. The building was squat, made of dark stone and clearly derelict, with a yawning hole in the roof and cracks in most of the windows.

'Sit down,' Robin advised Strike, pointing him towards a large tree stump just outside the cottage fence. In too much pain to argue, he did as she instructed, while Robin picked her way towards the front door and gave it a little push, but found it locked. Wading through knee-length grass, she peered one by one through the grimy windows. The rooms were thick with dust and empty. The only sign of any previous occupant was in the kitchen, where a filthy mug bearing a picture of Johnny Cash sat alone on a stained surface.

'Doesn't look as though anyone's lived here for years, and no sign of anyone sleeping rough,' she informed Strike, emerging from the other side of the cottage.

Strike, who had just lit a cigarette, made no answer. He was staring down into a large hollow in the woodland floor, around twenty feet square, bordered with trees and full of nettles, tangled thorn and towering weeds.

'Would you call that a dell?' he asked her.

Robin peered down into the basin-like indentation.

'I'd say it's more like a dell than anything else we've passed,' she said.

'"He strangled the kid and they buried it, down in the dell by our dad's house",' quoted Strike.

'I'll have a look,' said Robin. 'You stay here.'

'No,' said Strike, raising a hand to stop her, 'you're not going to find anything—'

But Robin was already sliding her way down the steep edges of the 'dell', the thorns snagging at her jeans as she descended.

It was extremely difficult to move around once she reached the bottom. Nettles came up almost to her waist and she held up her hands to avoid scratches and stings. Milk parsley and wood avens speckled the dark green with white and yellow. The long thorny branches of wild roses curled like barbed wire everywhere she trod.

'Watch yourself,' said Strike, feeling impotent as he watched her struggle along, scratching or stinging herself at every other step.

'I'm fine,' said Robin, peering at the ground beneath the wild vegetation. If anything had been buried here, it had long since been covered by plants, and digging would be a very difficult business. She said as much to Strike, as she bent low to see what lay underneath a dense patch of bramble.

'Doubt Kinvara would be happy with us digging, anyway,' said Strike, and as he said it, he remembered Billy's words: *She wouldn't let me dig, but she'd let you.*

'Wait,' said Robin, sounding tense.

In spite of the fact that he knew perfectly well she could not have found anything, Strike tensed.

'What?'

'There's something in there,' said Robin, moving her head from side to side, the better to see into a thick patch of nettles, right in the centre of the dell.

'Oh God.'

'What?' Strike repeated. Although far higher up than her, he could make out nothing whatsoever in the nettle patch. 'What can you see?'

'I don't know . . . I might be imagining it.' She hesitated. 'You haven't got gloves, I suppose?'

'No. Robin, don't—'

But she had already walked into the patch of nettles, her hands raised, stamping them down at the base wherever she could, flattening them as much as possible. Strike saw her bend over and pull something out of the ground. Straightening up, she stood quite still, her red-gold head bowed over whatever she had found, until Strike said impatiently:

'What is it?'

Her hair fell away from a face that looked pale against the morass of dark green in which she stood, as she held up a small, wooden cross.

'No, stay there,' she ordered him, as he moved automatically towards the edge of the dell to help her climb out. 'I'm fine.'

She was, in fact, covered in scratches and nettle stings, but deciding that a few more would hardly count, Robin pushed her way more forcefully out of the dell, using her hands to pull herself up the steep sides until she came close enough for Strike to reach out a hand and help her the last few feet.

'Thanks,' she said breathlessly.

'Looks like it's been there years,' she said, rubbing earth from the bottom, which was pointed, the better to stick into the ground. The wood was damp and stained.

'Something was written on it,' said Strike, taking it from her and squinting at the slimy surface.

'Where?' said Robin. Her hair grazed his cheek as they stood close beside each other, staring at the very faint residue of what looked like felt tip, long since washed away by rain and dew.

'That looks like a kid's writing,' said Robin quietly.

'That's an "S",' said Strike, 'and at the end . . . is that a "g" or a "y"?'

'I don't know,' whispered Robin.

They stood in silence, contemplating the cross, until the faint, echoing barks of Rattenbury the Norfolk terrier pierced their reverie.

'We're still on Kinvara's property,' said Robin nervously.

'Yeah,' said Strike, keeping hold of the cross as he began to lumber back the way they had come, teeth gritted against the pain in his leg. 'Let's find a pub. I'm starving.'

44

But there are so many sorts of white horses in this world, Mrs. Helseth . . .

Henrik Ibsen, *Rosmersholm*

'Of course,' said Robin, as they drove towards the village, 'a cross sticking out of the ground doesn't mean there's anything buried beneath it.'

'True,' said Strike, who had needed most of his breath on the return walk for the frequent obscenities he uttered as he stumbled and skidded on the forest floor, 'but it makes you think, doesn't it?'

Robin said nothing. Her hands on the steering wheel were covered in nettle stings that prickled and burned.

The country inn they reached five minutes later was the very image of picture-postcard England, a white, timbered building with leaded bay windows, moss-covered slates on the roof and climbing red roses around the door. A beer garden with parasols completed the picture. Robin turned the Land Rover into the small car park opposite.

'This is getting stupid,' muttered Strike, who had left the cross on the dashboard and was now climbing out of the car, staring at the pub.

'What is?' asked Robin, coming around the back of the car to join him.

'It's called the White Horse.'

'After the one up the hill,' said Robin, as they set off across the road together. 'Look at the sign.'

Painted on the board atop a wooden pole was the strange chalk figure they had seen earlier.

'The pub where I met Jimmy Knight the first time was called the White Horse, too,' said Strike.

'The White Horse,' said Robin, as they walked up the steps into the beer garden, Strike's limp now more pronounced than ever, 'is one of the ten most popular pub names in Britain. I read it in some article. Quick, those people are leaving – grab their table, I'll get the drinks.'

The low-ceilinged pub was busy inside. Robin headed first for the Ladies where she stripped off her jacket, tied it around her waist and washed her smarting hands. She wished that she had managed to find dock leaves on the journey back from Steda Cottage, but most of her attention on the return walk had been given to Strike who had nearly fallen twice more and hobbled on looking furious with himself, repelling offers of assistance with bad grace and leaning heavily on the walking stick she had fashioned from a branch.

The mirror showed Robin that she was dishevelled and grubby compared to the prosperous middle-aged people she had just seen in the bar, but being in a hurry to return to Strike and review the morning's activities, she merely dragged a brush through her hair, wiped a green stain off her neck and returned to queue for drinks.

'Cheers, Robin,' said Strike gratefully, when she returned to him with a pint of Arkell's Wiltshire Gold, shoving the menu across the table to her. 'Ah, that's good,' he sighed, taking a swig. 'So what's the most popular one?'

'Sorry?'

'The most popular pub name. You said the White Horse is in the top ten.'

'Oh, right . . . it's either the Red Lion or the Crown, I can't remember which.'

'The Victory's my real local,' said Strike reminiscently.

He had not been back to Cornwall in two years. He saw the pub now in his mind's eye, a squat building of whitewashed Cornish stone, the steps beside it winding down to the bay. It was the pub in which he had first managed to get served without ID, sixteen years old and dumped back at his uncle and aunt's for a few weeks, while his mother's life went through one of its regular bouts of upheaval.

'Ours is the Bay Horse,' said Robin, and she, too, had a sudden vision of a pub from what she would always think of as home, also white, standing on a street that led off the market square in Masham. It was there that she had celebrated her A-level results with her friends, the same night that Matthew and she had got into a stupid row, and he had left, and she had refused to follow, but remained with her friends.

'Why "bay"?' asked Strike, now halfway down his pint and luxuriating in the sunshine, his sore leg stretched out in front of him. 'Why not just "brown"?'

'Well, there *are* brown horses,' said Robin, 'but bay means something different. Black points: legs, mane and tail.'

'What colour was your pony – Angus, wasn't it?'

'How did you remember that?' asked Robin, surprised.

'Dunno,' said Strike. 'Same as you remembering pub names. Some things stick, don't they?'

'He was grey.'

'Meaning white. It's all just jargon to confuse non-riding plebs, isn't it?'

'No,' said Robin, laughing. 'Grey horses have black skin under the white hair. True whites—'

'—die young,' said Strike, as a barmaid arrived to take their order. Having ordered a burger, Strike lit another cigarette and as the nicotine hit his brain, felt a wave of something close to euphoria. A pint, a hot day in August, a well-paid job, food on the way and Robin, sitting across from him, their friendship restored, if not entirely to what it had been before her honeymoon, then perhaps as close as was possible, now that she was married. Right now, in this sunny beer garden, and in spite of the pain in his leg, his tiredness and the unresolved mess that was his relationship with Lorelei, life felt simple and hopeful.

'Group interviews are never a good idea,' he said, exhaling away from Robin's face, 'but there were some interesting crosscurrents among the Chiswells, weren't there? I'm going to keep working on Izzy. I think she might be a bit more forthcoming without the family around.'

Izzy will like being worked on, Robin thought, as she took out her mobile.

'I've got something to show you. Look.'

She brought up her photograph of Freddie Chiswell's birthday party.

'That,' she said, pointing at the girl's pale, unhappy face, 'is Rhiannon Winn. She was at Freddie Chiswell's eighteenth birthday party. Turns out—' she scrolled back a picture, to show the group in white tunics, 'they were on the British fencing team together.'

'Christ, of course,' said Strike, taking the phone from Robin. 'The sword – the sword in Ebury Street. I bet it was Freddie's!'

'Of course!' echoed Robin, wondering why she hadn't realised that before.

'That can't be long before she killed herself,' said Strike, scrutinising more closely the miserable figure of Rhiannon Winn at the birthday party. 'And – bloody hell, that's Jimmy Knight behind her. What's he doing at a public schoolboy's eighteenth?'

'Free drink?' suggested Robin.

Strike gave a small snort of amusement as he handed back Robin's phone.

'Sometimes the obvious answer is the right one. Was I imagining Izzy looking self-conscious when the story of Jimmy's teenage sex appeal came up?'

'No,' said Robin, 'I noticed that, too.'

'Nobody wants us to talk to Jimmy's old mates the Butcher brothers, either.'

'Because they know more than where their sister works?'

Strike sipped his beer, thinking back to what Chiswell had told him the first time they'd met.

'Chiswell said other people were involved in whatever he did to get blackmailed, but they had a lot to lose if it got out.'

He took out his notebook and contemplated his own spiky, hard-to-read handwriting, while Robin sat peacefully enjoying the quiet chatter of the beer garden. A lazy bee buzzed nearby, reminding her of the lavender walk at Le Manoir aux Quat'Saisons, where she and Matthew had spent their anniversary. It was best not to compare how she felt now to the way she had felt then.

'Maybe,' said Strike, tapping the open notebook with his pen, 'the Butcher brothers agreed to take on horse-slashing duties for Jimmy while he was in London? I always thought he might have mates back down here who could've taken care of that side of things. But we'll let Izzy get Tegan's whereabouts out of them before we approach them. Don't want to upset the client unless it's absolutely necessary.'

'No,' agreed Robin. 'I wonder . . . d'you think Jimmy met them when he came down here looking for Billy?'

'Could well have done,' said Strike, nodding over his notes. 'Very interesting, that. From what they said to each other on that march, Jimmy and Flick knew where Billy was at the time. They were off to see him when my hamstring went. Now they've lost him again . . . you know, I'd give a hell of a lot to find Billy. That's where all of this started and we're still—'

He broke off as their food arrived: a burger with blue cheese on it for Strike, and a bowl of chilli for Robin.

'We're still?' prompted Robin, as the barmaid moved away.

' . . . none the wiser,' said Strike, 'about the kid he claims he saw die. I didn't want to ask the Chiswells about Suki Lewis, or not yet. Best not to suggest I'm interested in anyone but Chiswell's death right now.'

He picked up his burger and took an enormous bite, his eyes unfocused, staring out over the road. After demolishing half of his burger, Strike turned back to his notes.

'Things to be done,' he announced, picking up his pen again. 'I want to find this cleaning woman Jasper Chiswell laid off. She had a key for a bit and she might be able to tell us how and when the helium got into the house.

'Hopefully Izzy will trace Tegan Butcher for us, and Tegan'll be able to shed some light on Raphael's trip down there on the morning his father died, because I'm still not buying that story.

'We'll leave Tegan's brothers for now, because the Chiswells clearly don't want us talking to them, but I might try and have a word with Henry Drummond, the art dealer.'

'Why?' asked Robin.

'He was an old friend, did Chiswell a favour hiring Raphael. They must've been reasonably close. You never know,

Chiswell might've told him what the blackmail was about. And he tried to reach Chiswell early on the morning Chiswell died. I'd like to know why.

'So, going forwards: you're going to have a bash at Flick at her jewellery shop, Barclay can stay on Jimmy and Flick, and I'll tackle Geraint Winn and Aamir Mallik.'

'They'll never talk to you,' said Robin at once. 'Never.'

'Want to bet?'

'Tenner says they won't.'

'I don't pay you enough for you to throw tenners around,' said Strike. 'You can buy me a pint.'

Strike took care of the bill and they headed back across the road to the car, Robin secretly wishing that there was somewhere else they needed to go, because the prospect of returning to Albury Street was depressing.

'We might be better off going back on the M40,' said Strike, reading a map on his phone. 'There's been an accident on the M4.'

'OK,' said Robin.

This would take them past Le Manoir aux Quat'Saisons. As she reversed out of the car park, Robin suddenly remembered Matthew's texts from earlier. He had claimed to have been messaging work, but she couldn't remember him ever contacting his office at a weekend before. One of his regular complaints about her job was that its hours and responsibilities bled into Saturday and Sunday, unlike his.

'What?' she said, becoming aware that Strike had just spoken to her.

'I said, they're supposed to be bad luck, aren't they?' repeated Strike, as they drove away from the pub.

'What are?'

'White horses,' he said. 'Isn't there a play where white horses appear as a death omen?'

'I don't know,' said Robin, changing gear. 'Death rides a white horse in Revelations, though.'

'A pale horse,' Strike corrected her, winding down the window so that he could smoke again.

'Pedant.'

'Says the woman who won't call a brown horse "brown",' said Strike.

He reached for the grubby wooden cross, which was sliding about on the dashboard. Robin kept her eyes on the road ahead, determinedly focused on anything but the vivid image that had occurred to her when she had first spotted it, almost hidden in the thick, whiskered stems of the nettles: that of a child, rotting in the earth at the bottom of that dark basin in the woods, dead and forgotten by everyone except a man they said was mad.

45

It is a necessity for me to abandon a false and equivocal position.

Henrik Ibsen, *Rosmersholm*

Strike paid in pain for the walk through the woods at Chiswell House the next morning. So little did he fancy getting up out of bed and heading downstairs to work on a Sunday that he was forced to remind himself that, like the character of Hyman Roth in one of his favourite films, he had chosen this business freely. If, like the Mafia, private detection made demands beyond the ordinary, certain concomitants had to be accepted along with the rewards.

He had had a choice, after all. The army had been keen to keep him, even with half his leg missing. Friends of friends had offered everything from management roles in the close protection industry to business partnerships, but the itch to detect, solve and reimpose order upon the moral universe could not be extinguished in him, and he doubted it ever would be. The paperwork, the frequently obstreperous clients, the hiring and firing of subordinates gave him no intrinsic satisfaction – but the long hours, the physical privations and the occasional risks of his job were accepted stoically and with occasional relish. And so he showered, put on his prosthesis and, yawning, made his painful way downstairs, remembering his brother-in-law's suggestion that his ultimate goal ought to be sitting in an office while others literally did the legwork.

Strike's thoughts drifted to Robin as he sat down at her computer. He had never asked her what her ultimate ambition for the agency was, assuming, perhaps arrogantly, that it was the same as his: build up a sufficient bank balance to ensure them both a decent income while they took the work that was most interesting, without fear of losing everything the moment they lost a client. But perhaps Robin was waiting for him to initiate a talk along the lines that Greg had suggested? He tried to imagine her reaction, if he invited her to sit down on the farting sofa while he subjected her to a PowerPoint display setting out long-term objectives and suggestions for branding.

As he set to work, thoughts of Robin metamorphosed into memories of Charlotte. He remembered how it had been on days like this while they had been together, when he had required uninterrupted hours alone at a computer. Sometimes Charlotte had taken herself out, often making an unnecessary mystery about where she was going, or invented reasons to interrupt him, or pick a fight that kept him pinned down while the precious hours trickled away. And he knew that he was reminding himself how difficult and exhausting that behaviour had been, because ever since he had seen her at Lancaster House, Charlotte had slid in and out of his disengaged mind like a stray cat.

A little under eight hours, seven cups of tea, three bathroom breaks, four cheese sandwiches, three bags of crisps, an apple and twenty-two cigarettes later, Strike had repaid all his subcontractors' expenses, ensured that the accountant had the firm's latest receipts, read Hutchins' updated report on Dodgy Doc and tracked several Aamir Malliks across cyberspace in search of the one he wanted to interview. By five o'clock he thought he had him, but the photograph was so far from 'handsome', which was how Mallik had been described in the blind item online, that he thought it best to email Robin a copy of the pictures he had found on Google Images, to confirm that this was the Mallik he sought.

Strike stretched, yawning, listening to a drum solo that a prospective purchaser was banging out in a shop below in Denmark Street. Looking forward to getting back upstairs and watching the day's Olympic highlights, which would include Usain Bolt running the hundred metres, he was on the point of shutting off his computer when a small 'ping' alerted him to the arrival of an email from Lorelei@VintageVamps.com, the subject line reading simply: 'You and me'.

Strike rubbed his eyes with the heels of his palms, as though the sight of the new email had been some temporary aberration of sight. However, there it sat at the top of his inbox when he raised his head and opened his eyes again.

'Oh, shit,' he muttered. Deciding that he might as well know the worst, he clicked on it.

The email ran to nearly a thousand words and gave the impression of having been carefully crafted. It was a methodical dissection of Strike's character, which read like the case notes for a psychiatric case that, while not hopeless, required urgent intervention. By Lorelei's analysis, Cormoran Strike was a fundamentally damaged and dysfunctional creature standing in the way of his own happiness. He caused pain to others due to the essential dishonesty of his emotional dealings. Never having experienced a healthy relationship, he ran from it when it was given to him. He took those who cared about him for granted and would probably only realise this when he hit rock bottom, alone, unloved and tortured by regrets.

This prediction was followed by a description of the soul-searching and doubts that had preceded Lorelei's decision to send the email, rather than simply tell Strike that their no-strings arrangement was at an end. She concluded that she thought it fairest to him to explain in writing why she, and by implication every other woman in the world, would find him unacceptable unless he changed his behaviour. She asked him to read and think about what she had said 'understanding that this doesn't come from a place of anger, but of sadness', and requested a further meeting so that they could 'decide whether you want this relationship enough to try a different way'.

After reaching the bottom of the email, Strike remained where he was, staring at the screen, not because he was contemplating a response, but because he was gathering himself for the physical pain he was anticipating upon standing up. At last he pushed himself up into a vertical position, flinching as he lowered his weight onto the prosthesis, then closed down his computer and locked up the office.

Why can't we end it by phone? he thought, heaving himself up the stairs by using the handrail. *It's obvious it's fucking dead, isn't it? Why do we have to have a post-mortem?*

Back in the flat, he lit another cigarette, dropped down onto a kitchen chair and called Robin, who answered almost immediately.

'Hi,' she said quietly. 'Just a moment.'

He heard a door close, footsteps, and another door closing.

'Did you get my email? Just sent you a couple of pictures.'

'No,' said Robin, keeping her voice low. 'Pictures of what?'

'I think I've found Mallik living in Battersea. Pudgy bloke with a monobrow.'

'That's not him. He's tall and thin with glasses.'

'So I've just wasted an hour,' said Strike, frustrated. 'Didn't he ever let slip where he was living? What he liked to do at the weekends? National Insurance number?'

'No,' said Robin, 'we barely spoke. I've already told you this.'

'How's the disguise coming along?'

Robin had already told Strike by text that she had an interview on Thursday with the 'mad Wiccan' who ran the jewellery shop in Camden.

'Not bad,' said Robin. 'I've been experimenting with—'

There was a muffled shout in the background.

'Sorry, I'm going to have to go,' Robin said hastily.

'Everything OK?'

'It's fine, speak tomorrow.'

She hung up. Strike remained with the mobile at his ear. He deduced that he had called during a difficult moment for Robin, possibly even a row, and lowered the mobile with faint disappointment at not having had a longer chat. For a moment or two, he contemplated the mobile in his hand. Lorelei would be expecting him to call as soon as he had read her email. Deciding that he could credibly claim not to have seen it yet, Strike put down his phone and reached instead for the TV remote control.

46

. . . I should have handled the affair more judiciously.

Henrik Ibsen, *Rosmersholm*

Four days later, at lunchtime, Strike was to be found leaning up against a counter in a tiny takeaway pizza restaurant, which was most conveniently situated for watching a house directly across the street. One of a pair of brown brick semi-detached houses, the name 'Ivy Cottages' was engraved in stone over the twin doors, which seemed to Strike more fitting for humbler dwellings than these houses, which had graceful arched windows and corniced keystones.

Chewing on a slice of pizza, Strike felt his phone vibrate in his pocket. He checked to see who was calling before answering, because he had already had one fraught conversation with Lorelei today. Seeing that it was Robin, he answered.

'I'm in,' said Robin. She sounded excited. 'Just had my interview. The owner's dreadful, I'm not surprised nobody wants to work for her. It's a zero-hours contract. Basically, she wants a couple of people to fill in whenever she fancies not working.'

'Flick still there?'

'Yes, she was manning the counter while I was talking to the shop owner. The woman wants to give me a trial tomorrow.'

'You weren't followed?'

'No, I think that journalist has given up. He wasn't here yesterday either. Mind you, he probably wouldn't have recognised me even if he'd seen me. You should see my hair.'

'Why, what have you done with it?'

'Chalk.'

'What?'

'Hair chalk,' said Robin. 'Temporary colour. It's black and blue. And I'm wearing a lot of eye make-up and some temporary tattoos.'

'Send us a selfie, I could do with some light relief.'

'Make your own. What's going on your end?'

'Bugger all. Mallik came out of Della's house with her this morning—'

'God, are they *living* together?'

'No idea. They went out somewhere in a taxi with the guide dog. They came back an hour ago and I'm waiting to see what happens next. One interesting thing, though: I've seen Mallik before. Recognised him the moment I saw him this morning.'

'Really?'

'Yeah, he was at Jimmy's CORE meeting. The one I went to, to try and find Billy.'

'How weird ... D'you think he was acting as a go-between for Geraint?'

'Maybe,' said Strike, 'but I can't see why the phone wouldn't have done if they wanted to keep in touch. You know, there's something funny about Mallik generally.'

'He's all right,' said Robin quickly. 'He didn't like me, but that was because he was suspicious. That just means he's sharper than most of the rest of them.'

'You don't fancy him as a killer?'

'Is this because of what Kinvara said?'

'"My husband provoked somebody, somebody I warned him he shouldn't upset",' Strike quoted.

'And why should anyone be particularly worried about upsetting Aamir? Because he's brown? I felt sorry for him, actually, having to work with—'

'Hang on,' said Strike, letting his last piece of pizza fall back onto the plate.

The front door of Della's house had opened again.

'We're off,' said Strike, as Mallik came out of the house alone, closed the door behind him, walked briskly down the garden path, and set off down the road. Strike headed out of the pizzeria in pursuit.

'Got a spring in his step now. He looks happy to be away from her . . .'

'How's your leg?'

'It's been worse. Hang on, he's turning left . . . Robin, I'm going to go, need to speed up a bit.'

'Good luck.'

'Cheers.'

Strike crossed Southwark Park Road as quickly as his leg permitted, then turned into Alma Grove, a long residential street with plane trees planted at regular intervals, and Victorian terraced houses on both sides. To Strike's surprise, Mallik stopped at a house on the right, with a turquoise door, and let himself inside. The distance between his place of residence and that of the Winns' was five minutes' walk at most.

The houses in Alma Grove were narrow and Strike could well imagine loud noises travelling easily through the walls. Giving Mallik what he judged to be sufficient time to remove his jacket and shoes, Strike approached the turquoise door and knocked.

After a few seconds' wait, Aamir opened up. His expression changed from pleasant enquiry to shock. Aamir evidently knew exactly who Strike was.

'Aamir Mallik?'

The younger man did not speak at first, but stood frozen with one hand on the door, the other on the hall wall, looking at Strike with dark eyes shrunken by the thickness of the lenses in his glasses.

'What do you want?'

'A chat,' said Strike.

'Why? What for?'

'Jasper Chiswell's family have hired me. They aren't sure he committed suicide.'

Appearing temporarily paralysed, Aamir neither moved nor spoke. Finally, he stood back from the door.

'All right, come in.'

In Aamir's position, Strike too would have wanted to know what the detective knew or suspected, rather than wondering through fretful nights why he had called. Strike entered and wiped his feet on the doormat.

The house was larger inside than it had appeared outside. Aamir led Strike through a door on the left into a sitting room. The décor was, very obviously, the taste of a person far older than Aamir. A thick, patterned carpet of swirling pinks and greens, a number of chintz-covered chairs, a wooden coffee table with a lace cloth laid over it and an ornamental edged mirror over the mantelpiece all spoke of geriatric occupants, while an ugly electric heater had been installed in the wrought iron fireplace. Shelves were bare, surfaces denuded of ornaments or other objects. A Stieg Larsson paperback lay on the arm of a chair.

Aamir turned to face Strike, hands in the pockets of his jeans.

'You're Cormoran Strike,' he said.

'That's right.'

'It was your partner who was pretending to be Venetia, at the Commons.'

'Right again.'

'What d'you want?' Aamir asked, for the second time.

'To ask you a few questions.'

'About what?'

'OK if I sit down?' asked Strike, doing so without waiting for permission. He noticed Aamir's eyes drop to his leg, and stretched out the prosthesis ostentatiously, so that a glint of the metal ankle could be seen above his sock. To a man so considerate of Della's disability, this might be sufficient reason not to ask Strike to get up again. 'As I said, the family doesn't think Jasper Chiswell killed himself.'

'You think I had something to do with his death?' asked Aamir, trying for incredulity and succeeding only in sounding scared.

'No,' said Strike, 'but if you want to blurt out a confession, feel free. It'll save me a lot of work.'

Aamir didn't smile.

'The only thing I know about you, Aamir,' said Strike, 'is that you were helping Geraint Winn blackmail Chiswell.'

'I wasn't,' said Aamir at once.

It was the automatic, ill-considered denial of a panicked man.

'You weren't trying to get hold of incriminating photographs to use against him?'

'I don't know what you're talking about.'

'The press are trying to break your bosses' super-injunction. Once the blackmail's out in the public domain, your part in it won't remain hidden for long. You and your friend Christopher—'

'He's not my friend!'

Aamir's vehemence interested Strike.

'D'you own this house, Aamir?'

'What?'

'Just seems a big place for a twenty-four-year-old on what can't be a big salary—'

'It's none of your business who owns this—'

'I don't care, personally,' said Strike, leaning forwards, 'but the papers will. You'll look beholden to the owners if you aren't paying a fair rent. It could seem like you owed them something, like you're in their pocket. The tax office will also consider it a benefit in kind if it's owned by your employers, which could cause problems for both—'

'How did you know where to find me?' Aamir demanded.

'Well, it wasn't easy,' Strike admitted. 'You don't have much of an online life, do you? But in the end,' he said, reaching for a sheaf of folded paper in the inside pocket of his jacket, and unfolding them, 'I found your sister's Facebook page. That *is* your sister, right?'

He laid the piece of paper, on which he had printed the Facebook post, on the coffee table. A plumply pretty woman in a hijab beamed up out of the poor reproduction of her photograph, surrounded by four young children. Taking Aamir's silence for assent, Strike said:

'I went back through a few years' worth of posts. That's you,' he said, laying a second printed page on top of the first. A younger Aamir stood smiling in academic robes, flanked by his parents. 'You took a first in politics and economics at LSE. Very impressive . . .

'And you got onto a graduate training programme at the Foreign Office,' Strike continued, placing a third sheet down on top of the first two. This showed an official, posed photograph of a small group of smartly dressed young men and women, all black or from other ethnic minorities, standing around a balding, florid-faced man. 'There you are,' said Strike, 'with senior civil servant Sir Christopher Barrowclough-Burns, who at that time was running a diversity recruitment drive.'

Aamir's eye twitched.

'And here you are again,' said Strike, laying down the last of his four printed Facebook pages, 'just a month ago, with your sister in that pizza place right opposite Della's house. Once I identified where it was and realised how close it was to the Winns' place, I thought it might be worth coming to Bermondsey to see whether I could spot you in the vicinity.'

Aamir stared down at the picture of himself and his sister. She had taken the selfie. Southwark Park Road was clearly visible behind them, through the window.

'Where were you at 6 a.m. on the thirteenth of July?' Strike asked Aamir.

'Here.'

'Could anyone corroborate that?'

'Yes. Geraint Winn.'

'Had he stayed the night?'

Aamir advanced a few steps, fists raised. It could not have been plainer that he had never boxed, but nevertheless, Strike tensed. Aamir looked close to breaking point.

'All I'm saying,' said Strike, holding up his hands pacifically, 'is that 6 a.m. is an odd time for Geraint Winn to be at your house.'

Aamir slowly lowered his fists, then, as though he did not know what else to do with himself, he backed away to sit down on the edge of the seat of the nearest armchair.

'Geraint came round to tell me Della had had a fall.'

'Couldn't he have phoned?'

'I suppose so, but he didn't,' said Aamir. 'He wanted me to help him persuade Della to go to casualty. She'd slipped down the last few stairs and her wrist was swelling up. I went round there – they only live round the corner – but I couldn't persuade her. She's stubborn. Anyway, it turned out to be only a sprain, not a break. She was fine.'

'So you're Geraint's alibi for the time Jasper Chiswell died?'

'I suppose so.'

'And he's yours.'

'Why would I want Jasper Chiswell dead?' asked Aamir.

'That's a good question,' said Strike.

'I barely knew the man,' said Aamir.

'Really?'

'Yes, really.'

'So what made him quote Catullus at you, and mention Fate, and intimate in front of a room full of people that he knew things about your private life?'

There was a long pause. Again, Aamir's eye twitched.

'That didn't happen,' he said.

'Really? My partner—'

'She's lying. Chiswell didn't know anything about my private life. Nothing.'

Strike heard the numb drone of a hoover next door. He had been right. The walls were not thick.

'I've seen you once before,' Strike told Mallik, who looked more frightened than ever. 'Jimmy Knight's meeting in East Ham, couple of months ago.'

'I don't know what you're talking about,' said Mallik. 'You've mistaken me for someone else.' Then, unconvincingly, 'Who's Jimmy Knight?'

'OK, Aamir,' said Strike, 'if that's how you want to play it, there's no point going on. Could I use your bathroom?'

'What?'

'Need a pee. Then I'll clear out, leave you in peace.'

Mallik clearly wanted to refuse, but seemed unable to find a reason to do so.

'All right,' said Aamir. 'But—'

A thought seemed to have occurred to him.

'—wait. I need to move – I was soaking some socks in the sink. Stay here.'

'Right you are,' said Strike.

Aamir left the room. Strike wanted an excuse to poke around upstairs for clues to the entity or activity that might have caused animal noises loud enough to disturb the neighbours, but the sound of Aamir's footsteps told him that the bathroom lay beyond the kitchen on the ground floor.

A couple of minutes later, Aamir returned.

'It's through here.'

He led Strike down the hall, through a nondescript, bare kitchen, and pointed him into the bathroom.

Strike entered, closed and locked the door, then placed his hand at the bottom of the sink. It was dry. The walls of the bathroom were pink and matched the pink bathroom suite. Grab rails beside the toilet and a floor-to-ceiling rail at the end of the bath suggested that this had been, some time in the recent past, the home of a frail or disabled person.

What was it that Aamir had wanted to remove or conceal before the detective entered? Strike opened the bathroom cabinet. It contained very little other than a young man's basic necessities: shaving kit, deodorant and aftershave.

Closing the cabinet, Strike saw his own reflection swing into view and, over his shoulder, the back of the door, where a thick navy towelling robe had been hung up carelessly, suspended from the arm hole rather than the loop designed for that purpose.

Flushing the toilet to maintain the fiction that he was too

busy to nose around, Strike approached the dressing gown and felt the empty pockets. As he did so, the precariously placed robe slid off the hook.

Strike took a step backwards, the better to appreciate what had just been revealed. Somebody had gouged a crude, four-legged figure into the bathroom door, splintering the wood and paint. Strike turned on the cold tap, in case Aamir was listening, took a picture of the carving with his mobile, turned off the tap and replaced the towelling robe as he had found it.

Aamir was waiting at the end of the kitchen.

'All right if I take those papers with me?' Strike asked, and without waiting for an answer he returned to the sitting room and picked up the Facebook pages.

'What made you leave the Foreign Office, anyway?' he asked casually.

'I . . . didn't enjoy it.'

'How did it come about, you working for the Winns?'

'We'd met,' said Aamir. 'Della offered me a job. I took it.'

It happened, very occasionally, that Strike felt scruples about what he was driven to ask during an interview.

'I couldn't help noticing,' he said, holding up the wad of printed material, 'that you seemed to drop out of sight of your family for quite a long time after you left the Foreign Office. No more appearances in group shots, not even on your mother's seventieth birthday. Your sister stopped mentioning you, for a long time.'

Aamir said nothing.

'It was as if you'd been disowned,' said Strike.

'You can get out, now,' said Aamir, but Strike didn't move.

'When your sister posted this picture of the pair of you in the pizza place,' Strike continued, unfolding the last sheet again, 'the responses were—'

'I want you to leave,' repeated Aamir, more loudly.

'"What you doing with that scumbag?" "Your dad know you still seeing him?"' Strike read aloud from the messages beneath the picture of Aamir and his sister. '"If my brother permitted *liwat*—"'

Aamir charged at him, sending a wild right-handed punch to the side of Strike's head that the detective parried. But the studious-looking Aamir was full of the kind of blind rage that could make a dangerous opponent of almost any man. Tearing a nearby lamp from its socket he swung it so violently that had Strike not ducked in time, the lamp base could have shattered, not on the wall that half-divided the sitting room, but on his face.

'Enough!' bellowed Strike, as Aamir dropped the remnants of the lamp and came at him again. Strike fended off the windmilling fists, hooked his prosthetic leg around the back of Aamir's leg, and threw him to the floor. Swearing under his breath, because this action had done his aching stump no good at all, Strike straightened up, panting, and said:

'Any more and I'll fucking deck you.'

Aamir rolled out of Strike's reach and got to his feet. His glasses were hanging from one ear. Hands shaking, he took them off and examined the broken hinge. His eyes were suddenly huge.

'Aamir, I'm not interested in your private life,' panted Strike, 'I'm interested in who you're covering up for—'

'Get out,' whispered Aamir.

'—because if the police decide it's murder, everything you're trying to hide will come out. Murder inquiries respect no one's privacy.'

'*Get out!*'

'All right. Don't say I didn't warn you.'

At the front door, Strike turned one last time to face

Aamir, who had followed him into the hall, and braced himself as Strike came to a halt.

'Who carved that mark on the inside of your bathroom door, Aamir?'

'*Out!*'

Strike knew there was no point persisting. As soon as he had crossed the threshold, the front door slammed behind him.

Several houses away, the wincing Strike leaned up against a tree to take the weight off his prosthesis, and texted Robin the picture he had just taken, along with the message:

Remind you of anything?

He lit a cigarette and waited for Robin's response, glad of an excuse to remain stationary, because quite apart from the pain in his stump, the side of his head was throbbing. In dodging the lamp he had hit it against the wall, and his back was aching because of the effort it had taken to throw the younger man to the floor.

Strike glanced back at the turquoise door. If he was honest, something else was hurting: his conscience. He had entered Mallik's house with the intention of shocking or intimidating him into the truth about his relationship with Chiswell and the Winns. While a private detective could not afford the doctor's dictum 'first, do no harm', Strike generally attempted to extract truth without causing unnecessary damage to the host. Reading out the comments at the bottom of that Facebook post had been a low blow. Brilliant, unhappy, undoubtedly tied to the Winns by something other than choice, Aamir Mallik's eruption into violence had been the reaction of a desperate man. Strike didn't need to consult the papers in his pocket to recall the picture of Mallik standing proudly in the Foreign Office, about to embark on a stellar career with his first-class degree, with his mentor, Sir Christopher Barrowclough-Burns, by his side.

His mobile rang.

'Where on earth did you find that carving?' said Robin.

'The back of Aamir's bathroom door, hidden under a dressing gown.'

'You're joking.'

'No. What does it look like to you?'

'The white horse on the hill over Woolstone,' said Robin.

'Well, that's a relief,' said Strike, elbowing himself off the supporting tree and limping off along the street again. 'I was worried I'd started hallucinating the bloody things.'

47

. . . I want to try and play my humble part in the struggles of life.

Henrik Ibsen, *Rosmersholm*

Robin emerged from Camden Town station at half past eight on Friday morning and set off for the jewellery shop where she was to have her day's trial, furtively checking her appearance in every window that she passed.

In the months following the trial of the Shacklewell Ripper, she had become adept at make-up techniques such as altering the shape of her eyebrows or over-painting her lips in vermillion, which made a significant difference to her appearance when coupled with wigs and coloured contact lenses, but she had never before worn as much make-up as today. Her eyes, in which she was wearing dark brown contact lenses, were heavily rimmed with black kohl, her lips painted pale pink, her nails a metallic grey. Having only one conventional hole in each earlobe, she had bought a couple of cheap ear cuffs to simulate a more adventurous approach to piercing. The short black second-hand dress she had bought at the local Oxfam shop in Deptford still smelled slightly fusty, even though she had run it through the washing machine the previous day, and she wore it with thick black tights and a pair of flat black lace-up boots in spite of the warmth of the morning. Thus attired, she hoped that she resembled the other goth and emo girls who frequented Camden, an area of London that Robin had rarely visited and which she associated mainly with Lorelei and her vintage clothes store.

She had named her new alter ego Bobbi Cunliffe. When undercover, it was best to assume names with a personal association, to which you responded instinctively. Bobbi sounded like Robin, and indeed people had sometimes tried to abbreviate her name that way, most notably her long-ago flirt in a temporary office, and her brother, Martin, when he wished to annoy her. Cunliffe was Matthew's surname.

To her relief, he had left for work early that day, because he was auditing an office out in Barnet, leaving Robin free to complete her physical transformation without undermining remarks and displeasure that she was, again, going undercover. Indeed, she thought she might derive a certain pleasure from using her married name – the first time she had ever offered it as her own – while embodying a girl whom Matthew would instinctively dislike. The older he got, the more Matthew was aggravated by and contemptuous of people who did not dress, think or live as he did.

The Wiccan's jewellery shop, Triquetra, was tucked away in Camden Market. Arriving outside at a quarter to nine, Robin found the stallholders of Camden Lock Place already busy, but the store locked up and empty. After a five-minute wait, her employer arrived, puffing slightly. A large woman whom Robin guessed to be in her late fifties, she had straggly dyed black hair that showed half an inch of silver root, had the same savage approach to eyeliner as Bobbi Cunliffe and wore a long green velvet dress.

During the cursory interview that had led to today's trial, the shop owner had asked very few questions, instead speaking at length about the husband of thirty years who had just left her to live in Thailand, the neighbour who was suing her over a boundary dispute and the stream of unsatisfactory and ungrateful employees who had walked out on Triquetra to take other jobs. Her undisguised desire to extract the maximum amount of work for the minimum amount of pay, coupled with her outpourings of self-pity, made Robin wonder why anybody had ever wanted to work for her in the first place.

'You're punctual,' she observed, when within earshot. 'Good. Where's the other one?'

'I don't know,' said Robin.

'I *don't need this*,' said the owner, with a slight note of hysteria. 'Not on the day I've got to meet Brian's lawyer!'

She unlocked the door and showed Robin into the shop, which was the size of a large kiosk, and as she raised her arms to start pulling up blinds, the smell of body odour and patchouli mingled with the dusty, incense-scented air. Daylight fell into the shop like a solid thing, rendering everything there more insubstantial and shabby by comparison. Dull silver necklaces and earrings hung in racks on the dark purple walls, many of them featuring pentagrams, peace symbols and marijuana leaves, while glass hookahs mingled with tarot cards, black candles, essential oils and ceremonial daggers on black shelves behind the counter.

'We've got *millions* of extra tourists coming through Camden right now,' said the owner, bustling around the back of the counter, 'and if she doesn't turn – *there you are*,' she said, as Flick, who looked sulky, sloped inside. Flick was wearing a yellow and green Hezbollah T-shirt and ripped jeans, and carrying a large leather messenger bag.

'Tube was late,' she said.

'Well, *I* managed to get here all right, and so did Bibi!'

'Bobbi,' Robin corrected her, deliberately broadening her Yorkshire accent.

She didn't want to pretend to be a Londoner this time. It was best not to have to talk about schools and locales that Flick might know.

'—well, I need you two to be on top of things *all – the – time,*' said the owner, beating out the last three words with one hand against the other. 'All right, Bibi—'

'—Bobbi—'

'—yes, come here and see how the till works.'

Robin had no difficulty grasping how the till worked, because she had had a Saturday job in her teens at a clothes shop in Harrogate. It was just as well that she did not need longer instruction, because a steady stream of shoppers began to arrive about ten minutes after they opened. To Robin's slight surprise, because there was nothing in the shop that she would have cared to buy, many visitors to Camden seemed to feel that their trip would be incomplete without a pair of pewter earrings, or a pentagram-embossed candle, or one of the small hessian bags that lay in a basket beside the till, each of which purported to contain a magic charm.

'All right, I need to be off,' the owner announced at eleven, while Flick was serving a tall German woman who was dithering between two packs of tarot cards. 'Don't forget: one of you needs to be focused on stock all the time, in case of pilfering. My friend Eddie will be keeping an eye out,' she said, pointing at the stall selling old LPs just outside. 'Twenty minutes each for lunch, taken separately. Don't forget,' she repeated ominously, 'Eddie's watching.'

She left in a whirl of velvet and body odour. The German

customer departed with her tarot cards and Flick slammed the till drawer shut, the noise echoing in the temporarily empty shop.

'Old Steady Eddie,' she said venomously. 'He doesn't give a shit. We could rob her blind and he wouldn't care. Cow,' added Flick for good measure.

Robin laughed and Flick seemed gratified.

'What's tha name?' asked Robin, in broad Yorkshire. 'She never said.'

'Flick,' said Flick. 'You're Bobbi, yeah?'

'Yeah,' said Robin.

Flick took out her mobile from her messenger bag, which she had stowed beneath the counter, checked it, appeared not to see what she had hoped to see, then stuffed it out of sight again.

'You must've been hard up for work, were you?' she asked Robin.

'Had to take what I could,' Robin said. 'I were sacked.'

'Yeah?'

'Fookin' Amazon,' said Robin.

'Those tax-dodging bastards,' said Flick, slightly more interested. 'What happened?'

'Didn't make my daily rate.'

Robin had lifted her story directly from a recent news report about working conditions in one of the retail company's warehouses: the relentless pressure to make targets, packing and scanning thousands of products a day under unforgiving pressure from supervisors. Flick's expression wavered between sympathy and anger as Robin talked.

'That's outrageous!' she said, when Robin had finished.

'Yeah,' said Robin, 'and no union or nothing, obviously. Me dad were a big trade union man back in Yorkshire.'

'Bet he was furious.'

'He's dead,' said Robin, unblushingly. 'Lungs. Ex-miner.'

'Oh, shit,' said Flick. 'Sorry.'

She was looking upon Robin with respect and interest now.

'See, you'll have been a worker, not an employee. That's how the bastards get away with it.'

'What's the difference?'

'Fewer statutory rights,' said Flick. 'You might have a case against them if they deducted from your wages, though.'

'Dunno if I could prove that,' said Robin. 'How come you know all this?'

'I'm pretty active in the labour movement,' said Flick, with a shrug. She hesitated, 'And my mother's an employment lawyer.'

'Yeah?' said Robin, allowing herself to sound politely surprised.

'Yeah,' said Flick, picking her nails, 'but we don't get on. I don't see any of my family, actually. They don't like my partner. Or my politics.'

She smoothed out the Hezbollah T-shirt and showed Robin.

'What, are they Tories?' asked Robin.

'Might as well be,' said Flick. 'They loved bloody Blair.'

Robin felt her phone vibrate in the pocket of her second-hand dress.

'Is there a bog anywhere here?'

'Through here,' said Flick, pointing to a well-hidden purple painted door with more racks of jewellery nailed to it.

Beyond the purple door Robin found a small cubbyhole with a cracked, dirty window. A safe sat beside a dilapidated kitchen unit with a kettle, a couple of cleaning products and a stiff J-cloth on top. There was no room to sit down and barely room to stand, because a grubby toilet had been plumbed into the corner.

Robin shut herself inside the chipboard cubicle, put down

the toilet lid and sat down to read the lengthy text that Barclay had just sent to both her and Strike.

Billy's been found. He was picked up off street 2 weeks ago. Psychotic episode, sectioned, hospital in north London, don't know which yet. Wouldn't tell docs his next of kin till yesterday. Social worker contacted Jimmy this morning. Jimmy wants me to go with him to persuade Billy to discharge himself. Scared what Billy's going to tell the doctors, says he talks too much. Also, Jimmy's lost bit of paper with Billy's name on & he's shitting himself about it. Asked me if I'd seen it. He says it's handwritten, no other details, I don't know why so important. Jimmy thinks Flick's nicked it. Things bad between them again.

As Robin was reading this for a second time, a response came in from Strike.

Barclay: find out visiting arrangements at the hospital, I want to see Billy. Robin: try and search Flick's bag.

Thanks, Robin texted back, exasperated. **I'd never have thought of that on my own.**

She got up, flushed the toilet and returned to the shop, where a gang of black-clad goths were picking over the stock like drooping crows. As she sidled past Flick, Robin saw that her messenger bag was sitting on a shelf beneath the counter. When the group had finally left in possession of essential oils and black candles, Flick took out her phone to check it again, before sinking once more into a morose silence.

Robin's experience in many temporary offices had taught her that little bonded women more than discovering that they were not alone in their particular man-related miseries. Taking out her own phone, she saw a further text from Strike:

That's why I get paid the big money. Brains.

Amused against her will, Robin suppressed a grin and said: 'He must think I'm fooking stupid.'

'Wassup?'

'Boyfriend. So-called,' said Robin, ramming her phone back into her pocket. 'S'posed to be separated from his wife. Guess where he was last night? Mate of mine saw him leaving hers this morning.' She exhaled loudly and slumped down on the counter.

'Yeah, my boyfriend likes old women and all,' said Flick, picking at her nails. Robin, who had not forgotten that Jimmy had been married to a woman thirteen years his senior, hoped for more confidences, but before she could ask more, another group of young women entered, chattering in a language that Robin did not recognise, though she thought it sounded Eastern European. They clustered around the basket of supposed charms.

'*Dziękuję ci*,' Flick said, as one of them handed over her money, and the girls laughed and complimented her on her accent.

'What did you just say?' asked Robin, as the party left. 'Was that Russian?'

'Polish. Learned a bit from my parents' cleaner.' Flick hurried on, as though she had given something away, 'Yeah, I always got on better with the cleaners than I did with my parents, actually, you can't call yourself a socialist and have a cleaner, can you? Nobody should be allowed to live in a house too big for them, we should have forcible repossessions, redistribution of land and housing to the people who need it.'

'Too right,' said Robin enthusiastically, and Flick seemed reassured to be forgiven her professional parents by Bobbi Cunliffe, daughter of a dead ex-miner and Yorkshire trade unionist.

'Want a tea?' she offered.

'Aye, that'd be great,' said Robin.

'Have you heard of the Real Socialist Party?' asked Flick, once she had come back into the shop with two mugs.

'No,' said Robin.

'It's not your normal political party,' Flick assured her. 'We're more like a proper community-based campaign, like, back to the Jarrow marchers, that kind of thing, the real spirit of labour movement, not an imperialist Tory-lite shower of shite like fucking "New Labour". We don't want to play the same old politics game, we want to change the rules of the game in favour of ordinary working—'

Billy Bragg's version of the 'Internationale' rang out. As Flick reached into her bag, Robin realised that this was Flick's ringtone. Reading the caller's name, Flick became tense.

'You be all right on your own for a bit?'

'Course,' said Robin.

Flick slid into the back room. As the door swung shut Robin heard her say:

'What's going on? Have you seen him?'

As soon as the door was securely shut, Robin hurried to where Flick had been standing, crouched down and slid her hand under the leather flap of the messenger bag. The interior resembled the depths of a bin. Her fingers groped through sundry bits of crumpled paper, sweet wrappers, a sticky lump of something Robin thought might be chewed gum, various lid-less pens and tubes of make-up, a tin with a picture of Che Guevara on it, a pack of rolling tobacco that had leaked over the rest of the contents, some Rizlas, some spare tampons and a small, twisted ball of fabric that Robin was afraid might be a pair of worn pants. Trying to flatten out, read and then re-crumple each piece of paper was time-consuming. Most seemed to be abandoned drafts of articles. Then, through the door behind her, she heard Flick say loudly:

'*Strike?* What the hell . . .'

Robin froze, listening.

' . . . paranoid . . . it alone now . . . tell them he's . . . '

'Excuse me,' said a woman peering over the counter. Robin jumped up. The portly, grey-haired customer in a tie-dyed T-shirt pointed up at the shelf on the wall, 'could I see that rather special *athame*?'

'Which?' asked Robin, confused.

'The *athame.* The ceremonial dagger,' said the elderly woman, pointing.

Flick's voice rose and fell in the room behind Robin.

' . . . it, didn't you? . . . member you . . . pay me back . . . Chiswell's money . . . '

'Mmm,' said the customer, weighing the knife carefully in her hand, 'have you anything larger?'

'*You had it, not me!*' said Flick loudly, from behind the door.

'Um,' said Robin, squinting up at the shelf, 'I think this is all we've got. That one might be a bit bigger . . . '

She stood on tiptoe to reach the longer knife, as Flick said:

'*Fuck off, Jimmy!*'

'There you are,' said Robin, handing over the seven-inch-dagger.

With a clatter of falling necklaces, the door behind Robin flew open, hitting her in the back.

'Sorry,' said Flick, seizing her bag and shoving the phone back inside it, breathing hard, her eyes bright.

'Yes, you see, I like the triple moon marking on the smaller one,' said the elderly witch, pointing at the decoration on the hilt of the first dagger, unfazed by Flick's dramatic reappearance, 'but I prefer the longer blade.'

Flick was in that febrile state between fury and tears that Robin knew was one of the most amenable to indiscretion and confession. Desperate to get rid of her tiresome customer, she said bluntly in Bobbi's thick Yorkshire:

'Well, that's all we've got.'

The customer chuntered a little more, weighing the two knives in her hands, and at last took herself off without buying either.

'Y'all right?' Robin asked Flick at once.

'No,' said Flick. 'I need a smoke.'

She checked her watch.

'Tell her I'm taking lunch if she comes back, all right?'

Damn, thought Robin, as Flick disappeared, taking her bag and her promising mood with her.

For over an hour, Robin minded the shop alone, becoming increasingly hungry. Once or twice, Eddie at the record stall peered vaguely into the shop at Robin, but showed no other interest in her activities. In a brief lull between more customers, Robin nipped into the back room to make sure that there wasn't any food there that she had overlooked. There wasn't.

At ten to one, Flick strolled back into the shop with a dark, thuggishly handsome man in a tight blue T-shirt. He subjected Robin to the hard, arrogant stare of a certain brand of womaniser, melding appreciation and disdain to signal that she might be good-looking, but she would have to try a little harder than that to arouse his interest. It was a strategy that Robin had seen work on other young women in offices. It had never worked on her.

'Sorry I was so long,' Flick told Robin. Her bad mood did

not seem entirely dissipated. 'Ran into Jimmy. Jimmy, this is Bobbi.'

'All right?' said Jimmy, holding out a hand.

Robin shook it.

'You go,' said Flick to Robin. 'Go and get something to eat.'

'Oh, right,' said Robin. 'Thanks.'

Jimmy and Flick waited while, under cover of checking her bag for money, Robin crouched down and, hidden by the counter, set her mobile to record before placing it carefully at the back of the dark shelf.

'See tha in a bit, then,' she said brightly, and strolled away into the market.

48

But what do you say to it all, Rebecca?

Henrik Ibsen, *Rosmersholm*

A whining wasp zigzagged from inner to outer rooms of Strike's office, passing between the two windows that were flung open to admit the fume-laden evening air. Barclay waved the insect away with the takeaway menu that had just arrived with a large delivery of Chinese food. Robin peeled lids off the cartons and laid them out on her desk. Over by the kettle, Strike was trying to find a third fork.

Matthew had been surprisingly accommodating when Robin had called him from Charing Cross Road three-quarters of an hour previously, to say that she needed to meet Strike and Barclay, and was likely to be back late.

'Fine,' he had said, 'Tom wants to go for a curry, anyway. I'll see you at home.'

'How was today?' Robin asked, before he could hang up. 'The office out in . . .'

Her mind went blank.

'Barnet,' he said. 'Games developer. Yeah, it was all right. How was yours?'

'Not bad,' said Robin.

Matthew was so determinedly uninterested in the details of the Chiswell job after their many arguments about it that there seemed no point in telling him where she had been, who she was impersonating, or what had happened that day. After they had said goodbye, Robin walked on through meandering tourists and Friday night drinkers, knowing that a casual listener would have taken the conversation to be that of two people connected merely by proximity or circumstance, with no particular liking for each other.

'Want a beer?' Strike asked her, holding up a four pack of Tennent's.

'Yes, please,' said Robin.

She was still wearing her short black dress and lace-up boots, but had tied back her chalked hair, cleaned her face of its thick make-up and removed her dark lenses. Seeing Strike's face in a patch of evening sunlight, she thought he looked unwell. There were deeper lines than usual around his mouth and across his forehead, lines etched there, she suspected, by grinding, daily pain. He was also moving awkwardly, using his upper body to turn and trying to disguise his limp as he returned to her desk with the beer.

'What've you been up to today?' she asked Strike, as Barclay heaped his plate with food.

'Following Geraint Winn. He's holed up in a miserable B&B five minutes away from the marital home. He led me all the way into central London and back to Bermondsey again.'

'Risky, following him,' commented Robin. 'He knows what you look like.'

'All three of us could've been behind him and he wouldn't have noticed. He's lost about a stone since I last saw him.'

'What did he do?'

'Went to eat in a place right by the Commons, called the Cellarium. No windows, like a crypt.'

'Sounds cheerful,' said Barclay, settling down on the fake leather sofa and starting on his sweet and sour pork balls.

'He's like a sad homing pigeon,' said Strike, tipping the whole tub of Singapore noodles onto his own plate, 'returning to the place of his former glories with the tourists. Then we went to King's Cross.'

Robin paused in the act of helping herself to beansprouts.

'Blow job in a dark stairwell,' said Strike matter-of-factly.

'Eurgh,' muttered Robin, continuing to help herself to food.

'Did ye see it, aye?' asked Barclay with interest.

'Back view. Elbowed my way through the front door, then backed out with apologies. He was in no state to recognise me. After that, he bought himself some new socks from Asda and went back to his B&B.'

'There are worse days out,' said Barclay, who had already eaten half the food on his plate. Catching Robin's eye, he said through a mouthful, 'Wife wants me home by half eight.'

'All right, Robin,' said Strike, lowering himself gingerly onto his own desk chair, which he had brought through to the outer office, 'let's hear what Jimmy and Flick had to say to each other when they thought no one was listening.'

He opened a notebook and took a pen from the pot on her desk, leaving his left hand free to fork Singapore noodles into his mouth. Still chewing vigorously, Barclay leaned forwards on the sofa, interested. Robin placed her mobile face up on the desk and pressed 'play'.

For a moment there was no sound except faint footsteps, which were Robin's, leaving the Wiccan's shop earlier in search of lunch.

'I thought you were here on your own?' said Jimmy's voice, faint but clear.

'She's having a day's trial,' said Flick. 'Where's Sam?'

'I told him I'll meet him at yours later. Right, where's your bag?'

'Jimmy, I haven't—'

'Maybe you picked it up by mistake.'

More footsteps, a scraping of wood and leather, clattering, thunks and furtive rustlings.

'This is a fucking tip.'

'I haven't got it, how many more times? And you've got no right to search that without my—'

'This is serious. I had it in my wallet. Where's it gone?'

'You've dropped it somewhere, haven't you?'

'Or someone's taken it.'

'Why would *I* take it?'

'Insurance policy.'

'That's a hell of an—'

'But if that's what you're thinking, you wanna remember, you fucking nicked it, so it incriminates you as much as me. More.'

'I was only there in the first place because of you, Jimmy!'

'Oh, *that's* going to be the story, is it? Nobody bloody made you. You're the one who started all this, remember.'

'Yeah and I wish I hadn't, now!'

'Too late for that. I want that paper back and so should you. It proves we had access to his place.'

'You mean it proves a connection between him and Bill – ouch!'

'Oh, fuck off, that didn't hurt! You demean women who really are knocked around, playing the victim. I'm not kidding, now. If you've taken it—'

'Don't threaten me—'

'What're you going to do, run off to Mummy and Daddy? How're they going to feel when they find out what their little girl's been up to?'

Flick's rapid breathing now became sobs.

'You nicked money from him, and all,' said Jimmy.

'You thought it was a laugh at the time, you said he deserved it—'

'Try that defence in court, see how far it gets you. If you try and save yourself by throwing me under the bus, I won't have any fucking problem telling the pigs you were in this thing *all the way*. So if that bit of paper turns up somewhere I don't want it to go—'

'I haven't got it, I don't know where it is!'

'—you've been fucking warned. Give me your front door key.'

'What? Why?'

'Because I'm going over to that shithole you call a flat right now and I'm searching it with Sam.'

'You're not going over there without me—'

'Why not? Got another Indian waiter sleeping off his hangover there, have you?'

'I never—'

'I don't give a shit,' said Jimmy. 'Screw whoever you like. Give me your key. *Give it me*.'

More footsteps; a tinkling of keys. The sound of Jimmy walking away and then a cascade of sobs that continued until Robin pressed pause.

'She cried until the shop owner came back,' said Robin, 'which was just before I did, and she hardly spoke this afternoon. I tried to walk back to the Tube with her, but she shook me off. Hopefully she'll be in a more talkative mood tomorrow.'

'So, did you and Jimmy search her flat?' Strike asked Barclay.

'Aye. Books, drawers, under her mattress. Nothing.'

'What exactly did he say you were looking for?'

'"Bit o' paper wi' handwriting an' Billy's name on", he says. "I had it in me wallet and it's gone". Claims it's somethin' tae do with a drugs deal. He thinks I'm some ned who'll believe anythin'.'

Strike put down his pen, swallowed a large mouthful of noodles and said:

'Well, I don't know about you two, but what jumps out at me is "it proves we had access".'

'I think I might know a bit more about that,' said Robin, who had so far successfully concealed her excitement about what she was about to reveal. 'I found out today that Flick can speak a bit of Polish, and we know she stole cash from her previous place of work. What if—?'

'"I do that cleaning",' said Strike, suddenly. 'That's what she said to Jimmy, on the march, when I was following them! "I do that cleaning, and it's disgusting" . . . Bloody hell – you think she was—?'

'Chiswell's Polish cleaner,' said Robin, determined not to be robbed of her moment of triumph. 'Yes. I do.'

Barclay was continuing to shovel pork balls into his mouth, though his eyes were suitably surprised.

'If that's true, it changes bloody everything,' said Strike. 'She'd have had access, been able to snoop around, take stuff into the house—'

'How'd she find out he wanted a cleaner?' asked Barclay.

'Must've seen the card he put in a newsagent's window.'

'They live miles apart. She's in Hackney.'

'Maybe Jimmy spotted it, snooping around Ebury Street, trying to collect his blackmail money,' suggested Robin, but Strike was now frowning.

'But that's back to front. If she found out about the blackmailable offence when she was a cleaner, her employment must've pre-dated Jimmy trying to collect money.'

'All right, maybe Jimmy didn't tip her off. Maybe they found out he wanted a cleaner while they were trying to dig dirt on him in general.'

'So they could run an exposé on the Real Socialist Party website?' suggested Barclay. 'That'd reach a good four or five people.'

Strike snorted in amusement.

'Main point is,' he said, 'this piece of paper's got Jimmy very worried.'

Barclay speared his last pork ball and stuck it in his mouth. 'Flick's taken it,' he said thickly. 'I guarantee it.'

'Why are you so sure?' asked Robin.

'She wants somethin' over him,' said Barclay, getting up to take his empty plate over to the sink. 'Only reason he's keepin' her around is because she knows too much. He told me the other day he'd be happy tae get shot of her if he could. I asked why he couldnae just dump her. He didnae answer.'

'Maybe she's destroyed it, if it's so incriminating?' suggested Robin.

'I don't think so,' said Strike. 'She's a lawyer's daughter, she's not going to destroy evidence. Something like that paper could be valuable, if the shit hits the fan and she decides she's going to cooperate with the police.'

Barclay returned to the sofa and picked up his beer.

'How's Billy?' Robin asked him, getting started at last on her own cooling meal.

'Poor wee bastard,' said Barclay. 'Skin and bone. The traffic cops caught him when he jumped a Tube barrier. He tried tae batter them, ended up bein' sectioned. The doctors say he's got delusions o' persecution. At first he thought he was bein' chased by the government and the medical staff were all part o' some giant conspiracy, but now he's back on his medication he's a wee bit more rational.

'Jimmy wanted tae take him home there and then, but the docs werenae gonna let that happen. What's really pissin' Jimmy off,' said Barclay, pausing to finish his can of Tennent's, 'is Billy's still obsessed wi' Strike. Keeps askin' for him. The doctors think it's part o' his delusion, that he's latched ontae the famous detective as part of his fantasy, like: the only person he can really trust. Couldnae tell them he and Strike have met. Not wi' Jimmy standin' there telling them it's all a load o' pish.

'The medics don't want anyone near him except family, and they're no keen on Jimmy any more, neither, not after he tried tae persuade Billy he's well enough to go home.'

Barclay crushed his beer can in his hand and checked his watch.

'Gotta go, Strike.'

'Yeah, all right,' said Strike. 'Thanks for staying. Thought it would be good to have a joint debrief.'

'Nae bother.'

With a wave to Robin, Barclay departed. Strike bent to pick up his own beer off the floor and winced.

'You all right?' asked Robin, who was helping herself to more prawn crackers.

'Fine,' he said, straightening up again. 'I did a lot of walking again today, and I could have done without the fight yesterday.'

'Fight? What fight?' asked Robin.

'Aamir Mallik.'

'What!'

'Don't worry. I didn't hurt him. Much.'

'You didn't tell me the argument got physical!'

'I wanted to do it in person, so I could enjoy you looking at me like I'm a complete bastard,' said Strike. 'How about a bit of sympathy for your one-legged partner?'

'You're an ex-boxer!' said Robin. 'And he probably weighs about nine stone soaking wet!'

'He came at me with a lamp.'

'*Aamir* did?'

She couldn't imagine the reserved, meticulous man she had known in the House of Commons using physical violence against anyone.

'Yeah. I was pushing him about Chiswell's "man of your habits" comment and he snapped. If it makes you feel any better, I don't feel good about it,' said Strike. 'Hang on a minute. Need a pee.'

He pulled himself awkwardly out of the chair and departed for the bathroom on the landing. As she heard the door close, Strike's mobile, which was charging on top of the filing cabinet beside Robin's desk, rang. She got up to check it and saw, through the cracked and sellotaped screen, the name 'Lorelei'. Wondering whether to answer it, Robin hesitated too long and the call went to voicemail. Just as she was about to sit down again, a small *ping* declared that a text had arrived.

If you want a hot meal and a shag with no human emotions involved, there are restaurants and brothels.

Robin heard the bang of the bathroom door outside and stumbled hastily back to her chair. Strike limped back inside the room, lowered himself into his chair and picked up his noodles.

'Your phone just rang,' said Robin. 'I didn't pick up—'

'Chuck it over,' said Strike.

She did so. He read the text with no change of expression, muted the phone and put it in his pocket.

'What were we saying?'

'That you didn't feel good about the fight—'

'I feel fine about the fight,' Strike corrected her. 'If I hadn't defended myself I'd have a face full of stitches.'

He pronged a forkful of noodles.

'The bit I don't feel great about is when I told him I know he's been ostracised by his family, barring one sister who's still talking to him. It's all on Facebook. It was when I mentioned his family dropping him that I nearly got my head taken off with a table lamp.'

'Maybe they're upset because they think he's with Della?' suggested Robin as Strike chewed his noodles.

He shrugged and made an expression indicative of 'maybe', swallowed, and said, 'Has it occurred to you that Aamir is literally the only person connected with this case who's got a motive? Chiswell threatened him, presumably with exposure. "A man of your habits." "Lachesis knew when everyone's time was up".'

'What happened to "forget about motive, concentrate on means"?'

'Yeah, yeah,' said Strike wearily. He set aside his plate, from which he had eaten nearly all the noodles, took out his cigarettes and lighter, and sat up a little straighter. 'OK, let's focus on means.

'Who had access to the house, to anti-depressants and helium? Who knew Jasper Chiswell's habits well enough to be sure he'd drink his orange juice that morning? Who had a key, or, who would he have trusted enough to let in in the early hours of the morning?'

'Members of his family.'

'Right,' said Strike, as his lighter flared, 'but we know Kinvara, Fizzy, Izzy and Torquil can't have done it, which leaves us with Raphael and his story of being ordered down to Woolstone that morning.'

'You really think he could have killed his father then

driven coolly down to Woolstone to wait with Kinvara until the police arrived?'

'Forget psychology or probability: we're considering opportunity,' said Strike, blowing out a long jet of smoke. 'Nothing I've heard so far precludes Raphael being at Ebury Street at six in the morning. I know what you're going to say,' he forestalled her, 'but it wouldn't be the first time a phone call had been faked by a killer. He could have called his own mobile with Chiswell's to make it seem as though his father had ordered him down to Woolstone.'

'Which means that either Chiswell didn't have a passcode on his mobile, or that Raphael knew it.'

'Good point. That needs checking.'

Clicking out the nib of his pen, Strike made a note on his pad. As he did it, he wondered whether Robin's husband, who had previously deleted her call history without her knowledge, knew her current passcode. These small matters of trust were often powerful indicators of the strength of a relationship.

'There's another logistical problem if Raphael was the killer,' Robin said. 'He didn't have a key, and if his father let him in, it would mean Chiswell was awake and conscious while Raphael pounded up anti-depressants in the kitchen.'

'Another good point,' said Strike, 'but the pounding up of the pills has to be explained away with all of our suspects.

'Take Flick. If she was posing as the cleaner, she probably knew the house in Ebury Street better than most of the family. Loads of opportunities to poke around, and she had a restricted key for a while. They're hard to get copied, but let's say she managed it, so she could still let herself in and out of the house whenever she fancied.

'She creeps in in the early hours to doctor the orange juice, but crushing pills in a pestle and mortar is a noisy job—'

'—unless,' said Robin, 'she brought the pills already crushed up, in a bag or something, and dusted them around the pestle and mortar to make it look as though Chiswell had done it.'

'OK, but we still need to explain why there were no traces of amitriptyline in the empty orange juice carton in the bin. Raphael could plausibly have handed his father a glass of juice—'

'—except that Chiswell's prints were the only ones on there—'

'—but would Chiswell not find it odd to come downstairs in the morning to a pre-poured glass of juice? Would *you* drink a glass of something you hadn't poured, and which appeared mysteriously in what you thought was an empty house?'

Down in Denmark Street, a group of young women's voices rose over the constant swish and rumble of traffic, singing Rihanna's 'Where Have You Been?'

'*Where have you been? All my life, all my life . . .*'

'Maybe it *was* suicide,' said Robin.

'That attitude won't get the bills paid,' said Strike, tapping his cigarette ash onto his plate. 'Come on, people who had the means to get into Ebury Street that day: Raphael, Flick—'

'—and Jimmy,' said Robin. 'Everything that applies to Flick applies to him, because she would've been able to give him all the information she had about Chiswell's habits and his house, and given him her copied key.'

'Correct. So those are three people we know could have got in that morning,' said Strike, 'but this took much more than simply being able to get in through the door. The killer also had to know which anti-depressants Kinvara was taking, and arrange for the helium canister and rubber tubing to be there, which suggests close contact with the Chiswells, access to the house to get the stuff inside, or insider knowledge of the fact that the helium and tubing were already in there.'

'As far as we know, Raphael hadn't been in Ebury Street lately and wasn't on terms with Kinvara to know what pills she was taking, though I suppose his father might have mentioned it to him,' said Robin. 'Judged on opportunity alone, the Winns and Aamir seem to be ruled out . . . so, assuming she *was* the cleaner, Jimmy and Flick go to the top of our suspect list.'

Strike heaved a sigh and closed his eyes.

'Bollocks to it,' he muttered, as he passed a hand across his face, 'I keep circling back to motive.'

Opening his eyes again, he stubbed out his cigarette on his dinner plate and immediately lit another one.

'I'm not surprised MI5 are interested, because there's no obvious gain here. Oliver was right – blackmailers don't generally kill their victims, it's the other way around. Hatred's a picturesque idea, but a hot-blooded hate killing is a hammer or a lamp to the head, not a meticulously planned fake suicide. If it was murder, it was more like a clinical execution, planned in every detail. Why? What did the killer get out of it? Which also makes me wonder, why *then?* Why did Chiswell die *then*?

'It was surely in Jimmy and Flick's best interests for Chiswell to stay alive until they could produce evidence that forced him to come across with the money they wanted. Same with Raphael: he'd been written out of the will, but his relationship with his father was showing some signs of improvement. It was in his interest for his father to stay alive.

'But Chiswell had covertly threatened Aamir with exposure of something unspecified, but probably sexual, given the Catullus quotation, and he'd recently come into possession of information about the Winns' dodgy charity. We shouldn't forget that Geraint Winn wasn't really a blackmailer: he didn't want money, he wanted Chiswell's resignation and disgrace. Is it beyond the realms of possibility that Winn or Mallik took a different kind of revenge when they realised the first plan had failed?'

Strike dragged heavily on his cigarette and said:

'We're missing something, Robin. The thing that ties all this together.'

'Maybe it doesn't tie together,' said Robin. 'That's life, isn't it? We've got a group of people who all had their own personal tribulations and secrets. Some of them had reason not to like Chiswell, to resent him, but that doesn't mean it all joins up neatly. Some of it must be irrelevant.'

'There's still something we don't know.'

'There's a lot we don't—'

'No, something big, something ... fundamental. I can smell it. It keeps almost showing itself. Why did Chiswell say he might have more work for us after he'd scuppered Winn and Knight?'

'I don't know,' said Robin.

'"One by one, they trip themselves up",' Strike quoted. 'Who'd tripped themselves up?'

'Geraint Winn. I'd just told him about the missing money from the charity.'

'Chiswell had been on the phone, trying to find a money clip, you said. A money clip that belonged to Freddie.'

'That's right,' said Robin.

'Freddie,' repeated Strike, scratching his chin.

And for a moment he was back in the communal TV room of a German military hospital, with the television muted in the corner and copies of the *Army Times* lying on a low table. The young lieutenant who had witnessed Freddie Chiswell's death had been sitting there alone when Strike found him, wheelchair-bound, a bullet still lodged in his spine.

'. . . the convoy stopped, Major Chiswell told me to get out, see what was going on. I told him I could see movement up on the ridge. He told me to fucking well do as I was told.

'I hadn't gone more than a couple of feet when I got the bullet in the back. The last thing I remember was him yelling out of the lorry at me. Then the sniper took the top of his head off.'

The lieutenant had asked Strike for a cigarette. He wasn't supposed to be smoking, but Strike had given him the half pack he had on him.

'Chiswell was a cunt,' said the young man in the wheelchair.

In Strike's imagination he saw tall, blond Freddie swaggering up a country lane, slumming it with Jimmy Knight and his mates. He saw Freddie in fencing garb, out on the piste, watched by the indistinct figure of Rhiannon Winn, who was perhaps already entertaining suicidal thoughts.

Disliked by his soldiers, revered by his father: could Freddie be the thing that Strike sought, the element that tied everything together, that connected two blackmailers and the story of a strangled child? But the notion seemed to dissolve as he examined it, and the diverse strands of the investigation fell apart once more, stubbornly unconnected.

'I want to know what the photographs from the Foreign Office show,' said Strike aloud, his eyes on the purpling sky beyond the office window. 'I want to know who hacked the Uffington white horse onto the back of Aamir Mallik's bathroom door, and I want to know why there was a cross in the ground on the exact spot Billy said a kid was buried.'

'Well,' said Robin, standing up and beginning to clear away the debris of their Chinese takeaway, 'nobody ever said you weren't ambitious.'

'Leave that. I'll do it. You need to get home.'

I don't want to go home.

'It won't take long. What are you up to tomorrow?'

'Got an afternoon appointment with Chiswell's art dealer friend, Drummond.'

Having rinsed off the plates and cutlery, Robin took her handbag down from the peg where she'd hung it, then turned back. Strike tended to rebuff expressions of concern, but she had to say it.

'No offence, but you look terrible. Maybe rest your leg before you have to go out again? See you soon.'

She left before Strike could answer. He sat lost in thought until, finally, he knew he must begin the painful journey back upstairs to his attic flat. Having heaved himself upright again, he closed the windows, turned off the lights and locked up the office.

As he placed his false foot on the bottom stair to the floor above, his phone rang again. He knew, without checking, that it was Lorelei. She wasn't about to let him go without at least attempting to hurt him as badly as he had hurt her. Slowly, carefully, keeping his weight off his prosthesis as much as was practical, Strike climbed the stairs to bed.

49

Rosmers of Rosmersholm – clergymen, soldiers, men who have filled high places in the state – men of scrupulous honour, every one of them . . .

Henrik Ibsen, *Rosmersholm*

Lorelei didn't give up. She wanted to see Strike face to face, wanted to know why she had given nearly a year of her life, as she saw it, to an emotional vampire.

'You owe me a meeting,' she said, when he finally picked up the phone at lunchtime next day. 'I want to see you. You owe me that.'

'And what will that achieve?' he asked her. 'I read your email, you've made your feelings clear. I told you from the start what I wanted and what I didn't want—'

'Don't give me that "I never pretended I wanted anything serious" line. Who did you call when you couldn't walk? You were happy enough for me to act like your wife when you were—'

'So let's both agree I'm a bastard,' he said, sitting in his combined kitchen-sitting room with his amputated leg stretched out on a chair in front of him. He was wearing only boxer shorts, but would soon need to get his prosthesis on and dress smartly enough to blend in at Henry Drummond's art gallery. 'Let's wish each other well and—'

'No,' she said, 'you don't get out of it that easily. I was happy, I was doing fine—'

'I never wanted to make you miserable. I like you—'

'You *like* me,' she repeated shrilly. 'A year together and you *like* me—'

'What do you want?' he said, losing his temper at last. 'Me to limp up the fucking aisle, not feeling what I should feel, not wanting it, wishing I was out of it? You're making me say what I don't want to say. I didn't want to hurt anyone—'

'But you did! You *did* hurt me! And now you want to walk away as though nothing happened!'

'Whereas you want a public scene in a restaurant?'

'I want,' she said, crying now, 'not to feel as though I could have been anyone. I want a memory of the end that doesn't make me feel disposable and cheap—'

'I never saw you that way. I don't see you like that now,' he said, eyes closed, wishing he had never crossed the room at Wardle's party. 'Truth is, you're too—'

'Don't tell me I'm too good for you,' she said. 'Leave us both with some dignity.'

She hung up. Strike's dominant emotion was relief.

No investigation had ever brought Strike so reliably back to the same small patch of London. The taxi disgorged him onto the gently sloping pavement of St James's Street a few hours later, with the red brick St James's Palace ahead and Pratt's on Park Place to his right. After paying off the driver, he headed for Drummond's Gallery, which lay between a wine dealer's and a hat shop on the left-hand side of the street. Although he had managed to put his prosthesis on, Strike was walking with the aid of a collapsible walking stick that Robin had bought him during another period when his leg had become almost too painful to bear his weight.

Even if it had marked the end of a relationship he wanted to escape, the call with Lorelei had left its mark. He knew in his heart that he was, in the spirit if not in the letter, guilty of some of the charges she had laid against him. While he had told Lorelei at the outset that he sought neither commitment nor permanence, he had known perfectly well that she had understood him to mean 'right now' rather than 'never' and he had not corrected that impression, because he wanted a distraction and a defence against the feelings that had dogged him after Robin's wedding.

However, the ability to section off his emotions, of which Charlotte had always complained, and to which Lorelei had dedicated a lengthy paragraph of the email dissecting his personality, had never failed him yet. Arriving two minutes early for his appointment with Henry Drummond, he transferred his attention with ease to the questions he intended to put to the late Jasper Chiswell's old friend.

Pausing beside the black marble exterior of the gallery, he saw himself reflected in the window and straightened his tie. He was wearing his best Italian suit. Behind his reflection, tastefully illuminated, a single painting in an ornate golden frame stood on an easel behind the spotless glass. It featured a pair of what, to Strike, looked like unrealistic horses with giraffe-like necks and staring eyes, ridden by eighteenth-century jockeys.

The gallery beyond the heavy door was cool and silent, with a floor of highly polished white marble. Strike walked carefully with his stick among the sporting and wildlife paintings, which were illuminated discreetly around the white walls, all of them in heavy gilded frames, until a well-groomed young blonde in a tight black dress emerged from a side door.

'Oh, good afternoon,' she said, without asking his name, and walked away towards the back of the gallery, her stilettos making a metallic click on the tiles. 'Henry! Mr Strike's here!'

A concealed door opened, and Drummond emerged: a curious-looking man, whose ascetic features of pinched nose and black brows were enclosed by rolls of fat around chin and neck, as though a puritan had been engulfed by the body of a jolly squire. With his mutton-chop whiskers and dark grey suit and waistcoat he had a timeless, irrefutably upper-class, appearance.

'How do you do?' he said, offering a warm, dry hand. 'Come into the office.'

'Henry, Mrs Ross just called,' said the blonde, as Strike walked into the small room beyond the discreet door, which was book-lined, mahogany-shelved and very tidy. 'She'd like to see the Munnings before we close. I've told her it's reserved, but she'd still like—'

'Let me know when she arrives,' said Drummond. 'And could we have some tea, Lucinda? Or coffee?' he enquired of Strike.

'Tea would be great, thank you.'

'Do sit down,' said Drummond, and Strike did so, grateful for a large and sturdy leather chair. The antique desk between them was bare but for a tray of engraved writing paper, a fountain pen and an ivory and silver letter opener. 'So,' said Henry Drummond heavily, 'you're looking into this appalling business for the family?'

'That's right. D'you mind if I take notes?'

'Carry on.'

Strike took out his notebook and pen. Drummond swivelled gently from side to side in his rotating chair.

'Terrible shock,' he said softly. 'Of course, one thought immediately of foreign interference. Government minister, eyes of the world on London with the Olympics and so forth . . . '

'You didn't think he could have committed suicide?' asked Strike.

Drummond sighed heavily.

'I knew him for forty-five years. His life had not been devoid of vicissitudes. To have come through everything – the divorce from Patricia, Freddie's death, resignation from the government, Raphael's ghastly car accident – to end it *now*, when he was Minister for Culture, when everything seemed back on track . . .

'Because the Conservative Party was his life's blood, you know,' said Drummond. 'Oh, yes. He'd bleed blue. Hated being out, delighted to get back in again, rise to minister . . . we joked of him becoming PM, in our younger days of course, but that dream was gone. Jasper always said, "Tory faithful likes bastards or buffoons", and that he was neither one nor the other.'

'So you'd say he was in generally good spirits around the time he died?'

'Ah . . . well, no, I couldn't say that. There were stresses, worries – but suicidal? Definitely not.'

'When was the last time you saw him?'

'The last time we met face to face was here, at the gallery,' said Drummond. 'I can tell you exactly what date it was: Friday the twenty-second of June.'

This, Strike knew, was the day that he had met Chiswell for the first time. He remembered the minister walking away towards Drummond's gallery after their lunch at Pratt's.

'And how did he seem to you that day?'

'Extremely angry,' said Drummond, 'but that was inevitable, given what he walked in on, here.'

Drummond picked up the letter opener and turned it delicately in his thick fingers.

'His son – Raphael – had just been caught, for the second time – ah—'

Drummond balked for a second.

'—*in flagrante*,' he said, 'with the other young person I employed at that time, in the bathroom behind me.'

He indicated a discreet black door.

'I had already caught them in there, a month prior to that. I hadn't told Jasper the first time, because I felt he had quite enough on his plate.'

'In what way?'

Drummond fingered the ornate ivory, cleared his throat and said:

'Jasper's marriage isn't – wasn't . . . I mean to say, Kinvara is a handful. Difficult woman. She was badgering Jasper to put one of her mares in foal to Totilas at the time.'

When Strike looked blank, Drummond elucidated:

'Top dressage stallion. Nigh on ten thousand for semen.'

'Christ,' said Strike.

'Well, quite,' said Drummond. 'And when Kinvara doesn't get what she wants . . . one doesn't know whether it's temperament or something deeper – actual mental instability – anyway, Jasper had a very difficult time with her.

'Then he'd been through the ghastly business of Raphael's, ah, accident – that poor young mother killed – the press, and so on and so forth, his son in jail . . . as a friend, I didn't want to add to his troubles.

'I'd told Raphael the first time it happened that I wouldn't inform Jasper, but I also said he was on a final warning and if he stepped out of line again, he would be out on his ear, old friend of his father's or not. I had Francesca to consider, too. She's my goddaughter, eighteen years old and completely smitten with him. I didn't want to have to tell her parents.

'So when I walked in and heard them, I really had no choice. I'd thought I was safe to leave Raphael in charge for an hour because Francesca wasn't at work that day, but of course, she'd sneaked in specially to see him, on her day off.

'Jasper arrived to find me pounding on the door. There was no way to hide what was going on. Raphael was trying to block my entrance to the bathroom here while Francesca climbed out of the window. She couldn't face me. I rang her parents, told them everything. She never came back.

'Raphael Chiswell,' said Drummond heavily, 'is a Bad Lot. Freddie, the son who died – my godchild too, incidentally – was worth a million of . . . well, well,' he said, turning the penknife over and over in his fingers, 'one shouldn't say it, I know.'

The office door opened and the young blonde in the black dress entered with a tea tray. Strike compared it mentally to the tea he had in the office as she set down two silver pots, one containing hot water, bone china cups and saucers and a sugar bowl complete with tongs.

'Mrs Ross has just arrived, Henry.'

'Tell her I'm tied up for the next twenty minutes or so. Ask her to wait, if she's got time.'

'So I take it,' said Strike, when Lucinda had left, 'that there wasn't much time for conversation that day?'

'Well, no,' said Drummond, unhappily. 'Jasper had come to see Raphael at work, believing that all was going splendidly, and to arrive in the middle of that scene . . . Totally on my side, obviously, once he grasped what was going on. He was the one who actually shoved the boy out of the way to get the bathroom door open. Then he turned a nasty colour. He had a heart problem, you know, it had been grumbling on for years. Sat down on the toilet rather suddenly. I was very worried, but he wouldn't let me call Kinvara . . .

'Raphael had the decency to be ashamed of himself, then. Tried to help his father. Jasper told him to get out of it, made me close the door, leave him in there . . . '

Now sounding gruff, Drummond broke off and poured himself and Strike tea. He was evidently in some distress. As he added three lumps to his own cup, the teaspoon rattled against the cup.

''Pologise. Last time I ever saw Jasper, you see. He came out of the bathroom, ghastly colour, still, shook my hand, apologised, said he'd let his oldest friend . . . let me down.'

Drummond coughed again, swallowed and continued with what seemed an effort:

'None of it was Jasper's fault. Raphael learned such morals as he's got from the mother, and she's best described as a high-class . . . well, well. Meeting Ornella was really the start of all Jasper's problems. If he'd only stayed with Patricia . . .

'Anyway, I never saw Jasper again. I had some difficulty bringing myself to shake Raphael's hand at the funeral, if you want the truth.'

Drummond took a sip of tea and Strike tried his own. It was far too weak.

'All sounds very unpleasant,' the detective said.

'You may well say so,' sighed Drummond.

'You'll appreciate that I have to ask about some sensitive matters.'

'Of course,' said Drummond.

'You've spoken to Izzy. Did she tell you that Jasper Chiswell was being blackmailed?'

'She mentioned it,' said Drummond, with a glance to check that the door was shut. 'He hadn't breathed a word to me. Izzy said it was one of the Knights . . . one remembers a family in the grounds. The father was an odd-job man, yes? As for the Winns, well, no, I don't think there was much liking between them and Jasper. Strange couple.'

'The Winns' daughter Rhiannon was a fencer,' said Strike. 'She was on the junior British fencing team with Freddie Chiswell—'

'Oh yes, Freddie was awfully good,' said Drummond.

'Rhiannon was a guest at Freddie's eighteenth birthday party, but she was a couple of years younger. She was only sixteen when she killed herself.'

'How ghastly,' said Drummond.

'You don't know anything about that?'

'How should I?' said Drummond, a fine crease between his dark eyes.

'You weren't at the eighteenth?'

'I was, as a matter of fact. Godfather, you know.'

'You can't remember Rhiannon?'

'Goodness, you can't expect me to remember all the names! There were upwards of a hundred young people there. Jasper had a marquee in the garden and Patricia ran a treasure hunt.'

'Really?' said Strike.

His own eighteenth birthday party, in a rundown pub in Shoreditch, had not included a treasure hunt.

'Just in the grounds, you know. Freddie always liked a competition. A glass of champagne at every clue, it was rather jolly, got things off with a swing. I was manning clue three, down by what the children always used to call the dell.'

'The hollow in the ground by the Knights' cottage?' asked Strike casually. 'It was full of nettles when I saw it.'

'We didn't put the clue *in* the dell, we put it under Jack o'Kent's doormat. He couldn't be trusted to take care of the champagne, because he had a drink problem. I sat on the edge of the dell in a deck chair and watched them hunt and everyone who found the clue got a glass of champagne and off they went.'

'Soft drinks for the under-eighteens?' asked Strike.

Faintly exasperated by this killjoy attitude, Drummond said:

'Nobody *had* to drink champagne. It was an eighteenth, a celebration.'

'So Jasper Chiswell never mentioned anything to you that he wouldn't want to get into the press?' asked Strike, returning to the main point.

'Nothing whatsoever.'

'When he asked me to find a way of countering his blackmailers, he told me that whatever he'd done happened six years ago. He implied to me that it wasn't illegal when he did it, but is now.'

'I've no idea what that could have been. Jasper was a very law-abiding type, you know. Whole family, pillars of the community, churchgoers, they've done masses for the local area . . . '

A litany of Chiswellian beneficence followed, which rolled on for a couple of minutes and did not fool Strike in the slightest. Drummond was obfuscating, he was sure, because Drummond knew exactly what Chiswell had done. He became almost lyrical as he extolled the innate goodness of Jasper, and of the entire family, excepting, always, the scapegrace Raphael.

' . . . and hand always in his pocket,' Drummond concluded, 'minibus for the local Brownies, repairs to the church roof, even after the family finances . . . well, well,' he said again, in a little embarrassment.

'The blackmailable offence,' Strike began again, but Drummond interrupted.

'There was no offence.' He caught himself. 'You just said

it yourself. Jasper told you he had done nothing illegal. No law was broken.'

Deciding that it would do no good to push Drummond harder about the blackmail, Strike turned a page in his notebook, and thought he saw the other relax.

'You called Chiswell on the morning he died,' said Strike.

'I did.'

'Would that have been the first time you'd spoken since sacking Raphael?'

'Actually, no. There had been a conversation a couple of weeks prior to that. M'wife wanted to invite Jasper and Kinvara over for dinner. I called him at DCMS, breaking the ice, you know, after the Raphael business. It wasn't a long conversation, but amicable enough. He said they couldn't make the night suggested. He also told me . . . well, to be frank, he told me he wasn't sure how much longer he and Kinvara would be together, that the marriage was in trouble. He sounded tired, exhausted . . . unhappy.'

'You had no more contact until the thirteenth?'

'We had no contact even then,' Drummond reminded him. 'I phoned Jasper, yes, but there was no answer. Izzy tells me—' He faltered. 'She tells me that he was probably already dead.'

'It was early for a call,' said Strike.

'I . . . had information I thought he should have.'

'Of what kind?'

'It was personal.'

Strike waited. Drummond sipped his tea.

'It related to the family finances, which as I imagine you know, were very poor at the time Jasper died.'

'Yes.'

'He'd sold off land and remortgaged the London property, offloaded all the good paintings through me. He was right down to the dregs, at the end, trying to sell me some of old Tinky's leavings. It was . . . a little embarrassing, actually.'

'How so?'

'I deal in Old Masters,' said Drummond. 'I do not buy paintings of spotted horses by unknown Australian folk artists. As a courtesy to Jasper, being an old friend, I had some of it valued with my usual man at Christie's. The only thing that had any monetary worth at all was a painting of a piebald mare and foal—'

'I think I've seen that,' said Strike.

'—but it was worth peanuts,' said Drummond. 'Peanuts.'

'How much, at a guess?'

'Five to eight thousand at a push,' said Drummond dismissively.

'Quite a lot of peanuts to some people,' said Strike.

'My dear fellow,' said Henry Drummond, 'that wouldn't have repaired a tenth of the roof at Chiswell House.'

'But he was considering selling it?' asked Strike.

'Along with half a dozen others,' said Drummond.

'I had the impression that Mrs Chiswell was particularly attached to that painting.'

'I don't think his wife's wishes were of much importance to him by the end . . . Oh dear,' sighed Drummond, 'this is all very difficult. I really don't wish to be responsible for telling the family something that I know will only cause hurt and anger. They're already suffering.'

He tapped his teeth with a nail.

'I assure you,' he said, 'that the reason for my call cannot have any bearing on Jasper's death.'

Yet he seemed in two minds.

'You must speak to Raphael,' he said, clearly choosing his words with care, 'because I think . . . possibly . . . I don't like Raphael,' he said, as though he had not already made that perfectly clear, 'but I think, actually, he did an honourable thing on the morning his father died. At least, I can't see what he personally had to gain by it, and I think he's keeping silent about it for the same reason as myself. Being in the family, he is better placed to decide what to do than I can be. Speak to Raphael.'

Strike had the impression that Henry Drummond would rather Raphael made himself unpopular with the family.

There was a knock on the office door. Blonde Lucinda put her head inside.

'Mrs Ross isn't feeling terribly well, Henry; she's going to go, but she'd like to say goodbye.'

'Yes, all right,' said Drummond, getting to his feet. 'I don't think I can be of more use, I'm afraid, Mr Strike.'

'I'm very grateful for you seeing me,' said Strike, also rising, though with difficulty, and picking up his walking stick again. 'Could I ask one last thing?'

'Certainly,' said Drummond, pausing.

'Do you understand anything by the phrase "he put the horse on them"?'

Drummond appeared genuinely puzzled.

'Who put *what* horse . . . where?'

'You don't know what that might mean?'

'I've really no idea. Terribly sorry, but as you've heard, I've got a client waiting.'

Strike had no alternative but to follow Drummond back into the gallery.

In the middle of the otherwise deserted gallery stood Lucinda, who was fussing over a dark, heavily pregnant woman sitting on a high chair, sipping water.

As he recognised Charlotte, Strike knew that this second encounter could not be a coincidence.

50

> *. . . you have branded me, once for all – branded me for life.*
>
> Henrik Ibsen, *Rosmersholm*

'Corm,' she said weakly, gaping at him over the rim of her glass. She was pale, but Strike, who would have put nothing past her to stage a situation that she could use to her advantage, including skipping food or applying white foundation, merely nodded.

'Oh, you know each other?' said Drummond, surprised.

'I must go,' mumbled Charlotte, getting to her feet while the concerned Lucinda hovered. 'I'm late, I'm meeting my sister.'

'Are you sure you're well enough?' said Lucinda.

Charlotte gave Strike a tremulous smile.

'Would you mind walking me up the road? It's only a block.'

Drummond and Lucinda turned to Strike, clearly delighted to offload responsibility for this wealthy, well-connected woman onto his shoulders.

'Not sure I'm the best person for the job,' said Strike, indicating his stick.

He felt Drummond and Lucinda's surprise.

'I'll give you plenty of warning if I think I'm actually going into labour,' said Charlotte. 'Please?'

He could have said 'No'. He might have said, 'Why don't you get your sister to meet you here?' A refusal, as she knew well, would make him appear churlish in front of people he might need to talk to again.

'Fine,' he said, keeping his voice just the right side of brusque.

'Thanks so much, Lucinda,' said Charlotte, sliding down from the chair.

She was wearing a beige silk trench coat over a black T-shirt, maternity jeans and sneakers. Everything she wore, even these casual things, was of fine quality. She had always favoured monochrome colours, stark or classic designs, against which her remarkable beauty was thrown into relief.

Strike held open the door for her, reminded by her pallor of the occasion when Robin had turned white and clammy at journey's end, after deftly steering a hire car out of what could have been a disastrous crash on black ice.

'Thank you,' he said to Henry Drummond.

'My pleasure,' said the art dealer formally.

'The restaurant's not far,' Charlotte said, pointing up the slope as the gallery door swung shut.

They walked side by side, passers-by perhaps assuming that he was responsible for her bulging stomach. He could smell what he knew was Shalimar on her skin. She had worn it ever since she was nineteen and he had sometimes bought it for her. Once again, he remembered walking this way towards the argument with her father in an Italian restaurant so many years ago.

'You think I arranged this.'

Strike said nothing. He had no desire to become enmeshed in disagreement or reminiscence. They had walked for two blocks before he spoke.

'Where is this place?'

'Jermyn Street. Franco's.'

The moment she said the name, he recognised it as the very same one in which they had met Charlotte's father all those years previously. The ensuing row had been short but exceedingly vicious, for a vein of incontinent spite ran right through every member of Charlotte's aristocratic family, but then she and Strike had gone back to her flat and made love with an intensity and urgency that he now wished he could expunge from his brain, the memory of her crying even as she climaxed, hot tears falling onto his face as she shouted with pleasure.

'Ouch. Stop,' she said sharply.

He turned. Cradling her belly with both hands, she backed into a doorway, frowning.

'Sit down,' he said, resenting even having to make suggestions to help her. 'On the step there.'

'No,' she said, taking deep breaths. 'Just get me to Franco's and you can go.'

They walked on.

The maître d'hôtel was all concern: it was clear that Charlotte was not well.

'Is my sister here?' Charlotte asked.

'Not yet,' said the maître d' anxiously, and like Henry Drummond and Lucinda, he looked to Strike to share responsibility for this alarming and unsought problem.

Barely a minute later, Strike was sitting in Amelia's seat at the table for two beside the window, and the waiter was bringing a bottle of water, and Charlotte was still taking deep breaths, and the maître d' was putting bread down between them, saying uncertainly that Charlotte might feel better if she ate something, but also suggesting quietly to Strike that he could call an ambulance at any moment, if that seemed desirable.

At last they were left alone. Still, Strike did not speak. He intended to leave the moment her colour improved, or her sister arrived. All around them sat well-heeled diners, enjoying wine and pasta amid tasteful wood, leather and glass, with black and white prints on the geometric white and red wallpaper.

'You think I arranged this,' mumbled Charlotte again.

Strike said nothing. He was keeping lookout for Charlotte's sister, whom he had not seen for years and who doubtless would be appalled to find them sitting together. Perhaps there would be another tight-lipped row, hidden from their fellow diners, in which fresh aspersions would be cast upon his personality, his background and his motives in escorting his wealthy, pregnant, married ex-girlfriend to her dinner date.

Charlotte took a breadstick and began to eat it, watching him.

'I really didn't know you were going to be there today, Corm.'

He didn't believe it for a second. The meeting at Lancaster House had been chance: he had seen her shock when their eyes met, but this was far too much of a coincidence. If he hadn't known it to be impossible, he would even have supposed that she knew he had split up with his girlfriend that morning.

'You don't believe me.'

'It doesn't matter,' he said, still scanning the street for Amelia.

'I got a real shock when Lucinda said you were there.'

Bollocks. She wouldn't have told you who was in the office. You already knew.

'This happens a lot lately,' she persisted. 'They call them Braxton Hicks contractions. I hate being pregnant.'

He knew he had not disguised his immediate thought when she leaned towards him and said quietly:

'I know what you're thinking. I didn't get rid of ours. I didn't.'

'Don't start, Charlotte,' he said, with the sensation that the firm ground beneath his feet was starting to crack and shift.

'I lost—'

'I'm not doing this again,' he said, a warning note in his voice. 'We're not going back over dates from two years ago. I don't care.'

'I took a test at my mother's—'

'*I said I don't care.*'

He wanted to leave, but she was if anything paler now, her lips trembling as she gazed at him with those horribly familiar, russet-flecked green eyes, now brimming with tears. The swollen belly still didn't seem part of her. He would not have been entirely surprised had she lifted her T-shirt to show a cushion.

'I wish they were yours.'

'Fuck's sake, Charlotte—'

'If they were yours, I'd be happy about it.'

'Don't give me that. You didn't want kids any more than I did.'

Tears now tipped over onto her cheeks. She wiped them away, her fingers shaking more violently than ever. A man at the next table was trying to pretend that he wasn't watching. Always hyperaware of the effect that she was having on those around her, Charlotte threw the eavesdropper a look that made him return hurriedly to his tortellini, then tore off a piece of bread and put it in her mouth, chewing while crying. Finally she gulped water to help her swallow, then pointed at her belly and whispered:

'I feel sorry for them. That's all I've got: pity. I feel sorry for them, because I'm their mother and Jago's their father. What a start in life. In the beginning I tried to think up ways of dying without killing them.'

'Don't be so fucking self-indulgent,' Strike said roughly. 'They're going to need you, aren't they?'

'I don't want to be needed, I never did. I want to be free.'

'To kill yourself?'

'Yes. Or to try and make you love me again.'

He leaned in towards her.

'You're married. You're having his children. We're finished, it's over.'

She leaned in, too, her tear-stained face the most beautiful he had ever seen. He could smell Shalimar on her skin.

'I'll always love you better than anyone in this world,' she said, stark white and stunning. 'You know that's the truth. I loved you better than anyone in my family, I'll love you better than my children, I'll love you on my deathbed. I think about you when Jago and I—'

'Keep this up and I'm leaving.'

She leaned back in her seat again and stared at him as though he were an approaching train and she was tied to the tracks.

'You know it's true,' she said hoarsely. 'You know it is.'

'Charlotte—'

'I know what you're going to say,' she said, 'that I'm a liar. I *am*. I *am* a liar, but not on the big things, never on the big ones, Bluey.'

'Don't call me that.'

'You didn't love me enough—'

'Don't you dare fucking blame me,' he said, in spite of

himself. Nobody else did this to him: nobody even came close. 'The end – that was all you.'

'You wouldn't compromise—'

'Oh, I compromised. I came to live with you, like you wanted—'

'You wouldn't take the job Daddy—'

'I had a job. I had the agency.'

'I was wrong about the agency, I know that now. You've done such incredible things . . . I read everything about you, all the time. Jago found it all on my search history—'

'Should have covered your tracks, shouldn't you? You were a damn sight more careful with me, when you were screwing him on the side.'

'I wasn't sleeping with Jago while I was with you—'

'You got engaged to him two weeks after we finished.'

'It happened fast because I made it happen fast,' she said fiercely. 'You said I was lying about the baby and I was hurt, furious – you and I would be married now if you hadn't—'

'Menus,' said a waiter suddenly materialising beside their table, handing one to each of them. Strike waved his away.

'I'm not staying.'

'Take it for Amelia,' Charlotte instructed him, and he pulled the menu out of the waiter's hand and slapped it down on the table in front of him.

'We have a couple of specials today,' said the waiter.

'Do we look like we want to hear specials?' Strike growled. The waiter stood for a second, frozen in astonishment, then wound his way back through the crowded tables, his back view affronted.

'All this romantic bullshit,' Strike said, leaning in to Charlotte. 'You wanted things I couldn't give you. Every single fucking time, you hated the poverty.'

'I acted like a spoiled bitch,' she said, 'I know I did, then I married Jago and I got all those things I thought I deserved and I want to fucking die.'

'It goes beyond holidays and jewellery, Charlotte. You wanted to break me.'

Her expression became rigid, as it so often had before the worst outbursts, the truly horrifying scenes.

'You wanted to stop me wanting anything that wasn't you. That'd be the proof I loved you, if I gave up the army, the agency, Dave Polworth, every-bloody-thing that made me who I am.'

'I never, ever wanted to break you, that's a terrible thing to—'

'You wanted to smash me up because that's what you do. You have to break it, because if you don't, it might fade away. You've got to be in control. If you kill it, you don't have to watch it die.'

'Look me in the eye and tell me you've loved anyone, since, like you loved me.'

'No, I haven't,' he said, 'and thank fuck for that.'

'We had incredible times together—'

'You'll have to remind me what they were.'

'That night on Benjy's boat in Little France—'

'—your thirtieth? Christmas in Cornwall? They were a whole lot of fucking fun.'

Her hand fell to her belly. Strike thought he saw movement through the thin black T-shirt, and it seemed to him again that there was something alien and inhuman beneath her skin.

'Sixteen years, on and off, I gave you the best I had to give, and it was never enough,' he said. 'There comes a point where you stop trying to save the person who's determined to drag you down with them.'

'Oh, *please*,' she said, and suddenly, the vulnerable and

desperate Charlotte vanished, to be replaced by somebody altogether tougher, cool-eyed and clever. 'You didn't want to save me, Bluey. You wanted to *solve* me. Big difference.'

He welcomed the reappearance of this second Charlotte, who was in every way as familiar as the fragile version, but whom he had far less compunction about hurting.

'I'm looking good to you now because I got famous and you married an arsehole.'

She absorbed the hit without blinking, though her face became a little pinker. Charlotte had always enjoyed a fight.

'You're so predictable. I knew you'd say I came back because you're famous.'

'Well, you do tend to resurface whenever there's drama, Charlotte,' Strike said. 'I seem to remember that the last time, I'd just got my leg blown off.'

'You bastard,' she said, with a cool smile. 'That's how you explain me taking care of you, all those months afterwards?'

His mobile rang: Robin.

'Hi,' he said, turning away from Charlotte to look out of the window. 'How's it going?'

'Hi, just telling tha I can't meet tha tonight,' said Robin, in a much thicker Yorkshire accent than usual. 'I'm going out with a friend. Party.'

'I take it Flick's listening?' said Strike.

'Yeah, well, why don't you try calling your wife if you're lonely?' said Robin.

'I'll do that,' said Strike, amused in spite of Charlotte's cool stare from across the table. 'D'you want me to yell at you? Give this some credibility?'

'No, *you* fook off,' said Robin loudly, and she hung up.

'Who was that?' asked Charlotte, eyes narrowed.

'I've got to go,' said Strike, pocketing the mobile and reaching for his walking stick, which had slipped and fallen under the table while he and Charlotte argued. Realising what he was after, she leaned sideways and succeeded in picking it up before he could reach it.

'Where's the cane I gave you?' she said. 'The Malacca one?'

'You kept it,' he reminded her.

'Who bought you this one? Robin?'

Amidst all of Charlotte's paranoid and frequently wild accusations, she had occasionally made uncannily accurate guesses.

'She did, as a matter of fact,' said Strike, but instantly regretted saying it. He was playing Charlotte's game and at once, she turned into a third and rare Charlotte, neither cold nor fragile, but honest to the point of recklessness.

'All that's kept me going through this pregnancy is the thought that once I've had them, I can leave.'

'You're going to walk out on your kids, the moment they exit the womb?'

'For another three months, I'm trapped. They all want the boy so much, they hardly let me out of their sight. Once I've given birth, it'll be different. I can go. We both know I'll be a lousy mother. They're better off with the Rosses. Jago's mother's already lining herself up as a surrogate.'

Strike held out his hand for the walking stick. She hesitated, then passed it over. He got up.

'Give my regards to Amelia.'

'She's not coming. I lied. I knew you'd be at Henry's. I was at a private viewing with him yesterday. He told me you were going to interview him.'

'Goodbye, Charlotte.'

'Wouldn't you rather have had advance warning that I want you back?'

'But I don't want you,' he said, looking down at her.

'Don't kid a kidder, Bluey.'

Strike limped out of the restaurant past the staring waiters, all of whom seemed to know how rude he had been to one of their colleagues. As he slammed his way out into the street, he felt as though he was pursued, as though Charlotte had projected after him a succubus that would tail him until they met again.

51

Can you spare me an ideal or two?

Henrik Ibsen, *Rosmersholm*

'You've been brainwashed to think it's got to be this way,' said the anarchist. 'See, you need to get your head around a world without leaders. No individual invested with more power than any other individual.'

'Right,' said Robin. 'So tha've *never* voted?'

The Duke of Wellington in Hackney was overflowing this Saturday evening, but the deepening darkness was still warm and a dozen or so of Flick's friends and comrades in CORE were happy to mill around on the pavement on Balls Pond Road, drinking before heading back to Flick's for a party. Many of the group were holding carrier bags containing cheap wine and beer.

The anarchist laughed and shook his head. He was stringy, blond and dreadlocked, with many piercings, and Robin thought she recognised him from the mêlée in the crowd on the night of the Paralympic reception. He had already shown her the squidgy lump of cannabis he had brought to contribute to the general amusement of the party. Robin, whose experience of drugs was restricted to a couple of long-ago tokes on a bong back in her interrupted university career, had feigned an intelligent interest.

'You're so naive!' he told her now. 'Voting's part of the great democratic con! Pointless ritual designed to make the masses think they've got a say and influence! It's a power-sharing deal between the Red and Blue Tories!'

'What's th'answer, then, if it's not voting?' asked Robin, cradling her barely touched half of lager.

'Community organisation, resistance and mass protest,' said the anarchist.

''Oo organises it?'

'The communities themselves. You've been bloody brain-washed,' repeated the anarchist, mitigating the harshness of the statement with a small grin, because he liked Yorkshire socialist Bobbi Cunliffe's plain-spokenness, 'to think you need leaders, but people can do it for themselves once they've woken up.'

'An' who's gonna wake 'em up?'

'Activists,' he said, slapping his own thin chest, 'who aren't in it for money or power, who want *empowerment* of the people, not *control*. See, even unions – no offence,' he said, because he knew that Bobbi Cunliffe's father had been a trade union man, 'same power structures, the leaders start aping management—'

'Y'all right, Bobbi?' asked Flick, pushing to her side through the crowd. 'We'll head off in a minute, that was last orders. What're you telling her, Alf?' she added, with a trace of anxiety.

After a long Saturday in the jewellery shop, and the exchange of many (in Robin's case, wholly imaginary) confidences about their love lives, Flick had become enamoured of Bobbi Cunliffe to the point that her own speech had become slightly tinged with a Yorkshire accent. Towards the end of the afternoon she had extended a two-fold invitation, firstly to that night's party, and secondly, pending her friend Hayley's approval, a rented half-share in the bedroom recently vacated by their ex-flatmate, Laura. Robin had accepted both offers, placed her phone call to Strike, and agreed to Flick's suggestion that, in the absence of the Wiccan, they lock up the shop early.

''E's just telling me 'ow me dad was no better'n a capitalist,' said Robin.

'Fuck's sake, Alf,' said Flick, as the anarchist laughingly protested.

Their group straggled out along the pavement as they headed off through the night towards Flick's flat. In spite of his obvious desire to continue instructing Robin in the rudiments of a leaderless world, the anarchist was ousted from Robin's side by Flick herself, who wanted to talk about Jimmy. Ten yards ahead of them, a plump, bearded and pigeon-toed Marxist, who had been introduced to Robin as Digby, walked alone, leading the way to the party.

'Doubt Jimmy'll come,' she told Robin, and the latter thought she was arming herself against disappointment. 'He's in a bad mood. Worried about his brother.'

'What's wrong wi' him?'

'It's schizophrenic affection something,' said Flick. Robin was sure that Flick knew the correct term, but that she thought it appropriate, faced with a genuine member of the working classes, to feign a lack of education. She had let slip the fact that she had started a university course during the afternoon, seemed to regret it, and ever since had dropped her 'h's a little more consistently. 'I dunno. 'E 'as delusions.'

'Like what?'

'Thinks there's government conspiracies against him and that,' said Flick, with a little laugh.

'Bloody 'ell,' said Bobbi.

'Yeah, he's in 'ospital. He's caused Jimmy a lot of trouble,' said Flick. She stuck a thin roll-up in her mouth and lit it. 'You ever heard of Cormoran Strike?'

She said the name as though it were another medical condition.

'Who?'

'Private detective,' said Flick. 'He's been in the papers a lot. Remember that model who fell out of a window, Lula Landry?'

'Vaguely,' said Robin.

Flick glanced over her shoulder to check that Alf the anarchist was out of earshot.

'Well, Billy went to see 'im.'

'The fook for?'

'Because Billy's mental, keep up,' said Flick, with another little laugh. 'He thinks he saw something years ago—'

'What?' said Robin, quicker than she meant to.

'A murder,' said Flick.

'Christ.'

'He didn't, obviously,' said Flick. 'It's all bollocks. I mean, he *saw* something, but nobody bloody died. Jimmy was there, he knows. Anyway, Billy goes to this detective prick and now we can't get rid of him.'

'What d'you mean?'

''E beat Jimmy up.'

'The detective did?'

'Yeah. Followed Jimmy on a protest we were doing, beat him up, got Jimmy fooking arrested.'

'Bloody 'ell,' said Bobbi Cunliffe again.

'Deep state, innit?' said Flick. 'Ex-army. Queen and the flag and all that fucking shit. See, Jimmy and me had something on a Conservative minister—'

'Did you?'

'Yeah,' said Flick. 'I can't tell you what, but it was big, and then Billy fucked everything up. Sent Strike sniffing around, and we reckon he got in touch with the gov—'

She broke off suddenly, her eyes following a small car that had just passed them.

'Thought that was Jimmy's for a moment. It isn't. I forgot, it's off the road.'

Her mood sagged again. During the slack periods in the shop that day, Flick had told Robin the history of her and Jimmy's relationship, which in its endless fights and truces and renegotiations might have been the story of some disputed territory. They seemed never to have reached an agreement on the relationship's status and every treaty had fallen apart in rows and betrayals.

'You're well shot of him, if you ask me,' said Robin, who all day had pursued a cautious policy of trying to prise Flick free of the loyalty she clearly felt she owed the faithless Jimmy, in the hope of extracting confidences.

'Wish it were that easy,' said Flick, lapsing into the cod-Yorkshire she had adopted towards the end of the day. 'It's not like I wanna be *married* or anything—' she laughed at the very idea, '—he can sleep with who he likes and so can I. That's the deal and I'm fine with it.'

She had already explained to Robin at the shop that she identified as both genderqueer and pansexual, while monogamy, properly looked at, was a tool of patriarchal oppression, a line that Robin suspected had been originally Jimmy's. They walked in silence for a while. In the denser darkness they entered an underpass, when Flick said with a flicker of spirit:

'I mean, I've had my own fun.'

'Glad to hear it,' said Robin.

'Jimmy wouldn't like it if he knew all of them, either.'

The pigeon-toed Marxist walking ahead of them turned his head at that and Robin saw, by the light of a streetlamp, his little smirk as he glanced back at Flick, whose words he had clearly caught. The latter, being engaged in trying to dig her door keys out of the bottom of her cluttered messenger bag, seemed not to notice.

'We're up there,' Flick said, pointing at three lit windows above a small sports shop. 'Hayley's back already. Shit, I hope she remembered to hide my laptop.'

The flat was reached from a back entrance, up a cold, narrow stairwell. Even from the bottom of the stairs, they could hear the persistent bass of 'Niggas in Paris', and on reaching the landing, they found the flimsy door standing open and a number of people leaning up against the walls outside, sharing an enormous joint.

'*What's fifty grand to a muh-fucka like me*,' rapped Jay-Z, from the dimly lit interior.

The dozen or so newcomers met a substantial number of people already inside. It was astonishing how many people could fit into such a small flat, which evidently comprised only two bedrooms, a minuscule shower room and a cupboard-sized kitchenette.

'We're using Hayley's room to dance in, it's the biggest, the one you'll share,' Flick shouted in Robin's ear as they forced their way towards the dark room.

Lit only by two strings of fairy lights, and the small rectangles of lights emanating from the phones of those checking their texts and social media, the room was already thick with the smell of cannabis and lined with people. Four young women and a man were managing to dance in the middle of the floor. Her eyes growing gradually accustomed to the darkness, Robin saw the skeletal frame of a bunk bed, already supporting a few people sharing a joint on the top mattress. She could just make out an LGBT rainbow flag and a poster of *True Blood*'s Tara Thornton on the wall behind them.

Jimmy and Barclay had already combed this flat for the piece of paper Flick had stolen from Chiswell and not found it, Robin reminded herself, peering through the darkness for likely hiding places. Robin wondered whether Flick kept it permanently on her person, but Jimmy would surely have thought of that, and in spite of Flick's avowed pansexuality, Robin thought Jimmy better placed than herself to persuade Flick to strip. Meanwhile, the darkness might be Robin's friend as she slid her hand beneath mattresses and rugs, but the party was so densely packed that she doubted it would be possible to do without alerting somebody to her odd behaviour.

'. . . find Hayley,' Flick bellowed in Robin's ear, pressing a can of lager into her hand, and they edged out of the room again into Flick's own bedroom, which seemed even smaller than it really was because every inch of the walls and ceiling had been covered in political flyers and posters, the orange of CORE and the black and red of the Real Socialist Party predominating. A gigantic Palestinian flag was pinned over the mattress on the floor.

Five people were already inside this room, which was lit by a solitary lamp. A pair of young women, one black, one white, lay entwined on the mattress on the floor, while podgy, bearded Digby had taken up a position on the floor, talking to them. Two teenage boys stood awkwardly against the wall, furtively watching the girls on the bed, their heads close together as they rolled a joint.

'Hayley, this is Bobbi,' said Flick. 'She's interested in Laura's half of the room.'

Both girls on the bed looked around: the tall, shaven-headed, sleepy-eyed peroxide blonde answered.

'I've already said Shanice can move in,' said the blonde, sounding stoned, and the petite black girl in her arms kissed her on the neck.

'Oh,' said Flick, turning in consternation to Robin. 'Shit. Sorry.'

'You're all right,' said Robin, feigning bravery in the face of disappointment.

'Flick,' someone called from the hall, 'it's Jimmy downstairs.'

'Oh, fuck,' said Flick, flustered, but Robin saw the pleasure flare in her face. 'Wait there,' she said to Robin, and left for the press of bodies in the hall.

'*Bougie girl, grab her hand*,' rapped Kanye West from the other room.

Pretending to be interested in the conversation between the girls on the bed and Digby, Robin slid down the wall to sit on the laminate floor, sipping her lager while she covertly surveyed Flick's bedroom. It had evidently been tidied for the party. There was no wardrobe, but a clothes rail holding coats and the occasional dress, while T-shirts and sweaters were half-heartedly folded in a dark corner. A small number of Beanie Babies sat on top of the chest of drawers, along with a clutter of make-up, while various placards stood jumbled in a corner. Jimmy and Barclay must surely have been thoroughly through this room. Robin wondered whether they had thought of searching behind all these flyers. Unfortunately, even if they hadn't, she could hardly start unpinning them now.

'Look, this is basic stuff,' said Digby, addressing the girls on the bed. 'You'll agree that capitalism depends in part on the poorly paid labour of women, right? So feminism, if it's to be effective, *must* also be Marxist, the one implies the other.'

'Patriarchy is about more than capitalism,' said Shanice.

Out of the corner of her eye, Robin saw Jimmy fighting his way through the narrow hall, his arm around Flick's neck. The latter appeared happier than she had all evening.

'Women's oppression is inextricably linked to their inability to enter the labour force,' announced Digby.

The drowsy-eyed Hayley disentangled herself from Shanice to extend her hand towards the black-clad teenagers in a silent request. Their joint passed over Robin's head.

'Sorry 'bout the room,' Hayley said vaguely to Robin, after taking a long toke. 'Bastard getting a place in London, innit?'

'Total bastard,' said Robin.

'—because you want to subsume feminism within the larger ideology of Marxism.'

'There's no *subsuming*, the aims are identical!' said Digby, with an incredulous little laugh.

Hayley tried to give Shanice the joint, but the impassioned Shanice waved it away.

'Where are you Marxists when we're challenging the ideal of the heteronormative family?' she demanded of Digby.

'Hear, hear,' said Hayley vaguely, snuggling closer to Shanice and shoving the teenagers' joint at Robin, who passed it straight back to the boys. Interested though they had been in the lesbians, they promptly left the bedroom before anybody else could offer their meagre supply of drugs around.

'I used to have some of them,' Robin said aloud, getting to her feet, but nobody was listening. Digby took the opportunity to peek up Robin's short black skirt as she passed close to him on her way to the chest of drawers. Under cover of the increasingly heated conversation about feminism and Marxism, and with the appearance of vaguely nostalgic interest, Robin picked up and put down each of Flick's Beanie Babies in turn, feeling through the thin plush to the plastic beads and stuffing within. None of them felt as though they had been opened up and re-sewn to conceal a piece of paper.

With a sense of slight hopelessness, she returned to the dark hall, where people stood pressed together, spilling out onto the landing.

A girl was hammering on the door of the bathroom.

'Stop shagging in there, I need a piss!' she said, to the amusement of various people standing around.

This is hopeless.

Robin slid into the kitchenette, which was hardly larger than two telephone boxes, where a couple was sitting on the side, the girl with her legs over the man's, who had his hand up her skirt, while the teenagers in black were now foraging with difficulty for something to eat. Under pretence of finding another drink, Robin sifted through empty cans and bottles, watching the progress of the teenagers through the cupboards and reflecting how insecure a hiding place a cereal box would make.

Alf the anarchist appeared in the kitchen doorway as Robin made to leave the room, now far more stoned than he had been in the pub.

'There she is,' he said loudly, trying to focus on Robin. 'Th' union leader's daughter.'

'That's me,' said Robin, as D'banj sang '*Oliver, Oliver, Oliver Twist*' from the second bedroom. She tried to duck under Alf's arm, but he lowered it, blocking her exit from the kitchen. The cheap laminate floor was vibrating with the stamping of the determined dancers in Hayley's room.

'You're hot,' said Alf. ''M'I allowed to say that? I mean it in a fucking feminist way.'

He laughed.

'Thanks,' said Robin, succeeding on her second pass in dodging around him and getting back into the tiny hall, where the desperate girl was still pounding on the bathroom door. Alf caught Robin's arm, bent down and said something incomprehensible in her ear. When he straightened up again, some of her hair chalk had left a black stain on the end of his sweaty nose.

'What?' said Robin.

'I said,' he shouted, '"wanna find somewhere quieter so we can talk more?"'

But then Alf noticed somebody standing behind her.

'All right, Jimmy?'

Knight had arrived in the hall. He smiled at Robin, then leaned up against the wall, smoking and holding a can of lager. He was ten years older than most of the people there, and some of the girls cast him sideways looks, in his tight black T-shirt and jeans.

'Waiting for the bog as well?' he asked Robin.

'Yeah,' said Robin, because that seemed the simplest way to extricate herself from both Jimmy and Alf the anarchist, should she need to. Through the open door of Hayley's room, she saw Flick dancing, now clearly delighted with life, laughing at whatever was said to her.

'Flick says your dad was a trade union man,' Jimmy said to Robin. 'Miner, yeah?'

'Yeah,' said Robin.

'Fuck's SAKE,' said the girl who had been hammering on the bathroom door. She danced on the spot in desperation for a few more seconds, then pushed her way out of the flat.

'There are bins to the left!' called one of the other girls after her.

Jimmy leaned closer to Robin, so that she could hear him over the thumping bass. His expression was, as far as she could see, sympathetic, even gentle.

'Died, though, didn't he?' he asked Robin. 'Your dad. Lungs, Flick said?'

'Yeah,' said Robin.

'I'm sorry,' said Jimmy, quietly. 'Been through something similar myself.'

'Really?' said Robin.

'Yeah, my mum. Lungs, as well.'

'Workplace related?'

'Asbestos,' said Jimmy, nodding as he dragged on his cigarette. 'Wouldn't happen now, they've brought in legislation. I was twelve. My brother was two, he can't even remember her. My old man drank himself to death without her.'

'That's really rough,' said Robin sincerely. 'I'm sorry.'

Jimmy blew smoke away from her face and pulled a grimace.

'Two of a kind,' said Jimmy, clinking his can of lager against Robin's. 'Class war veterans.'

Alf the anarchist lurched away, swaying slightly, and disappeared into the dark room pierced with fairy lights.

'Family ever get compensation?' asked Jimmy.

'Tried,' said Robin. 'Mum's still pursuing it.'

'Good luck to her,' said Jimmy, raising his can and drinking. 'Good bloody luck to her.'

He banged on the bathroom door.

'Fucking hurry up, people are waiting,' he shouted.

'Maybe someone's ill?' Robin suggested.

'Nah, it'll be someone having a quickie,' said Jimmy.

Digby emerged from Flick's bedroom, looking disgruntled.

'I'm a tool of patriarchal oppression, apparently,' he announced loudly.

Nobody laughed. Digby scratched his belly under his T-shirt, which Robin now saw featured a picture of Groucho Marx, and ambled into the room where Flick was dancing.

'He's a tool, all right,' Jimmy muttered to Robin. 'Rudolf Steiner kid. Can't get over the fact that nobody gives him stars for effort any more.'

Robin laughed, but Jimmy didn't. His eyes held hers just a fraction too long, until the bathroom door opened a crack and a plump, red-faced young girl peeked out. Behind her, Robin saw a man with a wispy grey beard replacing his Mao cap.

'Larry, you filthy old bastard,' said Jimmy, grinning as the red-faced girl scuttled past Robin and disappeared into the dark room after Digby.

'Evening, Jimmy,' said the elderly Trotskyist, with a prim smile, and he, too, left the bathroom to a couple of cheers from the young men outside.

'Go on,' Jimmy told Robin, holding open the door and blocking anyone else's attempts to push past her.

'Thanks,' she said, as she slid into the bathroom.

The glare of the strip light was dazzling after the dinginess of the rest of the flat. The bathroom barely had standing room between the smallest shower Robin had ever seen, with a grimy transparent curtain hanging off half its hooks, and a small toilet in which a large amount of sodden tissue and a cigarette end was floating. A used condom glistened in the wicker bin.

Above the sink were three rickety shelves crammed with half-used toiletries and general clutter, crammed together so that one touch seemed likely to dislodge everything.

Struck by a sudden idea, Robin moved closer to these shelves. She was remembering how she had relied on the squeamish ignorance and avoidance of most men towards matters pertaining to menstruation when she had hidden the listening devices in a box of Tampax. Her eyes ran swiftly over half-used bottles of supermarket-brand shampoo, an old tub of Vim, a dirty sponge, a pair of cheap deodorants and a few well-used toothbrushes in a chipped mug. Very carefully, because everything was so tightly packed together, Robin eased out a small box of Lil-Lets that proved to have only one sealed tampon inside it. As she reached up to replace the box, she spotted the corner of a small, squashy bundle, encased in a plastic wrapper and hidden behind the Vim and a bottle of fruity shower gel.

With a sudden stab of excitement, she reached up and wriggled the white polythene parcel carefully out of the place it had been wedged, trying not to knock everything over.

Somebody hammered on the door.

'I'm fucking bursting!' shouted a new girl.

'Won't be long!' Robin shouted back.

Two bulky sanitary towels had been rolled up in their own unromantic wrapping ('for Very Heavy Flow'): the sort of thing a young woman was unlikely to steal, especially if wearing skimpy clothing. Robin extracted them. There was nothing odd about the first. The second, however, emitted a small, crisp cracking noise as Robin bent it. Her excitement mounting, Robin turned it sideways and saw that it had been slit with what had probably been a razor blade. Wriggling her fingers into the tissue-like foam within, she felt a thick, folded piece of paper, which she eased out and unfolded.

The writing paper was exactly the same as that on which Kinvara had written her farewell note, with the name 'Chiswell' embossed across the top and a Tudor rose, like a drop of blood, beneath it. A few disjointed words and phrases were scrawled in the distinctive, cramped handwriting Robin had seen so often in Chiswell's office, and in the middle of the page one word had been circled many times.

251 Ebury Street
London
SW1W

Blanc de blanc

Suzuki ✓

~~*Mother?*~~

Odi et amo, quare id faciam, fortasse requiris?
Nescio, sed fieri sentio et excrucior.

Hardly breathing in her excitement, Robin took out her mobile, took several pictures of the note, then refolded it, replaced it in the sanitary towel and returned the package to the place it had been on the shelf. She attempted to flush the toilet, but it was clogged and all she achieved was that the water rose ominously in the bowl, refusing to subside, the cigarette butt bobbing there in swirling tissue.

'Sorry,' Robin said, opening the door. 'Loo's blocked.'

'Whatever,' said the impatient, drunk girl outside, 'I'll do it in the sink.'

She pushed past Robin and slammed the door.

Jimmy was still standing outside.

'Think I'm going to take off,' Robin told him. 'I only really came t'see if that room was vacant, but soombody's got in ahead of me.'

'Shame,' said Jimmy lightly. 'Come to a meeting some time. We could use a bit of Northern soul.'

'Yeah, I might,' said Robin.

'Might what?'

Flick had arrived, holding a bottle of Budweiser.

'Come to a meeting,' said Jimmy, taking a fresh cigarette out of his pack. 'You were right, Flick, she's the real deal.'

Jimmy reached out and pulled Flick to him, pressing her to his side, and kissed her on the top of the head.

'Yeah, sh'iz,' said Flick, smiling with real warmth as she wound her arm around Jimmy's waist. 'Come to the next one, Bobbi.'

'Yeah, I might,' said Bobbi Cunliffe, the trade unionist's daughter, and she bade them goodbye, pushed her way out of the hall and out into the cold stairwell.

Not even the sight and smell of one of the black-clad teenagers vomiting copiously on the pavement just outside the main door could dampen Robin's jubilation. Unable to wait, she texted Strike the picture of Jasper Chiswell's note while hurrying towards the bus stop.

52

I can assure you, you have been on the wrong scent entirely, Miss West.

Henrik Ibsen, *Rosmersholm*

Strike had fallen asleep, fully clothed, his prosthesis still attached, on top of the bedcovers in his attic bedroom. The cardboard folder containing everything pertaining to the Chiswell file was lying on his chest, vibrating gently as he snored, and he dreamed that he was walking hand in hand with Charlotte through an otherwise deserted Chiswell House, which they had bought together. Tall, slim and beautiful, she was no longer pregnant. She trailed Shalimar and black chiffon behind her, but their mutual happiness was evaporating in the damp chill of the shabby rooms through which they were wandering. What could have prompted the reckless, quixotic decision to purchase this draughty house, with the peeling walls and the wires dangling from the ceiling?

The loud buzz of a text arriving jerked Strike from sleep. For a fraction of a second he registered the fact that he was back in his attic room, alone, neither the owner of Chiswell House nor the lover of Charlotte Ross, before groping for the phone on which he was half lying in the full expectation that he was about to see a message from Charlotte.

He was wrong: it was Robin's name he saw when he peered groggily at the screen, and it was, moreover, one in the morning. Momentarily forgetting that she had been out at a party with Flick, Strike sat up hurriedly and the cardboard file that had been lying on his chest slid smoothly off him, scattering its various pages across the floorboards, while Strike squinted, blurry-eyed, at the photograph Robin had just sent him.

'Fuck me backwards.'

Ignoring the mess of notes at his feet, he called her back.

'Hi,' said Robin jubilantly, over the unmistakable sounds of a London night bus: the clatter and roar of the engine, the grinding of brakes, the tinny ding of the bell and the obligatory drunken laughter of what sounded like a gaggle of young women.

'How the *fuck* did you manage that?'

'I'm a woman,' said Robin. He could hear her smile. 'I know where we hide things when we really don't want them found. I thought you'd be asleep.'

'Where are you – a bus? Get off and grab a cab. We can charge it to the Chiswell account if you get a receipt.'

'There's no need—'

'Do as you're bloody told!' Strike repeated, a little more aggressively than he had intended, because while she had just pulled off quite a coup, she had also been knifed, out alone on the street after dark, a year previously.

'All right, all right, I'll get a cab,' said Robin. 'Have you read Chiswell's note?'

'Looking at it now,' said Strike, switching to speakerphone so that he could read Chiswell's note while talking to her. 'I hope you left it where you found it?'

'Yeah. I thought that was best?'

'Definitely. Where exactly—?'

'Inside a sanitary towel.'

'Christ,' said Strike, taken aback. 'I'd never've thought to—'

'No, nor did Jimmy and Barclay,' said Robin smugly. 'Can you read what it says at the bottom? The Latin?'

Squinting at the screen, Strike translated:

'"*I hate and I love. Why do I do it, you might ask? I don't know. I just feel it, and it crucifies me . . .*" that's Catullus again. A famous one.'

'Did you do Latin at university?'

'No.'

'Then how—?'

'Long story,' said Strike.

In fact, the story of his ability to read Latin wasn't long, merely (to most people) inexplicable. He didn't feel like telling it in the middle of the night, nor did he want to explain that Charlotte had studied Catullus at Oxford.

'"I hate and I love",' Robin repeated. 'Why would Chiswell have written that down?'

'Because he was feeling it?' Strike suggested.

His mouth was dry: he had smoked too much before falling asleep. He got up, feeling achy and stiff, and picked his way carefully around the fallen notes, heading for the sink in the other room, phone in hand.

'Feeling it for Kinvara?' asked Robin dubiously.

'Ever see another woman around while you were in close contact with him?'

'No. Of course, he might not have been talking about a woman.'

'True,' admitted Strike. 'Plenty of man love in Catullus. Maybe that's why Chiswell liked him so much.'

He filled a mug with cold tap water, drank it down in one, then threw in a tea bag and switched on the kettle, all the while peering down at the lit screen of his phone in the darkness.

'"Mother", crossed out,' he muttered.

'Chiswell's mother died twenty-two years ago,' said Robin. 'I've just looked her up.'

'Hmm,' said Strike. '"Bill", circled.'

'Not Billy,' Robin pointed out, 'but if Jimmy and Flick thought it meant his brother, people must sometimes call Billy "Bill".'

'Unless it's the thing you pay,' said Strike. 'Or a duck's beak, come to that . . . "Suzuki" . . . "Blanc de" . . . Hang on. Jimmy Knight's got an old Suzuki Alto.'

'It's off the road, according to Flick.'

'Yeah. Barclay says it failed its MOT.'

'There was a Grand Vitara parked outside Chiswell House when we visited, too. One of the Chiswells must own it.'

'Good spot,' said Strike.

He switched on the overhead light and crossed to the table by the window, where he had left his pen and notebook.

'You know,' said Robin thoughtfully, 'I think I've seen "Blanc de blanc" somewhere recently.'

'Yeah? Been drinking champagne?' asked Strike, who had sat down to make more notes.

'No, but . . . yeah, I suppose I must've seen it on a wine label, mustn't I? Blanc de blancs . . . what does it mean? "White from whites?"'

'Yeah,' said Strike.

For nearly a minute, neither of them spoke, both examining the note. 'You know, I hate to say this, Robin,' said Strike at last, 'but I think the most interesting thing about this is that Flick had it. Looks like a to-do list. Can't see anything here that proves wrongdoing or suggests grounds for blackmail or murder.'

'Mother, crossed out,' Robin repeated, as though determined to wring meaning out of the cryptic phrases. 'Jimmy Knight's mother died of asbestosis. He just told me so, at Flick's party.'

Strike tapped his notepad lightly with the end of his pen, thinking, until Robin voiced the question that he was grappling with.

'We're going to have to tell the police about this, aren't we?'

'Yeah, we are,' sighed Strike, rubbing his eyes. 'This proves she had access to Ebury Street. Unfortunately, that means we're going to have to pull you out of the jewellery shop. Once the police search her bathroom, it won't take her long to work out who must've tipped them off.'

'Bugger,' said Robin. 'I really felt like I was getting somewhere with her.'

'Yeah,' Strike agreed. 'This is the problem with having no official standing in an inquiry. I'd give a lot to have Flick in an interrogation room . . . This bloody case,' he said, yawning. 'I've been going through the file all evening. This note's like everything else: it raises more questions than it answers.'

'Hang on,' said Robin, and he heard sounds of movement, 'sorry – Cormoran, I'm going to get off here, I can see a taxi rank—'

'OK. Great work tonight. I'll call you tomorrow – later today, I mean.'

When she had hung up, Strike set his cigarette down in the ashtray, returned to his bedroom to pick up the scattered case notes off the floor, and took them back to the kitchen. Ignoring the freshly boiled kettle, he took a beer from the fridge, sat back down at the table with the file and, as an afterthought, opened the sash window beside him a few inches, to let some clean air into the room while he kept smoking.

The Military Police had trained him to organise interrogations and findings into three broad categories: people, places and things, and Strike had been applying this sound old principle to the Chiswell file before falling asleep on the bed. Now he spread the contents of the file out over the kitchen table and set to work again, while a cold night breeze laden with petrol fumes blew across the photographs and papers, so that their corners trembled.

'People,' Strike muttered.

He had written a list before he slept of the people who most interested him in connection with Chiswell's death. Now he saw that he had unconsciously ranked the names according to their degree of involvement in the dead man's blackmail. Jimmy Knight's name topped the list, followed by Geraint Winn's, and then by what Strike thought of as each man's respective deputy, Flick Purdue and Aamir Mallik. Next came Kinvara, who knew that Chiswell was being blackmailed, and why; Della Winn, whose super-injunction had kept the blackmail out of the press, but whose precise degree of involvement in the affair was otherwise unknown to Strike, and then Raphael, who had by all accounts been ignorant both of what his father had done, and of the blackmail itself. At the bottom of the list was Billy Knight, whose only known connection with the blackmail was the bond of blood between himself and the primary blackmailer.

Why, Strike asked himself, had he ranked the names in this particular order? There was no proven link between Chiswell's death and the blackmail, unless, of course, the threat of exposure of his unknown crime had indeed pushed Chiswell into killing himself.

It then occurred to Strike that a different hierarchy was revealed if he turned the list on its head. In this case Billy sat on top, a disinterested seeker, not of money or another man's disgrace, but of truth and justice. In the reversed order, Raphael came in second, with his strange and, to Strike, implausible story of being sent to his stepmother on the morning of his father's death, which Henry Drummond claimed grudgingly to have hidden some honourable motive as yet unknown. Della rose to third place, a widely admired woman of impeccable morality, whose true thoughts and feelings towards her blackmailing husband and to his victim remained inscrutable.

Read backwards, it seemed to Strike that each suspect's relation to the dead man became cruder, more transactional, until the list terminated with Jimmy Knight and his angry demand for forty thousand pounds.

Strike continued to pore over the list of names as though he might suddenly see something emerging out of his dense, spiky handwriting, the way unfocused eyes may spot the 3D image hidden in a series of brightly coloured dots. All that occurred to him, however, was the fact that there was an unusual number of pairs connected to Chiswell's death: couples – Geraint and Della, Jimmy and Flick; pairs of full siblings – Izzy and Fizzy, Jimmy and Billy; the duo of blackmailing collaborators – Jimmy and Geraint; and the subsets of each blackmailer and his deputy – Flick and Aamir. There was even the quasi-parental pairing of Della and Aamir. This left two people who formed a pair in being isolated within the otherwise close-knit family: the widowed Kinvara and Raphael, the unsatisfactory, outsider son.

Strike tapped his pen unconsciously against the notebook, thinking. *Pairs.* The whole business had begun with a pair of crimes: Chiswell's blackmail and Billy's allegation of infanticide. He had been trying to find the connection between them from the start, unable to believe that they could be entirely separate cases, even if on the face of it their only link was in the blood tie between the Knight brothers.

Turning the page, he examined the notes he had headed 'Places'. After a few minutes spent examining his own jottings concerning access to the house in Ebury Street, and the locations, in several cases unknown, of the suspects at the time of Chiswell's death, he made a note to remind himself that he still hadn't received from Izzy contact details for Tegan Butcher, the stable girl who could confirm that Kinvara had been at home in Woolstone while Chiswell was suffocating in a plastic bag in London.

He turned to the next page, headed 'Things', and now he set down his pen and spread Robin's photographs out so that they formed a collage of the death scene. He scrutinised the flash of gold in the pocket of the dead man, and then the bent sword, half hidden in shadow in the corner of the room.

It seemed to Strike that the case he was investigating was littered with objects that had been found in surprising places: the sword in the corner, the lachesis pills on the floor, the wooden cross found in a tangle of nettles at the bottom of the dell, the canister of helium and the rubber tubing in a house where no child's party had ever been held, but his tired mind could find neither answers nor patterns here.

Finally, Strike downed the rest of his beer, lobbed the empty can across the room into the kitchen bin, turned to a blank page in his notebook and began to write a to-do list for the Sunday of which two hours had already elapsed.

1. Call Wardle
Text note found in Flick's flat,
Update on police case if possible.

2. Call Izzy
Show her stolen note.
Ask: was Freddie's money clip ever found?
Tegan's details?
Need phone number for Raphael.
Also phone number, if poss, for Della Winn
3. Call Barclay
Give update.
Cover Jimmy & Flick again
When does Jimmy visit Billy?
4. Call hospital
Try and arrange interview with Billy when Jimmy not there.
5. Call Robin
Arrange interview with Raphael
6. Call Della
Try and arrange interview

After a little further thought, he finished the list with

7. Buy teabags/beer/bread

After tidying up the Chiswell file, tipping the overflowing ashtray into the bin, opening the window wider to admit more cold, fresh air, Strike went for a last pee, cleaned his teeth, switched off the lights and returned to his bedroom, where a single reading lamp still burned.

Now, with his defences weakened by beer and tiredness, the memories he had sought to bury in work forced their way to the forefront of his mind. As he undressed and removed his prosthetic leg, he found himself going back over every word Charlotte had said to him across the table for two in Franco's, remembering the expression of her green eyes, the scent of Shalimar reaching him through the garlic fumes of the restaurant, her thin white fingers playing with the bread.

He got into bed between the chilly sheets and lay, hands behind his head, staring up into the darkness. He wished he could feel indifferent, but in fact his ego had stretched luxuriously at the idea that she had read all about the cases that had made his name and that she thought about him while in bed with her husband. Now, though, reason and experience rolled up their sleeves, ready to conduct a professional post-mortem on the remembered conversation, methodically disinterring the unmistakable signs of Charlotte's perennial will to shock and her apparently insatiable need for conflict.

The abandonment of her titled husband and newborn children for a famous, one-legged detective would certainly constitute the crowning achievement of a career of disruption. Having an almost pathological hatred of routine, responsibility or obligation, she had sabotaged every possibility of permanence before she had to deal with the threats of boredom or compromise. Strike knew all this, because he knew her better than any other human being, and he knew that their final parting had happened at the exact moment where real sacrifice and hard choices had to be made.

But he also knew – and the knowledge was like ineradicable bacteria in a wound that stopped it ever healing – that she loved him as she had never loved anyone else. Of course, the sceptical girlfriends and wives of his friends, none of whom had liked Charlotte, had told him over and over again, 'That's not love, what she does to you', or, 'Not being funny, Corm, but how do you know she hasn't said exactly the same to all the others she's had?' Such women saw his confidence that Charlotte loved him as delusion or egotism. They had not been present for those times of total bliss and mutual understanding that remained some of the best of Strike's life. They had not shared jokes inexplicable to any other human being but himself and Charlotte, or felt the mutual need that had drawn them back together for sixteen years.

She had walked from him straight into the arms of the man she thought would hurt Strike worst, and indeed, it *had* hurt, because Ross was the absolute antithesis of him and had dated Charlotte before Strike had even met him. Yet Strike remained certain her flight to Ross had been self-immolation, done purely for spectacular effect, a Charlottian form of *sati*.

Difficile est longum subito deponere amorem,
Difficile est, verum hoc qua lubet efficias.

It is hard to abruptly shrug off a long-established love
Hard, but this, somehow, you must do.

Strike turned off the light, closed his eyes and sank, once more, into uneasy dreams of the empty house where squares of unfaded wallpaper bore witness to the removal of everything of value, but this time he walked alone, with the strange sensation that hidden eyes were watching.

53

And then, in the end, the poignant misery of her victory . . .

Henrik Ibsen, *Rosmersholm*

Robin arrived home just before 2 a.m. As she crept around the kitchen, making herself a sandwich, she noticed on the kitchen calendar that Matthew was planning to play five-a-side football later that morning. Accordingly, when she slipped into bed with him twenty minutes later, she set the alarm on her phone for eight o'clock before plugging it in to charge. As part of her effort to try and keep the atmosphere amicable, she wanted to get up to see him before he left.

He seemed happy that she'd made the effort to join him for breakfast, but when she asked whether he wanted her to come and cheer from the sidelines, or meet him for lunch afterwards, he declined both offers.

'I've got paperwork to do this afternoon. I don't want to drink at lunchtime. I'll come straight back,' he said, so Robin, secretly delighted, because she was so tired, told him to have a good time and kissed him goodbye.

Trying not to focus on how much lighter of heart she felt once Matthew had left the house, Robin occupied herself with laundry and other essentials until, shortly after midday, while she was changing the sheets on their bed, Strike called.

'Hi,' said Robin, gladly abandoning her task, 'any news?'

'Plenty. Ready to write some stuff down?'

'Yes,' said Robin, hurriedly grabbing notebook and pen off the top of her dressing table and sitting down on the stripped mattress.

'I've been making some calls. First off, Wardle. Very impressed with your work in getting hold of that note—'

Robin smiled at her reflection in the mirror.

'—though he's warned me the police won't take kindly to us, as he put it, "clodhopping all over an open case". I've asked him not to say where he got the tip-off about the note, but I expect they'll put two and two together, given that Wardle and I are mates. Still, that's unavoidable. The interesting bit is that the police are still worried about the same features of the death scene as we are and they've been going deeper into Chiswell's finances.'

'Looking for evidence of blackmail?'

'Yeah, but they haven't got anything, because Chiswell never paid out. Here's the interesting bit. Chiswell got an unexplained payment in cash of forty thousand pounds last year. He opened a separate bank account for it, then seems to have spent it all on house repairs and other sundries.'

'He *received* forty thousand pounds?'

'Yep. And Kinvara and the rest of the family are claiming total ignorance. They say they don't know where the money came from or why Chiswell would've opened a separate account to take receipt of it.'

'The same amount Jimmy asked for before he scaled down his request,' said Robin. 'That's odd.'

'Certainly is. So then I called Izzy.'

'You've been busy,' said Robin.

'You haven't heard the half of it. Izzy denies knowledge of where the forty grand came from, but I'm not sure I believe her. Then I asked her about the note Flick stole. She's appalled that Flick might've been posing as her father's cleaner. Very shaken up. I think for the first time she's considering the possibility that Kinvara isn't guilty.'

'I take it she never met this so-called Polish woman?'

'Correct.'

'What did she make of the note?'

'She thinks it looks like a to-do list, as well. She assumes "Suzuki" meant the Grand Vitara, which was Chiswell's. No thoughts on "mother". The one thing of interest I got from her was in relation to "blanc de blanc". Chiswell was allergic to champagne. Apparently it made him go bright red and hyperventilate. What's odd about that is, there was a big empty box labelled Moët & Chandon in the kitchen when I checked it, the morning Chiswell died.'

'You never told me that.'

'We'd just found the body of a government minister. An empty box seemed relatively uninteresting at the time, and it never occurred to me it might be relevant to anything until I spoke to Izzy today.'

'Were there bottles inside?'

'Nothing, so far as I could see, and according to the family, Chiswell never entertained there. If he wasn't drinking champagne himself, why was the box there?'

'You don't think—'

'That's exactly what I think,' said Strike. 'I reckon that box was how the helium and the rubber tubing got into the house, disguised.'

'Wow,' said Robin, lying back on the unmade bed and looking up at the ceiling.

'Quite clever. The killer could've sent it to him as a gift, couldn't they, knowing he was highly unlikely to open and drink it?'

'Bit slapdash,' said Robin. 'What was to stop him opening it up anyway? Or re-gifting it?'

'We need to find out when it was sent,' Strike was saying. 'Meanwhile, one minor mystery's been cleared up. Freddie's money clip was found.'

'Where?'

'Chiswell's pocket. That was the flash of gold in the photograph you took.'

'Oh,' said Robin, blankly. 'So he must have found it, before he died?'

'Well, it'd be hard for him to find it *after* he died.'

'Ha ha,' said Robin sarcastically. 'There *is* another possibility.'

'That the killer planted it on the corpse? Funny you should say that. Izzy says she was very surprised when it turned up on the body, because if he'd found it, she would have assumed he'd have told her. He made a massive fuss about losing it, apparently.'

'He did,' Robin agreed. 'I heard him on the phone, ranting on about it. They fingerprinted it, presumably?'

'Yeah. Nothing suspicious. Only his – but at this point, that means nothing. If there was a killer, it's clear they wore gloves. I also asked Izzy about the bent sword, and we were right. It was Freddie's old sabre. Nobody knows how it got bent, but Chiswell's fingerprints were the only ones on there. I suppose it's possible Chiswell got it off the wall while drunk and sentimental and accidentally trod on it, but again, there's nothing to say a gloved killer couldn't have handled it as well.'

Robin sighed. Her elation at finding the note appeared to have been premature.

'So, still no real leads?'

'Hold your horses,' said Strike bracingly, 'I'm leading up to the good stuff.

'Izzy managed to get a new phone number for that stable girl who can confirm Kinvara's alibi, Tegan Butcher. I want you to give her a ring. I think you'll seem less intimidating to her than I will.'

Robin jotted down the digits Strike read out.

'And after you've called Tegan, I want you to phone Raphael,' said Strike, giving her the second number he had got from Izzy. 'I'd like to clear up once and for all what he was really up to, the morning his father died.'

'Will do,' said Robin, glad of something concrete to do.

'Barclay's going to go back onto Jimmy and Flick,' said Strike, 'and I . . . '

He left a small pause, deliberately dramatic, and Robin laughed.

'And you're . . . '

' . . . am going to interview Billy Knight and Della Winn.'

'What?' said Robin, amazed. 'How're you going to get into the hosp – and *she'll* never agree—'

'Well, that's where you're wrong,' said Strike. 'Izzy dug Della's number out of Chiswell's records for me. I just rang her. I admit, I was expecting her to tell me to piss off—'

'—in slightly more elevated language, if I know Della,' Robin suggested.

'—and she sounded initially as though she wanted to,' admitted Strike, 'but Aamir's disappeared.'

'What?' said Robin, sharply.

'Calm down. "Disappeared" is Della's word. In reality, he resigned the day before yesterday and vacated his house, which hardly makes him a missing person. He's not picking up the phone to her. She's blaming me, because – her words again – I did "a fine job" on him when I went round to question him. She says he's very fragile and it'll be my fault if he ends up doing himself a mischief. So—'

'You've offered to find him in exchange for her answering questions?'

'Right in one,' said Strike. 'She jumped at the offer. Says I'll be able to reassure him that he's not in trouble and that nothing unsavoury I might have heard about him will go any further.'

'I hope he's all right,' said Robin, concerned. 'He *really* didn't like me, but that just proves he's smarter than any of the rest of them. When are you meeting Della?'

'Seven o'clock this evening, at her house in Bermondsey. And tomorrow afternoon, if all goes to plan, I'm going to be talking to Billy. I checked with Barclay, and Jimmy's got no plans to visit then, so I called the hospital. I'm waiting for Billy's psychiatrist to call me back now and confirm.'

'You think they'll let you question him?'

'Supervised, yeah, I think they will. They're interested in seeing how lucid he is if he gets to talk to me. He's back on his meds and greatly improved, but he's still telling the story of the strangled kid. If the psychiatric team's in agreement, I'm going to be visiting the locked ward tomorrow.'

'Well, great. It's good to have things to be getting on with. God knows, we could use a breakthrough – even if it is about the death we're not being paid to investigate,' she sighed.

'There might not be a death at the bottom of Billy's story at all,' said Strike, 'but it's going to bug me for ever unless we find out. I'll let you know how I get on with Della.'

Robin wished him luck, bade him goodbye and ended the call, though she remained lying on her half-made bed. After a few seconds, she said aloud:

'Blanc de blancs.'

Once again, she had the sense of a buried memory shifting, issuing a gust of low mood. Where on earth had she seen that phrase, while feeling miserable?

'Blanc de blancs,' she repeated, getting off the bed. 'Blanc d – *ow!*'

She had put her bare foot down on something small and very sharp. Bending down, she picked up a backless diamond stud earring.

At first, she merely stared at it, her pulse unaltered. The earring wasn't hers. She owned no diamond studs. She wondered why she hadn't trodden on it when she climbed into bed with a sleeping Matthew in the early hours of the morning. Perhaps her bare foot had missed it, or, more probably, the earring had been in the bed and displaced only when Robin pulled off the undersheet.

Of course, there were many diamond stud earrings in the world. The fact remained that the pair to which Robin's attention had most recently been drawn had been Sarah Shadlock's. Sarah had been wearing them the last time Robin and Matthew had gone to dinner, the night that Tom had attacked Matthew with sudden and apparently unwarranted ferocity.

For what felt like a very long time, but was in reality little over a minute, Robin sat contemplating the diamond in her hand. Then she laid the earring carefully on her bedside cabinet, picked up her mobile, entered 'Settings', removed her caller ID, then phoned Tom's mobile.

He answered within a couple of rings, sounding grumpy. In the background, a presenter was wondering aloud what the forthcoming Olympic closing ceremony would be like.

'Yah, hello?'

Robin hung up. Tom wasn't playing five-a-side football. She continued to sit, motionless, her phone in her hand, on the heavy matrimonial bed that had been so difficult to move up the narrow stairs of this lovely rented house, while her mind moved back over the clear signs that she, the detective, had wilfully ignored.

'I'm so stupid,' Robin said quietly to the empty, sunlit room. '*So* bloody stupid.'

54

Your gentle and upright disposition, your polished mind, your unimpeachable honour, are known to and appreciated by everyone . . .

Henrik Ibsen, *Rosmersholm*

Though the early evening was still bright, Della's front garden lay in shadow, which gave it a placid, melancholy air in contrast to the busy, dusty road that ran beyond the gates. As Strike rang the doorbell, he noted two large dog turds on the otherwise immaculate front lawn and he wondered who was helping Della with such mundane tasks now that her marriage was over.

The door opened, revealing the Minister for Sport in her impenetrable black glasses. She was wearing what Strike's elderly aunt back in Cornwall would have called a house-coat, a knee-length purple fleece robe that buttoned to the high neck, giving her a vaguely ecclesiastic air. The guide dog stood behind her, looking up at Strike with dark, mournful eyes.

'Hi, it's Cormoran Strike,' said the detective, without moving. Given that she could neither recognise him by sight nor examine any of the identification he carried, the only way she could know whom she was admitting to her house was by the sound of his voice. 'We spoke on the phone earlier and you asked me to come and see you.'

'Yes,' she said, unsmiling. 'Come in, then.'

She stepped back to let him pass, one hand on the Labrador's collar. Strike entered, wiping his feet on the doormat. A swell of music, loud strings and woodwind instruments, cut through by the pounding of a kettle drum, issued from what Strike assumed was the sitting room. Strike, who had been raised by a mother who listened mainly to metal bands, knew very little about classical music, but there was a looming, ominous quality about this music that he didn't particularly care for. The hall was dark, because the lights hadn't been turned on, and otherwise nondescript, with a dark brown patterned carpet that, while practical, was rather ugly.

'I've made coffee,' said Della. 'I'll need you to carry the tray into the sitting room for me, if you wouldn't mind.'

'No problem,' said Strike.

He followed the Labrador, which padded along at Della's heels, its tail wagging vaguely. The symphony grew louder as they passed the sitting room, the doorframe of which Della touched lightly as she passed, feeling for familiar markers to orientate herself.

'Is that Beethoven?' asked Strike, for something to say.

'Brahms. Symphony Number One, C Minor.'

The edges of every surface in the kitchen were rounded. The knobs on the oven, Strike noticed, had raised numbers stuck to them. On a cork noticeboard was a list of phone numbers headed IN CASE OF EMERGENCY, that he imagined were for the use of a cleaner or home help. While Della crossed to the worktop opposite, Strike extracted his mobile from his coat pocket and took a picture of Geraint

Winn's number. Della's outstretched hand reached the rim of the deep ceramic sink, and she moved sideways, where a tray sat already laden with a mug and a cafetière of freshly brewed coffee. Two bottles of wine stood beside it. Della felt for both of these, turned and held them out to Strike, still unsmiling.

'Which is which?' she asked.

'Châteauneuf-du-Pape, 2010, in your left hand,' said Strike, 'and Château Musar, 2006, in your right.'

'I'll have a glass of the Châteauneuf-du-Pape if you wouldn't mind opening the bottle and pouring it for me. I assumed that you wouldn't want a drink, but if you do, help yourself.'

'Thanks,' said Strike, picking up the corkscrew she had laid beside the tray, 'coffee will be fine.'

She set off silently for the sitting room, leaving him to follow with the tray. As he entered the room he caught the heavy scent of roses and was fleetingly reminded of Robin. While Della grazed furniture with her fingertips, feeling her way towards an armchair with wide wooden arms, Strike saw four large bunches of flowers positioned in vases around the room and punctuating the overall drabness with their vivid colours, red, yellow and pink.

Aligning herself by pressing the backs of her legs against the chair, Della sat down neatly, then turned her face towards Strike as he set the tray on the table.

'Would you put my glass here, on my right chair arm?' she said, patting it, and he did so, while the pale Labrador, which had flopped down beside Della's chair, watched him out of kind, sleepy eyes.

The strings of the violins in the symphony swooped and fell as Strike sat down. From the fawn carpet to the furniture, all of which might have been designed in the seventies, everything seemed to be in different shades of brown. Half of one wall was covered in built-in shelves holding what he thought must be at least a thousand CDs. On a table to the rear of the room was a stack of Braille manuscripts. A large, framed photograph of a teenage girl sat on the mantelpiece. It occurred to Strike that her mother could not even enjoy the bittersweet solace of looking at Rhiannon Winn every day, and he found himself filled with inconvenient compassion.

'Nice flowers,' he commented.

'Yes. It was my birthday a few days ago,' said Della.

'Ah. Many happy returns.'

'Are you from the West Country?'

'Partly. Cornwall.'

'I can hear it in your vowels,' said Della.

She waited while he dealt with the cafetière and poured himself coffee. When the sounds of clinking and pouring had ceased, she said:

'As I said on the phone, I'm very worried about Aamir. He'll still be in London, I'm sure, because it's all he's ever known. Not with his family,' she added, and Strike thought he heard a trace of contempt. 'I'm extremely concerned about him.'

She felt carefully for the wine glass next to her and took a sip.

'When you've reassured him that he isn't in any kind of trouble, and that anything Chiswell told you about him will go no further, you must tell him to contact me – urgently.'

The violins continued to screech and whine in what, to the untutored Strike, was a dissonant expression of foreboding. The guide dog scratched herself, her paw thudding off the carpet. Strike took out his notebook.

'Have you got the names or contact details of any friends Mallik might have gone to?'

'No,' said Della. 'I don't think he has many friends.

Latterly he mentioned someone from university but I don't remember a name. I doubt it was anyone particularly close.'

The thought of this distant friend seemed to make her uneasy.

'He studied at the LSE, so that's an area of London he knows well.'

'He's on good terms with one of his sisters, isn't he?'

'Oh, no,' said Della, at once. 'No, no, they all disowned him. No, he's got nobody, really, other than me, which is what makes this situation so dangerous.'

'The sister posted a picture on Facebook of the two of them fairly recently. It was in that pizza joint opposite your house.'

Della's expression betrayed not merely surprise, but displeasure.

'Aamir told me you'd been snooping online. Which sister was it?'

'I'd have to ch—'

'But I doubt he'd be staying with her,' said Della, talking over him. 'Not with the way the family as a whole has treated him. He *might* have contacted her, I suppose. You might see what she knows.'

'I will,' said Strike. 'Any other ideas about where he might go?'

'He really doesn't have anyone else,' she said. 'That's what worries me. He's vulnerable. It's essential I find him.'

'Well, I'll certainly do my best,' Strike promised her. 'Now, you said on the phone that you'd answer a few questions.'

Her expression became slightly more forbidding.

'I doubt I can tell you anything of interest, but go on.'

'Can we start with Jasper Chiswell, and you and your husband's relationship with him?'

By her expression, she managed to convey that she found the question both impertinent and slightly ludicrous. With a cold smile and raised eyebrows, she responded:

'Well, Jasper and I had a professional relationship, obviously.'

'And how was that?' asked Strike, adding sugar to his coffee, stirring it and taking a sip.

'Given,' said Della, 'that Jasper hired you to try and discover disreputable information about us, I think you already know the answer to that question.'

'You maintain that your husband wasn't blackmailing Chiswell, then, do you?'

'Of course I do.'

Strike knew that pushing on this particular point, when Della's super-injunction had already shown what lengths she would go to in her own defence, would only alienate her. A temporary retreat seemed indicated.

'What about the rest of the Chiswells? Did you ever run across any of them?'

'Some,' she said, a little warily.

'And how did you find them?'

'I barely know them. Geraint says Izzy was hardworking.'

'Chiswell's late son was on the junior British fencing team with your daughter, I think?'

The muscles of her face seemed to contract. He was reminded of an anemone shutting in on itself when it senses a predator.

'Yes,' she said.

'Did you like Freddie?'

'I don't think I ever spoke to him. Geraint was the one who ferried Rhiannon around to her tournaments. He knew the team.'

The shadow stems of the roses closest to the window

stretched like bars across the carpet. The Brahms symphony crashed stormily on in the background. Della's opaque lenses contributed to a feeling of inscrutable menace and Strike, though wholly unintimidated, was put in mind of the blind oracles and seers that peopled ancient myths, and the particular supernatural aura attributed by the able-bodied to this one particular disability.

'What was it that made Jasper Chiswell so eager to find out things to your disadvantage, would you say?'

'He didn't like me,' said Della simply. 'We disagreed frequently. He came from a background that finds anything that deviates from its own conventions and norms to be suspect, unnatural, even dangerous. He was a rich white Conservative male, Mr Strike, and he felt the corridors of power were best populated exclusively by rich white Conservative males. He sought, in everything, to restore a status quo he remembered in his youth. In pursuit of that objective, he was frequently unprincipled and certainly hypocritical.'

'In what way?'

'Ask his wife.'

'You know Kinvara, do you?'

'I wouldn't say I "know" her. I had an encounter with her a while ago that was certainly interesting in the light of Chiswell's public proclamations about the sanctity of marriage.'

Strike had the impression that beneath the lofty language, and in spite of her genuine anxiety about Aamir, Della was deriving pleasure from saying these things.

'What happened?' Strike asked.

'Kinvara turned up unexpectedly late one afternoon at the ministry, but Jasper had already left for Oxfordshire. I think it was her aim to surprise him.'

'When was this?'

'I should say ... a year ago, at least. Shortly before Parliament went into recess, I think. She was in a state of great distress. I heard a commotion outside and went to find out what was going on. I could tell by the silence of the outer office that they were all agog. She was very emotional, demanding to see her husband. Initially I thought she must have had dreadful news and perhaps needed Jasper as a source of comfort and support. I took her into my office.

'Once it was just the two of us, she broke down completely. She was barely coherent, but from the little I could understand,' said Della, 'she'd just found out there was another woman.'

'Did she say who?'

'I don't think so. She may have done, but she was – well, it was quite disturbing,' said Della austerely. 'More as though she had suffered a bereavement than the end of a marriage. "I was just part of his game", "He never loved me" and so forth.'

'What game did you take her to mean?' asked Strike.

'The political game, I suppose. She spoke of being humiliated, of being told, in so many words, that she had served her purpose ...

'Jasper Chiswell was a very ambitious man, you know. He'd lost his career once over infidelity. I imagine he cast around quite clinically for the kind of new wife who'd burnish his image. No more Italian fly-by-nights now he was trying to get back into the cabinet. He probably thought Kinvara would go down very well with the county Conservatives. Well-bred. Horsey.

'I heard, later, that Jasper had bundled her off into some kind of psychiatric clinic not long afterwards. That's how families like the Chiswells deal with excessive emotion, I suppose,' said Della, taking another sip of wine. 'Yet she stayed with him. Of course, people do stay, even when they're treated abominably. He talked about her within my hearing as though she was a deficient, needy child. I remember him saying Kinvara's mother would be "babysitting" her for her birthday, because he had to be in Parliament for a vote. He could have paired his vote, of course – found a Labour MP and struck a deal. Simply couldn't be bothered.

'Women like Kinvara Chiswell, whose entire self-worth is predicated on the status and success of marriage, are naturally shattered when everything goes wrong. I think all those horses of hers were an outlet, a substitute and – oh yes,' said Della, 'I've just remembered – the *very* last thing she said to me that day was that in addition to everything else, she now had to go home to put down a beloved mare.'

Della felt for the broad, soft head of Gwynn, who was lying beside her chair.

'I felt very sorry for her, there. Animals have been an enormous consolation to me in my life. One can hardly overstate the comfort they give, sometimes.'

The hand that caressed the dog still sported a wedding ring, Strike noticed, along with a heavy amethyst ring that matched her housecoat. Somebody, he supposed Geraint, must have told her that it was the same colour and again, he felt an unwelcome pang of pity.

'Did Kinvara tell you how or when she'd found out that her husband had been unfaithful?'

'No, no, she simply gave way to an almost incoherent outpouring of rage and grief, like a small child. Kept saying, "I loved him and he never loved me, it was all a lie". I've never heard such a raw explosion of grief, even at a funeral or a deathbed. I never spoke to her again except for hello. She acted as though she had no memory of what had passed between us.'

Della took another sip of wine.

'Can we return to Mallik?' Strike asked.

'Yes, of course,' she said at once.

'The morning that Jasper Chiswell died – the thirteenth – you were here, at home?'

There was a lengthy silence.

'Why are you asking me that?' Della said, in a changed tone.

'Because I'd like to corroborate a story I've heard,' said Strike.

'You mean, that Aamir was here with me, that morning?'

'Exactly.'

'Well, that's quite true. I'd slipped downstairs and sprained my wrist. I called Aamir and he came over. He wanted me to go to casualty, but there was no need. I could still move all my fingers. I simply needed some help managing breakfast and so on.'

'*You* called Mallik?'

'What?' she said.

It was the age-old, transparent 'what?' of the person who is afraid they've made a mistake. Strike guessed that some very rapid thinking was going on behind the dark glasses.

'*You* called Aamir?'

'Why? What does he say happened?'

'He says your husband went in person to fetch him from his house.'

'Oh,' said Della and then, 'of course, yes, I forgot.'

'Did you?' asked Strike gently. 'Or are you backing up their story?'

'I forgot,' Della repeated firmly. 'When I said I "called" him I wasn't talking about the telephone. I meant that I called "on" him. Via Geraint.'

'But if Geraint was here when you slipped, couldn't he have helped you with your breakfast?'

'I think Geraint wanted Aamir to help persuade me to go to casualty.'

'Right. So it was Geraint's idea to go to Aamir, rather than yours?'

'I can't remember now,' she said, but then, contradicting herself, 'I'd fallen rather heavily. Geraint has a bad back, naturally he wanted help and I thought of Aamir, and then the pair of them nagged me to go to A&E, but there was no need. It was a simple sprain.'

The light was now fading beyond the net curtains. Della's black lenses reflected the neon red of the dying sun above the rooftops.

'I'm extremely worried about Aamir,' she said again, in a strained voice.

'A couple more questions and I'm done,' Strike replied. 'Jasper Chiswell hinted in front of a roomful of people that he knew something disreputable about Mallik. Can you tell me anything about that?'

'Yes, well, it was that conversation,' said Della quietly, 'that first made Aamir think about resigning. I could feel him pulling away from me after it happened. And then *you* finished the job, didn't you? You went to his house, to taunt him further.'

'There was no taunting, Mrs Winn—'

'*Liwat*, Mr Strike, did you never learn what that meant all the time you were in the Middle East?'

'Yeah, I know what it means,' said Strike matter-of-factly. 'Sodomy. Chiswell seemed to be threatening Aamir with exposure—'

'Aamir wouldn't suffer from exposure of the truth, I assure you!' said Della fiercely. 'Not that it matters a jot, but he doesn't happen to be gay!'

The Brahms symphony continued on what, to Strike,

was its gloomy and intermittently sinister course, horns and violins competing to jar the nerves.

'You want the truth?' said Della loudly. 'Aamir objected to being groped and harassed, *felt up* by a senior civil servant, whose inappropriate touching of young men passing through his office is an open secret, even a joke! And when a comprehensive-educated Muslim boy loses his cool and smacks a senior civil servant, which of the two do you imagine finds themselves smeared and stigmatised? Which of them, do you think, becomes the subject of derogatory rumours, and is forced out of a job?'

'I'm guessing,' said Strike, '*not* Sir Christopher Barrowclough-Burns.'

'How did you know whom I was talking about?' said Della sharply.

'Still in the post, is he?' asked Strike, ignoring the question.

'Of course he is! Everybody knows about his *harmless* little ways, but nobody wants to go on the record. I've been trying to get something done about Barrowclough-Burns for years. When I heard Aamir had left the diversity programme in murky circumstances, I made it my business to find him. He was in a pitiable state when I first made contact with him, absolutely pitiable. Quite apart from the derailing of what should have been a stellar career, there was a malicious cousin who'd heard some gossip and spread the rumour that Aamir had been fired for homosexual activity at work.

'Well, Aamir's father isn't the sort of man to look kindly on a gay son. Aamir had been resisting his parents' pressure to marry a girl they thought suitable. There was a terrible row and a complete breach. This brilliant young man lost everything, family, home and job, in the space of a couple of weeks.'

'So you stepped in?'

'Geraint and I had an empty property around the corner. Both our mothers used to live there. Neither Geraint nor I have siblings. It had become too difficult to manage our mothers' care from London, so we brought them up from Wales and housed them together, around the corner. Geraint's mother died two years ago, mine this, so the house was empty. We didn't need the rent. It seemed only sensible to let Aamir stay there.'

'And this was nothing but disinterested kindness?' Strike said. 'You weren't thinking of how useful he might be to you, when you gave him a job and a house?'

'What d'you mean, "useful"? He's a very intelligent young man, any office would be—'

'Your husband was pressuring Aamir to get incriminating information on Jasper Chiswell from the Foreign Office, Mrs Winn. Photographs. He was pressuring Aamir to go to Sir Christopher for pictures.'

Della reached out for her glass of wine, missed the stem by inches and hit the glass with her knuckles. Strike lunged forwards to try and catch it, but too late: a whip-like trail of red wine described a parabola in the air and spattered the beige carpet, the glass falling with a thud beside it. Gwynn got up and approached the spill with mild interest, sniffing the spreading stain.

'How bad is it?' asked Della urgently, her fingers grasping the arms of her chair, her face inclined to the floor.

'Not good,' said Strike.

'Salt, please . . . put salt on it. In the cupboard to the right of the cooker!'

Turning on the light as he entered the kitchen, Strike's attention was caught for the first time by an odd something he had failed to spot on his previous entry into the room: an envelope stuck high up on a wall-mounted cabinet to the right, too high for Della to reach. Having grabbed the salt out of the cupboard he made a detour to read the single word written on it: *Geraint*.

'To the right of the cooker!' Della called a little desperately from the sitting room.

'Ah, the right!' Strike shouted back, as he tugged down the envelope and slit it open.

Inside was a receipt from 'Kennedy Bros. Joiners', for the replacement of a bathroom door. Strike licked his finger, dampened down the envelope flap, resealed it as best he could and stuck it back where he had found it.

'Sorry,' he told Della, re-entering the room. 'It was right in front of me and I didn't notice.'

He twisted the top of the cardboard tub and poured salt liberally over the purple stain. The Brahms symphony came to an end as he straightened up, dubious as to the likely success of the home remedy.

'Have you done it?' Della whispered into the silence.

'Yeah,' said Strike, watching the wine rising into the white and turning it a dirty grey. 'I think you're still going to need a carpet cleaner, though.'

'Oh dear . . . the carpet was new this year.'

She seemed deeply shaken, though whether this was entirely due to the spilled wine was, Strike thought, debatable. As he returned to the sofa and set down the salt beside the coffee, music started up again, this time a Hungarian air that was no more restful than the symphony, but weirdly manic.

'Would you like more wine?' he asked her.

'I – yes, I think I would,' she said.

He poured her another and passed it directly into her hand. She drank a little, then said shakily:

'How could you know what you just told me, Mr Strike?'

'I'd rather not answer that, but I assure you it's true.'

Clutching her wine in both hands Della said:

'You *have* to find Aamir for me. If he thought *I* sanctioned Geraint telling him to go to Barrowclough-Burns for favours, it's no wonder he—'

Her self-control was visibly disintegrating. She tried to set the wine down on the arm of her chair and had to feel for it with the other hand before doing so successfully, all the while shaking her head in little jerks of disbelief.

'No wonder he what?' asked Strike quietly.

'Accused me of . . . of smothering . . . controlling . . . well, of course, this explains everything . . . we were so close – you wouldn't understand – it's hard to explain – but it was remarkable, how soon we became – well, like family. Sometimes, you know, there's an instant affinity – a connection that years couldn't forge, with other people—

'But these past few weeks, it all changed – I could feel it – starting when Chiswell made that jibe in front of everyone – Aamir became distant. It was as though he no longer trusted me . . . I should have known . . . oh Lord, I should have known . . . you have to find him, you have to . . . '

Perhaps, Strike thought, the depth of her burning sense of need was sexual in origin, and perhaps on some subconscious level it had indeed been tinged with appreciation of Aamir's youthful masculinity. However, as Rhiannon Winn watched over them from her cheap gilt frame, wearing a smile that didn't reach her wide, anxious eyes, her teeth glinting with heavy braces, Strike thought it far more likely that Della was a woman possessed of that which Charlotte so conspicuously lacked: a burning, frustrated maternal drive tinged, in Della's case, with unassuageable regret.

'This as well,' she whispered. '*This as well.* What hasn't he ruined?'

'You're talking about—'

'My husband!' said Della numbly. 'Who else? My charity – our charity – but you know that, of course? It was you who told Chiswell about the missing twenty-five thousand, wasn't it? And the lies, the stupid lies, Geraint's been telling people? David Beckham, Mo Farah – all those impossible promises?'

'My partner found out.'

'Nobody will believe me,' said Della distractedly, 'but I didn't know, I had no idea. I've missed the last four board meetings – preparations for the Paralympics. Geraint only told me the truth after Chiswell threatened him with the press. Even then he claimed it was the accountant's fault, but he swore to me the other things weren't true. Swore it, on his mother's grave.'

She twisted the wedding ring on her finger, apparently distracted.

'I suppose your wretched partner tracked down Elspeth Lacey-Curtis, as well?'

'Afraid so,' lied Strike, judging that a gamble was indicated. 'Did Geraint deny that, too?'

'If he'd said anything to make the girls uncomfortable he felt awful, but he swore there was nothing else to it, no touching, just a couple of risqué jokes. But in this climate,' said Della furiously, 'a man ought to damned well think about what jokes he makes to a bunch of fifteen-year-old girls!'

Strike leaned forwards and grabbed Della's wine, which was in danger of being upended again.

'What are you doing?'

'Moving your glass onto the table,' said Strike.

'Oh,' said Della, 'thank you.' Making a noticeable effort to control herself, she continued, 'Geraint was representing *me* at that event, and it will go the way it always goes in the press when it all comes out: it will have been my fault, all of it! Because men's crimes are *always* ours in the final analysis, aren't they, Mr Strike? Ultimate responsibility *always* lies with the woman, who should have stopped it, who should have acted, who *must have known*. Your failings are really *our* failings, aren't they? Because the proper role of the woman is carer, and there's nothing lower in this whole world than a bad mother.'

Breathing hard, she pressed her trembling fingers to her temples. Beyond the net curtains night, deep blue, was inching like a veil over the glaring red of sunset and as the room grew darker, Rhiannon Winn's features faded gradually into the twilight. Soon all that would be visible was her smile, punctuated by the ugly braces.

'Give me back my wine, please.'

Strike did so. Della drank most of it down at once and continued to clasp the glass as she said bitterly:

'There are plenty of people ready to think all kinds of odd things about a blind woman. Of course, when I was younger, it was worse. There was often a prurient interest in one's private life. It was the first place some men's minds went. Perhaps you've experienced it, too, have you, with your one leg?'

Strike found that he didn't resent the blunt mention of his disability from Della.

'Yeah, I've had a bit of that,' he admitted. 'Bloke I was at school with. Hadn't seen him in years. It was my first time back in Cornwall since I got blown up. Five pints in, he asked me at what point I warned women my leg was going to come off with my trousers. He thought he was being funny.'

Della smiled thinly.

'Never occurs to some people that it is we who should be making the jokes, does it? But it will be different for you, as a man . . . most people seem to think it in the natural order of things that the able-bodied woman should look after the disabled man. Geraint had to deal with that for years ... people assuming there was something peculiar about him, because he chose a disabled wife. I think I may have tried to compensate for that. I wanted him to have a role ... status ... but it would have been better for both of us, in retrospect, if he had done something unconnected to me.'

Strike thought she was a little drunk. Perhaps she hadn't eaten. He felt an inappropriate desire to check her fridge. Sitting here with this impressive and vulnerable woman, it was easy to understand how Aamir had become so entangled with her both professionally and privately, without ever intending to become so.

'People assume I married Geraint because there was nobody else who wanted me, but they're quite wrong,' said Della, sitting up straighter in her chair. 'There was a boy I was at school with who was smitten with me, who proposed when I was nineteen. I had a choice and I chose Geraint. Not as a carer, or because, as journalists have sometimes implied, my limitless ambition made a husband necessary ... but because I loved him.'

Strike remembered the day he had followed Della's husband to the stairwell in King's Cross, and the tawdry things that Robin had told him about Geraint's behaviour at work, yet nothing that Della had just said struck him as incredible. Life had taught him that a great and powerful love could be felt for the most apparently unworthy people, a circumstance that ought, after all, to give everybody consolation.

'Are you married, Mr Strike?'

'No,' he said.

'I think marriage is nearly always an unfathomable entity, even to the people inside it. It took this ... all of this mess ... to make me realise I can't go on. I don't really know when I stopped loving him, but at some point after Rhiannon died, it slipped—'

Her voice broke.

'—slipped away from us.' She swallowed. 'Please will you pour me another glass of wine?'

He did so. The room was very dark now. The music had changed again, to a melancholy violin concerto which at last, in Strike's opinion, was appropriate to the conversation. Della had not wanted to talk to him, but now seemed reluctant to let the conversation end.

'Why did your husband hate Jasper Chiswell so much?' Strike asked quietly. 'Because of Chiswell's political clashes with you, or—?'

'No, no,' said Della Winn wearily. 'Because Geraint has to blame somebody other than himself for the misfortunes that befall him.'

Strike waited, but she merely drank more wine, and said nothing.

'What exactly—?'

'Never mind,' she said loudly. 'Never mind, it doesn't matter.'

But a moment later, after another large gulp of wine, she said:

'Rhiannon didn't really want to do fencing. Like most little girls, what she wanted was a pony, but we – Geraint and I – we didn't come from pony-owning backgrounds. We didn't have the first idea what one does with horses. As I think back, I suppose there were ways around that, but we were both terribly busy and felt it would be impractical, so she took up fencing instead, and very good she was at it, too . . .

'Have I answered enough of your questions, Mr Strike?' she asked a little thickly. 'Will you find Aamir?'

'I'll try,' Strike promised her. 'Could you give me his number? And yours, so I can keep you updated?'

She had both numbers off by heart, and he copied them down before closing his notebook and getting back to his feet.

'You've been very helpful, Mrs Winn. Thank you.'

'That sounds worrying,' she said, with a faint crease between the eyebrows. 'I'm not sure I meant to be.'

'Will you be—?'

'Perfectly,' said Della, enunciating over-clearly. 'You'll call me when you find Aamir, won't you?'

'If you don't hear from me before then, I'll update you in a week's time,' Strike promised. 'Er – is anyone coming in tonight, or—?'

'I see you aren't quite as hardened as your reputation would suggest,' said Della. 'Don't worry about me. My neighbour will be in to walk Gwynn for me shortly. She checks the gas dials and so forth.'

'In that case, don't get up. Good night.'

The near-white dog raised her head as he walked towards the door, sniffing the air. He left Della sitting in the darkness, a little drunk, with nothing else for company but the picture of the dead daughter she had never seen.

Closing the front door, Strike couldn't remember the last time he had felt such a strange mixture of admiration, sympathy and suspicion.

55

. . . let us at least fight with honourable weapons, since it seems we must fight.

Henrik Ibsen, *Rosmersholm*

Matthew, who had supposedly been out just for the morning, still hadn't come home. He had sent two texts since, one at three in the afternoon:

Tom got work troubles, wants to talk. Gone to pub with him (I'm on Cokes.) Back as soon as I can.

And then, at seven o'clock:

Really sorry, he's pissed, I can't leave him. Going to find him a taxi then come back. Hope you've eaten. Love you x

Still with her caller ID switched off, Robin had again phoned Tom's mobile. He had answered immediately. There was no background babble of a pub.

'Yes?' said Tom testily and apparently sober, 'who is this?'

Robin hung up.

Two bags were packed and waiting in the hall. She had

already phoned Vanessa and asked whether she could stay on her sofa for a couple of nights, before she got a new place to live. She found it strange that Vanessa didn't sound more surprised, but at the same time, was glad not to have to fend off pity.

Waiting in the sitting room, watching night fall outside the window, Robin wondered whether she would even have been suspicious had she not found the earring. Lately she had become simply grateful for time without Matthew, when she could relax, not having to hide anything, whether the work she was doing on the Chiswell case or the panic attacks that must be conducted quietly, without fuss, on the bathroom floor.

Sitting in the stylish armchair belonging to their absent landlord, Robin felt as though she were inhabiting a memory. How often were you aware, while it happened, that you were living an hour that would change the course of your life for ever? She would remember this room for a long time, and she gazed around it now, with the aim of fixing it in her mind, thereby trying to ignore the sadness, the shame and the pain that burned and twisted inside her.

At just past nine o'clock, she heard, with a wave of nausea, Matthew's key in the lock and the sound of the door opening.

'Sorry,' he shouted, before he'd even closed the door, 'he's a silly sod, I had a job persuading the taxi driver to take—'

Robin heard his small exclamation of surprise as he spotted the suitcases. Safe, now, to dial, she pressed the number she had ready on her phone. He walked into the sitting room, puzzled, in time to hear her booking a minicab. She hung up. They looked at each other.

'What's with the cases?'

'I'm leaving.'

There was a long silence. Matthew seemed not to understand.

'What d'you mean?'

'I don't know how to say it any more clearly, Matt.'

'Leaving *me*?'

'That's right.'

'Why?'

'Because,' said Robin, 'you're sleeping with Sarah.'

She watched Matthew struggling to find words that might save him, but the seconds slid by, and it was too late for real incredulity, for astonished innocence, for genuine incomprehension.

'What?' he said at last, with a forced laugh.

'Please don't,' she said. 'There's no point. It's over.'

He continued to stand in the doorway of the sitting room and she thought he looked tired, even haggard.

'I was going to go and leave a note,' said Robin, 'but that felt too melodramatic. Anyway, there are practical things we need to talk about.'

She thought she could see him thinking, *How did I give it away? Who have you told?*

'Listen,' he said urgently, dropping his sports bag beside him (full, no doubt, of clean, pressed kit), 'I know things haven't been good between us, you and me, but it's you I want, Robin. Don't throw us away. Please.'

He walked forwards, dropped into a crouch beside her chair and tried to take her hand. She pulled it away, genuinely astonished.

'You're sleeping with Sarah,' she repeated.

He got up, crossed to the sofa and sat down, dropped his face into his hands and said weakly:

'I'm sorry. I'm sorry. It's been so shit between you and me—'

'—that you had to sleep with your friend's fiancée?'

He looked up at that, in sudden panic.

'Have you spoken to Tom? Does he know?'

Suddenly unable to bear his proximity, she walked away towards the window, full of a contempt she had never felt before.

'Even now, worried about your promotion prospects, Matt?'

'No – fuck – you don't understand,' he said. 'It's over between me and Sarah.'

'Oh, really?'

'Yes,' he said. 'Yes! Fuck – this is so fucking ironic – we talked all day. We agreed it couldn't go on, not after – you and Tom – we've just ended it. An hour ago.'

'Wow,' said Robin, with a little laugh, feeling disembodied, '*isn't* that ironic?'

Her mobile rang. Dreamlike, she answered it.

'Robin?' said Strike. 'Update. I've just seen Della Winn.'

'How did it go?' she asked, trying to sound steady and bright, determined not to cut the call short. Her working life was now her entire life and Matthew would no longer impinge upon it. Turning her back on her fuming husband, she looked out onto the dark cobbled street.

'Very interesting on two counts,' said Strike. 'Firstly, she slipped up. I don't think Geraint was with Aamir the morning Chiswell died.'

'That *is* interesting,' said Robin, forcing herself to concentrate, aware of Matthew watching her.

'I've got a number for him and I tried it, but he's not picking up. I thought I'd see if he's still at the B&B down the road as I'm in the vicinity, but the owner says he's moved on.'

'Shame. What was the other interesting thing?' asked Robin.

'Is that Strike?' asked Matthew loudly, from behind her. She ignored him.

'What was that?' asked Strike.

'Nothing,' said Robin. 'Go on.'

'Well, the second interesting thing is that Della met Kinvara last year, who was hysterical because she thought Chiswell—'

Robin's mobile was pulled roughly out of her hand. She

wheeled around. Matthew ended the call with a stab of his finger.

'How *dare* you?' shouted Robin, holding out her hand. 'Give that back!'

'We're trying to save our fucking marriage and you're taking calls from him?'

'I'm not trying to save this marriage! *Give me back my phone!*'

He hesitated, then thrust it back at her, only to look outraged when she coolly phoned Strike back again.

'Sorry about that, Cormoran, we got cut off,' she said, with Matthew's wild eyes on her.

'Everything all right there, Robin?'

'It's fine. What were you saying about Chiswell?'

'That he was having an affair.'

'An affair!' said Robin, her eyes on Matthew's. 'Who with?'

'Christ knows. Have you had any luck getting hold of Raphael? We know he's not that bothered about protecting his father's memory. He might tell us.'

'I left a message for him, and for Tegan. Neither of them have called back.'

'OK, well, keep me posted. This all sheds an interesting light on the hammer round the head, though, doesn't it?'

'Certainly does,' said Robin.

'That's me at the Tube. Sure you're all right?'

'Yes, of course,' said Robin, with what she hoped sounded like workaday impatience. 'Speak soon.'

She hung up.

'"Speak soon",' Matthew imitated her, in the high-pitched, wispy voice he always used when impersonating women. '"Speak later, Cormoran. I'm running out on my marriage so I can be at your beck and call for ever, Cormoran. I don't mind working for minimum wage, Cormoran, not if I can be your skivvy".'

'Fuck off, Matt,' said Robin calmly. 'Fuck off back to

Sarah. The earring she left in our bed is upstairs on my bedside table, by the way.'

'Robin,' he said, suddenly earnest, 'we can get through this. If we love each other, we can.'

'Well, the problem with that, Matt,' said Robin, 'is that I don't love you any more.'

She had always thought the idea of eyes darkening was literary licence, but she saw his light eyes turn black as his pupils dilated in shock.

'You bitch,' he said quietly.

She felt a cowardly impulse to lie, to back away from the absolute statement, to protect herself, but something stronger in her held on: the need to tell the unvarnished truth, when she had been lying to him and herself for so long.

'No,' she said. 'I don't. We should have split up on the honeymoon. I stayed because you were ill. I felt sorry for you. No,' she corrected herself, determined to do the thing properly, 'actually, we should never have gone on the honeymoon. I ought to have walked out of the wedding once I knew you'd deleted those calls from Strike.'

She wanted to check her watch to see when her cab would arrive, but she was scared to take her eyes off her husband. There was something in his expression that recalled a snake peering out from under a rock.

'How do you think your life looks to other people?' he asked quietly.

'What d'you mean?'

'You bailed out on uni. Now you're bailing out on us. You even bailed on your therapist. You're a fucking flake. The only thing you haven't run out on is this stupid job that's half-killed you, and you got sacked from *that*. He only took you back because he wants to get into your pants. And he probably can't get anyone else so cheap.'

She felt as though he had punched her. Winded, her voice sounded weak.

'Thanks, Matt,' she said, moving towards the door. 'Thanks for making this so easy.'

But he moved quickly to block her exit.

'It was a temping job. He paid you attention, so you kidded yourself that was the career for you, even though it's the last fucking thing you should've been doing, with *your* history—'

She was fighting tears now, but determined not to succumb.

'I wanted to do police work for years and years—'

'No, you fucking didn't!' jeered Matthew, 'when did you ever—?'

'I had a life before you!' Robin shouted. 'I had a home life where I said things you never heard! I never told you, Matthew, because I knew you'd laugh, like my dickhead brothers! I did psychology hoping it would take me to some kind of forensic—'

'You never said this, you're trying to justify—'

'I didn't tell you because I knew you'd sneer—'

'Bullshit—'

'It isn't bullshit!' she shouted. 'I'm telling you the truth, this is the whole truth, and you're proving my point, you don't believe me! You liked it when I dropped out of uni—'

'The hell d'you mean?'

'"There's no hurry to go back", "you don't *have* to have a degree . . . "'

'Oh, so now I'm being fucking blamed for being sensitive!'

'You liked it, you liked me being stuck at home, why can't you admit it? Sarah Shadlock at uni and me underachieving back in Masham – it made up for me getting better A-levels than you, getting into my first choice of—'

'Oh!' he laughed humourlessly, 'oh, you got better fucking *A-levels* than me? Yeah, that keeps me up at night—'

'If I hadn't been raped, we'd have split up years ago!'

'Is this what you learned in therapy? To tell lies about the past, to justify all your bullshit?'

'I learned to tell the truth!' shouted Robin, driven to the point of brutality. 'And here's some more: I was falling out of love with you before the rape! You weren't interested in anything I was doing – my course, my new friends. All you wanted to know was whether any other blokes were making moves on me. But afterwards, you were so sweet, so kind . . . you seemed like the safest man in the world, the only one I could trust. That's why I stayed. We wouldn't be here, now, but for that rape.'

They both heard the car pull up outside. Robin tried to slide past him into the hall, but he moved to block her again.

'No, you don't. You're not getting out of it that bloody easily. You stayed because I was *safe*? Fuck off. You loved me.'

'I thought I did,' said Robin, 'but not any more. Get out of the way. I'm leaving.'

She tried to sidestep him, but he moved to block her again.

'No,' he said again, and now he moved forwards, jostling her back into the sitting room. 'You're staying here. We're having this out.'

The minicab driver rang the doorbell.

'Coming!' Robin shouted, but Matthew snarled:

'You're not running away this time, you're going to stay and sort out your mess—'

'No!' shouted Robin, as though to a dog. She came to a halt, refusing to be backed further into the room, even though he was so close she could feel his breath on her face, and she was suddenly reminded of Geraint Winn, and was overwhelmed with revulsion. 'Get away from me. *Now!*'

And like a dog Matthew took a step backwards, responding not to the order, but to something in her voice. He was angry, but scared, too.

'Right,' said Robin. She knew she was on the edge of a panic attack, but she held on, and every second she did not dissolve was giving her strength, and she stood her ground. 'I'm leaving. You try and stop me, I'll retaliate. I've fought off far bigger, meaner men than you, Matthew. You haven't even got a bloody knife.'

She saw his eyes turn blacker than ever, and suddenly she remembered how her brother, Martin, had punched Matthew in the face, at the wedding. No matter what was coming, she vowed, in a kind of dark exhilaration, she'd do better than Martin. She'd break his damn nose if she had to.

'Please,' he said, his shoulders suddenly sagging, 'Robin—'

'You're going to have to hurt me if you want to stop me leaving, but I warn you, I'll prosecute you for assault if you do. *That* won't go down too well at the office, will it?'

She held his gaze for a few more seconds then walked back towards him, her fists already curling, waiting for him to block or grab her, but he moved aside.

'Robin,' he said hoarsely. 'Wait. Seriously, wait, you said there were things we had to discuss—'

'The lawyers can do it,' she said, reaching the front door and pulling it open.

The cool night air touched her like a blessing.

A stocky woman was sitting at the wheel of a Vauxhall Corsa. Seeing Robin's cases, she got out to help her hoist them into the boot. Matthew had followed and was now standing in the doorway. As Robin made to get into the car, he called to her and her tears began to fall at last, but without looking at him, she slammed the door.

'Please, let's go,' she said thickly, to the driver, as Matthew came down the steps and bent to speak to her through the glass.

'I still fucking love you!'

The car moved away over the cobbles of Albury Street, past the moulded frontages of the pretty sea merchants' houses where she had never felt she belonged. At the top of the street she knew that if she looked back, she would see Matthew standing watching the vanishing car. Her eyes met those of the driver in the rear-view mirror.

'Sorry,' said Robin nonsensically, and then, bewildered by her own apology, she said, 'I've – I've just left my husband.'

'Yeah?' said the driver, switching on her indicator. 'I've left two. It gets easier with practice.'

Robin tried to laugh, but the noise turned into a loud wet hiccough, and as the car approached the lonely stone swan high on the corner pub, she began to cry in earnest.

'Here,' said the driver gently, and she passed back a plastic-wrapped pack of tissues.

'Thanks,' sobbed Robin, extracting one and pressing it to her tired, stinging eyes until the white tissue was sodden and streaked with the last traces of thick black eye make-up that she had worn to impersonate Bobbi Cunliffe. Avoiding the sympathetic gaze of the driver in the rear-view mirror, she looked down into her lap. The wrapper on the tissues was that of an unfamiliar American brand: 'Dr Blanc'.

At once, Robin's elusive memory dropped into view, as though it had been waiting for this tiny prod. Now she remembered exactly where she had seen the phrase 'Blanc de Blanc', but it had nothing to do with the case, and everything to do with her imploding marriage, with a lavender walk and a Japanese water garden, and the last time she had ever said 'I love you', and the first time she'd known she didn't mean it.

56

I cannot – I will not – go through life with a dead body on my back.

Henrik Ibsen, *Rosmersholm*

As Strike approached Henlys Corner on the North Circular Road the following afternoon, he saw, with a muttered oath, that traffic ahead had come to a halt. The junction, which was a notorious hotspot for congestion, had supposedly been improved earlier that year. As he joined the stationary queue, Strike wound down his window, lit a cigarette and glanced at his dashboard clock, with the familiar sensation of angry impotence that driving in London so often engendered. He had wondered whether it might be wiser to take the Tube north, but the psychiatric hospital lay a good mile from the nearest station, and the BMW was marginally easier on his still sore leg. Now he feared that he was going to be late for an interview that he was determined not to miss, firstly because he had no wish to disoblige the psychiatric team who were letting him see Billy Knight, and secondly because Strike didn't know when there would next be an opportunity to speak to the younger brother without fear of running into the older. Barclay had assured him that morning that Jimmy's plans for the day comprised writing a polemic on Rothschild's global influence for the Real Socialist website and sampling some of Barclay's new stash.

Scowling and tapping his fingers on the steering wheel, Strike fell back to ruminating on a question that had been nagging at him since the previous evening: whether or not the cut connection halfway through his call to Robin had really been due to Matthew snatching the phone out of her hand. He had not found Robin's subsequent assurances that all was well particularly convincing.

While heating himself baked beans on his one-ringed hob, because he was still attempting to lose weight, Strike had debated calling Robin back. Eating his meatless dinner unenthusiastically in front of the television, supposedly watching highlights of the Olympics closing ceremony, his attention was barely held by the sight of the Spice Girls zooming around on top of London cabs. *I think marriage is nearly always an unfathomable entity, even to the people inside it*, Della Winn had said. Perhaps Robin and Matthew were even now in bed together. Was pulling a phone out of her hand any worse than deleting her call history? She had stayed with Matthew after that. Where was her red line?

And Matthew was surely too careful of his own reputation and prospects to abandon all civilised norms. One of Strike's last thoughts before falling asleep the night before had been that Robin had successfully fought off the Shacklewell Ripper, a grisly reflection, perhaps, but one that brought a certain reassurance.

The detective was perfectly aware that the state of his junior partner's marriage ought to be the least of his worries, given that he so far had no concrete information for the client who was currently paying three full-time investigators to find out the facts about her father's death. Nevertheless, as the traffic finally moved on, Strike's thoughts continued to eddy around Robin and Matthew until at last he saw a signpost to the psychiatric clinic and, with an effort, focused his mind on the forthcoming interview.

Unlike the gigantic rectangular prism of concrete and black glass where Jack had been admitted a few weeks earlier, the hospital outside which Strike parked twenty minutes later boasted crocketed spires and byzantine windows covered with iron bars. In Strike's opinion it looked like the bastard offspring of a gingerbread palace and a gothic prison. A Victorian stonemason had carved the word 'Sanatorium' into the dirty redbrick arch over the double doorway.

Already five minutes late, Strike flung open the driver's door and, not bothering to change his trainers for smarter footwear, locked the BMW and hurried, limping, up the grubby front steps.

Inside he found a chilly hallway with high, off-white ceilings, churchlike windows and a general suspicion of decay barely kept at bay by the fug of disinfectant. Spotting the ward number he had been given by phone, he set off along a corridor to the left.

Sunlight falling through the barred windows cast striped patches onto the off-white walls, which were hung crookedly with art, some of which had been done by former patients. As Strike passed a series of collages depicting detailed farmyard scenes in felt, tinsel and yarn, a skeletal teenage girl emerged from a bathroom alongside a nurse. Neither of them seemed to notice Strike. Indeed, the girl's dull eyes were focused, it seemed to him, inward upon a battle she was waging far from the real world.

Strike was faintly surprised to discover the double doors to the locked ward at the end of the ground floor corridor. Some vague association with belfries and Rochester's first wife had led him to picture it on an upper floor, hidden perhaps in one of those pointed spires. The reality was entirely prosaic: a large green buzzer on the wall, which Strike pressed, and a male nurse with bright red hair peering through a small glass window, who turned to speak to somebody behind him. The door opened and Strike was admitted.

The ward had four beds and a seating area, where two patients in day clothes were sitting, playing draughts: an older, apparently toothless man and a pale youth with a thickly bandaged neck. A cluster of people were standing around a workstation just inside the door: an orderly, two more nurses, and what Strike assumed to be two doctors, one male, one female. All turned to stare at him as he entered. One of the nurses nudged the other.

'Mr Strike,' said the male doctor, who was short, rather foxy in appearance and had a strong Mancunian accent. 'How do you do? Colin Hepworth, we spoke on the phone. This is my colleague, Kamila Muhammad.'

Strike shook hands with the woman, whose navy trouser suit reminded him of a policewoman's.

'We're both going to be sitting in on your interview with Billy,' she said. 'He's just gone to the bathroom. He's quite excited about seeing you again. We thought we'd use one of our interview rooms. It's right here.'

She led him around the workstation, the nurses still watching avidly, into a small room containing four chairs and a desk that had been bolted to the floor. The walls were pale pink but otherwise bare.

'Ideal,' said Strike. It was like a hundred interview rooms he had used in the military police. There, too, third parties had often been present, usually lawyers.

'A quick word before we start,' said Kamila Muhammad,

pulling the door to on Strike and her colleague, so that the nurses couldn't hear their conversation. 'I don't know how much you know about Billy's condition?'

'His brother told me it's schizoid affective disorder.'

'That's right,' she said. 'He went off his medication and ended up in a full-blown psychotic episode, which by the sounds of it is when he came to see you.'

'Yeah, he seemed pretty disturbed at the time. He looked as though he'd been sleeping rough, as well.'

'He probably had been. His brother told us he'd been missing around a week at that point. We don't believe Billy's psychotic any more,' she said, 'but he's still quite closed down, so it's hard to gauge to what degree he's engaged with reality. It can be difficult to get an accurate picture of someone's mental state where there are paranoid and delusional symptoms.'

'We're hoping that you can help us disentangle some of the facts from the fiction,' said the Mancunian. 'You've been a recurring motif in his conversation ever since he was sectioned. He's been very keen to talk to you, but not so much to any of us. He's also expressed fear of – of repercussions if he confides in anyone and, again, it's difficult to know whether that fear is part of his illness or, ah, whether there's someone who he genuinely has reason to fear. Because, ah—'

He hesitated, as though trying to choose his words carefully. Strike said:

'I'd imagine his brother could be scary if he chose to be,' and the psychiatrist seemed relieved to have been understood without breaking confidentiality.

'You know his brother, do you?'

'I've met him. Does he visit often?'

'He's been in a couple of times, but Billy's often been more distressed and agitated after seeing him. If he seems to be similarly affected during your interview—' said the Mancunian.

'Understood,' said Strike.

'Funny, really, seeing you here,' said Colin, with a faint grin. 'We assumed that his fixation with you was all part of his psychosis. An obsession with a celebrity is quite common with these kinds of disorders ... As a matter of fact,' he said candidly, 'just a couple of days ago, Kamila and I were agreeing that his fixation with you would preclude an early discharge. Lucky you called, really.'

'Yeah,' said Strike drily, 'that is lucky.'

The redheaded male nurse knocked on the door and put his head in.

'That's Billy ready to talk to Mr Strike.'

'Great,' said the female psychiatrist. 'Eddie, could we get some tea in here? Tea?' she asked Strike over her shoulder. He nodded. She opened the door. 'Come in, Billy.'

And there he was: Billy Knight, wearing a grey sweatshirt and jogging pants, his feet in hospital slippers. The sunken eyes were still deeply shadowed, and at some point since he and Strike had last seen each other, he had shaven his head. The finger and thumb of his left hand were bandaged. Even through the tracksuit that somebody, presumably Jimmy, had brought him to wear, Strike could tell that he was underweight, but while his fingernails were bitten to bloody stubs and there was an angry sore at the corner of his mouth, there was no longer an animal stench about him. He shuffled inside the interview room, staring at Strike, then held out a bony hand, which Strike shook. Billy addressed the doctors.

'Are you two going to stay?'

'Yes,' said Colin, 'but don't worry. We're going to keep quiet. You can say whatever you like to Mr Strike.'

Kamila positioned two chairs against the wall and Strike

and Billy sat down opposite each other, the desk between them. Strike could have wished for a less formal configuration of furniture, but his experience in Special Investigation Branch had taught him that a solid barrier between questioner and interviewee was often useful, and doubtless this was just as true on a locked psychiatric ward.

'I've been trying to find you, since you first came to see me,' Strike said. 'I've been quite worried about you.'

'Yeah,' said Billy. 'Sorry.'

'Can you remember what you said to me at the office?'

Absently, it seemed, Billy touched his nose and his sternum, but it was a ghost of the tic he had exhibited in Denmark Street, and almost as though he sought to remind himself how he had felt then.

'Yeah,' he said, with a small, humourless smile. 'I told you about the kid, up by the horse. The one I saw strangled.'

'D'you still think you witnessed a child being strangled?' asked Strike.

Billy raised a forefinger to his mouth, gnawed at the nail and nodded.

'Yeah,' he said, removing the finger. 'I saw it. Jimmy says I imagined it because I'm – you know. Ill. You know Jimmy, don't you? Went to the White Horse after him, didn't you?' Strike nodded. 'He was fucking livid. White Horse,' said Billy, with a sudden laugh. 'That's funny. Shit, that's funny. I never even thought of that before.'

'You told me you saw a child killed "up by the horse". Which horse did you mean?'

'White Horse of Uffington,' said Billy. 'Big chalk figure, up on the hill, near where I grew up. Doesn't look like a horse. More like a dragon and it's on Dragon Hill, as well. I've never understood why they all say it's a horse.'

'Can you tell me exactly what you saw up there?'

Like the skeletal girl Strike had just passed, he had the impression that Billy was staring inside himself, and that outer reality had temporarily ceased to exist for him. Finally, he said quietly:

'I was a little kid, proper little. I think they'd given me something. I felt sick and ill, like I was dreaming, slow and groggy, and they kept trying to make me repeat words and stuff and I couldn't speak properly and they all thought it was funny. I fell over in the grass on the way up. One of them carried me for a bit. I wanted to sleep.'

'You think you'd been given drugs?'

'Yeah,' said Billy dully. 'Hash, probably, Jimmy usually had some. I think Jimmy took me up the hill with them to keep my father from knowing what they'd done.'

'Who do you mean by "they"?'

'I don't know,' said Billy simply. 'Grown-ups. Jimmy's ten years older'n me. Dad used to make him look after me all the time, if he was out with his drinking mates. This lot came to the house in the night and I woke up. One of them gave me a yoghurt to eat. There was another little kid there. A girl. And then we all went out in a car . . . I didn't want to go. I felt sick. I was crying but Jimmy belted me.

'And we went to the horse in the dark. Me and the little girl were the only kids. She was howling,' said Billy and the skin of his gaunt face seemed to shrink more tightly to his bones as he said it. 'Screaming for her mum and *he* said, "Your mum can't hear you now, she's gone."'

'Who said that?' asked Strike.

'Him,' whispered Billy. 'The one that strangled her.'

The door opened and a new nurse brought in tea.

'Here we go,' she said brightly, her eager eyes on Strike. The male psychiatrist frowned at her slightly and she withdrew, closing the door again.

'Nobody's ever believed me,' said Billy, and Strike heard the underlying plea. 'I've tried to remember more, I wish I could, if I've got to think about it all the time I wish I could remember more of it.

'He strangled her to stop her making a noise. I don't think he meant it to go that far. They all panicked. I can remember someone shouting "You've killed her!" . . . or him,' Billy said quietly. 'Jimmy said afterwards it was a boy, but he won't admit that now. Says I'm making it all up. "Why would I say it was a boy when none of it ever fucking happened, you're mental." It was a girl,' said Billy stubbornly. 'I don't know why he tried to say it wasn't. They called her a girl's name. I can't remember what it was, but it was a girl.

'I saw her fall. Dead. Limp on the ground. It was dark. And then they panicked.

'I can't remember anything about going back down the hill, can't remember anything after that except the burial, down in the dell by my dad's place.'

'The same night?' asked Strike.

'I think so, I think it was,' said Billy nervously. 'Because I remember looking out of my bedroom window and it was still dark and they were carrying it to the dell, my dad and *him*.'

'Who's "him"?'

'The one who killed her. I think it was him. Big guy. White hair. And they put a bundle in the ground, all wrapped up in a pink blanket, and they closed it in.'

'Did you ask your father about what you'd seen?'

'No,' said Billy. 'You didn't ask my dad questions about what he did for the family.'

'For which family?'

Billy frowned in what seemed to be genuine puzzlement.

'You mean, for your family?'

'No. The family he worked for. The Chiswells.'

Strike had the impression that this was the first time the dead minister's family name had been mentioned in front of the two psychiatrists. He saw two pens falter.

'How was the burial connected with them?'

Billy seemed confused. He opened his mouth to say something, appeared to change his mind, frowned around the pale pink walls and fell to gnawing his forefinger again. Finally, he said:

'I don't know why I said that.'

It didn't feel like a lie or a denial. Billy seemed genuinely surprised by the words that had fallen out of his mouth.

'You can't remember hearing anything, or seeing anything, that would make you think he was burying the child for the Chiswells?'

'No,' said Billy slowly, brow furrowed. 'I just . . . I thought then, when I said it . . . he was doing a favour for . . . like I heard something, after . . .'

He shook his head.

'Ignore that, I don't know why I said it.'

People, places and things, thought Strike, taking out his notebook and opening it.

'Other than Jimmy and the little girl who died,' said Strike, 'what can you remember about the group of people who went to the horse that night? How many of them would you say were there?'

Billy thought hard.

'I don't know. Maybe . . . maybe eight, ten people?'

'All men?'

'No. There were women, too.'

Over Billy's shoulder, Strike saw the female psychiatrist raise her eyebrows.

'Can you remember anything else about the group? I know

you were young,' Strike said, anticipating Billy's objection, 'and I know you might have been given something that disorientated you, but can you remember anything you haven't told me? Anything they did? Anything they were wearing? Can you remember anyone's hair or skin colour? Anything at all?'

There was a long pause, then Billy closed his eyes briefly and shook his head once, as though disagreeing firmly with a suggestion only he could hear.

'She was dark. The little girl. Like . . . '

By a tiny turn of his head, he indicated the female doctor behind him.

'Asian?' said Strike.

'Maybe,' said Billy, 'yeah. Black hair.'

'Who carried you up the hill?'

'Jimmy and one of the other men took turns.'

'Nobody talked about why they were going up there in the dark?'

'I think they wanted to get to the eye,' said Billy.

'The eye of the horse?'

'Yeah.'

'Why?'

'I don't know,' said Billy, and he ran his hands nervously over his shaven head. 'There are stories about the eye, you know. He strangled her in the eye, I know that. I can remember that, all right. She pissed herself as she died. I saw it spattering on the white.'

'And you can't remember anything about the man who did it?'

But Billy's face had crumpled. Hunched over, he heaved with dry sobs, shaking his head. The male doctor half rose from his seat. Billy seemed to sense the movement, because he steadied himself and shook his head.

'I'm all right,' he said, 'I want to tell him. I've got to know if it's real. All my life, I can't stand it any more, I've got to know. Let him ask me, I know he's got to. Let him ask me,' said Billy, 'I can take it.'

The psychiatrist sat slowly back down.

'Don't forget your tea, Billy.'

'Yeah,' said Billy, blinking away the tears in his eyes and wiping his nose on the back of his sleeve. 'All right.'

He took the mug between his bandaged hand and his good one, and took a sip.

'OK to continue?' Strike asked him.

'Yeah,' said Billy quietly. 'Go on.'

'Can you remember anyone ever mentioning a girl called Suki Lewis, Billy?'

Strike had expected a 'no'. He had already turned the page to the list of questions written under the heading 'Places' when Billy said:

'Yeah.'

'What?' said Strike.

'The Butcher brothers knew her,' said Billy. 'Mates of Jimmy's from home. They did a bit of work round the Chiswells' place sometimes, with Dad. Bit of gardening and help with the horses.'

'They knew Suki Lewis?'

'Yeah. She ran away, didn't she?' said Billy. 'She was on the local news. The Butchers were excited because they seen her picture on the telly and they knew her family. Her mum was a headcase. Yeah, she was in care and she ran away to Aberdeen.'

'Aberdeen?'

'Yeah. That's what the Butchers said.'

'She was twelve.'

'She had family up there. They let her stay.'

'Is that right?' said Strike.

He wondered whether Aberdeen had seemed unfathomably remote to the teenage Butchers of Oxfordshire, and whether they had been more inclined to believe this story because it was, to them, uncheckable and so, strangely, more believable.

'We're talking about Tegan's brothers, right?' asked Strike.

'You can see he's good,' Billy said naively over his shoulder, to the male psychiatrist, 'can't you? See how much he knows? Yeah,' he said, turning back to Strike. 'She's their little sister. They were like us, working for the Chiswells. There used to be a lot to do in the old days, but they sold off a lot of the land. They don't need so many people any more.'

He drank some more tea, the mug in both hands.

'Billy,' said Strike, 'd'you know where you've been since you came to my office?'

At once, the tic reappeared. Billy's right hand released the warm mug and touched his nose and chest in quick, nervous succession.

'I was . . . Jimmy doesn't want me to talk about that,' he said, setting the mug clumsily back on the desk. 'He told me not to.'

'I think it's more important you answer Mr Strike's questions than worry about what your brother thinks,' said the male doctor, from behind Strike. 'You know, you don't have to see Jimmy if you don't want to, Billy. We can ask him to give you some time here, to get better in peace.'

'Did Jimmy visit you where you've been staying?' Strike asked.

Billy chewed his lip.

'Yeah,' he said at last, 'and he said I had to stay there or I'd cock everything up for him again. I thought the door had explosives round it,' he said, with a nervy laugh. 'Thought if

I tried to go out the door I'd explode. Probably not right, is it?' he said, appearing to search Strike's expression for a clue. 'I get ideas about stuff sometimes, when I'm bad.'

'Can you remember how you got away from the place you were being kept?'

'I thought they switched off the explosives,' said Billy. 'The guy told me to run for it and I did.'

'What guy was this?'

'The one who was in charge of keeping me there.'

'Can you remember anything you did while you were being kept captive?' Strike asked. 'How you spent your time?'

The other shook his head.

'Can you remember,' said Strike, 'carving anything, into wood?'

Billy's gaze was full of fear and wonder. Then he laughed.

'You know it all,' he said, and held up his bandaged left hand. 'Knife slipped. Went right in me.'

The male psychiatrist added helpfully:

'Billy had tetanus when he came in. There was a very nasty infected gash on that hand.'

'What did you carve into the door, Billy?'

'I really did that, then, did I? Carved the white horse on the door? Because afterwards I didn't know if I really did that or not.'

'Yeah, you did it,' said Strike. 'I've seen the door. It was a good carving.'

'Yeah,' said Billy, 'well, I used to – do some of that. Carving. For my dad.'

'What did you carve the horse onto?'

'Pendants,' said Billy, surprisingly. 'On little circles of wood with leather through 'em. For tourists. Sold them in a shop over in Wantage.'

'Billy,' said Strike, 'can you remember how you ended up in

that bathroom? Did you go there to see someone, or did somebody take you there?'

Billy's eyes roamed around the pink walls again, a deep furrow between his eyes as he thought.

'I was looking for a man called Winner . . . no . . .'

'Winn? Geraint Winn?'

'Yeah,' said Billy, again surveying Strike with astonishment. 'You know *everything.* How do you know all this?'

'I've been looking for you,' said Strike. 'What made you want to find Winn?'

'Heard Jimmy talking about him,' said Billy, gnawing at his nail again. 'Jimmy said Winn was going to help find out all about the kid who was killed.'

'Winn was going to help find out about the child who was strangled?'

'Yeah,' said Billy, nervously. 'See, I thought you were one of the people trying to catch me and lock me up, after I saw you. Thought you were trying to trap me and – I get like that, when I'm bad,' he said hopelessly. 'So I went to Winner – Winn – instead. Jimmy had a phone number and address for him written down, so I went to find Winn and then I got caught.'

'Caught?'

'By the – brown-skinned bloke,' mumbled Billy, with a half-glance back at the female psychiatrist. 'I was scared of him, I thought he was a terrorist and he was going to kill me, but then he told me he was working for the government, so I thought the government wanted me kept there in his house and the doors and windows were wired with explosives . . . but I don't think they were, really. That was just me. He probably didn't want me in his bathroom. Probably wanted to get rid of me all along,' said Billy, with a sad smile. 'And I wouldn't go, because I thought I'd get blown up.'

His right hand crept absently back to his nose and chest.

'I think I tried to call you again, but you didn't answer.'

'You did call. You left a message on my answering machine.'

'Did I? Yeah ... I thought you'd help me get out of there ... sorry,' said Billy, rubbing his eyes. 'When I'm like that, I don't know what I'm doing.'

'But you're sure you saw a child strangled, Billy?' asked Strike quietly.

'Oh yeah,' said Billy bleakly, raising his face. 'Yeah, that never goes away. I know I saw it.'

'Did you ever try and dig where you thought—?'

'Christ, no,' said Billy. 'Go digging right by my dad's house? No. I was scared,' he said weakly. 'I didn't want to see it again. After they buried her, they let it grow over, nettles and weeds. I used to have dreams like you wouldn't believe. That she climbed up out of the dell in the dark, all rotting, and tried to climb in my bedroom window.'

The psychiatrists' pens moved scratchily across their papers.

Strike moved down to the category of 'Things' that he had written on his notebook. There were only two questions left.

'Did you ever put a cross in the ground where you saw the body buried, Billy?'

'No,' said Billy, scared at the very idea. 'I never went near the dell if I could avoid it, I never wanted to.'

'Last question,' Strike said. 'Billy, did your father do anything unusual for the Chiswells? I know he was a handyman, but can you think of anything else he—?'

'What d'you mean?' said Billy.

He seemed suddenly more frightened than he had seemed all interview.

'I don't know,' said Strike carefully, watching his reaction. 'I just wondered—'

'Jimmy warned me about this! He told me you were snooping around Dad. You can't blame us for that, we had nothing to do with it, we were kids!'

'I'm not blaming you for anything,' said Strike, but there was a clatter of chairs: Billy and the two psychiatrists had got to their feet, the female's hand hovering over a discreet button beside the door that Strike knew must be an alarm.

'Has this all been to get me to talk? You trying to get me and Jimmy in trouble?'

'No,' said Strike, hoisting himself to his feet, too. 'I'm here because I believe you saw a child strangled, Billy.'

Agitated, mistrustful, Billy's unbandaged hand touched his nose and chest twice in quick succession.

'So why're you asking what Dad did?' he whispered. 'That's not how she died, it was nothing to do with that! Jimmy'll fucking tan me,' he said in a broken voice. 'He told me you were after him for what Dad did.'

'Nobody's going to tan anyone,' said the male psychiatrist firmly. 'Time's up, I think,' he said briskly to Strike, pushing open the door. 'Go on, Billy, out you go.'

But Billy didn't move. The skin and bone might have aged, but his face betrayed the fear and hopelessness of a small, motherless child whose sanity had been broken by the men who were supposed to protect him. Strike, who had met countless rootless and neglected children during his rackety, unstable childhood, recognised in Billy's imploring expression a last plea to the adult world, to do what grown-ups were meant to do, and impose order on chaos, substitute sanity for brutality. Face to face, he felt a strange kinship with the emaciated, shaven-headed psychiatric patient, because he recognised the same craving for order in himself. In his case, it had led him to the official side of the desk, but perhaps the only difference between the two of them was that Strike's mother had lived long enough, and loved him well enough, to stop him breaking when life threw terrible things at him.

'I'm going to find out what happened to the kid you saw strangled, Billy. That's a promise.'

The psychiatrists looked surprised, even disapproving. It was not part of their profession, Strike knew, to make definitive statements or guarantee resolutions. He put his notebook back into his pocket, moved from behind the desk and held out his hand. After a few long moments' consideration, the animosity seemed to seep out of Billy. He shuffled back to Strike, took his proffered hand and held it overlong, his eyes filling with tears.

In a whisper, so that neither of the doctors could hear, he said:

'I hated putting the horse on them, Mr Strike. I hated it.'

57

Have you the courage and the strength of will for that, Rebecca?

Henrik Ibsen, *Rosmersholm*

Vanessa's one-bedroomed flat occupied the ground floor of a detached house a short distance from Wembley Stadium. Before leaving for work that morning, she had given Robin a spare key to her flat, along with a kindly assurance that she knew that it would take Robin longer than a couple of days to find a new place to live, and that she didn't mind her staying until she managed to do so.

They had sat up late drinking the night before. Vanessa had told Robin the full story of finding out that her ex-fiancé had cheated on her, a story full of twists and counter-twists that Vanessa had never told before, which included the setting up of two fake Facebook pages as bait for both her ex and his lover, which had resulted, after three months of patient coaxing, in Vanessa receiving nude pictures from both of them. As impressed as she was shocked, Robin had laughed as Vanessa re-enacted the scene in which she passed her ex the pictures, hidden inside the Valentine card she had handed across a table for two in their favourite restaurant.

'You're too nice, girl,' said Vanessa, steely-eyed over her Pinot Grigio. 'At a bare minimum I'd have kept her bleeding earring and turned it into a pendant.'

Vanessa was now at work. A spare duvet sat neatly folded at the end of the sofa on which Robin was sitting, with her laptop open in front of her. She had spent the entire afternoon scanning available rooms in shared properties, which were all she could possibly afford on the salary that Strike was paying her. The memory of the bunk bed in Flick's flat kept recurring as she scanned the adverts in her price range, some of which featured stark, barrack-like rooms with multiple beds inside them, others with photographs that looked as though they ought to feature attached to news stories about reclusive hoarders discovered dead by neighbours. Last night's laughter seemed remote now. Robin was ignoring the painful, hard lump in her throat that refused to dissolve, no matter how many cups of tea she consumed.

Matthew had tried to contact her twice that day. Neither time had she picked up and he hadn't left a message. She would need to contact a lawyer about divorce soon, and that would cost money she didn't have, but her first priority had to be finding herself a place to live and continuing to put in the usual number of hours on the Chiswell case, because if Strike had cause to feel she wasn't pulling her weight she would be endangering the only part of her life that currently had worth.

You bailed out on uni. Now you're bailing out on us. You even bailed on your therapist. You're a fucking flake.

The photographs of grim rooms in unknown flats kept dissolving before her eyes as she pictured Matthew and Sarah in the heavy mahogany bed that her father-in-law had bought, and when this happened Robin's insides seemed to turn to liquid lead and her self-control threatened to melt away and she wanted to phone Matthew back and scream at him, but she didn't, because she refused to be what he wanted to make her, the irrational, incontinent, uncontrolled woman, the *fucking flake.*

And anyway, she had news for Strike, news she was keen to impart once he had finished his interview with Billy. Raphael Chiswell had answered his mobile at eleven o'clock that morning and, after some initial coldness, had agreed to talk to her, but only at a place of his choosing. An hour later, she had received a call from Tegan Butcher, who had not required much persuasion to agree to an interview. Indeed, she seemed disappointed to be talking to the famous Strike's partner rather than the man himself.

Robin copied down the details of a room in Putney (*live-in landlady, vegetarian household, must like cats*), checked the time and decided to change into the only dress she had brought with her from Albury Street, which was hanging, ironed and ready, from the top of Vanessa's kitchen door. It would take her over an hour to get from Wembley to the restaurant in Old Brompton Road, where she and Raphael had agreed to meet, and she feared that she needed more time than usual to make herself presentable.

The face staring out of Vanessa's bathroom mirror was white, with eyes still puffy with lack of sleep. Robin was still trying to paint out the shadows with concealer when her mobile rang.

'Cormoran, hi,' said Robin, switching to speakerphone. 'Did you see Billy?'

His account of the interview with Billy took ten minutes, during which time Robin finished her make-up, brushed her hair and pulled on the dress.

'You know,' Strike finished, 'I'm starting to wonder whether we shouldn't do what Billy wanted us to do in the first place: dig.'

'Mm,' said Robin, and then, 'Wait – what? You mean . . . literally?'

'It might come to that,' said Strike.

For the first time all day, Robin's own troubles were entirely eclipsed by something else, something monstrous. Jasper Chiswell's had been the first body she had seen outside the comforting, sanitised context of the hospital and the funeral parlour. Even the memory of the shrink-wrapped turnip head with its dark, gasping cavity for a mouth paled beside the prospect of earth and worms, a decaying blanket and a child's rotting bones.

'Cormoran, if you think there's genuinely a child buried in the dell, we should be telling the police.'

'I might, if I thought Billy's psychiatrists would vouch for him, but they won't. I had a long talk with them after the interview. They can't say one hundred per cent that the child strangling *didn't* happen – the old impossible-to-prove-a-negative problem – but they don't believe it.'

'They think he's making it up?'

'Not in the normal sense. They think it's a delusion or, at best, that he misinterpreted something he saw when he was very young. Maybe even something on TV. It would be consistent with his overall symptoms. I think myself there's unlikely to be anything down there, but it would be good to know for sure.

'Anyway, how's your day been? Any news?'

'What?' Robin repeated numbly. 'Oh – yes. I'm meeting Raphael for a drink at seven o'clock.'

'Excellent work,' said Strike. 'Where?'

'Place called Nam something . . . Nam Long Le Shaker?'

'The place in Chelsea?' said Strike. 'I was there, a long time ago. Not the best evening I've ever had.'

'And Tegan Butcher rang back. She's a bit of a fan of yours, by the sound of it.'

'Just what this case needs, another mentally disturbed witness.'

'Tasteless,' said Robin, trying to sound amused. 'Anyway, she's living with her mum in Woolstone and working at a bar at Newbury Racecourse. She says she doesn't want to meet us in the village because her mum won't like her getting mixed up with us, so she wonders whether we could come and see her at Newbury.'

'How far's that from Woolstone?'

'Twenty miles or so?'

'All right,' said Strike, 'how about we take the Land Rover out to Newbury to interview Tegan and then maybe swing by the dell, just for another look?'

'Um ... yes, OK,' said Robin, her mind racing over the logistics of having to return to Albury Street for the Land Rover. She had left it behind because parking places required a permit on Vanessa's street. 'When?'

'Whenever Tegan can see us, but ideally this week. Sooner the better.'

'OK,' said Robin, thinking of the tentative plans she had made to view rooms over the next couple of days.

'Everything all right, Robin?'

'Yes, of course.'

'Ring me when you've spoken to Raphael then, OK?'

'Will do,' said Robin, glad to end the call. 'Speak later.'

58

. . . I believe two different kinds of will can exist at the same time in one person.

Henrik Ibsen, *Rosmersholm*

Nam Long Le Shaker had the feeling of a decadent, colonial-era bar. Dimly lit, with leafy plants and assorted paintings and prints of beautiful women, the décor mixed Vietnamese and European styles. When Robin entered the restaurant at five past seven, she found Raphael leaning up against the bar, wearing a dark suit and tieless white shirt, already halfway down a drink and talking to the long-haired beauty who stood in front of a glittering wall of bottles.

'Hi,' said Robin.

'Hello,' he responded with a trace of coolness, and then, 'Your eyes are different. Were they that colour at Chiswell House?'

'Blue?' asked Robin, shrugging off the coat she had worn because she felt shivery, even though the evening was warm. 'Yes.'

'S'pose I didn't notice because half the bloody light bulbs are missing. What are you drinking?'

Robin hesitated. She ought not to drink while conducting

an interview, but at the same time, she suddenly craved alcohol. Before she could decide, Raphael said with a slight edge in his voice:

'Been undercover again today, have we?'

'Why d'you ask?'

'Your wedding ring's gone again.'

'Were your eyes this sharp in the office?' asked Robin, and he grinned, reminding her why she had liked him, even against her will.

'I noticed your glasses were fake, remember?' he said. 'I thought at the time you were trying to be taken seriously, because you were too pretty for politics. So these,' he indicated his deep brown eyes, 'may be sharp, but this,' he tapped his head, 'not so much.'

'I'll have a glass of red,' said Robin, smiling, 'and I'll pay, obviously.'

'If this is all on Mr Strike, let's have dinner,' said Raphael at once. 'I'm starving and skint.'

'Really?'

After a day of trawling through the available rooms for rent on her agency salary, she was not in the mood to hear the Chiswell definition of poverty again.

'Yeah, really, little though you might believe it,' said Raphael, with a slightly acid smile, and Robin suspected he knew what she had been thinking. 'Seriously, are we eating, or what?'

'Fine,' said Robin, who had barely touched food all day, 'let's eat.'

Raphael took his bottle of beer off the bar and led her through to the restaurant where they took a table for two beside the wall. It was so early that they were the only diners.

'My mother used to come here in the eighties,' said Raphael. 'It was well known because the owner liked telling the rich and famous to sod off if they weren't dressed properly to come in, and they all loved it.'

'Really?' said Robin, her thoughts miles away. It had just struck her that she would never again have dinner with Matthew like this, just the two of them. She remembered the very last time, at Le Manoir aux Quat'Saisons. What had he been thinking while he ate in silence? Certainly he had been furious at her for continuing to work with Strike, but perhaps he had also been weighing in his mind the competing attractions of Sarah, with her well-paid job at Christie's, her endless fund of stories about other people's wealth, and her no doubt self-confident performance in bed, where the diamond earrings her fiancé had bought her snagged on Robin's pillow.

'Listen, if eating with me's going to make you look like that, I'm fine with going back to the bar,' said Raphael.

'What?' said Robin, surprised out of her thoughts. 'Oh – no, it isn't you.'

A waiter brought over Robin's wine. She took a large slug.

'Sorry,' she said. 'I was just thinking about my husband. I left him last night.'

As she watched Raphael freeze in surprise with the bottle at his lips, Robin knew herself to have crossed an invisible boundary. In her whole time at the agency, she had never used truths about her private life to gain another's confidence, never blended the private and the professional to win another person over. In turning Matthew's infidelity into a device to manipulate Raphael, she knew that she was doing something that would appal and disgust her husband. Their marriage, he would have thought, ought to be sacrosanct, a world apart from what he saw as her seedy, ramshackle job.

'Seriously?' said Raphael.

'Yes,' said Robin, 'but I don't expect you to believe me,

not after all the crap I told you when I was Venetia. Anyway,' she took her notebook out of her handbag, 'you said you were OK with me asking some questions?'

'Er – yeah,' he said, apparently unable to decide whether he was more amused or disconcerted. 'Is this real? Your marriage broke up last night?'

'Yes,' said Robin. 'Why are you looking so shocked?'

'I don't know,' said Raphael. 'You just seem so . . . Girl Guidey.' His eyes moved over her face. 'It's part of the appeal.'

'Could I just ask my questions?' said Robin, determinedly unfazed.

Raphael drank some beer and said:

'Always busy with the job. Turns a man's thoughts to what it would take to distract you.'

'Seriously—'

'Fine, fine, questions – but let's order first. Fancy some dim sum?'

'Whatever's good,' said Robin, opening her notebook.

Ordering food seemed to cheer Raphael up.

'Drink up,' he said.

'I shouldn't be drinking at all,' she replied, and indeed, she hadn't touched the wine since her first gulp. 'OK, I wanted to talk about Ebury Street.'

'Go on,' said Raphael.

'You heard what Kinvara said about the keys. I wondered whether—'

'—I ever had one?' asked Raphael with equanimity. 'Guess how many times I was ever in that house.'

Robin waited.

'Once,' said Raphael. 'Never went there as a kid. When I got out of – you know – Dad, who hadn't visited me once while I was inside, invited me down to Chiswell House to see him, so I did. Brushed my hair, put on a suit, got all the way down to that hellhole and he didn't bother turning up. Detained by a late vote at the House or some crap. Picture how happy Kinvara was to have me on her hands for the night, in that bloody depressing house that I've had bad dreams about ever since I was a kid. Welcome home, Raff.

'I took the early train back to London. Following week, no contact from Dad until I get another summons, this time to go to Ebury Street. I considered just not bloody turning up. Why did I go?'

'I don't know,' said Robin. 'Why did you?'

He looked directly into her eyes.

'You can bloody hate someone and still wish they gave a shit about you and hate yourself for wishing it.'

'Yes,' said Robin quietly, 'of course you can.'

'So round I trot to Ebury Street, thinking I might get – not a heart to heart, I mean, you met my father – but maybe, you know, some human emotion. He opened the door, said "There you are", shunted me into the sitting room and there was Henry Drummond and I realised I was there for a job interview. Drummond said he'd take me on, Dad barked at me not to fuck it up and shoved me back out onto the street. First and last time I was ever inside the place,' said Raphael, 'so I can't say I've got fond associations with it.'

He paused to consider what he'd just said, then let out a short laugh.

'And my father killed himself there, of course. I was forgetting that.'

'No key,' said Robin, making a note.

'No, among the many things I didn't get that day were a spare key and an invitation to let myself in whenever I fancied it.'

'I need to ask you something that might seem as though it's slightly out of left field,' said Robin cautiously.

'This sounds interesting,' said Raphael, leaning forwards.

'Did you ever suspect that your father was having an affair?'

'What?' he said, almost comically taken aback. 'No – but – *what?*'

'Over the last year or so?' said Robin. 'While he was married to Kinvara?'

He seemed incredulous.

'OK,' said Robin, 'if you don't—'

'What on *earth* makes you think he was having an affair?'

'Kinvara was always very possessive, very concerned about your father's whereabouts, wasn't she?'

'Yeah,' said Raphael, now smirking, 'but you know why that was. That was *you*.'

'I heard that she broke down months before I went to work in the office. She told somebody that your father had cheated on her. She was distraught, by all accounts. It was around the time her mare was put down and she—'

'—hit Dad with the hammer?' He frowned. 'Oh. I thought that was because of her not wanting the horse put down. Well, I suppose Dad was a ladies' man when he was younger. Hey – maybe that's what he was up to, the night I went down to Chiswell House and he stayed up in London? Kinvara was definitely expecting him back and she was furious when he cried off at the last minute.'

'Yes, maybe,' said Robin, making a note. 'Can you remember what date that was?'

'Er – yeah, as a matter of fact, I can. You don't tend to forget the day you're released from jail. I got out on Wednesday the sixteenth of February last year, and Dad asked me to go down to Chiswell House on the following Saturday, so . . . the nineteenth.'

Robin made a note.

'You never saw or heard signs there was another woman?'

'Come on,' said Raphael, 'you were there, at the Commons. You saw how little I had to do with him. Was he going to tell me he was playing around?'

'He told you about seeing the ghost of Jack o'Kent roaming the grounds at night.'

'That was different. He was drunk then, and – morbid. Weird. Banging on about divine retribution . . . I don't know, I suppose he could've been talking about an affair. Maybe he'd grown a conscience at last, three wives down the line.'

'I didn't think he married your mother?'

Raphael's eyes narrowed.

'Sorry. Momentarily forgot I'm the bastard.'

'Oh, come on,' said Robin gently, 'you know I didn't mean—'

'All right, sorry,' he muttered. 'Being touchy. Being left out of a parent's will does that to a person.'

Robin remembered Strike's dictum about inheritance: *It is the money, and it isn't*, and in an uncanny echo of her thoughts, Raphael said:

'It isn't the money, although God knows I could use the money. I'm jobless, and I don't think old Henry Drummond's going to give me a reference, do you? And now my mother looks like she's going to settle permanently in Italy, so she's talking about selling the London flat, which means I'll be homeless. It'll come to this, you know,' he said bitterly. 'I'll end up as Kinvara's bloody stable boy. No one else will work for her and no one else'll employ me . . .

'But it's not just the money. When you're left out of the will . . . well, *left out*, that says it all. The last statement of a dead man to his family and I didn't rate a single mention and now I've got fucking Torquil advising me to piss off to Siena with my mother and "start again". Tosser,' said Raphael, with a dangerous expression.

'Is that where your mother lives? Siena?'

'Yeah. She's shacked up with an Italian count these days, and believe me, the last thing he wants is her twenty-nine-year-old son moving in. He's showing no sign of wanting to marry her and she's starting to worry about her old age, hence the idea of flogging the flat here. She's getting a bit long in the tooth to pull the trick she did on my father.'

'What d'you—?'

'She got pregnant on purpose. Don't look so shocked. My mother doesn't believe in shielding me from the realities of life. She told me the story years ago. I'm a gamble that didn't come off. She thought he'd marry her if she got pregnant, but as you've just pointed out—'

'I said I'm sorry,' said Robin. 'I am. It was really insensitive and – and stupid.'

She thought perhaps Raphael was about to tell her to go to hell, but instead he said quietly:

'See, you *are* sweet. You weren't entirely acting, were you? In the office?'

'I don't know,' said Robin. 'I suppose not.'

Feeling his legs shift under the table, she moved very slightly backwards again.

'What's your husband like?' Raphael asked.

'I don't know how to describe him.'

'Does he work for Christie's?'

'No,' said Robin. 'He's an accountant.'

'Christ,' said Raphael, appalled. 'Is that what you like?'

'He wasn't an accountant when I met him. Can we go back over your father calling you on the morning he died?'

'If you like,' said Raphael, 'but I'd much rather talk about you.'

'Well, why don't you tell me what happened that morning and then you can ask me whatever you like,' said Robin.

A fleeting smile passed over Raphael's face. He took a swig of beer and said:

'Dad called me. Told me he thought Kinvara was about to do something stupid and told me to go straight down to Woolstone and stop it. I *did* ask why it had to be me, you know.'

'You didn't tell us that at Chiswell House,' said Robin, looking up from her notes.

'Of course I didn't, because the others were there. Dad said he didn't want to ask Izzy. He was quite rude about her on the phone . . . he was an ungrateful shit, really he was,' said Raphael. 'She worked her fingers to the bloody bone and you saw how he treated her.'

'What do you mean, rude?'

'He said she'd shout at Kinvara, upset her and make it worse or something. Pot and bloody kettle, but there you are. But the truth is,' said Raphael, 'that he saw me as a kind of upper servant and Izzy as proper family. He didn't mind me getting my hands dirty and it didn't matter if I pissed off his wife by barging into her house and stopping her—'

'Stopping her what?'

'Ah,' said Raphael, 'food.'

The dim sum placed on the table before them, the waitress retreated.

'What did you stop Kinvara doing?' Robin repeated. 'Leaving your father? Hurting herself?'

'I love this stuff,' said Raphael, examining a prawn dumpling.

'She left a note,' persisted Robin, 'saying she was leaving. Did your father send you down there to persuade her not to go? Was he afraid Izzy would egg her on to leave him?'

'D'you seriously think I could persuade Kinvara to stay in the marriage? Never having to lay eyes on me again would've been one more incentive to go.'

'Then why did he send you to her?'

'I've told you,' said Raphael. 'He thought she was going to do something stupid.'

'Raff,' said Robin, 'you can keep playing silly buggers—'

He corpsed.

'Christ, you sound Yorkshire when you say that. Say it again.'

'The police think there's something fishy about your story of what you were up to that morning,' said Robin. 'And so do we.'

That seemed to sober him up.

'How do you know what the police are thinking?'

'We've got contacts on the force,' said Robin. 'Raff, you've given everyone the impression that your father was trying to stop Kinvara hurting herself, but nobody really buys that. The stable girl was there. Tegan. She could have prevented Kinvara from hurting herself.'

Raphael chewed for a while, apparently thinking.

'All right,' he sighed. 'All right, here it is. You know how Dad had sold off everything that would raise a few hundred quid, or given it to Peregrine?'

'Who?'

'All right, *Pringle*,' said Raphael, exasperated. 'I prefer not to use their stupid bloody nicknames.'

'He didn't sell off everything of value,' said Robin.

'What d'you mean?'

'That picture of the mare and foal is worth five to eight—'

Robin's mobile rang. She knew from the ringtone that it was Matthew.

'Aren't you going to get that?'

'No,' said Robin.

She waited until the phone had stopped ringing, then took it out of her bag.

'"Matt",' said Raphael, reading the name upside down. 'That's the accountant, is it?'

'Yes,' said Robin, silencing the phone, but it immediately began to vibrate in her hand instead. Matthew had called back.

'Block him,' suggested Raphael.

'Yes,' said Robin, 'good idea.'

All that was important to her right now was keeping Raphael cooperative. He seemed to enjoy watching her block Matthew. She put the mobile back in her bag and said:

'Go on about the paintings.'

'Well, you know how Dad had offloaded all the valuable ones through Drummond?'

'Some of us think five thousand pounds' worth of picture is quite valuable,' said Robin, unable to help herself.

'Fine, Ms Lefty,' said Raphael, suddenly nasty. 'You can keep *sneering* about how people like me don't know the value of money—'

'Sorry,' said Robin quickly, cursing herself. 'I am, seriously. Look, I've – well, I've been trying to find a room to rent this morning. Five thousand pounds would change my life right now.'

'Oh,' said Raphael, frowning. 'I – OK. Actually, if it comes to that *I'd* leap at the chance of five grand in my pocket right now, but I'm talking about *seriously* valuable stuff, worth tens and hundreds of thousands, things that my father wanted to keep in the family. He'd already handed them on to little *Pringle* to avoid death duties. There was a Chinese lacquer cabinet, an ivory workbox and a couple of other things, but there was also the necklace.'

'Which—?'

'It's a big ugly diamond thing,' said Raphael, and with the hand not spearing dumplings he mimed a thick collar.

'Important *stones*. It's come down through five generations or something and the convention was that it went to the eldest daughter on her twenty-first, but my father's father, who as you might have heard was a bit of a playboy—'

'This is the one who married Tinky the nurse?'

'She was his third or fourth,' said Raphael, nodding. 'I can never remember. Anyway, he only had sons, so he let all his wives wear the thing in turn, then left it to my father, who kept the new tradition going. His wives got to wear it – even my mother got a shot – and he forgot about the handing on to the daughter on her twenty-first bit, Pringle didn't get it and he didn't mention it in his will.'

'So – wait, d'you mean it's now—?'

'Dad called me up that morning and told me I had to get hold of the bloody thing. Simple job, kind of thing anyone would enjoy,' he said, sarcastically. 'Bust in on a stepmother who hates my guts, find out where she's keeping a valuable necklace, then steal it from under her nose.'

'So you think your father believed that she was leaving him, and was worried that she was going to take it with her?'

'I suppose so,' said Raphael.

'How did he sound on the phone?'

'I told you this. Groggy. I thought it was a hangover. After I heard he'd killed himself,' Raphael faltered, '. . . well.'

'Well?'

'To tell you the truth,' said Raphael, 'I couldn't get it out of my head that the last thing Dad wanted to say to me in this life was, "run along and make sure your sister gets her diamonds". Words to treasure for ever, eh?'

At a loss for anything to say, Robin took another sip of wine, then asked quietly:

'Do Izzy and Fizzy realise the necklace is Kinvara's now?'

Raphael's lips twisted in an unpleasant smile.

'Well, they know it is legally, but here's the really funny thing: they think she's going to hand it over to them. After everything they've said about her, after calling her a gold-digger for years, slagging her off at every possible opportunity, they can't quite grasp that she won't hand the necklace over to Fizzy for Flopsy – damn it – *Florence* – because,' he affected a shrill upper-class voice, '"Darling, even *TTS* wouldn't do that, it belongs in *the family*, she *must realise* she can't sell it."

'Bullets would bounce off their self-regard. They think there's a kind of natural law in operation, where Chiswells get what they want and lesser beings just fall into line.'

'How did Henry Drummond know you were trying to stop Kinvara keeping the necklace? He told Cormoran you went to Chiswell House for noble reasons.'

Raphael snorted.

'Cat's really out of the bag, isn't it? Yeah, apparently Kinvara left a message for Henry the day before Dad died, asking where she could get a valuation on the necklace.'

'Is that why he phoned your father that morning?'

'Exactly. To warn him what she was up to.'

'Why didn't you tell the police all this?'

'Because once the others find out she's planning to sell it, the whole thing's going to turn nuclear. There'll be an almighty row and the family'll go to lawyers and expect me to join them in kicking the shit out of Kinvara, and meanwhile I'm still treated like a second-class citizen, like a fucking *courier*, driving all the old paintings up to Drummond in London and hearing how much Dad was getting for them, and not a penny of *that* did I ever see – I'm not getting caught up in the middle of the great necklace scandal, I'm not playing their bloody game. I should've told Dad to stuff it, the day he phoned,' said Raphael, 'but he didn't sound well, and I suppose I felt sorry for him, or something, which only goes to prove they're right, I'm *not* a proper bloody Chiswell.'

He had run out of breath. Two couples had joined them in the restaurant now. Robin watched in the mirror as a well-groomed blonde did a double take at Raphael as she sat down with her florid, overweight companion.

'So, why did you leave Matthew?' Raphael asked.

'He cheated,' said Robin. She didn't have the energy to lie.

'Who with?'

She had the impression he was seeking to redress some kind of power balance. However much anger and contempt he had displayed during the outburst about his family, she had heard the hurt, too.

'With a friend of his from university,' said Robin.

'How did you find out?'

'A diamond earring, in our bed.'

'Seriously?'

'Seriously,' said Robin.

She felt a sudden wave of depression and fatigue at the idea of travelling all the way back to that hard sofa in Wembley. She had not yet called her parents to tell them what had happened.

'Under normal circumstances,' said Raphael, 'I'd be putting the moves on you. Well, not right now. Not tonight. But give it a couple of weeks . . .

'Trouble is, I look at you,' he raised a forefinger, and pointed first to her, and then to an imaginary figure behind her, 'and I see your one-legged boss looming over your shoulder.'

'Is there any particular reason you feel the need to mention him being one-legged?'

Raphael grinned.

'Protective, aren't you?'

'No, I—'

'It's all right. Izzy fancies him, too.'

'I never—'

'Defensive, too.'

'Oh, for God's sake,' said Robin, half-laughing, and Raphael grinned.

'I'm having another beer. Drink that wine, why don't you?' he said, indicating her glass, which was still two-thirds full.

When he had procured another bottle, he said with a malevolent grin, 'Izzy's always liked bits of rough. Did you notice the charged look from Fizzy to Izzy when Jimmy Knight's name was mentioned?'

'I did, actually,' said Robin. 'What was that about?'

'Freddie's eighteenth birthday party,' said Raphael, smirking. 'Jimmy crashed it with a couple of mates and Izzy – how do I put this delicately? – *lost* something in his company.'

'Oh,' said Robin, astonished.

'She was blind drunk. It's passed into family legend. I wasn't there. I was too young.

'Fizzy's so amazed at the idea that her sister could have slept with the estate carpenter's son that she thinks he must have some sort of supernatural, demonic sex appeal. *That's* why she thinks Kinvara was slightly on his side, when he turned up asking for money.'

'What?' said Robin sharply, reaching for her notebook again, which had fallen closed.

'Don't get too excited,' said Raphael, 'I still don't know what he was blackmailing Dad about, I never did. Not a full member of the family, you see, so not to be fully trusted.

'Kinvara told you this at Chiswell House, don't you remember? She was alone at home, the first time Jimmy turned up. Dad was in London again. From what I've pieced together, when she and Dad first talked it over, she argued Jimmy's case. Fizzy thinks that's down to Jimmy's sex appeal. Would you say he's got any?'

'I suppose some people might think he has,' said Robin

indifferently, who was making notes. 'Kinvara thought your father should pay Jimmy his money, did she?'

'From what I understand,' said Raphael, 'Jimmy didn't frame it as blackmail on the first approach. She thought Jimmy had a legitimate claim and argued for giving him something.'

'When was this, d'you know?'

'Search me,' said Raphael, shaking his head. 'I think I was in jail at the time. Bigger things to worry about . . .

'Guess,' he said, for the second time, 'how often any of them have asked me what it was like in jail?'

'I don't know,' said Robin cautiously.

'Fizzy, never. Dad, never—'

'You said Izzy visited.'

'Yeah,' he acknowledged, with a tip of the bottle to his sister. 'Yeah, she did, bless her. Good old Torks has made a couple of jokes about not wanting to bend over in the shower. I suggested,' said Raphael, with a hard smile, 'that he'd know all about that kind of thing, what with his old pal Christopher sliding his hand between young men's legs at the office. Turns out it's serious stuff when some hairy old convict tries it, but harmless frolics for public schoolboys.'

He glanced at Robin.

'I suppose you know now why Dad was taunting that poor bloke Aamir?'

She nodded.

'Which Kinvara thought was a motive for murder,' said Raphael, rolling his eyes. 'Projection, pure projection – they're all at it.

'Kinvara thinks Aamir killed Dad, because Dad had been cruel to him in front of a room full of people. Well, you should have heard some of the things Dad was saying to Kinvara by the end.

'Fizzy thinks Jimmy Knight might've done it because he

was angry about money. *She's* bloody angry about all the family money that's vanished, but she can't say that in so many words, not when her husband's half the reason it's gone.

'Izzy thinks Kinvara must have killed Dad because Kinvara felt unloved and sidelined and disposable. Dad never thanked Izzy for a damn thing she did for him, and didn't give a toss when she said she was leaving. You get the picture?

'None of them have got the guts to say that they all felt like killing Dad at times, not now he's dead, so they project it all onto someone else. And *that*,' said Raphael, 'is why none of them are talking about Geraint Winn. He gets double protection, because Saint Freddie was involved in Winn's big grudge. It's staring them in the face that he had a real motive, but we're not supposed to mention that.'

'Go on,' said Robin, her pen at the ready. 'Mention.'

'No, forget it,' said Raphael, 'I shouldn't have—'

'I don't think you say much accidentally, Raff. Out with it.'

He laughed.

'I'm trying to stop fucking over people who don't deserve it. It's all part of the great redemption project.'

'Who doesn't deserve it?'

'Francesca, the little girl I – you know – at the gallery. She's the one who told me. She got it from her older sister, Verity.'

'Verity,' repeated Robin.

Sleep-deprived, she struggled to remember where she had heard that name. It was very like 'Venetia', of course . . . and then she remembered.

'Wait,' she said, frowning in her effort to concentrate. 'There was a Verity on the fencing team with Freddie and Rhiannon Winn.'

'Right in one,' said Raphael.

'You all know each other,' said Robin wearily, unknowingly echoing Strike's thought as she started writing again.

'Well, that's the joy of the public school system,' said Raphael. 'In London, if you've got the money, you meet the same three hundred people everywhere you go . . . Yeah, when I first arrived at Drummond's gallery, Francesca couldn't wait to tell me that her big sister had once dated Freddie. I think she thought that made the pair of us predestined, or something.

'When she realised I thought Freddie was a bit of a shit,' said Raphael, 'she changed tack and told me a nasty story.

'Apparently, at his eighteenth, Freddie, Verity and a couple of others decided to mete out some punishment to Rhiannon for having dared to replace Verity on the fencing team. In their view she was – I don't know – a bit common, a bit Welsh? – so they spiked her drink. All good fun. Sort of stuff that goes on in a dorm, you know.

'But she didn't react too well to neat vodka – or maybe, from their point of view, she reacted really well. Anyway, they managed to take some nice pictures of her, to pass around among themselves . . . this was in the early days of the internet. These days I suppose half a million people would have viewed them in the first twenty-four hours, but Rhiannon only had to endure the whole fencing team and most of Freddie's mates having a good gloat.

'Anyway,' said Raphael, 'about a month later, Rhiannon killed herself.'

'Oh my God,' said Robin quietly.

'Yeah,' said Raphael. 'After little Franny told me the story, I asked Izzy about it. She got very upset, told me not to repeat it, ever – but she didn't deny it. I got lots of "nobody kills themselves because of a silly joke at a party" bluster and she told me I mustn't talk about Freddie like that, it would break Dad's heart . . .

'Well, the dead don't have hearts to break, do they?

And personally, I think it's about time somebody pissed on Freddie's eternal flame. If he hadn't been born a Chiswell, the bastard would've been in borstal. But I suppose you'll say I can talk, after what I did.'

'No,' said Robin gently. 'That isn't what I was going to say.'

The pugnacious expression faded from his face. He checked his watch.

'I'm going to have to go. I've got to be somewhere at nine.'

Robin raised her hand to signal for the bill. When she turned back to Raphael, she saw his eyes moving in routine fashion over both the other women in the restaurant, and in the mirror she saw how the blonde tried to hold his gaze.

'You can go,' she said, handing over her credit card to the waitress. 'I don't want to make you late.'

'No, I'll walk you out.'

While she was still putting her credit card back into her handbag, he picked up her coat and held it up for her.

'Thank you.'

'No problem.'

Out on the pavement, he hailed a taxi.

'You take this one,' he said. 'I fancy a walk. Clear my head. I feel as though I've had a bad therapy session.'

'No, it's all right,' said Robin. She didn't want to charge a taxi all the way back to Wembley to Strike. 'I'm going to get the Tube. Goodnight.'

''Night, Venetia,' he said.

Raphael got into the taxi, which glided away, and Robin pulled her coat more tightly around herself as she walked off in the opposite direction. It had been a chaotic interview, but she had managed to get much more than she had expected out of Raphael. Taking out her mobile again, she phoned Strike.

59

We two go with each other . . .

Henrik Ibsen, *Rosmersholm*

When he saw Robin was calling him, Strike, who had taken his notebook out to the Tottenham for a drink, pocketed the former, downed the remainder of his pint in one and took the call out onto the street.

The mess that building works had made of the top of Tottenham Court Road – the rubble-strewn channel where a street had been, the portable railings and the plastic barricades, the walkways and planks that enabled tens of thousands of people to continue to pass through the busy junction – was so familiar to him now that he barely noticed it. He had not come outside for the view, but for a cigarette, and he smoked two while Robin relayed everything that Raphael had told her.

Once the call was over, Strike returned his mobile to his pocket and absent-mindedly lit himself a third cigarette from the tip of the second and continued to stand there, thinking deeply about everything she had said and forcing passers-by to navigate around him.

A couple of things that Robin had told him struck the detective as interesting. Having finished his third cigarette and flicked it into the open abyss in the road, Strike retreated inside the pub and ordered himself a second pint. A group of students had now taken his table, so he headed into the back, where high bar stools sat beneath a stained-glass cupola whose colours were dimmed by night. Here, Strike took out his notebook again and re-examined the list of names over which he had pored in the early hours of Sunday, while he sought distraction from thoughts of Charlotte. After gazing at it again in the manner of a man who knows something is concealed there, he turned a few pages to reread the notes he had made of his interview with Della.

Large, hunch-backed and motionless but for the eyes flicking along the lines he had scribbled in the blind woman's house, Strike unknowingly repelled a couple of timid backpackers who had considered asking whether they might share his table and take the weight off their blistered feet. Fearing the consequences of breaking his almost tangible concentration, they retreated before he noticed them.

Strike turned back to the list of names. Married couples, lovers, business partners, siblings.

Pairs.

He flicked further backwards through the pages to find the notes he had made during the interview with Oliver, who had taken them through the forensic findings. A two-part killing, this: amitriptyline and helium, each potentially fatal on its own, yet used together.

Pairs.

Two victims, killed twenty years apart, a strangled child and a suffocated government minister, the former buried on the latter's land.

Pairs.

Strike turned thoughtfully to a blank page and made a new note for himself.

Francesca – confirm story

60

... you really must give me some explanation of your taking this matter – this possibility – so much to heart.

Henrik Ibsen, *Rosmersholm*

The following morning, a carefully worded official statement about Jasper Chiswell appeared in all the papers. Along with the rest of the British public, Strike learned over his breakfast that the authorities had concluded that no foreign power or terrorist organisation had been involved in the untimely death of the Minister for Culture, but that no other conclusion had yet been reached.

The news that there was no news had been greeted online with barely a ripple of interest. The local postboxes of Olympic winners were still being painted gold, and the public was basking in the satisfied afterglow arising from a triumphant games, its unspent enthusiasm for all things athletic now concentrated on the imminent prospect of the Paralympics. Chiswell's death had been filed away in the popular mind as the vaguely inexplicable suicide of a wealthy Tory.

Keen to know whether this official statement indicated that the Met investigation was close to concluding, Strike called Wardle to find out what he knew.

Unfortunately, the policeman was no wiser than Strike himself. Wardle added, not without a certain irritability, that he had not had a single day off in three weeks, that the policing of the capital while the city heaved under the weight of millions of extra visitors was complex and onerous past Strike's probable understanding, and that he didn't have time to go ferreting for information on unrelated matters on Strike's behalf.

'Fair enough,' said Strike, unfazed. 'Only asking. Say hello to April for me.'

'Oh yeah,' said Wardle, before Strike could hang up. 'She wanted me to ask you what you're playing at with Lorelei.'

'Better let you go, Wardle, the country needs you,' said Strike, and he hung up on the policeman's grudging laugh.

In the absence of information from his police contacts, and with no official standing to secure him the interviews he desired, Strike was temporarily stymied at a crucial point in the case, a frustration no more pleasant for being familiar.

A few phone calls after breakfast informed him that Francesca Pulham, Raphael's sometime colleague and lover from Drummond's gallery, was still studying in Florence, where she had been sent to remove her from his pernicious influence. Francesca's parents were currently on holiday in Sri Lanka. The Pulhams' housekeeper, who was the only person connected with the family that Strike was able to reach, refused point blank to give him telephone numbers for any of them. From her reaction, he guessed the Pulhams might be the kind of people who'd run for lawyers at the very idea of a private detective calling their house.

Having exhausted all possible avenues to the holidaying Pulhams, Strike left a polite request for an interview on Geraint Winn's voicemail, the fourth he had made that week, but the day wore on and Winn didn't call back. Strike couldn't blame him. He doubted that he would have chosen to be helpful, had he been in Winn's shoes.

Strike had not yet told Robin that he had a new theory about the case. She was busy in Harley Street, watching Dodgy Doc, but on Wednesday she called the office with the welcome news that she had arranged an interview with Tegan Butcher on Saturday at Newbury Racecourse.

'Excellent!' said Strike, cheered by the prospect of action, and striding through to the outer office to bring up Google Maps on Robin's computer. 'OK, I think we're going to be looking at an overnighter. Interview Tegan, then head over to Steda Cottage once it gets dark.'

'Cormoran, are you serious about this?' said Robin. 'You genuinely want to go digging in the dell?'

'That sounds like a nursery rhyme,' said Strike vaguely, examining B roads on the monitor. 'Look, I don't think there's anything there. In fact, as of yesterday, I'm sure of it.'

'What happened yesterday?'

'I had an idea. I'll tell you when I see you. Look, I promised Billy I'd find out the truth about his strangled child. There's no other way to be totally sure, is there, other than digging? But if you're feeling squeamish, you can stay in the car.'

'And what about Kinvara? We'll be on her property.'

'We'll hardly be digging up anything important. That whole area's waste ground. I'm going to get Barclay to meet us there, after dark. I'm not much good for digging. Will Matthew be OK if you're away overnight Saturday?'

'Fine,' said Robin, with an odd inflection that made Strike suspect that he wouldn't be fine about it at all.

'And you're OK to drive the Land Rover?'

'Er – is there any chance we could take your BMW instead?'

'I'd rather not take the BMW up that overgrown track. Is there something wrong with the—?'

'No,' said Robin, cutting across him. 'That's fine, OK, we'll take the Land Rover.'

'Great. How's Dodgy?'

'In his consulting rooms. Any news on Aamir?'

'I've got Andy trying to find the sister he's still on good terms with.'

'And what are you up to?'

'I've just been reading the Real Socialist Party website.'

'Why?'

'Jimmy gives quite a lot away in his blog posts. Places he's been and things he's seen. You OK to stay on Dodgy until Friday?'

'Actually,' said Robin, 'I was going to ask whether I could take a couple of days off to deal with some personal business.'

'Oh,' said Strike, brought up short.

'I've got a couple of appointments I need – I'd rather not miss,' said Robin.

It wasn't convenient to Strike to have to cover Dodgy Doc himself, partly because of the continuing pain in his leg, but mainly because he was eager to continue chasing down confirmation of his theory on the Chiswell case. This was also very short notice to ask for two days' leave. On the other hand, Robin had just indicated a willingness to sacrifice her weekend to a probable wildgoose chase into the dell.

'Yeah, OK. Everything all right?'

'Fine, thanks. I'll let you know if anything interesting happens with Dodgy. Otherwise, we should probably leave London at elevenish on Saturday.'

'Barons Court again?'

'Would it be all right if you meet me at Wembley Stadium station? It would just be easier, because of where I'm going to be on Friday night.'

This, too, was inconvenient: a journey for Strike of twice the length and involving a change of Tube.

'Yeah, OK,' he said again.

After Robin had hung up, he remained in her chair for a while, pondering their conversation.

She had been noticeably tight-lipped about the nature of the appointments that were so important that she didn't want to miss them. He remembered how particularly angry Matthew had sounded in the background of his calls to Robin, to discuss their pressured, unstable and occasionally dangerous job. She had twice sounded distinctly underwhelmed about the prospect of digging in the hard ground at the bottom of the dell, and now being asked to drive the BMW rather than the tank-like Land Rover.

He had almost forgotten his suspicion of a couple of months ago, that Robin might be trying to get pregnant. Into his mind swam the vision of Charlotte's swollen belly at the dinner table. Robin wasn't the kind of woman who'd be able to walk away from her child as soon as it left the womb. If Robin was pregnant . . .

Logical and methodical as he usually was, and aware in one part of himself that he was theorising on scant data, Strike's imagination nevertheless showed him Matthew, the father-to-be, listening in on Robin's tense request for time off for scans and medical checks, gesticulating angrily at her that the time had come to stop, to go easy on herself, to take better care.

Strike turned back to Jimmy Knight's blog, but it took him a little longer than usual to discipline his troubled mind back into obedience.

61

Oh, you can tell me. You and I are such friends, you know.

Henrik Ibsen, *Rosmersholm*

Fellow Tube travellers gave Strike a slightly wider berth than was necessary on Saturday morning, even allowing for his kit bag. He generally managed to cut a path easily through crowds, given his bulk and his boxer's profile, but the way he was muttering and cursing as he struggled up the stairs at Wembley Stadium station – the lifts weren't working – made passers-by extra careful to neither jostle nor impede him.

The primary reason for Strike's bad mood was Mitch Patterson, whom he had spotted that morning from the office window, skulking in a doorway, dressed in jeans and a hoodie entirely unsuited to his age and bearing. Puzzled and angered by the private detective's reappearance, but having no route out of the building except by the front door, Strike had called a cab to wait for him at the end of the street, and left the building only once it was in position. Patterson's expression when Strike had said 'Morning, Mitch' might have amused Strike, if he hadn't been so insulted that Patterson had thought he could get away with watching the agency in person.

All the way to Warren Street station, where he asked the cab to drop him, Strike had been hyper-alert, worried that Patterson had been there as a distraction or decoy, enabling a second, less obtrusive tail to follow him. Even now, as he clambered, panting, off the top of the stairs at Wembley, he turned to scrutinise the travellers for the one who ducked down, turned back or hastily concealed their face. None of them did so. On balance, Strike concluded that Patterson had been working alone; victim, perhaps, of one of the man-power problems so familiar to Strike. The fact that Patterson had chosen to cover the job rather than forgo it suggested that somebody was paying him well.

Strike hoisted his kit bag more securely onto his shoulder and set off towards the exit.

Having pondered the question during his inconvenient journey to Wembley, Strike could think of three reasons why Patterson had reappeared. The first was that the press had got wind of some interesting new development in the Met investigation into Chiswell's death, and that this had led a newspaper to rehire Patterson, his remit to find out what Strike was up to and how much he knew.

The second possibility was that someone had paid Patterson to stalk Strike, in the hopes of impeding his movements or hampering his business. That suggested that Patterson's employer was somebody that Strike was currently investigating, in which case, Patterson doing the job himself made sense: the whole point would be to destabilise Strike by letting him know that he was being watched.

The third possible reason for Patterson's renewed interest in him was the one that bothered Strike most, because he had a feeling it was most likely to be the true one. He now knew that he had been spotted in Franco's with Charlotte. His informant was Izzy, whom he had called in the hope of fleshing out details of the theory he hadn't yet confided to anyone.

'So, I hear you had dinner with Charlotte!' she had blurted, before he had managed to pose a question.

'There was no dinner. I sat with her for twenty minutes because she was feeling ill, then left.'

'Oh – sorry,' said Izzy, cowed by his tone. 'I – I wasn't prying – Roddy Fforbes was in Franco's and he spotted the pair of you . . .'

If Roddy Fforbes, whoever he was, was spreading it around London that Strike was taking his heavily pregnant, married ex-fiancée out for dinner while her husband was in New York, the tabloids would definitely be interested, because wild, beautiful and aristocratic Charlotte was news. Her name had peppered gossip columns since she was sixteen years old, her various tribulations – running away from school, the stints in rehab and in psychiatric clinics – were well documented. It was even possible that Patterson had been hired by Jago Ross, who could certainly afford it. If the side effect of policing his wife's movements was ruining Strike's business, Ross would undoubtedly consider that a bonus.

Robin, who was sitting a short distance away from the station in the Land Rover, saw Strike emerge onto the pavement, kit bag over his shoulder, and registered that he looked as bad-tempered as she had ever seen him. He lit a cigarette, scanning the street until his eye found the Land Rover at the end of a series of parked vehicles, and he began to limp, unsmiling, towards her. Robin, whose own mood was perilously low, could only assume that he was angry at having to make the long trip to Wembley with what appeared to be a heavy bag and a sore leg.

She had been awake since four o'clock that morning, unable to get back to sleep, cramped and unhappy on Vanessa's hard sofa, thinking about her future, and about the row she had had with her mother by phone. Matthew had called the house in Masham, trying to reach her, and Linda was not only desperately worried, but furious that Robin hadn't told her what was going on first.

'Where are you staying? With Strike?'

'Of course I'm not staying with Strike, why on earth would I be—?'

'Where, then?'

'With a different friend.'

'Who? Why didn't you tell us? What are you going to do? I want to come down to London to see you!'

'Please don't,' said Robin through gritted teeth.

Her guilt about the expense of the wedding she and Matthew had put her parents to, and about the embarrassment her mother and father were about to endure in explaining to their friends that her marriage was over barely a year after it had begun, weighed heavily on her, but she couldn't bear the prospect of Linda badgering and cajoling, treating her as though she were fragile and damaged. The last thing she needed right now was her mother suggesting that she go back to Yorkshire, to be cocooned in the bedroom that had witnessed some of the worst times of her life.

After two days viewing a multitude of densely packed houses, Robin had put down a deposit on a box room in a house in Kilburn, where she would have five other housemates, and into which she would be able to move the following week. Every time she thought of the place, her stomach turned over in trepidation and misery. At the age of almost twenty-eight, she would be the oldest housemate.

Trying to propitiate Strike, she got out of the car and

offered to help him with the kit bag, but he grunted at her that he could manage. As the canvas hit the metal floor of the Land Rover she heard a loud clattering of heavy metal tools and experienced a nervous spasm in her stomach.

Strike, who had taken fleeting stock of Robin's appearance, had his worst suspicions strengthened. Pale, with shadows beneath her eyes, she managed to look both puffy and drawn and also seemed to have lost weight in the few days since he'd last seen her. The wife of his old army friend Graham Hardacre had been hospitalised in the early stages of pregnancy because of persistent vomiting. Perhaps one of Robin's important appointments had been to address that problem.

'You all right?' Strike asked Robin roughly, buckling up his seatbelt.

'Fine,' she said, for what felt like the umpteenth time, taking his shortness as annoyance at his long Tube journey.

They drove out of London without talking. Finally, when they had reached the M40, Strike said:

'Patterson's back. He was watching the office this morning.'

'You're kidding!'

'Has there been anyone round your place?'

'Not that I know of,' said Robin, after an almost imperceptible hesitation. Perhaps this was what Matthew had been calling her about, when he had tried to reach her in Masham.

'You didn't have any trouble getting away this morning?'

'No,' said Robin, honestly enough.

In the days that had elapsed since she'd walked out, she had imagined telling Strike that her marriage was over, but had not yet been able to find a form of words that she knew she would be able to deliver with the requisite calm. This frustrated her: it ought, she told herself, to be easy. He was the friend and colleague who had been there when she'd called off the wedding and who knew about Matthew's previous infidelity with Sarah.

She ought to be able to tell him casually mid-conversation, as she had with Raphael.

The problem was that on the rare occasions when she and Strike had shared revelations about their love lives, it had been when one of them had been drunk. Otherwise, a profound reserve on such matters had always lain between them, in spite of Matthew's paranoid conviction that they spent most of their working lives in flirtation.

But there was more to it than that. Strike was the man she had hugged on the stairs at her wedding reception, the man with whom she had imagined walking out on her husband before the marriage could be consummated, the man for whom she had spent nights of her honeymoon wearing a groove in the white sand as she paced alone, wondering whether she was in love with him. She was afraid of giving herself away, afraid of betraying what she had thought and felt, because she was sure that if he ever had the merest suspicion of what a disruptive factor he had been, in both the beginning and the end of her marriage, it would surely taint their working relationship, as certainly as it would surely prejudice her job if he ever knew about the panic attacks.

No, she must appear to be what he was – self-contained and stoic, able to absorb trauma and limp on, ready to face whatever life flung at her, even what lay at the bottom of the dell, without flinching or turning away.

'So what d'you think Patterson's up to?' she asked.

'Time will tell. Did your appointments go all right?'

'Yes,' said Robin, and to distract herself from the thought of her tiny new rented room, and the student couple who had shown her around, casting sideways glances at the strangely grown-up woman who was coming to live with them, she said, 'There are biscuits in the bag back there. No tea, sorry, but we can stop if you like.'

The thermos was back in Albury Street, one of the things she had forgotten to sneak out of the house when she had returned while Matthew was at work.

'Thanks,' said Strike, though without much enthusiasm. He was wondering whether the reappearance of snacks, given his self-proclaimed diet, might not be further proof of his partner's pregnancy.

Robin's phone rang in her pocket. She ignored it. Twice that morning, she had received calls from the same unknown number and she was afraid that it might be Matthew who, finding himself blocked, had borrowed another phone.

'D'you want to get that?' asked Strike, watching her pale, set profile.

'Er – not while I'm driving.'

'I can answer it, if you want.'

'No,' she said, a little too quickly.

The mobile stopped ringing but, almost at once, began again. More than ever convinced that it was Matthew, Robin took the phone out of her jacket, saying:

'I think I know who it is, and I don't want to talk to them just now. Once they hang up, could you mute it?'

Strike took the mobile.

'It's been put through from the office number. I'll turn it to speakerphone,' said Strike helpfully, given that the ancient Land Rover didn't have a functioning heater, let alone Bluetooth, and he did so, holding the mobile close to her mouth, so that she could make herself heard over the rattle and growl of the draughty vehicle.

'Hello, Robin here. Who's this?'

'Robin? Don't you mean *Venetia*?' said a Welsh voice.

'Is that Mr Winn?' said Robin, eyes on the road, while Strike held the mobile steady for her.

'Yes, you nasty little bitch, it is.'

Robin and Strike glanced at each other, startled. Gone was the unctuous, lascivious Winn, keen to charm and impress.

'Got what you were after, haven't you, eh? Wriggling up and down that corridor, sticking your tits in where they weren't wanted, "oh, Mr Winn—"' he imitated her the same way Matthew did, high-pitched and imbecilic, '"—oh, help me, Mr Winn, should I do charity or should I do politics, let me bend a bit lower over the desk, Mr Winn". How many men have you trapped that way, how far do you go—?'

'Have you got something to tell me, Mr Winn?' asked Robin loudly, talking over him. 'Because if you've just called to insult me—'

'Oh, I've got plenty to bloody tell you, *plenty to bloody tell you,*' shouted Winn. 'You are going to *pay*, Miss Ellacott, for what you've done to me, *pay* for the damage you've done to me and my wife, you don't get off that easily, you broke the law in this office and I'm going to see you in court, do you understand me?' He was becoming almost hysterical. 'We'll see how well your wiles work on a judge, shall we? Low-cut top and "oh, I think I'm overheating—"'

A white light seemed to be encroaching on the edges of Robin's vision, so that the road ahead turned tunnel-like.

'NO!' she shouted, taking both hands off the wheel before slamming them back down again, her arms shaking. It was the 'no' she had given Matthew, a 'no' of such vehemence and force that it brought Geraint Winn up short in exactly the same way.

'Nobody made you stroke my hair and pat my back and ogle my chest, Mr Winn, that wasn't what *I* wanted, though I'm sure it gives you a bit of a kick to think it was—'

'Robin!' said Strike, but he might as well have been one more creak of the car's ancient chassis, and she ignored, too, Geraint's sudden interjection, 'Who else is there? Was that Strike?'

'—you're a creep, Mr Winn, a *thieving* creep who stole from a charity and I'm not only happy I got the goods on you, I'll be delighted to tell the world you're flicking out pictures of your dead daughter while you're trying to peer down young women's shirts—'

'How dare you!' gasped Winn, 'are there no depths – you *dare* mention Rhiannon – it's all going to come out, Samuel Murape's family—'

'Screw you and screw your bloody grudges!' shouted Robin. 'You're a pervy, thieving—'

'If you've got anything else to say, I suggest you put it in writing, Mr Winn,' Strike shouted into the mobile, while Robin, hardly knowing what she was doing, continued to yell insults at Winn from a distance. Ending the call with a jab of the finger, Strike grabbed the wheel as Robin again removed both hands from it to gesticulate.

'Fuck's sake!' said Strike, 'pull over – pull over, now!'

She did as he told her automatically, the adrenaline disorientating her like alcohol, and when the Land Rover lurched to a halt she threw off her seat belt and got out on the hard shoulder, cars whizzing past her. Hardly knowing what she was doing she began to stumble away from the Land Rover, tears of rage sliding down her face, trying to outpace the panic now lapping at her, because she had just irrevocably alienated a man they might need to talk to again, a man who had already been talking about revenge, who might even be the one paying Patterson . . .

'Robin!'

Now, she thought, Strike, too, would think her a flake, a damaged fool who should never have taken on this line of work, the one who ran when things got tough. It was that which made her wheel around to face him as he hobbled along the hard shoulder after her, and she wiped her face roughly on her sleeve and said, before he could tell her off, 'I know I shouldn't have lost it, I know I've fucked up, I'm sorry.' But his answer was lost in the pounding in her ears and, as though it had been waiting for her to stop running, the panic now engulfed her. Dizzy, unable to order her thoughts, she collapsed on the verge, dry bristles of grass prickling through her jeans as, eyes shut and head in hands, she tried to breathe herself back to normality as the traffic zoomed past.

She wasn't quite sure whether one minute or ten had elapsed, but finally her pulse slowed, her thoughts became ordered and the panic ebbed away, to be replaced by mortification. After all her careful pretence that she was coping, she had blown it.

A whiff of cigarette smoke reached her. Opening her eyes, she saw Strike's legs sticking out on the ground to her right. He, too, had sat down on the verge.

'How long have you been having panic attacks?' he asked conversationally.

There seemed no point dissembling any more.

'About a year,' she muttered.

'Been getting help with them?'

'Yes. I was in therapy for a bit. Now I do CBT exercises.'

'Do you, though?' Strike asked mildly. 'Because I bought vegetarian bacon a week ago, but it's not making me any healthier, just sitting there in the fridge.'

Robin began to laugh and found that she couldn't stop. More tears leaked from her eyes. Strike watched her, not unkindly, smoking his cigarette.

'I could have been doing them a bit more regularly,' Robin admitted at last, mopping her face again.

'Anything else you fancy telling me, now we're getting into things?' asked Strike.

He felt he ought to know the worst now, before he gave her any advice on her mental condition, but Robin seemed confused.

'Any other health matters that might affect your ability to work?' he prompted her.

'Like what?'

Strike wondered whether a direct enquiry constituted some kind of infringement of her employment rights.

'I wondered,' he said, 'whether you might be, ah, pregnant.'

Robin began to laugh again.

'Oh God, that's funny.'

'Is it?'

'No,' she said, shaking her head, 'I'm not pregnant.'

Strike now noticed that her wedding and engagement rings were missing. He had become so used to seeing her without them as she impersonated Venetia Hall and Bobbi Cunliffe that it had not occurred to him that their absence today might be significant, yet he didn't want to pose a direct question, for reasons that had nothing at all to do with employment rights.

'Matthew and I have split up,' Robin said, frowning at the passing traffic in an effort not to cry again. 'A week ago.'

'Oh,' said Strike. 'Shit. I'm sorry.'

But his concerned expression was at total odds with his actual feelings. His dark mood had lightened so abruptly that it was akin to having moved from sober to three pints down. The smell of rubber and dust and burned grass recalled the car park where he had accidentally kissed her, and he drew on his cigarette again and tried hard not to let his feelings show in his face.

'I know I shouldn't have spoken to Geraint Winn like that,' said Robin, tears now falling again. 'I shouldn't have mentioned Rhiannon, I lost control and – it's just, *men*, bloody *men*, judging everyone by their bloody selves!'

'What happened with Matt—?'

'He's been sleeping with Sarah Shadlock,' said Robin savagely. 'His best friend's fiancée. She left an earring in our bed and I – oh *bugger*.'

It was no use: she buried her face in her hands and, with a sense of having nothing to lose now, cried in earnest, because she had thoroughly disgraced herself in Strike's eyes, and the one remaining piece of her life that she had been seeking to preserve had been tainted. How delighted Matthew would be to see her falling apart on a motorway verge, proving his point, that she was unfit to do the job she loved, forever limited by her past, by having, twice, been in the wrong place, at the wrong time, with the wrong men.

A heavy weight landed across her shoulders. Strike had put his arm around her. This was simultaneously comforting and ominous, because he had never done that before, and she was sure that this was the precursor to him telling her that she was unfit to work, that they would cancel the next interview and return to London.

'Where have you been staying?'

'Vanessa's sofa,' said Robin, trying frantically to mop her streaming eyes and nose: snot and tears had made the knees of her jeans soggy. 'But I've got a new place now.'

'Where?'

'Kilburn, a room in a shared house.'

'Bloody hell, Robin,' said Strike. 'Why didn't you tell me? Nick and Ilsa have got a proper spare room, they'd be delighted—'

'I can't sponge off your friends,' said Robin thickly.

'It wouldn't be sponging,' said Strike. He jammed his cigarette in his mouth and started searching his pockets with his free hand. 'They like you and you could stay there for a couple of weeks until – aha. I thought I had one. It's only creased, I haven't used it – don't think so, anyway—'

Robin took the tissue and, with one hearty blow of her nose, demolished it.

'Listen,' Strike began, but Robin interrupted at once:

'Don't tell me to take time off. Please don't. I'm fine, I'm fit to work, I hadn't had a panic attack in ages before that one, I'm—'

'—not listening.'

'All right, sorry,' she muttered, the sodden tissue clutched in her fist. 'Go on.'

'After I got blown up, I couldn't get in a car without doing what you've just done, panicking and breaking out in a cold sweat and half suffocating. For a while I'd do anything to avoid being driven by someone else. I've still got problems with it, to tell the truth.'

'I didn't realise,' said Robin. 'You don't show it.'

'Yeah, well, you're the best driver I know. You should see me with my bloody sister. Thing is, Robin – oh, bollocks.'

The traffic police had arrived, pulling up behind the abandoned Land Rover, apparently puzzled as to why the occupants were sitting fifty yards away on the verge, to all appearances unconcerned with the fate of their poorly parked vehicle.

'Not in too much of a hurry to get help, then?' said the portlier of the two sarcastically. He had the swagger of a man who thinks himself a joker.

Strike removed his arm from around Robin's shoulders and both stood up, in Strike's case, clumsily.

'Car sickness,' Strike told the officer blandly. 'Careful, or she might puke on you.'

They returned to the car. The first officer's colleague was peering at the tax disc on the ancient Land Rover.

'You don't see many of this age still on the roads,' he commented.

'It's never let me down yet,' said Robin.

'Sure you're all right to drive?' Strike muttered, as she turned the ignition key. 'We could pretend you're still feeling ill.'

'I'm fine.'

And this time, it was true. He had called her the best driver he knew, and it might not be much, but he had given her back some of her self-respect, and she steered seamlessly back onto the motorway.

There was a long silence. Strike decided that further discussion of Robin's mental health ought to wait until she wasn't driving.

'Winn said a name at the end of the call there,' he mused, taking out his notebook. 'Did you hear?'

'No,' muttered Robin, shamefaced.

'It was Samuel something,' Strike said, making a note. 'Murdoch? Matlock?'

'I didn't hear.'

'Cheer up,' said Strike bracingly, 'he probably wouldn't have blurted it out if you hadn't been yelling at him. Not that I recommend calling interviewees thieving perverts in future . . .'

He stretched around in his seat, reaching for the carrier bag in the back. 'Fancy a biscuit?'

62

. . . I do not want to see your defeat, Rebecca.

Henrik Ibsen, *Rosmersholm*

The car park at Newbury Racecourse was already jam-packed when they arrived. Many of the people heading for the ticket marquee were dressed for comfort, like Strike and Robin, in jeans and jackets, but others had donned fluttering silk dresses, suits, padded waistcoats, tweed hats and corduroy trousers in shades of mustard and puce that reminded Robin of Torquil.

They queued for tickets, each lost in their thoughts. Robin was afraid of what was coming once they reached the Crafty Filly, where Tegan Butcher worked. Certain that Strike had not yet had his full say on her mental health, she was afraid that he had merely postponed the announcement that he wanted her to return to a desk job in the office.

In fact, Strike's mind was temporarily elsewhere. The white railings glimpsed beyond the small marquee where the crowd queued for tickets, and the abundance of tweed and corduroy, were reminding him of the last time he had been at a racecourse. He had no particular interest in the sport. The one constant paternal figure in his life, his uncle Ted, had been a footballing and sailing man, and while a couple of Strike's friends in the army had enjoyed a bet on the horses, he had never seen the attraction.

Three years previously, though, he had attended the Epsom Derby with Charlotte and two of her favourite siblings. Like Strike, Charlotte came from a disjointed and dysfunctional family. In one of her unpredictable effusions of enthusiasm, Charlotte had insisted on accepting Valentine and Sacha's invitation, notwithstanding Strike's lack of interest in the sport and his barely cordial feelings towards both men, who considered him an inexplicable oddity in their sister's life.

He had been broke at the time, setting up the agency on a shoestring, already being chased by lawyers for repayment of the small loan he had taken from his biological father, when every bank had turned him down as a bad risk. Nevertheless, Charlotte had been incensed when, after losing a fiver on the nose on the favourite, Fame and Glory, who had come in second, he had refused to place another bet. She had refrained from calling him puritanical or sanctimonious, plebeian or penny-pinching, as she had done previously when he had refused to emulate the reckless and ostentatious spending of her family and friends. Egged on by her brothers, she had chosen to lay larger and larger bets herself, finally winning £2500 and insisting that they visit the champagne tent, where her beauty and high spirits had turned many heads.

As he walked with Robin up a wide tarmacked thoroughfare that ran parallel from the racetrack itself behind the towering stands, past coffee bars, cider stalls and ice cream vans, the jockeys' changing rooms and owners' and trainers' bar, Strike thought about Charlotte, and gambles that came off, and gambles that didn't, until Robin's voice pulled him back to the present.

'I think that's the place.'

A painted sign showed the head of a dark, winking filly in a snaffle bit hung on the side of a one-storey brick bar. The outdoor seating area was crowded. Champagne flutes clinked amid a buzz of talk and laughter. The Crafty Filly overlooked the paddock where horses would shortly be paraded, around which a further crowd had begun to congregate.

'Grab that high table,' Strike told Robin, 'and I'll get drinks and tell Tegan we're here.'

He disappeared into the building without asking her what she wanted.

Robin sat down at one of the tall tables with its metal bar-chairs, which she knew Strike preferred because getting on and off them would be easier on his amputated leg than the low wickerwork sofas. The whole outside area sat beneath a canopy of polyurethane to protect drinkers from non-existent rain. The sky was cloudless today, the day warm with a light breeze that barely moved the leaves of the topiary plants at the entrance to the bar. It would be a clear night for digging in the dell outside Steda Cottage, Robin thought, always assuming that Strike wasn't about to cancel the expedition, because he thought her too unstable and emotional to take along.

That thought turned her insides even colder and she fell to reading the printed lists of runners they had been given, along with their cardboard entry tags, until a half-bottle of Moët & Chandon landed unexpectedly in front of her and Strike sat down, holding a pint of bitter.

'Doom Bar on draught,' he said cheerfully, tipping his glass to her before taking a sip. Robin looked blankly at the little bottle of champagne, which she thought resembled bubble bath.

'What's this for?'

'Celebration,' said Strike, having taken a sizeable gulp of his beer. 'I know you're not supposed to say it,' he went on, rummaging through his pockets for cigarettes, 'but you're well shot of him. Sleeping with his mate's fiancée in the marital bed? He deserves everything that's coming to him.'

'I can't drink. I'm driving.'

'That's just cost me twenty-five quid, so you can take a token swig.'

'Twenty-five quid, for this?' said Robin, and taking advantage of Strike lighting his cigarette, she surreptitiously wiped her leaking eyes again.

'Tell me something,' said Strike, as he waved his match, extinguishing it. 'D'you ever think about where you see the agency going?'

'What d'you mean?' said Robin, looking alarmed.

'My brother-in-law was giving me the third degree about it, night the Olympics started,' said Strike. 'Banging on about reaching a point where I didn't have to go out on the street any more.'

'But you wouldn't want that, would y – wait,' said Robin, panicking. 'Are you trying to tell me I've got to go back to the desk and answering the phones?'

'No,' said Strike, blowing smoke away from her, 'I just wondered whether you give the future any thought.'

'You want me to leave?' asked Robin, still more alarmed. 'Go and do something el—?'

'Bloody hell, Ellacott, no! I'm asking you whether you think about the future, that's all.'

He watched as Robin uncorked the little bottle.

'Yes, of course I do,' she said uncertainly. 'I've been hoping we can get the bank balance a bit healthier, so we aren't living hand to mouth all the time, but I love the—' her voice wobbled, '—the job, you know I do. That's all I want. Do it, get better at it and . . . I suppose make the agency the best in London.'

Grinning, Strike clinked his beer glass against her champagne.

'Well, bear in mind we want exactly the same thing while I'm saying the next bit, all right? And you might as well drink. Tegan can't take a break for forty minutes, and we've got a lot of time to kill before we head over to the dell this evening.'

Strike watched her take a sip of champagne before going on.

'Pretending you're OK when you aren't isn't strength.'

'Well, that's where you're wrong,' Robin contradicted him. The champagne had fizzed on her tongue and seemed to give her courage even before it hit her brain. 'Sometimes, acting as though you're all right, makes you all right. Sometimes you've got to slap on a brave face and walk out into the world, and after a while it isn't an act any more, it's who you are. If I'd waited to feel ready to leave my room after – you know,' she said, 'I'd still be in there. I had to leave before I was ready. And,' she said, looking him directly in the eyes, her own bloodshot and swollen, 'I've been working with you for two years, watching you plough on no matter what, when we both know any doctor would have told you to put your leg up and rest.'

'And where did that get me, eh?' asked Strike reasonably. 'Invalided out for a week, with my hamstring screaming for mercy every time I walk more than fifty yards. You want to draw parallels, fine. I'm dieting, I've been doing my stretches—'

'And the vegetarian bacon, rotting away in the fridge?'

'Rotting? That stuff's like industrial rubber, it'll outlive me. Listen,' he said, refusing to be deflected, 'it'd be a bloody miracle if you hadn't suffered any after-effects from what happened last year.' His eyes sought the tip of the purple scar on her forearm, visible beneath the cuff of her shirt. 'Nothing in your past precludes you from doing this job, but you need to take care of yourself if you want to keep doing it. If you need time off—'

'—that's the last thing I want—'

'This isn't about what you want. It's about what you need.'

'Shall I tell you something funny?' said Robin. Whether because of the mouthful of champagne, or for some other reason, she had experienced a startling lift in mood that made her loose-tongued. 'You'd have thought I'd have had panic attacks galore over the last week, wouldn't you? I've been trying to find a place to live, looking round flats, travelling all over London, I've had loads of people coming up unexpectedly behind me – that's a major trigger,' she explained. 'People behind me, when I don't know they're there.'

'Don't think we need Freud to explain that one.'

'But I've been fine,' said Robin. 'I think it's because I haven't had to—'

She stopped short, but Strike thought he knew what the end of the sentence would have been. Taking a chance, he said:

'This job becomes well-nigh impossible if your home life's screwed up. I've been there. I know.'

Relieved to have been understood, Robin drank more champagne then said in a rush:

'I think it's made me worse, having to hide what's going on, having to do the exercises in secret, because any sign I wasn't a hundred per cent and Matthew would be yelling at me again for doing this job. I thought it was him trying to reach me on the phone this morning, that's why I didn't want to take the call. And when Winn started calling me those names, it – well, it felt as though I *had* taken the call. I don't need Winn to tell me I'm basically a pair of walking tits, a stupid, deluded girl who doesn't realise that's my only useful attribute.'

Matthew's been telling you that, has he? thought Strike, imagining a few corrective measures from which he thought Matthew might benefit. Slowly and carefully he said:

'The fact that you're a woman . . . I *do* worry about you more when you're out alone on a job than I would if you were a bloke. Hear me out,' he said firmly, as she opened her mouth in panic. 'We've got to be honest with each other, or we're screwed. Just listen, will you?

'You've escaped two killers using your wits and remembering your training. I'd lay odds bloody Matthew couldn't've managed that. But I don't want a third time, Robin, because you might not be so lucky.'

'You *are* telling me to go back to a desk job—'

'Can I finish?' he said sternly. 'I don't want to lose you, because you're the best I've got. Every case we've worked since you arrived, you've found evidence I couldn't have found and got round people I couldn't have persuaded to talk to me. We're where we are today largely because of you. But the odds are always going to be against you if you come up against a violent man and I've got responsibilities here. I'm the senior partner, I'm the one you could sue—'

'You're worried I'd *sue*—?'

'No, Robin,' he said harshly, 'I'm worried you'll end up fucking dead and I'll have to carry that on my conscience for the rest of my life.'

He took another swig of Doom Bar, then said:

'I need to know you're mentally healthy if I'm putting you out on the street. I want a cast-iron guarantee from you that you're going to address these panic attacks, because it isn't only you who has to live with the consequences if you're not up to it.'

'Fine,' muttered Robin, and when Strike raised his eyebrows, she said, 'I mean it. I'll do what it takes. I will.'

The crowd around the paddock was becoming ever denser. Evidently the runners in the next race were about to be paraded.

'How are things with Lorelei?' Robin asked. 'I like her.'

'Then I'm afraid I've got even more bad news for you, because you and Matthew aren't the only people who split up last weekend.'

'Oh, shit. Sorry,' said Robin, and she covered her embarrassment by drinking more champagne.

'For someone who didn't want that, you're getting through it quite fast,' said Strike, amused.

'I didn't tell you, did I?' said Robin, remembering suddenly, as she held up the little green bottle. 'I know where I saw Blanc de Blancs before, and it wasn't on a bottle – but it doesn't help us with the case.'

'Go on.'

'There's a suite at Le Manoir aux Quat'Saisons called that,' said Robin. 'Raymond Blanc, you know, the chef who started the hotel? Play on words. Blanc de Blanc – no "s".'

'Is that where you had your anniversary weekend?'

'Yeah. We weren't in "Blanc de Blanc", though. We couldn't afford a suite,' said Robin. 'I just remember walking past the sign. But yes . . . that's where we celebrated our paper anniversary. Paper,' she repeated, with a sigh, 'and some people make it to platinum.'

Seven dark thoroughbreds were appearing one by one in the paddock now, jockeys in their silks perched atop them like monkeys, stable girls and lads leading the nervy creatures, with their silken flanks and their prancing strides. Strike and Robin were some of the few not craning their necks for a better view. Before she had time to second-guess herself, Robin introduced the subject she most wanted to discuss.

'Was that Charlotte I saw you talking to at the Paralympic reception?'

'Yeah,' said Strike.

He glanced at her. Robin had had occasion before now to deplore how easily he seemed to read her thoughts.

'Charlotte had nothing to do with me and Lorelei splitting. She's married now.'

'So were Matthew and I,' Robin pointed out, taking another sip of champagne. 'Didn't stop Sarah Shadlock.'

'I'm not Sarah Shadlock.'

'Obviously not. If you were that bloody annoying I wouldn't be working for you.'

'Maybe you could put that on the next employee satisfaction review. "Not as bloody annoying as the woman who shagged my husband." I'll have it framed.'

Robin laughed.

'You know, I had an idea about Blanc de Blancs myself,' said Strike. 'I was going back over Chiswell's to-do list, trying to eliminate possibilities and substantiate a theory.'

'What theory?' said Robin sharply, and Strike noted that even halfway down the bottle of champagne, with her marriage in splinters and a box room in Kilburn to look forward to, Robin's interest in the case remained as acute as ever.

'Remember when I told you I thought there was something big, something fundamental, behind the Chiswell business? Something we hadn't spotted yet?'

'Yes,' said Robin, 'you said it kept "almost showing itself".'

'Well remembered. So, a couple of things Raphael said—'

'That's me on my break, now,' said a nervous female voice behind them.

63

It is a purely personal matter, and there is not the slightest necessity to go proclaiming it all over the countryside.

Henrik Ibsen, *Rosmersholm*

Short, square and heavily freckled, Tegan Butcher wore her dark hair scraped back in a bun. Even in her smart bar uniform, which comprised a grey tie and a black shirt on which a white horse and jockey were embroidered, she had the air of a girl more at home in muddy Wellington boots. She had brought a milky coffee out of the bar to drink while they questioned her.

'Oh – thanks very much,' she said, when Strike went to fetch an extra chair, clearly gratified that the famous detective would do as much for her.

'No problem,' said Strike. 'This is my partner, Robin Ellacott.'

'Yeah, it was you that contacted me, wasn't it?' said Tegan as she got up onto the bar chair, making slightly heavy weather of the climb, being so short. She seemed simultaneously excited and fearful.

'You haven't got long, I know,' said Strike, 'so we'll get straight to it, if you don't mind, Tegan?'

'No. I mean, yeah. That's fine. Go on.'

'How long did you work for Jasper and Kinvara Chiswell?'

'I was doing it part time for them while I was still at school, so counting that . . . two and a half years, yeah.'

'How did you like working for them?'

'It was all right,' said Tegan cautiously.

'How did you find the minister?'

'He was all right,' said Tegan. She appeared to realise that this wasn't particularly descriptive, and added, 'My family've known him for ages. My brothers done a bit of work up at Chiswell House for years, on and off.'

'Yeah?' said Strike, who was making notes. 'What did your brothers do?'

'Repairing fences, bit of gardening, but they've sold off most of the land now,' said Tegan. 'The garden's gone wild.'

She picked up her coffee and took a sip, then said anxiously:

'My mum would do her nut if she knew I was meeting you. She told me to keep well out of it.'

'Why's that?'

'"Least said, soonest mended", she always says. That and "least seen, most admired". That's what I got if I ever wanted to go to the young farmers' disco.'

Robin laughed. Tegan grinned, proud to have amused her.

'How did you find Mrs Chiswell as an employer?' asked Strike.

'All right,' said Tegan, yet again.

'Mrs Chiswell liked to have someone sleeping at the house if she was away for the night, is that right? To be near the horses?'

'Yeah,' said Tegan, and then, volunteering information for the first time, 'she's paranoid.'

'Wasn't one of her horses slashed?'

'You can call it slashed if you want,' said Tegan, 'but I'd

call it more of a scratch. Romano managed to get his blanket off in the night. He was a sod for doing that.'

'You don't know anything about intruders in the garden, then?' asked Strike, his pen poised over his notebook.

'Weelll,' said Tegan slowly, 'she *said* something about it, but . . . '

Her eyes had strayed to Strike's Benson & Hedges, which were lying beside his beer glass.

'Can I have a smoke?' she asked, greatly daring.

'Help yourself,' said Strike, taking out a lighter and pushing it towards her.

Tegan lit up, took a deep drag on the cigarette, and said:

'I don't think there was ever anyone in the gardens. That's just Mrs Chiswell. She's—' Tegan struggled to find the right word. 'Well, if she was a horse you'd call her spooky. *I* never heard anyone when I was there overnight.'

'You slept over at the house the night before Jasper Chiswell was found dead in London, didn't you?'

'Yeah.'

'Can you remember what time Mrs Chiswell got back?'

''Bout eleven. I got a right shock,' said Tegan. Now that her nerves were wearing off, a slight tendency to garrulity was revealed. 'Because she was s'posed to be staying up in London. She went off on one when she walked in, because I'd had a fag in front of the telly – she doesn't like smoking – and I'd had a couple of glasses of wine out the bottle in the fridge, as well. Mind, she'd told me to help myself to anything I wanted before she left, but she's like that, always shifting the goalposts. What was right one minute was wrong the next. You had to walk on eggshells, you really did.

'But she was already in a bad mood when she arrived. I could tell from the way she came stomping down the hall.

The fag and the wine, that just gave her an excuse to have a go at me. That's what she's like.'

'But you stayed the night, anyway?'

'Yeah. She said I was too drunk to drive, which was rubbish, I weren't drunk, and then she told me to go and check on the horses, because she had a phone call to make.'

'Did you hear her make the call?'

Tegan rearranged herself in the too-high chair, so that the elbow of her smoking arm was cupped in her free hand, her eyes slightly narrowed against the smoke, a pose she evidently thought appropriate while dealing with a tricky private detective.

'I dunno if I should say.'

'How about I suggest a name and you can nod if it's the right one?'

'Go on, then,' said Tegan, with the mingled mistrust and curiosity of one who has been promised a magic trick.

'Henry Drummond,' said Strike. 'She was leaving a message to say that she wanted a valuation on a necklace?'

Impressed against her will, Tegan nodded.

'Yeah,' she said. 'That's right.'

'So you went out to check on the horses . . . ?'

'Yeah, and when I got back Mrs Chiswell said I should stay over anyway, because she needed me early, so I did.'

'And where did *she* sleep?' asked Robin.

'Well – upstairs,' said Tegan, with a surprised laugh. 'Obviously. In her bedroom.'

'You're sure she was there all night?' asked Robin.

'Yeah,' said Tegan, with another little laugh. 'Her bedroom was next to mine. They're the only two with windows that face the stables. I could hear her going to bed.'

'You're sure she didn't leave the house during the night? Didn't drive anywhere, as far as you know?' asked Strike.

'No. I'd've heard the car. There are potholes everywhere round that house, you can't leave quietly. Anyway, I met her next morning on the landing, heading for the bathroom in her nightie.'

'What time would that have been?'

''Bout half-seven. We had breakfast together in the kitchen.'

'Was she still angry with you?'

'Bit ratty,' admitted Tegan.

'You didn't happen to hear her take another call, round about breakfast time?'

Frankly admiring, Tegan said:

'You mean, from Mr Chiswell? Yeah. She went out of the kitchen to take it. All I heard was "No, I mean it this time, Jasper". Sounded like a row. I've told the police this. I thought they must've argued in London and that's why she'd come home early instead of staying up there.

'Then I went outside to muck out, and she came out and she was schooling Brandy, that's one of her mares, and then,' said Tegan, with a slight hesitation, '*he* arrived. Raphael, you know. The son.'

'And what happened then?' asked Strike.

Tegan hesitated.

'They had a row, didn't they?' said Strike, mindful of how much of Tegan's break was slipping away.

'Yeah,' said Tegan, smiling in frank wonderment. 'You know *everything*!'

'D'you know what it was about?'

'Same thing she was phoning that bloke about, night before.'

'The necklace? Mrs Chiswell wanting to sell it?'

'Yeah.'

'Where were you when they were having the row?'

'Still mucking out. He got out of his car and went marching up to her in the outdoor school—'

Robin, seeing Strike's perplexity, muttered, 'Like a paddock where you train horses.'

'Ah,' he said.

'—yeah,' said Tegan, 'that's where she was schooling Brandy. First they were talking and I couldn't hear what they were saying and then it turned into a proper shouting match and she dismounted and yelled at me to come and untack Brandy – take off the saddle and bridle,' she added kindly, in case Strike hadn't understood, 'and they marched off into the house and I could hear them still having a go at each other as they disappeared.

'She never liked him,' said Tegan. 'Raphael. Thought he was spoiled. Always slagging him off. *I* thought he was all right, personally,' she said, with a would-be dispassionate air at odds with her heightened colour.

'Can you remember what they were saying to each other?'

'A bit,' said Tegan. 'He was telling her she couldn't sell it, that it belonged to his dad or something, and she told him to mind his own business.'

'Then what happened?'

'They went inside, I kept mucking out, and after a bit,' said Tegan, faltering slightly, 'I saw a police car coming up the drive and . . . yeah, it was awful. Policewoman come and asked me to go inside and help. I went in the kitchen and Mrs Chiswell was white as a sheet and all over the place. They wanted me to show them where the teabags were. I made her a hot drink and he – Raphael – made her sit down. He was really nice to her,' said Tegan, 'considering she'd just been calling him every name under the sun.'

Strike checked his watch.

'I know you haven't got long. Just a couple more things.'

'All right,' she said.

'There was an incident over a year ago,' said Strike, 'where Mrs Chiswell attacked Mr Chiswell with a hammer.'

'Oh, God, yeah,' said Tegan. 'Yeah ... she really lost it. That was right after Lady was put down, start of the summer. She was Mrs Chiswell's favourite mare and Mrs Chiswell come home and the vet had already done it. She'd wanted to be there when it happened and she went crazy when she come back and seen the knacker's van.'

'How long had she known that the mare would have to be put down?' asked Robin.

'Those last two, three days, I think we all knew, really,' said Tegan sadly. 'But she was such a lovely horse, we kept hoping she'd pull through. The vet had waited for hours for Mrs Chiswell to come home, but Lady was suffering and he couldn't wait around all day, so ...'

Tegan made a gesture of hopelessness.

'Any idea what made her go up to London that day, if she knew Lady was dying?' asked Strike.

Tegan shook her head.

'Can you talk us through exactly what happened, when she attacked her husband? Did she say anything first?'

'No,' said Tegan. 'She come into the yard, seen what had happened, ran towards Mr Chiswell, grabbed the hammer and just swung for him. Blood everywhere. It was horrible,' said Tegan, with patent sincerity. 'Awful.'

'What did she do after she'd hit him?' asked Robin.

'Just stood there. The expression on her face ... it was like a *demon* or something,' said Tegan unexpectedly. 'I thought he was dead, thought she'd killed him.

'They put her away for a couple of weeks, you know. She went off to some hospital. I had to do the horses alone ...

'We were all gutted about Lady. I loved that mare and I

thought she was going to make it, but she'd given up, she lay down and wouldn't eat. I couldn't blame Mrs Chiswell for being upset, but . . . she could've killed him. Blood everywhere,' she repeated. 'I wanted to leave. Told my mum. Mrs Chiswell scared me, that night.'

'So what made you stay?' asked Strike.

'I dunno, really . . . Mr Chiswell wanted me to, and I was fond of the horses. Then she came out of hospital and she was really depressed and I suppose I felt sorry for her. I kept finding her crying in Lady's empty stall.'

'Was Lady the mare that Mrs Chiswell wanted to – er – what's the right term?' Strike asked Robin.

'Put in foal?' Robin suggested.

'Yeah . . . put in foal to the famous stallion?'

'Totilas?' said Tegan, with the ghost of an eye roll. 'No, it was Brandy she wanted to breed from, but Mr Chiswell was having none of it. Totilas! He costs a fortune.'

'So I heard. She didn't by any chance mention using a different stallion? There's one called "Blanc de Blancs", I don't know whether—'

'Never heard of him,' said Tegan. 'No, it *had* to be Totilas, he was the best, she was fixated on using him. That's what she's like, Mrs Chiswell. When she gets an idea in her head you can't shift it. She was going to breed this beautiful Grand Prix horse and . . . you know she lost a baby, don't you?'

Strike and Robin nodded.

'Mum felt sorry for her, she thought the thing about getting a foal was, you know, a sort of substitute. Mum thinks it was all to do with the baby, how Mrs Chiswell's mood went up and down all the time.

'Like, one day, a few weeks after she came out of hospital, I remember, she was *manic*. I think it was the drugs they had her on. High as a kite. Singing in the yard. And I said to her,

"You're cheerful, Mrs C", and she laughed and said, "Oh, I've been working on Jasper and I think I'm nearly there, I think he's going to let me use Totilas after all." It was all rubbish. I asked him and he was really grumpy about it, said it was wishful thinking and he could hardly afford as many horses as she'd already got.'

'You don't think he might've surprised her,' said Strike, 'by offering her a different stallion to breed from? A cheaper one?'

'That would just've annoyed her,' said Tegan. 'It was Totilas or nothing.' She stubbed out the cigarette Strike had given her, checked her watch and said regretfully, 'I've only got a couple more minutes.'

'Two more things, and we're done,' said Strike. 'I've heard that your family knew a girl called Suki Lewis, years ago? She was a runaway from care—'

'You know *everything*!' said Tegan again, delightedly. 'How did you know that?'

'Billy Knight told me. D'you happen to know what happened to Suki?'

'Yeah, she went to Aberdeen. She was in our Dan's class at school. Her mum was a nightmare: drink and drugs and all sorts. Then the mum goes on a real bender and that's how Suki got put into care. She ran away to find her dad. He worked on the North Sea rigs.'

'And you think she found her father, do you?' asked Strike.

With a triumphant air, Tegan reached into her back pocket for her mobile. After a few clicks, she presented Strike with the Facebook page she had brought up for a beaming brunette, who stood posing with a posse of girlfriends in front of a swimming pool in Ibiza. Through the tan, the bleached smile and the false eyelashes, Strike discerned the palimpsest of the thin, buck-toothed girl from the old photograph. The page was captioned 'Susanna McNeil'.

'See?' said Tegan happily. 'Her dad took her in with his new family. "Susanna" was her proper name but her mum called her "Suki". My mum's friends with Susanna's auntie. Says she's doing great.'

'You're quite sure this is her?' asked Strike.

'Yeah, of course,' said Tegan. 'We were all pleased for her. She was a nice girl.'

She checked her watch again.

''M'sorry, but that's my break over, I've got to go.'

'One more question,' said Strike. 'How well did your brothers know the Knight family?'

'Quite well,' said Tegan. 'The boys were in different years at school but yeah, they knew them through working at Chiswell House.'

'What do your brothers do now, Tegan?'

'Paul's managing a farm over near Aylesbury now and Dan's up in London doing landscape – why are you writing this down?' she said, alarmed for the first time at the sight of Strike's pen moving across his notebook. 'You mustn't tell my brothers I've spoken to you! They'll go mad if they think I've talked about what went on up at the house!'

'Really? What *did* go on up there?' Strike asked.

Tegan looked uncertainly from him to Robin and back again.

'You already know, don't you?'

And when neither Strike nor Robin responded she said:

'Listen, Dan and Paul just helped out with transporting them. Loading them up and that. And it was legal back then!'

'What was legal?' asked Strike.

'I *know* you know,' said Tegan, half-worried, half-amused. 'Someone's been talking, haven't they? Is it Jimmy Knight? He was back not long ago, sniffing around, wanting to talk to Dan. Anyway, everyone knew, locally. It was supposed to be hush-hush, but we all knew about Jack.'

'Knew *what* about him?' asked Strike.

'Well . . . that he was the gallows maker.'

Strike absorbed the information without so much as a quiver of the eyelid. Robin wasn't sure her own expression had remained as impassive.

'But you already knew,' said Tegan. 'Didn't you?'

'Yeah,' said Strike, to reassure her. 'We knew.'

'Thought so,' said Tegan, relieved and sliding down, inelegantly, from her chair. 'But if you see Dan, don't tell him I said. He's like Mum. "Least said, soonest mended." Mind, none of us think there was anything wrong with it. This country'd be better with the death penalty, if you ask me.'

'Thanks for meeting us, Tegan,' said Strike. She blushed slightly as she shook first his hand, then Robin's.

'No problem,' she said, now seeming reluctant to leave them. 'Are you going to stay for the races? Brown Panther's running in the two-thirty.'

'We might,' said Strike, 'we've got a bit of time to kill before our next appointment.'

'I've got a tenner on Brown Panther,' Tegan confided. 'Well . . . bye, then.'

She had gone a few steps when she wheeled around and returned to Strike, now even pinker in the face.

'Can I have a selfie with you?'

'Er,' said Strike, carefully not catching Robin's eye, 'I'd rather not, if it's all the same to you.'

'Can I have your autograph, then?'

Deciding that this was the lesser of two evils, Strike wrote his signature on a napkin.

'Thanks.'

Clutching her napkin, Tegan departed at last. Strike

waited until she had disappeared into the bar before turning to Robin, who was already busy on her phone.

'Six years ago,' she said, reading from the mobile screen, 'an EU directive came in banning member states from exporting torture equipment. Until then, it was perfectly legal to export British-made gallows abroad.'

64

Speak so that I can understand you.

Henrik Ibsen, *Rosmersholm*

'"I acted within the law and in accordance with my conscience",' Strike quoted Chiswell's gnomic pronouncement back in Pratt's. 'So he did. Never hid the fact that he was pro-hanging, did he? I suppose he provided the wood from his grounds.'

'And the space for Jack o'Kent to build them – which is why Jack o'Kent warned Raff not to go into the barn, when he was a child.'

'And they probably split the profits.'

'Wait,' said Robin, remembering what Flick had shrieked after the minister's car, the night of the Paralympic reception. '"He put the horse on them" . . . Cormoran, d'you think—?'

'Yeah, I do,' said Strike, his thoughts keeping pace with hers. 'The last thing Billy said to me at the hospital was "I hated putting the horse on them". Even in the middle of a psychotic episode, Billy could carve a perfect White Horse of Uffington into wood . . . Jack o'Kent had his boys carving it onto trinkets for tourists and onto gallows for export . . . nice little father-son business he had going, eh?'

Strike clinked his beer glass against her little champagne bottle and downed the last dregs of his Doom Bar.

'To our first proper breakthrough. If Jack o'Kent was putting a little bit of local branding on the gallows, they were traceable back to him, weren't they? And not only to him: to the Vale of the White Horse, and to Chiswell. It all fits, Robin. Remember Jimmy's placard, with the pile of dead black children on it? Chiswell and Jack o'Kent were flogging them abroad – Middle East or Africa, probably. But Chiswell can't have known they had the horse carved into them – Christ, no, he *definitely* didn't,' said Strike, remembering Chiswell's words in Pratt's, 'because when he told me there were photographs, he said "there are no distinguishing marks, so far as I'm aware".'

'You know how Jimmy said he was owed?' said Robin, following her own train of thought. 'And how Raff said Kinvara thought he had a legitimate claim for money, at first? What d'you think are the chances that Jack o'Kent left some gallows ready for sale when he died—'

'—and Chiswell sold them without bothering to track down and pay off Jack's sons? Very smart,' said Strike, nodding. 'So for Jimmy, this all started as a demand for his rightful share of his father's estate. Then, when Chiswell denied he owed them anything, it turned into blackmail.'

'Not a very strong case for blackmail, though, when you think about it, is it?' said Robin. 'D'you really think Chiswell would have lost a lot of voters over this? It *was* legal at the time he sold them, and he was publicly pro-death penalty, so nobody could say he was a hypocrite. Half the country thinks we should bring back hanging. I'm not sure the kind of people who vote for Chiswell would have thought he did much wrong.'

'Another good point,' conceded Strike, 'and Chiswell could probably have brazened it out. He'd survived worse: impregnating his mistress, divorce, an illegitimate kid, Raphael's drugged-up car crash and imprisonment . . .

'But there were "unintended consequences", remember?' Strike asked thoughtfully. 'What did those pictures at the Foreign Office show, that Winn was so keen to get hold of? And who's that "Samuel" Winn just mentioned on the phone?'

Strike pulled out his notebook and jotted down a few sentences in his dense, hard-to-read handwriting.

'At least,' said Robin, 'we've got confirmation of Raff's story. The necklace.'

Strike grunted, still writing. When he'd finished, he said, 'Yeah, that was useful, as far as it went.'

'What d'you mean, "as far as it went"?'

'Him heading down to Oxfordshire to stop Kinvara running off with a valuable necklace is a better story than the trying-to-stop-her-topping-herself one,' said Strike, 'but I still don't think we're being told everything.'

'Why not?'

'Same objection as before. Why would Chiswell send Raphael down there as his emissary, when his wife hated him? Can't see why Raphael would be any more persuasive than Izzy.'

'Have you taken against Raphael, or something?'

Strike raised his eyebrows.

'I haven't got personal feelings for him one way or the other. You?'

'Of course not,' said Robin, a little too quickly. 'So, what was that theory you mentioned, before Tegan arrived?'

'Oh, yeah,' said Strike. 'Well, it might be nothing, but a couple of things Raphael said to you jumped out at me. Got me thinking.'

'What things?'

Strike told her.

'I can't see what's significant about any of that.'

'Maybe not in isolation, but try putting it together with what Della told me.'

'Which bit?'

But even when Strike reminded her what Della had said, Robin remained confused.

'I don't see the connection.'

Strike got up, grinning.

'Mull it over for a while. I'm going to ring Izzy and tell her Tegan's let the cat out of the bag about the gallows.'

He walked away and disappeared into the crowds in search of a quiet spot from which to make his call, leaving Robin to swill the now-tepid champagne around in the miniature bottle and ponder what Strike had just said. Nothing coherent emerged from her exhausted attempts to connect the disparate pieces of information, and after a few minutes she gave up and simply sat there, enjoying the warm breeze that lifted the hair from her shoulders.

In spite of her tiredness, the shattered state of her marriage and her very real apprehension about going digging in the dell later that night, it was pleasant to sit here, breathing in the smells of the racecourse, of soft air redolent of turf, leather and horse, catching trails of perfume from the women now moving away from the bar towards the stands, and the smoky whiff of venison burgers cooking in a van nearby. For the first time in a week, Robin realised that she was actually hungry.

She picked up the cork of the champagne bottle and turned it over in her fingers, remembering another cork, the one she had saved from her twenty-first birthday party, for which Matthew had come home from university with a bunch of new friends, Sarah among them. Looking back, she knew that her parents had wanted to throw a big party for her twenty-first in compensation for her not having the graduation party they had all been expecting.

Strike was taking a long time. Perhaps Izzy was spilling all the details, now that they knew what the substance of the blackmail had been about, or perhaps, Robin thought, she simply wanted to keep him on the phone.

Izzy isn't his type, though.

The thought startled her a little. She felt slightly guilty for giving it headspace and even more uncomfortable when it was jostled out of the way by another.

All his girlfriends have been beautiful. Izzy isn't.

Strike attracted remarkably good-looking women, when you considered his generally bearlike appearance and what he himself had referred to in her hearing as 'pube-like' hair.

I bet I look gross, was Robin's next, inconsequential thought. Puffy-faced and pale when she had got in the Land Rover that morning, she had cried a lot since. She was half-deliberating whether she had time to find a bathroom and at least brush her hair, when she spotted Strike walking back towards her holding a venison burger in each hand and a betting slip in his mouth.

'Izzy isn't picking up,' he informed her through clenched teeth. 'Left a message. Grab one of these and come on. I've just put a tenner each way on Brown Panther.'

'I didn't realise you're a betting man,' said Robin.

'I'm not,' said Strike, removing the betting slip from his teeth and pocketing it, 'but I'm feeling lucky today. Come on, we'll watch the race.'

As Strike turned away, Robin slid the champagne cork discreetly into her pocket.

'*Brown* Panther,' Strike said through a mouthful of burger, as they approached the track. 'Except he isn't, is he? Black mane, so he's—'

'—a bay, yes,' said Robin. 'Are you upset he isn't a panther, either?'

'Just trying to follow the logic. That stallion I found online – Blanc de Blancs – was chestnut, not white.'

'Not grey, you mean.'

'Fuck's sake,' muttered Strike, half-amused, half-exasperated.

65

I wonder how many there are who would do as much – who dare do it?

Henrik Ibsen, *Rosmersholm*

Brown Panther came in second. They spent Strike's winnings among the food and coffee tents, killing the hours of daylight until it was time to head for Woolstone and the dell. While panic fluttered in Robin's chest every time she thought of the tools in the back of the Land Rover and the dark basin full of nettles, Strike distracted her, whether intentionally or not, by a persistent refusal to explain how the testimony of Della Winn and Raphael Chiswell fitted together, or what conclusions he had drawn from it.

'Think,' he kept saying, 'just think.'

But Robin was exhausted, and it was easier to simply push him to explain over successive coffees and sandwiches, all the while savouring this unusual interlude in their working lives, for she and Strike had never before spent hours together unless at some time of crisis.

But as the sun sank ever closer to the horizon, Robin's thoughts darted more insistently towards the dell, and each time they did so her stomach did a small backflip. Noticing her increasingly preoccupied silences, Strike suggested for the second time that she stay in the Land Rover while he and Barclay dug.

'No,' said Robin tersely. 'I didn't come to sit in the car.'

It took them three-quarters of an hour to reach Woolstone. Colour was bleeding rapidly out of the sky to the west as they descended for the second time into the Vale of the White Horse, and by the time they had reached their destination a few feeble stars were spotting the dust-coloured heavens. Robin turned the Land Rover onto the overgrown track leading to Steda Cottage and the car rocked and pitched its way over the deep furrows and tangled thorns and branches, into the deeper darkness bestowed by the dense canopy above.

'Get as far in as you can,' Strike instructed her, checking the time on his mobile. 'Barclay's got to park behind us. He should've been here already, I told him nine o'clock.'

Robin parked and cut the engine, eyeing the thick woodland that lay between the track and Chiswell House. Unseen they might be, but they were still trespassing. Her anxiety about possible detection was as nothing, however, to her very real fear of what lay beneath the tangled nettles at the bottom of that dark basin outside Steda Cottage, and so she returned to the subject she had been using as a distraction all afternoon.

'I've told you – *think*,' said Strike, for the umpteenth time. 'Think about the lachesis pills. You're the one who thought they were significant. Think about all those odd things Chiswell kept doing: taunting Aamir in front of everyone, saying Lachesis "knew when everyone's number would be up", telling you "one by one, they trip themselves up", looking for Freddie's money clip, which turned up in his pocket.'

'I have thought about those things, but I still don't see how—'

'The helium and tubing entering the house disguised as a crate of champagne. Somebody knew he wouldn't want to drink it, because he was allergic. Ask yourself how Flick knew Jimmy had a claim on Chiswell. Think about Flick's row with her flatmate Laura—'

'How can *that* have anything to do with this?'

'Think!' said Strike, infuriatingly. 'No amitriptyline was found in the empty orange juice carton in Chiswell's bin. Remember Kinvara, obsessing over Chiswell's whereabouts. Have a guess what little Francesca at Drummond's art gallery is going to tell me if I ever get her on the phone. Think about that call to Chiswell's constituency office about people "pissing themselves as they die" – which isn't conclusive in itself, I grant you, but it's bloody suggestive when you stop to think about it—'

'You're winding me up,' said the incredulous Robin. 'Your idea connects all of that? And makes sense of it?'

'Yep,' said Strike smugly, 'and it also explains how Winn and Aamir knew there were photographs at the Foreign Office, presumably of Jack o'Kent's gallows in use, when Aamir hadn't worked there in months and Winn, so far as we know, had never set foot—'

Strike's mobile rang. He checked the screen.

'Izzy calling back. I'll take it outside. I want to smoke.'

He got out of the car. Robin heard him say, 'Hi,' before he slammed the door. She sat waiting for him, her mind buzzing. Either Strike had genuinely had a brainwave, or he was taking the mickey, and she slightly inclined to the latter, so utterly disconnected did the separate bits of information he had just listed seem.

Five minutes later, Strike returned to the passenger seat.

'Our client's unhappy,' he reported, slamming the door again. 'Tegan was supposed to be telling us that Kinvara crept back out that night to kill Chiswell, not confirming her alibi and blabbing about Chiswell flogging gallows.'

'Izzy admitted it?'

'Didn't have much choice, did she? But she didn't like it. Very insistent on telling me that exporting gallows was legal at the time. I put it to her that her father had defrauded Jimmy and Billy out of their money, and you were right. There were two sets of gallows built and ready to sell when Jack o'Kent died and nobody bothered to tell his sons. She liked admitting that even less.'

'D'you think she's worried they'll mount a claim on Chiswell's estate?'

'I can't see that it'd do Jimmy's reputation much good in the circles he moves in, accepting money made from hanging people in the Third World,' said Strike, 'but you never know.'

A car sped past on the road behind them and Strike craned around hopefully.

'Thought that might be Barclay . . . ' He checked his watch. 'Maybe he's missed the turning.'

'Cormoran,' said Robin, who was far less interested in either Izzy's mood or Barclay's whereabouts than in the theory Strike was withholding from her, 'have you *seriously* got an idea that explains everything you just told me?'

'Yeah,' said Strike, scratching his chin, 'I have. Trouble is, it brings us closer to *who*, but I'm still damned if I can see *why* they did it, unless it was done out of blind hatred – but this doesn't feel like a red-blooded crime of passion, does it? This wasn't a hammer round the head. This was a well-planned execution.'

'What happened to "means before motive"?'

'I've been concentrating on means. That's how I got here.'

'You won't even tell me "he" or "she"?'

'No good mentor would deprive you of the satisfaction of working it out for yourself. Any biscuits left?'

'No.'

'Lucky I've still got this, then,' Strike said, producing a Twix from his pocket, unwrapping it and handing her half, which she took with a bad grace that amused him.

Neither spoke until they had finished eating. Then Strike said, far more soberly than hitherto:

'Tonight's important. If there's nothing buried in a pink blanket at the bottom of the dell, the whole Billy business is finished: he imagined the strangling, we've set his mind at rest and I get to try and prove my theory about Chiswell's death, unencumbered by distractions, without worrying where a dead kid fits in and who killed her.'

'Or him,' Robin reminded Strike. 'You said Billy wasn't sure which it was.'

As she said it, her unruly imagination showed her a small skeleton wrapped in the rotten remains of a blanket. Would it be possible to tell whether the body had been male or female from what was left? Would there be a hair grip or a shoelace, buttons, a hank of long hair?

Let there be nothing, she thought. *God, let there be nothing there.*

But aloud, she asked:

'And if there *is* – something – someone – buried in the dell?'

'Then my theory's wrong, because I can't see how a child strangling in Oxfordshire fits with anything I've just mentioned.'

'It doesn't have to,' said Robin reasonably. 'You could be right about who killed Chiswell, and this could be an entirely separate—'

'No,' Strike said, shaking his head. 'It's too much of a coincidence. If there's something buried in the dell, it connects to everything else. One brother witnessing a murder as a child, the other blackmailing a murdered man twenty years later, the kid being buried on Chiswell's land . . . if there's a child buried in the dell, it fits in somewhere. But I'll lay odds there's nothing there. If I seriously thought there was a body in the dell, I'd've tried to persuade the police to do the job. Tonight's for Billy. I promised him.'

They sat watching the track fade gradually from sight in the darkness, Strike occasionally checking his mobile.

'Where's bloody Barclay got—? Ah!'

Headlights had just swung onto the track behind them. Barclay advanced an old Golf up the track and braked, turning off his lights. In her wing mirror, Robin watched his silhouette leave the car, turning into the flesh and blood Barclay as he reached Strike's window, carrying a kit bag just like the detective's.

'Evenin',' he said laconically. 'Nice night for a grave robbin'.'

'You're late,' said Strike.

'Aye, I know. Just got a call from Flick. Thought you'd want tae hear what she's got tae say.'

'Get in the back,' Strike suggested. 'You can tell us while we're waiting. We'll give it ten minutes, make sure it's properly dark.'

Barclay clambered into the back of the Land Rover and closed the doors. Strike and Robin twisted around in their seats to talk to him.

'So, she calls me, greetin'—'

'English translation, please.'

'Cryin', then – not to mention shittin' herself. The police came calling today.'

''Bout bloody time,' said Strike. 'And?'

'They searched the bathroom and found Chiswell's note. She's been interviewed.'

'What was her explanation for having it?'

'Didnae confide in me. All she wanted was to know where

Jimmy is. She's in a right fuckin' state. It was all "just tell Jimmy they've got it, he'll know whut I mean".'

'Where is Jimmy, d'you know?'

'Havenae a scooby. Saw him yesterday and he didnae mention any plans, but he told me he'd pissed off Flick by askin' if she had Bobbi Cunliffe's number. He took a liking to young Bobbi,' said Barclay, grinning at Robin. 'Flick told him she didnae know and wanted to know why he was so interested. Jimmy said he was jus' tryin' to get Bobbi along to a Real Socialist meetin', but, y'know, Flick's not that fuckin' dumb.'

'D'you think she realises it was me who tipped off the police?' asked Robin.

'Not yet,' said Barclay. 'She's panickin'.'

'All right,' said Strike, squinting up at the little of the sky they could see through the foliage overhead, 'I think we should get started. Grab that bag beside you, Barclay, I've got tools and gloves in there.'

'How're ye gonnae dig wi' your leg like that?' asked Barclay sceptically.

'You can't do it on your own,' said Strike, 'we'll still be here tomorrow night.'

'I'm digging, too,' said Robin firmly. She felt braver after Strike's assurances that they were highly unlikely to find anything in the dell. 'Pass me those wellies, Sam.'

Strike was already extracting torch and walking stick from his kit bag.

'I'll carry it,' offered Barclay, and there was a sound of heavy metal tools shifting as he hoisted Strike's bag onto his shoulder along with his own.

The three of them set off along the track, Robin and Barclay matching their pace to Strike's, who progressed carefully, focusing the beam of his torch on the ground and making regular use of the stick, both to lean on and push obstacles out of his way. Their footsteps were deadened by the soft ground, but the quiet night amplified the chink and clatter of the tools carried by Barclay, the rustling of tiny, unseen creatures fleeing the giants who had invaded their wilderness and, from the direction of Chiswell House, the barking of a dog. Robin remembered the Norfolk terrier, and hoped he wasn't loose.

When they reached the clearing, Robin saw that night had turned the derelict cottage into a witch's lair. It was easy to imagine figures lurking behind the cracked windows and, telling herself firmly that the situation was quite creepy enough without imagining fresh horrors, she turned away from it. With a soft 'ooft', Barclay let the kit bags fall onto the ground at the lip of the dell and unzipped both. By the light of the torch, Robin saw a wide array of tools: a pick, a mattock, two pinchbars, a fork, a small axe and three spades, one of them with a pointed head. There were also several pairs of thick gardening gloves.

'Aye, that should do us,' said Barclay, squinting into the dark basin below them. 'We'll want to clear that before we've got any chance o' breakin' the ground.'

'Right,' said Robin, reaching for a pair of gloves.

'Ye sure about this, big man?' Barclay asked Strike, who had done the same.

'I can pull up nettles, for Christ's sake,' said Strike irritably.

'Bring the axe, Robin,' said Barclay, grabbing the mattock and a pinchbar. 'Some o' those bushes'll need hacked down.'

The three of them slid and stumbled down the steep side of the dell and set to work. For nearly an hour they hacked at sinewy branches and tugged up nettles, occasionally swapping tools or returning to the upper ground to fetch different ones.

In spite of the gathering cool of the night, Robin was soon sweating, peeling off layers as she worked. Strike, on the other hand, was devoting a considerable amount of energy to pretending that the constant bending and twisting on slippery, uneven ground wasn't hurting the end of his stump. The darkness concealed his winces, and he was careful to rearrange his features whenever Barclay or Robin turned on the torch to check on their progress.

Physical activity was helping dispel Robin's fear of what could be hidden beneath their feet. Perhaps, she thought, this was what it was like in the army: hard manual work and the camaraderie of your colleagues helping you focus on something other than the grisly reality of what might lie ahead. The two ex-soldiers had bent to their task methodically and without complaint except for occasional curses as stubborn roots and branches tore at fabric and flesh.

'Time tae dig,' said Barclay at last, when the bottom of the basin was as clear as they could reasonably make it. 'Ye'll need to get out of it, Strike.'

'I'll start, Robin can take over,' said Strike. 'Go on,' he said to her, 'take a break, hold the torch steady for us and pass me down the fork.'

Growing up with three brothers had taught Robin valuable lessons about the male ego, and about picking her fights. Convinced that Strike's order was dictated more by pride than by sense, she nevertheless complied, clambering up the steep side of the dell, there to sit and hold the beam of the torch steady while they worked, occasionally passing down different tools to help them remove rocks and tackle particularly hard stretches of ground.

It was a slow job. Barclay dug three times as fast as Strike, who Robin could see was immediately struggling, especially with pressing the pointed head spade down into the earth with a foot, his prosthesis being unreliable if asked to support his entire weight on the uneven ground, and excruciating when pressed down against resistant metal. Minute by minute she held off intervening, until a muttered '*fuck*' escaped Strike, and he bent over, grimacing in pain.

'Shall I take over?' she suggested.

'Think you're going to have to,' he muttered ungraciously.

He dragged himself back out of the dell, trying not to put any more weight on his stump, taking the torch from a descending Robin and holding it steady for the other two as they worked, the end of his stump throbbing and, he suspected, rubbed raw.

Barclay had created a short channel a couple of feet deep before he took his first break, clambering out of the hole to fetch a bottle of water from his kit bag. While he drank and Robin took a rest, leaning on the handle of her spade, the sound of barking reached them again. Barclay squinted towards the unseen Chiswell House.

'What kind of dogs has she got in there?' he asked.

'Old Lab and a yappy bastard of a terrier,' said Strike.

'Don't like our chances if she lets them oot,' said Barclay, wiping his mouth on his arm. 'Terrier'll get straight through those bushes. They've got fuckin' good hearin', terriers.'

'Better hope she doesn't let them out, then,' said Strike, but he added, 'Give it five, Robin,' and turned off the torch.

Robin, too, climbed out of the basin and accepted a fresh bottle of water from Barclay. Now that she was no longer digging, the chill made her exposed flesh creep. The fluttering and scurrying of small creatures in the grass and trees seemed extraordinarily loud in the darkness. Still the dog barked, and, distantly, Robin thought she heard a woman shout.

'Did you hear that?'

'Aye. Sounded like she was telling it to shut up,' said Barclay.

They waited. At last, the terrier stopped barking.

'Give it a few more minutes,' said Strike. 'Let it fall asleep.'

They waited, the whispering of every leaf magnified in the darkness, until Robin and Barclay lowered themselves back into the dell and began to dig again.

Robin's muscles were now begging for mercy, her palms beginning to blister beneath the gloves. The deeper they dug, the harder the job became, the soil compacted and full of rocks. Barclay's end of the trench was considerably deeper than Robin's.

'Let me do a bit,' Strike suggested.

'No,' she snapped, too tired to be anything but blunt. 'You'll bugger your leg completely.'

'She's nae wrong, pal,' panted Barclay. 'Gie's another drink of water, I'm gaspin'.'

An hour later, Barclay was standing waist deep in soil and Robin's palms were bleeding beneath the overlarge gloves, which were rubbing away layers of skin as she used the blunt end of the mattock to try and prise a heavy rock out of the ground.

'Come – *on* – you – bloody – thing—'

'Want a hand?' offered Strike, readying himself to descend.

'Stay there,' she told him angrily. 'I'm not going to be able to help carry you back to the car, not after this—'

A final, involuntary yelp escaped her as she succeeded in overturning the small boulder. A couple of tiny, wriggling insects attached to the underside slid away from the torch-light. Strike directed the beam back on Barclay.

'Cormoran,' said Robin sharply.

'What?'

'I need light.'

Something in her voice made Barclay stop digging. Rather

than direct the beam back at her, and disregarding her warning of a moment ago, Strike slid back down into the pit, landing on the loose earth. The torchlight swung around, blinding Robin for a second.

'What've you seen?'

'Shine it here,' she said. 'On the rock.'

Barclay clambered towards them, his jeans covered from hem to pockets in soil.

Strike did as Robin asked. The three of them peered down at the encrusted surface of the rock. There, stuck to the mud, was a strand of what was plainly not vegetable matter, but wool fibres, faintly but distinctly pink.

They turned in unison to examine the indentation left in the ground where the rock had sat, Strike directing the torchlight into the hole.

'Oh, shit,' gasped Robin, and without thinking she clapped two muddy garden gloves to her face. A couple of inches of filthy material had been revealed, and in the strong beam of the torch, it, too, was pink.

'Give me that,' said Strike, tugging the mattock out of her hand.

'No—!'

But he almost pushed her aside. By the deflected torchlight she could see his expression, forbidding, furious, as though the pink blanket had grievously wronged him, as though he had suffered a personal affront.

'Barclay, you take this.'

He thrust the mattock at his subcontractor.

'Break this up, as much as you can. Try not to puncture the blanket. Robin, go to the other end. Use the fork. And mind my hands,' Strike told Barclay. Sticking the torch in his mouth so that he could see by its light, he fell to his knees in the dirt and began to move earth aside with his fingers.

'Listen,' whispered Robin, freezing.

The sound of the terrier's frenzied barking reached them once again through the night air.

'I yelled, didn't I, when I overturned the rock?' whispered Robin. 'I think I woke it up again.'

'Never mind that now,' said Strike, his fingers prising dirt away from the blanket. 'Dig.'

'But what if—?'

'We'll deal with that if it happens. *Dig.*'

Robin plied the fork. After a couple of minutes, Barclay swapped the mattock for a shovel. Slowly, the length of the pink blanket, its contents still buried too deep to remove, was revealed.

'That's no adult,' said Barclay, surveying the stretch of filthy blanket.

And still, the terrier continued to yap, distantly, from the direction of Chiswell House.

'We should call the polis, Strike,' said Barclay, pausing to wipe sweat and mud out of his eyes. 'Are we no disturbing a crime scene, here?'

Strike didn't answer. Feeling slightly sick, Robin watched his fingers feeling the shape of the thing that was hidden beneath the filthy blanket.

'Go up to my kit bag,' he told her. 'There's a knife in there. Stanley knife. Quickly.'

The terrier was still yapping distractedly. Robin thought it sounded louder. She clambered up the steep side of the dell, groped around in the dark depths of the bag, found the knife and slid back down to Strike.

'Cormoran, I think Sam's right,' she whispered. 'We should leave this to the—'

'Give me the knife,' he said, holding out his hand. 'Come on, quick, I can feel it. This is the skull. *Quickly!*'

Against her better instincts, she handed over the blade. There was a sound of puncturing fabric and then a ripping.

'What are you doing?' she gasped, watching Strike tugging at something in the ground.

'Jesus fuck, Strike,' said Barclay angrily, 'are ye tryin' to rip off its—?'

With a dreadful crunching noise, the earth gave up something large and white. Robin gave a small yelp, stepped backwards and fell, half-sitting, into the wall of the dell.

'Fuck,' repeated Barclay.

Strike shifted the torch to his free hand so as to shine it onto the thing he had just dragged out of the earth. Stunned, Robin and Barclay saw the discoloured and partially shattered skull of a horse.

66

Do not sit here musing and brooding over insoluble conundrums.

Henrik Ibsen, *Rosmersholm*

Protected through the years by the blanket, the skull shone pale in the torchlight, weirdly reptilian in the length of its nose and the sharpness of its mandibles. A few blunt teeth remained. There were cavities in the skull in addition to the eyeholes, one in the jaw, one to the side of the head, and around each, the bone was cracked and splintered.

'Shot,' said Strike, turning the skull slowly in his hands. A third indentation showed the course of another bullet, which had fractured but not penetrated the horse's head.

Robin knew she would have been feeling far worse had the skull been human, but she was nonetheless shaken by the noise it had made when released from the earth, and by the unexpected sight of this fragile shell of what had once lived and breathed, stripped bare by bacteria and insects.

'Vets euthanise horses with a single shot to the forehead,' she said. 'They don't spray them with bullets.'

'Rifle,' said Barclay authoritatively, clambering nearer to examine the skull. 'Someone's took pot shots at it.'

'Not that big, is it? Was it a foal?' Strike asked Robin.

'Maybe, but I think it looks more like a pony, or a miniature horse.'

He turned it slowly in his hands and all three of them watched the skull moving in the torchlight. They had expended so much pain and effort digging it out of the ground that it seemed to hold secrets beyond those of its mere existence.

'So Billy *did* witness a burial,' said Strike.

'But it wasn't a child. You won't have to rethink your theory,' said Robin.

'Theory?' repeated Barclay, and was ignored.

'I don't know, Robin,' said Strike, his face ghostly beyond the torchlight. 'If he didn't invent the burial, I don't think he invented—'

'Shit,' said Barclay. 'She's done it, she's let those fucking dogs out.'

The yapping of the terrier and the deeper, booming barks of the Labrador, no longer muffled by containing walls, came ringing through the night. Without ceremony, Strike dropped the skull.

'Barclay, grab all the tools and get out of here. We'll hold the dogs off.'

'What about—?'

'Leave it, there's no time to fill it in,' said Strike, already clambering out of the dell, ignoring the excruciating pain in the end of his stump. 'Robin, come on, you're with me—'

'What if she's called the police?' Robin said, reaching the top of the dell first and turning to help heave Strike up.

'We'll wing it,' he panted, 'come on, I want to stop the dogs before they get to Sam.'

The woods were dense and tangled. Strike had left his walking stick behind. Robin held his arm as he limped as fast as he could, grunting with pain every time he asked his stump to bear his weight. Robin glimpsed a pinprick of light through the trees. Somebody had come out of the house with a torch.

Suddenly, the Norfolk terrier burst through the undergrowth, barking ferociously.

'Good boy, yes, you found us!' Robin panted.

Ignoring her friendly overture it launched itself at her, trying to bite. She kicked out at it with her Wellingtoned foot, holding it at bay while sounds reached them of the heavier Labrador crashing towards them.

'Little fucker,' said Strike, trying to repel the Norfolk terrier as it darted around them, snarling, but seconds later the terrier had caught wind of Barclay: it turned its head towards the dell and, before either of them could stop it, took off again, yapping frenziedly.

'Shit,' said Robin.

'Never mind, keep going,' said Strike, though the end of his stump was burning and he wondered how much longer it would support him.

They had managed only a few more paces when the fat Labrador reached them.

'Good boy, yes, good boy,' Robin crooned, and the Labrador, less enthusiastic about the chase, allowed her to secure a tight grip on its collar. 'Come on, come with us,' said Robin, and she half dragged it, with Strike still leaning on her, towards the overgrown croquet lawn where they now saw a torch bobbing ever nearer through the darkness. A shrill voice called:

'Badger! Rattenbury! Who's that? Who's there?'

The silhouette behind the torchlight was female and bulky.

'It's all right, Mrs Chiswell!' called Robin. 'It's only us!'

'Who's "us"? Who are you?'

'Follow my lead,' Strike muttered to Robin, and he called, 'Mrs Chiswell, it's Cormoran Strike and Robin Ellacott.'

'What are you doing here?' she shouted, across the diminishing space between them.

'We were interviewing Tegan Butcher in the village, Mrs Chiswell,' called Strike, as he, Robin and the reluctant Badger made their laborious way through the long grass. 'We were driving back this way and we saw two people entering your property.'

'What two people? Where?'

'They entered the woods back there,' said Strike. From the depths of the trees, the Norfolk terrier was still frenziedly barking. 'We didn't have your number, or we'd have called to warn you.'

Within a few feet of her now, they saw that Kinvara was wearing a thick, padded coat over a short nightdress of black silk, her legs bare above Wellington boots. Her suspicion, shock and incredulity met Strike's total assurance.

'Thought we ought to do something, seeing as we were the only people who witnessed it,' he gasped, wincing a little as he hobbled up to her with Robin's assistance, self-deprecatingly heroic. 'Apologies,' he added, coming to a halt, 'for the state of us. Those woods are muddy and I fell over a couple of times.'

A cold breeze swept the dark lawn. Kinvara stared at him, flummoxed, suspicious, then turned her face in the direction of the terrier's continued barking.

'RATTENBURY!' she shouted. '*RATTENBURY!*'

She turned back to Strike.

'What did they look like?

'Men,' invented Strike, 'young and fit from the way they were moving. We knew you'd had trouble with trespassers before—'

'Yes. Yes, I have,' said Kinvara, sounding frightened. She

seemed to take in Strike's condition for the first time, as he leaned heavily on Robin, face contorted with pain.

'I suppose you'd better come in.'

'Thanks very much,' said Strike gratefully, 'very kind of you.'

Kinvara jerked the Labrador's collar out of Robin's grip and bellowed, 'RATTENBURY!' again, but the distantly barking terrier did not respond, so she dragged the Labrador, which was showing signs of rebellion, back towards the house, Robin and Strike following.

'What if she calls the police?' Robin muttered to Strike.

'Cross that bridge when we come to it,' he responded.

A floor-to-ceiling drawing room window stood open. Kinvara had evidently followed her frantic dogs through it, as the quickest route to the woods.

'We're pretty muddy,' Robin warned her, as they crunched their way across the gravel path that encircled the house.

'Just leave your boots outside,' said Kinvara, stepping into the drawing room without bothering to remove her own. 'I'm planning to change this carpet, anyway.'

Robin tugged off her wellies, followed Strike inside and closed the window.

The cold, dingy room was illuminated by a single lamp.

'Two men?' Kinvara repeated, turning again to Strike. 'Where exactly did you see them coming in?'

'Over the wall at the road,' said Strike.

'D'you think they knew you'd seen them?'

'Oh yeah,' said Strike. 'We pulled up, but they ran into the woods. Think they might've bottled it once we followed them, though, don't you?' he asked Robin.

'Yes,' said Robin, 'we think we heard them running back towards the road when you let the dogs out.'

'Rattenbury's still chasing someone – of course, that

could be a fox – he goes crazy about the foxes in the woods,' said Kinvara.

Strike's attention had just been caught by a change to the room since the last time he had seen it. There was a fresh square of dark crimson wallpaper over the mantelpiece, where the painting of the mare and foal had hung.

'What happened to your picture?' he asked.

Kinvara turned to see what Strike was talking about. She answered, perhaps a few seconds too late:

'I sold it.'

'Oh,' said Strike. 'I thought you were particularly fond of that one?'

'Not since what Torquil said that day. I didn't like having it hanging there, after that.'

'Ah,' said Strike.

Rattenbury's persistent barking continued to echo from the woods where, Strike was certain, it had found Barclay, struggling back to his car with two kit bags full of tools. Now that Kinvara had released her hold on its collar, the fat Labrador let out a single booming bark and trotted to the window, where it began whining and pawing at the glass.

'The police won't get here in time even if I call them,' said Kinvara, half worried, half angry. 'I'm never top priority. They think I make it all up, these intruders.

'I'm going to check on the horses,' she said, coming to a decision, but instead of going out through the window, she stomped out of the drawing room into the hall and from there, as far as they could hear, into a different room.

'I hope the dog hasn't got Barclay,' Robin whispered.

'Better hope he hasn't brained it with a spade,' muttered Strike.

The door reopened. Kinvara had returned, and to Robin's consternation, she was carrying a revolver.

'I'll take that,' said Strike, hobbling forwards and taking the revolver out of her startled grip. He examined it. 'Harrington & Richardson 7-shot? This is illegal, Mrs Chiswell.'

'It was Jasper's,' she replied, as though this constituted a special permit, 'and I'd rather take—'

'I'll come with you to check on the horses,' said Strike firmly, 'and Robin can stay here and keep an eye on the house.'

Kinvara might have liked to protest, but Strike was already opening the drawing room window. Seizing its opportunity, the Labrador lumbered back out into the dark garden, its deep barks echoing around the grounds.

'Oh, for God's sake – you shouldn't have let him out – Badger!' shouted Kinvara. She whipped back around to Robin, said, 'mind you stay in this room!' then followed the Labrador back into the garden, Strike limping after her with the revolver. Both disappeared into the darkness. Robin stood where they had left her, struck by the vehemence of Kinvara's order.

The open window had admitted plenty of night air into what was already a chilly interior. Robin approached the log basket beside the fire, which was temptingly full of newspaper, sticks, logs and firelighters, but she could hardly build a fire in Kinvara's absence. The room was as shabby in every respect as she remembered it, the walls now denuded of everything but four prints of Oxfordshire landscapes. Outside in the grounds the two dogs continued to bark, but inside the room the only sound, which Robin hadn't noticed on her last visit, due to the family's talking and bickering, was the loud ticking of an old grandfather clock in the corner.

Every muscle in Robin's body was starting to ache after the long hours of digging, and her blistered hands were smarting. She had just sat down on the sagging sofa, hugging herself for warmth, when she heard a creak overhead that sounded very like a footstep.

Robin stared up at the ceiling. She had probably imagined it. Old houses made strange noises that sounded human until they were familiar to you. Her parents' radiators made chugging noises in the night and their old doors groaned in the central heating. It was probably nothing.

A second creak sounded, several feet from where the first had occurred.

As she got to her feet, Robin scanned the room for anything she could use as a weapon. A small, ugly bronze frog ornament sat on a table beside the sofa. As her fingers closed over the cold pockmarked surface, she heard a third creak from overhead. Unless she was imagining it, the footsteps had now moved all the way across a room directly above the one in which she was.

Robin stood quite still for almost a minute, straining her ears. She knew what Strike would say: stay put. Then she heard another tiny movement overhead. Somebody, she was sure, was creeping around upstairs.

Moving as quietly as possible in her socked feet, Robin edged around the drawing room door without touching it, in case it creaked, and walked quietly into the middle of the stone-flagged hall, where the hanging lantern cast a patchy light. She came to a halt beneath it, straining her ears, heart bumping erratically, imagining an unknown person standing above her, also frozen, listening, waiting. Bronze frog still clutched in her right hand, she moved to the foot of the stairs. The landing above her was in darkness. The sound of the dogs' barking echoed from deep in the woods.

She was halfway towards the upper landing when she thought she heard another small noise above her: the scuff of a foot on carpet followed by the swish of a closing door.

She knew that there was no point calling out 'Who's there?' If the person hiding from her had been prepared to show their face, they would hardly have let Kinvara leave the house alone to face whatever had set off the dogs.

Reaching the top of the stairs, Robin saw that a vertical strip of light lay like a spectral finger across the dark floor, emanating from the only lit room. Her neck and scalp prickled as she crept towards it, afraid that the unknown lurker was watching from one of the three dark rooms with open doors she was passing. Constantly checking over her shoulder, she pushed the door of the lit bedroom with the tips of her fingers, raised the bronze frog high and entered.

This was clearly Kinvara's room: messy, cluttered and deserted. A single lamp burned on the bedside table nearest the door. The bed was unmade, with an air of having been left in a hurry, the cream quilted eiderdown lying crumpled on the floor. The walls were covered with many pictures of horses, all of them of significantly lesser quality, even to Robin's untutored eye, than the missing picture in the drawing room. The wardrobe doors stood open, but only a Lilliputian could have been hidden among the densely packed clothes within.

Robin returned to the dark landing. Taking a tighter grip on the bronze frog, she orientated herself. The sounds she had heard had come from a room directly overhead, which meant that it was probably the one with the closed door, facing her.

As she reached out her hand towards the doorknob, the terrifying sensation that unseen eyes were watching intensified. Pushing the door open, she felt around on the interior wall without entering, until she found a light switch.

The stark light revealed a cold, bare bedroom with a brass bedstead and a single chest of drawers. The heavy curtains on their old fashioned brass rings had been drawn, hiding the grounds. On the double bed lay the painting, 'Mare Mourning', the brown and white mare forever nosing the pure white foal curled up in the straw.

Groping in the pocket of her jacket with the hand not holding the bronze paperweight, Robin found her mobile and took several photographs of the painting lying on the bedspread. It had the appearance of having been hastily placed there.

She had a sudden feeling that something had moved behind her. She whipped around, trying to blink away the shining impression of the gilded frame burned into her retina by the flash on her camera. Then she heard Strike's and Kinvara's voices growing louder in the garden and knew that they were returning to the drawing room.

Slapping off the light in the spare room, Robin ran as quietly as possible back across the landing and down the stairs. Fearing that she wouldn't be able to reach the drawing room in time to greet them, she darted to the downstairs bathroom, flushed the toilet, and then ran back across the hall, reaching the drawing room just as her hostess re-entered it from the garden.

67

. . . I had good reason enough for so jealously drawing a veil of concealment over our compact.

Henrik Ibsen, *Rosmersholm*

The Norfolk terrier was struggling in Kinvara's arms, its paws muddy. At the sight of Robin, Rattenbury set up a volley of barking again and struggled to get free.

'Sorry, I was dying for the loo,' panted Robin, the bronze frog hidden behind her back. The old cistern backed up her story, making loud gushing and clanking noises that echoed through the stone-flagged hallway. 'Any luck?' Robin called to Strike, who was climbing back into the room behind Kinvara.

'Nothing,' said Strike, now haggard with pain. After waiting for the panting Labrador to hop back into the room, he closed the window, the revolver in his other hand. 'There were definitely people out there, though. The dogs knew it, but I think they've taken off. What were the odds of us passing just as they were climbing over the wall?'

'Oh, do *shut up*, Rattenbury!' shouted Kinvara.

She set the terrier down and, when it refused to stop yapping at Robin, she threatened it with a raised hand, at which it whimpered and retreated into a corner to join the Labrador.

'Horses OK?' Robin asked, moving to the end table from which she had taken the bronze paperweight.

'One of the stable doors wasn't fastened properly,' said Strike, wincing as he bent to feel his knee. 'But Mrs Chiswell thinks it might have been left like that. Would you mind if I sat down, Mrs Chiswell?'

'I – no, I suppose not,' Kinvara said gracelessly.

She headed to a table of bottles sitting in the corner of the room, uncorked some Famous Grouse and poured herself a stiff measure of whisky. While her back was turned, Robin slid the paperweight back onto the table. She tried to catch Strike's eyes, but he had sunk down onto the sofa with a faint groan, and now turned to Kinvara.

'I wouldn't say no, if you're offering,' he said shamelessly, wincing again as he massaged his right knee. 'Actually, I think this is going to have to come off, do you mind?'

'Well – no, I suppose not. What do you want?'

'I'll have a Scotch as well, please,' said Strike, setting the revolver down on the table beside the bronze frog, rolling up his trouser leg and signalling with his eyes that Robin, too, should sit down.

While Kinvara sloshed another measure into a glass, Strike started to remove the prosthesis. Turning to give him his drink, Kinvara watched in queasy fascination as Strike worked on the false leg, averting her eyes at the point it left the inflamed stump. Panting as he propped the prosthesis against the ottoman, Strike allowed his trouser leg to fall back over his amputated leg.

'Thanks very much,' he said, accepting the whisky from her and taking a swig.

Trapped with a man who couldn't walk, to whom she

ought in theory to be grateful, and to whom she had just given a drink, Kinvara sat down, too, her expression stony.

'Actually, Mrs Chiswell, I was going to phone you to confirm a couple of things we heard from Tegan earlier,' said Strike. 'We could go through them now if you like. Get them out of the way.'

With a slight shiver, Kinvara glanced at the empty fireplace, and Robin said helpfully, 'Would you like me to—?'

'No,' snapped Kinvara. 'I can do it.'

She went to the deep basket standing beside the fireplace, from which she grabbed an old newspaper. While Kinvara built a structure of small bits of wood over a mound of newspaper and a firelighter, Robin succeeded in catching Strike's eye.

'There's somebody upstairs,' she mouthed, but she wasn't sure he had understood. He merely raised his eyebrows quizzically, and turned back to Kinvara.

A match flared. Flames erupted around the little pile of paper and sticks in the fireplace. Kinvara picked up her glass and returned to the drinks table, where she topped it up with more neat Scotch, then, coat wrapped more tightly around herself, she returned to the log basket, selected a large piece of wood, dropped it on top of the burgeoning fire, then fell back onto the sofa.

'Go on, then,' she said sullenly to Strike. 'What do you want to know?'

'As I say, we spoke to Tegan Butcher today.'

'And?'

'And we now know what Jimmy Knight and Geraint Winn were blackmailing your husband about.'

Kinvara evinced no surprise.

'I told those stupid girls you'd find out,' she said with a shrug. 'Izzy and Fizzy. Everyone round here knew what

Jack o'Kent was doing in the barn. Of course somebody was going to talk.'

She took a gulp of whisky.

'I suppose you know all of it, do you? The gallows? The boy in Zimbabwe?'

'You mean Samuel?' asked Strike, taking a punt.

'Exactly, Samuel Mu – Mudrap or something.'

The fire caught suddenly, flames leaping up past the log, which shifted in a shower of sparks.

'Jasper was worried they were his gallows the moment we heard the boy had been hanged. You know all of it, do you? That there were two sets? But only one made it to the government. The other lot went astray, the lorry was hijacked or something. That's how they ended up in the middle of nowhere.

'The photographs are pretty grisly, apparently. The Foreign Office thinks it was probably a case of mistaken identity. Jasper didn't see how they could be traced to him, but Jimmy said he could prove they were.

'I *knew* you'd find out,' said Kinvara, with an air of bitter satisfaction. 'Tegan's a horrible gossip.'

'So, to be clear,' said Strike, 'when Jimmy Knight first came here to see you, he was asking for his and Billy's share for two sets of gallows his father had left completed when he died?'

'Exactly,' said Kinvara, sipping her whisky. 'They were worth eighty thousand for the pair. He wanted forty.'

'But presumably,' said Strike, who remembered that Chiswell had talked of Jimmy returning a week after his first attempt to get money, and asking for a reduced amount, 'your husband told him he'd only ever received payment for one of them, as one set got stolen en route?'

'Yes,' said Kinvara, with a shrug. 'So then Jimmy asked for twenty, but we'd spent it.'

'How did you feel about Jimmy's request, when he first came asking for money?' Strike asked.

Robin wasn't sure whether Kinvara had turned a little pinker in the face, or whether it was the effects of the whisky.

'Well, I saw his point, if you want the truth. I could see why he felt he had a claim. Half the proceeds of the gallows belonged to the Knight boys. That had been the arrangement while Jack o'Kent was alive, but Jasper took the view that Jimmy couldn't expect money for the stolen set, and given that he'd been storing them in his barn, and bearing all the costs of transportation and so on . . . and he said that Jimmy couldn't sue him even if he wanted to. He didn't like Jimmy.'

'No, well, I suppose their politics were very different,' said Strike.

Kinvara almost smirked.

'It was a bit more personal than that. Haven't you heard about Jimmy and Izzy? No . . . I suppose Tegan's too young to have heard that story. Oh, it was only once,' she said, apparently under the impression that Strike was shocked, 'but that was quite enough for Jasper. A man like Jimmy Knight, deflowering his darling daughter, you know . . .

'But Jasper couldn't have given Jimmy the money even if he'd wanted to,' she went on. 'He'd already spent it. It took care of our overdraft for a while and repaired the stable roof. I never knew,' she added, as though sensing unspoken criticism, 'until Jimmy explained it to me that night, what the arrangement between Jasper and Jack o'Kent had been. Jasper had told me the gallows were his to sell and I believed him. *Naturally* I believed him. He was my husband.'

She got up again and headed back to the drinks table as the fat Labrador, seeking warmth, left its distant corner, waddled around the ottoman and slumped down in front of the now roaring fire. The Norfolk terrier trotted after it, growling at Strike and Robin until Kinvara said angrily:

'*Shut up*, Rattenbury.'

'There are a couple more things I wanted to ask you about,' said Strike. 'Firstly, did your husband have a passcode on his phone?'

'Of course he did,' said Kinvara. 'He was very security-conscious.'

'So he didn't give it out to a lot of people?'

'He didn't even tell *me* what it was,' said Kinvara. 'Why are you asking?'

Ignoring the question, Strike said:

'Your stepson's now told us a different story to account for his trip down here, on the morning of your husband's death.'

'Oh, really? What's he saying this time?'

'That he was trying to stop you selling a necklace that's been in the family for—'

'Come clean, has he?' she interrupted, turning back towards them with a fresh whisky in her hands. With her long red hair tangled from the night air, and her flushed cheeks, she had a slight air of abandon now, forgetting to hold her coat closed as she headed back to the sofa, the black nightdress revealing a canyon of cleavage. She flopped back down on the sofa. 'Yes, he wanted to stop me doing a flit with the necklace, which, by the way, I'm *perfectly* entitled to do. It's mine under the terms of the will. Jasper should have been a bit more bloody careful writing it if he didn't want me to have it, shouldn't he?'

Robin remembered Kinvara's tears, the last time they had been in this room, and how she had felt sorry for her, unlikeable though she had shown herself to be in other ways. Her attitude now had little of the grief-stricken widow about it, but perhaps, Robin thought, that was the drink, and the recent shock of their intrusion into her grounds.

'So you're backing up Raphael's story that he drove down here to stop you taking off with the necklace?'

'Don't you believe him?'

'Not really,' said Strike. 'No.'

'Why not?'

'It rings false,' said Strike. 'I'm not convinced your husband was in a fit state that morning to remember what he had and hadn't put in his will.'

'He was well enough to call me and demand to know whether I was really walking out on him,' said Kinvara.

'Did you tell him you were going to sell the necklace?'

'Not in so many words, no. I said I was going to leave as soon as I could find somewhere else for me and the horses. I suppose he might have wondered how I'd manage that, with no real money of my own, which made him remember the necklace.'

'So Raphael came here out of simple loyalty to the father who'd cut him off without a penny?'

Kinvara subjected Strike to a long and penetrating look over her whisky glass, then said to Robin:

'Would you throw another log on the fire?'

Noting the lack of a 'please', Robin nevertheless did as she was asked. The Norfolk terrier, which had now joined the sleeping Labrador on the hearthrug, growled at her until she had sat down again.

'All right,' said Kinvara, with an air of coming to a decision. 'All right, here it is. I don't suppose it matters any more, anyway. Those bloody girls will find out in the end and serve Raphael right.

'He *did* come down to try and stop me taking the necklace, but it wasn't for Jasper, Fizzy or Flopsy's sake – I suppose,' she said aggressively to Robin, 'you know all the family nicknames, don't you? You probably had a good giggle at them, while you were working with Izzy?'

'Erm—'

'Oh, don't pretend,' said Kinvara, rather nastily, 'I know you'll have heard them. They call me "Tinky Two" or something, don't they? And behind his back, Izzy, Fizzy and Torquil call Raphael "Rancid". Did you know that?'

'No,' said Robin, at whom Kinvara was still glaring.

'Sweet, isn't it? And Raphael's mother is known to all of them as the Orca, because she dresses in black and white.

'Anyway . . . when the Orca realised Jasper wasn't going to marry her,' said Kinvara, now very red in the face, 'd'you know what she did?'

Robin shook her head.

'She took the famous family necklace to the man who became her *next* lover, who was a diamond merchant, and she had him prise out the really valuable stones and replace them with cubic zirconias. Man-made diamond substitutes,' Kinvara elucidated, in case Strike and Robin hadn't understood. 'Jasper never realised what she'd done and I certainly didn't. I expect Ornella's been having a jolly good laugh every time I've been photographed in the necklace, thinking I'm wearing a hundred thousand pounds' worth of stones.

'Anyway, when my darling stepson got wind of the fact that I was leaving his father, and heard that I'd talked about having enough money to buy land for the horses, he twigged that I might be about to get the necklace valued. So he came hotfooting it down here, because the last thing he wanted was for the family to find out what his mother had done. What would be the odds of him wheedling his way back into his father's good books after that?'

'Why haven't you told anyone this?' asked Strike.

'Because Raphael promised me that morning that if I didn't tell his father what the Orca had done, he'd maybe manage to persuade his mother to give the stones back. Or at least, give me their value.'

'And are you still trying to recover the missing stones?'

Kinvara squinted malevolently at Strike over the rim of her glass.

'I haven't done anything about it since Jasper died, but that doesn't mean I won't. Why should I let the bloody Orca waltz off with what's rightfully mine? It's down in Jasper's will, the contents of the house that haven't been spefi – specif – spe-cif-ically excluded,' she enunciated carefully, thick-tongued now, 'belong to me. So,' she said, fixing Strike with a gimlet stare, 'does *that* sound more like Raphael to you? Coming down here to try and cover up for his darling mama?'

'Yes,' said Strike, 'I'd have to say it does. Thank you for your honesty.'

Kinvara looked pointedly at the grandfather clock, which was now showing three in the morning, but Strike refused to take the hint.

'Mrs Chiswell, there's one last thing I want to ask and I'm afraid it's quite personal.'

'What?' she said crossly.

'I spoke to Mrs Winn recently. Della Winn, you know, the—'

'Della-Winn-the-Minister-for-Sport,' said Kinvara, just as her husband had done, the first time Strike met him. 'Yes, I know who she is. Very odd woman.'

'In what way?'

Kinvara wriggled her shoulders impatiently, as though it should be obvious.

'Never mind. What did she say?'

'That she met you in a state of considerable distress a year ago and that from what she could gather, you were upset because your husband had admitted to an affair.'

Kinvara opened her mouth then closed it again. She sat thus for a few seconds, then shook her head as though to clear it and said:

'I . . . thought he was being unfaithful, but I was wrong. I got it all wrong.'

'According to Mrs Winn, he'd said some fairly cruel things to you.'

'I don't remember what I said to her. I wasn't very well at the time. I was overemotional and I got everything wrong.'

'Forgive me,' said Strike, 'but, as an outsider, your marriage seemed—'

'What a dreadful job you've got,' said Kinvara shrilly. 'What a really nasty, *seedy* job you do. Yes, our marriage was going wrong, what of it? Do you think, now he's dead, now he's *killed himself*, I want to relive it all with the pair of *you*, perfect strangers whom my stupid stepdaughters have dragged in, to stir everything up and make it ten times worse?'

'So you've changed your mind, have you? You think your husband committed suicide? Because when we were last here, you suggested Aamir Mallik—'

'I don't know what I said then!' she said hysterically. 'Can you not understand what it's been like since Jasper killed himself, with the police and the family and *you*? I didn't think this would happen, I had no idea, it didn't seem real – Jasper was under enormous pressure those last few months, drinking too much, in an awful temper – the blackmail, the fear of it all coming out – yes, I think he killed himself and I've got to live with the fact that I walked out on him that morning, which was probably the final straw!'

The Norfolk terrier began to yap furiously again. The Labrador woke with a start and started barking, too.

'Please leave!' shouted Kinvara, getting to her feet. 'Get

out! I never wanted you mixed up in this in the first place! Just go, will you?'

'Certainly,' said Strike politely, setting down his empty glass. 'Would you mind waiting while I get my leg back on?'

Robin had already stood up. Strike strapped the false leg back on while Kinvara watched, chest heaving, glass in hand. At last, Strike was ready to stand, but his first attempt had him falling back onto the sofa. With Robin's assistance, he finally achieved a standing position.

'Well, goodbye, Mrs Chiswell.'

Kinvara's only answer was to stalk to the window and fling it open again, shouting at the dogs, which had got up excitedly, to stay put.

No sooner had her unwelcome guests stepped out onto the gravel path than Kinvara slammed the window behind them. While Robin put her Wellington boots back on, they heard the shriek of the brass curtain rings as Kinvara dragged the drapes shut, then called the dogs out of the room.

'Not sure I'm going to be able to make it back to the car, Robin,' said Strike, who wasn't putting weight on his prosthesis. 'In retrospect, the digging might've . . . might've been a mistake.'

Wordlessly, Robin took his arm and placed it over her shoulders. He didn't resist. Together they moved slowly off across the grass.

'Did you understand what I mouthed at you back there?' asked Robin.

'That there was someone upstairs? Yeah,' he said, wincing horribly every time he put down his false foot. 'I did.'

'You don't seem—'

'I'm not surpr – wait,' he said abruptly, still leaning on her as he came to a halt. 'You didn't go up there?'

'Yes,' said Robin.

'*For fuck's sake—*'

'I heard footsteps.'

'And what would've happened if you'd been jumped?'

'I took a weapon and I wasn't – and if I hadn't gone up there, I wouldn't have seen this.'

Taking out her mobile, Robin brought up the photo of the painting on the bed, and handed it to him.

'You didn't see Kinvara's expression, when she saw the blank wall. Cormoran, she didn't realise that painting had been moved until you asked about it. Whoever was upstairs tried to hide it while she was outside.'

Strike stared at the phone screen for what felt like a long time, his arm heavy on Robin's shoulders. Finally, he said:

'Is that a piebald?'

'Seriously?' said Robin, in total disbelief. 'Horse colours? Now?'

'Answer me.'

'No, piebalds are black and white, not brown and—'

'We need to go to the police,' said Strike. 'The odds on another murder just went up exponentially.'

'You aren't serious?'

'I'm completely serious. Get me back to the car and I'll tell you everything . . . but don't ask me to talk till then, because my leg's fucking killing me.'

68

I have tasted blood now . . .

Henrik Ibsen, *Rosmersholm*

Three days later, Strike and Robin received an unprecedented invitation. As a courtesy for having chosen to aid rather than upstage the police in passing on information about Flick's stolen note and 'Mare Mourning', the Met welcomed the detective partners into the heart of the investigation at New Scotland Yard. Used to being treated by the police as either inconveniences or showboaters, Strike and Robin were surprised but grateful for this unforeseen thawing of relations.

On arrival, the tall blonde Scot who was heading the team ducked out of an interrogation room for a minute to shake hands. Strike and Robin knew that the police had brought two suspects in for questioning, although nobody had yet been charged.

'We spent the morning on hysterics and flat denial,' DCI Judy McMurran told them, 'but I think we'll have cracked her by the end of the day.'

'Any chance we could give them a little look, Judy?' asked her subordinate, DI George Layborn, who had met Strike and Robin at the door and brought them upstairs. He was a pudgy man who reminded Robin of the traffic policeman who had thought he was such a card, back on the hard shoulder where she'd had her panic attack.

'Go on, then,' said DCI McMurran, with a smile.

Layborn led Strike and Robin around a corner and through the first door on their right into a dark and cramped area, of which half one wall was a two-way mirror into an interrogation room.

Robin, who had only ever seen such spaces in films and on TV, was mesmerised. Kinvara Chiswell was sitting on one side of a desk, beside a thin-lipped solicitor in a pinstriped suit. White-faced, devoid of make-up, wearing a pale grey silk blouse so creased she might have slept in it, Kinvara was weeping into a tissue. Opposite her sat another detective inspector in a far cheaper suit than the solicitor's. His expression was impassive.

As they watched, DCI McMurran re-entered the room and took the vacant chair beside her colleague. After what felt like a very long time, but was probably only a minute, DCI McMurran spoke.

'Still nothing to say about your night at the hotel, Mrs Chiswell?'

'This is like a nightmare,' whispered Kinvara. 'I can't believe this is happening. I can't believe I'm here.'

Her eyes were pink, swollen and apparently lashless now that she had wept her mascara away.

'Jasper killed himself,' she said tremulously. 'He was depressed! Everyone will tell you so! The blackmail was eating away at him . . . have you talked to the Foreign Office yet? Even the idea that there might be photographs of that boy who was hanged – can't you see how scared Jasper was? If that had come out—'

Her voice cracked.

'Where's your evidence against me?' she demanded. 'Where is it? *Where?*'

Her solicitor gave a dry little cough.

'To return,' said DCI McMurran, 'to the subject of the hotel. Why do you think your husband called them, trying to ascertain—'

'It isn't a crime to go to a hotel!' said Kinvara hysterically, and she turned to her solicitor, 'This is ridiculous, Charles, how can they make a case against me because I went to a—'

'Mrs Chiswell will answer any questions you've got about her birthday,' the solicitor told DCI McMurran, with what Robin thought was remarkable optimism, 'but equally—'

The door of the observation room opened and hit Strike.

'No problem, we'll shift,' Layborn told his colleague. 'Come on, gang, we'll go to the incident room. Got plenty more to show you.'

As they turned a second corner, they saw Eric Wardle walking towards them.

'Never thought I'd see the day,' he said, grinning as he shook Strike's hand. 'Actually invited in by the Met.'

'You staying, Wardle?' asked Layborn, who seemed faintly resentful at the prospect of another policeman sharing the guests he was keen to impress.

'Might as well,' said Wardle. 'Find out what I've been assisting in, all these weeks.'

'Must've taken its toll,' said Strike, as they followed Layborn into the incident room, 'passing on all that evidence we found.'

Wardle sniggered.

Used as she was to the cramped and slightly dilapidated offices in Denmark Street, Robin was fascinated to see the space that Scotland Yard devoted to the investigation into a high profile and suspicious death. A whiteboard on the wall carried a timeline for the killing. The adjacent wall bore a collage of photographs of the death scene and the corpse, the latter showing Chiswell freed from his plastic wrapping, so that his congested face appeared in awful close-up, with a livid scratch down one cheek, the cloudy eyes half open, the skin a dark, mottled purple.

Spotting her interest, Layborn showed her the toxicology reports and phone records that the police had used to build their case, then unlocked the large cupboard where physical evidence was bagged and tagged, including the cracked tube of lachesis pills, a grubby orange juice carton and Kinvara's farewell letter to her husband. Seeing the note that Flick had stolen, and a printout of the photograph of 'Mare Mourning' lying on a spare bed, both of which Robin knew had now become central to the police case, she experienced a rush of pride.

'Right then,' said DI Layborn, closing the cupboard and walking over to a computer monitor. 'Time to see the little lady in action.'

He inserted a video disc in the nearest machine, beckoning Strike, Robin and Wardle closer.

The crowded forecourt of Paddington station was revealed, jerky black and white figures moving everywhere. The time and date showed in the upper left corner.

'There she is,' said Layborn, hitting 'pause' and pointing a stubby finger at a woman. 'See her?'

Even though blurred, the figure was recognisable as Kinvara. A bearded man had been caught in the frame, staring, probably because her coat hung open, revealing the clinging black dress she had worn to the Paralympian reception. Layborn pressed 'play' again.

'Watch her, watch her – gives to the homeless—'

Kinvara had donated to a swaddled man holding a cup in a doorway.

'—watch her,' Layborn said unnecessarily, 'straight up to the railway worker – pointless question – shows him her ticket . . . watch her, now . . . off to the platform, stops and asks another bloke a question, making sure she's remembered every bloody step of the way, even if she's not caught on camera . . . *aaaand* . . . onto the train.'

The picture twitched and changed. A train was pulling into the station at Swindon. Kinvara got off, talking to another woman.

'See?' said Layborn. 'Still making damn sure people remember her, just in case. And—'

The picture changed again, to that of the car park at Swindon station.

'—there she is,' said Layborn, 'car's parked right near the camera, conveniently. In she gets and off she goes. Gets home, insists the stable girl stays overnight, sleeps in the next room, goes outside next morning to ride within sight of the girl . . . cast-iron alibi.

'Course, like you, we'd already come to the conclusion that if it was murder, it must have been a two-person job.'

'Because of the orange juice?' asked Robin.

'Mostly,' said Layborn. 'If Chiswell' (he said the name as it was spelled) 'had taken amitriptyline unknowingly, the most likely explanation was that he'd poured himself doctored juice out of a carton in the fridge, but the carton in the bin was undoctored and only had his prints on.'

'Easy to get his prints on small objects once he was dead, though,' said Strike. 'Just press his hand onto them.'

'Exactly,' said Layborn, striding over to the wall of photographs and pointing at a close-up of the pestle and mortar. 'So we went back to this. The way Chiswell's prints are positioned and the way the powdered residue was sitting there pointed to it being faked, which meant the doctored juice could have been fixed up hours in advance, by somebody who had a key, who knew which anti-depressants the wife was on, that Chiswell's sense of taste and smell were impaired and that he always drank juice in the mornings. Then all they'd need to do is have the accomplice plant an undoctored juice carton in the bin with his dead handprint on, and take away the one with the amitriptyline residue in it.

'Well, who's better positioned to know and do all of that, than the missus?' asked Layborn rhetorically. 'But here she was, with her cast-iron alibi for time of death, seventy-odd miles away when he was gulping down anti-depressants. Not to mention she's left that letter, trying to give us a nice clean story: husband already facing bankruptcy and blackmail realises his wife's leaving him, which tips him over the edge, so he tops himself.

'But,' said Layborn, pointing at the enlarged picture of the dead Chiswell's face, stripped of its plastic bag, revealing a deep red scrape on the cheek, 'we didn't like the look of *that*. We thought from the first that was suspicious. Amitriptyline in overdose can cause agitation as well as sleepiness. That mark looked as though somebody else forced the bag over his head.

'Then there was the open door. The last person in or out didn't know there was a trick to closing it properly, so it didn't look like Chiswell was the last person to touch it. Plus, the packaging on the pills being absent – that smelled wrong from the start. Why would Jasper Chiswell get rid of it?' asked Layborn. 'Just a few little careless mistakes.'

'It nearly came off,' said Strike. 'If only Chiswell had been put to sleep by the amitriptyline as intended, and if they'd thought the thing through right to the finest details – close the door properly, leave the pill packaging *in situ*—'

'But they didn't,' said Layborn, 'and *she's* not smart enough on her own to talk herself out of this.'

'"I can't believe this is happening",' Strike quoted. 'She's consistent. On Saturday night she told us "I didn't think this would happen", "it didn't seem real—"'

'Try that in court,' said Wardle quietly.

'Yeah, what were you expecting, love, when you crushed up a load of pills and put them in his orange juice?' said Layborn. 'Guilty is as guilty does.'

'Amazing, the lies people can tell themselves when they're drifting along in the wake of a stronger personality,' said Strike. 'I'll bet you a tenner that when McMurran finally breaks her, Kinvara'll say they started off hoping Chiswell would kill himself, then trying to pressure him into doing it, and finally reached a point when there didn't seem much difference between trying to push him into suicide, and putting the pills in his orange juice herself. I notice she's still trying to push the gallows business as the reason he'd top himself.'

'That was very good work of yours, connecting the dots on the gallows,' admitted Layborn. 'We were a bit behind you on that, but it explained a hell of a lot. This is highly confidential,' he added, taking a brown envelope off a nearby desk and tipping out a large photograph, 'but we had this from the Foreign Office this morning. As you can see—'

Robin, who had gone to look, half-wished she hadn't. What was there to be gained, really, from seeing the corpse of what seemed to be a teenage boy, whose eyes had been picked out by carrion birds, and hanging from a gallows in a rubble-strewn street? The boy's dangling feet were bare. Somebody, Robin guessed, had stolen his trainers.

'The lorry containing the second pair of gallows was hijacked. Government never took delivery and Chiswell never got payment for them. This picture suggests they ended up being used by rebels for extrajudicial killings. This poor lad, Samuel Murape, was in the wrong place at the wrong time. British student, gap year, out there to visit family. It's not particularly clear,' Layborn said, 'but see there, just behind his foot—'

'Yeah, that could be the mark of the white horse,' said Strike.

Robin's mobile, which was switched to silent, vibrated in her pocket. She was waiting for an important call, but it was only a text from an unknown number.

> **I know you've blocked my phone, but I need to meet you. An urgent situation's come up and it's to your advantage as much as mine to sort it out. Matt**

'It's nothing,' Robin told Strike, returning the mobile to her pocket.

This was the third message Matthew had left that day.

Urgent situation, my arse.

Tom had probably found out that his fiancée and his good friend had been sleeping together. Maybe Tom was threatening to call Robin, or drop in on the office in Denmark Street, to find out how much she knew. If Matthew thought that constituted an 'urgent situation' to Robin, who was currently standing beside multiple pictures of a drugged and suffocated government minister, he was wrong. With an effort, she refocused on the conversation in the incident room.

'. . . the necklace business,' Layborn was saying to Strike. 'Far more convincing story than the one he told us. All that guff about wanting to stop her hurting herself.'

'It was Robin who got him to change his story, not me,' said Strike.

'Ah – well, good work,' Layborn said to Robin, with a hint

of patronage. 'I thought he was an oily little bastard when I took his initial statement. Cocky. Just out of jail, and all. No bloody remorse for running over that poor woman.'

'How are you getting on with Francesca?' Strike asked. 'The girl from the gallery?'

'We managed to get hold of the father in Sri Lanka and he's not happy. Being quite obstructive, actually,' said Layborn. 'He's trying to buy time to get her lawyered up. Bloody inconvenient, the whole family being abroad. I had to get tough with him over the phone. I can understand why he doesn't want it all coming out in court, but too bad. Gives you a real insight into the mindset of the upper classes, eh, case like this? One rule for them . . . '

'On that subject,' said Strike, 'I assume you've spoken to Aamir Mallik?'

'Yeah, we found him exactly where your boy – Hutchins, is it? – said he was. At his sister's. He's got a new job—'

'Oh, I'm glad,' said Robin inadvertently.

'—and he wasn't overjoyed to have us turning up at first, but he ended up being very frank and helpful. Said he found that disturbed lad – Billy, is it? – on the street, wanting to see his boss, shouting about a dead child, strangled and buried on Chiswell's land. Took him home with the idea of getting him to hospital, but he asked Geraint Winn's advice first. Winn was furious. Told him on no account to call an ambulance.'

'Did he, now?' said Strike, frowning.

'From what Mallik's told us, Winn was worried association with Billy's story would taint his own credibility. He didn't want the waters muddied by a psychotic tramp. Blew up at Mallik for taking him into a house belonging to the Winns, told him to turf him out on the street again. Trouble was—'

'Billy wouldn't go,' said Strike.

'Exactly. Mallik says he was clearly out of his mind,

thought he was being held against his will. Curled up in the bathroom most of the time. Anyway,' Layborn took a deep breath, 'Mallik's had enough of covering up for the Winns. He's confirmed that Winn wasn't with him on the morning of Chiswell's death. Winn told Mallik afterwards, when he put pressure on Mallik to lie, he'd had an urgent phone call at 6 a.m. that day, which is why he left the marital home early.'

'And you've traced that call?' said Strike.

Layborn picked up the printout of phone records, rifled through them, then handed a couple of marked pages to Strike.

'Here you go. Burner phones,' he said. 'We've got three different numbers so far. There were probably more. Used once, never used again, untraceable except for the single instance we got on record. Months in the planning.

'A single-use phone was used to contact Winn that morning, and two more were used to call Kinvara Chiswell on separate occasions during the previous weeks. She "can't remember" who called her, but both times – see there? – she talked to whoever it was for over an hour.'

'What's Winn got to say for himself?' asked Strike.

'Closed up like an oyster,' said Layborn. 'We're working on him, don't worry. There are porn stars who've been fucked fewer different ways than Geraint W – sorry, love,' he said, grinning, to Robin, who found the apology more offensive than anything Layborn had said. 'But you take my point. He might as well tell us everything now. He's screwed every which w – well,' he said, floundering once more. 'What interests me,' he started up again, 'is how much the wife knew. Strange woman.'

'In what way?' asked Robin.

'Oh, you know. I think she plays on this a bit,' said

Layborn, with a vague gesture towards his eyes. 'Very hard to believe she didn't know what he was up to.'

'Speaking of people not knowing what their other halves are up to,' interposed Strike, who thought he detected a martial glint in Robin's eye, 'how's it going with our friend Flick?'

'Ah, we're making very good progress there,' said Layborn. 'The parents have been helpful in *her* case. They're both lawyers and they've been urging her to cooperate. She's admitted she was Chiswell's cleaner, that she stole the note and took receipt of the crate of champagne right before Chiswell told her he couldn't afford her any more. Says she put it in a cupboard in the kitchen.'

'Who delivered it?'

'She can't remember. We'll find out. Courier service, I shouldn't wonder, booked on another burner phone.'

'And the credit card?'

'That was another good spot of yours,' admitted Layborn. 'We didn't know a credit card had gone missing. We got details through from the bank this morning. The same day Flick's flatmate realised the card was gone, somebody charged a crate of champagne and bought a hundred quid's worth of stuff on Amazon, all to be sent to an address in Maida Vale. Nobody took delivery, so it was returned to the depot where it was picked up that afternoon by someone who had the failed delivery notice. We're trying to locate the staff who can identify the person who collected it and we're getting a breakdown on what was bought on Amazon, but my money's on helium, tubing and latex gloves.

'This was all planned months in advance. *Months*.'

'And that?' Strike asked, pointing to the photocopy of the note in Chiswell's handwriting, which was lying on the side in its polythene bag. 'Has she told you why she nicked it yet?'

'She says she saw "Bill" and thought it meant her boyfriend's brother. Ironic, really,' said Layborn. 'If she hadn't stolen it, we wouldn't have cottoned on nearly so fast, would we?'

The 'we', thought Robin, was daring, because it had been Strike who had 'cottoned on', Strike who had finally cracked the significance of Chiswell's note, as they drove back to London from Chiswell House.

'Robin deserves the bulk of the credit there, too,' said Strike. 'She found the thing, she noticed "Blanc de Blanc" and the Grand Vitara. I just pieced it together once it was staring me in the face.'

'Well, we were just behind you,' said Layborn, absent-mindedly scratching his belly. 'I'm sure we'd have got there.'

Robin's mobile vibrated in her pocket again: somebody was calling this time.

'I need to take this. Is there anywhere I can—?'

'Through here,' said Layborn helpfully, opening a side door.

It was a photocopier room, with a small window covered in a Venetian blind. Robin closed the door on the others' conversation and answered.

'Hi, Sarah.'

'Hi,' said Sarah Shadlock.

She sounded totally unlike the Sarah whom Robin had known for nearly nine years, the confident and bombastic blonde whom Robin had sensed, even in their teens, was hoping that some mischance might befall Matthew's long-distance relationship with his girlfriend. Always there through the years, giggling at Matthew's jokes, touching his arm, asking loaded questions about Robin's relationship with Strike, Sarah had dated other men, settling at last for poor tedious Tom, with his well-paid job and his bald patch, who had put diamonds on Sarah's finger and in her ears, but never quelled her yen for Matthew Cunliffe.

All her swagger had gone today.

'Well, I've asked two experts, but,' she said, sounding fragile and fearful, 'and they can't say for sure, not from a photograph taken on a phone—'

'Well, obviously not,' said Robin coolly. 'I said in my text, didn't I, that I wasn't expecting a definitive answer? We're not asking for a firm identification or valuation. All we want to know is whether somebody might have credibly believed—'

'Well, then, yes,' said Sarah. 'One of our experts is quite excited about it, actually. One of the old notebooks lists a painting done of a mare with a dead foal, but it's never been found.'

'What notebooks?'

'Oh, sorry,' said Sarah. She had never sounded so meek, so frightened, in Robin's vicinity. 'Stubbs.'

'And if it *is* a Stubbs?' asked Robin, turning to look out of the window at the Feathers, a pub where she and Strike had sometimes drunk.

'Well, this is entirely speculative, obviously . . . but *if* it's genuine, *if* it's the one he listed in 1760, it could be a lot.'

'Give me a rough estimate.'

'Well, his "Gimcrack" went for—'

'—twenty-two million,' said Robin, feeling suddenly light-headed. 'Yes. You said so at our house-warming party.'

Sarah made no answer. Perhaps the mention of the party, where she had brought lilies to her lover's wife's house, had scared her.

'So if "Mare Mourning" is a genuine Stubbs—'

'It'd probably make more than "Gimcrack" at auction. It's a unique subject. Stubbs was an anatomist, as much scientist as artist. If this is a depiction of a lethal white foal, it might be the first recorded instance. It could set records.'

Robin's mobile buzzed in her hand. Another text had arrived.

'This has been very helpful, Sarah, thanks. You'll keep this confidential?'

'Yes, of course,' said Sarah. And then, in a rush:

'Robin, listen—'

'No,' said Robin, trying to stay calm. 'I'm working a case.'

'—it's over, it's finished, Matt's in pieces—'

'Goodbye, Sarah.'

Robin hung up, then read the text that had just arrived.

Meet me after work or I'm giving a statement to the press.

Eager as she was to return to the group next door and relay the sensational information she had just received, Robin remained where she stood, temporarily flummoxed by the threat, and texted back:

Statement to the press about what?

His response came within seconds, littered with angry typos.

The mail called the office this morning g and left a message asking how I feel about my dive shacking up with Cornish Strike. The sun's been one this afternoon. You probably know he's two timing you but maybe you don't give a shit. I'm not having the papers calling me at work. Either meet me or I'm go give a statement to get them off my back.

Robin was rereading the message when yet another text arrived, this time with an attachment.

In case you haven't seen it

Robin enlarged the attachment, which was a screenshot of a diary item in the *Evening Standard*.

> THE CURIOUS CASE OF CHARLOTTE CAMPBELL AND CORMORAN STRIKE
>
> A staple of the gossip columns ever since she ran away from her first private school, Charlotte Campbell has lived out her life in a glare of publicity. Most people would choose a discreet spot for their consultation with a private detective, but the pregnant Ms Campbell – now Mrs Jago Ross – chose the window table of one of the West End's busiest restaurants.
>
> Were detective services under discussion during the intense heart-to-heart, or something more personal? The colourful Mr Strike, illegitimate son of rock star Jonny Rokeby, war hero and modern-day Sherlock Holmes, also happens to be Campbell's ex-lover.
>
> Campbell's businessman husband will doubtless be keen to solve the mystery – business or pleasure? – upon his return from New York.

A mass of uncomfortable feelings jostled inside Robin, of which the dominant ones were panic, anger and mortification at the thought of Matthew speaking to the press in such a way as to leave open, spitefully, the possibility that she and Strike were indeed sleeping together.

She tried to call the number, but it went straight to voicemail. Two seconds later, another angry text appeared.

I'M WITH A CLIENT I DON'T WANT TO TALK ABOUT THIS IN FRONT OF HIM JUST MEET ME

Angry now, Robin texted:

And I'm at New Scotland Yard. Find a quiet corner.

She could imagine Matthew's polite smile as the client watched, his smooth 'just the office, excuse me', while he hammered out his furious replies.

We've got stuff to sort out and you're acting like a child refusing to meet me. Either you come talk to me or I'm ringing the papers at eight. I notice you're not denying your sleeping with him, by the way

Furious, but feeling cornered, Robin typed back:

Fine, let's discuss it face to face, where?

He texted her directions to a bar in Little Venice. Still shaken, Robin pushed open the door to the incident room. The group was now huddled around a monitor showing a page of Jimmy Knight's blog, from which Strike was reading aloud:

' . . . "in other words, a single bottle of wine at Le Manoir aux Quat'Saisons can cost more than a single, out-of-work mother receives per week to feed, clothe and house her entire family." Now that,' said Strike, 'struck me as a weirdly specific choice of restaurant, if he wanted to rant about Tories and their spending. *That's* what made me think he'd been there recently. Then Robin tells me "Blanc de Blanc" is the name of one of their suites, but I didn't put that together as quickly as I should've done. It hit me a few hours later.'

'He's a hell of a bloody hypocrite on top of everything else, isn't he?' said Wardle, who was standing, arms folded, behind Strike.

'You've looked in Woolstone?' Strike asked.

'The shithole in Charlemont Road, Woolstone, everywhere,' said Layborn, 'but don't worry. We've got a line on one of his girlfriends down in Dulwich. Checking there right now. With luck, we'll have him in custody tonight.'

Layborn now noticed Robin, standing with her phone in her hand.

'I know you've already got people looking at it,' she told Layborn, 'but I've got a contact at Christie's. I sent her the picture of "Mare Mourning" and she's just called me back. According to one of their experts, it *might* be a Stubbs.'

'Even I've heard of Stubbs,' Layborn said.

'What would it be worth, if it is?' Wardle asked.

'My contact thinks upwards of twenty-two million.'

Wardle whistled. Layborn said, 'Fuck me.'

'Doesn't matter to us what it's worth,' Strike reminded them all. 'What matters is whether somebody might've spotted its potential value.'

'Twenty-two fucking million,' said Wardle, 'is a hell of a motive.'

'Cormoran,' said Robin, picking her jacket off the back of the chair where she'd left it, 'could I have a quick word outside? I'm going to have to leave, sorry,' she said to the others.

'Everything OK?' Strike asked, as they re-entered the corridor together and Robin had closed the door on the group of police.

'Yes,' said Robin, and then, 'Well – not really. Maybe,'

she said, handing him her phone, 'you'd better just read this.'

Frowning, Strike scrolled slowly through the interchange between Robin and Matthew, including the *Evening Standard* clip.

'You're going to meet him?'

'I've got to. This must be why Mitch Patterson's sniffing around. If Matthew fans the flames with the press, which he's more than capable of doing . . . They're already excited about you and—'

'Forget me and Charlotte,' he said roughly, 'that was twenty minutes that she coerced me into. He's trying to coerce *you*—'

'I know he is,' said Robin, 'but I *have* got to talk to him sooner or later. Most of my stuff's still in Albury Street. We've still got a joint bank account.'

'D'you want me to come?'

Touched, Robin said:

'Thanks, but I don't think that would help.'

'Then ring me later, will you? Let me know what happened.'

'I will,' she promised.

She headed off alone towards the lifts. She didn't even notice who had just walked past her in the opposite direction until somebody said, 'Bobbi?'

Robin turned. There stood Flick Purdue, returning from the bathroom with a policewoman, who seemed to have escorted her there. Like Kinvara, Flick had cried away her make-up. She appeared small and shrunken in a white shirt that Robin suspected her parents had insisted she wear, rather than her Hezbollah T-shirt.

'It's Robin. How are you, Flick?'

Flick seemed to be struggling with ideas too monstrous to utter.

'I hope you're cooperating,' said Robin. 'Tell them everything, won't you?'

She thought she saw a tiny shake of the head, an instinctive defiance, the last embers of loyalty not yet extinguished, even in the trouble Flick found herself.

'You must,' said Robin quietly. 'He'd have killed *you* next, Flick. You knew too much.'

69

I have foreseen all contingencies – long ago.

Henrik Ibsen, *Rosmersholm*

A twenty-minute Tube ride later, Robin emerged at Warwick Avenue underground station in a part of London she barely knew. She had always felt a vague curiosity about Little Venice, as her extravagant middle name, 'Venetia', had been given to her because she had been conceived in the real Venice. Doubtless she would henceforth associate this area with Matthew and the bitter, tense meeting she was sure awaited her, down by the canal.

She walked down a street named Clifton Villas, where plane trees spread leaves of translucent jade against square cream-coloured houses, the walls of which glowed gold in the evening sun. The quiet beauty of this soft summer evening made Robin feel suddenly, overwhelmingly melancholy, because it recalled just such a night in Yorkshire, a decade previously, when she had hurried up the road from her parents' house, barely seventeen years old and wobbling on her high heels, desperately excited about her first date with Matthew Cunliffe, who had just passed his driving test and would be taking her into Harrogate for the evening.

And here she was walking towards him again, to arrange the permanent disentanglement of their lives. Robin despised herself for feeling sad, for remembering, when it was preferable to concentrate on his unfaithfulness and unkindness, the joyful shared experiences that had led to love.

She turned left, crossed the street and walked on, now in the chilly shadow of the brick that bordered the right-hand side of Blomfield Road, parallel to the canal, and saw a police car speeding across the top of the street. The sight of it gave her strength. It felt like a friendly wave from what she knew now was her real life, sent to remind her what she was meant to be, and how incompatible that was with being the wife of Matthew Cunliffe.

A pair of high black wooden gates was set into the wall, gates that Matthew's text had told her led to the canal-side bar, but when Robin pushed at them, they were locked. She glanced up and down the road, but there was no sign of Matthew, so she reached into her bag for her mobile, which, though muted, was already vibrating with a call. As she took it out, the electric gates opened and she walked through them, raising the mobile to her ear as she did so.

'Hi, I'm just—'

Strike yelled in her ear.

'*Get out of there, it isn't Matthew—*'

Several things happened at once.

The phone was torn out of her hand. In one frozen second, Robin registered that there was no bar in sight, only an untidy patch of canal bank beneath a bridge, hemmed by overgrown shrubs, and a dark barge, *Odile*, sitting squat and shabby in the water below her. Then a fist hit her hard in the solar plexus, and she jack-knifed, winded. Doubled over, she heard a splash as her phone was lobbed into the canal, then somebody grabbed a fistful of her hair and the waistband of her trousers and dragged her, while she still had no air in her lungs to scream, towards the barge. Thrown through the open doorway of the boat, she hit a narrow wooden table and fell to the floor.

The door slammed shut. She heard the scrape of a lock.

'Sit down,' said a male voice.

Still winded, Robin pulled herself up onto a wooden bench at the table, which was covered in a thin cushioned pad, then turned, to find herself looking into the barrel of a revolver.

Raphael lowered himself into the chair opposite her.

'Who just rang you?' he demanded and she deduced that in the physical effort to get her on the boat, and his terror that she might make a noise that the caller could hear, he had not had time or opportunity to check the screen on her mobile.

'My husband,' lied Robin in a whisper.

Her scalp was burning where he had pulled her hair. The pain in her midriff was such that she wondered whether he had cracked one of her ribs. Still fighting to draw air into her lungs, Robin seemed for a few disorientated seconds to see her predicament in miniature, from far away, encased in a trembling bead of time. She foresaw Raphael tipping her weighted corpse into the dark water by night, and Matthew, who had apparently lured her to the canal, being questioned and maybe accused. She saw the distraught faces of her parents and her brothers at her funeral in Masham, and she saw Strike standing at the back of the church, as he had at her wedding, furious because the thing he had feared had come to pass, and she was dead due to her own failings.

But as each gasp re-inflated Robin's lungs, the illusion that she was watching from afar dissolved. She was here, now, on this dingy boat, breathing in its fusty smell, trapped within its wooden walls, with the dilated pupil of the revolver staring at her, and Raphael's eyes above it.

Her fear was a real, solid presence in the galley, but it must stand apart from her, because it couldn't help, and would only hinder. She must stay calm, and concentrate. She chose not to speak. It would give her back some of the power he had just taken from her if she refused to fill the silence. This was the trick of the therapist: let the pause unspool; let the more vulnerable person fill it.

'You're very cool,' Raphael said finally. 'I thought you might get hysterical and scream. That's why I had to punch you. I wouldn't have done that otherwise. For what it's worth, I like you, Venetia.'

She knew that he was trying to re-impersonate the man who had charmed her against her will at the Commons. Clearly, he thought the old mixture of ruefulness and remorse would make her forgive, and soften, even with her burning scalp, and her bruised ribs, and the gun in her face. She said nothing. His faint, imploring smile disappeared and he said bluntly:

'I need to know how much the police know. If I can still blag my way out of what they've got, then I'm afraid you,' he raised the gun a fraction to point directly at Robin's forehead (and she thought of vets and the one clean shot that the horse in the dell had been denied) 'are done for. I'll muffle the shot in a cushion and put you overboard once it's dark. But if they already know everything, then I'll end it, here, tonight, because I'm never going back to prison. So you can see how it's in your best interests to be honest, can't you? Only one of us is getting off this boat.'

And when she didn't speak, he said fiercely:

'Answer me!'

'Yes,' she said. 'I understand.'

'So,' he said quietly, 'were you really just at Scotland Yard?'

'Yes.'

'Is Kinvara there?'

'Yes.'

'Under arrest?'

'I think so. She's in an interrogation room with her solicitor.'

'Why have they arrested her?'

'They think the two of you are having an affair. That you were behind everything.'

'What's "everything"?'

'The blackmail,' said Robin, 'and the murder.'

He advanced the gun so that it was pressing against her forehead. Robin felt the small, cold ring of metal pressing into her skin.

'Sounds like a crock of shit to me. How're we supposed to have had an affair? She hated me. We were never alone together for two minutes.'

'Yes, you were,' said Robin. 'Your father invited you down to Chiswell House, right after you got out of jail. The night he was detained in London. You and she were alone together, then. That's when we think it started.'

'Proof?'

'None,' said Robin, 'but I think you could seduce anyone if you really put your—'

'Don't try flattery, it won't work. Seriously, "that's when we think it started"? Is that all you've got?'

'No. There were other signs of something going on.'

'Tell me the signs. All of them.'

'I'd be able to remember better,' said Robin steadily, 'without you pressing a gun into my forehead.'

He withdrew it, but still pointing the revolver at her face, he said:

'Go on. Quickly.'

Part of Robin wanted to succumb to her body's desire to

dissolve, to carry her off into blissful unconsciousness. Her hands were numb, her muscles felt like soft wax. The place where Raphael had pressed the gun into her skin felt cold, a ring of white fire for a third eye. He hadn't turned on the lights in the boat. They were facing each other in the deepening darkness and perhaps, by the time he shot her, she would no longer be able to see him clearly . . .

Focus, said a small, clear voice through the panic. *Focus. The longer you keep him talking, the more time they'll have to find you. Strike knows you were tricked.*

She suddenly remembered the police car speeding across the top of Blomfield Road and wondered whether it had been circling, looking for her, whether the police, knowing that Raphael had lured her to the area, had already dispatched officers to search for them. The fake address had been some distance away along the canal bank, reached, so Raphael's texts had said, through the black gates. Would Strike guess that Raphael was armed?

She took a deep breath.

'Kinvara broke down in Della Winn's office last summer and said that someone had told her she'd never been loved, that she was used as part of a game.'

She must speak slowly. Don't rush it. Every second might count, every second that she could keep Raphael hanging on her words, was another second in which somebody might come to her aid.

'Della assumed she was talking about your father, but we checked and Della can't remember Kinvara actually saying his name. We think you seduced Kinvara as an act of revenge towards your father, kept the affair going for a couple of months, but when she got clingy and possessive, you ditched her.'

'All supposition,' said Raphael harshly, 'and therefore bullshit. What else?'

'Why did Kinvara go up to town on the day her beloved mare was likely to be put down?'

'Maybe she couldn't face seeing the horse shot. Maybe she was in denial about how sick it was.'

'Or,' said Robin, 'maybe she was suspicious about what you and Francesca were up to in Drummond's gallery.'

'No proof. Next.'

'She had a kind of breakdown when she got back to Oxfordshire. She attacked your father and was hospitalised.'

'Still grieving her stillborn, excessively attached to her horses, generally depressed,' Raphael rattled off. 'Izzy and Fizzy will fight to take the stand and explain how unstable she is. What else?'

'Tegan told us that one day Kinvara was manically happy again, and she lied when asked why. She said your father had agreed to put her other mare in foal to Totilas. We think the real reason was that you'd resumed the affair with her, and we don't think the timing was coincidental. You'd just driven the latest batch of paintings up to Drummond's gallery for valuation.'

Raphael's face became suddenly slack, as though his essential self had temporarily vacated it. The gun twitched in his hand and the fine hairs on Robin's arms lifted gently as though a breeze had rippled over them. She waited for Raphael to speak, but he didn't. After a minute, she continued:

'We think that when you loaded up the paintings for valuation, you saw "Mare Mourning" close up for the first time and realised that it might be a Stubbs. You decided to substitute a different painting of a mare and foal for valuation.'

'Evidence?'

'Henry Drummond's now seen the photograph I took of "Mare Mourning" on the spare bed at Chiswell House. He's ready to testify that it wasn't among the pictures he valued for your father. The painting he valued at five to eight thousand pounds was by John Frederick Herring, and it showed a black and white mare and foal. Drummond's also ready to testify that you're sufficiently knowledgeable about art to have spotted that "Mare Mourning" might be a Stubbs.'

Raphael's face had lost its mask-like cast. Now his near-black irises swivelled fractionally from side to side, as though he were reading something only he could see.

'I must've accidentally taken the Frederick Herring inste—'

A police siren sounded a few streets away. Raphael's head turned: the siren wailed for a few seconds, then, as abruptly as it had started, was shut off.

He turned back to face Robin. He didn't seem overly worried by the siren now it had stopped. Of course, he thought that it had been Matthew on the phone when he grabbed her.

'Yeah,' he said, regaining the thread of his thought. 'That's what I'll say. I took the painting of the piebald to be valued by mistake, never saw "Mare Mourning", had no idea it might be a Stubbs.'

'You can't have taken the piebald picture by mistake,' said Robin quietly. 'It didn't come from Chiswell House and the family's prepared to say so.'

'The family,' said Raphael, 'don't notice what's under their fucking noses. A Stubbs has been hanging in a damp spare bedroom for nigh on twenty years and nobody noticed, and you know why? Because they're such fucking arrogant snobs . . . "Mare Mourning" was old Tinky's. She inherited it from the broken-down, alcoholic, gaga old Irish baronet she married before my grandfather. She had no idea what it was worth. She kept it because it was horsey and she loved horses.

'When her first husband died, she hopped over to England and pulled the same trick, became my grandfather's expensive private nurse and then his even more expensive wife. She died intestate and all her crap – it *was* mostly crap – got absorbed into the Chiswell estate. The Frederick Herring could easily have been one of hers and nobody noticed it, stuck away in some filthy corner of that bloody house.'

'What if the police trace the piebald picture?'

'They won't. It's my mother's. I'll destroy it. When the police ask me, I'll say my father told me he was going to flog it now he knew it was worth eight grand. "He must've sold it privately, officer."'

'Kinvara doesn't know the new story. She won't be able to back you up.'

'This is where her well-known instability and unhappiness with my father works in my favour. Izzy and Fizzy will line up to tell the world that she never paid much attention to what he was up to, because she didn't love him and was only in it for the money. Reasonable doubt is all I need.'

'What's going to happen when the police put it to Kinvara that you only restarted the affair because you realised she might be about to become fantastically wealthy?'

Raphael let out a long, slow hiss.

'Well,' he said quietly, 'if they can make Kinvara believe that, I'm fucked, aren't I? But right now, Kinvara believes her Raffy loves her more than anything in the world, and she's going to take a *lot* of convincing that's not true, because her whole life's going to fall apart otherwise. I drilled it into her: if they don't know about the affair, they can't touch us. I virtually had her reciting it while I fucked her. And I warned her they'd try and turn us against each other if either one of us was suspected. I've got her very well-schooled and I said, when in doubt, cry your eyes out, tell them nobody ever tells you anything and act bloody confused.'

'She's already told one silly lie to try and protect you, and the police know about it,' said Robin.

'What lie?'

'About the necklace, in the early hours of Sunday morning. Didn't she tell you? Maybe she realised you'd be angry.'

'*What did she say?*'

'Strike told her he didn't buy the new explanation for you going down to Chiswell House the morning your father died—'

'What d'you mean, he didn't buy it?' said Raphael, and Robin saw outraged vanity mingled with his panic.

'*I* thought it was convincing,' she assured him. 'Clever, to tell a story that you'd appear to give up only unwillingly. Everyone's always more disposed to believe something they believe they've uncovered for themsel—'

Raphael raised the gun so that it was close to her forehead again and even though the cold ring of metal had not yet touched her skin again, she felt it there.

'What lie did Kinvara tell?'

'She claimed you came to tell her that your mother removed diamonds from the necklace and replaced them with fakes.'

Raphael appeared horrified.

'What the fuck did she say that for?'

'Because she'd had a shock, I suppose, finding Strike and me in the grounds when you were hiding upstairs. Strike said he didn't believe the necklace story, so she panicked and made up a new version. The trouble is, this one's checkable.'

'The stupid cunt,' said Raphael quietly, but with a venom that made the back of Robin's neck prickle. 'That stupid, stupid cunt . . . why didn't she just stick to our story? And . . . no, wait . . . ' he said, with the air of a man suddenly making a welcome connection, and to Robin's mingled consternation and relief, he withdrew the gun from where it had been almost touching her, and laughed softly. '*That's* why she hid the necklace on Sunday afternoon. She gave me some fucking guff about not wanting Izzy or Fizzy to sneak in and take it . . . well, she's stupid, but she's not hopeless. Unless someone checks the stones, we're still in the clear . . . And they'll have to take apart the stable block to find it. OK,' he said, as though talking to himself, 'OK, I think all of that's recoverable.

'Is that it, Venetia? Is that all you've got?'

'No,' said Robin. 'There's Flick Purdue.'

'I don't know who that is.'

'Yes, you do. You picked her up months ago, and fed her the truth about the gallows, knowing she'd pass the information to Jimmy.'

'What a busy boy I've been,' said Raphael lightly. 'So what? Flick won't admit to shagging a Tory minister's son, especially if Jimmy might find out. She's as besotted with him as Kinvara is with me.'

'That's true, she didn't want to admit it, but somebody must have spotted you creeping out of her flat next morning. She tried to pretend you were an Indian waiter.'

Robin thought she saw a minute wince of surprise and displeasure. Raphael's *amour propre* was wounded at the thought that he could have been so described.

'OK,' he said, after a moment or two, 'OK, let's see . . . what if it *was* a waiter Flick shagged, but she's maliciously claiming it was me because of her class warrior bullshit and the grudge her boyfriend's got against my family?'

'You stole her flatmate's credit card out of her bag in the kitchen.'

She could tell by the tightening of his mouth that he had not expected this. Doubtless he had thought that given Flick's lifestyle, suspicion would fall on anyone passing through her tiny, overcrowded flat, and perhaps especially Jimmy.

'Proof?' he said again.

'Flick can provide the date you were at her flat and if Laura testifies her credit card went missing that night—'

'But with no firm evidence I was ever there—'

'How did Flick find out about the gallows? We know she told Jimmy about them, not the other way around.'

'Well, it can't have been me, can it? I'm the only member of the family who never knew.'

'You knew everything. Kinvara had the full story from your father, and she passed it all to you.'

'No,' said Raphael, 'I think you'll find Flick heard about the gallows from the Butcher brothers. I'm reliably informed that one of them lives in London now. Yeah, I think I've heard a rumour one of them shagged their mate Jimmy's girlfriend. And believe me, the Butcher brothers aren't going to come over well in court, pair of shifty oiks driving gallows around under cover of darkness. I'm going to look a lot more plausible and presentable than Flick and the Butchers if this comes to court, I really am.'

'The police have got phone records,' Robin persisted. 'They know about an anonymous call to Geraint Winn, which was made around the time Flick found out about the gallows. We think you tipped off Winn anonymously about Samuel Murape. You knew Winn had a grudge against the Chiswells. Kinvara told you everything.'

'I don't know anything about that phone call, Your Honour,' said Raphael, 'and I'm very sorry that my late brother was a prize cunt to Rhiannon Winn, but that's nothing to do with me.'

'We think *you* made that threatening call to Izzy's office, the first day you were there, talking about people pissing themselves as they die,' said Robin, 'and we think it was *your* idea for Kinvara to pretend she kept hearing intruders in the grounds. Everything was designed to create as many witnesses as possible to the fact that your father had reason to be anxious and paranoid, that he might crack under extreme pressure—'

'He *was* under extreme pressure. He *was* being blackmailed by Jimmy Knight. Geraint Winn *was* trying to force him out of his job. Those aren't lies, they're facts and they're going to be pretty sensational in a courtroom, especially once the Samuel Murape story gets out.'

'Except that you made stupid, avoidable mistakes.'

He sat up straighter and leaned forwards, his elbow sliding a few inches, so that the nozzle of the gun grew larger. His eyes, which had been smudges in the shadow, became clearly defined again, onyx black and white. Robin wondered how she had ever thought him handsome.

'What mistakes?'

As he said it, Robin saw, out of the corner of her eye, a flashing blue light glide over the bridge just visible through the window to her right, which was blocked from Raphael's view by the side of the boat. The light vanished and the bridge was reabsorbed by the deepening darkness.

'For one thing,' said Robin carefully, 'it was a mistake to keep meeting Kinvara in the lead-up to the murder. She kept pretending she'd forgotten where she was meeting your father, didn't she? Just to get a couple of minutes with you, just to see you and check up on you—'

'That's not proof.'

'Kinvara was followed to Le Manoir aux Quat'Saisons on her birthday.'

His eyes narrowed.

'Who by?'

'Jimmy Knight. Flick's confirmed it. Jimmy thought your father was with Kinvara and wanted to confront him publicly about not giving him his money. Obviously, your father wasn't there, so Jimmy went home and wrote an angry blog about how High Tories spend their money, mentioning Le Manoir aux Quat'Saisons by name.'

'Well, unless he saw me sneaking into Kinvara's hotel suite,' said Raphael, 'which he didn't, because I took fucking good care to make sure nobody did, that's all supposition, too.'

'All right,' said Robin, 'what about the *second* time you were overheard having sex in the gallery bathroom? That wasn't Francesca. You were with Kinvara.'

'Prove it.'

'Kinvara was in town that day, buying lachesis pills and pretending she was angry that your father was still seeing you, which was all part of the cover story that she hated you. She rang your father to check that he was having lunch elsewhere. Strike overheard that call. What you and Kinvara didn't realise was that your father was having lunch only a hundred yards away from where you were having sex.

'When your father forced his way into the bathroom, he found a tube of lachesis pills on the floor. That's why he nearly had a heart attack. He knew that's what she'd come to town for. He knew who'd just been having sex with you in the bathroom.'

Raphael's smile was more of a grimace.

'Yeah, that was a fuck-up. The day he came into our office, talking about Lachesis – "knows when everyone's number's up" – I realised later, he was trying to put the frighteners on me, wasn't he? I didn't know what the hell he was on about at the time. But when you and your crippled boss mentioned the pills at Chiswell House, Kinvara twigged: they fell out of her pocket while we were screwing.

We hadn't known what first tipped him off . . . it was only after I heard he was ringing Le Manoir about Freddie's money clip that I knew he must have realised something was going on. Then he invited me over to Ebury Street and I knew he was about to confront me about it, and we needed to get a move on, killing him.'

The entirely matter-of-fact way he discussed patricide chilled Robin. He might have been talking about wall-papering a room.

'He must've been planning to produce those pills during his big "I know you're fucking my wife" speech . . . why didn't I spot them on the floor? I tried to put the room straight afterwards, but they must've rolled out of his pocket or something . . . it's harder than you'd think,' said Raphael, 'tidying up around a corpse you've just dispatched. I was surprised, actually, how much it affected me.'

She had never heard his narcissism so clearly. His interest and sympathy was entirely for himself. His dead father was nothing.

'The police have taken statements from Francesca and her parents, now,' Robin said. 'She absolutely denies being in the bathroom with you that second time. Her parents never believed her, but—'

'They didn't believe her because she's even fucking dumber than Kinvara.'

'The police are combing through security camera footage from the shops she says she was in, while you and Kinvara were in the bathroom.'

'OK,' said Raphael, 'well, worst comes to the worst, and they can prove she wasn't with me, I might have to come clean about the fact that it was *another* young lady I was with in the bathroom that day, whose reputation I've been chivalrously trying to defend.'

'Will you really be able to find a woman to lie for you, in court, on a murder charge?' asked Robin, in disbelief.

'The woman who owns this houseboat is mad for me,' said Raphael softly. 'We had a thing going before I went inside. She visited me in jail and everything. She's in rehab right now. Crazy bitch, loves drama. Thinks she's an artist. She drinks too much, she's a real pain in the arse, actually, but she fucks like a rabbit. She never bothered taking the spare key to this place off me, and she keeps a key to her mummy's house in that drawer over there—'

'It wouldn't happen to be her mother's house where you had the helium, tubing and gloves delivered, would it?' asked Robin.

Raphael blinked. He hadn't expected that.

'You needed an address that didn't seem connected to you. You made sure it was delivered while the owners were away, or at work, then you could let yourself in, collect the failed delivery card . . .'

'Pick it up, disguised, and get it couriered off to dear old Dad's house, yeah.'

'And Flick took delivery and Kinvara made sure she hid it from your father until it was time to kill him?'

'That's right,' said Raphael. 'You pick up a lot of tips in jail. Fake IDs, vacant buildings, empty addresses, you can do a hell of a lot with them. Once you're dead—' Robin's scalp prickled – 'nobody's going to connect me with any of the addresses.'

'The owner of this barge—'

'Is going to be telling everyone she was having sex with me in Drummond's bathroom, remember? She's on my team, Venetia,' he said quietly, 'so it's not looking good for you, is it?'

'There were other mistakes,' said Robin, her mouth dry.

'Like?'

'You told Flick your father needed a cleaner.'

'Yeah, because it makes her and Jimmy look fishy as hell, that she wheedled her way into my father's house. The jury'll be focused on that, not how she found out he wanted a cleaner. I've already told you, she's going to look like a grubby little tart with a grudge in the dock. That's just one more lie.'

'But she stole a note from your father, a note he wrote while he was trying to check Kinvara's story with Le Manoir aux Quat'Saisons. I found it in her bathroom. She'd lied, told him her mother was going to the hotel with her. They'd never normally give out information about guests, but he was a government minister and he'd previously been there, so we think he managed to trick them into agreeing that they could remember the family vehicle there and that it was a shame her mother hadn't made it. He made a note of the suite Kinvara was in, probably pretending he'd forgotten it, and he was trying to get hold of the bill, to see whether there was any sign of two lots of breakfast or dinner, I suppose. When the prosecution produce the note and the bill in court—'

'*You* found that note, did you?' said Raphael.

Robin's stomach turned over. She had not meant to give Raphael another reason to shoot her.

'I knew I'd underestimated you after that dinner we had, at Nam Long Le Shaker,' said Raphael. It wasn't a compliment. His eyes were narrowed, his nostrils flared in dislike. 'You were a mess, but you were still asking fucking inconvenient questions. You and your boss were cosier with the police than I expected, too. And even after I tipped off the *Mail*—'

'That was *you*,' said Robin, wondering how she had never realised. '*You* put the press and Mitch Patterson back on us . . .'

'I told them you'd left your husband for Strike, but that he was still shagging his ex. Izzy had given me that bit of gossip. I thought you needed slowing down, you two, because you kept poking away at my alibi . . . but after I've shot you,' – an icy chill ran the length of Robin's body – 'your boss'll be busy answering the press's questions about how your body ended up in a canal, won't he? I think that's called killing two birds with one stone.'

'Even if I'm dead,' said Robin, her voice as steady as she could make it, 'there'll still be your father's note and the hotel's testimony—'

'OK, so he was worried about what Kinvara was doing at Le Manoir,' said Raphael roughly. 'I've just told you, nobody saw me on the premises. The stupid cow did ask for two glasses with the champagne, but she could've been with someone else.'

'You aren't going to have any opportunity to cook up a new story with her,' said Robin, her mouth drier than ever, her tongue sticking to the roof of her mouth as she tried to sound calm and confident. 'She's in custody now, she isn't as clever as you – and you made other mistakes,' Robin rushed on, 'stupid ones, because you had to enact the plan in a hurry once you realised your father was onto you.'

'Like?'

'Like Kinvara taking away the packaging on the amitriptyline, after she'd doctored the orange juice. Kinvara forgetting to tell you the trick to closing the front door properly. And,' said Robin, aware that she was playing her very last card, 'her throwing the front door key to you, at Paddington.'

In the wordless space that now stretched between them, Robin thought she heard footsteps close at hand. She didn't dare look out of the window in case she alerted Raphael, who appeared too appalled by what she had just said to take in anything else.

'"Throwing the front door key to me?"' repeated Raphael, with fragile bravado. 'What the hell are you talking about?'

'The keys to Ebury Street are restricted, almost impossible to copy. The pair of you only had access to one: hers, because your father was suspicious of you both by the time he died, and he'd made sure the spare was out of your reach.

'She needed the key to get into the house and doctor the orange juice and you needed it to go in early next morning and suffocate him. So you cobbled together a plan at the last minute: she'd pass you the key at a prearranged spot at Paddington, where you'd be disguised as a homeless person.

'You were caught on camera. The police have got people enlarging and clarifying the image right now. They think you must have bought things from a charity shop in haste, which might produce another useful witness. The police are now combing CCTV footage for your movements from Paddington onwards.'

Raphael said nothing at all for nearly a minute. His eyes were moving fractionally from left to right, as he tried to find a loophole, an escape.

'That's . . . inconvenient,' he said finally. 'I didn't think I was on camera, sitting there.'

Robin thought she could see hope slipping away from him now. Quietly, she continued, 'As per your plan, Kinvara arrived home in Oxfordshire, called Drummond and left a message that she wanted the necklace valued, to set up that whole back-up story.

'Early next morning, another burner phone was used to call both Geraint Winn and Jimmy Knight. Both were lured out of their houses, presumably with a promise of information on Chiswell. That was you, making sure they were in the frame if murder was suspected.'

'No proof,' muttered Raphael automatically, but still his

eyes darted this way and that, searching for invisible lifelines.

'You let yourself into the house very early in the morning, expecting to find your father almost comatose after his early morning orange juice, but—'

'He *was* out of it, at first,' said Raphael. His eyes had become glazed, and Robin knew that he was remembering what had happened, watching it, inside his head. 'He was slumped on the sofa, very groggy. I walked straight past him into the kitchen, opened my box of toys—'

For a sliver of a second, Robin saw again the shrink-wrapped head, the grey hair pressed around the face so that only the gaping black hole of the mouth was visible. Raphael had done that; Raphael, who currently had a gun pointing at her face.

'—but while I'm arranging everything, the old bastard wakes up, sees me fixing the tubing onto the helium canister and comes back to fucking life. He staggers up, grabs Freddie's sword off the wall and tries to fight, but I got it off him. Bent the blade doing it. Forced him down into the chair – he was still struggling – and—'

Raphael mimed putting the bag over his father's head.

'*Caput.*'

'And then,' said Robin, her mouth still dry, 'you made those phone calls from his phone that were supposed to establish your alibi. Kinvara had told you his passcode, of course. And you left, without closing the door properly.'

Robin didn't know whether she was imagining movement out of the porthole to her left. She kept her eyes fixed on Raphael, and the slightly wavering gun.

'Loads of this is circumstantial,' he muttered, eyes still glazed. 'Flick and Francesca have both got motives for lying about me . . . I didn't end it well with Francesca . . . I might still have a chance . . . I might . . .'

'There's no chance, Raff,' said Robin. 'Kinvara isn't going to lie for you much longer. When they tell her the truth about "Mare Mourning", she's going to put everything together for the first time. I think *you* insisted she move it into the drawing room, to protect it from the damp in the spare room. How did you manage that? Did you make up some rubbish about it reminding *you* of her dead mare? Then she's going to realise you started up the affair again once you knew its true value, and that all the dreadful things you said to her when you ended it were true. And worst of all,' said Robin, 'she's going to realise that when the two of you heard intruders in the grounds – real ones, this time – you let the woman you were supposedly madly in love with walk out into the grounds in the dark, in her nightdress, while you stayed behind to protect—'

'*All right!*' he shouted suddenly and he advanced the gun nozzle until it pressed into her forehead again. 'Stop fucking *talking*, will you?'

Robin sat quite still. She imagined how it would feel when he pressed the trigger. He had said he would shoot her through a cushion to muffle the sound, but perhaps he had forgotten, perhaps he was about to lose control.

'D'you know what it's like in jail?' he asked.

She tried to say 'no', but the sound wouldn't come.

'The noise,' he whispered. 'The smell. The ugly, dumb people – like animals, some of them. Worse than animals. I never knew there were people like it. The places they make you eat and shit. Watching your back all the time, waiting for violence. The clanging, the yelling and the fucking squalor. I'd rather be buried alive. I won't do it again . . .

'I was going to have a dream life. I was going to be free, totally free. I'd never have to kowtow to the likes of fucking Drummond again. There's a villa on Capri I've had my eye on for a long time. View out over the Gulf of Naples. Then I'd have a nice pad in London . . . new car, once my fucking ban's lifted . . . imagine walking along and knowing you could buy anything, do anything. A dream life . . .

'Couple of little problems to get out of the way before I was completely sorted . . . Flick, easy: late night, dark road, knife in the ribs, victim of street crime.

'And Kinvara . . . once she'd made a will in my favour, after a few years, she'd have broken her neck riding an unsuitable horse or drowned out in Italy . . . she's a terrible swimmer . . .

'And then all of them could fuck themselves, couldn't they? The Chiswells, my whore of a mother. I'd need nothing from anyone. I'd have everything . . .

'But that's all gone,' he said. Dark-skinned though he was, she saw that he had turned ashen, the dark shadows beneath his eyes hollow in the half-light. 'It's all gone. You know what, Venetia? I'm going to blow your fucking brains out, because I've decided I don't like you. I think I'd like to see your fucking head explode before mine comes off—'

'Raff—'

'*Raff . . . Raff . . .*' he bleated, imitating her, 'why do women all think they're different? You're not different, none of you.'

He was reaching for the limp cushion beside him.

'We'll go together. I'd like to arrive in hell with a sexy girl on my ar—'

With a great splintering of wood, the door crashed open. Raphael spun around, pointing the gun at the large figure that had just fallen inside. Robin launched herself over the table to grab his arm, but Raphael knocked her backwards with his elbow and she felt blood spurt as her lip split.

'Raff, no, don't – *don't!*'

He had stood up, stooped in the cramped space, the barrel

of the gun in his mouth. Strike, who had shouldered in the door, stood panting feet away from him, and behind Strike was Wardle.

'Go on and do it, then, you cowardly little fuck,' said Strike.

Robin wanted to protest, but couldn't make a noise.

There was a small, metallic click.

'Took out the bullets at Chiswell House, you stupid bastard,' said Strike, hobbling forwards and smacking the revolver out of Raphael's mouth. 'Not half as clever as you thought you were, eh?'

There was a great ringing in Robin's ears. Raphael was spitting oaths in English and Italian, screaming threats, thrashing and twisting as Strike helped bend him over the table for Wardle to cuff him, but she stumbled away from the group as though in a dream, backwards towards the kitchen area of the galley, where pots and pans were hanging and white kitchen roll sat, ludicrously ordinary, beside a tiny sink. She could feel her lip swelling where Raphael had hit her. She tore off some kitchen roll, ran it under the cold tap and pressed it to her bleeding mouth, while through the porthole she watched uniformed officers hurrying through the black gates, taking possession of the gun and of the struggling Raphael, whom Wardle had just dragged onto the bank.

She had just been held at gunpoint. Nothing seemed real. Now the police were stomping in and out of the barge, but it was all noise and echo, and now she realised that Strike was standing beside her, and he seemed the only person with any reality.

'How did you know?' she asked thickly, through the cold wodge of tissue.

'Twigged five minutes after you left. The last three digits on that number you showed me on those supposed texts from

Matthew were the same as one of the burner phone numbers. Went after you but you were already gone. Layborn sent panda cars out and I've been calling you nonstop ever since. Why didn't you pick up?'

'My phone was on silent in my bag. Now it's in the canal.'

She craved a stiff drink. Maybe, she thought vaguely, there really was a bar somewhere nearby . . . but of course, she wouldn't be allowed to go to a bar. She was facing hours back at New Scotland Yard. They would need a long statement. She would have to relive the last hour in detail. She felt exhausted.

'How did you know I was here?'

'Called Izzy and asked if Raphael knew anyone in the vicinity of that fake address he was trying to get you to. She told me he'd had some posh druggie girlfriend who owned a barge. He was running out of places to go. The police have been watching his flat for the last two days.'

'And you knew the gun was empty?'

'I *hoped* it was empty,' he corrected her. 'For all I knew, he'd checked it and reloaded.'

He groped in his pocket. His fingers shook slightly as he lit a cigarette. He inhaled, then said:

'You did bloody well to keep him talking that long, Robin, but next time you get a call from an unknown number, you bloody well call it back and check who's on the other end. And don't you ever – *ever* – tell a suspect anything about your personal life again.'

'Would it be OK if I have *two minutes*,' she asked, pressing the cold kitchen roll against her swollen and bleeding lip, 'to enjoy not being dead, before you start?'

Strike blew out a jet of smoke.

'Yeah, fair enough,' he said, and pulled her clumsily into a one-armed hug.

ONE MONTH LATER

EPILOGUE

Your past is dead, Rebecca. It has no longer any hold on you – has nothing to do with you – as you are now.

Henrik Ibsen, *Rosmersholm*

The Paralympics had been and gone, and September was doing its best to wash away the memory of the long, Union-Jacked summer days, when London had basked for weeks in the world's attention. Rain was pattering against the Cheyne Walk Brasserie's high windows, competing with Serge Gainsbourg as he crooned 'Black Trombone' from hidden speakers.

Strike and Robin, who had arrived together, had only just sat down when Izzy, who had chosen the restaurant for its proximity to her flat, arrived in a slightly dishevelled flapping of Burberry trench coat and sodden umbrella, the latter taking some time to collapse at the door.

Strike had only spoken to their client once since the case had been solved, and then briefly, because Izzy had been too shocked and distressed to say much. They were meeting today at Strike's request, because there was one last piece of unfinished business in the Chiswell case. Izzy had told Strike by phone, when they arranged lunch, that she had not been out much since Raphael's arrest. 'I can't face people. It's all so dreadful.'

'How are you?' she said anxiously, as Strike manoeuvred himself out from behind the white-clothed table to accept a damp embrace. 'And oh, poor Robin, I'm so sorry,' she added, hurrying around the other side of the table to hug Robin, before saying distractedly, 'Oh yes, please, thank you,' to the unsmiling waitress, who took her wet raincoat and umbrella.

Sitting down, Izzy said, 'I promised myself I wouldn't cry,' then grabbed a napkin from the table and pressed it firmly to her tear ducts. 'Sorry . . . keep doing this. *Trying* not to be embarrassing . . .'

She cleared her throat and straightened her back.

'It's just been such a shock,' she whispered.

'Of course it has,' said Robin, and Izzy gave her a watery smile.

'*C'est l'automne de ma vie,*' sang Gainsbourg. '*Plus personne ne m'étonne . . .*'

'You found this place OK, then?' Izzy said, scrabbling to find conventional conversational ground. 'Quite pretty, isn't it?' she said, inviting them to admire the Provençal restaurant which Strike had thought, as he entered, had a feeling of Izzy's flat about it, translated into French. Here was the same conservative mix of traditional and modern: black and white photographs hung on stark white walls, chairs and benches covered in scarlet and turquoise leather, and old-fashioned bronze and glass chandeliers with rose-coloured lampshades.

The waitress returned with menus and offered to take their drink order.

'Should we wait?' Izzy asked, gesturing at the empty seat.

'He's running late,' said Strike, who was craving beer. 'Might as well order drinks.'

After all, there was nothing more to find out. Today was about explanations. An awkward silence fell again as the waitress walked away.

'Oh, gosh, I don't know whether you've heard,' Izzy said suddenly to Strike, with an air of being relieved to have found what to her was standard gossip. 'Charlie's been admitted to hospital.'

'Really?' he said, with no sign of particular interest.

'Yah, bed rest. She had something – leak of amniotic fluid, I think – anyway, they want her under observation.'

Strike nodded, expressionless. Ashamed of herself for wishing to know more, Robin kept quiet. The drinks arrived. Izzy, who seemed too keyed up to have noticed Strike's unenthusiastic response to what was, for her, a safe subject of mutual interest, said:

'I heard Jago hit the roof when he saw that story about the two of you in the press. Probably delighted to have her where he can keep an eye—'

But Izzy caught something in Strike's expression that made her desist. She took a slug of wine, checked to see whether anyone at the few occupied tables was listening, and said:

'I suppose the police are keeping you informed? You know Kinvara's admitted everything?'

'Yeah,' said Strike, 'we heard.'

Izzy shook her head, her eyes filling with tears again.

'It's been so awful. One's friends don't know what to say . . . I still can't *believe* it. It's just so incredible. *Raff* . . . I wanted to go and see him, you know. I really *needed* to see him . . . but he refused. He won't see anyone.'

She gulped more wine.

'He must have gone mad or something. He must be ill, mustn't he? To have done it? Must be mentally ill.'

Robin remembered the dark barge, where Raphael had

spoken in holy accents of the life he wanted, of the villa in Capri, the bachelor pad in London, and the new car, once the ban imposed for running over a young mother had been lifted. She thought how meticulously he had planned his father's death, the errors made only because of the haste with which the murder was to be enacted. She pictured his expression over the gun, as he had asked her why women thought there was any difference between them: the mother whom he called a whore, the stepmother he had seduced, Robin, whom he was about to kill so that he didn't have to enter hell alone. Was he ill in any sense that would put him in a psychiatric institution rather than the prison that so terrified him? Or had his dream of patricide been spawned in the shadowy wasteland between sickness and irreducible malevolence?

'. . . he had an awful childhood,' Izzy was saying, and then, though neither Strike nor Robin had responded, 'he *did*, you know, he really did. I don't want to speak ill of Papa, but Freddie was *everything*. Papa wasn't kind to Raff and the Orca – I mean, Ornella, his mother – well, Torks always says she's more like a high-class hooker than anything else. When Raff wasn't at boarding school she dragged him around with her, always chasing some new man.'

'There are worse childhoods,' said Strike.

Robin, who had just been thinking that Raphael's life with his mother sounded not unlike the little she knew about Strike's early years, was nevertheless surprised to hear him express this view so bluntly.

'Plenty of people go through worse than having a party girl for a mother,' he said, 'and they don't end up committing murder. Look at Billy Knight. No mother at all for most of his life. Violent, alcoholic father, beaten and neglected, ends up with serious mental illness and he's never hurt anyone.

He came to my office in the throes of psychosis, trying to get justice for someone else.'

'Yes,' said Izzy hastily, 'yes, that's true, of course.'

But Robin had the impression that even now, Izzy could not equate the pain of Raphael and Billy. The former's suffering would always evoke more pity in her than the latter's, because a Chiswell was innately different to the kind of motherless boy whose beatings were hidden in the woods, where estate workers lived according to the laws of their kind.

'And here he is,' said Strike.

Billy Knight had just entered the restaurant, raindrops glittering on his shorn hair. Though still underweight, his face was fuller, his person and clothes cleaner. He had been released from hospital only a week previously, and was currently living in Jimmy's flat on Charlemont Road.

'Hello,' he said to Strike. 'Sorry I'm late. Tube took longer'n I thought.'

'No problem,' said the two women, at the same time.

'You're Izzy,' said Billy, sitting down beside her. 'Haven't seen you 'n a long time.'

'No,' said Izzy, a little over-heartily. 'It's been quite a while, hasn't it?'

Robin held out a hand across the table.

'Hi, Billy, I'm Robin.'

'Hello,' he said again, shaking it.

'Would you like some wine, Billy?' offered Izzy. 'Or beer?'

'Can't drink on my meds,' he told her.

'Ah, no, of course not,' said Izzy, flustered. 'Um . . . well, have some water, and there's your menu . . . we haven't ordered yet . . . '

Once the waitress had been and gone, Strike addressed Billy.

'I made you a promise when I visited you in hospital,' he

said. 'I told you I'd find out what happened to the child you saw strangled.'

'Yeah,' said Billy apprehensively. It was in the hopes of hearing the answer to the twenty-year-old mystery that he had travelled from East Ham to Chelsea in the rain. 'You said on the phone that you'd worked it out.'

'Yes,' said Strike, 'but I want you to hear it from someone who knew, who was there at the time, so you get the full story.'

'You?' Billy said, turning to Izzy. 'You were *there?* Up at the horse?'

'No, no,' said Izzy hastily. 'It happened during the school holidays.'

She took a fortifying gulp of wine, set down her glass, drew a deep breath and said:

'Fizz and I were both staying with school friends. I – I heard what happened, afterwards . . .

'What happened was . . . Freddie was home from university and he'd brought a few friends back with him. Papa left them in the house because he had some old regimental dinner to attend in London . . .

'Freddie could be . . . the truth is, he was awfully naughty sometimes. He brought up a lot of good wine from the cellar and they all got sloshed and then one of the girls said she'd wanted to try the truth of that story about the white horse . . . you know the one,' she said to Billy, the Uffington local. 'If you turn three times in the eye and make a wish . . .'

'Yeah,' said Billy, with a nod. His haunted eyes were huge.

'So they all left the house in the dark, but being Freddie . . . he *was* naughty . . . they made a detour through the woods to *your* house. Steda Cottage. Because Freddie wanted to buy some, ah, marijuana, was it, your brother grew?'

'Yeah,' said Billy, again.

'Freddie wanted to get some, so they could smoke it, up at the horse while the girls were making wishes. Of course, they shouldn't have been driving. They were already drunk.

'Well, when they got to your house, your father wasn't there—'

'He was in the barn,' said Billy suddenly. 'Finishing a set of . . . you know.'

The memory seemed to have forced its way to the front of his mind, triggered by her recital. Strike saw Billy's left hand holding tightly to his right, to prevent the recurrence of the tic that seemed for Billy to have something of the significance of warding off evil. Rain continued to lash the restaurant windows and Serge Gainsbourg sang, '*Oh, je voudrais tant que tu te souviennes . . .*'

'So,' said Izzy, taking another deep breath, 'the way I heard it, from one of the girls who was there . . . I don't want to say who,' she added a little defensively to Strike and Robin, 'it's a long time ago and she was traumatised by the whole thing . . . well, Freddie and his friends clattering into the cottage woke you up, Billy. There was quite a crowd of them in there, and Jimmy rolled them a joint before they set off . . . Anyway,' Izzy swallowed, 'you were hungry, and Jimmy . . . or maybe,' she winced, 'maybe it was Freddie, I don't know . . . they thought it would be funny to crumble up some of what they were smoking and put it in your yoghurt.'

Robin imagined Freddie's friends, some of them perhaps enjoying the exotic thrill of sitting in that dark workman's cottage with a local lad who sold drugs, but others, like the girl who had told Izzy the story, uneasy about what was going on, but too young, too scared of their laughing peers to intervene. They had seemed like adults to the five-year-old Billy, but now Robin knew that they had all been nineteen to twenty-one at most.

'Yeah,' said Billy quietly. 'I knew they'd gave me something.'

'So, then, Jimmy wanted to join them, going up the hill. I heard he'd taken a bit of a fancy to one of the girls,' said Izzy primly. 'But you weren't very well, after being fed that yoghurt. He couldn't leave you alone in that state, so he took you with him.

'You all piled into a couple of Land Rovers and off you went, to Dragon Hill.'

'But . . . no, this is wrong,' said Billy. The haunted expression had returned to his face. 'Where's the little girl? She was already there. She was with us in the car. I remember them taking her out when we got to the hill. She was crying for her mum.'

'It – it wasn't a girl,' said Izzy. 'That was just Freddie's – well, it was his idea of humour—'

'It *was* a girl. They called her by a girl's name,' said Billy. 'I remember.'

'Yes,' said Izzy miserably. 'Raphaela.'

'That's it!' said Billy loudly, and heads turned across the restaurant. 'That's it!' Billy repeated in a whisper, his eyes wide. 'Raphaela, that's what they called her—'

'It wasn't a girl, Billy . . . it was my little – it was my little—'

Izzy pressed the napkin to her eyes again.

'*So* sorry . . . it was my little brother, Raphael. Freddie and his friends were supposed to be babysitting him, with my father away from home. Raff was awfully cute when he was little. He'd been woken up by them, too, I think, and the girls said they couldn't leave him in the house, they should take him with them. Freddie didn't want to. He wanted to leave Raff there on his own, but the girls promised they'd take care of him.

'But once they were up there, Freddie was awfully drunk

and he'd had a lot of weed and Raff wouldn't stop crying and Freddie got angry. He said he was ruining everything and then . . . '

'He throttled him,' said Billy, with a panicked expression. 'It was real, he killed—'

'No, no, he didn't!' said Izzy, distressed. 'Billy, you know he didn't – you *must* remember Raff, he came to us every summer, he's alive!'

'Freddie put his hands round Raphael's neck,' said Strike, 'and squeezed until he was unconscious. Raphael urinated. He collapsed. But he didn't die.'

Billy's left hand was still gripping his right tightly.

'I *did* see it.'

'Yeah, you did,' said Strike, 'and, all things considered, you were a bloody good witness.'

The waitress returned with their meals. Once everyone was served, Strike with his rib-eye steak and chips, the two women with their quinoa salads and Billy with the soup, which was all he seemed to have felt confident ordering, Izzy continued her story.

'Raff told me what had happened when I got back from the holidays. He was so little, so upset, I tried to bring it up with Papa, but he wouldn't listen. He just sort of brushed me off. Said Raphael was whiny and always . . . always complaining . . .

'And I look back,' she said to Strike and Robin, her eyes filling with tears again, 'and I think about it all . . . how much hate Raff must've felt, after things like that . . . '

'Yeah, Raphael's defence team will probably try and use that kind of thing,' said Strike briskly, as he attacked his steak, 'but the fact remains, Izzy, that he didn't act on his desire to see your father dead until he found out there was a Stubbs hanging upstairs.'

'A disputed Stubbs,' Izzy corrected Strike, pulling a handkerchief out of her cuff and blowing her nose. 'Henry Drummond thinks it's a copy. The man from Christie's is hopeful, but there's a Stubbs aficionado in the States who's flying over to examine it, and he says it doesn't match the notes Stubbs made of the lost painting . . . but honestly,' she shook her head, 'I don't give a damn. What that thing's led to, what it's done to our family . . . it can go in a skip for all I care. There are more important things,' said Izzy croakily, 'than money.'

Strike had an excuse for making no reply, his mouth being full of steak, but he wondered whether it had occurred to Izzy that the fragile man beside her was living in a tiny two-roomed flat in East Ham with his brother, and that Billy was, properly speaking, owed money from the sale of the last set of gallows. Perhaps, once the Stubbs was sold, the Chiswell family might consider fulfilling that obligation.

Billy was eating his soup in an almost trancelike state, his eyes unfocused. Robin thought his deeply contemplative state seemed peaceful, even happy.

'So, I must've got confused, mustn't I?' Billy asked at last. He spoke now with the confidence of a man who feels firm footing in reality. 'I saw the horse being buried and thought it was the kid. I got mixed up, that's all.'

'Well,' said Strike, 'I think there might be a bit more to it than that. You knew that the man who'd throttled the child was the same one burying the horse in the dell with your father. I suppose Freddie wasn't around much, being so much older than you, so you weren't completely clear who he was . . . but I think you've blocked out a lot about the horse and how it died. You conflated two acts of cruelty, perpetrated by the same person.'

'What happened,' asked Billy, now slightly apprehensive, 'to the horse?'

'Don't you remember Spotty?' asked Izzy.

Amazed, Billy set down his soup spoon and held his hand horizontally perhaps three feet off the ground.

'That little – yeah . . . didn't it graze the croquet lawn?'

'She was an *ancient*, miniature spotted horse,' Izzy explained to Strike and Robin. 'She was the last of Tinky's lot. Tinky had awful, kitschy taste, even in horses . . .'

(. . . *nobody noticed, and you know why? Because they're such fucking arrogant snobs* . . .)

' . . . but Spotty was awfully sweet,' Izzy admitted. 'She'd follow you around like a dog if you were in the garden . . .

'I don't think Freddie *meant* to do it . . . but,' she said hopelessly, 'oh, I don't know any more. I don't know what he was thinking . . . he always had a terrible temper. Something had annoyed him. Papa was out, he took Papa's rifle out of the gun cabinet, went up on the roof and started shooting at birds and then . . . well, he told me afterwards he hadn't meant to hit Spotty, but he must have been aiming near her, mustn't he, to kill her?'

He was aiming at her, thought Strike. *You don't put two bullets in an animal's head from that distance without meaning to.*

'Then he panicked,' said Izzy. 'He got Jack o' – I mean, your father,' she told Billy, 'to help him bury the body. When Papa came home Freddie pretended Spotty had collapsed, that he'd called the vet who'd taken her away, but of course, that story didn't stand up for two minutes. Papa was *furious* when he found out the truth. He couldn't abide cruelty to animals.

'I was heartbroken when I heard,' said Izzy sadly. 'I loved Spotty.'

'You didn't by any chance put a cross in the ground where she'd been buried, did you, Izzy?' asked Robin, her fork suspended in mid-air.

'How on *earth* did you know that?' asked Izzy, astonished, as tears trickled out of her eyes again, and she reached again for her handkerchief.

The downpour continued as Strike and Robin walked away from the brasserie together, along Chelsea Embankment towards Albert Bridge. The slate-grey Thames rolled eternally onwards, its surface barely troubled by the thickening rain that threatened to extinguish Strike's cigarette, and soaked the few tendrils of hair that had escaped the hood of Robin's raincoat.

'Well, that's the upper classes for you,' said Strike. 'By all means throttle their kids, but don't touch their horses.'

'Not entirely fair,' Robin reproved him. 'Izzy thinks Raphael was treated appallingly.'

'Nothing to what he's got coming to him in Dartmoor,' said Strike indifferently. 'My pity's limited.'

'Yes,' said Robin, 'you made that abundantly clear.'

Their shoes smacked wetly on the shining pavement.

'CBT still going all right?' Strike asked, who was limiting the question to once weekly. 'Keeping up your exercises?'

'Diligently,' said Robin.

'Don't be flippant, I'm serious—'

'So am I,' said Robin, without heat. 'I'm doing what I've got to do. I haven't had a single panic attack for weeks. How's your leg?'

'Getting better. Doing my stretches. Watching my diet.'

'You just ate half a potato field and most of a cow.'

'That was the last meal I can charge to the Chiswells,' said Strike. 'Wanted to make the most of it. What are your plans this afternoon?'

'I need to get that file from Andy, then I'll ring the guy in Finsbury Park and see whether he'll talk to us. Oh, and

Nick and Ilsa said to ask if you want to come for a takeaway curry tonight.'

Robin had caved in to the combined insistence of Nick, Ilsa and Strike himself that going to live in a box room in a house full of strangers was undesirable in the immediate aftermath of being taken hostage at gunpoint. In three days' time, she would be moving into a room in a flat in Earl's Court, which she would share with a gay actor friend of Ilsa's whose previous partner had moved out. Her new flatmate's stated requirements were cleanliness, sanity and tolerance of irregular hours.

'Yeah, great,' said Strike. 'I'll have to head back to the office first. Barclay reckons he's got Dodgy bang to rights this time. Another teenager, going in and out of a hotel together.'

'Great,' said Robin. 'No, I don't mean great, I mean—'

'It *is* great,' said Strike firmly, as the rain splashed over and around them. 'Another satisfied client. The bank balance is looking uncharacteristically healthy. Might be able to hike your salary up a bit. Anyway, I'm going up here. See you at Nick and Ilsa's later, then.'

They parted with a wave, concealing from each other the slight smile that each wore once safely walking away, pleased to know that they would meet again in a few short hours, over curry and beer at Nick and Ilsa's. But soon Robin had given over her thoughts to the questions needing answers from a man in Finsbury Park.

Head bowed against the rain, she had no attention left to spare for the magnificent mansion past which she was walking, its rain-specked windows facing the great river, its front doors engraved with twin swans.

ACKNOWLEDGEMENTS

For reasons not entirely related to the complexity of the plot, *Lethal White* has been one of the most challenging books I've written, but it's also one of my favourites. I truly couldn't have done it without the help of the following people.

David Shelley, my wonderful editor, allowed me all the time I needed to make the novel exactly what I wanted it to be. Without his understanding, patience and skill, there might not be a *Lethal White* at all.

My husband Neil read the manuscript while I was writing it. His feedback was invaluable and he also supported me in a thousand practical ways, but I think I'm most grateful for the fact that he never once asked why I decided to write a large, complex novel while also working on a play and two screenplays. I know he knows why, but there aren't many people who would have resisted the temptation.

Mr Galbraith still can't quite believe his luck at having a fantastic agent who is also a dear friend. Thank you, The Other Neil (Blair).

Many people helped me research the various locations Strike and Robin visit during the course of this story and gave me the benefit of their experience and knowledge. My deepest thanks to:

Simon Berry and Stephen Fry, who took me for a fabulous, memorable lunch at Pratt's and enabled me to look at the betting book; Jess Phillips MP, who was incredibly helpful, gave me an insider's tour of the Commons and Portcullis House and, with Sophie Francis-Cansfield, David Doig and Ian Stevens, answered innumerable questions about life at Westminster; Baroness Joanna Shields, who was so kind and generous with her time, showed me inside DCMS, answered all my questions and enabled me to visit Lancaster House; Racquel Black, who couldn't have been more helpful, especially in taking pictures when I ran out of battery; Ian Chapman and James Yorke, who gave me a fascinating tour of Lancaster House; and Brian Spanner, for the daytrip to Horse Isle.

I'd be totally lost without my office and home support team. Huge thanks, therefore, to Di Brooks, Danni Cameron, Angela Milne, Ross Milne and Kaisa Tiensuu for their hard work and good humour, both of which are deeply appreciated.

After sixteen years together, I hope Fiona Shapcott knows exactly how much she means to me. Thank you, Fi, for everything you do.

My friend David Goodwin has been an unfailing source of inspiration and this book would not be what it is without him.

The QSC, on the other hand, have just got in the way.

To Mark Hutchinson, Rebecca Salt and Nicky Stonehill, thank you for holding everything together this year, especially those bits when you were holding *me* together.

Last but never, ever, least: thanks to my children, Jessica, David and Kenzie, for putting up with me. Having a writer for a mother isn't always an easy shift, but the real world wouldn't be worth living in without you and Dad.

CREDITS

Rosmersholm epigraphs *Complete Works of Henrik Ibsen* (Hastings: Delphi Classics, ebook), 2013. Translated by Robert Farquharson.

'Wherever You Will Go' (p 27 and p 30) Words and Music by Aaron Kamin & Alex Band. © 2001 Alex Band Music/Universal Music Careers/BMG Platinum Songs/Amedeo Music. Universal Music Publishing MGB Limited/BMG Rights Management (US) LLC. All Rights Reserved. Used by Permission of Hal Leonard Europe Limited.

'No Woman No Cry' (p 109 and p 110) Written by Vincent Ford. Published by Fifty Six Hope Road Music Limited/Primary Wave/Blue Mountain Music. All Rights Reserved.

'Hear the word of Lachesis, the daughter of Necessity' (p 223) *The Dialogues of Plato* (New York: Scribner, Armstrong & Co, ebook), 1873.

'Where Have You Been' (p 493) Words and Music by Lukasz Gottwald, Geoff Mack, Adam Wiles, Esther Dean & Henry Russell Walter. © 2012 Kasz Money Publishing/Dat Damn Dean Music/Prescription Songs/Songs Of Universal Inc/Oneirology Publishing/TSJ Merlyn Licensing BV/Hill And Range Southwind Mus S A. Carlin Music Corporation/Kobalt Music Publishing Limited/Universal/MCA Music Limited/EMI Music Publishing Limited. All Rights Reserved. Used by Permission of Hal Leonard Europe Limited.

'Niggas In Paris' (p 527 and p 529) Words & Music by Reverend W. A. Donaldson, Kanye West, Chauncey Hollis, Shawn Carter & Mike Dean. © 2011 Unichappell Music Inc. (BMI)/EMI Blackwood Music Inc./Songs Of Universal Inc./Please Gimme My Publishing Inc./U Can't Teach Bein' The Shhh Inc./Carter Boys Music (ASCAP)/Papa George Music (BMI). EMI Music Publishing Limited/Universal/MCA Music Limited. All rights on behalf of Papa George Music, Carter Boys Music and Unichappell Music Inc. administered by Warner/Chappell North America Ltd. All Rights Reserved. Used by Permission of Hal Leonard Europe Limited, Sony/ATV Music Publishing and Warner/Chappell North America Ltd.

'Black Trombone' (p 759 and p 760) Words and Music by Serge Gainsbourg. © 1962 Melody Nelson Publishing/Warner Chappell Music France. Imagem Music/Warner/Chappell Overseas Holdings Limited. Used by Permission of Hal Leonard Europe Limited and Warner/Chappell Overseas Holdings Limited.

'La Chanson de Prévert' (p 765) Words and Music by Serge Gainsbourg. © 1961 Melody Nelson Publishing/Warner Chappell Music France. Imagem Music/Warner/Chappell Overseas Holdings Limited. Used by Permission of Hal Leonard Europe Limited and Warner/Chappell Overseas Holdings Limited.

READ
THE FIRST NOVEL FEATURING CORMORAN STRIKE

'Reminds me why I fell in love with crime fiction in the first place'
Val McDermid

'A scintillating novel'
The Times

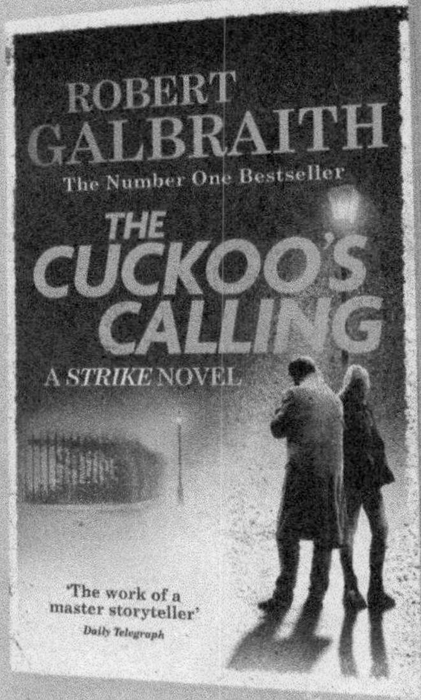

When a troubled model falls to her death from a snow-covered Mayfair balcony, it is assumed that she has committed suicide. However, her brother has his doubts, and calls in private investigator Cormoran Strike to look into the case.

Strike is a war veteran – wounded both physically and psychologically – and his life is in disarray. The case gives him a financial lifeline, but it comes at a personal cost: the more he delves into the young model's complex world, the darker things get – and the closer he gets to terrible danger . . .

A gripping, elegant mystery steeped in the atmosphere of London – from the hushed streets of Mayfair to the backstreet pubs of the East End to the bustle of Soho – *The Cuckoo's Calling* introduces Cormoran Strike in the acclaimed first crime novel by Robert Galbraith – J.K. Rowling's pseudonym.

READ
THE STARTLING NEW ADDITION TO THE STRIKE SERIES

'An ambitious, immersive mystery'
Heat

'Confident, utterly gripping, niftily plotted'
India Knight

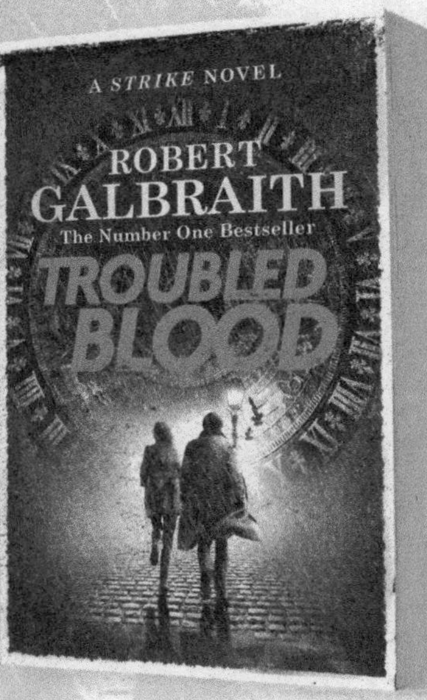

Private Detective Cormoran Strike is visiting his family in Cornwall when he is approached by a woman asking for help finding her mother, Margot Bamborough – who went missing in mysterious circumstances in 1974.

Strike has never tackled a cold case before, let alone one forty years old. But despite the slim chance of success, he is intrigued and takes it on; adding to the long list of cases that he and his partner in the agency, Robin Ellacott, are currently working on. And Robin herself is also juggling a messy divorce and unwanted male attention, as well as battling her own feelings about Strike.

As Strike and Robin investigate Margot's disappearance, they come up against a fiendishly complex case with leads that include tarot cards, a psychopathic serial killer and witnesses who cannot all be trusted. And they learn that even cases decades old can prove to be deadly . . .

A breathtaking, labyrinthine epic, *Troubled Blood* is the fifth Strike and Robin novel and the most gripping and satisfying yet.

Praise for *Career of Evil:*

'Quirkily different . . . let's hope the sardonic Strike is here to stay' ***Independent***

'The denouement is violent, unexpected and satisfying . . . [an] entertaining novel' ***The Times***

'As readable and exciting as ever' ***Daily Telegraph***

'A confident hold on a deliriously clever plot' ***Guardian***

'A page-turner with legs that will keep you up all night' ***Observer***

'Thoroughly enjoyable' ***Mail on Sunday***

'Criminally good stuff' ***Sun***

'[A] smart and addictive thriller' ***Sunday Mirror***

'A book that abounds with ideas' ***Scotland on Sunday***

'Oozes atmosphere . . . a rollicking good story' ***Metro***

'The real joy of this series comes from the originality of the characters' ***Morning Star***

By Robert Galbraith

The Cuckoo's Calling

The Silkworm

Career of Evil

Lethal White

Troubled Blood

CAREER OF EVIL

ROBERT
GALBRAITH

sphere

SPHERE

First published in Great Britain in 2015 by Sphere
Paperback edition published in 2016 by Sphere
This reissue published in 2018 by Sphere

21

A CIP catalogue record for this book is available from the British Library.

ISBN 978-0-7515-6359-7

Typeset in Bembo by M Rules
Printed and bound in Great Britain by Clays Ltd, Elcograf S.p.A.

Papers used by Sphere are from well-managed forests and other responsible sources.

Sphere
An imprint of
Little, Brown Book Group
Carmelite House
50 Victoria Embankment
London EC4Y 0DZ

An Hachette UK Company
www.hachette.co.uk

www.littlebrown.co.uk

See pages 575–579 for full credits.

Selected Blue Öyster Cult lyrics 1967–1994 by kind permission of Sony/ATV Music Publishing (UK) Ltd.

www.blueoystercult.com

'Don't Fear the Reaper: The Best of Blue Öyster Cult' from Sony Music Entertainment Inc available now via iTunes and all usual musical retail outlets.

To Séan and Matthew Harris,

Do whatever you want with this dedication,
but don't –
don't –
use it on your eyebrows.

I choose to steal what you choose to show
And you know I will not apologize –
You're mine for the taking.

I'm making a career of evil . . .

Blue Öyster Cult, 'Career of Evil'
Lyrics by Patti Smith

1

2011

This Ain't the Summer of Love

He had not managed to scrub off all her blood. A dark line like a parenthesis lay under the middle fingernail of his left hand. He set to digging it out, although he quite liked seeing it there: a memento of the previous day's pleasures. After a minute's fruitless scraping, he put the bloody nail in his mouth and sucked. The ferrous tang recalled the smell of the torrent that had splashed wildly onto the tiled floor, spattering the walls, drenching his jeans and turning the peach-coloured bath towels – fluffy, dry and neatly folded – into blood-soaked rags.

Colours seemed brighter this morning, the world a lovelier place. He felt serene and uplifted, as though he had absorbed her, as though her life had been transfused into him. They belonged to you once you had killed them: it was a possession way beyond sex. Even to know how they looked at the moment of death was an intimacy way past anything two living bodies could experience.

With a thrill of excitement he reflected that nobody knew what he had done, nor what he was planning to do next. He sucked his middle finger, happy and at peace, leaning up against the warm wall in the weak April sunshine, his eyes on the house opposite.

It was not a smart house. Ordinary. A nicer place to live, admittedly, than the tiny flat where yesterday's blood-stiffened clothing lay in black bin bags, awaiting incineration, and where his knives lay gleaming, washed clean with bleach, rammed up behind the U-bend under the kitchen sink.

This house had a small front garden, black railings and a lawn in need of mowing. Two white front doors had been crammed together side by side, showing that the three-storey building had been converted into upper and lower flats. A girl called Robin Ellacott lived on the ground floor. Though he had made it his business to find out her real name, inside his own head he called her The Secretary. He had just seen her pass in front of the bow window, easily recognisable because of her bright hair.

Watching The Secretary was an extra, a pleasurable add-on. He had a few hours spare so he had decided to come and look at her. Today was a day of rest, between the glories of yesterday and tomorrow, between the satisfaction of what had been done and the excitement of what would happen next.

The right-hand door opened unexpectedly and The Secretary came out, accompanied by a man.

Still leaning into the warm wall, he stared along the street with his profile turned towards them, so that he might appear to be waiting for a friend. Neither of them paid him any attention. They walked off up the street, side by side. After he had given them a minute's head start, he decided to follow.

She was wearing jeans, a light jacket and flat-heeled boots. Her long wavy hair was slightly ginger now that he saw her in the sunshine. He thought he detected a slight reserve between the couple, who weren't talking to each other.

He was good at reading people. He had read and charmed

the girl who had died yesterday among the blood-soaked peach towels.

Down the long residential street he tracked them, his hands in his pockets, ambling along as though heading for the shops, his sunglasses unremarkable on this brilliant morning. Trees waved gently in the slight spring breeze. At the end of the street the pair ahead turned left into a wide, busy thoroughfare lined with offices. Sheet glass windows blazed high above him in the sunlight as they passed the Ealing council building.

Now The Secretary's flatmate, or boyfriend, or whatever he was – clean-cut and square-jawed in profile – was talking to her. She returned a short answer and did not smile.

Women were so petty, mean, dirty and small. Sulky bitches, the lot of them, expecting men to keep them happy. Only when they lay dead and empty in front of you did they become purified, mysterious and even wonderful. They were entirely yours then, unable to argue or struggle or leave, yours to do with whatever you liked. The other one's corpse had been heavy and floppy yesterday after he had drained it of blood: his life-sized plaything, his toy.

Through the bustling Arcadia shopping centre he followed The Secretary and her boyfriend, gliding behind them like a ghost or a god. Could the Saturday shoppers even see him, or was he somehow transformed, doubly alive, gifted with invisibility?

They had arrived at a bus stop. He hovered nearby, pretending to look through the door of a curry house, at fruit piled high in front of a grocer's, at cardboard masks of Prince William and Kate Middleton hanging in a newsagent's window, watching their reflections in the glass.

They were going to get on the number 83. He did not have a lot of money in his pockets, but he was so enjoying watching her that he did not want it to end yet. As he climbed aboard behind them he heard the man mention Wembley Central. He bought a ticket and followed them upstairs.

The couple found seats together, right at the front of the bus. He took a place nearby, next to a grumpy woman whom he forced to move her bags of shopping. Their voices carried sometimes over the hum of the other passengers. When not talking, The Secretary looked out of the window, unsmiling. She did not want to go wherever they were going, he was sure of it. When she pushed a strand of hair out of her eyes he noticed that she was wearing an engagement ring. So she was going to be getting married . . . or so she thought. He hid his faint smile in the upturned collar of his jacket.

The warm midday sun was pouring through the dirt-stippled bus windows. A group of men got on and filled the surrounding seats. A couple of them were wearing red and black rugby shirts.

He felt, suddenly, as though the day's radiance had dimmed. Those shirts, with the crescent moon and star, had associations he did not like. They reminded him of a time when he had not felt like a god. He did not want his happy day spotted and stained by old memories, bad memories, but his elation was suddenly draining away. Angry now – a teenage boy in the group caught his eye, but looked hurriedly away, alarmed – he got up and headed back to the stairs.

A father and his small son were holding tight to the pole beside the bus doors. An explosion of anger in the pit of his stomach: *he* should have had a son. Or rather, he should *still* have had a son. He pictured the boy standing beside him, looking up at him, hero-worshipping him – but his son was long gone, which was entirely due to a man called Cormoran Strike.

He was going to have revenge on Cormoran Strike. He was going to wreak havoc upon him.

When he reached the pavement he looked up at the bus's

front windows and caught one last glimpse of The Secretary's golden head. He would be seeing her again in less than twenty-four hours. That reflection helped calm the sudden rage caused by the sight of those Saracens shirts. The bus rumbled off and he strode away in the opposite direction, soothing himself as he walked.

He had a wonderful plan. Nobody knew. Nobody suspected. And he had something very special waiting for him in the fridge at home.

2

> A rock through a window never comes with a kiss.
>
> Blue Öyster Cult, 'Madness to the Method'

Robin Ellacott was twenty-six years old and had been engaged for over a year. Her wedding ought to have taken place three months previously, but the unexpected death of her future mother-in-law had led to the ceremony's postponement. Much had happened during the three months since the wedding should have happened. Would she and Matthew have been getting on better if vows had been exchanged, she wondered. Would they be arguing less if a golden band was sitting beneath the sapphire engagement ring that had become a little loose on her finger?

Fighting her way through the rubble on Tottenham Court Road on Monday morning, Robin mentally relived the argument of the previous day. The seeds had been sown before they had even left the house for the rugby. Every time they met up with Sarah Shadlock and her boyfriend Tom, Robin and Matthew seemed to row, something that Robin had pointed out as the argument, which had been brewing since the match, dragged on into the small hours of the morning.

'Sarah was shit-stirring, for God's sake – can't you see it? *She* was the one asking all about him, going on and on, I didn't start it . . .'

The everlasting roadworks around Tottenham Court Road station had obstructed Robin's walk to work ever since she had started at the private detective agency in Denmark Street. Her mood was not improved by tripping on a large chunk of rubble; she staggered a few steps before recovering her balance. A barrage of wolf-whistles and lewd remarks issued from a deep chasm in the road full of men in hard hats and fluorescent jackets. Shaking long strawberry-blonde hair out of her eyes, red in the face, she ignored them, her thoughts returning irresistibly to Sarah Shadlock and her sly, persistent questions about Robin's boss.

'He is *strangely* attractive, isn't he? Bit beaten-up-looking, but I've never minded that. Is he sexy in the flesh? He's a big guy, isn't he?'

Robin had seen Matthew's jaw tightening as she tried to return cool, indifferent answers.

'Is it just the two of you in the office? Is it really? Nobody else at all?'

Bitch, thought Robin, whose habitual good nature had never stretched to Sarah Shadlock. *She knew exactly what she was doing.*

'Is it true he was decorated in Afghanistan? Is it? Wow, so we're talking a war hero too?'

Robin had tried her hardest to shut down Sarah's one-woman chorus of appreciation for Cormoran Strike, but to no avail: a coolness had crept into Matthew's manner towards his fiancée by the end of the match. His displeasure had not prevented him bantering and laughing with Sarah on the journey back from Vicarage Road, though, and Tom, whom Robin found boring and obtuse, had chortled away, oblivious to any undercurrents.

Jostled by passers-by also navigating the open trenches in

the road, Robin finally reached the opposite pavement, passing beneath the shadow of the concrete grid-like monolith that was Centre Point and becoming angry all over again as she remembered what Matthew had told her at midnight, when the argument had burst back into flame.

'You can't stop bloody talking about him, can you? I heard you, to Sarah—'

'I *did not* start talking about him again, it was *her*, you weren't listening—'

But Matthew had imitated her, using the generic voice that stood for all women, high-pitched and imbecilic: '*Oh, his hair's so lovely*—'

'For God's sake, you're completely bloody paranoid!' Robin had shouted. '*Sarah* was banging on about Jacques Burger's bloody hair, not Cormoran's, and all I said—'

'"*Not Cormoran's*,"' he had repeated in that moronic squeal. As Robin rounded the corner into Denmark Street she felt as furious as she had eight hours ago, when she had stormed out of the bedroom to sleep on the sofa.

Sarah Shadlock, bloody Sarah Shadlock, who had been at university with Matthew and had tried as hard as she could to win him away from Robin, the girl left behind in Yorkshire . . . If Robin could have been sure she would never see Sarah again she would have rejoiced, but Sarah would be at their wedding in July, Sarah would doubtless continue to plague their married life, and perhaps one day she would try to worm her way into Robin's office to meet Strike, if her interest was genuine and not merely a means of sowing discord between Robin and Matthew.

I will never *introduce her to Cormoran*, thought Robin savagely as she approached the courier standing outside the door to the office. He had a clipboard in one gloved hand and a long rectangular package in the other.

'Is that for Ellacott?' Robin asked as she came within

speaking distance. She was expecting an order of ivory cardboard-covered disposable cameras, which were to be favours at the wedding reception. Her working hours had become so irregular of late that she found it easier to send online orders to the office rather than the flat.

The courier nodded and held out the clipboard without taking off his motorcycle helmet. Robin signed and took the long package, which was much heavier than she had expected; it felt as though some single large object slid inside it as she put it under her arm.

'Thank you,' she said, but the courier had already turned away and swung a leg over his motorbike. She heard him ride away as she let herself inside the building.

Up the echoing metal staircase that wound around the broken birdcage lift she walked, her heels clanging on the metal. The glass door flashed as she unlocked and opened it and the engraved legend – C. B. STRIKE, PRIVATE INVESTIGATOR – stood out darkly.

She had arrived deliberately early. They were currently inundated with cases and she wanted to catch up with some paperwork before resuming her daily surveillance of a young Russian lap-dancer. From the sound of heavy footfalls overhead, she deduced that Strike was still upstairs in his flat.

Robin laid her oblong package on the desk, took off her coat and hung it, with her bag, on a peg behind the door, turned on the light, filled and switched on the kettle, then reached for the sharp letter-opener on her desk. Remembering Matthew's flat refusal to believe that it had been flanker Jacques Burger's curly mane she had been admiring, rather than Strike's short and frankly pube-like hair, she made an angry stab to the end of the package, slit it open and pulled the box apart.

A woman's severed leg had been crammed sideways in the box, the toes of the foot bent back to fit.

3

Half-a-hero in a hard-hearted game.

Blue Öyster Cult, 'The Marshall Plan'

Robin's scream reverberated off the windows. She backed away from the desk, staring at the obscene object lying there. The leg was smooth, slender and pale, and she had grazed it with her finger as she pulled its packaging open, felt the cold rubbery texture of the skin.

She had just managed to quell her scream by clamping her hands over her mouth when the glass door burst open beside her. Six foot three and scowling, Strike's shirt hung open, revealing a monkeyish mass of dark chest hair.

'What the—?'

He followed her stricken gaze and saw the leg. She felt his hand close roughly over her upper arm and he steered her out onto the landing.

'How did it arrive?'

'Courier,' she said, allowing him to walk her up the stairs. 'On a motorbike.'

'Wait here. I'll call the police.'

When he had closed the door of his flat behind her she stood quite still, heart juddering, listening to his footsteps returning downstairs. Acid rose in her throat. A leg. She had just been given a leg. She had just carried a leg calmly upstairs, a woman's leg in a box. Whose leg was it? Where was the rest of her?

She crossed to the nearest chair, a cheap affair of padded plastic and metal legs, and sat down, her fingers still pressed against her numb lips. The package, she remembered, had been addressed to her by name.

Strike, meanwhile, was at the office window that looked down into the road, scanning Denmark Street for any sign of the courier, his mobile pressed to his ear. By the time he returned to the outer office to scrutinise the open package on the desk, he had made contact with the police.

'A leg?' repeated Detective Inspective Eric Wardle on the end of the line. 'A fucking *leg*?'

'And it's not even my size,' said Strike, a joke he would not have made had Robin been present. His trouser leg was hitched up to reveal the metal rod that served as his right ankle. He had been in the process of dressing when he had heard Robin's scream.

Even as he said it, he realised that this was a right leg, like his own lost limb, and that it had been cut below the knee, which was exactly where he had been amputated. His mobile still clamped to his ear, Strike peered more closely at the limb, his nostrils filling with an unpleasant smell like recently defrosted chicken. Caucasian skin: smooth, pale and unblemished but for an old greenish bruise on the calf, imperfectly shaven. The stubbly hairs were fair and the unpainted toenails a little grubby. The severed tibia shone icy white against the surrounding flesh. A clean cut: Strike thought it likely to have been made by an axe or a cleaver.

'A woman's, did you say?'

'Looks like—'

Strike had noticed something else. There was scarring on

the calf where the leg had been severed: old scarring, unrelated to the wound that had taken it from the body.

How many times during his Cornish childhood had he been caught unawares as he stood with his back to the treacherous sea? Those who did not know the ocean well forgot its solidity, its brutality. When it slammed into them with the force of cold metal they were appalled. Strike had faced, worked with and managed fear all his professional life, but the sight of that old scarring rendered him temporarily winded by a terror all the worse for its unexpectedness.

'Are you still there?' said Wardle on the end of the line.

'What?'

Strike's twice-broken nose was within an inch of the place where the woman's leg had been cut off. He was remembering the scarred leg of a child he had never forgotten . . . how long was it since he had seen her? How old would she be now?

'You called me first . . . ?' Wardle prompted.

'Yeah,' said Strike, forcing himself to concentrate. 'I'd rather you did it than anyone else, but if you can't—'

'I'm on my way,' said Wardle. 'Won't be long. Sit tight.'

Strike turned off his phone and set it down, still staring at the leg. Now he saw that there was a note lying underneath it, a typed note. Trained by the British Army in investigative procedure, Strike resisted the powerful temptation to tug it out and read it: he must not taint forensic evidence. Instead he crouched down unsteadily so that he could read the address hanging upside down on the open lid.

The box had been addressed to Robin, which he did not like at all. Her name was correctly spelled, typed on a white sticker that bore the address of their office. This sticker overlay another. Squinting, determined not to reposition the box even to read the address more clearly, he saw that the sender had first addressed the box to 'Cameron Strike', then overlain it with the second sticker reading 'Robin Ellacott'. Why had they changed their mind?

'Fuck,' said Strike quietly.

He stood up with some difficulty, took Robin's handbag from the peg behind the door, locked the glass door and headed upstairs.

'Police are on their way,' he told her as he set her bag down in front of her. 'Want a cup of tea?'

She nodded.

'Want brandy in it?'

'You haven't got any brandy,' she said. Her voice was slightly croaky.

'Have you been looking?'

'Of course not!' she said, and he smiled at how indignant she sounded at the suggestion she might have been through his cupboards. 'You're just – you're not the sort of person who'd have medicinal brandy.'

'Want a beer?'

She shook her head, unable to smile.

Once the tea had been made, Strike sat down opposite her with his own mug. He looked exactly what he was: a large ex-boxer who smoked too much and ate too much fast food. He had heavy eyebrows, a flattened and asymmetrical nose and, when not smiling, a permanent expression of sullen crossness. His dense, dark curly hair, still damp from the shower, reminded her of Jacques Burger and Sarah Shadlock. The row seemed a lifetime ago. She had only briefly thought of Matthew since coming upstairs. She dreaded telling him what had happened. He would be angry. He did not like her working for Strike.

'Have you looked at – at it?' she muttered, after picking up and setting down the boiling tea without drinking it.

'Yeah,' said Strike.

She did not know what else to ask. It was a severed leg. The situation was so horrible, so grotesque, that every question that occurred to her sounded ridiculous, crass. *Do you recognise it? Why do you think they sent it?* And, most pressing of all, *why to me?*

'The police'll want to hear about the courier,' he said.

'I know,' said Robin. 'I've been trying to remember everything about him.'

The downstairs door buzzer sounded.

'That'll be Wardle.'

'Wardle?' she repeated, startled.

'He's the friendliest copper we know,' Strike reminded her. 'Stay put, I'll bring him to you here.'

Strike had managed to make himself unpopular among the Metropolitan Police over the previous year, which was not entirely his fault. The fulsome press coverage of his two most notable detective triumphs had understandably galled those officers whose efforts he had trumped. However, Wardle, who had helped him out on the first of those cases, had shared in some of the subsequent glory and relations between them remained reasonably amicable. Robin had only ever seen Wardle in the newspaper reports of the case. Their paths had not crossed in court.

He turned out to be a handsome man with a thick head of chestnut hair and chocolate-brown eyes, who was wearing a leather jacket and jeans. Strike did not know whether he was more amused or irritated by the reflexive look Wardle gave Robin on entering the room – a swift zigzag sweep of her hair, her figure and her left hand, where his eyes lingered for a second on the sapphire and diamond engagement ring.

'Eric Wardle,' he said in a low voice, with what Strike felt was an unnecessarily charming smile. 'And this is Detective Sergeant Ekwensi.'

A thin black female officer whose hair was smoothed back in a bun had arrived with him. She gave Robin a brief smile and Robin found herself taking disproportionate comfort from the presence of another woman. Detective Sergeant Ekwensi then let her eyes stray around Strike's glorified bedsit.

'Where's this package?' she asked.

'Downstairs,' said Strike, drawing the keys to the office out of his pocket. 'I'll show you. Wife OK, Wardle?' he added as he prepared to leave the room with Detective Sergeant Ekwensi.

'What do you care?' retorted the officer, but to Robin's relief he dropped what she thought of as his counsellor's manner as he took the seat opposite her at the table and flipped open his notebook.

'He was standing outside the door when I came up the street,' Robin explained, when Wardle asked how the leg had arrived. 'I thought he was a courier. He was dressed in black leather – all black except for blue stripes on the shoulders of his jacket. His helmet was plain black and the visor was down and mirrored. He must have been at least six feet tall. Four or five inches taller than me, even allowing for the helmet.'

'Build?' asked Wardle, who was scribbling in his notebook.

'Pretty big, I'd say, but he was probably padded out a bit by the jacket.'

Robin's eyes wandered inadvertently to Strike as he re-entered the room. 'I mean, not—'

'Not a fat bastard like the boss?' Strike, who had overheard, suggested and Wardle, never slow to make or enjoy a dig at Strike, laughed under his breath.

'And he wore gloves,' said Robin, who had not smiled. 'Black leather motorcycle gloves.'

'Of course he'd wear gloves,' said Wardle, adding a note. 'I don't suppose you noticed anything about the motorbike?'

'It was a Honda, red and black,' said Robin. 'I noticed the logo, that winged symbol. I'd say 750cc. It was big.'

Wardle looked both startled and impressed.

'Robin's a petrolhead,' said Strike. 'Drives like Fernando Alonso.'

Robin wished that Strike would stop being cheery and flippant. A woman's leg lay downstairs. Where was the rest of her? She must not cry. She wished she had had more sleep. That damn sofa . . . she had spent too many nights on the thing lately . . .

'And he made you sign for it?' asked Wardle.

'I wouldn't say "made" me,' said Robin. 'He held out a clipboard and I did it automatically.'

'What was on the clipboard?'

'It looked like an invoice or . . .'

She closed her eyes in the effort to remember. Now she came to think of it, the form had looked amateurish, as though it had been put together on someone's laptop, and she said as much.

'Were you expecting a package?' Wardle asked.

Robin explained about the disposable wedding cameras.

'What did he do once you'd taken it?'

'Got back on the bike and left. He drove off into Charing Cross Road.'

There was a knock on the door of the flat and Detective Sergeant Ekwensi reappeared holding the note that Strike had noticed lying beneath the leg, which was now enclosed in an evidence bag.

'Forensics are here,' she told Wardle. 'This note was in the package. It would be good to know whether it means anything to Miss Ellacott.'

Wardle took the polythene-covered note and scanned it, frowning.

'It's gibberish,' he said, then read aloud: '"*A harvest of limbs, of arms and of legs, of necks—*"'

'"*—that turn like swans,*"' interrupted Strike, who was leaning against the cooker and too far away to read the note, '"*as if inclined to gasp or pray.*"'

The other three stared at him.

'They're lyrics,' said Strike. Robin did not like the expression on his face. She could tell that the words meant something to him, something bad. With what looked like an effort, he elucidated: 'From the last verse of "Mistress of the Salmon Salt". By Blue Öyster Cult.'

Detective Sergeant Ekwensi raised finely pencilled eyebrows.

'Who?'

'Big seventies rock band.'

'You know their stuff well, I take it?' asked Wardle.

'I know that song,' said Strike.

'Do you think you know who sent this?'

Strike hesitated. As the other three watched him, a confused series of images and memories passed rapidly through the detective's mind. A low voice said, She wanted to die. She was the quicklime girl. The thin leg of a twelve-year-old girl, scarred with silvery criss-crossing lines. A pair of small dark eyes like a ferret's, narrowed in loathing. The tattoo of a yellow rose.

And then – lagging behind the other memories, puffing into view, although it might have been another man's first thought – he remembered a charge sheet that made mention of a penis cut from a corpse and mailed to a police informer.

'Do you know who sent it?' repeated Wardle.

'Maybe,' said Strike. He glanced at Robin and Detective Sergeant Ekwensi. 'I'd rather talk about it alone. Have you got everything you want from Robin?'

'We'll need your name and address and so on,' said Wardle. 'Vanessa, can you take those?'

Detective Sergeant Ekwensi moved forwards with her notebook. The two men's clanging footsteps faded from earshot. In spite of the fact that she had no desire to see the severed leg again, Robin felt aggrieved at being left behind. It had been *her* name on the box.

The grisly package was still lying on the desk downstairs. Two more of Wardle's colleagues had been admitted by Detective Sergeant Ekwensi: one was taking photographs, the other talking on his mobile when their senior officer and the private detective walked past. Both looked curiously at Strike, who had achieved a measure of fame during the period in which he had managed to alienate many of Wardle's colleagues.

Strike closed the door of his inner office and he and Wardle took the seats facing each other across Strike's desk. Wardle turned to a fresh page of his notebook.

'All right, who d'you know who likes chopping up corpses and sending them through the post?'

'Terence Malley,' said Strike, after a momentary hesitation. 'For a start.'

Wardle did not write anything, but stared at him over the top of his pen.

'Terence "Digger" Malley?'

Strike nodded.

'Harringay Crime Syndicate?'

'How many Terence "Digger" Malleys do you know?' asked Strike impatiently. 'And how many have got a habit of sending people body parts?'

'How the hell did you get mixed up with Digger?'

'Joint ops with Vice Squad, 2008. Drug ring.'

'The bust he went down for?'

'Exactly.'

'Holy shit,' said Wardle. 'Well, that's bloody it, isn't it? The guy's an effing lunatic, he's just out and he's got easy access to half of London's prostitutes. We'd better start dragging the Thames for the rest of her.'

'Yeah, but I gave evidence anonymously. He shouldn't ever have known it was me.'

'They've got ways and means,' said Wardle. 'Harringay Crime Syndicate – they're like the fucking mafia. Did you hear how he sent Hatford Ali's dick to Ian Bevin?'

'Yeah, I heard,' said Strike.

'So what's the story with the song? The harvest of whatever the fuck it was?'

'Well, that's what I'm worried about,' said Strike slowly. 'It seems pretty subtle for the likes of Digger – which makes me think it might be one of the other three.'

4

Four winds at the Four Winds Bar,
Two doors locked and windows barred,
One door left to take you in,
The other one just mirrors it . . .

Blue Öyster Cult, 'Astronomy'

'You know *four men* who'd send you a severed leg? *Four?*'

Strike could see Robin's appalled expression reflected in the round mirror standing beside the sink, where he was shaving. The police had taken away the leg at last, Strike had declared work suspended for the day and Robin remained at the little Formica table in his kitchen-cum-sitting room, cradling a second mug of tea.

'To tell you the truth,' he said, strafing stubble from his chin, 'I think it's only three. Think I might've made a mistake telling Wardle about Malley.'

'Why?'

Strike told Robin the story of his brief contact with the career criminal, who owed his last prison stretch, in part, to Strike's evidence.

'. . . so now Wardle's convinced the Harringay Crime Syndicate found out who I was, but I left for Iraq shortly after testifying and I've never yet known an SIB officer's cover blown because he gave evidence in court. Plus, the song lyrics don't smell like Digger. He's not one for fancy touches.'

'But he's cut bits off people he's killed before?' Robin asked.

'Once that I know of – but don't forget, whoever did this hasn't necessarily killed anyone,' temporised Strike. 'The leg could have come off an existing corpse. Could be hospital waste. Wardle's going to check all that out. We won't know much until forensics have had a look.'

The ghastly possibility that the leg had been taken from a still-living person, he chose not to mention.

In the ensuing pause, Strike rinsed his razor under the kitchen tap and Robin stared out of the window, lost in thought.

'Well, you *had* to tell Wardle about Malley,' said Robin, turning back to Strike, who met her gaze in his shaving mirror. 'I mean, if he's already sent someone a – what exactly *did* he send?' she asked, a little nervously.

'A penis,' said Strike. He washed his face clean and dried it on a towel before continuing. 'Yeah, maybe you're right. More I think about it, though, the surer I am it's not him. Back in a minute – I want to change this shirt. I ripped two buttons off it when you screamed.'

'Sorry,' said Robin vaguely, as Strike disappeared into the bedroom.

Sipping her tea, she took a look around the room in which she was sitting. She had never been inside Strike's attic flat before. The most she had done previously was knock on the door to deliver messages or, in some of their busiest and most sleep-deprived stretches, to wake him up. The kitchen-cum-sitting room was cramped but clean and orderly. There were virtually no signs of personality: mismatched mugs, a cheap tea towel folded beside the gas ring; no photographs and nothing decorative, save for a child's drawing of a soldier, which had been tacked up on one of the wall units.

'Who drew that?' she asked, when Strike reappeared in a clean shirt.

'My nephew Jack. He likes me, for some reason.'

'Don't fish.'

'I'm not fishing. I never know what to say to kids.'

'So you think you've met *three men* who would've—?' Robin began again.

'I want a drink,' said Strike. 'Let's go to the Tottenham.'

There was no possibility of talking on the way, not with the racket of pneumatic drills still issuing from the trenches in the road, but the fluorescent-jacketed workmen neither wolf-whistled nor cat-called with Strike walking at Robin's side. At last they reached Strike's favourite local pub, with its ornate gilded mirrors, its panels of dark wood, its shining brass pumps, the coloured glass cupola and the paintings of gambolling beauties by Felix de Jong.

Strike ordered a pint of Doom Bar. Robin, who could not face alcohol, asked for a coffee.

'So?' said Robin, once the detective had returned to the high table beneath the cupola. 'Who are the three men?'

'I could be barking up a forest of wrong trees, don't forget,' said Strike, sipping his pint.

'All right,' said Robin. 'Who are they?'

'Twisted individuals who've all got good reason to hate my guts.'

Inside Strike's head, a frightened, skinny twelve-year-old girl with scarring around her leg surveyed him through lop-sided glasses. Had it been her right leg? He couldn't remember. *Jesus, don't let it be her . . .*

'*Who*?' Robin said again, losing patience.

'There are two army guys,' said Strike, rubbing his stubbly chin. 'They're both crazy enough and violent enough to – to—'

A gigantic, involuntary yawn interrupted him. Robin waited for cogent speech to resume, wondering whether he had been out with his new girlfriend the previous evening. Elin was an ex-professional violinist, now a presenter on Radio Three, a stunning Nordic-looking blonde who reminded Robin of a more beautiful Sarah Shadlock. She supposed that this was one reason why she had taken an almost immediate dislike to Elin. The other was that she had, in Robin's hearing, referred to her as Strike's secretary.

'Sorry,' Strike said. 'I was up late writing up notes for the Khan job. Knackered.'

He checked his watch.

'Shall we go downstairs and eat? I'm starving.'

'In a minute. It's not even twelve. I want to know about these men.'

Strike sighed.

'All right,' he said, dropping his voice as a man passed their table on the way to the bathroom. 'Donald Laing, King's Own Royal Borderers.' He remembered again eyes like a ferret's, concentrated hatred, the rose tattoo. 'I got him life.'

'But then—'

'Out in ten,' said Strike. 'He's been on the loose since 2007. Laing wasn't your run-of-the-mill nutter, he was an animal, a clever, devious animal; a sociopath – the real deal, if you ask me. I got him life for something I shouldn't have been investigating. He was about to get off on the original charge. Laing's got bloody good reason to hate my guts.'

But he did not say what Laing had done or why he, Strike, had been investigating it. Sometimes, and frequently when talking about his career in the Special Investigation Branch, Robin could tell by Strike's tone when he had come to the point beyond which he did not wish to speak. She had never yet pushed him past it. Reluctantly, she abandoned the subject of Donald Laing.

'Who was the other army guy?'

'Noel Brockbank. Desert Rat.'

'Desert – what?'

'Seventh Armoured Brigade.'

Strike was becoming steadily more taciturn, his expression brooding. Robin wondered whether this was because he was hungry – he was a man who needed regular sustenance to maintain an equable mood – or for some darker reason.

'Shall we eat, then?' Robin asked.

'Yeah,' said Strike, draining his pint and getting to his feet.

The cosy basement restaurant comprised a red-carpeted room with a second bar, wooden tables and walls covered in framed prints. They were the first to sit down and order.

'You were saying, about Noel Brockbank,' Robin prompted Strike when he had chosen fish and chips and she had asked for a salad.

'Yeah, he's another one with good reason to hold a grudge,' said Strike shortly. He had not wanted to talk about Donald Laing and he was showing even more reluctance to discuss Brockbank. After a long pause in which Strike glared over Robin's shoulder at nothing, he said, 'Brockbank's not right in the head. Or so he claimed.'

'Did you put him in prison?'

'No,' said Strike.

His expression had become forbidding. Robin waited, but she could tell nothing more was coming on Brockbank, so she asked:

'And the other one?'

This time Strike did not answer at all. She thought he had not heard her.

'Who's—?'

'I don't want to talk about it,' grunted Strike.

He glowered into his fresh pint, but Robin refused to be intimidated.

'Whoever sent that leg,' she said, 'sent it to *me*.'

'All right,' said Strike grudgingly, after a brief hesitation. 'His name's Jeff Whittaker.'

Robin felt a thrill of shock. She did not need to ask how Strike knew Jeff Whittaker. She already knew, although they had never discussed him.

Cormoran Strike's early life was extensively documented on the internet and it had been endlessly rehashed by the press coverage of his detective triumphs. He was the illegitimate and unplanned offspring of a rock star and a woman always described as a supergroupie, a woman who had died of an overdose when Strike was twenty. Jeff Whittaker had been her much younger second husband, who had been accused and acquitted of her murder.

They sat in silence until their food arrived.

'Why are you only having a salad? Aren't you hungry?' asked Strike, clearing his plate of chips. As Robin had suspected, his mood had improved with the ingestion of carbohydrates.

'Wedding,' said Robin shortly.

Strike said nothing. Comments on her figure fell strictly outside the self-imposed boundaries he had established for their relationship, which he had determined from the outset must never become too intimate. Nevertheless, he thought she was becoming too thin. In his opinion (and even the thought fell outside those same boundaries), she looked better curvier.

'Aren't you even going to tell me,' Robin asked, after

several more minutes' silence, 'what your connection with that song is?'

He chewed for a while, drank more beer, ordered another pint of Doom Bar then said, 'My mother had the title tattooed on her.'

He did not fancy telling Robin exactly where the tattoo had been. He preferred not to think about that. However, he was mellowing with food and drink: Robin had never showed prurient interest in his past and he supposed she was justified in a request for information today.

'It was her favourite song. Blue Öyster Cult were her favourite band. Well, "favourite" is an understatement. Obsession, really.'

'Her favourite wasn't the Deadbeats?' asked Robin, without thinking. Strike's father was the lead singer of the Deadbeats. They had never discussed him, either.

'No,' said Strike, managing a half-smile. 'Old Jonny came a poor second with Leda. She wanted Eric Bloom, lead singer of Blue Öyster Cult, but she never got him. One of the very few who got away.'

Robin was not sure what to say. She had wondered before what it felt like to have your mother's epic sexual history online for anybody to see. Strike's fresh pint arrived and he took a swig before continuing.

'I was nearly christened Eric Bloom Strike,' he said and Robin choked on her water. He laughed as she coughed into a napkin. 'Let's face it, Cormoran's not much bloody better. Cormoran Blue—'

'*Blue?*'

'Blue Öyster Cult, aren't you listening?'

'God,' said Robin. 'You keep that quiet.'

'Wouldn't you?'

'What does it mean, "Mistress of the Salmon Salt"?'

'Search me. Their lyrics are insane. Science fiction. Crazy stuff.'

A voice in his head: She wanted to die. She was the quicklime girl.

He drank more beer.

'I don't think I've ever heard any Blue Öyster Cult,' said Robin.

'Yeah, you have,' Strike contradicted her. '"Don't Fear the Reaper".'

'Don't – what?'

'It was a monster hit for them. "Don't Fear the Reaper".'

'Oh, I – I see.'

For one startled moment, Robin had thought that he was giving her advice.

They ate in silence for a while until Robin, unable to keep the question down any longer, though hoping she did not sound scared, asked:

'Why do you think the leg was addressed to me?'

Strike had already had time to ponder this question.

'I've been wondering that,' he said, 'and I think we've got to consider it a tacit threat, so, until we've found out—'

'I'm not stopping work,' said Robin fiercely. 'I'm not staying at home. That's what Matthew wants.'

'You've spoken to him, have you?'

She had made the call while Strike was downstairs with Wardle.

'Yes. He's angry with me for signing for it.'

'I expect he's worried about you,' said Strike insincerely. He had met Matthew on a handful of occasions and disliked him more each time.

'He's not worried,' snapped Robin. 'He just thinks that this is it, that I'll have to leave now, that I'll be scared out. I won't.'

Matthew had been appalled at her news, but even so, she

had heard a faint trace of satisfaction in his voice, felt his unexpressed conviction that now, at last, she must see what a ridiculous choice it had been to throw in her lot with a rackety private detective who could not afford to give her a decent salary. Strike had her working unsociable hours that meant she had to have packages sent to work instead of the flat. ('I didn't get sent a leg because Amazon couldn't deliver to the house!' Robin had said hotly.) And, of course, on top of everything else, Strike was now mildly famous and a source of fascination to their friends. Matthew's work as an accountant did not carry quite the same cachet. His resentment and jealousy ran deep and, increasingly, burst their bounds.

Strike was not fool enough to encourage Robin in any disloyalty to Matthew that she might regret when she was less shaken.

'Addressing the leg to you instead of me was an afterthought,' he said. 'They put my name on there first. I reckon they were either trying to worry me by showing they knew your name, or trying to frighten you off working for me.'

'Well, I'm not going to be frightened off,' said Robin.

'Robin, this is no time for heroics. Whoever he is, he's telling us he knows a lot about me, that he knows your name and, as of this morning, exactly what you look like. He saw you up close. I don't like that.'

'You obviously don't think my counter-surveillance abilities are up to much.'

'Seeing as you're talking to the man who sent you on the best bloody course I could find,' said Strike, 'and who read that fulsome letter of commendation you shoved under my nose—'

'Then you don't think my self-defence is any good.'

'I've never seen any of it and I've got only your word that you ever learned any.'

'Have you ever known me lie about what I can and can't do?'

demanded Robin, affronted, and Strike was forced to acknowledge that he had not. 'Well then! I won't take stupid risks. You've trained me to notice anyone dodgy. Anyway, you can't afford to send me home. We're struggling to cover our cases as it is.'

Strike sighed and rubbed his face with two large hairy-backed hands.

'Nothing after dark,' he said. 'And you need to carry an alarm, a decent one.'

'Fine,' she said.

'Anyway, you're doing Radford from next Monday,' he said, taking comfort from the thought.

Radford was a wealthy entrepreneur who wanted to put an investigator, posing as a part-time worker, into his office to expose what he suspected were criminal dealings by a senior manager. Robin was the obvious choice, because Strike had become more recognisable since their second high-profile murder case. As Strike drained his third pint, he wondered whether he might be able to convince Radford to increase Robin's hours. He would be glad to know she was safe in a palatial office block, nine to five every day, until the maniac who had sent the leg was caught.

Robin, meanwhile, was fighting waves of exhaustion and a vague nausea. A row, a broken night, the dreadful shock of the severed leg – and now she would have to head home and justify all over again her wish to continue doing a dangerous job for a bad salary. Matthew, who had once been one of her primary sources of comfort and support, had become merely another obstacle to be navigated.

Unbidden, unwanted, the image of the cold, severed leg in its cardboard box came back to her. She wondered when she would stop thinking about it. The fingertips that had grazed it tingled unpleasantly. Unconsciously, she tightened her hand into a fist in her lap.

5

> Hell's built on regret.
>
> Blue Öyster Cult, 'The Revenge of Vera Gemini'
> Lyrics by Patti Smith

Much later, after he had seen Robin safely onto the Tube, Strike returned to the office and sat alone in silence at her desk, lost in thought.

He had seen plenty of dismembered corpses, seen them rotting in mass graves and lying, freshly blown apart, by roadsides: severed limbs, flesh pulped, bones crushed. Unnatural death was the business of the Special Investigation Branch, the plain-clothes wing of the Royal Military Police, and his and his colleagues' reflexive reaction had often been humour. That was how you coped when you saw the dead torn and mutilated. Not for the SIB the luxury of corpses washed and prettified in satin-lined boxes.

Boxes. It had looked quite ordinary, the cardboard box in which the leg had come. No markings to indicate its origin, no trace of a previous addressee, nothing. The whole thing had been so organised, so careful, so neat – and this was what unnerved him, not the leg itself, nasty object though it was.

What appalled him was the careful, meticulous, almost clinical *modus operandi*.

Strike checked his watch. He was supposed to be going out with Elin this evening. His girlfriend of two months was in the throes of a divorce that was proceeding with the chilly brinkmanship of a grandmaster chess tournament. Her estranged husband was very wealthy, something that Strike had not realised until the first night he had been permitted to come back to the marital home and found himself in a spacious, wood-floored apartment overlooking Regent's Park. The shared custody arrangements meant that she was only prepared to meet Strike on nights when her five-year-old daughter was not at home, and when they went out, they chose the capital's quieter and more obscure restaurants as Elin did not wish her estranged husband to know that she was seeing anyone else. The situation suited Strike perfectly. It had been a perennial problem in his relationships that the normal nights for recreation were often nights that he had to be out tailing other people's unfaithful partners, and he had no particular desire to kindle a close relationship with Elin's daughter. He had not lied to Robin: he did not know how to talk to children.

He reached for his mobile. There were a few things he could do before he left for dinner.

The first call went to voicemail. He left a message asking Graham Hardacre, his ex-colleague in the Special Investigation Branch, to call him. He was not sure where Hardacre was currently stationed. The last time they had spoken, he had been due a move from Germany.

To Strike's disappointment, his second call, which was to an old friend whose life path had run more or less in the opposite direction to that of Hardacre, was not picked up either. Strike left a second, almost identical message, and hung up.

Pulling Robin's chair closer to the computer, he turned it

on and stared at the homepage without seeing it. The image that was filling his mind, entirely against his will, was of his mother, naked. Who had known the tattoo was there? Her husband, obviously, and the many boyfriends who had woven in and out of her life, and anyone else who might have seen her undressed in the squats and the filthy communes in which they had intermittently lived. Then there was the possibility that had occurred to him in the Tottenham, but which he had not felt equal to sharing with Robin: that Leda had, at some point, been photographed in the nude. It would have been entirely in character.

His fingers hovered over the keyboard. He got as far as *Leda Strike nak* before deleting, letter by letter, with an angry, jabbing forefinger. There were places no normal man wanted to go, phrases you did not want to leave on your internet search history, but also, unfortunately, tasks you did not want to delegate.

He contemplated the search box he had emptied, the cursor blinking dispassionately at him, then typed fast in his usual two-fingered style: *Donald Laing*.

There were plenty of them, especially in Scotland, but he could rule out anyone who had been paying rent or voting in elections while Laing had been in jail. After careful elimination and bearing in mind Laing's approximate age, Strike narrowed his focus to a man who appeared to have been living with a woman called Lorraine MacNaughton in Corby in 2008. Lorraine MacNaughton was now registered as living there alone.

He deleted Laing's name and substituted *Noel Brockbank*. There were fewer of them in the UK than there had been Donald Laings, but Strike reached a similar dead end. There had been an N. C. Brockbank living alone in Manchester in 2006, but if that was Strike's man, it suggested that he had split up with his wife. Strike was not sure whether that would be a good or a bad thing . . .

Slumping back in Robin's chair, Strike moved on to considering the likely consequences of being sent an anonymous severed leg. The police would have to ask the public for information soon, but Wardle had promised to warn Strike before they gave a press conference. A story this bizarre and grotesque would always be news, but interest would be increased – and it gave him no pleasure to reflect on it – because the leg had been sent to his office. Cormoran Strike was newsworthy these days. He had solved two murders under the noses of the Met, both of which would have fascinated the public, even had a private detective not solved them: the first, because the victim had been a beautiful young woman, the second, because it had been a strange, ritualistic killing.

How, Strike wondered, would the sending of the leg affect the business he had been working so hard to build up? He could not help feeling that the consequences were likely to be serious. Internet searches were a cruel barometer of status. Some time soon, Googling *Cormoran Strike* would not return to the top of the page glowing encomiums on his two most famous and successful cases, but the brutal fact that he was a man in receipt of a body part, a man who had at least one very nasty enemy. Strike was sure he understood the public well enough, or at least the insecure, frightened and angry section of it that was the private investigator's bread and butter, to know they were unlikely to be drawn to a business that received severed legs in the post. At best, new clients would assume that he and Robin had troubles enough of their own; at worst, that they had, through recklessness or ineptitude, got into something way over their heads.

He was about to turn off the computer when he changed his mind and, with even more reluctance than he had brought to the job of searching for his mother in the nude, typed in *Brittany Brockbank.*

There were a few of them on Facebook, on Instagram, working for companies of which he had never heard, beaming out of selfies. He scrutinised the images. They were nearly all in their twenties, the age she would be now. He could discount those who were black, but there was no telling which of the others, brunette, blonde or redhead, pretty or plain, photographed beaming or moody or caught unawares, was the one he sought. None were wearing glasses. Was she too vain to wear them in a picture? Had she had her eyes lasered? Perhaps she eschewed social media. She had wanted to change her name, he remembered that. Or perhaps the reason for her absence was more fundamental – she was dead.

He looked at his watch again: time to go and change.

It can't be her, he thought, and then, *Let it not be her.*

Because if it was her, it was his fault.

6

Is it any wonder that my mind's on fire?

Blue Öyster Cult, 'Flaming Telepaths'

Robin was unusually vigilant on the journey home that evening, surreptitiously comparing every man in the carriage with her memory of the tall figure in black leathers who had handed her the gruesome package. A thin young Asian man in a cheap suit smiled hopefully as she caught his eye for the third time; after that, she kept her eyes on her phone, exploring – when reception permitted – the BBC website and wondering, like Strike, when the leg would become news.

Forty minutes after leaving work she entered the large Waitrose near her home station. The fridge at home had almost nothing in it. Matthew did not enjoy food shopping and (although he had denied it during their last row but one) she was sure that he thought she, who contributed less than a third of the household income, ought to bolster her contribution by performing those mundane tasks he did not like.

Single men in suits were filling their baskets and trolleys with ready meals. Professional women hurried past, grabbing pasta that would be quick to cook for the family. An exhausted-looking young mother with a tiny baby screaming in its buggy wove around the aisles like a groggy moth, unable to focus, a single bag of carrots in her basket. Robin moved slowly up and down the aisles, feeling oddly jumpy. There was nobody there who resembled the man in black motorcycle leathers, nobody who might be lurking, fantasising about cutting off Robin's legs ... *cutting off my legs* ...

'Excuse me!' said a cross middle-aged woman trying to reach the sausages. Robin apologised and moved aside, surprised to find that she was holding a pack of chicken thighs. Throwing it into her trolley, she hurried off to the other end of the supermarket where, among the wines and spirits, she found relative quiet. Here she pulled out her mobile and called Strike. He answered on the second ring.

'Are you all right?'

'Yes, of course—'

'Where are you?'

'Waitrose.'

A short, balding man was perusing the shelf of sherry just behind Robin, his eyes level with her breasts. When she moved aside, he moved with her. Robin glared; he blushed and moved away.

'Well, you should be OK in Waitrose.'

'Mm,' said Robin, her eyes on the bald man's retreating back. 'Listen, this might be nothing, but I've just remembered: we've had a couple of weird letters in the last few months.'

'Nutter letters?'

'Don't start.'

Robin always protested at this blanket term. They had attracted a significant increase in oddball correspondence since Strike had solved his second high-profile murder case. The most coherent of the writers simply asked for money, on the assumption that Strike was now immensely rich. Then came those who had strange personal grudges that they wished Strike to avenge, those whose waking hours seemed devoted to proving outlandish theories, those whose needs and wishes were so inchoate and rambling that the only message they conveyed was mental illness, and finally ('Now *these* seem nutty,' Robin had said) a sprinkling of people, both male and female, who seemed to find Strike attractive.

'Addressed to you?' Strike asked, suddenly serious.

'No, you.'

She could hear him moving around his flat as they talked. Perhaps he was going out with Elin tonight. He never talked about the relationship. If Elin had not dropped by the office one day, Robin doubted that she would have known that she existed – perhaps not until he turned up for work one day wearing a wedding ring.

'What did they say?' asked Strike.

'Well, one of them was from a girl who wanted to cut off her own leg. She was asking for advice.'

'Say that again?'

'She wanted to cut off her own leg,' Robin enunciated clearly, and a woman choosing a bottle of rosé nearby threw her a startled look.

'Jesus Christ,' muttered Strike. 'And I'm not allowed to call them nutters. You think she managed it and thought I'd like to know?'

'I thought a letter like that might be relevant,' said Robin repressively. 'Some people *do* want to cut bits of themselves off, it's a recognised phenomenon, it's called . . . *not* "being a nutter",' she added, correctly anticipating him, and he laughed. 'And there was another one, from a person who signed with their initials: a long letter, they went on and on about your leg and how they wanted to make it up to you.'

'If they were trying to make it up to me you'd think they would've sent a man's leg. I'd look pretty bloody stupid—'

'Don't,' she said. 'Don't joke. I don't know how you can.'

'I don't know how you can't,' he said, but kindly.

She heard a very familiar scraping noise followed by a sonorous clang.

'You're looking in the nutter drawer!'

'I don't think you should call it the "nutter drawer", Robin. Bit disrespectful to our mentally ill—'

'I'll see you tomorrow,' she said, smiling against her will, and hung up on his laughter.

The fatigue she had been fighting all day washed over her anew as she ambled around the supermarket. It was deciding what to eat that was effortful; she would have found it quite soothing merely to shop from a list that somebody else had prepared. Like the working mothers seeking anything quick to cook, Robin gave up and chose a lot of pasta. Queuing at the checkout, she found herself right behind the young woman whose baby had at last exhausted itself and now slept as though dead, fists flung out, eyes tight shut.

'Cute,' said Robin, who felt the girl needed encouragement.

'When he's asleep,' the mother replied with a weak smile.

By the time Robin had let herself in at home she was truly exhausted. To her surprise, Matthew was standing waiting for her in the narrow hall.

'*I* shopped!' he said when he saw the four bulging shopping bags in her hands and she heard his disappointment that the grand gesture had been undermined. 'I sent you a text that I was going to Waitrose!'

'Must've missed it,' said Robin. 'Sorry.'

She had probably been on the phone to Strike. They might even have been there at the same time, but of course she had spent half her visit skulking among the wine and spirits.

Matthew walked forward, arms outstretched, and pulled her into a hug with what she could not help but feel was infuriating magnanimity. Even so, she had to admit that he looked, as always, wonderfully handsome in his dark suit, his thick tawny hair swept back off his forehead.

'It must've been scary,' he murmured, his breath warm in her hair.

'It was,' she said, wrapping her arms around his waist.

They ate pasta in peace, without a single mention of Sarah Shadlock, Strike or Jacques Burger. The furious ambition of that morning, to make Matthew acknowledge that it had been Sarah, not she, who had voiced admiration of curly hair, had burned out. Robin felt that she was being rewarded for her mature forbearance when Matthew said apologetically:

'I'm going to have to do a bit of work after dinner.'

'No problem,' said Robin. 'I wanted an early night anyway.'

She took a low-calorie hot chocolate and a copy of *Grazia* to bed with her, but she could not concentrate. After ten minutes, she got up and fetched her laptop, took it back to bed with her and Googled Jeff Whittaker.

She had read the Wikipedia entry before, during one of her guilty trawls through Strike's past, but now she read with greater attention. It started with a familiar disclaimer:

> This article has multiple issues.
>
> This article needs additional citations for verification.
>
> This article possibly contains original research.

Jeff Whittaker

Jeff Whittaker (b.1969) is a musician best known for his marriage to 1970s supergroupie Leda Strike, whom he was charged with killing in 1994.[1] Whittaker is a grandson of diplomat Sir Randolph Whittaker KCMB DSO.

Early Life

Whittaker was raised by his grandparents. His teenage mother, Patricia Whittaker, was schizophrenic.[citation needed] Whittaker never knew who his father was.[citation needed] He was expelled from Gordonstoun School after drawing a knife on a member of staff.[citation needed] He claims that his grandfather locked him in a shed for three days following his expulsion, a charge his grandfather denies.[2] Whittaker ran away from home and lived rough for a period during his teens. He also claims to have worked as a gravedigger.[citation needed]

Musical Career

Whittaker played guitar and wrote lyrics for a succession of thrash metal bands in the late 80s and early 90s, including Restorative Art, Devilheart and Necromantic.[3][4]

Personal Life

In 1991 Whittaker met Leda Strike, ex-girlfriend of Jonny Rokeby and Rick Fantoni, who was working for the record company considering signing Necromantic.[citation needed] Whittaker and Strike were married in 1992. In December of that year she gave birth to a son, Switch LaVey Bloom Whittaker.[5] In 1993 Whittaker was sacked from Necromantic due to his drug abuse.[citation needed]

When Leda Whittaker died of a heroin overdose in 1994, Whittaker was charged with her murder. He was found not guilty.[6][7][8][9]

In 1995 Whittaker was re-arrested for assault and attempted kidnap of his son, who was in the custody of Whittaker's grandparents. He received a suspended jail sentence for the assault on his grandfather.[citation needed]

In 1998 Whittaker threatened a co-worker with a knife and received a three-month jail sentence.[10][11]

In 2002 Whittaker was jailed for preventing the lawful burial of a body. Karen Abraham, with whom he had been living, was found to have died of heart failure, but Whittaker had kept her body in their shared flat for a month.[12][13][14]

In 2005 Whittaker was jailed for dealing crack cocaine.[15]

Robin read the page twice. Her concentration was poor tonight. Information seemed to slide off the surface of her mind, failing to be absorbed. Parts of Whittaker's history stood out, glaringly strange. Why would anyone conceal a corpse for a month? Had Whittaker feared that he would be charged with murder again, or was there some other reason? Bodies, limbs, pieces of dead flesh . . . She sipped the hot chocolate and grimaced. It tasted of flavoured dust; in the pressure she felt to be slim in her wedding dress, she had foresworn chocolate in its true form for a month now.

She replaced the mug on her bedside cabinet, returned her fingers to the keyboard and searched for images of *Jeff Whittaker trial*.

A matrix of photographs filled the screen, showing two different Whittakers, photographed eight years apart and entering and exiting two different courts.

The young Whittaker accused of murdering his wife wore dreadlocks tied back in a ponytail. He had a certain seedy glamour in his black suit and tie, tall enough to see over the heads of most of the photographers crowding around him. His cheekbones were high, his skin sallow and his large eyes set unusually far apart: the kind of eyes that might have belonged to an opium-crazed poet, or a heretic priest.

The Whittaker who had been accused of preventing another woman's burial had lost his vagrant handsomeness. He was heavier, with a brutal crew cut and a beard. Only the wide-set eyes were unchanged, and the aura of unapologetic arrogance.

Robin scrolled slowly down through the photographs. Soon the pictures of what she thought of as 'Strike's Whittaker' became interspersed with pictures of other Whittakers who had been in trials. A cherubic-looking African-American called Jeff Whittaker had taken his neighbour to court for allowing his dog to repeatedly foul his lawn.

Why did Strike think his ex-stepfather (she found it odd to think of him in those terms, as he was only five years older than Strike) would have sent him the leg? She wondered when Strike had last seen the man he thought had murdered his mother. There was so much she did not know about her boss. He did not like to talk about his past.

Robin's fingers slid back to the keys and typed *Eric Bloom*.

The first thing that occurred to her, staring at the pictures of the leather-clad seventies rocker, was that he had Strike's exact hair: dense, dark and curly. This reminded her of Jacques Burger and Sarah Shadlock, which did nothing to improve her mood. She turned her attention to the other two men whom Strike had mentioned as possible suspects, but she could not remember what their names had been. Donald something? And a funny name beginning with B ... Her memory was usually excellent. Strike often complimented her on it. Why couldn't she remember?

On the other hand, would it matter if she could? There was little you could do on a laptop to find two men who might be anywhere. Robin had not worked for a detective agency for this long without being perfectly aware that those who used pseudonyms, lived rough, favoured squats, rented their accommodation or did not add their names to electoral rolls could easily fall through the wide mesh of Directory Enquiries.

After sitting in thought for several more minutes, and with a sense that she was somehow betraying her boss, Robin typed

Leda Strike into the search box and then, feeling guiltier than ever, *naked*.

The picture was black and white. The young Leda posed with her arms over her head, a long cloud of dark hair falling down over her breasts. Even in the thumbnail version, Robin could make out an arch of curly script set above the dark triangle of pubic hair. Squinting slightly, as though rendering the image a little fuzzy somehow mitigated her actions, Robin brought up the full-sized picture. She did not want to have to zoom in and nor did she need to. The words *Mistress of* were clearly legible.

The bathroom fan whirred into life next door. With a guilty start, Robin shut down the page she had been viewing. Matthew had lately developed a habit of borrowing her laptop and a few weeks previously she had caught him reading her emails to Strike. With this in mind, she reopened the web page, cleared her browsing history, brought up her settings and, after a moment's consideration, changed her password to DontFearTheReaper. That would scupper him.

As she slid out of bed to go and throw the hot chocolate down the kitchen sink it occurred to Robin that she had not bothered to look up any details about Terence 'Digger' Malley. Of course, the police would be far better placed than she or Strike to find a London gangster.

Doesn't matter, though, she thought sleepily, heading back to the bedroom. *It isn't Malley*.

7

Good To Feel Hungry

Of course, if he'd had the sense he was born with – that had been a favourite phrase of his mother's, vicious bitch that she'd been (*You haven't got the sense you were born with, have you, you stupid little bastard?*) – if he'd had the sense he was born with, he wouldn't have followed The Secretary the very day after handing her the leg. Only it had been difficult to resist the temptation when he did not know when he would next have a chance. The urge to tail her again had grown upon him in the night, to see what she looked like now that she had opened his present.

From tomorrow, his freedom would be severely curtailed, because It would be home and It required his attention when It was around. Keeping It happy was very important, not least because It earned the money. Stupid and ugly and grateful for affection, It had barely noticed that It was keeping him.

Once he'd seen It off to work that morning he had hurried out of the house to wait for The Secretary at her home station, which had been a smart decision, because she hadn't gone to the office at all. He had thought the arrival of the leg might disrupt her routine and he had been right. He was nearly always right.

He knew how to follow people. At some points today he had been wearing a beanie hat, at others he had been bareheaded. He had stripped to his T-shirt, then worn his jacket and then his jacket turned inside out, sunglasses on, sunglasses off.

The Secretary's value to him – over and above the value any female had to him, if he could get her alone – was in what he was going to do, through her, to Strike. His ambition to be avenged on Strike – permanently, brutally avenged – had grown in him until it became the central ambition of his life. He had always been this way. If someone crossed him they were marked and at some point, whenever opportunity presented itself, even if it took years, they would get theirs. Cormoran Strike had done him more harm than any other human being ever, and he was going to pay a just price.

He had lost track of Strike for several years and then an explosion of publicity had revealed the bastard: celebrated, heroic. This was the status *he* had always wanted, had craved. It had been like drinking acid, choking down the fawning articles about the cunt, but he had devoured everything he could, because you needed to know your target if you wanted to cause maximum damage. He intended to inflict as much pain on Cormoran Strike as was – not humanly possible, because he knew himself to be something more than human – as was superhumanly possible. It would go way beyond a knife in the ribs in the dark. No, Strike's punishment was going to be slower and stranger, frightening, tortuous and finally devastating.

Nobody would ever know he'd done it; why should they? He'd escaped without detection three times now: three women dead and nobody had a clue who'd done it. This knowledge enabled him to read today's *Metro* without the slightest trace of fear; to feel only pride and satisfaction at the hysterical accounts of the severed leg, to savour the whiff of fear and confusion that rose from each story, the bleating incomprehension of the sheep-like masses who scent a wolf.

All he needed now was for The Secretary to take one short walk down a deserted stretch of road . . . but London throbbed and teemed with people all day long and here he was, frustrated and wary, watching her as he hung around the London School of Economics.

She was tracking someone too, and it was easy to see who that was. Her target had bright platinum hair extensions and led The Secretary, mid-afternoon, all the way back to Tottenham Court Road.

The Secretary disappeared inside a pub opposite the lap-dancing club into which her mark had gone. He debated following her inside, but she seemed dangerously watchful today, so he entered a cheap Japanese restaurant with plate-glass windows opposite the pub, took a table near the window and waited for her to emerge.

It would happen, he told himself, staring through his shades into the busy road. He would get her. He had to hold on to that thought, because this evening he was going to have to return to It and the half-life, the lie-life, that allowed the real Him to walk and breathe in secret.

The smeared and dusty London window reflected his naked expression, stripped of the civilised coating he wore to beguile the women who had fallen prey to his charm and his knives. To the surface had risen the creature that lived within, the creature that wanted nothing except to establish its dominance.

8

I seem to see a rose,
I reach out, then it goes.

Blue Öyster Cult, 'Lonely Teardrops'

As Strike had been expecting ever since the news of the severed leg hit the media, his old acquaintance Dominic Culpepper of the *News of the World* had contacted him early on Tuesday morning in a state of advanced ire. The journalist refused to accept that Strike might have had legitimate reasons for choosing not to contact Culpepper the very second he had realised that he was in receipt of a severed limb, and Strike further compounded this offence by declining the invitation to keep Culpepper informed of every fresh development in the case, in return for a hefty retainer. Culpepper had previously put paid work Strike's way and the detective suspected, by the time the call terminated, that this source of income would henceforth be closed to him. Culpepper was not a happy man.

Strike and Robin did not speak until mid-afternoon. Strike, who was carrying a backpack, called from a crowded Heathrow Express train.

'Where are you?' he asked.

'Pub opposite Spearmint Rhino,' she said. 'It's called the Court. Where are you?'

'Coming back from the airport. Mad Dad got on the plane, thank Christ.'

Mad Dad was a wealthy international banker whom Strike was tailing on behalf of his wife. The couple were having an extremely contentious custody battle. The husband's departure for Chicago would mean that Strike would have a few nights' respite from observing him as he sat in his car outside his wife's house at four in the morning, night-vision goggles trained on his young sons' window.

'I'll come and meet you,' said Strike. 'Sit tight – unless Platinum cops off with someone, obviously.'

Platinum was the Russian economics student and lap-dancer. Their client was her boyfriend, a man whom Strike and Robin had nicknamed 'Two-Times', partly because this was the second time they had investigated a blonde girlfriend for him, and also because he seemed addicted to finding out where and how his lovers were betraying him. Robin found Two-Times both sinister and pitiable. He had met Platinum at the club Robin was now watching, and Robin and Strike had been given the job of finding out whether any other men were being granted the additional favours she was now giving Two-Times.

The odd thing was that, little though he might believe or like it, Two-Times seemed to have picked an atypically monogamous girlfriend this time. After watching her movements for several weeks, Robin had learned that she was a largely solitary creature, lunching alone with books and rarely interacting with her colleagues.

'She's obviously working at the club to help pay for her course,' Robin had told Strike indignantly, after a week's tailing. 'If Two-Times doesn't want other men ogling her, why doesn't he help her out financially?'

'The main attraction is that she gives other men lap dances,' Strike had replied patiently. 'I'm surprised it's taken him this long to go for someone like her. Ticks all his boxes.'

Strike had been inside the club shortly after they took the job and he had secured the services of a sad-eyed brunette by the unlikely name of Raven to keep an eye on his client's girlfriend. Raven was to check in once a day, to tell them what Platinum was up to and inform them immediately if the Russian girl appeared to be giving out her phone number or being over-attentive to any client. The rules of the club forbade touching or soliciting but Two-Times remained convinced ('Poor, sad bastard,' said Strike) that he was only one among many men taking her out to dinner and sharing her bed.

'I still don't understand why we have to watch the place,' Robin sighed into the phone, not for the first time. 'We could take Raven's calls anywhere.'

'You know why,' said Strike, who was preparing to disembark. 'He likes the photographs.'

'But they're only of her walking to and from work.'

'Doesn't matter. Turns him on. Plus, he's convinced that one of these days she's going to leave the club with some Russian oligarch.'

'Doesn't this stuff ever make you feel grubby?'

'Occupational hazard,' said Strike, unconcerned. 'See you shortly.'

Robin waited amidst the floral and gilt wallpaper. Brocade chairs and mismatched lampshades contrasted strongly with enormous plasma TVs showing football and Coke ads. The paintwork was the fashionable shade of greige in which Matthew's sister had recently painted her sitting room. Robin found it depressing. Her view of the club's entrance was slightly impeded by the wooden banisters of a staircase leading to an upper floor. Outside, a constant stream of traffic flooded left and right, plenty of red double-deckers temporarily obscuring her view of the front of the club.

Strike arrived looking irritable.

'We've lost Radford,' he said, dumping his backpack beside the high window table at which she was sitting. 'He's just phoned me.'

'No!'

'Yep. He thinks you're too newsworthy to plant in his office now.'

The press had had the story of the severed leg since six that morning. Wardle had kept his word to Strike and warned him ahead of time. The detective had been able to leave his attic flat in the small hours with enough clothes in his holdall for a few days' absence. He knew the press would soon be staking out the office, and not for the first time.

'And,' said Strike, returning to Robin with a pint in his hand and easing himself up onto a bar stool, 'Khan's bottled it too. He's going to go for an agency that doesn't attract body parts.'

'*Bugger*,' said Robin, and then: 'What are you smirking about?'

'Nothing.' He did not want to tell her that he always liked it when she said 'bugger'. It brought out the latent Yorkshire in her accent.

'They were good jobs!' said Robin.

Strike agreed, his eyes on the front of Spearmint Rhino.

'How's Platinum? Raven checked in?'

As Raven had just called, Robin was able to inform Strike that there was, as ever, no news. Platinum was popular with punters and had so far that day given three lap dances that had proceeded, judged by the rules of the establishment, in total propriety.

'Read the stories?' he asked, pointing at an abandoned *Mirror* on a nearby table.

'Only online,' said Robin.

'Hopefully it'll bring in some information,' said Strike. 'Someone must've noticed they're missing a leg.'

'Ha ha,' said Robin.

'Too soon?'

'Yes,' said Robin coldly.

'I did some digging online last night,' said Strike. 'Brockbank might've been in Manchester in 2006.'

'How d'you know it was the right man?'

'I don't, but the guy was around the right age, right middle initial—'

'You remember his middle initial?'

'Yeah,' said Strike. 'It doesn't look like he's there any more, though. Same story with Laing. I'm pretty sure he was at an address in Corby in 2008, but he's moved on. How long,' Strike added, staring across the street, 'has that bloke in the camouflage jacket and shades been in that restaurant?'

'About half an hour.'

As far as Strike could tell, the man in sunglasses was watching him back, staring out across the street through two windows. Broad-shouldered and long-legged, he looked too large for the silver chair. With the sliding reflections of traffic and passers-by refracting off the window Strike found it difficult to be sure, but he appeared to be sporting heavy stubble.

'What's it like in there?' Robin asked, pointing towards the double doors of Spearmint Rhino under their heavy metallic awning.

'In the strip club?' asked Strike, taken aback.

'No, in the Japanese restaurant,' said Robin sarcastically. 'Of course in the strip club.'

'It's all right,' he said, not entirely sure what he was being asked.

'What does it look like?'

'Gold. Mirrors. Dim lighting.' When she looked at him expectantly, he said, 'There's a pole in the middle, where they dance.'

'Not lap dances?'

'There are private booths for them.'

'What do the girls wear?'

'I dunno – not much—'

His mobile rang: Elin.

Robin turned her face away, toying with what looked like a pair of reading glasses on the table in front of her, but which actually contained the small camera with which she photographed Platinum's movements. She had found this gadget exciting when Strike first handed it to her, but the thrill had long since worn off. She drank her tomato juice and stared out of the window, trying not to listen to what Strike and Elin were saying to each other. He always sounded matter-of-fact when on the phone to his girlfriend, but then, it was difficult to imagine Strike murmuring endearments to anyone. Matthew called her both 'Robsy' and 'Rosy-Posy' when he was in the right mood, which was not often these days.

' . . . at Nick and Ilsa's,' Strike was saying. 'Yeah. No, I agree . . . yeah . . . all right . . . you too.'

He cut the call.

'Is that where you're going to stay?' Robin asked. 'With Nick and Ilsa?'

They were two of Strike's oldest friends. She had met and liked both of them on a couple of visits to the office.

'Yeah, they say I can stay as long as I want.'

'Why not with Elin?' asked Robin, risking rebuff, because

she was perfectly aware of the line Strike preferred to maintain between his personal and professional lives.

'Wouldn't work,' he said. He didn't seem annoyed that she had asked, but showed no inclination to elaborate. 'I forgot,' he added, glancing back across the street to the Japanese Canteen. The table where the man in camouflage jacket and shades had sat was now unoccupied. 'I got you this.'

It was a rape alarm.

'I've already got one,' said Robin, pulling it out of her coat pocket and showing him.

'Yeah, but this one's better,' said Strike, showing her its features. 'You want an alarm of at least 120 decibels and it sprays them with indelible red stuff.'

'Mine does 140 decibels.'

'I still think this one's better.'

'Is this the usual bloke thing of thinking any gadget you've chosen must be superior to anything I've got?'

He laughed and drained his pint.

'I'll see you later.'

'Where are you going?'

'I'm meeting Shanker.'

The name was unfamiliar to her.

'The bloke who sometimes gives me tip-offs I can barter with the Met,' Strike explained. 'The bloke who told me who'd stabbed that police informer, remember? Who recommended me as a heavy to that gangster?'

'Oh,' said Robin. 'Him. You've never told me what he was called.'

'Shanker's my best chance for finding out where Whittaker is,' said Strike. 'He might have some information on Digger Malley as well. He runs with some of the same crowd.'

He squinted across the road.

'Keep an eye out for that camouflage jacket.'

'You're jumpy.'

'Bloody right I'm jumpy, Robin,' he said, drawing out a pack of cigarettes ready for the short walk to the Tube. 'Someone sent us an effing leg.'

9

One Step Ahead of the Devil

Seeing Strike in the mutilated flesh, walking along the opposite pavement towards the Court, had been an unexpected bonus.

What a fat fucker he'd become since they had last seen each other, ambling up the road carrying his backpack like the dumb squaddie he had once been, without realising that the man who had sent him a leg was sitting barely fifty yards away. So much for the great detective! Into the pub he'd gone to join little Secretary. He was almost certainly fucking her. He hoped so, anyway. That would make what he was going to do to her even more satisfying.

Then, as he had stared through his sunglasses at the figure of Strike sitting just inside the pub window, he thought that Strike turned and looked back. Of course, he couldn't make out features from across the road, through two panes of glass and his own tinted lenses, but something in the distant figure's attitude, the full disc of its face turned in his direction, had brought him to a high pitch of tension. They had looked at each other across the road and the traffic growled past in either direction, intermittently blocking them from view.

He had waited until three double-deckers had come crawling end to end into the space between them, then slid out of his chair, through the glass doors of the restaurant and up the side street. Adrenalin coursed through him as he stripped off his camouflage jacket and turned it inside out. There could be no question of binning it: his knives were concealed inside the lining. Around another corner, he broke into a flat-out run.

10

With no love, from the past.

Blue Öyster Cult, 'Shadow of California'

The unbroken stream of traffic obliged Strike to stand and wait before crossing Tottenham Court Road, his eyes sweeping the opposite pavement. When he reached the other side of the street he peered through the window of the Japanese restaurant, but there was no camouflage jacket to be seen, nor did any of the men in shirts or T-shirts resemble the sunglasses-wearer in size or shape.

Strike felt his mobile vibrate and pulled it out of his jacket pocket. Robin had texted him:

Get a grip.

Grinning, Strike raised a hand of farewell towards the windows of the Court and headed off towards the Tube.

Perhaps he was just jumpy, as Robin had said. What were the odds that the nutter who had sent the leg would be sitting watching Robin in broad daylight? Yet he had not liked the fixed stare of the big man in the camouflage jacket, nor the fact that he had been wearing sunglasses: the day was not that bright. Had his disappearance while Strike's view was occluded been coincidental or deliberate?

The trouble was that Strike could place little reliance on his memories of what the three men who were currently preoccupying him looked like, because he had not seen Brockbank for eight years, Laing for nine and Whittaker for sixteen. Any of them might have grown fat or wasted in that time, lost their hair, become bearded or moustached, be incapacitated or newly muscled. Strike himself had lost a leg since he had last set eyes on any of them. The one thing that nobody could disguise was height. All three of the men Strike was concerned about had been six feet tall or over and Camouflage Jacket had looked at least that in his metal chair.

The phone in his pocket buzzed as he walked towards Tottenham Court Road station, and on pulling it out of his pocket he saw, to his pleasure, that it was Graham Hardacre. Drawing aside so as not to impede passers-by, he answered.

'Oggy?' said his ex-colleague's voice. 'What gives, mate? Why are people sending you legs?'

'I take it you're not in Germany?' said Strike.

'Edinburgh, been here six weeks. Just been reading about you in the *Scotsman*.'

The Special Investigation Branch of the Royal Military Police had an office in Edinburgh Castle: 35 Section. It was a prestigious posting.

'Hardy, I need a favour,' said Strike. 'Intel on a couple of guys. D'you remember Noel Brockbank?'

'Hard to forget. Seventh Armoured, if memory serves?'

'That's him. The other one's Donald Laing. He was before I knew you. King's Own Royal Borderers. Knew him in Cyprus.'

'I'll see what I can do when I get back to the office, mate. I'm in the middle of a ploughed field right now.'

A chat about mutual acquaintances was curtailed by the increasing noise of rush-hour traffic. Hardacre promised to ring back once he had had a look at the army records and Strike continued towards the Tube.

He got out at Whitechapel station thirty minutes later to find a text message from the man he was supposed to be meeting.

Sorry Bunsen cant do today ill give you a bell

This was both disappointing and inconvenient, but not a surprise. Considering that Strike was not carrying a consignment of drugs or a large pile of used notes, and that he did not require intimidation or beating, it was a mark of great esteem that Shanker had even condescended to fix a time and place for meeting.

Strike's knee was complaining after a day on his feet, but there were no seats outside the station. He leaned up against the yellow brick wall beside the entrance and called Shanker's number.

'Yeah, all right, Bunsen?'

Just as he no longer remembered why Shanker was called Shanker, he had no more idea why Shanker called him Bunsen. They had met when they were seventeen and the connection between them, though profound in its way, bore none of the usual stigmata of teenage friendship. In fact, it had not been a friendship in any usual sense, but more like an enforced brotherhood. Strike was sure that Shanker would mourn his passing were he to die, but he was equally certain that Shanker would rob his body of all valuables if left alone with it. What others might not understand was that Shanker would do so in the belief that Strike would be glad, in whatever afterworld he was dwelling, to think that it was Shanker who had his wallet, rather than some anonymous opportunist.

'You're busy, Shanker?' asked Strike, lighting a fresh cigarette.

'Yeah, Bunsen, no chance today. Woss 'appening?'

'I'm looking for Whittaker.'

'Gonna finish it, are you?'

The change in Shanker's tone would have alarmed anyone who had forgotten who Shanker was, what he was. To Shanker and his associates, there was no proper end to a grudge other than killing and, in consequence, he had spent half his adult life behind bars. Strike was surprised Shanker had survived into his mid-thirties.

'I just want to know where he is,' said Strike repressively.

He doubted that Shanker would have heard about the leg. Shanker lived in a world where news was of strictly personal interest and was conveyed by word of mouth.

'I can 'ave an ask around.'

'Usual rates,' said Strike, who had a standing arrangement with Shanker for useful bits of information. 'And – Shanker?'

His old friend had a habit of hanging up without warning when his attention was diverted.

''S'there more?' said Shanker, his voice moving from distant to close as he spoke; Strike had been right to think he had removed the mobile from his ear, assuming they were done.

'Yeah,' said Strike. 'Digger Malley.'

A silence on the end of the line eloquently expressed the fact that, just as Strike never forgot what Shanker was, nor did Shanker ever forget what Strike was.

'Shanker, this is between you and me, no one else. You've never discussed me with Malley, have you?'

After a pause, and in his most dangerous voice, Shanker said:

'The fuck would I do that for?'

'Had to ask. I'll explain when I see you.'

The dangerous silence continued.

'Shanker, when have I ever grassed you up?' asked Strike.

Another, shorter silence, and then Shanker said in what, to Strike, was his normal voice:

'Yeah, all right. Whittaker, huh? See what I can do, Bunsen.'

The line went dead. Shanker did not do goodbyes.

Strike sighed and lit up another cigarette. The journey had been pointless. He would get straight back on a train once he had finished his Benson & Hedges.

The station entrance gave onto a kind of concrete forecourt surrounded by the backs of buildings. The Gherkin, that giant black bullet of a building, glinted on the distant horizon. It had not been there twenty years previously, during Strike's family's brief sojourn in Whitechapel.

Looking around, Strike felt no sense of homecoming or nostalgia. He could not remember this patch of concrete, these nondescript rears of buildings. Even the station seemed only dimly familiar. The endless series of moves and upheavals that had characterised life with his mother had blurred memories of individual places; he sometimes forgot which corner shop had belonged to which rundown flat, which local pub had adjoined which squat.

He had meant to get back on the Tube and yet before he knew it, he was walking, heading for the one place in London he had avoided for seventeen years: the building where his mother had died. It had been the last of Leda's squats, two floors of a decrepit building on Fulbourne Street, which was barely a minute from the station. As he walked, Strike began to remember. Of course: he had walked over this metal bridge over the railway line during his A-level year. He remembered the name, Castlemain Street, too . . . surely one of his fellow A-level students, a girl with a pronounced lisp, had lived there . . .

He slowed to an amble as he reached the end of Fulbourne Street, experiencing a strange double impression. His vague memory of the place, weakened no doubt by his deliberate attempts to forget, lay like a faded transparency over the scene in front of his eyes. The buildings were as shabby as he remembered them, white plaster peeling away from the frontages, but the businesses and shops were totally unfamiliar. He felt as though he had returned to a dreamscape where the scene had shifted and mutated. Of course, everything was impermanent in the poor areas of London, where fragile, fairweather businesses grew up and faded away and were replaced: cheap signage tacked up and removed; people passing through, passing away.

It took him a minute or two to identify the door of what had once been the squat, because he had forgotten the number. At last he found it, beside a shop selling cheap clothing of both Asian and Western varieties, which he thought had been a West Indian supermarket in his day. The brass letter box brought back a strange stab of memory. It had rattled loudly whenever anyone went in or out of the door.

Fuck, fuck, fuck . . .

Lighting a second cigarette from the tip of the first, he walked briskly out onto Whitechapel Road, where market stalls stood: more cheap clothing, a multitude of gaudy plastic goods. Strike sped up, walking he was not sure where, and some of what he passed triggered more memories: that snooker hall had been there seventeen years ago . . . so had the Bell Foundry . . . and now the memories were rising to bite him as though he had trodden on a nest of sleeping snakes . . .

As she neared forty, his mother had begun to go for younger men, but Whittaker had been the youngest of the lot: twenty-one when she had started sleeping with him. Her son had been sixteen when she first brought Whittaker home. The musician had looked ravaged even then, with sallow hollows under his wide-apart eyes, which were a striking golden hazel. His dark hair fell in dreadlocks to his shoulders; he lived in the same T-shirt and jeans and consequently stank.

A well-worn phrase kept echoing in Strike's head, keeping pace with his footsteps as he trudged down Whitechapel Road.

Hiding in plain sight. Hiding in plain sight.

Of course people would think he was obsessed, biased, unable to let go. They would say his thoughts had jumped to Whittaker when he saw the leg in the box because he had never got over the fact that Whittaker had walked free on the charge of killing Strike's mother. Even if Strike explained his reasons for suspecting Whittaker, they would probably laugh at the notion that such an ostentatious lover of the perverse and the sadistic could have cut off a woman's leg. Strike knew how deeply ingrained was the belief that the evil conceal their dangerous predilections for violence and domination. When they wear them like bangles for all to see, the gullible populace laughs, calls it a pose, or finds it strangely attractive.

Leda had met Whittaker at the record company where she worked as a receptionist, a minor, living piece of rock history employed as a kind of totem on the front desk. Whittaker, who played the guitar and wrote lyrics for a succession of thrash metal bands that, one by one, threw him out because of his histrionics, substance abuse and aggression, claimed to have met Leda while pursuing a record deal. However, Leda had confided to Strike that their first encounter had happened while she was trying to persuade security not to be so rough with the young man they were throwing out. She had brought him home, and Whittaker had never left.

The sixteen-year-old Strike had not been sure whether or not Whittaker's gloating, open pleasure in everything that was sadistic and demonic was genuine or a pose. All he had known was that he hated Whittaker with a visceral loathing that had transcended anything he had felt for any of the other lovers whom Leda had taken up, then left behind. He had been forced to breathe in the man's stench as he did his homework of an evening in the squat; he had almost been able to taste him. Whittaker tried patronising the teenager – sudden explosions and waspish put-downs revealed an articulacy he was careful to hide when he wished to ingratiate himself with Leda's less educated friends – but Strike had been ready with put-downs and comebacks of his own and he had the advantage of being less stoned than Whittaker, or, at least, only as stoned as a person could be living in a constant fug of cannabis smoke. Out of Leda's hearing, Whittaker had jeered at Strike's determination to continue his oft-disrupted education. Whittaker was tall and wiry, surprisingly well muscled for one who lived an almost entirely sedentary life; Strike was already over six feet and boxing at a local club. The tension between the two stiffened the smoky air whenever both were present, the threat of violence constant.

Whittaker had driven Strike's half-sister Lucy away for good with his bullying, his sexual taunts and sneers. He had strutted around the squat naked, scratching his tattooed torso, laughing at the fourteen-year-old girl's mortification. One night she had run to the telephone box at the corner of the street and begged their aunt and uncle in Cornwall to come and fetch her. They had arrived at the squat at dawn next day, having driven overnight from St Mawes. Lucy was ready with her meagre possessions in a small suitcase. She had never lived with her mother again.

Ted and Joan had stood on the doorstep and pleaded with Strike to come too. He had refused, his resolve hardening with every plea Joan made, determined to sit Whittaker out, not to leave him alone with his mother. By now, he had heard

Whittaker talking lucidly about what it would feel like to take a life, as though it were an epicurean treat. He had not believed, then, that Whittaker meant it, but he had known him capable of violence, and had seen him threaten their fellow squatters. Once – Leda refused to believe it had happened – Strike had witnessed Whittaker attempt to bludgeon a cat that had inadvertently woken him from a doze. Strike had wrested the heavy boot from Whittaker's hand as he chased the terrified cat around the room, swinging at it, screaming and swearing, determined to make the animal pay.

The knee onto which the prosthesis was fitted was beginning to complain as Strike strode faster and faster along the street. The Nag's Head pub rose up on the right as though he had conjured it, squat, square and brick. Only at the door did he catch sight of the dark-clad bouncer and remember that the Nag's Head was another lap-dancing club these days.

'Bollocks,' he muttered.

He had no objection to semi-clad women gyrating around him while he enjoyed a pint, but he could not justify the exorbitant price of drinks in such an establishment, not when he had lost two clients in a single day.

He therefore entered the next Starbucks he encountered, found a seat and heaved his sore leg onto an empty chair while he moodily stirred a large black coffee. The squashy earth-coloured sofas, the tall cups of American froth, the wholesome young people working with quiet efficiency behind a clean glass counter: these, surely, were the perfect antidote to Whittaker's stinking spectre, and yet he would not be driven out. Strike found himself unable to stop reliving it all, remembering . . .

While he had lived with Leda and her son, Whittaker's teenage history of delinquency and violence had been known only to social services in the north of England. The tales he told about his past were legion, highly coloured and often contradictory. Only after he had been arrested for murder had the truth leaked out from people from his past who surfaced, some hoping for money from the press, some determined to revenge themselves on him, others trying in their own muddled fashion to defend him.

He had been born into a moneyed upper-middle-class family headed by a knighted diplomat whom Whittaker had believed, until the age of twelve, was his father. At that point he had discovered that his older sister, whom he had been led to believe was in London working as a Montessori teacher, was actually his mother, that she had serious alcohol and drug problems and that she was living in poverty and squalor, ostracised by her family. From this time onward, Whittaker, already a problem child prone to outbursts of extreme temper during which he lashed out indiscriminately, had become determinedly wild. Expelled from his boarding school, he had joined a local gang and soon became ringleader, a phase that culminated in a spell in a correctional facility because he had held a blade to a young girl's throat while his friends sexually assaulted her. Aged fifteen, he had run away to London, leaving a trail of petty crime in his wake and finally succeeding in tracking down his biological mother. A brief, enthusiastic reunion had deteriorated almost at once into mutual violence and animosity.

'Is anyone using this?'

A tall youth had bent over Strike, his hands already gripping the back of the chair on which Strike's leg was resting. He reminded Strike of Robin's fiancé Matthew, with his wavy brown hair and clean-cut good looks. With a grunt, Strike removed his leg, shook his head and watched the guy walk away carrying the chair, rejoining a group of six or more. The girls there were eager for his return, Strike could see: they straightened up and beamed as he placed the chair down and joined them. Whether because of the resemblance to Matthew, or because he had taken Strike's chair, or because Strike genuinely sensed a tosser when he saw one, Strike found the youth obscurely objectionable.

His coffee unfinished but resentful that he had been disturbed, Strike heaved himself back to his feet and left. Spots of rain hit him as he walked back along Whitechapel Road, smoking again and no longer bothering to resist the tidal wave of memory now carrying him along . . .

Whittaker had had an almost pathological need for attention. He resented Leda's focus being diverted from him at any time and for any reason – her job, her children, her friends – and he would turn his flashes of mesmeric charm on other women whenever he deemed her inattentive. Even Strike, who hated him like a disease, had to acknowledge that Whittaker possessed a powerful sex appeal which worked on nearly every woman who passed through the squat.

Thrown out of his most recent band, Whittaker continued to dream of stardom. He knew three guitar chords and covered every bit of paper not hidden from him with lyrics that drew heavily on the Satanic Bible, which Strike remembered lying, its black cover emblazoned with a pentagram and goat-head combined, on the mattress where Leda and Whittaker slept. Whittaker had an extensive knowledge of the life and career of the American cult leader Charles Manson. The scratchy sound of an old vinyl copy of Manson's album *LIE: The Love and Terror Cult* formed the soundtrack to Strike's GCSE year.

Whittaker had been familiar with Leda's legend when he met her, and liked to hear about the parties she had been at, the men she had slept with. Through her, he became connected to the famous, and as Strike got to know him better he came to conclude that Whittaker craved celebrity above almost anything else. He made no moral distinction between his beloved Manson and the likes of Jonny Rokeby, rock star. Both had fixed themselves permanently in the popular consciousness. If anything, Manson had achieved it more successfully, because his myth would not fluctuate with fashion: evil was always fascinating.

However, Leda's fame was not all that attracted Whittaker. His lover had borne children to two wealthy rock stars who provided child support. Whittaker had entered the squat under the clear impression that it was part of Leda's style to dwell in impoverished bohemia, but that somewhere nearby was a vast pool of money into which Strike and Lucy's fathers – Jonny Rokeby and Rick Fantoni respectively – were pouring money. He did not seem to understand or believe the truth: that years of Leda's financial mismanagement and profligacy had led both men to tie up the money in such a way that Leda could not fritter it away. Gradually, over the months, Whittaker's spiteful asides and jibes on the subject of Leda's reluctance to spend money on him had become more frequent. There were grotesque tantrums when Leda would not fork out for the Fender Stratocaster on which he had set his heart, would not buy him the Jean Paul Gaultier velvet jacket for which, stinking and shabby though he was, he suddenly had a yen.

He increased the pressure, telling outrageous and easily disprovable lies: that he needed urgent medical treatment, that he was ten thousand pounds in debt to a man threatening to break his legs. Leda was alternately amused and upset.

'Darling, I haven't got any dough,' she would say. 'Really, darling, I haven't, or I'd give you some, wouldn't I?'

Leda had fallen pregnant in Strike's eighteenth year, while he was applying for university. He had been horrified, but even then he had not expected her to marry Whittaker. She had always told her son that she had hated being a wife. Her first teenage essay into matrimony had lasted two weeks before she had fled. Nor did marriage seem at all Whittaker's style.

Yet it had happened, undoubtedly because Whittaker thought it would be the only sure way to get his hands on those mysteriously hidden millions. The ceremony took place at the Marylebone registry office, where two Beatles had previously married. Perhaps Whittaker had imagined that he would be photographed in the doorway like Paul McCartney, but nobody had been interested. It would take the death of his beaming bride to bring the photographers swarming to the court steps.

Strike suddenly realised that he had walked all the way to Aldgate East station without meaning to. This whole trip, he castigated himself, had been a pointless detour. If he had got back on the train at Whitechapel he would have been well on the way to Nick and Ilsa's by now. Instead, he had careered off as fast as he could in the wrong direction, timing his arrival perfectly to hit the rush-hour crush on the Tube.

His size, to which was added the offence of a backpack, caused unexpressed disgruntlement in those commuters forced to share the space with him, but Strike barely noticed. A head taller than anyone near him, he held on to a hand strap and watched his swaying reflection in the darkened windows, remembering the last part, the worst part: Whittaker in court, arguing for his liberty, because the police had spotted anomalies in his story of where he had been on the day that the needle entered his wife's arm, inconsistencies in his account of where the heroin had come from and what Leda's history of drug use had been.

A raggle-taggle procession of fellow squat-dwellers had given evidence about Leda and Whittaker's turbulent, violent relationship, about Leda's eschewal of heroin in all its forms, about Whittaker's threats, his infidelities, his talk of murder and of money, his lack of noticeable grief after Leda's body had been found. They had insisted over and again, with unwise hysteria, that they were sure Whittaker had killed her. The defence found them pathetically easy to discredit.

An Oxford student in the dock had come as a refreshing change. The judge had eyed Strike with approval: he was clean, articulate and intelligent, however large and intimidating he might be if not suited and tied. The prosecution had wanted him there to answer questions on Whittaker's preoccupation with Leda's wealth. Strike told the silent court about his stepfather's previous attempts to get his hands on a fortune that existed largely in Whittaker's own head, and about his increasing pleas to Leda for her to put him in her will as proof of her love for him.

Whittaker watched out of his gold eyes, almost entirely impassive. In the last minute of his evidence, Strike and Whittaker's eyes had met across the room. The corner of Whittaker's mouth had lifted in a faint, derisive smile. He had raised his index finger half an inch from the place where it rested on the bench in front of him and made a tiny sideways swiping motion.

Strike had known exactly what he was doing. The micro-gesture had been made just for him, a miniature copy of one with which Strike was familiar: Whittaker's mid-air, horizontal slash of the hand, directed at the throat of the person who had offended him.

'You'll get yours,' Whittaker used to say, the gold eyes wide and manic. 'You'll get yours!'

He had brushed up well. Somebody in his moneyed family had stumped up for a decent defence lawyer. Scrubbed clean, soft-spoken and wearing a suit, he had denied everything in quiet, deferential tones. He had his story straight by the time he appeared in court. Everything that the prosecution tried to pull in to draw a picture of the man he really was – Charles Manson on the ancient record player, the Satanic Bible on the bed, the stoned conversations about killing for pleasure – were batted away by a faintly incredulous Whittaker.

'What can I tell you . . . I'm a musician, your honour,' he said at one point. 'There's poetry in the darkness. *She* understood that better than anyone.'

His voice had cracked melodramatically and he broke into dry sobs. Counsel for the defence hastened to ask whether he needed to take a moment.

It was then that Whittaker had shaken his head bravely and offered his gnomic pronouncement on Leda's death:

'She wanted to die. She was the quicklime girl.'

Nobody else had understood the reference at the time, perhaps only Strike who had heard the song so many times through his childhood and adolescence. Whittaker was quoting from 'Mistress of the Salmon Salt'.

He had walked free. The medical evidence supported the view that Leda had not been an habitual heroin user, but her reputation was against her. She had done plenty of other drugs. She was an infamous party girl. To the men in curled wigs whose job it was to classify violent deaths, it seemed wholly in character that she would die on a dirty mattress in pursuit of pleasure her mundane life could not give her.

On the court steps, Whittaker announced that he intended to write a biography of his late wife, then vanished from view. The promised book had never appeared. Leda and Whittaker's son had been adopted by Whittaker's long-suffering grandparents and Strike had never seen him again. Strike had quietly left Oxford and joined the army; Lucy had gone off to college; life had carried on.

Whittaker's periodic reappearance in the newspapers, always connected with some criminal act, could never be a matter of indifference to Leda's children. Of course, Whittaker was never front-page news: he was a man who had married somebody famous for sleeping with the famous. Such limelight as he achieved was a weak reflection of a reflection.

'He's the turd that won't flush,' as Strike put it to Lucy, who did not laugh. She was less inclined even than Robin to embrace rough humour as a means of dealing with unpalatable facts.

Tired and increasingly hungry, swaying with the train, his knee aching, Strike felt low and aggrieved, mainly at himself. For years he had turned his face resolutely towards the future. The past was unalterable: he did not deny what had happened, but there was no need to wallow in it, no need to go seeking out the squat of nearly two decades ago, to recall the rattling of that letter box, to relive the screams of the terrified cat, the sight of his mother in the undertaker's, pale and waxen in her bell-sleeved dress . . .

You're a fucking idiot, Strike told himself angrily as he scanned the Tube map, trying to work out how many changes he would have to make to get to Nick and Ilsa's. *Whittaker never sent the leg. You're just looking for an excuse to get at him.*

The sender of that leg was organised, calculating and efficient; the Whittaker he had known nearly two decades previously had been chaotic, hot-headed and volatile.

And yet . . .

You'll get yours . . .

She was the quicklime girl . . .

'*Fuck!*' said Strike loudly, causing consternation all around him.

He had just realised that he had missed his connection.

11

Feeling easy on the outside,
But not so funny on the inside.

Blue Öyster Cult, 'This Ain't the Summer of Love'

Strike and Robin took turns tailing Platinum over the next couple of days. Strike made excuses to meet during the working day and insisted that Robin leave for home during daylight hours, when the Tube was still busy. On Thursday evening, Strike followed Platinum until the Russian was safely back under the ever-suspicious gaze of Two-Times, then returned to Octavia Street in Wandsworth, where he was still living to avoid the press.

This was the second time in his detective career that Strike had been forced to take refuge with his friends Nick and Ilsa. Theirs was probably the only place he could have borne to stay, but Strike still felt strangely undomesticated within the orbit of a dual-career married couple. Whatever the drawbacks of the cramped attic space above his office, he had total freedom to come and go as he pleased, to eat at 2 a.m. when he had come in from a surveillance job, to move up and down the clanging metal stairs without fear of waking housemates. Now he felt unspoken pressure to be present for the occasional shared meal, feeling anti-social when he helped himself from the fridge in the small hours, even though he had been invited to do so.

On the other hand, Strike had not needed the army to teach him to be tidy and organised. The years of his youth that had been spent in chaos and filth had caused an opposite reaction. Ilsa had already remarked on the fact that Strike moved around the house without leaving any real mark on it, whereas her husband, a gastroenterologist, might be found by the trail of discarded belongings and imperfectly closed drawers.

Strike knew from acquaintances back in Denmark Street that press photographers were still hanging around the door to his office and he was resigned to spending the rest of the week in Nick and Ilsa's guest room, which had bare white walls and a melancholy sense of awaiting its true destiny. They had been trying unsuccessfully for years to have a child. Strike never enquired as to their progress and sensed that Nick, in particular, was grateful for his restraint.

He had known them both for a long time, Ilsa for most of his life. Fair-haired and bespectacled, she came from St Mawes in Cornwall, which was the most constant home that Strike had ever known. He and Ilsa had been in the same primary school class. Whenever he had gone back to stay with Ted and Joan, as had happened regularly through his youth, they had resumed a friendship initially based on the fact that Joan and Ilsa's mother were themselves old schoolmates.

Nick, whose sandy hair had begun receding in his twenties, was a friend from the comprehensive in Hackney where Strike had finished his school career. Nick and Ilsa had met at Strike's eighteenth birthday party in London, dated for a year, then split up when they went off to separate universities. In their mid-twenties they had met again, by which time Ilsa was engaged to another lawyer and Nick dating a fellow doctor.

Within weeks both relationships were over; a year later, Nick and Ilsa had married, with Strike as best man.

Strike returned to their house at half past ten in the evening. As he closed the front door Nick and Ilsa greeted him from the sitting room and urged him to help himself to their still-plentiful takeaway curry.

'What's this?' he asked, looking around, disconcerted, at long lengths of Union Jack bunting, many sheets of scribbled notes and what looked like two hundred red, white and blue plastic cups in a large polythene bag.

'We're helping organise the street party for the royal wedding,' said Ilsa.

'Jesus Christ almighty,' said Strike darkly, heaping his plate with lukewarm Madras.

'It'll be fun! You should come.'

Strike threw her a look that made her snigger.

'Good day?' asked Nick, passing Strike a can of Tennent's.

'No,' said Strike, accepting the lager with gratitude. 'Another job cancelled. I'm down to two clients.'

Nick and Ilsa made sympathetic noises, and there followed a comradely silence while he shovelled curry into his mouth. Tired and dispirited, Strike had spent most of the journey home contemplating the fact that the arrival of the severed leg was having, as he had feared, the effect of a wrecking ball on the business he had been working so hard to build up. His photograph was currently proliferating online and in the papers, in connection with a horrible, random act. It had been a pretext for the papers to remind the world that he was himself one-legged, a fact of which he was not ashamed, but which he was hardly likely to use in advertising; a whiff of something strange, something perverse, was attached to him now. He was tainted.

'Any news about the leg?' asked Ilsa, once Strike had

demolished a considerable amount of curry and was halfway down the can of lager. 'Have the police got anything?'

'I'm meeting Wardle tomorrow night to catch up, but it doesn't sound like they've got much. He's been concentrating on the gangster.'

He had not given Nick and Ilsa details about three of the men he thought might be dangerous and vengeful enough to have sent him the leg, but he had mentioned that he had once run across a career criminal who had previously cut off and mailed a body part. Understandably, they had immediately taken Wardle's view that he was the likely culprit.

For the first time in years, sitting on their comfortable green sofa, Strike remembered that Nick and Ilsa had met Jeff Whittaker. Strike's eighteenth birthday party had taken place at the Bell pub in Whitechapel; his mother was by this time six months pregnant. His aunt's face had been a mask of mingled disapproval and forced jollity and his Uncle Ted, usually the peacemaker, had been unable to disguise his anger and disgust as a patently high Whittaker had interrupted the disco to sing one of his self-penned songs. Strike remembered his own fury, his longing to be away, to be gone to Oxford, to be rid of it all, but perhaps Nick and Ilsa would not remember much about that: they had been engrossed in each other that night, dazed and amazed by their sudden, profound mutual attraction.

'You're worried about Robin,' said Ilsa, more statement than question.

Strike grunted agreement, his mouth full of naan bread. He had had time to reflect on it over the last four days. In this extremity, and through no fault of her own, she had become a vulnerability, a weak spot, and he suspected that whoever had decided to re-address the leg to her had known it. If his employee had been male, he would not currently feel so worried.

Strike had not forgotten that Robin had hitherto been an almost unqualified asset. She was able to persuade recalcitrant witnesses to speak when his own size and naturally intimidating features inclined them to refuse. Her charm and ease of manner had allayed suspicion, opened doors, smoothed Strike's path a hundred times. He knew he owed her; he simply wished that, right now, she would bow out of the way, stay hidden until they had caught the sender of the severed leg.

'I like Robin,' said Ilsa.

'Everyone likes Robin,' said Strike thickly, through a second mouthful of naan. It was the truth: his sister Lucy, the friends who called in at the office, his clients – all made a point of telling Strike how much they liked the woman who worked with him. Nevertheless, he detected a note of faint enquiry in Ilsa's voice that made him keen to make any discussion of Robin impersonal, and he felt vindicated when Ilsa's next question was:

'How's it going with Elin?'

'All right,' said Strike.

'Is she still trying to hide you from her ex?' asked Ilsa, a faint sting in the enquiry.

'Don't like Elin, do you?' said Strike, taking the discussion unexpectedly into the enemy camp for his own amusement. He had known Ilsa on and off for thirty years: her flustered denial was exactly what he had expected.

'I do like – I mean, I don't really know her, but she seems – anyway, you're happy, that's what counts.'

He had thought that this would be sufficient to make Ilsa drop the subject of Robin – she was not the first of his friends to say that he and Robin got on so well, wasn't there a possibility . . . ? Hadn't he ever considered . . . ? – but Ilsa was a lawyer and not easily scared away from pursuing a line of questioning.

'Robin postponed her wedding, didn't she? Have they set a new—?'

'Yep,' said Strike. 'Second of July. She's taking a long weekend to go back to Yorkshire and – do whatever you do for weddings. Coming back on Tuesday.'

He had been Matthew's unlikely ally in insisting that Robin take Friday and Monday off, relieved to think that she would be two hundred and fifty miles away in her family home. She had been deeply disappointed that she would not be able to come along to the Old Blue Last in Shoreditch and meet Wardle, but Strike thought he had detected a faint trace of relief at the idea of a break.

Ilsa looked slightly aggrieved at the news that Robin still intended to marry someone other than Strike, but before she could say anything else Strike's mobile buzzed in his pocket. It was Graham Hardacre, his old SIB colleague.

'Sorry,' he told Nick and Ilsa, setting down his plate of curry and standing up, 'got to take this, important – Hardy!'

'Can you talk, Oggy?' asked Hardacre, as Strike headed back to the front door.

'I can now,' said Strike, reaching the end of the short garden path in three strides and stepping out into the dark street to walk and smoke. 'What've you got for me?'

'To be honest,' said Hardacre, who sounded stressed, 'it'd be a big help if you came up here and had a look, mate. I've got a Warrant Officer who's a real pain in the arse. We didn't get off on the right foot. If I start sending stuff out of here and she gets wind of it—'

'And if I come up?'

'Make it early in the morning and I could leave stuff open on the computer. Carelessly, y'know?'

Hardacre had previously shared information with Strike that, strictly speaking, he ought not to have done. He had only just moved to 35 Section: Strike was not surprised that he did not want to jeopardise his position.

The detective crossed the road, sat down on the low garden wall of the house opposite, lit a cigarette and asked: 'Would it be worth coming up to Scotland for?'

'Depends what you want.'

'Old addresses – family connections – medical and psychiatric records couldn't hurt. Brockbank was invalided out, what was it, 2003?'

'That's right,' said Hardacre.

A noise behind Strike made him stand and turn: the owner of the wall on which he had been sitting was emptying rubbish into his dustbin. He was a small man of around sixty, and by the light of the street lamp Strike saw his annoyed expression elide into a propitiatory smile as he took in Strike's height and breadth. The detective strolled away, past semi-detached houses whose leafy trees and hedges were rippling in the spring breeze. There would be bunting, soon, to celebrate the union of yet another couple. Robin's wedding day would follow not long after.

'You won't have much on Laing, I s'pose,' Strike said, his voice faintly interrogative. The Scot's army career had been shorter than Brockbank's.

'No – but Christ, he sounds a piece of work,' said Hardacre.

'Where'd he go after the Glasshouse?'

The Glasshouse was the military jail in Colchester, where all convicted military personnel were transferred before being placed in a civilian prison.

'HMP Elmley. We've got nothing on him after that; you'd need the probation service.'

'Yeah,' said Strike, exhaling smoke at the starry sky. He and Hardacre both knew that as he was no longer any kind of policeman, he had no more right than any other member of the public to access the probation service's records. 'Whereabouts in Scotland did he come from, Hardy?'

'Melrose. He put down his mother as next of kin when he joined up – I've looked him up.'

'Melrose,' repeated Strike thoughtfully.

He considered his two remaining clients: the moneyed idiot who got his kicks trying to prove he was a cuckold and the wealthy wife and mother who was paying Strike to gather evidence of the way her estranged husband was stalking their sons. The father was in Chicago and Platinum's movements could surely go uncharted for twenty-four hours.

There remained, of course, the possibility that none of the men he suspected had anything to do with the leg, that everything was in his mind.

A harvest of limbs . . .

'How far from Edinburgh is Melrose?'

''Bout an hour, hour and a half's drive.'

Strike ground out his cigarette in the gutter.

'Hardy, I could come up Sunday night on the sleeper, nip into the office early, then drive down to Melrose, see whether Laing's gone back to his family, or if they know where he is.'

'Nice one. I'll pick you up at the station if you let me know when you're getting in, Oggy. In fact,' Hardacre was gearing himself up for an act of generosity, 'if it's only a day trip you're after, I'll lend you my car.'

Strike did not immediately return to his curious friends and his cold curry. Smoking another cigarette, he strolled around the quiet street, thinking. Then he remembered that he was supposed to be attending a concert at the Southbank Centre with Elin on Sunday evening. She was keen to foster an interest in classical music that he had never pretended was more than lukewarm. He checked his watch. It was too late to ring and cancel now; he would need to remember to do so next day.

As he returned to the house, his thoughts drifted back to Robin. She spoke very little about the wedding that was now a mere two and a half months away. Hearing her tell Wardle about the disposable wedding cameras she had ordered had brought home to Strike how soon she would become Mrs Matthew Cunliffe.

There's still time, he thought. For what, he did not specify, even to himself.

12

. . . the writings done in blood.

Blue Öyster Cult, 'O.D.'d on Life Itself'

Many men might think it a pleasant interlude to receive cash for following a pneumatic blonde around London, but Strike was becoming thoroughly bored of trailing Platinum. After hours hanging around Houghton Street, where the LSE's glass and steel walkways occasionally revealed the part-time lap-dancer passing overhead on her way to the library, Strike followed her to Spearmint Rhino for her 4 p.m. shift. Here, he peeled away: Raven would call him if Platinum did anything that passed for untoward, and he was meeting Wardle at six.

He ate a sandwich in a shop near the pub chosen for their rendezvous. His mobile rang once, but on seeing that it was his sister, he let the call go to voicemail. He had a vague idea that it would soon be his nephew Jack's birthday and he had no intention of going to his party, not after the last time, which he remembered mainly for the nosiness of Lucy's fellow mothers and the ear-splitting screams of overexcited and tantrumming children.

The Old Blue Last stood at the top of Great Eastern Street in Shoreditch, a snub-nosed, imposing three-storey brick building curved like the prow of a boat. Within Strike's memory, it had been a strip club and brothel: an old school friend of his and Nick's had allegedly lost his virginity there to a woman old enough to be his mother.

A sign just inside the doors announced the Old Blue Last's rebirth as a music venue. From eight o'clock that evening, Strike saw, he would be able to enjoy live performances from Islington Boys' Club, Red Drapes, In Golden Tears and Neon Index. There was a wry twist to his mouth as he pushed his way into a dark wood-floored bar, where an enormous antique mirror behind the bar bore gilded letters advertising the pale ales of a previous age. Spherical glass lamps hung from the high ceiling, illuminating a crowd of young men and women, many of whom looked like students and most dressed with a trendiness that was beyond Strike.

Although she was in her soul a lover of stadium bands, his mother had taken him to many such venues in his youth, where bands containing her friends might scrape a gig or two before splitting up acrimoniously, re-forming and appearing at a different pub three months later. Strike found the Old Blue Last a surprising choice of meeting place for Wardle, who had previously only drunk with Strike in the Feathers, which was right beside Scotland Yard. The reason became clear when Strike joined the policeman, who was standing alone with a pint at the bar.

'The wife likes Islington Boys' Club. She's meeting me here after work.'

Strike had never met Wardle's wife, and while he had never given the matter much thought, he would have guessed her to be a hybrid of Platinum (because Wardle's eyes invariably followed fake tans and scanty clothing) and the only wife of a Met policeman that Strike knew, whose name was Helly and who was primarily interested in her children, her house and salacious gossip. The fact that Wardle's wife liked an indie band of whom Strike had never heard, notwithstanding the fact that he was already predisposed to despise that very band, made him think that she must be a more interesting person than the one he had expected.

'What've you got?' Strike asked Wardle, having secured himself a pint from an increasingly busy barman. By unspoken consent they left the bar and took the last free table for two in the place.

'Forensics are in on the leg,' said Wardle as they sat down. 'They reckon it came off a woman aged between mid-teens and mid-twenties and that she was dead when it was cut off – but not long dead, looking at the clotting – and it was kept in a freezer in between cutting it off and handing it to your friend Robin.'

Mid-teens to mid-twenties: by Strike's calculations, Brittany Brockbank would be twenty-one now.

'Can't they be any more precise on the age?'

Wardle shook his head.

'That's as far as they're prepared to go. Why?'

'I told you why: Brockbank had a stepdaughter.'

'Brockbank,' repeated Wardle in the non-committal tone that denotes lack of recall.

'One of the guys I thought might've sent the leg,' said Strike, failing to conceal his impatience. 'Ex-Desert Rat. Big dark guy, cauliflower ear—'

'Yeah, all right,' said Wardle, immediately nettled. 'I get passed names all the time, pal. Brockbank – he had the tattoo on his forearm—'

'That's Laing,' said Strike. 'He's the Scot I landed in jail for ten years. Brockbank was the one who reckoned I'd given him brain damage.'

'Oh, yeah.'

'His stepdaughter, Brittany, had old scarring on her leg. I told you that.'

'Yeah, yeah, I remember.'

Strike stifled a caustic retort by sipping his pint. He would have felt far more confident that his suspicions were being taken seriously had it been his old SIB colleague Graham Hardacre who sat opposite him, rather than Wardle. Strike's relationship with Wardle had been tinged from the first with wariness and, latterly, with a faint competitiveness. He rated Wardle's detective abilities higher than those of several other Met officers whom Strike had run across, but Wardle still regarded his own theories with paternal fondness that he never extended to Strike's.

'So have they said anything about the scarring on the calf?'

'Old. Long pre-dated the death.'

'Jesus fuck,' said Strike.

The old scarring might be of no particular interest to forensics, but it was of vital importance to him. This was what he had dreaded. Even Wardle, whose habit it was to take the mickey out of Strike on every possible occasion, appeared to be experiencing something like empathy at the sign of the detective's concern.

'Mate,' he said (and that, too, was new), 'it's not Brockbank. It's Malley.'

Strike had been afraid of this, afraid that the very mention of Malley would send Wardle careering after him to the exclusion of Strike's other suspects, excited at the thought of being the man who put away so notorious a gangster.

'Evidence?' Strike said bluntly.

'Harringay Crime Syndicate's been moving Eastern European prostitutes around London and up in Manchester. I've been talking to Vice. They bust into a brothel up the road last week and got two little Ukrainians out of there.' Wardle dropped his voice still lower. 'We've got female officers debriefing them. They had a friend who thought she was coming to the UK for a modelling job and never took kindly to the work, even when they beat the crap out of her. Digger dragged her out of the house by her hair two weeks ago and they haven't seen her since. They haven't seen Digger since, either.'

'All in a day's work for Digger,' said Strike. 'That doesn't mean it's her leg. Has anyone ever heard him mention me?'

'Yes,' said Wardle triumphantly.

Strike lowered the pint he had been about to sip. He had not expected an affirmative answer.

'They have?'

'One of the girls Vice got out of the house is clear she heard Digger talking about you not long ago.'

'In what context?'

Wardle uttered a polysyllable: the surname of a wealthy Russian casino owner for whom Strike had indeed done some work at the end of the previous year. Strike frowned. As far as he could see, Digger knowing that he had worked for the casino owner made it no more likely that Digger had found out that he owed his previous stretch of incarceration to Strike's evidence. All Strike took from this fresh information was that his Russian client moved in extremely insalubrious circles, something of which he had already been aware.

'And how does me taking Arzamastsev's coin affect Digger?'

'Well, where d'you wanna start?' said Wardle, with what Strike felt was vagueness masquerading as the wide view. 'The Syndicate's got fingers in a lot of pies. Basically, we've got a guy you've crossed with a history of sending people body parts, and he disappears with a young girl right before you get sent a young girl's leg.'

'You put it like that, it sounds convincing,' said Strike, who remained entirely unconvinced. 'Have you done anything about looking at Laing, Brockbank and Whittaker?'

'Course,' said Wardle. 'Got people trying to locate all of them.'

Strike hoped that was true, but refrained from questioning the statement on the basis that it would jeopardise his friendly relations with Wardle.

'We've got CCTV of the courier as well,' said Wardle.

'And?'

'Your colleague's a good witness,' said Wardle. 'It *was* a Honda. Fake plates. Clothes exactly as she described. He drove off south-west – heading towards a real courier depot, as it goes. Last time we caught him on camera was in Wimbledon. No sign of him or the bike since, but like I say, fake plates. Could be anywhere.'

'Fake plates,' repeated Strike. 'He did a hell of a lot of planning.'

The pub was filling up all around them. Apparently the band was going to play upstairs: people were squeezing towards the door that led to the first floor and Strike could hear the familiar scream of microphone feedback.

'I've got something else for you,' said Strike, without enthusiasm. 'I promised Robin I'd give you copies.'

He had returned to his office before daybreak that morning. The press had given up trying to catch him going in or out, though an acquaintance in the guitar shop opposite informed him that photographers had lingered until the previous evening.

Wardle took the two photocopied letters, looking mildly intrigued.

'They've both come in the last couple of months,' said Strike. 'Robin thinks you should take a look. Want another?' he asked, gesturing to Wardle's almost empty glass.

Wardle read the letters while Strike bought two more pints. He was still holding the note signed RL when he returned. Strike picked up the other one and read, in clearly legible, rounded schoolgirlish writing:

> . . . that I will only be truly me and truly complete when my leg is gone. Nobody gets that it isn't and never will be part of me. My need to be an amputee is very hard for my family to accept, they think it is all in my mind, but you understand . . .

You got that wrong, thought Strike, dropping the photocopy back onto the table top and noting as he did so that she had written her address in Shepherd's Bush as clearly and neatly as possible, so that his reply, advising her on how best to cut off her leg, would be in no danger of going astray. It was signed Kelsey, but with no surname.

Wardle, still deep in the second letter, let out a snort of mingled amusement and disgust.

'Fucking hell, have you *read* this?'

'No,' said Strike.

More young people were squeezing into the bar. He and Wardle were not the only people in their mid-thirties, but they were definitely at the older end of the spectrum. He watched a pretty, pale young woman made up like a forties starlet, with narrow black eyebrows, crimson lipstick and powder-blue hair pinned into victory rolls, look around for her date. 'Robin reads the nutter letters and gives me a précis if she thinks I need one.'

'"I want to massage your stump,"' read Wardle aloud. '"I want you to use me as a living crutch. I want—" Holy shit. That's not even physically—'

He flipped over the letter.

'"RL." Can you read that address?'

'No,' said Strike, squinting at it. The handwriting was dense and extremely difficult to read. The only legible word in the cramped address, on a first read, was 'Walthamstow'.

'What happened to "I'll be by the bar", Eric?'

The young woman with the pale blue hair and crimson lips had appeared at the table beside them, holding a drink. She wore a leather jacket over what looked like a forties summer dress.

'Sorry, babes, talking shop,' said Wardle, unperturbed. 'April, Cormoran Strike. My wife,' he added.

'Hi,' said Strike, extending a large hand. He would never have guessed Wardle's wife looked like this. For reasons he was too tired to analyse, it made him like Wardle better.

'Oh, it's *you*!' said April, beaming at Strike while Wardle slid the photocopied letters off the table, folded and pocketed them. 'Cormoran Strike! I've heard loads about *you*. Are you staying for the band?'

'I doubt it,' said Strike, though not unpleasantly. She was very pretty.

April seemed reluctant to let him go. They had friends joining them, she told him, and sure enough, within a few minutes of her arrival another six people turned up. There were two unattached women in the group. Strike allowed himself to be talked into moving upstairs with them, where there was a small stage and an already packed room. In response to his questions, April revealed that she was a stylist who had been working on a magazine shoot that very day, and – she said it casually – a part-time burlesque dancer.

'Burlesque?' repeated Strike at the top of his voice, as microphone feedback again screeched through the upper room, to shouts and groans of protest from the assembled drinkers. *Isn't that arty stripping?* he wondered, as April shared the information that her friend Coco – a girl with tomato-red hair who smiled at him and wiggled her fingers – was a burlesque dancer too.

They seemed a friendly group and none of the men were treating him with that tiresome chippiness that Matthew exhibited every time he came within Strike's orbit. He had not watched any live music in a long time. Petite Coco had already expressed a desire to be lifted up so she could see . . .

However, when Islington Boys' Club took to the stage Strike found himself forcibly transported back to times and people he strove not to think about. Stale sweat in the air, the familiar sound of guitars being tweaked and tuned, the humming of the open mic: he could have borne them all, had the lead singer's posture and his lithe androgyny not recalled Whittaker.

Four bars in and Strike knew he was leaving. There was nothing wrong with their brand of guitar-heavy indie rock: they played well and, in spite of his unfortunate resemblance to Whittaker, the lead singer had a decent voice. However, Strike had been in this environment too often and unable to leave: tonight, he was free to seek peace and clean air, and he intended to exercise that prerogative.

With a shouted farewell to Wardle and a wave and a smile to April, who winked and waved back, he left, large enough to carve an easy path through people already sweaty and breathless. He gained the door as Islington Boys' Club finished their first song. The applause overhead sounded like muffled hail on a tin roof. A minute later, he was striding away, with relief, into the swishing sound of traffic.

13

In the presence of another world.

Blue Öyster Cult, 'In the Presence of Another World'

On Saturday morning, Robin and her mother took the ancient family Land Rover from their small hometown of Masham to the dressmaker's in Harrogate where Robin's wedding dress was being altered. The design had been modified because it had initially been made for a wedding in January and was now to be worn in July.

'You've lost more weight,' said the elderly dressmaker, sticking pins down the back of the bodice. 'You don't want to go any thinner. This dress was meant for a bit of curve.'

Robin had chosen the fabric and design of the dress over a year ago, loosely based on an Elie Saab model that her parents, who would also be forking out for half of her elder brother Stephen's wedding in six months' time, could never have afforded. Even this cut-price version would have been impossible on the salary Strike paid Robin.

The lighting in the changing room was flattering, yet Robin's reflection in the gilt-framed mirror looked too pale, her eyes heavy and tired. She was not sure that altering the dress to make it strapless had been successful. Part of what she had liked about the design in the first place had been the long sleeves. Perhaps, she thought, she was simply jaded from having lived with the idea of the dress for so long.

The changing room smelled of new carpet and polish. While Robin's mother Linda watched the dressmaker pin, tuck and twitch the yards of chiffon Robin, depressed by her own reflection, focused instead on the little corner stand carrying crystal tiaras and fake flowers.

'Remind me, have we fixed on a headdress?' asked the dressmaker, who had the habit of using the first person plural so often found in nursing staff. 'We were leaning towards a tiara for the winter wedding, weren't we? I think it might be worth trying flowers with the strapless.'

'Flowers would be nice,' Linda agreed from the corner of the dressing room.

Mother and daughter closely resembled each other. Though her once slender waist had thickened and the faded red-gold hair piled untidily on top of her head was now laced with silver, Linda's blue-grey eyes were her daughter's and they rested now upon her second child with an expression of concern and shrewdness that would have been comically familiar to Strike.

Robin tried on an array of fake floral headdresses and liked none of them.

'Maybe I'll stick with the tiara,' she said.

'Or fresh flowers?' suggested Linda.

'Yes,' said Robin, suddenly keen to get away from the carpet smell and her pale, boxed-in reflection. 'Let's go and see whether the florist could do something.'

She was glad to have the changing room to herself for a few minutes. As she worked her way out of the dress and pulled her jeans and sweater back on, she tried to analyse her low mood. While she regretted that she had been forced to miss Strike's meeting with Wardle, she had been looking forward to putting a couple of hundred miles between her and the faceless man in black who had handed her a severed leg.

Yet she had no sense of escape. She and Matthew had rowed yet again on the train coming north. Even here, in the changing room in James Street, her multiplying anxieties haunted her: the agency's dwindling caseload, the fear of what would happen if Strike could no longer afford to employ her. Once dressed, she checked her mobile. No messages from Strike.

She was almost monosyllabic among the buckets of mimosa and lilies a quarter of an hour later. The florist fussed and fiddled, holding blooms against Robin's hair and accidentally letting drops of cold, greenish water fall from the long stem of a rose onto her cream sweater.

'Let's go to Bettys,' suggested Linda when a floral headdress had at last been ordered.

Bettys of Harrogate was a local institution, the spa town's long-established tearoom. There were hanging flower baskets outside, where customers queued under a black, gold and glass canopy, and within were tea-canister lamps and ornamental teapots, squashy chairs and waitresses in *broderie anglaise* uniforms. It had been a treat to Robin, ever since she was small, to peer through the glass counter at rows of fat marzipan pigs, to watch her mother buying one of the luxurious fruitcakes laced with alcohol that came in its own special tin.

Today, sitting beside the window staring out at primary-coloured flowerbeds resembling the geometric shapes cut out of plasticine by small children, Robin declined anything to eat, asked for a pot of tea and flipped over her mobile again. Nothing.

'Are you all right?' Linda asked her.

'Fine,' said Robin. 'I was just wondering if there was any news.'

'What kind of news?'

'About the leg,' said Robin. 'Strike met Wardle last night – the Met officer.'

'Oh,' said Linda and silence fell between them until their tea arrived.

Linda had ordered a Fat Rascal, one of Bettys' large scones. She finished buttering it before she asked:

'You and Cormoran are going to try and find out who sent that leg yourselves, are you?'

Something in her mother's tone made Robin proceed warily.

'We're interested in what the police are doing, that's all.'

'Ah,' said Linda, chewing, watching Robin.

Robin felt guilty for being irritable. The wedding dress was expensive and she had not been appreciative.

'Sorry for being snappy.'

'That's all right.'

'It's just, Matthew's on my case all the time about working for Cormoran.'

'Yes, we heard something about that last night.'

'Oh God, Mum, I'm sorry!'

Robin had thought they'd kept the row quiet enough not to wake her parents. They had argued on the way up to Masham, suspended hostilities while having supper with her parents, then resumed the argument in the living room after Linda and Michael had gone to bed.

'Cormoran's name came up a lot, didn't it? I assume Matthew's—?'

'He's not *worried*,' said Robin.

Matthew determinedly treated Robin's work as a kind of joke, but when forced to take it seriously – when, for instance, somebody sent her a severed leg – he became angry rather than concerned.

'Well, if he's not worried, he should be,' said Linda. 'Somebody sent you part of a dead woman, Robin. It's not so long ago that Matt called us to say you were in hospital with concussion. I'm not telling you to resign!' she added, refusing to be cowed by Robin's reproachful expression. 'I know this is what you want! Anyway' – she forced the larger half of her Fat Rascal into Robin's unresisting hand – 'I wasn't going to ask whether Matt was worried. I was going to ask whether he was jealous.'

Robin sipped her strong Bettys Blend tea. Vaguely she contemplated taking some of these teabags back to the office. There was nothing as good as this in Ealing Waitrose. Strike liked his tea strong.

'Yes, Matt's jealous,' she said at last.

'I'm assuming he's got no reason?'

'Of course not!' said Robin hotly. She felt betrayed. Her mother was always on her side, always—

'There's no need to get fired up,' said Linda, unruffled. 'I wasn't suggesting you'd done anything you shouldn't.'

'Well, good,' said Robin, eating the scone without noticing it. 'Because I haven't. He's my boss, that's all.'

'And your friend,' suggested Linda, 'judging by the way you talk about him.'

'Yes,' said Robin, but honesty compelled her to add, 'it's not like a normal friendship, though.'

'Why not?'

'He doesn't like talking about personal stuff. Blood out of a stone.'

Except for one notorious evening – barely mentioned between them since – when Strike had got so drunk he could hardly stand, voluntary information about his private life had been virtually non-existent.

'You get on well, though?'

'Yeah, really well.'

'A lot of men find it hard to hear how well their other halves get on with other men.'

'What am I supposed to do, only ever work with women?'

'No,' said Linda. 'I'm just saying: Matthew obviously feels threatened.'

Robin sometimes suspected that her mother regretted the fact that her daughter had not had more boyfriends before committing herself to Matthew. She and Linda were close; she was Linda's only daughter. Now, with the tearoom clattering and tinkling around them, Robin realised that she was afraid that Linda might tell her it wasn't too late to back out of the wedding if she wanted to. Tired and low though she was, and in spite of the fact that they had had several rocky months, she knew that she loved Matthew. The dress was made, the church was booked, the reception almost paid for. She must plough on, now, and get to the finishing line.

'I don't fancy Strike. Anyway, he's in a relationship: he's seeing Elin Toft. She's a presenter on Radio Three.'

She hoped that this information would distract her mother, an enthusiastic devourer of radio programmes while cooking and gardening.

'Elin Toft? Is she that very beautiful blonde girl who was on the telly talking about Romantic composers the other night?' asked Linda.

'Probably,' said Robin, with a pronounced lack of enthusiasm, and in spite of the fact that her diversionary tactic had been successful, she changed the subject. 'So you're getting rid of the Land Rover?'

'Yes. We'll get nothing for it, obviously. Scrap, maybe . . . unless,' said Linda, struck by a sudden thought, 'you and Matthew want it? It's got a year's tax left on it and it always scrapes through its MOT somehow.'

Robin chewed her scone, thinking. Matthew moaned constantly about their lack of car, a deficiency he attributed to her low salary. His sister's husband's A3 Cabriolet caused him almost physical pangs of envy. Robin knew he would feel very differently about a battered old Land Rover with its permanent smell of wet dog and Wellington boots, but at one o'clock that morning in the family sitting room, Matthew had listed his estimates of the salary of all their contemporaries, concluding with a flourish that Robin's pay lay right at the bottom of the league table. With a sudden spurt of malice, she imagined herself telling her fiancé, 'But we've got the Land Rover, Matt, there's no point trying to save for an Audi now!'

'It could be really useful for work,' she said aloud, 'if we need to go outside London. Strike won't need to hire a car.'

'Mm,' said Linda, apparently absently, but with her eyes fixed on Robin's face.

They drove home to find Matthew laying the table with his future father-in-law. He was usually more helpful in the kitchen at her parents' house than at home with Robin.

'How's the dress looking?' he asked in what Robin supposed was an attempt at conciliation.

'All right,' said Robin.

'Is it bad luck to tell me about it?' he said and then, when she did not smile, 'I bet you look beautiful, anyway.'

Softening, she reached out a hand and he winked, squeezing her fingers. Then Linda plonked a dish of mashed potato on the table between them and told him that she had given them the old Land Rover.

'What?' said Matthew, his face a study in dismay.

'You're always saying you want a car,' said Robin, defensive on her mother's behalf.

'Yeah, but – the Land Rover, in London?'

'Why not?'

'It'll ruin his image,' said her brother Martin, who had just entered the room with the newspaper in his hand; he had been examining the runners for that afternoon's Grand National. 'Suit you down to the ground, though, Rob. I can just see you and Hopalong, off-roading to murder scenes.'

Matthew's square jaw tightened.

'Shut up, Martin,' snapped Robin, glaring at her younger brother as she sat down at the table. 'And I'd love to see you call Strike Hopalong to his face,' she added.

'He'd probably laugh,' said Martin airily.

'Because you're peers?' said Robin, her tone brittle. 'Both of you with your stunning war records, risking life and limb?'

Martin was the only one of the four Ellacott siblings who had not attended university, and the only one who still lived with their parents. He was always touchy at the slightest hint that he underachieved.

'The fuck's that supposed to mean – I should be in the army?' he demanded, firing up.

'Martin!' said Linda sharply. 'Mind your language!'

'Does she have a go at you for still having both legs, Matt?' asked Martin.

Robin dropped her knife and fork and walked out of the kitchen.

The image of the severed leg was before her again, with its shining white tibia sticking out of the dead flesh, those slightly grubby toenails whose owner had meant, perhaps, to clean or paint before anybody else would see them . . .

And now she was crying, crying for the first time since she had taken the package. The pattern on the old stair carpet blurred and she had to grope for the doorknob of her bedroom. She crossed to the bed and dropped, face down, onto the clean duvet, her shoulders shaking and her chest heaving, her hands pressed over her wet face as she tried to muffle the sound of her sobs. She did not want any of them to come after her; she did not want to have to talk or explain; she simply wanted to be alone to release the emotion she had tamped down to get through the working week.

Her brother's glibness about Strike's amputation was an echo of Strike's own jokes about the dismembered leg. A woman had died in what were likely to have been terrible, brutal circumstances, and nobody seemed to care as much as Robin did. Death and a hatchet had reduced the unknown female to a lump of meat, a problem to be solved and she, Robin, felt as though she was the only person to remember that a living, breathing human being had been using that leg, perhaps as recently as a week ago . . .

After ten minutes' solid weeping she rolled over onto her back, opened her streaming eyes and looked around her old bedroom as though it might give her succour.

This room had once seemed like the only safe place on earth. For the three months after she had dropped out of university she had barely left it, even to eat. The walls had been shocking pink back then, a mistaken decorating choice she had made when she was sixteen. She had dimly recognised that it did not work, but had not wanted to ask her father to repaint, so she had covered the garish glare with as many posters as possible. There had been a large picture of Destiny's Child facing her at the foot of the bed. Though there was nothing there now but the smooth eau de nil wallpaper Linda had put up when Robin left home to join Matthew in London, Robin could still visualise Beyoncé, Kelly Rowland and Michelle Williams staring at her out of the cover of their album *Survivor*. The image was indelibly connected with the worst time of her life.

The walls bore only two framed photographs these days: one of Robin with her old sixth form on their last day of school (Matthew at the back of the shot, the most handsome boy in the year, refusing to pull a face or wear a stupid hat) and the other of Robin, aged twelve, riding her old Highland pony Angus, a shaggy, strong and stubborn creature who had lived on her uncle's farm and on whom Robin had doted, his naughtiness notwithstanding.

Depleted and exhausted, she blinked away more tears and wiped her wet face with the heels of her hands. Muffled voices rose from the kitchen below her room. Her mother, she was sure, would be advising Matthew to leave her alone for a while. Robin hoped that he would listen. She felt as though she would like to sleep through the rest of the weekend.

An hour later she was still lying on the double bed, staring drowsily out of the window at the top of the lime tree in the garden, when Matthew knocked and entered with a mug of tea.

'Your mum thought you could use this.'

'Thanks,' said Robin.

'We're all going to watch the National together. Mart's put a big bet on Ballabriggs.'

No mention of her distress or of Martin's crass comments; Matthew's manner implied that she had somehow embarrassed herself and he was offering her a way out. She knew at once that he had no conception of what the sight and feel of that woman's leg had stirred up in her. No, he was simply annoyed that Strike, whom none of the Ellacotts had ever met, was once again taking up space in weekend conversation. It was Sarah Shadlock at the rugby all over again.

'I don't like watching horses break their necks,' said Robin. 'Anyway, I've got some work to do.'

He stood looking down at her, then walked out, closing the door with a little too much force, so that it jumped open again behind him.

Robin sat up, smoothed her hair, took a deep breath and then went to fetch her laptop case from on top of the dressing table. She had felt guilty bringing it along on their trip home, guilty for hoping that she might find time for what she was privately calling her lines of enquiry. Matthew's air of generous forgiveness had put paid to that. Let him watch the National. She had better things to do.

Returning to the bed, she made a pile of pillows behind her, opened the laptop and navigated to certain bookmarked webpages that she had talked to nobody about, not even Strike, who would no doubt think she was wasting her time.

She had already spent several hours pursuing two separate but related lines of enquiry suggested by the letters that she had insisted Strike should take to Wardle: the communication from the young woman who wished to remove her own leg, and the missive from the person who wished to do things to Strike's stump that had made Robin feel faintly queasy.

Robin had always been fascinated by the workings of the human mind. Her university career, though cut short, had been dedicated to the study of psychology. The young woman who had written to Strike seemed to be suffering from body integrity identity disorder or BIID: the irrational desire for the removal of a healthy body part.

Having read several scientific papers online, Robin now knew that sufferers of BIID were rare and that the precise cause of their condition was unknown. Visits to support sites had already shown her how much people seemed to dislike sufferers of the condition. Angry comments peppered the message boards, accusing BIID sufferers of coveting a status that others had had thrust upon them by bad luck and illness, of wanting to court attention in a grotesque and offensive manner. Equally angry retorts followed the attacks: did the writer really think the sufferer *wanted* to have BIID? Did they not understand how difficult it was to be transabled – wanting, needing, to be paralysed or amputated? Robin wondered what Strike would think of the BIID sufferers' stories, were he to read them. She suspected that his reaction would not be sympathetic.

Downstairs, the sitting room door opened and she heard a brief snatch of a commentator's voice, her father telling their old chocolate Labrador to get out because it had farted and Martin's laughter.

To her own frustration, the exhausted Robin could not remember the name of the young girl who had written to Strike, asking for advice on cutting off her leg, but she thought it had been Kylie or something similar. Scrolling slowly down the most densely populated support site she had found, she kept an eye out for usernames that might in any way connect to her, because where else would a teenager with an unusual fixation go to share her fantasy, if not cyberspace?

The bedroom door, still ajar since Matthew's exit, swung open as the banished Labrador, Rowntree, came waddling into the bedroom. He reported to Robin for an absent-minded rub of his ears, then flopped down beside the bed. His tail bumped against the floor for a while and then he fell wheezily asleep. To the accompaniment of his snuffling snores, Robin continued to comb the message boards.

Quite suddenly, she experienced one of those jolts of excitement with which she had become familiar since starting work for Strike, and which were the immediate reward of looking for a tiny piece of information that might mean something, nothing or, occasionally, everything.

Nowheretoturn: Does anyone know anything about Cameron Strike?

Holding her breath, Robin opened the thread.

W@nBee: that detective with one leg? yeah, hes a veteran.
Nowheretoturn: I heard he might of done it himself.
W@nBee: No, if you look up he's was in Afganistan.

That was all. Robin combed more threads on the forum, but Nowheretoturn had not pursued their enquiry, nor did they appear again. That meant nothing; they might have changed their username. Robin searched until satisfied that she had probed every corner of the site, but Strike's name did not recur.

Her excitement ebbed away. Even assuming that the letter-writer and Nowheretoturn were the same person, her belief that Strike's amputation had been self-inflicted had been clear in the letter. There weren't many famous amputees on whom you might be able to pin the hope that their condition was voluntary.

Shouts of encouragement were now emanating from the sitting room below. Abandoning the BIID boards, Robin turned to her second line of enquiry.

She liked to think that she had developed a tougher skin since working at the detective agency. Nevertheless, her first forays into the fantasies of acrotomophiliacs – those who were sexually attracted to amputees – which had been accessed with only a few clicks of the mouse, had left her with a cringing feeling in her stomach that lingered long after she had left the internet. Now she found herself reading the outpourings of a man (she assumed he was a man) whose most exciting sexual fantasy was a woman with all four limbs amputated above the elbow and knee joints. The precise point at which limbs were cut seemed to be a particular preoccupation. A second man (they could not be women, surely) had masturbated since early youth over the idea of accidentally guillotining off his own and his best friend's legs. Everywhere was discussion of the fascination of the stumps themselves, of the restricted movement of amputees, of what Robin assumed was disability as an extreme manifestation of bondage.

While the distinctive nasal voice of the commentator on the Grand National gabbled incomprehensibly from below, and her brother's shouts of encouragement became louder, Robin scanned more message boards, seeking any mention of Strike and also searching for a connecting line between this paraphilia and violence.

Robin found it notable that none of the people pouring their amputee and amputation fantasies onto this forum seemed to be aroused by violence or pain. Even the man whose sexual fantasy involved him and his friend cutting off their own legs together was clear and articulate on that subject: the guillotining was merely the necessary precursor to the achievement of stumps.

Would a person aroused by Strike-as-amputee cut off a woman's leg and send it to him? That was the sort of thing Matthew might think would happen, Robin thought scornfully, because Matthew would assume that anyone odd enough to find stumps attractive would be crazy enough to dismember somebody else: indeed, he would think it likely. However, from what Robin remembered of the letter from RL, and after perusing the online outpourings of his fellow acrotomophiliacs, she thought it much more likely that what RL meant by 'making it up' to Strike was likely to mean practices that Strike would probably find a lot less appetising than the original amputation.

Of course, RL might be both an acrotomophiliac and a psychopath . . .

'YES! FUCKING YES! FIVE HUNDRED QUID!'

screamed Martin. From the rhythmic thumping emanating from the hall, it sounded as though Martin had found the sitting room inadequate for the full performance of a victory dance. Rowntree woke, jumped to his feet and let out a groggy bark. The noise was such that Robin did not hear Matthew approaching until he pushed the door open. Automatically, she clicked the mouse repeatedly, backtracking through the sites devoted to the sexual fetishisation of amputees.

'Hi,' she said. 'I take it Ballabriggs won.'

'Yeah,' said Matthew.

For the second time that day, he held out a hand. Robin slid the laptop aside and Matthew pulled her to her feet and hugged her. With the warmth of his body came relief, seeping through her, calming her. She could not stand another night's bickering.

Then he pulled away, his eyes fixed on something over her shoulder.

'What?'

She looked down at the laptop. There in the middle of a glowing white screen of text was a large boxed definition:

Acrotomophilia *noun*
A paraphilia in which sexual gratification is derived from fantasies or acts involving an amputee.

There was a brief silence.

'How many horses died?' asked Robin in a brittle voice.

'Two,' Matthew answered, and walked out of the room.

14

. . . you ain't seen the last of me yet,
I'll find you, baby, on that you can bet.

Blue Öyster Cult, 'Showtime'

Half past eight on Sunday evening found Strike standing outside Euston station, smoking what would be his last cigarette until he arrived in Edinburgh in nine hours' time.

Elin had been disappointed that he was going to miss the evening concert, and instead they had spent most of the afternoon in bed, an alternative that Strike had been more than happy to accept. Beautiful, collected and rather cool outside the bedroom, Elin was considerably more demonstrative inside it. The memory of certain erotic sights and sounds – her alabaster skin faintly damp under his mouth, her pale lips wide in a moan – added savour to the tang of nicotine. Smoking was not permitted in Elin's spectacular flat on Clarence Terrace, because her young daughter had asthma. Strike's post-coital treat had instead been to fight off sleep while she showed him a recording of herself talking about the Romantic composers on the bedroom television.

'You know, you look like Beethoven,' she told him thoughtfully, as the camera closed in on a marble bust of the composer.

'With a buggered nose,' said Strike. He had been told it before.

'And *why* are you going to Scotland?' Elin had asked as he reattached his prosthetic leg while sitting on the bed in her bedroom, which was decorated in creams and whites and yet had none of the depressing austerity of Ilsa and Nick's spare room.

'Following a lead,' said Strike, fully aware that he was overstating the case. There was nothing except his own suspicions to connect Donald Laing and Noel Brockbank to the severed leg. Nevertheless, and much though he might silently lament the nearly three hundred quid the round trip was costing him, he did not regret the decision to go.

Grinding the stub of his cigarette under the heel of his prosthetic foot, he proceeded into the station, bought himself a bag of food at the supermarket and clambered onto the overnight train.

The single berth, with its fold-down sink and its narrow bunk, might be tiny, but his army career had taken him to far more uncomfortable places. He was pleased to find that the bed could just accommodate his six foot three and after all, a small space was always easier to navigate once his prosthesis had been removed. Strike's only gripe was that the compartment was overheated: he kept his attic flat at a temperature every woman he knew would have deplored as icy, not that any woman had ever slept in his attic flat. Elin had never even seen the place; Lucy, his sister, had never been invited over lest it shatter her delusion that he was making plenty of money these days. In fact, now he came to think about it, Robin was the only woman who had ever been in there.

The train jolted into motion. Benches and pillars flickered past the window. Strike sank down on the bunk, unwrapped the first of his bacon baguettes and took a large mouthful, remembering as he did so Robin sitting at his kitchen table, white-faced and shaken. He was glad to think of her at home in Masham, safely out of the way of possible harm: at least he could stow one nagging worry.

The situation in which he now found himself was deeply familiar. He might have been back in the army, travelling the length of the UK as cheaply as possible, to report to the SIB station in Edinburgh. He had never been stationed there. The offices, he knew, were in the castle that stood on top of a jagged rock outcrop in the middle of the city.

Later, after swaying along the rattling corridor to pee, he undressed to his boxer shorts and lay on top of the thin blankets to sleep, or rather to doze. The side-to-side rocking motion was soothing, but the heat and the changing pace of the train kept jarring him out of sleep. Ever since the Viking in which he was being driven had blown up around him in Afghanistan, taking half his leg and two colleagues with it, Strike had found it difficult to be driven by other people. Now he discovered that this mild phobia extended to trains. The whistle of an engine speeding past his carriage in the opposite direction woke him like an alarm three times; the slight sway as the train cornered made him imagine the terror of the great metal monster overbalancing, rolling, crashing and smashing apart . . .

The train pulled into Edinburgh Waverley at a quarter past five, but breakfast was not served until six. Strike woke to the sound of a porter moving down the carriage, delivering trays. When Strike opened his door, balancing on one leg, the uniformed youth let out an uncontrolled yelp of dismay, his eyes on the prosthesis which lay on the floor behind Strike.

'Sorry, pal,' he said in a thick Glaswegian accent as he looked from the prosthesis to Strike's leg, realising that the passenger had not, after all, hacked off his own leg. 'Whit a reddy!'

Amused, Strike took the tray and closed the door. After a wakeful night he wanted a cigarette much more than a reheated, rubbery croissant, so he set about reattaching the leg and getting dressed, gulping black coffee as he did so, and was among the first to step out into the chilly Scottish early morning.

The station's situation gave the odd feeling of being at the bottom of an abyss. Through the concertinaed glass ceiling Strike could make out the shapes of dark Gothic buildings towering above him on higher ground. He found the place near the taxi rank where Hardacre had said he would pick him up, sat down on a cold metal bench and lit up, his backpack at his feet.

Hardacre did not appear for twenty minutes, and when he did so, Strike felt a profound sense of misgiving. He had been so grateful to escape the expense of hiring a car that he had felt it would be churlish to ask Hardacre what he drove.

A Mini. A fucking Mini . . .

'Oggy!'

They performed the American half-hug, half-handshake that had permeated even the armed forces. Hardacre was barely five foot eight, an amiable-looking investigator with thinning, mouse-coloured hair. Strike knew his nondescript appearance hid a sharp investigative brain. They had been together for the Brockbank arrest, and that alone had been enough to bond them, with the mess it had landed them in afterwards.

Only when he watched his old friend folding himself into the Mini did it seem to occur to Hardacre that he ought to have mentioned the make of car he drove.

'I forgot you're such a big bastard,' he commented. 'You gonna be all right to drive this?'

'Oh yeah,' said Strike, sliding the passenger seat as far back as it could go. 'Grateful for the lend, Hardy.'

At least it was an automatic.

The little car wound its way out of the station and up the hill to the soot-black buildings that had peered down at Strike through the glass roof. The early morning was a cool grey.

'S'posed to be nice later,' muttered Hardacre as they drove up the steep, cobbled Royal Mile, past shops selling tartan and flags of the lion rampant, restaurants and cafés, boards advertising ghost tours and narrow alleyways affording fleeting glimpses of the city stretched out below to their right.

At the top of the hill the castle came into view: darkly forbidding against the sky, surrounded by high, curved stone walls. Hardacre took a right, away from the crested gates where tourists keen to beat the queues were already lurking. At a wooden booth he gave his name, flashed his pass and drove on, aiming for the entrance cut in the volcanic rock, which led to a floodlit tunnel lined with thick power cables. Leaving the tunnel, they found themselves high above the city, cannons ranged on the battlements beside them, giving on to a misty view of the spires and rooftops of the black and gold city stretching out to the Firth of Forth in the distance.

'Nice,' said Strike, moving to the cannons for a better look.

'Not bad,' agreed Hardacre, with a matter-of-fact glance down at the Scottish capital. 'Over here, Oggy.'

They entered the castle through a wooden side door. Strike followed Hardacre along a chilly, narrow stone-flagged corridor and up a couple of flights of stairs that were not easy on the knee joint of Strike's right leg. Prints of Victorian military men in dress uniforms hung at unequal intervals on the walls.

A door on the first landing led into a corridor lined with offices, carpeted in shabby dark pink, with hospital-green walls. Though Strike had never been there before, it felt instantly familiar in a way that the old squat in Fulbourne Street could not touch. This had been his life: he could have settled down at an unoccupied desk and been back at work within ten minutes.

The walls bore posters, one reminding investigators of the importance of and procedures relating to the Golden Hour – that short period of time after an offence when clues and information were most plentiful and easiest to gather – another showing photographs of Drugs of Abuse. There were whiteboards covered with updates and deadlines for various live cases – 'awaiting phone & DNA analysis', 'SPA Form 3 required' – and metal file cases carrying mobile fingerprint kits. The door to the lab stood open. On a high metal table sat a pillow in a plastic evidence bag; it was covered in dark brown bloodstains. A cardboard box next to it contained bottles of spirits. Where there was bloodshed, there was always alcohol. An empty bottle of Bell's stood in the corner, supporting a red military cap, the very item of clothing after which the corps was nicknamed.

A short-haired blonde in a pin-striped suit approached, going in the opposite direction:

'Strike.'

He did not recognise her immediately.

'Emma Daniels. Catterick, 2002,' she said with a grin. 'You called our Staff Sergeant a negligent twat.'

'Oh yeah,' he said, while Hardacre sniggered. 'He was. You've had your hair cut.'

'And you've got famous.'

'I wouldn't go that far,' said Strike.

A pale young man in shirtsleeves put his head out of an office further down the corridor, interested in the conversation.

'Gotta get on, Emma,' said Hardacre briskly. 'Knew they'd be interested if they saw you,' he told Strike, once he had ushered the private detective into his office and closed the door behind them.

The room was rather dark, due largely to the fact that the window looked directly out onto a bare face of craggy rock. Photographs of Hardacre's kids and a sizeable collection of beer steins enlivened the decor, which comprised the same shabby pink carpet and pale green walls as the corridor outside.

'All right, Oggy,' said Hardacre, tapping at his keyboard, then standing back to let Strike sit down at his desk. 'Here he is.'

The SIB was able to access records across all three services. There on the computer monitor was a headshot of Noel Campbell Brockbank. It had been taken before Strike met him, before Brockbank had taken the hits to the face that had permanently sunken one of his eye sockets and enlarged one of his ears. A dark crew cut, a long, narrow face, tinged blue around the jaw and with an unusually high forehead: Strike had thought when they had first met that his elongated head and slightly lopsided features made it look as though Brockbank's head had been squeezed in a vice.

'I can't let you print anything out, Oggy,' said Hardacre as Strike sat down on the wheeled computer chair, 'but you could take a picture of the screen. Coffee?'

'Tea, if you've got any. Cheers.'

Hardacre left the room, closing the door carefully behind him, and Strike took out his mobile to take pictures of the screen. When he was confident he had a decent likeness he scrolled down to see Brockbank's full record, making a note of his date of birth and other personal details.

Brockbank had been born on Christmas Day in the year of Strike's own birth. He had given a home address in Barrow-in-Furness when he had joined the army. Shortly before serving in Operation Granby – better known to the public as the first Gulf war – he had married a military widow with two daughters, one of them Brittany. His son had been born while he was serving in Bosnia.

Strike went through the record, making notes as he did so, all the way down to the life-changing injury that had put paid to Brockbank's career. Hardacre re-entered the room with two mugs and Strike muttered thanks as he continued to peruse the digital file. There was no mention in here of the crime of which Brockbank had been accused, which Strike and Hardacre had investigated and of which they both remained convinced that Brockbank was guilty. The fact that he had eluded justice was one of the biggest regrets of Strike's military career. His most vivid memory of the man was Brockbank's expression, feral in its wildness, as he launched himself at Strike bearing a broken beer bottle. He had been around Strike's own size, perhaps even taller. The sound of Brockbank hitting the wall when Strike punched him had been, Hardacre said later, like a car ramming the side of the flimsy army accommodation.

'He's drawing a nice fat military pension, I see,' muttered Strike, scribbling down the various locations to which it had been sent since Brockbank had left the military. He had gone home first: Barrow-in-Furness. Then Manchester, for a little under a year.

'Ha,' said Strike quietly. 'So it *was* you, you bastard.'

Brockbank had left Manchester for Market Harborough, then returned to Barrow-in-Furness.

'What's this here, Hardy?'

'Psych report,' said Hardacre, who had sat down on a low chair by the wall and was perusing a file of his own. 'You shouldn't be looking at that at all. Very careless of me to have left it up there.'

'Very,' agreed Strike, opening it.

However, the psychiatric report did not tell Strike much that he did not already know. Only once he had been hospitalised had it become clear that Brockbank was an alcoholic. There had been much debate among his doctors as to which of his symptoms could be attributed to alcohol, which to PTSD and which to his traumatic brain injuries. Strike had to Google some of the words as he went: aphasia – difficulty finding the right word; dysarthria – disordered speech; alexithymia – difficulty understanding or identifying one's own emotions.

Forgetfulness had been very convenient to Brockbank around that time. How difficult would it have been for him to fake some of these classic symptoms?

'What they didn't take into account,' said Strike, who had known and liked several other men with traumatic brain injury, 'was that he was a cunt to start with.'

'True that,' said Hardacre, sipping his coffee while he worked.

Strike closed down Brockbank's files and opened Laing's. His photograph tallied exactly with Strike's memories of the Borderer, who had been only twenty when they had first met: broad and pale, his hair growing low on his forehead, with the small, dark eyes of a ferret.

Strike had good recall of the details of Laing's brief army career, which he himself had ended. Having taken a note of Laing's mother's address in Melrose, he skim-read the rest of the document and then opened the attached psychiatric report.

Strong indications of anti-social and borderline personality disorders . . . likely to present continuing risk of harm to others . . .

A loud knock on the office door caused Strike to close down the records on screen and get to his feet. Hardacre had barely reached the door when a severe-looking woman in a skirt suit appeared.

'Got anything for me on Timpson?' she barked at Hardacre, but she gave Strike a suspicious glare and he guessed that she had already been well aware of his presence.

'I'll cut away now, Hardy,' he said at once. 'Great to catch up.'

Hardacre introduced him briefly to the Warrant Officer, gave a potted version of his and Strike's previous association and walked Strike out.

'I'll be here late,' he said as they shook hands at the door. 'Ring me when you know what time you'll have the car back. Happy travels.'

As Strike made his way carefully down the stone stairs, it was impossible not to reflect that he could have been here, working alongside Hardacre, subject to the familiar routines and demands of the Special Investigation Branch. The army had wanted to keep him, even with his lower leg gone. He had never regretted his decision to leave, but this sudden, brief re-immersion in his old life gave rise to an inevitable nostalgia.

As he stepped out into the weak sunshine that was gleaming through a rupture in the thick clouds, he had never been more conscious of the change in his status. He was free, now, to walk away from the demands of unreasonable superiors and the confinement of a rock-bound office, but he had also been stripped of the might and status of the British Army. He was completely alone as he resumed what might well prove a wild goose chase, armed only with a few addresses, in pursuit of the man who had sent Robin a woman's leg.

15

Where's the man with the golden tattoo?

Blue Öyster Cult, 'Power Underneath Despair'

As Strike had expected, driving the Mini, even once he had made every possible adjustment to the seat, was extremely uncomfortable. The loss of his right foot meant that he operated the accelerator with his left. This required a tricky and uncomfortable angling of his body in such a cramped space. Not until he was out of the Scottish capital and safely on the quiet and straight A7 to Melrose did he feel able to turn his thoughts from the mechanics of driving the borrowed car to Private Donald Laing of the King's Own Royal Borderers, whom he had first met eleven years previously in a boxing ring.

The encounter had happened by evening in a stark, dark sports hall that rang with the raucous cries of five hundred baying squaddies. He had been Corporal Cormoran Strike of the Royal Military Police then, fully fit, toned and muscled with two strong legs, ready to show what he could do in the Inter-Regimental Boxing Tournament. Laing's supporters had outnumbered Strike's by at least three to one. It was nothing personal. The military police were unpopular on principle.

Watching a Red Cap being knocked senseless would be a satisfying end to a good night's boxing. They were two big men and this would be the last bout of the night. The roar of the crowd had thundered through both fighters' veins like a second pulse.

Strike remembered his opponent's small black eyes and his bristle cut, which was the dark red of fox fur. A tattoo of a yellow rose spanned the length of his left forearm. His neck was thicker by far than his narrow jaw and his pale, hairless chest was muscled like a marble statue of Atlas, the freckles that peppered his arms and shoulders standing out like gnat bites on his white skin.

Four rounds and they were evenly matched, the younger man perhaps faster on his feet, Strike superior in technique.

In the fifth, Strike parried, feinted to the face then struck Laing with a blow to the kidneys that floored him. The anti-Strike faction fell silent as his opponent hit the canvas, then boos echoed throughout the hall like the bellowing of elephants.

Laing was back on his feet by the count of six, but he had left some of his discipline behind him on the canvas. Wild punches; a temporary refusal to break that earned a stern reproof from the ref; an extra jab after the bell: a second warning.

One minute into the sixth round, Strike managed to capitalise on his opponent's disintegrating technique and forced Laing, whose nose was now pouring blood, onto the ropes. When the referee separated them, then signalled to continue, Laing shed the last thin membrane of civilised behaviour and attempted to land a headbutt. The referee tried to intervene and Laing became crazed. Strike narrowly avoided a kick to the crotch, then found himself locked in Laing's arms, with the other's teeth digging into his face. Indistinctly Strike heard the ref's shouts, the sudden drop in noise from the crowd as enthusiasm turned to unease at the ugly force emanating from Laing. The referee forced the boxers apart, bellowing at Laing, but he seemed to hear none of it, merely gathering himself again then swinging at Strike who sidestepped and landed a hard punch to Laing's gut. Laing doubled over, winded, and hit the floor on his knees. Strike left the ring to weak applause, blood trickling from the stinging bite on his cheekbone.

Strike, who finished the tournament as runner-up to a Sergeant from 3 Para, was rotated out of Aldershot two weeks later, but not before word had reached him that Laing had been confined to barracks for his display of ill discipline and violence in the ring. The punishment might have been worse, but Strike heard that his senior officer had accepted Laing's plea of mitigating circumstances. His story was that he had entered the ring deeply distressed by news of his fiancée's miscarriage.

Even then, years before he had gained the additional knowledge of Laing that had led Strike to this country road in a borrowed Mini, he had not believed that a dead foetus meant anything to the animal he had sensed seething beneath Laing's hairless, milk-white skin. Laing's incisor marks had still been visible on his face as he left the country.

Three years later, Strike had arrived in Cyprus to investigate an alleged rape. On entering the interrogation room he came face to face for the second time with Donald Laing, who was now carrying a little more weight and sporting a few new tattoos, his face heavily freckled from the Cyprus sun and creases etched around the deep-set eyes.

Unsurprisingly, Laing's lawyer objected to the investigation being undertaken by a man whom his client had once bitten, so Strike swapped cases with a colleague who was in Cyprus investigating a drugs ring. When he met this colleague for a drink a week later Strike found, to his surprise, that he was inclined to believe Laing's story, which was that he and the alleged victim, a local waitress, had had clumsy, drunken, consensual sex which she now regretted because her boyfriend had heard rumours that she had left her place of work with Laing. There were no witnesses to the alleged attack, which the waitress claimed had taken place at knifepoint.

'Real party girl,' was his fellow SIB man's assessment of the alleged victim.

Strike was in no position to contradict him, but he had not forgotten that Laing had once managed to gain the sympathy of a senior officer after a display of violence and insubordination witnessed by hundreds. When Strike asked for details of Laing's story and demeanour, his colleague had described a sharp, likeable man with a wry sense of humour.

'Discipline could be better,' the investigator admitted, having reviewed Laing's file, 'but I don't see him as a rapist. Married to a girl from home; she's out here with him.'

Strike returned to his drug case in the sweltering sun. A couple of weeks later, by now sporting the full beard that grew conveniently fast when he wished to look 'less army', as the military phrase had it, he was to be found lying on the floorboards of a smoke-filled loft, listening to an odd story. Given Strike's unkempt appearance, his Jesus sandals, baggy shorts and the sundry bracelets tied around his thick wrist, the stoned young Cypriot dealer beside him was perhaps justified in not suspecting that he was talking to a British military policeman. As they lounged side by side with spliffs in their hands, his companion confided the names of several soldiers dealing on the island, and not merely in cannabis. The youth's accent was thick and Strike was so busy memorising approximations of the real names, or indeed pseudonyms, that the new name of 'Dunnullung' did not immediately suggest anyone he knew. Only when his companion began to tell him how

'Dunnullung' tied up and tortured his wife did Strike connect Dunnullung with Laing. 'Crazy man,' said the ox-eyed boy in a detached voice. 'Because she try and leave.' Upon careful, casual questioning, the Cypriot confided that he had had the story from Laing himself. It seemed to have been told partly to amuse, partly to warn the young man with whom he was dealing.

The Seaforth Estate had been baking in the midday sun when Strike visited it the following day. The houses here were the oldest of the island's military accommodation, white-painted and a little shabby. He had chosen to visit while Laing, who had successfully eluded his charge of rape, was busy at work. When he rang the doorbell, he heard only a baby's distant cries.

'We think she's agoraphobic,' confided a gossipy female neighbour who had rushed outside to share her views. 'There's something a bit off there. She's really shy.'

'What about her husband?' asked Strike.

'Donnie? Oh, he's the life and soul, Donnie,' said the neighbour brightly. 'You should hear him imitating Corporal Oakley! Oh, it's spot on. So funny.'

There were rules, many of them, about entering another soldier's house without his express permission. Strike pounded on the door, but there was no answer. He could still hear the baby crying. He moved around to the rear of the house. The curtains were all closed. He knocked on the back door. Nothing.

His only justification, if he had to defend his actions, would be the sound of that baby crying. It might not be considered sufficient reason for forcing entry without a warrant. Strike mistrusted anyone who was over-reliant on instinct or intuition, but he was convinced that there was something wrong. He possessed a finely honed sense for the strange and the wicked. He had seen things all through his childhood that other people preferred to imagine happened only in films.

The door buckled and gave the second time he shouldered it. The kitchen smelled bad. Nobody had emptied the bin for days. He moved into the house.

'Mrs Laing?'

Nobody answered. The baby's feeble cries were coming from the upper floor. He climbed the stairs, calling out as he went.

The door to the main bedroom stood open. The room was in semi-darkness. It smelled horrible.

'Mrs Laing?'

She was naked, tied by one wrist to the headboard, partially covered by a heavily bloodstained sheet. The baby lay beside her on the mattress, wearing only a nappy. Strike could see that it looked shrunken, unhealthy.

As he bounded across the room to free her, his other hand already scrambling for the mobile to call an ambulance, she spoke in a cracked voice:

'No . . . go away . . . get out . . .'

Strike had rarely seen terror like it. In his inhumanity, her husband had come to seem almost supernatural. Even as Strike worked to release her wrist, which was bloody and swollen, she begged him to leave her there. Laing had told her that he would kill her if the baby was not happier when he returned. She did not seem able to conceive of a future where Laing was not omnipotent.

Donald Laing had been sentenced to sixteen years' imprisonment for what he had done to his wife, and Strike's evidence had put him away. To the last, Laing had denied everything, saying that his wife had tied herself up, that she liked it, that she was kinky that way, that she had neglected the baby, that she had tried to frame him, that it was all a put-up job.

The memories were as filthy as any he had. Strange to relive them while the Mini moved past sweeping slopes of green, sparkling in the strengthening sun. This scenery was of a kind that was not familiar to Strike. The sweeping masses of granite, these rolling hills, had an alien grandeur in their bareness, in their calm spaciousness. He had spent much of his childhood perched on the coast, with the taste of salt in the air: this was a place of woodland and river, mysterious and secretive in a different way from St Mawes, the little town with its long smuggling history, where colourful houses tumbled down to the beach.

As he passed a spectacular viaduct to his right, he thought about psychopaths, and how they were to be found everywhere, not only in run-down tenements and slums and squats, but even here, in this place of serene beauty. The likes of Laing resembled rats: you knew they were there, but you never gave them much thought until you came face to face with one.

A pair of miniature stone castles stood sentinel on either side of the road. As Strike drove into Donald Laing's hometown, the sun broke through, dazzlingly bright.

16

So grab your rose and ringside seat,
We're back home at Conry's bar.

Blue Öyster Cult, 'Before the Kiss, A Redcap'

Behind the glass door of a shop on the high street hung a tea towel. It was decorated with black line drawings of local landmarks, but what attracted Strike's attention were a number of stylised yellow roses exactly like the tattoo he remembered on Donald Laing's powerful forearm. He paused to read the verse in the middle:

It's oor ain toon
It's the best toon
That ever there be:
Here's tae Melrose,
Gem o' Scotland,
The toon o' the free.

He had deposited the Mini in a car park beside the abbey, with its dark red arches rising against a pale blue sky. Beyond, to the south-east, was the triple peak of Eildon Hill, which Strike had noted on the map and which added drama and distinction to the skyline. After a bacon roll purchased at a nearby coffee shop and eaten at an outside table, followed by a cigarette and his second strong tea of the day, Strike had set out on foot in search of the Wynd, the home address Laing had given sixteen years previously when he joined the army and which Strike was not entirely sure how to pronounce. Was it 'wind' as in breeze, or 'wind' as in clock?

The small town looked prosperous in the sunshine as Strike strolled up the sloping high street to the central square, where a unicorn-topped pillar stood in a basin of flowers. A round stone in the pavement bore the town's old Roman name, Trimontium, which Strike knew must refer to the triple-peaked hill nearby.

He seemed to have missed the Wynd, which according to the map on his phone led off the high street. He doubled back and found a narrow entrance in the walls to his right, only large enough for a pedestrian, which led to a dim inner courtyard. Laing's old family home had a bright blue front door and was reached by a short flight of steps.

Strike's knock was answered almost at once by a pretty, dark-haired woman far too young to be Laing's mother. When Strike explained his mission, she responded in a soft accent he found attractive:

'Mrs Laing? She's no' been here for ten years or more.'

Before his spirits had time to sink, she added:

'She stays up in Dingleton Road.'

'Dingleton Road? Is that far?'

'Just up the way.' She pointed behind her, to the right. 'I dinnae ken the number, sorry.'

'No problem. Thanks for your help.'

It occurred to him as he walked back along the dingy passageway to the sunlit square that, barring the obscenities the young soldier had muttered into Strike's ear in the boxing ring, he had never heard Donald Laing speak. Still working undercover on his drugs case, it had been imperative that Strike was not seen wandering in and out of HQ in his beard, so the interrogation of Laing after his arrest had been undertaken by others. Later, when he had successfully concluded the drugs case and was again clean-shaven, Strike had given evidence against Laing in court, but he had been on a plane out of Cyprus by the time that Laing had stood up to deny that he had tied up or tortured his wife. As he crossed Market Square, Strike wondered whether his Borders accent might have been one reason that people had been so willing to believe in Donnie Laing, to forgive him, to like him. The detective seemed to remember reading that advertisers used Scottish accents to suggest integrity and honesty.

The only pub he had spotted so far stood a short distance along a street Strike passed on the way to Dingleton Road. Melrose appeared to be fond of yellow: though the walls were white, the pub's doors and window were picked out in acid-bright lemon and black. To the Cornish-born Strike's amusement, given the landlocked situation of the town, the pub was called the Ship Inn. He walked on into Dingleton Road, which snaked under a bridge, became a steep hill and disappeared out of sight.

The term 'not far' was a relative one, as Strike had often had occasion to observe since losing his calf and foot. After ten minutes' walk up the hill he was beginning to regret that he had not returned to the abbey car park for the Mini. Twice he asked women in the street whether they knew where Mrs Laing lived, but though polite and friendly, neither could tell him. He trudged on, sweating slightly, past a stretch of white bungalows, until he met an elderly man coming the other way, wearing a tweed flat cap and walking a black and white Border collie.

'Excuse me,' said Strike. 'Do you happen to know where Mrs Laing lives? I've forgotten the number.'

'Messus Laing?' replied the dog walker, surveying Strike from beneath thick salt and pepper eyebrows. 'Aye, she's my next-door neighbour.'

Thank Christ.

'Three along,' said the man, pointing, 'wi' the stone wishing well oot front.'

'Thanks very much,' said Strike.

As he turned up Mrs Laing's drive he noticed, out of the corner of his eye, that the old man was still standing on the spot, watching him, in spite of the collie trying to tug him downhill.

Mrs Laing's bungalow looked clean and respectable. Stone animals of Disneyesque cuteness littered her lawn and peeped out from her flowerbeds. The front door lay at the side of the building, in shadow. Only as he raised his hand to the door-knocker did it occur to Strike that he might, within seconds, come face to face with Donald Laing.

For a whole minute after he knocked, nothing happened except that the elderly dog walker retraced his steps and stood at Mrs Laing's gate, unabashedly staring. Strike suspected that the man regretted giving out his neighbour's address and was checking that the large stranger meant the woman no harm, but he was wrong.

'She's in,' he called to Strike, who was deliberating as to whether to try again. 'But she's wud.'

'She's what?' Strike called back as he knocked for a second time.

'Wud. Doolally.'

The dog walker took a few steps down the drive towards Strike.

'Demented,' he translated for the Englishman.

'Ah,' said Strike.

The door opened, revealing a tiny, wizened, sallow-faced old woman wearing a deep blue dressing gown. She glared up at Strike with a kind of unfocused malevolence. There were several stiff whiskers growing out of her chin.

'Mrs Laing?'

She said nothing, but peered at him out of eyes that he knew, bloodshot and faded though they were, must have been beady and ferret-like in their day.

'Mrs Laing, I'm looking for your son Donald.'

'No,' she said, with surprising vehemence. 'No.'

She retreated and slammed the door.

'Bugger,' said Strike under his breath, which made him think of Robin. She would almost certainly have been better than him at charming the little old woman. Slowly he turned, wondering whether there was anyone else in Melrose who might help – he had definitely seen other Laings listed on 192.com – and found himself face to face with the dog walker, who had proceeded all the way down the drive to meet him and was looking cautiously excited.

'You're the detective,' he said. 'You're the detective that put her son away.'

Strike was astonished. He could not imagine how he was recognisable to an elderly Scottish man whom he had never met before. His so-called fame was of a very low order when it came to being identified by strangers. He walked the streets of London daily without anyone caring who he was, and unless somebody met him or heard his name in the context of an investigation, was rarely associated with the newspaper stories about his successful cases.

'Aye, you did!' said the elderly man, his excitement rising. 'My wife and I are friends of Margaret Bunyan's.' And in the face of Strike's mystification he elaborated: 'Rhona's mother.'

It took a few seconds for Strike's capacious memory to render up the information that Laing's wife, the young woman whom he had discovered tied to the bed beneath the blood-stained sheet, had been called Rhona.

'When Margaret seen you in the papers she said to us, "That's him, that's the lad that rescued our Rhona!" You've done very well for yourself, haven't you? Stop it, Wullie!' he added in a loud aside to the eager collie, which was still pulling on its lead, trying to regain the road. 'Oh, aye, Margaret follows everything you do, all the stories in the papers. You found out who killed that model girl – and that writer! Margaret's never forgot what you did for her girl, never.'

Strike muttered something indistinct, something he hoped sounded grateful for Margaret's appreciation.

'Wha' for are you wanting to talk to auld Mrs Laing? He's nae done something else, has he, Donnie?'

'I'm trying to find him,' said Strike evasively. 'D'you know if he's back in Melrose?'

'Och, no, I wouldnae think so. He came back to see his mother a few years back, but I dinnae know that he's been here since. It's a small toon: Donnie Laing back – we'd hear, ken?'

'D'you think Mrs – Bunyan, did you say? – might have any—?'

'She'd love tae meet you,' said the old man excitedly. '*No*, Wullie,' he added to the whining Border collie, which was trying to tug him to the gate. 'I'll ring her, will I? She's only over in Darnick. Next village. Will I ring?'

'That'd be very helpful.'

So Strike accompanied the old man next door and waited in a small, spotless sitting room while he gabbled excitedly into the phone over his dog's increasingly furious whines.

'She'll come over,' said the old man, with his hand over the receiver. 'D'ye want to meet her here? You're welcome. The wife'll make tea—'

'Thanks, but I've got a couple of things to do,' lied Strike, who doubted the possibility of a successful interview in the presence of this garrulous witness. 'Could you see whether she'd be free for lunch at the Ship Inn? In an hour?'

The collie's determination for its walk tipped the balance in Strike's favour. The two men left the house and walked back down the hill together, the collie tugging all the way so that Strike was forced into a faster gait than suited him on a steep downward slope. He said goodbye with relief to his helpful acquaintance in Market Square. With a cheery wave, the old man headed off in the direction of the River Tweed and Strike, now limping slightly, walked down the high street, killing time until he needed to return to the Ship.

At the bottom of the road he encountered another explosion of black and acid yellow which, Strike realised, explained the Ship Inn's colours. Here again was the yellow rose, on a sign announcing MELROSE RUGBY FOOTBALL CLUB. Strike paused, hands in pockets, looking over the low wall at a smooth, level expanse of viridian velvet surrounded by trees, the yellow rugby posts shining in the sun, stands to the right and softly undulating hills beyond. The pitch was as well maintained as any place of worship, and an extraordinarily well-appointed facility for such a small town.

Staring out across the expanse of velvety grass, Strike remembered Whittaker, stinking and smoking in the corner of the squat while Leda lay beside him, listening open-mouthed to the tales of his hard life – credulous and greedy as a baby bird, as Strike now saw it, for the yarns Whittaker spun her. From Leda's point of view, Gordonstoun might as well have been Alcatraz: it was nothing short of outrageous that her slender poet had been forced out into the harsh Scottish winter to be pummelled and knocked about in the mud and the rain.

'Not rugby, darling. Oh, poor baby . . . *you* playing rugby!'

And when the seventeen-year-old Strike (sporting a fat lip from the boxing club at the time) had laughed, softly, into his homework, Whittaker had staggered to his feet, shouting in his obnoxious mockney:

'What are you facking laughing about, meathead?'

Whittaker could not stand laughter at his expense. He needed, craved adulation; in its absence, he would take fear or even loathing as evidence of his power, but ridicule was evidence of another's assumed superiority and consequently unbearable.

'You'd facking love it, wouldn't you, you stupid little tit? Think you're facking officer class already, dontcha, out with the rugger buggers. Get his rich daddy to send him to facking Gordonstoun!' Whittaker had yelled at Leda.

'Calm down, darling!' she had said, and then, in slightly more peremptory terms: 'No, Corm!'

Strike had stood up, braced, ready and eager to hit Whittaker. That had been the closest he had ever come to doing it, but his mother had staggered between them, a thin, beringed hand on each heaving chest.

Strike blinked and the bright sunlit pitch, a place of innocent endeavour and excitement, seemed to come back into focus. He could smell leaves, grass and the warm rubber from the road beside him. Slowly he turned and headed back towards the Ship Inn, craving a drink, but his treacherous subconscious was not done with him yet.

The sight of that smooth rugby pitch had unleashed another memory: black-haired, dark-eyed Noel Brockbank, running at him with the broken beer bottle in his hand. Brockbank had been massive, powerful and fast: a flanker. Strike remembered his own fist rising around the side of that broken bottle, connecting just as the glass touched his own neck—

A basal skull fracture, that's what they had called it. Bleeding from the ear. A massive brain injury.

'Fuck, fuck, fuck,' mumbled Strike under his breath, in time with his own footsteps.

Laing, that's what you're here for. Laing.

He passed under the metal galleon with bright yellow sails that hung over the Ship Inn's door. A sign just inside read MELROSE'S ONLY PUB.

He found the place instantly calming: a glow of warm colour, shining glass and brass; a carpet that resembled a patchwork of faded browns, reds and greens; walls of warm peach and exposed stone. Everywhere were more indications of Melrose's sporting obsession: blackboards announcing upcoming matches, several enormous plasma screens and, above the urinal (it had been hours since Strike had last peed), a small wall-mounted television, just in case a try was pending at the point a full bladder could no longer be ignored.

Mindful of the journey back to Edinburgh in Hardacre's car, he bought himself half a pint of John Smith's and sat down on a leather-covered sofa facing the bar, perusing the laminated menu and hoping that Margaret Bunyan would be punctual, because he had just realised that he was hungry.

She appeared a mere five minutes later. Although he could barely remember what her daughter looked like and had never met Mrs Bunyan before, her expression of mingled apprehension and anticipation gave her away as she paused, staring at him, on the doormat.

Strike got up and she stumbled forwards, both hands gripping the strap of a large black handbag.

'It *is* you,' she said breathlessly.

She was around sixty, small and fragile-looking, wearing

metal-framed glasses, her expression anxious beneath tightly permed fair hair.

Strike held out a large hand and shook hers, which trembled slightly, cold and fine-boned.

'Her dad's over in Hawick today, he can't come, I rang him, he said to tell you we'll never forget what you did for Rhona,' she said on a single breath. She sank down beside Strike on the sofa, continuing to observe him with mingled awe and nerves. 'We've never forgot. We read about you in the papers. We were so sorry about your leg. What you did for Rhona! What you did—'

Her eyes were suddenly brimful of tears.

'—we were so . . . '

'I'm glad I was able to—'

Find her child tied naked and bloodstained on a bed? Talking to relatives about what the people they loved had endured was one of the worst parts of the job.

'—able to help her.'

Mrs Bunyan blew her nose on a handkerchief retrieved from the bottom of her black handbag. He could tell that she was of the generation of women who would never usually enter a pub alone and certainly not buy drinks at a bar if a man were there to undertake the ordeal for them.

'Let me get you something.'

'Just an orange juice,' she said breathlessly, dabbing at her eyes.

'And something to eat,' Strike urged, keen to order the beer-battered haddock and chips for himself.

When he had placed their order at the bar and returned to her, she asked what he was doing in Melrose and the source of her nervousness became apparent at once.

'He's not come back, has he? Donnie? Is he back?'

'Not as far as I know,' said Strike. 'I don't know where he is.'

'D'you think he's got something to do . . . ?'

Her voice had dropped to a whisper.

'We read in the paper . . . we saw that someone sent you a – a—'

'Yes,' said Strike. 'I don't know whether he's got anything to do with it, but I'd like to find him. Apparently he's been back here to see his mother since leaving jail.'

'Och, four or five years ago, that would've been,' said Margaret Bunyan. 'He turned up on her doorstep, forced his way into the bungalow. She's got Alzheimer's now. She couldn't stop him, but the neighbours called his brothers and they came and threw him out.'

'They did, did they?'

'Donnie's the youngest. He's got four older brothers. They're hard men,' said Mrs Bunyan, 'all of them. Jamie stays in Selkirk – he came tearing through to get Donnie out of his mother's house. They say he knocked him senseless.'

She took a tremulous sip of her orange juice and continued:

'We heard all about it. Our friend Brian, who you just met, he saw the fight happening out on the street. Four of them onto one, all of them shouting and yelling. Someone called the police. Jamie got a caution. He didn't care,' said Mrs Bunyan. 'They didn't want him anywhere near them, or their mother. They ran him out of town.

'I was terrified,' she continued. 'For Rhona. He'd always said he'd find her when he got out.'

'And did he?' asked Strike.

'Och, yes,' said Margaret Bunyan miserably. 'We knew he would. She'd moved tae Glasgow, got a job in a travel agent's. He still found her. Six months she lived in fear of him turning up and then one day he did. Came to her flat one night, but he'd been ill. He wasn't the same.'

'Ill?' repeated Strike sharply.

'I can't remember what it was he'd got, some kind of arthritis, I think, and Rhona said he'd put on a lot of weight. He turned up at her flat at night, he'd tracked her down, but thanks be to God,' said Mrs Bunyan fervently, 'her fiancé was staying over. His name's Ben,' she added, with a triumphal flourish, the colour high in her faded cheeks, 'and he's a *policeman*.'

She said it as though she thought Strike would be especially glad to hear this, as though he and Ben were co-members of some great investigative brotherhood.

'They're married now,' said Mrs Bunyan. 'No kids, because – well, you know why—'

And without warning, a torrent of tears burst forth, streaming down Mrs Bunyan's face behind her glasses. The horror of what had happened a decade ago was suddenly fresh and raw, as though a pile of offal had been dumped on the table in front of them.

'—Laing stuck a knife up inside her,' whispered Mrs Bunyan.

She confided in him as though Strike were a doctor or a priest, telling him the secrets that weighed on her, but which she could not tell her friends: he already knew the worst. As she groped again for the handkerchief in her square black bag, Strike remembered the wide patch of blood on the sheets, the excoriated skin on her wrist where Rhona had tried to free herself. Thank God her mother could not see inside his head.

'He stuck a knife inside – and they tried to – you know – repair—'

Mrs Bunyan took a deep, shuddering breath as two plates of food appeared in front of them.

'But she and Ben have lovely holidays,' she whispered frantically, dabbing repeatedly at her hollow cheeks, lifting her glasses to reach her eyes. 'And they breed – they breed German – German Shepherds.'

Hungry though he was, Strike could not eat in the

immediate aftermath of discussing what had been done to Rhona Laing.

'She and Laing had a baby, didn't they?' he asked, remembering its feeble whimpering from beside its bloodstained, dehydrated mother. 'The kid must be, what, ten by now?'

'He d-died,' she whispered, tears dripping off the end of her chin. 'C-cot death. He was always sickly, the bairn. It happened two d-days after they put D-Donnie away. And h-he – Donnie – he telephoned her out of the jail and told her he knew she'd killed – killed – the baby – and that he'd kill her when he got out—'

Strike laid a large hand briefly on the sobbing woman's shoulder, then hoisted himself to his feet and approached the young barmaid who was watching them with her mouth open. Brandy seemed too strong for the sparrow-like creature behind him. Strike's Aunt Joan, who was only a little older than Mrs Bunyan, always regarded port as medicinal. He ordered a glass and took it back to her.

'Here. Drink this.'

His reward was a recrudescence of tears, but after much more dabbing with the sodden handkerchief she said shakily, 'You're very kind,' sipped it, gave a little gasping sigh and blinked at him, her fair-lashed eyes pink like a piglet's.

'Have you got any idea where Laing went after turning up at Rhona's?'

'Yes,' she whispered. 'Ben put out feelers through work, through the probation office. Apparently he went to Gateshead, but I don't know whether he's still there.'

Gateshead. Strike remembered the Donald Laing he had found online. Had he moved from Gateshead to Corby? Or were they different men?

'Anyway,' said Mrs Bunyan, 'he's never bothered Rhona and Ben again.'

'I'll bet he hasn't,' said Strike, picking up his knife and fork. 'A copper and German Shepherds, eh? He's not stupid.'

She seemed to take courage and comfort from his words, and with a timid, tearful smile began to pick at her macaroni cheese.

'They married young,' commented Strike, who was keen to hear anything he could about Laing, anything that might give a lead on his associations or habits.

She nodded, swallowed and said:

'Far too young. She started seeing him when she was only fifteen and we didn't like it. We'd heard things about Donnie Laing. There was a young girl who said he'd forced himself on her at the Young Farmers' disco. It never came to anything: the police said there wasn't enough evidence. We tried to warn Rhona he was trouble,' she sighed, 'but that made her more determined. She was always headstrong, our Rhona.'

'He'd already been accused of rape?' asked Strike. His fish and chips were excellent. The pub was filling up, for which he was grateful: the barmaid's attention was diverted from them.

'Oh yes. They're a rough family,' said Mrs Bunyan, with the sort of prim small-town snobbery that Strike knew well from his own upbringing. 'All those brothers, they were always fighting, in trouble with the police, but he was the worst of them. His own brothers didn't like him. I don't think his mother liked him much, tae tell the truth. There was a rumour,' she said in a burst of confidence, 'that he wasnae the father's. The parents were always fighting and they separated round about the time she got pregnant with Donnie. They say she had a run-around with one of the local policemen, as a matter of fact. I don't know whether it's true. The policeman moved on and Mr Laing moved back in, but Mr Laing never liked Donnie, I know that. Never liked him at all. People said it was because he knew Donnie wasn't his.

'He was the wildest of all of them. A big lad. He got into the junior sevens—'

'Sevens?'

'The rugby sevens,' she said, and even this small, genteel lady was surprised that Strike did not immediately understand what, to Melrose, seemed more religion than sport. 'But they kicked him out. No discipline. *Someone* carved up Greenyards the week after they kicked him out. The pitch,' she added, in response to the Englishman's mystifying ignorance.

The port was making her talkative. Words were tumbling out of her now.

'He took up boxing instead. He had the gift of the gab, though, oh aye. When Rhona first took up with him – she was fifteen and he was seventeen – I had some folk telling me he wasn't a bad lad really. Oh, aye,' she repeated, nodding at Strike's look of disbelief. 'Folk that didn't know him so well were took in by him. He could be charming when he wanted to, Donnie Laing.

'But you just ask Walter Gilchrist whether he was charming. Walter sacked him off the farm – he was always being late – and *someone* set fire to his barn after. Oh, they never proved it was Donnie. They never proved it was him who wrecked the pitch, neither, but I know what I believe.

'Rhona wouldn't listen. She thought she knew him. He was misunderstood and I don't know what else. We were prejudiced, narrow-minded. He wanted tae join the army. Good riddance, I thought. I hoped she'd forget him if he left.

'Then he came back. He got her pregnant but she lost it. She was angry with me because I said—'.

She did not want to tell him what she had said, but Strike could imagine.

'—and then she wouldn't talk to me any more, and she went and married him on his next leave. Her dad and I weren't invited,' she said. 'Off to Cyprus together. But I know he killed our cat.'

'What?' said Strike, thrown.

'I know it was him. We'd told Rhona she was making an awful mistake, last time we saw her before she married him. That night we couldn't find Purdy. Next day she was on the back lawn, dead. The vet said she'd been strangled.'

On the plasma screen over her shoulder a scarlet-clad Dimitar Berbatov was celebrating a goal against Fulham. The air was full of Borders voices. Glasses clinked and cutlery tinkled as Strike's companion talked of death and mutilation.

'I know he did it, I know he killed Purdy,' she said feverishly. 'Look at what he did to Rhona and the baby. He's evil.'

Her hands fumbled with the catch on her bag and pulled out a small wad of photographs.

'My husband always says, "Why are you keeping them? Burn them." But I always thought we might need pictures of him one day. There,' she said, thrusting them into Strike's eager hands. 'You have them, you keep them. Gateshead. That's where he went next.'

Later, after she had left with renewed tears and thanks, after he had paid the bill, Strike walked to Millers of Melrose, a family butcher he had noticed on his stroll around the town. There he treated himself to some venison pies that he suspected would be far tastier than anything he would be able to purchase at the station before boarding the sleeper back to London.

Returning to the car park via a short street where golden roses bloomed, Strike thought again about the tattoo on that powerful forearm.

Once, years ago, it had meant something to Donnie Laing to belong to this lovely town, surrounded by farmland and overlooked by the triple peaks of Eildon Hill. Yet he had been no straightforward worker of the soil, no team player, no asset to a place that seemed to pride itself on discipline and honest endeavour. Melrose had spat out the burner of barns, the strangler of cats, the carver-up of rugby fields, so Laing had taken refuge in a place where many men had found either their salvation or their inevitable comeuppance: the British Army. When that had led to jail, and jail disgorged him, he had tried to come home, but nobody had wanted him.

Had Donald Laing found a warmer welcome in Gateshead? Had he moved from there to Corby? Or, Strike wondered, as he folded himself back into Hardacre's Mini, had these been mere stopping posts on his way to London and Strike?

17

The Girl That Love Made Blind

Tuesday morning. It was asleep after what It said had been a long, hard night. Like he fucking cared, although he had to act like he did. He had persuaded It to go and lie down, and when It began to breathe deeply and evenly he watched It for a while, imagining choking the fucking life out of It, seeing Its eyes open and Its struggle for breath, Its face slowly turning purple . . .

When he had been sure that he would not wake It, he had left the bedroom quietly, pulled on a jacket and slipped out into the early morning air to find The Secretary. This was his first chance of following her in days and he was too late to pick up the trail at her home station. The best he could do was to lurk around the mouth of Denmark Street.

He spotted her from a distance: that bright, wavy strawberry-blonde head was unmistakable. The vain bitch must like standing out in the crowd or she'd cover it or cut it or dye it. They all wanted attention, he knew that for a fact: all of them.

As she moved closer, his infallible instinct for other people's moods told him something had changed. She was looking down as she walked, hunch-shouldered, oblivious to the other workers swarming around her, clutching bags, coffees and phones.

He passed right by her in the opposite direction, drawing so close that he could have smelled her perfume if they had not been in that bustling street full of car fumes and dust. He might have been a traffic bollard. That annoyed him a little, even though it had been his intention to pass by her unnoticed. He had singled her out, but she treated him with indifference.

On the other hand, he had made a discovery: she had been crying for hours. He knew what it looked like when women did that; he had seen it plenty of times. Puffy and reddened and flabby-faced, leaking and whining: they all did it. They liked playing the victim. You'd kill them just to make them shut up.

He turned and followed her the short distance to Denmark Street. When women were in her state, they were often malleable in ways they would not be when less distressed or frightened. They forgot to do all the things that bitches did routinely to keep the likes of him at bay: keys between their knuckles, phones in their hands, rape alarms in their pockets, walking in packs. They became needy, grateful for a kind word, a friendly ear. That was how he had landed It.

His pace quickened as she turned into Denmark Street, which the press had at last given up as a bad job after eight days. She opened the black door of the office and went inside.

Would she come out again, or was she going to spend the day with Strike? He really hoped they were screwing each other. They probably were. Just the two of them in the office all the time – bound to be.

He withdrew into a doorway and pulled out his phone, keeping one eye on the second-floor window of number twenty-four.

18

I've been stripped, the insulation's gone.

Blue Öyster Cult, 'Lips in the Hills'

The first time that Robin had ever entered Strike's office had been on her first morning as an engaged woman. Unlocking the glass door today, she remembered watching the new sapphire on her finger darken, shortly before Strike had come hurtling out of the office and nearly knocked her down the metal staircase to her death.

There was no ring on her finger any more. The place where it had sat all these months felt hypersensitive, as though it had left her branded. She was carrying a small holdall that contained a change of outfit and a few toiletries.

You can't cry here. You mustn't cry here.

Automatically she performed the usual start-of-the-working-day tasks: took off her coat, hung it up with her handbag on a peg beside the door, filled and switched on the kettle, and stowed the holdall under her desk, where Strike would not see it. She kept turning back to check that she'd done what she had meant to do, feeling disembodied, like a ghost whose chilly fingers might slip through the handles of handbags and kettles.

It had taken four days to dismantle a relationship that had lasted nine years. Four days of mounting animosity, of grudges aired and accusations hurled. Some of it seemed so trivial, looking back. The Land Rover, the Grand National, her decision to take her laptop home. On Sunday there had been a petty squabble about whose parents were paying for the wedding cars, which had led yet again to an argument about her pitiful pay packet. By the time they had got into the Land Rover on Monday morning to drive back home, they had barely been speaking.

Then last night, at home in West Ealing, had come the explosive argument that had rendered all the squabbling that had gone before trivial, mere warning tremors of the seismic disaster that would lay waste to everything.

Strike would be down shortly. She could hear him moving around in the flat upstairs. Robin knew that she must not look shaky or unable to cope. Work was all she had now. She would have to find a room in somebody else's flat, which would be all she would be able to afford on the pittance Strike paid her. She tried to imagine future housemates. It would be like being back in halls of residence.

Don't think about that now.

As she made tea she realised that she had forgotten to bring in the tin of Bettys teabags she had bought shortly after trying on her wedding dress for the last time. The thought almost overset her, but by a powerful effort of will she restrained the urge to cry and took her mug to the computer, ready to trawl through the emails she had not been able to answer during their week of exile from the office.

Strike, she knew, had only just got back from Scotland: he had returned on the overnight train. She would make conversation about that when he appeared, so as to keep attention away from her red, swollen eyes. Before leaving the flat this morning she had tried to improve their appearance with ice and cold water, but with limited success.

Matthew had tried to block her path as she headed out of the flat. He had looked ghastly too.

'Look, we've got to talk. We've got to.'

Not any more, thought Robin, whose hands shook as she lifted the hot tea to her lips. *I haven't got to do anything I don't want to do any more.*

The brave thought was undermined by a single hot tear that leaked without warning down her cheek. Horrified, she brushed it away; she had not thought that she had any tears left to cry. Turning to her monitor she began typing a reply to a client who had queried his invoice, hardly knowing what she wrote.

Clanging footsteps on the stairs outside made her brace herself. The door opened. Robin looked up. The man who stood there was not Strike.

Primal, instinctive fear ripped through her. There was no time to analyse why the stranger had such an effect on her; she only knew that he was dangerous. In an instant she had calculated that she would not be able to reach the door in time, that her rape alarm was in her coat pocket and that her best weapon was the sharp letter-opener lying inches from her left hand.

He was gaunt and pale, his head was shaven, a few freckles were scattered across a broad nose and his mouth was wide and thick lipped. Tattoos covered his wrists, knuckles and neck. A gold tooth glinted on one side of his grinning mouth. A deep scar ran from the middle of his upper lip towards his cheekbone, dragging his mouth upwards in a permanent Elvis-style sneer. He wore baggy jeans and a tracksuit top and he smelled strongly of stale tobacco and cannabis.

''S'up?' he said. He repeatedly clicked the fingers of both hands hanging at his sides as he moved into the room. *Click, click, click.* 'You all alone, yeah?'

'No,' she said, her mouth completely dry. She wanted to grab the letter-opener before he came any closer. *Click, click, click*. 'My boss is just—'

'Shanker!' said Strike's voice from the doorway.

The stranger turned.

'Bunsen,' he said and stopped clicking his fingers, held out a hand and gave Strike a dap greeting. ''Ow you doin', bruv?'

Dear God, thought Robin, limp with relief. Why hadn't Strike told her that the man was coming? She turned away, busying herself with email so that Strike would not see her face. As Strike led Shanker into the inner office and closed the door behind them, she caught the word 'Whittaker'.

Ordinarily she would have wished that she could be in there, listening. She finished her email and supposed that she ought to offer them coffee. First she went to splash more cold water on her face in the tiny bathroom on the landing, which retained a strong smell of drains no matter how many air-fresheners she bought out of petty cash.

Strike, meanwhile, had seen just enough of Robin to be shocked by her appearance. He had never seen her face so pale, nor her eyes so puffy and bloodshot. Even as he sat down at his desk, eager to hear what information on Whittaker Shanker had brought to his office, the thought crossed his mind: *What's the bastard done to her?* And for a fraction of a second, before fixing all his attention on Shanker, Strike imagined punching Matthew and enjoying it.

'Why you lookin' so ugly, Bunsen?' asked Shanker, stretching himself out in the chair opposite and clicking his fingers enthusiastically. He had had the tic since his teens and Strike pitied the person who would try to make him stop.

'Knackered,' said Strike. 'Got back from Scotland a couple of hours ago.'

'Never been to Scotland,' said Shanker.

Strike was not aware that Shanker had ever been out of London in his life.

'So what've you got for me?'

''E's still around,' said Shanker, ceasing his finger-clicking to pull a pack of Mayfairs out of his pocket. He lit one with a cheap lighter without asking whether Strike minded. With a mental shrug, Strike took out his own Benson & Hedges and borrowed the lighter. 'Seen 'is dealer. Geezer says 'e's in Catford.'

'He's left Hackney?'

'Unless 'e's left a clone of 'imself behind 'e musta done, Bunsen. I didn't check for clones. Gimme another ton an' I'll go see.'

Strike gave a short snort of amusement. People underestimated Shanker at their peril. Given that he looked as though he had done every kind of illegal substance in his time, his restlessness often misled acquaintances into assuming he was on something. In fact, he was sharper and soberer than many a businessman at the end of their working day, if incurably criminal.

'Got an address?' said Strike, pulling a notebook towards him.

'Not yet,' said Shanker.

'Is he working?'

''E tells ev'ryone 'e's a road manager for some metal band.'

'But?'

''E's pimping,' said Shanker matter-of-factly.

There was a knock on the door.

'Anyone want coffee?' asked Robin. Strike could tell that she was deliberately keeping her face out of the light. His eyes found her left hand: the engagement ring was missing.

'Cheers,' said Shanker. 'Two sugars.'

'Tea would be great, thanks,' said Strike, watching her move away as he reached into his desk for the old tin ashtray he had swiped from a bar in Germany. He pushed it across to Shanker before the latter could tap his lengthening ash on the floor.

'How d'you know he's pimping?'

'I know this uvver geezer who met 'im with the brass,' said Shanker. Strike was familiar with the cockney slang: brass nail – 'tail'. 'Says Whittaker lives with 'er. Very young. Just legal.'

'Right,' said Strike.

He had dealt with prostitution in its various aspects ever since he had become an investigator, but this was different: this was his ex-stepfather, a man whom his mother had loved and romanticised, to whom she had borne a child. He could almost smell Whittaker in the room again: his filthy clothes, his animal stink.

'Catford,' he repeated.

'Yeah. I'll keep looking if you want,' said Shanker, disregarding the ashtray and flicking his ash onto the floor. ''Ow much is it wurf to you, Bunsen?'

While they were still negotiating Shanker's fee, a discussion that proceeded with good humour but the underlying seriousness of two men who knew perfectly well that he would do nothing without payment, Robin brought in the coffee. With the light full on her face, she looked ghastly.

'I've done the most important emails,' she told Strike, pretending not to notice his enquiring look. 'I'll head off and do Platinum now.'

Shanker looked thoroughly intrigued by this announcement, but nobody explained.

'You OK?' Strike asked her, wishing that Shanker were not present.

'Fine,' said Robin, with a pathetic attempt at a smile. 'I'll catch up with you later.'

'"'Ead off and do platinum"?' repeated Shanker curiously over the sound of the outer door closing.

'It's not as good as it sounds,' said Strike, leaning back in his seat to look out of the window. Robin left the building in her trench coat and headed off up Denmark Street and out of sight. A large man in a beanie hat came out of the guitar shop opposite and set off in the same direction, but Strike's attention had already been recalled by Shanker, who said:

'Someone really sent you a fucking leg, Bunsen?'

'Yep,' said Strike. 'Cut it off, boxed it up and delivered it by hand.'

'Fuck me backwards,' said Shanker, whom it took a great deal to shock.

After Shanker had left in possession of a wad of cash for services already rendered, and the promise of the same again for further details on Whittaker, Strike phoned Robin. She did not pick up, but that wasn't unusual if she was somewhere she couldn't easily talk. He texted her:

Let me know when you're somewhere I can meet you

then sat down in her vacated chair, ready to do his fair share of answering enquiries and paying invoices.

However, he found it hard to focus after the second night on a sleeper. Five minutes later he checked his mobile but Robin had not responded, so he got up to make himself another mug of tea. As he raised the mug to his lips he caught a faint whiff of cannabis, transferred from hand to hand as he and Shanker said farewell.

Shanker came originally from Canning Town but had cousins in Whitechapel who, twenty years previously, had become involved in a feud with a rival gang. Shanker's willingness to help out his cousins had resulted in him lying alone in the gutter at the end of Fulbourne Street, bleeding copiously from the deep gash to his mouth and cheek that disfigured him to this day. It was there that Leda Strike, returning from a late-evening excursion to purchase Rizlas, had found him.

To walk past a boy of her own son's age while he lay bleeding in the gutter would have been impossible for Leda. The fact that the boy was clutching a bloody knife, that he was screaming imprecations and clearly in the grip of some kind of drug made no difference at all. Shanker found himself being mopped up and talked to as he had not been talked to since his own mother had died when he was eight. When he refused point blank to let the strange woman call an ambulance, for fear of what the police would do to him (Shanker had just stuck his knife through the thigh of his attacker), Leda took what, to her, was the only possible course: she helped him home to the squat and looked after him personally. After cutting up Band Aids and sticking them clumsily over the deep cut in a semblance of stitches, she cooked him a sloppy mess full of cigarette ash and told her bemused son to find a mattress where Shanker could sleep.

Leda treated Shanker from the first as though he were a long-lost nephew, and in return he had worshipped her in the way that only a broken boy clinging to the memory of a loving mother could. Once healed, he availed himself of her sincere invitation to drop round whenever he felt like it. Shanker talked to Leda as he could talk to no other human being and was perhaps the only person who could see no flaw in her. To Strike, he extended the respect he felt for his mother. The two boys, who in almost every other regard were as different as it was possible to be, were further bonded by a silent but powerful hatred of Whittaker, who had been insanely jealous of the new element in Leda's life but wary of treating him with the disdain he showed Strike.

Strike was sure that Whittaker had recognised in Shanker the same deficit from which he himself suffered: a lack of normal boundaries. Whittaker had concluded, rightly, that his teenage stepson might well wish him dead, but that he was restrained by a desire not to distress his mother, a respect for the law and a determination not to make an irrevocable move that would forever blight his own prospects. Shanker, however, knew no such restraints and his long periods of cohabitation with the fractured family kept a precarious curb on Whittaker's growing tendency towards violence.

In fact, it had been the regular presence of Shanker in the squat that had made Strike feel he could safely leave for university. He had not felt equal to putting into words what he most feared when he took leave of Shanker, but Shanker had understood.

'No worries, Bunsen, mate. No worries.'

Nevertheless, he could not always be there. On the day that Leda had died, Shanker had been away on one of his regular, drug-related business trips. Strike would never forget Shanker's grief, his guilt, his uncontrollable tears when they next met. While Shanker had been negotiating a good price for a kilo of premium Bolivian cocaine in Kentish Town, Leda Strike had been slowly stiffening on a filthy mattress. The finding of the post-mortem was that she had ceased to breathe a full six hours before any of the other squat dwellers tried to rouse her from what they had thought was a profound slumber.

Like Strike, Shanker had been convinced from the first that Whittaker had killed her, and such was the violence of his grief and his desire for instant retribution that Whittaker might well have been glad he was taken into custody before Shanker could get his hands on him. Inadvisably allowed into the witness box to describe a maternal woman who had never touched heroin in her life, Shanker had screamed 'That fucker done it!', attempted to clamber over the barrier towards Whittaker and been bundled unceremoniously out of court.

Consciously pushing away these memories of the long-buried past, which smelled no better for being dug up again, Strike took a swig of hot tea and checked his mobile again. There was still no word from Robin.

19

Workshop of the Telescopes

He had known the second he laid eyes on The Secretary that morning that she was out of kilter, off-balance. Look at her, sitting in the window of the Garrick, the large students' restaurant serving the LSE. She was plain today. Puffy, red-eyed, pale. He could probably take the seat next to her and the stupid bitch wouldn't notice. Concentrating on the tart with the silver hair, who was working on a laptop a few tables away, she had no attention to spare for men. Suited him. She'd be noticing him before long. He'd be her last sight on earth.

He didn't need to look like Pretty Boy today; he never approached them sexually if they were upset. That was when he became the friend in need, the avuncular stranger. *Not all men are like that, darling. You deserve better. Let me walk you home. Come on, I'll give you a lift.* You could do almost anything with them if you made them forget you had a dick.

He entered the crowded restaurant, skulking around the counter, buying a coffee and finding himself a corner where he could watch her from behind.

Her engagement ring was missing. That was interesting.

It shone a new light on the holdall she had been alternately carrying over her shoulder and hiding under tables. Was she planning to sleep somewhere other than the flat in Ealing? Might she be heading down a deserted street for once, a short-cut with poor lighting, a lonely underpass?

The very first time he'd killed had been like that: a simple question of seizing the moment. He remembered it in snap-shots, like a slideshow, because it had been thrilling and new. That was before he had honed it to an art, before he had started playing it like the game it was.

She'd been plump and dark. Her mate had just left, got into a punter's car and disappeared. The bloke in the car had not known that he was choosing which of them would survive the night.

He, meanwhile, had been driving up and down the street with his knife in his pocket. When he had been sure that she was alone, completely alone, he had drawn up and leaned across the passenger seat to talk to her through the window. His mouth had been dry as he asked for it. She had agreed a price and got in the car. They had driven down a nearby dead end where neither streetlights nor passers-by would trouble them.

He got what he'd asked for, then, as she was straightening up, before he had even zipped up his flies, he had punched her, knocking her back into the car door, the back of her head banging off the window. Before she could make a sound he'd pulled out the knife.

The meaty thump of the blade in her flesh – the heat of her blood gushing over his hands – she did not even scream but gasped, moaned, sinking down in the seat as he pounded the blade into her again and again. He had torn the gold pendant from around her neck. He had not thought, then, about taking the ultimate trophy: a bit of her, but instead wiped his hands on her dress while she sat slumped beside him, twitching in her death throes. He had reversed out of the alleyway, trembling with fear and elation, and driven out of town with the body beside him, keeping carefully to the speed limit, looking in his rear-view mirror every few seconds. There was a place he had checked out just a few days previously, a stretch of deserted countryside and an overgrown ditch. She had made a heavy, wet thump when he rolled her into it.

He had her pendant still, along with a few other souvenirs. They were his treasure. What, he wondered, would he take from The Secretary?

A Chinese boy near him was reading something on a tablet. *Behavioural Economics*. Dumb psychological crap. *He* had seen a psychologist once, been forced to.

'Tell me about your mother.'

The little bald man had literally said it, the joke line, the cliché. They were supposed to be smart, psychologists. He'd played along for the fun of it, telling the idiot about his mother: that she was a cold, mean, screwed-up bitch. His birth had been an inconvenience, an embarrassment to her, and she wouldn't have cared if he'd lived or died.

'And your father?'

'I haven't got a father,' he'd said.

'You mean you never see him?'

Silence.

'You don't know who he is?'

Silence.

'Or you simply don't like him?'

He said nothing. He was tired of playing along. People were brain dead if they fell for this kind of crap, but he had long since realised that other people *were* brain dead.

In any case, he'd told the truth: he had no father. The man who had filled that role, if you wanted to call it that – the one who had knocked him around day in, day out ('a hard man, but a fair man') – had not fathered him. Violence and rejection, that was what family meant to him. At the same time, home was where he had learned to survive, to box clever. He had always known that he was superior, even when he'd been cowering under the kitchen table as a child. Yes, even then he'd known that he was made of better stuff than the bastard coming at him with his big fist and his clenched face . . .

The Secretary stood up, imitating the tart with the silver hair, who was just leaving with her laptop in a case. He downed his coffee in one and followed.

She was so easy today, so easy! She'd lost all her wariness; she barely had attention to spare for the platinum whore. He boarded the same Tube train as the pair of them, keeping his back to The Secretary but watching her reflection from between the reaching arms of a bunch of Kiwi tourists. He found it easy to slip into the crowd behind her when she left the train.

The three of them moved in procession, the silver-haired tart, The Secretary and him, up the stairs, onto the pavement, along the road to Spearmint Rhino . . . he was already late home, but he could not resist this. She had not stayed out after dark before and the holdall and the lack of engagement ring all added up to an irresistible opportunity. He would simply have to make up some story for It.

The silver-haired tart disappeared into the club. The Secretary slowed down and stood irresolute on the pavement. He slid out his mobile and pulled back into a shadowy doorway, watching her.

20

I never realized she was so undone.

Blue Öyster Cult, 'Debbie Denise'
Lyrics by Patti Smith

Robin had forgotten her promise to Strike that she would not stay out after dark. In fact, she had hardly registered the fact that the sun had gone down until she realised that headlights were swooping past her and that the shop windows were lit up. Platinum had changed her routine today. She would usually have been inside Spearmint Rhino for several hours already, gyrating half naked for the benefit of strange men, not striding along the road, fully dressed in jeans, high-heeled boots and a fringed suede jacket. Presumably she had changed her shift, but she would soon be safely gyrating around a pole, which left the question of where Robin was going to spend the night.

Her mobile had been vibrating inside the pocket of her coat all day. Matthew had sent more than thirty texts.

We've got to talk.
Ring me, please.
Robin, we can't sort anything out if you don't talk to me.

As the day had worn on and her silence had not broken, he had started trying to call. Then the tone of his texts had changed.

Robin, you know I love you.
I wish it hadn't happened. I wish I could change it, but I can't.
It's you I love, Robin. I always have and I always will.

She had not texted back, or picked up his calls, or rung him. All she knew was that she could not bear to go back to the flat, not tonight. What would happen tomorrow, or the next day, she had no idea. She was hungry, exhausted and numb.

Strike had become almost as importuning towards late afternoon.

Where are you? Ring me pls.

She had texted him back, because she could not face talking to him either.

Can't speak. Platinum's not at work.

She and Strike maintained a certain emotional distance, always, and she was afraid that if he were kind to her she would cry, revealing the sort of weakness that he would deplore in an assistant. With virtually no cases left, with the threat of the man who had sent the leg hanging over her, she must not give Strike another reason to tell her to stay at home.

He had not been satisfied with her response.

Call me asap.

She had ignored that one on the basis that she might easily have failed to receive it, being close to the Tube when he sent it and shortly afterwards having no reception as she and Platinum rode the Tube back to Tottenham Court Road. On emerging from the station Robin found another missed call from Strike on her phone, as well as a new text from Matthew.

I need to know whether you're coming home tonight. I'm worried sick about you. Just text to tell me you're alive, that's all I'm asking.

'Oh, don't flatter yourself,' muttered Robin. 'Like I'd kill myself over you.'

A strangely familiar paunchy man in a suit walked past Robin, illuminated by the glow of Spearmint Rhino's canopy. It was Two-Times. Robin wondered whether she imagined the self-satisfied smirk he gave her.

Was he going inside to watch his girlfriend gyrate for other men? Did he get a thrill out of having his sex life documented? Precisely what kind of weirdo was he?

Robin turned away. She needed to make a decision as to what to do tonight. A large man in a beanie hat appeared to be arguing into his mobile phone in a dark doorway a hundred yards away.

The disappearance of Platinum had robbed Robin of purpose. Where was she going to sleep? As she stood there, irresolute, a group of young men walked past her, deliberately close, one of them brushing against her holdall. She could smell Lynx and lager.

'Got your costume in there, darling?'

She became aware of the fact that she was standing outside a lap-dancing club. As she turned automatically in the direction of Strike's office, her mobile rang. Without thinking, she answered it.

'Where the hell have you been?' said Strike's angry voice in her ear.

She barely had time to be glad that he wasn't Matthew before he said:

'I've been trying to get hold of you all day! Where *are* you?'

'On Tottenham Court Road,' she said, walking fast away from the still-jeering men. 'Platinum's only just gone inside and Two—'

'What did I tell you about not staying out after dark?'

'It's well-lit,' said Robin.

She was trying to remember whether she had ever noticed a Travelodge near here. She needed somewhere clean and cheap. It must be cheap, because she was drawing on the joint account; she was determined not to spend more than she had put in.

'Are you all right?' asked Strike, slightly less aggressively.

A lump rose in her throat.

'Fine,' she said, as forcefully as she could. She was trying to be professional, to be what Strike wanted.

'I'm still at the office,' he said. 'Did you say you're on Tottenham Court Road?'

'I've got to go, sorry,' she said, in a tight, cold voice and hung up.

The fear of crying had become so overwhelming that she had to end the call. She thought he had been on the verge of offering to meet her, and if they met she would tell him everything, and she must not do that.

Tears were suddenly pouring down her face. She had no one else. There! She had admitted it to herself at last. The people they had meals with at weekends, the ones they went to watch rugby with: they were all Matthew's friends, Matthew's work colleagues, Matthew's old university friends. She had nobody of her own but Strike.

'Oh God,' she said, wiping her eyes and nose on the sleeve of her coat.

'You all right, sweetheart?' called a toothless tramp from a doorway.

She was not sure why she ended up in the Tottenham, except that the bar staff knew her, she was familiar with where the Ladies was, and it was somewhere that Matthew had never been. All she wanted was a quiet corner in which she could look up cheap places to stay. She was also craving a drink, which was most unlike her. After splashing her face with cold water in the bathroom she bought herself a glass of red wine, took it to a table and pulled out her phone again. She had missed another call from Strike.

Men at the bar were looking over at her. She knew what she must look like, tear-stained and alone, her holdall beside her. Well, she couldn't help that. She typed into her mobile: **Travelodges near Tottenham Court Road** and waited for the slow response, drinking her wine faster than perhaps she ought to have done on a virtually empty stomach. No breakfast, no lunch: a bag of crisps and an apple consumed at the student café where Platinum had been studying were all she had eaten that day.

There was a Travelodge in High Holborn. That would have to do. She felt slightly calmer for knowing where she was going to spend the night. Careful not to make eye contact with any of the men at the bar, she went up to get a second glass of wine. Perhaps she ought to call her mother, she thought suddenly, but the prospect made her feel tearful all over again. She could not face Linda's love and disappointment, not yet.

A large figure in a beanie hat entered the pub, but Robin was keeping her attention determinedly on her change and her wine, giving none of the hopeful men lurking at the bar the slightest reason to suppose that she wanted any of them to join her.

The second glass of wine made her feel much more relaxed. She remembered how Strike had got so drunk here, in this very pub, that he could barely walk. That had been the only night that he had ever shared personal information. Maybe that was the real reason she had been drawn here, she thought, raising her eyes to the colourful glass cupola overhead. This was the bar where you went to drink when you found out that the person you loved was unfaithful.

'You alone?' said a man's voice.

'Waiting for someone,' she said.

He was slightly blurred when she looked up at him, a wiry blond man with bleached blue eyes, and she could tell that he did not believe her.

'Can I wait with you?'

'No, you fucking can't,' said another, familiar voice.

Strike had arrived, massive, scowling, glaring at the stranger, who retreated with ill grace to a couple of friends at the bar.

'What are you doing here?' asked Robin, surprised to find that her tongue felt numb and thick after two glasses of wine.

'Looking for you,' said Strike.

'How did you know I was—?'

'I'm a detective. How many of those have you had?' he asked, looking down at her wine glass.

'Only one,' she lied, so he went to the bar for another, and a pint of Doom Bar for himself. As he ordered, a large man in a beanie hat ducked out of the door, but Strike was more interested in keeping an eye on the blond man who was still staring over at Robin and only seemed to give up on her once Strike reappeared, glowering, with two drinks and sat down opposite her.

'What's going on?'

'Nothing.'

'Don't give me that. You look like bloody death.'

'Well,' said Robin, taking a large slurp of wine, 'consider my morale boosted.'

Strike gave a short laugh.

'Why have you got a holdall with you?' When she did not answer, he said, 'Where's your engagement ring?'

She opened her mouth to answer but a treacherous desire to cry rose to drown the words. After a short inner struggle and another gulp of wine she said:

'I'm not engaged any more.'

'Why not?'

'This is rich, coming from you.'

I'm drunk, she thought, as though watching herself from outside her own body. *Look at me. I'm drunk on two and a half glasses of wine, no food and no sleep.*

'What's rich?' asked Strike, confused.

'We don't talk about personal . . . you don't talk about personal stuff.'

'I seem to remember spilling my guts all over you in this very pub.'

'Once,' said Robin.

Strike deduced from her pink cheeks and her thickened speech that she was not on her second glass of wine. Both amused and concerned, he said:

'I think you need something to eat.'

'That's 'zacktly what I said to you,' Robin replied, 'that night when you were . . . and we ended up having a kebab – and I do not,' she said with dignity, 'want a kebab.'

'Well,' said Strike, 'y'know, it's London. We can probably find you something that isn't a kebab.'

'I like crisps,' said Robin, so he bought her some.

'What's going on?' he repeated on his return. After a few

seconds of watching her attempting to open the crisps he took them from her to do it himself.

'Nothing. I'm going to sleep in a Travelodge tonight, that's all.'

'A Travelodge.'

'Yeah. There's one in . . . there's one . . .'

She looked down at her dead mobile and realised that she had forgotten to charge it the previous night.

'I can't remember where it is,' she said. 'Just leave me, I'm fine,' she added, groping in her holdall for something to blow her nose on.

'Yeah,' he said heavily, 'I'm totally reassured now I've seen you.'

'I *am* fine,' she said fiercely. 'I'll be at work as usual tomorrow, you wait and see.'

'You think I came to find you because I'm worried about work?'

'Don't be nice!' she groaned, burying her face in her tissues. 'I can't take it! Be normal!'

'What's normal?' he asked, confused.

'G-grumpy and uncommunic— uncommunica—'

'What do you want to communicate about?'

'Nothing in particular,' she lied. 'I just thought . . . keep things profess'nal.'

'What's happened between you and Matthew?'

'What's happening b'tween you and Elin?' she countered.

'How's that important?' he asked, nonplussed.

'Same thing,' she said vaguely, draining her third glass. 'I'd like 'nother—'

'You're having a soft drink this time.'

She examined the ceiling while waiting for him. There were theatrical scenes painted up there: Bottom cavorted with Titania amid a group of fairies.

'Things are going OK with Elin,' he told her when he sat back down, having decided that an exchange of information was the easiest way to make her talk about her own problems. 'It suits me, keeping it low key. She's got a daughter she doesn't want me getting too close to. Messy divorce.'

'Oh,' said Robin, blinking at him over her glass of Coke. 'How did you meet her?'

'Through Nick and Ilsa.'

'How do they know her?'

'They don't. They had a party and she came along with her brother. He's a doctor, works with Nick. They hadn't ever met her before.'

'Oh,' said Robin again.

She had briefly forgotten her own troubles, diverted by this glimpse into Strike's private world. So normal, so unremarkable! A party and he had gone along and got talking to the beautiful blonde. Women liked Strike – she had come to realise that over the months they had worked together. She had not understood the appeal when she had started working for him. He was so very different from Matthew.

'Does Ilsa like Elin?' asked Robin.

Strike was startled by this flash of perception.

'Er – yeah, I think so,' he lied.

Robin sipped her Coke.

'OK,' said Strike, restraining his impatience with difficulty, 'your turn.'

'We've split up,' she said.

Interrogation technique told him to remain silent, and after a minute or so the decision was vindicated.

'He . . . told me something,' she said. 'Last night.'

Strike waited.

'And we can't go back from that. Not that.'

She was pale and composed but he could almost feel the anguish behind the words. Still he waited.

'He slept with someone else,' she said in a small, tight voice.

There was a pause. She picked up her crisp packet, found that she had finished the contents and dropped it on the table.

'Shit,' said Strike.

He was surprised: not that Matthew had slept with another woman, but that he had admitted it. His impression of the handsome young accountant was of a man who knew how to run his life to suit himself, to compartmentalise and categorise where necessary.

'And not just once,' said Robin, in that same tight voice. 'He was doing it for months. With someone we both know. Sarah Shadlock. She's an old friend of his from university.'

'Christ,' said Strike. 'I'm sorry.'

He *was* sorry, genuinely sorry, for the pain she was in. Yet the revelation had caused certain other feelings – feelings he usually kept under tight rein, considering them both misguided and dangerous – to flex inside him, to test their strength against their restraining bonds.

Don't be a stupid fucker, he told himself. *That's one thing that can never happen. It'd screw everything up royally.*

'What made him tell you?' Strike asked.

She did not answer, but the question brought back the scene in awful clarity.

Their magnolia sitting room was far too tiny to accommodate a couple in such a state of fury. They had driven all the way home from Yorkshire in the Land Rover that Matthew had not wanted. Somewhere along the way, an incensed Matthew had asserted that it was a matter of time before Strike made a pass at Robin and what was more, he suspected that she would welcome the advance.

'He's my friend, that's all!' she had bellowed at Matthew from beside their cheap sofa, their weekend bags still in the hall. 'For you to suggest I'm *turned on* by the fact he's had his leg—'

'You're so bloody naive!' he had bellowed. 'He's your friend until he tries to get you into bed, Robin—'

'Who are you judging him by? Are you biding your time before you jump on your co-workers?'

'Of course I'm bloody not, but you're so frigging starry-eyed about him – he's a man, it's just the two of you in the office—'

'He's my *friend*, like you're *friends* with Sarah Shadlock but you've never—'

She had seen it in his face. An expression she had never noticed before passed across it like a shadow. Guilt seemed to slide physically over the high cheekbones, the clean jaw, the hazel eyes she had adored for years.

'—have you?' she said, her tone suddenly wondering. '*Have* you?'

He hesitated too long.

'No,' he had said forcefully, like a paused film jerking back into action. 'Of course n—'

'You have,' she said. 'You've slept with her.'

She could see it in his face. He did not believe in male-female friendships because he had never had one. He and Sarah had been sleeping together.

'When?' she had asked. 'Not . . . was it *then*?'

'I didn't—'

She heard the feeble protestation of a man who knows he has lost, who had even wanted to lose. That had haunted her all night and all day: on some level, he had wanted Robin to know.

Her strange calm, more stunned than accusatory, had led

him on to tell her everything. Yes, it had been *then*. He felt terrible about it, he always had – but he and Robin hadn't been sleeping together at the time and, one night, Sarah had been comforting him, and, well, things had got out of hand—

'She was *comforting* you?' Robin had repeated. Rage had come then, at last, unfreezing her from her state of stunned disbelief. 'She was comforting *you*?'

'It was a difficult time for me too, you know!' he had shouted.

Strike watched as Robin shook her head unconsciously, trying to clear it, but the recollections had turned her pink and her eyes were sparkling again.

'What did you say?' she asked Strike, confused.

'I asked what made him tell you.'

'I don't know. We were in the middle of a row. He thinks . . .' She took a deep breath. Two-thirds of a bottle of wine on an empty stomach was leading her to emulate Matthew's honesty. 'He doesn't believe you and I are just friends.'

This was no surprise to Strike. He had read suspicion in every look Matthew had ever given him, heard insecurity in every chippy comment thrown his way.

'So,' Robin went on unsteadily, 'I pointed out that we *are* just friends, and that he's got a platonic friend himself, dear old Sarah Shadlock. So then it all came out. He and Sarah had an affair at university while I was . . . while I was at home.'

'That long ago?' Strike said.

'You think I shouldn't mind if it was seven years ago?' she demanded. 'If he's lied about it ever since and we constantly see her?'

'I was just surprised,' said Strike evenly, refusing to be drawn into a fight, 'that he's owned up to it after all this time.'

'Oh,' said Robin. 'Well, he was ashamed. Because of when it happened.'

'At university?' said Strike, confused.

'It was right after I dropped out,' said Robin.

'Ah,' said Strike.

They had never discussed what had made her leave her psychology degree and return to Masham.

Robin had not intended to tell Strike the story, but all resolutions were adrift tonight on the little sea of alcohol with which she had filled her hungry and exhausted body. What did it matter if she told him? Without that information he would not have the full picture or be able to advise her what to do next. She was relying on him, she realised dimly, to help her. Whether she liked it or not – whether *he* liked it or not – Strike was her best friend in London. She had never looked that fact squarely in the face before. Alcohol buoyed you up and it washed your eyes clean. *In vino veritas*, they said, didn't they? Strike would know. He had an odd, occasional habit of quoting Latin.

'I didn't *want* to leave uni,' said Robin slowly, her head swimming, 'but something happened and afterwards I had problems . . .'

That was no good. That didn't explain it.

'I was coming home from a friend's, in another hall of residence,' she said. 'It wasn't that late . . . only eight o'clock or something . . . but there had been a warning out about him – on the local news—'

That was no good either. Far too much detail. What she needed was a bald statement of fact, not to talk him through every little bit of it, the way she'd had to in court.

She took a deep breath, looked into Strike's face and read dawning comprehension there. Relieved not to have to spell it out, she asked:

'Please could I have some more crisps?'

When he returned from the bar he handed them to her in silence. She did not like the look on his face.

'Don't go thinking – it doesn't make any difference!' she said desperately. 'It was twenty minutes of my life. It was something that happened to me. It isn't me. It doesn't *define* me.'

Strike guessed that they were phrases she had been led to embrace in some kind of therapy. He had interviewed rape victims. He knew the forms of words they were given to make sense of what, to a woman, was incomprehensible. A lot of things about Robin were explained now. The long allegiance to Matthew, for instance: the safe boy from home.

However, the drunken Robin read in Strike's silence the thing she had most feared: a shift in the way he saw her, from equal to victim.

'It doesn't make any difference!' she repeated furiously. 'I'm still the same!'

'I know that,' he said, 'but it's still one fucking horrible thing to have happened to you.'

'Well, yes . . . it was . . . ' she muttered, mollified. Then, firing up again: 'My evidence got him. I noticed things about him while . . . He had this patch of white skin under his ear – they call it vitiligo – and one of his pupils was fixed, dilated.'

She was gabbling slightly now, wolfing down her third packet of crisps.

'He tried to strangle me; I went limp and played dead and he ran for it. He'd attacked two other girls wearing the mask and neither of them could tell the police anything about him. My evidence got him put away.'

'That doesn't surprise me,' said Strike.

She found this response satisfactory. They sat in silence for a minute while she finished the crisps.

'Only, afterwards, I couldn't leave my room,' she said, as though there had been no pause. 'In the end, the university sent me home. I was only supposed to take a term off, but I – I never went back.'

Robin contemplated this fact, staring into space. Matthew had urged her to stay at home. When her agoraphobia had resolved, which had taken more than a year, she had begun visiting him at his university in Bath, wandering hand in hand among dwellings of soft Cotswold stone, down sweeping Regency crescents, along the tree-lined banks of the River Avon. Every time they had gone out with his friends Sarah Shadlock had been there, braying at Matthew's jokes, touching his arm, leading the conversation constantly to the good times they all enjoyed when Robin, the tedious girlfriend from home, was not present . . .

She was comforting me. It was a difficult time for me too, you know!

'Right,' said Strike, 'we've got to get you a place to spend tonight.'

'I'm going to the Travel—'

'No, you're not.'

He did not want her staying in a place where anonymous people might wander the corridors unchallenged, or could walk in off the street. Perhaps he was being paranoid, but he wanted her somewhere that a scream would not be lost in the raucous cries of hen parties.

'I could sleep in the office,' said Robin, swaying as she tried to stand; he grabbed her by the arm. 'If you've still got that camp—'

'You're not sleeping in the office,' he said. 'I know a good place. My aunt and uncle stayed there when they came up to see *The Mousetrap*. C'mon, give me the holdall.'

He had once before put his arm around Robin's shoulders

but that had been quite different: he had been using her as a walking stick. This time it was she who could barely move in a straight line. He found her waist and held her steady as they left the pub.

'Matthew,' she said, as they moved off, 'would *not* like this.'

Strike said nothing. In spite of everything he had heard, he was not as sure as Robin was that the relationship was over. They had been together nine years and there was a wedding dress ready and waiting in Masham. He had been careful to offer no criticism of Matthew that might be repeated to her ex-fiancé in the renewal of hostilities that was surely coming, because the accumulated ties of nine years could not be severed in a single night. His reticence was for Robin's sake rather than his own. He had no fear of Matthew.

'Who *was* that man?' asked Robin sleepily, after they had walked a hundred yards in silence.

'Which man?'

'That man this morning . . . I thought he might be the leg man . . . he scared the hell out of me.'

'Ah . . . that's Shanker. He's an old friend.'

'He's terrifying.'

'Shanker wouldn't hurt you,' Strike assured her. Then, as an afterthought: 'But don't ever leave him alone in the office.'

'Why not?'

'He'll nick anything that's not nailed down. He does nothing for nothing.'

'Where did you meet him?'

The story of Shanker and Leda took them all the way to Frith Street, where quiet townhouses looked down upon them, exuding dignity and order.

'Here?' said Robin, gazing open-mouthed up at Hazlitt's Hotel. 'I can't stay here – this'll be expensive!'

'I'm paying,' said Strike. 'Think of it as this year's bonus.

No arguments,' he added, as the door opened and a smiling young man stood back to let them in. 'It's my fault you need somewhere safe.'

The wood-panelled hall was cosy, with the feeling of a private house. There was only one way in and nobody could open the front door from outside.

When he had given the young man his credit card Strike saw the unsteady Robin to the foot of the stairs.

'You can take tomorrow morning off if you—'

'I'll be there at nine,' she said. 'Cormoran, thanks for – for—'

'Not a problem. Sleep well.'

Frith Street was quiet as he closed the Hazlitt's door behind him. Strike set off, his hands deep in his pockets, lost in thought.

She had been raped and left for dead. *Holy shit.*

Eight days previously some bastard had handed her a woman's severed leg and she had not breathed a word of her past, not asked for special dispensation to take time off, nor deviated in any respect from the total professionalism she brought to work every morning. It was he, without even knowing her history, who had insisted on the best rape alarm, on nothing after dark, on checking in with her regularly through the working day . . .

At the precise moment Strike became aware that he was walking away from Denmark Street rather than towards it, he spotted a man in a beanie hat twenty yards away, skulking on the corner of Soho Square. The amber tip of the cigarette swiftly vanished as the man turned and began to walk hurriedly away.

''Scuse me, mate!'

Strike's voice echoed through the quiet square as he sped up. The man in the hat did not look back, but broke into a run.

'Oi! Mate!'

Strike, too, began to run, his knee protesting with every jolting step. His quarry looked back once then took a sharp left, Strike moving as fast as he could in pursuit. Entering Carlisle Street, Strike squinted ahead at the crowd clustered around the entrance of the Toucan, wondering whether his man had joined it. Panting, he ran on past the pub drinkers, drawing up at the junction with Dean Street and revolving on the spot, looking for his quarry. He had a choice of taking a left, a right or continuing along Carlisle Street, and each offered a multitude of doorways and basement spaces in which the man in the beanie hat could have hidden, assuming he had not hailed a passing cab.

'Bollocks,' Strike muttered. His stump was sore against the end of his prosthesis. All he had was an impression of ample height and breadth, a dark coat and hat and the suspicious fact that he had run when called, run before Strike could ask him for the time, or a light, or directions.

He took a guess and headed right, up Dean Street. The traffic swooshed past him in either direction. For nearly an hour Strike continued to prowl the area, probing into dark doorways and basement cavities. He knew this was almost certainly a fool's errand, but if – if – they had been followed by the man who had sent the leg, he was clearly a reckless bastard who might not have been scared away from Robin's vicinity by Strike's ungainly pursuit.

Men in sleeping bags glared at him as he moved far closer than members of the public usually dared; twice he startled cats out from behind dustbins, but the man in the beanie hat was nowhere to be seen.

21

> . . . the damn call came,
> And I knew what I knew and didn't want to
> know.
>
> Blue Öyster Cult, 'Live for Me'

Robin woke next day to a sore head and a weight in the pit of her stomach. In the time it took to roll over on unfamiliar, crisp white pillows, the events of the previous evening seemed to come crashing down on her. Shaking her hair out of her face she sat up and looked around. Between the carved posts of her wooden four-poster she made out the dim outlines of a room barely illuminated by the line of brilliant light between brocade curtains. As her eyes became accustomed to the gilded gloom she made out the portrait of a fat gentleman with mutton-chop whiskers, framed in gilt. This was the kind of hotel in which you took an expensive city break, not where you slept off a hangover with a few hastily snatched clothes in a holdall.

Had Strike deposited her here in elegant, old-fashioned luxury as pre-emptive compensation for the serious talk he would initiate today? *You're obviously in a very emotional place . . . I think it would be good if you took a break from work.*

Two-thirds of a bottle of bad wine and she had told him everything. With a weak groan, Robin sank back on the pillows, covered her face with her arms and succumbed to the memories that had regained all their power now that she was weak and miserable.

The rapist had worn a rubber gorilla mask. He had held her down with one hand and the weight of a whole arm on her throat, telling her she was about to die as he raped her, telling her he was going to choke the fucking life out of her. Her brain a scarlet cavity of screaming panic, his hands tightening like a noose around her neck, her survival had hung on her ability to pretend that she was already dead.

Later there had been days and weeks when she had felt as though she had in fact died, and was trapped in the body from which she felt entirely disconnected. The only way to protect herself, it had seemed, was to separate herself from her own flesh, to deny their connection. It had been a long time before she had felt able to take possession again.

He had been soft-spoken in court, meek, 'yes, your honour', 'no, your honour', a nondescript middle-aged white man, florid in complexion except for that white patch under his ear. His pale, washed-out eyes blinked too often, eyes that had been slits viewed through the holes in his mask.

What he had done to her shattered her view of her place in the world, ended her university career and drove her back to Masham. It forced her through a gruelling court case in which the cross-examination had been almost as traumatic as the original attack, for his defence was that she had invited him into the stairwell for sex. Months after his gloved hands had reached out of the shadows and dragged her, gagging, into the cavity behind the stairs, she had not been able to stand physical contact, not even a gentle hug from a family member. He had polluted her first and only sexual relationship, so that she and

Matthew had had to start again, with fear and guilt attending them every step of the way.

Robin pressed her arms down over her eyes as though she might obliterate it all from her mind by force. Now, of course, she knew that the young Matthew, whom she had considered a selfless paragon of kindness and understanding, had in fact been cavorting with a naked Sarah in his student house in Bath while Robin lay on her lonely bed in Masham for hours at a stretch, staring blankly at Destiny's Child. Alone in the sumptuous quiet of Hazlitt's, Robin contemplated for the first time the question of whether Matthew would have left her for Sarah, had she been happy and unharmed, or even whether she and Matthew might have grown naturally apart if she had completed her degree.

She lowered her arms and opened her eyes. They were dry today; she felt as though she had no tears left to weep. The pain of Matthew's confession no longer pierced her. She felt it as a dull ache underlying the more urgent panic about the damage she feared she might have done to her work prospects. How could she have been so stupid as to tell Strike what had happened to her? Hadn't she already learned what happened when she was honest?

A year after the rape, when the agoraphobia had been overcome, when her weight was nearly back to normal, when she was itching to get back out into the world and make up the time she had lost, she had expressed a vague interest in 'something related' to criminal investigative work. Without her degree and with her confidence so recently shredded, she had not dared voice aloud her true desire to be some kind of investigator. A good thing too, because every single person she knew had tried to dissuade her even from her tentatively expressed desire to explore the outer reaches of police work, even her mother, usually the most understanding of creatures.

They had all taken what they thought a strange new interest as a sign of continuing sickness, a symptom of her inability to throw off what had happened to her.

It was not true: the desire had long pre-dated the rape. At the age of eight she had informed her brothers that she was going to catch robbers and had been roundly mocked, for no better reason than that she ought to be laughed at, given that she was a girl and their sister. Though Robin hoped that their response was not a true reflection of their estimate of her abilities, but based on a kind of collegiate male reflex, it had left her diffident about expressing her interest in detective work to three loud, opinionated brothers. She had never told anyone that she had chosen to study psychology with a secret eye towards investigative profiling.

Her pursuit of that goal had been utterly thwarted by the rapist. That was another thing he had taken from her. Asserting her ambition while recuperating from a state of intense fragility, at a time when everyone around her appeared to be waiting for her to fall apart again, had proved too difficult. Out of exhaustion and a feeling of obligation to the family that had been so protective and loving in her time of greatest need she had let a lifelong ambition fall by the wayside, and everyone else had been satisfied to see it go.

Then a temping agency had sent her by mistake to a private detective. She should have been there a week, but she had never left. It had felt like a miracle. Somehow, by luck, then through talent and tenacity, she had made herself valuable to the struggling Strike and ended up almost exactly where she had fantasised being before a total stranger had used her for his perverse enjoyment like a disposable, inanimate object, then beaten and throttled her.

Why, *why*, had she told Strike what had happened to her? He had been worried about her before she revealed her history:

now what? He would decide she was too fragile to work, Robin was sure of it, and from there it would be a swift, short step to the sidelines, because she was unable to take on all the responsibilities he needed a workmate to shoulder.

The calm Georgian room's silence and solidity was oppressive.

Robin struggled out from under the heavy covers and crossed the sloping wooden floorboards to a bathroom with a claw-footed bath and no shower. Fifteen minutes later, as she was dressing, her mobile, which she had mercifully remembered to charge the previous night, rang on the dressing table.

'Hi,' said Strike. 'How are you?'

'Fine,' she said, her voice brittle.

He had called to tell her not to come in, she knew it.

'Wardle's just phoned. They've found the rest of the body.'

Robin sat down hard on the needlepoint stool, both hands clutching the mobile to her ear.

'What? Where? Who is she?'

'Tell you when I pick you up. They want to talk to us. I'll be outside at nine. Make sure you eat something,' he added.

'Cormoran!' she said, to stop him hanging up.

'What?'

'I'm still . . . I've still got a job, then?'

There was a slight pause.

'What're you talking about? Of course you've still got a job.'

'You don't . . . I'm still . . . nothing's changed?' she said.

'Are you going to do as you're told?' he asked. 'When I say nothing after dark, you're going to listen from now on?'

'Yes,' she said, a little shakily.

'Good. I'll see you at nine.'

Robin breathed a deep, shuddering sigh of relief. She was not finished: he still wanted her. As she went to replace the mobile on the dressing table she noticed that the longest text message that she had ever received had arrived overnight.

Robin, I can't sleep for thinking about you. You don't know how much I wish it hadn't happened. It was a shitty thing to do and there's no defence. I was 21 and I didn't know then what I know now: that there's nobody like you and that I could never love anyone else as much as I love you. There's never been anyone apart from you since then. I've been jealous of you and Strike and you might say I don't have the right to feel jealous because of what I did but maybe on some level I think you deserve better than me and that's what's been getting to me. I only know I love you and I want to marry you and if that's not what you want now then I'll have to accept that but please Robin just text me and let me know you're OK, please. Matt xxxxxxx

Robin put the mobile back on the dressing table and continued dressing. She ordered a croissant and coffee from room service and was surprised how much better food and drink made her feel when they arrived. Only then did she read Matthew's text again.

. . . maybe on some level I think you deserve better than me and that's what's been getting to me . . .

This was touching, and most unlike Matthew, who frequently expressed the view that citing subconscious motivation was no more than chicanery. Hard on the heels of that thought, though, came the reflection that Matthew had never cut Sarah out of his life. She was one of his best friends from university: embracing him tenderly at his mother's funeral, dining out with them as part of a cosy foursome, still flirting with Matthew, still stirring between him and Robin.

After a brief inner deliberation, Robin texted back:

I'm fine.

She was waiting for Strike on the doorstep of Hazlitt's, neat as ever, when the black cab drew up at five to nine.

Strike had not shaved, and as his beard grew with vigour his jaw looked grimy.

'Have you seen the news?' he asked as soon as she had got into the cab.

'No.'

'Media have just got it. Saw it on the telly as I left.'

He leaned forward to slide shut the plastic divider between themselves and the driver.

'Who is she?' asked Robin.

'They haven't formally ID'd her yet, but they think she's a twenty-four-year-old Ukrainian woman.'

'Ukrainian?' said Robin, startled.

'Yeah.' He hesitated, then said, 'Her landlady found her dismembered in a fridge-freezer in what looks like her own flat. The right leg's missing. It's definitely her.'

The taste of Robin's toothpaste in her mouth turned chemical; croissant and coffee churned in her stomach.

'Where's the flat?'

'Coningham Road, Shepherd's Bush. Ring any bells?'

'No, I – oh God. *Oh God*. The girl who wanted to cut off her leg?'

'Apparently.'

'But she didn't have a Ukrainian name, did she?'

'Wardle thinks she might've been using a fake one. You know – hooker name.'

The taxi bore them down Pall Mall towards New Scotland Yard. White neoclassical buildings slid past the windows on both sides: august, haughty and impervious to the shocks of frail humanity.

'It's what Wardle expected,' said Strike after a long pause. 'His theory was that the leg belonged to a Ukrainian prostitute last seen with Digger Malley.'

Robin could tell that there was more. She looked at him anxiously.

'There were letters from me in her flat,' said Strike. 'Two letters, signed with my name.'

'But you didn't write back!'

'Wardle knows they're fake. Apparently they've spelled my name wrong – Cameron – but he's still got to get me in.'

'What do the letters say?'

'He wouldn't tell me over the phone. He's being pretty decent,' said Strike. 'Not being a dick about it.'

Buckingham Palace rose up ahead of them. The gigantic marble statue of Queen Victoria frowned down on Robin's confusion and her hangover, then slid out of view.

'They're probably going to ask us to look at pictures of the body to see whether we can ID her.'

'OK,' said Robin, more stoutly than she felt.

'How are you?' Strike asked.

'I'm fine,' she said. 'Don't worry about me.'

'I was going to call Wardle this morning anyway.'

'Why?'

'Last night, walking away from Hazlitt's, I saw a big guy in a black beanie hat lurking down a side street. There was something about his body language I didn't like. I called out to him – I was going to ask him for a light – and he scarpered. *Don't,*' said Strike, though Robin had not made a sound, 'tell me I'm jumpy or imagining things. I think he followed us, and I'll tell you something else – I think he was in the pub when I arrived. I didn't see his face, just the back of his head as he left.'

To his surprise, Robin did not dismiss him. Instead she frowned in concentration, trying to recall a vague impression.

'You know . . . I saw a big bloke in a beanie hat somewhere yesterday, too . . . yeah, he was in a doorway on Tottenham Court Road. His face was in shadow, though.'

Strike muttered another oath under his breath.

'Please don't tell me to stop working,' said Robin in a more high-pitched voice than usual. '*Please.* I love this job.'

'And if the fucker's stalking you?'

She could not repress a frisson of fear, but determination overrode it. To help catch this animal, whoever he was, would be worth almost anything . . .

'I'll be vigilant. I've got two rape alarms.'

Strike did not look reassured.

They disembarked at New Scotland Yard and were shown upstairs at once, into an open-plan office where Wardle stood in his shirtsleeves, talking to a group of subordinates. When he saw Strike and Robin he left his colleagues at once and led the detective and his partner into a small meeting room.

'Vanessa!' he called through the door as Strike and Robin took seats at an oval table, 'have you got the letters?'

Detective Sergeant Ekwensi appeared shortly afterwards with two typewritten sheets protected in plastic slips and a copy of what Strike recognised as one of the handwritten letters that he had given Wardle in the Old Blue Last. Detective Sergeant Ekwensi, who greeted Robin with a smile that the latter again found disproportionately reassuring, sat down beside Wardle with a notebook.

'You want coffee or anything?' Wardle asked. Strike and Robin shook their heads. Wardle slid the letters across the table to Strike. He read both before pushing them sideways to Robin.

'I didn't write either of them,' Strike told Wardle.

'I didn't think so,' said Wardle. 'You didn't answer on Strike's behalf, Miss Ellacott?'

Robin shook her head.

The first letter admitted that Strike had indeed arranged the removal of his own leg because he wished to be rid of it, confessing that the story of an Afghan IED was an elaborate cover-up, and that he did not know how Kelsey had found this out, but implored her not to tell anybody else. The fake Strike then agreed to help her with her own 'encumbrance' and asked where and when they could meet face to face.

The second letter was brief, confirming that Strike would come and visit her on the third of April at 7 p.m.

Both of the letters were signed *Cameron Strike* in thick black ink.

'That,' said Strike, who had pulled the second letter back towards him after Robin had finished reading it, 'reads as though she wrote back to me suggesting a time and place.'

'That was going to be my next question,' said Wardle. 'Did you get a second letter?'

Strike looked towards Robin, who shook her head.

'OK,' said Wardle, 'for the record: when did the original letter from—' he checked the photocopy '—Kelsey, she's signed herself – come in?'

Robin answered.

'I've got the envelope back in the nut—' The ghost of a smile passed over Strike's face '—in the drawer where we keep unsolicited letters. We can check the postmark, but as far as I can remember it was early this year. Maybe February.'

'OK, excellent,' said Wardle, 'we'll be sending someone over to retrieve that envelope.' He smiled at Robin, who was looking anxious. 'Calm down: I believe you. Some total nutter's trying to frame Strike. None of it hangs together. Why would he stab a woman, dismember her and then mail her leg to his own office? Why would he leave letters from himself in the flat?'

Robin tried to smile back.

'She was stabbed?' interposed Strike.

'They're working on what actually killed her,' said Wardle, 'but there are two deep wounds to the torso they're pretty sure would have done it before he started cutting her up.'

Beneath the table top, Robin made fists, her nails digging deep into her palms.

'Now,' said Wardle, and Detective Sergeant Ekwensi clicked out the nib of her pen and prepared to write, 'does the name Oxana Voloshina mean anything to either of you?'

'No,' said Strike and Robin shook her head.

'It looks like that was the victim's real name,' Wardle explained. 'That's how she signed her tenancy agreement and the landlady says she provided ID. She was claiming to be a student.'

'Claiming?' said Robin.

'We're looking into who she really was,' said Wardle.

Of course, thought Robin, *he's expecting her to be a prostitute.*

'Her English was good, judging by her letter,' commented Strike. 'That's if she genuinely wrote it.'

Robin looked at him, confused.

'If someone's faking letters from me, why couldn't they have faked the letter from her?' Strike asked her.

'To try and get you to genuinely communicate with her, you mean?'

'Yeah – lure me to a rendezvous or lay some kind of paper trail between us that would look incriminating once she was dead.'

'Van, go see if the photos of the body are viewable,' said Wardle.

Detective Sergeant Ekwensi left the room. Her posture was that of a model. Robin's insides began to crawl with panic. As though Wardle had sensed it, he turned to her and said:

'I don't think you'll need to look at them if Strike—'

'She should look,' said Strike.

Wardle looked taken aback and Robin, though she tried not to show it, found herself wondering whether Strike was trying to scare her into compliance with his nothing-after-dark rule.

'Yes,' she said, with a decent show of calm. 'I think I should.'

'They're – not nice,' said Wardle, with uncharacteristic understatement.

'The leg was sent to Robin,' Strike reminded him. 'There's as much chance that she's seen this woman previously as I have. She's my partner. We work the same jobs.'

Robin glanced sideways at Strike. He had never before described her as his partner to somebody else, or not within Robin's hearing. He was not looking at her. Robin switched her attention back to Wardle. Apprehensive though she was, after hearing Strike put her on equal professional footing with himself she knew that, whatever she was about to see, she would not let herself, or him, down. When Detective Sergeant Ekwensi returned holding a sheaf of photographs in her hand Robin swallowed hard and straightened her back.

Strike took them first and his reaction was not reassuring.

'Holy fucking shit.'

'The head's best preserved,' said Wardle quietly, 'because he put it in the freezer.'

Just as she would have withdrawn her hand instinctively from something red hot, Robin now had to fight a powerful urge to turn away, to close her eyes, to flip the photograph over. Instead she took it from Strike and looked down; her intestines became liquid.

The severed head sat on what remained of its neck, staring blindly into the camera, its eyes so frosted their colour was invisible. The mouth gaped darkly. Her brown hair was stiff, flecked with ice. The cheeks were full and chubby, the chin and forehead covered in acne. She looked younger than twenty-four.

'Do you recognise her?'

Wardle's voice sounded startlingly close to Robin. She had felt as though she had travelled a long distance as she stared at the severed head.

'No,' said Robin.

She put the picture down and took the next from Strike. A left leg and two arms had been rammed into the fridge, where they had begun to decompose. Having steeled herself for the head she had not thought anything else could be as bad and she was ashamed of the small bleat of distress that escaped her.

'Yeah, it's bad,' said Detective Sergeant Ekwensi quietly. Robin met her eyes with gratitude.

'There's a tattoo on the wrist of the left arm,' Wardle pointed out, handing them a third picture in which the relevant arm lay outstretched on a table. Now feeling definitely nauseated, Robin looked and made out '1D' in black ink.

'You don't need to see the torso,' said Wardle, shuffling the photographs and handing them back to Detective Sergeant Ekwensi.

'Where was it?' asked Strike.

'In the bath,' said Wardle. 'That's where he killed her, the bathroom. It looked like an abattoir in there.' He hesitated. 'The leg wasn't the only thing he cut off her.'

Robin was glad that Strike did not ask what else had gone. She did not think she could stand to hear.

'Who found her?' asked Strike.

'The landlady,' said Wardle. 'She's elderly and she collapsed right after we got there. Looks like a heart attack. They took her to Hammersmith Hospital.'

'What made her go round?'

'Smell,' said Wardle. 'Downstairs had rung her. She decided to pop in early before doing her shopping, try and catch this Oxana at home. When she didn't answer the landlady let herself in.'

'Downstairs hadn't heard anything – screams – anything?'

'It's a converted house full of students. Less than bloody useless,' said Wardle. 'Loud music, mates coming and going all hours, they gaped like sheep when we asked them if they'd heard anything from upstairs. The girl who'd rung the landlady had total hysterics. She said she'd never forgive herself for not phoning up when she first smelled something bad.'

'Yeah, that would've changed everything,' said Strike. 'You could've stuck her head back on and she'd have been fine.'

Wardle laughed. Even Detective Sergeant Ekwensi smiled.

Robin stood up abruptly. Last night's wine and this morning's croissant were churning horribly in her guts. Excusing herself in a small voice, she moved briskly towards the door.

22

I don't give up but I ain't a stalker,
I guess I'm just an easy talker.

Blue Öyster Cult, 'I Just Like To Be Bad'

'Thank you, I *get* the concept of gallows humour,' said Robin an hour later, part exasperated, part amused. 'Can we move on?'

Strike regretted his witticism in the meeting room, because Robin had returned from a twenty-minute bathroom trip looking white and slightly clammy, a whiff of peppermint revealing that she had cleaned her teeth again. Instead of taking a taxi he had suggested they take a short walk in the fresh air along Broadway to the Feathers, the closest pub, where he ordered them a pot of tea. Personally, he was ready for a beer, but Robin had not been trained up to consider alcohol and bloodshed natural fellows and he felt a pint might reinforce her impression of his callousness.

The Feathers was quiet at half past eleven on a Wednesday morning. They took a table at the back of the large pub, away from a couple of plain-clothes officers who were talking in soft voices near the window.

'I told Wardle about our friend in the beanie while you

were in the bathroom,' Strike told Robin. 'He says he's going to put a plainclothes man around Denmark Street to keep an eye out for a few days.'

'D'you think the press are going to come back?' asked Robin, who had not yet had time to worry about this.

'I hope not. Wardle's going to keep the fake letters under wraps. He says it's playing into this nutter's hands to release them. He inclines to the view that the killer's genuinely trying to frame me.'

'You don't?'

'No,' said Strike. 'He's not that unhinged. There's something weirder going on here.'

He fell silent and Robin, respecting his thought process, maintained her own silence.

'Terrorism, that's what this is,' said Strike slowly, scratching his unshaven chin. 'He's trying to put the wind up us, disrupt our lives as much as possible; and let's face it, he's succeeding. We've got police crawling over the office and calling us into the Yard, we've lost most of our clients, you're—'

'Don't worry about me!' said Robin at once, 'I don't want you to worry—'

'For fuck's sake, Robin,' said Strike on a flash of temper, 'both of us saw that guy yesterday. Wardle thinks I should tell you to stay home and I—'

'Please,' she said, her early-morning fears swarming back upon her, 'don't make me stop work—'

'It's not worth being murdered to escape your home life!'

He regretted saying it immediately, as he saw her wince.

'I'm not using it as an escape,' she muttered. 'I love this job. I woke up this morning feeling sick about what I told you last night. I was worried you – might not think I'm tough enough any more.'

'This hasn't got anything to do with what you told me last

night and nothing to do with being tough. It's about a psycho who might be following you, who's already hacked a woman to bits.'

Robin drank her lukewarm tea and said nothing. She was ravenous. However, the thought of eating pub food containing any form of meat made sweat break out over her scalp.

'It can't have been a first murder, can it?' Strike asked rhetorically, his dark eyes fixed on the hand-painted names of beers over the bar. 'Beheading her, cutting off her limbs, taking bits of her away? Wouldn't you work up to that?'

'You'd think so,' Robin agreed.

'That was done for the pleasure of doing it. He had a one-man orgy in that bathroom.'

Robin was now unsure whether she was experiencing hunger or nausea.

'A sadistic maniac who's got a grudge against me and has decided to unite his hobbies,' Strike mused aloud.

'Does that fit any of the men you suspect?' Robin asked. 'Have any of them killed before, that you know of?'

'Yeah,' said Strike. 'Whittaker. He killed my mother.'

But in a very different way, thought Robin. It had been a needle, not knives, that had dispatched Leda Strike. Out of respect for Strike, who was looking grim, she did not voice the thought. Then she remembered something else.

'I suppose you know,' she said cautiously, 'that Whittaker kept another woman's dead body in his flat for a month?'

'Yeah,' said Strike. 'I heard.'

The news had filtered through to him while he was out in the Balkans, passed on by his sister Lucy. He had found a picture online of Whittaker walking into court. His ex-stepfather had been almost unrecognisable, crew-cutted and bearded, but still with those staring gold eyes. Whittaker's story, if Strike remembered correctly, had been that he had been afraid of 'another false accusation' of murder, so he had attempted to mummify the dead woman's body, binding it up in bin bags and hiding it under floorboards. The defence had claimed to an unsympathetic judge that their client's novel approach to his problem was due to heavy drug use.

'He hadn't murdered her, though, had he?' Robin asked, trying to remember exactly what Wikipedia had said.

'She'd been dead a month, so I doubt it was an easy post-mortem,' said Strike. The look that Shanker had described as ugly had returned. 'Personally, I'd lay odds he killed her. How unlucky does a man get, two of his girlfriends dropping dead at home while he's sitting there doing nothing?

'He liked death, Whittaker; he liked bodies. He claimed he'd been a gravedigger when he was a teenager. He had a thing about corpses. People took him for a hardcore goth or some ten-a-penny poseur – the necrophiliac lyrics, the Satanic Bible, Aleister Crowley, all that crap – but he was an evil, amoral bastard who told everyone he met he was an evil, amoral bastard and what happened? Women fell over themselves to get at him.

'I need a drink,' said Strike. He got up and headed for the bar.

Robin watched him go, slightly taken aback by his sudden rush of anger. His opinion that Whittaker had murdered twice was unsupported by either the courts or, as far as she knew, police evidence. She had become used to Strike's insistence on the meticulous collection and documentation of facts, his oft-repeated reminders that hunches and personal antipathies might inform, but must never be allowed to dictate, the direction of an investigation. Of course, when it was a case of Strike's own mother . . .

Strike returned with a pint of Nicholson's Pale Ale and a couple of menus.

'Sorry,' he muttered when he had sat back down and taken a long pull on the pint. 'Thinking about stuff I haven't thought about for a long time. Those bloody lyrics.'

'Yes,' said Robin.

'For fuck's sake, it *can't* be Digger,' said Strike in frustration, running a hand through his dense, curly hair and leaving it entirely unchanged. 'He's a professional gangster! If he'd found out I gave evidence against him and wanted retribution he'd have bloody shot me. He wouldn't fanny about with severed legs and song lyrics, knowing it'd bring the police down on him. He's a businessman.'

'Does Wardle still think it's him?'

'Yeah,' said Strike, 'but he should know as well as anyone the procedures on anonymous evidence are watertight. You'd have coppers lying dead all over town if they weren't.'

He refrained from further criticism of Wardle, though it cost him an effort. The man was being considerate and helpful when he could be causing Strike difficulties. Strike had not forgotten that the last time he had tangled with the Met they had kept him in an interrogation room for five solid hours on what appeared to be the whim of resentful officers.

'What about the two men you knew in the army?' asked Robin, dropping her voice because a group of female office workers were settling themselves at a table nearby. 'Brockbank and Laing. Had either of them killed anyone? I mean,' she added, 'I know they were soldiers, but outside combat?'

'It wouldn't surprise me to hear Laing had done someone in,' said Strike, 'but he hadn't, as far as I know, before he went down. He used a knife on his ex-wife, I know that – tied her up and cut her. He spent a decade inside and I doubt they managed to rehabilitate him. He's been out over four years: plenty of time to commit murder.

'I haven't told you – I met his ex-mother-in-law in Melrose. She reckons he went to Gateshead when he got out of the nick and we know he might have been in Corby in 2008 . . . but,' said Strike, 'she also told me he was ill.'

'What kind of ill?'

'Some form of arthritis. She didn't know the details. Could an unfit man have done what we saw in those photos?' Strike picked up the menu. 'Right. I'm bloody starving and you haven't eaten anything except crisps for two days.'

When Strike had ordered pollock and chips and Robin a ploughman's, he made another conversational swerve.

'Did the victim look twenty-four to you?'

'I – I couldn't tell,' said Robin, trying and failing to block the image of the head with its smooth chubby cheeks, its frosted-white eyes. 'No,' she said, after a brief pause. 'I thought it – she – looked younger.'

'Me too.'

'I might . . . bathroom,' said Robin, standing up.

'You OK?'

'I just need a pee – too much tea.'

He watched her go, then finished his pint, following a train of thought he had not yet confided to Robin, or indeed anyone else.

The child's essay had been shown to him by a female investigator in Germany. Strike could still remember the last line, written in neat girlish handwriting on a sheet of pale pink paper.

> The lady changed her name to Anastassia and died her hair and nobody ever found out were she went, she vanished.

'Is that what you'd like to do, Brittany?' the investigator had asked quietly on the tape Strike had watched later. 'You'd like to run away and vanish?'

'It's just a story!' Brittany had insisted, trying for a scornful laugh, her little fingers twisting together, one leg almost wrapped around the other. Her thin blonde hair had hung lank around her pale, freckly face. Her spectacles had been wonky. She had reminded Strike of a yellow budgerigar. 'I only made it up!'

DNA testing would find out soon enough who the woman in the fridge had been, and then the police would trawl backwards to see who Oxana Voloshina – if that was her name – really was. Strike could not tell whether he was being paranoid or not in continuing to worry that the body belonged to Brittany Brockbank. Why had the name Kelsey been used on the first letter to him? Why did the head look so young, still smooth with puppy fat?

'I should be on Platinum by now,' said Robin sadly, checking her watch as she sat back down at the table. One of the office workers beside them seemed to be celebrating her birthday: with much raucous laughter from her colleagues she had just unwrapped a red and black basque.

'I wouldn't worry about it,' Strike said absently, as his fish and chips and Robin's ploughman's descended in front of them. He ate silently for a couple of minutes, then set down his knife and fork, pulled out his notebook, looked something up in the notes he had made back in Hardacre's Edinburgh office and picked up his phone. Robin watched him key in words, wondering what he was doing.

'Right,' said Strike, after reading the results, 'I'm going to Barrow-in-Furness tomorrow.'

'You're – what?' asked Robin, bewildered. 'Why?'

'Brockbank's there – or he's supposed to be.'

'How do you know?'

'I found out in Edinburgh that his pension's being sent there and I've just looked up the old family address. Someone called Holly Brockbank's living in the house now. Obviously a relative. She should know where he is. If I can establish that he's been in Cumbria for the last few weeks, we'll know he hasn't been delivering legs or stalking you in London, won't we?'

'What aren't you telling me about Brockbank?' Robin asked, her blue-grey eyes narrowing.

Strike ignored the question.

'I want you to stay at home while I'm out of town. Sod Two-Times, he's got only himself to blame if Platinum cops off with another punter. We can live without his money.'

'That'll leave us with a single client,' Robin pointed out.

'I've got a feeling we'll have none at all unless this nutter's caught,' said Strike. 'People aren't going to want to come near us.'

'How are you going to get to Barrow?' asked Robin.

A plan was dawning. Hadn't she foreseen this very eventuality?

'Train,' he said, 'you know I can't afford a hire car right now.'

'How about,' said Robin triumphantly, 'I drive you in my new – well, it's ancient, but it goes fine – Land Rover!'

'Since when have you had a Land Rover?'

'Since Sunday. It's my parents' old car.'

'Ah,' he said. 'Well, that sounds great—'

'But?'

'No, it'd be a real help—'

'*But?*' repeated Robin, who could tell that he had some reservations.

'I don't know how long I'll be up there.'

'That doesn't matter. You've just told me I'll be mouldering at home in any case.'

Strike hesitated. How much of her desire to drive him was rooted in the hope of wounding Matthew, he wondered. He could well imagine how the accountant would view an open-ended trip north, the two of them alone, staying overnight. A clean and professional relationship ought not to include using each other to make partners jealous.

'Oh shit,' he said suddenly, plunging his hand into his pocket for his mobile.

'What's the matter?' asked Robin, alarmed.

'I've just remembered – I was supposed to be meeting Elin last night. Fuck – totally forgot. Wait there.'

He walked out into the street, leaving Robin to her lunch. Why, she wondered, her eyes on Strike's large figure as he paced up and down outside the floor-to-ceiling windows, phone pressed to his ear, hadn't Elin called or texted to ask where Strike was? From there it was an easy step to wondering – for the first time, no matter what Strike had suspected – what Matthew was going to say if she returned home only to pick up the Land Rover and disappeared with several days' worth of clothes in a bag.

He can't complain, she thought, with a bold attempt at defiance. *It's nothing to do with him any more.*

Yet the thought of having to see Matthew, even briefly, was unnerving.

Strike returned, rolling his eyes.

'Doghouse,' he said succinctly. 'I'll meet her tonight instead.'

Robin did not know why the announcement that Strike was off to meet Elin should lower her spirits. She supposed that she was tired. The various strains and emotional shocks of the last thirty-six hours were not to be overcome in one pub lunch. The office workers nearby were now screeching with laughter as a pair of fluffy handcuffs fell out of another package.

It isn't her birthday, Robin realised. *She's getting married.*

'Well, am I driving you, or what?' she asked curtly.

'Yeah,' said Strike, who appeared to be warming to the idea (or was he merely cheered by the thought of his date with Elin?). 'You know what, that'd be great. Thanks.'

23

Moments of pleasure, in a world of pain.

Blue Öyster Cult, 'Make Rock Not War'

Mist lay in thick, soft layers like cobweb over the treetops of Regent's Park next morning. Strike, who had swiftly silenced his alarm so as not to wake Elin, stood balancing on his single foot at the window, the curtain behind him to block out the light. For a minute he looked out upon the ghostly park and was transfixed by the effect of the rising sun on leafy branches rising from the sea of vapour. You could find beauty nearly anywhere if you stopped to look for it, but the battle to get through the days made it easy to forget that this totally cost-free luxury existed. He carried memories like this from his childhood, especially those parts of it that he had spent in Cornwall: the glitter of the sea as you first saw it on a morning as blue as a butterfly's wing; the mysterious emerald-and-shadow world of the Gunnera Passage at Trebah Garden; distant white sails bobbing like seabirds on blustery gunmetal waves.

Behind him in the dark bed, Elin shifted and sighed. Strike moved carefully out from behind the curtain, took the prosthesis leaning against the wall and sat down on one of her bedroom chairs to attach it. Then, still moving as quietly as possible, he headed for the bathroom with the day's clothes in his arms.

They'd had their first row the previous evening: a landmark in every relationship. The total absence of communication when he failed to turn up for their date on Tuesday ought to have been a warning, but he had been too busy with Robin and a dismembered body to give it much thought. True, she had been frosty when he had phoned to apologise, but the fact that she had so readily agreed to a rescheduled date had not prepared him for a near-glacial reception when he had turned up in person twenty-four hours later. After a dinner eaten to the accompaniment of painful, stilted conversation he had offered to clear out and leave her to her resentment. She had become briefly angry as he reached for his coat, but it was the feeble spurt of a damp match; she had then crumbled into a tearful, semi-apologetic tirade in which he learned, firstly, that she was in therapy, secondly, that her therapist had identified a tendency towards passive aggression and, thirdly, that she had been so deeply wounded by his failure to turn up on Tuesday that she had drunk an entire bottle of wine alone in front of the television.

Strike had apologised again, offering in extenuation a difficult case, a tricky and unexpected development, expressing sincere remorse for having forgotten their date, but added that if she could not forgive, he had better clear out.

She had flung herself into his arms; they had gone straight to bed and had the best sex of their brief relationship.

Shaving in Elin's immaculate bathroom with its sunken lights and snow-white towels, Strike reflected that he had got off pretty lightly. If he had forgotten to turn up to a date with Charlotte, the woman with whom he had been involved, on and off, for sixteen years, he would have been carrying physical wounds right now, searching for her in the cold dawn, or perhaps trying to restrain her from throwing herself from the high balcony.

He had called what he felt for Charlotte love and it remained the most profound feeling he had had for any woman. In the pain it had caused him and its lasting after-effects it had more resembled a virus that, even now, he was not sure he had overcome. Not seeing her, never calling her, never using the new email address she had set up to show him her distraught face on the day of her wedding to an old boyfriend: this was his self-prescribed treatment, which was keeping the symptoms at bay. Yet he knew he had been left impaired, that he no longer had the capacity to feel in the way that he had once felt. Elin's distress of the previous evening had not touched him at his core in the way Charlotte's had once done. He felt as though his capacity for loving had been blunted, the nerve endings severed. He had not intended to wound Elin; he did not enjoy seeing her cry; yet the ability to feel empathetic pain seemed to have closed down. A small part of him, in truth, had been mentally planning his route home as she sobbed.

Strike dressed in the bathroom then moved quietly back into the dimly lit hall, where he'd stowed his shaving things in the holdall he had packed for Barrow-in-Furness. A door stood ajar to his right. On a whim, he pushed it wider.

The little girl whom he had never met slept here when not at her father's. The pink and white room was immaculate, with a ceiling mural of fairies around the cornice. Barbies sat in a neat line on a shelf, their smiles vacant, their pointy breasts covered in a rainbow of gaudy dresses. A fake-fur rug with a polar bear's head lay on the floor beside a tiny white four-poster.

Strike knew hardly any little girls. He had two godsons, neither of whom he had particularly wanted, and three nephews. His oldest friend back in Cornwall had daughters, but

Strike had virtually nothing to do with them; they rushed past him in a blur of ponytails and casual waves: 'Hi Uncle Corm, bye Uncle Corm.' He had grown up, of course, with a sister, although Lucy had never been indulged with sugar-pink-canopied four-posters, much as she might have wanted them.

Brittany Brockbank had had a cuddly lion. It came back to him suddenly, out of nowhere, looking at the polar bear on the floor: a cuddly lion with a comical face. She had dressed it in a pink tutu and it had been lying on the sofa when her stepfather came running at Strike, a broken beer bottle in his hand.

Strike turned back to the hall, feeling in his pocket. He always carried a notebook and pen on him. He scribbled a brief note to Elin, alluding to the best part of the previous night, and left it on the hall table so as not to risk waking her. Then, as quietly as he had done everything else, he hoisted his holdall onto his shoulder and let himself out of the flat. He was meeting Robin at West Ealing station at eight.

The last traces of mist were lifting from Hastings Road when Robin left her house, flustered and heavy-eyed, a carrier bag of food in one hand and a holdall full of clean clothes in the other. She unlocked the rear of the old grey Land Rover, swung the clothes into it and hurried around to the driver's seat with the food.

Matthew had just tried to hug her in the hall and she had forcibly resisted, two hands on his smooth warm chest, pushing him away, shouting at him to get off. He had been wearing only boxer shorts. Now she was afraid that he might be struggling into some clothes, ready to give chase. She slammed the car door and dragged on her seatbelt, eager to be gone, but as she turned the key in the ignition Matthew burst out of the house, barefoot, in T-shirt and tracksuit bottoms. She had never seen his expression so naked, so vulnerable.

'Robin,' he called as she stepped on the accelerator and pulled away from the kerb. 'I love you. *I love you!*'

She spun the wheel and moved precariously out of the parking space, missing their neighbour's Honda by inches. She could see Matthew shrinking in the rear-view mirror; he, whose self-possession was usually total, was proclaiming his love at the top of his voice, risking the neighbours' curiosity, their scorn and their laughter.

Robin's heart thumped painfully in her chest. A quarter past seven; Strike would not be at the station yet. She turned left at the end of the road, intent only on putting distance between herself and Matthew.

He had risen at dawn, while she was trying to pack without waking him.

'Where are you going?'

'To help Strike with the investigation.'

'You're going away overnight?'

'I expect so.'

'Where?'

'I don't know exactly.'

She was afraid to tell him their destination in case he came after them. Matthew's behaviour when she had arrived home the previous evening had left her shaken. He had cried and begged. She had never seen him like that, not even after his mother's death.

'Robin, we've got to talk.'

'We've talked enough.'

'Does your mother know where you're going?'

'Yes.'

She was lying. Robin had not told her mother about the ruptured engagement yet, nor that she was heading off north with Strike. After all, she was twenty-six; it was none of her mother's business. She knew, though, that Matthew was really asking whether she had told her mother that the wedding was off, because they were both aware that she would not have been getting in the Land Rover to drive off to an undisclosed location with Strike if their engagement had still been intact. The sapphire ring was lying exactly where she had left it, on a bookshelf loaded with his old accountancy textbooks.

'Oh shit,' Robin whispered, blinking away tears as she turned at random through the quiet streets, trying not to focus on her naked finger, or on the memory of Matthew's anguished face.

One short walk took Strike much further than simple physical distance. This, he thought as he smoked his first cigarette of the day, was London: you started in a quiet, symmetrical Nash terrace that resembled a sculpture in vanilla ice-cream. Elin's pin-striped Russian neighbour had been getting into his Audi, and Strike had received a curt nod in response to his 'Morning'. A short walk past the silhouettes of Sherlock Holmes at Baker Street station and he was sitting on a grimy Tube train surrounded by chattering Polish workmen, fresh and businesslike at 7 a.m. Then bustling Paddington, forcing a path through commuters and coffee shops, holdall over shoulder. Finally a few stops on the Heathrow Connect, accompanied by a large West Country family who were already dressed for Florida in spite of the early morning chill. They watched the station signs like nervous meerkats, their hands gripping their suitcase handles as though expecting an imminent mugging.

Strike arrived at West Ealing station fifteen minutes early and desperate for a cigarette. Dropping the holdall by his feet he lit up, hoping that Robin would not be too prompt, because he doubted that she would want him smoking in the Land Rover. He had only taken a couple of satisfying drags, however, when the box-like car rounded the corner, Robin's bright red-gold head clearly visible through the windscreen.

'I don't mind,' she called over the running engine as he hoisted his holdall back onto his shoulder and made to extinguish the cigarette, 'as long as you keep the window open.'

He climbed inside, shoved his bag into the back and slammed the door.

'You can't make it smell worse than it already does,' said Robin, managing the stiff gears with her usual expertise. 'It's pure dog in here.'

Strike pulled on a seatbelt as they accelerated away from the pavement, looking around at the interior of the car. Shabby and scuffed, a pungent fug of Wellington boot and Labrador certainly pervaded. It reminded Strike of military vehicles that he had driven across all terrains in Bosnia and Afghanistan, but at the same time it added something to his picture of Robin's background. This Land Rover spoke of muddy tracks and ploughed fields. He remembered her saying that an uncle had a farm.

'Did you ever have a pony?'

She glanced at him, surprised. In that fleeting full-face look he noted the heaviness of her eyes, her pallor. She had clearly not slept much.

'What on earth do you want to know that for?'

'This feels like the kind of car you'd take to the gymkhana.'

Her reply had a touch of defensiveness:

'Yes, I did.'

He laughed, pushing the window down as far as it would go and resting his left hand there with the cigarette.

'Why is that funny?'

'I don't know. What was it called?'

'Angus,' she said, turning left. 'He was a bugger. Always carting me off.'

'I don't trust horses,' said Strike, smoking.

'Have you ever been on one?'

It was Robin's turn to smile. She thought it might be one of the few places where she would see Strike truly discomforted, on the back of a horse.

'No,' said Strike. 'And I intend to keep it that way.'

'My uncle's got something that'd carry you,' said Robin. 'Clydesdale. It's massive.'

'Point taken,' said Strike drily, and she laughed.

Smoking in silence as she concentrated on navigating through the increasingly heavy morning traffic, Strike noted how much he liked making her laugh. He also recognised that he felt much happier, much more comfortable, sitting here in this ramshackle Land Rover talking inconsequential nonsense with Robin than he had felt last night at dinner with Elin.

He was not a man who told himself comfortable lies. He might have argued that Robin represented the ease of friendship; Elin, the pitfalls and pleasures of a sexual relationship. He knew that the truth was more complicated, and certainly made more so by the fact that the sapphire ring had vanished from Robin's finger. He had known, almost from the moment they had met, that Robin represented a threat to his peace of mind, but endangering the best working relationship of his life would be an act of wilful self-sabotage that he, after years of a destructive on-off relationship, after the hard graft and sacrifice that had gone into building his business, could not and would not let happen.

'Are you ignoring me on purpose?'

'What?'

It was just plausible that he had not heard her, so noisy was the old Land Rover's engine.

'I said, how are things with Elin?'

She had never asked him outright about a relationship

before. Strike supposed the confidences of two nights ago had moved them onto a different level of intimacy. He would have avoided this, if he could.

'All right,' he said repressively, throwing away his cigarette butt and pulling up the window, which marginally reduced the noise.

'She forgave you, then?'

'What for?'

'For completely forgetting that you had a date!' said Robin.

'Oh, that. Yeah. Well, no – then, yeah.'

As she turned onto the A40, Strike's ambiguous utterance brought to Robin a sudden, vivid mental image: of Strike, with his hairy bulk and his one and a half legs, entangled with Elin, blonde and alabaster against pure white sheets . . . she was sure that Elin's sheets would be white and Nordic and clean. She probably had somebody to do her laundry. Elin was too upper middle class, too wealthy, to iron her own duvet covers in front of the TV in a cramped sitting room in Ealing.

'How about Matthew?' Strike asked her as they moved out onto the motorway. 'How'd that go?'

'Fine,' said Robin.

'Bollocks,' said Strike.

Though another laugh escaped her, Robin was half inclined to resent his demand for more information when she was given so little about Elin.

'Well, he wants to get back together.'

'Course he does,' said Strike.

'Why "of course"?'

'If I'm not allowed to fish, you aren't.'

Robin was not sure what to say to that, though it gave her a small glow of pleasure. She thought it might be the very first time that Strike had ever given any indication that he saw her as a woman, and she silently filed away the exchange to pore over later, in solitude.

'He apologised and kept asking me to put my ring back on,' Robin said. Residual loyalty to Matthew prevented her mentioning the crying, the begging. 'But I . . .'

Her voice trailed away, and although Strike wanted to hear more, he asked no further questions, but pulled down the window and smoked another cigarette.

They stopped for a coffee at Hilton Park Services. Robin went to the bathroom while Strike queued for coffees in Burger King. In front of the mirror she checked her mobile. As she had expected, a message from Matthew was waiting, but the tone was no longer pleading and conciliatory.

> **If you sleep with him, we're over for good. You might think it'll make things even but it's not like for like. Sarah was a long time ago, we were kids and I didn't do it to hurt you. Think about what you're throwing away, Robin. I love you.**

'Sorry,' Robin muttered, moving aside to allow an impatient girl access to the hand-dryer.

She read Matthew's text again. A satisfying gush of anger obliterated the mingled pity and pain engendered by that morning's pursuit. Here, she thought, was the authentic Matthew: **if you sleep with him, we're over for good.** So he did not really believe that she had meant it when she took off her ring and told him she no longer wished to marry him? It would be over 'for good' only when he, Matthew, said so? **It's not like for like.** Her infidelity would be worse than his by definition. To him, her journey north was simply an exercise in retaliation: a dead woman and a killer loose mere pretext for feminine spite.

Screw you, she thought, ramming the mobile back into her

pocket as she returned to the café, where Strike sat eating a double Croissan'Wich with sausage and bacon.

Strike noted her flushed face, her tense jaw, and guessed that Matthew had been in touch.

'Everything all right?'

'Fine,' said Robin and then, before he could ask anything else, 'So are you going to tell me about Brockbank?'

The question came out a little more aggressively than she had intended. The tone of Matthew's text had riled her, as had the fact that it had raised in her mind the question of where she and Strike were actually going to sleep that night.

'If you want,' said Strike mildly.

He drew his phone out of his pocket, brought up the picture of Brockbank that he had taken from Hardacre's computer and passed it across the table to Robin.

Robin contemplated the long, swarthy face beneath its dense dark hair, which was unusual, but not unattractive. As though he had read her mind, Strike said:

'He's uglier now. That was taken when he'd just joined up. One of his eye sockets is caved in and he's got a cauliflower ear.'

'How tall is he?' asked Robin, remembering the courier standing over her in his leathers, his mirrored visor.

'My height or bigger.'

'You said you met him in the army?'

'Yep,' said Strike.

She thought for a few seconds that he was not going to tell her anything more, until she realised that he was merely waiting for an elderly couple, who were dithering about where to sit, to pass out of earshot. When they had gone Strike said:

'He was a major, Seventh Armoured Brigade. He married a dead colleague's widow. She had two small daughters. Then they had one of their own, a boy.'

The facts flowed, having just re-read Brockbank's file, but in truth Strike had never forgotten them. It had been one of those cases that stayed with you.

'The eldest stepdaughter was called Brittany. When she was twelve, Brittany disclosed sexual abuse to a school friend in Germany. The friend told her mother, who reported it. We were called in – I didn't interview her personally, that was a female officer. I just saw the tape.'

What had crucified him was how grown-up she had tried to be, how together. She was terrified of what would happen to the family now she had blabbed, and was trying to take it back.

No, of course she hadn't told Sophie that he had threatened to kill her little sister if she told on him! No, Sophie wasn't lying, exactly – it had been a joke, that was all. She'd asked Sophie how to stop yourself having a baby because – because she'd been curious, everyone wanted to know stuff like that. Of course he hadn't said he'd carve up her mum in little pieces if she told – the thing about her leg? Oh, that – well, that was a joke, too – it was all joking – he told her she had scars on her leg because he'd nearly cut her leg off when she was little, but her mum had walked in and seen him. He'd said he did it because she'd trodden on his flowerbeds when she was a toddler, but of course it was a joke – ask her mum. She'd got stuck in some barbed wire, that was all, and badly cut trying to pull herself free. They could ask her mum. He hadn't cut her. He'd never cut her, not Daddy.

The involuntary expression she had made when forcing herself to say 'Daddy' was with Strike still: she had looked like a child trying to swallow cold tripe, under threat of punishment. Twelve years old and she had learned life was only bearable for her family if she shut up and took whatever he wanted to do without complaint.

Strike had taken against Mrs Brockbank from their first

interview. She had been thin and over made-up, a victim, no doubt, in her way, but it seemed to Strike that she had voluntarily jettisoned Brittany to save the other two children, that she turned two blind eyes to the long absences from the house of her husband and eldest child, that her determination not to know was tantamount to collaboration. Brockbank had told Brittany that he would strangle both her mother and her sister if she ever spoke about what he did to her in the car when he took her on lengthy excursions into nearby woods, into dark alleyways. He would cut all of them up into little bits and bury them in the garden. Then he'd take Ryan – Brockbank's small son, the only family member whom he seemed to value – and go where no one would ever find them.

'It was a joke, just a joke. I didn't mean any of it.'

Thin fingers twisting, her glasses lopsided, her legs not long enough for her feet to reach the floor. She was still refusing point blank to be physically examined when Strike and Hardacre went to Brockbank's house to bring him in.

'He was pissed when we got there. I told him why we'd come and he came at me with a broken bottle.

'I knocked him out,' said Strike without bravado, 'but I shouldn't've touched him. I didn't need to.'

He had never admitted this out loud before, even though Hardacre (who had backed him to the hilt in the subsequent inquiry) had known it as well.

'If he came at you with a bottle—'

'I could've got the bottle off him without decking him.'

'You said he was big—'

'He was pretty pissed. I could've managed him without punching him. Hardacre was there, it was two on one.

'Truth is, I was glad he came at me. I wanted to punch him. Right hook, literally knocked him senseless – which is how he got away with it.'

'Got away with—'

'Got off,' said Strike. 'Got clean away.'

'How?'

Strike drank more coffee, his eyes unfocused, remembering.

'He was hospitalised after I hit him because he had a massive epileptic seizure when he came out of the concussion. Traumatic brain injury.'

'Oh God,' said Robin.

'He needed emergency surgery to stop the bleeding from his brain. He kept having fits. They diagnosed TBI, PTSD and alcoholism. Unfit to stand trial. Lawyers came stampeding in. I was put on an assault charge.

'Luckily, my legal team found out that, the weekend before I hit him, he'd played rugby. They dug around a bit and found out he'd taken a knee to the head from an eighteen-stone Welshman and been stretchered off the field. A junior medic had missed the bleeding from his ear because he was covered in mud and bruises, and just told him to go home and take it easy. As it turned out, they'd missed a basal skull fracture, which my legal team found out when they got doctors to look at the post-match X-ray. The skull fracture had been done by a Welsh forward, not me.

'Even so, if I hadn't had Hardy as a witness to the fact that he'd come at me with the bottle, I'd have been in it up to my neck. In the end, they accepted that I'd acted in self-defence. I couldn't have known his skull was already cracked, or how much damage I'd do by punching him.

'Meanwhile, they found child porn on his computer. Brittany's story tallied with frequent sightings of her being driven out, alone, by her stepfather. Her teacher was interviewed and said she was getting more and more withdrawn at school.

'Two years he'd been assaulting her and warning her he'd

kill her, her mother and her sister if she told anyone. He had her convinced that he'd already tried to cut her leg off once. She had scarring all around her shin. He'd told her he was just sawing it off when the mother came in and stopped him. In her interview, the mother said the scarring was from an accident when she was a toddler.'

Robin said nothing. Both hands were over her mouth and her eyes were wide. Strike's expression was frightening.

'He lay in hospital while they tried to get his fits under control, and whenever anyone tried to interview him he faked confusion and amnesia. He had lawyers swarming all over him, smelling a big fat payout: medical neglect, assault. He claimed he'd been a victim of abuse himself, that the child porn was just a symptom of his mental issues, his alcoholism. Brittany was insisting she'd made everything up, the mother was screaming to everyone that Brockbank had never laid a finger on any of the kids, that he was a perfect father, that she'd lost one husband and now she was going to lose another. Top brass just wanted the accusation to go away.

'He was invalided out,' said Strike, his dark eyes meeting Robin's blue-grey ones. 'He got off scot-free, with a payout and pension to boot, and off he went, Brittany in tow.'

24

Step into a world of strangers
Into a sea of unknowns . . .

Blue Öyster Cult, 'Hammer Back'

The rattling Land Rover devoured the miles with stoic competence, but the journey north had begun to seem interminably long before the first signs to Barrow-in-Furness appeared. The map had not adequately conveyed how far away the seaport was, how isolated. Barrow-in-Furness was not destined to be passed through, or visited incidentally; an end unto itself, it constituted a geographical cul-de-sac.

Through the southernmost reaches of the Lake District they travelled, past rolling fields of sheep, dry stone walls and picturesque hamlets that reminded Robin of her Yorkshire home, through Ulverston ('Birthplace of Stan Laurel'), until they achieved their first glimpse of a wide estuary that hinted at their approach to the coast. At last, past midday, they found themselves in an unlovely industrial estate, the road flanked by warehouses and factories, which marked the periphery of the town.

'We'll grab something to eat before we go to Brockbank's,' said Strike, who had been examining a map of Barrow for the past five minutes. He disdained using electronic devices to navigate on the basis that you did not need to wait for paper to download, nor did the information disappear under adverse conditions. 'There's a car park up here. Take a left at the roundabout.'

They passed a battered side entrance to Craven Park, home ground of the Barrow Raiders. Strike, whose eyes were peeled for a sighting of Brockbank, drank in the distinct character of the place. He had expected, Cornish-born as he was, to be able to see the sea, to taste it, but they might have been miles inland for all he could tell. The initial impression was of a gigantic out-of-town retail centre, where the garish façades of high-street outlets confronted them on all sides, except that here and there, standing proud and incongruous between the DIY stores and pizza restaurants, were architectural gems that spoke of a prosperous industrial past. The art deco customs house had been turned into a restaurant. A Victorian technical college embellished with classical figures bore the legend *Labor Omnia Vincit.* A little further and they came across rows and rows of terraced housing, the kind of cityscape Lowry painted, the hive where workers lived.

'Never seen so many pubs,' said Strike as Robin turned into the car park. He fancied a beer, but with *Labor Omnia Vincit* in mind, agreed to Robin's suggestion of a quick bite to eat in a nearby café.

The April day was bright, but the breeze carried with it a chill off the unseen sea.

'Not overselling themselves, are they?' he muttered as he saw the name of the café: The Last Resort. It stood opposite Second Chance, which sold old clothing, and a flourishing pawnbroker's. Notwithstanding its unpropitious name, The Last Resort was cosy and clean, full of chattering old ladies, and they returned to the car park feeling pleasantly well fed.

'His house won't be easy to watch if no one's home,' said Strike, showing Robin the map when they were back in the Land Rover. 'It's in a dead straight dead end. Nowhere to lurk.'

'Has it occurred to you,' said Robin, not entirely flippantly, as they drove away, 'that Holly *is* Noel? That he's had a sex change?'

'If he has, he'll be a cinch to find,' said Strike. 'Six foot eight in high heels, with a cauliflower ear. Take a right here,' he added as they passed a nightclub called Skint. 'Christ, they tell it like it is in Barrow, don't they?'

Ahead, a gigantic cream building with the name BAE SYSTEMS on it blocked any view of the seafront. The edifice was windowless and seemed to stretch a mile across, blank, faceless, intimidating.

'I think Holly's going to turn out to be a sister, or maybe a new wife,' said Strike. 'Hang a left . . . she's the same age as him. Right, we're looking for Stanley Road . . . we're going to end up right by BAE Systems, by the look of it.'

As Strike had said, Stanley Road ran in a straight line with houses on one side and a high brick wall topped with barbed wire on the other. Beyond this uncompromising barrier rose the strangely sinister factory building, white and windowless, intimidating in its sheer size.

'"Nuclear Site Boundary"?' Robin read from a sign on the wall, slowing the Land Rover to a crawl as they proceeded up the road.

'Building submarines,' said Strike, looking up at the barbed wire. 'Police warnings everywhere – look.'

The cul-de-sac was deserted. It terminated in a small parking area beside a children's play park. As she parked, Robin noticed a number of objects stuck in the barbed wire on top of the wall. The ball had undoubtedly landed there by accident, but there was also a small pink doll's pushchair, tangled up and irretrievable. The sight of it gave her an uncomfortable feeling: somebody had deliberately thrown that out of reach.

'What are you getting out for?' asked Strike, coming around the back of the vehicle.

'I was—'

'I'll deal with Brockbank, if he's in there,' said Strike, lighting up. 'You're not going anywhere near him.'

Robin got back into the Land Rover.

'Try not to punch him, won't you?' she muttered at Strike's retreating figure as he walked with a slight limp towards the house, his knee stiff from the journey.

Some of the houses had clean windows and ornaments neatly arranged behind the glass; others had net curtains in various states of cleanliness. A few were shabby and, on the evidence of grimy interior windowsills, dirty. Strike had almost reached a maroon door when he suddenly stopped in his tracks. Robin noticed that a group of men in blue overalls and hard hats had appeared at the end of the street. Was one of them Brockbank? Was that why Strike had stopped?

No. He was merely taking a phone call. Turning his back on both the door and the men, he moved slowly back towards Robin, his stride no longer purposeful but with the aimless ramble of a man intent only on the voice in his ear.

One of the men in the overalls was tall, dark and bearded. Had Strike seen him? Robin slipped out of the Land Rover again and, on pretext of texting, took several photographs of the workmen, zooming in on them as closely as she could. They turned a corner and walked out of sight.

Strike had paused ten yards away from her, smoking and listening to the person talking on his mobile. A grey-haired woman was squinting at the pair of them from an upstairs window of the nearest house. Thinking to allay her suspicions, Robin turned away from the houses and took a picture of the huge nuclear facility, playing the tourist.

'That was Wardle,' said Strike, coming up behind her. He looked grim. 'The body isn't Oxana Voloshina's.'

'How do they know?' asked Robin, stunned.

'Oxana's been home in Donetsk for three weeks. Family wedding – they haven't spoken to her personally, but they've talked to her mother on the phone and she says Oxana's there. Meanwhile, the landlady's recovered enough to tell police that she was especially shocked when she found the body because she thought Oxana had gone back to Ukraine for a holiday. She also mentioned that the head didn't look very like her.'

Strike slid his phone back into his pocket, frowning. He hoped this news would focus Wardle's mind on someone other than Malley.

'Get back in the car,' said Strike, lost in thought, and he set off towards Brockbank's house again.

Robin returned to the driver's seat of the Land Rover. The woman in the upper window was still staring.

Two policewomen in high-visibility tabards came walking down the street. Strike had reached the maroon door. The rap of metal on wood echoed down the street. Nobody answered. Strike was preparing to knock again when the policewomen reached him.

Robin sat up, wondering what on earth the police wanted with him. After a brief conversation all three of them turned and headed towards the Land Rover.

Robin pushed down the window, feeling suddenly and unaccountably guilty.

'They want to know,' Strike called, when within earshot, 'whether I'm Mr Michael Ellacott.'

'What?' said Robin, completely confused by the mention of her father's name.

The ludicrous thought came to her that Matthew had sent the police after them – but why would he have told them that Strike was her father? And then the realisation came to her, voiced as soon as understood.

'The car's registered in Dad's name,' she said. 'Have I done something wrong?'

'Well, you're parked on a double yellow line,' said one of the policewomen drily, 'but that's not why we're here. You've been taking photographs of the facility. It's all right,' she added, as Robin looked panicked. 'People do it every day. You were caught on the security cameras. Can I see your driving licence?'

'Oh,' said Robin weakly, aware of Strike's quizzical look. 'I only – I thought it would make an arty picture, you know? The barbed wire and the white building and – and the clouds . . .'

She handed over her documentation, studiously avoiding Strike's eye, mortified.

'Mr Ellacott's your father, is he?'

'He lent us the car, that's all,' said Robin, dreading the idea of the police contacting her parents and them finding out that she was in Barrow, without Matthew, ring-less and single . . .

'And where do you two live?'

'We don't – not together,' said Robin.

They gave their names and addresses.

'You're visiting someone, are you, Mr Strike?' asked the second policewoman.

'Noel Brockbank,' said Strike promptly. 'Old friend. Passing, thought I'd look him up.'

'Brockbank,' repeated the policewoman, handing Robin her licence, and Robin hoped that the woman might know him, which would surely go a long way to repairing her gaffe. 'Good Barrovian surname, that. All right, on you go. No more photos round here.'

'I'm. So. Sorry,' Robin mouthed at Strike as the policewomen walked away. He shook his head, grinning through his annoyance.

'"Arty photo"... the wire ... the sky ...'

'What would you have said?' she demanded. 'I could hardly tell them I was taking pictures of workmen because I thought one of them might be Brockbank – look—'

But when she brought up the picture of the workmen she realised that the tallest of them, with his ruddy cheeks, short neck and large ears, was not the man they sought.

The door of the nearest house opened. The grey-haired woman who had been watching from the upper window appeared, pulling a tartan shopping trolley. Her expression was now cheery. Robin was sure that the woman had observed the police arrive and depart, and was satisfied that they were not spies.

'It's always 'appening,' she called loudly, her voice ringing across the street. She pronounced 'always' 'orlwuz'. The accent was unfamiliar to Robin, who had thought she knew Cumbrian, hailing from the next county. 'They've gor camеraz orl awwer. Teeking registrations. We're orl used to it.'

'Spot the Londoners,' said Strike pleasantly, which made her pause, curious.

'From London? Wha' brings th'all the way to Barra?'

'Looking for an old friend. Noel Brockbank,' said Strike, pointing down the street, 'but there's no answer at his house. He'll be at work, I expect.'

She frowned a little.

'Noel, did th'say? Not Holly?'

'We'd love to see Holly, if she's around,' said Strike.

'She'll be at work noo,' said the neighbour, checking her watch. 'Bak'ry awwer in Vickerstown. Or,' said the woman, with a trace of grim humour, 'tha can try the Crow's Nest tonight. She's usually there.'

'We'll try the bakery – surprise her,' said Strike. 'Where is it exactly?'

'Little white one, just up the road from Vengeance Street.'

They thanked her and she set off along the road, pleased to have been helpful.

'Did I hear that right?' Strike muttered, shaking open his map once they were safely back in the Land Rover. '"Vengeance Street"?'

'That's what it sounded like,' said Robin.

The short journey took them across a bridge spanning the estuary, where sailing boats bobbed on dirty-looking water or sat marooned on mudflats. Utilitarian, industrial buildings along the shore gave way to more streets of terraced houses, some pebble-dashed, some of red brick.

'Ships' names,' guessed Strike as they drove up Amphitrite Street.

Vengeance Street ran up a hill. A few minutes' exploration of its vicinities revealed a little white-painted bakery.

'That's her,' said Strike at once, as Robin pulled in with a clear view of the glass door. 'Got to be his sister, look at her.'

The bakery worker looked, thought Robin, harder than most men. She had the same long face and high forehead as Brockbank; her flinty eyes were outlined in thick kohl, her jet-black hair scraped back into a tight, unflattering ponytail. The cap-sleeved black T-shirt, worn under a white apron, revealed thick bare arms that were covered in tattoos from shoulder to wrist. Multiple gold hoops hung from each ear. A vertical frown line between her eyebrows gave her a look of perpetual bad temper.

The bakery was cramped and busy. Watching Holly bag up pasties, Strike remembered his venison pies from Melrose and his mouth watered.

'I could eat again.'

'You can't talk to her in there,' said Robin. 'We'd do better to approach her at home, or in the pub.'

'You could nip in and get me a pasty.'

'We had rolls less than an hour ago!'

'So? I'm not on a bloody diet.'

'Nor am I, any more,' said Robin.

The brave words brought to mind the strapless wedding dress still waiting for her in Harrogate. Did she really not intend to fit into it? The flowers, the catering, the bridesmaids, the choice of first dance – would none of it be needed any more? Deposits lost, presents returned, the faces of stunned friends and relatives when she told them . . .

The Land Rover was chilly and uncomfortable, she was very tired after hours of driving and for a few seconds – the time it took for a weak, treacherous lurch of her heart – the thought of Matthew and Sarah Shadlock made her want to cry all over again.

'D'you mind if I smoke?' said Strike, pushing down the window and letting in the cold air without waiting for an answer. Robin swallowed an affirmative answer; he had forgiven her for the police, after all. Somehow the chilly breeze helped brace her for what she needed to tell him.

'You can't interview Holly.'

He turned to her, frowning.

'Taking Brockbank by surprise is one thing, but if Holly recognises you she'll warn him you're after him. I'll have to do it. I've thought of a way.'

'Yeah – that's not going to happen,' said Strike flatly. 'Odds are he's either living with her or a couple of streets away. He's a nutcase. If he smells a rat he'll turn nasty. You're not doing it alone.'

Robin drew her coat more tightly around her and said coolly:

'D'you want to hear my idea or not?'

25

There's a time for discussion and a time for a fight.

Blue Öyster Cult, 'Madness to the Method'

Strike didn't like it, but he was forced to concede that Robin's plan was a good one and that the danger of Holly tipping off Noel outweighed the probable risk to Robin. Accordingly, when Holly left work with a colleague at five o'clock, she was followed on foot by Strike, although unaware of his presence. Robin, meanwhile, drove to a deserted stretch of road beside a wide stretch of marshy wasteland, retrieved her holdall from the back of the car, wriggled out of her jeans and dragged on a smarter, though creased, pair of trousers.

She was driving back across the bridge towards central Barrow when Strike called to inform her that Holly had not returned home, but headed straight to the pub at the end of her street.

'Great, I think that'll be easier anyway,' shouted Robin in the direction of her mobile, which was lying on the front passenger seat, set to speakerphone. The Land Rover vibrated and rattled around her.

'What?'

'I said, I think – never mind, I'm nearly there!'

Strike was waiting outside the Crow's Nest car park. He had just opened the passenger door when Robin gasped:

'Get down, get down!'

Holly had appeared in the doorway of the pub, pint in hand. She was taller than Robin and twice as broad in her black cap-sleeved T-shirt and jeans. Lighting a cigarette, she squinted around at what must have been a view she knew by heart, and her narrowed eyes rested briefly on the unfamiliar Land Rover.

Strike had scrambled into the front seat as best he could, keeping his head low. Robin put her foot down and drove away at once.

'She didn't give me a second look when I was following her,' Strike pointed out, hoisting himself into a sitting position.

'You still shouldn't let her see you if you can help it,' said Robin sententiously, 'in case she noticed you and it reminds her.'

'Sorry, forgot you're Highly Commended,' said Strike.

'Oh sod off,' said Robin with a flash of temper. Strike was surprised.

'I was joking.'

Robin turned into a parking space further up the street, out of sight of the Crow's Nest entrance, then checked her handbag for a small package she had bought earlier in the afternoon.

'You wait here.'

'The hell I will. I'll be in the car park, keeping an eye out for Brockbank. Give me the keys.'

She handed them over with ill grace and left. Strike watched her walking towards the pub, wondering about that sudden spurt of temper. Perhaps, he thought, Matthew belittled what he probably saw as meagre achievements.

The Crow's Nest stood where Ferry and Stanley Roads met and formed a hairpin bend: a large, drum-shaped building of red brick. Holly was still standing in the doorway, smoking and drinking her pint. Nerves fluttered in the pit of Robin's stomach. She had volunteered for this: now hers was the sole responsibility for finding out where Brockbank was. Her stupidity at bringing the police down on them earlier had made her touchy, and Strike's ill-timed humour had reminded her of Matthew's subtly belittling comments about her counter-surveillance training. After formal congratulations on her top marks Matthew had implied that what she had learned was, after all, no more than common sense.

Robin's mobile rang in her coat pocket. Aware of Holly's eyes on her as she approached, Robin pulled out the phone to check the caller's name. It was her mother. On the basis that it would look slightly more unusual to switch off the call than to take it, she raised it to her ear.

'Robin?' came Linda's voice as Robin passed Holly in the doorway without looking at her. 'Are you in Barrow-in-Furness?'

'Yes,' said Robin. Confronted by two inner doors, she chose the one on the left, which brought her into a large, high-ceilinged and dingy bar room. Two men in the now-familiar blue overalls were playing pool at a table just inside the door. Robin sensed, rather than saw, the turning of several heads towards the stranger. Avoiding all eye contact, she drifted towards the bar as she continued her call.

'What are you doing there?' asked Linda and, without waiting for a response, 'We've had the police on the phone, checking whether Dad lent you the car!'

'It was all a misunderstanding,' said Robin. 'Mum, I can't really talk now.'

The door opened behind her and Holly walked past, thickly tattooed arms folded, giving Robin a sideways look of appraisal and, she sensed, animosity. Apart from the short-haired barmaid, they were the only two females in the place.

'We called the flat,' her mother went on, unheeding, 'and Matthew said you'd gone away with Cormoran.'

'Yes,' said Robin.

'And when I asked whether you'd have time to drop round for lunch this weekend—'

'Why would I be in Masham this weekend?' Robin asked, confused. Out of the corner of her eye she saw Holly taking a bar stool and chatting to several more blue-overalled men from the BAE factory.

'It's Matthew's dad's birthday,' said her mother.

'Oh, of course it is,' said Robin. She had completely forgotten. There was to be a party. It had been on the calendar so long that she had got used to the sight of it and forgotten that the trip back to Masham was actually going to happen.

'Robin, is everything all right?'

'Like I said, Mum, I can't really talk right now,' said Robin.

'*Are you all right?*'

'Yes!' said Robin impatiently. 'I'm absolutely fine. I'll ring you later.'

She hung up and turned to the bar. The barmaid, who was waiting to take her order, wore the same look of shrewd appraisal as the watching neighbour in Stanley Road. There was an extra layer to their caginess around here, but Robin understood, now, that theirs was not the chauvinistic antagonism of the local for the stranger. Rather, it was the protectiveness of a people whose business was confidential. With her heart beating slightly faster than usual, Robin said with an air of forced confidence:

'Hi, I don't know whether you can help me. I'm looking for Holly Brockbank. I was told she might be in here.'

The barmaid considered Robin's request, then said, unsmiling:

'Tha's 'er, down the bar. Can A get th'somethin'?'

'Glass of white wine, please,' said Robin.

The woman whom she was impersonating would drink wine, Robin knew. She would also be unfazed by the edge of mistrust she saw in the barmaid's eyes, by Holly's reflexive antagonism, by the up-and-down stares of the pool players. The woman whom she was pretending to be was cool, clear-headed and ambitious.

Robin paid for her drink then headed directly for Holly and the three men chatting to her at the bar. Curious but cagey, they fell silent when it became clear that they were Robin's destination.

'Hello,' said Robin, smiling. 'Are you Holly Brockbank?'

'Yeah,' said Holly, her expression grim. 'Whee're thoo?'

'Sorry?'

Aware of several pairs of amused eyes on her, Robin kept her smile in place by sheer force of will.

'Who – are – yew?' asked Holly, in a mock London accent.

'My name's Venetia Hall.'

'Ooh, unlucky,' said Holly with a broad grin at the closest workman, who sniggered.

Robin pulled a business card out of her handbag, freshly printed that afternoon on a machine in a shopping centre, while Strike remained behind, keeping an eye on Holly in the bakery. It had been Strike's suggestion that she use her middle name. ('Makes you sound like a poncy southerner.')

Robin handed over the business card, looked boldly into Holly's heavily kohled eyes and repeated: 'Venetia Hall. I'm a lawyer.'

Holly's grin evaporated. Scowling, she read the card, one of two hundred Robin had had printed for £4.50.

Hardacre and Hall
PERSONAL INJURY LAWYERS
Venetia Hall
Senior Partner
Tel: 0888 789654
Fax: 0888 465877 Email: venetia@h&hlegal.co.uk

'I'm looking for your brother Noel,' said Robin. 'We—'

''Ow did thoo know A was 'ere?'

In her mistrust she seemed to be swelling, bristling like a cat.

'A neighbour said you might be.'

Holly's blue-overalled companions smirked.

'We might have some good news for your brother,' Robin ploughed on bravely. 'We're trying to find him.'

'A dunno where 'e is and A don' care.'

Two of the workmen slid away from the bar towards a table, leaving only one behind, who smiled faintly as he observed Robin's discomfiture. Holly drained her pint, slid a fiver sideways at the remaining man and told him to get her another, clambered off her barstool and strode away towards the Ladies, her arms held stiffly like a man's.

''Er boyo an' 'er don' speak,' said the barmaid, who had drifted up the bar to eavesdrop. She seemed to feel vaguely sorry for Robin.

'I don't suppose *you* know where Noel is?' Robin asked, feeling desperate.

''E's not been in 'ere for a year or more,' said the barmaid vaguely. 'You know where 'e is, Kev?'

Holly's friend answered only with a shrug and ordered Holly's pint. His accent revealed him to be Glaswegian.

'Well, it's a pity,' said Robin, and her clear, cool voice did not betray the frantic pounding of her heart. She dreaded going back to Strike with nothing. 'There could be a big payout for the family, if only I can find him.'

She turned to go.

'For the family, or for him?' asked the Glaswegian sharply.

'It depends,' said Robin coolly, turning back. She did not imagine that Venetia Hall would be particularly chummy with people unconnected to the case she was building. 'If family members have had to take on a carer role – but I'd need details to judge. Some relatives,' lied Robin, 'have had very significant compensation.'

Holly was coming back. Her expression turned thunderous when she saw Robin talking to Kevin. Robin walked off to the Ladies herself, her heart pounding in her chest, wondering whether the lie she had just told would bear fruit. By the look on Holly's face as they passed each other, Robin thought there was an outside chance that she might be cornered by the sinks and beaten up.

However, when she came out of the bathroom she saw Holly and Kevin nose to nose at the bar. Robin knew not to push any harder: either Holly bit, or she did not. She tied her coat belt more tightly and walked, unhurriedly but purposefully, back past them towards the door.

'Oi!'

'Yes?' Robin said, still a little coolly, because Holly had been rude and Venetia Hall was used to a certain level of respect.

'Orlrigh', wha's it all abou'?'

Though Kevin seemed keen to participate in their conversation, his relationship with Holly was apparently not far enough advanced to permit listening in on private financial matters. He drifted away to a fruit machine looking disgruntled.

'We can yatter over 'ere,' Holly told Robin, taking her fresh pint and pointing Robin to a corner table beside a piano.

The pub's windowsill bore ships in bottles: pretty, fragile things compared to the huge, sleek monsters that were being constructed beyond the windows, behind that high perimeter wall. The heavily patterned carpet would conceal a thousand stains; the plants behind the curtains looked droopy and sad, yet the mismatched ornaments and sporting trophies gave a homey feel to the large room, the bright blue overalls of its customers an impression of brotherhood.

'Hardacre and Hall is representing a large group of servicemen who suffered serious and preventable injury outside the field of combat,' said Robin, sliding into her pre-rehearsed spiel. 'While we were reviewing records we came across your brother's case. We can't be sure until we talk to him, of course, but he'd be very welcome to add his name to our pool of litigants. His would be very much the type of case we're expecting to win. If he joins us, it'll add to the pressure on the army to pay. The more complainants we can get, the better. It would be at no cost to Mr Brockbank, of course. No win,' she said, mimicking the TV adverts, 'no fee.'

Holly said nothing. Her pale face was hard and set. There were cheap rings of yellow gold on every digit except her wedding-ring finger.

'Kevin said summa' abou' the family gettin' money.'

'Oh yes,' said Robin blithely. 'If Noel's injuries have impacted you, as a family—'

'Ower righ' they 'ave,' snarled Holly.

'How?' asked Robin, taking a notebook out of her shoulder bag and waiting, pencil poised.

She could tell that alcohol and a sense of grievance were going to be her greatest allies in extracting maximum information from Holly, who was now warming to the idea of telling the story she thought the lawyer wanted to hear.

The first thing to be done was to soften that first impression of animosity towards her injured brother. Carefully she took Robin over Noel joining the army at sixteen. He had given it everything: it had been his life. Oh yeah, people didn't realise the sacrifices soldiers made . . . did Robin know Noel was her twin? Yeah, born on Christmas Day . . . Noel and Holly . . .

To tell this bowdlerised story of her brother was to elevate herself. The man with whom she had shared a womb had sallied forth into the world, travelled and fought and been promoted through the ranks of the British Army. His bravery and sense of adventure reflected back on her, left behind in Barrow.

'. . . 'n 'e married a woman called Irene. Widow. Took 'er on with two kids. Jesus. No good turn goes unpunished, don't they say?'

'What do you mean?' asked Venetia Hall politely, clasping half an inch of warm vinegary wine.

'Married 'er, 'ad a son with 'er. Lovely little boy . . . Ryan . . . Lovely. We've not seen him for . . . six years, is it? Seven years? Bitch. Yeah, Irene jus' fucked off when 'e was at the doctor's one day. Took the kids – and his son was everything to Noel, mind. Everything – so much for in sickness and in fuckin' health, eh? Some fuckin' wife. When 'e needed support most. Bitch.'

So Noel and Brittany had long since parted company. Or had he made it his business to track down the stepdaughter whom he surely blamed as much as Strike for his life-changing injuries? Robin maintained an impassive expression, although her heart was racing. She wished she could text Strike right there and then.

After his wife had left, Noel had turned up uninvited at the old family home, the tiny two up, two down on Stanley Road in which Holly had lived all her life and which she had occupied alone since her stepfather had died.

'A took 'im in,' said Holly, straightening her back. 'Family's family.'

There was no mention of Brittany's allegation. Holly was playing the concerned relative, the devoted sister, and if it was a ham performance Robin was experienced enough, now, to know that there were usually nuggets of truth to be sifted from even the most obvious dross.

She wondered whether Holly knew about the accusation of child abuse: it had happened in Germany, after all, and no charges had been brought. Yet if Brockbank had been truly brain damaged on his discharge, would he have been canny enough to remain silent about the reason for his ignominious exit from the army? If he had been innocent and not of sound mind, wouldn't he have talked, perhaps endlessly, of the injustice that had brought him to such a low ebb?

Robin bought Holly a third pint and turned her deftly to the subject of what Noel had been like after he had been invalided out.

''E wasn' 'imself. Fits. Seizures. 'E was on a load o' medication. I jus' go'rover nursin' my stepfather – 'e 'ad a stroke – an' then A gets Noel comin' 'ome, with 'is convulsions and . . .'

Holly buried the end of her sentence in her pint.

'That's tough,' said Robin, who was now writing in the small notebook. 'Any behavioural difficulties? Families often mention those kinds of challenges as the worst.'

'Yeah,' said Holly. 'Well. 'Is temper wasn' improved by gettin' 'is brain knocked outta his skull for 'im. 'E smashed up the 'ouse for us twice. 'E was orlwuz ragin' at us.

''E's famous now, tha knows,' said Holly darkly.

'Sorry?' said Robin, thrown.

'The gadgee that beat 'im up!'

'The gadg—'

'Cameron fuckin' Strike!'

'Ah, yes,' said Robin. 'I think I've heard of him.'

'Oh yeah! Fuckin' private detective now, in orl the papers! Fuckin' military policeman when 'e beat the shit outta Noel . . . fuckin' damaged him for fuckin' life . . . '

The rant went on for some time. Robin made notes, waiting for Holly to tell her why the military police had come for her brother, but she either did not know or was determined not to say. All that was certain was that Noel Brockbank had attributed his epilepsy entirely to the actions of Strike.

After what sounded like a year of purgatory, during which Noel had treated both his twin sister and her house as convenient outlets for his misery and his temper, he left for a bouncer's job in Manchester obtained for him by an old Barrovian friend.

'He was well enough to work, then?' asked Robin, because the picture Holly had painted was of a man totally out of control, barely able to contain explosions of temper.

'Yeah, well, 'e was orlrigh' by then as long as 'e didn't drink and took his meds. A were glad to see the back of 'im. Took it outta me, 'avin' 'im 'ere,' said Holly, suddenly remembering that there was a payout promised to those whose lives had been badly affected by their relative's injuries. 'I 'ad panic attacks. Wen' to my GP. It's in my records.'

The full impact of Brockbank's bad behaviour on Holly's life filled the next ten minutes, Robin nodding seriously and sympathetically and interjecting encouraging phrases such as 'Yes, I've heard that from other relatives,' and 'Oh yes, that would be very valuable in a submission.' Robin offered the now-tractable Holly a fourth pint.

'A'll ge' you one,' said Holly, with a vague show of getting to her feet.

'No, no, this is all on expenses,' said Robin. As she waited for the fresh pint of McEwan's to be poured, she checked her mobile. There was another text from Matthew, which she did not open, and one from Strike, which she did.

All OK?

Yes, she texted back.

'So your brother's in Manchester?' she asked Holly on her return to the table.

'No,' said Holly, after taking a large swig of McEwan's. ''E was sacked.'

'Oh, really?' said Robin, pencil poised. 'If it was as a result of his medical condition, you know, we can help with an unfair dismissal—'

'It weren't coz of tha',' said Holly.

A strange expression crossed the tight, sullen face: a flash of silver between storm clouds, of something powerful trying to break through.

''E come back 'ere,' said Holly, 'an' it all started again—'

More stories of violence, irrational rages, broken furniture, at the end of which Brockbank had secured another job, vaguely described as 'security', and taken off for Market Harborough.

'An' then he come back again,' said Holly, and Robin's pulse quickened.

'So he's here in Barrow?' she asked.

'No,' said Holly. She was drunk now and finding it harder to retain a hold on the line she was supposed to be peddling. ''E jus' come back for a coupla weeks but this time A told him A'd 'ave the police on 'im if 'e come back again an' 'e lef' f'r good. Need a slash,' said Holly, 'an' a fag. D'you smoke?'

Robin shook her head. Holly got a little unsteadily to her feet and proceeded to the Ladies, leaving Robin to pull her mobile out of her pocket and text Strike.

Says he's not in Barrow, not with family. She's drunk. Still working on her. She's about to go outside for a cig, lie low.

She regretted the last two words as soon as she had pressed 'send', in case they elicited another sarcastic reference to her counter-surveillance course, but her phone buzzed almost immediately and she saw two words:

Will do.

When Holly finally returned to the table, smelling strongly of Rothmans, she was carrying a white wine, which she slid across to Robin, and her fifth pint.

'Thanks very much,' said Robin.

'See,' said Holly plaintively, as though there had been no break in the conversation, 'it was havin' a real impact on me 'ealth, 'aving 'im 'ere.'

'I'm sure,' said Robin. 'So does Mr Brockbank live—?'

''E was violent. A told you abou' the time he shoved me head into the fridge door.'

'You did, yes,' said Robin patiently.

'An' 'e blacked me eye when A tried to stop him smashing up me mam's plates—'

'Awful. You'd certainly be in line for some kind of payout,' lied Robin and, ignoring a tiny qualm of guilt, she plunged straight towards the central question. 'We assumed Mr Brockbank was here in Barrow because this is where his pension's being paid.'

Holly's reactions were slower after four and a half pints. The promise of compensation for her suffering had given her a glow: even the deep line that life had graven between her eyebrows, and which gave her a look of permanent fury, seemed to have diminished. However, the mention of Brockbank's pension turned her muzzily defensive.

'No, it's not,' said Holly.

'According to our records, it is,' said Robin.

The fruit machine played a synthetic jingle and flashed in the corner; the pool balls clicked and thudded off the baize; Barrovian accents mingled with Scots. Robin's flash of intuition came to her like certain knowledge. Holly was helping herself to the military pension.

'Of course,' said Robin, with a convincing lightness, 'we know Mr Brockbank might not be picking it up for himself. Relatives are sometimes authorised to collect money when the pensioner is incapacitated.'

'Yeah,' said Holly at once. A blush was creeping blotchily up her pale face. It made her look girlish, notwithstanding the tattoos and multiple piercings. 'A collected it for 'im when 'e was first out. When 'e was 'avin' fits.'

Why, thought Robin, *if he was so incapacitated, did he transfer the pension to Manchester, and then to Market Harborough, and then back to Barrow again?*

'So are you sending it on to him now?' asked Robin, her heart beating fast again. 'Or can he pick it up for himself now?'

'Lissen,' said Holly.

There was a Hell's Angels tattoo on her upper arm, a wing-helmeted skull that rippled as she leaned in towards Robin. Beer, cigarettes and sugar had turned her breath rancid. Robin did not flinch.

'Lissen,' she said again, 'you get people payouts, like, if they've been . . . if they've been hurt, like, or . . . wharrever.'

'That's right,' said Robin.

'Wharriff someone'd been . . . wharriff social services shoulda . . . shoulda done somethin' an' they never?'

'It would depend on the circumstances,' said Robin.

'Our mam lef' when we was nine,' said Holly. 'Lef' us with oor stepfather.'

'I'm sorry,' said Robin. 'That's tough.'

'Nineteen-seventies,' said Holly. 'Nobody gave a shit. Child abuse.'

A lead weight dropped inside Robin. Holly's bad breath was in her face, her mottled face close. She had no idea that the sympathetic lawyer who had approached her with the promise of sacks of free cash was only a mirage.

''E done it to both of us,' said Holly. 'Me step. Noel gorrit an' all. From when we wuz tiny. We useter hide under ower beds together. An' then Noel did it to me. Mind,' she said, suddenly earnest, ''e could be orlright, Noel. We wuz close and tha' when we wuz little. Anyway,' her tone revealed a sense of double betrayal, 'when 'e wor sixteen, he lef' us to join the army.'

Robin, who had not meant to drink any more, picked up her wine and took a large slug. Holly's second abuser had also been her ally against her first: the lesser of two evils.

'Bastard, he wor,' she said, and Robin could tell she meant the stepfather, not the twin who had abused her then disappeared abroad. 'He had an accident at work when A was sixteen, though, an' after tha' A could manage 'im better. Industrial chemicals. Fucker. Couldn't get it up after that. On so many painkillers an' shit. An' then 'e 'ad his stroke.'

The look of determined malice on Holly's face told Robin exactly what kind of care the stepfather might have received at her hands.

'Fucker,' she said quietly.

'Have you received counselling at all?' Robin heard herself ask.

I do *sound like a poncy southerner.*

Holly snorted.

'Fuck, no. You're the firs' person A've ever told. S'pose you've heard a lot of stories like this?'

'Oh, yes,' said Robin. She owed Holly that.

'A told Noel, last time 'e come back,' said Holly, five pints to the bad now and slurring her words badly, 'fuck off an' stay away from us. You leave or A'm going to the p'lice about what you did to us before, an' see what they think o' that, after all these little girls keep sayin' you've fiddled with 'em.'

The phrase turned the warm wine rancid in Robin's mouth.

'Tha's 'ow he lost the job in Manchester. Groped a thirteen-year-ould. Prob'bly the same in Market 'Arborough. 'E wouldn' tell me why 'e was back, but A know 'e'll've done summat like that again. 'E learned from the best,' said Holly. 'So, could A sue?'

'I think,' said Robin, fearful of giving advice that would cause further damage to the wounded woman beside her, 'that the police would probably be your best bet. Where *is* your brother?' she asked, desperate, now, to extract the information she wanted and leave.

'Dunno,' said Holly. 'When A told 'im A'd go to the p'lice 'e wen' beserk, bu' then . . .'

She mumbled something indistinct, something in which the word 'pension' was just audible.

He told her she could keep the pension if she didn't go to the police.

So there she sat, drinking herself into an early grave with the money her brother had given her not to reveal his abuse. Holly knew he was almost certainly still 'fiddling' with other young girls . . . had she ever known about Brittany's accusation? Did she care? Or had the scar tissue grown so thick over her own wounds that it rendered her impervious to other little girls' agony? She was still living in the house where it had all happened, with the front windows facing out on barbed wire and bricks . . . why hadn't she run, Robin wondered. Why hadn't she escaped, like Noel? Why stay in the house facing the high, blank wall?

'You haven't got a number for him, or anything like that?' Robin asked.

'No,' said Holly.

'There could be big money in this if you can find me any kind of contact,' said Robin desperately, throwing finesse to the wind.

''S'old place,' Holly slurred, after a few minutes' muddled thought and fruitless staring at her phone, ''n Market 'Arborough . . .'

It took a long time to locate the telephone number of Noel's last place of work, but at last they found it. Robin made a note, then dug ten pounds out of her own purse and thrust it into Holly's willing hand.

'You've been very helpful. Very helpful indeed.'

'It's jus' gadgees, isn't i'? All th'same.'

'Yes,' said Robin, without a clue what she was agreeing to. 'I'll be in touch. I've got your address.'

She stood up.

'Yeah. See thoo. Jus' gadgees. All th'same.'

'She means men,' said the barmaid, who had come over to collect some of Holly's many empty glasses, and was smiling at Robin's clear bewilderment. 'A gadgee is a man. She's saying men are all the same.'

'Oh yes,' said Robin, barely aware of what she was saying. 'So true. Thanks very much. Goodbye, Holly . . . take care of yourself . . .'

26

Desolate landscape,
Storybook bliss . . .

Blue Öyster Cult, 'Death Valley Nights'

'Psychology's loss,' said Strike, 'is private detection's gain. That was bloody good going, Robin.'

He raised his can of McEwan's and toasted her. They were sitting in the parked Land Rover, eating fish and chips a short distance away from the Olympic Takeaway. Its bright windows intensified the surrounding darkness. Silhouettes passed regularly across the rectangles of light, metamorphosed into three-dimensional humans as they entered the bustling chip shop, and turned back into shadows as they left.

'So his wife left him.'

'Yep.'

'And Holly says he hasn't seen the kids since?'

'Right.'

Strike sipped his McEwan's, thinking. He wanted to believe that Brockbank really had lost contact with Brittany, but what if the evil bastard had somehow tracked her down?

'We still don't know where he is, though,' Robin sighed.

'Well, we know he isn't here and that he hasn't been here for around a year,' said Strike. 'We know he still blames me for what's wrong with him, that he's still abusing little girls and that he's a fuck sight saner than they thought he was in the hospital.'

'Why d'you say that?'

'Sounds like he's kept the accusation of child abuse quiet. He's holding down jobs when he could be sitting at home claiming disability benefit. I suppose working gives him more opportunities to meet young girls.'

'Don't,' murmured Robin as the memory of Holly's confession suddenly gave way to that of the frozen head, looking so young, so plump, so dimly surprised.

'That's Brockbank and Laing both at large in the UK, both hating my guts.'

Chomping chips, Strike rummaged in the glove compartment, extracted the road atlas and for a while was quiet, turning pages. Robin folded the remainder of her fish and chips in its newspaper wrappings and said:

'I've got to ring my mother. Back in a bit.'

Leaning against a street lamp a short distance away she called her parents' number.

'Are you all right, Robin?'

'Yes, Mum.'

'What's going on between you and Matthew?'

Robin looked up at the faintly starry sky.

'I think we've split up.'

'You *think*?' said Linda. She sounded neither shocked nor sad, merely interested in the full facts.

Robin had been worried that she might cry when she had to say it aloud, yet no tears stung her eyes, nor did she need to force herself to speak calmly. Perhaps she was toughening up. The desperate life story of Holly Brockbank and the gruesome end of the unknown girl in Shepherd's Bush certainly gave a person perspective.

'It only happened on Monday night.'

'Was this because of Cormoran?'

'No,' said Robin. 'Sarah Shadlock. It turns out Matt was sleeping with her while I was . . . at home. When – you know when. After I dropped out.'

Two young men meandered out of the Olympic, definitely the worse for drink, shouting and swearing at each other. One of them spotted Robin and nudged the other. They veered towards her.

'Thoo orlrigh', darlin'?'

Strike got out of the car and slammed the door, looming darkly, a head taller than both of them. The youths swayed away in sudden silence. Strike lit a cigarette leaning up against the car, his face in shadow.

'Mum, are you still there?'

'He told you this on Monday night?' asked Linda.

'Yes,' said Robin.

'Why?'

'We were rowing about Cormoran again,' Robin muttered, aware of Strike yards away. 'I said, "It's a platonic relationship, like you and Sarah" – and then I saw his face – and then he admitted it.'

Her mother gave a long, deep sigh. Robin waited for words of comfort or wisdom.

'Dear God,' said Linda. There was another long silence. 'How are you really, Robin?'

'I'm all right, Mum, honestly. I'm working. It's helping.'

'Why are you in Barrow, of all places?'

'We're trying to trace one of the men Strike thinks might've sent him the leg.'

'Where are you staying?'

'We're going to go to the Travelodge,' said Robin. 'In separate rooms, obviously,' she hastened to add.

'Have you spoken to Matthew since you left?'

'He keeps sending me texts telling me he loves me.'

As she said it, she realised that she had not read his last. She had only just remembered it.

'I'm sorry,' Robin told her mother. 'The dress and the reception and everything . . . I'm so sorry, Mum.'

'They're the last things I'm worried about,' said Linda and she asked yet again: 'Are you all right, Robin?'

'Yes, I promise I am.' She hesitated, then said, almost defiantly, 'Cormoran's been great.'

'You're going to have to talk to Matthew, though,' said Linda. 'After all this time . . . you can't not talk to him.'

Robin's composure broke; her voice trembled with rage and her hands shook as the words poured out of her.

'We were at the rugby with them just two weekends ago, with Sarah and Tom. She's been hanging around ever since they were at uni – they were sleeping together while I was – while I – he's never cut her out of his life, she's always hugging him, flirting with him, shit-stirring between him and me – at the rugby it was Strike, *oh, he's so attractive, just the two of you in the office, is it?* – and all this time I've thought it just went one way, I *knew* she'd tried to get him into bed at uni but I never – eighteen months, they were sleeping together – and you know what he said to me? She was *comforting* him . . . I had to give in and say she could come to the wedding because I'd asked Strike without telling Matt, that was my punishment, because I didn't want her there. Matt has lunch with her whenever he's near her offices—'

'I'm going to come down to London and see you,' said Linda.

'No, Mum—'

'For a day. Take you out for lunch.'

Robin gave a weak laugh.

'Mum, I don't take a lunch hour. It isn't that kind of job.'

'I'm coming to London, Robin.'

When her mother's voice became firm like that, there was no point arguing.

'I don't know when I'll be back.'

'Well, you can let me know and I'll book the train.'

'I . . . oh, OK,' said Robin.

When they had bidden each other goodbye she realised that she had tears in her eyes at last. Much as she might pretend otherwise, the thought of seeing Linda brought much comfort.

She looked over at the Land Rover. Strike was still leaning up against it, and he too was on the phone. Or was he merely pretending? She had been talking loudly. He could be tactful when he chose.

She looked down at the mobile in her hands and opened Matthew's message.

Your mother called. I told her you're away with work. Let me know whether you want me to tell Dad you're not going to his birthday thing. I love you, Robin. Mxxxxxx

There he went again: he did not really believe that the relationship was at an end. **Let me know whether you want me to tell Dad** . . . as though it were a storm in a teacup, as though she would never take it so far as not to attend his father's party . . . *I don't even like your bloody father* . . .

Angry, she typed and sent the response.

Of course I'm not coming.

She got back into the car. Strike seemed to be genuinely talking on the phone. The road atlas lay open on the passenger seat: he had been looking at the Leicestershire town of Market Harborough.

'Yeah, you too,' she heard Strike say. 'Yeah. See you when I get back.'

Elin, she thought.

He climbed back into the car.

'Was that Wardle?' she asked innocently.

'Elin,' he said.

Does she know you've gone away with me? Just the two of us?

Robin felt herself turn red. She did not know where that thought had come from. It wasn't as though . . .

'You want to go to Market Harborough?' she asked, holding up the map.

'Might as well,' said Strike, taking another swig of beer. 'It's the last place Brockbank worked. Could get a lead; we'd be stupid not to check it out . . . and if we're going through there . . .'

He lifted the book out of her hands and flicked over a few pages.

'It's only twelve miles from Corby. We could swing by and see whether the Laing who was shacked up with a woman there in 2008 is our Laing. She's still living there: Lorraine MacNaughton's the name.'

Robin was used to Strike's prodigious memory for names and details.

'OK,' she said, pleased to think that the morning would bring more investigation, not simply a long drive back to London. Perhaps, if they found something interesting, there would be a second night on the road and she need not see Matthew for another twelve hours – but then she remembered that Matthew would be heading north the following night, for his father's birthday. She would have the flat to herself in any case.

'Could he have tracked her down?' Strike wondered aloud, after a silence.

'Sorry – what? Who?'

'Could Brockbank have tracked Brittany down and killed her after all this time? Or am I barking up the wrong tree because I feel so fucking guilty?'

He gave the door of the Land Rover a soft thump with his fist.

'The leg, though,' said Strike, arguing against himself. 'It's scarred just like hers was. That was a thing between them: "I tried to saw off your leg when you were little and your mum walked in." Fucking evil bastard. Who else would send me a scarred leg?'

'Well,' said Robin slowly, 'I can think of a reason a leg was chosen, and it might not have anything at all to do with Brittany Brockbank.'

Strike turned to look at her.

'Go on.'

'Whoever killed that girl could have sent you any part of her and achieved the same result,' said Robin. 'An arm, or – or a breast –' she did her best to keep her tone matter-of-fact, '– would have meant the police and the press swarming all over us just the same. The business would still have been compromised and we'd have been just as shaken up – but he chose to send a right leg, cut exactly where your right leg was amputated.'

'I suppose it ties in with that effing song. Although—' Strike reconsidered. 'No, I'm talking crap, aren't I? An arm would've worked just as well for that. Or a neck.'

'He's making clear reference to your injury,' Robin said. 'What does your missing leg mean to him?'

'Christ knows,' said Strike, watching her profile as she talked.

'Heroism,' said Robin.

Strike snorted.

'There's nothing heroic about being in the wrong place at the wrong time.'

'You're a decorated veteran.'

'I wasn't decorated for being blown up. That happened before.'

'You've never told me that.'

She turned to face him, but he refused to be sidetracked.

'Go on. Why the leg?'

'Your injury's a legacy of war. It represents bravery, adversity overcome. Your amputation's mentioned every single time they talk about you in the press. I think – for him – it's tied up with fame and achievement and – and honour. He's trying to denigrate your injury, to tie it to something horrible, divert the public's perception away from you as hero towards you as a man in receipt of part of a dismembered girl. He wants to cause you trouble, yes, but he wants to diminish you in the process. He's somebody who wants what you've got, who wants recognition and importance.'

Strike bent down and took a second can of McEwan's out of the brown bag at his feet. The crack of the ring pull reverberated in the cold air.

'If you're right,' said Strike, watching his cigarette smoke curl away into the darkness, 'if what's riling this maniac is that I got famous, Whittaker goes to the top of the list. That was all he ever wanted: to be a celebrity.'

Robin waited. He had told her virtually nothing about his stepfather, although the internet had supplied her with many of the details that Strike had withheld.

'He was the most parasitic fucker I've ever met,' said Strike. 'It'd be like him to try and siphon off a bit of fame from someone else.'

She could feel him becoming angry again beside her in the small space. He reacted consistently at every mention of each of the three suspects: Brockbank made him guilty, Whittaker angry. Laing was the only one he discussed with anything like objectivity.

'Hasn't Shanker come up with anything yet?'

'Says he's in Catford. Shanker'll track him down. Whittaker'll be there, somewhere, in some filthy corner. He's definitely in London.'

'Why are you so sure?'

'Just London, isn't it?' said Strike, staring across the car park at the terraced houses. 'He came from Yorkshire originally, Whittaker, you know, but he's pure cockney now.'

'You haven't seen him for ages, have you?'

'I don't need to. I know him. He's part of the junk that washes up in the capital looking for the big time and never leaves. He thought London was the only place that deserved him. Had to be the biggest stage for Whittaker.'

Yet Whittaker had never managed to claw his way out of the dirty places of the capital where criminality, poverty and violence bred like bacteria, the underbelly where Shanker still dwelled. Nobody who had not lived there would ever understand that London was a country unto itself. They might resent it for the fact that it held more power and money than any other British city, but they could not understand that poverty carried its own flavour there, where everything cost more, where the relentless distinctions between those who had succeeded and those who had not were constantly, painfully visible. The distance between Elin's vanilla-columned flat in Clarence Terrace and the filthy Whitechapel squat where his mother had died could not be measured in mere miles. They were separated by infinite disparities, by the lotteries of birth and chance, by faults of judgement and lucky breaks. His mother and Elin, both beautiful women, both intelligent, one sucked down into a morass of drugs and human filth, the other sitting high over Regent's Park behind spotless glass.

Robin, too, was thinking about London. It had Matthew in its spell, but he had no interest in the labyrinthine worlds she probed daily during her detective work. He looked excitedly towards the surface glitter: the best restaurants, the best areas to live, as though London were a huge Monopoly board. He had always had a divided allegiance to Yorkshire, to their hometown Masham. His father was Yorkshire-born, while his late mother had come from Surrey and had carried with her an air of having gone north on sufferance. She had persistently corrected any Yorkshire turns of speech in Matthew and his sister Kimberley. His carefully neutral accent had been one of the reasons that Robin's brothers had not been impressed when they had started dating: in spite of her protestations, in spite of his Yorkshire name, they had sensed the wannabe southerner.

'It'd be a strange place to come from, this, wouldn't it?' said Strike, still looking out over the terraces. 'It's like an island. I've never heard that accent before either.'

A man's voice sounded somewhere nearby, singing a rousing song. Robin thought at first that the tune was a hymn. Then the man's unique voice was joined by more voices and the breeze changed direction so that they heard a few lines quite distinctly:

> 'Friends to share in games and laughter
> Songs at dusk and books at noon . . .'

'School song,' said Robin, smiling. She could see them now, a group of middle-aged men in black suits, singing loudly as they walked up Buccleuch Street.

'Funeral,' guessed Strike. 'Old schoolmate. Look at them.'

As the black-suited men drew level with the car, one of them spotted Robin looking.

'Barrow Boys' Grammar School!' he shouted at her, fist raised as though he had just scored a goal. The men cheered, but there was melancholy to their drink-fuelled swagger. They began singing the song again as they passed out of sight.

'Harbour lights and clustered shipping
Clouds above the wheeling gulls . . .'

'Hometowns,' said Strike.

He was thinking about men like his Uncle Ted, a Cornishman to his bones, who lived and would die in St Mawes, part of the fabric of the place, remembered as long as there were locals, beaming out of fading photographs of the Life Boat on pub walls. When Ted died – and Strike hoped it would be twenty, thirty years hence – they would mourn him as the unknown Barrovian Grammar boy was being mourned: with drink, with tears, but in celebration that he had been given to them. What had dark, hulking Brockbank, child rapist, and fox-haired Laing, wife-torturer, left behind in the towns of their birth? Shudders of relief that they had gone, fear that they had returned, a trail of broken people and bad memories.

'Shall we go?' Robin asked quietly and Strike nodded, dropping the burning stub of his cigarette into his last inch of McEwan's, where it emitted a small, satisfying hiss.

27

A dreadful knowledge comes . . .

Blue Öyster Cult, 'In the Presence of Another World'

They were given rooms five doors apart in the Travelodge. Robin had dreaded the man behind the desk offering a double room, but Strike had headed that off with a peremptory 'two singles' before he had time to open his mouth.

Ridiculous, really, to feel suddenly self-conscious, because they had been physically closer all day in the Land Rover than they were in the lift. It felt odd saying goodnight to Strike when she reached the door of her room; not that he lingered. He merely said ''night' and walked on to his own room, but he waited outside his door until she managed to work the key card and let herself inside with a flustered wave.

Why had she had waved? Ridiculous.

She dropped her holdall on the bed and moved to the window, which offered only a bleak view of the same industrial warehouses they had passed on their way into town a few hours earlier. It felt as though they had been away from London for much longer than they had.

The heating was turned up too high. Robin forced open a stiff window, and the cool night air surged inside, eager to invade the stuffy square box of a room. After putting her phone on to charge, she undressed, pulled on a nightshirt, brushed her teeth and slid down between the cool sheets.

She still felt strangely unsettled, knowing that she was sleeping five rooms away from Strike. That was Matthew's fault, of course. *If you sleep with him, we're over for good.*

Her unruly imagination suddenly presented her with the sound of a knock on the door, Strike inviting himself in on some slim pretext . . .

Don't be ridiculous.

She rolled over, pressing her flushed face into the pillow. What was she thinking? Damn Matthew, putting things in her head, judging her by himself . . .

Strike, meanwhile, had not yet made it into bed. He was stiff all over from the long hours of immobility in the car. It felt good to get the prosthesis off. Even though the shower was not particularly handy for a man with one leg, he used it, carefully holding on to the bar inside the door, trying to relax his sore knee with hot water. Towel-dried, he navigated his way carefully back to the bed, put his mobile on to charge and climbed, naked, beneath the covers.

Lying with his hands behind his head he stared up at the dark ceiling and thought about Robin, lying five rooms away. He wondered whether Matthew had texted again, whether they were on the phone together, whether she was capitalising on her privacy to cry for the first time all day.

The sounds of what was probably a stag party reached him through the floor: loud male laughter, shouting, whoops, slamming doors. Somebody put on music and the bass pounded through his room. It reminded him of the nights he had slept in his office, when the music playing in the 12 Bar Café below had vibrated through the metal legs of his camp bed. He hoped the noise was not as loud in Robin's room. She needed her rest – she had to drive another two hundred and fifty miles tomorrow. Yawning, Strike rolled over and, in spite of the thudding music and yells, fell almost immediately asleep.

They met by agreement in the dining room next morning, where Strike blocked Robin from view as she surreptitiously refilled their flask from the urn at the buffet and both loaded their plates with toast. Strike resisted the full English and rewarded himself for his restraint by sliding several Danish pastries into his backpack. At eight o'clock they were back in the Land Rover, driving through the glorious Cumbrian countryside, a rolling panorama of heather moors and peat lands under a hazy blue sky, and joining the M6 South.

'Sorry I can't share the driving,' said Strike, who was sipping coffee. 'That clutch would kill me. It'd kill both of us.'

'I don't care,' said Robin. 'I love driving, you know that.'

They sped on in companionable silence. Robin was the only person whom Strike could stand to be driven by, notwithstanding the fact that he had an ingrained prejudice against women drivers. This was something that he generally kept quiet, but which had its roots in many a negative passenger experience, from his Cornish aunt's nervous ineptitude, to his sister Lucy's distractibility, to Charlotte's reckless courting of danger. An ex-girlfriend from the SIB, Tracey, had been competent behind the wheel and yet had become so paralysed with fear on a high, narrow alpine road that she had stopped, on the verge of hyperventilating, refusing to cede the wheel to him but unable to drive further.

'Matthew like the Land Rover?' Strike asked as they trundled over a flyover.

'No,' said Robin. 'He wants an A3 Cabriolet.'

'Course he does,' said Strike under his breath, inaudible in the rattling car. 'Wanker.'

It took them four hours to reach Market Harborough, a town which, as they established en route, neither Strike nor Robin had ever visited. The approach wound through a number of pretty little villages with thatched roofs, seventeenth-century churches, topiary gardens and residential streets with names like Honeypot Lane. Strike remembered the stark, blank wall, barbed wire and looming submarine factory that had formed the view from Noel Brockbank's childhood home. What could have brought Brockbank here, to bucolic prettiness and charm? What kind of business owned the telephone number that Holly had given Robin, and which was now residing in Strike's wallet?

The impression of genteel antiquity only increased when they reached Market Harborough itself. The ornate and aged church of St Dionysius rose proudly in the heart of the town, and beside it, in the middle of the central thoroughfare, stood a remarkable structure resembling a small timbered house on wooden stilts.

They found a parking space to the rear of this peculiar building. Keen to smoke and to stretch his knee, Strike got out, lit up and went to examine a plaque that informed him the stilted edifice was a grammar school that had been built in 1614. Biblical verses painted in gold ran around the structure.

Man looketh on the outward appearance, but the Lord looketh on the heart.

Robin had remained in the Land Rover, examining the map for the best route to Corby, their next stop. When Strike had finished his cigarette he hoisted himself back into the passenger seat.

'OK, I'm going to try the number. If you fancy stretching your legs, I'm nearly out of fags.'

Robin rolled her eyes, but took the proffered tenner and left in search of Benson & Hedges.

The number was engaged the first time Strike tried it. On his second attempt, a heavily accented female voice answered:

'Thai Orchid Massage, how can I help you?'

'Hi,' said Strike. 'I've been given your number by a friend. Whereabouts are you?'

She gave him a number in St Mary's Road, which he saw, after a brief consultation of the map, was mere minutes away.

'Any of your ladies free for me this morning?' he asked.

'What kind you like?' said the voice.

He could see Robin coming back in the wing mirror, her strawberry-blonde hair blowing freely in the breeze, a gold pack of Benson & Hedges glinting in her hand.

'Dark,' said Strike, after a fractional hesitation. 'Thai.'

'We have two Thai ladies free for you. What service you look for?'

Robin pulled open the driver's door and got back in.

'What have you got?' asked Strike.

'One-lady sensual massage with oils, ninety pound. Two-lady sensual massage with oil, one hundred twenty. Full body-to-body naked massage with oil, one hundred fifty. You negotiate extras with lady, OK?'

'OK, I'd like the – er – one lady,' said Strike. 'Be with you in a bit.'

He hung up.

'It's a massage parlour,' he told Robin, examining the map, 'but not the kind you'd take your bad knee to.'

'Really?' she said, startled.

'They're everywhere,' he said. 'You know that.'

He understood why she was disconcerted. The scene beyond the windscreen – St Dionysius, the godly grammar school on stilts, a busy and prosperous high street, a St George's Cross rippling in the breeze outside a nearby pub – might have appeared on a poster advertising the town.

'What are you going to – where is it?' asked Robin.

'Not far away,' he said, showing her on the map. 'I'm going to need a cashpoint first.'

Was he actually going to pay for a massage? Robin wondered, startled, but she did not know how to frame the question, and nor was she sure that she wanted to hear the answer. After pulling in at a cashpoint to enable Strike to increase his overdraft by another two hundred pounds, she followed his directions onto St Mary's Road, which lay at the end of the main street. St Mary's Road proved to be a perfectly respectable-looking thoroughfare lined with estate agents, beauty spas and solicitors, most of them in large detached buildings.

'That's it,' said Strike, pointing, as they drove past a discreet establishment that sat on a corner. A glossy purple and gold sign read THAI ORCHID MASSAGE. Only the dark blinds on the windows hinted at activities beyond the medically sanctioned manipulation of sore joints. Robin parked in a side street and watched Strike until he passed out of sight.

Approaching the massage parlour's entrance, Strike noticed that the orchid depicted on the glossy sign overhead looked remarkably like a vulva. He rang the bell and the door was opened instantly by a long-haired man almost as tall as himself.

'I just phoned,' Strike said.

The bouncer grunted and nodded Strike through a pair of thick black inner curtains. Immediately inside was a small, carpeted lounge area with two sofas, where an older Thai woman sat along with two Thai girls, one of whom looked about fifteen. A TV in the corner was showing *Who Wants to Be a Millionaire?* The girls' expressions changed from bored to alert as he entered. The older woman stood up. She was vigorously chewing gum.

'You call, yeah?'

'That's right,' said Strike.

'You want drink?'

'No thanks.'

'You like Thai girl?'

'Yep,' said Strike.

'Who you want?'

'Her,' said Strike, pointing at the younger girl, who was dressed in a pink halterneck, suede miniskirt and cheap-looking patent stilettos. She smiled and stood up. Her skinny legs reminded him of a flamingo's.

'OK,' said his interlocutor. 'You pay now, go private booth after, OK?'

Strike handed over ninety pounds and his chosen girl beckoned, beaming. She had the body of an adolescent boy except for the clearly fake breasts, which reminded him of the plastic Barbies on Elin's daughter's shelf.

The private booth was accessed down a short corridor: a small room with a single black-blinded window and low lighting, it was suffused with the smell of sandalwood. A shower had been crammed into the corner. The massage table was of fake black leather.

'You want shower first?'

'No thanks,' said Strike.

'OK, you take off clothes in there,' she said, pointing at a tiny curtained-off corner in which Strike would have had great difficulty concealing his six foot three frame.

'I'm happier with my clothes on. I want to talk to you.'

She did not seem fazed. She had seen all sorts.

'You want top off?' she offered brightly, reaching for the bow behind her neck. 'Ten pound extra, top off.'

'No,' said Strike.

'Hand relief?' she offered, eyeing his flies. 'Hand relief with oil? Twenty extra.'

'No, I just want to talk to you,' said Strike.

Doubt crossed her face, and then a sudden flash of fear.

'You police.'

'No,' said Strike, holding up his hands as though surrendering to her. 'I'm not police. I'm looking for a man called Noel Brockbank. He used to work here. On the door, I expect – probably the bouncer.'

He had chosen this particular girl because she looked so young. Knowing Brockbank's proclivities, he thought Brockbank might have sought contact with her rather than any of the other girls, but she shook her head.

'He gone,' she said.

'I know,' said Strike. 'I'm trying to find out where he went.'

'Mama sack him.'

Was the owner her mother, or was it an honorary title? Strike preferred not to involve Mama in this. She looked shrewd and tough. He had an idea he would be forced to pay well for what might turn out to be no information at all. There was a welcome naivety about his chosen girl. She could have charged him for confirmation that Brockbank had once worked there, that he had been sacked, but it had not occurred to her.

'Did you know him?' Strike asked.

'He sacked week I come,' she said.

'Why was he sacked?'

The girl glanced at the door.

'Would anyone here have a contact number for him, or know where he went?'

She hesitated. Strike took out his wallet.

'Twenty,' he said, 'if you can introduce me to someone who's got information on where he is now. That's yours to keep.'

She stood playing with the hem of her suede skirt like a

child, staring at him, then tweaked the tenners out of his hand and tucked them deep into her skirt pocket.

'Wait here.'

He sat down on the fake-leather massage table and waited. The little room was as clean as any spa, which Strike liked. He found dirt deeply anaphrodisiac; it always reminded him of his mother and Whittaker in that fetid squat, of stained mattresses and the miasma of his stepfather thick in his nostrils. Here beside the oils neatly lined up on a side cabinet, erotic thoughts could hardly fail to occur. The idea of a full body-to-body naked massage with oil was far from unpleasing.

For no reason that he could think of, his thoughts jumped to Robin, sitting outside in the car. He got briskly to his feet again, as though he had been discovered doing something compromising, and then angry Thai voices sounded close at hand. The door burst open to reveal Mama and his chosen girl, who looked frightened.

'You pay for one girl massage!' said Mama angrily.

Like her protégée, her eyes found his flies. She was checking to see whether any business had already been done, whether he was trying to get more on the cheap.

'He change mind,' said the girl desperately. 'He want two girl, one Thai, one blonde. We do nothing. He change mind.'

'You pay for one girl only,' shouted Mama, pointing at Strike with a talon-tipped finger.

Strike heard heavy footsteps and guessed that the long-haired doorman was approaching.

'I'm happy,' he said, inwardly cursing, 'to pay for the two-girl massage as well.'

'One hundred twenty more?' Mama shouted at him, unable to believe her ears.

'Yes,' he said. 'Fine.'

She made him come back out into the lounge area to pay.

An overweight redhead was sitting there in a cut-out black lycra dress. She looked hopeful.

'He want blonde,' said Strike's accomplice as he handed over another hundred and twenty pounds, and the redhead's face fell.

'Ingrid with client,' said Mama, shoving Strike's cash in a drawer. 'You wait here 'til she finish.'

So he sat between the skinny Thai girl and the redhead and watched *Who Wants to Be a Millionaire?* until a small, suited man with a white beard came scurrying out of the corridor and, avoiding eye contact with everybody, disappeared through the black curtains and escaped onto the street. Five minutes later a slim peroxide blonde who, Strike thought, must be around his own age appeared in purple lycra and thigh-high boots.

'You go with Ingrid,' said Mama and Strike and the Thai girl traipsed obediently back to the private parlour.

'He no want massage,' Strike's first girl told the blonde breathlessly when the door was closed. 'He want know where Noel went.'

The blonde eyed Strike, frowning. She might be more than twice the age of her companion, but she was good-looking, with dark brown eyes and high cheekbones.

'What d'you want *'im* for?' she asked in pure Essex and then, calmly, 'Are you police?'

'No,' said Strike.

Sudden comprehension was illuminating her pretty face.

''Ang on,' she said slowly. 'I know 'oo you are – you're that Strike! You're Cameron Strike! The detective 'oo solved the Lula Landry case and – Jesus – didn't someone just send you a *leg*?'

'Er – yeah, they did.'

'Noel was fucking *obsessed* with you!' she said. 'All I ever heard 'im talk about, practically. After you was on the news.'

'Is that right?'

'Yeah, 'e kept saying you give 'im a brain injury!'

'I can't take full credit. You knew him well, did you?'

'Not *that* well!' she said, correctly interpreting Strike's meaning. 'I knew 'is friend from up north, John. He was a great guy, one of my regular punters before 'e went off to Saudi. Yeah, they was at school together, I fink. 'E felt sorry for Noel 'cause 'e was ex-forces and 'e'd 'ad a few problems, so 'e recommended him for 'ere. Said 'e was down on his luck. 'E got me to rent Noel a room at my place an' all.'

Her tone said plainly that she felt John's sympathy for Brockbank had been misplaced.

'How did that go?'

''E was all right at first, but once 'is guard come down 'e just ranted all the time. About the army, about you, about 'is son – 'e's obsessed with 'is son, getting 'is son back. 'E says it's your fault he can't see 'im, but I don't see 'ow 'e works that out. Anyone could see why his ex-wife didn't want 'im near the kid.'

'And why's that?'

'Mama found 'im with 'er granddaughter on 'is lap and 'is 'and up 'er skirt,' said Ingrid. 'She's six.'

'Ah,' said Strike.

''E left owing me two weeks' rent and that's the last I ever saw of 'im. Good bloody riddance.'

'D'you know where he went after he was sacked?'

'No idea.'

'So you haven't got any contact details?'

'I've prob'bly still got his mobile number,' she said. 'I don't know whether 'e'll still be using it.'

'Could you give—?'

'Do I look like I've got a mobile on me?' she asked, raising her arms high. The lycra and boots outlined every curve.

Her erect nipples were clearly visible through the thin fabric. Invited to look, Strike forced himself to maintain eye contact.

'Could you meet me later and give it to me?'

'We're not allowed to exchange contact details with punters. Terms and conditions, sweet'art: why we're not allowed to carry phones. Tell you what,' she said, eyeing him up and down, 'seeing as it's you and seeing as 'ow I know you punched the bastard and you're a war 'ero and everyfing, I'll meet you up the road when I clock off.'

'That,' said Strike, 'would be great. Thanks very much.'

He did not know whether he imagined a flirtatious glint in her eye. Possibly he was distracted by the smell of massage oil and his recent thoughts of warm, slippery bodies.

Twenty minutes later, having waited long enough for Mama to assume that relief had been sought and given, Strike left the Thai Orchid and crossed the road to where Robin was waiting in the car.

'Two hundred and thirty quid for an old mobile number,' he said as she pulled away from the kerb and accelerated towards the town centre. 'I hope it's bloody worth it. We're looking for Adam and Eve Street – she says it's just up here on the right – the café's called Appleby's. She's going to meet me there in a bit.'

Robin found a parking space and they waited, discussing what Ingrid had said about Brockbank while eating the Danish pastries that Strike had stolen from the breakfast buffet. Robin was starting to appreciate why Strike was carrying extra weight. She had never before undertaken an investigation that lasted more than twenty-four hours. When every meal had to be sourced in passing shops and eaten on the move, you descended quickly to fast food and chocolate.

'That's her,' said Strike forty minutes later, clambering out of the Land Rover and heading for the interior of Appleby's.

Robin watched the blonde approach, now in jeans and a fake-fur jacket. She had the body of a glamour model and Robin was reminded of Platinum. Ten minutes passed, then fifteen; neither Strike nor the girl reappeared.

'How long does it take to hand over a telephone number?' Robin asked the interior of the Land Rover crossly. She felt chilly in the car. 'I thought you wanted to get on to Corby?'

He had told her nothing had happened, but you never knew. Perhaps it had. Perhaps the girl had covered Strike in oil and . . .

Robin drummed her fingers on the steering wheel. She thought about Elin, and how she would feel if she knew what Strike had done that day. Then, with a slight jolt, she remembered that she had not checked her phone to see whether Matthew had been in contact again. She took it out of her coat pocket and saw no new messages. Since telling him she was definitely not going to his father's birthday party, he had gone quiet.

The blonde and Strike emerged from the café. Ingrid did not seem to want to let Strike go. When he waved farewell she leaned forward and kissed him on the cheek, then sashayed away. Strike caught Robin watching and got back into the car with a kind of bashful grimace.

'That looked interesting,' said Robin.

'Not really,' said Strike, showing her the number now keyed into his phone: **NOEL BROCKBANK MOBILE**. 'She was just chatty.'

If Robin had been a male colleague he would have found it impossible not to add: 'I was in there.' Ingrid had flirted shamelessly across the table, scrolling slowly through the contacts on her phone, wondering aloud whether she still had the number so that he started to feel anxious that she had nothing, asking him whether he had ever had a proper Thai massage, probing about what he wanted Noel for, about the cases he had solved, especially that of the beautiful dead model, which had first brought him to public notice, and finally insisting, with a warm smile, that he take her number too, 'just in case'.

'D'you want to try Brockbank's number now?' Robin asked, recalling Strike's attention from the back view of Ingrid as she walked away.

'What? No. That wants thinking about. We might only have one shot if he picks up.' He checked his watch. 'Let's get going, I don't want to be too late in Cor—'

The phone in his hand rang.

'Wardle,' said Strike.

He answered, putting the phone onto speaker so that Robin could listen.

'What's going on?'

'We've ID'd the body,' said Wardle. A note in his voice warned them that they were about to recognise a name. The tiny pause that followed allowed the image of that little girl with her small bird-like eyes to slide in panic through Strike's mind.

'She's called Kelsey Platt and she's the girl who wrote to you for advice on how to cut off her leg. She was genuine. Sixteen years old.'

Equal amounts of relief and disbelief crashed over Strike. He groped for a pen, but Robin was already writing.

'She was doing a City and Guilds in childcare at some vocational college, which is where she met Oxana Voloshina. Kelsey usually lived in Finchley with her half-sister and the sister's partner. She told them she was going away on a college placement for two weeks. They didn't report her missing – they weren't worried. She wasn't expected back until tonight.

'Oxana says Kelsey didn't get on with her sister and asked whether she could stay there for a couple of weeks, get some space. Looks like the girl had it all planned out, writing to you from that address. The sister's a total mess, understandably. I can't get much sense out of her yet, but she's confirmed the handwriting on the letter was genuine and the thing the girl had about wanting to get rid of her leg didn't seem to come as a total shock to her. We got DNA samples off the girl's hair-brush. It matches. It's her.'

With a creak of the passenger seat, Strike leaned closer to Robin to read her notes. She could smell the cigarette smoke on his clothes and a tiny whiff of sandalwood.

'There's a partner living with the sister?' he asked. 'A man?'

'You won't pin it on him,' said Wardle, and Strike could tell that Wardle had already had a good try. 'Forty-five, retired fireman, not in great nick. Knackered lungs and a watertight alibi for the weekend in question.'

'The weekend—?' began Robin.

'Kelsey left her sister's on the night of April first. We know she must've died on the second or third – you got handed her leg on the fourth. Strike, I'm going to need you back in here for more questions. Routine, but we're going to have to take a formal statement about those letters.'

There seemed little else to be said. After accepting Strike's thanks for letting them know, Wardle rang off, leaving a silence that seemed to Robin to quiver with aftershocks.

28

. . . oh Debbie Denise was true to me,
She'd wait by the window, so patiently.

Blue Öyster Cult, 'Debbie Denise'
Lyrics by Patti Smith

'This whole trip's been a wasted detour. It isn't Brittany. It can't be Brockbank.'

Strike's relief was stupendous. The colours of Adam and Eve Street seemed suddenly washed clean, the passers-by brighter, more likeable than they had been before he had taken the call. Brittany must, after all, be alive somewhere. This was not his fault. The leg had not been hers.

Robin said nothing. She could hear the triumph in Strike's voice, feel his release. She, of course, had never met or seen Brittany Brockbank, and while she was glad the girl was safe, the fact remained that a girl had died in horrific circumstances. The guilt that had tumbled from Strike seemed to have fallen heavily into her own lap. She was the one who had skim-read Kelsey's letter and simply filed it in the nutter drawer without response. Would it have made a difference, Robin wondered, if she had contacted Kelsey and advised her to get help? Or if Strike had called her and told her that he had lost his leg in battle, that whatever she had been told about his injury was a lie? Robin's insides ached with regret.

'Are you sure?' she said aloud after a full minute's silence, both of them lost in their own private thoughts.

'Sure about what?' asked Strike, turning to look at her.

'That it can't be Brockbank.'

'If it's not Brittany—' began Strike.

'You've just told me that girl—'

'Ingrid?'

'Ingrid,' said Robin, with a trace of impatience, 'yes. You've just told me she says Brockbank's obsessed with you. He holds you accountable for his brain damage and the loss of his family.'

Strike watched her, frowning, thinking.

'Everything I said last night about the killer wanting to denigrate you and belittle your war record would sit comfortably with everything we know about Brockbank,' Robin went on, 'and don't you think that meeting this Kelsey and perhaps seeing the scarring on her leg that was like Brittany's, or hearing that she wanted to get rid of it could have – I don't know – triggered something in him? I mean,' said Robin tentatively, 'we don't know exactly how the brain damage—'

'He's not that fucking brain damaged,' snapped Strike. 'He was faking in the hospital. I know he was.'

Robin said nothing, but sat behind the wheel and watched shoppers moving up and down Adam and Eve Street. She envied them. Whatever their private preoccupations, they were unlikely to include mutilation and murder.

'You make some good points,' said Strike at last. Robin could tell that she had taken the edge off his private celebration. He checked his watch. 'C'mon, we'd better get off to Corby if we're going to do it today.'

The twelve miles between the two towns were swiftly covered. Robin guessed from his surly expression that Strike was mulling over their discussion about Brockbank. The road was nondescript, the surrounding countryside flat, hedgerows and occasional trees lining the route.

'So, Laing,' said Robin, trying to move Strike out of what seemed an uncomfortable reverie. 'Remind me—?'

'Laing, yeah,' said Strike slowly.

She was right to think that he had been lost in thoughts of Brockbank. Now he forced himself to focus, to regroup.

'Well, Laing tied up his wife and used a knife on her; accused of rape twice that I know of, but never done for it – and he tried to bite half my face off in the boxing ring. Basically, a violent, devious bastard,' said Strike, 'but, like I told you, his mother-in-law reckons he was ill when he got out of jail. She says he went to Gateshead, but he can't have stayed there long if he was living in Corby with this woman in 2008,' he said, checking the map again for Lorraine MacNaughton's road. 'Right age, right time frame . . . we'll see. If Lorraine's not in, we'll go back after five o'clock.'

Following Strike's directions, Robin drove through the very centre of Corby town, which proved to be a sprawl of concrete and brick dominated by a shopping centre. A massive block of council offices, on which aerials bristled like iron moss, dominated the skyline. There was no central square, no ancient church and certainly no stilted, half-timbered grammar school. Corby had been planned to house its explosion of migrant workers in the 1940s and 1950s; many of the buildings had a cheerless, utilitarian air.

'Half the street names are Scottish,' said Robin as they passed Argyll Street and Montrose Street.

'Used to call it Little Scotland, didn't they?' said Strike, noting a sign for Edinburgh House. He had heard that in its industrial heyday, Corby had had the largest Scottish population south of the border. Saltires and lions rampant fluttered from balconies of flats. 'You can see why Laing might've felt more at home here than in Gateshead. Could've had contacts in the area.'

Five minutes later they found themselves in the old part of town, whose pretty stone buildings retained traces of the village that Corby had been before the steelworks arrived. Shortly afterwards they came upon Weldon Road, where Lorraine MacNaughton lived.

The houses stood in solid blocks of six, each pair a mirror image of the other, so that their front doors sat side by side and the layout of the windows was reversed. Carved into the stone lintel over each door was a name.

'That's hers,' said Strike, pointing at Summerfield, which was twinned with Northfield.

Summerfield's front garden had been covered in fine gravel. Northfield's grass needed mowing, which reminded Robin of her own flat back in London.

'I think we'd both better go in,' Strike said, unbuckling his seatbelt. 'She'll probably be more comfortable with you there.'

The doorbell seemed to be out of order. Strike therefore rapped sharply on the door with his knuckles. An explosion of furious barking told them that the house had at least one living inhabitant. Then they heard a woman's voice, angry but somehow ineffectual.

'Shh! Be quiet! Stop it! Shh! No!'

The door opened and Robin had just caught a glimpse of a hard-faced woman of around fifty when a rough-coated Jack Russell came pelting out, growling and barking with ferocity, and sank its teeth into Strike's ankle. Fortunately for Strike, but less so for the Jack Russell, its teeth connected with steel. It yelped and Robin capitalised on its shock by stooping swiftly, grabbing it by the scruff of the neck and lifting it up. So surprised was the dog at finding itself dangling in mid-air that it simply hung there.

'No biting,' said Robin.

Apparently deciding that a woman brave enough to pick it up was worthy of respect, the dog allowed her to take a firmer grip, twisted in mid-air and attempted to lick her hand.

'Sorry,' said the woman. 'He was my mother's. He's a bloody nightmare. He likes you, look. Miracle.'

Her shoulder-length brown hair had grey roots. Deep marionette lines lay either side of a thin-lipped mouth. She was leaning on a stick, one of her ankles swollen and bandaged, the foot encased in a sandal that displayed yellowing toenails.

Strike introduced himself, then showed Lorraine his driving licence and a business card.

'Are you Lorraine MacNaughton?'

'Yeah,' she said hesitantly. Her eyes flickered to Robin, who smiled reassuringly over the Jack Russell's head. 'You're a – what did you say?'

'A detective,' said Strike, 'and I was wondering whether you could tell me anything about Donald Laing. Telephone records show he was living here with you a couple of years ago.'

'Yeah, he was,' she said slowly.

'Is he still here?' Strike asked, although he knew the answer.

'No.'

Strike indicated Robin.

'Would it be all right if my colleague and I come in and ask you a few questions? We're trying to find Mr Laing.'

There was a pause. Lorraine chewed her inner lip, frowning. Robin cradled the Jack Russell, which was now enthusiastically licking her fingers where, no doubt, it could taste traces of Danish pastry. Strike's torn trouser leg flapped in a light breeze.

'All right, come in,' said Lorraine, and she backed away on her crutches to admit them.

The frowzy front room smelled strongly of stale cigarette smoke. There were countless old-ladyish touches: crocheted tissue-box covers, cheap frilled cushions and an array of fancily dressed teddy bears arranged on a polished sideboard. One wall was dominated by a painting of a saucer-eyed child dressed as a pierrot. Strike could no more imagine Donald Laing living here than he could visualise a bullock bedded down in the corner.

Once inside, the Jack Russell scrabbled to get down out of Robin's arms, then started barking at Strike again.

'Oh, shut up,' groaned Lorraine. Sinking down onto the faded brown velvet sofa, she used both arms to lift her bandaged ankle back onto a leather pouffe, reached sideways to retrieve her packet of Superkings and lit up.

'I'm supposed to keep it raised,' she explained, cigarette waggling in her mouth as she picked up a full cut-glass ashtray and set it on her lap. 'District nurse is in every day to change the dressings. Sit down.'

'What have you done?' asked Robin, squeezing past the coffee table to sit beside Lorraine on the sofa. The Jack Russell immediately jumped up beside her and, mercifully, stopped barking.

'I got a load of chip fat dropped on me,' said Lorraine. 'At work.'

'Christ,' said Strike, settling himself in the armchair. 'That must've been agony.'

'Yeah, it was. They say I'll be off at least a month. Least it wasn't far to go to casualty.'

Lorraine, it transpired, worked in the canteen of the local hospital.

'So what's Donnie done?' Lorraine muttered, puffing smoke, once the subject of her injury had been thoroughly aired. 'Robbery again, is it?'

'Why do you say that?' asked Strike carefully.

'He robbed me,' she said.

Robin saw, now, that the brusqueness was a façade. Lorraine's long cigarette trembled as she said it.

'When was this?' asked Strike.

'When he walked out. Took all my jewellery. Mum's wedding ring, everything. He knew what that meant to me. She'd not been dead a year. Yeah, one day he just walks out of the house and never comes back. I called the police, I thought he'd had an accident. Then I realised my purse was empty and my jewellery was gone.'

The humiliation had not left her. Her sunken cheeks flushed as she said it.

Strike felt in the inside pocket of his jacket.

'I want to make sure we're talking about the same man. Does this picture look familiar?'

He handed her one of the photographs Laing's ex-mother-in-law had given him in Melrose. Big and broad in his blue and yellow kilt, with his dark ferret-like eyes and that low-sprouting crop of fox-red hair, Laing was standing outside a registry office. Rhona clung to his arm, less than half his width in what looked like a poorly fitting, possibly second-hand wedding gown.

Lorraine examined the photograph for what seemed like a very long time. At last she said:

'I *think* it's him. It could be.'

'You can't see it, but he had a big tattoo of a yellow rose on his left forearm,' said Strike.

'Yeah,' said Lorraine heavily. 'That's right. He did.'

She smoked, staring at the picture.

'He'd been married, had he?' she asked, with a slight quaver in her voice.

'Didn't he tell you?' asked Robin.

'No. Told me he'd never been.'

'How did you meet him?' asked Robin.

'Pub,' said Lorraine. 'He didn't look much like that when I knew him.'

She turned in the direction of the sideboard behind her and made a vague attempt to get up.

'Can I help?' Robin offered.

'In that middle drawer. There might be a picture.'

The Jack Russell began barking again as Robin opened a drawer containing an assortment of napkin rings, crocheted doilies, souvenir teaspoons, toothpicks and loose photographs. Robin extracted as many of the latter as she could and brought them back to Lorraine.

'That's him,' said Lorraine, after sorting through many pictures that mostly featured a very elderly woman whom Robin assumed to be Lorraine's mother. Lorraine passed the picture straight to Strike.

He would not have recognised Laing if he had passed him in the street. The former boxer was massively swollen, especially around the face. His neck was no longer visible; his skin seemed tight, his features distorted. One arm was around a smiling Lorraine's shoulders, the other hung loose at his side. He was not smiling. Strike peered closer. The yellow rose tattoo was visible, but partially obscured by angry red skin plaques that mottled the whole expanse of his forearm.

'Is there something wrong with his skin?'

'Psoriatic arthritis,' said Lorraine. 'He was bad with it. That's why he was on the sick benefit. Had to stop work.'

'Yeah?' said Strike. 'What had he been working as before?'

'He come down here as a manager for one of the big construction firms,' she said, 'but then he got ill and couldn't work. He'd had his own building company up in Melrose. He was the managing director.'

'Really?' said Strike.

'Yeah, family business,' said Lorraine, searching her stack of photographs. 'He inherited it from his dad. There he is again, look.'

They were holding hands in this picture, which looked as though it had been taken in a beer garden. Lorraine beamed and Laing looked blank, his moon face shrinking his dark eyes to slits. He had the characteristic look of a man on medically prescribed steroids. The hair like a fox's pelt was the same, but otherwise Strike was hard pressed to make out the features of the fit young boxer who had once bitten his face.

'How long were you together?'

'Ten months. I met him right after Mum died. She was ninety-two – she lived here with me. I was helping with Mrs Williams next door and all; she was eighty-seven. Senile. Her son's in America. Donnie was good to her. He mowed her lawn and got shopping.'

Bastard knew which side his bread was buttered, thought Strike. Ill, unemployed and broke as Laing had been at the time, a lonely middle-aged woman without dependents who could cook, who had her own house, who had just inherited money from her mother, must have been a godsend. It would have been worth faking a bit of compassion to get his feet under the table. Laing had had charm when he chose to use it.

'He seemed all right when we met,' said Lorraine morosely. 'Couldn't do enough for me then. He wasn't well himself. Joints swollen and everything. He had to have injections off the doctor . . . He got a bit moody later, but I thought that was just his health. You don't expect ill people to be always cheerful, do you? Not everyone's like Mum. She was a bloody marvel, her health was that bad and she was always smiling and . . . and . . . '

'Let me get you a tissue,' said Robin and she leaned slowly towards the crochet-covered box, so as not to disarrange the Jack Russell, which had its head on her lap.

'Did you report the theft of your jewellery?' Strike asked, once Lorraine had received her tissue, which she plied between deep drags on her Superking.

'No,' she said gruffly. 'What was the point? They were never going to find it.'

Robin guessed that Lorraine had not wanted to draw official attention to her humiliation, and sympathised.

'Was he ever violent?' Robin asked gently.

Lorraine looked surprised.

'No. Is that why you're here? Has he hurt someone?'

'We don't know,' said Strike.

'I don't think he'd *hurt* anyone,' she said. 'He wasn't that kind of man. I said that to the police.'

'Sorry,' said Robin, stroking the now-dozing Jack Russell's head. 'I thought you didn't report the robbery?'

'This was later,' said Lorraine. 'Month or so after he'd gone. Somebody broke into Mrs Williams's place, knocked her out and robbed the house. The police wanted to know where Donnie was. I said, "He's long gone, moved out." Anyway, he wouldn't do that, I told them. He'd been good to her. He wouldn't punch an old lady.'

They had once held hands in a beer garden. He had mowed the old lady's lawn. She refused to believe Laing had been all bad.

'I assume your neighbour couldn't give the police a description?' Strike asked.

Lorraine shook her head.

'She never came back, after. Died in a home. Got a family in Northfield now,' said Lorraine. 'Three little kids. You should hear the noise – and they've got the bloody cheek to complain about the dog!'

They had hit a complete dead end. Lorraine had no idea where Laing had gone next. She could not remember him mentioning any place to which he was connected other than Melrose and she had never met any of his friends. Once she had realised that he was never coming back, she had deleted his mobile number from her phone. She agreed to let them take the two photographs of Laing, but other than that, had no more help to offer.

The Jack Russell protested loudly at Robin withdrawing her warm lap and showed every sign of wishing to take his displeasure out on Strike as the detective rose from his chair.

'*Stop it*, Tigger,' said Lorraine crossly, holding the struggling dog on the sofa with difficulty.

'We'll see ourselves out,' Robin shouted over the dog's frenzied barking. 'Thanks so much for all your help!'

They left her there in her cluttered, smoky sitting room, bandaged ankle raised, probably a little sadder and more uncomfortable for their visit. The sound of the hysterical dog followed them all the way up the garden path.

'I feel like we could at least have made her a cup of tea or something,' said Robin guiltily as they got back into the Land Rover.

'She doesn't know what a lucky escape she's had,' said Strike bracingly. 'Think about the poor old dear in there,' he pointed at Northfield, 'beaten to shit for a couple of extra quid.'

'You think that was Laing?'

'Of course it was bloody Laing,' said Strike as Robin turned on the engine. 'He'd cased the joint while he was supposedly helping her out, hadn't he? And you notice that, for all he was supposed to be so ill with his arthritis, he was still capable of mowing lawns and half killing old women.'

Hungry and tired, her head aching from the stale cigarette smoke, Robin nodded and said that she supposed so. It had been a depressing interview and the prospect of a further two and a half hours' drive to get back home was not appealing.

'D'you mind if we get going?' said Strike, checking his watch. 'I told Elin I'll be over tonight.'

'No problem,' said Robin.

Yet for some reason – perhaps due to her headache, perhaps because of the lonely woman sitting in Summerfield among the memories of loved ones who had left her – Robin could easily have wept all over again.

29

I Just Like To Be Bad

Sometimes he found it hard to be with the people who thought themselves his friends: the men with whom he associated when he needed money. Theft was their main occupation, tomming of a Saturday night their recreation; he was popular among them, a mate, so they thought, a fellow, an equal. An equal!

The day the police had found her, all he had wanted was to be alone to savour the coverage. The stories in the paper made good reading. He felt proud: this was the first time he'd been able to kill in private, to take his time, to organise things as he'd wanted. He intended to do the same with The Secretary; to have time to enjoy her alive before he killed her.

His one frustration was there was no mention of the letters that were supposed to point the police to Strike, to make them interrogate and badger the fucker, drag his name through the mud in the papers, make the dumb public think he'd had something to do with it.

However, there were columns and columns of coverage, photographs of the flat where he'd done her, interviews with the pretty-boy police officer. He saved the stories: they were souvenirs, just like the bits of her he had taken for his private collection.

Of course, his pride and enjoyment had to be hidden from It, because It required very careful handling at the moment. It wasn't happy, not happy at all. Life wasn't panning out the way It had expected and he had to pretend to give a flying fuck, to be concerned, be a nice guy, because It was useful to him: It brought in money and It might have to give him alibis. You never knew whether they might be needed. He'd had a close call once before.

That had been the second time he had killed, in Milton Keynes. You didn't shit on your own doorstep: that had always been one of his guiding principles. He had never been to Milton Keynes before or since and had no connection with the place. He had stolen a car, away from the boys, a solo job. He had had fake plates ready for a while. Then he had simply driven, wondering whether he would get lucky. There had been a couple of failed attempts since his first murder: trying to chat up girls in pubs, in clubs, trying to isolate them, was not working as well as it had in the past. He didn't look as good as he once had, he knew that, but he didn't want to establish a pattern of doing prostitutes. The police started to put two and two together if you went for the same type every time. Once he had managed to track a tipsy girl down an alleyway, but before he'd even drawn his knife out a pack of giggling kids had burst into view and he had taken off. After that he had given up on trying to pick up a girl in the usual way. It would have to be force.

He had driven for hours in increasing frustration; not a whiff of a victim in Milton Keynes. At ten to midnight he was on the verge of caving and sniffing out a hooker when he'd spotted her. She was arguing with her boyfriend on a roundabout in the middle of the road, a short-haired brunette in jeans. As he passed he kept an eye on the couple in his rear-view mirror. He watched her storm away, as good as intoxicated by her own anger and tears. The infuriated man she had left behind shouted after her, then, with a gesture of disgust, stumbled off in the opposite direction.

He did a U-turn and drove back up the road towards her. She was sobbing as she walked, wiping her eyes on her sleeve.

He had wound down the window.

'You all right, love?'

'Piss off!'

She sealed her fate by plunging angrily into bushes beside the road to get away from his crawling car. Another hundred yards would have taken her to a well-lit stretch of road.

All he had to do was turn off the road and park. He pulled on the balaclava before getting out of the car, the knife ready in his hand, and walked calmly back to the place where she had disappeared. He could hear her trying to fight her way back out of the dense patch of trees and shrubs, placed there by town planners to soften the contours of the wide grey dual carriageway. There was no street lamp here. He was invisible to passing drivers as he skirted the dark foliage. As she beat her way back onto the pavement, he was standing ready to force her back in at knifepoint.

He had spent an hour in the bushes before leaving the body. He ripped her earrings from her lobes and then wielded his knife with abandon, hacking off bits of her. A gap in the traffic and he scurried, panting, back to the stolen car in the darkness, balaclava still in place.

He drove away, every particle of him elated and sated, his pockets seeping. Only then did the mist lift.

Last time, he had used a car from work, which he had subsequently cleaned thoroughly in full view of his workmates. He doubted anyone would be able to get the blood out of these cloth seats and his DNA would be on everything. What was he going to do? That was the closest he had ever come to panicking.

He drove miles north before abandoning the car in a lonely field far from the main road, not overlooked by any buildings. Here, shivering in the cold, he took off the fake plates, soaked one of his socks in the petrol tank, then chucked it into the bloody front seat and lit it. It took a long time for the car to properly catch; he had to re-approach it several times to help it along until finally, at three in the morning while he watched, shivering, from the cover of trees, it exploded. Then he ran.

It was winter, which meant at least that the balaclava did not look out of place. He buried the fake plates in a wood and hurried on, head bowed, hands in his pockets on his treasured souvenirs. He had considered burying them too, but he could not bring himself to do it. He had covered the bloodstains on his trousers with mud, kept his balaclava on at the station, acting drunk in a corner of the train carriage to keep people away from him, muttering to himself, projecting that aura of menace and madness that acted like a cordon when he wished to be left alone.

By the time he reached home they had found her body. He watched it on the TV that night, eating off a tray in his lap. They found the burnt-out car, but not the plates and – this really was proof of his own inimitable luck, the strange protective blessing the cosmos gave him – the boyfriend with whom she had argued was arrested, charged and, though the evidence against him was transparently weak, convicted! The thought of that dickhead serving his time still made him laugh sometimes . . .

Nevertheless, those long hours of driving through the darkness when he had known an encounter with the police might be fatal, when he had feared a request to turn out his pockets or a shrewd-eyed passenger noticing dried blood on him had taught him a powerful lesson. Plan every detail. Leave nothing to chance.

That was why he needed to nip out for some Vicks VapoRub. The number-one priority right now was to make sure that Its stupid new scheme did not interfere with his own.

30

I am gripped, by what I cannot tell . . .

Blue Öyster Cult, 'Lips in the Hills'

Strike was inured to the shifts between frenetic activity and enforced passivity demanded by investigations. Nevertheless, the weekend following their round trip to Barrow, Market Harborough and Corby found him in a strange state of tension.

The gradual re-immersion in civilian life that had taken place over the past couple of years had brought with it pressures from which he had been protected while in the military. His half-sister Lucy, the only sibling with whom he had shared a childhood, called early on Saturday morning to ask why he had not responded to her invitation to his middle nephew's birthday party. He explained that he had been away, unable to access mail sent to the office, but she barely listened.

'Jack hero-worships you, you know,' she said. 'He really wants you to come.'

'Sorry, Lucy,' said Strike, 'can't make it. I'll send him a present.'

Had Strike still been in the SIB, Lucy would not have felt entitled to exert emotional blackmail. It had been easy to avoid family obligations then, while he was travelling the world. She had seen him as an inextricable part of the army's immense and implacable machine. When he steadily refused to yield to her word picture of a desolate eight-year-old nephew looking in vain for Uncle Cormoran at the garden gate, she desisted, asking instead how the hunt for the man who had sent the leg was progressing. Her tone implied that there was something disreputable about being sent a leg. Keen to get her off the phone, Strike told her untruthfully that he was leaving everything up to the police.

Fond as he was of his younger sister, he had come to accept that their relationship rested almost entirely on shared and largely traumatic memories. He never confided in Lucy unless forced to do so by external events, for the simple reason that confidences usually elicited alarm or anxiety. Lucy lived in a state of perennial disappointment that he was still, at the age of thirty-seven, holding out against all those things that she believed necessary to make him happy: a job with regular hours, more money, a wife and children.

Glad to have got rid of her, Strike made himself his third mug of tea of the morning and laid back down on the bed with a pile of newspapers. Several of them displayed a photograph of MURDER VICTIM KELSEY PLATT, wearing a navy school uniform, a smile on her plain, pimply face.

Dressed only in boxers, his hairy belly no smaller for the plentiful takeaways and chocolate bars that had filled it in the last fortnight, he munched his way through a packet of Rich Tea biscuits and skimmed several of the stories, but they told him nothing he did not already know, so he turned instead to the anticipatory comment about the next day's Arsenal–Liverpool match.

His mobile rang while he was reading. He had not realised how tightly wound he was: he reacted so fast that Wardle was taken by surprise.

'Bloody hell, that was quick. What were you doing, sitting on it?'

'What's going on?'

'We've been over to Kelsey's sister's place – name's Hazel, she's a nurse. We're looking into all Kelsey's day-to-day contacts, we've gone through her room and we've got her laptop. She'd been online, on some message board for people who want to hack bits off themselves, and she was asking about you.'

Strike scratched his dense, curly hair, staring at the ceiling, listening.

'We've got personal details for a couple of the people she was interacting with regularly on the boards. I should have pictures by Monday – where will you be?'

'Here, in the office.'

'Her sister's boyfriend, the ex-fireman, says Kelsey kept asking him about people trapped in buildings and car accidents and all sorts. She really wanted to get rid of that leg.'

'Jesus,' muttered Strike.

After Wardle had hung up, Strike found himself unable to focus on the backroom reshuffles at the Emirates. After a few minutes he abandoned the pretence that he was absorbed in the fate of Arsène Wenger's management team and resumed his staring at the cracks in the ceiling, absently turning his mobile over and over.

In the blinding relief that the leg had not been Brittany Brockbank's, he had given less thought to the victim than he would ordinarily have done. Now, for the first time, he wondered about Kelsey and the letter that she had sent him, which he had not bothered to read.

The idea of anybody seeking amputation was repugnant to Strike. Round and round in his hand he turned his mobile, marshalling everything he knew about Kelsey, trying to build a mental picture out of a name and mingled feelings of pity and distaste. She had been sixteen; she had not got on with her sister; she had been studying childcare ... Strike reached for his notebook and began to write: *Boyfriend at college? Lecturer?* She had gone online, asking about him. Why? Where had she got the idea that he, Strike, had amputated his own leg? Or had she evolved a fantasy out of newspaper reports about him?

Mental illness? Fantasist? he wrote.

Wardle was already looking into her online contacts. Strike paused in his writing, remembering the photograph of Kelsey's head with its full cheeks in the freezer, staring out of its frosted eyes. Puppy fat. He had thought all along that she looked far too young for twenty-four. In truth, she had looked young for sixteen.

He let his pencil fall and continued to turn his mobile over and over in his left hand, thinking ...

Was Brockbank a 'true' paedophile, as a psychologist Strike had met in the context of another military rape case had put it? Was he a man who was only sexually attracted to children? Or was he a different kind of violent abuser, a man who targeted young girls merely because they were most readily available and easiest to cow into silence, but who had wider sexual tastes if an easy victim became available? In short, was a babyish-looking sixteen-year-old too old to appeal sexually to Brockbank, or would he rape any easily silenced female if he got the chance? Strike had once had to deal with a nineteen-year-old soldier who had attempted to rape a sixty-seven-year-old. Some men's violent sexual nature required only opportunity.

Strike had not yet called the number that Ingrid had given him for Brockbank. His dark eyes drifted to the tiny window that showed a feebly sunlit sky. Perhaps he should have passed Brockbank's number to Wardle. Perhaps he ought to call it now ...

Yet even as Strike began to scroll down the list of contacts, he reconsidered. What had he achieved so far by confiding his suspicions to Wardle? Nothing. The policeman was busy in his operations room, doubtless sifting leads, busy with his own lines of enquiry and giving Strike's – as far as the private detective could tell – only slightly more credence than he would have given anyone who had hunches but no proof. The fact that Wardle, with all his resources, had not yet located Brockbank, Laing or Whittaker, did not suggest that he was prioritising the men.

No, if Strike wanted to find Brockbank he ought surely to maintain the cover that Robin had created: that of the lawyer looking to win the ex-major compensation. The traceable backstory they had created with his sister in Barrow might prove valuable. In fact, thought Strike, sitting up on the bed, it might be an idea to call Robin right now and give her Brockbank's number. She was alone, he knew, in the Ealing flat, while Matthew was home in Masham. He could call and perhaps—

Oh no you don't, you silly fucker.

A vision of himself and Robin in the Tottenham had bloomed in his head, a vision of where a phone call might lead. They were both at a loose end. A drink to discuss the case . . .

On a Saturday night? Piss off.

Strike got up suddenly, as though the bed had become painful to lie on, dressed and headed out to the supermarket.

On his way back into Denmark Street carrying bulging plastic bags he thought he spotted Wardle's plain-clothes policeman, stationed in the area to keep an eye out for large men in beanie hats. The young man in a donkey jacket was hyperaware, his eyes lingering a tad too long on the detective as he walked past, his shopping swinging.

Elin called Strike much later, after he had eaten a solitary evening meal in his flat. As usual, Saturday night was out of bounds for a meeting. He could hear her daughter playing in the background as she talked. They had already arranged to see each other for dinner on Sunday, but she had called to ask whether he fancied meeting her earlier. Her husband was determined to force the sale of the valuable flat in Clarence Terrace and she had started looking for a new property.

'Do you want to come and look at it with me?' she asked. 'I've got an appointment at the show flat tomorrow at two.'

He knew, or thought he knew, that the invitation sprang, not from some eager hope that he would one day be living with her there – they had only been dating for three months – but because she was a woman who would always choose company when possible. Her air of cool self-sufficiency was misleading. They might never have met had she not preferred to attend a party full of her brother's unknown colleagues and friends rather than spend a few hours alone. There was nothing wrong with that, of course, nothing wrong with being sociable, except that for a year now Strike had organised his life to suit himself and the habit was hard to break.

'Can't,' he said, 'sorry. I'm on a job until three.'

The lie convincingly told. She took it reasonably well. They agreed to meet at the bistro on Sunday evening as previously planned, which meant that he would be able to watch Arsenal–Liverpool in peace.

After he had hung up, he thought again of Robin, alone in the flat she shared with Matthew. Reaching for a cigarette, he turned on the TV and sank back onto his pillows in the dark.

Robin was having a strange weekend. Determined not to sink into moroseness just because she was alone and Strike had gone off to Elin's (where had that thought come from? Of course he had gone; after all, it was the weekend, and it was no business of hers where he chose to spend it), she had spent hours on her laptop, doggedly pursuing one old line of enquiry, and one new.

Late on Saturday night she made an online discovery that caused her to jog three victory laps of the tiny sitting room and almost phone Strike to tell him. It took several minutes, with her heart thumping and her breath coming fast, to calm down, and to tell herself that the news would keep until Monday. It would be much more satisfying to tell him in person.

Knowing that Robin was alone, her mother called her twice over the weekend, both times pressing for a date when she could come down to London.

'I don't know, Mum, not just now,' sighed Robin on Sunday morning. She was sitting in her pyjamas on the sofa, laptop open in front of her again, trying to hold an online conversation with a member of the BIID community who called themselves **<<Δēvōţėė>>**. She had only picked up her mother's call because she was afraid ignoring it might result in an unannounced visit.

<<Δēvōţėė>>: where do you want to be cut?
TransHopeful: mid-thigh
<<Δēvōţėė>>: both legs?

'What about tomorrow?' asked Linda.

'No,' said Robin at once. Like Strike, she lied with fluent conviction, 'I'm midway through a job. The following week's better.'

TransHopeful: Yes, both. Do you know anyone who's done it?
<<Δēvōţėė>>: Can't share that on msj board. Where you live?

'I haven't seen him,' said Linda. 'Robin, are you typing?'

'No,' lied Robin again, her fingers suspended over the keyboard. 'Who haven't you seen?'

'Matthew, of course!'

'Oh. Well, no, I didn't think he'd come calling this weekend.'

She tried typing more quietly.

TransHopeful: London
<<Δēvōtėė>>: Me too. Got a pic?

'Did you go to Mr Cunliffe's birthday party?' she asked, trying to drown out the sound of the laptop keys.

'Of course we didn't!' said Linda. 'Well, let me know what day's best week after next, and I'll book my ticket. It's Easter; it'll be busy.'

Robin agreed, returned Linda's affectionate goodbye and directed her full attention to **<<Δēvōtėė>>**. Unfortunately, after Robin had refused to give him or her (she was almost positive that he was male) a picture, **<<Δēvōtėė>>** lost interest in their back and forth on the noticeboards and went quiet.

She had expected Matthew to return from his father's on Sunday evening, but he did not. When she checked the calendar in the kitchen at eight, she realised that he had always intended to take Monday off. Presumably she had agreed to this, back when the weekend had been planned, and told Matthew that she would ask Strike for a day's holiday, too. It was lucky that they had split up, really, she told herself bracingly: she had dodged one more row about her working hours.

However, she cried later, alone in the bedroom that was thick with relics of their shared past: the fluffy elephant he had given her on their first Valentine's Day together – he had not been so suave in those days; she could remember him turning red as he had produced it – and the jewellery box he had given her for her twenty-first. Then there were all the photographs showing them beaming during holidays in Greece and Spain, and dressed up at Matthew's sister's wedding. The biggest picture of the lot showed them arm in arm on Matthew's graduation day. He was in his academic gown and Robin stood beside him in a summer dress, beaming as she celebrated an achievement of which she had been robbed by a man in a gorilla mask.

31

Nighttime flowers, evening roses,
Bless this garden that never closes.

Blue Öyster Cult, 'Tenderloin'

Robin's mood was buoyed next day by the glorious spring morning that greeted her outside her front door. She did not forget to remain aware of her surroundings as she travelled by Tube towards Tottenham Court Road, but saw no sign of any large man in a beanie hat. What leapt to the eye on her morning commute was the mounting journalistic excitement about the royal wedding. Kate Middleton seemed to be on the front of virtually every newspaper held by her fellow travellers. It made Robin hyperaware all over again of that naked, sensitive place on her third finger where an engagement ring had sat for a year. However, excited as she was about sharing the results of her solo investigative work with Strike, Robin refused to be downcast.

She had just left Tottenham Court Road station when she heard a man shout her name. For a split-second she feared an ambush by Matthew, then Strike appeared, forging a path through the crowd, backpack on his shoulder. Robin deduced that he had spent the night with Elin.

'Morning. Good weekend?' he asked. Then, before she could answer: 'Sorry. No. Crap weekend, obviously.'

'Bits of it were all right,' said Robin as they wended their way through the usual obstacle course of barriers and holes in the road.

'What have you got?' Strike asked loudly over the interminable drills.

'Sorry?' she shouted.

'What. Have. You. Found. Out?'

'How do you know I've found anything out?'

'You've got that look,' he said. 'The look you get when you're dying to tell me something.'

She grinned.

'I need a computer to show you.'

They turned the corner into Denmark Street. A man dressed all in black stood outside their office door, holding a gigantic bunch of red roses.

'Oh, for God's sake,' breathed Robin.

A spasm of fear receded: her mind had momentarily edited out the armful of blooms and seen only the man in black – but it wasn't the courier, of course. This, she saw as they approached him, was a youth with long hair, an Interflora deliveryman wearing no helmet. Strike doubted the boy had ever handed over fifty red roses to a less enthusiastic recipient.

'His father's put him up to this,' Robin said darkly, as Strike held open the door for her and she pushed her way inside, being none too gentle with the quivering floral display. '"All women love roses," he'll have said. That's all it takes – a bunch of bloody flowers.'

Strike followed her up the metal staircase, amused but careful not to show it. He unlocked the office door and Robin crossed to her desk and dropped the roses unceremoniously onto it, where they quivered in their beribboned polythene bag of greenish water. There was a card. She did not want to open it in front of Strike.

'Well?' he asked, hanging his backpack on the peg beside the door. 'What have you found out?'

Before Robin could say a word there was a rap on the door. Wardle's shape was easily recognisable through the frosted glass: his wavy hair, his leather jacket.

'I was in the area. Not too early, is it? Bloke downstairs let me in.'

Wardle's eyes travelled immediately to the roses on Robin's desk.

'Birthday?'

'No,' she said shortly. 'Do either of you want coffee?'

'I'll do it,' said Strike, moving over to the kettle and still speaking to Robin. 'Wardle's got some stuff to show us.'

Robin's spirits sank: was the policeman about to pre-empt her? Why hadn't she called Strike on Saturday night, when she'd found it?

Wardle sat down on the mock-leather sofa that always emitted loud farting noises whenever anyone over a certain weight sat on it. Clearly startled, the policeman repositioned himself gingerly and opened a folder.

'It turns out Kelsey was posting on a website for other people who wanted to get limbs taken off,' Wardle told Robin.

Robin sat down in her usual seat behind her desk. The roses impeded her view of the policeman; she picked them up impatiently and deposited them on the floor beside her.

'She mentioned Strike,' Wardle went on. 'Asked if anyone else knew anything about him.'

'Was she using the name Nowheretoturn?' asked Robin, trying to keep her voice casual. Wardle looked up, astonished, and Strike turned, a coffee spoon suspended in mid-air.

'Yeah, she was,' said the policeman, staring. 'How the hell did you know that?'

'I found that message board last weekend,' said Robin. 'I thought Nowheretoturn might be the girl who wrote the letter.'

'Christ,' said Wardle, looking from Robin to Strike. 'We should offer her a job.'

'She's got a job,' said Strike. 'Go on. Kelsey was posting . . .'

'Yeah, well, she ended up exchanging email addresses with these two. Nothing particularly helpful, but we're looking to establish whether they actually met her – you know, in Real Life,' said Wardle.

Strange, thought Strike, how that phrase – so prevalent in childhood to differentiate between the fantasy world of play and the dull adult world of fact – had now come to signify the life that a person had outside the internet. He handed Wardle and Robin their coffees, then went through to his inner office to fetch a chair, preferring not to share the farting sofa with Wardle.

When he returned, Wardle was showing Robin printed screenshots of the Facebook pages of two people.

She examined each of them carefully, then passed them on to Strike. One was a thick-set young woman with a round, pale face, bobbed black hair and glasses. The other was a light-haired man in his twenties with lopsided eyes.

'*She* blogs about being "transabled", whatever the fuck that is, and *he's* all over message boards asking for help in hacking bits off himself. Both of them have got serious issues, if you ask me. Recognise either of them?'

Strike shook his head, as did Robin. Wardle sighed and took the pictures back.

'Long shot.'

'What about other men she's been knocking around with?

Any boys or lecturers at college?' asked Strike, thinking of the questions that had occurred to him on Saturday.

'Well, the sister says Kelsey claimed to have a mysterious boyfriend they were never allowed to meet. Hazel doesn't believe he existed. We've spoken to a couple of Kelsey's college friends and none of them ever saw a boyfriend, but we're following it up.

'Speaking of Hazel,' Wardle went on, picking up his coffee and drinking some before continuing, 'I've said I'll pass on a message. She'd like to meet you.'

'Me?' said Strike, surprised. 'Why?'

'I dunno,' said Wardle. 'I think she wants to justify herself to everyone. She's in a real state.'

'Justify herself?'

'She's guilt-ridden because she treated the leg thing as weird and attention-seeking, and feels that's why Kelsey went looking for someone else to help her with it.'

'She understands I never wrote back? That I never had actual contact with her?'

'Yeah, yeah, I've explained that to her. She still wants to talk to you. I dunno,' said Wardle slightly impatiently, 'you got sent her sister's leg – you know what people are like when they're in shock. Plus, it's you, isn't it?' said Wardle, with a faint edge in his voice. 'She probably thinks the Boy Wonder will solve it while the police are blundering.'

Robin and Strike avoided looking at each other and Wardle added grudgingly:

'We could've handled Hazel better. Our guys interrogated her partner a bit more aggressively than she liked. It put her on the defensive. She might like the idea of having you on the books: the detective who's already saved one poor innocent from the nick.'

Strike decided to ignore the defensive undertone.

'Obviously, we had to question the bloke who was living with her,' Wardle added for Robin's benefit. 'That's routine.'

'Yes,' said Robin. 'Of course.'

'No other men in her life, except the sister's partner and this alleged boyfriend?' asked Strike.

'She was seeing a male counsellor, a skinny black guy in his fifties who was visiting family in Bristol on the weekend she died, and there's a church youth group leader called Darrell,' said Wardle, 'fat guy in dungarees. He cried his eyes out all through the interview. He was present and correct at the church on the Sunday; nothing checkable otherwise, but I can't see him wielding a cleaver. That's everyone we know about. Her course is nearly all girls.'

'No boys in the church youth group?'

'They're nearly all girls as well. Oldest boy's fourteen.'

'How would the police feel about me seeing Hazel?' Strike asked.

'We can't stop you,' Wardle said, shrugging. 'I'm for it, on the understanding that you'll pass on anything useful, but I doubt there's anything else there. We've interviewed everyone, we've been through Kelsey's room, we've got her laptop and personally I'd bet none of the people we've talked to knew anything. They all thought she was off on a college placement.'

After thanks for the coffee and a particularly warm smile for Robin, which was barely returned, Wardle left.

'Not a word about Brockbank, Laing or Whittaker,' Strike grumbled as Wardle's clanging footsteps faded from earshot. 'And you never told me you'd been ferreting around on the net,' he added to Robin.

'I had no proof she was the girl who'd written the letter,' said Robin, 'but I did think Kelsey might have gone online looking for help.'

Strike heaved himself to his feet, took her mug from

her desk and was heading for the door when Robin said indignantly:

'Aren't you interested in what I was going to tell you?'

He turned, surprised.

'That wasn't it?'

'No!'

'Well?'

'I think I've found Donald Laing.'

Strike said nothing at all, but stood looking blank, a mug in each hand.

'You've – what? How?'

Robin turned on her computer, beckoned Strike over and began typing. He moved around to look over her shoulder.

'First,' she said, 'I had to find out how to spell psoriatic arthritis. Then . . . look at this.'

She had brought up a JustGiving charity page. A man glared out of the small picture at the top.

'Bloody hell, that's him!' said Strike, so loudly that Robin jumped. He set the mugs down and dragged his chair around the desk to look at the monitor. In doing so, he knocked over Robin's roses.

'Shit – sorry—'

'I don't care,' said Robin. 'Sit here, I'll clear them up.'

She moved out of the way and Strike took her place on the swivel chair.

It was a small photograph, which Strike enlarged by clicking on it. The Scot was standing on what seemed to be a cramped balcony with a balustrade of thick, greenish glass, unsmiling, with a crutch under his right arm. The short, bristly hair still grew low on his forehead, but it seemed to have darkened over the years, no longer red as a fox's pelt. Clean-shaven, his skin looked pockmarked. He was less swollen in the face than he had been in Lorraine's picture, but he had put on weight since the days when he had been muscled like a marble Atlas and had bitten Strike on the face in the boxing ring. He was wearing a yellow T-shirt and on his right forearm was the rose tattoo, which had undergone a modification: a dagger now ran through it, and drops of blood fell out of the flower towards the wrist. Behind Laing on his balcony was what looked like a blurry, jagged pattern of windows in black and silver.

He had used his real name:

Donald Laing Charity Appeal

I am a British veteran now suffering from psoriatic arthritis.

I am raising money for Arthritis Research. Please give what you can.

The page had been created three months previously. He had raised 0 per cent of the one thousand pounds he was hoping to meet.

'No rubbish about doing anything for the money,' Strike noted. 'Just "gimme".'

'Not give *me*,' Robin corrected him from the floor, where she was mopping up spilled flower water with bits of kitchen roll. 'He's giving it to the charity.'

'So he says.'

Strike was squinting at the jagged pattern behind Laing on the balcony.

'Does that remind you of anything? Those windows behind him?'

'I thought of the Gherkin at first,' said Robin, throwing the sodden towels in the bin and getting to her feet, 'but the pattern's different.'

'Nothing about where he's living,' said Strike, clicking everywhere he could on the page to see what further information he might uncover. 'JustGiving must have his details somewhere.'

'You somehow never expect evil people to get ill,' said Robin.

She checked her watch.

'I'm supposed to be on Platinum in fifteen. I'd better get going.'

'Yeah,' said Strike, still staring at Laing's picture. 'Keep in touch and – oh yeah: I need you to do something.'

He pulled his mobile out of his pocket.

'Brockbank.'

'So you *do* still think it might be him?' Robin said, pausing in the act of putting on her jacket.

'Maybe. I want you to call him, keep the Venetia Hall, personal injury lawyer thing going.'

'Oh. OK,' she said, pulling out her own mobile and keying in the number that he had shown her, but beneath her matter-of-fact manner she was quietly elated. Venetia had been her own idea, her creation, and now Strike was turning the whole line of enquiry over to her.

She was halfway up Denmark Street in the sunshine before Robin remembered that there had been a card with the now-battered roses, and that she had left it behind, unread.

32

What's that in the corner?
It's too dark to see.

Blue Öyster Cult, 'After Dark'

Surrounded all day long by the sounds of traffic and loud voices, Robin did not have a good opportunity to call Noel Brockbank until five o'clock that afternoon. Having seen Platinum to work as usual, she turned into the Japanese restaurant beside the lap-dancing club and took her green tea to a quiet corner table. There, she waited for five minutes to satisfy herself that any background noises Brockbank might hear could plausibly belong to a busy office situated on a main road, and keyed in the number, her heart hammering.

It was still in service. Robin listened to it ringing for twenty seconds and then, just when she had guessed that nobody was going to pick up, somebody did.

Very heavy breathing roared down the line. Robin sat still, the mobile tight against her ear. Then she jumped, as a shrill toddler's voice said:

'HELLO!'

'Hello?' said Robin cautiously.

In the background a woman's muffled voice said:

'What've you got, Zahara?'

A scraping noise and then, much louder:

'That's Noel's, he's been look—'

The line went dead. Robin lowered the phone slowly, her heart still racing. She could almost see the sticky little finger that had accidentally cut the call.

The phone began to vibrate in her hand: Brockbank's number, calling back. She took a steadying breath and answered.

'Hello, Venetia Hall.'

'What?' said a woman's voice.

'Venetia Hall – Hardacre and Hall,' said Robin.

'What?' said the woman again. 'Did you just call this number?'

She had a London accent. Robin's mouth was dry.

'Yes, I did,' said Robin-as-Venetia. 'I'm looking for Mr Noel Brockbank.'

'Why?'

After an almost imperceptible pause Robin said:

'Could I ask who I'm speaking to, please?'

'Why?' The woman was sounding increasingly belligerent. 'Who are you?'

'My name's Venetia Hall,' said Robin, 'and I'm a lawyer specialising in personal injury compensation.'

A couple sat down in front of her and began to talk loudly in Italian.

'What?' said the woman on the end of the line again.

Inwardly cursing her neighbours, Robin raised her voice and gave the same story that she had told Holly back in Barrow.

'Money for *him*?' said the unknown woman, with a degree less animosity.

'Yes, if his case is successful,' said Robin. 'Can I ask—?'

'How did you find out about him?'

'We came across Mr Brockbank's records while we were researching other—'

'How much money?'

'That depends.' Robin took a deep breath. 'Where is Mr Brockbank?'

'At work.'

'Can I ask where—?'

'I'll get him to call you. This number, yeah?'

'Yes, please,' said Robin. 'I'll be here in the office tomorrow from nine.'

'Vene – Ven – what was your name?'

Robin spelled Venetia for her.

'Yeah, all right, then. I'll get him to call. Bye, then.'

Robin rang Strike to tell him what had happened as she walked towards the Tube, but his number was engaged.

Her spirits ebbed as she descended into the Underground. Matthew would be at home by now. It felt as though it had been a long time since she had seen her ex-fiancé and she dreaded their reunion. Her mood sank still further as she travelled home, wishing she had a valid reason to stay away, but grudgingly obedient to her promise to Strike that she would not stay out after dark.

Forty minutes later she arrived at West Ealing station. Walking towards the flat with dread in her heart, her second attempt to call Strike went through.

'Bloody good work!' he said when she told him that she had successfully contacted Brockbank's phone. 'You say this woman had a London accent?'

'I think so,' said Robin, feeling that Strike was missing a more important point, 'and a small daughter, by the sounds of it.'

'Yeah. Expect that's why Brockbank's there.'

She had expected him to show more concern for a child in

close proximity with a man he knew to be a child rapist, but no; he briskly changed the subject.

'I've just been on the phone to Hazel Furley.'

'Who?'

'Kelsey's sister, remember? Who wants to meet me? I'm going to see her on Saturday.'

'Oh,' said Robin.

'Can't do it before then – Mad Dad's back from Chicago. Just as well. Two-Times won't support us for ever.'

Robin did not respond. She was still thinking about the toddler who had answered the phone. Strike's reaction to that news had disappointed her.

'Are you all right?' asked Strike.

'Yes,' said Robin.

She had reached the end of Hastings Road.

'Well, I'll see you tomorrow,' she said.

He agreed to it and hung up. Feeling unexpectedly worse for having spoken to Strike, she headed with some trepidation towards her front door.

She need not have worried. The Matthew who had returned from Masham was no longer the man who begged Robin hourly to talk to him. He slept on the sofa. Over the next three days they moved carefully around each other, Robin with cool politeness, he with an air of ostentatious devotion that tipped, at times, into parody. He hurried to wash up cups as soon as she had finished drinking from them and on Thursday morning asked her respectfully how work was going.

'Oh, *please*,' was Robin's only response as she strode past him to the front door.

His family, she guessed, had told him to back off, to give her time. They had not yet discussed how they were going to tell everyone else that the wedding was off: Matthew clearly did not wish to have that discussion. Day to day, Robin stopped short of initiating the conversation. Sometimes she asked herself whether this cowardice revealed her own secret desire to put her ring back on. At others, she was sure that her reluctance sprang from exhaustion, disinclination for what she knew would be the worst and most painful confrontation yet, and a need to marshal her forces before the final break. Little though she had encouraged her mother's forthcoming visit, Robin was subconsciously hoping to draw enough strength and comfort from Linda to do what had to be done.

The roses on her desk shrivelled slowly. Nobody had bothered to put them in fresh water, so they died quietly in the wrappings in which they had arrived, but Robin was not there to throw them out and Strike, who visited the office infrequently to fetch things, felt it would be out of place for him to dispose of them, or of the still-unopened card.

After the previous week of regular contact Robin and Strike had resumed a work pattern that meant they rarely saw each other, taking it in turns to follow Platinum and Mad Dad, who had returned from America and immediately resumed the stalking of his young sons. On Thursday afternoon they discussed by phone the question of whether Robin should try Noel Brockbank again, because he had still not called her back. After consideration, Strike told her that Venetia Hall, busy lawyer, would have other fish to fry.

'If he hasn't contacted you by tomorrow you can try again. That'll be a full working week. Course, his lady friend might have lost the number.'

When Strike had hung up, Robin resumed her wanderings in Edge Street in Kensington, which was where Mad Dad's family lived. The location did nothing to lift Robin's spirits. She had begun looking online for somewhere else to live, but the places she would be able to afford on the salary Strike paid her were even worse than she had feared, single rooms in shared houses the best she could expect.

The beautiful Victorian mews houses that surrounded her, with glossy front doors, leafy climbing plants, window boxes and bright sash windows, spoke of the comfortable, prosperous existence to which Matthew had aspired back in the days that Robin seemed ready to embrace a more lucrative career. She had told him all along that she did not care about money, or at least not as much as he did, and that remained true, but it would be a strange human being, she thought, who could linger among these pretty, quiet houses and not compare them, to the others' detriment, with 'small room in strictly vegan household, mobile phone tolerated if used in bedroom' that was just within her price range, or the cupboard-sized room in Hackney in 'friendly and respectful household ready to TAKE YOU ON BOARD!'

Her mobile rang again. She tugged the phone out of her jacket pocket, expecting Strike, and her stomach turned over: Brockbank. Taking a deep breath, she answered.

'Venetia Hall.'

'You th'lawyer?'

She did not know what she had expected him to sound like. He had taken monstrous form in her mind, this rapist of children, the long-jawed thug with his broken bottle and what Strike believed to be fake amnesia. His voice was deep and his accent, though by no means as thick as his twin's, remained distinctly Barrovian.

'Yes,' said Robin. 'Is that Mr Brockbank?'

'Aye, tha's righ'.'

The quality of his silence was somehow threatening. Robin hastened to tell her fictitious story of the compensation that might await him if he were happy to meet her. When she had finished, he said nothing. Robin held her nerve, because

Venetia Hall had the self-confidence not to rush to fill a silence, but the crackling of the slack line between them unnerved her.

'An' where did you find ou' abou' us, eh?'

'We came across your case notes while we were investigating—'

'Investigatin' wha'?'

Why did she have such a feeling of menace? He couldn't be anywhere near her, but she scanned her surroundings all the same. The sunny, gracious street was deserted.

'Investigating similar non-combat-related injuries to other servicemen,' she said, wishing that her voice had not risen to such a high pitch.

More silence. A car rolled towards her round the corner.

Damn it, Robin thought desperately as she realised that the driver was the obsessive father she was supposed to be observing covertly. He had looked her full in the face as she turned towards his car. She ducked her head and walked slowly away from the school.

'So wha' do I 'ave ter do then, eh?' asked Noel Brockbank in her ear.

'Could we meet and have a chat about your history?' Robin asked, her chest actually painful, so fast was her heart pounding.

'I though' you'd read our 'istory?' he said and the hairs on the back of Robin's neck stood up. 'A cun' called Cameron Strike gave us brain damage.'

'Yes, I saw that in your file,' said Robin breathlessly, 'but it's important to take a statement so we can—'

'Take a statemen'?'

There was a pause that felt suddenly dangerous.

'Sure you're no' a horney?'

Robin Ellacott, northerner, understood; Venetia Hall, Londoner, almost certainly would not. 'Horney' was the Cumbrian word for policeman.

'Not a what – I'm sorry?' she said, doing her best to sound politely confused.

Mad Dad had parked outside his estranged wife's house. Any moment now, his sons would be leaving with their nanny for a play date. If he accosted them, Robin needed to photograph the encounter. She was falling down on the paying job: she ought to be photographing Mad Dad's movements.

'Police,' said Brockbank aggressively.

'Police?' she said, still striving for that tone of mingled disbelief and amusement. 'Of course not.'

'You sure abou' tha', are you?'

The front door of Mad Dad's wife's house had opened. Robin saw the nanny's red hair and heard a car door open. She forced herself to sound offended and confused.

'Yes, of course I am. Mr Brockbank, if you're not interested—'

Her hand was slightly damp on the phone. Then, taking her by surprise, he said:

'All right, I'll mee' you.'

'Excellent,' said Robin as the nanny led the two little boys onto the pavement. 'Whereabouts are you?'

'Shoreditch,' said Brockbank.

Robin felt every nerve tingle. He was in London.

'So, where would be convenient to—?'

'Wha's tha' noise?'

The nanny was screaming at Mad Dad, who was advancing on her and the boys. One of his sons began wailing.

'Oh, I'm actually – it's just my day for picking up my son from school,' said Robin loudly over the background shrieks and shouts.

Silence again on the end of the line. Matter-of-fact Venetia Hall would surely break it, but Robin found herself paralysed by what she tried to tell herself was an irrational fear.

Then he spoke in a voice more menacing than Robin had ever heard, the more so because he half crooned the words, so close to the receiver that he seemed to be breathing into her ear.

'Do A know you, little girl?'

Robin tried to speak, but no sound came out. The line went dead.

33

> Then the door was open and the wind
> appeared . . .
>
> Blue Öyster Cult, '(Don't Fear) The Reaper'

'I messed up with Brockbank,' said Robin. 'I'm really sorry – but I don't know *how* I messed up! Plus I didn't dare take pictures of Mad Dad, because I was too close.'

It was nine o'clock on Friday morning and Strike had arrived, not from the upstairs flat but from the street, fully dressed and carrying his backpack again. Robin had heard him humming as he came up the stairs. He had stayed overnight at Elin's. Robin had called him the previous evening to tell him about the Brockbank call, but Strike had not been at liberty to talk for long and had promised that they would do so today.

'Never mind Mad Dad. We'll get him another day,' said Strike, busy at the kettle. 'And you did great with Brockbank. We know he's in Shoreditch, we know I'm on his mind and we know he was suspicious that you might be police. So is that because he's been fiddling with kids up and down the country, or because he's recently hacked a teenager to death?'

Ever since Brockbank had spoken his last six words into her ear, Robin had felt slightly shaken. She and Matthew had barely talked to each other the previous evening and, having no outlet for a sudden feeling of vulnerability that she did not entirely understand, she had placed all her reliance on seeing Strike face to face and getting to discuss the meaning of those six ominous words: *Do A know you, little girl?* Today, she would have welcomed the serious, cautious Strike who had taken the sending of the leg as a threat and warned her about staying out after dark. The man now cheerfully making himself coffee and talking about child abuse and murder in a matter-of-fact tone was bringing her no comfort. He could have no idea what Brockbank had sounded like, crooning inside her ear.

'We know something else about Brockbank,' she said in a tight voice. 'He's living with a little girl.'

'He might not be living with her. We don't know where he left the phone.'

'All right, then,' said Robin, feeling even more tightly wound. 'If you want to be pedantic: we know he's in close contact with a little girl.'

She turned away on the pretext of dealing with the mail she had scooped from the doormat on her arrival. The fact that he had arrived humming had irked her. Presumably his night with Elin had been a welcome distraction, providing recreation and recuperation. Robin would have loved a respite from her hypervigilant days and evenings of frigid silence. The knowledge that she was being unreasonable did nothing to diminish her resentment. She scooped the dying roses in their dry plastic bag off the desk and pushed them headfirst into the bin.

'There's nothing we can do about that kid,' said Strike.

A most enjoyable stab of anger shot through Robin.

'I won't worry about her, then,' she snapped.

Trying to extract a bill from an envelope, she accidentally ripped the whole thing in two.

'You think she's the only child at risk from an abuser? There'll be hundreds of them, right now, just in London.'

Robin, who had half expected him to soften now that she had revealed how angry she was, looked round. He was watching her, eyes slightly narrowed, with no air of sympathy.

'Keep worrying all you want, but it's wasted energy. There's nothing you or I can do about that kid. Brockbank's not on any registers. He hasn't got any convictions. We don't even know where she is or what she's—'

'Her name's Zahara,' said Robin.

To her horror, her voice turned to a strangled squeal, her face flooded with colour and tears started in her eyes. She turned away again, although not fast enough.

'Hey,' said Strike kindly, but Robin made a wild flapping gesture with her hand to stop him talking. She refused to break down; all that was holding her together was her ability to keep moving forwards, to keep doing the job.

'I'm fine,' she said through clenched teeth. 'I am. Forget it.'

She could not now confess how menacing she had found Brockbank's sign-off. 'Little girl', he had called her. She was *not* a little girl. She was not broken or childlike – not any more – but Zahara, whoever she was . . .

She heard Strike leave for the landing, and a moment later a large wad of toilet paper appeared in her swimming sights.

'Thank you,' she said thickly, taking it from Strike's hand and blowing her nose.

Several silent minutes passed while Robin periodically dabbed at her eyes and blew her nose, avoiding looking at

Strike, who was perversely remaining in her part of the office rather than heading for his own.

'*What?*' Robin said at last, anger rising again at the fact that he was simply standing there watching her.

He grinned. In spite of everything, she experienced a sudden desire to laugh.

'Are you going to stand there all morning?' she asked, trying to sound cross.

'No,' said Strike, still grinning, 'I just wanted to show you something.'

He ferreted in his backpack and pulled out a glossy property brochure.

'Elin's,' he said. 'She went to see it yesterday. She's thinking of buying a flat there.'

All desire to laugh fled. How exactly did Strike think that it would cheer Robin up, to know that his girlfriend was thinking of buying a ludicrously expensive flat? Or was he about to announce (Robin's fragile mood began to collapse in on itself) that he and Elin were moving in together? Like a film flickering rapidly before her eyes she saw the upstairs flat empty, Strike living in luxury, herself in a tiny box room on the edge of London, whispering into her mobile so that her vegan landlady did not hear her.

Strike laid the brochure on the desk in front of her. The cover showed a tall modern tower topped by a strange shield-like face in which wind turbines were set like three eyes. The legend read: 'Strata SE1, London's most desirable residential property'.

'See?' said Strike.

His triumphant air was aggravating Robin beyond measure, not least because it seemed so unlike him to gloat about the prospect of borrowed luxury, but before she could respond there was a knock on the glass door behind him.

'Bloody hell,' said Strike in frank astonishment as he opened the door to Shanker, who walked in, clicking his fingers and bringing with him the usual fug of cigarette smoke, cannabis and body odour.

'I was in the area,' said Shanker, unconsciously echoing Eric Wardle. 'I've found him for you, Bunsen.'

Shanker dropped down onto the mock-leather sofa, legs spread out in front of him, and took out a packet of Mayfairs.

'You've found Whittaker?' asked Strike, whose dominant emotion was astonishment that Shanker was awake so early in the morning.

''Oo else did you ask me to find?' said Shanker, inhaling deeply on his cigarette and clearly enjoying the effect he was creating. 'Catford Broadway. Flat over a chip shop. The brass lives with 'im.'

Strike held out his hand and shook Shanker's. Notwithstanding his gold tooth and the scar that twisted his upper lip, their visitor's grin was strangely boyish.

'Want a coffee?' Strike asked him.

'Yeah, go on then,' said Shanker, who seemed disposed to bask in his triumph. 'All right?' he added cheerfully to Robin.

'Yes, thanks,' she said with a tight smile, returning to the unopened mail.

'Talk about on a roll,' Strike said quietly to Robin while the kettle boiled loudly and an oblivious Shanker smoked and checked texts on his phone. 'That's all three of them in London. Whittaker in Catford, Brockbank in Shoreditch and now we know Laing's in Elephant and Castle – or he was three months ago.'

She had agreed to it before doing a double-take.

'How do we know Laing was in Elephant and Castle?'

Strike tapped the glossy brochure of the Strata on her desk.

'What d'you think I'm showing you that for?'

Robin had no idea what he meant. She looked blankly at the brochure for several seconds before its significance struck her. Panels of silver punctuated the long jagged lines of darkened windows all down the rounded column: this was the background visible behind Laing as he stood on his concrete balcony.

'*Oh*,' she said weakly.

Strike wasn't moving in with Elin. She did not know why she was blushing again. Her emotions seemed totally out of control. What on earth was wrong with her? She turned on her swivel chair to concentrate on the post yet again, hiding her face from both men.

'I dunno if I've got enough dosh on me to pay you, Shanker,' Strike said, looking through his wallet. 'I'll walk you down to a cashpoint.'

'Fair enough, Bunsen,' said Shanker, leaning over to Robin's bin to dispose of the ash trickling from his cigarette. 'You need 'elp wiv Whittaker, y'know where I am.'

'Yeah, cheers. I can probably handle it, though.'

Robin reached for the last envelope in the post pile, which felt stiff and had an additional thickness at one corner, as though it contained a card with some kind of novelty attached. On the point of opening it, Robin noticed that it had been addressed to her, not Strike. She paused, uncertain, looking at it. Her name and the address of the office had been typed. The postmark was from central London and the letter had been sent the previous day.

Strike and Shanker's voices rose and fell but she could not have said what they were saying.

It's nothing, she told herself. *You're overwrought. It couldn't happen again.*

Swallowing hard, she opened the envelope and gingerly removed the card.

The image showed a Jack Vettriano painting of a blonde sitting in profile on a chair, which was draped in a dustsheet. The blonde was holding a teacup and her elegant black stockinged, stilettoed legs were crossed and raised on a footstool. There was nothing pinned to the front of the card. The object that she had felt through the card was taped inside it.

Strike and Shanker were still talking. A whiff of decay caught her nostrils through the fug of Shanker's body odour.

'Oh God,' said Robin quietly, but neither man heard her. She flipped over the Vettriano print.

A rotting toe was Sellotaped to the inner corner of the card. Carefully printed in capital letters were the words:

SHE'S AS BEAUTIFUL AS A FOOT

She dropped it onto the desk and stood up. In slow motion, it seemed, she turned to Strike. He looked from her stricken face to the obscene object lying on the desk.

'Get away from it.'

She obeyed, sick and trembling and wishing that Shanker was not there.

'What?' Shanker kept saying. 'What? What is it? What?'

'Somebody's sent me a severed toe,' said Robin in a collected voice that was not her own.

'You're fucking kidding me,' said Shanker, moving forwards with eager interest.

Strike physically restrained Shanker from picking up the card, which lay where it had fallen from Robin's hand. Strike recognised the phrase 'She's as Beautiful as a Foot'. It was the title of another Blue Öyster Cult song.

'I'll call Wardle,' Strike said, but instead of taking out his mobile he scribbled a four-digit code on a Post-it note and extracted his credit card from his wallet. 'Robin, go and get the rest of Shanker's money out for him, then come back here.'

She took the note and the credit card, absurdly grateful for the prospect of fresh air.

'And Shanker,' said Strike sharply, as the two of them reached the glass door, 'you walk her back here, all right? Walk her back to the office.'

'You got it, Bunsen,' said Shanker, energised, as he always had been, by strangeness, by action, by the whiff of danger.

34

> The lies don't count, the whispers do.
>
> Blue Öyster Cult, 'The Vigil'

Strike sat alone at the kitchen table in his attic flat that night. The chair was uncomfortable and the knee of his amputated leg aching after several hours tailing Mad Dad, who had taken time out of work today to stalk his younger son on a trip to the Natural History Museum. The man owned his own company or he would surely have been fired for the working hours he spent intimidating his children. Platinum, however, had gone unwatched and unphotographed. On learning that Robin's mother was due to visit that evening, Strike had insisted on Robin taking three days off, overriding all her objections, walking her to the Tube and insisting that she text him once safely back at her flat.

Strike yearned for sleep, yet felt too weary to get up and go to bed. He had been more disturbed by the second communication from the killer than he had been prepared to admit to his partner. Appalling though the arrival of the leg had been, he now acknowledged that he had nourished a vestige of hope that the addressing of the package to Robin had been a nasty embellishment, but an afterthought. The second communication with her, sly sideways wink at Strike notwithstanding ('She's As Beautiful As a Foot'), had told him for certain that this man, whoever he was, had Robin in his sights. Even the name of the painting on the front of the card he had selected – the image of the solitary, leggy blonde – was ominous: *In Thoughts of You*.

Rage burgeoned in the motionless Strike, chasing away his tiredness. He remembered Robin's white face and knew that he had witnessed the death of her faint hope that the sending of the leg had not been the random act of a madman. Even so, she had argued vociferously against taking time off, pointing out that their only two paying jobs frequently clashed: Strike would be unable to cover both properly on his own and would consequently have to choose on a daily basis whether to follow Platinum or Mad Dad. He had been adamant: she should return to work only when her mother returned to Yorkshire.

Their persecutor had now succeeded in reducing Strike's business to two clients. He had just endured a second incursion of police into his office and was worried that the press would get wind of what had happened, even though Wardle had promised not to release news of the card and the toe. Wardle agreed with Strike that one of the killer's objectives was to focus press and police attention on the detective, and that it was playing into the killer's hands to alert the media.

His mobile rang loudly in the small kitchen. Glancing at his watch, he saw that it was twenty past ten. He seized it, barely registering Wardle's name as he raised it to his ear, because his mind had been on Robin.

'Good news,' Wardle told him. 'Well, of a kind. He hasn't killed another woman. The toe's Kelsey's. Off the other leg. Waste not, want not, eh?'

Strike, who was not in the mood for humour, replied brusquely. After Wardle had hung up, he continued to sit at his kitchen table, lost in thought while the traffic growled past in Charing Cross Road below. Only the recollection that he had to get to Finchley the next morning to meet Kelsey's sister finally motivated him to begin the usual onerous process of dealing with his prosthesis before bed.

Strike's knowledge of London was, thanks to his mother's peripatetic habits, extensive and detailed, but there were gaps, and Finchley was one of them. All he knew about the area was that it had been Margaret Thatcher's constituency in the 1980s, while he, Leda and Lucy had been moving between squats in places like Whitechapel and Brixton. Finchley would have been too far away from the centre to suit a family entirely reliant on public transport and takeaways, too expensive for a woman who frequently ran out of coins for the electricity meter: the kind of place, as his sister Lucy might once have wistfully put it, where proper families lived. In marrying a quantity surveyor and producing three impeccably turned-out sons, Lucy had fulfilled her childhood yearning for neatness, order and security.

Strike took the Tube to West Finchley and endured a long walk to Summers Lane rather than find a taxi, because his finances were so bad. Sweating slightly in the mild weather, he moved through road after road of quiet detached houses, cursing the place for its leafy quiet and its lack of landmarks. Finally, thirty minutes after he had left the station, he found Kelsey Platt's house, smaller than many of its fellows, with a whitewashed exterior and a wrought-iron gate.

He rang the doorbell and immediately heard voices through the pane of frosted glass like the one in his own office door.

'Ah think it's the detective, pet,' said a Geordie voice.

'You get it!' said a woman's high-pitched voice.

A large red mass bloomed behind the glass and the door opened onto the hall, which was mostly concealed by a burly, barefoot man in a scarlet towelling robe. He was bald, but his bushy grey beard, coupled with the scarlet robe, would have suggested Santa had he looked jolly. However, he was frantically mopping his face with the sleeve of his dressing gown. The eyes behind his glasses were swollen into bee-stung slits and his ruddy cheeks were shining with tears.

'Sorry,' he said gruffly, moving aside to let Strike in. 'Working nights,' he added in explanation of his attire.

Strike sidled past. The man smelled strongly of Old Spice and camphor. Two middle-aged women were locked in a tight embrace at the foot of the stairs, one blonde, the other dark, both sobbing. They broke apart as Strike watched, wiping their faces.

'Sorry,' gasped the dark-haired woman. 'Sheryl's our neighbour. She's been in Magaluf, she's only just h-heard about Kelsey.'

'Sorry,' echoed red-eyed Sheryl. 'I'll give you space, Hazel. Anything you need. Anything, Ray – anything.'

Sheryl squeezed past Strike – 'sorry' – and hugged Ray. They swayed together briefly, both big people, their bellies pressed together, arms stretched around each other's necks. Ray began sobbing again, his face in her broad shoulder.

'Come through,' hiccoughed Hazel, dabbing at her eyes as she led the way into the sitting room. She had the look of a Bruegel peasant, with her rounded cheeks, prominent chin and wide nose. Eyebrows as thick and bushy as tiger moth caterpillars overhung her puffy eyes. 'It's been like this all week. People hearing and coming over and . . . sorry,' she finished on a gasp.

He had been apologised to half a dozen times in the space of two minutes. Other cultures would have been ashamed of an insufficient display of grief; here in quiet Finchley, they were ashamed to have him witness it.

'Nobody knows what to say,' Hazel whispered, pressing

away her tears as she gestured him to the sofa. 'It's not like she was hit by a car, or was ill. They don't know what you say when someone's been—' She hesitated, but baulked at the word and her sentence ended in a gargantuan sniff.

'I'm sorry,' said Strike, taking his turn. 'I know this is a terrible time for you.'

The sitting room was immaculate and somehow unwelcoming, perhaps because of its chilly colour scheme. A three-piece suite covered in striped silvery-grey cloth, white wallpaper with a thin grey stripe, cushions angled on their points, ornaments on the mantelpiece perfectly symmetrical. The dust-free television screen gleamed with reflected light from the window.

Sheryl's misty form trotted past on the other side of the net curtains, wiping her eyes. Ray shuffled past the sitting-room door on his bare feet, dabbing under his glasses with the end of his towelling-robe belt, his shoulders stooped. As though she had read Strike's mind, Hazel explained:

'Ray broke his back trying to get a family out of a boarding house that caught fire. Wall gave way and his ladder fell. Three storeys.'

'Christ,' said Strike.

Hazel's lips and hands were trembling. Strike remembered what Wardle had said: that the police had mishandled Hazel. Suspicion or rough questioning of her Ray would have seemed unforgivable cruelty to her in this state of shock, an inexcusable exacerbation of their appalling ordeal. Strike knew a lot about the brutal intrusion of officialdom into private devastation. He had been on both sides of the fence.

'Anyone want a brew?' Ray called huskily from what Strike assumed was the kitchen.

'Go to bed!' Hazel called back, clutching a sodden ball of tissues. 'I can make 'em! Go to bed!'

'You sure?'

'Get to bed, I'll wake you at three!'

Hazel wiped her whole face with a fresh tissue, as though it were a face cloth.

'He's not one for disability pay and all that, but nobody wants to give him a proper job,' she told Strike quietly as Ray shuffled, sniffing, back past the door. 'Not with his back and his age and his lungs not being the best. Cash in hand . . . shift work . . . '

Her voice trailed away, her mouth trembled, and for the first time she looked Strike directly in the eye.

'I don't really know why I asked you to come,' she confessed. 'It's all confused in my head. They said she wrote to you but you never wrote back and then you got sent her – her—'

'It must have been an appalling shock to you,' said Strike, fully aware that anything he could say would understate the case.

'It's been –' she said feverishly '– terrible. Terrible. We didn't know anything, anything at all. We thought she was on a college placement. When the police came to the door – she said she was going away with college and I believed her, some residential placement at a school. It sounded right – I never thought – but she was such a liar. She lied all the time. Three years she's been living with me and I still haven't – I mean, I couldn't get her to stop.'

'What did she tell lies about?' asked Strike.

'Anything,' said Hazel, with a slightly wild gesture. 'If it was Tuesday she'd say it was Wednesday. Sometimes there was no point to it at all. I don't know why. I don't know.'

'Why was she living with you?' Strike asked.

'She's my – she was my half-sister. Same mum. We lost Dad when I was twenty. Mum married a guy from work and had Kelsey. There were twenty-four years between us – I'd left home – I was more like an auntie to her than a sister. Then Mum and Malcolm had a car crash out in Spain three years ago. Drunk driver. Malcolm died outright, Mum was in a coma for four days and then she passed, too. There isn't any other family, so I took Kelsey in.'

The extreme tidiness of their surroundings, the cushions on their points, surfaces clear and highly polished, made Strike wonder how a teenager had fitted in here.

'Me and Kelsey didn't get on,' said Hazel, again seeming to read Strike's thoughts. Tears flowed once more as she pointed upstairs, where Ray had gone to bed. 'He was much more patient with all her moodiness and her sulks. He's got a grown-up son who's working abroad. He's better with kids than me. Then the police come jack-booting in here,' she said on a sudden rush of fury, 'and tell us she's been – they start questioning Ray like he'd – like he'd *ever*, in a million *years* – I said to him, it's like a nightmare. You see people on the news, don't you, appealing for kids to come home – people put on trial for things they never did – you never think . . . you never think . . . but we never even knew she was missing. We'd have looked. We never knew. The police asking Ray questions – where he was and I don't know what—'

'They've told me he didn't have anything to do with it,' Strike said.

'Yeah, they believe that *now*,' said Hazel through angry tears, 'after three men told them he was with them every minute of the stag weekend and showed them the bloody photos to prove it . . .'

She would never think it reasonable that the man who had been living with Kelsey should be questioned about her death. Strike, who had heard the testimony of Brittany Brockbank and Rhona Laing and many others like them, knew that most women's rapists and killers were not strangers in masks who reached out of the dark space under the stairs. They were the father, the husband, the mother's or the sister's boyfriend . . .

Hazel wiped the tears away as fast as they fell onto her round cheeks, then suddenly asked:

'What did you do with her silly letter anyway?'

'My assistant put it in the drawer where we keep unusual correspondence,' said Strike.

'The police said you never wrote back to her. They say they was forged, the letters they found.'

'That's right,' said Strike.

'So whoever done it must've known she was interested in you.'

'Yes,' said Strike.

Hazel blew her nose vigorously, then asked:

'D'you want a cuppa, then?'

He accepted only because he thought she wanted a chance to pull herself together. Once she had left the room he looked around openly. The only photograph stood on a small nest of tables in the corner beside him. It showed a beaming woman in her sixties wearing a straw hat. This, he assumed, was Hazel and Kelsey's mother. A slightly darker stripe on the surface of the table beside the picture suggested that another had stood beside it, preventing the sun bleaching that small strip on the cheap wood. Strike guessed that this had been the school photograph of Kelsey, the picture that all the papers had printed.

Hazel returned carrying a tray bearing mugs of tea and a plate of biscuits. After she had carefully positioned his tea on a coaster beside her mother's photograph, Strike said:

'I hear Kelsey had a boyfriend.'

'Rubbish,' retorted Hazel, dropping back into her armchair. 'More porkies.'

'What makes you—?'

'She said his name was Niall. Niall. *Honestly*.'

Her eyes leaked more tears. Strike was at a loss to understand why Kelsey's boyfriend might not have been called Niall and his incomprehension showed.

'One Direction,' she said over the top of her tissue.

'Sorry,' said Strike, completely at sea. 'I don't—'

'The band. They're a band that came third on *The X Factor*. She's obsessed – she was obsessed – and Niall was her favourite. So when she says she's met a boy called Niall and he's eighteen and he's got a motorbike, I mean, what were we supposed to think?'

'Ah. I see.'

'She said she met him at the counsellor's. She's been seeing a counsellor, see. Claimed she met Niall in the waiting room, that he was there because his mum and dad died, like hers. *We* never saw hide nor hair of him. I said to Ray, "She's at it again, she's fibbing," and Ray said to me, "Let it go, it keeps her happy," but I didn't like her lying,' said Hazel with a fanatic glare. 'She lied *all* the time, came home with a plaster on her wrist, said it was a cut and it turned out to be a One Direction tattoo. Look at her saying she was going away on a college placement, look at that . . . she kept lying and lying and look where it got her!'

With an enormous, visible effort she controlled a fresh eruption of tears, holding her trembling lips together and pressing the tissues hard across her eyes. Taking a deep breath, she said:

'Ray's got a theory. He wanted to tell the police, but *they* didn't care, they were more interested in where *he'd* been when she was – but Ray's got a friend called Ritchie who puts a bit of gardening his way, see, and Kelsey met Ritchie—'

The theory was rolled out with a huge amount of extraneous detail and repetition. Strike, who was well used to the rambling style of unpractised witnesses, listened attentively and politely.

A photograph was produced out of a dresser drawer, which did double duty in proving to Strike that Ray had been with three friends on a stag weekend in Shoreham-by-Sea when Kelsey was killed, and also revealed young Ritchie's injuries. Ritchie and Ray sat on the shingle beside a patch of sea holly, grinning, holding beers and squinting in the sunlight. Sweat glistened on Ray's bald pate and illuminated young Ritchie's swollen face, his stitches and bruising. His leg was in a surgical boot.

'—and, see, Ritchie came round here right after he'd had his smash and Ray thinks it put the idea in her head. He thinks she was planning to do something to her leg and then pretend she'd had a traffic accident.'

'Ritchie couldn't be the boyfriend, could he?' asked Strike.

'Ritchie! He's a bit simple. He'd have told us. Anyway, she barely knew him. It was all a fantasy. I think Ray's right. She was planning to do something to her leg again and pretend she'd come off some boy's bike.'

It would have been an excellent theory, thought Strike, if Kelsey had been lying in hospital, pretending to have suffered a motorbike accident and refusing to give more details under the pretence of protecting a fictitious boyfriend. He did Ray the credit of agreeing that this was exactly the kind of plan a sixteen-year-old might have come up with, mingling grandiosity and short-sightedness in dangerous measure. However, the point was moot. Whether or not Kelsey had once planned a fake motorbike crash, the evidence showed that she had abandoned the plan in preference for asking Strike for instructions on leg removal.

On the other hand, this was the first time that anyone had drawn any connection between Kelsey and a motorcyclist, and Strike was interested in Hazel's absolute conviction that any boyfriend must be fictional.

'Well, there was hardly any boys on her childcare course,' said Hazel, 'and where else was she going to meet him? *Niall.* She'd never had a boyfriend at school or anything. She went to the counsellor and sometimes she went to the church up the road, they've a youth group, but there's no Niall-with-a-motorbike *there*,' said Hazel. 'The police checked, asked her friends if they knew anything. Darrell who runs the group, he was that upset. Ray saw him this morning on his way home. Says Darrell burst into tears when he saw him from across the road.'

Strike wanted to take notes, but knew it would change the atmosphere of confidence he was trying to nurture.

'Who's Darrell?'

'He didn't have anything to do with it. Youth worker at the church. He's from Bradford,' said Hazel obscurely, 'and Ray's sure he's gay.'

'Did she talk about her—' Strike hesitated, unsure what to call it. 'Her problem with her leg at home?'

'Not to me,' said Hazel flatly. 'I wouldn't have it, I didn't want to hear it, I hated it. She told me when she was fourteen and I told her exactly what I thought. Attention-seeking, that's all it was.'

'There was old scarring on her leg. How did that—?'

'She did it right after Mum died. Like I didn't have enough to worry about. She tied wire round it, tried to cut off the circulation.'

Her expression revealed a mixture, it seemed to Strike, of revulsion and anger.

'She was in the car when Mum and Malcolm died, in the back. I had to get a counsellor and all that for her. He thought it was a cry for help or something, what she did to her leg. Grief. Survivors' guilt, I can't remember. She said not, though, said she'd wanted the leg gone for a while . . .

I don't know,' said Hazel, shaking her head vigorously.

'Did she talk to anyone else about it? Ray?'

'A bit, yeah. I mean, he knew what she was like. When we first got together, when he moved in, she told him some real whoppers – her dad being a spy, that was one of them, and that was why their car had crashed, and I don't know what else. So he knew what she was like, but he didn't get angry with her. He just used to change the subject, chat to her about school and that . . .'

She had turned an unattractive dark red.

'I'll tell you what she wanted,' she burst out. 'To be in a wheelchair – pushed around like a baby and to be pampered and the centre of attention. That's what it was all about. I found a diary, must have been a year or so ago. The things she'd written, what she liked to imagine, what she fantasised about. Ridiculous!'

'Such as?' asked Strike.

'Such as having her leg cut off and being in a wheelchair and being pushed to the edge of the stage and watching One Direction and having them come and make a big fuss of her afterwards because she was disabled,' said Hazel on a single breath. 'Imagine that. It's disgusting. There are people who are really disabled and they never wanted it. I'm a nurse. I know. I see them. Well,' she said, with a glance at Strike's lower legs, '*you* don't need telling.

'You didn't, did you?' she asked suddenly, point blank. 'You *didn't* – you *didn't* cut – do it – yourself?'

Was that why she had wanted to see him, Strike wondered. In some confused, subconscious manner, trying to find her moorings in the sea on which she was suddenly adrift, had she wanted to prove a point – even though her sister was gone and beyond understanding – that people didn't *do* that, not in the real world where cushions stood neatly on points and disability came only by mischance, through crumbling walls or roadside explosives?

'No,' he said. 'I was blown up.'

'There you are, you see!' she said, tears erupting again, savagely triumphant. 'I could have told her that – I could have told her if she'd only . . . if she'd asked me . . . but what she claimed,' said Hazel, gulping, 'was that her leg felt like it shouldn't be there. Like it was wrong to have it and it needed to come off – like a tumour or something. I wouldn't listen. It was all nonsense. Ray says he tried to talk sense into her. He told her she didn't know what she was asking for, that she wouldn't want to be in hospital like he was after he broke his back, laid up for months in plaster, skin sores and infections and all the rest of it. He didn't get angry with her, though. He'd say to her, come and help me in the garden or something, distract her.

'The police told us she was talking to people online who were like her. We had no idea. I mean, she was sixteen, you can't go looking on their laptops, can you? Not that I'd know what to look for.'

'Did she ever mention me to you?' Strike asked.

'The police asked that. No. I can't remember her ever talking about you and nor can Ray. I mean, no offence, but – I remember the Lula Landry trial, but I wouldn't have remembered your name from that, or recognised you. If she'd brought you up I'd remember. It's a funny name – no offence.'

'What about friends? Did she go out much?'

'She hardly had any friends. She wasn't the popular sort. She lied to all the kids at school too, and nobody likes that, do they? They bullied her for it. Thought she was strange. She hardly ever went out. When she was meeting this supposed *Niall*, I don't know.'

Her anger did not surprise Strike. Kelsey had been an

unplanned addition to her spotless household. Now, for the rest of her life, Hazel would carry guilt and grief, horror and regret, not least that her sister's life had been ended before she could grow out of the peculiarities that had helped estrange them.

'Would it be all right if I used your bathroom?' Strike asked.

Dabbing her eyes, she nodded.

'Straight ahead, top of the stairs.'

Strike emptied his bladder while reading a framed citation for 'brave and meritorious conduct', awarded to firefighter Ray Williams, which was hanging over the cistern. He strongly suspected that Hazel had hung that there, not Ray. Otherwise the bathroom displayed little of interest. The same meticulous attention to cleanliness and neatness displayed in the sitting room extended all the way to the inside of the medicine cabinet, where Strike learned that Hazel was still menstruating, that they bulk-bought toothpaste and that one or both of the couple had haemorrhoids.

He left the bathroom as quietly as he could. Faintly, from behind a closed door, came a soft rumbling indicating that Ray was asleep. Strike took two decisive steps to the right and found himself in Kelsey's box room.

Everything matched, covered in the same shade of lilac: walls, duvet, lampshade and curtains. Strike thought he might have guessed that order had been forcibly imposed on chaos in here, even had he not seen the rest of the house.

A large cork noticeboard ensured that there would be no unsightly pin marks on the walls. Kelsey had plastered the cork with pictures of five pretty young boys whom Strike assumed were One Direction. Their heads and legs protruded outside the frame of the board. There was a particular recurrence of a blond boy. Other than the pictures of One Direction, she had cut out puppies, mostly shih-tzus, random words and acronyms: OCCUPY, FOMO and AMAZEBALLS, and many recurrences of the name NIALL, often stuck onto hearts. The slapdash, random collage told of an attitude completely at odds with the precision with which the duvet had been laid on the bed and the exactly square position of the lilac rug.

Prominent on the narrow bookshelf was what looked like a new *One Direction: Forever Young – Our Official X Factor Story*. Otherwise the shelves held the *Twilight* series, a jewellery box, a mess of small trinkets that not even Hazel had managed to make look symmetrical, a plastic tray of cheap make-up and a couple of cuddly toys.

Banking on the fact that Hazel was heavy enough to make a noise coming upstairs, Strike swiftly opened drawers. The police would have taken away anything of interest, of course: the laptop, any scrap of scribbled paper, any telephone number or jotted name, any diary, if she had continued to keep one after Hazel had gone snooping. A mishmash of belongings remained: a box of writing paper like that on which she had written to him, an old Nintendo DS, a pack of false nails, a small box of Guatemalan worry dolls and, in the very bottom drawer of her bedside table, tucked inside a fluffy pencil case, several stiff foil-covered strips of pills. He pulled them out: ovoid capsules in mustard yellow labelled Accutane. He took one of the strips and pocketed it, closed the drawer and headed to her wardrobe, which was untidy and slightly fusty. She had liked black and pink. He felt swiftly among the folds of material, rifling through the pockets of the clothes, but found nothing until he tried a baggy dress in which he found what looked like a crumpled raffle or coat check ticket, numbered 18.

Hazel had not moved since Strike had left her. He guessed that he could have stayed away longer and she would not have noticed. When he re-entered the room she gave a little start. She had been crying again.

'Thank you for coming,' she said thickly, getting to her feet. 'I'm sorry, I—'

And she began to sob in earnest. Strike put a hand on her shoulder and before he knew it, she had her face on his chest, sobbing, gripping the lapels of his coat, with no trace of coquettishness, but in pure anguish. He put his arms around her shoulders and they stood so for a full minute until, with several heaving breaths, she stepped away again and Strike's arms fell back to his sides.

She shook her head, no words left, and walked him to the door. He reiterated his condolences. She nodded, her face ghastly in the daylight now falling into the dingy hall.

'Thanks for coming,' she gulped. 'I just needed to see you. I don't know why. I'm ever so sorry.'

35

Dominance and Submission

Since leaving home, he had cohabited with three women, but this one – It – was testing him to his limits. All three dirty bitches had claimed to love him, whatever that was supposed to mean. Their so-called love had turned the first two tractable. At heart, of course, all women were cheating cunts, determined to take more than they gave, but the first two hadn't been anything like It. He was forced to put up with more than he'd ever put up with before, because It was an essential part of his grand plan.

Nevertheless, he constantly fantasised about killing It. He could imagine Its stupid face slackening as the knife sank deep into her belly, unable to believe that Baby (It called him Baby) was killing her, even as the hot blood began pouring over his hands, the rusty smell filling the air still shivering with her screams . . .

Having to play nice was playing havoc with his self-control. Switching on the charm, drawing them in and keeping them sweet was easy, second nature to him, always had been. Sustaining the pose over long periods, though, was something else. The pretence was bringing him to breaking point. Sometimes, even the sound of Its breathing was enough to make him want to grab his knife and puncture her fucking lungs . . .

Unless he got to do one soon, he'd fucking explode.

Early on Monday morning he made an excuse to get out, but as he approached Denmark Street, intending to pick up The Secretary's trail as she arrived for work, something quivered in him, like the twitching of a rat's whiskers.

He paused beside a telephone box on the opposite side of the road, squinting at a figure standing on the corner of Denmark Street, right outside an instrument shop painted in the garish colours of a circus poster.

He knew the police, knew their moves, their games. The young man standing with his hands in the pockets of his donkey jacket was pretending to be casual, a mere bystander . . .

He'd invented that fucking game. He could make himself practically invisible. Look at that dickhead, standing on the corner thinking his donkey jacket made him one of the lads . . . *never shit a shitter, pal.*

Slowly he turned and walked out of sight behind the telephone box, where he slid the beanie hat off his head . . . He'd been wearing it when Strike chased him. Donkey Jacket might have a description. He should have thought of that, should have guessed Strike would call in his police mates, cowardly fucker . . .

There's been no photofit issued, though, he thought, his self-esteem rising again as he walked back down the street. Strike had come within feet of him, though he didn't realise it, and still had no fucking idea who he was. God, it would feel good, after he'd done The Secretary, to watch Strike and his fucking business sinking out of sight under the mudslide of the publicity, police and press crawling all over him, tainted by association, unable to protect his staff, suspected of her death, utterly ruined . . .

He was already planning his next move. He would go to the LSE, where The Secretary often followed the other blonde tart around, and hook up with her there. In the meantime, he'd need a different hat and, perhaps, new sunglasses. He felt in his pockets for money. He had hardly any, as fucking usual. He'd need to force It back out to work. He'd had enough of It whining and bleating and making excuses at home.

In the end he bought two new hats, a baseball cap and a grey woollen beanie to replace the black fleece version he put in a bin at Cambridge Circus. Then he caught the Tube to Holborn.

She wasn't there. Nor were any students. After searching fruitlessly for a glimpse of red-gold hair, he remembered that today was Easter Monday. The LSE was closed for the bank holiday.

After a couple of hours he returned to Tottenham Court Road, looked for her in the Court and skulked for a while near the entrance to Spearmint Rhino, but could not find her anywhere.

After a run of days when he had been unable to get out and look for her, the disappointment caused him almost physical pain. Agitated, he began walking quiet side streets, hoping that some girl would stroll across his path, any woman at all, it didn't have to be The Secretary; the knives beneath his jacket would be happy with anything now.

Perhaps she had been so shaken up by his little greetings card that she had resigned. That wasn't what he wanted at all. He wanted her terrified and off balance, but working for Strike, because she was his means of getting the bastard.

In bitter disappointment, he returned in the early evening to It. He knew he was going to have to remain with It for the next two days and the prospect was draining him of his last vestiges of control. If he could have used It in the way he planned to use The Secretary, it would have been a different matter, a release: he would have hurried home, knives at the ready – but he dared not. He needed It alive and in thrall to him.

Before forty-eight hours had passed, he was ready to explode with rage and violence. On Wednesday evening he told It that he would have to leave early next day to do a job and advised It bluntly that it was time It got back to work too. The resultant whining and mewling wore at him until he became angry. Cowed by his sudden rage, It tried to placate him. It needed him, It wanted him, It was sorry . . .

He slept apart from It on the pretence of still being angry. This left him free to masturbate, but that left him unsatisfied. What he wanted, what he needed, was contact with female flesh through sharp steel, to feel his dominance as the blood spurted, to hear total submission in her screams, her pleas, her dying gasps and whimpers. Memories of the times when he had done it were no comfort; they merely inflamed his need. He burned to do it again: he wanted The Secretary.

He rose on Thursday morning at a quarter to five, got dressed, pulled on his baseball cap and left to make his way across London to the flat that she shared with Pretty Boy. The sun had risen by the time he reached Hastings Road. An ancient Land Rover parked a short way from the house gave him cover. He leaned against it, keeping watch through the windscreen at the windows of her flat.

There was movement behind the sitting-room windows at seven and shortly afterwards Pretty Boy left in his suit. He looked drawn and unhappy. *You think you're unhappy now, you silly bastard . . . wait until I've had my fun with your girlfriend . . .*

Then at last she appeared, accompanied by an older woman who greatly resembled her.

For fuck's sake.

What was she doing, going on outings with her fucking mother? It felt like mockery. Sometimes the whole world seemed like it was out to get him, to stop him doing things he wanted, to keep him down. He fucking hated this feeling that his omnipotence was seeping away, that people and circumstances were hemming him in, reducing him to just another thwarted, seething mortal. Somebody was going to pay for this.

36

> I have this feeling that my luck is none too good . . .
>
> Blue Öyster Cult, 'Black Blade'

When his alarm went off on Thursday morning, Strike extended one heavy arm and slapped the button on top of the old clock so hard that it toppled off his bedside table onto the floor. Squinting, he had to concede that the sunlight glowing through his thin curtains seemed to confirm the alarm's raucous assertion. The temptation to roll over and sink back into sleep was almost overwhelming. He lay with his forearm over his eyes for a few more seconds, blocking out the day, then, with a mingled sigh and groan, he threw back the covers. As he groped for the handle of the bathroom door shortly afterwards, he reflected that he must have averaged three hours' sleep over the preceding five nights.

As Robin had foreseen, sending her home had meant he had to choose between tailing Platinum and Mad Dad. Having recently witnessed the latter jumping out at his small sons unexpectedly, and seen their tears of fright, Strike had decided that Mad Dad ought to be prioritised. Leaving Platinum to her blameless routine, he had spent large parts of the week covertly photographing the skulking father, racking up image after image of the man spying on his boys and accosting them whenever their mother was not present.

When not covering Mad Dad, Strike had been busy with his own investigations. The police were moving far too slowly for his liking so, still without the slightest proof that Brockbank, Laing or Whittaker had any connection with Kelsey Platt's death, Strike had packed almost every free hour of the preceding five days with the kind of relentless, round-the-clock police work that he had previously only given the army.

Balanced on his only leg, he wrenched the dial on the shower clockwise and allowed the icy water to pummel him awake, cooling his puffy eyes and raising gooseflesh through the dark hair on his chest, arms and legs. The one good thing about his tiny shower was that, if he slipped, there was no room to fall. Once clean, he hopped back to the bedroom, where he towelled himself roughly and turned on the TV.

The royal wedding would take place the following day and the preparations dominated every news channel he could find. While he strapped on his prosthesis, dressed and consumed tea and toast, presenters and commentators kept up a constant, excitable stream of commentary about the people who were already sitting out in tents along the route and outside Westminster Abbey, and the numbers of tourists pouring into London to witness the ceremony. Strike turned off the television and headed downstairs to the office, yawning widely and wondering how this multimedia barrage of wedding talk would be affecting Robin, whom he had not seen since the previous Friday, when the Jack Vettriano card containing a grisly little surprise had arrived.

In spite of the fact that he had just finished a large mug of tea upstairs, Strike automatically switched on the kettle when he arrived in the office, then put down on Robin's desk the list of strip joints, lap-dancing clubs and massage parlours he had begun compiling in his few free hours. When Robin arrived, he intended to ask her to continue researching and telephoning all the places she could find in Shoreditch, a job she could do safely from her own home. If he could have enforced her cooperation, he would have sent her back to Masham with her mother. The memory of her white face had haunted him all week.

Stifling a second enormous yawn, he slumped down at Robin's desk to check his emails. In spite of his intention to send her home, he was looking forward to seeing her. He missed her presence in the office, her enthusiasm, her can-do attitude, her easy, unforced kindness, and he wanted to tell her about the few advances he had made during his dogged pursuit of the three men currently obsessing him.

He had now notched up nearly twelve hours in Catford, trying to glimpse Whittaker entering or leaving his flat over the chip shop, which stood on a busy pedestrian street running along the rear of the Catford Theatre. Fishmongers, wig shops, cafés and bakeries curved around the perimeter of the theatre, and each had a flat above it boasting three arched windows in triangular formation. The thin curtains of the flat where Shanker believed Whittaker to be living were constantly closed. Market stalls filled the street by day, providing Strike with useful cover. The mingled smells of incense from the dream-catcher stall and the slabs of raw fish lying on ice nearby filled his nostrils until he barely noticed them.

For three evenings Strike had watched from the stage door of the theatre, opposite the flat, seeing nothing but shadowy forms moving behind the flat's curtains. Then, on Wednesday evening, the door beside the chip shop had opened to reveal an emaciated teenage girl.

Her dark, dirty hair was pulled back off a sunken, rabbity face, which had the violet-shadowed pallor of a consumptive. She wore a crop top, a zip-up grey hoodie and leggings that gave her thin legs the look of pipe cleaners. Arms crossed tightly across her thin torso, she entered the chip shop by leaning on the door until it gave, then half falling into it. Strike hurried across the road so fast that he caught the door as it swung closed and took a place immediately behind her in the queue.

When she reached the counter the man serving addressed her by name.

'All right, Stephanie?'

'Yeah,' she said in a low voice. 'Two Cokes, please.'

She had multiple piercings in her ears, nose and lip. After counting out payment in coins she left, head bowed, without looking at Strike.

He returned to his darkened doorway across the road where he ate the chips he had just bought, his eyes never moving from the lit windows above the chippy. Her purchase of two Cokes suggested that Whittaker was up there, perhaps sprawled naked on a mattress, as Strike had so often seen him in his teens. Strike had thought himself detached, but the awareness as he had stood in the chip-shop queue that he might be mere feet from the bastard, separated only by a flimsy wood and plaster ceiling, had made his pulse race. Stubbornly he watched the flat until the lights in the windows went off around one in the morning, but there had been no sign of Whittaker.

He had been no luckier with Laing. Careful perusal of Google Street View suggested that the balcony on which the fox-haired Laing had posed for his JustGiving photograph belonged to a flat in Wollaston Close, a squat, shabby block of flats that stood a short distance from the Strata. Neither phone nor voter registration records for the property revealed any trace of Laing, but Strike still held out hope that he might be living there as the guest of another, or renting and living without a landline. He had spent hours on Tuesday evening keeping watch over the flats, bringing with him a pair of night-vision goggles that enabled him to peer through uncurtained windows once darkness fell, but saw no hint of the Scot entering, leaving or moving around inside any of the flats. Having no wish to tip Laing off that he was after him, Strike had decided against door-to-door enquiries, but had lurked by day near the brick arches of a railway bridge nearby, which had been filled in to create tunnel-like spaces. Small businesses lived here: an Ecuadorian café, a hairdresser's. Eating and drinking silently among cheerful South Americans, Strike had been conspicuous by his silence and moroseness.

Strike's fresh yawn turned into another groan of tiredness as he stretched in Robin's computer chair, so that he did not hear the first clanging footsteps on the stairs in the hallway. By the time he had realised that somebody was approaching and checked his watch – it was surely too early for Robin, who had told him her mother's train would leave at eleven – a shadow was climbing the wall outside the frosted glass. A knock on the door, and to Strike's astonishment, Two-Times entered the office.

A paunchy middle-aged businessman, he was considerably wealthier than his crumpled, nondescript appearance would suggest. His face, which was entirely forgettable, neither handsome nor homely, was today screwed up in consternation.

'She's dumped me,' he told Strike without preamble.

He dropped onto the mock-leather sofa in an eruption of fake flatulence that took him by surprise; for the second time, Strike assumed, that day. It must have been a shock to the man to be dumped, when his usual procedure was to collect evidence of infidelity and present it to the blonde in question, thus severing the connection. The better Strike had got to know his client, the more he had understood that, for Two-Times, this constituted some kind of satisfying sexual climax. The man appeared to be a peculiar mixture of masochist, voyeur and control freak.

'Really?' said Strike, getting to his feet and heading towards the kettle; he needed caffeine. 'We've been keeping a very close eye on her and there hasn't been a hint of another man.'

In fact, he had done nothing about Platinum all week except to take Raven's calls, a few of which he had allowed to go to voicemail while he had been tailing Mad Dad. He now wondered whether he had listened to all of them. He hoped to Christ that Raven had not been warning him that another rich man had shown up, ready to defray some of Platinum's student expenses in return for exclusive privileges, or he would have to say goodbye to Two-Times's cash for good.

'Why's she dumped me then?' demanded Two-Times.

Because you're a fucking weirdo.

'Well, I can't swear there isn't someone else,' said Strike, choosing his words carefully as he poured instant coffee into a mug. 'I'm just saying she's been bloody clever about it if there is. We've been tailing her every move,' he lied. 'Coffee?'

'I thought you were supposed to be the best,' grumbled Two-Times. 'No, I don't drink instant.'

Strike's mobile rang. He pulled it out of his pocket and checked the caller: Wardle.

'Sorry, I need to take this,' he told his disgruntled client, and did so.

'Hi, Wardle.'

'Malley's ruled out,' said Wardle.

It was a mark of Strike's exhaustion that these words meant nothing to him for a second or two. Then the realisation dawned that Wardle was talking about the gangster who had once cut off a man's penis, and of whose probable guilt in the matter of the leg Wardle had seemed convinced.

'Digger – right,' said Strike, to show that he was paying attention. 'He's out, is he?'

'It can't've been him. He was in Spain when she was killed.'

'Spain,' repeated Strike.

Two-Times drummed his thick fingers on the arm of the sofa.

'Yeah,' said Wardle, 'bloody Menorca.'

Strike took a swig of coffee so strong he might as well have emptied boiling water straight into the jar. A headache was building in the side of his skull. He rarely got headaches.

'But we've made progress with those two whose pictures I showed you,' said Wardle. 'The bloke and the girl who were posting on that freaks' website where Kelsey was asking questions about you.'

Strike dimly remembered the pictures Wardle had shown him of a young man with lopsided eyes and a woman with black hair and glasses.

'We've interviewed them and they never met her; they only had online contact. Plus, *he's* got a rock-solid alibi for the date she died: he was doing a double shift at Asda – in Leeds. We've checked.

'But,' said Wardle, and Strike could tell he was leading up to something he thought promising, 'there's a bloke who's been hanging round the forum, calls himself "Devotee", who's been freaking them all out a bit. He's got a thing for amputees. He liked to ask the women where they wanted to be amputated and apparently he tried to meet a couple of them. He's gone very quiet lately. We're trying to track him down.'

'Uh huh,' said Strike, very conscious of Two-Times's mounting irritation. 'Sounds hopeful.'

'Yeah, and I haven't forgotten that letter you got from the bloke who liked your stump,' said Wardle. 'We're looking into him, too.'

'Great,' said Strike, hardly aware of what he was saying, but holding up a hand to show Two-Times – who was on the verge of getting up from the sofa – that he was almost done. 'Listen, I can't talk now, Wardle. Maybe later.'

When Wardle had hung up, Strike attempted to placate Two-Times, who had worked himself up into a state of weak anger while forced to wait for the phone call to end. Precisely what he thought Strike could do about the fact that his girlfriend had chucked him was a question that the detective, who could not afford to jettison possible repeat business, did not ask. Swigging tar-black coffee while the pain built in his head, Strike's dominant emotion was a fervent wish that he was in a position to tell Two-Times to fuck off.

'So what,' asked his client, 'are you going to do about it?'

Strike was unsure whether he was being asked to force Platinum back into the relationship, track her all over London in the hopes of discovering another boyfriend or refund Two-Times's money. Before he could answer, however, he heard more footsteps on the metal stairs, and female voices. Two-Times barely had time for more than a startled, questioning look at Strike before the glass door opened.

Robin looked taller to Strike than the Robin he kept in his memory: taller, better-looking and more embarrassed. Behind her – and under normal circumstances he would have been interested and amused by the fact – was a woman who could only be her mother. Though a little shorter and definitely broader, she had the same strawberry-blonde hair, the same blue-grey eyes and an expression of beneficent shrewdness that was deeply familiar to Robin's boss.

'I'm so sorry,' said Robin, catching sight of Two-Times and halting abruptly. 'We can wait downstairs – come on, Mum—'

Their unhappy client got to his feet, definitely cross.

'No, no, not at all,' he said. 'I didn't have an appointment. I'll go. Just my final invoice, then, Strike.'

He pushed his way out of the office.

An hour and a half later, Robin and her mother were sitting in silence as their taxi moved towards King's Cross, Linda's suitcase swaying a little on the floor.

Linda had been insistent that she wanted to meet Strike before she left for Yorkshire.

'You've been working for him for over a year. Surely he won't mind if I look in to say hello? I'd like to see *where* you work, at least, so I can picture it when you're talking about the office . . .'

Robin had resisted as hard as she could, embarrassed by the very idea of introducing her mother to Strike. It felt childish, incongruous and silly. She was particularly concerned that appearing with her mother in tow would reinforce Strike's evident belief that she was too shaken up to deal with the Kelsey case.

Bitterly did Robin now regret betraying her distress when the Vettriano card had arrived. She ought to have known better than to let any hint of fear show, especially after telling him about the rape. He said it had made no difference, but she knew better: she'd had plenty of experience of people telling her what was, and wasn't, good for her.

The taxi bowled along the Inner Circle and Robin had to remind herself that it was not her mother's fault that they had blundered in on Two-Times. She ought to have called Strike first. The truth was that she had hoped that Strike would be out, or upstairs; that she would be able to show Linda around the office and take her away without having to introduce them. She had been afraid that, if she phoned him, Strike would make a point of being there to meet her mother, out of a characteristic blend of mischief and curiosity.

Linda and Strike had chatted away while Robin made tea, keeping deliberately quiet. She strongly suspected that one of the reasons Linda wanted to meet Strike was to assess the precise degree of warmth that existed between him and her daughter. Helpfully, Strike looked appalling, a good ten years older than his real age, with that blue-jawed, sunken-eyed look that he got when he forfeited sleep for work. Linda would surely be hard pressed to imagine that Robin was nursing a secret infatuation now she had seen her boss.

'I liked him,' said Linda as the red-brick palace of St Pancras came into view, 'and I have to say, he might not be pretty, but he's got something about him.'

'Yes,' said Robin coldly. 'Sarah Shadlock feels the same way.'

Shortly before they had left for the station, Strike had asked for five minutes with her alone in the inner office. There, he had handed her the beginnings of a list of massage parlours, strip joints and lap-dancing clubs in Shoreditch and asked her to begin the laborious process of ringing them all in search of Noel Brockbank.

'The more I think about it,' Strike had said, 'the more I think he'll still be working as a heavy or a bouncer. What else is there for him, big bloke with brain damage and his history?'

Out of deference to the listening Linda, Strike had omitted

to add that he was sure Brockbank would still be working in the sex industry, where vulnerable women might be most easily found.

'OK,' Robin had replied, leaving Strike's list where he had put it on her desk. 'I'll see Mum off and come back—'

'No, I want you to do it from home. Keep a record of all the calls; I'll reimburse you.'

A mental picture of the Destiny's Child *Survivor* poster had flickered in Robin's mind.

'When do I come back into the office?'

'Let's see how long that takes you,' he said. Correctly reading her expression, he had added: 'Look, I think we've just lost Two-Times for good. I can cover Mad Dad alone—'

'What about Kelsey?'

'You're trying to trace Brockbank,' he said, pointing at the list in her hand. Then (his head was pounding, though Robin did not know it), 'Look, everyone'll be off work tomorrow, it's a bank holiday, the royal wedding—'

It could not have been clearer: he wanted her out of the way. Something had changed while she had been out of the office. Perhaps Strike was remembering that, after all, she had not been trained by the military police, had never seen dismembered limbs before a leg was delivered to their door, that she was not, in short, the kind of partner who was of use to him in this extremity.

'I've just had five days off—'

'For Christ's sake,' he said, losing patience, 'you're only making lists and phone calls – why d'you have to be in here to do it?'

You're only making lists and phone calls.

She remembered how Elin had called her Strike's secretary.

Sitting in the taxi with her mother, a lava slide of anger and resentment swept away rationality. He had called her his partner in front of Wardle, back when he had needed her to look at the photographs of a dismembered body. There had been no new contract, though, no formal renegotiation of their working relationship. She was a faster typist than Strike, with his wide hairy fingers: she dealt with the bulk of the invoices and emails. She did most of the filing too. Perhaps, Robin thought, Strike himself had told Elin that she was his secretary. Perhaps calling her partner had been a sop to her, a mere figure of speech. Maybe (she was deliberately inflaming her own resentment now, and she knew it) Strike and Elin discussed Robin's inadequacies during their sneaky dinners away from Elin's husband. He might have confided in Elin how much he now regretted taking on a woman who, after all, had been a mere temp when she had come to him. He had probably told Elin about the rape too.

It was a difficult time for me too, you know.

You're only making lists and phone calls.

Why was she crying? Tears of rage and frustration were trickling down her face.

'Robin?' said Linda.

'It's nothing, nothing,' said Robin savagely, wiping under her eyes with the heels of her hands.

She had been desperate to get back to work after five days in the house with her mother and Matthew, after the awkward three-cornered silences in the tiny space, the whispered conversations she knew that Linda had had with Matthew while she was in the bathroom, and about which she had chosen not to ask. She did not want to be trapped at home all over again. Irrational though it might have been, she felt safer in the middle of London, keeping an eye out for that large figure in the beanie hat, than she did in her flat in Hastings Road.

They pulled up at last outside King's Cross. Robin was

trying hard to keep her emotions under control, conscious of Linda's sideways looks as they crossed the crowded station towards her platform. She and Matthew would be alone again tonight, with the looming prospect of that final, definitive talk. She had not wanted Linda to come and stay, yet her imminent departure forced Robin to admit that there had been a comfort in her mother's presence that she had barely acknowledged.

'Right,' said Linda once her case had been safely stowed in the luggage rack and she had returned to the platform to spend the last couple of minutes with her daughter. 'This is for you.'

She was holding out five hundred pounds.

'Mum, I can't take—'

'Yes, you can,' said Linda. 'Put it towards a deposit on a new place to live – or a pair of Jimmy Choos for the wedding.'

They had gone window-shopping in Bond Street on Tuesday, staring through the shop windows at flawless jewels, at handbags that cost more than second-hand cars, at designer clothing to which neither woman could even aspire. It felt a long way from the shops of Harrogate. Robin had gazed most covetously through the shoe-shop windows. Matthew did not like her to wear very high heels; defiantly, she had voiced a hankering for some five-inch spikes.

'I can't,' repeated Robin as the station echoed and bustled around them. Her parents were sharing the expense of her brother Stephen's wedding later in the year. They had already paid a sizeable deposit on her reception, which had been postponed once; they had bought the dress and paid for its alterations, lost one deposit on the wedding cars . . .

'I want you to,' said Linda sternly. 'Either invest it in your single life or buy wedding shoes.'

Fighting more tears, Robin said nothing.

'You've got Dad's and my full support whatever you decide,' said Linda, 'but I want you to ask yourself why you haven't let anyone else know why the wedding's off. You can't keep living in limbo like this. It's not good for either of you. Take the money. Decide.'

She wrapped Robin in a tight embrace, kissed her just beneath the ear and got back on the train. Robin managed to smile all the time she was waving goodbye, but when the train had finally pulled away, taking her mother back to Masham, to her father, to Rowntree the Labrador and everything that was friendly and familiar, Robin dropped down on a cold metal bench, buried her face in her hands and wept silently into the banknotes Linda had given her.

'Cheer up, darling. Plenty more fish in the sea.'

She looked up. An unkempt man stood in front of her. His belly spilled widely over his belt and his smile was lascivious.

Robin got slowly to her feet. She was as tall as he was. Their eyes were on a level.

'Sod off,' she said.

He blinked. His smile turned to a scowl. As she strode away, stuffing Linda's money into her pocket, she heard him shout something after her, but she neither knew nor cared what it had been. A vast unfocused rage rose in her, against men who considered displays of emotion a delicious open door; men who ogled your breasts under the pretence of scanning the wine shelves; men for whom your mere physical presence constituted a lubricious invitation.

Her fury billowed to encompass Strike, who had sent her home to Matthew because he now considered her a liability; who would rather endanger the business that she had helped build up, soldiering on single-handedly, than let her do what she was good at, what she sometimes outshone him at, because of the permanent handicap she had in his eyes acquired by being in the wrong stairwell at the wrong time, seven years previously.

So yes, she would ring his bloody lap-dancing clubs and his strip joints in search of the bastard who had called her 'little girl', but there was something else she would do too. She had been looking forward to telling Strike about it, but there had been no time with Linda's train due, and she had felt no inclination after he told her to stay at home.

Robin tightened her belt and marched on, frowning, feeling fully justified in continuing to follow one lead, unbeknownst to Strike, alone.

37

This ain't the garden of Eden.

Blue Öyster Cult, 'This Ain't the Summer of Love'

If she had to be at home, she supposed she would watch the wedding. Robin staked out a position on the sitting-room sofa early next morning, her laptop open on her knees, her mobile beside her, the TV on in the background. Matthew, too, had the day off work, but he was in the kitchen, keeping out of her way. There had been no solicitous offers of tea today, no questions about her work, no obsequious attentiveness. Robin sensed a change in him since her mother had left. He seemed anxious, wary, more serious. Somehow, during their quiet conversations, Linda appeared to have convinced Matthew that what had happened might never be reparable.

Robin knew perfectly well that she needed to deliver the *coup de grâce*. Linda's parting words had increased her sense of urgency. She had not yet found another place to live, but she must nevertheless tell Matthew that she was moving out and agree a form of words to issue to their friends and family. Yet here she sat on the sofa, working rather than dealing with the subject that seemed to fill the small flat, pressing against the walls, keeping the atmosphere perpetually stiff with tension.

Commentators wearing buttonholes and corsages were babbling on screen about the decorations in Westminster Abbey. Famous guests snaked towards the entrance and Robin half listened as she noted down the telephone numbers for lap-dancing clubs, strip joints and massage parlours in and around Shoreditch. Every now and then she scrolled down a page to look through the client reviews on the remote chance that somebody might have mentioned a bouncer called Noel, but no individual was named except the women who worked there. Punters often recommended them on the basis of their reported enthusiasm for their jobs. Mandy from one massage parlour 'gives full thirty minutes' with 'never any sense of being rushed'; the gorgeous Sherry of Beltway Strippers was always 'willing, accommodating and up for a laugh'. 'I can thoroughly recommend Zoe,' said one punter, 'gorgeous figure and a very "happy ending"!!!'

In a different mood – or, perhaps, in a different life – Robin might have found the way they talked about the women funny. So many of the men handing over cash for sex needed to believe that the women's enthusiasm was real, that they took their time for pleasure, that they were really laughing at punters' jokes, genuinely enjoying the body-to-body massages and the hand jobs. One reviewer had posted a poem about his favourite girl.

Even as she diligently compiled her list of numbers, Robin thought it unlikely that Brockbank, with his insalubrious record, would have been hired by any of the more upmarket places, whose websites featured artistically lit, airbrushed naked girls and invitations for couples to attend together.

Brothels, Robin knew, were illegal, but you did not have to travel too far into cyberspace to find mention of them. She had become adept at nosing information from out-of-the-way corners of the internet since going to work for Strike and was soon painstakingly cross-referencing mentions of local establishments on ramshackle sites dedicated to the exchange of such information. Here, at the cheapest end of the market, there were no poems: '£60 for anal going rate round here' 'All forigen girls ,no english.' 'Very young probably still clean. Wouldn put your dick in some of wht you see.'

Often, only an approximate location was available. She knew that Strike would not let her go looking for any of these basements and tenements where 'mostly east european grils' or 'all Chinese tail' were working.

Taking a break and subconsciously hoping to loosen the tight knot in her chest, she looked up at the television. Princes William and Harry were walking up the aisle together. As Robin watched, the door to the sitting room opened and Matthew walked in, carrying a mug of tea. He had not offered to make her one. He sat down in the armchair, saying nothing, and stared at the television screen.

Robin returned to her work, hyperconscious of Matthew beside her. Joining her without talking was a departure. Acceptance of her separateness – not interrupting her, even with the offer of tea – was also new. So was the fact that he did not pick up the remote control and change the channel.

The cameras returned to the outside of the Goring Hotel, where they were keeping vigil for the first glimpse of Kate Middleton in her wedding dress. Robin took covert glimpses over the top of her laptop while scrolling slowly down a series of barely literate comments about a brothel near Commercial Road.

An outburst of excitable comment and cheering made Robin look up in time to see Kate Middleton climbing into a limousine. Long lace sleeves, just like the ones she had removed from her own wedding dress . . .

The limousine moved slowly away. Kate Middleton was

just visible beside her father in the car. So she had chosen to wear her hair down. Robin had planned to keep her hair down too. Matthew liked it that way. Not that that mattered any more . . .

The crowds were cheering all the way down the Mall, Union Jacks as far as the eye could see.

As Matthew turned towards her, Robin pretended to be immersed in her laptop again.

'D'you want tea?'

'No,' she said. 'Thanks,' she added grudgingly, aware how aggressive she had sounded.

Her mobile beeped beside her. Matthew often scowled or sulked when this happened on her days off: he expected it to be Strike, which it sometimes was. Today he merely turned back to watch the television.

Robin picked up her mobile and read the text that had just arrived:

How do I know you're not press?

It was the lead she was pursuing without Strike's knowledge and she had her answer ready. While the crowds cheered the limousine's slow progress on screen, she typed in:

If the press knew about you, they'd already be outside your house. I told you to look me up online. There's a picture of me going into court to give evidence in Owen Quine's murder case.
Have you found it?

She put the mobile down again, her heart beating faster.

Kate Middleton was getting out of her limousine at the Abbey. Her waist looked tiny in the lace dress. She looked so happy . . . genuinely happy . . . Robin's heart hammered as she watched the beautiful woman in a tiara proceed towards the Abbey entrance.

Her mobile beeped again.

Yes I've seen the picture. So?

Matthew made a peculiar noise into his mug of tea. Robin ignored him. He probably thought that she was texting Strike, usually the cause of his little grimaces and noises of exasperation. Switching her mobile to camera mode, Robin held it up in front of her face and took a photo.

The flash startled Matthew, who looked around. He was crying.

Robin's fingers trembled as she sent the photograph of herself off in a text. After that, not wanting to look at Matthew, she watched the television again.

Kate Middleton and her father were now walking slowly up the scarlet-carpeted aisle that divided a sea of hatted guests. The culmination of a million fairy tales and fables was being played out in front of her: the commoner walking slowly towards her prince, beauty moving inexorably towards high rank . . .

Against her will, Robin remembered the night that Matthew had proposed under the statue of Eros at Piccadilly Circus. There had been tramps sitting on the steps, jeering as Matthew sank to his knees. She had been caught completely off guard by that unexpected scene on the grimy steps, Matthew risking his best suit on the damp, dirty stone, alcoholic fumes wafting towards them over the smell of exhaust fumes: the little blue velvet box and then the winking sapphire, smaller and paler than Kate Middleton's. Matthew later told her he'd chosen it because it matched her eyes. One of the tramps had got to his feet and applauded drunkenly when she said yes. She remembered the flashing neon lights of Piccadilly reflected on Matthew's beaming face.

Nine years of shared life, of growing up together, of arguing and reconciling, of loving. Nine years, holding fast to each other through trauma that ought to have broken them apart.

She remembered the day after the proposal, the day she had been sent by the temping agency to Strike. It seemed much, much longer ago than it was. She felt like a different person ... at least, she *had* felt like a different person, until Strike told her to stay at home and copy down phone numbers, evading the question of when she would return to work as his partner.

'*They* split up.'

'What?' said Robin.

'*They* did,' said Matthew, and his voice broke. He nodded at the screen. Prince William had just turned to look at his bride. 'They broke up for a bit.'

'I know they did,' said Robin.

She tried to speak coldly, but Matthew's expression was bereft.

Maybe on some level I think you deserve better than me.

'Is it – are we really over?' he asked.

Kate Middleton had drawn level with Prince William at the altar. They looked delighted to be reunited.

Staring at the screen, Robin knew that today her answer to Matthew's question would be taken as definitive. Her engagement ring was still lying where she had left it, on top of old accountancy textbooks on the bookcase. Neither of them had touched it since she had taken it off.

'Dearly beloved ...' began the Dean of Westminster on screen.

She thought of the day that Matthew had asked her out for the very first time and remembered walking home from school, her insides on fire with excitement and pride. She remembered Sarah Shadlock giggling, leaning against him in a pub in Bath, and Matthew frowning slightly and pulling away. She thought of Strike and Elin . . . *what have they got to do with anything?*

She remembered Matthew, white-faced and shaking, in the hospital where they had kept her for twenty-four hours after the rape. He had missed an exam to be with her, simply taken off without leaving word. His mother had been annoyed about that. He had had to re-sit in the summer.

I was twenty-one and I didn't know then what I know now: that there's nobody like you and that I could never love anyone else as much as I love you . . .

Sarah Shadlock, arms around him when he was drunk, no doubt, while he poured out his confused feelings about Robin, agoraphobic, unable to be touched . . .

The mobile beeped. Automatically, Robin picked it up and looked at it.

All right, I believe it's you.

Robin could not take in what she was reading and set the mobile down on the sofa without responding. Men looked so tragic when they cried. Matthew's eyes were scarlet. His shoulders heaved.

'Matt,' she said in a low voice over his silent sobs. 'Matt . . .' She held out her hand.

38

Dance on Stilts

The sky was marbled pink, but the streets were still heaving with people. A million Londoners and out-of-towners swarmed the pavements: red, white and blue hats, Union Jacks and plastic crowns, beer-swilling buffoons clutching the hands of children with painted faces, all of them bobbing and eddying on a tide of mawkish sentiment. They filled the Tube, they packed the streets, and as he forced his way through them, looking for what he needed, he heard more than once the refrain of the national anthem, sung tunelessly by the tipsy, and once with virtuosity by a gaggle of rollicking Welsh women who blocked his way out of the station.

He had left It sobbing. The wedding had lifted It temporarily out of Its misery, led to cloying affection and self-pitying tears, to plaintive hints about commitment and companionship. He had kept his temper only because his every nerve, every atom of his being focused on what he was going to do tonight. Focused on the release that was coming, he had been patient and loving, but his reward had been It taking the biggest liberty yet and trying to prevent him leaving.

He had already put on the jacket that accommodated his knives, and he had cracked. Although he had not laid a finger on It, he knew how to terrify and intimidate with words alone, with body language, with a sudden revelation of the beast inside. He had slammed his way out of the house, leaving It cowed and appalled behind him.

He would have to work hard to make up for that, he reflected as he pushed his way through a crowd of drinkers on a pavement. A bunch of poxy flowers, some fake regret, some bullshit about being stressed . . . the thought turned his expression mean. Nobody dared challenge him, not with his size and demeanour, though he knocked into several of them ploughing his way through them. They were like skittles, fleshy ninepins, and they had about as much life and meaning to him. People had significance in his life only in what they could do for him. That was how The Secretary had come to assume such importance. He had never tracked a woman for so long.

Yes, the last one had taken a while too, but that had been different: that dumb little bitch had toppled so gleefully into his clutches you'd have thought getting hacked to pieces was her life's ambition. Which, of course, it had been . . .

The thought of it made him smile. The peach towels and the stink of her blood . . . He was starting to get the feeling again, that feeling of omnipotence. He was going to get one tonight, he could feel it . . .

Headin' for a meeting, shining up my greeting . . .

He was on the lookout for a girl who had become separated from the massing throngs, addled with drink and sentimentality, but they moved in herds through the streets, so he was starting to think he'd be better with a whore after all.

Times had changed. It wasn't how it had been in the old days. Hookers didn't need to walk the streets any more, not with mobile phones and the internet. Buying yourself a woman was as easy as dialling up a takeaway nowadays, but he didn't want to leave a trail online or on some bitch's mobile records. Only the dregs were left on the streets and he knew all the areas, but it had to be somewhere that he had no association with, somewhere a long way from It . . .

By ten to midnight he was in Shacklewell, walking the streets with his lower face concealed by the upturned collar of his jacket, his hat low on his forehead, the knives bouncing heavily against his chest as he walked, one a straightforward carving knife, the other a compact machete. Lit windows of curry houses and more pubs, Union Jack bunting everywhere . . . if it took all night, he would find her . . .

On a dark corner stood three women in tiny skirts, smoking, talking. He passed by on the other side of the street and one of them called out to him, but he ignored her, passing on into the darkness. Three was too many: two witnesses left.

Hunting was both easier and more difficult on foot. No worries about number plates caught on camera, but the difficulty was where he took her, not to mention the getaway being so much harder.

He prowled the streets for another hour until he found himself back on that stretch of road where the three whores had stood. Only two of them now. More manageable. A single witness. His face was almost entirely covered. He hesitated, and as he did so a car slowed and the driver had a brief conversation with the girls. One of them got in and the car drove away.

The glorious poison flooded his veins and his brain. It was exactly like the first time he'd killed: then, too, he had been left with the uglier one, to do with whatever he wanted.

No time for hesitation. Either of her mates could come back.

'Back again, babes?'

Her voice was guttural, although she looked young, with red hennaed hair in a shabby bob, piercings in both ears and her nose. Her nostrils were wet and pink, as though she had a cold. Along with her leather jacket and rubber miniskirt, she wore vertiginous heels on which she seemed to have trouble balancing.

'How much?' he asked, barely listening to her answer. What mattered was where.

'We can go to my place if you want.'

He agreed, but he was tense. It had better be a self-contained room or a bedsit: nobody on the stairs, no one to hear or see, just some dirty, dark little nook where a body begged to be. If it turned out to be a communal place, some actual brothel, with other girls and a fat old bitch in charge or, worse, a pimp . . .

She wobbled out onto the road before the pedestrian light turned green. He seized her arm and yanked her back as a white van went hurtling past.

'My saviour!' she giggled. 'Ta, babes.'

He could tell she was on something. He'd seen plenty like her. Her raw, weeping nose disgusted him. Their reflection in the dark shop windows they passed could have been father and daughter, she was so short and skinny and he so large, so burly.

'See the wedding?' she asked.

'What?'

'Royal wedding? She looked lovely.'

Even this dirty little whore was wedding-crazy. She babbled on about it as they walked, laughing far too often, teetering on her cheap stilettos, while he remained entirely silent.

'Shame 'is mum never saw 'im marry, though, innit? 'Ere we go,' said the girl, pointing to a tenement a block ahead. 'That's my gaff.'

He could see it in the distance: there were people standing

around the lit door, a man sitting on the steps. He stopped dead.

'No.'

''Smatter? Don't worry about them, babes, they know me,' she said earnestly.

'No,' he said again, his hand tight around her thin arm, suddenly furious. What was she trying to pull? Did she think he was born yesterday?

'Down there,' he said, pointing to a shadowy space between two buildings.

'Babes, there's a bed—'

'Down there,' he repeated angrily.

She blinked at him out of heavily made-up eyes, a little fazed, but her thought processes were fogged, the silly bitch, and he convinced her silently, by sheer force of personality.

'Yeah, all right, babes.'

Their footsteps crunched on a surface that seemed to be part gravel. He was afraid there might be security lights or sensors, but a thicker, deeper darkness awaited them twenty yards off the road.

He handed over the notes. She unzipped his trousers for him. He was still soft. While she was busy on her knees in the darkness, trying to persuade him into tumescence, he was pulling his knives silently from their hiding place inside his jacket. A slither of nylon lining, one in each hand, his palms sweaty on the plastic handles . . .

He kicked her so hard in the stomach that she flew backwards through the air. A choking, wheezing gasp then a crunch of gravel told him where she had landed. Lurching forward, his flies still open, his trousers sliding down his hips, he found her by tripping over her and was on her.

The carving knife plunged and plunged: he hit bone, probably rib, and stabbed again. A whistle from her lungs and then, shocking him, she screamed.

Though he was straddling her she was fighting and he could not find her throat to finish her. He gave a mighty left-handed swing with the machete, but incredibly she still had enough life in her to shriek again—

A stream of obscenities poured from his mouth – stab, stab and stab again with the carving knife – he punctured her palm as she tried to stop him and that gave him an idea – slamming her arm down, kneeling on it, he raised his knife—

'You fucking little cocksucking . . . '

'Who's down there?'

Fucking hell and shit.

A man's voice, coming out of the dark from the direction of the street, said again:

'Who's there?'

He scrambled off her, pulling up his pants and his trousers, backing away as quietly as he could, two knives in his left hand and what he thought were two of her fingers in his right, still warm, bony and bleeding . . . She was still moaning and whimpering . . . then, with a last long wheeze, she fell silent . . .

He hobbled away into the unknown, away from her motionless form, every sense as sharp as a cat's to the distant approach of a hound.

'Everything all right down there?' said an echoing male voice.

He had reached a solid wall. He felt his way along it until it turned into wire mesh. By the distant light of a street lamp he saw the outlines of what looked like a ramshackle car repair shop beyond the fence, the hulking forms of vehicles eerie in the gloom. Somewhere in the space he had just left he heard footsteps: the man had come to investigate the screams.

He must not panic. He must not run. Noise would be fatal. Slowly he edged along the wire enclosure containing the old cars, towards a patch of darkness that might be either an opening onto an adjoining street or a dead end. He slid the bloody knives back inside his jacket, dropped her fingers into his pocket and crept along, trying not to breathe.

An echoing shout from the alleyway:

'Fucking hell! Andy – ANDY!'

He began to run. They would not hear him now, not with their yells echoing off the walls, and as though the universe were once again his friend, it laid soft grassy ground beneath his feet as he lumbered into the new darkness of the opening . . .

A dead end, a six-foot wall. He could hear traffic on the other side. Nothing else for it: panting, scrambling, wishing he were what he had once been, fit and strong and young, he tried to hoist himself up, his feet trying to find some purchase, his muscles screaming in protest . . .

Panic can do wonderful things. He was on top of the wall and down again. He landed heavily; his knees protested, but he staggered then regained his balance.

Walk on, walk on . . . normal . . . normal . . . normal . . .

Cars whooshed past. Surreptitiously he wiped his bloody hands on his jacket. Distant shouting, too muffled to hear . . . he needed to get away from here as quickly as possible. He would go to the place that It didn't know about.

A bus stop. He jogged a short distance and joined the queue. It didn't matter where he went as long as it took him out of here.

His thumb made a bloody mark on the ticket. He pushed it deep into his pocket and made contact with her severed fingers.

The bus rumbled away. He took long slow breaths, trying to calm himself.

Somebody upstairs began singing the national anthem again. The bus sped up. His heart jolted. Slowly his breathing returned to normal.

Staring at his own reflection in the filthy window, he rolled her still-warm little finger between his own. As panic receded, elation took its place. He grinned at his dark reflection, sharing his triumph with the only one who could understand.

39

The door opens both ways . . .

Blue Öyster Cult, 'Out of the Darkness'

'Look at this,' said Elin on Monday morning, standing aghast in front of the television with a bowl of granola in her hands. 'Can you believe it!'

Strike had just entered the kitchen, freshly washed and dressed, after their usual Sunday night rendezvous. The spotless cream and white space was full of stainless steel surfaces and subdued lighting, like a space age operating theatre. A plasma TV hung on the wall behind the table. President Obama was on screen, standing at a podium, talking.

'They've killed Osama bin Laden!' said Elin.

'Bloody hell,' said Strike, stopping dead to read the ticker-tape running across the bottom of the screen.

Clean clothes and a shave had made little difference to his hangdog look of exhaustion. The hours he was putting in trying to catch a glimpse of Laing or Whittaker were beginning to take their painful toll: his eyes were bloodshot and his skin was tinged with grey.

He crossed to the coffee maker, poured himself a mugful and gulped it down. He had almost fallen asleep on top of Elin last night, and counted it among the week's few small achievements that he had finished that job, at least. Now he leaned against the steel-topped island, watching the immaculate President and envying him from his soul. He, at least, had got his man.

The known details of bin Laden's death gave Elin and Strike something to talk about while she was dropping him off at the Tube.

'I wonder how sure they were it was him,' she said, pulling up outside the station, 'before they went in.'

Strike had been wondering that, too. Bin Laden had been physically distinctive, of course: well over six feet tall . . . and Strike's thoughts drifted back to Brockbank, Laing and Whittaker, until Elin recalled them.

'I've got work drinks on Wednesday, if you fancy it.' She sounded slightly self-conscious. 'Duncan and I have nearly agreed everything. I'm sick of sneaking around.'

'Sorry, no can do,' he said. 'Not with all these surveillance jobs on, I told you.'

He had to pretend to her that the pursuit of Brockbank, Laing and Whittaker were paid jobs, because she would never have understood his so far fruitless persistence otherwise.

'OK, well, I'll wait for you to ring me, then,' she said, and he caught, but chose to ignore, a cool undertone in her voice.

Is it worth it? he asked himself as he descended into the Underground, backpack over his shoulder, with reference not to the men he was pursuing but to Elin. What had begun as an agreeable diversion was starting to assume the status of onerous obligation. The predictability of their rendezvous – same restaurants, same nights – had started to pall, yet now that she offered to break the pattern he found himself unenthusiastic. He could think offhand of a dozen things he would rather do with a night off than have drinks with a bunch of Radio Three presenters. Sleep headed the list.

Soon – he could feel it coming – she would want to introduce him to her daughter. In thirty-seven years, Strike had successfully avoided the status of 'Mummy's boyfriend'. His memories of the men who had passed through Leda's life, some of them decent, most of them not – the latter trend reaching its apotheosis in Whittaker – had left him with a distaste that was almost revulsion. He had no desire to see in another child's eyes the fear and mistrust that he had read in his sister Lucy's every time the door opened onto yet another male stranger. What his own expression had been, he had no idea. For as long as he had been able to manage it, he had closed his mind wilfully to that part of Leda's life, focusing on her hugs and her laughter, her maternal delight in his achievements.

As he climbed out of the Tube at Notting Hill Gate on his way to the school, his mobile buzzed: Mad Dad's estranged wife had texted.

> **Just checking you know boys not at school today because of bank holiday. They're with grandparents. He won't follow them there.**

Strike swore under his breath. He had indeed forgotten about the bank holiday. On the plus side, he was now free to return to the office, catch up with some paperwork, then head out to Catford Broadway by daylight for a change. He only wished that the text could have arrived before he made the detour to Notting Hill.

Forty-five minutes later, Strike was tramping up the metal staircase towards his office and asking himself for the umpteenth time why he had never contacted the landlord about getting the birdcage lift fixed. When he reached the glass door of his office, however, a far more pressing question presented itself: why were the lights on?

Strike pushed open the door so forcefully that Robin, who had heard his laborious approach, nevertheless jumped in her chair. They stared at each other, she defiant, he accusing.

'What are you doing here?'

'Working,' said Robin.

'I told you to work from home.'

'I've finished,' she said, tapping a sheaf of papers that lay on the desk beside her, covered with handwritten notes and telephone numbers. 'Those are all the numbers I could find in Shoreditch.'

Strike's eyes followed her hand, but what caught his attention was not the small stack of neatly written papers she was showing him, but the sapphire engagement ring.

There was a pause. Robin wondered why her heart was pummelling her ribs. How ridiculous to feel defensive . . . it was up to her whether she married Matthew . . . ludicrous even to feel she had to state that to herself . . .

'Back on, is it?' Strike said, turning his back on her as he hung up his jacket and backpack.

'Yes,' said Robin.

There was a short pause. Strike turned back to face her.

'I haven't got enough work for you. We're down to one job. I can cover Mad Dad on my own.'

She narrowed her grey-blue eyes.

'What about Brockbank and Laing and Whittaker?'

'What about them?'

'Aren't you still trying to find them?'

'Yes, but that's not the—'

'So how are you going to cover four cases?'

'They're not cases. No one's paying—'

'So they're a kind of hobby, are they?' said Robin. 'That's why I've been looking for numbers all weekend?'

'Look – I want to trace them, yes,' said Strike, trying to marshal his arguments through heavy fatigue and other, less easily definable emotions (the engagement was back on . . . he had suspected all along that it might happen . . . sending her home, giving her time with Matthew would have helped, of course) 'but I don't—'

'You were happy enough to let me drive you to Barrow,' said Robin, who had come prepared for argument. She had known perfectly well he didn't want her back in the office. 'You didn't mind me questioning Holly Brockbank and Lorraine MacNaughton, did you? So what's changed?'

'*You got sent another fucking body part, that's what's fucking changed, Robin!*'

He had not intended to shout, but his voice echoed off the filing cabinets.

Robin remained impassive. She had seen Strike angry before, heard him swear, seen him punch those very metal drawers. It didn't bother her.

'Yes,' she said calmly, 'and it shook me up. I think most people would have been shaken up by getting a toe stuck inside a card. You looked pretty sick about it yourself.'

'Yeah, which is why—'

'—you're trying to cover four cases single-handedly and you sent me home. I didn't ask for time off.'

In the euphoric aftermath of replacing her ring, Matthew had actually helped her rehearse her case for returning to work. It had been quite extraordinary, looking back on it, he pretending to be Strike and she putting her arguments, but Matthew had been ready to help her do anything at all, so long as she agreed to marry him on the second of July.

'I wanted to get straight back to—'

'Just because you wanted to get back to work,' said Strike, 'doesn't mean it was in your best interests to do so.'

'Oh, I didn't realise you're a qualified occupational therapist,' said Robin, delicately sarcastic.

'Look,' said Strike, more infuriated by her aloof rationality than he would have been with rage and tears (the sapphire sparkling coolly from her finger again), 'I'm your employer and it's down to me if—'

'I thought I was supposed to be your partner,' said Robin.

'Makes no difference,' said Strike, 'partner or not, I've still got a responsibility—'

'So you'd rather see this business fail than let me work?' said Robin, an angry flush rising in her pale face, and while Strike felt he was losing on points he took an obscure pleasure in the fact that she was losing her cool. 'I helped you build it up! You're playing right into his hands, whoever he is, sidelining me, neglecting paying cases and working yourself into the—'

'How do you know I've—?'

'Because you look like shit,' said Robin baldly and Strike, caught off guard, almost laughed for the first time in days.

'Either,' she resumed, 'I'm your partner or I'm not. If you're going to treat me like some piece of special-occasion china that gets taken out when you don't think I'll get hurt, we're – we're doomed. The business is doomed. I'd do better to take Wardle up on—'

'On what?' said Strike sharply.

'On his suggestion that I apply to the police,' said Robin, looking Strike squarely in the face. 'This isn't a game to me, you know. I'm not a little girl. I've survived far worse than being sent a toe. So –' she screwed up her courage. She had hoped it would not come to an ultimatum '– decide. Decide whether I'm your partner or a – a liability. If you can't rely on me – if you can't let me run the same risks you do – then I'd rather—'

Her voice nearly broke, but she forced herself onwards.

'—rather get out,' she finished.

In her emotion, she swung her chair round to face her computer a little too forcefully and found herself facing the wall.

Mustering what dignity she felt she had left, she adjusted her seat to face the monitor and continued opening emails, waiting for his answer.

She had not told him about her lead. She needed to know whether she was reinstated as his partner before she either shared her spoils or gave it to him as a farewell gift.

'Whoever he is, he butchers women for pleasure,' said Strike quietly, 'and he's made it clear he'd like to do the same to you.'

'I've grasped that,' said Robin in a tight voice, her eyes on the screen, 'but have *you* grasped the fact that if he knows where I work, he probably also knows where I live, and if he's that determined he'll follow me anywhere I go? Can't you understand that I'd much rather help catch him than sit around waiting for him to pounce?'

She was not going to beg. She had emptied the inbox of twelve spam emails before he spoke again, his voice heavy.

'All right.'

'All right what?' she asked, looking around cautiously.

'All right . . . you're back at work.'

She beamed. He did not return the smile.

'Oh, cheer up,' she said, getting to her feet and moving around the desk.

For one crazy moment Strike thought she might be about to hug him, she looked so happy (and with the protective ring back on her finger, perhaps he had become a safely huggable figure, a de-sexed non-competitor), but she was merely heading for the kettle.

'I've got a lead,' she told him.

'Yeah?' he said, still struggling to make sense of the new situation. (What was he going to ask her to do that wasn't too dangerous? Where could he send her?)

'Yes,' she said. 'I've made contact with one of the people on the BIID forum who was talking to Kelsey.'

Yawning widely, Strike dropped down into the fake-leather sofa, which made its usual flatulent noises under his weight, and tried to remember whom she was talking about. He was so sleep-deprived that his usually capacious and accurate memory was becoming unreliable.

'The . . . bloke or the woman?' he asked, with the vague remembrance of the photographs Wardle had shown them.

'The man,' said Robin, pouring boiling water onto teabags.

For the first time in their relationship Strike found himself relishing an opportunity to undermine her.

'So you've been going onto websites without telling me? Playing games with a bunch of anonymous punters without knowing who you're messing with?'

'I told you I'd been on there!' said Robin indignantly. 'I saw Kelsey asking questions about you on a message board, remember? She was calling herself Nowheretoturn. I *told* you all this when Wardle was here. *He* was impressed,' she added.

'He's also way ahead of you,' said Strike. 'He's questioned both of those people she was talking to online. It's a dead end. They never met her. He's working on a guy called Devotee now, who was trying to meet women off the site.'

'I already know about Devotee.'

'How?'

'He asked to see my picture and when I didn't send it, he went quiet—'

'So you've been flirting with these nutters, have you?'

'Oh, for God's sake,' said Robin impatiently, 'I've been pretending I've got the same disorder they have, it's hardly flirting – and I don't think Devotee's anything to worry about.'

She passed Strike a mug of tea, which was precisely his preferred shade of creosote. Perversely, this aggravated rather than soothed him.

'So you don't think Devotee's anything to worry about? What are you basing that on?'

'I've been doing some research into acrotomophiliacs ever since that letter came in addressed to you – the man who was fixated on your leg, remember? As paraphilias go, it's hardly ever associated with violence. I think Devotee's much more likely to be masturbating over his keyboard at the idea of all the wannabes.'

Unable to think of any response to this, Strike drank some tea.

'Anyway,' said Robin (his lack of thanks for his tea had rankled), 'the guy Kelsey was talking to online – he wants to be an amputee too – lied to Wardle.'

'What do you mean, he lied?'

'He *did* meet Kelsey in real life.'

'Yeah?' said Strike, determinedly casual. 'How do you know that?'

'He's told me all about it. He was terrified when the Met contacted him – none of his family or his friends knows about his obsession with getting rid of his leg – so he panicked and said he'd never met Kelsey. He was afraid that if he admitted he had, there would be publicity and he'd have to give evidence in court.

'Anyway, once I'd convinced him that I am who I am, that I'm not a journalist or a policewoman—'

'You told him the truth?'

'Yes, which was the best thing I could have done, because once he was convinced I was really me, he agreed to meet.'

'And what makes you think he's genuinely going to meet you?' asked Strike.

'Because we've got leverage with him that the police haven't.'

'Like what?'

'Like,' she said coldly, wishing that she could have returned a different answer, 'you. Jason's absolutely desperate to meet you.'

'Me?' said Strike, completely thrown. 'Why?'

'Because he believes you cut your leg off yourself.'

'*What?*'

'Kelsey convinced him that you did it yourself. He wants to know how.'

'Jesus fucking Christ,' said Strike, 'is he mentally ill? Of course he is,' he answered himself immediately. 'Of course he's mentally ill. He wants to cut his fucking leg off. Jesus fucking Christ.'

'Well, you know, there's debate about whether BIID is a mental illness or some kind of brain abnormality,' said Robin. 'When you scan the brain of someone suffering—'

'Whatever,' said Strike, waving the topic away. 'What makes you think this nutter's got anything useful—?'

'*He met Kelsey,*' said Robin impatiently, 'who must have told him why she was so convinced you were one of them. He's nineteen years old, he works in an Asda in Leeds, he's got an aunt in London and he's going to come down, stay with her and meet me. We're trying to find a date. He needs to find out when he can get the time off.

'Look, he's two removes from the person who convinced Kelsey you were a voluntary amputee,' she went on, both disappointed and annoyed by Strike's lack of enthusiasm for the results of her solo work, but still holding out a faint hope that he would stop being so tetchy and critical, 'and that person is almost certainly the killer!'

Strike drank more tea, allowing what she had told him to percolate slowly through his exhausted brain. Her reasoning was sound. Persuading Jason to meet her was a significant achievement. He ought to offer praise. Instead he sat in silence, drinking his tea.

'If you think I should call Wardle and pass this over to him—' said Robin, her resentment palpable.

'No,' said Strike, and the haste with which he answered gave Robin some small satisfaction. 'Until we've heard what he's . . . we won't waste Wardle's time. We'll let him know once we've heard what this Jason's got. When did you say he's coming to London?'

'He's trying to get time off; I don't know yet.'

'One of us could go up to Leeds and meet him.'

'He wants to come down. He's trying to keep all this away from anyone who knows him.'

'OK,' said Strike gruffly, rubbing his bloodshot eyes and trying to formulate a plan that would keep Robin simultaneously busy and out of harm's way. 'You keep the pressure on him, then, and start ringing round those numbers, see whether you can get a lead on Brockbank.'

'I've already started doing that,' she said and he heard the latent rebelliousness, the imminent insistence that she wanted to be back on the street.

'And,' said Strike, thinking fast, 'I want you to stake out Wollaston Close.'

'Looking for Laing?'

'Exactly. Keep a low profile, don't stay there after dark and if you see the beanie bloke you get out of there or set off your bloody rape alarm. Preferably both.'

Even Strike's surliness could not douse Robin's delight that she was back on board, a fully equal partner in the business.

She could not know that Strike believed and hoped that he was sending her up a dead end. By day and by night he had watched the entrances to the small block of flats, shifting position regularly, using night-vision goggles to scan the balconies and windows. Nothing he had seen indicated that Laing was lurking within: no broad shadow moving behind a curtain, no hint of a low-growing hairline or dark ferret-like eyes, no massive figure swaying along on crutches or (because Strike took nothing for granted when it came to Donald Laing) swaggering along like the ex-boxer he was. Every man who had passed in and out of the building had been scrutinised by Strike for a hint of resemblance to Laing's JustGiving photograph or to the faceless figure in the beanie hat, and none of them had come close to a match.

'Yeah,' he said, 'you get onto Laing and – give me half those Brockbank numbers – we'll divide them up. I'll stick with Whittaker. Make sure you check in regularly, OK?'

He heaved himself out of the sofa.

'Of course,' said Robin, elated. 'Oh, and – Cormoran—'

He was already on the way to the inner office, but turned.

'—what are these?'

She was holding up the Accutane pills that he had found in Kelsey's drawer and which he had left in Robin's in-tray after looking them up online.

'Oh, them,' he said. 'They're nothing.'

Some of her cheeriness seemed to evaporate. A faint guilt stirred. He knew he was being a grumpy bastard. She didn't deserve it. He tried to pull himself together.

'Acne medication,' he said. 'They were Kelsey's.'

'Of course – you went to the house – you saw her sister! What happened? What did she say?'

Strike did not feel equal to telling her all about Hazel Furley now. The interview felt a long time ago, he was exhausted and still felt unreasonably antagonistic.

'Nothing new,' he said. 'Nothing important.'

'So why did you take these pills?'

'I thought they might be birth control . . . maybe she was up to something her sister didn't know about.'

'Oh,' said Robin. 'So they really are nothing.'

She tossed them into the bin.

Ego made Strike go on: ego, pure and simple. She had found a good lead and he had nothing except a vague idea about the Accutane.

'And I found a ticket,' he said.

'A what?'

'Like a coat check ticket.'

Robin waited expectantly.

'Number eighteen,' said Strike.

Robin waited for a further explanation, but none came. Strike yawned and conceded defeat.

'I'll see you later. Keep me posted on what you're up to and where you are.'

He let himself into his office, closed the door, sat down at his desk and slumped backwards in his chair. He had done all he could to stop her getting back on the street. Now, he wanted nothing more than to hear her leave.

40

. . . love is like a gun
And in the hands of someone like you
I think it'd kill.

Blue Öyster Cult, 'Searchin' for Celine'

Robin was a decade younger than Strike. She had arrived in his office as a temporary secretary, unsought and unwelcome, at the lowest point of his professional life. He had only meant to keep her on for a week, and that because he had almost knocked her to her death down the metal stairs when she arrived, and he felt he owed her. Somehow she had persuaded him to let her stay, firstly for an extra week, then for a month and, finally, for ever. She had helped him claw his way out of near insolvency, worked to make his business successful, learned on the job and now asked nothing more than to be allowed to stand beside him while that business crumbled again, and to fight for its survival.

Everyone liked Robin. *He* liked Robin. How could he fail to like her, after everything they had been through together? However, from the very first he had told himself: this far and no further. A distance must be maintained. Barriers must remain in place.

She had entered his life on the very day that he had split from Charlotte for good, after sixteen years of an on-off relationship that he still could not say had been more pleasurable than painful. Robin's helpfulness, her solicitousness, her fascination with what he did, her admiration for him personally (if he was going to be honest with himself, he should do it thoroughly) had been balm to those wounds that Charlotte had inflicted, those internal injuries that had long outlasted her parting gifts of a black eye and lacerations.

The sapphire on Robin's third finger had been a bonus, then: a safeguard and a full stop. In preventing the possibility of anything more, it set him free to . . . what? Rely on her? Befriend her? Allow barriers to become imperceptibly eroded, so that as he looked back it occurred to him that they had each shared personal information that hardly anybody else knew. Robin was one of only three people (he suspected) who knew about that putative baby that Charlotte claimed to have lost, but which might never have existed, or was aborted. He was one of a mere handful who knew that Matthew had been unfaithful. For all his determination to keep her at arm's length, they had literally leaned on each other. He could remember exactly what it felt like to have his arm around her waist as they had meandered towards Hazlitt's Hotel. She was tall enough to hold easily. He did not like having to stoop. He had never fancied very small women.

Matthew would *not* like this, she had said.

He would have liked it even less had he known how much Strike had liked it.

She was nowhere near as beautiful as Charlotte. Charlotte had had the kind of beauty that made men forget themselves mid-sentence, that stunned them into silence. Robin, as he could hardly fail to notice when she bent over to turn off her PC at the wall, was a very sexy girl, but men were not struck dumb in her presence. Indeed, remembering Wardle, she seemed to make them more loquacious.

Yet he liked her face. He liked her voice. He liked being around her.

It wasn't that he wanted to *be* with her – that would be insanity. They could not run the business together and have an affair. In any case, she wasn't the kind of girl you had an affair with. He had only ever known her engaged or else bereft at the demise of her engagement and therefore saw her as the kind of woman who was destined for marriage.

Almost angrily, he added together those things he knew and had observed that marked her as profoundly different from him, as embodying a safer, more cloistered, more conventional world. She had had the same pompous boyfriend since sixth form (although he understood that a little better now), a nice middle-class family back in Yorkshire, parents married for decades and apparently happy, a Labrador and a Land Rover and a *pony*, Strike reminded himself. A bloody pony!

Then other memories intruded and a different Robin peeled away from this picture of a safe and ordered past: and there in front of him stood a woman who would not have been out of place in the SIB. This was the Robin who had taken advanced driving courses, who had concussed herself in the pursuit of a killer, who had calmly wrapped her coat like a tourniquet around his bleeding arm after he was stabbed and taken him to hospital. The Robin who had improvised so successfully in interrogating suspects that she had winkled out information that the police had not managed to get, who had invented and successfully embodied Venetia Hall, who had persuaded a terrified young man who wanted his leg amputated to confide in her, who had given Strike a hundred other examples of initiative, resourcefulness and courage that might have turned her into a plain-clothes police officer by now, had she not once walked into a dark stairwell where a bastard in a mask stood waiting.

And that woman was going to marry Matthew! Matthew, who had been banking on her working in human resources, with a nice salary to complement his own, who sulked and bitched about her long, unpredictable hours and her lousy pay check . . . couldn't she *see* what a stupid bloody thing she was doing? Why the fuck had she put that ring back on? Hadn't she tasted freedom on that drive up to Barrow, which Strike looked back on with a fondness that discomposed him?

She's making a fucking huge mistake, that's all.

That was all. It wasn't personal. Whether she was engaged, married or single, nothing could or ever would come of the weakness he was forced to acknowledge that he had developed. He would re-establish the professional distance that had somehow ebbed away with her drunken confessions and the camaraderie of their trip up north, and temporarily shelve his half-acknowledged plan to end the relationship with Elin. It felt safer just now to have another woman within reach, and a beautiful one at that, whose enthusiasm and expertise in bed ought surely to compensate for an undeniable incompatibility outside it.

He fell to wondering how long Robin would continue working for him after she became Mrs Cunliffe. Matthew would surely use every ounce of his husbandly influence to prise her away from a profession as dangerous as it was poorly paid. Well, that was her lookout: her bed, and she could lie in it.

Except that once you had broken up, it was much easier to do so again. He ought to know. How many times had he and Charlotte split? How many times had their relationship fallen to pieces, and how many times had they tried to reassemble the wreckage? There had been more cracks than substance by the end: they had lived in a spider's web of fault lines, held together by hope, pain and delusion.

Robin and Matthew had just two months to go before the wedding.

There was still time.

41

> See there a scarecrow who waves through the mist.
>
> Blue Öyster Cult, 'Out of the Darkness'

It happened quite naturally that Strike saw Robin very little over the following week. They were staking out different locations and exchanged information almost exclusively over their mobiles.

As Strike had expected, neither Wollaston Close nor its environs had revealed any trace of the ex-King's Own Royal Borderer, but he had been no more successful in spotting his man in Catford. The emaciated Stephanie entered and left the flat over the chip shop a few more times. Although he could not be there around the clock, Strike was soon pretty sure that he had seen her entire wardrobe: a few pieces of dirty jersey and one tatty hoodie. If, as Shanker had confidently asserted, she was a prostitute, she was working infrequently. While he took care never to let her see him, Strike doubted that her hollow eyes would retain much of an impression even if he had moved into plain view. They had become shuttered, full of inner darkness, no longer taking in the outside world.

Strike had tried to ascertain whether Whittaker was almost

permanently inside or almost constantly absent from the flat in Catford Broadway, but there was no landline registered for the address and the property was listed online as owned by a Mr Dareshak, who was either renting it or unable to get rid of his squatters.

The detective was standing smoking beside the stage door one evening, watching the lit windows and wondering whether he was imagining movement behind them, when his mobile buzzed and he saw Wardle's name.

'Strike here. What's up?'

'Bit of a development, I think,' said the policeman. 'Looks like our friend's struck again.'

Strike moved the mobile to his other ear, away from the passing pedestrians.

'Go on.'

'Someone stabbed a hooker down in Shacklewell and cut off two of her fingers as a souvenir. Deliberately cut 'em off – pinned her arm down and hacked at them.'

'Jesus. When was this?'

'Ten days ago – twenty-ninth of April. She's only just come out of an induced coma.'

'She survived?' said Strike, now taking his eyes entirely off the windows behind which Whittaker might or might not have been lurking, his attention all Wardle's.

'By a fucking miracle,' said Wardle. 'He stabbed her in the abdomen, punctured her lung, then hacked off her fingers. Miracle he missed major organs. We're pretty sure he thought she was dead. She'd taken him down a gap between two buildings for a blow job, but they were disturbed: two students walking down Shacklewell Lane heard her scream and went down the alley to see what was going on. If they'd been five minutes later she'd've been a goner. It took two blood transfusions to keep her alive.'

'And?' said Strike. 'What's she saying?'

'Well, she's drugged up to the eyeballs and can't remember the actual attack. She thinks he was a big, beefy white guy wearing a hat. Dark jacket. Upturned collar. Couldn't see much of his face, but she thinks he was a northerner.'

'She does?' said Strike, his heart pounding faster than ever.

'That's what she said. She's groggy, though. Oh, and he stopped her getting run over, that's the last thing she can remember. Pulled her back off the road when a van was coming.'

'What a gent,' said Strike, exhaling smoke at the starry sky.

'Yeah,' said Wardle. 'Well, he wanted his body parts pristine, didn't he?'

'Any chance of a photofit?'

'We're going to get the artist in to see her tomorrow, but I haven't got high hopes.'

Strike stood in the darkness, thinking hard. He could tell that Wardle had been shaken by the new attack.

'Any news on any of my guys?' he asked.

'Not yet,' said Wardle tersely. Frustrated, Strike chose not to push it. He needed this open line into the investigation.

'What about your Devotee lead?' Strike asked, turning back to look at the windows of Whittaker's flat, where nothing seemed to have changed. 'How's that coming along?'

'I'm trying to get the cybercrime lot after him, but I'm being told they've got bigger fish to fry just now,' said Wardle, not without bitterness. 'Their view is he's just a common or garden pervert.'

Strike remembered that this had also been Robin's opinion. There seemed little else to say. He said goodbye to Wardle, then sank back into his niche in the cold wall, smoking and watching Whittaker's curtained windows as before.

*

Strike and Robin met in the office by chance the following morning. Strike, who had just left his flat with a cardboard file of pictures of Mad Dad under his arm, had intended to head straight out without entering the office, but the sight of Robin's blurred form through the frosted glass changed his mind.

'Morning.'

'Hi,' said Robin.

She was pleased to see him and even more pleased to see that he was smiling. Their recent communication had been full of an odd constraint. Strike was wearing his best suit, which made him look thinner.

'Why are you so smart?' she asked.

'Emergency lawyer's appointment: Mad Dad's wife wants me to show them everything I've got, all the pictures of him lurking outside the school and jumping out at the kids. She called me late last night; he'd just turned up at the house pissed and threatening: she's going to throw the book at him, try and get an injunction out.'

'Does this mean we're stopping surveillance on him?'

'I doubt it. Mad Dad won't go quietly,' said Strike, checking his watch. 'Anyway, forget that – I've got ten minutes and I've got news.'

He told her about the attempted murder of the prostitute in Shacklewell. When he had finished, Robin looked sober and thoughtful.

'He took fingers?'

'Yeah.'

'You said – when we were in the Feathers – you said you didn't see how Kelsey could have been his first murder. You said you were sure he'd worked up to – what he did to her.'

Strike nodded.

'Do you know whether the police have looked for any other killings where a bit of the woman was cut off?'

'Bound to have,' said Strike, hoping he was right and making a mental note to ask Wardle. 'Anyway,' he said, 'after this one, they will.'

'And she doesn't think she'd recognise him again?'

'Like I said, he'd obscured his face. Big white guy, black jacket.'

'Did they get any DNA evidence from her?' asked Robin.

Simultaneously, both of them thought of what Robin herself had been subjected to in hospital after her attack. Strike, who had investigated rapes, knew the form. Robin had a sudden miserable memory of having to pee into a sample bottle, one eye completely closed from where he had punched her, aching all over, her throat swollen from the strangulation, then having to lie down on the examination couch, and the female doctor's gentleness as she parted Robin's knees . . .

'No,' said Strike. 'He didn't – no penetration. Anyway, I'd better get going. You can forget about tailing Mad Dad today: he'll know he's blotted his copybook, I doubt he'll show up at school. If you can keep an eye on Wollaston—'

'Wait! I mean, if you've got time,' she added.

'Couple more minutes,' he said, checking his watch again. 'What's up? You haven't spotted Laing?'

'No,' she said, 'but I think – just possibly – we might have a lead on Brockbank.'

'You're kidding!'

'It's a strip club off Commercial Road; I've had a look at it on Google Street View. Looks pretty grotty. I called and asked for Noel Brockbank and a woman said "Who?" and then, "Nile, you mean?" And she put her hand over the mouthpiece and had a bit of discussion with another woman about what the new bouncer was called. He's obviously only just arrived. So I described him physically and she said "Yeah, that's Nile."

Of course,' said Robin self-deprecatingly, 'it might not be him at all, it *could* be a dark man who really is called Nile, but when I described the long jaw, she said immediately—'

'You've played your usual blinder,' said Strike, checking his watch. 'Gotta go. Text me the details of this strip club, will you?'

'I thought I might—'

'No, I want you to stick to Wollaston Close,' said Strike. 'Keep in touch.'

As the glass door closed behind him and he clanged away down the metal stairs, she tried to feel pleased that he had said she'd played a blinder. Nevertheless, she had hoped for a chance to do something other than stare pointlessly at the flats of Wollaston Close for hours. She was starting to suspect that Laing was not there and, worse still, that Strike knew it.

The visit to the lawyers was brief but productive. The solicitor was delighted with the copious evidence that Strike had laid in front of him, which vividly documented Mad Dad's constant violations of the custody agreements.

'Oh, excellent,' he beamed over an enlarged picture of the youngest son cowering tearfully behind his nanny as his father snarled and pointed, almost nose to nose with the defiant woman. 'Excellent, excellent . . . '

And then, catching sight of his client's expression, he had hurried to conceal his glee at this vision of her child's distress and offered tea.

An hour later Strike, still in his suit but with his tie now stuffed in his pocket, was following Stephanie into Catford shopping centre. This meant passing under a gigantic fibreglass sculpture of a grinning black cat, which sat on top of the girder that spanned the alley leading into the mall. Two storeys high from its dangling paw to the tip of its jaunty tail, which pointed skywards, it seemed poised to pounce upon or scoop up shoppers as they passed beneath.

Strike had decided to follow Stephanie on a whim, never having tracked her before, and intended to return to keep watch over the flat once he had satisfied himself as to where she was going and whom she might be meeting. She walked, as she almost always did, with her arms wrapped tightly around her torso, as though holding herself together, wearing the familiar grey hoodie on top of a black miniskirt and leggings. The slenderness of her twig-like legs was emphasised by her clumpy trainers. She visited a pharmacy and Strike watched through the window as she sat huddled in a chair waiting for a prescription, making eye contact with nobody, staring at her feet. Once she had collected her white paper bag she left the way she had come, passing back beneath the giant cat with its dangling paw, apparently returning to the flat. However, she walked straight past the chippy in Catford Broadway and shortly afterwards took a right at the Afro Caribbean Food Centre and disappeared into a small pub called the Catford Ram, which was built into the rear of the shopping centre. The pub, which appeared to have only one window, had a wood-clad exterior that would have given it the look of a large Victorian kiosk had it not been plastered with signs advertising fast food, Sky Sports and a Wi-Fi connection.

The entire area was paved for pedestrians, but a battered grey transit van had been parked a short distance from the pub entrance, giving Strike useful cover as he lurked, debating his options. No purpose would be served at this juncture by coming face to face with Whittaker and the pub looked too small to avoid being seen by his ex-stepfather, if that was whom Stephanie was meeting. All he really wanted was a chance to measure Whittaker's current appearance against that of the figure in the beanie hat and, perhaps, the man in the camouflage jacket who had been watching the Court.

Strike leaned up against the van and lit a cigarette. He had just resolved to find a vantage point that was a little further away, so that he might observe whom Stephanie left the pub with, when the rear doors of the van behind which he was lurking suddenly opened.

Strike took several hasty steps backwards as four men clambered out of the back, along with a smoky haze that gave out a powerful, acrid smell of burned plastic that the ex-SIB man recognised immediately as crack.

All four were unkempt, their jeans and T-shirts filthy, their age hard to gauge because each of them was sunken-faced and prematurely wrinkled. The mouths of two of them had collapsed inwards onto gums that had lost teeth. Momentarily taken aback to find the clean-suited stranger at such close quarters, they seemed to understand from his startled expression that he had not known what was happening inside and slammed the van doors.

Three of them swaggered off towards the pub, but the fourth man did not leave. He was staring at Strike, and Strike was staring right back at him. It was Whittaker.

He was bigger than Strike remembered. Although he had known that Whittaker was almost as tall as he was, he had forgotten the scale of him, the breadth of his shoulders, the heft of the bones beneath his heavily tattooed skin. His thin T-shirt, emblazoned with the logo of the band Slayer, which was both militaristic and occult, blew back against him as they stood facing each other, revealing the outline of ribs.

His yellow face looked freeze-dried like an old apple, the flesh wasted, the skin shrunken against the bone, with cavities beneath the high cheekbones. His matted hair was thinning at the temples: it hung in rats' tails around his stretched earlobes, each of which was adorned with a silver flesh tunnel. There they stood, Strike in his Italian suit, abnormally well groomed, and Whittaker, stinking of crack fumes, his heretic priest's golden eyes now set beneath wrinkled, sagging lids.

Strike could not have said how long they stared at each other, but a stream of perfectly coherent thoughts passed through his mind while they did . . .

If Whittaker were the killer, he might be panicked but not too surprised to see Strike. If he were not the killer, his shock at finding Strike right outside his van ought to be extreme. Yet Whittaker had never behaved like other people. He always liked to appear unshockable and omniscient.

Then Whittaker reacted and Strike felt at once that it would have been unreasonable to expect him to do anything other than what he did. Whittaker grinned, revealing blackened teeth, and instantly the hatred of twenty years ago rose in Strike, and he yearned to put his fist through Whittaker's face.

'Looky look,' said Whittaker quietly. 'It's Sergeant Sherlock facking Holmes.'

He turned his head and Strike saw scalp shining through the thinning roots and took some petty pleasure in the fact that Whittaker was going bald. He was a vain fucker. He wouldn't like that.

'Banjo!' shouted Whittaker at the last of his three companions, who had only just reached the pub. 'Bring 'er out 'ere!'

His smile remained insolent, although the mad eyes flickered from the van to Strike and back to the pub. His filthy fingers were flexing. For all his assumed insouciance, he was edgy. Why didn't he ask why Strike was there? Or did he already know?

The friend called Banjo reappeared, dragging Stephanie out of the pub by her thin wrist. In her free hand she was still clutching the pharmacist's white paper bag. It looked glaringly pristine against her and Banjo's cheap and dirty clothes. A gold necklace bounced around her neck.

'Why're you—? What—?' she whimpered, uncomprehending.

Banjo deposited her beside Whittaker.

'Go get us a pint,' Whittaker instructed Banjo, who shuffled obediently away. Whittaker slid a hand around the back of Stephanie's thin neck and she looked up at him with the slavish adoration of a girl who, like Leda before her, saw in Whittaker wonderful things that were totally invisible to Strike. Then Whittaker's fingers gripped her neck until the skin around them went white and began to shake her, not so vigorously as to attract the attention of a passer-by, but with sufficient force to change her expression instantly to one of abject fear.

'Know anything about this?'

''Bout w-what?' she stammered. The pills were rattling in her white paper bag.

''Im!' said Whittaker quietly. ''Im that you're so interested in, you filthy little bitch—'

'Get off her,' said Strike, speaking for the first time.

'Do I take orders?' Whittaker asked Strike quietly, his grin wide, his eyes manic.

With sudden, shocking strength, he seized Stephanie around the neck with both hands and lifted her bodily into the air, so that she dropped the white bag on the pavement to try to fight free, her feet scrabbling, her face growing purple.

No thought, no reflection. Strike punched Whittaker hard in the gut and he fell backwards, taking Stephanie with him; before Strike could do anything to prevent it, he heard the smack of her head on the concrete. Temporarily winded, Whittaker tried to get to his feet, a stream of whispered filth pouring from between his black teeth, while out of the corner of his eye Strike saw Whittaker's three friends, Banjo at the fore, pushing their way out of the pub: they had seen everything through its one dingy window. One of them was holding a short, rusty blade.

'Do it!' Strike taunted them, standing his ground and opening his arms wide. 'Bring the cops round your mobile crack den!'

The winded Whittaker made a gesture from the ground that had the effect of holding his friends at bay, which was the most common sense Strike had ever known him show. Faces were peering out of the pub window.

'You fucking mother . . . you motherfucker . . .' Whittaker wheezed.

'Yeah, let's talk about mothers,' Strike said, jerking Stephanie to her feet. The blood was pounding in his ears. He itched to punch Whittaker until the yellow face was pulp. 'He killed mine,' he told the girl, looking into her hollow eyes. Her arms were so thin that his hands almost met around them. 'Did you hear that? He's already killed one woman. Maybe more.'

Whittaker tried to grab Strike around his knees and bring him down; Strike kicked him off, still holding Stephanie. Whittaker's red handprints stood out on her white neck, as did the imprint of the chain, from which hung the outline of a twisted heart.

'Come with me, now,' Strike told her. 'He's a fucking killer. There are women's refuges. Get away from him.'

Her eyes were like boreholes into a darkness he had never known. He might have been offering her a unicorn: his proposal was madness, outside the realm of the possible, and incredibly, though Whittaker had squeezed her throat until she could not speak, she wrenched away from Strike as if he were a kidnapper, stumbled over to Whittaker and crouched protectively over him, the twisted heart swinging.

Whittaker allowed Stephanie to help him to his feet and turned to face Strike, rubbing his stomach where the punch had landed and then, in his manic way, he began cackling like an old woman. Whittaker had won: they both knew it. Stephanie was clinging to him as though he had saved her. He pushed his filthy fingers deep into the hair at the back of her head and pulled her hard towards him, kissing her, his tongue down her throat, but with his free hand he gestured to his still-watching friends to get back in the van. Banjo climbed into the driver's seat.

'See ya, mummy's boy,' Whittaker whispered to Strike, pushing Stephanie in front of him into the back of the van. Before the doors shut on the obscenities and jeers of his male companions, Whittaker looked directly into Strike's eyes and made the familiar throat-slashing gesture in mid-air, grinning. The van moved away.

Strike became suddenly aware that a number of people were standing around him, staring, all gazing at him with the vacant yet startled expressions of an audience when the lights go up unexpectedly. Faces were still pressed up against the pub window. There was nothing left for him to do except memorise the registration number of the battered old van before it turned the corner. As he departed the scene, furious, the onlookers scattered, clearing his way.

42

I'm living for giving the devil his due.

Blue Öyster Cult, 'Burnin' For You'

Fuck-ups happen, Strike told himself. His military career had not been entirely devoid of mishap. You could train as hard as you liked, check every piece of equipment, plan for every contingency and still some random mischance would screw you. Once, in Bosnia, a faulty mobile phone had unexpectedly dumped all its power, triggering a train of mishaps that culminated in a friend of Strike's barely escaping with his life after driving up the wrong street in Mostar.

None of this altered the fact that if a subordinate in the SIB had been running surveillance and leaned up against the back of a carelessly parked van without first checking that it was empty, Strike would have had a lot to say about it, and loudly. He had not meant to confront Whittaker, or so he told himself, but a period of sober reflection forced him to admit that his actions told a different story. Frustrated by the long hours watching Whittaker's flat, he had taken few pains to hide himself from the pub windows, and while he could not have known that Whittaker was inside the van, there was a savage retrospective pleasure in knowing that, at last, he had punched the fucker.

God, he had wanted to hurt him. The gloating laugh, the rat's-tail hair, the Slayer T-shirt, the acrid smell, the clutching fingers around the thin white neck, the taunting talk of mothers: the feelings that had erupted in Strike at the unexpected sight of Whittaker had been those of his eighteen-year-old self, eager to fight, careless of consequences.

Setting aside the pleasure it had been to hurt Whittaker, the encounter had not produced much meaningful information. Try though he might to effect a retrospective comparison, he could neither identify nor rule out Whittaker as the large figure in the beanie hat on looks alone. While the dark silhouette that Strike had chased through Soho had not had Whittaker's matted locks, long hair can be tied back or tucked into a hat; it had looked burlier than Whittaker, but padded jackets easily add substance. Nor had Whittaker's reaction on finding Strike outside his van given the detective real clues. The more he thought about it, the less he could decide whether he had read triumph in Whittaker's gloating expression, or whether the last gesture, the dirty fingers slashing through the air, had been his usual play-acting, a toothless threat, the infantile retaliation of a man determined at all costs to be the worst, the scariest.

In brief, their encounter had revealed that Whittaker remained narcissistic and violent, and given Strike two small pieces of additional information. The first was that Stephanie had aggravated Whittaker by showing curiosity about Strike, and while Strike assumed that this was merely because he had once been Whittaker's stepson, he did not entirely rule out the possibility that it had been triggered by Whittaker mentioning a desire for retribution, or letting slip that he was seeking it. Secondly, Whittaker had managed to make himself some male friends. While he had always had a, to Strike, incomprehensible attraction for certain women, Whittaker had been almost universally disliked and despised by men in the days that Strike had known him. His own gender had tended to deplore his histrionics, the Satanic bullshit, his craving to be first in all company and, of course, to resent his strange magnetic pull over females. Now, though, Whittaker seemed to have found a crew of sorts, men who shared drugs with him and allowed him to boss them around.

Strike concluded that the one thing he could profitably do in the short term was tell Wardle what had happened and give him the registration number of the van. He did this in the hope that the police would think it worth their while to check for drugs and any other incriminating evidence within the vehicle or, even better, inside that flat over the chippy.

Wardle listened to Strike's insistence that he had smelled crack fumes without any form of enthusiasm. Strike was forced to admit, when their call had concluded, that if he were in Wardle's position he would not have considered his own evidence grounds for a search warrant. The policeman clearly thought that Strike had it in for his ex-stepfather, and no amount of pointing out the Blue Öyster Cult connection between himself and Whittaker seemed likely to change Wardle's mind.

When Robin phoned that night with her usual progress report, Strike found relief and solace in telling her what had happened. Although she had news of her own, she was instantly distracted by the announcement that he had come face to face with Whittaker, and listened to the whole story in eager silence.

'Well, I'm glad you hit him,' she said when Strike had finished castigating himself for allowing the altercation to happen.

'You are?' said Strike, taken aback.

'Of course I am. He was strangling the girl!'

The moment the words left Robin's mouth she wished she had not said them. She did not want to give Strike any further reason for remembering the thing that she wished she had never told him.

'As knights errant go, I was on the crap side. She fell over with him and cracked her head on the pavement. What I don't get,' he added, after a short pause for reflection, 'is *her*. That was her chance. She could've left: I'd've got her to a refuge, I'd've seen her right. Why the fuck did she go back to him? Why do women do that?'

In the fractional hesitation before Robin replied, Strike realised that a certain personal interpretation could be put on these words.

'I suppose,' began Robin, and simultaneously Strike said, 'I didn't mean—'

Both stopped.

'Sorry, go on,' said Strike.

'I was only going to say that abused people cling to their abusers, don't they? They've been brainwashed to believe there's no alternative.'

I was the bloody alternative, standing there, right in front of her!

'Any sign of Laing today?' Strike asked.

'No,' said Robin. 'You know, I *really* don't think he's there.'

'I still think it's worth—'

'Look, I know who's in every flat except for one of them,' said Robin. 'People go in and out of all the others. The last one's either unoccupied, or someone's lying in there dead, because the door never opens. I haven't even seen carers or nurses visit.'

'We'll give it another week,' said Strike. 'It's the only lead we've got for Laing. Listen,' he added irritably, as she tried to protest, 'I'll be in the same position, staking out that strip club.'

'Except we know that Brockbank's there,' said Robin sharply.

'I'll believe it when I see him,' retorted Strike.

They said goodbye a few minutes later in poorly concealed mutual dissatisfaction.

All investigations had their slumps and droughts, when information and inspiration ran dry, but Strike was finding it difficult to take a philosophical view. Thanks to the unknown sender of the leg, there was no longer any money coming in to the business. His last paying client, Mad Dad's wife, no longer needed him. In the hope of persuading a judge that the restraining order was not required, Mad Dad was actually complying with it.

The agency could not survive much longer if the twin stenches of failure and perversity continued to emanate from his office. As Strike had foreseen, his name was now multiplying across the internet in connection with the killing and dismemberment of Kelsey Platt, and the gory details were not only obliterating all mention of his previous successes, they were also eclipsing the simple advertisement of his detective services. Nobody wanted to hire a man so notorious; nobody liked the idea of a detective so intimately connected with unsolved murder.

It was therefore in a mood of determination and slight desperation that Strike set out for the strip club where he hoped to find Noel Brockbank. It turned out to be another converted old pub, which lay on a side street off Commercial Road in Shoreditch. The brick façade was crumbling in parts; its windows had been blacked out and crude white silhouettes of naked women painted upon them. The original name ('The Saracen') was still picked out in wide golden letters across the peeling black paint over the double doors.

The area had a large proportion of Muslim residents. Strike passed them in their hijabs and taqiyahs, browsing the many cheap clothes shops, all bearing names like International Fashion and Made in Milan and displaying sad mannequins in synthetic wigs wearing nylon and polyester. Commercial Road was crammed with Bangladeshi banks, tatty estate agents, English schools and ramshackle grocers that sold past-its-prime fruit behind grimy windows, but it had no benches to sit on, not even a low, cold wall. Even though he frequently changed his vantage point, Strike's knee soon began to complain about long stretches spent standing, waiting for nothing, because Brockbank was nowhere to be seen.

The man on the door was squat and neckless, and Strike saw nobody enter or leave the place except punters and strippers. The girls came and went, and like their place of employment, they were shabbier and less polished than those who worked at Spearmint Rhino. Some were tattooed or pierced; several were overweight, and one, who looked drunk as she entered the building at eleven in the morning, appeared distinctly grubby viewed through the window of the kebab shop that lay directly opposite the club. After watching the Saracen for three days, Strike, whose hopes had been high, whatever he had said to Robin, reluctantly concluded that either Brockbank had never worked there, or that he had already been sacked.

Friday morning arrived before the depressing pattern of no leads changed. As he was lurking in the doorway of an especially dismal clothing store named World Flair, Strike's mobile rang and Robin spoke in his ear:

'Jason's coming to London tomorrow. The leg guy. From the wannabe amputee website.'

'Great!' said Strike, relieved at the mere prospect of interviewing someone. 'Where are we meeting him?'

'It's "them",' said Robin, with a definite note of reservation in her voice. 'We're meeting Jason *and* Tempest. She's—'

'Excuse me?' interrupted Strike. '*Tempest?*'

'I doubt it's her birth name,' said Robin drily. 'She's the woman Kelsey was interacting with online. Black hair and glasses.'

'Oh, yeah, I remember,' repeated Strike, supporting the mobile between jaw and shoulder while he lit a cigarette.

'I've just got off the phone with her. She's a big activist in the transabled community and she's pretty overwhelming, but Jason thinks she's wonderful and he seems to feel safer with her there.'

'Fair enough,' said Strike. 'So where are we meeting Jason and Tempest?'

'They want to go to Gallery Mess. It's the café at the Saatchi Gallery.'

'Really?' Strike seemed to remember that Jason worked in an Asda, and was surprised that his first craving on arriving in London was contemporary art.

'Tempest's in a wheelchair,' said Robin, 'and apparently it's got really good disabled access.'

'OK,' said Strike. 'What time?'

'One,' said Robin. 'She – er – asked whether we'd be paying.'

'I suppose we'll have to.'

'And listen – Cormoran – would it be all right if I took the morning off?'

'Yeah, of course. Everything OK?'

'Everything's fine, I've just got some – some wedding stuff to sort out.'

'No problem. Hey,' he added, before she could hang up, 'shall we meet up somewhere first, before we question them? Agree our interviewing strategy?'

'That'd be great!' said Robin, and Strike, touched by her enthusiasm, suggested they meet in a sandwich shop on the King's Road.

43

Freud, have mercy on my soul.

Blue Öyster Cult, 'Still Burnin''

The next day, Strike had been in Pret A Manger on the King's Road for five minutes when Robin arrived, carrying a white bag over her shoulder. He was as uninformed about female fashion as most male ex-soldiers, but even he recognised the name Jimmy Choo.

'Shoes,' he said, pointing, after he had ordered her a coffee.

'Well done,' said Robin, grinning. 'Shoes. Yes. For the wedding,' she added, because after all, they ought to be able to acknowledge that it was happening. A strange taboo had seemed to exist around the subject since she had resumed her engagement.

'You're still coming, right?' she added as they took a table beside the window.

Had he ever agreed that he was attending her wedding, Strike wondered. He had been given the reissued invitation, which like the first had been of stiff cream card engraved in black, but he could not remember telling her that he would be there. She watched him expectantly for an answer, and he was reminded of Lucy and her attempts to coerce him into attending his nephew's birthday party.

'Yeah,' he said unwillingly.

'Shall I RSVP for you?' Robin asked.

'No,' he said. 'I'll do it.'

He supposed that it would entail calling her mother. This, he thought, was how women roped you in. They added you to lists and forced you to confirm and commit. They impressed upon you that if you didn't show up a plate of hot food would go begging, a gold-backed chair would remain unoccupied, a cardboard place name would sit shamefully upon a table, announcing your rudeness to the world. Offhand, he could think of literally nothing he wanted to do less than watch Robin marry Matthew.

'D'you want – would you like me to invite Elin?' Robin asked valiantly, hoping to see his expression become a degree or two less surly.

'No,' said Strike without hesitation, but he read in her offer a kind of plea, and his real fondness for her caused his better nature to reassert itself. 'Let's see the shoes then.'

'You don't want to see the—!'

'I asked, didn't I?'

Robin lifted the box out of its bag with a reverence that amused Strike, took off the lid and unfolded the tissue paper inside. They were high, glittery champagne-coloured heels.

'Bit rock 'n' roll for a wedding,' said Strike. 'I thought they'd be . . . I dunno . . . flowery.'

'You'll hardly see them,' she said, stroking one of the stilettos with a forefinger. 'They had some platforms, but—'

She did not finish the sentence. The truth was that Matthew did not like her too tall.

'So how are we going to handle Jason and Tempest?' she said, pushing the lid back down on the shoes and replacing them in the bag.

'You're going to take the lead,' said Strike. 'You're the one who's had contact with them. I'll jump in if necessary.'

'You realise,' said Robin awkwardly, 'that Jason's going to ask you about your leg? That he thinks you – you lied about how you lost it?'

'Yeah, I know.'

'OK. I just don't want you to get offended or anything.'

'I think I can handle it,' said Strike, amused by her look of concern. 'I'm not going to hit him, if that's what's worrying you.'

'Well, good,' said Robin, 'because from his pictures you'd probably break him in two.'

They walked side by side up the King's Road, Strike smoking, to the place where the entrance to the gallery sat a little retired from the road, behind the statue of a bewigged and stockinged Sir Hans Sloane. Passing through an arch in the pale brick wall, they entered a grassy square that might, but for the noise of the busy street behind them, have belonged to a country estate. Nineteenth-century buildings on three sides surrounded the square. Ahead, contained in what might once have been barracks, was Gallery Mess.

Strike, who had vaguely imagined a canteen tacked on to the gallery, now realised that he was entering a far more upmarket space and remembered with some misgivings both his overdraft and his agreement to pay for what was almost certainly going to be lunch for four.

The room they entered was long and narrow, with a second, wider area visible through arched openings to their left. White tablecloths, suited waiters, high-vaulted ceilings and contemporary art all over the walls increased Strike's dread of how much this was going to cost him as they followed the maître d' into the inner portion of the room.

The pair they sought was easy to spot among the tastefully

dressed, mostly female clientele. Jason was a stringy youth with a long nose who wore a maroon hoodie and jeans and looked as though he might take flight at the slightest provocation. Staring down at his napkin, he resembled a scruffy heron. Tempest, whose black bob had certainly been dyed and who wore thick, square black-rimmed spectacles, was his physical opposite: pale, dumpy and doughy, her small, deep-set eyes like raisins in a bun. Wearing a black T-shirt with a multi-coloured cartoon pony stretched across an ample chest, she was sitting in a wheelchair adjacent to the table. Both had menus open in front of them. Tempest had already ordered herself a glass of wine.

When she spotted Strike and Robin approaching, Tempest beamed, stretched out a stubby forefinger and poked Jason on the shoulder. The boy looked around apprehensively; Strike registered the pronounced asymmetry of his pale blue eyes, one of which was a good centimetre higher than the other. It gave him an oddly vulnerable look, as though he had been finished in a hurry.

'Hi,' said Robin, smiling and reaching out a hand to Jason first. 'It's nice to meet you at last.'

'Hi,' he muttered, proffering limp fingers. After one quick glance at Strike he looked away, turning red.

'Well, hello!' said Tempest, sticking her own hand out to Strike, still beaming. Deftly she reversed her wheelchair a few inches and suggested that he pull up a chair from a neighbouring table. 'This place is great. It's so easy to get around in, and the staff are really helpful. Excuse me!' she said loudly to a passing waiter, 'Could we have two more menus, please?'

Strike sat down beside her, while Jason shunted up to make room for Robin beside him.

'Lovely space, isn't it?' said Tempest, sipping her wine, 'And the staff are wonderful about the wheelchair. Can't help you enough. I'm going to be recommending it on my site; I do a list of disability-friendly venues.'

Jason drooped over his menu, apparently afraid to make eye contact with anyone.

'I've told him not to mind what he orders,' Tempest told Strike comfortably. 'He didn't realise how much you'll have made from solving those cases. I've told him: the press will have paid you loads just for your story. I suppose that's what you do now, try and solve the really high-profile ones?'

Strike thought of his plummeting bank balance, his glorified bedsit over the office and the shattering effect the severed leg had had on his business.

'We try,' he said, avoiding looking at Robin.

Robin chose the cheapest salad and a water. Tempest ordered a starter as well as a main course, urged Jason to imitate her, then collected in the menus to return them to the waiter with the air of a gracious hostess.

'So, Jason,' Robin began.

Tempest at once talked over Robin, addressing Strike.

'Jason's nervous. He hadn't really thought through what the repercussions of meeting you might be. I had to point them out to him; we've been on the phone day and night, you should see the bills – I should charge you, ha, ha! But seriously—'

Her expression became suddenly grave.

'—we'd really like your assurance up front that we're not going to be in trouble for not telling the police everything. Because it wasn't as though we had any useful information. She was just a poor kid with problems. We don't know anything. We only met up with her once, and we haven't got a clue who killed her. I'm sure you know much more about it than we do. I was pretty worried when I heard Jason had been talking to your partner, to be honest, because I don't think anyone really appreciates how much we're persecuted as a community. I've had death threats myself – I should hire you to investigate them, ha ha.'

'Who's made death threats against you?' asked Robin in polite surprise.

'It's *my* website, you see,' said Tempest, ignoring Robin and addressing Strike. 'I run it. It's like I'm den mother – or Mother Superior, ha ha . . . anyway, I'm the one everyone confides in and comes to for advice, so obviously, *I'm* the one who gets attacked when ignorant people target us. I suppose I don't help myself. I fight other people's battles a lot, don't I, Jason? Anyway,' she said, pausing only to take a greedy sip of wine, 'I can't advise Jason to talk to you without a guarantee he's not going to get in any trouble.'

Strike wondered what possible authority she thought he had in the matter. The reality was that both Jason and Tempest had concealed information from the police and, whatever their reasons for doing so, and whether or not the information turned out to be valuable, their behaviour had been foolish and potentially harmful.

'I don't think either of you will be in trouble,' he lied easily.

'Well, OK, that's good to hear,' said Tempest with some complacency, 'because we *do* want to help, obviously. I mean, I said to Jason, if this man's preying on the BIID community, which is possible – I mean, bloody hell, it's our *duty* to help. It wouldn't surprise me, either, the abuse we get on the website, the hatred. It's unbelievable. I mean, obviously it stems from ignorance, but we get abuse from people you'd expect to be on our side, who know exactly what it's like to be discriminated against.'

Drinks arrived. To Strike's horror, the Eastern European waiter upended his bottle of Spitfire beer into a glass containing ice.

'Hey!' said Strike sharply.

'The beer isn't cold,' said the waiter, surprised by what he clearly felt was Strike's overreaction.

'For fuck's sake,' muttered Strike, fishing the ice out of his glass. It was bad enough that he was facing a hefty lunch bill, without ice in his beer. The waiter gave Tempest her second glass of wine with a slightly huffy air. Robin seized her chance:

'Jason, when you first made contact with Kelsey—'

But Tempest set down her glass and drowned Robin out.

'Yeah, I checked all my records, and Kelsey first visited the site back in December. Yeah, I told the police that, I let them see everything. She asked about *you*,' Tempest told Strike in a tone that suggested he ought to be flattered to have secured a mention on her website, 'and then she got talking to Jason and they exchanged email addresses, and from then on they were in direct contact, weren't you, Jason?'

'Yeah,' he said weakly.

'Then she suggested meeting up and Jason got in touch with me – didn't you, Jason? – and basically he thought he'd feel more comfortable if I came along, because after all, it's the internet, isn't it? You never know. She could've been anyone. She could've been a man.'

'What made you want to meet Kel—?' Robin began to ask Jason, but again, Tempest talked over her.

'They were both interested in *you*, obviously,' said Tempest to Strike. 'Kelsey got Jason interested, didn't she, Jason? She knew *all* about you,' said Tempest, smiling slyly as though they shared disreputable secrets.

'So what did Kelsey tell you about me, Jason?' Strike asked the boy.

Jason turned scarlet at being addressed by Strike and Robin wondered suddenly whether he could be gay. From her extensive perusal of the message boards she had detected an erotic undertone to some, though not all, of the posters' fantasies, <<Δēvōtėė>> being the most blatant of them.

'She said,' mumbled Jason, 'her brother knew you. That he'd worked with you.'

'Really?' said Strike. 'Are you sure she said her brother?'

'Yeah.'

'Because she didn't have one. Only a sister.'

Jason's lopsided eyes travelled nervously over the objects on the table before returning to Strike.

'I'm pretty sure she said brother.'

'Worked with me in the army, did he?'

'No, not in the army, I don't think. Later.'

She lied all the time . . . If it was Tuesday she'd say it was Wednesday.

'Now, *I* thought she said her boyfriend told her,' said Tempest. 'She told us she had a boyfriend called Neil, Jason – remember?'

'Niall,' mumbled Jason.

'Oh, was it? All right, Niall. He picked her up after we had coffee, remember?'

'Hang on,' said Strike, raising a hand, and Tempest paused obediently. 'You *saw* Niall?'

'Yes,' said Tempest. 'He picked her up. On his motorbike.'

There was a brief silence.

'A man on a motorbike picked her up from – where did you meet her?' asked Strike, his calm tone belying his suddenly pounding pulse.

'Café Rouge on Tottenham Court Road,' said Tempest.

'That's not far from our office,' said Robin.

Jason turned an even darker red.

'Oh, Kelsey and Jason knew that, ha ha! You were hoping to see Cormoran pop in, weren't you, Jason? Ha ha ha,' laughed Tempest merrily as the waiter returned with her starter.

'A man on a motorbike picked her up, Jason?'

Tempest's mouth was full and, at last, Jason was able to speak.

'Yeah,' he said with a furtive look at Strike. 'He was waiting for her along the road.'

'Could you see what he looked like?' asked Strike, correctly anticipating the answer.

'No, he was sort of – sort of tucked around the corner.'

'He kept his helmet on,' said Tempest, washing down a mouthful with wine, the quicker to rejoin the conversation.

'What colour was the motorbike, can you remember?' Strike asked.

Tempest rather thought it had been black and Jason was sure it had been red, but they agreed that it had been parked far too far away to recognise the make.

'Can you remember anything else Kelsey said about her boyfriend?' asked Robin.

Both shook their heads.

Their main courses arrived midway through a lengthy explanation by Tempest of the advocacy and support services offered by the website she had developed. Only with her mouth full of chips did Jason finally find the courage to address Strike directly.

'Is it true?' he said suddenly. His face again grew bright red as he said it.

'Is what true?' asked Strike.

'That you – that—'

Chewing vigorously, Tempest leaned towards Strike in her wheelchair, placed her hand on his forearm and swallowed.

'That you did it yourself,' she whispered, with the ghost of a wink.

Her thick thighs had subtly re-adjusted themselves as she lifted them off the chair, bearing their own weight, instead of hanging behind the mobile torso. Strike had been in Selly Oak Hospital with men left paraplegic and quadriplegic by the injuries they had sustained in war, seen their wasted legs, the compensations they had learned to make in the movement of their upper bodies to accommodate the dead weight below. For the first time, the reality of what Tempest was doing hit him forcibly. She did not need the wheelchair. She was entirely able-bodied.

Strangely, it was Robin's expression that kept Strike calm and polite, because he found vicarious release in the look of distaste and fury she threw Tempest. He addressed Jason.

'You'll need to tell me what you've been told before I can tell you whether it's true or not.'

'Well,' said Jason, who had barely touched his Black Angus burger, 'Kelsey said you went to the pub with her brother and you got – got drunk and told him the truth. She reckoned you walked off your base in Afghanistan with a gun and you went as far as you could in the dark, then you – shot yourself in the leg, and then you got a doctor to amputate it for you.'

Strike took a large swig of beer.

'And I did this why?'

'What?' said Jason, blinking confusedly.

'Was I trying to get invalided out of the army, or—?'

'Oh, no!' said Jason, looking strangely hurt. 'No, you were—' He blushed so hard it seemed unlikely that there was enough blood left in the rest of his body '—like us. You needed it,' he whispered. 'You needed to be an amputee.'

Robin suddenly found that she could not look at Strike and pretended to be contemplating a curious painting of a hand holding a single shoe. At least, she thought it showed a hand holding a shoe. It might equally have been a brown plant pot with a pink cactus growing out of it.

'The – brother – who told Kelsey all about me – did he know she wanted to take off her own leg?'

'I don't think so, no. She said I was the only one she'd ever told.'

'So you think it was just coincidence he mentioned—?'

'People keep it quiet,' said Tempest, shoehorning herself back into the conversation at the first opportunity. 'There's a lot of shame, a *lot* of shame. I'm not out at work,' she said blithely, waving towards her legs. 'I have to say it's a back injury. If they knew I'm transabled they'd never understand. And don't get me started on the prejudice from the medical profession, which is absolutely unbelievable. I've changed GPs twice; I wasn't going to put up with being offered bloody psychiatric help *again*. No, Kelsey told us she'd never been able to tell anyone, poor little love. She had nobody to turn to. Nobody understood. That's why she reached out to us – and to you, of course,' she told Strike, smiling with a little condescension because, unlike her, he had ignored Kelsey's appeal. 'You're not alone, mind. Once people have successfully achieved what they're after they tend to leave the community. We get it – we understand – but it would mean a lot if people hung around just to describe what it feels like to finally be in the body you're meant to be in.'

Robin was worried that Strike might explode, here in this polite white space where art lovers conversed in soft voices. However, she had reckoned without the self-control that the ex-Special Investigation Branch officer had learned through long years of interrogations. His polite smile to Tempest might have been a little grim, but he merely turned again to Jason and asked:

'So you don't think it was Kelsey's brother's idea for her to contact me?'

'No,' said Jason, 'I think that was all her own idea.'

'So what exactly did she want from me?'

'Well, *obviously*,' interposed Tempest, half-laughing, 'she wanted advice on how to do what you'd done!'

'Is that what you think, Jason?' asked Strike and the boy nodded.

'Yeah . . . she wanted to know how badly she'd have to injure her leg to get it taken off, and I think she had a sort of idea you'd introduce her to the doctor who did yours.'

'That's the perennial problem,' said Tempest, clearly oblivious to the effect she was having on Strike, 'finding reliable surgeons. They're usually completely unsympathetic. People have died trying to do it themselves. There was a wonderful surgeon in Scotland who performed a couple of amputations on BIID sufferers, but then they stopped him. That was a good ten years ago. People go abroad, but if you can't pay, if you can't afford travel . . . you can see why Kelsey wanted to get her mitts on your contact list!'

Robin let her knife and fork fall with a clatter, feeling on Strike's behalf all the offence that she assumed him to be experiencing. *His contact list!* As though his amputation was a rare artefact that Strike had bought on the black market . . .

Strike questioned both Jason and Tempest for another fifteen minutes before concluding that they knew nothing more of any use. The picture they painted of their one meeting with Kelsey was of an immature and desperate girl whose urge to be amputated was so powerful that she would, by the consent of both of her cyberfriends, have done anything to achieve it.

'Yeah,' sighed Tempest, 'she was one of those. She'd already had a go when she was younger, with some wire. We've had people so desperate they've put their legs on train tracks. One guy tried to freeze his leg off in liquid nitrogen. There was a girl in America who deliberately botched a ski jump, but the danger with that is you might not get exactly the degree of disability you're after—'

'So what degree are *you* after?' Strike asked her. He had just put up a hand for the bill.

'I want my spinal cord severed,' said Tempest with total composure. 'Paraplegic, yeah. Ideally I'll have it done by a surgeon. In the meantime, I just get on with it,' she said, gesturing again to her wheelchair.

'Using the disabled bathrooms and stairlifts, the works, eh?' asked Strike.

'Cormoran,' said Robin in a warning voice.

She had thought this might happen. He was stressed and sleep-deprived. She supposed she ought to be glad that they had got all the information they needed first.

'It's a need,' said Tempest composedly. 'I've known ever since I was a child. I'm in the wrong body. I need to be paralysed.'

The waiter had arrived; Robin held out her hand for the bill, because Strike hadn't noticed him.

'Quickly, please,' she said to the waiter, who looked sullen. He was the man Strike had barked at for putting ice in his beer glass.

'Know many disabled people, do you?' Strike was asking Tempest.

'I know a couple,' she said. 'Obviously we've got a lot in—'

'You've got fuck all in common. Fuck all.'

'I knew it,' muttered Robin under her breath, snatching the chip and pin machine out of the waiter's grip and shoving in her Visa card. Strike stood up, towering over Tempest, who looked suddenly unnerved, while Jason shrank back in his seat, looking as though he wanted to disappear inside his hoodie.

'C'mon, Corm—' said Robin, ripping her card out of the machine.

'Just so you know,' said Strike, addressing both Tempest and Jason as Robin grabbed her coat and tried to pull him away from the table, 'I was in a car that blew up around me.' Jason had put his hands over his scarlet face, his eyes full of tears. Tempest merely gaped. 'The driver was ripped in two – *that'd* get you some attention, eh?' he said savagely to Tempest. 'Only he was dead, so not so fucking much. The other guy lost half his face – I lost a leg. There was nothing voluntary about—'

'OK,' said Robin, taking Strike's arm. 'We're off. Thanks very much for meeting us, Jason—'

'Get some help,' said Strike loudly, pointing at Jason as he allowed Robin to pull him away, diners and waiters staring. 'Get some fucking help. With your *head*.'

They were out in the leafy road, nearly a block away from the gallery, before Strike's breathing began to return to normal.

'OK,' he said, though Robin had not spoken. 'You warned me. I'm sorry.'

'That's all right,' she said mildly. 'We got everything we wanted.'

They walked on in silence for a few yards.

'Did you pay? I didn't notice.'

'Yes. I'll take it out of petty cash.'

They walked on. Well-dressed men and women passed them, busy, bustling. A bohemian-looking girl with dreadlocks floated past in a long paisley dress, but a five-hundred-pound handbag revealed that her hippy credentials were as fake as Tempest's disability.

'At least you didn't punch her,' said Robin. 'In her wheelchair. In front of all the art lovers.'

Strike began to laugh. Robin shook her head.

'I knew you'd lose it,' she sighed, but she was smiling.

44

Then Came the Last Days of May

He had thought she was dead. It had not troubled him that he hadn't seen a news report, because she'd been a hooker. He'd never seen anything in the papers about the first one he'd done either. Prostitutes didn't fucking count, they were nothing, no one cared. The Secretary was the one who was going to make the big splash, because she was working for that bastard – a clean-living girl with her pretty fiancé, the kind the press went wild for . . .

He didn't understand how the whore could still be alive, though. He remembered the feeling of her torso beneath the knife, the popping, puncturing sound of the metal slitting her skin, the grating of steel on bone, the blood gushing. Students had found her, according to the newspaper. Fucking students.

He still had her fingers, though.

She'd produced a photofit. What a fucking joke! The police were shaven monkeys in uniforms, the lot of them. Did they think this picture would help? It looked nothing like him, nothing at all; it could have been anyone, white or black. He would have laughed out loud if It hadn't been there, but It wouldn't like him laughing over a dead hooker and a photofit . . .

It was pretty bolshy at the moment. He had had to work hard to make up for the fact that he had treated It roughly, had to apologise, play the nice guy. 'I was upset,' he had said. 'Really upset.' He'd had to cuddle It and buy It fucking flowers and stay home, to make up for being angry, and now It was taking advantage, the way women always did, trying to take more, as much as It could get.

'I don't like it when you go away.'

I'll make YOU *fucking go away if you keep this up.*

He had told her a cock-and-bull story about the chance of a job, but for the first time ever she actually fucking dared question him: who told you about it? How long will you be gone?

He watched It talking and he imagined drawing back a fist and punching It so hard in Its ugly fucking face that the bones splintered . . .

Yet he needed It a little while longer, at least until he did The Secretary.

It still loved him, that was the trump card: he knew he could bring It back into line with the threat of leaving for good. He didn't want to overplay that one, though. So he pressed on with the flowers, the kisses, the kindness that made the memory of his rage soften and dissolve in It's stupid, addled memory. He liked to add a little emollient to her drinks, a little extra something to keep her off balance, weeping into his neck, clinging to him.

Patient, kind, but determined.

At last she agreed: a week away, completely away, free to do as he liked.

45

Harvester of eyes, that's me.

Blue Öyster Cult, 'Harvester of Eyes'

Detective Inspector Eric Wardle was far from delighted that Jason and Tempest had lied to his men, but Strike found him less angry than he might have expected when they met for a pint, at Wardle's invitation, on Monday evening in the Feathers. The explanation for his surprising forbearance was simple: the revelation that Kelsey had been picked up from her rendezvous in Café Rouge by a man on a motorbike fitted perfectly with Wardle's new pet theory.

'You remember the guy called Devotee who was on their website? Got a fetish for amputees, went quiet after Kelsey was killed?'

'Yeah,' said Strike, who recalled Robin saying that she had had an interaction with him.

'We've tracked him down. Guess what's in his garage?'

Strike assumed, from the fact that no arrest had been made, that they had not found body parts, so he obligingly suggested: 'Motorbike?'

'Kawasaki Ninja,' said Wardle. 'I know we're looking for a

Honda,' he added, forestalling Strike, 'but he crapped himself when we came calling.'

'So do most people when CID turn up on their doorstep. Go on.'

'He's a sweaty little guy, name of Baxter, a sales rep with no alibi for the weekend of the second and third, or for the twenty-ninth. Divorced, no kids, claims he stayed in for the royal wedding, watching it. Would you have watched the royal wedding without a woman in the house?'

'No,' said Strike, who had only caught footage on the news.

'He claims the bike's his brother's and he's just looking after it, but after a bit of questioning he admitted he's taken it out a few times. So we know he can ride one, and he could have hired or borrowed the Honda.'

'What did he say about the website?'

'He downplayed that completely, says he's only pissing around, doesn't mean anything by it, he's not turned on by stumps, but when we asked whether we could have a look at his computer he didn't like it at all. Asked to talk to his lawyer before he gave an answer. That's where we've left it, but we're going back to see him again tomorrow. Friendly chat.'

'Did he admit to talking to Kelsey online?'

'Hard for him to deny it when we've got her laptop and all Tempest's records. He asked Kelsey about her plans for her leg and offered to meet her and she brushed him off – online, anyway. Bloody hell, we've got to look into him,' said Wardle in response to Strike's sceptical look, 'he's got no alibi, a motorbike, a thing for amputation and he tried to meet her!'

'Yeah, of course,' said Strike. 'Any other leads?'

'That's why I wanted to meet you. We've found your Donald Laing. He's in Wollaston Close, in Elephant and Castle.'

'He is?' said Strike, genuinely taken aback.

Savouring the fact that he had surprised Strike for once, Wardle smirked.

'Yeah, and he's a sick man. We found him through a JustGiving page. We got on to them and got his address.'

That was the difference between Strike and Wardle, of course: the latter still had badges, authority and the kind of power Strike had relinquished when he left the army.

'Have you seen him?' asked Strike.

'Sent a couple of guys round and he wasn't in, but the neighbours confirmed it's his flat. He rents, lives alone and he's pretty ill, apparently. They said he's gone home to Scotland for a bit. Friend's funeral. Supposed to be back soon.'

'Likely bloody story,' muttered Strike into his pint. 'If Laing's got a friend left in Scotland I'll eat this glass.'

'Have it your own way,' said Wardle, half amused, half impatient. 'I thought you'd be pleased we're chasing up your guys.'

'I am,' said Strike. 'Definitely ill, is he?'

'The neighbour reckons he needs sticks. He's been in and out of hospital a lot, apparently.'

The leather-padded screen overhead was showing last month's Arsenal–Liverpool match with the sound turned down. Strike watched as van Persie sank the penalty that he had thought, watching back on his tiny portable at the flat, might help Arsenal to a desperately needed win. It hadn't happened, of course. The Gunners' fortunes were currently sinking with his own.

'You seeing anyone?' asked Wardle abruptly.

'What?' said Strike, startled.

'Coco liked the look of you,' said Wardle, making sure that Strike saw him smirking as he said it, the better to impress upon Strike that he thought this ludicrous. 'The wife's friend, Coco. Red hair, remember?'

Strike remembered that Coco was a burlesque dancer.

'I said I'd ask,' said Wardle. 'I've told her you're a miserable bastard. She says she doesn't mind.'

'Tell her I'm flattered,' said Strike, which was the truth, 'but yeah, I'm seeing someone.'

'Not your work partner, is it?' asked Wardle.

'No,' said Strike. 'She's getting married.'

'You missed a trick there, mate,' said Wardle, yawning. '*I* would.'

'So, let me get this straight,' said Robin in the office next morning. 'As soon as we find out that Laing actually *does* live in Wollaston Close, you want me to stop watching it.'

'Hear me out,' said Strike, who was making tea. 'He's away, according to the neighbours.'

'You've just told me you don't think he's really gone to Scotland!'

'The fact that the door of his flat's been closed ever since you've been watching it suggests he's gone *somewhere.*'

Strike dropped teabags into two mugs.

'I don't buy the friend's funeral bit, but it wouldn't surprise me if he'd popped back to Melrose to try and beat some cash out of his demented mother. That could easily be our Donnie's idea of holiday fun.'

'One of us should be there for when he comes back—'

'One of us *will* be there,' said Strike soothingly, 'but in the meantime, I want you to switch to—'

'Brockbank?'

'No, I'm doing Brockbank,' said Strike. 'I want you to have a bash at Stephanie.'

'Who?'

'Stephanie. Whittaker's girl.'

'Why?' asked Robin loudly, as the kettle boiled in its usual crescendo of rattling lid and rambunctious bubbles, condensation steaming up the window behind it.

'I want to see whether she can tell us what Whittaker was doing the day Kelsey was killed, and on the night that girl got her fingers hacked off in Shacklewell. The third and the twenty-ninth of April, to be precise.'

Strike poured water on the teabags and stirred in milk, the teaspoon pinging off the sides of the mug. Robin was not sure whether she was pleased or aggrieved by the suggested change to her routine. On balance, she thought she was glad, but her recent suspicions that Strike was trying to sideline her were not easily dispelled.

'You definitely still think Whittaker could be the killer?'

'Yep,' said Strike.

'But you haven't got any—'

'I haven't got any evidence for any of them, have I?' said Strike. 'I'm just going to keep going until I either get some or clear all of them.'

He handed her a mug of tea and sank down on the mock-leather sofa, which for once did not fart beneath him. A minor triumph, but in the absence of others, better than nothing.

'I hoped I'd be able to rule out Whittaker on how he's looking these days,' said Strike, 'but, you know, it *could've* been him in that beanie hat. I know one thing: he's exactly the same bastard he was when I knew him. I've blown it completely with Stephanie, she's not going to talk to me now, but you might be able to do something with her. If she can give him an alibi for those dates, or point us towards someone else who can, we'll have to rethink. If not, he stays on the list.'

'And what are you going to be doing while I'm on Stephanie?'

'Sticking with Brockbank. I've decided,' said Strike, stretching out his legs and taking a fortifying drink of tea, 'I'm going into the strip club today, find out what's happened to him. I'm tired of eating kebabs and hanging round clothes shops waiting for him to show up.'

Robin did not say anything.

'What?' said Strike, watching her expression.

'Nothing.'

'Come off it.'

'OK . . . what if he *is* there?'

'I'll cross that bridge – I'm not going to hit him,' said Strike, correctly reading her thoughts.

'OK,' said Robin, but then, 'you hit Whittaker, though.'

'That was different,' said Strike, and when she did not respond, 'Whittaker's special. He's family.'

She laughed, but reluctantly.

When Strike withdrew fifty pounds from a cashpoint prior to entering the Saracen off Commercial Road, the machine churlishly showed him a negative balance in his current account. His expression grim, Strike handed over a tenner to the short-necked bouncer on the door and pushed his way through the strips of black plastic masking the interior, which was dimly lit, but insufficiently to mask the overall impression of shabbiness.

The interior of the old pub had been ripped out in its entirety. The refashioned decor gave the impression of a community centre gone bad, dimly lit and soulless. The floor was of polished pine, which reflected the wide neon strip running the length of the bar that took up one side of the room.

It was shortly after midday, but there was already a girl gyrating on a small stage at the far end of the pub. Bathed in red light and standing in front of angled mirrors so that every inch of dimpled flesh could be appreciated, she was removing her bra to the Rolling Stones' 'Start Me Up'. A grand total of four men were sitting on high stools, one to each elevated table, dividing their attention between the girl now swinging clumsily around a pole and a big-screen TV showing Sky Sports.

Strike headed straight for the bar, where he found himself facing a sign that read 'Any customer caught masturbating will be ejected'.

'What can I get you, love?' asked a girl with long hair, purple eye-shadow and a nose ring.

Strike ordered a pint of John Smith's and took a seat at the bar. Other than the bouncer, the only other male employee on view was the man sitting behind a turntable beside the stripper. He was stocky, blond, middle-aged and did not remotely resemble Brockbank.

'I was hoping to meet a friend here,' Strike told the barmaid, who, having no further customers, was leaning on the bar, staring dreamily at the television and picking her long nails.

'Yeah?' she said, sounding bored.

'Yeah,' said Strike. 'He said he was working here.'

A man in a fluorescent jacket approached the bar and she moved away to serve him without another word.

'Start Me Up' ended and so did the stripper's act. Naked, she hopped off the stage, grabbed a wrap and disappeared through a curtain at the back of the pub. Nobody clapped.

A woman in a very short nylon kimono and stockings slid out from behind the curtain and began walking around the pub, holding out an empty beer glass to punters, who one by one put their hands in their pockets and gave her some change. She reached Strike last. He dropped in a couple of quid. She headed straight for the stage, where she put her pint glass of coins carefully beside the DJ's turntable, wriggled out of her kimono and stepped on to the stage in bra, pants, stockings and heels.

'Gentlemen, I think you're going to enjoy this . . . Big welcome, please, for the lovely Mia!'

She began to jiggle to Gary Numan's 'Are "Friends" Electric?' There was not the remotest synchronicity between her movements and the track.

The barmaid resumed her lounging position near Strike. The view of the TV was clearest from where he sat.

'Yeah, like I was saying,' Strike began again, 'a friend of mine told me he's working here.'

'Mm-hm,' she said.

'Name of Noel Brockbank.'

'Yeah? I don't know him.'

'No,' said Strike, making a show of scanning the place, although he had already established that Brockbank was nowhere to be seen. 'Maybe I've got the wrong place.'

The first stripper pushed her way out from behind the curtain, having changed into a bubblegum-pink spaghetti-strapped minidress that barely skimmed her crotch, and was somehow more indecent than her previous nakedness. She approached the man in the fluorescent jacket and asked him something, but he shook his head. Looking around, she caught Strike's eye, smiled and approached him.

'Hiya,' she said. Her accent was Irish. Her hair, which he had thought blonde in the red light of the stage, turned out to be vivid copper. Beneath the thick orange lipstick and the thick false eyelashes hid a girl who looked as though she should still have been at school. 'I'm Orla. Who're you?'

'Cameron,' said Strike, which was what people usually called him after failing to grasp his first name.

'D'ya fancy a private dance then, Cameron?'

'Where does that happen?'

'Troo there,' she said, pointing towards the curtain where she had changed. 'I've never seen you in here before.'

'No. I'm looking for a friend.'

'What's her name?'

'It's a him.'

'Yeh've come to the wrong place fer hims, darlin',' she said.

She was so young he felt mildly dirty just hearing her call him darling.

'Can I buy you a drink?' Strike asked.

She hesitated. There was more money in a private dance, but perhaps he was the kind of guy who needed warming up first.

'Go on, then.'

Strike paid an exorbitant amount for a vodka and lime, which she sipped primly on a seat beside him, most of her breasts hanging out of the dress. The texture of her skin reminded him of the murdered Kelsey: smooth and firm, with plenty of youthful fat. There were three small blue stars inked on her shoulder.

'Maybe you know my friend?' Strike said. 'Noel Brockbank.'

She was no fool, little Orla. Suspicion and calculation mingled in the sharp sideways look she gave him. She was wondering, like the masseuse back in Market Harborough, whether he was police.

'He owes me money,' said Strike.

She continued to scrutinise him for a moment, her smooth forehead furrowed, then apparently swallowed the lie.

'Noel,' she repeated. 'I tink he's gone. Hang on – Edie?'

The bored barmaid did not take her eyes from the TV.

'Hmm?'

'What was the name of yer man that Des sacked the other week? Guy who only lasted a few days?'

'Dunno what he was called.'

'Yeah, I tink it was Noel who was sacked,' Orla told

Strike. Then, with a sudden and endearing bluntness, she said: 'Gimme a tenner an' I'll make sure for ya.'

With a mental sigh, Strike handed over a note.

'Wait there, now,' said Orla cheerfully. She slipped off her bar stool, tucked the tenner into the elastic of her pants, tugged her dress down inelegantly and sauntered over to the DJ, who scowled over at Strike while Orla spoke to him. He nodded curtly, his jowly face glowing in the red light, and Orla came trotting back looking pleased with herself.

'I tort so!' she told Strike. 'I wasn't here when it happened, but he had a fit or sometin'.'

'A fit?' repeated Strike.

'Yeah, it was only his first week on the job. Big guy, wasn't he? Wit a big chin?'

'That's right,' said Strike.

'Yeah, an' he was late, and Des wasn't happy. Dat's Des, over dare,' she added unnecessarily, pointing out the DJ who was watching Strike suspiciously while changing the track from 'Are "Friends" Electric?' to Cyndi Lauper's 'Girls Just Wanna Have Fun'. 'Des was givin' out to him about being late and your man just dropped to the floor an' started writhin' around. They say,' added Orla, with relish, 'he pissed himself.'

Strike doubted that Brockbank would have urinated over himself to escape a dressing down from Des. It sounded as though he had genuinely had an epileptic fit.

'Then what happened?'

'Your mate's gorlfriend come runnin' out the back—'

'What girlfriend's this?'

'Hang on – Edie?'

'Hm?'

'Who's dat black gorl, now, with the extensions? The one with the great knockers? The one Des doesn't like?'

'Alyssa,' said Edie.

'Alyssa,' Orla told Strike. 'She come runnin' out the back and was screamin' at Des to phone an ambulance.'

'Did he?'

'Yeah. Dey took yer man away, and Alyssa went with him.'

'And has Brock – has Noel been back since?'

'He's no bloody use as a bouncer if he's gonna fall down and piss himself just 'cause someone's shoutin' at him, is he?' said Orla. 'I heard Alyssa wanted Des to give him a second chance, but Des doesn't give second chances.'

'So Alyssa called Des a tight cunt,' said Edie, emerging suddenly from her listlessness, 'and he sacked her too. Silly bitch. She needs the money. She's got kids.'

'When did all this happen?' Strike asked Orla and Edie.

'Couple of weeks ago,' said Edie. 'But he was a creep, that guy. Good riddance.'

'In what way was he a creep?' asked Strike.

'You can always tell,' said Edie with a kind of hard-bitten weariness. 'Always. Alyssa's got fucking terrible taste in men.'

The second stripper was now down to her thong and twerking enthusiastically towards her scanty audience. Two older men had just entered the club and hesitated before approaching the bar, their eyes on the thong, which was clearly about to come off.

'You don't know where I'd find Noel, do you?' Strike asked Edie, who seemed too bored to demand money for the information.

'He's living with Alyssa, somewhere in Bow,' said the barmaid. 'She got herself a council house but she was always bitching about the place. I don't know exactly where it is,' she said, forestalling Strike's question. 'I never went round or nothing.'

'I tort she liked it,' said Orla vaguely. 'She said there was a good nursery.'

The stripper had wriggled out of her thong and was waving it over her head, lasso-style. Having seen all there was to see, the two new punters drifted to the bar. One of them, a man old enough to be Orla's grandfather, fixed his rheumy eyes on her cleavage. She sized him up, businesslike, then turned to Strike.

'So, you wanna private dance or not?'

'I don't think I will,' said Strike.

Before the words were even fully out of his mouth she had put down her glass, wriggled off the chair and slid towards the sixty-year-old, who grinned, revealing more gaps than teeth.

A hulking figure appeared at Strike's side: the neckless bouncer.

'Des wants a word,' he said in what would have been a menacing tone had his voice not been surprisingly high-pitched for a man so broad.

Strike looked around. The DJ, who was glaring across the room at him, beckoned.

'Is there a problem?' Strike asked the bouncer.

'Des'll tell you, if there is,' was the faintly ominous answer.

So Strike crossed the room to speak to the DJ, and stood like a massive schoolboy summoned to the headmaster at his lectern. Fully alive to the absurdity of the situation, he had to wait while a third stripper deposited her glass of coins safely beside the turntable, wriggled out of her purple robe and ascended the stage in black lace and Perspex heels. She was heavily tattooed and, beneath thick make-up, spotty.

'Gentlemen, tits, ass and class from – Jackaline!'

'Africa' by Toto began. Jackaline began to spin around the pole, at which she was far more accomplished than either of her colleagues, and Des covered the microphone with his hand and leaned forwards.

'Right, pal.'

He appeared both older and harder than he had in the red light of the stage, his eyes shrewd, a scar as deep as Shanker's running along his jaw.

'What are you asking about that bouncer for?'

'He's a friend of mine.'

'He never had a contract.'

'I never said he had.'

'Unfair dismissal my fucking arse. He never told me he had fucking fits. Have you been sent here by that Alyssa bitch?'

'No,' said Strike. 'I was told Noel worked here.'

'She's a mad fucking cow.'

'I wouldn't know. It's him I'm looking for.'

Scratching an armpit, Des glowered at Strike while, four feet away, Jackaline slipped her bra straps from her shoulders and glared over her shoulder at the half-dozen punters watching.

'*Bollocks* was that bastard ever in the Special Forces,' said Des aggressively, as though Strike had insisted he had been.

'Is that what he told you?'

'It's what *she* said. Alyssa. They wouldn't take a fucking wreck like that. Anyway,' said Des, eyes narrowed, 'there was other stuff I didn't like.'

'Yeah? Like what?'

'That's my business. You tell her that from me. It wasn't just his fucking fit. You tell her to ask Mia why I didn't want him back, and you tell Alyssa if she does one more stupid fucking thing to my car, or sends one more of her friends round trying to get something on me, I'll fucking have her in court. You tell her that!'

'Fair enough,' said Strike. 'Got an address?'

'Fuck off, all right?' snarled Des. 'Fuck off out of here.'

He leaned into the microphone.

'Nice,' he said, with a kind of professional leer, as Jackaline jiggled her breasts rhythmically in the scarlet light. Des made a 'hop it' gesture to Strike and returned to his stack of old vinyl records.

Accepting the inevitable, Strike allowed himself to be escorted to the door. Nobody paid any attention; the audience's attention remained divided between Jackaline and Lionel Messi on the widescreen TV. At the door, Strike stood aside for a group of young men in suits to enter, all of whom seemed already a little worse for drink.

'Tits!' yelled the first of them, pointing at the stripper. '*Tits!*'

The bouncer took exception to this mode of entry. A mild altercation ensued, with the shouter cowed by his friends and the bouncer's strictures, which were delivered with several jabs of a forefinger to his chest.

Strike waited patiently for the matter to be adjusted. When the young men had finally been allowed to enter, he took his departure to the opening strains of 'The Only Way Is Up' by Yazz.

46

Subhuman

Alone with his trophies, he felt himself entirely whole. They were proof of his superiority, his astonishing ability to glide through the ape-like police and the sheep-like masses, taking whatever he wanted, like a demigod.

Of course, they gave him something else too.

He never seemed to get hard when he was actually killing. Thinking about it beforehand, yes: sometimes he could drive himself into an onanistic frenzy with ideas of what he was going to do, refining and restaging the possibilities in his mind. Afterwards – now, for instance, holding in his hand the chilly, rubbery, shrunken breast he had hacked from Kelsey's torso, already turning slightly leathery with its repeated exposure to the air outside the fridge – then he had no problem at all. He was like a flagpole *now*.

He had the new one's fingers in the icebox. He took one out, pressed it against his lips then bit down on it, hard. He imagined her still connected to it, screaming in agony. He chewed deeper, relishing the feeling of the cold flesh splitting, his teeth pressing hard into the bone. One hand fumbled with the string of his tracksuit bottoms . . .

Afterwards he put it all back in the fridge, closed the door and gave it a little pat, grinning to himself. There'd be a lot more than that in there, soon. The Secretary wasn't small: five foot seven or eight by his reckoning.

One minor problem . . . he didn't know where she was. He'd lost the trail. She hadn't been to the office this morning. He'd gone to the LSE, where he'd spotted the platinum bitch, but seen no sign of The Secretary. He'd looked in the Court; he'd even checked the Tottenham. This was a temporary setback, though. He'd sniff her out. He'd pick her up again tomorrow morning at West Ealing station, if he had to.

He made himself a coffee and poured a slug of whisky into it from a bottle he'd had here for months. There was hardly anything else in the dirty hidey-hole where he hid his treasures, in his secret sanctuary: a kettle, a few chipped mugs, the fridge – the altar of his profession – an old mattress to sleep on and a docking port for him to place his iPod on. That was important. It had become part of his ritual.

He had thought they were shit when he'd first heard them, but as his obsession with bringing down Strike had grown, so had his liking for their music. He liked to listen to it through earphones while he was stalking The Secretary, while he was cleaning his knives. It was sacred music to him now. Some of their lyrics stayed with him like fragments of a religious service. The more he listened, the more he felt they understood.

Women were reduced to the elemental when they were facing the knife. They became cleansed by their terror. There was a kind of purity to them as they begged and pleaded for their lives. The Cult (as he privately called them) seemed to understand. They got it.

He put his iPod into the dock and selected one of his

favourite tracks, 'Dr. Music'. Then he headed to the sink and the cracked shaving mirror he kept there, razor and scissors at the ready: all the tools a man needed to totally transform himself.

From the single speaker of the dock, Eric Bloom sang:

Girl don't stop that screamin'
You're sounding so sincere . . .

47

I sense the darkness clearer . . .

Blue Öyster Cult, 'Harvest Moon'

Today – June the first – Robin was able to say for the first time: 'I'm getting married next month'. July the second suddenly seemed very close. The dressmaker back in Harrogate wanted a final fitting, but she had no idea when she would be able to fit in a trip home. At least she had her shoes. Her mother was taking the RSVPs and updating her regularly on the guest list. Robin felt strangely disconnected from it all. Her tedious hours of surveillance in Catford Broadway, staking out the flat over the chip shop, were a world away from queries on the flowers, who should sit beside whom at the reception, and (this last from Matthew) whether or not she had yet asked Strike for the fortnight off for the honeymoon, which Matthew had booked and which was to be a surprise.

She did not know how the wedding could have come so close without her realising. Next month, the very next month, she would become Robin Cunliffe – at least, she supposed she would. Matthew certainly expected her to take his name. He was incredibly cheerful these days, hugging her wordlessly when he passed her in the hall, raising not a single objection to the long hours she was working, hours that bled into their weekends.

He had driven her to Catford on the last few mornings because it was on the way to the company he was auditing in Bromley. He was being nice about the despised Land Rover now, even while he crashed the gears and stalled it at junctions, saying what a wonderful gift it had been, how kind Linda was to have given it to them, how useful a car was when he was sent somewhere out of town. During yesterday's commute he had offered to remove Sarah Shadlock from the wedding guest list. Robin could tell that he had had to screw up his courage even to ask the question, afraid that mentioning Sarah's name might provoke a row. She had thought about it for a while, wondering how she really felt, and finally said no.

'I don't mind,' she said. 'I'd rather she came. It's fine.'

Removing Sarah from the list would tell Sarah that Robin had found out what had happened years before. She would rather pretend that she had always known, that Matthew had confessed long ago, that it was nothing to her; she had her pride. However, when her mother, who had also queried Sarah's attendance, asked whom Robin wanted to put on Sarah's free side, now that Sarah and Matthew's mutual university friend Shaun couldn't make it, Robin answered with a question.

'Has Cormoran RSVPed?'

'No,' said her mother.

'Oh,' said Robin. 'Well, he says he's going to.'

'You want to put him next to Sarah, do you?'

'No, of course not!' snapped Robin.

There was a short pause.

'Sorry,' said Robin. 'Sorry, Mum . . . stressed . . . no, could you sit Cormoran next to . . . I don't know . . . '

'Is his girlfriend coming?'

'He says not. Put him anywhere, just not near bloody – I mean, not by Sarah.'

So, Robin settled in to wait for a glimpse of Stephanie on the warmest morning so far. The shoppers on Catford Broadway were wearing T-shirts and sandals; black women passed in brightly coloured head wraps. Robin, who had put on a sundress under an old denim jacket, leaned back into one of her accustomed nooks in the theatre building, pretending that she was talking on the mobile and killing time before she pretended to peruse the scented candles and incense sticks on the nearest stall.

It was difficult to maintain concentration when you were convinced that you had been sent on a wild goose chase. Strike might insist that he still thought Whittaker a suspect in Kelsey's killing, but Robin was quietly unconvinced. She increasingly inclined to Wardle's view that Strike had it in for his ex-stepfather and that his usually sound judgement was clouded by old grievances. Glancing up periodically at the unmoving curtains of Whittaker's flat, she remembered that Stephanie had last been seen being bundled into the back of a transit van by Whittaker, and wondered whether she was even inside the flat.

From faint resentment that this was going to be another wasted day, she fell easily to dwelling on the main grudge she currently felt against Strike: his appropriation of the search for Noel Brockbank. Somehow Robin had come to feel that Brockbank was particularly her own suspect. Had she not successfully impersonated Venetia Hall, they would never have known that Brockbank was living in London, and if she had not had the wit to recognise that Nile was Noel, they would never have traced him to the Saracen. Even the low voice in her ear – *do A know you, little girl?* – creepy as it had been, constituted a strange kind of connection.

The mingled smells of raw fish and incense that had come

to represent Whittaker and Stephanie filled her nostrils as she leaned back against chilly stone and watched the unmoving door of his flat. Like foxes to a dustbin, her unruly thoughts slunk back to Zahara, the little girl who had answered Brockbank's mobile. Robin had thought of her every day since they had spoken and had asked Strike for every detail about the little girl's mother on his return from the strip club.

He had told Robin that Brockbank's girlfriend was called Alyssa and that she was black, so Zahara must be too. Perhaps she looked like the little girl with stiff pigtails now waddling along the street, holding tight to her mother's forefinger and staring at Robin with solemn dark eyes. Robin smiled, but the little girl did not: she merely continued to scrutinise Robin as she and her mother passed. Robin kept smiling until the little girl, twisting almost 180 degrees so as not to break eye contact with Robin, tripped over her tiny sandaled feet. She hit the ground and began to wail; her impassive mother scooped her up and carried her. Feeling guilty, Robin resumed her observation of Whittaker's windows as the fallen toddler's wails reverberated down the street.

Zahara almost certainly lived in the flat in Bow that Strike had told her about. Zahara's mother complained about the flat, apparently, although Strike said that one of the girls . . .

One of the girls had said . . .

'Of course!' Robin muttered excitedly. '*Of course!*'

Strike wouldn't have thought of that – of course he wouldn't, he was a man! She began to press the keys on her phone.

There were seven nurseries in Bow. Absently replacing her mobile in her pocket and energised by her train of thought, Robin began her usual drift through the market stalls, casting the occasional glance up at the windows of Whittaker's flat and at the perennially closed door, her mind entirely given over to the pursuit of Brockbank. She could think of two possible courses of action: stake out each of these seven nurseries, watching for a black woman picking up a girl called Zahara (and how would she know which was the right mother and daughter?) or . . . or . . . She paused beside a stall selling ethnic jewellery, barely seeing it, preoccupied by thoughts of Zahara.

Entirely by chance, she looked up from a pair of feather and bead earrings as Stephanie, whom Strike had accurately described, came out of the door beside the chip shop. Pale, red-eyed and blinking in the bright light like an albino rabbit, Stephanie leaned on the chip-shop door, toppled inside and proceeded to the counter. Before Robin could collect her wits, Stephanie had brushed past her holding a can of Coke and gone back into the building through the white door.

Shit.

'Nothing,' she told Strike on the phone an hour later. 'She's still in there. I didn't have a chance to do anything. She was in and out in about three minutes.'

'Stick with it,' said Strike. 'She might come out again. At least we know she's awake.'

'Any luck with Laing?'

'Not while I was there, but I've had to come back to the office. Big news: Two-Times has forgiven me. He's just left. We need the money – I could hardly refuse.'

'Oh, for God's sake – how can he have another girlfriend *already*?' asked Robin.

'He hasn't. He wants me to check out some new lap-dancer he's flirting with, see whether she's already in a relationship.'

'Why doesn't he just *ask* her?'

'He has. She says she isn't seeing anyone, but women are devious, cheating scum, Robin, you know that.'

'Oh yes, of course,' sighed Robin. 'I forgot. Listen, I've had an idea about Br— Wait, something's happening.'

'Everything all right?' he asked sharply.

'Fine . . . hang on . . .'

A transit van had rolled up in front of her. Keeping the mobile to her ear, Robin ambled around it, trying to see what was going on. As far as she could make out, the driver had a crew cut, but the sun on the windscreen dazzled her eyes, obscuring his features. Stephanie had appeared on the pavement. Arms wrapped tightly around herself, she trooped across the street and climbed into the back of the van. Robin stepped back to allow it to pass, pretending to talk into her mobile. Her eyes met those of the driver; they were dark and hooded.

'She's gone, got in the back of an old van,' she told Strike. 'The driver didn't look like Whittaker. Could've been mixed race or Mediterranean. Hard to see.'

'Well, we know Stephanie's on the game. She's probably off to earn Whittaker some money.'

Robin tried not to resent his matter-of-fact tone. He had, she reminded herself, freed Stephanie from Whittaker's stranglehold with a punch to the gut. She paused, looking into a newsagent's window. Royal wedding ephemera was still very much in evidence. A Union Jack was hanging on the wall behind the Asian man at the till.

'What do you want me to do? I could go and cover Wollaston Close for you, if you're off after Two-Times' new girl. It makes – oof,' she gasped.

She had turned to walk away and collided with a tall man sporting a goatee, who swore at her.

'Sorry,' she gasped automatically as the man shoved his way past her into the newsagent's.

'What just happened?' asked Strike.

'Nothing – I bumped into someone – listen, I'm going to go to Wollaston Close,' she said.

'All right,' said Strike after a perceptible pause, 'but if Laing turns up, just try and get a picture. Don't go anywhere near him.'

'I wasn't intending to,' said Robin.

'Call me if there's any news. Or even if there isn't.'

The brief spurt of enthusiasm she had felt at the prospect of going back to Wollaston Close had faded by the time she had reached Catford station. She was not sure why she felt suddenly downcast and anxious. Perhaps she was hungry. Determined to break herself of the chocolate habit that was jeopardising her ability to fit into the altered wedding dress, she bought herself an unappetising-looking energy bar before boarding the train.

Chewing the sawdusty slab as the train carried her towards Elephant and Castle, she found herself absent-mindedly rubbing her ribs where she had collided with the large man in the goatee. Being sworn at by random people was the price you paid for living in London, of course; she could not ever remember a stranger swearing at her in Masham, not even once.

Something made her suddenly look all around her, but there did not seem to be any large man in her vicinity, neither in the sparsely occupied carriage nor peering at her from the neighbouring ones. Now she came to think of it, she had jettisoned some of her habitual vigilance that morning, lulled by the familiarity of Catford Broadway, distracted by her thoughts of Brockbank and Zahara. She wondered whether she would have noticed somebody else there, watching her . . . but that, surely, was paranoia. Matthew had dropped her off in the Land Rover that morning; how could the killer have followed her to Catford unless he had been waiting in some kind of vehicle at Hastings Road?

Nevertheless, she thought, she must guard against complacency. When she got off the train she noticed a tall dark man walking a little behind her, and deliberately stopped to let him pass. He did not give her a second look. *I'm definitely being paranoid*, she thought, dropping the unfinished energy bar into a bin.

It was half past one before she reached the forecourt of Wollaston Close, the Strata building looming over the shabby old flats like an emissary from the future. The long sundress and the old denim jacket that had fitted in so well in the market in Catford felt a little studentish here. Yet again pretending to be on her mobile, Robin looked casually upwards and her heart gave a little skip.

Something had changed. The curtains had been pulled back.

Hyperaware now, she maintained her course in case he was looking out of the window, intending to find a place in shadow where she could keep an eye on his balcony. So intent was she on finding the perfect place to lurk, and on maintaining the appearance of a natural conversation, that she had no attention to spare for where she was treading.

'*No!*' Robin squealed as her right foot skidded out from under her, her left became caught in the hem of her long skirt and she slid into an undignified half-splits before toppling sideways and dropping her mobile.

'Oh bugger,' she moaned. Whatever she had slipped in looked like vomit or even diarrhoea: some was clinging to her dress, to her sandal, and she had grazed her hand on landing, but it was the precise identity of the thick, yellow-brown, glutinous lumpy stuff that worried her most.

Somewhere in her vicinity a man burst out laughing. Cross and humiliated, she tried to get up without spreading the muck further over her clothes and shoes and did not look immediately for the source of the jeering noise.

'Sorry, hen,' said a soft Scottish voice right behind her. She looked around sharply and several volts of electricity seemed to pass through her.

In spite of the warmth of the day, he was wearing a windstopper hat with long earflaps, a red and black check jacket and jeans. A pair of metal crutches supported most of his substantial weight as he looked down at her, still grinning. Deep pockmarks disfigured his pale cheeks, his chin and the pouches beneath his small, dark eyes. The flesh on his thick neck spilled over his collar.

A plastic bag containing what looked like a few groceries hung from one hand. She could just see the tattooed dagger tip that she knew ran through a yellow rose higher on his forearm. The drops of tattooed blood running down his wrist looked like injuries.

'Ye'll need a tap,' he said, grinning broadly as he pointed at her foot and the hem of her dress, 'and a scrubbing brush.'

'Yes,' said Robin shakily. She bent to pick up her mobile. The screen was cracked.

'I live up there,' he said, nodding towards the flat she had been watching on and off for a month. 'Ye can come up if y'want. Clean yerself up.'

'Oh no – that's all right. Thanks very much, though,' said Robin breathlessly.

'Nae problem,' said Donald Laing.

His gaze slithered down her body. Her skin prickled, as though he had run a finger down her. Turning on his crutches, he began to move away, the plastic bag swinging awkwardly. Robin stood where he had left her, conscious of the blood pounding in her face.

He did not look back. The earflaps of his hat swayed like spaniel's ears as he moved painfully slowly around the side of the flats and out of sight.

'Oh my God,' whispered Robin. Hand and knee smarting

where she had fallen, she absent-mindedly pushed her hair out of her face. Only then did she realise, with relief, from the smell on her fingers, that the slippery substance had been curry. Hurrying to a corner out of sight of Donald Laing's windows, she pressed the keys of the cracked mobile and called Strike.

48

Here Comes That Feeling

The heatwave that had descended on London was his enemy. There was nowhere to hide his knives in a T-shirt, and the hats and high collars on which he relied for disguise looked out of place. He could do nothing but wait, fuming and impotent, in the place that It did not know about.

At last, on Sunday, the weather broke. Rain swept the parched parks, windscreen wipers danced, tourists donned their plastic ponchos and trudged on through the puddles regardless.

Full of excitement and determination, he pulled on a hat worn low over his eyes and donned his special jacket. As he walked, the knives bounced against his chest in the long makeshift pockets he'd ripped in the lining. The capital's streets were hardly less crowded now than when he'd knifed the tart whose fingers sat in his icebox. Tourists and Londoners were still swarming everywhere like ants. Some of them had bought Union Jack umbrellas and hats. He barged into some of them for the simple pleasure of knocking them aside.

His need to kill was becoming urgent. The last few wasted days had slid past, his leave of absence from It slowly expiring, but The Secretary remained alive and free. He had searched for hours, trying to trace her and then, shockingly, she had been right there in front of him, the brazen bitch, in broad daylight – but there had been witnesses everywhere . . .

Poor impulse control, that fucking psychiatrist would have said, knowing what he'd done at the sight of her. Poor impulse control! He could control his impulses fine when he wanted – he was a man of superhuman cleverness, who had killed three women and maimed another without the police being any the wiser, so fuck the psychiatrist and his dumb diagnoses – but when he'd seen her right in front of him after all those empty days, he'd wanted to scare her, wanted to get up close, *really* close, close enough to smell her, speak to her, look into her frightened eyes.

Then she'd strutted away and he had not dared follow her, not then, but it had almost killed him to let her go. She ought to be lying in parcels of meat in his fridge by now. He ought to have witnessed her face in that ecstasy of terror and death, when he owned them completely and they were his to play with.

So here he was, walking through the chilly rain, burning inside because it was Sunday and she had gone again, back to the place where he could never get near her, because Pretty Boy was always there.

He needed more freedom, a lot more freedom. The real obstacle was having It at home all the time, spying on him, clinging to him. All that would have to change. He'd already pushed It unwillingly back into work. Now he had decided that he would have to pretend to It that he had a new job. If necessary, he'd steal to get cash, pretend he'd earned it – he'd done that plenty of times before. Then, freed up, he'd be able to put in the time he really needed to make sure he was close at hand when The Secretary dropped her guard, when nobody was looking, when she turned the wrong corner . . .

The passers-by had as little life as automata to him. Stupid, stupid, stupid . . . Everywhere he walked he looked for her, the one he'd do next. Not The Secretary, no, because the bitch was back behind her white front door with Pretty Boy, but any woman stupid enough, drunk enough, to walk a short way with a man and his knives. He had to do one before he went back to It, he had to. It would be all that could keep him going, once he was back pretending to be the man It loved. His eyes flickered from under his hat, sorting them, discarding them: the women with men, the women with kids clutching them, but no women alone, none the way he needed them . . .

He walked for miles until darkness fell, past lit pubs where men and women laughed and flirted, past restaurants and cinemas, looking, waiting, with a hunter's patience. Sunday night and the workers were returning home early, but it did not matter: there were still tourists everywhere, out-of-towners, drawn by the history and mystery of London . . .

It was nearly midnight when they leapt to his practised eye like a cluster of plump mushrooms in long grass: a bunch of squawking, tiddly girls cackling and weaving along the pavement. They were on one of those miserable, rundown streets that were his especial delight, where a drunken tussle and a shrieking girl would be nothing out of the ordinary. He followed, ten yards behind them, watching them pass under street lamps, elbowing each other and cackling, all except for one of them. She was the drunkest and youngest-looking of them all: ready to throw up, if he knew anything about it. She stumbled on her heels, falling slightly behind her friends, the silly little tart. None of her friends had realised what a state she was in. They were just the right side of legless, snorting and guffawing as they staggered along.

He drifted after them, casual as you please.

If she threw up in the street the noise would attract her

friends, who would stop and rally around her. While she fought the urge to vomit, she could not speak. Slowly, the distance between her and her friends increased. She swayed and wobbled, reminding him of the last one, with her stupid high heels. This one must not survive to help make photofits.

A taxi was approaching. He saw the scenario play out before it did. They hailed it loudly, screeching and waving their arms, and in they piled, one by one, fat arse after fat arse. He sped up, head down, face hidden. The street lamps reflected in the puddles, the 'for hire' light extinguished, the growl of the engine . . .

They had forgotten her. She swayed right into the wall, holding up an arm to support herself.

He might only have seconds. One of her friends would realise any time now that she wasn't with them.

'You all right, darling? You feeling bad? Come here. This way. You'll be all right. Just down here.'

She began to retch as he tugged her down a side street. Feebly she tried to pull her arm away, heaving; the vomit splattered down her, gagging her.

'Filthy bitch,' he snarled, one hand already on the handle of his knife under the jacket. He was dragging her forcibly towards a darkened recess between an adult video store and a junk shop.

'No,' she gasped, but she choked on her vomit, heaving.

A door opened across the street, light rippling down a flight of steps. People burst out onto the pavement, laughing.

He slammed her up against the wall and kissed her, pinning her flat while she tried to struggle. She tasted foul, of sick. The door opposite closed, the gaggle of people passed by, their voices echoing in the quiet night, the light extinguished.

'Fucking hell,' he said in disgust, releasing her mouth but keeping her pinned to the wall with his body.

She drew breath to scream, but he had the knife ready and it sank deep between her ribs with ease, nothing like the last one, who'd fought so hard and so stubbornly. The noise died on her stained lips as the hot blood poured over his gloved hand, soaking the material. She jerked convulsively, tried to speak, her eyes rolled upwards into whiteness and her entire body sagged, still pinned by the knife.

'Good girl,' he whispered, pulling the carving knife free as she fell, dying, into his arms.

He dragged her deeper into the recess, where a pile of rubbish sat waiting for collection. Kicking the black bags aside, he dumped her in a corner then pulled out his machete. Souvenirs were imperative, but he only had seconds. Another door might open, or her dozy bitches of friends might come back in their taxi . . .

He slashed and sawed, put his warm, oozing trophies in his pocket, then piled up the rubbish over and on her.

It had taken less than five minutes. He felt like a king, like a god. Away he walked, knives safely stowed, panting in the cool, clean night air, jogging a little once he was on the main road again. He was already a block away when he heard raucous female voices shouting in the distance.

'Heather! *Heather, where are you, you silly cow?*'

'Heather can't hear you,' he whispered into the darkness.

He tried to stop himself laughing, burying his face in his collar, but he could not restrain his jubilation. Deep in his pockets, his sopping fingers were playing with the rubbery cartilage and skin to which her earrings – little plastic ice-cream cones – were still attached.

49

It's the time in the season for a maniac at night.

Blue Öyster Cult, 'Madness to the Method'

The weather remained cool, rain-flecked and faintly blustery as June entered its second week. The blaze of sunlit pageantry that had surrounded the royal wedding had receded into memory: the giddy high tide of romantic fervour had ebbed, the wedding merchandise and congratulatory banners had been removed from shop windows and the capital's newspapers returned to more mundane matters, including an imminent Tube strike.

Then horror exploded across Wednesday's front pages. The mutilated body of a young woman had been uncovered beneath bin bags, and within a few hours of the first police appeal for information the world had been informed that a twenty-first-century Jack the Ripper was stalking the streets of London.

Three women had been attacked and mutilated, but the Met appeared to have no leads. In their stampede to cover every possible aspect of the story – maps of London showing the location of each attack, pictures of the three victims – the journalists revealed themselves determined to make up for lost time, aware that they might have arrived a little late at the party. They had previously treated the killing of Kelsey Platt as a lone act of madness and sadism, and the subsequent attack on Lila Monkton, the eighteen-year-old prostitute, had gained virtually no media coverage. A girl who had been selling herself for sex on the day of the royal wedding could hardly expect to oust a new-minted duchess from the front pages.

The murder of Heather Smart, a twenty-two-year-old building society employee from Nottingham, was an entirely different matter. The headlines virtually wrote themselves, for Heather was a wonderfully relatable heroine with her steady job, her innocent desire to see the capital's landmarks and a boyfriend who was a primary school teacher. Heather had been to see *The Lion King* the night before her death, had eaten dim sum in Chinatown and posed for photographs in Hyde Park with the Life Guards riding past in the background. Endless column inches could be spun out of the long weekend to celebrate her sister-in-law's thirtieth birthday, which had culminated in a brutal, sordid death in the back lot of an adult entertainment store.

The story, like all the best stories, split like an amoeba, forming an endless series of new stories and opinion pieces and speculative articles, each spawning its own counter chorus. There were discussions of the deplorable drunken tendencies of the young British woman, with reciprocal accusations of victim-blaming. There were horror-struck articles about sexual violence, tempered with reminders that these attacks were far less common than in other countries. There were interviews with the distraught, guilt-stricken friends who had accidentally abandoned Heather, which in turn spawned attacks and vilifications on social media, leading back to a defence of the grieving young women.

Overlaying every story was the shadow of the unknown killer, the madman who was hacking women's bodies apart. The press again descended upon Denmark Street in search of the man who had received Kelsey's leg. Strike decided that the time had come for Robin to take that much-discussed but daily postponed trip to Masham for a final fitting of her wedding dress, then decamped yet again to Nick and Ilsa's with a backpack and a crushing sense of his own impotence. A plain-clothes officer remained stationed in Denmark Street in case anything suspicious turned up in the post. Wardle was concerned lest another body part addressed to Robin arrived.

Weighed down by the demands of an investigation that was being conducted under the full glare of the national media, Wardle was unable to meet Strike face to face for six days after the discovery of Heather's body. Strike journeyed again to the Feathers in the early evening, where he found Wardle looking haggard, but looking forward to talking things over with a man who was both inside and outside the case.

'Been a fucker of a week,' sighed Wardle, accepting the pint Strike had bought him. 'I've started bloody smoking again. April's really pissed off.'

He took a long draught of lager, then shared with Strike the truth about the discovery of Heather's body. The press stories, as Strike had already noted, conflicted in many possibly important essentials, though all blamed the police for not finding her for twenty-four hours.

'She and her friends were all shitfaced,' said the policeman, setting the scene with bluntness. 'Four of them got into a cab, so ratted they forgot about Heather. They were a street away when they realised she wasn't with them.

'The cabbie's hacked off because they're loud and obnoxious. One of them starts swearing at him when he says he can't do a U-turn in the middle of the road. There's a big argument, so it's a good five minutes before he agrees to go back for Heather.

'When they finally reach the street where they think they left her – they're from Nottingham, remember, they don't know London at all – Heather's nowhere to be seen. They crawl up the road in the cab, shouting for her out of the open window. Then one of them thinks she sees Heather in the distance, getting onto a bus. So two of them get out – there's no bloody logic to it, they were out of their skulls – and go running down the road screaming after the bus to stop while the other two lean out of the cab screaming at them to get back in, they should follow the bus in the cab. Then the one who got into an argument with the cabbie earlier calls him a stupid Paki, he tells them to get the fuck out of his cab and drives away.

'So basically,' said Wardle wearily, 'all this shit we're taking for not finding her within twenty-four hours is down to alcohol and racism. The silly bitches were convinced Heather had got on that bus so we wasted a day and a half trying to track a woman wearing a similar coat. Then the owner of the Adult Entertainment Centre goes to put his bins out and finds her lying there under a load of bags, nose and ears cut off.'

'So that bit was true,' said Strike.

Her mutilated face had been the one detail all of the papers had agreed on.

'Yeah, that bit was true,' said Wardle heavily. '"The Shacklewell Ripper". It's got a great ring to it.'

'Witnesses?'

'Nobody saw a bloody thing.'

'What about Devotee and his motorbike?'

'Ruled out,' Wardle admitted, his expression grim. 'He's got a firm alibi for Heather's killing – family wedding – and we couldn't make anything stick for either of the other two attacks.'

Strike had the impression that Wardle wanted to tell him something else, and waited receptively.

'I don't want the press to get wind of this,' Wardle said, dropping his voice, 'but we think he might've done two more.'

'Jesus,' said Strike, genuinely alarmed. 'When?'

'Historic,' said Wardle. 'Unsolved murder in Leeds, 2009. Prostitute, originally from Cardiff. Stabbed. He didn't cut anything off her, but he took a necklace she always wore and dumped her in a ditch out of town. The body wasn't found for a fortnight.

'Then, last year, a girl was killed and mutilated in Milton Keynes. Sadie Roach, her name was. Her boyfriend went down for it. I've looked it all up. The family campaigned hard for his release and he got out on appeal. There was nothing to tie him to it, except that they'd rowed and he once threatened a bloke with a penknife.

'We've got the psychologist and forensics on to all five attacks and the conclusion is they've got enough features in common to suggest the same perpetrator. It looks like he uses two knives, a carving knife and a machete. The victims were all vulnerable – prostitutes, drunk, emotionally off balance – and all picked up off the street except for Kelsey. He took trophies from all of them. It's too soon to say whether we've got any similar DNA off the women. Odds are, not. It doesn't look like he had sex with any of them. He gets his kicks a different way.'

Strike was hungry, but something told him not to interrupt Wardle's moody silence. The policeman drank more beer then said, without quite meeting Strike's eyes, 'I'm looking into all your guys. Brockbank, Laing and Whittaker.'

About fucking time.

'Brockbank's interesting,' said Wardle.

'You've found him?' asked Strike, freezing with his pint at his lips.

'Not yet, but we know he was a regular attendee at a church in Brixton until five weeks ago.'

'Church? Are you sure it's the same bloke?'

'Tall ex-soldier, ex-rugby player, long jaw, one of his eyes sunken, cauliflower ear, dark crew cut,' reeled off Wardle. 'Name Noel Brockbank. Six foot three or four. Strong northern accent.'

'That's him,' said Strike. 'A bloody *church*?'

'Hang on,' said Wardle, getting up. 'Need a slash.'

And yet, why not a church? Strike thought as he went to the bar for a couple of fresh pints. The pub was filling up around him. He took a menu back to the table as well as the beers, but could not concentrate on it. *Young girls in the choir . . . he wouldn't be the first . . .*

'Needed that,' said Wardle, rejoining Strike. 'I might go out for a fag, join you back—'

'Finish about Brockbank first,' said Strike, pushing the fresh pint across the table.

'To tell you the truth, we found him by accident,' said Wardle, sitting back down and accepting the pint. 'One of our guys has been tailing the mother of a local drug lord. We don't think Mum's as innocent as she's claiming to be, so our guy follows her to church and there's Brockbank standing on the door handing out hymnbooks. He got talking to the copper without knowing who he was, and our guy didn't have a clue Brockbank was wanted in connection with anything.

'Four weeks later our guy hears me talking about looking for a Noel Brockbank on the Kelsey Platt case and tells me he met a bloke with the same name a month ago in Brixton. See?' said Wardle, with a ghost of his usual smirk. 'I *do* pay attention to your tip-offs, Strike. Be silly not to, after the Landry case.'

You pay attention when you've got nothing out of Digger Malley and Devotee, thought Strike, but he made impressed and grateful noises before returning to the main point.

'Did you say Brockbank's stopped attending church?'

'Yeah,' sighed Wardle. 'I went down there yesterday, had a word with the vicar. Young guy, enthusiastic, inner-city church – you know the sort,' said Wardle – inaccurately, because Strike's contact with the clergy had been mostly limited to military chaplains. 'He had a lot of time for Brockbank. Said he'd had a rough deal in life.'

'Brain damage, invalided out of the army, lost his family, all that crap?' asked Strike.

'That was the gist,' said Wardle. 'Said he misses his son.'

'Uh huh,' said Strike darkly. 'Did he know where Brockbank was living?'

'No, but apparently his girlfriend—'

'Alyssa?'

Frowning slightly, Wardle reached into the inside pocket of his jacket, pulled out a notebook and consulted it.

'Yeah, it is, as it goes,' he said. 'Alyssa Vincent. How did you know that?'

'They've both just been sacked from a strip club. I'll explain in a bit,' said Strike hurriedly, as Wardle showed signs of becoming sidetracked. 'Go on about Alyssa.'

'Well, she's managed to get a council house in east London near her mother. Brockbank told the vicar he was going to move in with her and the kids.'

'Kids?' said Strike, his thoughts flying to Robin.

'Two little girls, apparently.'

'Do we know where this house is?' asked Strike.

'Not yet. The vicar was sorry to see him go,' said Wardle, glancing restlessly towards the pavement, where a couple of men were smoking. 'I did get out of him that Brockbank was in church on Sunday the third of April, which was the weekend Kelsey died.'

In view of Wardle's increasing restlessness, Strike passed no comment except to suggest that they both adjourn to the pavement for a cigarette.

They lit up and smoked side by side for a couple of minutes. Workers walked past in both directions, weary from late hours at the office. Evening was drawing in. Directly above them, between the indigo of approaching night and the neon coral of the setting sun, was a narrow stretch of no-coloured sky, of vapid and empty air.

'*Christ*, I've missed this,' said Wardle, dragging on the cigarette as though it was mother's milk before picking up the thread of their conversation once more. 'Yeah, so Brockbank was in church that weekend, making himself useful. Very good with the kids, apparently.'

'I'll bet he is,' muttered Strike.

'Take some nerve, though, wouldn't it?' said Wardle, blowing smoke towards the opposite side of the road, his eyes on Epstein's sculpture *Day*, which adorned the old London Transport offices. A boy stood before a throned man, his body contorted so that he both managed to embrace the king behind him and display his own penis to onlookers. 'To kill and dismember a girl, then turn up in church as though nothing had happened?'

'Are you Catholic?' Strike asked.

Wardle looked startled.

'I am, as it goes,' he said suspiciously. 'Why?'

Strike shook his head, smiling slightly.

'I know a psycho wouldn't care,' said Wardle with a trace of defensiveness. 'I'm just saying ... anyway, we've got people trying to find out where he's living now. If it's a council house, and assuming Alyssa Vincent's her real name, it shouldn't be too difficult.'

'Great,' said Strike. The police had resources that he and Robin could not match; perhaps now, at last, some definitive information would be forthcoming. 'What about Laing?'

'Ah,' said Wardle, grinding out his first cigarette and immediately lighting another, 'we've got more on him. He's been living alone in Wollaston Close for eighteen months now. Survives on disability benefits. He had a chest infection over the weekend of the second and third and his friend Dickie came in to help him out. He couldn't get to the shops.'

'That's bloody convenient,' said Strike.

'Or genuine,' said Wardle. 'We checked with Dickie and he confirmed everything Laing told us.'

'Was Laing surprised the police were asking about his movements?'

'Seemed pretty taken aback at first.'

'Did he let you in the flat?'

'Didn't arise. We met him crossing the car park on his sticks and we ended up talking to him in a local café.'

'That Ecuadorian place in a tunnel?'

Wardle subjected Strike to a hard stare that the detective returned with equanimity.

'You've been staking him out as well, have you? Don't mess this up for us, Strike. We're on it.'

Strike might have responded that it had taken press scrutiny and the failure to make anything of his preferred leads to make Wardle commit serious resources to the tracking of Strike's three suspects. He chose to hold his silence.

'Laing's not stupid,' Wardle continued. 'We hadn't been questioning him long when he twigged what it was about. He knew you must've given us his name. He'd seen in the papers you got sent a leg.'

'What was his view on the matter?'

'There might've been an undertone of "couldn't've happened to a nicer bloke",' said Wardle with a slight grin, 'but on balance, about what you'd expect. Bit of curiosity, bit of defensiveness.'

'Did he look ill?'

'Yeah,' said Wardle. 'He didn't know we were coming, and we met him shambling along on his sticks. He doesn't look good close up. Bloodshot eyes. His skin's kind of cracked. Bit of a mess.'

Strike said nothing. His mistrust of Laing's illness lingered. In spite of the clear photographic evidence of steroid use, skin plaques and lesions that Strike had seen with his own eyes, he found himself stubbornly resistant to the idea that Laing was genuinely ill.

'What was he doing when the other women were killed?'

'Says he was home alone,' said Wardle. 'Nothing to prove or disprove it.'

'Hmn,' said Strike.

They turned back into the pub. A couple had taken their table so they found another beside the floor-to-ceiling window onto the street.

'What about Whittaker?'

'Yeah, we caught up with him last night. He's roadying for a band.'

'Are you sure about that?' said Strike suspiciously, remembering Shanker's assertion that Whittaker claimed to be doing so, but was in fact living off Stephanie.

'Yeah, I'm sure. We called in on the druggie girlfriend—'

'Get inside the flat?'

'She talked to us at the door, unsurprisingly,' said Wardle. 'The place stinks. Anyway, she told us he was off with the boys, gave us the address of the concert and there he was. Old transit van parked outside and an even older band. Ever heard of Death Cult?'

'No,' said Strike.

'Don't bother, they're shit,' said Wardle. 'I had to sit through half an hour of the stuff before I could get near Whittaker. Basement of a pub in Wandsworth. I had tinnitus all the next day.

'Whittaker seemed to be half expecting us,' said Wardle. 'Apparently he found you outside his van a few weeks ago.'

'I told you about that,' said Strike. 'Crack fumes—'

'Yeah, yeah,' said Wardle. 'Look, I wouldn't trust him as far as I could throw him, but he reckons Stephanie can give him an alibi for the whole day of the royal wedding, so that would rule out the attack on the hooker in Shacklewell, and he claims he was off with Death Cult when both Kelsey and Heather were killed.'

'All three killings covered, eh?' said Strike. 'That's neat. Do Death Cult agree he was with them?'

'They were pretty vague about it, to be honest,' said Wardle. 'The lead singer's got a hearing aid. I don't know whether he caught everything I asked him. Don't worry, I've got guys checking all their witness statements,' he added in the face of Strike's frown. 'We'll find out whether he was really there or not.'

Wardle yawned and stretched.

'I've got to get back to the office,' he said. 'This could be an all-nighter. We've got a load of information coming in now the papers are on to it.'

Strike was extremely hungry now, but the pub was noisy

and he felt he would rather eat somewhere he could think. He and Wardle headed up the road together, both lighting fresh cigarettes as they walked.

'The psychologist raised something,' said Wardle as the curtain of darkness unrolled across the sky above them. 'If we're right, and we're dealing with a serial killer, he's usually an opportunist. He's got a bloody good m.o. – he must be a planner to a degree, or he couldn't have got away with it so often – but there was a change in the pattern with Kelsey. He knew exactly where she was staying. The letters and the fact that he knew there wouldn't be anyone there: it was totally premeditated.

'Trouble is, we've had a bloody good look, but we can't find any evidence that any of your guys have ever been in proximity with her. We virtually took her laptop apart, and there was nothing there. The only people she ever talked to about her leg were those oddballs Jason and Tempest. She had hardly any friends, and the ones she did have were all girls. There was nothing suspicious on her phone. As far as we know, none of your guys has ever lived or worked in Finchley or Shepherd's Bush, let alone gone anywhere near her school or college. They've got no known connection with any of her associates. How the hell could any of them get close enough to manipulate her without her family noticing?'

'We know she was duplicitous,' said Strike. 'Don't forget the pretend boyfriend who turned out to be pretty real when he picked her up from Café Rouge.'

'Yeah,' sighed Wardle. 'We've still got no leads on that bloody bike. We've put out a description in the press, but nothing.

'How's your partner?' he added, pausing outside the glass doors of his place of work, but apparently determined to smoke the cigarette down to the last millimetre. 'Not too shaken up?'

'She's fine,' said Strike. 'She's back in Yorkshire for a wedding dress fitting. I made her take the time off: she's been working through the weekend a lot lately.'

Robin had left without complaint. What was there to stay for, with the press staking out Denmark Street, one lousy paying job and the police now covering Brockbank, Laing and Whittaker more efficiently than the agency ever could?

'Good luck,' said Strike as he and Wardle parted. The policeman raised a hand in acknowledgement and farewell, and disappeared into the large building behind the slowly revolving prism glittering with the words New Scotland Yard.

Strike strolled back towards the Tube, craving a kebab and inwardly deliberating the problem that Wardle had just put to him. How could any of his suspects have got close enough to Kelsey Platt to know her movements or gain her trust?

He thought about Laing, living alone in his grim Wollaston Close flat, claiming his disability benefit, overweight and infirm, looking far older than his real age of thirty-four. He had been a funny man, once. Did he still have it in him to charm a young girl to the point that she would have ridden on motorbikes with him or taken him trustingly to a flat in Shepherd's Bush, about which her family knew nothing?

What about Whittaker, stinking of crack, with his blackened teeth and his thinning, matted hair? True, Whittaker had once had mesmeric charm, and emaciated, drug-addicted Stephanie seemed to find him appealing, but Kelsey's only known passion had been for a clean-cut blond boy just a few years older than herself.

Then there was Brockbank. To Strike, the massive, swarthy ex-flanker was downright repulsive, as unlike pretty

Niall as it was possible to be. Brockbank had been living and working miles from Kelsey's home and work, and while both had attended churches, their places of worship were on opposite banks of the Thames. The police would surely have unearthed any contact between the two congregations by now.

Did the absence of any known connection between Kelsey and Strike's three suspects rule each of them out as the killer? While logic seemed to urge the answer yes, something stubborn inside Strike continued to whisper no.

50

I'm out of my place, I'm out of my mind . . .

Blue Öyster Cult, 'Celestial the Queen'

Robin's trip home was tinged throughout with the strangest sense of unreality. She felt out of step with everybody, even her mother, who was preoccupied with the wedding arrangements and, while sympathetic to Robin's constant checking of her phone for any development on the Shacklewell Ripper, a little harassed.

Back in the familiar kitchen where Rowntree snoozed at her feet, the seating plan for the reception spread out on the scrubbed wooden table between them, Robin began to appreciate how fully she had abnegated responsibility for her wedding. Linda was constantly firing questions at her about favours, speeches, the bridesmaids' shoes, her headdress, when it would be convenient to speak to the vicar, where she and Matt wanted the presents sent, whether Matthew's Auntie Sue ought to be on the top table or not. Robin had imagined that being at home would be restful. Instead she was required to deal, on the one hand, with a tidal wave of trivial queries from her mother; on the other, a series of questions from her brother Martin, who pored over accounts of the discovery of Heather

Smart's body until Robin lost her temper with what she saw as his ghoulishness, whereupon an overwrought Linda banned all mention of the killer from their house.

Matthew, meanwhile, was angry, though trying not to show it, that Robin had not yet asked Strike for two weeks off for the honeymoon.

'I'm sure it'll be fine,' said Robin at dinner. 'We've got hardly any work on and Cormoran says the police have taken over all our leads.'

'He still hasn't confirmed,' said Linda, who had been beadily watching how little Robin was eating.

'Who hasn't?' asked Robin.

'Strike. No RSVP.'

'I'll remind him,' said Robin, taking a large slug of wine.

She had not told any of them, not even Matthew, that she kept having nightmares that woke her gasping in the darkness, back in the bed where she had slept in the months following her rape. A massive man kept coming for her in these dreams. Sometimes he burst into the office where she worked with Strike. More frequently he loomed out of the darkness in the back streets of London, knives shining. That morning he had been on the point of gouging out her eyes when she woke, gasping, to the sound of Matthew drowsily asking her what she had said.

'Nothing,' she had said, pushing sweaty hair off her forehead. 'Nothing.'

Matthew had to return to work on Monday. He seemed pleased to leave her behind in Masham, helping Linda with preparations for the wedding. Mother and daughter met the vicar at St Mary the Virgin for a final discussion about the form of the service on Monday afternoon.

Robin tried hard to concentrate on the minister's cheerful suggestions, his ecclesiastical pep talk, but all the time he was talking her eyes kept drifting to the large stone crab that appeared to be clinging to the church wall on the right of the aisle.

This crab had fascinated her in her childhood. She had not been able to understand why there was a big carved crab crawling up the stones of their church, and her curiosity on the point had ended up infecting Linda, who had gone to the local library, looked up the records and triumphantly informed her daughter that the crab had been the emblem of the ancient Scrope family, whose memorial sat above it.

Nine-year-old Robin had been disappointed by the answer. In a way, an explanation had never been the point. She had simply liked being the only one who wanted to find out the truth.

She was standing in the dressmaker's box-like changing room, with its gilt-framed mirror and its new-carpet smell, when Strike called next day. Robin knew that it was Strike because of the unique ringtone that she had attached to his calls. She lunged for her handbag, causing the dressmaker to emit a little cry of annoyance and surprise as the folds of chiffon that she was dextrously re-pinning were torn from her hands.

'Hello?' said Robin.

'Hi,' said Strike.

The single syllable told her that something bad had happened.

'Oh God, has someone else been killed?' Robin blurted out, forgetting the dressmaker crouching at the hem of her wedding dress. The woman stared at her in the mirror, her mouth full of pins.

'Sorry, could you give me a moment? Not you!' she added to Strike, in case he hung up.

'Sorry,' she repeated as the curtain closed behind the

dressmaker and she sank down onto the stool in the corner in her wedding dress, 'I was with someone. *Has* someone else died?'

'Yes,' said Strike, 'but it's not what you think. It's Wardle's brother.'

Robin's tired and overwrought brain tried to join dots that refused to connect.

'It's nothing to do with the case,' said Strike. 'He was knocked down on a zebra crossing by a speeding van.'

'God,' said Robin, utterly fazed. She had temporarily forgotten that death came in any manner other than at the hands of a maniac with knives.

'It's a fucker, all right. He had three kids, and a fourth on the way. I've just spoken to Wardle. Bloody terrible thing to happen.'

Robin's brain seemed to grind back into gear again.

'So is Wardle—?'

'Compassionate leave,' said Strike. 'Guess who's taken over from him?'

'Not Anstis?' Robin asked, suddenly worried.

'Worse than that,' said Strike.

'Not – not Carver?' said Robin, with a sudden presentiment of doom.

Of the policemen whom Strike had managed to offend and upstage during his two most famous detective triumphs, Detective Inspector Roy Carver had been the most comprehensively outclassed and was consequently the most deeply embittered. His failings during the investigation into a famous model's fall from her penthouse flat had been extensively documented and, indeed, exaggerated in the press. A sweaty man with dandruff and a mottled, purple face like corned beef, he had had an antipathy towards Strike even before the detective had publicly proven that the policeman had failed to spot murder.

'Right in one,' said Strike. 'I've just had him here for three hours.'

'Oh, God – why?'

'Come off it,' said Strike, 'you know why. This is a wet dream for Carver, having an excuse to interrogate me about a series of murders. He stopped just short of asking me for alibis, and he spent a hell of a lot of time on those fake letters to Kelsey.'

Robin groaned.

'Why on earth would they let Carver—? I mean, with his record—'

'Hard though it might be for us to believe, he hasn't been a dickhead his entire career. His bosses must think he was unlucky with Landry. It's supposed to be only temporary, while Wardle's off, but he's already warned me to stay well away from the investigation. When I asked how enquiries into Brockbank, Laing and Whittaker were going, he as good as told me to fuck off with my ego and my hunches. We'll be getting no more inside information on the progress of the case, I can promise you that.'

'He'll have to follow up Wardle's lines of investigation, though,' said Robin, 'won't he?'

'Given that he'd clearly rather chop off his own knob than let me solve another of his cases, you'd think he'd be careful to follow up all my leads. Trouble is, I can tell he's rationalised the Landry case as me getting lucky, and I reckon he thinks me coming up with three suspects in this case is pure showboating. I wish to hell,' said Strike, 'we'd got an address for Brockbank before Wardle had to leave.'

As Robin had been silent for a whole minute while she listened to Strike, the dressmaker clearly thought it reasonable to check whether she was ready to resume the fitting, and poked her head in through the curtain. Robin, whose expression was suddenly beatific, waved her away impatiently.

'We *have* got an address for Brockbank,' Robin told Strike in a triumphant voice as the curtains swung closed again.

'What?'

'I didn't tell you, because I thought Wardle would already have got it, but I thought, just in case – I've been ringing round the local nurseries, pretending I was Alyssa, Zahara's mum. I said I wanted to check they had our new address right. One of them read it out to me off the parent contact sheet. They're living on Blondin Street in Bow.'

'Jesus Christ, Robin, that's fucking brilliant!'

When the dressmaker returned to her job at last, she found a considerably more radiant bride than she had left. Robin's lack of enthusiasm for the process of altering her dress had been diminishing the seamstress's pleasure in her job. Robin was easily the best-looking client on her books and she had hoped to get a photograph for advertising purposes once the dress was finished.

'That's wonderful,' said Robin, beaming at the seamstress as she tugged the last seam straight and together they contemplated the vision in the mirror. 'That's absolutely wonderful.'

For the first time, she thought that the dress really didn't look bad at all.

51

Don't turn your back, don't show your profile,
You'll never know when it's your turn to go.

Blue Öyster Cult, 'Don't Turn Your Back'

'The public response has been overwhelming. We're currently following up over twelve hundred leads, some of which look promising,' said Detective Inspector Roy Carver. 'We continue to appeal for information on the whereabouts of the red Honda CB750 used to transport part of Kelsey Platt's body and we remain interested in speaking to anybody who was in Old Street on the night of 5th June, when Heather Smart was killed.'

The headline POLICE FOLLOW NEW LEADS IN HUNT FOR SHACKLEWELL RIPPER was not really justified, in Robin's view, by anything in the brief report beneath, although she supposed that Carver would not share details of genuine new developments with the press.

Five photographs of the women now believed to have been victims of the Ripper filled most of the page, their identities and their brutal fates stamped across their chests in black typeface.

Martina Rossi, 28, prostitute, stabbed to death, necklace stolen.

Martina was a plump, dark woman wearing a white tank top. Her blurry photograph looked as though it had been a selfie. A small heart-shaped-harp charm hung from a chain around her neck.

> Sadie Roach, 25, admin assistant, stabbed to death, mutilated, earrings taken.

She had been a pretty girl with a gamine haircut and hoops in her ears. Judging by cropped figures at the edges of her picture, it had been taken at a family gathering.

> Kelsey Platt, 16, student, stabbed to death and dismembered.

Here was the familiar chubby, plain face of the girl who had written to Strike, smiling in her school uniform.

> Lila Monkton, 18, prostitute, stabbed, fingers cut off, survived.

A blurred picture of a gaunt girl whose bright red hennaed hair was cut into a shaggy bob, her multiple piercings glinting in the camera flash.

> Heather Smart, 22, financial services worker, stabbed to death, nose and ears removed.

She was round-faced and innocent-looking, with wavy mouse-brown hair, freckles and a timid smile.

Robin looked up from the *Daily Express* with a deep sigh. Matthew had been sent to audit a client in High Wycombe, so he had been unable to give Robin a lift today. It had taken her a full hour and twenty minutes to get to Catford from Ealing on trains crammed with tourists and commuters sweating in the London heat. Now she left her seat and headed for the door, swaying with the rest of the commuters as the train slowed and stopped, yet again, at Catford Bridge station.

Her week back at work with Strike had been strange. Strike, who clearly had no intention to comply with the instruction to keep out of Carver's investigation, was nevertheless taking the investigating officer seriously enough to be cautious.

'If he can make a case that we've buggered up the police investigation, we're finished as a business,' he said. 'And we know he'll try and say I've screwed things up, whether I have or not.'

'So why are we carrying on?'

Robin had been playing devil's advocate, because she would have been deeply unhappy and frustrated had Strike announced that they were abandoning their leads.

'Because Carver thinks my suspects are bullshit, and I think he's an incompetent tit.'

Robin's laugh had ended prematurely when Strike had told her he wanted her to return to Catford and stake out Whittaker's girlfriend.

'Still?' she asked. 'Why?'

'You know why. I want to see whether Stephanie can give him alibis for any of the key dates.'

'You know what?' said Robin, plucking up her courage. 'I've been in Catford a lot. If it's all the same to you, I'd rather do Brockbank. Why don't I try and get something out of Alyssa?'

'There's Laing as well, if you want a change,' said Strike.

'He saw me up close when I fell over,' Robin countered at once. 'Don't you think it would be better if you did Laing?'

'I've been watching his flat while you've been away,' Strike said.

'And?'

'And he mostly stays in, but sometimes he goes to the shops and back.'

'You don't think it's him any more, do you?'

'I haven't ruled him out,' said Strike. 'Why are you so keen to do Brockbank?'

'Well,' said Robin bravely, 'I feel like I've done a lot of the running on him. I got the Market Harborough address out of Holly and I got Blondin Street out of the nursery—'

'And you're worried about the kids who're living with him,' said Strike.

Robin remembered the little black girl with the stiff pigtails who had tripped over, staring at her, in Catford Broadway.

'So what if I am?'

'I'd rather you stuck to Stephanie,' said Strike.

She had been annoyed; so annoyed that she had promptly asked for two weeks off rather more bluntly than she might otherwise have done.

'Two weeks off?' he said, looking up in surprise. He was far more used to her begging to stay at work than asking to leave it.

'It's for my honeymoon.'

'Oh,' he said. 'Right. Yeah. I suppose that'll be soon, will it?'

'Obviously. The wedding's on the second.'

'Christ, that's only – what – three weeks or something?'

She had been annoyed that he had not realised that it was so close.

'Yes,' she had said, getting to her feet and reaching for her jacket. 'And would you mind RSVPing if you're coming?'

So she returned to Catford and the busy market stalls, to the smell of incense and raw fish, to pointless hours of standing beneath the crouching stone bears over the stage door of the Broadway Theatre.

Robin had hidden her hair under a straw hat today and was wearing sunglasses, but she still wondered whether she did not see a hint of recognition in the eyes of stallholders as she settled once more to lurk opposite the triple windows of Whittaker and Stephanie's flat. She had only had a couple of glimpses of the girl since she had resumed her surveillance on her, and on neither occasion had there been the slightest chance of speaking to her. Of Whittaker, there had been no hint at all. Robin settled back against the cool grey stone of the theatre wall, prepared for another long day of tedium, and yawned.

By late afternoon she was hot, tired and trying not to resent her mother, who had texted repeatedly throughout the day with questions about the wedding. The last, telling her to ring the florist, who had yet another finicky question for her, arrived just as Robin had decided she needed something to drink. Wondering how Linda would react if she texted back and said she'd decided to have plastic flowers everywhere – on her head, in her bouquet, all over the church – anything to stop having to make decisions – she crossed to the chip shop, which sold chilled fizzy drinks.

She had barely touched the door handle when somebody collided with her, also aiming for the chip-shop door.

'Sorry,' said Robin automatically, and then, 'oh my God.'

Stephanie's face was swollen and purple, one eye almost entirely closed.

The impact had not been hard, but the smaller girl had been bounced off her. Robin reached out to stop her stumbling.

'Jesus – what happened?'

She spoke as though she knew Stephanie. In a sense, she felt she did. Observing the girl's little routines, becoming familiar with her body language, her clothing and her liking for Coke had fostered a one-sided sense of kinship. Now she found it natural and easy to ask a question hardly any British stranger would ask of another: 'Are you all right?'

How she managed it, Robin hardly knew, but two minutes

later she was settling Stephanie into a chair in the welcome shade of the Stage Door Café, a few doors along from the chip shop. Stephanie was obviously in pain and ashamed of her appearance, but at the same time she had become too hungry and thirsty to remain upstairs in the flat. Now she had simply bowed to a stronger will, thrown off balance by the older woman's solicitude, by the offer of a free meal. Robin gabbled nonsensically as she ushered Stephanie down the street, maintaining the fiction that her quixotic offer of sandwiches was due to her guilt at having almost knocked Stephanie over.

Stephanie accepted a cold Fanta and a tuna sandwich with mumbled thanks, but after a few mouthfuls she put her hand to her cheek as though in pain and set the sandwich down.

'Tooth?' asked Robin solicitously.

The girl nodded. A tear trickled out of her unclosed eye.

'Who did this?' Robin said urgently, reaching across the table for Stephanie's hand.

She was playing a character, growing into the role as she improvised. The straw hat and the long sundress she was wearing had unconsciously suggested a hippyish girl full of altruism who thought that she could save Stephanie. Robin felt a tiny reciprocal squeeze of her fingers even as Stephanie shook her head to indicate that she was not going to give away her attacker.

'Somebody you know?' Robin whispered.

More tears rolled down Stephanie's face. She withdrew her hand from Robin's and sipped her Fanta, wincing again as the cold liquid made contact with what Robin thought was probably a cracked tooth.

'Is he your father?' Robin whispered.

It would have been an easy assumption to make. Stephanie could not possibly be older than seventeen. She was so thin that she barely had breasts. Tears had washed away any trace of the kohl that usually outlined her eyes. Her grubby face was infantile, with the suggestion of an overbite, but all was dominated by the purple and grey bruising. Whittaker had pummelled her until the blood vessels in her right eye had burst: the sliver that was visible was scarlet.

'No,' whispered Stephanie. 'Boyfriend.'

'Where is he?' Robin asked, reaching again for Stephanie's hand, now chilly from contact with the cold Fanta.

'Away,' said Stephanie.

'Does he live with you?'

Stephanie nodded and tried to drink more Fanta, keeping the icy liquid away from the damaged side of her face.

'I didn't wan' 'im to go,' whispered Stephanie.

As Robin leaned in, the girl's restraint suddenly dissolved in the face of kindness and sugar.

'I aksed to go wiv 'im and 'e wouldn't take me. I know 'e's out tomming, I know 'e is. 'E's got someone else, I 'eard Banjo saying sumfing. 'E's got anuvver girl somewhere.'

To Robin's disbelief, Stephanie's primary source of pain, far worse than that of her cracked tooth and her bruised and broken face, was the thought that filthy, crack-dealing Whittaker might be somewhere else, sleeping with another woman.

'I on'y wan'ed to go wiv 'im,' Stephanie repeated, and tears slid more thickly down her face, stinging that slit of an eye into a more furious redness.

Robin knew that the kind, slightly dippy girl she had been impersonating would now earnestly beseech Stephanie to leave a man who had beaten her so badly. The trouble was, she was sure that would be the surest way to make Stephanie walk out on her.

'He got angry because you wanted to go with him?' she repeated. 'Where has he gone?'

'Says 'e's wiv the Cult like last – they're a band,' mumbled Stephanie, wiping her nose on the back of her hand. ''E roadies for 'em – bur it's just an excuse,' she said, crying harder, 'to go places an' find girls to fuck. I said I'd go an' – 'cause last time 'e wanted me to – an' I done the 'ole band for 'im.'

Robin did her very best not to look as though she understood what she had just been told. However, some flicker of anger and revulsion must have contaminated the look of pure kindliness she was trying to project, because Stephanie seemed suddenly to withdraw. She did not want judgement. She met that every day of her life.

'Have you been to a doctor?' Robin asked quietly.

'Wha'? No,' said Stephanie, folding her thin arms around her torso.

'When's he due back, your boyfriend?'

Stephanie merely shook her head and shrugged. The temporary sympathy Robin had kindled between them seemed to have cooled.

'The Cult,' said Robin, improvising rapidly, her mouth dry, 'that isn't Death Cult, is it?'

'Yeah,' said Stephanie, dimly surprised.

'Which gig? I saw them the other day!'

Don't ask me where, for God's sake . . .

'This was in a pub called the – Green Fiddle, or sumfing. Enfield.'

'Oh, no, it wasn't the same gig,' said Robin. 'When was yours?'

'Need a pee,' mumbled Stephanie, looking around the café.

She shuffled off towards the bathroom. When the door had closed behind her, Robin frantically keyed search terms into her mobile. It took her several attempts to find what she was looking for: Death Cult had played a pub called the Fiddler's Green in Enfield on Saturday the fourth of June, the day before Heather Smart had been murdered.

The shadows were lengthening outside the café now, which

had emptied apart from themselves. Evening was drawing in. The place would surely close soon.

'Cheers for the sandwich an' ev'rything,' said Stephanie, who had reappeared beside her. 'I'm gonna—'

'Have something else. Some chocolate or something,' Robin urged her, even though the waitress mopping table tops looked ready to throw them out.

'Why?' asked Stephanie, showing the first sign of suspicion.

'Because I really want to talk to you about your boyfriend,' said Robin.

'Why?' repeated the teenager, a little nervous now.

'Please sit down. It isn't anything bad,' Robin coaxed her. 'I'm just worried about you.'

Stephanie hesitated, then sank slowly back into the seat she had vacated. For the first time, Robin noticed the deep red mark around her neck.

'He didn't – he didn't try and strangle you, did he?' she asked.

'Wha'?'

Stephanie felt her thin neck and tears welled again in her eyes.

'Oh, tha's – tha' was my necklace. 'E give it me an' then 'e . . . 'cause I ain't makin' enough money,' she said, and began to cry in earnest. ''E's sold it.'

Unable to think what else to do, Robin stretched her other hand across the table and held on to Stephanie's with both of her own, holding tightly, as though Stephanie were on some moving plateau that was drifting away.

'Did you say he made you . . . with the whole band?' Robin asked quietly.

'That were f'free,' said Stephanie tearfully, and Robin understood that Stephanie was still thinking of her money-making abilities. 'I only blew 'em.'

'After the gig?' asked Robin, releasing one hand to press paper napkins into Stephanie's.

'No,' said Stephanie, wiping her nose, 'next night. We stayed over in the van at the lead singer's 'ouse. 'E lives in Enfield.'

Robin would not have believed that it was possible to feel simultaneously disgusted and delighted. If Stephanie had been with Whittaker on the night of the fifth of June, Whittaker could not have killed Heather Smart.

'Was he – your boyfriend – was he there?' she asked in a quiet voice. 'All the time, while you were – you know—?'

'The fuck's going on 'ere?'

Robin looked up. Stephanie snatched her hand away, looking frightened.

Whittaker was standing over them. Robin recognised him immediately from the pictures she had seen online. He was tall and broad-shouldered, yet scrawny. His old black T-shirt was washed out almost to grey. The heretic priest's golden eyes were fascinating in their intensity. In spite of the matted hair, the sunken, yellowing face, in spite of the fact that he repulsed her, she could yet feel the strange, manic aura of him, a magnetic pull like the reek of carrion. He woke the urge to investigate provoked by all dirty, rotten things, no less powerful because it was shameful.

''Oo are *you*?' he asked, not aggressively, but with something close to a purr in his voice. He was looking unabashedly right down the front of her sundress.

'I bumped into your girlfriend outside the chippy,' said Robin. 'I bought her a drink.'

'Didjoo now?'

'We're closing,' said the waitress loudly.

The appearance of Whittaker had been a little too much for her, Robin could tell. His flesh tunnels, his tattoos, his maniac's eyes, his smell would be desirable in very few establishments selling food.

Stephanie looked terrified, even though Whittaker was ignoring her completely. His attention was entirely focused on Robin, who felt absurdly self-conscious as she paid the bill, then stood and walked, Whittaker just behind her, out onto the street.

'Well – goodbye then,' she said weakly to Stephanie.

She wished that she had Strike's courage. He had urged Stephanie to come away with him right underneath Whittaker's nose, but Robin's mouth was suddenly dry. Whittaker was staring at her as though he had spotted something fascinating and rare on a dung heap. Behind them, the waitress was bolting the doors. The sinking sun was throwing cold shadows across the street that Robin only knew as hot and smelly.

'Jus' bein' kind, were you, darlin'?' Whittaker asked softly, and Robin could not tell whether there was more malice or sweetness in his voice.

'I suppose I was worried,' said Robin, forcing herself to look into those wide-apart eyes, 'because Stephanie's injuries look quite serious.'

'That?' said Whittaker, putting out a hand to Stephanie's purple and grey face. 'Come off a pushbike, din'choo, Steph? Clumsy little cow.'

Robin suddenly understood Strike's visceral hatred for this man. She would have liked to hit him too.

'I hope I'll see you again, Stephanie,' she said.

She did not dare give the girl a number in front of Whittaker. Robin turned and began to walk away, feeling like the worst kind of coward. Stephanie was about to walk back upstairs with the man. She ought to have done more, but what? What could she say that would make a difference? Could she report the assault to the police? Would that constitute an interference with Carver's case?

Only when she was definitely out of sight of Whittaker did she lose the sensation that invisible ants were crawling up her spine. Robin pulled out her mobile and called Strike.

'I know,' she said, before Strike could start telling her off, 'it's getting late but I'm on my way to the station right now and when you've heard what I've got, you'll understand.'

She walked fast, chilly in the increasing cool of the evening, telling him everything that Stephanie had said.

'So he's got an alibi?' said Strike slowly.

'For Heather's death, yes, if Stephanie's telling the truth, and I honestly think she is. She was with him – and the whole of Death Cult, as I say.'

'She definitely said Whittaker was there while she was servicing the band?'

'I think so. She was just answering that when Whittaker turned up and – hang on.'

Robin stopped and looked around. Busy talking, she had taken a wrong turning somewhere on the way back to the station. The sun was setting now. Out of the corner of her eye, she thought she saw a shadow move behind a wall.

'Cormoran?'

'Still here.'

Perhaps she had imagined the shadow. She was on a stretch of unfamiliar residential road, but there were lit windows and a couple walking along in the distance. She was safe, she told herself. It was all right. She just needed to retrace her steps.

'Everything OK?' asked Strike sharply.

'Fine,' she said. 'I've taken a wrong turn, that's all.'

'Where are you exactly?'

'Near Catford Bridge station,' she said. 'I don't know how I've ended up here.'

She did not want to mention the shadow. Carefully she crossed the darkening road, so that she would not have to walk past the wall where she thought she had seen it, and after transferring her mobile into her left hand she took a tighter hold of the rape alarm in her right pocket.

'I'm going back the way I came,' she told Strike, wanting him to know where she was.

'Have you seen something?' he demanded.

'I don't kn— maybe,' she admitted.

Yet when she drew level with the gap between houses where she had thought she had seen the figure, there was nobody there.

'I'm jumpy,' she said, speeding up. 'Meeting Whittaker wasn't fun. There's definitely something – nasty – about him.'

'Where are you now?'

'About twenty feet away from where I was the last time you asked me. Hang on, I can see a street name. I'm crossing back over, I can see where I've gone wrong, I should've turned—'

She heard the footsteps only when they were right behind her. Two massive black-clad arms closed around her, pinning hers to her sides, squeezing the air from her lungs. Her mobile slipped out of her hand and fell with a crack onto the pavement.

52

Do not envy the man with the x-ray eyes.

Blue Öyster Cult, 'X-Ray Eyes'

Strike, who had been standing in the shadow of a warehouse in Bow, keeping watch on Blondin Street, heard Robin's sudden gasp, the thud of the mobile on the pavement and then the scuffling and skidding of feet on asphalt.

He began to run. The phone connection to Robin was still open, but he could hear nothing. Panic sharpened his mental processes and obliterated all perception of pain as he sprinted down a darkening street in the direction of the nearest station. He needed a second phone.

'Need to borrow that, mate!' he bellowed at a pair of skinny black youths walking towards him, one of whom was chuckling into a mobile. 'Crime's being committed, need to borrow that phone!'

Strike's size and his aura of authority as he pelted towards them made the teenager surrender the phone with a look of fear and bewilderment.

'Come with me!' Strike bellowed at the two boys, running on past them towards busier streets where he might be able to find a cab, his own mobile still pressed to his other ear.

'Police!' Strike yelled into the boy's phone as the stunned teenagers ran alongside him like bodyguards. 'There's a woman being attacked near Catford Bridge station, I was on the line to her when it happened! It's happening right – no, I don't know the street but it's one or two away from the station – right now, I was on the line to her when he grabbed her, I heard it happen – yeah – and fucking hurry!

'Cheers, mate,' Strike panted, throwing the mobile back into the hands of its owner, who continued to run alongside him for several yards without realising that he no longer needed to.

Strike hurtled around a corner; Bow was a totally unfamiliar area of London to him. On he ran past the Bow Bells pub, ignoring the red-hot jabs of the ligaments in his knee, moving awkwardly with only one free arm to balance himself, his silent phone still clamped to his ear. Then he heard a rape alarm going off at the other end of the line.

'TAXI!' he bellowed at a distant glowing light. 'ROBIN!' he yelled into the phone, sure she could not hear him over the screeching alarm. 'ROBIN, I'VE CALLED THE POLICE! THE POLICE ARE ON THEIR WAY. ARE YOU LISTENING, YOU FUCKER?'

The taxi had driven off without him. Drinkers outside the Bow Bells stared at the lunatic hobbling past at high speed, yelling and swearing into his phone. A second taxi appeared.

'TAXI! TAXI!' Strike bellowed and it turned, heading towards him, just as Robin's voice spoke in his ear, gasping.

'Are . . . you there?'

'JESUS CHRIST! WHAT'S HAPPENED?'

'Stop . . . shouting . . .'

With enormous difficulty he modulated his volume.

'*What's happened?*'

'I can't see,' she said. 'I can't . . . see anything . . .'

Strike wrenched open the back door of the cab and threw himself inside.

'Catford Bridge station, hurry! What d'you mean, you can't—? What's he done to you? NOT YOU!' he bellowed at the confused cabbie. 'Go! Go!'

'No . . . it's your bloody . . . rape alarm . . . stuff . . . in my face . . . oh . . . shit . . . '

The taxi was speeding along, but Strike had to physically restrain himself from urging the driver to floor it.

'What happened? Are you hurt?'

'A – a bit . . . there are people here . . . '

He could hear them now, people surrounding her, murmuring, talking excitedly amongst themselves.

' . . . hospital . . . ' he heard Robin say, away from the phone.

'Robin? ROBIN?'

'Stop shouting!' she said. 'Listen, they've called an ambulance, I'm going to—'

'WHAT'S HE DONE TO YOU?'

'Cut me . . . up my arm . . . I think it'll need stitching . . . God, it stings . . . '

'Which hospital? Let me speak to someone! I'll meet you there!'

Strike arrived at the Accident and Emergency Department at University Hospital Lewisham twenty-five minutes later, limping heavily and wearing such an anguished expression that a kindly nurse reassured him that a doctor would be with him shortly.

'No,' he said, waving her away as he clumped towards the reception desk, 'I'm here with someone – Robin Ellacott, she's been knifed—'

His eyes travelled frantically over the packed waiting room where a young boy was whimpering on his mother's lap and a groaning drunk cradled his bloodied head in his hands. A male nurse was showing a breathless old lady how to use an inhaler.

'Strike . . . yes . . . Miss Ellacott said you'd be coming,' said the receptionist, who had checked her computer records with what Strike felt was unnecessary and provocative deliberation. 'Down the corridor and to the right . . . first cubicle.'

He slipped a little on the shining floor in his haste, swore and hurried on. Several people's eyes followed his large, ungainly figure, wondering whether he was quite right in the head.

'Robin? Fucking hell!'

Scarlet spatters disfigured her face; both eyes were swollen. A young male doctor, who was examining an eight-inch wound in her forearm, barked:

'Out until I've finished!'

'It isn't blood!' Robin called as Strike retreated behind the curtain. 'It's the damn spray stuff in your rape alarm!'

'Stay still, please,' Strike heard the doctor say.

He paced a little outside the cubicle. Five other curtained beds hid their secrets along the side ward. The nurses' rubber soles squeaked on the highly polished grey floor. God, how he hated hospitals: the smell of them, the institutional cleanliness underlaid with that faint whiff of human decomposition, immediately transported him back to those long months in Selly Oak after his leg had been blown off.

What had he done? *What had he done?* He had let her work, knowing the bastard had her in his sights. She could have died. She *should* have died. Nurses rustled past in their blue scrubs. Behind the curtain, Robin gave a small gasp of pain and Strike ground his teeth.

'Well, she's been extremely lucky,' said the doctor, ripping the curtains open ten minutes later. 'He could have severed the brachial artery. There's tendon damage, though, and we won't know how much until we get her into theatre.'

He clearly thought they were a couple. Strike did not put him right.

'She needs surgery?'

'To repair the tendon damage,' said the doctor, as though Strike were a bit slow. 'Plus, that wound needs a proper clean. I want to X-ray her ribs as well.'

He left. Bracing himself, Strike entered the cubicle.

'I know I screwed up,' said Robin.

'Holy shit, did you think I was going to tell you off?'

'Maybe,' she said, pulling herself up a little higher on the bed. Her arm was bound up in a temporary crêpe bandage. 'After dark. I wasn't paying attention, was I?'

He sat down heavily beside the bed on the chair that the doctor had vacated, accidentally knocking a metal kidney dish to the floor. It clanged and rattled; Strike put his prosthetic foot on it to silence it.

'Robin, how the fuck did you get away?'

'Self-defence,' she said. Then, correctly reading his expression, she said crossly, 'I *knew* you didn't believe I'd done any.'

'I did believe you,' he said, 'but Jesus fucking Christ—'

'I had lessons from this brilliant woman in Harrogate who was ex-army,' said Robin, wincing a little as she re-adjusted herself on her pillows again. 'After – you know what.'

'Was this before or after the advanced driving tests?'

'After,' she said, 'because I was agoraphobic for a while. It was the driving that really got me back out of my room and then, after that, I did self-defence classes. The first one I signed to was run by a man and he was an idiot,' said Robin. 'All judo moves and – just useless. But Louise was brilliant.'

'Yeah?' said Strike.

Her composure was unnerving him.

'Yeah,' said Robin. 'She taught us it's not about clever throws when you're an ordinary woman. It's about reacting smartly and fast. Never let yourself get taken to a second location. Go for the weak spots and then run like hell.

'He grabbed me from behind but I heard him just before he got to me. I practised it loads with Louise. If they grab you from behind, you bend over.'

'Bend over,' repeated Strike numbly.

'I had the rape alarm in my hand. I bent right over and slammed it into his balls. He was wearing tracksuit pants. He let go for a couple of seconds and I tripped on this damn dress again – he pulled out the knife – I can't remember exactly what happened then – I know he cut me as I was trying to get up – but I managed to press the button on the alarm and it went off and that scared him – the ink went all over my face and must've gone in his as well, because he was close to me – he was wearing a balaclava – I could hardly see – but I got in a good jab at his carotid artery as he bent over me – that's the other thing Louise taught us, side of the neck, you can make them collapse if you do it right – and he staggered, and then I think he realised people were coming and he ran.'

Strike was speechless.

'I'm really hungry,' said Robin.

Strike felt in his pockets and pulled out a Twix.

'Thanks.'

But before she could take a bite, a nurse escorting an old man past the foot of her bed said sharply:

'Nil by mouth, you're going to theatre!'

Robin rolled her eyes and handed the Twix back to Strike. Her mobile rang. Strike watched, dazed, as she picked it up.

'Mum . . . hi,' said Robin.

Their eyes met. Strike read Robin's unexpressed desire to save her mother, at least temporarily, from what had just happened, but no diversionary tactics were necessary because Linda was gabbling without allowing Robin to speak. Robin laid the mobile on her knees and switched it to speakerphone, her expression resigned.

'... let her know as soon as possible, because lily of the valley is out of season, so if you want it, it'll be a special order.'

'OK,' said Robin. 'I'll skip lily of the valley.'

'Well, it would be great if you could call her directly and tell her what you *do* want, Robin, because it isn't easy being the intermediary. She says she's left you loads of voicemails.'

'Sorry, Mum,' said Robin. 'I'll call her.'

'You're not supposed to be using that in here!' said a second cross nurse.

'Sorry,' said Robin again. 'Mum, I'll have to go. I'll speak to you later.'

'Where are you?' Linda asked.

'I'm . . . I'll ring you later,' said Robin, and cut the call.

She looked at Strike and asked:

'Aren't you going to ask me which of them I think it was?'

'I'm assuming you don't know,' said Strike. 'If he was wearing a balaclava and your eyes were full of ink.'

'I'm sure about one thing,' said Robin. 'It wasn't Whittaker. Not unless he changed into sweatpants the moment I left him. Whittaker was wearing jeans and he was – his physique wasn't right. This guy was strong, but soft, you know? Big, though. As big as you.'

'Have you told Matthew what's happened?'

'He's on his w—'

He thought, when her expression changed to one of near horror, that he was about to turn and see a livid Matthew bearing down upon them. Instead, the dishevelled figure of Detective Inspector Roy Carver appeared at the foot of Robin's bed, accompanied by the tall, elegant figure of Detective Sergeant Vanessa Ekwensi.

Carver was in shirtsleeves. Large wet patches of sweat

radiated out from his armpits. The constantly pink whites of his bright blue eyes always made him look as though he had been swimming in heavily chlorinated water. His thick, greying hair was full of large flakes of dandruff.

'How are—?' began Detective Sergeant Ekwensi, her almond-shaped eyes on Robin's forearm, but Carver interrupted with an accusatory bark.

'What've *you* been up to, then, eh?'

Strike stood up. Here at last was the perfect target for his so far suppressed desire to punish somebody, anybody, for what had just happened to Robin, to divert his feelings of guilt and anxiety onto a worthy target.

'I want to talk to you,' Carver told Strike. 'Ekwensi, you take her statement.'

Before anyone could speak or move, a sweet-faced young nurse stepped obliviously between the two men, smiling at Robin.

'Ready to take you to X-ray, Miss Ellacott,' she said.

Robin got stiffly off the bed and walked away, looking back over her shoulder at Strike, trying to convey warning and restraint with her expression.

'Out here,' Carver growled at Strike.

The detective followed the policeman back through A&E. Carver had commandeered a small visitors' room where, Strike assumed, news of imminent or actual death was conveyed to relatives. It contained several padded chairs, a box of tissues on a small table and an abstract print in shades of orange.

'I told you to stay out of it,' Carver said, taking up a position in the middle of the room, arms folded, feet wide apart.

With the door closed, Carver's body odour filled the room. He did not stink in the same way as Whittaker: not of ingrained filth and drugs, but of sweat that he could not contain through the working day. His blotchy complexion was not improved by the overhead strip lighting. The dandruff, the wet shirt, the mottled skin: he seemed to be visibly falling to pieces. Strike had undoubtedly helped him on his way, humiliating him in the press over the murder of Lula Landry.

'Sent her to stake out Whittaker, didn't you?' asked Carver, his face growing slowly redder, as though he were being boiled. 'You did this to her.'

'Fuck you,' said Strike.

Only now, with his nose full of Carver's sweat, did he admit to himself that he had known it for a while: Whittaker was not the killer. Strike had sent Robin after Stephanie because, in his soul, he had thought it the safest place to put her, but he had kept her on the streets, and he had known for weeks that the killer was tailing her.

Carver knew that he had hit a nerve. He was grinning.

'You've been using murdered women to pay off your fucking grudge against your stepdaddy,' he said, taking pleasure in Strike's rising colour, grinning to see the large hands ball into fists. Carver would enjoy nothing more than running Strike in for assault; they both knew it. 'We've checked out Whittaker. We checked all three of your fucking hunches. There's nothing in any of them. Now you listen to me.'

He took a step closer to Strike. Though a head shorter, he projected the power of a furious, embittered but powerful man, a man with much to prove, and with the full might of the force behind him. Pointing at Strike's chest, he said:

'Stay out of it. You're fucking lucky you haven't got your partner's blood on your hands. If I find you anywhere near our investigation again, I'll fucking run you in. Understand me?'

He poked his stubby fingertip into Strike's sternum. Strike resisted the urge to knock it away, but a muscle in his jaw twitched. For a few seconds they eyeballed each other. Carver grinned more widely, breathing as though he had just triumphed in a wrestling match, then strutted to the door and left, leaving Strike to stew in rage and self-loathing.

He was walking slowly back through A&E when tall, handsome Matthew came running through the double doors in his suit, wild-eyed, his hair all over the place. For the first time in their acquaintanceship, Strike felt something other than dislike for him.

'Matthew,' he said.

Matthew looked at Strike as though he did not recognise him.

'She went for an X-ray,' said Strike. 'She might be back by now. That way,' he pointed.

'Why's she need—?'

'Ribs,' said Strike.

Matthew elbowed him aside. Strike did not protest. He felt he deserved it. He watched as Robin's fiancé tore off in her direction, then, after hesitating, turned to the double doors and walked out into the night.

The clear sky was now dusted with stars. Once he reached the street he paused to light a cigarette, dragging on it as Wardle had done, as though the nicotine were the stuff of life. He began to walk, feeling the pain in his knee now. With every step, he liked himself less.

'RICKY!' bawled a woman down the street, imploring an escaping toddler to return to her as she struggled with the weight of a large bag. 'RICKY, COME BACK!'

The little boy was giggling manically. Without really thinking what he was doing, Strike bent down automatically and caught him as he sped towards the road.

'Thank you!' said the mother, almost sobbing her relief as she jogged towards Strike. Flowers toppled off the bag in her arms. 'We're visiting his dad – oh God—'

The boy in Strike's arms struggled frantically. Strike put

him down beside his mother, who was picking up a bunch of daffodils off the pavement.

'Hold them,' she told the boy sternly, who obeyed. 'You can give them to Daddy. Don't drop them! Thanks,' she said again to Strike and marched away, keeping a tight grip on the toddler's free hand. The little boy walked meekly beside his mother now, proud to have a job to do, the stiff yellow flowers upright in his hand like a sceptre.

Strike walked on a few paces and then, quite suddenly, stopped dead in the middle of the pavement, staring as though transfixed by something invisible hanging in the cold air in front of him. A chilly breeze tickled his face as he stood there, completely indifferent to his surroundings, his focus entirely inward.

Daffodils . . . lily of the valley . . . flowers out of season.

Then the sound of the mother's voice echoed through the night again – 'Ricky, no!' – and caused a sudden explosive chain reaction in Strike's brain, lighting a landing strip for a theory that he knew, with the certainty of a prophet, would lead to the killer. As the steel joists of a building are revealed as it burns, so Strike saw in this flash of inspiration the skeleton of the killer's plan, recognising those crucial flaws that he had missed – that everyone had missed – but which might, at last, be the means by which the murderer and his macabre schemes could be brought down.

53

> You see me now a veteran of a thousand psychic wars . . .
>
> Blue Öyster Cult, 'Veteran of the Psychic Wars'

It had been easy to feign insouciance in the brightly lit hospital. Robin had drawn strength, not merely from Strike's amazement and admiration at her escape, but from listening to her own account of fighting off the killer. She had been the calmest of them all in the immediate aftermath of the attack, consoling and reassuring Matthew when he began to cry at the sight of her ink-stained face and the long wound in her arm. She had drawn strength from everyone else's weakness, hoping that her adrenalin-fuelled bravery would carry her safely back to normality, where she would find a sure footing and move on unscathed, without having to pass through the dark mire where she had lived so long after the rape . . .

However, during the week that followed she found it almost impossible to sleep, and not only because of the throbbing of her injured forearm, which was now in a protective half-cast. In the short dozes she managed at night or by day, she felt her attacker's thick arms around her again and heard him breathing in her ear. Sometimes the eyes she had not seen became the eyes of the rapist when she was nineteen: pale, one pupil fixed. Behind their black balaclava and gorilla mask, the nightmare figures merged, mutated and grew, filling her mind day and night.

In the worst dreams, she watched him doing it to somebody else and was waiting her turn, powerless to help or escape. Once, the victim was Stephanie with her pulverised face. On another unbearable occasion, a little black girl screamed for her mother. Robin woke from that one shouting in the dark, and Matthew became so worried about her that he called in sick to work the following day so that he could stay with her. Robin did not know whether she was grateful or resentful.

Her mother came, of course, and tried to make her come home to Masham.

'You've got ten days until the wedding, Robin, why don't you just come home with me now and relax before—'

'I want to stay here,' said Robin.

She was not a teenager any more: she was a grown woman. It was up to her where she went, where she stayed, what she did. Robin felt as though she were fighting all over again for the identities she had been forced to relinquish the last time a man had lunged at her out of the darkness. He had transformed her from a straight-A student into an emaciated agoraphobic, from an aspiring forensic psychologist into a defeated girl who agreed with her overbearing family that police work would only exacerbate her mental problems.

That was not going to happen again. She would not let it. She could barely sleep, she did not want to eat, but furiously she dug in, denying her own needs and fears. Matthew was frightened of contradicting her. Weakly he agreed with her that there was no need for her to go home, yet Robin heard him whispering with her mother in the kitchen when they thought she could not hear them.

Strike was no help at all. He had not bothered to say

goodbye to her at the hospital, nor he had come to see how she was doing, merely speaking to her on the phone. He, too, wanted her to go back to Yorkshire, safely out of the way.

'You must have a load of stuff to do for the wedding.'

'Don't patronise me,' said Robin furiously.

'Who's patronising—?'

'Sorry,' she said, dissolving into silent tears that he could not see and doing everything in her power to keep her voice normal. 'Sorry . . . uptight. I'm going home on the Thursday before; there's no need to go earlier.'

She was no longer the person who had lain on her bed staring at Destiny's Child. She refused to be that girl.

Nobody could understand why she was so determined to remain in London, nor was she ready to explain. She threw away the sundress in which he had attacked her. Linda entered the kitchen just as Robin was shoving it into the bin.

'Stupid bloody thing,' said Robin, catching her mother's eye. 'I've learned *that* lesson. Don't run surveillance in long dresses.'

She spoke defiantly. *I'm going back to work. This is temporary.*

'You're not supposed to be using that hand,' said her mother, ignoring the unspoken challenge. 'The doctor said to rest and elevate it.'

Neither Matthew nor her mother liked her reading about the progress of the case in the press, which she did obsessively. Carver had refused to release her name. He said he did not want the media descending on her, but she and Strike both suspected that he was afraid that Strike's continued presence in the story would give the press a delicious new twist: Carver versus Strike all over again.

'In fairness,' Strike said to Robin over the phone (she tried to limit herself to one call to him a day), 'that's the last bloody thing anyone needs. It won't help catch the bastard.'

Robin said nothing. She was lying on her and Matthew's bed with a number of newspapers that she had bought against Linda and Matthew's wishes spread around her. Her eyes were fixed on a double-page spread in the *Mirror*, where the five supposed victims of the Shacklewell Ripper were again pictured in a row. A sixth black silhouette of a woman's head and shoulders represented Robin. The legend beneath the silhouette read '26-year-old office worker, escaped'. Much was made of the fact that the 26-year-old office worker had managed to spray the killer with red ink during the attack. She was praised by a retired policewoman in a side column for her foresight in carrying such a device, and there was a separate feature on rape alarms over the page.

'You've really given up on it?' she asked.

'It's not a question of giving up,' said Strike. She could hear him moving around the office, and she wished she were there, even if only making tea or answering emails. 'I'm leaving it to the police. A serial killer's out of our league, Robin. It always was.'

Robin was looking down at the gaunt face of the only other woman who had survived the killing spree. 'Lila Monkton, prostitute.' Lila, too, knew what the killer's pig-like breathing sounded like. He had cut off Lila's fingers. Robin would only have a long scar on her arm. Her brain buzzed angrily in her skull. She felt guilty that she had got off so lightly.

'I wish there was something—'

'Drop it,' said Strike. He sounded angry, just like Matthew. 'We're done, Robin. I should never have sent you to Stephanie. I've let my grudge against Whittaker colour my judgement ever since that leg arrived and it nearly got you—'

'Oh for God's sake,' said Robin impatiently. '*You* didn't try and kill me, *he* did. Let's keep the blame where it belongs. You had good reason for thinking it was Whittaker – the lyrics. Anyway, that still leaves—'

'Carver's looked into Laing and Brockbank and he doesn't think there's anything there. We're staying out of it, Robin.'

Ten miles away in his office, Strike hoped that he was convincing her. He had not told Robin about the epiphany that had occurred to him after his encounter with the toddler outside the hospital. He had tried to contact Carver the following morning, but a subordinate had told him that Carver was too busy to take his call and advised him not to try again. Strike had insisted on telling the irritable and faintly aggressive subordinate what he had hoped to tell Carver. He would have bet his remaining leg that not a word of his message had been passed on.

The windows in Strike's office were open. Hot June sunshine warmed the two rooms now devoid of clients and soon, perhaps, to be vacated due to an inability to afford the rent. Two-Times's interest in the new lap-dancer had petered out. Strike had nothing to do. Like Robin, he yearned for action, but he did not tell her that. All he wanted was for her to heal and be safe.

'Police still in your street?'

'Yes,' she sighed.

Carver had placed a plain-clothes officer in Hastings Road around the clock. Matthew and Linda took immense comfort in the fact that he was out there.

'Cormoran, listen. I know we can't—'

'Robin, there's no "we" just now. There's me, sitting on my arse with no work, and there's you, staying at bloody home until that killer's caught.'

'I wasn't talking about the case,' she said. Her heart was banging hard and fast against her ribs again. She had to say it aloud, or she would burst. 'There's one thing we – *you* can do, then. Brockbank might not be the killer, but we know he's a rapist. You could go to Alyssa and warn her she's living with—'

'Forget it,' said Strike's voice harshly in her ear. 'For the last fucking time, Robin, you can't save everyone! He's never been convicted! If we go blundering in there, Carver will string us up.'

There was a long silence.

'Are you crying?' Strike asked anxiously, because he thought her breathing had become ragged.

'No, I'm not crying,' said Robin truthfully.

An awful coldness had spread through her at Strike's refusal to help the young girls living in Brockbank's vicinity.

'I'd better go, it's lunch,' she said, though nobody had called her.

'Look,' he said, 'I get why you want—'

'Speak later,' she said and hung up.

There's no 'we' just now.

It had happened all over again. A man had come at her out of the darkness and had ripped from her not only her sense of safety, but her status. She had been a partner in a detective agency . . .

Or had she? There had never been a new contract. There had never been a pay rise. They had been so busy, so broke, that it had never occurred to her to ask for either. She had simply been delighted to think that that was how Strike saw her. Now even that was gone, perhaps temporarily, perhaps for ever. *There's no 'we' any more.*

Robin sat in thought for a few minutes, then got off the bed, the newspapers rustling. She approached the dressing table where the white shoebox sat, engraved with the silver words Jimmy Choo, reached out a hand and stroked the pristine surface of the cardboard.

The plan did not come to her like Strike's epiphany outside the hospital, with the exhilarating force of flame. Instead it rose slowly, dark and dangerous, born of the hateful enforced passivity of the past week and out of ice-cold anger at Strike's stubborn refusal to act. Strike, who was her friend, had joined the enemy's ranks. He was a six-foot-three ex-boxer. He would never know what it was like to feel yourself small, weak and powerless. He would never understand what rape did to your feelings about your own body: to find yourself reduced to a thing, an object, a piece of fuckable meat.

Zahara had sounded three at most on the telephone.

Robin remained quite still in front of her dressing table, staring down at the box containing her wedding shoes, thinking. She saw the risks plainly spread beneath her, like the rocks and raging waters beneath a tightrope walker's feet.

No, she could not save everyone. It was too late for Martina, for Sadie, for Kelsey and for Heather. Lila would spend the rest of her days with two fingers on her left hand and a grisly scar across her psyche that Robin understood only too well. However, there were also two young girls who faced God knows how much more suffering if nobody acted.

Robin turned away from the new shoes, reached for her mobile and dialled a number she had been given voluntarily, but which she had never imagined she would use.

54

And if it's true it can't be you,
It might as well be me.

Blue Öyster Cult, 'Spy in the House of the Night'

She had three days in which to plan, because she had to wait for her accomplice to get hold of a car and find a gap in his busy schedule. Meanwhile she told Linda that her Jimmy Choos were too tight for her, the style too flashy, and allowed her mother to accompany her as she exchanged them for cash. Then she had to decide what lie she was going to tell Linda and Matthew, to buy sufficient time away from them to put her plan into action.

She ended up telling them that she was to have another police interview. Insisting that Shanker remain in the car when he picked her up was key to maintaining that illusion, as was getting Shanker to pull up alongside the plain-clothes policeman still patrolling their street and telling him that she was off to get her stitches out, which in reality would not happen for another two days.

It was now seven o'clock on a cloudless evening and apart from Robin, who was leaning up against the warm brick wall of the Eastway Business Centre, the scene was deserted. The sun was making its slow progress towards the west and on the distant, misty horizon, at the far end of Blondin Street, the Orbit sculpture was rising into existence. Robin had seen plans in the papers: it would soon look like a gigantic candlestick telephone wrapped in its own twisted cord. Beyond it, Robin could just make out the growing outline of the Olympic stadium. The distant view of the gigantic structures was impressive and somehow inhuman, worlds and worlds away from the secrets she suspected were hidden behind the newly painted front door she knew to be Alyssa's.

Perhaps because of what she had come to do, the silent stretch of houses she was watching unnerved her. They were new, modern and somehow soulless. Barring the grandiose edifices being constructed in the distance, the place lacked character and was devoid of any sense of community. There were no trees to soften the outlines of the low, square houses, many of them sporting 'To Let' signs, no corner shop, neither pub nor church. The warehouse against which she was leaning, with its upper windows hung with shroud-like white curtains and its metal garage doors heavily graffitied, offered no cover. Robin's heart was thudding as though she had been running. Nothing would turn her back now, yet she was afraid.

Footsteps echoed nearby and Robin whipped around, her sweaty fingers tight on her spare rape alarm. Tall, loose-limbed and scarred, Shanker was loping towards her carrying a Mars bar in one hand and a cigarette in the other.

'She's comin',' he said thickly.

'Are you sure?' said Robin, her heart pounding faster than ever. She was starting to feel light-headed.

'Black girl, two kids, comin' up the road now. Seen 'er when I was buyin' this,' he said, waving the Mars bar. 'Wan' some?'

'No thanks,' said Robin. 'Er – d'you mind getting out of the way?'

'Sure you don't wan' me to come in wiv ya?'

'No,' said Robin. 'Only come if you see – him.'

'You sure the cunt's not already in there?'

'I rang twice. I'm sure he's not.'

'I'll be round the corner, then,' said Shanker laconically and he ambled off, alternately taking drags on his cigarette and bites of his Mars bar, to a position out of sight of Alyssa's door. Robin, meanwhile, hurried off down Blondin Street so that Alyssa would not pass her as she entered the house. Drawing in beneath the overhanging balcony of a block of dark red flats, Robin watched as a tall black woman turned into the street, one hand gripping that of a toddler and trailed by an older girl whom Robin thought must be around eleven. Alyssa unlocked the front door and let herself and her daughters inside.

Robin headed back up the street towards the house. She had dressed in jeans and trainers today: there must be no tripping, no falling over. The newly reconnected tendons throbbed beneath the cast.

Her heart was thumping so hard that it hurt as she knocked on Alyssa's front door. The older daughter peeped out of the bow window to her right as she stood waiting. Robin smiled nervously. The girl ducked out of sight.

The woman who appeared less than a minute later was, by any standards, gorgeous. Tall, black and with a bikini model's figure, she wore her hair in waist-length twists. The first thought that shot through Robin's mind was that if a strip joint had been prepared to fire Alyssa, she must indeed be a tricky character.

'Yeah?' she said, frowning at Robin.

'Hi,' said Robin, her mouth dry. 'Are you Alyssa Vincent?'

'Yeah. Who're you?'

'My name's Robin Ellacott,' said Robin, her mouth dry. 'I wonder – could I have a quick word with you about Noel?'

'What about him?' demanded Alyssa.

'I'd rather tell you inside,' said Robin.

Alyssa had the wary, defiant look of one perpetually braced to take the next punch life was going to throw her.

'Please. It's important,' said Robin, her tongue sticking to the roof of her mouth because it was so dry. 'I wouldn't ask otherwise.'

Their eyes locked: Alyssa's a warm caramel brown, Robin's a clear grey-blue. Robin was sure that Alyssa was going to refuse. Then the thick-lashed eyes widened suddenly and a strange flicker of excitement passed over Alyssa's face, as though she had just experienced a pleasurable revelation. Without another word, Alyssa stepped backwards into the dimly lit hall and made a strangely extravagant flourish, pointing Robin inside.

Robin did not know why she felt a lurch of misgiving. Only the thought that the two little girls were in there pushed her over the threshold.

A minuscule hall opened onto the sitting room. A TV and a single sofa constituted the only furnishings. A table lamp sat on the floor. There were two photographs in cheap gilt frames hanging on the wall, one showing chubby Zahara, the toddler, who was wearing a turquoise dress with matching butterfly clips in her hair, the other of her big sister in a maroon school uniform. The sister was the image of her beautiful mother. The photographer had not managed to induce a smile.

Robin heard a lock being turned on the front door. She turned, her trainers screeching on the polished wood floor. Somewhere nearby a loud ping announced that a microwave had just finished its work.

'Mama!' said a shrill voice.

'Angel!' shouted Alyssa, walking into the room. 'Get it out for her! All right,' she said, arms folded, 'what d'you wanna tell me about Noel, then?'

Robin's impression that Alyssa was gloating over some private piece of intelligence was reinforced by the nasty smirk that disfigured the lovely face. The ex-stripper stood with her arms crossed, so that her breasts were thrust up like the figurehead of a ship, the long ropes of hair hanging to her waist. She was taller than Robin by two inches.

'Alyssa, I work with Cormoran Strike. He's a—'

'I know who he is,' said Alyssa slowly. The secret satisfaction she seemed to have gleaned from Robin's appearance had suddenly gone. 'He's the bastard that give Noel epilepsy! Fucking hell! You've gone to *him,* have you? In it together, are you? Why didn't you go to the pigs, you lying bitch, if he – *really*—'

She smacked Robin hard in the shoulder and before Robin could defend herself, began punching her with every subsequent word.

'—done – *anything* – *TO* – *YOU!*'

Alyssa was suddenly pummelling her wherever she could land a punch: Robin threw up her left arm to defend herself, trying to protect her right, and kicked out at Alyssa's knee. Alyssa shrieked in pain and hopped backwards; from somewhere behind Robin the toddler screamed and her older sister came sliding into the room.

'Fucking bitch!' screamed Alyssa, 'attacking me in front of my kids—'

And she launched herself at Robin, grabbing her hair and slamming her head into the curtainless window. Robin felt Angel, who was thin and wiry, trying to force the two women apart. Abandoning restraint, Robin managed to land a smack to Alyssa's ear, causing her to gasp in pain and retreat. Robin seized Angel under the armpits, swung her out of the way, put her own head down and charged at Alyssa, knocking her backwards onto the sofa.

'Leave my mum – *leave my mum alone!*' shouted Angel, grabbing Robin's injured forearm and yanking it so that Robin, too, yelled in pain. Zahara was screaming from the doorway, a sippy cup of hot milk held upside down in her hand.

'YOU'RE LIVING WITH A PAEDOPHILE!' Robin roared over the racket as Alyssa tried to push herself back off the sofa to renew the fight.

Robin had imagined herself imparting the devastating news in a whisper and watching Alyssa crumble in shock. Not once had she visualised Alyssa looking up at her and snarling:

'Yeah, whatever. D'you think I don't know who you are, you fucking bitch? Are you not happy ruining his fucking life—'

She launched herself at Robin again: the space was so small that Robin hit the wall again. Locked together they slid sideways into the TV, which toppled off its stand with an ominous crash. Robin felt the wound on her forearm twist and let out another shriek of pain.

'Mama! Mama!' wailed Zahara, while Angel seized the back of Robin's jeans, hampering her ability to fend Alyssa off.

'Ask your daughters!' shouted Robin as fists and elbows flew and she tried to twist free of Angel's stubborn grip. 'Ask your daughters whether he's—'

'Don't you – dare – fucking – bring – my kids—'

'Ask them!'

'Lying fucking bitch – you and your fucking mother—'

'My *mother*?' said Robin, and with an almighty effort she elbowed Alyssa so hard in the midriff that the taller woman doubled over and collapsed onto the sofa again. 'Angel, get off me!' Robin roared, wrenching the girl's fingers off her jeans, sure that she had seconds before Alyssa returned to the attack. Zahara continued to wail from the doorway. '*Who*,' Robin panted, standing over Alyssa, 'd'you think I am?'

'Very fucking funny!' gasped Alyssa, whom Robin had winded. 'You're fucking Brittany! Phoning him and persecuting him—'

'*Brittany?*' said Robin in astonishment. 'I'm not Brittany!'

She yanked her purse out of her jacket pocket. 'Look at my credit card – look at it! I'm Robin Ellacott and I work with Cormoran Strike—'

'The fucker who gave him brain dam—'

'D'you know why Cormoran went to arrest him?'

''Cause his fucking wife framed—'

'Nobody framed him! He raped Brittany and he's been sacked from jobs all over the country because he interferes with little girls! He did it to his own sister – I've met her!'

'Fucking liar!' shouted Alyssa, making to get up from the sofa again.

'I – am – not – LYING!' roared Robin, shoving Alyssa back against the cushions.

'You mad bitch,' gasped Alyssa, 'get out of my fucking house!'

'Ask your daughter whether he's hurt her! Ask her! Angel?'

'*Don't you* dare *talk to my kids, you bitch!*'

'Angel, tell your mother whether he's—'

'Th'fook's going on?'

Zahara had been screaming so loudly that they had not heard the key in the lock.

He was massive, dark-haired and bearded, wearing an all-black tracksuit. One eye socket was sunken, caved in towards his nose, making his stare intense and unnerving. His dark, shadowed eyes on Robin, he bent down slowly and picked up the toddler, who beamed and cuddled close to him. Angel, on the other hand, shrank backwards into the wall. Very slowly, his eyes on Robin, Brockbank lowered Zahara into her mother's lap.

'Nice t'see thoo,' he said with a smile that was no smile, but a promise of pain.

Cold all over, Robin tried to slide her hand discreetly into her pocket for her rape alarm, but Brockbank was on her in seconds, seizing her wrist and compressing her stitches.

'You're fookin' phonin' no one, sneakly larl bitch – thought A didn' know it was thoo, din't thoo—'

She tried to twist away from him, her stitches pulling under his grasp, and screamed:

'SHANKER!'

'A shoulda fuckin' killed thoo when A 'ad th'chance, larl bitch!'

And then came a splintering crash of wood that was the front door caving in. Brockbank released Robin and whirled around to see Shanker hurtling into the room, knife to the fore.

'*Don't stab him!*' gasped Robin, clutching her forearm.

The six people crammed into the small bare box of a room froze for a fraction of a second, even the toddler clinging to her mother. Then a thin voice piped up, desperate, trembling, but liberated at last by the presence of a scarred, gold-toothed man whose tattooed knuckles were tight around a knife.

'He done it to me! He done it to me, Mum, he did! He done it to me!'

'What?' said Alyssa, looking towards Angel. Her face was suddenly slack with shock.

'He done it to me! What that lady said. He done it to me!'

Brockbank made a small, convulsive movement, swiftly curbed as Shanker raised his knife, pointing it at the bigger man's chest.

'You're all right, babes,' Shanker said to Angel, his free hand shielding her, his gold tooth glinting in the sun falling slowly behind the houses opposite. ''E ain't gonna do that no more. You fuckin' nonce,' he breathed into Brockbank's face. 'I'd like to skin ya.'

'Whatchoo talkin' abou', Angel?' said Alyssa, still clutching Zahara, her face now a study in dread. 'He never—?'

Brockbank suddenly put his head down and charged Shanker like the flanker he had once been. Shanker, who was less than half his width, was knocked aside like a dummy; they heard Brockbank pushing his way past the caved-in door as Shanker, swearing furiously, gave chase.

'Leave him – *leave him*!' Robin screamed, watching through the window as the two men streaked off down the street. 'Oh God – SHANKER! – the police will – where's Angel—?'

Alyssa had already left the room in pursuit of her daughter, leaving behind her the much-tried toddler to wail and scream on the sofa. Robin, who knew she could not hope to catch the two men, felt suddenly so shivery that she dropped into a crouch, holding her head as waves of sickness passed over her.

She had done what she had meant to do and she had been aware all along that there would almost certainly be collateral damage. Brockbank escaping or being stabbed by Shanker had been possibilities she had foreseen. Her only present certainty was that she could do nothing to prevent either. After taking a couple of deep breaths she stood up again and moved to the sofa to try to comfort the terrified toddler, but unsurprisingly, given that Robin was associated in the little girl's mind with scenes of violence and hysteria, Zahara screamed harder than ever, and lashed out at Robin with a tiny foot.

'I never knew,' said Alyssa. 'Oh God. Oh God. Why didn't you tell me, Angel? Why didn't you tell me?'

Evening was drawing in. Robin had turned on the lamp,

which threw pale grey shadows up onto the magnolia walls. Three flat hunchbacked ghosts seemed to crouch on the back of the sofa, mimicking Alyssa's every movement. Angel was curled, sobbing, on her mother's lap as the pair of them rocked backwards and forwards.

Robin, who had already made two rounds of tea and had cooked spaghetti hoops for Zahara, was sitting on the hard floor beneath the window. She had felt obliged to stay until they could get an emergency joiner to fix the door that Shanker had shouldered in. Nobody had yet called the police. Mother and daughter were still confiding in each other and Robin felt like an interloper, yet could not leave the family until she knew that they had a secure door and a new lock. Zahara was asleep on the sofa beside her mother and sister, curled up with her thumb in her mouth, one chubby hand still clutching the sippy cup.

'He said he'd kill Zahara if I told you,' said Angel into her mother's neck.

'Oh, sweet Jesus,' moaned Alyssa, tears splattering down her daughter's back. 'Oh, sweet Lord.'

The ominous feeling inside Robin was like having a bellyful of crawling, prickle-footed crabs. She had texted her mother and Matthew to say that the police needed to show her more photofits, but both were getting worried about her long absence and she was running out of plausible reasons to stop them coming to meet her. Again and again she checked the mute button on her phone in case somehow she had stopped it ringing. Where was Shanker?

The joiner arrived at last. Once Robin had given him her credit card details to pay for the damage, she told Alyssa that she had better get going.

Alyssa left Angel and Zahara curled up together on the sofa and accompanied Robin out into the dusky street.

'Listen,' said Alyssa.

There were still tear tracks down her face. Robin could tell that Alyssa was unused to thanking people.

'Thanks, all right?' she said, almost aggressively.

'No problem,' said Robin.

'I never – I mean – I met him at fucking *church*. I thought I'd found a good bloke at last, y'know . . . he was really good with the – with the kids—'

She began to sob. Robin considered reaching out to her, but decided against it. She was bruised all over her shoulders where Alyssa had pummelled her and her knife wound was throbbing more than ever.

'Has Brittany really been phoning him?' Robin asked.

''S'what he told me,' said Alyssa, wiping her eyes on the back of her hand. 'He reckoned his ex-wife framed him, got Brittany to lie . . . said if ever a young blonde bird turned up she was talking shit and I wasn't to believe anything she said.'

Robin remembered the low voice in her ear:

Do A know you, little girl?

He had thought that she was Brittany. *That* was why he had hung up and never called back.

'I'd better be off,' said Robin, worried about how long it would take her to get back to West Ealing. Her body ached all over. Alyssa had landed some powerful blows. 'You'll call the police, right?'

'I s'pose,' said Alyssa. Robin suspected that the idea was a novel one to Alyssa. 'Yeah.'

As Robin walked away in the darkness, her fist clenched tightly around her second rape alarm, she wondered what Brittany Brockbank had found to say to her stepfather, and thought she knew: 'I haven't forgotten. Do it again and I'll report you.' Perhaps it had been a salve to her conscience. She had been frightened that he was still doing to others what he had done to her, but could not face the consequences of a historical accusation.

I put it to you, Miss Brockbank, that your stepfather never touched you, that this story was concocted by yourself and your mother . . .

Robin knew how it worked. The defence barrister she had faced had been cold and sardonic, his expression vulpine.

You were coming back from the student bar, Miss Ellacott, where you had been drinking, yes?

You had made a public joke about missing the – ah – attentions of your boyfriend, yes?

When you met Mr Trewin—

I didn't—

When you met Mr Trewin outside the halls of residence—

I didn't meet—

You told Mr Trewin you were missing—

We never talked—

I put it to you, Miss Ellacott, that you are ashamed of inviting Mr Trewin—

I didn't invite—

You had made a joke, Miss Ellacott, hadn't you, in the bar, about missing the, ah, sexual attentions of—

I said I missed—

How many drinks had you had, Miss Ellacott?

Robin understood only too well why people were scared of telling, of owning up to what had been done to them, of being told that the dirty, shameful, excruciating truth was a figment of their own sick imagination. Neither Holly nor Brittany had been able to face the prospect of open court, and perhaps Alyssa and Angel would be scared away too. Yet nothing, Robin was sure, short of death or incarceration would ever stop Noel Brockbank raping little girls. Even so, she would be glad to know that Shanker had not killed him, because if he had . . .

'Shanker!' she shouted as a tall, tattooed figure in a shell suit passed under a street lamp ahead.

'Couldn't fucking find the bastard, Rob!' came Shanker's echoing voice. He did not seem to realise that Robin had been sitting on a hard floor in terror for two whole hours, praying for his return. 'He can move for a big fucker, can't 'e?'

'The police'll find him,' said Robin, whose knees were suddenly weak. 'Alyssa's going to call them, I think. Shanker, will you . . . please will you drive me home?'

55

Came the last night of sadness
And it was clear she couldn't go on.

Blue Öyster Cult, '(Don't Fear) The Reaper'

For twenty-four hours Strike remained in ignorance of what Robin had done. She did not answer when he phoned at lunchtime the next day, but as he was wrestling with his own dilemmas and believed her to be safe at home with her mother he neither found this strange nor troubled to call back. His injured partner was one of the few problems that he believed temporarily solved and he did not intend to encourage her in thoughts of returning to his side by confiding in her the revelation he had experienced outside the hospital.

This, however, was now his overriding preoccupation. After all, there was no longer any competition for his time or attention in the solitary, silent room where no clients called or visited. The only sound was the buzzing of a fly zooming between the open windows in the hazy sunlight, as Strike sat chain-smoking Benson & Hedges.

As he looked back over the almost three months since the severed leg had been delivered, the detective saw his mistakes only too clearly. He ought to have known the identity of the killer after visiting Kelsey Platt's home. If he had only realised, then – if he had not allowed himself to be taken in by the killer's misdirection, not been distracted by the competing scents of other deranged men – Lila Monkton would still have all ten fingers and Heather Smart might be safe at work in her Nottingham building society, vowing, perhaps, never again to be as drunk as she had been on her sister-in-law's birthday jaunt to London.

Strike had not come up through the Special Investigation Branch of the Royal Military Police without learning to manage the emotional consequences of an investigation. The previous evening had been full of self-directed anger, but even as he castigated himself for not seeing what was right in front of him he had acknowledged the killer's brazen brilliance. There had been artistry in the way that he had used Strike's background against him, forcing Strike to second guess and question himself, undermining his trust in his own judgement.

The fact that the killer was indeed one of the men whom he had suspected from the first was cold comfort. Strike could not remember ever being in such agony of mind over an investigation as he was now. Alone in his deserted office, convinced that the conclusion he had reached had neither been given credence by the officer in whom he had confided it, nor passed on to Carver, Strike felt, however unreasonably, that if another killing occurred it would indeed be his fault.

Yet if he went near the investigation again – if he started staking out or tailing his man – Carver would almost certainly see him in court for interfering with the course of a police investigation or obstructing the police in their enquiries. He would have felt the same way himself, had he been in Carver's shoes – except, thought Strike with a rush of pleasurable anger, that he would have listened to anyone, however infuriating, if he thought they had a shred of credible evidence. You did not solve a case as complex as this by discriminating against witnesses on the grounds that they have previously outwitted you.

Only when his stomach rumbled did Strike remember that he was supposed to be going out for dinner with Elin that night. The divorce settlement and custody arrangements had now been finalised, and Elin had announced over the phone that it was about time they enjoyed a decent dinner for a change and that she had booked Le Gavroche – 'My treat.'

Alone, smoking in his office, Strike contemplated the forthcoming evening with a dispassion he was no longer able to bring to the thought of the Shacklewell Ripper. On the plus side, there would be excellent food, which was an enticing prospect given the fact that he was skint and had last night dined on baked beans on toast. He supposed that there would be sex too, in the pristine whiteness of Elin's flat, the soon-to-be-vacated home of her disintegrating family. On the minus side – he found himself staring the bald fact in the face as he had never done before – he would have to talk to her, and talking to Elin, he had finally admitted to himself, was far from one of his favourite pastimes. He always found the conversation especially effortful when it came to his own work. Elin was interested, yet strangely unimaginative. She had none of the innate interest in and easy empathy for other people that Robin displayed. His would-be humorous word portraits of the likes of Two-Times left her perplexed rather than amused.

Then there were those two ominous words 'my treat'. The increasing imbalance in their respective incomes was about to become painfully obvious. When Strike had met Elin, he had at least been in credit. If she thought that he was going to be able to return the treat with dinner at Le Gavroche on another night, she was destined to be sorely disappointed.

Strike had spent sixteen years with another woman who had been far richer than he was. Charlotte had alternately brandished money as a weapon and deplored Strike's refusal to live beyond his means. Memories of Charlotte's occasional fits of pique that he could not or would not fund treats on which she had set her capricious heart made his hackles rise when Elin spoke of having a decent dinner 'for a change'. It had mostly been he who had footed the bills for French and Indian meals in out-of-the-way bistros and curry houses where Elin's ex-husband had been unlikely to see them. He did not appreciate the fruits of his hard-earned cash being disparaged.

His state of mind was not entirely propitious, therefore, when he headed off to Mayfair at eight o'clock that evening, wearing his best Italian suit, thoughts of a serial killer still chasing each other around his overtired brain.

Upper Brook Street comprised grand eighteenth-century houses and the frontage of Le Gavroche, with its wrought iron canopy and ivy-covered railings, the expensive solidity and security implied by its heavy mirrored front door, was dissonant to Strike's uneasy frame of mind. Elin arrived shortly after he had been seated in the green and red dining room, which was artfully lit so that puddles of light fell only where needed onto snow-white tablecloths, over gilt-framed oil paintings. She looked stunning in a pale blue form-fitting dress. As he rose to kiss her, Strike momentarily forgot his latent unease, his disgruntlement.

'This makes a nice change,' she said, smiling, as she sank down onto the curved, upholstered bench at their round table.

They ordered. Strike, who craved a pint of Doom Bar, drank burgundy of Elin's choosing and wished, despite having smoked more than a pack that day, that he could have a cigarette. Meanwhile, his dinner companion launched into a barrage of property talk: she had decided against the Strata penthouse and had now looked at a property in Camberwell, which seemed promising. She showed him a picture on her phone: another columned and porticoed vision of Georgian whiteness met his tired eyes.

As Elin discussed the various pros and cons of a move to Camberwell, Strike drank in silence. He even begrudged the wine's deliciousness, throwing it back like the cheapest plonk, trying to blunt the edges of his resentment with alcohol. It did not work: far from dissolving, his sense of alienation deepened. The comfortable Mayfair restaurant with its low lighting and its deep carpet felt like a stage set: illusory, ephemeral. What was he doing here, with this gorgeous but dull woman? Why was he pretending to be interested in her expensive lifestyle, when his business was in its death throes and he alone in London knew the identity of the Shacklewell Ripper?

Their food arrived and the deliciousness of his fillet of beef did something to assuage his resentment.

'So what have you been up to?' asked Elin, punctiliously polite as usual.

Strike now found himself presented with a stark choice. Telling her the truth about what he had been up to would necessitate an admission that he had not kept her abreast of any of the recent events that would have been deemed enough news for a decade in most people's lives. He would be forced to reveal that the girl in the newspapers who had survived the Ripper's latest attack was his own business partner. He would have to tell her that he had been warned off the case by a man whom he had previously humiliated over another high-profile murder. If he were making a clean breast of all that he had been up to, he ought also to add that he now knew exactly who the killer was. The prospect of relating all this bored and oppressed him. He had not once thought to call her while any of these events had unfolded, which was revealing enough in itself.

Playing for time while he took another sip of wine, Strike came to the decision that the affair had to end. He would make an excuse not to go back to Clarence Terrace with her tonight, which ought to give her early warning of his intentions; the sex had been the best part of the relationship all along. Then, next time they met, he'd tell her it was over. Not only did he feel it would be churlish to end things over a meal for which she was paying, there was a remote chance that she would walk out, leaving him with a bill that his credit card company would undoubtedly refuse to process.

'I haven't been up to much, to be honest,' he lied.

'What about the Shackle—'

Strike's mobile rang. He pulled it out of his jacket pocket and saw that the number had been withheld. Some sixth sense told him to answer it.

'Sorry,' he said to Elin, 'I think I need to—'

'Strike,' said Carver's unmistakable South London voice. 'Did you send her to do it?'

'What?' said Strike.

'Your fucking partner. Did you send her to Brockbank?'

Strike stood up so suddenly that he hit the edge of the table. A spray of bloodied brown liquid spattered across the heavy white tablecloth, his fillet of beef slid over the edge of the plate and his wine glass toppled, splashing Elin's pale blue dress. The waiter gaped, as did the refined couple at the next table.

'Where is she? What's happened?' asked Strike loudly, oblivious to everything except the voice on the end of the line.

'I warned you, Strike,' said Carver, his voice crackling with rage. 'I fucking warned you to stay away. You have fucked up royally this time—'

Strike lowered the mobile. A disembodied Carver bellowed into the restaurant, the 'cunts' and 'fucks' clearly audible to anybody standing nearby. He turned to Elin in her purple-stained dress, with her beautiful face screwed up in mingled perplexity and anger.

'I've got to go. I'm sorry. I'll call you later.'

He did not stay to see how she took it; he did not care.

Limping slightly, because he had twisted his knee in his haste to get up, Strike hurried out of the restaurant, phone to his ear again. Carver was now virtually incoherent, shouting Strike down whenever he attempted to speak.

'Carver, listen,' Strike shouted as he regained Upper Brook Street, 'there's something I want to – fucking listen, will you!'

But the policeman's obscenity-strewn soliloquy merely became louder and filthier.

'You fucking stupid fucking cunt, he's gone to ground – I know what you were fucking up to – we've found it, you bastard, we found the church connection! If you ever – shut your fucking mouth, I'm talking! – if you *ever* come near one of my fucking investigations again . . .'

Strike slogged on through the warm night, his knee protesting, frustration and fury mounting with every step he took.

It took him nearly an hour to reach Robin's flat in Hastings Road, by which time he was in full possession of the facts. Thanks to Carver, he knew that the police had been with Robin this evening and were perhaps still there, interrogating her about the intrusion into Brockbank's house that had led to a report of child rape and the flight of their suspect. Brockbank's photograph had been widely disseminated across the force, but he had not, as yet, been apprehended.

Strike had not warned Robin that he was coming. Turning into Hastings Road as fast as his limp would allow, he saw through the fading light that all the windows of her flat were lit. As he approached, two police officers, unmistakable even in plain clothes, emerged from the front entrance. The sound of the front door closing echoed down the quiet street. Strike moved into the shadows as the police crossed the road to their car, talking quietly to each other. Once they had pulled safely away, he proceeded to the white front door and rang the bell.

'. . . thought we were done,' said Matthew's exasperated voice behind the door. Strike doubted that he knew that he could be heard, because when he opened it Robin's fiancé was wearing an ingratiating smile that vanished the moment he realised who it was.

'What d'you want?'

'I need to talk to Robin,' said Strike.

As Matthew hesitated, with every appearance of wishing to block Strike's entrance, Linda came out into the hall behind him.

'Oh,' she said at the sight of Strike.

He thought she looked both thinner and older than the previous time he had met her, no doubt because her daughter had nearly got herself killed, then turned up voluntarily at a violent sexual predator's house and got attacked all over again. Strike could feel the fury building beneath his diaphragm. If necessary, he would shout for Robin to come and meet him on the doorstep, but he had no sooner formed this resolution than she appeared behind Matthew. She too looked paler and thinner than usual. As always, he found her better-looking in the flesh than in the memory he had of her when not present. This did not make him feel any more kindly towards her.

'Oh,' she said in exactly the same colourless tone as her mother.

'I'd like a word,' said Strike.

'All right,' said Robin with a slightly defiant upwards jerk of her head that made her red-gold hair dance around her shoulders. She glanced at her mother and Matthew, then back at Strike. 'D'you want to come into the kitchen, then?'

He followed her down the hall into the small kitchen where

a table for two stood crammed into the corner. Robin closed the door carefully behind them. Neither sat down. Dirty dishes were piled by the sink; they had apparently been eating pasta before the police arrived to interrogate Robin. For some reason, this evidence that Robin had been behaving so prosaically in the wake of the chaos she had unleashed increased the rage now battling with Strike's desire not to lose control.

'I told you,' he said, 'not to go anywhere near Brockbank.'

'Yes,' said Robin in a flat voice that aggravated him still further. 'I remember.'

Strike wondered whether Linda and Matthew were listening at the door. The small kitchen smelled strongly of garlic and tomatoes. An England Rugby calendar hung on the wall behind Robin. The thirtieth of June was circled thickly, the words HOME FOR WEDDING written beneath the date.

'But you decided to go anyway,' said Strike.

Visions of violent, cathartic action – picking up the pedal bin and throwing it through the steamy window, for instance – were rising chaotically in his mind's eye. He stood quite still, large feet planted on the scuffed lino, staring at her white and stubborn face.

'I don't regret it,' she said. 'He was raping—'

'Carver's convinced I sent you. Brockbank's vanished. You've driven him underground. How're you going to feel if he decides he'd better cut the next one into pieces before she can blab?'

'Don't you dare put that on me!' said Robin, her voice rising. 'Don't you dare! You're the one who punched him when you went to arrest him! If you hadn't hit him he might've gone down for Brittany!'

'That makes what you did right, does it?'

He refrained from shouting only because he could hear Matthew lurking in the hall, however quiet the accountant thought he was being.

'I've stopped Angel being abused and if that's a bad thing to do—'

'You've driven my business off the edge of a fucking cliff,' said Strike in a quiet voice that stopped her in her tracks. 'We were warned away from those suspects, from the whole investigation, but you went storming in and now Brockbank's gone to ground. The press'll be all over me for this. Carver'll tell them I've fucked it all up. They'll bury me. And even if you don't give a shit about any of that,' said Strike, his face rigid with fury, 'how about the fact the police have just found a connection between Kelsey's church and the one in Brixton where Brockbank was attending?'

She looked stricken.

'I – I didn't know—'

'Why wait for the facts?' asked Strike, his eyes dark shadows in the harsh overhead lighting. 'Why not just blunder in and tip him off before the police can take him in?'

Appalled, Robin said nothing. Strike was looking at her now as though he never liked her, as though they had never shared any of the experiences that, to her, had constituted a bond like no other. She had been prepared for him to punch walls and cupboards again, even, in the heat of his anger, to—

'We're finished,' said Strike.

He took some satisfaction from the shrinking movement she could not hide, from the sudden blanching of her face.

'You don't—'

'I don't mean it? You think I need a partner who won't take instruction, who does what I've explicitly told her not to do, who makes me look like a trouble-making egotistical prick in front of the police and causes a murder suspect to disappear under the force's nose?'

He said it in a single breath and Robin, who had taken a step backwards, knocked the England Rugby calendar off the wall with a rustle and thud she failed to hear, so loudly was the blood pounding in her ears. She thought she might faint. She had imagined him shouting 'I ought to fire you!' but not once had she considered that he might actually do it, that everything she had done for him – the risks, the injuries, the insights and the inspirations, the long hours of discomfort and inconvenience – would be washed away, rendered negligible by this one act of well-intentioned disobedience. She could not even get enough breath into her lungs to argue, because his expression was such that she knew all she could expect was further icy condemnation of her actions and an exposition of how badly she had screwed up. The memory of Angel and Alyssa holding each other on the sofa, the reflection that Angel's suffering was finished and that her mother believed and supported her, had comforted Robin through the hours of suspense during which she waited for this blow to fall. She had not dared tell Strike what she had done. Now she thought it might have been better if she had.

'What?' she said stupidly, because he had asked her something. The noises had been meaningless.

'*Who was the man you took with you?*'

'That's none of your business,' she whispered after a short hesitation.

'They said he threatened Brockbank with a kni— Shanker!' said Strike, light dawning only now, and in that instant she saw a trace of the Strike she knew in the reanimated, infuriated face. '*How the fuck did you get Shanker's number?*'

But she could not speak. Nothing mattered beside the fact that she was fired. She knew that Strike did not relent when he decided that a relationship had run its course. His girlfriend of sixteen years had never heard from him again after he had ended it, although Charlotte had tried to initiate contact since.

He was already leaving. She followed him into the hall on

numb legs, feeling herself to be acting like a beaten dog who still slinks after the punisher, hoping desperately for forgiveness.

'Goodnight,' Strike called to Linda and Matthew, who had retreated into the sitting room.

'Cormoran,' Robin whispered.

'I'll send your last month's salary on,' he said without looking at her. 'Quick and clean. Gross misconduct.'

The door closed behind him. She could hear his size fourteens moving away up the path. With a gasp, she began to cry. Linda and Matthew both came hurrying into the hall, but too late: Robin had fled to the bedroom, unable to face their relief and delight that, at last, she would have to give up her dream of being a detective.

56

When life's scorned and damage done
To avenge, this is the pact.

Blue Öyster Cult, 'Vengeance (The Pact)'

Half past four the following morning found Strike awake after virtually no sleep. His tongue ached from the amount of smoking he had done overnight at the Formica table in his kitchen, while contemplating the decimation of his business and his prospects. He could barely bring himself to think about Robin. Fine cracks, like those in thick ice during a thaw, were starting to appear in what had been implacable fury, but what lay beneath was scarcely less cold. He could understand the impulse to save the child – who couldn't? Hadn't he, as she had so injudiciously pointed out, knocked Brockbank out cold after viewing Brittany's taped evidence? – but the thought of her heading off with Shanker, without telling him, and after Carver had warned them not to go anywhere near the suspects, made rage thunder through his veins all over again as he upended his cigarette pack and found it empty.

He pulled himself to his feet, picked up his keys and left the flat, still wearing the Italian suit in which he had dozed. The sun was coming up as he trudged down Charing Cross Road in a dawn that made everything look dusty and fragile, a grey light full of pale shadows. He bought cigarettes in a corner shop in Covent Garden and continued to walk, smoking and thinking.

After two hours spent walking the streets, Strike reached a decision about his next move. Heading back towards the office, he saw a waitress in a black dress unlocking the doors to the Caffè Vergnano 1882 on Charing Cross Road, realised how hungry he was and turned inside.

The small coffee shop smelled of warm wood and espresso. As Strike sank gratefully onto a hard oak chair he became uncomfortably aware that for the past thirteen hours he had smoked ceaselessly, slept in his clothes and eaten steak and drunk red wine without cleaning his teeth. The man in the reflection beside him looked crumpled and grimy. He tried not to give the young waitress any opportunity to smell his breath as he ordered a ham and cheese panini, a bottle of water and a double espresso.

As the copper-domed coffee maker on the counter hissed into life, Strike sank into a reverie, searching his conscience for a truthful answer to an uncomfortable question.

Was he any better than Carver? Was he contemplating a high-risk and dangerous course of action because he really thought it the only way to stop the killer? Or was he inclining to the higher-stakes option because he knew that if he brought it off – if he were the one to catch and incriminate the murderer – it would reverse all the damage done to his reputation and his business, restoring to him the lustre of a man who succeeded where the Met failed? Was it, in short, necessity or ego that was driving him towards what many would say was a reckless and foolish measure?

The waitress set his sandwich and coffee in front of him and

Strike began to eat with the glazed stare of a man too preoccupied even to taste what he was chewing.

This was as well-publicised a series of crimes as Strike had ever come into contact with: the police would currently be flooded with information and leads, all of which needed following up and none of which (Strike was prepared to bet) would lead anywhere near the real devious and successful killer.

He still had the option of trying to make contact with one of Carver's superiors, although he was now in such poor odour with the police that he doubted he would be allowed direct speech with a superintendent, whose first loyalty would of course be to his own men. Trying to circumnavigate Carver would do nothing to diminish the impression that he was trying to undermine the head of the investigation.

What was more, Strike did not have evidence, merely a theory about where the evidence was. While there was a remote chance that somebody at the Met might take Strike seriously enough to go looking for what he promised they would find, Strike feared that further delay might cost another life.

He was surprised to find that he had finished his panini. Still extremely hungry, he ordered a second.

No, he thought, with sudden resolve, *this is the way it's got to be.*

This animal needed to be stopped as soon as possible. It was time to get out ahead of him for the first time. However, as a sop to his conscience, as a proof to himself that he was motivated primarily by catching a killer rather than by glory, Strike took out his mobile again and called Detective Inspector Richard Anstis, his oldest acquaintance on the force. He was not on the best terms with Anstis these days, but Strike wanted to be certain in his own mind that he had done all he could to allow the Met the chance to do the job for him.

After a long pause, a foreign dialling tone sounded in his ear. Nobody picked up. Anstis was on holiday. Strike debated leaving a voicemail and decided against. Leaving such a message on Anstis's phone when there was nothing the man could do would definitely ruin his holiday, and from what Strike knew of Anstis's wife and three children, the man needed one.

Hanging up, he scrolled absent-mindedly through his recent calls. Carver had not left his number. Robin's name sat a few rows beneath. The sight of it stabbed the tired and desperate Strike to the heart because he was simultaneously furious with her and longing to talk to her. Setting the mobile resolutely back onto the table, he shoved his hand into his inside jacket pocket and pulled out a pen and notebook.

Eating his second sandwich as fast as his first, Strike began to write a list.

1) Write to Carver.

This was partly a further sop to his own conscience and partly what he generally termed 'arse-covering'. He doubted the ability of an email to find its way to Carver, whose direct address he did not have, through the tsunami of tip-offs now sure to be pouring into Scotland Yard. People were culturally disposed to take ink and paper seriously, especially when it had to be signed for: an old-fashioned letter, sent recorded delivery, would be sure to find its way to Carver's desk. Strike would then have laid a trail just as the killer had done, demonstrating very clearly that he had tried every possible route to tell Carver how the killer might be stopped. This was likely to be useful when they all found themselves in court, which Strike did not doubt would happen whether or not the plan he had formulated, walking through the dawn in sleepy Covent Garden, was successful.

2) Gas canister (propane?)
3) Fluorescent jacket
4) Woman – who?

He paused, arguing with himself, scowling over the paper. After much thought, he reluctantly wrote:

5) Shanker

This meant that the next item had to be:

6) £500 (from where?)

And finally, after a further minute's thought:

7) Advertise for Robin replacement.

57

> Sole survivor, cursed with second sight,
> Haunted savior, cried into the night.
>
> Blue Öyster Cult, 'Sole Survivor'

Four days passed. Numb with shock and misery, Robin at first hoped and even believed that Strike would call her, that he would regret what he had said to her, that he would realise what a mistake he had made. Linda had left, kind and supportive to the last, but, Robin suspected, secretly happy to think that Robin's association with the detective had ended.

Matthew had expressed enormous sympathy in the face of Robin's devastation. He said that Strike did not know how lucky he had been. He had enumerated for her all the things she had done for the detective, foremost of which was accepting a laughably small salary for unreasonably long hours. He reminded Robin that her status as partner in the agency had been entirely illusory, and totted up all the proofs of Strike's lack of respect for her: the absence of a partnership agreement, the lack of overtime pay, the fact that she always seemed to be the one who made tea and went out to buy sandwiches.

A week previously, Robin would have defended Strike

against all such accusations. She would have said that the nature of the work necessitated long hours, that the moment to demand a pay rise was not when the business was fighting for its very survival, that Strike made her mugs of tea quite as often as she made them for him. She might have added that Strike had spent money he could ill afford training her in surveillance and counter-surveillance, and that it was unreasonable to expect him, as senior partner, sole investor and founding member of the agency, to place her on absolutely equal legal footing with himself.

Yet she said none of those things, because the last two words that Strike had spoken to her were with her every day like the sound of her own heartbeat: *gross misconduct*. The memory of Strike's expression in that last moment helped her pretend that she saw things exactly as Matthew did, that her dominant emotion was anger, that the job which had meant everything to her could be easily replaced, that Strike had no integrity or moral sense if he could not appreciate that Angel's safety trumped all other considerations. Robin had neither the will or the energy to point out that Matthew had performed an abrupt volte-face on the last point, because he had been furious, initially, when he had found out that she had gone to Brockbank's.

As the days went by without any contact from Strike, she felt unspoken pressure from her fiancé to pretend that the prospect of their wedding on Saturday not only made up for her recent sacking, but consumed all her thoughts. Having to fake excitement while he was present made Robin relieved to be alone during the day while Matthew worked. Every evening, before he returned, she deleted the search history on her laptop, so that he would not see that she was constantly looking for news about the Shacklewell Ripper online and – just as often – Googling Strike.

On the day before she and Matthew were due to leave for

Masham, he arrived home holding a copy of the *Sun*, which was not his usual read.

'Why have you got that?'

Matthew hesitated before answering and Robin's insides twisted.

'There hasn't been another—?'

But she knew there had not been another killing: she had been following the news all day.

He opened the paper, folded it to a page about ten in, and handed it to her, his expression hard to read. Robin found herself staring at her own photograph. She was walking with her head down in the picture, dressed in her trench coat, leaving court after giving evidence at the well-publicised trial of the murderer of Owen Quine. Two smaller pictures were set into her own: one of Strike, looking hungover, the other of the spectacularly beautiful model whose killer they had worked together to catch. Beneath the photo spread were the words:

LANDRY DETECTIVE SEEKS NEW GIRL FRIDAY

Cormoran Strike, the detective who solved the murder cases of both supermodel Lula Landry and author Owen Quine, has parted company with glamorous assistant Robin Ellacott, 26.

The detective has placed an advertisement for the position online: 'If you have a background in police or military investigative work and would like to pursue—

There were several more paragraphs, but Robin could not bear to read them. Instead, she looked at the byline, which was that of Dominic Culpepper, a journalist whom Strike knew personally. Possibly he had called Culpepper, who often badgered Strike for stories, and let him have this one, to make sure his need for a new assistant was disseminated as widely as possible.

Robin had not thought that she could feel any worse, but now she discovered that she had been mistaken. She really was sacked, after everything that she had done for him. She had been a disposable 'Girl Friday', an 'assistant' – never a partner, never an equal – and now he was already looking for somebody with a background in the police or the military: somebody disciplined, someone who would take orders.

Rage gripped her; everything blurred, the hall, the newspaper, Matthew standing there trying to look sympathetic, and Robin had to physically resist the impulse to dive into the sitting room, where her mobile sat charging on a side table, and call Strike. She had thought of doing so many times in the last four days, but then it had been to ask – to beg – him to reconsider.

Not any more. Now she wanted to shout at him, belittle him, accuse him of base ingratitude, hypocrisy, lack of honour—

Her burning eyes met Matthew's and she saw, before he rearranged his expression, how delighted he was that Strike had put himself so dramatically in the wrong. Matthew, she could tell, had looked forward to showing her the newspaper. Her anguish was nothing compared to his ecstasy at her separation from Strike.

She turned away, heading for the kitchen, resolving that she would not shout at Matthew. If they rowed it would feel like a triumph for Strike. She refused to allow her ex-boss to sully her relationship with the man whom she had to – the man whom she *wanted* to marry in three days' time. Clumsily dumping a saucepan of spaghetti into a colander, Robin spattered herself with boiling water and swore.

'Pasta again?' said Matthew.

'Yes,' said Robin coldly. 'Is that a problem?'

'God, no,' said Matthew, approaching her from behind

and putting his arms around her. 'I love you,' he said into her hair.

'I love you too,' said Robin mechanically.

The Land Rover was packed with everything they would need for their stay up north, for the wedding night at Swinton Park Hotel and for their honeymoon 'somewhere hot', which was all that Robin knew about the destination. They set off at ten o'clock the following morning, both wearing T-shirts in the bright sunshine, and as Robin got into the car she remembered that misty morning in April when she had driven away, Matthew in hot pursuit, when she had been desperate to get away, to get to Strike.

She was a much better driver than Matthew, but when the two of them made a journey together, he always took the wheel. Matthew sang Daniel Bedingfield's 'Never Gonna Leave Your Side' as he turned onto the M1. An old song, it dated from the year that they had both started university.

'Could you not sing that?' said Robin suddenly, unable to bear it any longer.

'Sorry,' he said, startled. 'It seemed appropriate.'

'Maybe it's got happy memories for you,' said Robin, turning to look out of the window, 'but it hasn't for me.'

Out of the corner of her eye she saw Matthew look at her, then turn back to the road. After another mile or so she wished she had not said anything.

'That doesn't mean you can't sing something else.'

'That's all right,' he said.

The temperature had fallen slightly by the time they reached Donington Park Services, where they stopped for a coffee. Robin left her jacket hanging over the back of her chair when she went to the bathroom. Alone, Matthew stretched, his T-shirt riding up out of his jeans to reveal a few inches of flat stomach and drawing the attention of the girl serving behind the Costa Coffee bar. Feeling good about himself and life, Matthew grinned and winked at her. She turned red, giggled and turned to her smirking fellow barista, who had seen.

The phone in Robin's jacket rang. Assuming that it was Linda trying to find out how close they were to home, Matthew reached lazily across – conscious of the girls' eyes upon him – and tugged the phone out of Robin's pocket.

It was Strike.

Matthew looked at the vibrating device as though he had inadvertently picked up a tarantula. The phone continued to ring and vibrate in his hand. He looked around: Robin was nowhere to be seen. He answered the call, then immediately cut it. Now *Corm Missed Call* was written across the screen.

The big ugly bastard wanted Robin back, Matthew was sure of it. Strike had had five long days to realise he'd never get anyone better. Maybe he'd started interviewing people for the position and nobody had come close, or maybe all of them had laughed in his face at the pitiful salary he was offering.

The phone rang again: Strike was calling back, trying to make sure that the hanging up had been deliberate rather than accidental. Matthew looked at the mobile, paralysed with indecision. He dared not answer on Robin's behalf or tell Strike to fuck off. He knew Strike: he'd keep calling back until he spoke to Robin.

The call went to voicemail. Now Matthew realised that a recorded apology was the worst thing that could happen: Robin could listen to it again and again and finally be worn down and softened by it . . .

He looked up: Robin was returning from the Ladies. With her phone in his hand he stood up and pretended to be talking into it.

'It's Dad,' he lied to Robin, placing a hand over the

mouthpiece and praying that Strike would not call back again while he was standing in front of her. 'Mine's out of battery . . . listen, what's your passcode? I need to look something up for the honeymoon flights – it's to tell Dad—'

She gave it to him.

'Give me a sec, I don't want you to hear anything about the honeymoon,' he said and walked away from her, torn between guilt and pride in his own quick thinking.

Once safe inside the men's bathroom, he opened up her phone. Getting rid of any record of Strike's calls meant deleting her entire call history – this he did. Then he called voicemail, listened to Strike's recorded message and deleted that too. Finally, he went into the settings on Robin's phone and blocked Strike.

Breathing deeply he turned to his handsome reflection in the mirror. Strike had said on the voicemail message that if he did not hear back from her he would not call again. The wedding was in forty-eight hours' time, and the anxious, defiant Matthew was counting on Strike keeping his word.

58

Deadline

He was pumped up, on edge, pretty sure he had just done something stupid. As the Tube train rattled south, his knuckles whitened because he was clutching the hanging strap so tightly. Behind his shades, his puffy, reddened eyes squinted at the station signs.

Its shrill voice still seemed to be piercing his eardrum.

'I don't believe you. Where's the money, then, if you've got night work? No – I want to talk to you – no – you're not going out again—'

He had hit her. He shouldn't have done it, he knew that: the vision of her appalled face was taunting him now, her eyes wide with shock, her hand clamped over the cheek where his fingermarks were turning red against the white.

It was her own fucking fault. He hadn't been able to stop himself, not after the last couple of weeks, during which It had become more and more strident. After he'd come home with his eyes full of red ink he'd pretended to have had an allergic reaction, but there'd been no sympathy from the cold bitch. All It had done was carp about where he'd been and – for the first time – ask where the money was that he claimed to be earning. There hadn't been much time for theft with the boys lately, not with all his time devoted to hunting.

She'd brought home a newspaper with a news story in it about the fact that the Shacklewell Ripper might now have red ink stains around his eyes. He had burned the paper in the garden, but he couldn't stop her reading the story elsewhere. The day before yesterday, he thought he'd surprised It watching him with an odd expression on her face. It wasn't stupid, not really; was It starting to wonder? This anxiety was the last thing he needed when his attempt on The Secretary had left him almost humiliated.

There was no point going after The Secretary any more, because she had left Strike for ever. He had seen the story online, in the internet café where he sometimes whiled away an hour, just to get away from It. He took some consolation from the idea that his machete had frightened her off, that she would bear for ever the long scar down her forearm that he had carved there, but that wasn't good enough.

His months and months of careful planning had all been with the intention of entangling Strike in murder, tarring him with suspicion. Firstly, embroil him in the death of the stupid little bitch who'd wanted her leg cut off, so that the police swarmed all over him and the dumb public thought he'd had something to do with it. Then, murder his Secretary. Let him try and limp away from that untainted. Let him try and be the famous detective after that.

But the bastard kept wriggling free. There had been no mention of the letters in the press, the letter he had carefully written out 'from' Kelsey, and which had been supposed to turn Strike into suspect number one. Then the press had colluded with the fucker, not giving out The Secretary's name, not drawing the connection between her and Strike.

Perhaps it might be wise to stop now . . . except that he could not stop. He had come too far. He had never in his life put so much planning into anything as he had into the ruination of Strike. The fat, crippled bastard had already advertised for somebody to replace The Secretary, and that didn't look like a man who was about to go out of business.

One good thing, though: there was no sign of a police presence around Denmark Street any more. Someone had called them off. They probably thought nobody was needed now that The Secretary had gone.

Perhaps he ought not to have returned to Strike's place of work, but he had hoped to see the frightened Secretary leaving with a box in her hands, or get a glimpse of a downcast, beaten Strike, but no – shortly after he'd taken up a well-concealed position to watch the street, the bastard had come striding along Charing Cross Road with a stunning-looking woman, apparently completely unperturbed.

The girl had to be a temp, because Strike had not had time to interview and hire a permanent replacement. No doubt the Big Man needed somebody to open his mail. She wore heels that would not have disgraced that little hooker, teetering along, waggling a fine arse. He liked them dark, he always had. In fact, given the choice, he'd have taken someone like her any time over The Secretary.

She hadn't had surveillance training; that much was clear. He had watched Strike's office all morning after his first glimpse of her, watched her nipping out to the post and back, nearly always on the phone, oblivious to her surroundings, so busy tossing her long hair over her shoulders that she was unable to keep eye contact with anyone for long, dropping her keys, gabbling at the top of her voice on her phone or to anyone else with whom she came into casual contact. At one o'clock he had slipped into the sandwich shop behind her and heard her making noisy plans to go to Corsica Studios the following evening.

He knew what Corsica Studios was. He knew *where* it was. Excitement ripped through him: he had to turn his back on her, pretending to look out of the window, because he thought the expression on his face would give it away to all of them . . . If he did her while she was still working for Strike, he'd have fulfilled his plan: Strike would be connected to two hacked-up women and nobody, police or public, would ever trust him again.

This would be so much easier too. The Secretary had been a fucking nightmare to pick off, always alert and streetwise, going home by crowded, well-lit paths every evening to her pretty boyfriend, but The Temp was offering herself up on a plate. After telling the whole sandwich shop where she would be meeting her mates, she had strutted back to work on her Perspex heels, dropping Strike's sandwiches once on the way. He noticed that there was no wedding or engagement ring on her finger as she bent to pick them up. He had been hard pressed to suppress his jubilation as he peeled away, formulating his plan.

If only he hadn't slapped It, he'd be feeling good now, excited, elated. The slap hadn't been an auspicious start to the evening. No wonder he felt jumpy. There had been no time to stay and calm her down, turn her sweet: he had simply walked out, determined to get to The Temp, but he still felt jumpy . . . What if It called the police?

She wouldn't. It had only been a slap. She loved him, she told him so all the time. When they loved you, they let you get away with fucking murder . . .

He experienced a tickling sensation at the back of his neck and looked around with the wild idea that he would see Strike looking at him from the corner of the carriage, but nobody remotely resembling that fat bastard was there, only several ill-kempt men grouped together. One of them, who had a scarred face and a gold tooth, was indeed watching him, but as he squinted back through his shades the man ceased his scrutiny and returned to fiddling with his mobile . . .

Perhaps he should call It when he got off the Tube, before heading for Corsica Studios, and tell It he loved her.

59

With threats of gas and rose motif.

Blue Öyster Cult, 'Before the Kiss'

Strike was standing in shadow, his mobile in his hand, waiting. The deep pocket of his second-hand jacket, which was far too heavy in the warmth of this June evening, bulged and sagged with the weight of an object he was keen to conceal. What he planned would be best accomplished under cover of darkness, but the sun was taking its time to sink behind the ill-assorted rooftops visible from his hiding place.

He knew he ought to be concentrating only upon the dangerous business of the night, but his thoughts kept slinking back to Robin. She had not returned his call. He had set a mental deadline for himself: if she doesn't ring by the end of this evening, she's never calling. At twelve o'clock the following day she would be getting married to Matthew in Yorkshire, and Strike was sure that constituted a fatal cut-off point. If they did not speak before that ring landed on her finger, he thought that they were unlikely ever to speak again. If anything in the world had been calculated to make him recognise what he had lost, it had been the truculent, noisy presence of the woman with whom he had shared his office for the last few days, staggeringly good-looking though she was.

To the west, the sky over the rooftops blazed with colours as bright as a parakeet's wing: scarlet, orange, even a faint trace of green. Behind this flamboyant show came a pale wash of violet faintly strewn with stars. Almost time to move.

As though Shanker had heard his thought, Strike's mobile vibrated and he looked to see a message:

Pint tomorrow?

They had agreed on a code. If all of this came to court, which Strike thought overwhelmingly likely, his intention was to keep Shanker well away from the witness box. There must be no incriminating messages between them tonight. 'Pint tomorrow?' meant 'he's in the club'.

Strike slid the mobile back into his pocket and emerged from his hiding place, crossing the dark car park that lay beneath the deserted flat of Donald Laing. The Strata building looked down upon him as he walked, vast and black, its jagged windows reflecting the last traces of bloody light.

Fine netting had been stretched over the front of the balconies of Wollaston Close to prevent birds landing on them and flying in through open doors and windows. Strike moved around to the side entrance, which he had earlier wedged open after a group of teenage girls had left it. Nobody had tampered with the arrangement. People assumed that somebody needed their hands free and feared triggering their wrath. An angry neighbour could be quite as dangerous as an intruder round here, and you had to live with them afterwards.

Halfway up the stairs, Strike stripped off his jacket to reveal a fluorescent one. Carrying the first so that it concealed the canister of propane inside, he proceeded on his way, emerging onto the balcony of Laing's flat.

Lights shone from the homes sharing the balcony. Laing's neighbours had opened their windows on this warm summer evening, so that their voices and the sounds of their TVs floated out into the night. Strike walked quietly past towards the dark, empty flat at the end. Outside the door he had so often watched from the car park, he shifted the gas canister wrapped in his jacket into the crook of his left arm and withdrew from his pocket firstly a pair of latex gloves, which he put on, then a mismatched assortment of tools, some of which belonged to Strike himself, but many of which had been lent for the occasion by Shanker. These included a mortice skeleton key, two sets of jigglers and assorted comb picks.

As Strike set to work on the two locks on Laing's front door a female, American voice floated out into the night through the neighbouring window.

'There's the law and there's what's right. I'm gonna do what's right.'

'What wouldn't I give to fuck Jessica Alba?' asked a stoned male voice, to laughter and agreement from what sounded like two other men.

'Come on, you bastard,' breathed Strike, fighting with the lower of the two locks and keeping a tight grip on the concealed propane canister. 'Move . . . *move* . . . '

The lock turned with a loud click. He pushed the door open.

As he had expected, the place smelled bad. Strike could make out very little in what looked like a dilapidated and unfurnished room. He needed to close the curtains before turning on the lights. Turning left, he immediately knocked into what felt like a box. Something heavy fell off the top and landed with a crash on the floor.

Fuck.

'Oi!' shouted a voice audible through the flimsy dividing wall. 'That you, Donnie?'

Strike hastened back to the door, felt frantically up and down the wall beside the doorjamb and found the light switch. Flooded suddenly with light, the room proved to contain nothing except an old, stained double mattress and an orange box on which an iPod dock had clearly been standing, because it now lay on the ground where it had fallen.

'Donnie?' said the voice, now coming from the balcony outside.

Strike pulled out the propane canister, discharged it and shoved it underneath the orange box. Footsteps from the balcony outside were followed by a knock on the door. Strike opened it.

A spotty, greasy-haired man looked hazily at him. He appeared extremely stoned and was holding a can of John Smith's.

'Jesus,' he said blearily, sniffing. ''S'that fucking smell?'

'Gas,' said Strike in his fluorescent jacket, stern representative of the National Grid. 'We've had a report from upstairs. Looks like this is where it's coming from.'

'Bloody hell,' said the neighbour, looking sick. 'Not going to blow up, are we?'

'That's what I'm here to find out,' Strike said sententiously. 'You haven't got any naked flames next door? Not smoking, are you?'

'I'll go make sure,' said the neighbour, looking suddenly terrified.

'All right. I might be in to check your place when I've finished here,' said Strike. 'I'm waiting for back-up.'

He regretted that phrase as soon as it had escaped him, but his new acquaintance did not seem to find such language odd from a gas man. As he turned away, Strike asked:

'Owner's name's Donnie, is it?'

'Donnie Laing,' said the jittery neighbour, clearly desperate to go and hide his stash and extinguish all naked flames. 'He owes me forty quid.'

'Ah,' said Strike. 'Can't help with that.'

The man scuttled off and Strike closed the door thanking his lucky stars that he'd had the forethought to provide himself with a cover. All he needed was for the police to be tipped off now, before he could prove anything . . .

He lifted up the orange box, shut off the hissing propane and then replaced the iPod in its dock on top of the box. About to move deeper into the flat, he had a sudden thought and turned back to the iPod. One delicate poke of his latex-covered forefinger and the tiny screen lit up. 'Hot Rails to Hell' by – as Strike knew only too well – Blue Öyster Cult.

60

Vengeance (The Pact)

The club was heaving with people. It had been constructed in two railway arches, just like those opposite his flat, and had a subterranean feel enhanced by the curved corrugated iron roof. A projector was throwing psychedelic lights across the ridges of metal. The music was deafening.

They had not been overly keen on letting him in. He'd had a bit of attitude from the bouncers: he had experienced a fleeting fear that they would pat him down, in his jacket with the knives concealed inside it.

He looked older than anybody else he could see and he resented it. That was what the psoriatic arthritis had done to him, leaving him pockmarked and blown up with steroids. His muscle had run to fat since his boxing days; he had pulled with ease back in Cyprus, but not any more. He knew he'd have no chance with any of these hundreds of giddy little bitches crammed together beneath the glitter ball. Hardly any of them were dressed the way he expected of a club. Many of them were in jeans and T-shirts, like a bunch of lesbians.

Where was Strike's temp, with her gorgeous arse and her

delicious distractibility? There weren't that many tall black women here; she ought to be easy to spot, yet he had combed bar and dance floor and seen no sign of her. It had seemed like providence, her mentioning this club so very close to his flat; he had thought it meant a return of his godlike status, the universe arranging itself once more for his benefit, but that feeling of invincibility had been fleeting and almost entirely dispelled by the argument with It.

The music thumped inside his head. He would rather have been back at home, listening to Blue Öyster Cult, masturbating over his relics, but he had *heard* her planning to be here ... fuck, it was so crowded that he might be able to press up against her and stab her without anyone noticing or hearing her scream ... Where was the bitch?

The tosser in the Wild Flag T-shirt had jostled him so many times he yearned to give him a good kicking. Instead he elbowed his way out of the bar to look at the dance floor again.

The shifting lights panned across a swaying carpet of arms and sweaty faces. A glint of gold – a scarred and sneering mouth—

He cleaved his way through onlookers, not caring how many little tarts he knocked aside.

That scarred guy had been on the Tube. He looked back. The man appeared to have lost someone; he was standing on tiptoe looking all around.

There was something wrong. He could feel it. Something fishy. Bending his knees slightly, the better to mingle with the crowd, he forced his way towards a fire exit.

'Sorry, mate, I need you to use the—'

'Fuck off.'

He was out of it before anyone could stop him, forcing the bar across the fire door, plunging out into the night. He jogged along the exterior wall and around a corner where, alone, he breathed deeply, considering his options.

You're safe, he told himself. *You're safe. No one's got anything on you.*

But was it true?

Of all the clubs she could have mentioned, she had chosen the one two minutes from his house. What if that had not been a gift from the gods but something entirely different? What if someone was trying to set him up?

No. It couldn't be. Strike had sent the pigs to him and they hadn't been interested. He was safe for sure. There was nothing to connect him to any of them . . .

Except that that guy with the scarred face had been on the Tube from Finchley. The implications of that temporarily jammed his thought processes. If somebody was following not Donald Laing but a completely different man, he was totally fucked . . .

He began to walk, every now and then breaking into a short run. The crutches that were so useful a prop were no longer necessary except for gaining the sympathy of gullible women, fooling the disability office and, of course, maintaining his cover as a man too sick and ill to go looking for little Kelsey Platt. His arthritis had burned itself out years back, though it had proved a pleasant little earner and kept the flat in Wollaston Close ticking over . . .

Hurrying across the car park, he looked up at his flat. The curtains were closed. He could have sworn he had left them open.

61

And now the time has come at last
To crush the motif of the rose.

Blue Öyster Cult, 'Before the Kiss, A Redcap'

The bulb was out in the only bedroom. Strike turned on the small torch he had brought with him and advanced slowly towards the only piece of furniture, a cheap pine wardrobe. The door creaked as he opened it.

The interior was plastered with articles from the newspapers about the Shacklewell Ripper. Taped above all of them was a picture that had been printed on a piece of A4 paper, possibly from the internet. Strike's young mother, naked, arms over her head, her long cloud of dark hair not quite covering her breasts proudly displayed, an arch of curly script clearly visible over the dark triangle of pubic hair: *Mistress of the Salmon Salt.*

He looked down at the floor of the wardrobe where a pile of hard-core pornography sat beside a black bin bag. Putting the torch under his arm, Strike opened the latter with his latex-gloved hands. Inside was a small selection of women's underclothing, some of it stiff with old brown blood. At the very bottom of the bag his fingers closed on a fine chain and a hoop earring. A heart-shaped harp charm glinted in the light of his torch. There was a trace of dry blood on the hoop.

Strike replaced everything in the black bin bag, closed the wardrobe door and continued to the kitchenette, which was clearly the source of the rotting smell that pervaded the entire place.

Somebody had turned up the TV next door. An echoing tirade of gunshots sounded through the thin wall. Strike heard faint, stoned laughter.

Beside the kettle sat a jar of instant coffee, a bottle of Bell's, a magnifying mirror and a razor. The oven was thick with grease and dust, and looked as though it had not been used for a long time. The fridge door had been wiped down with a dirty cloth that had left behind it sweeping arcs of a pinkish residue. Strike had just reached for the handle when his mobile vibrated in his pocket.

Shanker was calling him. They had agreed not to phone each other, but only to text.

'Fucking hell, Shanker,' said Strike, raising the mobile to his ear. 'I thought I said—'

He heard the breathing behind him a bare second before a machete came swinging through the air at his neck. Strike dived sideways, the mobile flying out of his hand, and slipped on the dirty floor. As he fell, the slashing blade sliced into his ear. The hulking shadow raised the machete again to attack Strike as he landed on the floor; Strike kicked out at its crotch and the killer grunted in pain, backed off a couple of paces, then raised the machete once more.

Scrambling to his knees, Strike punched his assailant hard in the balls. The machete slid out of Laing's fingers and fell onto Strike's back, causing him to shout out in pain even as he put his arms around Laing's knees and toppled him. Laing's head collided with the cooker door but his thick fingers were scrabbling for Strike's throat. Strike tried to land a punch but was pinned down by Laing's considerable weight. The man's large, powerful hands were closing on his windpipe. With a gigantic effort Strike mustered enough force to headbutt Laing, whose skull again clanged off the oven door—

They rolled over, Strike now on top. He tried to punch Laing in the face but the other's reactions were as quick as they had been in the ring: one hand deflected the blow and his other was under Strike's chin, forcing his face upwards – Strike swung again, unable to see where he was aiming, hit bone and heard it crack—

Then Laing's large fist came out of nowhere, bang into the middle of Strike's face, and he felt his nose shatter; blood spurted everywhere as he rocked backwards with the force of the punch, his eyes watering so that everything blurred: groaning and panting, Laing threw him off – from nowhere, like a conjuror, he produced a carving knife—

Half blinded, blood pouring into his mouth, Strike saw it glimmer in the moonlight and kicked out with his prosthetic leg – there was a muffled chink of metal on metal as the knife hit the steel rod of his ankle and was raised again—

'*No, you don't, you fucker!*'

Shanker had Laing in a headlock from behind. Ill-advisedly, Strike grabbed for the carving knife and got his palm sliced open. Shanker and Laing were wrestling, the Scot by far the larger of the two and rapidly getting the better of it. Strike took another powerful kick at the carving knife with his prosthetic foot and this time knocked it clean out of Laing's hand. Now he could help Shanker wrestle him to the ground.

'Give it up or I'll fuckin' knife ya!' bellowed Shanker, arms around Laing's neck as the Scot writhed and swore, his heavy fists still clenched, his broken jaw sagging. 'You ain't the only one with a fucking blade, you fat piece of shit!'

Strike tugged out the handcuffs that were the most expensive piece of equipment he had taken away with him from the SIB. It took the combined force of both Strike and Shanker to force Laing into a position where he could be cuffed, securing the thick wrists behind his back while Laing struggled and swore non-stop.

Freed of the necessity to hold Laing down, Shanker kicked him so hard in the diaphragm that the killer emitted a long faint wheeze and was rendered temporarily speechless.

'You all right, Bunsen? Bunsen, where'd he get you?'

Strike had slumped back against the oven. The cut to his ear was bleeding copiously, as was his slashed right palm, but his rapidly swelling nose troubled him most, because the blood pouring out of it into his mouth was making it difficult to breathe.

'There y'go, Bunsen,' said Shanker, returning from a brief search of the small flat with a roll of toilet paper.

'Cheers,' said Strike thickly. He stuffed his nostrils with as much paper as they would hold, then looked down at Laing. 'Nice to see you again, Ray.'

The still-winded Laing said nothing. His bald pate was shining faintly in the moonlight that had illuminated his knife.

'Fort you said 'is name was Donald?' asked Shanker curiously as Laing shifted on the ground. Shanker kicked him in the stomach again.

'It is,' said Strike, 'and stop bloody kicking him; if you rupture anything I'll have to answer for it in court.'

'So why you callin' 'im—?'

'Because,' said Strike, '– and don't touch anything, either, Shanker, I don't want your fingerprints in here – because Donnie's been using a borrowed identity. When he's not here,' Strike said, approaching the fridge and putting his left hand, with its still-intact latex glove, on the handle, 'he's heroic retired firefighter Ray Williams, who lives in Finchley with Hazel Furley.'

Strike pulled open the fridge door and, still using his left hand, opened the freezer compartment.

Kelsey Platt's breasts lay inside, dried up now like figs, yellow and leathery. Beside them lay Lila Monkton's fingers, the nails varnished purple, Laing's teeth marks imprinted deeply upon them. At the back lay a pair of severed ears from which little plastic ice-cream cones still hung, and a mangled piece of flesh in which nostrils were still distinguishable.

'Holy shit,' said Shanker, who had also bent over to look, from behind him. 'Holy shit, Bunsen, they're bits—'

Strike closed both icebox and fridge door and turned to look at his captive.

Laing lay quiet now. Strike was sure that he was already using that devious fox-like brain to see how he could work this desperate situation to his advantage, how he would be able to argue that Strike had framed him, planted or contaminated evidence.

'Should've recognised you, shouldn't I, Donnie?' said Strike, wrapping his right hand in toilet paper to stem the bleeding. Now, by the dim moonlight falling through the grubby window, Strike could just make out the features of Laing beneath the stones of extra weight that steroids and a lack of regular exercise had packed onto his once thickly muscled frame. His fatness, his dry, lined skin, the beard he had doubtless grown to hide his pockmarks, the carefully shaven head and the shuffling walk he had affected added up to a man at least ten years older than his real age. 'Should've recognised you the moment you opened the front door to me at Hazel's,' Strike said. 'But you kept your face covered, dabbing away at your fucking tears, didn't you? What had you done, rubbed something in them to make them swell up?'

Strike offered his pack to Shanker before lighting up.

'The Geordie accent was a bit overdone, now I think about it. You'll have picked that up in Gateshead, did you? He's always been a good mimic, our Donnie,' he told Shanker. 'You should have heard his Corporal Oakley. Life and soul, Donnie was, apparently.'

Shanker was staring from Strike to Laing, apparently fascinated. Strike continued to smoke, looking down at Laing. His nose was stinging and throbbing so badly it was making his own eyes water. He wanted to hear the killer speak, once, before he rang the police.

'Beat up and robbed a demented old lady in Corby, didn't you, Donnie? Poor old Mrs Williams. You took her son's award for bravery and I bet you got a good bit of old documentation of his as well. You knew he'd gone abroad. It's not too hard to steal someone's identity if you've got a bit of ID to start with. Easy to parlay that into enough current identification to hoodwink a lonely woman and a careless policeman or two.'

Laing lay silent on the dirty floor, but Strike could almost feel the frantic workings of his filthy, desperate mind.

'I found Accutane in the house,' Strike told Shanker. 'It's a drug for acne, but it's for psoriatic arthritis too. I should've known then. He kept it hidden in Kelsey's room. Ray Williams didn't have arthritis.

'I bet you had lots of little secrets together, didn't you, Donnie, you and Kelsey? Winding her up about me, getting her exactly where you wanted her? Taking her for motorbike rides to lurk near my office . . . pretending to post letters for her . . . bringing her my fake notes . . .'

'You sick bastard,' said the disgusted Shanker. He leaned over Laing with his cigarette tip close to Laing's face, clearly yearning to hurt him.

'You're not burning him either, Shanker,' said Strike, pulling out his mobile. 'You'd better get out of here, I'm going to call the cops.'

He rang 999 and gave the address. His story would be that he had followed Laing to the club and back to his flat, that there had been an argument and that Laing had attacked him. Nobody needed to know that Shanker had been involved, nor that Strike had picked Laing's locks. Of course, the stoned neighbour might talk, but Strike thought it likely that the young man might prefer to stay well out of it rather than have his sobriety and drug history assessed in a court of law.

'Take all this and get rid of it,' Strike told Shanker, peeling off the fluorescent jacket and handing it to him. 'And the gas canister through there.'

'Right y'are, Bunsen. Sure you're gonna be all right with him?' Shanker added, eyes on Strike's broken nose, his bleeding ear and hand.

'Yeah, course I will,' said Strike, vaguely touched.

He heard Shanker picking up the metal canister in the next room and, shortly afterwards, saw him passing the kitchen window on the balcony outside.

'SHANKER!'

His old friend was back in the kitchen so fast that Strike knew he must have sprinted; the heavy gas canister was raised, but Laing still lay handcuffed and quiescent on the floor, and Strike stood smoking beside the cooker.

'Fuckin' 'ell, Bunsen, I fort 'e'd jumped you!'

'Shanker, could you get hold of a car and drive me somewhere tomorrow morning? I'll give you—'

Strike looked down at his bare wrist. He had sold his watch yesterday for the cash that had paid for Shanker's help tonight. What else did he have to flog?

'Listen, Shanker, you know I'm going to make money out of this one. Give me a few months and I'll have clients queuing up.'

''S'all right, Bunsen,' said Shanker, after brief consideration. 'You can owe me.'

'Seriously?'

'Yeah,' said Shanker, turning to go. 'Gimme a bell when you're ready to leave. I'll go get us a car.'

'Don't nick one!' Strike called after him.

Mere seconds after Shanker had passed the window for the second time, Strike heard the distant sound of a police siren.

'Here they come, Donnie,' he said.

It was then that Donald Laing spoke in his true voice to Strike, for the first and last time.

'Your mother,' he said, in a deep Borders accent, 'was a fucking whore.'

Strike laughed.

'Maybe so,' he said, bleeding and smoking in the darkness as the sirens grew louder, 'but she loved me, Donnie. I heard yours didn't give a shit about you, little policeman's bastard that you were.'

Laing began to thrash around, trying fruitlessly to free himself, but he merely spun on his side, arms still pinned behind his back.

62

A redcap, a redcap, before the kiss . . .

Blue Öyster Cult, 'Before the Kiss, A Redcap'

Strike did not meet Carver that night. He suspected the man would have shot off his own kneecaps rather than face Strike now. A pair of CID officers he had never met interrogated him in a side room in Accident and Emergency, between the various medical procedures his injuries warranted. His ear had been stitched back together, his slashed palm bandaged, a dressing had been applied to his back, which the falling machete had nicked, and for the third time in his life his nose had been painfully manipulated back into approximate symmetry. At convenient intervals, Strike had given the police a lucid exposition of the line of reasoning that had led him to Laing. He was careful to tell them that he had phoned that information through to a subordinate of Carver's two weeks previously and had also tried to tell Carver directly the last time they had spoken.

'Why aren't you writing that down?' he asked the officers who sat in silence, staring at him. The younger man made a cursory note.

'I also,' Strike continued, 'wrote a letter and sent it to DI Carver, recorded delivery. He should have got it yesterday.'

'You sent it recorded delivery?' repeated the older of the two officers, a sad-eyed man with a moustache.

'That's right,' said Strike. 'Thought I'd make sure it was good and hard to lose.'

The policeman made a far more detailed note.

Strike's story was that, suspecting the police weren't convinced by his suspicions about Laing, he had never stopped watching him. He had followed Laing to the nightclub, worried about whether he was going to try to pick up a woman, then tailed him to his flat where he had decided to confront him. About Alyssa, who had played the part of his temp with such aplomb, and Shanker, whose enthusiastic intervention had certainly spared Strike several more stab wounds, he said nothing.

'The clincher,' Strike told the officers, 'is going to be finding this guy Ritchie, sometimes known as Dickie, whose motorbike Laing's been borrowing. Hazel will be able to tell you all about him. He's been giving Laing alibis all over the shop. I reckon he's a petty criminal himself and probably thought he was just helping Laing cheat on Hazel or do a bit of benefit fraud. He doesn't sound like a smart guy. I think he'll crack pretty quickly once he realises it was murder.'

The doctors and police finally decided that they needed nothing more from Strike at five o'clock in the morning. He refused the policemen's offer of a lift, which he suspected was made partly to keep tabs on him as long as they could.

'We wouldn't want this to get out before we've had a chance to speak to the families,' said the younger officer, whose white-blond hair stood out in the drab dawn on the forecourt where the three men were taking leave of one another.

'I'm not going to the press,' said Strike, yawning widely as he felt in his pockets for his remaining cigarettes. 'I've got other stuff to do today.'

He had begun to walk away when a thought occurred to him.

'What was the church connection? Brockbank – what made Carver think it was him?'

'Oh,' said the moustached officer. He did not seem particularly eager to share the information. 'There was a youth worker who'd transferred from Finchley to Brixton . . . didn't lead anywhere, but,' he added, with an air of faint defiance, 'we've got him. Brockbank. Got a tip-off from a homeless hostel yesterday.'

'Nice one,' said Strike. 'Press love a paedophile. I'd lead with that when you talk to them.'

Neither officer smiled. Strike bade them good morning and left, wondering whether he had any money on him for a taxi, smoking left-handed because the local anaesthetic was wearing off in his right hand, his broken nose stinging in the cool morning air.

'Fuckin' Yorkshire?' Shanker said over the phone when he called to tell Strike he had a car and the detective had told him where he wanted to go. '*Yorkshire?*'

'Masham,' Strike had replied. 'Look, I've already told you: I'll pay you anything you like when I get the money. It's a wedding and I don't want to miss it. Time's going to be tight as it is – anything you like, Shanker, you've got my word on it, and I'll pay you when I can.'

''Oo's gettin' married?'

'Robin,' said Strike.

'Ah,' said Shanker. He had sounded pleased. 'Yeah, well, in that case, Bunsen, I'll drive ya. I toldja you shouldn't've—'

'—yeah—'

'—Alyssa toldja—'

'Yeah, she did, bloody loudly too.'

Strike had a strong suspicion that Shanker was now sleeping with Alyssa. He could think of few other explanations for the speed with which he had suggested her when Strike had explained the need for a woman to play a safe but essential part in the entrapment of Donald Laing. She had demanded a hundred pounds for doing the job and had assured Strike that it would have been considerably more had she not considered herself deep in his partner's debt.

'Shanker, we can talk about all this on the way. I need food and a shower. We're going to be bloody lucky to make it.'

So here they were, speeding north in the Mercedes Shanker had borrowed; from where, Strike did not enquire. The detective, who had had barely any sleep in the previous couple of nights, dozed for the first sixty miles, waking with a snort only when his mobile buzzed in his suit pocket.

'Strike,' he said sleepily.

'Bloody good job, mate,' said Wardle.

His tone did not match his words. After all, Wardle had been in charge of the investigation when Ray Williams had been cleared of all suspicion in relation to Kelsey's death.

'Cheers,' said Strike. 'You realise you're now the only copper in London still prepared to talk to me.'

'Ah well,' said Wardle, rallying slightly. 'Quality over quantity. I thought you'd like to know: they've already found Richard and he's sung like a canary.'

'Richard . . .' mumbled Strike.

He felt as though his exhausted brain had been purged of the details that had obsessed him for months. Trees poured soothingly past the passenger window in a rush of summer greenery. He felt as though he could sleep for days.

'Ritchie – Dickie – motorbike,' said Wardle.

'Oh yeah,' said Strike, absent-mindedly scratching his

stitched ear, then swearing. 'Shit, that hurt – sorry – he's talked already, has he?'

'He's not what you'd call a bright boy,' said Wardle. 'We found a bunch of stolen gear at his place as well.'

'I thought that might be how Donnie was funding himself. He's always been a handy thief.'

'There was a little gang of them. Nothing major, just a lot of petty pilfering. Ritchie was the only one who knew Laing had a double identity; he thought he was working a benefits scam. Laing asked three of them to back him up and pretend their camping trip to Shoreham-by-Sea had been the weekend he killed Kelsey. Apparently he told them he had another bird somewhere and Hazel wasn't to know.'

'He could always get people on side, Laing,' said Strike, remembering the investigating officer in Cyprus who had been so ready to clear him of rape.

'How did you realise they weren't there that weekend?' asked Wardle curiously. 'They had photos and everything . . . how did you know they weren't on the stag the weekend she died?'

'Oh,' said Strike. 'Sea holly.'

'What?'

'Sea holly,' repeated Strike. 'Sea holly isn't in bloom in April. Summer and autumn – I spent half my childhood in Cornwall. The picture of Laing and Ritchie on the beach . . . there was sea holly. I should've realised then . . . but I kept getting sidetracked.'

After Wardle had hung up, Strike stared through the windscreen at the passing fields and trees, thinking back over the past three months. He doubted that Laing had ever known about Brittany Brockbank, but he had probably dug around enough to know the story of Whittaker's trial, the quoting of 'Mistress of the Salmon Salt' from the dock. Strike felt as though Laing had laid drag trails for him, without any idea how successful they would be.

Shanker turned on the radio. Strike, who would have preferred to go back to sleep, did not complain, but wound down the window and smoked out of it. In the steadily brightening sunshine he realised that the Italian suit he had pulled on automatically was flecked with small amounts of gravy and red wine. He rubbed off the worst of the dried-on stains, until reminded suddenly of something else.

'Oh, fuck.'

'Whassamatter?'

'I forgot to ditch someone.'

Shanker began to laugh. Strike smiled ruefully, which was painful. His whole face ached.

'Are we tryina stop this wedding, Bunsen?'

'Course not,' said Strike, pulling out another cigarette. 'I was invited. I'm a friend. A guest.'

'You sacked 'er,' said Shanker. 'Which ain't a mark of friendship where I come from.'

Strike refrained from pointing out that Shanker knew hardly anyone who had ever had a job.

'She's like your mum,' said Shanker, after a long silence.

'Who is?'

'Your Robin. Kind. Wanted to save that kid.'

Strike found it difficult to defend a refusal to save a child to a man who had been rescued, bleeding, from the gutter at the age of sixteen.

'Well, I'm going to try and get her back, aren't I? But the next time she calls you – if she calls you—'

'Yeah, yeah, I'll tell ya, Bunsen.'

The wing mirror showed Strike a face that might have belonged to the victim of a car crash. His nose was enormous and purple and his left ear looked black. By daylight he saw that his hasty attempt to shave using his left hand had not been entirely successful. As he imagined himself sliding into the back of the church he realised how conspicuous he was going to be, what a scene it would make if Robin decided she did not want him there. He didn't want to spoil her day. At the first request to leave, he vowed inwardly, he would do so.

'BUNSEN!' shouted Shanker excitedly, making Strike jump. Shanker turned up the radio.

'*. . . arrest has been made in the case of the Shacklewell Ripper. After a thorough search of a flat in Wollaston Close, London, police have charged thirty-four-year-old Donald Laing with the murders of Kelsey Platt, Heather Smart, Martina Rossi and Sadie Roach, the attempted murder of Lila Monkton and a serious assault on a sixth, unnamed woman . . .*'

'They didn't mention you!' said Shanker when the report ended. He sounded disappointed.

'They wouldn't,' said Strike, fighting an uncharacteristic nervousness. He had just seen the first sign to Masham. 'But they will. Good thing too: I need the publicity if I'm gonna get my business back off the ground.'

He automatically checked his wrist, forgetting that there was no watch there, and instead consulted the dashboard clock.

'Put your foot down, Shanker. We're going to miss the start as it is.'

Strike became increasingly anxious as they approached their destination. The service had been scheduled to start twenty minutes before they finally tore up the hill to Masham, Strike checking his phone for the location of the church.

'It's over there,' he said, pointing frantically to the opposite side of the broadest market square he had ever seen, which was packed with people at food stalls. As Shanker drove none too slowly around the periphery of the market several bystanders scowled and one man in a flat cloth cap shook his fist at the scarred man driving so dangerously in the sedate heart of Masham.

'Park here, anywhere here!' said Strike, spotting two dark blue Bentleys adorned with white ribbons parked at the far end of the square, the chauffeurs talking with their hats off in the sunshine. They looked around as Shanker braked. Strike threw off his seatbelt; he could see the church spire over the treetops now. He felt almost sick, due, no doubt, to the forty cigarettes he must have smoked overnight, the lack of sleep and Shanker's driving.

Strike had hurried several steps away from the car before dashing back to his friend.

'Wait for me. I might not be staying.'

He hurried away again past the staring chauffeurs, nervously straightened his tie, then remembered the state of his face and suit and wondered why he bothered.

Through the gates and into the deserted churchyard Strike limped. The impressive church reminded him of St Dionysius in Market Harborough, back when he and Robin had been friends. The hush over the sleepy, sunlit graveyard felt ominous. He passed a strange, almost pagan-looking column covered in carvings to his right as he approached the heavy oak doors.

Grasping the handle with his left hand he paused for a second.

'Fuck it,' he breathed to himself, and opened it as quietly as he could.

The smell of roses met him: white roses of Yorkshire blooming in tall stands and hanging in bunches at the ends of the packed queues. A thicket of brightly coloured hats stretched away towards the altar. Hardly anybody looked around at Strike as he shuffled inside, although those that did stared. He edged along the rear wall, staring at the far end of the aisle.

Robin was wearing a coronet of white roses in her long, wavy hair. He could not see her face. She was not wearing her cast. Even at this distance, he could see the long, purple scar running down the back of her forearm.

'Do you,' came a ringing voice from an unseen vicar, 'Robin Venetia Ellacott, take this man, Matthew John Cunliffe, to be your lawful wedded husband, to have and to hold, from this day forward—'

Exhausted, tense, his gaze fixed on Robin, Strike had not realised how near he was to the flower arrangement that stood on a fine, tulip-like bronze stand.

'—for better, for worse, for richer, for poorer, in sickness and in health, until death—'

'Oh shit,' said Strike.

The arrangement he had hit toppled as though in slow motion and fell with a deafening clang to the floor. Congregation and couple turned and looked back.

'I'm – Christ, I'm sorry,' said Strike hopelessly.

Somewhere in the middle of the congregation a man laughed. Most returned their gazes to the altar at once, but a few guests continued to glare at Strike before remembering themselves.

'—do you part,' said the vicar with saintly tolerance.

The beautiful bride, who had not once smiled in the entire service, was suddenly beaming.

'I do,' said Robin in a ringing voice, looking straight into the eyes, not of her stony-faced new husband, but of the battered and bloodied man who had just sent her flowers crashing to the floor.

Acknowledgements

I can't remember ever enjoying writing a novel more than *Career of Evil*. This is odd, not only on account of the grisly subject matter, but also because I've rarely been busier than over the last twelve months and have had to keep switching between projects, which is not my favourite way to work. Nevertheless, Robert Galbraith has always felt like my own private playground, and he didn't let me down on this occasion.

I have to thank my usual team for ensuring that my once-secret identity remains such fun: my peerless editor, David Shelley, who has now been godfather to four of my novels and who makes the editing process so rewarding; my wonderful agent and friend Neil Blair, who has been Robert's stalwart supporter from the first; Deeby and SOBE, who have allowed me to pick their military brains clean; the Back Door Man, for reasons best left undisclosed; Amanda Donaldson, Fiona Shapcott, Angela Milne, Christine Collingwood, Simon Brown, Kaisa Tiensu and Danni Cameron, without whose hard work I would not have any time left over to do my own, and the dream team of Mark Hutchinson, Nicky Stonehill and Rebecca Salt, without whom I would, frankly, be a wreck.

Particular thanks are due to MP, who enabled me to make a fascinating visit to 35 Section SIB (UK) RMP in Edinburgh Castle. Thanks are also due to the two policewomen who didn't arrest me for taking photographs of the perimeter of a nuclear facility in Barrow-in-Furness.

To all the lyricists who have worked with and for Blue Öyster Cult, thank you for writing such great songs and for letting me use some of your words in this novel.

To my children, Decca, Davy and Kenz: I love you beyond words and I want to thank you for being so understanding about the times when the writing bug is particularly active.

Lastly and mostly: thank you, Neil. Nobody helped more when it came to this book.

'**Career of Evil**' (pvii) Words by Patti Smith. Music by Patti Smith and Albert Bouchard © 1974, Reproduced by permission of Sony/ATV Tunes LLC, London W1F 9LD '**This Ain't The Summer of Love**' (p1, p73, p354) Words and Music by Albert Bouchard, Murray Krugman and Donald Waller © 1975, Reproduced by permission of Sony/ATV Music Publishing (UK) Ltd, Sony/ATV Tunes LLC, London W1F 9LD and Peermusic (UK) Ltd. '**Madness to the Method**' (p6, p223, p455) Words and Music by D Trismen and Donald Roeser © 1985, Reproduced by permission of Sony/ATV Music Publishing (UK) Ltd, Sony/ATV Tunes LLC, London W1F 9LD '**The Marshall Plan**' (p10) Words and Music by Albert Bouchard, Joseph Bouchard, Eric Bloom, Allen Lainer and Donald Roeser © 1980, Reproduced by permission of Sony/ATV Music Publishing (UK) Ltd, Sony/ATV Tunes LLC, London W1F 9LD '**Mistress of The Salmon Salt (Quicklime Girl)**' (p17 and p80) Words and Music by Albert Bouchard and Samuel Pearlman © 1973, Reproduced by permission of Sony/ATV Tunes LLC, London W1F 9LD '**Astronomy**' (p20) Words and Music by Albert Bouchard, Joseph Bouchard and Samuel Pearlman © 1974, Reproduced by permission of Sony/ATV Music Publishing (UK) Ltd, Sony/ATV Tunes LLC, London W1F 9LD '**The Revenge of Vera Gemini**' (p30) Words by Patti Smith. Music by Albert Bouchard and Patti Smith © 1976, Reproduced by permission of Sony/ATV Music Publishing (UK) Ltd, Sony/ATV Tunes LLC, London W1F 9LD '**Flaming Telepaths**' (p35) Words and Music by Albert Bouchard, Eric Bloom, Samuel Pearlman and Donald Roeser, © 1974, Reproduced by permission of Sony/ATV Music Publishing (UK) Ltd, Sony/ATV Tunes LLC, London W1F 9LD '**Good to Feel Hungry**' (p44) (Eric Bloom, Danny Miranda, Donald B. Roeser, Bobby Rondinelli, John P. Shirley). Reproduced by permission of Six Pound Dog Music and Triceratops Music '**Lonely Teardrops**' (p47) Words and Music by Allen Lanier © 1980, Reproduced by permission of Sony/ATV Music Publishing (UK) Ltd, Sony/ATV Tunes LLC, London W1F 9LD '**One Step Ahead of the Devil**' (p55) (Eric Bloom, Danny Miranda, Donald B. Roeser, Bobby Rondinelli, John P. Shirley). Reproduced by permission of Six Pound Dog Music and Triceratops Music '**Shadow of California**' (p57) Words and Music by Samuel Pearlman and Donald Roeser © 1983, Reproduced by permission of Sony/ATV Music Publishing (UK) Ltd/Sony/ATV Tunes LLC, London W1F 9LD '**O.D.'D On Life Itself**' (p82) Words and Music by Albert Bouchard, Eric Bloom, Samuel Pearlman and Donald Roeser © 1973, Reproduced by permission of Sony/ATV Music Publishing (UK) Ltd, Sony/ATV Tunes LLC, London W1F 9LD '**In The Presence Of Another World**' (p91 and p251) Words and Music by Joseph Bouchard and Samuel Pearlman © 1988, Reproduced by permission of Sony/ATV Music Publishing (UK) Ltd, Sony/ATV Tunes LLC, London W1F 9LD '**Showtime**' (p106) (Eric Bloom, John P. Trivers). Reproduced by permission of Six Pound Dog Music '**Power Underneath Despair**' (p116) (Eric Bloom, Donald B. Roeser, John P. Shirley). Reproduced by permission of Six Pound Dog Music and Triceratops Music '**Before the Kiss, A Redcap**' (p123, p548, p556, p564) Words and Music by Donald Roeser and Samuel Pearlman © 1972, Reproduced by permission of Sony/ATV Music Publishing (UK) Ltd, Sony/ATV Tunes LLC, London W1F 9LD Words taken from '**Here's Tae Melrose**' (p123) by Jack Drummond (Zoo Music Ltd) '**The Girl That Love Made Blind**' (p140) Lyrics by Albert Bouchard '**Lips In The Hills**' (p142 and p283) Words and Music by Eric Bloom,

Donald Roeser and Richard Meltzer © 1980, Reproduced by permission of Sony/ATV Music Publishing (UK) Ltd, Sony/ATV Tunes LLC, London W1F 9LD '**Workshop of the Telescopes**' (p152) (Albert Bouchard, Allen Lanier, Donald Roeser, Eric Bloom, Sandy Pearlman) '**Debbie Denise**' (p156 and p266) Words by Patti Smith. Music by Albert Bouchard and Patti Smith © 1976, Reproduced by permission of Sony/ATV Music Publishing (UK) Ltd, Sony/ATV Tunes LLC, London W1F 9LD '**Live For Me**' (p174) (Donald B. Roeser, John P. Shirley). Reproduced by permission of Triceratops Music '**I Just Like To Be Bad**' (p188 and p278) (Eric Bloom, Brian Neumeister, John P. Shirley). Reproduced by permission of Six Pound Dog Music '**Make Rock Not War**' (p198) Words and Music by Robert Sidney Halligan Jr. © 1983, Reproduced by permission of Screen Gems-EMI Music Inc/ EMI Music Publishing Ltd, London W1F 9LD '**Hammer Back**' (p213) (Eric Bloom, Donald B. Roeser, John P. Shirley). Reproduced by permission of Six Pound Dog Music and Triceratops Music '**Death Valley Nights**' (p240) Words and Music by Albert Bouchard and Richard Meltzer © 1977, Reproduced by permission of Sony/ATV Music Publishing (UK) Ltd, Sony/ATV Tunes LLC, London W1F 9LD '**Outward Bound (A Song for the Grammar School, Barrow-in-Furness)**' (p249, 250) Words by Dr Thomas Wood '**Tenderloin**' (p292) Words and Music by Allen Lainer © 1976, Reproduced by permission of Sony/ATV Music Publishing (UK) Ltd/ Sony/ATV Tunes LLC, London W1F 9LD '**After Dark**' (p301) Words and Music by Eric Bloom, L Myers and John Trivers © 1981, Reproduced by permission of Sony/ATV Music Publishing (UK) Ltd, Sony/ATV Tunes LLC, London W1F 9LD '**(Don't Fear) The Reaper**' (p310 and p519) Words and Music by Donald Roeser © 1976, Reproduced by permission of Sony/ATV Music Publishing (UK) Ltd, Sony/ATV Tunes LLC, London W1F 9LD '**She's As Beautiful As A Foot**' (p316) (Albert Bouchard, Richard Meltzer, Allen Lanier) '**The Vigil**' (p318) Words and Music by Donald Roeser and S Roeser © 1979,

Reproduced by permission of Sony/ATV Music Publishing (UK) Ltd, Sony/ATV Tunes LLC, London W1F 9LD '**Dominance and Submission**' (p334) (Albert Bouchard, Eric Bloom, Sandy Pearlman) '**Black Blade**' (p339)Words and Music by Eric Bloom, John Trivers and Michael Moorcock © 1980, Reproduced by permission of Sony/ ATV Music Publishing (UK) Ltd, Sony/ATV Tunes LLC and Action Green Music Ltd/EMI Music Publishing Ltd, London W1F 9LD '**Dance on Stilts**' (p361 and p362) (Donald B. Roeser, John P. Shirley). Reproduced by permission of Triceratops Music '**Out of the Darkness**' (p369 and p387) (Eric Bloom, Danny Miranda, Donald Roeser, John D. Shirley). Reproduced by permission of Six Pound Dog Music and Triceratops Music '**Searchin' For Celine**' (p382) Words and Music by Allen Lainer © 1977, Reproduced by permission of Sony/ATV Music Publishing (UK) Ltd, Sony/ATV Tunes LLC, London W1F 9LD '**Burnin' For You**' (p399) Words and Music by Donald Roeser and Richard Meltzer © 1981, Reproduced by permission of Sony/ATV Music Publishing (UK) Ltd, Sony/ATV Tunes LLC, London W1F 9LD '**Still Burnin'**' (p407) (Donald B. Roeser, John S. Rogers). Reproduced by permission of Triceratops Music '**Then Came The Last Days of May**' (p421) Words and Music by Donald Roeser © 1972, Reproduced by permission of Sony/ ATV Music Publishing (UK) Ltd, Sony/ATV Tunes LLC, London W1F 9LD '**Harvester of Eyes**' (p423) Words and Music by Eric Bloom, Donald Roeser and Richard Meltzer © 1974, Reproduced by permission of Sony/ATV Music Publishing (UK) Ltd, Sony/ATV Tunes LLC, London W1F 9LD '**Subhuman**' (p437) (Eric Bloom, Sandy Pearlman) '**Dr. Music**' (p439) Words and Music by Joseph Bouchard, R Meltzer, Donald Roeser © 1979, Reproduced by permission of Sony/ATV Music Publishing (UK) Ltd, Sony/ATV Tunes LLC, London W1F 9LD '**Harvest Moon**' (p440) (Donald Roeser). Reproduced by permission of Triceratops Music '**Here Comes That Feeling**' (p450) (Donald B. Roeser, Dick Trismen). Reproduced by permission of Triceratops Music '**Celestial the**

Queen' (p469) Words and Music by Joseph Bouchard and H Robbins © 1977, Reproduced by permission of Sony/ATV Music Publishing (UK) Ltd, Sony/ATV Tunes LLC, London W1F 9LD '**Don't Turn Your Back**' (p475) Words and Music by Allen Lainer and Donald Roeser © 1981, Reproduced by permission of Sony/ ATV Music Publishing (UK) Ltd, Sony/ATV Tunes LLC, London W1F 9LD '**X-Ray Eyes**' (p488) (Donald B. Roeser, John P. Shirley). Reproduced by permission of Triceratops Music '**Veteran of the Psychic Wars**' (p499) Words and Music by Eric Bloom and Michael Moorcock © 1981, Reproduced by permission of Sony/ ATV Music Publishing (UK) Ltd, Sony/ATV Tunes LLC and Action Green Music Ltd/ EMI Music Publishing Ltd, London W1F 9LD '**Spy in the House of the Night**' (p506) Words and Music by Richard Meltzer and Donald Roeser © 1985, Reproduced by permission of Sony/ATV Music Publishing (UK) Ltd, Sony/ATV Tunes LLC, London W1F 9LD '**Vengeance (The Pact)**' (p531 and p533) Words and Music by Albert Bouchard and Joseph Bouchard © 1981, Reproduced by permission of Sony/ATV Music Publishing (UK) Ltd, Sony/ATV Tunes LLC, London W1F 9LD '**Sole Survivor**' (p536) Words and Music by Eric Bloom, L Myers and John Trivers © 1981, Reproduced by permission of Sony/ATV Music Publishing (UK) Ltd, Sony/ATV Tunes LLC, London W1F 9LD '**Deadline**' (p543) (Donald Roeser)

READ
THE FIRST NOVEL FEATURING CORMORAN STRIKE

'Reminds me why I fell in love with crime fiction in the first place'
Val McDermid

'A scintillating novel'
The Times

When a troubled model falls to her death from a snow-covered Mayfair balcony, it is assumed that she has committed suicide. However, her brother has his doubts, and calls in private investigator Cormoran Strike to look into the case.

Strike is a war veteran – wounded both physically and psychologically – and his life is in disarray. The case gives him a financial lifeline, but it comes at a personal cost: the more he delves into the young model's complex world, the darker things get – and the closer he gets to terrible danger . . .

A gripping, elegant mystery steeped in the atmosphere of London – from the hushed streets of Mayfair to the backstreet pubs of the East End to the bustle of Soho – *The Cuckoo's Calling* introduces Cormoran Strike in the acclaimed first crime novel by Robert Galbraith – J.K. Rowling's pseudonym.

READ

STRIKE AND ROBIN'S SECOND CASE

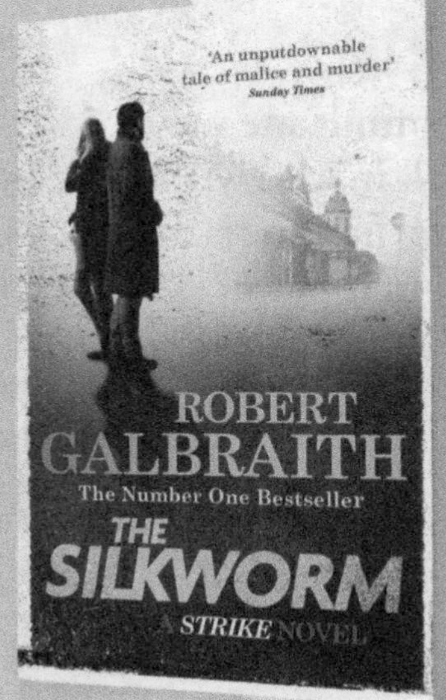

'An unputdownable tale of malice and murder'
Sunday Times
ROBERT GALBRAITH
The Number One Bestseller
THE SILKWORM
A STRIKE NOVEL

'Galbraith has pulled off a thoroughly enjoyable classic'

Peter James

'A superb and polished thriller . . . an ingenious whodunit'

Sunday Mirror

When novelist Owen Quine goes missing, his wife calls in private detective Cormoran Strike. At first, she just thinks he has gone off by himself for a few days – as he has done before – and she wants Strike to find him and bring him home.

But as Strike investigates, it becomes clear that there is more to Quine's disappearance than his wife realises. The novelist has just completed a manuscript featuring poisonous pen-portraits of almost everyone he knows. If the novel were published it would ruin lives - so there are a lot of people who might want to silence him.

And when Quine is found brutally murdered in bizarre circumstances, it becomes a race against time to understand the motivation of a ruthless killer, a killer unlike any he has encountered before . . .

A compulsively readable crime novel with twists at every turn, *The Silkworm* is the second in the highly acclaimed series featuring Cormoran Strike and his determined young assistant Robin Ellacott.

READ
THE MOST EPIC STRIKE NOVEL YET

'Come for the twists and turns and stay for the beautifully drawn central relationship'
Independent

'An obsessive reading experience'
Observer

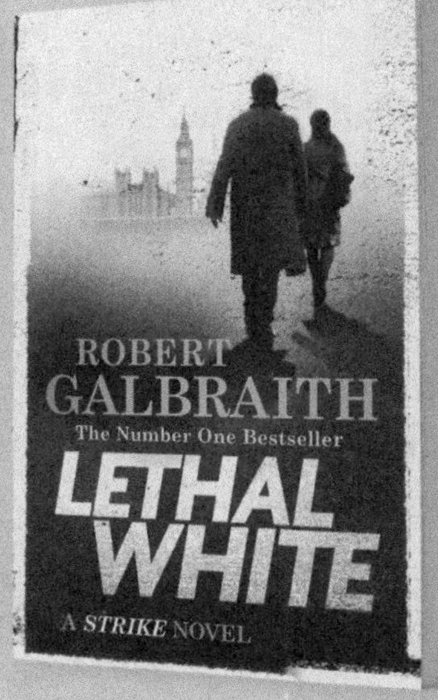

When Billy, a troubled young man, comes to private eye Cormoran Strike's office to ask for his help investigating a crime he thinks he witnessed as a child, Strike is left deeply unsettled. But before Strike can question him further, Billy bolts from his office in a panic.

Trying to get to the bottom of Billy's story, Strike and Robin Ellacott – once his assistant, now a partner in the agency – set off on a twisting trail that leads them through the backstreets of London, into a secretive inner sanctum within Parliament, and to a beautiful but sinister manor house deep in the countryside.

And during this labyrinthine investigation, Strike's own life is far from straightforward: his relationship with his former assistant is more fraught than it ever has been – Robin is now invaluable to Strike in the business, but their personal relationship is much, much more tricky than that . . .

***Lethal White* is both a gripping mystery and a page-turning next instalment in the ongoing story of Cormoran Strike and Robin Ellacott.**

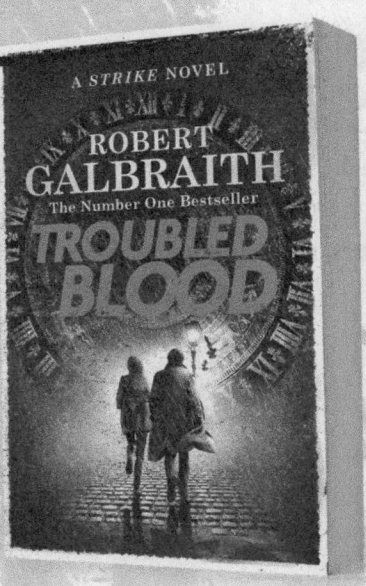

Praise for *Troubled Blood*

'A scrupulous plotter and master of misdirection, Galbraith keeps the pages turning . . . Strike and Ellacott remain one of crime's most engaging duos'
Guardian

'The best one yet . . . confident, utterly gripping, niftily plotted, clearly meticulously researched . . . and heavy on satisfying characterisation'
The Sunday Times

'A finely honed, superbly constructed tale'
Daily Mail

'An ambitious, immersive mystery that also reveals ever more about the enigmatic Cormoran'
Heat

'Complex and enjoyable'
Sunday Mirror

'The new Galbraith is possibly her finest Strike outing yet, emblazoned with the rich vein of characterisation of the detective and his assistant Robin Ellacott'
i

'A mix of supernatural eeriness and head-scratching mystery with a juicy whodunnit at its core'
Sun

'The real charm lies in the star-crossed relationship between Strike and his assistant Robin'
Mail on Sunday

'I'm a huge fan of Cormoran Strike . . . *Troubled Blood* is terrific'
Richard & Judy
Daily Express

'Galbraith is fluent in invention of incident, characters, conversation and confrontations'
The Scotsman

ROBERT
GALBRAITH

TROUBLED BLOOD

A *STRIKE* NOVEL

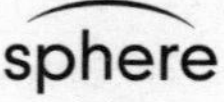

sphere

SPHERE

First published in Great Britain in 2020 by Sphere
This paperback edition published in 2021 by Sphere

5 7 9 10 8 6 4

All illustrations by the author.

All characters and events in this publication, other than those clearly in the public domain, are fictitious and any resemblance to real persons, living or dead, is purely coincidental.

A CIP catalogue record for this book is available from the British Library.

ISBN 978-0-7515-7995-6

Typeset in Bembo by M Rules
Printed and bound in Great Britain by Clays Ltd, Elcograf S.p.A.

Papers used by Sphere are from well-managed forests and other responsible sources.

Sphere
An imprint of
Little, Brown Book Group
Carmelite House
50 Victoria Embankment
London EC4Y 0DZ

An Hachette UK Company
www.hachette.co.uk

www.littlebrown.co.uk

To Barbara Murray,
social worker, WEA worker, teacher,
wife, mother, grandmother,
demon bridge player
and
world's best mother-in-law

There they her sought, and euery where inquired,
Where they might tydings get of her estate;
Yet found they none. But by what haplesse fate,
Or hard misfortune she was thence conuayd,
And stolne away from her beloued mate,
Were long to tell . . .

Edmund Spenser
The Faerie Queene

For, if it were not so, there would be something disappearing into nothing, which is mathematically absurd.

Aleister Crowley
The Book of Thoth

PART ONE

Then came the iolly Sommer . . .

Edmund Spenser
The Faerie Queene

1

And such was he, of whom I haue to tell,
The champion of true Iustice, Artegall . . .

Edmund Spenser
The Faerie Queene

'You're a Cornishman, born and bred,' said Dave Polworth irritably. '"Strike" isn't even your proper name. By rights, you're a Nancarrow. You're not going to sit here and say you'd call yourself English?'

The Victory Inn was so crowded on this warm August evening that drinkers had spilled outside onto the broad stone steps which led down to the bay. Polworth and Strike were sitting at a table in the corner, having a few pints to celebrate Polworth's thirty-ninth birthday. Cornish nationalism had been under discussion for twenty minutes, and to Strike it felt much longer.

'Would I call myself English?' he mused aloud. 'No, I'd probably say British.'

'Fuck off,' said Polworth, his quick temper rising. 'You wouldn't. You're just trying to wind me up.'

The two friends were physical opposites. Polworth was short and spare as a jockey, weathered and prematurely lined, his sunburned scalp visible through his thinning hair. His T-shirt was crumpled, as though he had pulled it off the floor or out of a washing basket, and his jeans were ripped. On his left forearm was tattooed the black and white cross of St Piran; on his right hand was a deep scar, souvenir of a close encounter with a shark.

His friend Strike resembled an out-of-condition boxer, which in fact he was; a large man, well over six feet tall, with a slightly crooked nose, his dense dark hair curly. He bore no tattoos and, in spite of the perpetual shadow of the heavy beard, carried about him that well-pressed and fundamentally clean-cut air that suggested ex-police or ex-military.

'You were born here,' Polworth persisted. 'So you're Cornish.'

'Trouble is, by that standard, you're a Brummie.'

'Fuck off!' yelped Polworth again, genuinely stung. 'I've been here since I was two months old and my mum's a Trevelyan. It's identity – what you feel here,' and Polworth thumped his chest over his heart. 'My mum's family goes back centuries in Cornwall—'

'Yeah, well, blood and soil's never been my—'

'Did you hear about the last survey they done?' said Polworth, talking over Strike. '"What's your ethnic origin?" they asked, and half – *half* – ticked "Cornish" instead of "English". Massive increase.'

'Great,' said Strike. 'What next? Boxes for Dumnones and Romans?'

'Keep using that patronising fucking tone,' said Polworth, 'and see where it gets you. You've been in London too fucking long, boy ... There's nothing wrong with being proud of where you came from. Nothing wrong with communities wanting some power back from Westminster. The Scots are gonna lead the way, next year. You watch. When they get independence, that'll be the trigger. Celtic peoples right across the country are going to make their move.

'Want another one?' he added, gesturing towards Strike's empty pint glass.

Strike had come out to the pub craving a respite from tension and worry, not to be harangued about Cornish politics. Polworth's allegiance to Mebyon Kernow, the nationalist party he'd joined at sixteen, appeared to have gained a greater hold over him in the year or so since they had last seen each other. Dave usually made Strike laugh like almost nobody else, but he brooked no jokes upon Cornish independence, a subject that for Strike had all the appeal of soft furnishings or trainspotting. For a second Strike considered saying that he needed to get back to his aunt's house, but the prospect of that was almost more depressing than his old friend's invective against supermarkets that resisted putting the cross of St Piran on goods of Cornish origin.

'Great, thanks,' he said, passing his empty glass to Dave, who headed up to the bar, nodding left and right to his many acquaintances.

Left alone at the table, Strike's eyes roamed absently over the pub he'd always considered his local. It had changed over the years, but was still recognisably the place in which he and his Cornish mates had met in their late teens. He had an odd double impression of being exactly where he belonged, and where he'd never belonged, of intense familiarity and of separateness.

As his gaze moved aimlessly from timber floor to nautical prints, Strike found himself looking directly into the large, anxious eyes of a woman standing at the bar with a friend. She had a long, pale face and her dark, shoulder-length hair was streaked with grey. He didn't recognise her, but he'd been aware for the past hour that certain locals were craning their necks to look at him, or else trying to catch his eye. Looking away, Strike took out his mobile and pretended to be texting.

Acquaintances had a ready excuse for conversation, if he showed the slightest sign of encouraging them, because everyone in St Mawes seemed to know that his aunt Joan had received a diagnosis of advanced ovarian cancer ten days previously, and that he, his half-sister, Lucy, and Lucy's three sons had hastened at once to Joan and Ted's house to offer what support they could. For a week now he'd been fielding enquiries, accepting sympathy and politely declining offers of help every time he ventured out of the house. He was tired of finding fresh ways of saying 'Yes, it looks terminal and yes, it's shit for all of us.'

Polworth pushed his way back to the table, carrying two fresh pints.

'There you go, Diddy,' he said, resuming his bar stool.

The old nickname hadn't been bestowed, as most people assumed, in ironic reference to Strike's size, but derived from 'didicoy', the Cornish word for gypsy. The sound of it softened Strike, reminding him why his friendship with Polworth was the most enduring of his life.

Thirty-five years previously, Strike had entered St Mawes Primary School a term late, unusually large for his age and with an accent that was glaringly different from the local burr. Although he'd been born in Cornwall, his mother had spirited him away as soon as she'd recovered from the birth, fleeing into the night, baby in her arms, back to the London life she loved, flitting from flat to squat to party. Four years after Strike's birth, she'd returned to St Mawes with her son and with her two-year-old daughter, Lucy, only to take off again in the early hours of the morning, leaving Strike and his half-sister behind.

Precisely what Leda had said in the note she left on the kitchen table, Strike had never known. Doubtless she'd been having a spell of difficulty with a landlord or a boyfriend, or perhaps there was a music festival she particularly wanted to attend: it became difficult to live exactly as she pleased with two children in tow. Whatever the reason for her lengthening absence, Leda's sister-in-law, Joan, who was as conventional and orderly as Leda was flighty and chaotic, had bought Strike a uniform and enrolled him in the local school.

The other four-and-a-half-year-olds had gawped when he was introduced to the class. A few of them giggled when the teacher said his first name, Cormoran. He was worried by this school business, because he was sure that his mum had said she was going to 'home school' him. He'd tried to tell Uncle Ted that he didn't think his mum would want him to go, but Ted, normally so understanding, had said firmly that he had to, so there he was, alone among strangers with funny accents. Strike, who'd never been a great crier, had sat down at the old roll-top desk with a lump like an apple in his throat.

Why Dave Polworth, pocket don of the class, had decided to befriend the new boy had never been satisfactorily explained, even to Strike. It couldn't have been out of fear of Strike's size, because Dave's two best friends were hefty fishermen's sons, and Dave was in any case notorious as a fighter whose viciousness was inversely proportional to his height. By the end of that first day Polworth had become both friend and champion, making it his business to impress upon their classmates all the reasons that Strike was worthy of their respect: he was a Cornishman born, a nephew to Ted Nancarrow of the local lifeguard, he didn't know where his mum was and it wasn't his fault if he spoke funny.

Ill as Strike's aunt was, much as she had enjoyed having her nephew to stay for a whole week and even though he'd be leaving the following morning, Joan had virtually pushed him out of the house to celebrate 'Little Dave's' birthday that evening. She placed immense value on old ties and delighted in the fact that Strike and Dave Polworth were still mates, all these years later. Joan counted the fact of their friendship as proof that she'd been right to send him to school over his feckless mother's wishes and proof that Cornwall was Strike's true home, no matter how widely he might have wandered since, and even though he was currently London-based.

Polworth took a long pull on his fourth pint and said, with a sharp glance over his shoulder at the dark woman and her blonde friend, who were still watching Strike,

'Effing emmets.'

'And where would your garden be,' asked Strike, 'without tourists?'

'Be ansom,' said Polworth promptly. 'We get a ton of local visitors, plenty of repeat business.'

Polworth had recently resigned from a managerial position in an engineering firm in Bristol to work as head gardener in a large public garden a short distance along the coast. A qualified diver, an accomplished surfer, a competitor in Ironman competitions, Polworth had been relentlessly physical and restless since childhood, and time and office work hadn't tamed him.

'No regrets, then?' Strike asked.

'Fuck, no,' said Polworth fervently. 'Needed to get my hands dirty again. Need to get back outside. Forty next year. Now or never.'

Polworth had applied for the new job without telling his wife what he was doing. Having been offered the position, he'd quit his job and gone home to announce the fait accompli to his family.

'Penny come round, has she?' Strike asked.

'Still tells me once a week she wants a divorce,' Polworth answered indifferently. 'But it was better to present her with the fact, than argue the toss for five years. It's all worked out great. Kids love the new school, Penny's company let her transfer to the office in the Big City', by which Polworth meant Truro, not London. 'She's happy. Just doesn't want to admit it.'

Strike privately doubted the truth of this statement. A disregard for inconvenient facts tended to march hand in hand with Polworth's love of risk and romantic causes. However, Strike had problems enough of his own without worrying about Polworth's, so he raised his fresh pint and said, hoping to keep Polworth's mind off politics:

'Well, many happy returns, mate.'

'Cheers,' said Polworth, toasting him back. 'What d'you reckon to Arsenal's chances, then? Gonna qualify?'

Strike shrugged, because he feared that discussing the likelihood of his London football club securing a place in the Champions League would lead back to a lack of Cornish loyalties.

'How's your love life?' Polworth asked, trying a different tack.

'Non-existent,' said Strike.

Polworth grinned.

'Joanie reckons you're gonna end up with your business partner. That Robin girl.'

'Is that right?' said Strike.

'Told me all about it when I was round there, weekend before last. While I was fixing their Sky Box.'

'They didn't tell me you'd done that,' said Strike, again tipping his pint towards Polworth. 'That was good of you, mate, cheers.'

If he'd hoped to deflect his friend, he was unsuccessful.

'Both of 'em. Her and Ted,' said Polworth, 'both of 'em reckon it's Robin.'

And when Strike said nothing, Polworth pressed him, 'Nothing going on, then?'

'No,' said Strike.

'How come?' asked Polworth, frowning again. As with Cornish independence, Strike was refusing to embrace an obvious and desirable objective. 'She's a looker. Seen her in the paper. Maybe not on a par with Milady Berserko,' Polworth acknowledged. It was the nickname he had long ago bestowed on Strike's ex-fiancée. 'But on the other hand, she's not a fucking nutcase, is she, Diddy?'

Strike laughed.

'Lucy likes her,' said Polworth. 'Says you'd be perfect together.'

'When were you talking to Lucy about my love life?' asked Strike, with a touch less complaisance.

'Month or so ago,' said Polworth. 'She brought her boys down for the weekend and we had them all over for a barbecue.'

Strike drank and said nothing.

'You get on great, she says,' said Polworth, watching him.

'Yeah, we do,' said Strike.

Polworth waited, eyebrows raised and looking expectant.

'It'd fuck everything up,' said Strike. 'I'm not risking the agency.'

'Right,' said Polworth. 'Tempted, though?'

There was a short pause. Strike carefully kept his gaze averted from the dark woman and her companion, who he was sure were discussing him.

'There might've been moments,' he admitted, 'when it crossed my mind. But she's going through a nasty divorce, we spend half our lives together as it is and I like having her as a business partner.'

Given their longstanding friendship, the fact that they'd already clashed over politics and that it was Polworth's birthday, he was trying not to let any hint of resentment at this line of questioning show. Every married person he knew seemed desperate to chivvy others into matrimony, no matter how poor an advertisement they themselves were for the institution. The Polworths, for instance, seemed to exist in a permanent state of mutual animosity. Strike had more often heard Penny refer to her husband as 'that twat' than by his name, and many was the night when Polworth had regaled his friends in happy detail of the ways in which he'd managed to pursue his own ambitions and interests at the expense of, or over the protests of, his wife. Both seemed happiest and most relaxed in the company of their own sex, and on those rare occasions when Strike had enjoyed hospitality at their home, the gatherings always seemed to follow a pattern of natural segregation, the women congregating in one area of the home, the men in another.

'And what happens when Robin wants kids?' asked Polworth.

'Don't think she does,' said Strike. 'She likes the job.'

'They all say that,' said Polworth dismissively. 'What age is she now?'

'Ten years younger than us.'

'She'll want kids,' said Polworth confidently. 'They all do. And it happens quicker for women. They're up against the clock.'

'Well, she won't be getting kids with me. I don't want them. Anyway, the older I get, the less I think I'm the marrying kind.'

'Thought that myself, mate,' said Polworth. 'But then I realised I'd got it all wrong. Told you how it happened, didn't I? How I ended up proposing to Penny?'

'Don't think so,' said Strike.

'I never told you about the whole Tolstoy thing?' asked Polworth, surprised at this omission.

Strike, who'd been about to drink, lowered his glass in amazement. Since primary school, Polworth, who had a razor-sharp intelligence but despised any form of learning he couldn't put to immediate, practical use, had shunned all printed material except technical manuals. Misinterpreting Strike's expression, Polworth said,

'Tolstoy. He's a writer.'

'Yeah,' said Strike. 'Thanks. How does Tolstoy—?'

'Telling you, aren't I? I'd split up with Penny the second time. She'd been banging on about getting engaged, and I wasn't feeling it. So I'm in this bar, telling my mate Chris about how I'm sick of her telling me she wants a ring – you remember Chris? Big guy with a lisp. You met him at Rozwyn's christening.

'Anyway, there's this pissed older guy at the bar on his own, bit of a ponce in his corduroy jacket, wavy hair, and he's pissing me off, to be honest, because I can tell he's listening, and I ask him what the fuck he's looking at and he looks me straight in the eye,' said Polworth, 'and he says: "You can only carry a weight and use your hands, if you strap the weight to your back. Marry, and you get the use of your hands back. Don't marry, and you'll never have your hands free for anything else. Look at Mazankov, at Krupov. They've ruined their careers for the sake of women."

'I thought Mazankov and Krupov were mates of his. Asked him what the fuck he was telling me for. Then he says he's quoting this writer, Tolstoy.

'And we got talking and I tell you this, Diddy, it was a life-changing moment. The light bulb went on,' said Polworth, pointing at the air over his balding head. 'He made me see it clearly. The male predicament, mate. There I am, trying to get my hole on a Thursday night, heading home alone again, poorer, bored shitless; I thought of the money I've spent chasing gash, and the hassle, and whether I want to be watching porn alone at forty, and I thought, this is the whole point.

What marriage is for. Am I going to do better than Penny? Am I enjoying talking shit to women in bars? Penny and me get on all right. I could do a hell of a lot worse. She's not bad-looking. I'd have my hole already at home, waiting for me, wouldn't I?'

'Pity she can't hear this,' said Strike. 'She'd fall in love with you all over again.'

'I shook that poncey bloke's hand,' said Polworth, ignoring Strike's sarcasm. 'Made him write me down the name of the book and all. Went straight out that bar, got a taxi to Penny's flat, banged on the door, woke her up. She was fucking livid. Thought I'd come round because I was pissed, couldn't get anything better and wanted a shag. I said, "No, you dozy cow, I'm here because I wanna marry you."'

'And I'll tell you the name of the book,' said Polworth. '*Anna Karenina.*' He drained his pint. 'It's shit.'

Strike laughed.

Polworth belched loudly, then checked his watch. He was a man who knew a good exit line and had no more time for prolonged leave-taking than for Russian literature.

'Gonna get going, Diddy,' he said, getting to his feet. 'If I'm back before half eleven, I'm on for a birthday blowie – which is the whole point I'm making, mate. Whole point.'

Grinning, Strike accepted Polworth's handshake. Polworth told Strike to convey his love to Joan and to call him next time he was down, then squeezed his way out of the pub, and disappeared from view.

2

Heart, that is inly hurt, is greatly eas'd
With hope of thing, that may allay his Smart . . .

Edmund Spenser
The Faerie Queene

Still grinning at Polworth's story, Strike now realised that the dark woman at the bar was showing signs of wanting to approach him. Her spectacled blonde companion appeared to be advising against it. Strike finished his pint, gathered up his wallet, checked his cigarettes were still in his pocket and, with the assistance of the wall beside him, stood up, making sure his balance was everything it should be before trying to walk. His prosthetic leg was occasionally uncooperative after four pints. Having assured himself that he could balance perfectly well, he set off towards the exit, giving unsmiling nods to those few locals whom he could not ignore without causing offence, and reached the warm darkness outside without being importuned.

The wide, uneven stone steps that led down towards the bay were still crowded with drinkers and smokers. Strike wove his way between them, pulling out his cigarettes as he went.

It was a balmy August night and tourists were still strolling around the picturesque seafront. Strike was facing a fifteen-minute walk, part of it up a steep slope, back to his aunt and uncle's house. On a whim he turned right, crossed the street and headed for the high stone wall separating the car park and ferry point from the sea. Leaning against it, he lit a cigarette and stared out over the smoke grey and silver ocean, becoming just one more tourist in the darkness, free to smoke quietly without having to answer questions about cancer, deliberately postponing the moment when he'd have to return to the uncomfortable sofa that had been his bed for the past six nights.

On arrival, Strike had been told that he, the childless single man and ex-soldier, wouldn't mind sleeping in the sitting room 'because *you'll* sleep anywhere'. She'd been determined to shut down the possibility, mooted by Strike on the phone, that he might check into a bed and breakfast rather than stretch the house to capacity. Strike's visits were rare, especially in conjunction with his sister and nephews, and Joan wanted to enjoy his presence to the full, wanted to feel that she was, once again, the provider and nurturer, currently weakened by her first round of chemotherapy though she might be.

So the tall and heavy Strike, who'd have been far happier on a camp bed, had lain down uncomplainingly every night on the slippery, unyielding mass of satin-covered horsehair, to be woken each morning by his young nephews, who routinely forgot that they had been asked to wait until eight o'clock before barging into the sitting room. At least Jack had the decency to whisper apologies every time he realised that he'd woken his uncle. The eldest, Luke, clattered and shouted his way down the narrow stairs every morning and merely sniggered as he dashed past Strike on his way to the kitchen.

Luke had broken Strike's brand-new headphones, which the detective had felt obliged to pretend didn't matter in the slightest. His eldest nephew had also thought it amusing to run off into the garden with Strike's prosthetic leg one morning, and to stand waving it at his uncle through the window.

When Luke finally brought it back, Strike, whose bladder had been very full and who was incapable of hopping up the steep stairs to the only toilet, had delivered Luke a quiet telling-off that had left the boy unusually subdued for most of the morning.

Meanwhile, Joan told Strike every morning, 'you slept well', without a hint of enquiry. Joan had a lifelong habit of subtly pressurising the family into telling her what she wanted to hear. In the days when Strike was sleeping in his office and facing imminent insolvency (facts that he had admittedly not shared with his aunt and uncle), Joan had told him happily 'you're doing awfully well' over the phone, and it had felt, as it always did, unnecessarily combative to challenge her optimistic declaration. After his lower leg had been blown off in Afghanistan, a tearful Joan had stood at his hospital bed as he tried to focus through a fog of morphine, and told him 'You feel comfortable, though. You aren't in pain.' He loved his aunt, who'd raised him for significant chunks of his childhood, but extended periods in her company made him feel stifled and suffocated. Her insistence on the smooth passing of counterfeit social coin from hand to hand, while uncomfortable truths were ignored and denied, wore him out.

Something gleamed in the water – sleek silver and a pair of soot-black eyes: a seal was turning lazily just below Strike. He watched its revolutions in the water, wondering whether it could see him and, for reasons he couldn't have explained, his thoughts slid towards his partner in the detective agency.

He was well aware that he hadn't told Polworth the whole truth about his relationship with Robin Ellacott, which, after all, was nobody else's business. The truth was that his feelings contained nuances and complications that he preferred not to examine. For instance, he had a tendency, when alone, bored or low-spirited, to want to hear her voice.

He checked his watch. She was having a day off, but there was an outside chance she'd still be awake and he had a decent pretext for texting: Saul Morris, their newest subcontractor, was owed his month's expenses, and Strike had left no instructions for sorting this out. If he texted about Morris, there was a good chance that Robin would call him back to find out how Joan was.

'Excuse me?' a woman said nervously, from behind him.

Strike knew without turning that it was the dark woman from the pub. She had a Home Counties accent and her tone contained that precise mixture of apology and excitement that he usually encountered in those who wanted to talk about his detective triumphs.

'Yes?' he said, turning to face the speaker.

Her blonde friend had come with her: or perhaps, thought Strike, they were more than friends. An indefinable sense of closeness seemed to bind the two women, whom he judged to be around forty. They wore jeans and shirts and the blonde in particular had the slightly weather-beaten leanness that suggests weekends spent hill walking or cycling. She was what some would call a 'handsome' woman, by which they meant that she was bare faced. High-cheekboned, bespectacled, her hair pulled back into a ponytail, she also looked stern.

The dark woman was slighter in build. Her large grey eyes shone palely in her long face. She had an air of intensity, even of fanaticism, about her in the half-light, like a medieval martyr.

'Are you . . . are you Cormoran Strike?' she asked.

'Yes,' he said, his tone uninviting.

'Oh,' she breathed, with an agitated little hand gesture. 'This is – this is so strange. I know you probably don't want to be – I'm sorry to bother you, I know you're off duty,' she gave a nervous laugh, 'but – my name's Anna, by the way – I wondered,' she took a deep breath, 'whether I could come – whether I could come and talk to you about my mother.'

Strike said nothing.

'She disappeared,' Anna went on. 'Margot Bamborough's her name. She was a GP. She finished work one evening, walked out of her practice and nobody's seen her since.'

'Have you contacted the police?' asked Strike.

Anna gave an odd little laugh.

'Oh yes – I mean, they knew – they investigated. But they never found anything. She disappeared,' said Anna, 'in 1974.'

The dark water lapped the stone and Strike thought he could hear the seal clearing its damp nostrils. Three drunk youths went weaving past, on their way to the ferry point. Strike wondered whether they knew the last ferry had been and gone at six.

'I just,' said the woman in a rush, 'you see – last week – I went to see a medium.'

Fuck, thought Strike.

He'd occasionally bumped up against the purveyors of paranormal insights during his detective career and felt nothing but contempt for them: leeches, or so he saw them, of money from the pockets of the deluded and the desperate.

A motorboat came chugging across the water, its engine grinding the night's stillness to pieces. Apparently this was the lift the three drunk boys were waiting for. They now began laughing and elbowing each other at the prospect of imminent seasickness.

'The medium told me I'd get a "leading",' Anna pressed on. 'She told me, "You're going to find out what happened to your mother. You'll get a leading and you must follow it. The way will become clear very soon." So when I saw you just now in the pub – *Cormoran Strike*, in the Victory – it just seemed such an incredible coincidence and I thought – I had to speak to you.'

A soft breeze ruffled Anna's dark, silver-streaked hair. The blonde said crisply,

'Come on, Anna, we should get going.'

She put an arm around the other's shoulders. Strike saw a wedding ring shining there.

'We're sorry to have bothered you,' she told Strike.

With gentle pressure, the blonde attempted to turn Anna away. The latter sniffed and muttered,

'Sorry. I . . . probably had too much wine.'

'Hang on.'

Strike often resented his own incurable urge to know, his inability to leave an itch unscratched, especially when he was as tired and aggravated as he was tonight. But 1974 was the year of his own birth. Margot Bamborough had been missing as long as he'd been alive. He couldn't help it: he wanted to know more.

'Are you on holiday here?'

'Yes.' It was the blonde who had spoken. 'Well, we've got a second home in Falmouth. Our permanent base is in London.'

'I'm heading back there tomorrow,' said Strike (*What the fuck are you doing?* asked a voice in his head), 'but I could probably swing by and see you tomorrow morning in Falmouth, if you're free.'

'Really?' gasped Anna. He hadn't seen her eyes fill with tears, but he knew they must have done, because she now wiped them. 'Oh, that'd be *great*. Thank you. *Thank you!* I'll give you the address.'

The blonde showed no enthusiasm at the prospect of seeing Strike again. However, when Anna started fumbling through her handbag, she said, 'It's all right, I've got a card', pulled a wallet out of her back pocket, and handed Strike a business card bearing the name 'Dr Kim Sullivan, BPS Registered Psychologist', with an address in Falmouth printed below it.

'Great,' said Strike, inserting it into his own wallet. 'Well, I'll see you both tomorrow morning, then.'

'I've actually got a work conference call in the morning,' said Kim. 'I'll be free by twelve. Will that be too late for you?'

The implication was clear: you're not speaking to Anna without me present.

'No, that'll be fine,' said Strike. 'I'll see you at twelve, then.'

'Thank you so much!' said Anna.

Kim reached for Anna's hand and the two women walked away. Strike watched them pass under a street light before turning back towards the sea. The motorboat carrying the young drinkers had now chugged away again. It already looked tiny, dwarfed by the wide bay, the roar of its engine gradually deadened into a distant buzz.

Forgetting momentarily about texting Robin, Strike lit a second cigarette, took out his mobile and Googled Margot Bamborough.

Two different photographs appeared. The first was a grainy head-and-shoulders shot of an attractive, even-featured face with wide-set eyes, her wavy, dark blonde hair centre-parted. She was wearing a long-lapelled blouse under what appeared to be a knitted tank top.

The second picture showed the same woman looking younger and wearing the famous black corset of a Playboy Bunny, accessorised with black ears, black stockings and white tail. She was holding a tray of what looked like cigarettes, and smiling at the camera. Another young woman, identically dressed, stood beaming behind her, slightly bucktoothed and curvier than her willowy friend.

Strike scrolled down until he read a famous name in conjunction with Margot's.

. . . young doctor and mother, Margaret **'Margot' Bamborough**, whose disappearance on 11 October 1974 shared certain features with Creed's abductions of Vera Kenny and Gail Wrightman.

Bamborough, who worked at the St John's Medical Practice in Clerkenwell, had arranged to meet a female friend in the local Three Kings pub at six o'clock. She never arrived.

Several witnesses saw a small white van driving at speed in the area around the time that **Bamborough** would have been heading for her rendezvous.

DI Bill Talbot, who led the investigation into **Bamborough**'s disappearance, was convinced from an early stage that the young doctor had fallen victim to the serial killer known to be at large in the south east area. However, no trace of **Bamborough** was discovered in the basement flat where Dennis Creed imprisoned, tortured and killed seven other women.

Creed's trademark of beheading the corpses of his victims . . .

3

But now of Britomart it here doth neede,
The hard aduentures and strange haps to tell

Edmund Spenser
The Faerie Queene

Had her day gone as planned, Robin Ellacott would have been tucked up in bed in her rented flat in Earl's Court at this moment, fresh from a long bath, her laundry done, reading a new novel. Instead, she was sitting in her ancient Land Rover, chilly from sheer exhaustion despite the mild night, still wearing the clothes she'd put on at four-thirty that morning, as she watched the lit window of a Pizza Express in Torquay. Her face in the wing mirror was pale, her blue eyes bloodshot, and the strawberry blonde hair currently hidden under a black beanie hat needed a wash.

From time to time, Robin dipped her hand into a bag of almonds sitting on the passenger seat beside her. It was only too easy to fall into a diet of fast food and chocolate when you were running surveillance, to snack more often than needed out of sheer boredom. Robin was trying to eat healthily in spite of her unsociable hours, but the almonds had long since ceased to be appetising, and she craved nothing more than a bit of the pizza she could see an overweight couple enjoying in the restaurant window. She could almost taste it, even though the air around her was tangy with sea salt and underlain by the perpetual fug of old Wellington boots and wet dog that imbued the Land Rover's ancient fabric seats.

The object of her surveillance, whom she and Strike had nicknamed 'Tufty' for his badly fitting toupee, was currently out of view. He'd disappeared into the pizzeria an hour and a half previously with three companions, one of whom, a teenager with his arm in a cast, was visible if Robin craned her head sideways into the space above the front passenger seat. This she did every five minutes or so, to check on the progress of the foursome's meal. The last time she had looked, ice cream was being delivered to the table. It couldn't, surely, be much longer.

Robin was fighting a feeling of depression which she knew was at least partly down to utter exhaustion, to the stiffness all over her body from many hours in the driving seat, and to the loss of her long-awaited day off. With Strike unavoidably absent from the agency for an entire week, she'd now worked a twenty-day stretch without breaks. Their best subcontractor, Sam Barclay, had been supposed to take over the Tufty job today in Scotland, but Tufty hadn't flown to Glasgow as expected. Instead, he'd taken a surprise detour to Torquay, leaving Robin with no choice but to follow him.

There were other reasons for her low spirits, of course, one of which she acknowledged to herself; the other, she felt angry with herself for dwelling on.

The first, admissible, reason was her ongoing divorce, which was becoming more contentious by the week. Following Robin's discovery of her estranged husband's affair, they'd had one last cold and bitter meeting, coincidentally in a Pizza Express near Matthew's place of work, where they'd agreed to seek a no-fault divorce following a two-year separation. Robin was too honest not to admit that she, too, bore responsibility for the failure of their relationship. Matthew might have been unfaithful, but she knew that she'd never fully committed to the marriage, that she'd prioritised her job over Matthew on almost every occasion and that, by the end, she had been waiting for a reason to leave. The affair had been a shock, but a release, too.

However, during the twelve months that had elapsed since her pizza with Matthew, Robin had come to realise that far from seeking a 'no-fault' resolution, her ex-husband saw the end of the marriage as entirely Robin's responsibility and was determined to make her pay, both emotionally and financially, for her offence. The joint bank account, which held the proceeds of the sale of their old house, had been frozen while the lawyers wrangled over how much Robin could reasonably expect when she had been earning so much less than Matthew, and had – it had been strongly hinted in the last letter – married him purely with a view to obtaining a pecuniary advantage she could never have achieved alone.

Every letter from Matthew's lawyer caused Robin additional stress, rage and misery. She hadn't needed her own lawyer to point out that Matthew appeared to be trying to force her to spend money she didn't have on legal wrangling, to run down the clock and her resources until she walked away with as close to nothing as he could manage.

'I've never known a childless divorce be so contentious,' her lawyer had told her, words that brought no comfort.

Matthew continued to occupy almost as much space in Robin's head as when they'd been married. She thought she could read his thoughts across the miles and silence that separated them in their widely divergent new lives. He'd always been a bad loser. He had to emerge from this embarrassingly short marriage the winner, by walking away with all the money, and stigmatising Robin as the sole reason for its failure.

All of this was ample reason for her present mood, of course, but then there was the other reason, the one that was inadmissible, that Robin was annoyed with herself for fretting about.

It had happened the previous day, at the office. Saul Morris, the agency's newest subcontractor, was owed his month's expenses, so, after seeing Tufty safely back into the marital home in Windsor, Robin had driven back to Denmark Street to pay Saul.

Morris had been working for the agency for six weeks. He was an ex-police officer, an undeniably handsome man, with black hair and bright blue eyes, though something about him set Robin's teeth on edge. He had a habit of softening his voice when he spoke to her; arch asides and over-personal comments peppered their most mundane interactions, and no double entendre went unmarked if Morris was in the room. Robin rued the day when he'd found out that both of them were currently going through divorces, because he seemed to think this gave him fertile new ground for assumed intimacy.

She'd hoped to get back from Windsor before Pat Chauncey, the agency's new office manager, left, but it was ten past six by the time Robin climbed the stairs and found Morris waiting for her outside the locked door.

'Sorry,' Robin said, 'traffic was awful.'

She'd paid Morris back in cash from the new safe, then told him briskly she needed to get home, but he clung on like gum stuck in her hair, telling her all about his ex-wife's latest late-night texts. Robin tried to unite politeness and coolness until the phone rang on her old desk. She'd ordinarily have let it go to voicemail, but so keen was she to curtail Morris's conversation that she said,

'I've got to get this, sorry. Have a nice evening,' and picked up the receiver.

'Strike Detective Agency, Robin speaking.'

'Hi, Robin,' said a slightly husky female voice. 'Is the boss there?'

Given that Robin had only spoken to Charlotte Campbell once, three years previously, it was perhaps surprising that she'd known instantly who was on the line. Robin had analysed these few words of Charlotte's to a perhaps ludicrous degree since. Robin had detected an undertone of laughter, as though Charlotte found Robin amusing. The easy use of Robin's first name and the description of Strike as 'the boss' had also come in for their share of rumination.

'No, I'm afraid not,' Robin had said, reaching for a pen while her heart beat a little faster. 'Can I take a message?'

'Could you ask him to call Charlotte Campbell? I've got something he wants. He knows my number.'

'Will do,' said Robin.

'Thanks very much,' Charlotte had said, still sounding amused. 'Bye, then.'

Robin had dutifully written down 'Charlotte Campbell called, has something for you' and placed the message on Strike's desk.

Charlotte was Strike's ex-fiancée. Their engagement had been terminated three years previously, on the very day that Robin had come to work at the agency as a temp. Though Strike was far from communicative on the subject, Robin knew that they'd been together for sixteen years ('on and off', as Strike tended to emphasise, because the relationship had faltered many times before its final termination), that Charlotte had become engaged to her present husband just two weeks after Strike had left her and that Charlotte was now the mother of twins.

But this wasn't all Robin knew, because after leaving her husband, Robin had spent five weeks living in the spare room of Nick and Ilsa Herbert, who were two of Strike's best friends.

Robin and Ilsa had struck up their own friendship during that time, and still met regularly for drinks and coffees. Ilsa made very little secret of the fact that she hoped and believed that Strike and Robin would one day, and preferably soon, realise that they were 'made for each other'. Although Robin regularly asked Ilsa to desist from her broad hints, asserting that she and Strike were perfectly happy with a friendship and working relationship, Ilsa remained cheerfully unconvinced.

Robin was very fond of Ilsa, but her pleas for her new friend to forget any idea of matchmaking between herself and Strike were genuine. She was mortified by the thought that Strike might think she herself was complicit in Ilsa's regular attempts to engineer foursomes that increasingly had the appearance of double dates. Strike had declined the last two proposed outings of this type and, while the agency's current workload certainly made any kind of social life difficult, Robin had the uncomfortable feeling that he was well aware of Ilsa's ulterior motive. Looking back on her own brief married life, Robin was sure she'd never been guilty of treating single people as she now found herself treated by Ilsa: with a cheerful lack of concern for their sensibilities, and sometimes ham-fisted attempts to manage their love lives.

One of the ways in which Ilsa attempted to draw Robin out on the subject of Strike was to tell her all about Charlotte, and here, Robin felt guilty, because she rarely shut the Charlotte conversations down, even though she never left one of them without feeling as though she had just gorged on junk food: uncomfortable, and wishing she could resist the craving for more.

She knew, for instance, about the many me-or-the-army ultimatums, two of the suicide attempts ('The one on Arran wasn't a proper one,' said Ilsa scathingly. 'Pure manipulation') and about the ten days' enforced stay in the psychiatric clinic.

She'd heard stories that Ilsa gave titles like cheap thrillers: the Night of the Bread Knife, the Incident of the Black Lace Dress and the Blood-Stained Note. She knew that in Ilsa's opinion, Charlotte was bad, not mad, and that the worst rows Ilsa and her husband Nick had ever had were on the subject of Charlotte, 'and she'd have bloody loved knowing that, too,' Ilsa had added.

And now Charlotte was phoning the office, asking Strike to call her back, and Robin, sitting outside the Pizza Express, hungry and exhausted, was pondering the phone call yet again, much as a tongue probes a mouth ulcer. If she was phoning the office, Charlotte clearly wasn't aware that Strike was in Cornwall with his terminally ill aunt, which didn't suggest regular contact between them. On the other hand, Charlotte's slightly amused tone had seemed to hint at an alliance between herself and Strike.

Robin's mobile, which was lying on the passenger seat beside the bag of almonds, buzzed. Glad of any distraction, she picked it up and saw a text message from Strike.

Are you awake?

Robin texted back:

No

As she'd expected, the mobile rang immediately.

'Well, you shouldn't be,' said Strike, without preamble. 'You must be knackered. What's it been, three weeks straight on Tufty?'

'I'm still on him.'

'What?' said Strike, sounding displeased. 'You're in Glasgow? Where's Barclay?'

'In Glasgow. He was ready in position, but Tufty didn't get on the plane. He drove down to Torquay instead. He's having pizza right now. I'm outside the restaurant.'

'The hell's he doing in Torquay, when the mistress is in Scotland?'

'Visiting his original family,' said Robin, wishing she could see Strike's face as she delivered the next bit of news. 'He's a bigamist.'

Her announcement was greeted with total silence.

'I was outside the house in Windsor at six,' said Robin, 'expecting to follow him to Stansted, see him safely onto the plane and let Barclay know he was on the way, but he didn't go to the airport. He rushed out of the house looking panicky, drove to a lock-up, took his case inside and came out with an entirely different set of luggage and minus his toupee. Then he drove all the way down here.

'Our client in Windsor's about to find out she's not legally married,' said Robin. 'Tufty's had this wife in Torquay for twenty years. I've been talking to the neighbours. I pretended I was doing a survey. One of the women along the street was at the original wedding. Tufty travels a lot for business, she said, but he's a lovely man. Devoted to his sons.

'There are two boys,' Robin continued, because Strike's stunned silence continued unabated, 'students, both in their late teens and both the absolute spit of him. One of them came off his motorbike yesterday – I got all this out of the neighbour – he's got his arm in a cast and looks quite bruised and cut up. Tufty must've got news of the accident, so he came haring down here instead of going to Scotland.

'Tufty goes by the name of Edward Campion down here, not John – turns out John's his middle name, I've been searching the online records. He and the first wife and sons live in a really nice villa, view of the sea, massive garden.'

'Bloody hell,' said Strike. 'So our pregnant friend in Glasgow—'

'—is the least of Mrs-Campion-in-Windsor's worries,' said Robin. 'He's leading a triple life. Two wives and a mistress.'

'And he looks like a balding baboon. There's hope for all of us. Did you say he's having dinner right now?'

'Pizza with the wife and kids. I'm parked outside. I didn't manage to get pictures of him with the sons earlier, and I want to, because they're a total giveaway. Mini-Tuftys, just like the two in Windsor. Where d'you think he's been pretending to have been?'

'Oil rig?' suggested Strike. 'Abroad? Middle East? Maybe that's why he's so keen on keeping his tan topped up.'

Robin sighed.

'The client's going to be shattered.'

'So's the mistress in Scotland,' said Strike. 'That baby's due any minute.'

'His taste's amazingly consistent,' said Robin. 'If you lined them up side by side, the Torquay wife, the Windsor wife and the mistress in Glasgow, they'd look like the same woman at twenty-year intervals.'

'Where are you planning to sleep?'

'Travelodge or a B&B,' said Robin, yawning again, 'if I can find anything vacant at the height of the holiday season. I'd drive straight back to London overnight, but I'm exhausted. I've been awake since four, and that's on top of a ten-hour day yesterday.'

'No driving and no sleeping in the car,' said Strike. 'Get a room.'

'How's Joan?' asked Robin. 'We can handle the workload if you want to stay in Cornwall a bit longer.'

'She won't sit still while we're all there. Ted agrees she needs some quiet. I'll come back down in a couple of weeks.'

'So, were you calling for an update on Tufty?'

'Actually, I was calling about something that just happened. I've just left the pub . . .'

In a few succinct sentences, Strike described the encounter with Margot Bamborough's daughter.

'I've just looked her up,' he said. 'Margot Bamborough, twenty-nine-year-old doctor, married, one-year-old daughter. Walked out of her GP practice in Clerkenwell at the end of a day's work, said she was going to have a quick drink with a female friend before heading home. The pub was only five minutes' walk away. The friend waited, but Margot never arrived and was never seen again.'

There was a pause. Robin, whose eyes were still fixed on the window of the pizza restaurant, said,

'And her daughter thinks you're going to find out what happened, nearly four decades later?'

'She seemed to be putting a lot of store on the coincidence of spotting me in the boozer right after the medium told her she'd get a "leading".'

'Hmm,' said Robin. 'And what do *you* think the chances are of finding out what happened after this length of time?'

'Slim to non-existent,' admitted Strike. 'On the other hand, the truth's out there. People don't just vaporise.'

Robin could hear a familiar note in his voice that indicated rumination on questions and possibilities.

'So you're meeting the daughter again tomorrow?'

'Can't hurt, can it?' said Strike.

Robin didn't answer.

'I know what you're thinking,' he said, with a trace of defensiveness. 'Emotionally overwrought client – medium – situation ripe for exploitation.'

'I'm not suggesting *you'd* exploit it—'

'Might as well hear her out, then, mightn't I? Unlike a lot

of people, I wouldn't take her money for nothing. And once I'd exhausted all avenues—'

'I know you,' said Robin. 'The less you found out, the more interested you'd get.'

'Think I'd have her wife to deal with unless I got results within a reasonable period. They're a gay couple,' he elaborated. 'The wife's a psychol—'

'Cormoran, I'll call you back,' said Robin, and without waiting for his answer, she cut the call and dropped the mobile back onto the passenger seat.

Tufty had just ambled out of the restaurant, followed by his wife and sons. Smiling and talking, they turned their steps towards their car, which lay five behind where Robin sat in the Land Rover. Raising her camera, she took a burst of pictures as the family drew nearer.

By the time they passed the Land Rover, the camera was lying in her lap and Robin's head was bowed over her phone, pretending to be texting. In the rear-view mirror she watched as the Tufty family got into their Range Rover and departed for the villa beside the sea.

Yawning yet again, Robin picked up her phone and called Strike back.

'Get everything you wanted?' he asked.

'Yeah,' said Robin, checking the photographs one-handedly with the phone to her ear, 'I've got a couple of clear ones of him and the boys. God, he's got strong genes. All four kids have got his exact features.'

She put the camera back into her bag.

'You realise I'm only a couple of hours away from St Mawes?'

'Nearer three,' said Strike.

'If you like—'

'You don't want to drive all the way down here, then back to London. You've just told me you're knackered.'

But Robin could tell that he liked the idea. He'd travelled down to Cornwall by train, taxi and ferry, because since he had lost a leg, long drives were neither easy nor particularly pleasurable.

'I'd like to meet this Anna. Then I could drive you back.'

'Well, if you're sure, that'd be great,' said Strike, now sounding cheerful. 'If we take her on, we should work the case together. There'd be a massive amount to sift through, cold case like this, and it sounds like you've wrapped up Tufty tonight.'

'Yep,' sighed Robin. 'It's all over except for the ruining of half a dozen lives.'

'*You* didn't ruin anyone's life,' said Strike bracingly. 'He did that. What's better: all three women find out now, or when he dies, with all the effing mess that'll cause?'

'I know,' said Robin, yawning again. 'So, do you want me to come to the house in St M—'

His 'no' was swift and firm.

'They – Anna and her partner – they're in Falmouth. I'll meet you there. It's a shorter drive for you.'

'OK,' said Robin. 'What time?'

'Could you manage half eleven?'

'Easily,' said Robin.

'I'll text you a place to meet. Now go and get some sleep.'

As she turned the key in the ignition, Robin became conscious that her spirits had lifted considerably. As though a censorious jury were watching, among them Ilsa, Matthew and Charlotte Campbell, she consciously repressed her smile as she reversed out of the parking space.

4

Begotten by two fathers of one mother,
Though of contrarie natures each to other . . .

Edmund Spenser
The Faerie Queene

Strike woke shortly before five the following morning. Light was already streaming through Joan's thin curtains. Every night the horsehair sofa punished a different part of his body, and today he felt as though he had been punched in a kidney. He reached for his phone, noted the time, decided that he was too sore to fall back asleep, and raised himself to a sitting position.

After a minute spent stretching and scratching his armpits while his eyes acclimatised to the odd shapes rising on all sides in the gloom of Joan and Ted's sitting room, he Googled Margot Bamborough for a second time and, after a cursory examination of the picture of the smiling, wavy-haired doctor with widely spaced eyes, he scrolled through the results until he found a mention of her on a website devoted to serial killers. Here he found a long article punctuated with pictures of Dennis Creed at various ages, from pretty, curly-haired blond toddler all the way through to the police mugshot of a slender man with a weak, sensual mouth and large, square glasses.

Strike then turned to an online bookstore, where he found

an account of the serial killer's life, published in 1985 and titled *The Demon of Paradise Park.* It had been written by a well-respected investigative journalist, now dead. Creed's nondescript face appeared in colour on the cover, superimposed over ghostly black and white images of the seven women he was known to have tortured and killed. Margot Bamborough's face wasn't among them. Strike ordered the second-hand book, which cost £1, to be delivered to the office.

He returned his phone to its charging lead, put on his prosthetic leg, picked up his cigarettes and lighter, navigated around a rickety nest of tables with a vase of dried flowers on it and, being careful not to nudge any of the ornamental plates off the wall, passed through the doorway and down three steep steps into the kitchen. The lino, which had been there since his childhood, was icy cold on his remaining foot.

After making himself a mug of tea, he let himself out of the back door, still clad in nothing but boxers and a T-shirt, there to enjoy the cool of early morning, leaning up against the wall of the house, breathing in salt-laden air between puffs on his cigarette, and thinking about vanished mothers. Many times over the past ten days had his thoughts turned to Leda, a woman as different to Joan as the moon to the sun.

'Have you tried smoking yet, Cormy?' she'd once asked vaguely, out of a haze of blue smoke of her own creation. 'It isn't good for you, but God, I love it.'

People sometimes asked why social services never got involved with Leda Strike's family. The answer was that Leda had never stayed still long enough to present a stable target. Often her children remained in a school for mere weeks before a new enthusiasm seized her, and off they went, to a new city, a new squat, crashing on her friends' floors or, occasionally, renting. The only people who knew what was going on, and who might have contacted social services, were Ted and Joan, the one fixed point in the children's lives, but whether because Ted feared damaging the relationship between himself and his wayward sister, or because Joan worried that the children might not forgive her, they'd never done so.

One of the most vivid memories of Strike's childhood was also one of the rare occasions he could remember crying, when Leda had made an unannounced return, six weeks into Strike's first term at St Mawes Primary School. Amazed and angry that such definitive steps as enrolling him in school had been taken in her absence, she'd ushered him and his sister directly onto the ferry, promising them all manner of treats up in London. Strike had bawled, trying to explain to her that he and Dave Polworth had been going to explore smugglers' caves at the weekend, caves that might well have had no existence except in Dave's imagination, but which were no less real to Strike for that.

'You'll see the caves,' Leda had promised, plying him with sweets once they were on the train to London. 'You'll see what's-his-name soon, I promise.'

'Dave,' Strike had sobbed, 'he's called D-Dave.'

Don't think about it, Strike told himself, and he lit a second cigarette from the tip of his first.

'Stick, you'll catch your death, out there in boxers!'

He looked around. His sister was standing in the doorway, wrapped in a woollen dressing gown and wearing sheepskin slippers. They were physically so unalike that people struggled to believe that they were related, let alone half-siblings. Lucy was small, blonde and pink-faced, and greatly resembled her father, a musician not quite as famous as Strike's, but far more interested in maintaining contact with his offspring.

'Morning,' he said, but she'd already disappeared, returning with his trousers, sweatshirt, shoes and socks.

'Luce, it's not cold—'

'You'll get pneumonia. Put them on!'

Like Joan, Lucy had total confidence in her own judgement of her nearest and dearest's best interests. With slightly better grace than he might have mustered had he not been about to return to London, Strike took his trousers and put them on, balancing awkwardly and risking a fall onto the gravel path. By the time he'd added a shoe and sock to his real foot, Lucy had made him a fresh mug of tea along with her own.

'I couldn't sleep, either,' she told him, handing over the mug as she sat down on the stone bench. It was the first time they'd been entirely alone all week. Lucy had been glued to Joan's side, insisting on doing all the cooking and cleaning while Joan, who found it inconceivable that she should sit down while the house was full of guests, hovered and fussed. On the rare moments that Joan wasn't present, one or more of Lucy's sons had generally been there, in Jack's case wanting to talk to Strike, the other two generally badgering Lucy for something.

'It's awful, isn't it?' said Lucy, staring out over the lawn and Ted's carefully tended flower-beds.

'Yeah,' sighed Strike. 'But fingers crossed. The chemo—'

'But it won't cure her. It'll just prolong – pro—'

Lucy shook her head and dabbed at her eyes with a crumpled piece of toilet roll she pulled out of her dressing-gown pocket.

'I've rung her twice a week for nigh on twenty years, Stick. This place is a second home for our boys. She's the only mother I've ever known.'

Strike knew he oughtn't to rise to the bait. Nevertheless, he said,

'Other than our actual mother, you mean.'

'Leda wasn't my mother,' said Lucy coldly. Strike had never heard her say it in so many words, though it had often been implied. 'I haven't considered her my mother since I was fourteen years old. Younger, actually. *Joan's* my mother.'

And when Strike made no response, she said,

'You chose Leda. I know you love Joan, but we have entirely different relationships with her.'

'Didn't realise it was a competition,' Strike said, reaching for another cigarette.

'I'm only telling you how I feel!'

And telling me how I *feel.*

Several barbed comments about the infrequency of Strike's visits had already dropped from his sister's lips during their week of enforced proximity. He'd bitten back all irritable retorts. His primary aim was to leave the house without rowing with anyone.

'I always hated it when Leda came to take us away,' said Lucy now, 'but you were glad to go.'

He noted the Joan-esque statement of fact, the lack of enquiry.

'I wasn't always glad to go,' Strike contradicted her, thinking of the ferry, Dave Polworth and the smugglers' caves, but Lucy seemed to feel that he was trying to rob her of something.

'I'm just saying, you lost *your* mother years ago. Now I'm – I might be – losing mine.'

She mopped her eyes again with the damp toilet roll.

Lower back throbbing, eyes stinging with tiredness, Strike stood smoking in silence. He knew that Lucy would have liked to excise Leda for ever from her memory, and sometimes, remembering a few of the things Leda had put them through, he sympathised. This morning, though, the wraith of Leda seemed to drift on his cigarette smoke around him. He could hear her saying to Lucy, 'Go on and have a good cry, darling, it always helps', and 'Give your old mum a fag, Cormy'. He couldn't hate her.

'I can't *believe* you went out with Dave Polworth last night,' said Lucy suddenly. 'Your last night here!'

'Joan virtually shoved me out of the house,' said Strike, nettled. 'She loves Dave. Anyway, I'll be back in a couple of weeks.'

'Will you?' said Lucy, her eyelashes now beaded with tears. 'Or will you be in the middle of some case and just forget?'

Strike blew smoke out into the constantly lightening air, which had that flat blue tinge that precedes sunrise. Far to the right, hazily visible over the rooftops of the houses on the slope that was Hillhead, the division between sky and water was becoming clearer on the horizon.

'No,' he said, 'I won't forget.'

'Because you're good in a crisis,' said Lucy, 'I don't deny that, but it's keeping a commitment going that you seem to have a problem with. Joan'll need support for months and months, not just when—'

'I know that, Luce,' said Strike, his temper rising in spite of himself. 'I understand illness and recuperation, believe it or—'

'Yeah, well,' said Lucy, 'you were great when Jack was in hospital, but when everything's fine you simply don't bother.'

'I took Jack out two weeks ago, what're you—?'

'You couldn't even make the effort to come to Luke's birthday party! He'd told all his friends you were going to be there—'

'Well, he shouldn't have done, because I told you *explicitly* over the phone—'

'You said you'd try—'

'No, *you* said I'd try,' Strike contradicted her, temper rising now, in spite of his best intentions. '*You* said "You'll make it if you can, though." Well, I couldn't make it, I told you so in advance and it's not my fault you told Luke differently—'

'I appreciate you taking Jack out every now and then,' said Lucy, talking over him, 'but has it never occurred to you that it would be nice if the other two could come, too? Adam *cried* when Jack came home from the War Rooms! And then you come down here,' said Lucy, who seemed determined to get everything off her chest now she'd started, 'and you only bring a present for Jack. What about Luke and Adam?'

'Ted called with the news about Joan and I set straight off. I'd been saving those badges for Jack, so I brought them with me.'

'Well, how do you think that makes Luke and Adam feel? Obviously they think you don't like them as much as Jack!'

'I don't,' said Strike, finally losing his temper. 'Adam's a whiny little prick and Luke's a complete arsehole.'

He crushed out his cigarette on the wall, flicked the stub into the hedge and headed back inside, leaving Lucy gasping for air like a beached fish.

Back in the dark sitting room, Strike blundered straight into the table nest: the vase of dried flowers toppled heavily onto the patterned carpet and before he knew what he was doing he'd crushed the fragile stems and papery heads to dust beneath his false foot. He was still tidying up the fragments as best he could when Lucy strode silently past him towards the door to the stairs, emanating maternal outrage. Strike set the now empty vase back on the table and, waiting until he heard Lucy's bedroom door close, headed upstairs for the bathroom, fuming.

Afraid to use the shower in case he woke Ted and Joan, he peed, pulled the flush and only then remembered how noisy the old toilet was. Washing as best he could in tepid water while the cistern refilled with a noise like a cement mixer, Strike thought that if anyone slept through that, they'd have to be drugged.

Sure enough, on opening the bathroom door, he came face to face with Joan. The top of his aunt's head barely came up to Strike's chest. He looked down on her thinning grey hair, into once forget-me-not blue eyes now bleached with age. Her frogged and quilted red dressing gown had the ceremonial dignity of a kabuki robe.

'Morning,' Strike said, trying to sound cheerful and achieving only a fake bonhomie. 'Didn't wake you, did I?'

'No, no, I've been awake for a while. How was Dave?' she asked.

'Great,' said Strike heartily. 'Loving his new job.'

'And Penny and the girls?'

'Yeah, they're really happy to be back in Cornwall.'

'Oh good,' said Joan. 'Dave's mum thought Penny might not want to leave Bristol.'

'No, it's all worked out great.'

The bedroom door behind Joan opened. Luke was standing there in his pyjamas, rubbing his eyes ostentatiously.

'You woke me up,' he told Strike and Joan.

'Oh, sorry, love,' said Joan.

'Can I have Coco Pops?'

'Of course you can,' said Joan fondly.

Luke bounded downstairs, stamping on the stairs to make as much noise as possible. He was gone barely a minute before he came bounding back towards them, glee etched over his freckled face.

'Granny, Uncle Cormoran's broken your flowers.'

You little shit.

'Yeah, sorry. The dried ones,' Strike told Joan. 'I knocked them over. The vase is fine—'

'Oh, they couldn't matter less,' said Joan, moving at once to the stairs. 'I'll fetch the carpet sweeper.'

'No,' said Strike at once, 'I've already—'

'There are still bits all over the carpet,' Luke said. 'I trod on them.'

I'll tread on you in a minute, arsehole.

Strike and Luke followed Joan back to the sitting room,

where Strike insisted on taking the carpet sweeper from Joan, a flimsy, archaic device she'd had since the seventies. As he plied it, Luke stood in the kitchen doorway watching him, smirking while shovelling Coco Pops into his mouth. By the time Strike had cleaned the carpet to Joan's satisfaction, Jack and Adam had joined the early morning jamboree, along with a stony-faced Lucy, now fully dressed.

'Can we go to the beach today, Mum?'

'Can we swim?'

'Can I go out in the boat with Uncle Ted?'

'Sit down,' Strike told Joan. 'I'll bring you a cup of tea.'

But Lucy had already done it. She handed Joan the mug, threw Strike a filthy look, then turned back to the kitchen, answering her sons' questions as she went.

'What's going on?' asked Ted, shuffling into the room in pyjamas, confused by this break-of-dawn activity.

He'd once been nearly as tall as Strike, who greatly resembled him. His dense, curly hair was now snow white, his deep brown face more cracked than lined, but Ted was still a strong man, though he stooped a little. However, Joan's diagnosis seemed to have dealt him a physical blow. He seemed literally shaken, a little disorientated and unsteady.

'Just getting my stuff together, Ted,' said Strike, who suddenly had an overpowering desire to leave. 'I'm going to have to get the first ferry to make the early train.'

'Ah,' said Ted. 'All the way back up to London, are you?'

'Yep,' said Strike, chucking his charging lead and deodorant back into the kit bag where the rest of his belongings were already neatly stowed. 'But I'll be back in a couple of weeks. You'll keep me posted, right?'

'You can't leave without breakfast!' said Joan anxiously. 'I'll make you a sandwich—'

'It's too early for me to eat,' lied Strike. 'I've had a cup of tea and I'll get something on the train. Tell her,' he said to Ted, because Joan wasn't listening, but scurrying for the kitchen.

'Joanie!' Ted called. 'He doesn't want anything!'

Strike grabbed his jacket off the back of a chair and hoisted the kit bag out to the hall.

'You should go back to bed,' he told Joan, as she hurried to bid him goodbye. 'I really didn't want to wake you. Rest, all right? Let someone else run the town for a few weeks.'

'I wish you'd stop smoking,' she said sadly.

Strike managed a humorous eye roll, then hugged her. She clung to him the way she had done whenever Leda was waiting impatiently to take him away, and Strike squeezed her back, feeling again the pain of divided loyalties, of being both battleground and prize, of having to give names to what was uncategorisable and unknowable.

'Bye, Ted,' he said, hugging his uncle. 'I'll ring you when I'm home and we'll fix up a time for the next visit.'

'I could've driven you,' said Uncle Ted feebly. 'Sure you don't want me to drive you?'

'I like the ferry,' lied Strike. In fact, the uneven steps leading down to the boat were almost impossible for him to navigate without assistance from the ferryman, but because he knew it would give them pleasure, he said, 'Reminds me of you two taking us shopping in Falmouth when we were kids.'

Lucy was watching him, apparently unconcerned, through the door from the sitting room. Luke and Adam hadn't wanted to leave their Coco Pops, but Jack came wriggling breathlessly into the tiny hall to say,

'Thanks for my badges, Uncle Corm.'

'It was a pleasure,' said Strike, and he ruffled the boy's hair. 'Bye, Luce,' he called. 'See you soon, Jack,' he added.

5

He little answer'd, but in manly heart
His mightie indignation did forbeare,
Which was not yet so secret, but some part
Thereof did in his frouning face appeare . . .

Edmund Spenser
The Faerie Queene

The bedroom in the bed and breakfast where Robin spent the night barely had room for a single bed, a chest of drawers and a rickety sink plumbed into the corner. The walls were covered in a mauve floral wallpaper that Robin thought must surely have been considered tasteless even in the seventies, the sheets felt damp and the window was imperfectly covered by a tangled Venetian blind.

In the harsh glare of a single light bulb unsoftened by its shade of open wickerwork, Robin's reflection looked exhausted and ill-kempt, with purple shadows beneath her eyes. Her backpack contained only those items she always carried on surveillance jobs – a beanie hat, should she need to conceal her distinctive red-blonde hair, sunglasses, a change of top, a credit card and ID in a couple of different names. The fresh T-shirt she'd just pulled out of her backpack was heavily creased and her hair in urgent need of a wash; the sink was soapless and she'd omitted to pack toothbrush or toothpaste, unaware that she was going to be spending the night away from home.

Robin was back on the road by eight. In Newton Abbot she stopped at a chemist and a Sainsbury's, where she purchased, in addition to basic toiletries and dry shampoo, a small, cheap bottle of 4711 cologne. She cleaned her teeth and made herself as presentable as possible in the supermarket bathroom. While brushing her hair, she received a text from Strike:

I'll be in the Palacio Lounge café in The Moor, middle of Falmouth. Anyone will tell you where The Moor is.

The further west Robin drove, the lusher and greener the landscape became. Yorkshire-born, she'd found it extraordinary to see palm trees actually flourishing on English soil, back in Torquay. These twisting, verdant lanes, the luxuriance of the vegetation, the almost sub-tropical greenness was a surprise to a person raised among bare, rolling moors and hillside. Then there were the glints to her left of a quicksilver sea, as wide and gleaming as plate glass, and the tang of the salt now mixed with the citrus of her hastily purchased cologne. In spite of her tiredness she found her spirits buoyed by the glorious morning, and the idea of Strike waiting at journey's end.

She arrived in Falmouth at eleven o'clock, and drove in search of a parking space through streets packed with tourists and past shop doorways accreted in plastic toys and pubs covered in flags and multicoloured window boxes. Once she'd parked in The Moor itself – a wide open market square in the heart of the town – she saw that beneath the gaudy summertime trappings, Falmouth boasted some grand old nineteenth-century buildings, one of which housed the Palacio Lounge café and restaurant.

The high ceilings and classical proportions of what looked

like an old courthouse had been decorated in a self-consciously whimsical style, which included garish orange floral wallpaper, hundreds of kitschy paintings in pastel frames, and a stuffed fox dressed as a magistrate. The clientele, which was dominated by students and families, sat on mismatched wooden chairs, their chatter echoing through the cavernous space. After a few seconds Robin spotted Strike, large and surly-looking at the back of the room, seeming far from happy beside a pair of families whose many young children, most of whom were wearing tie-dyed clothing, were racing around between tables.

Robin thought she saw the idea of standing to greet her cross Strike's mind as she wound her way through the tables towards him, but if she was right, he decided against. She knew how he looked when his leg was hurting him, the lines around his mouth deeper than usual, as though he had been clenching his jaw. If Robin had looked tired in the dusty bed and breakfast mirror three hours previously, Strike looked utterly drained, his unshaven jaw appearing dirty, the shadows under his eyes dark blue.

'Morning,' he said, struggling to make himself heard over the merry shrieking of the hippy children. 'Get parked OK?'

'Just round the corner,' she said, sitting down.

'I chose this place because I thought it would be easy to find,' he said.

A small boy knocked into their table, causing Strike's coffee to slop over onto his plate, which was littered with croissant flakes, and ran off again. 'What d'you want?'

'Coffee would be great,' said Robin loudly, over the cries of the children beside them. 'How're things in St Mawes?'

'Same,' said Strike.

'I'm sorry,' said Robin.

'Why? It's not your fault,' grunted Strike.

This was hardly the greeting Robin had expected after a two-and-a-half hour drive to pick him up. Possibly her annoyance showed, because Strike added,

'Thanks for doing this. Appreciate it. *Oh, don't pretend you can't see me, dipshit*,' he added crossly, as a young waiter walked away without spotting his raised hand.

'I'll go to the counter,' said Robin. 'I need the loo anyway.'

By the time she'd peed and managed to order a coffee from a harassed waiter, a tension headache had begun to pound on the left-hand side of her head. On her return to the table she found Strike looking like thunder, because the children at the next tables were now shrieking louder than ever as they raced around their oblivious parents, who simply shouted over the din. The idea of giving Strike Charlotte's telephone message right now passed through Robin's mind, only to be dismissed.

In fact, the main reason for Strike's foul mood was that the end of his amputated leg was agony. He'd fallen (*like a total tit*, as he told himself) while getting onto the Falmouth ferry. This feat required a precarious descent down worn stone steps without a handhold, then a step down into the boat with only the boatman's hand for assistance. At sixteen stone, Strike was hard to stabilise when he slipped, and slip he had, with the result that he was now in a lot of pain.

Robin took paracetamol out of her bag.

'Headache,' she said, catching Strike's eye.

'I'm not bloody surprised,' he said loudly, looking at the parents shouting at each other over the raucous yells of their offspring, but they didn't hear him. The idea of asking Robin for painkillers crossed Strike's mind, but this might engender enquiries and fussing, and he'd had quite enough of those in the past week, so he continued to suffer in silence.

'Where's the client?' she asked, after downing her pills with coffee.

'About five minutes' drive away. Place called Wodehouse Terrace.'

At this point, the smallest of the children racing around nearby tripped and smacked her face on the wooden floor. The child's shrieks and wails of pain pounded against Robin's eardrums.

'Oh, Daffy!' said one of the tie-dyed mothers shrilly, '*what* have you done?'

The child's mouth was bloody. Her mother crouched beside their table, loudly castigating and soothing, while the girl's siblings and friends watched avidly. The ferry-goers this morning had worn similar expressions when Strike had hit the deck.

'He's got a false leg,' the ferryman had shouted, partly, Strike suspected, in case anyone thought the fall was due to his negligence. The announcement had in no way lessened Strike's mortification or the interest of his fellow travellers.

'Shall we get going?' Robin asked, already on her feet.

'Definitely,' said Strike, wincing as he stood and picked up his holdall. 'Bloody kids,' he muttered, limping after Robin towards the sunlight.

6

Faire Lady, hart of flint would rew
The vndeserued woes and sorrowes, which ye shew.

Edmund Spenser
The Faerie Queene

Wodehouse Terrace lay on a hill, with a wide view of the bay below. Many of the houses had had loft conversions, but Anna and Kim's, as they saw from the street, had been more extensively modified than any other, with what looked like a square glass box where once there had been roof.

'What does Anna do?' asked Robin, as they climbed the steps towards the deep blue front door.

'No idea,' said Strike, 'but her wife's a psychologist. I got the impression she isn't keen on the idea of an investigation.'

He pressed the doorbell. They heard footsteps on what sounded like bare wood, and the door was opened by Dr Sullivan, tall, blonde and barefoot in jeans and a shirt, the sun glinting off her spectacles. She looked from Strike to Robin, apparently surprised.

'My partner, Robin Ellacott,' Strike explained.

'Oh,' said Kim, looking displeased. 'You do realise – this is only supposed to be an exploratory meeting.'

'Robin happened to be just up the coast on another case, so—'

'I'm more than happy to wait in the car,' said Robin politely, 'if Anna would rather speak to Cormoran alone.'

'Well – we'll see how Anna feels.'

Standing back to admit them, Kim added, 'Straight upstairs, in the sitting room.'

The house had clearly been remodelled throughout and to a high standard. Everywhere was bleached wood and glass. The bedroom, as Robin saw through an open door, had been relocated to the ground floor, along with what looked like a study. Upstairs, in the glass box they'd seen from the street, was an open-plan area combining kitchen, dining and sitting room, with a dazzling view of the sea.

Anna was standing beside a gleaming, expensive coffee machine, wearing a baggy blue cotton jumpsuit and white canvas shoes, which to Robin looked stylish and to Strike, frumpy. Her hair was tied back, revealing the delicacy of her bone structure.

'Oh, hello,' she said, starting at the sight of them. 'I didn't hear the door over the coffee machine.'

'Annie,' said Kim, following Strike and Robin into the room, 'this is Robin Ellacott, er – Cameron's partner. She's happy to go if you'd rather just talk to—'

'Cormoran,' Anna corrected Kim. 'Do people get that wrong a lot?' she asked Strike.

'More often than not,' he said, but with a smile. 'But it's a bloody stupid name.'

Anna laughed.

'I don't mind you staying,' she told Robin, advancing and offering a handshake. 'I think I read about you, too,' she added, and Robin pretended that she didn't notice Anna glancing down at the long scar on her forearm.

'Please, sit down,' said Kim, gesturing Strike and Robin to an inbuilt seating area around a low Perspex table.

'Coffee?' suggested Anna, and both of them accepted.

A ragdoll cat came prowling into the room, stepping delicately through the puddles of sunlight on the floor, its clear blue eyes like Joan's across the bay. After subjecting both Strike and Robin to dispassionate scrutiny, it leapt lightly onto the sofa and into Strike's lap.

'Ironically,' said Kim, as she carried a tray laden with cups and biscuits to the table, 'Cagney absolutely *loves* men.'

Strike and Robin laughed politely. Anna brought over the coffee pot, and the two women sat down side by side, facing Strike and Robin, their faces in the full glare of the sun until Anna reached for a remote control, which automatically lowered cream-coloured sun blinds.

'Wonderful place,' said Robin, looking around.

'Thanks,' said Kim. '*Her* work,' she said, patting Anna's knee. 'She's an architect.'

Anna cleared her throat.

'I want to apologise,' she said, looking steadily at Strike with her unusual silver-grey eyes, 'for the way I behaved last night. I'd had a few glasses of wine. You probably thought I was a crank.'

'If I'd thought that,' said Strike, stroking the loudly purring cat, 'I wouldn't be here.'

'But mentioning the medium probably gave you entirely the wrong . . . because, believe me, Kim's already told me what a fool I was to go and see her.'

'I don't think you're a fool, Annie,' Kim said quietly. 'I think you're vulnerable. There's a difference.'

'May I ask what the medium said?' asked Strike.

'Does it matter?' asked Kim, looking at Strike with what Robin thought was mistrust.

'Not in an investigative sense,' said Strike, 'but as he – she? – is the reason Anna approached me—'

'It was a woman,' said Anna, 'and she didn't really tell me anything useful . . . not that I . . .'

With a nervous laugh, she shook her head and started again.

'I know it was a stupid thing to do. I – I've been through a difficult time recently – I left my firm and I'm about to turn forty and . . . well, Kim was away on a course and I – well, I suppose I wanted—'

She waved her hands dismissively, took a deep breath and said,

'She's quite an ordinary-looking woman who lives in Chiswick. Her house was full of angels – made of pottery and glass, I mean, and there was a big one painted on velvet over the fireplace.

'Kim,' Anna pressed on, and Robin glanced at the psychologist, whose expression was impassive, 'Kim thinks she – the medium – knew who my mother was – that she Googled me before I arrived. I'd given her my real name. When I got there, I simply said that my mother died a long time ago – although of course,' said Anna, with another nervous wave of her thin hands, 'there's no proof that my mother's dead – that's half the – but anyway, I told the medium she'd died, and that nobody had ever been clear with me about how it happened.

'So the woman went into a – well, I suppose you'd call it a trance,' Anna said, looking embarrassed, 'and she told me that people thought they were protecting me for my own good, but that it was time I knew the truth and that I would soon have a "leading" that would take me to it. And she said "your mother's very proud of you" and "she's always watching over you", and things like that, I suppose they're boilerplate – and then, at the end, "she lies in a holy place".

'"Lies in a holy place"?' repeated Strike.

'Yes. I suppose she thought that would be comforting, but I'm not a churchgoer. The sanctity or otherwise of my mother's final resting place – if she's buried – I mean, it's hardly my primary concern.'

'D'you mind if I take notes?' Strike asked.

He pulled out a notebook and pen, which Cagney the cat appeared to think were for her personal amusement. She attempted to bat the pen around as Strike wrote the date.

'Come here, you silly animal,' said Kim, getting up to lift the cat clear and put her back on the warm wooden floor.

'To begin at the beginning,' said Strike. 'You must've been very young when your mother went missing?'

'Just over a year old,' said Anna, 'so I can't remember her at all. There were no photographs of her in the house while I was growing up. I didn't know what had happened for a long time. Of course, there was no internet back then – anyway, my mother kept her own surname after marriage. I grew up as Anna Phipps, which is my father's name. If anybody had said "Margot Bamborough" to me before I was eleven, I wouldn't have known she had any connection to me.

'I thought Cynthia was my mum. She was my childminder when I was little,' she explained. 'She's a third cousin of my father's and quite a bit younger than him, but she's a Phipps, too, so I assumed we were a standard nuclear family. I mean – why wouldn't I?

'I do remember, once I'd started school, questioning why I was calling Cyn "Cyn" instead of "Mum". But then Dad and Cyn decided to get married, and they told me I could call her "Mum" now if I wanted to, and I thought, oh, I see, I had to use her name before, because they weren't married. You fill in the gaps when you're a child, don't you? With your own weird logic.

'I was seven or eight when a girl at school said to me, "That's not your real mum. Your real mum disappeared." It sounded mad. I didn't ask Dad or Cyn about it. I just locked it away, but I think, on some deep level, I sensed I'd just been handed the answer to some of the strange things I'd noticed and never been given answers to.

'I was eleven when I found out properly. By then, I'd heard other things from other kids at school. "Your real mum ran away" was one of them. Then one day, this really *poisonous* boy said to me, "Your mum was killed by a man who cut off her head."'

'I went home and I told my father what that boy had said. I wanted him to laugh, to say it was ridiculous, what a horrible little boy . . . but he turned white.

'That same evening he and Cynthia called me downstairs out of my bedroom, sat me down in the sitting room and told me the truth.

'And everything I thought I knew crumbled away,' said Anna quietly. 'Who thinks something like this has happened in their own family? I adored Cyn. I got on better with her than with my father, to tell you the truth. And then I found out that she wasn't my mum at all, and they'd both lied – lied in fact, lied by omission.

'They told me my mother walked out of her GP's practice one night and vanished. The last person to see her alive was the receptionist. She said she was off to the pub, which was five minutes up the road. Her best friend was waiting there. When my mother didn't turn up, the friend, Oonagh Kennedy, who'd waited an hour, thought she must have forgotten. She called my parents' house. My mother wasn't there. My father called the practice, but it was closed. It got dark. My mother didn't come home. My father called the police.

'They investigated for months and months. Nothing. No clues, no sightings – at least, that's what my father and Cyn said, but I've since read things that contradict that.

'I asked Dad and Cyn where my mother's parents were.

They said they were dead. That turned out to be true. My grandfather died of a heart attack a couple of years after my mother disappeared and my grandmother died of a stroke a year later. My mother was an only child, so there were no other relatives I could meet or talk to about her.

'I asked for photographs. My father said he'd got rid of them all, but Cyn dug some out for me, a couple of weeks after I found out. She asked me not to tell my father she'd done it; to hide them. I did: I had a pyjama case shaped like a rabbit and I kept my mother's photographs in there for years.'

'Did your father and stepmother explain to you what *might* have happened to your mother?' Strike asked.

'Dennis Creed, you mean?' said Anna. 'Yes, but they didn't tell me details. They said there was a chance she'd been killed by a – by a bad man. They had to tell me that much, because of what the boy at school had said.

'It was an appalling idea, thinking she might have been killed by Creed – I found out his name soon enough, kids at school were happy to fill me in. I started having nightmares about her, headless. Sometimes she came into my bedroom at night. Sometimes I dreamed I found her head in my toy chest.

'I got really angry with my father and Cyn,' said Anna, twisting her fingers together. 'Angry that they'd never told me, obviously, but I also started wondering what else they were hiding, whether they were involved in my mother disappearing, whether they'd wanted her out of the way, so they could marry. I went a bit off the rails, started playing truant . . . one weekend I took off and was brought home by the police. My father was livid. Of course, I look back, and after what had happened to my mother . . . obviously, me going missing, even for a few hours . . .

'I gave them hell, to tell you the truth,' said Anna shamefacedly. 'But all credit to Cyn, she stuck by me. She never gave up. She and Dad had had kids together by then – I've got a younger brother and sister – and there was family therapy and holidays with bonding activities, all led by Cyn, because my father certainly didn't want to do it. The subject of my mother just makes him angry and aggrieved. I remember him yelling at me, didn't I realise how terrible it was for *him* to have it all dragged up again, how did I think *he* felt . . .

'When I was fifteen I tried to find my mother's friend, Oonagh, the one she was supposed to be meeting the night she disappeared. They were Bunny Girls together,' said Anna, with a little smile, 'but I didn't know that at the time. I tracked Oonagh down in Wolverhampton, and she was quite emotional to hear from me. We had a couple of lovely phone calls. She told me things I really wanted to know, about my mother's sense of humour, the perfume she wore – Rive Gauche, I went out and blew my birthday money on a bottle next day – how she was addicted to chocolate and was an obsessive Joni Mitchell fan. My mother came more alive to me when I was talking to Oonagh than through the photographs, or anything Dad or Cyn had told me.

'But my father found out I'd spoken to Oonagh and he was furious. He made me give him Oonagh's number and called her and accused her of encouraging me to defy him, told her I was troubled, in therapy and what I didn't need was people "stirring". He told me not to wear the Rive Gauche, either. He said he couldn't stand the smell of it.

'So I never did meet Oonagh, and when I tried to reconnect with her in my twenties, I couldn't find her. She might have passed away, for all I know.'

'I got into university, left home and started reading everything I could about Dennis Creed. The nightmares came back, but it didn't get me any closer to finding out what really happened.

'Apparently the man in charge of the investigation into my mother's disappearance, a detective inspector called Bill Talbot, always thought Creed took her. Talbot will be dead by now; he was coming up for retirement anyway.

'Then, a few years out of uni, I had the bright idea of starting a website,' said Anna. 'My girlfriend at the time was tech-savvy. She helped me set it up. I was very naive,' she sighed. 'I said who I was and begged for information about my mother.

'You can probably imagine what happened. All kinds of theories: psychics telling me where to dig, people telling me my father had obviously done it, others telling me I wasn't really Margot's daughter, that I was after money and publicity, and some really malicious messages as well, saying my mother had probably run off with a lover and worse. A couple of journalists got in touch, too. One of them ran an awful piece in the *Daily Express* about our family: they contacted my father and that was just about the final nail in the coffin for our relationship.

'It's never really recovered,' said Anna bleakly. 'When I told him I'm gay, he seemed to think I was only doing it to spite him. And Cyn's gone over to his side a bit, these last few years. She always says, "I've got a loyalty to your dad, too, Anna." So,' said Anna, 'that's where we are.'

There was a brief silence.

'Dreadful for you,' said Robin.

'It is,' agreed Kim, placing her hand on Anna's knee again, 'and I'm wholly sympathetic to Anna's desire for resolution, of course I am. But is it realistic,' she said, looking from Robin to Strike, 'and I mean this with no offence to you two, to think that you'll achieve what the police haven't, after all this time?'

'Realistic?' said Strike. 'No.'

Robin noticed Anna's downward look and the sudden rush of tears into her large eyes. She felt desperately sorry for the older woman, but at the same time she respected Strike's honesty, and it seemed to have impressed the sceptical Kim, too.

'Here's the truth,' Strike said, tactfully looking at his notes until Anna had finished drying her eyes with the back of her hand. 'I think we'd have a reasonable chance of getting hold of the old police file, because we've got decent contacts at the Met. We can sift right through the evidence again, revisit witnesses as far as that's possible, basically make sure every stone's been turned over twice.

'But it's odds on that after all this time, we wouldn't find any more than the police did, and we'd be facing two major obstacles.

'Firstly, zero forensic evidence. From what I understand, literally no trace of your mother was ever found, is that right? No items of clothing, bus pass – nothing.'

'True,' mumbled Anna.

'Secondly, as you've just pointed out, a lot of the people connected with her or who witnessed anything that night are likely to have died.'

'I know,' said Anna, and a tear trickled, sparkling, down her nose onto the Perspex table. Kim reached out and put an arm around her shoulders. 'Maybe it's turning forty,' said Anna, with a sob, 'but I can't stand the idea that I'll go to my grave never knowing what happened.'

'I understand that,' said Strike, 'but I don't want to promise what I'm unlikely to be able to deliver.'

'Have there,' asked Robin, 'been any new leads or developments over the years?'

Kim answered. She seemed a little shaken by Anna's naked distress, and kept her arm around her shoulders.

'Not as far as we know, do we, Annie? But any information of that kind would probably have gone to Roy – Anna's father. And he might not have told us.'

'He acts as though none of it ever happened; it's how he copes,' said Anna, wiping her tears away. 'He pretends my mother never existed – except for the inconvenient fact that if she hadn't, I wouldn't be here.

'Believe it or not,' she said, 'it's the possibility that she just went away of her own accord and never came back, never wanted to see how I was doing, or let us know where she was, that really haunts me. That's the thing I can't bear to contemplate. My grandmother on my father's side, who I never loved – she was one of the meanest women I've ever met – took it upon herself to tell me that it had always been her private belief that my mother had simply run away. That she didn't like being a wife and a mother. That hurt me more than I can tell you, the thought that my mother would let everyone go through the horror of wondering what had happened to her, and never check that her daughter was all right . . .

'Even if Dennis Creed killed her,' said Anna, 'it would be terrible – awful – but it would be over. I could mourn rather than live with the possibility that she's out there somewhere, living under a different name, not caring what happened to us all.'

There was a brief silence, in which both Strike and Robin drank coffee, Anna sniffed, and Kim left the sofa area to tear off some kitchen roll, which she handed to her wife.

A second ragdoll cat entered the room. She subjected the four humans to a supercilious glare before lying down and stretching in a patch of sunlight.

'That's Lacey,' said Kim, while Anna mopped her face. 'She doesn't really like anyone, even us.'

Strike and Robin laughed politely again.

'How would this work?' asked Kim abruptly. 'How d'you charge?'

'By the hour,' said Strike. 'You'd get an itemised monthly

bill. I can email you our rates,' he offered, 'but I'd imagine you two will want to talk this over properly before coming to a decision.'

'Yes, definitely,' said Kim, but as she gave Strike her email address she looked with concern again at Anna, who was sitting with head bowed, still pressing kitchen roll to her eyes at regular intervals.

Strike's stump protested at being asked to support his weight again so soon after sitting down, but there seemed little more to discuss, especially as Anna had regressed into a tearful silence. Slightly regretting the untouched plate of biscuits, the detective shook Anna's cool hand.

'Thanks, anyway,' she said, and he had the feeling that he had disappointed her, that she'd hoped he would make her a promise of the truth, that he would swear upon his honour to do what everyone else had failed to do.

Kim showed them out of the house.

'We'll call you later,' she said. 'This afternoon. Will that be all right?'

'Great, we'll wait to hear from you,' said Strike.

Robin glanced back as she and Strike headed down the sunlit garden steps towards the street, and caught Kim giving them a strange look, as though she'd found something in the pair of visitors that she hadn't expected. Catching Robin's eye, she smiled reflexively, and closed the blue door behind them.

7

Long they thus traueiled in friendly wise,
Through countreyes waste, and eke well edifyde . . .

Edmund Spenser
The Faerie Queene

As they headed out of Falmouth, Strike's mood turned to cheerfulness, which Robin attributed mainly to the interest of a possible new case. She'd never yet known an intriguing problem to fail to engage his attention, no matter what might be happening in his private life.

She was partially right: Strike's interest had certainly been piqued by Anna's story, but he was mainly cheered by the prospect of keeping weight off his prosthesis for a few hours, and by the knowledge that every passing minute put further distance between himself and his sister. Opening the car window, allowing the familiar sea air to rush bracingly inside the old car, he lit a cigarette and, blowing smoke away from Robin, asked,

'Seen much of Morris while I've been away?'

'Saw him yesterday,' said Robin. 'Paid him for his month's expenses.'

'Ah, great, cheers,' said Strike, 'I meant to remind you that needed doing. What d'you think of him? Barclay says he's good at the job, except he talks too much in the car.'

'Yeah,' said Robin noncommittally, 'he does like to talk.'

'Hutchins thinks he's a bit smarmy,' said Strike, subtly probing.

He'd noticed the special tone Morris reserved for Robin. Hutchins had also reported that Morris had asked him what Robin's relationship status was.

'Mm,' said Robin, 'well, I haven't really had enough contact with him to form an opinion.'

Given Strike's current stress levels and the amount of work the agency was struggling to cover, she'd decided not to criticise his most recent hire. They needed an extra man. At least Morris was good at the job.

'Pat likes him,' she added, partly out of mischief, and was amused to see, out of the corner of her eye, Strike turn to look at her, scowling.

'That's no bloody recommendation.'

'Unkind,' said Robin.

'You realise in a week's time it's going to be harder to sack her? Her probation period's nearly up.'

'I don't want to sack her,' said Robin. 'I think she's great.'

'Well, then, on your head be it if she causes trouble down the line.'

'It won't be on my head,' said Robin. 'You're not pinning Pat on me. Hiring her was a joint decision. You were the one who was sick of temps— '

'And you were the one who said "it might not be a bad idea to get a more traditional manager in" and "we shouldn't discount her because of her age"—'

'—I know what I said, and I stand by the age thing. We *do* need someone who understands a spreadsheet, who's organised, but you were the one who—'

'—I didn't want you accusing me of ageism.'

'*—you were the one who offered her the job*,' Robin finished firmly.

'Dunno what I was bloody thinking,' muttered Strike, flicking ash out of the window.

Patricia Chauncey was fifty-six and looked sixty-five. A thin woman with a deeply lined, monkeyish face and implausibly jet-black hair, she vaped continually in the office, but was to be seen drawing deeply on a Superking the moment her feet touched the pavement at the end of the day's work. Pat's voice was so deep and rasping that she was often mistaken for Strike on the phone. She sat at what once had been Robin's desk in the outer office and had taken over the bulk of the agency's phone-answering and administrative duties now that Robin had moved to full-time detection.

Strike and Pat's relationship had been combative from the start, which puzzled Robin, who liked them both. Robin was used to Strike's intermittent bouts of moodiness, and prone to give him the benefit of the doubt, especially when she suspected he was in pain, but Pat had no compunction about snapping 'Would a "thanks" kill you?' if Strike showed insufficient gratitude when she passed him his phone messages. She evidently felt none of the reverence some of their temps had displayed towards the now famous detective, one of whom had been sacked on the spot when Strike realised she was surreptitiously filming him on her mobile from the outer office. Indeed, the office manager's demeanour suggested that she lived in daily expectation of finding out things to Strike's discredit, and she'd displayed a certain satisfaction on hearing that the dent in one of the filing cabinets was due to the fact that he'd once punched it.

On the other hand, the filing was up to date, the accounts were in order, all receipts were neatly docketed, the phone was answered promptly, messages were passed on accurately, they never ran out of teabags or milk, and Pat had never once arrived late, no matter the weather and irrespective of Tube delays.

It was true, too, that Pat liked Morris, who was the recipient of most of her rare smiles. Morris was always careful to pay Pat his full tribute of blue-eyed charm before turning his attention to Robin. Pat was already alert to the possibility of romance between her younger colleagues.

'He's lovely-looking,' she'd told Robin just the previous week, after Morris had phoned in his location so that the temporarily unreachable Barclay could be told where to take over surveillance on their biggest case. 'You've got to give him that.'

'I haven't got to give him anything,' Robin had said, a little crossly.

It was bad enough having Ilsa badger her about Strike in her leisure time without Pat starting on Morris during her working hours.

'Quite right,' Pat had responded, unfazed. 'Make him earn it.'

'Anyway,' said Strike, finishing his cigarette and crushing the stub out in the tin Robin kept for that purpose in the glove compartment, 'you've wrapped up Tufty. Bloody good going.'

'Thanks,' Robin said. 'But there's going to be press. Bigamy's always news.'

'Yeah,' said Strike. 'Well, it's going to be worse for him than us, but it's worth trying to keep our name out of it if we can. I'll have a word with Mrs-Campion-in-Windsor. So that leaves us,' he counted the names on his thick fingers, 'with Two-Times, Twinkletoes, Postcard and Shifty.'

It had become the agency's habit to assign nicknames to their targets and clients, mainly to avoid letting real names slip in public or in emails. Two-Times was a previous client of the agency, who'd recently resurfaced after trying other private detectives and finding them unsatisfactory. Strike and Robin had previously investigated two of his girlfriends. At a superficial glance, he seemed most unlucky in love, a man whose partners, initially attracted by his fat bank balance, seemed incapable of fidelity. Over time, Strike and Robin had come to believe that he derived obscure emotional or sexual satisfaction from being cheated on, and that they were being paid to provide evidence that, far from upsetting him, gave him pleasure. Once confronted with photographic evidence of her perfidy, the girlfriend of the moment would be confronted, dismissed and another found, and the whole pattern repeated. This time round, he was dating a glamour model who thus far, to Two-Times' poorly concealed disappointment, seemed to be faithful.

Twinkletoes, whose unimaginative nickname had been chosen by Morris, was a twenty-four-year-old dancer who was currently having an affair with a thirty-nine-year-old double-divorcee, notable mainly for her history of drug abuse and her enormous trust fund. The socialite's father was employing the agency to discover anything they could about Twinkletoes' background or behaviour, which could be used to prise his daughter away from him.

Postcard was, so far, an entirely unknown quantity. A middle-aged and, in Robin's opinion, fairly unattractive television weather forecaster had come to the agency after the police had said there was nothing they could do about the postcards that had begun to arrive at his place of work and, most worryingly, hand delivered to his house in the small hours. The cards made no threats; indeed, they were often no more than banal comments on the weatherman's choice of tie, yet they gave evidence of knowing far more about the man's movements and private life than a stranger should have. The use of postcards was also a peculiar choice, when persecution was so much easier, these days, online. The agency's subcontractor, Andy Hutchins, had now spent two solid weeks' worth of nights parked outside the weatherman's house, but Postcard hadn't yet shown themselves.

Last, and most lucrative, was the interesting case of Shifty, a young investment banker whose rapid rise through his company had generated a predictable amount of resentment among overlooked colleagues, which had exploded into full-blown suspicion when he'd been promoted to the second-in-command job ahead of three undeniably better qualified candidates. Exactly what leverage Shifty had on the CEO (known to the agency as Shifty's Boss or SB) was now a matter of interest not only to Shifty's subordinates, but to a couple of suspicious board members, who'd met Strike in a dark bar in the City to lay out their concerns. Strike's current strategy was to try to find out more about Shifty through his personal assistant, and to this end Morris had been given the job of chatting her up after hours, revealing neither his real name nor his occupation, but trying to gauge how deep her loyalty to Shifty ran.

'D'you need to be back in London by any particular time?' Strike asked, after a brief silence.

'No,' said Robin, 'why?'

'Would you mind,' said Strike, 'if we stop for food? I didn't have breakfast.'

Despite remembering that he had, in fact, had a plate full of croissant crumbs in front of him when she arrived at the Palacio Lounge, Robin agreed. Strike seemed to read her mind.

'You can't count a croissant. Mostly air.'

Robin laughed.

By the time they reached Subway at Cornwall Services, the atmosphere between the two of them had become almost light-hearted, notwithstanding their tiredness. Once Robin, mindful of her resolution to eat more healthily, had started on her salad and Strike had taken a few satisfying mouthfuls of his steak and cheese sandwich, he emailed Kim Sullivan their form letter about billing clients, then said,

'I had a row with Lucy this morning.'

Robin surmised that it must have been a bad one, for Strike to mention it.

'Five o'clock, in the garden, while I was having a quiet smoke.'

'Bit early for conflict,' said Robin, picking unenthusiastically through lettuce leaves.

'Well, it turns out we're competing in the Who Loves Joan Best Handicap Stakes. Didn't even know I'd been entered.'

He ate in silence for a minute, then went on,

'It ended with me telling her I thought Adam's a whiny prick and Luke's an arsehole.'

Robin, who'd been sipping her water, inhaled, and was seized by a paroxysm of coughs. Diners at nearby tables glanced round as Robin spluttered and gasped. Grabbing a paper napkin from the table to mop her chin and her streaming eyes, she wheezed,

'What – on *earth* – did you say that for?'

'Because Adam's a whiny prick and Luke's an arsehole.'

Still trying to cough water out of her windpipe, Robin laughed, eyes streaming, but shook her head.

'Bloody hell, Cormoran,' she said, when at last she could talk properly.

'You haven't just had a solid week of them. Luke broke my new headphones, then ran off with my leg, the little shit. Then Lucy accuses me of favouring Jack. Of course I favour him – he's the only decent one.'

'Yes, but telling their *mother*—'

'Yeah, I know,' said Strike heavily. 'I'll ring and apologise.'

There was a brief pause. 'But for fuck's sake,' he growled, 'why do I have to take all three of them out together? Neither of the others give a toss about the military. "Adam cried when you came back from the War Rooms", my arse. The little bastard didn't like that I'd bought Jack stuff, that's all. If Lucy had her way, I'd be taking them on group outings every weekend, and they'd *take turns* to choose; it'll be the zoo and effing go-karting, and everything that was good about me seeing Jack'll be ruined. I *like* Jack,' said Strike, with what appeared to be surprise. 'We're interested in the same stuff. What's with this mania for treating them all the same? Useful life lesson, I'd have thought, realising you aren't owed. You don't get stuff automatically because of who you're related to.

'But fine, she wants me to buy the other two presents,' and he framed a square in mid-air with his hands. '"Try Not Being a Little Shit". I'll get that made up as a plaque for Luke's bedroom wall.'

They bought a bag of snacks, then resumed their drive. As they turned out onto the road again, Strike expressed his guilt that he couldn't share the driving, because the old Land Rover was too much of a challenge with his false leg.

'It doesn't matter,' said Robin. 'I don't mind. What's funny?' she added, seeing Strike smirking at something he had found in their bag of food.

'English strawberries,' he said.

'And that's comical, why?'

He explained about Dave Polworth's fury that goods of Cornish origin weren't labelled as such, and his commensurate glee that more and more locals were putting their Cornish identity above English on forms.

'Social identity theory's very interesting,' said Robin. 'That and self-categorisation theory. I studied them at uni. There are implications for businesses as well as society, you know . . . '

She talked happily for a couple of minutes before realising, on glancing sideways, that Strike had fallen fast asleep. Choosing not to take offence, because he looked grey with tiredness, Robin fell silent, and other than the occasional grunting snore, there was no more communication to be had from Strike until, on the outskirts of Swindon, he suddenly jerked awake again.

'Shit,' he said, wiping his mouth with the back of his hand, 'sorry. How long was I asleep?'

'About three hours,' said Robin.

'Shit,' he said again, 'sorry,' and immediately reached for a cigarette. 'I've been kipping on the world's most uncomfortable sofa and the kids have woken me up at the crack of fucking dawn every day. Want anything from the food bag?'

'Yes,' said Robin, throwing the diet to the winds. She was in urgent need of a pick-me-up. 'Chocolate. English or Cornish, I don't mind.'

'Sorry,' Strike said for a third time. 'You were telling me about a social theory or something.'

Robin grinned.

'You fell asleep around the time I was telling you my fascinating application of social identity theory to detective practice.'

'Which is?' he said, trying to make up in politeness now what he had lost earlier.

Robin, who knew perfectly well that this was why he had asked the question, said,

'In essence, we tend to sort each other and ourselves into groupings, and that usually leads to an overestimation of similarities between members of a group, and an underestimation of the similarities between insiders and outsiders.'

'So you're saying all Cornishmen aren't rugged salt-of-the-earthers and all Englishmen aren't pompous arseholes?'

Strike unwrapped a Yorkie and put it into her hand.

'Sounds unlikely, but I'll run it past Polworth next time we meet.'

Ignoring the strawberries, which had been Robin's purchase, Strike opened a can of Coke and drank it while smoking and watching the sky turn bloody as they drew nearer to London.

'Dennis Creed's still alive, you know,' said Strike, watching trees blur out of the window. 'I was reading about him online this morning.'

'Where is he?' asked Robin.

'Broadmoor,' said Strike. 'He went to Wakefield initially, then Belmarsh, and was transferred to Broadmoor in '95.'

'What was the psychiatric diagnosis?'

'Controversial. Psychiatrists disagreed about whether or not he was sane at his trial. Very high IQ. In the end the jury decided he was capable of knowing what he was doing was wrong, hence prison, not hospital. But he must've developed symptoms since that to justify medical treatment.

'On a very small amount of reading,' Strike went on, 'I can see why the lead investigator thought Margot Bamborough might have been one of Creed's victims. Allegedly, there was a small van seen speeding dangerously in the area, around the time she should have been walking towards the Three Kings. Creed used a van,' Strike elucidated, in response to Robin's questioning look, 'in some of the other known abductions.'

The lamps along the motorway had been lit before Robin, having finished her Yorkie, quoted:

'"She lies in a holy place".'

Still smoking, Strike snorted.

'Typical medium bollocks.'

'You think?'

'Yes, I bloody think,' said Strike. 'Very convenient, the way people can only speak in crossword clues from the afterlife. Come off it.'

'All right, calm down. I was only thinking out loud.'

'You could spin almost anywhere as "a holy place" if you wanted. Clerkenwell, where she disappeared – that whole area's got some kind of religious connection. Monks or something. Know where Dennis Creed was living in 1974?'

'Go on.'

'Paradise Park, Islington,' said Strike.

'Oh,' said Robin. 'So you think the medium *did* know who Anna's mother was?'

'If I was in the medium game, I'd sure as hell Google clients' names before they showed up. But it could've been a fancy touch designed to sound comforting, like Anna said. Hints at a decent burial. However bad her end was, it's purified by where her remains are. Creed admitted to scattering bone fragments in Paradise Park, by the way. Stamped them into the flower-beds.'

Although the car was still stuffy, Robin felt a small, involuntary shudder run through her.

'Fucking ghouls,' said Strike.

'Who?'

'Mediums, psychics, all those shysters . . . preying on people.'

'You don't think some of them believe in what they're doing? Think they really are getting messages from the beyond?'

'I think there are a lot of nutters in the world, and the less we reward them for their nuttery, the better for all of us.'

The mobile rang in Strike's pocket. He pulled it out.

'Cormoran Strike.'

'Yes, hello – it's Anna Phipps. I've got Kim here, too.'

Strike turned the mobile to speakerphone.

'Hope you can hear us all right,' he said, over the rumble and rattle of the Land Rover. 'We're still in the car.'

'Yes, it is noisy,' said Anna.

'I'll pull over,' said Robin, and she did so, turning smoothly onto the hard shoulder.

'Oh, that's better,' said Anna, as Robin turned off the engine. 'Well, Kim and I have talked it over, and we've decided: we *would* like to hire you.'

Robin felt a jolt of excitement.

'Great,' said Strike. 'We're very keen to help, if we can.'

'But,' said Kim, 'we feel that, for psychological and – well, candidly, financial – reasons we'd like to set a term on the investigation, because if the police haven't solved this case in nigh on forty years – I mean, you could be looking for the next forty and find nothing.'

'That's true,' said Strike. 'So—'

'We think a year,' said Anna, sounding nervous. 'What do you – does that seem reasonable?'

'It's what I would have suggested,' said Strike. 'To be honest, I don't think we've got much chance in anything under twelve months.'

'Is there anything more you need from me to get started?' Anna asked, sounding both nervous and excited.

'I'm sure something will occur to me,' said Strike, taking out his notebook to check a name, 'but it would be good to speak to your father and Cynthia.'

The other end of the line became completely silent. Strike and Robin looked at each other.

'I don't think there's any chance of that,' said Anna. 'I'm sorry, but if my father knew I was doing this, I doubt he'd ever forgive me.'

'And what about Cynthia?'

'The thing is,' came Kim's voice, 'Anna's father's been unwell recently. Cynthia is the more reasonable of the two on this subject, but she won't want anything to upset Roy just now.'

'Well, no problem,' said Strike, raising his eyebrows at Robin. 'Our first priority's got to be getting hold of the police file. In the meantime, I'll email you one of our standard contracts. Print it out, sign it and send it back, we'll get going.'

'Thank you,' said Anna and, with a slight delay, Kim said, 'OK, then.'

They hung up.

'Well, well,' said Strike. 'Our first cold case. This is going to be interesting.'

'And we've got a year,' said Robin, pulling back out onto the motorway.

'They'll extend that if we look as though we're onto something,' said Strike.

'Good luck with that,' said Robin sardonically. 'Kim's prepared to give us a year so she can tell Anna they've tried everything. I'll bet you a fiver right now we don't get any extensions.'

'I'll take that bet,' said Strike. 'If there's a hint of a lead, Anna's going to want to see it through to the end.'

The remainder of the journey was spent discussing the agency's four current investigations, a conversation that took them all the way to the top of Denmark Street, where Strike got out.

'Cormoran,' said Robin, as he lifted the holdall out of the back of the Land Rover, 'there's a message on your desk from Charlotte Campbell. She called the day before yesterday and asked you to ring her back. She said she's got something you want.'

There was a brief moment where Strike simply looked at Robin, his expression unreadable.

'Right. Thanks. Well, I'll see you tomorrow. No, I won't,' he instantly contradicted himself, 'you've got time off. Enjoy.'

And with a slam of the rear door he limped off towards the office, head down, carrying his holdall over his shoulder, leaving an exhausted Robin no wiser as to whether he did or didn't want whatever it was that Charlotte Campbell had.

PART TWO

Then came the Autumne all in yellow clad . . .

Edmund Spenser
The Faerie Queene

8

Full dreadfull thinges out of that balefull booke
He red . . .

Edmund Spenser
The Faerie Queene

When Strike and Robin broke the news of her husband's bigamy, the white-faced woman they now called the Second Mrs Tufty had sat in silence for a couple of minutes. Her small but charming house in central Windsor was quiet that Tuesday morning, her son and daughter at primary school, and she'd cleaned before they arrived: there was a smell of Pledge in the air and Hoover marks on the carpet. Upon the highly polished coffee table lay ten photographs of Tufty in Torquay, minus his toupee, laughing as he walked out of the pizza restaurant with the teenage boys who so strongly resembled the young children he'd fathered in Windsor, his arm around a smiling woman who might have been their client's older sister.

Robin, who could remember exactly how she'd felt when Sarah Shadlock's diamond earring had fallen out of her own marital bed, could only guess at the scale of pain, humiliation and shame behind the taut face. Strike was speaking conventional words of sympathy, but Robin would have bet her entire bank account that Mrs Tufty hadn't heard a word – and knew she'd been right when Mrs Tufty suddenly stood up, shaking so badly that Strike also struggled to his feet, mid-sentence, in case she needed catching. However, she walked jerkily past him out of the room. Shortly afterwards, they heard the front door open and spotted their client through the net curtain, approaching a red Audi Q3 parked in front of the house with a golf club in her hand.

'Oh shit,' said Robin.

By the time they reached her, the Second Mrs Tufty had smashed the windscreen and put several deep dents in the roof of the car. Gawping neighbours had appeared at windows and a pair of Pomeranians were yapping frenziedly behind glass in the house opposite. When Strike grabbed the four iron out of her hand, Mrs Tufty swore at him, tried to wrestle it back, then burst into a storm of tears.

Robin put her arm around their client and steered her firmly back into the house, Strike bringing up the rear, holding the golf club. In the kitchen, Robin instructed Strike to make strong coffee and find brandy. On Robin's advice, Mrs Tufty called her brother and begged him to come, quickly, but when she'd hung up and begun scrolling to find Tufty's number, Robin jerked the mobile out of her well-manicured hand.

'Give it back!' said Mrs Tufty, wild-eyed and ready to fight. 'The bastard . . . the bastard . . . I want to talk to him . . . give it back!'

'Bad idea,' said Strike, putting coffee and brandy in front of her. 'He's already proven he's adept at hiding money and assets from you. You need a shit-hot lawyer.'

They remained with the client until her brother, a suited HR executive, arrived. He was annoyed that he'd been asked to leave work early, and so slow at grasping what he was being told that Strike became almost irate and Robin felt it necessary to intervene to stop a row.

'Fuck's sake,' muttered Strike, as they drove back towards

London. '*He was already married to someone else when he married your sister.* How hard is that to grasp?'

'Very hard,' said Robin, an edge to her voice. 'People don't expect to find themselves in these kinds of situations.'

'D'you think they heard me when I asked them not to tell the press we were involved?'

'No,' said Robin.

She was right. A fortnight after they'd visited Windsor, they woke to find several tabloids carrying front-page exposés of Tufty and his three women, a picture of Strike in all the inside pages and his name in one of the headlines. He was news in his own right now, and the juxtaposition of famous detective and squat, balding, wealthy man who'd managed to run two families and a mistress was irresistible.

Strike had only ever given evidence at noteworthy court cases while sporting the full beard that grew conveniently fast when he needed it, and the picture the press used most often was an old one that showed him in uniform. Nevertheless, it was an ongoing battle to remain as inconspicuous as his chosen profession demanded, and being badgered for comment at his offices was an inconvenience he could do without. The storm of publicity was prolonged when both Mrs Tuftys formed an offensive alliance against their estranged husband. Showing an unforeseen taste for publicity, they not only granted a women's magazine a joint interview, but appeared on several daytime television programmes together to discuss their long deception, their shock, their newfound friendship, their intention to make Tufty rue the day he'd met either of them and to issue a thinly veiled warning to the pregnant mistress in Glasgow (who, astonishingly, seemed disposed to stand by Tufty) that she had another think coming if she imagined he'd have two farthings to rub together once his wives had finished with him.

September proceeded, cool and unsettled. Strike called Lucy

to say sorry for being rude about her sons, but she remained cold even after the apology, doubtless because he'd merely expressed regret for voicing his opinion out loud, and hadn't retracted it. Strike was relieved to discover that her boys had weekend sporting fixtures now that school had started again, which meant he didn't have to sleep on the sofa on the next visit to St Mawes, and could devote himself to Ted and Joan without the distraction of Lucy's tense, accusatory presence.

Though as desperate to cook for him as ever, his aunt was already enfeebled by the chemotherapy. It was painful to watch her dragging herself around the kitchen, but she wouldn't sit down, even when Ted implored her to do so. On Saturday night, his uncle broke down after Joan had gone to bed, and sobbed into Strike's shoulder. Ted had once seemed an unperturbable, invulnerable bastion of strength to his nephew, and Strike, who could normally sleep under almost any conditions, lay awake past two in the morning, staring into the darkness that was deeper by far than a London night, wondering whether he should stay longer, and despising himself for deciding that it was right that he should return to London.

In truth, the agency was so busy that he felt guilty about the burden it was placing on Robin and his subcontractors by taking a long weekend in Cornwall. In addition to the five open cases still on the agency's books, he and Robin were juggling increased management demands made by the expanded workforce, and negotiating a year's extension on the office lease with the developer who'd bought their building. They were also trying, though so far without luck, to persuade one of the agency's police contacts to find and hand over the forty-year-old file on Margot Bamborough's disappearance. Morris was ex-Met, as was Andy Hutchins, their most longstanding subcontractor, a quiet, saturnine man whose MS was thankfully in remission, and both had tried to call in favours from former colleagues as well, but so far, responses to the agency's requests had ranged from 'mice have probably had it' to 'fuck off, Strike, I'm busy'.

One rainy afternoon, while tailing Shifty through the City, trying not to limp too obviously and inwardly cursing the second pavement seller of cheap umbrellas who'd got in his way, Strike's mobile rang. Expecting to be given another problem to sort out, he was caught off guard when the caller said,

'Hi, Strike. George Layborn here. Heard you're looking at the Bamborough case again?'

Strike had only met DI Layborn once before, and while it had been in the context of a case where Strike and Robin had given material assistance to the Met, he hadn't considered their association close enough to ask Layborn for help on getting the Bamborough file.

'Hi, George. Yeah, you heard right,' said Strike, watching Shifty turn into a wine bar.

'Well, I could meet you tomorrow evening, if you fancy it. Feathers, six o'clock?' said Layborn.

So Strike asked Barclay to swap jobs, and headed to the pub near Scotland Yard the following evening, where he found Layborn already at the bar, waiting for him. A paunchy, grey-haired, middle-aged man, Layborn bought both of them pints of London Pride, and they removed themselves to a corner table.

'My old man worked the Bamborough case, under Bill Talbot,' Layborn told Strike. 'He told me all about it. What've you got so far?'

'Nothing. I've been looking back at old press reports, and I'm trying to trace people who worked at the practice she disappeared from. Not much else I can do until I see the police file, but nobody's been able to help with that so far.'

Layborn, who had demonstrated a fondness for colourfully

obscene turns of phrase on their only previous encounter, seemed oddly subdued tonight.

'It was a fucking mess, the Bamborough investigation,' he said quietly. 'Anyone told you about Talbot yet?'

'Go on.'

'He went off his rocker,' said Layborn. 'Proper mental breakdown. He'd been going funny before he took on the case, but you know, it was the seventies – looking after the work-force's mental health was for poofs. He'd been a good officer in his day, mind you. A couple of junior officers noticed he was acting odd, but when they raised it, they were told to eff off.

'He'd been heading up the Bamborough case six months before his wife called an ambulance in the middle of the night and got him sectioned. He got his pension, but it was too late for the case. He died a good ten years ago, but I heard he never got over fucking up the investigation. Once he recovered he was mortified about how he'd behaved.'

'How was that?'

'Putting too much stock in his own intuitions, didn't take evidence properly, had no interest in talking to witnesses if they didn't fit his theory—'

'Which was that Creed abducted her, right?'

'Exactly,' said Layborn. 'Although Creed was still called the Essex Butcher back then, because he dumped the first couple of bodies in Epping Forest and Chigwell.' Layborn took a long pull on his pint. 'They found most of Jackie Aylett in an industrial bin. He's an animal, that one. Animal.'

'Who took over the case after Talbot?'

'Bloke called Lawson, Ken Lawson,' said Layborn, 'but he'd lost six months, the trail had gone cold and he'd inherited a right balls-up. Added to which, she was unlucky in her timing, Margot Bamborough,' Layborn continued. 'You know what happened a month after she vanished?'

'What?'

'Lord Lucan disappeared,' said Layborn. 'You try and keep a missing GP on the front pages after a peer of the realm's nanny gets bludgeoned to death and he goes on the run. They'd already used the Bunny Girl pictures – did you know Bamborough was a Bunny Girl?'

'Yeah,' said Strike.

'Helped fund her medical degree,' said Layborn, 'but according to my old man, the family didn't like that being dragged up. Put their backs right up, even though those pictures definitely got the case a bit more coverage. Way of the world,' he said, 'isn't it?'

'What did your dad think happened to her?' asked Strike.

'Well, to be honest,' sighed Layborn, 'he thought Talbot was probably right: Creed had taken her. There were no signs she meant to disappear – passport was still in the house, no case packed, no clothes missing, stable job, no money worries, young child.'

'Hard to drag a fit, healthy twenty-nine-year-old woman off a busy street without someone noticing,' said Strike.

'True,' said Layborn. 'Creed usually picked them off when they were drunk. Having said that, it was a dark evening and rainy. He'd pulled that trick before. And he was good at lulling women's suspicions and getting their sympathy. A couple of them walked into his flat of their own accord.'

'There was a van like Creed's seen speeding in the area, wasn't there?'

'Yeah,' said Layborn, 'and from what Dad told me it was never checked out properly. Talbot didn't want to hear that it might have been someone trying to get home for their tea, see. Routine work just wasn't done. For instance, I heard there was an old boyfriend of Bamborough's hanging around. I'm not saying the boyfriend killed her, but Dad told me Talbot spent half the interview trying to find out where this boyfriend had been on the night Helen Wardrop got attacked.'

'Who?'

'Prostitute. Creed tried to abduct her in '73. He had his failures, you know. Peggy Hiskett, she got away from him and gave the police a description in '71, but that didn't help them much. She said he was dark and stocky, because he was wearing a wig at the time and all padded out in a woman's coat. They caught him in the end because of Melody Bower. Nightclub singer, looked like Diana Ross. Creed got chatting to her at a bus stop, offered her a lift, then tried to drag her into the van when she said no. She escaped, gave the police a proper description and told them he'd said his house was off Paradise Park. He got careless towards the end. Arrogance did for him.'

'You know a lot about this, George.'

'Yeah, well, Dad was one of the first into Creed's basement after they arrested him. He wouldn't ever talk about what he saw in there, and he'd seen gangland killings, you name it . . . Creed's never admitted to Bamborough, but that doesn't mean he didn't do it. That cunt will keep people guessing till he's dead. Evil fucking bastard. He's played with the families of his known victims for years. Likes hinting he did more women, without giving any details. Some journalist interviewed him in the early eighties, but that was the last time they let anyone talk to him. The Ministry of Justice clamped down. Creed uses publicity as a chance to torment the families. It's the only power he's got left.'

Layborn drained the last of his pint and checked his watch.

'I'll do what I can for you with the file. My old man would've wanted me to help. It never sat right with him, what happened with that case.'

The wind was picking up by the time Strike returned to his attic flat. His rain-speckled windows rattled in their loose frames as he sorted carefully through the receipts in his wallet for those he needed to submit to the accountant.

At nine o'clock, after eating dinner cooked on his single-ringed hob, he lay down on his bed and picked up the second-hand biography of Dennis Creed, *The Demon of Paradise Park,* which he'd ordered a month ago and which had so far lain unopened on his bedside table. Having undone the button on his trousers to better accommodate the large amount of spaghetti he'd just consumed, he emitted a loud and satisfying belch, lit a cigarette, laid back against his pillows and opened the book to the beginning, where a timeline laid out the bare bones of Creed's long career of rape and murder.

1937	Born in Greenwell Terrace, Mile End.
1954	April: began National Service. November: raped schoolgirl **Vicky Hornchurch**, 15. Sentenced to 2 years, Feltham Borstal.
1955–61	Worked in a variety of short-lived manual and office jobs. Frequented prostitutes.
1961	July: raped and tortured shop assistant **Sheila Gaskins**, 22. Sentenced to 5 years, HMP Pentonville.
1968	April: abducted, raped, tortured and murdered schoolgirl **Geraldine Christie**, 16.
1969	September: abducted, raped, tortured and murdered secretary and mother of one **Jackie Aylett**, 29. Killer dubbed 'The Essex Butcher' by press.
1970	January: moved to Vi Cooper's basement in Liverpool Road, near Paradise Park. Gained job as dry-cleaning delivery man. February: abducted dinner lady and mother of

	three **Vera Kenny**, 31. Kept in basement for three weeks. Raped, tortured and murdered. November: abducted estate agent **Noreen Sturrock**, 28. Kept in basement for four weeks. Raped, tortured and murdered.
1971	August: failed to abduct pharmacist **Peggy Hiskett**, 34.
1972	September: abducted unemployed **Gail Wrightman**, 30. Kept imprisoned in basement. Raped and tortured.
1973	January: murdered Wrightman. December: failed to abduct prostitute and mother of one **Helen Wardrop**, 32.
1974	September: abducted hairdresser **Susan Meyer**, 27. Kept imprisoned in basement. Raped and tortured.
1975	February: abducted PhD student **Andrea Hooton**, 23. Hooton and Meyer were held concurrently in basement for 4 weeks. March: murdered Susan. April: murdered Andrea.
1976	January 25th: attempted to abduct nightclub singer **Melody Bower**, 26. January 31st: landlady Vi Cooper recognises Creed from description and photofit. February 2nd: Creed arrested.

Strike turned over the page and skim-read the introduction, which featured the only interview ever granted by Creed's mother, Agnes Waite.

. . . She began by telling me that the date given on Creed's birth certificate was false.

'It says he was born December 20th, doesn't it?' she asked me. 'That's not right. It was the night of November 19th. He lied about it when he registered the birth, because we were outside the time you were supposed to do it.'

'"He" was Agnes's stepfather, William Awdry, a man notorious in the local area for his violent temper . . .

'He took the baby out of my arms as soon as I'd had it and said he was going to kill it. Drown it in the outside toilet. I begged him not to. I pleaded with him to let the baby live. I hadn't known till then whether I wanted it to live or die, but once you've seen them, held them . . . and he was strong, Dennis, he wanted to live, you could tell.

'It went on for weeks, the threats, Awdry threatening to kill him. But by then the neighbours had heard the baby crying and probably heard what [Awdry] was threatening, as well. He knew there was no hiding it; he'd waited too long. So he registered the birth, but lied about the date, so nobody would ask why he'd done it so late. There wasn't nobody to say it had happened earlier, not anybody who'd count. They never got me a midwife or a nurse or anything . . .'

Creed often wrote me fuller answers than we'd had time for during face-to-face interviews. Months later he sent me the following, concerning his own suspicions about his paternity:

'I saw my supposed step-grandfather looking at me out of the mirror. The resemblance grew stronger as I got older. I had his eyes, the same shaped ears, his sallow complexion, his long neck. He was a bigger man than I was, a more masculine-looking man, and I think part of his great dislike of me came from the fact that he hated to see his own features in a weak and girlish form. He despised vulnerability . . .'

'Yeah, of course Dennis was his,' Agnes told me. 'He [Awdry] started on me when I was thirteen. I was never allowed out, never had a boyfriend. When my mother realised I was expecting, Awdry told her I'd been sneaking out to meet someone. What else was he going to say? And Mum believed him. Or she pretended to.'

Agnes fled her stepfather's overcrowded house shortly before Dennis's second birthday, when she was sixteen-and-a-half.

'I wanted to take Dennis with me, but I left in the middle of the night and I couldn't afford to make noise. I had nowhere to go, no job, no money. Just a boyfriend who said he'd look after me. So I went.'

She was to see her firstborn only twice more. When she found out William Awdry was serving nine months in jail for assault, she returned to her mother's house in hopes of snatching Dennis away.

'I was going to tell Bert [her first husband] he was my nephew, because Bert didn't know anything about that whole mess. But Dennis didn't remember me, I don't think. He wouldn't let go of my mum, wouldn't talk to me, and my mum told me it was too late now and I shouldn't have left him if I wanted him so bad. So I went away without him.'

The last time Agnes saw her son in the flesh was when she made a trip to his primary school and called him over to the fence to speak to her. Though he was barely five, Creed claimed in our second interview to remember this final meeting.

'She was a thin, plain little woman, dressed like a tart,' he told me. 'She didn't look like the other boys' mothers. You could tell she wasn't a respectable person. I didn't want the other children to see me talking to her. She said she was my mother and I told her it wasn't true, but I knew it was, really. I ran away from her.'

'He didn't want nothing to do with me,' said Agnes. 'I gave up after that. I wasn't going to go to the house if Awdry was there. Dennis was in school, at least. He looked clean . . .

'I used to wonder about him, how he was and that,' Agnes said. 'Obviously, you do. Kids come out of you. Men don't understand what that is. Yeah, I used to wonder, but I moved north with Bert when he got the job with the GPO and I never went back to London, not even when my mum died, because Awdry had put it about that if I turned up he'd kick off.'

When I told Agnes I'd met Dennis a mere week before visiting her in Romford, she had only one point of curiosity.

'They say he's very clever, is he?'

I told her that he was, undoubtedly, very clever. It was the one point on which all his psychiatrists agreed. Warders told me he read extensively, especially books of psychology.

'I don't know where he got that from. Not me . . .

'I read it all in the papers. I saw him on the news, heard everything he did. Terrible, just terrible. What would make a person do that?

'After the trial was over, I thought back to him, all naked and bloody on the lino where I'd had him, with my stepfather standing over us, threatening to drown him, and I swear to you now,' said Agnes Waite, 'I wish I'd let it happen.'

Strike stubbed out his cigarette and reached for the can of Tennent's sitting beside the ashtray. A light rain pattered against his windows as he flicked a little further on in the book, pausing midway through chapter two.

. . . grandmother, Ena, was unwilling or unable to protect the youngest member of the household from her husband's increasingly sadistic punishments.

Awdry took a particular satisfaction in humiliating Dennis for his persistent bedwetting. His step-grandfather would pour a bucket of water over his bed, then force the boy to sleep in it. Creed recalled several occasions on which he was forced to walk to the corner shop without trousers, but still wearing sodden pyjama bottoms, to buy Awdry cigarettes.

'One took refuge in fantasy,' Creed wrote to me later. 'Inside my head I was entirely free and happy. But there were, even then, props in the material world that I enjoyed incorporating into my secret life. Items that attained a totemic power in my fantasies.'

By the age of twelve, Dennis had discovered the pleasures of voyeurism.

'It excited me,' he wrote, after our third interview, 'to watch a woman who didn't know she was being observed. I'd do it to my sisters, but I'd creep up to lit windows as well. If I got lucky, I'd see women or girls undressing, adjusting themselves or even a glimpse of nudity. I was aroused not only by the obviously sensual aspects, but by the sense of power. I felt I stole something of their essence from them, taking that which they thought private and hidden.'

He soon progressed to stealing women's underwear from neighbours' washing lines and even from his grandmother, Ena. These he enjoyed wearing in secret, and masturbating in . . .

Yawning, Strike flicked on, coming to rest on a passage in chapter four.

... a quiet member of the mailroom staff at Fleetwood Electric, who astonished his colleagues when, on a works night out, he donned the coat of a female co-worker to imitate singer Kay Starr.

'There was little Dennis, belting out "Wheel of Fortune" in Jenny's coat,' an anonymous workmate told the press after Creed's arrest. 'It made some of the older men uncomfortable. A couple of them thought he was, you know, queer, after. But the younger ones, we all cheered him like anything. He came out of his shell a bit after that.'

But Creed's secret fantasy life didn't centre on a life of amateur theatrics or pub singing. Unbeknownst to anyone watching the tipsy sixteen-year-old onstage, his elaborate fantasies were becoming ever more sadistic ...

Colleagues at Fleetwood Electric were appalled when 'little Dennis' was arrested for the rape and torture of Sheila Gaskins, 22, a shop assistant whom he'd followed off a late night bus. Gaskins, who survived the attack only because Creed was scared away by a nightwatchman who heard sounds down an alleyway, was able to provide evidence against him.

Convicted, he served five years in HMP Pentonville. This was the last time Creed would give way to sudden impulse.

Strike paused to light himself a fresh cigarette, then flicked ten chapters on through the book, until a familiar name caught his eye.

... Dr Margot Bamborough, a Clerkenwell GP, on October 11th 1974.

DI Bill Talbot, who headed the investigation, immediately noted suspicious similarities between the disappearance of the young GP and those of Vera Kenny and Gail Wrightman.

Both Kenny and Wrightman had been abducted on rainy nights, when the presence of umbrellas and rainwashed windscreens provided handy impediments to would-be witnesses. There was a heavy downpour on the evening Margot Bamborough disappeared.

A small van with what were suspected to be fake number plates had been seen in both Kenny's and Wrightman's vicinities shortly before they vanished. Three separate witnesses came forward to say that a small white van of similar appearance had been seen speeding away from the vicinity of Margot Bamborough's practice that night.

Still more suggestive was the eyewitness account of a driver who saw two women in the street, one of whom seemed to be infirm or faint, the other supporting her. Talbot at once made the connection both with the drunk Vera Kenny, who'd been seen getting into a van with what appeared to be another woman, and the testimony of Peggy Hiskett, who'd reported the man dressed as a woman at a lonely bus stop, who'd tried to persuade her to drink a bottle of beer with him, becoming aggressive before, fortunately, she managed to attract the attention of a passing car.

Convinced that Bamborough had fallen victim to the serial killer now dubbed the Essex Butcher, Talbot—

Strike's mobile rang. Trying not to lose his page, Strike groped for it and answered it without looking at the caller's identity.

'Strike.'

'Hello, Bluey,' said a woman, softly.

Strike set the book on the bed, pages down. There was a pause, in which he could hear Charlotte breathing.

'What d'you want?'

'To talk to you,' she said.

'What about?'

'I don't know,' she half-laughed. 'You choose.'

Strike knew this mood. She was halfway into a bottle of wine or had perhaps enjoyed a couple of whiskies. There was a moment of drunkenness – not even of drunkenness, of alcohol-induced softening – where a Charlotte emerged who was endearing, even amusing, but not yet combative or maudlin. He'd asked himself once, towards the end of their engagement, when his own innate honesty was forcing him to face facts and ask hard questions, how realistic or healthy it was to wish for a wife forever very slightly drunk.

'You didn't call me back,' said Charlotte. 'I left a message with your Robin. Didn't she give it to you?'

'Yeah, she gave it to me.'

'But you didn't call.'

'What d'you want, Charlotte?'

The sane part of his brain was telling him to end the call, but still he held the phone to his ear, listening, waiting. She'd been like a drug to him for a long time: a drug, or a disease.

'Interesting,' said Charlotte dreamily. 'I thought she might have decided not to pass on the message.'

He said nothing.

'Are the two of you together yet? She's quite good-looking. And always there. On tap. So conven—'

'Why are you calling?'

'I've told you, I wanted to talk to you . . . d'you know what day it is today? The twins' first birthday. The entire *famille Ross* has turned up to fawn over them. This is the first moment I've had to myself all day.'

He knew, of course, that she'd had twins. There'd been an announcement in *The Times*, because she'd married into an aristocratic family that routinely announced births, marriages and deaths in its columns, although Strike had not, in fact, read the news there. It was Ilsa who'd passed the information on, and Strike had immediately remembered the words Charlotte had said to him, over a restaurant table she had tricked him into sharing with her, more than a year previously.

All that's kept me going through this pregnancy is the thought that once I've had them, I can leave.

But the babies had been born prematurely and Charlotte had not left them.

Kids come out of you. Men don't understand what that is.

There'd been two previous tipsy phone calls to Strike like this one in the past year, both made late at night. He'd ended the first one mere seconds in, because Robin was trying to reach him. Charlotte had hung up abruptly a few minutes into the second.

'Nobody thought they'd live, did you know that?' Charlotte said now. 'It's,' she whispered, '*a miracle*.'

'If it's your kids' birthday, I should let you go,' said Strike. 'Goodnight, Char—'

'Don't go,' she said, suddenly urgent. 'Don't go, please don't.'

Hang up, said the voice in his head. He didn't.

'They're asleep, fast asleep. They don't know it's their birthday, the whole thing's a joke. Commemorating the anniversary of that fucking nightmare. It was hideous, they cut me open—'

'I've got to go,' he said. 'I'm busy.'

'*Please*,' she almost wailed. 'Bluey, I'm so unhappy, you don't know, I'm so fucking miserable—'

'You're a married mother of two,' he said brutally, 'and I'm not an agony aunt. There are anonymous services you can call if you need them. Goodnight, Charlotte.'

He cut the call.

The rain was coming down harder. It drummed on his dark

windows. Dennis Creed's face was now the wrong way up on the cast-aside book. His light-lashed eyes seemed reversed in the upside-down face. The effect was unsettling, as though the eyes were alive in the photograph.

Strike opened the book again and continued to read.

9

Faire Sir, of friendship let me now you pray,
That as I late aduentured for your sake,
The hurts whereof me now from battell stay,
Ye will me now with like good turne repay.

Edmund Spenser
The Faerie Queene

George Layborn still hadn't managed to lay hands on the Bamborough file when Robin's birthday arrived.

For the first time in her life, she woke on the morning of October the ninth, remembered what day it was and experienced no twinge of excitement, but a lowering sensation. She was twenty-nine years old today, and twenty-nine had an odd ring to it. The number seemed to signify not a landmark, but a staging post: 'Next stop: THIRTY'. Lying alone for a few moments in her double bed in her rented bedroom, she remembered what her favourite cousin, Katie, had said during Robin's last trip home, while Robin had been helping Katie's two-year-old son make Play-Doh monsters to ride in his Tonka truck.

'It's like you're travelling in a different direction to the rest of us.'

Then, seeing something in Robin's face that made her regret her words, Katie had hastily added,

'I don't mean it in a bad way! You seem really happy. Free, I mean! Honestly,' Katie had said, with hollow insincerity, 'I really envy you sometimes.'

Robin hadn't known a second's regret for the termination of a marriage that, in its final phase, had made her deeply unhappy. She could still conjure up the mood, mercifully not experienced since, in which all colour seemed drained from her surroundings – and they had been pretty surroundings, too: she knew that the sea captain's house in Deptford where she and Matthew had finally parted had been a most attractive place, yet it was strange how few details she could remember about it now. All she could recall with any clarity was the deadened mood she'd suffered within those walls, the perpetual feelings of guilt and dread, and the dawning horror which accompanied the realisation that she had shackled herself to somebody whom she didn't like, and with whom she had next to nothing in common.

Nevertheless, Katie's blithe description of Robin's current life as 'happy' and 'free' wasn't entirely accurate. For several years now, Robin had watched Strike prioritise his working life over everything else – in fact, Joan's diagnosis had been the first occasion she'd known him to reallocate his jobs, and make something other than detection his top concern – and these days Robin, too, felt herself becoming taken over by the job, which she found satisfying to the point that it became almost all-consuming. Finally living what she'd wanted ever since she first walked through the glass door of Strike's office, she now understood the potential for loneliness that came with a single, driving passion.

Having sole possession of her bed had been a great pleasure at first: nobody sulking with their back to her, nobody complaining that she wasn't pulling her weight financially, or droning on about his promotion prospects; nobody demanding sex that had become a chore rather than a pleasure. Nevertheless, while she missed Matthew not at all, she could envisage a time (if she was honest, was perhaps already living it) when the lack of physical contact, of affection and even of sex – which for Robin was a more complicated prospect than for many women – would become, not a boon, but a serious absence in her life.

And then what? Would she become like Strike, with a succession of lovers relegated firmly to second place, after the job? No sooner had she thought this than she found herself wondering, as she'd done almost daily since, whether her partner had called Charlotte Campbell back. Impatient with herself, she threw back the covers and, ignoring the packages lying on top of her chest of drawers, went to take a shower.

Her new home in Finborough Road occupied the top two floors of a terraced house. The bedrooms and bathroom were on the third floor, the public rooms on the fourth. A small terraced area lay off the sitting room, where the owner's elderly rough-coated dachshund, Wolfgang, liked to lie outside on sunny days.

Robin, who was under no illusions about property available in London for single women on an average wage, especially one with legal bills to pay, considered herself immensely fortunate to be living in a clean, well-maintained and tastefully decorated flat, with a double room to herself and a flatmate she liked. Her live-in landlord was a forty-two-year-old actor called Max Priestwood, who couldn't afford to run the place without a tenant. Max, who was gay, was what Robin's mother would have called ruggedly handsome: tall and broad-shouldered, with a full head of thick, dark blond hair and a perpetually weary look about his grey eyes. He was also an old friend of Ilsa's, who'd been at university with his younger brother.

In spite of Ilsa's assurances that 'Max is absolutely lovely', Robin had spent the first few months of her tenancy wondering whether she'd made a huge mistake in moving in with him, because he seemed sunk in what seemed perpetual gloom. Robin tried her very best to be a good flatmate: she was naturally tidy, she never played music loudly or cooked anything very smelly; she made a fuss of Wolfgang and remembered to feed him if Max was out; she was punctilious when it came to replacing washing-up liquid and toilet roll; and she made a point of being polite and cheery whenever they came into contact, yet Max rarely if ever smiled, and when she first arrived, he'd seemed to find it an immense effort to talk to her. Feeling paranoid, Robin had wondered at first whether Ilsa had strong-armed Max into accepting her as a tenant.

Conversation had become slightly easier between them over the months of her tenancy, yet Max was never loquacious. Sometimes Robin was grateful for this monosyllabic tendency, because when she came in after working a twelve-hour stretch of surveillance, stiff and tired, her mind fizzing with work concerns, the last thing she wanted was small talk. At other times, when she might have preferred to go upstairs to the open-plan living area, she kept to her room rather than feel she was intruding upon Max's private space.

She suspected the main reason for Max's perennially low mood was his state of persistent unemployment. Since the West End play in which he had had a small part had ended four months ago, he hadn't managed to get another job. She'd learned quickly not to ask him whether he had any auditions lined up. Sometimes, even saying 'How was your day?' sounded unnecessarily judgemental. She knew he'd previously shared his flat with a long-term boyfriend, who by coincidence was also called Matthew. Robin knew nothing about Max's break-up except that his Matthew had signed over his half of the flat to

Max voluntarily, which to Robin seemed remarkably generous compared with the behaviour of her own ex-husband.

Having showered, Robin pulled on a dressing gown and returned to her bedroom to open the packages that had arrived in the post over the past few days, and which she'd saved for this morning. She suspected her mother had bought the aromatherapy bath oils that were ostensibly from her brother Martin, that her veterinarian sister-in-law (who was currently pregnant with Robin's first niece or nephew) had chosen the homespun sweater, which was very much Jenny's own style, and that her brother Jonathan had a new girlfriend, who'd probably chosen the dangly earrings. Feeling slightly more depressed than she had before she'd opened the presents, Robin dressed herself all in black, which could take her through a day of paperwork at the office, a catch-up meeting with the weatherman whom Postcard was persecuting, all the way to birthday drinks that evening with Ilsa and Vanessa, her policewoman friend. Ilsa had suggested inviting Strike, and Robin had said that she would prefer it to be girls only, because she was trying to avoid any further occasions on which Ilsa might try and matchmake.

On the point of leaving her room, Robin's eye fell on a copy of *The Demon of Paradise Park* which she, like Strike, had bought online. Her copy was slightly more battered than his and had taken longer to arrive. She hadn't yet read much of it, partly because she was generally too tired of an evening to do anything other than fall into bed, but partly because what she had read had already caused a slight recurrence of the psychological symptoms she had carried with her ever since her forearm had been sliced open one dark night. Today, however, she stuffed it into her bag to read on the Tube.

A text from her mother arrived while Robin was walking to the station, wishing her a happy birthday and telling her to check her email account. This she did, and saw that her parents had sent her a one-hundred-and-fifty-pound voucher for Selfridges. This was a most welcome gift, because Robin had virtually no disposable income left, once her legal bills, rent and other living expenses had been paid, to spend on anything that might be considered self-indulgent.

Feeling slightly more cheerful as she settled into a corner of the train, Robin took *The Demon of Paradise Park* from her bag and opened it to the page she had last reached.

The coincidence of the first line caused her an odd inward tremor.

Chapter 5

Little though he realised it, Dennis Creed was released from prison on his true 29th birthday, 19th November, 1966. His grandmother, Ena, had died while he was in Feltham Borstal, and there was no question of him returning to live with his step-grandfather. He had no close friends to call on, and anyone who might have been well disposed to him prior to his second rape conviction was, unsurprisingly, in no rush to meet or help him. Creed spent his first night as a free man in a hostel near King's Cross.

After a week sleeping in hostels or on park benches, Creed managed to find himself a single room in a boarding house. For the next four years, Creed would move between a series of rundown rooms and short-term, cash-in-hand jobs, interspersed with periods of rough living. He admitted to me later that he frequented prostitutes a good deal at this time, but in 1968 he killed his first victim.

Schoolgirl Geraldine Christie was walking home—

Robin skipped the next page and a half. She had no particular desire to read the particulars of the harm Creed had visited upon Geraldine Christie.

. . . until finally, in 1970, Creed secured himself a permanent home in the basement rooms of the boarding house run by Violet Cooper, a fifty-year-old ex-theatre dresser who, like his grandmother, was an incipient alcoholic. This now demolished house would, in time, become infamous as Creed's 'torture chamber'. A tall, narrow building of grubby brick, it lay in Liverpool Road, close to Paradise Park.

Creed presented Cooper with forged references, which she didn't bother to follow up, and claimed he'd recently been dismissed from a bar job, but that a friend had promised him employment in a nearby restaurant. Asked by defending counsel at his trial why she'd been happy to rent a room to an unemployed man of no fixed abode, Cooper replied that she was 'tender-hearted' and that Creed seemed 'a sweet boy, bit lost and lonely'.

Her decision to rent, first a room, then the entire basement, to Dennis Creed, would cost Violet Cooper dearly. In spite of her insistence during the trial that she had no idea what was happening in the basement of her boarding house, suspicion and opprobrium have been attached to the name Violet Cooper ever since. She has now adopted a new identity, which I agreed not to disclose.

'I thought he was a pansy,' Cooper says today. 'I'd seen a bit of it in the theatre. I felt sorry for him, that's the truth.'

A plump woman whose face has been ravaged by both time and drink, she admits that she and Creed quickly struck up a close friendship. At times during our conversation she seemed to forget that young 'Den' who spent many evenings with her upstairs in her private sitting room, both of them tipsy and singing along to her collection of records, was the serial killer who dwelled in her basement.

'I wrote to him, you know,' she says. 'After he was convicted. I said, "If you ever felt anything for me, if any of it was real, tell me whether you did any of them other women. You've got nothing to lose now, Den," I says, "and you could put people's minds at rest."'

But the letter Creed wrote back admitted nothing.

'Sick, he is. I realised it, then. He'd just copied out the lyrics from an old Rosemary Clooney song we used to sing together, "Come On-A My House". You know the one . . . "*Come on-a my house, my house, I'm-a gonna give you candy* . . . " I knew then he hated me as much as he hated all them other women. Taunting me, he was.'

However, back in 1970, when Creed first moved into her basement, he'd been keen to ingratiate himself with his landlady, who admits he swiftly became a combination of son and confidant. Violet persuaded her friend Beryl Gould, who owned a dry-cleaner's, to give young Den a job as a delivery man, and this gave him access to the small van that would soon become notorious in the press . . .

Twenty minutes after boarding the train, Robin got out at Leicester Square. As she emerged into daylight, her mobile phone vibrated in her pocket. She pulled it out and saw a text from Strike. Drawing aside from the crowd emerging from the station, she opened it.

News: I've found Dr Dinesh Gupta, GP who worked with Margot at the Clerkenwell Practice in 1974. He's 80-odd but sounds completely compos mentis and is happy to meet me this afternoon at his house in Amersham. Currently watching Twinkletoes having breakfast in Soho. I'll get Barclay to take over from me at lunchtime and go straight to Gupta's. Any chance you could put off your meeting with Weatherman and come along?

Robin's heart sank. She'd already had to change the time of the weatherman's catch-up meeting once and felt it unfair to do so a second time, especially at such short notice. However, she'd have liked to meet Dr Dinesh Gupta.

I can't mess him around again, she typed back. **Let me know how it goes.**

Right you are, replied Strike.

Robin watched her mobile screen for a few more seconds. Strike had forgotten her birthday last year, realising his omission a week late and buying her flowers. Given that he'd seemed to feel guilty about the oversight, she'd imagined that he might make a note of the date and perhaps set an alert on his mobile this year. However, no 'Happy birthday, by the way!' appeared, so she put her mobile back in her pocket and, unsmiling, walked on towards the office.

10

And if by lookes one may the mind aread,
He seemd to be a sage and sober syre . . .

Edmund Spenser
The Faerie Queene

'You are thinking,' said the small, spectacled, elderly doctor, who was dwarfed by both his suit and his upright armchair, 'that I look like Gandhi.'

Strike, who'd been thinking exactly that, was surprised into a laugh.

The eighty-one-year-old doctor appeared to have shrunk inside his suit; the collar and cuffs of his shirt gaped and his ankles were skinny in their black silk socks. Tufts of white hair appeared both in and over his ears, and he wore horn-rimmed spectacles. The strongest features in his genial brown face were the aquiline nose and dark eyes, which alone appeared to have escaped the ageing process, and were as bright and knowing as a wren's.

No speck of dust marred the highly polished coffee table between them, in what bore the appearance of a seldom-used, special occasion room. The deep gold of wallpaper, sofa and chairs glowed, pristine, in the autumn sunshine diffused by the net curtains. Four gilt-framed photographs hung in pairs on the wall on either side of the fringed drapes. Each picture showed a different dark-haired young woman, all wearing mortarboards and gowns, and holding degree certificates.

Mrs Gupta, a tiny, slightly deaf, grey-haired woman, had already told Strike what degrees each of her daughters had taken – two medicine, one modern languages and one computing – and how well each was doing in her chosen career. She'd also shown him pictures of the six grandchildren she and her husband had been blessed with so far. Only the youngest girl remained childless, 'but she will have them,' said Mrs Gupta, with a Joan-ish certainty. 'She'll never be happy without.'

Having provided Strike and her husband with tea served in china cups, and a plate of fig rolls, Mrs Gupta retreated to the kitchen, where *Escape to the Country* was playing with the sound turned up high.

'As it happens, my father met Gandhi as a young man when Gandhi visited London in 1931,' said Dr Gupta, selecting a fig roll. 'He, too, had studied law in London, you see, but a while after Gandhi. But ours was a wealthier family. Unlike Gandhi, my father could afford to bring his wife to England with him. My parents decided to remain in the UK after Daddy qualified as a barrister.

'So my immediate family missed partition. Very fortunate for us. My grandparents and two of my aunts were killed as they attempted to leave East Bengal. Massacred,' said Dr Gupta, 'and both my aunts were raped before being killed.'

'I'm sorry,' said Strike, who, not having anticipated the turn the conversation had taken, had frozen in the act of opening his notebook and now sat feeling slightly foolish, his pen poised.

'My father,' said Dr Gupta, nodding gently as he munched his fig roll, 'carried the guilt with him to his grave. He thought he should have been there to protect them all, or to have died alongside them.

'Now, *Margot* didn't like hearing the truth about partition,' said Dr Gupta. 'We all wanted independence, naturally, but the transition was handled very badly, very badly indeed. Nearly three million went missing. Rapes. Mutilation. Families torn asunder. Dreadful mistakes made. Appalling acts committed.

'Margot and I had an argument about it. A friendly argument, of course,' he added, smiling. 'But Margot romanticised uprisings of people in distant lands. She didn't judge brown rapists and torturers by the same standards she would have applied to white men who drowned children for being the wrong religion. She believed, I think, like Suhrawardy, that "bloodshed and disorder are not necessarily evil in themselves, if resorted to for a noble cause".'

Dr Gupta swallowed his biscuit and added,

'It was Suhrawardy, of course, who incited the Great Calcutta Killings. Four thousand dead in a single day.'

Strike allowed a respectful pause to fill the room, broken only by the distant sound of *Escape to the Country*. When no further mention of bloodshed and terror was forthcoming, he took the opening that had been offered to him.

'Did you like Margot?'

'Oh yes,' said Dinesh Gupta, still smiling. 'Although I found some of her beliefs and her attitudes shocking. I was born into a traditional, though Westernised, family. Before Margot and I went into practice together, I had never been in daily proximity to a self-proclaimed *liberated* lady. My friends at medical school, and the partners in my previous practice, had all been men.'

'A feminist, was she?'

'Oh, very much so,' said Gupta, smiling. 'She would tease me about what she thought were my regressive attitudes. She was a great improver of people, Margot – whether they wished to be improved or not,' said Gupta, with a little laugh. 'She volunteered at the WEA, too. The Workers' Educational

Association, you know? She'd come from a poor family, and she was a great proponent of adult education, especially for women.

'She would certainly have approved of my girls,' said Dinesh Gupta, turning in his armchair to point at the four graduation photographs behind him. 'Jheel still laments that we had no son, but I have no complaints. No complaints,' he repeated, turning back to face Strike.

'I understand from the General Medical Council records,' said Strike, 'that there was a third GP at the St John's practice, a Dr Joseph Brenner. Is that right?'

'Dr Brenner, yes, quite right,' said Gupta. 'I doubt he's still alive, poor fellow. He'd be over a hundred now. He'd worked alone in the area for many years before he came in with us at the new practice. He brought with him Dorothy Oakden, who'd done his typing for twenty-odd years. She became our practice secretary. An older lady – or so she seemed to me at the time,' said Gupta, with another small chuckle. 'I don't suppose she was more than fifty. Married late and widowed not long afterwards. I have no idea what became of her.'

'Who else worked at the practice?'

'Well, let's see . . . there was Janice Beattie, the district nurse, who was the best nurse I ever worked with. An Eastender by birth. Like Margot, she understood the privations of poverty from personal experience. Clerkenwell at that time was by no means as smart as it's become since. I still receive Christmas cards from Janice.'

'I don't suppose you have her address?' asked Strike.

'It's possible,' said Dr Gupta. 'I'll ask Jheel.'

He made to get up.

'Later, after we've talked, will be fine,' said Strike, afraid to break the chain of reminiscence. 'Please, go on. Who else worked at St John's?'

'Let's see, let's see,' said Dr Gupta again, sinking slowly back into his chair. 'We had two receptionists, young women, but I'm afraid I've lost touch with both of them . . . now, what were their names . . . ?'

'Would that be Gloria Conti and Irene Bull?' asked Strike, who'd found both names in old press reports. A blurry photograph of both young women had shown a slight, dark girl and what he thought was probably a peroxide blonde, both of them looking distressed to be photographed as they entered the practice. The accompanying article in the *Daily Express* quoted 'Irene Bull, receptionist, aged 25', as saying *'It's terrible. We don't know anything. We're still hoping she'll come back. Maybe she's lost her memory or something.'* Gloria was mentioned in every press report he'd read, because she'd been the last known person to see Margot alive. *'She just said "Night, Gloria, see you tomorrow." She seemed normal, well, a bit tired, it was the end of the day and we'd had an emergency patient who'd kept her longer than she expected. She was a bit late to meet her friend. She put up her umbrella in the doorway and left.'*

'Gloria and Irene,' said Dr Gupta, nodding. 'Yes, that's right. They were both young, so they should still be with us, but I'm afraid I haven't the faintest idea where they are now.'

'Is that everyone?' asked Strike.

'Yes, I think so. No, wait,' said Gupta, holding up a hand. 'There was the cleaner. A West Indian lady. What was her name, now?'

He screwed up his face.

'I'm afraid I can't remember.'

The existence of a practice cleaner was new information to Strike. His own office had always been cleaned by him or by Robin, although lately, Pat had pitched in. He wrote down 'Cleaner, West Indian'.

'How old was she, can you remember?'

'I really couldn't tell you,' said Gupta. He added delicately, 'Black ladies – they are much harder to *age*, aren't they? They look younger for longer. But I think she had several children, so not *very* young. Mid-thirties?' he suggested hopefully.

'So, three doctors, a secretary, two receptionists, a practice nurse and a cleaner?' Strike summarised.

'That's right. We had,' said Dr Gupta, 'all the ingredients of a successful business – but it was an unhappy practice, I'm afraid. Unhappy from the start.'

'Really?' said Strike, interested. 'Why was that?'

'Personal chemistry,' said Gupta promptly. 'The older I've grown, the more I've realised that the team is everything. Qualifications and experience are important, but if the team doesn't *gel* . . .' He interlocked his bony fingers, '. . . forget it! You'll never achieve what you should. And so it was at St John's.

'Which was a pity, a very great pity, because we had potential. The practice was popular with ladies, who usually prefer consulting members of their own sex. Margot and Janice were both well liked.

'But there were internal divisions from the beginning. Dr Brenner joined us for the conveniences of a newer practice building, but he never acted as though he was part of the team. In fact, over time he became openly hostile to some of us.'

'Specifically, who was he hostile to?' asked Strike, guessing the answer.

'I'm afraid,' said Dr Gupta, sadly, 'he didn't like Margot. To be quite frank, I don't think Joseph Brenner liked *ladies*. He was rude to the girls on reception, as well. Of course, they were easier to bully than Margot. I think he respected Janice – she was very efficient, you know, and less combative than Margot – and he was always polite to Dorothy, who was fiercely loyal to him. But he took against Margot from the start.'

'Why was that, do you think?'

'Oh,' said Dr Gupta, raising his hands and letting them fall in a gesture of hopelessness, 'the truth is that Margot – now, I liked her, you understand, our discussions were always good-humoured – but she was a *Marmite* sort of person. Dr Brenner was no feminist. He thought a woman's place was at home with her children, and Margot leaving a baby at home and coming back out to work full time, he disapproved of that. Team meetings were very uncomfortable. He'd wait for Margot to start talking and then talk over her, very loudly.

'He was something of a bully, Brenner. He thought our receptionists were no better than they should be. Complained about their skirt lengths, their hairstyles.

'But actually, although he was *especially* rude to ladies, it's my opinion that he didn't really like *people*.'

'Odd,' said Strike. 'For a doctor.'

'Oh,' said Gupta, with a chuckle, 'that's by no means as unusual as you might think, Mr Strike. We doctors are like everybody else. It is a popular myth that all of us must love humanity in the round. The *irony* is that our biggest liability as a practice was Brenner himself. He was an addict!'

'Really?'

'Barbiturates,' said Gupta. 'Barbiturates, yes. A doctor couldn't get away with it these days, but he over-ordered them in massive quantities. Kept them in a locked cupboard in his consulting room. He was a very difficult man. Emotionally shut down. Unmarried. And this secret addiction.'

'Did you talk to him about it?' asked Strike.

'No,' said Gupta sadly. 'I put off doing so. I wanted to be sure of my ground before I broached the subject. From quiet enquiries I made, I suspected that he was still using his old practice address in addition to ours, doubling his order and using multiple pharmacies. It was going to be tricky to prove what he was up to.

'I might never have realised if Janice hadn't come to me and said she'd happened to walk in on him when his cupboard was open, and seen the quantities he'd amassed. She then admitted that she'd found him slumped at his desk in a groggy state one evening after the last patient had left. I don't think it ever affected his judgement, though. Not *really*. I'd noticed that at the end of the day he might have been a little glazed, and so on, but he was nearing retirement. I assumed he was tired.'

'Did Margot know about this addiction?' asked Strike.

'No,' said Gupta, 'I didn't tell her, although I should have done. She was my partner and the person I ought to have confided in, so we could decide what to do.

'But I was afraid she'd storm straight into Dr Brenner's consulting room and confront him. Margot wasn't a woman to back away from doing what she thought was right, and I did sometimes wish that she would exercise a little more *tact*. The fallout from a confrontation with Brenner was likely to be severe. Delicacy was required – after all, we had no absolute proof – but then Margot went missing, and Dr Brenner's barbiturate habit became the least of our worries.'

'Did you and Brenner continue working together after Margot disappeared?' asked Strike.

'For a few months, yes, but he retired not long afterwards. I continued to work at St John's for a short while, then got a job at another practice. I was glad to go. The St John's practice was full of bad associations.'

'How would you describe Margot's relationships with the other people at work?' Strike asked.

'Well, let's see,' said Gupta, taking a second fig roll. 'Dorothy the secretary never liked her, but I think that was out of loyalty to Dr Brenner. As I say, Dorothy was a widow. She was one of those *fierce* women who attach themselves to an employer they can defend and champion. Whenever Margot or I displeased or challenged Joseph in any way, our letters and reports were sure to go straight to the bottom of the typing pile. It was a joke between us. No computers in those days, Mr Strike. Nothing like nowadays – Aisha,' he said, indicating the top right-hand picture on the wall behind him, 'she types everything herself, a computer in her consulting room, everything computerised, which is much more efficient, but we were at the mercy of the typist for all our letters and reports.

'No, Dorothy didn't like Margot. Civil, but cold. Although,' said Gupta, who had evidently just remembered something, 'Dorothy *did* come to the barbecue, which was a surprise. Margot held a barbecue at her house one Sunday, the summer before she disappeared,' he explained. 'She knew that we weren't pulling together as a team, so she invited us all around to her house. The barbecue was supposed to . . . ' and, wordlessly this time, he again illustrated the point by interlacing his fingers. 'I remember being surprised that Dorothy attended, because Brenner had declined. Dorothy brought her son, who was thirteen or fourteen, I think. She must have given birth late, especially for the seventies. A boisterous boy. I remember Margot's husband telling him off for smashing a valuable bowl.'

A fleeting memory of his nephew Luke carelessly treading on Strike's new headphones in St Mawes crossed the detective's mind.

'Margot and her husband had a very nice house out in Ham. The husband was a doctor too, a haematologist. Big garden. Jheel and I took our girls, but as Brenner didn't go, and Dorothy was offended by Margot's husband telling off her son, Margot's objective wasn't achieved, I'm afraid. The divisions remained entrenched.'

'Did everyone else attend?'

'Yes, I think so. No – wait. I don't think the cleaning lady – *Wilma*!' said Dr Gupta, looking delighted. 'Her name was Wilma! I had no idea I still knew it . . . but her surname . . . I'm not even sure I knew it back then . . . No, Wilma didn't come. But everyone else, yes.

'Janice brought her own little boy – he was younger than Dorothy's and far better behaved, as I remember. My girls spent the afternoon playing badminton with the little Beattie boy.'

'Was Janice married?'

'Divorced. Her husband left her for another woman. She got on with it, raised her son alone. Women like Janice always do get on with it. Admirable. Her life wasn't easy when I knew her, but I believe she married again, later, and I was glad when I heard about it.'

'Did Janice and Margot get along?'

'Oh yes. They had the gift of being able to disagree without taking personal offence.'

'Did they disagree often?'

'No, no,' said Gupta, 'but decisions must be made in a working environment. We were – or tried to be – a democratic business . . .

'No, Margot and Janice were able to have rational disagreements without taking offence. I think they liked and respected each other. Janice was hit hard by Margot's disappearance. She told me the day I left the practice that a week hadn't passed since it happened that she hadn't dreamed about Margot.

'But none of us were ever quite the same afterwards,' said Dr Gupta quietly. 'One does not expect a friend to vanish into thin air without leaving a single trace behind them. There is something – uncanny about it.'

'There is,' agreed Strike. 'How did Margot get along with the two receptionists?'

'Well, now, Irene, the older of the two,' sighed Gupta, 'could be a handful. I remember her being – not rude, but a little cheeky – to Margot, at times. At the practice Christmas party – Margot organised that, as well, still trying to force us all to get along, you know – Irene had rather a lot to drink. I remember a slight *contretemps*, but I really couldn't tell you what it was all about. I doubt it was anything serious. They seemed as amicable as ever the next time I saw them. Irene was quite hysterical after Margot disappeared.'

There was a short pause.

'*Some* of that may have been theatrics,' Gupta admitted, 'but the underlying distress was genuine, I'm sure.

'Gloria – poor little Gloria – *she* was devastated. Margot was more than an employer to Gloria, you know. She was something of an older sister figure, a mentor. It was Margot who wanted to hire her, even though Gloria had almost no relevant experience. And I must admit,' said Gupta judiciously, 'she turned out to be a good appointment. Hard worker. Learned fast. You only had to correct her once. I believe she was from an impoverished background. I know Dorothy looked down on Gloria. She could be quite unkind.'

'And what about Wilma, the cleaner?' asked Strike, reaching the bottom of his list. 'How did she get on with Margot?'

'I'd be lying if I said I could remember,' said Gupta. 'She was a quiet woman, Wilma. I never heard that they had any kind of problem.'

After a slight pause, he added,

'I hope I'm not inventing things, but I *seem* to remember that Wilma's husband was something of a bad lot. I *think* Margot told me that Wilma ought to divorce him. I don't know whether she said that directly to Wilma's face – though she probably did, knowing Margot . . . as a matter of fact,' he continued, 'I heard, after I left the practice, that Wilma had been fired. There was an allegation of drinking at work. She always had a Thermos with her. But I may be misremembering that, so please don't set too much store by it. As I say, I'd already left.'

The door to the sitting room opened.

'More tea?' enquired Mrs Gupta, and she removed the tray and the now-cooling teapot, telling Strike, who had risen to help her, to sit back down and not to be silly. When she'd left, Strike said,

'Could I take you back to the day Margot disappeared, Dr Gupta?'

Appearing to brace himself slightly, the little doctor said,

'Of course. But I must warn you: what I mostly remember about that day now is the account of it I gave the police at the time. Do you see? My actual memories are hazy. Mostly, I remember what I told the investigating officer.'

Strike thought this an unusually self-aware comment for a witness. Experienced in taking statements, he knew how wedded people became to the first account they gave, and that valuable information, discarded during that first edit, was often lost for ever beneath the formalised version that now stood in for actual memory.

'That's all right,' he told Gupta. 'Whatever you can remember.'

'Well, it was an entirely ordinary day,' said Gupta. 'The *only* thing that was *slightly* different was that one of the girls on reception had a dental appointment and left at half past two – Irene, that was.'

'We doctors were working as usual in our respective consulting rooms. Until half past two, both girls were on reception, and after Irene left, Gloria was there alone. Dorothy was at her desk until five, which was her regular departure time. Janice was at the practice until lunchtime, but off making house calls in the afternoon, which was quite routine. I saw Margot a couple of times in the back, where we had, not exactly a kitchen, but a sort of nook where we had a kettle and a fridge. She was pleased about Wilson.'

'About who?'

'Harold Wilson,' said Gupta, smiling. 'There'd been a general election the day before. Labour got back in with a majority. He'd been leading a minority government since February, you see.'

'Ah,' said Strike. 'Right.'

'I left at half past five,' said Gupta. 'I said goodbye to Margot, whose door was open. Brenner's door was closed. I assumed he was with a patient.

'Obviously, I can't speak with authority about what happened after I left,' said Gupta, 'but I can tell you what the others told me.'

'If you wouldn't mind,' said Strike. 'I'm particularly interested in the emergency patient who kept Margot late.'

'Ah,' said Gupta, now placing his fingertips together and nodding, 'you know about the mysterious dark lady. Everything I know about *her* came from little Gloria.

'We operated on a first-come, first-served basis at St John's. Registered patients came along and waited their turn, unless it was an emergency, of course. But this lady walked in off the street. She wasn't registered with the practice, but she had severe abdominal pain. Gloria told her to wait, then went to see whether Joseph Brenner would see her, because he was free, whereas Margot was still with her last registered patient of the day.

'Brenner made heavy weather of the request. While Gloria and Brenner were talking, Margot came out of her consulting room, seeing off her last patients, a mother and child, and offered to see the emergency herself as she was going from the practice to the pub with a friend, which was just up the road. Brenner, according to Gloria, said "good of you" or something like that – which was friendly, for Brenner – and he put on his coat and hat and left.

'Gloria went back into the waiting room to tell the lady Margot would see her. The lady went into the consulting room and stayed there longer than Gloria expected. Fully twenty-five, thirty minutes, which took the time to a quarter past six, and Margot was supposed to be meeting her friend at six.

'At last the patient came out of the consulting room and left. Margot came out shortly afterwards in her coat. She told Gloria that she was late for the pub, and asked Gloria to lock up. She walked out into the rain . . . and was never seen again.'

The door of the sitting room opened and Mrs Gupta reappeared with fresh tea. Again, Strike stood to help her, and was again shooed back into his chair. When she'd left, Strike asked,

'Why did you call the last patient "mysterious"? Because she was unregistered, or—?'

'Oh, you didn't know about that business?' said Gupta. 'No, no. Because there was much discussion afterwards as to whether or not she was actually a lady.'

Smiling at Strike's look of surprise, he said,

'Brenner started it. He'd walked out past her and told the investigating officer that he'd thought, on the brief impression he had of her, that she was a man and was surprised afterwards to hear that she was female. Gloria said she was a thickset young lady, dark – gypsy-ish, was her word – not a very *politically correct* term, but that's what Gloria said. Nobody else saw her, of course, so we couldn't judge.

'An appeal was put out for her, but nobody came forward, and in the absence of any information to the contrary, the investigating officer put a great deal of pressure on Gloria to say that she thought the patient was really a man in disguise, or at least, that she could have been mistaken in thinking she was a lady. But Gloria insisted that she knew a lady when she saw one.'

'This officer being Bill Talbot?' asked Strike.

'Precisely,' said Gupta, reaching for his tea.

'D'you think he wanted to believe the patient was a man dressed as a woman because—'

'Because Dennis Creed sometimes cross-dressed? Yes,' said Gupta. 'Although we called him the Essex Butcher back then. We didn't know his real name until 1976. And the only physical description of the Butcher at the time said he was dark and squat – I suppose I see why Talbot was suspicious but . . . '

'Strange for the Essex Butcher to walk into a doctor's surgery in drag and wait his turn?'

'Well . . . quite,' said Dr Gupta.

There was a brief silence while Gupta sipped tea and Strike flicked back through his notes, checking that he had asked everything he wanted to know. It was Gupta who spoke first.

'Have you met Roy? Margot's husband?'

'No,' said Strike. 'I've been hired by her daughter. How well did you know him?'

'Only very slightly,' said Gupta.

He put the teacup down on the saucer. If ever Strike had seen a man with more to say, that man was Dinesh Gupta.

'What was your impression of him?' asked Strike, surreptitiously clicking the nib back out of his pen.

'Spoiled,' said Gupta. 'Very spoiled. A handsome man, who'd been made a prince by his mother. We Indian boys know something about that, Mr Strike. I met Roy's mother at the barbecue I mentioned. She singled me out for conversation. A snob, I should say. She didn't consider receptionists or secretaries worth her time. I had the strong impression that she thought her son had married beneath him. Again, this opinion is not unknown among Indian mothers. He's a haemophiliac, isn't he?' asked Gupta.

'Not that I've heard,' said Strike, surprised.

'Yes, yes,' said Gupta 'I think so, I think he is. He was a haematologist by profession, and his mother told me that he had chosen the specialty because of his own condition. You see? The clever, fragile little boy and the proud, overprotective mother.

'But then the little prince chose for a wife somebody utterly unlike his mother. Margot wasn't the kind of woman to leave her patients, or her adult learners, to rush home and cook Roy's dinner for him. Let him get his own, would have been her attitude . . . or the little cousin could have cooked, of course,' Gupta went on, with something of the delicacy he had brought to the mention of 'black ladies'. 'The young woman they paid to look after the baby.'

'Was Cynthia at the barbecue?'

'That was her name, was it? Yes, she was. I didn't talk to her. She was carrying Margot's daughter around, while Margot mingled.'

'Roy was interviewed by the police, I believe,' said Strike, who in fact took this for granted rather than knowing it for certain.

'Oh yes,' said Gupta. 'Now, *that* was a curious thing. Inspector Talbot told me at the start of my own police interview that Roy had been completely ruled out of their enquiries – which I've always thought was an odd thing to tell me. Don't you find it so? This was barely a week after Margot's disappearance. I suppose it was only just dawning on us all that there really was no mistake, no innocent explanation. We'd all had our hopeful little theories in the first couple of days. She'd maybe felt stressed, unable to cope, and gone off alone somewhere. Or perhaps there'd been an accident, and she was lying unconscious and unidentified in a hospital. But as the days went by, and the hospitals had been checked, and her photograph had been in all the papers and still there was no news, everything started to look more sinister.

'I found it most peculiar that Inspector Talbot informed me, unasked, that Roy wasn't under suspicion, that he had a complete alibi. Talbot struck all of us as peculiar, actually. Intense. His questions jumped around a lot.

'I *think* he was trying to reassure me,' said Gupta, taking a third fig roll and examining it thoughtfully as he continued. 'He wanted me to know that my brother doctor was in the clear, that I had nothing to fear, that he knew no doctor could have done anything so terrible as to abduct a woman, or – by then, we were all starting to fear it – to kill her . . .

'But Talbot thought it was Creed, of course, from the very start – and he was probably right,' sighed Gupta, sadly.

'What makes you think so?' asked Strike. He thought Gupta might mention the speeding van or the rainy night, but the answer was, he thought, a shrewd one.

'It's very difficult to dispose of a body as completely and cleanly as Margot's seems to have been hidden. Doctors know how death smells and we understand the legalities and procedures surrounding a dead human. The ignorant might imagine it is nothing more than disposing of a table of equivalent weight, but it is a very different thing, and a very difficult one. And even in the seventies, before DNA testing, the police did pretty well with fingerprints, blood groups and so forth.

'How has she remained hidden for so long? Somebody did the job very cleverly and if we know anything about Creed, it's that he's very clever, isn't that so? It was living ladies who betrayed him in the end, not dead. He knew how to render his corpses mute.'

Gupta popped the end of the fig roll in his mouth, sighed,

brushed his hands fastidiously clean of crumbs, then pointed at Strike's legs and said,

'Which one is it?'

Strike didn't resent the blunt question, from a doctor.

'This one,' he said, shifting his right leg.

'You walk very naturally,' said Gupta, 'for a big man. I might not have known, if I hadn't read about you in the press. The prosthetics were not nearly as good in the old days. Wonderful, what you can buy now. Hydraulics reproducing natural joint action! Marvellous.'

'The NHS can't afford those fancy prosthetics,' said Strike, slipping his notebook back into his pocket. 'Mine's pretty basic. If it's not too much trouble,' he continued, 'could I ask you for the practice nurse's current address?'

'Yes, yes, of course,' said Gupta. He succeeded in rising from his armchair on the third attempt.

It took the Guptas half an hour to find, in an old address book, the last address they had for Janice Beattie.

'I can't swear it's current,' said Gupta, handing the slip of paper to Strike in the hall.

'It'll give me a head start on finding her, especially if she's got a different married name now,' said Strike. 'You've been very helpful, Dr Gupta. I really appreciate you taking the time to talk to me.'

'Of course,' said Dr Gupta, considering Strike with his shrewd, bright brown eyes, 'it would be a miracle if you found her, after all this time. But I'm glad somebody's looking again. Yes, I'm very glad somebody's looking.'

11

It fortuned forth faring on his way,
He saw from far, or seemed for to see
Some troublous vprore or contentious fray

Edmund Spenser
The Faerie Queene

Strike walked back towards Amersham station, past the box hedges and twin garages of the professional middle classes, thinking about Margot Bamborough. She'd emerged from the old doctor's reminiscences as a vivid and forceful personality and, irrationally, this had been a surprise. In vanishing, Margot Bamborough had assumed in Strike's mind the insubstantiality of a wraith, as though it had always been predestined that she would one day disperse into the rainy dusk, never to return.

He remembered the seven women depicted on the front cover of *The Demon of Paradise Park*. They lived on in ghostly black and white, sporting the hairstyles that had become gradually more unfashionable with every day they'd been absent from their families and their lives, but each of those negative images represented a human whose heart had once beaten, whose ambitions and opinions, triumphs and disappointments had been as real as Margot Bamborough's, before they ran into the man who was paid the compliment of full colour in the cover photograph of the dreadful story of their deaths.

Strike still hadn't finished the book, but knew that Creed had been responsible for the deaths of a diverse array of victims, including a schoolgirl, an estate agent and a pharmacist. That had been part of the terror of the Essex Butcher, according to the contemporary press: he wasn't confining his attacks to prostitutes who, it was implied, were a killer's natural prey. In fact, the only working girl who was known to have been attacked by him had survived.

Helen Wardrop, the woman in question, had told her story in a television documentary about Creed, which Strike had watched on YouTube a few nights previously while eating a Chinese takeaway. The programme had been salacious and melodramatic, with many poorly acted reconstructions and music lifted from a seventies horror movie. At the time of filming, Helen Wardrop had been a slack-faced, slow-spoken woman with dyed red hair and badly applied fake eyelashes, whose glazed affect and monotone suggested either tranquillisers or neurological damage. Creed had struck the drunk and screaming Helen what might have been a fatal blow to the head with a hammer in the course of trying to force her into the back of his van. She turned her head obligingly for the interviewer, to show the viewers a still-depressed area of skull. The interviewer told her she must feel very lucky to have survived. There was a tiny hesitation before she agreed with him.

Strike had turned off the documentary at that point, frustrated by the banality of the questioning. He, too, had once been in the wrong place at the wrong time, and bore the lifelong consequences, so he perfectly understood Helen Wardrop's hesitation. In the immediate aftermath of the explosion that had taken Strike's foot and shin, not to mention the lower half of Sergeant Gary Topley's body and a chunk of Richard Anstis's face, Strike had felt a variety of emotions which included guilt, gratitude, confusion, fear, rage, resentment and loneliness, but he couldn't remember feeling lucky. 'Lucky' would have been the bomb not detonating. 'Lucky' would have meant still having both his legs. 'Lucky' was what people who couldn't bear to contemplate horrors needed to hear maimed and terrorised survivors call themselves. He recalled his aunt's tearful assertion that he wasn't in pain as he lay in his hospital bed, groggy with morphine, her words standing in stark contrast to the first Polworth had spoken to him, when he visited Strike in Selly Oak Hospital.

'Bit of a fucker, this, Diddy.'

'It is, a bit,' Strike had said, his amputated leg stretched in front of him, nerve endings insisting that the calf and foot were still there.

Strike arrived at Amersham station to discover he'd just missed a train back to London. He therefore sat down on a bench outside in the feeble autumn sunshine of late afternoon, took out his cigarettes, lit one, then examined his phone. Two texts and a missed call had come in while he'd been interviewing Gupta, his mobile on mute.

The texts were from his half-brother Al and his friend Ilsa, and could therefore wait, whereas the missed call was from George Layborn, whom he immediately phoned back.

'That you, Strike?'

'Yeah. You just phoned me.'

'I did. I've got it for you. Copy of the Bamborough file.'

'You're kidding!' said Strike, exhaling on a rush of exhilaration. 'George, that's phenomenal, I owe you big time for this.'

'Buy me a pint and mention me to the press if you ever find out who did it. "Valuable assistance." "Couldn't have done it without him." We can decide the wording after. Might remind this lot I deserve promotion. Listen,' added Layborn, more seriously, 'it's a mess. The file. Real mess.'

'In what way?'

'Old. Bits missing, from what I've seen, though they might just be in the wrong order – I haven't had time to go systematically through the whole thing, there's four boxes' worth here – but Talbot's record-keeping was all over the place and Lawson coming in and trying to make sense of it hasn't really helped. Anyway, for what it's worth, it's yours. I'll be over your way tomorrow and drop it in at the office, shall I?'

'Can't tell you how much I appreciate this, George.'

'My old man would've been dead happy to know someone was going to take another look,' said Layborn. 'He'd've loved to see Creed nailed for another one.'

Layborn rang off and Strike immediately lit a cigarette and called Robin to give her the good news, but his call went straight to voicemail. Then he remembered that she was in a meeting with the persecuted weatherman, so he turned his attention to the text from Al.

Hey bruv, it began, chummily.

Al was the only sibling on his father's side with whom Strike maintained any kind of ongoing relationship, spasmodic and one-sided though it was, Al making all the running. Strike had a total of six Rokeby half-siblings, three of whom he'd never even met, a situation which he felt no need to remedy, finding the stresses of his known relatives quite sufficient to be going on with.

As you know, the Deadbeats are celebrating 50 years together next year—

Strike hadn't known this. He'd met his father, Jonny Rokeby, who was lead singer of the Deadbeats, exactly twice in his life and most of the information he had about his rock-star father had come either from his mother Leda, the woman with whom he had carelessly fathered a child in the semi-public corner of a party in New York, or from the press.

As you know, the Deadbeats are celebrating 50 years together next year and (super confidential) they're going to drop a surprise new album on 24th May. We (families) are throwing them a big London bash that night at Spencer House to celebrate the launch. Bruv, it would mean the world to all of us, especially Dad, if you came. Gaby's had the idea of getting a picture taken of all the kids together, to give him as a present on the night. First ever. Getting it framed, as a surprise. Everyone's in. We just need you. Think about it, bruv.

Strike read this text through twice, then closed it without replying and opened Ilsa's, which was far shorter.

It's Robin's birthday, you total dickhead.

12

With flattering wordes he sweetly wooed her,
And offered faire guiftes, t'allure her sight,
But she both offers and the offerer
Despysde, and all the fawning of the flatterer.

Edmund Spenser
The Faerie Queene

The television weatherman brought his wife to the catch-up meeting with Robin. Once ensconced in the agency's inner office, the couple proved hard to shift. The wife had arrived with a new theory to present to Robin, triggered by the most recent anonymous postcard to arrive by post at the television studio. It was the fifth card to feature a painting, and the third to have been bought at the National Portrait Gallery shop, and this had caused the weatherman's thoughts to turn to an ex-girlfriend, who'd been to art school. He didn't know where the woman was now, but surely it was worth looking for her?

Robin thought it was highly unlikely that an ex-girlfriend would choose anonymous postcards to reconnect with a lost love, given the existence of social media and, indeed, the publicly available contact details for the weatherman, but she agreed diplomatically that this was worth looking into, and took down as many details of this long-vanished love interest as the weatherman could remember. Robin then ran through all the measures the agency was so far taking to trace the sender of the cards, and reassured husband and wife that they were continuing to watch the house at night, in the hopes that Postcard would show themselves.

The weatherman was a small man with reddish-brown hair, dark eyes and a possibly deceptive air of apology. His wife, a thin woman several inches taller than her husband, seemed frightened by the late-night hand deliveries, and slightly annoyed by her husband's half-laughing assertions that you didn't expect this sort of thing when you were a weatherman, because, after all, he was hardly the *film star* type, and who knew what this woman was capable of?

'Or man,' his wife reminded him. 'We don't *know* it's a woman, do we?'

'No, that's true,' said her husband, the smile fading slowly from his face.

When at last the couple had left, walking out past Pat, who was stoically typing away at her desk, Robin returned to the inner office and re-examined the most recent postcard. The painting on the front featured the portrait of a nineteenth-century man in a high cravat. *James Duffield Harding.* Robin had never heard of him. She flipped the card over. The printed message read:

HE ALWAYS REMINDS ME OF YOU.

She turned the card over again. The mousy man in side-whiskers *did* resemble the weatherman.

A yawn caught her by surprise. She'd spent most of the day clearing paperwork, authorising payment of bills and tweaking the rota for the coming fortnight to accommodate Morris's request for Saturday afternoon off, so that he could go and watch his three-year-old daughter perform in a ballet show. Checking her watch, Robin saw that it was already five o'clock. Fighting the low mood that had been held at bay by hard work, she tidied away the Postcard file, and switched her mobile ringer back on. Within seconds, it had rung: Strike.

'Hello,' said Robin, trying not to sound peeved, because as the hours had rolled by it had become clear to her that Strike had indeed forgotten her birthday yet again.

'Happy birthday,' he said, over the sound of what Robin could tell was a train.

'Thanks.'

'I've got something for you, but I won't be back for an hour, I've only just got on the train back from Amersham.'

Have you hell got something, thought Robin. *You forgot. You're just going to grab flowers on the way back to the office.*

Robin was sure Ilsa must have tipped Strike off, because Ilsa had called her just before the client had arrived, to tell Robin that she might be unavoidably late for drinks. She'd also asked, with unconvincing casualness, what Strike had bought her, and Robin had answered truthfully, 'Nothing'.

'That's nice, thanks,' Robin said now, 'but I'm just leaving. Going out for a drink tonight.'

'Oh,' said Strike. 'Right. Sorry – couldn't be helped, you know, with coming out here to meet Gupta.'

'No,' said Robin, 'well, you can leave them here in the office—'

'Yeah,' said Strike, and Robin noted that he didn't dispute the word 'them'. It was definitely going to be flowers.

'Anyway,' said Strike, 'big news. George Layborn's got hold of a copy of the Bamborough file.'

'Oh, that's great!' said Robin, enthusiastic in spite of herself.

'Yeah, isn't it? He's going to bring it over tomorrow morning.'

'How was Gupta?' asked Robin, sitting down on her side of the partners' desk which had replaced Strike's old single one.

'Interesting, especially about Margot herself,' said Strike, who became muffled as, Robin guessed, the train went through a tunnel. Robin pressed the mobile closer to her ear and said,

'In what way?'

'Dunno,' said Strike distantly. 'From the old photo, I wouldn't have guessed an ardent feminist. She sounds much more of a personality than I'd imagined, which is stupid, really – why shouldn't she have a personality, and a strong one?'

But Robin knew, somehow, what he meant. The hazy picture of Margot Bamborough, frozen in blurry time with her seventies middle parting, her wide, rounded lapels, her knitted tank top, seemed to belong to a long-gone, two-dimensional world of faded colour.

'Tell you the rest tomorrow,' said Strike, because their connection was breaking up. 'Reception's not great here. I can hardly hear you.'

'OK, fine,' said Robin loudly. 'Speak tomorrow.'

She opened the door into the outer office again. Pat was just turning off Robin's old PC, electronic cigarette sticking out of her mouth.

'Was that Strike?' she asked, crow-like, with her jet-black hair and her croak, the fake cigarette waggling.

'Yep,' said Robin, reaching for her coat and bag. 'He's on his way back from Amersham. Lock up as usual though, Pat, he can let himself in if he needs to.'

'Has he remembered your birthday yet?' asked Pat, who seemed to have taken sadistic satisfaction in news of Strike's forgetfulness that morning.

'Yes,' said Robin, and out of loyalty to Strike she added, 'he's got a present for me. I'll get it tomorrow.'

Pat had bought Robin a new purse. 'That old one was

coming apart at the seams,' she said, when Robin unwrapped it. Robin, touched in spite of the fact that she might not have chosen bright red, had expressed warm thanks and at once transferred her money and cards across into the new one.

'Good thing about having one in a nice bright colour, you can always find it in your bag,' Pat had said complacently. 'What's that Scottish nutter got you?'

Barclay had left a small wrapped package with Pat to give to Robin that morning.

'Cards,' said Robin, smiling as she unwrapped the package. 'Sam was telling me all about these, look, when we were out on surveillance the other night. Cards showing Al-Qaeda's most wanted. They gave packs out to the American troops during the Iraq War.'

'What's he given you those for?' said Pat. 'What are you supposed to do with them?'

'Well, because I was interested, when he told me,' said Robin, amused by Pat's disdain. 'I can play poker with them. They've got all the right numbers and everything, look.'

'Bridge,' Pat had said. 'That's a proper game. I like a nice game of bridge.'

As both women pulled on their coats, Pat asked,

'Going anywhere nice tonight?'

'For a drink with a couple of friends,' said Robin. 'But I've got a Selfridges voucher burning a hole in my pocket. Think I might treat myself first.'

'Lovely,' croaked Pat. 'What d'you fancy?'

Before Robin could answer, the glass door behind her opened and Saul Morris entered, handsome, smiling and a little breathless, his black hair sleek, his blue eyes bright. With some misgiving, she saw the wrapped present and card clutched in his hand.

'Happy birthday!' he said. 'Hoped I'd catch you.'

And before Robin could prevent it, he'd bent down and kissed her on the cheek; no air kiss, this, but proper contact of lips and skin. She took half a step backwards.

'Got you a little something,' he said, apparently sensing nothing amiss, but holding out to her the gift and card. 'It's nothing really. And how's Moneypenny?' he said, turning to Pat, who had already removed her electronic cigarette to smile at him, displaying teeth the colour of old ivory.

'*Moneypenny*,' repeated Pat, beaming. 'Get on with you.'

Robin tore the paper from her gift. Inside was a box of Fortnum & Mason salted caramel truffles.

'Oh, *very* nice,' said Pat approvingly.

Chocolates, it seemed, were a far more appropriate gift for a young woman than a pack of cards with Al-Qaeda members on them.

'Remembered you like a bit of salted caramel,' said Morris, looking proud of himself.

Robin knew exactly where he'd got this idea, and it didn't make her any more appreciative.

A month previously, at the first meeting of the entire expanded agency, Robin had opened a tin of fancy biscuits that had arrived in a hamper sent by a grateful client. Strike had enquired why everything these days was salted caramel flavour, and Robin had replied that it didn't seem to be stopping him eating them by the handful. She'd expressed no personal fondness for the flavour, but Morris had evidently paid both too little and too much attention, treasuring up his lazy assumption for use at some later date.

'Thanks very much,' she said, with a bare minimum of warmth. 'I'm afraid I've got to dash.'

And before Pat could point out that Selfridges would still be there in a half an hour, Robin had slid past Morris and started down the metal stairs, his card still unopened in her hand.

Exactly why Morris grated on her so much, Robin was still pondering as she moved slowly around Selfridges' great perfume hall half an hour later. She'd decided to buy herself some new perfume, because she'd been wearing the same scent for five years. Matthew had liked it, and never wanted her to change, but her last bottle was down to the dregs, and she had a sudden urge to douse herself in something that Matthew wouldn't recognise, and possibly wouldn't even like. The cheap little bottle of 4711 cologne she'd bought on the way to Falmouth was nowhere near distinctive enough for a new signature scent, and so she wandered through a vast maze of smoked mirrors and gilded lights, between islands of seductive bottles and illuminated pictures of celebrities, each little domain presided over by black-clad sirens offering squirts and testing strips.

Was it pompous of her, she wondered, to think that Morris the subcontractor ought not to assume the right to kiss an agency partner? Would she mind if the generally reserved Hutchins kissed her on the cheek? No, she decided, she wouldn't mind at all, because she'd now known Andy over a year, and in any case, Hutchins would do the polite thing and make the greeting a matter of brief proximity of two faces, not a pressing of lips into her face.

And what about Barclay? He'd never kissed her, though he had recently called her 'ya numpty' when, on surveillance, she had accidentally spilled hot coffee all over him in her excitement at seeing their target, a civil servant, leaving a known brothel at two o'clock in the morning. But she hadn't minded Barclay calling her a numpty in the slightest. She'd *been* a numpty.

Turning a corner, Robin found herself facing the Yves Saint Laurent counter, and with a sudden sharpening of interest, her eyes focused on a blue, black and silver cylinder bearing the name Rive Gauche. Robin had never knowingly smelled Margot Bamborough's favourite perfume before.

'It's a classic,' said the bored-looking salesgirl, watching Robin spraying Rive Gauche onto a fresh testing strip and inhaling.

Robin tended to rate perfumes according to how well they reproduced a familiar flower or foodstuff, but this wasn't a smell from nature. There was a ghostly rose there, but also something strangely metallic. Robin, who was used to fragrances made friendly with fruit and candy, set down the strip with a smile and a shake of her head and walked on.

So that was how Margot Bamborough had smelled, she thought. It was a far more sophisticated scent than the one Matthew had loved on Robin, which was a natural-smelling concoction of figs, fresh, milky and green.

Robin turned a corner and saw, standing on a counter directly ahead of her, a faceted glass bottle full of pink liquid: Flowerbomb, Sarah Shadlock's signature scent. Robin had seen it in Sarah and Tom's bathroom whenever she and Matthew had gone over for dinner. Since leaving Matthew, Robin had had ample time to realise that the occasions on which he had changed the sheets mid-week, because he'd 'spilled tea' or 'thought I'd do it today, save you doing it tomorrow' must have been as much to wash away that loud, sweet scent, as any other, more obviously incriminating traces that might have leaked from careful condoms.

'It's a modern classic,' said the hopeful salesgirl, who'd noticed Robin looking at the glass hand grenade. With a perfunctory smile, Robin shook her head and turned away. Now her reflection in the smoked glass looked simply sad, as she picked up bottles and smelled strips in a joyless hunt for something to improve this lousy birthday. She suddenly wished that she were heading home, and not out for drinks.

'What are you looking for?' said a sharp-cheekboned black girl, whom Robin passed shortly afterwards.

Five minutes later, after a brief, professional interchange, Robin was heading back towards Oxford Street with a rectangular black bottle in her bag. The salesgirl had been highly persuasive.

' . . . and if you want something *totally* different,' she'd said, picking up a fifth bottle, spraying a little onto a strip and wafting it around, 'try Fracas.'

She'd handed the strip to Robin, whose nostrils were now burning from the rich and varied assault of the past half hour.

'Sexy but grown-up, you know? It's a real classic.'

And in that moment, Robin, breathing in heady, luscious, oily tuberose, had been seduced by the idea of becoming, in her thirtieth year, a sophisticated woman utterly different from the kind of fool who was too stupid to realise that what her husband told her he loved, and what he liked taking into his bed, bore about as much resemblance as a fig to a hand grenade.

13

Thence forward by that painfull way they pas,
Forth to an hill, that was both steepe and hy;
On top whereof a sacred chappell was,
And eke a little hermitage thereby.

Edmund Spenser
The Faerie Queene

In retrospect, Strike regretted the first gift he'd ever given Robin Ellacott. He'd bought the expensive green dress in a fit of quixotic extravagance, feeling safe in giving her something so personal only because she was engaged to another man and he was never going to see her again, or so he'd thought. She'd modelled it for Strike in the course of persuading a saleswoman into indiscretions, and that girl's evidence, which Robin had so skilfully extracted, had helped solve the case that had made Strike's name and saved his agency from bankruptcy. Buoyed by a tide of euphoria and gratitude, he'd returned to the shop and made the purchase as a grand farewell gesture. Nothing else had seemed to encapsulate what he wanted to tell her, which was 'look what we achieved together', 'I couldn't have done it without you' and (if he was being totally honest with himself) 'you look gorgeous in this, and I'd like you to know I thought so when I saw you in it'.

But things hadn't panned out quite as Strike had expected,

because within an hour of giving her the green dress he'd hired her as a full-time assistant. Doubtless the dress accounted for at least some of the profound mistrust Matthew, her fiancé, had henceforth felt towards the detective. Worse still, from Strike's point of view, it had set the bar uncomfortably high for future gifts. Whether consciously or not, he'd lowered expectations considerably since, either by forgetting to buy Robin birthday and Christmas gifts, or by making them as generic as was possible.

He purchased stargazer lilies at the first florist he could find when he got off the train from Amersham, and bore them into the office for Robin to find next day. He'd chosen them for their size and powerful fragrance. He felt he ought to spend more money than he had on the previous year's belated bunch, and these looked impressive, as though he hadn't skimped. Roses carried an unwelcome connotation of Valentine's Day, and nearly everything else in the florist's stock – admittedly depleted at half past five in the afternoon – looked a little bedraggled or underwhelming. The lilies were large and yet reassuringly impersonal, sculptural in quality and heavy with fragrance, and there was safety in their very boldness. They came from a clinical hothouse; there was no romantic whisper of quiet woods or secret garden about them: they were flowers of which he could say robustly 'nice smell', with no further justification for his choice.

Strike wasn't to know that Robin's primary association with stargazer lilies, now and for evermore, would be with Sarah Shadlock, who'd once brought an almost identical bouquet to Robin and Matthew's housewarming party. When she walked into the office the day after her birthday and saw the flowers standing there on the partners' desk, stuck in a vase full of water but still in their cellophane, with a large magenta bow on them and a small card that read 'Happy birthday from

Cormoran' (no kiss, he never put kisses), she was affected exactly the same way she'd been by the hand-grenade-shaped bottle in Selfridges. She didn't want these flowers; they were a double irritant in reminding her of Strike's forgetfulness and Matthew's infidelity, and if she had to look at or smell them, she resolved, it wouldn't be in her own home.

So she'd left the lilies at the office, where they stubbornly refused to die, Pat conscientiously refilling their water every morning and taking such good care of them that they lived for nearly two weeks. Even Strike was sick of them by the end: he kept getting wafts of something that reminded him of his ex-girlfriend Lorelei's perfume, an unpleasant association.

By the time the waxy pink and white petals began to shrivel and fall, the thirty-ninth anniversary of Margot Bamborough's disappearance had passed unmarked and probably unnoticed by anyone except, perhaps, her family, Strike and Robin, who both registered the fateful date. Copies of the police records had been brought to the office as promised by George Layborn, and now lay in four cardboard boxes under the partners' desk, which was the only place the agency had room for them. Strike, who was currently the least encumbered by the agency's other cases, because he was holding himself in readiness to go back down to Cornwall should the need arise, set himself to work systematically through these files. Once he'd digested their contents, he intended to visit Clerkenwell with Robin, and retrace the route between the old St John's practice where Margot had last been seen alive, and the pub where her friend had waited for her in vain.

So, on the last day of October, Robin left the office at one o'clock and hurried, beneath a threatening sky and with her umbrella ready in her hand, onto the Tube. She was quietly excited by the prospect of this afternoon, the first she and Strike would spend working the Bamborough case together.

It was already drizzling slightly when Robin caught sight of Strike, standing smoking as he surveyed the frontage of a building halfway down St John's Lane. He turned at the sound of her heels on the wet pavement.

'Am I late?' she called, as she approached.

'No,' said Strike, 'I was early.'

She joined him, still holding her umbrella, and looked up at the tall, multi-storey building of brown brick, with large, metal-framed windows. It appeared to house offices, but there was no indication of what kind of businesses were operating inside.

'It was right here,' said Strike, pointing at the door numbered 29. 'The old St John's Medical Practice. They've remodelled the front of the building, obviously. There used to be a back entrance,' he said. 'We'll go round and have a shufti in a minute.'

Robin turned to look up and down St John's Lane, which was a long, narrow one-way street, bordered on either side by tall, multi-windowed buildings.

'Very overlooked,' commented Robin.

'Yep,' said Strike. 'So, let's begin with what Margot was wearing when she disappeared.'

'I already know,' said Robin. 'Brown corduroy skirt, red shirt, knitted tank top, beige Burberry raincoat, silver necklace and earrings, gold wedding ring. Carrying a leather shoulder bag and a black umbrella.'

'You should take up detection,' said Strike, mildly impressed. 'Ready for the police records?'

'Go on.'

'At a quarter to six on the eleventh of October 1974 only three people are known to have been inside this building: Margot, who was dressed exactly as you describe, but hadn't yet put on her raincoat; Gloria Conti, who was the younger of the two receptionists; and an emergency patient with abdominal pain, who'd walked in off the street. The patient, according to the hasty note Gloria took, was called "Theo question mark". In spite of the male name, and Dr Joseph Brenner's assertion that he thought the patient looked like a man, and Talbot trying hard to persuade her that Theo was a man dressed as a woman, Gloria never wavered in her assertion that "Theo" was a woman.

'All the other employees had left before a quarter to six, except Wilma the cleaner, who hadn't been there at all that day, because she didn't work Fridays. More of Wilma later.

'Janice, the nurse, was here until midday, then making house visits the rest of the afternoon and didn't return. Irene, the receptionist, left at half past two for a dental appointment and didn't come back. According to their statements, each of which were corroborated by some other witness, the secretary, Dorothy, left at ten past five, Dr Gupta at half past and Dr Brenner at a quarter to six. Police were happy with the alibis all three gave for the rest of the evening: Dorothy went home to her son and spent the evening watching TV with him. Dr Gupta attended a large family dinner to celebrate his mother's birthday and Dr Brenner was with the spinster sister he shared his house with. Both Brenners were seen through the sitting-room window later that evening, by a dog walker.

'The last registered patients, a mother and child, were Margot's, and they left the practice shortly before Brenner did. The patients testified that Margot was fine when they saw her.

'From that point on, Gloria is the only witness. According to Gloria, Theo went into Margot's consulting room and stayed there longer than expected. At a quarter past six, Theo left, never to be seen at the practice again. A police appeal was subsequently put out for her, but nobody came forward.

'Margot left no notes about Theo. The assumption is that

she intended to write up the consultation the following day, because her friend had now been waiting for her in the pub for a quarter of an hour and she didn't want to make herself even later.

'Shortly after Theo left, Margot came hurrying out of her consulting room, put on her raincoat, told Gloria to lock up with the emergency key, walked out into the rain, put up her umbrella, turned right and disappeared from Gloria's sight.'

Strike turned and pointed up the road towards a yellow stone arch of ancient appearance, which lay directly ahead of them.

'Which means she was heading in that direction, towards the Three Kings.'

For a moment, both of them looked towards the old arch that spanned the road, as though some shadow of Margot might materialise. Then Strike ground out his cigarette underfoot and said,

'Follow me.'

He walked the length of number 28, then paused to point up a dark passageway the width of a door, called Passing Alley.

'Good hiding place,' said Robin, pausing to look up and down the dark, vaulted corridor through the buildings.

'Certainly is,' said Strike. 'If somebody wanted to lie in wait for her, this is tailor made. Catch her by surprise, drag her up here – but after that, it'd get problematic.'

They walked along the short passage and emerged into a sunken garden area of concrete and shrubs that lay between two parallel streets.

'The police searched this whole garden area with sniffer dogs. Nothing. And if an assailant dragged her onwards, through there,' Strike pointed to the road that ran parallel to St John's Lane, 'onto St John Street, it would've been well-nigh impossible to go undetected. The street's far busier than St John's Lane. And that's assuming a fit, tall twenty-nine-year-old wouldn't have shouted and fought back.'

He turned to look at the back entrance.

'The district nurse sometimes went in the back, rather than going through the waiting room. She had a little room to the rear of the building where she kept her own stuff and sometimes saw patients. Wilma the cleaner sometimes went out the back door as well. Otherwise it was usually locked.'

'Are we interested in people being able to enter or leave the building through a second door?' asked Robin.

'Not especially, but I want to get a feel for the layout. It's been nearly forty years: we've got to go back over everything.'

They walked back through Passing Alley to the front of the building.

'We've got one advantage over Bill Talbot,' said Strike. 'We know the Essex Butcher turned out to be slim and blond, not a swarthy thickset person of gypsy-ish appearance. Theo, whoever she was, wasn't Creed. Which doesn't necessarily make her irrelevant, of course.

'One last thing, then we're done with the practice itself,' said Strike, looking up at number 29. 'Irene, the blonde receptionist, told the police that Margot received two threatening, anonymous notes shortly before she disappeared. They're not in the police file, so we've only got Irene's statement to go on. She claims she opened one, and that she saw another on Margot's desk when bringing her tea. She says the one she read mentioned hellfire.'

'You'd think it was the secretary's job to open mail,' commented Robin. 'Not a receptionist's.'

'Good point,' said Strike, pulling out his notebook and scribbling, 'we'll check that . . . It seems relevant to add here that Talbot thought Irene was an unreliable witness: inaccurate and prone to exaggeration. Incidentally, Gupta said Irene and

Margot had what he called a "contretemps" at a Christmas party. He didn't think it was a particularly big deal, but he'd remembered it.'

'And is Talbot—?'

'Dead? Yes,' said Strike. 'So's Lawson, who took over from him. Talbot's got a son, though, and I'm thinking of getting in touch with him. Lawson never had kids.'

'Go on, about the anonymous notes.'

'Well, Gloria, the other receptionist, said Irene showed her one of the notes, but couldn't remember what was in it. Janice, the nurse, confirmed that Irene had told her about them at the time, but said she hadn't personally seen them. Margot didn't tell Gupta about them – I called him to check.

'Anyway,' said Strike, giving the street one last sweeping look through the drizzle, 'assuming nobody abducted Margot right outside the practice, or that she didn't get in a car yards from the door, she headed towards the Three Kings, which takes us this way.'

'D'you want to come under this umbrella?' Robin asked.

'No,' said Strike. His densely curling hair looked the same wet or dry: he had very little vanity.

They continued up the street and passed through St John's Gate, the ancient stone arch decorated with many small heraldic shields, emerging onto Clerkenwell Road, a bustling two-way street, which they crossed, arriving beside an old-fashioned scarlet phone box which stood at the mouth of Albemarle Way.

'Is that the phone box where the two women were seen struggling?' asked Robin.

Strike did a double take.

'You've read the case notes,' he said, almost accusingly.

'I had a quick look,' Robin admitted, 'while I was printing out Two-Times' bill last night. I didn't read everything; didn't have time. Just looked at a few bits and pieces.'

'Well, that *isn't* the phone box,' said Strike. 'The important phone box – or boxes – come later. We'll get to them in due course. Now follow me.'

Instead of proceeding into a paved pedestrian area that Robin, from her own scant research, knew Margot must have crossed if she had been heading for the Three Kings, Strike turned left, up Clerkenwell Road.

'Why are we going this way?' asked Robin, jogging to keep up.

'Because,' said Strike, stopping again and pointing up at a top window on the building opposite, which looked like an old brick warehouse, 'some time after six o'clock on the evening in question, a fourteen-year-old schoolgirl called Amanda White swore she saw Margot at the top window, second from the right, banging her fists against the glass.'

'I haven't seen *that* mentioned online!' said Robin.

'For the good reason that the police concluded there was nothing in it.

'Talbot, as is clear from his notes, disregarded White because her story couldn't be fitted into his theory that Creed had abducted Margot. But Lawson went back to Amanda when he took over, and actually walked with her along this stretch of road.

'Amanda's account had a few things going for it. For one thing, she told the police unprompted that this had happened the evening after the general election, which she remembered because she had an argument with a Tory schoolfriend. The pair of them had been kept back after school for a detention. They'd then gone for a coffee together, over which the schoolfriend went into a huff when Mandy said it was good that Wilson had won, and refused to walk home with her.

'Amanda said she was still angry about her friend getting stroppy when she looked up and saw a woman pounding on the glass with her fists. The description she gave was a good one, although by this time, a full description of Margot's appearance and clothing had been in the press.

'Lawson contacted the business owner who worked on the top floor. It was a paper design company run by a husband and wife. They produced small runs of pamphlets, posters and invitations, that kind of stuff. No connection to Margot. Neither of them were registered with the St John's practice, because they lived out of the area. The wife said she sometimes had to thump the window frame to make it close. However, the wife in no way resembled Margot, being short, tubby and ginger-haired.'

'And someone would've noticed Margot on her way up to the third floor, surely?' said Robin, looking from the top window to the front door. She moved back from the kerb: cars were splashing through the puddles in the gutter. 'She'd have climbed the stairs or used the lift, and maybe rung the doorbell to get in.'

'You'd think so,' agreed Strike. 'Lawson concluded that Amanda had made an innocent mistake and thought the printer's wife was Margot.'

They returned to the point where they had deviated from what Robin thought of as 'Margot's route'. Strike paused again, pointing up the gloomy side road called Albemarle Way.

'Now, disregard the phone box, but note that Albemarle Way is the first side street since Passing Alley I think she could plausibly have entered – voluntarily or not – without necessarily being seen by fifty-odd people. Quieter, as you can see – but not *that* quiet,' admitted Strike, looking towards the end of Albemarle Way, where traffic was passing at a steady rate. Albemarle Way was narrower than St John's Lane, but similar in being bordered by tall buildings in unbroken lines, which kept it permanently in shadow. 'Still a risk for an abductor,' said Strike, 'but if Dennis Creed was lurking somewhere in his van, waiting for a lone woman – any woman – to walk past in the rain, this is the place I can see it happening.'

It was at this moment, as a cold breeze whistled up Albemarle Way, that Strike caught a whiff of what he had thought were the dying stargazer lilies, but now realised was coming from Robin herself. The perfume wasn't exactly the same as the one that Lorelei had worn; his ex's had been strangely boozy, with overtones of rum (and he'd liked it when the scent had been an accompaniment to easy affection and imaginative sex; only later had he come to associate it with passive-aggression, character assassination and pleas for a love he could not feel). Nevertheless, this scent strongly resembled Lorelei's; he found it cloying and sickly.

Of course, many would say it was rich for him to have opinions about how women smelled, given that his signature odour was that of an old ashtray, overlain with a splash of Pour Un Homme on special occasions. Nevertheless, having spent much of his childhood in conditions of squalor, Strike found cleanliness a necessary trait in anyone he could find attractive. He'd liked Robin's previous scent, which he'd missed when she wasn't in the office.

'This way,' he said, and they proceeded through the rain into an irregular pedestrianised square. A few seconds later, Strike suddenly became aware that he'd left Robin behind, and walked back several paces to join her in front of St John Priory Church, a pleasingly symmetrical building of red brick, with long windows and two white stone pillars flanking the entrance.

'Thinking about her lying in a holy place?' he asked, lighting up again while the rain beat down on him. Exhaling, he held the cigarette cupped in his hand, to prevent its extinguishment.

'No,' said Robin, a little defensively, but then, 'yes, all right, maybe a bit. Look at this . . .'

Strike followed her through the open gates into a small garden of remembrance, open to the public and full (as Robin read off a small sign on the inner wall) of medicinal herbs, including many used in medieval times, in the Order of St John's hospitals. A white figure of Christ hung on the back wall, surrounded with the emblems of the four evangelists: the bull, the lion, the eagle and the angel. Fronds and leaves undulated gently beneath the rain. As Robin's eyes swept the small, walled garden, Strike, who'd followed her, said,

'I think we can agree that if somebody buried her in here, a cleric would have noticed disturbed earth.'

'I know,' said Robin. 'I'm just looking.'

As they returned to the street, she added,

'There are Maltese crosses everywhere, look. They were on that archway we just passed through, too.'

'It's the cross of the Knights Hospitaller. Knights of St John. Hence the street names and the emblem of St John ambulance; they've got their headquarters back in St John's Lane. If that medium Googled the area Margot went missing, she can't have missed Clerkenwell's associations with the Order of St John. I'll bet you that's where she got the idea for that little bit of "holy place" padding. But bear it in mind, because the cross is going to come up again once we reach the pub.'

'You know,' said Robin, turning to look back at the Priory, 'Peter Tobin, that Scottish serial killer – he attached himself to churches. He joined a religious sect at one point, under an assumed name. Then he got a job as a handyman at a church in Glasgow, where he buried that poor girl beneath the floorboards.'

'Churches are good cover for killers,' said Strike. 'Sex offenders, too.'

'Priests and doctors,' said Robin thoughtfully. 'It's hard-wired in most of us to trust them, don't you think?'

'After the Catholic Church's many scandals? After Harold Shipman?'

'Yes, I think so,' said Robin. 'Don't you think we tend to invest some categories of people with unearned goodness? I suppose we've all got a need to trust people who seem to have power over life and death.'

'Think you're onto something there,' said Strike, as they entered a short pedestrian lane called Jerusalem Passage. 'I told Gupta it was odd that Joseph Brenner didn't like people. I thought that might be a basic job requirement for a doctor. He soon put me right.

'Let's stop here a moment,' Strike said, doing so. 'If Margot got this far – I'm assuming she'd've taken this route, because it's the shortest and most logical way to the Three Kings – this is the first time she'd have passed residences rather than offices or public buildings.'

Robin looked at the buildings around them. Sure enough, there were a couple of doors whose multiple buzzers indicated flats above.

'Is there a chance,' said Strike, 'however remote, that someone living along this lane could have persuaded or forced her inside?'

Robin looked up and down the street, the rain pattering onto her umbrella.

'Well,' she said slowly, 'obviously it *could* have happened, but it seems unlikely. Did someone wake up that day and decide they wanted to abduct a woman, reach outside and grab one?'

'Have I taught you nothing?'

'OK, fine: *means before motive*. But there are problems with the means, too. This is really overlooked as well. Does nobody see or hear her being abducted? Doesn't she scream or fight?

And I assume the abductor lives alone, unless their housemates are also in on the kidnapping?'

'All valid points,' admitted Strike. 'Plus, the police went door to door here. Everyone was questioned, though the flats weren't searched.

'But let's think this through ... She's a doctor. What if someone shoots out of a house and begs her to come inside to look at an injured person – a sick relative – and once inside, they don't let her go? That'd be a good ploy for getting her inside, pretending there was a medical emergency.'

'OK, but that presupposes they knew she was a doctor.'

'The abductor could've been a patient.'

'But how did they know she'd be passing their house at that particular time? Had she alerted the whole neighbourhood that she was about to go to the pub?'

'Maybe it was a random thing, they saw her passing, they knew she was a doctor, they ran out and grabbed her. Or – I dunno, let's say there really was a sick or dying person inside, or someone's had an accident – perhaps there's an argument – she disagrees with the treatment or refuses to help – the fight becomes physical – she's accidentally killed.'

There was a short silence, while they moved aside for a group of chattering French students. When these had passed, Strike said,

'It's a stretch, I grant you.'

'We can find out how many of these buildings are occupied by the same people they were thirty-nine years ago,' said Robin, 'but we've still got the problem of how they've kept her body hidden for nearly four decades. You wouldn't dare move, would you?'

'That's a problem, all right,' admitted Strike. 'As Gupta said, it's not like disposing of a table of equivalent weight. Blood, decomposition, infestation ... plenty have tried keeping bodies on the premises. Crippen. Christie. Fred and Rose West. It's generally considered a mistake.'

'Creed managed it for a while,' said Robin. 'Boiling down severed hands in the basement. Burying heads apart from bodies. It wasn't the corpses that got him caught.'

'Are you reading *The Demon of Paradise Park*?' asked Strike sharply.

'Yes,' said Robin.

'D'you want that stuff in your head?'

'If it helps us with the case,' said Robin.

'Hmm. Just thinking of my health and safety responsibilities.'

Robin said nothing. Strike gave the houses a last, sweeping look, then invited Robin to walk on, saying,

'You're right, I can't see it. Freezers get opened, gas men visit and notice a smell, neighbours notice blocked drains. But in the interests of thoroughness, we should check who was living here at the time.'

They now emerged onto the busiest road they had yet seen. Aylesbury Street was a wide road, lined with more office blocks and flats.

'So,' said Strike, pausing again on the pavement, 'if Margot's still walking to the pub, she would've crossed here and turned left, into Clerkenwell Green. But we're pausing to note that it was *there*,' Strike pointed some fifty yards to the right, 'that a small white van nearly knocked down two women as it sped away from Clerkenwell Green that evening. The incident was witnessed by four or five onlookers. Nobody got the registration number— '

'But Creed was putting fake licence plates on the delivery van he was using,' said Robin, 'so that might not help anyway.'

'Correct. The van seen by witnesses on the eleventh of October 1974 had a design on the side. The onlookers didn't all agree what it was, but two of them thought a large flower.'

'And we also know,' said Robin, 'that Creed was using removable paint on the van to disguise its appearance.'

'Correct again. So, on the surface, this looks like our first proper hint that Creed might've been in the area. Talbot, of course, wanted to believe that, so he was uninterested in the opinion of one of the witnesses that the van actually belonged to a local florist. However, a junior officer, presumably one of those who'd realised that his lead investigator was going quietly off his onion, went and questioned the florist, a man called Albert Shimmings, who absolutely denied driving a speeding van in this area that night. He claimed he'd been giving his young son a lift in it, miles away.'

'Which doesn't necessarily mean it *wasn't* Shimmings,' said Robin. 'He might have been worried about being done for dangerous driving. No CCTV cameras . . . nothing to prove it one way or the other.'

'My thoughts exactly. If Shimmings is still alive, I think we should check his story. He might've decided it's worth telling the truth now a speeding charge can't stick. In the meantime,' said Strike, 'the matter of the van remains unresolved and we have to admit that one possible explanation is that Creed was driving it.'

'But where did he abduct Margot, if it *was* Creed in the van?' asked Robin. 'It can't've been back in Albemarle Way, because this isn't how he'd have left the area.'

'True. If he'd grabbed her in Albemarle Way, he'd've joined Aylesbury Street much further down and he definitely wouldn't have come via Clerkenwell Green – which leads us neatly to the Two Struggling Women by the Phoneboxes.'

They proceeded through the drizzle into Clerkenwell Green, a wide rectangular square which boasted trees, a pub and a café. Two telephone boxes stood in the middle, near parked cars and a bike stand.

'Here,' said Strike, coming to a halt between the phone boxes, 'is where Talbot's craziness really starts messing with the case. A woman called Ruby Elliot, who was unfamiliar with the area, but trying to find her daughter and son-in-law's new house in Hayward's Place, was driving around in circles in the rain, lost.

'She passed these phone boxes and noticed two women struggling together, one of whom seemed, in her word, "tottery". She has no particularly distinct memory of them – remember, it's pouring with rain and she's anxiously trying to spot street signs and house numbers, because she's lost. All she can tell the police is that one of them was wearing a headscarf and the other a raincoat.

'The day after this detail appeared in the paper, a middle-aged woman of sound character came forward to say that the pair of women Ruby Elliot had seen had almost certainly been her and her aged mother. She told Talbot she'd been walking the old dear across Clerkenwell Green that night, taking her home after a little walk. The mother, who was infirm and senile, was wearing a rainhat, and she herself was wearing a raincoat similar to Margot's. They didn't have umbrellas, so she was trying to hurry her mother along. The old lady didn't take kindly to being rushed and there was a slight altercation here, right by the phone boxes. I've got a picture of the two of them, incidentally: the press got hold of it – "sighting debunked".

'But Talbot wasn't having it. He flat-out refused to accept that the two women hadn't been Margot and a man dressed like a woman. The way he sees it: Margot and Creed meet here by the phone boxes, Creed wrestles her into his van, which presumably was parked *there* –' Strike pointed to the short line of parked cars nearby, 'then Creed takes off at speed, with her screaming and banging on the sides of the van, exiting down Aylesbury Street.'

'But,' said Robin, 'Talbot thought *Theo* was Creed. Why would Creed come to Margot's surgery dressed as a woman, then walk out, leaving her unharmed, walk to Clerkenwell Green and grab her here, in the middle of the most public, overlooked place we've seen?'

'There's no point trying to make sense of it, because there isn't any. When Lawson took over the case, he went back to Fiona Fleury, which was the respectable middle-aged woman's name, questioned her again and came away completely satisfied that she and her mother had been the women Ruby Elliot saw. Again, the general election was useful, because Fiona Fleury remembered being tired and not particularly patient with her difficult mother, because she'd sat up late the night before, watching election coverage. Lawson concluded – and I'm inclined to agree with him – that the matter of the two struggling women had been resolved.'

The drizzle had thickened: raindrops were pounding on Robin's umbrella and rendering the hems of her trousers sodden. They now turned up Clerkenwell Close, a curving street that rose towards a large and impressive church with a high, pointed steeple, set on higher ground.

'Margot can't have got this far,' said Robin.

'You say that,' said Strike, and to her surprise he paused again, looking ahead at the church, 'but we now reach one last alleged sighting.

'A church handyman – yeah, I know,' he added, in response to Robin's startled look, 'called Willy Lomax claims he saw a woman in a Burberry raincoat walking up the steps to St James-on-the-Green that evening, around the time Margot should've been arriving at the pub. He saw her from behind. These were the days, of course, when churches weren't locked up all the time.

'Talbot, of course, disregarded Lomax's evidence, because

if Margot was alive and walking into churches, she couldn't have been speeding away in the Essex Butcher's van. Lawson couldn't make much of Lomax's evidence. The bloke stuck fast to his story: he'd seen a woman matching Margot's description go inside but, being a man of limited curiosity, didn't follow her, didn't ask her what she was up to and didn't watch to see whether she ever came out of the church again.

'And now,' said Strike, 'we've earned a pint.'

14

In which there written was with cyphres old . . .

Edmund Spenser
The Faerie Queene

On the opposite side of the road from the church hung the sign of the Three Kings. The pub's curved, tiled exterior wall mirrored the bend in the road.

As she followed Strike inside, Robin had the strange sensation of walking back in time. Most of the walls were papered in pages from old music papers dating back to the seventies: a jumble of reviews, adverts for old stereo systems and pictures of pop and rock stars. Hallowe'en decorations hung over the bar, Bowie and Bob Marley looking down from framed prints, and Bob Dylan and Jimi Hendrix looked back at them from the opposite wall. As Robin sat down at a free table for two and Strike headed to the bar, she spotted a newspaper picture of Jonny Rokeby in tight leather trousers in the collage around the mirror. The pub looked as though it hadn't changed in many years; it might even have had these same frosted windows, these mismatched wooden tables, bare floorboards, round glass wall lamps and candles in bottles back when Margot's friend sat waiting for her in 1974.

For the first time, looking around this quirky, characterful pub, Robin found herself wondering exactly what Margot Bamborough had been like. It was odd how professional people's jobs defined them in the imagination. 'Doctor' felt, in many ways, like a complete identity. Waiting for her companion to buy the drinks, her eyes drifting from the skulls hanging from the bar to the pictures of dead rock stars, Robin was struck by the odd idea of a reverse nativity. The three Magi had journeyed towards a birth; Margot had set out for the Three Kings and, Robin feared, met death along the way.

Strike set Robin's wine in front of her, took a satisfying mouthful of Sussex Best, sat down and then reached inside his overcoat and pulled out a roll of papers. Robin noticed photocopied newspaper reports among the typed and handwritten pages.

'You've been to the British Library.'

'I was there all day yesterday.'

He took the top photocopy and showed it to Robin. It showed a small clipping from the *Daily Mail*, featuring a picture of Fiona Fleury and her aged mother beneath the caption: *Essex Butcher Sighting 'Was Really Us'*. Neither woman would have been easy to mistake for Margot Bamborough: Fiona was a tall, broad woman with a cheery face and no waist; her mother was shrivelled with age and stooped.

'This is the first inkling that the press were losing confidence in Bill Talbot,' said Strike. 'A few weeks after this appeared, they were baying for his blood, which probably didn't help his mental health . . . Anyway,' he said, his large, hairy-backed hand lying flat on the rest of the photocopied paper. 'Let's go back to the one, incontrovertible fact we've got, which is that Margot Bamborough was still alive and inside the practice at a quarter to six that night.'

'At a quarter *past* six, you mean,' said Robin.

'No, I don't,' said Strike. 'The sequence of departures goes: ten past five, Dorothy. Half past five, Dinesh Gupta, who catches sight of Margot inside her consulting room before he leaves, and walks out past Gloria and Theo.

'Gloria goes to ask Brenner if he'll see Theo. He refuses. Margot comes out of her consulting room and her last scheduled patients, a mother and child, come out at the same time and leave, also walking out past Theo in the waiting room. Margot tells Gloria she's happy to see Theo. Brenner says "good of you" and leaves, at a quarter to six.

'From then on, we've only got Gloria's uncorroborated word for anything that happened. She's the only person claiming Theo and Margot left the surgery alive.'

Robin paused in the act of taking a sip of wine.

'Come on. You aren't suggesting they never left? That Margot's still there, buried under the floorboards?'

'No, because sniffer dogs went all over the building, as well as the garden behind it,' said Strike. 'But how's this for a theory? The reason Gloria was so insistent that Theo was a woman, not a man, was because he was her accomplice in the murder or abduction of Margot.'

'Wouldn't it have been more sensible to write down a girl's name instead of "Theo" if she wanted to hide a man's identity? And why would she ask Dr Brenner if he could see Theo, if she and Theo were planning to kill Margot?'

'Both good points,' admitted Strike, 'but maybe she knew perfectly well Brenner would refuse, because he was a cantankerous old bastard, and was trying to make the thing look natural to Margot. Humour me for a moment.

'Inert bodies are heavy, hard to move and difficult to hide. A living, fighting woman is even harder. I've seen press photographs of Gloria and she was what my aunt would call a "slip of a girl", whereas Margot was a tall woman. I doubt Gloria could have killed Margot without help, and she definitely couldn't have lifted her.'

'Didn't Dr Gupta say Margot and Gloria were close?'

'*Means before motive.* The closeness could've been a front,' said Strike. 'Maybe Gloria didn't like being "improved" after all, and only acted the grateful pupil to allay Margot's suspicions.

'Be that as it may, the last time there are multiple witnesses to Margot's whereabouts was half an hour before she supposedly left the building. After that, we've only got Gloria's word for what happened.'

'OK, objection sustained,' said Robin.

'So,' said Strike, as he took his hand off the pile of paper, 'having granted me that, forget for a moment any alleged sightings of her at windows or walking into churches. Forget the speeding van. It's entirely possible that *none* of that had anything to do with Margot.

'Go back to the one thing we know for certain: Margot Bamborough was still alive at a quarter to six.

'So now we turn to three men the police considered plausible suspects at the time and ask ourselves where they were at a quarter to six on the eleventh of October 1974.'

'There you go,' he said, passing Robin a photocopy of a tabloid news story dated 24 October 1974. 'That's Roy Phipps, otherwise known as Margot's husband and Anna's dad.'

The photograph showed a handsome man of around thirty, who strongly resembled his daughter. Robin thought that if she had been looking to cast a poet in a cheesy movie, she'd have put Roy Phipps's headshot to the top of the pile. This was where Anna had got her long, pale face, her high forehead and her large, beautiful eyes. Phipps had worn his dark hair down to his long-lapelled collar in 1974, and he stared up out of this old newsprint harrowed, facing the camera, looking up from the card in his hand. The caption read: *Dr Roy Phipps, appealing to the public for help.*

'Don't bother reading it,' said Strike, already placing a second news story over the first. 'There's nothing in there you don't already know, but *this* one will give you a few titbits you don't.'

Robin bent obediently over the second news story, of which Strike had photocopied only half.

> her husband, Dr Roy Phipps, who suffers from von Willebrand Disease, was ill at home and confined to bed at the marital home in Ham on the 11th October.
>
> 'Following several inaccurate and irresponsible press reports, we would like to state clearly that we are satisfied that Dr Roy Phipps had nothing to do with his wife's disappearance,' DI Bill Talbot, the detective in charge of the investigation, told newsmen. 'His own doctors have confirmed that walking and driving would both have been beyond Dr Phipps on the day in question and both Dr Phipps' nanny and his cleaner have given sworn statements confirming that Dr Phipps did not leave the house on the day of his wife's disappearance.'

'What's von Willebrand Disease?' asked Robin.

'A bleeding disorder. I looked it up. You don't clot properly. Gupta remembered that wrong; he thought Roy was a haemophiliac.

'There are three kinds of von Willebrand Disease,' said Strike. 'Type One just means you'd take a bit longer than normal to clot, but it shouldn't leave you bedbound, or unable to drive. I'm assuming Roy Phipps is Type Three, which can be as serious as haemophilia, and could lay him up for a while. But we'll need to check that.

'Anyway,' said Strike, turning over the next page. 'This is Talbot's record of his interview with Roy Phipps.'

'Oh God,' said Robin quietly.

The page was covered in small, slanting writing, but the most distinctive feature of the record were the stars Talbot had drawn all over it.

'See there?' said Strike, running a forefinger down a list of dates that were just discernible amid the scrawls. 'Those are the dates of the Essex Butcher abductions and attempted abductions.

'Talbot loses interest halfway down the list, look. On the twenty-sixth of August 1971, which is when Creed tried to abduct Peggy Hiskett, Roy was able to prove that he and Margot were on holiday in France.

'So that was that, as far as Talbot was concerned. If Roy hadn't tried to abduct Peggy Hiskett, he wasn't the Essex Butcher, and if he wasn't the Essex Butcher, he couldn't have had anything to do with Margot's disappearance.

'But there's a funny thing at the bottom of Talbot's list of dates. All refer to Creed's activities except that last one. He's circled December twenty-seventh, with no year. No idea why he was interested in December twenty-seventh.'

'Or, presumably, why he went Vincent van Gogh all over his report?'

'The stars? Yeah, they're a feature on all Talbot's notes. Very strange. Now,' said Strike, 'let's see how a statement *should* be taken.'

He turned the page and there was a neatly typewritten, double-spaced statement, four pages long, which DI Lawson had taken from Roy Phipps, and which had been duly signed on the final page by the haematologist.

'You needn't read the whole thing now,' said Strike. 'Bottom line is, he stuck to it that he'd been laid up in bed all day, as the cleaner and his nanny would testify.

'But now we go to Wilma Bayliss, the Phippses' cleaner. She also happened to be the St John's practice's cleaner. The rest of the practice didn't know at the time that she'd been doing some private work for Margot and Roy. Gupta told me that he thought Margot might've been encouraging Wilma to leave her husband, and giving her a bit of extra work might've been part of that scheme.'

'Why did she want Wilma to leave her husband?'

'I'm glad you asked that,' said Strike, and he turned over another piece of paper to show a tiny photocopied news clipping, which was dated in Strike's spiky and hard-to-read handwriting: 6 November 1972.

Rapist Jailed

Jules Bayliss, 36, of Leather Lane, Clerkenwell was today sentenced at the Inner London Crown Court to 5 years' jail for 2 counts of rape. Bayliss, who previously served two years in Brixton for aggravated assault, pleaded Not Guilty.

'Ah,' said Robin. 'I see.'

She took another slug of wine.

'Funnily enough,' she added, though she didn't sound amused, 'Creed got five years for his second rape as well. After they let him out, he started killing women as well as raping them.'

'Yeah,' said Strike. 'I know.'

For the second time, he considered questioning the advisability of Robin reading *The Demon of Paradise Park*, but decided against.

'I haven't yet managed to find out what became of Jules Bayliss,' he said, 'and the police notes regarding him are incomplete, so I can't be sure whether he was still in the nick when Margot was abducted.

'What's relevant to us is that Wilma told a different story to Lawson to the one she told Talbot – although Wilma claimed she had, in fact, told Talbot, and that he didn't record it, which is possible, because, as you can see, his note-taking left a lot to be desired.

'Anyway, one of the things she told Lawson was that she'd sponged blood off the spare-room carpet the day Margot disappeared. The other was that she'd seen Roy walking through the garden on the day he was supposedly laid up in bed. She also admitted to Lawson that she hadn't actually seen Roy in bed, but she'd heard him talking from the master bedroom that day.'

'Those are . . . pretty major changes of story.'

'Well, as I say, Wilma's position was that she wasn't changing her story, Talbot simply hadn't recorded it properly. But Lawson seems to have given Wilma a very hard time about it, and he re-interviewed Roy on the strength of what she'd said, too. However, Roy still had Cynthia the nanny as his alibi, who was prepared to swear to the fact that he'd been laid up all day, because she was bringing him regular cups of tea in the master bedroom.

'I know,' he said, in response to Robin's raised eyebrows. 'Lawson seems to have had the same kind of dirty mind as us. He questioned Phipps on the precise nature of his relationship with Cynthia, which led to an angry outburst from Phipps, who said she was twelve years younger than he was and a cousin to boot.'

It flitted across both Strike's and Robin's minds at this point that there were ten years separating them in age. Both suppressed this unbidden and irrelevant thought.

'According to Roy, the age difference and the blood relationship ought to have constituted a total prohibition on the relationship in the minds of all decent people. But as we know, he managed to overcome those qualms seven years later.

'Lawson also interrogated Roy about the fact that Margot had met an old flame for a drink three weeks before she died. In his rush to exonerate Roy, Talbot hadn't paid too much attention to the account of Oonagh Kennedy—'

'The friend Margot was supposed to be meeting in here?' said Robin.

'Exactly. Oonagh told both Talbot and Lawson that when Roy found out Margot had been for a drink with this old boyfriend, he'd been furious, and that he and Margot weren't talking to each other when she disappeared.

'According to Lawson's notes, Roy didn't like any of this being brought up—'

'Hardly surprising—'

'—and got quite aggressive. However, after speaking to Roy's doctors, Lawson was satisfied that Roy had indeed had a serious episode of bleeding after a fall in a hospital car park, and would have found it well nigh impossible to drive to Clerkenwell that evening, let alone kill or kidnap his wife.'

'He could have hired someone,' suggested Robin.

'They checked his bank accounts and couldn't find any suspicious payments, but that obviously doesn't mean he didn't find a way. He's a haematologist; he won't be lacking in brains.'

Strike took a further swig of beer.

'So that's the husband,' he said, flipping over the four pages of Roy's statement. 'Now for the old flame.'

'God above,' said Robin, looking down at another press photograph.

The man's thick, wavy hair reached well past his shoulders. He stood, unsmiling, with his hands on his narrow hips beside a painting of what appeared to be two writhing lovers. His shirt was open almost to his navel and his jeans were skin tight at the crotch and extremely wide at the ankle.

'I thought you'd enjoy that,' said Strike, grinning at

Robin's reaction. 'He's Paul Satchwell, an artist – though not a very highbrow one, by the sounds of it. When the press got onto him, he was designing a mural for a nightclub. He's Margot's ex.'

'She's just gone *right* down in my estimation,' muttered Robin.

'Don't judge her too harshly. She met him when she was a Bunny Girl, so she was only nineteen or twenty. He was six years older than her and probably seemed like the height of sophistication.'

'In *that* shirt?'

'That's a publicity photo for his art show,' said Strike. 'It says so below. Possibly he didn't show as much chest hair in day-to-day life. The press got quite excited at the thought an ex-lover might be involved, and let's face it, a bloke who looked like that was a gift to the tabloids.'

Strike turned to another example of Talbot's chaotic note-taking, which like the first was covered in five-pointed stars and had the same list of dates, with scribbled annotations beside them.

'As you can see, Talbot didn't start with anything as mundane as "Where were you at a quarter to six on the night Margot disappeared?" He goes straight into the Essex Butcher dates, and when Satchwell told him he was celebrating a friend's thirtieth birthday on September the eleventh, which was when Susan Meyer was abducted, Talbot basically stopped asking him questions. But once again, we've got a date unconnected with Creed heavily circled at the bottom, with a gigantic cross beside it. April the sixteenth this time.'

'Where was Satchwell living when Margot disappeared?'

'Camden,' said Strike, turning the page to reveal, again, a conventional typewritten statement. 'There you go, look, it's in his statement to Lawson. Not all that far from Clerkenwell.

'To Lawson, Satchwell explained that after a gap of eight years, he and Margot met by chance in the street and decided to go for a catch-up drink. He was quite open with Lawson about this, presumably because he knew Oonagh or Roy would already have told them about it. He even told Lawson he'd have been keen to resume an affair with Margot, which seems a bit *too* helpful, although it was probably meant to prove he had nothing to hide. He said he and Margot had a volatile relationship for a couple of years when she was much younger, and that Margot finally ended it for good when she met Roy.

'Satchwell's alibi checked out. He told Lawson he was alone in his studio, which was also in Camden, for most of the afternoon on the day Margot disappeared, but took a phone call there round about five. Landlines – far harder to monkey about with than mobiles when you're trying to set up an alibi. Satchwell ate in a local café, where he was known, at half past six, and witnesses agreed they'd seen him. He then went home to change before meeting some friends in a bar around eight. The people he claimed to have been with confirmed it all and Lawson was satisfied that Satchwell was in the clear.

'Which brings us to the third, and, I'd have to say, most promising suspect – always excepting Dennis Creed. This,' said Strike, moving Satchwell's statement from the top of a now greatly diminished pile of paper, 'is Steve Douthwaite.'

If Roy Phipps would have been a lazy casting director's idea of a sensitive poet, and Paul Satchwell the very image of a seventies rock star, Steve Douthwaite would have been hired without hesitation to play the cheeky chap, the wisecracking upstart, the working-class Jack the Lad. He had dark, beady eyes, an infectious grin and a spiky mullet that reminded Robin of the young men featured on an old Bay City Rollers LP which Robin's mother, to her children's hilarity, still cherished. Douthwaite was holding a pint in one hand, and his other arm was slung around the shoulder of a man whose face had been cropped from the picture, but whose suit, like Douthwaite's, looked cheap, creased and shiny. Douthwaite had loosened his kipper tie and undone his top shirt button to reveal a neck chain.

'Ladykiller' Salesman Sought Over Missing Doctor

Police are anxious to trace the whereabouts of double-glazing salesman Steve Douthwaite, who has vanished following routine questioning over the disappearance of Dr Margot Bamborough, 29.

Douthwaite, 28, left no forwarding address after quitting his job and his flat in Percival Street, Clerkenwell.

A former patient of the missing doctor's, Douthwaite raised suspicion at the medical practice because of his frequent visits to see the pretty blonde doctor. Friends of the salesman describe him as 'smooth talking' and do not believe Douthwaite suffered any serious health issues. Douthwaite is believed to have sent Dr Bamborough gifts.

Douthwaite, who was raised in foster care, has had no contact with friends since February 7th. Police are believed to have searched Douthwaite's home since he vacated it.

Tragic Affair

'He caused a lot of trouble round here, a lot of bad feeling,' said a co-worker at Diamond Double Glazing, who asked not to be named. 'Real Jack the Lad. He had an affair with another guy's wife. She ended up taking an overdose, left her kids without a mum. Nobody was sorry when Douthwaite took off, to be honest. We were happy to see the back of him. Too interested in booze and girls and not much cop at the job.'

Doctor Would Be 'A Challenge'

Asked what he thought Douthwaite's relationship with the missing doctor had been, his co-worker said,

'Chasing girls is all Steve cares about. He'd think a doctor was a challenge, knowing him.'

Police are eager to speak to Douthwaite again and appeal to any members of the public who might know his whereabouts.

When Robin had finished reading, Strike, who'd just finished his first pint, said,

'Want another drink?'

'I'll get these,' said Robin.

She went to the bar, where she waited beneath the hanging skulls and fake cobwebs. The barman had painted his face like Frankenstein's monster. Robin ordered drinks absent-mindedly, thinking about the Douthwaite article.

When she'd returned to Strike with a fresh pint, a wine and two packets of crisps, she said,

'You know, that article isn't fair.'

'Go on.'

'People don't necessarily tell their co-workers about their medical problems. Maybe Douthwaite *did* seem fine to his mates when they were all down the pub. That doesn't mean he didn't have anything wrong with him. He might have been mentally ill.'

'Not for the first time,' said Strike, 'you're bang on the money.'

He searched the small number of photocopied papers remaining in his pile and extracted another handwritten document, far neater than Talbot's and devoid of doodles and random dates. Somehow Robin knew, before Strike had said a word, that this fluid, rounded handwriting belonged to Margot Bamborough.

'Copies of Douthwaite's medical records,' said Strike. 'The police got hold of them. "Headaches, upset stomach, weight loss, palpitations, nausea, nightmares, trouble sleeping",' Strike read out. 'Margot's conclusion, on visit four – see there? – is "personal and employment-related difficulties, under severe strain, exhibiting signs of anxiety".'

'Well, his married girlfriend had killed herself,' said Robin. 'That'd knock anyone except a psychopath for six, wouldn't it?'

Charlotte slid like a shadow across Strike's mind.

'Yeah, you'd think. Also, look there. He'd been the victim of an assault shortly before his first visit to Margot. "Contusions, cracked rib." I smell angry, bereaved and betrayed husband.'

'But the paper makes it sound as though he was stalking Margot.'

'Well,' said Strike, tapping the photocopy of Douthwaite's medical notes, 'there are a hell of a lot of visits here. He saw her three times in one week. He's anxious, guilty, feeling unpopular, probably didn't expect his bit of fun to end in the woman's death. And there's a good-looking doctor offering no judgement, but kindness and support. I don't think it's beyond the realms of possibility to think he might have developed feelings for her.

'And look at this,' Strike went on, turning over the medical records to show Robin more typed statements. 'These are from Dorothy and Gloria, who both said Douthwaite came out of her room the last time he saw Margot, looking – well, this is Dorothy,' he said, and he read aloud, '"*I observed Mr Douthwaite leaving Dr Bamborough's surgery and noticed that he looked as though he had had a shock. I thought he also looked angry and distressed. As he walked out, he tripped over the toy truck of a boy in the waiting room and swore loudly. He seemed distracted and unaware of his surroundings.*" And Gloria,' said Strike, turning over the page, 'says: "*I remember Mr Douthwaite leaving because he swore at a little boy. He looked as though he had just been given bad news. I thought he seemed scared and angry.*"

'Now, Margot's notes of her last consultation with Douthwaite don't mention anything but the same old stress-related symptoms,' Strike went on, turning back to the medical records, 'so she definitely hadn't just diagnosed him with anything life-threatening. Lawson speculated that she might've felt he was getting over-attached, and told him he had to stop taking up valuable time that could be given to other patients, which Douthwaite didn't like hearing. Maybe he'd convinced himself his feelings were reciprocated. All the evidence suggests he was in a fragile mental state at the time.

'Anyway, four days after Douthwaite's last appointment, Margot vanishes. Tipped off by the surgery that there was a patient who seemed a bit over-fond of her, Talbot called him in for questioning. Here we go.'

Once again, Strike extracted a star-strewn scrawl from amid the typewritten pages.

'As usual, Talbot starts the interrogation by running through the list of Creed dates. Trouble is, Douthwaite doesn't seem to remember what he was doing on any of them.'

'If he was already ill with stress—' began Robin.

'Well, exactly,' said Strike. 'Being interrogated by a police officer who thinks you might be the Essex Butcher wouldn't help your anxiety, would it?

'And look at this, Talbot adds a random date again: twenty-first February. But he also does something else. Can you make anything of that?'

Robin took the page from Strike and examined the last three lines of writing.

'Pitman shorthand,' said Robin.

'Can you read it?'

'No. I know a bit of Teeline; I never learned Pitman. Pat can do it, though.'

'You're saying she might be useful for once?'

'Oh sod off, Strike,' said Robin, crossly. 'You want to go back to temps, fine, but I like getting accurate messages and knowing the filing's up to date.'

She took a photograph on her phone and texted it to Pat, along with a request to translate it. Strike, meanwhile, was reflecting that Robin had never before called him 'Strike' when annoyed. Perversely, it had sounded more intimate than the use of his first name. He'd quite enjoyed it.

'Sorry for impugning Pat,' he said.

'I just told you to sod off,' said Robin, failing to suppress a smile. 'What did Lawson make of Douthwaite?'

'Well, unsurprisingly, when he tried to interview him and found out he'd left his flat and job, leaving no forwarding address, he got quite interested in him. Hence the tip-off to the papers. They were trying to flush him out.'

'And did it work?' asked Robin, now eating crisps.

'It did. Douthwaite turned up at a police station in Waltham Forest the day after the "Ladykiller" article appeared, probably terrified he'd soon have Fleet Street and Scotland Yard on his doorstep. He told them he was unemployed and living in a bedsit. Local police called Lawson, who went straight over there to interview him.

'There's a full account here,' said Strike, pushing some of the last pages of the roll he had brought with him towards Robin. 'All written by Lawson: "appears scared" – "evasive" – "nervous" – "sweating" – and the alibi's not good. Douthwaite says that on the afternoon of Margot's disappearance he was out looking for a new flat.'

'He claims he was already looking for a new place when she disappeared?'

'Coincidence, eh? Except that upon closer questioning he couldn't say which flats he'd seen and couldn't come up with the name of anyone who'd remember seeing him. In the end he said his flat-hunting had involved sitting in a local café and circling ads in the paper. Trouble was, nobody in the café remembered him being there.

'He said he'd moved to Waltham Forest because he had bad associations with Clerkenwell after being interviewed by Talbot and made to feel as though he was under suspicion, and that, in any case, things hadn't been good for him at work since his affair with the co-worker's suicidal wife.'

'Well, that's credible enough,' said Robin.

'Lawson interviewed him twice more, but got nothing else out of him. Douthwaite came lawyered up to interview three. At that point, Lawson backed off. After all, they had nothing on Douthwaite, even if he was the fishiest person they interviewed. And it was – just – credible that the reason nobody had noticed him in the café was because it was a busy place.'

A group of drinkers in Hallowe'en costumes now entered the pub, giggling and clearly already full of alcohol. Robin noticed Strike casting an automatic eye over a young blonde in a rubber nurse's uniform.

'So,' she said, 'is that everything?'

'Almost,' said Strike, 'but I'm tempted not to show you this.'

'Why not?'

'Because I think it's going to feed your obsession with holy places.'

'I'm not—'

'OK, but before you look at it, just remember that nutters are always attracted by murders and missing person cases, all right?'

'Fine,' said Robin. 'Show me.'

Strike flipped over the piece of paper. It was a photocopy of the crudest kind of anonymous note, featuring letters cut out of magazines.

If YOU WaNt TO kNOw WhEre MargOt BamBorOuGh IS bURied DiG hERe

'Another St John's Cross,' said Robin.

'Yep. That arrived at Scotland Yard in 1985, addressed to Lawson, who'd already retired. Nothing else in the envelope.'

Robin sighed and leaned back in her chair.

'Nutter, obviously,' said Strike, now tapping his photocopied articles and statements back into a pile and rolling them up again. 'If you really knew where a body was buried, you'd include a bloody map.'

It was nearly six o'clock now, close to the hour at which a doctor had once left her practice and had never been seen again. The frosted pub windows were inky blue. Up at the bar, the blonde in the rubber uniform was giggling at something a man dressed as the Joker had told her.

'You know,' said Robin, glancing down at the papers sitting beside Strike's pint, 'she was late . . . it was pouring with rain . . . '

'Go on,' said Strike, wondering whether she was about to say exactly what he'd been thinking.

'Her friend was waiting in here, alone. Margot's late. She would've wanted to get here as quickly as possible. The simplest, most plausible explanation I can think of is that somebody offered her a lift. A car pulled up—'

'Or a van,' said Strike. Robin had, indeed, reached the same conclusion he had. 'Someone she knew—'

'Or someone who seemed safe. An elderly man—'

'Or what she thinks is a woman.'

'Exactly,' said Robin.

She turned a sad face to Strike.

'That's it. She either knew the driver, or the stranger seemed safe.'

'And who'd remember that?' said Strike. 'She was wearing a nondescript raincoat, carrying an umbrella. A vehicle pulls up. She bends down to the window, then gets in. No fight. No conflict. The car drives away.'

'And only the driver would know what happened next,' said Robin.

Her mobile rang: it was Pat Chauncey.

'She always does that,' said Strike. 'Text her, and she doesn't text back, she calls—'

'Does it matter?' said Robin, exasperated, and answered.

'Hi, Pat. Sorry to bother you out of hours. Did you get my text?'

'Yeah,' croaked Pat. 'Where did you find that?'

'It's in some old police notes. Can you translate it?'

'Yeah,' said Pat, 'but it doesn't make much sense.'

'Hang on, Pat, I want Cormoran to hear this,' said Robin, and she changed to speakerphone.

'Ready?' came Pat's rasping voice.

'Yes,' said Robin. Strike pulled out a pen and flipped over his roll of paper so that he could write on the blank side.

'It says: *"And that is the last of them, comma, the twelfth, comma, and the circle will be closed upon finding the tenth, comma"* – and then there's a word I can't read, I don't think it's proper Pitman – and after that another word, which phonetically says Ba – fom – et, full stop. Then a new sentence, "*Transcribe in the true book.*"'

'Baphomet,' repeated Strike.

'Yeah,' said Pat.

'That's a name,' said Strike. 'Baphomet is an occult deity.'

'OK, well, that's what it says,' said Pat, matter-of-factly.

Robin thanked her and rang off.

'"*And that is the last of them, the twelfth, and the circle will be closed upon finding the tenth – unknown word – Baphomet. Transcribe in the true book,*"' Strike read back.

'How d'you know about Baphomet?' asked Robin.

'Whittaker was interested in all that shit.'

'Oh,' said Robin.

Whittaker was the last of Strike's mother's lovers, the man Strike believed had administered the overdose that had killed her.

'He had a copy of *The Satanic Bible*,' said Strike. 'It had a picture of Baphomet's head in a penta – shit,' he said, rifling back through the loose pages to find one of those on which Talbot had doodled many five-pointed stars. He frowned at it for a moment, then looked up at Robin.

'I don't think these are stars. They're pentagrams.'

PART THREE

. . . Winter, clothëd all in frieze . . .

Edmund Spenser
The Faerie Queene

15

Wherein old dints of deepe woundes did remaine . . .

Edmund Spenser
The Faerie Queene

In the second week of November, Joan's chemotherapy caused her white blood cell count to plummet dangerously, and she was admitted to hospital. Strike left Robin in charge of the agency, Lucy left her three sons in the care of her husband, and both hurried back to Cornwall.

Strike's fresh absence coincided with the monthly team meeting, which for the first time Robin led alone, the youngest and arguably least experienced investigator at the agency, and the only woman.

Robin wasn't sure whether she had imagined it, but she thought Hutchins and Morris, the two ex-policemen, put up slightly more disagreement about the next month's rota, and about the line they ought to take on Shifty, than they would have done had Strike been there. It was Robin's opinion that Shifty's PA, who'd now been extensively wined and dined at the agency's expense without revealing anything about the hold her boss might have over his CEO, ought to be abandoned as a possible source. She'd decided that Morris ought to see her one last time to wrap things up, allaying any suspicion about what he'd been after, after which Robin thought it time to try and infiltrate Shifty's social circle with a view to getting information direct from the man they were investigating. Barclay was the only subcontractor who agreed with Robin, and backed her up when she insisted that Morris was to leave Shifty's PA well alone. Of course, as Robin was well aware, she and Barclay had once gone digging for a body together, and such things create a bond.

The memory of the team meeting was still bothering her as she sat with her legs up on the sofa in the flat in Finborough Road later, now in pyjamas and a dressing gown, working on her laptop. Wolfgang the dachshund was curled at her bare feet, keeping them warm.

Max was out. He'd suddenly announced the previous weekend that he feared he was in danger of passing from 'introvert' to 'recluse', and had accepted an invitation to go to dinner with some actor friends, even though, in his bitter words on parting, 'They'll all be pitying me, but I suppose they'll enjoy that'. Robin had taken Wolfgang for a quick walk around the block at eleven, but otherwise had spent her evening on the Bamborough case, for which she'd had no time while Strike had been in St Mawes, because the other four cases on the agency's books were absorbing all working hours.

Robin hadn't been out since her birthday drinks with Ilsa and Vanessa, which hadn't been as enjoyable as she'd hoped. The conversation had revolved entirely around relationships, because Vanessa had arrived with a brand-new engagement ring on her finger. Since then, Robin had used pressure of work during Strike's absence to avoid nights out with either of her friends. Her cousin Katie's words, *it's like you're travelling in a different direction to the rest of us*, were hard to forget, but the truth was that Robin didn't want to stand in a bar while Ilsa and Vanessa encouraged her to respond to the advances of some overfamiliar, Morris-like man with a line in easy patter and bad jokes.

She and Strike had now divided between them the people they wished to trace and re-interview in the Bamborough case. Unfortunately, Robin now knew that at least four of her allocated people had passed beyond the reach of questioning.

After careful cross-referencing of old records, Robin had managed to identify the Willy Lomax who'd been the long-serving handyman of St James's Church, Clerkenwell. He'd died in 1989 and Robin had so far been unable to find a single confirmed relative.

Albert Shimmings, the florist and possible driver of the speeding van seen on the night of Margot's disappearance, had also passed away, but Robin had emailed two men she believed to be his sons. She sincerely hoped she'd correctly identified them, otherwise an insurance agent and a driving instructor were both about to get truly mystifying messages. Neither had yet responded to her request to talk to them.

Wilma Bayliss, the ex-practice cleaner, had died in 2003. A mother of two sons and three daughters, she'd divorced Jules Bayliss in 1975. By the time she died, Wilma hadn't been a cleaner, but a social worker, and she'd raised a high-achieving family, including an architect, a paramedic, a teacher, another social worker and a Labour councillor. One of the sons now lived in Germany, but Robin nevertheless included him in the emails and Facebook messages she sent out to all five siblings. There'd been no response so far.

Dorothy Oakden, the practice secretary, had been ninety-one when she died in a North London nursing home. Robin hadn't yet managed to trace Carl, her only child.

Meanwhile, Margot's ex-boyfriend, Paul Satchwell, and the receptionist, Gloria Conti, were proving strangely and similarly elusive. At first Robin had been relieved when she'd failed to find a death certificate for either of them, but after combing telephone directories, census records, county court judgments, marriage and divorce certificates, press archives, social media and lists of company staff, she'd come up with nothing. The only possible explanations Robin could think of were changes of name (in Gloria's case, possibly by marriage) and emigration.

As for Mandy White, the schoolgirl who'd claimed to have seen Margot at a rainy window, there were so many Amanda Whites of approximately the right age to be found online that Robin was starting to despair of ever finding the right one. Robin found this line of inquiry particularly frustrating, firstly because there was a good chance that White was no longer Mandy's surname, and secondly because, like the police before her, Robin thought it highly unlikely that Mandy had actually seen Margot at the window that night.

Having examined and discounted the Facebook accounts of another six Amanda Whites, Robin yawned, stretched and decided she was owed a break. Setting her laptop down on a side table, she swung her legs carefully off the sofa so as not to disturb Wolfgang, and crossed the open-plan area that combined kitchen, dining and living rooms, to make herself one of the low-calorie hot chocolates she was trying to convince herself was a treat, because she was still, in the middle of this long, sedentary stretch of surveillance, trying to keep an eye on her waistline.

As she stirred the unappetising powder into boiling water, a whiff of tuberose mingled with the scent of synthetic caramel. In spite of her bath, Fracas still lingered in her hair and on her pyjamas. This perfume, she'd finally decided, had been a costly mistake. Living in a dense cloud of tuberose made her feel not only perpetually on the verge of a headache, but also as though she were wearing fur and pearls in broad daylight.

Robin's mobile, which was lying on the sofa beside Wolfgang, rang as she picked up her laptop again. Startled from his sleep, the disgruntled dog rose on arthritic legs. Robin lifted him to safety before picking up her phone and seeing, to her disappointment, that it wasn't Strike, but Morris.

'Hi, Saul.'

Ever since the birthday kiss, Robin had tried to keep her manner on the colder side of professional when dealing with Morris.

'Hey, Robs. You said to call if I had anything, even if it was late.'

'Yes, of course.' *I never said you could call me 'Robs', though.* 'What's happened?' asked Robin, looking around for a pen.

'I got Gemma drunk tonight. Shifty's PA, you know. Under the influence, she told me she thinks Shifty's got something on his boss.'

Well, that's hardly news, thought Robin, abandoning the fruitless search for a writing implement.

'What makes her think so?'

'Apparently he's said stuff to her like, "Oh, he'll always take *my* calls, don't worry", and "I know where all the bodies are buried".'

An image of a cross of St John slid across Robin's mind and was dismissed.

'As a joke,' Morris added. 'He passed it off like he was joking, but it made Gemma think.'

'But she doesn't know any details?'

'No, but listen, seriously, give me a bit more time and I reckon I'll be able to persuade her to wear a wire for us. Not to blow my own horn here – can't reach, for one thing – no, seriously,' he said, although Robin hadn't laughed, 'I've got her properly softened up. Just give me a bit more time—'

'Look, I'm sorry, Saul, but we went over this at the meeting,' Robin reminded Morris, suppressing a yawn, which made her eyes water. 'The client doesn't want us to tell any of the employees we're investigating this, so we can't tell her who you are. Pressuring her to investigate her own boss is asking her to risk her job. It also risks blowing the whole case if she decides to tell him what's going on.'

'But again, not to toot—'

'Saul, it's one thing her confiding in you when she's drunk,' said Robin (why wasn't he listening? They'd been through this endlessly at the team meeting). 'It's another asking a girl with no investigative training to work for us.'

'She's all over me, Robin,' said Morris earnestly. 'It'd be crazy not to use her.'

Robin suddenly wondered whether Morris had slept with the girl. Strike had been quite clear that that wasn't to happen. She sank back down on the sofa. Her copy of *The Demon of Paradise Park* was warm, she noticed, from the dachshund lying on it. The displaced Wolfgang was now gazing at Robin from under the dining table, with the sad, reproachful eyes of an old man.

'Saul, I really think it's time for Hutchins to take over, to see what he can do with Shifty himself,' said Robin.

'OK, but before we make that decision, let me ring Strike and—'

'You're not ringing Strike,' said Robin, her temper rising. 'His aunt's – he's got enough on his plate in Cornwall.'

'You're so sweet,' said Morris, with a little laugh, 'but I promise you, Strike would want a say in this—'

'He left me in charge,' said Robin, anger rising now, 'and I'm telling you, you've taken it as far as you can with that girl. She doesn't know anything useful and trying to push her further could backfire badly on this agency. I'm asking you to give it up now, please. You can take over on Postcard tomorrow night, and I'll tell Andy to get to work on Shifty.'

There was a pause.

'I've upset you, haven't I?' said Morris.

'No, you haven't upset me,' said Robin. After all, 'upset' wasn't quite the same as 'enrage'.

'I didn't want to—'

'You haven't, Saul, I'm only reminding you what we agreed at the meeting.'

'OK,' he said. 'All right. Hey – listen. Did you hear about the boss who told his secretary the company was in trouble?'

'No,' said Robin, through clenched teeth.

'He said, "I'm going to have to lay you or Jack off." She said, "Well, you'll have to jack off, because I've got a headache."'

'Ha ha,' said Robin. 'Night, Saul.'

Why did I say 'ha ha'?' she asked herself furiously, as she set down her mobile. *Why didn't I just say, 'Stop telling me crap jokes?' Or say nothing! And why did I say sorry when I was asking him to do what we all agreed at the meeting? Why am I cossetting him?*

She thought of all those times she'd pretended with Matthew. Faking orgasms had been nothing compared to pretending to find him funny and interesting through all those twice-told tales of rugby club jokes, through every anecdote designed to show him as the cleverest or the funniest man in the room. *Why do we do it?* she asked herself, picking up *The Demon of Paradise Park* without considering what she was doing. *Why do we work so hard to keep the peace, to keep them happy?*

Because, suggested the seven ghostly black and white faces behind Dennis Creed's, *they can turn nasty, Robin. You know just how nasty they can turn, with your scar up your arm and your memory of that gorilla mask.*

But she knew that wasn't why she'd humoured Morris, not

really. She didn't expect him to become abusive or violent if she refused to laugh at his stupid jokes. No, this was something else. The only girl in a family of boys, Robin had been raised, she knew, to keep everyone happy, in spite of the fact that her own mother had been quite the women's libber. Nobody had meant to do it, but she'd realised during the therapy she'd undertaken after the attack that had left her forearm forever scarred, that her family role had been that of 'easy child', the non-complainer, the conciliator. She'd been born just a year before Martin, who had been the Ellacotts' 'problem child': the most scattered and impetuous, the least academic and conscientious, the son who still lived at home at twenty-eight and the brother with whom she had least in common. (Though Martin had punched Matthew on the nose on her wedding day, and the last time she'd been home she'd found herself hugging him when he offered, on hearing how difficult Matthew was being about the divorce, to do it again.)

Wintry specks of rain were dotting the window behind the dining table. Wolfgang was fast asleep again. Robin couldn't face perusing the social media accounts of another fifty Amanda Whites tonight. As she picked up *The Demon of Paradise Park*, she hesitated. She'd made a rule for herself (because it had been a long, hard journey to reach the place where she was now, and she didn't want to lose her current good state of mental health) not to read this book after dark, or right before bed. After all, the information it contained could be found summarised online: there was no need to hear in his own words what Creed had done to each of the women he'd tortured and killed.

Nevertheless, she picked up her hot chocolate, opened the book to the page she had marked with a Tesco receipt, and began to read at the point she'd left off three days previously.

Convinced that Bamborough had fallen victim to the serial killer now dubbed the Essex Butcher, Talbot made enemies among his colleagues with what they felt was his obsessive focus on one theory.

'They called it early retirement,' said a colleague, 'but it was basically dismissal. They said he wasn't interested in anything other than the Butcher, but here we are, 9 years on, and no-one's ever found a better explanation, have they?'

Margot Bamborough's family failed to positively identify any of the unclaimed jewellery and underwear found in Creed's basement flat when he was arrested in 1976, although Bamborough's husband, Dr Roy Phipps, thought a tarnished silver locket which had been crushed, possibly by blunt force, might have resembled one that the doctor was believed to have been wearing when she disappeared.

However, a recently published account of Bamborough's life, *Whatever Happened to Margot Bamborough?* [4] written by the son of a close friend of the doctor, contains revelations about the doctor's private life which suggest a new line of enquiry – and a possible connection with Creed. Shortly before her disappearance, Margot Bamborough booked herself into the Bride Street Nursing Home in Islington, a private facility which in 1974 provided discreet abortions.

16

Behold the man, and tell me Britomart,
If ay more goodly creature thou didst see;
How like a Gyaunt in each manly part
Beares he himselfe with portly maiestee . . .

Edmund Spenser
The Faerie Queene

Four days later, at a quarter past five in the morning, the 'Night Riviera' sleeper train pulled into Paddington station. Strike, who'd slept poorly, had spent long stretches of the night watching the ghostly grey blur of the so-called English Riviera slide past his compartment window. Having slept on top of the covers with his prosthesis still attached, he turned down the proffered breakfast on its plastic tray, and was among the first passengers to disembark into the station, kit bag over his shoulder.

There was a nip of frost in the early morning air and Strike's breath rose in a cloud before him as he walked down the platform, Brunel's steel arches curving above him like the ribs of a blue whale's skeleton, cold dark sky visible through the glass ceiling. Unshaven and slightly uncomfortable on the stump that had missed its usual nightly application of soothing cream, Strike headed for a bench, sat down, lit a much-needed cigarette, pulled out his mobile and phoned Robin.

He knew she'd be awake, because she'd just spent the night

parked in Strike's BMW outside the house of the weatherman, watching for Postcard. They'd communicated mostly by text while he'd been in Cornwall, while he divided his time between the hospital in Truro and the house in St Mawes, taking it in turns with Lucy to sit with Joan, whose hair had now fallen out and whose immune system appeared to have collapsed under the weight of the chemotherapy, and to minister to Ted, who was barely eating. Before returning to London, Strike had cooked a large batch of curry, which he left in the freezer, alongside shepherd's pies made by Lucy. When he raised his cigarette to his mouth he could still smell a trace of cumin on his fingers, and if he concentrated, he could conjure up the deadly smell of hospital disinfectant underlain with a trace of urine, instead of cold iron, diesel and the distant waftings of coffee from a nearby Starbucks.

'Hi,' said Robin, and at the sound of her voice Strike felt, as he had known he would, a slight easing of the knot of tension in his stomach. 'What's happened?'

'Nothing,' he said, slightly surprised, before he recollected that it was half past five in the morning. 'Oh – yeah, sorry, this isn't an emergency call, I've just got off the sleeper. Wondered whether you fancied getting breakfast before you head home to bed.'

'Oh, that'd be wonderful,' said Robin, with such genuine pleasure that Strike felt a little less tired, 'because I've got Bamborough news.'

'Great,' said Strike, 'so've I. Be good to have a catch-up.'

'How's Joan?'

'Not great. They let her go home yesterday. They've assigned her a Macmillan nurse. Ted's really low. Lucy's still down there.'

'You could've stayed,' said Robin. 'We can cope.'

'It's fine,' he said, screwing his eyes up against his own smoke. A shaft of wintry sunlight burst through a break in the clouds and illuminated the fag butts on the tiled floor. 'I've told them I'll go back for Christmas. Where d'you want to meet?'

'Well, I was planning to go to the National Portrait Gallery before I went home, so—'

'You were what?' said Strike.

'Planning to go to the National Portrait Gallery. I'll explain when I see you. Would you mind if we meet somewhere near there?'

'I can get anywhere,' said Strike, 'I'm right by the Tube. I'll head that way and whoever finds a café first can text the other.'

Forty-five minutes later, Robin entered Notes café, which lay on St Martin's Lane and was already crowded, though it was so early in the morning. Wooden tables, some of them as large as the one in her parents' kitchen in Yorkshire, were crammed with young people with laptops and businessmen grabbing breakfast before work. As she queued at the long counter, she tried to ignore the various pastries and cakes spread out beneath it: she'd taken sandwiches with her to her overnight surveillance of the weatherman's house, and those, she told herself sternly, ought to suffice.

Having ordered a cappuccino, she headed for the back of the café, where Strike sat reading *The Times* beneath an iron chandelier that resembled a large spider. She seemed to have forgotten over the previous six days how large he was. Hunched over the newspaper, he reminded her of a black bear, stubble thick on his face, tucking into a bacon and egg ciabatta roll, and Robin felt a wave of liking simply for the way he looked. Or perhaps, she thought, she was merely reacting against clean-jawed, slim and conventionally handsome men who, like tuberose perfumes, seemed attractive until prolonged exposure made you crave escape.

'Hi,' she said, sliding into the seat opposite him.

Strike looked up, and in that moment, her long shining hair

and her aura of good health acted upon him like an antidote to the fug of clinical decay in which he had spent the past five days.

'You don't look knackered enough to have been up all night.'

'I'll take that as a compliment and not as an accusation,' said Robin, eyebrows raised. 'I *was* up all night and Postcard still hasn't shown herself – or himself – but another card came yesterday, addressed to the television studio. It said Postcard loved the way he smiled at the end of Tuesday's weather report.'

Strike grunted.

Robin said, 'D'you want to go first on Bamborough, or shall I?'

'You first,' said Strike, still chewing, 'I'm starving.'

'OK,' said Robin. 'Well, I've got good news and bad. The bad news is nearly everyone I've been trying to trace is dead, and the rest might as well be.'

She filled Strike in on the deceased status of Willy Lomax, Albert Shimmings, Wilma Bayliss and Dorothy Oakden, and on the steps she'd taken, so far, to contact their relatives.

'Nobody's got back in touch except one of Shimmings' sons, who seems worried that we're journalists trying to pin Margot's disappearance on his father. I've written a reassuring email back. Hope it works.'

Strike, who had paused in his steady demolition of the roll to drink half a mug of tea, said,

'I've been having similar problems. That "two women struggling by the phone boxes" sighting is going to be nigh on impossible to check. Ruby Elliot, who saw them, and the Fleury mother and daughter, who almost certainly *were* them, are all dead as well. But they've both got living descendants, so I've fired off a few messages. Only one response so far, from a Fleury grandson who doesn't know what the hell I'm talking about. And Dr Brenner doesn't seem to have a single living relative that I can see. Never married, no kids, and a dead sister who didn't marry, either.'

'D'you know how many women there are out there called Amanda White?' sighed Robin.

'I can imagine,' said Strike, taking another large bite of roll. 'That's why I gave her to you.'

'You—?'

'I'm kidding,' he said, smirking at her expression. 'What about Paul Satchwell and Gloria Conti?'

'Well, if they're dead, they didn't die in the UK. But here's something really weird: I can't find a single mention of either of them after '75.'

'Coincidence,' said Strike, raising his eyebrows. 'Douthwaite, he of the stress headaches and the dead mistress, has disappeared as well. He's either abroad, or he's changed his identity. Can't find any address for him after '76, and no death certificate, either. Mind you, if I were in his shoes, I might've changed my name, as well. His press reviews weren't good, were they? Crap at his job, sleeping with a colleague's wife, sending flowers to a woman who then disappears—'

'We don't know it was flowers,' said Robin, into her coffee cup.

Other kinds of presents are available, Strike.

'Chocolates, then. Same applies. Harder to see why Satchwell and Conti took themselves off the radar, though,' said Strike, running his hand over his unshaven chin. 'The press interest in them died away fairly fast. And you'd have found Conti online if it was a simple case of a married name. There can't be as many Gloria Contis as there are Amanda Whites.'

'I've been wondering whether she went to live in Italy,' said Robin. 'Her dad's first name was Ricardo. She could've had relatives there. I've sent off a few Facebook enquiries to some Contis, but the only people who've responded so far don't know a Gloria. I'm pretending I'm doing genealogical research, because I'm worried she might not respond if I mention Margot straight off.'

'Think you're probably right,' said Strike, adding more sugar to his tea. 'Yeah, Italy's a good idea. She was young, might've fancied a change of scene. Satchwell disappearing's odd, though. That photo didn't suggest a shy man. You'd think he'd have popped up somewhere by now, advertising his paintings.'

'I've checked art exhibitions, auctions, galleries. It really is as though he dematerialised.'

'Well, I've made *some* progress,' said Strike, swallowing the last mouthful of his roll and pulling out his notebook. 'You can get a surprising amount of work done, sitting around in a hospital. I've found four living witnesses, and one of them's already agreed to talk: Gregory Talbot, son of Bill who went off his rocker and drew pentagrams all over the case file. I explained who I am and who hired me, and Gregory's quite amenable to a chat. I'm going over there on Saturday, if you want to come.'

'I can't,' said Robin, disappointed. 'Morris and Andy have both got family stuff on. Barclay and I have got to cover the weekend.'

'Ah,' said Strike, 'shame. Well, I've also found two of the women who worked with Margot at the practice,' said Strike, turning a page in his notebook. 'The nurse, Janice, is still going by her first married name, which helped. The address Gupta gave me was an old one, but I traced her from there. She's now in Nightingale Grove—'

'Very appropriate,' said Robin.

'—in Hither Green. And Irene Bull's now Mrs Irene Hickson, widow of a man who ran a successful building contractor's. She's living in Circus Street, Greenwich.'

'Have you phoned them?'

'I decided to write first,' said Strike. 'Older women, both living alone – I've set out who we are and who's hired us, so they've got time to check us out, make sure we're kosher, maybe check with Anna.'

'Good thinking,' said Robin.

'And I'm going to do the same with Oonagh Kennedy, the woman waiting for Margot in the pub that night, once I'm sure I've got the right one. Anna said she was in Wolverhampton, but the woman I've found is in Alnwick. She's the right age, but she's a retired *vicar*.'

Robin grinned at Strike's expression, which was a mixture of suspicion and distaste.

'What's wrong with vicars?'

'Nothing,' he said, adding a moment later, 'much. Depends on the vicar. But Oonagh was a Bunny Girl back in the sixties. She was standing beside Margot in one of the pictures the press used, named in one of the captions. Don't you think the transition from Bunny Girl to vicar is fairly unlikely?'

'Interesting life trajectory,' Robin admitted, 'but you're speaking to a temporary secretary who became a full-time detective. And speaking of Oonagh,' she added, drawing her copy of *The Demon of Paradise Park* out of her handbag and opening it. 'I wanted to show you something. There,' she said, holding it out to him. 'Read the bit I've marked with pencil.'

'I've already read the whole book,' said Strike. 'Which bit—?'

'Please,' Robin insisted, 'just read where I've marked.'

Strike wiped his hand on a paper napkin, took the book from Robin and read the paragraphs next to which she had made a thick pencil line.

Shortly before her disappearance, Margot Bamborough booked herself into the Bride Street Nursing Home in

Islington, a private facility which in 1974 provided discreet abortions.

The Bride Street Nursing Home closed its doors in 1978 and no records exist to show whether Bamborough had the procedure. However, the possibility that she allowed a friend to use her name is mooted by the author of *Whatever Happened to Margot Bamborough?*, who notes that the Irish woman and fellow Bunny Girl Bamborough was supposedly meeting in the pub that night might have had good reason for maintaining the pub story, even after Bamborough's death.

Bride Street Nursing Home lay a mere eight minutes' walk from Dennis Creed's basement flat on Liverpool Road. The possibility remains, therefore, that Margot Bamborough never intended to go to the pub that night, that she told the lie to protect herself, or another woman, and that she may have been abducted, not from a street in Clerkenwell, but a short distance from Creed's house near Paradise Park.

'What the—?' began Strike, looking thunderstruck. 'My copy hasn't got this bit. You've got an extra three paragraphs!'

'I *thought* you hadn't read it,' said Robin, sounding satisfied. 'Yours can't be a first edition. Mine is. Look here,' she said, flicking to a place at the back of the book, while Strike still held it. 'See there, the endnote? "*Whatever Happened to Margot Bamborough?* by C. B. Oakden, published 1985." Except it wasn't published,' said Robin. 'It was pulped. The author of this,' she said, tapping *The Demon of Paradise Park*, 'must've got hold of an advance copy. I've been digging,' Robin went on. 'All this happened pre-internet, obviously, but I found a couple of mentions of it online, in legal articles about suing for libel to stop publication.

'Basically, Roy Phipps and Oonagh Kennedy brought a joint action against C. B. Oakden and won. Oakden's book was pulped and there was a hasty reprint of *The Demon of Paradise Park*, without the offending passage.'

'C. B. Oakden?' repeated Strike. 'Is he—?'

'Dorothy-the-practice-secretary's son. Exactly. Full name: Carl Brice Oakden. The last address I've got for him was in Walthamstow, but he's moved and I haven't managed to track him down yet.'

Strike re-read the paragraphs relating to the abortion clinic, then said,

'Well, if Phipps and Kennedy succeeded in suing to stop publication, they must have convinced a judge that this was partly or completely false.'

'Horrible thing to lie about, isn't it?' said Robin. 'Bad enough if he was saying Margot had the abortion, but hinting that Oonagh had it, and was covering up where Margot was that night—'

'I'm surprised he got it past lawyers,' said Strike.

'Oakden's publisher was a small press,' said Robin. 'I looked them up, too. They went out of business not long after he had his book pulped. Maybe they didn't bother with lawyers.'

'More fool them,' said Strike, 'but unless they had some kind of death wish, this can't have been *entirely* invented. He must've had something to base it on. And *this* bloke,' he held up *The Demon of Paradise Park*, 'was a proper investigative journalist. He wouldn't have theorised without seeing some proof.'

'Can we check with him, or is he—?'

'Dead,' said Strike, who sat for a moment, thinking, then went on:

'The appointment must've been made in Margot's name. The question is whether she had the procedure, or whether somebody used her name without her knowing.' Strike re-read the first few lines of the passage. 'And the date of the appointment isn't given, either. "Shortly before her disappearance" . . . weasel words. If the appointment had been made for the day she disappeared, the author would say so. That'd be a major revelation and it'd have been investigated by the police. "Shortly before her disappearance" is open to wide interpretation.'

'Coincidence, though, isn't it?' said Robin. 'Her making an appointment so close to Creed's house?'

'Yeah,' said Strike, but after a moment's consideration he said, 'I don't know. Is it? How many abortion clinics were there in London in 1974?'

Handing the book back to Robin, he continued,

'This might explain why Roy Phipps was jumpy about his daughter talking to Oonagh Kennedy. He didn't want her telling his teenage daughter her mother might've aborted her sibling.'

'I thought of that, too,' said Robin. 'It'd be an awful thing to hear. Especially when she's lived most of her life wondering whether her mother ran out on her.'

'We should try and get hold of a copy of *Whatever Happened to Margot Bamborough?*' said Strike. 'There might still be copies in existence if they got as far as printing them. He could've given some away. Review copies and the like.'

'I'm already on it,' said Robin. 'I've emailed a few different second-hand book places.'

This wasn't the first time she had found herself doing something for the agency that made her feel grubby.

'Carl Oakden was only fourteen when Margot disappeared,' she continued. 'Writing a book about her, milking the connection, claiming Margot and his mother were close friends—'

'Yeah, he sounds a common-or-garden shit,' Strike agreed. 'When did he leave his address in Walthamstow?'

'Five years ago.'

'Had a look on social media?'

'Yes. Can't find him.'

Strike's mobile vibrated in his pocket. Robin thought she saw a flicker of panic in his face as he fumbled to find it, and knew that he was thinking of Joan.

'Everything all right?' she asked, watching his expression darken as he looked down at his mobile screen.

Strike had just seen:

Bruv, can we please talk this over face to face? The launch and the new album are a big deal for Dad. All we're asking—

'Yeah, fine,' he said, stuffing the phone back in his pocket, the rest of the message unread. 'So, you wanted to go to—?'

For a moment, he couldn't remember the unlikely place Robin had told him she wanted to visit, and which was the reason they were currently sitting in this particular café.

'The National Portrait Gallery,' she said. 'Three of Postcard's postcards were bought in their gift shop.'

'Three of – sorry, what?'

He was distracted by what he'd just read. He'd been quite clear with his half-brother that he had no wish either to attend the party celebrating his father's new album, or to feature in the photograph with his half-siblings which was to be their congratulatory gift to him.

'Postcard's postcards – the person who's persecuting our weatherman,' she reminded him, before mumbling, 'it doesn't matter, it was just an idea I had.'

'Which was?'

'Well, the last-but-one picture Postcard sent was of a portrait they said "always reminded" them of our weatherman. So I thought . . . maybe they see that painting a lot. Maybe they work at the gallery. Maybe they secretly want him to know that, to come looking for them?'

Even as she said it, she thought the theory sounded far-fetched, but the truth was that they had absolutely no leads on Postcard. He or she had failed to turn up at the weatherman's house since they'd been watching it. Three postcards bought in a single place might mean something, or perhaps nothing at all. What else did they have?

Strike grunted. Unsure whether this indicated a lack of enthusiasm for her theory about Postcard, Robin returned her copy of *The Demon of Paradise Park* to her handbag and said,

'Heading for the office after this?'

'Yeah. I told Barclay I'll take over watching Twinkletoes at two.' Strike yawned. 'Might try and get a couple of hours' kip first.'

He pushed himself into a standing position.

'I'll call you and let you know how I get on with Gregory Talbot. And thanks for holding the fort while I was away. Really appreciate it.'

'No problem,' said Robin.

Strike hoisted his kit bag onto his shoulder and limped out of the café. With a slight feeling of anti-climax, Robin watched him pause outside the window to light a cigarette, then walk out of sight. Checking her watch, Robin saw that there was still an hour and a half before the National Portrait Gallery opened.

There were doubtless more pleasurable ways of whiling away that time than in wondering whether the text that Strike had just received had come from Charlotte Campbell, but that was the distraction that occurred to Robin, and it occupied her for a surprising proportion of the time she had left to kill.

17

But thou . . . whom frowning froward fate
Hath made sad witnesse of thy fathers fall . . .

Edmund Spenser
The Faerie Queene

Jonny Rokeby, who'd been almost entirely absent from his eldest son's life, had nevertheless been a constant, intangible presence, especially during Strike's childhood. Friends' parents had owned his father's albums, had Rokeby's poster on their bedroom walls as teenagers and regaled Strike with their fond memories of Deadbeats' concerts. A mother at the school gate had once begged the seven-year-old Strike to take a letter from her to his father. His mother had burned it later, at the squat where they were then staying.

Until he joined the army, where, by his choice, nobody knew either his father's name or his profession, Strike regularly found himself contemplated like a specimen in a jar, bothered by questions that under normal conditions would be considered personal and intrusive, and dealing with unspoken assumptions that had their roots in envy and spite.

Rokeby had demanded Leda take a paternity test before he'd accept that Strike was his son. When the test came back positive, a financial settlement had been reached which ought to have ensured that his young son would never again have to sleep on a dirty mattress in a room shared with near-strangers. However, a combination of his mother's profligacy and her regular disputes with Rokeby's representatives had merely ensured that Strike's life became a series of confusing bouts of affluence that usually ended in abrupt descents back into chaos and squalor. Leda was prone to giving her children wildly extravagant treats, which they enjoyed while wearing too-small shoes, and to taking off on trips to the Continent or to America to see her favourite bands in concert, leaving her children with Ted and Joan while she rode around in chauffeured cars and stayed in the best hotels.

He could still remember lying in the spare room in Cornwall, Lucy asleep in the twin bed beside him, listening to his mother and Joan arguing downstairs, because the children had arrived back at their aunt and uncle's in the middle of winter, without coats. Strike had twice been enrolled in private schools, but Leda had both times pulled him out again before he'd completed more than a couple of terms, because she'd decided that her son was being taught the wrong values. Every month, Rokeby's money melted away on handouts to friends and boyfriends, and in reckless ventures – Strike remembered a jewellery business, an arts magazine and a vegetarian restaurant, all of which failed, not to mention the commune in Norfolk that had been the worst experience of his young life.

Finally, Rokeby's lawyers (to whom the rock star had delegated all matters concerning the well-being of his son) tied up the paternity payments in such a way that Leda could no longer fritter the money away. The only difference this made to the teenage Strike's day-to-day life had been that the treats had stopped, because Leda wasn't prepared to have her spending scrutinised in the manner demanded by the new arrangement. From that point onwards, the paternity payments had sat accumulating quietly in an account, and the family had survived on the smaller financial contributions made by Lucy's father.

Strike had only met his father twice and had unhappy memories of both encounters. For his part, Rokeby had never asked why Strike's money remained unspent. A tax exile of long standing, he had a band to front, several homes to maintain, two exes and a current wife to keep happy, five legitimate and two illegitimate children. Strike, whose conception had been an accident, whose positive paternity test had broken up Rokeby's second marriage and whose whereabouts were usually uncertain, came low on his list of priorities.

Strike's uncle had provided the model of manhood to which Strike had aspired through his mother's many changes of lover, and a childhood spent in the long shadow cast by his biological father. Leda had always blamed Ted, the ex-military policeman, for Strike's unnatural interest in the army and investigation. Speaking from the middle of a blue haze of cannabis smoke, she would earnestly attempt to dissuade her son from a career in the army, lecturing him on Britain's shameful military history, on the inextricable links between imperialism and capitalism, and trying, without success, to persuade him to learn the guitar or, at the very least, to let his hair grow.

Yet with all the disadvantages and pain they had brought, Strike knew that the peculiar circumstances of his birth and upbringing had given him a head start as an investigator. He'd learned early how to colour himself according to his environment. From the moment he learned that penalties attached to not sounding like everyone else, his accent had switched between London and Cornwall. Before the loss of a leg had hampered his full range of physical movement, he'd been able, in spite of his distinctive size, to move and talk in ways that made him appear smaller than he really was. He'd also learned the value of concealing personal information, and of editing the stories you told about yourself, to avoid becoming entangled in other people's notions of who you must be. Most importantly of all, Strike had developed a sensitive radar for the changes in behaviour that marked the sudden realisation that he was a famous man's son. He'd been wise to the ways of manipulators, flatterers, liars, chancers and hypocrites ever since he was a child.

These dubious gifts were the best his father had given him, for, apart from child support, there'd never been a birthday card or a Christmas present. It had taken his leg being blown off in Afghanistan for Rokeby to send Strike a handwritten note. Strike had asked Charlotte, who had been sitting next to his hospital bed when he received it, to put it in the bin.

Since Strike had become of interest to the newspapers in his own right, Rokeby had made further tentative attempts to reconnect with his estranged son, going so far as to suggest in recent interviews that they were on good terms. Several of Strike's friends had sent him links to a recent online interview with Rokeby in which he'd spoken of his pride in Strike. The detective had deleted the messages without a response.

Strike was grudgingly fond of Al, the half-brother whom Rokeby had recently used as an emissary. Al's dogged pursuit of a relationship with Strike had been maintained in spite of his older brother's initial resistance. Al appeared to admire in Strike those qualities of self-reliance and independence that the latter had had no choice but to develop. Nevertheless, Al was showing an antagonising bull-headedness in continuing to push Strike into celebrating an anniversary which meant nothing to Strike, except in serving as yet another reminder of how much more important Rokeby's band had always been to him than his illegitimate son. The detective resented the time he spent on Saturday morning, crafting a response to Al's latest text message on the subject. He finally chose brevity over further argument:

> **Haven't changed my mind, but no hard feelings or bitterness this end. Hope all goes well & let's get a beer when you're next in town.**

Having taken care of this irksome bit of personal business, Strike made himself a sandwich, put on a clean shirt over his T-shirt, extracted from the Bamborough case file the page on which Bill Talbot had written his cryptic message in Pitman shorthand, and set off by car for West Wickham, where he had an appointment with Gregory Talbot, son of the late Bill.

Driving through intermittent sun and rain, and smoking as he went, Strike refocused his mind on business, mulling not only the questions he planned to ask the policeman's son, but also the various concerns related to the agency that had arisen since his return. Certain issues that needed his personal attention had been raised by Barclay the previous day. The Scot, who Strike was inclined to rate as his best investigator after Robin, had firstly expressed himself with characteristic bluntness on the subject of the West End dancer on whom they were supposed to be finding dirt.

'We're not gonnae get anythin' on him, Strike. If he's shaggin' some other bird, she must be livin' in his fuckin' wardrobe. I ken e's wi' oor lassie for her credit card, but he's too smart tae fuck up a good thing.'

'Think you're probably right,' said Strike, 'but I said we'd give the client three months, so we keep going. How're you getting on with Pat?' he added. He was hoping that somebody else found the new secretary as much of a pain in the arse as he did, but was disappointed.

'Aye, she's great. I ken she sounds like a bronchial docker, but she's very efficient. But if we're havin' an honest talk aboot new hires, here . . . ' Barclay said, his large blue eyes looking up at his boss from under thick brows.

'Go on,' said Strike. 'Morris not pulling his weight?'

'I wouldnae say that, exactly.'

The Glaswegian scratched the back of his prematurely grey head, then said,

'Robin not mentioned anything to ye?'

'Has there been trouble between them?' asked Strike, more sharply.

'Not tae say trouble, exactly,' said Barclay slowly, 'but he doesnae like takin' orders from her. Makes that plain behind her back.'

'Well, that'll have to change. I'll have a word.'

'An' he's got his own ideas aboot the Shifty case.'

'Is that right?' said Strike.

'He still thinks he's gonnae win over the PA. Robin told him it wus time tae let it go, time tae put Hutchins in. She's found oot—'

'That Shifty belongs to Hendon Rifle Club, yeah, she emailed me. And she wants to get Hutchins in there, to try and befriend him. Smart plan. Shifty fancies himself a bit of a macho man, from all we know about him.'

'But Morris wants tae do it his way. He said tae her face he was happy wi' the new plan, but—'

'You think he's still seeing the PA?'

'"Seein'" might be a polite way o' puttin' it,' said Barclay.

So Strike had called Morris into the office and laid it down in plain language that he was to leave Shifty's PA alone, and concentrate for the next week on Two-Times' girlfriend. Morris had raised no objections: indeed, his capitulation had been tinged with obsequiousness. The encounter had left a slightly unpleasant aftertaste. Morris was, in nearly all respects, a desirable hire, with many good contacts in the force, but there had been something in his manner as he hurried to agree that denoted a slipperiness Strike couldn't like. Later that night, while Strike was following the taxi containing Twinkletoes and his girlfriend through the West End, he remembered Dr Gupta's interlaced fingers, and the old doctor's verdict that what made a successful business was the smooth functioning of a team.

Entering West Wickham, he found rows of suburban houses with bay windows, broad drives and private garages. The Avenue, where Gregory Talbot lived, was lined with solid family residences that spoke of conscientious middle-class owners who mowed their lawns and remembered bin day. The houses weren't as palatial as the detached houses on Dr Gupta's street, but were many times more spacious than Strike's attic flat over the office.

Turning into Talbot's drive, Strike parked his BMW behind a skip that blocked the front of the garage. As he switched off his engine, a pale, entirely bald man with large ears and steel-rimmed glasses opened his door looking cautiously excited. Strike knew from his online research that Gregory Talbot was a hospital administrator.

'Mr Strike?' he called, while the detective was getting carefully out of the BMW (the drive was slick with rain and the memory of tripping on the Falmouth ferry, still fresh).

'That's me,' said Strike, closing his car door and holding out his hand as Talbot came walking towards him. Talbot was shorter than Strike by a good six inches.

'Sorry about the skip,' he said. 'We're doing a loft conversion.'

As they approached the front door, a pair of twin girls Strike guessed to be around ten years old came bursting outside, almost knocking Gregory aside.

'Stay in the garden, girls,' called Gregory, though Strike thought the more pressing problem was surely that they had bare feet, and that the ground was cold and wet.

'*Thtay in the garden, girlth*,' imitated one of the twins. Gregory looked mildly over the top of his glasses at the twins.

'Rudeness isn't funny.'

'It bloody is,' said the first twin, to the raucous laughter of the second.

'Swear at me again, and there'll be no chocolate pudding for you tonight, Jayda,' said Gregory. 'Nor will you borrow my iPad.'

Jayda pulled a grotesque face but did not, in fact, swear again.

'We foster,' Gregory told Strike as they stepped inside. 'Our own kids have left home. Through to the right and have a seat.'

To Strike, who lived in a slightly Spartan minimalism by choice, the cluttered and very untidy room was unappealing. He wanted to accept Gregory's invitation to sit down, but there was nowhere he could do so without having to first shift a large quantity of objects, which felt rude. Oblivious to Strike's plight, Gregory glanced through the window at the twins. They were already running back indoors, shivering.

'They learn,' he said, as the front door slammed and the twins ran upstairs. Turning back to face the room, he became aware that none of the seats were currently useable.

'Oh, yeah, sorry,' he said, though with none of the embarrassment that Strike's Aunt Joan would have displayed had a casual visitor found her house in this state of disorder. 'The girls were in here this morning.'

Gregory swiftly cleared a leaking bubble-gun, two naked Barbie dolls, a child's sock, a number of small bits of brightly coloured plastic and half a satsuma off the seat of an armchair to allow Strike to sit down. He dumped the homeless objects onto a wooden coffee table that was already piled high with magazines, a jumble of remote controls, several letters and empty envelopes and further small plastic toys, including a good deal of Lego.

'Tea?' he offered. 'Coffee? My wife's taken the boys swimming.'

'Oh, there are boys, too?'

'Hence the loft conversion,' said Gregory. 'Darren's been with us nearly five years.'

While Gregory fetched hot drinks, Strike picked up the official sticker album of this year's Champions League, which he'd spotted lying on the floor beneath the coffee table. He turned the pages with a feeling of nostalgia for the days when he, too, had collected football stickers. He was idly pondering Arsenal's chances of winning the cup when a series of crashes directly overhead, which made the pendant light sway very slightly, made him look up. It sounded as though the twins were jumping on and off their bed. Setting the sticker book down, he pondered, without finding an answer, the question of what could have motivated Talbot and his wife to bring into their home children with whom they had no biological relationship. By the time Gregory reappeared with a tray, Strike's thoughts had travelled to Charlotte, who had always declared herself entirely unmaternal, and whose premature twins she'd vowed, while pregnant, to abandon to the care of her mother-in-law.

'Would you mind shifting—?' Gregory asked, eyes on the coffee table.

Strike hastened to move handfuls of objects off it, onto the sofa.

'Cheers,' said Gregory, setting down the tray. He scooped yet another mound of objects off the second armchair, dumped them, too, onto the now considerable pile on the sofa, picked up his mug, sat down and said,

'Help yourself,' indicating a slightly sticky sugar bowl and an unopened packet of biscuits.

'Thanks very much,' said Strike, spooning sugar into his tea.

'So,' said Gregory, looking mildly excited. 'You're trying to prove Creed killed Margot Bamborough.'

'Well,' said Strike, 'I'm trying to find out what happened to her and one possibility, obviously, is Creed.'

'Did you see, in the paper last weekend? One of Creed's drawings, selling for over a grand?'

'Missed that,' said Strike.

'Yeah, it was in the *Observer.* Self-portrait in pencil, done when he was in Belmarsh. Sold on a website where you can buy serial-killer art. Crazy world.'

'It is,' agreed Strike. 'Well, as I said on the phone, what I'd really like to talk to you about is your father.'

'Yes,' said Gregory, and some of his jauntiness left him. 'I, er, I don't know how much you know.'

'That he took early retirement, following a breakdown.'

'Well, yes, that's it in a nutshell,' said Gregory. 'His thyroid was at the bottom of it. Overactive and undiagnosed, for ages. He was losing weight, not sleeping . . . There was a lot of pressure on him, you know. Not just from the force; the press, as well. People were very upset. Well, you know – a missing doctor – Mum put him acting a bit oddly down to stress.'

'In what way was he acting oddly?'

'Well, he took over the spare room and wouldn't let anyone in there,' said Gregory, and before Strike could ask for more details, he continued: 'After they found out about his thyroid and got him on the right drugs, he went back to normal, but it was too late for his career. He got his pension, but he felt guilty about the Bamborough case for years. He blamed himself, you know, thinking that if he hadn't been so ill, he might've got him.

'Because Margot Bamborough wasn't the last woman Creed took – I suppose you'll know all about that? He abducted Andrea Hooton after he took Bamborough. When they arrested him and went into the house and saw what was in the basement – the torture equipment and the photos he'd taken of the women – he admitted he'd kept some of them alive for months before he killed them.

'Dad was really upset when he heard that. He kept going back over it in his head, thinking if he'd caught him earlier, Bamborough and Hooton might've still been alive. He beat himself up for getting fixated—'

Gregory cut himself off.

'—distracted, you know.'

'So, even once your father had recovered, he still thought Creed had taken Margot?'

'Oh yeah, definitely,' said Gregory, looking mildly surprised that this was in question. 'They ruled out all the other possibilities, didn't they? The ex-boyfriend, that dodgy patient who had a thing for her, they all came up clean.'

Rather than answering this with his honest view, which was that Talbot's unfortunate illness had allowed valuable months to pass in which all suspects, Creed included, had had time to hide a body, cover up evidence, refine their alibis, or all three, Strike took from an inside pocket the piece of paper on which Talbot had written his Pitman message, and held it out to Gregory.

'Wanted to ask you about something. I think that's your father's handwriting?'

'Where did you get this?' asked Gregory, taking the paper cautiously.

'From the police file. It says: "*And that is the last of them, the twelfth, and the circle will be closed upon finding the tenth*" – and then there's an unknown word – "*Baphomet. Transcribe in the true book*",' said Strike, 'and I was wondering whether that meant anything to you?'

At that moment, there came a particularly loud crash from overhead. With a hasty 'excuse me', Gregory laid the paper on top of the tea tray and hurried from the room. Strike heard him climbing the stairs, and then a telling-off. It appeared that one of the twins had overturned a chest of drawers. Soprano voices united in exculpation and counter-accusation.

Through the net curtains, Strike now saw an old Volvo pulling up outside the house. A plump middle-aged brunette in a navy raincoat got out, followed by two boys, whom he guessed to be around fourteen or fifteen. The woman went to the boot of the car and took out two sports bags and several bags of shopping from Aldi. The boys, who'd begun to slouch towards the house, had to be called back to assist her.

Gregory arrived back at the sitting-room door just as his wife entered the hall. One of the teenage boys shoved his way past Gregory to survey the stranger with the amazement appropriate to spotting an escaped zoo animal.

'Hi,' said Strike.

The boy turned in astonishment to Gregory.

'Who's he?' he asked, pointing.

The second boy appeared beside the first, eyeing Strike with precisely the same mixture of wonder and suspicion.

'This is Mr Strike,' said Gregory.

His wife now appeared between the boys, placed a hand on their shoulders and steered them bodily away, smiling at Strike as she did so.

Gregory closed the door behind him and returned to his armchair. He appeared to have momentarily forgotten what he and Strike had been talking about before he had gone upstairs, but then his eye fell upon the piece of paper scrawled all over with his father's handwriting, dotted with pentagrams and with the cryptic lines in Pitman shorthand.

'D'you know why Dad knew Pitman shorthand?' he said, with forced cheerfulness. 'My mother was learning it at secretarial college, so he learned it as well, so he could test her. He was a good husband – and a good dad, too,' he added, a little defiantly.

'Sounds it,' said Strike.

There was another pause.

'Look,' said Gregory, 'they kept the – the specifics of Dad's illness out of the press at the time. He was a good copper and it wasn't his fault he got ill. My mother's still alive. She'd be devastated if it all got out now.'

'I can appreciate—'

'Actually, I'm not sure you can,' said Gregory, flushing slightly. He seemed a polite and mild man, and it was clear that this assertive statement cost him some effort. 'The families of some of Creed's victims, afterwards – there was a lot of ill feeling towards Dad. They blamed him for not getting Creed, for screwing it all up. People wrote to the house, telling him he was a disgrace. Mum and Dad ended up moving . . . From what you said on the phone, I thought you were interested in Dad's theories, not in – not in stuff like that,' he said, gesturing at the pentagram-strewn paper.

'I'm very interested in your father's theories,' said Strike. Deciding that a little duplicity was called for, or at least a little reframing of the facts, the detective added, 'Most of what your father wrote in the case file is entirely sound. He was asking all the right questions and he'd noticed—'

'The speeding van,' said Gregory quickly.

'Exactly,' said Strike.

'Rainy night, exactly like when Vera Kenny and Gail Wrightman were abducted.'

'Right,' said Strike, nodding.

'The two women who were struggling together,' said Gregory. 'That last patient, the woman who looked like a man. I mean, you've got to admit, you add all that together—'

'This is what I'm talking about,' said Strike. 'He might've been ill, but he still knew a clue when he saw one. All I want to know is whether the shorthand means anything I should know about.'

Some of Gregory's excitement faded from his face.

'No,' he said, 'it doesn't. That's just his illness talking.'

'You know,' said Strike slowly, 'your father wasn't the only one who saw Creed as satanic. The title of the best biography of him—'

'*The Demon of Paradise Park*.'

'Exactly. Creed and Baphomet have a lot in common,' said Strike.

In the pause that followed, they heard the twins running downstairs and loudly asking their foster mother whether she'd bought chocolate mousse.

'Look – I'd love you to prove it was Creed,' said Gregory at last. 'Prove Dad was right all along. There'd be no shame in Creed being too clever for him. He was too clever for Lawson, as well; he's been too clever for everyone. I know there wasn't any sign of Margot Bamborough in Creed's basement, but he never revealed where he'd put Andrea Hooton's clothes and jewellery, either. He was varying the way he disposed of bodies at the end. He was unlucky with Hooton, chucking her off the cliffs; unlucky the body was found so quickly.'

'All true,' said Strike.

Strike drank his tea while Gregory absent-mindedly chewed off a hangnail. A full minute passed before Strike decided that further pressure was required.

'This business about transcribing in the true book—'

He knew by Gregory's slight start that he'd hit the bullseye.

'—I wondered whether your father kept separate records from the official file – and if so,' said Strike, when Gregory didn't answer, 'whether they're still in existence.'

Gregory's wandering gaze fixed itself once more on Strike.

'Yeah, all right,' he said, 'Dad thought he was looking for something supernatural. We didn't know that until near the end, until we realised how ill he was. He was sprinkling salt outside our bedroom doors every night, to keep out Baphomet. He'd made himself what Mum thought was a home office in the spare room, but he was keeping the door locked.

'The night he was sectioned,' said Gregory, looking miserable, 'he came running out of it, ah, shouting. He woke us all up. My brother and I came out onto the landing. Dad had left the door to the spare room open, and we saw pentagrams all over the walls and lit candles. He'd taken up the carpet and made a magic circle on the floor to perform some kind of ritual, and he claimed . . . well, he thought he'd conjured some kind of demonic creature . . .

'Mum called 999 and an ambulance came and . . . well, you know the rest.'

'Must've been very distressing for all of you,' said Strike.

'Well, yeah. It was. While Dad was in hospital, Mum cleaned out the room, took away his tarot cards and all the occult books, and painted over the pentagrams and the magic circle. It was all the more upsetting for her, because both had been committed churchgoers before Dad had his breakdown . . . '

'He was clearly very ill,' said Strike, 'which wasn't his fault, but he was still a detective and he still had sound copper sense. I can see it in the official record. If there's another set of records anywhere, especially if it contains stuff that isn't in the official file, it's an important document.'

Gregory chewed his nail again, looking tense. Finally, he seemed to reach a decision:

'Ever since we spoke on the phone, I've been thinking that maybe I should give you this,' he said, standing up and heading over to an overflowing bookcase in the corner. From the top, he took a large leather-bound notebook of old-fashioned type, which had a cord wrapped around it.

'This was the only thing that didn't get thrown away,' said Gregory, looking down at the notebook, 'because Dad wouldn't let go of it when the ambulance arrived. He said he had to record what the, ah, spirit had looked like, the thing he'd conjured . . . so the notebook got taken to hospital with him. They let him draw the demon, which helped the doctors understand what had been going on in his head, because at first he didn't want to talk to them. I found all this out afterwards; they protected me and my brother from it while it was going on. After Dad got well, he kept the notebook, because he said if anything was a reminder to take his medicine, this was it. But I wanted to meet you before I made a decision.'

Resisting the urge to hold out his hand, Strike sat trying to look as sympathetic as his naturally surly features would allow. Robin was far better at conveying warmth and empathy; he'd watched her persuading recalcitrant witnesses many times since they'd gone into business together.

'You understand,' said Gregory, still clutching the notebook, and evidently determined to hammer the point home, 'he'd had a complete mental breakdown.'

'Of course,' said Strike. 'Who else have you shown that to?'

'Nobody,' said Gregory. 'It's been up in our attic for the last ten years. We had a couple of boxes of stuff from Mum and Dad's old house up there. Funny, you turning up just as the loft was being mucked out . . . maybe this is all Dad's doing? Maybe he's trying to tell me it's OK to pass this over?'

Strike made an ambiguous noise designed to convey agreement that the Talbots' decision to clear out their loft had been somehow prompted by Gregory's dead father, rather than the need to accommodate two extra children.

'Take it,' said Gregory abruptly, holding out the old notebook. Strike thought he looked relieved to see it pass into someone else's possession.

'I appreciate your trust. If I find anything in here I think you can help with, would it be all right to contact you again?'

'Yeah, of course,' said Gregory. 'You've got my email address . . . I'll give you my mobile number . . . '

Five minutes later, Strike was standing in the hall, shaking hands with Mrs Talbot as he prepared to return to his office.

'Lovely to meet you,' she said. 'I'm glad he's given you that thing. You never know, do you?'

And with the notebook in his hand, Strike agreed that you never did.

18

So the fayre Britomart hauing disclo'ste
Her clowdy care into a wrathfull stowre,
The mist of griefe dissolu'd . . .

Edmund Spenser
The Faerie Queene

Robin, who'd recently given up many weekends to cover the agency's workload, took the following Tuesday and Wednesday off at Strike's insistence. Her suggestion that she come into the office to look at the notebook Gregory Talbot had given Strike, and to go systematically through the last box of the police file, which neither of them had yet had time to examine, had been sternly vetoed by the senior partner. Strike knew there was no time left this year for Robin to take all the leave she was owed, but he was determined that she should take as much as she could.

However, if Strike imagined that Robin derived much pleasure from her days off, he was wrong. She spent Tuesday dealing with mundanities such as laundry and food shopping, and on Wednesday morning, set off for a twice-postponed appointment with her solicitor.

When she'd broken the news to her parents that she and Matthew were to divorce a little over a year after they'd married, her mother and father had wanted her to use a solicitor in Harrogate, who was an old family friend.

'I live in London. Why would I use a law firm in Yorkshire?'

Robin had chosen a lawyer in her late forties called Judith, whose dry humour, spiky grey hair and thick black-rimmed glasses had endeared her to Robin when first they met. Robin's feeling of warmth had abated somewhat over the ensuing twelve months. It was hard to maintain fondness for the person whose job it was to pass on the latest intransigent and aggressive communications from Matthew's lawyer. As the months rolled past, Robin noticed that Judith occasionally forgot or misremembered information pertinent to the divorce. Robin, who always took care to give her own clients the impression that their concerns were uppermost in her mind at all times, couldn't help wondering whether Judith would have been more meticulous if Robin had been richer.

Like Robin's parents, Judith had initially assumed that this divorce would be quick and easy, a matter of two signatures and a handshake. The couple had been married a little over a year and there were no children, not even a pet to argue over. Robin's parents had gone so far as to imagine that Matthew, whom they'd known since he was a child, must feel such shame at his infidelity that he'd want to compensate Robin by being generous and reasonable over the divorce. Her mother's growing fury towards her ex-son-in-law was starting to make Robin dread her phone calls home.

The offices of Stirling and Cobbs were a twenty-minute walk away from Robin's flat, on North End Road. Zipping herself into a warm coat, umbrella in hand, Robin chose to walk that morning purely for the exercise, because she'd spent so many long hours in her car of late, sitting outside the weatherman's house, waiting for Postcard. Indeed, the last time she'd walked for a whole hour had been inside the National Portrait Gallery, a trip that had been fruitless, except for one tiny incident that Robin had discounted, because Strike had taught her to mistrust the hunches so romanticised by the non-investigative public, which, he said, were more often than not born of personal biases or wishful thinking.

Tired, dispirited and knowing full well that nothing she was about to hear from Judith was likely to cheer her up, Robin was passing a bookie's when her mobile rang. Extracting it from her pocket took a little longer than usual, because she was wearing gloves, and she consequently sounded a little panicky when she finally managed to answer the unknown number.

'Yes, hello? Robin Ellacott speaking.'

'Oh, hi. This is Eden Richards.'

For a moment, Robin couldn't for the life of her think who Eden Richards was. The woman on the end of the line seemed to divine her dilemma, because she continued,

'Wilma Bayliss's daughter. You sent me and my brothers and sisters messages. You wanted to talk to us about Margot Bamborough.'

'Oh, yes, of course, thank you for calling me back!' said Robin, backing into the bookie's doorway, her finger in the ear not pressed against the phone, to block out the sound of traffic. Eden, she now remembered, was the oldest of Wilma's offspring, a Labour councillor from Lewisham.

'Yeah,' said Eden Richards, 'well, I'm afraid we don't want to talk to you. And I'm speaking for all of us here, OK?'

'I'm sorry to hear that,' said Robin, watching abstractedly as a passing Doberman Pinscher squatted and defecated on the pavement while its scowling owner waited, a plastic bag hanging from his hand. 'Can I ask why—?'

'We just don't want to,' said Eden. 'OK?'

'OK,' said Robin, 'but to be clear, all we're doing is checking statements that were made around the time Margot—'

'We can't speak for our mother,' said Eden. 'She's dead. We feel sorry for Margot's daughter, but we don't want to drag up stuff that – it's something we don't particularly want to relive, any of our family. We were young when she disappeared. It was a bad time for us. So the answer's no, OK?'

'I understand,' said Robin, 'but I wish you'd reconsider. We aren't asking you to talk about anything pers—'

'You are, though,' said Eden. 'Yeah, you are. And we don't want to, OK? You aren't police. And by the way: my youngest sister's going through chemotherapy, so leave her alone, please. She doesn't need the grief. I'm going to go now. The answer's no, OK? Don't contact any of us again, please.'

And the line went dead.

'Shit,' said Robin out loud.

The owner of the Doberman Pinscher, who was now scooping a sizeable pile of that very substance off the pavement, said, 'You and me both, love.'

Robin forced a smile, stuffed her mobile back into her pocket and walked on. Shortly afterwards, still wondering whether she could have handled the call with Eden better, Robin pushed open the glass door of Stirling and Cobbs, Solicitors.

'*Well*,' said Judith five minutes later, once Robin was sitting opposite her in the tiny office full of filing cabinets. The monosyllable was followed by silence as Judith glanced over the documents in the file in front of her, clearly reminding herself of the facts of the case while Robin sat watching. Robin would much rather have sat for another five minutes in the waiting room than witness this casual and hasty revision of what was causing her so much stress and pain.

'Umm,' said Judith, 'yes . . . just checking that . . . yes, we had a response to ours on the fourteenth, as I said in my email, so you'll be aware that Mr Cunliffe isn't prepared to shift his position on the joint account.'

'Yes,' said Robin.

'So, I really think it's time to go to mediation,' said Judith Cobbs.

'And as I said in my reply to your email,' said Robin, wondering whether Judith had read it, 'I can't see mediation working.'

'Which is why I wanted to speak to you face to face,' said Judith, smiling. 'We often find that when the two parties have to sit down in the same room, and answer for themselves, especially with impartial witnesses present – I'd be with you, obviously – they become far less intransigent than they are by letter.'

'You said yourself,' Robin replied (blood was thumping in her ears: the sensation of not being heard was becoming increasingly common during these interactions), 'the last time we met – you agreed that Matthew seems to be trying to force this into court. He isn't really interested in the joint account. He can outspend me ten times over. He just wants to beat me. He wants a judge to agree that I married him for his bank account. He'll think it money well spent if he can point to some ruling that says the divorce was all my fault.'

'It's easy,' said Judith, still smiling, 'to attribute the worst possible motives to ex-partners, but he's clearly an intelligent—'

'Intelligent people can be as spiteful as anyone else.'

'True,' said Judith, still with an air of humouring Robin, 'but refusing to even *try* mediation is a bad move for both of you. No judge will look kindly on anyone who refuses to at least *try* and settle matters without recourse to the courts.'

The truth, as perhaps Judith and Robin both equally knew, was that Robin dreaded having to sit face to face with Matthew and the lawyer who had authored all those cold, threatening letters.

'I've *told* him I don't want the inheritance he got from his mother,' said Robin. 'All I want back out of that joint account is the money *my* parents put into our first property.'

'Yes,' said Judith, with a hint of boredom: Robin knew that she'd said exactly this, every time they'd met each other. 'But as you're aware, *his* position—'

'Is that I contributed virtually nothing to our finances, so he ought to keep the whole lot, because he went into the marriage out of love and I'm some kind of gold-digger.'

'This is obviously upsetting you,' said Judith, no longer smiling.

'We were together ten years,' said Robin, trying, with little success, to remain calm. 'When he was a student and I was working, I paid for everything. Should I have kept the receipts?'

'We can certainly make that point in mediation—'

'That'll just infuriate him,' said Robin.

She raised a hand to her face purely for the purpose of hiding it. She felt suddenly and perilously close to tears.

'OK, fine. We can try mediation.'

'I think that's the sensible thing to do,' said Judith Cobbs, smiling again. 'So, I'll contact Brophy, Shenstone and—'

'I suppose I'll get a chance to tell Matthew he's a total shit, at least,' said Robin, on a sudden wave of fury.

Judith gave a small laugh.

'Oh, I wouldn't advise *that*,' she said.

Oh, wouldn't you really? thought Robin, as she hitched on another fake smile, and got up to leave.

A blustery, damp wind was blowing when she left the solicitor's. Robin trudged back towards Finborough Road, until finally, her face numb, her hair whipping into her eyes, she turned into a small café where, in defiance of her own healthy eating rules, she bought a large latte and a chocolate brownie. She sat and stared out at the rainswept street, enjoying the comfort of cake and coffee, until her mobile rang again.

It was Strike.

'Hi,' she said, through a mouthful of brownie. 'Sorry. Eating.'

'Wish I was,' he said. 'I'm outside the bloody theatre again. I think Barclay's right: we're not going to get anything on Twinkletoes. I've got Bamborough news.'

'So've I,' said Robin, who had managed to swallow the mouthful of brownie, 'but it isn't good news. Wilma Bayliss's children don't want to talk to us.'

'The cleaner's kids? Why not?'

'Wilma wasn't a cleaner by the time she died,' Robin reminded him. 'She was a social worker.'

Even as she said it, Robin wondered why she felt the need to correct him. Perhaps it was simply that if Wilma Bayliss was to be forever referred to as a cleaner, she, Robin, might as well be forever called 'the temp'.

'All right, why don't the *social worker's* kids want to talk to us?' asked Strike.

'The one who called me – Eden, she's the eldest – said they didn't want to drag up what had been a difficult time for the family. She said it had nothing to do with Margot – but then she contradicted herself, because when I said we only wanted to talk about Margot – I can't remember her exact words, but the sense was that talking about Margot's disappearance would involve them talking about the family's personal stuff.'

'Well, their father was in jail in the early seventies and Margot was urging Wilma to leave him,' said Strike. 'It's probably that. Think it's worth calling her back? Trying a bit more persuasion?'

'I don't think she's going to change her mind.'

'And she said she was speaking for her brothers and sisters, as well?'

'Yes. One of them's having chemotherapy. She warned me specifically away from her.'

'OK, avoid her, but one of the others might be worth a shot.'

'That'll annoy Eden.'

'Probably, but we've got nothing to lose now, have we?'

'S'pose not,' said Robin. 'So what's *your* news?'

'The practice nurse and the receptionist, the one who isn't Gloria Conti—'

'Irene Bull,' said Robin.

'Irene Bull, now Hickson, exactly – they're both happy to talk to us. Turns out they've been friends since the St John's practice days. Irene will be delighted to host Janice and us at her house on Saturday afternoon. I think we should both go.'

Robin turned her mobile to speakerphone so that she could check the rota she kept on her phone. The entry for Saturday read: *Strike's birthday/TT girlfriend.*

'I'm supposed to be following Two-Times' girlfriend,' said Robin, switching back from speakerphone.

'Sod that, Morris can do it,' said Strike. 'You can drive us – if you don't mind,' he added, and Robin smiled.

'No, I don't mind,' she said.

'Well, great,' said Strike. 'Enjoy the rest of your day off.'

He rang off. Robin picked up the rest of the brownie and finished it slowly, savouring every bite. In spite of the prospect of mediation with Matthew, and doubtless because of a much-needed infusion of chocolate, she felt a good deal happier than she had ten minutes previously.

19

There did I finde mine onely faithfull frend
In heauy plight and sad perplexitie;
Whereof I sorie, yet my selfe did bend,
Him to recomfort with my companie.

Edmund Spenser
The Faerie Queene

Strike never told anyone that his birthday was imminent and avoided announcing it on the day itself. It wasn't that he didn't appreciate people remembering: indeed, he tended to be far more touched when they did than he ever let show, but he had an innate dislike of scheduled celebration and forced jollity, and of all inane practices, having 'Happy Birthday' sung to him was one of his least favourites.

As far back as he could remember, the day of his birth had brought up unhappy memories on which he chose, usually successfully, not to dwell. His mother had sometimes forgotten to buy him anything when he was a child. His biological father had never acknowledged the date. Birthdays were inextricably linked with the knowledge, which had long since become part of him, that his existence was accidental, that his genetic inheritance had been contested in court, and that the birth itself had been 'fucking hideous, darling, if men had to do it the human race would be extinct in a year'.

To his sister, Lucy, it would have been almost cruel to let a loved one's birthday pass without a card, a gift, a phone call or, if she could manage it, a party or at the very least a meal. This was why he usually lied to Lucy, pretending to have plans so as to avoid having to go all the way out to her house in Bromley and participate in a family dinner that she'd enjoy far more than he would. Not long ago, he'd happily have celebrated with a takeaway at his friends Nick and Ilsa's, but Ilsa had suggested Robin accompany Strike, and as Strike had decided many weeks ago that Ilsa's increasingly open attempts at matchmaking could only be successfully countered by a blanket refusal to cooperate, he'd pretended that he was going to Lucy's instead. The one joyless hope Strike had for his thirty-ninth birthday was that Robin would have forgotten it, because, if she did, his own omission would be cancelled out: they'd be quits.

He descended the metal stairs to the office on Friday morning and saw, to his surprise, two packages and four envelopes sitting beside the usual pile of mail on Pat's desk. The envelopes were all of different colours. Apparently, friends and family had decided to make sure birthday greetings reached him in time for the weekend.

'Is it your birthday?' Pat asked in her deep, gravelly voice, still staring at her monitor and typing, electronic cigarette jammed between her teeth as usual.

'Tomorrow,' said Strike, picking up the cards. He recognised the handwriting on three of them, but not the fourth.

'Many happy returns,' grunted Pat, over the clacking of her keyboard. 'You should've said.'

Some spirit of mischief prompted Strike to ask,

'Why? Would you've baked me a cake?'

'No,' said Pat indifferently. 'Might've got you a card, though.'

'Lucky I didn't say, then. One fewer tree's died.'

'It wouldn't have been a *big* card,' said Pat, unsmiling, her fingers still flying over the keyboard.

Grinning slightly, Strike removed himself, his cards and packages into the inner office, and later that evening took them upstairs with him, still unopened.

He woke on the twenty-third with his mind full of his trip to Greenwich with Robin later, and only remembered the significance of the day when he saw the presents and cards on the table. The packages contained a sweater from Ted and Joan, and a sweatshirt from Lucy. Ilsa, Dave Polworth and his half-brother Al had all sent joke cards which, while not actually making him laugh, were vaguely cheering.

He slipped the fourth card out of its envelope. It had a photograph of a bloodhound on the front, and Strike considered this for a second or two, wondering why it had been chosen. He'd never owned a dog, and while he had a mild preference for dogs over cats, having worked alongside a few in the military, he wouldn't have said dog-loving was one of his salient characteristics. Flicking the card open, he saw the words:

Happy birthday Cormoran,
Best,
Jonny (Dad)

For a few moments, Strike merely looked at the words, his mind as blank as the rest of the card. The last time he'd seen his father's writing, he'd been full of morphine after his leg had been blown off. As a child, he'd occasionally caught a glimpse of his father's signature on legal documents sent to his mother. Then, he'd stared awestruck at the name, as though he were glimpsing an actual part of his father, as though the ink were blood, and solid proof that his father was a real human being, not a myth.

Quite suddenly, and with a force that shocked Strike, he

found himself full of rage, rage on behalf of the small boy who would once have sold his soul to receive a birthday card from his father. He'd grown well beyond any desire to have contact with Jonny Rokeby, but he could still recall the acute pain his father's continual and implacable absence had so often caused him as a child: while the primary class was making Father's Day cards, for instance, or when strange adults questioned him about why he never saw Rokeby, or other children jeered at him, singing Deadbeats songs or telling him his mother had got pregnant with him purely to get Rokeby's money. He remembered the longing that was almost an ache, always most acute around birthdays and Christmas, for his father to send something, or phone: anything, to show that he knew Strike was alive. Strike hated the memory of these fantasies more than he hated remembering the pain caused by their eternal unfulfillment, but most of all he hated remembering the hopeful lies he'd told himself when, as a very young boy, he'd made excuses for his father, who probably didn't know that the family had moved yet again, who'd sent things to the wrong address, who wanted to know him but simply couldn't find him.

Where had Rokeby been when his son was a nobody? Where had Rokeby been every time Leda's life came off the rails, and Ted and Joan rode, again, to the rescue? Where had he been on any of the thousands of occasions when his presence might have meant something real, and genuine, rather than an attempt to look good to the papers?

Rokeby knew literally nothing about his son except that he was a detective, and *that* explained the fucking bloodhound. *Fuck you and fuck your fucking card.* Strike tore the card in half, then into quarters, and threw the pieces into the bin. But for a disinclination to trigger the fire alarm, he might have put a match to them.

Anger pulsed like a current through Strike all morning. He

hated his own rage, as it showed that Rokeby still had some emotional hold on him, and by the time he set out for Earl's Court, where Robin was picking him up, he was not far off wishing that birthdays had never been invented.

Sitting in the Land Rover just outside the station entrance some forty-five minutes later, Robin watched Strike emerge onto the pavement, carrying a leather-bound notebook, and noted that he looked as grumpy as she'd ever seen him.

'Happy birthday,' she said, when he opened the passenger door. Strike immediately noticed the card and the small wrapped package lying on the dashboard.

Fuck.

'Cheers,' and climbed in beside her, looking even grumpier.

As Robin pulled out onto the road, she said,

'Is it turning thirty-nine that's upset you, or has something else happened?'

Having no desire to talk about Rokeby, Strike decided an effort was required.

'No, I'm just knackered. I was up late last night, going through the last box of the Bamborough file.'

'I wanted to do that on Tuesday, but you wouldn't let me!'

'You were owed time off,' said Strike shortly, tearing open the envelope of her card. 'You're *still* owed time off.'

'I know, but it would've been a lot more interesting than doing my ironing.'

Strike looked down at the front of Robin's card, which featured a watercolour picture of St Mawes. She must, he thought, have gone to some trouble to find it in London. 'Nice,' he said, 'thanks.'

Flipping it open, he read,

Many happy returns, love Robin x

She'd never put a kiss on any message to him before, and he liked it being there. Feeling slightly more cheerful, he unwrapped the small package that accompanied the card, and found inside a pair of replacement headphones of the kind Luke had broken while he'd been in St Mawes over the summer.

'Ah, Robin, that's – thanks. That's great. I hadn't replaced them, either.'

'I know,' said Robin, 'I noticed.'

As Strike put her card back in its envelope, he reminded himself that he really did need to get her a decent Christmas present.

'Is that Bill Talbot's secret notebook?' Robin asked, glancing sideways at the leather-bound book in Strike's lap.

'The very same. I'll show you after we've talked to Irene and Janice. Batshit crazy. Full of bizarre drawings and symbols.'

'What about the last box of police records? Anything interesting?' Robin asked.

'Yes, as it goes. A chunk of police notes from 1975 had got mixed in with a bunch of later stuff. There were a few interesting bits.

'For instance, the practice cleaner, Wilma, was sacked a couple of months after Margot disappeared, but for petty theft, not drinking, which is what Gupta told me. Small amounts of money disappearing out of people's purses and pockets. I also found out a call was made to Margot's marital home on Anna's second birthday, from a woman claiming to be Margot.'

'Oh my God, that's horrible,' said Robin. 'A prank call?'

'Police thought so. They traced it to a phone box in Marylebone. Cynthia, the childminder-turned-second-wife, answered. The woman identified herself as Margot and told Cynthia to look after her daughter.'

'Did Cynthia think it was Margot?'

'She told police she was too shocked to really take in what

the caller said. She thought it sounded a bit like her, but on balance it sounded more like someone imitating her.'

'What makes people do things like that?' Robin asked, in genuine perplexity.

'They're shits,' said Strike. 'There were also a bunch of alleged sightings of Margot after the day she disappeared, in the last box. They were all disproven, but I've made a list and I'll email them to you. Mind if I smoke?'

'Carry on,' said Robin, and Strike wound down the window. 'I actually emailed *you* a tiny bit of information last night, too. *Very* tiny. Remember Albert Shimmings, the local florist—'

'—whose van people thought they saw speeding away from Clerkenwell Green? Yeah. Did he leave a note confessing to murder?'

'Unfortunately not, but I've spoken to his eldest son, who says that his dad's van *definitely* wasn't in Clerkenwell at half past six that evening. It was waiting outside his clarinet teacher's house in Camden, where his dad drove him every Friday. He says they told the police that at the time. His dad used to wait outside for him in the van and read spy novels.'

'Well, the clarinet lessons aren't in the records, but both Talbot and Lawson believed Shimmings when they spoke to him. Good to have it confirmed, though,' he added, lest Robin think he was being dismissive of her routine work. 'Well, that means there's still a possibility the van was Dennis Creed's, doesn't it?'

Strike lit up a Benson & Hedges, exhaled out of the window, and said,

'There was some interesting material on these two women we're about to meet, in that last box of notes. More stuff that came out when Lawson took over.'

'Really? I thought Irene had a dental appointment and Janice had house visits on the afternoon Margot disappeared?'

'Yeah, that's what their original statements said,' said Strike, 'and Talbot didn't check either woman's story. Took both at their word.'

'Presumably because he didn't think a woman could be the Essex Butcher?'

'Exactly.'

Strike pulled his own notebook out of his coat pocket and opened it to the pages he'd scribbled on Tuesday.

'Irene's first statement, which she gave to Talbot, said she'd had a grumbling toothache for a few days before Margot disappeared. Her friend Janice the nurse thought it might be an abscess, so Irene made an emergency appointment for three o'clock, leaving the practice at two-thirty. She and Janice were planning to go to the cinema that evening, but Irene's face was sore and swollen after having a tooth removed, so when Janice phoned her to see how the dentist's had gone, and to check whether she still wanted to go out that night, she said she'd rather stay at home.'

'No mobile phones,' mused Robin. 'Different world.'

'Exactly what I thought when I was going over this,' said Strike. 'These days Irene's mates would've expected a minute-by-minute commentary. Selfies from the dental chair.

'Talbot gave his officers to understand that he'd personally contacted the dentist to check this story, but he hadn't. Wouldn't put it past him to have consulted a crystal ball.'

'Ha ha.'

'I'm not kidding. Wait till you see his notebook.'

Strike turned a page.

'Anyway, six months later, Lawson takes over the case and goes systematically back through every single witness and suspect in the file. Irene told the dentist story again, but half an hour after she left him, she panicked and asked to see him again. This time she admitted she'd lied.

'There'd never been any tooth pain. She hadn't visited the dentist. She said she'd been forced to do a lot of unpaid overtime at the surgery and resented it, and felt she was owed an afternoon off, so she faked toothache, pretended to have got an emergency appointment, then left the practice and went to the West End to do some shopping.

'She told Lawson that it was only when she got home – she was still living with her parents, incidentally – that it occurred to her that if she went out to meet Janice the nurse that evening, Janice might ask to see the place where the tooth had been extracted, or at least expect to see some swelling. So when Janice rang her to check they were still going to the cinema, she lied and said she didn't feel up to it.

'Lawson gave Irene quite a hard time, judging from his notes. Didn't she understand what a serious matter it was, lying to the police, people had been arrested for less, et cetera. He also put it to her that the new story showed she had no alibi for any point of the afternoon and evening, other than around half past six in the evening, when Janice rang her at home.'

'Where did Irene live?'

'Street called Corporation Row, which as it happens lies very close to the Three Kings, although not on the route Margot would have taken from the practice.

'Anyway, at the point alibis were mentioned, Irene became hysterical. She poured out a load of stuff about Margot having a lot of enemies, without being able to say who these enemies were, although she referred Lawson back to the anonymous letters Margot received.

'The next day, Irene went back to Lawson yet again, this time accompanied by her very angry father, who did her no favours by losing his temper at Lawson for daring to upset his daughter. In the course of this third interview, Irene presented Lawson with a receipt from Oxford Street, which was marked 3.10 p.m. on the day Margot disappeared. The receipt was for cash. Lawson probably took a lot of pleasure in telling Irene and her dad that all the receipt proved was that *somebody* had gone shopping on Oxford Street that day.'

'Still – a receipt for the right day, right time—'

'Could've been her mother's. A friend's.'

'Why would they have kept it for six months?'

'Why would she?'

Robin considered the matter. She regularly kept receipts, but these were matters of expenses while doing surveillance, to be presented to the accountant.

'Yeah, maybe it is odd she still had it,' she conceded.

'But Lawson never managed to get anything further out of her. I don't think he genuinely suspected her, mind you. I get the impression he just didn't like her. He pressed her very hard on the anonymous notes she claimed to have seen, the ones mentioning hellfire. I don't think he believed in them.'

'I thought the other receptionist confirmed she'd seen one?'

'She did. Nothing to say they weren't in cahoots, though. No trace of the notes was ever found.'

'But that'd be a serious lie,' said Robin. 'With the fake dental appointment, I can see why she fibbed and why she'd have been frightened to admit it afterwards. Lying about anonymous notes in the context of a missing person, though . . .'

'Ah, but don't forget, Irene was already telling the story of the anonymous notes before Margot went missing. It's more of the same, isn't it? The two receptionists could've invented these threatening notes for the pleasure of starting a malicious rumour, then found it impossible to back away from the lie after Margot disappeared.

'Anyway,' said Strike, flicking over a couple of pages, 'so much for Irene. Now for her best buddy, the practice nurse.

'Janice's original statement was that she drove around all afternoon, making house calls. The last visit, which was to an old lady with multiple health issues, kept her longer than she expected. She left there around six and hurried straight to a call box to ring Irene at home, to see whether they were still on for the cinema that evening. Irene said she didn't feel up to it, but Janice had already got herself a babysitter, and was desperate to see the movie – James Caan, *The Gambler* – so she went anyway. Watched the movie alone, then went back to the neighbour's, picked up her son and went home.

'Talbot didn't bother to check any of this, but a zealous junior officer did, on his own initiative, and it all checked out. All the patients confirmed that Janice had been at their houses at the right times. The babysitter confirmed that Janice returned to pick up her son when expected. Janice also produced a half-torn ticket for the movie out of the bottom of her handbag. Given that this was less than a week after Margot disappeared, it doesn't seem particularly fishy, her still having it. On the other hand, a torn ticket is no more proof that she sat through the movie than the receipt is proof Irene went shopping.'

He threw his cigarette end out of the window.

'Where did Janice's last patient of the day live?' asked Robin, and Strike knew that her mind was running on distances and timings.

'Gopsall Street, which is about a ten-minute drive from the practice. It would've been *just* possible for a woman in a car to have intercepted Margot on the way to the Three Kings, assuming Margot was walking very slowly, or was delayed somewhere along the route, or left the practice later than Gloria said she did. But it would've required luck, because as we know, some of the path Margot would've taken was pedestrianised.'

'And I can't really see why you'd make arrangements with a friend to go to the cinema if you were planning to abduct someone,' said Robin.

'Nor can I,' said Strike. 'But I'm not finished. When Lawson takes over the case he finds out that Janice lied to Talbot as well.'

'You're kidding.'

'Nope. Turned out she didn't actually have a car. Six weeks before Margot disappeared, Janice's ancient Morris Minor gave up the ghost and she sold it for scrap. From that time onwards, she was making all her house calls by public transport and on foot. She hadn't wanted to tell anyone at the practice that she was carless, in case they told her she couldn't do her job. Her husband had walked out, leaving her with a kid. She was saving up to get a new car, but she knew it was going to take a while, so she pretended the Morris Minor was in the garage, or that it was easier to get the bus, if anyone asked.'

'But if that's true—'

'It is. Lawson checked it all out, questioned the scrap yard and everything.'

'—then that surely puts her completely out of the frame for an abduction.'

'I'm inclined to agree,' said Strike. 'She could've got a cab, of course, but the cabbie would've had to be in on the abduction, too. No, the interesting thing about Janice is that in spite of believing she was entirely innocent, Talbot interviewed her a total of seven times, more than any other witness or suspect.'

'*Seven times?*'

'Yep. He had a kind of excuse at first. She was a neighbour of Steve Douthwaite's, Margot's acutely stressed patient. Interviews two and three were all about Douthwaite, who Janice knew to say hello to. Douthwaite was Talbot's preferred candidate for the Essex Butcher, so you can follow his thought processes – you *would* question neighbours if you thought someone might be butchering women at home. But Janice wasn't able to tell Talbot anything about Douthwaite beyond what we already know, and Talbot still kept going back to her. After the third interview, he stopped asking her about Douthwaite and things got very strange indeed. Among other things, Talbot asked whether she'd ever been hypnotised, whether she'd be prepared to try it, asked her all about her dreams and urged her to keep a diary of them so he could read it, and also to make him a list of her most recent sexual partners.'

'He did *what*?'

'There's a copy of a letter from the Commissioner in the file,' said Strike drily, 'apologising to Janice for Talbot's behaviour. All in all, you can see why they wanted him off the force as fast as possible.'

'Did his son tell you any of that?'

Strike remembered Gregory's earnest, mild face, his assertion that Bill had been a good father and his embarrassment as the conversation turned to pentagrams.

'I doubt he knew about it. Janice doesn't seem to have made a fuss.'

'Well,' said Robin, slowly. 'She *was* a nurse. Maybe she could tell he was ill?'

She considered the matter for a few moments, then said,

'It'd be frightening, though, wouldn't it? Having the investigating officer coming back to your house every five minutes, asking you to keep a dream diary?'

'It'd put the wind up most people. I'm assuming the explanation is the obvious one – but we should ask her about it.'

Strike glanced into the back and saw, as he'd hoped, a bag of food.

'Well, it is your birthday,' said Robin, her eyes still on the road.

'Fancy a biscuit?'

'Bit early for me. You carry on.'

As he leaned back to fetch the bag, Strike noticed that Robin smelled again of her old perfume.

20

And if that any ill she heard of any,
She would it eeke, and make much worse by telling,
And take great ioy to publish it to many,
That euery matter worse was for her melling.

Edmund Spenser
The Faerie Queene

Irene Hickson's house lay in a short, curving Georgian terrace of yellow brick, with arched windows and fanlights over each black front door. It reminded Robin of the street where she'd spent the last few months of her married life, in a rented house that had been built for a sea merchant. Here, too, were traces of London's trading past. The lettering over an arched window read *Royal Circus Tea Warehouse.*

'Mr Hickson must've made good money,' said Strike, looking up at the beautifully proportioned frontage as he and Robin crossed the street. 'This is a long way from Corporation Row.'

Robin rang the doorbell. They heard a shout of 'Don't worry, I'll get it!' and a few seconds later, a short, silver-haired woman opened the door to them. Dressed in a navy sweater, and trousers of the kind that Robin's mother would have called 'slacks', she had a round pink and white face. Blue eyes peeked out from beneath a blunt fringe that Robin suspected she might have cut herself.

'Mrs Hickson?' asked Robin.

'Janice Beattie,' said the older woman. 'You're Robin, are you? An' you're—'

The retired nurse's eyes swept down over Strike's legs in what looked like professional appraisal.

'—Corm'ran, is that 'ow you say it?' she asked, looking back up into his face.

'That's right,' said Strike. 'Very good of you to see us, Mrs Beattie.'

'Oh, no trouble at all,' she said, backing away to let them in. 'Irene'll be wiv us in a mo.'

The naturally upturned corners of the nurse's mouth and the dimples in her full cheeks gave her a cheerful look even when she wasn't smiling. She led them through a hall that Strike found oppressively over-decorated. Everything was dusky pink: the flowered wallpaper, the thick carpet, the dish of pot-pourri that sat on the telephone table. The distant sound of a flush told them exactly where Irene was.

The sitting room was decorated in olive green, and everything that could be swagged, flounced, fringed or padded had been. Family photographs in silver frames were crowded on side tables, the largest of which showed a heavily tanned forty-something blonde who was cheek to cheek over fruit-and-umbrella-laden cocktails with a florid gentlemen who Robin assumed was the late Mr Hickson. He looked quite a lot older than his wife. A large collection of porcelain figurines stood upon purpose-built mahogany shelves against the shiny olive-green wallpaper. All represented young women. Some wore crinolines, others twirled parasols, still others sniffed flowers or cradled lambs in their arms.

'She collects 'em,' said Janice, smiling as she saw where Robin was looking. 'Lovely, aren't they?'

'Oh yes,' lied Robin.

Janice didn't seem to feel she had the right to invite them to sit down without Irene present, so the three of them remained standing beside the figurines.

'Have you come far?' she asked them politely, but before they could answer, a voice that commanded attention said,

'Hello! Welcome!'

Like her sitting room, Irene Hickson presented a first impression of over-embellished, over-padded opulence. Just as blonde as she'd been at twenty-five, she was now much heavier, with an enormous bosom. She'd outlined her hooded eyes in black, pencilled her sparse brows into a high, Pierrot-ish arch and painted her thin lips in scarlet. In a mustard-coloured twinset, black trousers, patent heels and a large quantity of gold jewellery, which included clip-on earrings so heavy that they were stretching her already long lobes, she advanced on them in a potent cloud of amber perfume and hairspray.

'How d'you do?' she said, beaming at Strike as she offered her hand, bracelets jangling. 'Has Jan told you? What happened this morning? *So* strange, with you coming today; *so* strange, but I've lost *count* of the number of times things like that happen to me.' She paused, then said dramatically, '*My Margot shattered*. My Margot Fonteyn, on the top shelf,' she said, pointing to a gap in the china figurines. 'Fell apart into a million pieces when I ran the feather duster over her!'

She paused, waiting for astonishment.

'That *is* odd,' said Robin, because it was clear Strike wasn't going to say anything.

'*Isn't it?*' said Irene. 'Tea? Coffee? Whatever you want.'

'I'll do it, dear,' said Janice.

'Thank you, my love. Maybe make both?' said Irene. She waved Strike and Robin graciously towards armchairs. 'Please, sit down.'

The armchairs placed Strike and Robin within view of

a window framed in tasselled curtains, through which they could see a garden with intricate paving and raised beds. It had an Elizabethan air, with low box hedges and a wrought iron sundial.

'Oh, the garden was all my Eddie,' said Irene, following their gaze. 'He *loved* his garden, bless his heart. *Loved* this house. It's why I'm still here, although it's too big for me now, really . . . Excuse me. I haven't been well,' she added in a loud whisper, making quite a business of lowering herself onto the sofa and placing cushions carefully around herself. 'Jan's been a *saint*.'

'I'm sorry to hear that,' said Strike. 'That you've been unwell, I mean, not that your friend's a saint.'

Irene gave a delighted peal of laughter and Robin suspected that if Strike had been sitting slightly nearer, Irene might have playfully cuffed him. With an air of giving Strike privileged information, she half-mouthed:

'Irritable bowel syndrome. It flares up. The pain is sometimes – *well*. The funny thing is, I was *fine* all the time I was away – I've been staying with my eldest daughter, they're in Hampshire, that's why I didn't get your letter straight away – but the moment I got home, I called Jan, I said, you'll have to come, I'm in *that much pain* – and my GP's no use,' she added, with a little moue of disgust. '*Woman*. All my own fault, according to her! I should be cutting out everything that makes life worth living – I was telling them, Jan,' she said, as her friend backed into the room with a laden tea tray, 'that you're a *saint*.'

'Oh, carry on. Everyone likes a good review,' said Janice cheerfully. Strike was halfway out of his chair to help her with the tray, on which stood both teapot and cafetière, but like Mrs Gupta she refused help, depositing it on a padded ottoman. An assortment of chocolate biscuits, some foil-wrapped, lay on a doily; the sugar bowl had tongs and the flowered fine bone china suggested 'for best'. Janice joined her friend on the sofa and poured out the hot drinks, serving Irene first.

'Help yourself to biscuits,' Irene told her visitors, and then, eyeing Strike hungrily, 'So – the famous Cameron Strike! I nearly had a *heart attack* when I saw your name at the bottom of the letter. And you're going to try and crack Creed, are you? Will he talk to you, do you think? Will they let you go and see him?'

'We're not that far along yet,' said Strike with a smile, as he took out his notebook and uncapped his pen. 'We've got a few questions, mainly background, that you two might be able—'

'Oh, *anything* we can do to help,' said Irene eagerly. '*Anything.*'

'We've read both your police statements,' said Strike, 'so unless—'

'Oh dear,' interrupted Irene, pulling a mock-fearful expression. 'You know all about me being a naughty girl, then? About the dentist and that, do you? There'll be young girls out there doing it, right now, fibbing to get a few hours off, but just my luck I picked the day Margot – sorry, I don't mean that,' Irene said, catching herself. 'I don't. This is how I get myself in trouble,' she said, with a little laugh. '*Steady, girl*, Eddie would've said, wouldn't he Jan?' she said, tapping her friend on the arm. 'Wouldn't he have said, *steady, girl*?'

'He would,' said Janice, smiling and nodding.

'I was going to say,' Strike continued, 'that unless either of you have got anything to add—'

'Oh, don't think we haven't thought about it,' interrupted Irene again. 'If we'd remembered anything else we'd have been *straight* down the police station, wouldn't we, Jan?'

'—I'd like to clarify a few points.

'Mrs Beattie,' said Strike, looking at Janice, who was absent-mindedly stroking the underside of her wedding ring, which was the only piece of jewellery she wore, 'one thing that struck me when I read the police notes was how many times Inspector Talbot—'

'Oh, you and me both, Cameron,' Irene interrupted eagerly, before Janice could open her mouth. 'You and me both! I know *exactly* what you're going to ask – *why did he keep pestering Jan?* I told her at the time – didn't I, Jan? – I said, this isn't right, you should report it, but you didn't, did you? I mean, I know he was having a breakdown, blah blah blah – *you'll* know all about that,' she said, with a nod towards Strike, that simultaneously conveyed a compliment and an eagerness to fill him in should he require it, 'but ill men are still *men*, aren't they?'

'Mrs Beattie,' repeated Strike, slightly louder, 'why do *you* think Talbot kept interviewing you?'

Irene took the broad hint and allowed Janice to answer, but her self-restraint lasted only until Janice hit her stride, at which point she set up a murmured counterpoint, echoing Janice's words, adding agreement and emphasis, and giving the general impression that she feared that if she did not make a noise every few seconds, Strike might forget she was there.

'I dunno, in all honesty,' said Janice, still fiddling with her wedding ring. 'The first few times 'e saw me it was straightforward questions—'

'At first it was, yeah,' murmured Irene, nodding along.

'—about what I done that day, you know, what I could tell 'im about people coming to see Margot, because I knew a lot of the patients—'

'We got to know them all, working at the practice,' said Irene, nodding.

'—but then, it was like 'e thought I 'ad . . . well, *special powers*. I know that sounds bonkers, but I don't fink—'

'Oho, well, *I* do,' said Irene, her eyes on Strike.

'—no, I honestly *don't* fink 'e was – you know –' Janice

seemed embarrassed even to say it, '*keen* on me. 'E *did* ask inappropriate things, but I could tell 'e wasn't right, you know – in the 'ead. It was an 'orrible position to be in, honestly,' Janice said, switching her gaze to Robin. 'I didn't feel like I could *tell* anyone. 'E was police! I just 'ad to keep sitting there while 'e asked me about me *dreams*. And after the first few interviews that's all he wanted to talk about, me past boyfriends and stuff, nothing about Margot or the patients—'

'He was interested in *one* patient, though, wasn't—?' began Robin.

'Duckworth!' piped up Irene excitedly.

'Douthwaite,' said Strike.

'Douthwaite, yes, that's who I meant,' muttered Irene, and to cover a slight embarrassment she helped herself to a biscuit, which meant that for a few moments, at least, Janice was able to talk uninterrupted.

'Yeah, 'e did ask me about Steve,' said Janice, nodding, ''cause 'e lived in my block of flats, down Percival Street.'

'Did you know Douthwaite well?' asked Robin.

'Not really. Ackshly, I never knew 'im at all until 'e got beaten up. I come 'ome late and found a load of people on the landing with 'im. People knew I was a nurse so – there's me wiv my son Kevin under one arm and shopping in the other hand – but Steve was in a right state, so I 'ad to 'elp. 'E didn't want the police called, but 'e'd 'ad the sort of beating that can leave you wiv internal injuries. The ovver geezer 'ad used a bat. Jealous 'usband —'

'Who had *completely* the wrong end of the stick, didn't he?' interrupted Irene. 'Because Douthwaite was queer!' she said, with a shout of laughter. 'He was only *friends* with the wife, but this jealous idiot thinks—'

'Well, I don't *know* if Steve was queer—' began Janice, but there was no stopping Irene.

'—man – woman – two and two makes five! My Eddie was *exactly the same* – Jan, bear me out, what was Eddie like?' she said, tapping Janice's arm again. '*Exactly* the same, wasn't he? I remember once, I said, "Eddie, you think if I so much *look* at a man – he can be queer, he can be Welsh –" But after you told me, Jan, I thought, yeah, that Duckworth – Douth-thing – *is* a bit camp. When he came in the surgery afterwards, I could see it. Good-looking, but a bit soft.'

'But I don't know wevver 'e *was* queer, Irene, I didn't know 'im well enough to—'

'He kept coming back to see you,' Irene chided her. 'You told me he did. Kept coming back to your place for tea and sympathy and telling you all his problems.'

'It were only a couple of times,' said Janice. 'We'd chat, passing on the stairs, and one time 'e 'elped me with my shopping and come in for a cup of tea.'

'But he asked you—' prompted Irene.

'I'm getting to that, dear,' said Janice, with what Strike thought was remarkable patience. ''E was getting 'eadaches,' she told Strike and Robin, 'an' I told 'im 'e needed to go and see a doctor for 'eadaches, I couldn't diagnose 'im. I mean, I felt a bit sorry for 'im, but I didn't want to get in the 'abit of 'olding out-of-hours clinics in me flat. I 'ad Kevin to look after.'

'So you think Douthwaite's visits to Margot were because of his health?' asked Robin. 'Not because he had a romantic interest in—?'

'He *did* send her chocolates one time,' said Irene, 'but if you ask me, it was more like she was an agony aunt.'

'Well, 'e 'ad these 'ead pains and 'e was def'nitely nervous. Depressed, maybe,' said Janice. 'Everyone 'ad blamed him for what happened to that poor girl 'oo killed 'erself, but I don't know . . . and some of me ovver neighbours told me there were young men coming in and out of his flat—'

'There you are,' said Irene triumphantly. 'Queer!'

'Might not've been that,' said Janice. 'Coulda just been 'is mates, or drugs, or stuff falling off the back of a lorry . . . One fing I do know, 'cause people talked, locally: the 'usband of that girl who killed 'erself was knockin' twelve bells out of 'er. Tragedy, really. But the papers pinned it all on Steve an' 'e ran. Well, sex sells better'n domestic violence, doesn't it? If you find Steve,' she added, 'tell 'im I said 'ello. It wasn't fair, what the papers did.'

Robin had been trained by Strike to organise her interviews and notes into the categories of people, places and things. She now asked both women,

'Were there any other patients you can ever remember giving cause for alarm at the practice, or perhaps having an unusual relationship with Marg—?'

'*Well*,' said Irene, '*remember*, Jan, there was that one with the beard down to here . . . ' She placed her hand at waist level, ' . . . remember? *What* was he called? Apton? Applethorpe? Jan, you remember. You *do* remember, Jan, he stank like a tramp and you had to go round his house once. He used to wander around near St John's. I think he lived on Clerkenwell Road. Sometimes he had his kid with him. Really *funny*-looking kid. Massive ears.'

'Oh, *them*,' said Janice, her frown disappearing. 'But they weren't Margot's—'

'Well, *he* was stopping people on the street, afterwards, telling them he'd killed Margot!' Irene told Strike excitedly. 'Yeah! He was! He stopped Dorothy! Of course, *Dorothy* wasn't going to tell the police, not Dorothy, she was all "load of stuff and nonsense", "he's a lunatic", but I said to her, "What if he actually *did* do it, Dorothy, and you haven't told anyone?" Now, Applethorpe was a proper nutcase. He had a girl locked up—'

'She weren't *locked up*, Irene,' said Janice, for the first time showing a trace of impatience. 'Social work said she were agoraphobic, but she weren't being kept there against 'er *will*—'

'She was peculiar,' said Irene stubbornly. 'You told me she was. I think someone should've taken the kid away, personally. You said the flat was filthy—'

'You can't take people's children off them because they 'aven't cleaned the 'ouse!' said Janice firmly. She turned back to Strike and Robin. 'Yeah, I visited the Applethorpes, just the once, but I don't fink they ever met Margot. See, it was diff'rent then: doctors 'ad their own lists, and the Applethorpes were registered with Brenner. 'E asked me to go round for 'im, check on the kid.'

'Do you remember the address? Street name?'

'Oh gawd,' said Janice, frowning. 'Yeah, I think it was Clerkenwell Road. I think so. See, I only visited the once. The kid 'adn't been well and Dr Brenner wanted 'im checked and 'e'd never make an 'ouse call if 'e could avoid it. Anyway, the kid was on the mend, but I spotted right off the dad was—'

'Nutcase—' said Irene, nodding along.

'—jittery, bit out of it,' said Janice. 'I went in the kitchen to wash my 'ands and there was a load of benzedrine lying in full view on the worktop. I warned both the parents, now the kid was walking, to put it away somewhere safe—'

'*Really* funny-looking kid,' interposed Irene.

'—and I went to Brenner after, an' I said, "Dr Brenner, that man's abusing benzedrine." It was proper addictive, we all knew it by then, even in '74. 'Course, Brenner thought I was being *presumptuous*, queryin' 'is prescriptions. But I was worried, so I called social work wivout telling Brenner, and they were very good. They were already keeping a close eye on the family.'

'But the mother—' said Irene.

'You can't decide for other people what makes 'em 'appy, Irene!' said Janice. 'The mum loved that kid, even if the dad was – well, 'e *was* odd, poor sod,' Janice conceded. ''E thought 'e was a kind of – I don't know what you'd call it – a guru, or a magic man. Thought 'e could put the evil eye on people. 'E told me that durin' the 'ouse call. You do meet people wiv weird ideas, nursin'. I just used to say, "Really? 'Ow interesting." There's no point challenging 'em. But Applethorpe thought he could ill-wish people – that's what we used to call it, in the old days. 'E was worried 'is little boy 'ad got German measles because he'd got cross with 'im. 'E said 'e could do that to people . . . He died 'imself, poor sod. Year after Margot vanished.'

'Did he?' said Irene, with a trace of disappointment.

'Yeah. It would've been after you left, after you married Eddie. I remember, street cleaners found him early in the morning, curled up and dead under the Walter Street bridge. 'Eart attack. Keeled over and there was nobody there to 'elp him. Wasn't that old, neither. I remember Dr Brenner being a bit twitchy about it.'

'Why was that?' asked Strike.

'Well, 'e'd prescribed the Bennies the man was abusin', 'adn't 'e?'

To Robin's surprise, a fleeting smile passed over Strike's face.

'But it weren't just Applethorpe,' Janice went on, who didn't seem to have noticed anything odd in Strike's response. 'There was—'

'Oh, *tons* of people swore blind they'd heard something, or had a hunch, blah blah blah,' said Irene, rolling her eyes, 'and there was us, you know, who were actually *involved*, it was terrible, just – excuse me,' she said, putting her hand on her stomach, 'I must just nip to the – sorry.'

Irene left the room in something of a hurry. Janice looked after her, and it was hard, given her naturally smiley face, to tell whether she was more concerned or amused.

'She'll be fine,' she told Strike and Robin quietly. 'I 'ave *told* 'er the doc's probably right tellin' 'er to lay off the spicy food, but she wanted a curry last night . . . she gets lonely. Rings me up to come over. I stayed overnight. Eddie only died last year. Nearly ninety, bless 'im. 'E *adored* Irene and the girls. She misses 'im something rotten.'

'Were you about to tell us somebody else had claimed to know what happened to Margot?' Strike prompted her gently.

'What? Oh, yeah . . . Charlie Ramage. 'E 'ad an 'ot tub and sauna business. Wealfy man, so you'd think 'e 'ad better things to do with 'is time than make up stories, but there you go, people are funny.'

'What did he say?' asked Robin.

'Well, see, motorbikes were Charlie's 'obby. 'E 'ad loads of 'em, and 'e used to go on these long rides all over the country. 'E 'ad a bad smash and 'e was at 'ome wiv two broken legs, so I was droppin' in sev'ral times a week . . . this would've been a good two years after Margot disappeared. Well, Charlie was a man 'oo liked to talk, and one day, out of a clear blue sky, 'e swears blind 'e met Margot, about a week after she went missing, in Leamington Spa. But, you know,' Janice said, shaking her head. 'I didn't take it very serious. Lovely man, but like I say, 'e liked to talk.'

'What exactly did he tell you?' asked Robin.

'Said 'e'd been on one of 'is bike trips up north, and 'e stopped outside this big church in Leamington Spa, and 'e was leaning against the wall 'avin' a cup of tea an' a sandwich, an' there was this woman walking in the graveyard on the other side of the railings, lookin' at the graves. Not like she was in mourning or anyfing, just interested. Black 'air, accordin' to

Charlie. An' 'e called out to 'er, "Nice place, innit?" and she turned to look at 'im and – well, 'e swore blind it was Margot Bamborough, wiv 'er 'air dyed. 'E said 'e told 'er she looked familiar and she looked upset and hurried off.'

'And he claimed this happened a week after she disappeared?' asked Robin.

'Yeah, 'e said 'e recognised 'er because 'er picture was still all over the papers at the time. So I says, "Did you go to the police about this, Charlie?" And 'e says, "Yeah, I did," an' 'e told me 'e was friends with a policeman, quite an 'igh up bloke, an' 'e told 'is friend. But I never saw or 'eard anyfing about it after, so, you know . . . '

'Ramage told you this story in 1976?' Strike asked, making a note.

'Yeah, musta been,' said Janice, frowning in an effort to remember, as Irene walked back into the room. 'Because they'd got Creed by then. That's 'ow it came up. 'E'd been reading about the trial in the papers and then 'e says, cool as you like, "Well, I don't fink 'e done anyfing to Margot Bamborough, because I reckon I seen 'er after she disappeared."'

'Did Margot have any connection with Leamington Spa, as far as you know?' asked Robin.

'What's this?' said Irene sharply.

'Nuffing,' said Janice. 'Just a stupid story some patient told me. Margot in a graveyard wiv dyed hair. *You* know.'

'In Leamington Spa?' said Irene, looking displeased. Robin had the impression that she greatly resented having left Janice in the spotlight while she was forced back to the bathroom. 'You never told me that. Why didn't you tell me?'

'Oh . . . well, it was in '76,' said Janice, looking slightly cowed. 'You must've just 'ad Sharon. You 'ad better fings to fink about than Charlie Ramage telling porkies.'

Irene helped herself to another biscuit, frowning slightly.

'I'd like to move on to the practice itself,' said Strike. 'How did you find Margot to—'

'To work with?' said Irene, loudly, who seemed to feel it was her turn, having missed out on several minutes of Strike's attention. 'Well, speaking *personally*—'

Her pause was that of an epicure, savouring the prospect of coming pleasure.

'—to be *totally* honest, she was one of those people who think they know best about *everything*. She'd tell you how to live your life, how to do the filing, how to make a cup of tea, blah blah blah—'

'Oh, Irene, she weren't *that* bad,' muttered Janice. 'I liked—'

'Jan, *come on*,' said Irene loftily. 'She'd never got over being the clever clogs in her family and thought all the rest of us were thick as mince! Well, maybe she didn't think *you* were,' said Irene, with an eye roll, as her friend shook her head, 'but she did me. Treated me like a moron. *Patronising* isn't it. Now, I didn't dislike her!' Irene added quickly. 'Not *dislike*. But she was *picky*. Veee-ry pleased with herself. We'd *completely* forgotten we came from a two-up, two-down in Stepney, put it that way.'

'How did *you* find her?' Robin asked Janice.

'Well—' began Janice, but Irene talked over her.

'*Snobby*. Jan, *come on*. She marries herself a rich consultant – *that* was no two-up, two-down, that place out in Ham! Proper eye-opener it was, seeing what she'd married into, and then she has the gall to come into work preaching the liberated life to the rest of us: marriage isn't the be all and end all, don't stop your career, blah blah blah. And *always* finding fault.'

'What did she—?'

'How you answered the phone, how you spoke to patients, how you dressed, even – *"Irene, I don't think that top's appropriate for work."* She was a bloody Bunny Girl! The hypocrisy of her! I didn't dislike her,' Irene insisted. 'I didn't, truly, I'm just trying to give you the full – oh, and she wouldn't let us make her hot drinks, would she, Jan? Neither of the *other* two doctors ever complained we didn't know what to do with a teabag.'

'That's not why—' began Janice.

'Jan, *come on*, you *remember* how fussy—'

'Why would *you* say she didn't like people making her drinks?' Strike asked Janice. Robin could tell that his patience was wearing thin with Irene.

'Oh, that was 'cause of when I was washing up mugs one day,' said Janice. 'I tipped the dregs out of Dr Brenner's and I found an—'

'*Atomal* pill, wasn't it?' asked Irene.

'—Amytal capsule, stuck to the bottom. I knew what it was from the col—'

'Blue,' interjected Irene, nodding, 'weren't they?'

'Blue 'Eavens, they used to call them on the street, yeah,' said Janice. 'Downers. I always made sure everyone knew I didn't 'ave nuffing like that in me nurse's bag, when I was out makin' 'ouse calls. You 'ad to be careful, in case you got mugged.'

'How did you know it was Dr Brenner's cup?' asked Strike.

''E always used the same one, wiv his old university's coat of arms on,' said Janice. 'There'd 'ave been 'ell to pay if anyone else touched it.' She hesitated, 'I don't know wevver – if you've talked to Dr Gupta—'

'We know Dr Brenner was addicted to barbiturates,' Strike said. Janice looked relieved.

'Right – well, I knew 'e must've dropped it in there, accidental, when he was taking some. Probably didn't realise, thought it 'ad rolled away on the floor. There'd have been a lot of questions asked, usually, at a doctor's surgery, finding drugs in a drink. If something gets into someone's tea by accident, that's serious.'

'How much harm would a single capsule—?' Robin began.

'Oh, no *real* harm,' said Irene knowledgeably, 'would it, Jan?'

'No, a single capsule, that's not even a full dose,' said Janice. 'You'd've felt a bit sleepy, that's all. Anyway, Margot come out the back to make the tea when I was tryin' to get the pill off the bottom of the mug with a teaspoon. We 'ad a sink and a kettle and a fridge just outside the nurse's room. She saw me trying to scrape the pill out. So it weren't *fussiness*, 'er making 'er own drinks after that. It were precautionary. I took extra care to make sure I was drinking out of me own mug, as well.'

'Did you tell Margot how you thought the pill had got in the tea?' asked Robin.

'No,' said Janice, 'because Dr Gupta 'ad asked me not to mention Brenner's problem, so I just said "must've been an accident", which was *technically* true. I expected her to call a staff meeting and hold an enquiry—'

'Ah, well, you know my theory about why she didn't do that,' said Irene.

'Irene,' said Janice, shaking her head. 'Honestly—'

'*My* theory,' said Irene, ignoring Janice, 'is Margot thought someone *else* had put the pill in Brenner's drink, and if you're asking me *who*—'

'*Irene*,' said Janice again, clearly urging restraint, but Irene was unstoppable.

'—I'll tell you – *Gloria*. That girl was as rough as hell and she came from a criminal background – no, I'm saying it, Jan, I'm sure Cameron wants to know *everything* what was going on at that practice—'

''Ow can Gloria putting something in Brenner's tea – and by the way,' Janice said to Strike and Robin, '*I* don't fink she did—'

'Well, as I was on the desk with Gloria every day, Jan,' said Irene loftily, '*I* knew what she was really like—'

'— but even if she *did* put the pill in 'is tea, Irene, 'ow could that 'ave anything to do with Margot disappearin'?'

'*I* don't know,' said Irene, who seemed to be getting cross, 'but they're interested in who was working there and what went on – aren't you?' she demanded of Strike, who nodded. With a '*See?*' to Janice, Irene plunged on, 'So: Gloria came from a really rough family, a Little Italy family—'

Janice tried to protest, but Irene overrode her again.

'She *did*, Jan! One of her brothers was drug dealing, that sort of thing, she told me so! That Atomal capsule might not've come from Brenner's store at all! She could've got it off one of her brothers. Gloria *hated* Brenner. He was a miserable old sod, all right, always having a go at us. She said to me once, "Imagine living with him. If I was his sister I'd poison the old bastard's food," and Margot heard her, and told her off, because there were patients in the waiting room, and it wasn't professional, saying something like that about one of the doctors.

'Anyway, when Margot never did anything about the pill in Brenner's mug, I thought, *that's because she knows who did it*. She didn't want her little pet in trouble. Gloria was her *project*, see. Gloria spent half her time in Margot's consulting room being lectured on feminism while I was left to hold the fort on reception . . . she'd've let Gloria away with murder, Margot would. Total blind spot.'

'Do either of you know where Gloria is now?' asked Strike.

'No idea. She left not long after Margot disappeared,' said Irene.

'I never saw her again after she left the practice,' said Janice, who looked uncomfortable, 'but Irene, I don't fink we should be flinging accusations—'

'Do me a favour,' said Irene abruptly to her friend, a hand

on her stomach, 'and fetch that medicine off the top of the fridge for me, will you? I'm still not right. And would anyone like more tea or coffee while Jan's there?'

Janice got up uncomplainingly, collected empty cups, loaded the tray and set off for the kitchen. Robin got up to open the door for her, and Janice smiled at her as she passed. While Janice's footsteps padded away down the thickly carpeted hall, Irene said, unsmiling,

'*Poor* Jan. She's had an awful life, really. Like something out of Dickens, her childhood. Eddie and I helped her out financially a few times, after Beattie left her. She calls herself "Beattie", but he never married her, you know,' said Irene. 'Awful, isn't it? And they had a kid, too. I don't think he ever really wanted to be there, and then he walked out. Larry, though – I mean, he wasn't the brightest tool in the box,' Irene laughed a little, 'but he thought the world of her. I think she thought she could do better at first – Larry worked for Eddie, you know – not on the management side, he was just a builder, but in the end, I think she realised – well, you know, not everyone's prepared to take on a kid . . . '

'Could I ask you about the threatening notes to Margot you saw, Mrs Hickson?'

'Oh, yes, of course,' said Irene, pleased. 'So *you* believe me, do you? Because the police didn't.'

'There were two, you said in your statement?'

'That's right. I wouldn't've opened the first one, only Dorothy was off, and Dr Brenner told me to sort out the post. Dorothy was *never* off usually. It was because her son was having his tonsils out. Spoiled little so-and-so, he was. That was the *only* time I ever saw her upset, when she told me she was taking him into hospital the next day. Hard as nails, usually – but she was a widow, and he was all she had.'

Janice reappeared with refilled teapot and cafetière. Robin

got up and took the heavy teapot and cafetière off the tray for her. Janice accepted her help with a smile and a whispered 'thanks', so that she didn't interrupt Irene.

'What did the note say?' Strike asked.

'Well, it's *ages* ago, now,' said Irene. Janice handed her a packet of indigestion tablets, which Irene took with a brief smile, but no thanks. 'But from what I remember . . .' she popped pills out of the blister pack, 'let me see, I want to get this right . . . it was *very* rude. It called Margot the c-word, I remember *that*. And said hellfire waited for women like her.'

'Was it typed? Printed?'

'Written,' said Irene. She took a couple of tablets with a sip of tea.

'What about the second one?' said Strike.

'I don't know what that said. I had to go into her consulting room to give her a message, see, and I saw it lying on her desk. Same writing, I recognised it at once. She didn't like me seeing it, I could tell. Screwed it up and threw it in the bin.'

Janice passed round fresh cups of tea and coffee. Irene helped herself to another chocolate biscuit.

'I doubt you'll know,' said Strike, 'but I wondered if you ever had any reason to suspect that Margot was pregnant before she—'

'How d'you know about that?' gasped Irene, looking thunderstruck.

'She *was*?' said Robin.

'Yes!' said Irene. 'See – Jan, don't look like that, honestly – I took a call from a nursing home, while she was out on a house call! They called the practice to confirm she'd be in next day . . .' and she mouthed the next few words, '*for an abortion!*'

'They told you what procedure she was going in for, over the phone?' asked Robin.

For a moment, Irene looked rather confused.

'They – well, no – actually, I – well, I'm not proud of it, but I called the clinic back. Just nosy. You do that kind of thing when you're young, don't you?'

Robin hoped her reciprocal smile looked sincerer than Irene's.

'When was this, Mrs Hickson, can you remember?' Strike asked.

'Not long before she disappeared. Four weeks? Something like that?'

'Before or after the anonymous notes?'

'I don't – after, I think,' said Irene. 'Or was it? I can't remember . . .'

'Did you talk to anyone else about the appointment?'

'Only Jan, and she told me off. Didn't you, Jan?'

'I know you didn't mean any 'arm,' muttered Janice, 'but patient confidentiality—'

'Margot wasn't *our* patient. It's a different thing.'

'And you didn't tell the police about this?' Strike asked her.

'No,' said Irene, 'because I – well, I shouldn't've known, should I? Anyway, how could it have anything to do with her disappearing?'

'Apart from Mrs Beattie, did you tell anyone else about it?'

'No,' said Irene defensively, 'because – I mean, I wouldn't have told anyone *else* – you kept your mouth shut, working at a doctor's surgery. I could've told all kinds of people's secrets, couldn't I? Being a receptionist, I saw files, but of course you didn't say anything, I knew how to keep secrets, it was part of the job . . .'

Expressionless, Strike wrote 'protesting too much' in his notebook.

'I've got another question, Mrs Hickson, and it might be a sensitive one,' Strike said, looking up again. 'I heard you and Margot had a disagreement at the Christmas party.'

'*Oh*,' said Irene, her face falling. '*That*. Yes, well—'

There was a slight pause.

'I was cross about what she'd done to Kevin. Jan's son. Remember, Jan?'

Janice looked confused.

'Come on, Jan, you *do*,' said Irene, tapping Janice's arm again. 'When she took him into her consulting room and blah blah blah.'

'*Oh*,' said Janice. For a moment, Robin had the distinct impression that Janice was truly cross with her friend this time. 'But—'

'You remember,' said Irene, glaring at her.

'I . . . yeah,' said Janice. 'Yeah, I *was* angry about that, all right.'

'Jan had kept him off school,' Irene told Strike. 'Hadn't you, Jan? How old was he, six? And then—'

'What exactly happened?' Strike asked Janice.

'Kev had a tummy ache,' said Janice. 'Well, schoolitis, really. My neighbour 'oo sometimes looked after 'im wasn't well—'

'Basically,' interrupted Irene, 'Jan brought Kevin to work and—'

'Could Mrs Beattie tell the story?' Strike asked.

'Oh – yes, of course!' said Irene. She put her hand back on her abdomen again and stroked it, with a long-suffering air.

'Your usual childminder was ill?' Strike prompted Janice.

'Yeah, but I was s'posed to be at work, so I took Kev wiv me to the practice and give 'im a colouring book. Then I 'ad to change a lady's dressing in the back room, so I put Kev in the waiting room. Irene and Gloria were keeping an eye on him for me. But then Margot – well, she took 'im into her consulting room and examined 'im, stripped 'im off to the waist and everything. She *knew* 'e was my son an' she *knew* why 'e was there, but she took it upon herself . . . I was angry,

I can't lie,' said Janice quietly. 'We 'ad words. I said, "All you 'ad to do was wait until I'd seen the patient and I'd've come in wiv 'im while you looked at him."

'And I've got to say, when I put it to her straight, she backed down right away and apologised. No,' Janice said, because Irene had puffed herself up, 'she *did*, Irene, she apologised, said I was quite right, she shouldn't have seen him without me, but 'e'd been holding his tummy and she acted on instinct. It wasn't badly intentioned. She just, sometimes—'

'—put people's backs up, that's what I'm saying,' said Irene. 'Thought she was above everyone else, she knew best—'

'—rushed in, I was going to say. But she were a good doctor,' said Janice, with quiet firmness. 'You 'ear it all, when you're in people's 'ouses, you 'ear what the patients think of them, and Margot was well liked. She took time. She was kind – she *was*, Irene, I know she got on your wick, but that's what the patients—'

'Oh, well, maybe,' said Irene, with an if-you-say-so inflection. 'But she didn't have much competition at St John's, did she?'

'Were Dr Gupta and Dr Brenner unpopular?' Strike asked.

'Dr Gupta was lovely,' said Janice. 'A very good doctor, although some patients didn't want to see a brown man, and that's the truth. But Brenner was an 'ard man to like. It was only after he died that I understood why he might've—'

Irene gave a huge gasp and then began, unexpectedly, to laugh.

'*Tell them what you collect, Janice.* Go on!' She turned to Strike and Robin. 'If this isn't the *creepiest,* most *morbid*—'

'I don't *collect* 'em,' said Janice, who had turned pink. 'They're just something I like to *save*—'

'*Obituaries!* What d'you think of that? The rest of us collect china or snow globes, blah blah blah, but Janice collects—'

'*It isn't a collection*,' repeated Janice, still pink-faced. 'All it is—' She addressed Robin with a trace of appeal. 'My mum couldn't read—'

'*Imagine*,' said Irene complacently, stroking her stomach. Janice faltered for a moment, then said,

'—yeah, so . . . Dad wasn't bothered about books, but 'e used to bring the paper 'ome, and that's 'ow I learned to read. I used to cut out the best stories. 'Uman interest, I s'pose you'd call them. I've never been that interested in fiction. I can't see the point, things somebody's made up.'

'Oh, I *love* a good novel,' breathed Irene, still rubbing her stomach.

'Anyway . . . I dunno . . . when you read an obituary, you find out 'oo people've *really* been, don't you? If it's someone I know, or I nursed, I keep 'em because, I dunno, I felt like *somebody* should. You get your life written up in the paper – it's an achievement, isn't it?'

'Not if you're Dennis Creed, it isn't,' said Irene. Looking as though she'd said something very clever she reached forwards to take another biscuit, and a deafening fart ripped through the room.

Irene turned scarlet. Robin thought for one horrible moment that Strike was going to laugh, so she said loudly to Janice,

'Did you keep Dr Brenner's obituary?'

'Oh, yeah,' said Janice, who seemed completely unperturbed by the loud noise that had just emanated from Irene. Perhaps she was used to far worse, as a nurse. 'An' it explained *a lot*.'

'In what way?' asked Robin, determinedly not looking at either Strike or Irene.

''E'd been into Bergen-Belsen, one of the first medical men in there.'

'God,' said Robin, shocked.

'I know,' said Janice. ''E never talked about it. I'd never 'ave known, if I 'adn't read it in the paper. What 'e must have seen . . . mounds of bodies, dead kids . . . I read a library book about it. Dreadful. Maybe that's why 'e was the way 'e was, I dunno. I felt sorry, when I read it. I 'adn't seen 'im in years by the time 'e died. Someone showed me the obituary, knowing I'd been at St John's, and I kept it as a record of him. You could forgive Brenner a lot, once you saw what 'e'd witnessed, what 'e'd been through . . . but that's true of everyone, really, innit? Once you know, ev'rything's explained. It's a shame you often *don't* know until it's too late to – you all right, love?' she said to Irene.

In the wake of the fart, Robin suspected that Irene had decided the only dignified cover-up was to emphasise that she was unwell.

'D'you know, I think it's stress,' she said, her hand down the waistband of her trousers. 'It always flares up when I'm . . . sorry,' she said with dignity to Strike and Robin, 'but I'm afraid I don't think I . . . '

'Of course,' said Strike, closing his notebook. 'I think we've asked everything we came for, anyway. Unless there's anything else,' he asked the two women, 'that you've remembered that seems odd, in retrospect, or out of place?'

'We've fort, 'aven't we?' Janice asked Irene. 'All these years . . . we've talked about it, obviously.'

'It *must've* been Creed, mustn't it?' said Irene, with finality. 'What other explanation is there? Where else could she have gone? *Do* you think they'll let you in to see him?' she asked Strike again, with a last flicker of curiosity.

'No idea,' he said, getting to his feet. 'Thanks very much for your hospitality, anyway, and for answering our questions . . . '

Janice saw them out. Irene waved wordlessly as they left the room. Robin could tell that the interview had fallen short of her expectation of enjoyment. Awkward and uncomfortable admissions had been forced from her; the picture she'd painted of her young self had not been, perhaps, everything she would have wished – and nobody, Robin thought, shaking hands with Janice at the door, would particularly enjoy farting loudly in front of strangers.

21

Well then, sayd Artegall, let it be tride.
First in one ballance set the true aside.
He did so first; and then the false he layd
In th'other scale . . .

Edmund Spenser
The Faerie Queene

'Well, I'm no doctor,' said Strike, as they crossed the road back to the Land Rover, 'but I blame the curry.'

'Don't,' said Robin, laughing against her will. She couldn't help but feel a certain vicarious embarrassment.

'You weren't sitting as near her as I was,' said Strike, as he got back into the car. 'I'm guessing lamb bhuna—'

'Seriously,' said Robin, half-laughing, half-disgusted, 'stop.'

As he drew his seatbelt back over himself, Strike said,

'I need a proper drink.'

'There's a decent pub not far from here,' said Robin. 'I looked it up. The Trafalgar Tavern.'

Looking up the pub was doubtless yet another Nice Thing that Robin had chosen to do for his birthday, and Strike wondered whether it was her intention to make him feel guilty. Probably not, he thought, but that, nevertheless, was the effect, so he passed no comment other than to ask,

'What did you think of all that?'

'Well, there were a few cross-currents, weren't there?' said Robin, steering out of the parking space. 'And I think we were told a couple of lies.'

'Me too,' said Strike. 'Which ones did you spot?'

'Irene and Margot's row at the Christmas party, for starters,' said Robin, turning out of Circus Street. 'I don't think it was really about Margot examining Janice's son – although I *do* think Margot examined Kevin without permission.'

'So do I,' said Strike. 'But I agree: I don't think that's what the row was about. Irene forced Janice to tell that story, because she didn't want to admit the truth. Which makes me wonder . . . Irene getting Janice to come to her house, so we can interview them both together: was that so Irene could make sure Janice didn't tell us anything she wouldn't want told? That's the trouble with friends you've had for decades, isn't it? They know too much.'

Robin, who was busy trying to remember the route to the Trafalgar she'd memorised that morning, thought at once about all those stories Ilsa had told her about Strike and Charlotte's relationship. Ilsa had told her Strike had refused an invitation to go over to their house that evening for dinner, claiming that he had a prior arrangement with his sister. Robin found it hard to believe this, given Strike's and Lucy's recent row. Perhaps she was being paranoid, but she'd also wondered whether Strike wasn't avoiding being in her company outside work hours.

'You don't suspect Irene, do you?'

'Only of being a liar, a gossip and a compulsive attention-seeker,' said Strike. 'I don't think she's bright enough to have abducted Margot Bamborough and not given herself away in forty years. On the other hand, lies are always interesting. Anything else catch your interest?'

'Yes. There was something funny about that Leamington Spa story, or rather, Irene's reaction when she heard Janice talking about it . . . I think Leamington Spa meant something to her. And it was odd that Janice *hadn't* told her what that patient said. You'd think she definitely would have done, given that they're best friends, and they both knew Margot, and they've stayed in touch all these years. Even if Janice thought that man Ramage was making it all up, why wouldn't she tell Irene?'

'Another good point,' said Strike, looking thoughtfully at the neo-classical façade of the National Maritime Museum as they drove past wide stretches of beautifully manicured emerald lawn. 'What did you think of Janice?'

'Well, when we were allowed to hear her speak, she seemed quite decent,' said Robin cautiously. 'She seemed fair-minded about Margot and Douthwaite. Why she puts up with being treated as Irene's skivvy, though . . .'

'Some people need to be needed . . . and there might be a sense of obligation, if Irene was telling the truth about her and her husband helping Janice out financially when she needed it.'

Strike spotted the pub Robin had chosen from a distance. Large and opulent-looking, with many balconies and awnings, not to mention window-baskets and coats of arms, it stood on the bank of the Thames. Robin parked and they proceeded past black iron bollards to the paved area where many wooden tables afforded a view over the river, in the midst of which a life-size black statue of the diminutive Lord Nelson faced the water.

'See?' said Robin, 'you can sit outside and smoke.'

'Isn't it a bit cold?' said Strike.

'This coat's padded. I'll get the—'

'No, I will,' said Strike firmly. 'What d'you want?

'Just a lime and soda, please, as I'm driving.'

As Strike walked into the pub, there was a sudden chorus of 'Happy Birthday to You'. For a split-second, seeing helium balloons in the corner, he was horror-struck, thinking that Robin had brought him here for a surprise party; but a bare heartbeat later, it registered that he didn't recognise a single face, and that the balloons formed the figure 80. A tiny woman with lavender hair was beaming at the top of a table full of family: flashes went off as she blew out the candles on a large chocolate cake. Applause and cheers followed, and a toddler blew a feathered whistle.

Strike headed towards the bar, still slightly shaken, taking himself to task for having imagined, for a moment, that Robin would have arranged a surprise party for him. Even Charlotte, with whom he'd had the longest and closest relationship of his life, had never done that. Indeed, Charlotte had never allowed anything as mundane as his birthday to interfere with her own whims and moods. On Strike's twenty-seventh, when she'd been going through one of her intermittent phases of either rampant jealousy, or rage at his refusal to give up the army (the precise causes of their many scenes and rows tended to blur in his mind), she'd thrown his wrapped gift out of a third-floor window in front of him.

But, of course, there were other memories. His thirty-third birthday, for instance. He'd just been discharged from Selly Oak hospital, and was walking for the first time on a prosthesis, and Charlotte had taken him back to her flat in Notting Hill, cooked for him, and returned from the kitchen at the end of the meal holding two cups of coffee, stark naked and more beautiful than any woman he had ever seen. He'd laughed and gasped at the same time. He hadn't had sex for nearly two years. The night that had followed would probably never be forgotten by him, nor the way she had sobbed in his arms afterwards, telling him that he was the only man for her, that she was afraid of what she felt, afraid that she was evil for not regretting his missing lower leg if it brought her back to him, if it meant that, at last, she could look after him as he had always looked after her. And close to midnight, Strike had proposed to her, and they'd made love again, and then talked through to dawn about how he was going to start his detective agency, and she'd told him she didn't want a ring, that he was to save his money for his new career, at which he would be magnificent.

Drinks and crisps purchased, Strike returned to Robin, who was sitting on an outside bench, hands in her pockets, looking glum.

'Cheer up,' said Strike, speaking to himself as much as to her.

'Sorry,' said Robin, though she didn't really know why she was apologising.

He sat down beside her, rather than opposite, so both of them faced the river. There was a small shingle beach below them, and waves lapped the cold pebbles. On the opposite bank rose the steel-coloured office blocks of Canary Wharf; to their left, the Shard. The river was the colour of lead on this cold November day. Strike tore one of the crisp packets down the middle so that both could help themselves. Wishing she'd asked for coffee instead of a cold drink, Robin took a sip of her lime and soda, ate a couple of crisps, returned her hands to her pockets, then said,

'I know this isn't the attitude, but honestly . . . I don't think we're going to find out what happened to Margot Bamborough.'

'What's brought this on?'

'I suppose Irene misremembering names . . . Janice going along with her, covering up the reason for the Christmas party row . . . it's such a long time ago. People are under no obligation to tell the truth to us now, even if they can remember it. Factor in people getting wedded to old theories, like that whole thing about Gloria and the pill in Brenner's mug, and people wanting to make themselves important, pretending to know things and . . . well, I'm starting to think we're attempting the impossible here.'

A wave of tiredness had swept over Robin while sitting

in the cold, waiting for Strike, and in its wake had come hopelessness.

'Pull yourself together,' said Strike bracingly. 'We've already found out two big things the police never knew.' He pulled out his cigarettes, lit one, then said, 'Firstly: there was a big stock of barbiturates on the premises where Margot worked. Secondly: Margot Bamborough might well have had an abortion.

'Taking the barbiturates first,' he said, 'are we overlooking something very obvious, which is that there were means on the premises to put someone to sleep?'

'Margot wasn't put to sleep,' said Robin, gloomily munching crisps. 'She walked out of there.'

'Only if we assume—'

'—Gloria wasn't lying. I know,' said Robin. 'But how do she and Theo – because Theo's still got to be in on it, hasn't she? How did Gloria and Theo administer enough barbiturates to render Margot unconscious? Don't forget, if Irene's telling the truth, Margot wasn't letting anyone else make her drinks at that point. And from what Janice said about dosage, you'd need a lot of pills to make someone actually unconscious.'

'Well reasoned. So, going back to that little story about the pill in the tea—'

'Didn't you believe it?'

'I did,' said Strike, 'because it seems a totally pointless lie. It's not interesting enough to make an exciting anecdote, is it, a single pill? It does reopen the question of whether Margot knew about or suspected Brenner's addiction, though. She might've noticed him being odd in his manner. Downers would make him drowsy. Perhaps she'd seen he was slow on the uptake. Everything we've found out about Margot suggests that if she thought Brenner was behaving unprofessionally, or might be dangerous to patients, she'd have waded straight in and confronted him. And we've just heard a lot of interesting background on Brenner, who sounds like a traumatised, unhappy and lonely man. What if Margot threatened him with being struck off? Loss of status and prestige, to a man who has virtually nothing else in his life? People have killed for less.'

'He left the surgery before she did, that night.'

'What if he waited for her? Offered her a lift?'

'If he did, I think she'd have been suspicious,' said Robin. 'Not that he wanted to hurt her, but that he was going to shout at her, which would've been in character, from what we know of *him*. I'd rather have walked in the rain, personally. And she was a lot younger than him, and tall and fit. I can't remember now where he lived . . .'

'With his unmarried sister, about twenty minutes' drive from the practice. The sister said he'd arrived home at the usual time. A dog-walking neighbour confirmed they'd seen him through the window round about eleven . . .

'But I can think of one other possibility regarding those barbiturates,' Strike went on. 'As Janice pointed out, they had street value, and by the sounds of it, Brenner had amassed a big stock of them. We've got to consider the possibility that some outsider knew there were valuable drugs on the premises, set out to nick them, and Margot got in the way.'

'Which takes us back to Margot dying on the premises, which means—'

'Gloria and Theo come back into the frame. Gloria and Theo might have planned to take the drugs themselves. And we've just heard—'

'—about the drug-dealing brother,' said Robin.

'Why the sceptical tone?'

'Irene was determined to have a go at Gloria, wasn't she?'

'She was, yeah, but the fact that Gloria had a drug-dealing brother is information worth knowing, as is the fact that there were a stack of drugs on the premises that were ripe for nicking. Brenner wouldn't have wanted to admit he had them in the first place, so probably wouldn't have reported the theft, which makes for a situation open to exploitation.'

'A criminal brother doesn't make a person criminal in themselves.'

'Agreed, but it makes me even keener to find Gloria. The term "person of interest" fits her pretty accurately . . .

'And then there's the abortion,' said Strike. 'If Irene's telling the truth about the nursing home calling to confirm the appointment—'

'*If*,' said Robin.

'I don't think that was a lie,' said Strike. 'For the opposite reason to the pill in Brenner's cup. That lie's too big. People don't make things like that up. Anyway, she told Janice about it at the time, and their little row about patient confidentiality rings true. And C. B. Oakden must've based the story on something. I wouldn't be at all surprised if that tip-off came from Irene. She doesn't strike me as a woman who'd turn down a chance to speculate or gossip.'

Robin said nothing. She'd only once in her life had to face the possibility that she might be pregnant, and could still remember the relief that had flooded her when it became clear that she wasn't, and wouldn't have to face still more contact with strangers, and another intimate procedure, more blood, more pain.

Imagine aborting your husband's child, she thought. Could Margot really have done that, when she already had that child's sister at home? What had been going through her mind, a month before she disappeared? Perhaps she'd been quietly breaking down, like Talbot? The past few years had taught Robin how very mysterious human beings were, even to those who thought they knew them best. Infidelity and bigamy, kinks and fetishes, theft and fraud, stalking and harassment:

she'd now delved into so many secret lives she'd lost count. Nor did she hold herself superior to any of the deceived and duped who came to the agency, craving truth. Hadn't she thought she knew her own husband back to front? How many hundreds of nights had they lain entwined like Siamese twins, whispering confidences and sharing laughter in the dark? She'd spent nearly half her life with Matthew, and not until a hard, bright diamond ear stud had appeared in their bed had she realised that he was living a life apart, and was not, and perhaps never had been, the man she thought she knew.

'You don't want to think she had an abortion,' said Strike, correctly deducing at least part of the reason for Robin's silence. She didn't answer, instead asking,

'You haven't heard back from her friend Oonagh, have you?'

'Didn't I tell you?' said Strike. 'Yeah, I got an email yesterday. She *is* a retired vicar, and she'd be delighted to meet us when she comes down to London to do some Christmas shopping. Date to be confirmed.'

'That's good,' said Robin. 'You know, I'd like to talk to someone who actually *liked* Margot.'

'Gupta liked her,' said Strike. 'And Janice, she's just said so.'

Robin ripped open the second bag of crisps.

'Which is what you'd expect, isn't it?' she said. 'That people would at least *pretend* they liked Margot, after what happened. But Irene didn't. Don't you find it a bit ... *excessive* ... to be holding on to that much resentment, forty years later? She really put the boot in. Wouldn't you think it was ... I don't know, more *politic* ... '

'To claim to be friends?'

'Yes ... but maybe Irene knew there were far too many witnesses to the fact that they *weren't* friends. What did you think of the anonymous notes? True or false?'

'Good question,' said Strike, scratching his chin. 'Irene really enjoyed telling us Margot had been called "the c-word", but "hellfire" doesn't sound like the kind of thing she'd invent. I'd have expected something more in the "uppity bitch" line.'

He drew out his notebook again, and scanned the notes he'd made of the interview.

'Well, we still need to check these leads out, for what they're worth. Why don't you follow up Charlie Ramage and Leamington Spa, and I'll look into the Bennie-abusing Applethorpe?'

'You just did it again,' said Robin.

'Did what?'

'Smirked when you said "Bennies". What's so funny about benzedrine?'

'Oh—' Strike chuckled. 'I was just reminded of something my Uncle Ted told me. Did you ever watch *Crossroads*?'

'What's *Crossroads*?'

'I always forget how much younger you are,' Strike said. 'It was a daytime soap opera and it had a character in it called Benny. He was – well, these days you'd call him special needs. Simple. He wore a woolly hat. Iconic character, in his way.'

'You were thinking of him?' said Robin. It didn't seem particularly amusing.

'No, but you need to know about him to understand the next bit. I assume you know about the Falklands War.'

'I'm younger than you, Strike. I'm not pig-ignorant.'

'OK, right. So, the British troops who went over there – Ted was there, 1982 – nicknamed the locals "Bennies", after the character on *Crossroads*. Command gets wind of this, and the order comes down the line, "Stop calling these people we've just liberated Bennies". So,' said Strike, grinning, 'They started calling them "Stills".'

'"Stills"? What does "Stills" mean?'

'"Still Bennies,"' said Strike, and he let out a great roar of laughter. Robin laughed, too, but mostly at Strike's amusement. When his guffaws had subsided, both watched the river for a few seconds, drinking and, in Strike's case, smoking, until he said,

'I'm going to write to the Ministry of Justice. Apply for permission to visit Creed.'

'Seriously?'

'We've got to try. The authorities always thought Creed assaulted or killed more women than he was done for. There was jewellery in his house and bits of clothing nobody ever identified. Just because everyone thinks it's Creed—'

'—doesn't mean it isn't,' agreed Robin, who followed the tortured logic perfectly.

Strike sighed, rubbed his face, cigarette still poking out of his mouth, then said,

'Want to see exactly how crazy Talbot was?'

'Go on.'

Strike pulled the leather-bound notebook out of the inside pocket of his coat and handed it to her. Robin opened it and turned the pages in silence.

They were covered in strange drawings and diagrams. The writing was small, meticulously neat but cramped. There was much underlining and circling of phrases and symbols. The pentagram recurred. The pages were littered with names, but none connected with the case: Crowley, Lévi, Adams and Schmidt.

'Huh,' she said quietly, stopping on a particularly heavily embellished page on which a goat's head with a third eye looked balefully up at her. 'Look at this . . . '

She bent closer.

'He's using astrological symbols.'

'He's what?' said Strike, frowning down at the page she was perusing.

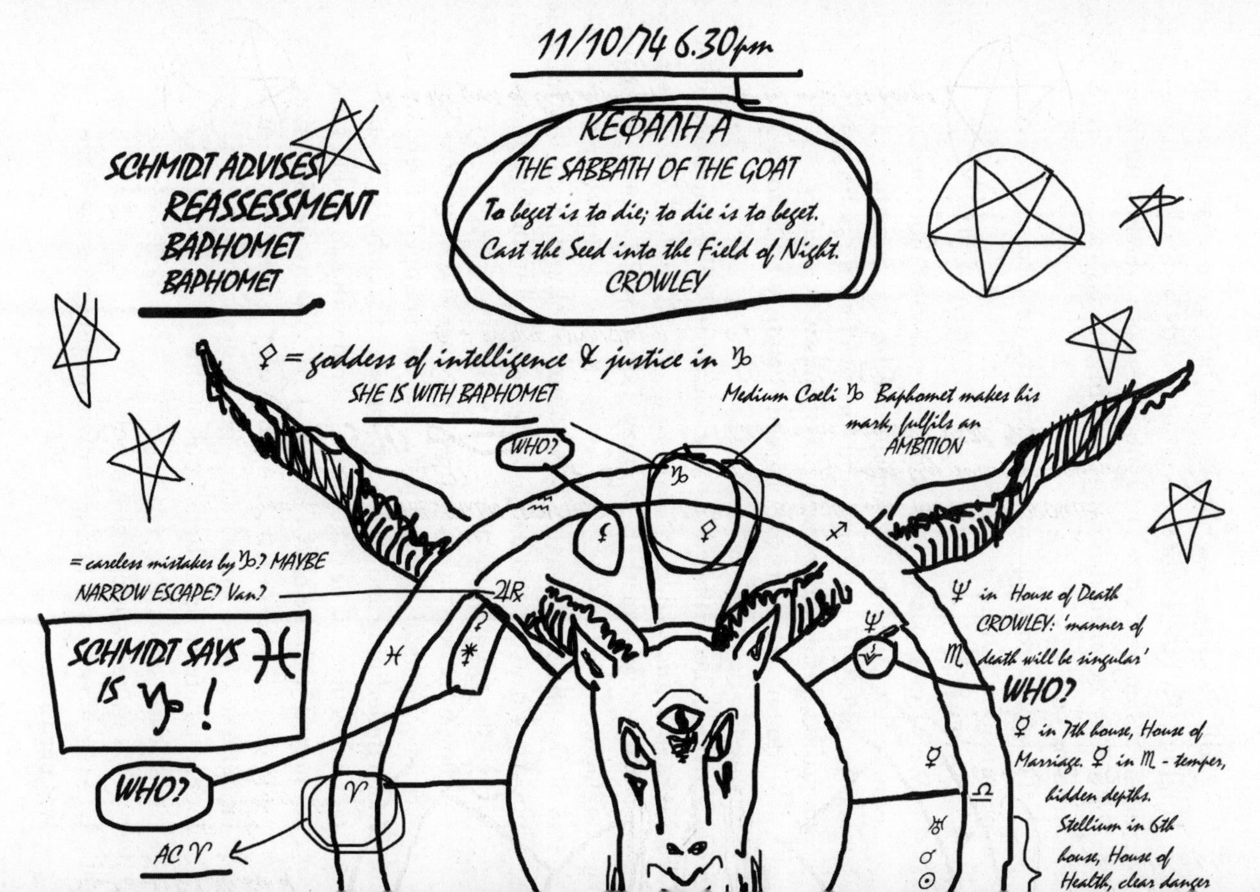

11/10/74 6.30pm
ΚΕΦΑΛΗ Α
THE SABBATH OF THE GOAT
To beget is to die; to die is to beget.
Cast the Seed into the Field of Night.
CROWLEY
SCHMIDT ADVISES
REASSESSMENT
BAPHOMET
BAPHOMET
♀ = goddess of intelligence & justice in ♑
SHE IS WITH BAPHOMET
Medium Coeli ♑ Baphomet makes his mark, fulfils an AMBITION
WHO?
= careless mistakes by ♑? MAYBE NARROW ESCAPE? Van?
SCHMIDT SAYS ♓ IS ♑ !
WHO?
AC ♈
♆ in House of Death
CROWLEY: 'manner of death will be singular'
WHO?
♀ in 7th house, House of Marriage. ♀ in ♏ - temper, hidden depths.
Stellium in 6th house, House of Health, clear danger

Significant? But 'the sign of ♑ is rough, harsh, dark, even blind; It is divinely unscrupulous, sublimely careless of result' CROWLEY
♈ the hair is often light brown or reddish; the eyes are somewhat blue and cold – body well-formed, very rarely accumulates fat' ADAMS so ♈ true subject and clearly not ♑
BUT CLOSE TO SCENE OF ABDUCTION?
for all medical people. Baphomet fakes illness? Medical emergency?
6th House also SERVANTS
☽ in 4th DEVOTED MOTHER
Indication of overbearing/conceited/bullying individual ♌3
WHO?
Southern node in ♊
Cauda Draconis: CROWLEY says SUDDEN LOSSES
2nd House, House of Possessions: TROPHIES TAKEN FROM HER
ADAMS: ♊ in speech is logical and clear – ♊2??
SCHMIDT CORRECTS TO
Baphomet's ruler in ♋
'Holy, holy, holy, unto One Hundred and Fifty Six times holy be OUR LADY that rideth upon THE BEAST!' CROWLEY
♋ knows something, possibly subconscious, has had prior contact with ♑?
She disappeared during ♎ SIGNIFICANT?
♎ = JUSTICE /ADJUSTMENT Was she pursuing justice?
Dr ♎ perfect example of type. ADAMS says head is long-skulled, features small, regular and pleasing, hair very dark brown or black, tendency to grow low on forehead – gentleness – amiability – 'things may be very wrong without people perceiving it. ♎ is the one who discovers the trouble and proceeds to adjust it.' 'A disruption gives him the most terrible agony of spirit.' '♎ IS THE MOST TRUSTWORTHY OF THE SIGNS' ... but also Crowley?
♑
It is the sign of antagonism and fatality.
It is the goat of lust attacking the heavens with its horns.
- Eliphas Levi

'That's Libra,' said Robin, pointing at a symbol towards the bottom of the page. 'It's my sign, I used to have a keyring with that on it.'

'He's using bloody *star signs*?' said Strike, pulling the book back towards him, looking so disgusted that Robin started to laugh again.

Strike scanned the page. Robin was right. The circles drawn around the goat's head told him something else, too.

'He's calculated the full horoscope for the moment he thought she was abducted,' he said. 'Look at the date there. The eleventh of October 1974. Half past six in the evening . . . fuck's sake. *Astrology* . . . he was out of his tree.'

'What's your sign?' asked Robin, trying to work it out.

'No idea.'

'Oh sod off,' said Robin.

He looked at her, taken aback.

'You're being affected!' she said. 'Everyone knows their star sign. Don't pretend to be above it.'

Strike grinned reluctantly, took a large drag on his cigarette, exhaled, then said,

'Sagittarius, Scorpio rising, with the sun in the first house.'

'You're—' Robin began to laugh. 'Did you just pull that out of your backside, or is it real?'

'Of course, it's not fucking *real*,' said Strike. '*None* of it's real, is it? But yeah. That's what my *natal horoscope* says. Stop bloody laughing. Remember who my mother was. She loved all that shit. One of her best mates did my full horoscope for her when I was born. I should have recognised that straight off,' he said, pointing at the goat drawing. 'But I haven't been through this properly yet, haven't had time.'

'So what does having the sun in the first house mean?'

'It means nothing, it's all bollocks.'

Robin could tell that he didn't want to admit that he'd

remembered, which made her laugh some more. Half-annoyed, half-amused, he muttered,

'Independent. Leadership.'

'Well—'

'It's all bollocks, and we've got enough mystic crap swimming round this case without adding star signs. The medium and the holy place, Talbot and Baphomet—'

'—Irene and her broken Margot Fonteyn,' said Robin.

'Irene and her broken fucking Margot Fonteyn,' Strike muttered, rolling his eyes.

A fine shower of icy rain began to fall, speckling the table top and over Talbot's notebook, which Strike closed before the ink could run. In unspoken agreement, both got up and headed back towards the Land Rover.

The lavender-haired old lady who shared Strike's birthday was now being helped into a nearby Toyota by what looked like two daughters. All around her car stood family, smiling and talking under umbrellas. Just for a moment, as he pulled himself back inside the Land Rover, Strike wondered where he'd be if he lived to eighty, and who'd be there with him.

22

And later times thinges more vnknowne shall show.
Why then should witlesse man so much misweene
That nothing is but that which he hath seene?
What if within the Moones fayre shining spheare,
What if in euery other starre vnseene
Of other worldes he happily should heare?

Edmund Spenser
The Faerie Queene

Strike got himself a takeaway that night, to eat alone in his attic flat. As he upended the Singapore noodles onto his plate, he inwardly acknowledged the irony that, had Ilsa not been so keen to act as midwife to a romantic relationship between himself and Robin, he might now have been sitting in Nick and Ilsa's flat in Octavia Road, enjoying a laugh with two of his old friends and indeed with Robin herself, whose company had never yet palled on him, through the many long hours they had worked together.

Strike's thoughts lingered on his partner while he ate, on the kiss on the well-chosen card, on the headphones and the fact that she was now calling him Strike in moments of annoyance, or when the two of them were joking, all of them clear signs of increasing intimacy. However stressful the divorce proceedings, of which she'd shared few details, however little she might consciously be seeking romance, she was nevertheless a free agent.

Not for the first time, Strike wondered exactly how egotistical it was to suspect that Robin's feelings towards him might be warmer than those of pure friendship. He got on with her better than he'd ever got on with any woman. Their mutual liking had survived all the stresses of running a business together, the personal trials each had endured since they had met, even the major disagreement that had once seen him sack her. She'd hurried to the hospital when he had found himself alone with a critically ill nephew, brooking, he had no doubt, the displeasure of the ex-husband Strike never forgot to call 'that arsehole' inside his own head.

Nor was Strike unconscious of Robin's good looks: indeed, he'd been fully aware of them ever since she'd taken off her coat in his office for the first time. But her physical appeal was less of a threat to his peace of mind than the deep, guilty liking for being, currently, the main man in her life. Now that the possibility of something more lay in front of him, now that her husband was gone, and she was single, he found himself seriously wondering what would happen, should they act upon what he was beginning to suspect was a mutual attraction. Could the agency, for which they'd both sacrificed so much, which for Strike represented the culmination of all his ambitions, survive the partners falling into bed together? However he reframed this question, the answer always came back 'no', because he was certain, for reasons that had to do with past trauma, not from any particularly puritanical streak, that what Robin sought, ultimately, was the security and permanence of marriage.

And he wasn't the marrying kind. No matter the inconveniences, what he craved at the end of a working day was his private space, clean and ordered, organised exactly as he liked it, free of emotional storms, from guilt and recriminations, from demands to service Hallmark's idea of romance, from a life where someone else's happiness was his responsibility. The truth was that he'd always been responsible for some woman: for Lucy, as they grew up together in squalor and chaos; for Leda, who lurched from lover to lover, and whom he had sometimes had to physically protect as a teenager; for Charlotte, whose volatility and self-destructive tendencies had been given many different names by therapists and psychiatrists, but whom he had loved in spite of it all. He was alone now, and at a kind of peace. None of the affairs or one-night stands he'd had since Charlotte had touched the essential part of him. He'd sometimes wondered since whether Charlotte had not stunted his ability to feel deeply.

Except that, almost against his will, he did care about Robin. He felt familiar stirrings of a desire to make her happy that irked him far more than the habit he'd developed of looking determinedly away when she bent over a desk. They were friends, and he hoped they'd always be friends, and he suspected the best way to guarantee that was never see each other naked.

When he'd washed up his plate, Strike opened the window to admit the cold night air, reminding himself that every woman he knew would have been complaining immediately about the draught. He then lit a cigarette, opened the laptop he'd brought upstairs and drafted a letter to the Ministry of Justice, explaining that he'd been hired by Anna Phipps, setting out his proven credentials as an investigator both within the army and outside it, and requesting permission to visit and question Dennis Creed in Broadmoor.

Once finished, he yawned, lit his umpteenth cigarette of the day and went to lie down on his bed, as usual undoing his trousers first. Picking up *The Demon of Paradise Park*, he turned to the final chapter.

The question that haunts the officers who entered Creed's basement in 1976 and saw for themselves the combination of jail and torture chamber that he'd constructed there, is whether the 12 women he is known to have assaulted, raped and/or killed represent the total tally of his victims.

In our final interview, Creed, who that morning had been deprived of privileges following an aggressive outburst against a prison officer, was at his least communicative and most cryptic.

Q: People suspect there may have been more victims.
A: Is that right?
Q: Louise Tucker. She was sixteen, she'd run away—
A: You journalists love putting ages on people, don't you? Why is that?
Q: Because it paints a picture. It's a detail we can all identify with. D'you know anything about Louise Tucker?
A: Yeah. She was sixteen.
Q: There was unclaimed jewellery in your basement. Unclaimed pieces of clothing.
A: . . .
Q: You don't want to talk about the unclaimed jewellery?
A: . . .
Q: Why don't you want to talk about those unclaimed items?
A: . . .
Q: Does any part of you think, "I've got nothing to lose, now. I could put people's minds at rest. Stop families wondering"?
A: . . .
Q: You don't think, it would be a kind of reparation? I could repair something of my reputation?

A: [laughs] "Reputation" . . . you think I spend my days worrying about my reputation? You people really don't [indistinguishable]
Q: What about Kara Wolfson? Disappeared in '73.
A: How old was she?
Q: Twenty-six. Club hostess in Soho.
A: I don't like whores.
Q: Why's that?
A: Filthy.
Q: You frequented prostitutes.
A: When there was nothing else on offer.
Q: You tried – Helen Wardrop was a prostitute. And she got away from you. Gave a description to the police.
A: . . .
Q: You tried to abduct Helen in the same area Kara was last seen.
A: . . .
Q: What about Margot Bamborough?
A: . . .
Q: A van resembling your van was seen speeding in the area she disappeared.
A: . . .
Q: If you abducted Bamborough, she'd have been in your basement at the same time as Susan Meyer, wouldn't she?
A: . . . Nice for her.
Q: Was it nice for her?
A: Someone to talk to.
Q: Are you saying you were holding both Bamborough and Meyer at the same time?
A: [smiles]
Q: What about Andrea Hooton? Was Bamborough dead when you abducted Andrea?

A: . . .
Q: You threw Andrea's body off cliffs. That was a change in your m.o. Was she the first body you threw off there?
A: . . .
Q: You don't want to confirm whether you abducted Margot Bamborough?
A: [smiles]

Strike put down the book and lay for a while, smoking and thinking. Then he reached for Bill Talbot's leather-bound notebook, which he'd earlier thrown onto his bed when taking off his coat.

Flicking through the densely packed pages, looking for something comprehensible, something he could connect with a solid fact or reference point, he suddenly placed a thick finger in the book to stop the pages turning, his attention caught by a sentence written mostly in English that seemed familiar.

12th (♓) found. Therefore AS EXPECTED killer is ♑

It was an effort to get up and fetch his own notebook, but this he did. Slumping back onto his bed, he found the sentence that Pat had translated for him from Pitman shorthand:

And that is the last of them, the twelfth, and the circle will be closed upon finding the tenth – unknown word – Baphomet. Transcribe in the true book.

The unknown word, Strike realised, was the same symbol that followed the word 'Killer' in Talbot's notebook.

With a feeling of both exasperation and curiosity, Strike picked up his phone and Googled 'astrological symbols'.

A few minutes later, having read a couple of astrological web pages with an expression of mild distaste, he'd successfully

12th (♓) found. Therefore AS EXPECTED killer is ♑

'Capricornus is divinely unscrupulous, sublimely careless of result... thou hast no right but to do thy will. Do that, and no other shall say nay. For pure will, unassuaged of purpose, delivered from the lust of result, is every way perfect.' – Crowley

Husband can't be true ♑, Adams says ♑ materialistic, severe, hard-bitten, thin lipped, 'eyes small and piercing'

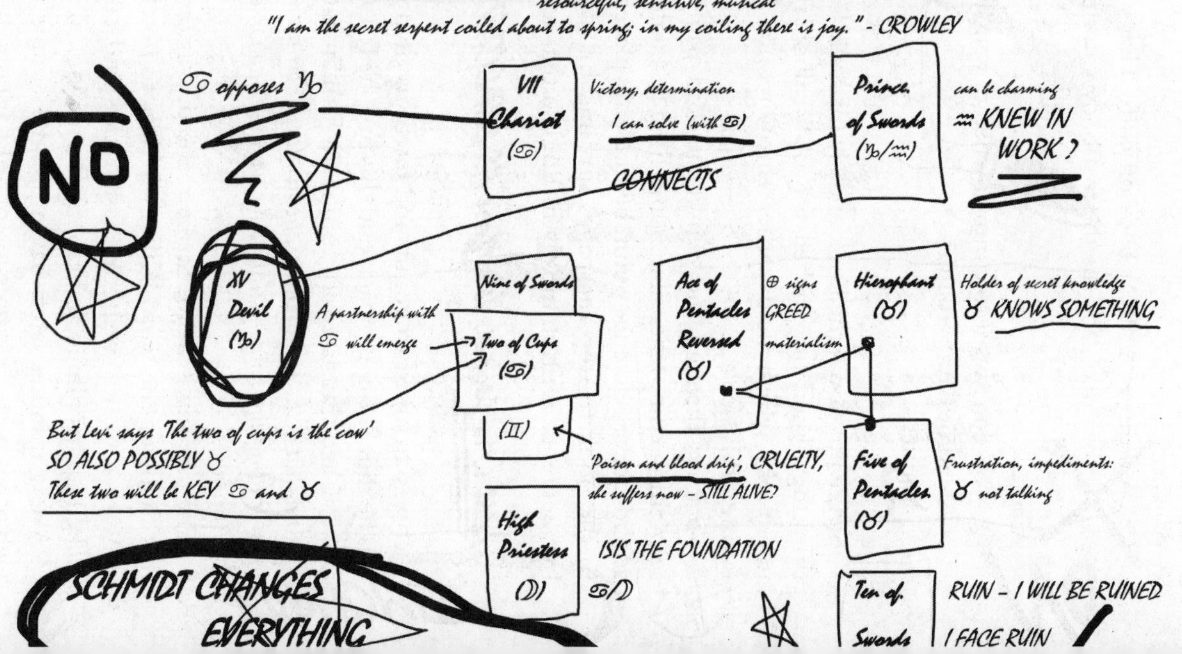

BAPHOMET
V
(II)
NO
♋
QUESTION ♋ AGAIN :- PSYCHIC, intuitions, re-interview,
nature is GOOD :- nurtures, protects, opposes EVIL,
Adams: 'the face is round and flat – the eyes are large and pale'.
Remember also ♄ in ♋,
therefore ♋ may have had contact with Baphomet/ ♑
MIGHT BE IN DANGER,
♉
whereas ♉ nature is LIKE BAPHOMET'S
'the hierophant will say to you: —
"Turn round!" and, in the shadow which you throw
in the presence of this sun of intelligences, these
will appear to you the devil, that black phantom' - Levi
UNTRUSTWORTHY. HIDING THINGS. KNOWS MORE
♏ MOLE (ADAMS)
Falsehoods, broken mirrors, troubled waters – Crowley
WATER CONNECTION: ALL SIGNS ARE WATER RELATED
ALSO RAIN WHEN SHE WAS TAKEN
NO
WATER WATER WATER WATER WATER WATER EVERYWHERE
♒ worried about how ♏ died?
SCHMIDT AGREES W ADAMS
Did ♒ challenge ♓ about ♏? Was ♋ there, did ♋ witness? ♋ is kind, instinct is to protect, INTERVIEW AGAIN.
♏ and ♒ are connected WATER WATER also ♋ and ♑ HAS A FISH'S TAIL.
The monster Cetus, Leviathan, the biblical whale
Superficial charm, evil in depths
Headstrong, enjoys spotlight
A performer, a liar

interpreted Talbot's sentence. It read: '*Twelfth (Pisces) found. Therefore AS EXPECTED killer is Capricorn.*'

Pisces was the twelfth sign of the zodiac, Capricorn the tenth. Capricorn was also the sign of the goat, which Talbot, in his manic state, appeared to have connected with Baphomet, the goat-headed deity.

'Fuck's sake,' muttered Strike, turning to a fresh page in his notebook and writing something.

An idea now occurred to him: those strange, unexplained dates with crosses beside them on all the male witnesses' statements. He wondered whether he could be bothered to get up and go downstairs to fetch the relevant pages from the boxes of police records. With a sigh, he decided that the answer was yes. He did up his flies, heaved himself to his feet, and fetched the office keys from their hook by the door.

Ten minutes later, Strike returned to his bedroom with both his laptop and a fresh notebook. As he settled down on top of the duvet again, he noticed that the screen of his mobile, which was lying on the duvet, was now lit up. Somebody had tried to call him while he'd been downstairs. Expecting it to be Lucy, he picked up the phone and looked at it.

He'd just missed a call from Charlotte. Strike lay the phone back down again and opened his laptop. Slowly and painstakingly, he set to work matching the unexplained dates on each male suspect's witness statements with the relevant sign of the zodiac. If his hunch that Talbot had been checking the men's star signs was correct, Steven Douthwaite was a Pisces, Paul Satchwell was an Aries and Roy Phipps, who'd been born on the twenty-seventh of December . . . was a Capricorn. Yet Talbot had cleared Roy Phipps of involvement early in the case.

'So that makes no fucking sense,' muttered Strike to the empty room.

He put down his laptop and picked up Talbot's notebook

again, reading on from the assertion that Margot's killer must be Capricorn.

'Christ almighty,' Strike muttered, trying, but not entirely succeeding, to find sense among the mass of esoteric ramblings with the aid of his astrological websites. As far as he could tell, Talbot appeared to have absolved Roy Phipps from suspicion on the grounds that he wasn't really a Capricorn, but some sign that Strike couldn't make head nor tail of, and which he suspected Talbot might have invented.

Returning to the notebook, Strike recognised the Celtic cross layout of tarot cards from his youth. Leda fancied herself a reader of tarot; many times had he seen her lay out the cards in the very formation Talbot had sketched in the middle of the page. He had never, however, seen the cards given astrological meanings before, and wondered whether this, too, had been Talbot's own invention.

His mobile buzzed again. He picked it up.

Charlotte had sent him a photograph. A naked photograph, of herself holding two coffees. The accompanying message said **6 years ago tonight. I wish it was happening again. Happy Birthday, Bluey x**

Against his will, Strike stared at the body no sentient heterosexual man could fail to desire, and at the face Venus would envy. Then he noticed the blurring along her lower stomach, where she'd airbrushed out her Caesarean scar. This took care of his burgeoning erection. Like an alcoholic pushing away brandy, he deleted the picture and returned to Talbot's notebook.

23

It is the mynd, that maketh good or ill,
That maketh wretch or happie, rich or poore:
For some, that hath abundance at his will,
Hath not enough, but wants in greatest store;
And other, that hath litle, askes no more,
But in that litle is both rich and wise.

Edmund Spenser
The Faerie Queene

Eleven days later, Robin was woken at 8 a.m. by her mobile ringing, after barely an hour's sleep. She'd spent the night on another pointless vigil outside the house of the persecuted weatherman, and had returned to her flat in Earl's Court to grab a couple of hours' sleep before hurrying out again to interview Oonagh Kennedy with Strike, in the café at Fortnum & Mason. Completely disorientated, she knocked a couple of items off the bedside table as she groped in the dark for her phone.

''Lo?'

'Robin?' said a happy shout in her ear. 'You're an aunt!'

'I'm what, sorry?' she muttered.

Wisps of her dreams still clung about her: Pat Chauncey had been asking her out to dinner, and had been deeply hurt that she didn't want to go.

'You're an aunt! Jenny's just had the baby!'

'Oh,' said Robin, and very slowly her brain computed that this was Stephen, her elder brother, on the line. 'Oh, that's wonderful . . . what—?'

'A girl!' said Stephen jubilantly. 'Annabel Marie. Eight pounds eight ounces!'

'Wow,' said Robin, 'that's – is that big? It seems—'

'I'm sending you a picture now!' said Stephen. 'Got it?'

'No – hang on,' said Robin, sitting up. Bleary-eyed, she switched to speakerphone to check her messages. The picture arrived as she was peering at the screen: a wrinkled, bald red baby swaddled in a hospital robe, fists balled up, looking furious to have been forced from a place of quiet, padded darkness into the brightness of a hospital ward.

'Just got it. Oh, Stephen, she's . . . she's beautiful.'

It was a lie, but nevertheless, tears prickled in the exhausted Robin's eyes.

'My God, Button,' she said quietly; it was Stephen's childhood nickname. 'You're a dad!'

'I know!' he said. 'Insane, isn't it? When are you coming home to see her?'

'Soon,' Robin promised. 'I'm back for Christmas. Give Jenny all my love, won't you?'

'I will, yeah. Gonna call Jon now. See you soon, Robs.'

The call was cut. Robin lay in darkness, staring at the brightly lit picture of the crumpled baby, whose puffy eyes were screwed up against a world she seemed to have decided already was not much of a place. It was quite extraordinary to think of her brother Stephen as a father, and that the family now had one more member.

Robin seemed to hear her cousin Katie's words again: *It's like you're travelling in a different direction to the rest of us*. In the old days with Matthew, before she'd started work at the agency, she'd expected to have children with him. Robin had no strong feelings *against* having children, it was simply that she knew, now, that the job she loved would be impossible if she were a mother, or at least, that it would stop being the job she loved. Motherhood, from her limited observation of those her age who were doing it, seemed to demand as much from a woman as she could possibly give. Katie had talked of the perennial tug on her heart when she wasn't with her son, and Robin had tried to imagine an emotional tether even stronger than the guilt and anger with which Matthew had tried to retain her. The problem wasn't that Robin didn't think she'd love her child. On the contrary, she thought it likely that she would love that child to the extent that this job, for which she had voluntarily sacrificed a marriage, her safety, her sleep and her financial security, would have to be sacrificed in return. And how would she feel, afterwards, about the person who'd made that sacrifice necessary?

Robin turned on the light and bent to pick up the things she had knocked off her bedside table: an empty glass, thankfully unbroken, and the thin, flimsy paperback entitled *Whatever Happened to Margot Bamborough?* by C. B. Oakden, which Robin had received in the post the previous morning, and which she'd already read.

Strike didn't yet know that she had managed to get hold of a copy of Oakden's book and Robin had been looking forward to showing him. She had a couple more fragments of Bamborough news, too, but now, perhaps because of her sheer exhaustion, the feeling of anticipation at sharing them had disappeared. Deciding that she wouldn't be able to get back to sleep, she got out of bed.

As she showered, Robin realised, to her surprise, that she was crying.

This is ridiculous. You don't even want a baby. Get a grip of yourself.

When Robin arrived upstairs, dressed, with her hair blow-dried and concealer applied to the shadows under her eyes, she found Max eating toast in the kitchen.

'Morning,' he said, looking up from a perusal of the day's news on his phone. 'You all right?'

'Fine,' said Robin, with forced brightness. 'Just found out I'm an aunt. My brother Stephen's wife gave birth this morning.'

'Oh. Congratulations,' said Max, politely interested. 'Um . . . boy or girl?'

'Girl,' said Robin, turning on the coffee machine.

'I've got about eight godchildren,' said Max gloomily. 'Parents love giving the job to childless people. They think we'll put more effort in, having no kids of our own.'

'True,' said Robin, trying to maintain her cheery tone. She'd been made godmother to Katie's son. The christening had been the first time she'd been in the church in Masham since her wedding to Matthew.

She took a mug of black coffee back to her bedroom, where she opened up her laptop and decided to set down her new information on the Bamborough case in an email to Strike before they met. They might not have much time together before Oonagh Kennedy's interview, so this would expedite discussion.

Hi,

Few bits and pieces on Bamborough before I see you:

- Charles Ramage, the hot tub millionaire, is dead. I've spoken to his son, who couldn't confirm the story about the Margot sighting, but remembered Janice nursing his father after his crash and said Ramage Snr liked her and 'probably told her all his stories, he had loads of them'. Said his father never minded exaggerating if it made a story better, but was not a liar and 'had a good heart. Wouldn't have told a lie about a missing woman.' Also confirmed that his father was close friends with a 'senior police officer' (couldn't remember rank or first name) called Greene. Ramage Snr's widow is still alive and living in Spain, but she's his second wife and the son doesn't get on with her. I'm trying to get a contact number/email address for her.

- I'm 99% sure I've found the right Amanda White, who's now called Amanda Laws. Two years ago she posted a piece on Facebook about people disappearing, which included Margot. She said in the comment that she'd been personally involved in the Margot disappearance. I've sent her a message but nothing back yet.
- I've got hold of a copy of *Whatever Happened to Margot Bamborough?* and read it (it's not long). Judging by what we know about Margot so far, it looks full of inaccuracies. I'll bring it with me this morning.

See you in a bit x

Sleep-deprived, Robin had added the kiss automatically and had sent the email before she could retract it. It was one thing to put a kiss on a birthday card, quite another to start adding them to work emails.

Shit.

She could hardly write a PS saying 'Ignore that kiss, my fingers did it without me meaning to.' That would draw attention to the thing if Strike hadn't thought anything of it.

As she closed her laptop, her mobile screen lit up: she'd received a long, excited text from her mother about baby Annabel Marie's perfection, complete with a photograph of herself cradling her new granddaughter, Robin's father beaming over his wife's shoulder. Robin texted back:

She's gorgeous!

even though the baby was quite as unprepossessing in the new photograph as she'd been in the old. Yet she wasn't really lying: the fact of Annabel's birth *was* somehow gorgeous, an everyday miracle, and Robin's mysterious shower tears had been partly in acknowledgement of the fact.

As the Tube sped her towards Piccadilly Circus, Robin took out her copy of C. B. Oakden's book, which she'd found at a second-hand bookshop in Chester, and flicked through it again. The dealer had said the book had been in his shop for several years, and had arrived in a job lot of books he'd taken off the hands of the family of an elderly local woman who'd died. Robin suspected that the dealer hadn't known of the book's murky legal status before Robin's email enquiry, but he appeared to have no particular moral qualms about selling it. As long as Robin guaranteed by phone that she wouldn't reveal where she'd got it, he was happy to part with it, for a hefty mark-up. Robin only hoped Strike would think the price justified, once he'd read it.

Robin's particular copy appeared to have escaped pulping because it had been one of the author's free copies, which must have been given to him before the court decision. An inscription on the fly-leaf read: *To Auntie May, with every good wish, CB Oakden (Carl).* To Robin, 'with every good wish' seemed an affected, grandiose message to send an aunt.

Barely a hundred pages long, the flimsy paperback had a

photograph of Margot as a Bunny Girl on the cover, a picture familiar to Robin because it had appeared in so many newspaper reports of her disappearance. Half cut off in this enlarged picture was a second Bunny Girl, who Robin knew to be Oonagh Kennedy. The photograph was reproduced in its entirety in the middle of the paperback, along with other pictures which Robin thought Strike would agree were the most valuable part of the book, though only, she feared, in terms of putting faces to names rather than helping the investigation.

Robin got off the Tube at Piccadilly Circus and walked in a strong wind up Piccadilly, beneath swaying Christmas lights, wondering where she might find a baby present for Stephen and Jenny. Having passed no appropriate shops, she arrived outside Fortnum & Mason with an hour to spare before the projected meeting with Oonagh Kennedy.

Robin had often passed the famous store since she had lived in London, but never gone inside. The ornate frontage was duck-egg blue and the windows, dressed for Christmas, some of the most beautiful in the city. Robin peered through clear circles of glass surrounded by artificial snow, at heaps of jewel-like crystallised fruits, silk scarves, gilded tea canisters, and wooden nutcrackers shaped like fairy-tale princes. A gust of particularly cold, rain-flecked wind whipped at her, and, without conscious thought, Robin allowed herself to be swept inside the sumptuous seasonal fantasy, through a door flanked by a doorman in an overcoat and top hat.

The store was carpeted in scarlet. Everywhere were mountains of duck-egg blue packaging. Close at hand she saw the very truffles that Morris had bought her for her birthday. Past marzipan fruits and biscuits she walked, until she glimpsed the café at the back of the ground floor where they'd agreed to meet Oonagh. Robin turned back. She didn't want to see the retired vicar before the allotted time, because she wanted to reason herself into a more business-like frame of mind before an interview.

'Excuse me,' she asked a harried-looking woman selecting marzipan fruits for a client, 'd'you sell anything for children in—?'

'Third floor,' said the woman, already moving away.

The small selection of children's goods available were, in Robin's view, exorbitantly priced, but as Annabel's only aunt, and only London-based relative, she felt a certain pressure to give a suitably metropolitan gift. Accordingly, she purchased a large, cuddly Paddington bear.

Robin was walking away from the till with her duck-egg carrier bag when her mobile rang. Expecting it to be Strike, she saw instead an unknown number.

'Hi, Robin here.'

'Hi, Robin. It's Tom,' said an angry voice.

Robin couldn't for the life of her think who Tom was. She mentally ran through the cases the agency was currently working on – Two-Times, Twinkletoes, Postcard, Shifty and Bamborough – trying in vain to remember a Tom, while saying with what she intended to be yes-of-course-I-know-who-you-are warmth,

'Oh, hi!'

'*Tom Turvey*,' said the man, who didn't appear fooled.

'Oh,' said Robin, her heart beginning to beat uncomfortably fast, and she drew back into an alcove where pricey scented candles stood on shelves.

Tom Turvey was Sarah Shadlock's fiancé. Robin had had no contact with him since finding out that their respective partners had been sleeping together. She'd never particularly liked him, nor had she ever found out whether he knew about the affair.

'Thanks,' said Tom. 'Thanks a *fucking bunch*, Robin!'

He was close to shouting. Robin distanced the mobile a little from her ear.

'Excuse me?' she said, but she suddenly seemed to have become all nerves and pulse.

'Didn't bother fucking telling me, eh? Just walked away and washed your hands, did you?'

'Tom—'

'She's told me *fucking* everything, and you knew a year ago and I find out today, *four weeks before my wedding*—'

'Tom, I—'

'Well, I hope you're fucking happy!' he bellowed. Robin removed the phone from her ear and held it at arm's length. He was still clearly audible as he yelled, 'I'm the only one of us who hasn't been fucking around, and I'm the one who's been *fucked over*—'

Robin cut him off. Her hands were shaking.

'*Excuse me*,' said a large woman, who was trying to see the candles on the shelves behind Robin, who mumbled an apology and walked away, until she reached a curving iron banister, beyond which was a large, circular expanse of thin air. Looking down, she saw the floors had been cut out, so that she was able to see right into the basement, where compressed people were criss-crossing the space with baskets laden with expensive hams and bottles of wine. Head spinning, hardly aware of what she was doing, Robin turned and headed blindly back towards the department exit, trying not to bump into tables piled with fragile china. Down the red carpeted stairs she walked, trying to breathe herself back to calm, trying to make sense of what she'd just heard.

'Robin.'

She walked on, and only when somebody said '*Robin*' again did she turn and realise Strike had just entered the store via a side door from Duke Street. The shoulders of his overcoat were studded with glimmering raindrops.

'Hi,' she said, dazed.

'You all right?'

For a split-second she wanted to tell him everything: after all, he knew about Matthew's affair, he knew how her marriage had ended and he'd met Tom and Sarah. However, Strike himself looked tense, his mobile gripped in his hand.

'Fine. You?'

'Not great,' he said.

The two of them moved aside to allow a group of tourists into the store. In the shadow of the wooden staircase Strike said,

'Joan's taken a turn for the worse. They've readmitted her to hospital.'

'Oh God, I'm so sorry,' said Robin. 'Listen – go to Cornwall. We'll cope. I'll interview Oonagh, I'll take care of everything—'

'No. She specifically told Ted she didn't want us all dashing down there again. But that's not like her . . .'

Strike seemed every bit as scattered and distracted as Robin felt, but now she pulled herself together. *Screw Tom, screw Matthew and Sarah.*

'Seriously, Cormoran, go. I can take care of work.'

'They're expecting me in a fortnight for Christmas. Ted says she's desperate to have us all at home. It's supposed to be just for a couple of days, the hospital thing.'

'Well, if you're sure . . .' said Robin. She checked her watch. 'We've got ten minutes until Oonagh's supposed to be here. Want to go to the café and wait for her?'

'Yeah,' said Strike. 'Good thinking, I could use a coffee.'

'God Rest Ye Merry, Gentlemen' trilled from the speakers as they entered the realm of crystallised fruits and expensive teas, both lost in painful thought.

24

. . . my delight is all in ioyfulnesse,
In beds, in bowres, in banckets, and in feasts:
And ill becomes you with your lofty creasts,
To scorne the ioy, that Ioue is glad to seeke . . .

Edmund Spenser
The Faerie Queene

The café was reached by a flight of stairs that placed it on a higher level than the shop floor, which it overlooked. Once he and Robin had sat down at a table for four by the window, Strike sat silently looking down into Jermyn Street, where passers-by were reduced to moving mushrooms, eclipsed by their umbrellas. He was a stone's throw from the restaurant in which he'd last seen Charlotte.

He'd received several more calls from her since the nude photograph on his birthday, plus several texts, three of which had arrived the previous evening. He'd ignored all of them, but somewhere at the back of his anxiety about Joan scuttled a familiar worry about what Charlotte's next move was going to be, because the texts were becoming increasingly overwrought. She had a couple of suicide attempts in her past, one of which had almost succeeded. Three years after he'd left her, she was still trying to make him responsible for her safety and her happiness, and Strike found it equally infuriating and saddening. When Ted had called Strike that morning with the news about Joan, the detective had been in the process of looking up the telephone number of the merchant bank where Charlotte's husband worked. If Charlotte threatened suicide, or sent any kind of final message, Strike intended to call Jago.

'Cormoran,' Robin said.

He looked round. A waiter had arrived at the table. When both had ordered coffee, and Robin some toast, each relapsed into silence. Robin was looking away from the window towards the shoppers stocking up on fancy groceries for Christmas down on the shop floor and re-running Tom Turvey's outburst in her head. The aftershocks were still hitting her. *Four weeks before my fucking wedding.* It must have been called off. Sarah had left Tom for Matthew, the man she'd wanted all along, and Robin was sure she wouldn't have left Tom unless Matthew had shown himself ready to offer her what Tom had: diamonds and a change of name. *I'm the only one of us who hasn't been fucking around.* Everyone had been unfaithful, in Tom's opinion, except poor Tom . . . so Matthew must have told his old friend that she, Robin, had been sleeping with someone else (which meant Strike, of course, of whom Matthew had been perennially jealous and suspicious from the moment Robin had gone to work for him). And even now that Tom knew about Matthew and Sarah, after his old friend's duplicity and treachery had been revealed, Tom still believed the lie about Robin and Strike. Doubtless he thought his current misery was all Robin's fault, that if she hadn't succumbed to Strike, the domino effect of infidelity would never have been started.

'You sure you're all right?'

Robin started and looked around. Strike had come out of his own reverie and was looking at her over his coffee cup.

'Fine,' she said. 'Just knackered. Did you get my email?'

'Email?' said Strike, reaching for the phone in his pocket. 'Yeah, but I haven't read it, sorry. Dealing with other—'

'Don't bother now,' said Robin hastily, inwardly cringing at the thought of that accidental kiss, even in the midst of her new troubles. 'It isn't particularly important, it'll keep. I did find this, though.'

She took the copy of *Whatever Happened to Margot Bamborough?* out of her bag and passed it over the table, but before Strike could express his surprise, she muttered,

'Give it back, give it back now,' tugged it back out of his hand and stuffed it into her bag.

A stout woman was heading towards them across the café. Two bulging bags of Christmas fare were dangling from her hands. She had the full cheeks and large square front teeth of a cheerful-looking chipmunk, an aspect that in her youthful photos had added a certain cheeky charm to her prettiness. The hair that once had been long, dark and glossy was now chin-length and white, except at the front, where a dashing bright purple streak had been added. A large silver and amethyst cross bounced on her purple sweater.

'Oonagh?' said Robin.

'Dat's me,' she panted. She seemed nervous. 'The *queues*! Well, what do I expect, Fortnum's at Christmas? But fair play, dey *do* a lovely mustard.'

Robin smiled. Strike drew out the chair beside him.

'T'anks very much,' said Oonagh, sitting down.

Her Irish accent was attractive, and barely eroded by what Robin knew had been a longer residence in England than in the country of her birth.

Both detectives introduced themselves.

'Very nice to meet you,' Oonagh said, shaking hands before clearing her throat nervously. 'Excuse me. I was *made up* to get yer message,' she told Strike. 'Years and years I've spent, wondering why Roy never hired someone, because he's got the money to do it and the police never got anywhere. So little Anna called you in, did she? God bless that gorl, *what* she must've gone through . . . Oh, hello,' she said to the waiter, 'could I have a cappuccino and a bit of that carrot cake? T'ank you.'

When the waiter had gone, Oonagh took a deep breath and said,

'I know I'm rattlin' on. I'm nervous, that's the truth.'

'There's nothing to be—' began Strike.

'Oh, there is,' Oonagh contradicted him, looking sober. 'Whatever happened to Margot, it can't be anything good, can it? Nigh on forty years I've prayed for that girl, prayed for the truth and prayed God would look after her, alive or dead. She was the best friend I ever had and – sorry. I knew this would happen. Knew it.'

She picked up her unused cloth napkin and mopped her eyes.

'Ask me a question,' she said, half-laughing. 'Save me from meself.'

Robin glanced at Strike, who handed the interview to her with a look as he pulled out his notebook.

'Well, perhaps we can start with how you and Margot met?' Robin suggested.

'We can, o' course,' said Oonagh. 'That would've been '66. We were both auditioning to be Bunny Girls. You'll know all about that?'

Robin nodded.

'I had a decent figure then, believe it or not,' said Oonagh, smiling as she gestured down at her tubby torso, although she seemed to feel little regret for the loss of her waist.

Robin hoped Strike wasn't going to take her to task later for not organising her questions according to the usual categories of *people, places and things*, but she judged it better to make this feel more like a normal conversation, at least at first, because Oonagh was still visibly nervous.

'Did you come over from Ireland, to try and get the job?' asked Robin.

'Oh no,' said Oonagh. 'I was already in London. I kinda run away from home, truth be told. You're lookin' at a convent gorl with a mammy as strict as a prison warder. I had a week's wages from a clothes shop in Derry in my pocket, and my mammy gave me one row too many. I walked out, got on the ferry, came to London and sent a postcard home to tell 'em I was alive and not to worry. My mammy didn't speak to me for t'irty years.

'I was waitressing when I heard they were opening a Playboy Club in Mayfair. Well, the money was *crazy* good compared to what you could earn in a normal place. T'irty-five pounds a week, we started on. That's near enough six hundred a week, nowadays. There was nowhere else in London was going to pay a working-class gorl that. It was more than most of our daddies earned.'

'And you met Margot at the club?'

'I met her at the audition. Knew *she'd* get hired the moment I looked at her. She had the figure of a model: all legs, and the girl *lived* on sugar. She was t'ree years younger than me, and she lied about her age so they'd take – oh, t'ank you very much,' said Oonagh, as the waiter placed her cappuccino and carrot cake in front of her.

'Why was Margot auditioning?' Robin asked.

'Because her family had nothing – and I mean, *nothing*, now,' Oonagh said. 'Her daddy had an accident when she was four. Fell off a step-ladder, broke his back. Crippled. That's why she had no brothers and sisters. Her mammy used to clean people's houses. *My* family had more than the Bamboroughs and nobody ever got rich farming a place the size of ours. But the Bamboroughs were not-enough-to-eat poor.

'She was such a clever girl, but the family needed help. She got herself into medical school, told the university she'd have to defer for a year, then headed straight for the Playboy Club. We took to each other straight away, in the audition, because she was *so funny*.'

'Was she?' said Robin. Out of the corner of her eye, she saw Strike look up from his notebook in surprise.

'Oh, Margot Bamborough was the funniest person I ever knew in my life,' said Oonagh. 'In my *loife*, now. We used to laugh till we cried. I've never laughed like that since. Proper cockney accent and she could just make you laugh until you *dropped*.

'So we started work together, and they were *strict*, mind you,' said Oonagh, now forking cake into her mouth as she talked. 'Inspected before you walked out on the floor, uniform on properly, nails done, and then there were *rules* like you've no idea. They used to put plain-clothes detectives in the club to catch us out, make sure we weren't giving out our full names or our phone numbers.

'If you were any good at it, you could put a tidy bit of money away. Margot graduated to cigarette girl, selling them out of a little tray. She was popular with the men because she was so funny. She hardly spent a penny on herself. She split the lot between a savings account for medical school and the rest she gave her mammy. Worked every hour they'd let her. Bunny Peggy, she called herself, because she didn't want any of the punters to know her real name. I was Bunny *Una*, because nobody knew how to say "Oonagh". We got all kinds of offers – you had to say no, of course. But it was nice to be asked, right enough,' said Oonagh, and perhaps picking up on Robin's surprise, she smiled and said,

'Don't think Margot and I didn't know *exactly* what we were doin', corseted up with bunny ears on our heads. What you maybe don't realise is a woman couldn't get a mortgage in dose days without a man co-signing the forms. Same with credit cards. I squandered my money at first, but I learned better, learned from Margot. I got smart, I started saving. I ended up buying my own flat with cash. Middle-class gorls, with their mammies and daddies paying their way, they could afford to burn their bras and have hairy armpits. Margot and I, we did what we had to.

'Anyway, the Playboy Club was sophisticated. It wasn't a knocking shop. It had licences it would've lost if things got seedy. We had women guests, too. Men used to bring their wives, their dates. The worst we had was a bit of tail-pulling, but if a club member got really handsy, he lost his membership. You should've seen what I had to put up with in my job before that: hands up my skirt when I bent over a table, and worse. They looked after us at the Playboy Club. Members weren't allowed to date Bunny Girls – well, in t'eory. It happened. It happened to Margot. I was angry at her for that, I said, you're risking everything, you fool.'

'Was this Paul Satchwell?' asked Robin.

'It was indeed,' said Oonagh. 'He'd come to the club as someone's guest, he wasn't a member, so Margot t'ought it was a grey area. I was still worried she was going to lose the job.'

'You didn't like him?'

'No, I didn't like him,' said Oonagh. 'T'ought he was Robert Plant, so he did, but Margot fell for him hook, line and sinker. She didn't go out a lot, see, because she was saving. I'd been round the nightclubs in my first year in London; I'd met plenty of Satchwells. He was six years older than she was, an artist and he wore his jeans so tight you could see his cock and balls right through them.'

Strike let out an involuntary snort of laughter. Oonagh looked at him.

'Sorry,' he muttered. 'You're, ah, not like most vicars I've met.'

'I don't t'ink the Good Lord will mind me mentioning cocks and balls,' said Oonagh airily. 'He made 'em, didn't he?'

'So they started dating?' asked Robin.

'They did,' said Oonagh. '*Mad* passion, it was. You could *feel* the heat off the two of them. For Margot – see, before Satchwell, she'd always had *tunnel vision* about life, you know, eyes on the prize: become a doctor and save her family. She was cleverer than any of the boys she knew, and men don't like that much *nowadays*. She was taller than half of them, as well. She told me she'd never had a man interested in her brains before Satchwell. *Interested in her brains*, my aunt Nelly. The girl had a body like Jane Birkin. Oh, and it wasn't only *his* looks, either, she said. He'd read t'ings. He could talk about art. He could talk for the *hour* about art, right enough. I heard him. Well, *I* don't know a Monet from a poster of Margate, so I'm no judge, but it sounded a load of old bollocks to me.

'But he'd take Margot out to a gallery and educate her about art, then he'd take her home to bed. Sex makes fools of us all,' sighed Oonagh Kennedy. 'And he was her very first and it was obvious, you know,' she nodded at Robin, 'he knew what he was doing, so it was all that much more important to her. Mad in love, she was. *Mad*.

'Then, one night, just a couple o' weeks before she was supposed to be starting medical school, she turns up at my flat *howling*. She'd dropped in on Paul unexpected after work and there was another woman at the flat with him. Naked. *Modelling*, he told her. Modelling – at midnight. She turned round and ran. He went chasin' after her, but she jumped in a taxi and came to mine.

'*Heartbroken*, she was. All night, we sat up talking, me saying "You're better off without him", which was no more than the truth. I said to her, "Margot, you're about to start medical school. The place'll be *wall to wall* with handsome, clever boys training to be doctors. You won't remember Satchwell's *name* after a week or two."

'But then, near dawn, she told me a t'ing I've never told anyone before.'

Oonagh hesitated. Robin tried to look politely but warmly receptive.

'She'd let him take pictures of her. You know. *Pictures.* And she was scared, she wanted them back. I said to her, why in God's name would you let him do such a t'ing, Margot? Because it would've *killed* her mother. The pride they had in her, their only daughter, their brilliant gorl. If those photos turned up anywhere, a magazine or I don't know what, they'd have never lived it down, boastin' up and down their street about their Margot, the genius.

'So I said, I'll come with you and we'll get them back. So we went round there early and banged on his door. The bastard – excuse me, now,' she said. 'You'll rightly say, that's not a Christian attitude, but wait till you hear. Satchwell said to Margot, "I'll speak to you, but not your nanny." Your *nanny.*

'Well, now. I spent ten years working with domestic abuse survivors in Wolverhampton and it's one of the *hallmarks* of an abuser, if their victim isn't compliant, it's because she's under someone *else's* control. Her *nanny.*

'Before I know what's going on, she's inside and I'm stuck on the other side of a closed door. He'd pulled her in and slammed it in my face. I could hear them shouting at each other. Margot was giving as good as she got, God bless her.

'And then, and this is what I *really* wanted to tell you,' said Oonagh, 'and I want to get it right. I told that Inspector Talbot and he didn't listen to a word I was saying, and I told the one who took over, what was his name—?'

'Lawson?' asked Robin.

'Lawson,' said Oonagh, nodding. 'I told both of 'em: I could hear Margot and Paul screaming at each other through the door, Margot telling him to give her the pictures and the negatives – different world, you see. Negatives, you had to get, if you didn't want more copies made. But he refused. He said they were *his copyright*, the dirty bastard – so then I heard Margot say, and this is the important bit, "If you show those pictures to anyone, if they ever turn up in print, I'll go straight to the police and I'll tell them all about your little *pillow* dream—"'

'"Pillow dream"?' repeated Robin.

'That's what she said. And he hit her. A smack loud enough to hear through solid wood, and I heard her shriek. Well, I started hammering and kicking the door. I said, unless he opened it I was going for the police *right now. That* put the fear o' God into him. He opened the door and Margot comes out, hand to her face, it was bright red, you could see his finger marks, and I pulled her behind me and I said to Satchwell, "Don't you *ever* come near her again, and you heard what she said. There'll be trouble if those pictures turn up anywhere."

'And I swear to you, he looked murderous. He stepped right up to me, the way a man will when he wants to remind you what he could do, if he wanted. Almost standing on my toes, he was. I didn't shift,' said Oonagh Kennedy. 'I stood my ground, but I was scared, I won't deny it. And he said to Margot, "Have you told her?" And Margot says, "She doesn't know anything. Yet." And he says, "Well, you know what'll happen if I find out you've talked." And he mimed – well, never mind. It was an – an obscene pose, I suppose you'd say. One of the pictures he'd taken. And he walked back into his flat and slammed the door.'

'Did Margot ever tell you what she meant by the "pillow dream"?' asked Robin.

'She wouldn't. You might t'ink she was scared, but ... you know, I t'ink it's just women,' sighed Oonagh. 'We're socialised that way, but maybe Mother Nature's got a hand in it. How many kids would survive to their first birthday if their mammies couldn't forgive 'em?

'Even that day, with his handprint across her face, she didn't want to tell me, because there was a bit of her that didn't want to hurt him. I saw it all the bloody time with my domestic abuse survivors. Women still protecting them. Still worrying about them! Love dies hard in some women.'

'Did she see Satchwell after that?'

'I wish to *God* I could say she didn't,' said Oonagh, shaking her head, 'but yes, she did. They couldn't stay away from each other.

'She started her degree course, but she was that popular at the club, they let her go part time, so I was still seeing a lot of her. One day, her mammy called the club because her daddy had taken sick, but Margot hadn't come in. I was terrified: where was Margot, what had happened to her, why wasn't she there? I've often t'ought back to that moment, you know, because when it happened for real, I was so sure at first she'd turn up, like she had the first time.

'Anyway, when she saw how upset I'd been, t'inking she'd gone missing, she told me the truth. She and Satchwell had started things up again. She had all the old excuses down: he swore he'd never hit her again, he'd cried his eyes out about it, it was the worst mistake of his life, and anyway, she'd provoked him. I told her, "If you can't see him now for what he is, after what he did to you first time round ..." Anyway, they split again and, surprise, surprise, he not only knocked her around again, he kept her locked in his flat all day, so she couldn't get to work. That was the first shift she'd ever missed. She nearly lost the job over it, and had to make up some cock-and-bull story.

'So then at last,' said Oonagh, 'she tells me she's learned her lesson, I was right all along, she's never going back to him, that's it, *finito*.'

'Did she get the photographs back?' asked Robin.

'First t'ing I asked, when I found out they were back together. She said he'd told her he'd destroyed them. She believed it, too.'

'You didn't?'

'O' course I didn't,' said Oonagh. 'I'd seen him, when she t'reatened him with his *pillow dream*. That was a frightened man. He'd never have destroyed anyt'ing that gave him bargaining power over her.

'Would it be all right if I get another cappuccino?' asked Oonagh apologetically. 'My t'roat's dry, all this talking.'

'Of course,' said Strike, hailing a waiter, and ordering fresh coffees all round.

Oonagh pointed at Robin's Fortnum's bag.

'Been stocking up for Christmas, too?'

'Oh, no, I've been buying a present for my new niece. She was born this morning,' said Robin, smiling.

'Congratulations,' said Strike, who was surprised Robin hadn't already told him.

'Oh, how lovely,' said Oonagh. 'My fifth grandchild arrived last month.'

The interval while waiting for the fresh coffees was filled by Oonagh showing Robin pictures of her grandchildren, and Robin showing Oonagh the two pictures she had of Annabel Marie.

'*Gorgeous*, isn't she?' said Oonagh, peering through her purple reading glasses at the picture on Robin's phone. She included Strike in the question, but, seeing only an angry-looking, bald monkey, his acquiescence was half-hearted.

When the coffees had arrived and the waiter moved away again, Robin said,

'While I remember . . . would you happen to know if Margot had family or friends in Leamington Spa?'

'Leamington Spa?' repeated Oonagh, frowning. 'Let's see . . . one of the gorls at the club was from . . . no, that was King's Lynn. They're similar sorts of names, aren't they? I can't remember anyone from there, no . . . Why?'

'We've heard a man claimed to have seen her there, a week after she disappeared.'

'There were a few sightings after, right enough. Nothing in any of them. None of them made sense. Leamington Spa, that's a new one.'

She took a sip of her cappuccino. Robin asked,

'Did you still see a lot of each other, once Margot went off to medical school?'

'Oh yeah, because she was still working at the club part time. How she did it all, studying, working, supporting her family . . . living on nerves and chocolate, skinny as ever. And then, at the start of her second year, she met Roy.'

Oonagh sighed.

'Even the cleverest people can be bloody *stupid* when it comes to their love lives,' she said. 'In fact, I sometimes t'ink, the cleverer they are with books, the stupider they are with sex. Margot t'ought she'd learned her lesson, that she'd grown up. She couldn't see that it was *classic* rebound. He might've *looked* as different from Satchwell as you could get, but really, it was more of the same.

'Roy had the kind of background Margot would've loved. Books, travel, culture, you know. See, there were gaps in what Margot knew. She was insecure about not knowing about the right fork, the right words. "Napkin" instead of "serviette". All that snobby English stuff.

'Roy was mad for her, mind you. It wasn't all one way. I could see what the appeal was: she was like nothing he'd ever known before. She shocked him, but she fascinated him: the Playboy Club and her work ethic, her feminist ideas, supporting her mammy and daddy. They had arguments, intellectual arguments, you know.

'But there was something *bloodless* about the man. Not *wet* exactly, but—' Oonagh gave a sudden laugh. '"Bloodless" – you'll know about his bleeding problem?'

'Yes,' said Robin. 'Von Something Disease?'

'Dat's the one,' said Oonagh. 'He'd been cossetted and wrapped up in cotton wool all his life by his mother, who was a *horror.* I met her a few times. That woman gave me the respect you'd give something you'd got stuck on your shoe.

'And Roy was . . . still waters run deep, I suppose sums it up. He didn't show a lot of emotion. *Their* flirtation wasn't all sex, it really *was* ideas with them. Not that he wasn't good-looking. He was handsome, in a kind of . . . *limp* way. As different from Satchwell as you could imagine. Pretty boy, all eyes and floppy hair.

'But he was a manipulator. A little bit of disapproval here, a cold look there. He loved how different Margot was, but it still made him uncomfortable. He wanted a woman the exact opposite to his mother, but he wanted Mammy to approve. So the fault lines were dere from the beginning.

'And he could *sulk*,' said Oonagh. 'I *hate* a sulker, now. My mother was the same. T'irty years she wouldn't talk to me, because I moved to London. She finally gave in so she could meet her grandchildren, but then my sister got tipsy at Christmas and let it slip I'd left the church and joined the

Anglicans, we were finished for ever. Playboy, she could forgive. Proddy, never.

'Even when they were dating, Roy would stop talking to Margot for days at a time. She told me once he cut her off for a week. She lost patience, she said, "I'm off." That brought him round sharp enough. I said, what was he sulking about? And it was the club. He hated her working there. I said, "Is *he* offering to support your family, while you study?" "Oh, he doesn't like the idea of other men ogling me," she says. Girls like that idea, that little bit of possessiveness. They t'ink it means he only wants her, when o' course, it's the other way round. He only wants her available to *him*. *He's* still free to look at other girls, and Roy had other people interested in him, girls from his own background. He was a pretty boy with a lot of family money. Well,' said Oonagh, 'look at little cousin Cynthia, lurking in the wings.'

'Did you know Cynthia?' asked Robin.

'Met her once or twice, at their house. Mousy little thing. She never spoke more than two words to me,' said Oonagh. 'But she made Roy feel good about himself. Laughing loike a drain at all his jokes. Such as they were.'

'Margot and Roy must have married right after medical school, did they?'

'Dat's right. I was a bridesmaid. She went into general practice. Roy was a high-flier, he went into one of the big teaching hospitals, I can't remember which.

'Roy's parents had this very nice big house with huge lawns and all the rest of it. After his father died, which was just before they had Anna, the mother made it over to Roy. Margot's name wasn't on the deeds, I remember her telling me dat. But Roy loved the idea of bringing up his family in the same house he'd grown up in, and it was beautiful, right enough, out near Hampton Court. So the mother-in-law moved out and Roy and Margot moved in.

'Except, of course, the mother-in-law felt she had the right to walk back in any time she felt like it, because she'd given it to them and she still looked on it as more hers than Margot's.'

'Did you and Margot still see a lot of each other?' asked Robin.

'We did,' said Oonagh. 'We used to try and meet at least once every couple of weeks. Real best friends, we were. Even after she married Roy, she wanted to hold on to me. They had their middle-class friends, o' course, but I t'ink,' said Oonagh, her voice thickening, 'I t'ink she knew I'd always be on her side, you see. She was moving in circles where she felt alone.'

'At home, or at work, too?' asked Robin.

'At home, she was a fish out of water,' said Oonagh. 'Roy's house, Roy's family, Roy's friends, Roy's everyt'ing. She *saw* her own mammy and daddy plenty, but it was hard, the daddy being in his wheelchair, to get him out to the big house. I t'ink the Bamboroughs felt intimidated by Roy and his mother. So Margot used to go back to Stepney to see them. She was still supporting them financially. Ran herself ragged between all her different commitments.'

'And how were things at work?'

'Uphill, all the way,' said Oonagh. 'There weren't that many women doctors back then, and she was young and working class and that practice she ended up at, the St John's one, she felt alone. It wasn't a happy place,' said Oonagh, echoing Dr Gupta. 'Being Margot, she wanted to try and make it better. That was Margot's whole ethos: make it better. Make it work. Look after everyone. Solve the problem. She tried to bring them together as a team, even though she was the one being bullied.'

'Who was bullying her?'

'The old fella,' said Oonagh. 'I can't remember the names,

now. There were two other doctors, isn't that right? The old one and the Indian one. She said *he* was all right, the Indian fella, but she could feel the disapproval off him, too. They had an argument about the pill, she told me. GPs could give it to unmarried women if they wanted – when it was first brought out, it was married women only – but the Indian lad, he still wouldn't hand it out to unmarried women. The first family planning clinics started appearing the same year Margot disappeared. We talked about them. Margot said, t'ank God for it, because she was sure the women coming to their clinic weren't able to get it from either of the other doctors.

'But it wasn't only them. She had trouble with the other staff. I don't t'ink the nurse liked her, either.'

'Janice?' said Robin.

'Was it Janice?' said Oonagh, frowning.

'Irene?' suggested Strike.

'She was blonde,' said Oonagh. 'I remember, at the Christmas party—'

'You were there?' said Robin, surprised.

'Margot *begged* me to go,' said Oonagh. 'She'd set it up and she was afraid it was going to be awful. Roy was working, so *he* couldn't go. This was just a few months after Anna was born. Margot had been on maternity leave and they'd got another doctor in to cover for her, a man. She was convinced the place had worked better without her. She was hormonal and tired and dreading going back. Anna would only have been two or three months old. Margot brought her to the party, because she was breastfeeding. She'd organised the Christmas party to try and make a bit of a fresh start with them all, break the ice before she had to go back in.'

'Go on about Irene,' said Robin, conscious of Strike's pen hovering over his notebook.

'Well, she got drunk, if she's the blonde one. She'd brought some man with her to the party. Anyway, towards the end of the night, Irene accused Margot of *flirting* with the man. Did you ever in your loife hear anything more ridiculous? There's Margot standing there with her new baby in her arms, and the girl having a *proper* go at her. Was she not the nurse? It's so long ago . . .'

'No, Irene was the receptionist,' said Robin.

'I t'ought that was the little Italian girl?'

'Gloria was the other one.'

'Oh, Margot *loved* her,' said Oonagh. 'She said the girl was very clever but in a bad situation. She never gave me details. I t'ink the girl had seen her for medical advice and o' course, Margot wouldn't have shared anything about her health. She took all of dat very seriously. No priest in his confessional treated other people's secrets with more respect.'

'I want to ask you about something sensitive,' said Robin tentatively. 'There was a book about Margot, written in 1985, and you—'

'Joined with Roy to stop it,' said Oonagh at once. 'I did. It was a pack o' lies from start to finish. You know what he wrote, obviously. About—'

Oonagh might have left the Catholic Church, but she baulked at the word.

'—the termination. It was a filthy lie. I never had an abortion and nor did Margot. She'd have told me, if she was thinking about it. We were best friends. Somebody used her name to make dat appointment. I don't know who. The clinic didn't recognise her picture. She'd never been there. The very best t'ing in her life was Anna and she'd *never* have got rid of another baby. *Never.* She wasn't religious, but she'd have t'ought that was a sin, all right.'

'She wasn't a churchgoer?' Robin asked.

'At'eist t'rough and t'rough,' said Oonagh. 'She t'ought it

was all superstition. Her mammy was chapel, and Margot reacted against it. The church kept women down, was the way Margot looked at it, and she said to me, "If there's a God, why'd my daddy, who's a good man, have to fall off that step-ladder? Why's my family have to live the life we've had?" Well, Margot couldn't tell me anything about hypocrisy and religion I didn't already know. I'd left the Catholics by then. Doctrine of papal infallibility. No contraception, no matter if women died having their eleventh.

'My own mammy t'ought she was God's deputy on this earth, so she did, and some of the nuns at my school were pure bitches. Sister Mary Theresa – see there?' said Oonagh, pushing her fringe out of her eyes to reveal a scar the size of a five-pence piece. 'She hit me round the head wit' a metal set square. Blood everywhere. "I expect you deserved it," Mammy said.

'Now, I'll tell you who reminded me of Sister Mary Theresa,' said Oonagh. 'Would *she* have been the nurse, now? The older one at Margot's practice?'

'D'you mean Dorothy?'

'She was a widow, the one I'm t'inking of.'

'Yes, that was Dorothy, the secretary.'

'Spit image of Sister Mary Theresa, the eyes on her,' said Oonagh. 'I got cornered by her at the party. They're drawn to the church, women like dat. Nearly every congregation's got a couple. Outward observance, inward poison. They say the words, you know "Father forgive me, for I have sinned", but the Dorothys of this world, they don't believe they *can* sin, not really.

'One t'ing life's taught me: where there's no capacity for joy, there's no capacity for goodness,' said Oonagh Kennedy. 'She had it in for Margot, that Dorothy. I told her I was Margot's best friend and she started asking nosy questions.

How we'd met. Boyfriends. How Margot met Roy. None of her bloody business.

'Then she started talking about the old doctor, whatever his name was. There was a bit of Sister Mary Theresa in her, all right, but dat woman's god was sitting a desk away. I told Margot about the talk I'd had with her afterwards, and Margot said I was right. Dorothy was a mean one.'

'It was Dorothy's son who wrote the book about Margot,' said Robin.

'*Was it her son*?' gasped Oonagh. 'Was it? Well, *there you are.* Nasty pieces of work, the pair of them.'

'When was the last time you saw Margot?' Robin asked.

'Exactly two weeks before the night she disappeared. We met at The T'ree Kings then, too. Six o'clock, I had a night off from the club. There were a couple of bars nearer the practice, but she didn't want to run into anyone she worked with after hours.'

'Can you remember what you talked about that night?'

'I remember everyt'ing,' said Oonagh. 'You'll think that's an exaggeration, but it isn't. I started by giving her a row about going for a drink with Satchwell, which she'd told me about on the phone. They'd bumped into each other in the street.

'She said he seemed different to how he used to be and that worried me, I'm not going to lie. She wasn't built for an affair, but she was unhappy. Once we got to the pub, she told me the whole story. He'd asked to see her again and she'd said no. I believed her, and I'll tell you why: because she looked so damn miserable that she'd said no.

'She seemed worn down, that night. Unhappy like I'd never seen her before. She said Roy hadn't been talking to her for ten days when she ran into Satchwell. They'd had a row about his mother walking in and out of the house like she owned it. Margot wanted to redecorate, but Roy said it'd break his mother's heart if they got rid of any of the things his father loved. So there was Margot, an outsider in her own home, not even allowed to change the ornaments.

'Margot said she'd had a line from *Court and Spark* running through her head, all day long. Joni Mitchell's album, *Court and Spark*,' she said, seeing Robin's puzzlement. '*That* was Margot's religion. Joni Mitchell. She *raved* about that album. It was a line from the song "The Same Situation". "*Caught in my struggle for higher achievements, And my search for love that don't seem to cease.*" I can't listen to that album to this day. It's too painful.

'She told me she went straight home after havin' the drink with Paul and told Roy what had just happened. I think partly she felt guilty about going for the drink, but partly she wanted to jolt him awake. She was tired and miserable and she was saying *someone else wanted me, once.* Human nature, isn't it? "Wake up," she was saying. "You can't just ignore me and cut me off and refuse all compromises. I can't live like this."

'Well, being Roy, he wasn't the type to fire up and start throwing things. I t'ink she'd have found it easier if he had. He was furious, all right, but he showed it by gettin' colder and more silent.

'I don't t'ink he said another word to her until the day she disappeared. She told me on the phone when we arranged the drink for the eleventh, "I'm still living in a silent order." She sounded hopeless. I remember thinking then, "She's going to leave him."

'When we met in the pub that last time, I said to her, "Satchwell's not the answer to whatever's wrong with you and Roy."

'We talked about Anna, too. Margot would've given anything to take a year or two out and concentrate on Anna, and that's exactly what Roy and his mother had wanted her to do, stay home with Anna and forget working.

'But she couldn't. She was still supporting her parents. Her mammy was ill now, and Margot didn't want her out cleaning houses any more. While she was working, she could look Roy in the face and justify all the money she was giving them, but his mother wasn't going to let her precious, delicate son work for the benefit of a pair o' chain-smokin' Eastenders.'

'Can you remember anything else you talked about?'

'We talked about the Playboy Club, because I was leaving. I'd got my flat and I was thinking of going and studying. Margot was all for it. What I didn't tell her was, I was thinking of a t'eology degree, what with her attitude to religion.

'We talked about politics, a bit. We both wanted Wilson to win the election. And I told her I was worried I still hadn't found The One. Over t'irty, I was. That was old, then, for finding a husband.

'Before we said goodbye that night, I said, "Don't forget, there's always a spare room at my place. Room for a bassinet, as well."'

Tears welled again in Oonagh's eyes and trickled down her cheeks. She picked up her napkin and pressed it to her face.

'I'm sorry. Forty years ago, but it feels like yesterday. They don't disappear, the dead. It'd be easier if they did. I can see her so clearly. If she walked up those steps now, part of me wouldn't be surprised. She was such a *vivid* person. For her to disappear like that, just thin air where she was . . .'

Robin said nothing until Oonagh had wiped her face dry, then asked,

'What can you remember about arranging to meet on the eleventh?'

'She called me, asked to meet same place, same time. I said yes, o' course. There was something funny in the way she said it. I said, "Everything all right?" She said, "I need to ask your advice about something. I might be going mad. I shouldn't really talk about it, but I t'ink you're the only one I can trust."'

Strike and Robin looked at each other.

'Was that not written down anywhere?'

'No,' said Strike.

'No,' said Oonagh, and for the first time she looked angry. 'Well, I can't say I'm surprised.'

'Why not?' asked Robin.

'Talbot was away with the fairies,' said Oonagh. 'I could see it in the first five minutes of my interview. I called Roy, I said, "That man isn't right. Complain, tell them you want someone else on the case." He didn't, or if he did, nothing was done.

'And Lawson t'ought I was some silly little Bunny Girl,' said Oonagh. 'Probably t'ought I was tellin' fibs, trying to make myself interesting off the back of my best friend disappearing. Margot Bamborough was more like a sister than a friend to me,' said Oonagh fiercely, 'and the on'y person I've ever really talked to about her is my husband. I cried all over him, two days before we got married, because she should've been there. She should've been my matron of honour.'

'Have you got any idea what she was going to ask your advice about?' asked Robin.

'No,' said Oonagh. 'I've t'ought about it often since, whether it could have had anything to do with what happened. Something about Roy, perhaps, but then why would she say she shouldn't talk about it? We'd already talked about Roy. I'd told her as plain as I could, the last time we met, she could come and live with me if she left, Anna as well.

'Then I t'ought, maybe it's something a patient has told her, because like I said, she was scrupulous about confidentiality.

'Anyway, I walked up that hill in the rain to the pub on the eleventh. I was early, so I went to have a look at that church there, over the road, big—'

'Wait,' said Strike sharply. 'What kind of coat were you wearing?'

Oonagh didn't seem surprised by the question. On the contrary, she smiled.

'You're t'inking of the old gravedigger, or whoever he was? The one who t'ought he saw Margot going in there? I *told* them at the time it was me,' said Oonagh. 'I wasn't wearing a raincoat, but it was beige. My hair was darker than Margot's, but it was the same kind of length. I *told* them, when they asked me, did I think Margot might've gone into the church before meeting me – I said, no, she hated church. *I* went there! That was me!'

'Why?' asked Strike. 'Why did you go in there?'

'I was being called,' said Oonagh simply.

Robin repressed a smile, because Strike looked almost embarrassed at the answer.

'God was calling me back,' said Oonagh. 'I kept going into Anglican churches, t'inking, is this the answer? There was so much about the Catholics I couldn't take, but still, I could feel the pull back towards Him.'

'How long d'you think you were in the church?' asked Robin, to give Strike time to recover himself.

'Five minutes or so. I said a little prayer. I was asking for guidance. Then I walked out again, crossed the road and went into the pub.

'I waited nearly the full hour before I called Roy. At first I t'ought, she's been delayed by a patient. Then I t'ought, no, she must've forgotten. But when I called the house, Roy said she wasn't there. He was quite short with me. I wondered whether somethin' more had happened between them. Maybe Margot had snapped. Maybe I was going to get home and find her on the doorstep with Anna. So I went dashin' home, but she wasn't there.

'Roy called at nine to see whether I'd had any contact. That's when I started to get really worried. He said he was going to call the police.

'You'll know the rest,' said Oonagh quietly. 'It was like a nightmare. You put all your hopes on t'ings that are less and less likely. Amnesia. Knocked down by a car and unconscious somewhere. She's run away somewhere to t'ink.

'But I knew, really. She'd never've left her baby girl, and she'd *never* have left without telling me. I knew she was dead. I could tell the police t'ought it was the Essex Butcher, but me . . .'

'But you?' prompted Robin gently.

'Well, I kept t'inking, t'ree weeks after Paul Satchwell comes back into her life, she vanishes for ever. I know he had his little alibi, all his arty friends backing him up. I said to Talbot and Lawson: ask him about the pillow dream. Ask him what that means, the pillow dream he was so frightened Margot would tell people about.

'Is that in the police notes?' she asked Strike, turning to look at him. 'Did either of them ask Satchwell about the pillow dream?'

'No,' said Strike slowly. 'I don't think they did.'

25

All those were idle thoughtes and fantasies,
Deuices, dreames, opinions vnsound,
Shewes, visions, sooth-sayes, and prophesies;
And all that fained is, as leasings, tales, and lies.

Edmund Spenser
The Faerie Queene

Three evenings later, Strike was to be found sitting in his BMW outside a nondescript terraced house in Stoke Newington. The Shifty investigation, now in its fifth month, had so far yielded no results. The restive trustees who suspected that their CEO was being blackmailed by the ambitious Shifty were making ominous noises of discontent, and were clearly considering taking their business elsewhere.

Even after being plied with gin by Hutchins, who'd succeeded in befriending him at the rifle club, Shifty had remained as close lipped as ever about the hold he had over his boss, so it was time, Strike had decided, to start tailing SB himself. It was just possible that the CEO, a rotund, pinstriped man with a bald patch like a monk's tonsure, was still indulging in the blackmailable behaviour that Shifty had uncovered and that had leveraged him into a promotion that neither Shifty's CV, nor his personality, justified.

Strike was sure Shifty wasn't exploiting a simple case of

infidelity. SB's current wife had the immaculate, plastic sheen of a doll newly removed from cellophane and Strike suspected it would take more than her husband having an affair to make her relinquish her taloned grip on a black American Express card, especially as she'd been married barely two years and had no children to guarantee a generous settlement.

Christmas tree lights twinkled in almost every window surrounding Strike. The roof of the house beside him had been hung with brilliant blue-white icicles that burned the retina if looked at too long. Wreaths on doors, glass panels decorated with fake snow and the sparkle of orange, red and green reflected in the dirty puddles all reminded Strike that he really did need to start buying Christmas gifts to take to Cornwall.

Joan had been released from hospital that morning, her drugs adjusted, and determined to get home and start preparing for the family festivities. Strike would need to buy presents not only for Joan and Ted but for his sister, brother-in-law and nephews. This was an irksome extra chore, given the amount of work the agency currently had on its books. Then he reminded himself that he had to buy something for Robin, too, something better than flowers. Strike, who disliked shopping in general, and buying gifts in particular, reached for his cigarettes to ward off a dim sense of persecution.

Having lit up, Strike took from his pocket the copy of *Whatever Happened to Margot Bamborough?* which Robin had given him, but which he hadn't yet had time to read. Small tags marked the places Robin thought might be of some interest to the investigation.

With a quick glance at the still-closed front door of the house he was watching, Strike opened the book and skim-read a couple of pages, looking up at regular intervals to check that SB hadn't yet emerged.

The first chapter, which Robin hadn't marked, but which

Strike flicked through anyway, dealt summarily with Margot's childhood and adolescence. Unable to gain access to anybody with particularly clear memories of his subject, Oakden had to fall back on generalities, supposition and a good deal of padding. Thus Strike learned that Margot Bamborough 'would have dreamed of leaving poverty behind', 'would have been caught up in the giddy atmosphere of the 1960s' and 'would have been aware of the possibilities for consequence-free sex offered by the contraceptive pill'. Word count was boosted by the information that the mini-skirt had been popularised by Mary Quant, that London was the heart of a thriving music scene and that the Beatles had appeared on America's *Ed Sullivan Show* around the time of Margot's nineteenth birthday. 'Margot would have been excited by the possibilities offered to the working classes in this new, egalitarian era,' C. B. Oakden informed his readers.

Chapter two ushered in Margot's arrival at the Playboy Club, and here, the sense of strain that had suffused the previous chapter vanished. C. B. Oakden evidently found Playboy Bunny Margot a far more inspiring subject than child Margot, and he devoted many paragraphs to the sense of freedom and liberation she would have felt on lacing herself tightly into her Bunny costume, putting on false ears and judiciously padding the cups of her costume to ensure that her breasts appeared of sufficient fullness to satisfy her employer's stringent demands. Writing eleven years after her disappearance, Oakden had managed to track down a couple of Bunny Girls who remembered Margot. Bunny Lisa, who was now married with two children, reminisced about having 'a good laugh' with her, and being 'devastated' by her disappearance. Bunny Rita, who ran her own marketing business, said that she was 'really bright, obviously going places', and thought 'it must've been dreadful for her poor family'.

Strike glanced up again at the front of the house into which SB had disappeared. Still no sign of him. Turning back to C. B. Oakden, the bored Strike skipped ahead to the first place Robin had marked as of interest.

> After her successful stint at the Playboy Club, the playful and flirtatious Margot found it hard to adapt to the life of a general practitioner. At least one employee at the St John's practice says her manner was out of place in the setting of a consulting room.
>
> "She didn't keep them at a proper distance, that was the trouble. She wasn't from a background that had a lot of professional people. A doctor's got to hold himself above the patients.
>
> "She recommended that book *The Joy of Sex*, to a woman who went to see her. I heard people in the waiting room talking about it, after. Giggling, you know. A doctor shouldn't be telling people to read things like that. It reflects poorly on the whole practice. I was embarrassed for her.
>
> "The one who was keen on her, the young fellow who kept coming back to see her, buying her chocolates and what have you – if she was telling people about different sex positions, you can see how men got the wrong idea, can't you?"

There followed several paragraphs that had clearly been cribbed from the press, covering the suicide of Steve Douthwaite's married ex-girlfriend, his sudden flight from his job and the fact that Lawson had re-interviewed him several times. Making the most of his scant material, Oakden managed to suggest that Douthwaite had been at best disreputable, at worst, dangerous: a feckless drifter and an unprincipled lady's man, in whose vicinity women had a habit of dying or disappearing. It was with a slight snort of sudden amusement, therefore, that Strike read the words,

> Now calling himself Stevie Jacks, Douthwaite currently works at Butlin's holiday camp in Clacton-on-Sea—

After glancing up again to check that SB hadn't yet emerged, Strike read on:

> where he runs events for the campers by day and performs in the cabaret by night. His "Longfellow Serenade" is a particular hit with the ladies. Dark-haired Douthwaite/Jacks remains a handsome man, and clearly popular with female campers.
>
> "I've always liked singing," he tells me in the bar after the show. 'I was in a band when I was younger but it broke up. I came to Butlin's once when I was a kid, with my foster family. I always thought it looked a laugh, being a Redcoat. Plenty of big-time entertainers got their start here, you know."
>
> When talk turns to Margot Bamborough, however, a very different side to this cheeky cabaret singer appears.
>
> "The press wrote a load of balls. I never bought her chocolates or anything else, that was just made up to make me look like some kind of creep. I had a stomach ulcer and headaches. I'd been through a bad time."
>
> After refusing to explain why he'd changed his name, Douthwaite left the bar.
>
> His colleagues at the holiday camp expressed their shock that "Stevie" had been questioned by the police over the disappearance of the young doctor.
>
> "He never told us anything about it," said Julie Wilkes, 22. "I'm quite shocked, actually. You'd think he'd have told us. He never said 'Jacks' wasn't his real name, either."

Oakden treated his readers to a brief history of Butlin's, and ended the chapter with a paragraph of speculation on the opportunities a predatory man might find at a holiday camp.

Strike lit another cigarette, then flicked ahead to the second of Robin's markers, where a short passage dealt with Jules Bayliss, husband of the office-cleaner-turned-social-worker, Wilma. The only piece of new information here was that convicted rapist Bayliss had been released on bail in January 1975, a full three months after Margot went missing. Nevertheless, Oakden asserted that Bayliss 'would have got wind' of the fact that Margot was trying to persuade his wife to leave him, 'would have been angry that the doctor was pressurising his wife to break up the family' and 'would have had many criminal associations in his own community'. The police, Oakden informed his readers, 'would have looked carefully into the movements of any of Bayliss's friends or relatives on the eleventh of October, so we must conclude,' he finished, anticlimactically, 'that no suspicious activity was uncovered.'

Robin's third tab marked the pages dealing with the abortion at Bride Street Nursing Home. Oakden ushered in this part of his story with considerable fanfare, informing his readers that he was about to reveal facts that had never before been made public.

What followed was interesting to Strike only in as far as it proved that an abortion had definitely taken place on the fourteenth of September 1974, and that the name given by the patient had been Margot Bamborough. As proof, Oakden reprinted photographs of the Bride Street medical records that had been provided by an unidentified employee of the nursing home, which had closed down in 1978. Strike supposed the unnamed employee would no longer have been fearful for their job when Oakden had come offering money for information in the eighties. The unnamed employee also told

Oakden that the woman who had had the procedure didn't resemble the picture of Margot that had subsequently appeared in the papers.

Oakden then posed a series of rhetorical questions that he and his foolhardy publishers appeared to think circumvented libel laws. Was it possible that the woman who had the abortion had used Margot's name with her support and consent? In which case, who might Margot have been most eager to assist? Was it not most likely that a Roman Catholic would be particularly worried about anyone finding out she had had an abortion? Was it not also the case that complications could arise from such a procedure? Might Margot have returned to the vicinity of the Bride Street Nursing Home on the eleventh of October to visit somebody who had been readmitted to the clinic? Or to ask advice on behalf of that person? Could Margot possibly have been abducted, not from Clerkenwell, but from a street or two away from Dennis Creed's basement?

To which Strike answered mentally, *no, and you deserved to have your book pulped, pal.* The string of events suggested by Oakden had clearly been put together in a determined attempt to place Margot in the vicinity of Creed's basement on the night she disappeared. 'Complications' were necessary to explain Margot returning to the nursing home a month after the abortion, but they couldn't be Margot's own, given that she was fit, well and working at the St John's practice all the way up to her disappearance. Once attributed to a best friend, however, undefined 'complications' could serve two purposes: to give Margot a reason to head back to the clinic to visit Oonagh, and Oonagh a reason to lie about both women's whereabouts that night. All in all, Strike considered Oakden lucky not to have been sued, and surmised that fear of the resultant publicity was all that had held Roy and Oonagh back.

He flicked forward to Robin's fourth tab and, after checking again that the front door of the house he was watching remained closed, read the next marked passage.

> "I saw her as clearly as I can see you now. She was standing at that window, *pounding* on it, as if she wanted to attract attention. I especially remember, because I was reading *The Other Side of Midnight* at the time and just thinking about women and what they go through, you know, and I looked up and I saw her.
>
> "If I close my eyes, she's there, it's like a snapshot in my head and it's haunted me ever since, to be honest. People have said to me since, 'you're making it up' or 'you need to let it go', but I'm not changing my story just because other people don't believe it. What would that make me?"
>
> The small printers who then occupied the top floor of the building was run by husband and wife team Arnold and Rachel Sawyer. Police accepted their assurance that Margot Bamborough had never set foot on the premises, and that the woman seen by Mandy that night was probably Mrs Sawyer herself, who claimed one of the windows needed to be hit to close properly.
>
> However, an odd connection between A&R Printing and Margot Bamborough went unnoticed by police. A&R's first major printing job was for the now-closed nightclub Drudge – the very nightclub for which Paul Satchwell, Margot's lover, had designed a risqué mural. Satchwell's designs subsequently featured on flyers printed by A&R Printing, so it is likely that he and the Sawyers would have been in touch with each other.
>
> Might this suggest . . .

'Fuck's sake,' muttered Strike, turning the page and dropping his eyes to a brief paragraph Robin had marked with a thick black line.

> However, ex-neighbour Wayne Truelove thinks that Paul Satchwell subsequently went abroad.
>
> "He talked to me about going travelling. I don't think he was making a lot of money from his art and after the police questioned him, he told me he was thinking of clearing out for a bit. Probably smart, going away."

Robin's fifth and final tab came towards the end of the book, and after again checking that SB's car was parked where he had left it, and that the front door of the house had not opened, Strike read:

> A month after Margot's disappearance, her husband Roy visited the St John's practice. Roy, who had been unable to conceal his bad temper at the practice barbecue that summer, was unsurprisingly subdued on this visit.
>
> Dorothy remembers: "He wanted to speak to us all, to thank us for cooperating with the police. He looked ill. Hardly surprising.
>
> "We'd boxed up her personal effects because we had a locum working out of her room. The police had already searched it. We put her personal effects together. There was hand cream and her framed degree certificate and a photo of him, Roy, holding their daughter. He looked through the box and got a bit emotional, but then he picked up this thing that she'd had on her desk. It was one of those little wooden figures, like a Viking. He said 'Where did this come from? Where did she get this?' None of us knew, but I thought he seemed upset by it.

"He probably thought a man had given it her. Of course, the police were looking into her love life by then. Awful thing, not to be able to trust your wife."

Strike glanced up yet again at the house, saw no change, and flicked to the end of the book, which concluded in a final burst of speculation, supposition and half-baked theory. On the one hand, Oakden implied that Margot had brought tragedy on herself, that fate had punished her for being too sexual and too bold, for cramming herself into a corset and bunny ears, for hoisting herself hubristically out of the class into which she had been born. On the other hand, she seemed to have lived her life surrounded by would-be killers. No man associated with Margot escaped Oakden's suspicion, whether it was 'charming but feckless Stevie Douthwaite-turned-Jacks', 'domineering blood specialist Roy Phipps', 'resentful rapist Jules Bayliss', 'hot-tempered womaniser Paul Satchwell' or 'notorious sex monster Dennis Creed'.

Strike was on the point of closing the book when he noticed a line of darker page edges in the middle, suggesting photographs, and opened it again.

Other than the familiar press headshot and the picture of Margot and Oonagh in their Bunny Girl costumes – Oonagh curvaceous and grinning broadly, Margot statuesque, with a cloud of fair hair – there were only three photos. All were of poor quality and featured Margot only incidentally.

The first was captioned: 'The author, his mother and Margot'. Square-jawed, iron-grey-haired, and wearing winged glasses, Dorothy Oakden stood facing the camera with her arm around a skinny freckle-faced boy with a pageboy haircut, who had screwed up his face into a grimace that distorted his features. Strike was reminded of Luke, his eldest nephew. Behind the Oakdens was a long expanse of striped lawn and, in the distance, a sprawling house with many pointed gables. Objects appeared to be protruding out of the lawn close to the house: upon closer examination, Strike concluded that they were the beginnings of walls or columns: it looked as though a summerhouse was under construction.

Walking across the lawn behind Dorothy and Carl, unaware that she was being photographed, was Margot Bamborough, barefooted, wearing denim shorts and a T-shirt, carrying a plate and smiling at somebody out of shot. Strike deduced that this picture had been taken at the staff barbecue Margot had organised. The Phipps house was certainly grander than he'd imagined.

After looking up once more to check that SB's car remained parked where he'd left it, Strike turned to the last two pictures, both of which featured the St John's practice Christmas party.

Tinsel had been draped over the reception desk and the waiting room cleared of chairs, which had been stacked in corners. Strike searched for Margot in both pictures and found her, baby Anna in her arms, talking to a tall black woman he assumed was Wilma Bayliss. In the corner of the picture was a slim, round-eyed woman with feathered brown hair, who Strike thought might be a young Janice.

In the second picture, all heads were turned away from the camera or partially obscured, except one. A gaunt, unsmiling older man in a suit, with his hair slicked back, was the only person who seemed to have been given notice that the picture was about to be taken. The flash had turned his eyes red. The picture was captioned 'Margot and Dr Joseph Brenner', though only the back of Margot's head was visible.

In the corner of this picture were three men who, judging from their coats and jackets, had just arrived at the party. The darkness of their clothing made a solid block of black on the right-hand side of the photo. All had their backs to the camera, but the largest, whose face was slightly turned to the left, displayed one long black sideburn, a large ear, the tip of a fleshy nose and a drooping eye. His left hand was raised in the act of scratching his face. He was wearing a large gold ring featuring a lion's head.

Strike examined this picture until noises out on the street made him look up. SB had just emerged from the house. A plump blonde in carpet slippers was standing on her doormat. She raised a hand and patted SB gently on the top of the head, as you would pet a child or a dog. Smiling, SB bade her farewell, then turned and walked back towards his Mercedes.

Strike threw the copy of *Whatever Happened to Margot Bamborough?* into the passenger seat. Waiting for SB to pull out into the road, he set off in pursuit.

After five minutes or so, it became clear that his quarry was driving back to his home in West Brompton. One hand on the steering wheel, Strike groped for his mobile, then pressed the number of an old friend. The call went straight to voicemail.

'Shanker, it's Bunsen. Need to talk to you about something. Let me know when I can buy you a pint.'

26

All were faire knights, and goodly well beseene,
But to faire Britomart they all but shadowes beene.

Edmund Spenser
The Faerie Queene

With five active cases on the agency's books, and only four days to go until Christmas, two of the agency's subcontractors succumbed to seasonal flu. Morris fell first: he blamed his daughter's nursery, where the virus had swept like wildfire through toddlers and parents alike. He continued to work until a high temperature and joint pain forced him to telephone in his apologies, by which time he'd managed to pass the bug to a furious Barclay, who in turn had transmitted it to his own wife and young daughter.

'Stupid arsehole shoulda stayed at home instead o' breathin' all over me in the car,' Barclay ranted hoarsely over the phone to Strike early on the morning of the twentieth, while Strike was opening up the office. The last full team meeting before Christmas was to have taken place at ten o'clock, but as two of the team were now unable to attend, Strike had decided to cancel. The only person he hadn't been able to reach was Robin, who he assumed was on the Tube. Strike had asked her to come in early so they could catch up with the Bamborough case before everyone else arrived.

'We're supposedtae be flying to Glasgow the morra,' Barclay

rasped, while Strike put on the kettle. 'The wean's in that much pain wi' her ears—'

'Yeah,' said Strike, who was feeling sub-standard himself, doubtless due to tiredness, and too much smoking. 'Well, feel better and get back whenever you can.'

'Arsehole,' growled Barclay, and then, 'Morris, I mean. Not you. Merry fuckin' Christmas.'

Trying to convince himself that he was imagining the tickle in his throat, the slight clamminess of his back and the pain behind his eyes, Strike made himself a mug of tea, then moved through to the inner office and pulled up the blinds. Wind and heavy rain were causing the Christmas lights strung across Denmark Street to sway on their cables. Just as they'd done on the five previous mornings, the decorations reminded Strike that he still hadn't started his Christmas shopping. He took a seat on his accustomed side of the partners' desk, knowing that he'd now left the job so late that he would be forced to execute it within a couple of hours, which at least obviated the tedious preliminary of carefully considering what anyone might like. Rain lashed the window behind him. He'd have liked to go back to bed.

He heard the glass door open and close.

'Morning,' Robin called from the outer office. 'It's *vile* out there.'

'Morning,' Strike called back. 'Kettle's just boiled and team meeting's cancelled. That's Barclay down with flu as well.'

'Shit,' said Robin. 'How're *you* feeling?'

'Fine,' said Strike, now sorting out his various Bamborough notes.

But when Robin entered the inner office, carrying tea in one hand and her own notebook in the other, she didn't think Strike looked fine at all. He was paler than usual, his forehead looked shiny and there were grey shadows around his eyes. She closed the office door and sat down opposite him without passing comment.

'Not much point to a team meeting anyway,' muttered Strike. 'Fuck-all progress on any of the cases. Twinkletoes is clean. The worst you can say about him is he's with her for the money, but her dad knew that from the start. Two-Times' girlfriend isn't cheating and Christ only knows what Shifty's got on SB. You saw my email about the blonde in Stoke Newington?'

'Yes,' said Robin, whose face had been whipped into high colour by the squally weather. She was trying to comb her hair back into some semblance of tidiness with her fingers. 'Nothing come up on the address?'

'No. If I had to guess, I'd say she's a relative. She patted him on the head as he left.'

'Dominatrix?' suggested Robin.

There wasn't much she hadn't learned about the kinks of powerful men since joining the agency.

'It occurred to me, but the way he said goodbye . . . they looked . . . cosy. But he hasn't got a sister and she looked younger than him. Would cousins pat each other on the head?'

'Well, Sunday night's all wrong for a normal counsellor or a therapist, but patting's quasi-parental . . . life coach? Psychic?'

'That's a thought,' said Strike, stroking his chin. 'Stockholders wouldn't be impressed if he's making business decisions based on what his fortune teller in Stoke Newington's telling him. I was going to put Morris on to the woman over Christmas, but he's out of action, Hutchins is on Two-Times' girl and I'm supposed to be leaving for Cornwall day after tomorrow. You're off to Masham when – Tuesday?'

'No,' said Robin, looking anxious. 'Tomorrow – Saturday. We did discuss this back in September, remember? I swapped with Morris so I could—'

'Yeah, yeah, I remember,' lied Strike. His head was starting to throb, and the tea wasn't making his throat feel much more comfortable. 'No problem.'

But this, of course, meant that if he was going to give Robin a Christmas present, he'd have to buy it and get it to her by the end of the day.

'I'd try and get a later train,' said Robin, 'but obviously, with it being Christmas—'

'No, you're owed time off,' he said brusquely. 'You shouldn't be working just because those careless bastards got flu.'

Robin, who had a strong suspicion that Barclay and Morris weren't the only people at the agency with flu, said,

'D'you want more tea?'

'What? No,' said Strike, feeling unreasonably resentful at her for, as he saw it, forcing him to go shopping. 'And Postcard's a washout, we've got literally noth—'

'I might – *might* – have something on Postcard.'

'What?' said Strike, surprised.

'Our weatherman got another postcard yesterday, sent to the television studio. It's the fourth one bought in the National Portrait Gallery shop, and it's got an odd message on it.'

She pulled the postcard from her bag and handed it over the desk to Strike. The picture on the front reproduced a self-portrait of Joshua Reynolds, his hand shading his eyes in the stereotypical pose of one staring at something indistinct. On the back was written:

> I hope I'm wrong, but I think you sent someone to my work, holding some of my letters. Have you let someone else see them? I really hope you haven't. Were you trying to scare me? You act like you're so kind and down-to-earth, no airs and graces. I'd have thought you'd have the decency to come yourself if you've got something to say to me. If you don't understand this, ignore.

Strike looked up at Robin.

'Does this mean . . . ?'

Robin explained that she'd bought the same three postcards that Postcard had previously sent from the gallery shop, then roamed the gallery's many rooms, holding the postcards so that they were visible to all the guides she passed, until an owlish woman in thick-lensed glasses had appeared to react at the sight of them, and disappeared through a door marked 'Staff Only'.

'I didn't tell you at the time,' Robin said, 'because I thought I might've imagined it, and she also looked exactly like the kind of person I'd imagined Postcard to be, so I was worried I was doing a Talbot, chasing my own mad hunches.'

'But you're not off your rocker, are you? That was a bloody good idea, going to the shop, and this,' he brandished the postcard of the Reynolds, 'suggests you hit the bullseye first throw.'

'I didn't manage to get a picture of her,' said Robin, trying not to show how much pleasure Strike's praise had given her, 'but she was in Room 8 and I can describe her. Big glasses, shorter than me, thick brown hair, bobbed, probably fortyish.'

Strike made a note of the description.

'Might nip along there myself before I head for Cornwall,' he said. 'Right, let's get on with Bamborough.'

But before either could say another word, the phone rang in the outer office. Glad to have something to complain about, Strike glanced at his watch, heaved himself to his feet and said,

'It's nine o'clock, Pat should—'

But even as he said it, they both heard the glass door open, Pat's unhurried tread and then, in her usual rasping baritone,

'Cormoran Strike Detective Agency.'

Robin tried not to smile as Strike dropped back into his chair. There was a knock on the door, and Pat stuck her head inside,

'Morning. Got a Gregory Talbot on hold for you.'

'Put him through,' said Strike. 'Please,' he added, detecting a martial look in Pat's eye, 'and close the door.'

She did so. A moment later, the phone rang on the partners' desk and Strike switched it to speakerphone.

'Hi, Gregory, Strike here.'

'Yes, hello,' said Gregory, who sounded anxious.

'What can I do for you?'

'Er, well, you know how we were clearing out the loft?'

'Yes,' said Strike.

'Well, yesterday I unpacked an old box,' said Gregory, sounding tense, 'and I found something hidden under Dad's commendations and his uniform—'

'Not *hidden*,' said a querulous female voice in the background.

'I didn't know it was there,' said Gregory. 'And now my mother—'

'Let me talk to him,' said the woman in the background.

'My mother would like to talk to you,' said Gregory, sounding exasperated.

A defiant, elderly female voice replaced Gregory's.

'Is this Mr Strike?'

'It is.'

'Gregory's told you all about how the police treated Bill at the end?'

'Yes,' said Strike.

'He could have kept working once he got treatment for his thyroid, but they didn't let him. He'd given them *everything*, the force was his *life*. Greg says he's given you Bill's notes?'

'That's right,' said Strike.

'Well, after Bill died I found this *can* in a box in the shed and it had the Creed mark on it – you've read the notes, you know Bill used a special symbol for Creed?'

'Yes,' said Strike.

'I couldn't take everything with me into sheltered accommodation, they give you virtually *no* storage space, so I put it into the boxes to go in Greg and Alice's attic. I quite forgot it was there until Greg started looking through his dad's things yesterday. The police have made it *quite* clear they weren't interested in Bill's theories, but Greg says you are, so you should have it.'

Gregory came back on the line. They heard movement that seemed to indicate that Gregory was moving away from his mother. A door closed.

'It's a can containing a reel of old 16mm film,' he told Strike, his mouth close to the receiver. 'Mum doesn't know what's on there. I haven't got a camera to run it, but I've held a bit up to the light and . . . it looks like a dirty movie. I was worried about putting it out for the binmen—'

Given that the Talbots were fostering children, Strike understood his qualms.

'If we give it to you – I wonder—'

'You'd rather we didn't say where we got it?' Strike said, eyes on Robin's. 'I can't see why we'd need to.'

Robin noticed that he hadn't promised, but Gregory seemed happy.

'I'll drop it off, then,' he said. 'I'm coming up West this afternoon. Taking the twins to see Father Christmas.'

When Gregory had rung off, Strike said,

'You notice the Talbots are still convinced, forty years on—'

The phone rang in the outer office again.

'—that Margot was killed by Creed? I think I know what the symbol on this can of film is going to be, because—'

Pat knocked on the door of the inner office.

'Fuck's sake,' muttered Strike, whose throat was starting to burn. '*What?*'

'Charming,' said Pat, coldly. 'There's a Mister Shanker on

the line for you. It diverted from your mobile. He says you wanted to—'

'Yeah, I do,' said Strike. 'Transfer it back to my mobile – please,' he added, and turning to Robin, he said, 'sorry, can you give me a moment?'

Robin left the room, closing the door behind her, and Strike pulled out his mobile.

'Shanker, hi, thanks for getting back to me.'

He and Shanker, whose real name he'd have been hard pressed to remember, had known each other since they were teenagers. Their lives had been moving in diametrically different directions even then, Strike heading for university, army and detective work, Shanker pursuing a career of ever-deepening criminality. Nevertheless, a strange sense of kinship had continued to unite them and they were, occasionally, useful to each other, Strike paying Shanker in cash for information or services that he could get no other way.

'What's up, Bunsen?'

'I wanted to buy you a pint and show you a photo,' said Strike.

'Up your way later today, as it goes. Going to Hamleys. Got the wrong fackin' Monster High doll for Zahara.'

Everything except 'Hamleys' had been gibberish to Strike.

'OK, call me when you're ready for a drink.'

'Fair dos.'

The line went dead. Shanker didn't tend to bother with goodbyes.

Robin returned carrying two fresh mugs of tea and closed the door with her foot.

'Sorry about that,' said Strike, absent-mindedly wiping sweat off his top lip. 'What was I saying?'

'That you think you know what symbol's on Talbot's can of old film.'

'Oh, yeah,' said Strike. 'Symbol for Capricorn. I've been having a go at deciphering these notes,' he added, tapping the leather-bound notebook sitting beside him, and he took Robin through the reasons Bill Talbot had come to believe that Margot had been abducted by a man born under the sign of the goat.

'Talbot was ruling out suspects on the basis that they weren't Capricorns?' asked Robin in disbelief.

'Yeah,' said Strike, frowning, his throat burning worse than ever. He took a sip of tea. 'Except that Roy Phipps is a Capricorn, and Talbot ruled him out, too.'

'Why?'

'I'm still trying to decipher it all, but he seems to have been using a weird symbol for Phipps that I haven't been able to identify on any astrological site so far.

'But the notes explain why he kept interviewing Janice. Her star sign's Cancer. Cancer is Capricorn's "opposing" sign and Cancerians are psychic and intuitive, according to Talbot's notes. Talbot concluded that, as a Cancerian, Janice was his natural ally against Baphomet, and that she might have supernatural insights into Baphomet's identity, hence the dream diary.

'Even more significant in his mind was that Saturn, Capricorn's ruler—'

Robin hid a smile behind her mug of tea. Strike's expression, as he outlined these astrological phenomena, would have been appropriate to a man asked to eat weeks'-old seafood.

'—was in Cancer on the day of Margot's disappearance. From this, Talbot deduced that Janice knew or had had contact with Baphomet. Hence the request for a list of her sexual partners.'

'Wow,' said Robin quietly.

'I'm just giving you a hint of the nuttery, but there's plenty more. I'll email you the important points when I've finished deciphering it. But what's interesting is that there are hints of an actual detective trying to fight through his illness.

'He had the same idea that occurred to me: that Margot might've been lured somewhere on the pretext of someone needing medical assistance, although he dresses it all up in mumbo-jumbo – there was a stellium in the sixth house, the House of Health, which he decided meant danger associated with illness.'

'What's a stellium?'

'Group of more than three planets. The police did check out patients she'd seen a lot of in the run-up to the disappearance. There was Douthwaite, obviously, and a demented old woman on Gopsall Street, who kept ringing the surgery for something to do, and a family who lived on Herbal Hill, whose kid had had a reaction to his polio vaccination.'

'Doctors,' said Robin, 'have contact with *so many* people.'

'Yeah,' said Strike, 'and I think that's part of what went wrong in this case. Talbot took in a huge amount of information and couldn't see what to discard. On the other hand, the possibility of her being lured into a house on a medical pretext, or attacked by an angry patient isn't crazy. Medics walk unaccompanied into all kinds of people's houses . . . and look at Douthwaite. Lawson really fancied him as Margot's abductor or killer, and Talbot was very interested in him, too. Even though Douthwaite was a Pisces, Talbot tries to make him a Capricorn. He says "Schmidt" thinks Douthwaite's really a Capricorn—'

'Who's Schmidt?'

'No idea,' said Strike, 'but he or she is all over the notes, correcting signs.'

'All the chances to get actual evidence lost,' said Robin quietly, 'while Talbot was checking everyone's horoscope.'

'Exactly. It'd be funny if it wasn't so serious. But his interest in Douthwaite still smacks of sound copper instinct. Douthwaite seems pretty bloody fishy to me, as well.'

'Ha ha,' said Robin.

Strike looked blank.

'Pisces,' she reminded him.

'Oh. Yeah,' said Strike, unsmiling. The throbbing behind his eyes was worse than ever, his throat complaining every time he swallowed, but he couldn't have flu. It was impossible. 'I read that bit you marked in Oakden's book,' he continued. 'The stuff about Douthwaite changing his name when he went to Clacton to sing at a holiday camp, but I can't find any trace of a Steve, Steven or Stevie Jacks after 1976, either. One name change might be understandable after a lot of police attention. Two starts to look suspicious.'

'You think?' said Robin. 'We know he was the nervous type, judging from his medical records. Maybe he was spooked by Oakden turning up at Butlin's?'

'But Oakden's book was pulped. Nobody beyond a couple of Butlin's Redcoats ever knew Stevie Jacks had been questioned about Margot Bamborough.'

'Maybe he went abroad,' said Robin. 'Died abroad. I'm starting to think that's what happened to Paul Satchwell, as well. Did you see, Satchwell's ex-neighbour said he went off travelling?'

'Yeah,' said Strike. 'Any luck on Gloria Conti yet?'

'Nothing,' sighed Robin. 'But I have got a *couple* of things,' she went on, opening her notebook. 'They don't advance us much, but for what they're worth . . .

'I've now spoken to Charlie Ramage's widow in Spain. The hot-tub millionaire who thought he saw Margot in the Leamington Spa graveyard?'

Strike nodded, glad of a chance to rest his throat.

'I think Mrs Ramage has either had a stroke or likes a lunchtime drink. She sounded slurred, but she confirmed that Charlie thought he'd seen Margot in a graveyard, and that he discussed it afterwards with a policeman friend, whose name she couldn't remember. Then suddenly she said, "No, wait – Mary Flanagan. It was Mary Flanagan he thought he saw." I took her back over the story and she said, yes, that was all correct, except that it was Mary Flanagan, not Margot Bamborough, he thought he'd seen. I've looked up Mary Flanagan,' said Robin, 'and she's been missing since 1959. It's Britain's longest ever missing person case.'

'Which of them would you say seemed more confused?' asked Strike. 'Mrs Ramage, or Janice?'

'Mrs Ramage, definitely,' said Robin. 'Janice definitely wouldn't have confused the two women, would she? Whereas Mrs Ramage might have done. She had no personal interest: to her, they were just two missing people whose names began with "M".'

Strike sat frowning, thinking it over. Finally he said, his tonsils burning,

'If Ramage was a teller of tall tales generally, his policeman mate can't be blamed for not taking him seriously. This is at least confirmation that Ramage believed he'd once met a missing woman.'

He frowned so intensely that Robin said,

'Are you in pain?'

'No. I'm wondering whether it'd be worth trying to see Irene and Janice separately. I'd hoped never to have to talk to Irene Hickson again. At the very least, we should keep looking for a connection between Margot and Leamington Spa. Did you say you had another lead?'

'Not much of one. Amanda Laws – or Amanda White, as she was when she supposedly saw Margot at that window on

Clerkenwell Road – answered my email. I'll forward her reply if you want to read it, but basically she's angling for money.'

'Is she, now?'

'She dresses it up a bit. Says she told the police and nobody believed her, told Oakden and he didn't give her a penny, and she's tired of not being taken seriously and if we want her story she'd like to be paid for it this time. She claims she's endured a lot of negative attention, being called a liar and a fantasist, and she's not prepared to go through all of that again unless she gets compensated.'

Strike made a second note.

'Tell her it isn't the agency's practice to pay witnesses for their cooperation,' said Strike. 'Appeal to her better nature. If that doesn't work, she can have a hundred quid.'

'I think she's hoping for thousands.'

'And I'm hoping for Christmas in the Bahamas,' said Strike, as rain dotted the window behind him. 'That all you've got?'

'Yes,' said Robin, closing her notebook.

'Well, I've drawn a blank on the Bennie-abusing patient who claimed to have killed Margot, Applethorpe. I think Irene must've got the name wrong. I've tried all the variants that've occurred to me, but nothing's coming up. I might *have* to call her back. I'll try Janice first, though.'

'You haven't told me what you thought of the Oakden book.'

'Bog-standard opportunist,' said Strike, 'who did well to squeeze ten chapters out of virtually nothing. But I'd like to track him down if we can.'

'I'm trying,' sighed Robin, 'but he's another one who seems to have vanished off the face of the planet. His mother seemed to be his primary source, didn't she? I don't think he persuaded anyone who *really* knew Margot to talk to him.'

'No,' said Strike. 'You'd highlighted nearly all the interesting bits.'

'Nearly?' said Robin sharply.

'All,' Strike corrected himself.

'You spotted something else?'

'No,' said Strike, but seeing that she was unconvinced, he added, 'I've just been wondering whether someone might've put a hit on her.'

'Her husband?' said Robin, startled.

'Maybe,' said Strike.

'Or are you thinking about the cleaner's husband? Jules Bayliss, and his alleged criminal connections?'

'Not really.'

'Then why—'

'I just keep coming back to the fact that if she was killed, it was done very efficiently. Which might suggest—'

'—a contract killer,' said Robin. 'You know, I read a biography of Lord Lucan recently. They think he hired someone to kill his wife—'

'—and the killer got the nanny by mistake,' said Strike, who was familiar with the theory. 'Yeah. Well, if that's what happened to Margot, we're looking at an assassin a damn sight more efficient than Lucan's. Not a trace of her left behind, not so much as a drop of blood.'

There was a momentary silence, while Strike glanced behind him to see the rain and wind still buffeting the Christmas lights outside, and Robin's thoughts flew to Roy Phipps, the man whom Oonagh had called bloodless, conveniently bedridden on the day of Margot's disappearance.

'Well, I need to get going,' said Strike, pushing himself up out of his chair.

'I should, too,' sighed Robin, collecting her things.

'You're coming back into the office later, though?' Strike asked.

He needed to give her the as-yet-unbought Christmas present before she left for Yorkshire.

'I wasn't planning to,' said Robin. 'Why?'

'Come back in,' Strike said, trying to think of a reason. He opened the door into the outer office. 'Pat?'

'Yes?' said Pat, without looking round. She was once more typing fast and accurately, her electronic cigarette waggling between her teeth.

'Robin and I both need to head out now, but a man called Gregory Talbot's about to drop off a can of 16mm film. D'you think you can track down a projector that'll play it? Ideally before five o'clock?'

Pat swung slowly around on her desk chair to look at Strike, her monkey-ish face set, her eyes narrowed.

'You want me to find a vintage film projector by five o'clock?'

'That's what I said.' Strike turned to Robin. 'Then we can have a quick look at whatever Talbot had hiding in the attic before you leave for Masham.'

'OK,' said Robin, 'I'll come back at four.'

27

His name was Talus, made of yron mould,
Immoueable, resistlesse, without end.
Who in his hand an yron flale did hould,
With which he thresht out falshood, and did truth vnfould.

Edmund Spenser
The Faerie Queene

Some two and a half hours later, Strike stood beneath the awning of Hamleys on Regent Street, shopping bags by his feet, telling himself firmly that he was fine in spite of ample empirical evidence that he was, in fact, shivering. Cold rain was spattering all around him onto the dirty pavements, where it was kicked out of puddles by the marching feet of hundreds of passing pedestrians. It splashed over kerbs in the wake of passing vehicles and dripped down the back of Strike's collar, though he stood, theoretically, beneath shelter.

While checking his phone yet again for some sign that Shanker hadn't forgotten they were supposed to be meeting for a drink, he lit a cigarette, but his raw throat didn't appreciate the sudden ingestion of smoke. With a foul taste in his mouth, he ground out the cigarette after one drag. There was no message from Shanker, so Strike picked up his bulky shopping bags and set off again, his throat burning every time he swallowed.

He'd imagined optimistically that he might have finished all his shopping within two hours, but midday had come and gone and he still wasn't done. How did people decide what to buy, when the speakers were all shrieking Christmas tunes at you, and the shops were full of too much choice, and all of it looked like junk? Endless processions of women kept ranging across his path, choosing items with apparently effortless ease. Were they genetically programmed to seek and find the right gift? Was there nobody he could pay to do this for him?

His eyes felt heavy, his throat ached and his nose had started running. Unsure where he was going, or what he was looking for, he walked blindly onwards. He, who usually had an excellent sense of direction, kept turning the wrong way, becoming disorientated. Several times he knocked into carefully stacked piles of Christmas merchandise, or buffeted smaller people, who scowled and muttered and scurried away.

The bulky bags he was carrying contained three identical Nerf blasters for his nephews; large plastic guns which shot foam bullets, which Strike had decided to buy on the dual grounds that he would have loved one when he was eleven, and the assistant had assured him they were one of the must-have gifts of the year. He'd bought his Uncle Ted a sweater because he couldn't think of anything else, his brother-in-law a box of golf balls and a bottle of gin on the same principle, but he still had the trickiest gifts to buy – the ones for the women: Lucy, Joan and Robin.

His mobile rang.

'Fuck.'

He hobbled sideways out of the crowd and, standing beside a mannequin wearing a reindeer sweater, shook himself free from a few of his bags so that he could pull out his mobile.

'Strike.'

'Bunsen, I'm near Shakespeare's 'Ead on Great Marlborough Street. See you there in twenty?'

'Great,' said Strike, who was becoming hoarse. 'I'm just round the corner.'

Another wave of sweat passed over him, soaking scalp and chest. It was, some part of his brain acknowledged, just possible that he had caught Barclay's flu, and if that was the case, he mustn't give it to his severely immunosuppressed aunt. He picked up his shopping bags again and made his way back to the slippery pavement outside.

The black and white timbered frontage of Liberty rose up to his right as he headed along Great Marlborough Street. Buckets and boxes of flowers lay all around the main entrance, temptingly light and portable, and already wrapped; so easy to carry to the Shakespeare's Head and take on to the office afterwards. But, of course, flowers wouldn't do this time. Sweating worse than ever, Strike turned into the store, dumped his bags once more on the floor beside an array of silk scarves, and called Ilsa.

'Hey, Oggy,' said Ilsa.

'What can I get Robin for Christmas?' he said. It was becoming difficult to talk: his throat felt raw.

'Are you all right?'

'I'm fantastic. Give me an idea. I'm in Liberty.'

'Um . . . ' said Ilsa. 'Let's th . . . ooh, I know what you can get her. She wants some new perfume. She didn't like the stuff she—'

'I don't need backstory,' said Strike ungraciously. 'That's great. Perfume. What does she wear?'

'I'm trying to tell you, Oggy,' said Ilsa. 'She wants a change. Choose her something new.'

'I can't smell,' said Strike, impatiently, 'I've got a cold.'

But this basic problem aside, he was afraid that a perfume

he'd personally picked out was too intimate a gift, like that green dress of a few years back. He was looking for something like flowers, but not flowers, something that said 'I like you', but not 'this is what I'd like you to smell like'.

'Just go to an assistant and say "I want to buy a perfume for someone who wears Philosykos but wants a—"'

'She what?' said Strike. 'She wears what?'

'Philosykos. Or she did.'

'Spell it,' said Strike, his head thumping. Ilsa did so.

'So I just ask an assistant, and they'll give me something like it?'

'That's the idea,' said Ilsa patiently.

'Great,' said Strike. 'Appreciate it. Speak soon.'

The assistant thought you'd like it.

Yeah, he'd say that. *The assistant thought you'd like it* would effectively de-personalise the gift, turn it into something almost as mundane as flowers, but it would still show he'd taken some care, given it some thought. Picking up his carrier bags again, he limped towards an area he could see in the distance that looked as though it was lined with bottles.

The perfume department turned out to be small, about the size of Strike's office. He sidled into the crowded space, passing beneath a cupola painted with stars, to find himself surrounded by shelves laden with fragile cargos of glass bottles, some of which wore ruffs, or patterns like lace; others which looked like jewels, or the kind of phial suitable for a love potion. Apologising as he forced people aside with his Nerf guns, his gin and his golf balls, he met a slim, black-clad man who asked, 'Can I help you?' At this moment Strike's eye fell on a range of bottled scents which were identically packed with black labels and tops. They looked functional and discreet, with no overt suggestion of romance.

'I'd like one of those,' he croaked, pointing.

'Right,' said the assistant. 'Er—'

'It's for someone who used to wear Philosykos. Something like that.'

'OK,' said the assistant, leading Strike over to the display. 'Well, what about—'

'No,' said Strike, before the assistant could remove the top of the tester. The perfume was called Carnal Flower. 'She said she didn't like that one,' Strike added, with the conscious aim of appearing less strange. 'Are any of the others like Philo—'

'She might like Dans Tes Bras?' suggested the assistant, spraying a second bottle onto a smelling strip.

'Doesn't that mean—?'

'"In your arms",' said the assistant.

'No,' said Strike, without taking the smelling strip. 'Are any of the others like Phi—?'

'Musc Ravageur?'

'You know what, I'll leave it,' said Strike, sweat prickling anew beneath his shirt. 'Which exit is nearest the Shakespeare's Head?'

The unsmiling assistant pointed Strike towards the left. Muttering apologies, Strike edged back out past women who were studying bottles and spraying on testers, turned a corner and saw, with relief, the pub where he was meeting Shanker, which lay just beyond the glass doors of a room full of chocolates.

Chocolates, he thought, slowing down and incidentally impeding a group of harried women. *Everyone likes chocolates.* Sweat was now coming over him in waves, and he seemed to feel simultaneously hot and cold. He approached a table piled high with chocolate boxes, looking for the most expensive one, one that would show appreciation and friendship. Trying to choose a flavour, he thought he recalled a conversation about salted caramel, so he took the largest box he could find and headed for the till.

Five minutes later, another bag hanging from his hands, Strike emerged at the end of Carnaby Street, where music-themed Christmas decorations hung between the buildings. In Strike's now fevered state, the invisible heads suggested by giant headphones and sunglasses seemed sinister rather than festive. Struggling with his bags, he backed into the Shakespeare's Head, where fairy lights twinkled and chatter and laughter filled the air.

'Bunsen,' said a voice, just inside the door.

Shanker had secured a table. Shaven-headed, gaunt, pale and heavily tattooed, Shanker had an upper lip that was fixed in a permanent Elvis-style sneer, due to the scar that ran up towards his cheekbone. He was absent-mindedly clicking the fingers of the hand not holding his pint, a tic he'd had since his teens. No matter where he was, Shanker managed to emanate an aura of danger, projecting the idea that he might, on the slightest provocation, resort to violence. Crowded as the pub was, nobody had chosen to share his table. Incongruously, or so it seemed to Strike, Shanker, too, had shopping bags at his feet.

'What's wrong wiv ya?' Shanker said, as Strike sank down opposite him and disposed of his own bags beneath the table. 'Ya look like shit.'

'Nothing,' said Strike, whose nose was now running profusely and whose pulse seemed to have become erratic. 'Cold or something.'

'Well, keep it the fuck away from me,' said Shanker. 'Last fing we fuckin' need at home. Zahara's only just got over the fuckin' flu. Wanna pint?'

'Er – no,' said Strike. The thought of beer was currently repellent. 'Couldn't get me some water, could you?'

'Fuck's sake,' muttered Shanker, as he got up.

When Shanker had returned with a glass of water and sat down again, Strike said, without preamble,

'I wanted to ask you about an evening, must've been round about '92, '93. You needed to get into town, you had a car, but you couldn't drive it yourself. You'd done something to your arm. It was strapped up.'

Shanker shrugged impatiently, as much as to say, who could be expected to remember something so trivial? Shanker's life had been an endless series of injuries received and inflicted, and of needing to get places to deliver cash, drugs, threats or beatings. Periods of imprisonment had done nothing but temporarily change the environment in which he conducted business. Half the boys with whom he had associated in his teens were dead, most killed by knives or overdoses. One cousin had died in a police car chase, and another had been shot through the back of the head, his killer never caught.

'You had to make a delivery,' Strike went on, trying to jog Shanker's memory. 'Jiffy bag full of something – drugs, cash, I don't know. You came round the squat looking for someone to drive you, urgently. I said I'd do it. We went to a strip club in Soho. It was called Teezers.'

'Teezers, yeah,' said Shanker. 'Long gone, Teezers. Closed ten, fifteen year ago.'

'When we got there, there was a group of men standing on the pavement, heading inside. One of them was a bald black guy—'

'Your fucking memory,' said Shanker, amused. 'You could do a stage act. "Bunsen, the Amazing Memory Man"—'

'—and there was a big Latin-looking bloke with dyed black hair and sideburns. We pulled up, you wound down the window and he came over and put his hand on the door to talk to you. He had eyes like a basset hound and he was wearing a massive gold ring with a lion's—'

'Mucky Ricci,' said Shanker.

'You remember him?'

'Just said 'is name, Bunsen, d'in I?'

'Yeah. Sorry. What was his real name, d'you know?'

'Nico, Niccolo Ricci, but everyone called 'im "Mucky". Old-school villain. Pimp. 'E owned a few strip clubs, ran a couple of knocking shops. Real bit of old London, 'e was. Got his start as part of the Sabini gang, when 'e was a kid.'

'How're you spelling Ricci? R – I – C – C – I, right?'

'What's this about?'

Strike tugged the copy of *Whatever Happened to Margot Bamborough?* out of his coat pocket, turned to the photographs of the practice Christmas party and held it out to Shanker, who took it suspiciously. He squinted for a moment at the partial picture of the man with the lion ring, then passed the book back to Strike.

'Well?' said Strike.

'Yeah, looks like 'im. Where's that?'

'Clerkenwell. A doctors' Christmas party.'

Shanker looked mildly surprised.

'Well, Clerkenwell, that was the old Sabini stamping ground, warn't it? And I s'pose even gangsters need doctors sometimes.'

'It was a party,' said Strike. 'Not a surgery. Why would Mucky Ricci be at a doctors' party?'

'Dunno,' said Shanker. 'Anyone need killing?'

'Funny you should ask that,' said Strike. 'I'm investigating the disappearance of a woman who was there that night.'

Shanker looked sideways at him.

'Mucky Ricci's gaga,' he said quietly. 'Old man now, innit.'

'Still alive, though?'

'Yer. 'E's in an 'ome.'

'How d'you know that?'

'Done a bit o' business wiv 'is eldest, Luca.'

'Boys in the same line of work as their old man?'

'Well, there ain't no Little Italy gang any more, is there? But they're villains, yeah,' said Shanker. Then he leaned across the table and said quietly, 'Listen to me, Bunsen. You do not wanna screw wiv Mucky Ricci's boys.'

It was the first time Shanker had ever given Strike such a warning.

'You go fuckin' wiv their old man, you try pinnin' anyfing on 'im, the Ricci boys'll skin ya. Understand? They don't fuckin' care. They'll torch your fuckin' office. They'll cut up your girl.'

'Tell me about Mucky. Anything you know.'

'Did you 'ear what I just said, Bunsen?'

'Just tell me about him, for fuck's sake.'

Shanker scowled.

''Ookers. Porn. Drugs, but girls was 'is main thing. Same era as George Cornell, Jimmy Humphreys, all those boys. That gold ring 'e wore, 'e used to say Danny the Lion gave it 'im. Danny Leo, the mob boss in New York. Claimed they were related. Dunno if it's true.'

'Ever run across anyone called Conti?' Strike asked. 'Probably a bit younger than Ricci.'

'Nope. But Luca Ricci's a fuckin' psycho,' said Shanker. 'When did this bint disappear?'

'1974,' said Strike.

He expected Shanker to say 'Nineteen seventy fucking four?', to pour scorn on the likelihood of finding any kind of solution after all this time, but his old friend merely frowned at him, his clicking fingers recalling the relentless progress of the deathwatch beetle, and it occurred to the detective that Shanker knew more about old crimes and the long shadows they cast than many policemen.

'Name of Margot Bamborough,' said Strike. 'She vanished on her way to the pub. Nothing ever found, no handbag, door keys, nothing. Never seen again.'

Shanker sipped his beer.

'Professional job,' he said.

'That occurred to me,' said Strike. 'Hence—'

'Fuck your fucking "hence",' said Shanker fiercely. 'If the bint was taken out by Mucky Ricci or any of his boys, she's past fuckin' savin', in't she? I know you like bein' the boy scout, mate, but the last guy who pissed off Luca Ricci, his wife opened the door few days later and got acid thrown in her face. Blind in one eye, now.

'You wanna drop this, Bunsen. If Mucky Ricci's the answer, you need to stop askin' the question.'

28

Greatly thereat was Britomart dismayd,
Ne in that stownd wist, how her selfe to beare . . .

Edmund Spenser
The Faerie Queene

Somehow, Pat had managed to track down a vintage film projector. It had been promised for delivery at four, but Strike and Robin were still waiting for it at a quarter to six, at which time Robin told Strike she really did need to leave. She hadn't yet packed for her trip home to Yorkshire, she wanted an early night before catching the train and, if she was honest, she was feeling insulted by Strike's gift of unwrapped salted caramel chocolates, which he'd pulled hastily out of a Liberty bag when he saw her, and which she now suspected was the whole lousy reason he had forced her to come back to the office in the first place. As this had necessitated a long trip back to Denmark Street on a packed Tube, it was hard not to feel resentful about the time and trouble she had taken to find and wrap the DVD of two old Tom Waits concerts he'd mentioned wanting to watch, a few weeks previously. Robin had never heard of the singer: it had taken her some trouble to identify the man Strike had been talking about, and the concerts he'd never seen as those on *No Visitors After Midnight*. And in return, she got chocolates she was sure had been grabbed at random.

She left Strike's present behind, untouched, in Max's kitchen, before boarding the crowded train to Harrogate next morning. As she travelled north in her mercifully pre-booked seat, Robin tried to tell herself that her feeling of emptiness was merely tiredness. Christmas at home would be a wonderful break. She'd be meeting her new niece for the first time; there'd be lie-ins and home-cooked food and hours in front of the telly.

A toddler was shouting at the back of the carriage, his mother trying just as loudly to entertain and subdue him. Robin pulled out her iPod and put on headphones. She'd downloaded Joni Mitchell's album, *Court and Spark*, which Oonagh had mentioned as Margot Bamborough's favourite. Robin hadn't yet had time to listen to it, or, indeed, to any other music, for weeks.

But *Court and Spark* didn't soothe or cheer her. She found it unsettling, unlike anything she had ever listened to before. Expecting melodies and hooks, Robin was disappointed: everything felt unfinished, left open, unresolved. A beautiful soprano voice tumbled and swooped over piano or guitar chords that never led to anything as mundane as a chorus that you could settle into, or tap your foot to. You couldn't hum along, you couldn't have joined in unless you, too, could sing like Mitchell, which Robin certainly couldn't. The words were strange, and evoked responses she didn't like: she wasn't sure she'd ever felt the things Mitchell sang about, and this made her feel defensive, confused and sad: *Love came to my door, with a sleeping roll and a madman's soul . . .*

A few seconds into track three, she turned off the iPod and reached instead for the magazine she had brought with her. At the back of the carriage, the toddler was now howling.

Robin's mood of mild despondency persisted until she got off the train, but when she saw her mother standing on the platform, ready to drive her back to Masham, she was overtaken by a wave of genuine warmth. She hugged Linda, and for almost ten minutes afterwards, while they wended their way, chatting, towards the car, passing a café out of which jangling Christmas music was emanating, even the dour grey Yorkshire skies and the car interior, which smelled of Rowntree the Labrador, felt comforting and cheery in their familiarity.

'I've got something to tell you,' Linda said, when she had closed the driver's door. Instead of turning the key in the ignition, Linda turned to Robin, looking almost fearful.

A sickening jolt of panic turned Robin's stomach upside down.

'What's happened?' she said.

'It's all right,' Linda said hastily, 'everyone's well. But I want you to know before we get back to Masham, in case you see them.'

'See who?'

'Matthew,' said Linda, 'has brought … he's brought that woman home with him. Sarah Shadlock. They're staying with Geoffrey for Christmas.'

'*Oh*,' said Robin. 'Christ, Mum, I thought someone had died.'

She hated the way Linda was looking at her. Though her insides had just grown cold, and the fragile happiness that had briefly kindled inside her had been snuffed out, she forced a smile and a tone of unconcern.

'It's fine. I knew. Her ex-fiancé called me. I should've guessed,' she said, wondering why she hadn't, 'they might be here for Christmas. Can we get home, please? I'm dying for a cup of tea.'

'You *knew*? Why didn't you tell us?'

But Linda herself supplied the answer to that, as they drove. It neither soothed nor comforted Robin to have Linda storming about how outraged she'd been, when a neighbour told her that Matthew had been strolling hand in hand with Sarah through the middle of town. She didn't feel comforted by strictures against her ex-husband's morals and manners, nor did she appreciate having each family member's reaction detailed to her ('Martin was all for *punching* him again'). Then Linda moved on to the divorce: what was going on? Why wasn't it all settled yet? Did Robin *honestly* think mediation would work? Didn't Matthew's behaviour, *flaunting* this woman in front of the whole of Masham, *show* how utterly lost to shame and reason he was? Why, oh why, hadn't Robin agreed to let Harveys of Harrogate deal with it all, was she *sure* this London woman was up to it, because Corinne Maxwell had told Linda that when *her* daughter divorced without children it was all *completely* straightforward . . .

But at least there was little Annabel Marie, was the conclusion of Linda's monologue, as they turned onto Robin's parents' street.

'*Wait* till you see her, Robin, just *wait* . . . '

The front door opened before the car came to a halt. Jenny and Stephen were standing on the threshold, looking so excited that an onlooker might have suspected it was they who were about to see their baby daughter for the first time, not Robin. Realising what was expected of her, Robin hitched an eager smile onto her face, and within minutes found herself sitting on the sofa in her parents' living room, a warm little sleeping body in her arms, wrapped up in wool, surprisingly solid and heavy, and smelling of Johnson's baby powder.

'She's gorgeous, Stephen,' Robin said, while Rowntree's tail thumped against the coffee table. He was nosing at her, thrusting his head repeatedly under Robin's hand, confused as to why he wasn't receiving the fuss and love he was used to. 'She's gorgeous, Jenny,' Robin said, as her sister-in-law took photos of 'Auntie Robin' meeting Annabel for the first time. 'She's gorgeous, Mum,' Robin said to Linda, who had come back with a tea tray and a craving to hear what Robin thought of their twenty-inch-long marvel.

'Evens things out, doesn't it, having another girl?' said Linda delightedly. Her anger at Matthew was over now: her granddaughter was everything.

The sitting room was more cramped than usual, not only with Christmas tree and cards, but with baby equipment. A changing mat, a Moses basket, a pile of mysterious muslin cloths, a bag of nappies and an odd contraption that Jenny explained was a breast pump. Robin rhapsodised, smiled, laughed, ate biscuits, heard the story of the birth, admired some more, held her niece until she woke, then, after Jenny had taken back possession of the baby and, with a touch of new self-importance, settled herself down to breastfeed, said that she would nip upstairs and unpack.

Robin carried her bag upstairs, her absence unnoticed and unregretted by those below, who were lost in adoration of the baby. Robin closed the door of her old room behind her, but instead of unpacking, lay down on her old bed. Facial muscles aching from all her forced smiling, she closed her eyes, and allowed herself the luxury of exhausted misery.

29

Thus warred he long time against his will,
Till that through weakness he was forced at last
To yield himself unto the mighty ill,
Which, as a victor proud, 'gan ransack fast
His inward parts and all his entrails waste . . .

Edmund Spenser
The Faerie Queene

With three days to go before Christmas, Strike was forced to abandon the pretence that he didn't have flu. Concluding that the only sensible course was to hole up in his attic flat while the virus passed through his system, he took himself to a packed Sainsbury's where, feverish, sweating, breathing through his mouth and desperate to get away from the crowds and the canned carols, he grabbed enough food for a few days, and bore it back to his two rooms above the office.

Joan took the news that he wouldn't be joining the festivities in Cornwall predictably hard. She went so far as to suggest that it would be fine for him to come, as long as they sat at opposite ends of the dinner table, but to Strike's relief, Ted overruled her. Strike didn't know whether he was being paranoid, but he suspected Lucy didn't believe he was genuinely ill. If she did, her tone suggested that he might have caught flu deliberately. He thought he heard a trace of accusation when she informed him that Joan was now entirely bald.

By five o'clock in the afternoon of Christmas Eve, Strike had developed a cough that made his lungs rattle and his ribs ache. Drowsing on his bed in a T-shirt and boxer shorts, his prosthetic leg propped against a wall, he was woken abruptly by a loud noise. Footsteps seemed to be moving down the stairs, away from his attic door. A paroxysm of coughing seized him before he could call out to the person he thought had woken him. Struggling back into a sitting position to clear his lungs, he didn't hear the second approach of footsteps until somebody knocked on his door. He greatly resented the effort it took to shout, 'What?'

'D'you need anything?' came Pat's deep, gravelly voice.

'No,' Strike shouted. The syllable emerged as a croak.

'Have you got food?'

'Yes.'

'Painkillers?'

'Yes.'

'Well, I'm leaving some things outside the door for you.' He heard her setting objects down. 'There are a couple of presents. Eat the soup while it's still hot. See you on the twenty-eighth.'

Her footsteps were clanging down the metal stairs before he could respond.

He wasn't sure whether he'd imagined the mention of hot soup, but the possibility was enough to make him drag his crutches towards himself and make his way laboriously to the door. The chill of the stairwell added gooseflesh to his fever sweats. Pat had somehow managed to carry the old video projector upstairs for him, and he suspected that it was the sound of her setting this down that had woken him. Beside it lay the can of film from Gregory Talbot's attic, a small pile of wrapped Christmas gifts, a handful of cards and two polystyrene tubs of hot chicken soup that he knew she must have walked to Chinatown to fetch. He felt quite pathetically grateful.

Leaving the heavy projector and the can of film where they were, he pulled and prodded the Christmas gifts and card across the floor into the flat with one of his crutches, then slowly bent down to pick up the tubs of soup.

Before eating, he took his mobile from the bedside table and texted Pat:

Thanks very much. Hope you have a good Christmas.

He then wrapped the duvet around himself and ate the soup straight out of the tubs, tasting nothing. He'd hoped the hot liquid would soothe his raw throat, but the cough persisted, and once or twice he thought he was going to choke everything back up again. His intestines also seemed unsure whether they welcomed food. Having finished the two tubs, he settled back down beneath the duvet, sweating while he looked at the black sky outside, guts churning, and wondering why he wasn't yet on the mend.

After a night of intermittent dozing interrupted by prolonged coughing fits, Strike woke on Christmas morning to find his fever unabated, and sweaty sheets tangled about him. His normally noisy flat was unnaturally quiet. Tottenham Court Road was suddenly, weirdly devoid of traffic. He supposed most of the taxi drivers were at home with their families.

Strike was not a self-pitying man, but lying alone in bed, coughing and sweating, his ribs sore and his fridge now virtually empty, he was unable to prevent his thoughts roaming back over Christmases past, especially those spent at Ted and Joan's in St Mawes, where everything proceeded as it did on the television and in story books, with turkey and crackers and stockings.

Of course, today was far from the first Christmas he'd spent away from family and friends. There'd been a couple such in the army, when he'd eaten foil trays of tasteless turkey in field canteens, among camouflage-wearing colleagues wearing Santa hats. The structure he'd enjoyed in the military had then consoled him in the absence of other pleasures, but there was no camaraderie to sustain him today, only the dismal fact that he was alone, ill and one-legged, stuck up in a draughty attic, forced to endure the consequences of his own firm repudiation of any relationship that might offer support in moments of illness or sadness.

The memory of Pat's kindness became, this Christmas morning, still more touching in retrospect. Turning his head, he saw the few gifts that she'd brought upstairs still lying on the floor just inside the door.

He got up from his bed, still coughing, reached for his crutches and swung himself towards the bathroom. His urine was dark, his unshaven face in the mirror ashen. Though dismayed by his own debility and exhaustion, habits ingrained in him by the military prevented Strike from returning to bed. He knew that lying unwashed with his leg off would merely increase his hovering feeling of depression. He therefore showered, moving more carefully than usual to guard against the risk of falls, dried himself off, put on a clean T-shirt, boxers and dressing gown and, still racked with coughs, prepared himself a tasteless breakfast of porridge made with water, because he preferred to conserve his last pint of milk for his tea. As he'd expected to be well on the mend by now, his stocks of food had dwindled to some limp vegetables, a couple of bits of uncooked chicken two days out of date and a small chunk of hard Cheddar.

After breakfast Strike took painkillers, put on his prosthesis and then, determined to use what small amount of physical strength he could muster before the illness dragged him under again, stripped and remade his bed with clean sheets, removed his Christmas presents from the floor to his kitchen table, and carried the projector and roll of film inside from the landing where he had left them. The can, as he'd expected, bore the mark of Capricorn upon it, drawn in faded but clearly legible marker pen.

His mobile buzzed as he propped the can against the wall beneath his kitchen window. He picked it up, expecting a text from Lucy asking when he was going to call and wish everyone in St Mawes a Merry Christmas.

Merry Christmas, Bluey. Are you happy? Are you with someone you love?

It had been a fortnight since Charlotte had last texted him, almost as though she'd telepathically heard his resolution to contact her husband if her messages became any more self-destructive.

It would be so easy to answer; so easy to tell her he was alone, ill, unsupported. He thought of the naked photo she'd sent on his birthday, which he'd forced himself to delete. But he'd come such a long way, to a place of lonely security against emotional storms. However much he'd loved her, however much she could still disturb his serenity with a few typed words, he forced himself, standing beside his small Formica table, to recall the only occasion on which he'd taken her back to St Mawes for Christmas. He remembered the row heard all through the tiny house, remembered her storming out past the family assembled around the turkey, remembered Ted and Joan's faces, because they'd so looked forward to the visit, having not seen Strike for over a year, because he was at that time stationed in Germany with the Special Investigation Branch of the Royal Military Police.

He set his mobile to mute. Self-respect and self-discipline had always been his bulwarks against lethargy and misery. What was Christmas Day, after all? If you disregarded the fact that other people were enjoying feasts and fun, merely a winter's day like any other. If he was currently bodily weak, why shouldn't he use his mental faculties, at least, to continue work on the Bamborough case?

Thus reasoning, Strike made himself a fresh cup of strong tea, added a very small amount of milk, opened his laptop and, pausing regularly for coughing fits, re-read the document he'd been working on before he'd fallen ill: a summary of the contents of Bill Talbot's symbol-laden, leather-bound notebook, which Strike had now spent three weeks deciphering. His intention was to send the document to Robin for her thoughts.

Talbot's Occult Notes

1. Overview
2. Symbol key
3. Possible leads
4. Probably irrelevant
5. Action points

Overview

Talbot's breakdown manifested itself in a belief that he could solve the Bamborough case by occult means. In addition to astrology, he consulted Aleister Crowley's Thoth tarot, which has an astrological dimension. He immersed himself in several occult writers, including Crowley, Éliphas Lévi and astrologer Evangeline Adams, and attempted magic rituals.

Talbot was a regular churchgoer before his mental health broke down. While ill, he thought he was hunting a literal embodiment of evil/the devil. Aleister Crowley, who seems to have influenced Talbot more than anyone else, called himself 'Baphomet' and also connected Baphomet both with the devil and the sign of Capricorn. This is probably where Talbot got the idea that Margot's killer was a Capricorn.

Most of what's in the notebook is worthless, but I think Talbot left three

Strike now deleted the number 'three' and substituted 'four'. As ever, when immersed in work, he felt a craving for a cigarette. As though in rebellion against the very idea, his lungs immediately treated him to a violent fit of coughing that necessitated the grabbing of kitchen roll to catch what they were trying to expel. Suitably chastened and shivering slightly, Strike drew his dressing gown more tightly around him, took a sip of tea he couldn't taste and continued to work.

Most of what's in the notebook is worthless, but I think Talbot left four possibly genuine leads out of the official police record, only recording them in 'the true book', ie, his leather notebook.

<u>Symbol key</u>
There are no names in the notebook, only zodiacal signs. I'm not listing unidentified eye witnesses – we've got no chance of tracing them on their star signs and nothing else – but by cross-referencing corroborative details, these are my best guesses at the identity of people Talbot thought were important to the investigation.

♈	Aries	Paul Satchwell (ex-boyfriend)
♉	Taurus	Wilma Bayliss (office cleaner)
♊	Gemini	Oonagh Kennedy
♊2	Gemini 2	Amanda Laws (saw M at window)
♋	Cancer	Janice Beattie (nurse)
♋2	Cancer 2	Cynthia Phipps (Anna's nanny/stepmother)
♌	Leo	Dinesh Gupta (GP)
♌2	Leo 2	Willy Lomax (saw M entering church)

♌3	Leo 3	? (from Talbot's notes, ♌3 seems to have been seen coming out of the practice by a member of the public. Hints that ♌3 is known to police and that ♌3 was there at night)

Strike now deleted the last paragraph and substituted a name and a new note.

♌3	Leo 3	Nico 'Mucky' Ricci (gangster who attended practice Christmas party. Nobody seems to have recognised him except an unnamed passer-by)
♍	Virgo	Dorothy Oakden (practice secretary)
♎	Libra	Joseph Brenner (GP)
♎2	Libra 2	Ruby Elliot (saw 2 struggling women)
♏	Scorpio	? (dead person)*
♏2	Scorpio 2	Mrs Fleury (was leading elderly mother across Clerkenwell Green on evening of Margot's disappearance)
♐	Sagittarius	Gloria Conti (receptionist)
♐2	Sagittarius 2	Jules Bayliss (husband of cleaner)
♒	Aquarius	Margot Bamborough (victim)
♑	Capricorn	The Essex Butcher/Baphomet
♓	Pisces	Steven Douthwaite (patient)
	no idea	Roy Phipps (husband) **
	no idea	Irene Bull/Hickson (receptionist)**

* I suggest an identity for Scorpio below, but could be someone we haven't yet heard of.

** No idea what either of these symbols mean. Can't find them on any astrological website. Talbot seems to have invented them. If he'd stuck to birth signs, Irene would have been one of the Geminis and Roy would have been Capricorn. Talbot writes that Phipps 'can't be true Capricorn' (because he's resourceful, sensitive, musical) then comes up with this new symbol for him, on the advice of Schmidt.

Schmidt
The name 'Schmidt' is all over the notebook. 'Schmidt corrects to (different star sign)', 'Schmidt changes everything', 'Schmidt disagrees'. Schmidt mostly wants to change people's star signs, which you'd think would be one certainty, given that birth dates don't change. I've checked with Gregory Talbot, and he can't remember his father ever knowing anyone of the name. My best guess is that Schmidt might have been a figment of Talbot's increasingly psychotic imagination. Perhaps he couldn't help noticing people weren't matching the star signs' supposed qualities and Schmidt was his rational side trying to reassert itself.

<u>Possible leads</u>

Joseph Brenner
In spite of Talbot's early determination to clear Brenner of suspicion on the basis of his star sign (Libra is 'the most trustworthy of the signs' according to Evangeline Adams), he later records in the notebook that an unidentified patient of the practice told Talbot that he/she saw Joseph Brenner inside a block of flats on Skinner Street on the evening Margot disappeared. This directly contradicts Brenner's own story (he went straight home), his sister's corroboration of that story, and possibly the story of the dog-walking neighbour who claims to have seen Brenner through the window at home at 11 in the evening. No time is given for Brenner's alleged sighting in Michael Cliffe House, which was a 3-minute drive from the St John's practice and consequently far nearer Margot's route than Brenner's own house, which was a 20-minute drive away. <u>None of this is in the police notes and it doesn't seem to have been followed up</u>.

Death of Scorpio

Talbot seems to suggest that somebody died, and that Margot may have found the death suspicious. Scorpio's death is connected to Pisces (Douthwaite) and Cancer (Janice), which makes the most likely candidate for Scorpio Joanna Hammond, the married woman Douthwaite had an affair with, who allegedly committed suicide.

The Hammond/Douthwaite/Janice explanation fits reasonably well: Margot could have voiced suspicions about Hammond's death to Douthwaite the last time she saw him, which gives us the reason he stormed out of her surgery. And as a friend/neighbour of Douthwaite's, Janice might have had her own suspicions about him.

The problem with this theory is that I've looked up Joanna Hammond's birth certificate online and she was born under Sagittarius. Either she isn't the dead person in question, or Talbot mistook her date of birth.

Blood at the Phipps house/Roy walking

When Lawson took over the case, Wilma the cleaner told him she'd seen Roy walking in the garden on the day Margot disappeared, when he was supposed to be bedbound. She also claimed she found blood on the spare bedroom carpet and cleaned it up.

Lawson thought this was the first time Wilma had mentioned either fact to the police and suspected she was trying to make trouble for Roy Phipps.

However, turns out Wilma <u>did</u> tell Talbot the story, but instead of recording it in the official police record, he put it in his astrological notebook.

Even though Wilma had already given him what you'd think is significant information, Talbot's notes indicate that he was sure she was concealing something else. He seems to have developed a fixation with Wilma having occult powers/secret knowledge. He speculates that Taurus might have 'magick' and even suggests the blood on the carpet might have been put there by Wilma herself, for some ritual purpose.

Tarot cards associated with Taurus, Wilma's sign, came up a lot when he was using them and he seems to have interpreted them to mean she knew more than she was letting on. He underlined the phrase 'black phantom' in regard to her, and associated her with 'Black Lilith', which is some astrological fixed point associated with taboos and secrets. In the absence of any other explanation, I suspect a good slug of old-fashioned racism.

Out on Charing Cross Road, a car passed, blaring from its radio 'Do They Know It's Christmas?' Frowning, Strike added another bullet point to 'possibly genuine new information', and began to type.

Nico 'Mucky' Ricci

According to Talbot, Leo 3 was seen leaving the practice one night by an unnamed passer-by, who told Talbot about it afterwards. Nico 'Mucky' Ricci was caught on camera in one of Dorothy Oakden's photos of the practice Christmas party in 1973. The picture's reproduced in her son's book. Ricci was a Leo (confirmed by d.o.b. in press report from 1968).

Ricci was a professional gangster, pornographer and pimp who in 1974 was living in Leather Lane, Clerkenwell, a short walk from the St John's practice, so should have been registered with one of the doctors there. He's now in his 90s and living in a nursing home, according to Shanker.

The fact that Ricci was at the party isn't in the official

record. Talbot found the fact Ricci was at the practice significant enough to write down in the astrological notebook, but there's no sign he ever followed it up or told Lawson about it. Possible explanations: 1) as Ricci was Leo, not Capricorn, Talbot concluded he couldn't be Baphomet, 2) Talbot didn't trust the person who said he'd seen Ricci leaving the building, 3) Talbot knew, but didn't record in his book, that Ricci had an alibi for that night Margot disappeared, 4) Talbot knew Ricci had alibis for other Essex Butcher abductions.

Whichever applies, the presence of Ricci at that party needs looking into. He's a man who had the contacts to arrange a permanent disappearance. See action points below.

It cost Strike far more effort than it would usually have done to organise his thoughts on Mucky Ricci and set them down. Tired now, his throat raw and his intercostal muscles aching from coughing, he read through the rest of the document, which in his opinion contained little of real value other than the action points. After correcting a couple of typos, he attached the lot to an email and sent it to Robin.

Only after this had gone did it occur to him that some people might think emailing work colleagues on Christmas Day was unacceptable. However, he shrugged off any momentary qualms by telling himself that Robin was currently enjoying a family Christmas, and would be highly unlikely to check her email until tomorrow at the earliest.

He picked up his mobile and checked it. Charlotte hadn't texted again. Of course, she had twins, aristocratic in-laws and a husband to keep happy. He set the phone down again.

Little energy though he had, Strike found the absence of anything to do still more enervating. Without much curiosity, he examined a couple of the Christmas presents lying beside him, both of which were clearly from grateful clients, as they were addressed to both him and Robin. Shaking the larger one, he deduced that it contained chocolates.

He returned to his bedroom and watched a bit of television, but the relentless emphasis on Christmas depressed him and he switched off midway through a continuity announcer's wish that everyone was having a wonderful—

Strike returned to the kitchen and his gaze fell on the heavy projector and can of film lying just inside the door. After a moment's hesitation, he heaved the heavy machine onto his kitchen table, facing a blank stretch of kitchen wall and plugged it in. It seemed to be in working order. He then prised the lid off the tin to reveal a large roll of 16mm film, which he took out and fitted into the projector.

Doubtless because he wasn't thinking as clearly as usual, and also because of the need to stop regularly to cough up more sputum into kitchen roll, it took Strike nearly an hour to work out how to operate the old projector, by which time he realised that he had regained something of an appetite. It was now nearly two o'clock. Trying not to imagine what was going on in St Mawes, where a large turkey with all the trimmings was doubtless reaching the peak of bronzed perfection, but seeing this flicker of returned appetite as a sign of returning health, he took the pack of out-of-date chicken and the limp vegetables out of the fridge, chopped it all, boiled up some dried noodles and made a stir fry.

He could taste nothing, but this second ingestion of food made him feel slightly more human, and ripping the paper and cellophane off the box of chocolates, he ate several of them, too, before flicking the switch on the projector.

Onto the wall, pale in the sunlight, flickered the naked figure of a woman. Her head was covered in a hood. Her hands were bound behind her. A man's black-trousered leg entered the shot. He kicked her: she stumbled and fell to her knees. He continued to kick until she was prone on the ground of what looked like a warehouse.

She'd have screamed, of course, she couldn't have failed to scream, but there was no soundtrack. A thin scar ran from beneath her left breast down to her ribs, as though this wasn't the first time knives had touched her. All the men involved had covered their faces with scarves or balaclavas. She alone was naked: the men merely pulled down their jeans.

She stopped moving long before they had finished with her. At one point, close to the end, when she was barely moving, when blood still dripped from her many stab wounds, the left hand of a man who seemed to have watched, but not participated, slid in front of the camera. It bore something large and gold.

Strike flicked off the projector. He was suddenly drenched in cold sweat. His stomach was cramping. He barely made it to the bathroom before he vomited, and there he remained, heaving until he was empty, until dusk fell beyond the attic windows.

30

Ah dearest Dame, quoth then the Paynim bold,
Pardon the error of enraged wight,
Whome great griefe made forgett the raines to hold
Of reasons rule . . .

Edmund Spenser
The Faerie Queene

Annabel was wailing in Stephen's old bedroom, which was next door to Robin's own. Her niece had cried through a substantial portion of Christmas night and Robin had been awake along with her, listening to Joni Mitchell on her headphones to block out the noise.

Four days stuck in her parents' house in Masham had driven Robin back to Mitchell's sprawling, wandering tunes and the lyrics that had made her feel strangely lost. Margot Bamborough had found something there she had needed, and hadn't Margot Bamborough's life been far more complicated than her own? Ailing parents to support, a new daughter to love and to miss, a workplace full of cross currents and bullying, a husband who wouldn't talk to her, another man lurking in the background, promising that he'd changed. What were Robin's troubles, compared to those?

So Robin lay in the dark and listened as she hadn't on the train. Then, she had heard an alienating sophistication in the words the beautiful voice had sung. Robin hadn't had glamorous love affairs she could anatomise or lament: she'd had one proper boyfriend and one marriage, which had gone horribly wrong, and now she was home at her parents' house, a childless twenty-nine-year-old who was 'travelling in a different direction to the rest of us': in other words, backwards.

But in the darkness, really listening, she began to hear melodies among the suspended chords, and as she stopped comparing the music to anything she would usually have listened to, she realised that the images she had found alienating in their strangeness were confessions of inadequacy and displacement, of the difficulty of merging two lives, of waiting for the soulmate who never arrived, of craving both freedom and love.

It was with a literal start that she heard the words, at the beginning of track eight, *'I'm always running behind the times, just like this train . . .'*

And when, later in the song, Mitchell asked: 'what are you going to do now? You got no one to give your love to', tears started in Robin's eyes. Not a mile from where she lay, Matthew and Sarah would be lying in bed in her ex-father-in-law's spare room, and here was Robin, alone again in a room that for her would forever have a hint of prison cell about it. This was where she had spent months after leaving university, pinioned within four walls by her own memories of a man in a gorilla mask, and the worst twenty minutes of her life.

Since arriving home, everyone in the house had been keen to accompany her into Masham, 'because you shouldn't have to hide'. The implication, no matter their kind intention, was that it would be a natural response for a woman whose ex-husband had found a new partner to hide. There was shame in being single.

But listening to *Court and Spark*, Robin thought that it was perfectly true that she was travelling in a different direction to anyone she knew. She was fighting her way back to the person she should have been before a man in a mask reached for her from the darkness beneath a stairwell. The reason nobody else understood was that they assumed that her true self was to be the wife Matthew Cunliffe had wanted: a woman who worked quietly in HR and stayed home safely after dark. They didn't realise that that woman had been the result of those twenty minutes, and that the authentic Robin might never have emerged if she hadn't been sent, by mistake, to a shabby office in Denmark Street.

With a strange sense of having spent her sleepless hours fruitfully, Robin turned off her iPod. Four o'clock on Boxing Day morning and the house was silent at last. Robin took out her earbuds, rolled over and managed to fall asleep.

Two hours later, Annabel woke again, and this time, Robin got up and crept downstairs, bare-footed, to the big wooden table beside the Aga, carrying her notebook, her laptop and her phone.

It was pleasant to have the kitchen to herself. The garden beyond the window, covered in a hard frost, was dark blue and silver in the winter pre-dawn. Setting her laptop and phone on the table, she greeted Rowntree, who was too arthritic these days for early morning frolicking, but wagged his tail lazily from his basket beside the radiator. She made herself a cup of tea, then took a seat at the table and opened her laptop.

She hadn't yet read Strike's document summarising the horoscope notes, which had arrived while she was busy helping her mother cook Christmas lunch. Robin had been adding the Brussels sprouts to the steamer when she saw, out of the corner of her eye, the notification on her phone, which was charging on one of the few power points that wasn't taken up by some piece of baby equipment: bottle steriliser, baby alarm or breast pump. Seeing Strike's name, her heart had momentarily lifted, because she was sure that she was about to read thanks for the gift of the Tom Waits DVD, and the fact that he'd emailed on Christmas Day was an indicator of friendship such as she had perhaps never received from him.

However, when she opened the email she simply read:

FYI: summary of Talbot's horoscope notes and action points.

Robin knew her face must have fallen when she looked up and saw Linda watching her.

'Bad news?'

'No, just Strike.'

'On Christmas Day?' said Linda sharply.

And Robin had realised in that instant that Geoffrey, her ex-father-in-law, must have been spreading it around Masham that if Matthew had been unfaithful, it was only after being heinously betrayed himself. She read the truth in her mother's face, and in Jenny's sudden interest in Annabel, whom she was jiggling in her arms, and in the sharp look flung at her by Jonathan, her youngest brother, who was tipping bottled cranberry sauce into a dish.

'It's work,' Robin had said coldly. Each of her silent accusers had returned hastily to their tasks.

It was, therefore, with very mixed feelings towards the author that Robin now settled down to read Strike's document. Emailing her on Christmas Day had felt reproachful, as though she'd let him down by going back to Masham instead of remaining in London and single-handedly running the agency while he, Barclay and Morris were down with flu. Moreover, if he was going to email at all on Christmas Day, some kind of personal message might be seen as common politeness. Perhaps he'd simply treated her Christmas present with the same indifference she'd treated his.

Robin had just read to the bottom of 'Possible leads' and was digesting the idea that a professional gangster had been, on at least one occasion, in close proximity to Margot Bamborough, when the kitchen door opened, admitting baby Annabel's distant wails. Linda entered the room, wearing a dressing gown and slippers.

'What are you doing down here?' she asked, sounding disapproving, as she crossed to the kettle.

Robin tried not to show how irked she felt. She'd spent the last few days smiling until her face ached, helping as much as was physically possible, admiring baby Annabel until she doubted that a pore had been left unpraised; she'd joined in charades and poured drinks and watched films and unwrapped chocolates or cracked nuts for Jenny, who was constantly pinned to the sofa by the demands of breastfeeding. She'd shown an intelligent and sympathetic interest in Jonathan's university friends' exploits; she'd listened to her father's opinions on David Cameron's agricultural policy and she'd noticed, but shown no resentment about, the fact that not a single member of her family had asked what she was doing at work. Was she not allowed to sit quietly in the kitchen for half an hour, while Annabel rendered sleep impossible?

'Reading an email,' said Robin.

'They think,' said Linda (and Robin knew 'they' must be the new parents, whose thoughts and wishes were of all-consuming importance just now) 'it was the sprouts. She's been colicky all night. Jenny's exhausted.'

'Annabel didn't have sprouts,' said Robin.

'She gets it all through the breast milk,' explained Linda, with what felt to Robin like condescension for being excluded from the mysteries of motherhood.

Bearing two cups of tea for Stephen and Jenny, Linda left the room again. Relieved, Robin opened her notebook and jotted down a couple of thoughts that had occurred to her while reading 'Possible leads,' then returned to Strike's document to read his short list of 'Probably irrelevant' items gleaned from Talbot's notebook.

Paul Satchwell

After a few months, Talbot's mental state clearly deteriorated, judging by his notes, which become progressively more detached from reality.

Towards the end of the notebook he goes back to the other two horned signs of the zodiac, Aries and Taurus, presumably because he's still fixated on the devil. As stated above, Wilma comes in for a lot of unfounded suspicion, but he also goes to the trouble of calculating Satchwell's complete birth horoscope, which means he must have got a birth time from him. Probably means nothing, but strange that he went back to Satchwell and spent this much time on his birth chart, which he didn't do for any other suspect. Talbot highlights aspects of the chart that supposedly indicate aggression, dishonesty and neuroses. Talbot also keeps noting that various parts of Satchwell's chart are 'same as AC' without explanation.

Roy Phipps and Irene Hickson

As mentioned above, the signs Talbot uses for Roy Phipps and Irene Hickson (who was then Irene Bull) haven't ever been used in astrology and seem to be inventions of Talbot's.

Roy's symbol looks like a headless stickman. Exactly what it's supposed to represent I can't find out – presumably a constellation? Quotations about snakes recur around Roy's name.

Irene's invented sign looks like a big fish and—

The kitchen door opened again. Robin looked around. It was Linda again.

'You still here?' she said, still with a slight sense of disapproval.

'No,' said Robin, 'I'm upstairs.'

Linda's smile was reluctant. As she took more mugs from the cupboard, she asked,

'D'you want another tea?'

'No thanks,' said Robin, closing her laptop. She'd decided to finish reading Strike's document in her room. Maybe she was imagining it, but Linda seemed to be making more noise than usual.

'He's got you working over Christmas as well, then?' said Linda.

For the past four days, Robin had suspected that her mother wanted to talk to her about Strike. The looks she'd seen on her surprised family's faces yesterday had told her why. However, she felt under no obligation to make it easy for Linda to interrogate her.

'As well as what?' asked Robin.

'You know what I mean,' said Linda. 'Christmas. I'd have thought you were owed time off.'

'I get time off,' said Robin.

She took her empty mug over to the sink. Rowntree now struggled to his feet and Robin let him out of the back door, feeling the icy air on every bit of exposed skin. Over the garden hedge she could see the sun turning the horizon green as it made its way steadily up through the icy heavens.

'Is he seeing anyone?' Linda asked. 'Strike?'

'He sees lots of people,' said Robin, wilfully obtuse. 'It's part of the job.'

'You know what I mean,' said Linda.

'Why the interest?'

She expected her mother to back off, but was surprised.

'I think you know why,' she said, turning to face her daughter.

Robin was furious to find herself blushing. She was a twenty-nine-year-old woman. At that very moment, her mobile emitted a beep on the kitchen table. She was convinced that it would be Strike texting her, and so, apparently, was Linda, who, being nearer, picked up the phone to hand it to Robin, glancing at the sender's name as she did so.

It wasn't Strike. It was Saul Morris. He'd written:

Hope you're not having as shit a Christmas as I am.

Robin wouldn't normally have answered. Resentment at her family, and something else, something she didn't particularly want to admit to, made her text back, while Linda watched:

Depends how shit yours is. Mine's fairly shit.

She sent the message, then looked up at Linda.

'Who's Saul Morris?' her mother asked.

'Subcontractor at the agency. Ex-police,' said Robin.

'Oh,' said Linda.

Robin could tell that had given Linda fresh food for thought. If she was honest with herself, she'd meant to do exactly that. Picking her laptop off the table, she left the kitchen.

The bathroom was, of course, occupied. Robin returned to her room. By the time she lay back down on her bed, laptop open again, Morris had texted her again.

Tell me your troubles and I'll tell you mine. Problem shared and all that.

Slightly regretting that she'd answered him, Robin turned the mobile face down on her bed and continued reading Strike's document.

Irene's invented sign looks like a big fish and Talbot's blunt about what he thinks it represents: 'the monster Cetus, Leviathan, the biblical whale, superficial charm, evil in depths. Headstrong, enjoys spotlight, a performer, a liar.' Talbot seems to have suspected Irene was a liar even before she was proven to have lied about her trip to the dentist, which Talbot never found out about, although there's no indication as to what he thinks she was lying about.

Margot as Babalon

This is only of relevance in as much as it shows just how ill Talbot was.

On the night he was finally sectioned, he attempted some kind of magic ritual. Judging by his notes, he was trying to conjure Baphomet, presumably because he thought Baphomet would take the form of Margot's killer.

According to Talbot, what manifested in the room wasn't Baphomet, but the spirit of Margot 'who blames me, who attacks me'. Talbot believed she'd become Babalon in death, Babalon being Baphomet's second-in-command/consort. The demon he 'saw' was carrying a cup of blood and a sword. There are repeated mentions of lions scribbled round the picture of the demon. Babalon rides a seven-headed lion on the card representing Lust in the Thoth tarot.

At some point after Talbot drew the demon, he went back and drew Latin crosses over some of the notes and on the demon itself, and wrote a biblical quotation warning against witchcraft across the picture. The appearance of the demon seems to have pushed him back towards religion, and that's where his notes end.

Robin heard the bathroom door open and close. Now desperate for a pee, she jumped up and headed out of her room.

Stephen was crossing the landing, holding his washbag, puffy-eyed and yawning.

'Sorry about last night, Rob,' he said. 'Jenny thinks it was the sprouts.'

'Yeah, Mum said,' Robin replied, edging around him. 'No problem. Hope she feels better.'

'We're going to take her out for a walk. I'll see if I can buy you some ear plugs.'

Once she'd showered, Robin returned to her room. Her phone beeped twice while she was dressing.

Brushing her hair in the mirror, her eyes fell on the new perfume she'd received as a Christmas present from her mother. Robin had told her she was looking for a new fragrance, because the old one reminded her too much of Matthew. She'd been touched that Linda remembered the conversation when she opened the gift.

The bottle was round; not an orb, but a flattish circle: Chanel Chance Eau Fraîche. The liquid was pale green. An unfortunate association of ideas now made Robin think of sprouts. Nevertheless, she sprayed some on her wrists and behind her ears, filling the air with the scent of sharp lemon and nondescript flowers. What, she wondered, had made her mother choose it? What was it about the perfume that made her think 'Robin'? To Robin's nostrils it smelled like a deodorant, generic, clean and totally without romance. She remembered her unsuccessful purchase of Fracas, and the desire to be sexy and sophisticated that had ended only in headaches. Musing about the disparity between the way people would like to be seen, and the way others prefer to see them, Robin sat back down on her bed beside her laptop and flipped over her phone.

Morris had texted twice more.

Lonely and hungover this end. Not being with the kids at Christmas is shit.

When Robin hadn't answered this, he'd texted again.

Sorry, being a maudlin dickhead. Feel free to ignore.

Calling himself a dickhead was the most likeable thing she'd ever known Morris do. Feeling sorry for him, Robin replied,

It must be tough, I'm sorry.

She then returned to her laptop and the last bit of Strike's document, detailing actions to be taken, and with initials beside each to show which of them should undertake it.

<u>Action points</u>

Talk to Gregory Talbot again – CS
I want to know why, even after he got well, Bill Talbot never told colleagues about the leads in this notebook he'd withheld from colleagues during the investigation, ie, sighting of Brenner in Skinner Street the night Margot disappeared/blood on the Phippses' carpet/a death Margot might have been worried about/Mucky Ricci leaving the practice one night.

Speak to Dinesh Gupta again – CS
He might know who Brenner was visiting in Skinner Street

that night. Could have been a patient. He might also be able to shed light on Mucky Ricci appearing at the party. Will also ask him about 'Scorpio' in case this refers to a patient whose death seemed suspicious to Margot.

Interview Roy Phipps – CS/RE
We've tiptoed around Phipps too long. Time to ring Anna and see whether she can persuade him to give us an interview.

Try and secure interview with one of Wilma Bayliss's children – CS/RE
Especially important if we can't get to Roy. Want to re-examine Wilma's story (Roy walking, blood on the carpet).

Find C. B. Oakden – CS/RE
Judging from his book, he's full of shit, but there's an outside possibility he knows things about Brenner we don't, given that his mother was the closest person to Brenner at the practice.

Find & interview Paul Satchwell – CS/RE

Find & interview Steven Douthwaite – CS/RE

Robin couldn't help but feel subtly criticised. Strike had now added his initials to action points that had previously been Robin's alone, such as finding Satchwell, and persuading Wilma Bayliss's children to give them interviews. She set the laptop down again, picked up her phone and headed back to the kitchen for breakfast.

An abrupt silence fell when she walked into the room.

Linda, Stephen and Jenny all wore self-conscious looks of those who fear they might have been overheard. Robin put bread in the toaster, trying to tamp down her rising resentment. She seemed to sense mouthed speech and gesticulations behind her back.

'Robin, we just ran into Matthew,' said Stephen suddenly. 'When we were walking Annabel round the block.'

'Oh,' said Robin, turning to face them, trying to look mildly interested.

It was the first time Matthew had been spotted. Robin had avoided midnight mass out of conviction that he and Sarah would be there, but her mother had reported that none of the Cunliffes had attended. Now Linda, Stephen and Jenny were all looking at her, worried, pitying, waiting for her reaction and her questions.

Her phone beeped.

'Sorry,' she said, picking it up, delighted to have a reason to look away from them all.

Morris had texted:

Why's your Christmas so shit?

While the other three watched, she typed back:

My ex-father-in-law lives locally and my ex has brought his new girlfriend home. We're currently the local scandal.

She didn't like Morris, but at this moment he felt like a welcome ally, a lifeline from the life she had forged, with difficulty, away from Matthew and Masham. Robin was on the point of setting down the phone when it beeped again and, still with the other three watching her, she read:

That stinks.

It does, she texted back.

Then she looked up at her mother, Stephen and Jenny, forcing herself to smile.

'D'you want to tell me about it?' Robin asked Stephen. 'Or do I have to ask?'

'No,' he said hurriedly, 'it wasn't much – we were just pushing Annabel up to the Square and back, and we saw them coming towards us. Him and that—'

'Sarah,' supplied Robin. She could just imagine them hand in hand, enjoying the wintry morning, the picturesque town, sleepy in the frost and early sunshine.

'Yeah,' said Stephen. 'He looked like he wanted to double back when he saw us, but he didn't. Said, "Congratulations in order, I see."'

Robin could hear Matthew saying it.

'And that was it, really,' said Stephen.

'I'd've liked to have kicked him in the balls,' said Jenny suddenly. 'Smug bastard.'

But Linda's eyes were on Robin's phone.

'Who are you texting back and forth on Boxing Day?' she asked.

'I've just told you,' said Robin. 'Morris. He works for the agency.'

She knew exactly what impression she was giving Linda, but she had her pride. Perhaps there was no shame in being single, but the pity of her family, the thought of Matthew and Sarah walking through Masham, everyone's suspicion of her and Strike, and the fact that there was nothing whatsoever to tell about her and Strike, except that he thought he'd better start taking over some of her leads because she'd got no results: all made her want to clutch some kind of fig leaf to her threadbare dignity. Smarmy and overfamiliar as he might be, Morris was today, perhaps, more to be pitied than censured, and was offering himself up to save Robin's face.

She saw her mother and brother exchange looks and had the empty satisfaction of knowing that they were already haring after her false scent. Miserable, she opened the fridge and took out half a bottle of carefully re-corked champagne left over from Christmas Day.

'What are you doing?' asked Linda.

'Making myself a mimosa,' said Robin. 'Still Christmas, isn't it?'

One more night and she'd be back on the train to London. Almost as though she had heard Robin's antisocial thought, a cry of anguish issued through the baby monitor just behind her, making Robin jump, and what she was starting to think of as the baby circus relocated from the kitchen to the sitting room, Linda bringing a glass of water for Jenny to drink while breastfeeding and turning on the TV for her, while Stephen ran upstairs to fetch Annabel.

Drink, Robin decided, was the answer. If you splashed in enough orange juice, nobody had to know you were finishing off a bottle of champagne single-handedly, and those feelings of misery, anger and inadequacy that were writhing in the pit of your stomach could be satisfactorily numbed. Mimosas carried her through to lunchtime, when everyone had a glass of red, although Jenny drank 'just a mouthful' because of Annabel, and ignored Robin's suggestion that alcoholic breast milk might help her sleep. Morris was still texting, mostly stupid Christmas knock-knock jokes and updates on his day, and Robin was replying in the same mindless manner that she sometimes continued eating crisps, with a trace of self-loathing.

My mother's just arrived. Send sherry and excuses not to talk to her WI group about policework.

What's your mother's name? Robin texted back. She was definitely a little bit drunk.

Fanny, said Morris.

Robin was unsure whether to laugh or not, or, indeed, whether it was funny.

'Robs, d'you want to play Pictionary?' asked Jonathan.

'What?' she said.

She was sitting on an uncomfortable hard-backed chair in the corner of the sitting room. The baby circus occupied at least half the room. *The Wizard of Oz* was on the television but nobody was really watching.

'Pictionary,' repeated Jonathan, holding up the box. 'Oh, yeah, and Robs, could I come and stay with you for a weekend in February?'

I'm only kidding, texted Morris. **Frances.**

'What?' Robin said again, under the impression somebody had asked her something.

'Morris is obviously a very interesting man,' said Linda archly, and everyone looked around at Robin, who merely said,

'Pictionary, yes, fine.'

Got to play Pictionary, she texted Morris.

Draw a dick, came back the instant answer.

Robin set down her phone again. The drink was wearing off now, leaving in its wake a headache that throbbed behind her right temple. Luckily, Martin arrived at that moment with a tray full of coffees and a bottle of Baileys.

Jonathan won Pictionary. Baby Annabel screamed some more. A cold supper was laid out on the kitchen table, to which neighbours had been invited to admire Annabel. By eight o'clock in the evening, Robin had taken paracetamol and started to drink black coffee to clear her head. She needed to pack. She also needed, somehow, to shut down her day-long conversation with Morris, who, she could tell, was now very drunk indeed.

Mohter gone home, complaining not seeing grandchioldren enough. What shall we talk about now? What are you wearing?

She ignored the text. Up in her bedroom, she packed her case, because she was catching an early train. *Please, God, let Matthew and Sarah not be on it.* She resprayed herself with her mother's Christmas gift. Smelling it again, she decided that the only message it conveyed to bystanders was 'I have washed'. Perhaps her mother had bought her this boring floral antiseptic out of a subconscious desire to wipe her daughter clean of the suggestion of adultery. There was certainly nothing of the seductress about it, and it would forever remind her of this lousy Christmas. Nevertheless, Robin packed it carefully among her socks, having no wish to hurt her mother's feelings by leaving it behind.

By the time she returned downstairs, Morris had texted another five times.

I was joking.Tell me u know I was joking.Fukc have I offended uHave I?Answer me either way fuck's sake

Slightly riled, and embarrassed now by her stupid, adolescent pretence to her family that she, like Matthew, had found another partner, she paused in the hall to text back,

I'm not offended. Got to go. Need an early night.

She entered the sitting room, where her family were all sitting, sleepy and overfed, watching the news. Robin moved a muslin cloth, half a pack of nappies and one of the Pictionary boards from the sofa, so she could sit down.

'Sorry, Robin,' said Jenny, yawning as she reached out for the baby things and put them by her feet.

Robin's phone beeped yet again. Linda looked over at her. Robin ignored both her mother and the phone, because she was looking down at the Pictionary board where Martin had tried to draw 'Icarus'. Nobody had guessed it. They'd thought Icarus was a bug hovering over a flower.

But something about the picture held Robin fixated. Again, her phone beeped. She looked at it.

Are you in bed?

Yes and so should you be, she texted back, her mind still on the Pictionary board. The flower that looked like a sun. The sun that looked like a flower.

Her phone beeped yet again. Exasperated, she looked at it.

Morris had sent her a picture of his erect dick. For a moment, and even while she felt appalled and repulsed, Robin continued to stare at it. Then, with a suddenness that made her father start awake in his chair, she got up and almost ran out of the room.

The kitchen wasn't far enough. Nowhere would be far enough. Shaking with rage and shock, she wrenched open the back door and strode out into the icy garden, with the water in the birdbath she'd unfrozen with boiling water already milky hard in the moonlight. Without stopping to pause for thought, she called Morris's number.

'Hey—'

'How fucking dare you – *how fucking dare you send me that?'*

'Fuck,' he said thickly, 'I di'n – I thought – "wish you were here" or—'

'I said I was going to bloody bed!' Robin shouted. 'I did not ask to see your fucking dick!'

She could see the neighbours' heads bobbing behind their kitchen blinds. The Ellacotts were providing rich entertainment this Christmas, all right: first a new baby, then a shouting match about a penis.

'Oh shit,' gasped Morris. 'Oh fuck ... no ... listen, I di'n' mean—'

'Who the fuck does that?' shouted Robin. 'What's wrong with you?'

'No ... shit ... fuck ... I'm s'rry ... I thought ... I'm so f'king sorry ... Robin, don't ... oh Jesus ... '

'*I don't want to see your dick!*'

A storm of dry sobs answered her, then Robin thought she heard him lay down the phone on some hard surface. At a distance from the mouthpiece he emitted moans of anguish interspersed with weeping. Heavy objects seemed to be falling over. Then there was a clatter and he picked up his mobile again.

'Robin, I'm so fuckin' sorry ... what've I done, what've I ... ? I thought ... I should fucking kill myself ... don't ... don't tell Strike, Robin ... I'm fuckin' begging you ... if I lose this job ... don't tell, Robin ... I lose this, I lose fuckin' everything ... I can't lose my little girls, Robin ... '

He reminded her of Matthew, the day that she'd found out he was cheating. She could see her ex-husband as clearly as though he was there on the ice-crusted lawn, face in his hands as he gasped his apologies, then looking up at her in panic. '*Have you spoken to Tom? Does he know?*'

What was it about her that made men demand that she keep their dirty secrets?

'I won't tell Strike,' she said, shaking more with rage than with cold, 'because his aunt's dying and we need an extra man. But you'd better never send me anything other than an update on a case again.'

'Oh God, Robin . . . thank you . . . thank you . . . you are such a decent person . . . '

He'd stopped sobbing. His gushing offended her almost as much as the picture of his dick.

'I'm going.'

She stood in the dark, barely feeling the cold, her mobile hanging at her side. As the light in the neighbour's kitchen went off, her parents' back door opened. Rowntree came lolloping over the frozen lawn, delighted to find her outside.

'You all right, love?' Michael Ellacott asked his daughter.

'Fine,' said Robin, crouching to fuss Rowntree to hide her sudden rush of tears. 'It's all fine.'

PART FOUR

Great enemy . . . is wicked Time . . .

Edmund Spenser
The Faerie Queene

31

Deare knight, as deare, as euer knight was deare,
That all these sorrowes suffer for my sake,
High heuen behold the tedious toyle, ye for me take . . .

Edmund Spenser
The Faerie Queene

Strike's gastric upset added days to his illness, and he spent New Year's Eve in bed, reliant on takeaway pizzas but hardly able to touch them when they arrived. For the first time in his life he didn't fancy chocolate, because the truffles he'd consumed after his out-of-date chicken had been the first things to reappear during his prolonged vomiting. The only enjoyable thing he did was to watch the DVD of Tom Waits's *No Visitors After Midnight*, the taped concerts Robin had bought him for Christmas, which he finally unwrapped on New Year's Day. His text thanking her elicited a short 'you're welcome'.

By the time he felt fit enough to travel down to Cornwall, clutching his belated Christmas gifts, Strike had lost over a stone, and this was the first thing an anxious Joan commented on when he finally appeared at her house in St Mawes, full of apologies for his absence at Christmas.

If he'd waited one more day to come down to Joan and Ted's, he'd have been unable to reach them, because no sooner had he arrived than a vicious weather front crashed over the south of Britain. Storms lashed the Cornish coast, train services were suspended, tons of sand washed off the beaches and flooding turned the roads of coastal towns into freezing canals. The Cornish peninsula was temporarily cut off from the rest of England, and while St Mawes had not fared as badly as Mevagissey and Fowey along the coast, sandbags had appeared at the entrances of buildings on the seafront. Waves smashed against the harbour wall, khaki and gunmetal grey. The tourists had melted out of sight like the seals: locals in sodden oilskins greeted each other with nods as they made their way in and out of local shops. All the gaudy prettiness of summertime St Mawes was wiped away and, like an actress when the stage-paint is removed, the town's true self was revealed, a place of hard stone and stiff backbone.

Though pelted with rain and pummelled by gales, Ted and Joan's house was, mercifully, set on high ground. Trapped there, Strike remembered Lucy telling him he was better suited to a crisis than to keeping a commitment going, and knew that there was truth in the accusation. He was well suited to emergencies, to holding his nerve, to quick thinking and fast reactions, but found the qualities demanded by Joan's slow decline harder to summon.

Strike missed the absence of an overriding objective, in pursuit of which he could shelve his sadness; missed the imperative to dismiss pain and distress in the service of something greater, which had sustained him in the military. None of his old coping strategies were admissible in Joan's kitchen, beside the flowered casserole dishes and her old oven gloves. Dark humour and stoicism would be considered unfeeling by the kindly neighbours who wanted him to share and show his pain. Craving diversionary action, Strike was instead expected to provide small talk and homely acts of consideration.

Joan was quietly delighted: hours and days alone with her nephew were compensation for the Christmas he'd missed. Resigned, Strike gave her what she wanted: as much companionship as possible, sitting with her and talking to her all day long. Chemotherapy had been discontinued, because Joan wasn't strong enough for it: she wore a headscarf over the wispy hair she had left, and her husband and nephew watched anxiously as she picked at food, and held themselves constantly ready to assist her when she moved between rooms. Either of them could have carried her with ease, now.

As the days went by, Strike noticed another change in his aunt that surprised him. Just as her storm-ravaged birthplace had revealed a different aspect in adversity, so an unfamiliar Joan was emerging, a Joan who asked open-ended questions that were not designed to elicit confirmation of her own biases, or thinly veiled requests for comforting lies.

'Why haven't you ever married, Cormoran?' she asked her nephew at midday on Saturday morning, when they sat together in the sitting room, Joan in the comfiest armchair, Strike on the sofa. The lamp beside her, which they'd turned on because of the overcast, rainy day, made her skin look as finely translucent as tissue paper.

Strike was so conditioned to tell Joan what she wanted to hear that he was at a loss for an answer. The honest response he'd given Dave Polworth seemed impossible here. She'd probably take it as her fault if he told her that he wasn't the marrying kind; she must have done something wrong, failed to teach him that love was essential to happiness.

'Dunno,' he said, falling back on cliché. 'Maybe I haven't met the right woman.'

'If you're waiting for perfection,' said the new Joan, 'it doesn't exist.'

'You don't wish I'd married Charlotte, do you?' he asked

her. He knew perfectly well that both Joan and Lucy considered Charlotte little short of a she-devil.

'I most certainly don't,' said Joan, with a spark of her old fight, and they smiled at each other.

Ted popped his head around the door.

'That's Kerenza here, love,' he said. 'Her car's just pulled up.'

The Macmillan nurse, whom Strike had met on his first day there, was a blessing such as he could never have imagined. A slender, freckled woman his age, she brought into the house no aura of death, but of life continuing, simply with more comfort and support. Strike's own prolonged exposure to the medical profession had inured him to a certain brand of hearty, impersonal cheerfulness, but Kerenza seemed to see Ted and Joan as individuals, not as simple-minded children, and he heard her talking to Ted, the ex-lifeguard, about people trying to take selfies with their backs to the storm waves while she took off her raincoat in the kitchen.

'Exactly. Don't understand the sea, do they? Respect it, or stay well away, my dad would've said . . . Morning, Joan,' she said, coming into the room. 'Hello, Cormoran.'

'Morning, Kerenza,' said Strike, getting to his feet. 'I'll get out of the way.'

'And how're you feeling today, my love?' the nurse asked Joan.

'Not too bad,' said Joan. 'I'm just a bit . . . '

She paused, to let her nephew pass out of earshot. As Strike closed the door on the two women, he heard more crunching footsteps on the gravel path outside. Ted, who was reading the local paper at the table, looked up.

'Who's that, now?'

A moment later, Dave Polworth appeared at the glass panel in the back door, a large rucksack on his back. He entered, rainswept and grinning.

'Morning, Diddy,' he said, and they exchanged the

handshake and hug that had become the standard greeting in their later years. 'Morning, Ted.'

'What're you doing here?' asked Ted.

Polworth swung his rucksack off, undid it and lifted out a couple of polythene-wrapped, frozen dishes onto the table.

'Penny baked a couple of casseroles. I'm gonna get some provisions in, wanted to know what you needed.'

The flame of pure, practical kindness that burned in Dave Polworth had never been more clearly visible to Strike, except perhaps on his very first day at primary school, when the diminutive Polworth had taken Strike under his protection.

'You're a good lad,' said Ted, moved. 'Say thanks very much to Penny, won't you?'

'Yeah, she sent her love and all that,' said Polworth dismissively.

'Wanna keep me company while I have a smoke?' Strike asked him.

'Go on, then,' said Polworth.

'Use the shed,' suggested Ted.

So Strike and Polworth headed together across the waterlogged garden, heads bowed against the strong wind and rain, and entered Ted's shed. Strike lit up with relief.

'You been on a diet?' asked Polworth, looking Strike up and down.

'Flu and food poisoning.'

'Oh, yeah, Lucy said you'd been ill.' Polworth jerked his head in the direction of Joan's window. 'How is she?'

'Not great,' said Strike.

'How long you down for?'

'Depends on the weather. Listen, seriously, I really appreciate everything you've been—'

'Shut up, you ponce.'

'Can I ask another favour?'

'Go on.'

'Persuade Ted to get a pint with you this lunchtime. He needs to get out of this house for a bit. He'll do it if he knows I'm with her, but otherwise he won't leave.'

'Consider it done,' said Polworth.

'You're—'

'—a prince among men, yeah, I know I am. Arsenal through to the knockout stages, then?'

'Yeah,' said Strike. 'Bayern Munich next, though.'

He'd missed watching his team qualify before Christmas, because he'd been tailing Shifty through the West End. The Champions League, which should have been a pleasure and a distraction, was failing to grip him as it usually did.

'Robin running things in London while you're down here?'

'Yeah,' said Strike.

She'd texted him earlier, asking for a brief chat about the Bamborough case. He'd replied that he'd call her when he had a moment. He, too, had news on the case, but Margot Bamborough had been missing for nearly forty years and, like Kerenza the nurse, Strike was currently prioritising the living.

When he'd finished his cigarette, they returned to the house to find Ted and Kerenza in conversation in the kitchen.

'She'd rather talk to you than to me today,' said Kerenza, smiling at Strike as she shrugged on her raincoat. 'I'll be back tomorrow morning, Ted.'

As she moved towards the back door, Polworth said,

'Ted, come and have a pint.'

'Oh, no, thanks, lad,' said Ted. 'I'll bide here just now.'

Kerenza stopped with her hand on the door knob.

'That's a very good idea. Get a bit of fresh air, Ted – fresh water, today, I should say,' she added, as the rain clattered on the roof. 'Bye-bye, now.'

She left. Ted required a little more persuasion, but finally agreed that he'd join Polworth for a sandwich at the Victory. Once they'd gone, Strike took the local paper off the table and carried it back into the sitting room.

He and Joan discussed the flooding, but the pictures of waves battering Mevagissey meant far less to her than they would have a couple of months ago. Strike could tell that Joan's mind was on the personal, not the general.

'What does my horoscope say?' she asked, as he turned the page of the paper.

'I didn't know you believed in that stuff, Joan.'

'Don't know whether I do or not,' said Joan. 'I always look, though.'

'You're . . .' he said, trying to remember her birthday. He knew it was in the summer.

'Cancer,' she said, and then she gave a little laugh. 'In more ways than one.'

Strike didn't smile.

'"Good time for shaking up your routine,"' he informed her, scanning her horoscope so he could censor out anything depressing, '"so don't dismiss new ideas out of hand. Jupiter retrograde encourages spiritual growth."'

'Huh,' said Joan. After a short pause, she said, 'I don't think I'll be here for my next birthday, Corm.'

The words hit him like a punch in the diaphragm.

'Don't say that.'

'If I can't say it to you, who can I say it to?'

Her eyes, which had always been a pale forget-me-not blue, were faded now. She'd never spoken to him like this before, as an equal. Always, she'd sought to stand slightly above him, so that from her perspective the six-foot-three soldier might still be her little boy.

'I can't say it to Ted or Lucy, can I?' she said. 'You know what they're like.'

'Yeah,' he said, with difficulty.

'Afterwards . . . you'll look after Ted, won't you? Make sure you see him. He does love you so much.'

Fuck.

For so long, she'd demanded a kind of falseness from all around her, a rose-tinted view of everything, and now at last she offered simple honesty and plain-speaking and he wished more than anything that he could be simply nodding along to news of some neighbourhood scandal. Why hadn't he visited them more often?

'I will, of course,' he said.

'I want the funeral at St Mawes church,' she said quietly, 'where I was christened. But I don't want to be buried, because it'd have to be in the cemetery all the way up in Truro. Ted'll wear himself out, travelling up and down, taking me flowers. I know him.

'We always said we wanted to be together, afterwards, but we never made a plan and he won't talk to me about it now. So, I've thought about it, Corm, and I want to be cremated. You'll make sure this happens, won't you? Because Ted starts crying every time I try and talk about it and Lucy just won't listen.'

Strike nodded and tried to smile.

'I don't want the family at the cremation. I hate cremations, the curtains and the conveyor belt. You say goodbye to me at the church, then take Ted to the pub and let the undertakers deal with the crematorium bit, all right? Then, after, you can pick up my ashes, take me out on Ted's boat and scatter me in the sea. And when his turn comes, you can do the same for Ted, and we'll be together. You and Lucy won't want to be worrying about looking after graves all the way from London. All right?'

The plan had so much of the Joan he knew in it: it was full of practical kindness and forethought, but he hadn't expected the final touch of the ashes floating away on the tide, no tombstone, no neat dates, instead a melding with the element that had dominated her and Ted's lives, perched on their seaside town, in thrall to the ocean, except during that strange interlude where Ted, in revolt against his own father, had disappeared for several years into the military police.

'All right,' he said, with difficulty.

She sank back a little in her chair with an air of relief at having got this off her chest, and smiled at him.

'It's so lovely, having you here.'

Over the past few days he'd become used to her short reveries and her non-sequiturs, so it was less of a surprise than it might have been to hear her say, a minute later,

'I wish I'd met your Robin.'

Strike, whose mind's eye was still following Joan's ashes into the sunset, pulled himself together.

'I think you'd like her,' he said. 'I'm sure she'd like you.'

'Lucy says she's pretty.'

'Yeah, she is.'

'Poor girl,' murmured Joan. He wondered why. Of course, the knife attack had been reported in the press, when Robin had given evidence against the Shacklewell Ripper.

'Funny, you talking about horoscopes,' Strike said, trying to ease Joan off Robin, and funerals, and death. 'We're investigating an old disappearance just now. The bloke who was in charge of the case . . .'

He'd never before shared details of an investigation with Joan, and he wondered why not, now he saw her rapt attention.

'But I remember that doctor!' she said, more animated than he had seen her in days. 'Margot Bamborough, yes! She had a baby at home . . .'

'Well, that baby's our client,' said Strike. 'Her name's Anna. She and her partner have got a holiday home in Falmouth.'

'That poor family,' said Joan. 'Never knowing . . . and so the officer thought the answer was in the stars?'

'Yep,' said Strike. 'Convinced the killer was a Capricorn.'

'Ted's a Capricorn.'

'Thanks for the tip-off,' said Strike seriously, and she gave a little laugh. 'D'you want more tea?'

While the kettle boiled, Strike checked his texts. Barclay had sent an update on Two-Times' girlfriend, but the most recent message was from an unknown number, and he opened it first.

Hi Cormoran, it's your half-sister, Prudence Donleavy, here. Al gave me your number. I do hope you'll take this in the spirit it's meant. Let me firstly say that I absolutely understand and sympathise with your reasons for not wanting to join us for the Deadbeats anniversary/album party. You may or may not know that my own journey to a relationship with Dad has been in many ways a difficult one, but ultimately I feel that connecting with him – and, yes, forgiving him – has been an enriching experience. We all hope very much that you'll reconsider —

'What's the matter?' said Joan.

She'd followed him into the kitchen, shuffling, slightly stooped.

'What are you doing? I can fetch anything you want—'

'I was going to show you where I hide the chocolate biscuits. If Ted knows, he scoffs the lot, and the doctor's worried about his blood pressure. What were you reading? I know that look. You were angry.'

He didn't know whether her new appreciation for honesty would stretch as far as his father, but somehow, with the wind and rain whipping around them, an air of the confessional had descended upon the house. He told her about the text.

'Oh,' said Joan. She pointed at a Tupperware box on a top shelf. 'The biscuits are in there.'

They returned to the sitting room with the biscuits, which she'd insisted he put on a plate. Some things never changed.

'You've never met Prudence, have you?' asked Joan, when she was resettled in her chair.

'Haven't met Prudence, or the eldest, Maimie, or the youngest, Ed,' said Strike, trying to sound matter of fact.

Joan said nothing for a minute or so, then a great sigh inflated, then collapsed, her thin chest, and she said,

'I think you should go to your father's party, Corm.'

'Why?' said Strike. The monosyllable rang in his ears with an adolescent, self-righteous fury. To his slight surprise, she smiled at him.

'I know what went on,' she said. 'He behaved very badly, but he's still your father.'

'No, he isn't,' said Strike. 'Ted's my dad.'

He'd never said it out loud before. Tears filled Joan's eyes.

'He'd love to hear you say that,' she said softly. 'Funny, isn't it . . . years ago, years and years, I was just a girl, and I went to see a proper gypsy fortune teller. They used to camp up the road. I thought she'd tell me lots of nice things. You expect them to, don't you? You've paid your money. D'you know what she said?'

Strike shook his head.

'"You'll never have children." Just like that. Straight out.'

'Well, she got that wrong, didn't she?' said Strike.

Tears started again in Joan's bleached eyes. Why had he never said these things before, Strike asked himself. It would have been so easy to give her pleasure, and instead he'd held tightly to his divided loyalties, angry that he had to choose, to label, and in doing so, to betray. He reached for her hand and she squeezed it surprisingly tightly.

'You should go to that party, Corm. I think your father's at the heart of . . . of a lot of things. I wish,' she added, after a short pause, 'you had someone to look after you.'

'Doesn't work that way these days, Joan. Men are supposed to be able to look after themselves – in more ways than one,' he added, smiling.

'Pretending you don't need things . . . it's just silly,' she said quietly. 'What does *your* horoscope say?'

He picked up the paper again and cleared his throat.

'"Sagittarius: with your ruler retrograde, you may find you aren't your usual happy-go-lucky self . . ."'

32

Where euer yet I be, my secrete aide
Shall follow you.

Edmund Spenser
The Faerie Queene

It was three o'clock in the afternoon and Robin, who was sitting in her Land Rover close to the nondescript house in Stoke Newington that Strike had watched before Christmas, had seen nothing of interest since arriving in the street at nine o'clock that morning. As rain drizzled down her windscreen she half-wished she smoked, just for something to do.

She'd identified the blonde owner-occupier of the house online. Her name was Elinor Dean, and she was a divorcee who lived alone. Elinor was definitely home, because Robin had seen her pass in front of a window two hours previously, but the squally weather seemed to be keeping her inside. Nobody had visited the house all day, least of all Shifty's Boss. Perhaps they were relatives, after all, and his pre-Christmas visit was simply one of those things you did in the festive season: pay social debts, give presents, check in. The patting on the head might have been a private joke. It certainly didn't seem to suggest anything sexual, criminal or deviant, which was what they were looking for.

Robin's mobile rang.

'Hi.'

'Can you talk?' asked Strike.

He was walking down the steeply sloping street where Ted and Joan's house lay, leaning on the collapsible walking stick he'd brought with him, knowing that the roads would be wet and possibly slippery. Ted was back in the house; they'd just helped Joan upstairs for a nap, and Strike, who wanted to smoke and didn't much fancy the shed again, had decided to go for a short walk in the relentless rain.

'Yes,' said Robin. 'How's Joan?'

'Same,' said Strike. He didn't feel like talking about it. 'You said you wanted a Bamborough chat.'

'Yeah,' said Robin. 'I've got good news, no news and bad news.'

'Bad first,' said Strike.

The sea was still turbulent, spray exploding into the air above the wall of the dock. Turning right, he headed into the town.

'The Ministry of Justice isn't going to let you interview Creed. The letter arrived this morning.'

'Ah,' said Strike. The teeming rain ripped through the blueish haze of his cigarette smoke, destroying it. 'Well, can't say I'm surprised. What's it say?'

'I've left it back at the office,' said Robin, 'but the gist is that his psychiatrists agree non-cooperation isn't going to change at this stage.'

'Right,' said Strike. 'Well, it was always a long shot.'

But Robin could hear his disappointment, and empathised. They were five months into the case, they had no new leads worth the name, and now that the possibility of interviewing Creed had vanished, she somehow felt that she and Strike were pointlessly searching rockpools, while yards away the great white slid away, untouchable, into dark water.

'And I went back to Amanda White, who's now Amanda

Laws, who thought she saw Margot at the printers' window. She wanted money to talk, remember? I offered her expenses if she wants to come to the office – she's in London, it wouldn't be much – and she's thinking it over.'

'Big of her,' grunted Strike. 'What's the good news?' he asked.

'Anna's persuaded her stepmother to speak to us. Cynthia.'

'Really?'

'Yes, but alone. Roy still doesn't know anything about us,' said Robin. 'Cynthia's meeting us behind his back.'

'Well, Cynthia's something,' said Strike. 'A lot, actually,' he added, after a moment's reflection.

His feet were taking him automatically towards the pub, his wet trouser leg chilly on his remaining ankle.

'Where are we going to meet her?'

'It can't be at their house, because Roy doesn't know. She's suggesting Hampton Court, because she works part time as a guide there.'

'A guide, eh? Reminds me: any news of Postcard?'

'Barclay's at the gallery today,' said Robin. 'He's going to try and get pictures of her.'

'And what're Morris and Hutchins up to?' Strike asked, now walking carefully up the wide, slippery steps that led to the pub.

'Morris is on Two-Times' girl, who hasn't put a foot wrong – Two-Times really is out of luck this time – and Hutchins is on Twinkletoes. Speaking of which, you're scheduled to submit a final report on Twinkletoes next Friday. I'll see the client for you, shall I?'

'That'd be great, thanks,' said Strike, stepping inside the Victory with a sense of relief. The rain dripped off him as he removed his coat. 'I'm not sure when I'm going to be able to get back. You probably saw, the trains have been suspended.'

'Don't worry about the agency. We've got everything

covered. Anyway, I haven't finished giving you the Bamborough – oh, hang on,' said Robin.

'D'you need to go?'

'No, it's fine,' said Robin.

She'd just seen Elinor Dean's front door open. The plump blonde emerged wearing a hooded coat which, conveniently, circumscribed her field of vision. Robin slid out of the Land Rover, closed the door and set off in pursuit, still speaking on her mobile.

'Our blonde friend's on the move,' she said quietly.

'Did you just say you've got more good news on Bamborough?' asked Strike.

He'd reached the bar, and by simply pointing, was able to secure himself a pint, which he paid for, then carried to the corner table at which he'd sat with Polworth in the summer.

'I have,' said Robin, turning the corner at the end of the road, the oblivious blonde walking ahead of her. 'Wish I could say I'd found Douthwaite or Satchwell, but the last person to see Margot alive is something, right?'

'You've found Gloria Conti?' said Strike sharply.

'Don't get too excited,' said Robin, still trudging along in the rain. Elinor seemed to be heading for the shops. Robin could see a Tesco in the distance. 'I haven't managed to speak to her yet, but I'm almost sure it's her. I found the family in the 1961 census: mother, father, one older son and a daughter, Gloria, middle name Mary. By the looks of things, Gloria's now in France, Nîmes, to be precise, and married to a Frenchman. She's dropped the "Gloria", and she's now going by Mary Jaubert. She's got a Facebook page, but it's private. I found her through a genealogical website. One of her English cousins is trying to put together a family tree. Right date of birth and everything.'

'Bloody good work,' said Strike. 'You know, I'm not sure

she isn't even more interesting than Satchwell or Douthwaite. Last to see Margot alive. Close to her. The only living person to have seen Theo, as well.'

Strike's enthusiasm did much to allay Robin's suspicion that he'd added himself to her action points because he thought she wasn't up to the job.

'I've tried to "friend" her on Facebook,' Robin continued, 'but had no response yet. If she doesn't answer, I know the company her husband works for, and I thought I might email him to get a message to her. I thought it was more tactful to try the private route first, though.'

'I agree,' said Strike. He took a sip of Doom Bar. It was immensely consoling to be in the warm, dry pub, and to be talking to Robin.

'And there's one more thing,' said Robin. 'I think I might have found out which van was seen speeding away from Clerkenwell Green the evening Margot disappeared.'

'What? How?' said Strike, stunned.

'It occurred to me over Christmas that what people thought might've been a flower painted on the side could have been a sun,' she said. 'You know. The planet.'

'It's technically a st—'

'Sod off, I know it's a star.'

The hooded blonde, as Robin had suspected, was heading into Tesco. Robin followed, enjoying the warm blast of heat as she entered the shop, though the floor underfoot was slippery and dirty.

'There was a wholefoods shop in Clerkenwell in 1974 whose logo was a sun. I found an ad for it in the British Library newspaper archive, I checked with Companies House and I've managed to talk to the director, who's still alive. *I know I couldn't talk to him if he weren't*,' she added, forestalling any more pedantry.

'Bloody hell, Robin,' said Strike, as the rain battered the window behind him. Good news and Doom Bar were certainly helping his mood. 'This is excellent work.'

'Thank you,' said Robin. 'And get this: he sacked the bloke he had making deliveries, he thinks in mid-1975, because the guy got done for speeding while driving the van. He remembered his name – Dave Underwood – but I haven't had time to—'

Elinor turned abruptly, midway up the aisle of tinned foods, and walked back towards her. Robin pretended to be absorbed in choosing a packet of rice. Letting her quarry pass, she finished her sentence.

'—haven't had time to look for him yet.'

'Well, you're putting me to shame,' admitted Strike, rubbing his tired eyes. Though he now had a spare bedroom to himself rather than the sofa, the old mattress was only a small step up in terms of comfort, its broken springs jabbing him in the back and squealing every time he turned over. 'The best I've done is to find Ruby Elliot's daughter.'

'Ruby-who-saw-the-two-women-struggling-by-the-phone-boxes?' Robin recited, watching her blonde target consulting a shopping list before disappearing down a new aisle.

'That's the one. Her daughter emailed to say she's happy to have a chat, but we haven't fixed up a time yet. And I called Janice,' said Strike, 'mainly because I couldn't face Irene, to see whether she can remember the so-called Applethorpe's real name, but she's in Dubai, visiting her son for six weeks. Her answer machine message literally says "Hi, I'm in Dubai, visiting Kevin for six weeks". Might drop her a line advising her it's not smart to advertise to random callers that you've left your house empty.'

'So did you call Irene?' Robin asked. Elinor, she saw, was now looking at baby food.

'Not yet,' said Strike. 'But I have—'

At that very moment, a bleeping on his phone told him that someone else was trying to reach him.

'Robin, that might be him. I'll call you back.'

Strike switched lines.

'Cormoran Strike.'

'Yes, hello,' said Gregory Talbot. 'It's me – Greg Talbot. You asked me to call.'

Gregory sounded worried. Strike couldn't blame him. He'd hoped to divest himself of a problem by handing the can of old film to Strike.

'Yeah, Gregory, thanks very much for calling me back. I had a couple more questions, hope that's OK.'

'Go on.'

'I've been through your father's notebook and I wanted to ask whether your father happened to know, or mention, a man called Niccolo Ricci? Nicknamed "Mucky"?'

'Mucky Ricci?' said Gregory. 'No, he didn't really *know* him. I remember Dad talking about him, though. Big in the Soho sex shop scene, if that's the one I'm thinking of?'

It sounded as though talking about the gangster gave Gregory a small frisson of pleasure. Strike had met this attitude before, and not just in members of the fascinated public. Even police and lawyers were not immune to the thrill of coming within the orbit of criminals who had money and power to rival their own. He'd known senior officers talk with something close to admiration of the organised crime they were attempting to prevent, and barristers whose delight at drinking with high-profile clients went far beyond the hope of an anecdote to tell at a dinner party. Strike suspected that to Gregory Talbot, Mucky Ricci was a name from a fondly remembered childhood, a romantic figure belonging to a lost era, when his father was a sane copper and a happy family man.

'Yeah, that's the bloke,' said Strike. 'Well, it looks as though Mucky Ricci was hanging around Margot Bamborough's practice, and your father seems to have known about it.'

'Really?'

'Yes,' said Strike, 'and it seems odd that information never made it into the official records.'

'Well, Dad was ill,' said Gregory defensively. 'You've seen the notebook. He didn't know what he was up to, half the time.'

'I appreciate that,' said Strike, 'but once he'd recovered, what was his attitude to the evidence he'd collected while on the case?'

'What d'you mean?'

Gregory sounded suspicious now, as though he feared Strike was leading him somewhere he might not want to go.

'Well, did he think it was all worthless, or—?'

'He'd been ruling out suspects on the basis of their star signs,' said Gregory quietly. 'He thought he saw a demon in the spare room. What d'you *think* he thought? He was ... he was ashamed. It wasn't his fault, but he never got over it. He wanted to go back and make it right, but they wouldn't let him, they forced him out. The Bamborough case tainted everything for him, all his memories of the force. His mates were all coppers and he wouldn't see them any more.'

'He felt resentful at the way he was treated, did he?'

'I wouldn't say – I mean, he was justified, I'd say, to feel they hadn't treated him right,' said Gregory.

'Did he ever look over his notes, afterwards, to make sure he'd put everything in there in the official record?'

'I don't know,' said Gregory, a little testy now. 'I think his attitude was, they've got rid of me, they think I'm a big problem, so let Lawson deal with it.'

'How did your father get on with Lawson?'

'Look, what's all this about?' Before Strike could answer, Gregory said, 'Lawson made it quite clear to my father that his day was done. He didn't want him hanging around, didn't want him anywhere near the case. Lawson did his best to completely discredit my father, I don't mean just because of his illness. I mean, as a man, and as the officer he'd been before he got ill. He told everyone on the case they were to stay away from my father, even out of working hours. So if information didn't get passed on, it's down to Lawson as much as him. Dad might've tried and been rebuffed, for all I know.'

'I can certainly see it from your father's point of view,' said Strike. 'Very difficult situation.'

'Well, exactly,' said Gregory, slightly placated, as Strike had intended.

'To go back to Mucky Ricci,' Strike said, 'as far as you know, your father never had direct dealings with him?'

'No,' said Gregory, 'but Dad's best mate on the force did, name of Browning. He was Vice Squad. He raided one of Mucky's clubs, I know that. I remember Dad talking about it.'

'Where's Browning now? Can I talk to him?'

'He's dead,' said Gregory. 'What exactly—?'

'I'd like to know where that film you passed to me came from, Gregory.'

'I've no idea,' said Gregory. 'Dad just came home with it one day, Mum says.'

'Any idea when this was?' asked Strike, hoping not to have to find a polite way of asking whether Talbot had been quite sane at the time.

'It would've been while Dad was working on the Bamborough case. Why?'

Strike braced himself.

'I'm afraid we've had to turn the film over to the police.'

Hutchins had volunteered to take care of this, on the

morning that Strike had headed down to Cornwall. As an ex-policeman who still had good contacts on the force, he knew where to take it and how to make sure it got seen by the right people. Strike had asked Hutchins not to talk to Robin about the film, or to tell her what he'd done with it. She was currently in ignorance of the contents.

'What?' said Gregory, horrified. 'Why?'

'It isn't porn,' said Strike, muttering now, in deference to the elderly couple who had just entered the Victory and stood, disorientated by the storm outside, dripping and blinking mere feet from his table. 'It's a snuff movie. Someone filmed a woman being gang-raped and stabbed.'

There was another silence on the end of the phone. Strike watched the elderly couple shuffle to the bar, the woman taking off her plastic rain hat as she went.

'Actually killed?' said Gregory, his voice rising an octave. 'I mean . . . it's definitely real?'

'Yeah,' said Strike.

He wasn't about to give details. He'd seen people dying and dead: the kind of gore you saw on horror movies wasn't the same, and even without a soundtrack, he wouldn't quickly forget the hooded, naked woman twitching on the floor of the warehouse, while her killers watched her die.

'And I suppose you've told them where you got it?' said Gregory, more panicked than angry.

'I'm afraid I had to,' said Strike. 'I'm sorry, but some of the men involved could still be alive, could still be charged. I can't sit on something like that.'

'I wasn't concealing anything, I didn't even know it was—'

'I wasn't meaning to suggest you knew, or you meant to hide it,' said Strike.

'If they think – we *foster kids*, Strike—'

'I've told the police you handed it over to me willingly,

without knowing what was on there. I'll stand up in court and testify that I believe you were in total ignorance of what was in your attic. Your family's had forty-odd years to destroy it and you didn't. Nobody's going to blame you,' said Strike, even though he knew perfectly well that the tabloids might not take that view.

'I was afraid something like this was going to happen,' said Gregory, now sounding immensely stressed. 'I've been worried, ever since you came round for coffee. Dragging all this stuff up again . . .'

'You told me your father would want to see the case solved.'

There was another silence, and then Gregory said,

'He would. But not at the cost of my mother's peace of mind, or me and my wife having our foster kids taken off us.'

A number of rejoinders occurred to Strike, some of them unkind. It was far from the first time he'd encountered the tendency to believe the dead would have wanted whatever was most convenient to the living.

'I had a responsibility to hand that film over to the police once I'd seen what was on it. As I say, I'll make it clear to anyone who asks that you weren't trying to hide anything, that you handed it over willingly.'

There was little more to say. Gregory, clearly still unhappy, rang off, and Strike called Robin back.

She was still in Tesco, now buying a packet of nuts and raisins, chewing gum and some shampoo for herself while, two tills away, the object of her surveillance bought baby powder, baby food and dummies along with a range of groceries.

'Hi,' Robin said into her mobile, turning to look out of the shopfront window while the blonde walked past her.

'Hi,' said Strike. 'That was Gregory Talbot.'

'What did he—? Oh yes,' said Robin with sudden interest, turning to follow the blonde out of the store, 'what was on that can of film? I never asked. Did you get the projector working?'

'I did,' said Strike. 'I'll tell you about the film when I see you. Listen, there's something else I wanted to say. Leave Mucky Ricci to me, all right? I've got Shanker putting out a few feelers. I don't want you looking for him, or making enquiries.'

'Couldn't I—?'

'*Did you not hear me?*'

'All right, calm down!' said Robin, surprised. 'Surely Ricci must be ninety-odd by—?'

'He's got sons,' said Strike. 'Sons *Shanker's* scared of.'

'*Oh*,' said Robin, who fully appreciated the implication.

'Exactly. So we're agreed?'

'We are,' Robin assured him.

After Strike had hung up, Robin followed Elinor back out into the rain, and back to her terraced house. When the front door had closed again, Robin got back into her Land Rover and ate her packet of dried fruit and nuts, watching the front door.

It had occurred to her in Tesco that Elinor might be a child-minder, given the nature of her purchases, but as the afternoon shaded into evening, no parents came to drop off their charges, and no baby's wail was heard on the silent street.

33

For he the tyrant, which her hath in ward
By strong enchauntments and blacke Magicke leare,
Hath in a dungeon deepe her close embard . . .
There he tormenteth her most terribly,
And day and night afflicts with mortall paine . . .

Edmund Spenser
The Faerie Queene

Now that the blonde in Stoke Newington had also become a person of interest, the Shifty case became a two-to-three-person job. The agency was watching Elinor Dean's house in addition to tracking the movements of Shifty's Boss and Shifty himself, who continued to go about his business, enjoying the fat salary to which nobody felt he was entitled, but remaining tight-lipped about the hold he had over his boss. Meanwhile, Two-Times was continuing to pay for surveillance on his girlfriend more, it seemed, out of desperation than hope, and Postcard had gone suspiciously quiet. Their only suspect, the owlish guide at the National Portrait Gallery, had vanished from her place of work.

'I hope to God it's flu, and she hasn't killed herself,' Robin said to Barclay on Friday afternoon, when their paths crossed at the office. Strike was still stuck in Cornwall and she'd just seen the Twinkletoes client out of the office. He'd paid his sizeable final bill grudgingly, having found out only that the West

End dancer with whom his feckless daughter was besotted was a clean-living, monogamous and apparently heterosexual young man.

Barclay, who was submitting his week's receipts to Pat before heading out to take over surveillance of Shifty overnight, looked surprised.

'The fuck would she've killed herself?'

'I don't know,' said Robin. 'That last message she wrote sounded a bit panicky. Maybe she thought I'd come to confront her, holding the postcards she'd sent.'

'You need tae get some sleep,' Barclay advised her.

Robin moved towards the kettle.

'No fer me,' Barclay told her, 'I've gottae take over from Andy in thirty. We're back in Pimlico, watchin' Two-Times' bird never cop off wi' any fucker.'

Pat counted out tenners for Barclay, towards whom her attitude was tolerant rather than warm. Pat's favourite member of the agency, apart from Robin, remained Morris, whom Robin had met only three times since New Year: twice when swapping over at the end of a surveillance shift and once when he'd come into the office to leave his week's report. He'd found it difficult to meet her eye and talked about nothing but work, a change she hoped would be permanent.

'Who's next on the client waiting list, Pat?' she asked, while making coffee.

'We havenae got the manpower for another case the noo,' said Barclay flatly, pocketing his cash. 'Not wi' Strike off.'

'He'll be back on Sunday, as long as the trains are running,' said Robin, putting Pat's coffee down beside her. They'd arranged to meet Cynthia Phipps the following Monday, at Hampton Court Palace.

'I need a weekend back home, end o' the month,' Barclay told Pat, who in Strike's absence was in charge of the rota. As she opened it up on her computer, Barclay added, 'Migh' as well make the most of it, while I dinnae need a passport.'

'What d'you mean?' asked the exhausted Robin, sitting down on the sofa in the outer office with her coffee. She was, technically, off duty at the moment, but couldn't muster the energy to go home.

'Scottish independence, Robin,' said Barclay, looking at her from beneath his heavy eyebrows. 'I ken you English've barely noticed, but the union's about tae break up.'

'It won't really, will it?' said Robin.

'Every fucker I know's gonna vote Yes in September. One o' me mates from school called me an Uncle Tam last time I wus home. Arsehole won't be doin' that again,' growled Barclay.

When Barclay had left, Pat asked Robin,

'How's his aunt?'

Robin knew Pat was referring to Strike, because she never referred to her boss by name if she could help it.

'Very ill,' said Robin. 'Not fit for more chemotherapy.'

Pat jammed her electronic cigarette between her teeth and kept typing. After a while, she said,

'He was on his own at Christmas, upstairs.'

'I know,' said Robin. 'He told me how good you were to him. Buying him soup. He was really grateful.'

Pat sniffed. Robin drank her coffee, hoping for just enough of an energy boost to get her off this sofa and onto the Tube. Then Pat said,

'I'd've thought *he'd*'ve had somewhere to go, other than the attic.'

'Well, he had flu really badly,' said Robin. 'He didn't want to give it to anyone else.'

But as she washed up her mug, put on her coat, bade Pat farewell and set off downstairs, Robin found herself musing on this brief exchange. She'd often pondered the, to her, inexplicable animosity that Pat seemed to feel towards Strike. It had been clear from her tone that Pat had imagined Strike somehow immune to loneliness or vulnerability, and Robin was puzzled as to why, because Strike had never made any secret of where he was living or the fact that he slept there alone.

Robin's mobile rang. Seeing an unknown number, and remembering that Tom Turvey had been on the other end of the line the last time she'd answered one, she paused outside Tottenham Court Road station to answer it, with slight trepidation.

'Is this Robin Ellacott?' said a Mancunian voice.

'It is,' said Robin.

'Hiya,' said the woman, a little nervously. 'You wanted to talk to Dave Underwood. I'm his daughter.'

'Oh, yes,' said Robin. 'Thank you so much for getting back to me.'

Dave Underwood was the man who'd been employed to drive a wholefoods shop van at the time that Margot Bamborough went missing. Robin, who'd found his address online and written him a letter three days previously, hadn't expected such a quick response. She'd become inured to people ignoring her messages about Margot Bamborough.

'It was a bit of a shock, getting your letter,' said the woman on the phone. 'The thing is, Dad can't talk to you himself. He had a tracheotomy three weeks ago.'

'Oh, I'm so sorry to hear that,' said Robin, one finger in the ear not pressed to the phone, to block out the rumbling traffic.

'Yeah,' said the woman. 'He's here with me now, though, and he wants me to say . . . look . . . he's not going to be in trouble, is he?'

'No, of course not,' said Robin. 'As I said in my letter, it really is just about eliminating the van from enquiries.'

'All right then,' said Dave's daughter. 'Well, it *was* him.

Amazing, you working it out, because they all swore it was a flower on the side of the van, didn't they? He was glad at the time, because he thought he'd get in trouble, but he's felt bad about it for years. He went the wrong way on a delivery and he was speeding through Clerkenwell Green to try and put himself right. He didn't want to say, because the boss had had a go at him that morning for not getting deliveries out on time. He saw in the paper they were thinking maybe he'd been Dennis Creed and he just . . . well, you know. Nobody likes getting mixed up with stuff like that, do they? And the longer he kept quiet, the worse he thought it would look, him not coming forward straight away.'

'I see,' said Robin. 'Yes, I can understand how he felt. Well, this is very helpful. And after he'd made his delivery, did he—?'

'Yeah, he went back to the shop and he got a right telling-off anyway, because they opened the van and saw he'd delivered the wrong order. He had to go back out again.'

So Margot Bamborough clearly hadn't been in the back of the wholefoods van.

'Well, thanks very much for getting back to me,' said Robin, 'and please thank your father for being honest. That's going to be a great help.'

'You're welcome,' said the woman, and then, quickly, before Robin could hang up. 'Are you the girl the Shacklewell Ripper stabbed?'

For a moment, Robin considered denying it, but she'd signed the letter to Dave Underwood with her real name.

'Yes,' she said, but with less warmth than she'd put into her thank you for the information about the van. She didn't like being called 'the girl the Shacklewell Ripper stabbed'.

'Wow,' said the woman, 'I told Dad I thought it was you. Well, at least Creed can't get you, eh?'

She said it almost jauntily. Robin agreed, thanked her again for her cooperation, hung up the phone and proceeded down the stairs into the Tube.

At least Creed can't get you, eh?

The cheery sign-off stayed with Robin as she descended to the Tube. That flippancy belonged only to those who had never felt blind terror, or come up against brute strength and steel, who'd never heard pig-like breathing close to their ear, or seen defocused eyes through balaclava holes, or felt their own flesh split, yet barely registered pain, because death was so close you could smell its breath.

Robin glanced over her shoulder on the escalator, because the careless commuter behind her kept touching the backs of her upper thighs with his briefcase. Sometimes she found casual physical contact with men almost unbearable. Reaching the bottom of the escalator she moved off fast to remove herself from the commuter's vicinity. *At least Creed can't get you, eh?* As though being 'got' was nothing more than a game of tag.

Or was it being in the newspaper had somehow made Robin seem less human to the woman on the end of the phone? As Robin settled herself into a seat between two women on the Tube, her thoughts returned to Pat, and to the secretary's surprise that Strike had nowhere to go when he was ill, and nobody to look after him. Was that at the root of her antipathy? An assumption that newsworthiness meant invulnerability?

When Robin let herself into the flat forty minutes later, carrying a bag of groceries and looking forward to an early night, she found the place empty except for Wolfgang, who greeted her exuberantly, then whined in a way that indicated a full bladder. With a sigh, Robin found his lead and took him downstairs for a quick walk around the block. After that, too tired to cook a proper meal, she scrambled herself some eggs and ate them with toast while watching the news on TV.

She was running herself a bath when her mobile rang

again. Her heart sank a little when she saw that it was her brother Jonathan, who was in his final year of university in Manchester. She thought she knew what he was calling about.

'Hi, Jon,' she said.

'Hey, Robs. You didn't answer my text.'

She knew perfectly well that she hadn't. He'd sent it that morning, while she'd been watching Two-Times' girlfriend having a blameless coffee, alone with a Stieg Larsson novel. Jon wanted to know whether he and a female friend could come and stay at her flat on the weekend of the fourteenth and fifteenth of February.

'Sorry,' said Robin, 'I know I didn't, it's been a busy day. I'm not sure, to be honest, Jon. I don't know what Max's plans—'

'He wouldn't mind us crashing in your room, would he? Courtney's never been to London. There's a comedy show we want to see on Saturday. At the Bloomsbury Theatre.'

'Is Courtney your girlfriend?' asked Robin, smiling now. Jonathan had always been quite cagey with the family about his love life.

'Is she my *girlfriend*,' repeated Jonathan mockingly, but Robin had an idea that he was quite pleased with the question really, and surmised that the answer was 'yes'.

'I'll check with Max, OK? And I'll ring you back tomorrow,' said Robin.

Once she'd disposed of Jonathan, she finished running the bath and headed into her bedroom to fetch pyjamas, dressing gown and something to read. *The Demon of Paradise Park* lay horizontally across the top of her neat shelf of novels. After hesitating for a moment, she picked it up and took it back to the bathroom with her, trying as she did so to imagine getting ready for bed with her brother and an unknown girl in the room, as well. Was she prudish, stuffy and old before her time? She'd never finished her university degree: 'crashing' on floors in the houses of strangers had never been part of her life, and in the wake of the rape that had occurred in her halls of residence, she'd never had any desire to sleep anywhere except in an environment over which she had total control.

Sliding into the hot bubble bath, Robin let out a great sigh of pleasure. It had been a long week, sitting in the car for hours or else trudging through the rainy streets after Shifty or Elinor Dean. Eyes closed, enjoying the heat and the synthetic jasmine of her cheap bubble bath, her thoughts drifted back to Dave Underwood's daughter.

At least Creed can't get you, eh? Setting aside the offensively jocular tone, it struck her as significant that a woman who'd known for years that Creed hadn't been driving the sun-emblazoned van was nevertheless certain that he'd abducted Margot.

Because, of course, Creed hadn't *always* used a van. He'd killed two women before he ever got the job at the dry cleaner's, and managed to persuade women to walk into his basement flat even after he'd acquired the vehicle.

Robin opened her eyes, reached for *The Demon of Paradise Park* and turned to the page where she had last left it. Holding the book clear of the hot, foamy water, she continued to read.

> One night in September 1972, Dennis Creed's landlady spotted him bringing a woman back to the basement flat for the first time. She testified at Creed's trial that she heard the front gate 'squeak' at close to midnight, glanced down from her bedroom window at the steps into the basement and saw Creed and a woman who 'seemed a bit drunk but was walking OK', heading into the house.
>
> When she asked Dennis who the woman was, he told her the implausible story that she was a regular client of the dry cleaner's. He claimed he'd met the drunk woman by

chance in the street, and that she had begged him to let her come into his flat to phone a taxi.

In reality, the woman Violet had seen Dennis steering into the flat was the unemployed Gail Wrightman, who'd been stood up that evening by a boyfriend. Wrightman left the Grasshopper, a bar in Shoreditch, at half past ten in the evening, after consuming several strong cocktails. A woman matching Wrightman's description was seen getting into a white van at a short distance from the bar. Barring Cooper's glimpse of a brunette in a light-coloured coat entering Creed's flat that night, there were no further sightings of Gail Wrightman after she left the Grasshopper.

By now, Creed had perfected a façade of vulnerability that appealed particularly to older women like his landlady, and a convivial, sexually ambiguous persona that worked well with the drunk and lonely. Creed subsequently admitted to meeting Wrightman in the Grasshopper, adding Nembutal to her drink and lying in wait outside the bar where, confused and unsteady on her feet, she was grateful for his offer of a lift home.

Cooper accepted his explanation of the dry-cleaning client who'd wanted to call a taxi 'because I had no reason to doubt it'.

In reality, Gail Wrightman was now gagged and chained to a radiator in Creed's bedroom, where she would remain until Creed killed her by strangulation in January 1973. This was the longest period he kept a victim alive, and demonstrates the degree of confidence he had that his basement flat was now a place of safety, where he could rape and torture without fear of discovery.

However, shortly before Christmas that year, his landlady visited him on some trivial pretext, and she recalled in the witness box that 'he wanted to get rid of me, I could tell. I thought there was a nasty smell about the place, but we'd had problems with next door's drains before. He told me he couldn't chat because he was waiting for a phone call.

'I know it was Christmastime when I went down there, because I remember asking him why he hadn't put any cards up. I knew he didn't have many friends but I thought someone must have remembered him and I thought it was a shame. The radio was playing 'Long-Haired Lover from Liverpool', and it was loud, I remember that, but that wasn't anything unusual. Dennis liked music.'

Cooper's surprise visit to the basement almost certainly sealed Wrightman's death warrant. Creed later told a psychiatrist that he'd been toying with the idea of simply keeping Wrightman 'as a pet' for the foreseeable future, to spare himself the risks that further abductions would entail, but that he reconsidered and decided to 'put her out of her misery'.

Creed murdered Wrightman on the night of January 9th 1973, a date chosen to coincide with a three-day absence of Vi Cooper to visit a sick relative. Creed cut off Wrightman's head and hands in the bath before driving the rest of the corpse in his van to Epping Forest by night, wrapped in tarpaulin, and burying it in a shallow grave. Back at home, he boiled the flesh off Wrightman's head and hands and smashed up the bones, as he'd done to the corpses of both Vera Kenny and Noreen Sturrock, adding the powdered bone to the inlaid ebony box he kept under his bed.

On her return to Liverpool Road, Violet Cooper noted that the 'bad smell' had gone from the basement flat and concluded that the drains had been sorted out.

Landlady and lodger resumed their convivial evenings, drinking and singing along to records. It's likely that Creed experimented with drugging Vi at this time. She later testified that she often slept so soundly on nights that Dennis joined her for a nightcap that she found herself still groggy the next morning.

Wrightman's grave remained undisturbed for nearly four months, until discovered by a dog walker whose terrier dug and retrieved a thigh bone. Decomposition, the absence of head and hands or any clothing rendered identification almost impossible given the difficulties of tissue typing in such circumstances. Only after Creed's arrest, when Wrightman's underwear, pantyhose and an opal ring her family identified as having belonged to her were found under the floorboards of Creed's sitting room, were detectives able to add Wrightman's murder to the list of charges against him.

Gail's younger sister had never lost hope that Gail was still alive. 'I couldn't believe it until I saw the ring with my own eyes. Until that moment, I honestly thought there'd been a mistake. I kept telling Mum and Dad she'd come back. I couldn't believe there was wickedness like that in the world, and that my sister could have met it.

'He isn't human. He played with us, with the families, during the trial. Smiling and waving at us every morning. Looking at the parents or the brother or whoever, whenever their relative was mentioned. Then, afterwards, after he was convicted, he keeps telling a bit more, and a bit more, and we've had to live with that hanging over us for years, what Gail said, or how she begged him. I'd murder him with my own bare hands if I could, but I could never make him suffer the way he made Gail suffer. He isn't capable of human feeling, is he? It makes you—'

There was a loud bang from the hall and Robin jumped so severely that water slopped over the edge of the bath.

'Just me!' called Max, who sounded uncharacteristically

cheerful, and she heard him greeting Wolfgang. 'Hello, you. Yes, hello, hello . . . '

'Hi,' called Robin. 'I took him out earlier!'

'Thanks very much,' said Max, 'Come join me, I'm celebrating!'

She heard Max climbing the stairs. Pulling out the plug, she continued to sit in the bath as the water ebbed away, crisp bubbles still clinging to her as she finished the chapter.

> It makes you pray there's a hell.'
>
> In 1976, Creed told prison psychiatrist Richard Merridan that he tried to 'lie low' following the discovery of Wrightman's remains. Creed admitted to Merridan that he felt a simultaneous desire for notoriety and a fear of capture.
>
> 'I liked reading about the Butcher in the papers. I buried her in Epping Forest like the others because I wanted people to know that the same person had done them all, but I knew I was risking everything, not varying the pattern. After that, after Vi had seen me with her, and come in the flat with her there, I thought I'd better just do whores for a bit, lie low.'
>
> But the choice to 'do whores' would lead, just a few months later, to Creed's closest brush with capture yet.

The chapter ended here. Robin got out of the bath, mopped up the spilled water, dressed in pyjamas and dressing gown, then headed upstairs to the living area where Max sat watching television, looking positively beatific. Wolfgang seemed to have been infected by his owner's good mood: he greeted Robin as though she'd been away on a long journey and set to work licking the bath oil off her ankles until she asked him kindly to desist.

'I've got a job,' Max told Robin, muting the TV. Two champagne glasses and a bottle were sitting on the coffee table in front of him. 'Second lead, new drama, BBC One. Have a drink.'

'Max, that's fantastic!' said Robin, thrilled for him.

'Yeah,' he said, beaming. 'Listen. D'you think your Strike would come over for dinner? I'm playing a veteran. It'd be good to speak to someone who's actually ex-army.'

'I'm sure he would,' said Robin, hoping she was right. Strike and Max had never met. She accepted a glass of champagne, sat down and held up her glass in a toast. 'Congratulations!'

'Thanks,' he said, clinking his glass against hers. 'I'll cook, if Strike comes over. It'll be good, actually. I need to meet more people. I'm turning into one of those "he always kept himself to himself" blokes you see on the news.'

'And I'll be the dumb flatmate,' said Robin, her thoughts still with Vi Cooper, 'who thought you were lovely and never questioned why I kept coming across you hammering the floorboards back down.'

Max laughed.

'And they'll blame you more than me,' said Max, 'because they always do. The women who didn't realise ... mind you, some of them ... who was that guy in America who made his wife call him on an intercom before he'd let her into the garage?'

'Jerry Brudos,' said Robin. Brudos had been mentioned in *The Demon of Paradise Park*. Like Creed, Brudos had been wearing women's clothing when he abducted one of his victims.

'I need to get a bloody social life going again,' said Max, more expansive than Robin had ever known him under the influence of alcohol and good news. 'I've been feeling like hell ever since Matthew left. Kept wondering whether I shouldn't just sell this place and move on.'

Robin thought her slight feeling of panic might have shown in her face, because Max said,

'Don't worry, I'm not going to. But it's half-killed me, keeping it going. I really only bought the place because of him. "Put it all into property, you can't lose with property," he said.'

He looked as though he was going to say something else, but if so, decided against it.

'Max, I wanted to ask you something,' said Robin, 'but it's totally fine if the answer's no. My younger brother and a girlfriend are looking for a place to stay in London for the weekend of the fourteenth and fifteenth of February. But if you don't—'

'Don't be silly,' said Max. 'They can sleep on this,' he said, patting the sofa. 'It folds out.'

'Oh,' said Robin, who hadn't known this. 'Well, great. Thanks, Max.'

The champagne and the hot bath had made Robin feel incredibly sleepy, but they talked on for a while about Max's new drama, until at last Robin apologised and said she really did need to go to bed.

As she pulled the duvet over herself, Robin decided against starting a new chapter on Creed. It was best not to have certain things in your head if you wanted to get to sleep. However, once she'd turned out her bedside lamp she found her mind refusing to shut down, so she reached for her iPod.

She never listened to music on headphones unless she knew Max was in the flat. Some life experiences made a person forever conscious of their ability to react, to have advance warning. Now, though, with the front door safely double-locked (Robin had checked, as she always did), and with her flatmate and a dog mere seconds away, she inserted her earbuds and pressed shuffle on the four albums of Joni Mitchell's she'd now bought, choosing music over another bottle of perfume she didn't like.

Sometimes, when listening to Mitchell, which Robin was doing frequently these days, she could imagine Margot Bamborough smiling at her through the music. Margot was forever frozen at twenty-nine, fighting not to be defeated by a life more complicated than she had ever imagined it would be, when she conceived the ambition of raising herself out of poverty by brains and hard work.

An unfamiliar song began to play. The words told the story of the end of a love affair. It was a simpler, more direct lyric than many of Mitchell's, with little metaphor or poetry about it. *Last chance lost/The hero cannot make the change/Last chance lost/The shrew will not be tamed.*

Robin thought of Matthew, unable to adapt himself to a wife who wanted more from life than a steady progression up the property ladder, unable to give up the mistress who had always, in truth, been better suited to his ideals and ambitions than Robin. So did that make Robin the shrew, fighting for a career that everyone but she thought was a mistake?

Lying in the dark, listening to Mitchell's voice, which was deeper and huskier on her later albums, an idea that had been hovering on the periphery of Robin's thoughts for a couple of weeks forced its way into the forefront of her mind. It had been lurking ever since she'd read the letter from the Ministry of Justice, refusing Strike permission to see the serial killer.

Strike had accepted the Ministry of Justice's decision, and indeed, so had Robin, who had no desire to increase the suffering of the victims' families. And yet the man who might save Anna from a lifetime of continued pain and uncertainty was still alive. If Irene Hickson had been bursting to talk to Strike, how much more willing might Creed be, after decades of silence?

Last chance lost/the hero cannot make the change.

Robin sat up abruptly, pulled out her earphones, turned the lamp back on and reached for the notebook and pen she always kept beside her bed these days.

There was no need to tell Strike what she was up to. The possibility that her actions might backfire on the agency must be taken. If she didn't try, she'd forever wonder whether there hadn't been a chance of reaching Creed, after all.

34

. . . no Art, nor any Leach's Might . . .
Can remedy such hurts; such hurts are hellish Pain.

Edmund Spenser
The Faerie Queene

The train service between Cornwall and London resumed at last. Strike packed his bags, but promised his aunt and uncle he'd be back soon. Joan clung to him in silence at parting. Incredibly, Strike would have preferred one of the emotional-blackmail-laden farewells that had previously antagonised him.

Riding the train back to London, Strike found his mood mirrored in the monochrome winter landscape of mud and shivering trees he was watching through the dirt-streaked window. Joan's slow decline was a different experience to the deaths with which Strike was familiar, which had almost all been of the unnatural kind. As a soldier and an investigator, he'd become inured to the need to assimilate, without warning, the sudden, brutal extinction of a human being, to accept the sudden vacuum where once a soul had flickered. Joan's slow capitulation to an enemy inside her own body was something new to him. A small part of Strike, of which he was ashamed, wanted everything to be over, and for the mourning to begin in earnest, and, as the train bore him east, he looked forward to the temporary sanctuary of his empty flat, where he was free to feel miserable without either the need to parade his sadness for the neighbours, or to sport a veneer of fake cheerfulness for his aunt.

He turned down two invitations for dinner on Saturday night, one from Lucy, one from Nick and Ilsa, preferring to deal with the agency's books and review case files submitted by Barclay, Hutchins and Morris. On Sunday he spoke again to Dr Gupta and to a couple of relatives of deceased witnesses in the Bamborough case, preparatory to a catch-up with Robin the following day.

But on Sunday evening, while standing beside the spaghetti boiling on his single hob, he received a second text from his unknown half-sister, Prudence.

> **Hi Cormoran, I don't know whether you received my first text. Hopefully this one will reach you. I just wanted to say (I think) I understand your reasons for not wanting to join us for Dad's group photo, or for the party. There's a little more behind the party than a new album. I'd be happy to talk to you about that in person, but as a family we're keeping it confidential. I hope you won't mind me adding that, like you, I'm the result of one of Dad's briefer liaisons (!) and I've had to deal with my own share of hurt and anger over the years. I wonder whether you'd like to have a coffee to discuss this further? I'm in Putney. Please do get in touch. It would be great to meet. Warmest wishes, Pru**

His spaghetti now boiling noisily, Strike lit a cigarette. Pressure seemed to be building behind his eyeballs. He knew he was smoking too much: his tongue ached, and ever since his Christmas flu, his morning cough had been worse than ever. Barclay had been extolling the virtues of vaping the last time they'd met. Perhaps it was time to try that, or at least to cut down on the cigarettes.

He read Prudence's text a second time. What confidential reason could be behind the party, other than his father's new album? Had Rokeby finally been given his knighthood, or was he making a fuss over the Deadbeats' fiftieth anniversary in an attempt to remind those who gave out honours that he hadn't yet had one? Strike tried to imagine Lucy's reaction, if he told her he was off to meet a host of new half-siblings, when her small stock of relatives was about to be diminished by one. He tried to picture this Prudence, of whom he knew nothing at all, except that her mother had been a well-known actress.

Turning off the hob, he left the spaghetti floating in its water, and began to text a response, cigarette between his teeth.

Thanks for the texts. I've got no objection to meeting you, but now's not a good time. Appreciate that you're doing what you think is the right thing but I've never been much for faking feelings or maintaining polite fictions to suit public celebrations. I don't have a relationship with—

Strike paused for a full minute. He never referred to Jonny Rokeby as 'Dad' and he didn't want to say 'our father', because that seemed to bracket himself and Prudence together in a way that felt uncomfortable, as she was a total stranger.

And yet some part of him didn't feel she was a stranger. Some part of him felt a tug towards her. What was it? Simple curiosity? An echo of the longing he'd felt as a child, for a father who never turned up? Or was it something more primitive: the calling of blood to blood, an animal sense of connection that couldn't quite be eradicated, no matter how much you tried to sever the tie?

—Rokeby and I've got no interest in faking one for a few hours just because he's putting out a new album. I hold no ill will towards you and, as I say, I'd be happy to meet when my life is less—

Strike paused again. Standing in the steam billowing from his saucepan, his mind roved over the dying Joan, over the open cases on the agency's books, and, inexplicably, over Robin.

—complicated. Best wishes, Cormoran.

He ate his spaghetti with a jar of shop-bought sauce, and fell asleep that night to the sound of rain hammering on the roof slates, to dream that he and Rokeby were having a fist fight on the deck of a sailing ship, which pitched and rolled until both of them fell into the sea.

Rain was still falling at ten to eleven the following morning, when Strike emerged from Earl's Court Tube station to wait for Robin, who was going to pick him up before driving to meet Cynthia Phipps at Hampton Court Palace. Standing beneath the brick overhang outside the station exit, yet another cigarette in his mouth, Strike read two recently arrived emails off his phone: an update from Barclay on Two-Times, and one from Morris on Shifty. He'd nearly finished them when the mobile rang. It was Al, and rather than let the call go to voicemail, Strike decided to put an end to this badgering once and for all.

'Hey, bruv,' said Al. 'How're you?'

'Been better,' said Strike.

He deliberately didn't reciprocate the polite enquiry.

'Look,' said Al, 'um . . . Pru's just rung me. She told me what you sent her. Thing is, we've got a photographer booked for next Saturday, but if you're not going to be in the picture – the whole point is that it's from all of us. First time ever.'

'Al, I'm not interested,' said Strike, tired of being polite.

There was a brief silence. Then Al said,

'You know, Dad keeps trying to reach out—'

'Is that right?' said Strike, anger suddenly piercing the fog of fatigue, of his worry about Joan, and the mass of probable irrelevancies he'd found out on the Bamborough case, which he was trying to hold in his head, so he could impart them to Robin. 'When would this be? When he set his lawyers on me, chasing me for money that was legally mine in the first—?'

'If you're talking about Peter Gillespie, Dad didn't know how heavy he was getting with you, I swear he didn't. Pete's retired now—'

'I'm not interested in celebrating his new fucking album,' said Strike. 'Go ahead and have fun without me.'

'Look,' said Al, 'I can't explain right now – if you can meet me for a drink, I'll tell you – there's a reason we want to do this for him now, the photo and the party—'

'The answer's no, Al.'

'You're just going to keep sticking two fingers up at him for ever, are you?'

'Who's sticking two fingers up? I haven't said a word about him publicly, unlike him, who can't give a fucking interview without mentioning me these days—'

'He's trying to put things right, and you can't give an inch!'

'He's trying to tidy up a messy bit of his public image,' said Strike harshly. 'Tell him to pay his fucking taxes if he wants his knighthood. I'm not his pet fucking black sheep.'

He hung up, angrier than he'd expected, his heart thumping uncomfortably hard beneath his coat. Flicking his cigarette butt into the road, his thoughts travelled inescapably back to Joan, with her headscarf hiding her baldness, and Ted weeping into his tea. Why, he thought, furiously, couldn't it have been Rokeby who lay dying, and his aunt who was well and happy, confident she'd reach her next birthday, striding through St Mawes, chatting to lifelong friends, planning dinners for Ted, nagging Strike over the phone about coming to visit?

When Robin turned the corner in the Land Rover a few minutes later, she was taken aback by Strike's appearance. Even though he'd told her by phone about the flu and the out-of-date chicken, he looked noticeably thinner in the face, and so enraged she automatically checked her watch, wondering whether she was late.

'Everything all right?' she asked, when he opened the passenger seat door.

'Fine,' he said shortly, climbing into the passenger seat and slamming the door.

'Happy New Year.'

'Haven't we already said that?'

'No, actually,' said Robin, somewhat aggravated by his surliness. 'But please don't feel pressured into saying it back. I'd hate you to feel railroaded—'

'Happy New Year, Robin,' muttered Strike.

She pulled out into the road, her windscreen wipers working hard to keep the windscreen clear, with a definite sense of déjà vu. He'd been grumpy when she'd picked him up on his birthday, too, and in spite of everything he was going through, she too was tired, she too had personal worries, and would have appreciated just a little effort.

'What's up?' she asked.

'Nothing.'

They drove for a few minutes in silence, until Robin said,

'Did you see Barclay's email?'

'About Two-Times and his girlfriend? Yeah, just read it,'

said Strike. 'Ditched, and she'll never realise it was because she was too faithful.'

'He's such a freak,' said Robin, 'but as long as he pays his bill . . . '

'My thoughts exactly,' said Strike, making a conscious effort to throw off his bad temper. After all, none of it – Joan, Pru, Al, Rokeby – was Robin's fault. She'd been holding the agency together while he dealt with matters in Cornwall. She was owed better.

'We've got room for another waiting list client now,' he said, trying for a more enthusiastic tone. 'I'll call that commodities broker who thinks her husband's shagging the nanny, shall I?'

'Well,' said Robin, 'the Shifty job's taking a lot of manpower at the moment. We're covering him, his boss and the woman in Stoke Newington. The boss went back to Elinor Dean yesterday evening, you know. Same thing all over again, including the pat on the head.'

'Really?' said Strike, frowning.

'Yeah. The clients are getting quite impatient for proper evidence, though. Plus, we haven't got any resolution on Postcard yet and Bamborough's taking up quite a bit of time.'

Robin didn't want to say explicitly that with Strike moving constantly between London and Cornwall, she and the subcontractors were covering the agency's existing cases by forfeiting their days off.

'So you think we should concentrate on Shifty and Postcard, do you?'

'I think we should accept that Shifty's currently a three-person-job and not be in a hurry to take anything else on just now.'

'All right, fair enough,' grunted Strike. 'Any news on the guide at the National Portrait Gallery? Barclay told me you were worried she might've topped herself.'

'What did he tell you that for?' Robin said. She regretted blurting out her anxiety now: it felt soft, unprofessional.

'He didn't mean anything by it. Has she reappeared?'

'No,' said Robin.

'Any more postcards to the weatherman?'

'No.'

'Maybe you've scared her off.'

Strike pulled his notebook out of his pocket and opened it, while the rain continued to drum against the windscreen.

'I've got a few bits and pieces on Bamborough, before we meet Cynthia Phipps. That was great work of yours, eliminating the wholefoods van, by the way.'

'Thanks,' said Robin.

'But there's a whole new van on the scene,' said Strike.

'What?' said Robin sharply.

'I spoke to the daughter of Ruby Elliot yesterday. You remember Ruby—'

'The woman who saw the two women struggling from her car.'

'That's the one. I also spoke to a nephew of Mrs Fleury, who was crossing Clerkenwell Green, trying to get her senile mother home out of the rain.'

Strike cleared his throat, and said, reading from his notes:

'According to Mark Fleury, his aunt was quite upset by the description in the papers of her "struggling" and even "grappling" with her mother, because it suggested she'd been rough with the old dear. She said she was chivvying her mother along, not forcing her, but admitted that otherwise the description fitted them to a tee: right place, right time, rain hat, raincoat, etc.

'But Talbot leapt on the "we weren't grappling" discrepancy and tried to pressure Mrs Fleury into retracting her story and admitting that she and the old lady couldn't have been the people Ruby Elliot saw. Mrs Fleury wasn't having that, though. The description of them was too good: she was sure they were the right people.

'So Talbot went back to Ruby and tried to force her to change *her* story. You'll remember that there was another phone box at the opening of Albemarle Way. Talbot tried to persuade Ruby that she'd seen two people struggling in front of *that* phone box instead.

'Which is where things get mildly interesting,' said Strike, turning a page in his notebook. 'According to Ruby's daughter, Ruby was an absent-minded woman, a nervous driver and a poor map reader, with virtually no sense of direction. On the other hand, her daughter claims she had a very retentive memory for small visual details. She might not remember what street she'd met an acquaintance on, but she could describe down to the colour of a shoelace what they'd been wearing. She'd been a window dresser in her youth.

'Given her general vagueness, Talbot should have found it easy to persuade her she'd mistaken the phone box, but the harder he pushed, the firmer she stood, and the reason she stood firm, and said the two women couldn't have been in front of the Albemarle phone box, was because she'd seen *something else* happen beside that particular phone box, something she'd forgotten all about until Talbot mentioned the wedge-shaped building. Don't forget, she didn't know Clerkenwell at all.

'According to her daughter, Ruby kept driving around in a big circle that night, continually missing Hayward's Place, where her daughter's new house was. When he said, "Are you sure you didn't see these two struggling women beside the *other* phone box, near the wedge-shaped building on the corner of Albemarle Way?" Ruby suddenly remembered that she'd had to brake at that point in the road, because a transit van ahead of her had stopped beside the wedge-shaped building without warning. It was picking up a dark, stocky young woman who was standing in the pouring rain, beside the phone box. The woman—'

'Wait a moment,' said Robin, momentarily taking her eyes off the rainy road to glance at Strike. '"Dark and stocky?" It wasn't *Theo*?'

'Ruby thought it was, once she compared her memory of the girl in the rain with the artist's impressions of Margot's last patient. Dark-skinned, solid build, thick black hair – plastered to her face because it was so wet – and wearing a pair of—'

Strike sounded the unfamiliar name out, reading from his notebook.

'—*Kuchi* earrings.'

'What are Kuchi earrings?'

'Romany-style, according to Ruby's daughter, which might account for Gloria calling Theo "gypsyish". Ruby knew clothes and jewellery. It was the kind of detail she noticed.

'The transit van braked without warning to pick up the-girl-who-could-have-been-Theo, temporarily holding up traffic. Cars behind Ruby were tooting their horns. The dark girl got into the front passenger seat, the transit van moved off in the direction of St John Street and Ruby lost sight of it.'

'And she didn't tell Talbot?'

'Her daughter says that by the time she remembered the second incident, she was exhausted by the whole business, sick to death of being ranted at by Talbot and told she must have been mistaken in thinking the two struggling women hadn't been Margot and Creed in drag, and regretting she'd ever come forward in the first place.

'After Lawson took over the case, she was afraid of what the police and the press would say to her if she suddenly came up with a story of seeing someone who resembled Theo. Rightly or wrongly, she thought it might look as though, having had her first sighting proven to be worthless, she wanted another shot at being important to the inquiry.'

'But her daughter felt OK about telling you all this?'

'Well, Ruby's dead, isn't she? It can't hurt her now. Her daughter made it clear she doesn't think any of this is going to amount to anything, so she might as well tell me the lot. And when all's said and done,' said Strike, turning a page in his notebook, 'we don't know the girl *was* Theo . . . although personally, I think she was. Theo wasn't registered with the practice, so probably wasn't familiar with the area. That corner would make an easily identifiable place to meet the transit van after she'd seen a doctor. Plenty of space for it to pull over.'

'True,' said Robin slowly, 'but if that girl really *was* Theo, this lets her out of any involvement with Margot's disappearance, doesn't it? She clearly left the surgery alone, got a lift and drove—'

'Who was driving the van?'

'I don't know. Anyone. Parent, friend, sibling . . .'

'Why didn't Theo come forward after all the police appeals?'

'Maybe she was scared. Maybe she had a medical problem she didn't want anyone to know about. Plenty of people would rather not get mixed up with the police.'

'Yeah, you're not wrong,' admitted Strike. 'Well, I still think it's worth knowing that one of the last people to see Margot alive might've left the area in a vehicle big enough to hide a woman in.

'And speaking of the last person to see Margot alive,' Strike added, 'any response from Gloria Conti?'

'No,' said Robin. 'If nothing's happened by the end of next week, I'll try and contact her through her husband.'

Strike turned a page in his notebook.

'After I spoke to Ruby's daughter and the Fleury bloke, I

called Dr Gupta back. Dunno whether you remember, but in my summary of the horoscope notes I mentioned "Scorpio", whose death, according to Talbot, worried Margot.'

'Yes,' said Robin. 'You speculated Scorpio might be Steve Douthwaite's married friend, who killed herself.'

'Well remembered,' said Strike. 'Well, Gupta can't remember any patient dying in unexplained circumstances, or in a way that troubled Margot, although he emphasised that all this is forty years ago and he can't swear there wasn't such a patient.

'Then I asked him whether he knew who Joseph Brenner might have been visiting in a block of flats on Skinner Street on the evening Margot disappeared. Gupta says they had a number of patients in Skinner Street, but he can't think of any reason why Brenner would have lied about going on a house call there.

'Lastly, and not particularly helpfully, Gupta remembers that a couple of men came to pick Gloria up at the end of the practice Christmas party. He remembers one of the men being a lot older, and says he assumed that was Gloria's father. The name "Mucky Ricci" meant nothing to him.'

Midway across Chiswick Bridge, the sun sliced suddenly through a chink in the rain clouds, dazzling their eyes. The dirty Thames beneath the bridge and the shallow puddles flashed laser bright, but, seconds later, the clouds closed again and they were driving again through rain, in the dull grey January light, along a straight dual carriageway bordered by shrubs slick with rain and naked trees.

'What about that film?' said Robin, glancing sideways at Strike. 'The film that came out of Gregory Talbot's attic? You said you'd tell me in person.'

'Ah,' said Strike. 'Yeah.'

He hesitated, looking past the windscreen wipers at the long straight road ahead, glimmering beneath a diagonal curtain of rain.

'It showed a hooded woman being gang-raped and killed.'

Robin experienced a slight prickling over her neck and scalp.

'And people get off on that,' she muttered, in disgust.

He knew from her tone that she hadn't understood, that she thought he was describing a pornographic fiction.

'No,' he said, 'it wasn't porn. Someone filmed . . . the real thing.'

Robin looked around in shock, before turning quickly back to face the road. Her knuckles whitened on the steering wheel. Repulsive images were suddenly forcing their way into her mind. What had Strike seen, that made him look so closed up, so blank? Had the hooded woman's body resembled Margot's, the body Oonagh Kennedy had said was 'all legs'?

'You all right?' asked Strike.

'Fine,' she almost snapped. 'What – what did you see, how—?'

But Strike chose to answer a question she hadn't asked.

'The woman had a long scar over the ribcage. There was never any mention of Margot having a scarred ribcage in press reports or police notes. I don't think it was her.'

Robin said nothing but continued to look tense.

'There were four men, ah, involved,' Strike continued, 'all Caucasian, and all with their faces hidden. There was also a fifth man looking on. His arm came briefly into shot. It could've been Mucky Ricci. There was an out-of-focus big gold ring.'

He was trying to reduce the account to a series of dry facts. His leg muscles had tensed up quite as much as Robin's hands, and he was primed to grab the wheel. She'd had a panic attack once before while they were driving.

'What are the police saying?' Robin asked. 'Do they know where it came from?'

'Hutchins asked around. An ex-Vice Squad guy thinks it's part of a batch they seized in a raid made on a club in Soho in '75. The club was owned by Ricci. They took a load of hardcore pornography out of the basement.

'One of Talbot's best mates was also Vice Squad. The best guess is that Talbot nicked or copied it, after his mate showed it to him.'

'Why would he do that?' said Robin, a little desperately.

'I don't think we're going to get a better answer than "because he was mentally ill",' said Strike. 'But the starting point must have been his interest in Ricci. He'd found out Ricci was registered with the St John's practice and attended the Christmas party. In the notes, he called Ricci—'

'—Leo three,' said Robin. 'Yes, I know.'

Strike's leg muscles relaxed very slightly. This degree of focus and recall on Robin's part didn't suggest somebody about to have a panic attack.

'Did you learn my email off by heart?' he asked her.

It was Robin's turn to remember Christmas, and the brief solace it had been, to bury herself in work at her parents' kitchen table.

'I pay attention when I'm reading, that's all.'

'Well, I still don't understand why Talbot didn't chase up this Ricci lead, although judging by the horoscope notes, there was a sharp deterioration in his mental state over the six months he was in charge of the case. I'm guessing he stole that can of film not long before he got kicked off the force, hence no mention of it in the police notes.'

'And then hid it so nobody else could investigate the woman's death,' said Robin. Her sympathy for Bill Talbot had just been, if not extinguished, severely dented. 'Why the hell didn't he take the film back to the police when he was back in his right mind?'

'I'd guess because he wanted his job back and, failing that, wanted to make sure he got his pension. Setting aside basic integrity, I can't see that he had a great incentive to admit he'd tampered with evidence on another case. Everyone was already pissed off at him: victims' families, press, the force, all blaming him for having fucked up the investigation. And then Lawson, a bloke he doesn't like, takes over and tells him to stay the fuck out of it. He probably told himself the dead woman was only a prostitute or—'

'Jesus,' said Robin angrily.

'*I'm* not saying "only a prostitute",' Strike said quickly. 'I'm guessing at the mindset of a seventies policeman who'd already been publicly shamed for buggering up a high-profile case.'

Robin said nothing, but remained stony-faced for the rest of the journey, while Strike, the muscles of his one-and-a-half legs so tense they ached, tried not to make it too obvious that he was keeping a covert eye on the hands gripping the steering wheel.

35

. . . fayre Aurora, rysing hastily,
Doth by her blushing tell, that she did lye
All night in old Tithonus frosen bed,
Whereof she seemes ashamed inwardly.

Edmund Spenser
The Faerie Queene

'Ever been here before?' Strike asked Robin, as she parked in the Hampton Court car park. She'd been silent since he'd told her about the film, and he was trying to break the tension.

'No.'

They got out of the Land Rover and set off across the car park in the chilly rain.

'Where exactly are we meeting Cynthia?'

'The Privy Kitchen Café,' said Robin. 'I expect they'll give us a map at the ticket office.'

She knew that the film hidden in Gregory Talbot's attic wasn't Strike's fault. He hadn't put it there, hadn't hidden it for forty years, couldn't have known, when he inserted it in the projector, that he was about to watch a woman's last, terrified, excruciating moments. She wouldn't have wanted him to withhold the truth about what he'd seen. Nevertheless, his dry and unemotional description had grated on Robin.

Reasonably or not, she'd wanted some sign that he had been repulsed, or disgusted, or horrified.

But perhaps this was unrealistic. He'd been a military policeman long before Robin had known him, where he'd learned a detachment she sometimes envied. Beneath her determinedly calm exterior, Robin felt shaken and sick, and wanted to know that when Strike had watched the recording of the woman's dying moments, he'd recognised her as a person as real as he was.

Only a prostitute.

Their footsteps rang out on the wet tarmac as the great red-brick palace rose up before them, and Robin, who wanted to drive dreadful images out of her mind, tried to remember everything she knew about Henry VIII, that cruel and corpulent Tudor king who'd beheaded two of his six wives, but somehow found herself thinking about Matthew, instead.

When Robin had been brutally raped by a man in a gorilla mask who'd been lurking beneath the stairs of her hall of residence, Matthew had been kind, patient and understanding. Robin's lawyer might be mystified by the source of Matthew's vindictiveness over what should have been a straightforward divorce, but Robin had come to believe that the end of the marriage had been a profound shock to Matthew, because he thought he was owed infinite credit for having helped her through the worst period of her life. Matthew, Robin felt sure, thought she was forever in his debt.

Tears prickled in Robin's eyes. Angling her umbrella so that Strike couldn't see her face, she blinked hard until her eyes were clear again.

They walked across a cobbled courtyard in silence until Robin came to a sudden halt. Strike, who never enjoyed navigating uneven surfaces with his prosthesis, wasn't sorry to pause, but he was slightly worried that he was about to be on the receiving end of an outburst.

'Look at that,' Robin said, pointing down at a shining cobblestone.

Strike looked closer and saw, to his surprise, a small cross of St John engraved upon a small square brick.

'Coincidence,' he said.

They walked on, Robin looking around, forcing herself to take in her surroundings. They passed into a second courtyard, where a school party in hooded raincoats was being addressed by a guide in a medieval jester's costume.

'Oh wow,' said Robin quietly, looking over her shoulder and then walking backwards for a few paces, the better to see the object set high in the wall above the archway. 'Look at *that*!'

Strike did as he was bidden and saw an enormous, ornate, sixteenth-century astronomical clock of blue and gold. The signs of the zodiac were marked on the perimeter, both with the glyphs with which Strike had become unwillingly familiar, and with pictures representing each sign. Robin smiled at Strike's expression of mingled surprise and annoyance.

'What?' he said, catching her look of amusement.

'You,' she said, turning to walk on. 'Furious at the zodiac.'

'If you'd spent three weeks wading through all Talbot's bollocks, you wouldn't be keen on the zodiac, either,' said Strike.

He stood back to allow Robin to enter the palace first. Following the map Strike had been given, they headed along a flagged, covered walkway towards the Privy Kitchen Café.

'Well, I think there's a kind of poetry to astrology,' said Robin, who was consciously trying to keep her mind off Talbot's old can of film, and her ex-husband. 'I'm not saying it works, but there's a kind of – of symmetry to it, an order . . . '

Through a door to the right, a small Tudor garden came into view. Brightly coloured heraldic beasts stood sentinel over square beds full of sixteenth-century herbs. The sudden appearance of the spotted leopard, the white hart and the red dragon seemed to Robin to cheer her on, asserting the potency and allure of symbol and myth.

'It makes a kind of – not literal sense,' Robin said, as the whimsically strange creatures passed out of sight, 'but it's survived for a reason.'

'Yeah,' said Strike. 'People will believe any old shit.'

Slightly to his relief, Robin smiled. They entered the white-walled café, which had small leaded windows and dark oak furniture.

'Find us a discreet table, I'll get the drinks in. What d'you want, coffee?'

Choosing a deserted side room, Robin sat down at a table beneath one of the leaded windows and glanced through the potted history of the palace they'd received with their tickets. She learned that the Knights of St John had once owned the land on which the palace stood, which explained the cross on the cobblestone, and that Cardinal Wolsey had given Henry VIII the palace in a futile bid to stave off his own decline in influence. However, when she read that the ghost of nineteen-year-old Catherine Howard was supposed to run, screaming, along the Haunted Gallery, eternally begging her fifty-year-old-husband, the King, not to have her beheaded, Robin closed the pamphlet without reading the rest. Strike arrived with the coffees to find her with her arms folded, staring into space.

'Everything all right?'

'Yes,' she said. 'Just thinking about star signs.'

'Still?' said Strike, with a slight eye roll.

'Jung says it was man's first attempt at psychology, did you know that?'

'I didn't,' said Strike, sitting down opposite her. Robin, as he knew, had been studying psychology at university before she dropped out. 'But there's no excuse to keep using it now we've got actual psychology, is there?'

'Folklore and superstition haven't gone away. They'll never go away. People need them,' she said, taking a sip of coffee. 'I think a purely scientific world would be a cold place. Jung also talked about the collective unconscious, you know. The archetypes lurking in all of us.'

But Strike, whose mother had ensured that he'd spent a large portion of his childhood in a fug of incense, dirt and mysticism, said shortly,

'Yeah, well. I'm Team Rational.'

'People like feeling connected to something bigger,' said Robin, looking up at the rainy sky outside. 'I think it makes you feel less lonely. Astrology connects you to the universe, doesn't it? And to ancient myths and ideas—'

'—and incidentally feeds your ego,' said Strike. 'Makes you feel less insignificant. "Look how special the universe is telling me I am." I don't buy the idea that I've got anything more in common with other people born on November the twenty-third than I think being born in Cornwall makes me a person better than someone born in Manchester.'

'I never said—'

'You might not, but my oldest mate does,' said Strike. 'Dave Polworth.'

'The one who gets ratty when Cornish flags aren't on strawberries?'

'That's him. Committed Cornish nationalist. He gets defensive about it if you challenge him – "I'm not saying we're better than anyone else" – but he thinks you shouldn't be able to buy property down there unless you can prove Cornish ethnicity. Don't remind him he was born in Birmingham if you value your teeth.'

Robin smiled.

'Same kind of thing, though, isn't it?' said Strike. '"I'm special and different because I was born on this bit of rock."

"I'm special and different because I was born on June the twelfth—"'

'Where you're born *does* influence who you are, though,' said Robin. 'Cultural norms and language have an effect. And there have been studies showing people born at different times of the year are more prone to certain health conditions.'

'So Roy Phipps bleeds a lot because he was born—? Hello there!' said Strike, breaking off suddenly, his eyes on the door.

Robin turned and saw, to her momentary astonishment, a slender woman wearing a long green Tudor gown and headdress.

'I'm *so sorry*!' said the woman, gesturing at her costume and laughing nervously as she advanced on their table. 'I thought I'd have time to change! I've been doing a school group – we finished late—'

Strike stood up and held out a hand to shake hers.

'Cormoran Strike,' he said. Eyes on her reproduction pearl necklace with its suspended initial 'B', he said, 'Anne Boleyn, I presume?'

Cynthia's laughter contained a couple of inadvertent snorts, which increased her odd resemblance, middle-aged though she was, to a gawky schoolgirl. Her movements were unsuited to the sweeping velvet gown, being rather exaggerated and ungainly.

'Hahaha, yes, that's me! Only my second time as Anne. You think you've thought of *all* the questions the kids might ask you, then one of them says "How did it feel to get your head cut off?", hahahaha!'

Cynthia wasn't at all what Robin had expected. She now realised that her imagination had sketched in a young blonde, the stereotypical idea of a Scandinavian au pair . . . or was that because Sarah Shadlock had almost white hair?

'Coffee?' Strike asked Cynthia.

'Oh – coffee, yes please, wonderful, thank you,' said Cynthia, over-enthusiastically. When Strike had left, Cynthia made a small pantomime of dithering over which seat to take until Robin, smiling, pulled out the seat beside her and offered her own hand, too.

'Oh, yes, hello!' said Cynthia, sitting down and shaking hands. She had a thin, sallow face, currently wearing an anxious smile. The irises of her large eyes were heavily mottled, an indeterminate colour between blue, green and grey, and her teeth were rather crooked.

'So you lead the tour in character?' asked Robin.

'Yes, exactly, as poor Anne, hahaha,' said Cynthia, with another nervous, snorting laugh. '"I couldn't give the King a son! They said I was a witch!" Those are the sort of things children like to hear; I have to work quite hard to get the politics in, hahaha. Poor Anne.' Her thin hands fidgeted.

'Oh, I'm still – I can take this off, at least, hahaha!'

Cynthia set to work unpinning her headdress. Even though she could tell that Cynthia was very nervous, and that her constant laughter was more of a tic than genuine amusement, Robin was again reminded of Sarah Shadlock, who tended to laugh a lot, and loudly, especially in the vicinity of Matthew. Wittingly or not, Cynthia's laughter imposed a sort of obligation: smile back or seem hostile. Robin remembered a documentary on monkeys she had watched one night when she was too tired to get up and go to bed: chimps, too, laughed back at each other to signal social cohesion.

When Strike returned to the table with Cynthia's coffee, he found her newly bare-headed. Her dark hair was fifty per cent grey, and smoothed back into a short, thin ponytail.

'It's very good of you to meet us, Mrs Phipps,' he said, sitting back down.

'Oh, no, not at all, not at all,' said Cynthia, waving her

thin hands and laughing some more. 'Anything I can do to help Anna with – but Roy hasn't been well, so I don't want to worry him just now.'

'I'm sorry to hear—'

'Yes, thank you, no, it's prostate cancer,' said Cynthia, no longer laughing. 'Radiation therapy. Not feeling too chipper. Anna and Kim came over this morning to sit with him, or I wouldn't have been able – I don't like leaving him at the moment, but the girls are there, so I thought I'd be fine to . . .'

The end of the sentence was lost as she took a sip of coffee. Her hand trembled slightly as she replaced the cup onto the saucer.

'Your stepdaughter's probably told—' Strike began, but Cynthia immediately interrupted him.

'*Daughter.* I don't ever call Anna my stepdaughter. Sorry, but I feel *just* the same about her as I do about Jeremy and Ellie. No difference at all.'

Robin wondered whether that was true. She was uncomfortably aware that part of her was standing aside, watching Cynthia with judgemental eyes. *She isn't Sarah*, Robin reminded herself.

'Well, I'm sure Anna's told you why she hired us, and so on.'

'Oh, yes,' said Cynthia. 'No, I must admit, I've been expecting something like this for a while. I hope it isn't going to make things worse for her.'

'Er – well, we hope that, too, obviously,' said Strike, and Cynthia laughed and said, 'Oh, no, of course, yes.'

Strike took out his notebook, in which a few photocopied sheets were folded, and a pen.

'Could we begin with the statement you gave the police?'

'You've got it?' said Cynthia, looking startled. 'The original?'

'A photocopy,' he said, unfolding it.

'How . . . funny. Seeing it again, after all this time. I was eighteen. Eighteen! It seems a century ago, hahaha!'

The signature at the bottom of the uppermost page, Robin saw, was rounded and rather childish. Strike handed the photocopied pages to Cynthia, who took them looking almost frightened.

'I'm afraid I'm awfully dyslexic,' she said. 'I was forty-two before I was diagnosed. My parents thought I was bone idle, hahaha . . . um, so . . .'

'Would you rather I read it to you?' Strike suggested. Cynthia handed it back to him at once.

'Oh, thank you – this is how I learn all my guiding notes, by listening to audio discs, hahaha . . .'

Strike flattened out the photocopied papers on the table.

'Please interrupt if you want to add or change anything,' he told Cynthia, who nodded and said that she would.

'"Name, Cynthia Jane Phipps . . . date of birth, July the twentieth 1957 . . . address, "The Annexe, Broom House, Church Road" . . . that would be Margot's—?'

'I had self-contained rooms over the double garage,' said Cynthia. Robin thought she laid slight emphasis on 'self-contained'.

'"I am employed as nanny to Dr Phipps and Dr Bamborough's infant daughter, and I live in their house—"'

'Self-contained studio,' said Cynthia. 'It had its own entrance.'

'"My hours . . ." Don't think we need any of that,' muttered Strike. 'Here we go. "On the morning of the eleventh of October I began work at 7 a.m. I saw Dr Bamborough before she left for work. She seemed entirely as usual. She reminded me that she would be late home because she was meeting her friend Miss Oonagh Kennedy for drinks near her place of work. As Dr Phipps was bedbound due to his recent accident—"'

'Anna told you about Roy's von Willebrand Disease?' said Cynthia anxiously.

'Er – I don't think *she* told us, but it's mentioned in the police report.'

'Oh, didn't she say?' said Cynthia, who seemed unhappy to hear it. 'Well, he's a Type Three. That's serious, as bad as haemophilia. His knee swelled up and he was in a lot of pain, could hardly *move*,' said Cynthia.

'Yes,' said Strike, 'it's all in the police—'

'No, because he'd had an accident on the seventh,' said Cynthia, who seemed determined to say this. 'It was a wet day, pouring with rain, you can check that. He was walking around a corner of the hospital, heading for the car park, and an out-patient rode right into him on a pushbike. Roy got tangled up in the front wheel, slipped, hit his knee and had a major bleed. These days he has prophylactic injections so it doesn't happen the way it used to, but back then, if he injured himself, it could lay him up for weeks.'

'Right,' said Strike, and judging it to be the most tactful thing to do, he made careful note of all these details, which he'd already read in Roy's own statements and police interviews.

'No, Anna knows her dad was ill that day. She's always known,' Cynthia added.

Strike continued reading the statement aloud. It was a retelling of facts Strike and Robin already knew. Cynthia had been in charge of baby Anna at home. Roy's mother had come over during the day. Wilma Bayliss had cleaned for three hours and left. Cynthia had taken occasional cups of tea to the invalid and his mother. At 6 p.m., Evelyn Phipps had gone home to her bungalow to play bridge with friends, leaving a tray of food for her son.

'"At 8 p.m. in the evening I was watching television in the

sitting room downstairs when I heard the phone ring in the hall. I would usually only ever answer the phone if both Dr Phipps and Dr Bamborough were out. As Dr Phipps was in, and could answer the phone from the extension beside his bed, I didn't answer.

'"About five minutes later, I heard the gong that Mrs Evelyn Phipps had placed beside Dr Phipps's bed, in case of emergency. I went upstairs. Dr Phipps was still in bed. He told me that it had been Miss Kennedy on the phone. Dr Bamborough hadn't turned up at the pub. Dr Phipps said he thought she must have been delayed at work or forgotten. He asked me to tell Dr Bamborough to go up to their bedroom as soon as she came in.

'"I went back downstairs. About an hour later, I heard the gong again and went upstairs and found Dr Phipps now quite worried about his wife. He asked me whether she'd come in yet. I said that she hadn't. He asked me to stay in the room while he phoned Miss Kennedy at home. Miss Kennedy still hadn't seen or heard from Dr Bamborough. Dr Phipps hung up and asked me what Dr Bamborough had been carrying when she left the house that morning. I told him just a handbag and her doctor's bag. He asked me whether Dr Bamborough had said anything about visiting her parents. I said she hadn't. He asked me to stay while he called Dr Bamborough's mother.

'"Mrs Bamborough hadn't heard from her daughter or seen her. Dr Phipps was now quite worried and asked me to go downstairs and look in the drawer in the base of the clock on the mantelpiece in the sitting room and see whether there was anything in there. I went and looked. There was nothing there. I went back upstairs and told Dr Phipps that the clock drawer was empty. Dr Phipps explained that this was a place he and his wife sometimes left each other private notes. I hadn't known about this previously.

'"He asked me to stay with him while he called his mother, because he might have something else for me to do. He spoke to his mother and asked her advice. It was a brief conversation. When he hung up, Dr Phipps asked me whether I thought he ought to call the police. I said I thought he should. He said he was going to. He told me to go downstairs and let the police in when they arrived and show them up to his bedroom. The police arrived about half an hour later and I showed them up to Dr Phipps's bedroom.

'"I didn't find Dr Bamborough to be unusual in her manner when she left the house that morning. Relations between Dr Phipps and Dr Bamborough seemed completely happy. I'm very surprised at her disappearance, which is out of character. She is very attached to her daughter and I cannot imagine her ever leaving the baby, or going away without telling her husband or me where she was going.

'"Signed and dated Cynthia Phipps, 12 October 1974."'

'Yes, no, that's . . . I haven't got anything to add to that,' said Cynthia. 'Odd to hear it back!' she said, with another little snorting laugh, but Robin thought her eyes were frightened.

'This is obviously, ah, sensitive, but if we could go back to your statement that relations between Roy and Margot—'

'Yes, sorry, no, I'm not going to talk about their marriage,' said Cynthia. Her sallow cheeks became stained with a purplish blush. 'Everyone rows, everyone has ups and downs, but it's not up to me to talk about their marriage.'

'We understand that your husband couldn't have—' began Robin.

'*Margot's* husband,' said Cynthia. 'No, you see, they're two completely different people. Inside my head.'

Convenient, said a voice inside Robin's.

'We're simply exploring the possibility that she went away,' said Strike, 'maybe to think or—'

'No, Margot wouldn't have just walked out without saying anything. That wouldn't have been like her.'

'Anna told us her grandmother—' said Robin.

'Evelyn had early onset Alzheimer's and you couldn't take what she said seriously,' said Cynthia, her tone higher and more brittle. 'I've always told Anna that, I've *always* told her that Margot would never have left her. I've *always* told her that,' she repeated.

Except, continued the voice inside Robin's head, *when you were pretending to be her real mother, and hiding Margot's existence from her.*

'Moving on,' said Strike, 'you received a phone call on Anna's second birthday, from a woman purporting to be Margot?'

'Um, yes, no, that's right,' said Cynthia. She took another shaky sip of coffee. 'I was icing the birthday cake in the kitchen when the phone rang, so not in any danger of forgetting what day it was, hahaha. When I picked up, the woman said, "Is that you, Cynthia?" I said "Yes", and she said "It's Margot here. Wish little Annie a happy birthday from her mummy. And make sure you look after her." And the line went dead.

'I just stood there,' she mimed holding an invisible implement in her hand, and tried to laugh again, but no sound came out, 'holding the spatula. I didn't know what to do. Anna was playing in the sitting room. I was . . . I decided I'd better ring Roy at work. He told me to call the police, so I did.'

'Did you think it was Margot?' asked Strike.

'No. It wasn't – well, it *sounded* like her, but I don't think it *was* her.'

'You think somebody was imitating it?'

'Putting it on, yes. The accent. Cockney, but . . . no, I didn't get that feeling you get when you just *know* who it is . . . '

'You're sure it was a woman?' said Strike. 'It couldn't have been a man imitating a woman?'

'I don't think so,' said Cynthia.

'Did Margot ever call Anna "little Annie"?' asked Robin.

'She called her all kinds of pet names,' said Cynthia, looking glum. 'Annie Fandango, Annabella, Angel Face ... somebody could have guessed, or maybe they'd just got the name wrong ... But the timing was ... they'd just found bits of Creed's last victim. The one he threw off Beachy Head—'

'Andrea Hooton,' said Robin. Cynthia looked slightly startled that she had the name on the tip of her tongue.

'Yes, the hairdresser.'

'No,' said Robin. 'That was Susan Meyer. Andrea was the PhD student.'

'Oh, yes,' said Cynthia. 'Of course ... I'm so bad with names ... Well, Roy had just been through the whole identification business with, um, you know, the bits of the body that washed up, so we'd had our hopes – not our hopes!' said Cynthia, looking terrified at the word that had escaped her, 'I don't mean that! No, we were obviously relieved it wasn't Margot, but you think, you know, maybe you're going to get an answer ... '

Strike thought of his own guilty wish that Joan's slow and protracted dying would be over soon. A corpse, however unwelcome, meant anguish could find both expression and sublimation among flowers, speeches and ritual, consolation drawn from God, alcohol and fellow mourners; an apotheosis reached, a first step taken towards grasping the awful fact that life was extinct, and life must go on.

'We'd already been through it once when they found the other body, the one in Alexandra Lake,' said Cynthia.

'Susan Meyer,' muttered Robin.

'Roy was shown pictures, both times ... And then this

phone call, coming right after he'd had to . . . for the second time . . . it was . . .'

Cynthia was suddenly crying, not like Oonagh Kennedy, with her head up and tears sparkling on her cheeks, but hunched over the table, hiding her face, her shaking hands supporting her forehead.

'I'm so sorry,' she sobbed. 'I knew this would be awful . . . we never talk about her any – any more . . . I'm sorry . . .'

She sobbed for a few more seconds, then forced herself to look up again, her large eyes now pink and wet.

'Roy wanted to believe it had been Margot on the phone. He kept saying "Are you sure, are you *sure*, it didn't sound like her?" He was on tenterhooks while the police traced the call . . .

'You're being very polite,' she said, and her laugh this time was slightly hysterical, 'but I know what you want to know, and what Anna wants to know, too, even though I've *told* her and *told* her . . . There was *nothing* going on between me and Roy before Margot disappeared, and not for *four years* afterwards . . . Did she tell you that Roy and I are related?'

She said it as though forcing herself to say it, although a third cousin was not, after all, a very close relationship. But Robin, thinking of Roy's bleeding disorder, wondered whether the Phippses, like the Romanovs, mightn't be well advised not to marry their cousins.

'Yes, she did,' said Strike.

'I was sick of the sound of his name before I went to work for them, actually. It was all, "Just look at Cousin Roy, with all his health problems, getting into St Barts and studying medicine. If you'd only *work harder*, Cynthia . . ." I used to hate the very idea of him, hahaha!'

Robin recalled the picture of young Roy in the press: the sensitive face, the floppy hair, the poet's eyes. Many women found injury and illness romantic in a handsome man. Hadn't Matthew, in his worst effusions of jealousy against Strike, invoked his amputated leg, the warrior's wound against which he, whole-bodied and fit, felt unable to compete?

'You might not believe this, but as far as I was concerned at seventeen, the best thing about Roy was Margot! No, I thought she was *marvellous*, so – so fashionable and, you know, lots of opinions and things . . .

'She asked me over for dinner, after she heard I ploughed all my exams. Well, I hero-worshipped her, so I was thrilled. I poured my heart out, told her I couldn't face resits, I just wanted to get out in the real world and earn my own money. And she said, "Look, you're wonderful with children, how about coming and looking after my baby when I go back to work? I'll get Roy to do up the rooms over the garage for you."

'My parents were *livid*,' said Cynthia, with another brave but unsuccessful stab at a laugh. 'They were furious with her, *and* Roy, although actually, he didn't want me there in the first place, because he wanted Margot to stay at home and look after Anna herself. Mummy and Daddy said she was just after cheap labour. These days I do see it more from their point of view. I'm not sure *I'd* have been delighted if a woman had persuaded one of my girls to leave school and move in with them, and look after their baby. But no, I loved Margot. I was excited.'

Cynthia fell silent for a moment, a faraway look in her doleful eyes, and Robin wondered whether she was thinking about the huge and unalterable consequences of accepting the job as nanny, which instead of being a springboard to her own independent life had placed her in a house she would never leave, led to her raising Margot's child as her own, sleeping with Margot's husband, forever stuck in the shadow of the doctor she claimed to have loved. What was it like to live with an absence that huge?

'My parents wanted me to go away after Margot disappeared. They didn't like me being alone at the house with Roy, because people were starting to gossip. There were even hints in the press, but I swear to you on the lives of my children,' said Cynthia, with a kind of dull finality, 'there was *nothing* between Roy and me, ever, before Margot disappeared, and not for a long time afterwards, either. I stayed for Anna, because I couldn't bear to leave her . . . she'd become my daughter!'

She hadn't, said the implacable voice in Robin's head. *And you should have told her so.*

'Roy didn't date anyone for a long time after Margot disappeared. Then there was a colleague at work for a while,' Cynthia's thin face flushed again, 'but it only lasted a few months. Anna didn't like her.

'I had a kind of on-off boyfriend, but he packed me in. He said it was like dating a married woman with a child, because I put Anna and Roy first, always.

'And then I suppose . . .' said Cynthia shakily, one hand balled in a fist, the other clutching it, ' . . . over time . . . I realised I'd fallen in love with Roy. I never dreamed he'd want to be with me, though. Margot was so clever, such a – such a big personality, and he was so much older than me, so much more intelligent and sophisticated . . .

'One evening, after I'd put Anna to bed, I was about to go back to my rooms and he asked me what had happened with Will, my boyfriend, and I said it was over, and he asked what had happened, and we got talking, and he said . . . he said, "You're a very special person and you deserve far better than him." And then . . . then, we had a drink . . .

'That was *four years* after she'd disappeared,' Cynthia repeated. 'I was eighteen when she vanished and I was twenty-two when Roy and I . . . admitted we had feelings for each other. We kept it secret, obviously. It was another three years before Roy could get a death certificate for Margot.'

'That must have been very hard,' said Strike.

Cynthia looked at him for a moment, unsmiling. She seemed to have aged since arriving at the table.

'I've had nightmares about Margot coming back and throwing me out of the house for nearly forty years,' she said, and she tried to laugh. 'I've never told Roy. I don't want to know whether he dreams about her, too. We don't talk about her. It's the only way to cope. We'd said everything we had to say to the police, to each other, to the rest of the family. We'd raked it all over, hours and hours of talking. "It's time to close the door", that's how Roy put it. He said, "We've left the door open long enough. She's not coming back."

'There were a couple of spiteful things said in the press, you know, when we got married. "Husband of vanished doctor marries young nanny." It's always going to sound sordid, isn't it? Roy said not to mind them. My parents were appalled by the whole thing. It was only when I had Jeremy that they came around.

'We never *meant* to mislead Anna. We were waiting . . . I don't know . . . trying to find the right moment, to explain . . . but how are you supposed to do it? She used to call me "Mummy",' whispered Cynthia, 'she was h- happy, she was a completely happy little girl, but then those children at school told her about Margot and it ruined *every*—'

From somewhere close by came a loud synthesiser version of 'Greensleeves'. All three of them looked startled until Cynthia, laughing her snorting laugh, said, 'It's my phone!' She pulled the mobile from a deep pocket in her dress and answered it.

'Roy?' she said.

Robin could hear Roy talking angrily from where she sat. Cynthia looked suddenly alarmed. She tried to get up, but stepped on the hem of her dress and tripped forwards. Trying to disentangle herself, she said,

'No, I'm – oh, she hasn't. Oh, God – Roy, I didn't want to tell you because – no – yes, I'm still with them!'

Finally managing to free herself from both dress and table, Cynthia staggered away and out of the room. The headdress she'd been wearing slid limply off her seat. Robin stooped to pick it up, put it back on the seat of Cynthia's chair and looked up to see Strike watching her.

'What?' asked Robin.

He was about to answer when Cynthia reappeared. She looked stricken.

'Roy knows – Anna's told him. He wants you to come back to Broom House.'

36

He oft finds med'cine who his grief imparts;
But double griefs afflict concealing hearts,
As raging flames who striveth to suppress.

Edmund Spenser
The Faerie Queene

Cynthia hurried away to change out of her Anne Boleyn costume and reappeared ten minutes later in a pair of poorly fitting jeans, a grey sweater and trainers. She appeared extremely anxious as they walked together back through the palace, setting a fast pace that Strike found challenging on cobblestones still slippery with the rain which had temporarily ceased, but the heavy grey clouds, gilt-edged though they were, promised an imminent return. Glancing upwards as they passed back through the gatehouse of the inner court, Robin's eye was caught by the gleaming gold accents on the astronomical clock, and noticed that the sun was in Margot's sign of Aquarius.

'I'll see you there,' said Cynthia breathlessly, as they approached the car park, and without waiting for an answer she half-ran towards a blue Mazda3 in the distance.

'This is going to be interesting,' said Robin.

'Certainly is,' said Strike.

'Grab the map,' said Robin, once both were back in the car.

The old Land Rover didn't have a functioning radio, let alone satnav. 'You'll have to navigate.'

'What d'you think of her?' asked Strike, while he looked up Church Road in Ham.

'She seems all right.'

Robin became aware that Strike was looking at her, as he had in the café, a slightly quizzical expression on his face.

'What?' she said again.

'I had the impression you weren't keen.'

'No,' said Robin, with a trace of defensiveness, 'she's fine.'

She reversed out of the parking space, remembering Cynthia's snorting laughter and her habit of jumbling affirmatives and negatives together.

'Well—'

'Thought so,' said Strike, smugly.

'Given what might've happened to Margot, I wouldn't have kicked off the conversation with cheery decapitation jokes.'

'She's lived with it for forty years,' said Strike. 'People who live with something that massive stop being able to see it. It's the backdrop of their lives. It's only glaringly obvious to everyone else.'

It started to rain again as they left the car park: a fine veil laying itself swiftly over the windscreen.

'OK, I'm prejudiced,' Robin admitted, switching on the wipers. 'Feeling a bit sensitive about second wives right now.'

She drove on for a few moments before becoming aware that Strike was looking at her again.

'What?' she asked, for a third time.

'Why're you sensitive about second wives?'

'Because – oh, I didn't tell you, did I? I told Morris.' She'd tried not to think, since, about her drunken Boxing Day spent texting, of the small amount of comfort she had derived from it, or the immense load of discomfort. 'Matthew and Sarah Shadlock are together officially now. She left her fiancé for him.'

'Shit,' said Strike, still watching her profile. 'No, you didn't tell me.'

But he mentally docketed the fact that she'd told Morris, which didn't fit with the idea that he'd formed of Robin and Morris's relationship. From what Barclay had told him about Morris's challenges to Robin's authority, and from Robin's generally lukewarm comments on his new hire, he'd assumed that Morris's undoubted sexual interest in Robin had fizzled out for lack of a return. And yet she'd told Morris this painful bit of personal information, and not told him.

As they drove in silence towards Church Road, he wondered what had been going on in London while he had been in Cornwall. Morris was a good-looking man and he, like Robin, was divorcing. Strike wondered why he hadn't previously considered the implications of this obvious piece of symmetry. Comparing notes on lawyers, on difficult exes, on the mechanics of splitting two lives: they'd have plenty to talk about, plenty of opportunities for mutual sympathy.

'Straight up here,' he said, and they drove in silence across the Royal Paddocks, between high, straight red walls.

'Nice street,' commented Robin, twenty minutes after they'd left Hampton Court Palace, as she turned the Land Rover into a road that might have been deep in countryside. To their left was dense woodland, to the right, several large, detached houses that stood back from the road behind high hedges.

'It's that one,' said Strike, pointing at a particularly sprawling house with many pointed, half-timbered gables. The double gates stood open, as did the front door. They turned into the drive and parked behind the blue Mazda3.

As soon as Robin switched off the engine, they heard

shouting coming from inside the house: a male voice, intemperate and high pitched. Anna Phipps's wife, Kim, tall, blonde and wearing jeans and a shirt as before, came striding out of the house towards them, her expression tense.

'Big scenes,' she said, as Strike and Robin got out of the car into the mist of rain.

'Would you like us to wait—?' Robin began.

'No,' Kim said, 'he's determined to see you. Come in.'

They walked across the gravel and entered Broom House. Somewhere inside, male and female voices continued to shout.

Every house has its own deep ingrained smell, and this one was redolent of sandalwood and a not entirely unpleasant fustiness. Kim led them through a long, large-windowed hall that seemed frozen in the mid-twentieth century. There were brass light fittings, watercolours and an old rug on polished floorboards. With a sudden frisson, Robin thought that Margot Bamborough had once walked this very floor, her metallic rose perfume mingling with the scents of polish and old carpet.

As they approached the door of the drawing room, the argument taking place inside became suddenly comprehensible.

'—and if I'm to be talked about,' a man was shouting, 'I should have right of reply – my family deciding to investigate me behind my back, charming, *charming*, it really is—'

'Nobody's investigating *you*, for God's sake!' they heard Anna say. 'Bill Talbot was incompetent—'

'Oh, was he really? Were you there? Did you know him?'

'I didn't *have* to be there, Dad—'

Kim opened the door. Strike and Robin followed Kim inside.

It was like coming upon a tableau. The three people standing inside froze at their entrance. Cynthia's thin fingers were pressed to her mouth. Anna stood facing her father across a small antique table.

The romantic-looking poet of 1974 was no more. Roy Phipps's remaining hair was short, grey and clung only around his ears and the back of his head. In his knitted sweater vest, with his high, domed, shining pate and his wild eyes, slightly sunken in a blotchy face, he'd now be better suited to the role of mad scientist.

So furious did Roy Phipps look, that Robin quite expected him to start shouting at the newcomers, too. However, the haematologist's demeanour changed when his eyes met Strike's. Whether this was a tribute to the detective's bulk, or to the aura of gravity and calm he managed to project in highly charged situations, Robin couldn't tell, but she thought she saw Roy decide against yelling. After a brief hesitation, the doctor accepted Strike's proffered hand, and as the two men shook, Robin wondered how aware men were of the power dynamics that played out between them, while women stood watching.

'Dr Phipps,' said Strike.

Roy appeared to have found the gear change between intemperate rage and polite greeting a difficult one, and his immediate response was slightly incoherent.

'So you're – you're the detective, are you?' he said. Bluish-red blotches lingered in his pale cheeks.

'Cormoran Strike – and this is my partner, Robin Ellacott.'

Robin stepped forwards.

'How d'you do?' Roy said stiffly, shaking her hand, too. His was hot and dry.

'Shall I make tea?' said Cynthia, in a half-whisper.

'Yes – no, why not,' said Roy, his ill-temper clearly jockeying with the nervousness that seemed to increase while Strike stood, large and unmoving, watching him. 'Sit, sit,' he said, pointing Strike to a sofa, at right angles to another.

Cynthia hurried out of the room to make tea, and Strike and Robin sat where they'd been instructed.

'Going to help Cyn,' muttered Anna and she hurried out of the room, and Kim, after a moment's hesitation, followed her, leaving Strike and Robin alone with Roy. The doctor settled himself into a high-backed velvet armchair and glared around him. He didn't look well. The flush of temper receded, leaving him looking wan. His socks had bunched up around his skinny ankles.

There ensued one of the most uncomfortable silences Robin had ever endured. Mainly to avoid looking at Roy, she allowed her eyes to roam around the large room, which was as old fashioned as the hall. A grand piano stood in the corner. More large windows looked out onto an enormous garden, where a long rectangular fish pond lay just beyond a paved area, at the far end of which lay a covered, temple-like stone structure where people could either sit and watch the koi carp, now barely visible beneath the rain-flecked surface of the water, or look out over the sweeping lawn, with its mature trees and well-tended flower-beds.

An abundance of leather-bound books and bronzes of antique subjects filled bookcases and cabinets. A tambour frame stood between the sofas, on which a very beautiful piece of embroidery was being worked in silks. The design was Japanese influenced, of two koi swimming in opposite directions. Robin was debating whether to pass polite comment on it, and to ask whether Cynthia was responsible, when Strike spoke.

'Who was the classicist?'

'What?' said Roy. 'Oh. My father.'

His crazy-looking eyes roamed over the various small bronzes and marbles dotted around the room. 'Took a first in Classics at Cambridge.'

'Ah,' said Strike, and the glacial silence resumed.

A squall of wind threw more rain at the window. Robin was

relieved to hear the tinkling of teaspoons and the footsteps of the three returning women.

Cynthia, who re-entered the room first, set a tea tray down on the antique table standing between the sofas. It rocked a little with the weight. Anna added a large cake on a stand.

Anna and Kim sat down side by side on the free sofa, and when Cynthia had drawn up spindly side tables to hold everyone's tea, and cut slices of cake for those who wanted some, she sat herself down beside her stepdaughter-in-law, looking scared.

'Well,' said Roy at last, addressing Strike. 'I'd be interested to hear what you think your chances are of finding out what the Metropolitan Police has been unable to discover in four decades.'

Robin was sure Roy had been planning this aggressive opening during the long and painful silence.

'Fairly small,' said Strike matter-of-factly, once he'd swallowed a large piece of the cake Cynthia had given him, 'though we've got a new alleged sighting of your first wife I wanted to discuss with you.'

Roy looked taken aback.

'*Alleged* sighting,' Strike emphasised, setting down his plate and reaching inside his jacket for his notebook. 'But obviously ... Excellent cake, Mrs Phipps,' he told Cynthia.

'Oh, thank you,' she said in a small voice. 'Coffee and walnut was Anna's favourite when she was little – wasn't it, love?' she said, but Anna's only response was a tense smile.

'We heard about it from one of your wife's ex-colleagues, Janice Beattie.'

Roy shook his head and shrugged impatiently, to convey non-recognition of the names.

'She was the practice nurse at the St John's surgery,' said Strike.

'Oh,' said Roy. 'Yes. I think she came here once, for a barbecue. She seemed quite a decent woman . . . Disaster, that afternoon. Bloody disaster. Those children were atrocious – d'you remember?' he shot at Cynthia.

'Yes,' said Cynthia quickly, 'no, there was one boy who was really—'

'Spiked the punch,' barked Roy. 'Vodka. Someone was sick.'

'Gloria,' said Cynthia.

'I don't remember all their names,' said Roy, with an impatient wave of the hand. 'Sick all over the downstairs bathroom. Disgusting.'

'This boy would've been Carl Oakden?' asked Strike.

'That's him,' said Roy. 'We found the vodka bottle empty, later, hidden in a shed. He'd sneaked into the house and taken it out of the drinks cabinet.'

'Yes,' said Cynthia, 'and then he smashed—'

'Crystal bowl of my mother's and half a dozen glasses. Hit a cricket ball right across the barbecue area. The nurse cleaned it all up for me, because – decent of her. She knew I couldn't – broken glass,' said Roy, with an impatient gesture.

'On the bright side,' said Cynthia, with the ghost of a laugh, 'he'd smashed the punch, so nobody else got sick.'

'That bowl was art deco,' said Roy, unsmiling. 'Bloody disaster, the whole thing. I said to Margot,' and he paused for a second after saying the name, and Robin wondered when he'd last spoken it, '"I don't know what you think this is going to achieve." Because *he* didn't come, the one she was trying to conciliate – the doctor she didn't get on with, what was his—?'

'Joseph Brenner,' said Robin.

'Brenner, exactly. *He'd* refused the invitation, so what was the point? But no, we still had to give up our Saturday to entertain this motley collection of people, and our reward was to have our drink stolen and our possessions smashed.'

Roy's fists lay on the arms of his chair. He uncoiled the long fingers for a moment in a movement like a hermit crab unflexing its legs, then curled them tightly in upon themselves again.

'That same boy, Oakden, wrote a book about Margot later,' he said. 'Used a photograph from that damn barbecue to add credibility to the notion that he and his mother knew all about our private lives. So, yes,' said Roy coldly, '*not* one of Margot's better ideas.'

'Well, she was trying to make the practice work better together, wasn't she?' said Anna. 'You've never really needed to manage different personalities at work—'

'Oh, you know all about my work, too, do you, Anna?'

'Well, it wasn't the same as being a GP, was it?' said Anna. 'You were lecturing, doing research, you didn't have to manage cleaners and receptionists and a whole bunch of non-medics.'

'They *were* quite badly behaved, Anna,' said Cynthia, hurrying loyally to support Roy. 'No, they really were. I never told – I didn't want to cause trouble – but one of the women sneaked upstairs into your mum and dad's bedroom.'

'What?' barked Roy.

'Yes,' said Cynthia, nervously. 'No, I went upstairs to change Anna's nappy and I heard movement in there. I walked in and she was looking at Margot's clothes in the wardrobe.'

'Who was this?' asked Strike.

'The blonde one. The receptionist who wasn't Gloria.'

'Irene,' said Strike. 'Did she know you'd seen her?'

'Oh yes. I walked in, holding Anna.'

'What did she say when she saw you?' asked Robin.

'Well, she was a bit embarrassed,' said Cynthia. 'You would be, wouldn't you? She laughed and said "just being nosy" and walked back out past me.'

'Good God,' said Roy Phipps, shaking his head. 'Who *hired* these people?'

'Was she really just looking?' Robin asked Cynthia. 'Or d'you think she'd gone in there to—'

'Oh, I don't think she'd *taken* anything,' said Cynthia. 'And you never – Margot never missed anything, did she?' she asked Roy.

'No, but you should still have told me this at the time,' said Roy crossly.

'I didn't want to cause trouble. You were already . . . well, it was a stressful day, wasn't it?'

'About this alleged sighting,' said Strike, and he told the family the third-hand tale of Charlie Ramage, who claimed to have seen Margot wandering among graves in a churchyard in Leamington Spa.

'. . . and Robin's now spoken to Ramage's widow, who confirmed the basic story, though she couldn't swear to it that it was Margot he thought he'd seen, and not another missing woman. The sighting doesn't seem to have been passed to the police, so I wanted to ask whether Margot had any connection with Leamington Spa that you know of?'

'None,' said Roy, and Cynthia shook her head.

Strike made a note.

'Thank you. While we're on the subject of sightings,' said Strike, 'I wonder whether we could run through the rest of the list?'

Robin thought she knew what Strike was up to. However uncomfortable the idea that Margot was still alive might be for the people in this room, Strike wanted to start the interview from a standpoint that didn't presume murder.

'The woman at the service station in Birmingham, the mother in Brighton, the dog walker down in Eastbourne,' Roy rattled off, before Strike could speak. 'Why would she have been out and about, driving cars and walking dogs? If she'd disappeared voluntarily, she clearly didn't want to be found. The same goes for wandering around graveyards.'

'True,' said Strike. 'But there was one sighting—'

'Warwick,' said Roy. 'Yes.'

A look passed between husband and wife. Strike waited. Roy set down his cup and saucer on the table in front of him and looked up at his daughter.

'You're quite sure you want to do this, Anna, are you?' he asked, looking at his silent daughter. 'Quite, *quite* sure?'

'What d'you mean?' she snapped back. 'What d'you think I hired detectives for? Fun?'

'All right, then,' said Roy, 'all right. That sighting caught . . . caught my attention, because my wife's ex-boyfriend, a man called Paul Satchwell, hailed originally from Warwick. This was a man she'd . . . reconnected with, before she disappeared.'

'Oh for God's sake,' said Anna, with a tight little laugh, 'did you *honestly* think I don't know about Paul Satchwell? Of course I do!' Kim reached out and put a hand on her wife's leg, whether in comfort or warning, it was hard to tell. 'Have you never heard of the internet, Dad, or press archives? I've seen Satchwell's ridiculous photograph, with all his chest hair and his medallions, and I know my mother went for a drink with him three weeks before she vanished! But it was only one drink—'

'Oh, was it?' said Roy nastily. 'Thanks for your reassurance, Anna. Thanks for your expert knowledge. How marvellous to be all-knowing—'

'Roy,' whispered Cynthia.

'What are you saying, that it was more than a drink?' said Anna, looking shaken. 'No, it wasn't, that's a horrible thing to say! Oonagh says—'

'Oh, right, yes, I see!' said Roy loudly, his sunken cheeks turning purple as his hands gripped the arms of his chair, '*Oonagh* says, does she? Everything is explained!'

'What's explained?' demanded Anna.

'This!' he shouted, pointing a trembling, rope-veined, swollen-knuckled hand at Strike and Robin. 'Oonagh Kennedy's behind it all, is she? I should have *known* I hadn't heard the last of her!'

'For God's sake, Roy,' said Kim loudly, 'that's a preposterous—'

'*Oonagh Kennedy wanted me arrested!*'

'Dad, that's simply not true!' said Anna, forcibly removing Kim's restraining hand from her leg. 'You've got a morbid fixation about Oonagh—'

'Badgering me to complain about Talbot—'

'Well, why the bloody hell *didn't* you?' said Anna loudly. 'The man was in the middle of a fully fledged breakdown!'

'Roy!' whimpered Cynthia again, as Roy leaned forwards to face his daughter across the too-small circular table, with its precariously balanced cake. Gesticulating wildly, his face purple, he shouted,

'Police swarming all over the house going through your mother's things – sniffer dogs out in the garden – they were looking for any reason to arrest me, and I should lodge a formal complaint against the man in charge? *How would that have looked?*'

'He was incompetent!'

'Were you there, Miss Omniscient? Did you know him?'

'Why did they replace him? Why does everything written about the case say he was incompetent? The truth is,' said Anna, stabbing the air between her and her father with a forefinger, 'you and Cyn loved Bill Talbot because he thought you were innocent from the off and—'

'*Thought* I was innocent?' bellowed Roy. 'Well, thank you, it's good to know that nothing's changed since you were thirteen years old—'

'Roy!' said Cynthia and Kim together.

'—and accused me of building the koi pond over the place I'd buried her!'

Anna burst into tears and fled the room, almost tripping over Strike's legs as she went. Suspecting there was about to be a mass exodus, he retracted his feet.

'When,' Kim said coldly to her father-in-law, 'is Anna going to be forgiven for things she said when she was a confused child, going through a dreadful time?'

'And *my* dreadful time is nothing, of course? Nothing!' shouted Roy, and as Strike expected, he, too, left the room at the fastest pace he could manage, which was a speedy hobble.

'Christ's sake,' muttered Kim, striding after Roy and Anna and almost colliding at the door with Cynthia, who'd jumped up to follow Roy.

The door swung shut. The rain pattered on the pond outside. Strike blew out his cheeks, exchanged looks with Robin, then picked up his plate and continued eating his cake.

'Starving,' he said thickly, in response to Robin's look. 'No lunch. And it's good cake.'

Distantly they heard shouting, and the slamming of another door.

'D'you think the interview's over?' muttered Robin.

'No,' said Strike, still eating. 'They'll be back.'

'Remind me about the sighting in Warwick,' said Robin.

She'd merely skimmed the list of sightings that Strike had emailed her. There hadn't seemed anything very interesting there.

'A woman asked for change in a pub, and the landlady thought she was Margot. A mature student came forward two days later to identify herself, but the landlady wasn't convinced that was who she'd seen. The police were, though.'

Strike took another large mouthful of cake before saying,

'I don't think there's anything in it. Well . . . ' he swallowed and shot a meaningful look at the sitting room door, 'there's a bit more *now*.'

Strike continued to eat cake, while Robin's eyes roamed the room and landed on an ormolu mantel clock of exceptional ugliness. With a glance at the door, she got up to examine it. A gilded classical goddess wearing a helmet sat on top of the ornate, heavy case.

'Pallas Athena,' said Strike, watching her, pointing his fork at the figure.

In the base of the clock was a drawer with a small brass handle. Remembering Cynthia's statement about Roy and Margot leaving notes for each other here, she pulled the drawer open. It was lined in red felt and empty.

'D'you think it's valuable?' she asked Strike, sliding the drawer shut.

'Dunno. Why?'

'Because why else would you keep it? It's horrible.'

There were two distinct kinds of taste on view in this room and they didn't harmonise, Robin thought, as she looked around, all the time listening out for the return of the family. The leather-bound copies of Ovid and Pliny, and the Victorian reproductions of classical statues, among them a pair of miniature Medici lions, a reproduction Vestal virgin and a Hermes poised on tiptoe on his heavy bronze base, presumably represented Roy's father's taste, whereas she suspected that his mother had chosen the insipid watercolour landscapes and botanical subjects, the dainty antique furniture and the chintz curtains.

Why had Roy never made a clean sweep and redecorated, Robin wondered. Reverence for his parents? Lack of imagination? Or had the sickly little boy, housebound no doubt for much of his childhood, developed an attachment to these objects that he couldn't put aside? He and Cynthia seemed to have made little impression on the room other than in adding a few family pictures to faded black and white photos featuring Roy's parents and Roy as a child. The only one to hold Robin's interest was a family group that looked as though it had been taken in the early nineties, when Roy had still had all his hair, and Cynthia's had been thick and wavy. Their two biological children, a boy and a girl, looked like Anna. Nobody would have guessed that she'd had a different mother.

Robin moved to the window. The surface of the long, formal koi pond outside, with its stone pavilion at the end, was now so densely rain-pocked that the vivid red, white and black shapes moving beneath the surface were barely discernible as fish. There was one particularly big creature, pearl white and black, that looked as though it might be over two feet long. The miniature pavilion would normally be reflected in the pond's smooth surface, but today it merely added an extra layer of diffuse grey to the far end of the pond. It had a strangely familiar design on the floor.

'Cormoran,' Robin said, at the exact moment Strike said, 'Look at this.'

Both turned. Strike, who'd finished his cake, was now standing beside one of Roy's father's statuettes, which Robin had overlooked. It was a foot-high bronze of a naked man with a cloth around his shoulders, holding a snake. Momentarily puzzled, Robin realised after a second or two why Strike was pointing at it.

'Oh . . . the snaky invented sign Talbot gave Roy?'

'Precisely. This is Asclepius,' said Strike. 'Greek god of medicine. What've you found?'

'Look on the floor of the gazebo thing. Inlaid in the stone.'

He joined her at the window.

'Ah,' he said. 'You can see the beginnings of that in one

of the photographs of Margot's barbecue. It was under construction.'

A cross of St John lay on the floor of the gazebo, inlaid in darker granite. 'Interesting choice of design,' said Strike.

'You know,' said Robin, turning to look at the room, 'people who're manic often think they're receiving supernatural messages. Things the sane would call coincidences.'

'I was thinking exactly that,' said Strike, turning to look at the figure of Pallas Athena, on top of the ugly mantel clock. 'To a man in Talbot's state of mental confusion, I'm guessing this room would've seemed crammed with astrological—'

Roy's voice sounded in the hall outside.

'—then don't blame me—'

The door opened and the family filed back inside.

'—if she hears things she doesn't like!' Roy finished, addressing Cynthia, who was immediately behind him, and looked scared. Roy's face was an unhealthy purple again, though the skin around his eyes remained a jaundiced yellow.

He seemed startled to see Strike and Robin standing at the window.

'Admiring your garden,' said Strike, as he and Robin returned to their sofa.

Roy grunted and took his seat again. He was breathing heavily.

'Apologies,' he said, after a moment or two. 'You aren't seeing the family at its best.'

'Very stressful for everyone,' said Strike, as Anna and Kim re-entered the room and resumed their seats on the sofa, where they sat holding hands. Cynthia perched herself beside them, watching Roy anxiously.

'I want to say something,' Roy told Strike. 'I want to make it perfectly clear—'

'Oh for God's sake, I've had *one* phone call with her!' said Anna.

'I'd appreciate it, Anna,' said Roy, his chest labouring, 'if I could finish.'

Addressing Strike, he said,

'Oonagh Kennedy disliked me from the moment Margot and I first met. She was possessive towards Margot, and she also happened to have left the church, and she was one of those who had to make an enemy of everyone still in it. Moreover—'

'Dr Phipps,' interrupted Strike, who could foresee the afternoon degenerating into a long row about Oonagh Kennedy. 'I think you should know that when we interviewed Oonagh, she made it quite clear that the person she thought we should be concentrating our energies on is Paul Satchwell.'

For a second or two, Roy appeared unable to fully grasp what had just been said to him.

'*See?*' said Anna furiously. 'You just implied that there was more between my mother and Satchwell than one drink. What did you mean? Or were you,' she said, and Robin heard the underlying hope, 'just angry and lashing out?'

'People who insist on opening cans of worms, Anna,' said Roy, 'shouldn't complain when they get covered in slime.'

'Well, go on then,' said Anna, 'spill your slime.'

'Anna,' whispered Cynthia, and was ignored.

'All right,' said Roy. 'All right, then.' He turned back to Strike and Robin. 'Early in our relationship, I saw a note of Satchwell's Margot had kept. "Dear Brunhilda" it said – it was his pet name for her. The Valkyrie, you know. Margot was tall. Fair.'

Roy paused and swallowed.

'Some three weeks before she disappeared, she came home and told me she'd run into Satchwell in the street and that they'd gone for an . . . *innocent* drink.'

He cleared his throat. Cynthia poured him more tea.

'After she – after she'd disappeared, I had to go and

collect her things from the St John's practice. Among them I found a small—'

He held his fingers some three inches apart.

'—wooden figure, a stylised Viking which she'd been keeping on her desk. Written in ink on this figure's base was "Brunhilda", with a small heart.'

Roy took a sip of tea.

'I'd never seen it before. Of course, it's *possible* that Satchwell was carrying it around with him for years, on the off chance that he'd one day bump into Margot in the street. However, I concluded that they'd seen each other again and that he'd given her this – this token – on a subsequent occasion. All I know is, I'd never seen it before I collected her things from her surgery.'

Robin could tell that Anna wanted to suggest an alternative explanation, but it was very difficult to find a flaw in Roy's reasoning.

'Did you tell the police what you suspected?' Strike asked.

'Yes,' said Phipps, 'and I believe Satchwell claimed that there'd been no second meeting, that he'd given the figurine to Margot years before, when they were first involved. They couldn't prove it either way, of course. But *I'd* never seen it before.'

Robin wondered which would be more hurtful: finding out that a spouse had hidden a love token from a former partner, and taken to displaying it many years later, or that they'd been given it recently.

'Tell me,' Strike was saying, 'did Margot ever tell you anything about a "pillow dream"?'

'A what?' said Roy.

'Something Satchwell had told her, concerning a pillow?'

'I don't know what you're talking about,' said Roy, suspiciously.

'Did Inspector Talbot ever happen to mention that he

believed Satchwell lied about his whereabouts on the eleventh of October?'

'No,' said Roy, now looking very surprised. 'I understood the police were entirely satisfied with his alibi.'

'We've found out,' Strike said, addressing Anna, 'that Talbot kept his own separate case notes – separate from the official police record, I mean. After appearing to rule out Aries, he went back to him and started digging for more information on him.'

'"Aries"?' repeated Anna, confused.

'Sorry,' said Strike, irritated by his own lapse into astrological speak. 'Talbot's breakdown manifested itself as a belief he could solve the case by occult means. He started using tarot cards and looking at horoscopes. He referred to everyone connected with the case by their star signs. Satchwell was born under the sign of Aries, so that's what he's called in Talbot's private notes.'

There was a brief silence, and then Kim said,

'Jesus wept.'

'Astrology?' said Roy, apparently confounded.

'You *see*, Dad?' said Anna, thumping her knee with her fist. 'If Lawson had taken over earlier—'

'Lawson was a fool,' said Roy, who nevertheless looked shaken. 'An idiot! He was more interested in proving that Talbot had been inept than in finding out what happened to Margot. He insisted on going back over *everything*. He wanted to personally interview the doctors who'd treated me for the bleed on my knee, even though they'd given signed statements. He went back to my bank to check my accounts, in case I'd paid someone to kill your mother. He put pressure . . .'

He stopped and coughed, thumping his chest. Cynthia began to rise off the sofa, but Roy indicated with an angry gesture that she should stay put.

'... put pressure on Cynthia, trying to get her to admit she'd lied about me being in bed all that day, but he never found out a shred of new information about what had happened to your mother. He was a jobsworth, a bullying, unimaginative jobsworth whose priority wasn't finding *her*, it was proving that Talbot messed up. Bill Talbot may have been ... he clearly *was*,' Roy added, with a furious glance at Strike, 'unwell, but the simple fact remains: nobody's ever found a better explanation than Creed, have they?'

And with the mention of Creed, the faces of the three women on the sofa fell. His very name seemed to conjure a kind of black hole in the room, into which living women had disappeared, never to be seen again; a manifestation of almost supernatural evil. There was a finality in the very mention of him: the monster, now locked away for life, untouchable, unreachable, like the women locked up and tortured in his basement. And Robin's thoughts darted guiltily to the email she had now written, and sent, without telling Strike what she'd done, because she was afraid he might not approve.

'Do any of you know,' Roy asked abruptly, 'who Kara Wolfson and Louise Tucker were?'

'Yes,' said Robin, before Strike could answer. 'Louise was a teenage runaway and Kara was a nightclub hostess. Creed was suspected of killing both of them, but there was no proof.'

'Exactly,' said Roy, throwing her the kind of look he might once have given a medical student who had made a correct diagnosis. 'Well, in 1978 I met up with Kara's brother and Louise's father.'

'I never knew you did that!' said Anna, looking shocked.

'Of course not. You were five years old,' snapped Roy. He turned back to Strike and Robin. 'Louise's father had made his own study of Creed's life. He'd gone to every place Creed had ever lived or worked and interviewed as many people who'd admit to knowing him. He was petitioning Merlyn-Rees, the then Home Secretary, to let him go and dig in as many of these places as possible.

'The man was half-insane,' said Roy. 'I saw then what living with something like this could do to you. The obsession had taken over his entire life. He wanted buildings dismantled, walls taken down, foundations exposed. Fields where Creed might once have walked, dug up. Streams dragged, which some schoolboy friend said Creed might have once gone fishing in. Tucker was shaking as he talked, trying to get me and Wolfson, who was a lorry driver, to join him in a TV campaign. We were to chain ourselves to the railings outside Downing Street, get ourselves on the news . . . Tucker's marriage had split up. He seemed on bad terms with his living children. Creed had become his whole life.'

'And you didn't want to help?' asked Anna.

'If,' said Roy quietly, 'he'd had actual evidence – any solid clue that linked Margot and Creed—'

'I've read you thought one of the necklaces in the basement might've been—'

'If you will get your information from sensationalist books, Anna—'

'Because you've always made it so *easy* for me to talk to you about my mother,' said Anna. 'Haven't you?'

'Anna,' whispered Cynthia again.

'The locket they found in Creed's basement wasn't Margot's, and I should know, because I gave it to her,' said Roy. His lips trembled, and he pressed them together.

'Just a couple more questions, if you wouldn't mind,' said Strike, before Anna could say anything else. He was determined to avert further conflict if he could. 'Could we talk for a moment about Wilma, the cleaner who worked at the practice and did housework for you here, as well?'

'It was all Margot's idea, hiring her, but she wasn't very good,' said Roy. 'The woman was having some personal difficulties and Margot thought the solution was more money. After Margot disappeared, she walked out. Never turned up again. No loss. I heard afterwards she'd been sacked from the practice. Pilfering, I heard.'

'Wilma told police—'

'That there was blood on the carpet upstairs, the day Margot went missing,' interrupted Roy. From Anna and Kim's startled expressions, Robin deduced that this was entirely new information to them.

'Yes,' said Strike.

'It was menstrual,' said Roy coldly. 'Margot's period had started overnight. There were sanitary wrappers in the bathroom, my mother told me. Wilma sponged the carpet clean. This was in the spare room, at the opposite end of the house to the marital bedroom. Margot and I were sleeping apart at that time, because of,' there was a slight hesitation, 'my injury.'

'Wilma also said that she thought she'd seen you—'

'Walking across the garden,' said Roy. 'It was a lie. If she saw anyone, it would have been one of the stonemasons. We were finishing the gazebo at that time,' he said, pointing towards the stone folly at the end of the fishpond.

Strike made a note and turned over a page in his notebook.

'Can either of you remember Margot talking about a man called Niccolo Ricci? He was a patient at the St John's practice.'

Both Roy and Cynthia shook their heads.

'What about a patient called Steven Douthwaite?'

'No,' said Roy. 'But we heard about him afterwards, from the press.'

'Someone at the barbecue mentioned that Margot had been sent chocolates by a patient,' said Cynthia. 'That was him, wasn't it?'

'We think so. She never talked about Douthwaite, then? Never mentioned him showing an inappropriate interest in her, or told you he was gay?'

'No,' said Roy again. 'There's such a thing as patient confidentiality, you know.'

'This might seem an odd question,' said Strike, 'but did Margot have any scars? Specifically, on her ribcage?'

'No,' said Roy, unsettled. 'Why are you asking that?'

'To exclude one possibility,' said Strike, and before they could ask for further details, he said,

'Did Margot ever tell you she'd received threatening notes?'

'Yes,' said Roy. 'Well, not notes in the plural. She told me she'd got *one*.'

'She did?' said Strike, looking up.

'Yes. It accused her of encouraging young women into promiscuity and sin.'

'Did it threaten her?'

'I don't know,' said Roy. 'I never saw it.'

'She didn't bring it home?'

'No,' said Roy shortly. He hesitated, then said, 'We had a row about it.'

'Really?'

'Yes. There can be serious consequences,' said Roy, turning redder, '*societal* consequences, when you start enabling things that don't take place in nature—'

'Are you worried she told some girl it was OK to be gay?' asked Anna, and yet again Cynthia whispered, '*Anna!*'

'I'm talking,' said Roy, his face congested, 'about giving reckless advice that might lead to marital breakdown. I'm talking about facilitating promiscuity, behind the backs of parents. Some very angry man had sent her that note, and she never seemed to have considered – considered—'

Roy's face worked. For a moment, it looked as though he was going to shout, but then, most unexpectedly, he burst into noisy tears.

His wife, daughter and daughter-in-law sat, stunned, in a row on the sofa; nobody, even Cynthia, went to him. Roy was suddenly crying in great heaving gulps, tears streaming down over his sunken cheeks, trying and failing to master himself, and finally speaking through the sobs.

'She – never seemed – to remember – that I couldn't – protect her – couldn't – do anything – if somebody tried – to hurt – because I'm a useless – bleeder . . . *useless* . . . *bloody* . . . *bleeder* . . .'

'Oh *Dad*,' whispered Anna, horrified, and she slid off the sofa and walked to her father on her knees. She tried to place her hands on his leg, but he batted her consoling hands away, shaking his head, still crying.

'No – no – I don't deserve it – you don't know everything – you don't know—'

'What don't I know?' she said, looking scared. 'Dad, I know more than you think. I know about the abortion—'

'There was never – never – *never* an abortion!' said Roy, gulping and sobbing. 'That was the one – one thing Oonagh Kennedy and I – we both knew – she'd *never* – *never* – not after you! She told me – Margot told me – after she had you – changed her views completely. *Completely!*'

'Then what don't I know?' whispered Anna.

'I was – I was c- cruel to her!' wailed Roy. 'I was! I made things difficult! Showed no interest in her work. I drove her away! She was going to l- leave me . . . I know what happened. I know. I've always known. The day before – before she went – she left a message – in the clock – silly – thing we used to – and the note said – *Please t- talk to me* . . .'

Roy's sobs overtook him. As Cynthia got up and went

to kneel on Roy's other side, Anna reached for her father's hand, and this time, he let her hold it. Clinging to his daughter, he said,

'I was waiting – for an apology. For going to drink – with Satchwell. And because she hadn't – written an apology – I didn't t- talk to her. And the next day—

'I know what happened. She liked to walk. If she was upset – long walks. She forgot about Oonagh – went for a walk – trying to decide what to do – leave me – because I'd made her – so – so sad. She wasn't – paying attention – and Creed – and Creed – must have . . .'

Still holding his hand, Anna slid her other arm around her father's shaking shoulders and drew her to him. He cried inconsolably, clinging to her. Strike and Robin both pretended an interest in the flowered rug.

'Roy,' said Kim gently, at last. 'Nobody in this room hasn't said or done things they don't bitterly regret. Not one of us.'

Strike, who'd got far more out of Roy Phipps than he'd expected, thought it was time to draw the interview to a close. Phipps was in such a state of distress that it felt inhumane to press him further. When Roy's sobs had subsided a little, Strike said formally,

'I want to thank you very much for talking to us, and for the tea. We'll get out of your hair.'

He and Robin got to their feet. Roy remained entangled with his wife and daughter. Kim stood up to show them out.

'*Well*,' Kim said quietly, as they approached the front door, 'I have to tell you, that was . . . well, close to a miracle. He's never talked about Margot like that, *ever*. Even if you don't find out anything else . . . thank you. That was . . . healing.'

The rain had ceased and the sun had come out. A double rainbow lay over the woods opposite the house. Strike and Robin stepped outside, into clean fresh air.

'Could I ask you one last thing?' said Strike, turning back to Kim who stood in the doorway.

'Yes, of course.'

'It's about that summer house thing in the garden, beside the koi pond. I wondered why it's got a cross of St John on the floor,' said Strike.

'*Oh*,' said Kim. 'Margot chose the design. Yes, Cynthia told me, ages ago. Margot had just got the job at St John's – and funnily enough, this area's got a connection to the Knights Hospitaller, too—'

'Yes,' said Robin. 'I read about that, at Hampton Court.'

'So, she thought it would be a nice allusion to the two things ... You know, now you mention it, I'm surprised nobody ever changed it. Every other trace of Margot's gone from the house.'

'Expensive, though,' said Strike, 'to remove slabs of granite.'

'Yes,' said Kim, her smile fading a little. 'I suppose it would be.'

37

Spring-headed Hydres, and sea-shouldring Whales,
Great whirlpooles, which all fishes make to flee,
Bright Scolopendraes, arm'd with siluer scales
Mighty Monoceros, with immeasured tayles . . .
The dreadfull Fish, that hath deseru'd the name
Of Death . . .

Edmund Spenser
The Faerie Queene

Rain fell almost ceaselessly into February. On the fifth, the most savage storm yet hit the south. Thousands of homes lost power, part of the sea wall supporting the London–South West railway line collapsed, swathes of farmland disappeared under flood water, roads became rivers and the nightly news featured fields turned to seas of grey water and houses waist-deep in mud. The Prime Minister promised financial assistance, the emergency services scrambled to help the stranded, and high on her hill above the flooded St Mawes, Joan was deprived of a promised visit from Strike and Lucy, because they were unable to reach her either by road or train.

Strike sublimated the guilt he felt for not heading to Cornwall before the weather rendered the journey impossible by working long hours and skimping on sleep. Masochistically, he chose to work back-to-back shifts, so that Barclay and

Hutchins could take some of the leave due to them because of his previous trips to see Joan. In consequence, it was Strike, not Hutchins, who was sitting in his BMW in the everlasting rain outside Elinor Dean's house in Stoke Newington on Wednesday evening the following week, and Strike who saw a man in a tracksuit knock on her door and be admitted.

Strike waited all night for the man to reappear. Finally, at six in the morning, he emerged onto the still dark street with his hand clamped over his lower face. Strike, who was watching him through night vision glasses, caught a glimpse of Elinor Dean in a cosy quilted dressing gown, waving him off. The tracksuited man hurried back to his Citroën with his right hand still concealing his mouth and set off in a southerly direction.

Strike tailed the Citroën until they reached Risinghill Street in Pentonville, where Strike's target parked and entered a modern, red-brick block of flats, both hands now in his pockets and nothing unusual about his mouth as far as the detective could see. Strike waited until the man was safely inside, took a note of which window showed a light five minutes later, then drove away, parking shortly afterwards in White Lion Street.

Early as it was, people were already heading off to work, umbrellas angled against the continuing downpour. Strike wound down the car window, because even he, inveterate smoker though he was, wasn't enjoying the smell of his car after a night's surveillance. Then, though his tongue ached from too much smoking, he lit up again and phoned Saul Morris.

'All right, boss?'

Strike, who didn't particularly like Morris calling him 'boss', but couldn't think of any way to ask him to stop without sounding like a dickhead, said,

'I want you to switch targets. Forget Shifty today; I've just followed a new guy who spent the night at Elinor Dean's.' He gave Morris the address. 'He's second floor, flat on the far left as you're looking at the building. Fortyish, greying hair, bit of a paunch. See what you can find out about him – chat up the neighbours, find out where he works and have a dig around online, see if you can find out what his interests are. I've got a hunch he and SB are visiting that woman for the same reason.'

'See, this is why you're the head honcho. You take over for one night and crack the case.'

Strike wished Morris would stop brown-nosing him, too. When he'd hung up, he sat smoking for a while, while the wind nipped at his exposed flesh, and rain hit his face in what felt like icy needle pricks. Then, after checking the time to make sure his early-rising uncle would be awake, he phoned Ted.

'All right, boy?' said his uncle, over the crackling phone line.

'Fine. How are you?'

'Oh, I'm fine,' said Ted. 'Just having some breakfast. Joanie's still asleep.'

'How is she?'

'No change. Bearing up.'

'What about food, have you got enough?'

'We're fine for food, don't you worry about that,' said Ted. 'Little Dave Polworth come over yesterday with enough to feed us for a week.'

'How the hell did he get to you?' asked Strike, who knew that a large chunk of the land between his aunt and uncle and Polworth's house was under several feet of water.

'Rowed part of the way,' said Ted, sounding amused. 'He made it sound like one of his Ironman competitions. All covered in oilskins he was when he got here. Big backpack full of shopping. He's all right, that Polworth.'

'Yeah, he is,' said Strike, momentarily closing his eyes. It oughtn't to be Polworth looking after his aunt and uncle. It should be him. He ought to have left earlier, knowing the weather was looking bad, but for months now he'd been juggling guilt about his aunt and uncle with the guilt he felt about the load he was putting on his subcontractors, and Robin especially. 'Ted, I'll be there as soon as they put the trains back on.'

'Aye, I know you will, lad,' said Ted. 'Don't worry about us. I won't take you to her, because she needs her rest, but I'll tell her you called. She'll be chuffed.'

Tired, hungry and wondering where he might get some breakfast, Strike typed out a text to Dave Polworth, his cigarette jammed between his teeth, using the nickname he'd had for Polworth ever since the latter had got himself bitten by a shark at the age of eighteen.

Ted's just told me what you did yesterday. I'll never be able to repay all this, Chum. Thank you.

He flicked his cigarette end out of the car, wound up the window and had just turned on the engine when his mobile buzzed. Expecting to see a response from Polworth, doubtless asking him when he'd turned into such a poof or a big girl (Polworth's language being always as far from politically correct as you could get), he looked down at the screen, already smiling in anticipation, and read:

Dad wants to call you. When would be a good time?

Strike read the text twice before understanding that it was from Al. At first, he felt only blank surprise. Then anger and profound resentment rose like vomit.

'Fuck off,' he told his phone loudly.

He turned out of the side street and drove away, jaw clenched, wondering why he should be hounded by Rokeby now, of all times in his life, when he was so worried about relatives who'd cared about him when there'd been no kudos to be gained from the association. The time for amends had passed; the damage was irreparable; blood wasn't thicker than fucking water. Consumed by thoughts of frail Joan, with whom he shared no shred of DNA, marooned in her house on the hill amid floods, anger and guilt writhed inside him.

A matter of minutes later, he realised he was driving through Clerkenwell. Spotting an open café on St John Street he parked, then headed through the rain into warmth and light, where he ordered himself an egg and tomato sandwich. Choosing a table by the window, he sat down facing the street, eye to eye with his own unshaven and stony-faced reflection in the rain-studded window.

Hangovers apart, Strike rarely got headaches, but something resembling one was starting to build on the left side of his skull. He ate his sandwich, telling himself firmly that food was making him feel better. Then, after ordering a second mug of tea, he pulled out his mobile again and typed out a response to Al, with the dual objective of shutting down Rokeby once and for all, and of concealing from both his half-brother and his father how much their persistence was disturbing his peace.

I'm not interested. It's too late. I don't want to fall out with you, but take this 'no' as final.

He sent the text and then cast around immediately for something else to occupy his tired mind. The shops opposite were ablaze with red and pink: February the fourteenth was almost here. It now occurred to him that he hadn't heard from Charlotte since he'd ignored her text at Christmas. Would she send him a message on Valentine's Day? Her desire for contact seemed to be triggered by special occasions and anniversaries.

Automatically, without considering what he was doing, but with the same desire for comfort that had pushed him into this café, Strike pulled his phone out of his pocket again and called Robin, but the number was engaged. Shoving the mobile back in his pocket, stressed, anxious and craving action, he told himself he should make use of being in Clerkenwell, now he was here.

This café was only a short walk from the old St John's surgery. How many of these passers-by, he wondered, had lived in the area forty years previously? The hunched old woman in her raincoat with her tartan shopping trolley? The grey-whiskered man trying to flag down a cab? Perhaps the ageing Sikh man in his turban, texting as he walked? Had any of them consulted Margot Bamborough? Could any of them remember a dirty, bearded man called something like Applethorpe, who'd roamed these very streets, insisting to strangers that he'd killed the doctor?

Strike's absent gaze fell on a man walking with a strange, rolling gait on the opposite side of the road. His fine, mousy hair was rain-soaked and plastered to his head. He had neither coat nor umbrella, but wore a sweatshirt with a picture of Sonic the Hedgehog on the front. The lack of coat, the slightly lumbering walk, the wide, childlike stare, the slightly gaping mouth, the stoic acceptance of becoming slowly drenched to the skin: all suggested some kind of cognitive impairment. The man passed out of Strike's line of vision as the detective's mobile rang.

'Hi. Did you just call me?' said Robin, and Strike felt a certain release of tension, and decided the tea was definitely soothing his head.

'I did, yeah. Just for an update.'

He told her the story of the tracksuited man who'd visited Elinor Dean overnight.

'And he was covering up his mouth when he left? That's weird.'

'I know. There's definitely something odd going on in that house. I've asked Morris to dig a bit on the new bloke.'

'Pentonville's right beside Clerkenwell,' said Robin.

'Which is where I am right now. Café on St John Street. I th – think,' a yawn overtook Strike, 'sorry – I think, seeing as I'm in the area, I might have another dig around on the late Applethorpe. Try and find someone who remembers the family, or knows what might've happened to them.'

'How're you going to do that?'

'Walk the area,' said Strike, and he became conscious of his aching knee even as he said it, 'have an ask around in any businesses that look long-established. I kn – know,' he yawned again, 'it's a long shot, but we haven't got anyone else claiming to have killed Margot.'

'Aren't you knackered?'

'Been worse. Where are you right now?'

'Office,' said Robin, 'and I've got a bit of Bamborough news, if you've got time.'

'Go on,' said Strike, happy to postpone the moment when he had to go back out into the rain.

'Well, firstly, I've had an email from Gloria Conti's husband. You know, the receptionist who was the last to see Margot? It's short. "*Dear Mr Ellacott—*"'

'Mister?'

'"Robin" often confuses people. "*I write for my wife, who is been very afflicted by your communications. She has not proofs or information that concern Margot Bamborough and it is not convenient that you contact her at my offices. Our family is private and desires to remain like that. I would like your assurances that you will not contact my wife another time. Yours sincerely, Hugo Jaubert.*"'

'Interesting,' agreed Strike, scratching his unshaven chin. 'Why isn't Gloria emailing back herself? Too afflicted?'

'I wonder why she's so affli – upset, I mean? Maybe,' Robin said, answering her own question, 'because I contacted her through her husband's office? But I tried through Facebook and she wouldn't answer.'

'You know, I think it might be worth getting Anna to contact Gloria. Margot's daughter might tug at her heartstrings better than we can. Why don't you draft another request and send it over to Anna, see whether she'd be comfortable letting you put her name to it?'

'Good thinking,' said Robin, and he heard her scribbling a note. 'Anyway, in better news, when you called me just now, I was talking to Wilma Bayliss's second-oldest daughter, Maya. She's the deputy headmistress. I think I'm close to persuading her to talk to us. She's worried about her older sister's reaction, but I'm hopeful.'

'Great,' said Strike, 'I'd like to hear more about Wilma.'

'And there's one other thing,' said Robin. 'Only, you might think this is a bit of a long shot.'

'I've just told you I'm about to go door to door asking about a dead nutter who definitely wasn't called Applethorpe,' said Strike, and Robin laughed.

'OK, well, I was back online last night, having another look for Steve Douthwaite, and I found this old "Memories of Butlin's" website, where ex-Redcoats chat to each other and reminisce and organise reunions and stuff – you know the kind of thing. Anyway, I couldn't find any mention of Douthwaite, or Jacks, as he was calling himself in Clacton-on-Sea, but I did find – I know it's probably totally irrelevant,' she said, 'and I don't know whether you remember, but a girl called Julie Wilkes was quoted in *Whatever Happened to Margot Bamborough?* She said she was shocked that Stevie Jacks hadn't told his friends that he'd been caught up in a missing woman case.'

'Yeah, I remember,' said Strike.

'Well . . . that girl drowned,' said Robin. 'Drowned at the holiday camp at the end of the 1985 holiday season. Her body was found one morning in the camp swimming pool. A group of them were discussing her death on the message boards on the website. They think she got drunk, slipped, hit her head and slid into the pool.

'Maybe it's horrible luck,' said Robin, 'but women do have a habit of dying in Douthwaite's vicinity, don't they? His married girlfriend kills herself, his doctor goes missing, and then there's this co-worker who drowns . . . Everywhere he goes, unnatural death follows . . . it's just odd.'

'Yeah, it is,' said Strike, frowning out at the rain. He was about to wonder aloud where Douthwaite had hidden himself, when Robin said in a slight rush,

'Listen, there's something else I wanted to ask you, but it's absolutely fine if the answer's no. My flatmate Max – you know he's an actor? Well, he's just been cast in a TV thing as an ex-soldier and he doesn't know anyone else to ask. He wondered whether you'd come over to dinner so he can ask you some questions.'

'Oh,' said Strike, surprised but not displeased. ' . . . yeah, OK. When?'

'I know it's short notice, but would tomorrow suit you? He really needs it soon.'

'Yeah, that should be all right,' said Strike. He was holding himself ready to travel down to St Mawes as soon as it became practicable, but the sea wall looked unlikely to be repaired by the following day.

When Robin had hung up, Strike ordered a third mug of tea. He was procrastinating, and he knew why. If he was genuinely going to have a poke around Clerkenwell for anyone who remembered the dead man who claimed to have killed Margot Bamborough, it would help if he knew the man's real name, and as Janice Beattie was still in Dubai, his only recourse was Irene Hickson.

The rain was as heavy as ever. Minute to minute, he postponed the call to Irene, watching traffic moving through the rippling sheets of rain, pedestrians navigating the puddle-pocked street, and thinking about the long-ago death of a young Redcoat, who'd slipped, knocked her head and drowned in a swimming pool.

Water everywhere, Bill Talbot had written in his astrological notebook. It had taken Strike some effort to decipher that particular passage. He'd concluded that Talbot was referring to a cluster of water signs apparently connected with the death of the unknown Scorpio. Why, Strike asked himself now, sipping his tea, was Scorpio a water sign? Scorpions lived on land, in heat; could they even swim? He remembered the large fish sign Talbot had used in the notebook for Irene, which at one point he'd described as 'Cetus'. Picking up his mobile, Strike Googled the word.

The constellation Cetus, he read, known also as the whale, was named for a sea monster slain by Perseus when saving Andromeda from the sea god Poseidon. It resided in a region of the sky known as 'The Sea', due to the presence there of many other water-associated constellations, including Pisces, Aquarius the water bearer, and Capricorn, the fish-tailed goat.

Water everywhere.

The astrological notes were starting to tangle themselves around his thought processes, like an old net snagged in a propeller. A pernicious mixture of sense and nonsense, they mirrored, in Strike's opinion, the appeal of astrology itself, with its flattering, comforting promise that your petty concerns were of interest to the wide universe, and that the stars or the spirit world would guide you where your own hard work and reason couldn't.

Enough, he told himself sternly. Pressing Irene's number on his mobile, he waited, listening to her phone ringing and visualising it beside the bowl of pot-pourri, in the over-decorated hall, with the pink flowered wallpaper and the thick pink carpet. At exactly the point where he'd decided, with a mixture of relief and regret, that she wasn't in, she answered.

'Double four five nine,' she trilled, making it into a kind of jingle. Joan, too, always answered her landline by telling the caller the number they'd just dialled.

'Is that Mrs Hickson?'

'Speaking.'

'It's Cormoran Strike here, the—'

'Oh, hello!' she yelped, sounding startled.

'I wondered whether you might be able to help me,' said Strike, taking out his notebook and opening it. 'When we last met, you mentioned a patient of the St John's practice who you thought might've been called Apton or Applethorpe—'

'Oh, yes?'

'—who claimed to have—'

'—killed Margot, yes,' she interrupted him. 'He stopped Dorothy in broad daylight—'

'Yes—'

'—but she thought it was a load of rubbish. I said to her, "What if he really did, Dorothy—?"'

'I haven't been able to find anyone of that name who lived in the area in 1974,' said Strike loudly, 'so I wondered whether you might've misremembered his na—'

'Possibly, yes, I might have done,' said Irene. 'Well, it's been a long time, hasn't it? Have you tried directory enquiries? Not directory enquiries,' she corrected herself immediately. 'Online records and things.'

'It's difficult to do a search with the wrong name,' said Strike, just managing to keep his tone free of exasperation or sarcasm. 'I'm right by Clerkenwell Road at the moment. I think you said he lived there?'

'Well, he was always hanging around there, so I assumed so.'

'He was registered with your practice, wasn't he? D'you remember his first—?'

'Um, let me think ... It was something like ... Gilbert, or – no, I can't remember, I'm afraid. Applethorpe? Appleton? Apton? *Everyone* knew him locally by sight because he looked so peculiar: long beard, filthy, blah blah blah. And sometimes he had his kid with him,' said Irene, warming up, 'really *funny*-looking kid—'

'Yes, you said—'

'—with *massive* ears. *He* might still be alive, the son, but he's probably – *you* know ...'

Strike waited, but apparently he was supposed to infer the end of the sentence by Irene's silence.

'Probably—?' he prompted.

'Oh, *you* know. In a place.'

'In—?'

'A home or something!' she said, a little impatiently, as though Strike were being obtuse. 'He was never going to be *right*, was he? – with a druggie father and a retarded mother, I don't care what Jan says. Jan hasn't got the same – well, it's not her fault – her family was – different standards. And she likes to look – in front of strangers – well, we all do – but after all, you're after the truth, aren't you?'

Strike noted the fine needle of malice directed at her friend, glinting among the disconnected phrases.

'Have you found Duckworth?' Irene asked, jumping subject.

'Douthwaite?'

'Oh, what am I like, I keep doing that, hahaha.' However little pleased she'd been to hear from him, he was at least someone to talk to. 'I'd *love* to know what happened to him,

I really would, *he* was a fishy character if ever there was one. Jan played it down with you, but she was a bit disappointed when he turned out to be gay, you know. She had a soft spot for him. Well, she was very lonely when I first knew her. We used to try and set her up, Eddie and I—'

'Yes, you said—'

'—but men didn't want to take on a kid and Jan was a bit *you* know, when a woman's been alone, I don't mean *desperate*, but clingy – Larry didn't mind, but Larry wasn't exactly—'

'I had one other thing I wanted to ask—'

'—only *he* wouldn't marry her, either. He'd been through a bad divorce—'

'It's about Leamington Spa—'

'You'll have checked Bognor Regis?'

'Excuse me?' said Strike.

'For Douthwaite? Because he went to Bognor Regis, didn't he? To a holiday camp?'

'Clacton-on-Sea,' said Strike. 'Unless he went to Bognor Regis as well?'

'As well as what?'

Jesus fucking Christ.

'What makes you think Douthwaite was ever in Bognor Regis?' Strike asked, slowly and clearly, rubbing his forehead.

'I thought – wasn't he there, at some point?'

'Not as far as I'm aware, but we know he worked in Clacton-on-Sea in the mid-eighties.'

'Oh, it must've been that – yes, someone must've told me that, they're all – old-fashioned seaside – *you* know.'

Strike seemed to remember he'd asked both Irene and Janice whether they had any idea where Douthwaite had gone after he left Clerkenwell, and that both had said they didn't know.

'How did you know he went to work in Clacton-on-Sea?' he asked.

'Jan told me,' said Irene, after a tiny pause. 'Yes, Jan would've told me. *She* was his neighbour, you know, *she* was the one who knew him. Yes, I think she tried to find out where he'd gone after he left Percival Road, because she was worried about him.'

'But this was eleven years later,' said Strike.

'What was?'

'He didn't go to Clacton-on-Sea until eleven years after he left Percival Road,' said Strike. 'When I asked you both if you knew where he'd gone—'

'Well, you meant *now*, didn't you?' said Irene, 'where he is *now*? I've no idea. Have you looked into that Leamington Spa business, by the way?' Then she laughed, and said, 'All these seaside places! No, wait – it isn't seaside, is it, not Leamington Spa? But you know what I mean – *water* – I do *love* water, it's – Greenwich, Eddie knew I'd love this house when he spotted it for sale – *was* there anything in that Leamington Spa thing, or was Jan making it up?'

'Mrs Beattie wasn't making it up,' said Strike. 'Mr Ramage definitely saw a missing—'

'Oh, I didn't mean Jan would make it up, no, I don't mean that,' said Irene, instantly contradicting herself. 'I just mean, you know, odd place for Margot to turn up, Leamington – have you found any connection,' she asked airily, 'or—?'

'Not yet,' said Strike. '*You* haven't remembered anything about Margot and Leamington Spa, have you?'

'Me? Goodness, no, how should I know why she'd go there?'

'Well, sometimes people do remember things after we've talked to—'

'Have you spoken to Jan since?'

'No,' said Strike. 'D'you know when she's back from Dubai?'

'No,' said Irene. 'All right for some, isn't it? I wouldn't mind some sunshine, the winter we're – but it's wasted on Jan, she doesn't sunbathe, and I wouldn't fancy the flight all that way in Economy, which is how she has to – I wonder how she's getting on, six weeks with her daughter-in-law! Doesn't matter how well you get on, that's a long—'

'Well, I'd better let you get on, Mrs Hickson.'

'Oh, all right,' she said. 'Yes, well. Best of luck with everything.'

'Thank you,' he said, and hung up.

The rain pattered on the window. With a sigh, Strike retired to the café bathroom for a long overdue pee.

He was just paying his bill when he spotted the man in the Sonic the Hedgehog sweatshirt walking past the window, now on the same side of the street as the café. He was heading back the way he'd come, two bulging bags of Tesco shopping hanging from his hands, moving with that same odd, rocking, side-to-side gait, his soaking hair flat to his skull, his mouth slightly open. Strike's eyes followed him as he passed, watching the rain drip off the bottom of his shopping bags and from the lobes of his particularly large ears.

38

So long in secret cabin there he held
Her captive to his sensual desire;
Till that with timely fruit her belly swell'd,
And bore a boy unto that salvage sire . . .

Edmund Spenser
The Faerie Queene

Asking himself whether he could possibly have got as lucky as he hoped, Strike threw a tip on the table and hurried outside into the driving rain, pulling on his coat as he went.

If the mentally impaired adult in the sopping Sonic sweatshirt was indeed the big-eared child once marched around these streets by his eccentric parent, he'd have been living in this corner of Clerkenwell for forty years. Well, people did that, of course, Strike reflected, particularly if they had support there and if their whole world was a few familiar streets. The man was still within sight, heading stolidly towards Clerkenwell Road in the pelting rain, neither speeding up, nor making any attempt to prevent himself becoming progressively more sodden. Strike turned up his coat collar and followed.

A short distance down St John Street, Strike's target turned right past a small ironmonger's on the corner, and headed into Albemarle Way, the short street with an old red telephone box at the other end, and tall, unbroken buildings on either side. Strike's interest quickened.

Just past the ironmonger's, the man set down both of his shopping bags on the wet pavement and took out a door key. Strike kept walking, because there was nowhere to hide, but made a note of the door number as he passed. Was it possible that the late Applethorpe had lived in this very flat? Hadn't Strike thought that Albemarle Way presented a promising place to lie in wait for a victim? Not, perhaps, as good as Passing Alley, nor as convenient as the flats along Jerusalem Passage, but better by far than busy Clerkenwell Green, where Talbot had been convinced that Margot had struggled with a disguised Dennis Creed.

Strike heard the front door close behind the large-eared man and doubled back. The dark blue door needed painting. A small push-button bell was beside it, beneath which was stuck the printed name 'Athorn'. Could this be the name Irene had misremembered as Applethorpe, Appleton or Apton? Then Strike noticed that the man had left the key in the lock.

With a feeling that he might have been far too dismissive of the mysterious ways of the universe, Strike pulled out the key and pressed the doorbell, which rang loudly inside. For a moment or two, nothing happened, then the door opened again and there stood the man in the wet Sonic sweatshirt.

'You left this in the lock,' said Strike, holding out the key.

The man addressed the third button of Strike's overcoat rather than look him in eye.

'I did that before and Clare said not to again,' he mumbled, holding out his hand for the key, which Strike gave him. The man began to close the door.

'My name's Cormoran Strike. I wonder whether I could come in and talk to you about your father?' Strike said, not quite putting his foot in the door, but preparing to do so should it be required.

The other's big-eared face stood out, pale, against the dark hall.

'My-Dad-Gwilherm's dead.'

'Yes,' said Strike, 'I know.'

'He carried me on his shoulders.'

'Did he?'

'Yeah. Mum told me.'

'D'you live alone?'

'I live with Mum.'

'Is her name Clare?'

'No. Deborah.'

'I'm a detective,' said Strike, pulling a card out of his pocket. 'My name's Cormoran Strike and I'd really like to talk to your mum, if that's OK.'

The man didn't take the card, but looked at it out of the corner of his eye. Strike suspected that he couldn't read.

'Would that be all right?' Strike asked, as the cold rain continued to fall.

'Yer, OK. You can come in,' said the other, still addressing Strike's coat button, and he opened the door fully to admit the detective. Without waiting to see whether Strike was following, he headed up the dark staircase inside.

Strike felt some qualms about capitalising on the vulnerabilities of a man like Athorn, but the prospect of looking around what he now strongly suspected was the flat in which the self-proclaimed killer of Margot Bamborough had been living in 1974 was irresistible. After wiping his feet carefully on the doormat, Strike closed the door behind him, spotting as he did so a couple of letters lying on the floor, which the son of the house had simply walked over; one of them carried a wet footprint. Strike picked up the letters, then climbed the bare wooden stairs, over which hung a naked, non-functioning light bulb.

As he climbed, Strike indulged himself with the fantasy of a flat which nobody other than the inhabitants had entered for forty years, with locked cupboards and rooms, or even – it had been known to happen – a skeleton lying in open view. For a split-second, as he stepped out onto the landing, his hopes surged: the oven in the tiny kitchen straight ahead looked as though it dated from the seventies, as did the brown wall tiles, but unfortunately, from a detective point of view, the flat looked neat and smelled fresh and clean. There were even recent Hoover marks on the old carpet, which was patterned in orange and brown swirls. The Tesco bags sat waiting to be unpacked on lino that was scuffed, but that had been recently washed.

To Strike's right stood an open door onto a small sitting room. The man he'd followed was standing there, facing a much older woman, who was sitting crocheting in an armchair beside the window. She looked, as well she might, shocked to see a large stranger standing in her hall.

'He wants to talk to you,' announced the man.

'Only if you're comfortable with that, Mrs Athorn,' Strike called from the landing. He wished Robin was with him. She was particularly good at putting nervous women at their ease. He remembered that Janice had said that this woman was agoraphobic. 'My name's Cormoran Strike and I wanted to ask a few questions about your husband. But if you're not happy, of course, I'll leave immediately.'

'I'm cold,' said the man loudly.

'Change your clothes,' his mother advised him. 'You've got wet. Why don't you wear your coat?'

'Too tight,' he said, 'you silly woman.'

He turned and walked out of the room past Strike, who

stood back to let him pass. Gwilherm's son disappeared into a room opposite, on the door of which the name 'Samhain' appeared in painted wooden letters.

Samhain's mother didn't appear to enjoy eye contact any more than her son did. At last, addressing Strike's knees, she said,

'All right. Come in, then.'

'Thanks very much.'

Two budgerigars, one blue, one green, chirruped in a cage in the corner of the sitting room. Samhain's mother had been crocheting a patchwork blanket. A number of completed woollen squares were piled on the wide windowsill beside her and a basket of wools sat at her feet. A huge jigsaw mat was spread out on a large ottoman in front of the sofa. It bore a two-thirds completed puzzle of unicorns. As far as tidiness went, the sitting room compared very favourably with Gregory Talbot's.

'You've got some letters,' Strike said, and he held up the damp envelopes to show her.

'You open them,' she said.

'I don't think—'

'You open them,' she repeated.

She had the same big ears as Samhain and the same slight underbite. These imperfections notwithstanding, there was a prettiness in her soft face and in her dark eyes. Her long, neatly plaited hair was white. She had to be at least sixty, but her smooth skin was that of a much younger woman. There was a strangely otherworldly air about her as she sat, plying her crochet hook beside the rainy window, shut away from the world. Strike wondered whether she could read. He felt safe to open the envelopes that were clearly junk mail, and did so.

'You've been sent a seed catalogue,' he said, showing her, 'and a letter from a furniture shop.'

'I don't want them,' said the woman beside the window, still talking to Strike's legs. 'You can sit down,' she added.

He sidled carefully between the sofa and the ottoman which, like Strike himself, was far too big for this small room. Having successfully avoided nudging the enormous jigsaw, he took a seat at a respectful distance from the crocheting woman.

'This one,' said Strike, referring to the last letter, 'is for Clare Spencer. Do you know her?'

The letter didn't have a stamp. Judging by the address on the back, the letter was from the ironmonger downstairs.

'Clare's our social worker,' she said. 'You can open it.'

'I don't think I should do that,' said Strike. 'I'll leave it for Clare. You're Deborah, is that right?'

'Yes,' she murmured.

Samhain reappeared in the door. He was now barefoot but wearing dry jeans and a fresh sweatshirt with Spider-Man on the front.

'I'm going to put things in the fridge,' he announced, and disappeared again.

'Samhain does the shopping now,' Deborah said, with a glance at Strike's shoes. Though timid, she didn't seem averse to talking to him.

'Deborah, I'm here to ask you about Gwilherm,' Strike said.

'He's not here.'

'No, I—'

'He died.'

'Yes,' said Strike. 'I'm sorry. I'm really here because of a doctor who used to work—'

'Dr Brenner,' she said at once.

'You remember Dr Brenner?' said Strike, surprised.

'I didn't like him,' she said.

'Well, I wanted to ask you about a *different* doc—'

Samhain reappeared at the sitting room door and said loudly to his mother,

'D'you want a hot chocolate, or not?'

'Yes,' she said.

'Do *you* want a hot chocolate, or not?' Samhain demanded of Strike.

'Yes please,' Strike said, on the principle that all friendly gestures should be accepted in such situations.

Samhain lumbered out of sight. Pausing in her crocheting, Deborah pointed at something straight ahead of her and said,

'That's Gwilherm, there.'

Strike looked around. An Egyptian ankh, the symbol of eternal life, had been drawn on the wall behind the old TV. The walls were pale yellow everywhere except behind the ankh, where a patch of dirty green survived. In front of the ankh, on top of the flat-topped television set, was a black object which Strike at first glance took for a vase. Then he spotted the stylised dove on it, realised that it was an urn and understood, finally, what he was being told.

'Ah,' said Strike. 'Those are Gwilherm's ashes, are they?'

'I told Tudor to get the one with the bird, because I like birds.'

One of the budgerigars fluttered suddenly across the cage in a blur of bright green and yellow.

'Who painted that?' asked Strike, pointing at the ankh.

'Gwilherm,' said Deborah, continuing to dextrously ply her crochet hook.

Samhain re-entered the room, holding a tin tray.

'Not on my jigsaw,' his mother warned him, but there was no other free surface.

'Should I—?' offered Strike, gesturing towards the puzzle, but there was no space anywhere on the floor to accommodate it.

'You close it,' Deborah told him, with a hint of reproach, and Strike saw that the jigsaw mat had wings, which could be fastened to protect the puzzle. He did so, and Samhain laid the tray on top. Deborah stuck her crochet hook carefully in the ball of wool and accepted a mug of instant hot chocolate and a Penguin biscuit from her son. Samhain kept the Batman mug for himself. Strike sipped his drink and said, 'Very nice,' not entirely dishonestly.

'I make good hot chocolate, don't I, Deborah?' said Samhain, unwrapping a biscuit.

'Yes,' said Deborah, blowing on the surface of the hot liquid.

'I know this was a long time ago,' Strike began again, 'but there was another doctor, who worked with Dr Brenner—'

'Old Joe Brenner was a dirty old man,' said Samhain Athorn, with a cackle.

Strike looked at him in surprise. Samhain directed his smirk at the closed jigsaw.

'Why was he a dirty old man?' asked the detective.

'My Uncle Tudor told me,' said Samhain. '*Dirty* old man. Hahahaha. Is this mine?' he asked, picking up the envelope addressed to Clare Spencer.

'No,' said his mother. 'That's Clare's.'

'Why is it?'

'I think,' said Strike, 'it's from your downstairs neighbour.'

'He's a bastard,' said Samhain, putting the letter back down. 'He made us throw everything away, didn't he, Deborah?'

'I like it better now,' said Deborah mildly. 'It's good now.'

Strike allowed a moment or two to pass, in case Samhain had more to add, then asked,

'Why did Uncle Tudor say Joseph Brenner was a dirty old man?'

'Tudor knew everything about everyone,' said Deborah placidly.

'Who was Tudor?' Strike asked her.

'Gwilherm's brother,' said Deborah. 'He always knew about people round here.'

'Does he still visit you?' asked Strike, suspecting the answer.

'Passed-away-to-the-other side,' said Deborah, as though it was one long word. 'He used to buy our shopping. He took Sammy to play football and to the swimming.'

'I do all the shopping now,' piped up Samhain. 'Sometimes I don't want to do the shopping but if I don't, I get hungry, and Deborah says, "It's your fault there's nothing to eat." So then I go shopping.'

'Good move,' said Strike.

The three of them drank their hot chocolate.

'Dirty old man, Joe Brenner,' repeated Samhain, more loudly. 'Uncle Tudor used to tell me some stories. Old Betty and the one who wouldn't pay, hahahaha. Dirty old Joe Brenner.'

'I didn't like him,' said Deborah quietly. 'He wanted me to take my pants off.'

'Really?' said Strike.

While this had surely been a question of a medical examination, he felt uncomfortable.

'Yes, to look at me,' said Deborah. 'I didn't want it. Gwilherm wanted it, but I don't like men I don't know looking at me.'

'No, well, I can understand that,' said Strike. 'You were ill, were you?'

'Gwilherm said I had to,' was her only response.

If he'd still been in the Special Investigation Branch, there would have been a female officer with him for this interview. Strike wondered what her IQ was.

'Did you ever meet Dr Bamborough?' he asked. 'She was,' he hesitated, 'a lady doctor.'

'I've never seen a lady doctor,' said Deborah, with what sounded like regret.

'D'you know whether Gwilherm ever met Dr Bamborough?'

'She died,' said Deborah.

'Yes,' said Strike, surprised. 'People think she died, but no one knows for s—'

One of the budgerigars made the little bell hanging from the top of its cage tinkle. Both Deborah and Samhain looked around, smiling.

'Which one was it?' Deborah asked Samhain.

'Bluey,' he said. 'Bluey's cleverer'n Billy Bob.'

Strike waited for them to lose interest in the budgerigars, which took a couple of minutes. When both Athorns' attention had returned to their hot chocolates, he said,

'Dr Bamborough disappeared and I'm trying to find out what happened to her. I've been told that Gwilherm talked about Dr Bamborough, after she went missing.'

Deborah didn't respond. It was hard to know whether she was listening, or deliberately ignoring him.

'I heard,' said Strike – there was no point not saying it; this was the whole reason he was here, after all – 'that Gwilherm told people he killed her.'

Deborah glanced at Strike's left ear, then back at her hot chocolate.

'You're like Tudor,' she said. 'You know what's what. He probably did,' she added placidly.

'You mean,' said Strike carefully, 'he told people about it?'

She didn't answer.

'. . . or you think he killed the doctor?'

'Was My-Dad-Gwilherm doing magic on her?' Samhain enquired of his mother. 'My-Dad-Gwilherm didn't kill that lady. My uncle Tudor told me what really happened.'

'What did your uncle tell you?' asked Strike, turning from

mother to son, but Samhain had just crammed his mouth full of chocolate biscuit, so Deborah continued the story.

'He woke me up one time when I was asleep,' said Deborah, 'and it was dark. He said, "I killed a lady by mistake." I said, "You've had a bad dream." He said, "No, no, I've killed her, but I didn't mean it."'

'Woke you up to tell you, did he?'

'Woke me up, all upset.'

'But you think it was just a bad dream?'

'Yes,' said Deborah, but then, after a moment or two, she said, 'but maybe he did kill her, because he could do magic.'

'I see,' said Strike untruthfully, turning back to Samhain. 'What did your Uncle Tudor say happened to the lady doctor?'

'I can't tell you that,' said Samhain, suddenly grinning. 'Uncle Tudor said not to tell. Never.' But he grinned with a Puckish delight at having a secret. 'My-Dad-Gwilherm did that,' he went on, pointing at the ankh on the wall.

'Yes,' said Strike, 'your mum told me.'

'I don't like it,' said Deborah placidly, looking at the ankh. 'I'd like it if the walls were all the same.'

'I like it,' said Samhain, 'because it's different from the other walls . . . you silly woman,' he added abstractedly.

'Did Uncle Tudor—' began Strike, but Samhain, who'd finished his biscuit, now got to his feet and left the room, pausing in the doorway to say loudly,

'Clare says it's nice I still got things of Gwilherm's!'

He disappeared into his bedroom and closed the door firmly behind him. With the feeling he'd just seen a gold sovereign bounce down a grate, Strike turned back to Deborah.

'Do *you* know what Tudor said happened to the doctor?'

She shook her head, uninterested. Strike looked hopefully back towards Samhain's bedroom door. It remained closed.

'Can you remember *how* Gwilherm thought he'd killed the doctor?' he asked Deborah.

'He said his magic killed her, then took her away.'

'Took her away, did it?'

Samhain's bedroom door suddenly opened again and he trudged back into the room, holding a coverless book in his hand.

'Deborah, is this My-Dad-Gwilherm's magic book, is it?'

'That's it,' said Deborah.

She'd finished her hot chocolate, now. Setting down the empty mug, she picked up her crochet again.

Samhain held the book wordlessly out to Strike. Though the cover had come off, the title page was intact: *The Magus* by Francis Barrett. Strike had the impression that being shown this book was a mark of esteem, and he therefore flicked through it with an expression of deep interest, his main objective to keep Samhain happy and close at hand for further questioning.

A few pages inside was a brown smear. Strike halted the cascade of pages to examine it more closely. It was, he suspected, dried blood, and had been wiped across a few lines of writing.

> This I will say more, to wit, that those who walk in their sleep, do, by no other guide than the spirit of the blood, that is, of the outward man, walk up and down, perform business, climb walls and manage things that are otherwise impossible to those that are awake.

'You can do magic, with that book,' said Samhain. 'But it's my book, because it was My-Dad-Gwilherm's, so it's mine now,' and he held out his hand before Strike could examine it any further, suddenly jealous of his possession. When Strike handed it back, Samhain clutched the book to his chest with one hand and bent to take a third chocolate biscuit.

'No more, Sammy,' said Deborah.

'I went in the rain and got them,' said Samhain loudly. 'I can have what I want. Silly woman. *Stupid* woman.'

He kicked the ottoman, but it hurt his bare foot, and this increased his sudden, childish anger. Pink-faced and truculent, he looked around the room: Strike suspected he was looking for something to disarrange, or perhaps break. His choice landed on the budgies.

'I'll open the cage,' he threatened his mother, pointing at it. He let *The Magus* fall onto the sofa as he clambered onto the seat, looming over Strike.

'No, don't,' said Deborah, immediately distressed. 'Don't do that, Sammy!'

'And I'll open the window,' said Samhain, now trying to walk his way along the sofa seats, but blocked by Strike. 'Hahaha. You stupid woman.'

'No – Samhain, don't!' said Deborah, frightened.

'You don't want to open the cage,' said Strike, standing up and moving in front of it. 'You wouldn't want your budgies to fly away. They won't come back.'

'I know they won't,' said Samhain. 'The last ones didn't.'

His anger seemed to subside as fast as it had come, in the face of rational opposition. Still standing on the sofa, he said grumpily, 'I went out in the rain. I got them.'

'Have you got Clare's phone number?' Strike asked Deborah.

'In the kitchen,' she said, without asking why he wanted it.

'Can you show me where that is?' Strike asked Samhain, although he knew perfectly well. The whole flat was as big as Irene Hickson's sitting room. Samhain frowned at Strike's midriff for a few moments, then said,

'All right, then.'

He walked the length of the sofa, jumped off the end with a crash that made the bookcase shake, and then lunged for the biscuits.

'Hahaha,' he taunted his mother, both hands full of Penguins. 'I got them. Silly woman. *Stupid* woman.'

He walked out of the room.

As Strike inched back out of the space between ottoman and sofa, he stooped to pick up *The Magus*, which Samhain had dropped, and slid it under his coat. Crocheting peacefully by the window, Deborah Athorn noticed nothing.

A short list of names and numbers was attached to the kitchen wall with a drawing pin. Strike was pleased to see that several people seemed interested in Deborah and Samhain's welfare.

'Who're these people?' he asked, but Samhain shrugged and Strike was confirmed in his suspicion that Samhain couldn't read, no matter how proud he was of *The Magus*. He took a photo of the list with his phone, then turned to Samhain.

'It would really help me if you could remember what your Uncle Tudor said happened to the lady doctor.'

'Hahaha,' said Samhain, who was unwrapping another Penguin. 'I'm not telling.'

'Your Uncle Tudor must have really trusted you, to tell you.'

Samhain chewed in silence for a while, then swallowed and said, with a proud little upwards jerk of the chin, 'Yer.'

'It's good to have people you can trust with important information.'

Samhain seemed pleased with this statement. He ate his biscuit and, for the first time, glanced at Strike's face. The detective had the impression that Samhain was enjoying another man's presence in the flat.

'I did that,' he said suddenly and, walking to the sink, he

picked up a small clay pot, which was holding a washing-up brush and a sponge. 'I go to class on Tuesdays and we make stuff. Ranjit teaches us.'

'That's excellent,' said Strike, taking it from him and examining it. 'Where were you, when your uncle told you what happened to Dr Bamborough?'

'At the football,' said Samhain. 'And I made this,' he told Strike, prising a wooden photo frame off the fridge, where it had been attached with a magnet. The framed picture was a recent one of Deborah and Samhain, both of whom had a budgerigar perched on their finger.

'That's very good,' said Strike, admiring it.

'Yer,' said Samhain, taking it back from him and slapping it on the fridge. 'Ranjit said it was the best one. We were at the football and I heard Uncle Tudor telling his friend.'

'Ah,' said Strike.

'And then he said to me, "Don't you tell no one."'

'Right,' said Strike. 'But if you tell me, I can maybe help the doctor's family. They're really sad. They miss her.'

Samhain cast another fleeting look at Strike's face.

'She can't come back now. People can't be alive again when they're dead.'

'No,' said Strike. 'But it's nice when their families know what happened and where they went.'

'My-Dad-Gwilherm died under the bridge.'

'Yes.'

'My Uncle Tudor died in the hospital.'

'You see?' said Strike. 'It's good you know, isn't it?'

'Yer,' said Samhain. 'I know what happened.'

'Exactly.'

'Uncle Tudor told me it was Nico and his boys done it.'

It came out almost indifferently.

'You can tell her family,' said Samhain, 'but nobody else.'

'Right,' said Strike, whose mind was working very fast. 'Did Tudor know how Nico and the boys did it?'

'No. He just knew they did.'

Samhain picked up another biscuit. He appeared to have no more to say.

'Er – can I use your bathroom?'

'The bog?' said Samhain, with his mouth full of chocolate.

'Yes. The bog,' said Strike.

Like the rest of the flat, the bathroom was old but perfectly clean. It was papered in green, with a pattern of pink flamingos on it, which doubtless dated from the seventies and now, forty years later, was fashionably kitsch. Strike opened the bathroom cabinet, found a pack of razor blades, extracted one and cut the blood-stained page of *The Magus* out with one smooth stroke, then folded it and slipped it in his pocket.

Out on the landing, he handed Samhain the book back.

'You left it on the floor.'

'Oh,' said Samhain. 'Ta.'

'You won't do anything to the budgies if I leave, will you?'

Samhain looked up at the ceiling, grinning slightly.

'*Will* you?' asked Strike.

'No,' sighed Samhain at last.

Strike returned to the doorway of the sitting room.

'I'll be off now, Mrs Athorn,' he said. 'Thanks very much for talking to me.'

'Goodbye,' said Deborah, without looking at him.

Strike headed downstairs, and let himself back onto the street. Once outside, he stood for a moment in the rain, thinking hard. So unusually still was he, that a passing woman turned to stare back at him.

Reaching a decision, Strike turned left, and entered the ironmonger's which lay directly below the Athorns' flat.

A sullen, grizzled and aproned man behind the counter

looked up at Strike's entrance. One of his eyes was larger than the other, which gave him an oddly malevolent appearance.

'Morning,' said Strike briskly. 'I've just come from the Athorns, upstairs. I gather you want to talk to Clare Spencer?'

'Who're you?' asked the ironmonger, with a mixture of surprise and aggression.

'Friend of the family,' said Strike. 'Can I ask why you're putting letters to their social worker through their front door?'

'Because they don't pick up their phones at the bloody social work department,' snarled the ironmonger. 'And there's no point talking to *them*, is there?' he added, pointing his finger at the ceiling.

'Is there a problem I can help with?'

'I doubt it,' said the ironmonger shortly. 'You're probably feeling pretty bloody pleased with the situation, are you, if you're a friend of the family? Nobody has to put their hand in their pocket except me, eh? Quick bit of a cover-up and let someone else foot the bill, eh?'

'What cover-up would this be?' asked Strike.

The ironmonger was only too willing to explain. The flat upstairs, he told Strike, had long been a health risk, crammed with the hoarded belongings of many years and a magnet for vermin, and in a just world, it ought not to be *he* who was bearing the costs of living beneath a pair of actual morons—

'You're talking about friends of mine,' said Strike.

'*You* do it, then,' snarled the ironmonger. '*You* pay a bleeding fortune to keep the rats down. My ceiling's sagging under the weight of their filth—'

'I've just been upstairs and it's perfectly—'

'Because they mucked it out last month, when I said I was going to bloody court!' snarled the ironmonger. 'Cousins come down from Leeds when I threaten legal action – nobody give a shit until then – and I come back Monday morning and they've cleaned it all up. Sneaky bastards!'

'Didn't you want the flat cleaned?'

'I want compensation for the money I've had to spend! Structural damage, bills to Rentokil – that pair shouldn't be living together without supervision, they're not fit, they should be in a home! If I have to take it to court, I will!'

'Bit of friendly advice,' said Strike, smiling. 'If you behave in any way that could be considered threatening towards the Athorns, their friends will make sure it's *you* who ends up in court. Have a nice day,' he added, heading for the door.

The fact that the Athorns' flat had recently been mucked out by helpful relatives tended to suggest that Margot Bamborough's remains weren't hidden on the premises. On the other hand, Strike had gained a bloodstain and a rumour, which was considerably more than he'd had an hour ago. While still disinclined to credit supernatural intervention, he had to admit that deciding to eat breakfast on St John Street that morning had been, at the very least, a most fortuitous choice.

39

. . . they thus beguile the way,
Vntill the blustring storme is ouerblowne . . .
They cannot finde that path, which first was showne,
But wander too and fro in waies vnknowne . . .

Edmund Spenser
The Faerie Queene

Robin's alarm went off at half past six on Friday morning, in the middle of a dream about Matthew: he'd come to her in the Earl's Court flat, and begged her to return to him, saying that he'd been a fool, promising he'd never again complain about her job, imploring her to admit that she missed what they'd once had. He'd asked her whether she honestly liked living in a rented flat, without the security and companionship of marriage, and in the dream Robin felt a pull back towards her old relationship, before it had become complicated by her job with Strike. He was a younger Matthew in the dream, a far kinder Matthew, and Sarah Shadlock was dismissed as a mistake, a blip, a meaningless error. In the background hovered Robin's flatmate, no longer the disengaged and courteous Max, but a pale, simpering girl who echoed Matthew's persuasions, who giggled when he looked at her and urged Robin to give him what he wanted. Only when she'd managed to silence her alarm, and dispel the fog of sleep, did Robin, who was lying face down on her pillow, realise how closely the dream-flatmate had resembled Cynthia Phipps.

Struggling to understand why she'd set her alarm so early, she sat up in bed, the cream walls of her bedroom a blueish mauve in the dawn light, then remembered that Strike had planned a full team meeting, the first in two months, and that he'd asked her to come in an hour earlier than the others again, so that they could discuss the Bamborough case before everyone else got there.

Extremely tired, as she always seemed to be these days, Robin showered and dressed, fumbling over buttons, forgetting where she'd put her phone, realising there was a stain on her sweater only when halfway upstairs to the kitchen and generally feeling disgruntled at life and early starts. When she reached the upper floor, she found Max sitting at the dining table in his dressing gown, poring over a cookbook. The TV was on: the breakfast television presenter was asking whether Valentine's Day was an exercise in commercial cynicism or an opportunity to inject some much-needed romance into a couple's life.

'Has Cormoran got any special dietary requirements?' Max asked her, and when Robin looked blank, he said, 'For tonight. Dinner.'

'Oh,' said Robin, 'no. He'll eat anything.'

She checked her emails on her phone as she drank a mug of black coffee. With a small stab of dread, she saw one from her lawyer titled 'Mediation'. Opening it, she saw that an actual date was being proposed: Wednesday March the nineteenth, over a month away. She pictured Matthew talking to his own lawyer, consulting his diary, asserting his power, as ever. *I'm tied up for the whole of next month.* Then she imagined facing him across a boardroom table, their lawyers beside them, and felt panic mixed with rage.

'You should eat breakfast,' said Max, still reading cookbooks.

'I'll get something later,' said Robin, closing her email.

She picked up the coat she'd left draped over the arm of the sofa and said,

'Max, you haven't forgotten my brother and his friend are spending the weekend, have you? I doubt they'll be around much. It's just a base.'

'No, no, all good,' said Max vaguely, lost in recipes.

Robin headed out into the cool, damp early morning, getting all the way to the Tube before she realised that she didn't have her purse on her.

'*Shit!*'

Robin was usually tidy, efficient and organised; she rarely made this kind of mistake. Hair flying, she ran back to the flat, asking herself what the hell she could have done with it, and wondering, now panicking, whether she'd dropped it in the street or had it stolen out of her bag.

Meanwhile, in Denmark Street, the groggy Strike was hopping on his one foot out of the shower, eyes puffy, and similarly exhausted. The after-effects of a week spent covering Barclay's and Hutchins's shifts were now catching up with him, and he slightly regretted having asked Robin to come into work so early.

However, just after pulling on his trousers, his mobile rang and with a stab of fear, he saw Ted and Joan's number.

'Ted?'

'Hi, Corm. There's no need to panic, now,' said Ted. 'I just wanted to give you an update.'

'Go on,' said Strike, standing bare-chested and frozen in the cold grey light filtered by the too-thin curtains of his attic flat.

'She's not looking too clever. Kerenza was talking about trying to get her to hospital, but Joanie doesn't want to go. She's still in bed, she – didn't get up, yesterday,' said Ted, his voice cracking. 'Couldn't manage it.'

'Shit,' muttered Strike, sinking down onto his bed. 'Right, Ted, I'm coming.'

'You can't,' said his uncle. 'We're surrounded by flood water. It's dangerous. Police are telling everyone to stay put, not to travel. Kerenza can . . . she says she can manage her pain at home. She's got drugs they can inject . . . because she's not eating a lot now. Kerenza doesn't think it's . . . you know . . . she thinks it'll be . . . '

He began to cry in earnest.

' . . . not immediate, but . . . she says . . . not long.'

'I'm coming,' said Strike firmly. 'Does Lucy know how bad Joan is?'

'I called you first,' said Ted.

'I'll tell her, don't worry about that. I'll ring you when we've put a plan together, all right?'

Strike hung up and called Lucy.

'Oh God, no,' his sister gasped, when he'd given her an unemotional summary of what Ted had said. 'Stick, I can't leave right now – Greg's stuck in Wales!'

'The hell's Greg doing in Wales?'

'It's for work – oh God, what are we going to do?'

'When's Greg back?'

'Tomorrow night.'

'Then we'll go down Sunday morning.'

'How? The trains are all off, the roads are flooded—'

'I'll hire a jeep or something. Polworth'll meet us the other end with a boat if we have to. I'll ring you back when I've got things sorted.'

Strike dressed, made himself tea and toast, carried them downstairs to the partners' desk in the inner office and called Ted back, overriding his objections, telling him that, like it or not, he and Lucy were coming on Sunday. He could hear his uncle's yearning for them, his desperate need for company to share the burden of dread and grief. Strike then called Dave Polworth, who thoroughly approved of the plan and promised to be ready with boat, tow ropes and scuba equipment if necessary.

'I've got fuck all else to do. My place of work's underwater.'

Strike called a few car hire companies, finally finding one that had a jeep available. He was giving his credit card details when a text arrived from Robin.

Really sorry, I lost my purse, just found it, on my way now.

Strike had entirely forgotten that they were supposed to be catching up on the Bamborough case before the team meeting. Having finished hiring the jeep, he began to assemble the items he'd intended to discuss with Robin: the blood-smeared page he'd cut out of *The Magus*, which he'd now put into a plastic pouch, and the discovery he'd made the previous evening on his computer, which he brought up on his monitor, ready to show her.

He then opened up the rota, to check what shifts he'd have to reallocate now that he was heading back to Cornwall, and saw 'Dinner with Max' written in for that evening.

'*Bollocks*,' he said. He didn't suppose he could get out of it now, having agreed to it the previous day, but this was the last thing he needed.

At that very moment, Robin, who was climbing the escalator at Tottenham Court Road two steps at a time, heard her mobile ringing in her bag.

'Yes?' she gasped into the phone, as she emerged into the station, one among many bustling commuters.

'Hey, Robs,' said her younger brother.

'Hi,' she said, using her Oyster card at the barrier. 'Everything OK?'

'Yeah, fine,' said Jonathan, though he didn't sound quite as cheerful as the last time they'd spoken. 'Listen, is it all right if I bring another guy with me to crash at yours?'

'What?' said Robin, as she emerged into the blustery rain and controlled chaos of the intersection of Tottenham Court Road and Charing Cross Road, at which there had now been building works for three and a half years. She hoped she'd misheard what Jonathan had said.

'Another guy,' he repeated. 'Is that OK? He'll sleep anywhere.'

'Oh Jon,' Robin moaned, half-jogging along Charing Cross Road now, 'we've only got one sofa bed.'

'Kyle'll sleep on the floor, he doesn't care,' said Jonathan. 'It's not that big a deal is it? One more person?'

'OK, fine,' sighed Robin. 'You're still planning on getting here at ten, though?'

'I'm not sure. We might get an earlier train, we're thinking of skipping lectures.'

'Yeah, but the thing is,' said Robin, 'Cormoran's coming over to dinner to talk to Max—'

'Oh great!' said Jonathan, sounding slightly more enthusiastic. 'Courtney'd love to meet him, she's obsessed with crime!'

'No – Jon, I'm trying to tell you, Max needs to interview Cormoran about a part he's playing. I don't think there'll be enough food for another three—'

'Don't worry about that, if we get there earlier, we'll just order ourselves a takeaway.'

How was she supposed to say, 'Please don't come during dinner'? After he'd hung up, Robin broke into a jog, hoping that Jonathan's time management, which she knew from experience could use improvement, might see him miss enough trains south to delay his arrival.

Taking the corner into Denmark Street at a run, she saw,

with a sinking feeling, Saul Morris ahead of her, walking towards the office and carrying a small, wrapped bunch of pink gerberas.

They'd better not be for me.

'Hey, Robs,' he said, turning as she ran up behind him. 'Oh dear,' he added, grinning, 'someone overslept. Pillow face,' he said, pointing at the spot on his cheek where, Robin surmised, her own still bore a faint crease from the way she'd slept, face down and unmoving, because she was so tired. 'For Pat,' he added, displaying his straight white teeth along with the gerberas. 'Says her husband never gets her anything on Valentine's.'

God, you're smarmy, Robin thought, as she unlocked the door. She noticed that he was calling her 'Robs' again, yet another sign that his discomfort in her presence post-Christmas had evaporated over the succeeding seven weeks. She wished she could as easily shrug off the lingering, unreasonable but no less potent sense of shame she felt, forever having seen his erection on her phone.

Upstairs, the harassed Strike was checking his watch when his mobile rang. It was unusually early for his old friend Nick Herbert to be calling him, and Strike, now sensitised to expect bad news, picked up with a sense of foreboding.

'All right, Oggy?'

Nick sounded hoarse, as though he'd been shouting.

'I'm fine,' said Strike, who thought he could hear footsteps and voices on the metal stairs outside. 'What's up?'

'Nothing much,' said Nick. 'Wondered whether you fancied a pint tonight. Just you and me.'

'Can't,' said Strike, very much regretting that this was so. 'Sorry, I've got something on.'

'Ah,' said Nick. 'OK. What about lunchtime, you free then?'

'Yeah, why not?' said Strike, after a slight hesitation. God knew he could use a pint away from work, from family, from his hundred other problems.

Through the open door he saw Robin enter the outer office, followed by Saul Morris, who was holding a bunch of flowers. He closed the dividing door on them, then his tired brain processed the flowers and the date.

'Hang on. Aren't you busy with Valentine's shit?' he asked Nick.

'Not this year,' said Nick.

There was a short silence. Strike had always considered Nick and Ilsa, a gastroenterologist and a lawyer respectively, the happiest couple he knew. Their house on Octavia Street had often been a place of refuge to him.

'I'll explain over a pint,' said Nick. 'I need one. I'll come to you.'

They agreed a pub and a time and rang off. Strike checked his watch again: he and Robin had fifteen minutes left of what he'd hoped would be an hour on Bamborough. Opening the door, he said,

'Ready? We haven't got long.'

'Sorry,' said Robin, hurrying inside. 'You got my text, didn't you? About the purse?'

'Yeah,' said Strike, closing the door on Morris and pointing at the page from *The Magus*, which he'd laid in front of Robin's seat. 'That's the page from the book in the Athorns' house.'

He'd called Robin about finding the Athorns straight after leaving the ironmonger, and she'd responded with excitement and congratulations. His present grumpiness aggravated her. Presumably it was due to her lateness, but was she not allowed a little human fallibility, after all the extra hours she'd put in lately, covering her own work and Strike's, managing the subcontractors, trying as hard as she could not to put extra stress on him when his aunt was dying? However, outside she could hear Barclay and Hutchins entering the outer office, which reminded her that not so very long ago, she'd been the temp, that Strike had laid down his expectations of a partner in uncompromising terms at the start of their professional relationship. There were three men outside who undoubtedly considered themselves better qualified for her position than she was. So, Robin simply sat down, picked up the page and read the passage beneath the smear.

'The writing mentions blood.'

'I know.'

'How fresh does blood have to be, to analyse?'

'The oldest sample I've heard of that was successfully analysed was twenty-something years old,' said Strike. 'If this is blood, and it dates from when Gwilherm Athorn was alive, it's a good decade older. On the other hand, it's been kept away from light and damp, inside that book, which might help. Anyway, I'm going to call Roy Phipps and ask him what Margot's blood group was and then I'll try and find someone to analyse it for us. Might try that bloke your friend Vanessa used to date in forensics, what was his name?'

'Oliver,' said Robin, 'and he's now her fiancé.'

'Well, him, yeah. One other interesting thing came out of my conversation with Samhain . . . '

He told her about Uncle Tudor's belief that 'Nico and his boys' had killed Margot Bamborough.

'"Nico" – d'you think—?'

'Niccolo "Mucky" Ricci? Odds on,' said Strike. 'He wasn't living far away and he must've been a local personality, although no one from the practice seems to have realised who'd walked into their Christmas party.

'I've left a message with the Athorns' social worker, because I want to know how much store we can put in Deborah and Samhain's memories. Shanker's supposed to be digging around on Ricci for me, but I've heard sod all from him. Might give him a prod.'

He held out his hand and Robin passed the blood-smeared page back.

'Anyway, the only other development is that I've found C. B. Oakden,' said Strike.

'What? How?'

'Last night,' said Strike. 'I was thinking about names. Irene getting them wrong – Douthwaite and Duckworth, Athorn and Applethorpe. Then I started thinking about how people often don't stray too far from their original name if they change it.'

He swung his computer monitor around to face her, and Robin saw a picture of a man in early middle age. He was slightly freckled, his eyes fractionally too close together and his hair thinning, though he still had enough to sweep across his narrow forehead. He was still just recognisable as the boy screwing up his face at the camera, at Margot Bamborough's barbecue.

The story below read:

SERIAL SWINDLER GETS JAIL SENTENCE

'Despicable Betrayal of Trust'

A serial fraudster who conned over £75,000 from elderly widows over a two-year period has been jailed for four years, nine months.

Brice Noakes, 49, of Fortune Street, Clerkenwell, who was born Carl Oaken, persuaded a total of nine 'vulnerable and trusting women' to part with jewellery and cash, which in one case amounted to £30,000 of life savings.

Noakes was described by Lord Justice McCrieff as 'a cunning and unscrupulous man who capitalised shamelessly on his victims' vulnerability.'

Smartly dressed and well-spoken Noakes targeted widows living alone, usually offering valuations on jewellery. Noakes persuaded his victims to allow him to remove valuable items from their houses, promising to return with an expert assessment.

On other occasions he posed as a representative from the council, who claimed that the householder was in arrears with council tax and about to be prosecuted.

'Using plausible but entirely fraudulent paperwork, you pressured and bullied vulnerable women into transferring money into an account set up for your own benefit,' said Lord Justice McCrieff, while sentencing.

'Some of the women concerned were initially too embarrassed to tell their families that they'd let this individual into their homes,' said Chief Inspector Grant. 'We believe there may be many more victims who are too ashamed to admit that they've been defrauded, and we would urge them, if they recognise Noakes' picture, to contact us.'

'The paper's misspelled his real name,' said Robin. 'They've printed "Oaken", not Oakden.'

'Which is why he wouldn't have shown up on a basic Google search,' said Strike.

Feeling subtly criticised, because she was the one who was supposed to be looking for Oakden, Robin glanced at the date on the news story, which was five years old.

'He'll be out of jail by now.'

'He is,' said Strike, turning the monitor back towards himself, typing another couple of words and turning it to face Robin again. 'I did a bit more searching on variations of his name, and . . . '

She saw an author page of the Amazon website, listing the books written by an author called Carl O. Brice. The photograph showed the same man from the newspaper, a little older, a little balder, a little more creased around the eyes. His thumbs hooked in his jeans pockets, he wore a black T-shirt with a white logo on it: a clenched fist inside the Mars symbol.

Carl O. Brice

Carl O. Brice is a life coach, entrepreneur and award-winning writer on men's issues including masculism, fathers' rights, gynocentrism, men's mental health, female privilege and toxic feminism. Carl's personal experience of the gynocentric family court system, cultural misandry and male exploitation give him the tools and skills to guide men from all walks of life to healthier, happier lives. In his award-winning book series, Carl examines the catastrophic impact that modern feminism has had on freedom of speech, the workplace, men's rights and the nuclear family.

Robin glanced down the list of books beneath the author biography. The covers were cheap and amateurish. All featured pictures of women in various slightly pornified costumes and poses. A scantily dressed blonde wearing a crown was sitting on a throne for *From Courtly Love to Family Courts, A History of Gynocentrism*, whereas a brunette dressed in a rubber stormtrooper outfit pointed at the camera for *Shamed: The Modern War on Masculinity*.

'He's got his own website,' said Strike, turning the monitor back to himself. 'He self-publishes books, offers to coach men on how to get access to their kids, and flogs protein shakes and vitamins. I don't think he'll pass up the chance to talk to us. He seems the type to come running at the sniff of notoriety or money.

'Speaking of which,' said Strike, 'how're you getting on with that woman who thinks she saw Margot at the window on—?'

'Amanda Laws,' said Robin. 'Well, I went back to her offering her expenses if she'll come into the office, and she hasn't answered yet.'

'Well, chase her,' said Strike. 'You realise we're now six months in—?'

'Yes, I do realise that,' said Robin, unable to help herself. 'I learned counting at school.'

Strike raised his eyebrows.

'Sorry,' she muttered. 'I'm just tired.'

'Well, so am I, but I'm also mindful of the fact we still haven't traced some fairly important people yet. Satchwell, for instance.'

'I'm working on him,' said Robin, glancing at her watch and getting to her feet. 'I think they're all out there, waiting for us.'

'Why's Morris brought flowers?' said Strike.

'They're for Pat. For Valentine's Day.'

'Why the hell?'

Robin paused at the door, looking back at Strike.

'Isn't it obvious?'

She let herself out of the room, leaving Strike to frown after her, wondering what was obvious. He could imagine only two reasons to buy a woman flowers: because you were hoping to sleep with her, or to avoid being criticised for not buying flowers on a day when flowers might be expected. Neither seemed to apply in this case.

The team was sitting in a cramped circle outside, Hutchins and Barclay on the fake leather sofa, Morris on one of the fold-up plastic chairs that had been bought when the team outgrew the existing seats, and Pat on her own wheeled desk chair, which left another two uncomfortable plastic chairs for the partners. Robin noticed how all three men stopped talking when Strike emerged from the inner office: when she'd led the meeting alone, she'd had to wait until Hutchins and Morris finished discussing a mutual police acquaintance who'd been caught taking bribes.

The bright pink daisy-like gerberas sat in a small vase on Pat's desk now. Strike glanced at them before saying,

'All right, let's start with Shifty. Morris, did you get anywhere with that bloke in the tracksuit?'

'Yeah, I did,' said Morris, consulting his notes. 'His name's Barry Fisher. He's divorced with one kid and he's a manager at Shifty's gym.'

Appreciative, low-toned growls of approval and interest issued from Strike, Barclay and Hutchins. Robin contented herself with a slight eyebrow raise. It was her experience that the slightest hint of warmth or approval from her was interpreted by Morris as an invitation to flirtation.

'So, I've booked myself in for a trial session with one of their trainers,' said Morris.

Bet it's with a woman, thought Robin.

'While I was talking to her, I saw him wandering about talking to some of the other girls. He's definitely hetero, judging by how he was looking at one of the women on the cross-trainer. I'm going back Monday for a workout, if that's all right with you, boss. Try and find out more about him.'

'Fine,' said Strike. 'Well, this looks like our first solid lead: a link between Shifty and whatever's going on inside Elinor Dean's house.'

Robin, who'd spent the night before last sitting in her Land Rover outside Elinor's house, said,

'It might not be relevant, but Elinor took an Amazon delivery yesterday morning. Two massive boxes. They looked quite light, but—'

'We should open a book,' Morris told Strike, talking over Robin. 'Twenty on dominatrix.'

'Never seen the appeal in bein' whipped,' said Barclay thoughtfully. 'If I want pain, I jus' forget to put the bins oot.'

'Bit mumsy-looking, though, isn't she?' said Hutchins. 'If I had SB's money, I'd go for something a bit more—'

He sketched a slimmer figure in mid-air. Morris laughed.

'Ach, there's no accountin' for taste,' said Barclay. 'Army mate o' mine wouldnae look at anythin' under thirteen stone. We usedtae call him the Pork Whisperer.'

The men laughed. Robin smiled, mainly because Barclay was looking at her, and she liked Barclay, but she felt too tired and demoralised to be truly amused. Pat was wearing a 'boys will be boys' expression of bored tolerance.

'Unfortunately, I've got to go back to Cornwall on Sunday,' said Strike, 'which I appreciate—'

'The fuck are ye gonna get tae Cornwall?' asked Barclay, as the office windows shook with the wind.

'Jeep,' said Strike. 'My aunt's dying. Looks like she's got days.'

Robin looked at Strike, startled.

'I appreciate that leaves us stretched,' Strike continued matter-of-factly, 'but it can't be helped. I think it's worth continuing to keep an eye on SB himself. Morris'll do some digging with this bloke at the gym and the rest of you can divvy up shifts on Elinor Dean. Unless anyone's got anything to add,' said Strike, pausing for comments. The men all shook their heads and Robin, too tired to mention the Amazon boxes again, remained silent. 'Let's have a look at Postcard.'

'I've got news,' said Barclay laconically. 'She's back at work. I've talked tae her. Yer woman,' he added, to Robin, 'short. Big round glasses. Ambled over and started askin' questions.'

'What about?' asked Morris, a smirk playing around his lips.

'Light effects in the landscapes o' James Duffield Harding,' said Barclay. 'What d'ye think I asked, who she fancied for the Champions League?'

Strike laughed, and so did Robin, this time, glad to see Morris looking foolish.

'Yeah, I read the notice by his portrait an' looked him up on my phone round the corner,' said Barclay. 'Wanted a way o' gettin' ontae the subject o' weather wi' her. Anyway,' said the Glaswegian, 'coupla minutes intae the conversation, talkin' light effects an' broodin' skies an' that, she brought up oor weatherman friend. Turned pink when she mentioned him. Said he'd described a viewer's picture as "Turneresque" last week.

'It's her,' said Barclay, addressing Robin. 'She wanted tae mention him for the pleasure of sayin' his name. She's Postcard.'

'Bloody well done,' Strike told Barclay.

'It's Robin's win,' said Barclay. 'She made the pass. I jus' tapped it in.'

'Thanks, Sam,' said Robin, pointedly, not looking at Strike, who registered both the tone and her expression.

'Fair point,' said Strike, 'well done, both of you.'

Aware that he'd been short with Robin during their meeting about the Bamborough case, Strike sought to make amends by asking her opinion on which of the waiting list clients they ought to contact, now that the Postcard case was as good as wrapped up, and she said she thought the commodities broker who thought her husband was sleeping with their nanny.

'Great,' said Strike. 'Pat, can you get in touch and tell her we're ready to roll if she still wants him under surveillance? If nobody's got anything else—'

'I have,' said Hutchins, generally the quietest person in the agency. 'It's about that roll of film you wanted passed to the Met.'

'Oh yeah?' said Strike. 'Is there news?'

'My mate rang last night. There's nothing to be done with it. You won't get any prosecutions now.'

'Why not?' said Robin.

She sounded angrier than she'd meant to. The men all looked at her.

'Perpetrators' faces all hidden,' said Hutchins. 'That arm that appears for a moment: you can't build a prosecution case on an out-of-focus ring.'

'I thought your contact said the roll had come out of a raid on one of Mucky Ricci's brothels?' said Robin.

'He *thinks* it did,' Hutchins corrected her. 'You won't get DNA evidence off a can that old, that's been kept in a shed and an attic and handled by a hundred people. It's a no-go. Shame,' he said indifferently, 'but there you are.'

Strike now heard his mobile ringing back on the partners' desk, where he'd left it. Worried it might be Ted, he excused himself from the meeting and retreated into the inner office, closing the door behind him.

There was no caller ID on the number ringing his mobile.

'Cormoran Strike.'

'Hello, Cormoran,' said an unfamiliar, husky voice. 'It's Jonny.'

There was a brief silence.

'Your father,' Rokeby added.

Strike, whose tired mind was full of Joan, of the agency's three open cases, of guilt about being grumpy with his partner, and the logistical demands he was placing on his employees by disappearing to Cornwall again, said nothing at all. Through the dividing door, he could hear the team still discussing the roll of film.

'Wanted a chat,' said Rokeby. 'Is that all right?'

Strike felt suddenly disembodied; completely detached from everything, from the office, from his fatigue, from the concerns that had seemed all-important just seconds ago. It was as though he and his father's voice existed alone and nothing else was fully real, except Strike's adrenalin, and a primal desire to leave a mark that Rokeby wouldn't quickly forget.

'I'm listening,' he said.

Another silence.

'Look,' said Rokeby, sounding slightly uneasy, 'I don't wanna do this by phone. Let's meet. It's been too fucking long. Water under the bridge. Let's meet, let's . . . I wanna – this can't go on. This fucking – feud, or whatever it is.'

Strike said nothing.

'Come to the house,' said Rokeby. 'Come over. Let's talk, and . . . you're not a kid any more. There are two sides to every story. Nothing's black and white.'

He paused. Strike still said nothing.

'I'm proud of you, d'you know that?' said Rokeby. 'I'm really fucking proud of you. What you've done and . . . '

The sentence petered out. Strike stared, motionless, at the blank wall in front of him. Beyond the partition wall, Pat was laughing at something Morris had said.

'Look,' repeated Rokeby, with just a tiny hint of temper now, because he was a man used to getting his own way. 'I get it, I do, but what the fuck can I do? I can't time travel. Al's told me what you've been saying, and there's a bunch of stuff you don't know, about your mother and all her fucking men. If you just come over, we can have a drink, we can have it all out. And,' said Rokeby, quietly insinuating, 'maybe I can help you out a bit, maybe there's something you want I can help out with, peace offering, I'm open to suggestions ... '

In the outer office, Hutchins and Barclay were taking their leave, ready to get back to their separate jobs. Robin was thinking only about how much she wanted to go home. She was supposed to have the rest of the day off, but Morris was hanging around, and she was sure he was waiting because he wanted to walk with her to the Tube. Pretending to have paperwork to look at, she was rifling through a filing cabinet while Morris and Pat chatted, hoping he'd leave. She'd just opened an old file on a prolific adulterer, when Strike's voice filled the room from the inner office. She, Pat and Morris turned their heads. Several pages of the file Robin was balancing on top of the drawer slid to the floor.

'... so GO FUCK YOURSELF!'

Before Robin could exchange looks with Morris or Pat, the dividing door between inner and outer offices opened. Strike looked alarming: white, livid, his breath coming fast. He stormed through the outer office, grabbed his coat and could be heard heading down the metal staircase outside.

Robin picked up the fallen pages.

'Shit,' said Morris, grinning. 'Wouldn't have wanted to be on the end of *that* call.'

'Nasty temper,' said Pat, who looked weirdly satisfied. 'Knew it, the moment I laid eyes on him.'

40

Thus as they words amongst them multiply,
They fall to strokes, the frute of too much talke . . .

Edmund Spenser
The Faerie Queene

Robin found no polite way of avoiding walking to the Tube with Morris and in consequence was obliged to listen to two off-colour jokes, and to lie about her Valentine's plans, because she could just imagine Morris's response if she told him Strike was coming over. Pretending that she hadn't heard or registered Morris's suggestion that they should get together one night to compare notes on lawyers, she parted from him at the bottom of the escalator with relief.

Tired and mildly depressed, Robin's thoughts lingered on Morris as the Tube sped her back towards Earl's Court. Was he so used to women responding readily to his undeniable handsomeness that he took it for granted he was eliciting a positive response? Or did the fault lie in Robin herself, who, for the sake of politeness, for the cohesion of the team, because she didn't want to make trouble when the agency was so busy, continued to smile at his stupid jokes and chose not to say, loudly and clearly, 'I don't like you. We're never going to date.'

She arrived home to find the flat full of the cheering and delicious smell of simmering beef and red wine. Max appeared to have gone out, but a casserole was sitting in the oven and Wolfgang was lying as close to the hot door as he could manage without burning himself, reminding Robin of fans who camped out overnight in hope of catching a glimpse of pop stars.

Instead of lying down on her bed and trying to get a few hours' sleep before dinner, Robin, who'd been stung by Strike's reminders that she hadn't chased up Amanda Laws or found Paul Satchwell, made herself more coffee, opened her laptop and sat down at the small dining table. After sending Amanda Laws another email, she opened Google. When she did so, each letter of the logo turned one by one into a pastel-coloured, heart-shaped candy with a slogan on it: MR RIGHT, PUPPY LUV and BLIND DATE, and for some reason, her thoughts moved to Charlotte Campbell. It would, of course, be very difficult for a married woman to meet her lover tonight. And who, she wondered, had Strike been telling to fuck off over the phone?

Robin set to work on Satchwell, trying to emulate Strike's success in finding C. B. Oakden. She played around with Satchwell's three names, reversing Paul and Leonard, trying initials and deliberate misspellings, but the men who appeared in answer to her searches didn't look promising.

Was it possible that Margot's tight-jeaned, hairy-chested artist had turned, over the space of four decades, into classic car collector Leo Satchwell, a rotund man with a goatee who wore tinted glasses? Unlikely, Robin decided, after wasting ten minutes on Leo: judging by the photographs on his Facebook page, in which he stood alongside other enthusiasts, he was barely five feet tall. There was a Brian Satchwell in Newport, but he had a lazy eye and was five years too young, and a Colin Satchwell in Eastbourne who ran an antiques business. She was still trying to find an image of Colin when she heard the front door open. A few minutes later, Max walked into the kitchen, with a bag of shopping in his hand.

'How's the casserole doing?' he asked.

'Great,' said Robin, who hadn't checked it.

'Get out of the way, Wolfgang, unless you want to be burned,' said Max, as he opened the oven door. To Robin's relief, the casserole appeared to be doing well, and Max shut the door again.

Robin closed her laptop. A feeling that it was rude to sit typing while someone else was cooking in her vicinity persisted from the days when she'd lived with a husband who'd always resented her bringing work home.

'Max, I'm really sorry about this, but my brother's bringing another friend with him tonight.'

'That's fine,' said Max, unpacking his shopping.

'And they might be arriving early. They aren't expecting to eat with us—'

'They're welcome. This casserole serves eight. I was going to freeze the rest, but we can eat the lot tonight, I don't mind.'

'That's really nice of you,' said Robin, 'but I know you want to talk to Cormoran alone, so I could take them—'

'No, the more the merrier,' said Max, who seemed mildly cheerful at the prospect of company. 'I told you, I've decided to give up the recluse life.'

'Oh,' said Robin. 'OK, then.'

She had some misgivings about what she feared might be quite an ill-assorted group, but telling herself her tiredness was making her pessimistic, she retired to her bedroom, where she spent the rest of the afternoon trying to find a photograph of Colin Satchwell. Finally, at six o'clock, after a great deal of cross-referencing, she located a picture on the website of a local church, where he appeared to be an alderman. Portly, with a low hairline, he in no way resembled the artist she sought.

Aware that she really ought to change and go upstairs to help Max, she was on the point of closing her laptop when a new email arrived. The subject line was one word: 'Creed', and with a spurt of nervous excitement, Robin opened it.

Hi Robin,

Quick update: I've passed the Creed request to the two people I mentioned. My Ministry of Justice contact was a bit more hopeful than I thought he'd be. This is confidential, but another family's been lobbying for Creed to be interviewed again. Their daughter was never found, but they've always believed a pendant in Creed's house belonged to her. My contact thinks something might be achievable if the Bamborough family joined forces with the Tuckers. I don't know whether Cormoran would be allowed to conduct the interview, though. That decision would be taken by the Broadmoor authorities, the Ministry of Justice and the Home Office and my MoJ contact thinks it more likely to be police. I'll let you know what's going on as soon as I hear anything else.

Best, Izzy

Robin read this email through and allowed herself a flicker of optimism, though she didn't intend to tell Strike what she was up to just yet. With luck, they'd be allowed to talk to the police interviewer before he or she went into Broadmoor. She typed an email of thanks, then began to get ready for dinner.

Her slightly improved mood survived looking in the mirror and seeing how tired she looked, with grey shadows under her slightly bloodshot eyes, and hair that definitely needed washing. Making do with dry shampoo, Robin tied back her hair, changed into clean jeans and her favourite top, applied undereye concealer and was on the point of leaving her room when her mobile rang.

Afraid that it would be Strike cancelling, she was positively relieved to see Ilsa's name.

'Hi, Ilsa!'

'Hi, Robin. Are you with Corm?'

'No,' said Robin. Instead of leaving her bedroom, she sat back down on the bed. 'Are you OK?'

Ilsa sounded odd: weak and numb.

'D'you know where Corm is?'

'No, but he should be here in ten minutes. D'you want me to give him a message?'

'No. I – d'you know whether he's been with Nick today?'

'No,' said Robin, now worried. 'What's going on, Ilsa? You sound terrible.'

Then she remembered that it was Valentine's Day and registered the fact that Ilsa didn't know where her husband was. Something more than worry overtook Robin: it was fear. Nick and Ilsa were the happiest couple she knew. The five weeks she'd lived with them after leaving Matthew had restored some of Robin's battered faith in marriage. They couldn't split up: not Nick and Ilsa.

'It's nothing,' said Ilsa.

'Tell me,' Robin insisted. 'What—?'

Wrenching sobs issued through the phone.

'Ilsa, what's happened?'

'I . . . I miscarried.'

'Oh God,' gasped Robin. 'Oh no. Ilsa, I'm so sorry.'

She knew that Nick and Ilsa had been trying for some years to have a child. Nick never talked about it and Ilsa, only rarely. Robin had had no idea she was pregnant. She suddenly remembered Ilsa not drinking, on the night of her birthday.

'It happened – in the – in the supermarket.'

'Oh no,' whispered Robin. 'Oh God.'

'I started bleeding . . . at court . . . we're in the middle of a . . . massive case . . . couldn't leave . . .' said Ilsa. 'And then . . . and then . . . heading home . . .'

She became incoherent. Tears started in Robin's eyes as she sat with the phone clamped to her ear.

' . . . knew . . . something bad . . . so I got out of the cab . . . and I went . . . into the supermarket . . . and I was in . . . the loo . . . and I felt . . . felt . . . and then . . . a little . . . blob . . . a tiny bod – bod – body . . .'

Robin put her face in her hands.

'And . . . I didn't know . . . what to do . . . but . . . there was a woman . . . in the loo with . . . and she . . . it had happened . . . to her . . . so kind . . .'

She dissolved again into incoherence. Snorts, gulps and hiccups filled Robin's ear before words became intelligible again.

'And Nick said . . . it was my fault. Said . . . all my fault . . . working . . . too hard . . . I didn't take . . . enough care . . . didn't put . . . the baby first.'

'He didn't,' said Robin. She liked Nick. She couldn't believe he'd have said such a thing to his wife.

'He did, he said I should've . . . come home . . . that I . . . put w – work . . . before the b – baby—'

'Ilsa, listen to me,' said Robin. 'If you got pregnant once, you can get pregnant again.'

'No, no, no, I can't,' said Ilsa, dissolving again into tears, 'it was our third go at IVF. We agreed . . . agreed . . . no more after this. No more.'

The doorbell rang.

'Ilsa, I've got to get the door, it might be Cormoran—'

'Yes, yes, go . . . it's fine . . . it's all fine.'

Before Robin could stop her, Ilsa had hung up. Hardly

knowing what she was doing, Robin ran downstairs and flung open the door.

But naturally, it wasn't Strike. He'd never arrived on time for any out-of-work event to which she'd invited him, whether drinks, house-warming party or even her wedding. Instead she found herself facing Jonathan, the brother who most resembled her: tall and slender, with the same strawberry blond hair and blue eyes. The resemblance was even closer this evening, because both siblings looked peaky. Jonathan, too, had shadows under his eyes, not to mention a slightly grey cast to his skin.

'Hey, Robs.'

'Hi,' said Robin, accepting Jonathan's hug and trying to act pleased to see him, 'come in.'

'This is Courtney,' said Jonathan, 'and that's Kyle.'

'Hiya,' giggled Courtney, who was holding a can. She was an exquisitely pretty girl, with large dark eyes and long black hair, and she seemed slightly tipsy. Kyle, who accidentally bashed Robin with his large rucksack on entering, was a couple of inches taller than she was, skinny, with a high-fade haircut, large, bloodshot eyes and a neatly groomed beard.

'Hi there,' he said, holding out his hand and smiling down at Robin. A stranger might have thought he was welcoming her to his flat, rather than the other way around. 'Robin, yeah?'

'Yes,' said Robin, forcing a smile. 'Lovely to meet you. Come upstairs; we're eating on the top floor.'

Lost in thoughts of Ilsa, she followed the three students. Courtney and Kyle were giggling and whispering together, Courtney a little clumsy on her feet. On reaching the living area, Robin introduced all three guests to Max, while Kyle dumped his none-too-clean rucksack on their host's cream sofa.

'Thanks very much for letting us stay,' said Jonathan to Max, who'd laid the table for six. 'Something smells really good.'

'I'm vegan,' piped up Courtney. 'But I can just eat, like, pasta, or whatever.'

'I'll do some pasta, don't you worry about that,' Robin told Max hastily, as she surreptitiously lifted Kyle's dirty rucksack off the sofa, trying not to make a big deal of what she was doing. Courtney promptly knelt on the sofa with her damp trainers still on, and said to Robin,

'Is this the sofa bed?'

Robin nodded.

'We'll have to sort out who sleeps where,' said Courtney, with a glance at Kyle. Robin thought she saw her brother's smile falter.

'Actually, why don't we put all the bags in my bedroom for now?' Robin suggested, as Jonathan swung his holdall onto the sofa, too. 'And keep this area clear for after dinner?'

Neither Courtney nor Kyle showed any inclination to move, so Robin and Jonathan took the bags downstairs together. Once they were in Robin's room, Jonathan took a box of chocolates out of his holdall and gave them to his sister.

'Thanks, Jon, that's lovely. D'you feel OK? You look a bit pale.'

'I was blunted last night. Listen, Robs . . . don't say anything to Courtney about her being, like, my girlfriend or whatever.'

'I wasn't going to.'

'Good, because . . . '

'You've split up?' Robin suggested sympathetically.

'We weren't ever – we hooked up a couple of times,' muttered Jonathan, 'but – I dunno, I think she might be into Kyle now.'

Courtney's laugh rang out from the upper floor. With a perfunctory smile at his sister, Jonathan returned to his friends.

Robin tried to call Ilsa back, but her number was engaged. Hoping this meant that she'd located Nick, Robin texted:

Just tried to call you. Please let me know what's going on. I'm worried about you. Robin xxx

She went back upstairs and started cooking pumpkin ravioli for Courtney. Apparently sensing that the casserole would soon be leaving the oven, Wolfgang slunk around Max's and Robin's ankles. Checking her watch, Robin noted that Strike was already fifteen minutes late. His record was an hour and a half. She tried, without much success, not to feel angry. After the way he'd treated her for being late this morning . . .

Robin was just draining the ravioli when the doorbell finally rang.

'D'you want me—?' said Max, who was pouring drinks for Jonathan, Courtney and Kyle.

'No, I'll do it,' said Robin shortly.

When she opened the door, she knew immediately that Strike, who was peering down at her with unfocused eyes, was drunk.

'Sorry I'm late,' he said thickly. 'Can I have a pee?'

She stood back to let him pass. He reeked of Doom Bar and cigarettes. Tense as she was, Robin noted that he hadn't thought to bring Max a bottle of anything, in spite of the fact he'd apparently spent all afternoon in the pub.

'The bathroom's there,' she said, pointing. He disappeared inside. Robin waited on the landing. He seemed to take a very long time.

'We're eating up here,' she said, when at last he emerged.

'More stairs?' mumbled Strike.

When they reached the open-plan living area, he seemed to pull himself together. He shook hands with Max and Jonathan in turn and said quite coherently that he was pleased to meet them. Courtney temporarily abandoned Kyle and bounced over to say hello to the famous detective, and Strike looked positively enthusiastic as he took in her looks. Suddenly very conscious of her own washed-out and puffy-eyed appearance, Robin turned back to the kitchen area to put Courtney's ravioli in a bowl for her. Behind her, she heard Courtney saying,

'And this is Kyle.'

'Oh, yeah, you're the detective?' Kyle said, determinedly unimpressed.

Jonathan, Courtney, Kyle and Max already had drinks, so Robin poured herself a large gin and tonic. While she was adding ice, a cheerful Max came back into the kitchen to fetch Strike a beer, then got the casserole out of the oven and on to the table. Wolfgang whined as the object of his devotion was lifted out of his reach.

While Max served everyone at the table, Robin set Courtney's ravioli down in front of her.

'Oh God, no, wait,' said Courtney. 'Is this vegan? Where's the packet?'

'In the bin,' said Robin.

'Tuh,' said Courtney, and she got up and walked into the kitchen. Max and Robin were the only two people at the table whose eyes didn't automatically follow Courtney. Robin downed half her gin before picking up her knife and fork.

'No, it's OK,' called Courtney, from beside the bin. 'It's vegan.'

'Oh good,' said Robin.

To Robin's left, Max began asking Strike's opinion on various aspects of his character's personality and past. Courtney returned to the table and began to wolf down her pasta, drinking and topping up her wine regularly as she went while telling Jonathan and Kyle her plans about a protest march at university. Robin joined in neither conversation, but ate and drank in silence, one eye on the mobile beside her plate in case Ilsa texted or rang back.

'... couldn't happen,' Strike was saying. 'He wouldn't've been allowed to join up in the first place, conviction for possession with intent to supply. Total bollocks.'

'Really? The writers did quite a lot of research—'

'Should've known that, then.'

'... *so* yeah, basically, you dress up in your underwear and short skirts and stuff,' Courtney was saying, and when Kyle and Jon laughed she said, '*Don't*, it's serious—'

'... no, this is useful,' said Max, scribbling in a notebook. 'So if he'd been in jail before the army—'

'If he'd done more than thirty months, the army wouldn't've taken him ... '

'I'm not wearing *suspenders*, Kyle – anyway, Miranda doesn't want—'

'I don't know how long he's supposed to have done,' said Max. 'I'll check. Tell me about drugs in the army, how common—?'

'—so she says, "D'you not understand how problematic the word 'slut' is, Courtney?" And I'm like, "Er, what d'you think—"'

'"What d'you think a fucking SlutWalk's *for*?"' said Kyle, talking over Courtney. He had a deep voice and the air of a young man who was used to being listened to.

The screen of Robin's mobile lit up. Ilsa had texted back.

'Excuse me,' she muttered, though nobody was paying her any attention, and she headed into the kitchen area to read what Ilsa had said.

Didn't mean to worry you. Nick home, shitfaced. He's been in the pub with Corm. We're talking. He says he didn't mean it the way I took it. What other way was there? X

Robin, who felt entirely on Ilsa's side, nevertheless texted back:

He's a dickhead but I know he really loves you. Xxx

As she poured herself another double gin and tonic, Max called to her, asking her to bring Strike another beer from the fridge. When Robin set the open bottle down in front of Strike he didn't thank her, but merely took a long pull on it and raised his voice, because he was having difficulty trying to make himself heard over Kyle and Courtney, whose conversation had now migrated to the unknown Miranda's views on pornography.

'... so I'm, like, you *do* understand that women can actually *choose* what to do with their own bodies, Miran – Oh shit, sorry—'

Courtney's expansive gesture had knocked over her wine glass. Robin jumped up to get the kitchen roll. By the time she got back, Courtney's glass had been refilled by Kyle. Robin mopped up the wine while the two separate conversations grew steadily louder on either side of her, binned the sodden kitchen roll, then sat back down, wishing she could just go to bed.

'... troubled background, that's fucking original, guess what, plenty of people join the army because they want to serve, not to escape ...'

'Pure whorephobia,' boomed Kyle. 'I s'pose she thinks waitresses love every fucking minute of their jobs, does she?'

'... and he can't have been in 1 Rifles if he's your age. The battalion was only formed ...'

'... labour for hire, where's the fucking difference?'

'... think it was end 2007 ... '

'... and some women enjoy *watching* porn, too!'

Courtney's words fell loudly into a temporary lull. Everyone looked round at Courtney, who'd blushed and was giggling with her hand over her mouth.

'It's all right, we're talking feminism,' said Kyle, with a smirk. 'Courtney isn't suggesting, y'know – after-dinner entertainment.'

'*Kyle!*' gasped Courtney, slapping his upper arm and dissolving into further giggles.

'Who wants pudding?' Robin asked, standing up to collect the empty plates. Max, too, got to his feet.

'I'm sorry Strike's so pissed,' Robin murmured to Max, as she tipped a few uneaten pieces of ravioli into the bin.

'Are you kidding?' said Max, with a slight smile. 'This is pure gold. My character's an alcoholic.'

He'd gone, bearing a homemade cheesecake to the table, before Robin could tell him that Strike didn't usually drink this much; indeed, this was only the second time she'd ever known him drunk. The first time he'd been sad and quite endearing, but tonight there was a definite undercurrent of aggression. She remembered the shouted 'Go fuck yourself' she'd heard through the office door that afternoon and again wondered to whom Strike had been talking.

Robin followed Max back to the table, carrying a lemon tart and a third large gin and tonic. Kyle was now treating the entire table to his views on pornography. Robin didn't much like the expression on Strike's face. He'd often displayed an instinctive antipathy towards the kind of young man you could least imagine in the army; she trusted he was going to keep his feelings to himself tonight.

'... form of entertainment, just like any other,' Kyle was saying, with an expansive gesture. Fearful of more accidents, Robin discreetly moved the almost empty wine bottle out of hitting range. 'When you look at it objectively, strip it from all the puritanical bullshit—'

'Yeah, exactly,' said Courtney, 'women have got agency over their own—'

'—movies, gaming, it all stimulates the pleasure centres in your brain,' said Kyle, now pointing at his own immaculately groomed head. 'You could make an argument that movies are emotional pornography. All this moralistic, manufactured outrage about porn—'

'I can't eat either of those if they've got dairy in them,' Courtney whispered to Robin, who pretended she hadn't heard.

'—women want to make a living out of their own bodies, that's the literal definition of female empowerment and you could argue it has more societal benefit than—'

'When I was in Kosovo,' said Strike unexpectedly and all three students turned to look at him, with startled expressions. Strike paused, fumbling to get his cigarettes out of his pocket.

'Cormoran,' said Robin, 'you can't smo—'

'No problem,' said Max, getting up, 'I'll bring an ashtray.'

It took Strike three attempts to make his lighter work and in the meantime everybody watched him in silence. Without raising his voice, he'd dominated the room.

'Who'd like cheesecake?' Robin said into the silence, her voice artificially cheery.

'I can't,' said Courtney, with a slight pout. 'But I might be able to have the lemon tart, if it's—?'

'When I was in Kosovo,' Strike repeated, exhaling as Max returned, placed an ashtray in front of him and sat back down again, ' – cheers – I investigated a porn case – well, human trafficking. Coupla soldiers had paid for sex with underage girls. They were filmed without their knowledge an' the videos ended up on PornHub. Case ended up part of an international civilian investigation. Whole load of pre-pubescent boys and girls had been trafficked into porn. The youngest was seven.'

Strike took a large drag of his cigarette, squinting through the smoke at Kyle.

'What societal benefit would you say that had?' he asked.

There was a short, nasty silence in which the three students stared at the detective.

'Well, obviously,' said Kyle, with a small half-laugh, 'that's – that's a completely different thing. Nobody's talking about kids – that's not – that's illegal, isn't it? I'm talking about—'

'Porn industry's full of trafficking,' said Strike, still watching Kyle through his smoke. 'Women and kids from poor countries. One of the little girls in my case was filmed with a plastic bag over her head, while a bloke anally raped her.'

Out of the corner of her eye, Robin saw Kyle and Courtney throw her darting looks and knew, with an elevator drop in the area of her solar plexus, that her brother must have shared her history with his friends. Max was the only person at the table who seemed entirely relaxed. He was watching Strike with the dispassionate attention of a chemist checking an ongoing experiment.

'The video of that kid was viewed over a hundred thousand times online,' said Strike. Cigarette jammed in his mouth, he now helped himself to a large piece of cheesecake, effectively demolishing it to get a third of it onto his plate. 'Plenty of pleasure centres stimulated there, eh?' he went on, looking up at Kyle.

'No, but that's completely different, though,' said Courtney, rallying to Kyle's defence. 'We were talking about women who – it's up to women, grown women, to decide what they want to do with their own bod—'

'Did you cook all this?' Strike asked Max through a mouthful of cheesecake. He still had a lit cigarette in his left hand.

'Yes,' said Max.

'Bloody good,' said Strike. He turned back to Kyle. 'How many waitresses d'you know who got trafficked into it?'

'Well, obviously none but – I mean, you're bound to've seen that bad stuff, aren't you, being police—'

'As long as you don't have to see it, all good, eh?'

'Well, if you feel like that . . . ' said Kyle, red in the face now, 'if you're so against it, you must never've – you've never used porn, then, you don't—?'

'If nobody else wants pudding,' said Robin loudly, standing up and pointing towards the sofa area, 'shall we have coffee over there?'

Without waiting for an answer, she headed for the kitchen area. Behind her, she heard the scraping of a couple of chairs. After switching on the kettle, she headed downstairs to the bathroom, where, after she'd peed, she sat for five minutes on the toilet with her face in her hands.

Why had Strike turned up drunk? Why did they have to talk about rape and porn? Her attacker had been a voracious consumer of violent pornography, with a particular emphasis on choking, but his internet search history had been deemed inadmissible evidence by the judge. Robin didn't want to know whether Strike used porn; she didn't want to think about trafficked children being filmed, just as she didn't want to remember Morris's dick pic on her phone, or the snuff movie Bill Talbot had stolen. Tired and low, she asked herself why Strike couldn't leave the students alone, if not out of consideration for his host, then for her, his partner.

She headed back upstairs. Halfway to the living area she heard Kyle's heated voice and knew the argument had escalated. Arriving on the top floor, Robin saw the other five sitting around the coffee table, on which stood a cafetière, a bottle and the chocolates Jonathan had brought. Strike and

Max were both holding glasses of brandy while Courtney, who was now very obviously drunk, though nowhere near as much as Strike, was nodding along with Kyle's argument, a cup of coffee balanced precariously in her hands. Robin sat back down at the abandoned dining table, away from the rest of the group, took a piece of beef out of the casserole and fed it to a pathetically grateful Wolfgang.

'The *point* is to destigmatise and reclaim derogatory language about women,' Kyle was saying to Strike. 'That's the *point*.'

'And that'll be 'chieved by a bunch'f nice middle-class girls going f'ra walk in their underwear, will it?' said Strike, his voice thick with alcohol.

'Well, not necessar'ly *under*—' began Courtney.

'It's about ending victim-blaming,' said Kyle loudly. 'Surely you can—?'

'An' how's it end victim-blaming?'

'Well, *obv'sly*,' said Courtney loudly, 'by changing the adertu – the underlying attitudes—'

'You think rapists'll see you all marching 'long and think "better jack in the raping", do you?'

Courtney and Kyle both began shouting at Strike. Jonathan glanced anxiously at his sister, who felt another of those sickening drops in her stomach.

'It's about destigmatising—'

'Oh, don't get me wrong, plen'y of men will enjoy watching you all strut past in your bras,' said Strike, taking a sloppy gulp of brandy, ''n 'I'm sure you'll look great on Instagram—'

'It's not about Instagram!' said Courtney, who sounded almost tearful now. 'We're making a serious point about—'

'Men who call women sluts, yeah, you said,' said Strike, talking over her again. 'I'm sure they'll feel properly rebuked, watching you prounce – prance by in your mini-skirt.'

'It's not about *rebuking*,' said Kyle, 'you're missing the—'

'I'm not missing your super-subtle fucking point,' snapped Strike. 'I'm telling you that in the *real* world, this f'cking Whore Walk—'

'SlutWalk,' said Kyle and Courtney loudly.

'—'ll make fuck-all difference. The kind of man who calls women sluts'll look at your fucking sideshow and think "there go a load of sluts, look". Reclaim fucking language all you fucking like. You don't change real altit – att – real-world attitudes by deciding slurs aren't derug – derogat'ry.'

Wolfgang, who was still quivering at Robin's ankle in the hope of getting more beef, emitted a loud whimper, which made Strike glance around. He saw Robin sitting there, pale and impassive.

'What *d'you* think 'bout all this?' Strike asked her loudly, waving his glass in the direction of the students, so that brandy slopped over the rim onto the carpet.

'I think it would be a good idea to change the subject,' said Robin, whose heart was beating so fast it hurt.

'Would *you* go on a fucking Whore—?'

'I don't know, maybe,' said Robin, blood thumping in her ears, wanting only for the conversation to end. Her rapist had grunted 'whore' over and over again during the attack. If her would-be killer had squeezed her neck for another thirty seconds, it would have been the last word she heard on earth.

'She's b'ng polite,' said Strike, turning back to the students.

'Talking for women now, are you?' sneered Kyle.

'For an *actual* rape victim!' said Courtney.

The room seemed to warp. A clammy silence descended. On the edge of Robin's field of vision she saw Max turn to look at her.

Strike got to his feet at the second attempt. Robin knew he was saying something to her, but it was all noise: her ears felt full of cotton wool. Strike lurched off towards the door: he was leaving. He bounced off the doorframe and disappeared from sight.

Everyone continued to stare at Robin.

'Oh God, I'm really sorry if I shouldn't have said that,' whispered Courtney through the fingers she'd pressed to her mouth. Her eyes were brimming with tears. From downstairs came the sound of the door slamming.

'It's fine,' said a distant voice that sounded quite like Robin's own. 'Excuse me a moment.'

She got to her feet, and followed Strike.

41

With that they gan their shiuering speares to shake,
And deadly points at eithers breast to bend,
Forgetfull each to haue bene euer others frend.

Edmund Spenser
The Faerie Queene

The dark, unfamiliar road took the exceptionally drunk Strike by surprise. Rain and high winds battered him as he stood, swaying, wondering which direction the Tube was. His usually reliable sense of direction was telling him to turn right, so he lurched off that way, searching his pockets for cigarettes as he went, savouring the delicious release of tension and temper he'd just enjoyed. The memory of what had just happened presented itself in a few scattered fragments: Kyle's angry red face. *Tosser. Fucking students.* Max laughing at something Strike had said. Lots of food. Even more drink.

Rain sparkled in the street lights and blurred Strike's vision. Objects seemed to shrink and enlarge around him, particularly the parked car that suddenly put itself in his path as he attempted to walk in a straight line down the street. His thick fingers fumbled fruitlessly in his pockets. He couldn't find his cigarettes.

That last brandy might have been a mistake. He could still taste it. He didn't like brandy, and he'd had a hell of a lot of Doom Bar with Nick in the pub.

It was a mighty effort to walk in these high winds. His glow of well-being was wearing off, but he definitely didn't feel sick, even after all that beef casserole and a sizeable bit of cheesecake, though he didn't really want to think about them, nor about the forty or so cigarettes he'd consumed in the past twenty-four hours, nor about the brandy he could still taste.

Without warning, his stomach contracted. Strike staggered to a gap between two cars, bent double and vomited as copiously as he'd done at Christmas, over and over, for several minutes, until he was standing with his hands on his knees, still heaving, but bringing nothing else up.

Sweaty-faced, he stood up, wiping his mouth on the back of his hand, pistons banging in his head. It was several seconds before he became aware of the pale figure standing watching him, its fair hair blowing wildly in the wind.

'Wh—? Oh,' he said, as Robin came into focus. 'It's you.'

It occurred to him that she might have followed him to bring his forgotten cigarettes and looked hopefully at her hands, but they were empty. Strike moved away from the puddle of vomit in the gutter and leaned up against another parked car.

'I was in the pub with Nick all afternoon,' he said thickly, under the impression that Robin might be concerned about him.

Something hard was pressing into his buttock. Now he realised that he did have his cigarettes on him, after all, and he was glad of this, because he'd rather taste tobacco than vomit. He tugged the pack out of his back pocket and, after a few false starts, managed to light up.

At last, it penetrated his consciousness that Robin's demeanour was unusual. Focusing on her face, he registered it as white and oddly pinched.

'What?'

'"What?"' she repeated. 'Fucking "*what?*"'

Robin swore far less often than Strike did. The damp night air, which felt icy on Strike's sweaty face, was rapidly sobering him up. Robin appeared to be angry: angrier, in fact, than he'd ever seen her. But drink was still slowing his reactions, and nothing better occurred to him than to repeat,

'What?'

'You arrive late,' she said, 'because of *course* you do, because when have you ever shown me the common *fucking* courtesy of turning up on time—'

'Wha—?' said Strike again, this time less because he was looking for information than in disbelief. She was the unique woman in his life who'd never tried to change him. This wasn't the Robin he knew.

'You arrive *rat-arsed*, because of *course* you do, because what do I matter? It's only *Robin* who'll be embarrassed, and *my* flatmate, and *my* fam—'

'He wasn't bothered,' Strike managed to say. His memories of the evening weren't particularly distinct, but he was sure of that, at least: Max hadn't minded him being drunk. Max had given him more booze. Max had laughed at a joke he'd made, which he couldn't now remember. He liked Max.

'And then you launch an attack on my guests. And then,' said Robin, 'you lay me open to having something I wanted to keep priv – to keep—'

Her eyes were suddenly wet, her fists clenched, her body rigid.

'—to keep private bandied about in a fucking argument, in front of strangers. Did it *once* occur—'

'Hang on,' said Strike, 'I never—'

'—*once* occur to you that I might not want *rape* discussed, in front of people I barely know?'

'*I* never—'

'Why were you asking me whether I think SlutWalks are a good idea?'

'Well, obv'sly b'cause—'

'Did we need to talk about child rape over dinner?'

'I was making a p—'

'And then you *walk out*, and leave me to—'

'Well,' said Strike, 'by the sounds of it, the sooner I left, the bett—'

'Better for *you*,' she said, advancing on him, her teeth bared: he'd never seen her like this before, 'because you got to dump all your aggression at my house, then walk out and let me clean up your fucking mess, as per usual!'

'"As per fucking usual?"' said Strike, eyebrows raised. 'Wait a—'

'Now I've got to go back in there, and make it all right, soothe everyone's feelings—'

'No, you haven't,' Strike contradicted her. 'Go to fucking bed if you—'

'It's. What. I. DO!' shouted Robin, thumping herself hard on the sternum with each word. Shocked into silence, Strike stared at her. 'Like I remember to say *please* and *thank you* to the secretary, when you don't give a toss! Like I excuse your bad moods to other people when they get offended! Like I suck up a ton of shit on your behalf—'

'Whoa,' said Strike, pushing himself off the stationary car, and looking down at her from his full height. 'Where's all this—?'

'—and you can't be *fucking* bothered, with all I do for you, to arrive sober for *one dinner*—'

'If you must know,' said Strike, temper rising anew from the ashes of his previous euphoria, 'I was in the pub with Nick, who—'

'—whose wife just lost their baby! I know – and what the *fuck* was he doing in the pub with you, leaving her to—'

'She threw him out!' barked Strike. 'Did she tell you that, during the Great Sisterhood Grievance Meeting? And I'm not going to apologise for wanting some fucking R&R after the week I've just had—'

'—whereas *I* don't need R&R, do I? *I* haven't forfeited half my annual leave—'

'How many times have I thanked you for covering for me when I'm in Corn—?'

'So what was with you being an arsehole to me this morning, when I was late for the *first fucking time ever*—'

'I'd had three and a half hours' sleep—'

'You live over the bloody office!'

'Fuck this,' said Strike, throwing his cigarette down. He began to walk away from her, certain now of the direction to the Tube, thinking of the things he could have said: that it was guilt about the pressure he was putting on Robin that had kept him in London, when he should be in St Mawes with his dying aunt; Jonny Rokeby on the phone that morning; and Nick's tears in the pub, and the relief it had been to sit with an old mate and drink, and listen to someone else's troubles instead of fret about his own.

'And *don't*,' bellowed Robin from behind him, 'buy me any more *fucking flowers*!'

'No danger of that!' yelled Strike over his shoulder, as he strode away into the darkness.

42

. . . his late fight
With Britomart, so sore did him offend,
That ryde he could not, till his hurts he did amend.

Edmund Spenser
The Faerie Queene

When Strike woke on Saturday morning, with a thumping headache and a foul-tasting mouth, it took him a while to piece together exactly what had happened the previous evening. Aside from the memory of vomiting, which he felt he'd done far too much of lately, all he could at first recall were Kyle's bright red face and Robin's pinched white one.

But then, slowly, he reconstructed Robin's complaints: arriving late and drunk, being rude to her brother and upsetting a dinner party by telling a couple of students what he considered home truths about the real world. He also thought there'd been mention of him being insufficiently touchy-feely with staff.

Gingerly, he got out of bed and, with the aid of the furniture, hopped his way to the bathroom and then into the shower.

As Strike washed, two separate impulses did battle within him. One was the urge to self-justify, which patted him on the back and awarded him a win for what he could remember of his argument with the students. The other was an innate honesty about his motives that forced him to recognise that his instant antagonism to Robin's guests had been rooted in their resemblance to the kinds of people towards whom his mother would have instantly gravitated.

Leda Strike's whole life had been a battle against constraint of any kind: going for a march in her underwear would have seemed to her just one more fabulous blow against limitations. Strike, who never forgot Leda's generous heart or her ineradicable love of the underdog, was nevertheless clear-eyed about the fact her activism had mostly taken the form of enthusiastic exhibitionism. Not for Leda the tedious toil of door-to-door canvassing, the difficult business of compromise, or the painstaking work structural change entailed. Never a deep or critical thinker, she'd been a sucker for what Strike thought of as intellectual charlatans. The basis for her life's philosophy, if such a word could be used for the loose collection of whims and kneejerk reactions she called beliefs, was that everything of which the bourgeoisie disapproved must be good and right. Naturally, she'd have sided with Kyle and Courtney in championing pornography and SlutWalks, and she'd have seen her son's quibbles as something he must have picked up from her killjoy sister-in-law.

While Strike dried himself and put on his prosthesis, moving cautiously in deference to his throbbing head, the idea of phoning Robin occurred, only to be dismissed. His long-established habit, in the aftermath of a row with a woman, was to wait for her to make the next move, which he considered mere common sense. If she apologised, all well and good; if she wanted further discussion, there was a chance she'd be calmer after a spell of reflection; if she was still angry, it was simply masochistic to volunteer for further grief until she came looking for it. While Strike wasn't in principle opposed to offering an unsolicited apology in the event that he felt himself to have been in the wrong, in practice his apologies tended to be delivered late, and only when it became clear that resolution would come no other way.

This modus operandi owed much to his experiences with Charlotte. Attempting to make up with Charlotte before every last ounce of her fury had been spent had been like trying to rebuild a house during an earthquake. Sometimes, after he refused to accede to some new demand – usually leaving the army, but sometimes giving up contact with another female friend or refusing to spend money he didn't have, all of which were seen by Charlotte as proof he didn't love her – Charlotte would walk out, and only after she came back, by which time Strike might well have met or slept with someone else, would the row be discussed. Their arguments had often lasted a week or more. A couple of times, Strike had returned to postings abroad before anything was resolved.

Yet, as he ate a much-needed bacon roll, drank coffee and downed a couple of Nurofen; after he'd called Ted, heard that Joan was still holding out, and assured him that he and Lucy would be there the following day; while opening a couple of bits of post, and ripping up a large gilt-edged invitation to the Deadbeats' fiftieth anniversary party in May; while food shopping in the everlasting wind and rain, stocking up for what might be a journey of many hours; while he packed clothes for the trip, spoke to Lucy and checked the weather forecast, his thoughts kept returning to Robin.

Gradually he realised that what was bothering him most was the fact that he'd got used to Robin being on his side, which was one of the main reasons he tended to seek reasons to call her if he was at a loose end or feeling low. Over time, they'd developed a most soothing and satisfying camaraderie, and Strike hadn't imagined it could be disrupted by what he categorised as a dinner party row.

When his phone rang at four o'clock in the afternoon, he surprised himself by snatching it up in the hope that it was his partner, only to see yet another unknown number. Wondering whether he was about to hear Rokeby again, or some other unknown blood relative, he answered.

'Strike.'

'What?' said a sharp, middle-class female voice.

'Cormoran Strike here. Who's this?'

'Clare Spencer, the Athorns' social worker. You left a message for me.'

'Oh, yes,' said Strike, pulling out a kitchen chair and sitting down. 'Thanks for getting back to me, Mrs – er – Ms Spencer.'

'Mrs,' she said, sounding very slightly amused. 'Can I just ask – are you *the* Cormoran Strike?'

'I doubt there are many others,' said Strike.

He reached for his cigarettes, then pushed them away again. He really did need to cut down.

'I see,' said Clare Spencer. 'Well, it was a bit of a shock to get a message from you. How d'you know the Athorns?'

'Their name came up,' said Strike, thinking how very inaccurate a statement that was, 'in the course of a case I'm investigating.'

'Was it *you* who went into their downstairs neighbour's shop, and threatened him?'

'I didn't threaten him,' said Strike. 'But his attitude seemed aggressive, so I pointed out that they had friends who might take it amiss if he bullied them.'

'Ha,' said Clare, sounding warmer. 'He's a horror, that man. He's been trying to get them out of that flat for ages. Wants to buy the whole building. He removed a supporting wall, then tried to blame Deborah and Samhain for his ceiling sagging. He's caused them a lot of stress.'

'The flat was –' Strike almost said 'mucked out', but tried to find a politer way of saying it, '– thoroughly cleaned recently, he said?'

'Yes. I'm not denying it was pretty messy, but we've sorted that out now, and as for saying they've caused structural damage, we got a surveyor in who went through the whole place and agreed there's nothing wrong with it. *What* a chancer the man is. Anyway, you did a good thing, there, warning him off. He thinks because they haven't got many close relatives, he can get away with browbeating them. So, what's this case you're investigating?'

Briefly, Strike told her about Margot Bamborough, her disappearance in 1974, and the information that had led him to the Athorns' door.

'... and so,' he concluded, 'I wanted to talk to someone who could tell me how much reliance I can put on what they've told me.'

There was a brief silence.

'I see,' said Clare, who sounded a little more guarded now. 'Well, I'm afraid I've got a duty of confidentiality as their social worker, so—'

'Could I ask you some questions? And if you can't answer, obviously I'll accept that.'

'All right,' she said. He had the impression that his actions with regard to the bullying ironmonger had put her on his side.

'They're clearly competent to live alone,' said Strike.

'With support, yes,' said Clare. 'They've done very well, actually. They've got a strong mutual bond. It's probably kept both of them out of institutionalised care.'

'And what exactly—?' Strike wondered how to word the question sensitively. Clare came to his aid.

'Fragile X syndrome,' she said. 'Deborah's relatively

high-functioning, although she's got some social difficulties, but she can read and so forth. Samhain copes better socially, but his cognitive impairment's greater than his mother's.'

'And the father, Gwilherm—?'

Clare laughed.

'I've only been their social worker for a couple of years. I never knew Gwilherm.'

'You can't tell me how sane he was?'

There was a longer pause.

'Well,' she said, 'I suppose . . . it seems to be common knowledge that he was very odd. Various family members have spoken to me about him. Apparently he thought he could hex people. With black magic, you know.'

'Deborah told me something I found . . . slightly concerning. It involved a doctor called Dr Brenner, who was a partner of Dr Bamborough's at the St John's practice. She might've been referring to a medical examination, but—'

He thought Clare had said something.

'Sorry?'

'No, nothing. What exactly did she tell you?'

'Well,' said Strike, 'she mentioned having to take her pants off, and not wanting to, but she said Gwilherm told her she had to. I assumed—'

'This was a doctor?'

'Yes,' said Strike.

There was another, longer pause.

'I don't really know what to tell you,' said Clare finally. 'It's possible that was a medical examination, but . . . well, a lot of men used to visit that flat.'

Strike said nothing, wondering whether he was being told what he thought he was being told.

'Gwilherm had to get drink and drugs money somewhere,' said Clare. 'From what Deborah's disclosed to social workers over the years, we think he was – well, not to put too fine a point on it, we think he was pimping her out.'

'Christ,' muttered Strike, in disgust.

'I know,' said Clare. 'From bits and pieces she's told caregivers, we think Gwilherm used to take Samhain out whenever she was with a client. It *is* dreadful. She's so vulnerable. On balance, I can't be sorry Gwilherm died young. But please – don't mention any of this to Deborah's family, if you speak to them. I've no idea how much they know, and she's happy and settled these days. There's no need to upset anyone.'

'No, of course not,' said Strike, and he remembered Samhain's words: *old Joe Brenner was a dirty old man.*

'How reliable would you say Samhain's memory is?'

'Why? What's he told you?'

'A couple of things his Uncle Tudor said.'

'Well, people with Fragile X usually have quite good long-term memories,' said Clare cautiously. 'I'd say he'd be more reliable about things his Uncle Tudor told him than on many subjects.'

'Apparently Uncle Tudor had a theory about what happened to Margot Bamborough. It involved some people called "Nico and his boys".'

'Ah,' said Clare, 'yes. D'you know who that is?'

'Go on.'

'There was an old gangster who used to live in Clerkenwell,' said Clare, 'called Niccolo Ricci. Samhain likes talking about "Nico and his boys". Like they're folk heroes, or something.'

They talked for a couple more minutes, but Clare had nothing more of interest to tell.

'Well, thanks very much for getting back to me,' said Strike. 'Social workers work Saturdays as well as detectives, I see.'

'People don't stop needing help at weekends,' she said

drily. 'Good luck. I hope you find out what happened to that poor doctor.'

But he could tell by her tone, however friendly, that she thought it highly unlikely.

Strike's headache had now settled into a dull throb that increased if he bent over or stood up too suddenly. He returned to his methodical arrangements for next day's departure to Cornwall, emptying his fridge of perishables, making sandwiches for the trip; listening to the news, which told him that three people had died that day as a result of the adverse weather conditions; packing his kit bag; ensuring his emails were up to date, setting up an out-of-office message redirecting potential clients to Pat, and checking the rota, to make sure it had been altered to accommodate his absence. Through all these tasks he kept an ear out for his mobile, in case a text from Robin arrived, but nothing came.

Finally, at eight o'clock, while he was finishing cooking the fry-up he felt he was owed given his hangover and how hard he'd worked all day, his mobile buzzed at last. From across the table, he saw that three long consecutive texts had arrived. Knowing that he was leaving the following morning without any clear idea of when he'd be back, Robin appeared to have begun the reconciliation process as women were wont to do, with an essay on her various grievances. He opened the first message, magnanimously prepared to accept almost any terms for a negotiated peace, and only then realised that it was from an unknown number.

I thought today was Valentine's day but I've just realised it's the 15th. They've got me on so many drugs in here I can hardly remember my name. I'm in a place again. This isn't my phone. There's another woman here who's allowed one & she lent it to me. Yours is the only mobile number I know by heart. Why

didn't you ever change it? Was it because of me or is that my vanity. I'm so full of drugs I cant feel anything but I know I love you. I wonder how much they'd have to give me before that went too. Engouh to kill me I suppose.

The next message, from the same number, read:

How did you spent valentines day. Did you have sex. I'm here partly because I don't want sex. I cant stand him touching me and I know he wants more kids. Id rather die than have more. Actually I'd rather die than most things. But you know that about me. Will I ever see you again? You could come and see me here. Today I imagined you walking in, like I did when your leg. I imagined you telling them to let me go because you loved me and you'd look after me. I cried and

The third message continued:

the psychiatrist was pleased to see me crying because they like emotion. I don't know what the whole address is but it's called Symonds House. I love you don't forget me whatever hpapens to me. I love you.

A fourth and final message read:

It's Charlotte in case that isn't obvious.

Strike read the entire thread through twice. Then he closed his eyes, and like millions of his fellow humans, wondered why troubles could never come singly, but in avalanches, so that you became increasingly destabilised with every blow that hit you.

43

And you faire Ladie knight, my dearest Dame,
Relent the rigour of your wrathfull will,
Whose fire were better turn'd to other flame;
And wiping out remembrance of all ill,
Graunt him your grace . . .

Edmund Spenser
The Faerie Queene

To Robin's relief, her three guests got up early the next morning, because they wanted to spend a full day in London. All were subdued after what Robin thought of as the Nightmare Dinner. She dreaded a tearful plea for forgiveness from Courtney, who seemed especially low, so Robin faked a cheery briskness she certainly didn't feel, making recommendations for cheap places to eat and good things to see before waving the students off. As Robin was due to run surveillance on Elinor Dean overnight, she'd given Jonathan a spare key, and wasn't sorry that she'd probably still be in Stoke Newington when the students returned to Manchester, because they intended to catch a mid-morning Sunday train.

Not wanting to be alone with Max, in case he wanted a post-mortem on the previous evening, Robin made herself a voluntary prisoner in her own bedroom all day, where she continued to work on her laptop, attempting to block out waves of anger towards Strike, and a tearfulness that kept threatening to overcome her. Hard as she tried to concentrate on finding out who'd been living in Jerusalem Passage when Margot had disappeared, however, her thoughts kept returning to her partner.

Robin wasn't in the least surprised not to have heard from him, but was damned if she'd initiate contact. She couldn't in good conscience retract a word of what she'd said after watching him vomit in the gutter, because she was tired of being taken for granted in ways Strike didn't recognise.

But as the afternoon wore on, and the rain continued to fall outside her window, and while she hadn't been nearly as drunk as Strike, she developed a dull headache. Equal parts of misery and rage dragged at her every time she remembered last night's dinner, and all the things she'd shouted at Strike in the street. She wished she could cry, but the tightness in her chest prevented her doing so. Her anger boiled anew every time she remembered the drunk Strike attacking her guests, but then she found herself re-running Courtney and Kyle's arguments in her head. She was sure none of the students had ever brushed up against the ugliness Robin had encountered, not merely under that dark stair in her hall of residence, but during her work with Strike: battered women, raped girls, death. They didn't want to hear Strike's stories, because it was so much more comforting to believe that language alone could remake the world. But none of that made her feel more kindly to her partner: on the contrary, she resented agreeing with him. He'd been looking for someone or something to attack, and it was she who'd paid the price.

Robin forced herself to keep working, because work was her one constant, her salvation. By eight in the evening, Robin was as sure as a thorough perusal of online records could make her that nobody living in Jerusalem Passage had been there for forty years. By this time, she was so hungry that she really did need to eat something, which she feared meant facing Max, and discussing Strike.

Sure enough, when she reached the living area, she found Max sitting watching TV with Wolfgang on his lap. He muted the news the moment he saw her, and Robin's heart sank.

'Evening.'

'Hi,' said Robin. 'I'm going to make myself something to eat. D'you want anything?'

'There's still a bit of casserole, if you want it.'

'Strike didn't finish it all, then?'

She mentioned him first in the spirit of getting it over with. She could tell that Max had things to say.

'No,' said Max. He lifted the sleepy Wolfgang onto the sofa beside him, stood up and moved to the kitchen. 'I'll heat it up for you.'

'There's no need, I can—'

But Max did so, and when Robin was settled at the table with her food and a drink, he sat down at the table with her with a beer. This was highly unusual and Robin felt suddenly nervous. Was she being softened up for some kind of unwelcome announcement? Had Max decided, after all, to sell up?

'Never told you how I ended up in such a nice flat, did I?' he said.

'No,' said Robin cautiously.

'I had a big payout, five years ago. Medical negligence.'

'Oh,' said Robin.

There was a pause. Max smiled.

'People usually say, "Shit, what went wrong?" But you never probe, do you? I've noticed that. You don't ask a lot of questions.'

'Well, I have to do a lot of that at work,' said Robin.

But that wasn't why she hadn't asked Max about his

finances, and it wasn't why she didn't ask now what had gone wrong with his body or his treatment, either. Robin had too many things in her own past that she didn't want endlessly probed to want to cause other people discomfort.

'I was having palpitations seven years ago,' Max said, examining the label on his beer. 'Arrhythmia. I got referred to a heart specialist and he operated: opened me up and ablated my sinus node. You probably don't know what that is,' he said, glancing up at Robin, and she shook her head. 'I didn't either, until they ballsed mine up. Basically, they knackered my heart's ability to beat for itself. I ended up having to be fitted with a pacemaker.'

'Oh no,' said Robin, a bit of beef suspended in mid-air on her fork.

'And the best bit was,' said Max, 'none of it was necessary. There wasn't anything wrong with my sinus node in the first place. Turned out I hadn't been suffering from atrial tachycardia at all. It was stage fright.'

'I – Max, I'm so sorry.'

'Yeah, it wasn't good,' said Max, taking a sip of his beer. 'Two unnecessary open-heart surgeries, endless complications. I lost jobs, I was unemployed for four years and I'm still on anti-depressants. Matthew said I *had* to pursue a claim against the doctors. I probably wouldn't have done, if he hadn't nagged me. Lawyers' fees. Ton of stress. But I won in the end, got a big payout, and he persuaded me to sink it all into a decent property. He's a barrister, he earns great money. Anyway, we bought this place.'

Max pushed his thick blond hair out of his face and glanced down at Wolfgang, who'd trotted to the table to savour the smell of casserole once more.

'A week after we moved in, he sat me down and told me he was leaving. The ink was barely dry on the mortgage. He said he'd struggled against it, because he felt a loyalty to me, because of what I'd been through, but he couldn't fight his feelings any longer. He told me,' said Max, with a hollow smile, 'he'd realised pity wasn't love. He wanted me to keep the flat, didn't want me to buy him out – as if I could have done – so he signed over his half. That was to make him feel less guilty, obviously. And off he went with Tiago. He's Brazilian, the new guy. Owns a restaurant.'

'That,' said Robin quietly, 'sounds like hell.'

'Yeah, it was . . . I really need to stop looking at their bloody Instagram accounts.' Max heaved a deep sigh and absent-mindedly rubbed the shirt over the scars on his chest. 'Obviously I thought of just selling up, but we barely lived here together, so it's not as though it's got a ton of memories. I didn't have the energy to go through more house-hunting and moving, so here I've stayed, struggling to make the mortgage every month.'

Robin thought she knew why Max was telling her all this, and her hunch was confirmed when he looked directly at her and said,

'Anyway, I just wanted to say, I'm sorry about what happened to you. I had no idea. Ilsa only told me you were held at gunpoint—'

'Oh, I didn't get raped *then*,' said Robin, and to Max's evident surprise, she started to laugh. Doubtless it was her tiredness, but it was a relief to find dark comedy in this litany of terrible things humans did to each other, though none of it was really funny at all: his mutilated heart, the gorilla mask in her nightmares. 'No, the rape happened ten years ago. That's why I dropped out of university.'

'Shit,' said Max.

'Yeah,' said Robin, and echoing Max, she said, 'it wasn't good.'

'So when did the knife thing happen?' asked Max, eyes on Robin's forearm, and she laughed again. Really, what else was there to do?

'That was a couple of years ago.'

'Working for Strike?'

'Yes,' said Robin, and she stopped laughing now. 'Listen, about last night—'

'I enjoyed last night,' said Max.

'You can't be serious,' said Robin.

'I'm completely serious. It was really useful for building my character. He's got some proper big man, take-no-bullshit energy about him, hasn't he?'

'You mean he acts like a dick?'

Max laughed and shrugged.

'Is he very different sober?'

'Yes,' said Robin, 'well – I don't know. Less of a dick.' And before Max could ask anything else about her partner, she said quickly, 'He's right about your cooking, anyway. That was fantastic. Thanks so much, I really needed that.'

Having cleared up, Robin returned downstairs, where she showered before changing for the night's surveillance. With an hour to go before she needed to take over from Hutchins, she sat back down on her bed and idly typed variations on the name Paul Satchwell into Google. *Paul L Satchwell. LP Satchwell. Paul Leonard Satchwell. Leo Paul Satchwell.*

Her mobile rang. She glanced down. It was Strike. After a moment or two, she picked it up, but said nothing.

'Robin?'

'Yes.'

'Are you OK to talk?'

'Yes,' she said again, her heart beating faster than usual as she frowned up at the ceiling.

'Calling to apologise.'

Robin was so astonished, she said nothing for several seconds. Then she cleared her throat and said,

'Can you even remember what you're apologising for?'

'Er . . . yeah, I think so,' said Strike. 'I . . . didn't mean *that* to get dragged up. Should've realised it wasn't a subject you'd want discussed over dinner. Didn't think.'

Tears started in Robin's eyes at last.

'OK,' she said, trying to sound casual.

'And I'm sorry for being rude to your brother and his friends.'

'Thank you,' said Robin.

There was a silence. The rain still fell outside. Then Strike said,

'Have you heard from Ilsa?'

'No,' said Robin. 'Have you heard from Nick?'

'No,' said Strike.

There was another silence.

'So, we're OK, yeah?' said Strike.

'Yes,' said Robin, wondering whether it was true.

'If I've taken you for granted,' said Strike, 'I'm sorry. You're the best I've got.'

'Oh, for *fuck's* sake, Strike,' said Robin, abandoning the pretence that she wasn't crying as she snorted back tears.

'What?'

'You just . . . you're bloody infuriating.'

'Why?'

'Saying that. Now.'

'That's not the first time I've said it.'

'It is, actually.'

'I've told other people.'

'Yeah, well,' said Robin, now laughing and crying simultaneously as she reached for tissues, 'you see how that isn't the same thing as telling *me*?'

'Yeah, I s'pose,' said Strike. 'Now you mention it.'

He was smoking at his small Formica kitchen table while the eternal rain fell outside his attic window. Somehow, the texts from Charlotte had made him realise he had to call Robin, had to make things right with her before he set off for Cornwall and Joan. Now the sound of her voice, and her laughter, acted on him as it usually did, by making everything seem fractionally less awful.

'When are you leaving?' Robin asked, drying her eyes.

'Tomorrow at eight. Lucy's meeting me at the car hire. We've got a jeep.'

'Well, be careful,' said Robin. She'd heard on the news that day about the three people who'd died, trying to travel through the wind and the floods.

'Yeah. Can't pretend I don't wish you were driving. Lucy's bloody terrible behind the wheel.'

'You can stop flattering me now. I've forgiven you.'

'I'm serious,' said Strike, his eyes on the relentless rain. 'You and your advanced driving course. You're the only person who doesn't scare the shit out of me behind the wheel.'

'D'you think you'll make it?'

'Possibly not all the way in the jeep. But Polworth's standing by to rescue us. He's got access to dinghies. We've got to do it. Joan might only have days.'

'Well, I'll be thinking about you,' said Robin. 'Keeping everything crossed.'

'Cheers, Robin. Keep in touch.'

After Strike had hung up, Robin sat for a while, savouring the sudden feeling of lightness that had filled her. Then she pulled her laptop towards her, ready to shut it down before she left for her night's surveillance in the Land Rover. Casually, as she might have thrown the dice one last time before turning away from the craps table, she typed 'Paul Satchwell artist' into Google.

. . . **artist Paul Satchwell** has spent most of his career on the Greek island of . . .

'*What?*' said Robin aloud, as though the laptop had spoken to her. She clicked on the result, and the website of the Leamington Spa Museum and Art Gallery filled the screen. She hadn't once seen it, in all her hours of searching for Satchwell. This page had either just been created or amended.

Temporary Exhibition March 3rd – 7th 2014

Local Artists

The Leamington Spa Museum and Art Gallery will be hosting a temporary exhibition of artists from the Warwickshire area. Entrance free.

Robin scrolled down the page past sundry artists' photos until she saw him.

It was, without a doubt, the same man. His face might be leathery and cracked, his teeth might have yellowed, his thick, curly hair turned whiter and thinner, but it still hung to his shoulders, while his open shirt showed thick white chest hair.

Born in Leamington Spa and raised in Warwick, artist Paul Satchwell has spent most of his career on the Greek island of Kos. Working mainly in oils, Paul's Hellenic-influenced exploration of myths challenge the viewer to face primal fears and examine preconceptions through sensual use of line and colour . . .

44

Huge sea of sorrow, and tempestuous griefe,
Wherein my feeble barke is tossed long,
Far from the hoped hauen of reliefe,
Why doe thy cruel billowes beat so strong,
And thy moyst mountaines each on others throng,
Threatning to swallow vp my fearefull lyfe?

Edmund Spenser
The Faerie Queene

The storm water, rain and gales they faced were real enough, yet Strike and Lucy's battle to reach St Mawes had a strange, dreamlike quality. Both knew death lay at the end; both were resolved that if they managed to reach Joan alive, they would stay with her until she died.

Trees swayed and creaked as they sped along the motorway. They had to divert around great wide lakes where lately there had been fields, forcing them miles out of their way. Twice they were halted at roadblocks and told, by irate police, to turn back. They pressed on, at one point driving fifty miles to progress fifteen, listening to every weather update on the radio and becoming progressively more certain that there would come a point where they had to abandon the jeep. Rain lashed the car, high winds lifted the windscreen wipers from the glass, and brother and sister took it in turns to drive, bound by a single objective, and temporarily freed from all other concerns.

To Strike's grateful surprise, the crisis had revealed a different Lucy, just as illness had uncovered a different Joan. His sister was focused entirely on what needed to be done. Even her driving was different, without three noisy sons in the back seat, squabbling and thumping each other if the journey lasted longer than twenty minutes. He'd forgotten how efficient and practical Lucy could be, how patient, how resolute. Her calm determination only broke when they reached an impasse thirty miles from St Mawes, where flooding and fallen trees had rendered the road impassable.

While Lucy sat slumped at the steering wheel, sobbing with her face in her arms, Strike left the jeep to stand outside under a tree, where, sheltering from the perennial rain and taking the opportunity to smoke, he called Dave Polworth, who was holding himself ready to assist them.

'Yeah, we thought that's where you'd have to stop,' said Polworth, when Strike had given him their position.

'Who's "we"?'

'Well, I can't fucking do this alone, can I, Diddy? Should be with you in an hour. Stay in the car.'

And an hour later, true to his word, Dave Polworth and five other men, two of them members of the local lifeguard, three old schoolfriends of Strike's, emerged out of the gathering gloom. Dressed in waterproofs, and carrying waders ready for the worst passages, the men took charge of Strike and Lucy's bags. Leaving the jeep parked up a side street, the party set off on foot.

The end of Strike's stump began to chafe long before they had walked for two hours solid over boggy ground and slippery tarmac. Soon, he had to abandon pride and allow two of his old schoolfriends to support him on either side. Darkness fell before they reached a couple of dinghies that Polworth had arranged to carry them over flooded fields. Using oars to alternately row and punt themselves along, they navigated with the aid of torches and compasses.

Polworth had called on every friend and acquaintance he knew to arrange Strike and Lucy's passage across the storm-ravaged peninsula. They covered several miles by tractor pulling a trailer, but at some passages were forced to wade through feet of icy flood water, the diminutive Lucy accepting a piggyback from the largest lifeboat man.

Four hours after they'd abandoned the jeep, they reached St Mawes. At the gate of Ted and Joan's house, brother and sister hugged each of their escorts goodbye.

'Don't start,' said Polworth, as the weary and sore Strike tried to put into words what he felt to be incommunicable. 'Get inside, or what the fuck was it all for?'

Ted, whom they'd updated regularly through their journey, greeted them in pyjamas at the back door, tears running down the deep folds in his craggy face.

'I never thought you'd get here,' he kept saying, as he made them tea. '*Never* thought you'd make it.'

'How is she?' asked the shivering Lucy, as the three of them sat in the kitchen, their hands around mugs of tea, eating toast.

'She managed a bit of soup today,' said Ted. 'She's still . . . she sleeps a lot. But when she's awake, she likes to talk. Oh, she'll be over the moon to have you two here . . . '

And so began days that had the same strange, outside-time quality of their journey. Initially Strike, the end of whose stump was rubbed raw after the painful exigencies of their journey, abandoned his prosthesis and navigated the small house by hopping and holding onto chair backs and walls. He read and responded to Robin's emails about the agency's work, but her news seemed to come from a place far more remote than London.

Joan was now bird-like in her frailty, her bones visible through the translucent skin. She'd made it clear that she wished to die at home, not in the hospital in Truro, so she lay, tiny and shrunken, in the large double bed that dominated the bedroom, a bed that had been purchased to accommodate Ted's bulk back when he'd been a tall, fit and muscular man, late of the Royal Military Police and subsequently a stalwart member of the local lifeguard.

By day, Strike, Ted and Lucy took it in turns to sit beside Joan's bed, because awake or asleep, she liked to know that one of them was nearby. Kerenza came morning and afternoon, and these were the only times when her family left the room. Joan was no longer able to swallow medication, so Kerenza began injecting the morphine through a syringe driver. Strike knew that she washed his aunt, and helped her perform still more private functions: the long convalescence after his amputation had left him under no illusion about what nurses dealt with. Kind, efficient and humane, Kerenza was one of the few people Strike welcomed gladly into the draughty kitchen.

And still Joan clung on. Three days after their arrival, four: she slept almost constantly, but still she clung to life.

'It's you two,' said Ted. 'She doesn't want to go while you two are here.'

Strike was coming to dread silences too large for human voices to fill. His nerves were stretched by the constant clinking of teaspoons in hot drinks made for something to do, by the tears shed by Uncle Ted when he thought nobody was looking, by the hushed enquiries of well-meaning neighbours.

On the fifth day, Lucy's husband Greg arrived with their three boys. Husband and wife had debated how sensible it was to take the boys out of school, and risk a journey that remained tricky, though the storms had at last subsided, but Lucy could bear their absence no longer. When Greg arrived, the boys came running out of the car towards their mother and the whole family clung to each other, while Strike and Ted looked on, united in their aloneness, unmarried man and soon-to-be widower. The boys were led up to Joan's bedroom to see her, and she managed smiles for all of them. Even Luke was subdued afterwards, and Jack cried.

Both spare rooms were now needed to accommodate the new arrivals, so Strike returned, uncomplaining, to sleep on the sofa.

'You look like shit,' Polworth informed him bluntly on day six, and indeed Strike, who'd woken every hour on the horsehair sofa, felt it. 'Let's get a pint.'

'Can I come?' asked Jack hopefully. He was showing a tendency to hang around Strike rather than his father, while Lucy sat upstairs with Joan.

'You can if your dad says it's OK,' said Strike.

Greg, who was currently walking around the garden with his phone clamped to his ear, trying to contribute to a conference call with his London office while Luke and Adam played football around him, agreed with a thumbs up.

So Strike, Polworth and Jack walked down into St Mawes together. Though the sky was dark and the roads still wet, the winds had at last dropped. As they reached the seafront, Strike's mobile rang. He answered it, still walking.

'Strike.'

'It's Shanker. Got your message.'

'I left that ten days ago,' said Strike.

'I've been busy, you ungrateful piece of shit.'

'Sorry,' said Strike.

He waved the other two on and paused again at the harbour wall, looking out at the green-grey sea and the hazy horizon.

'I've nosed around a bit,' said Shanker, 'and you're not gonna find out 'oo that bint was, Bunsen. The one on the film. Nobody knows. She'll 'ave done somethin' fucking serious to get that, though.'

'Deserved it, you reckon,' said Strike, as he surveyed the flat sea. It didn't look capable, now, of the violence it had inflicted upon the town.

'I'm not saying she *deserved* – I'm sayin' even Mucky Ricci didn't make 'an 'abit of *that*,' said Shanker impatiently. 'Are you in solitary?'

'What?'

'Where the fuck are you? There's no noise.'

'In Cornwall.'

For a moment, Strike expected Shanker to ask where that was. Shanker was almost impressively ignorant of the country that lay beyond London.

'The fuck are you doin' in Cornwall?'

'My aunt's dying.'

'Oh shit,' said Shanker. 'Sorry.'

'Where is he now?'

''Oo?'

'Ricci.'

''E's in an 'ome. I told you.'

'All right. Thanks for trying, Shanker. Appreciate it.'

For perhaps the first time ever, it was Shanker who shouted at Strike to stop him hanging up.

'Oi – oi!'

'What?' said Strike, raising the mobile to his ear again.

'Why d'you wanna know where 'e is? You ain't gonna go talkin' to Ricci. You're done.'

'I'm not done,' said Strike, eyes screwed up against the sea breeze. 'I haven't found out what happened to the doctor, yet.'

'*Fuck's* sake. D'you wanna get shot through the fuckin' 'ead?'

'See you, Shanker,' said Strike, and before his old friend could say anything else, he cut the call and muted his phone.

Polworth was already at a table with Jack when Strike reached the Victory, two pints and a Coke on the table.

'Just been telling Jack,' Polworth told Strike, as the detective sat down. 'Haven't I, eh?' he asked Jack, who nodded, beaming. 'For when he's older. *This* is his local.'

'A pub three hundred miles from where he lives?'

'He was born in Cornwall. He was just telling me.'

'Oh yeah,' said Strike. 'I forgot about that.'

The family had been staying with Ted and Joan when Lucy went into labour a month early. Jack had been born in the same Truro hospital as Strike himself.

'And you're a Nancarrow on your mum's side,' Polworth told Jack, who was greatly enjoying Polworth's approval. 'So that makes you a Cornishman, born and bred.'

Polworth turned to Strike.

'Who was the pearly king on the phone there? We could hear his cockney a mile off.'

'Guy called Shanker,' said Strike. 'I've told you about him. My mum scraped him off the street one night when he'd been stabbed. He adopted us.'

Strike sipped his pint, wondering how Polworth and Shanker would get on, in the unlikely event of them ever meeting. He fancied they might end up punching each other. They seemed to Strike like pieces from entirely different jigsaw puzzles: no point of connection. At the mention of stabbing, Polworth had glanced at Jack, but lowering his pint Strike said,

'Don't worry about him. He wants to be a Red Cap, like me and Ted.'

Jack beamed some more. He was having a great time.

'Can I try some of that beer?' he asked his uncle.

'Don't push it,' said Strike.

'Look at this,' said Polworth, pointing at a page in the newspaper he'd picked up. 'Westminster trying to bully the Scots, the bast—'

Strike cleared his throat. Jack giggled.

'Sorry,' said Polworth. 'But come on. Telling them they can't keep the pound if they vote for independence? 'Course they'll keep the pound. It's in everyone's interests . . .'

He talked on for the next ten minutes about small nationalism, the obvious arguments for both Scottish and Cornish independence and the idiocy of those who opposed them, until Jack looked glazed and Strike, as a last resort, dragged the conversation back to football. Arsenal, as he'd foreseen, had lost to defending champions Bayern Munich, and he didn't doubt the second leg would see them knocked out. He and Ted had watched the game together and done a good job of pretending they cared about the result. Strike permitted Polworth to pass censorious comment on the foul that had seen Szczęsny sent off, and politics was mercifully dropped.

Strike thought about Polworth later that night, as he lay in the dark on the horsehair sofa again, unable to sleep. His tiredness now had a feverishness about it, exacerbated by the aching of his body, the perpetual strain of being here, in this overcrowded house, waiting for the tiny body upstairs to give up.

In this near fever state, a jumble of ideas circulated in Strike's mind. He thought of categories and boundaries, of those we want to create and enforce, and those we seek to escape or destroy. He remembered the fanatic glint in Polworth's eye as he argued for a harder boundary between his county and the rest of England. He fell asleep thinking about the spurious groupings of astrology, and dreamed of Leda, laying out her tarot cards in the Norfolk commune of long ago.

Strike was woken at five by his own aching body. Knowing that Ted would be awake soon, he got up and dressed, ready to take over the bedside vigil while his uncle ate breakfast.

Sure enough, hearing Strike's footstep on the upstairs landing, Ted emerged from the bedroom in his dressing gown.

'Just made you tea,' whispered Strike. 'It's in the pot in the kitchen. I'll sit with her for a bit.'

'You're a good lad,' whispered Ted, clapping Strike on the arm. 'She's asleep now, but I had a little chat with her at four. Most she's said for days.'

The talk with his wife seemed to have cheered him. He set off downstairs for his tea and Strike let himself quietly into the familiar room, taking up his position on the hard-backed chair beside Joan.

The wallpaper hadn't been changed, so far as Strike knew, since Ted and Joan had moved into the house, their only home since he'd left the army, in the town where both had grown up. Ted and Joan seemed not to notice that the house had grown shabby over the decades: for all that Joan was meticulous about cleanliness, she'd equipped and decorated the house once and seemed never to have seen any need to do so again. The paper was decorated with small bunches of purple flowers, and Strike could remember tracing geometric shapes between them with his forefinger as a small child, when he climbed into bed with Ted and Joan early in the morning, when both were still sleepy and he wanted breakfast and a trip to the beach.

Twenty minutes after he'd sat down, Joan opened her eyes and looked at Strike so blankly that he thought she didn't know him.

'It's me, Joan,' he said quietly, moving his chair a little closer to her bed and switching on the lamp, with its fringed shade. 'Corm. Ted's having breakfast.'

Joan smiled. Her hand was a tiny claw, now. The fingers

twitched. Strike took it into his own. She said something he couldn't hear, and he lowered his large head to her face.

'What did you say?'

'. . . you're . . . good man.'

'Oh, I don't know about that,' muttered Strike.

He held her hand in a light clasp, scared of putting pressure on it. The *arcus senilis* outlining the irises of her pale eyes made the blue seem more faded than ever. He thought of all the times he could have visited, and hadn't. All those missed opportunities to call. All those times he'd forgotten her birthday.

'. . . helping people . . . '

She peered up at him and then, making a supreme effort, she whispered,

'I'm proud of you.'

He wanted to speak, but something was blocking his throat. After a few seconds, he saw her eyelids drooping.

'I love you, Joan.'

The words came out so hoarsely they were almost inaudible, but he thought she smiled as she sank back into a sleep from which she was never to wake.

45

Of auncient time there was a springing well,
From which fast trickled forth a siluer flood,
Full of great vertues, and for med'cine good.

Edmund Spenser
The Faerie Queene

Robin was still at the office when Strike called that evening with the news that Joan had died.

'I'm sorry about this, but I think I'm going to have to stay down here until we get this funeral sorted,' said Strike. 'There's a lot to do and Ted's in pieces.'

He'd just shared Joan's plan for her funeral with Ted and Lucy, thereby reducing both of them to sobs at the kitchen table. Ted's tears were for the poignancy of his wife making arrangements for his own comfort and relief, as she'd done for the fifty years of their marriage, and for the news that she'd wanted, at the end, to enter the sea and wait for him there. In Lucy's case, the sobs were for the lost possibility of a grave she'd hoped to visit and tend. Lucy filled her days with voluntary obligations: they gave purpose and form to a life she was determined would never be like her flighty biological mother's.

'No problem,' Robin reassured him. 'We're coping fine.'

'You're sure?'

'Completely sure.'

'There's a backlog at the crematorium, because of the floods,' said Strike. 'Funeral's pencilled in for March the third.'

This was the day Robin was planning to spend in Leamington Spa, so she could attend the opening of Paul Satchwell's exhibition. She didn't tell Strike this: she could tell that he had limited mental capacity right now for anything other than Joan, and his life in Cornwall.

'Don't worry,' she repeated. 'I'm so sorry, Cormoran,' she added.

'Thanks,' said Strike. 'I'd forgotten what it's like. Planning a funeral. I've already had to referee one argument.'

After he'd shared Joan's plans for her send-off, and Lucy and Ted had mopped up their tears, Ted had suggested they ask mourners for donations to the Macmillan Cancer Support in lieu of flowers.

'... but Lucy says Joan would've wanted flowers,' Strike told Robin. 'I've suggested we say either. Ted says that'll mean people do both and they can't afford it, but fuck it. Lucy's right. Joan *would* want flowers, and as many as possible. That's how she always judged other people's funerals.'

After they'd bidden each other goodbye, Robin sat for a while at the partners' desk, wondering whether it would be appropriate for the agency to send flowers to Strike's aunt's funeral. She'd never met Joan: she worried that it would seem odd, or intrusive, to send condolences. She remembered how, when she'd offered to pick Strike up from Joan's house in St Mawes the previous summer, he'd quickly cut her off, erecting, as ever, a firm boundary between Robin and his personal life.

Yawning, Robin shut down the computer, closed the completed file on Postcard, which she'd been updating, got to her feet and went to get her coat. At the outer door she stopped, her reflection blank-faced in the dark glass. Then, as though responding to an unheard command, she returned to the inner office, switched the computer back on and, before she could second-guess herself, ordered a sheaf of dark pink roses to be delivered to St Mawes church on March the third, with the message 'With deepest sympathy from Robin, Sam, Andy, Saul and Pat'.

Robin spent the rest of the month working without respite. She conducted a final meeting with the persecuted weatherman and his wife, in which she revealed Postcard's identity, gave them Postcard's real name and address, and took their final payment. She then had Pat contact their waiting list client, the commodities broker who suspected her husband of sleeping with their nanny and, next day, welcomed the woman to the office to take down her details and receive a down payment.

The commodities broker didn't bother to hide her disappointment that she was meeting Robin instead of Strike. She was a thin, colourless blonde of forty-two, whose over-highlighted hair had the texture, close up, of fine wire. Robin found her unlikeable until the end of the interview, when she talked about her husband, whose business had gone bankrupt and who now worked from home, giving him many long hours alone with the nanny.

'Fourteen years,' said the broker. 'Fourteen years, three kids and now . . .'

She hid her eyes behind her shaking hands and Robin, who'd been with Matthew since she was at school, felt, in spite of the woman's brittle façade, an unexpected glow of sympathy.

After the new client had left, Robin called Morris into the office and gave him the job of the first day's surveillance of the nanny.

'Okey-doke,' he said. 'Hey, what d'you say we call the client "RB"?'

'What does that stand for?' Robin asked.

'Rich Bitch,' said Morris, grinning. 'She's loaded.'

'No,' said Robin, unsmiling.

'Whoops,' said Morris, eyebrows raised. 'Feminist alert?'

'Something like that.'

'OK, how about—?'

'We'll call her Mrs Smith, after the street they live on,' said Robin coldly.

Over the next few days, Robin took her turn tailing the nanny, a glossy-haired brunette who somewhat reminded her of Strike's ex-girlfriend Lorelei. The commodities broker's children certainly seemed to adore their nanny, and so, Robin feared, did their father. While he didn't once touch the nanny in any amorous way, he showed every sign of a man completely smitten: mirroring her body language, laughing excessively at her jokes, and hurrying to open doors and gates for her.

A couple of nights later, Robin dozed off at the wheel for a few seconds while driving towards Elinor Dean's house in Stoke Newington. Jerking awake, she immediately turned on the radio and opened the window, so that her eyes streamed with the cold, sooty night air, but the incident scared her. Over the next few days, she increased her caffeine consumption in an effort to keep awake. This made her slightly jittery, and she found it hard to sleep even on the rare occasions the chance presented itself.

Robin had always been as careful with the firm's money as Strike himself, treating every penny spent as though it were to be deducted from her own take-home pay. The habit of parsimony had stayed with her, even though the agency's survival no longer depended on extracting money from clients before the final demands came in. Robin was well aware that Strike took very little money out of the business for his own needs, preferring to plough profits back into the agency. He continued to live a Spartan existence in the two and a half rooms over the office, and there were months when she, the salaried partner, took home more pay than the senior partner and founder of the firm.

All of this added to her feeling of guilt at booking herself into a Premier Inn in Leamington Spa on the Sunday night before Satchwell's art exhibition. The town was only a two-hour drive away; Robin knew she could have got up early on Monday morning instead of sleeping over in the town. However, she was so exhausted, she feared dozing off at the wheel again.

She justified the hotel room to herself by leaving twenty-four hours ahead of the exhibition's opening, thus giving herself time to take a look at the church where Margot had allegedly been sighted a week after her disappearance. She also packed photocopies of all the pages of Talbot's horoscope notes that mentioned Paul Satchwell, with the intention of studying them in the quiet of her hotel room. To these, she added a second-hand copy of Evangeline Adams's *Your Place in the Sun*, a pack of unopened tarot cards and a copy of *The Book of Thoth*. She hadn't told Strike she'd bought any of these items and didn't intend claiming expenses for them.

Much as she loved London, Yorkshire-born Robin sometimes pined for trees, moors and hills. Her drive up the nondescript M40, past hamlets and villages with archaic names like Middleton Cheney, Temple Herdewyke and Bishop's Itchington, gave her glimpses of flat green fields. The cool, damp day bore a welcome whiff of spring on the air, and in the breaks between scudding white clouds, hard, bright sunshine filled the old Land Rover with a light that made a pale grey ghost of Robin's reflection in the dusty window beside her. She really needed to clean the car: in fact, there were sundry small, personal chores piling up while she worked non-stop for the agency, such as ringing her mother, whose calls she'd been avoiding, and her lawyer, who'd left a message about the upcoming mediation, not to mention plucking her eyebrows, buying herself a new pair of flat shoes and sorting out a bank transfer to Max, covering her half of the council tax.

As the hedgerows flashed by, Robin consciously turned her thoughts away from these depressing mundanities to Paul Satchwell. She doubted she'd find him in Leamington Spa, being unable to imagine why the seventy-five-year-old would want to leave his home on Kos merely to visit the provincial art gallery. Satchwell had probably sent his paintings over from Greece, or else given permission for them to be exhibited. Why would he leave what Robin imagined as a dazzling white-walled villa, an artist's studio set among olive groves? Her plan was to pretend an interest in buying or commissioning one of his paintings, so as to get his home address. For a moment or two, she indulged herself in a little fantasy of flying out to Greece with Strike, to interrogate the old artist. She imagined the oven-blast of heat that would hit them on leaving the plane in Athens, and saw herself in a dress and sandals, heading up a dusty track to Satchwell's front door. But when her imagination showed her Strike in shorts, with the metal rod of his prosthetic leg on display, she felt suddenly embarrassed by her own imaginings, and closed the little fantasy down before it took her to the beach, or the hotel.

On the outskirts of Leamington Spa, Robin followed the sign to All Saints church, which she knew from her research was the only possible candidate for the place where Charlie Ramage had seen Margot. Janice had mentioned a 'big church'; All Saints was a tourist attraction due to its size. None of the other churches in Leamington Spa had graveyards attached to them. Moreover, All Saints was situated directly on the route of anyone travelling north from London. Although Robin found it hard to understand why Margot would have been browsing headstones in Leamington Spa, while her husband begged for information of her whereabouts in the national press and her Leamington-born lover remained in London, she had a strange feeling that seeing the church for herself would give her a better idea as to whether Margot had ever been there. The missing doctor was becoming very real to Robin.

She managed to secure a parking space in Priory Terrace, right beside the church, and set off on foot around the perimeter, marvelling at the sheer scale of the place. It was a staggering size for a relatively small town; in fact, it looked more like a cathedral, with its long, arched windows. Turning right into Church Street, she noted the further coincidence of the street name being so similar to Margot's home address. On the right, a low wall topped with railings provided an ideal spot for a motorbike rider to park, and enjoy a cup of tea from his Thermos, looking at the graveyard.

Except that there was no graveyard. Robin came to an abrupt standstill. She could only see two tombs, raised stone caskets whose inscriptions had been eroded. Otherwise, there was simply a wide stretch of grass intersected with two footpaths.

'Bomb fell on it.'

A cheery-looking mother was walking towards Robin, pushing a double pushchair containing sleeping boy twins. She'd correctly interpreted Robin's sudden halt.

'Really?' said Robin.

'Yeah, in 1940,' said the woman, slowing down. 'Luftwaffe.'

'Wow. Awful,' said Robin, imagining the smashed earth, the broken tombstones and, perhaps, fragments of coffin and bone.

'Yeah – but they missed them two,' said the woman, pointing at the aged tombs standing in the shadow of a yew tree. One of the twin toddlers gave a little stretch in his sleep and his eyelids flickered. With a comical grimace at Robin, the mother took off again at a brisk walk.

Robin walked into the enclosed area that had once been a graveyard, looking around and wondering what to make of Ramage's story, now. There hadn't been a graveyard here in

1974, when he claimed to have seen Margot browsing among tombstones. Or had an intact cemetery been assumed by Janice Beattie, when she heard that Margot was looking at graves? Robin turned to look at the two surviving tombs. Certainly, if Margot had been examining these, she'd have been brought within feet of a motorcyclist parked beside the church.

Robin placed her hands on the cold black bars that kept the curious from actually touching the old tombs, and examined them. What could have drawn Margot to them? The inscriptions etched on the mossy stone were almost illegible. Robin tilted her head, trying to make them out.

Was she seeing things? Did one of the words say 'Virgo', or had she spent too much time dwelling on Talbot's horoscope notes? Yet the more she studied it, the more like 'Virgo' the name looked.

Robin associated that star sign with two people, these days: her estranged husband, Matthew, and Dorothy Oakden, the widowed practice secretary at Margot's old place of work. Robin had become so adept at reading Talbot's horoscope notes, that she routinely heard 'Dorothy' in her head when looking at the glyph for Virgo. Now she took out her phone, looked up the tomb and felt mildly reassured to discover that she wasn't seeing things: this was the last resting place of one James Virgo Dunn.

But why should it have been of interest to Margot? Robin scrolled down a genealogy page for the Virgos and the Dunns and learned that the man whose bones now lay in dust a few feet from her had been born in Jamaica, where he'd been the owner of forty-six slaves.

'No need to feel sorry for *you*, then,' Robin muttered, returning her phone to her pocket, and she walked on around the perimeter to the front of the church, until she reached the great oak and iron double front doors. As she headed up the stone steps towards them, she heard the low hum of a hymn. Of course: it was Sunday morning.

After a moment's hesitation, Robin opened the door as quietly as possible and peered inside. An immense, sombre space was revealed: chilly parabolas of grey stone, a hundred feet of cold air between congregation and ceiling. Doubtless a church of this gigantic size had been deemed necessary back in Regency times, when people had flocked to the spa town to drink its waters, but the modern congregation didn't come close to filling it. A black-robed verger looked around at her; Robin smiled apologetically, quietly closed the door and returned to the pavement, where a large modern steel sculpture, part squiggle, part coil, was evidently supposed to represent the medicinal spring around which the town had been built.

A pub nearby was just opening its doors and Robin fancied a coffee, so she crossed the road and entered the Old Library.

The interior was large but hardly less gloomy than the church, the décor mostly shades of brown. Robin bought herself a coffee, settled herself in a tucked-away corner where she couldn't be observed, and sank into abstraction. Her glimpse of the church's interior had told her nothing. Margot had been an atheist, but churches were some of the few places a person could sit and think, undisturbed. Might Margot have been drawn to All Saints out of that unfocused, inchoate need that had once driven Robin herself into an unknown graveyard, there to sit on a wooden bench and contemplate the parlous state of her marriage?

Robin set down her coffee cup, opened the messenger bag she'd brought with her and took out the wad of photocopies of those pages of Talbot's notebook that mentioned Paul Satchwell. Smoothing them flat, she glanced up casually at the two men who'd just sat down at a nearby table. The one with his back to her was tall and broad, with dark, curly hair, and before she could remind herself that he couldn't be Strike, because her partner was in St Mawes, a thrill of excitement and happiness passed through her.

The stranger seemed to have felt Robin looking at him, because he turned before she could avert her eyes. She caught a glimpse of eyes as blue as Morris's, a weak chin and a short neck before she bowed her head to examine the horoscope notes, feeling herself turning red and suddenly unable to take in the mass of drawings and symbols in front of her.

Waves of shame were crashing over her, entirely disproportionate to catching a stranger's eye. In the pit of her stomach, the last sparks of the excitement she'd felt on thinking that she was looking at Strike glimmered and died.

It was a momentary error of perception, she told herself. *There's absolutely nothing to worry about. Calm down.*

But instead of reading the notes, Robin put her face in her hands. In this strange bar, her resistance lowered by exhaustion, Robin knew she'd been avoiding the question of what she really felt about Strike for the past year. Busy trying to disentangle herself from Matthew, familiarising herself with a new flat and a new flatmate, managing and deflecting her parents' anxiety and judgement, fending off Morris's constant badgering, dodging Ilsa's infuriating determination to matchmake and working twice as hard as ever before, it had been easy not to think about anything else, even a question as fraught as what she really felt for Cormoran Strike.

Now, in the corner of this dingy brown pub, with nothing else to distract her, Robin found herself thinking back to those honeymoon nights spent pacing the fine white sand after Matthew had gone to bed, when Robin had interrogated herself about whether she was in love with the man who'd then been her boss, not her partner. She'd worn a deep channel on the beach as she walked up and down in the dark, finally deciding that the answer was 'no', that what she felt was a mixture of friendship, admiration and gratitude for the opportunity he'd given her to embark on a once-dreamed-of career, which she'd thought was closed to her forever. She liked her partner; she admired him; she was grateful to him. That was it. That was all.

Except . . . she remembered how much pleasure it had given her to see him sitting in Notes Café, after a week's absence, and how happy she was, no matter the circumstances, to see Strike's name light up her phone.

Almost scared now, she forced herself to think about how bloody aggravating Strike could be: grumpy, taciturn and ungrateful, and nowhere near as handsome, with his broken nose and hair he himself described as 'pube-like', as Matthew, or even Morris . . .

But he was her best friend. This admission, held at bay for so long, caused an almost painful twist in Robin's heart, not least because she knew it would be impossible ever to tell Strike so. She could just imagine him lumbering away from her like a startled bison at such a naked statement of affection, redoubling the barriers he liked to erect if ever they got too close to each other. Nevertheless, there was a kind of relief in admitting the painful truth: she cared deeply for her partner. She trusted him on the big things: to do the right thing for the right reasons. She admired his brains and appreciated his doggedness, not to mention the self-discipline all the more admirable because many whole-bodied men had never mastered it. She was often astonished by his almost total lack of self-pity. She loved the drive for justice that she shared, that unbreakable determination to settle and to solve.

And there was something more, something highly unusual. Strike had never once made her feel physically uncomfortable. Two of them in the office, for a long time the only workers at the agency, and while Robin was a tall woman, he was far bigger, and he'd never made her feel it, as so many men did, not even in an attempt to intimidate, but because they enjoy the Parade, as a peacock spreads its tail. Matthew hadn't been able to get past the idea of them together all the time, in a small office space, hadn't been able to believe that Strike wasn't capitalising on the situation to make advances, however subtle.

But Robin, who'd forever be hypersensitive to the uninvited touch, the sidelong, lecherous glance, the invasion of personal space, the testing of conventional limits, had never once experienced, with Strike, that shrinking sensation within her own skin evoked by attempts to push a relationship into a different space. A deep reserve lay over Strike's private life, and while that sometimes frustrated her (had he, or had he not, called Charlotte Campbell back?), his love of privacy extended to a respect for other people's boundaries. Never had there been an ostensibly helpful but unnecessary touch, no hand on the small of the back, no grasping of the arm, no look that made her skin prickle, or made her want to cover herself: the legacy of those violent encounters with men that had left her scarred in more ways than the visible.

In truth (why not admit everything to herself now, when she was so tired, her defences lowered?) she was aware of only two moments in four years where she'd been sure that Strike had seen her as a desirable woman, not as a friend, or an apprentice, or a younger sister.

The first had been when she'd modelled that green Cavalli dress for him, in the course of their first investigation together, when he'd looked away from her as a man would if shunning too-bright light. She'd been embarrassed by her own behaviour, afterwards: she hadn't meant to make him think she was trying to be seductive or provocative; all she'd been trying to do was get information out of the sales assistant. But when he'd subsequently given her the green dress, thinking he'd never see her again, she'd wondered whether part of the message Strike had been trying to convey was that he didn't disavow that look, that she had, indeed, looked wonderful in the dress, and this suspicion hadn't made her feel uncomfortable, but happy and flattered.

The second moment, far more painful to remember, had been when she'd stood at the top of the stairs at her wedding venue, Strike below her, and he'd turned when she called his name, and looked up at her, the new bride. He'd been injured and exhausted, and again, she'd seen a flicker of something in his face that wasn't mere friendship, and they'd hugged, and she'd felt . . .

Best not to think about it. Best not to dwell on that hug, on how like home it had felt, on how a kind of insanity had gripped her at that moment, and she'd imagined him saying 'come with me' and known she'd have gone if he had.

Robin swept the horoscope papers off the pub table, stuffed them back into her messenger bag and went outside, leaving half her coffee undrunk.

Trying to walk off her memories, she crossed a small stone bridge spanning the slow-flowing River Leam, which was spotted with clumps of duckweed, and passed the colonnade of the Royal Pump Rooms, where Satchwell's exhibition would open the following day. Striding briskly, her hands in her pockets, Robin tried to focus on the Parade, where shopfronts disfigured what had once been a sweeping white Regency terrace.

But Leamington Spa did nothing to raise her spirits. On the contrary, it reminded her too much of another spa town: Bath, where Matthew had gone to university. For Robin, long, symmetrical curves of Regency buildings, with their plain, classical façades, would forever conjure once-fond memories disfigured by later discoveries: visions of herself and Matthew strolling hand in hand, overlain by the knowledge that, even then, he'd been sleeping with Sarah.

'Oh, bugger everything,' Robin muttered, blinking tears out of her eyes. She turned abruptly and headed all the way back to the Land Rover.

Having parked the car closer to the hotel, she made a detour into the nearby Co-op to buy a small stash of food, then checked in at a self-service machine in her Premier Inn and headed upstairs to her single room. It was small, bare but perfectly clean and comfortable, and overlooked a spectacularly ugly town hall of red and white brick, which was over-embellished with scrolls, pediments and lions.

A couple of sandwiches, a chocolate éclair, a can of Diet Coke and an apple made Robin feel better. As the sun sank slowly behind the buildings on the Parade, she slipped off her shoes and reached into her bag for the photocopied pages of Talbot's notebook and her pack of Thoth tarot cards, which Aleister Crowley had devised, and in which Bill Talbot had sought the solution to Margot's disappearance. Sliding the pack out of the box into her hand, she shuffled through the cards, examining the images. Just as she'd suspected, Talbot had copied many motifs into his notebook, presumably from those cards which had come up during his frequent attempts to solve the case by consulting the tarot.

Robin now flattened a photocopy of what she thought of as the 'horns page', on which Talbot had dwelled on the three horned signs of the zodiac: Capricorn, Aries and Taurus. This page came in the last quarter of the notebook, in which quotations from Aleister Crowley, astrological symbols and strange drawings appeared far more often than concrete facts.

Here on the horns page was evidence of Talbot's renewed interest in Satchwell, whom he'd first ruled out on the basis that he was an Aries rather than a Capricorn. Talbot had evidently

Note St John's cross
"And the Light
shineth in Darkness
and the Darkness.
comprehended
it not"
St John
1:5
The Emperor = ♈
sudden, violent
activity
Crowley
equates
Baphomet
SCHMIDT CHANGES
♓ AND ♒ TO ♑
Change ♒ to ♀
But ♀ and ♅ both in 12th with ♓
♀ IN 10th HOUSE: ELEVATION
Solve et Coagula
No resolution without
BREAKING DOWN
?
nurturing
and protective
denies contact
with ♅
(wives and
infidelity)
Is ∞ right?
But
♆ in
in 7th – House
of Marriage
FITS and ♀ in
11th – House
of Career? At
work?
'LUST/BABALON
'yet of their own poison
do they
perish'

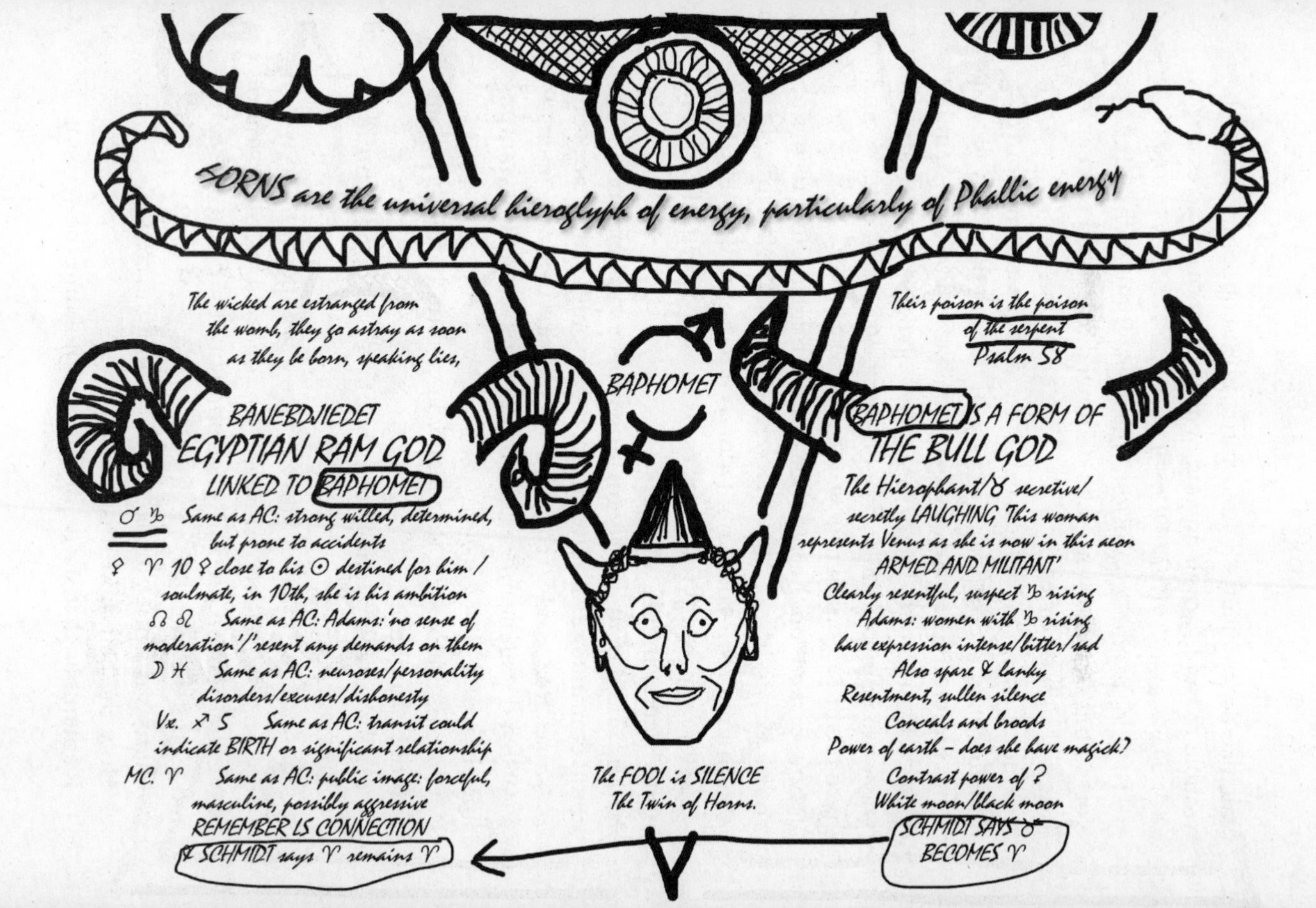
HORNS are the universal hieroglyph of energy, particularly of Phallic energy
The wicked are estranged from the womb, they go astray as soon as they be born, speaking lies,
Their poison is the poison of the serpent
Psalm 58
BAPHOMET
BANEBDJIEDET
EGYPTIAN RAM GOD
LINKED TO BAPHOMET
♂ ♑ Same as AC: strong willed, determined, but prone to accidents
☿ ♈ 10 ♀ close to his ☉ destined for him / soulmate, in 10th, she is his ambition
☊ ♌ Same as AC: Adams: 'no sense of moderation'/'resent any demands on them
☽ ♓ Same as AC: neuroses/personality disorders/excuses/dishonesty
Vx. ♐ 5 Same as AC: transit could indicate BIRTH or significant relationship
MC. ♈ Same as AC: public image: forceful, masculine, possibly aggressive
REMEMBER LS CONNECTION
☿ SCHMIDT says ♈ remains ♈
BAPHOMET IS A FORM OF
THE BULL GOD
The Hierophant/♉ secretive/ secretly LAUGHING 'This woman represents Venus as she is now in this aeon ARMED AND MILITANT'
Clearly resentful, suspect ♑ rising
Adams: women with ♑ rising have expression intense/bitter/sad
Also spare & lanky
Resentment, sullen silence
Conceals and broods
Power of earth – does she have magick?
Contrast power of ?
White moon/black moon
SCHMIDT SAYS ♉ BECOMES ♈
The FOOL is SILENCE
The Twin of Horns.

calculated Satchwell's whole birth horoscope and taken the trouble to note various aspects, which he noticed were *same as AC. Same as AC. AND DON'T FORGET LS connection.*

To add to the confusion, the mysterious Schmidt kept correcting signs, although he'd allowed Satchwell to keep his original sign of Aries.

And then an odd idea came to Robin: the notion of a fourteen-sign zodiac was clearly ludicrous (but why was it more ludicrous than a twelve-sign zodiac? asked a voice in her head, which sounded remarkably like Strike's), but certainly if you were going to squeeze in an extra two signs, dates would have to shift, wouldn't they?

She picked up her mobile and Googled 'fourteen-sign zodiac Schmidt'.

'Oh my God,' said Robin aloud, into her still hotel room.

Before she could fully process what she'd read, the mobile in her hand rang. It was Strike.

'Hi,' said Robin, hastily turning him to speakerphone so she could continue reading what she'd just found. 'How are you?'

'Knackered,' said Strike, who sounded it. 'What's happened?'

'What d'you mean?' asked Robin, her eyes rapidly scanning lines of text.

'You sound like you do when you've found something out.'

Robin laughed.

'OK, you won't believe this, but I've just found Schmidt.'

'You've what?'

'Schmidt, first name, Steven. He's a real person! He wrote a book in 1970 called *Astrology 14*, proposing the inclusion of two extra signs in the zodiac, Ophiuchus the Serpent-Bearer, and Cetus the Whale!'

There was a brief silence, then Strike muttered,

'How the hell did I miss that?'

'Remember that statue of the man holding the serpent, at

Margot's old house?' said Robin, falling back on her pillows among the scattered tarot cards.

'Asclepius,' said Strike. 'Ophiuchus was the Roman form. God of healing.'

'Well, this explains all the changing dates, doesn't it?' said Robin, 'and why poor Talbot got so confused! He was trying to put everyone into Schmidt's adjusted dates, but they didn't seem to fit. And all the other astrologers he was consulting were still using the twelve-sign system, so—'

'Yeah,' said Strike, talking over her, 'that'd make a crazy man crazier, all right.'

His tone said, 'This is interesting, but not important.' Robin removed the Three of Disks from beneath her and examined it absent-mindedly. Robin was now so well-versed in astrological symbols that she didn't need to look up the glyphs to know that it also represented Mars in Capricorn.

'How are things with you?' she asked.

'Well, the church isn't going to hold everyone who's coming tomorrow, which Joan would've been thrilled about. I just wanted to let you know I'll be heading back up the road again on Tuesday.'

'Are you sure you don't need to stay longer?'

'The neighbours are all promising they're going to look after Ted. Lucy's trying to get him to come up to London for a bit afterwards. Any other news your end?'

'Er . . . let's see . . . I wrapped up Postcard,' said Robin. 'I think our weatherman was quite disappointed when he saw who his stalker was. His wife cheered up no end, though.'

Strike gave a grunt of laughter.

'So, we've taken on the commodities broker,' Robin continued. 'We haven't got pictures of anything incriminating between the husband and nanny yet, but I don't think it's going to be long.'

'You're owed a long stretch off for all this, Robin,' said Strike gruffly. 'I can't thank you enough.'

'Don't be silly,' she said.

They hung up shortly afterwards.

Robin's room seemed to have become suddenly much darker. The sun had gone down; in silhouette, the town hall resembled a monstrous Gothic palace. She turned on her bedside lamp and looked around at the bed strewn with astrological notes and tarot cards. Seen in the light of Strike's lack of enthusiasm, Talbot's doodles looked like the determinedly weird drawings in the back of a teenager's jotter, leading nowhere, done purely for the love of strangeness.

Yawning, she refolded the photocopied notes and put them back in her bag, went for a shower, returned in her pyjamas to the bed and gathered up the tarot cards, putting them in order as she did so, to make sure none of them were missing. She didn't particularly want the cleaner to think of her as the kind of person who left tarot cards strewn in her wake.

On the point of replacing the deck in its box, Robin suddenly sat down on the bed and began to shuffle it instead. She was too tired to attempt the fifteen-card layout advocated in the little booklet that accompanied the tarot, but she knew from her exhaustive examination of his notes that Talbot had sometimes tried to see his way through the investigation by laying out just three cards: the first representing 'the nature of the problem', the second, 'the cause', and the third, 'the solution'.

After a minute's shuffling, Robin turned over the top card and laid it down in the pool of light cast by her bedside lamp: the Prince of Cups. A naked blueish-green man rode an eagle, which was diving towards water. He held a goblet containing a snake in one hand and a lotus flower in the other. Robin pulled *The Book of Thoth* out of her bag and looked up the meaning.

> The moral characteristics of the person pictured in this card are subtlety, secret violence, and craft. He is intensely secret, an artist in all his ways.

She thought immediately of Dennis Creed. A master of murder, in his way.

She turned over the next card: the Four of Cups, or Luxury. Another lotus was pouring water over four more goblets, golden this time. Robin turned to the book.

> The card refers to the Moon in Cancer, which is her own house; but Cancer itself is so placed that this implies a certain weakness, an abandonment to desire.

Was the tarot criticising her for soft living? Robin glanced around her little box of a room, then turned over the last card.

More cups and yet more lotuses, and two entwined fish, pouring out water into two more golden chalices which stood on a green lake.

> Love . . . The card also refers to Venus in Cancer. It shows the harmony of the male and the female: interpreted in the largest sense. It is perfect and placid harmony . . .

Robin inspected the card for a few more seconds, before laying it down beside the other two. They were all cups. As she knew from her study of the Thoth tarot, cups meant water. Well, here she was in a spa town . . .

Robin shook her head, though nobody was there to see her do it, returned the tarot cards to their box, climbed into bed, set her alarm and turned out the light.

46

Whereas that Pagan proud him selfe did rest,
In secret shadow by a fountaine side:
Euen he it was, that earst would haue supprest
Faire Vna . . .

Edmund Spenser
The Faerie Queene

Robin's night was punctuated with sudden wakings from a succession of anxious dreams: that she'd fallen asleep at the wheel again, or had overslept and arrived at the gallery to find Satchwell's exhibition gone. When the alarm on her mobile rang at 7 a.m., she forced herself immediately out of bed, showered, dressed and, glad to leave the impersonal bedroom, headed downstairs with her packed holdall to eat muesli and drink coffee in the dining room, which was painted an oppressive sludge green.

The day outside was fresh but overcast, a cold silver sun trying to penetrate the cloud. Having returned her holdall to the parked Land Rover, she headed on foot towards the Royal Pump Rooms, which housed the gallery where Satchwell's exhibition was about to open. To her left lay the ornamental Jephson Gardens, and a fountain of pinkish stone that might have been the model for one of Crowley's tarot cards. Four scallop-patterned basins sat at the top.

. . . a certain weakness, an abandonment to desire . . .

You're getting like Talbot, Robin told herself crossly. Speeding up, she arrived at the Pump Rooms with time to spare.

The building had just been opened; a young woman in black was walking away from the glass doors, holding a bunch of keys. Robin entered, to find little trace of the Regency pump rooms left inside: the floor was covered in modern grey tiles, the ceiling supported by metal columns. A café took up one wing of the open-plan space, a shop another. The gallery, Robin saw, lay across opposite, through more glass doors.

It comprised one long room, brick-walled and wooden-floored, which had been temporarily given over to an exhibition of local artists. There were only three people inside: a stocky, grey-bobbed woman in an Alice band, a small man with a hang-dog air whom Robin suspected was her husband, and another young woman in black, who she assumed worked there. The grey-haired woman's voice was echoing around the room as though it was a gymnasium.

'I *told* Shona that Long Itchington needs an accent light! You can barely *see* it, this corner's so dark!'

Robin walked slowly around, looking at canvases and sketches. Five local artists had been given space for the temporary exhibition, but she identified Paul Satchwell's work without difficulty: it had been given a prominent position and stood out boldly among the studies of local landmarks, portraits of pallid Britons standing at bus stops, and still lifes.

Naked figures twisted and cavorted in scenes from Greek mythology. Persephone struggled in the arms of Hades as he carried her down into the underworld; Andromeda strained against chains binding her to rock as a dragonish creature rose from the waves to devour her; Leda lay supine in bulrushes as Zeus, in the form of a swan, impregnated her.

Two lines of Joni Mitchell floated back to Robin as she

looked at the paintings: '*When I first saw your gallery, I liked the ones of ladies . . .*'

Except that Robin wasn't sure she liked the paintings. The female figures were all black-haired, olive-skinned, heavy-breasted and partially or entirely naked. The paintings were accomplished, but Robin found them slightly lascivious. Each of the women wore a similar expression of vacant abandon, and Satchwell seemed to have a definite preference for those myths that featured bondage, rape or abduction.

'Striking, aren't they?' said the meek-faced husband of the angry painter of Long Itchington, appearing at Robin's side to contemplate a picture of a totally naked Io, whose hair streamed behind her and whose breasts gleamed with sweat as she fled a bull with a gargantuan erection.

'Mm,' said Robin. 'I was wondering whether he was going to come to the exhibition. Paul Satchwell, I mean.'

'I think he said he's going to pop back in,' said the man.

'Back—? You mean he's here? In England?'

'Well, yes,' said the man, looking somewhat surprised. 'He was here yesterday, anyway. Came to see them hung.'

'Visiting family, I think he said,' said the young woman in black, who seemed glad of a reason to talk to somebody other than the fuming artist in the hairband.

'You haven't got contact details for him, have you?' asked Robin. 'Maybe the address of where he's staying?'

'No,' said the young woman, now looking intrigued. Evidently local artists didn't usually engender this much excitement. 'You can leave your name and address, though, if you like, and I'll tell him you want to speak to him if he drops by?'

So Robin accompanied the young woman back to the reception area, where she scribbled her name and phone number onto a piece of paper and then, her heart still beating fast in excitement, went to the café, bought herself a cappuccino and positioned herself beside a long window looking out onto the Pump Room Gardens, where she had a good view of people entering the building.

Should she book back into the Premier Inn and wait here in Leamington Spa until Satchwell showed himself? Would Strike think it worth neglecting their other cases to remain here in the hope of Satchwell turning up? It was Joan's funeral today: she couldn't burden him with the question.

She wondered what her partner was doing now. Perhaps already dressing for the service. Robin had only ever attended three funerals. The first had been her maternal grandfather's, who'd died just before she dropped out of university: she'd gone home for the funeral and never gone back. She remembered very little of the occasion: it had taken everything she'd had to preserve a fragile façade of well-being, and she remembered the strange sense of disembodiment that underlay the eggshell brittleness with which she'd met the half-scared enquiries of family members who knew what had happened to her. She remembered, too, Matthew's hand around hers. He hadn't once dropped it, skipping lectures and an important rugby game to come and be with her.

The only other funeral she'd attended had been four years previously, when she and Strike had attended the cremation of a murdered girl in the course of their first murder investigation, standing together at the back of the sparsely populated, impersonal crematorium. That had been before Strike had agreed to take her on permanently, when she'd been nothing but a temp whom Strike had allowed to inveigle her way into his investigation. Thinking back to Rochelle Onifade's funeral, Robin realised that even then, the ties binding her to Matthew had been loosening. Robin hadn't yet realised it, but she'd found something she wanted more than she'd wanted to be Matthew's wife.

Her coffee finished, Robin made a quick trip to the bathroom, then returned to the gallery in the hope that Satchwell might have entered it while she wasn't watching, but there was no sign of him. A few people had drifted in to wander around the temporary exhibition. Satchwell's paintings were attracting the most interest. Having walked the room once more, Robin pretended an interest in an old water fountain in the corner. Covered in swags and lion's heads with gaping mouths, it had once dispensed the health-giving spa waters.

Beyond the font lay another a room, which presented a total contrast to the clean, modern space behind her. It was octagonal and made of brick, with a very high ceiling and windows of Bristol blue glass. Robin stepped inside: it was, or had once been, a Turkish *hammam* or steam room, and had the appearance of a small temple. At the highest point of the vaulted ceiling was a cupola decorated with an eight-pointed star in glass, with a lantern hanging from it.

'Nice to see a bit of *pagan* influence, innit?'

The voice was a combination of self-conscious cockney, overlain with the merest whiff of a Greek accent. Robin spun around and there, planted firmly in the middle of the *hammam*, in jeans and an old denim shirt, was an elderly man with his left eye covered in a surgical dressing, which stood out, stark white against skin as brown as old terracotta. His straggly white hair fell to his stooping shoulders; white chest hair grew in the space left by his undone buttons, a silver chain hung around his crêpe-skinned throat, and silver and turquoise rings decorated his fingers.

'You the young lady 'oo wanted to talk to me?' asked Paul Satchwell, revealing yellow-brown teeth as he smiled.

'Yes,' said Robin, 'I am. Robin Ellacott,' she added, holding out her hand.

His uncovered eye swept Robin's face and figure with

unconcealed appreciation. He held her hand a little too long after shaking it but Robin continued to smile as she withdrew it, and delved in her handbag for a card, which she gave him.

'Private detective?' said Satchwell, his smile fading a little as he read the card, one-eyed. 'The 'ell's all this?'

Robin explained.

'Margot?' said Satchwell, looking shocked. 'Christ almighty, that's, what . . . forty years ago?'

'Nearly,' said Robin, moving aside to let some tourists claim her spot in the middle of the *hammam*, and read its history off the sign on the wall. 'I've come up from London in hopes of talking to you about her. It'd mean a lot to the family if you could tell me whatever you remember.'

'*Éla ré*, what d'you expect me to remember after all this time?' said Satchwell.

But Robin was confident he was going to accept. She'd discovered that people generally wanted to know what you already knew, why you'd come to find them, whether they had any reason to worry. And sometimes they wanted to talk, because they were lonely or felt neglected, and it was flattering to have somebody hang on your words, and sometimes, as now (elderly as he was, the single eye, which was a cold, pale blue, swept her body and back to her face) they wanted to spend more time with a young woman they found attractive.

'All right, then,' said Satchwell slowly, 'I don't know what I can tell you, but I'm hungry. Let me take you to lunch.'

'That'd be great, but I'll be taking you,' said Robin, smiling. 'You're doing *me* the favour.'

47

. . . the sacred Oxe, that carelesse stands,
With gilden hornes, and flowry girlonds crownd . . .
All suddeinly with mortall stroke astownd,
Doth groueling fall . . .
The martiall Mayd stayd not him to lament,
But forward rode, and kept her ready way . . .

Edmund Spenser
The Faerie Queene

Satchwell bade the attendant in the art gallery farewell by clasping her hands in a double handshake and assuring her he'd look in later in the week. He even took fulsome leave of the disgruntled painter of Long Itchington, who scowled after him as he left.

'Provincial galleries,' he said, chuckling, as he and Robin headed out of the Pump Rooms. 'Funny, seeing my stuff next to that old bat's postcard pictures, though, wasn't it? And a bit of a kick to be exhibited where you were born. I haven't been back here in, Christ, must be fifty-odd years. You got a car? Good. We'll get out of here, go froo to Warwick. It's just up the road.'

Satchwell kept up a steady stream of talk as they walked towards the Land Rover.

'Never liked Leamington.' With only one eye at his service,

he had to turn his head in exaggerated fashion to look around. 'Too *genteel* for the likes of me . . .'

Robin learned that he'd lived in the spa town only until he was six, at which point he and his single mother had moved to Warwick. He had a younger half-sister, the result of his mother's second marriage, with whom he was currently staying, and had decided to have his cataract removed while in England.

'Still a British citizen, I'm entitled. So when they asked me,' he said, with a grand wave backwards at the Royal Pump Rooms, 'if I'd contribute some paintings, I thought, why not? Brought them over with me.'

'They're wonderful,' said Robin insincerely. 'Have you got just the one sister?' She had no aim other than making polite conversation, but out of the corner of her eye, she saw Satchwell's head turn so that his unbandaged eye could look at her.

'No,' he said, after a moment or two. 'It was . . . I 'ad an older sister, too, but she died when we were kids.'

'Oh, I'm sorry,' said Robin.

'One of those things,' said Satchwell. 'Severely disabled. Had fits and stuff. She was older than me. I can't remember much about it. Hit my mum hard, obviously.'

'I can imagine,' said Robin.

They had reached the Land Rover. Robin, who'd already mentally calculated the risk to herself, should Satchwell prove to be dangerous, was confident that she'd be safe by daylight, and given that she had control of the car. She unlocked the doors and climbed into the driver's seat, and Satchwell succeeded in hoisting himself into the passenger seat on his second attempt.

'Yeah, we moved froo to Warwick from 'ere after Blanche died,' he said, buckling up his seatbelt. 'Just me and my mum. Not that Warwick's much better, but it's *aufentic*. Aufentic medieval buildings, you know?'

Given that he was Midlands born and raised, Robin thought his cockney accent must be a longstanding affectation. It came and went, mingled with an intonation that was slightly foreign after so many years in Greece.

'Whereas this place . . . the Victorians 'ad their wicked way with it,' he said, and as Robin reversed out her parking space he said, looking up at the moss-covered face of a stone Queen Victoria, 'there she is, look, miserable old cow,' and laughed. 'State of that building,' he added, as they passed the town hall. 'That's somefing me and Crowley had in common, for sure. Born 'ere, hated it 'ere.'

Robin thought she must have misheard.

'You and . . . ?'

'Aleister Crowley.'

'Crowley?' she repeated, as they drove up the Parade. 'The occult writer?'

'Yeah. 'E was born here,' said Satchwell. 'You don't see that in many of the guidebooks, because they don't like it. 'Ere, turn left. Go on, it's on our way.'

Minutes later, he directed her into Clarendon Square, where tall white terraced houses, though now subdivided into flats, retained a vestige of their old grandeur.

'That's it, where he was born,' said Satchwell with satisfaction, pointing up at number 30. 'No plaque or nothing. They don't like talking about him, the good people of Leamington Spa. I had a bit of a Crowley phase in my youth,' said Satchwell, as Robin looked up at the large, square windows. 'You know he tortured a cat to death when he was a boy, just to see whether it had nine lives?'

'I didn't,' said Robin, putting the car into reverse.

'Probably 'appened in there,' said Satchwell with morbid satisfaction.

Same as AC. Same as AC. Another moment of enlightenment

had hit Robin. Talbot had gone looking for identical components between Satchwell's horoscope and Crowley's, the self-proclaimed Beast, Baphomet, the wickedest man in the West. *LS connection.* Of course: Leamington Spa.

Why had Talbot decided, months into the investigation, that Satchwell deserved a full horoscope, the only one of the suspects to be so honoured? His alibi appeared watertight, after all. Had the return of suspicion been a symptom of Talbot's illness, triggered by the coincidence of Satchwell and Crowley's place of birth, or had he uncovered some unrecorded weakness in Satchwell's alibi? Satchwell continued to talk about his life in Greece, his painting and about his disappointment in how old England was faring, and Robin made appropriate noises at regular intervals while mentally reviewing those features of Satchwell's horoscope that Talbot had found so intriguing.

Mars in Capricorn: strong-willed, determined, but prone to accidents.

Moon in Pisces: neuroses/personality disorders/dishonesty

Leo rising: no sense of moderation. Resents demands on them.

They reached Warwick within half an hour and, as Satchwell had promised, found themselves in a town that could hardly have presented a greater contrast to the wide, sweeping white-faced crescents of Leamington. An ancient stone arch reminded Robin of Clerkenwell. They passed timber and beam houses, cobbles, steep sloping streets and narrow alleyways.

'We'll go to the Roebuck,' said Satchwell, when Robin had parked in the market square. 'It's been there for ever. Oldest pub in town.'

'Wherever you like,' said Robin, smiling as she checked that she had her notebook in her handbag.

They walked together through the heart of Warwick, Satchwell pointing out such landmarks as he deemed worth looking at. He was one of those men who felt a need to touch, tapping Robin unnecessarily upon the arm to draw her attention, grasping her elbow as they crossed a street, and generally assuming a proprietorial air over her as they wove their way towards Smith Street.

'D'you mind?' asked Satchwell, as they drew level with Picturesque Art Supplies, and without waiting for an answer he led her into the shop where, as he selected brushes and oils, he talked with airy self-importance of modern trends in art and the stupidity of critics. *Oh, Margot*, Robin thought, but then she imagined the Margot Bamborough she carried with her in her head judging her, in turn, by Matthew, with his endless store of anecdotes of his own sporting achievements, and his increasingly pompous talk of pay rises and bonuses, and felt humbled and apologetic.

At last, they made it into the Roebuck Inn, a low-beamed pub with a sign of a deer's head hanging outside, and secured a table for two towards the rear of the pub. Robin couldn't help but notice the coincidence: the wall behind Satchwell was dotted with horned animal heads, including a stuffed deer and bronze-coloured models of an antelope and a ram. Even the menus had silhouettes of antlered stag heads upon them. Robin asked the waitress for a Diet Coke, all the while trying to repress thoughts of the horned signs of the zodiac.

'Would it be all right,' she asked, smiling, when the waitress had departed for the bar, 'if I ask a few questions about Margot now?'

'Yeah, of course,' said Satchwell, with a smile that revealed his stained teeth again, but he immediately picked up the menu card and studied it.

'And d'you mind if I take notes?' Robin asked, pulling out her notebook.

'Go ahead,' he said, still smiling, watching her over the

top of his menu with his uncovered eye, which followed her movements as she opened the book and clicked out the nib of her pen.

'So, I apologise if any of these questions—'

'Are you sure you don't want a proper drink?' asked Satchwell, who had ordered a beer. 'I 'ate drinking on me own.'

'Well, I'm driving, you see,' said Robin.

'You could stay over. Not with me, don't worry,' he said quickly, with a grin that on a man so elderly, resembled a satyr's leer, 'I mean, go to an 'otel, file expenses. I s'pect you're taking a good chunk of money from Margot's family for this, are you?'

Robin merely smiled, and said,

'I need to get back to London. We're quite busy. It would be really useful to get some background on Margot,' she continued. 'How did you meet?'

He told her the story she already knew, about how he'd been taken to the Playboy Club by a client and seen there the leggy nineteen-year-old in her bunny ears and tail.

'And you struck up a friendship?'

'Well,' said Satchwell, 'I don't know that I'd call it *that*.'

With his cold eye upon Robin he said,

'We 'ad a very strong *sexual* connection. She was a virgin when we met, y'know.'

Robin kept smiling formally. He wasn't going to embarrass her.

'She was nineteen. I was twen'y-five. Beau'iful girl,' he sighed. 'Wish I'd kept the pictures I took of her, but after she disappeared I felt wrong about 'aving them.'

Robin heard Oonagh again. 'He took pictures of her. *You* know. *Pictures*.' It must be those revealing or obscene photos Satchwell was talking about, because after all, he'd hardly have felt guilty about having a snapshot.

The waitress came back with Satchwell's beer and Robin's Diet Coke. They ordered food; after swiftly scanning the menu, Robin asked for a chicken and bacon salad; Satchwell ordered steak and chips. When the waitress had gone Robin asked, though she knew the answer,

'How long were you together?'

'Coupla years, all told. We broke up, then got back togevver. She didn't like me using other models. Jealous. Not cut out for an artist's muse, Margot. Didn't like sitting still and not talking, haha . . . no, I fell hard for Margot Bamborough. Yeah, there was a damn sight more to her than being a Bunny Girl.'

Of course there was, thought Robin, though still smiling politely. *She became a bloody doctor.*

'Did you ever paint her?'

'Yeah,' said Satchwell. 'Few times. Some sketches and one full-size picture. I sold them. Needed the cash. Wish I 'adn't.'

He fell into a momentary abstraction, his uncovered eye surveying the pub, and Robin wondered whether old memories were genuinely resurfacing behind the heavily tanned face, which was so deeply lined and dark it might have been carved from teak, or whether he was playing the part that was expected of him when he said quietly,

'Hell of a girl, Margot Bamborough.'

He took a sip of his beer, then said,

'It's her 'usband who's hired you, is it?'

'No,' said Robin. 'Her daughter.'

'Oh,' said Satchwell, nodding. 'Yeah, of course: there was a kid. She didn't look as though she'd 'ad a baby, when I met her after they got married. Slim as ever. Both my wives put on about a stone with each of our kids.'

'How many children have you got?' asked Robin, politely.

She wanted the food to hurry up. It was harder to walk out

once food was in front of you, and some instinct told her that Paul Satchwell's whimsical mood might not last.

'Five,' said Satchwell. 'Two with me first wife, and three with me second. Didn't mean to: we got twins on the last throw. All pretty much grown up now, thank Christ. Kids and art don't mix. I love 'em,' he said roughly, 'but Cyril Connolly had it right. The enemy of promise is the pram in the bloody 'all.'

He threw her a brief glance out of his one visible eye and said abruptly,

'So 'er 'usband still thinks I had something to do with Margot disappearing, does 'e?'

'What d'you mean by "still"?' enquired Robin.

''E gave my name to the police,' said Satchwell. 'The night she disappeared. Thought she might've run off with me. Did you know Margot and I bumped into each other a coupla weeks before she disappeared?'

'I did, yes,' said Robin.

'It put ideas into what's-'is-name's head,' he said. 'I can't blame him, I s'pose it did look fishy. I'd've probably thought the same, if my bird had met up with an old flame right before they buggered off – disappeared, I mean.'

The food arrived: Satchwell's steak and chips looked appetising, but Robin, who'd been too busy concentrating on her questions, hadn't read the small print on the menu. Expecting a plate of salad, she received a wooden platter bearing various ramekins containing hot sausage slices, hummous and a sticky mess of mayonnaise-coated leaves, a challenging assortment to eat while taking notes.

'Want some chips?' offered Satchwell, pushing the small metal bucket that contained them towards her.

'No thanks,' said Robin, smiling. She took a bite of a breadstick and continued, her pen in her right hand,

'Did Margot talk about Roy, when you bumped into her?'

'A bit,' said Satchwell, his mouth full of steak. 'She put up a good front. What you do, when you meet the ex, isn't it? Pretend you think you did the right thing. No regrets.'

'Did you think she had regrets?' asked Robin.

'She wasn't 'appy, I could tell. I thought, nobody's paying you attention. She tried to put a brave face on it, but she struck me as miserable. Knackered.'

'Did you only see each other the once?'

Satchwell chewed his steak, looking at Robin thoughtfully. At last he swallowed, then said,

'Have you read my police statement?'

'Yes,' said Robin.

'Then you know perfectly well,' said Satchwell, waggling his fork at her, 'that it was just the once. *Don't* you?'

He was smiling, trying to pass off the implied admonition as waggish, but Robin felt the spindle-thin spike of aggression.

'So you went for a drink, and talked?' said Robin, smiling, as though she hadn't noticed the undertone, daring him to become defensive, and he continued, in a milder tone,

'Yeah, we went to some bar in Camden, not far from my flat. She'd been on an 'ouse call to some patient.'

Robin made a note.

'And can you remember what you talked about?'

'She told me she'd met 'er husband at medical school, 'e was an 'igh-flier and all that. What was 'e?' said Satchwell, with what seemed to Robin a forced unconcern. 'A cardiologist or something?'

'Haematologist,' said Robin.

'What's that, blood? Yeah, she was always impressed by clever people, Margot. Didn't occur to 'er that they can be shits like anyone else.'

'Did you get the impression Dr Phipps was a shit?' asked Robin lightly.

'Not really,' said Satchwell. 'But I was told 'e had a stick up his arse and was a bit of a mummy's boy.'

'Who told you that?' asked Robin, pausing with her pen suspended over her notebook.

'Someone 'oo'd met him,' he replied with a slight shrug. 'You not married?' he went on, his eyes on Robin's bare left hand.

'Living with someone,' said Robin, with a brief smile. It was the answer she'd learned to give, to shut down flirtation from witnesses and clients, to erect barriers. Satchwell said, 'Ah. I always know, if a bird's living with a bloke without marriage, she must be really keen on him. Nothing but 'er feelings holding her, is there?'

'I suppose not,' said Robin, with a brief smile. She knew he was trying to disconcert her. 'Did Margot mention anything that might be worrying her, or causing her problems? At home or at work?'

'Told you, it was all window dressing,' said Satchwell, munching on fries. 'Great job, great 'usband, nice kid, nice 'ouse: she'd made it.' He swallowed. 'I did the same thing back: told her I was having an exhibition, won an award for one of me paintings, in a band, serious girlfriend . . . which was a lie,' he added, with a slight snort. 'I only remember that bird because we split up later that evening. Don't ask me her name now. We 'adn't been together long. She had long black hair and a massive tattoo of a spider's web round her navel, that's what I mainly remember – yeah, anyway, I ended it. Seeing Margot again—'

He hesitated. His uncovered eye unfocused, he said,

'I was thirty-five. It's a funny age. It starts dawning on you forty's really gonna happen to you, not just to other people. What are you, twenty-five?'

'Twenty-nine,' said Robin.

'Happens earlier for women, that worrying about getting old thing,' said Satchwell. 'Got kids yet?'

'No,' said Robin, and then, 'so Margot didn't say anything to you that might suggest a reason for disappearing voluntarily?'

'Margot wouldn't have gone away and left everyone in the lurch,' said Satchwell, as positive on the point as Oonagh. 'Not Margot. Responsible was her middle name. She was a good girl, you know? School prefect sort.'

'So you didn't make any plans to meet again?'

'No plans,' said Satchwell, munching on chips. 'I mentioned to 'er my band was playing at the Dublin Castle the following week. Said, "drop in if you're passing", but she said she wouldn't be able to. Dublin Castle was a pub in Camden,' Satchwell added. 'Might still be there.'

'Yes,' said Robin, 'it is.'

'I told the investigating officer I'd mentioned the gig to her. Told 'im I'd've been up for seeing her again, if she'd wanted it. I 'ad nothing to hide.'

Robin remembered Strike's opinion that Satchwell volunteering this information seemed almost too helpful, and, trying to dissemble her sudden suspicion, asked:

'Did anyone spot Margot at the pub, the night you were playing?'

Satchwell took his time before swallowing, then said,

'Not as far as I know.'

'The little wooden Viking you gave her,' said Robin, watching him carefully, 'the one with "Brunhilda" written on the foot—'

'The one she had on her desk at work?' he said, with what Robin thought might have been a whiff of gratified vanity. 'Yeah, I gave her that in the old days, when we were dating.'

Could it be true, Robin wondered. After the acrimonious way Margot and Satchwell had broken up, after he'd locked her in his flat so she couldn't get out to work, after he'd hit her, after she'd married another man, would Margot really have kept Satchwell's silly little gift? Didn't private jokes and nicknames become dead and rotten things after a painful break-up, when the thought of them became almost worse than memories of rows and insults? Robin had given most of Matthew's gifts to charity after she'd found out about his infidelity, including the plush elephant that had been his first Valentine's present and the jewellery box he'd given her for her twenty-first. However, Robin could tell Satchwell was going to stick to his story, so she moved to the next question in her notebook.

'There was a printers on Clerkenwell Road I think you had an association with.'

'Come again?' said Satchwell, frowning. 'A printers?'

'A schoolgirl called Amanda White claims she saw Margot in an upper window belonging to this printers on the night—'

'Really?' said Satchwell. 'I never 'ad no association with no printers. 'Oo says I did?'

'There was a book written in the eighties about Margot's disappearance—'

'Yeah? I missed that.'

'—it said the printers produced flyers for a nightclub you'd painted a mural for.'

'For crying out loud,' said Satchwell, half-amused, half-exasperated. 'That's not an association. It'd be a stretch to call it a coincidence. I've never heard of the bloody place.'

Robin made a note and moved to her next question.

'What did you think of Bill Talbot?'

'Who?'

'The investigating officer. The first one,' said Robin.

'Oh yeah,' said Satchwell, nodding. 'Very odd bloke. When I 'eard afterwards he'd had a breakdown or whatever, I wasn't surprised. Kept asking me what I was doing on random dates. Afterwards, I worked out 'e was trying to decide wevver I was the Essex Butcher. He wanted to know my time of birth, as well, and what the hell that had to do with anything . . . '

'He was trying to draw up your horoscope,' said Robin, and she explained Talbot's preoccupation with astrology.

'*Dén tó pistévo!*' said Satchwell, looking annoyed. 'Astrology? That's not funny. He was in charge of the case – how long?'

'Six months,' said Robin.

'Jesus,' said Satchwell, scowling so that the clear tape holding the dressing over his eye crinkled.

'I don't think the people around him realised how ill he was until it got too obvious to ignore,' said Robin, now pulling a few tagged sheets of paper out of her bag: photocopies of Satchwell's statements to both Talbot and Lawson.

'What's all that?' he said sharply.

'Your statements to the police,' said Robin.

'Why are there – what are they, stars? – all over—'

'They're pentagrams,' said Robin. 'This is the statement Talbot took from you. It's just routine,' she added, because Satchwell was now looking wary. 'We've done it with everyone the police interviewed. I know your statements were double-checked at the time, but I wondered if I could run over them again, in case you remember anything useful?'

Taking his silence for consent, she continued:

'You were alone in your studio on the afternoon of the eleventh of October, but you took a call there at five from a Mr . . . Hendricks?'

'Hendricks, yeah,' said Satchwell. 'He was my agent at the time.'

'You went out to eat at a local café around half past six, where you had a conversation with the woman behind the till, which she remembered. Then you went back home to change, and out again to meet a few friends in a bar called Joe Bloggs around eight o'clock. All three friends you were drinking with confirmed your story . . . nothing to add to any of that?'

'No,' said Satchwell, and Robin thought she detected a slight sense of relief. 'That all sounds right.'

'Was it one of those friends who'd met Roy Phipps?' Robin asked casually.

'No,' said Satchwell, unsmiling, and then, changing the subject, he said, 'Margot's daughter must be knocking on forty now, is she?'

'Forty last year,' said Robin.

'*Éla*,' said Satchwell, shaking his head. 'Time just—'

One of the mahogany brown hands, wrinkled and embellished with heavy silver and turquoise rings, made a smooth motion, as of a paper aeroplane in flight.

'—and then one day you're old and you never saw it sneaking up on you.'

'When did you move abroad?'

'I didn't mean to move, not at first. Went travelling, late '75,' said Satchwell. He'd nearly finished his steak, now.

'What made you—?'

'I'd been thinking of travelling for a bit,' said Satchwell. 'But after Creed killed Margot – it was such a bloody 'orrible thing – such a shock – I dunno, I wanted a change of scene.'

'That's what you think happened to her, do you? Creed killed her?'

He put the last bit of steak into his mouth, chewed it and swallowed before answering.

'Well, yeah. Obviously at first I 'oped she'd just walked out on 'er husband and was 'oled up somewhere. But then it went on and on and . . . yeah, everyone thought it was the Essex Butcher, including the police. Not just the nutty one, the second one, the one who took over.'

'Lawson,' said Robin.

Satchwell shrugged, as much to say as the officer's name didn't matter, and asked,

'Are you going to interview Creed?'

'Hopefully.'

'Why would he tell the truth, now?'

'He likes publicity,' said Robin. 'He might like the idea of making a splash in the newspapers. So Margot disappearing was a shock to you?'

'Well, obviously it was,' said Satchwell, now probing his teeth with his tongue. 'I'd just seen her again and . . . I'm not going to pretend I was still *in love* with her, or anything like that, but . . . have *you* ever been caught up in a police investigation?' he asked her, with a trace of aggression.

'Yes,' said Robin. 'Several. It was stressful and intimidating, every time.'

'Well, there you are,' said Satchwell, mollified.

'What made you choose Greece?'

'I didn't, really. I 'ad an inheritance off my grandmother and I thought, I'll take some time off, do Europe, paint . . . went through France and Italy, and in '76 I arrived in Kos. Worked in a bar. Painted in my free hours. Sold quite a few pictures to tourists. Met my first wife . . . never left,' said Satchwell, with a shrug.

'Something else I wanted to ask you,' said Robin, moving the police statements to the bottom of her small stack. 'We've found out about a possible sighting of Margot, a week after she disappeared. A sighting that wasn't ever reported to the police.'

'Yeah?' said Satchwell, looking interested. 'Where?'

'In Leamington Spa,' said Robin, 'in the graveyard of All Saints church.'

Satchwell's thick white eyebrows rose, putting strain on the clear tape that was holding the dressing to his eye.

'In All Saints?' he repeated, apparently astonished.

'Looking at graves. Allegedly, she had her hair dyed black.'

''Oo saw this?'

'A man visiting the area on a motorbike. Two years later, he told the St John's practice nurse about it.'

'He told the *nurse*?'

Satchwell's jaw hardened.

'And what else has the *nurse* told you?' he said, searching Robin's face. He seemed suddenly and unexpectedly angry.

'Do you know Janice?' asked Robin, wondering why he looked so angry.

'That's her name, is it?' said Satchwell. 'I couldn't remember.'

'You *do* know her?'

Satchwell put more chips in his mouth. Robin could see that he was trying to decide what to tell her, and she felt that jolt of excitement that made all the long, tedious hours of the job, the sitting around, the sleeplessness, worthwhile.

'She's shit-stirring,' said Satchwell abruptly. 'She's a shit-stirrer, that one, that nurse. She and Margot didn't like each other. Margot told me she didn't like her.'

'When was this?'

'When we ran into each other, like I told you, in the street—'

'I thought you said she didn't talk about work?'

'Well, she told me that. They'd had a row or something. I don't know. It was just something she said in passing. She told me she didn't like the nurse,' repeated Satchwell.

It was as though a hard mask had surfaced under the leather dark skin: the slightly comical, crêpey-faced charmer had been replaced by a mean old one-eyed man. Robin remembered how Matthew's lower face had tautened when angry, giving him the look of a muzzled dog, but she wasn't intimidated. She sensed in Satchwell the same wily instinct for self-preservation as in her ex-husband. Whatever Satchwell might have meted out to Margot, or to the wives who'd left him, he'd think better of slapping Robin in a crowded pub, in the town where his sister still lived.

'You seem angry,' Robin said.

'*Gia chári tou*, of course I am – that nurse, what's her name? Trying to implicate me, isn't she? Making up a story to make it look like Margot ran away to be with me—'

'Janice didn't invent the story. We checked with Mr Ramage's widow and she confirmed that her late husband told other people he'd met a missing woman—'

'What else has *Janice* told you?' he said again.

'She never mentioned you,' said Robin, now immensely curious. 'We had no idea you knew each other.'

'But she claims Margot was seen in Leamington Spa after she disappeared? No, she knows exactly what she's bloody doing.'

Satchwell took another chip, ate it, then suddenly got to his feet and walked past Robin, who looked over her shoulder to see him striding into the gents. His back view was older than his front: she could see the pink scalp through the thin white hair and there was no backside filling out his jeans.

Robin guessed he considered the interview finished. However, she had something else up her sleeve: a dangerous something, perhaps, but she'd use it rather than let the interview end here, with more questions raised than answered.

It was fully five minutes before he reappeared and she could tell that he'd worked himself up in his absence. Rather than sitting back down, he stood over her as he said,

'I don't think you're a fucking detective. I think you're press.'

Seen from below, the tortoise's neck was particularly striking. The chain, the turquoise and silver rings and the long hair now seemed like fancy dress.

'You can call Anna Phipps and check if you like,' said

Robin. 'I've got her number here. Why d'you think the press would be interested in you?'

'I had enough of them last time. I'm off. I don't need this. I'm supposed to be recuperating.'

'One last thing,' said Robin, 'and you're going to want to hear it.'

She'd learned the trick from Strike. Stay calm, but assertive. Make them worry what else you've got.

Satchwell turned back, his one uncovered eye hard as flint. No trace of flirtation remained, no attempt to patronise her. She was an equal now; an adversary.

'Why don't you sit down?' said Robin. 'This won't take long.'

After a slight hesitation, Satchwell eased himself back into his seat. His hoary head now blocked the stuffed deer head that hung on the brick wall behind him. From Robin's point of view, the horns appeared to rise directly out of the white hair that fell in limp curls to his shoulders.

'Margot Bamborough knew something about you that you didn't want to get out,' said Robin. 'Didn't she?'

He glared at her.

'The pillow dream?' said Robin.

Every line of his face hardened, turning him vulpine. The sunburned chest, wrinkled beneath its white hair, caved as he exhaled.

'Told someone, did she? Who?' Before Robin could answer, he said, ''Er husband, I suppose? Or that fucking Irish girl, was it?'

His jaws worked, chewing nothing.

'I should never 'ave told her,' he said. 'That's what you do when you're drunk and you're in love, or whatever the fuck we were. Then I 'ad it playing on my mind for years that she was gonna . . . '

The sentence ended in silence.

'Did she mention it, when you met again?' asked Robin, feeling her way, pretending she knew more than she did.

'She asked after my poor mother,' said Satchwell. 'I fort at the time, are you 'aving a go? But I don't think she was. Maybe she'd learned better, being a doctor, maybe she'd changed her views. She'll have seen people like Blanche. A life not worth living.

'Anyway,' he said, leaning forwards slightly, 'I still think it was a dream. All right? I was six years old. I dreamed it. And even if it wasn't a dream, they're both dead and gone now and nobody can say no different. My old mum died in '89. You can't get 'er for anything now, poor cow. Single mother, trying to cope with us all on 'er own. It's merciful,' said Satchwell, 'putting someone out of their misery. A mercy.'

He got up, drained beneath his tan, his face sagging, turned and walked away, but at the moment he was about to disappear he suddenly turned and tottered back to her, his jaw working.

'I think,' he said, with as much malevolence as he could muster, 'you're a nasty little bitch.'

He left for good this time.

Robin's heart rate was barely raised. Her dominant emotion was elation. Pushing her unappetising ramekins aside, she pulled the little metal bucket he'd left behind towards her, and finished the artist's chips.

48

Sir Artegall, long hauing since,
Taken in hand th'exploit . . .
To him assynd, her high beheast to doo,
To the sea shore he gan his way apply . . .

Edmund Spenser
The Faerie Queene

Joan's funeral service finished with the hymn most beloved of sailors, 'Eternal Father, Strong to Save'. While the congregation sang the familiar words, Ted, Strike, Dave Polworth and three of Ted's comrades in the lifeboat service shouldered the coffin back down the aisle of the simple cream-walled church, with its wooden beams and its stained-glass windows depicting purple-robed St Maudez, for whom both village and church were named. Flanked by an island tower and a seal on a rock, the saint watched the coffin-bearers pass out of the church.

O Saviour, whose almighty word
The winds and waves submissive heard,
Who walked upon the foaming deep,
And calm amidst the rage did sleep . . .

Polworth, by far the shortest of the six men, walked directly behind Strike, doing his best to bear a fair share of the load.

The mourners, many of whom had had to stand at the back of the packed church, or else listen as best they could from outside, formed a respectful circle around the hearse outside as the shining oak box was loaded onto it. Barely a murmur was heard as the rear doors slammed shut on Joan's earthly remains. As the straight-backed undertaker in his thick black overcoat climbed back into the driver's seat, Strike put an arm around Ted's shoulders. Together, they watched the hearse drive out of sight. Strike could feel Ted trembling.

'Look at all these flowers, Ted,' said Lucy, whose eyes were swollen shut, and the three of them turned back to the church to examine the dense bank of sprays, wreaths and bunches that created a jubilant blaze against the exterior wall of the tiny church.

'Beautiful lilies, Ted, look . . . from Marion and Gary, all the way from Canada . . .'

The congregation was still spilling out of the church to join those outside. All kept a distance from the family while they moved crabwise along the wall of the church. Joan would surely have delighted in the mass of floral tributes and Strike drew unexpected consolation from messages that Lucy was reading aloud to Ted, whose eyes, like hers, were puffy and red.

'Ian and Judy,' she told her uncle. 'Terry and Olive . . .'

'Loads, aren't there?' said Ted, marvelling.

The now-whispering, milling crowd of mourners were doubtless wondering whether it would be heartless to set out immediately for the Ship and Castle, where the wake was to be held, Strike thought. He couldn't blame them; he too was craving a pint and perhaps a chaser too.

'"With deepest sympathy, from Robin, Sam, Andy, Saul and Pat",' Lucy read aloud. She turned to look at Strike, smiling. 'How lovely. Did you tell Robin pink roses were Joan's favourite?'

'Don't think so,' said Strike, who hadn't known himself.

The fact that his agency was represented here among the tributes to Joan meant a great deal to him. Unlike Lucy, he'd be travelling back to London alone, by train. Even though he'd been craving solitude for the past ten days, the prospect of his silent attic room was cheerless, after these long days of dread and loss. The roses, which were for Joan, were also for him: they said, you won't be alone, you have something you've built, and all right, it might not be a family, but there are still people who care about you waiting in London. Strike told himself 'people', because there were five names on the card, but he turned away thinking only of Robin.

Lucy drove Ted and Strike to the Ship and Castle in Ted's car, leaving Greg to follow with the boys. None of them talked in the car; a kind of emotional exhaustion had set in.

Joan had known what she was doing, Strike thought, as he watched the familiar streets slide past. He was grateful they weren't following to the crematorium, that they would reclaim the body in a form that could be clutched to the chest and borne on a boat, in the quiet of a sunny afternoon to come, just the family, to say their last, private farewell.

The Ship and Castle's dining-room windows looked out over St Mawes Bay, which was overcast but tranquil. Strike bought Ted and himself pints, saw his uncle safely into a chair among a knot of solicitous friends, returned to the bar for a double Famous Grouse, which he downed in one, then carried his pint to the window.

The sea was Quaker grey, sparkling occasionally where the silvered fringes of the clouds caught it. Viewed from the hotel window, St Mawes was a study in mouse and slate, but the little rowing boats perched on the mudflats below provided welcome dabs of cheerful colour.

'Y'all right, Diddy?'

He turned: Ilsa was with Polworth, and she reached up and hugged Strike. All three of them had been at St Mawes Primary School together. In those days, as Strike remembered it, Ilsa hadn't liked Polworth much. He'd always been unpopular with female classmates. Over Dave's shoulder, Strike could see Polworth's wife, Penny, chatting with a group of female friends.

'Nick really wanted to be here, Corm, but he had to work,' said Ilsa.

'Of course,' said Strike. 'It was really good of you to come, Ilsa.'

'I loved Joan,' she said simply. 'Mum and Dad are going to have Ted over on Friday night. Dad's taking him for a round of golf on Tuesday.'

The Polworths' two daughters, who weren't renowned for their good behaviour, were playing tag among the mourners. The smaller of the two – Strike could never remember which was Roz and which Mel – dashed around them and clung, momentarily, to the back of Strike's legs, as though he were a piece of furniture, looking out at her sister, before sprinting off again, giggling.

'And we're having Ted over Saturday,' said Polworth, as though nothing had happened. Neither Polworth ever corrected their children unless they were directly inconveniencing their parents. 'So don't worry, Diddy, we'll make sure the old fella's all right.'

'Cheers, mate,' said Strike, with difficulty. He hadn't cried in church, hadn't cried all these last horrible days, because there'd been so much to organise, and he found relief in activity. However, the kindness shown by his old friends was seeping through his defences: he wanted to express his gratitude properly, because Polworth hadn't yet permitted him to say all he wanted about the way he'd enabled Strike and Lucy to reach the dying Joan. Before Strike could make a start, however, Penny Polworth joined their group, followed by two women Strike didn't recognise, but who were both beaming at him.

'Hi, Corm,' said Penny, who was dark-eyed and blunt-nosed, and who'd worn her hair pulled back into a practical ponytail since she was five. 'Abigail and Lindy really want to meet you.'

'Hello,' said Strike, unsmiling. He held out his hand and shook both of theirs, sure that they were about to talk about his detective triumphs and already annoyed. Today, of all days, he wanted to be nothing but Joan's nephew. He assumed that Abigail was Lindy's daughter, because if you removed the younger woman's carefully pencilled, geometrically precise eyebrows and fake tan, they had the same round, flat faces.

'She was ever so proud of you,' said Lindy.

'We follow everything about you in the papers,' said plump Abigail, who seemed to be on the verge of giggling.

'What are you working on now? I don't suppose you can say, can you?' said Lindy, devouring him with her eyes.

'D'you ever get involved with the royals, at all?' asked Abigail.

Fuck's sake.

'No,' said Strike. 'Excuse me, need a smoke.'

He knew he'd offended them, but didn't care, though he could imagine Joan's disapproval as he walked away from the group by the window. What would it have hurt him, she'd have said, to entertain her friends by talking about his job? Joan had liked to show him off, the nephew who was the closest thing she'd ever have to a son, and it suddenly came back to him, after these long days of guilt, why he'd avoided coming back to the little town for so long: because he'd found himself slowly stifling under the weight of teacups and doilies and carefully curated conversations, and Joan's suffocating pride, and the neighbours' curiosity, and the sidelong glances at his false leg when nobody thought he could see them looking.

As he stumped down the hall, he pulled out his mobile and pressed Robin's number without conscious thought.

'Hi,' she said, sounding mildly surprised to hear from him.

'Hi,' said Strike, pausing on the doorstep of the hotel to pull a cigarette out of the packet with his teeth. He crossed the road and lit it, looking out over the mudflats at the sea. 'Just wanted to check in, and to thank you.'

'What for?'

'The flowers from the agency. They meant a lot to the family.'

'Oh,' said Robin, 'I'm glad . . . How was the funeral?'

'It was, you know . . . a funeral,' said Strike, watching a seagull bobbing on the tranquil sea. 'Anything new your end?'

'Well, yes, actually,' said Robin, after a fractional hesitation, 'but now's probably not the moment. I'll tell you when you're—'

'Now's a great moment,' said Strike, who was yearning for normality, for something to think about that wasn't connected to Joan, or loss, or St Mawes.

So Robin related the story of her interview with Paul Satchwell, and Strike listened in silence.

' . . . and then he called me a nasty little bitch,' Robin concluded, 'and left.'

'Christ almighty,' said Strike, genuinely amazed, not only that Robin had managed to draw so much information from Satchwell, but at what she'd found out.

'I've just been sitting here looking up records on my phone – I'm back in the Land Rover, going to head home in a bit. Blanche Doris Satchwell, died 1945, aged ten. She's buried in a cemetery outside Leamington Spa. Satchwell called it a mercy killing. Well,' Robin corrected herself, 'he called it a dream, which was his way of telling Margot, while retaining some plausible deniability, wasn't it? It's a traumatic memory to carry around with you from age six, though, isn't it?'

'Certainly is,' said Strike, 'and it gives him a motive of sorts, if he thought Margot might tell the authorities . . .'

'Exactly. And what d'you think about the Janice bit? Why didn't she tell us she knew Satchwell?'

'Very good question,' said Strike. 'Go over it again, what he said about Janice?'

'When I told him Janice was the one who said Margot was spotted in Leamington Spa, he said she was a shit-stirrer and that she was trying to implicate him somehow in Margot's disappearance.'

'Very interesting indeed,' said Strike, frowning at the bobbing seagull, which was staring at the horizon with concentrated intent, its cruel, hooked beak pointing towards the horizon. 'And what was that thing about Roy?'

'He said somebody had told him Roy was a "mummy's boy" who "had a stick up his arse",' said Robin. 'But he wouldn't tell me who'd said it.'

'Doesn't sound much like Janice, but you never know,' said Strike. 'Well, you've done bloody well, Robin.'

'Thanks.'

'We'll have a proper catch-up on Bamborough when I get back,' said Strike. 'Well, we'll need a catch-up on everything.'

'Great. I hope the rest of your stay's OK,' said Robin, with that note of finality that indicated the call was about to end. Strike wanted to keep her on the line, but she evidently thought she oughtn't monopolise his time in his last afternoon with the grieving family, and he could think of no pretext to keep her talking. They bade each other goodbye, and Strike returned his mobile to his pocket.

'Here you go, Diddy.'

Polworth had emerged from the hotel carrying a couple of fresh pints. Strike accepted his with thanks, and both turned to face the bay as they drank.

'You back up to London tomorrow, are you?' said Polworth.

'Yeah,' said Strike. 'But not for long. Joan wanted us to take her ashes out on Ted's boat and scatter them at sea.'

'Nice idea,' said Polworth.

'Listen, mate – thanks for everything.'

'Shut up,' said Polworth. 'You'd do it for me.'

'You're right,' said Strike. 'I would.'

'Easy to say, you cunt,' said Polworth, without skipping a beat, 'seeing as my mum's dead and I don't know where the fuck my dad is.'

Strike laughed.

'Well, I'm a private detective. Want me to find him for you?'

'Fuck, no,' said Polworth. 'Good riddance.'

They drank their pints. There was a brief break in the cloud and the sea was suddenly a carpet of diamonds and the bobbing seagull, a paper-white piece of origami. Strike was wondering idly whether Polworth's passionate devotion to Cornwall was a reaction against his absent Birmingham-born father when Polworth spoke up again:

'Speaking of fathers . . . Joan told me yours was looking for a reunion.'

'She did, did she?'

'Don't be narked,' said Polworth. 'You know what she was like. Wanted me to know you were going through a tough time. Nothing doing, I take it?'

'No,' said Strike. 'Nothing doing.'

The brief silence was broken by the shrieks and yells of Polworth's two daughters sprinting out of the hotel. Ignoring their father and Strike, they wriggled under the chain separating road from damp shingle and ran out to the water's edge, pursued a moment later by Strike's nephew Luke, who was holding a couple of cream buns in his hand and clearly intent on throwing them at the girls.

'OI,' bellowed Strike. 'NO!'

Luke's face fell.

'They started it,' he said, turning to show Strike a white smear down the back of his black suit jacket, newly purchased for his great-aunt's funeral.

'And I'm finishing it,' said Strike, while the Polworth girls giggled, peeking out over the rim of the rowing boat behind which they had taken refuge. 'Put those back where you got them.'

Glaring at his uncle, Luke took a defiant bite out of one of the buns, then turned and headed back into the hotel.

'Little shit,' muttered Strike.

Polworth watched in a detached way as his girls began to kick cold seawater and sand at each other. Only when the younger girl overbalanced and fell backwards into a foot of icy sea, eliciting a scream of shock, did he react.

'Fuck's sake . . . get inside. Come on – don't bloody whine, it's your own fault – come on, inside, now!'

The three Polworths headed back into the Ship and Castle, leaving Strike alone again.

The bobbing seagull, which was doubtless used to a tide of tourists, to the chugging and grinding of the Falmouth ferry and the fishing boats passing in and out of the bay every day, had been unfazed by the shrieks and yells of the Polworth girls. Its sharp eyes were fixed upon something Strike couldn't see, far out at sea. Only when the clouds closed again and the sea darkened to iron, did the bird take off at last. Strike's eyes followed it as it soared on wide, curved wings into the distance, away from the shelter of the bay for open sea, ready to resume the hard but necessary business of survival.

PART FIVE

. . . lusty Spring, all dight in leaues of flowres . . .

Edmund Spenser
The Faerie Queene

49

After long storms and tempests overblown,
The sun at length his joyous face doth clear;
So whenas fortune all her spite hath shown,
Some blissful hours at last must needs appear;
Else would afflicted wights oft-times despair . . .

Edmund Spenser
The Faerie Queene

At 8 a.m. on the morning she should have been meeting her estranged husband for mediation, Robin emerged from Tottenham Court Road station beneath a cerulean sky. The sunshine felt like a minor miracle after the long months of rain and storms and Robin, who had no surveillance to do today, had put on a dress, glad to be out of her everlasting jeans and sweatshirts.

Angry as she felt at Matthew for calling off the session with only twenty-four hours' notice ('My client regrets that an urgent matter of a personal nature has arisen. Given my own unavailability for the latter part of March, I suggest we find a mutually convenient date in April'), suspicious as she was that Matthew was dragging out the process merely to demonstrate his power and add pressure to give up her claim on their joint account, her spirits were raised by the dusty glow of the early morning sunshine illuminating the eternal roadworks at the top of Charing Cross Road. The truth, which had been borne forcibly upon Robin during the five days off that Strike had insisted she take, was that she was happier at work. With no desire to go home to Yorkshire and face the usual barrage of questions from her mother about the divorce and her job, and insufficient funds to get out of London to take a solitary mini-break, she'd spent most of her time taking care of her backlog of chores, or working on the Bamborough case.

She had, if not precisely leads, then ideas, and was now heading into the office early in the hope of catching Strike before the business of the day took over. The pneumatic drills drowned out the shouts of workmen in the road as Robin passed, until she reached the shadowy calm of Denmark Street, where the shops hadn't yet opened.

Almost at the top of the metal staircase, Robin heard voices emanating from behind the glass office door. In spite of the fact that it was not quite eight-fifteen, the light was already on.

'Morning,' said Strike, when she opened the door. He was standing beside the kettle and looked mildly surprised to see her so early. 'I thought you weren't going to be in until lunchtime?'

'Cancelled,' said Robin.

She wondered whether Strike had forgotten what she'd had on that morning, or whether he was being discreet because Morris was sitting on the fake leather sofa. Though as handsome as ever, Morris's bright blue eyes were bloodshot and his jaw dark with stubble.

'Hello, stranger,' he said. 'Look at you. Proper advert for taking it easy.'

Robin ignored this comment, but as she hung up her jacket, she found herself wishing she hadn't worn the dress. She greatly resented Morris making her feel self-conscious, but it would have been easier just to have worn jeans as usual.

'Morris has caught Mr Smith at it, with the nanny,' said Strike.

'That was quick!' said Robin, trying to be generous, wishing Morris hadn't been the one to do it.

'Red-handed, ten past one this morning,' said Morris, passing Robin a night vision digital camera. 'Hubby was pretending to be out with the boys. Nanny always has a night off on Tuesdays. Silly fuckers said goodbye on the doorstep. Rookie error.'

Robin scrolled slowly through the pictures. The voluptuous nanny who so resembled Strike's ex Lorelei was standing in the doorway of a terraced house, locked in the arms of Mrs Smith's husband. Morris had captured not only the clinch, but the street name and door number.

'Where's this place?' Robin asked, flicking past pictures of the clinch.

'Shoreditch. Nanny's best mate rents it,' said Morris. 'Always useful to have a friend who'll let you use their place for a sneaky shag, eh? I've got her name and details, too, so she's about to get dragged into it all, as well.'

Morris stretched luxuriously on the sofa, arms over his head, and said through a yawn,

'Not often you get the chance to make three women miserable at once, is it?'

'Not to mention the husband,' said Robin, looking at the handsome profile of the commodity broker's husband, silhouetted against a streetlamp as he made his way back to the family car.

'Well, yeah,' said Morris, holding his stretch, 'him too.'

His T-shirt had ridden up, exposing an expanse of toned abdomen, a fact of which Robin thought he was probably well aware.

'Don't fancy a breakfast meeting, do you?' Strike asked

Robin. He'd just opened the biscuit tin and found it empty. 'We're overdue a Bamborough catch-up. And I haven't had breakfast.'

'Great,' said Robin, immediately taking down her jacket again.

'You never take *me* out for breakfast,' Morris told Strike, getting up off the sofa. Ignoring this comment, Strike said,

'Good going on Smith, Morris. I'll let the wife know later. See you tomorrow.'

'Terrible, isn't it,' said Robin, as she and Strike walked back out of the black street door onto the cool of Denmark Street, where sunlight still hadn't penetrated, 'this missing plane?'

Eleven days previously, Malaysia Airlines flight 370 had taken off from Kuala Lumpur and disappeared without trace. More than two hundred people were missing. Competing theories about what had happened to the plane had dominated the news for the last week: hijack, crew sabotage and mechanical failure among them. Robin had been reading about it on the way into work. All those relatives, waiting for news. It must, surely, come soon? An aircraft holding nearly two hundred and fifty people wasn't as easily lost as a single woman, melting away into the Clerkenwell rain.

'Nightmare for the families,' agreed Strike, as they headed out into the sun on Charing Cross Road. He paused, looking up and down the road. 'I don't want to go to Starbucks.'

So they walked to Bar Italia in Frith Street, which lay opposite Ronnie Scott's jazz club, five minutes from the office. The small metal tables and chairs outside on the pavement were all unoccupied. In spite of its sunny promise, the March morning air still carried a chill. Every high stool at the counter inside the café bore a customer gulping down coffee before starting their working day, while reading news off their phones or else examining the shelves of produce reflected in the mirror that faced them.

'You going to be warm enough if we sit out here?' asked Strike doubtfully, looking from Robin's dress to the counter inside. She was starting to really wish she'd worn her jeans.

'I'll be fine,' said Robin. 'And I only want a cappuccino, I already ate.'

While Strike was buying food and drink, Robin sat down on the cold metal chair, drew her jacket more tightly around her and opened her bag, with the intention of taking out Talbot's leather notebook, but after a moment's hesitation, she changed her mind and left it where it was. She didn't want Strike to think that she'd been concentrating on Talbot's astrological musings over the last few days, even though she had, in fact, spent many hours poring over the book.

'Cappuccino,' said Strike, returning to her and setting the coffee in front of her. He'd bought himself a double espresso and a mozzarella and salami roll. Sitting down next to her, he said,

'How come mediation was cancelled?'

Pleased he'd remembered, Robin said:

'Matthew claims something urgent came up.'

'Believe him?'

'No. I think it's more mind games. I wasn't looking forward to it, but at least it would've been over. So,' she said, not wanting to talk about Matthew, 'have you got anything new on Bamborough?'

'Not much,' said Strike, who'd been working flat out on other cases since his return from Cornwall. 'We've got forensics back on that blood smear I found in the book in the Athorns' flat.'

'And?'

'Type O positive.'

'And did you call Roy to find out . . . ?'

'Yeah. Margot was A positive.'

'Oh,' said Robin.

'My hopes weren't high,' said Strike, with a shrug. 'It looked like a smear from a paper cut, if anything.

'I've found Mucky Ricci, though. He's in a private nursing home called St Peter's, in Islington. I had to do a fair bit of impersonation on the phone to get confirmation.'

'Great. D'you want me to—?'

'No. I told you, Shanker issued stern warnings about upsetting the old bastard, in case his sons got wind of it.'

'And you feel, of the two of us, I'm the one who upsets people, do you?'

Strike smirked slightly while chewing his roll.

'There's no point rattling Luca Ricci's cage unless we have to. Shanker told me Mucky was gaga, which I hoped meant he was a bit less sharp than he used to be. Might even have worked in our favour. Unfortunately, from what I managed to wheedle out of the nurse, he doesn't talk any more.'

'Not at all?'

'Apparently not. She mentioned it in passing. I tried to find out whether that's because he's depressed, or had a stroke, or whether he's demented, in which case questioning him is obviously pointless, but she didn't say.

'I went to check out the home. I was hoping for some big institutional place where you might slip in and out unnoticed, but it's more like a B&B. They've only got eighteen residents. I'd say the chances of getting in there undetected or passing yourself off as a distant cousin are close to zero.'

Irrationally, now that Ricci seemed unreachable, Robin, who hadn't been more interested in him than in any of the other suspects, immediately felt as though something crucial to the investigation had been lost.

'I'm not saying I won't take a bash at him, eventually,' said Strike. 'But right now, the possible gains don't justify making a bunch of professional gangsters angry at us. On the other hand, if we've got nothing else come August, I might have to see whether I can get a word or two out of Ricci.'

From his tone, Robin guessed that Strike, too, was well aware that more than half their allotted year on the Bamborough case had already elapsed.

'I've also,' he continued, 'made contact with Margot's biographer, C. B. Oakden, who's playing hard to get. He seems to think he's far more important to the investigation than I do.'

'Is he after money?'

'I'd say he's after anything he can get,' said Strike. 'He seemed as interested in interviewing me as letting me interview him.'

'Maybe,' suggested Robin, 'he's thinking of writing a book about you, like the one he did on Margot?'

Strike didn't smile.

'He comes across as equal parts wily and stupid. It doesn't seem to have occurred to him that I must know a lot about his dodgy past, given that I managed to track him down after multiple name changes. But I can see how he conned all those old women. He puts up a good show over the phone of knowing and remembering everyone around Margot. There was a real fluency to it: "Yes, Dr Gupta, lovely man", "Oh yes, Irene, bit of a handful". It's convincing until you remember he was fourteen when Margot disappeared, and probably met them all a couple of times, tops.

'But he wouldn't tell me anything about Brenner, which is who I'm really interested in. "I'll need to think about that," he said. "I'm not sure I want to go into that." I've called him twice so far. Both times he tried to divert the conversation back onto me, I dragged it back to Brenner, and he cut the call short, pretending he had something urgent to take care of. Both times, he promised to phone me back but didn't.'

'You don't think he's recording the calls, do you?' asked Robin. 'Trying to get stuff about you he can sell to the papers?'

'It occurred to me,' Strike admitted, tipping sugar into his coffee.

'Maybe I should talk to him next time?'

'Might not be a bad idea,' said Strike. 'Anyway,' he took a gulp of coffee, 'that's all I've done on Bamborough since I got back. But I'm planning to drop in on Nurse Janice the moment I've got a couple of clear hours. She'll be back from Dubai by now, and I want to know why she never mentioned she knew Paul Satchwell. Don't think I'll warn her I'm coming, this time. There's something to be said for catching people unawares. So, what's new your end?'

'Well,' said Robin, 'Gloria Conti, or Jaubert, as she is these days, hasn't answered Anna's email.'

'Pity,' said Strike, frowning. 'I thought she'd be more likely to talk to us if Anna asked.'

'So did I. I think it's worth giving it another week, then getting Anna to prod her. The worst that can happen is another definite "no". In slightly better news, I'm supposed to be speaking to Amanda White, who's now Amanda Laws, later today.'

'How much is that costing us?'

'Nothing. I appealed to her better nature,' said Robin, 'and she pretended to be persuaded, but I can tell she's quite enamoured of the idea of publicity, and she likes the idea of you, and of getting her name in the papers again as the plucky schoolgirl who stuck to her woman-in-the-window story even when the police didn't believe her. That's in spite of the fact that her whole shtick, when I first contacted her, was that she didn't want to go through all the stress of press interest again unless she got money out of it.'

'She still married?' asked Strike, taking his cigarettes out of his pocket. 'Because she and Oakden sound like a good match. Mightn't be a bad sideline for us, setting grifters up with each other.'

Robin laughed.

'So they can have dodgy children together, thus keeping us in business for ever?'

Strike lit his cigarette, exhaled and then said,

'Not a perfect business plan. There's no guarantee breeding two shits together will produce a third shit. I've known decent people who were raised by complete bastards, and vice versa.'

'You're nature over nurture, are you?' asked Robin.

'Maybe,' said Strike. 'My three nephews were all raised the same, weren't they? And—'

'—one's lovely, one's a prick and one's an arsehole,' said Robin.

Strike's loud burst of laughter seemed to offend the harried-looking suited man who was hurrying past with a mobile pressed to his ear.

'Well remembered,' Strike said, still grinning as he watched the scowling man march out of sight. Lately he, too, had had moods where the sound of other people's cheerfulness grated, but at this moment, with the sunshine, the good coffee and Robin beside him, he suddenly realised he was happier than he'd been in months.

'People are never raised the same way, though,' said Robin, 'not even in the same house, with the same parents. Birth order matters, and all kinds of other things. Speaking of which, Wilma Bayliss's daughter Maya has definitely agreed to talk to us. We're trying to find a convenient date. I think I told you, the youngest sister is recovering from breast cancer, so I don't want to hassle them.

'And there's something else,' said Robin, feeling self-conscious.

Strike, who'd returned to his sandwich, saw, to his surprise, Robin drawing from her bag Talbot's leather-bound notebook, which Strike had assumed was still in the locked filing cabinet in the office.

'I've been looking back through this.'

'Think I missed something, do you?' said Strike, through a mouthful of bread.

'No, I—'

'It's fine,' he said. 'Perfectly possible. Nobody's infallible.'

Sunshine was slowly making its way into Frith Street now, and the pages of the old notebook glowed yellow as Robin opened it.

'Well, it's about Scorpio. You remember Scorpio?'

'The person whose death Margot might have been worried about?'

'Exactly. You thought Scorpio might be Steve Douthwaite's married girlfriend, who killed herself.'

'I'm open to other theories,' said Strike. His sandwich finished, he brushed off his hands and took out another cigarette. 'The notes ask whether Aquarius confronted Pisces, don't they? Which I assumed meant Margot confronted Douthwaite.'

In spite of his neutral tone, Strike resented remembering these star signs. The laborious and ultimately unrewarding task of working out which suspects and witnesses were represented by each astrological glyph had been far from his favourite bit of research.

'Well,' said Robin, taking out two folded photocopies, which she'd been keeping in the notebook, 'I've been wondering . . . look at these.'

She passed the two documents to Strike, who opened them and saw copies of two birth certificates, one for Olive Satchwell, the other for Blanche Satchwell.

'Olive was Satchwell's mother,' said Robin, as Strike,

smoking, examined the documents. 'And Blanche was his sister, who died aged ten – possibly with a pillow over her face.'

'If you're expecting me to deduce their star signs from these birthdays,' said Strike, 'I haven't memorised the whole zodiac.'

'Blanche was born on the twenty-fifth of October, which makes her a Scorpio,' said Robin. 'Olive was born on the twenty-ninth of March. Under the traditional system, she'd be Aries, like Satchwell . . . '

To Strike's surprise, Robin now took out a copy of *Astrology 14* by Steven Schmidt.

'It was quite hard to track this down. It's been out of print for ages.'

'A masterwork like that? You amaze me,' said Strike, watching Robin turn to a page listing the dates of revised signs according to Schmidt. Robin smiled, but refusing to be deflected said,

'Look here. By Schmidt's system, Satchwell's mother was a Pisces.'

'We're mixing up the two systems now, are we?' asked Strike.

'Well, Talbot did,' Robin pointed out. 'He decided Irene and Roy should be given their Schmidt signs, but other people were allowed to keep the traditional ones.'

'But,' said Strike, well aware that he was trying to impose logic on what was essentially illogical, 'Talbot made massive, sweeping assumptions on the basis of people's original signs. Brenner was ruled out as a suspect solely because he was—'

'—Libra, yes,' said Robin.

'Well, what happens to Janice being psychic and the Essex Butcher being a Capricorn if all the dates start sliding around?'

'Wherever there was a discrepancy between the traditional sign and Schmidt sign, he seems to have gone with the sign he thought suited the person best.'

'Which makes a mockery of the whole business. And also,'

said Strike, 'calls all my identifications of signs and suspects into question.'

'I know,' said Robin. 'Even Talbot seems to have got very stressed trying to work across both systems, which is when he began concentrating mainly on asteroids and the tarot.'

'OK,' said Strike, blowing smoke away from her, 'go on with what you were saying – if Satchwell's sister was a Scorpio, and her mother was Pisces . . . remind me,' said Strike, 'exactly what that passage about Scorpio says?'

Robin flicked backwards through Talbot's notebook until she found the passage decorated with doodles of the crab, the fish, the scorpion, the fish-tailed goat and the water-bearer's urn.

'"Aquarius worried about how Scorpio died, question mark",' she read aloud. 'And – written in capitals – "SCHMIDT AGREES WITH ADAMS". Then, "Did Aquarius challenge Pisces about Scorpio? Was Cancer there, did Cancer witness? Cancer is kind, instinct is to protect," then, in capitals, "INTERVIEW AGAIN. Scorpio and Aquarius connected, water, water, also Cancer, and Capricorn," in capitals, "HAS A FISH'S TAIL".'

Brow furrowed, Strike said:

'We're assuming Cancer still means Janice, right?'

'Well, Janice and Cynthia are the only two Cancerians connected with the case, and Janice seems to fit this better,' said Robin. 'Let's say Margot decided she was going to act on her suspicion that Satchwell's mother killed his sister. If she phoned Olive from the surgery, Janice might have overheard a phone call, mightn't she? And if Janice knew the Satchwell family, or was involved with them in some way we don't know about, she mightn't have wanted to tell the police what she'd overheard, for fear of incriminating Olive.'

'Why would Margot have waited years to check out her

suspicions about the pillow dream?' asked Strike, but before Robin could supply an answer, he did it himself. 'Of course, people do sometimes take years to decide what action to take on something like that. Or to muster up the courage to do it.'

He handed Robin back the two photocopies.

'Well, if that's the story behind the Scorpio business, Satchwell's still a prime suspect.'

'I never got his address in Greece,' said Robin guiltily.

'We'll get at him through his surviving sister if we have to.'

Strike took a swig of coffee then, slightly against his better judgement, asked,

'What did you say about asteroids?'

Robin flicked further on through the notebook, to show Strike the page she'd pored over in Leamington Spa, which she thought of as the 'horns page'.

'As the case went on, he seemed to give up on normal astrology. I think Schmidt had confused him so much he couldn't work it any more, so he starts inventing his own system. He's calculated the asteroids' positions for the evening Margot disappeared. See here—'

Robin was pointing to the symbol ⚴ . . .

'That symbol stands for the asteroid Pallas Athena – remember that ugly clock at the Phippses' house? – and he's using it to mean Margot. The asteroid Pallas Athena was in the tenth house of the zodiac on the night Margot disappeared, and the tenth house is ruled by Capricorn. It's also supposed to govern businesses, upper classes and upper floors.'

'You think Margot's still in someone's attic?'

Robin smiled, but refused to be deflected.

'And see here . . .' She angled the notebook towards him, 'assuming the other asteroids also refer to living people, we've got Ceres, Juno and Vesta.

'I think he's using Vesta, "keeper of the hearth", to represent

Cynthia. Vesta was in the seventh house, which is the house of marriage. Talbot's written "FITS" – so I think he's saying Cynthia was in Margot's marital home, Broom House.

'I think "nurturing, protective Ceres" sounds like Janice again. She's in the twelfth house, and so's Juno, who's associated with "wives and infidelity", which might take us back to Joanna Hammond, Douthwaite's married girlfriend . . .'

'What's the twelfth house represent?'

'Enemies, secrets, sorrows and undoing.'

Strike looked at her, eyebrows raised. He'd indulged Robin because it was sunny, and he was enjoying her company, but his tolerance for astrology was now wearing very thin.

'It's also Pisces' house,' said Robin, 'which is Douthwaite's sign, so maybe—'

'You think Janice and Joanna Hammond were both in Douthwaite's flat when Margot was abducted, do you?'

'No, but—'

'Because that'd be tricky, given that Joanna Hammond died weeks before Margot disappeared. Or are you suggesting her ghost was haunting Douthwaite?'

'All right, I know it might mean nothing,' said Robin, half-laughing as she ploughed on, 'but Talbot's written something else here: "Ceres denies contact with Juno. Could Cetus be right?"'

She was pointing at the whale symbol representing Irene.

'I find it hard to imagine Irene Hickson being right about very much,' said Strike. He pulled the leather notebook towards him to look more closely at Talbot's small, obsessive writing, then pushed the notes away again with a slightly impatient shrug. 'Look, it's easy to get sucked into this stuff. When I was going through the notes I started making connections while I was trying to follow his train of thought, but he was ill, wasn't he? Nothing leads anywhere concrete.'

'I was just intrigued by that "Could Cetus be right?" because Talbot mistrusted Irene from the start, didn't he? Then he starts wondering whether she could have been right about . . . about something connected to enemies, secrets and undoing . . .'

'If we ever find out what happened to Margot Bamborough,' said Strike, 'I'll bet you a hundred quid you'll be able to make equally strong cases for Talbot's occult stuff being bang on the money, and completely off beam. You can always stretch this symbolic stuff to fit the facts. One of my mother's friends used to guess everyone's star signs and she was right *every single time*.'

'She was?'

'Oh yeah,' said Strike. 'Because even when she was wrong, she was right. Turned out they had a load of planets in that sign or, I dunno, the midwife who delivered them was that sign. Or their dog.'

'All right,' said Robin, equably. She'd expected Strike's scepticism, after all, and now put both the leather-bound notebook and *Astrology 14* back into her bag. 'I know it might mean nothing at all, I'm only—'

'If you want to go and see Irene Hickson again, be my guest. Tell her Talbot thought she might've had profound insight into something connected to asteroids and – I dunno – cheese—'

'The twelfth house doesn't govern *cheese*,' said Robin, trying to look severe.

'What number's the house of dairy?'

'Oh, bugger off,' she said, laughing against her will.

Robin's mobile vibrated in her pocket, and she pulled it out. A text had just arrived.

Hi Robin, if you want I can talk now? I've just agreed to work a later shift, so I'm not needed at work for a few hours. Otherwise it'll have to be after 8 tonight – Amanda

'Amanda White,' she told Strike. 'She wants to talk now.'

'Works for me,' said Strike, relieved to be back on firm investigative ground. Liar or not, Amanda White would at least be talking about an actual woman at a real window.

Robin pressed Amanda's number, switched the mobile to speakerphone and laid it on the table between her and Strike.

'Hi,' said a confident female voice, with a hint of North London. 'Is that Robin?'

'Yes,' said Robin, 'and I'm with Cormoran.'

'Morning,' said Strike.

'Oh, it's *you*, is it?' said Amanda, sounding delighted. 'I *am* honoured. I've been dealing with your assistant.'

'She's actually my partner,' said Strike.

'Really? Business, or the other?' said Amanda.

'Business,' said Strike, not looking at Robin. 'I understand Robin's been talking to you about what you saw on the night Margot Bamborough disappeared?'

'That's right,' said Amanda.

'Would you mind if we take a recording of this interview?'

'No, I s'pose not,' said Amanda. 'I mean, I want to do the right thing, although I won't pretend it hasn't been a bit of a dilemma, because it was really stressful, last time. Journalists, two police interviews, and I was only fourteen. But I've always been a stubborn girl, haha, and I stuck to my guns . . .'

So Amanda told the story with which Strike and Robin were already familiar: of the rain, and the angry schoolfriend, and the upper window, and the retrospective recognition of Margot, when Amanda saw her picture in the paper. Strike asked a couple of questions, but he could tell that nothing would ever change Amanda's story. Whether she truly believed she'd seen Margot Bamborough at the window that night or not, she was evidently determined never to relinquish her association with the forty-year-old mystery.

'. . . and I suppose I've been haunted ever since by the idea that I didn't do anything, but I was fourteen and it only hit me later, I could've been the one to save her,' she ended the story.

'Well,' said Robin, as Strike nodded at her, signalling he had everything he wanted, 'thank you so much for talking to us, Amanda. I really—'

'There's something else, before you go,' said Amanda. 'Wait until you hear this. It's just an amazing coincidence, and I don't think even the police know about this, because they're both dead.'

'Who're dead?' asked Robin, while Strike lit himself another cigarette.

'*Well*,' said Amanda, 'how's this for strange? My last job, this young girl at the office's great-aunt—'

Strike rolled his eyes.

'—was in a hospice with, guess who?'

'I don't know,' said Robin politely.

'Violet Cooper,' said Amanda. 'You probably don't—'

'Dennis Creed's landlady,' said Robin.

'*Exactly!*' said Amanda, sounding pleased that Robin appreciated the significance of her story. 'So, anyway, isn't that just *weird*, that I saw Margot at that window, and then, all those years later, I work with someone whose relative met Vi Cooper? Only she was calling herself something different by then, because people hated her.'

'That *is* a coincidence,' said Robin, making sure not to look at Strike. 'Well, thank—'

'That's not all!' said Amanda, laughing. 'No, there's more to it than that! So, this girl's great-aunt said Vi told her she wrote to Creed, once, asking if he'd killed Margot Bamborough.'

Amanda paused, clearly wanting a response, so Robin, who'd already read about this in *The Demon of Paradise Park*, said,

'Wow.'

'*I know*,' said Amanda. 'And apparently, Vi said – this is on her deathbed, so you know, she was telling the truth, because you would, wouldn't you? – Vi said the letter she got back, said he *had* killed her.'

'Really?' said Robin. 'I thought the letter—'

'No, but this is direct from Violet,' Amanda said, while Strike rolled his eyes again, 'and she said, he definitely did, he as good as told her so. He said it in a way only she'd understand, but she knew *exactly* what he meant.

'*Crazy*, though, isn't it? I see Margot at the window, and then, years later—'

'Amazing,' said Robin. 'Well, thanks very much for your time, Amanda, this has been really . . . er . . . '

It took Robin another couple of minutes, and much more insincere gratitude, to get Amanda off the line.

'What d'you think?' Robin asked Strike, when at last she'd succeeded in getting rid of Amanda.

He pointed a finger at the sky.

'What?' said Robin, looking up into the blue haze.

'If you look carefully,' said Strike, 'you might just see an asteroid passing through the house of bollocks.'

50

Aye me (said she) where am I, or with whom?
Emong the liuing, or emong the dead?

Edmund Spenser
The Faerie Queene

Agency work unconnected with the Bamborough case consumed Strike for the next few days. His first attempt to surprise Nurse Janice Beattie at home was fruitless. He left Nightingale Grove, a nondescript street that lay hard against the Southeastern railway line, without receiving any answer to his knock.

His second attempt, on the following Wednesday, was made on a breezy afternoon that kept threatening showers. Strike approached Janice's house from Hither Green station, along a pavement bordered to the right with railings and hedge, separating the road from the rail tracks. He was thinking about Robin as he trudged along, smoking, because she'd just turned down the opportunity of joining him to interview Janice, saying that there was 'something else' she needed to do, but not specifying what that something was. Strike thought he'd detected a trace of caginess, almost amounting to defensiveness, in Robin's response to the suggestion of a joint interview, where usually there'd have been only disappointment.

Since she'd left Matthew, Strike had become used to more

ease and openness between him and Robin, so this refusal, coupled with her tone and lack of an explanation, made him curious. While there were naturally matters he might not have expected her to tell him about – trips to the gynaecologist sprang to mind – he would have expected her to say 'I've got a doctor's appointment', at least.

The sky darkened as Strike approached Janice's house, which was considerably smaller than Irene Hickson's. It stood in a terrace. Net curtains hung at all the windows, and the front door was dark red. Strike didn't immediately register the fact that a light was shining from behind the net curtains at the sitting-room window until he was halfway across the road. When he realised that his quarry must be in, however, he successfully pushed all thoughts about his business partner out of his mind, crossed the road at a quicker pace and knocked firmly on the front door. As he stood waiting, he heard the muffled sounds of a TV on high volume through the glass of the downstairs window. He was just considering knocking again, in case Janice hadn't heard the first time, when the dooropened.

In contrast to the last time they'd met, the nurse, who was wearing steel-rimmed spectacles, looked shocked and none too pleased to see Strike. From behind her, two female American voices rang out from the out-of-sight TV: '*So you love the bling?*' '*I love the bling!*'

'Er – 'ave I missed a message, or—?'

'Sorry for the lack of warning,' said Strike insincerely, 'but as I was in the area, I wondered whether you could give me a couple of minutes?'

Janice glanced back over her shoulder. A camp male voice was now saying, '*The dress that Kelly is in love with is a one-of-a-kind runway sample . . .*'

Clearly disgruntled, Janice turned back to Strike.

'Well . . . all right,' she said, 'but the place is in a mess – and can you please wipe your feet properly, because the last bloke who turned up 'ere unannounced brought dog shit in wiv 'im. You can close the door be'ind you.'

Strike stepped over the threshold, while Janice strode out of sight into the sitting room. Strike expected her to turn off the TV but she didn't. While Strike wiped his feet on the coconut mat inside the door, a male voice said: '*This one-of-a-kind runway gown might be impossible to find, so Randy's on the search . . .*' After hesitating for a moment on the doormat, Strike decided that Janice expected him to follow her, and entered the small sitting room.

Having spent a significant part of his youth in squats with his mother, Strike had a very different idea of 'mess' to Janice's. Although cluttered, with something on almost every surface, the only signs of actual disorder in the room were a copy of the *Daily Mirror* lying in one armchair, some crumpled packaging lying beside an open packet of dates on the low coffee table and a hairdryer, which was lying incongruously on the floor beside the sofa, and which Janice was currently unplugging.

'*. . . Antonella's pulling the closest gown to Kelly's pick, a blinged-out $15,000 dress . . .*'

'The mirror down 'ere's better for drying my 'air,' Janice explained, straightening up, pink in the face, hairdryer in her hand and looking slightly cross, as though Strike was forcing her to justify herself. 'I would've appreciated some warning, you know,' she added, looking as stern as such a naturally smiley-looking woman could. 'You've caught me on the 'op.'

Strike was unexpectedly and poignantly reminded of Joan, who'd always been flustered if guests dropped in while the Hoover or the ironing board were still out.

'Sorry. As I say, I happened to be in the area . . . '

'*Even as Kelly steps into dress number one, she still can't get her dream dress off her mind*,' said the narrator loudly, and both Strike and Janice glanced towards the TV, where a young woman was wriggling into a clinging, semi-transparent white dress covered in silver rhinestones.

'*Say Yes to the Dress*,' said Janice, who was wearing the same navy jumper and slacks as the last time Strike had seen her. 'My guilty pleasure . . . D'you want a cup of tea?'

'Only if it's no trouble,' said Strike.

'Well, it's always *some* trouble, innit?' Janice said, with her first glimmer of a smile. 'But I was going to make myself some at the first advert break, so you might as well 'ave some.'

'In that case, thanks very much,' said Strike.

'*If I don't find this dress*,' said the camp male wedding consultant on-screen, rifling urgently through racks of white dresses, his eyebrows so sharply plucked they looked drawn on, '*it's not gonna be—*'

The screen went blank. Janice had turned it off with her remote control.

'Wanna date?' she asked Strike, holding out the box.

'No thanks,' said Strike.

'Got boxes of 'em in Dubai,' she said. 'I was gonna give 'em as presents, but I just can't stop eating 'em. 'Ave a seat. I won't be two ticks.'

Strike thought he caught another downward glance towards his lower legs as she marched out of the room, hairdryer in one hand, dates in the other, leaving Strike to take an armchair, which creaked beneath his weight.

Strike found the small sitting room oppressive. Predominantly red, the carpet was decorated in a scarlet, swirling pattern, on top of which lay a cheap crimson Turkish rug. Dried flower pictures hung on the red walls, between old photographs, some black and white, and the coloured ones faded, displayed in wooden frames. A china cabinet was full of cheap spun-glass ornaments. The largest, a Cinderella carriage pulled by six glass horses, stood in pride of place on the mantelpiece over the electric fire. Evidently, beneath Janice's no-nonsense clothing, there beat a romantic heart.

She returned a few minutes later, holding a wicker-handled tray bearing two mugs of tea with the milk already added, and a plate of chocolate Hobnobs. The act of making tea seemed to have put her into slightly better humour with her guest.

'That's my Larry,' she said, catching Strike looking towards a double frame on the small side table beside him. On one side was a sleepy-eyed, overweight man with a smoker's teeth. On the other was a blonde woman, heavy but pretty.

'Ah. And is this—?'

'My little sister, Clare. She died '97. Pancreatic cancer. They got it late.'

'Oh, I'm sorry to hear that,' said Strike.

'Yeah,' said Janice, with a deep sigh. 'Lost 'em both around the same time. To tell you the truth,' she said, as she sat down on the sofa and her knees gave audible clicks, 'I walked back in 'ere after Dubai and I fort, I really need to get some new pictures up. It was depressing, coming back in 'ere, the number of dead people . . .

'I got some gorgeous ones of Kev and the grandkids on 'oliday, but I 'aven't got 'em printed out yet. The lad next door's going to do it for me. All my old ones of Kev and the kids are two years out of date. I gave the boy the memory . . . *board*, is it?'

'Card?' suggested Strike.

'That's the one. The kids next door just laugh at me. Mind you, Irene's worse'n I am. She can 'ardly change a battery. So,' she said, 'why d'you want to see me again?'

Strike, who had no intention of risking an immediate rebuff, was planning to ask his questions about Satchwell last. Drawing out his notebook and opening it, he said,

'A couple of things that have come up since I last saw you. I asked Dr Gupta about this first one, but he couldn't help, so I hoped you might be able to. Would you happen to know anything about a man called Niccolo Ricci, sometimes nicknamed "Mucky"?'

'Old gangster, weren't 'e?' said Janice. 'I knew 'e lived local, in Clerkenwell, but I never met 'im. Why d'you want – oh, 'as Irene been telling you about the foundations thing?'

'The what?' asked Strike.

'Oh, it's nuffing, really. There was this rumour, back when they were doing a load of redevelopment round Clerkenwell in the early seventies, that some builders 'ad found a body buried in concrete under one of the demolished buildings. The story was that Little Italy gangsters 'ad hidden it there, back in the forties. But Eddie – this is Irene's Eddie, the builder she ended up marrying – that's 'ow they met, local pub, when 'is firm was doing a lot of the redevelopment – Eddie told us it was all cobblers. *I* 'adn't ever believed it. I fink Irene 'ad, a bit,' Janice added, dunking a biscuit in her tea.

'How does this tie in with Margot?' Strike asked.

'Well, after Margot disappeared, there was a theory 'er body 'ad been put into one o' the open foundations and covered in concrete. They was still doing a bit of building round there in '74, see.'

'Were people suggesting Ricci had killed her?' asked Strike.

'Gawd, no!' said Janice, with a shocked little laugh. 'What would Mucky Ricci 'ave to do with Margot? It was only because of that old rumour. It put the idea in people's minds, you know, burying bodies in concrete. People can be bloody silly. My Larry said to me – 'e was a builder, you know – it's not like workmen wouldn't've noticed a load of fresh concrete when they turned up for work.'

'Were you aware that Ricci attended the St John's practice Christmas party?'

''E what?' said Janice, with her mouth full.

'He and another couple of men arrived towards the end of the party, possibly to escort Gloria home.'

'They – *what*?' Janice said, looking unaffectedly astonished. 'Mucky Ricci and *Gloria*? Come off it. Is this because – no, look, you don't wanna pay no attention to Irene, not about Gloria. Irene . . . she gets carried away. She never much liked Gloria. And she gets the wrong end of the stick sometimes. *I* never 'eard Gloria's family 'ad any criminal connections. Irene watched way too many *Godfather* movies,' said Janice. 'We saw the first one togevver, at the cinema, and I went back and saw it again twice more on me own. James Caan, you know,' she sighed. 'My dream man.'

'Ricci was definitely at the practice party,' said Strike. 'From what I can tell, he turned up right at the end.'

'Well then, I'd already left. I needed to get 'ome to Kev. Is 'e still alive, Ricci?'

'Yes,' said Strike.

'Must be really getting on, is 'e?'

'He is,' said Strike.

'That's odd, though. What on earth would Ricci be doing at St John's?'

'I'm hoping to find out,' said Strike, flipping over a page of his notebook. 'The next thing I wanted to ask you was about Joseph Brenner. You remember the family you thought might be called Applethorpe? Well, I found—'

'You never tracked 'em down!' said Janice, looking impressed. 'What *was* their name?'

'Athorn.'

'Athorn!' said Janice, with an air of relief. 'I *knew* it wasn't Applethorpe. That bugged me for days, after . . . 'Ow are they? It's Fragile X they've got, isn't it? They're not in an 'ome, or—?'

'Still living together in the old flat,' said Strike, 'and getting on reasonably well, I think.'

'I 'ope they're being well supported, are they?'

'There's a social worker involved, who seems very much on their side, which brings me to what I was going to ask you.

'The social worker says that since Gwilherm's death, Deborah's disclosed . . .' Strike hesitated, ' . . . well, the way the social worker put it, was that Gwilherm was, er, pimping Deborah out.'

''E was what?' said Janice, the smile sliding off her face.

'It's an unpleasant idea, I know,' said Strike unemotionally. 'When I was talking to her, Deborah told me about Dr Brenner visiting her at home. She said he'd – er – asked her to take off her pants—'

'No!' said Janice, in what seemed instinctive revulsion. 'No, I'm sure – no, that's not right. That's not 'ow it would've 'appened, if she'd needed an intimate examination. It would have 'appened at the surgery.'

'You said she was agoraphobic?'

'Well – yeah, but . . .'

'Samhain, the son, said something about Dr Brenner being a "dirty old man".'

''E . . . but . . . no, it . . . it *must've* been an examination . . . maybe after the baby was born? But that should've been me, the nurse . . . that's upset me, now,' said Janice, looking distressed. 'You think you've 'eard everything, but . . . no, that's really upset me. I mean, I was in the 'ouse that one time to see the kid and she never said a word to me . . . but of course, *'e* was there, the father, telling me all about 'is bloody magic powers. She was probably too scared to ... no, that's really upset me, that 'as.'

'I'm sorry,' said Strike, 'but I have to ask: did you ever hear that Brenner used prostitutes? Ever hear any rumours about him, locally?'

'Not a word,' said Janice. 'I'd've told someone, if I'd 'eard that. It wouldn't be ethical, not in our catchment area. All the women there were registered to our practice. She'd've been a patient.'

'According to Talbot's notes,' said Strike, 'somebody claimed they saw Brenner in Michael Cliffe House on the evening Margot disappeared. The story Brenner gave the police was that he went straight home.'

'Michael Cliffe 'Ouse ... that's the tower block on Skinner Street, innit?' said Janice. 'We 'ad patients in there, but otherwise ...' Janice appeared sickened. 'You've upset me,' she said again. ''Im and that poor Athorn woman ... and there's me defending 'im to all and sundry, because of 'is experiences in the war. Not two weeks back, I 'ad Dorothy's son sitting exactly where you are now—'

'Carl Oakden was here?' said Strike sharply.

'Yeah,' said Janice, 'and 'e didn't wipe 'is feet, neither. Dog shit all up my 'all carpet.'

'What did he want?' asked Strike.

'Well, 'e *pretended* it was a nice catch-up,' said Janice. 'You'd think I might not recognise 'im after all this time, but actually, 'e don't look that much diff'rent, not really. Anyway, 'e sat in that chair where you are, spouting all sorts of rubbish about old times and 'is mum remembering me fondly – ha! Dorothy Oakden, remember me fondly? Dorothy thought Irene and me were a pair of hussies, skirts above our knees, going out to the pub togevver ...

''E mentioned *you*,' said Janice, with a beady look. 'Wanted to know if I'd met you, yet. 'E wrote a book about Margot, you know, but it never made it into the shops, which 'e's angry about. 'E told me all about it when 'e was 'ere. 'E's finking of writing another one and it's *you* what's got 'im interested in it. The famous detective solving the case – or the famous detective *not* solving the case. Either one'll do for Carl.'

'What was he saying about Brenner?' asked Strike. There would be time enough later to consider the implications of an amateur biographer tramping all over the case.

'Said Dr Brenner was a sadistic old man, and there I was, sort of sticking up for Dr Brenner . . . but now you're telling me this about Deborah Athorn . . .'

'Oakden said Brenner was sadistic, did he? That's a strong word.'

'I fort so, too. Carl said 'e'd never liked 'im, said Dr Brenner used to go round Dorothy's 'ouse a lot, which I never realised, for Sunday lunch and that. I always fort they were just work-mates. You know, Dr Brenner probably told Carl off, that's all. 'E was an 'oly terror when 'e was a kid, Carl, and 'e comes across as the kind of man 'oo 'olds a grudge.'

'If Oakden comes round here again,' said Strike, 'I'd advise you not to let him in. He's done time, you know. For conning . . .' He just stopped himself saying 'old' ' . . . single women out of their money.'

'*Oh*,' said Janice, taken aback. 'Blimey. I'd better warn Irene. 'E said 'e was going to try 'er next.'

'And he seemed primarily interested in Brenner, did he, when he came round here?'

'Well, no,' said Janice. ''E seemed mostly interested in *you*, but yeah, we talked about Brenner more'n anyone else at the practice.'

'Mrs Beattie, you wouldn't happen to still have that

newspaper obituary of Brenner you mentioned? I think you said you kept it?'

'Oh,' said Janice, glancing towards the drawer at the base of her china cabinet, 'yeah . . . Carl wanted to see that, too, when 'e 'eard I 'ad it . . . '

She pushed herself out of the sofa and crossed to the china cabinet. Gripping the mantelpiece to steady herself, she knelt down, opened the drawer and began rummaging.

'They're all in a bit of a state, my clippings. Irene finks I'm bonkers, me and my newspapers,' she added, wrist-deep in the contents of the drawer. 'She's never been much for the news or politics or any of that, but I've always saved interesting bits and pieces, you know: medical fings, and I won't lie, I do like a story on the royals and . . . '

She began tugging on what looked like the corner of a cardboard folder.

' . . . and Irene can fink it's strange all she likes, but I don't see what's wrong – with saving – the story of . . . '

The folder came free.

' . . . a life,' said Janice, walking on her knees to the coffee table. 'Why's that morbid? No worse'n keeping a photo.'

She flipped open the folder and began looking through the clippings, some of them yellow with age.

'See? I saved that for 'er, for Irene,' said Janice, holding up an article about holy basil. 'Supposed to 'elp with digestive problems, I fort Eddie could plant some in the garden for 'er. She takes too many pills for 'er bowels, they do as much 'arm as good, but Irene's one of those 'oo, if it doesn't come in a tablet, she don't wanna know . . .

'Princess Diana,' said Janice with a sigh, flashing a commemorative front page at Strike. 'I was a fan . . . '

'May I?' asked Strike, reaching for a couple of pieces of newsprint.

''Elp yourself,' said Janice, looking over her spectacles at the pieces of paper in Strike's hand. 'That article on diabetes is very interesting. Care's changed so much since I retired. My godson's Type One. I like to keep up with it all . . . and that'll be the fing about the kid 'oo died of peritonitis, in your other 'and, is it?'

'Yes,' said Strike, looking at the clipping, which was brown with age.

'Yeah,' said Janice darkly, still turning over bits of newspaper, ''e's the reason I'm a nurse. That's what put the idea in me 'ead. 'E lived two doors down from me when I was a kid. I cut that out an' kept it, only photo I was ever gonna 'ave . . . bawled my bloody eyes out. The doctor,' said Janice, with a hint of steel, 'was called out and 'e never bloody turned up. 'E would've come out for a middle-class kid, we all knew that, but little Johnny Marks from Bethnal Green, 'oo cared . . . and the doctor was criticised, but never struck off . . . If there's one thing I *'ate*, it's treating people diff'rent because of where they were born.'

With no apparent sense of irony, she shifted more pictures of the royals out of the way, looking puzzled.

'Where's Dr Brenner's thing?' she muttered.

Still clutching several clippings, she walked on her knees back towards the open drawer and rummaged in there again.

'No, it *really* isn't 'ere,' said Janice, returning to the coffee table. 'That's very odd . . . '

'You don't think Oakden took it, do you?' Strike suggested.

Janice looked up.

'That cheeky sod,' she said slowly. ''E could of bloody asked.'

She swept her clippings back into their folder, returned it to her drawer, used the mantelpiece to pull herself back up, knees clicking loudly again, then sat back down on the sofa with a sigh of relief and said,

'You know, 'e was always light-fingered, that boy.'

'What makes you say that?'

'Money went missing, back at the practice.'

'Really?' said Strike.

'Yeah. It all come to 'an 'ead after Margot disappeared. Little bits of money kept going missing and they fort it was Wilma, the cleaner – ev'ryone except me. *I* always fort it was Carl. 'E used to drop in after school, and in the school 'olidays. I dropped a word in Dr Gupta's ear, but I dunno, probably 'e didn't want to upset Dorothy, and it was easier to push Wilma out. True, there were ovver issues wiv Wilma . . . she drank,' said Janice, 'and 'er cleaning wasn't the best. She couldn't prove she never nicked it, and after there was a staff meeting about it, she resigned. She could see the way it was going.'

'And did the thefts stop?'

'Yeah,' said Janice, 'but so what? Carl might've thought 'e'd better give it rest, after nearly being found out.'

Strike, who tended to agree, said,

'Just a couple more questions. The first's about a woman called Joanna Hammond.'

'I should know 'oo that is, should I?'

'She was Steve Douthwaite's—'

'—girlfriend, 'oo killed 'erself,' said Janice. 'Oh yeah.'

'Can you remember whether she was registered with the St John's practice?'

'No, she weren't. I fink they lived over in Hoxton.'

'So Margot wouldn't have been involved with the coroner, or had any other professional connection with her death?'

'No, she'll 'ave been same as me: never knew the woman existed till she was already dead and Steve come looking for 'elp. I bet I know why you're asking, though,' said Janice. 'Talbot was dead set on Steve being the Essex Butcher, wasn't 'e? On and on about Steve, in all those interviews I 'ad with 'im. But honestly, Steve Douthwaite was a gentle soul. I grew up wiv a couple of proper violent men. Me father was one. I know the type, and Steve definitely weren't it.'

Remembering how endearing some women had found the apparent vulnerability of Dennis Creed, Strike merely nodded.

'Talbot asked wevver I'd ever visited that Joanna, as a nurse. I told 'im she wasn't a St John's patient, but that didn't put 'im off. Did I think there was anything fishy about 'er death, even so? I kept saying, "I never met the woman. 'Ow do I know?" I was getting worn down wiv it all by then, honestly, being treated like I was Gypsy bloody Rose Lee. I told Talbot, go see what the coroner said!'

'And you don't know whether there *was* a death Margot was worried about?' Strike asked. 'A death that was maybe categorised as natural, or accidental, but where she thought there might have been foul play?'

'What makes you ask that?' said Janice.

'Just trying to clear up something Talbot left in his notes. He seemed to think Margot might've had suspicions about the way somebody died. You were mentioned in connection with the death.'

Janice's round blue eyes widened behind her glasses.

'Mentioned as having witnessed something, or perhaps been present,' Strike elaborated. 'There was no hint of accusation.'

'I should bloody well 'ope not!' said Janice. 'No, I never *witnessed* nothing. I'd've said if I 'ad, wouldn't I?'

There was a short pause, which Strike judged it prudent not to break, and sure enough, Janice piped up again.

'Look, I can't speak for Margot forty years on. She's gone, i'n't she? It isn't fair on either of us. I don't wanna be casting suspicion round, all these years later.'

'I'm just trying to eliminate possible lines of inquiry,' said Strike.

There was a longer pause. Janice's eyes drifted over the tea tray and on to the picture of her late partner, with his stained teeth and his kind, sleepy eyes. Finally, she sighed and said,

'All right, but I want you to write down that this was *Margot's* idea, not mine, all right? I'm not accusing no one.'

'Fair enough,' said Strike, pen poised over his notebook.

'All right then, well – it was very sensitive, because of us working wiv 'er – Dorothy, I mean.

'Dorothy and Carl lived wiv Dorothy's mother. 'Er name was Maud, though I wouldn't remember that if Carl 'adn't been 'ere the ovver day. We were talking and I mentioned 'is gran, and 'e called 'er "bloody Maud", not "Grandma" or nothing.

'Anyway, Maud 'ad an infection on 'er leg, a sore what was taking its time 'ealing. It needed dressing and looking after, so I was visiting the 'ouse a lot. Ev'ry time I was in there, she told me *she* owned the 'ouse, not Dorothy. She was letting 'er daughter and grandson live wiv 'er. She liked saying it, you know. Feeling the power.

'I wouldn't say she'd be much fun to live with. Sour old lady. Nothing ever right for 'er. She moaned a lot about 'er grandson being spoiled – but like I said, 'e was an 'oly terror when 'e was younger, so I can't blame 'er there.

'Anyway,' said Janice, 'before the sore on 'er leg was 'ealed, she died, after falling downstairs. Now, 'er walking wasn't great, because she'd been laid up for a bit with this sore leg, and she needed a stick. People *do* fall downstairs, and if you're elderly, obviously that can 'ave serious consequences, but . . .

'Well, a week afterwards, Margot asked me into 'er consulting room for a word, and . . . well, yeah, I got the impression Margot was maybe a bit uneasy about it. She never said anyfing outright, just asked me what I fort. I knew what she was saying . . . but what could we do? We weren't there when she fell and the family said they was downstairs and just 'eard 'er take the tumble, and there she was at the bottom of the stairs, knocked out cold, and she died two nights later in 'ospital.

'Dorothy never showed no emotion about it, but Dorothy never *did* show much emotion about anything. What could we do?' Janice repeated, her palms turned upwards. 'Obviously I could see the way Margot's mind was working, because she knew Maud owned the 'ouse, and now Dorothy and Carl were sitting pretty, and . . . well, it's the kind of thing doctors consider, of course they do. It'll come back on them, if they've missed anything. But in the end, Margot never done nothing about it and as far as I know there was never any bother.

'There,' Janice concluded, with a slight air of relief at having got this off her chest. 'Now you know.'

'Thank you,' said Strike, making a note. 'That's very helpful. Tell me: did you ever mention this to Talbot?'

'No,' said Janice, 'but someone else mighta done. Ev'ryone knew Maud 'ad died, and 'ow she died, because Dorothy took a day off for the funeral. I'll be honest, by the end of all my interviews wiv Talbot, I just wanted to get out of there. Mostly 'e wanted me to talk about me dreams. It was creepy, honestly. Weird, the 'ole thing.'

'I'm sure it was,' said Strike. 'Well, there's just one more thing I wanted to ask, and then I'm done. My partner managed to track down Paul Satchwell.'

'Oh,' said Janice, with no sign of embarrassment or discomfort. 'Right. That was Margot's old boyfriend, wasn't it?'

'Yes. Well, we were surprised to find out you know each other.'

Janice looked at him blankly.

'What?'

'That you know each other,' Strike repeated.

'Me and Paul Satchwell?' said Janice with a little laugh. 'I've never even met the man!'

'Really?' said Strike, watching her closely. 'When he heard you'd told us about the sighting of Margot in Leamington Spa, he got quite angry. He said words to the effect,' Strike read off his notebook, 'that you were trying to cause trouble for him.'

There was a long silence. A frown line appeared between Janice's round blue eyes. At last she said,

'Did 'e mention me by name?'

'No,' said Strike. 'As a matter of fact, he seemed to have forgotten it. He just remembered you as "the nurse". He also told Robin that you and Margot didn't like each other.'

''E said Margot didn't like *me*?' said Janice, with the emphasis on the last word.

'I'm afraid so,' said Strike, watching her.

'But ... no, sorry, that's not right,' said Janice. 'We used to get on great! Ovver than that one time wiv Kev and 'is tummy ... all right, I *did* get shirty wiv 'er then, but I knew she *meant* it kindly. She fort she was doing me a favour, examining 'im ... I took offence because ... well, you do get a bit defensive, as a mother, if you fink another woman's judging you for not taking care of your kids properly. I was on me own with Kev and ... you just feel it more, when you're on your own.'

'So why,' Strike asked, 'would Satchwell say he knew you, and that you wanted to get him into trouble?'

The silence that followed was broken by the sound of a train passing beyond the hedge: a great rushing rumble built and subsided, and the quiet of the sitting room closed like a bubble in its wake, holding the detective and the nurse in suspension as they looked at each other.

'I fink you already know,' said Janice at last.

'Know what?'

'Don't give me that. All them fings you've solved – you're

not a stupid man. I fink you already know, and all this is to try and scare me into telling you.'

'I'm certainly not trying to *scare*—'

'I know you didn't like 'er,' said Janice abruptly. 'Irene. Don't bovver pretending, I know she annoyed you. If I couldn't read people I wouldn't 'ave been any good at my job, going in and out of strangers' 'ouses all the time, would I? And I was *very* good at my job,' said Janice, and somehow the remark didn't seem arrogant. 'Listen: you saw Irene in one of 'er show-off moods. She was so excited to meet you, she put on a big act.

'It's not easy for women, living alone when they're used to company, you know. Even me, coming back from Dubai, it's been a readjustment. You get used to 'aving family around you and then you're back in the empty 'ouse again, alone . . . Me, I don't mind me own company, but Irene 'ates it.

'She's been a very good friend to me, Irene,' said Janice, with a kind of quiet ferocity. 'Very kind. She 'elped me out financially, after Larry died, back when I 'ad nothing. I've always been welcome in 'er 'ouse. We're company for each other, we go back a long way. So she might 'ave a few airs and graces, so what? So 'ave plenty of people . . . '

There was another brief pause.

'Wait there,' said Janice firmly. 'I need to make a phone call.'

She got up and left the room. Strike waited. Beyond the net curtains, the sun suddenly slid out from behind a bullet-coloured cloud, and turned the glass Cinderella coach on the mantelpiece neon bright.

Janice reappeared with a mobile in her hand.

'She's not picking up,' she said, looking perturbed.

She sat back down on the sofa. There was another pause.

'*Fine*,' said Janice at last, as though Strike had harangued her into speech, 'it wasn't me 'oo knew Satchwell – it was Irene. But don't you go thinking she's done anyfing she shouldn't've!

I mean, not in a *criminal* sense. It worried 'er like 'ell, after. I was worried *for* 'er . . . Oh Gawd,' said Janice.

She took a deep breath then said,

'All right, well . . . she was engaged to Eddie at the time. Eddie was a lot older'n Irene. 'E worshipped the ground she walked on, an' she loved 'im, too. She *did*,' said Janice, though Strike hadn't contradicted her. 'And she was *really* jealous if Eddie so much as looked at anyone else . . .

'But she always liked a drink and a flirt, Irene. It was 'armless. *Mostly* 'armless . . . that bloke Satchwell 'ad a band, didn't 'e?'

'That's right,' said Strike.

'Yeah, well, Irene saw 'em play at some pub. I wasn't wiv 'er the night she met Satchwell. I never knew a fing about it till after Margot 'ad gone missing.

'So she watched Satchwell and – well, she fancied 'im. And after the band 'ad finished, she sees Satchwell come into the bar, and 'e goes right to the back of the room to Margot, 'oo's standing there in a corner, in 'er raincoat. Irene fort Satchwell must've seen 'er from the stage. Irene 'adn't spotted Margot before, because she was up the front, wiv 'er friends. Anyway, she watched 'em, and Satchwell and Margot 'ad a short chat – really short, Irene said – and it looked like it turned into an argument. And then Irene reckoned Margot spotted 'er, and that's when Margot walked out.

'So then, Irene goes up to that Satchwell and tells 'im she loved the band and everything and, well, one thing led to another, and . . . yeah.'

'Why would Satchwell think she was a nurse?' asked Strike.

Janice grimaced.

'Well, to tell you the truth, that's what the silly girl used to tell blokes she was, when they were chatting 'er up. She used to pretend to be a nurse because the fellas liked it. As long as they knew naff all about medical stuff she managed to fool 'em, because she'd 'eard the names of drugs and all that at work, though she got most of 'em wrong, God love 'er,' said Janice, with a small eye roll.

'So was this a one-night stand, or . . . ?'

'No. It was a two-, three-week thing. But it didn't last. Margot disappearing . . . well, that put the kibosh on it. You can imagine.

'But for a couple of weeks there, Irene was . . . infatuated, I s'pose you'd say. She *did* love Eddie, you know . . . it was a bit of a feather in 'er cap to 'ave this older man, Eddie, successful business and everything, wanting to marry 'er, but . . . it's funny, isn't it?' said Janice quietly. 'We're all animals, when you take everything else away. She *totally* lost 'er 'ead over Paul Satchwell. Just for a few weeks. Tryin' to see 'im as much as she could, sneaking around . . . I bet she scared the life out of 'im, actually,' said Janice soberly, 'because from what she told me later, I fink 'e only took 'er to bed to spite Margot. Margot was 'oo 'e really wanted . . . and Irene realised that too late. She'd been used.'

'So the story of Irene's sore tooth,' said Strike, 'which then became the story of a shopping trip . . . '

'Yeah,' said Janice quietly. 'She was with Satchwell that afternoon. She took that receipt off 'er sister to use with the police. *I* never knew till afterwards. I 'ad her in floods of tears in my flat, pouring 'er 'eart out. Well, 'oo else could she tell? Not Eddie or 'er parents! She was terrified of it coming out, and losing Eddie. She'd woken up by then. All she wanted was Eddie, and she was scared 'e'd drop 'er if 'e found out about Satchwell.

'See, Satchwell as good as told Irene, the last time they met, 'e was using 'er to get back at Margot. 'E'd been angry at Margot for saying she'd only come to watch the band outta curiosity, and for getting shirty when 'e tried to persuade 'er to go back to 'is flat. 'E gave 'er that little wooden Viking thing, you know. 'E'd 'ad it on 'im, 'oping she'd turn up, and I fink 'e thought she'd just *melt* or somefing when 'e did that, and that'd be the end of Roy . . . like that's all it takes, to walk out on a kid and a marriage, a little wooden doll . . . 'E said some nasty stuff about Margot to Irene . . . prick tease was the least of it . . .

'Anyway, after Margot went missing and the police got called in, Satchwell rings Irene up and says not to mention anyfing 'e'd said about being angry at Margot, and she begged 'im never to tell anyone about the both of 'em, and that's 'ow they left it. And I was the only one 'oo knew, and I kept me mouth shut, too, because . . . well, that's what you do when it's a friend, isn't it?'

'So when Charlie Ramage said he'd seen Margot in Leamington Spa,' said Strike, 'were you aware—?'

'—that that's where Satchwell come from? Not then, I wasn't, not when Charlie first told me. But not long after, there was a news story about some old geezer in Leamington Spa what 'ad put up a sign in 'is front garden. "Whites united against coloured invasion" or some such 'orrible thing. Me and Larry was out for dinner with Eddie and Irene, and Eddie's talking about this old racist in the news, and then, when Irene and I went to the loo, she says to me, "Leamington Spa, that's where Paul Satchwell was from." She 'adn't mentioned 'im to me in ages.

'I won't lie, it give me a proper uncomfortable feeling, 'er telling me that, because I thought, oh my Gawd, what if Charlie really did see Margot? What if Margot ran off to be with 'er ex? But then I fort, 'ang on, though: if Margot only went as far as Leamington Spa, 'ow come she 'asn't never been seen since? I mean, it's 'ardly Timbuktu, is it?'

'No,' said Strike. 'It isn't. And is that all Irene's ever told you about Margot and Satchwell?'

'It's enough, innit?' said Janice. Her pink and white complexion seemed more faded than when Strike had arrived, the veins beneath her eyes darker. 'Look, *don't* give Irene an 'ard time. Please. She don't seem it, but she's soft under all that silly stuff. She worries, you know.'

'I can't see why I'd have to give her a hard time,' said Strike. 'Well, you've been very helpful, Mrs Beattie. Thank you. That clears up quite a few points for me.'

Janice slumped backwards on the sofa, frowning at Strike.

'You smoke, don't you?' she said abruptly. 'I can smell it off you. Didn't they stop you smoking after you 'ad that amputation?'

'They tried,' said Strike.

'Very bad for you,' she said. 'Won't 'elp wiv your mobility, either, as you get older. Bad for your circulation *and* your skin. You should quit.'

'I know I should,' said Strike, smiling at her as he returned his notebook to his pocket.

'Hmm,' said Janice, her eyes narrowed. '"'Appened to be in the area", my Aunt Fanny.'

51

. . . neuer thinke that so
That Monster can be maistred or destroyd:
He is not, ah, he is not such a foe,
As steele can wound, or strength can ouerthroe.

Edmund Spenser
The Faerie Queene

The domed turrets of the Tower of London rose behind the wall of dirty yellow brick, but Robin had no attention to spare for ancient landmarks. Not only was the meeting she'd set up without Strike's knowledge supposed to start in thirty minutes' time, she was miles from where she'd expected to be at one o'clock, and completely unfamiliar with this part of London. She ran with her mobile in her hand, glancing intermittently at the map on its screen.

Within a few paces, the phone rang. Seeing that it was Strike, she answered the call.

'Hi. Just seen Janice.'

'Oh good,' said Robin, trying not to pant as she scanned her surroundings for either a Tube sign or a taxi. 'Anything interesting?'

'Plenty,' said Strike, who was strolling back along Nightingale Grove. Notwithstanding his recent exchange with the nurse, he'd just lit a Benson & Hedges. As he walked into the cool breeze, the smoke was snatched from his lips every time he exhaled. 'Where are you at the moment?'

'Tower Bridge Road,' said Robin, still running, still looking around in vain for a Tube sign.

'Thought you were on Shifty's Boss this morning?'

'I was,' said Robin. It was probably best that Strike knew immediately what had just happened. 'I've just left him on Tower Bridge with Barclay.'

'When you say "with" Barclay—'

'They might be talking by now, I don't know,' said Robin. Unable to talk normally while jogging, she slowed to a fast walk. 'Cormoran, SB looked as though he was thinking of jumping.'

'Off Tower Bridge?' asked Strike, surprised.

'Why not Tower Bridge?' said Robin, as she rounded a corner onto a busy junction. 'It was the nearest accessible high structure . . .'

'But his office isn't anywhere near—'

'He got off at Monument as usual but he didn't go into work. He looked up at the office for a bit, then walked away. I thought he was just stretching his legs, but then he headed out onto Tower Bridge and stood there, staring down at the water.'

Robin had spent forty anxious minutes watching SB stare down at the cement-coloured river below, his briefcase hanging limply by his side, while traffic rumbled along the bridge behind him. She doubted that Strike could imagine how nerve-racking she'd found the wait for Barclay to come and relieve her.

There was still no sign of a Tube station. Robin broke into a jog again.

'I thought of approaching him,' she said, 'but I was worried I'd startle him into jumping. You know how big he is, I couldn't have held him back.'

'You really think he was—?'

'Yes,' said Robin, trying not to sound triumphant: she'd just caught sight of a circular red Tube sign through a break in the traffic and started running. 'He looked utterly hopeless.'

'Are you running?' asked Strike, who could now hear her feet hitting the ground even over the growl of traffic.

'Yes,' said Robin, and then, 'I'm late for a dental appointment.'

She'd regretted not coming up with a solid reason earlier for not being able to interview Janice Beattie, and had decided on this story, should Strike ask again.

'Ah,' said Strike. 'Right.'

'Anyway,' Robin said, weaving around passers-by, 'Barclay arrived to take over – he agreed SB looked like he was thinking of jumping – and he said—'

She was developing a stitch in her side now.

'—said – he'd go and try – and talk to him – and that's when I left. At least – Barclay's big enough – to hold him back if he tries anything,' she finished breathlessly.

'But it also means SB will recognise Barclay in future,' Strike pointed out.

'Well, yeah, I know that,' said Robin, slowing to a walk again as she was almost at the Underground steps, and massaging the stitch in her side, 'but given that we thought he might be about to kill himself—'

'Understood,' said Strike, who had paused in the shadow of Hither Green station to finish his cigarette. 'Just thinking logistics. 'Course, if we're lucky, he might spill the beans to Barclay about what Shifty's got on him. Desperate men are sometimes willing to—'

'Cormoran, I'm going to have to go,' said Robin, who'd reached the Underground entrance. 'I'll see you back at the office after my appointment and you can fill me in about Janice.'

'Right you are,' said Strike. 'Hope it doesn't hurt.'

'What doesn't hu—? Oh, the dentist, no, it's just a check-up,' said Robin.

Really convincing, Robin, she thought, angry at herself, as she shoved her mobile back into her pocket and ran down the steps into the Underground.

Once on the train, she stripped off her jacket, because she was sweating from running, and neatened her hair with the aid of her reflection in the dirty dark window opposite her. Between SB and his possibly suicidal ideation, lying to Strike, her feeble cover story and the potential risks of the meeting she was about to have, she felt jittery. There'd been another occasion, a couple of years previously, when Robin had chosen to pursue a line of inquiry while keeping it secret from Strike. It had resulted in Strike sacking her.

This is different, she tried to reassure herself, smoothing sweaty strands of hair off her forehead. *He won't mind, as long as it works. It's what he wants, too.*

She emerged at Tottenham Court Road station twenty minutes later and hurried with her jacket over her shoulder into the heart of Soho.

Only when she was approaching the Star café, and saw the sign over the door, did she register the coincidence of the name. Trying not to think about asteroids, horoscopes or omens, Robin entered the café, where round wooden tables stood on a red-brick floor. The walls were decorated with old-fashioned tin signs, one of which was advertising ROBIN CIGARETTES. Directly beneath this, perhaps deliberately, sat an old man wearing a black windcheater, his face ruddy with broken veins and his thick grey hair oiled into a quiff that had the appearance of not having changed since the fifties. A walking stick was propped against the wall beside him. On his other side sat a teenage girl with long neon-yellow hair, who was texting on her phone and didn't look up until Robin had approached their table.

'Mr Tucker?' said Robin.

'Yeah,' said the man hoarsely, revealing crooked brown teeth. 'Miss Ellacott?'

'Robin,' she said, smiling as they shook hands.

'This is my granddaughter, Lauren,' said Tucker.

'Hiya,' said Lauren, glancing up from her phone, then back down again.

'I'll just get myself a coffee,' said Robin. 'Can I buy either of you anything?'

They declined. While Robin bought herself a flat white, she sensed the eyes of the old man on her. During their only previous conversation, which had been by phone, Brian Tucker had talked for a quarter of an hour, without pause, about the disappearance of his eldest daughter, Louise, in 1972, and his lifelong quest to prove that Dennis Creed had murdered her. Roy Phipps had called Tucker 'half-insane'. While Robin wouldn't have gone that far on the evidence to date, there was no doubt that he seemed utterly consumed by Creed, and with his quest for justice.

When Robin returned to the Tuckers' table and sat down with her coffee, Lauren put her phone away. Her long neon extensions, the unicorn tattoo on her forearm, her blatantly false eyelashes and her chipped nail varnish all stood in contrast to the innocent, dimpled face just discernible beneath her aggressively applied contouring.

'I came to help Grandad,' she told Robin. 'He doesn't walk so well these days.'

'She's a good girl,' said Tucker. 'Very good girl.'

'Well, thanks very much for meeting me,' Robin told both of them. 'I really appreciate it.'

Close to, Tucker's swollen nose had a strawberry-like appearance, flecked as it was with blackheads.

'No, I appreciate it, Miss Ellacott,' he said in his low, hoarse voice. 'I think they're really going to let it happen this time, I do. And like I said on the phone, if they don't, I'm ready to break into the television studio—'

'Well,' said Robin, 'hopefully we won't need to do anything that dras—'

'—and I've told them that, and it's shaken them up. Well, that, and your contact nudging the Ministry of Justice,' he conceded, gazing at Robin through small, bloodshot eyes. 'Mind you, I'm starting to think I should've threatened them with the press years ago. You don't get anywhere with these people playing by the rules, they just fob you off with their bureaucracy and their so-called expert opinions.'

'I can only imagine how difficult it's been for you,' said Robin, 'but given that we might be in with a chance to interview him, we don't want to do anything—'

'I'll have justice for Louise if it kills me,' said Tucker. 'Let them arrest me. It'll just mean more publicity.'

'But we wouldn't want—'

'She don't want you to do nothing silly, Grandad,' said Lauren. 'She don't want you to mess things up.'

'No, I won't, I won't,' said Tucker. His eyes were small, flecked and almost colourless, set in pouches of purple. 'But this might be our one and only chance, so it must be done in the right way *and by the right interrogator.*'

'Is he not coming?' said Lauren. 'Cormoran Strike? Grandad said he might be coming.'

'No,' said Robin, and seeing the Tuckers' faces fall, she added quickly, 'He's on another case just now, but anything you'd say to Cormoran, you can say to me, as his part—'

'It's got to be him who interviews Creed,' Tucker said. 'Not you.'

'I under—'

'No, love, you don't,' said Tucker firmly. 'This has been my whole life. I understand Creed better than any of the morons who've written books about him. I've studied him. He's been cut off from any kind of attention for years, now. Your boss is a famous man. Creed'll want to meet him. Creed'll think he's cleverer, of course he will. He'll want to beat your boss, want to come out of it on top, but the temptation of seeing his name in the papers again? He's always thrived on the publicity. I think he'll be ready to talk, as long as your boss can make him believe it's worth his while . . . he's kosher, your boss, is he?'

Under almost any other circumstances, Robin would have said 'he's actually my partner', but today, understanding what she was being asked, she said,

'Yes, he's kosher.'

'Yeah, I thought he seemed it, I thought so,' said Brian Tucker. 'When your contact got in touch, I went online, I looked it all up. Impressive, what he's done. He doesn't give interviews, does he?'

'No,' said Robin.

'I like that,' said Tucker, nodding. 'In it for the right reasons. But the name's known, now, and that'll appeal to Creed, and so will the fact your boss has had contact with famous people. Creed likes all that. I've told the Ministry of Justice and I told your contact, I want this Strike to do it, I don't want the police interviewing him. They've had their go and we all know how well *that* went. And no more bloody *psychiatrists*, thinking they're so smart and they can't even agree on whether the bastard's sane or not.

'I know Creed. I understand Creed. I've made a lifelong study of his psychology. I was there every day in court, during the trial. They didn't ask him about Lou in court, not by name, but he made eye contact with me plenty of times. He'll have recognised me, he'll have known who I was, because Lou was my spitting image.

'When they asked him in court about the jewellery – you know about the pendant, Lou's pendant?'

'Yes,' said Robin.

'She got it a couple of days before she disappeared. Showed it to her sister Liz, Lauren's mother – didn't she?' he asked Lauren, who nodded. 'A butterfly on a chain, nothing expensive, and because it was mass-produced, the police said it could have been anyone's. Liz remembered the pendant differently – that's what threw the police off, she wasn't sure at first that it was Lou's – but she admitted she only saw it briefly. And when they mentioned the jewellery, Creed looked straight at me. He knew who I was. Lou was my spit image,' repeated Tucker. 'You know his explanation for having a stash of jewellery under the floorboards?'

'Yes,' said Robin, 'he said he'd bought it because he liked to cross-dress—'

'That he'd bought it,' said Tucker, talking over Robin, 'to dress up in.'

'Mr Tucker, you said on the phone—'

'Lou nicked it from that shop they all used to go to, what was it—?'

'Biba,' said Lauren.

'Biba,' said Tucker. 'Two days before she disappeared, she played truant and that evening she showed Lauren's mum, Liz, what she'd stolen. She was a handful, Lou. Didn't get on with my second wife. The girls' mum died when Lou was ten. It affected Lou the worst, more than the other two. She never liked my second wife.'

He'd told Robin all of this on the phone, but still, she nodded sympathetically.

'My wife had a row with Lou the morning before she disappeared, and Lou bunked off school again. We didn't realise until she didn't come home that night. Rang round all her friends, none of them had seen her, so we called the cops. We found out later, one of her friends had lied. She'd smuggled Lou upstairs and not told her parents.

'Lou was spotted three times next day, still in her school uniform. Last known sighting was outside a launderette in Kentish Town. She asked some geezer for a light. We knew she'd started smoking. That was partly what she rowed with my wife about.

'Creed picked up Vera Kenny in Kentish Town, too,' said Tucker, hoarsely. 'In 1970, right after he'd moved into the place by Paradise Park. Vera was the first woman he took back to that basement. He chained them up, you know, and kept them alive while he—'

'Grandad,' said Lauren plaintively, 'don't.'

'No,' Tucker muttered, dipping his head, 'sorry, love.'

'Mr Tucker,' said Robin, seizing her chance, 'you said on the phone you had information about Margot Bamborough nobody else knows.'

'Yeah,' said Tucker, groping inside his windcheater for a wad of folded papers, which he unfolded with shaking hands. 'This top one, I got through a warder at Wakefield, back in '79. I used to hang round there every weekend in the late seventies, watch them all coming in and out. Found out where they liked to drink and everything.

'Anyway, this particular warder, I won't say his name, but we got chummy. Creed was on a high-security wing, in a single cell, because all the other cons wanted to take a pop at him. One geezer nearly took out Creed's eye in '82, stole a spoon from the canteen and sharpened the handle to a point in his cell. Tried to stab Creed through the eyeball. Just missed, because Creed dodged. My mate told me he screamed like a little girl,' said Tucker, with relish.

'Anyway, I said to my mate, I said, anything you can find

out, anything you can tell me. Things Creed's saying, hints he gives, you know. I paid him for it. He could've lost his job if anyone had found out. And my mate got hold of this and smuggled it out to me. I've never been able to admit to having it, because both of us would be in trouble if it got out, but I called up Margot Bamborough's husband, what was his name—?'

'Roy Phipps.'

'Roy Phipps, yeah. I said, "I've got a bit of Creed's writing here you're going to want to see. It proves he killed your wife."'

A contemptuous smile revealed Tucker's toffee-brown teeth again.

'But he didn't want to know,' said Tucker. 'Phipps thought I was a crank. A year after I called him, I read in the paper he'd married the nanny. Creed did Dr Phipps a good turn, it seems.'

'Grandad!' said Lauren, shocked.

'All right, all right,' muttered Tucker. 'I never liked that doctor. He could've done us a lot of good, if he'd wanted to. Hospital consultant, he was the kind of man the Home Secretary would've listened to. We could've kept up the pressure if he'd helped us, but he wasn't interested, and when I saw he was off with the nanny I thought, ah, right, everything's explained.'

'Could I—?' Robin began, gesturing towards the paper Tucker was still holding flat to the table, but he ignored her.

'So it was just me and Jerry for years,' said Tucker. 'Jerry Wolfson, Kara's brother. You know who that is?' he shot at Robin.

'Yes, the nightclub hostess—'

'Nightclub hostess, hooker on the side, and a drug habit as well. Jerry had no illusions about her, he wasn't naive, but it was still his sister. She raised him, after their mother left. Kara was all the family he had.

'February 1973, three months after my Lou, Kara disappeared as well. Left her club in Soho in the early hours of the morning. Another girl left at exactly the same time. It wasn't far from here, as a matter of fact,' said Tucker, pointing out of the door. 'The two girls go different ways up the street. The friend looks back and sees Kara bending down and talking to a van driver at the end of the road. The friend assumed that Kara knew the driver. She walks off. Kara's never seen again.

'Jerry spoke to all Kara's friends at the club, after, but nobody knew anything. There was a rumour going round, after Kara disappeared, that she'd been a police informer. That club was run by a couple of gangland figures. Suited them, to say she was an informer, see? Scare the other girls into keeping shtum about anything they'd seen or heard in the club.

'But Jerry never believed Kara was a snitch. He thought it was the Essex Butcher from the start – the van was the give-away. So we joined forces.

'He tried to get permission to visit Creed, same as me, but the authorities wouldn't let us. Jerry gave up, in the end. Drank himself to death. Something like this happens to someone you love, it marks you. You can't get out from under it. The weight of it crushes some people.

'My marriage broke up. My other two daughters didn't speak to me for years. Wanted me to stop going on about Lou, stop talking about Creed, pretend it never—'

'That's not fair, Grandad,' said Lauren, sternly.

'Yeah, all right,' mumbled Tucker. 'All right, I grant you, Lauren's mum, she's come round lately. I said to Liz, "Think of all the time I should've spent with Lou, like I've spent with you and Lisa. Add it all up. Family meals and holidays. Helping her with her homework. Telling her to clean her room. Arguing with her—" My God, she could be bolshie. Watching her graduate, I expect, because she was clever, Lou, even if she did get in trouble at school with all the bunking off. I said to Liz, "I never got to walk her up the aisle, did I? Never got to visit her in hospital when her kids were born. Add up all the time I would've given her if she'd lived—"'

Tucker faltered. Lauren put a plump hand over her grandfather's, which had swollen, purple joints.

'—add all that time together,' Tucker croaked, his eyes filmy with tears, 'and that's what I owe her, to find out what happened to her. That's all I'm doing. Giving her her due.'

Robin felt tears prickle behind her own eyelids.

'I'm so sorry,' she said quietly.

'Yeah, well,' said Tucker, wiping his eyes and nose roughly on the sleeve of his windcheater. He now took the top sheet of writing and thrust it at Robin. 'There you are. That shows you what we're up against.'

Robin took the paper, on which was written two short paragraphs in clear, slanting writing, every letter separate and distinct, and began to read.

She attempts to control through words and sometimes with flattery. Tells me how clever I am, then talks about 'treatment'. The strategy is laughably transparent. Her 'qualifications' and her 'training' are, compared to my self-knowledge, my self-awareness, the flicker of a damp match beside the light of the sun.

She promises a diagnosis of madness will mean gentler treatment for me. This she tells me between screams, as I whip her face and breasts. Bleeding, she begs me to see that she could be of use to me. Would testify for me. Her arrogance and her thirst for dominance have been fanned by the societal approval she gained from the position of 'doctor'. Even chained, she believes herself superior. This belief will be corrected.

'You see?' said Tucker in a fierce whisper. 'He had Margot Bamborough chained in his basement. He's enjoying writing about it, reliving it. But the psychiatrists didn't think it was an admission, they reckoned Creed was just churning out these bits of writing to try and draw more attention to himself. They said it was all a game to try and get more interviews, because he liked pitting his wits against the police, and reading about himself in the press, seeing himself on the news. They said that was just a bit of fantasy, and that taking it serious would give Creed what he wanted, because talking about it would turn him on.'

'Gross,' said Lauren, under her breath.

'But my warder mate said – because you know, there was three women they thought Creed had done whose bodies were never found: my Lou, Kara Wolfson and Margot Bamborough – and my warder mate said, it was the doctor he really liked being asked about. Creed likes high-status people, see. He thinks he could've been the boss of some multinational, or some professor or something, if he hadn't of turned to killing. My mate told me all this. He said, Creed sees himself on that sort of level, you know, just in a different field.'

Robin said nothing. The impact of what she'd just read wasn't easily dispelled. Margot Bamborough had become real to Robin, and she'd just been forced to imagine her, brutalised and bleeding, attempting to persuade a psychopath to spare her life.

'Creed got transferred to Belmarsh in '91,' Tucker continued, patting the papers still laid in front of him, and Robin forced herself to concentrate, 'and they started drugging him so he couldn't get a – you know, couldn't maintain . . .

'And that's when I got permission to write to him, and have him write back to me. Ever since he was convicted, I'd been lobbying the authorities to let me question him directly, and let him write back. I wore them down in the end. I had to swear I'd never publicise what he wrote me, or give the letter to the press, but I'm the only member of a victim's family he's ever been allowed direct contact with . . . and there,' he said, turning the next two sheets of paper towards Robin. 'That's what I got back.'

The letter was written on prison writing paper. There was no 'Dear Mr Tucker'.

Your letter reached me three weeks ago, but I was placed in solitary confinement shortly afterwards and deprived of writing materials, so have been unable to answer. Ordinarily I'm not permitted to respond to enquiries like yours, but I gather your persistence has worn the authorities down. Unlikely as it may seem, I admire you for this, Mr Tucker. Resilience in the face of adversity is one of my own defining characteristics.

During my three weeks of enforced solitude, I've wondered how I could possibly explain to you what not one man in ten thousand might hope to understand. Although you think I must be able to recall the names, faces and personalities of my various 'victims', my memory shows me only the many-limbed, many-breasted monster with whom I cavorted, a foul-smelling thing that gave tongue to pain and misery. Ultimately, my monster was never much of a companion, though there was fascination in its contortions. Given sufficient stimulus, it could be raised to an ecstasy of pain, and then it knew it lived, and stood tremulously on the edge of the abyss, begging, screaming, pleading for mercy.

How many times did the monster die, then live again? Too few to satisfy me. Even though its face and voice mutated, its reactions never varied. Richard Merridan, my old psychiatrist, gave what possessed me other names, but the truth is that I was in the grip of a divine frenzy.

Colleagues of Merridan's disputed his conclusion that I'm sane. Regrettably, their opinions were dismissed by the judge. In conclusion: I might have killed your daughter, or I might not. Either I did so in the grip of some madness which still occludes my memory, and which a more skilful doctor might yet penetrate, or I never met her, and little Louise is out there somewhere, laughing at her daddy's attempts to find her, or perhaps enduring a different hell to the one in which my monster lived.

Doubtless the additional psychiatric support available at Broadmoor would help me recover as much memory as possible. For their own inscrutable reasons, however, the authorities prefer to keep me here at Belmarsh. Only this morning I was threatened under the noses of warders. Regardless of the obvious fact that a cachet attaches to anyone who attacks me, I'm exposed, daily, to intimidation and physical danger. How anyone expects me to regain sufficient mental health to assist police further is a mystery.

Exceptional people ought to be studied only by those who can appreciate them. Rudimentary analysis, such as I've been subjected to thus far, merely entrenches my inability to recollect all that I did. Maybe you, Mr Tucker, can help me. Until I'm in a hospital environment where I can be given the assistance I require, what incentive do I have to dredge my fragmented memory for details that may help you discover what happened to your daughter? My safety is being compromised on a daily basis. My mental faculties are being degraded.

You will naturally be disappointed not to receive confirmation of what happened to Louise. Be assured that, when the frenzy is not upon me, I am not devoid of human sympathy. Even my worst critics concede that I actually understand others much more easily than they understand me! For instance, I can appreciate what it would mean to you to recover Louise's body *and give her the funeral you so desire. On the other hand, my small store of human empathy is being rapidly depleted by the conditions in which I am currently living. Recovery from the last attack upon me, which nearly removed my eye, was delayed due to the refusal of the authorities to let me attend a civilian hospital. 'Evil men forfeit the right to fair treatment!' Such seems to be the public's view. However, brutality breeds brutality. Even the most dim-witted psychiatrists agree, there.*

Do you have a merciful soul, Mr Tucker? If so, the first letter you'll write upon receiving this will be to the authorities, requesting that the remainder of my sentence will be served in Broadmoor, where the secrets my unruly memory still holds may be coaxed to the surface at last.

Ever yours,

Dennis

Robin finished reading, and looked up.

'You can't see it, can you?' said Tucker, with an oddly hungry expression. 'No, of course you can't. It isn't obvious. I didn't see it myself, at first. Nor did the prison authorities. They were too busy warning me they weren't going to transfer him to Broadmoor, so I needn't ask.'

He jabbed the bottom of the letter with a yellow-nailed finger.

'The clue's there. Last line. *First letter. My sentence.* Put together the first letter of every sentence, and see what you get.'

Robin did as she was bidden.

'Y – O – U – R – D – A – U – G – H – T – E – R . . .' Robin read out loud, until, fearing where the message was going to end, she fell silent, until she reached the last sentence, when the taste of milky coffee seemed to turn rancid in her mouth, and she said, 'Oh God.'

'What's it say?' asked Lauren, frowning and straining to see.

'Never you mind,' said Tucker shortly, taking the letter back. 'There you are,' he told Robin, folding up the papers and shoving them back into his inside pocket. 'Now you see what he is. He killed Lou like he killed your doctor and he's gloating about it.'

Before Robin could say anything, Tucker spun his next bit of paper to face her, and she saw a photocopied map of Islington, with a circle inked around what looked like a large house.

'Now,' he said, 'there are two places nobody's ever looked, where I think he might've hid bodies. I've been back over everywhere what had a connection with him, kid or adult. Police checked all the obvious, flats he'd lived and that, but never bothered with these.

'When Lou disappeared in November '72, he wouldn't've been able to bury her in Epping Forest, because—'

'They'd just found Vera Kenny's body there,' said Robin.

Tucker looked grudgingly impressed.

'You do your homework at that agency, don't you? Yeah, exactly. There was still a police presence in the forest at the time.

'But see that, there?' said Tucker, tapping on the marked building. 'That's a private house, now, but in the seventies it was the Archer Hotel, and guess who used to do their laundry? Creed's dry cleaner's. He used to pick up stuff from them once a week in his van, and bring it back again, sheets and bedspreads and what have you . . .

'Anyway, after he was arrested, the woman who owned the Archer Hotel gave a quote to the *Mail*, saying he always seemed so nice and polite, always chatty when he saw her . . .

'That isn't marked on modern maps,' said Tucker, now moving his finger to a cross marked in the grounds of the property, 'but it's on the old deeds. There's a well out the back of that property. Just a shaft into the ground that collects rainwater. Predated the current building.

'I tracked the owner down in '89, after she'd sold up. She told me the well was boarded up in her time, and she planted bushes round it, because she didn't want no kid going down it accidental. But Creed used to go through that garden to deliver laundry, right past the place where the well was. He'll have known it was there. She couldn't remember telling him,' said Tucker quickly, forestalling Robin's question, 'but that's neither here nor there, is it? She wasn't going to remember every word they said to her, was she, after all that time?

'Dead of night, Creed could've pulled up a van by the rear entrance, gone in through the back gate . . . but by the time I realised all this,' said Tucker, gritting his brown teeth in frustration, 'the Archer'd gone back to being a private property, and now there's been a bloody conservatory built over the old well.'

'Don't you think,' said Robin cautiously, 'when they built over it, they might have noticed—'

'Why would they?' said Tucker aggressively. 'I never knew a builder who went looking for work when he could just slap concrete over it. Anyway, Creed's not stupid. He'd've thrown rubbish down there on top of the body, wouldn't he? Cover it up. So *that's* a possibility,' he said firmly. 'And then you've got this.'

Tucker's last piece of paper was a second map.

'That there,' he said, tapping his swollen-knuckled finger on another circled building, 'is Dennis Creed's great-grandmother's house. It's mentioned in *The Demon of Paradise Park*. Creed said, in one of his interviews, the only time he ever saw countryside when he was a kid was when he got taken there.

'And look here,' said Tucker, pointing on a large patch of green. 'The house backs right onto Great Church Wood. Acres of woodland, acres and acres. Creed knew the way there. He had a van. He'd played in those woods as a child.

'We know he chose Epping Forest for most of the bodies, because he had no known connection with the place, but by '75, police were regularly checking Epping Forest by night, weren't they? But here's a different wood he knows, and it's not so far away from London, and Creed's got his van and his spades ready in the back.

'My best guess,' said Tucker, 'is my Lou and your doc are in the well or in the woods. And they've got different technology now to what they had in the seventies. Ground-penetrating radar and what have you. It wouldn't be difficult to see if there was a body in either of those places, not if the will was there.

'But,' said Tucker, sweeping the two maps off the table and folding them up with his shaking hands, 'there's no will, or there hasn't been, not for years. Nobody in authority cares. They think it's all over, they think Creed'll never talk. So that's why it's got to be your boss who interviews him. I wish it could be me,' said Tucker, 'but you've seen what Creed thought I was worth . . . '

As Tucker slid his papers back inside his windcheater, Robin became aware that the café around them had filled up during their conversation. At the nearest table sat three young men, all with amusingly Edwardian beards. So long attuned only to Tucker's low, hoarse voice, Robin's ears seemed suddenly full of noise. She felt as though she'd suddenly been transported from the distant past into a brash and indifferent present. What would Margot Bamborough, Louise Tucker and Kara Wolfson make of the mobile phones in almost every hand, or the sound of Pharrell Williams's 'Happy' now playing somewhere nearby, or the young woman carrying a coffee back from the counter, her hair in high bunches, wearing a T-shirt that read GO F#CK YOUR #SELFIE?

'Don't cry, Grandad,' said yellow-haired Lauren softly, putting her arm around her grandfather as a fat tear rolled down his swollen nose and fell upon the wooden table. Now that he'd stopped talking about Louise and Creed, he seemed to have become smaller.

'It's affected our whole family,' Lauren told Robin. 'Mum and Auntie Lisa are always scared if me and my cousins go out after dark—'

'Quite right!' said Tucker, who was now mopping his eyes on his sleeve again.

'—and all of us grew up knowing it's something that can *really happen*, you know?' said the innocent-faced Lauren. 'People *really do* disappear. They *really do* get murdered.'

'Yes,' said Robin. 'I know.'

She reached across the table and briefly gripped the old man's forearm.

'We'll do everything we can, Mr Tucker, I promise. I'll be in touch.'

As she left the café, Robin was aware that she'd just spoken for Strike, who knew absolutely nothing of the plan to interview Creed, let alone to try and find out what had happened to Louise Tucker, but she had no energy left to worry about that just now. Robin drew her jacket more closely around her and walked back to the office, her thoughts consumed by the terrible vacuum left in the wake of the vanished.

52

Oft Fire is without Smoke.

Edmund Spenser
The Faerie Queene

It was one o'clock in the morning, and Strike was driving towards Stoke Newington to relieve Robin, who was currently keeping watch over the terraced house that Shifty's Boss was again visiting, and where he was almost certainly indulging in another bout of the blackmailable behaviour Shifty had somehow found out about. Even though Shifty's hold on his boss had driven the latter onto Tower Bridge, SB didn't appear able or willing to give up whatever it was he was doing inside the house of Elinor Dean.

The night was crisp and clear, although the stars overhead were only dimly visible from brightly lit Essex Road, and Barclay's voice was currently issuing from the speaker of the BMW. A week had passed since the Scot had managed to persuade SB to leave Tower Bridge and get a coffee with him.

'He cannae help himself, the poor bastard.'

'Clearly,' said Strike. 'This is his third visit in ten days.'

'He said to me, "Ah cannae stop." Says it relieves his stress.'

'How does he square that with the fact he's suicidal?'

'It's the blackmail that's makin' him suicidal, Strike, no' whatever he gets up tae in Stoke Newington.'

'And he didn't give *any* indication what he does in there?'

'I told ye, he said he doesnae shag her, but that his wife'll leave him if it gets oot. Could be rubber,' added Barclay, thoughtfully.

'What?'

'Rubber,' repeated Barclay. 'Like that guy we had who liked wearin' latex to work under his suit.'

'Oh yeah,' said Strike. 'I forgot about him.'

The various sexual predilections of their clients often blurred in Strike's memory. He could hear the hum of the casino in the background. Shifty had been in there for hours and Barclay had been keeping him company, unnoticed, from across the floor.

'Anyway,' said Barclay, 'ye want me tae stay in here, do ye? Because it's costin' a small fortune and ye said the client's gettin' pissy aboot how much we're chargin'. I could watch when the slimy bastard leaves, from ootside on the street.'

'No, stay on him, keep photographing him, and try and get something incriminating,' said Strike.

'Shifty's coked oot o' his head,' said Barclay.

'Half his colleagues will be cokeheads, as well. We're going to need something worse than that to nail the bastard for blackmailing people onto high bridges . . . '

'You're goin' soft, Strike.'

'Just try and get something on the fucker and don't place large bets.'

'It's no' the gamblin' that'll bankrupt us,' said Barclay, 'it's the drinks.'

He hung up, and Strike wound down the window and lit a cigarette, trying to ignore the pain in his stiff neck and shoulders.

Like SB, Strike could have used a respite from life's problems and challenges, but such outlets were currently non-existent.

Over the past year, Joan's illness had taken from him that small sliver of time that wasn't given over to work. Since his amputation, he no longer played any kind of sport. He saw friends infrequently due to the demands of the agency, and derived many more headaches than pleasures from his relatives, who were being particularly troublesome just now.

Tomorrow was Easter Sunday, meaning that Joan's family would be gathering together in St Mawes to scatter her ashes at sea. Quite apart from the mournful event itself, Strike wasn't looking forward to yet another long journey to Cornwall, or to further enforced contact with Lucy, who'd made it clear over the course of several phone calls that she was dreading this final farewell. Again and again she returned to her sadness at not having a grave to visit, and Strike detected an undertone of blame, as though she thought Strike ought to have overruled Joan's dying wishes. Lucy had also expressed disappointment that Strike wasn't coming down for the whole weekend, as she and Greg were, and added bluntly that he'd better remember to bring Easter eggs for all three of his nephews, not just Jack. Strike could have done without transporting three fragile chocolate eggs all the way to Truro on the train, with a holdall to manage and his leg sore from days and weeks of non-stop work.

To compound his stress, both his unknown half-sister, Prudence, and his half-brother Al had started texting him again. His half-siblings seemed to imagine that Strike, having enjoyed a moment of necessary catharsis by shouting at Rokeby over the phone, was probably regretting his outburst, and more amenable to attending his father's party to make up. Strike hadn't answered any of their texts, but he'd experienced them as insect bites: determined not to scratch, they were nevertheless the source of a niggling aggravation.

Overhanging every other worry was the Bamborough case which, for all the hours he and Robin were putting into it, was proving as opaque as it had when first they'd agreed to tackle the forty-year-old mystery. The year's deadline was coming ever closer, and nothing resembling a breakthrough had yet occurred. If he was honest, Strike had low hopes of the interview with Wilma Bayliss's daughters, which he and Robin would be conducting later that morning, before Strike boarded the train to Truro.

All in all, as he drove towards the house of the middle-aged woman for whom SB seemed to feel such an attraction, Strike had to admit he felt a glimmer of sympathy for any man in desperate search of what the detective was certain was some form of sexual release. Recently it had been brought home to Strike that the relationships he'd had since leaving Charlotte, casual though they'd been, had been his only unalloyed refuge from the job. His sex life had been moribund since Joan's diagnosis of cancer: all those lengthy trips to Cornwall had eaten up time that might have been given to dates.

Which wasn't to say he hadn't had opportunities. Ever since the agency had become successful, a few of the rich and unhappy women who'd formed a staple of the agency's work had shown a tendency to size up Strike as a potential palliative for their own emotional pain or emptiness. Strike had taken on a new client of exactly this type the previous day, Good Friday. As she'd replaced Mrs Smith, who'd already initiated divorce proceedings against her husband on the basis of Morris's pictures of him with their nanny, they'd nicknamed the thirty-two-year-old brunette Miss Jones.

She was undeniably beautiful, with long legs, full lips and skin of expensive smoothness. She was of interest to the gossip columns partly because she was an heiress, and partly because she was involved in a bitter custody battle with her estranged boyfriend, on whom she was seeking dirt to use in court. Miss Jones had crossed and re-crossed her long legs while she told

Strike about her hypocritical ex-partner's drug use, the fact that he was feeding stories about her to the papers, and that he had no interest in his six-month-old daughter other than as a means to make Miss Jones unhappy. While he was seeing her to the door, their interview concluded, she'd repeatedly touched his arm and laughed longer than necessary at his mild pleasantries. Trying to usher her politely out of the door under Pat's censorious eye, Strike had had the sensation of trying to prise chewing gum off his fingers.

Strike could well imagine Dave Polworth's comments had he been privy to the scene, because Polworth had trenchant theories about the sort of women who found his oldest friend attractive, and of whom Charlotte was the purest example of the type. The women most readily drawn to Strike were, in Polworth's view, neurotic, chaotic and occasionally dangerous, and their fondness for the bent-nosed ex-boxer indicated a subconscious desire for something rocklike to which they could attach themselves like limpets.

Driving through the deserted streets of Stoke Newington, Strike's thoughts turned naturally to his ex-fiancée. He hadn't responded to the desperate text messages she'd sent him from what he knew, having Googled the place, to be a private psychiatric clinic. Not only had they arrived on the eve of his departure for Joan's deathbed, he hadn't wanted to fuel her vain hopes that he would appear to rescue her. Was she still there? If so, it would be her longest ever period of hospitalisation. Her one-year-old twins were doubtless in the care of a nanny, or the mother-in-law Charlotte had once assured him was ready and willing to take over maternal duties.

A short distance away from Elinor Dean's street, Strike called Robin.

'Is he still inside?'

'Yes. You'll be able to park right behind me, there's a space.

I think number 14 must've gone away for Easter with the kids. Both cars are gone.

'See you in five.'

When Strike turned into the street, he saw the old Land Rover parked a few houses down from Elinor's front door, and was able to park without difficulty in the space directly behind it. As he turned off his engine, Robin jumped down out of her Land Rover, closed the door quietly, and walked around the BMW to the passenger's side, a messenger bag over her shoulder.

'Morning,' she said, sliding into the seat beside him.

'Morning. Aren't you keen to get away?'

As he said it, the screen of the mobile in her hand lit up: somebody had texted her. Robin didn't even look at the message, but turned the phone over on her knee, to hide its light.

'Got a few things to tell you. I've spoken to C. B. Oakden.'

'Ah,' said Strike.

Given that Oakden seemed primarily interested in Strike, and that Strike suspected Oakden was recording his calls, the two detectives had agreed that it should be Robin who warned him away from the case.

'He didn't like it,' said Robin. 'There was a lot of "it's a free country", and "I'm entitled to talk to anyone I like". I said to him, "Trying to get in ahead of us and talk to witnesses could hamper our investigation." He said, as an experienced biographer—'

'Oh, fuck off,' said Strike under his breath.

'—he knows how to question people to get information out of them, and it might be a good idea for the three of us to pool our resources.'

'Yeah,' said Strike. 'That's exactly what this agency needs, a convicted con man on the payroll. How did you leave it?'

'Well, I can tell he *really* wants to meet you and I think he's determined to withhold everything he knows about Brenner until he comes face to face with you. He wants to keep Brenner as bait.'

Strike reached for another cigarette.

'I'm not sure Brenner's worth C. B. Oakden.'

'Even after what Janice said?'

Strike took a drag on the cigarette, then blew smoke out of the window, away from Robin. 'I grant you, Brenner looks a lot fishier now than he did when we started digging, but what are the odds Oakden's actually got useful information? He was a kid when all this happened and nicking that obituary smacks of a man trying to scrape up things to say, rather than—'

He heard a rustling beside him and turned to see Robin opening her messenger bag. Slightly to his surprise, Robin was pulling out Talbot's notebook again.

'Still carrying that around with you, are you?' said Strike, trying not to sound exasperated.

'Apparently I am,' she said, moving her mobile onto the dashboard so that she could open the book in her lap. Watching the phone, Strike saw a second text arrive, lighting up the screen, and this time, he caught sight of the name: Morris.

'What's Morris texting you about?' Strike said, and even to his ears, the question sounded critical.

'Nothing. He's just bored, sitting outside Miss Jones's boyfriend's house,' said Robin, who was flicking through Talbot's notebook. 'I want to show you something. There, look at that.'

She passed him the book, open to a page Strike remembered from his own perusal of the notes. It was close to the end of the notebook, where the pages were most heavily embellished with strange drawings. In the middle of this page danced a black skeleton holding a scythe.

'Ignore all the weird tarot drawings,' said Robin. 'Look

there, though. That sentence between the skeleton's legs. The little symbol, the circle with the cross in it, stands for the Part of Fortune . . .'

'What's that?' asked Strike.

'It's a point in the horoscope that's supposed to be about worldly success. "Part of Fortune in Second, MONEY AND POSSESSIONS." And "Mother's House", underlined. The Oakdens lived on Fortune Street, remember? And the Part of Fortune was in the house of money and possessions when Margot disappeared, and he's connecting that with the fact that Dorothy inherited her mother's house, and saying that wasn't a tragedy, but a stroke of luck for Dorothy.'

'You think?' said Strike, rubbing his tired eyes.

'Yes, because look, he then starts rambling about Virgo – which is Dorothy's sign under both systems – being petty and having an axe to grind, which from what we know about her fits. Anyway,' said Robin, 'I've been looking at dates of birth, and guess what? Under both the traditional and Schmidt's systems, Dorothy's mother was a Scorpio.'

'Christ's sake, how many more Scorpios are we going to find?'

'I know what you mean,' said Robin, unfazed, 'but from what I've read, Scorpio's one of the most common birth signs. Anyway, this is the important bit: Carl Oakden was born on the sixth of April. That means he's Aries under the traditional system, but Pisces under Schmidt's.'

A short silence followed.

'How old was Oakden when his grandmother fell downstairs?' asked Strike.

'Fourteen,' said Robin.

Strike turned his face away from Robin to blow smoke out of the window again.

'You think he pushed his grandmother, do you?'

'It might not have been deliberate,' said Robin. 'He could've pushed past her and she lost her balance.'

'"Margot confronted Pisces." It'd be a hell of a thing to accuse a child of—'

'Maybe she never confronted him at all. The confrontation might have been something Talbot suspected, or imagined. Either way—'

'—it's suggestive, yeah. It *is* suggestive . . .' Strike let out a slight groan. 'We're going to *have* to interview bloody Oakden, aren't we? There's a bit of a hotspot developing around that little grouping, isn't there? Brenner and the Oakdens, outward respectability—'

'—inward poison. Remember? That's what Oonagh Kennedy said about Dorothy.'

The detectives sat for a moment or two, watching Elinor Dean's front door, which remained closed, her dark garden silent and still.

'How many murders,' Robin asked, 'd'you think go undetected?'

'Clue's in the question, isn't it? "Undetected" – impossible to know. But yeah, it's those quiet, domestic deaths you wonder about. Vulnerable people picked off by their own families, and everyone thinking it was ill health—'

'—or a mercy that they've gone,' said Robin.

'Some deaths *are* a mercy,' said Strike.

And with these words, in both of their mind's eyes rose an image of horror. Strike was remembering the corpse of Sergeant Gary Topley, lying on the dusty road in Afghanistan, eyes wide open, his body missing from the waist down. The vision had recurred in Strike's nightmares ever since he'd seen it, and occasionally, in these dreams, Gary talked to him, lying in the dust. It was always a comfort to remember, on waking, that Gary's consciousness had been snuffed out instantly,

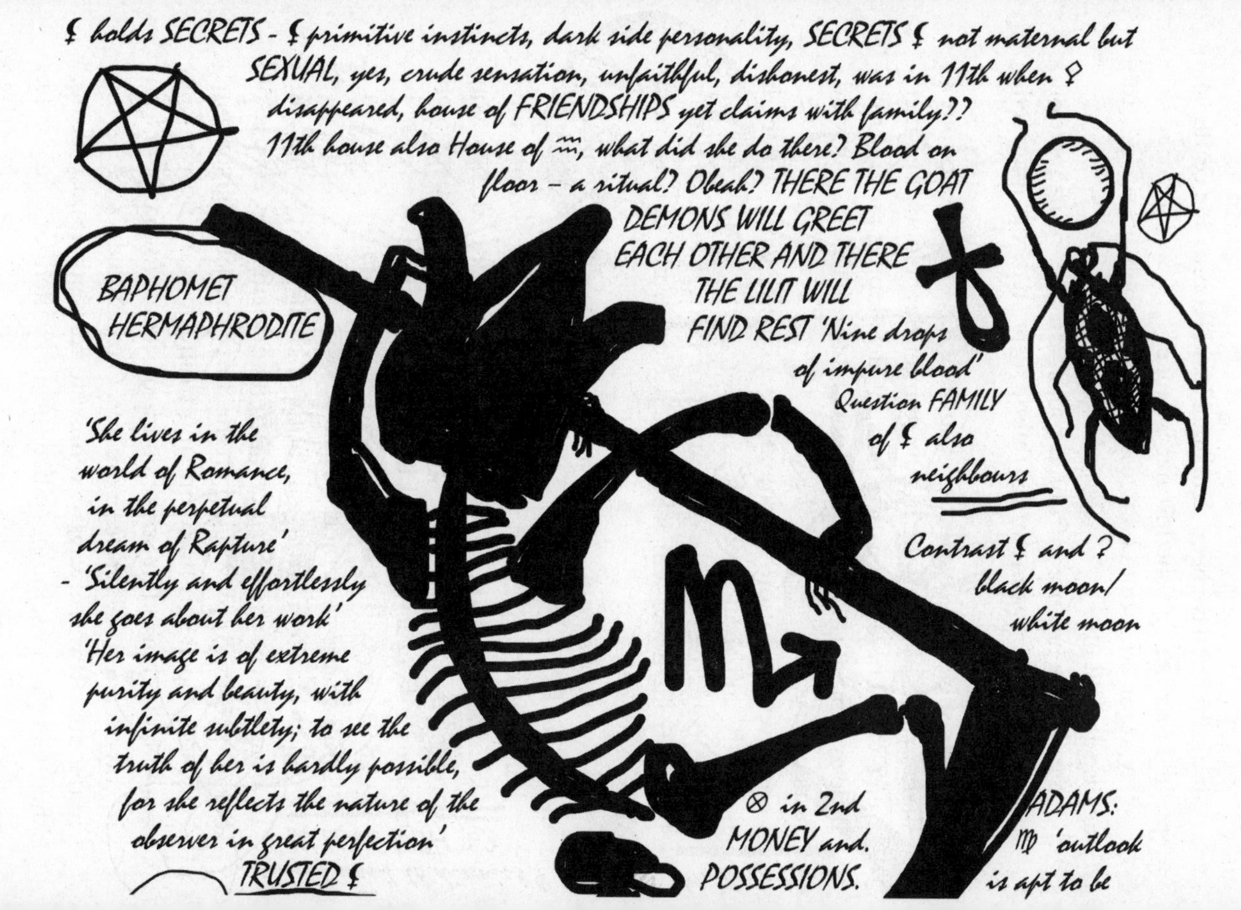

⚸ holds SECRETS - ⚸ primitive instincts, dark side personality, SECRETS ⚸ not maternal but
SEXUAL, yes, crude sensation, unfaithful, dishonest, was in 11th when ♀
disappeared, house of FRIENDSHIPS yet claims with family??
11th house also House of ♒, what did she do there? Blood on
floor - a ritual? Obeah? THERE THE GOAT
DEMONS WILL GREET
EACH OTHER AND THERE
THE LILIT WILL
FIND REST 'Nine drops
of impure blood'
Question FAMILY
of ⚸ also
neighbours
BAPHOMET
HERMAPHRODITE
'She lives in the
world of Romance,
in the perpetual
dream of Rapture'
- 'Silently and effortlessly
she goes about her work'
'Her image is of extreme
purity and beauty, with
infinite subtlety; to see the
truth of her is hardly possible,
for she reflects the nature of the
observer in great perfection'
TRUSTED ⚸
Contrast ⚸ and ?
black moon/
white moon
♏
⊗ in 2nd
MONEY and.
POSSESSIONS.
ADAMS:
♍ 'outlook
is apt to be

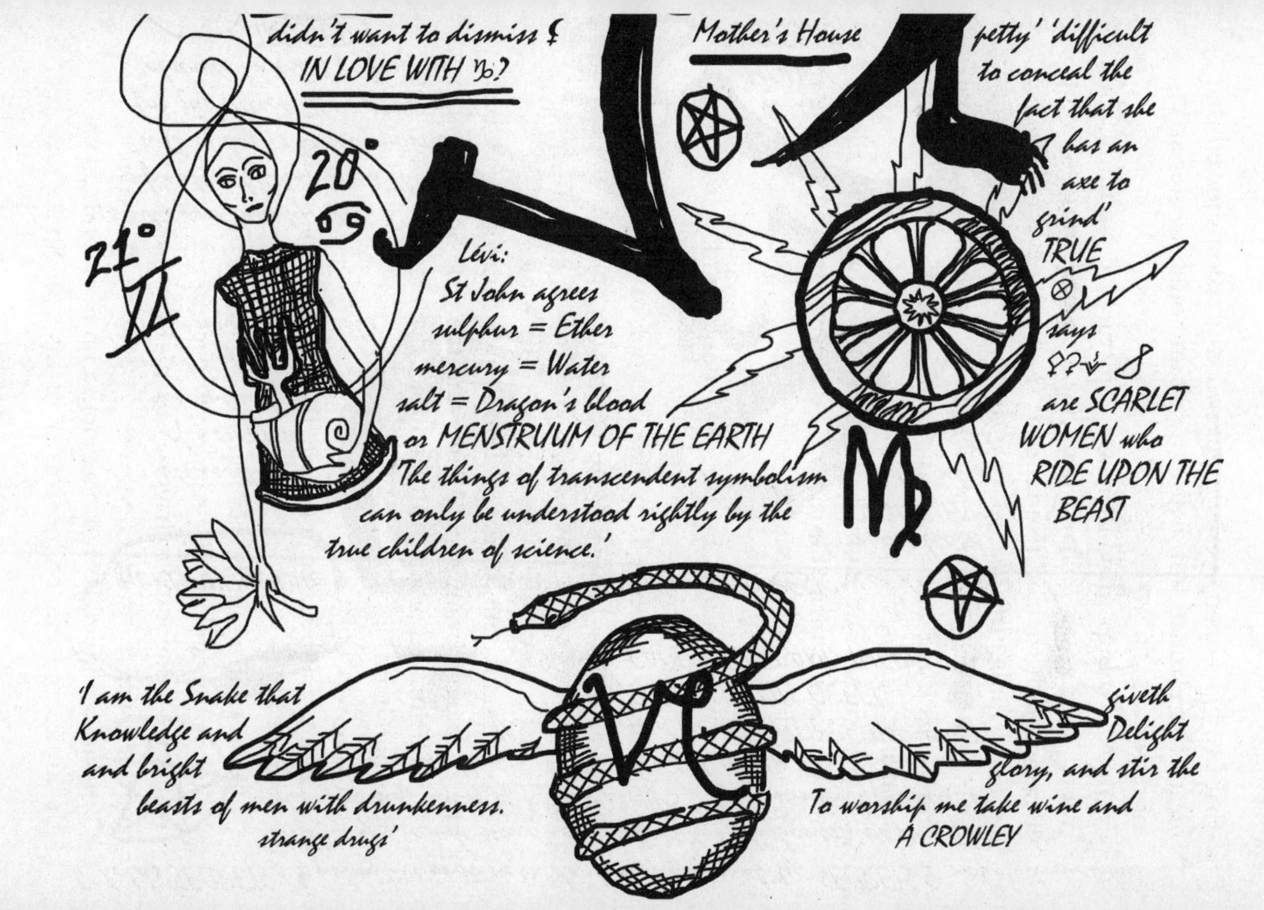
didn't want to dismiss &
IN LOVE WITH ♑?
Mother's House
petty' 'difficult
to conceal the
fact that she
has an
axe to
grind'
TRUE
⊗
says
♀?♆ ♉
are SCARLET
WOMEN who
RIDE UPON THE
BEAST
20°
♋
21°
♊
Lévi:
St John agrees
sulphur = Ether
mercury = Water
salt = Dragon's blood
or MENSTRUUM OF THE EARTH
The things of transcendent symbolism
can only be understood rightly by the
true children of science.'
♍
'I am the Snake that
giveth
Knowledge and
Delight
and bright
glory, and stir the
beasts of men with drunkenness.
To worship me take wine and
strange drugs'
A CROWLEY

that his wide-open eyes and puzzled expression showed that death had claimed him before his brain could register agony or terror.

But in Robin's mind there was a picture of something she wasn't sure had ever happened. She was imagining Margot Bamborough chained to a radiator (*I whip her face and breasts)*, pleading for her life (*the strategy is laughably transparent)*, and suffering torments (*it could be raised to an ecstasy of pain, and then it knew it lived, and stood tremulously on the edge of the abyss, begging, screaming, pleading for mercy)*.

'You know,' said Robin, talking partly to break the silence and dispel that mental image, 'I'd quite like to find a picture of Dorothy's mother, Maud.'

'Why?'

'For confirmation, because – I don't think I told you, look . . . '

She flicked backwards in the notebook to the page littered with water signs. In small writing beneath a picture of a scorpion were the words 'MOLE (Adams).'

'Is that a new sign?' asked Strike. 'The Mole?'

'No,' said Robin, smiling, 'Talbot's alluding to the fact that the astrologer Evangeline Adams said the true Scorpio often has a birthmark, or a prominent mole. I've read her book, got it second hand.'

There was a pause.

'What?' said Strike, because Robin was looking at him expectantly.

'I was waiting for you to jeer.'

'I lost the will to jeer some way back,' said Strike. 'You realise we're supposed to have solved this case in approximately fourteen weeks' time?'

'I know,' sighed Robin. She picked up her mobile to check the time, and out of the corner of his eye, Strike saw yet another text from Morris. 'Well, we're meeting the Bayliss sisters later. Maybe they'll have something useful to tell us ... are you sure you want to interview them with me? I'd be fine to do it alone. You're going to be really tired after sitting here all night.'

'I'll sleep on the train to Truro afterwards,' said Strike. 'You got any plans for Easter Sunday?'

'No,' said Robin. 'Mum wanted me to go home but ... '

Strike wondered what the silent sequel to the sentence was, and whether she'd made plans with someone else, and didn't want to tell him about it. Morris, for instance.

'OK, I swear this is the last thing I'm going to bring up from Talbot's notebook,' Robin said, 'but I want to flag something up before we meet the Baylisses.'

'Go on.'

'You said yourself, he seemed racist, from his notes.'

'"Black phantom",' Strike quoted, 'yeah.'

'And "Black Moon Lilith—"'

'—and wondering whether she was a witch.'

'Exactly. I think he really harassed her, and probably the family, too,' Robin said. 'The language he uses for Wilma – "crude", "dishonest" ... ' Robin flicked back to the page featuring the three horned signs, 'and "woman as she is now in this aeon ... armed and militant".'

'A radical feminist witch.'

'Which sounds quite cool when you say it,' said Robin, 'but I don't think Talbot meant it that way.'

'You think this is why the daughters didn't want to talk to us?'

'Maybe,' said Robin. 'So I think we need to be ... you know. Sensitive to what might have gone on. Definitely not go in there looking as though we suspect Wilma of anything.'

'Point well made, and taken,' said Strike.

'Right then,' said Robin with a sigh, as she put the notebook back into her messenger bag. 'I'd better get going ... What *is* he doing in there?' Robin asked quietly, looking at Elinor Dean's front door.

'Barclay thinks it might be a rubber fetish.'

'He'd need a lot of talcum powder to wriggle himself into anything made of rubber, the size of that belly.'

Strike laughed.

'Well, I'll see you in ... ' Robin checked the time on her mobile, 'seven hours, forty-five minutes.'

'Sleep well,' said Strike.

As she walked away from the BMW, Strike saw her looking at her mobile again, doubtless reading Morris's texts. He watched as she got into the ancient Land Rover, then turned the tank-like vehicle in a three-point turn, raising a hand in farewell as she passed him, heading back to Earl's Court.

As Strike reached for the Thermos of tea under his seat, he remembered the supposed dental appointment of the other day, about which Robin had sounded strangely flustered, and which had taken place (though Strike hadn't previously made the connection) on Morris's afternoon off. A most unwelcome possibility crossed his mind: had Robin lied, like Irene Hickson, and for the same reason? His mind darted to what Robin had said a few months previously, when she'd mentioned her ex-husband having a new partner: 'Oh, I didn't tell you, did I? I told Morris.'

As he unscrewed his Thermos, Strike mentally reviewed Robin's behaviour around Morris in the last few months. She'd never seemed to particularly like him, but might that have been an act, designed to deflect attention? Were his partner and his subcontractor actually in a relationship which he, busy with his own troubles, had failed to spot?

Strike poured himself tea, settled back in his seat, and

glowered at Elinor Dean's closed door through the steam rising from plastic-tasting tea the colour of mud. He was angry, he told himself, because he should have established a work rule that partners weren't allowed to date subcontractors, and for another reason which he preferred not to examine, because he knew perfectly well what it was, and no good could come of brooding upon it.

53

Like three faire branches budding farre and wide,
That from one roote deriu'd their vitall sap:
And like that roote that doth her life diuide,
Their mother was . . .

Edmund Spenser
The Faerie Queene

Seven hours later, in the cool, flat daylight of an overcast morning, Robin, who was back in her Land Rover, took a detour on her way to the café where she and Strike would be meeting the three Bayliss sisters.

When Maya, the middle sister, had suggested meeting in Belgique in Wanstead, Robin had realised how close she'd have to drive to the Flats where Dennis Creed had disposed of his second-to-last known victim, twenty-seven-year-old hairdresser Susan Meyer.

Half an hour ahead of the planned interview, Robin parked the Land Rover beside a stretch of shops on Aldersbrook Road, then crossed the street and headed up a short footpath, which led her to the reedy bank of the man-made Alexandra Lake, a wide stretch of water on which various wildfowl were bobbing. A couple of ducks came paddling hopefully towards Robin, but when she failed to produce bread or other treats, they glided away again, compact, self-sufficient, their onyx eyes scanning both water and bank for other possibilities.

Thirty-nine years ago, Dennis Creed had driven to this lake under cover of night, and rolled the headless, handless corpse of Susan Meyer into it, bound up in black plastic and rope. Susan Meyer's distinctive wedge cut and shy smile had earned her a prominent place on the cover of *The Demon of Paradise Park*.

The milky sky looked as opaque as the shallow lake, which resembled jade silk in which the gliding wildfowl made rippling creases. Hands in her pockets, Robin looked out over the water and the rustling weeds, trying to imagine the scene when a park worker had spotted the black object in the water, which he'd assumed initially was a tarpaulin swollen with air, until he hooked it with a long pole, felt the grisly weight and made an instant connection (or so he told the television crew who arrived shortly after the police and ambulance) with the bodies that kept turning up in Epping Forest, barely ten miles away.

Creed had abducted Susan exactly a month before Margot disappeared. Had they overlapped in Creed's basement? If so, Creed had, for a brief period, held three women there simultaneously. Robin preferred not to think about what Andrea, or Margot, if she'd been there, must have felt on being dragged into Creed's basement, seeing a fellow woman chained there, and knowing that she, too, would be reduced to that emaciated and broken-boned state before she died.

Andrea Hooton was the last woman Creed was known to have killed, and he'd varied the pattern when it came to disposing of her body, driving eighty miles from his house in Liverpool Road to throw the corpse off Beachy Head. Both Epping Forest and Wanstead Flats had become too heavily patrolled by then, and in spite of Creed's evident wish to make sure the Essex Butcher was credited with every kill, as evidenced by the secret store of press clippings he kept beneath the floorboards in his basement flat, he'd never wanted to be caught.

Robin checked her watch: it was time to head to the interview with the Bayliss sisters. Walking back to the Land Rover, she pondered the divide between normalcy and insanity. On the surface, Creed had been far saner than Bill Talbot. Creed had left no half-crazed scribblings behind him to explain his thought processes; he'd never plotted the course of asteroids to guide him: his interviews with psychiatrists and police had been entirely lucid. Not for Creed the belief in signs and symbols, a secret language decipherable only by initiates, a refuge in mystery or magic. Dennis Creed had been a meticulous planner, a genius of misdirection in his neat little white van, dressed in the pink coat he'd stolen from Vi Cooper, and sometimes wearing a wig that, from a distance, to a drunk victim, gave his hazy form a feminine appearance just long enough for his large hands to close over a gasping mouth.

When Robin arrived in the street where the café stood, she spotted Strike getting out of his BMW a short distance away from the entrance. Noticing the Land Rover in turn, Strike raised a hand in greeting and headed up the street towards her, while finishing what looked like a bacon and egg McMuffin, his chin stubbly, the shadows beneath his eyes purple.

'Have I got time for a fag?' were the first words he spoke, checking his watch as Robin got down out of the car and slammed the door. 'No,' he answered himself, with a sigh. 'Ah well . . .'

'You can take the lead on this interview,' he told Robin, as they headed together towards the café. 'You've done all the legwork. I'll take notes. Remind me what their names are?'

'Eden's the eldest. She's a Labour councillor from Lewisham.

Maya's the middle one, and she's deputy headmistress of a primary school. The youngest is Porschia Dagley, and she's a social worker—'

'—like her mother—'

'Exactly, and she lives just up the road from here. I think we've come to her neck of the woods because she's been ill, so the others didn't want her to have to travel.'

Robin pushed open the door of the café and led the way inside. The interior was sleekly modern, with a curved counter, a wooden floor and a bright orange feature wall. Close to the door at a table for six sat three black women. Robin found it easy to identify which sister was which, because of the photographs she'd seen on the family's Facebook pages, and on the Lewisham Council website.

Eden, the councillor, sat with her arms folded, a wavy bob casting a shadow over most of her face, so that only a carefully lipsticked, unsmiling plum mouth was clearly visible. She wore a well-tailored black jacket and her demeanour was suggestive of a businesswoman who'd been interrupted during an important meeting.

Maya, the deputy headmistress, wore a cornflower blue sweater and jeans. A small silver cross hung around her neck. She was smaller in build than Eden, the darkest skinned and, in Robin's opinion, the prettiest of the sisters. Her long, braided hair was tied back in a thick ponytail, she wore square-framed glasses over her large, wide-set eyes and her full mouth, with its naturally up-tilted corners, conveyed warmth. A leather handbag sat in Maya's lap, and she was gripping it with both hands as though afraid it might otherwise escape.

Porschia, the youngest sister and the social worker, was also the heaviest. Her hair had been cropped almost to her skull, doubtless because of her recent chemotherapy. She'd pencilled in the eyebrows that were just beginning to grow back; they arched over hazel eyes that shone gold against her skin. Porschia was wearing a purple smock top with jeans and long beaded earrings, which swung like miniature chandeliers as she looked around at Strike and Robin. As they approached the table Robin spotted a small tattoo on the back of Porschia's neck: the trident from the Barbadian flag. Robin knew that Eden and Maya were both well into their fifties, and that Porschia was forty-nine, but all three sisters could have passed for at least ten years younger than their real ages.

Robin introduced herself and Strike. Hands were shaken, Eden unsmiling throughout, and the detectives sat down, Strike at the head of the table, Robin between him and Porschia, facing Maya and Eden. Everyone but Eden made laboured small talk about the local area and the weather, until the waiter came to take their order. Once he'd left, Robin said,

'Thanks very much for meeting us, we really do appreciate it. Would you mind if Cormoran takes notes?'

Maya and Porschia shook their heads. Strike tugged his notebook out of his coat pocket and opened it.

'As I said on the phone,' Robin began, 'we're really after background, building up a complete picture of Margot Bamborough's life in the months—'

'Could *I* ask a couple of questions?' interrupted Eden.

'Of course,' said Robin politely, though expecting trouble.

Eden swept her hair back out of her face, revealing ebony-dark eyes.

'Did you two know there's a guy phoning around everyone who was connected to St John's, saying he's going to write a book about you investigating Bamborough's disappearance?'

Shit, thought Robin.

'Would this be a man called Oakden?' asked Strike.

'No, Carl Brice.'

'It's the same bloke,' said Strike.

'Are you connected to him or—?'

'No,' said Strike, 'and I'd strongly advise you not to talk to him.'

'Yeah, we worked that out for ourselves,' said Eden, coolly. 'But this means there'll be publicity, won't there?'

Robin looked at Strike, who said,

'If we solve the case, there'll be publicity even without Oakden – or Brice, or whatever he's calling himself these days – but that's a big "if". To be frank, the odds are we're not going to solve it, in which case I think Oakden's going to find it very hard to sell any books, and whatever you tell us will never go any further.'

'What if we know something that might help you solve the case, though?' asked Porschia, leaning forwards, so that she could look past Robin at Strike.

There was an infinitesimal pause in which Robin could almost feel Strike's interest sharpening, along with her own.

'Depends what that information is,' Strike answered slowly. 'It *might* be possible not to divulge where we got it, but if the source is important to getting a conviction . . .'

There was a long pause. The air between the sisters seemed charged with silent communications.

'Well?' said Porschia at last, on an interrogative note.

'We *did* decide to,' Maya mumbled to Eden, who continued to sit in silence, arms folded.

'OK, *fine*,' said Eden, with a don't-blame-me-later inflection.

The deputy headmistress reached absently for the little silver cross around her neck, and held it as she began to talk.

'I need to explain a bit of background, first,' she said. 'When we were kids – Eden and I were already teenagers, but Porschia was only nine—'

'Eight,' Porschia corrected her.

'Eight,' Maya said obediently, 'our dad was convicted of – of rape and sent to prison.'

'He didn't do it, though,' said Eden.

Robin reached automatically for her coffee cup and took a sip, so as to hide her face.

'He didn't, OK?' said Eden, watching Robin. 'He had a white girlfriend for a couple of months. The whole of Clerkenwell knew. They'd been seen together in bars all over the place. He tried to end it, and she cried rape.'

Robin's stomach lurched as though the floor had tilted. She very much wanted this story to be untrue. The idea of any woman lying about rape was repugnant to her. She'd had to talk through every moment of her own assault in court. Her soft-spoken fifty-three-year-old rapist and would-be murderer had taken the stand afterwards to explain to the jury how the twenty-year-old Robin had invited him into the stairwell of her hall of residence for sex. In his account, everything had been consensual: she'd whispered that she liked it rough, which had accounted for the heavy bruising around her neck, she'd enjoyed it so much she'd asked him back the following night, and yes (with a little laugh in the dock), of course he'd been surprised, nicely spoken young girl like her, coming on to him like that, out of nowhere . . .

'Easy thing for a white woman to do to a black man,' said Eden, ''specially in 1972. Dad already had a record, because he'd got into a fight a few years before that. He went down for five years.'

'Must've been hard on the family,' said Strike, not looking at Robin.

'It was,' said Maya. 'Very hard. The other kids at school . . . well, you know what kids are like . . .'

'Dad had been bringing in most of the money,' said Porschia. 'There were five of us, and Mum had never had much schooling. Before Dad got arrested, she'd been studying, trying to pass some exams, better herself. We were just about making ends meet while Dad was bringing in a wage, but once he was gone, we struggled.'

'Our mum and her sister married two brothers,' said Maya. 'Nine children between them. The families were really close, right up until Dad got arrested – but then everything changed. My Uncle Marcus went to court every day while Dad was on trial, but Mum wouldn't go and Uncle Marcus was really angry at her.'

'Well, he knew it would've made a big difference, if the judge had seen Dad had the family united behind him,' snapped Eden. '*I* went. I bunked off school to go. I knew he was innocent.'

'Well, good for you,' said Porschia, though her tone was far from congratulatory, 'but Mum didn't want to sit in open court listening to her husband talk about how often he had sex with his girlfriend—'

'That woman was trash,' said Eden curtly.

'*Dirty water does cool hot iron*,' said Porschia, with a Bajan inflection. 'His choice.'

'So, anyway,' said Maya hastily, 'the judge believed the woman, and Dad got put away. Mum never went to visit him inside, and she wouldn't take me or Porschia or our brothers, either.'

'I went,' piped up Eden again. 'I got Uncle Marcus to take me. He was still our dad. Mum had no right to stop us seeing him.'

'Yeah, so,' continued Maya, before Porschia could say anything, 'Mum wanted a divorce, but she had no money for legal advice. So Dr Bamborough put her in touch with this feminist lawyer, who'd give legal help to women in difficult circumstances, for a reduced fee. When Uncle Marcus told Dad that

Mum had managed to get herself a lawyer, Dad wrote to her from prison, begging her to change her mind. He said he'd found God, that he loved her and he'd learned his lesson and all he wanted was his family.'

Maya took a sip of her coffee.

'About a week after Mum got Dad's letter, she was cleaning Dr Bamborough's consulting room one evening after everyone had left, and she noticed something in the bin.'

Maya unfastened the handbag she'd been holding on her lap, and took out a pale blue piece of heavily creased paper, which had clearly been crumpled up into a ball at some point in the past. She held it out to Robin, who laid it flat on the table so that Strike could read it, too.

The faded handwriting was a distinctive mix of capitals and lower-case letters.

LEaVE my gIRL aLOnE yOU CUnT OR I'LL maKE SURE yOU gO TO HELL SLOW anD PaInFUL.

Robin glanced sideways at Strike and saw her own, barely disguised astonishment mirrored there. Before either of them could say anything, a group of young women passed their table, forcing Strike to push his chair in. Chatting and giggling, the women sat down at the table behind Maya and Eden.

'When Mum read that,' said Maya, speaking more quietly so that the newcomers couldn't hear her, 'she thought Dad had sent it. Not *literally*, because the prison censor would never have let that go out – she thought someone had done it for him.'

'Specifically, Uncle Marcus,' said Eden, arms folded and expression pinched. 'Uncle Marcus, who was a lay preacher and never used the c-word in his life.'

'Mum took the note over to Uncle Marcus and Auntie Carmen's,' said Maya, ignoring this interjection, 'and asked

Marcus straight out if he was behind it. He denied it, but Mum didn't believe him. It was the mention of hell: Marcus was a fire-and-brimstone kind of preacher back then—'

'—and he didn't believe Mum really wanted a divorce,' said Porschia. 'He blamed Dr Bamborough for persuading Mum to leave Dad, because, you know, Mum *really* needed a white woman to point out her life was shit. She'd never have noticed otherwise.'

'Going for a cigarette, OK?' said Eden abruptly. She pushed herself up and walked out, her heels rapping on the wooden floorboards.

Both younger sisters seemed to exhale in relief with her departure.

'She was Dad's favourite,' Maya told Strike and Robin quietly, watching through the window as Eden took out a packet of Silk Cut, shook her hair out of her face and lit herself a cigarette. 'She really loved him, even if he was a womaniser.'

'And she never got on with Mum,' said Porschia. 'Their rows would've woken the dead.'

'In fairness,' said Maya, 'them splitting up hit Eden hardest. She left school at sixteen, got herself a job at Marks & Spencer to help support—'

'Mum never wanted her to drop out of school,' said Porschia. 'That was Eden's choice. Eden likes to claim it was a sacrifice she made for the family, but come on. She couldn't *wait* to get out of school, because Mum put so much pressure on her to get good grades. She likes to claim she was a second mother to all of us, but that's not how I remember it. *I* mostly remember her whacking merry hell out of me if I so much as looked at her wrong.'

On the other side of the window, Eden stood smoking with her back to them.

'The whole situation was a nightmare,' said Maya sadly.

'Mum and Uncle Marcus never made it up, and with Mum and Carmen being sisters . . . '

'Let's just tell them now, while she can't stick her oar in,' Porschia urged Maya, and turning to Strike and Robin, she said, 'Auntie Carmen was helping Mum get the divorce, behind Uncle Marcus's back.'

'How?' asked Robin, as a waiter passed their table on the way to the group of women at the next table.

'See, when the lawyer Dr Bamborough had recommended told Mum what she charged, Mum knew she'd never be able to afford her, not even at the reduced rates,' said Porschia.

'Mum came home afterwards and cried,' said Maya, 'because she was desperate to have the divorce done and dusted before Dad got out of jail. She knew otherwise he'd just move right back in and she'd be trapped. Anyway, a few days later, Dr Bamborough asked her how things had gone with the lawyer, and Mum admitted she wasn't going to go through with the divorce, for lack of funds, so,' Maya sighed, 'Dr Bamborough offered to pay the lawyer, in exchange for Mum doing a few hours a week cleaning the house out in Ham.'

The women at the table behind theirs were now flirting with the young waiter, wondering whether it was too early for a cream cake, giggling about breaking their diets.

'Mum didn't feel she could refuse,' said Maya. 'But what with the costs of getting all the way out to Ham, and the time it would take her to get out there, when she already had two other jobs and exams coming up . . . '

'Your Aunt Carmen agreed to do the cleaning for her,' guessed Robin, and out of the corner of her eye she saw Strike glance at her.

'Yeah,' said Maya, eyes widening in surprise. 'Exactly. It seemed like a good solution. Auntie Carmen was a housewife and Uncle Marcus and Dr Bamborough were both out at work all day, so Mum thought neither of them would ever know the wrong woman was turning up.'

'There was one sticky moment,' said Porschia, 'remember, M? When Dr Bamborough asked us all over to a barbecue at her house?' She turned to Robin. 'We couldn't go, because Dr Bamborough's nanny would've realised Mum wasn't the woman turning up once a week to clean. My Auntie Carmen didn't like that nanny,' Porschia added. 'Didn't like her at all.'

'Why was that?' asked Strike.

'She thought the girl was after Dr Bamborough's husband. Went red every time she said his name, apparently.'

The door of the café opened and Eden walked back inside. As she sat down, Robin caught a whiff of smoke mingling with her perfume.

'Where've you got to?' she asked, looking cold.

'Auntie Carmen cleaning instead of Mum,' said Maya.

Eden re-folded her arms, ignoring her coffee.

'So the statement your mother gave the police, about the blood and Dr Phipps walking across the garden—' said Strike.

'—was really her telling him everything Carmen had told *her*, yeah,' said Maya, feeling again for the cross around her neck. 'She couldn't own up that her sister had been going there instead of her, because my Uncle Marcus would've gone *crazy* if he'd found out. Auntie Carmen *begged* Mum not to tell the police and Mum agreed.

'So she had to pretend she was the one who'd seen the blood on the carpet and Dr Phipps walking across the lawn.'

'Only,' interrupted Porschia, with a humourless laugh, 'Carmen changed her mind about Dr Phipps, after. Mum went back to her after her first police interview and said, "They're asking whether I couldn't have got confused and mistaken one of the workmen for Dr Phipps." Carmen said, "Oh. Yeah. I forgot there were workmen round the back. Maybe I did."'

Porschia let out a short laugh, but Robin knew she wasn't truly amused. It was the same kind of laughter Robin had taken refuge in, the night she'd discussed rape with Max over the kitchen table.

'I know it isn't funny,' said Porschia, catching Maya's eye, 'but come on. Carmen was always ditzy as hell, but you'd think she might've made sure of her facts *then*, wouldn't you? Mum was literally sick with stress, like, *retching* if she ate anything. And then that old bitch of a secretary at work found her having a dizzy spell . . . '

'Yeah,' said Eden, suddenly coming to life. 'Next thing was, Mum was accused of being a thief and a drunk and the practice fired her. The old secretary claimed she'd had a secret sniff of Mum's Thermos and smelled booze in it. Total fabrication.'

'That was a few months after Margot Bamborough disappeared, wasn't it?' asked Strike, his pen poised over his notebook.

'Oh, I'm sorry,' Eden said with icy sarcasm, 'did I go off topic? Back to the missing white lady, everyone. Never mind what the black woman went through, who gives a shit?'

'Sorry, I didn't—' began Strike.

'D'you know who Tiana Medaini is?' Eden shot at him.

'No,' he admitted.

'*No*,' said Eden, 'of course you bloody don't. Forty years after Margot Bamborough went missing, here we all are, fussing over her and where she went. Tiana Medaini's a black teenager from Lewisham. She went missing last year. How many front pages has Tiana been on? Why wasn't she top of the news, like Bamborough was? Because we're not worth the same, are we, to the press or to the bloody police?'

Strike appeared unable to find an adequate response; doubtless, Robin thought, because Eden's point was unarguable. The picture of Dennis Creed's only black victim, Jackie Aylett, a secretary and mother of one, was the smallest and the least distinct of the ghostly black and white images of Creed's victims on the cover of *The Demon of Paradise Park*. Jackie's dark skin showed up worst on the gloomy cover. The greatest prominence had been given to sixteen-year-old Geraldine Christie and twenty-seven-year-old Susan Meyer, both of them pale and blonde.

'When Margot Bamborough went missing,' Eden said fiercely, 'the white women at her practice were treated like bone china by the police, OK? Practically mopping their bloody tears for them – but not our mum. They treated her like a hardened con. That policeman in charge, what was his name—?'

'Talbot?' suggested Robin.

'"What are you hiding? Come on, I know you're hiding something."'

The mysterious figure of the Hierophant rose up in Robin's mind. The keeper of secrets and mysteries in the Thoth tarot wore saffron robes and sat upon a bull ('the card is referred to Taurus') and in front of him, half his size, stood a black priestess, her hair braided like Maya's ('Before him is the woman girt with a sword; she represents the Scarlet Woman . . . '). Which had come first, the laying out of tarot cards signifying secrecy and concealment, or the policeman's instinct that the terrified Wilma was lying to him?

'When he interviewed me—' began Eden.

'Talbot interviewed *you*?' asked Strike sharply.

'Yeah, he came to Marks & Spencer unannounced, to my work,' said Eden, and Robin realised that Eden's eyes were suddenly bright with tears. 'Someone else at the practice had seen that anonymous note Bamborough got. Talbot found out Dad was inside and he'd heard Mum was cleaning for the doctor. He went to every man in our family, accusing them of writing the threatening letters, and then he came to me, asking me really strange questions about all my male relatives, wanting to know what they'd been up to on different dates, asking whether Uncle Marcus often stayed out overnight. He even asked me about Dad and Uncle Marcus's—'

'—star signs?' asked Robin.

Eden looked astounded.

'The hell did you know that?'

'Talbot left a notebook. It's full of occult writing. He was trying to solve the case using tarot cards and astrology.'

'Astrology?' repeated Eden. 'Effing *astrology*?'

'Talbot shouldn't have been interviewing you without an adult present,' Strike told Eden. 'What were you, sixteen?'

Eden laughed in the detective's face.

'That might be how it works for white girls, but we're different, aren't you listening? We're hardy. We're *tough*. That occult stuff,' Eden said, turning back to Robin, 'yeah, that makes sense, because he asked me about *obeah*. You know what that is?'

Robin shook her head.

'Kind of magic they used to practise in the Caribbean. Originated in West Africa. We were all born in Southwark, but, you know, we were all black pagans to Inspector Talbot. He had me alone in the back room and he was asking me stuff about rituals using blood, about black magic. I was terrified, I didn't know what he was on about. I thought he meant Mum and the blood on the carpet, hinting she'd done away with Dr Bamborough.'

'He was having a psychotic breakdown,' said Robin. 'That's why they took him off the case. He thought he was hunting a devil. Your mum wasn't the only woman he thought might have supernatural power – but he was definitely racist,' Robin added quietly. 'That's clear from his notes.'

'You never told us about the police coming to Marks & Spencer,' said Porschia. 'Why didn't you tell us?'

'Why would I?' said Eden, angrily blotting her damp eyes. 'Mum was already ill with the stress of it all, I had Uncle Marcus shouting at me that Mum had put the police onto him and his boys, and I was really scared, if Uncle Marcus found out about the officer coming to my work, he'd report him, which was the last thing we needed. God, it was a mess,' said Eden, pressing her hands briefly against her wet eyes, 'such a bloody mess.'

Porschia looked as though she'd like to say something comforting to her elder sister, but Robin had the impression that this would be such a departure from their usual relationship, she didn't know quite how to set about it. After a moment or two, Porschia muttered,

'Need the loo,' pushed her chair away from the table and disappeared into the bathroom.

'I didn't want Porsh to come today,' said Maya, as soon as the bathroom door swung shut behind her younger sister. She was tactfully not looking at her elder sister, who was trying to pretend she wasn't crying, while surreptitiously wiping more tears from her eyes. 'She doesn't need this stress. She's only just finished chemo.'

'How's she doing?' asked Strike.

'She was given the all-clear last week, thank God. She's talking about going back to work on reduced hours. I think it's too early.'

'She's a social worker, isn't she?' asked Robin.

'Yeah,' sighed Maya. 'A backlog of a hundred desperate messages every morning, and you know you're in the firing line if anything goes wrong with a family you haven't been able to reach. I don't know how she does it. But she's like Mum. Two peas in a pod. She was always Mum's baby, and Mum was her hero.'

Eden let out a soft 'huh', which might have been agreement or disparagement. Maya ignored it. There was a short pause, in which Robin reflected on the tangled ties of family. A proxy war between Jules and Wilma Bayliss seemed still to be playing out in the next generation.

The bathroom door swung open again and Porschia reappeared. Instead of taking her seat beside Robin, she swivelled her wide hips around Strike at the end of the table, and edged in behind a startled Maya, who pulled her chair in hastily, until she reached Eden. After thrusting a handful of toilet roll into her elder sister's hand, Porschia slid her plump arms around Eden's neck and dropped a kiss on the top of her head.

'What are you doing?' said Eden huskily, reaching up to clasp her youngest sister's arms, not to remove them, but to hold them there. Strike, Robin saw out of the corner of her eye, was pretending to examine his notebook.

'Thanking you,' said Porschia softly, dropping another kiss on the top of her eldest sister's head before letting her go. 'For agreeing to do this. I know you didn't want to.'

Everyone sat in slightly startled silence while Porschia squeezed her way back around the table and resumed her seat next to Robin.

'Have you told them the last bit?' Porschia asked Maya, while Eden blew her nose. 'About Mum and Betty Fuller?'

'No,' said Maya, who appeared shell-shocked by the act of reconciliation she'd just witnessed. 'You're the one Mum told it to, I thought you should.'

'Right,' said Porschia, turning to look at Strike and Robin. 'This really is the last thing we know, and there might be nothing in it, but you might as well have it, now you know the other stuff.'

Strike waited, pen poised.

'Mum told me this not long after she retired. She shouldn't

have, really, because it was about a client, but when you hear what it was, you'll understand.

'Mum kept working in Clerkenwell after she'd qualified as a social worker. It was where all her friends were; she didn't want to move. So she really got to know the local community.

'One of the families she was working with lived in Skinner Street, not that far from the St John's practice—'

'Skinner Street?' repeated Strike. The name rang a bell, but, exhausted as he was, he couldn't immediately remember why that was. Robin, on the other hand, knew immediately why Skinner Street sounded familiar.

'Yeah. The family was called Fuller. They had just about every problem you can think of, Mum said: addiction, domestic abuse, criminality, the lot. The sort of head of the family was a grandmother who was only in her forties, and this woman's main source of income was prostitution. Betty was her name, and Mum said she was like a local news service, if you wanted to know about the underworld, anyway. The family had been in the area for generations.

'Anyway, one day, Betty says to Mum, bit sly, to see her reaction: "Marcus never sent no threatening notes to that doctor, you know."

'Mum was gobsmacked,' said Porschia. 'Her first thought was that Marcus was visiting the woman, you know, as a client – *I know he wasn't*,' said Porschia quickly, holding up a hand to forestall Eden, who'd opened her mouth. 'Mum and Marcus hadn't spoken for years at this point. Anyway, it was all innocent: Betty had met Marcus because the church was doing a bit of outreach in the local area. He'd brought round some Harvest Festival stuff for the family, and tried to persuade Betty to come along to a church service.

'Betty had worked out Marcus's connection with Mum, because Mum was still going by "Bayliss", and Betty claimed she knew who *really* wrote the threatening notes to Margot Bamborough, and that the person who wrote the notes was the same person who killed her. Mum said, "Who was it?" And Betty said if she ever told, Margot's killer would kill her, too.'

There was a short silence. The café clattered around them, and one of the women at the next table, who was eating a cream slice, said loudly, with unctuous pleasure,

'*God* that's good.'

'Did your mother believe Betty?' asked Robin.

'She didn't know what to think,' said Porschia. 'Betty knew some very rough people, so it was possible she'd heard something on the grapevine, but who knows? People talk, don't they, and they like making themselves important,' and Robin remembered Janice Beattie saying exactly this, as she passed on the rumour of Margot Bamborough appearing in a graveyard. 'But if there was anything in it, a woman like Betty, she'd go to the moon before she went to the cops.

'She might well be dead by now,' said Porschia, 'given her lifestyle, but for what it's worth, there it is. Shouldn't be hard to find out whether she's still alive.'

'Thanks very much for telling us,' said Strike. 'That's definitely worth following up.'

Having told all they knew, the three sisters now lapsed into a pained silence. It wasn't the first time that Robin had had cause to consider how much collateral damage each act of violence left in its wake. The disappearance of Margot Bamborough had evidently wreaked havoc in the lives of the Bayliss girls, and now she knew the full extent of the grief it had brought them, and the painful nature of the memories associated with it, she perfectly understood Eden's initial refusal to talk to detectives. If anything, she had to ask herself why the sisters had changed their minds.

'Thank you so much for this,' she said sincerely. 'I know

Margot's daughter will be incredibly grateful that you agreed to talk to us.'

'Oh, it's the daughter who's hired you, is it?' said Maya. 'Well, you can tell her from me, Mum felt guilty all her life that she didn't come clean with the police. She liked Dr Bamborough, you know. I mean, they weren't close friends or anything, but she thought she was a decent person.'

'It weighed on her,' said Porschia. 'Right up until her death, it weighed on her. That's why she kept that note. She'd have wanted us to do this. There's always handwriting analysis and stuff, isn't there?'

Strike agreed that there was. He went to pay the bill and Robin waited at the table with the sisters, who she could tell wanted the detectives gone, and as quickly as possible. They'd disclosed their personal trauma and their family's secrets, and now a thin layer of polite small talk was too onerous to sustain, and any other form of conversation impossible. Robin was relieved when Strike re-joined her, and after brief farewells, the two of them left the café.

The moment he hit clean air, Strike paused to pull his Benson & Hedges out of his pocket and lit one.

'Needed that,' he muttered, as they walked on. 'So . . . Skinner Street . . .'

'. . . is where Joseph Brenner was seen on the night Margot Bamborough disappeared,' said Robin.

'Ah,' muttered Strike, briefly closing his eyes. 'I *knew* there was something.'

'I'll look into Betty Fuller as soon as I get home,' said Robin. 'What did you think of the rest of it?'

'The Bayliss family really went through it, didn't they?' said Strike, pausing beside the Land Rover and glancing back at the café. His BMW lay another fifty yards ahead. He took another drag on his cigarette, frowning. 'Y'know . . . it gives us another angle on Talbot's bloody notebook,' he admitted. 'Strip away all the occult shit, and he was right, wasn't he? Wilma *was* hiding stuff from him. A lot of stuff, actually.'

'I thought that, too,' said Robin.

'You realise that threatening note's the first piece of physical evidence we've found?'

'Yes,' said Robin, checking her watch. 'What time are you heading to Truro?'

Strike didn't answer. Looking up, Robin saw that he was staring so fixedly across the open park on the other side of the road that she turned, too, to see what had captured his attention, but saw nothing except a couple of gambolling West Highland terriers and their male owner, who was walking along, swinging a pair of leads.

'Cormoran?'

Strike appeared to recall his attention from a long way away.

'What?' he said, and then, 'Yeah. No, I was just . . .'

He turned to look back at the café, frowning.

'Just thinking. But it's nothing, I think I'm doing a Talbot. Seeing meaning in total coincidence.'

'What coincidence?'

But Strike didn't answer until the café doors opened, and the three Bayliss sisters emerged in their coats.

'We should get going,' he said. 'They must be sick of the sight of us by now. I'll see you Monday. Let me know if you find out anything interesting on Betty Fuller.'

54

But nothing new to him was that same pain;
Nor pain at all; for he so oft had tried
The power thereof, and lov'd so oft in vain.

Edmund Spenser
The Faerie Queene

The train gave a lurch: the sleeping Strike's head rolled sideways and hit the cold window. He woke, feeling drool on his chin. Wiping it on his coat sleeve, he peered around. The elderly couple opposite him were politely immersed in their reading material, but across the aisle, four teenagers were enjoying paroxysms of silent laughter, carefully not looking at him, their shoulders shaking as they feigned interest in the fields out of the window. Apparently he'd been snoring with his mouth wide open, because it was now unpleasantly dry. Checking his watch, he saw that he'd been asleep at least two hours.

Strike reached for the tartan Thermos sitting on the table in front of him, which he'd rinsed out and refilled in McDonald's earlier, and poured himself a black coffee while the teenagers continued to gasp and snort with laughter. Doubtless they thought him comically odd and old, with his snores and his tartan Thermos, but a year of navigating swaying train carriages had taught him that his prosthetic leg appreciated as few trips to the catering car as possible. He drank a cup of plastic-tainted coffee, then re-settled himself comfortably, arms folded, looking out at the fields gliding past, bestridden with power pylons, the flat white cloud given a glaucous glow by the dust on the glass. The landscape registered only incidentally: Strike's attention was focused inwards on the odd idea that had occurred to him after the interview with the Bayliss sisters.

Of course, the idea might be nothing but the product of an overburdened mind making spurious connections between simple coincidences. He mentally turned it this way and that, examining it from different angles, until finally, yawning, he inched sideways over into the empty seat beside him, and laboriously pulled himself up into a standing position in the aisle, so he could access the holdall in the luggage rack overhead. Beside his holdall sat a Waitrose bag, because he'd made a detour into the supermarket on the way to Paddington station, where he'd grabbed three Easter eggs for his nephews, or rather, three chocolate hedgehogs ('Woodland Friends') because they were relatively compact. Now, groping in his holdall for *The Demon of Paradise Park*, he accidentally knocked over the carrier bag containing the chocolate. The uppermost hedgehog fell out: in his attempt to catch it, he accidentally batted it up into the air; the box bounced off the back of the elderly woman's seat, causing her to squeak in surprise, and the box hit the floor.

The teenagers for whom Strike was unintentionally mounting a one-man comedy show were now openly gasping and crying with laughter. Only when Strike bent down awkwardly to pick up the now cracked chocolate hedgehog, one hand on the teenagers' table to steady himself, did one of the young women spot the metal rod that served as his right ankle. He knew what she'd seen by the abrupt cessation of her laughter, and the frantic, whispered shushing of her friends. Panting, sweating and now aware of half the carriage's eyes on him, he shoved the damaged hedgehog back into its bag, found *The Demon of Paradise Park* in his holdall and then, sweating slightly, but taking malicious pleasure in the po-faced shock of the teenagers beside him, sidled back into his window seat.

After flicking through the book in search of the part he wanted to re-read, Strike finally found the chapter two-thirds of the way through the book, entitled 'Capture'.

> Thus far, Creed's relationship with landlady Violet Cooper had been key to his continuing safety. Violet herself admits that for the first five years of his tenancy, she'd never have believed harm of 'Den', who she saw as a lonely and gentle soul, fond of their singalong evenings, and probably gay.
>
> However, the pains he'd once taken to keep Violet happy had begun to irk Creed. Where once he'd drugged her because he was planning to pound bones to dust in the basement, or needed to load a corpse into the van by night, he now began lacing her gin-and-oranges with barbiturates purely to avoid the tedium of her company.
>
> Creed's manner towards Violet also changed. He became 'mean' to her, 'taking the Mickey when there was no need, saying nasty things, laughing at me for using the wrong words and stuff, treating me like I was stupid, which he'd never done before.
>
> 'I remember one time, I was telling him about the place my brother bought when he retired, cottage in the country, everything lovely, and I said, "You should've seen the garden, his roses and a gazebo," and he laughed at me, Dennis, well, jeered, really, because I'd said it wrong. *Gazz*ybo, I said, and I've never forgotten it, he said, "Don't use words if you can't say 'em, you just look thick."
>
> 'It hurt my feelings. I hadn't seen that nasty side of him.

I knew he was clever, he used to do the *Times* crossword every day. Knew all the answers on *Mastermind*, when we watched it together, but he'd never put me down before.

'Then, one night, he starts going on about my will. He wants to know who I'm going to leave the house to. He as good as asked me to leave it to him.

'I didn't like that. I wasn't an old woman, I wasn't planning to die any time soon. I changed the subject, but he started on it again a few nights later. I said, "Look, how d'you think that makes me feel, Dennis, you going on like this, like I'm on my last legs? You're making me feel like you're going to do away with me."

'He got uppity and said it was all right for me, but he had nothing, no security or nothing, and what if he got turfed out on the street by whoever I left the house to? And he flounced out. We made it up, later, but it left a nasty taste.'

It would seem the height of foolhardiness for Creed to persuade Violet into changing her will and then kill her. Quite apart from having an obvious motive, he'd be risking the ingression of police into the basement where he was concealing the remains and belongings of at least five women. However, Creed's arrogance and sense of inviolability seem to have known no bounds by this time. He was also stockpiling pills in larger quantities than ever, which brought him into contact with more than one street dealer. This made him more widely recognisable.

One of his new drugs contacts was Michael Cleat, who sold barbiturates stolen from a contact at a pharmaceutical company. Cleat would later cut a deal with police in exchange for his testimony at the killer's trial. Creed, he testified, had asked Cleat whether he or his contact could procure a doctor's prescription pad. Police suspected that

Creed was hoping to fake a prescription for Violet, to explain her possession of the means to overdose . . .

In spite of the coffee, Strike's eyelids began to droop again. After another couple of minutes, his head sank sideways and the book slipped out of his slack grasp.

When he woke up again, the sky outside had turned coral pink, the laughing teenagers were gone, and he found himself ten minutes from Truro station. Stiffer than ever and in no mood for the family reunion, he wished he was heading back to his attic flat for a shower and some peace. Nevertheless, his heart lifted slightly when he saw Dave Polworth waiting for him on the platform. The bag of chocolate hedgehogs rattled slightly as Strike clambered laboriously off the train. He'd have to remember to give the broken one to Luke.

'All right, Diddy?' said Polworth, as they shook hands and patted each other on the back, Strike's Waitrose bag impeding a hug.

'Thanks for picking me up, Chum, really appreciate it.'

They drove to St Mawes in Polworth's Dacia Duster, discussing plans for the following day. Polworth and his family had been invited to the scattering of the ashes, along with Kerenza the Macmillan nurse.

' . . . except it's not going to be a scattering,' said Polworth, driving through country lanes, as the sun turned into a burning coal on the horizon, 'more like a floating.'

'How's that?'

'Lucy's got an urn,' said Polworth. 'Water soluble, cotton and clay. She was showing me last night. It's supposed to look like a flower. You put the ashes inside and the whole thing bobs away and dissolves.'

'Nice idea,' said Strike.

'Prevents stupid accidents,' said Polworth, pragmatically.

'Remember Ian Restarick, from school? His grandad wanted his ashes thrown off Land's End. The dozy fuckers chucked them off in a high wind and ended up with their mouths full of the old boy. Restarick told me he was blowing ash out of his nose for a week after.'

Laughing, Strike felt his phone buzz in his pocket, and pulled it out. He was hoping the text might be Robin, perhaps telling him she'd already located Betty Fuller. Instead, he saw an unknown number.

I hated you as much as I did because I loved you so much. My love never ended but yours did. It wore out. I wore it out

Polworth was still talking, but Strike was no longer listening. He read the text through several times, frowning slightly, then put the phone back in his pocket and tried to concentrate on his old friend's anecdotes.

At Ted's house there were cries of welcome, and hugs from his uncle, Lucy and Jack. Strike tried to look delighted to be there, in spite of his fatigue, and knowing he'd have to wait to sleep until everyone else had gone to bed. Lucy had made pasta for everyone, and when she wasn't tending to everybody else's needs, telling Luke off for kicking Adam or picking at her own plate, she teetered on the verge of tears.

'It's so strange, isn't it?' she whispered to her brother after dinner, while Greg and the boys, at Greg's insistence, were clearing the table, 'Being here without her?' And without a pause she hurried on, 'We've decided we're going to do the ashes in the morning, because the weather looks good, and then come back here for Easter lunch.'

'Sounds great,' said Strike.

He knew how much importance Lucy placed on arrangements and plans, on having everything done in the right way.

She fetched the urn and admired the stylised white lily. Ted had already placed Joan's ashes inside.

'That's great. Joan would have loved it,' he said, with no idea whether that was true or not.

'And I've bought pink roses for all of us to throw into the water with it,' said Lucy, tears welling again.

'Nice touch,' said Strike, suppressing a yawn. He really did just want to shower, then lie down and sleep. 'Thanks for sorting all this out, Luce. Oh, and I brought Easter eggs for the boys, where do you want them?'

'We can put them in the kitchen. Did you remember to get some for Roz and Mel, too?'

'Who?'

'Dave and Penny's girls, they'll be coming tomorrow, too.'

Fuck's sake.

'I didn't think—'

'Oh, Stick,' said Lucy, 'aren't you their godfather?'

'No, I'm not,' said Strike, doing his very best not to sound short tempered, 'but fine, yeah, I'll nip down the shops tomorrow morning and buy some more.'

Later, when he was at last alone in the dark sitting room, lying on the sofa with which he'd become so unwillingly familiar over the past year, his prosthetic leg propped against the coffee table, he checked his phone again. There were, he was pleased to see, no more messages from the unknown number, and, exhausted as he was, he managed to fall asleep quickly.

However, at shortly before four in the morning, the phone rang. Jerked out of a profound sleep, Strike groped for it, registered the time then raised it to his ear.

'Hello?'

There was a long silence, although he could hear breathing on the end of the line.

'Who is this?' he said, suspecting the answer.

'Bluey,' came a tiny whisper. 'It's me.'

'It's four in the morning, Charlotte.'

'I know,' she whispered, and gave what might have been a giggle or a sob. She sounded strange; possibly manic. Strike stared up at the dark ceiling, his aunt's ashes a mere twelve feet away.

'Where are you?'

'In hell.'

'Charlotte—'

She hung up.

Strike could hear his own heart beating with ominous force, like a kettle drum deep inside a cave. Red-hot threads of panic and dread darted through him.

How many more burdens was he supposed to bear? Had he not paid enough, given enough, sacrificed enough – loved enough? Joan seemed very close just now, in the darkness of her own sitting room, with her ornamental plates and her dried flowers, closer even than her dusty remains, in that vaguely ludicrous white lily, which would look so puny and insignificant bobbing away on the wide sea, like a discarded paper plate. He seemed to hear her last words as he lay there: 'You're a good man . . . helping people . . . I'm proud of you . . .'

Charlotte had called him from the same unknown number she'd texted from earlier. Strike's exhausted mind now eddied around the known facts, which were that Charlotte had suicide attempts in her past, that she was married with children, and that she'd recently been committed to a mental facility. He remembered his resolution of weeks ago, to phone her husband if she sent him any more self-destructive messages, but Jago Ross wouldn't be at his merchant bank at 4 a.m. on an Easter weekend. He wondered whether it would be cruelty or kindness to ignore the call, and how he'd bear the knowledge that she'd overdosed, if he didn't respond. After a very long ten minutes, during which he half expected her to call him back, Strike sat up to compose a text.

I'm in Cornwall. My aunt's just died. I think you need help, but I'm the wrong person to give it to you. If you're alone, you need to get hold of someone and tell them how you're feeling.

The terrible thing was how well he and Charlotte knew each other. Strike knew just how pusillanimous, how disingenuous, Charlotte would find this bland response. She'd know that some small part of him (shrunken by determined abstinence, though never eradicated) felt a pull back towards her, especially in this extremity, not only because he'd assumed responsibility for her happiness for years, but because he could never forget that she'd come to him when he was at his lowest ebb, lying in a hospital bed with a freshly amputated leg, wondering what possible life there was for him now. He could still remember her appearing in the doorway, the most beautiful woman he'd ever seen, and how she'd walked down the ward towards him and kissed him wordlessly on the mouth, and that moment, more than any other, had told him that life would continue, would contain glorious moments of beauty and pleasure, that he wasn't alone any more, and that his missing leg didn't matter to the woman he couldn't forget.

Sitting in the darkness, atypically cold because of his exhaustion, Strike typed four more words –

It will get better

– and sent the message. Then he lay back down and waited for the phone to vibrate again, but it remained silent, and eventually he fell asleep.

He was woken, inevitably, by Luke bursting into the sitting room. While he listened to Luke clattering around the kitchen, Strike reached for his phone and looked at it. Charlotte had sent two more texts, one an hour previously, the next half an hour later.

Bluey I'm sorry about your aunt. is it the one I met?

And then, when Strike hadn't answered:

Am I evil? Jago says I am. I used to think I couldn't be, because you loved me

At least she wasn't dead. With a vice-like sensation in his belly, Strike sat up, put on his prosthesis and attempted to shut Charlotte out of his mind.

Breakfast wasn't a particularly relaxing affair. The table was so crowded with Easter eggs, it was like being in some cartoonish nest. Strike ate off a plate on his lap. Lucy had bought Strike and Ted an egg each, and the detective now gathered that he should have bought his sister one, as well. All three boys had tottering piles.

'What's a hedgehog got to do with Easter?' Adam asked Strike, holding up his uncle's offering.

'Eastertime's spring, isn't it?' said Ted, from the end of the table. 'It's when hibernating animals wake up.'

'Mine's all broken,' said Luke, shaking the box.

'That's a shame,' said Strike, and Lucy shot him a sharp look.

She was tense, telling off her sons for looking at their phones during the meal, glaring at Strike when he checked his own, constantly glancing out of the window, to check the state of the weather. The detective was glad of an excuse to get out of the house to buy Polworth's daughters Easter eggs, but he'd walked barely ten yards down the sloping road, cigarette in hand, when the family pulled up in their Dacia. When Strike confided his errand in an undertone, Polworth said,

'Fuck that, they've got enough chocolate for a year at home. Leave it.'

At eleven o'clock, with a leg of lamb left in the oven and the timer set, after Luke had been told that no, he couldn't take his iPad on the boat, and one false start, due to the need to return to the house for the Polworths' younger daughter to have the pee she'd insisted she didn't need before they left, the party made its way successfully down to the harbour, where they met Kerenza the nurse, and boarded Ted's old sailing boat, *Jowanet*.

Strike, who'd once been his uncle's proud helpmeet, no longer had the balance to work either sails or rudder. He sat with the women and children, spared the necessity of making conversation by the noise of wind against canvas. Ted shouted commands to Polworth and Jack. Luke was eating chocolate, his eyes screwed up against the cold breeze; Polworth's daughters were huddled, shivering, beside their mother, who had her arms around them. Tears were already trickling down Lucy's cheeks as she cradled the flat white urn in her lap. Beside her, Kerenza held a bunch of dark pink roses loosely wrapped in cellophane, and it was left to Greg and Polworth to shout at the children to watch out for the boom as they tacked around the peninsula where St Mawes Castle stood sentinel.

The surface of the sea changed from second to second, from rippling plain of sage and grey, to mesh of diamond-bright sparkles. The smell of ozone was as familiar and comforting to Strike as that of beer. He was just thinking how glad he was that Joan had chosen this, and not a grave, when he felt his phone vibrate against his chest. Unable to resist the temptation to read what he knew would be a text from Charlotte, he pulled it out and read it.

> **I thought you'd come back I thought you'd stop me marrying him I didn't think you'd let me do it**

He put the phone back into his pocket. Luke was watching him and Strike thought he saw the idea occur of asking why Uncle Cormoran could look at his phone, whereas he was banned from bringing his iPad, but the look his uncle gave him seemed to make him think better of the idea, and he merely stuffed more chocolate in his mouth.

A feeling of constraint seemed to fall over everyone, even Luke, as Ted turned the boat into the wind and brought the boat slowly to a halt, the sail flapping loudly in the wind, St Mawes Castle now the size of a sandcastle in the distance. Kerenza handed around the roses, one for everyone except Ted, who took the remainder of the bouquet between the hands that were forever sunburned. Nobody spoke, and yet the moment didn't feel anticlimactic. While the sails flapped angrily overhead, Ted bent low over the side of the boat and dropped the urn gently into the sea, murmuring his farewell, and the object Strike had imagined would look inadequate and tawdry became, precisely because of its smallness as it bobbed gallantly on the ocean, affecting, and strangely noble. Soon, the last earthly remains of Joan Nancarrow would dissolve into the sea, and only the pink roses, tossed one by one into the sea by each of them, would remain to show the place where she'd disappeared.

Strike put his arm around Lucy, who rested her head on his shoulder, as they sailed back to shore. Rozwyn, the elder of Polworth's daughters, broke into sobs initially provoked by the sight of the urn vanishing in the distance, but sustained by her enjoyment of her own grief and the sympathy of her mother. Strike watched until he could no longer see the white dot, then turned his eyes towards shore, thinking of the leg of lamb waiting for them back at the house.

His phone vibrated yet again, minutes after he'd regained firm ground. While Polworth helped Ted tie up the boat, Strike lit a cigarette and turned away from the group to read the new text.

I want to die speaking the truth people are such liars everyone I know lies in such if them swant to stop pretending

'I'll walk back,' he told Lucy.

'You can't,' she said at once, 'lunch'll be ready for us—'

'I'm going to want another one of these,' Strike said firmly, holding up his cigarette in her disapproving face. 'I'll meet you up there.'

'Want company, Diddy?' asked Polworth. 'Penny can take the girls back up to the house.'

'No, you're all right, mate,' said Strike. 'Need to make a work call,' he added quietly, so that Lucy couldn't hear. As he said it, he felt his mobile vibrate again.

'Goodbye, Corm,' said Kerenza, her freckled face kindly as ever. 'I'm not coming for lunch.'

'Great,' said Strike, 'no, sorry, I mean – thanks for coming, Kerenza, Joan was so fond of you.'

When Kerenza had finally got into her Mini, and the family's cars were driving away, Strike pulled out his phone again.

Never forget that I loved you goodbye blues x

Strike called the number. After a few rings, it went to voicemail.

'Charlotte, it's me,' said Strike. 'I'm going to keep ringing till you pick up.'

He hung up and dialled again. The number went to voicemail for a second time.

Strike began to walk, because his anxiety required action. The streets around the harbour weren't busy. Most people would be sitting down to Easter lunch. Over and again he dialled Charlotte's number, but she didn't answer.

It was as though a wire was tightening around his skull. His neck was rigid with tension. From second to second his feelings fluctuated between rage, resentment, frustration and fear. She'd always been an expert manipulator. She'd also narrowly escaped death by her own hand, twice.

The phone might be going unanswered because she was already dead. There could be sporting guns at the Castle of Croy, where her husband's family had lived for generations. There'd be heavy-duty medications at the clinic: she might have stockpiled them. She might even have taken a razor blade to herself, as she'd once tried to do during one of her and Strike's more vicious rows.

After calling the number for the tenth time, Strike came to a halt, looking out over the railings at the pitiless sea, which breathed no consolation as it rushed to and then retreated from the shore. Memories of Joan, and the way she'd clung so fiercely to life, flooded his mind: his anxiety about Charlotte was laced with fury, for throwing life away.

And then his phone rang.

'Where are you?' he almost shouted.

'Bluey?'

She sounded drunk, or very stoned.

'*Where are you?*'

'. . . told you,' she mumbled. 'Bluey, d'you 'member . . . '

'Charlotte, WHERE ARE YOU?'

'Told you, S'monds . . . '

He turned and began to half-run, half-hobble back the way he'd come: there was an old-fashioned red telephone box twenty yards back, and with his free hand he was already pulling coins from his trouser pocket.

'Are you in your room? *Where are you?*'

The telephone box smelled urinous, of cigarette butts and dirt from a thousand silt-clogged soles.

'C'n see sky . . . Bluey, I'm so . . . '

She was still mumbling, her breathing slow.

'One one eight, one one eight?' said a cheery voice through the receiver in his left hand.

'Symonds House, it's a residential psychiatric clinic in Kent.'

'Shall I connect—?'

'Yes, connect me . . . Charlotte, are you still there? Talk to me. Where are you?'

But she didn't answer. Her breathing was loud and becoming guttural.

'Symonds House,' said a bright female voice in his other ear.

'Have you got an in-patient there called Charlotte Ross?'

'I'm sorry, sir,' said the receptionist, 'we don't disclose—'

'She's overdosed. She's just called me from your facility, and she's overdosed. You need to find her – she might be outside, have you got grounds there?'

'Sir, can I ask you—?'

'*Check Charlotte Ross's whereabouts, now, I've got her on another line and she's overdosed.*'

He heard the woman speaking to someone away from the phone.

' . . . Mrs Ross . . . first floor, just to make . . . '

The voice spoke in his ear again, still professionally bright, but anxious now.

'Sir, what number is Mrs Ross calling from? She – in-patients don't have their own mobiles.'

'She's got one from somewhere,' said Strike, 'as well as a shitload of drugs.'

Somewhere in the background of the call he heard shouting, then loud footsteps. He tried to insert another coin into the slot, but it fell straight through and came out at the bottom.

'Fuck—'

'Sir, I'm going to ask you not to talk to me like that—'

'No, I just—'

The line went dead. Charlotte's breath was now barely audible.

Strike slammed as much change as he had in his pockets into the slot, then redialled telephone enquiries. Within a minute, he was again connected to the female voice at Symonds House.

'Symonds House—'

'Have you found her? I got cut off. Have you found her?'

'I'm afraid I can't disclose—' said the harassed-sounding woman.

'She got hold of a mobile and the means to kill herself on your watch,' said Strike, 'so you can bloody well disclose whether she's dead—'

'Sir, I'd appreciate you not shouting at me—'

But then Strike heard distant male voices through the mobile clamped to his other ear. There was no point hanging up and ringing: Charlotte hadn't heard his ten previous calls. She must have the mobile on silent.

'SHE'S HERE!' he bellowed, and the woman on the payphone line shrieked in shock. 'FOLLOW MY VOICE, SHE'S HERE!'

Strike was bellowing into the phone, well aware of the almost impossible odds of searchers hearing him: he could hear swishing and cracking, and knew that Charlotte was outside, probably in undergrowth.

Then, through the mobile, he heard a man shout.

'Shit, she's here – SHE'S HERE! Fuck . . . get an ambulance!'

'Sir,' said the shell-shocked woman, now that Strike had stopped yelling, 'could I have your name?'

But Strike hung up. Over the sound of his change clattering into the returned coin box, he continued to listen to the two men who'd found Charlotte, one of them shouting details of her overdose to the emergency services, the other repeatedly calling Charlotte's name, until somebody noticed that the mobile beside her was active, and turned it off.

55

Of louers sad calamities of old,
Full many piteous stories doe remaine . . .

Edmund Spenser
The Faerie Queene

As a noted beauty and socialite with a tantalising number of celebrity connections and a rebellious, self-destructive past, Charlotte was an old staple of the gossip columns. Naturally, her emergency hospitalisation out of a private psychiatric clinic made news.

The tabloids ran photo-heavy stories, showing Charlotte at the ages of fourteen (when she'd first run away from her private school and sparked a police hunt), eighteen (arm in arm with her well-known broadcaster father, a thrice-married heavy drinker), twenty-one (with her model-turned-socialite mother, at a cocktail party) and thirty-eight, where, as beautiful as ever, she smiled blankly alongside her white-blond husband, twin babies in her arms, an exquisite drawing room in the background. Nobody had been able to find a picture of her with Cormoran Strike, but the fact that they'd once dated, which Charlotte herself had been careful to mention to the press when she got engaged to Jago, ensured that his name appeared in print alongside hers. 'Emergency hospitalisation', 'history of addiction issues', 'troubled past': though the tabloids didn't say so explicitly, only the most naive reader could be left in doubt that Charlotte had attempted to take her own life. The story gained a second wind when an unnamed 'inside source' at Symonds House confided that the future Viscountess Ross had 'allegedly' been found face down in a shrubbery, right behind an old summer house.

The broadsheets' stories led with the questionable practices of the exorbitantly priced Symonds House, 'which' (said the *Telegraph*) 'has a reputation for being the last resort of the wealthy and well-connected. Controversial treatments include transcranial magnetic stimulation and the hallucinogen psilocybin (more commonly known as magic mushrooms).' They, too, used large photographs of Charlotte to embellish their stories, so Robin, who furtively read all of them and felt guilty afterwards, was reminded constantly how very beautiful Strike's ex had always been.

Strike hadn't mentioned a word of the business to Robin, and she hadn't asked. A moratorium had lain over Charlotte's name ever since that night, four years previously, when Robin had still been the temp, and an extremely drunk Strike confided in her that Charlotte had lied about being pregnant with his child. All Robin knew right now was that Strike had returned from Cornwall in a particularly buttoned-up mood, and while she knew that the disposal of his aunt's ashes must have been a sad occasion, she couldn't help suspecting this other source for his moodiness.

Out of loyalty to Strike, she refused to gossip about his ex, even though everyone around her seemed to want to talk about it. A week after Strike returned from Cornwall, Robin entered the office, already in a bad mood because Matthew had again postponed mediation. On seeing the door open, Pat the secretary hastily tried to hide a copy of the *Daily Mail* she'd been poring over with Morris. On realising that the new arrival was Robin rather than Strike, Pat had given her raven's caw of laughter and slapped the paper back onto her desk.

'Caught red-handed,' said Morris with a wink at Robin. 'Seen all this about the boss's ex?'

He's not my boss, he's my partner, thought Robin, but she merely said, 'Yes.'

'Talk about punching above his bloody weight,' said Morris, examining a picture of Charlotte at twenty-one in a beaded mini-dress. 'The fuck did a bloke who looks like him end up with that?'

Robin wasn't even safe from it at home. Max, whose floppy hair had been cropped short to play the ex-army officer, had begun shooting his TV series, and was more cheerful than she'd ever known him. Max was also thoroughly intrigued to know that Strike had been involved with Charlotte for sixteen years.

'I met her once,' he told Robin, who'd come upstairs after several hours in her room, combing online records for Betty Fuller. The one-time prostitute was proving harder to find than she'd anticipated.

'Really?' said Robin, who both wanted and didn't want to hear the story.

'Yeah, I was in a play years ago with her half-brother. Simon Legard? He starred in that mini-series about the financial crash, what was it called? She came to watch our play and took us all out for dinner afterwards. I liked her, actually, she was a real laugh. Some of those posh girls are a lot funnier than you'd think.'

'Mm,' said Robin noncommittally, and she returned immediately to her room with her cup of tea.

'I bet she tried to call Corm before she did it,' was Ilsa's cool comment on the phone, two weeks after Easter, by which time Robin had succeeded, through patient cross-referencing, in identifying the woman she thought was most likely to be the Betty Fuller who'd lived in Skinner Street at the time of Margot Bamborough's disappearance. Betty was now living in sheltered housing in Sans Walk, not far from her original flat, and Robin planned to pay her a visit the following afternoon, after the mediation with Matthew which seemed at last to be going ahead.

Ilsa had rung to wish Robin good luck. Robin had been trying not to think about having to see Matthew, telling herself that the ordeal would be over in a couple of hours, but it had become progressively harder to focus on her list of questions for Betty Fuller as the evening progressed, and she'd been glad, initially, to be interrupted by Ilsa.

'What's Corm saying about the whole Charlotte thing?' Ilsa asked.

'Nothing,' said Robin truthfully.

'No, he never talks about her any more,' said Ilsa. 'I wonder how much longer her marriage is going to last. Must be hanging by a thread. I'm quite surprised it's limped on this long, actually. She only did it to get back at Corm.'

'Well, she's had children with Jago,' Robin pointed out, then instantly regretted it. Ilsa had already told her that she and Nick had decided not to try a fourth round of IVF.

'She never wanted kids,' said Ilsa. 'That was something she and Corm had in common. That, and having really similar mothers. Drink, drugs and a million men each, except Charlotte's is still alive. So, you haven't spoken to him about it all?'

'No,' said Robin, who was feeling marginally worse for this conversation, in spite of Ilsa's kind intentions. 'Ilsa, sorry, but I'd better go. I've got work to do for tomorrow.'

'Can't you take the afternoon off? We could meet for a

coffee, you'll probably need some R&R afterwards. Corm wouldn't mind, would he?'

'I'm sure he wouldn't,' said Robin, 'but we're so busy, and I'm following up a lead. Anyway, work gives me something to think about other than Matthew. Let's catch up at the weekend, if you're free.'

Robin slept badly that night. It wasn't Charlotte who wove her way in and out of her dreams, but Miss Jones, the agency's client who, as everyone had now noticed, had taken such a shine to Strike that he'd had to ask Pat to stop putting her calls through. Robin woke before her alarm went off, glad to escape a complicated dream in which it was revealed that Miss Jones had been Matthew's wife all along, and that Robin was defending herself against a charge of fraud at the end of a long, polished table in a dark boardroom.

Wanting to look professional and confident, she dressed in black trousers and jacket, even though Matthew knew perfectly well that she spent most of her investigative life in jeans. Casting one last look in her mirror before leaving her room, she thought she looked washed-out. Trying not to think about all those pictures of Charlotte Ross, who rarely dressed in anything but black, but whose porcelain beauty merely shone brighter in contrast, Robin grabbed her handbag and left her room.

While waiting for the Tube, Robin tried to distract herself from the squirming feeling of nerves in her stomach by checking her emails.

Dear Miss Ellacott,

As previously stated I'm not prepared to talk to anyone except Mr Strike. This is not intended as any slight on you but I would feel more comfortable speaking man to man. Unfortunately, I will be unavailable from the end of next week due to work commitments which will be taking me out of the country. However I can make space on the evening of the 24th. If this is agreeable to Mr Strike, I suggest the American Bar in the Stafford hotel as a discreet meeting place. Kindly let me know if this is acceptable.

Sincerely,

CB Oakden

Twenty minutes later, when she'd emerged from Holborn Tube station and had reception again, Robin forwarded this message to Strike. She had a comfortable quarter of an hour to spare before her appointment and there were plenty of places to grab a coffee in her vicinity, but before she could do so, her mobile rang: it was Pat, at the office.

'Robin?' said the familiar croaking voice. 'D'you know where Cormoran is? I've tried his phone but he's not picking up. I've got his brother Al here in the office, wanting to see him.'

'Really?' said Robin, startled. She'd met Al a couple of years previously, but knew that he and Strike weren't close. 'No, I don't know where he is, Pat. Have you left a message? He's probably somewhere he can't pick up.'

'Yeah, I've left a voicemail,' said Pat. 'All right, I'll keep trying him. Bye.'

Robin walked on, her desire for a coffee forgotten in her curiosity about Al turning up at the office. She'd quite liked Al when she'd met him; he seemed in slight awe of his older half-brother, which Robin had found endearing. Al didn't look much like Strike, being shorter, with straight hair, a narrow jaw and the slight divergent squint he'd inherited from their famous father.

Thinking about Strike's family, she turned the corner and saw, with a thrill of dread that brought her to a halt, Matthew climbing out of a taxi, wearing an unfamiliar dark overcoat over his suit. His head turned, and for a moment they were looking at each other, fifty yards apart like gunslingers ready to fire. Then Robin's mobile rang; she reached for it automatically, and when she'd put it to her ear and looked up, Matthew had disappeared into the building.

'Hello?'

'Hi,' said Strike, 'just got the email from Oakden. "Out of the country", my arse.'

Robin glanced at her watch. She still had five minutes, and her lawyer, Judith, was nowhere in sight. She drew back against the cold stone wall and said,

'Yeah, I thought that, too. Have you rung Pat back?'

'No, why?'

'Al's at the office.'

'Al who?'

'Your brother, Al,' said Robin.

There was a brief pause.

'Fuck's sake,' said Strike under his breath.

'Where are you?' asked Robin.

'At a B&Q in Chingford. Our blonde friend in Stoke Newington's shopping.'

'What for?'

'Rubber foam and MDF, for starters,' said Strike. 'That bloke from Shifty's gym's helping her. Where are you?'

'Waiting outside Matthew's lawyers. It's mediation morning,' said Robin.

'Shit,' said Strike, 'I forgot. Best of luck. Listen – take the rest of the day off, if you'd—'

'I don't want time off,' said Robin. She'd just spotted Judith in the distance, walking briskly towards her in a red coat. 'I'm planning to go and see Betty Fuller afterwards. I'd better go, Cormoran. Speak later.'

She hung up and walked forwards to meet Judith, who smiled broadly.

'All right?' she asked, patting Robin on the arm with the hand not holding her briefcase. 'Should be fine. You let me do the talking.'

'Right,' said Robin, smiling back with as much warmth as she could muster.

They walked up the steps together into a small lobby area, where a stocky, suited man with a haircut like Caesar's came forward with a perfunctory smile, his hand outstretched to Judith.

'Ms Cobbs? Andrew Shenstone. Ms Ellacott? How d'you do?'

His handshake left Robin's hand throbbing. He and Judith walked ahead of Robin through double doors, chatting about London traffic, and Robin followed, dry-mouthed and feeling like a child trailing its parents. After a short walk up a dark corridor, they turned left into a small meeting room with an oval table and a shabby blue carpet. Matthew was sitting there alone, still wearing his overcoat. He readjusted himself in his chair when they entered. Robin looked directly into his face as she sat down, diagonally opposite him. To her surprise, Matthew looked instantly away. She'd imagined him glaring across the table, with that strange muzzle-like whitening around his mouth he'd worn during arguments towards the end of their marriage.

'Right then,' said Andrew Shenstone, with another smile, as Judith Cobbs opened the file she'd brought with her. He had a leather document holder sitting, closed, in front of him. 'Your client's position remains as stated in your letter of the fourteenth, Judith, is that correct?'

'That's right,' said Judith, her thick black glasses perched on the end of her nose as she scanned a copy of said letter.

'Ms Ellacott's perfectly happy to forgo any claim on your client, except in respect of the proceeds from the sale of the flat in – um—'

Hastings Road, thought Robin. She remembered moving into the cramped conversion with Matthew, excitedly carrying boxes of pot plants and books up the short path, Matthew plugging in the coffee machine that had been one of their first joint purchases, the fluffy elephant he'd given her so long ago, sitting on the bed.

'—Hastings Road, yes,' said Judith, scanning her letter, 'from which she'd like the ten thousand pounds her parents contributed to the deposit, upon purchase.'

'Ten thousand,' repeated Andrew Shenstone. He and Matthew looked at each other. 'In that case, we're agreeable.'

'You're ... agreeable?' said Judith Cobbs, as surprised as Robin herself.

'My client's circumstances have changed,' said Shenstone. 'His priority now is securing the divorce as speedily as possible, which I think your client has indicated is also preferable to her, excepting the ten thousand pounds? Of course,' added Shenstone, 'we're almost at the requisite two years, so ... '

Judith looked at Robin, who nodded, her mouth still dry.

'Then I think we can conclude things today. Very good indeed,' said Andrew Shenstone complacently, and it was impossible to escape the suspicion that he was addressing himself. 'I've taken the liberty of drawing up ... '

He opened his document holder, spun it around on the polished table top and pushed it towards Judith, who read the document inside carefully.

'Yes,' she said finally, sliding the document sideways to Robin, who learned that Matthew was promising to transfer the money to Robin's account within seven days of signature. 'Happy?' Judith added in an undertone to Robin.

'Yes,' said Robin, slightly dazed.

What, she wondered, had been the point of dragging her here? Had it been one last demonstration of power, or had Matthew only decided that morning to give in? She reached into her handbag, but Judith was already holding out her own fountain pen, so Robin took it and signed. Judith passed the document back to Andrew Shenstone, who slid it over to Matthew, who scrawled a hasty signature. He glanced up at Robin when he'd done so, then looked quickly away again, and in that moment, Robin knew what had happened, and why he'd given her what she wanted.

'Very good,' said Andrew Shenstone again, and he slapped the table with his thick hand and laughed. 'Well, short and sweet, eh? I think we're . . . ?'

'Yes,' said Judith, with a little laugh, 'I think we are!'

Matthew and Robin rose and watched their lawyers gathering up their things and, in Judith's case, pulling her coat back on. Disorientated by what had just happened, Robin again had the sensation of being a child with its parents, unsure how to quit the situation, waiting for the lawyers to release her.

Andrew Shenstone held the door open for Robin and she passed back into the corridor, heading towards the lobby. Behind her, the lawyers were talking about traffic again. When they paused in the lobby to take leave of each other, Matthew, after a brief word of thanks to Shenstone, walked straight out past Robin, into the street.

Robin waited for Andrew Shenstone to disappear inside the building again before addressing Judith.

'Thanks so much,' she said.

'Well, I didn't really do much, did I?' said Judith, laughing. 'But mediation often brings people to their senses, I've seen it happen before. Much harder to justify yourself in a room with objective observers.'

They shook hands, and Robin headed out into a spring breeze that blew her hair into her mouth. She felt slightly unsettled. Ten thousand pounds. She'd offered to give it back to her parents, knowing that they'd struggled to match Matthew's parents' contribution, but they'd told her to keep it. She'd have to settle her bill with Judith, of course, but the remainder would give her a buffer, maybe even help her back towards her own place.

She turned a corner and there, right in front of her, standing at the kerb, his arm raised in his attempt to hail a taxi, was Matthew.

Catching sight of her, he stood frozen for a moment, his hand still raised, and the taxi he'd been trying to hail slowed ten yards away, and picked up a couple instead.

'Sarah's pregnant, isn't she?' said Robin.

He looked down at her, not quite as tall as Strike, but as good-looking as he'd been at seventeen, on the day he'd asked her out.

'Yeah.' He hesitated. 'It was an accident.'

Was it hell, thought Robin. Sarah had always known how to get what she wanted. Robin realised at last how long a game Sarah had played: always present, giggling, flirting, prepared to settle for Matthew's best friend to keep him close. Then, as her clutch tightened, but Matthew threatened to slip through it, there'd been the diamond earring she'd left in Robin's bed and now, still more valuable, a pregnancy to make sure of him, before he could enter a dangerous state of singledom. Robin had a strong suspicion that this was what had lain behind the two postponements of mediation. Had a newly hormonal and insecure Sarah made scenes, frightened of Matthew coming face to face with Robin while he hadn't yet decided whether he wanted either the baby or its mother?

'And she wants to be married before she has it?'

'Yeah,' said Matthew. 'Well, so do I.'

Did the image of their own wedding flash across his mind, as it flashed across Robin's? The church in Masham that both of them had attended since primary school, the reception in that beautiful hotel, with the swans in the lake that refused to swim together, and the disastrous reception, during which Robin had known, for a few terrifying seconds, that if Strike had asked her to leave with him, she'd have gone.

'How're things with you?'

'Great,' said Robin.

She put up a good front. What you do, when you meet the ex, isn't it? Pretend you think you did the right thing. No regrets.

'Well,' he said, as the traffic rolled past, 'I need to . . . '

He began to walk away.

'Matt.'

He turned back.

'What?'

'I'll never forget . . . how you were, when I really needed you. Whatever else . . . I'll never forget that part.'

For a fraction of a second, his face worked slightly, like a small boy's. Then he walked back to her, bent down, and before she knew what was happening, he'd hugged her quickly, then let go as though she was red hot.

'G'luck, Robs,' he said thickly, and walked away for good.

56

Whereas this Lady, like a sheepe astray,
Now drowned in the depth of sleepe all fearlesse lay.

Edmund Spenser
The Faerie Queene

At the precise moment Matthew turned to walk away from Robin in Holborn, Strike, who was sitting in his parked car three miles away, outside the familiar terraced house in Stoke Newington, decided to call his brother, lest Al sit in wait for him at the office all day. The detective's anger was shot through with other, less easily identifiable feelings, of which the least painful to acknowledge was grudging admiration for Al's persistence. Strike didn't doubt that Al had come to the office for a last-ditch attempt to persuade Strike into some form of reconciliation with his father, preferably before or during the party to celebrate his father's new album. Having always considered Al a fairly weak and sybaritic character, Strike had to admit he was showing guts, risking his older brother's fury.

Strike waited until Elinor Dean had unloaded the foam and the cheap wood from her car and carried it all inside with the aid of her friend from Shifty's gym, watched the front door close, then called Al's number.

'Hi,' said Al, picking up after a single ring.

'Why are you in my office?' asked Strike.

'Wanted to see you, bruv. Talk face to face.'

'Well, I won't be back there today,' lied Strike. 'So I suggest you say whatever it is you've got to say now.'

'Bruv—'

'Who's there with you?'

'Er – your secretary – Pat, is it?' Strike heard Al turn away from his mobile to check, and heard Pat's caw of agreement, 'and a bloke called—'

'Barclay,' said the Scot loudly, in the background.

'Right, well, go into my office for some privacy,' said Strike. He listened while Al told Pat what Strike had asked him to do, heard the familiar sound of his own office door closing, then said,

'If this is about what I think it's about—'

'Cormoran, we didn't want to tell you this, but Dad's got cancer.'

Oh, for fuck's sake.

Strike leaned forwards momentarily and rested his forehead on the steering wheel of his car, before he sat up again.

'Prostate,' Al continued. 'They reckon they've caught it early. But we thought you should know, because this party isn't just about celebrating the band's anniversary, and the new album. It's about giving him something to look forward to.'

There was a silence.

'We thought you should know,' Al repeated.

Why should I fucking know? thought Strike, eyes on the closed door of Elinor Dean's house. He had no relationship with Rokeby. Did Al expect him to weep, to rush to Rokeby's side, to express compassion or pity? Rokeby was a multimillionaire. Doubtless he'd enjoy the very best treatment. The memory of Joan's lily urn bobbing away on the sea recurred as Strike said,

'OK, well, I don't really know how to respond to that. I'm sure it's a bugger for everyone who cares about him.'

Another long silence followed.

'We thought this might make a difference,' said Al quietly.

'To what?'

'To your attitude.'

'As long as they've caught it early, he'll be fine,' said Strike bracingly. 'Probably live to father another couple of kids he never sees.'

'Jesus Christ!' said Al, really angry now. 'You might not give a shit, but he happens to be my dad—'

'I give a shit about people who've ever given a shit about me,' said Strike, 'and keep your fucking voice down, those are my employees you're airing my private business in front of.'

'*That's* your priority?'

Strike thought of Charlotte who, according to the papers, remained in hospital, and of Lucy, who was agitating to know whether Strike would be able to take the weekend off, to join Ted at her house in Bromley for the weekend. He thought of the clients in the Shifty case, who were hinting they'd terminate payment in a week's time unless the agency found out what hold Shifty had on his boss. He thought of Margot Bamborough, and the rapidly vanishing year they'd been allotted to find out what had happened to her. Inexplicably, he thought of Robin, and the fact that he'd forgotten that today was her mediation session with Matthew.

'I've got a life,' said Strike, keeping a curb on his temper only by exercising maximum self-control, 'which is hard and complicated, just like everyone else's. Rokeby's got a wife and half a dozen kids and I'm at maximum capacity for people who need me. I'm not coming to his fucking party, I'm not interested in hearing from him, I don't want a relationship with him. I don't know how much clearer I can make this, Al, but I'm—'

The line went dead. Without regretting anything he'd

said, but nevertheless breathing heavily, Strike threw his mobile onto the passenger seat, lit a cigarette and watched Elinor Dean's front door for another fifteen minutes until, on a sudden whim, he snatched up the phone from beside him again, and called Barclay.

'What are you doing right now?'

'Filin' my expenses,' said the Scot laconically. 'That casino cost ye a fortune.'

'Is my brother still there?'

'No, he left.'

'Good. I need you to come and take over in Stoke Newington.'

'I havenae got my car wi' me.'

'OK, well, fuck it, then,' said Strike angrily.

'I'm sorry, Strike,' said Barclay, 'but I'm s'posed tae have this afternoon off—'

'No, *I'm* sorry,' said Strike, closing his eyes. He had the same sensation of a wire tightening around his forehead that he'd experienced in St Mawes. 'Getting frustrated. Enjoy your afternoon off. Seriously,' he added, in case Barclay thought he was being sarcastic.

Having hung up on Barclay, Strike rang Robin.

'How did mediation go?'

'Fine,' said Robin, though she sounded strangely flat. 'We've settled.'

'Great!'

'Yeah. It's a relief.'

'Did you say you're going to Betty Fuller's?'

'Yes, I was just about to head into the Tube.'

'Remind me where she lives?'

'Sheltered housing on Sans Walk in Clerkenwell.'

'OK, I'll meet you there,' said Strike.

'Really? I'm fine to—'

'I know, but I want to be there,' Strike cut across her.

He pulled away from Elinor Dean's house knowing that he'd just been abrasive towards his two favourite colleagues. If he was going to vent his temper, it could at least have been at Pat and Morris's expense.

Twenty minutes later, Strike entered Clerkenwell via Percival Street. To his right were the nondescript red-brick flats where Janice Beattie and Steve Douthwaite had once lived, and he wondered yet again what had become of Margot's one-time patient, whose whereabouts, in spite of his and Robin's best efforts, remained unknown.

Sans Walk was a narrow pedestrianised one-way street. Strike parked his BMW as close to it as possible. The day was surprisingly warm, in spite of a good amount of cloud. As he approached Sans Walk, he saw Robin waiting for him at the entrance.

'Hi,' she said. 'It's up the other end, that red-brick modern building with the circular tower thing on top.'

'Great,' said Strike, as they set off together. 'Sorry for earlier, I—'

'No, it's fine,' said Robin, 'I know we really need results soon.'

But Strike thought he detected a slight coolness.

'Al pissed me off,' he explained. 'So I might've been a bit—'

'Cormoran, it's fine,' repeated Robin, but with a smile that reassured Strike.

'Great news about the mediation,' he said.

'Yes,' said Robin, though she didn't look particularly pleased. 'So, what d'you think's the best tack to take with Betty Fuller?'

'Be honest and direct about who we are and what we're investigating,' said Strike, 'and then play it by ear, I think. And hope to Christ she's not demented . . .'

Priory House was a modern, multi-level building with a shared garden at the back. As they approached the front doors, a middle-aged couple came out; they had the relieved look of people who'd just done their duty, and, smiling at Strike and Robin, they held open the door to let them walk inside.

'Thanks very much,' said Robin, smiling at them, and as the couple walked on, she heard the woman say,

'At least she remembered who we are, this time . . .'

Had it not been for the mobility scooters, the place would have resembled a hall of residence, with its hardy dark grey carpet underfoot, its bulletin board bristling with pamphlets and a depressing smell of communal cooking hanging in the air.

'She's on the ground floor,' said Robin, pointing towards a corridor. 'I checked the names on the buzzer.'

They passed a number of identical pine doors until they reached the one with 'Elizabeth Fuller' printed on a card in a metal holder. Through the wood came the muffled sounds of voices. Just as it had been when he'd visited Janice Beattie, the TV was turned up very high inside. Strike rapped hard on the door.

After a lengthy wait, the door opened very slowly to reveal a panting old lady wearing a nasal cannula, who'd pulled her oxygen tank to the door with her. Over her shoulder, Strike saw a TV blaring the reality show *The Only Way is Essex.*

'*I'm fine. You just upset me, Arg,*' a heavily made-up girl in bright blue was saying onscreen.

Betty Fuller looked as though she'd been subject to heavier gravity than the rest of humankind. Everything about her had sagged and drooped: the corners of her lipless mouth, her papery eyelids, her loose jowls, the tip of her thin nose. It appeared that the flesh had been sucked down out of her upper body into her lower: Betty had almost no bust, but her hips were broad and her poor bare legs were immensely swollen, both ankles thicker than her neck. She wore what looked like a pair of men's slippers and a dark green knitted dress on which there were several stains. A yellowish scalp was clearly visible through the sparse grey hair slicked back off her face and a hearing aid was prominent in her left ear.

'Who're you?' she wheezed, looking from Robin to Strike.

'Afternoon, Mrs Fuller,' said Strike loudly and clearly, 'my name's Cormoran Strike and this is Robin Ellacott.'

He pulled his driver's licence out of his pocket and showed it to her, with his card. She made an impatient gesture, to show she couldn't read them; her eyes were milky with glaucoma.

'We're private detectives,' said Strike, voice still raised over the arguing pair on-screen (*'At the end of the day, Lucy, she slept, on a one-night stand, wiv a boy—' 'Arg – Arg – Arg – this is irrelevant—'*).

'We've been hired to try and find out what happened to Margot Bamborough. She was a doctor who—'

''Oo?'

'Dr Margot Bamborough,' Strike repeated, still more loudly. 'She went missing from Clerkenwell in 1974. We heard you—'

'Oh yeah . . . ' said Betty Fuller, who appeared to need to draw breath every few words. 'Dr Bamborough . . . yeah.'

'Well, we wondered whether we could talk to you about her?'

Betty Fuller stood there for what seemed a very long twenty seconds, thinking this over, while onscreen a young man in a maroon suit said to the over-made-up girl, *'I didn't wanna bring it up but you come over to me—'*

Betty Fuller made an impatient gesture, turned and shuffled back inside. Strike and Robin glanced at each other.

'Is it all right to come in, Mrs Fuller?' asked Strike loudly.

She nodded. Having carefully positioned her oxygen tank, she fell back into her armchair, then tugged the knitted dress in an effort to make it cover her knees. Strike and Robin entered the room and Strike closed the door. Watching the old lady struggle to pull her dress down, Robin had an urge to take a blanket off the unmade bed, and place it decorously over her lap.

Robin had discovered during her research that Betty was eighty-four. The old lady's physical state shocked her. The small room smelled of BO and urine. A door showed a small toilet leading off the single bedroom. Through the open wardrobe door, Robin saw crumpled clothes which had been thrown there, and two empty wine bottles, half hidden in underwear. There was nothing on the walls except a cat calendar: the month of May showed a pair of ginger kittens peeking out from between pink geranium blossoms.

'Would it be all right to turn this down?' Strike shouted over the TV, where the couple onscreen continued to argue, the woman's eyelashes as thick as woolly bear caterpillars.

'Turn it . . . off,' said Betty Fuller. ''S a recording.'

The Essex voices were suddenly extinguished. The two detectives looked around. There were only two choices for seats: the unmade bed and a hard, upright chair, so Robin took the former, Strike the latter. Removing his notebook from his pocket, Strike said,

'We've been hired by Dr Bamborough's daughter, Mrs Fuller, to try and find out what happened to her.'

Betty Fuller made a noise like 'hurhm', which sounded disparaging, although Strike thought it might also have been an attempt to clear phlegm out of her throat. She rocked slightly to one side in her chair and pulled ineffectually at the back of her dress. Her swollen lower legs were knotted with varicose veins.

'So, you remember Dr Bamborough disappearing, do you, Mrs Fuller?'

'... 'es,' she grunted, still breathing heavily. In spite of her incapacity and unpromising manner, Strike had the impression of somebody both more alert than they might appear at first glance, and happier to have company and attention than the unprepossessing exterior might suggest.

'You were living in Skinner Street then, weren't you?'

She coughed, which seemed to clear her lungs, and in a slightly steadier voice, she said,

'Was there till ... last year. Michael Cliffe ... 'Ouse. Top floor. Couldn't manage, no more.'

Strike glanced at Robin; he'd expected her to lead the interrogation, assumed Betty would respond better to a woman, but Robin seemed oddly passive, sitting on the bed, her gaze wandering over the small room.

'Were you one of Dr Bamborough's patients?' Strike asked Betty.

'Yeah,' wheezed Betty. 'I was.'

Robin was thinking, is this where single people end up, people without children to look out for them, without double incomes? In small boxes, living vicariously through reality stars?

Next Christmas, no doubt, she'd run into Matthew, Sarah and their new baby in Masham. She could just imagine Sarah's proud strut through the streets, pushing a top-of-the-range pushchair, Matthew beside her, and a baby with Sarah's white-blonde hair peeking over the top of the blankets. Now, when Jenny and Stephen ran into them, there'd be common ground, the shared language of parenthood. Robin decided there and then, sitting on Betty Fuller's bed, to make sure she didn't go home next Christmas. She'd offer to work through it, if necessary.

'Did you like Dr Bamborough?' Strike was asking Betty.

'She were ... all right,' said Betty.

'Did you ever meet any of the other doctors at the practice?' asked Strike.

Betty Fuller's chest rose and fell with her laboured breathing. Though it was hard to tell with the nasal cannula in the way, Strike thought he saw a thin smile.

'Yeah,' she said.

'Which ones?'

'Brenner,' she said hoarsely, and coughed again. 'Needed an 'ouse call . . . 'mergency . . . she weren't available.'

'So Dr Brenner came out to see you?'

'Hurhm,' said Betty Fuller. 'Yeah.'

There were a few small, cheaply framed photographs on the windowsill, Robin noticed. Two of them showed a fat tabby cat, presumably a lamented pet, but there were also a couple showing toddlers, and one of two big-haired teenaged girls, wearing puff-sleeved dresses from the eighties. So you could end up alone, in near squalor, even if you had children? Was it solely money, then, that made the difference? She thought of the ten thousand pounds she'd be receiving into her bank account later that week, which would be reduced immediately by legal bills and council tax. She'd need to be careful not to fritter it away. She really needed to start saving, to start paying into a pension.

'You must have been seriously unwell, were you?' Strike was asking Betty. 'To need a house call?'

He had no particular reason for asking, except to establish a friendly conversational atmosphere. In his experience of old ladies, there was little they enjoyed more than discussing their health.

Betty Fuller suddenly grinned at him, showing chipped yellow teeth.

'You ever taken it . . . up the shitter . . . with a nine-inch cock?'

Only by exercising the utmost restraint did Robin prevent herself letting out a shocked laugh. She had to hand it to Strike: he didn't so much as grin as he said,

'Can't say I have.'

'Well,' wheezed Betty Fuller, 'you can . . . take it from me . . . fuckin' . . . agony . . . geezer went at me . . . like a fucking power drill . . . split my arsehole open.'

She gasped for air, half-laughing.

'My Cindy 'ears me moanin' . . . blood . . . says "Mum, you gotta . . . get that seen to . . ." called . . . doctor.'

'Cindy's your—?'

'Daughter,' said Betty Fuller. 'Yeah . . . got two. Cindy and Cathy . . .'

'And Dr Brenner came out to see you, did he?' asked Strike, trying not to dwell on the mental image Betty had conjured.

'Yeah . . . takes a look . . . sends me to A&E, yeah . . . nineteen stitches,' said Betty Fuller. 'And I sat on . . . an ice pack . . . for a week . . . and no fuckin' money . . . comin' in . . . After that,' she panted, 'no anal . . . unless they was . . . payin' double and nuthin' over . . . six inches . . . neither.'

She let out a cackle of laughter, which ended in coughs. Strike and Robin were carefully avoiding looking at each other.

'Was that the only time you met Dr Brenner?' asked Strike, when the coughing had subsided.

'No,' croaked Betty Fuller, thumping her chest. 'I seen 'im regular . . . ev'ry Friday night . . . for monfs . . . after.'

She didn't seem to feel any qualms about telling Strike this. On the contrary, Strike thought she seemed to be enjoying herself.

'When did that arrangement start?' asked Strike.

'Couple o' weeks . . . after 'e seen me . . . for me arse,' said Betty Fuller. 'Knocked on me door . . . wiv 'is doctor's bag . . .

pretendin' 'e'd . . . come to check . . . then 'e says . . . wants a regular 'pointment. Friday night . . . 'alf past six . . . tell the neighbours . . . medical . . . if they ask . . .'

Betty paused to cough noisily. When she'd quelled her rattling chest, she went on,

'. . . and if I told anyone . . . 'e'd go to the cops . . . say I was . . . extorting 'im . . .'

'Threatened you, did he?'

'Yeah,' panted Betty Fuller, though without rancour, 'but 'e wasn't . . . try'na get it . . . free . . . so I kep' . . . me mouf shut.'

'You never told Dr Bamborough what was going on?' asked Robin.

Betty looked sideways at Robin who, in Strike's view, had rarely looked as out of place as she did sitting on Betty's bed: young, clean and healthy, and perhaps Betty's drooping, occluded eyes saw his partner the same way, because she seemed to resent both question and questioner.

''Course I fuckin' . . . didn't. She tried ta get me to . . . stop working . . . Brenner . . . easiest job of the week.'

'Why was that?' asked Strike.

Betty laughed wheezily again.

''E liked me . . . lyin' still, like I was . . . coma . . . playin' dead. 'E fucked me . . . sayin' 'is dirty words . . . I pretended . . . couldn't 'ear . . . except once,' said Betty, with a half-chuckle, half-cough, 'the bleedin' fire alarm . . . went off 'alfway . . . I said . . . in 'is ear . . . "I'm not stayin' dead . . . if we're on fuckin' fire . . . I've got kids . . . next room . . ." 'E was livid . . . turned out it was . . . false alarm . . .'

She cackled, then coughed again.

'D'you think Dr Bamborough suspected Dr Brenner of visiting you?' asked Robin.

'No,' said Betty, testily, with another sideways glance. ''Course she fuckin' didn't . . . was eivver of us gonna tell 'er?'

'Was Brenner with you,' asked Strike, 'the night she went missing?'

'Yeah,' said Betty Fuller indifferently.

'He arrived and left at the usual times?'

'Yeah,' said Betty again.

'Did he keep visiting you, after Dr Bamborough disappeared?'

'No,' said Betty. 'Police . . . all over the surgery . . . no, 'e stopped comin' . . . I 'eard . . . 'e retired, not long after . . . Dead now, I s'pose?'

'Yes,' said Strike, 'he is.'

The ruined face bore witness to past violence. Strike, whose own nose had been broken, was sure Betty's hadn't originally been the shape it was now, with its crooked tip.

'Was Brenner ever violent to you?'

'Never.'

'While your – arrangement was going on,' said Strike, 'did you ever mention it to anyone?'

'Nope,' said Betty.

'What about after Brenner retired?' asked Strike. 'Did you happen to tell a man called Tudor Athorn?'

'Clever, aincha?' said Betty, with a cackle of mild surprise. 'Yeah, I told Tudor . . . 'e's long gawn, 's well . . . used to drink . . . wiv Tudor. 'Is nephew's . . . still round 'ere . . . grown up . . . I seen 'im . . . about. Retarded,' said Betty Fuller.

'In your opinion,' said Strike, 'given what you know about Brenner, d'you think he'd have taken advantage of a patient?'

There was a pause. Betty's milky eyes surveyed Strike.

'On'y . . . if she was out cold.'

'Not otherwise?' said Strike.

Taking a deep breath of oxygen through her crooked nose, Betty said,

'Man like that . . . when there's one fing . . . what really . . . gets 'im off . . . that's all 'e wants . . . '

'Did he ever want to drug you?' asked Strike.

'No,' said Betty, 'didn't need to . . . '

'D'you remember,' asked Strike, turning a page in his notebook, 'a social worker called Wilma Bayliss?'

'Coloured girl?' said Betty. 'Yeah . . . you smoke, dontcha?' she added. 'Can smell it . . . give us one,' she said, and out of the wrecked old body came a whiff of flirtatiousness.

'I don't think that's a good idea,' said Strike, smiling. 'Seeing as you're on oxygen.'

'Oh fuck off, then,' said Betty.

'Did you like Wilma?'

''Oo?'

'Wilma Bayliss, your social worker.'

'She were . . . like they all are,' said Betty, with a shrug.

'We spoke to Mrs Bayliss's daughters recently,' said Strike. 'They were telling us about the threatening notes that were sent to Dr Bamborough, before she disappeared.'

Betty breathed in and out, her collapsed chest doing its valiant best for her, and a small squeak issued from her ruined lungs.

'Do you know anything about those notes?'

'No,' said Betty. 'I 'eard . . . they'd bin sent. Everyone 'eard, round 'ere.'

'Who did they hear it from?'

'Probably that Irene Bull . . . '

'You remember Irene, do you?'

With many more pauses to catch her breath, Betty Fuller explained that her youngest sister had been in the same year as Irene at school. Irene's family had lived in a road off Skinner Street: Corporation Row.

'Thought . . . 'er shit . . . smelled of roses . . . that one,' said

Betty. She laughed, but then broke yet again into a volley of hoarse coughs. When she'd recovered, she said, 'The police . . . asked 'em all . . . not to talk . . . but the mouth on . . . that girl . . . everyone knew . . . there'd been threats made.'

'According to Wilma's daughters,' said Strike, watching for Betty's reaction, 'you knew who sent those notes.'

'No, I never,' said Betty Fuller, no longer smiling.

'You were sure Marcus Bayliss hadn't sent them, though?'

'Marcus never . . . 'e was a lovely . . . y'know, I always liked . . . a darkie, me,' said Betty Fuller, and Robin, hoping Betty hadn't seen her wince, looked down at her hands. 'Very 'andsome . . . I'd've given it . . . 'im for free . . . hahaha . . . big, tall man,' said Betty wistfully, ' . . . kind man . . . no, *'e* never freatened no doctor.'

'So who d'you think—?'

'My second girl . . . my Cathy . . . ' continued Betty, determinedly deaf, ''er dad was a darkie . . . dunno *'oo* 'e was . . . condom split . . . I kept 'er 'cause . . . I like kids, but . . . she don't give a shit . . . about me. Smackhead!' said Betty fiercely. '*I* never touched it . . . seen too many . . . go that way . . . stole from me . . . I told 'er . . . keep the fuck . . . my 'ouse . . .

'Cindy's good,' gasped Betty. She was fighting her breathlessness now, though still relishing Strike's captive attention. 'Cindy . . . drops by. Earning . . . decent money . . . '

'Really?' said Strike, playing along, waiting for his opportunity. 'What does Cindy do?'

'Escort,' wheezed Betty. 'Lovely figure . . . up West . . . makin' more'n I ever . . . Arabs an' whatnot . . . but she says . . . "Ma, you wouldn't . . . like it these days . . . all they want . . . is anal."' Betty cackled, coughed and then, without warning, turned her head to look at Robin perched on the bed and said with vitriol: '*She* don't find it . . . funny, this one . . . do you?' she demanded of Robin, who was taken aback.

''S'pect . . . you give it away . . . for meals an' jewellery . . . an' fink it's . . . fink it's free . . . look at 'er face,' wheezed Betty, eyeing Robin with dislike, 'you're the same as . . . the sniffy fuckin' . . . social worker . . . we 'ad round . . . when I . . . minding Cathy's kids . . . gorn now,' said Betty, angrily. 'Took into care . . .

'"*New*, Mrs Fuller",' said Betty, adopting a grotesquely genteel accent, '"*new*, it meks . . . *new* diff'rence to *me . . . 'ow* yew ladies mek . . . ends meet . . . *sex work is work*" . . . they'll tell yer that . . . patronisin' . . . fuckin' . . . but would they . . . want *their* daughters . . . doin' it? *Would they fuck*,' said Betty Fuller, and she paid for her longest speech yet with her most severe spate of coughing.

'Cindy does . . . too much coke,' Betty wheezed, her eyes watering, when she could talk again. ' . . . keeps the weight off . . . Cathy, it was smack . . . boyfriend . . . workin' for 'im . . . beat 'er blue . . . pregnant and lost it . . . '

'I'm sorry to hear that,' said Strike.

'It's all kids . . . on the street . . . these days,' said Betty, and a glimmer of what Strike thought was real distress showed through the determinedly tough exterior. 'Fifteen, fourteen . . . children . . . my day . . . we'd've marched 'em . . . right back 'ome . . . it's all right, grown women, but kids – whatchew fucking starin' at?' she barked to Robin.

'Cormoran, I might—' said Robin, standing up and gesturing towards the door.

'Yeah, off you fuck,' said Betty Fuller, watching with satisfaction as Robin left her room. 'You doin' 'er, are you?' she wheezed at Strike, once the door had clicked shut behind Robin.

'No,' he said.

'What the fuck's . . . point, then?'

'She's very good at the job,' said Strike. 'When she's not up against someone like you, that is,' and Betty Fuller grinned, displaying her Cheddar-yellow teeth.

'Hahaha . . . I know . . . 'er type . . . knows fuckin' nothing . . . 'bout real life . . .'

'There was a man living in Leather Lane, back in Margot Bamborough's day,' said Strike. 'Name of Niccolo Ricci? "Mucky", they used to call him.'

Betty Fuller said nothing, but the milky eyes narrowed.

'What d'you know about Ricci?' asked Strike.

'Same as . . . ev'ryone,' said Betty.

Out of the corner of his eye, Strike saw Robin emerge into the daylight. She lifted her hair briefly off her neck, as though needing to remove weight from herself, then walked out of sight with her hands in her jacket pockets.

'It warn't Mucky . . . what freatened 'er,' said Betty. ''E wouldn't . . . write notes. Not 'is . . . style.'

'Ricci turned up at the St John's practice Christmas party,' said Strike. 'Which seemed odd.'

'Don't know . . . nuffin' 'bout that . . . '

'Some of the people at the party assumed he was Gloria Conti's father.'

'Never 'eard of 'er,' wheezed Betty.

'According to Wilma Bayliss's daughters,' said Strike, 'you told their mother you were scared of the person who wrote the notes. You said the writer of the notes killed Margot Bamborough. You told Wilma he'd kill you, too, if you said who he was.'

Betty's milky eyes were expressionless. Her thin chest laboured to get enough oxygen into her lungs. Strike had just concluded that she definitely wasn't going to talk, when she opened her mouth.

'Local girl I knew,' she said, 'friend o' mine . . . *she* met Mucky . . . 'e come cruisin' . . . our corner . . . 'e says to Jen . . .

"You're better'n this ... workin' the street ... body like yours ... I could get you ... five times what ... you're earnin' 'ere ..." so off Jen goes,' said Betty, 'up West ... Soho ... strippin' for punters ... sex wiv 'is mates ...'

'I met 'er ... coupla years later ... visitin' 'er mum ... and she tole me a story.

'Girl at their club ... gorgeous girl, Jen said ... got raped ... knifepoint. Cut ... ' said Betty Fuller, indicating her own sagging torso, 'right down the ribs ... by a mate ... of Ricci's ...

'Some people,' said the old woman, 'fink a hooker ... being raped ... it just means she never ... got paid ... 'spect your Miss Stick-Up-'Er-Arse,' said Betty, glancing at the window, 'finks that ... but it ain't that ...

'This girl ... angry ... wants revenge ... get back ... at Ricci ... so the silly bitch ... turns police informer ...

'And Mucky found out,' wheezed Betty Fuller, 'and 'e filmed it ... as they killed 'er. My mate Jen was told ... by someone ... what 'ad seen ... the film ... Ricci kept it ... in the safe ... show people ... if they needed ... scaring ...

'Jen's dead now,' said Betty Fuller. 'Overdosed ... firty-odd years ago ... fort she'd be better ... up West ... and 'ere's me ... workin' the streets ... still alive.

'I ain't got nuffing ... to say ... about no notes ... it warn't Marcus ... that's all ... That's my meals on wheels,' said Betty, her head turning, and Strike saw a man heading towards the outside door, with a pile of foil trays in his arms.

'I'm done,' Betty said, who seemed suddenly tired and cross. 'You can turn ... telly back on ... and move ... that table over ... pass me that knife and fork ... in the loo ...'

She'd rinsed them off in the bathroom sink, but they were still dirty. Strike washed them again before taking them to her. After arranging the table in front of her armchair, and turning *The Only Way is Essex* back on, he opened the door to the meals-on-wheels man, who was grey-haired and cheery.

'Oh hello,' said the newcomer in a loud voice. 'This your son, Betty?'

'Is he fuck,' wheezed Betty Fuller. 'Whatchew got?'

'Chicken casserole and jelly and custard, love . . .'

'Thanks very much for talking to me, Mrs Fuller,' said Strike, but Betty's stock of goodwill had plainly been exhausted, and she was now far more interested in her food.

Robin was leaning against a nearby wall, reading something off her phone, when Strike emerged from the building.

'I thought it was best to clear out,' she said, in a flat voice. 'How did it go?'

'She won't talk about the notes,' said Strike, as the pair of them headed back down Sans Walk, 'and if you ask me why, I'd say it's because she thinks Mucky Ricci wrote them. I've found out a bit more about that girl in the snuff movie.'

'You're joking?' said Robin, looking worried.

'Apparently she was a police informer in one of Ricci's—'

Robin gasped.

'Kara Wolfson!'

'What?'

'Kara Wolfson. One of the women they thought Creed might have killed. Kara worked at a nightclub in Soho – the owners put it about after she disappeared that she'd been a police informer!'

'How did you know that?' asked Strike, taken aback. He couldn't remember this information from *The Demon of Paradise Park*.

Robin suddenly remembered that she'd heard this from Brian Tucker, back at the Star Café. She hadn't yet heard back from the Ministry of Justice about the possibility of interviewing Creed, and as Strike still had no inkling what she was up to, she said,

'Think I read it online . . . '

But with a new heaviness pressing on her heart, Robin remembered that Kara's only remaining close relative, the brother she'd raised, had drunk himself to death. Hutchins had said the police weren't able to do anything about that film. Kara Wolfson's body might be anywhere. Some stories didn't have neat endings: there was nowhere to lay flowers for Kara Wolfson, unless it was on the corner near the strip joint where she'd last been seen.

Fighting the depression now threatening to overwhelm her, Robin raised her phone to show Strike what she'd been looking up, and said in a determinedly matter-of-fact voice,

'I was just reading about somnophilia, otherwise known as sleeping princess syndrome.'

'Which, I take it—?'

'Was Brenner's kink,' said Robin, and reading off her phone, she said, '"Somnophilia is a paraphilia in which the individual is sexually aroused by someone non-responsive . . . some psychologists have linked somnophilia with necrophilia." Cormoran . . . you know how he had barbiturates stocked up in his office?'

'Yeah,' said Strike slowly, as they walked back towards his car. 'Well, this is going to give us something to talk to Dorothy's son about, isn't it? I wonder whether she was game for playing dead? Or whether she found herself sleeping a long time, after Brenner had been round for lunch?'

Robin gave a small shudder.

'I know,' Strike continued, as he lit up, 'I said he'd be a last resort, but we've only got three months left. I'm starting to think I'm going to have to pay Mucky Ricci a visit.'

57

But all his mind is set on mucky pelfe,
To hoord vp heapes of euill gotten masse,
For which he others wrongs, and wreckes himself.

Edmund Spenser
The Faerie Queene

Adding daytime surveillance of St Peter's Roman Catholic Nursing Home to the rota meant that as May progressed, the agency was again struggling to cover all open cases. Strike wanted to know how many visitors were going in and out, and at what times, so that he might ascertain when he'd have the best chance of entering the building without running into one of the old gangster's relatives.

The nursing home lay in a quiet Georgian street on the very edge of Clerkenwell, in a quiet, leafy enclave where dun-coloured brick houses sported neo-classical pediments and glossy black front doors. A dark wood plaque on the exterior wall of the nursing home was embellished with a cross, and a biblical quotation, in gold:

For you know that it was not with perishable things such as silver or gold that you were redeemed from the empty way of life handed down to you from your ancestors, but with the precious blood of Christ, a lamb without blemish or defect.

Peter 1:18–19

'Nice sentiment,' as Strike commented to Robin, on one of their handovers, 'but nobody's getting in there without a good bit of cash.'

The private nursing home was small and clearly expensive. The staff, all of whom the agency quickly grew to know by sight, wore dark blue scrubs and hailed mostly from abroad. There was a black male nurse who sounded as though he'd come from Trinidad, and two blondes who talked Polish to each other every morning as they passed whichever agency member happened to be loitering in the area at the time, feigning a call on their mobile, reading a newspaper or appearing to wait, slightly impatiently, for a friend who never showed up.

A podiatrist and a hairdresser went regularly in and out of the home, but after two weeks' daytime surveillance, the agency tentatively concluded that Ricci only received visits on Sundays, when his two sons appeared, wearing the resigned looks of people for whom this was an unwelcome chore. It was easy to identify which brother was which from pictures that had appeared in the press. Luca looked, in Barclay's phrase, 'like a piano fell oan his heid', having a bald, flat, noticeably scarred skull. Marco was smaller, slighter and hairier, but gave off an air of barely contained violence, slamming his hand repeatedly on the nursing home's doorbell if the door wasn't opened immediately, and slapping a grandson around the back of the head for dropping a chocolate bar on the pavement. Both the brothers' wives had a hard-boiled look about them, and none of the family had the good looks Robin associated with Italians. The great-grandfather sitting mutely behind the doors of the nursing home might have been a true Latin, but his descendants were disappointingly pallid and Saxon in appearance, right down to the little ginger-haired boy who dropped his chocolate.

It was Robin who first laid eyes on Ricci himself, on the

third Saturday the agency was watching the home. Beneath her raincoat, Robin was wearing a dress, because she was meeting Strike later at the Stafford hotel in Mayfair, to interview C. B. Oakden. Robin, who'd never been to the hotel, had looked it up and learned that the five-star establishment, with its bowler-hatted doormen, was one of the oldest and smartest hotels in London, hence her atypical choice of surveillance wear. As she'd previously disguised herself while lurking outside St Peter's (alternately beanie hat, hair up, dark contact lenses and sunglasses), she felt safe to look like herself for once as she strolled up and down the street, pretending to talk on the phone, although she'd added clear-lensed glasses she'd remove for the Stafford.

The elderly residents of St Peter's were occasionally escorted or wheeled down the street in the afternoon to the nearby square, which had a central private garden enclosed by railings, open only to keyholders, there to doze or enjoy the lilac and pansies while well wrapped up against the cold. Hitherto, the agency had seen only elderly women taken on the outings, but today, for the first time, an old man was among the group coming down a ramp at the side of the building.

Robin recognised Ricci instantly, not by his lion ring, which, if he was wearing it, was well hidden beneath a tartan rug, but by the profile that time might have exaggerated, but could not disguise. His thick black hair was now dark grey and his nose and earlobes enormous. The large eyes that reminded Strike of a Basset hound had an even more pronounced droop these days. Ricci's mouth hung slightly open as one of the Polish nurses pushed him towards the square, talking to him brightly, but receiving no response.

'You all right, Enid, love?' the black male nurse called ahead to a frail-looking old lady wearing a sheepskin hat, and she laughed and nodded.

Robin gave the group a head start, then followed, watching as one of the nurses unlocked the gate to the garden, and the party disappeared inside. Walking around the square with her phone clamped to her ear, pretending to be in conversation, Robin thought how typical it was that today, of all days, she'd worn heels, never imagining that there might have been a possibility of approaching Ricci and chatting to him.

The group from the nursing home had come to a halt beside flower-beds of purple and yellow, Ricci parked in his wheelchair beside an empty park bench. The nurses chatted amongst themselves, and to those old ladies capable of doing so, while the old man stared vacantly across the lawns.

If she'd been wearing her usual trainers, Robin thought, she might possibly have been able to scale the railings and get into the garden unseen: there was a clump of trees that would provide cover from the nurses, and she could have sidled over to Ricci and found out, at the very least, whether he had dementia. Unfortunately, she had absolutely no chance of managing that feat in her dress and high heels.

As she completed her walk around the square, Robin spotted Saul Morris walking towards her. Morris was early, as he always tended to be, whenever it was Robin from whom he was taking over.

He's going to mention either the glasses or the heels first, Robin thought.

'High heels,' said Morris, as soon as he was within earshot, his bright blue eyes sweeping over her. 'Don't think I've ever seen you in heels before. Funny, I never think of you as tall, but you are, aren't you? Sexy specs, too.'

Before Robin could stop him, he'd stooped and kissed her on the cheek.

'I'm the guy you're meeting on a blind date,' he told her, straightening up again and winking.

'How do we account for the fact that I'm about to leave you standing here?' Robin asked, unsmiling, and Morris laughed too hard, just as he did at Strike's mildest jokes.

'Dunno – what would it take to make you walk out on a blind date?' asked Morris.

You turning up, thought Robin, but ignoring the question she checked her watch and said,

'If you're OK to take over now, I'll head—'

'Here they come,' said Morris quietly. 'Oh, the old fella's outside this time, is he? I wondered why you'd abandoned the front door.'

The comment aggravated Robin almost as much as his flirtatious manner. Why did he think she'd leave the front door, unless the target had moved? Nevertheless, she waited beside him while the small group of nurses and residents, having decided that twenty minutes was enough fresh air, passed them on the other side of the street, heading back to the home.

'My kids were taken out like that at nursery,' said Morris quietly, watching the group pass. 'All bundled up in pushchairs, the helpers wheeling them out. Some of that lot are probably wearing nappies, too,' he said, his bright blue eyes following the St Peter's party. 'Christ, I hope I never end up like that. Ricci's the only man, too, poor sod.'

'I think they're very well looked after,' Robin said, as the Trinidadian nurse shouted,

'Up we go, Enid!'

'Like being a kid again, though, isn't it?' said Morris, as they watched the wheelchairs rolling along in procession. 'But with none of the perks.'

'S'pose so,' said Robin. 'I'll head off, then, if you're ready to take over.'

'Yeah, no problem,' said Morris, but he immediately added, 'where're you going, all dressed up like that?'

'I'm meeting Strike.'

'*Oh*,' said Morris, eyebrows raised, 'I see—'

'No,' said Robin, 'you don't. We're interviewing someone at a really smart hotel.'

'Ah,' said Morris. 'Sorry.'

But there was a strange complacency, bordering on complicity, about the way Morris bade her goodbye, and it wasn't until Robin had reached the end of the street that the unwelcome thought occurred to her that Morris had entirely misread the sharpness of her denial that she was going on a date with Strike; that he might, in fact, have interpreted it as Robin wanting to make it quite clear that her affections weren't engaged elsewhere.

Was Morris – *could* he be – so deluded as to think that Robin was secretly hoping that his unsubtle flirtation might lead to something happening between them? Even after what had happened on Boxing Day, when she'd shouted at him for sending her that dick pic? Little though she wanted to believe it, she was afraid that the answer was 'yes'. Morris had been extremely drunk when she'd shouted at him, and possibly incapable of judging just how truly angry and disgusted she'd been. He'd seemed sincerely ashamed of himself in the immediate aftermath, so she'd forced herself to be friendlier than she wanted to be, purely out of a desire to foster team cohesion. The result had been that Morris had returned to his pre-dick pic ways. She only answered his late-night texts, mostly containing jokes and attempts at banter, to stop him pestering her with 'have I offended you?' follow-ups. Now it occurred to her that what she considered professionalism Morris took as encouragement. Everything he said to her about work suggested that he saw her as less able and less experienced than the rest of the agency: perhaps he also thought her naive enough to be flattered by the attentions of a man she actually found condescending and slimy.

Morris, Robin thought, as she headed towards the Tube, didn't actually like women. He desired them, but that, of course, was an entirely different matter: Robin, who was forever marked by the ineradicable memory of the man in the gorilla mask, knew better than most that desire and liking were different, and sometimes mutually exclusive, things. Morris gave himself away constantly, not only in the way he spoke to Robin, but in his desire to call Mrs Smith 'Rich Bitch', his attribution of venal or provocative motives to every woman under surveillance, in the barely disguised disgust with which he noted that Mucky Ricci was now forced to live in a houseful of females. *Christ, I hope I never end up like that.*

Robin walked another few steps, and suddenly stopped dead, earning herself a curious glance from a passing traffic warden. She'd had an idea, triggered by what Morris had just said to her: or rather, the idea had slammed its way into the forefront of her mind and she knew that it had been there in her subconscious all along, waiting for her to admit it.

Moving aside so as not to get in the way of passers-by, Robin pulled out her phone and checked the list of paraphilias she'd last consulted when looking up sleeping princess syndrome.

Autonepiophilia.

'Oh God,' Robin muttered. 'That's it. That's got to be it.'

Robin called Strike, but his number went to voicemail; he was doubtless already on the Tube, heading for the Stafford. After a moment or two's thought, she called Barclay.

'Hiya,' said the Scot.

'Are you still outside Elinor Dean's?'

'Yeah.'

'Is there anyone in there with her?'

'No.'

'Sam, I think I know what she's doing for those men.'

'Whut?'

Robin told him. The only answer was a long silence. Finally, Barclay said,

'You're aff yer heid, Robin.'

'Maybe,' said Robin, 'but the only way to know for sure is to knock on her door and ask if she'll do it for you. Say you were recommended to her by SB.'

'Will I fuck,' said Barclay. 'Does Strike know ye're asking me tae do this?'

'Sam, we've got a week left before the client pulls the plug. The worst that can happen is that she denies it. We're not going to have many more chances.'

She heard Barclay exhale, hard.

'All right, but it's on ye if ye're wrong.'

Robin hurried onwards towards the Tube station, second-guessing herself as she went. Would Strike think she was wrong to tell Barclay to go in, on her hunch? But they had a week left before the client withdrew funding: what was there, now, to lose?

It was Saturday evening, and Robin arrived on the crowded Tube platform to find she'd just missed a train. By the time she exited at Green Park station, she'd lost the chance of arriving at the American Bar early, which she'd hoped to do, so that she and Strike could have a few words together before Oakden arrived. Worse still, when she hurried down St James's Street, she saw, with a sense of déjà vu, a large crowd blocking the bottom of the road, being marshalled by police. As Robin slowed down, wondering whether she'd be able to get through the dense mass of people to the Stafford, a couple of sprinting paparazzi overtook her, in pursuit of a series of black Mercedeses. As Robin watched them pressing their lenses against windows, she became aware that the crowd in the distance was chanting '*Jonn-ny! Jonn-ny!*' Through the windows of one of the cars heading towards the event, Robin glimpsed a woman in a Marie Antoinette wig. Only when she was nearly knocked sideways by a sprinting pair of autograph hunters, both of them holding Deadbeats posters, did Robin realise with a thrill of shock that Strike's father was the Jonny whose name was being chanted.

'Shit,' she said aloud, wheeling around and hurrying back up the road, pulling out her mobile as she went. She knew there was another entrance to the Stafford via Green Park. Not only was she going to be late, but a horrible suspicion had just hit her. Why had Oakden been so determined to meet on this specific evening? And why had it had to be this bar, so close to what she was afraid was an event involving Strike's father? Did Strike know, had he realised, what was happening close by?

She called him, but he didn't pick up. Still walking, she typed out a text:

Cormoran I don't know whether you know this, but Jonny Rokeby's having an event around the corner. I think it's possible Oakden's trying to set you up.

Breaking into a jog, because she was already five minutes late, she knew she'd just told Strike, for the very first time, that she knew who his father was.

On her arrival in Green Park, she saw from a distance a policeman at the rear entrance, who, with one of the hotel's bowler-hatted attendants, was politely but firmly turning away two men with long-lensed cameras.

'Not this way, sorry,' said the policeman. 'Only for tonight. If it's the hotel you want, you'll have to go round the front.'

'What's going on?' demanded a suited man hand in hand with a beautiful Asian woman in a cheongsam. 'We've got a dinner booking! Why can't we go through?'

'Very sorry, sir, but there's an event on at Spencer House,' explained the doorman, 'and police want us to stop people using this as a short cut.'

The two men with cameras swore and turned away, jogging back the way Robin had come. She lowered her head as they passed her, glad that she was still wearing her unneeded glasses, because her picture had appeared in the press during a court case a couple of years back. Maybe she was being paranoid, but Robin was worried the pressmen had been trying to use the Stafford not as a short cut to Rokeby and his guests, but as a means of getting to his estranged son.

Now that the photographers had gone, the bowler-hatted attendant permitted the woman in the cheongsam and her companion to enter, and after giving Robin a shrewd up-and-down glance, evidently decided she wasn't a photographer and allowed her to proceed through the gate into a courtyard, where well-dressed drinkers were smoking beneath exterior heaters. After checking her mobile and seeing that Strike hadn't answered her text, she hurried up the steps into the American Bar.

It was a comfortable, elegant space of dark wood and leather, with pennants and baseball caps from many American states and universities hanging from the ceiling. Robin immediately spotted Strike standing in a suit at the bar, his surly expression lit by the rows of illuminated bottles on the wall.

'Cormoran, I just—'

'If you're about to tell me my father's just round the corner,' said Strike tersely, 'I know. This arsehole doesn't realise I'm wise to his attempted set-up, yet.'

Robin glanced into the far corner. Carl Oakden was sitting there, legs spread wide, an arm along the back of the leather bench. He was wearing a suit, but no tie, and his attitude was clearly meant to suggest a man at ease in these cosmopolitan surroundings. With his slightly too-close-together eyes and his narrow forehead, he still resembled the boy who'd smashed Roy's mother's crystal bowl all those years ago.

'Go and talk to him. He wants some food, I'm getting menus,' muttered Strike. 'We'd just got started on Steve Douthwaite. Apparently, Dorothy always thought the bloke was suspicious.'

Heading towards Oakden, Robin prayed that Strike was going to keep his temper. She'd only once seen him lose his cool with a witness, and had no desire to see it happen again.

'Mr Oakden?' she said, smiling as she reached him and extending her hand. 'I'm Robin Ellacott, we've emailed—'

'I know,' said Oakden, turning his head slowly to look her up and down with a smirk. He ignored her outstretched hand and Robin could tell he did so deliberately. Refusing to show that she realised that he was trying to be offensive, she shrugged off her raincoat.

'Nice bar,' she said pleasantly, sitting down opposite him. 'I've never been here before.'

'Normally takes you cheaper places, does he?' asked Oakden.

'Cormoran was just telling me you remember your mother talking about Steve Douth—'

'Love,' said Oakden, legs still wide apart, arm along the back of the leather bench, 'I told you all along, I'm not interested in being palmed off with assistants or secretaries. I'll talk to him, or nobody.'

'I'm actually Cormoran's—'

'I'll bet you are,' said Oakden, with a snigger. 'Don't suppose he can get rid of you now, can he?'

'Sorry?'

'Not now you've been knifed, trying to do a man's job,' said Oakden, with a glance towards her forearm as he raised his cocktail to his lips. 'You'd probably sue the shit out of him, if he tried.'

Oakden, who'd evidently done his homework on the detectives, was clearly revelling in his rudeness. Robin could only suppose that the con man assumed she was too desperate for his information to take offence at his manner. He seemed determined to derive maximum pleasure from this encounter: to enjoy free alcohol and food, and bait a woman who was unlikely to walk away. Robin wondered which paper or picture agency he'd contacted, to propose luring Strike within a few hundred yards of his father's party, and how much Oakden stood to gain, if they could get a picture of Strike apparently publicly snubbing his father, or catch the detective on record saying something angry and quotable.

'There you go,' said Strike, throwing a couple of leather-bound menus onto the table and sitting down. He hadn't thought to bring Robin anything to drink. Oakden picked up a menu and perused it slowly, and he seemed to enjoy keeping them waiting.

'I'll have the club sandwich,' he said at last, and Strike hailed a waiter. The order given, Strike turned back to Oakden and said,

'Yeah, so you were saying, your mother found Douthwaite—'

'Oh, she definitely thought he was a charmer,' said Oakden. His eyes, Robin noted, kept moving to the entrance of the bar, and she was sure Oakden was waiting for photographers to burst in. 'Wide boy, you know the type. Chatting up the slags on reception. The old woman said he tried it on with everyone. The nurse got all giggly when he was around and all.'

Robin remembered the gambolling black skeleton of Talbot's notebook, and the words written beside Crowley's figure of death: *Fortuna says Pallas Athena, Ceres, Vesta and Cetus are SCARLET WOMEN who RIDE UPON THE BEAST . . .*

'And did your mother think he fancied Dr Bamborough?'

Oakden took a sip of his cocktail and smacked his lips.

'Well, I mean, Margot,' he said, with a small snort of laughter, and Robin found herself irrationally resentful of Oakden using the missing doctor's first name, 'you know, she was the classic wanted-it-all-ways, wasn't she?'

'What ways were those?' said Strike.

'Bunny Girl,' said Oakden, taking another sip of his drink, 'legs out, tits out. Then, quick, get the white coat on—'

'Don't think GPs wear white coats,' said Strike.

'I'm talking metaphorically,' said Oakden airily. 'Child of her time, wasn't she?'

'How's that?'

'The rise of gynocentric society,' said Oakden, with a slight bow towards Robin, who suddenly thought his narrow head resembled a stoat's. 'Late sixties, early seventies, it's when it all started changing, isn't it? You've got the pill: consequence-free fucking. Looks like it benefits the male, but by enabling women to avoid or subvert the reproductive function, you're repressing natural and healthy patterns of sex behaviour. You've got a gynocentric court system, which favours the female even if she didn't want the kids in the first place. You've got misandrist authoritarianism masquerading as a campaign for equal rights, policing men's thoughts and speech and natural behaviour. And you've got widespread sexual exploitation of men. Playboy Club, that's all bullshit. Look, but don't touch. It's the old courtly love lie. The woman's there to be worshipped, the man's there to spew cash, but never get satisfaction. Suckers, the men who hang round those places.

'Bamborough didn't look after her own kid,' said Oakden, his eyes again darting to the entrance and back to Strike, 'didn't fuck her own husband, from what I heard, he was nearly always too ill to perform. He had plenty of cash though, so she gets a nanny and goes lording it over men at work.'

'Who, specifically, did she lord it over?' asked Strike.

'Well, Douthwaite ran out of there practically crying last time he saw her, my old woman said. But that's been our culture since the sixties, hasn't it? Male suffering, nobody gives a shit. People whine when men break, when they can't handle it any more, when they lash out. If Douthwaite did her in – I don't *personally* think he did,' said Oakden with an expansive gesture, and Robin reminded herself that Carl Oakden had almost certainly never laid eyes on Steven Douthwaite, and that he'd been fourteen years old when Margot disappeared, 'but *if* he did, I'd lay odds it's because she kicked his pain back in his teeth. Only women bleed,' said Oakden, with a contemptuous little laugh, 'isn't that right?' he shot at Robin. 'Ah, there's my sandwich.'

While the waiter served him, Robin got up and headed to the bar, where the beautiful woman in the cheongsam, whose hair hung like black silk in the light of the banked bottles of spirits, was standing with her partner. Both were ordering cocktails and looked delighted to be in each other's company. For a few seconds Robin suddenly wondered whether she'd ever again feel as they did. Her job reminded her almost daily of the many ways in which men and women could hurt each other.

As she ordered herself a tonic water, Robin's phone rang. Hoping it was Barclay, she instead saw her mother's name. Perhaps Linda had got wind of Sarah's pregnancy. Matthew might have taken his wife-to-be back to Masham by now, to share the good news. Robin muted the phone, paid for her drink, wishing it was alcoholic, and carried it back to the table in time to hear Oakden say to Strike,

'No, that didn't happen.'

'You didn't add vodka to the punch at Dr Bamborough's barbecue?'

Oakden took a large bite of his free sandwich, and chewed it insolently. In spite of his thin hair and the many wrinkles around his eyes, Robin could clearly see the spoiled teenager inside the fifty-four-year-old.

'Nicked some,' said Oakden thickly, 'then drank it in the shed. Surprised they missed it, but the rich are tight. How they stay minted, isn't it?'

'We heard the punch made someone sick.'

'Not my fault,' said Oakden.

'Dr Phipps was pretty annoyed, I hear.'

'Him,' said Oakden, with a smirk. 'Things worked out all right for old Phipps, didn't they?'

'In what way?' asked Strike.

'Wife out the way, marrying the nanny. All very convenient.'

'Didn't like Phipps, did you?' said Strike. 'That came across in your book.'

'You've read it?' said Oakden, momentarily startled. 'How come?'

'Managed to track down an advance copy,' said Strike. 'It should've come out in '85, right?'

'Yeah,' said Oakden.

'D'you remember the gazebo that was under construction in the garden when the barbecue happened?'

One of Oakden's eyelids flickered. He raised a hand quickly to his face and made a sweep of his forehead, as though he felt a hair tickling him.

'No,' he said.

'It's in the background of one of your photos. They'd just started building the columns. I expect they'd already put down the floor.'

'I can't remember that,' said Oakden.

'The shed where you took the vodka wasn't near there, then?'

'Can't've been,' said Oakden.

'While we're on the subject of nicking things,' said Strike, 'would you happen to have the obituary of Dr Brenner you took from Janice Beattie's house?'

'I never stole no obituary from her house,' said Oakden, with a display of disdain. 'What would I want that for?'

'To get some information you could try and pass off as your own?'

'I don't need to look up old Joe Brenner, I know plenty about him. He came round our house for his dinner every other Sunday. My old woman used to cook better than his sister, apparently.'

'Go on, then,' said Strike, his tone becoming combative, 'amaze us.'

Oakden raised his sparse eyebrows. He chewed another bite of sandwich and swallowed it, before saying,

'Hey, this was all your idea. You don't want the information, I'm happy to go.'

'Unless you've got more than you put in your book—'

'Brenner wanted Margot Bamborough struck off the bloody medical register. Come round our house one Sunday full of it. Couple of weeks before she disappeared. There,' said Oakden pugnaciously, 'I kept that out of the book, because my mother didn't want it in there.'

'Why was that?'

'Still loyal to him,' said Oakden, with a little snort of laughter. 'And I wanted to keep the old dear happy at the time, because noises had been made about writing me out of the will. Old women,' said the convicted con man, 'are a bit too persuadable if you don't keep an eye on them. She'd got chummy with the local vicar by the eighties. I was worried it was all going to go to rebuild the bloody church steeple unless I kept an eye on her.'

'Why did Brenner want Bamborough struck off?'

'She examined some kid without parental permission.'

'Was this Janice's son?' asked Robin.

'Was I talking to you?' Oakden shot at her.

'You,' growled Strike, 'want to keep a civil tongue in your bloody head. Was it Janice's son, yes or no?'

'Maybe,' said Oakden, and Robin concluded that he couldn't remember. 'Point is, that's unethical behaviour, looking at a kid without a parent there, and old Joe was all worked up about it. "I'll have her struck off for this," he kept saying. There. Didn't get *that* from no obituary, did I?'

Oakden drank the rest of his cocktail straight off, then said,

'I'll have another one of those.'

Strike ignored this, saying,

'And this was two weeks before Bamborough disappeared?'

'About that, yeah. Never seen the old bastard so excited. He loved disciplining people, old Joe. Vicious old bastard, actually.'

'In what way?'

'Told my old woman in front of me she wasn't hitting me enough,' said Oakden. 'She bloody listened, too. Tried to lay about me with a slipper a couple of days later, silly cow. She learned not to do that again.'

'Yeah? Hit her back, did you?'

Oakden's too-close-together eyes raked Strike, as though trying to ascertain whether he was worth educating.

'If my father had lived, he'd've had the right to punish me, but her trying to humiliate me because Brenner told her to? I wasn't taking that.'

'Exactly how close were your mother and Brenner?'

Oakden's thin brows contracted.

'Doctor and secretary, that's all. There wasn't anything else between them, if that's what you're implying.'

'They didn't have a little lie down after lunch, then?' said Strike. 'She didn't come over sleepy, after Brenner had come over?'

'You don't want to judge everyone's mother by yours,' said Oakden.

Strike acknowledged the jibe with a dark smile and said,

'Did your mother ask Brenner to sign the death certificate for your grandmother?'

'The hell's that got to do with anything?'

'Did she?'

'I dunno,' said Oakden, his eyes darting once again towards the bar's entrance. 'Where did you get that idea? What're you even asking that for?'

'Your grandmother's doctor was Margot Bamborough, right?'

'I dunno,' said Oakden.

'You can remember every word your mother told you about Steve Douthwaite, right down to him flirting with receptionists and looking tearful the last time he left the surgery, but you can't remember details of your own grandmother falling downstairs and killing herself?'

'I wasn't there,' said Oakden. 'I was out at a mate's house when it happened. Come home and seen the ambulance.'

'Just your mother at home, then?'

'The hell's this relevant to—?'

'What's the name of the mate whose house you were at?' asked Strike, for the first time taking out his notebook.

'What're you doing?' said Oakden, with an attempt at a laugh, dropping the last portion of his sandwich on his plate. 'What are you fucking implying?'

'You don't want to give us his name?'

'Why the fuck should – he was a schoolmate—'

'Convenient for you and your mother, old Maud falling downstairs,' said Strike. 'My information is she shouldn't have been trying to navigate stairs alone, in her condition. Inherited the house, didn't you?'

Oakden began to shake his head very slowly, as though marvelling at the unexpected stupidity of Cormoran Strike.

'Seriously? You're trying to . . . wow. *Wow.*'

'Not going to tell me the name of your schoolfriend, then?'

'*Wow,*' said Oakden, attempting a laugh. 'You think you can—'

'—drop a word in a friendly journalist's ear, to the effect that your long career of screwing over old ladies started with a good hard push in the small of your grandmother's back? Oh yeah, I definitely can.'

'Now you wait a fucking—'

'I know you think it's me being set up tonight,' said Strike, leaning in. His body language was unmistakeably menacing, and out of the corner of her eye, Robin saw the black-haired woman in the cheongsam and her partner watching warily, both with their drinks at their lips. 'But the police have still got a note written to them in 1985, telling them to dig beneath the cross of St John. DNA techniques have moved on a lot since then. I expect they'll be able to get a good match from the saliva under the envelope flap.'

Oakden's eyelid twitched again.

'You thought you were going to stir up a bit of press interest in the Bamborough case, to get people interested in your shitty book, didn't you?'

'I never—'

'I'm warning you. You go talking to the papers about me and my father, or about me working the Bamborough case, and I'll make sure you get nailed for that note. And if by chance that doesn't work, I'll put my whole agency onto turning over every part of your miserable fucking life, until I've got something else on you to take to the police. Understand?'

Oakden, who looked momentarily unnerved, recovered himself quickly. He even managed another little laugh.

'You can't stop me writing about whatever I want. That's freedom of—'

'I'm warning you,' repeated Strike, a little more loudly, 'what'll happen if you get in the way of this case. And you can pay for your own fucking sandwich.'

Strike stood up and Robin, caught off guard, hastened to grab her raincoat and get up, too.

'Cormoran, let's go out the back,' she said, thinking of the two photographers lurking at the front of the building, but they hadn't gone more than two steps when they heard Oakden call after them.

'You think I'm scared of your fucking agency? Some fucking detective you are!' he said, and now most of the heads in their vicinity turned. Glancing back, Robin saw that Oakden had got up, too: he'd come out from behind the table and was planted in the middle of the bar, clearly set on making a scene.

'Strike, please, let's just go,' said Robin, who now had a presentiment of real trouble. Oakden was clearly determined to come out of the encounter with something sellable, or at the very least, a narrative in which he'd come out on top. But Strike had already turned back towards their interviewee.

'You didn't even know your own fucking father's having a party round the corner,' said Oakden loudly, pointing in the direction of Spencer House. 'Not going to pop in, thank him for fucking your mother on a pile of beanbags while fifty people watched?'

Robin watched what she had dreaded unfold in apparent slow motion: Strike lunged for Oakden. She made a grab for the arm Strike had drawn back for a punch, but too late: his elbow slammed into Robin's forehead, breaking her glasses in two. Dark spots popped in front of Robin's eyes and the next thing she knew, she'd fallen backwards onto the floor.

Robin's attempted intervention had given the con man a few seconds in which to dodge, and instead of receiving what might have been a knockout punch, he suffered no worse than a glancing blow to the ear. Meanwhile the enraged Strike, who'd barely registered his arm being impeded, realised what he'd done only when he saw drinkers all over the bar jumping to their feet, their eyes on the floor behind him. Turning, he saw Robin lying there, her hands over her face, a trickle of blood issuing from her nose.

'Shit!' Strike bellowed.

The young barman had run out from behind the bar. Oakden was shouting something about assault. Still slightly dizzy, tears of pain streaming from her eyes, the humiliated Robin was assisted back onto her feet by a couple of affluent-looking grey-haired Americans, who were fussing about getting her a doctor.

'I'm absolutely fine,' she heard herself saying. She'd taken the full force of Strike's elbow between her eyebrows, and she realised her nose was bleeding only when she accidentally sprayed blood onto the kind American's white shirt front.

'Robin, shit—' Strike was saying.

'Sir, I'm going to have to—'

'Yes, we're *absolutely* going to leave,' Robin told the waiter, absurdly polite, while her eyes watered and she tried to stem the bleeding from her nostrils. 'I just need – oh, thank you so much,' she said to the American woman, who'd handed Robin her raincoat.

'Call the police!' Oakden was shouting. Thanks to Robin's intervention, he was entirely unmarked. 'Someone call the bloody police!'

'I won't be pressing charges,' Robin said to nobody in particular.

'Robin – I'm so—'

Grabbing a handful of Strike's sleeve, warm blood still trickling down onto her chin, Robin muttered,

'Let's just go.'

She trod on the cracked lens of her glasses as they headed out of the silent bar, the drinkers staring after them.

58

His louely words her seemd due recompence
Of all her passed paines: one louing howre
For many yeares of sorrow can dispence:
A dram of sweete is worth a pound of sowre:
Shee has forgott, how many, a woeful stowre
For him she late endurd; she speakes no more
Of past . . .
Before her stands her knight, for whom she toyld so sore.

Edmund Spenser
The Faerie Queene

'Robin—'

'*Don't* tell me I shouldn't have tried to stop you,' she said through gritted teeth, as they hurried through the outside courtyard. Her vision was blurred with tears of pain. Smokers turned to gape as she passed, trying to staunch her bleeding nose. 'If that punch had connected, we'd be back there waiting for the police.'

To Robin's relief, there were no paparazzi waiting for them as they headed into Green Park, but she was scared that it wouldn't take long, after the scene Strike had just made, for them to come hunting again.

'We'll get a cab,' said Strike, who was currently consumed with a mixture of total mortification and rage against

Oakden, his father, the press and himself. 'Listen, you're right—'

'I know I'm right, thanks!' she said, a little wildly.

Not only was her face throbbing, she was now wondering why Strike hadn't warned her about Rokeby's party; why, in fact, he'd let himself get lured there by a second-rate chancer like Oakden, careless of consequences for their case and for the agency.

'TAXI!' bellowed Strike, so loudly that Robin jumped. Somewhere nearby, she heard running footsteps.

A black cab pulled up and Strike pushed Robin inside.

'Denmark Street,' he yelled at the cabbie, and Robin heard the shouts of photographers as the taxi sped up again.

'It's all right,' said Strike, twisting to look out of the back window, 'they're on foot. Robin . . . I'm so fucking sorry.'

She'd pulled a mirror out of her bag to try and clean up her smarting face, wiping blood from her upper lip and chin. It looked as though she was going to have two black eyes: both were rapidly swelling.

'D'you want me to take you home?' said Strike.

Furious at him, fighting the urge to cry out of pain, Robin imagined Max's surprise and curiosity at seeing her in this state; imagined having to make light, again, of the injuries she'd sustained while working for the agency. She also remembered that she hadn't gone food shopping in days.

'No, I want you to give me something to eat and a strong drink.'

'You've got it,' said Strike, glad to have a chance to make reparations. 'Will a takeaway do?'

'No,' said Robin sarcastically, pointing at her rapidly blackening eyes, 'I'd like to go to the Ritz, please.'

Strike started to laugh but cut himself off, appalled at the state of her face.

'Maybe we should go to casualty.'

'Don't be ridiculous.'

'Robin—'

'You're sorry. I know. You said.'

Strike's phone rang. He glanced down: Barclay could wait, he decided, and muted it.

Three-quarters of an hour later, the taxi dropped them at the end of Denmark Street, with a takeaway curry and a couple of clinking bottles. Once upstairs, Robin repaired to the toilet on the landing, where she washed dried blood from her nostrils and chin with a wad of wet toilet paper. Two increasingly swollen, red-purplish mounds containing her eyes looked back at her out of the cracked mirror. A blue bruise was spreading over her forehead.

Inside the office, Strike, who'd normally have eaten the curry straight out of the foil tray it had come in, had brought out mis-matched plates, knives and forks, then, because Robin wanted a strong drink, went upstairs to his flat where he had a bottle of his favourite whisky. There was a small freezer compartment in his fridge, where he kept ice packs for his stump in addition to an ice tray. The cubes within this had been there for over a year, because although Strike enjoyed the odd drink of spirits, he generally preferred beer. About to leave the flat with the ice tray, he had second thoughts, and doubled back for one of the ice packs, as well.

'Thank you,' muttered Robin, when Strike reappeared, accepting the proffered ice pack. She was sitting in Pat's seat, behind the desk where she'd once answered the phone, where Strike had laid out the curry and plates. 'And you'd better re-do next week's rota,' she added, applying the ice pack gingerly to her left eye first, 'because there isn't a concealer in the world that's going to cover up this mess. I'm not going to have much chance of going unnoticed on surveillance with two black eyes.'

'Robin,' said Strike yet again, 'I'm so fucking sorry. I was a tit, I just . . . What d'you want, vodka, whisky—?'

'Whisky,' she said. 'On the rocks.'

Strike poured both of them a triple measure.

'I'm sorry,' he said, yet again, while Robin took a welcome gulp of Scotch, then began helping herself to curry. Strike sat down on the fake leather sofa opposite the desk. 'Hurting you's the last thing – there's no excuse for – I saw red, I lost it. My father's other kids have been pestering me for months to go to that fucking party,' said Strike, running his hand through the thick, curly hair that never looked disarranged. He felt she was owed the whole story now: the reason, if not the excuse, that he'd fucked up so badly. 'They wanted us to get a group photo taken together for a present. Then Al tells me Rokeby's got prostate cancer – which doesn't seem to have prevented him having four hundred mates over for a good old knees-up . . . I ripped up the invitation without registering where the thing was being held. I should've realised Oakden was up to something, I took my eye off the ball, and—'

He downed half his drink in one.

'There's no excuse for trying to punch him, but everything – these last few months – Rokeby rang me in February. First time ever. Tried to bribe me into meeting him.'

'He tried to *bribe* you?' said Robin, pressing the ice pack to her other eye, remembering the shouted 'go fuck yourself' from the inner office, on Valentine's Day.

'As good as,' said Strike. 'He said he was open to suggestions for helping me out . . . well, it's forty years too fucking late for that.'

Strike downed the rest of his whisky, reached for the bottle and poured the same again into his glass.

'When did you last see him?' Robin asked.

'When I was eighteen. I've met him twice,' Strike said. 'First time was when I was a kid. My mother tried to ambush him with me, outside a recording studio.'

He'd only ever told Charlotte this. Her family was at least as dysfunctional and peculiar as his own, riven with scenes that to other people might've been epoch defining – 'it was a month before Daddy torched Mummy's portrait in the hall, and the panelling caught fire, and the fire brigade came, and we all had to be evacuated via the upstairs windows' – but to the Campbells were so normalised they seemed routine.

'I thought he wanted to see me,' said Strike. The shock of what he'd done to Robin, and the whisky scorching his throat, had liberated memories he usually kept locked up tight inside him. 'I was seven. I was so fucking excited. I wanted to look smart, so he'd be – so he'd be proud of me. Told my mum to put me in my best trousers. We got outside this studio – my mother had music industry contacts, someone had tipped her off he was going to be there – and they wouldn't let us in. I thought there'd been some mistake. The bloke on the door obviously didn't realise my dad wanted to see me.'

Strike drank again. The curry lay cooling between them.

'My mother kicked off. They were threatening her when the band's manager got out of his car behind us. He knew who my mother was and he didn't want a public scene. He took us inside, into a room away from the studio.

'The manager tried to tell her it was a dumb move, turning up. If she wanted more money, she should go through lawyers. That's when I realised my father hadn't invited us at all. She was just trying to force her way in. I started crying,' said Strike roughly. 'Just wanted to go . . .

'And then, while my mother and Rokeby's manager are going at it hammer and tongs, Rokeby walks in. He heard shouting on the way back from the bathroom. Probably just done a line; I realised that later. He was already wound up when he came in the room.

'And I tried to smile,' said Strike. 'Snot all over my face. I didn't want him to think I was a whiner. I'd been imagining a hug. "There you are, at last." But he looked at me like I was nothing. Some fan's kid, in too-short trousers. My trousers were always too fucking short . . . I grew too fast . . .

'Then he clocked my mother, and he twigged. They started rowing. I can't remember everything they said. I was a kid. The gist was how dare she butt in, she had his lawyer's contact details, he was paying enough, it was her problem if she pissed it all away, and then he said, "This was a fucking accident." I thought he meant, he'd come to the studio accidentally or something. But then he looked at me, and I realised, he meant me. *I* was the accident.'

'Oh God, Cormoran,' said Robin quietly.

'Well,' said Strike, 'you've got to give him points for honesty. He walked out. We went home.

'For a while afterwards, I held out a bit of hope he'd regretted what he'd said. It was hard to let go of the idea he wanted to see me, deep down. But nothing.'

While the sun was far from setting, the room was becoming steadily darker. The high buildings of Denmark Street cast the outer office into shadow at this time of the evening, and neither detective had turned on the interior lights.

'Second time we met,' said Strike, 'I made an appointment with his management. I was eighteen. Just got into Oxford. We hadn't touched any of Rokeby's money for years. They'd been back to court to put restrictions on what my mother could do with it, because she was a nightmare with cash, just threw it away. Anyway, unbeknownst to me, my aunt and uncle had informed Rokeby I'd got into Oxford. My mother got a letter saying he had no obligations to me now I'd turned eighteen, but reminding her I could use the money that had been accumulating in the bank account.

'I arranged to see him at his manager's office. He was there with his long-time lawyer, Peter Gillespie. Got a smile off Rokeby this time. Well, I was off his hands financially now, but old enough to talk to the press. Oxford had clearly been a bit of a shock to him. He'd probably hoped, with a background like mine, I'd slide quietly out of sight for ever.

'He congratulated me on getting into Oxford and said I had a nice little nest egg all built up now, because my mother hadn't spent any of it for six, seven years.

'I told him,' said Strike, 'to stick his fucking money up his arse and set fire to it. Then I walked out.

'Self-righteous little prick, I was. Didn't occur to me that Ted and Joan were going to have to stump up if Rokeby didn't, which is what they did . . . I only realised that later. But I didn't take their money long. After my mother died, midway through my second year, I left Oxford and enlisted.'

'Didn't he contact you after your mum died?' asked Robin quietly.

'No,' said Strike, 'or if he did, I never got it. He sent me a note when my leg got blown off. I'll bet that put the fear of God into him, hearing I'd been blown up. Probably worried sick about what the press might make of it all.

'Once I was out of Selly Oak, he tried to give me the money again. He'd found out I was trying to start the agency. Charlotte's friends knew a couple of his kids, which is how he got wind of it.'

Robin felt something flip in her stomach at the sound of Charlotte's name. Strike so rarely acknowledged her existence.

'I said no, at first. I didn't want to take the money, but no other fucker wanted to lend a one-legged ex-soldier without a house or any savings enough money to set up a detective agency. I told his prick of a lawyer I'd take just enough money to start the agency and pay it back in instalments. Which I did.'

'That money was yours all along?' said Robin, who could remember Gillespie pressing Strike for repayment every few weeks, when she'd first joined the agency.

'Yeah, but I didn't want it. Resented even having to borrow a bit of it.'

'Gillespie acted as though—'

'You get people like Gillespie round the rich and famous,' said Strike. 'His whole ego was invested in being my father's enforcer. The bastard was half in love with my old man, or with his fame, I dunno. I was pretty blunt on the phone about what I thought about Rokeby, and Gillespie couldn't forgive it. I'd insisted on a loan agreement between us, and Gillespie was going to hold me to it, to punish me for telling him exactly what I thought of the pair of them.'

Strike pushed himself off the sofa, which made its usual farting noises as he did so, and began helping himself to curry. When they both had full plates, he went to fetch two glasses of water. He'd already got through a third of the whisky.

'Cormoran,' said Robin, once he was settled back on the sofa and had started eating. 'You do realise, I'm never going to gossip about your father to other people? I'm not going to talk to *you* about him if you don't want to, but . . . we're partners. You could have told me he was hassling you, and let off steam that way, instead of punching a witness.'

Strike chewed some of his chicken jalfrezi, swallowed, then said quietly,

'Yeah, I know.'

Robin ate a bit of naan. Her bruised face was aching less now: the ice pack and the whisky had both numbed her, in different ways. Nevertheless, it took a minute to marshal the courage to say,

'I saw Charlotte's been hospitalised.'

Strike looked up at her. He knew, of course, that Robin was well aware who Charlotte was. Four years previously, he'd got almost too drunk to walk, and told her a lot more than he'd ever meant to, about the alleged pregnancy Charlotte had insisted was his, which had broken them apart for ever.

'Yeah,' said Strike.

And he told Robin the story of the farewell text messages, and his dash to the public payphone, and how he'd listened until they'd found Charlotte lying in undergrowth in the grounds of her expensive clinic.

'Oh my Christ,' said Robin, setting down her fork. 'When did you know she was alive?'

'Knew for sure two days later, when the press reported it,' said Strike. He heaved himself back out of his chair, topped up Robin's whisky, then poured himself more before sitting back down again. 'But I'd concluded she must be alive before that. Bad news travels faster than good.'

There was a long silence, in which Robin hoped to hear more about how being drawn into Charlotte's suicide attempt, and by the sounds of it, saving her life, had made him feel, but Strike said nothing, merely eating his curry.

'Well,' said Robin at last, 'again, in future, maybe we could try that talking thing, before you die of a stress-induced heart attack or, you know, end up killing someone we need to question?'

Strike grinned ruefully.

'Yeah. We could try that, I s'pose . . . '

Silence closed around them again, a silence that seemed to the slightly drunk Strike to thicken like honey, comforting and sweet, but slightly dangerous if you sank too far into it. Full of whisky, contrition and a powerful feeling he preferred at all times not to dwell upon, he wanted to make some kind of statement about Robin's kindness and her tact, but all the words that occurred to him seemed clumsy and unserviceable: he wanted to express something of the truth, but the truth was dangerous.

How could he say, look, I've tried not to fancy you since you first took off your coat in this office. I try not to give names to what I feel for you, because I already know it's too much, and I want peace from the shit that love brings in its wake. I want to be alone, and unburdened, and free.

But I don't want you to be with anyone else. I don't want some other bastard to persuade you into a second marriage. I like knowing the possibility's there, for us to, maybe . . .

Except it'll go wrong, of course, because it always goes wrong, because if I were the type for permanence, I'd already be married. And when it goes wrong, I'll lose you for good, and this thing we've built together, which is literally the only good part of my life, my vocation, my pride, my greatest achievement, will be forever fucked, because I won't find anyone I enjoy running things with, the way I enjoy running them with you, and everything afterwards will be tainted by the memory of you.

If only she could come inside his head and see what was there, Strike thought, she'd understand that she occupied a unique place in his thoughts and in his affections. He felt he owed her that information, but was afraid that saying it might move this conversation into territory from which it would be difficult to retreat.

But, from second to second, sitting here, now with more than half a bottle of neat whisky inside him, a different spirit seemed to move inside him, asking himself for the first time whether determined solitude was what he really wanted, for evermore.

Joanie reckons you're gonna end up with your business partner. That Robin girl.

All or nothing. See what happens. Except that the stakes involved in making any kind of move would be the highest of his life; higher by far than when he'd staggered across a student party to chat up Charlotte Campbell, when, however much agony he'd endured for her later, he'd risked nothing more than minor humiliation, and a good story to tell.

Robin, who'd eaten as much curry as she could handle, had now resigned herself to not hearing what Strike felt for Charlotte. She supposed it had been a forlorn hope, but it was something she was very keen to know. The neat whisky she'd drunk had given the night a slight fuzziness, like a rain haze, and she felt slightly wistful. She knew that if it hadn't been for the alcohol, she might feel simply unhappy.

'I suppose,' said Strike, with the fatalistic daring of a trapeze artist, swinging out into the spotlight, only black air beneath him, 'Ilsa's been trying to matchmake, your end, as well?'

Across the room, sitting in shadow, Robin experienced something like an electric shock through her body. That Strike would even allude to a third party's idea of them being romantically involved was unprecedented. Didn't they always act as though nothing of the sort could be further from anyone's mind? Hadn't they always pretended certain dangerous moments had never happened, such as when she'd modelled that green dress for him, and hugged him while wearing her wedding dress, and felt the idea of running away together pass through his mind, as well as hers?

'Yes,' she said, at last. 'I've been worried . . . well, embarrassed about it, because I haven't . . .'

'No,' said Strike quickly, 'I never thought *you* were . . .'

She waited for him to say something else, suddenly acutely aware, as she'd never been before, that a bed lay directly above them, barely two minutes from where they sat. And, like Strike, she thought, everything I've worked and sacrificed for is in jeopardy if I take this conversation to the wrong place. Our relationship will be forever marred by awkwardness and embarrassment.

But worse than that, by far: she was scared of giving herself away. The feelings she'd been denying to Matthew, to her mother, to Ilsa and to herself must remain hidden.

'Well, sorry,' said Strike.

What did that mean, Robin wondered, her heart thumping very hard: she took another large gulp of whisky before she said,

'Why are you apologising? You're not—'

'She's *my* friend.'

'She's mine, too, now,' said Robin. 'I . . . don't think she can help herself. She sees two friends of the opposite sex getting on . . .'

'Yeah,' said Strike, all antennae now: was that all they were? Friends of the opposite sex? Not wanting to leave the subject of men and women, he said,

'You never told me how mediation went. How come he settled, after dragging it out all this time?'

'Sarah's pregnant. They want to get married before she has it . . . or before she gets too big for a designer dress, knowing Sarah.'

'Shit,' said Strike quietly, wondering how upset she was. He couldn't read her tone or see her clearly: the office was now full of shadow, but he didn't want to turn on the lights. 'Is he – did you expect that?'

'S'pose I should have,' said Robin, with a smile Strike couldn't see, but which hurt her bruised face. 'She was probably getting annoyed with the way he was dragging out our divorce. When he was about to end their affair, she left an earring in our bed for me to find. Probably getting worried he wasn't going to propose, so she forgot to take her pill. It's the one way women can control men, isn't it?' she said, momentarily forgetting Charlotte, and the baby she claimed to have lost. 'I've got a feeling she'd just told him she was pregnant when he cancelled mediation the first time. Matthew said it was an accident . . . maybe he didn't want to have it, when she first told him . . . '

'Do you want kids?' Strike asked Robin.

'I used to think so,' said Robin slowly. 'Back when I thought Matthew and I were . . . you know. For ever.'

As she said it, memories of old imaginings came to her: of a family group that had never existed, but which had once seemed quite vivid to her. The night that Matthew had proposed, she'd formed a clear mental picture of the pair of them with three children (a compromise between his family, where there had been two children, and her own, which had had four). She'd seen it all quite clearly: Matthew cheering on a young son who was learning to play rugby, as he'd done himself; Matthew watching his own little girl onstage, playing Mary in the school nativity play. It struck her now how very conventional her imaginings had been, and how much Matthew's expectations had become her own.

Sitting here in the darkness with Strike, Robin thought that Matthew would, in fact, be a very good father to the kind of child he'd be expecting: in other words, a little boy who wanted to play rugby, or a little girl who wanted to dance in a tutu. He'd carry their pictures around in his wallet, he'd get involved at their schools, he'd hug them when they needed it, he'd care about their homework. He wasn't devoid of kindness: he felt guilty when he did wrong. It was simply that what Matthew considered right was so heavily coloured by what other people did, what other people considered acceptable and desirable.

'But I don't know, any more,' said Robin, after a short pause.

'I can't see myself having kids while doing this job. I think I'd be torn . . . and I don't ever want to be torn again. Matthew was always trying to guilt me out of this career: I didn't earn enough, I worked too many hours, I took too many risks . . . but I love it,' said Robin, with a trace of fierceness, 'and I don't want to apologise for that any more . . .

'What about you?' she asked Strike. 'Do *you* want children?'

'No,' said Strike.

Robin laughed.

'What's funny?'

'I give a whole soul-searching speech on the subject and you're just: *no*.'

'I shouldn't be here, should I?' said Strike, out of the darkness. 'I'm an accident. I'm not inclined to perpetuate the mistake.'

There was a pause, then Robin said, with asperity,

'Strike, that's just bloody self-indulgent.'

'Why?' said Strike, startled into a laugh. When he'd said the same to Charlotte, she'd both understood and agreed with him. Early in her teens, her drunken mother had told Charlotte she'd considered aborting her.

'Because . . . for God's sake, you can't let your whole life be coloured by the circumstances of your conception! If everyone who was conceived accidentally stopped having kids—'

'We'd all be better off, wouldn't we?' said Strike robustly. 'The world's overpopulated as it is. Anyway, none of the kids I know make me particularly keen to have my own.'

'You like Jack.'

'I do, but that's one kid out of God knows how many. Dave Polworth's kids – you know who Polworth is?'

'Your best mate,' said Robin.

'He's my oldest mate,' Strike corrected her. 'My best mate . . .'

For a split-second he wondered whether he was going to say it, but the whisky had lifted the guard he usually kept upon himself: why not say it, why not let go?

'... is you.'

Robin was so amazed, she couldn't speak. Never, in four years, had Strike come close to telling her what she was to him. Fondness had had to be deduced from offhand comments, small kindnesses, awkward silences or gestures forced from him under stress. She'd only once before felt as she did now, and the unexpected gift that had engendered the feeling had been a sapphire and diamond ring, which she'd left behind when she walked out on the man who'd given it to her.

She wanted to make some kind of return, but for a moment or two, her throat felt too constricted.

'I ... well, the feeling's mutual,' she said, trying not to sound too happy.

Over on the sofa, Strike dimly registered that somebody was on the metal staircase below their floor. Sometimes the graphic designer in the office beneath worked late. Mostly Strike was savouring the pleasure it had given him to hear Robin return his declaration of affection.

And now, full of whisky, he remembered holding her on the stairs at her wedding. This was the closest they'd come to that moment in nearly two years, and the air seemed thick with unspoken things, and again, he felt as though he stood on a small platform, ready to swing out into the unknown. *Leave it there*, said the surly self that coveted a solitary attic space, and freedom, and peace. *Now*, breathed the flickering demon the whisky had unleashed, and like Robin a few minutes previously, Strike was conscious that they were sitting mere feet from a double bed.

Footsteps reached the landing outside the glass outer door. Before either Strike or Robin could react, it had opened.

'Is the power oot?' said Barclay, and he flicked on the light. After a moment in which the three blinked at each other in surprise, Barclay said,

'You're a friggin' genius, R – the fuck happened tae yer face?'

59

The warlike Britonesse . . .
. . . with such vncouth welcome did receaue
Her fayned Paramour, her forced guest,
That being forst his saddle soone to leaue,
Him selfe he did of his new loue deceaue:
And made him selfe then ample of his follie.
Which done, she passed forth not taking leaue,
And left him now as sad, as whilome iollie,
Well warned to beware with whom he dar'd to dallie.

Edmund Spenser
The Faerie Queene

Blinking in the bright light, Robin reached again for the ice pack.

'Strike hit me. Accidentally.'

'Jesus,' said Barclay. 'Wouldnae wanna see what he can do deliberately. How'd that happen?'

'My face got in the way of his elbow,' said Robin.

'Huh,' said Barclay, hungrily eyeing the almost empty curry cartons, 'what wus that? Compensation?'

'Exactly,' said Robin.

'Tha' why neither of yiz have been answerin' yer phones fer the last three hours?'

'Shit, sorry, Sam,' said Robin, pulling out her mobile and looking at it. She'd had fifteen missed calls from Barclay since muting her mother in the American Bar. She was also pleased to see that she'd missed a couple of texts from Morris, one of which seemed to have a picture attached.

'Beyond the call of duty to come in person,' said the slightly drunk Strike. He wasn't sure whether he was more glad or annoyed that Barclay had interrupted, but on balance, he thought annoyance was uppermost.

'The wife's at her mother's wi' the bairn overnight,' said Barclay. 'So I thought I'd come deliver the good news in person.'

He helped himself to a poppadum and sat down on the arm of the sofa at the other end to Strike.

'I've found oot what SB gets up tae in Stoke Newington. All down tae Robin. You ready for this?'

'What?' said Strike, looking between Barclay and Robin. 'When—?'

'Earlier,' said Robin, 'before I met you.'

'Rang the doorbell,' said Barclay, 'said I'd bin recommended by SB, wondered whether she could help me oot. She didnae believe me. I had to get a foot in the door to stop her slammin' it on me. Then she says SB told her a Scottish guy talked him doon off Tower Bridge the other day.

'So I decide it's cut our losses time,' said Barclay. 'I said, yeah, that wuz me. I'm a friend. We know what ye're up to in here. You're gonnae wanna talk to me, if ye care aboot your client.

'So she let me in.'

Barclay ate a bit of poppadum.

'Sorry, starvin'. Anyway, she takes me in the back room, and there it all is.'

'There what all is?'

'Giant playpen she's knocked up, out o' some foam an' MDF,' said Barclay, grinning. 'Big old changin' mat. Stack of adult nappies. Johnson's baby powder.'

Strike appeared to have been struck momentarily speechless. Robin began to laugh, but stopped quickly, because it made her face hurt.

'Poor old SB gets aff on bein' a baby. She's only got one other client, that guy at the gym. Doesnae need any more, because SB pays her so much. She dresses 'em up. Changes 'em. Powders their fucking arses—'

'You're having a laugh,' said Strike. 'This can't be real.'

'It is real,' said Robin, with the ice pack pressed to her face. 'It's called . . . hang on . . . '

She brought up the list of paraphilias on her phone again.

'Autonepiophilia. "Being aroused by the thought of oneself as an infant."'

'How the hell did you—?'

'I was watching the old people being wheeled out of the nursing home,' said Robin. 'Morris said they were like kids, that some of them were probably wearing nappies and it just . . . *clicked*. I saw her buying a ton of baby powder and dummies in the supermarket, but we've never once seen a child go in or out of that house. Then there was that patting on the head business, like the men were little kids . . .'

Strike remembered following the gym manager home, the man's hand over his lower face as he left Elinor Dean's house, as though he'd had something protruding from his mouth that he wanted to conceal.

'. . . and big boxes being delivered, of something really light,' Robin was saying.

'That'll be the adult nappies,' said Barclay. 'Anyway . . . she's no' a bad woman. Made me a cup of tea. She kens aboot the blackmail, but here's something interestin': she and SB don't think Shifty knows what's really goin' on inside that hoose.'

'How come?'

'The gym manager let it slip tae Shifty he knew a big man

at Shifty's company. SB and the gym guy sometimes go in the playpen together, see. Like it's a nurs – like it's a nurser—'

Barclay suddenly broke into peals of laughter and Strike followed suit. Robin pressed the ice pack to her face and joined in. For a minute, all three of them roared with laughter at the mental image of the two men in nappies, sitting in their MDF playpen.

'—like it's a nursery,' said Barclay in a falsetto, wiping tears out of his eyes. 'Fuck me, it takes all sorts, eh? Anyway, the tit at the gym lets this slip, an' Shifty, knowin' old SB never went tae a gym in his life, an' that he lives on the other side o' London, probes a wee bit, and notices the other guy gettin' uncomfortable. So Shifty follows SB. Watches him going in and oot Elinor's place. Draws the obvious conclusion: she's a hooker.

'Shifty then walks intae SB's office, closes the door, gives him Elinor's address, and says he kens what's goin' on in there. SB was shittin' himself, but he's no fool. He reckons Shifty thinks it's just straight sex, but he's worried Shifty might do more diggin'. See, SB found Elinor online, advertisin' her services in some dark corner o' the net. SB's scared Shifty'll go looking for whut she really does if he denies it's sex, an' if anyone finds oot whut really goes on in there, SB's gonna be straight back up Tower Bridge.

'So, that bit's no' so funny,' said Barclay, more soberly. 'The guy at the gym only came clean tae SB and Elinor a coupla months ago, about talking tae Shifty. He's aboot ready tae kill himself, for what he's done. Elinor's taken her ad down, but the internet never forgets, so that's no bloody use . . .

'The worst thing, Elinor says, is Shifty himself is a right cock. SB's told her all aboot him. Apparently Shifty takes his coke habit tae work and he's always feelin' up his PA, but SB cannae do anything about it, for fear of retribution. So,' said

Barclay, 'what are we gonnae do, eh? Tell the board SB's suit troosers dinnae fit him properly because he's wearin' a nappy underneath?'

Strike didn't smile. The amount of whisky he'd consumed didn't particularly help his mental processes. It was Robin who spoke first.

'Well, we can tell the board everything, and accept that's going to ruin a few lives . . . or we can let them terminate our contract without telling them what's going on, and accept that Shifty's going to keep blackmailing SB . . . or . . . '

'Yeah,' said Strike heavily, 'that's the question, isn't it? Where's the third option, where Shifty gets his comeuppance and SB doesn't end up in the Thames?'

'It sounds,' said Robin to Barclay, 'as though Elinor would back SB up, if he claimed it was just an affair? Of course, SB's wife mightn't be happy.'

'Aye, Elinor'd back him up,' said Barclay. 'It's in her interests.'

'I'd like to nail Shifty,' said Strike. 'That'd please the client no end, if we helped them get rid of Shifty without the company's name getting splashed all over the papers . . . which it definitely will if it gets out their CEO likes having his arse powdered . . .

'If that PA's being sexually harassed,' Strike said, 'and watching him do coke at work, why isn't she complaining?'

'Fear of not being believed?' Robin suggested. 'Of losing her job?'

'Could you,' Strike said to Robin, 'ring Morris for me? He'll still have the girl's contact details. And, Barclay,' Strike added, getting up from the sofa on the third attempt, and heading for the inner office, 'come in here, we're going to have to change next week's rota. Robin can't follow people looking like she just did three rounds with Tyson Fury.'

The other two went into Strike's office. Robin stayed sitting at Pat's desk for a moment, thinking not about what Barclay had just told them, but about the moments before he'd arrived, when she and Strike had been sitting in semi-darkness. The memory of Strike telling her she was his best friend made her heart feel immeasurably lightened, as though something she hadn't realised was weighing on it had been removed for ever.

After a moment's pleasurable savouring of this feeling, she pulled out her mobile, and opened the texts Morris had sent her earlier. The first, which had the picture attached, said '**lol**'. The image was of a sign reading: 'Viagra Shipment Stolen. Cops Looking For Gang of Hardened Criminals.' The second text said, '**Not funny?**'

'No,' Robin muttered. 'Not funny.'

Getting to her feet, she pressed Morris's number, and began to clear up the curry one-handed, while she held the phone to her ear.

'Evening,' said Morris, after a couple of rings. 'Calling to tell me you've found a hardened criminal?'

'Are you driving?' asked Robin, ignoring the witticism.

'On foot. Just seen the old folks' home locked up for the night. I'm actually right by the office, I'm on my way to relieve Hutchins. He's outside the Ivy, keeping an eye on Miss Jones's boyfriend.'

'Well, we need the details of Shifty's PA,' said Robin.

'What? Why?'

'We've found out what he's blackmailing SB about, but,' she hesitated, imagining the jokes she'd have to hear at SB's expense, if she told Morris what Elinor Dean was doing for him, 'it's nothing illegal and he's not hurting anyone. We want to talk to Shifty's PA again, so we need her contact details.'

'No, I don't think we should go back to her,' said Morris. 'Bad idea.'

'Why?' Robin asked, as she dropped the foil tins into the pedal bin, suppressing her frown because it made her bruised face ache.

'Because ... fuck's sake,' said Morris, who usually avoided swearing to Robin. 'You were the one who said we shouldn't use her.'

Behind Robin, in the inner office, Barclay laughed at something Strike had said. For the third time that evening, Robin had a feeling of impending trouble.

'Saul,' she said, 'you aren't still seeing her, are you?'

He didn't answer immediately. Robin picked up the plates from the desk and put them in the sink, waiting for his answer.

'No, of course I'm not,' he said, with an attempt at a laugh. 'I just think this is a bad idea. You were the one who said, before, that she had too much to lose—'

'But we wouldn't be asking her to entrap him or set him up this time—'

'I'll need to think about this,' said Morris.

Robin put the knives and forks into the sink, too.

'Saul, this isn't up for debate. We need her contact details.'

'I don't know whether I kept them,' said Morris, and Robin knew he was lying. 'Where's Strike right now?'

'Denmark Street,' said Robin. Not wanting another sly joke about her and Strike being together after dark, she purposely didn't say she was there, too.

'OK, I'll ring him,' said Morris, and before Robin could say anything else, he'd hung up.

The whisky she'd drunk was still having a slightly anaesthetic effect. Robin knew that if she were entirely sober, she'd be feeling still more incensed at yet another example of

Morris treating her not as a partner in the firm, but as Strike's secretary.

Turning on the taps in the cramped kitchen area, she began rinsing off the plates and forks, and as curry sauce dripped down the drain, her thoughts drifted again to those moments before Barclay had arrived, while she and Strike had still been sitting in semi-darkness.

Out on Charing Cross Road, a car passed, blaring Rita Ora's 'I Will Never Let You Down', and softly, under her breath, Robin sang along:

'Tell me baby what we gonna do
I'll make it easy, got a lot to lose . . . '

Putting the plug into the sink, she began to fill it, squirting washing-up liquid on top of the cutlery. Singing, her eyes fell on the unopened vodka Strike had bought, but which neither of them had touched. She thought of Oakden stealing vodka at Margot's barbecue . . .

'You've been tired of watching me
forgot to have a good time . . . '

. . . and claiming that he hadn't spiked the punch. Yet Gloria had vomited . . . At the very moment Robin drew breath into her lungs to call to Strike, and tell him her new idea, two hands closed on her waist.

Twice in Robin's life, a man had attacked her from behind: without conscious thought, she simultaneously stamped down hard with her high heel on the foot of the man behind her, threw back her head, smashing it into his face, grabbed a knife in the sink and spun around as the grip at her waist disappeared.

'FUCK!' bellowed Morris.

She hadn't heard him coming up the stairs over the noise of water splashing into the sink and her own singing. Morris was now doubled up, hands clamped over his nose.

'FUCK!' he shouted again, taking his hands away from his face, to reveal that his nose was bleeding. He hopped backwards, the imprint of her stiletto imprinted in his shoe, and collapsed onto the sofa.

'What's going on?' said Strike, emerging at speed from the inner office and looking from Morris on the sofa to Robin, who was still holding the knife. She turned off the taps, breathing hard.

'He grabbed me,' she said, as Barclay emerged from the inner room behind Strike. 'I didn't hear him coming.'

'It – was – a – fucking – *joke*,' said Morris, examining the blood smeared on his hands. 'I only meant to make you jump – fuck's *sake*—'

But adrenalin and whisky had suddenly unleashed an anger in Robin such as she hadn't felt since the night she'd left Matthew. Light-headed, she advanced on Morris.

'Would you sneak up on Strike and grab him round the waist? D'you creep up on Barclay and hug him? *D'you send either of them pictures of your dick?*'

There was a silence.

'You bitch,' said Morris, the back of his hand pressed to his nostrils. 'You said you wouldn't—'

'He did what?' said Strike.

'Sent me a dick pic,' snapped the furious Robin, and turning back to Morris, she said, 'I'm not some sixteen-year-old work experience girl who's scared of telling you to stop. I don't want your hands on me, OK? I don't want you kissing me—'

'He sent you—?' began Strike.

'I didn't tell you because you were so stressed,' said Robin.

'Joan was dying, you were up and down to Cornwall, you didn't need the grief, but I'm done. I'm not working with him any more. I want him gone.'

'Christ's sake,' said Morris again, dabbing at his nose, 'it was a *joke*—'

'Ye need tae learn tae read the fuckin' room, mate,' said Barclay, who was standing against the wall, arms folded, and seemed to be enjoying himself.

'You can't fucking fire me over—'

'You're a subcontractor,' said Strike. 'We're not renewing your contract. Your non-disclosure agreement remains in operation. One word of anything you've found out working here, and I'll make sure you never get another detective job. Now get the fuck out of this office.'

Wild-eyed, Morris stood up, still bleeding from his left nostril.

'Fine. You want to keep her on because you've got a hard-on for her, fine.'

Strike took a step forwards; Morris nearly fell over the sofa, backing away.

'Fine,' he said again.

He turned and walked straight out of the office, slamming the glass door behind him. While the door vibrated, and Morris's footsteps clanged away down the metal stairs, Barclay pushed himself off the wall, plucked the knife Robin was still holding out of her hand and went to drop it into the sink with the dirty crockery.

'Never liked that tosser,' he said.

Strike and Robin looked at each other, then at the worn carpet, where a couple of drops of Morris's blood still glistened.

'One all, then,' said Strike, clapping his hands together. 'What say, first to break Barclay's nose wins the night?'

PART SIX

So past the twelue Months forth, and their dew places found.

Edmund Spenser
The Faerie Queene

60

Fortune, the foe of famous cheuisaunce
Seldome (said Guyon) yields to vertue aide,
But in her way throwes mischiefe and mischaunce,
Whereby her course is stopt, and passage staid.

Edmund Spenser
The Faerie Queene

What would have happened had Sam Barclay not opened the door that evening and switched on the light was a question that preoccupied both detective partners over the weekend, each of them re-running the conversation in their head, wondering what the other was thinking, and whether too much had been said, or given away.

Sober now, Strike had to be glad he hadn't done what whisky had been urging him to do. Had he acted on that alcohol-fuelled impulse, he might now be in a state of bitter remorse, with no way back to the friendship that was unique in his life. Yet in his free moments, he wondered whether Robin had known how dangerously close he'd come to pushing the conversation into territory that had previously been fenced around with barbed wire, or that, seconds before Barclay flicked the light switch, Strike had been trying to remember when he'd last changed his sheets.

Robin, meanwhile, had woken on Sunday morning with

her face aching as though it had been trodden on, a slight hangover, and a volatile mixture of pleasure and anxiety. She went back over everything she'd said to Strike, hoping she hadn't betrayed any of those feelings she habitually denied, even to herself. The memory of him telling her she was his best friend caused a little spurt of happiness every time she returned to it, but as the day wore on, and her bruising worsened, she wished she'd been brave enough to ask him directly how he now felt about Charlotte Campbell.

An image of Charlotte hung permanently in Robin's head these days, like a shadowy portrait she'd never wanted hung. The picture had acquired shape and form in the four years since they'd passed on the stairs in the Denmark Street office, because of the many details Ilsa had given her, and the snippets she'd read in the press. Last night, though, that image had become stark and fixed: a darkly romantic vision of a lost and dying love, breathing her final words in Strike's ear as she lay among trees.

And this was, however you looked at it, an extraordinarily powerful image. Strike had once, when extremely drunk, told Robin that Charlotte was the most beautiful woman he'd ever seen, and as she hovered between life and death, that beautiful woman had chosen to contact Strike, to tell him she loved him still. What did prosaic Robin Ellacott have to offer that was in any way equal to such high-stakes drama, such extremity of emotion? An up-to-date rota, neatly docketed invoices and cups of strong tea? Doubtless because of the pain in her face, Robin's mood vacillated between diminishing cheerfulness and a tendency to brood. Finally, she gave herself a stern talking to: Strike had given her an unprecedented assurance of affection, and she'd never have to see Saul Morris again, and she should be delighted about both.

Predictably, it was Pat who took the sudden firing of Saul Morris hardest. Strike delivered the news on Monday morning, as he and the secretary narrowly missed colliding in the doorway onto Denmark Street, Strike on his way out, Pat on her way in. Both of them were preparing for the ingestion of nicotine, Pat having just taken out the electronic cigarette she used during work hours, Strike already holding the Benson & Hedges he rarely smoked in the office.

'Morning,' said Strike. 'I've left a note on your desk, couple of things I'd like you to do while I'm out. Robin'll be in at ten. Oh—'

He'd taken a couple of steps before turning back.

'—and can you calculate Morris's pay up to Friday and transfer it into his account right away? He's not coming back.'

He didn't wait for a reaction, so it was Robin who took the brunt of their secretary's disappointment when she arrived at ten to ten. Pat had Radio Two playing, but turned it off the moment the door handle turned.

'Morning. Why – what 'appened to you?' said Pat.

Robin's face looked worse, two days on, than it had on Saturday. While the swelling had subsided, both eyes were ringed in dark grey tinged with red.

'It was an accident. I bumped into something,' said Robin, stripping off her coat and hanging it on a peg. 'So I won't be on surveillance this week.'

She took a book out of her handbag and crossed to the kettle, holding it. She hadn't particularly enjoyed the covert staring on the Tube that morning, but wasn't going to mention Strike's elbow to Pat, because she tried, wherever possible, not to fuel Pat's antipathy for her partner.

'Why won't Saul be coming back?' Pat demanded.

'He didn't work out,' said Robin, her back to Pat as she took down two mugs.

'What d'you mean?' said Pat indignantly. 'He caught that man who was having it away with the nanny. He always kept his paperwork up to date, which is more'n you can say for that Scottish nutter.'

'I know,' said Robin. 'But he wasn't a great team player, Pat.'

Pat took a deep drag of nicotine vapour, frowning.

'He,' she nodded towards the empty chair where Strike usually sat, 'could take a few lessons from Morris!'

Robin knew perfectly well that it wasn't Pat's decision who the partners hired and fired, but unlike Strike, she also thought that in such a small team, Pat deserved the truth.

'It wasn't Cormoran who wanted him gone,' she said, turning to face the secretary, 'it was me.'

'You!' said Pat, astounded. 'I thought the pair of you were keen on each other!'

'No. I didn't like him. Apart from anything else, he sent me a picture of his erect penis at Christmas.'

Pat's deeply lined face registered an almost comical dismay.

'In . . . in the post?'

Robin laughed.

'What, tucked inside a Christmas card? No. By text.'

'You didn't—?'

'Ask for it? No,' said Robin, no longer smiling. 'He's a creep, Pat.'

She turned back to the kettle. The untouched bottle of vodka was still standing beside the sink. As Robin's eyes fell on it, she remembered the idea that had occurred to her on Saturday night, shortly before Morris's hands closed around her waist. After giving the secretary her coffee, she carried her own into the inner office, along with the book she'd taken from her bag. Pat called after her,

'Shall I update the rota, or will you?'

'I'll do it,' said Robin, closing the door, but instead, she called Strike.

'Morning,' he said, answering on the second ring.

'Hi. I forgot to tell you an idea I had on Saturday night.'

'Go on.'

'It's about Gloria Conti. Why did she vomit in the bathroom at Margot's barbecue, if Oakden didn't spike the punch?'

'Because he's a liar, and he *did* spike the punch?' suggested Strike. He was currently in the same Islington square that Robin had patrolled on Friday, but he paused now and reached for his cigarettes, eyes on the central garden, which today was deserted. Beds densely planted with purple pansies looked like velvet cloaks spread upon the glistening grass.

'Or did she throw up because she was pregnant?' said Robin.

'I thought,' said Strike, after a pause while lighting a cigarette, 'that only happens in the mornings? Isn't that why it's called—'

On the point of saying 'morning sickness', Strike remembered the expectant wife of an old army friend, who'd been hospitalised for persistent, round-the-clock vomiting.

'My cousin threw up any time of the day when she was pregnant,' said Robin. 'She couldn't stand certain food smells. And Gloria was at a barbecue.'

'Right,' said Strike, who was suddenly remembering the odd notion that had occurred to him after talking to the Bayliss sisters. Robin's theory struck him as stronger than his. In fact, his idea was weakened if Robin's was true.

'So,' he said, 'you're thinking it might've been Gloria who—'

'—had the abortion at the Bride Street clinic? Yes,' said Robin. 'And that Margot helped her arrange it. Irene mentioned Gloria being closeted in Margot's consulting room, remember? While Irene was left on reception?'

The lilac bush in the central garden was casting out such a heavy scent that Strike could smell it even over the smoke of his cigarette.

'I think you could be on to something here,' said Strike slowly.

'I also thought this might explain—'

'Why Gloria doesn't want to talk to us?'

'Well, yes. Apart from it being a traumatic memory, her husband might not know what happened,' said Robin. 'Where are you just now?'

'Islington,' said Strike. 'I'm about to have a crack at Mucky Ricci.'

'What?' said Robin, startled.

'Been thinking about it over the weekend,' said Strike, who, unlike Robin, had had no time off, but had run surveillance on Shifty and Miss Jones's boyfriend. 'We're nearly ten months into our year, and we've got virtually nothing. If he's demented, obviously it'll be no-go, but you never know, I could be able to get something out of him. He might even,' said Strike, 'get a kick out of reliving the good old days . . . '

'And what if his sons find out?'

'He can't talk, or not properly. I'm banking on him being unable to tell them I've been in. Look,' said Strike, in no particular hurry to hang up, because he wanted to finish his cigarette, and would rather do it talking to Robin, 'Betty Fuller thinks Ricci killed her, I could tell. So did Tudor Athorn; he told his nephew so, and they were the kind of people who were plugged into local gossip and knew about local low life.

'I keep going back to the thing Shanker said, when I told him about Margot vanishing without a trace. "Professional job." When you take a step back and look at it,' said Strike, now down to the last centimetre of his cigarette, 'it seems borderline impossible for every trace of her to have disappeared, unless someone with plenty of practice handled it.'

'Creed had practice,' said Robin quietly.

'D'you know what I did last night?' said Strike, ignoring this interjection. 'Looked up Kara Wolfson's birth certificate online.'

'Why? Oh,' said Robin, and Strike could hear her smiling, 'star sign?'

'Yeah. I know it breaks the means before motive rule,' he added, before Robin could point it out, 'but it struck me that someone might've told Margot about Kara's murder. Doctors know things, don't they? In and out of people's houses, having confidential consultations. They're like priests. They hear secrets.'

'You were checking whether Kara was a Scorpio,' said Robin. It was a statement rather than a question.

'Exactly. And wondering whether Ricci looked into that party to show his goons which woman they were going to pick off.'

'Well?'

'Well what?'

'*Was* Kara a Scorpio?'

'Oh. No. Taurus – seventeenth of May.'

Strike now heard pages turning at Robin's end of the call.

'Which means, according to Schmidt . . .' said Robin, and there was a brief pause, '. . . she was Cetus.'

'Huh,' said Strike, who'd now finished his cigarette. 'Well, wish me luck. I'm going in.'

'Good l—'

'*Cormoran Strike!*' said somebody gleefully, behind him.

As Strike hung up on Robin, a slender black woman in a cream coat came alongside him, beaming.

'You don't remember me, do you?' she said. 'Selly Oak. I'm—'

'Marjorie!' said Strike, the memory coming back to him. 'Marjorie the physiotherapist. How are you? What're you—?'

'I do a few hours in the old folks' home up the road!' said Marjorie. 'And look at *you*, all famous . . .'

Fuck.

It took Strike twenty-five minutes to extricate himself from her.

'. . . so that's bloody that,' he told Robin later at the office. 'I pretended I was in the area to visit my accountant, but if she's working at St Peter's, there's no chance of us getting in to see Ricci.'

'No chance of *you* getting in there—'

'I've already told you,' said Strike sharply. The state of Robin's face was a visible warning against recklessness, of the perils of failing to think through consequences. 'You're not going anywhere near him.'

'I've got Miss Jones on the line,' Pat called from the outer office.

'Put her through to me,' said Robin, as Strike mouthed 'thanks'.

Robin talked to Miss Jones while continuing to readjust the rota on her computer, which, given Robin's own temporary unavailability for surveillance, and Morris's permanent absence, was like trying to balance a particularly tricky linear equation. She spent the next forty minutes making vague sounds of agreement whenever Miss Jones paused to draw breath. Their client's objective, Robin could tell, was staying on the line long enough for Strike to come back to the office. Finally, Robin got rid of her by pretending to get a message from Pat saying Strike would be out all day.

It was her only lie of the day, Robin thought, while Strike and Pat discussed Barclay's expenses in the outer office. Given that Strike was adept himself at avoiding pledging his own word when he didn't want to, he really ought to have noticed that Robin had made no promises whatsoever about staying away from Mucky Ricci.

61

Then when the second watch was almost past,
That brasen dore flew open, and in went Bold
Britomart . . .

Edmund Spenser
The Faerie Queene

In the first week of June, a blind item appeared in the *Metro*, concerning Strike's presence in the American Bar on the night of his father's party.

> Which famous son of a famous father preferred to spend the night of his old man's celebrations brawling in a bar five hundred yards from the party, rather than hobnobbing with his family? Our spies tell us a punch was thrown, and his faithful assistant was unable to *Hold it Back.* A father-son competition for publicity? Dad definitely won this round.

As *Hold it Back* was the name of one of Jonny Rokeby's albums, nobody could really be in much doubt which father and son were in question. A couple of journalists called Strike's office, but as neither he nor Rokeby were disposed to comment, the story fizzled out for lack of details. 'Could've been worse,' was Strike's only comment. 'No photos, no mention of Bamborough. Looks like Oakden's been frightened out of the idea of selling stories about us.'

Feeling slightly guilty, Robin had already scrolled through the pictures of Jonny Rokeby's party on her phone, while on surveillance outside Miss Jones's boyfriend's house. Rokeby's guests, who included celebrities from both Hollywood and the world of rock 'n' roll, had all attended in eighteenth-century costumes. Buried in the middle of all the famous people was a single picture of Rokeby surrounded by six of his seven adult children. Robin recognised Al, grinning from beneath a crooked powdered wig. She could no more imagine Strike there, trussed up in brocade, with patches on his face, than she could imagine him pole-vaulting.

Relieved as she was that Oakden appeared to have given up the idea of discussing the agency with the press, Robin's anxiety mounted as June progressed. The Bamborough case, which mattered to her more than almost anything else, had come to a complete standstill. Gloria Conti had met Anna's request for her cooperation with silence, Steve Douthwaite remained as elusive as ever, Robin had heard no news about the possibility of interviewing Dennis Creed, and Mucky Ricci remained cloistered inside his nursing home, which, owing to the agency's reduced manpower, nobody was watching any more.

Even temporary replacements for Morris were proving impossible to find. Strike had contacted everyone he knew in the Special Investigation Branch, Hutchins had asked his Met contacts, and Robin had canvassed Vanessa, but nobody was showing any interest in joining the agency.

'Summer, isn't it?' said Barclay, as he and Robin crossed paths in the office one Saturday afternoon. 'People don't want tae start a new job, they want a holiday. I ken how they feel.'

Both Barclay and Hutchins had booked weeks off with their

wives and children months in advance, and neither partner could begrudge their subcontractors a break. The result was that by mid-July, Strike and Robin were the only two left working at the agency.

While Strike devoted himself to following Miss Jones's boyfriend, still trying to find out anything that might prove that he was an unsuitable person to have custody of his daughter, Robin was trying to kindle an acquaintance with Shifty's PA, which wasn't proving easy. So far that month, wearing a different wig and coloured contacts each time, Robin had tried to engage her in conversation in a bar, deliberately tripped over her in a nightclub, and followed her into the ladies in Harvey Nichols. While the PA didn't seem to have the slightest idea that it was the same woman opportuning or inconveniencing her, she showed no inclination to chat, let alone confess that her boss was a lech or a coke user.

Having tried and failed to sit next to the PA in a sandwich bar in Holborn one lunchtime, Robin, who today had dark hair and dark brown eyes courtesy of hair chalk and contact lenses, decided the moment had come to try and wheedle information out of a very old man, instead of a pretty young woman.

She hadn't reached this decision lightly, nor did she approach it in any casual spirit. While Robin was vaguely fond of Strike's old friend Shanker, she was under no illusions about how evil a person would have to be to scare a man who'd been steeped in criminal violence since the age of nine. Accordingly, she'd worked out a plan, of which the first step was to have a full and effective disguise. Today's happened to be particularly good: she'd learned a lot about make-up since starting the job with Strike, and she'd sometimes had the satisfaction of seeing her partner double-take before he realised who she was. After checking her reflection carefully in the mirror of a McDonald's bathroom, and reassuring herself that she not only looked utterly unlike Robin Ellacott, but that nobody would guess she'd recently had two black eyes, she set off for the Tube, and just under twenty minutes later, arrived at Angel station.

The garden where the old residents of St Peter's sometimes sat was empty as she passed it, in spite of the warm weather. The pansies were gone, replaced by pink asters and the broad, sunny street where the nursing home lay was almost deserted.

The quotation from St Peter gleamed gold in the sunshine as Robin approached the front door.

. . . it was not with perishable things such as silver or gold that you were redeemed . . . but with the precious blood of Christ . . .

Robin rang the bell. After a few moments, a chubby black-haired woman in the familiar blue uniform opened it.

'Afternoon,' she said, sounding Spanish.

'Hi,' said Robin, her North London accent copied from her friend Vanessa. 'I'm here to visit Enid? I'm her great-granddaughter.'

She'd stored up the only first name she'd heard for any of the old ladies in the home. Her great fear had been that Enid might have died before she got to use it, or that Enid had no family.

'Oh, that's nice,' said the nurse, smiling and gesturing towards a visitors' book just inside the door. 'Sign in, please, and don't forget to sign out when you leave. She's in her room. Might be asleep!'

Robin stepped into a dark, wood-panelled hall. She deliberately hadn't asked which number Enid's room was, because she intended to get lost finding it.

A number of walking frames and a couple of collapsible wheelchairs were lined up against the wall. The hall was dominated by an enormous crucifix facing the door, on which a pallid plaster Jesus hung, his six-pack rendered with startling precision, scarlet blood dripping from hands, feet and the punctures left by his crown of thorns. The home smelled better than Betty Fuller's sheltered accommodation: though there was a definite undertone of old cooking smells, it mingled with that of furniture wax.

Sunlight poured through the fan window behind Robin as she bent over the visitors' book and wrote in the date, the time she'd entered the building and the fake name she'd decided on: *Vanessa Jones*. Over the table where the visitors' book lay hung a board showing the name of each resident. Beside each was a little sliding door, which could be adjusted to show whether the occupant was 'in' or 'out'. Niccolo Ricci was currently – and, Robin suspected, almost permanently – 'in'.

There was a lift, but she chose to take the red-carpeted and wooden-banistered stairs, passing the Trinidadian nurse she'd often seen while on surveillance, who was descending. He smiled and wished her a good afternoon, his arms laden with packs of incontinence pads.

A doorway led off the first landing, a small sign beside it announcing that this way lay bedrooms 1 to 10. Robin set off along the corridor, reading names off doors. Unfortunately, 'Mrs Enid Billings' lived behind door number 2 and, as Robin swiftly discovered, Ricci wasn't on her floor. Aware that this was going to make any claim of having got lost on the way to Enid's room implausible in the extreme, Robin doubled back, and climbed up to the second floor.

A few steps along an identical corridor to the one below, she heard a woman with a strong Polish accent in the distance, and backed hastily into an alcove where a sink and cupboard had been placed.

'D'you need the bathroom? *Do – you – need – the – bathroom, Mister – Ricci?*'

A low moan answered.

'*Yes?*' said the voice. '*Or no?*'

There was a second, answering moan.

'*No?* All right then . . . '

Footsteps grew louder: the nurse was about to pass the alcove, so Robin stepped boldly out from it, smiling.

'Just washing my hands,' she told the approaching nurse, who was blonde and flat-footed and merely nodded as she passed, apparently preoccupied with other matters.

Once the nurse had disappeared, Robin proceeded down the corridor, until she reached the door of number 15, which bore the name 'Mr Nico Ricci'.

Unconsciously holding her breath, Robin knocked gently, and pushed. There was no lock on the inside of the door; it swung open at once.

The room inside, while small, faced south, getting plenty of sun. A great effort had been made to make the room homely: watercolour pictures hung on the walls, including one of the Bay of Naples. The mantelpiece was covered in family photographs, and a number of children's paintings had been taped up on the wardrobe door, including one captioned 'Grandpa and Me and a Kite'.

The elderly occupant was bent almost double in an armchair beside the window. In the minute that had elapsed since the nurse left him, he'd fallen fast asleep. Robin let the door close quietly behind her, crept across to Ricci and sat down on the end of his single bed, facing the one-time pimp, pornographer and orchestrator of gang-rape and murder.

There was no doubt that the staff looked after their charges well. Ricci's dark grey hair and his fingernails were as clean as his bright white shirt collar. In spite of the warmth of the room, they'd dressed him in a pale blue sweater. On one of the veiny hands lying limp on the chair beside him glistened the gold lion's head ring. The fingers were curled up in a way that made Robin wonder whether he could still use them. Perhaps he'd had a stroke, which would account for his inability to talk.

'Mr Ricci?' said Robin quietly.

He made a little snorting snuffle, and slowly raised his head, his mouth hanging open. His enormous, drooping eyes, though not as filmy as Betty Fuller's, nevertheless looked dull, and like his ears and nose seemed to have grown while the rest of him shrank, leaving loose folds of dark skin.

'I've come to ask you some questions,' said Robin quietly. 'About a woman called Margot Bamborough.'

He gaped at her, open-mouthed. Could he hear her? Could he understand? There was no hearing aid in either of his over-large ears. The loudest noise in the room was the thumping of Robin's heart.

'Do you remember Margot Bamborough?' she asked.

To her surprise, Ricci made his low moan. Did that mean yes or no?

'You do?' said Robin.

He moaned again.

'She disappeared. D'you know—?'

Footsteps were coming along the corridor outside. Robin got up hastily and smoothed away the impression she'd left on the bedspread.

Please God, don't let them be coming in here.

But God, it seemed, wasn't listening to Robin Ellacott. The footsteps grew louder, and then the door opened to reveal a very tall man whose face was pitted with acne scars and whose knobbly bald head looked, as Barclay had said, as though something heavy had been dropped on it: Luca Ricci.

'Who're you?' he said. His voice, which was far softer and

higher than she'd imagined, made the hairs on the back of her neck prickle. For a second or two, Robin's terror threatened to derail her carefully worked out contingency plan. The very worst she'd expected to have to deal with was a nurse. None of the Riccis should have been here; it wasn't Sunday. And of all the Riccis she would have wanted to meet, Luca was the last.

'You his relative?' Robin asked in her North London accent. 'Oh, fank Gawd! He was making a weird moaning noise. I've just been visiting my gran, I fort he was ill or somefing.'

Still standing in the doorway, Luca looked Robin up and down.

'He doesthn't mean anything by it,' said Luca, who had a lisp. 'He moanth a bit, but it don't mean nothing, do it, eh, Dad?' he said loudly to the old man, who merely blinked at his eldest son.

Luca laughed.

'What'th your name?' he asked Robin.

'Vanessa,' she said promptly. 'Vanessa Jones.'

She took half a step forwards, hoping he'd move aside, but he remained planted exactly where he was, though smiling a little more widely. She knew he'd understood that she wanted to leave, but couldn't tell whether his evident determination to keep her inside was done for the simple pleasure of keeping her momentarily trapped, or because he hadn't believed her reason for being in his father's room. Robin could feel sweat under her armpits and over her scalp, and hoped to God that her hair chalk wouldn't come off.

'Never theen you around here before,' said Luca.

'No, it's my first time,' said Robin, forcing herself to smile. 'They look after 'em well, don't they?'

'Yeah,' said Luca, 'not bad. I usually come Thundayth, but we're off to Florida tomorrow. Gonna mith hith birthday.

Not that he knowth it'th hith birthday – do you, eh?' he said, addressing his father, whose mouth continued to hang open, his eyes fixed vacantly on his son.

Luca took a small wrapped package from under his jacket, leaned over to the chest of drawers and laid it on top without moving his large feet so much as an inch.

'Aw, that's nice,' said Robin.

She could feel the sweat on her breastbone now, where it would be visible to Luca. The room was as warm as a greenhouse. Even had she not known who Luca was, she'd have known *what* he was. She could feel the potential for violence coming off him like radiation. It was in the greedy smile he was giving her, in the way he was now leaning up against the door jamb, revelling in the silent exercise of power.

'It'th only chocolateth,' said Luca. 'Who'th your granny?'

'Great-granny, really, but I call her "Gran",' Robin said, playing for time, trying to remember any of the names she'd passed on the way to Ricci's room. 'Sadie.'

'Where'th she?'

'Couple of rooms that way,' said Robin, pointing left. She hoped he couldn't hear how dry her mouth was. 'Promised my mum I'd pop in and visit her while she's on holiday.'

'Yeah?' said Luca. 'Where'th your Mum gone?'

'Florence,' Robin invented wildly. 'Art galleries.'

'Yeah?' said Luca again. 'Our family'th from Napleth, originally. Innit, Dad?' he called over Robin's head at the gaping old man, before looking Robin up and down again. 'Know what my old man uthed to be?'

'No,' said Robin, trying to maintain her smile.

'He owned thtrip clubth,' said Luca Ricci. 'Back in the old dayth, he'd've had your pantieth right off you.'

She tried to laugh, but couldn't, and saw that Luca was delighted to see her discomfort.

'Oh yeah. Girl like you? He'd've offered you a hothtess job. It wath good money, too, even if you did have to blow thome of Dad'th mateth, hahaha.'

His laugh was as high-pitched as a woman's. Robin couldn't join in. She was remembering Kara Wolfson.

'Well,' she said, feeling the sweat trickling down her neck, 'I really need—'

'Don't worry,' said Luca, smiling, still standing firmly between her and the door, '*I'm* not in that game.'

'What do you do?' asked Robin, who'd been on the verge of asking him to move aside, but lost her nerve.

'I'm in inthuranthe,' said Luca, smiling broadly. 'What about you?'

'Nursery nurse,' said Robin, taking the idea from the children's daubs on the wardrobe door.

'Yeah? Like kidth, do you?'

'I love them,' said Robin.

'Yeah,' said Luca. 'Me too. I got thix.'

'Wow,' said Robin. 'Six!'

'Yeah. And I'm not like him,' said Luca, looking over Robin's head again, at his gaping father. 'He wathn't interethted in uth until we were grown up. I like the littl'unth.'

'Oh, me too,' said Robin fervently.

'You needed to get knocked down by a car to get *hith* attention, when we were kidth,' said Luca. 'Happened to my brother Marco, when he wath twelve.'

'Oh no,' said Robin politely.

He was playing with her, demanding that she give him appropriate responses, while both of them were equally aware that she was too scared to ask him to move aside, afraid of what he might do. Now he smiled at her feigned concern for his brother Marco's long-ago car accident.

'Yeah, Dad thtayed at the hothpital with Marco for three

weekth tholid, till Marco wath out of danger,' said Luca. 'At leatht, I think it wath Marco he wath thtaying for. Might've been the nurtheth. In the old dayth,' said Luca, looking Robin up and down again, 'they wore black thtockingth.'

Robin could hear footsteps again, and this time she prayed, *please be coming in here*, and her prayer was answered. The door behind Luca opened, hitting him in the back. The flat-footed blonde nurse was back.

'Oh, sorry, Mr Ricci,' she said, as Luca stepped aside. 'Oh,' she repeated, becoming aware of Robin's presence.

''E was moaning,' Robin said again, pointing at Mucky, in his chair. 'Sorry, I shouldn't've – I fort he might be in pain or something.'

And right on cue, Mucky Ricci moaned, almost certainly to contradict her.

'Yeah, he does a bit of that, if he wants something,' said the nurse. 'Probably ready for the bathroom now, are you, Mr Ricci?'

'I'm not thtaying to watch him crap,' said Luca Ricci, with a little laugh. 'I only came to drop off hith prethent for Thurthday.'

Robin was already halfway out of the door, but to her horror, she'd walked barely three steps when Luca appeared behind her, taking one stride to her every two.

'Not going to thay goodbye to Thadie?' he asked, as they passed the door of Mrs Sadie O'Keefe.

'Oh, she fell asleep while I was in there, bless her,' said Robin. 'Flat out.'

They walked down the stairs, Luca slightly behind her all the way. She could feel his eyes, like lasers, on the nape of her neck, on her legs and her backside.

After what felt like ten minutes, though it was barely three, they reached the ground floor. The almost life-size plaster Jesus looked sadly down upon the killer and the impostor as they headed towards the door. Robin had just placed her hand on the handle when Luca said,

'Hang on a moment, Vanetha.'

Robin turned, a pulse thrumming in her neck.

'You've got to thign out,' said Luca, holding out a pen to her.

'Oh, I forgot,' said Robin, with a breathless giggle. 'I told you – it's my first time here.'

She bent over the visitors' book. Directly below the signature she'd written on entering the building was Luca's.

LUCA RICCI

In the space left for 'Comments' he'd written,

BROUGHT HIM SOME CHOCOLATES FOR HIS BIRTHDAY ON THURSDAY. PLEASE GIVE HIM THEM ON THE MORNING OF THE 25TH JULY.

Robin scrawled the time beside her signature, then turned back to the door. He was holding it open for her.

'Fanks very much,' she said breathlessly, sidling past him into the fresh air.

'Give you a lift anywhere?' Luca asked her, pausing at the top of the steps to the street. 'My car'th round the corner. Athton Martin.'

'Oh, no, fanks very much, though,' said Robin. 'I'm meeting my boyfriend.'

'Be good, then,' said Luca Ricci. 'And if you can't be good, be thafe, hahaha.'

'Yes,' said Robin, a little wildly. 'Oh, and enjoy Florida!'

He raised a hand to her and began to walk away, whistling 'Begin the Beguine'. Light-headed with relief, Robin walked off in the opposite direction. It took the utmost restraint to stop herself breaking into a run.

Once she'd reached the square, she slid behind the lilac bush and watched the front of the nursing home for a full half an hour. Once she was certain that Luca Ricci had genuinely left, she doubled back.

62

Oftimes it haps, that sorrowes of the mynd
Find remedie vnsought, which seeking cannot fynd.

Edmund Spenser
The Faerie Queene

The row, for which Robin was braced, was one of the worst she and Strike had ever had. His fury that she'd approached Mucky Ricci, after his clear warnings and instructions not to, remained unabated even after a solid hour's argument in the office that evening, which culminated in Robin seizing her bag and walking out while Strike was mid-sentence, leaving him facing the vibrating glass door, wishing it had shattered, so he could bill her.

A night's sleep only slightly mitigated Strike's anger. Yes, there were major differences between Robin's actions this time, and those that had seen him sack her three years previously: she hadn't, for instance, spooked a suspect into hiding. Nor was there any indication, at least in the first twenty-four hours following her visit, that either the Ricci family or the nursing home suspected 'Vanessa Jones' of being anyone other than she'd claimed to be. Above all (but this fact rankled, rather than soothed), Robin was now a partner in the firm, rather than a lowly subcontractor. For the first time, Strike was brought up against the hard fact that if they ever parted ways, a legal and financial tangle would engulf him. It would, in fact, be akin to a divorce.

He didn't want to split from Robin, but his newly awakened awareness that he'd made it very difficult to do so increased his ire. The atmosphere between them remained strained for a fortnight after her visit to St Peter's until, on the first morning in August, Robin received a terse text from Strike asking her to abandon her fresh attempt to befriend Shifty's PA, and come back to the office.

When she entered the inner room, she found Strike sitting at the partners' desk, with bits and pieces of the Bamborough police file laid out in front of him. He glanced up at her, noted that her eye and hair colour were her own, then said brusquely,

'The Shifty clients have just rung up. They've terminated the job, for lack of results.'

'Oh no,' said Robin, sinking into the chair opposite him. 'I'm sorry, I really tried with Shifty's PA—'

'And Anna and Kim want to talk to us. I've set up a conference call at four o'clock.'

'They aren't—?'

'Winding things up?' said Strike unemotionally. 'Probably. Apparently they've had a spur-of-the-moment invitation from a friend to join them on holiday in Tuscany. They want to talk to us before they go, because they'll still be away on the fifteenth.'

There was a long silence. Strike didn't appear to have anything else to say, but resumed his perusal of various bits of the case file.

'Cormoran,' said Robin.

'What?'

'Can we please talk about St Peter's?'

'I've said everything I've got to say,' said Strike, picking up Ruby Elliot's statement about the two women struggling together in the rain, and pretending to read it again.

'I don't mean about me *going* there. I've already said—'

'You said you wouldn't approach Ricci—'

'I "agreed" not to go near Ricci,' said Robin, sketching quotation marks in the air, 'just like you "agreed" with Gregory Talbot not to tell the police where you got that roll of film.' Hyperaware of Pat typing away in the outer office, Robin was speaking quietly. 'I didn't set out to *defy* you; I left him up to you, remember? But it needed doing, and you couldn't. In case you hadn't noticed, I'm a damn sight better than you are at disguising my appearance.'

'That's not in question,' said Strike, throwing aside Ruby Elliot's statement and picking up Gloria's description of Theo, instead. 'What bugs me, as you *bloody well know*, is that you didn't tell me you were going to—'

'D'you ring *me* every three seconds and tell me what you're going to do next? You're happy enough for me to work on my own initiative when it suits—'

'Luca Ricci's done time for putting electrodes on people's genitals, Robin!' said Strike, dropping the pretence that the description of Theo had his attention.

'How many times are we going to go over this? D'you think I was *pleased* when he walked in the room? I'd *never* have gone in there if I'd known he was about to make a surprise appearance! The fact remains—'

'—it's not a fact—'

'—if I hadn't—'

'—this theory—'

'*It isn't a bloody theory, Strike, it's reality, and you're just being pig-headed about it.*' Robin pulled her mobile out of her back pocket and brought up the photo she'd taken on her second visit to the nursing home, which had lasted barely two minutes, and involved her taking a quick, unwitnessed photograph of Luca Ricci's handwriting in the visitors' book.

'Give me the anonymous note,' she ordered Strike, holding out her hand for the piece of crumpled blue paper they'd taken away from their meeting with the Bayliss sisters. '*There*.'

She set them side by side, facing Strike. To Robin, the similarities were undeniable: the same odd mixture of capital and lower-case letters, all distinct and separate, but with odd and unnecessary little flourishes, rather like the incongruous lisp of a tall, dangerous-looking man whose skin was as pitted as a partly peeled orange.

'You can't prove it's the same writing from a photograph,' said Strike. He knew he was being ungracious, but his anger wasn't yet fully spent. 'Expert analysis relies on pen pressure, apart from anything else.'

'OK, fine,' said Robin, who now had a hard, angry lump in her throat. She got up and walked out, leaving the door slightly ajar. Through the gap, Strike heard her talking to Pat, followed by the tinkle of mugs. Annoyed though he was, he still hoped she was going to get him a cup of tea, as well.

Frowning slightly, he pulled Robin's mobile and the anonymous note towards him and looked again from one to the other. She was right, and he'd known, though not acknowledged it, from the moment she'd shown him the picture on her phone, on her return from St Peter's. Though he hadn't told Robin so, Strike had forwarded a picture of both the anonymous note and Luca Ricci's visitors' book message to an expert handwriting analyst he'd reached through his police contacts. The woman had expressed caution about reaching a hard and fast conclusion without having the original samples in front of her, but said that, on the evidence, she was 'seventy to eighty per cent certain' that both had been written by the same person.

'Does handwriting remain that consistent, forty years apart?' Strike asked.

'Not always,' the expert replied. 'You expect changes, typically. Mostly, people's handwriting deteriorates with age because of physical factors. Mood can have an influence, too. My research tends to show that handwriting alters least in people who write infrequently, compared with those who write a lot. Occasional writers seem to stick with the style they adopted early, possibly in school. In the case of these two samples, there are certainly distinctive features that seem to have hung around from youth.'

'I think it's fair to say this guy doesn't write a lot in his line of work,' said Strike.

Luca's last spell in jail, as Shanker had told him, had been for ordering and overseeing a stabbing. The victim had been knifed in the balls. By a miracle, he'd survived, 'but 'e won't be 'avin' any more kids, poor cunt,' Shanker had informed Strike, two nights previously. 'Can't get a fuckin' 'ard-on wiv-vout agony. Not worf living, is it, after that? The knife sliced straight through the right bollock, I 'eard – course, they 'ad him pinned down—'

'No need for details,' Strike had said. He'd just experienced a nasty sensation radiating out of his own balls up to his chest.

Strike had called Shanker on some slight pretext, purely to see whether any rumour had reached his old friend of Luca Ricci being concerned that a female detective had turned up in his father's nursing home. As Shanker hadn't mentioned anything, Strike had to conclude that no such whispers were abroad.

While this was a relief, it wasn't really a surprise. Once he'd calmed down, Strike had been forced to admit to himself that he was sure Robin had got away with it. Everything Strike knew about Luca Ricci suggested he'd never have let her walk away unscathed if he'd believed she was there to investigate any member of his family. The kinds of people whose darkest impulses were kept in check by their own consciences, the dictates of the law, by social norms and common sense might find it hard to believe anyone would be so foolish or reckless as to hurt Robin inside a nursing home bedroom, or march her out of the building with a knife to her back. *He wouldn't do it in broad daylight*, they'd say. *He wouldn't dare, with witnesses all around!* But Luca's fearsome reputation rested on his propensity for brazen violence, no matter where he was, or who was watching. He operated on an assumption of impunity, for which he had much justification. For every prison term he'd served, there'd been many incidents that should have seen him convicted, but which he'd managed to escape by intimidating witnesses, or terrifying others into taking the rap.

Robin returned to the inner office, stony-faced, but carrying two mugs of tea. She pushed the door closed with her foot, then set down the darker of the two teas in front of Strike.

'Thanks,' muttered Strike.

'You're welcome,' she replied stiffly, checking her watch as she sat down again. They had twenty minutes to go, before the conference call with Anna and Kim.

'We can't,' said Strike, 'tell Anna we think Luca Ricci wrote the anonymous notes.'

Robin simply looked at him.

'We can't have two nice middle-class women walking around telling people Ricci threatened Margot, and maybe killed her,' said Strike. 'We'd be putting them in danger, quite apart from ourselves.'

'Can't we at least show the samples to an expert?'

'I have,' said Strike, and he explained what the woman had said.

'Why didn't you tell—?'

'Because I was still bloody angry,' said Strike, sipping his tea. It was exactly the way he liked it, strong, sweet and the colour of creosote. 'Robin, the reality is, if we take the photo and the note to the police, whether or not anything comes of it, you'll have painted a giant target on your back. Ricci'll start digging around on who could have photographed his handwriting in that visitors' book. It won't take him long to find us.'

'He was twenty-two when Margot went missing,' said Robin quietly. 'Old enough and big enough to abduct a woman. He had contacts to help with the disposal of a body. Betty Fuller thought the person who wrote the notes was the killer, and she's still scared of telling us who it was. That could imply the son, just as well as the father.'

'I grant you all that,' said Strike, 'but it's time for a reality check. We haven't got the resources to go up against organised criminals. You going to St Peter's was reckless enough—'

'Could you explain to me why it was reckless when I did it, but not when you were planning to do it?' said Robin.

Strike was momentarily stymied.

'Because I'm less experienced?' said Robin. 'Because you think I'll mess it up, or panic? Or that I can't think on my feet?'

'None of those,' said Strike, though it cost him some pain to admit it.

'Well then—'

'Because my chances of surviving if Luca Ricci comes at me with a baseball bat are superior to yours, OK?'

'But Luca doesn't come at people with baseball bats,' said Robin reasonably. 'He comes at them with knives, electrodes and acid, and I don't see how you'd withstand any of them better than I would. The truth is, you're happy to take risks you don't want me to take. I don't know whether it's lack of confidence in me, or chivalry, or one dressed up as the other—'

'Look—'

'No, *you* look,' said Robin. 'If you'd been recognised in there, the whole agency would have paid the price. I've read up on Ricci, I'm not stupid. He goes for people's families and associates and even their *pets* as often as he goes for them personally. Like it or not, there are places I can go more easily than you. I'm less distinctive-looking, I'm easier to disguise, and people trust women more than men, especially around kids and old people. We wouldn't know *any* of this if I hadn't gone to St Peter's—'

'We'd be better off not knowing it,' Strike snapped back. 'Shanker said to me months back, "If Mucky's the answer, you need to stop asking the question." Same goes for Luca, in spades.'

'You don't mean that,' said Robin. 'I know you don't. You'd never choose not to know.'

She was right, but Strike didn't want to admit it. Indeed, one of the things that had kept his anger simmering for the past two weeks was that he knew there was a fundamental lack of logic in his own position. If trying to get information on the Ricci family had been worth doing at all, it should have been done, and as Robin had proven, she'd been the best person for the job. While he resented the fact that she hadn't warned him what she was about to do, he knew perfectly well that if she'd done so, he'd have vetoed it, out of a fundamentally indefensible desire to keep her out of harm's way, when the logical conclusion of that line of thinking was that she oughtn't to be doing this job at all. He wanted her to be open and direct with him, but knew that his own incoherent position on her taking physical risks was the reason she hadn't been honest about her intentions. The long scar on her forearm reproached him every time he looked at it, even though the mistake that had led to the attack had been entirely her own. He knew too much about her past; the relationship had become too personal: he didn't want to visit her in hospital again. He felt precisely that irksome sense of responsibility that kept him determinedly single, but without any of the compensatory pleasures. None of this was her fault, but it had taken a fortnight for him to look these facts clearly in the face.

'OK,' he muttered at last. 'I wouldn't choose not to know.' He made a supreme effort. 'You did bloody well.'

'Thank you,' said Robin, as startled as she was gratified.

'Can we agree, though – please? That in future, we talk these things through?'

'If I'd asked you—'

'Yeah, I might've said no, and I'd've been wrong, and I'll bear that in mind next time, OK? But as you keep reminding me, we're partners, so I'd be grateful—'

'All right,' said Robin. 'Yes. We'll discuss it. I'm sorry I didn't.'

At that moment, Pat knocked on the door and opened it a few inches.

'I've got a Ms Phipps and a Ms Sullivan on the line for you.'

'Put them through, please,' said Strike.

Feeling as though she was sitting in on the announcement of bad medical news, Robin let Strike do the talking to Anna and Kim. He took the couple systematically through every interview the agency had conducted over the past eleven and a half months, telling them the secrets he and Robin had unearthed, and the tentative conclusions they'd drawn.

He revealed that Irene Hickson had been briefly involved with Margot's ex-boyfriend, and that both had lied about it, and explained that Satchwell might have been worried that Margot would tell the authorities about the way his sister died; that Wilma the cleaner had never set foot in Broom House, and that the story of Roy walking was almost certainly false;

that the threatening notes had been real, but (with a glance at Robin) that they hadn't managed to identify the writer; that Joseph Brenner had been a more unsavoury character than anyone had realised, but that there was nothing to tie him to Margot's disappearance; that Gloria Conti, the last person to see Margot alive, was living in France, and didn't want to talk to them; and that Steve Douthwaite, Margot's suspicious patient, had vanished without trace. Lastly, he told them that they believed they'd identified the van seen speeding away from Clerkenwell Green on the night that Margot disappeared, and were confident that it hadn't been Dennis Creed's.

The only sound to break the silence when Strike first stopped talking was the soft buzzing emitted by the speaker on his desk, which proved the line was still open. Waiting for Anna to speak, Robin suddenly realised that her eyes were full of tears. She'd so very much wanted to find out what had happened to Margot Bamborough.

'Well . . . we knew it would be difficult,' said Anna at last. 'If not impossible.'

Robin could tell that Anna was crying, too. She felt wretched.

'I'm sorry,' said Strike formally. 'Very sorry, not to have better news for you. However, Douthwaite remains of real interest, and—'

'No.'

Robin recognised Kim's firm negative.

'No, I'm sorry,' said the psychologist. 'We agreed a year.'

'We're actually two weeks short,' said Strike, 'and if—'

'Have you got any reason to believe you can find Steve Douthwaite in the next two weeks?'

Strike's slightly bloodshot eyes met Robin's wet ones.

'No,' he admitted.

'As I said in my email, we're about to go on holiday,' said

Kim. 'In the absence of actually finding Margot's body, there was always bound to be another angle you could try, one more person who might know something, and as I said at the start of this, we haven't got the money, or, frankly, the emotional stamina, to keep this going for ever. I think it's better – cleaner – if we accept that you've done your best, and thank you for the trouble you've clearly taken. This has been a worthwhile exercise, even if – I mean, Anna and Roy's relationship's better than it's been in years, thanks to your visit. He'll be glad to hear that the cleaner accepted he wasn't able to walk that day.'

'Well, that's good,' said Strike. 'I'm only sorry—'

'I knew,' said Anna, her voice wavering, 'that it was going to be . . . almost impossible. At least I know I tried.'

After Anna had hung up, there was a silence in the room. Finally Strike said 'Need a pee', pulled himself up and left the room.

Robin got up, too, and began to gather together the photocopied pages from the police file. She couldn't believe it was all over. Having put the records into a neat pile, she sat down and began to flick through them one more time, knowing that she was hoping to see something – anything – they'd overlooked.

From Gloria Conti's statement to Lawson:

> She was a short, dark, stocky woman who looked like a gypsy. I judged her to be in her teens. She came in alone and said she was in a lot of pain. She said her name was Theo. I didn't catch her surname and I didn't ask her to repeat it because I thought she needed urgent attention. She was clutching her abdomen. I told her to wait and I went to ask Dr Brenner if he'd see her, because Dr Bamborough was still with patients.

From Ruby Elliot's statement to Talbot:

I saw them beside a telephone box, two women sort of struggling together. The tall one in the raincoat was leaning on the short one, who wore a plastic rain hood. They looked like women to me, but I didn't see their faces. It looked to me like one was trying to make the other walk quicker.

From Janice Beattie's statement to Lawson:

I've been on speaking terms with Mr Douthwaite since he was assaulted at the flats, but I wouldn't call him a friend. He did tell me how upset he was his friend had killed herself. He told me he had headaches. I thought it was tension. I know he grew up in foster care, but he never told me the names of any of his foster mothers. He never talked to me about Dr Bamborough except to say he'd gone to her about his headaches. He didn't tell me he was leaving Percival House. I don't know where he's gone.

From Irene Hickson's second statement to Lawson:

The attached receipt proves that I was in Oxford Street on the afternoon in question. I deeply regret not being honest about my whereabouts, but I was ashamed of lying to get the afternoon off.

And beneath the statement was the photocopy of Irene's receipt: Marks & Spencer, three items, which came to a total of £4.73.

From Joseph Brenner's statement to Talbot:

> I left the practice at my usual time, having promised my sister that I'd be home in time for dinner. Dr Bamborough kindly agreed to see the emergency patient, as she had a later appointment with a friend in the area. I have no idea whether Dr Bamborough had personal troubles. Our relationship was entirely professional. I have no knowledge of anyone who wanted to do her harm. I remember one of her patients sending her a small box of chocolates, although I can't say for certain that it was from Steven Douthwaite. I don't know Mr Douthwaite. I remember Dr Bamborough seemed displeased when Dorothy handed the chocolates to her, and asked Gloria, the receptionist, to throw them straight in the bin, although she later took them back out of the bin. She had a very sweet tooth.

Strike re-entered the office and dropped a five-pound note onto the table in front of Robin.

'What's that for?'

'We had a bet,' he said, 'about whether they'd extend the year if we had any outstanding leads. I said they would. You said they wouldn't.'

'I'm not taking that,' said Robin, leaving the fiver where it lay. 'There are still two more weeks.'

'They've just—'

'They've paid till the end of the month. I'm not stopping.'

'Did I not make myself clear just now?' said Strike, frowning down at her. 'We're leaving Ricci.'

'I know,' said Robin.

She checked her watch again.

'I'm supposed to be taking over from Andy in an hour. I'd better go.'

After Robin had left, Strike returned the photocopied papers to the boxes of old police records that still lay underneath the desk, then went out into the office where Pat sat, electronic cigarette between her teeth as always.

'We've lost two clients,' he told her. 'Who's next on the waiting list?'

'That footballer,' said Pat, bringing up the encrypted file on her monitor to show Strike a well-known name. 'And if you want to replace both of them, there's that posh woman who's got the chihuahua.'

Strike hesitated.

'We'll just take the footballer for now. Can you ring his assistant and say I'm available to take details any time tomorrow?'

'It's Saturday,' said Pat.

'I know,' said Strike. 'I work weekends and I doubt he'll want anyone to see him coming in here. Say I'm happy to go to his place.'

He returned to the inner office and pushed up the window, allowing the afternoon air, heavy with exhaust fumes and London's particular smell of warm brick, soot and, today, a faint trace of leaves, trees and grass, to permeate the office. Tempted to light up, he restrained himself out of deference to Pat, because he'd asked her not to smoke in the office. Clients these days were nearly all non-smokers and he felt it gave a poor impression to have the place reeking like an ashtray. He leaned on the windowsill and watched the Friday-night drinkers and shoppers walking up and down Denmark Street, half-listening to Pat's conversation with the Premier League footballer's assistant, but mostly thinking about Margot Bamborough.

He'd known all along there was only the remotest chance of finding out what had happened to her, but where had fifty weeks gone? He remembered all the time spent with Joan in Cornwall, and the other clients who'd come and gone, and asked himself if they might have found out what had happened to Margot Bamborough if none of these things had got in the way. Tempting though it was to blame distractions, he believed the outcome would have been the same. Perhaps Luca Ricci was the answer they weren't ever going to be able to admit. A plausible answer, in many ways: a professional hit, done for some inscrutable underworld reason, because Margot had got too close to a secret, or interfered in the gangsters' business. *Leave my girl alone* . . . she'd been the type to advise a stripper, or a hooker, or a porn actress, or an addict, to choose a different life, to give evidence against men who abused her . . .

'Eleven tomorrow,' rasped Pat, from behind Strike. 'At 'is place. I've left his address on the desk for you.'

'Thanks very much,' he said, turning to see her already in her coat. It was five o'clock. She looked vaguely surprised to hear his thanks, but ever since Robin had shouted at him for being rude to Pat, Strike had been consciously trying to be politer to the secretary. For a moment she hesitated, electronic cigarette between her yellow teeth, then removed it to say,

'Robin told me what that Morris did. What he sent her.'

'Yeah,' said Strike. 'Sleazy bastard.'

'Yeah,' said Pat. She was scrutinising him closely, as though seeing things she hadn't ever expected to find. ''Orrible. And 'e always reminded me,' she said surprisingly, 'of a young Mel Gibson.'

'Really?' said Strike.

'Funny fing, looks,' she said. 'You make assumptions.'

'I s'pose,' said Strike.

'You've got a real look of my first 'usband,' Pat told him.

'Is that right?' said Strike, startled.

'Yeah. Well . . . I'll be off. 'Ave a good weekend.'

'You too,' said Strike.

He waited until her footsteps had died away on the metal staircase, before pulling out his cigarettes, lighting one and returning to the inner office, where the window was still open. Here, he took an old ashtray out of the desk drawer and Talbot's leather notebook out of the top drawer of the filing cabinet, and settled down in his usual chair to flick through it once more, stopping at the final page.

Strike had never given Talbot's final jottings more than cursory attention, partly because his patience had run out by the time he got there, partly they were among the most shambolic and incoherent parts of the notes. Tonight, though, he had a melancholy reason for examining the last page of Talbot's notebook, because Strike, too, had come to the end of the case. So he examined Talbot's drawing of the demon he believed he'd conjured before the ambulance came to take him away: the spirit of Margot Bamborough, returned from some astral plane to haunt him in the form of Babalon, the Mother of Abominations.

There was no pressure to understand any more. Strike defocused his mind as he'd have relaxed his eyes, the better to spot one of those apparently three-dimensional images hidden in what appeared to be a flat pattern. His eyes glided over the phrases and fragments Talbot had half-remembered from Crowley's writings, and of consultation of the Thoth tarot. As he scrutinised the picture of the heavy-breasted demon, on whose belly the penitent Talbot had subsequently inscribed a Christian cross, he remembered Robin's words all those months previously in Hampton Court Palace, about the allure of myth and symbol, and the idea of the collective unconscious, where archetypes lurked. This demon, and the disconnected phrases that had seemed pertinent to Talbot in his psychotic state, had sprung from the policeman's own subconscious: it was too easy, too simplistic, to blame Crowley and Lévi for what Talbot's own mind had chosen to retain. This was what it generated, in a last spasm of madness, in a final attempt at

Having performed the ritual of the mark of the BEAST I conjured
BABALON the MOTHER OF ABOMINATIONS
SHE BLAMES ME SHE ATTACKS ME, THIS IS THE SPIRIT OF ♀ NOW THE MATE OF BAPHOMET ♑ IN HELL
Witch Moon turns BLOOD
she rides upon LION
the lion serpent
BLIND groping in
the poisoned darkness of
the BLACK MOON
Lust and strange drugs
SEVEN around her neck and
the seal of BABALON
POISONED DARKNESS
in the
MAGICK CUP
blood and
bitterness
SEVEN veils SEVEN
heads
streams SEVEN
her name
SEVEN
letters in
SEVEN
times
The moon
has no air
7

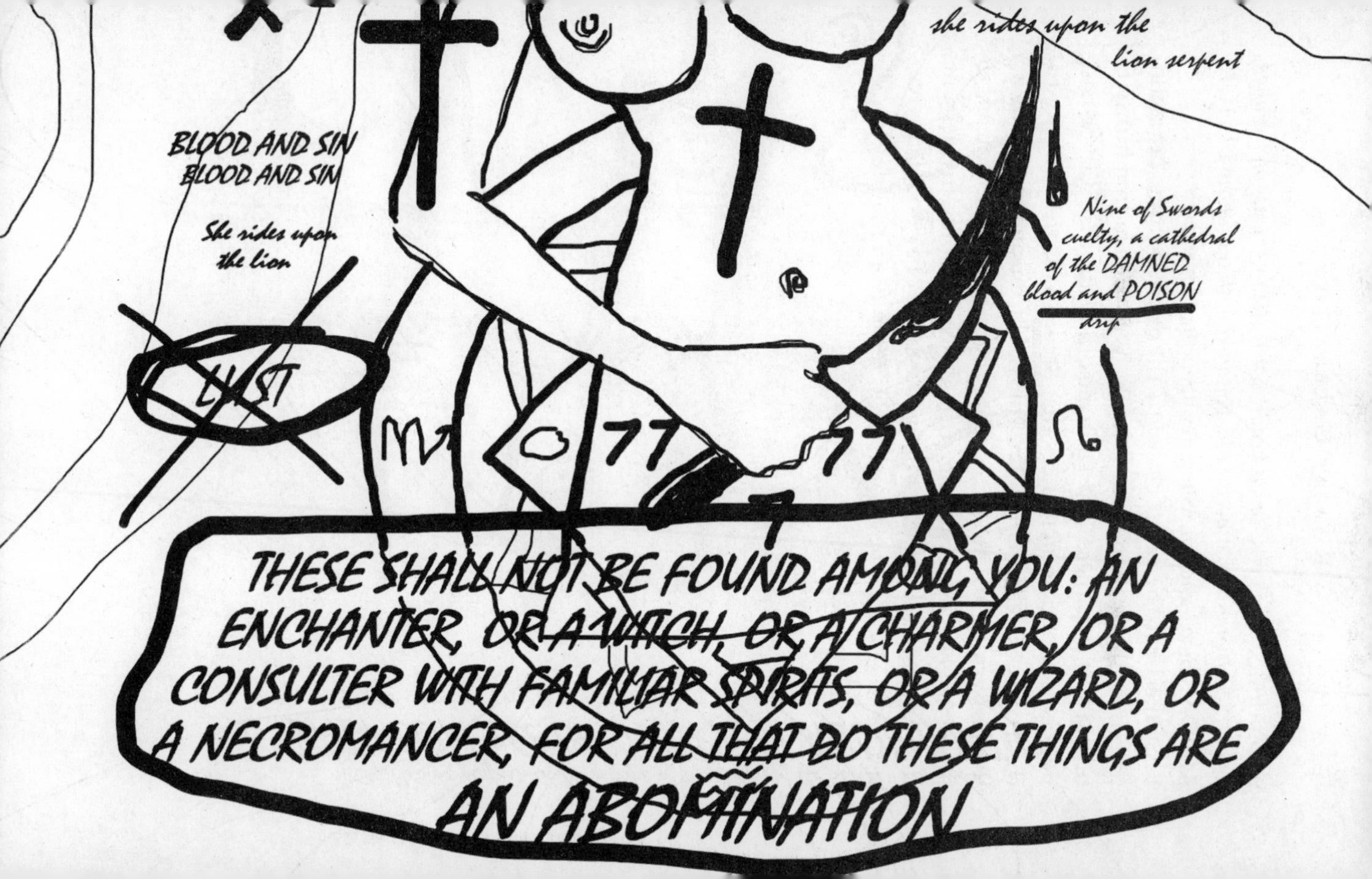
she rides upon the
lion serpent
BLOOD AND SIN
BLOOD AND SIN
She rides upon
the lion
Nine of Swords
cuelty, a cathedral
of the DAMNED
blood and POISON
drip
LUST
THESE SHALL NOT BE FOUND AMONG YOU: AN
ENCHANTER, OR A WITCH, OR A CHARMER, OR A
CONSULTER WITH FAMILIAR SPIRITS, OR A WIZARD, OR
A NECROMANCER, FOR ALL THAT DO THESE THINGS ARE
AN ABOMINATION

resolution. *Seven veils, seven heads, seven streams. Lust and strange drugs. Seven around her neck. The poisoned darkness of the BLACK MOON. Blood and sin. She rides upon the lion serpent.*

Strike bent the lamp closer to the page, so that he could scrutinise the drawing more closely. Was he deluding himself, or did some of these crazy jottings indicate that Talbot had noticed the odd coincidences that Strike had, after talking to the Bayliss sisters? As his gaze moved from one fragment of mystic writing to another, Strike thought he saw, not just a penitent churchgoer trying to make amends for his descent into witchcraft, but the last desperate effort of a good detective, trying to salvage clues from chaos, sense from madness.

63

At last resoluing forward still to fare,
Till that some end they finde or in or out,
That path they take, that beaten seemd most bare,
And like to lead the labyrinth about . . .

Edmund Spenser
The Faerie Queene

Over the next couple of weeks, Robin noticed that *Astrology 14* by Steven Schmidt, the second-hand book she'd left at the office, kept changing position. One morning it was on top of the filing cabinet where she'd left it, a few days later on Strike's half of the desk, and the following evening lying beside the kettle. Similarly, various bits of the Bamborough police records kept appearing, then disappearing again, while Bill Talbot's leather-bound notebook had vanished from the filing cabinet and, she suspected, made its way upstairs to Strike's attic flat.

The agency was once again very busy. The new client, a Premier League footballer, had sunk two million pounds into a proposed nightclub which had failed to materialise. His partner in the venture had now disappeared, along with all the money. The footballer, nicknamed Dopey by an unsympathetic Barclay, feared press exposure almost as much as not getting his cash back.

Meanwhile, Miss Jones's boyfriend continued to live a

frustratingly law-abiding life, but she appeared happy to keep paying the agency's bills, as long as Strike endured twice-weekly phone calls with her. During these supposed catch-ups, she told Strike all her problems, and hinted broadly that a dinner invitation would be happily accepted.

In addition to these clients, and leapfrogging those on the waiting list, was Shifty's Boss, who'd been forced into early retirement by the board. SB walked in off Denmark Street one morning looking for Barclay, who'd left his contact details with Elinor Dean. To Strike's surprise, early retirement seemed not to have spurred SB into despair, but liberated him.

'If you can believe it, I was genuinely thinking of killing myself, just a few months back,' he told Strike. 'But I'm out from under that bastard's thumb now. Now I've told my wife about Elinor—'

'Told her, have you?' said Strike, surprised.

'And she's been very understanding,' said SB. 'In my previous marriage, my – well, my needs – were taken care of by my ex-wife, but since we split . . . anyway, Portia and I have talked it all through, and she's perfectly happy for my arrangement with Elinor to continue, as long as there's no infidelity.'

Strike hid his expression behind his mug. He could well imagine that Portia, with her inch-long nails and her professional blow-dries, her thrice-yearly holidays, her black American Express card and her six-bedroomed house with swimming pool in West Brompton, preferred someone else to change SB's nappy.

'No, all I want *now*,' said SB, his satisfied smile replaced by a hard glare, 'is to make sure that shifty bastard gets what's coming to him. And I'm prepared to pay.'

So the agency had resumed surveillance on both Shifty and his PA.

The upshot of three demanding cases meant that most of

the communication between the two partners was done by phone for the rest of the month. Their paths finally crossed one Thursday afternoon in late August, when Strike entered the office as Robin was about to leave it.

Pat, who was listening to the radio while paying a slew of bills, offered to turn it off on seeing Strike, whose attention had just been caught by the figure-hugging blue dress Robin was wearing.

'No, it's fine,' he said. 'Nice to hear some music.'

'Cormoran, can I have a quick word before I go?' Robin asked, beckoning him into the inner office.

'... next up, in our hundred hits of the seventies, an oldie but goodie from one-hit-wonder Middle of the Road: "Chirpy Chirpy Cheep Cheep ..."'

'Where're you off to?' said Strike, closing the internal door on Pat. He'd spent most of the previous night on his feet, watching Shifty get drunk and coked up in a nightclub, and today driving between the various addresses Dopey's business partner had used over the previous two years. Unshaven and aching all over, he grunted in relief as he sank into his usual chair.

'The Vintry. Wine bar in the City,' said Robin. 'Gemma's going to be there later, Andy heard her arranging it. I'm hoping she's with girlfriends. I'm going to try and infiltrate the group somehow.'

Gemma was Shifty's PA. Through the closed door they now heard strains of a jaunty song playing on the radio, with its incongruous lyric,

'*Where's your mamma gone?*'

'You're still working on Bamborough, aren't you?' Robin asked.

'Just going back over a few things,' Strike admitted.

'And?'

'And nothing. It's like a maze. Moment I start thinking I'm getting somewhere, I turn a corner and come up against a dead end. Or find myself back where I started. Why are you looking so pleased?'

'I'm just glad you haven't given up,' said Robin.

'You won't say that when they cart me off to the same asylum as Bill Talbot. If I never see another fucking star sign, it'll be too soon . . . Where the *hell* is Douthwaite? What happened to him?'

'You think—?'

'I think he's bloody fishy, I always did. His alibi amounts to fuck all. Then he changes his name. Then, as you found out, another young woman dies in his vicinity – that drowned Redcoat. Then he vanishes again.

'If I could just speak to Douthwaite,' said Strike, drumming his fingers on the desk, 'I'd give it up.'

'Really?' said Robin.

He glanced at her, then, frowning, looked away. She was looking particularly sexy in that blue dress, which he'd never seen before.

'Yeah, if I could speak to Douthwaite, that'd do me.'

'*Last night I heard my mamma singing a song . . .* '

'And maybe Gloria Conti,' said Strike.

'*Woke up this morning, and my mamma was gone . . .* '

'And Creed,' said Strike. 'I'd like to talk to Dennis Creed.'

Robin felt a little skip of excitement. She'd received an email earlier, telling her to expect a decision by the end of the day on whether or not Creed could be re-interviewed.

'I'd better get going,' she said. 'Gemma's supposed to be there at six. It was nice of you,' she added, as she reached for the door handle, 'to let Pat keep the radio on.'

'Yeah, well,' said Strike, with a shrug. 'Trying to be friendly.'

As Robin was putting on her coat in the outer office, Pat said, 'That's a very good colour on you.'

'Thanks. It's quite old. Miracle it still fits, all the chocolate I've been eating lately.'

'Would he like a cuppa, d'you think?'

'I'm sure he would,' said Robin, surprised. Apparently Strike wasn't the only one who was trying to be friendly.

'Oooh, I used to love this,' said Pat, as the opening bars of 'Play That Funky Music' filled the office, and as Robin walked down the stairs, she heard Pat singing along, in her raspy baritone:

Once I was a funky singer,
Playin' in a rock and roll band . . .

The Vintry, which Robin reached twenty minutes later, lay near Cannon Street Tube station in the heart of the financial district, and was precisely the kind of place her ex-husband had most enjoyed. Undemandingly modern in a conventional, high-spec manner, with its sleek mixture of steel beams, large windows and wooden floors, it had a hint of open-plan office about it, in spite of the long bar with padded stools. There was the odd quirky touch, such as the two stuffed rabbits on a windowsill, which carried model guns and wore shooting caps, but in the main the clientele, which consisted overwhelmingly of men in suits, were cocooned in an atmosphere of tasteful beige blandness. They stood in cliques, fresh from the day's work, drinking, laughing together, reading newspapers or their phones, or eyeing up the few female customers – to Robin they seemed to exude not just confidence, but self-satisfaction. She received a number of appreciative looks as she sidled between stockbrokers, bankers and traders on her way to the bar.

Looking carefully around the large open-plan area, Robin gathered that Gemma hadn't yet arrived, so she took a free bar stool, ordered a tonic water and pretended to be reading the day's news off her phone, purely to avoid the open staring of the two young men to her right, one of whom seemed determined to make Robin look up, if only to ascertain where the annoying, braying laugh was coming from. To her left, a pair of older men were discussing the imminent Scottish independence referendum.

'Polls are looking shaky,' said the first man. 'Hope Cameron knows what he's doing.'

'They'd be bloody mad to do it. Mad.'

'There's opportunity in madness – for a few, anyway,' said the first man. 'I remember, when I was in Hong Kong – oh, I think that's our table free . . . '

The two speakers departed for their dinner. Robin glanced around again, carefully avoiding meeting the eyes of the young man with the braying laugh, and a patch of scarlet at the far end of the bar caught her eye. Gemma had arrived, and was standing alone, trying to catch the barman's eye. Robin slid off her bar stool, and carried her drink over to Gemma, whose long dark hair fell in gypsyish curls to the middle of her back.

'Hi – Linda?'

'What?' said Gemma, startled. 'No, sorry.'

'Oh,' said Robin, looking crestfallen. 'Maybe I've got the wrong bar. Has this place got other branches?'

'I've no idea, sorry,' said Gemma, still with her hand raised, trying to attract the barman's attention.

'She said she'd be wearing red,' said Robin, looking around at the sea of suits.

Gemma glanced at Robin, mildly interested.

'Blind date?'

'I wish,' said Robin, rolling her eyes. 'No, it's a friend of a friend who thinks there might be an opening at Winfrey and Hughes. The woman said she'd meet me for a quick drink.'

'Winfrey and Hughes? That's where I work.'

'You're kidding!' said Robin, with a laugh. 'Hey – you're not really Linda, are you? And pretending to be someone different, because you don't like the look of me or something?'

'No,' said the other woman, smiling. 'I'm Gemma.'

'Oh. Are you meeting someone, or—?'

'S'posed to be,' said Gemma, 'yeah.'

'D'you mind me sitting here with you? Just till they arrive? I was getting some properly lechy looks over there.'

'Tell me about it,' said Gemma, as Robin climbed up onto the barstool beside her. The barman now approached a pinstriped, grey-haired man who'd just arrived.

'Oi,' Robin called, and half a dozen businessmen's heads turned, as well as the barman's. 'She was here first,' said Robin, pointing sideways at Gemma, who laughed again.

'Wow. *You* don't mess around, do you?'

'No point, is there?' said Robin, taking a sip of her water. She'd subtly broadened her Yorkshire accent, as she often did when pretending to be a bolder, brasher character than she really felt herself to be. 'Gotta take charge, or they'll walk all bloody over you.'

'You're not wrong there,' sighed Gemma.

'Winfrey and Hughes isn't like that, is it?' said Robin. 'Full of tossers?'

'Well . . . '

The barman arrived at that moment to take Gemma's order. Once the PA had her large glass of red wine, she took a swig and said,

'It's OK, actually. Depends which bit you're working in. I'm PA to one of the high-ups. The work's interesting.'

'Nice guy?' asked Robin casually.

Gemma drank several mouthfuls of wine before saying,

'He's ... all right. Devil you know, isn't it? I like the job and the company. I've got a great salary and a ton of friends there ... oh damn—'

Her handbag had slipped off the barstool. As Gemma bent to retrieve it, Robin, whose eyes had roamed across the vista of cream, grey and beige in front of her, suddenly spotted Saul Morris.

He'd just walked into the bar, wearing a suit, an open-necked shirt and a remarkably smug smile. He glanced around, picked out Gemma and Robin by the bright colours of their dresses, and froze. For a second or two, he and Robin simply stared at each other; then Morris turned abruptly and hurried back out of the bar.

Gemma settled herself back onto her barstool, bag safely on her lap. The mobile phone she'd left lying on the counter now lit up.

'Andy?' said Gemma, answering quickly. 'Yeah ... no, I'm here already ...'

There was a long silence. Robin could hear Morris's voice. He was using the same wheedling tone in which he'd tried to talk her into bed, with all those puerile jokes and have-I-upset-yous.

'Fine,' said Gemma, her expression hardening. 'Fine. I just ... I'm going to take your number off my phone now and I'd like you ... no, actually, I ... oh just *fuck off*!'

She hung up, flushed, her lips trembling.

'Why,' she said, 'do they always want to be told they're still nice guys, after they've been total shits?'

'Often wondered that meself,' said Yorkshire Robin. 'Boyfriend?'

'Yeah,' said the shaken Gemma. 'For six months. Then he just stands me up one night, with no explanation. *Then* he comes back a couple of times – booty calls, basically,' she said, taking another big swig of wine. 'And finally he just ghosts me. I texted him yesterday, I said, look, I just wanna meet, just want an explanation—'

'Sounds like a right twat,' said Robin, whose heart was racing with excitement at this perfect opportunity to have a heart-to-heart. 'Hey,' she called to the barman, 'can we have a couple more wines and a menu, please?'

And after that, Robin found getting confidences out of Gemma as easy as shelling peas. With three large glasses of wine inside her, and her new friend from Yorkshire being so funny, supportive and understanding, a plate of chicken and polenta to eat, and a bottle of wine ('Yeah, why the hell not?'), she moved seamlessly from the misdemeanours of 'Andy' to the inappropriate and unsolicited groping by her boss that had escalated until she was on the verge of quitting.

'Can't you go to HR?' asked Robin.

'He says nobody'll believe me because of what happened when we were on a course last year . . . although . . . To tell you the truth, I don't really know *what* happened,' said Gemma, and looking away from Robin she mumbled, 'I mean . . . we had sex . . . but I was so out of it . . . so drunk . . . I mean, it wasn't, you know . . . it wasn't *rape* . . . I'm not saying *that* . . .'

'Were you in a fit state to give consent?' said Robin, no longer laughing. She'd only drunk half a glass of wine.

'Well, not . . . but . . . no, I'm not putting myself through *that*,' said Gemma, flushed and tearful. 'Not the police and everything, God no . . . he's a big shot, he could afford great lawyers . . . an' if I didn't win, how'm I gonna get another job in the City? . . . Court, and the papers . . . anyway, it's too late now . . . people saw me . . . coming out of his room. I pretended it was all OK. I had to, I was so embarrassed . . . rumour mill's been in overdrive since. We both denied anything happened, so how would it look if I . . .

'Andy told me I shouldn't report it,' said Gemma, pouring the last of the bottle into her glass.

'Did he?'

'Yeah . . . I told him about it, firs' time we had sex . . . see, it was the firs' time I'd slept with anyone since . . . and he said, "Yeah, you'll want to keep that quiet . . . be loads of grief for you, an' he'll probably get off" . . . He was ex-police, Andy, he knew all about that kind of thing.'

You total shit, Morris.

'No, if I was going to tell about *anything*,' said Gemma, hazily, 'it'd be the insider bloody trading . . . Oh yeah . . . nobody knows 'cept me . . .'

One hour later, Robin and Gemma emerged into the darkening street, Robin almost holding Gemma up, because she showed a tendency to sag if unsupported. After a ten-minute wait, she succeeded in flagging down a taxi, and loaded the very drunk Gemma into it.

'Le's go out Saturday!' Gemma called to Robin, trying to stop her closing the door.

'Fantastic!' said Robin, who'd given the PA a fake number. 'Ring me!'

'Yeah, I will . . . thanks so much for dinner!'

'No problem!' said Robin, and she succeeded at last in slamming the door on Gemma, who waved at her until the cab turned the corner.

Robin turned away and walked quickly back past the Vintry. A young man in a suit wolf-whistled as she passed.

'Oh bugger off,' muttered Robin, pulling out her phone to call Strike.

To her surprise, she saw she'd missed seven calls from him. She'd also received an email whose subject line read: Creed.

'Oh my God,' said Robin out loud.

She sped up, wanting to get away from the hordes of suited

men still walking the streets, to be alone and able to concentrate. Retreating at last into the dark doorway of a grey stone office block, she opened the email. After reading it through three times, to make absolutely sure her eyes weren't deceiving her, she called Strike back.

'There you are!' he said, answering on the first ring. 'Guess what?'

'What?'

'I've found Douthwaite!'

'You've *what*?' gasped Robin, attracting the startled attention of a sober-looking City gent shuffling past in the dark, holding a tightly furled umbrella. '*How?*'

'Names,' said Strike, who sounded elated. 'And Pat listening to hits of the seventies.'

'I don't—'

'He called himself Jacks first time, right? Well, Terry Jacks had a massive hit with a song called "Seasons in the Sun" in '74. They played it this afternoon. We know Douthwaite fancied himself a singer, so I thought, bet that's where he got the idea for "Jacks" . . . '

Robin could hear Strike pacing. He was evidently as excited as she felt.

'So then I went back to Oakden's book. He said Douthwaite's "Longfellow Serenade" was a particular hit with the ladies. I looked it up. That was one of Neil Diamond's. So then,' said Strike, 'I start Googling Steve Diamond . . .

'I'm about to text you a picture,' said Strike. 'Stand by.'

Robin took the phone away from her ear and waited. Within a few seconds, the text arrived, and she opened the accompanying picture.

A sweaty, red-faced, balding man in his sixties was singing into a microphone. He wore a turquoise T-shirt stretched over a sizeable belly. A chain still hung around his neck, but the only other resemblance to the picture of the spiky-haired, cheeky chap in his kipper tie were the eyes, which were as dark and bright as ever.

'It's him,' Robin said.

'That picture came off the website of a pub in Skegness,' said Strike. 'He's still a karaoke king and he co-owns and runs a bed and breakfast up there, with his wife Donna. I wonder,' said Strike, 'whether she realises his name hasn't always been Diamond?'

'This is *amazing*!' said Robin, so jubilant that she began to walk down the street again, purely to use the energy now surging through her. 'You're brilliant!'

'I know,' said Strike, with a trace of smugness. 'So, we're going to Skegness. Tomorrow.'

'I'm supposed to be—'

'I've changed the rota,' said Strike. 'Can you pick me up early? Say, eight o'clock? I'll come out to Earl's Court.'

'Definitely,' said Robin.

'Then I'll see you—'

'Wait,' said Robin.

'Oh, shit, yeah,' said Strike politely. 'Should've asked. How'd it go with Gemma?'

'Great,' said Robin. 'Shifty's insider trading, but never mind that now.'

'He's—?'

'Strike, I don't want to upstage you or anything,' she said, failing to suppress the note of triumph in her voice, 'because finding Douthwaite's incredible, but I think you ought to know . . . you're going to be allowed to interview Dennis Creed in Broadmoor, on September the nineteenth.'

64

. . . his hand did quake,
And tremble like a leafe of Aspin greene,
And troubled blood through his pale face was seene
To come, and goe with tidings from the heart,
As it a ronning messenger had beene.

Edmund Spenser
The Faerie Queene

'*Well*,' said Strike, getting into the Land Rover next morning.

They beamed at each other: for a moment, Robin thought she saw the idea of hugging her cross Strike's mind, but instead he held out his hand, and shook hers.

'My Christ, you wait a year for a breakthrough . . .'

Robin laughed, put the Land Rover into gear and pulled out onto the road. The day was unusually hot: she was driving in sunglasses, yet Strike noted a scarf protruding from the bag behind her seat.

'Don't think you're going to need that. Proper summer weather,' he said, looking out at the clear sky.

'We'll see,' said Robin sceptically. 'We used to visit Skegness when we were kids. Mum's sister used to live in Boston, up the road. There's usually a bracing breeze off the North Sea.'

'So, I read the email,' said Strike, referring to the message Robin had forwarded him, which laid out both the terms and conditions of him interviewing Dennis Creed, and the reasoning which had led the authorities to permit Strike to do it.

'What did you think?' Robin asked.

'Other than being bloody astounded you pulled this off—'

'It took ages.'

'I'm not surprised. Other than that, I won't lie . . . I'm feeling the pressure.'

'You mean, because of the Tuckers?'

'Yeah,' said Strike, opening the window so he could light a cigarette. 'Anna doesn't know I'm getting this shot, so she won't get their hopes up, but that poor bastard Tucker . . . '

Absolute secrecy about the interview, including signing a non-disclosure agreement that guaranteed Strike would never talk to the press about it, had been the first precondition set by the authorities.

'He really wants it to be you,' said Robin. 'Tucker. He says Creed's got a big ego and he'll want to meet you. And the psychiatrists must agree, mustn't they, or they wouldn't be allowing it? Brian Tucker says Creed always saw himself as high status, and deserving of associating with famous, successful people.'

'It isn't a psychiatrist's job to decide whether I'll be able to get anything out of him,' said Strike. 'I'd imagine all they'll care about is whether I'm going to rile him up. You don't get put in Broadmoor for being mildly eccentric.'

Strike was silent for a long time, looking out of the window, and Robin too remained quiet, not wanting to interrupt his train of thought. When at last Strike spoke again, he sounded matter of fact, and focused on the plan for Skegness.

'I looked up the B&B on TripAdvisor. It's called the Allardice, which is his wife's maiden name. We won't walk in there cold, because if he isn't there and the wife smells a rat, she can call him and warn him not to come back, so we'll park, get ourselves into a position where we can see the building, and ring him. If he's there, we walk straight in before he's got a chance to run – or catch him as he leaves, as the case might be. And if he isn't in, we wait.'

'For how long?' said Robin.

'I'd like to say "as long as it takes",' said Strike, 'but we're not actually being paid for this, so I've got to be back in town on Monday.'

'I could stay behind,' suggested Robin.

'I don't think so,' said Strike.

'Sorry,' said Robin, immediately regretting the suggestion, afraid that Strike might think she was simply after another weekend away in a hotel. 'I know we're short-staffed—'

'It isn't that. You were the one who pointed out women have a habit of dying or disappearing around Steve Douthwaite. Could be a case of bad luck, but on the other hand . . . three different surnames is a lot for a man with nothing to hide. I'm taking the lead on this one.'

They arrived in the small seaside town at eleven, leaving the Land Rover in a car park beside Skegness Bowl, an enormous red-walled seafront bowling alley. Strike could smell and taste the sea as he got out of the car, and turned instinctively towards it, but the ocean was invisible from where he stood. Instead he found himself looking at a manmade waterway of a murky green, along which a laughing young woman and her boyfriend were pedalling a dinghy-sized boat. The driver's door slammed and Strike turned to see Robin, still in sunglasses, wrapping the scarf around her neck.

'Told you,' she said to the mystified Strike, to whom the day felt unequivocally hot. Not for the first time wondering what it was about women and their bizarre ability to feel non-existent chills, Strike lit up, waited beside the Land Rover while Robin bought a parking permit, then walked with her up to Grand Parade, a wide street that ran along the seafront.

'"The Savoy",' said Strike, smirking as he read the names of the larger hotels, whose upper windows could surely see the distant sea. '"The Quorn". "The Chatsworth".'

'Don't jeer,' said Robin. 'I used to love coming to Skegness when I was a kid.'

'The Allardice should be up there,' Strike said, as they crossed the road, pointing up broad Scarbrough Avenue. 'Yeah, that's it, the one with the blue awning.'

They paused on the corner, beside an enormous mock Tudor hotel which boasted the Jubilee Carvery and Café. Early-morning drinkers of both beer and coffee were sitting at outside tables, enjoying the sunshine.

'Perfect place to keep an eye out,' said Strike, pointing at one of these pavement tables. 'I could use a cup of tea.'

'OK, I'll order,' said Robin. 'I need the loo, anyway. Are you going to call him or d'you want me to do it?'

'I will,' said Strike, already sinking onto one of the chairs, and taking out his mobile.

As Robin disappeared into the bar, Strike lit a cigarette, then keyed in the Allardice's number, his eyes on the front of the B&B. It stood in a row of eight tall red buildings, several of which had been converted into small boarding houses and had similar scalloped PVC awnings over the entrances. Spotless white net curtains hung at almost every window.

'Morning, the Allardice,' said a Scottish woman, who sounded on the irritable side of brisk.

'Steve there?' said Strike, faking casualness and confidence.

'That you, Barry love?'

'Yeah,' said Strike.

'He's on his way now,' she said. 'We only had a small, sorry. But do me a favour, Barry, and don't hold him up, because there are four beds to change here and he's supposed to be getting me more milk.'

'Righto,' said Strike, and not wanting to speak another syllable that might reveal him to be anyone other than Barry, he hung up.

'Is he there?' asked Robin anxiously, dropping into the seat opposite Strike. She'd washed her hands in the bathroom, but they were still damp, because she'd been in such a hurry to get back to Strike.

'No,' said Strike, knocking his cigarette ash into the small pink metal bucket placed on the table for that purpose. 'He's delivering something to a bloke up the road and will be back shortly, bringing milk.'

'Oh,' said Robin quietly, turning to look over her shoulder at the Allardice's royal blue awning, on which the name was inscribed in curly white lettering.

The barman brought out two metal pots and china teacups, and the detectives drank their tea in silence, Strike keeping a watchful eye on the Allardice, Robin on Grand Parade. The sea was blocked from her view by the wide, multicoloured frontage of the entrance to Skegness Pier, which advertised, among other attractions, the optimistically named Hollywood Bar and Diner. Elderly people rode mobility scooters up and down Grand Parade. Families strolled past, eating ice cream. Plume-tailed Maltese, fat pugs and panting chihuahuas trotted over the hot pavements alongside their owners.

'Cormoran,' muttered Robin suddenly.

A man had just turned the corner into Scarbrough Avenue, a heavy carrier bag dangling from his hand. His grey hair was close cropped around the ears, but a few strands had been combed over a wide expanse of sweaty forehead. His round shoulders and hangdog look gave him the air of a man whom life had ground down to a sullen obedience. The same turquoise T-shirt he'd worn in the karaoke picture was stretched tightly over his beer belly. Douthwaite crossed the road, climbed the three steps leading to the Allardice's front door and, with a flash of sun on glass, disappeared from view.

'Have you paid for this?' Strike asked, downing the rest of his tea and putting his empty cup back onto the saucer.

'Yes.'

'Then let's go,' said Strike, dropping his cigarette into the metal bucket and pulling himself to his feet, 'before he can disappear upstairs and start changing beds.'

They crossed the road as fast as Strike could walk and headed up the front steps, which had been painted pale blue. Baskets of purple petunias hung beneath the ground-floor windows and an assortment of stickers adorned the glass portion of the front door, one of which announced that this was a three-star residence, another asking guests to wipe their feet.

A tinkling bell announced their arrival. The deserted hall was narrow, its stairs carpeted in dark blue and green tartan. They waited beside a table laden with leaflets about local attractions, breathing in a combination of fried food and a powerful rose-scented air-freshener.

'... and Paula's got new tubes in her sunbeds,' said a Scottish voice, and a woman with short hair dyed canary yellow emerged through a door to the right. A deep vertical line was graven down the middle of her forehead. Barelegged, she wore an apron decorated with a Highland cow over her T-shirt and denim skirt, and a pair of Dr Scholl's sandals.

'We've no vacancies, sorry,' she said.

'Are you Donna?' asked Strike. 'We were hoping for a word with Steve.'

'What about?'

'We're private detectives,' said Strike, pulling out his wallet to hand her a card, 'and we're investigating—'

A hugely obese old lady came into view on the landing

above them. She was clad in shocking-pink leggings and a T-shirt bearing the slogan 'The More People I Meet, The More I Like My Dog'. Panting audibly, she began a sideways descent, both hands clutching the banister.

'—a missing person case,' Strike finished quietly, as he handed Donna his card.

At that moment, Steve Douthwaite emerged from behind his wife, a pile of towels in his arms. Close up, his dark eyes were bloodshot and puffy. Every feature had coarsened with age and, possibly, drink. His wife's demeanour, the card in her hand and the presence of the two strangers now looking at him brought him to a halt, the dark eyes frightened above his pile of towels.

'Cormoran Strike?' murmured Donna, reading the card. 'Aren't you the one . . . ?'

The old lady, who was barely halfway down the stairs, was now audibly wheezing.

'Get in here,' muttered Donna, pointing Strike and Robin towards the room from which she'd just emerged. 'And you,' she snapped at her husband.

They entered a small public sitting room, with a wall-mounted TV, a sparsely stocked bookcase and a miserable-looking spider plant sitting in a pedestalled urn. Through an arch was a breakfast room, where five tightly packed dining tables were being wiped down by a discontented-looking young woman in glasses, who sped up appreciably when she realised Donna had returned. Robin guessed that they were mother and daughter. Though the younger woman was dark rather than blonde, life had carved an identical groove of dissatisfaction in her forehead.

'Leave that, Kirsty,' said Donna abruptly. 'Take these towels upstairs, will you? And close the door.'

Kirsty relieved Douthwaite silently of his pile of towels and left the room, her slides slapping the bottoms of her sockless feet. The door clicked shut behind her.

'Sit down,' Donna instructed Strike and Robin, who did so, on a small sofa.

Douthwaite took up a standing position, arms folded, with his back to the TV. Frowning slightly, his eyes flickered over Strike and Robin and back to his wife. The sunlight filtering through the net curtains cast an unforgiving light over his hair, which looked like wispy strands of steel wool.

'He's the one who caught that Shacklewell Ripper,' Donna said to her husband, jerking her head at Strike. 'Why's he after you?' Her voice rose in both pitch and volume. 'Been dicking around with the wrong woman again, have you? *Have you?*'

'What?' said Douthwaite, but it was obvious this was a stalling tactic: he had understood well enough. His right forearm was tattooed with an hourglass, and around it was wrapped a ribbon with the words 'Never Enough'.

'Mr Douthwaite,' Strike began, but Douthwaite said quickly,

'Diamond! It's Diamond!'

'Why're you calling him Douthwaite?' asked Donna.

'I'm sorry,' said Strike insincerely. 'My mistake. Your husband was born Steven Douthwaite, as I'm sure you—'

But Donna clearly hadn't known this. She turned, astonished, from Strike to Douthwaite, who'd frozen, mouth slightly open.

'*Douthwaite?*' repeated Donna. She turned on her husband. 'You told me your name used to be Jacks!'

'I—'

'When were you *Douthwaite*?'

'—ages—'

'Why didn't you tell me?'

'I – what's it matter?'

The bell tinkled again and a group of people was heard out

in the hall. Still looking shocked and angry, Donna strode outside to see what was needed, her wooden-soled sandals banging over the tiles. The moment she'd disappeared, Douthwaite addressed Strike.

'What d'you want?'

'We've been hired by Dr Margot Bamborough's daughter, to look into her disappearance,' said Strike.

The parts of Douthwaite's face that weren't ruddy with broken veins blanched.

The enormous old lady who'd been descending the stairs now walked into the room, her wide, innocent face demonstrating total immunity to the atmosphere within.

'Which way's the seal sanctuary?'

'End of the road,' said Douthwaite hoarsely. 'Turn left.'

She sidled out of the room again. The bell outside tinkled.

'Listen,' said Douthwaite quickly, as the sound of his wife's footsteps grew louder again. 'You're wasting your time. I don't know anything about Margot Bamborough.'

'Perhaps you could have a look over your old police statement, at least,' asked Strike, taking a copy out of his inside pocket.

'What?' said Donna, now back in the room. 'What police statement? Oh, for *Christ's* sake,' she said, as the bell tinkled again, and she clunked back out of the room and bellowed up the stairs, 'Kirsty! *KIRSTY!*'

'That doctor,' Douthwaite said, looking at Strike through bloodshot eyes, his forehead sweaty, 'it all happened forty-odd years ago, I don't know anything about what happened, I never did.'

The harried Donna reappeared.

'Kirsty'll mind the front door,' she said, glaring at her husband. 'We'll go upstairs. Lochnagar's empty. We can't go in ours,' she added to Strike and Robin, pointing towards the basement, 'me grandkids are down there, playing computer games.'

Douthwaite hitched up his waistband and threw a wild look outside the net curtains, as though contemplating flight.

'Come on,' said Donna fiercely, and with a return to his hangdog look, he followed his wife out of the door.

Kirsty passed them, heading for the ground floor, as they climbed the steep tartan stairs, Strike making liberal use of the banister to haul himself up. He'd hoped Lochnagar might be on the first floor, but he was disappointed. It lay, as the name might have suggested, right at the top of the B&B, and faced out of the rear of the building.

The furniture inside was made of cheap pine. Kirsty had arranged towels in the shape of kissing swans on the maroon bedspread, which matched the patterned wallpaper of maroon and deep purple. Leads dangled from behind the wall-mounted TV. A plastic kettle sat in the corner on a low table, beside the Corby trouser press. Through the window Strike glimpsed the sea at last: a gleaming golden bar lying low between buildings, in the misty haze created by the net curtains.

Donna crossed the room and took the only chair. Her hands were gripping her own upper arms so tightly that the flesh showed white.

'You can sit down,' she told Strike and Robin.

Having nowhere else to do it, both sat down on the end of the double bed, with its slippery maroon cover. Douthwaite remained at the door, back against it, arms folded, displaying the hourglass tattoo.

'Diamond, Jacks, Douthwaite,' Donna recited. 'How many other names have you had?'

'None,' said Douthwaite, trying for a laugh, but failing.

'Why'd you change your name from Douthwaite to Jacks?' she demanded. 'Why were the police after you?'

'They weren't after me,' croaked Douthwaite. 'This was ages ago. I wanted a fresh start, that's all.'

'How many fresh starts does one man need?' said Donna. 'What did you do? Why'd you have to give a police statement?'

'A doctor went missing,' said Douthwaite, with a glance at Strike.

'What doctor? When?'

'Her name was Margot Bamborough.'

'Bamborough?' repeated Donna, her forehead bifurcated by that deep frown line, 'But that ... that was all over the news ...'

'They interviewed all the patients she'd seen before she disappeared,' Douthwaite said quickly. 'It was routine! They didn't have anything on me.'

'You must think I was born bloody yesterday,' said Donna. '*They*,' she pointed at Strike and Robin, 'haven't tracked you down because it was *routine enquiries*, have they? You didn't change your bloody name because it was *routine enquiries*! Screwing her, were you?'

'No, I wasn't bloody screwing her!' said Douthwaite, with his first sign of fight.

'Mr Douthwaite,' began Strike.

'Diamond!' said Douthwaite, more in desperation than in anger.

'I'd be grateful if you'd read through your police statement, see whether you've got anything to add.'

Douthwaite looked as though he'd have liked to refuse, but after a slight hesitation he took the pieces of paper and began to read. The statement was a long one, covering as it did the suicide of Joanna Hammond, his married ex-lover, the beating he'd endured at the hands of her husband, the anxiety and depression which had led to so many visits to the St John's surgery, his assertion that he'd felt nothing more for Margot

Bamborough than mild gratitude for her clinical expertise, his denial that he'd ever brought or sent her gifts and his feeble alibi for the time of her disappearance.

'Yeah, I've got nothing to add to that,' Douthwaite said at last, holding the pieces of paper back out to Strike.

'I want to read it,' said Donna at once.

'It's got nothing to do with – it's forty years ago, it's nothing,' said Douthwaite.

'Your real name's Douthwaite and I never knew till five minutes ago! I've got a right to know who you are,' she said fiercely, 'I've got a right to know, so I can decide whether I was a bloody mug to stay with you, after the last—'

'Fine, read it, go on,' said Douthwaite with unconvincing bravado, and Strike handed the statement over to Donna.

She'd read for barely a minute when she burst out,

'You were sleeping with a married – and she *killed* herself?'

'I wasn't – we weren't – once, it happened, once! Nobody kills themselves over that!'

'Why'd she do it, then? Why?'

'Her husband was a bastard.'

'*My* husband's a bastard. I haven't topped myself!'

'Christ's sake, Donna—'

'*What happened?*'

'It was nothing!' said Douthwaite. 'We used to hang out together, few of the lads at work and their wives and whatever, and one night I was out with some other mates and ran into Joanna, who was with some girlfriends and . . . some cunt tipped off her husband we'd left the pub together and—'

'And then this doctor disappeared and all, and the police came calling?'

Donna got to her feet, Douthwaite's crumpled statement quivering in her hand. Still sitting on the slippery maroon coverlet, Robin remembered the day she'd found Sarah Shadlock's diamond earring in her bed, and thought she knew a little, a very little, of what Donna was experiencing.

'I knew you were a bloody cheat and a liar, but *three girlfriends dead*? One's a tragedy,' said Donna furiously, and Strike wondered whether they were about to hear a Wildean epigram, 'but *three*? How bloody unlucky can one man get?'

'I never had anything going on with that doctor!'

'You'll try it on with anyone!' shrieked Donna, and addressing Robin, she said, 'Year before last, I catch him in a guest bedroom with one of my best friends—'

'Christ's sake, Donna!' whimpered Douthwaite.

'—and six months ago—'

'*Donna*—'

'—I find out he's been sneaking around with one of our regulars – and now –' said Donna, advancing on Douthwaite, his statements clutched in her fist. 'You creepy bastard, *what happened to all these women*?'

'I had nothing to do with any of them *dying*, fuck's sake!' said Douthwaite, trying for an incredulous laugh and merely looking terrified. 'Donna, come on – you think I'm some kind of *murderer?*'

'You expect me to believe—'

To Strike's surprise, Robin suddenly jumped to her feet. Taking Donna by the shoulders, she guided her back into her chair.

'Put your head down,' Robin was saying, 'head down.'

When Robin moved to untie Donna's apron, which was tight around her waist, and Strike saw that Donna's forehead, which was all he could see now she had sunk her face into her hands, was as white as the net curtain behind her.

'Donna?' said Douthwaite feebly, but his wife whispered,

'You stay away from me, you bastard.'

'Breathe,' Robin was saying, crouching beside Donna's

chair. 'Get her some water,' she told Strike, who got up and went into the tiny shower room, where a plastic beaker sat in a holder over the sink.

Almost as pale as his wife, Douthwaite watched as Robin persuaded Donna to drink.

'Stay there, now,' Robin told the landlady, one hand resting on her shoulder. 'Don't get up.'

'Did he have something to do with them dying?' Donna whispered, looking sideways at Robin, her pupils enormous with shock.

'That's what we're here to find out,' Robin murmured back.

She turned and looked meaningfully at Strike, who silently agreed that the best thing he could do for the stricken Donna was to get information out of Douthwaite.

'We've got a number of questions we'd like to ask you,' Strike told him. 'Obviously you're not obliged to answer them, but I'd put it to you that it would be in the best interests of everyone, yourself included, to cooperate.'

'What questions?' said Douthwaite, still flat against the door. Then, in a torrent of words, he said, 'I've never hurt anyone, never, I'm not a violent man. Donna will tell you, I've never laid a finger on her in anger, that's not who I am.'

But when Strike merely continued to look at him, Douthwaite said pleadingly,

'Look, I've told you – with Joanna – it was a one-night stand. I was just a kid,' he said, and in an echo of Irene Hickson, he said, 'You do those kinds of things when you're young, don't you?'

'And when you're old,' whispered Donna. 'And all the bloody years in between . . .'

'Where were you,' Strike asked Douthwaite, 'when Joanna killed herself?'

'In Brent,' said Douthwaite. 'Miles away! And I had

witnesses to prove it. We used to work in pairs, selling, each do one side of the street, and I was out with a bloke called Tadger,' and he tried to laugh again. Nobody smiled. 'Tadger, you can imagine the grief he . . . well, he was with me all day . . .

'Got back to the office late in the afternoon, and there was a group of lads in there, and they told us Hammond had just got the message his wife had topped herself . . .

'Terrible,' said the pale and sweating Douthwaite, 'but except for that one night together, I had nothing to do with it. But her old man – well, it was easier to blame me,' said Douthwaite, 'wasn't it, than think about his own bloody behaviour?

'I got home a couple of nights later and he was lying in wait. Ambush. He beat the shit out of me.'

'Good!' said Donna, on a half-sob.

'And your neighbour, Janice the nurse, looked after—'

'Straight off with the neighbour, were you, Steve?' said Donna, with a hollow laugh. 'Get the nurse to mop you up?'

'It wasn't like that!' said Douthwaite with surprising vehemence.

'It's his little trick,' the white-faced Donna told Robin, who was still kneeling by her chair. 'Always got a sob story on the go. Fell for it myself. Heartbroken after the love of his life drowned . . . oh my God,' Donna whispered, slowly shaking her head. 'And she was the third.' With a hysterical little laugh, she said, 'As far as we know. Maybe there are others. Who knows?'

'Christ's sake, Donna!' said Douthwaite, yet again. Patches of underarm sweat were visible through his thin turquoise T-shirt: Strike could literally smell his fear. 'Come on, you know me, you know I'd never hurt anyone!'

'Janice says she advised you to see the doctor about your symp—'

'*She* never told me to go to the doctor!' snapped Douthwaite, one eye on his wife. 'I didn't need telling, I went off my own bat because I was just getting worried about the . . . headaches and . . . mostly headaches. I felt really bad.'

'You visited Margot six times in one two-week period,' said Strike.

'I felt ill, stomach pains and what have you . . . I mean, it obviously affected me, Joanna dying, and then people talking about me . . . '

'Oh, poor you, poor you,' murmured Donna. 'Jesus effing Christ. You hate going to the doctor. Six times in two weeks?'

'Donna, come on,' said Douthwaite imploringly, 'I was feeling like shit! And then the bloody police come and make out like I was stalking her or something. It was all my health!'

'Did you buy her—?' began Strike.

'—chocolates? No!' said Douthwaite, who suddenly seemed very agitated. 'If someone sent her chocolates, maybe you should find *them*. But it wasn't me! I told the police I never bought her anything, it weren't like that—'

'Witnesses said you seemed distressed and possibly angry, the last time you left Dr Bamborough's surgery,' said Strike. 'What happened during that last visit?'

Douthwaite's breath was coming fast now. Suddenly, almost aggressively, he looked directly into Strike's eyes.

Experienced in the body language of suspects who yearn for the release and relief of unburdening themselves, no matter the consequences, Strike suddenly knew that Douthwaite was teetering on the brink of a disclosure. He'd have given almost anything to spirit the man away now, to a quiet interrogation room, but exactly as he'd feared, the precious moment was snatched away by Donna.

'Turned you down, did she? What did you think, Steve – a scrubby little failed salesman had a chance with a doctor?'

'*I wasn't bloody looking for a chance!*' said Douthwaite, rounding on his wife, 'I was there for my health, I was in a state!'

'He's like a bloody tomcat,' Donna told Robin, 'slinking around behind everyone's backs. He'll use anything to get his end away, anything. His girlfriend's topped herself and he's using it to chat up nurses and doctors—'

'I wasn't, I was ill!'

'That last meeting—' Strike began again.

'I don't know what you're on about, it was nothing,' Douthwaite said, now avoiding looking Strike in the face. 'The doc was just telling me to take it easy.'

'Like you ever needed telling that, you lazy bastard,' spat Donna.

'Perhaps,' said Strike, 'as you're feeling unwell, Mrs Diamond, I could speak to Steve somewhere sep—'

'Oh no you don't!' said Donna. 'No way! I want—'

She exploded into tears, shoulders sagging, face in her hands.

'I'm going to hear it all now . . . last chance . . .'

'Donna—' said Douthwaite plaintively.

'Don't,' she sobbed into her fingers. 'Don't you dare.'

'Perhaps,' said Strike, hoping to return to the last visit with Margot in due course, 'we could go over your alibi for the time Dr Bamborough disappeared?'

Donna was sobbing, tears and mucus flowing freely now. Robin grabbed a paper napkin off the tray beside the kettle and handed it to her.

Cowed by his wife's distress, Douthwaite allowed Strike to lead him back over his shaky alibi for the evening in question, sticking to the story that he'd been sitting unnoticed in a café, scanning the newspapers for flats to rent.

'I wanted to clear out, get away from all the gossip about Joanna. I just wanted to get away.'

'So the desire to move wasn't triggered by anything that

passed between you and Dr Bamborough during your last visit?' Strike asked.

'No,' said Douthwaite, still not looking at Strike. 'How could it be?'

'Given up on her?' Donna asked from behind the wet napkin with which she was blotting her eyes. 'Knew he'd made a fool of himself. Same as with that young lassie from Leeds, eh, Steve?'

'Donna, for *fuck's* sake—'

'He forgets,' Donna said to Robin, 'he's not that cocky little sod in his twenties any more. Deluded, b – baldy bastard,' she sobbed.

'*Donna*—'

'So you moved to Waltham Forest . . .' prompted Strike.

'Yeah. Police. Press. It was a nightmare,' said Douthwaite. 'I thought of ending it, to tell you the—'

'Shame you didn't,' said Donna savagely. 'Save us all a lot of time and trouble.'

As though he hadn't heard this, and ignoring Douthwaite's look of outrage, Strike asked,

'What made you go to Clacton-on-Sea? Did you have family there?'

'I haven't got family, I grew up in care—'

'Oh, someone pass him a bloody violin,' said Donna.

'Well, it's true, isn't it?' said Douthwaite, displaying unvarnished anger for the first time. 'And I'm allowed to tell the truth about my own bloody life, aren't I? I just wanted to be a Redcoat, because I sing a bit and it looked like a fun way to earn a living—'

'Fun,' muttered Donna, 'oh yeah, as long as *you're* having fun, Steve—'

'—get away from people treating me like I'd killed someone—'

'And *whoops*!' said Donna. 'There's another one gone, in the pool—'

'You know *bloody well* I had nothing to do with Julie drowning!'

'How could I know?' said Donna, 'I wasn't there! It was before we even met!'

'I showed you the story in the paper!' said Douthwaite. 'I *showed* you, Donna, come on!' He turned to Strike. 'A bunch of us were drinking in our chalet. Me and some mates were playing poker. Julie was tired. She left before we finished our game, walked back to her chalet. She walked round the pool, slipped in the dark, knocked herself out and—'

For the first time, Douthwaite showed real distress.

'—she drowned. I won't ever forget it. Never. I ran outside in me underpants next morning, when I heard the shouting. I saw her body when they were taking her out of the pool. You don't forget something like that. She was a kid. Twenty-two or something. Her parents came and . . . it was a horrible thing. Horrible. I never . . . that someone can go like that. A slip and a trip . . .

'Yeah, so . . . that's when I applied for a job at the Ingoldmells Butlin's up the road from here. And that's where I met Donna,' he said, with an apprehensive glance at his wife.

'So you leaving Clacton-on-Sea and changing your name again had nothing to do with a man called Oakden coming to question you about Margot Bamborough?' asked Strike.

Donna's head jerked up.

'Oh my God,' she said, 'so even the *Julie* bit's a lie?'

'It's not a lie!' said Douthwaite loudly. 'I *told* you Julie and I had an argument a couple of days before she died, I *told* you that, because I felt so guilty after! This man, this – what did you say his name was? Oakden? – yeah, he turned up, saying he was writing a book about Dr Bamborough disappearing.

Went round all the other Redcoats talking to them about me, telling them all I'd been a suspect and how I'd changed my name afterwards, making me sound dodgy as hell. And Julie was really pissed off with me because I hadn't told her—'

'Well, you really learned *that* lesson, didn't you, Steve?' said Donna. 'Run and hide, that's all you know, and when you're found out, you just sneak off and find some other woman to whine to, until she finds you out, and then—'

'Mr Douthwaite,' said Strike, cutting across Donna, 'I want to thank you for your time. I know it's been a shock, having all this raked up again.'

Robin looked up at Strike, astonished. He couldn't be leaving the interview here, surely? The Douthwaites (or Diamonds, as they thought of themselves), looked similarly taken aback. Strike extracted a second card from his pocket and held it out to Douthwaite.

'If you remember anything,' the detective said, 'you know where to find me. It's never too late.'

The hourglass tattoo on Douthwaite's forearm rippled as he held out his hand for the card.

'Who else've you talked to?' Douthwaite asked Strike.

Now that his ordeal was over, he seemed curiously averse to it ending. Perhaps, thought Robin, he feared being alone with his wife.

'Margot's husband and family,' said Strike, watching Douthwaite's reactions. 'The co-workers who're still alive – Dr Gupta. One of the receptionists, Irene Hickson. Janice Beattie, the nur—'

'That's nice,' piped up Donna, 'the nurse is still available, Steve—'

'—an ex-boyfriend of Margot's, her best friend, and a few other people.'

Douthwaite, who'd flushed at his wife's interjection, said,

'Not Dennis Creed?'

'Not yet,' said Strike. 'Well,' he looked from husband to wife, 'thanks for your time. We appreciate it.'

Robin got to her feet.

'I'm sorry,' she said quietly to Donna. 'I hope you feel better.'

'Thanks,' mumbled Donna.

As Strike and Robin reached the top of the stairs, they heard shouting break out again behind the door of Lochnagar.

'Donna, babes—'

'Don't you dare call me babes, you fucking bastard!'

'No point carrying on,' said Strike quietly, setting off down the steep tartaned stairs as slowly as the obese old lady had moved. 'He's not going to say it with her there.'

'Say what?'

'Well, that,' said Strike, as the Douthwaites' shouts echoed down the stairs, 'is the question, isn't it?'

65

Like as a ship, that through the Ocean wyde
Directs her course vnto one certaine cost,
Is met of many a counter winde and tyde,
With which her winged speed is let and crost,
And she her selfe in stormie surges tost;
Yet making many a borde, and many a bay,
Still winneth way, ne hath her compasse lost:
Right so it fares with me in this long way,
Whose course is often stayd, yet neuer is astray.

Edmund Spenser
The Faerie Queene

'I'm hungry,' Strike announced, once they stepped down onto the sunny pavement outside the Allardice.

'Let's get some fish and chips,' said Robin.

'Now you're talking,' said Strike enthusiastically, as they headed off towards the end of Scarbrough Avenue.

'Cormoran, what makes you think Douthwaite knows something?'

'Didn't you see the way he looked at me, when I asked him about his last appointment with Margot?'

'I must've been looking at Donna. I was seriously worried she was going to pass out.'

'Wish she had,' said Strike.

'Strike!'

'He was definitely thinking about telling me something, then she bloody ruined it.' As they reached the end of the road, he said, 'That was a scared man, and I don't think he's only scared of his wife . . . Do we go left or right?'

'Right,' said Robin, so they headed off along Grand Parade, passing a long open-fronted building called Funland, which was full of beeping and flashing video games, claw machines and coin-operated mechanical horses for children to ride. 'Are you saying Douthwaite's guilty?'

'I think he feels it,' Strike said, as they wove their way in and out of cheerful, T-shirted families and couples. 'He looked at me back there as though he was bursting to tell me something that's weighing on him.'

'If he had actual evidence, why didn't he tell the police? It would've got them off his back.'

'I can think of one reason.'

'He was scared of the person he thought had killed her?'

'Exactly.'

'So . . . Luca Ricci?' said Robin.

At that moment, a male voice from the depths of Funland called, 'White seven and four, *seventy-four.*'

'Possibly,' said Strike, though he didn't sound entirely convinced. 'Douthwaite and Ricci were living in the same area at the time. Maybe going to the same pubs. I suppose he might've heard a rumour about Ricci being out to get her. But that doesn't fit with the eye-witness accounts, does it? If Douthwaite was issuing the warning, you'd think it'd be Margot looking distressed afterwards, whereas we know *he* was the one who came running out of there looking scared and worried . . . but my gut feeling is that Douthwaite thinks whatever happened between them at that last appointment is relevant to her disappearance.'

The entrance to a well-maintained park on their right was

ablaze with petunias. Ahead, on an island in the middle of a traffic island, stood a sixty-foot-high clock tower of brick and stone, with a faintly Gothic appearance, and faces like a miniature Big Ben.

'Exactly how many chippies has Skegness got?' Strike asked, as they came to a halt on the busy intersection beside the clock tower. They were standing right beside two establishments which had tables spilling out onto the pavement, and he could see a further two fish and chip shops on the other side of the junction.

'I never counted,' said Robin. 'I was always more interested in the donkeys. Shall we try here?' she asked, pointing at the nearest free table, which was pistachio green and belonged to Tony's Chippy ('We Sell on Quality not Price').

'Donkeys?' repeated Strike, grinning, as he sat down on the bench.

'That's right,' said Robin. 'Cod or haddock?'

'Haddock, please,' said Strike, and Robin headed into the chip shop to order.

After a minute or so, looking forward to his chips and enjoying the feeling of sun on his back, Strike became aware that he was still watching Robin, and fixed his eyes instead on a fluttering mass just above him. Even though the top of the yellow railings separating Tony's from Harry Ramsbottom's had been fitted with fine spikes to stop birds landing on them, a handful of speckled starlings were doing just that, delicately poised between the needles, and balanced in the iron circles just below them, waiting for the chance to swoop on an abandoned chip.

Watching the birds, Strike wondered what the chances were of Douthwaite ringing the number on his card. He was a man with a long track record of hiding from his past, but Strike had definitely read in his face a desperation he'd only ever seen in the faces of men who could no longer bear the pressure of a terrible secret. Idly rubbing his chin, Strike decided to give the man a short period of grace, then either call him again, or even return, unannounced, to Skegness, where he might waylay Douthwaite in the street or a pub, where Donna couldn't interfere.

Strike was still watching the starlings when Robin set down two polystyrene trays, two small wooden forks and two cans of Coke on the table.

'Mushy peas,' said Strike, looking at Robin's tray, where a hefty dollop of what looked like green porridge sat alongside her fish and chips.

'Yorkshire caviar,' said Robin, sitting down. 'I didn't think you'd want any.'

'You were right,' said Strike, picking up a sachet of tomato sauce while watching with something like revulsion as Robin dipped a chip into the green sludge and ate it.

'Soft Southerner, you are,' she said, and Strike laughed.

'Don't ever let Polworth hear you say that,' he said, breaking off a bit of fish with his fingers, dipping it in ketchup and eating it. He then, without warning, broke into song:

A good sword and a trusty hand!
A merry heart and true!
King James's men shall understand,
What Cornish lads can do.

'What on earth's that?' asked Robin, laughing.

'First verse of "The Song of the Western Men",' said Strike. 'The gist is that Cornishmen are the antithesis of soft bastards. Bloody hell, this is good.'

'I know. You don't get fish and chips like this in London,' said Robin.

For a few minutes they ate in silence. The greaseproof paper in which the trays of chips were wrapped was printed with old pages of the *Mirror* newspaper. *Paul Quits the Beatles.* There were cartoons too, of the dirty postcard type: a busty blonde in bed with her elderly boss was saying 'Business must be booming. You've never given me so much overtime.' It reminded her of Gemma the PA, who'd perhaps already called the fake number Robin had given her, and realised that it wasn't only her ex, 'Andy', who wasn't all he appeared to be. But Robin had a recording on her phone of everything Gemma knew about Shifty's insider trading and Pat, at that moment, was transcribing it into a document shorn of anything that might identify the informant. Shifty, Robin hoped, would soon be jobless and, with any luck, in court.

A long stretch of fairground rides on the other side of the road hid the sea from her sight. The seats of the distant Ferris wheel were enclosed in casings shaped like pastel-coloured hot-air balloons. Nearby stood a gigantic climbing frame for adults, with ropes and swinging tyres, a hundred feet up in the air. Watching the harnessed people navigating the obstacles, Robin felt a strange mixture of contentment and melancholy: the possibility of an unknown development in the Bamborough case, the delicious chips and peas, the companionship of Strike and the sunshine were all cheering, but she was also remembering chasing along the out-of-sight beach as a small child, trying to outrun her brother Stephen to reach the donkeys and have first pick. Why did the memory of innocence sting so much, as you got older? Why did the memory of the child who'd thought she was invulnerable, who'd never known cruelty, give her more pain than pleasure?

Her childhood had been happy, unlike Strike's; it ought not to hurt. Over the space of summer weekends spread years apart, Robin and her brothers had competed to ride the black donkey called Noddy, who was doubtless long gone. Was it mortality, then, which turned cheerful memories bittersweet? Maybe, Robin thought, she'd bring Annabel here when she was old enough, and treat her to her first donkey ride. It was a nice idea, but she doubted Stephen and Jenny would see Skegness as a desirable weekend destination. Annabel's great-aunt had moved away from Boston: there was no longer any family connection to the area. Times changed, and so did childhoods.

'You all right?' said Strike, watching Robin's face.

'Fine,' she said. 'Just thinking . . . I'm going to be thirty in a few weeks.'

Strike snorted.

'Well, you're getting no sympathy from me,' he said. 'I'll be forty the month after.'

He snapped open his can of Coke and drank. Robin watched a family pass, all four eating ice creams, accompanied by a waddling dachshund that was nosing the Union Jack carrier bag which swung from the father's hand.

'D'you think Scotland's going to leave?'

'Go for independence? Maybe,' said Strike. 'The polls are close. Barclay thinks it could happen. He was telling me about some old mates of his at home. They sound just like Polworth. Same hate figures, same promises everything'll be rainbows and unicorns if only they cut themselves free of London. Anyone pointing out pitfalls or difficulties is scaremongering. Experts don't know anything. Facts lie. "Things can't be any worse than they are."'

Strike put several chips in his mouth, chewed, swallowed, then said,

'But life's taught me things can always get worse than they are. I thought I had it hard, then they wheeled a bloke onto the ward who'd had both his legs and his genitals blown off.'

He'd never before talked to Robin about the aftermath of

his life-changing injury. Indeed, he rarely mentioned his missing leg. A barrier had definitely fallen, Robin thought, since their whisky-fuelled talk in the dark office.

'Everyone wants a single, simple solution,' he said, now finishing his last few chips. '*One weird trick to lose belly fat.* I've never clicked on it, but I understand the appeal.'

'Well, reinvention's such an inviting idea, isn't it?' said Robin, her eyes on the fake hot-air balloons, circling on their prescribed course. 'Look at Douthwaite, changing his name and finding a new woman every few years. Reinventing a whole country would feel amazing. Being part of that.'

'Yeah,' said Strike. 'Of course, people think if they subsume themselves in something bigger, and that changes, they'll change too.'

'Well, there's nothing wrong with wanting to be better, or different, is there?' asked Robin. 'Nothing wrong with wanting to improve things?'

'Not at all,' said Strike. 'But *people* who fundamentally change are rare, in my experience, because it's bloody hard work compared to going on a march or waving a flag. Have we met a single person on this case who's radically different to the person they were forty years ago?'

'I don't know . . . I think *I've* changed,' said Robin, then felt embarrassed to have said it out loud.

Strike looked at her without smiling for the space it took him to chew and swallow a chip, then said,

'Yeah. But you're exceptional, aren't you?'

And before Robin had time for anything other than a slight blush, Strike said,

'Are you not finishing those chips?'

'Help yourself,' said Robin, shoving the tray towards him. She pulled her phone out of her pocket. 'I'll look up that one weird tip to lose belly fat.'

Strike smirked. After wiping her hands on her paper napkin, Robin checked her emails.

'Have you seen this from Vanessa Ekwensi? She's copied you in.'

'What?'

'She might know someone who could replace Morris . . . woman called Michelle Greenstreet . . . she wants to leave the police. She's been in eight years,' said Robin, scrolling slowly down the email, 'not enjoying response policing . . . she's in Manchester . . . wants to relocate to London, very keen on the detective side . . . '

'Sounds promising,' said Strike. 'Let's schedule an interview. She's already cleared the first hurdle with flying colours.'

'What hurdle?' said Robin, looking up.

'Doubt she's ever sent a dick pic.'

He patted his pockets, pulled out his packet of Benson & Hedges but found it empty.

'I need more fags, let's—'

'Wait,' said Robin, who was still staring down at her mobile. 'Oh my God. Cormoran – Gloria Conti's emailed me.'

'You're kidding,' said Strike. Having partly risen, he now let himself fall back onto the bench.

'"Dear Miss Ellacott,"' Robin read aloud, '"I'm sorry I haven't answered your emails. I wasn't aware you were trying to contact me and have only just found out. If convenient, I'd be available to talk to you tomorrow evening at 7pm. Yours sincerely . . . " and she's given her phone number,' said Robin, looking up at Strike, astonished. 'How can she only just have found out? It's been *months* of me emailing her without any response . . . unless Anna's prompted her?'

'Could be,' said Strike. 'Which doesn't suggest someone who wants the investigation over.'

'Of *course* she doesn't,' said Robin. 'But for sanity's sake, you'd have to draw the line somewhere.'

'So what does that make us?'

Robin smiled and shook her head.

'Dedicated?'

'Conti: last person to see Margot alive. Closest person to Margot at the practice . . .'

'I'm thanking her,' said Robin, who was typing fast onto her mobile, 'and agreeing to the call tomorrow.'

'We could do it from the office, together,' said Strike. 'Maybe FaceTime her, if she's agreeable?'

'I'll ask,' said Robin, still typing.

They set off a few minutes later in search of cigarettes, Robin reflecting on how casually she'd just agreed to go into work on a Saturday evening, so she could conduct Gloria's interview with Strike. There was no angry Matthew at home any more, furious about her committing herself to long hours, suspicious about what she and Strike were up to, alone in the office in the evening. And she thought back to Matthew's refusal to look her in the eye across the table at the mediation. He'd changed his partner, and his firm; he'd soon be a father. His life had changed, but had he?

They turned the corner to find themselves facing what Strike mentally categorised as 'acres of tat'. As far as the eye could see were racks of merchandise laid out on the pavement: beach balls, keyrings, cheap jewellery, sunglasses, buckets of candyfloss, fudge and plush toys.

'Look at that,' said Robin suddenly, pointing to her right. A bright yellow sign read: *Your Life Within Your Hands*. On the dark glass of the door below was written: *Palm Reader. Clairvoyant*, along with a circular chart, all twelve signs of the zodiac represented by the glyphs around a central sun.

'What?' said Strike.

'Well, you've had your chart done. Maybe I'd like mine.'

'Fuck's sake,' muttered Strike, and they walked on, Robin smiling to herself.

She waited outside, examining postcards, while Strike entered the newsagent's to buy cigarettes.

Waiting to be served, Strike was seized by a sudden, quixotic impulse (stimulated no doubt by the gaudy colour all around him, by the sunshine and sticks of rock, the rattle and clang of amusement arcades and a stomach full of some of the best fish and chips he'd ever eaten) to buy Robin a toy donkey. He came to his senses almost before the idea had formed: what was he, a kid on a daytime date with his first girlfriend? Emerging again into the sunlight as he left the shop, he noted that he couldn't have bought a donkey if he'd wanted to. There wasn't a single one in sight: the bins full of plushes held only unicorns.

'Back to the car, then?' said Robin.

'Yeah,' said Strike, ripping the cellophane off his cigarettes, but then he said, 'we'll go down to the sea before we head off, shall we?'

'OK,' said Robin, surprised. 'Er – why?'

'Just fancy it. It's wrong, being by the sea without actually laying eyes on it.'

'Is this a Cornish thing?' asked Robin, as they headed back to Grand Parade.

'Maybe,' said Strike, lighting the cigarette between his teeth. He took a drag on his cigarette, exhaled then sang,

And when we come to London Wall,
A pleasant sight to view,
Come forth! come forth! ye cowards all:
Here's men as good as you.

'"The Song of the Western Men?"'

'That's the one.'

'Why d'you think they feel the need to tell Londoners they're just as good? Isn't that a given?'

'Just London, isn't it?' said Strike, as they crossed the road. 'Pisses everyone off.'

'I love London.'

'Me too. But I can see why it pisses everyone off.'

They passed a fountain with a statue in the middle of the Jolly Fisherman, that rotund, bearded sailor skipping along in high wind, who'd been used on posters advertising Skegness for nearly a century, and progressed across a smooth paved area towards the beach.

At last they saw what Strike had felt the need to see: a wide expanse of flat ocean, the colour of chalcedony, beneath a periwinkle sky. Far out at sea, spoiling the horizon, were an army of tall white wind turbines, and while Strike personally enjoyed the chill breeze coming off the wide ocean, he understood at last why Robin had brought a scarf.

Strike smoked in silence, the cool wind making no difference whatsoever to his curly hair. He was thinking about Joan. It hadn't occurred to him until this moment that her plan for her final resting place had given them a grave to visit any time they were at the British coast. Cornish-born, Cornish-bred, Joan had known that this need to reconnect with the sea lived in all of them. Now, every time they made their way to the coast they paid her tribute, along with the obeisance due to the waves.

'They were Joan's favourites, pink roses,' he said, after a while. 'What you sent, to the funeral.'

'Oh, really?' said Robin. 'I . . . well, I had a kind of picture in my head of Joan, from things you'd told me, and . . . pink roses seemed to suit her.'

'If the agency ever fails,' said Strike, as they both turned away from the sea, 'you could come back to Skegness and set yourself up as a clairvoyant.'

'Bit niche,' said Robin, as they walked back towards the car park. 'Guessing dead people's favourite flowers.'

'No donkeys,' said Strike, glancing back over his shoulder at the beach.

'Never mind,' said Robin kindly. 'I think you'd have been a bit heavy.'

66

Speak, thou frail woman, speak with confidence.

Edmund Spenser
The Faerie Queene

The following evening, Strike and Robin sat down together on the same side of the partners' desk. They were alone in the office for the first time since the night Strike had given her two black eyes. The lights were on this time, there were no glasses of whisky in their hands, but each of them was very conscious of what had happened on the previous occasion, and both felt a slight self-consciousness, which manifested itself, on Strike's side, in a slightly brisker tone as they set up the computer monitor so that both could see it well, and on Robin's, in focusing herself on all the questions she wanted to ask Gloria.

At six o'clock – which was seven o'clock, Gloria's time – Strike dialled Gloria's number, and after a moment's suspense, they heard ringing, and a woman appeared onscreen, looking slightly nervous, in what looked like a book-lined study. Framed on the wall behind her was a large photograph of a family: Gloria herself, a distinguished-looking husband and three adult children, all wearing white shirts, all of them notably attractive.

Of all the people they'd met and interviewed in connection with Margot Bamborough, Gloria Conti, Robin thought, looked most like her younger self, although she hadn't made any obvious efforts to disguise the ageing process. Her hair, which was pure white, had been cut into a short and flattering bob. Although there were fine lines on her brow and around her eyes, her fair complexion seemed never to have been exposed to much sun. She was slim and high-cheekboned, so that the structure of her face was much as it had been when she was younger, and her high-necked navy shirt, small gold earrings and square-framed glasses were stylish and simple. Robin thought that Gloria looked far more like her idea of a college professor than the scion of a criminal family, but perhaps she was being influenced by the lines of books on the shelves behind her.

'Good evening,' said Gloria nervously.

'Good evening,' said Strike and Robin together.

'It's very good of you to talk to us, Mrs Jaubert,' said Strike. 'We appreciate it.'

'Oh, not at all,' she said, politely.

Robin hadn't imagined received pronunciation from Irene Hickson's descriptions of a girl from a rough background, but of course, as with Paul Satchwell, Gloria had now spent longer outside the country of her birth than in it.

'We've been hoping to talk to you for a long time,' said Robin.

'Yes, I'm very sorry about that,' said Gloria. 'My husband, Hugo, didn't tell me about any of your messages, you see. I found your last email in the trash folder, by accident. That's how I realised you were trying to contact me. Hugo – well, he thought he was doing the right thing.'

Robin was reminded of that occasion when Matthew had deleted a voicemail from Strike on Robin's phone in an attempt to stop Robin going back to work at the agency. She was surprised to see Gloria didn't seem to hold her husband's intervention against him. Perhaps Gloria could read her mind, because she said:

'Hugo assumed I wouldn't want to talk about what happened with strangers. He didn't realise that, actually, you're the only people I'd ever want to talk to, because you're trying to find out what really happened, and if you succeed, it'll be – well, it would lift a huge weight off me.'

'D'you mind if I take notes?' Strike asked her.

'No, not at all,' said Gloria politely.

As Strike clicked out the nib of his pen, Gloria reached out of shot for a large glass of red wine, took a sip, appeared to brace herself and said rather quickly,

'Please – if you don't mind – could I explain some things first? Since yesterday, I've been going over it, in my head, and I think if I tell you my story it will save you a lot of time. It's key to understanding my relationship with Margot and why I behaved . . . as I behaved.'

'That'd be very helpful,' said Strike, pen poised. 'Please, go on.'

Gloria took another sip of wine, put her glass back where they couldn't see it, drew a deep breath and said,

'Both my parents died in a house fire when I was five.'

'How awful,' said Robin, startled. The 1961 census record had shown a complete family of four. 'I'm so sorry.'

Strike gave a kind of commiserative growl.

'Thank you,' said Gloria. 'I'm only telling you that to explain – you see, I survived because my father threw me out of the window into a blanket the neighbours were holding. My mother and father didn't jump, because they were trying to reach my elder brother, who was trapped. All three of them died, so I was raised by my mother's parents. They were adorable people. They'd have sold their own souls for me, which makes everything I'm about to say even worse . . .

'I was quite a shy girl. I really envied the girls at school who had parents who were – you know – *with it*. My poor granny didn't really understand the sixties and seventies,' said Gloria, with a sad smile. 'My clothes were always a bit old-fashioned. No mini-skirts or eye make-up, you know . . .

'I reacted by developing a very elaborate fantasy life. I know most teenagers are fantasists, but I was . . . extreme. Everything sort of spun out of control when I was sixteen, and I went to see the movie *The Godfather* . . .

'It's ridiculous,' said Gloria soberly, 'but it's the truth. I . . . *cleaved* to that movie. I became *obsessed* with it. I don't know how many times I saw it; at least twenty, I expect. I was an English schoolgirl from seventies Islington, but what I *really* wanted was to be Apollonia from forties Sicily, and meet a handsome American Mafioso, and *not* to be blown up by a car bomb, but go and live with Michael Corleone in New York and be beautiful and glamorous while my husband did glamorously violent, criminal things, all underpinned, you know, by a strict moral code.'

Strike and Robin both laughed, but Gloria didn't smile. On the contrary, she looked sad and ashamed.

'I somehow thought all this might be achievable,' she went on, 'because I had an Italian surname. I'd never really cared about that, before *The Godfather.* Now, out of nowhere, I asked my grandparents to take me to the Italian church on Clerkenwell Road for mass, instead of their regular church – and bless them, they did it. I wish they hadn't. I wish they'd told me not to be so selfish, because their regular church gave them a lot of support and it was the centre of their social life.

'I'd always felt entirely English, which I *was* on my mum's side, but now I started trying to find out as much as I could about my dad's family. I hoped to find out I was descended from Mafiosi. Then I could get my grandparents to give me the money to go and meet them all in Sicily and maybe marry a distant cousin. But all I found out was that my Italian grandfather immigrated to London to work in a coffee shop. I already knew my dad had worked for London Transport. Everyone I found out about, no matter how far back I went, was completely respectable and law-abiding. It was a real disappointment,' said Gloria, with a sigh.

'Then one Sunday, at St Peter's, somebody pointed out a man called Niccolo Ricci, sitting at the back of the Italian church. They said he was one of the very last of the Little Italy gangsters.'

Gloria paused to take another mouthful of wine, replaced the glass out of shot again, then said,

'Anyway . . . Ricci had sons.'

Strike now set pen to paper for the first time.

'There wasn't much resemblance, really, between Luca Ricci and Al Pacino,' said Gloria drily, 'but I managed to find one. He was four years older than I was, and everyone I asked about him said he was trouble, which was exactly what I wanted to hear. It started with a few smiles in passing . . .

'We went on our first date a couple of months before I was due to sit my exams. I told Granny and Gramps I was revising at a schoolfriend's house. I'd always been such a good girl; they never dreamed I could be fibbing.

'I *desperately* wanted to like Luca, because this was my way into my fantasy. He had a car, and he was definitely criminal. He didn't tell me anything about summit meetings between heads of crime families, though . . . mostly he talked about his Fiat, and drugs and beating people up.

'After a few dates, it was obvious Luca was quite keen on me, or . . . no,' said Gloria, unsmiling, 'not keen, because that implies genuine affection. He really just wanted to fix me down, to keep me his. I was so stupid and lost to my fantasy, I found that quite exciting, because it seemed – you know – the proper Mafioso attitude. But I liked Luca best when I wasn't actually with him, when I was mixing him up with Michael Corleone in my head, in my bed at night.

'I stopped studying. My fantasy life took me over completely. Gangsters' molls didn't need A-levels. Luca didn't think I needed A-levels, either. I failed all of them.

'My grandparents were really disappointed, although they were so kind about it,' said Gloria. For the first time, her voice quivered slightly. 'Then – I think it was the following week – they found out about me seeing Luca. They were desperately worried and upset, but by this time, I didn't really care. I told them I'd given up on the idea of college. I wanted to go out to work.

'I only applied for the job at the St John's practice because it was in the heart of Little Italy, even though Little Italy didn't really exist any more. Luca's father was one of the very last relics. But it was all part of my fantasy: I was a Conti, I should be there, where my forefathers had been. It made it easier to see Luca, too, because he lived there.

'I should never have got that receptionist's job. I was far too young and I had no experience. It was Margot who wanted me to have it.'

Gloria paused, and Robin was sure it was because she'd just had to say Margot's name for the first time. Drawing another deep breath, she said,

'So, there I was, on reception with Irene all day. My grandparents weren't registered at St John's, because they lived in Islington, so I got away with telling Irene a bunch of lies about my background.

'I'd created a whole persona by now. I told her the Contis were an old Sicilian family, how my grandfather and father had been part of a crime family and I don't know what else.

Sometimes I used bits and pieces Luca had told me about the Riccis. Some of it was straight out of *The Godfather.* Ironically,' said Gloria, with a slight eye roll, 'the one authentically criminal thing I could have told her, I didn't. I kept my mouth shut about my boyfriend. Luca had told me never to talk about him and his family to other people, so I didn't. I took him seriously.

'I remember, a few months after I got the job, a rumour went round the local area that they'd found a body buried in concrete in one of the builder's sites up the road. I pretended I knew all about that through my underworld contacts. I told Irene I had it on good authority that the corpse had been a member of the Sabini gang. I really was a fool,' said Gloria quietly. 'A little idiot . . .

'But I always had the feeling Margot could see right through me. She told me not long after I started there that she'd "seen something" in me, at the interview. I didn't like that, I felt as though she was patronising me. She never treated me the way I wanted to be treated, as some street-smart Mafia girl with dark secrets, but always as though I was just a sweet young girl. Irene didn't like Margot, either, and we used to moan about her all the time on reception. Margot had a big thing about education and keeping your career, and we used to say what a hypocrite she was, because she'd married this rich consultant. When you're living a lie, nothing's more threatening than people who tell the truth . . .

'I'm sorry,' said Gloria, with an impatient shake of the head, 'this probably doesn't seem relevant at all, but it is, if you just bear with me . . .'

'Take your time,' said Strike.

'Well . . . the day after my eighteenth birthday, Luca and I got into a row. I can't remember what it was about, but he put his hand round my throat and pushed me up against the wall until I couldn't breathe. I was terrified.

'He let go, but there was this horrible look in his eye. He said, "You've got only yourself to blame." And he said, "You're starting to sound like that doctor."

'I'd talked to him quite a lot about Margot, you see. I'd told him she was a complete killjoy, really bossy and opinionated. I kept repeating things she'd said, to denigrate them, to tell myself there was nothing in them.

'She quoted Simone de Beauvoir once, during a staff meeting. She'd sworn when she dropped her pen, and Dr Brenner said, "People are always asking me what it's like working with a lady doctor, and if I ever meet one, I'll be able to tell them." Dorothy laughed – she hardly ever laughed – and Margot snapped right back at him – I know the quotation off by heart now, in French, too – "Man is defined as a human being and a woman as a female – whenever she behaves as a human being she is said to imitate the male."

'Irene and I talked about it afterwards. We called her a show-off for quoting some French woman, but things like that got in my head and I couldn't get them out again. I thought I wanted to be a fifties Mafia housewife, but sometimes Margot was really funny, and I watched her never backing down to Brenner, and you couldn't help admiring her for it . . . '

Gloria took yet another gulp of wine.

'Anyway, the evening Luca half-throttled me, I went home and lay awake crying half the night. The next morning, I put on a polo-neck for work to hide the bruises, and at five o'clock that afternoon, when I left work, I went straight to a call box near the surgery, rang Luca and finished with him. I told him he'd scared me and that I didn't want to see him any more.

'He took it quite quietly. I was surprised, but so relieved . . . for three or four days I thought it was all over, and I felt amazing. It was like waking up, or coming up for air after being underwater. I still wanted to be a mobster's girlfriend, but the fantasy version was fine. I'd had a little bit too much contact with reality.

'Then, at the end of our practice Christmas party, in walked Luca, with his father and one of his cousins.

'I was absolutely *terrified* to see them there. Luca said to me, "Dad just wanted to meet my girlfriend." And – I don't know why, except I was petrified of there being a scene – I just said, "Oh, OK." And I grabbed my coat and left with the three of them, before anyone could talk to them.

'They walked me to my bus stop. On the way, Nico said, "You're a nice girl. Luca was very upset by what you said to him on the phone. He's very fond of you, you know. You don't want to make him unhappy, do you?" Then he and Luca's cousin walked away. Luca said, "You didn't mean what you said, did you?" And I . . . I was so scared. Him bringing his father and cousin along . . . I told myself I'd be able to get out of it later. Just keep him happy for now. So I said, "No, I didn't mean it. You won't do anything like that ever again, though, will you?" And he said, "Like what?" As if he'd never pressed on my windpipe till I couldn't breathe. As though I'd imagined it.

'So, we carried on seeing each other,' said Gloria. 'Luca started talking about getting married. I kept saying I felt too young. Every time I came close to ending it, he'd accuse me of cheating on him, which was the worst crime of all, and there was no way of proving I wasn't, except to keep going out with him.'

Now Gloria looked away from them, her eyes on something off screen.

'We were sleeping together by then. I didn't want to. I'm not saying he forced me – not really,' said Gloria, and Robin thought of Shifty's PA, Gemma, 'but keeping him happy was the only way to keep going. Otherwise there'd be a slap or worse. One time, he made some comment about hurting my grandmother if I didn't behave. I went crazy at him, and he laughed, and said it was an obvious joke, but he wanted to plant the idea in my mind, and he succeeded.

'And he didn't believe in contraception. We were supposed to be using the ... you know, the rhythm method,' said Gloria, reaching again for her wine. 'But he was ... let's say, he was careless, and I was sure he wanted me pregnant, because then he'd have me cornered, and I'd marry him. My grandparents would probably have backed him up. They were devout people.

'So, without telling Luca, I went to Margot for the pill. She said she was happy to give it to me, but she didn't know I had a boyfriend, even, I'd never said ...

'And even though I didn't really like her,' said Gloria, 'I told her some of it. It was the only place I could drop the pretence, I suppose. I knew she couldn't tell anyone outside her consulting room. She tried to talk sense into me. Tried to show me there were ways out of the situation, apart from just giving in to Luca all the time. I thought it was all right for her, with all her money and her big safe house ...

'But she gave me a bit of hope, I suppose. Once, after he'd hit me, and told me I'd asked for it, and told me I should be grateful I had someone offering me a way out of living at home with two old people, I said, "There are other places I could go," and I think he got worried someone had offered to help me get away. I'd stopped making fun of Margot by this time, and Luca wasn't a stupid man ...

'That's when he wrote her threatening notes. Anonymously, you know – but I knew it was him,' said Gloria. 'I knew his writing. Dorothy was off one day because her son was having his tonsils out, so Irene was opening the post and she unfolded one of the notes, right at the desk beside me. She was gloating about it, and I had to pretend to find it funny, but not to recognise the handwriting.

'I confronted Luca about it. He told me not to be so stupid, of course he hadn't written the notes, but I knew he had . . .

'Anyway – I think it was right after the second note – I found out what I'd been terrified about happening had happened. I was pregnant. I hadn't realised that the pill wouldn't work if you'd had a stomach upset, and I'd had a bug, a month before. I knew I was cornered, and it was too late, I'd have to marry Luca. The Riccis would want it, and my grandparents wouldn't want me to be an unwed mother.

'That's when I admitted it to myself for the first time,' said Gloria, looking directly at Strike and Robin. 'I absolutely hated Luca Ricci.'

'Gloria,' said Robin quietly, 'I'm sorry to interrupt, but could I ask you: when you were sick at Margot's barbecue—?'

'You heard about that, did you? Yes, that was when I had the tummy bug. People said one of the kids had spiked the punch, but I don't think so. Nobody else was as ill as I was.'

Out of the corner of Robin's eye, she saw Strike writing something in his notebook.

'I went back to Margot to find out for sure whether I was pregnant,' said Gloria. 'I knew I could trust her. I broke down again in her surgery, and cried my eyes out, when she confirmed it. And then . . . well, she was just lovely. She held my hand and talked to me for ages.

'I thought abortion was a sin,' said Gloria. 'That's the way I was raised. She didn't think it was a sin, not Margot. She talked to me about the life I was likely to have with Luca, if I had the baby. We discussed me keeping it, alone, but we both knew Luca wouldn't want that, that he'd be in my life for ever if I had his kid. It was hard, then, being on your own with a child. I was watching Janice the nurse doing it. Always juggling her son and the job.

'I didn't tell Luca, obviously,' said Gloria. 'I knew that if I was going to – to *do anything* – I had to do it quickly, before he noticed my body change, but most of all, before the baby could feel it or . . .'

Gloria suddenly bowed her head, and covered her face with her hands.

'I'm so sorry,' said Robin. 'It must have been awful for you . . .'

'No – well –' said Gloria, straightening up and again pushing back her white hair, her eyes wet. 'Never mind that. I'm only telling you, so you understand . . .

'Margot made the appointment for me. She gave the clinic her name and contact details and she bought us both wigs, because if she was recognised, someone might recognise me by association. And she came with me – it was a Saturday – to this place in Bride Street. I've never forgotten the name of the street, because a bride is exactly what I *didn't* want to be, and that's why I was there.

'The clinic had been using Margot's name as the referring doctor, and I think somewhere there were crossed wires, because they thought "Margot Bamborough" was the one having the procedure. Margot said, "It doesn't matter, nobody'll ever know, all these records are confidential." And she said, in a way it was convenient, if there was any follow-up needed, they could contact her and arrange it.

'She held my hand on the way in, and she was there when I woke up,' said Gloria, and now tears leaked from her dark eyes, and she brushed them quickly away. 'When I was ready to go home, she took me to the end of my grandparents' street in a taxi. She told me what to do afterwards, how to take care of myself . . .

'I wasn't like Margot,' said Gloria, her voice breaking. 'I didn't believe it was right, what I did. September the fourteenth: I don't think that date's come by once, since, that I haven't remembered, and thought about that baby.

'When I went back to work after a couple of days off, she took me into her office and asked me how I was feeling, and then she said, "Now, Gloria, you've got to be brave. If you stay with Luca, this will happen again." She said, "We need to find you a job away from London, and make sure he doesn't know where you've gone." And she said something that's stayed with me always, "We aren't our mistakes. It's what we do *about* the mistake that shows who we are."

'But I wasn't like Margot,' said Gloria again. 'I wasn't brave, I couldn't imagine leaving my grandparents. I pretended to agree, but ten days after the abortion I was sleeping with Luca again, not because I wanted to, but because there didn't seem any other choice.

'And then,' said Gloria, 'about a month after we'd been to the clinic, it happened. Margot disappeared.'

A muffled male voice was now heard at Gloria's end of the call. She turned towards the door behind her and said,

'*Non, c'est toujours en cours!*'

Turning back to her computer she said,

'*Pardon.* I mean, sorry.'

'Mrs Jaubert – Gloria,' said Strike, 'could we please take you back through the day Margot disappeared?'

'The whole day?'

Strike nodded. Gloria took a slow inward breath, like somebody about to dive into deep water, then said,

'Well, the morning was all normal. Everyone was there except Wilma the cleaner. She didn't come in on Fridays.

'I remember two things about the morning: meeting Janice by the kettle at the back, and her going on about the sequel to *The Godfather* coming out soon, and me pretending to be excited about it, and actually feeling as though I'd run a mile rather than go and see it . . . and Irene being quite smug and pleased because Janice had just been on a date with some man she'd been trying to set Janice up with for ages.

'Irene was funny about Janice,' said Gloria. 'They were supposed to be such great friends, but she was always going on about Janice being a bit of a man-eater, which was funny if you'd known Irene. She used to say that Janice needed to learn to cut her cloth, that she was deluded, waiting for someone like James Caan to show up and sweep her off her feet, because she was a single mother and not that great a catch. Irene thought the best she could hope for was this man from Eddie's work, who sounded a bit simple. Irene was always laughing about him getting things wrong . . .

'We were quite busy, as I remember it, all three doctors coming in and out of the waiting room to call for their patients. I can't remember anything unusual about the afternoon except that Irene left early. She claimed she had toothache, but I thought it was a fib at the time. She hadn't seemed in pain to me, when she was going on about Janice's love life.

'I knew Margot was meeting her friend later in the pub. She told me, because she had a doughnut in cling film in the fridge, and she asked me to bring it through to her, right before she saw her last patient, to keep her going. She loved sugar. She was always in the biscuit tin at five o'clock. She had one of those metabolisms, never put on weight, full of nervous energy.

'I remember the doughnut, because when I took it in to her, I said, "Why didn't you just eat those chocolates?" She had a box she'd taken out of the bin, I think it was the day before. I mean, they were still in their cellophane when she took them out of the bin, it wasn't unhygienic. Someone had sent them to her—'

'Someone?' repeated Strike.

'Well, we all thought it was that patient the police were so interested in, Steve Douthwaite,' said Gloria. 'Dorothy thought that, anyway.'

'Wasn't there a message attached?'

'There was a card saying "Thank you",' said Gloria, 'and Dorothy might've made the assumption it was Steve Douthwaite, because we all thought he was turning up a lot. I don't think the card was signed, though.'

'So Margot threw the box in the bin, and then took it out again, afterwards?'

'Yes, because I laughed at her about it,' said Gloria. 'I said, "I knew you couldn't resist," and she laughed, too. And next day, when I said, "Why don't you eat them?" she said, "I have, I've finished them."'

'But she still had the box there?'

'Yes, on the shelf with her books. I went back to the front desk. Dr Brenner's patient left, but Brenner didn't, because he was writing up the notes.'

'Could I ask you whether you knew about Dr Brenner's barbiturate addiction?' asked Strike.

'His what?' said Gloria.

'Nobody ever told you about that?'

'No,' she said, looking surprised. 'I had no idea.'

'You never heard that Janice had found an Amytal capsule in the bottom of a cup of tea?'

'No . . . oh. Is that why Margot started making her own tea? She told me Irene made it too milky.'

'Let's go back to the order in which everyone left.'

'OK, so, Dr Gupta's patient was next, and Dr Gupta left

immediately afterwards. He had some family dinner he needed to attend, so off he went.

'And then, just when I was thinking we were done for the day, in walked that girl, Theo.'

'Tell us about Theo,' said Strike.

'Long black hair . . . dark-skinned. She looked Romanian or Turkish. Ornate earrings, you know: gypsy-ish. I actually thought she looked like a gypsy. I'd never seen her before, so I knew she wasn't registered with us. She looked as though she was in a lot of pain, with her stomach. She came up to the desk and asked to see a doctor urgently. I asked her name, and she said Theo . . . something or other. I didn't ask her again because she was obviously suffering, so I told her to wait and went to see whether a doctor was free. Margot's door was still closed, so I asked Dr Brenner. He didn't want to see her. He was always like that, always difficult. I never liked him.

'Then Margot's door opened, and the mother and child who'd been seeing her left, and she said she'd see the girl who was waiting.'

'And Theo was definitely a girl?' asked Strike.

'Without any doubt at all,' said Gloria firmly. 'She was broad-shouldered, I noticed that when she came to the desk, but she was definitely a woman. Maybe it was the shoulders that made Dr Brenner say, afterwards, she looked like a man, but honestly . . .

'I was thinking about him last night, knowing I was going to be talking to you. Brenner was probably the biggest misogynist I ever met. He'd denigrate women for not looking feminine or talking "like a lady", but he also despised Irene, who was giggly and blonde and very feminine, you know. I suppose what he wanted was for us all to be like Dorothy, subordinate and respectful, high collars, low hemlines. Dorothy was like a really humourless nun.'

Robin thought of Betty Fuller, lying on a bed, pretending to be comatose, while Brenner poured filthy words into her ear.

'Women patients really didn't like Brenner. We were always having them asking to switch to Margot, but we had to turn most of them down, because her list was so full. But Brenner was coming up for retirement and we were hoping we'd get someone better when he went.

'So, yes, he left, and Theo went in to see Margot. I kept checking the time, because I was supposed to be meeting Luca, and if I kept him waiting, there was always trouble. But Theo's appointment just went on and on. At a quarter past six, Theo finally came back out of the surgery and left.

'Margot came through just a couple of minutes later. She seemed absolutely exhausted. It had been a full day. She said, "I'm going to write her notes up tomorrow, I've got to go, Oonagh's waiting. Lock up with the spare key." I didn't really answer,' said Gloria, 'because I was so worried about Luca getting angry with me. So, I never said goodbye, or have a good evening, to this woman who saved my life . . .

'Because she did, you know. I never said it to her, but she did . . .'

A tear trickled down her face. Gloria paused to wipe it away, then said,

'I remember, as she put her umbrella up, she slipped. Turned over on her heel. It was raining, the pavement was wet. Then she straightened up and walked out of sight.

'I started dashing round, turning off lights, locking the records up in the filing cabinets. Then I made sure the back door was locked, which it was – the police asked me about that. I closed and locked the front door, and ran straight up Passing Alley, which was right beside the surgery, to meet Luca in St John Street.

'And that was the last time I ever saw Margot.'

Gloria reached again for her almost empty wine glass, and drained it.

'Did you have any idea what might have happened to her?' asked Strike.

'Of course,' said Gloria quietly. 'I was terrified Luca had got someone to hurt her, or kidnap her. She'd become a bugbear to him. Every time I stood up for myself, he'd say horrible things about Margot influencing me. He was convinced she was trying to persuade me to leave him, which, of course, she was. My greatest fear was that he'd somehow find out what she'd helped me do . . . you know. In Bride Street.

'I knew he couldn't have abducted her personally, because I met him on St John Street, not five minutes after she left the surgery, and I know it can't have been his father, because his brother Marco was in hospital at the time, and the parents were with him round the clock. But Luca had friends and cousins.

'I couldn't tell the police. Luca had stopped pretending he was joking, when he threatened my grandparents. I asked him whether he was behind it, though. The anxiety was too much: I had to ask. He got really angry, called me names – dumb bitch, things like that. He said, of course he hadn't. But he'd told me stories about his father "making people disappear", so I just didn't know . . .'

'Did you ever have reason to suppose he knew . . .' Robin hesitated ' . . . what happened in Bride Street?'

'I'm absolutely positive he never knew,' said Gloria. 'Margot was too good for him. The wigs and using her name and giving me a plausible story for why I couldn't have sex with him for a while . . . She's the reason I got away with it. No, I don't believe he ever knew. So, in my best moments, I thought, he didn't really have a strong enough reason—'

The door behind Gloria opened, and in walked a handsome aquiline-nosed, grey-haired man in a striped shirt and jeans, carrying a bottle of red wine. A large German Shepherd dog followed him into the room, its tail wagging.

'*Je m'excuse*,' he said, smiling at Strike and Robin onscreen. 'I am sorry for … *Comment dit-on "interrompre"?*' he asked his wife.

'Interrupt,' she said.

'*Oui*. I am sorry for interrupt.'

He refilled his wife's glass, handed it back to her, patted her on the shoulder, then walked out again, calling the dog.

'*Viens, Obélix*.'

When both man and dog had disappeared, Gloria said, with a little laugh,

'That was Hugo.'

'How long did you stay at the St John's practice, after Margot disappeared?' asked Strike, although he knew the answer.

'Six, seven months, I think,' said Gloria. 'Long enough to see the new policeman take over. We were all pleased, because the first – Talbot, wasn't it? – was quite strange. He bullied the life out of Wilma and Janice. I think that's what made Wilma ill, actually. She had quite enough on her plate without the police hounding her.'

'You don't think she drank, then?' asked Robin.

'Drank? That was all Dorothy's malice,' said Gloria, shaking her head. 'Dorothy was trying to pin the thefts on Wilma. Have you heard about that?'

Strike and Robin nodded.

'When she couldn't prove that Wilma was taking money out of people's bags, she put it about that she was drinking and the poor woman resigned. She was probably glad to leave, but it was still losing a salary, wasn't it?

'I wanted to leave myself,' said Gloria, 'but I was paralysed. I had this really strange feeling that, if I just stayed there, the world would right itself. Margot would come back. It was only after she disappeared that I realised . . . what she'd been to me . . .

'Anyway,' sighed Gloria, 'one night, months after she'd disappeared, Luca was *really* violent to me. I'd smiled at a man who opened a door for me as I left the pub with Luca, that's what sparked it. He beat me like he'd never beaten me before, at his place – he had this little flat.

'I remember saying "I'm sorry, I'm sorry, I shouldn't have smiled at him". And all the time I was saying it, I could see – in here –' Gloria tapped her head, 'Margot watching me, and even while I was begging Luca to stop, and agreeing I'd behaved like a little slut, and I shouldn't ever smile at strange men, I was thinking, *I'm going, Margot. I'm going where he'll never find me.*

'Because it had clicked in my head at last. She'd told me I needed to be brave. It was no good waiting for anyone else to save me. *I* had to save me.

'After he'd calmed down, he let me go home to my grandparents' house, but he wanted to see me again later. It was always like that after he'd been really violent. He wanted extra contact.

'He hadn't beaten me in the face. He never did, he never lost control like that, so I went back to my grandparents' and acted as though everything was fine. Went out to meet Luca that night, and he took me out for dinner, and that was the night he proposed, with a ring and everything.

'And I said yes,' said Gloria, with a strange smile and a shrug. 'I put that ring on, and I looked down at it, and I didn't even have to act happy, because I genuinely was. I thought *That'll buy some of my plane ticket.* Mind you, I'd never flown before in my life. The idea of it scared me. But all the time, I could see Margot in my head. *You've got to be brave, Gloria.*

'I had to tell my grandparents I was engaged. I couldn't tell them what I was really planning, because I was scared they wouldn't be able to act, or that they'd try and confront Luca or, worse, go to the police. Anyway, Luca came round to the house to meet them properly, pretending to be a nice guy, and it was awful, and I had to act as though I was thrilled about all of it.

'Every single day after that, I bought all the newspapers, and circled all of the jobs abroad that I might have a chance of getting. I had to do all of it in secret. Typed up a CV at work and got a bus to the West End to post all the applications, because I was scared someone who knew Luca would see me putting lots of envelopes in the post.

'After a few weeks, I got an interview with a French woman who was looking for an English home help, to teach her kids English. What really got me the job was being able to type. She ran her own business from home, so I could do a bit of admin for her while the kids were at nursery. The job came with room and board, and my employer would buy my plane ticket, so I didn't have to sell Luca's ring, and pretend I'd lost it . . .

'You know, the day I went into St John's and told them I was resigning, a funny thing happened. Nobody had mentioned Margot for weeks. Immediately after she disappeared, it was all any of us could talk about, but then it became taboo, somehow. We had a new locum doctor in her room. I can't remember his name. A new cleaner, too. But this day, Dorothy arrived, quite flustered, and she never showed any emotion, usually . . .

'This local . . . what's the word?' said Gloria, clicking her fingers, for the first time lost in her native language. 'We'd say *un dingue* . . . oh, you know, a crazy man, a loon . . . harmless, but strange. Big long beard, dirty, you used to see him wandering up and down Clerkenwell Road with his son. Anyway, he'd sort of accosted Dorothy in the middle of the street, and told her he killed Margot Bamborough.

'It had shaken Dorothy up, but in an odd way . . . please

don't think this is awful . . . I hoped it was true. Because although I'd have given *anything* to know Margot was alive, I was sure she was dead. She wasn't the type to run away. And my worst nightmare was that Luca was responsible, because that meant it was all my fault.'

Robin shook her head, but Gloria ignored her.

'I only told my grandparents the truth the night before I was due to leave for France. I hadn't let them spend any money on the wedding that wasn't going to happen, but even so, it was a huge shock to them. I sat them down, and told them everything, except for the termination.

'Of course, they were appalled. At first, they didn't want me to leave, they wanted me to go to the police. I had to explain why that was a terrible idea, tell them about the threats Luca had made, and all of that. But they were so glad I wasn't marrying him, they accepted it in the end. I told them it would all die down, and I'd be back soon . . . even though I wasn't sure that was true, or if it would be possible.

'My grandfather took me to the airport, early next day. We'd worked out a story, for when Luca came asking where I was. They were to say I'd been having doubts, because he'd been violent, and that I'd gone over to Italy to stay with some of Dad's relatives, to think things over. We even concocted a fake address to give him. I don't know whether he ever wrote to it.

'And that's everything,' said Gloria, sitting back in the desk chair. 'I stayed with my first employer for seven years, and ended up with a junior position in her firm. I didn't visit London again until I heard Luca was safely married.' She took another sip of wine from the glass her husband had refilled. 'His first wife drank herself to death at the age of thirty-nine. He used to beat her badly. I found all that out later.

'And I've never told another lie about myself,' said Gloria, raising her chin. 'Never exaggerated, never pretended, only ever told the absolute truth, except on one point. Until tonight, the only person who knew about the abortion was Hugo, but now you two know, too.

'Even if you find out Luca was behind what happened to Margot, and I have to have that on my conscience for ever, I owe her the truth. That woman saved me, and I've never, ever forgotten her. She was one of the bravest, kindest people I've ever known.'

67

There by th'vncertaine glims of starry night,
And by the twinkling of their sacred fire,
He mote perceiue a litle dawning sight . . .

Edmund Spenser
The Faerie Queene

They thanked Gloria for her time and her honesty. Having bidden her goodbye, Strike and Robin sat at the partners' desk, each of them sunk in thought, until Strike offered Robin one of the pots of dehydrated noodles he kept for snacks in the office. She declined, instead taking a bag of mixed nuts unenthusiastically out of her bag, and opening it. Once Strike had added boiling water to the plastic pot, he returned to the desk, stirring the noodles with a fork.

'It's the efficiency,' he said, sitting down again. 'That's what's bugging me. Literally no trace of her anywhere. Somebody was either extraordinarily clever, or unprecedentedly lucky. And Creed still fits that picture best, with Luca Ricci a close second.'

'Except it can't have been Luca. He's got an alibi: Gloria.'

'But as she says, he knew people who could take care of making someone disappear – because what are the odds, if Margot was abducted off the street, that this was a *truly* one-person job? Even Creed had his unwitting accomplices. The dozy landlady, giving him that safe basement, and the dry cleaner letting him have the van that day and n—'

'Don't,' said Robin sharply.

'Don't what?'

'Blame them.'

'I'm not blaming them, I'm—'

'Max and I were talking about this,' said Robin. 'About the way people – women, usually – get blamed for not knowing, or seeing – but everyone's guilty of that kind of bias. Everyone does it.'

'You think?' said Strike thickly, through his first mouthful of noodles.

'Yes,' said Robin. 'We've all got a tendency to generalise from our own past experiences. Look at Violet Cooper. She thought she knew who Creed really was, because she'd met a couple of men who behaved like him, in her theatre days.'

'Men who wouldn't let anyone in their basement flats because they were boiling down skulls?'

'You know what I mean, Strike,' said Robin, refusing to be amused. 'Soft-spoken, apparently gentle, slightly feminine. Creed liked putting on her feather boa, and he pretended to like show tunes, so she thought he was a gay man. But if the only gay man she'd met had been Max, my flatmate . . . '

'He's gay, is he?' said Strike, whose memories of Max were indistinct.

'Yes, and he isn't remotely camp, and hates musicals. Come to that, if she'd met a couple of Matt's straight mates down the rugby club, who couldn't wait to shove oranges up their T-shirts and prance around, she might've drawn a different conclusion, mightn't she?'

'S'pose so,' said Strike, chewing noodles and considering this point. 'And in fairness, most people don't know any serial killers.'

'Exactly. So even if somebody's got some unusual habits, our direct experience tends to suggest they're just eccentric. Vi had never met a man who fetishised women's clothing or . . . sorry, I'm boring you,' Robin added, because Strike's eyes seemed to have glazed over.

'No, you aren't,' he muttered. 'You're actually making me think . . . I had an idea, you know. I thought I'd spotted some coincidences, and it got me wondering . . .'

He set down the pot of noodles, reached under the desk and pulled one of the boxes of police evidence towards him, on top of which lay the pages he'd last been re-examining. He now took these bits of paper out, spread them in front of himself again, and resumed his noodle-eating.

'Are you going to tell me about the coincidences?' said Robin with a trace of impatience.

'Hang on a minute,' said Strike, looking up at her. 'Why was Theo standing *outside* the phone box?'

'What?' said Robin, confused.

'I don't think we can doubt, now, can we, that Ruby Elliot saw Theo by that phone box near Albemarle Way? Her description and Gloria's tally exactly . . . so why was Theo standing *outside* the phone box?'

'She was waiting for the van to pick her up.'

'Right. But, not to state the bleeding obvious, the sides of the old red telephone boxes have windows. It was pissing down with rain. Theo didn't have an umbrella, and Ruby said Theo's hair was plastered down – so why didn't she shelter in the telephone box, and keep watch for her lift? Clerkenwell Road's long and straight. She'd've had a perfectly good view from that telephone box, and plenty of time to come out and show herself to the van driver. Why,' said Strike for the third time, 'was she standing *outside* the phone box?'

'Because . . . there was someone in it?'

'That would seem the obvious explanation. And that phone box at the end of Albemarle Way would give you a view of the top of St John's Lane.'

'You think someone was lying in wait for Margot? Watching out from that phone box?'

Strike hesitated.

'Do me a favour and look up Fragile X syndrome?'

'OK . . . why?' said Robin, setting down her almonds and beginning to type.

'That phone box is at the end of the Athorns' street.'

While Robin brought up the search results, Strike pulled the copy of Irene Hickson's receipt towards him. It had the time 3.10 p.m. on it. Eating noodles, Strike was still looking at the slip of paper when Robin said, reading off her screen,

'"First called Martin-Bell syndrome . . . the FMR1 gene on the X chromosome was sequenced in 1991" . . . Sorry, what exactly do you need?'

'What specific disabilities does it cause?'

'"Social anxiety",' said Robin, reading again, '"lack of eye contact . . . challenges forming relationships . . . anxiety with unfamiliar situations and people . . . poor ability to recognise faces you've seen before", but "good long-term memory, good imitation skills and good visual learning". Men are more severely affected than women . . . good sense of humour, usually . . . "can be creative, especially visually" . . .'

She looked around the computer monitor.

'Why d'you want to know all this?'

'Just thinking.'

'About Gwilherm?'

'Yeah,' said Strike. 'Well, about the whole family.'

'*He* didn't have Fragile X, though, did he?'

'No, I don't know what Gwilherm's problem was. Maybe just the Bennies.'

He didn't smile as he said the name this time.

'Cormoran, what coincidences did you notice?'

Instead of answering, Strike pulled a couple of pages of police notes towards him and read through them again. Out of force of habit, Robin reached out for Talbot's notebook, and turned to the first page. For a couple of minutes, there was silence in the office, and neither partner noticed any of the noises that were as familiar to them as their own breathing: the traffic rolling down Charing Cross Road, occasional shouts and snatches of music from Denmark Street below.

The very first page of Bill Talbot's notebook began with untidy jottings of what Robin knew to be genuine evidence and observations. It was the most coherent part of the notes but the first pentagrams appeared at the very bottom of the page, as did the first astrological observation.

(Theo? MALE?) white van speeding Aylesbury St away from Clerkenwell Green
Two women struggling by phone boxes, smaller in rainhat, taller in raincoat,
seems unsteady on feet, then VAN speeding away from Clerkenwell Green
♃ is currently retrograde in ♓ meaning planet of OBJECTIVE TRUTH
in sign of ILLUSION and FANTASY

Robin re-read this final paragraph twice, frowning slightly. Then she set aside her bag of almonds to delve in the nearest box of police evidence. It took her five minutes to find the original police record of Ruby Elliot's statement, and while she searched, Strike remained deeply immersed in his own portion of the notes.

> I saw them beside a telephone box, two women sort of struggling together. The tall one in the raincoat was leaning on the short one, who was in a plastic rain hood. They both looked like women to me, but I didn't see their faces.

> It looked to me like one was trying to make the other walk quicker.

Pulse now quickened, Robin set aside this piece of paper, got back onto her knees and began to search for the record of Ruby's statement to Lawson, which took her another five minutes.

> I saw them beside the two telephone boxes in Clerkenwell Green, two women struggling with each together. The tall one in the raincoat was trying to make the little one in the rain hood walk faster.

'Cormoran,' said Robin urgently.

Strike looked up.

'The heights are round the wrong way.'

'What?'

'In Ruby's very first statement to Talbot,' Robin said, 'she said, "I saw them beside a telephone box, two women sort of struggling together. The tall one in the raincoat was leaning on the short one, who was in a plastic rain hood. They both looked like women to me, but I didn't see their faces. It looked to me like one was trying to make the other walk quicker."'

'Right,' said Strike, frowning slightly.

'And that's what Talbot wrote in his horoscope notes, too,' said Robin. 'But that's not how it should have been, if those two women were the Fleurys. Where's that picture?'

'Box one,' said Strike, shoving it towards Robin with his real foot.

She crouched down beneath the desk and began searching the photocopied papers until she found the sheaf of newspaper clippings Strike had shown her, months previously, in the Three Kings.

'There,' said Robin. 'Look. *There.*'

And there was the old picture, of the two women who'd come forward to say that they were Ruby's struggling women: the tall, broad, younger woman with her cheery face, and her aged mother, who was tiny and stooped.

'It's the wrong way round,' repeated Robin. 'If Fiona Fleury had leaned on her mother, she'd have flattened her . . . ' Robin scanned the few lines beneath the picture. 'Cormoran, *it doesn't fit.* Fiona says *she* was wearing the rain hat, but Ruby says it was the short woman who had the rainhat on.'

'Ruby was vague,' said Strike, but Robin could see his interest sharpening as he reached out for these pieces of paper. 'She could've been confused . . . '

'Talbot never thought the Fleurys were the people Ruby saw, and this is why!' said Robin. 'The heights were reversed. It was the taller woman Ruby saw who was unsteady, not the little one . . . '

'So how come she didn't tell Lawson the Fleurys couldn't be the people she saw?'

'Same reason she never told anybody she'd seen Theo? Because she'd been flustered by Talbot trying to force her to bend her story to fit his theories? Because she lost confidence in herself, and didn't know what she'd really seen? It was raining, she was lost, she was panicked . . . by the time it got to Lawson, maybe she just wanted to agree she'd seen the Fleurys and be left alone?'

'Plausible,' admitted Strike.

'How tall was Margot?'

'Five nine,' said Strike.

'And Creed?' said Robin.

'Five seven.'

'Oh God,' said Robin quietly.

There was another minute's silence, while Strike sat lost

in thought and Robin re-read the statements laid out in front of her.

'The phone boxes,' said Strike, at last. 'Those bloody phone boxes . . .'

'What about them?'

'Talbot wanted Ruby to have seen the two struggling women beside the two boxes in Clerkenwell Green, right? So he could tie them to the van that was speeding away up Aylesbury Street, which was supposed to contain Creed.'

'Right,' said Robin.

'But after the Fleurys came forward, Talbot tried to get Ruby to agree she'd seen the two struggling women beside the first phone box, the one at the end of Albemarle Way.'

'But she wouldn't change her story,' said Robin, 'because she'd seen Theo there.'

'Precisely,' said Strike, 'but that doesn't make sense.'

'I don't—'

'She's driving round in an enormous circle in the rain, right, looking for this house she can't find, right?'

'Yes . . .'

'Well, just because Ruby saw Theo get into a van by the phone box on one of her circuits doesn't mean she can't have seen two struggling women on her second or third circuit. We know she was hazy about landmarks, unfamiliar with the area and with no sense of direction, her daughter was very clear about that. But she had this very retentive visual memory, she's somebody who notices clothes and hairstyles . . .'

Strike looked down at the desk again, and for the second time, picked up Irene Hickson's receipt and examined it. Then, so suddenly that Robin jumped, Strike let the receipt fall and stood up, both hands clasped over the back of his head.

'Shit,' he said. '*Shit! Never* trust a phone call whose provenance you haven't checked!'

'What phone call?' said Robin nervously, casting her mind back over any phone calls she'd taken over the course of the case.

'Fuck's sake,' said Strike, walking out of the room into the outer office and then back again, still clasping the back of his head, apparently needing to pace, just as Robin had needed to walk when she'd found out Strike could interview Creed. '*How did I not fucking see it?*'

'Cormoran, what—?'

'Why did Margot keep an empty chocolate box?' said Strike.

'I don't know,' said Robin, confused.

'You know what?' said Strike slowly. 'I think I do.'

68

. . . an Hyena was,
That feeds on wemens flesh, as others feede on gras.

Edmund Spenser
The Faerie Queene

The high-security mental hospital that is Broadmoor lies slightly over an hour outside London, in the county of Berkshire. The word 'Broadmoor' had long since lost all bucolic associations in the collective mind of the British public, and Strike was no exception to this rule. Far from connoting a wide stretch of grassland or heath, the name spoke to Strike only of violence, heinous crimes and two hundred of the most dangerous men in Britain, whom the tabloids called monsters. Accordingly, and in spite of the fact that Strike knew he was visiting a hospital and not a prison, he took all the common sense measures he'd have taken for a high-security jail: he wore no tie, ensured that neither he or his car was carrying anything likely to trigger a burdensome search, brought two kinds of photographic ID and a copy of his letter from the Ministry of Justice, set out early, certain, though he'd never been there before, that getting inside the facility would be time-consuming.

It was a golden September morning. Sunshine pouring down upon the road ahead from between fluffy white clouds, and as Strike drove through Berkshire in his BMW, he listened to the news on the radio, the lead item of which was that Scotland had voted, by 55 per cent to 45 per cent, to remain in the United Kingdom. He was wondering how Dave Polworth and Sam Barclay were taking the news, when his mobile rang.

'It's Brian, Brian Tucker,' said the hoarse voice. 'Not interrupting, am I? Wanna wish you good luck.'

'Thanks, Brian,' said Strike.

They'd finally met three days previously, at Strike's office. Tucker had shown Strike the old letter from Creed, described the butterfly pendant taken from the killer's basement, which he believed was his daughter's, shared his theories and trembled with emotion and nerves at the thought of Strike coming face to face with the man he believed had murdered his eldest daughter.

'I'll let you go, I won't keep you,' said Tucker. 'You'll ring me when it's over, though?'

'I will, of course,' said Strike.

It was hard to concentrate on the news now that he'd heard Tucker's anxiety and excitement. Strike turned off the radio, and turned his thoughts instead to what lay ahead.

Gratifying though it would be to believe that he, Cormoran Strike, might trick or persuade Creed into confessing where all others had failed, Strike wasn't that egotistical. He'd interviewed plenty of suspects in his career; the skill lay in making it easier for a suspect to disclose the truth than to continue lying. Some were worn down by patient questioning, others resistant to all but intense pressure, still others yearned to unburden themselves, and the interrogator's methods had to change accordingly.

However, in talking to Creed, half of Strike's interrogatory arsenal would be out of commission. For one thing, he was there at Creed's pleasure, because the patient had had to give his consent for the interview. For another, it was hard to see how Strike could paint a frightening picture of the consequences of silence, when his interviewee was already serving life in Broadmoor. Creed's secrets were the only power he had left, and Strike was well aware that persuading him to relinquish any of them might prove a task beyond any human investigator. Standard appeals to conscience, or to the desire to figure as a better person to the self or to others, were likewise useless. As Creed's entire life demonstrated, his primary sources of enjoyment were inflicting pain and establishing dominance, and it was doubtful that anything else would persuade him into disclosures.

Strike's first glimpse of the infamous hospital was of a fortress on raised ground. It had been built by the Victorians in the middle of woodland and meadows, a red-brick edifice with a clocktower the highest point in the compound. The surrounding walls were twenty feet high, and as Strike drove up to the front gates, he could see the heads of hundreds of Cyclopean security cameras on poles. As the gates opened, Strike experienced an explosion of adrenalin, and for a moment the ghostly black and white images of seven dead women, and the anxious face of Brian Tucker, seemed to swim before him.

He'd sent his car registration number in advance. Once through the first set of double gates he encountered an inner wire fence, as tall as the wall he'd just passed through. A white-shirted, black-trousered man of military bearing unlocked a second set of gates once the first had closed behind the BMW, and directed Strike to a parking space. Before leaving his car, and wanting to save time going through the security he was about to face, the detective put his phone, keys, belt, cigarettes, lighter and loose change into the glove compartment and locked it.

'Mr Strike, is it?' said the smiling, white-shirted man, whose accent was Welsh and whose profile suggested a boxer. 'Got your ID there?'

Strike showed his driver's licence, and was led inside, where he encountered a scanner of the airport security type. Good-humoured, inevitable amusement ensued when the scanner announced shrill disapproval of Strike's metal lower leg, and his trousers had to be rolled up to prove he wasn't carrying a weapon. Having been patted down, he was free to join Dr Ranbir Bijral, who was waiting for him on the other side of the scanners, a slight, bearded psychiatrist whose open-necked yellow shirt struck a cheerful note against the dull green-grey tiled floors, the white walls and the unfresh air of all medical institutions, part disinfectant, part fried food, with a trace of incarcerated human.

'We've got twenty minutes until Dennis will be ready for you,' said Dr Bijral, leading Strike off along an eerily empty corridor, through many sets of turquoise swing doors. 'We coordinate patient movements carefully and it's always a bit of a feat moving him around. We have to make sure he never comes into contact with patients who have a particular dislike for him, you see. He's not popular. We'll wait in my office.'

Strike was familiar with hospitals, but had never been inside one with so little bustle or shuffle of patients in the corridors. The emptiness was slightly unnerving. They passed many locked doors. A short female nurse in navy scrubs marched past. She smiled at Strike, who smiled back.

'You've got women working here,' he said, slightly surprised.

'Of course,' said Dr Bijral.

Strike had somehow imagined an all-male staff, even though he knew that male prisons had female warders. Dr Bijral pushed open a door to a small office that had the air of a converted treatment room, with chipped paint on the walls and bars on the windows.

'Have a seat,' said Dr Bijral, waving his hand at the chair opposite his desk, and with slightly forced politeness, he asked, 'Did you have a good journey? Come up from London?'

'Yeah, it was a nice drive,' said Strike.

As he sat down behind the desk, Dr Bijral became business-like.

'All right, so: we're going to give you forty-five minutes with Creed.'

'Forty-five minutes,' repeated Strike.

'If Dennis wants to admit to another killing, that should be ample time,' said Dr Bijral, 'but . . . may I be honest with you, Mr Strike?'

'Of course.'

'If it had been down to Dennis's treatment team, we probably wouldn't have permitted this visit. I know the MoJ feel the Bamboroughs and the Tuckers ought to be given a last chance to ask Dennis about their relatives, but—'

Dr Bijral leaned back in his seat and sighed.

'—he's a classic sociopath, you see, a pure example of the type. He scores very highly on the dark triad: narcissism, Machiavellianism and psychopathy. Devious, sadistic, unrepentant and extremely egotistical.'

'Not a fan, then?' said Strike, and the doctor permitted himself a perfunctory smile.

'The problem, you see, is if he admitted to another murder under your questioning, you'd get the credit. And Dennis can't have that, he can't allow somebody else to come out on top. He had to give his consent to meeting you, of course, and I think he's agreed because it feeds his ego to be questioned, especially by a man who's been in the papers, and I think he'd like to manipulate you into being an advocate for him in some way. He's been lobbying to get out of Broadmoor and back into prison for a long time now.'

'I thought he was desperate to get in here?'

'He was, once,' said Bijral. 'High-profile sex offenders are usually under risk of attack in the prison system, as you probably know. You might have seen in the papers, one man nearly took his eye out with a sharpened spoon handle. Dennis wanted to come to Broadmoor when he was first convicted, but there were no grounds to admit him to hospital back then. Psychopathy isn't, in itself, treatable.'

'What changed?'

'He was exceptionally difficult to manage in the prison system. He managed to talk a young offender with Asperger's syndrome into killing himself. For that, he was put into solitary confinement. They ended up keeping him there for almost a year. By night, he took to re-enacting what had happened in the basement in Liverpool Road, screaming through the night, doing his voice and the women's. Warders couldn't stand hearing it, let alone prisoners.

'After eleven months in solitary, he became suicidal. First he went on hunger strike. Then he began trying to bite his own wrists open, and smashing his head against the wall. He was assessed, judged psychotic and transferred here.

'Once we'd had him a couple of months, he claimed he'd been faking his mental illness, which is pure Dennis. Nobody else can be cleverer than he is. But actually, his mental health was very poor when he came to us, and it took many months of medication and therapy to stop him self-harming and trying to kill himself.'

'And now he wants to leave?'

'Once he was well enough to fully appreciate the difference between jail and hospital, I think it's fair to say he was disappointed. He had more freedom in Belmarsh. He did a lot of writing and drawing before he got ill. I read the autobiography he'd been working on, when he was admitted. It was useful in assessing him. He writes very well for a man who had hardly any education, but . . .' Dr Bijral laced his fingers together, and Strike was reminded of another doctor, who'd talked of teamwork while eating fig rolls. 'You see, persuading patients to discuss their crimes is usually an important part of the therapeutic process. You're trying to find a pathway to accountability and remorse, but Dennis feels no remorse. He's still aroused by the thought of what he did to those women, and he enjoys talking and writing about it. He used to draw episodes from the basement, as well; essentially producing his own hardcore pornography. So when he came here, we confiscated all writing and drawing materials.

'Dennis blames us for his deteriorating mental faculties, although in fact, for a seventy-seven-year-old man, he's remarkably sharp. Every patient is different, and we manage Dennis on a strict reward and penalty system. His chosen rewards are unusual. He enjoys chess; he taught himself in Belmarsh, so sometimes I'll give him a game. He likes crosswords and logic puzzles, too. We allow him access to those when he's behaving himself.

'But you mustn't think he's typical of our patients,' added Dr Bijral earnestly. 'The vast majority of mentally ill people pose absolutely no risk of violence, as I'm sure you know. And people do leave Broadmoor, they do get better. People's behaviour can change, if they're motivated, if they're given the right help. Our aim is always recovery. One can hate the crime, but feel compassion for the perpetrator. Many of the men in here had appallingly abusive childhoods. Dennis's childhood was pure hell – though, of course, other people have upbringings as bad and never do what Dennis did. In fact, one of our former patients—'

There was a knock on the door and a cheery blonde poked her head inside.

'That's Dennis ready in the room, Ranbir,' she said, and withdrew.

'Shall we?' said Dr Bijral, getting to his feet. 'I'll be sitting in on the interview, and so will Dennis's primary nurse.'

The woman who'd announced Dennis's arrival in the meeting room walked with Strike and the psychiatrist down another couple of corridors. Now there were doors that had to be unlocked and relocked at every passage. Through the third set of locked doors, Strike saw an obese man shuffling along in Nike tracksuit bottoms, flanked by a pair of nurses, each of whom held one of the patient's stiff arms behind his back. The patient gave Strike a glazed look as the trio passed in silence.

Finally, Strike's party reached a deserted open-plan area, with armchairs and a switched-off TV. Strike had assumed the blonde woman was Creed's nurse, but he was wrong: a burly man with tattoos down both arms, and a prominent, square jaw, was introduced as 'Marvin, Dennis's lead nurse', and the blonde woman smiled at Strike, wished him luck and walked away.

'Well, shall we?' said Dr Bijral, and Marvin opened the door onto a Spartan meeting room, with a single window and a whiteboard on the wall.

The only occupant, a small, obese, bespectacled man, wore jeans and a black sweatshirt. He had a triple chin, and his belly kept him a foot and a half away from the white Formica-topped table at which he was sitting. Transplanted to a bus stop, Dennis Creed would have been just another old man, a little unkempt, his light grey hair in need of a trim.

(He'd pressed hot-irons to the bare breasts of secretary Jackie Aylett. He'd pulled out all of hairdresser Susan Meyer's finger and toenails. He'd dug the eyeballs out of estate agent Noreen Sturrock's face while she was still alive and manacled to a radiator.)

'Dennis, this is Cormoran Strike,' said Dr Bijral, as he sat down in a chair against the wall. Marvin stood, tattooed arms folded, beside him.

'Hello, Dennis,' said Strike, sitting down opposite him.

'Hello, Cormoran,' said Creed, in a flat voice which retained its working-class, East London accent.

The sunlight fell like a gleaming pane across the table between them, highlighting the smears on the lenses of Creed's wire-rimmed glasses and the dust motes in the air. Behind the dirt, Strike saw irises of such pale grey that they faded into the sclera, so that the enormous pupils seemed surrounded by whiteness. Close to, Strike could see the jagged scar which ran from temple to nose, dragging at his left lower eyelid, a relic of the attack that had almost taken half Creed's sight. The plump, pale hands on the table were slightly shaking and the slack mouth trembled: side-effects, Strike guessed, of Creed's medication.

'Who're you working for?' Creed asked.

''Spect you'll be able to work that out, from my questions,' said Strike.

'Why not say, then?' asked Creed, and when Strike didn't answer, he said, 'Sign of narcissism, withholding information to make yourself feel powerful, you know.'

Strike smiled.

'It's not a question of trying to feel powerful. I'm simply familiar with the King's Gambit.'

Creed pushed his wire-rimmed glasses back up his nose.

'Told you I play chess, did they?'

'Yeah.'

'D'you play?'

'Badly.'

'So how does the King's Gambit apply to this situation?'

'Your opening move appears to open an easy route to your king. You're offering to jump straight into discussing the missing woman I'm investigating.'

'But you think that's a ploy?'

'Maybe.'

There was a short pause. Then Creed said,

'I'll tell you who I think sent you, then, shall I?'

'Go on.'

'Margot Bamborough's daughter,' said Dennis Creed, watching carefully for Strike's reaction. 'The husband gave up on her long since, but her daughter'll be forty-odd now and she'll be well-heeled. Whoever hired you's got money. You won't come cheap. I've read all about you, in the paper.

'The second possibility,' said Creed, when Strike didn't respond, 'is old Brian Tucker. He pops up every few years, making a spectacle of himself. Brian's skint, though ... or did he put out the begging bowl on the internet? Get on the computer and whine out some hard-luck story, so mugs send in cash? But I think, if he'd done that, it would've been in the papers.'

'D'you get online much?' asked Strike.

'We're not allowed, in here,' said Creed. 'Why are you wasting time? We've only got forty-five minutes. Ask a question.'

'That was a question, what I just asked you.'

'Why won't you tell me which so-called victim you're interested in?'

'"So-called" victim?'

'Arbitrary labels,' said Creed. '"Victim". "Patient". *This* one deserves pity ... *this* one gets caged. Maybe those women I killed were the real patients, and I'm the true victim?'

'Novel point of view,' said Strike.

'Yeah, well, does people good to hear novel points of view,' said Creed, pushing his glasses up his nose again. 'Wake them up, if they're capable of it.'

'What would you say you were curing those women of?'

'The infection of life? Diagnosis: life. Terminal. "Pity not the fallen! I never knew them. I am not for them. I console not: I hate the consoled and the consoler . . ."'

(He'd slit open the corners of schoolgirl Geraldine Christie's mouth, and photographed her crying and screaming, before, as he told her parents from the dock, slitting her throat because she was making so much noise.)

'" . . . I am unique and conqueror. I am not of the slaves that perish." Know who said that?'

'Aleister Crowley,' said Strike.

'Unusual reading matter,' said Creed, 'for a decorated soldier in the British army.'

'Oh, we're all satanists on the sly,' said Strike.

'You think you're joking,' said Creed, whose expression had become intense, 'but you kill and you get given a medal and called a hero. I kill and get called evil and locked up for ever. Arbitrary categories. Know what's just down the road from here?'

'Sandhurst,' said Strike.

'Sandhurst,' repeated Creed, as though Strike hadn't spoken. 'Institutions for killers, side by side, one to make them, one to break them. Explain to me why's it more moral to murder little brown children on Tony Blair's say-so, than to do what I did? I'm made the way I am. Brain scans will show you, they've studied people like me. It's how we're wired. Why's it more evil to kill because you've got to, because it's your nature, than to blow up poor brown people because we want oil? Properly looked at, I'm the innocent, but *I* get fattened up and drugged like a captive pig, and you get a state pension.'

'Interesting argument,' said Strike. 'So you had no control over what you did?'

'Control,' scoffed Creed, shaking his head. 'That shows how far removed – I can't explain it in terms someone like you would understand. "You have your way. I have my ways. As for the right way, the correct way, and the only way, it does not exist." Know who said that?'

'Sounds like Nietzsche,' said Strike.

'Nietzsche,' said Creed, talking over him. 'Obviously, yes. I read a lot in Belmarsh, back before I got stuffed full of so many drugs I couldn't concentrate from one end of the sentence to another.

'I've got diabetes now, did you know that?' Creed continued. 'Yeah. Hospital-acquired diabetes. They took a thin, fit man, and piled the weight on me, with these drugs I don't need and the pig-swill we're forced to eat. Eight hundred so-called healers leeching a living off us. They need us ill, because we're their livelihoods. Morlocks. Understand that word?'

'Fictional underbeings,' said Strike, 'in *The Time—*'

'Obviously, yes,' said Creed again, who seemed irritated that Strike understood his references. 'H. G. Wells. Primitive beings preying on the highly evolved species, who don't realise they're being farmed to eat. Except *I* realise it, *I* know what's going on.'

'See yourself as one of the Eloi, do you?' asked Strike.

'Interesting thing about the Eloi,' said Creed, 'is their total lack of conscience. The higher race is intellectual, refined, with no so-called remorse . . . I was exploring all this in my book, the book I was writing before they took it off me. Wells's thing was only a superficial allegory, but he was groping towards a truth . . . What I was writing, part autobiography, part scientific treatise – but it was taken away from me, they've confiscated my manuscript. It could be an invaluable resource, but no, because it's mine, it's got to be destroyed. I've got an IQ of 140, but they want my brain flabby like my body.'

'You seem pretty alert to me. What drugs have they got you on?'

'I shouldn't be on any drugs at all. I should be in assertive rehab but they won't let me out of high dependency. They let the little schizophrenics loose in the workshops with knives over there, and I can't have a pencil. When I came here, I thought I'd meet intelligent people . . . any child who can memorise a seven times table could be a doctor, it's all rote learning and dogma. The patient's supposed to be a partner in this therapeutic process, and I say I'm well enough to go back to prison.'

'Certainly seem sane to me,' said Strike.

'Thank you,' said Creed, who'd become flushed. 'Thank you. *You're* an intelligent man, it appears. I thought you would be. That's why I agreed to this.'

'But you're still on medication—'

'I know all about their drugs, and they're giving me too much. I could prescribe better for myself than they know how to, here.'

'How d'you know about that stuff?' asked Strike.

'Obvious, easy,' said Creed, with a grandiose gesture. 'I used myself as a guinea pig, developed my own series of standardised tests. How well I could walk and talk on twenty milligrams, thirty milligrams . . . made notes on disorientation, drowsiness, differences in side-effects . . .'

'What kinds of drugs were these?' asked Strike.

'Amobarbital, pentobarbital, phenobarbital,' rattled off Creed: the names of barbiturates of the early seventies, mostly replaced, now, by other drugs.

'Easy to buy on the street?'

'I only bought off the street occasionally, I had other channels, that were never widely known . . .'

And Creed launched into a meandering speech that couldn't properly be called a story, because the narrative was disjointed and full of mysterious hints and oblique allusions, but the gist seemed to be that Creed had been associating with many unnamed but powerful people in the sixties and seventies, and that a steady supply of prescription drugs had been an incidental perk, either of working for gangsters, or spying on them for the authorities. He hinted at having been recruited by the security services, spoke of flights to America there was no evidence he'd ever taken, of barbiturate-addicted politicians and celebrities, and the dangerous desire of humans from all walks of life to dope themselves to cope with the cruel realities of the world, a tendency and temptation which Dennis Creed deplored and had always resisted.

Strike surmised that these fake reminiscences were designed to feed Creed's overweening craving for status. No doubt his decades in high-security prisons and mental hospitals had taught him that rape and torture were considered almost as contemptible there as they'd been on the outside. He might continue to derive sexual pleasure from reliving his crimes, but in others, they elicited only contempt. Without a fantasy career in which he was part-spy, part-gangster, the man with the 140 IQ was merely a dry-cleaning delivery man, a sexual deviant buying handfuls of downers from street dealers who'd exploited, then betrayed him.

'. . . see all that security all round me, at the trial? There were other forces at play, that's all I'll say . . .'

There'd been a solid cordon of police around Creed on his way in and out of court because the crowd had wanted to tear him apart. The details of his torture chamber had leaked: police had found the hot-irons and the pliers, the ball gags and the whips, the photographs Creed had taken of his victims, alive and dead, and the decomposing head and hands of Andrea Hooton, sitting in his bathroom sink. But the image of himself Creed now presented Strike turned murder into something incidental to a much more prestigious criminal life, a hobby that for some reason the public continued to harp on, when there was so much more to tell, and admire.

'. . . because they like salivating over dirty little things that excite them, as an outlet for their own unacceptable urges,' said Creed. 'I could've been a doctor, probably should have been, actually . . .'

(He'd poured cooking oil over dinner lady Vera Kenny's head, then set her hair on fire and photographed her while it burned, a ball gag in her mouth. He'd cut out unemployed Gail Wrightman's tongue. He'd murdered hairdresser Susan Meyer by stamping repeatedly on her head.)

'Never killed anyone by overdose, did you?' said Strike.

'It takes far more skill to disorientate them but keep them on their feet. Any fool can shove an overdose down someone's throat. The other takes knowledge and experience. That's how I know they're using too much on me in here, because I understand side-effects.'

'What were you giving the women in the basement?'

'I never drugged a woman, once I had her at home. Once she was inside, I had other ways of keeping her quiet.'

Andrea Hooton's mouth had been sewn shut by Creed while she was still alive: the traces of thread had still been present on the rotting head.

The psychiatrist glanced at his watch.

'What if a woman was already drunk?' asked Strike. 'Gail Wrightman: you picked her up in a bar, right? Wasn't there a danger of overdose, if you drugged her on top of the drink?'

'Intelligent question,' said Creed, drinking Strike in with

his enormous pupils. 'I can usually tell what a woman's had to the exact unit. Gail was on her own, sulking. Some man had stood her up . . . '

Creed was giving nothing away: these weren't secrets. He'd admitted to it all already, in the dock, where he'd enjoyed relaying the facts, watching the reaction of the victims' relatives. The photographs hidden under the floorboards, of Gail and Andrea, Susan and Vera, Noreen, Jackie and Geraldine, bound, burned and stabbed, alive and maimed, their mutilated and sometimes headless corpses posed in pornographic attitudes, had damned him before he opened his mouth, but he'd insisted on a full trial, pleading guilty by reason of insanity.

' . . . in a wig, bit of lipstick . . . they think you're harmless, odd . . . maybe queer. Talked to her for a minute or two, little dark corner. You act concerned . . .

'Bit of Nembutal in her drink . . . tiny amount, tiny,' said Creed, holding his trembling fingers millimetres apart. 'Nembutal and alcohol, potentially dangerous, if you don't know what you're doing, but I did, obviously . . .

'So I say, "Well, I got to go now, sweetheart, you be careful." "Be careful!" It always worked.' Creed affected squeaky tones to imitate Gail, '"Aw, don't go, have a drink!" "No, darling, I need my beauty sleep." That's when you prove you're not a threat. You make as if you want to leave, or actually walk away. Then, when they call you back, or run into you ten minutes later, when they're starting to feel like shit, they're relieved, because you're the nice man who's safe . . .

'It was all in my book, the different ways I got them. Instructive for women who want to keep out of trouble, you'd think, to read how a highly efficient killer works, but the authorities won't let it be published, which makes you question, are they happy for slags to be picked off on the streets? Maybe they are.

'Why're there people like me at all, Cormoran? Why's evolution let it happen? Because humans are so highly developed, we can only thin ourselves out with intraspecies predators. Pick off the weak, the morally depraved. It's a good thing that degenerate, drunk women don't breed. That's just a fact, it's a fact,' said Dennis Creed.

'I'd wind down my window. "Want a lift, love?" Swaying all over the place. Glad to see me. Got in the van, no trouble, grateful to sit down . . .

'I used to say to Gail, once I had her in the basement: "Should've gone to the bathroom instead, you dirty little bitch, shouldn't you? I bet you're the type to piss in the street. Filthy, that is, filthy" . . . Why're you so interested in drugging?'

The flow of talk had suddenly dried up. Creed's blank grey and black eyes darted left and right between each of Strike's.

'You think Dr Bamborough would be too clever to get herself drugged by the likes of me, do you?'

'Doctors can make mistakes, like anyone else,' said Strike. 'You met Noreen Sturrock on a bus, right?'

Creed considered Strike for several seconds, as though trying to work something out.

'Buses, now, is it? How often did Margot Bamborough take the bus?'

'Frequently, I'd imagine,' said Strike.

'Would she've taken a can of Coke from a stranger?'

'That's what you offered Noreen, right? And the Coke was full of phenobarbital?'

'Yeah. She was almost asleep by the time we came to my stop. I said, "You've missed yours, darling. Come on, I'll take you to a taxi rank." Walked her straight off the bus, arm round her. She wasn't a big girl, Noreen. That was one of the easiest.'

'Did you adjust dosage for weight?'

There was another slight pause.

'Buses and cans of pop, and adjusting drugs for weight? . . . You know what, Cormoran? I think my second guess was right. You're here for little Louise Tucker.'

'No,' said Strike with a sigh, settling back in his chair. 'As it happens, you were spot on first time round. I was hired by Margot Bamborough's daughter.'

There was a longer silence now, and the psychiatrist again checked his watch. Strike knew that his time was nearly up, and he thought Creed knew it, too.

'I want to go back to Belmarsh, Cormoran,' said Creed, leaning in now that Strike had leaned back. 'I want to finish my book. I'm sane, you know it, too, you just said it. I'm not ill. It's costing the taxpayer five times as much to keep me in here as it would in jail. Where would the British public say I should be, eh?'

'Oh, they'd want you back in prison,' said Strike.

'Well, I agree with them,' said Creed. 'I agree.'

He looked sideways at Dr Bijral, who had the look of a man about to call a halt.

'I'm sane and if I'm treated like it, I'll act like it,' said Creed.

He leaned further forwards.

'I killed Louise Tucker,' said Creed in a soft voice, and in Strike's peripheral vision the psychiatrist and the nurse both froze, astonished. 'Picked her up off a street corner in my van, November 1972. Freezing cold that night. She wanted to go home and she had no money. I couldn't resist, Cormoran,' said Creed, those big black pupils boring into Strike's. 'Little girl in her school uniform. No man could resist. Did it on impulse . . . no planning . . . no wig, no drugged Coke, nothing . . . '

'Why wasn't there any trace of her in the basement?' said Strike.

'There was. I had her necklace. But I never had *her* in the basement, see? You want proof, I'll give you proof: she called her stepmother "Claws". Tell Tucker she told me that, all right? Yeah, we had a five-minute chat about how pissed off she was at home, before she realised we were going the wrong way. Then she starts screaming and banging on the windows.

'I turned into a dark car park,' said Creed quietly, 'put my hand over her mouth, dragged her into the back of the van, fucked her and throttled her. I'd've liked to keep her longer, but she was loud, too loud.

'Dumb thing to do, but I couldn't resist, Cormoran. No planning – school uniform! But I had work next day, I needed the van empty. I wanted to take the body back to the basement, but old Vi Cooper was wide awake when I drove back up Liverpool Road. She was looking down at me out the top window when I drove past, so I didn't stop. Told her later she'd imagined it was me. The old bitch used to sit up to see what time I came in. I usually drugged her if I was off on the prowl, but this was a spur-of-the-moment treat . . .'

'What did you do with the body?' said Strike.

'Ah,' said Creed, sitting back in his seat. The wet lips slid over each other, and the wide pupils gaped. 'I think I'm going to need a transfer back to Belmarsh before I tell anyone that. You go and tell the newspapers I've decided to confess to killing Louise, and that I'm sane, and I should be in Belmarsh, and if I'm transferred, I'll tell old Brian Tucker where I put his little girl. You go tell the authorities, that's my offer . . .

'You never know, I might even feel up to talking about Margot Bamborough when I'm out of here. Let's get these drugs out of my system, and maybe I'll remember better.'

'You're full of shit,' said Strike, getting to his feet, looking angry. 'I'm not passing this on.'

'Don't be like that, because it's not the one you came for,' said Creed, with a slow smile. 'You're coming across like a proper narcissist, Cormoran.'

'I'm ready to go,' Strike told Dr Bijral.

'Don't be like that,' said Creed. 'Oi!'

Strike turned back.

'All right ... I'll give you a little clue about where I put Louise's body, and we'll see whether you're as clever as you think you are, all right? We'll see whether you or the police work it out first. If they find the body, they'll know I'm sane, and I'm ready to talk about Margot Bamborough, as long as I get moved where I want to go. And if nobody can figure out the clue, someone'll have to come back and talk to me, won't they? Maybe even you. We could play chess for more clues, Cormoran.'

Strike could tell that Creed was imagining weeks of front pages, as he laid a trail for investigators to follow. Psychological torture for the Tuckers, manipulation of public opinion, Strike, perhaps, at his beck and call: it was a sadist's wet dream.

'Go on then,' said Strike, looking down at him. 'What's the clue?'

'You'll find Louise Tucker's body where you find M54,' said Creed, and Strike knew Creed had thought out the clue well ahead of time, and was certain that it would have been a clue about Margot, had Strike said he'd been hired by the Tuckers. Creed needed to believe he hadn't given Strike what he really wanted. He had to come out on top.

'Right,' said Strike. He turned to Dr Bijral. 'Shall we?'

'M54, all right, Cormoran?' called Creed.

'I heard you,' said Strike.

'Sorry not to be able to help with Dr Bamborough!' called Creed, and Strike could hear his pleasure at the idea that he'd thwarted the detective.

Strike turned back one last time, and now he stopped pretending to be angry, and grinned, too.

'I was here for Louise, you silly fucker. I know you never

met Margot Bamborough. She was murdered by a far more skilful killer than you ever were. And just so you know,' Strike added, as the nurse's keys jangled, and Creed's slack, fat face registered dismay, 'I think you're a fucking lunatic, and if anyone asks me, I'll say you should be in Broadmoor till you rot.'

69

Beare ye the picture of that Ladies head?
Full liuely is the semblaunt, though the substance dead.

Edmund Spenser
The Faerie Queene

After almost an hour's debrief with Dr Bijral, during which the shaken psychiatrist phoned Scotland Yard, the detective left the hospital feeling as though he'd been there twice as long as he really had. The village of Crowthorne didn't lie on Strike's route back to London, but he was hungry, he wanted to call Robin and he felt a powerful need to place himself among ordinary people going about their lives, to expel the memory of those empty, echoing corridors, the jangle of keys and the widely dilated pupils of Dennis Creed.

He parked outside a pub, lit himself the cigarette he'd been craving for the past two and a half hours, then turned his phone back on. He'd already missed two calls from Brian Tucker, but instead of phoning the old man back, he pressed Robin's number. She answered on the second ring.

'What happened?'

Strike told her. When he'd finished, there was a short silence.

'Say the clue again,' said Robin, who sounded tense.

'"You'll find her where you find M54."'

'Not *the* M54? Not the motorway?'

'He could've meant that, but he left out the definite article.'

'The M54's twenty-odd miles long.'

'I know.'

Reaction was setting in: Strike should have felt triumphant, but in fact he was tired and tense. His phone beeped at him and he glanced at the screen.

'That's Brian Tucker again, trying to ring me,' he told Robin.

'What are you going to tell him?'

'The truth,' said Strike heavily, exhaling smoke out of his open window. 'Dr Bijral's already called Scotland Yard. Trouble is, if that clue's meaningless, or unsolvable, it leaves Tucker knowing Creed killed his daughter, but never getting the body back. This could well be Creed's idea of the ultimate torture.'

'It's something to have a confession, though, isn't it?' said Robin.

'Tucker's been convinced Creed killed her for decades. Confession without a body just keeps the wound open. Creed'll still have the last laugh, knowing where she is and not telling . . . How've you got on in the British Library?'

'Oh. Fine,' said Robin. 'I found Joanna Hammond a couple of hours ago.'

'And?' said Strike, now alert.

'She had a large mole on her face. Left cheek. You can see it in the picture of her wedding in the local paper. I'll text it to you now.'

'And the holy—?'

'It would've been on the back of her obituary. Same local paper.'

'Jesus Christ,' said Strike.

There was a longer silence. Strike's phone beeped again, and he saw that Robin had texted him a picture.

Opening it, he saw a couple on their 1969 wedding day: a blurry black and white picture of a toothy, beaming brunette bride, her hair worn in ringlets, in a high-necked lace dress, a pillbox hat on top of her veil, a large mole on her left cheekbone. The blond husband loomed over her shoulder, unsmiling. Even minutes into married life, he had the air of a man ready to wield a baseball bat.

'She wasn't Sagittarius under Schmidt,' said Robin, and Strike put the phone back up to his ear, 'she was Scorpio—'

'—which Talbot thought fitted her better, because of the mole,' said Strike, with a sigh. 'I should've gone back through all the identifications once you found out about Schmidt. We might've got here sooner.'

'What are we going to do about Douthwaite?'

'I'll ring him,' said Strike, after a moment's pause. 'Now. Then I'll call you back.'

His stomach rumbled as he called the Allardice boarding house in Skegness, and heard the familiar cross Scottish accent of Donna, Douthwaite's wife.

'Oh Christ,' she said, when Strike identified himself. 'What now?'

'Nothing to worry about,' lied Strike, who could hear a radio playing in the background. 'Just wanted to double-check a couple of points.'

'Steve!' he heard her yell, away from the receiver. 'It's *him*! . . . What d'you mean, "Who?", who d'you bloody think?'

Strike heard footsteps and then Douthwaite, who sounded half-angry, half-scared.

'What d'you want?'

'I want to tell you what I think happened during your last appointment with Margot Bamborough,' said Strike.

He spoke for two minutes, and Douthwaite didn't interrupt, though Strike knew he was still there, because of the distant sounds of the boarding house still reaching him over the line. When Strike had finished his reconstruction of Douthwaite's final consultation, there was silence but for the distant radio, which was playing 'Blame' by Calvin Harris.

So blame it on the night . . . don't blame it on me . . .

'Well?' said Strike.

He knew Douthwaite didn't want to confirm it. Douthwaite was a coward, a weak man who ran away from problems. He could have prevented further deaths had he had the courage to tell what he knew, but he'd been scared for his own skin, scared he'd be seen as complicit, stupid and shabby, in the eyes of newspaper readers. And so he'd run, but that had made things worse, and nightmarish consequences had ensued, and he'd run from those, too, barely admitting to himself what he feared, distracting himself with drink, with karaoke, with women. And now Strike was presenting him with a dreadful choice that was really no choice at all. Like Violet Cooper, Steve Douthwaite was facing a lifetime of opprobrium from the censorious public, and how much better would it have been if he'd come clean to Talbot forty years previously, when Margot Bamborough's body could have been found quickly, and a killer could have been brought to justice before others had to die.

'Am I right?' Strike said.

'Yes,' said Douthwaite, at last.

'OK, well, if you'll take my advice, you'll go straight to your wife and tell her, before the press do it. There's going to be no hiding from this one.'

'Shit,' said Douthwaite quietly.

'See you in court, then,' said Strike briskly, and he hung up, and called Robin straight back.

'He's confirmed it.'

'Cormoran,' said Robin.

'I advised him to tell Donna—'

'Cormoran,' said Robin, again.

'What?'

'I think I know what M54 is.'

'Not—'

'—the motorway? No. M54 is a globular cluster—'

'A what?'

'A spherical cluster of stars.'

'Stars?' said Strike, with a sinking sensation. 'Hang on—'

'Listen,' said Robin. 'Creed thought he was being clever, but it only takes a Google search—'

'They haven't got internet in there,' said Strike. 'He was whining about it—'

'Well, M54 is a cluster of stars in the constellation Sagittarius,' said Robin.

'Not astrology again,' said Strike, closing his eyes. 'Robin—'

'*Listen to me.* He said "You'll find her where you find M54", right?'

'Yeah—'

'The constellation Sagittarius is also known as the Archer.'

'So?'

'Brian showed us the map, Strike! Dennis Creed was a regular visitor to the Archer Hotel in Islington in the early seventies, when he was delivering their dry cleaning. There was a well on the property, in the back garden. Boarded up, and now covered over with a conservatory.'

A pair of jolly men with matching beer bellies walked into the pub across the road. Strike barely registered them. He'd even forgotten to take drags of the cigarette burning between his fingers.

'Think this through,' said Robin in his ear. 'Creed's got a body he didn't expect in the van, but he can't take it to Epping Forest, because there was still an active crime scene there.

They'd just found the remains of Vera Kenny. I don't know why he didn't take the body to the basement—'

'I do,' said Strike. 'He's just told me. He drove past the house and Vi Cooper was awake and at the window.'

'OK – right – so he's got to empty the van before work. He knows his way around the Archer garden, and he knows there's a back gate. He's got tools in the back of the van, he could prise those boards up easily. Cormoran, I'm *sure* she's in the old Archer well.'

There was a brief pause, then hot ash fell into Strike's lap from his neglected cigarette.

'Bollocks—'

He flicked the end out of the window, earning himself a look of disapproval from a passing old woman pulling a tartan shopping trolley.

'All right, here's what we're going to do,' he told Robin. 'I'll phone Tucker and tell him what's just happened, including your deduction. You call George Layborn and tell him about the well at the Archer. The quicker the police search it, the better for the Tuckers, especially if the news leaks that Creed's confessed.'

'OK, I'll get on to that right—'

'Hang on, I haven't finished,' said Strike. He'd closed his eyes now, and he was rubbing his temples as he thought through everything the agency needed to do, and quickly. 'When you've spoken to Layborn, I want you to ring Barclay and tell him he's going on a job with you, tomorrow morning. He can forget Miss Jones's boyfriend for a few hours. Or, most probably, all day, if what I think's going to happen happens.'

'What job are Barclay and I doing?' asked Robin.

'Isn't it obvious?' said Strike, opening his eyes again. 'We're up against the clock if Douthwaite talks to anyone.'

'So Barclay and I are . . . ?'

'Finding Margot's body,' said Strike. 'Yes.'

There was a long silence. Strike's stomach rumbled again. Now a pair of young women entered the pub, giggling at something one had shown the other on her phone.

'You really think she's there?' said Robin, a little shaken.

'I'm sure of it,' said Strike.

'And you're—?'

'I'm going to call Brian Tucker, eat some chips, make that long-distance phone call – I think they're three hours ahead of us, so that should work fine – then drive back to the office. I'll be back late afternoon and we can talk it all over properly.'

'Right,' said Robin, 'good luck.'

She rang off. Strike hesitated for a moment before calling Brian Tucker: he'd have liked to do it with a pint in his hand, but he still needed to drive back to London, and being arrested for drink driving on the eve of catching Margot Bamborough's killer was a complication he really didn't want to risk. Instead, he lit himself a second cigarette, and prepared to tell a grieving father that after a forty-two year wait, he might soon be in a position to bury his daughter.

70

. . . and lastly Death;
Death with most grim and griesly visage seene . . .

Edmund Spenser
The Faerie Queene

The morning was so mild it might have been summer, but the leaves of the plane trees beside the telephone box at the mouth of Albemarle Way were starting to turn yellow. A patchwork blue and white sky gave and withdrew warmth as the sun slid in and out behind clouds, and Robin felt shivery in spite of the sweater she was wearing beneath her raincoat, as though a cold wind was blowing up Albemarle Way, the short side street whose tall, unbroken buildings kept it forever in shadow.

She was standing beside the telephone box where once, nearly forty years previously, the killer of Margot Bamborough had waited and watched, feeling, Robin imagined, much as she did now. There must have been fear, and nervousness, and doubt that the plan could possibly work, and terror of the consequences of failure. But this sense of kinship didn't make Robin feel any more kindly to the killer. Looking across the road at the ancient arch of St John's Gate, she could imagine Margot Bamborough walking through it on a rainy evening forty years previously, or perhaps weaving, feeling strangely groggy and not knowing why . . . or had she realised? Possibly.

Margot was a clever woman, and that was why she'd had to die . . .

Clerkenwell Road was busy with traffic and pedestrians. Robin felt entirely isolated from all of them. Nobody passing Robin could have the slightest idea of what she was about to try and do. How bizarre they'd think her morning's plans, how macabre . . . a trickle of panic ran down Robin's spine . . .

Think about something else.

There'd been a picture in the *Metro* that morning of Charlotte Ross wearing sunglasses and a long dark coat, walking along a street in Mayfair with her sister, Amelia. There had been no sign of Charlotte's husband or young twins, and the short non-story beneath the picture had told Robin nothing she wanted to know.

> Charlotte Campbell was spotted enjoying a morning walk in London with her sister, Amelia Crichton, yesterday. Charlotte, who is married to Jago, heir to the Viscountcy of Croy, was recently released from hospital, following a prolonged stay in Symonds House, an addiction and mental health facility much favoured by the rich and famous.
>
> Charlotte, who once topped *Tatler*'s list of 100 Most Beautiful Londoners, has been a favourite of the gossip columns since she first ran away from school, aged 14. Daughter of . . .

Think about something else, Robin told herself, and consciously groped around for another subject.

It was September the twentieth. A person born today would be born under the sign of Virgo. Robin wondered how long it was going to take to rid herself of the mental tic of tying dates to star signs. She thought of Matthew, who was the Virgoan she knew best. The sign was supposed to be clever, and organised, and nervous. He was certainly organised, and bright in a book-smart way . . . she remembered Oonagh Kennedy saying, 'I sometimes t'ink, the cleverer they are with books, the stupider they are with sex,' and wondered whether he was now happy about the pregnancy he'd said was accidental . . .

Think about something else.

She checked her watch. Where was Barclay? True, Robin had arrived very early, and technically Barclay wasn't late, but she didn't like standing here alone, trying to distract herself from thoughts of what they were about to do.

Theo had once stood almost exactly where Robin now was, watching the traffic roll up and down Clerkenwell Road, dark-haired Theo of the Kuchi earrings and the painful abdomen, waiting for the silver van that would take her away. Why Theo had never come forward afterwards, why she'd never felt enough gratitude to the woman who'd seen her at short notice, at least to rule herself out of suspicion and stop Talbot haring after a delusion, remained a minor mystery. But of course, that assumed that Theo felt grateful. Nobody ever really knew what happened between a doctor and patient: it was the secular equivalent of the confession box. Robin's thoughts had moved to Douthwaite when, at last, she spotted Barclay, who was approaching, carrying a holdall. When he got close enough, Robin heard the tools inside it clinking.

'Havin' a wee bit o' déjà vu, here,' he said, coming to halt beside her. 'Didn't we once go diggin' fer a body before?'

'I don't think this qualifies as digging,' said Robin.

'What's the latest?'

'He's gone out,' said Robin. 'Strike says we've got to wait until he comes back.'

'What's in there?' asked Barclay, nodding at the carrier bag in Robin's hand.

'Chocolate biscuits,' said Robin.

'Bribe?'

'Basically.'

'And has Strike—?'

'Not yet. He's in position. He wants us to . . .'

Robin waited for a group of what looked like students to walk out of earshot.

'. . . do our bit, first. Were you pleased,' Robin continued, still trying not to think about what they were about to do until it was absolutely necessary, 'about the referendum result?'

'Aye, but don't kid yerself oan,' said Barclay darkly, 'this isn't finished. That stupid fucker Cameron's playing right into the nats' hands. "English votes for English laws", the day after Scotland decides to stay? You don't fight fuckin' nationalism with more fuckin' nationalism. He wants tae get his head out of Farage's arse – is this oor wee fella now?'

Robin looked around. Silhouetted against the end of Albemarle Way was a man walking along with a strange, rolling gait, who was carrying two full carrier bags. He stopped at a door, set down his shopping, put his key in the lock, picked up his shopping bags, stepped over the threshold and vanished from sight.

'That's him,' said Robin, as her insides seemed to wobble. 'Let's go.'

They walked side by side down the street to the dark blue front door.

'He's left the key in the lock,' said Barclay, pointing.

Robin was about to ring the bell when the door opened, and Samhain Athorn reappeared. Pale, big-eared and mousy-haired, he gaped slightly. He was wearing a Batman sweatshirt. Disconcerted to find two people on his doorstep, he blinked, then addressed Robin's left shoulder.

'I left the key.'

He reached around to pull it out of the lock. As he made to close the door, Barclay dextrously inserted a foot.

'You're Samhain, aren't you?' said Robin, smiling at him, while Samhain gaped. 'We're friends of Cormoran Strike's. You were very helpful to him, a few months ago.'

'I need to put the shopping away,' said Samhain. He tried to close the front door, but Barclay's foot was in the way.

'Could we come in?' asked Robin. 'Just for a little while? We'd like to talk to you and your mum. You were so helpful, before, telling Cormoran about your Uncle Tudor—'

'My Uncle Tudor's dead,' said Samhain.

'I know. I'm sorry.'

'He died in the hospital,' said Samhain.

'Really?' said Robin.

'My-Dad-Gwilherm died under the bridge,' said Samhain.

'That's so sad,' said Robin. 'Could we come in, please, just for a moment? Cormoran wanted me to bring you these,' she added, pulling the tin of chocolate biscuits out of her bag. 'As a thank you.'

'What's them?' asked Samhain, looking at the tin out of the corner of his eye.

'Chocolate biscuits.'

He took the tin out of her hand.

'Yeah. You can come in,' he said, and turning his back, he marched up the dark interior stairs.

With a glance at Barclay, Robin led the way inside. She heard her companion close the door behind her, and the clinking of the tools in his holdall. The staircase was steep, narrow and dark after daylight, the light bulb overhead dead. When Robin reached the landing she saw, through the open door, a white-haired woman with big ears like Samhain's, wiping the surfaces of a brown-tiled kitchen while Samhain, who had his back to her, eagerly peeled the plastic wrapper off the tin of chocolate biscuits.

Deborah turned, her neat white plait sliding over her shoulder, to fix her dark eyes on the two strangers.

'Hello, Mrs Athorn,' said Robin, coming to a halt in the hall.

'Are you from the social work department?' asked Deborah slowly. 'I phoned Clare . . .'

'We can help wi' anythin' Clare can,' said Barclay, before Robin could answer. 'What's the problem?'

'Him downstairs is a bastard,' said Samhain, who was now digging busily in the tin of chocolate biscuits, and selecting the one wrapped in gold foil. 'These are the best ones, in the shiny paper, that's how you know.'

'Is the man downstairs complaining again?' asked Robin, with a sudden upswell of excitement that bordered on panic.

'Can we have a look at whut the problem is?' asked Barclay. 'Where's he think his ceilin's crackin'?'

Deborah pointed towards the sitting room.

'I'll have a wee look,' said Barclay confidently, and he set off towards the sitting room.

'Don't eat all of them, Sammy,' said Deborah, who'd returned to the methodical wiping of the kitchen sides.

'They gave them to me, you silly woman,' said Samhain, his mouth full of chocolate.

Robin followed, fighting a sense of utter unreality. Could what Strike suspected really be true?

Two budgerigars were twittering in a cage in the corner of the small sitting room, which, like the hall, was carpeted in swirls of brown and orange. A crocheted blanket had been spread over the back of the sofa. Barclay was looking down at the almost completed jigsaw of unicorns leaping over a rainbow. Robin glanced around. The place was sparsely furnished. Apart from the sofa and the budgies' cage, there was only a small armchair, a television set on top of which stood an urn, and a small shelving unit on which sat a few old paperbacks and some cheap ornaments. Her eyes lingered on the Egyptian symbol of eternal life painted on a patch of dirty green wall.

She lies in a holy place.

'Floorboards?' she murmured to Barclay.

He shook his head, looked meaningfully down at the jigsaw of the unicorns, then pointed with his foot at the overlarge ottoman on which it lay.

'Oh God, no,' whispered Robin, before she could stop herself. 'You think?'

'Otherwise the carpet would've had tae come up,' murmured Barclay. 'Move furniture, take up floorboards . . . and would it make the ceilin' crack, down below? An' what aboot the smell?'

Samhain now came ambling into the room, eating his second foil-wrapped biscuit.

'D'you want a hot chocolate, or not?' he asked, looking at Robin's knees.

'Um . . . no, thank you,' said Robin, smiling at him.

'Does he want a hot chocolate, or not?'

'No thanks, mate,' said Barclay. 'Can we move this jigsaw? Need tae have a look beneath it.'

'Deborah don't like her jigsaw touched,' said Samhain sternly.

'We need to prove the man downstairs is lying, though,' said Robin. 'About his ceiling cracking.'

'Deborah,' called Samhain. 'They want to move your jigsaw.'

He walked out of the room with his rocking gait, and his mother took his place at the door, eyeing Robin's shoes as she said,

'You can't move my unicorns.'

'We need to have a little look underneath it,' said Robin.

'I promise we'll take very good care of it, and not break it. We could move it . . . '

She looked around, but there was no stretch of floor big enough to accommodate it.

'In my bedroom, you can put it,' said Samhain, bobbing back into sight. 'On my bed, they can put it, Deborah.'

'Excellent idea,' said Barclay heartily, bending to pick it up.

'Close it up first,' said Robin hastily, and she folded the wings of the jigsaw mat over the puzzle, containing all the pieces.

'Good job,' said Barclay, and he carried the jigsaw mat carefully out through the sitting-room door, followed by Deborah, who looked both anxious and alarmed, and by the self-important Samhain, who seemed proud to have had his plan adopted by this new man in the flat.

For a few seconds, Robin stood alone in the sitting room, looking down at the ottoman that was far too big for this small room. It had been covered with a cloth that Robin suspected dated from the sixties, being of thin, faded purple cotton, and carrying the design of a mandala. If a tall woman curled herself up, she might fit inside that ottoman, as long as she was thin, of course.

I don't want to look, Robin thought suddenly, panic rising again. *I don't want to see . . .*

But she had to look. She had to see. That was what she was there for.

Barclay returned, followed by both an interested-looking Samhain and a troubled Deborah.

'That doesn't open,' said Deborah, pointing at the exposed ottoman. 'You can't open that. You leave that alone.'

'I had my toys in there,' said Samhain. 'Didn't I, Deborah? Once I did. But My-Dad-Gwilherm didn't want me to keep them there no more.'

'You can't open that,' repeated Deborah, now distressed. 'Leave it, don't touch that.'

'Deborah,' said Robin quietly, walking towards the older woman, 'we've got to find out why the ceiling downstairs is cracking. You know how the man downstairs is always complaining, and saying he'd like you and Samhain to move out?'

'I don't want to go,' said Deborah at once, and for a split-second her dark eyes almost met Robin's, before darting back to the swirly carpet. 'I don't want to move. I'm going to ring Clare.'

'No,' said Robin, moving quickly around Deborah and blocking her way back to the kitchen, with its old wall-mounted phone beside the fridge. She hoped Deborah hadn't heard her panic. 'We're here instead of Clare, you see? To help you with the man downstairs. But we think – Sam and I—'

'My-Dad-Gwilherm called me Sam,' said Samhain. 'Didn't he, Deborah?'

'That's nice,' said Robin, and she pointed at Barclay. 'This man's called Sam, too.'

'Is his name Sam, is it?' said Samhain gleefully, and boldly he raised his eyes to Barclay's face before looking away again, grinning. 'Two Sams. Deborah! Two Sams!'

Robin addressed the perplexed Deborah, who was now shifting from foot to foot in a manner reminiscent of her son's rolling walk.

'Sam and I want to sort this out, Deborah, so you don't have any more trouble with the man downstairs.'

'Gwilherm didn't want that opened,' said Deborah, reaching nervously for the end of her white plait. 'He didn't want that opened, he wanted that kept shut.'

'Gwilherm would want you and Samhain to be allowed to stay here, though, wouldn't he?'

Deborah put the end of her plait in her mouth and sucked

at it, as though it was an ice lolly. Her dark eyes wandered as though in search of help.

'I think,' said Robin gently, 'it would be good if you and Samhain wait in his bedroom while we have a look at the ottoman.'

'Knotty man,' said Samhain, and he cackled again. 'Sam! Hey – Sam! Knotty man!'

'Good one,' said Barclay, grinning.

'Come on,' said Robin, sliding an arm around Deborah. 'You wait in the bedroom with Samhain. You haven't done anything wrong, we know that. Everything's going to be fine.'

As she led Deborah slowly across the landing, she heard Samhain say cheerily,

'I'm staying here, though.'

'No, mate,' Barclay replied, as Robin and Deborah entered Samhain's tiny bedroom. Every inch of wall was covered in pictures of superheroes and gaming characters. Deborah's gigantic jigsaw took up most of the bed. The floor around the PlayStation was littered with chocolate wrappers.

'Look after yer mam and, after, I'll teach ye a magic trick,' Barclay was saying.

'My-Dad-Gwilherm could do magic!'

'Aye, I know, I heard. That make it easy fer you tae do magic, if yer dad could do it, eh?'

'We won't be long,' Robin told Samhain's frightened mother. 'Just stay in here for now, all right? Please, Deborah?'

Deborah simply blinked at her. Robin was particularly afraid of the woman trying to reach the phone on the kitchen wall, because she didn't want to have to physically restrain her. Returning to the sitting room, she found Barclay still bargaining with Samhain.

'Do it now,' Samhain was saying, grinning, looking from Barclay's hands to his chin to his ear. 'Go on, show me now.'

'Sam can only do magic after we've done our job,' said Robin. 'Samhain, will you wait in the bedroom with your mum, please?'

'Go on, mate,' said Barclay. 'Just fer a bit. Then I'll teach ye the trick.'

The smile faded off Samhain's face.

'Silly woman,' he said sulkily to Robin. 'Stupid woman.'

He walked out of the room, but instead of going into his bedroom, he made for the kitchen.

'Shit,' Robin muttered, 'don't do anything yet, Sam—'

Samhain reappeared, holding the tin of chocolate biscuits, walked into his bedroom and slammed the door behind him.

'Now,' said Robin.

'Stay by the door,' said Sam, 'keep an eye on them.'

Robin closed the sitting-room door, leaving a tiny crack through which she could spy on Samhain's bedroom, and gave Barclay the thumbs up.

He pulled the mandala covering off the ottoman, bent down, gripped the edge of the lid and heaved. The lid wouldn't budge. He put all his strength into it, but still it didn't shift. From Samhain's room came the sound of raised voices. Deborah was telling Samhain not to eat any more chocolate biscuits.

'It's like – it's locked – on the inside,' said Barclay, panting and letting go.

He unzipped his holdall and, after some rummaging, pulled out a crowbar, which he wedged the end of into the crack separating the lid from the body of the ottoman. '*Come – oan – you – fucker*,' he gasped, as the end of the crowbar lost its grip and nearly hit Barclay in the face. 'Somethin's stickin' it doon.'

Robin peeked back at Samhain's bedroom door. It remained closed. Mother and son were still arguing about the chocolate biscuits. The budgerigars chirruped. Beyond the window,

Robin could see an aeroplane trail, a fuzzy white pipe cleaner stretched across the sky. Everyday things became so strange, when you were waiting for something dreadful to happen. Her heart was pounding fast.

'Help me,' said Barclay through gritted teeth. He'd managed to get the end of the crowbar deeper into the crack in the ottoman. 'It's gonnae take two.'

After another glance at Samhain's closed door, Robin hurried over to Barclay and gripped the crowbar alongside him. Using all their weight and force, both pushed the handle towards the floor.

'Jesus,' panted Robin. 'What's holding it?'

'Where's – Strike – when you need—'

There was a loud crunching, cracking noise. The crowbar suddenly gave way as the lid of the ottoman opened. Robin turned and saw a cloud of dust rising into the air. Barclay pushed the lid up.

The ottoman had been filled with concrete, which had stuck the lid down upon itself. The grey matter was lumpy and looked as though it might have been badly mixed. In two places, something smooth broke through the uneven, ashen surface: one resembling a few inches of walrus tusk, the other, a curved surface that hinted at a dark ivory globe. Then Robin saw, stuck to a bit of the concrete that had adhered to the lid of the ottoman, a few fair hairs.

They heard footsteps on the landing. Barclay slammed the lid of the ottoman down as Samhain opened the door. He was followed by Deborah.

'I'll teach you that magic trick now,' said Barclay, walking towards Samhain. 'Come in the kitchen, we'll do it there.'

The two men left. Deborah shuffled into the room, and picked up the faded purple throw that Robin had cast aside.

'Did you open it?' she mumbled, eyes on the old carpet.

'Yes,' said Robin, far more calmly than she felt. She sat down on the ottoman, even though she felt sacrilegious doing it. *I'm sorry, Margot. I'm so sorry.*

'I need to make a phone call now, Deborah. Then I think we should all have some hot chocolate.'

71

Such is the face of falshood, such the sight
Of fowle Duessa, when her borrowed light
Is laid away, and counterfesaunce knowne.

Edmund Spenser
The Faerie Queene

A train came roaring and rattling along the Southeastern railway line. Strike, who was standing on the opposite side of the road, felt his mobile vibrate in his pocket and pulled it out, but for a few seconds the din was such that he couldn't immediately hear Robin.

'. . . found her.'

'Say that again?' he shouted, as the train rumbled away.

'We've – found – her. Inside the ottoman inside the sitting room. Concrete was poured in all around her, but we can see a bit of her skull and maybe a femur.'

'Shit.'

Strike had expected the presence of the body in the Athorns' flat, but there was nothing routine, ever, about finding a dead human. 'Concrete?' he repeated.

'Yes. It doesn't look that well mixed. Amateurish. But it's done the job. It probably killed most of the smell.'

'Hell of a weight on a supporting beam.'

'Well, exactly. Where are you?'

'Outside, about to go in. Right: call 999, then call Layborn and tell him where I am, and why. That should speed things up.'

'OK. Good luck.'

Strike hung up. The nondescript street of terraced houses was quiet now the train had gone, birdsong replacing its thunderous clamour. Strike, who'd been waiting where he couldn't be seen, now walked up the street, passing three small houses, and at the fourth, turned left up a short garden path, then beat a tattoo on the dark red front door.

The net curtains twitched, and Janice Beattie's cross face appeared. Strike raised a hand in greeting. The curtain fell.

After a slightly longer wait than might have been expected, given the short distance from sitting room to hall, Janice opened the door. She was dressed all in black today, with sheepskin carpet slippers on her feet. Her clear china-blue eyes, rimmed in steel, looked as kind and innocent as ever. Silver-haired, apple-cheeked, she frowned up at the detective, but didn't speak.

'Can I come in?' asked Strike.

There was a long pause. The wild birds tweeted, and Strike thought fleetingly of the budgies in the Athorns' flat, where part of his mind was dwelling on the image of a skull and a femur, poking up through concrete.

'If you must,' said Janice slowly.

He followed Janice into the red sitting room, with its cheap crimson Turkish rug, its dried-flower pictures and its faded photographs. The sun was making the spun-glass Cinderella carriage and its six horses twinkle on top of the fire, which Janice had on, in spite of the mildness of the September day.

'Wanna cup of tea?' said Janice.

'That'd be great,' said Strike, fully alive to the unreality of the situation.

He listened to her sheepskin-muffled footsteps receding and the sound of the kitchen door opening. Taking out his mobile phone, he switched it to record and laid it on the arm of the chair in which he'd sat last time. He then pulled on a pair of latex gloves and followed Janice quietly out of the room, the worn carpet muffling his footsteps.

At the door, he paused, listening to the soft bubbling of boiling water against a kettle lid, and the tinkle of teaspoons, and the opening of a cupboard. With one fingertip, he pushed open the kitchen door.

Janice spun round, eyes wide. On seeing him, she grabbed one of the china mugs on the tray and raised it hurriedly to her lips, but Strike had already taken a stride towards her. Gripping the thin wrist with his latex-gloved hand, forcing the mug away from her mouth, he felt bone beneath the soft flesh and the papery skin of the elderly. With his free hand, he pulled the mug out of hers, and examined it. A good inch of viscous white liquid was swimming in the bottom of it. Still holding Janice's wrist, he looked into the teapot, which contained more of the same, then opened the cupboard over the kettle.

It was jammed with bottles of pills, weedkiller, bleach and jam jars full of what looked like home-dried plants, leaves and fungus: a poisoner's storehouse, a testimony to a lifetime's careful study of the means by which death could be delivered in the guise of healing.

'Think I'll skip tea,' said Strike. 'Let's have a chat, shall we?'

She offered no resistance as he led her by the wrist back through to the sitting room and pushed her down onto the sofa.

'A murder-suicide would be a hell of a way to go out,' said Strike, standing over her, 'but I don't much fancy being victim number . . . how many is it?'

Janice said nothing. Her round blue eyes registered only shock.

Strike looked up at the wall of old photographs. One showed a toothy, beaming brunette bride, her hair worn in ringlets, in a high-necked lace dress, a pillbox hat on top of her veil, a large mole on her left cheekbone. Just above it was a picture of a young blonde with her hair worn in a frizzy eighties perm. She was wearing a red coat. He hadn't noticed, hadn't seen, because he'd walked into the room with certain expectations, making assumptions no less sweeping than Talbot had, with his conviction that Cancerians were intuitive, gentle and perceptive. Nurses were angels, ministering to the vulnerable: he'd been as guilty of bias as Vi Cooper, seeing Janice through the prism of his grateful memories of the nurses in Selly Oak who'd helped him manage pain and depression, and of Kerenza down in Cornwall, bringing comfort and kindness every single day. And on top of it all, he'd been fooled by a veritable genius for lies and misdirection.

'I thought,' said Strike, 'I should come and tell the Athorns' social worker in person that a body's been found in their flat. You do a very good middle-class accent, Janice. I s'pose the phone Clare uses is round here somewhere?'

He looked around. Possibly she'd hidden it when she'd seen who was at the door. He suddenly spotted the hairdryer, tucked away behind the sofa, but with its lead protruding. He sidled past the coffee table, bent down and pulled it out, along with a roll of cellophane, a small phial with the label pulled off, a syringe and some chocolates.

'Leave them,' said Janice suddenly and angrily, but he laid the items on the coffee table instead.

'How ill would I have been if I'd eaten one of those dates you were doctoring when I arrived last time?' he asked. 'You use the hairdryer to fix the cellophane back round them, right?' When she didn't answer, he said, 'I haven't thanked you for those chocolates you sent Robin and me at Christmas. I had flu. Only managed to eat a couple before puking my guts up. Chucked the rest away, because they had bad associations. Lucky for me, eh?'

Strike now sat down in the armchair, beside his mobile, which was still recording.

'Did you kill *all* these people?' Strike asked, gesturing up at the wall of photographs, 'Or do some of them just have recurrent bowel problems around you? No,' he said, scrutinising the wall, 'Irene's not up there, is she?'

She blinked at him through the lenses of her round silver glasses, which were far cleaner than Dennis Creed's.

A car came trundling up the road beyond the net curtains. Janice watched it pass, and Strike thought she was half expecting to see a police car. Perhaps she wasn't going to talk at all. Sometimes, people didn't. They preferred to leave it all up to the lawyers.

'I spoke to your son on the phone last night,' said Strike.

'You never!'

The words had burst out of her, in shock.

'I did,' said Strike. 'Kevin was quite surprised to hear you'd been visiting him in Dubai, because he hasn't seen you in nearly seven years. Why d'you pretend you're visiting him? To get a break from Irene?'

She pressed her lips together. One hand was playing with the worn wedding ring on the other.

'Kevin told me he's had barely any contact with you, since leaving home. You weren't ever close, he said. But he paid for you to fly out there seven years ago, because he thought he should give you "another chance", as he put it . . . and his young daughter managed to ingest quite a lot of bleach while you were looking after her. She survived – just – and since then, he's cut you off completely.

'We ended up talking for nearly two hours,' said Strike,

watching Janice's colour fluctuate. 'It was hard for Kevin to say out loud what he's suspected all these years. Who wants to believe their own mum's been poisoning people? He preferred to think he was paranoid about all those "special drinks" you used to give him. And apparently your first husband—'

'He wasn't my 'usband,' muttered Janice. 'We were never married.'

'—left because he thought you were doing things to his meals, too. Kevin used to think his father was making it all up. But after our chat last night, I think he's seeing things very differently. He's ready to come over and testify against you.'

Janice gave a small convulsive jerk. For almost a minute there was silence.

'You're recording this,' she whispered at last, looking at the mobile lying on the arm of Strike's chair.

'I am, yeah,' said Strike.

'If you turn that off, I'll talk to you.'

'I'll still be able to testify to whatever you tell me.'

'I'm sure a lawyer would tell me not to let meself be recorded, though.'

'Yeah,' Strike acknowledged, 'you're probably right.'

He picked up the mobile, turned it to face her so she could watch, switched off the recording, then laid it down on the small coffee table beside the chocolates, the empty phial, the syringe, the cellophane and the hairdryer.

'Why d'you do it, Janice?'

She was still stroking the underside of her wedding ring.

'I don't know why,' she said. 'I just . . . like it.'

Her eyes wandered over the wall of photographs.

'I like seeing what 'appens to them, if they take poison or too many drugs. Sometimes I like 'elping 'em and 'aving them be grateful, and sometimes I like watching 'em suffer, and sometimes I like watching 'em go . . . ' A prickle ran up the back of Strike's neck. 'I don't know why,' she said again. 'I sometimes fink it's because I 'ad a bang on the 'ead, when I was ten. My dad knocked me downstairs. I was out for fifteen minutes. Ever since then, I've 'ad 'eadaches . . . 'Ead trauma can do fings to you, you know. So maybe it's not my fault, but . . . I dunno . . .

'Wiv me granddaughter,' said Janice, frowning slightly, 'I just wanted 'er gone, honestly . . . spoiled and whiny . . . I don't like kids,' she said, looking directly back at Strike. 'I've never liked kids. I never wanted 'em, never wanted Kev, but I fort if I 'ad it, 'is dad might marry me . . . but 'e never, 'e wouldn't . . .

'It was 'aving a baby what killed my mum,' said Janice. 'I was eight. She 'ad it at 'ome. Placenta previa, it was. Blood everywhere, me trying to 'elp, no doctor, my father drunk, screaming at everyone . . .

'I took this,' said Janice quietly, showing Strike the wedding ring on her finger, 'off Mum's dead 'and. I knew my father would sell it for drink. I took it and 'id it so 'e couldn't get it. It's all I got of 'er. I loved my mum,' said Janice Beattie, stroking the wedding ring, and Strike wondered whether it was true, whether head trauma and early abuse had made Janice what she was, and whether Janice had the capacity to love at all.

'Is that really your little sister, Clare?' Strike asked, pointing at the double frame beside Janice, where the sleepy-eyed, overweight man with smoker's teeth faced the heavy but pretty blonde.

'No,' said Janice, looking at the picture. After a short pause, she said, 'She was Larry's mistress. I killed both of 'em. I'm not sorry. They deserved it. 'E was wiv me, 'e wasn't much of a catch, but 'e was wiv me, the pair of 'em carryin' on be'ind my back. Bitch,' said Janice quietly, looking at the picture of the plump blonde.

'I assume you kept the obituaries?'

She got slowly up from the sofa, and Strike heard her knees click as she walked towards the china cabinet in the corner which housed most of her cheap spun-glass ornaments, and knelt down, again steadying herself with one hand on the mantelpiece. But now, instead of one folder, she tugged two out of the drawer in the base of the cabinet, and Strike remembered how she'd shifted things around in the drawer last time, doubtless removing those things she didn't want him to see.

'That one,' she said, showing him the fatter of the two folders, 'is all the stuff about Margot. I cut out everyfing I could find. Needed a second folder for all 'er clippings . . . '

She opened the thinner folder, which was the one Strike had seen before, and extracted an old work newsletter headed *Hickson & Co.* The blonde's colour photograph featured prominently at the top.

'Clare Martin,' said Janice. ''Eavy drinker, she was. "Accidental overdose" . . . liver failure. I knew she was taking too many paracetamol for 'er endometriosis, I watched 'er doing it. Me and Larry 'ad a bunch of people over to the 'ouse. They fort I was stupid. Eye contact between 'em all night long. Thick as mince, the pair of 'em. I was mixing drinks. Every cocktail I gave 'er was 'alf liquid paracetamol. She died eight days later . . .

'And there's Larry's,' she said indifferently, holding up a second newsletter from Hickson & Co.

'I waited six, seven monfs. That was easy. 'E was a walkin' timebomb, Larry, the doctors 'ad warned 'im, 'is 'eart was wrecked. Pseudoephedrine, that was. They never even checked 'im for drugs in 'is system. They knew what it was: smoking and eating like a pig. Nobody looked further than 'is dodgy ticker . . . '

Strike detected not the slightest sign of remorse as she

shuffled the obituaries of her victims as though they were so many knitting patterns. Her fingers trembled, but Strike thought that was down to shock, not shame. Mere minutes ago she'd thought of suicide. Perhaps that cool and clever brain was working very hard beneath the apparently frank surface, and Strike suddenly reached out and removed the drugged chocolates from the table beside Janice, and put them down on the floor beside his chair. Her eyes followed them, and he was sure he'd been right to suspect she was thinking of eating them. Now he leaned forwards again and picked up the old yellow clipping he'd examined last time, showing little Johnny Marks from Bethnal Green.

'He was your first, was he?'

Janice took a deep breath and exhaled. A couple of the cuttings fluttered.

'Yeah,' she said heavily. 'Pesticide. You could get all sorts in them days, buy it over the counter. Organophosphates. I fancied 'im something rotten, Johnny Marks, but 'e made fun of me. Yeah, so they fort it was peritonitis and 'e died. It's true the doctor didn't turn up, mind. People didn't care, when it was kids from a slum . . . That was a bad death, 'e 'ad. I was allowed to go in and look at 'im, after 'e died. I give 'im a little kiss on the cheek,' said Janice. ''E couldn't stop me then, could 'e? Shouldn't of made fun of me.'

'Marks,' said Strike, examining the clipping, 'gave you the idea for Spencer, right? It was the name that first connected her with you, but I should've twigged when Clare phoned me back so promptly. Social workers never do that. Too overworked.'

'Huh,' said Janice, and she almost smiled. 'Yeah. That's where I got the name: Clare Martin and Johnny Marks.'

'You didn't keep Brenner's obituary, did you?'

'No,' said Janice.

'Because you didn't kill him?'

'No. 'E died of old age somewhere in Devon. I never even read 'is obituary, but I 'ad to come up wiv somefing, didn't I, when you asked for it? So I said Oakden took it.'

She was probably the most accomplished liar Strike had ever met. Her ability to come up with falsehoods at a moment's notice, and the way she interwove her plausible lies with truth, never attempting too much, and delivering everything with such an air of authenticity and honesty, placed her in a class apart.

'Was Brenner really addicted to barbiturates?'

'No,' said Janice.

She was shuffling the obituaries back into their folder now, and Strike spotted the clipping about holy basil, on the reverse of which was Joanna Hammond's death notice.

'No,' she repeated, as she put the obituaries back into her bottom drawer and closed it, as though it mattered any more whether she tidied these things away, as though they wouldn't soon be used in evidence against her. Knees clicking, she got slowly to her feet again, and returned to the sofa.

'I was getting Brenner to sign for drugs for me,' she said. ''E fort I was selling them on the street, dopey old sod.'

'How did you persuade him to over-order drugs? Blackmail?'

'S'pose you'd call it that, yeah,' she said. 'I found out 'e was going to see a prostitute locally. One of 'er kids told me Brenner was visiting 'er once a week. I fort, right, I'll get you, you dirty old bastard. 'E was coming up for retirement. I knew 'e didn't want to end 'is career in disgrace. I went in to see 'im one day in his consulting room and told 'im I knew. 'E nearly 'ad an 'eart attack,' said Janice, with a malicious smile. 'I told 'im I knew 'ow to keep me mouf shut, and then I asked 'im to get me some drugs. 'E signed like a lamb. I was using stuff Brenner got me for years, after.'

'The prostitute was Betty Fuller, right?

'Yeah,' said Janice. 'I fort you'd find that out.'

'Did Brenner really assault Deborah Athorn?

'No. 'E checked 'er stitches after she had Samhain, that's all.'

'Why did Clare Spencer tell me that story? Just blowing a bit more smoke around?'

Janice shrugged.

'I dunno. I fort maybe you'd fink Brenner was a sex pest and Margot found out 'e was fiddling with patients.'

'Was there ever really an Amytal capsule in Brenner's mug?'

'No,' said Janice. 'It was in Irene's mug . . . that was stupid,' she said, her pink and white brow furrowed. The wide blue eyes drifted over her wall of victims' photographs, to the window and back to Strike. 'I shouldn't of done that. Sometimes I sailed a bit close to the wind. Took silly risks. Irene was pissing me off one day on reception, flirting wiv – just flirting,' said Janice, 'so I took 'er a mug of tea wiv a couple of capsules in it. She talks till you could throttle 'er, I just wanted 'er to shut the hell up for a bit. But she let it go cold . . .

'I was sort of glad, after I'd calmed down. I got the mug and took it out the back to wash up, but Margot come creepin' up behind me in 'er flat shoes. I tried to 'ide it, but she saw.

'I fort she'd go tellin' tales, so I 'ad to get in first. I went straight to Dr Gupta and said I'd found a capsule in Dr Brenner's tea, and told 'im I fort 'e was over-ordering drugs and was addicted. What else could I do? Gupta was a nice man but he was a coward. Bit scared of Brenner. I fort 'e probably wouldn't confront 'im, and 'e didn't, but honestly, I knew even if 'e 'ad, Brenner would rather pretend to be an addict than risk me tellin' anyone about 'is dirty little fing wiv Betty Fuller.'

'And was Margot really worried about how Dorothy Oakden's mother died?'

'No,' said Janice again. 'But I 'ad to tell you somefing, didn't I?'

'You're a genius of misdirection,' said Strike, and Janice turned slightly pink.

'I've always been clever,' she mumbled, 'but that don't 'elp a woman. It's better to be pretty. You 'ave a better life if you're good-looking. Men always went for Irene, not me. She talked shit all night long, but they liked 'er better. I wasn't bad-looking . . . I just didn't 'ave what men liked.'

'When we first met the two of you,' said Strike, ignoring this, 'I thought Irene might've wanted you interviewed together to make sure you didn't spill her secrets, but it was the other way round, wasn't it? You wanted to be there to control what *she* said.'

'Yeah, well,' said Janice, with another sigh, 'I didn't do that well, did I? She was blabbing left, right and centre.'

'Tell me, did Charlie Ramage really see a missing woman in Leamington Spa?'

'No. I just needed to give you somefing to fink about instead of Margot prodding Kev in the tummy. Charlie Ramage told me 'e saw Mary Flanagan in a country churchyard in . . . Worcestershire somewhere, I fink it was. I knew nobody could say no diff'rent, I knew 'e was dead and I knew 'e talked such bollocks, nobody round 'im would remember one more tall story.'

'Was the mention of Leamington Spa supposed to nudge me towards Irene and Satchwell?'

'Yeah,' said Janice.

'Did you put drugs in Wilma Bayliss's Thermos? Is that why she seemed drunk to people at the surgery?'

'I did, yeah.'

'Why?'

'I already told you,' said Janice restlessly, 'I don't know why

I do it, I just do . . . I wanted to see what would 'appen to 'er. I like knowing why fings are 'appening, when nobody else does . . .

''Ow did you work all this out?' she demanded. 'Talbot and Lawson never suspected.'

'Lawson might not have done,' said Strike, 'but I think Talbot did.'

''E never,' said Janice, at once. 'I 'ad 'im eating out me 'and.'

'I'm not so sure,' said Strike. 'He left a strange set of notes, and all through them he kept circling back to the death of Scorpio, or Juno, which are the names he gave Joanna Hammond. Seven interviews, Janice. I think he subconsciously knew there was something off about you. He mentions poison a lot, which I think had stuck in his mind because of the way Joanna died. At one point – I was reading the notes again, last night – he copies out a long description of the tarot card the Queen of Cups. Words to the effect that she reflects the observer back at themselves. "To see the truth of her is almost impossible." And on the night they hauled him off to hospital, he hallucinated a female demon with a cup in her hand and a seven hanging round her neck. He was too ill to string his suspicions together, but his subconscious kept trying to tell him you weren't all you seemed. At one point, he wrote: "Is Cetus right?" – he called Irene Cetus – and eventually I asked myself what she could've been right about. Then I remembered that the first time we met the pair of you, she told us she thought you were "sweet on" Douthwaite.'

At the sound of Douthwaite's name, Janice winced slightly.

'Oakden said you got giggly around Douthwaite, too,' Strike continued, watching her closely. 'And Dorothy bracketed you with Irene and Gloria as some kind of scarlet woman, which implies you'd done some flirting in front of her.'

'Is that all you went on: me flirting once, and being the

Queen of Cups?' said Janice, managing to get a note of scorn into her voice, though he thought she seemed shaken.

'No,' said Strike, 'there were plenty of other things. Strange anomalies and coincidences. People kept telling me Margot didn't like "the nurse", but they got you confused with Irene a lot, so it took me a while to twig that they really did mean you.

'Then there was Fragile X. When I saw you that first time, with Irene, you claimed you'd only been to visit the Athorns once, but the second time I met you, you seemed to know a hell of a lot about them. Fragile X was called Martin-Bell syndrome back in the early seventies. If you'd only seen them that one time, it seemed odd you knew exactly what was wrong with them, and used the modern term . . .

'And then I started noticing how many people were getting stomach upsets or acting drugged. Did you put something in the punch at Margot and Roy's barbecue?'

'I did, yeah,' she said. 'Ipecac syrup, that was. I fort it would be funny if they all thought they'd got food poisoning from the barbecue, but then Carl broke the bowl, and I was glad, really . . . I just wanted to see 'em all ill, and maybe look after 'em all, and ruin 'er party, but it was stupid, wasn't it? . . . That's what I mean, I sailed close to the wind sometimes, they were doctors, what if they'd known? . . . It was only Gloria who 'ad a big glassful and was sick. Margot's 'usband didn't like that . . . ruined their smart house . . . '

And Strike saw the almost indiscriminate desire for disruption that lay behind the meek exterior.

'Gloria throwing up at the barbecue,' said Strike. 'Irene and her irritable bowel syndrome – Kevin and his constant stomach aches – Wilma swaying on her feet and vomiting while she was working at St John's – me, puking up my Christmas chocolates – and, of course, Steve Douthwaite and his vision problems, his headaches and his churning guts . . .

I'm assuming it was Douthwaite Irene was flirting with, the day you put Amytal capsules in her tea?'

Janice pressed her lips together, eyes narrowed.

'I suppose you told her he was gay to try and get her to back off?'

'She already 'ad Eddie gagging to marry 'er,' Janice burst out. 'She 'ad all these blokes down the pub flirting with 'er. If I'd told 'er 'ow much I liked Steve, she'd've taken 'im for the fun of it, that's what she was. So yeah, I told 'er 'e was queer.'

'What are you drugging her with, these days?'

'It varies,' said Janice quietly. 'Depends 'ow much she's pissing me off.'

'So tell me about Steve Douthwaite.'

Suddenly, Janice was breathing deeply. Her face was flushed again: she looked emotional.

''E was . . . such a beautiful man.'

The passionate throb in her voice took Strike aback, almost more than the full stock of poisons she was keeping in her kitchen. He thought of the cheeky chap in his kipper tie, who'd become the puffy, bloodshot-eyed proprietor of the Allardice in Skegness, with his strands of greying hair stuck to his sweating forehead, and not for the first time, Strike had reason to reflect on the extraordinarily unpredictable nature of human love.

'I've always been one to fall 'ead over 'eels,' said Janice, and Strike thought of Johnny Marks dying in agony, and Janice kissing him farewell on his cold dead cheek. 'Oh, Steve could make you laugh. I *love* a man what can make you laugh. *Really* 'andsome. I used to walk past 'is flat ten times a day just to get an 'ello . . . we got friendly . . .

''E started dropping in, telling me all 'is problems . . . and 'e tells me 'ow 'e's mad about this married woman. Fallen for 'is mate's wife. On and on and on about 'ow 'ard 'er life is, and there's me sitting there wiv a kid on me own. What about *my* 'ard life? She 'ad an 'usband, didn't she? But no, I could tell I wasn't gonna get nowhere wiv 'im unless she was out the way, so I fort, right, well, she'll 'ave to go . . .

'She was no better lookin' than I was,' muttered Janice, pointing at the picture of Joanna Hammond on the wall. 'State of that fing on 'er face . . .

'So I looked 'er up in the phone book and I just went round 'er 'ouse when I knew 'er 'usband was at work. I used to 'ave this wig I wore to parties. Put that on, and me uniform, and a pair of glasses I used to 'ave, but I didn't need. Rang the doorbell, told 'er I'd 'ad a tip-off about 'er domestic situation.

'People will always let a nurse in,' said Janice. 'She was desperate to talk to someone. I got 'er good and emotional, cryin' and all that. She told me about sleeping with Steve, and 'ow she fort she was in love wiv 'im . . .

'I made 'er a drink wiv latex gloves on. ''Alf of it was weedkiller. She knew, the moment she tasted it, but I grabbed 'er 'air from be'ind,' Janice mimed the motion in mid-air, 'pulled 'er 'ead back, forced it down 'er fuckin' throat. Oh yeah. Once she was on the floor, chokin', I poured some more down, neat.

''Ad to stay a while, to make sure she didn't try an' phone anyone. Once I knew she was too far gone to recover, I took off me uniform an' left.

'It takes nerve,' said Janice Beattie, her colour high and her eyes bright, 'but act normal and people don't see nothing strange . . . you just got to 'old your nerve. And maybe I wasn't showy-looking when I was young, but that 'elped. I wasn't the kind people remembered . . .

'Next day, near enough, I 'ad Steve crying 'is eyes out round my place. It was all going great,' said the woman who'd poured neat weedkiller down her rival's throat, 'I saw 'im loads after that, 'e was round my place all the time. There was somefing there between us, I could feel it.

'I never drugged 'im a lot,' said Janice, as though this was true evidence of affection. 'Only enough to stop 'im going out, make 'im feel 'e needed me. I used to look after 'im really well. Once, 'e slept on my sofa, and I wiped 'is face for 'im, while 'e was asleep,' she said, and again, Strike thought of the kiss she'd given the dead Johnny Marks.

'But sometimes,' said Janice, with bitterness, 'men fort I was the mumsy type and didn't see me as anyfing else. I could tell Steve liked me, but I fort 'e might not be seeing me the right way, you know, wiv bein' a nurse, and Kev always dragging round after me. One evening, Steve come over, and Kev was 'aving a tantrum, and Steve said, he thought 'e'd be off, let me look after Kev . . . and I could tell, I fort, you're not gonna want me wiv a kid. So I fort, Kev needs to go.'

She said it as though talking about taking out the bins.

'But you gotta be careful when it's your own kid,' said Janice. 'I needed to get an 'istory going. 'E couldn't just die, not after being perfectly 'ealthy. I started experimenting wiv stuff, I was finking, maybe a salt overdose, claim 'e did it on a dare or somefing. I started putting stuff in 'is food 'ere and there. Get 'im complaining to teachers about stomach aches an' that, and then I'd say, "Oh, I know, I think it's a bit of schoolitis" . . .'

'But then Margot examined him,' said Strike.

'But then,' repeated Janice slowly, nodding, 'that hoity-toity bitch takes 'im into 'er surgery and examines 'im. And I knew she was suspicious. She asked me after, what drinks it was I'd given 'im, because the little bastard 'ad told 'er Mummy was givin' 'im special drinks . . .

'Not a week later,' said Janice, twisting the old wedding ring on her finger, 'I realise Steve's going to see 'er about 'is 'ealf, instead of coming to see me. Next fing I know, Margot's asking me all about Joanna's death, out the back by the kettle, and Dorothy and Gloria were listening in. I said, "'Ow the 'ell should I know what 'appened?" but I was worried. I fort, what's Steve been telling 'er? 'As 'e said 'e finks there was somefing wrong wiv it? 'As someone said they saw a nurse leaving the 'ouse?

'I was getting worried. I sent 'er chocolates full of phenobarbital. Irene 'ad told me Margot 'ad 'ad freatening notes, and I'm not surprised, interfering bitch, she was . . . I fort, they'll fink it's 'ooever sent them notes, sent the chocolates . . .

'But she never ate 'em. She frew 'em in the bin in front of me, but after, I 'eard she'd taken 'em out the bin and kept 'em. And that's when I knew, I really knew. I fort, she's gonna get 'em tested . . . '

'And that's when you finally agreed to go on a date with simple old Larry,' said Strike.

''Oo says 'e was simple?' said Janice, firing up.

'Irene,' said Strike. 'You needed access to concrete, didn't you? Didn't want to be seen buying it, I'd imagine. What did you do, tell Larry to take some and not mention it to anyone?'

She simply looked at him out of those round blue eyes that nobody who hadn't heard this conversation could possibly mistrust.

'What gave you the idea of concrete?' Strike asked. 'That rumour of the body in the foundations?'

'Yeah,' said Janice, finally. 'It seemed like the way to stop the body smelling. I needed 'er to disappear. It was too near 'ome, what wiv 'er examining Kev, and asking me about Joanna, and keeping those chocolates. I wanted people to fink maybe the Essex Butcher got 'er, or the bloke 'oo sent the threatening notes.'

'How many times had you visited the Athorns before you killed Margot?'

'A few.'

'Because they needed a nurse? Or for some other reason?'

The longest pause yet ensued, long enough for the sun to slide out from a cloud, and the glass Cinderella coach to burn briefly like white fire, and then turn back into the tawdry gewgaw it really was.

'I sort of fort of killing them,' said Janice slowly. 'I don't know why, really. Just from the time I met 'em . . . they were odd and nobody ever went there. Those cousins of theirs visited once every ten years. I met 'em back in January, those cousins, when the flat needed cleaning out, to stop that man downstairs going to court . . . they stayed an hour and let "Clare" do all the rest . . .

'Yeah, I just fort I might kill the Athorns one day,' she said, with a shrug. 'That's why I kept visiting. I liked the idea of watching an 'ole family die togevver, and waiting to see when people realised, and then it'd be on the news, probably, and I'd know what 'appened when everyone was gossiping, local . . .

'I did a bit of experimenting on 'em. Vitamin injections, I told them it was. Special treatments. And I used to hold their noses while they were asleep. Used to pull up their eyelids and look at their eyes, while they were unconscious. Nurses don't never give anaesthetics, see, but Dr Brenner was letting me 'ave all sorts, and the Athorns just let me do stuff to 'em, even Gwilherm. 'E loved me coming over. 'E'd spend days on benzedrine and then 'e'd get sedatives off me. Proper junkie.

'I used to say to 'im, now, don't you go telling anyone what we're doing. These are expensive treatments. It's only because I like your family.

'Some days, I used to fink, I'll kill the kid and then give evidence against Gwilherm. That was one idea I 'ad. I fort, I'll get in the papers, all dressed up, give evidence against 'im, you know. My picture on the front page . . . and I fort that'd be somefing interesting to talk to Steve about, when 'e seen my picture in the paper. Men love nurses. That was the on'y fing I 'ad going for me when I was out wiv Irene, and then the bitch starts pretending she's a nurse an' all . . .

'Only fank Gawd I never did any of that, fank Gawd I saved the Athorns, because what would I 'ave done wiv Margot if I 'adn't 'ad them up the road? I'd nicked their spare key by then. They never noticed.

'I never fort it would work,' said Janice, ''cause I 'ad to frow the plan togevver in about five minutes. I knew she was onto me, when she saved the chocolates, and I was up all night, finking, worrying . . . and it was the next day, or maybe the day after, Steve went charging out of her surgery that last time. I was scared she'd warned 'im about me, because when I went round that night, 'e made some excuse not to let me in . . . I mean, 'e never went to the police, so now I know I was being paranoid, but at the time—'

'You weren't being paranoid,' said Strike. 'I spoke to him yesterday. Margot told him he ought to stop eating anything you prepared him. Just that. He understood what she was saying, though.'

Janice's face grew redder.

'That bitch,' she said venomously. 'What did she do that for? She 'ad a rich 'usband and a lover wanting her back, why's she got to take Steve off me?'

'Go on,' said Strike, 'about how you did it.'

A subtle change now came over Janice. Previously, she'd seemed diffident, matter-of-fact, or even ashamed of her own impetuousness, but now, for the first time, she seemed to enjoy what she was saying, as though she killed Margot Bamborough all over again, in the telling.

'Went out wiv Larry. Told 'im some bullshit about this poor family what needed to concrete over somefing on their roof terrace. Said they were dirt-poor. 'E was so keen to impress me, silly sod, 'e wanted to go do the building work for 'em.'

She rolled her eyes.

'I 'ad to give 'im all this crap about 'ow that would made the dad feel inadequate . . . I said just nicking a few bags of concrete mix off the building site'd be enough.

'Larry drove it to Albemarle Way for me and carried it up to their landing. I wouldn't let 'im come any further, said it would be uneffical for 'im to see patients. 'E was silly, Larry, you could tell 'im anyfing . . . But he wouldn't marry me,' said Janice suddenly. 'Why is that? Why wouldn't anyone marry me? What 'aven't I got, that ovver women 'ave?' asked the nurse who'd pulled back the eyelids from her drugged victims to stare into their unseeing eyes. 'Nobody ever wanted to marry me . . . never . . . I wanted to be in the paper in a white dress. I wanted my day in church and I never got it. Never . . . '

'You needed an alibi as well as concrete, presumably?' said Strike, ignoring her question. 'I assume you chose the demented old lady in Gopsall Street because she couldn't say one way or another whether you'd been with her when Margot disappeared?'

'Yeah,' said Janice, returning to her story, 'I went to see 'er late morning and I left drugs there and a note, to prove I'd been in. I knew she'd agree I was there early evening. She didn't 'ave no family, she'd agree with anyfing you said to 'er . . .

'I went from 'er place to buy a cinema ticket for the late-night show, and I called up my babysitter and told 'er I'd be later than I fort because we were getting the last viewing. I knew Irene wouldn't wanna go wiv me. She'd been makin' noises about not feelin' up to it all morning. I knew she didn't 'ave no bad toof, but I pretended to go along wiv it. Irene never wanted to go anywhere we weren't gonna meet men.'

'So, you went back to the surgery that afternoon – in through the back door, I suppose?'

'Yeah,' said Janice, her eyes slightly unfocused now. 'Nobody saw me. I knew Margot 'ad a doughnut in the fridge, because I'd been in there that morning and seen it, but there was people around all the time, so I couldn't do nuffing. I injected it wiv Nembutal sodium solution, froo the cellophane.'

'You must've been well practised by now? You knew how much to give her, so she could still walk up the road?'

'Nuffing's certain,' said the nurse. Unlike Creed, she didn't pretend omnipotence, but then, she'd also been, however reluctantly, in the business of healing as well as killing. 'I 'ad a good feeling for dosages, but you can't never be an 'undred per cent sure. I'd 'eard she was going to meet some friend in a pub up the road, and she usually ate somefing before she went, but I couldn't be sure she'd eat it, or still be able to walk up the road after, or when it would really hit 'er . . .

'All the time I was doing it, getting the concrete and drugging the doughnut, I was finking, this won't work, it can't work. You're gonna go to prison, Janice . . . And you know somefing?' said the nurse, now pink cheeked and fierce, 'By then, I didn't even care. Not if she'd told Steve about me. I fort, I'll go on trial and I'll tell 'em 'ow 'e treated me like a mum and a nurse and took advantage, round my flat all hours. 'E'll 'ave to bloody notice me and 'ear me then, won't 'e? I didn't care. I just fort, I want you dead, lady. I want you dead, you wiv your 'usband and your boyfriend on the side, and my man coming to see you three times a week . . .

'Eivver she dies, I fort, and I get away wiv it, or I'll be famous, I'll be in the papers . . . and I liked the idea, then.'

She looked around her small sitting room, and Strike was certain that she wondered what her cell would be like.

'I left the surgery and went round the long way to the

Athorns', but when I let myself in, Gwilherm wasn't there. I fort, OK, that's a problem. Where is 'e?

'And then Deborah and Samhain started moaning. They didn't want their vitamin injections. I 'ad to get strict wiv 'em. I said to Deborah, it's these injections what's keeping you well. You don't take 'em, I'll have to ring an ambulance and get 'em to take you into 'ospital for an assessment . . . You could scare 'er into anyfing if you told 'er she'd 'ave to go outside. I give Deborah and Samhain their vitamin injections, lying side by side in the double bedroom. Rolled 'em onto their sides. They were out for the count.

'So then I goes outside, and I waits in the phone box, pretending to be on the phone, keepin' watch.

'It didn't feel real, none of it. I didn't fink it'd work. Probably I'd go into work next day and 'ear Margot passed out in the street, and then she'd start yelling the place down saying she was drugged, and I knew she'd point the finger at me . . .

'She didn't come for ages. I fort, it's over. She's eaten the doughnut and got ill in the surgery. She's called an ambulance. She's guessed, she's got sick. There was this girl, standing in front of the phone box, and I'm trying to see round 'er, trying to see . . .

'And then I saw Margot coming up the road. I fort, well, this is it. It was raining hard. People weren't watchin'. It was all umbrellas and cars splashing. She crossed the road and I could see she was in a bad way. Wobbling all over the place. She got to my side of the road and leaned up against the wall. 'Er legs were about to go. I come out the phone box and I says, "Come on, love, you need to sit down." Kept my face down. She come wiv me, a few steps, then she realised it was me. We 'ad a bit of a struggle. I got 'er a few more feet, just inside Albemarle Way, but she was a tall girl . . . and I fort, this is where it ends . . .

'And then I seen Gwilherm coming up the other way. It was

me only chance. I called 'im to 'elp me. 'E fort 'e was 'elping 'er. 'E 'elped me drag 'er up the stairs. There wasn't much fight in 'er by then. I told Gwilherm some rubbish to stop 'im phoning the ambulance. Said I could treat 'er myself . . . said 'e didn't want no police coming up, looking round the flat . . . 'E was a very paranoid man about the auforities, so that worked . . .

'I says, you go and see if Deborah and Samhain are still asleep. They've both been very worried about where you've been, and I 'ad to give 'em a little sedative.

'I suffocated 'er while 'e was out of the room. It didn't take much. 'Eld 'er nose, kept 'er mouth shut. Did to Margot what I'd been planning to do to the Athorns.

'When I knew she was dead,' said Janice, 'I left 'er sitting on the sofa and I went into the barfroom. I sat on the bog, looking at the flamingos on the wallpaper and I fort, now what? Gwilherm's here. 'E's seen 'er . . . and the on'y fing I could fink of was, let 'im fink 'e's done it. 'E's crazy enough. I fort, I'll probably 'ave to kill 'im, too, in the end, but I'll worry about that later . . .

'So I waited in the bog and let 'im go in the room and find 'er.

'I give 'im five minutes alone wiv the body, then I walk back in, talkin' to Margot, like I left 'er alive. "You feeling all right now, Margot, love?" And then I says, "What've you done, Gwilherm? What've you done?"

'And he says, "Nuffing, nuffing, I ain't done nuffing," and I'm saying, "You told me you can kill people with your powers. P'rhaps we better call the police," and 'e's begging me not to, 'e didn't mean to, it was all a mistake. So in the end I says, all right, I won't give you away. I'll make it disappear. I'll take care of it.

''E was crying like a baby and he asked me for one of

my sedatives. 'E *asked* me to put 'im out, can you believe that? I give 'im some downers. Left 'im curled up asleep on Samhain's bed.

'It was really 'ard, putting her in that big box fing all on me own. I 'ad to take out all the crap they kept in there. Folded 'er up. Once I 'ad 'er in there, I checked on all the Athorns. Made sure the airways weren't obstructed. Then I ran back outside to the phone box. I says to Irene, are we still on for the cinema? And she says no, like I fort she would, fank Gawd.

'So I go back inside. I was there till midnight, near enough. I 'ad to mix the concrete bit by bit, by 'and, in a bucket. It took ages. Margot filled up most of that box fing, but it took a long time to get all the concrete round her. Then I closed the lid. It stuck to the concrete. I couldn't get it up again, so that was good.

'When they was all awake, I told Gwilherm I'd taken care of it. I said to 'im quietly, the lid on that box thing 'as jammed. Best find somewhere else to put Samhain's toys.

''E knew, obviously. I fink 'e pretended to 'imself 'e didn't, but 'e did. I was there free times a week, afterwards. I 'ad to be. Keeping 'im happy. One time I went round and 'e'd painted all those symbols on the walls, like it was some sort of pagan temple or something.

'Weeks after, monfs after, I was worried sick. I knew 'e was tellin' people 'e'd killed 'er. Luckily, everyone fort 'e was a nutcase, local. But it got bad, towards the end. 'E 'ad to go. I still can't believe I waited a year to get rid of 'im . . .'

'And around the time you killed him, you phoned Cynthia Phipps and pretended to be Margot, didn't you? To give the police another lead to hare after, and distract from Gwilherm, in case anyone had taken him seriously?'

'Yeah. That's right,' mumbled Janice, twisting the old wedding ring.

'And you kept visiting Deborah and Samhain as Clare Spencer?'

'Well, yeah,' said Janice. 'I 'ad to. They needed watching. Last fing I wanted was real social workers fiddling around in there.'

'And Deborah and Samhain never realised Clare was the same as Janice the nurse?'

'People with Fragile X don't recognise faces easy,' said Janice. 'I changed me 'air colour and used me glasses. I done a lot to keep 'em 'ealfy, you know. Vitamin D for Deborah, cause she never goes outside. She's younger'n me . . . I fort, I might well be dead before anyone finds the body. Longer it went on, less likely it was anyone would ever know I 'ad anyfing to do wiv it . . .'

'And what about Douthwaite?'

''E scarpered,' said Janice, her smile fading. 'That near enough broke my 'eart. There was me 'aving to go out on foursomes wiv Irene and Eddie, and act like I was 'appy wiv Larry, and the love of my life's disappeared. I asked ev'ryone where Steve 'ad gone, and no one knew.'

'So why's Julie Wilkes on your wall?' asked Strike.

''Oo?' said Janice, lost in her self-pitying reverie.

'The Redcoat who worked at Clacton-on-Sea,' said Strike, pointing at the young blonde with her frizzy hair, who was framed on Janice's wall.

'Oh . . . 'er,' said Janice, with a sigh. 'Yeah . . . I ran into someone 'oo knew someone 'oo'd met Steve at Butlin's, few years later . . . oh, I was excited. Gawd, I was bored wiv Larry by then. I really wanted to see Steve again. I *love* a man 'oo can make me laugh,' repeated the woman who'd planned the murder of a family, for the pleasure of watching them die. 'I *knew* there'd been somefing there between us, I *knew* we coulda bin a couple. So I booked me and Larry an 'oliday at

Butlin's. Kev didn't wanna come – suited me. I got meself a perm and I went on a diet. Couldn't wait. You build things up in your mind, don't you?

'And we went to the club night and there 'e was,' said Janice quietly. 'Oh, 'e looked gorgeous. "Longfellow Serenade". All the girls went crazy for 'im when 'e finished singing. There's Larry boozing . . . After Larry went to bed in the chalet I went back out again. Couldn't find 'im.

'Took me free days to get a word wiv 'im. I said, "Steve, it's me. Janice. Your neighbour. The nurse!"'

She turned slowly redder than she'd been all interview. Her eyes watered with the intensity of her blush.

'He goes "Oh yeah. All right, Janice?" And 'e walks away. And I seen 'im,' said Janice, and her jaw quivered, 'kiss that girl, that Julie, and look back at me, like 'e wanted me to see . . .

'And I fort, *no.* After all what I've done for you, Steve? *No.*

'I did it on the last night but one of our 'oliday. Larry snoring 'is 'ead off as usual. 'E never noticed I wasn't in bed.

'They all used to go to Steve's chalet after work, I found that out, following 'em. She come out on 'er own. Pissed. Two in the morning.

'It wasn't 'ard. There wasn't anyone round. They didn't 'ave cameras around like they do nowadays. I pushed 'er, and I jumped in after 'er, and I 'eld 'er under. It was the surprise what killed 'er. She took in a load of water on the way down. That was the only one I ever did wivvout drugs, but I was angry, see . . .

'Got out, towelled meself off. Mopped up all the footprints, but it was a warm night, you couldn't see nuffing by morning.

'Next day, I seen 'im. I says, "Terrible fing, that girl, Steve. You look awful. Wanna get a drink?"

'E went white as a sheet, but I fort, well, you used me, Steve, and then you left me high and dry, didn't you?'

A police siren sounded somewhere in the distance, and Strike, glancing at his watch, thought it was likely to be heading here, for Nightingale Grove.

'You took my sympafy and my kindness and you let me cook for you,' said Janice, still addressing an imaginary Steve Douthwaite. 'I was even ready to kill my kid for you! And then you go off messing around wiv ovver women? *No.* Actions 'ave consequences,' said Janice, her cheeks still burning. 'Men need to learn that, and take some responsibility. Women 'ave to,' she said, as the police siren grew ever louder. 'Well, I'll see 'im again in court, won't I? You know, I'm quite looking forward to it, now I'm finking about it,' said Janice. 'It's not fun, living 'ere all on me own. It'll be funny seeing Irene's face. I'll be all over the papers, won't I? And maybe some men will read about why I done it, and realise they want to be careful 'oo they lead on. Useful lesson for men everywhere, if you ask me. Actions,' repeated Janice Beattie, as the police car drew to a halt outside her front door, and she squared her shoulders, ready to accept her fate, ''ave consequences.'

PART SEVEN

Then came October full of merry glee . . .

Edmund Spenser
The Faerie Queene

72

. . . they for nought would from their worke refraine . . .

Edmund Spenser
The Faerie Queene

Success, as Cormoran Strike had long since learned, is a much more complex business than most people suppose.

It wasn't the first time that the press had turned its sights upon the detective agency, and while the acclaim was undoubtedly flattering and a good advert for the business, it was, as ever, severely prejudicial to the partners' ability to keep working. Robin, whose home address was swiftly discovered by the press, took refuge at the house of Vanessa Ekwensi, and with the aid of a number of wigs and some skilful make-up, managed to continue to cover a certain amount of work, so that Barclay and Hutchins didn't have to do everything themselves. Strike, on the other hand, was forced back into Nick and Ilsa's spare room, where he let his beard grow, and lay low, directing the agency's subcontractors by phone. Pat Chauncey alone remained based at the office in Denmark Street, taking care of administrative matters, stolidly opening and closing up each morning and evening.

'I've got no comment. You'd all do better sodding off,' she croaked twice a day at the knot of journalists hanging around Denmark Street.

The eruption of publicity that followed the twin discoveries of a woman's body encased in concrete in a quiet flat in Clerkenwell, and a teenager's skeleton hidden beneath debris in the depths of an underground well in Islington, showed no sign of abating quickly. There were far too many exciting angles to this story: the separate excavations and positive identifications of the bones of Margot Bamborough and Louise Tucker, the comments from two bereaved families, who scarcely knew whether they felt more relief or grief, the profiles of two very different killers and, of course, the private detectives now widely acclaimed as the capital's most talented.

Gratifying though this was, Strike took no satisfaction in the way the press hounded either Gregory Talbot ('What would you say to people who say your father had blood on his hands?') or Dinesh Gupta ('Do you regret giving Janice Beattie that glowing reference, doctor?') nor in seeing the Athorns led out of their flat by genuine social workers, frightened, displaced and uncomprehending. Carl Oakden made a brief appearance in the *Daily Mail*, trying to sell himself as an expert on both Strike and Margot Bamborough, but as the article began with the words 'Convicted con man Carl Brice, son of the old practice secretary, Dorothy . . . ' it was perhaps unsurprising that Oakden soon slunk back into the shadows. Strike's father, on the other hand, was happy to continue associating his name with Strike's, issuing a fulsome statement of pride in his eldest son through his publicist. Fuming quietly, Strike ignored all requests for comment.

Dennis Creed, who for so long had received top billing in any news story including him, was relegated almost to a footnote in this one. Janice Beattie had outdone him, not only in the number of her suspected victims, but in remaining undetected for decades longer. Photographs of her sitting room in Nightingale Grove were leaked to the press, who highlighted the framed pictures of the dead on the walls, the folder of obituaries kept in her china cabinet, and the syringe, the cellophane and the hairdryer that Strike had found behind the sofa. The store of drugs and poisons retrieved from her kitchen were carried out of her house by forensics experts, and the rosy-cheeked, silver-haired nurse dubbed 'the Poisoner Granny' blinked impassively at news cameras as she was led into court and remanded in custody.

Meanwhile, Strike could barely open a newspaper or switch on the TV without seeing Brian Tucker, who was giving interviews to anybody who'd speak to him. In a cracked voice he wept, exulted, praised Strike and Robin, told the world they deserved knighthoods ('Or the other thing, what is it for women?' 'Damehood,' murmured the sympathetic blonde presenter, who was holding the emotional Tucker's hand), cried as he reminisced about his daughter, described the preparations for her funeral, criticised the police and informed the world that he'd suspected all along that Louise was hidden in the well. Strike, who was happy for the old man, nevertheless wished, both for his own sake and for Tucker's, that he'd go and grieve quietly somewhere, rather than taking up space on an endless succession of daytime television sofas.

A trickle of relatives, suspicious about the way their loved ones had died under Janice's care, soon turned into a tide. Exhumation orders were made, and Irene Hickson, the contents of whose food cupboards had been removed and analysed by the police, was profiled in the *Daily Mail*, sitting in her swagged and flounced sitting room, flanked by two voluptuous daughters who closely resembled her.

'I mean, Jan was always a bit of a man-eater, but I never suspected anything like this, never. I'd've called her my best friend. I don't know how I could've been such a fool! She used to offer to go food shopping for me, before I came back from staying at my daughter's. Then I'd eat some of the stuff she'd put in the fridge, get ill, call her and ask her to come over. I suppose this is a comfier house than hers, and she liked staying here, and I sometimes gave her money, so that's why I'm not dead. I don't know whether I'll ever get over the shock, honestly. I can't sleep, I feel sick all the time, I can't stop thinking about it. I look back now, and ask myself, *how did I never see*? And if it turns out she killed Larry, poor Larry who Eddie and I introduced her to, I don't know how I'm going to live with myself, honestly, it's all just a nightmare. You don't expect this from a nurse, do you?'

And on this count, if no other, Strike was forced to agree with Irene Hickson. He asked himself why it had taken him so long to look closer at an alibi he'd known from the first was barely adequate, and why he'd taken Janice's word at face value, when he'd challenged almost everyone else's. He was forced to conclude that, like the women who'd climbed willingly into Dennis Creed's van, he'd been hoodwinked by a careful performance of femininity. Just as Creed had camouflaged himself behind an apparently fey and gentle façade, so Janice had hidden behind the persona of the nurturer, the selfless giver, the compassionate mother. Strike had preferred her apparent modesty to Irene's garrulity and her sweetness to her friend's spite, yet knew he'd have been far less ready to take those traits at face value, had he met them in a man. *Ceres is nurturing and protective. Cancer is kind, instinct is to protect.* A hefty dose of self-recrimination tempered Strike's celebrations, which puzzled Ilsa and Nick, who were inclined to gloat over the newspaper reports of their friend's latest and most celebrated detective triumph.

Meanwhile, Anna Phipps was longing to thank Strike and Robin in person, but the detective partners postponed a meeting until the first effusion of press attention died down.

The hypercautious Strike, whose beard was now coming along nicely, finally agreed to a meeting over two weeks after Margot's body had been found. Though he and Robin had been in daily contact by phone, this would also be the first time they'd met since solving the case.

Rain pattered against the window of Nick and Ilsa's spare bedroom as Strike dressed that morning. He was pulling a sock over his false foot when his mobile beeped from the bedside table. Expecting to see a message from Robin, possibly warning him that press were on the prowl outside Anna and Kim's house, he saw, instead, Charlotte's name.

Hello Bluey. I thought Jago had thrown this phone away, but I've just found it hidden at the back of a cupboard. So, you've done another amazing thing. I've been reading all about you in the press. I wish they had some decent pictures of you, but I suppose you're glad they don't? Congratulations, anyway. It must feel good to prove everyone who didn't believe in the agency wrong. Which includes me, I suppose. I wish I'd been more supportive, but it's too late now. I don't know whether you'll be glad to hear from me or not. Probably not. You never called the hospital, or if you did, nobody told me. Maybe you'd have been secretly glad if I'd died? A problem solved, and you like solving things . . . Don't think I'm not grateful. I suppose I am, or I will be, one day. But I know you'd have done what you did for anyone. That's your code, isn't it? And I always wanted something particular from you, something you wouldn't give anyone else. Funny, I've started to appreciate people who're decent to everyone, but it's too late for that, too, isn't it? Jago and I are separating, only he doesn't want to call it that yet, because leaving your suicidal wife isn't a good look and nobody would believe it's me leaving him. I still mean the thing I said to you at the end. I always will.

Strike sat back down on the spare bed, mobile in his hands, one sock on, one off. The rainy daylight illuminated the phone's screen, reflecting his bearded face back at him as he scowled at a text so Charlottian he could have written it himself: the apparent resignation to her fate, the attempts to provoke him into reassurance, the vulnerability wielded like a weapon. Had she really left Jago? Where were the now two-year-old twins? He thought of all the things he could have told her, which would have given her hope: that he'd wanted to call the hospital, that he'd dreamed about her since the suicide attempt, that she retained a potent hold over his imagination that he'd tried to exorcise but couldn't. He considered ignoring the message, but then, on the point of setting the mobile back down, changed his mind, and, character by careful character, typed out his brief response.

You're right, I'd have done what I did for anyone. That doesn't mean I'm not glad you're alive, because I am. But you need to stay alive for yourself and your kids now. I'm about to change my number. Look after yourself.

He re-read his words before sending. She'd doubtless experience the words as a blow, but he'd done a lot of thinking since her suicide attempt. Having always told himself that he'd never changed his number because too many contacts had it, he'd lately admitted to himself that he'd wanted to keep a channel of communication open between himself and Charlotte, because he wanted to know she couldn't forget him, any more than he could forget her. It was time to cut that last, thin thread. He pressed 'send' on the text, then finished dressing.

Having made sure that both of Nick and Ilsa's cats were shut up in the kitchen, he left the house. Another text from Charlotte arrived as he was walking up the road in the rain.

> **I don't think I've ever felt so envious in my life as I am of that girl Robin.**

And this, Strike decided to ignore.

He'd set off for Clapham South station deliberately early, because he wanted time for a cigarette before Robin picked him up and drove them the short distance to Anna and Kim's flat. Standing beneath the overhang outside the station, he lit up, looking out over a row of bicycles at a muddy corner of Clapham Common, where ochre-leaved trees shivered in the downpour. He'd only taken a couple of drags on his cigarette when his mobile rang in his pocket. Resolving not to answer if it was Charlotte, he pulled it out and saw Polworth's name.

'All right, Chum?'

'Still got time for the little people, then, Sherlock?'

'I can spare you a minute or two,' said Strike, watching the rain. 'Wouldn't want people to think I've lost the common touch. How's things?'

'We're coming up to London for a weekend.'

Polworth sounded about as excited as a man facing a colonoscopy.

'I thought London was the heart of all evil?'

'Not my choice. It's Roz's birthday. She wants to see the fucking *Lion King* and Trafalgar Square and shit.'

'If you're looking for somewhere to stay, I've only got one bedroom.'

'We're booked into an Airbnb. Weekend after next. Just wondered if you were up for a pint. Could bring your Robin along, so Penny's got someone to talk to. Unless, I dunno, the fucking Queen's got a job for you.'

'Well, she has, but I told her the waiting list's full. That'd be great,' said Strike. 'What else is new?'

'Nothing,' said Polworth. 'You saw the Scots bottled it?'

The old Land Rover had appeared in a line of traffic. Having no desire to get onto the subject of Celtic nationalism, Strike said,

'If "bottling"'s what you want to call it, yeah. Listen, I'm gonna have to go, mate, Robin's about to pick me up in the car. I'll ring you later.'

Chucking his cigarette end down a nearby storm drain, he was ready to climb into the Land Rover as soon as Robin pulled up.

'Morning,' she said, as Strike hoisted himself into the passenger seat. 'Am I late?'

'No, I was early.'

'Nice beard,' said Robin, as she pulled away from the kerb in the rain. 'You look like a guerrilla leader who's just pulled off a successful coup.'

'Feel like one,' said Strike, and in fact, right now, reunited with Robin, he felt the straightforward sense of triumph that had eluded him for days.

'Was that Pat you were just talking to?' asked Robin. 'On the phone?'

'No, Polworth. He's coming up to London weekend after next.'

'I thought he hated London?'

'He does. One of his kids wants to visit. He wants to meet you, but I wouldn't advise it.'

'Why not?' asked Robin, who was mildly flattered.

'Women don't usually like Polworth.'

'I thought he was married?'

'He is. His wife doesn't like him.'

Robin laughed.

'Why did you think Pat would be calling me?' asked Strike.

'I've just had her on the phone. Miss Jones is upset at not getting updates from you personally.'

'I'll FaceTime her later,' said Strike, as they drove across the common, windscreen wipers working. 'Hopefully the beard'll put her off.'

'Some women like them,' said Robin, and Strike couldn't help wondering whether Robin was one of them.

'Sounds like Hutchins and Barclay are closing in on Dopey's partner,' he said.

'Yes,' said Robin. 'Barclay's offering to go out to Majorca and have a look around.'

'I'll bet he is. Are you still on for interviewing the new subcontractor together, Monday?'

'Michelle? Yes, definitely,' said Robin

'Hopefully we'll be back in the office by then.'

Robin turned into Kyrle Road. There was no sign of press, so she parked outside a Victorian terraced house divided into two flats.

When Strike rang the bell labelled 'Phipps/Sullivan', they heard footsteps on stairs through the door, which opened to reveal Anna Phipps, who was wearing the same baggy blue cotton jumpsuit and white canvas shoes as the first time they'd met her, in Falmouth.

'Come in,' she said, smiling as she retreated so that they could enter a small square of space at the bottom of the staircase. The walls were painted white: a series of abstract, monochrome prints covered the walls, and the fanned window over the door cast pools of light onto the uncarpeted stairs, reminding Robin of the St Peter's nursing home, and the life-size Jesus watching over the entrance.

'I'm going to try not to cry,' said Anna quietly, as though scared of being overheard, but in spite of her resolution, her eyes were already full of tears. 'I'm sorry, but I – I'd really like to hug you,' she said, and she promptly did so, embracing first Robin, then Strike. Stepping back, she shook her head, half-laughing, and wiped her eyes.

'I can't ever express to you how grateful . . . how grateful I am. What you've given me . . . ' She made an ineffable gesture and shook her head. 'It's just so . . . so strange. I'm incredibly happy and relieved, but at the same time, I'm grieving . . . Does that make sense?'

'Totally,' said Robin. Strike grunted.

'Everyone's here,' said Anna, gesturing upstairs. 'Kim, Dad, Cyn, and Oonagh, too. I invited her down for a few days. We're planning the funeral, you see – Dad and Cyn are really leaving it up to me – anyway . . . come up, everyone wants to thank you . . . '

As they followed Anna up the steep stairs, Strike using the banister to heave himself along, he remembered the tangle of emotions that had hit him when he'd received the phone call telling him of his own mother's death. Amid the engulfing wave of grief had been a slight pinprick of relief, which had shocked and shamed him, and which had taken a long time to process. Over time, he'd come to understand that in some dark corner of his mind, he'd been dreading and half-expecting the news. The axe had fallen at last, suspense was forever over: Leda's appalling taste in men had culminated in a sordid death on a dirty mattress, and while he'd missed her ever since, he'd be a liar if he claimed to miss the toxic mixture of anxiety, guilt and dread he'd endured over her last couple of years of life.

He could only imagine the mixture of emotions currently possessing Margot's husband, or the nanny who'd taken Margot's place in the family. As he reached the upper landing, he glimpsed Roy Phipps sitting in an armchair in the sitting room. Their eyes met briefly, before Kim came out of the room, blocking Strike's view of the haematologist. The blonde psychologist was smiling broadly: she, at least, seemed to feel unalloyed pleasure.

'Well,' she said, shaking first Strike's hand, then Robin's, 'what can we say, really? Come through ...'

Strike and Robin followed Anna and Kim into the sitting room, which was as large and airy as their Falmouth holiday home, with long gauze curtains at the windows, stripped floorboards, a large white rug and pale grey walls. The books had been arranged by colour. Everything was simple and well designed; very different from the house in which Anna had grown up, with its ugly Victorian bronzes and chintz-covered chairs. The only art on the walls was over the fireplace: a black and white photograph of sea and sky.

Rain was beating on the large bay window behind Roy, who was already on his feet. He wiped his hand nervously on his trousers before holding it out to Strike.

'How are you?' he asked jerkily.

'Very well, thanks,' said Strike.

'Miss Ellacott,' said Roy, holding out his hand to Robin in turn. 'I understand *you* actually ...?'

The unspoken words *found her* seemed to ring around the room.

'Yes,' said Robin, and Roy nodded and pursed his lips, his large eyes leaving her to focus on one of the ragdoll cats, which had just prowled into the room, its aquamarine eyes shrewd.

'Sit down, Dad,' said Anna gently, and Roy did as he was told.

'I'll just go and see whether Oonagh's found everything; she's making tea,' said Kim cheerfully, and left.

'Please, have a seat,' said Anna to Strike and Robin, who sat down side by side on the sofa. The moment Strike was settled, the ragdoll cat leapt up lightly beside him and stepped into his lap. Robin, meanwhile, had noticed the ottoman that stood in place of a coffee table. It was upholstered in grey and white striped canvas, and far smaller than the one in the Athorns' flat, too small for a woman to curl up in, but even so, it was a piece of furniture Robin doubted she'd ever own, no matter how useful they might be. She'd never forget the dusty mass of hardened concrete, and the skull of Margot Bamborough curving up out of it.

'Where's Cyn?' Anna asked her father.

'Bathroom,' said Roy, a little hoarsely. He threw a nervous glance at the empty landing beyond the door, before addressing the detective:

'I – I have to tell you how ashamed I am that I never hired anybody myself. Believe me, the thought that we could have known all this ten, twenty years ago . . . '

'Well, that's not very good for our egos, Roy,' said Strike, stroking the purring cat. 'Implying that anyone could have done what we did.'

Roy and Anna both laughed harder than the comment deserved, but Strike understood the need for the release of jokes, after a profound shock. Mere days after he'd been airlifted out of the bloody crater where he'd lain after his leg had been blown off, fading in and out of consciousness with Gary Topley's torso beside him, he seemed to remember Richard Anstis, the other survivor, whose face had been mangled in the explosion, making a stupid joke about the savings Gary could have made on trousers, had he lived. Strike could still remember laughing at the idiotic, tasteless joke, and enjoying a few seconds' relief from shock, grief and agony.

Women's voices now came across the landing: Kim had returned with a tea tray, followed by Oonagh Kennedy, who was bearing a large chocolate cake. She was beaming from beneath her purple-streaked fringe, her amethyst cross bouncing on her chest as before, and when she'd put down the cake, she said,

'Here dey are, then, the heroes of the hour! I'm going to hug the pair of you!'

Robin stood to receive her tribute, but Strike, not wanting to disarrange the cat, received his hug awkwardly while sitting.

'And here I go again!' said Oonagh, laughing as she straightened up, and wiping her eyes. 'I swear to God, it's loike being on a rollercoaster. Up one minute, down the next—'

'I did the same, when I saw them,' said Anna, laughing at Oonagh. Roy's smile, Robin noticed, was nervous and a little fixed. What did it feel like, she wondered, to be face to face with his dead wife's best friend, after all these years? Did the physical changes in Oonagh make him wonder what Margot would have looked like, had she lived to the age of seventy? Or was he wondering anew, as he must have done over all the intervening years, whether his marriage would have survived the long stretch of icy silence that had followed her drink with Paul Satchwell, whether the strains and tensions in the relationship could have been overcome, or whether Margot would have taken Oonagh up on her offer of refuge in her flat?

They'd have divorced, Robin thought, with absolute certainty, but then she wondered whether she wasn't tangling up Margot with herself, as she'd tended to do all through the case.

'Oh, hello,' said a breathless voice, from the doorway, and everyone looked around to see Cynthia, on whose thin, sallow face was a smile that didn't quite reach her anxious, mottled eyes. She was wearing a black dress, and Robin wondered whether she'd consciously put it on to suggest mourning. 'Sorry, I was – how are you both?'

'Fine,' said Robin.

'Great,' said Strike.

Cynthia let out one of her nervous, breathless laughs, and said,

'Yes, no – so wonderful—'

Was it wonderful for Cynthia, Robin wondered, as Anna's stepmother pulled up a chair, and she declined a piece of the cake which, it transpired, Oonagh had gone out in the rain to purchase. How did it feel to have Margot Bamborough back, even in the form of a skeleton in a box? Did it hurt to see her husband so shaken and emotional, and to have to receive Oonagh, Margot's best friend, into the heart of the family, like a newly discovered aunt? Robin, who seemed to be on something of a clairvoyant streak, felt sure that if Margot had never been killed, but had simply divorced Roy, Cynthia would never have been the haematologist's choice of second wife. Margot would probably have begged the young Cynthia to accompany her into her new life, and continue looking after Anna. Would Cynthia have agreed, or would her loyalties have lain with Roy? Where would she have gone, and who would she have married, once there was no place for her at Broom House?

The second cat now entered the room, staring at the unusually large group it found inside. She picked her way past the armchairs, the ottoman and the sofa, jumped up onto the windowsill and sat with her back to them, watching the raindrops sliding down the window.

'Now, listen,' said Kim, from the upright chair she'd brought out of a corner of the room, 'we really do want to pay you for the extra month you put in. I know you said no—'

'It was our choice to keep working on the case,' said Strike. 'We're glad to have helped and we definitely don't want more money.'

He and Robin had agreed that, as the Margot Bamborough case looked likely to pay for itself three times over in terms of publicity and extra work, and as Strike felt he really should have solved it sooner, taking more cash from Anna and Kim felt unnecessarily greedy.

'Then we'd like to make a donation to charity,' said Kim. 'Is there one you'd like us to support?'

'Well,' said Strike, clearing his throat, 'if you're serious, Macmillan nurses . . .'

He saw a slight look of surprise on the family's faces.

'My aunt died this year,' he explained, 'and the Macmillan nurse gave her a lot of support.'

'Oh, I see,' said Kim, with a slight laugh, and there was a little pause, in which the spectre of Janice Beattie seemed to rise up in the middle of them, like the wisp of steam issuing from the teapot spout.

'A nurse,' said Anna quietly. 'Who'd suspect a nurse?'

'Margot,' said Roy and Oonagh together.

They caught each other's eye, and smiled: a rueful smile, doubtless surprised at finding themselves in agreement at long last, and Robin saw Cynthia look away.

'She didn't like that nurse. She told me so,' said Oonagh, 'but I got the woman confused with that blonde at the Christmas party who made a scene.'

'No, she never took to the nurse,' said Roy. 'She told me, too, when she joined the practice. I didn't take much notice . . .'

He seemed determined to be honest, now, however much it hurt.

'. . . I thought it was a case of two women being too similar: both working class, both strong characters. When I met the woman at the barbecue, I actually thought she seemed quite . . . well . . . decent. Of course, Margot never told me her suspicions . . .'

There was another silence, and everyone in the room, Strike

was sure, was remembering that Roy hadn't spoken to his wife at all in those few weeks before her murder, which was precisely the time period during which Margot's suspicions of Janice must have crystallised.

'Janice Beattie's probably the best liar I've ever met,' Strike said, into the tense atmosphere, 'and a hell of an actress.'

'I've had the most extraordinary letter,' said Anna, 'from her son, Kevin. Did you know he's coming over from Dubai to testify against her?'

'We did,' said Strike, who George Layborn was briefing regularly on the progress of the police investigation.

'He wrote that he thinks Mum examining him saved his life,' said Anna.

Robin noticed how Anna was now calling Margot 'Mum', when previously she'd only said 'my mother'.

'It's a remarkable letter,' said Kim, nodding. 'Full of apologies, as though it's somehow his fault.'

'Poor man,' said Oonagh quietly.

'He says he blames himself for not going to the police about her, but what child would believe his mother's a serial killer? I really *can't*,' said Anna again, over the purring of Cagney the cat in Strike's lap, 'explain adequately to you both what you've done for me . . . for all of us. The not knowing's been so terrible, and now I know for sure that Mum didn't leave willingly and that she went . . . well, quite peacefully . . .'

'As deaths go,' said Strike, 'it was almost painless.'

'And I know for sure she loved me,' said Anna.

'We always—' began Cynthia, but her stepdaughter said quickly,

'I know you always told me she did, Cyn, but without knowing what really happened, there was always going to be a doubt, wasn't there? But when I compare my situation with Kevin Beattie's, I actually feel lucky . . . D'you know,' Anna asked Strike and Robin, 'what they found when they – you know – got Mum out of the concrete?'

'No,' said Strike.

Cynthia's thin hands were playing with her wedding ring, twisting it around her finger.

'The locket Dad gave her,' said Anna. 'It's tarnished, but when they opened it up, it had a picture of me in it, which was as good as new,' said Anna, and her eyes suddenly shone with tears again. Oonagh reached out and patted Anna on the knee. 'They say I'll be able to have it back, once they've completed all the forensics.'

'How lovely,' said Robin quietly.

'And did you hear what was in her handbag?' asked Kim.

'No,' said Strike.

'Notes from her consultation on Theo,' said Kim. 'They're completely legible – protected by the leather, you know. Her full name was Theodosia Loveridge and she was from a traveller family. Margot suspected an ectopic pregnancy and wanted to ring an ambulance, but Theo said her boyfriend would take her. Margot's notes suggest Theo was scared of her family knowing she was pregnant. They don't seem to have approved of the boyfriend.'

'So that's why she never came forward, afterwards?' said Robin.

'I suppose so,' said Kim. 'Poor girl. I hope she was OK.'

'May I ask,' said Roy, looking at Strike, 'how strong you think the case against Janice Beattie is? Because – I don't know what your police contacts have told you – but the latest we've heard is that forensics haven't been able to prove Margot was drugged.'

'Not so far,' said Strike, who'd spoken to George Layborn the previous evening, 'but I've heard they're going to try some new-fangled way of getting traces of drugs and chemicals out of the concrete surrounding the body. No guarantees, but it was used successfully in a case in the States recently.'

'But if they can't prove she was drugged,' said Roy, his expression intense, 'the case against Janice is entirely circumstantial, isn't it?'

'Her lawyer's certainly trying to get her off, judging by his comments to the press,' said Kim.

'He'll have his work cut out for him,' said Strike. 'The defence has got to come up with reasons the police found a phone belonging to a non-existent social worker in her house, and why the Athorns had the number. The Athorns' cousins in Leeds can identify her as the woman who helped them muck out the flat. Gloria Conti's willing to come over to testify about the doughnut in the fridge and the vomiting attacks she and Wilma suffered, and Douthwaite's going to take the stand—'

'He is?' said Oonagh, her expression clearing. 'Oh, that's good, we've been worried about him—'

'I think he finally realises the only way out of this is going through with it,' said Strike. 'He's ready to testify that from the moment he started eating food prepared by Janice, he had symptoms of poisoning, and, most importantly, that during their last consultation, Margot advised him not to eat anything else prepared by Janice.

'Then we've got Kevin Beattie testifying that his daughter drank bleach while Janice was supposedly looking after her, and that his mother used to feed him "special drinks" that made him feel ill . . . What else?' said Strike, inviting Robin to continue, mainly so he could eat some cake.

'Well, there are all the lethal substances they've taken out of Janice's kitchen,' said Robin, 'not to mention the fact that she tried to poison Cormoran's tea when he went round there to confront her. There's also the drugged food the police have found at Irene's, and the framed photographs on her wall, including Joanna Hammond, who she claimed never to have met, and Julie Wilkes, who drowned at the Clacton-on-Sea Butlin's. And the police are confident they're going to be able to get forensic evidence out of other victims' graves, even if Margot's results are inconclusive. Janice had her ex-partner, Larry, cremated, but his lover Clare was buried and she's being exhumed.'

'Personally,' said Strike, who'd managed to eat half his slice of chocolate cake while Robin was talking, 'I think she's going to die in jail.'

'Well, that's good to hear,' said Roy, looking relieved, and Cynthia said breathlessly,

'Yes, no, definitely.'

The cat at the window looked around and then, slowly, turned to face the rain again, while its twin pawed idly at Strike's sweater.

'You two will come to the funeral, won't you?' asked Anna.

'We'd be honoured,' said Robin, because Strike had just taken another big mouthful of cake.

'We're, ah, leaving the arrangements up to Anna,' said Roy. 'She's taking the lead.'

'I'd like Mum to have a proper grave,' said Anna. 'Somewhere to visit, you know . . . all these years, without knowing where she is. I want her where I can find her.'

'I can understand that,' said Strike.

'You really *don't* know what you've given me,' said Anna, for the third time. She'd reached out a hand to Oonagh, but she was looking at Cynthia. 'I've got Oonagh, now, as well as Cyn, who's been the most wonderful mother . . . Mum certainly chose the right person to raise me . . . '

As Cynthia's face crumpled, Strike and Robin both looked tactfully away, Robin at the cat at the window and Strike at the seascape over the mantelpiece. The rain drummed against the window, the cat in his lap purred, and he remembered the lily urn bobbing away. With a twist in his chest, and in spite of his satisfaction at having done what he'd set out to do, he wished he could have called Joan, and told her the end of Margot Bamborough's story, and heard her say she was proud of him, one last time.

73

For naturall affection soone doth cesse,
And quenched is with Cupids greater flame:
But faithfull friendship doth them both suppresse,
And them with maystring discipline doth tame,
Through thoughts aspyring to eternall fame.
For as the soule doth rule the earthly masse,
And all the seruice of the bodie frame,
So loue of soule doth loue of bodie passe,
No lesse then perfect gold surmounts the meanest brasse.

Edmund Spenser
The Faerie Queene

Robin woke a few days later to autumn sunshine streaming through the gap in her curtains. Glancing at her mobile, she saw to her amazement that it was ten in the morning, which meant she'd just enjoyed the longest sleep she'd had all year. Then she remembered why she was having a lie-in: today was the ninth of October, and it was her birthday.

Ilsa had arranged a dinner in her honour the following evening, which was a Friday. Ilsa had chosen and booked the smart restaurant, to which she and Nick, Vanessa and her fiancé Oliver, Barclay, Hutchins and their wives, Max, his new boyfriend (the lighting director on his TV show) and Strike were all invited. Robin had no plans for today, her actual birthday, which Strike had insisted she take off. She now sat up in bed, yawning, and looked at the packages lying on her chest of drawers opposite, which were all from her family. The small package from her mother had the appearance of a piece of jewellery, doubtless in tribute to this milestone birthday. Just as she was about to get out of bed, her phone beeped and she saw a text from Strike.

> **I know you're supposed to be having a day off but something's come up. Please can you meet me at the Shakespeare's Head, Marlborough St, 5pm. Dress smart, might need to go on somewhere upmarket.**

Robin read this twice, as though she might have missed a 'happy birthday'. Surely – *surely* – he hadn't forgotten again? Or did he think that, by planning to turn up at the dinner Ilsa had planned, he was doing all that was required, and the actual day of her birth required no acknowledgement? True, she felt at a slightly loose end without work and with none of her friends available, but Strike wasn't to know that, so it was with very mixed feelings that she texted back: **OK**.

However, when she arrived upstairs in her dressing gown to fetch a cup of tea, Robin found a large box sitting on the kitchen table, with a card on top of it, her name on the envelope in Strike's unmistakeable cramped, hard-to-read writing. Max, she knew, had left the flat early to film outdoor scenes in Kent, taking Wolfgang with him, who'd sleep in the car and enjoy a lunchtime walk. As she hadn't heard the doorbell, she had to conclude that Strike had somehow transferred both box and card to Max ahead of time, to surprise her with this morning. This argued degrees of planning and effort that seemed highly uncharacteristic. Moreover, she'd never received a proper card from Strike, not even when he'd bought her the green dress after solving their first case.

The front of the birthday card was somewhat generic and featured a large glittery pink number thirty. Inside, Strike had written:

Happy birthday. This isn't your real present,
you'll get that later. (Not flowers)
Love Strike x

Robin looked at this message for far longer than it warranted. Many things about it pleased her, including the kiss and the fact that he'd called himself 'Strike'. She set the card on the table and picked up the large box which, to her surprise, was so light it felt empty. Then she saw the product name on the side: Balloon in a Box.

Opening the lid, she pulled out a balloon in the shape of a donkey's head, tied by a thick ribbon to a weighted base. Grinning, she set it down on the table, made herself tea and breakfast, then texted Strike.

Thanks for the balloon donkey. Perfect timing. My old one's nearly deflated.

She received an answer sixty seconds later.

Great. I was worried it was so obvious, everybody would've got you one. See you at 5.

Light-hearted now, Robin drank tea, ate her toast and returned downstairs to open her family's presents. Everybody had bought her slightly more expensive versions of last year's gifts, except for her parents, who'd sent a beautiful pendant: a single round opal, which was her birthstone, shimmering green and blue, surrounded by tiny diamonds. The accompanying card read: 'Happy thirtieth, Robin. We love you, Mum and Dad x.'

Robin felt her luck, these days, at having two loving parents. Her work had taught her how many people weren't that fortunate, how many people had families that were broken beyond repair, how many adults walked around carrying invisible scars from their earliest childhood, their perceptions and associations forever altered by lack of love, by violence, by cruelty. So she called Linda to thank her, and ended up talking to her mother for over an hour: inconsequential chatter, most of it, but cheering, nevertheless. It was easier to ring home now that her divorce was over. Robin hadn't told her mother that Matthew and Sarah were expecting a baby: she'd let Linda find that out in her own time, and work off her initial outrage out of Robin's earshot.

Towards the end of the call, Linda, who'd disapproved of Robin's dramatic change of career ever since her first injury incurred on the job, mentioned the continuing press coverage concerning Margot Bamborough.

'You really did an incredible thing, there,' said Linda. 'You and, er . . . Cormoran.'

'Thanks, Mum,' said Robin, as surprised as she was touched.

'How's Morris?' her mother asked, in a would-be casual tone.

'Oh, we sacked him,' said Robin cheerfully, forgetting that she hadn't told her mother that, either. 'His replacement's starting next week. Woman called Michelle Greenstreet. She's great.'

After showering, Robin returned to her bedroom to blow dry her hair properly, ate lunch watching TV, then returned downstairs to change into the figure-hugging blue dress that she'd last worn when persuading Shifty's PA to give up her secrets. She added the opal necklace, which, since she'd left her engagement ring behind when leaving Matthew, was now the most valuable piece of jewellery she owned. The beautiful stone, with its iridescent flecks, lifted the appearance of the old dress, and for once pleased with her appearance, Robin picked up the second of her handbags, which was slightly smarter than the one she usually took to the office, and went to pick up her mobile phone from her bedside table.

The drawer of the bedside table was slightly open and, looking down, Robin glimpsed the Thoth tarot pack, sitting inside. For a moment, she hesitated; then, under the smiling eyes of the balloon donkey she'd installed in the corner of her bedroom, she checked the time on her phone. It was still early to leave the house, if she wanted to meet Strike in Marlborough Street at five. Setting down her bag, she took out the tarot pack, sat down on her bed and began shuffling the cards before turning the first card over and laying it down in front of her.

Two swords intersected a blue rose against a green background. She consulted the *Book of Thoth*.

> Peace ... The Two of Swords. It represents a general shaking-up, resulting from the conflict of Fire and Water in their marriage ... This comparative calm is emphasized by the celestial attribution: the Moon in Libra ...

Robin now remembered that this first card was supposed to represent 'the nature of the problem'.

'Peace isn't a problem,' she muttered, to the empty room. 'Peace is good.'

But of course, she hadn't actually asked the cards a question; she'd simply wanted them to tell her something today, on the day of her birth. She turned over the second card, the supposed cause of the problem.

A strange green masked female figure stood beneath a pair of scales, holding a green sword.

> Adjustment ... This card represents the sign of Libra ... she represents The Woman Satisfied. Equilibrium stands apart from any individual prejudices ... She is therefore to be understood as assessing the virtue of every act and demanding exact and precise satisfaction ...

Robin raised her eyebrows and turned over the third and last card: the solution. Here again were the two entwined fish, which poured out water into two golden chalices floating on a green lake: it was the same card she'd turned over in Leamington Spa, when she still didn't know who'd killed Margot Bamborough.

> Love ... The card also refers to Venus in Cancer. It shows the harmony of the male and the female: interpreted in the largest sense. It is perfect and placid harmony ...

Robin took a deep breath, then returned all the cards to their pack and the pack to her bedside drawer. As she stood and picked up her raincoat, the balloon donkey swayed slightly on its ribbon.

Robin could feel the new opal resting in the hollow of the base of her throat as she walked towards the Tube station along the road, and having slept properly for once, and having clean hair, and carrying a feeling of lightness with her that had persisted ever since she took the balloon donkey out of his box, she attracted many pairs of male eyes in the street and on the train. But Robin ignored all of them, heading up the stairs at Oxford Circus, and then proceeded down Regent Street and, finally, to the Shakespeare's Head where she saw Strike standing outside, wearing a suit.

'Happy birthday,' he said, and after a brief hesitation he bent down and kissed her on the cheek. He smelled, Robin noticed, not only of cigarettes, but of a subtle lavender after-shave, which was unusual.

'Thanks . . . aren't we going into the pub?'

'Er – no,' said Strike. 'I want to buy you some new perfume.' He pointed towards the rear entrance of Liberty, which lay a mere ten yards away. 'It's your real birthday present – unless you've already bought some?' he added. He really hoped not. He couldn't think of anything else to offer her that didn't take them back into the realm of awkwardness and possible misunderstanding.

'I . . . no,' said Robin. 'How did you know I've . . . ?'

'Because I phoned Ilsa, last Christmas . . .'

As he held open the glass door for her, which led to a chocolate department now full of Hallowe'en treats, Strike explained about his failed attempt to buy Robin perfume, the previous December.

' . . . so I asked the assistant, but he kept showing me things with names like . . . I dunno . . . "Shaggable You" . . . '

The laugh Robin failed to repress was so loud that people turned to look at her. They moved past tables stacked with expensive truffles.

' . . . and I panicked,' Strike admitted, 'which is why you ended up with chocolates. Anyway,' he said, as they came to the threshold of the perfume room, with its cupola painted with moon and stars, 'you choose whatever you want and I'll pay.'

'Strike,' said Robin, 'this is . . . this is *thoughtful*.'

'Yeah, well,' said her partner, with a shrug. 'People can change. Or so a psychiatrist in Broadmoor told me. I'm going to stand here,' he said, pointing at a corner where he hoped his bulk wouldn't impede anyone. 'Take your time.'

So Robin spent a pleasurable quarter of an hour browsing among bottles, spraying testers onto strips, enjoying a brief consultation with the helpful assistant, and finally narrowing her choice down to two perfumes. Now she hesitated, wondering whether she dare do what she wanted . . . but surely, if they were best friends, it was all right?

'OK, there are two I really like,' Robin said, reappearing at Strike's side. 'Give me your opinion. You've got to live with it, in the Land Rover.'

'If they're strong enough to cover up the smell of that car, they aren't fit for human inhalation,' he said, but nevertheless, he took the two smelling strips.

The first smelled of vanilla, which reminded him of cake, and he liked it. The second put him in mind of warm, musky skin, with a suggestion of bruised flowers.

'That one. The second one.'

'Huh. I thought you'd prefer the first.'

'Because it smells like food?'

She grinned as she sniffed the smelling strips.

'Yes . . . I think I prefer two, as well. It isn't cheap.'

'I'll cope.'

So he carried a heavy cube of white glass which bore the unexceptional name 'Narciso' to the desk.

'Yeah, it's a gift,' Strike said when asked, and he waited patiently as the price sticker was peeled off and a ribbon and wrapping added. He couldn't personally see the point, but he felt that Robin was owed a little ceremony, and her smile as she took the bag from him told him he'd answered correctly. Now they walked together back through the store and out of the main entrance, where buckets of flowers surrounded them.

'So where—?' asked Robin.

'I'm taking you to the Ritz for champagne,' said Strike.

'Are you serious?'

'Yeah. It's why I'm wearing a suit.'

For a moment Robin simply looked at him, then she

reached up and hugged him tightly. Surrounded by banked flowers, both remembered the hug they'd shared at the top of the stairs on her wedding day, but this time, Robin turned her face and kissed Strike deliberately on the cheek, lips to stubble.

'Thanks, Strike. This really means a lot.'

And that, thought her partner, as the two of them headed away towards the Ritz in the golden glow of the early evening, really was well worth sixty quid and a bit of an effort . . .

Out of his subconscious rose the names Mazankov and Krupov, and it was a second or two before he remembered where he'd heard them, why they sounded Cornish, and why he thought of them now. The corners of his mouth twitched, but as Robin didn't see him smiling, he felt no compulsion to explain.

ACKNOWLEDGEMENTS

My thanks, as ever, to my superb editor David Shelley, who always makes the job a pleasure; to my wonderful agent Neil Blair; to the management team who keep me sane, Mark Hutchinson, Rebecca Salt and Nicky Stonehill; to my home and office team, without whom this book would never have been finished: Di Brooks, Simon Brown, Danny Cameron, Angela Milne, Ross Milne, Fi Shapcott and Kaisa Tiensuu; to Neil Murray, the world's best reader of works-in-progress; to Kenzie, for spotting that cross of the Knights of St John where I didn't expect to find one; to William Leone and Lynne Corbett, for inspiration and for checking my calculations; to Russell Townsend, for helping me check out all these locations and for saving my dead laptop; and to Tom Burke, for fascinating Crowleyana and the Atlantis bookshop.

CREDITS

'Come On-A My House' (p 91) Words and Music by Ross Bagdasarian and William Saroyan. © 1957 Songs Of Universal, Inc. International Copyright Secured. All Rights Reserved. Printed by Permission of Hal Leonard Europe Ltd & Bagdasarian Productions.

'Same Situation' (p 276) Words and Music by Joni Mitchell. © 1973 (Renewed) Crazy Crow Music. All Rights Administered by Sony/ATV Tunes LLC, 424 Church St., Suite 1200, Nashville, TN 37219. Exclusive Print Rights Administered by Alfred Music. All Rights Reserved. Used By Permission of Alfred Music.

'Court and Spark' (p 276, p 313 & p 329) Words and Music by Joni Mitchell. © 1973 (Renewed) Crazy Crow Music. All Rights Administered by Sony/ATV Tunes LLC, 424 Church St., Suite 1200, Nashville, TN 37219. Exclusive Print Rights Administered by Alfred Music. All Rights Reserved. Used By Permission of Alfred Music.

'Just Like This Train' (p 329) Words and Music by Joni Mitchell. © 1973 (Renewed) Crazy Crow Music. All Rights Administered by Sony/ATV Tunes LLC, 424 Church St., Suite 1200, Nashville, TN 37219. Exclusive Print Rights

'Blame' (p 862) Words and Music by Calvin Harris, John Newman and James Newman. © 2014 TSJ Merlyn Licensing B.V, B-Unique Music Ltd. and Black Butter Music Publishing Ltd. All Rights on behalf of TSJ Merlyn Licensing B.V Administered by EMI Music Publishing Ltd. All Rights on behalf of B-Unique Music Ltd. Administered Worldwide by Songs of Kobalt Music Publishing. All Rights on behalf of Black Butter Music Publishing Ltd. Administered by BMG Rights Management (UK) Ltd. International Copyright Secured. All Rights Reserved. Printed by Permission of Hal Leonard Europe Ltd & EMI Music Publishing Ltd.

Help us make the next generation of readers

We – both author and publisher – hope you enjoyed this book. We believe that you can become a reader at any time in your life, but we'd love your help to give the next generation a head start.

Did you know that 9% of children don't have a book of their own in their home, rising to 12% in disadvantaged families*? We'd like to try to change that by asking you to consider the role you could play in helping to build readers of the future.

We'd love you to think of sharing, borrowing, reading, buying or talking about a book with a child in your life and spreading the love of reading. We want to make sure the next generation continue to have access to books, wherever they come from.

And if you would like to consider donating to charities that help fund literacy projects, find out more at www.literacytrust.org.uk and www.booktrust.org.uk.

Thank you.

little, brown
BOOK GROUP

*As reported by the National Literacy Trust

Praise for *The Silkworm*

'Teems with sly humour, witty asides and intelligence …
A pleasure to read'
The Times

'An intelligent and captivating drama driven by fascinatingly real characters. This is storytelling at its very best'
Heat

'*The Silkworm* is a deeply satisfying work of crime fiction, more complex and darker than its predecessor'
The Australian

'Irresistible reading' Val McDermid,
Guardian

'A superb and polished thriller … an ingenious whodunit'
Sunday Mirror

By Robert Galbraith

The Cuckoo's Calling

The Silkworm

Career of Evil

Lethal White

Troubled Blood

THE SILKWORM

ROBERT
GALBRAITH

sphere

SPHERE

First published in Great Britain in 2014 by Sphere
Paperback edition published in 2015 by Sphere
This reissue published in 2018 by Sphere

27

A CIP catalogue record for this book is available from the British Library.

ISBN 978-0-7515-4926-3

Typeset in Bembo by M Rules
Printed and bound in Great Britain by Clays Ltd, Elcograf S.p.A.

Papers used by Sphere are from well-managed forests and other responsible sources.

Sphere
An imprint of
Little, Brown Book Group
Carmelite House
50 Victoria Embankment
London EC4Y 0DZ

An Hachette UK Company
www.hachette.co.uk

www.littlebrown.co.uk

To Jenkins,
without whom …
he knows the rest

. . . blood and vengeance the scene, death the story,
a sword imbrued with blood, the pen that writes,
and the poet a terrible buskined tragical fellow,
with a wreath about his head of burning match instead
of bays.

The Noble Spanish Soldier
Thomas Dekker

THE SILKWORM

1

QUESTION
What dost thou feed on?
ANSWER
Broken sleep.

Thomas Dekker, *The Noble Spanish Soldier*

'Someone bloody famous,' said the hoarse voice on the end of the line, 'better've died, Strike.'

The large unshaven man tramping through the darkness of pre-dawn, with his telephone clamped to his ear, grinned.

'It's in that ballpark.'

'It's six o'clock in the fucking morning!'

'It's half past, but if you want what I've got, you'll need to come and get it,' said Cormoran Strike. 'I'm not far away from your place. There's a—'

'How d'you know where I live?' demanded the voice.

'You told me,' said Strike, stifling a yawn. 'You're selling your flat.'

'Oh,' said the other, mollified. 'Good memory.'

'There's a twenty-four-hour caff—'

'Fuck that. Come into the office later—'

'Culpepper, I've got another client this morning, he pays

better than you do and I've been up all night. You need this now if you're going to use it.'

A groan. Strike could hear the rustling of sheets.

'It had better be shit-hot.'

'Smithfield Café on Long Lane,' said Strike and rang off.

The slight unevenness in his gait became more pronounced as he walked down the slope towards Smithfield Market, monolithic in the winter darkness, a vast rectangular Victorian temple to meat, where from four every weekday morning animal flesh was unloaded, as it had been for centuries past, cut, parcelled and sold to butchers and restaurants across London. Strike could hear voices through the gloom, shouted instructions and the growl and beep of reversing lorries unloading the carcasses. As he entered Long Lane, he became merely one among many heavily muffled men moving purposefully about their Monday-morning business.

A huddle of couriers in fluorescent jackets cupped mugs of tea in their gloved hands beneath a stone griffin standing sentinel on the corner of the market building. Across the road, glowing like an open fireplace against the surrounding darkness, was the Smithfield Café, open twenty-four hours a day, a cupboard-sized cache of warmth and greasy food.

The café had no bathroom, but an arrangement with the bookies a few doors along. Ladbrokes would not open for another three hours, so Strike made a detour down a side alley and in a dark doorway relieved himself of a bladder bulging with weak coffee drunk in the course of a night's work. Exhausted and hungry, he turned at last, with the pleasure that only a man who has pushed himself past his physical limits can ever experience, into the fat-laden atmosphere of frying eggs and bacon.

Two men in fleeces and waterproofs had just vacated a table. Strike manoeuvered his bulk into the small space and sank, with a grunt of satisfaction, onto the hard wood and steel chair. Almost before he asked, the Italian owner placed tea in front of him in a tall white mug, which came with triangles of white buttered bread. Within five minutes a full English breakfast lay before him on a large oval plate.

Strike blended well with the strong men banging their way in and out of the café. He was large and dark, with dense, short, curly hair that had receded a little from the high, domed forehead that topped a boxer's broad nose and thick, surly brows. His jaw was grimy with stubble and bruise-coloured shadows enlarged his dark eyes. He ate gazing dreamily at the market building opposite. The nearest arched entrance, numbered two, was taking substance as the darkness thinned: a stern stone face, ancient and bearded, stared back at him from over the doorway. Had there ever been a god of carcasses?

He had just started on his sausages when Dominic Culpepper arrived. The journalist was almost as tall as Strike but thin, with a choirboy's complexion. A strange asymmetry, as though somebody had given his face a counterclockwise twist, stopped him being girlishly handsome.

'This better be good,' Culpepper said as he sat down, pulled off his gloves and glanced almost suspiciously around the café.

'Want some food?' asked Strike through a mouthful of sausage.

'No,' said Culpepper.

'Rather wait till you can get a croissant?' asked Strike, grinning.

'Fuck off, Strike.'

It was almost pathetically easy to wind up the ex-public

schoolboy, who ordered tea with an air of defiance, calling the indifferent waiter (as Strike noted with amusement) 'mate'.

'Well?' demanded Culpepper, with the hot mug in his long pale hands.

Strike fished in his overcoat pocket, brought out an envelope and slid it across the table. Culpepper pulled out the contents and began to read.

'Fucking hell,' he said quietly, after a while. He shuffled feverishly through the bits of paper, some of which were covered in Strike's own writing. 'Where the hell did you get this?'

Strike, whose mouth was full of sausage, jabbed a finger at one of the bits of paper, on which an office address was scribbled.

'His very fucked-off PA,' he said, when he had finally swallowed. 'He's been shagging her, as well as the two you know about. She's only just realised she's not going to be the next Lady Parker.'

'How the hell did you find *that* out?' asked Culpepper, staring up at Strike over the papers trembling in his excited hands.

'Detective work,' said Strike thickly, through another bit of sausage. 'Didn't your lot used to do this, before you started outsourcing to the likes of me? But she's got to think about her future employment prospects, Culpepper, so she doesn't want to appear in the story, all right?'

Culpepper snorted.

'She should've thought about that before she nicked—'

With a deft movement, Strike tweaked the papers out of the journalist's fingers.

'She didn't nick them. He got her to print this lot off for him this afternoon. The only thing she's done wrong is show it to me. But if you're going to splash her private life all over the papers, Culpepper, I'll take 'em back.'

'Piss off,' said Culpepper, making a grab for the evidence of wholesale tax evasion clutched in Strike's hairy hand. 'All right, we'll leave her out of it. But he'll know where we got it. He's not a complete tit.'

'What's he going to do, drag her into court where she can spill the beans about every other dodgy thing she's witnessed over the last five years?'

'Yeah, all right,' sighed Culpepper after a moment's reflection. 'Give 'em back. I'll leave her out of the story, but I'll need to speak to her, won't I? Check she's kosher.'

'*Those* are kosher. You don't need to speak to her,' said Strike firmly.

The shaking, besotted, bitterly betrayed woman whom he had just left would not be safe left alone with Culpepper. In her savage desire for retribution against a man who had promised her marriage and children she would damage herself and her prospects beyond repair. It had not taken Strike long to gain her trust. She was nearly forty-two; she had thought that she was going to have Lord Parker's children; now a kind of bloodlust had her in its grip. Strike had sat with her for several hours, listening to the story of her infatuation, watching her pace her sitting room in tears, rock backwards and forwards on her sofa, knuckles to her forehead. Finally she had agreed to this: a betrayal that represented the funeral of all her hopes.

'You're going to leave her out of it,' said Strike, holding the papers firmly in a fist that was nearly twice the size of Culpepper's. 'Right? This is still a fucking massive story without her.'

After a moment's hesitation and with a grimace, Culpepper caved in.

'Yeah, all right. Give me them.'

The journalist shoved the statements into an inside pocket and gulped his tea, and his momentary disgruntlement at Strike seemed to fade in the glorious prospect of dismantling the reputation of a British peer.

'Lord Parker of Pennywell,' he said happily under his breath, 'you are well and truly screwed, mate.'

'I take it your proprietor'll get this?' Strike asked, as the bill landed between them.

'Yeah, yeah . . . '

Culpepper threw a ten-pound note down onto the table and the two men left the café together. Strike lit up a cigarette as soon as the door had swung closed behind them.

'How did you get her to talk?' Culpepper asked as they set off together through the cold, past the motorbikes and lorries still arriving at and departing the market.

'I listened,' said Strike.

Culpepper shot him a sideways glance.

'All the other private dicks I use spend their time hacking phone messages.'

'Illegal,' said Strike, blowing smoke into the thinning darkness.

'So how—?'

'You protect your sources and I'll protect mine.'

They walked fifty yards in silence, Strike's limp more marked with every step.

'This is going to be massive. Massive,' said Culpepper gleefully. 'That hypocritical old shit's been bleating on about corporate greed and he's had twenty mill' stashed in the Cayman Islands . . . '

'Glad to give satisfaction,' said Strike. 'I'll email you my invoice.'

Culpepper threw him another sideways look.

'See Tom Jones's son in the paper last week?' he asked.

'Tom Jones?'

'Welsh singer,' said Culpepper.

'Oh, him,' said Strike, without enthusiasm. 'I knew a Tom Jones in the army.'

'Did you see the story?'

'No.'

'Nice long interview he gave. He says he's never met his father, never had a word from him. I bet he got more than your bill is going to be.'

'You haven't seen my invoice yet,' said Strike.

'Just saying. One nice little interview and you could take a few nights off from interviewing secretaries.'

'You're going to have to stop suggesting this,' said Strike, 'or I'm going to have to stop working for you, Culpepper.'

'Course,' said Culpepper, 'I could run the story anyway. Rock star's estranged son is a war hero, never knew his father, working as a private—'

'Instructing people to hack phones is illegal as well, I've heard.'

At the top of Long Lane they slowed and turned to face each other. Culpepper's laugh was uneasy.

'I'll wait for your invoice, then.'

'Suits me.'

They set off in different directions, Strike heading towards the Tube station.

'Strike!' Culpepper's voice echoed through the darkness behind him. 'Did you fuck her?'

'Looking forward to reading it, Culpepper,' Strike shouted wearily, without turning his head.

He limped into the shadowy entrance of the station and was lost to Culpepper's sight.

2

> How long must we fight? for I cannot stay,
> Nor will not stay! I have business.
>
> Francis Beaumont and Philip Massinger,
> *The Little French Lawyer*

The Tube was filling up already. Monday-morning faces: sagging, gaunt, braced, resigned. Strike found a seat opposite a puffy-eyed young blonde whose head kept sinking sideways into sleep. Again and again she jerked herself back upright, scanning the blurred signs of the stations frantically in case she had missed her stop.

The train rattled and clattered, speeding Strike back towards the meagre two and a half rooms under a poorly insulated roof that he called home. In the depths of his tiredness, surrounded by these blank, sheep-like visages, he found himself pondering the accidents that had brought all of them into being. Every birth was, viewed properly, mere chance. With a hundred million sperm swimming blindly through the darkness, the odds against a person becoming themselves were staggering. How many of this Tube-full had been planned, he wondered, lightheaded with tiredness. And how many, like him, were accidents?

There had been a little girl in his primary school class who had a port-wine stain across her face and Strike had always felt a secret kinship with her, because both of them had carried something indelibly different with them since birth, something that was not their fault. They couldn't see it, but everybody else could, and had the bad manners to keep mentioning it. The occasional fascination of total strangers, which at five years old he had thought had something to do with his own uniqueness, he eventually realised was because they saw him as no more than a famous singer's zygote, the incidental evidence of a celebrity's unfaithful fumble. Strike had only met his biological father twice. It had taken a DNA test to make Jonny Rokeby accept paternity.

Dominic Culpepper was a walking distillation of the prurience and presumptions that Strike met on the very rare occasions these days that anybody connected the surly-looking ex-soldier with the ageing rock star. Their thoughts leapt at once to trust funds and handsome hand-outs, to private flights and VIP lounges, to a multi-millionaire's largesse on tap. Agog at the modesty of Strike's existence and the punishing hours he worked, they asked themselves: what must Strike have done to alienate his father? Was he faking penury to wheedle more money out of Rokeby? What had he done with the millions his mother had surely squeezed out of her rich paramour?

And at such times, Strike would think nostalgically of the army, of the anonymity of a career in which your background and your parentage counted for almost nothing beside your ability to do the job. Back in the Special Investigation Branch, the most personal question he had faced on introduction was a request to repeat the odd pair of names with which his extravagantly unconventional mother had saddled him.

Traffic was already rolling busily along Charing Cross Road by the time Strike emerged from the Tube. The November dawn was breaking now, grey and half-hearted, full of lingering shadows. He turned into Denmark Street feeling drained and sore, looking forward to the short sleep he might be able to squeeze in before his next client arrived at nine thirty. With a wave at the girl in the guitar shop, with whom he often took cigarette breaks on the street, Strike let himself in through the black outer door beside the 12 Bar Café and began to climb the metal staircase that curled around the broken birdcage lift inside. Up past the graphic designer on the first floor, past his own office with its engraved glass door on the second; up to the third and smallest landing where his home now lay.

The previous occupant, manager of the bar downstairs, had moved on to more salubrious quarters and Strike, who had been sleeping in his office for a few months, had leapt at the chance to rent the place, grateful for such an easy solution to the problem of his homelessness. The space under the eaves was small by any standards, and especially for a man of six foot three. He scarcely had room to turn around in the shower; kitchen and living room were uneasily combined and the bedroom was almost entirely filled by the double bed. Some of Strike's possessions remained boxed up on the landing, in spite of the landlord's injunction against this.

His small windows looked out across rooftops, with Denmark Street far below. The constant throb of the bass from the bar below was muffled to the point that Strike's own music often obliterated it.

Strike's innate orderliness was manifest throughout: the bed was made, the crockery clean, everything in its place. He needed a shave and shower, but that could wait; after hanging up his overcoat, he set his alarm for nine twenty and stretched out on the bed fully clothed.

He fell asleep within seconds and within a few more – or so it seemed – he was awake again. Somebody was knocking on his door.

'I'm sorry, Cormoran, I'm really sorry—'

His assistant, a tall young woman with long strawberry-blonde hair, looked apologetic as he opened the door, but at the sight of him her expression became appalled.

'Are you all right?'

'Wuzassleep. Been 'wake all night – two nights.'

'I'm really sorry,' Robin repeated, 'but it's nine forty and William Baker's here and getting—'

'Shit,' mumbled Strike. 'Can't've set the alarm right – gimme five min—'

'That's not all,' said Robin. 'There's a woman here. She hasn't got an appointment. I've told her you haven't got room for another client, but she's refusing to leave.'

Strike yawned, rubbing his eyes.

'Five minutes. Make them tea or something.'

Six minutes later, in a clean shirt, smelling of toothpaste and deodorant but still unshaven, Strike entered the outer office where Robin was sitting at her computer.

'Well, better late than never,' said William Baker with a rigid smile. 'Lucky you've got such a good-looking secretary, or I might have got bored and left.'

Strike saw Robin flush angrily as she turned away, ostensibly organising the post. There had been something inherently offensive in the way that Baker had said 'secretary'. Immaculate in his pinstriped suit, the company director was employing Strike to investigate two of his fellow board members.

'Morning, William,' said Strike.

'No apology?' murmured Baker, his eyes on the ceiling.

'Hello, who are you?' Strike asked, ignoring him and addressing instead the slight, middle-aged woman in an old brown overcoat who was perched on the sofa.

'Leonora Quine,' she replied, in what sounded, to Strike's practised ear, like a West Country accent.

'I've got a very busy morning ahead, Strike,' said Baker.

He walked without invitation into the inner office. When Strike did not follow, he lost a little of his suavity.

'I doubt you got away with shoddy time-keeping in the army, Mr Strike. Come along, please.'

Strike did not seem to hear him.

'What exactly is it you were wanting me to do for you, Mrs Quine?' he asked the shabby woman on the sofa.

'Well, it's my husband—'

'Mr Strike, I've got an appointment in just over an hour,' said William Baker, more loudly.

'—your secretary said you didn't have no appointments but I said I'd wait.'

'Strike!' barked William Baker, calling his dog to heel.

'Robin,' snarled the exhausted Strike, losing his temper at last. 'Make up Mr Baker's bill and give him the file; it's up to date.'

'What?' said William Baker, thrown. He re-emerged into the outer office.

'He's sacking you,' said Leonora Quine with satisfaction.

'You haven't finished the job,' Baker told Strike. 'You said there was more—'

'Someone else can finish the job for you. Someone who doesn't mind tossers as clients.'

The atmosphere in the office seemed to become petrified. Wooden-faced, Robin retrieved Baker's file from the outer cabinet and handed it to Strike.

'How *dare*—'

'There's a lot of good stuff in that file that'll stand up in court,' said Strike, handing it to the director. 'Well worth the money.'

'You haven't finished—'

'He's finished with *you*,' interjected Leonora Quine.

'Will you shut up, you stupid wom—' William Baker began, then took a sudden step backwards as Strike took a half-step forwards. Nobody said anything. The ex-serviceman seemed suddenly to be filling twice as much space as he had just seconds before.

'Take a seat in my office, Mrs Quine,' said Strike quietly.

She did as she was told.

'You think she'll be able to afford you?' sneered a retreating William Baker, his hand now on the door handle.

'My fees are negotiable,' said Strike, 'if I like the client.'

He followed Leonora Quine into his office and closed the door behind him with a snap.

3

. . . left alone to bear up all these ills . . .

Thomas Dekker, *The Noble Spanish Soldier*

'He's a right one, isn't he?' commented Leonora Quine as she sat down in the chair facing Strike's desk.

'Yeah,' agreed Strike, sinking heavily into the seat opposite her. 'He is.'

In spite of a barely crumpled pink-and-white complexion and the clear whites of her pale blue eyes, she looked around fifty. Fine, limp, greying hair was held off her face by two plastic combs and she was blinking at him through old-fashioned glasses with over-large plastic frames. Her coat, though clean, had surely been bought in the eighties. It had shoulder pads and large plastic buttons.

'So you're here about your husband, Mrs Quine?'

'Yeah,' said Leonora. 'He's missing.'

'How long's he been gone?' asked Strike, reaching automatically for a notebook.

'Ten days,' said Leonora.

'Have you been to the police?'

'I don't need the police,' she said impatiently, as though she was tired of explaining this to people. 'I called them once before and everyone was angry at me because he was only with a friend. Owen just goes off sometimes. He's a writer,' she said, as though this explained everything.

'He's disappeared before?'

'He's emotional,' she said, her expression glum. 'He's always going off on one, but it's been ten days and I know he's really upset but I need him home now. There's Orlando and I've got things to do and there's—'

'Orlando?' repeated Strike, his tired mind on the Florida resort. He did not have time to go to America and Leonora Quine, in her ancient coat, certainly did not look as though she could afford a ticket for him.

'Our daughter, Orlando,' said Leonora. 'She needs looking after. I've got a neighbour in to sit with her while I'm here.'

There was a knock on the door and Robin's bright gold head appeared.

'Would you like coffee, Mr Strike? You, Mrs Quine?'

When they had given Robin their orders and she had withdrawn, Leonora said:

'It won't take you long, because I think I know where he is, only I can't get hold of the address and nobody'll take my calls. It's been ten days,' she repeated, 'and we need him home.'

It seemed to Strike a great extravagance to resort to a private detective in this circumstance, especially as her appearance exhaled poverty.

'If it's a simple question of making a phone call,' he said gently, 'haven't you got a friend or a—?'

'Edna can't do it,' she said and he found himself disproportionately touched (exhaustion sometimes laid him raw in this way) at her tacit admission that she had one friend in the world.

'Owen's told them not to say where he is. I need,' she said simply, 'a man to do it. Force them to say.'

'Your husband's name's Owen, is it?'

'Yeah,' she replied, 'Owen Quine. He wrote *Hobart's Sin*.'

Neither name nor title meant anything to Strike.

'And you think you know where he is?'

'Yeah. We was at this party with a load of publishers and people – he didn't want to take me, but I says, "I got a babysitter already, I'm coming" – so I hears Christian Fisher telling Owen about this place, this writer's retreat place. And afterwards I says to Owen, "What was that place he was telling you about?" and Owen says, "I'm not telling you, that's the whole bloody point, getting away from the wife and kids."'

She almost invited Strike to join her husband in laughing at her; proud, as mothers sometimes pretend to be, of their child's insolence.

'Who's Christian Fisher?' asked Strike, forcing himself to concentrate.

'Publisher. Young, trendy bloke.'

'Have you tried phoning Fisher and asking him for the address of this retreat?'

'Yeah, I've called him every day for a week and they said they'd taken a message and he'd get back to me, but he hasn't. I think Owen's told him not to say where he is. But *you'll* be able to get the address out of Fisher. I know you're good,' she said. 'You solved that Lula Landry thing, when the police never.'

A mere eight months previously, Strike had had but a single client, his business had been moribund and his prospects desperate. Then he had proven, to the satisfaction of the Crown Prosecution Service, that a famous young woman had not committed suicide but had been pushed to her death from a fourth-floor balcony. The ensuing publicity had brought a tide of business; he had been, for a few weeks, the best-known private detective in the metropolis. Jonny Rokeby had become a mere footnote to his story; Strike had become a name in his own right, albeit a name most people got wrong . . .

'I interrupted you,' he said, trying hard to hold on to the thread of his thoughts.

'Did you?'

'Yeah,' said Strike, squinting at his own crabbed writing on the notebook. 'You said, "There's Orlando, I've got things to do and there's—"'

'Oh yeah,' she said, 'there's funny stuff happening since he left.'

'What kind of funny stuff?'

'Shit,' said Leonora Quine matter-of-factly, 'through our letter box.'

'Someone's put excrement through your letter box?' Strike said.

'Yeah.'

'Since your husband disappeared?'

'Yeah. Dog,' said Leonora, and it was a split-second before Strike deduced that this applied to the excrement, not her husband. 'Three or four times now, at night. Nice thing to find in the morning, I don't think. And there was a woman come to the door and all, who was weird.'

She paused, waiting for Strike to prompt her. She seemed to enjoy being questioned. Many lonely people, Strike knew, found it pleasant to be the focus of somebody's undivided attention and sought to prolong the novel experience.

'When did this woman come to the door?'

'Last week it was, and she asks for Owen and when I says, "He's not here," she says, "Tell him Angela died," and walks off.'

'And you didn't know her?'

'Never seen her before.'

'Do you know an Angela?'

'No. But he gets women fans going funny over him, sometimes,' said Leonora, suddenly expansive. 'Like, he had this woman once that wrote him letters and sent him photos of herself dressed up like one of his characters. Some of these women who write to him think he understands them or something because of his books. Silly, innit?' she said. 'It's all made up.'

'Do fans usually know where your husband lives?'

'No,' said Leonora. 'But she could've bin a student or something. He teaches writing as well, sometimes.'

The door opened and Robin entered with a tray. After putting black coffee in front of Strike and a tea in front of Leonora Quine, she withdrew again, closing the door behind her.

'Is that everything strange that's happened?' Strike asked Leonora. 'The excrement through the door, and this woman coming to the house?'

'And I think I've been followed. Tall, dark girl with round shoulders,' said Leonora.

'This is a different woman to the one—?'

'Yeah, the one that come to the house was dumpy. Long red hair. This one's dark and bent over, like.'

'You're sure she was following you?'

'Yeah, I think so. I seen her behind me two, three times now. She isn't local, I've never seen her before and I've lived in Ladbroke Grove thirty-odd years.'

'OK,' said Strike slowly. 'You said your husband's upset? What happened to upset him?'

'He had a massive row with his agent.'

'What about, do you know?'

'His book, his latest. Liz – that's his agent – tells him it's the best thing he's ever done, and then, like, a day later, she takes him out to dinner and says it's unpublishable.'

'Why did she change her mind?'

'Ask *her*,' said Leonora, showing anger for the first time. 'Course he was upset after that. Anyone would be. He's worked on that book for two years. He comes home in a right state and he goes into his study and grabs it all—'

'Grabs what?'

'His book, the manuscript and his notes and everything, swearing his head off, and he shoves them in a bag and he goes off and I haven't seen him since.'

'Has he got a mobile? Have you tried calling him?'

'Yeah and he's not picking up. He never does, when he goes off like this. He chucked his phone out the car window once,' she said, again with that faint note of pride at her husband's spirit.

'Mrs Quine,' said Strike, whose altruism necessarily had its limits, whatever he had told William Baker, 'I'll be honest with you: I don't come cheap.'

'That's all right,' said Leonora implacably. 'Liz'll pay.'

'Liz?'

'*Liz* – Elizabeth Tassel. Owen's agent. It's her fault he's gone away. She can take it out of her commission. He's her best client. She'll want him back all right, once she realises what she's done.'

Strike did not set as much store by this assurance as Leonora herself seemed to. He added three sugars to the coffee and gulped it down, trying to think how best to proceed. He felt vaguely sorry for Leonora Quine, who seemed inured to her erratic husband's tantrums, who accepted the fact that nobody would deign to return her calls, who was sure that the only help she could expect must be paid for. Her slight eccentricity of manner aside, there was a truculent honesty about her. Nevertheless, he had been ruthless in taking on only profitable cases since his business had received its unexpected boost. Those few people who had come to him with hard-luck stories, hoping that his own personal difficulties (reported and embellished in the press) would predispose him to helping them free of charge, had left disappointed.

But Leonora Quine, who had drunk her tea quite as quickly as Strike had downed his coffee, was already on her feet, as though they had agreed terms and everything was settled.

'I'd better get going,' she said, 'I don't like leaving Orlando too long. She's missing her daddy. I've told her I'm getting a man to go find him.'

Strike had recently helped several wealthy young women rid themselves of City husbands who had become much less attractive to them since the financial crash. There was something appealing about restoring a husband to a wife, for a change.

'All right,' he said, yawning as he pushed his notebook towards her. 'I'll need your contact details, Mrs Quine. A photograph of your husband would be handy too.'

She wrote her address and telephone number out for him in a round, childish hand, but his request for a photo seemed to surprise her.

'What d'you need a picture for? He's at that writer's retreat. Just make Christian Fisher tell you where it is.'

She was through the door before Strike, tired and sore, could emerge from behind his desk. He heard her say briskly to Robin: 'Ta for the tea,' then the glass door onto the landing opened with a flash and closed with a gentle judder, and his new client had gone.

4

Well, 'tis a rare thing to have an ingenious friend . . .

William Congreve, *The Double-Dealer*

Strike dropped onto the sofa in the outer office. It was almost new, an essential expense as he had broken the second-hand one with which he had initially furnished the office. Covered in mock leather that he had thought smart in the showroom, it made farting noises if you moved on it in the wrong way. His assistant – tall, curvaceous, with a clear, brilliant complexion and bright blue-grey eyes – scrutinised him over her coffee cup.

'You look terrible.'

'Spent all night weaselling details of a peer of the realm's sexual irregularities and financial malfeasance out of a hysterical woman,' said Strike, on a massive yawn.

'Lord Parker?' gasped Robin.

'That's the one,' said Strike.

'He's been—?'

'Shagging three women simultaneously and salting millions away offshore,' said Strike. 'If you've got a strong stomach, try the *News of the World* this Sunday.'

'How on earth did you find all that out?'

'Contact of a contact of a contact,' intoned Strike.

He yawned again, so widely that it looked painful.

'You should go to bed,' said Robin.

'Yeah, I should,' said Strike, but he did not move.

'You haven't got anyone else till Gunfrey this afternoon at two.'

'Gunfrey,' sighed Strike, massaging his eye sockets. 'Why are all my clients shits?'

'Mrs Quine doesn't seem like a shit.'

He peered blearily at her through his thick fingers.

'How d'you know I took her case?'

'I knew you would,' said Robin with an irrepressible smirk. 'She's your type.'

'A middle-aged throwback to the eighties?'

'Your kind of client. And you wanted to spite Baker.'

'Seemed to work, didn't it?'

The telephone rang. Still grinning, Robin answered.

'Cormoran Strike's office,' she said. 'Oh. Hi.'

It was her fiancé, Matthew. She glanced sideways at her boss. Strike had closed his eyes and tilted his head back, his arms folded across his broad chest.

'Listen,' said Matthew in Robin's ear; he never sounded very friendly when calling from work. 'I need to move drinks from Friday to Thursday.'

'Oh Matt,' she said, trying to keep both disappointment and exasperation out of her voice.

It would be the fifth time that arrangements for these particular drinks had been made. Robin alone, of the three people involved, had not altered time, date or venue, but had shown herself willing and available on every occasion.

'Why?' she muttered.

A sudden grunting snore issued from the sofa. Strike had fallen asleep where he sat, his large head tilted back against the wall, arms still folded.

'Work drinks on the nineteenth,' said Matthew. 'It'll look bad if I don't go. Show my face.'

She fought the urge to snap at him. He worked for a major firm of accountants and sometimes he acted as though this imposed social obligations more appropriate to a diplomatic posting.

She was sure that she knew the real reason for the change. Drinks had been postponed repeatedly at Strike's request; on each occasion he had been busy with some piece of urgent, evening work, and while the excuses had been genuine, they had irritated Matthew. Though he had never said it aloud, Robin knew that Matthew thought Strike was implying that his time was more valuable than Matthew's, his job more important.

In the eight months that she had worked for Cormoran Strike, her boss and her fiancé had not met, not even on that infamous night when Matthew had picked her up from the casualty department where she had accompanied Strike, with her coat wrapped tightly around his stabbed arm after a cornered killer had tried to finish him. When she had emerged, shaken and bloodstained, from the place where they were stitching Strike up, Matthew had declined her offer to introduce him to her injured boss. He had been furious about the whole business, even though Robin had reassured him that she herself had never been in any danger.

Matthew had never wanted her to take a permanent job with Strike, whom he had regarded with suspicion from the first, disliking his penury, his homelessness and the profession that Matthew seemed to find absurd. The little snatches of information that Robin brought home – Strike's career in the Special Investigation Branch, the plain-clothes wing of the Royal Military Police, his decoration for bravery, the loss of his lower right leg, the expertise in a hundred areas of which Matthew – so used to being expert in her eyes – knew little or nothing – had not (as she had innocently hoped) built a bridge between the two men, but had somehow reinforced the wall between them.

Strike's burst of fame, his sudden shift from failure to success, had if anything deepened Matthew's animosity. Robin realised belatedly that she had only exacerbated matters by pointing out Matthew's inconsistencies: 'You don't like him being homeless and poor and now you don't like him getting famous and bringing in loads of work!'

But Strike's worst crime in Matthew's eyes, as she well knew, was the clinging designer dress that her boss had bought her after their trip to the hospital, the one that he had intended as a gift of gratitude and farewell, and which, after showing it to Matthew with pride and delight, and seeing his reaction, she had never dared wear.

All of this Robin hoped to fix with a face-to-face meeting, but repeated cancellations by Strike had merely deepened Matthew's dislike. On the last occasion, Strike had simply failed to turn up. His excuse – that he had been forced to take a detour to shake off a tail set on him by his client's suspicious spouse – had been accepted by Robin, who knew the intricacies of that particularly bloody divorce case, but it had reinforced Matthew's view of Strike as attention-seeking and arrogant.

She had had some difficulty in persuading Matthew to commit to a fourth attempt at drinks. Time and venue had both been picked by Matthew, but now, after Robin had secured Strike's agreement all over again, Matthew was changing the night and it was impossible not to feel that he was doing it to make a point, to show Strike that he too had other commitments; that he too (Robin could not help herself thinking it) could piss people around.

'Fine,' she sighed into the phone, 'I'll check with Cormoran and see whether Thursday's OK.'

'You don't sound like it's fine.'

'Matt, don't start. I'll ask him, OK?'

'I'll see you later, then.'

Robin replaced the receiver. Strike was now in full throat, snoring like a traction engine with his mouth open, legs wide apart, feet flat on the floor, arms folded.

She sighed, looking at her sleeping boss. Strike had never shown any animosity towards Matthew, had never passed comment on him in any way. It was Matthew who brooded over the existence of Strike, who rarely lost an opportunity to point out that Robin could have earned a great deal more if she had taken any of the other jobs she had been offered before deciding to stay with a rackety private detective, deep in debt and unable to pay her what she deserved. It would ease her home life considerably if Matthew could be brought to share her opinion of Cormoran Strike, to like him, even admire him. Robin was optimistic: she liked both of them, so why could they not like each other?

With a sudden snort, Strike was awake. He opened his eyes and blinked at her.

'I was snoring,' he stated, wiping his mouth.

'Not much,' she lied. 'Listen, Cormoran, would it be all right if we move drinks from Friday to Thursday?'

'Drinks?'

'With Matthew and me,' she said. 'Remember? The King's Arms, Roupell Street. I did write it down for you,' she said, with a slightly forced cheeriness.

'Right,' he said. 'Yeah. Friday.'

'No, Matt wants – he can't do Friday. Is it OK to do Thursday instead?'

'Yeah, fine,' he said groggily. 'I think I'm going to try and get some sleep, Robin.'

'All right. I'll make a note about Thursday.'

'What's happening on Thursday?'

'Drinks with – oh, never mind. Go and sleep.'

She sat staring blankly at her computer screen after the glass door had closed, then jumped as it opened again.

'Robin, could you call a bloke called Christian Fisher,' said Strike. 'Tell him who I am, tell him I'm looking for Owen Quine and that I need the address of the writer's retreat he told Quine about?'

'Christian Fisher . . . where does he work?'

'Bugger,' muttered Strike. 'I never asked. I'm so knackered. He's a publisher . . . trendy publisher.'

'No problem, I'll find him. Go and sleep.'

When the glass door had closed a second time, Robin turned her attention to Google. Within thirty seconds she had discovered that Christian Fisher was the founder of a small press called Crossfire, based in Exmouth Market.

As she dialled the publisher's number, she thought of the wedding invitation that had been sitting in her handbag for a week now. Robin had not told Strike the date of her and

Matthew's wedding, nor had she told Matthew that she wished to invite her boss. If Thursday's drinks went well . . .

'*Crossfire*,' said a shrill voice on the line. Robin focused her attention on the job in hand.

5

> There's nothing of so infinite vexation
> As man's own thoughts.
>
> John Webster, *The White Devil*

Twenty past nine that evening found Strike lying in a T-shirt and boxers on top of his duvet, with the remnants of a takeaway curry on the chair beside him, reading the sports pages while the news played on the TV he had set up facing the bed. The metal rod that served as his right ankle gleamed silver in the light from the cheap desk lamp he had placed on a box beside him.

There was to be an England–France friendly at Wembley on Wednesday night, but Strike was much more interested in Arsenal's home derby against Spurs the following Saturday. He had been an Arsenal fan since his earliest youth, in imitation of his Uncle Ted. Why Uncle Ted supported the Gunners, when he had lived all his life in Cornwall, was a question Strike had never asked.

A misty radiance, through which stars were struggling to twinkle, filled the night sky beyond the tiny window beside him. A few hours' sleep in the middle of the day had done virtually nothing to alleviate his exhaustion, but he did not feel quite ready to turn in yet, not after a large lamb biryani and a pint of beer. A note in Robin's handwriting lay beside him on the bed; she had given it to him as he had left the office that evening. Two appointments were noted there. The first read:

Christian Fisher, 9 a.m. tomorrow, Crossfire Publishing, Exmouth Market EC1

'Why's he want to see me?' Strike had asked her, surprised. 'I only need the address of that retreat he told Quine about.'

'I know,' said Robin, 'that's what I told him, but he sounded really excited to meet you. He said he could do nine tomorrow and wouldn't take no for an answer.'

What, Strike asked himself irritably, staring at the note, *was I playing at?*

Exhausted, he had allowed temper to get the better of him that morning and ditched a well-heeled client who might well have put more work his way. Then he had allowed Leonora Quine to steamroller him into accepting her as a client on the most dubious promise of payment. Now that she was not in front of him, it was hard to remember the mixture of pity and curiosity that had made him take her case on. In the stark, cold quiet of his attic room, his agreement to find her sulking husband seemed quixotic and irresponsible. Wasn't the whole point of trying to pay off his debts that he could regain a sliver of free time: a Saturday afternoon at the Emirates, a Sunday lie-in? He was finally making money after working almost non-stop for months, attracting clients not only because of that first glaring bout of notoriety but because of a quieter word-of-mouth. Couldn't he have put up with William Baker for another three weeks?

And what, Strike asked himself, looking down at Robin's

handwritten note again, was this Christian Fisher so excited about that he wanted to meet in person? Could it be Strike himself, either as the solver of the Lula Landry case or (much worse) as the son of Jonny Rokeby? It was very difficult to gauge the level of your own celebrity. Strike had assumed that his burst of unexpected fame was on the wane. It had been intense while it lasted, but the telephone calls from journalists had subsided months ago and it was almost as long since he had given his name in any neutral context and heard Lula Landry's back. Strangers were once again doing what they had done most of his life: calling him some variation on 'Cameron Strick'.

On the other hand, perhaps the publisher knew something about the vanished Owen Quine that he was eager to impart to Strike, although why, in this case, he had refused to tell Quine's wife, Strike could not imagine.

The second appointment that Robin had written out for him was beneath Fisher's:

Thursday November 18th, 6.30 p.m., The King's Arms, 25 Roupell Street, SE1

Strike knew why she had written the date out so clearly: she was determined that this time – was it the third or fourth time they'd tried? – he and her fiancé would finally meet.

Little though the unknown accountant might believe it, Strike was grateful for Matthew's mere existence, and for the sapphire and diamond ring that shone from Robin's third finger. Matthew sounded like a dickhead (Robin little imagined how accurately Strike remembered each of her casual asides about her fiancé), but he imposed a useful barrier between Strike and a girl who might otherwise disturb his equilibrium.

Strike had not been able to guard against warm feelings for Robin, who had stuck by him when he was at his lowest ebb and helped him turn his fortunes around; nor, having normal eyesight, could he escape the fact that she was a very good-looking woman. He viewed her engagement as the means by which a thin, persistent draught is blocked up, something that might, if allowed to flow untrammelled, start to seriously disturb his comfort. Strike considered himself to be in recovery after a long, turbulent relationship that had ended, as indeed it had begun, in lies. He had no wish to alter his single status, which he found comfortable and convenient, and had successfully avoided any further emotional entanglements for months, in spite of his sister Lucy's attempts to fix him up with women who sounded like the desperate dregs of some dating site.

Of course, it was possible that once Matthew and Robin were actually married, Matthew might use his improved status to persuade his new wife to leave the job that he clearly disliked her doing (Strike had correctly interpreted Robin's hesitations and evasions on that score). However, Strike was sure that Robin would have told him, had the wedding date been fixed, so he considered that danger, at present, remote.

With yet another huge yawn, he folded the newspaper and threw it onto the chair, turning his attention to the television news. His one personal extravagance since moving into the tiny attic flat had been satellite TV. His small portable set now sat on top of a Sky box and the picture, no longer reliant on a feeble indoor aerial, was sharp instead of grainy. Kenneth Clarke, the Justice Secretary, was announcing plans to slash £350 million from the legal aid budget. Strike watched through his haze of tiredness as the florid, paunchy man told Parliament that he wished to 'discourage people from resorting to lawyers whenever they face a problem, and instead encourage them to consider more suitable methods of dispute resolution'.

He meant, of course, that poor people ought to relinquish the services of the law. The likes of Strike's average client would still avail themselves of expensive barristers. Most of his work these days was undertaken on behalf of the mistrustful, endlessly betrayed rich. His was the information that fed their sleek lawyers, that enabled them to win better settlements in their vitriolic divorces and their acrimonious business disputes. A steady stream of well-heeled clients was passing his name on to similar men and women, with tediously similar difficulties; this was the reward for distinction in his particular line of work, and if it was often repetitive, it was also lucrative.

When the news ended he clambered laboriously off the bed, removed the remnants of his meal from the chair beside him and walked stiffly into his small kitchen area to wash everything up. He never neglected such things: habits of self-respect learned in the army had not left him in the depths of his poverty, nor were they entirely due to military training. He had been a tidy boy, imitating his Uncle Ted, whose liking for order everywhere from his toolbox to his boathouse had contrasted so starkly with the chaos that had surrounded Strike's mother Leda.

Within ten minutes, after a last pee in the toilet that was always sodden because of its proximity to the shower, and cleaning his teeth at the kitchen sink where there was more room, Strike was back on his bed, removing his prosthesis.

The weather forecast for the next day was rounding off the news: sub-zero temperatures and fog. Strike rubbed powder into the end of his amputated leg; it was less sore tonight than it had been a few months ago. Today's full English breakfast and takeaway curry notwithstanding, he had lost a bit of weight since he had been able to cook for himself again, and this had eased the pressure on his leg.

He pointed the remote control at the TV screen; a laughing blonde and her washing powder vanished into blankness. Strike manoeuvred himself clumsily beneath the covers.

Of course, if Owen Quine was hiding at his writer's retreat it would be easy enough to winkle him out. Egotistical bastard, he sounded, flouncing off into the darkness with his precious book . . .

The hazy mental image of a furious man storming away with a holdall over his shoulder dissolved almost as quickly as it had formed. Strike was sliding into a welcome, deep and dreamless sleep. The faint pulse of a bass guitar far below in the subterranean bar was swiftly drowned by his own rasping snores.

6

Oh, Mr Tattle, every thing is safe with you, we know.

William Congreve, *Love for Love*

Wads of icy mist were still clinging to the buildings of Exmouth Market when Strike turned into it at ten to nine the following morning. It did not feel like a London street, not with pavement seating outside its many cafés, pastel-painted façades and a basilica-like church, gold, blue and brick: Church of Our Most Holy Redeemer, wreathed in smoky vapour. Chilly fog, shops full of curios, kerb-side tables and chairs; if he could have added the tang of salt water and the mournful screech of seagulls he might have thought himself back in Cornwall, where he had spent the most stable parts of his childhood.

A small sign on a nondescript door beside a bakery announced the offices of Crossfire Publishing. Strike buzzed the bell promptly at nine o'clock and was admitted to a steep white-washed staircase, up which he clambered with some difficulty and with liberal use of the handrail.

He was met on the top landing by a slight, dandyish and bespectacled man of around thirty. He had wavy, shoulder-length hair and wore jeans, a waistcoat and a paisley shirt with a touch of frill around the cuffs.

'Hi there,' he said. 'I'm Christian Fisher. Cameron, isn't it?'

'Cormoran,' Strike corrected him automatically, 'but—'

He had been about to say that he answered to Cameron, a stock response to years of the mistake, but Christian Fisher came back at once:

'Cormoran – Cornish giant.'

'That's right,' said Strike, surprised.

'We published a kids' book on English folklore last year,' said Fisher, pushing open white double doors and leading Strike into a cluttered, open-plan space with walls plastered in posters and many untidy bookshelves. A scruffy young woman with dark hair looked up curiously at Strike as he walked past.

'Coffee? Tea?' offered Fisher, leading Strike into his own office, a small room off the main area with a pleasant view over the sleepy, foggy street. 'I can get Jade to nip out for us.' Strike declined, saying truthfully that he had just had coffee, but wondering, too, why Fisher seemed to be settling in for a longer meeting than Strike felt the circumstances justified. 'Just a latte, then, Jade,' Fisher called through the door.

'Have a seat,' Fisher said to Strike, and he began to flit around the bookshelves that lined the walls. 'Didn't he live in St Michael's Mount, the giant Cormoran?'

'Yeah,' said Strike. 'And Jack's supposed to have killed him. Of beanstalk fame.'

'It's here somewhere,' said Fisher, still searching the shelves. '*Folk Tales of the British Isles*. Have you got kids?'

'No,' said Strike.

'Oh,' said Fisher. 'Well, I won't bother, then.'

And with a grin he took the chair opposite Strike.

'So, am I allowed to ask who's hired you? Am I allowed to guess?'

'Feel free,' said Strike, who on principle never forbade speculation.

'It's either Daniel Chard or Michael Fancourt,' said Fisher. 'Am I right?'

The lenses on his glasses gave his eyes a concentrated, beady look. Though giving no outward sign, Strike was taken aback. Michael Fancourt was a very famous writer who had recently won a major literary prize. Why exactly would he be interested in the missing Quine?

'Afraid not,' said Strike. 'It's Quine's wife, Leonora.'

Fisher looked almost comically astonished.

'His wife?' he repeated blankly. 'That mousy woman who looks like Rose West? What's *she* hired a private detective for?'

'Her husband's disappeared. He's been gone eleven days.'

'Quine's *disappeared*? But – but then . . .'

Strike could tell Fisher had been anticipating a very different conversation, one to which he had been eagerly looking forward.

'But why's she sent you to me?'

'She thinks you know where Quine is.'

'How the hell would I know?' asked Fisher, and he appeared genuinely bewildered. 'He's not a friend of mine.'

'Mrs Quine says she heard you telling her husband about a writer's retreat, at a party—'

'*Oh*,' said Fisher, 'Bigley Hall, yeah. But Owen won't be *there*!' When he laughed, he was transformed into a bespectacled Puck: merriment laced with slyness. 'They wouldn't let Owen Quine in if he paid them. Born shit-stirrer. And one of the women who runs the place hates his guts. He wrote a stinking review of her first novel and she's never forgiven him.'

'Could you give me the number anyway?' asked Strike.

'I've got it on here,' said Fisher, pulling a mobile out of the back pocket of his jeans. 'I'll call now . . .'

And he did so, setting the mobile on the desk between them and switching it on to speakerphone for Strike's benefit. After a full minute of ringing, a breathless female voice answered:

'Bigley Hall.'

'Hi, is that Shannon? It's Chris Fisher here, from Crossfire.'

'Oh, hi Chris, how's it going?'

The door of Fisher's office opened and the scruffy dark girl from outside came in, wordlessly placed a latte in front of Fisher and departed.

'I'm phoning, Shan,' Fisher said, as the door clicked shut, 'to see if you've got Owen Quine staying. He hasn't turned up there, has he?'

'*Quine?*'

Even reduced to a distant and tinny monosyllable, Shannon's dislike echoed scornfully around the book-lined room.

'Yeah, have you seen him?'

'Not for a year or more. Why? He's not thinking of coming here, is he? He won't be bloody welcome, I can tell you that.'

'No worries, Shan, I think his wife's got hold of the wrong end of the stick. Speak soon.'

Fisher cut off her farewells, keen to return to Strike.

'See?' he said. 'Told you. He couldn't go to Bigley Hall if he wanted to.'

'Couldn't you have told his wife that, when she phoned you up?'

'Oh, *that's* what she kept calling about!' said Fisher with an air of dawning comprehension. 'I thought *Owen* was making her call me.'

'Why would he make his wife phone you?'

'Oh, come on,' said Fisher, with a grin, and when Strike did not grin back, he laughed shortly and said, 'Because of *Bombyx Mori*. I thought it'd be typical of Quine to try to get his wife to call me and sound me out.'

'*Bombyx Mori*,' repeated Strike, trying to sound neither interrogative nor puzzled.

'Yeah, I thought Quine was pestering me to see whether there was still a chance I'd publish it. It's the sort of thing he'd do, make his wife ring. But if anyone's going to touch *Bombyx Mori* now, it won't be me. We're a small outfit. We can't afford court cases.'

Gaining nothing from pretending to know more than he did, Strike changed tack.

'*Bombyx Mori*'s Quine's latest novel?'

'Yeah,' said Fisher, taking a sip of his takeaway latte, following his own train of thought. 'So he's disappeared, has he? I'd've thought he'd want to stick around and watch the fun. I'd've thought that was the whole point. Or has he lost his nerve? Doesn't sound like Owen.'

'How long have you published Quine?' asked Strike. Fisher looked at him incredulously.

'I've never published him!' he said.

'I thought—'

'He's been with Roper Chard for his last three books – or is it four? No, what happened was, I was at a party with Liz Tassel, his agent, a few months ago, and she told me in confidence – she'd had a few – that she didn't know how much longer Roper Chard were going to put up with him, so I said I'd be happy to have a look at his next one. Quine's in the so-bad-he's-good category these days – we could've done something offbeat with the marketing. Anyway,' said Fisher, 'there *was Hobart's Sin*. That was a good book. I figured he might still have something in him.'

'Did she send you *Bombyx Mori*?' asked Strike, feeling his way and inwardly cursing himself for the lack of thoroughness with which he had questioned Leonora Quine the previous day. This was what came of taking on clients when you were three parts dead of exhaustion. Strike was used to coming to interviews knowing more than the interviewee and he felt curiously exposed.

'Yeah, she biked me over a copy Friday before last,' said Fisher, his Puckish smirk slyer than ever. 'Biggest mistake of poor Liz's life.'

'Why?'

'Because she obviously hadn't read it properly, or not all the way to the end. About two hours after it arrived I got this very panicky message on my phone: "Chris, there's been a mistake, I've sent the wrong manuscript. Please don't read it, could you just send it straight back, I'll be at the office to take it." I've never heard Liz Tassel like that in my life. Very scary woman usually. Makes grown men cower.'

'And did you send it back?'

'Course not,' said Fisher. 'I spent most of Saturday reading it.'

'And?' asked Strike.

'Hasn't anyone told you?'

'Told me . . . ?'

'What's in there,' said Fisher. 'What he's done.'

'What has he done?'

Fisher's smile faded. He put down his coffee.

'I've been warned,' he said, 'by some of London's top lawyers not to disclose that.'

'Who's employing the lawyers?' asked Strike. When Fisher

didn't answer, he added, 'Anyone apart from Chard and Fancourt?'

'It's just Chard,' said Fisher, toppling easily into Strike's trap. 'Though I'd be more worried about Fancourt if I were Owen. He can be an evil bastard. Never forgets a grudge. Don't quote me,' he added hastily.

'And the Chard you're talking about?' said Strike, groping in semi-darkness.

'Daniel Chard, CEO of Roper Chard,' said Fisher, with a trace of impatience. 'I don't understand how Owen thought he'd get away with screwing over the man who runs his publisher, but that's Owen for you. He's the most monumentally arrogant, deluded bastard I've ever met. I suppose he thought he could depict Chard as—'

Fisher broke off with an uneasy laugh.

'I'm a danger to myself. Let's just say I'm surprised that even Owen thought he'd get away with it. Maybe he lost his nerve when he realised everyone knew exactly what he was hinting at and that's why he's done a runner.'

'It's libellous, is it?' Strike asked.

'Bit of a grey area in fiction, isn't it?' asked Fisher. 'If you tell the truth in a grotesque way – not that I'm suggesting,' he added hastily, 'that the stuff he's saying is *true*. It couldn't be *literally* true. But everyone's recognisable; he's done over quite a few people and in a very clever way . . . It feels a lot like Fancourt's early stuff, actually. Load of gore and arcane symbolism . . . you can't see quite what he's getting at in some places, but you want to know, what's in the bag, what's in the fire?'

'What's in the—?'

'Never mind – it's just stuff in the book. Didn't Leonora tell you any of this?'

'No,' said Strike.

'Bizarre,' said Christian Fisher, 'she must *know*. I'd've thought Quine's the sort of writer who lectures the family on his work at every mealtime.'

'Why did you think Chard or Fancourt would hire a private detective, when you didn't know Quine was missing?'

Fisher shrugged.

'I dunno. I thought maybe one of them was trying to find out what he's planning to do with the book, so they could stop him, or warn the new publisher they'll sue. Or that they might be hoping to get something on Owen – fight fire with fire.'

'Is that why you were so keen to see me?' asked Strike. 'Have you got something on Quine?'

'No,' said Fisher with a laugh. 'I'm just nosy. Wanted to know what's going on.'

He checked his watch, turned over a copy of a book cover in front of him and pushed out his chair a little. Strike took the hint.

'Thanks for your time,' he said, standing up. 'If you hear from Owen Quine, will you let me know?'

He handed Fisher a card. Fisher frowned at it as he moved around his desk to show Strike out.

'Cormoran Strike ... *Strike* ... I know that name, don't I ...?'

The penny dropped. Fisher was suddenly reanimated, as though his batteries had been changed.

'Bloody hell, you're the Lula Landry guy!'

Strike knew that he could have sat back down, ordered a latte and enjoyed Fisher's undivided attention for another hour or so. Instead, he extricated himself with firm friendliness and, within a few minutes, re-emerged alone on the cold misty street.

7

I'll be sworn, I was ne'er guilty of reading the like.

Ben Jonson, *Every Man in His Humour*

When informed by telephone that her husband was not, after all, at the writer's retreat, Leonora Quine sounded anxious.

'Where is he, then?' she asked, more of herself, it seemed, than Strike.

'Where does he usually go when he walks out?' Strike asked.

'Hotels,' she said, 'and once he was staying with some woman but he don't know her no more. Orlando,' she said sharply, away from the receiver, 'put that *down*, it's mine. I said, it's *mine*. What?' she said, loudly in Strike's ear.

'I didn't say anything. D'you want me to keep looking for your husband?'

'Course I do, who else is gonna bloody find him? I can't leave Orlando. Ask Liz Tassel where he is. She found him before. Hilton,' said Leonora unexpectedly. 'He was at the Hilton once.'

'Which Hilton?'

'I dunno, ask Liz. She made him go off, she should be bloody helping bring him back. She won't take my calls. Orlando, *put it down*.'

'Is there anyone else you can think—?'

'No, or I'd've bloody asked them, wouldn't I?' snapped Leonora. 'You're the detective, you find him! *Orlando!*'

'Mrs Quine, we've got—'

'Call me Leonora.'

'Leonora, we've got to consider the possibility that your husband might have done himself an injury. We'd find him more quickly,' said Strike, raising his voice over the domestic clamour at the other end of the line, 'if we involved the police.'

'I don't wanna. I called them that time he was gone a week and he turned up at his lady friend's and they weren't happy. He'll be angry if I do that again. Anyway, Owen wouldn't – *Orlando, leave it!*'

'The police could circulate his picture more effectively and—'

'I just want him home quietly. Why doesn't he just come back?' she added pettishly. 'He's had time to calm down.'

'Have you read your husband's new book?' Strike asked.

'No. I always wait till they're finished and I can read 'em with proper covers on and everything.'

'Has he told you anything about it?'

'No, he don't like talking about work while he's – *Orlando, put it down!*'

He was not sure whether she had hung up deliberately or not.

The fog of early morning had lifted. Rain was speckling his office windows. A client was due imminently, yet another divorcing woman who wanted to know where her soon-to-be-ex husband was burying assets.

'Robin,' said Strike, emerging into the outer office, 'will you print me out a picture of Owen Quine off the internet, if you can find one? And call his agent, Elizabeth Tassel, and see if she's willing to answer a few quick questions.'

About to return to his own office, he thought of something else.

'And could you look up "bombyx mori" for me, and see what it means?'

'How are you spelling that?'

'God knows,' said Strike.

The soon-to-be divorcée arrived on time, at eleven thirty. She was a suspiciously youthful-looking forty-something who exuded fluttery charm and a musky scent that always made the office feel cramped to Robin. Strike disappeared into his office with her, and for two hours Robin heard only the gentle rise and fall of their voices over the steady thrumming of the rain and the tapping of her fingers on the keyboard; calm and placid sounds. Robin had become used to hearing sudden outbreaks of tears, moans, even shouting from Strike's office. Sudden silences could be the most ominous of all, as when a male client had literally fainted (and, they had learned later, suffered a minor heart attack) on seeing the photographs of his wife and her lover that Strike had taken through a long lens.

When Strike and his client emerged at last, and she had taken fulsome farewell of him, Robin handed her boss a large picture of Owen Quine, taken from the website of the Bath Literature Festival.

'Jesus Christ almighty,' said Strike.

Owen Quine was a large, pale and portly man of around sixty, with straggly yellow-white hair and a pointed Van Dyke beard. His eyes appeared to be of different colours, which gave a peculiar intensity to his stare. For the photograph he had wrapped himself in what seemed to be a Tyrolean cape and was wearing a feather-trimmed trilby.

'You wouldn't think he'd be able to stay incognito for long,' commented Strike. 'Can you make a few copies of this, Robin? We might have to show it around hotels. His wife thinks he once stayed at a Hilton, but she can't remember which one, so could you start ringing round to see if he's booked in? Can't imagine he'd use his own name, but you could try describing him . . . Any luck with Elizabeth Tassel?'

'Yes,' said Robin. 'Believe it or not, I was just about to call her when she called me.'

'She called here? Why?'

'Christian Fisher's told her you've been to see him.'

'And?'

'She's got meetings this afternoon, but she wants to meet you at eleven o'clock tomorrow at her office.'

'Does she, now?' said Strike, looking amused. 'More and more interesting. Did you ask her if she knows where Quine is?'

'Yes; she says she hasn't got a clue, but she was still adamant she wants to meet you. She's very bossy. Like a headmistress. And *Bombyx mori*,' she finished up, 'is the Latin name for a silkworm.'

'A silkworm?'

'Yeah, and you know what? I always thought they were like spiders spinning their webs, but you know how they get silk from the worms?'

'Can't say I do.'

'They boil them,' said Robin. 'Boil them alive, so that they don't damage their cocoons by bursting out of them. It's the cocoons that are made of silk. Not very nice, really, is it? Why did you want to know about silkworms?'

'I wanted to know why Owen Quine might have called his novel *Bombyx Mori*,' said Strike. 'Can't say I'm any the wiser.'

He spent the afternoon on tedious paperwork relating to a

surveillance case and hoping the weather might improve: he would need to go out as he had virtually nothing to eat upstairs. After Robin had left, Strike continued working while the rain pounding his window became steadily heavier. Finally he pulled on his overcoat and walked, in what was now a downpour, down a sodden, dark Charing Cross Road to buy food at the nearest supermarket. There had been too many takeaways lately.

On the way back up the road, with bulging carrier bags in both hands, he turned on impulse into a second-hand bookshop that was about to close. The man behind the counter was unsure whether they had a copy of *Hobart's Sin*, Owen Quine's first book and supposedly his best, but after a lot of inconclusive mumbling and an unconvincing perusal of his computer screen, offered Strike a copy of *The Balzac Brothers* by the same author. Tired, wet and hungry, Strike paid two pounds for the battered hardback and took it home to his attic flat.

Having put away his provisions and cooked himself pasta, Strike stretched out on his bed as night pressed dense, dark and cold at his windows, and opened the missing man's book.

The style was ornate and florid, the story gothic and surreal. Two brothers by the names of Varicocele and Vas were locked inside a vaulted room while the corpse of their older brother decayed slowly in a corner. In between drunken arguments about literature, loyalty and the French writer Balzac, they attempted to co-author an account of their decomposing brother's life. Varicocele constantly palpated his aching balls, which seemed to Strike to be a clumsy metaphor for writer's block; Vas seemed to be doing most of the work.

After fifty pages, and with a murmur of 'Bollocks is right', Strike threw the book aside and began the laborious process of turning in.

The deep and blissful stupor of the previous night eluded him. Rain hammered against the window of his attic room and his sleep was disturbed; confused dreams of catastrophe filled the night. Strike woke in the morning with the uneasy aftermath clinging over him like a hangover. The rain was still pounding on his window, and when he turned on his TV he saw that Cornwall had been hit by severe flooding; people were trapped in cars, or evacuated from their homes and now huddled in emergency centres.

Strike snatched up his mobile phone and called the number, familiar to him as his own reflection in the mirror, that all his life had represented security and stability.

'Hello?' said his aunt.

'It's Cormoran. You all right, Joan? I've just seen the news.'

'We're all right at the moment, love, it's up the coast it's bad,' she said. 'It's wet, mind you, blowing up a storm, but nothing like St Austell. Just been watching it on the news ourselves. How are you, Corm? It's been ages. Ted and I were just saying last night, we haven't heard from you, and we were wanting to say, why don't you come for Christmas as you're on your own again? What do you think?'

He was unable to dress or to fasten on his prosthesis while holding the mobile. She talked for half an hour, an unstoppable gush of local chat and sudden, darting forays into personal territory he preferred to leave unprobed. At last, after a final blast of interrogation about his love life, his debts and his amputated leg, she let him go.

Strike arrived in the office late, tired and irritable. He was wearing a dark suit and tie. Robin wondered whether he was going to meet the divorcing brunette for lunch after his meeting with Elizabeth Tassel.

'Heard the news?'

'Floods in Cornwall?' Strike asked, switching on the kettle, because his first tea of the day had grown cold while Joan gabbled.

'William and Kate are engaged,' said Robin.

'Who?'

'Prince William,' said Robin, amused, 'and Kate Middleton.'

'Oh,' said Strike coldly. 'Good for them.'

He had been among the ranks of the engaged himself until a few months ago. He did not know how his ex-fiancée's new engagement was proceeding, nor did he enjoy wondering when it was going to end. (Not as theirs had ended, of course, with her clawing her betrothed's face and revealing her betrayal, but with the kind of wedding he could never have given her; more like the one William and Kate would no doubt soon enjoy.)

Robin judged it safe to break the moody silence only once Strike had had half a mug of tea.

'Lucy called just before you came down, to remind you about your birthday dinner on Saturday night, and to ask whether you want to bring anyone.'

Strike's spirits slipped several more notches. He had forgotten all about the dinner at his sister's house.

'Right,' he said heavily.

'Is it your birthday on Saturday?' Robin asked.

'No,' said Strike.

'When is it?'

He sighed. He did not want a cake, a card or presents, but her expression was expectant.

'Tuesday,' he said.

'The twenty-third?'

'Yeah.'

After a short pause, it occurred to him that he ought to reciprocate.

'And when's yours?' Something in her hesitation unnerved him. 'Christ, it's not today, is it?'

She laughed.

'No, it's gone. October the ninth. It's all right, it was a Saturday,' she said, still smiling at his pained expression. 'I wasn't sitting here all day expecting flowers.'

He grinned back. Feeling he ought to make a little extra effort, because he had missed her birthday and never considered finding out when it was, he added:

'Good thing you and Matthew haven't set a date yet. At least you won't clash with the Royal Wedding.'

'Oh,' said Robin, blushing, 'we have set a date.'

'You have?'

'Yes,' said Robin. 'It's the – the eighth of January. I've got your invitation here,' she said, stooping hurriedly over her bag (she had not even asked Matthew about inviting Strike, but too late for that). 'Here.'

'The eighth of January?' Strike said, taking the silver envelope. 'That's only – what? – seven weeks away.'

'Yes,' said Robin.

There was a strange little pause. Strike could not remember immediately what else he wanted her to do; then it came back to him, and as he spoke he tapped the silver envelope against his palm, businesslike.

'How's it going with the Hiltons?'

'I've done a few. Quine isn't there under his own name and nobody's recognised the description. There are loads of them, though, so I'm just working my way through the list. What are you up to after you see Elizabeth Tassel?' she asked casually.

'Pretending I want to buy a flat in Mayfair. Looks like somebody's husband's trying to realise some capital and take it offshore before his wife's lawyers can stop him.

'Well,' he said, pushing the unopened wedding invitation deep into his overcoat pocket, 'better be off. Got a bad author to find.'

8

I took the book and so the old man vanished.

John Lyly, *Endymion: or, the Man in the Moon*

It occurred to Strike as he travelled, standing, the one Tube stop to Elizabeth Tassel's office (he was never fully relaxed on these short journeys, but braced to take the strain on his false leg, wary of falls) that Robin had not reproached him for taking on the Quine case. Not, of course, that it was her place to reproach her employer, but she had turned down a much higher salary to throw her lot in with his and it would not have been unreasonable for her to expect that once the debts were paid, a raise might be the least he could do for her. She was unusual in her lack of criticism, or critical silence; the only female in Strike's life who seemed to have no desire to improve or correct him. Women, in his experience, often expected you to understand that it was a measure of how much they loved you that they tried their damnedest to change you.

So she was marrying in seven weeks' time. Seven weeks left until she became Mrs Matthew . . . but if he had ever known her fiancé's surname, he could not recall it.

As he waited for the lift at Goodge Street, Strike experienced a sudden, crazy urge to call his divorcing brunette client – who had made it quite clear that she would welcome such a development – with a view to screwing her tonight in what he imagined would be her deep, soft, heavily perfumed bed in Knightsbridge. But the idea occurred only to be instantly dismissed. Such a move would be insanity; worse than taking on a missing-person case for which he was unlikely ever to see payment . . .

And why *was* he wasting time on Owen Quine? he asked himself, head bowed against the biting rain. Curiosity, he answered inwardly after a few moments' thought, and perhaps something more elusive. As he headed down Store Street, squinting through the downpour and concentrating on maintaining his footing on the slippery pavements, he reflected that his palate was in danger of becoming jaded by the endless variations on cupidity and vengefulness that his wealthy clients kept bringing him. It had been a long time since he had investigated a missing-person case. There would be satisfaction in restoring the runaway Quine to his family.

Elizabeth Tassel's literary agency lay in a mostly residential mews of dark brick, a surprisingly quiet cul-de-sac off busy Gower Street. Strike pressed a doorbell beside a discreet brass plaque. A light thumping sound ensued and a pale young man in an open-necked shirt opened the door at the foot of red-carpeted stairs.

'Are you the private detective?' he asked with what seemed to be a mixture of trepidation and excitement. Strike followed him, dripping all over the threadbare carpet, up the stairs to a mahogany door and into a large office space that had once, perhaps, been a separate hall and sitting room.

Aged elegance was slowly disintegrating into shabbiness. The windows were misty with condensation and the air heavy with old cigarette smoke. A plethora of overstocked wooden bookcases lined the walls and the dingy wallpaper was almost obscured by framed literary caricatures and cartoons. Two heavy desks sat facing each other across a scuffed rug, but neither was occupied.

'Can I take your coat?' the young man asked, and a thin and frightened-looking girl jumped up from behind one of the desks. She was holding a stained sponge in one hand.

'I can't get it out, Ralph!' she whispered frantically to the young man with Strike.

'Bloody thing,' Ralph muttered irritably. 'Elizabeth's decrepit old dog's puked under Sally's desk,' he confided, *sotto voce*, as he took Strike's sodden Crombie and hung it on a Victorian coat-stand just inside the door. 'I'll let her know you're here. Just keep scrubbing,' he advised his colleague as he crossed to a second mahogany door and opened it a crack.

'That's Mr Strike, Liz.'

There was a loud bark, followed immediately by a deep, rattling human cough that could have plausibly issued from the lungs of an old coal miner.

'Grab him,' said a hoarse voice.

The door to the agent's office opened, revealing Ralph, who was holding tight to the collar of an aged but evidently still feisty Dobermann pinscher, and a tall, thick-set woman of around sixty, with large, uncompromisingly plain features. The geometrically perfect steel-grey bob, a black suit of severe cut and a slash of crimson lipstick gave her a certain dash. She emanated that aura of grandeur that replaces sexual allure in the successful older woman.

'You'd better take him out, Ralph,' said the agent, her olive-dark eyes on Strike. The rain was still pelting against the windows. 'And don't forget the poo bags, he's a bit soft today.'

'Come in, Mr Strike.'

Looking disgusted, her assistant dragged the big dog, with its head like a living Anubis, out of her office; as Strike and the Dobermann passed each other, it growled energetically.

'Coffee, Sally,' the agent shot at the frightened-looking girl who had concealed her sponge. As she jumped up and vanished through a door behind her desk, Strike hoped she would wash her hands thoroughly before making drinks.

Elizabeth Tassel's stuffy office was a kind of concentration of the outer room: it stank of cigarettes and old dog. A tweed bed for the animal sat under her desk; the walls were plastered with old photographs and prints. Strike recognised one of the largest: a reasonably well-known and elderly writer of illustrated children's books called Pinkelman, whom he was not sure was still alive. After indicating wordlessly that Strike should take the seat opposite her, from which he had first to remove a stack of papers and old copies of the *Bookseller*, the agent took a cigarette from a box on the desk, lit it with an onyx lighter, inhaled deeply then broke into a protracted fit of rattling, wheezing coughs.

'So,' she croaked when these had subsided and she had returned to the leather chair behind the desk, 'Christian Fisher tells me that Owen's put in another of his famous vanishing acts.'

'That's right,' said Strike. 'He disappeared the night that you and he argued about his book.'

She began to speak, but the words disintegrated immediately into further coughs. Horrible, tearing noises issued from deep in her torso. Strike waited in silence for the fit to pass.

'Sounds nasty,' he said at last, when she had coughed herself into silence again and, incredibly, taken another deep drag of her cigarette.

'Flu,' she rasped. 'Can't shake it. When did Leonora come to you?'

'The day before yesterday.'

'Can she afford you?' she croaked. 'I wouldn't have thought you come cheap, the man who solved the Landry case.'

'Mrs Quine suggested that you might pay me,' said Strike.

The coarse cheeks purpled and her dark eyes, watery from so much coughing, narrowed.

'Well, you can go straight back to Leonora' – her chest began to heave beneath the smart black jacket as she fought off the desire to cough again – 'and tell her that I won't pay a p-penny to get that bastard back. He's no – no longer my client. Tell her – tell her—'

She was overtaken by another giant explosion of coughing.

The door opened and the thin female assistant entered, struggling under the weight of a heavy wooden tray laden with cups and a cafetière. Strike got up to take it from her; there was barely room on the desk to set it down. The girl attempted to make a space. In her nerves, she knocked over a stack of papers.

A furious admonitory gesture from the coughing agent sent the girl scuttling from the room in fright.

'Use-useless – little—' wheezed Elizabeth Tassel.

Strike put the tray down on the desk, ignoring the scattered papers all over the carpet, and resumed his seat. The agent was a bully in a familiar mould: one of those older women who capitalised, whether consciously or not, on the fact that they awoke in those who were susceptible, childhood memories of demanding and all-powerful mothers. Strike was immune to such intimidation. For one thing, his own mother, whatever her faults, had been young and openly adoring; for another, he sensed vulnerability in this apparent dragon. The chain-smoking, the fading photographs and the old dog basket suggested a more sentimental, less self-assured woman than her young hirelings might think.

When at last she had finished coughing, he handed her a cup of coffee he had poured.

'Thank you,' she muttered gruffly.

'So you've sacked Quine?' he asked. 'Did you tell him so, the night you had dinner?'

'I can't remember,' she croaked. 'Things got heated very quickly. Owen stood up in the middle of the restaurant, the better to shout at me, then flounced out leaving me to pay the bill. You'll find plenty of witnesses to what was said, if you're interested. Owen made sure it was a nice, public scene.'

She reached for another cigarette and, as an afterthought, offered Strike one. After she had lit both, she said:

'What's Christian Fisher told you?'

'Not much,' said Strike.

'I hope for both your sakes that's true,' she snapped.

Strike said nothing, but smoked and drank his coffee while Elizabeth waited, clearly hoping for more information.

'Did he mention *Bombyx Mori*?' she asked.

Strike nodded.

'What did he say about it?'

'That Quine's put a lot of recognisable people in the book, thinly disguised.'

There was a charged pause.

'I hope Chard *does* sue him. That's his idea of keeping his mouth shut, is it?'

'Have you tried to contact Quine since he walked out of –

where was it you were having dinner?' Strike asked.

'The River Café,' she croaked. 'No, I haven't tried to contact him. There's nothing left to say.'

'And he hasn't contacted you?'

'No.'

'Leonora says you told Quine his book was the best thing he'd ever produced, then changed your mind and refused to represent it.'

'She says *what*? That's *not* what – *not* – what I s—'

It was her worst paroxysm of coughing yet. Strike felt a strong urge to forcibly remove the cigarette from her hand as she hacked and spluttered. Finally the fit passed. She drank half a cup of hot coffee straight off, which seemed to bring her some relief. In a stronger voice, she repeated:

'That's *not* what I said. "The best thing he'd ever written" – is that what he told Leonora?'

'Yes. What did you really say?'

'I was ill,' she said hoarsely, ignoring the question. 'Flu. Off work for a week. Owen rang the office to tell me the novel was finished; Ralph told him I was at home in bed, so Owen couriered the manuscript straight to my house. I had to get up to sign for it. Absolutely typical of him. I had a temperature of a hundred and four and could barely stand. His book was finished so I was expected to read it *immediately*.'

She slugged down more coffee and said:

'I chucked the manuscript on the hall table and went straight back to bed. Owen started ringing me, virtually on the hour, to see what I thought. All through Wednesday and Thursday he badgered me . . .

'I've never done it before in thirty years in the business,' she croaked. 'I was supposed to be going away that weekend. I'd been looking forward to it. I didn't want to cancel and I didn't want Owen calling me every three minutes while I was away. So . . . just to get him off my back . . . I was still feeling awful . . . I skim-read it.'

She took a deep drag on her cigarette, coughed routinely, composed herself and said:

'It didn't look any worse than his last couple. If anything, it was an improvement. Quite an interesting premise. Some of the imagery was arresting. A Gothic fairy tale, a grisly *Pilgrim's Progress*.'

'Did you recognise anyone in the bits you read?'

'The characters seemed mostly symbolic,' she said, a touch defensively, 'including the hagiographic self-portrait. Lots of p-perverse sex.' She paused to cough again. 'The mixture as usual, I thought . . . but I – I wasn't reading carefully, I'd be the first to admit that.'

He could tell that she was not used to admitting fault.

'I – well, I skimmed the last quarter, the bits where he writes about Michael and Daniel. I glanced at the ending, which was grotesque and a bit silly . . .

'If I hadn't been so ill, if I'd read it properly, naturally I'd have told him straight away that he wouldn't be able to get away with it. Daniel's a st-strange man, very t-touchy' – her voice was breaking up again; determined to finish her sentence she wheezed, 'and M-Michael's the nastiest – the nastiest—' before exploding again into coughs.

'Why would Mr Quine try and publish something that was bound to get him sued?' Strike asked when she had stopped coughing.

'Because Owen doesn't think he's subject to the same laws as the rest of society,' she said roughly. 'He thinks himself a genius, an *enfant terrible*. He takes pride in causing offence. He thinks it's brave, heroic.'

'What did you do with the book when you'd looked at it?'

'I called Owen,' she said, closing her eyes momentarily in what seemed to be fury at herself. 'And said, "Yes, jolly good," and I got Ralph to pick the damn thing up from my house, and asked him to make two copies, and send one to Jerry Waldegrave, Owen's editor at Roper Chard and the other, G-God help me, to Christian Fisher.'

'Why didn't you just email the manuscript to the office?' asked Strike curiously. 'Didn't you have it on a memory stick or something?'

She ground out her cigarette in a glass ashtray full of stubs.

'Owen insists on continuing to use the old electric typewriter on which he wrote *Hobart's Sin*. I don't know whether it's affectation or stupidity. He's remarkably ignorant about technology. Maybe he tried to use a laptop and couldn't. It's just another way he contrives to make himself awkward.'

'And why did you send copies to two publishers?' asked Strike, although he already knew the answer.

'Because Jerry Waldegrave might be a blessed saint and the nicest man in publishing,' she replied, sipping more coffee, 'but even *he's* lost patience with Owen and his tantrums lately. Owen's last book for Roper Chard barely sold. I thought it was only sensible to have a second string to our bow.'

'When did you realise what the book was really about?'

'Early that evening,' she croaked. 'Ralph called me. He'd sent off the two copies and then had a flick through the original. He phoned me and said, "Liz, have you actually read this?"'

Strike could well imagine the trepidation with which the pale young assistant had made the call, the courage it had taken, the agonised deliberation with his female colleague before he had reached his decision.

'I had to admit I hadn't . . . or not thoroughly,' she muttered. 'He read me a few choice excerpts I'd missed and . . .'

She picked up the onyx lighter and flicked it absently before looking up at Strike.

'Well, I panicked. I phoned Christian Fisher, but the call went straight to voicemail, so I left a message telling him that the manuscript that had been sent over was a first draft, that he wasn't to read it, that I'd made a mistake and would he please return it as soon as – as soon as p-possible. I called Jerry next, but I couldn't reach him either. He'd told me he was going away for an anniversary weekend with his wife. I hoped he wouldn't have any time for reading, so I left a message along the lines of the one I'd left for Fisher.

'Then I called Owen back.'

She lit yet another cigarette. Her large nostrils flared as she inhaled; the lines around her mouth deepened.

'I could barely get the words out and it wouldn't have mattered if I had. He talked over me as only Owen can, absolutely delighted with himself. He said we ought to meet to have dinner and celebrate the completion of the book.

'So I dragged myself into clothes, and I went to the River Café and I waited. And in came Owen.

'He wasn't even late. He's usually late. He was virtually floating on air, absolutely elated. He genuinely thinks he's done something brave and marvellous. He'd started to talk about film adaptations before I managed to get a word in edgeways.'

When she expelled smoke from her scarlet mouth she looked truly dragonish, with her shining black eyes.

'When I told him that I think what he's produced is vile,

malicious and unpublishable, he jumped up, sent his chair flying and began screaming. After insulting me both personally and professionally, he told me that if I wasn't brave enough to represent him any more, he'd self-publish the thing – put it out as an ebook. Then he stormed out, parking me with the bill. N-not,' she snarled, 'that that's anything un-un-unus—'

Her emotion triggered an even worse coughing fit than before. Strike thought she might actually choke. He half-rose out of his chair, but she waved him away. Finally, purple in the face, her eyes streaming, she said in a voice like gravel:

'I did everything I could to put it right. My whole weekend by the sea ruined; I was on the phone constantly, trying to get hold of Fisher and Waldegrave. Message after message, stuck out on the bloody cliffs at Gwithian trying to get reception—'

'Is that where you're from?' Strike asked, mildly surprised, because he heard no echo of his Cornish childhood in her accent.

'It's where one of my authors lives. I told her I hadn't been out of London in four years and she invited me for the weekend. Wanted to show me all the lovely places where she sets her books. Some of the m-most beautiful scenery I've ever seen but all I could think about was b-bloody *Bombyx Mori* and trying to stop anyone reading it. I couldn't sleep. I felt dreadful . . .

'I finally heard back from Jerry at Sunday lunchtime. He hadn't gone on his anniversary weekend after all, and he claims he'd never got my messages, so he'd decided to read the bloody book.

'He was disgusted and furious. I assured Jerry that I'd do everything in my power to stop the damn thing . . . but I had to admit that I'd also sent it to Christian, at which Jerry slammed the phone down on me.'

'Did you tell him that Quine had threatened to put the book out over the internet?'

'No, I did not,' she said hoarsely. 'I was praying that was an empty threat, because Owen really doesn't know one end of a computer from the other. But I was worried . . .'

Her voice trailed away.

'You were worried?' Strike prompted her.

She did not answer.

'This self-publishing explains something,' said Strike casually. 'Leonora says Quine took his own copy of the manuscript and all his notes with him when he disappeared into the night. I did wonder whether he was intending to burn it or throw it in a river, but presumably he took it with a view to turning it into an ebook.'

This information did nothing to improve Elizabeth Tassel's temper. Through clenched teeth she said:

'There's a girlfriend. They met on a writing course he taught. She's self-published. I know about her because Owen tried to interest me in her bloody awful erotic fantasy novels.'

'Have you contacted her?' Strike asked.

'Yes, as a matter of fact, I have. I wanted to frighten her off, tell her that if Owen tried to rope her in to help him reformat the book or sell it online she'd probably be party to a lawsuit.'

'What did she say?'

'I couldn't get hold of her. I tried several times. Maybe she's not at that number any more, I don't know.'

'Could I take her details?' Strike asked.

'Ralph's got her card. I asked him to keep ringing her for me. *Ralph!*' she bellowed.

'He's still out with Beau!' came the girl's frightened squeak from beyond the door. Elizabeth Tassel rolled her eyes and got heavily to her feet.

'There's no point asking *her* to find it.'

When the door had swung shut behind the agent, Strike got at once to his feet, moved behind the desk and bent down to examine a photograph on the wall that had caught his eye, which necessitated the removal of a double portrait on the bookcase, featuring a pair of Dobermanns.

The picture in which he was interested was A4-sized, in colour but very faded. Judging by the fashions of the four people it featured, it had been taken at least twenty-five years previously, outside this very building.

Elizabeth herself was clearly recognisable, the only woman in the group, big and plain with long, windswept dark hair and wearing an unflattering drop-waisted dress of dark pink and turquoise. On one side of her stood a slim, fair-haired young man of extreme beauty; on the other was a short, sallow-skinned, sour-looking man whose head was too large for his body. He looked faintly familiar. Strike thought he might have seen him in the papers or on TV.

Beside the unidentified but possibly well-known man stood a much younger Owen Quine. The tallest of the four, he was wearing a crumpled white suit and a hairstyle best described as a spiky mullet. He reminded Strike irresistibly of a fat David Bowie.

The door swished open on its well-oiled hinges. Strike did not attempt to cover up what he was doing, but turned to face the agent, who was holding a sheet of paper.

'That's Fletcher,' she said, her eyes on the picture of the dogs in his hand. 'He died last year.'

He replaced the portrait of her dogs on the bookcase.

'Oh,' she said, catching on. 'You were looking at the other one.'

She approached the faded picture; shoulder to shoulder with Strike, he noted that she was nearly six feet tall. She smelled of John Player Specials and Arpège.

'That's the day I started my agency. Those are my first three clients.'

'Who's he?' asked Strike of the beautiful blond youth.

'Joseph North. The most talented of them, by far. Unfortunately, he died young.'

'And who's—?'

'Michael Fancourt, of course,' she said, sounding surprised.

'I thought he looked familiar. D'you still represent him?'

'No! I thought . . . '

He heard the rest of the sentence, even though she did not say it: *I thought everyone knew that.* Worlds within worlds: perhaps all of literary London *did* know why the famous Fancourt was no longer her client, but he did not.

'Why don't you represent him any more?' he asked, resuming his seat.

She passed the paper in her hand across the desk to him; it was a photocopy of what looked like a flimsy and grubby business card.

'I had to choose between Michael and Owen, years ago,' she said. 'And like a b-bloody fool' – she had begun to cough again; her voice was disintegrating into a guttural croak – 'I chose Owen.

'Those are the only contact details I've got for Kathryn Kent,' she added firmly, closing down further discussion of Fancourt.

'Thank you,' he said, folding the paper and tucking it inside his wallet. 'How long has Quine been seeing her, do you know?'

'A while. He brings her to parties while Leonora's stuck at home with Orlando. Utterly shameless.'

'No idea where he might be hiding? Leonora says you've found him, the other times he's—'

'I don't "find" Owen,' she snapped. 'He rings me up after a week or so in a hotel and asks for an advance – which is what he calls a gift of money – to pay the minibar bill.'

'And you pay, do you?' asked Strike. She seemed very far from a pushover.

Her grimace seemed to acknowledge a weakness of which she was ashamed, but her response was unexpected.

'Have you met Orlando?'

'No.'

She opened her mouth to continue but seemed to think better of it and merely said:

'Owen and I go back a very long way. We were good friends . . . once,' she added, on a note of deep bitterness.

'Which hotels has he stayed at before this?'

'I can't remember all of them. The Kensington Hilton once. The Danubius in St John's Wood. Big faceless hotels with all the creature comforts he can't get at home. Owen's no citizen of Bohemia – except in his approach to hygiene.'

'You know Quine well. You don't think there's any chance that he might have—?'

She finished the sentence for him with a faint sneer.

'—"done something silly"? Of course not. He'd never dream of depriving the world of the genius of Owen Quine. No, he's out there plotting his revenge on all of us, thoroughly aggrieved that there isn't a national manhunt going on.'

'He'd expect a manhunt, even when he makes such a practice of going missing?'

'Oh yes,' said Elizabeth. 'Every time he puts in one of these little vanishing acts he expects it to make the front page. The trouble is that the very first time he did it, years and years ago, after an argument with his first editor, it worked. There *was* a little flurry of concern and a smattering of press. He's lived in the hope of that ever since.'

'His wife's adamant that he'd be annoyed if she called the police.'

'I don't know where she gets that idea,' said Elizabeth, helping herself to yet another cigarette. 'Owen would think helicopters and sniffer dogs the least the nation could do for a man of his importance.'

'Well, thanks for your time,' said Strike, preparing to stand. 'It was good of you to see me.'

Elizabeth Tassel held up a hand and said:

'No, it wasn't. I want to ask you something.'

He waited receptively. She was not used to asking favours, that much was clear. She smoked for a few seconds in silence, which brought on another bout of suppressed coughs.

'This – this . . . *Bombyx Mori* business has done me a lot of harm,' she croaked at last. 'I've been disinvited from Roper Chard's anniversary party this Friday. Two manuscripts I had on submission with them have been sent back without so much as a thank you. And I'm getting worried about poor Pinkelman's latest.' She pointed at the picture of the elderly children's writer on the wall. 'There's a disgusting rumour flying around that I was in cahoots with Owen; that I egged him on to rehash an old scandal about Michael Fancourt, whip up some controversy and try to get a bidding war going for the book.

'If you're going to trawl around everyone who knows Owen,' she said, coming to the point, 'I'd be very grateful if you could tell them – especially Jerry Waldegrave, if you see him – that I had no idea what was in that novel. I'd never have sent it out, least of all to Christian Fisher, if I hadn't been so ill. I was,' she hesitated, '*careless*, but no more than that.'

This, then, was why she had been so anxious to meet him. It did not seem an unreasonable request in return for the addresses of two hotels and a mistress.

'I'll certainly mention that if it comes up,' said Strike, getting to his feet.

'Thank you,' she said gruffly. 'I'll see you out.'

When they emerged from the office, it was to a volley of barks. Ralph and the old Dobermann had returned from their walk. Ralph's wet hair was slicked back as he struggled to restrain the grey-muzzled dog, which was snarling at Strike.

'He's never liked strangers,' said Elizabeth Tassel indifferently.

'He bit Owen once,' volunteered Ralph, as though this might make Strike feel better about the dog's evident desire to maul him.

'Yes,' said Elizabeth Tassel, 'pity it—'

But she was overtaken by another volley of rattling, wheezing coughs. The other three waited in silence for her to recover.

'Pity it wasn't fatal,' she croaked at last. 'It would have saved us all a lot of trouble.'

Her assistants looked shocked. Strike shook her hand and said a general goodbye. The door swung shut on the Dobermann's growling and snarling.

9

Is Master Petulant here, mistress?

William Congreve, *The Way of the World*

Strike paused at the end of the rain-sodden mews and called Robin, whose number was busy. Leaning against a wet wall with the collar of his overcoat turned up, hitting 'redial' every few seconds, his gaze fell on a blue plaque fixed to a house opposite, commemorating the tenancy of Lady Ottoline Morrell, literary hostess. Doubtless scabrous *romans à clef* had once been discussed within those walls, too . . .

'Hi Robin,' said Strike when she picked up at last. 'I'm running late. Can you ring Gunfrey for me and tell him I've got a firm appointment with the target tomorrow. And tell Caroline Ingles there hasn't been any more activity, but I'll call her tomorrow for an update.'

When he had finished tweaking his schedule, he gave her the name of the Danubius Hotel in St John's Wood and asked her to try to find out whether Owen Quine was staying there.

'How're the Hiltons going?'

'Badly,' said Robin. 'I've only got two left. Nothing. If he's at any of them he's either using a different name or a disguise – or the staff are very unobservant, I suppose. You wouldn't think they could miss him, especially if he's wearing that cloak.'

'Have you tried the Kensington one?'

'Yes. Nothing.'

'Ah well, I've got another lead: a self-published girlfriend called Kathryn Kent. I might visit her later. I won't be able to pick up the phone this afternoon; I'm tailing Miss Brocklehurst. Text me if you need anything.'

'OK, happy tailing.'

But it was a dull and fruitless afternoon. Strike was running surveillance on a very well-paid PA who was believed by her paranoid boss and lover to be sharing not only sexual favours but also business secrets with a rival. However, Miss Brocklehurst's claim that she wanted to take an afternoon off to be better waxed, manicured and fake-tanned for her lover's delectation appeared to be genuine. Strike waited and watched the front of the spa through a rain-speckled window of the Caffè Nero opposite for nearly four hours, earning himself the ire of sundry women with pushchairs seeking a space to gossip. Finally Miss Brocklehurst emerged, Bisto-brown and presumably almost hairless from the neck down, and after following her for a short distance Strike saw her slide into a taxi. By a near miracle given the rain, Strike managed to secure a second cab before she had moved out of view, but the sedate pursuit through the clogged, rainwashed streets ended, as he had expected from the direction of travel, at the suspicious boss's own flat. Strike, who had taken photographs covertly all the way, paid his cab fare and mentally clocked off.

It was barely four o'clock and the sun was setting, the endless rain becoming chillier. Christmas lights shone from the window of a trattoria as he passed and his thoughts slid to Cornwall, which he felt had intruded itself on his notice three times in quick succession, calling to him, whispering to him.

How long had it been since he had gone home to that beautiful little seaside town where he had spent the calmest parts of his childhood? Four years? Five? He met his aunt and uncle whenever they 'came up to London', as they self-consciously put it, staying at his sister Lucy's house, enjoying the metropolis. Last time, Strike had taken his uncle to the Emirates to watch a match against Manchester City.

His phone vibrated in his pocket: Robin, following instructions to the letter as usual, had texted him instead of calling.

Mr Gunfrey is asking for another meeting tomorrow at his office at 10, got more to tell you. Rx

Thanks, Strike texted back.

He never added kisses to texts unless to his sister or aunt.

At the Tube, he deliberated his next moves. The whereabouts of Owen Quine felt like an itch in his brain; he was half irritated, half intrigued that the writer was proving so elusive. He pulled the piece of paper that Elizabeth Tassel had given him out of his wallet. Beneath the name Kathryn Kent was the address of a tower block in Fulham and a mobile number. Printed along the bottom edge were two words: *indie author*.

Strike's knowledge of certain patches of London was as detailed as any cabbie's. While he had never penetrated truly upmarket areas as a child, he had lived in many other addresses around the capital with his late, eternally nomadic mother: usually squats or council accommodation, but occasionally, if her boyfriend of the moment could afford it, in more salubrious surroundings. He recognised Kathryn Kent's address: Clement Attlee Court comprised old council blocks, many of which had now been sold off into private hands. Ugly square brick towers with balconies on every floor, they sat within a few hundred yards of million-pound houses in Fulham.

There was nobody waiting for him at home and he was full of coffee and pastries after his long afternoon in Caffè Nero. Instead of boarding the Northern line, he took the District line to West Kensington and set out in the dark along North End Road, past curry houses and a number of small shops with boarded windows, folding under the weight of the recession. By the time Strike had reached the tower blocks he sought, night had fallen.

Stafford Cripps House was the block nearest the road, set just behind a low, modern medical centre. The optimistic architect of the council flats, perhaps giddy with socialist idealism, had given each one its own small balcony space. Had they imagined the happy inhabitants tending window boxes and leaning over the railings to call cheery greetings to their neighbours? Virtually all of these exterior areas had been used by the occupants for storage: old mattresses, prams, kitchen appliances, what looked like armfuls of dirty clothes sat exposed to the elements, as though cupboards full of junk had been cross-sectioned for public view.

A gaggle of hooded youths smoking beside large plastic recycling bins eyed him speculatively as he passed. He was taller and broader than any of them.

'Big fucker,' he caught one of them saying as he passed out of their sight, ignoring the inevitably out-of-order lift and heading for the concrete stairs.

Kathryn Kent's flat was on the third floor and was reached via a windswept brick balcony that ran the width of the building. Strike noted that, unlike her neighbours, Kathryn had hung real curtains in the windows, before rapping on the door.

There was no response. If Owen Quine was inside, he was determined not to give himself away: there were no lights on, no sign of movement. An angry-looking woman with a cigarette jammed in her mouth stuck her head out of the next door with almost comical haste, gave Strike one brief searching stare, then withdrew.

The chilly wind whistled along the balcony. Strike's overcoat was glistening with raindrops but his uncovered head, he knew, would look the same as ever; his short, tightly curling hair was impervious to the effects of rain. He drove his hands deep inside his pockets and there found a stiff envelope he had forgotten. The exterior light beside Kathryn Kent's front door was broken, so Strike ambled two doors along to reach a functioning bulb and opened the silver envelope.

Mr and Mrs Michael Ellacott

request the pleasure of your company
at the wedding of their daughter

Robin Venetia

to

Mr Matthew John Cunliffe

at the church of St Mary the Virgin, Masham

on Saturday 8th January 2011

at two o'clock
and afterwards at
Swinton Park

The invitation exuded the authority of military orders: this wedding will take place in the manner described hereon. He and Charlotte had never got as far as the issuing of stiff cream invitations engraved with shining black cursive.

Strike pushed the card back into his pocket and returned to wait beside Kathryn's dark door, digging into himself, staring out over dark Lillie Road with its swooshing double lights, headlamps and reflections sliding along, ruby and amber. Down on the ground the hooded youths huddled, split apart, were joined by others and regrouped.

At half past six the expanded gang loped off together in a pack. Strike watched them until they were almost out of sight, at which point they passed a woman coming in the opposite direction. As she moved through the light puddle of a street lamp, he saw a thick mane of bright red hair flying from beneath a black umbrella.

Her walk was lopsided, because the hand not holding the umbrella was carrying two heavy carrier bags, but the impression she gave from this distance, regularly tossing back her thick curls, was not unattractive; her windblown hair was eye-catching and her legs beneath the loose overcoat were slender. Closer and closer she moved, unaware of his scrutiny from three floors up, across the concrete forecourt and out of sight.

Five minutes later she had emerged onto the balcony where Strike stood waiting. As she drew nearer, the straining buttons on the coat betrayed a heavy, apple-shaped torso. She did not notice Strike until she was ten yards away, because her head was bowed, but when she looked up he saw a lined and puffy face much older than he had expected. Coming to an abrupt halt, she gasped.

'*You!*'

Strike realised that she was seeing him in silhouette because of the broken lights.

'You fucking *bastard*!'

The bags hit the concrete floor with a tinkle of breaking glass: she was running full tilt at him, hands balled into fists and flailing.

'You bastard, you *bastard*, I'll never forgive you, *never*, you get away from me!'

Strike was forced to parry several wild punches. He stepped backwards as she screeched, throwing ineffectual blows and trying to break past his ex-boxer's defences.

'You wait – Pippa's going to fucking kill you – you wait—'

The neighbour's door opened again: there stood the same woman with a cigarette in her mouth.

'Oi!' she said.

Light from the hall flooded onto Strike, revealing him. With a half gasp, half yelp, the red-headed woman staggered backwards, away from him.

'The fuck's going on?' demanded the neighbour.

'Case of mistaken identity, I think,' said Strike pleasantly.

The neighbour slammed her door, plunging the detective and his assailant back into darkness.

'Who are you?' she whispered. 'What do you want?'

'Are you Kathryn Kent?'

'*What do you want?*'

Then, with sudden panic, 'If it's what I think it is, I don't work in that bit!'

'Excuse me?'

'Who are you, then?' she demanded, sounding more frightened than ever.

'My name's Cormoran Strike and I'm a private detective.'

He was used to the reactions of people who found him unexpectedly on their doorsteps. Kathryn's response – stunned silence – was quite typical. She backed away from him and almost fell over her own abandoned carrier bags.

'Who's set a private detective on me? It's *her*, is it?' she said ferociously.

'I've been hired to find the writer Owen Quine,' said Strike. 'He's been missing for nearly a fortnight. I know you're a friend of his—'

'No, I'm not,' she said and bent to pick up her bags again; they clinked heavily. 'You can tell her that from me. She's welcome to him.'

'You're not his friend any more? You don't know where he is?'

'I don't give a shit where he is.'

A cat stalked arrogantly along the edge of the stone balcony.

'Can I ask when you last—?'

'No, you can't,' she said with an angry gesture; one of the bags in her hand swung and Strike flinched, thinking that the cat, which had drawn level with her, would be knocked off the ledge into space. It hissed and leapt down. She aimed a swift, spiteful kick at it.

'Damn thing!' she said. The cat streaked away. 'Move, please. I want to get into my house.'

He took a few steps back from the door to let her approach it. She could not find her key. After a few uncomfortable seconds of trying to pat her own pockets while carrying the bags she was forced to set them down at her feet.

'Mr Quine's been missing since he had a row with his agent about his latest book,' said Strike, as Kathryn fumbled in her coat. 'I was wondering whether—'

'I don't give a shit about his book. I haven't read it,' she added. Her hands were shaking.

'Mrs Kent—'

'Ms,' she said.

'Ms Kent, Mr Quine's wife says a woman called at his house looking for him. By the description, it sounded—'

Kathryn Kent had found the key but dropped it. Strike bent to pick it up for her; she snatched it from his grasp.

'I don't know what you're talking about.'

'You didn't go looking for him at his house last week?'

'I told you, I don't know where he is, I don't know anything,' she snapped, ramming the key into the lock and turning it.

She caught up the two bags, one of which clinked heavily again. It was, Strike saw, from a local hardware store.

'That looks heavy.'

'My ballcock's gone,' she told him fiercely.

And she slammed her door in his face.

10

VERDONE: We came to fight.
CLEREMONT: Ye shall fight, Gentlemen,
And fight enough; but a short turn or two . . .

Francis Beaumont and Philip Massinger,
The Little French Lawyer

Robin emerged from the Tube the following morning, clutching a redundant umbrella and feeling sweaty and uncomfortable. After days of downpours, of Tube trains full of the smell of wet cloth, of slippery pavements and rain-speckled windows, the sudden switch to bright, dry weather had taken her by surprise. Other spirits might have lightened in the respite from the deluge and lowering grey clouds, but not Robin's. She and Matthew had had a bad row.

It was almost a relief, when she opened the glass door engraved with Strike's name and job title, to find that her boss was already on the telephone in his own office, with the door closed. She felt obscurely that she needed to pull herself together before she faced him, because Strike had been the subject of last night's argument.

'You've invited him to the wedding?' Matthew had said sharply.

She had been afraid that Strike might mention the invitation over drinks that evening, and that if she did not warn Matthew first, Strike would bear the brunt of Matthew's displeasure.

'Since when are we just asking people without telling each other?' Matthew had said.

'I meant to tell you. I thought I had.'

Then Robin had felt angry with herself: she never lied to Matthew.

'He's my boss, he'll expect to be invited!'

Which wasn't true; she doubted that Strike cared one way or the other.

'Well, I'd like him there,' she said, which, at last, was honesty. She wanted to tug the working life that she had never enjoyed so much closer to the personal life that currently refused to meld with it; she wanted to stitch the two together in a satisfying whole and to see Strike in the congregation, approving (approving! Why did he have to approve?) of her marrying Matthew.

She had known that Matthew would not be happy, but she had hoped that by this time the two men would have met and liked each other, and it was not her fault that that had not happened yet.

'After all the bloody fuss we had when I wanted to invite Sarah Shadlock,' Matthew had said – a blow, Robin felt, that was below the belt.

'Invite her then!' she said angrily. 'But it's hardly the same thing – Cormoran's never tried to get me into bed – what's that snort supposed to mean?'

The argument had been in full swing when Matthew's father telephoned with the news that a funny turn Matthew's mother had suffered the previous week had been diagnosed as a mini-stroke.

After this, she and Matthew felt that squabbling about Strike was in bad taste, so they went to bed in an unsatisfactory state of theoretical reconciliation, both, Robin knew, still seething.

It was nearly midday before Strike finally emerged from his office. He was not wearing his suit today, but a dirty and holey sweater, jeans and trainers. His face was thick with the heavy stubble that accrued if he did not shave every twenty-four hours. Forgetting her own troubles, Robin stared: she had never, even in the days when he was sleeping in the office, known Strike to look like a down-and-out.

'Been making calls for the Ingles file and getting some numbers for Longman,' Strike told Robin, handing her the old-fashioned brown card folders, each with a handwritten serial number on the spine, that he had used in the Special Investigation Branch and which remained his favourite way of collating information.

'Is that a – a deliberate look?' she asked, staring at what looked like grease marks on the knees of his jeans.

'Yeah. It's for Gunfrey. Long story.'

While Strike made them both tea, they discussed details of three current cases, Strike updating Robin on information received and further points to be investigated.

'And what about Owen Quine?' Robin asked, accepting her mug. 'What did his agent say?'

Strike lowered himself onto the sofa, which made its usual farting noises beneath him, and filled her in on the details of his interview with Elizabeth Tassel and his visit to Kathryn Kent.

'When she first saw me, I could swear she thought I was Quine.'

Robin laughed.

'You're not *that* fat.'

'Cheers, Robin,' he said drily. 'When she realised I wasn't

Quine, and before she knew who I was, she said, "I don't work in that bit." Does that mean anything to you?'

'No . . . but,' she added diffidently, 'I did manage to find out a bit about Kathryn Kent yesterday.'

'How?' asked Strike, taken aback.

'Well, you told me she's a self-published writer,' Robin reminded him, 'so I thought I'd look online and see what's out there and' – with two clicks of her mouse she brought up the page – 'she's got a blog.'

'Good going!' said Strike, moving gladly off the sofa and round the desk to read over Robin's shoulder.

The amateurish web page was called 'My Literary Life', decorated with drawings of quills and a very flattering picture of Kathryn that Strike thought must be a good ten years out of date. The blog comprised a list of posts, arranged by date like a diary.

'A lot of it's about how traditional publishers wouldn't know good books if they were hit over the head with them,' said Robin, scrolling slowly down the web page so he could look at it. 'She's written three novels in what she calls an erotic fantasy series, called the Melina Saga. They're available for download on Kindle.'

'I don't want to read any more bad books; I had enough with the Brothers Ballsache,' said Strike. 'Anything about Quine?'

'Loads,' said Robin, 'assuming he's the man she calls The Famous Writer. TFW for short.'

'I doubt she's sleeping with two authors,' said Strike. 'It must be him. "Famous" is stretching it a bit, though. Had you heard of Quine before Leonora walked in?'

'No,' admitted Robin. 'Here he is, look, on the second of November.'

Great talk with TFW about Plot and Narrative tonight which are of course not the same thing. For those wondering:- Plot is what happens, Narrative is how much you show your readers and **how** you show it to them.

An example from my second Novel 'Melina's Sacrifice.'

As they made their way towards the Forest of Harderell Lendor raised his handsome profile to see how near they were to it. His well-maintained body, honed by horseback-riding and archery skills –

'Scroll up,' said Strike, 'see what else there is about Quine.'

Robin obliged, pausing on a post from 21 October.

So TFW calls and he can't see me (again.) Family problems. What can I do except say that I understand? I knew it would be complicated when we fell in love. I can't be openly explicit on this but Ill just say he's stuck with a wife he doesn't love because of a Third Party. Not his fault. Not the Third Party's fault. The wife won't let him go even if it's the best thing for everyone so we're locked into what sometimes feels like it's Purgatory

The Wife knows about me and pretend's not to. I don't know how she can stnad living with a man who wants to be with someone else because I know I couldn't do it. TFW says she's always put the Third Party before everything else including HIm. Strange how often being a 'Carer' masks deep Selfishness.

Some people will say its all my fault for falling in love with a Married man. Your not telling me anything my friends, mySsister and my own Mother don't tell me all the time. I've tried to call it off and what can I say except The Heart has it's reasons, which Reasons don't know. And now tonight I'm crying over him all over again for a brand new Reason. He tells me he's nearly finished his

Masterpiece, the book he says is the Best he's ever written. 'I hope you'll like it. You're in it.'

What do you say when a Famous Writer writes you into what he says is his best book? I understand what he's giving me in way's a Non-Writer can't. It makes you feel proud and humble. Yes there are people we Writer's let into our hearts, but into our Books?! That's special. That's different.

Can't help loving TFW. The Heart has it's Reasons.

There was an exchange of comments below.

What would you say if I told you he'd read a bit to me? Pippa2011
You'd better be joking Pip he won't read me any!!! Kath
You wait. Pippa2011 xxxx

'Interesting,' said Strike. 'Very interesting. When Kent attacked me last night, she assured me that someone called Pippa wanted to kill me.'

'Look at this, then!' said Robin in excitement, scrolling down to 9 November.

The first time I ever met TFW he said to me "Your not writing properly unless someone is bleeding, probably you". As follower's of this Blog know I've Metaphorically opened my veins both here and also in my novels. But today I feel like I have been Fatally stabbed by somebodywho I had learned to trust.

'O Macheath! thou hast robb'd me of my Quiet—to see thee tortur'd would give me Pleasure.'

'Where's that quotation from?' asked Strike.
Robin's nimble fingers danced across the keyboard.

'*The Beggar's Opera*, by John Gay.'

'Erudite, for a woman who confuses "you're" and "your" and goes in for random capitalisation.'

'We can't all be literary geniuses,' said Robin reproachfully.

'Thank Christ for that, from all I'm hearing about them.'

'But look at the comment under the quotation,' said Robin, returning to Kathryn's blog. She clicked on the link and a single sentence was revealed.

I'll turn the handle on the f*@%ing rack for you Kath.

This comment, too, had been made by Pippa2011.

'Pippa sounds a handful, doesn't she?' commented Strike. 'Anything about what Kent does for a living on here? I'm assuming she's not paying the bills with her erotic fantasies.'

'That's a bit odd, too. Look at this bit.'

On 28 October, Kathryn had written:

Like most Writers I also have a day job. I can't say to much about it for secuty reasons. This week security has been tightened at our Facility again which means in consequence that my officious Co-Worker (born again Christian, sanctimnious on the subject of my private life) an excuse to suggest to management that blogs e.tc should be viewed in case sensitive Information is revealed. Frotunately it seems sense has prevailed and no action is being taken.

'Mysterious,' said Strike. 'Tightened security . . . women's prison? Psychiatric hospital? Or are we talking industrial secrets?'

'And look at this, on the thirteenth of November.'

Robin scrolled right down to the most recent post on the blog, which was the only entry after that in which Kathryn claimed to have been fatally stabbed.

> My beloved sister has lost her long battle with breast cancer three days ago. Thank you all for your good wishes and support.

Two comments had been added below this, which Robin opened.

Pippa2011 had written:

> So sorry to hear this Kath. Sending you all the love in the world xxx.

Kathryn had replied:

> Thanks Pippa your a real friend xxxx

Kathryn's advance thanks for multiple messages of support sat very sadly above the short exchange.

'Why?' asked Strike heavily.

'Why what?' said Robin, looking up at him.

'Why do people do this?'

'Blog, you mean? I don't know . . . didn't someone once say the unexamined life isn't worth living?'

'Yeah, Plato,' said Strike, 'but this isn't examining a life, it's exhibiting it.'

'Oh God!' said Robin, slopping tea down herself as she gave a guilty start. 'I forgot, there's something else! Christian Fisher called just as I was walking out the door last night. He wants to know if you're interested in writing a book.'

'He *what*?'

'A book,' said Robin, fighting the urge to laugh at the expression of disgust on Strike's face. 'About your life. Your experiences in the army and solving the Lula Landry—'

'Call him back,' Strike said, 'and tell him no, I'm not interested in writing a book.'

He drained his mug and headed for the peg where an ancient leather jacket now hung beside his black overcoat.

'You haven't forgotten tonight?' Robin said, with the knot that had temporarily dissolved tight in her stomach again.

'Tonight?'

'Drinks,' she said desperately. 'Me. Matthew. The King's Arms.'

'No, haven't forgotten,' he said, wondering why she looked so tense and miserable. ''Spect I'll be out all afternoon, so I'll see you there. Eight, was it?'

'Six thirty,' said Robin, tenser than ever.

'Six thirty. Right. I'll be there . . . Venetia.'

She did a double-take.

'How did you know—?'

'It's on the invitation,' said Strike. 'Unusual. Where did that come from?'

'I was – well, I was conceived there, apparently,' she said, pink in the face. 'In Venice. What's your middle name?' she asked over his laughter, half amused, half cross. 'C. B. Strike – what's the B?'

'Got to get going,' said Strike. 'See you at eight.'

'*Six thirty!*' she bellowed at the closing door.

Strike's destination that afternoon was a shop that sold electronic accessories in Crouch End. Stolen mobile phones and laptops were unlocked in a back room, the personal information therein extracted, and the purged devices and the information were then sold separately to those who could use them.

The owner of this thriving business was causing Mr Gunfrey, Strike's client, considerable inconvenience. Mr Gunfrey, who was every bit as crooked as the man whom Strike had tracked to his business headquarters, but on a larger and more flamboyant scale, had made a mistake in treading on the wrong toes. It was Strike's view that Gunfrey needed to clear out while he was ahead. He knew of what this adversary was capable; they had an acquaintance in common.

The target greeted Strike in an upstairs office that smelled as bad as Elizabeth Tassel's, while two shell-suited youths lolled around in the background picking their nails. Strike, who was impersonating a thug for hire recommended by their mutual acquaintance, listened as his would-be employer confided that he was intending to target Mr Gunfrey's teenage son, about whose movements he was frighteningly well informed. He went so far as to offer Strike the job: five hundred pounds to cut the boy. ('I don't want no murder, jussa message to his father, you get me?')

It was gone six before Strike managed to extricate himself from the premises. His first call, once he had made sure he had not been followed, was to Mr Gunfrey himself, whose appalled silence told Strike that he had at last realised what he was up against.

Strike then phoned Robin.

'Going to be late, sorry,' he said.

'Where are you?' she asked, sounding strained. He could hear the sounds of the pub behind her: conversation and laughter.

'Crouch End.'

'Oh God,' he heard her say under her breath. 'It'll take you ages—'

'I'll get a cab,' he assured her. 'Be as quick as I can.'

Why, Strike wondered, as he sat in the taxi rumbling along Upper Street, had Matthew chosen a pub in Waterloo? To make sure that Strike had to travel a long way? Payback for Strike having chosen pubs convenient to him on their previous attempts to meet? Strike hoped the King's Arms served food. He was suddenly very hungry.

It took forty minutes to reach his destination, partly because the row of nineteenth-century workers' cottages where the pub stood was blocked to traffic. Strike chose to get out and end the curmudgeonly taxi driver's attempt to make sense of the street numbering, which appeared not to follow a logical sequence, and proceeded on foot, wondering whether the difficulty of finding the place had influenced Matthew's choice.

The King's Arms turned out to be a picturesque Victorian corner pub the entrances of which were surrounded by a mixture of professional young men in suits and what looked like students, all smoking and drinking. The small crowd parted easily as he approached, giving him a wider berth than was strictly necessary even for a man of his height and breadth. As he crossed the threshold into the small bar Strike wondered, not without a faint hope that it might happen, whether he might be asked to leave on account of his filthy clothes.

Meanwhile, in the noisy back room, which was a glass-ceilinged courtyard self-consciously crammed with bric-a-brac, Matthew was looking at his watch.

'It's nearly a quarter past,' he told Robin.

Clean cut in his suit and tie, he was – as usual – the handsomest man in the room. Robin was used to seeing women's eyes swivel as he walked past them; she had never quite managed to make up her mind how aware Matthew was of their swift, burning glances. Sitting at the long wooden bench that they had been forced to share with a party of cackling students, six foot one, with a firm cleft chin and bright blue eyes, he looked like a thoroughbred kept in a paddock of Highland ponies.

'That's him,' said Robin, with a surge of relief and apprehension.

Strike seemed to have become larger and rougher-looking since he had left the office. He moved easily towards them through the packed room, his eyes on Robin's bright gold head, one large hand grasping a pint of Hophead. Matthew stood up. It looked as though he braced himself.

'Cormoran – hi – you found it.'

'You're Matthew,' said Strike, holding out a hand. 'Sorry I'm so late, I tried to get away earlier but I was with the sort of bloke you wouldn't want to turn your back on without permission.'

Matthew returned an empty smile. He had expected Strike to be full of those kinds of comments: self-dramatising, trying to make a mystery of what he did. By the look of him, he'd been changing a tyre.

'Sit down,' Robin told Strike nervously, moving along the bench so far that she was almost falling off the end. 'Are you hungry? We were just talking about ordering something.'

'They do reasonably decent food,' said Matthew. 'Thai. It's not the Mango Tree, but it's all right.'

Strike smiled without warmth. He had expected Matthew to be like this: name-dropping restaurants in Belgravia to prove, after a single year in London, that he was a seasoned metropolitan.

'How did it go this afternoon?' Robin asked Strike. She

thought that if Matthew only heard about the sort of things that Strike did, he would become as fascinated as she was by the process of detection and his every prejudice would fall away.

But Strike's brief description of his afternoon, omitting all identifying details of those involved, met barely concealed indifference on the part of Matthew. Strike then offered them both a drink, as they were holding empty glasses.

'You could show a bit of interest,' Robin hissed at Matthew once Strike was out of earshot at the bar.

'Robin, he met a man in a shop,' said Matthew. 'I doubt they'll be optioning the film rights any time soon.'

Pleased with his own wit, he turned his attention to the blackboard menu on the opposite wall.

When Strike had returned with drinks, Robin insisted on battling her way up to the bar with their food order. She dreaded leaving the two men alone together, but felt that they might, somehow, find their own level without her.

Matthew's brief increase in self-satisfaction ebbed away in Robin's absence.

'You're ex-army,' he found himself telling Strike, even though he had been determined not to permit Strike's life experience to dominate the conversation.

'That's right,' said Strike. 'SIB.'

Matthew was not sure what that was.

'My father's ex-RAF,' he said. 'Yeah, he was in same time as Jeff Young.'

'Who?'

'Welsh rugby union player? Twenty-three caps?' said Matthew.

'Right,' said Strike.

'Yeah, Dad made Squadron Leader. Left in eighty-six and he's run his own property management business since. Done all right for himself. Nothing like your old man,' said Matthew, a little defensively, 'but all right.'

Tit, thought Strike.

'What are you talking about?' Robin said anxiously, sitting back down.

'Just Dad,' said Matthew.

'Poor thing,' said Robin.

'Why poor thing?' snapped Matthew.

'Well – he's worried about your mum, isn't he? The mini-stroke?'

'Oh,' said Matthew, 'that.'

Strike had met men like Matthew in the army: always officer class, but with that little pocket of insecurity just beneath the smooth surface that made them overcompensate, and sometimes overreach.

'So how are things at Lowther-French?' Robin asked Matthew, willing him to show Strike what a nice man he was, to show the real Matthew, whom she loved. 'Matthew's auditing this really odd little publishing company. They're quite funny, aren't they?' she said to her fiancé.

'I wouldn't call it "funny", the shambles they're in,' said Matthew, and he talked until their food arrived, littering his chat with references to 'ninety k' and 'a quarter of a mill', and every sentence was angled, like a mirror, to show him in the best possible light: his cleverness, his quick thinking, his besting of slower, stupider yet more senior colleagues, his patronage of the dullards working for the firm he was auditing.

'. . . trying to justify a Christmas party, when they've barely broken even in two years; it'll be more like a wake.'

Matthew's confident strictures on the small firm were followed by the arrival of their food and silence. Robin, who had been hoping that Matthew would reproduce for Strike some of the kinder, more affectionate things he had found to tell her about the eccentrics at the small press, could think of nothing to say. However, Matthew's mention of a publishing party had just given Strike an idea. The detective's jaws worked more slowly. It had occurred to him that there might be an excellent opportunity to seek information on Owen Quine's whereabouts, and his capacious memory volunteered a small piece of information he had forgotten he knew.

'Got a girlfriend, Cormoran?' Matthew asked Strike directly; it was something he was keen to establish. Robin had been vague on the point.

'No,' said Strike absently. ''Scuse me – won't be long, got to make a phone call.'

'Yeah, no problem,' said Matthew irritably, but only once Strike was once again out of earshot. 'You're forty minutes late and then you piss off during dinner. We'll just sit here waiting till you deign to come back.'

'*Matt!*'

Reaching the dark pavement, Strike pulled out cigarettes and his mobile phone. Lighting up, he walked away from his fellow smokers to the quiet end of the side street to stand in darkness beneath the brick arches that bore the railway line.

Culpepper answered on the third ring.

'Strike,' he said. 'How's it going?'

'Good. Calling to ask a favour.'

'Go on,' said Culpepper non-committally.

'You've got a cousin called Nina who works for Roper Chard—'

'How the hell do you know that?'

'You told me,' said Strike patiently.

'When?'

'Few months ago when I was investigating that dodgy dentist for you.'

'Your fucking memory,' said Culpepper, sounding less impressed than unnerved. 'It's not normal. What about her?'

'Couldn't put me in touch with her, could you?' asked Strike. 'Roper Chard have got an anniversary party tomorrow night and I'd like to go.'

'Why?'

'I've got a case,' said Strike evasively. He never shared with Culpepper details of the high-society divorces and business ruptures he was investigating, in spite of Culpepper's frequent requests to do so. 'And I just gave you the scoop of your bloody career.'

'Yeah, all right,' said the journalist grudgingly, after a short hesitation. 'I suppose I could do that for you.'

'Is she single?' Strike asked.

'What, you after a shag, too?' said Culpepper, and Strike noted that he seemed amused instead of peeved at the thought of Strike trying it on with his cousin.

'No, I want to know whether it'll look suspicious if she takes me to the party.'

'Oh, right. I think she's just split up with someone. I dunno. I'll text you the number. Wait till Sunday,' Culpepper added with barely suppressed glee. 'A tsunami of shit's about to hit Lord Porker.'

'Call Nina for me first, will you?' Strike asked him. 'And tell her who I am, so she understands the gig?'

Culpepper agreed to it and rang off. In no particular hurry

to return to Matthew, Strike smoked his cigarette down to the butt before moving back inside.

The packed room, he thought, as he made his way across it, bowing his head to avoid hanging pots and street signs, was like Matthew: it tried too hard. The decor included an old-fashioned stove and an ancient till, multiple shopping baskets, old prints and plates: a contrived panoply of junk-shop finds.

Matthew had hoped to have finished his noodles before Strike returned, to underline the length of his absence, but had not quite managed it. Robin was looking miserable and Strike, wondering what had passed between them while he had been gone, felt sorry for her.

'Robin says you're a rugby player,' he told Matthew, determined to make an effort. 'Could've played county, is that right?'

They made laborious conversation for another hour: the wheels turned most easily while Matthew was able to talk about himself. Strike noticed Robin's habit of feeding Matthew lines and cues, each designed to open up an area of conversation in which he could shine.

'How long have you two been together?' he asked.

'Nine years,' said Matthew, with a slight return of his former combative air.

'That long?' said Strike, surprised. 'What, were you at university together?'

'School,' said Robin, smiling. 'Sixth form.'

'Wasn't a big school,' said Matthew. 'She was the only girl with any brains who was fanciable. No choice.'

Tosser, thought Strike.

Their way home lay together as far as Waterloo station; they walked through the darkness, continuing to make small talk, then parted at the entrance to the Tube.

'There,' said Robin hopelessly, as she and Matthew walked away towards the escalator. 'He's nice, isn't he?'

'Punctuality's shit,' said Matthew, who could find no other charge to lay against Strike that did not sound insane. 'He'll probably arrive forty minutes bloody late and ruin the service.'

But it was tacit consent to Strike's attendance and, in the absence of genuine enthusiasm, Robin supposed it could have been worse.

Matthew, meanwhile, was brooding in silence on things he would have confessed to nobody. Robin had accurately described her boss's looks – the pube-like hair, the boxer's profile – but Matthew had not expected Strike to be so big. He had a couple of inches on Matthew, who enjoyed being the tallest man in his office. What was more, while he would have found it distasteful showboating if Strike had held forth about his experiences in Afghanistan and Iraq, or told them how his leg had been blown off, or how he had earned the medal that Robin seemed to find so impressive, his silence on these subjects had been almost more irritating. Strike's heroism, his action-packed life, his experiences of travel and danger had somehow hovered, spectrally, over the conversation.

Beside him on the train, Robin too sat in silence. She had not enjoyed the evening one bit. Never before had she known Matthew quite like that; or at least, never before had she *seen* him like that. It was Strike, she thought, puzzling over the matter as the train jolted them. Strike had somehow made her see Matthew through his eyes. She did not know quite how he had done it – all that questioning Matthew about rugby – some people might have thought it was polite, but Robin knew better . . . or was she just annoyed that he had been late, and blaming him for things that he had not intended?

And so the engaged couple sped home, united in unexpressed irritation with the man now snoring loudly as he rattled away from them on the Northern line.

11

Let me know
Wherefore I should be thus neglected.

John Webster, *The Duchess of Malfi*

'Is that Cormoran Strike?' asked a girlish upper-middle-class voice at twenty to nine the following morning.

'It is,' said Strike.

'It's Nina. Nina Lascelles. Dominic gave me your number.'

'Oh yeah,' said Strike, who was standing bare-chested in front of the shaving mirror he usually kept beside the kitchen sink, the shower room being both dark and cramped. Wiping shaving foam from around his mouth with his forearm, he said:

'Did he tell you what it was about, Nina?'

'Yeah, you want to infiltrate Roper Chard's anniversary party.'

'"Infiltrate" is a bit strong.'

'But it sounds much more exciting if we say "infiltrate".'

'Fair enough,' he said, amused. 'I take it you're up for this?'

'Oooh, yes, fun. Am I allowed to guess why you want to come and spy on everyone?'

'Again, "spy" isn't really—'

'Stop spoiling things. Am I allowed a guess?'

'Go on then,' said Strike, taking a sip from his mug of tea, his eyes on the window. It was foggy again; the brief spell of sunshine extinguished.

'*Bombyx Mori*,' said Nina. 'Am I right? I am, aren't I? Say I'm right.'

'You're right,' said Strike and she gave a squeal of pleasure.

'I'm not even supposed to be talking about it. There's been a lockdown, emails round the company, lawyers storming in and out of Daniel's office. Where shall we meet? We should hook up somewhere first and turn up together, don't you think?'

'Yeah, definitely,' said Strike. 'Where's good for you?'

Even as he took a pen from the coat hanging behind the door he thought longingly of an evening at home, a good long sleep, an interlude of peace and rest before an early start on Saturday morning, tailing his brunette client's faithless husband.

'D'you know Ye Olde Cheshire Cheese?' asked Nina. 'On Fleet Street? Nobody from work'll be in there, and it's walking distance to the office. I know it's corny but I love it.'

They agreed to meet at seven thirty. As Strike returned to his shaving, he asked himself how likely it was that he would meet anyone who knew Quine's whereabouts at his publisher's party. *The trouble is*, Strike mentally chided the reflection in the circular mirror as the pair of them strafed stubble from their chins, *you keep acting like you're still SIB. The nation's not paying you to be thorough any more, mate.*

But he knew no other way; it was part of a short but inflexible personal code of ethics that he had carried with him all his adult life: do the job and do it well.

Strike was intending to spend most of the day in the office, which under normal circumstances he enjoyed. He and Robin shared the paperwork; she was an intelligent and often helpful sounding board and as fascinated now with the mechanics of an investigation as she had been when she had joined him. Today, however, he headed downstairs with something bordering on reluctance and, sure enough, his seasoned antennae detected in her greeting a self-conscious edge that he feared would shortly break through into 'What did you think of Matthew?'

This, Strike reflected, retiring to the inner office and shutting the door on the pretext of making phone calls, was exactly why it was a bad idea to meet your only member of staff outside working hours.

Hunger forced him to emerge a few hours later. Robin had bought sandwiches as usual, but she had not knocked on the door to let him know that they were there. This, too, seemed to point to feelings of awkwardness after the previous evening. To postpone the moment when it must be mentioned, and in the hope that if he kept off the subject long enough she might never bring it up (although he had never known the tactic to work on a woman before), Strike told her truthfully that he had just got off the phone with Mr Gunfrey.

'Is he going to go to the police?' asked Robin.

'Er – no. Gunfrey isn't the type of bloke who goes to the police if someone's bothering him. He's nearly as bent as the bloke who wants to cut his son. He's realised he's in over his head this time, though.'

'Didn't you think of recording what that gangster was paying you to do and taking it to the police yourself?' asked Robin, without thinking.

'No, Robin, because it'd be obvious where the tip-off came from and it'll put a strain on business if I've got to dodge hired killers while doing surveillance.'

'But Gunfrey can't keep his son at home for ever!'

'He won't have to. He's going to take the family off for a

surprise holiday in the States, phone our knife-happy friend from LA and tell him he's given the matter some thought and changed his mind about interfering with his business interests. Shouldn't look too suspicious. The bloke's already done enough shitty stuff to him to warrant a cooling off. Bricks through his windscreen, threatening calls to his wife.

'S'pose I'll have to go back to Crouch End next week, say the boy never showed up and give his monkey back.' Strike sighed. 'Not very plausible, but I don't want them to come looking for me.'

'He gave you a—?'

'Monkey – five hundred quid, Robin,' said Strike. 'What do they call that in Yorkshire?'

'Shockingly little to stab a teenager,' said Robin forcefully and then, catching Strike off guard, 'What did you think of Matthew?'

'Nice bloke,' lied Strike automatically.

He refrained from elaboration. She was no fool; he had been impressed before now by her instinct for the lie, the false note. Nevertheless, he could not help hurrying them on to a different subject.

'I'm starting to think, maybe next year, if we're turning a proper profit and you've already had your pay rise, we could justify taking someone else on. I'm working flat out here, I can't keep going like this for ever. How many clients have you turned down lately?'

'A couple,' Robin responded coolly.

Surmising that he had been insufficiently enthusiastic about Matthew but resolute that he would not be any more hypocritical than he had already been, Strike withdrew shortly afterwards into his office and shut the door again.

However, on this occasion, Strike was only half right.

Robin had indeed felt deflated by his response. She knew that if Strike had genuinely liked Matthew he would never have been as definitive as 'nice bloke'. He'd have said 'Yeah, he's all right,' or 'I s'pose you could do worse.'

What had irritated and even hurt was his suggestion of bringing in another employee. Robin turned back to her computer monitor and started typing fast and furiously, banging the keys harder than usual as she made up this week's invoice for the divorcing brunette. She had thought – evidently wrongly – that she was here as more than a secretary. She had helped Strike secure the evidence that had convicted Lula Landry's killer; she had even collected some of it alone, on her own initiative. In the months since, she had several times operated way beyond the duties of a PA, accompanying Strike on surveillance jobs when it would look more natural for him to be in a couple, charming doormen and recalcitrant witnesses who instinctively took offence at Strike's bulk and surly expression, not to mention pretending to be a variety of women on the telephone that Strike, with his deep bass voice, had no hope of impersonating.

Robin had assumed that Strike was thinking along the same lines that she was: he occasionally said things like 'It's good for your detective training' or 'You could use a counter-surveillance course.' She had assumed that once the business was on a sounder footing (and she could plausibly claim to have helped make it so) she would be given the training she knew she needed. But now it seemed that these hints had been mere throwaway lines, vague pats on the head for the typist. So what was she doing here? Why had she thrown away something much better? (In her temper, Robin chose to forget how little she had wanted that human resources job, however well paid.)

Perhaps the new employee would be female, able to perform these useful jobs, and she, Robin, would become receptionist and secretary to both of them, and never leave her desk again. It was not for that that she had stayed with Strike, given up a much better salary and created a recurring source of tension in her relationship.

At five o'clock on the dot Robin stopped typing in mid-sentence, pulled on her trench coat and left, closing the glass door behind her with unnecessary force.

The bang woke Strike up. He had been fast asleep at his desk, his head on his arms. Checking his watch he saw that it was five and wondered who had just come into the office. Only when he opened the dividing door and saw that Robin's coat and bag were gone and her computer monitor dark did he realise that she had left without saying goodbye.

'Oh, for fuck's sake,' he said impatiently.

She wasn't usually sulky; it was one of the many things he liked about her. What did it matter if he didn't like Matthew? He wasn't the one marrying him. Muttering irritably under his breath, Strike locked up and climbed the stairs to his attic room, intending to eat and change before meeting Nina Lascelles.

12

She is a woman of an excellent assurance, and an extraordinary happy wit, and tongue.

Ben Jonson, *Epicoene, or The Silent Woman*

Strike proceeded along the dark, cold Strand towards Fleet Street that evening with his hands balled deep in his pockets, walking as briskly as fatigue and an increasingly sore right leg would permit. He regretted leaving the peace and comfort of his glorified bedsit; he was not sure that anything useful would come of this evening's expedition and yet, almost against his will, he was struck anew in the frosty haze of this winter's night by the aged beauty of the old city to which he owed a divided childhood allegiance.

Every taint of the touristic was wiped away by the freezing November evening: the seventeenth-century façade of the Old Bell Tavern, with its diamond windowpanes aglow, exuded a noble antiquity; the dragon standing sentinel on top of the Temple Bar marker was silhouetted, stark and fierce, against the star-studded blackness above; and in the far distance the misty dome of St Paul's shone like a rising moon. High on a brick wall above him as he approached his destination were names that spoke of Fleet Street's inky past – the *People's Friend*, the *Dundee*

Courier – but Culpepper and his journalistic ilk had long since been driven out of their traditional home to Wapping and Canary Wharf. The law dominated the area now, the Royal Courts of Justice staring down upon the passing detective, the ultimate temple of Strike's trade.

In this forgiving and strangely sentimental mood, Strike approached the round yellow lamp across the road that marked the entrance to Ye Olde Cheshire Cheese and headed up the narrow passageway that led to the entrance, stooping to avoid hitting his head on the low lintel.

A cramped wood-panelled entrance lined with ancient oil paintings opened on to a tiny front room. Strike ducked again, avoiding the faded wooden sign 'Gentlemen only in this bar', and was greeted at once with an enthusiastic wave from a pale, petite girl whose dominant feature was a pair of large brown eyes. Huddled in a black coat beside the log fire, she was cradling an empty glass in two small white hands.

'Nina?'

'I knew it was you, Dominic described you to a T.'

'Can I get you a drink?'

She asked for a white wine. Strike fetched himself a pint of Sam Smith and edged onto the uncomfortable wooden bench beside her. London accents filled the room. As though she had read his mood, Nina said:

'It's still a real pub. It's only people who never come here who think it's full of tourists. And Dickens came here, and Johnson and Yeats . . . I love it.'

She beamed at him and he smiled back, mustering real warmth with several mouthfuls of beer inside him.

'How far's your office?'

'About a ten-minute walk,' she said. 'We're just off the

Strand. It's a new building and there's a roof garden. It's going to be bloody freezing,' she added, giving a pre-emptive shiver and drawing her coat more tightly around her. 'But the bosses had an excuse not to hire anywhere. Times are hard in publishing.'

'There's been some trouble about *Bombyx Mori*, you said?' asked Strike, getting down to business as he stretched out his prosthetic leg as far as it would go under the table.

'Trouble,' she said, 'is the understatement of the century. Daniel Chard's livid. You *don't* make Daniel Chard the baddie in a dirty novel. Not done. No. Bad idea. He's a strange man. They say he got sucked into the family business, but he really wanted to be an artist. Like Hitler,' she added with a giggle.

The lights over the bar danced in her big eyes. She looked, Strike thought, like an alert and excited mouse.

'Hitler?' he repeated, faintly amused.

'He rants like Hitler when he's upset – we've found *that* out this week. Nobody's ever heard Daniel speak above a mumble before this. Shouting and screaming at Jerry; we could hear him through the walls.'

'Have you read the book?'

She hesitated, a naughty grin playing around her mouth.

'Not officially,' she said at last.

'But unofficially . . . '

'I might have had a sneaky peek,' she said.

'Isn't it under lock and key?'

'Well, yeah, it's in Jerry's safe.'

A sly sideways glance invited Strike to join her in gentle mockery of the innocent editor.

'The trouble is, he's told everyone the combination because he keeps forgetting it and that means he can ask us to remind him. Jerry's the sweetest, straightest man in the world and I don't think it would have occurred to him that we'd have a read if we weren't supposed to.'

'When did you look at it?'

'The Monday after he got it. Rumours were really picking up by then, because Christian Fisher had rung about fifty people over the weekend and read bits of the book over the phone. I've heard he scanned it and started emailing parts around, as well.'

'This would have been before lawyers started getting involved?'

'Yeah. They called us all together and gave us this ridiculous speech about what would happen if we talked about the book. It was just nonsense, trying to tell us the company's reputation would suffer if the CEO's ridiculed – we're about to go public, or that's the rumour – and ultimately our jobs would be imperilled. I don't know how the lawyer kept a straight face saying it. My dad's a QC,' she went on airily, 'and he says Chard'll have a hard time going after any of us when so many people outside the company know.'

'Is he a good CEO, Chard?' asked Strike.

'I suppose so,' she said restlessly, 'but he's quite mysterious and dignified so . . . well, it's just funny, what Quine wrote about him.'

'Which was . . . ?'

'Well, in the book Chard's called Phallus Impudicus and—'

Strike choked on his pint. Nina giggled.

'He's called "Impudent Cock"?' Strike asked, laughing, wiping his mouth on the back of his hand. Nina laughed; a surprisingly dirty cackle for one who looked like an eager schoolgirl.

'You did Latin? I gave it up, I hated it – but we all know what "phallus" is, right? I had to look it up and *Phallus impudicus* is actually the proper name for a toadstool called stinkhorn. Apparently they smell vile and . . . well,' she giggled some more, 'they look like rotting knobs. Classic Owen: dirty names and everyone with their bits out.'

'And what does Phallus Impudicus get up to?'

'Well, he walks like Daniel, talks like Daniel, looks like Daniel and he enjoys a spot of necrophilia with a handsome writer he's murdered. It's really gory and disgusting. Jerry always said Owen thinks the day wasted if he hasn't made his readers gag at least twice. Poor Jerry,' she added quietly.

'Why "poor Jerry"?' asked Strike.

'He's in the book as well.'

'And what kind of phallus is he?'

Nina giggled again.

'I couldn't tell you, I didn't read the bit about Jerry. I just flicked through to find Daniel because everyone said it was so gross and funny. Jerry was only out of his office half an hour, so I didn't have much time – but we all know he's in there, because Daniel hauled Jerry in, made him meet the lawyers and add his name to all the stupid emails telling us the sky will fall in if we talk about *Bombyx Mori*. I suppose it makes Daniel feel better that Owen's attacked Jerry too. He knows everyone loves Jerry, so I expect he thinks we'll all keep our mouths shut to protect him.

'God knows why Quine's gone for Jerry, though,' Nina added, her smile fading a little. 'Because Jerry hasn't got an enemy in the world. Owen *is* a bastard, really,' she added as a quiet afterthought, staring down at her empty wine glass.

'Want another drink?' Strike asked.

He returned to the bar. There was a stuffed grey parrot in a glass case on the wall opposite. It was the only bit of genuine whimsy he could see and he was prepared, in his mood of tolerance for this authentic bit of old London, to do it the courtesy of assuming that it had once squawked and chattered within these walls and had not been bought as a mangy accessory.

'You know Quine's gone missing?' Strike asked, once back beside Nina.

'Yeah, I heard a rumour. I'm not surprised, the fuss he's caused.'

'D'you know Quine?'

'Not really. He comes into the office sometimes and tries to flirt, you know, with his stupid cloak draped round him, showing off, always trying to shock. I think he's a bit pathetic, and I've always hated his books. Jerry persuaded me to read *Hobart's Sin* and I thought it was dreadful.'

'D'you know if anyone's heard from Quine lately?'

'Not that I know of,' said Nina.

'And no one knows why he wrote a book that was bound to get him sued?'

'Everyone assumes he's had a major row with Daniel. He rows with everyone in the end; he's been with God knows how many publishers over the years.

'I heard Daniel only publishes Owen because he thinks it makes it look as though Owen's forgiven him for being awful to Joe North. Owen and Daniel don't really like each other, that's common knowledge.'

Strike remembered the image of the beautiful blond young man hanging on Elizabeth Tassel's wall.

'How was Chard awful to North?'

'I'm a bit vague on the details,' said Nina. 'But I know he *was*. I know Owen swore he'd never work for Daniel, but then he ran through nearly every other publisher so he had to pretend he'd been wrong about Daniel and Daniel took him on because he thought it made him look good. That's what everyone says, anyway.'

'And has Quine rowed with Jerry Waldegrave, to your knowledge?'

'No, which is what's so bizarre. Why attack Jerry? He's lovely! Although from what I've heard, you can't really—'

For the first time, as far as Strike could tell, she considered what she was about to say before proceeding a little more soberly:

'Well, you can't really tell what Owen's getting at in the bit about Jerry, and as I say, I haven't read it. But Owen's done over loads of people,' Nina went on. 'I heard his own wife's in there, and apparently he's been *vile* about Liz Tassel, who might be a bitch, but everyone knows she's stuck by Owen through thick and thin. Liz'll never be able to place anything with Roper Chard again; everyone's furious at her. I know she was disinvited for tonight on Daniel's orders – pretty humiliating. And there's supposed to be a party for Larry Pinkelman, one of her other authors, in a couple of weeks and they *can't* uninvite her from that – Larry's such an old sweetheart, everyone loves him – but God knows what reception she'll get if she turns up.

'Anyway,' said Nina, shaking back her light brown fringe and changing the subject abruptly, 'how are you and I supposed to know each other, once we get to the party? Are you my boyfriend, or what?'

'Are partners allowed at this thing?'

'Yeah, but I haven't told anyone I'm seeing you, so we can't have been going out long. We'll say we got together at a party last weekend, OK?'

Strike heard, with almost identical amounts of disquiet and gratified vanity, the enthusiasm with which she suggested a fictional tryst.

'Need a pee before we go,' he said, raising himself heavily from the wooden bench as she drained her third glass.

The stairs down to the bathroom in Ye Olde Cheshire Cheese were vertiginous and the ceiling so low that he smacked his head even while stooping. As he rubbed his temple, swearing under his breath, it seemed to Strike that he had just been given a divine clout over the head, to remind him what was, and what was not, a good idea.

13

It is reported, you possess a book
Wherein you have quoted by intelligence
The names of all notorious offenders,
Lurking about the city.

John Webster, *The White Devil*

Experience had taught Strike that there was a certain type of woman to whom he was unusually attractive. Their common characteristics were intelligence and the flickering intensity of badly wired lamps. They were often attractive and usually, as his very oldest friend Dave Polworth liked to put it, 'total fucking flakes'. Precisely what it was about him that attracted the type, Strike had never taken the time to consider, although Polworth, a man of many pithy theories, took the view that such women ('nervy, overbred') were subconsciously looking for what he called 'carthorse blood'.

Strike's ex-fiancée, Charlotte, might have been said to be queen of the species. Beautiful, clever, volatile and damaged, she had returned again and again to Strike in the face of familial opposition and her friends' barely veiled disgust. He had finally put an end to sixteen years of their on-again, off-again relationship in March and she had become engaged almost immediately to the ex-boyfriend from whom Strike, so many years ago in Oxford, had won her. Barring one exceptional night since, Strike's love life had been voluntarily barren. Work had filled virtually every waking hour and he had successfully resisted advances, subtle or overt, from the likes of his glamorous brunette client, soon-to-be divorcées with time to kill and loneliness to assuage.

But there was always the dangerous urge to submit, to brave complications for a night or two of consolation, and now Nina Lascelles was hurrying along beside him in the dark Strand, taking two strides to his one, and informing him of her exact address in St John's Wood 'so it looks like you've been there'. She barely came up to his shoulder and Strike had never found very small women attractive. Her torrent of chat about Roper Chard was laden with more laughter than was strictly necessary and once or twice she touched his arm to emphasise a point.

'Here we are,' she said at last, as they approached a tall modern building with a revolving glass door and the words 'Roper Chard' picked out in shining orange Perspex across the stonework.

A wide lobby dotted with people in evening dress faced a line of metal sliding doors. Nina pulled an invitation out of her bag and showed it to what looked like hired help in a badly fitting tuxedo, then she and Strike joined twenty others in a large mirrored lift.

'This floor's for meetings,' Nina shouted up to him as they debouched into a crowded open-plan area where a band was playing to a sparsely populated dance floor. 'It's usually partitioned. So – who do you want to meet?'

'Anyone who knew Quine well and might have an idea where he is.'

'That's only Jerry, really . . . '

They were buffeted by a fresh consignment of guests from the lift behind them and moved into the crowd. Strike thought he felt Nina grab the back of his coat, like a child, but he did not reciprocate by taking her hand or in any way reinforce the impression that they were boyfriend and girlfriend. Once or twice he heard her greet people in passing. They eventually won through to the far wall, where tables manned by white-coated waiters groaned with party food and it was possible to make conversation without shouting. Strike took a couple of dainty crab cakes and ate them, deploring their minuscule size, while Nina looked around.

'Can't see Jerry anywhere, but he's probably up on the roof, smoking. Shall we try up there? Oooh, look there – Daniel Chard, mingling with the herd!'

'Which one?'

'The bald one.'

A respectful little distance had been left around the head of the company, like the flattened circle of corn that surrounds a rising helicopter, as he talked to a curvaceous young woman in a tight black dress.

Phallus Impudicus; Strike could not repress a grin of amusement, yet Chard's baldness suited him. He was younger and fitter-looking than Strike had expected and handsome in his way, with thick dark eyebrows over deep-set eyes, a hawkish nose and a thin-lipped mouth. His charcoal suit was unexceptional but his tie, which was pale mauve, was much wider than the average and bore drawings of human noses. Strike, whose dress sense had always been conventional, an instinct honed by the sergeants' mess, could not help but be intrigued by this small but forceful statement of non-conformity in a CEO, especially as it was drawing the occasional glance of surprise or amusement.

'Where's the drink?' Nina said, standing pointlessly on tiptoe.

'Over there,' said Strike, who could see a bar in front of the windows that showed a view of the dark Thames. 'Stay here, I'll get them. White wine?'

'Champers, if Daniel's pushed the boat out.'

He took a route through the crowd so that he could, without ostentation, bring himself in close proximity to Chard, who was letting his companion do all the talking. She had that air of slight desperation of the conversationalist who knows that they are failing. The back of Chard's hand, which was clutching a glass of water, Strike noticed, was covered in shiny red eczema. Strike paused immediately behind Chard, ostensibly to allow a party of young women to pass in the opposite direction.

'. . . and it really was awfully funny,' the girl in the black dress was saying nervously.

'Yes,' said Chard, who sounded deeply bored, 'it must have been.'

'And was New York wonderful? I mean – not wonderful – was it useful? Fun?' asked his companion.

'Busy,' said Chard and Strike, though he could not see the CEO, thought he actually yawned. 'Lots of digital talk.'

A portly man in a three-piece suit who appeared drunk already, though it was barely eight thirty, stopped in front of Strike and invited him, with overdone courtesy, to proceed. Strike had no choice but to accept the elaborately mimed invitation and so passed out of range of Daniel Chard's voice.

'Thanks,' said Nina a few minutes later, taking her champagne from Strike. 'Shall we go up to the roof garden, then?'

'Great,' said Strike. He had taken champagne too, not because he liked it, but because there had been nothing else there he cared to drink. 'Who's that woman Daniel Chard's talking to?'

Nina craned to see as she led Strike towards a helical metal staircase.

'Joanna Waldegrave, Jerry's daughter. She's just written her first novel. Why? Is that your type?' she asked, with a breathy little laugh.

'No,' said Strike.

They climbed the mesh stairs, Strike relying heavily once more on the handrail. The icy night air scoured his lungs as they emerged on to the top of the building. Stretches of velvety lawn, tubs of flowers and young trees, benches dotted everywhere; there was even a floodlit pond where fish darted, flame-like, beneath the black lily pads. Outdoor heaters like giant steel mushrooms had been placed in groups between neat square lawns and people were huddled under them, their backs turned to the synthetic pastoral scene, looking inwards at their fellow smokers, cigarette tips glowing.

The view over the city was spectacular, velvet black and jewelled, the London Eye glowing neon blue, the Oxo Tower with its ruby windows, the Southbank Centre, Big Ben and the Palace of Westminster shining golden away to the right.

'Come on,' said Nina, and she boldly took Strike's hand and led him towards an all-female trio, whose breath rose in gusts of white mist even when they were not exhaling smoke.

'Hi guys,' said Nina. 'Anyone seen Jerry?'

'He's pissed,' said a redhead baldly.

'*Oh no*,' said Nina. 'And he was doing so well!'

A lanky blonde glanced over her shoulder and murmured:

'He was half off his face in Arbutus last week.'

'It's *Bombyx Mori*,' said an irritable-looking girl with short dark hair. 'And the anniversary weekend in Paris didn't come off. Fenella had another tantrum, I think. *When* is he going to leave her?'

'Is she here?' asked the blonde avidly.

'Somewhere,' said the dark girl. 'Aren't you going to introduce us, Nina?'

There was a flurry of introduction that left Strike none the wiser as to which of the girls was Miranda, Sarah or Emma, before the four women plunged again into a dissection of the unhappiness and drunkenness of Jerry Waldegrave.

'He should have ditched Fenella years ago,' said the dark girl. 'Vile woman.'

'Shh!' hissed Nina and all four of them became unnaturally still as a man nearly as tall as Strike ambled up to them. His round, doughy face was partly concealed by large horn-rimmed glasses and a tangle of brown hair. A brimming glass of red wine was threatening to spill over his hand.

'Guilty silence,' he noted with an amiable smile. His speech had a sonorous over-deliberation that to Strike declared a practised drunk. 'Three guesses what you're talking about: *Bombyx* – *Mori* – Quine. Hi,' he added, looking at Strike and stretching out a hand: their eyes were on a level. 'We haven't met, have we?'

'Jerry – Cormoran, Cormoran – Jerry,' said Nina at once. 'My date,' she added, an aside directed more at the three women beside her than at the tall editor.

'Cameron, was it?' asked Waldegrave, cupping a hand around his ear.

'Close enough,' said Strike.

'Sorry,' said Waldegrave. 'Deaf on one side. And have you ladies been gossiping in front of the tall dark stranger,' he said, with rather ponderous humour, 'in spite of Mr Chard's very clear instructions that nobody outside the company should be made privy to our guilty secret?'

'You won't tell on us, will you, Jerry?' asked the dark girl.

'If Daniel really wanted to keep that book quiet,' said the redhead impatiently, though with a swift glance over her shoulder to check that the boss was nowhere near by, 'he shouldn't be sending lawyers all over town trying to hush it up. People keep calling me, asking what's going on.'

'Jerry,' said the dark girl bravely, 'why did you have to speak to the lawyers?'

'Because I'm in it, Sarah,' said Waldegrave, with a wave of his glass that sent a slug of the contents slopping onto the manicured lawn. 'In it up to my malfunctioning ears. In the book.'

The women all made sounds of shock and protestation.

'What could Quine possibly say about you, when you've been so decent to him?' demanded the dark girl.

'The burden of Owen's song is that I'm gratuitously brutal to his masterpieces,' said Waldegrave, and he made a scissor-like gesture with the hand not grasping the glass.

'Oh, is that all?' said the blonde, with the faintest tinge of disappointment. 'Big deal. He's lucky to have a deal at all, the way he carries on.'

'Starting to look like he's gone underground again,' commented Waldegrave. 'Not answering any calls.'

'Cowardly bastard,' said the redhead.

'I'm quite worried about him, actually.'

'Worried?' repeated the redhead incredulously. 'You can't be serious, Jerry.'

'You'd be worried too, if you'd read that book,' said Waldegrave, with a tiny hiccup. 'I think Owen's cracking up. It reads like a suicide note.'

The blonde let out a little laugh, hastily repressed when Waldegrave looked at her.

'I'm not joking. I think he's having a breakdown. The subtext, under all the usual grotesquerie, is: everyone's against me, everyone's out to get me, everyone hates me—'

'Everyone *does* hate him,' interjected the blonde.

'No rational person would have imagined it could be published. And now he's disappeared.'

'He's always doing that, though,' said the redhead impatiently. 'It's his party piece, isn't it, doing a runner? Daisy Carter at Davis-Green told me he went off in a huff twice when they were doing *The Balzac Brothers* with him.'

'I'm worried about him,' said Waldegrave stubbornly. He took a deep drink of wine and said, 'Might've slit his wrists—'

'Owen wouldn't kill himself!' scoffed the blonde. Waldegrave looked down at her with what Strike thought was a mixture of pity and dislike.

'People *do* kill themselves, you know, Miranda, when they think their whole reason for living is being taken away from them. Even the fact that other people think their suffering is a joke isn't enough to shake them out of it.'

The blonde girl looked incredulous, then glanced around the circle for support, but nobody came to her defence.

'Writers are different,' said Waldegrave. 'I've never met one who was any good who wasn't screwy. Something bloody Liz Tassel would do well to remember.'

'She claims she didn't know what was in the book,' said Nina. 'She's telling everyone she was ill and didn't read it properly—'

'I know Liz Tassel,' growled Waldegrave and Strike was interested to see a flash of authentic anger in this amiable, drunken editor. 'She knew what she was bloody doing when she put that book out. She thought it was her last chance to make some money off Owen. Nice bit of publicity off the back of the scandal about Fancourt, whom she's hated for years . . . but now the shit's hit the fan she's disowning her client. Bloody outrageous behaviour.'

'Daniel disinvited her tonight,' said the dark girl. 'I had to ring her and tell her. It was horrible.'

'D'you know where Owen might've gone, Jerry?' asked Nina.

Waldegrave shrugged.

'Could be anywhere, couldn't he? But I hope he's all right, wherever he is. I can't help being fond of the silly bastard, in spite of it all.'

'What *is* this big Fancourt scandal that he's written about?' asked the redhead. 'I heard someone say it was something to do with a review . . . '

Everyone in the group apart from Strike began to talk at once, but Waldegrave's voice carried over the others' and the women fell silent with the instinctive courtesy women often show to incapacitated males.

'Thought everyone knew that story,' said Waldegrave on another faint hiccup. 'In a nutshell, Michael's first wife Elspeth wrote a very bad novel. An anonymous parody of it appeared in a literary magazine. She cut the parody out, pinned it to the front of her dress and gassed herself, *à la* Sylvia Plath.'

The redhead gasped.

'She *killed* herself?'

'Yep,' said Waldegrave, swigging wine again. 'Writers: screwy.'

'Who wrote the parody?'

'Everyone's always thought it was Owen. He denied it, but

then I suppose he would, given what it led to,' said Waldegrave. 'Owen and Michael never spoke again after Elspeth died. But in *Bombyx Mori*, Owen finds an ingenious way of suggesting that the real author of the parody was Michael himself.'

'*God*,' said the redhead, awestruck.

'Speaking of Fancourt,' said Waldegrave, glancing at his watch, 'I'm supposed to be telling you all that there's going to be a grand announcement downstairs at nine. You girls won't want to miss it.'

He ambled away. Two of the girls ground out their cigarettes and followed him. The blonde drifted off towards another group.

'Lovely, Jerry, isn't he?' Nina asked Strike, shivering in the depths of her woollen coat.

'Very magnanimous,' said Strike. 'Nobody else seems to think that Quine didn't know exactly what he was doing. Want to get back in the warm?'

Exhaustion was lapping at the edges of Strike's consciousness. He wanted passionately to go home, to begin the tiresome process of putting his leg to sleep (as he described it to himself), to close his eyes and attempt eight straight hours' slumber until he had to rise and place himself again in the vicinity of another unfaithful husband.

The room downstairs was more densely packed than ever. Nina stopped several times to shout and bawl into the ears of acquaintances. Strike was introduced to a squat romantic novelist who appeared dazzled by the glamour of cheap champagne and the loud band, and to Jerry Waldegrave's wife, who greeted Nina effusively and drunkenly through a lot of tangled black hair.

'She always sucks up,' said Nina coldly, disengaging herself and leading Strike closer to the makeshift stage. 'She comes from money and makes it clear that she married down with Jerry. Horrible snob.'

'Impressed by your father the QC, is she?' asked Strike.

'Scary memory you've got,' said Nina, with an admiring look. 'No, I think it's . . . well, I'm the Honourable Nina Lascelles really. I mean, who gives a shit? But people like Fenella do.'

An underling was now angling a microphone at a wooden lectern on a stage near the bar. Roper Chard's logo, a rope knot between the two names, and '100th Anniversary' were emblazoned on a banner.

There followed a tedious ten-minute wait during which Strike responded politely and appropriately to Nina's chatter, which required a great effort, as she was so much shorter, and the room was increasingly noisy.

'Is Larry Pinkelman here?' he asked, remembering the old children's writer on Elizabeth Tassel's wall.

'Oh no, he hates parties,' said Nina cheerfully.

'I thought you were throwing him one?'

'How did you know that?' she asked, startled.

'You just told me so, in the pub.'

'Wow, you really pay attention, don't you? Yeah, we're doing a dinner for the reprint of his Christmas stories, but it'll be very small. He hates crowds, Larry, he's really shy.'

Daniel Chard had at last reached the stage. The talk faded to a murmur and then died. Strike detected tension in the air as Chard shuffled his notes and then cleared his throat.

He must have had a great deal of practice, Strike thought, and yet his public speaking was barely competent. Chard looked up mechanically to the same spot over the crowd's head at regular intervals; he made eye contact with nobody; he was, at times, barely audible. After taking his listeners on a brief journey through the illustrious history of Roper Publishing, he made a modest detour into the antecedents of Chard Books, his grandfather's company, described their amalgamation and his own humble delight and pride, expressed in the same flat monotone as the rest, in finding himself, ten years on, as head of the global company. His small jokes were greeted with exuberant laughter fuelled, Strike thought, by discomfort as much as alcohol. Strike found himself staring at the sore, boiled-looking hands. He had once known a young private in the army whose eczema had become so bad under stress that he had had to be hospitalised.

'There can be no doubt,' said Chard, turning to what Strike, one of the tallest men in the room and close to the stage, could see was the last page of his speech, 'that publishing is currently undergoing a period of rapid changes and fresh challenges, but one thing remains as true today as it was a century ago: content is king. While we boast the best writers in the world, Roper Chard will continue to excite, to challenge and to entertain. And it is in that context' – the approach of a climax was declared not by any excitement, but by a relaxation in Chard's manner induced by the fact that his ordeal was nearly over – 'that I am honoured and delighted to tell you that we have this week secured the talents of one of the finest authors in the world. Ladies and gentlemen, please welcome Michael Fancourt!'

A perceptible intake of breath rolled like a breeze across the crowd. A woman yelped excitedly. Applause broke out somewhere to the rear of the room and spread like crackling fire to the front. Strike saw a distant door open, the glimpse of an over-large head, a sour expression, before Fancourt was swallowed by the enthusiastic employees. It was several minutes before he emerged onto the stage to shake Chard's hand.

'Oh my God,' an excitedly applauding Nina kept saying. 'Oh my *God*.'

Jerry Waldegrave, who like Strike rose head and shoulders above the mostly female crowd, was standing almost directly opposite them on the other side of the stage. He was again holding a full glass, so could not applaud, and he raised it to his lips, unsmiling, as he watched Fancourt gesture for quiet in front of the microphone.

'Thanks, Dan,' said Fancourt. 'Well, I certainly never expected to find myself here,' he said, and these words were greeted by a raucous outbreak of laughter, 'but it feels like a homecoming. I wrote for Chard and then I wrote for Roper and they were good days. I was an angry young man' – widespread titters – 'and now I'm an angry old man' – much laughter and even a small smile from Daniel Chard – 'and I look forward to raging for you' – effusive laughter from Chard as well as the crowd; Strike and Waldegrave seemed to be the only two in the room not convulsed. 'I'm delighted to be back and I'll do my best to – what was it, Dan? – keep Roper Chard exciting, challenging and entertaining.'

A storm of applause; the two men were shaking hands amid camera flashes.

'Half a mill', I reckon,' said a drunken man behind Strike, 'and ten k to turn up tonight.'

Fancourt descended the stage right in front of Strike. His habitually dour expression had barely varied for the photographs, but he looked happier as hands stretched out towards him. Michael Fancourt did not disdain adulation.

'*Wow*,' said Nina to Strike. 'Can you *believe* that?'

Fancourt's over-large head had disappeared into the crowd. The curvaceous Joanna Waldegrave appeared, trying to make her way towards the famous author. Her father was suddenly behind her; with a drunken lurch he reached out a hand and took her upper arm none too gently.

'He's got other people to talk to, Jo, leave him.'

'Mummy's made a beeline, why don't you grab *her*?'

Strike watched Joanna stalk away from her father, evidently angry. Daniel Chard had vanished too; Strike wondered whether he had slipped out of a door while the crowd was busy with Fancourt.

'Your CEO doesn't love the limelight,' Strike commented to Nina.

'They say he's got a lot better,' said Nina, who was still gazing towards Fancourt. 'He could barely look up from his notes ten years ago. He's a good businessman, though, you know. Shrewd.'

Curiosity and tiredness tussled inside Strike.

'Nina,' he said, drawing his companion away from the throng pressing around Fancourt; she permitted him to lead her willingly, 'where did you say the manuscript of *Bombyx Mori* is?'

'In Jerry's safe,' she said. 'Floor below this.' She sipped champagne, her huge eyes shining. 'Are you asking what I think you're asking?'

'How much trouble would you be in?'

'Loads,' she said insouciantly. 'But I've got my keycard on me and everyone's busy, aren't they?'

Her father, Strike thought ruthlessly, was a QC. They would be wary of how they dismissed her.

'D'you reckon we could run off a copy?'

'Let's do it,' she said, throwing back the last of her drink.

The lift was empty and the floor below dark and deserted. Nina opened the door to the department with her keycard and led him confidently between blank computer monitors and deserted desks towards a large corner office. The only light came from perennially lit London beyond the windows and the occasional tiny orange light indicating a computer on standby.

Waldegrave's office was not locked but the safe, which stood behind a hinged bookcase, operated on a keypad. Nina input a four-number code. The door swung open and Strike saw an untidy stack of pages lying inside.

'That's it,' she said happily.

'Keep your voice down,' Strike advised her.

Strike kept watch while she ran off a copy for him at the photocopier outside the door. The endless swish and hum was strangely soothing. Nobody came, nobody saw; fifteen minutes later, Nina was replacing the manuscript in the safe and locking it up.

'There you go.'

She handed him the copy, with several strong elastic bands holding it together. As he took it she leaned in for a few seconds; a tipsy sway, an extended brush against him. He owed her something in return, but he was shatteringly tired; both the idea of going back to that flat in St John's Wood and of taking her to his attic in Denmark Street were unappealing. Would a drink, tomorrow night perhaps, be adequate repayment? And then he remembered that tomorrow night was his birthday dinner at his sister's. Lucy had said he could bring someone.

'Want to come to a tedious dinner party tomorrow night?' he asked her.

She laughed, clearly elated.

'What'll be tedious about it?'

'Everything. You'd cheer it up. Fancy it?'

'Well – why not?' she said happily.

The invitation seemed to meet the bill; he felt the demand for some physical gesture recede. They made their way out of the dark department in an atmosphere of friendly camaraderie, the copied manuscript of *Bombyx Mori* hidden beneath Strike's overcoat. After noting down her address and phone number, he saw her safely into a taxi with a sense of relief and release.

14

There he sits a whole afternoon sometimes, reading of these same abominable, vile, (a pox on them, I cannot abide them!) rascally verses.

Ben Jonson, *Every Man in His Humour*

They marched against the war in which Strike had lost his leg the next day, thousands snaking their way through the heart of chilly London bearing placards, military families to the fore. Strike had heard through mutual army friends that the parents of Gary Topley – dead in the explosion that had cost Strike a limb – would be among the demonstrators, but it did not occur to Strike to join them. His feelings about the war could not be encapsulated in black on a square white placard. Do the job and do it well had been his creed then and now, and to march would be to imply regrets he did not have. And so he strapped on his prosthesis, dressed in his best Italian suit and headed off to Bond Street.

The treacherous husband he sought was insisting that his estranged wife, Strike's brunette client, had lost, through her own drunken carelessness, several pieces of very valuable jewellery while the couple were staying at a hotel. Strike happened to know that the husband had an appointment in Bond Street this morning, and had a hunch that some of that allegedly lost jewellery might be making a surprise reappearance.

His target entered the jewellers while Strike examined the windows of a shop opposite. Once he had left, half an hour later, Strike took himself off for a coffee, allowed two hours to elapse, then strode inside the jewellers and proclaimed his wife's love of emeralds, which pretence resulted, after half an hour's staged deliberation over various pieces, in the production of the very necklace that the brunette had suspected her errant husband of having pocketed. Strike bought it at once, a transaction only made possible by the fact that his client had advanced him ten thousand pounds for the purpose. Ten thousand pounds to prove her husband's deceit was as nothing to a woman who stood to receive a settlement of millions.

Strike picked up a kebab on his way home. After locking the necklace in a small safe he had installed in his office (usually used for the protection of incriminating photographs) he headed upstairs, made himself a mug of strong tea, took off the suit and put on the TV so that he could keep an eye on the build-up to the Arsenal–Spurs match. He then stretched out comfortably on his bed and started to read the manuscript he had stolen the night before.

As Elizabeth Tassel had told him, *Bombyx Mori* was a perverse *Pilgrim's Progress*, set in a folkloric no-man's-land in which the eponymous hero (a young writer of genius) set out from an island populated by inbred idiots too blind to recognise his talent on what seemed to be a largely symbolic journey towards a distant city. The richness and strangeness of the language and imagery were familiar to Strike from his perusal of *The Balzac Brothers*, but his interest in the subject matter drew him on.

The first familiar character to emerge from the densely

written and frequently obscene sentences was Leonora Quine. As the brilliant young Bombyx journeyed through a landscape populated by various dangers and monsters he came across Succuba, a woman described succinctly as a 'well-worn whore', who captured and tied him up and succeeded in raping him. Leonora was described to the life: thin and dowdy, with her large glasses and her flat, deadpan manner. After being systematically abused for several days, Bombyx persuaded Succuba to release him. She was so desolate at his departure that Bombyx agreed to take her along: the first example of the story's frequent strange, dream-like reversals, whereby what had been bad and frightening became good and sensible without justification or apology.

A few pages further on, Bombyx and Succuba were attacked by a creature called the Tick, which Strike recognised easily as Elizabeth Tassel: square-jawed, deep-voiced and frightening. Once again Bombyx took pity on the thing once it had finished violating him, and permitted it to join him. The Tick had an unpleasant habit of suckling from Bombyx while he slept. He started to become thin and weak.

Bombyx's gender appeared strangely mutable. Quite apart from his apparent ability to breast-feed, he was soon showing signs of pregnancy, despite continuing to pleasure a number of apparently nymphomaniac women who strayed regularly across his path.

Wading through ornate obscenity, Strike wondered how many portraits of real people he was failing to notice. The violence of Bombyx's encounters with other humans was disturbing; their perversity and cruelty left barely an orifice unviolated; it was a sadomasochistic frenzy. Yet Bombyx's essential innocence and purity were a constant theme, the simple statement of his genius apparently all the reader needed to absolve him of the crimes in which he colluded as freely as the supposed monsters around him. As he turned the pages, Strike remembered Jerry Waldegrave's opinion that Quine was mentally ill; he was starting to have some sympathy with his view . . .

The match was about to start. Strike set the manuscript down, feeling as though he had been trapped for a long time inside a dark, grubby basement, away from natural light and air. Now he felt only pleasurable anticipation. He was confident Arsenal were about to win – Spurs had not managed to beat them at home in seventeen years.

And for forty-five minutes Strike lost himself in pleasure and frequent bellows of encouragement while his team went two-nil up.

At half time, and with a feeling of reluctance, he muted the sound and returned to the bizarre world of Owen Quine's imagination.

He recognised nobody until Bombyx drew close to the city that was his destination. Here, on a bridge over the moat that surrounded the city walls, stood a large, shambling and myopic figure: the Cutter.

The Cutter sported a low cap instead of horn-rimmed glasses, and carried a wriggling, bloodstained sack over his shoulder. Bombyx accepted the Cutter's offer to lead him, Succuba and the Tick to a secret door into the city. Inured by now to sexual violence, Strike was unsurprised that the Cutter turned out to be intent on Bombyx's castration. In the ensuing fight, the bag rolled off the Cutter's back and a dwarfish female creature burst out of it. The Cutter let Bombyx, Succuba and the Tick escape while he pursued the dwarf; Bombyx and his companions managed to find a chink in the city's walls and looked back to see the Cutter drowning the little creature in the moat.

Strike had been so engrossed in his reading that he had not realised the match had restarted. He glanced up at the muted TV.

'*Fuck!*'

Two-all: unbelievably Spurs had drawn level. Strike threw the manuscript aside, appalled. Arsenal's defence was crumbling before his eyes. This should have been a win. They had been set to go top of the league.

'*FUCK!*' Strike bellowed ten minutes later as a header soared past Fabiański.

Spurs had won.

He turned off the TV with several more expletives and checked his watch. There was only half an hour in which to shower and change before picking up Nina Lascelles in St John's Wood; the round trip to Bromley was going to cost him a fortune. He contemplated the prospect of the final quarter of Quine's manuscript with distaste, feeling much sympathy for Elizabeth Tassel, who had skimmed the final passages.

He was not even sure why he was reading it, other than curiosity.

Downcast and irritable, he moved off towards the shower, wishing that he could have spent the night at home and feeling, irrationally, that if he had not allowed his attention to be distracted by the obscene, nightmarish world of *Bombyx Mori*, Arsenal might have won.

15

I tell you 'tis not modish to know relations in town.

William Congreve, *The Way of the World*

'So? What did you think of *Bombyx Mori*?' Nina asked him as they pulled away from her flat in a taxi he could ill afford. If he had not invited her, Strike would have made the journey to Bromley and back by public transport, time-consuming and inconvenient though that would have been.

'Product of a diseased mind,' said Strike.

Nina laughed.

'But you haven't read any of Owen's other books; they're nearly as bad. I admit this one's got a *serious* gag factor. What about Daniel's suppurating knob?'

'I haven't got there yet. Something to look forward to.'

Beneath yesterday evening's warm woollen coat she was wearing a clinging, strappy black dress, of which Strike had had an excellent view when she had invited him into her St John's Wood flat while she collected bag and keys. She was also clutching a bottle of wine that she had seized from her kitchen when she saw that he was empty-handed. A clever, pretty girl with nice manners, but her willingness to meet him the very night following their first introduction, and that night a Saturday to boot, hinted at recklessness, or perhaps neediness.

Strike asked himself again what he thought he was playing at as they rolled away from the heart of London towards a realm of owner-occupiers, towards spacious houses crammed with coffee makers and HD televisions, towards everything that he had never owned and which his sister assumed, anxiously, must be his ultimate ambition.

It was like Lucy to throw him a birthday dinner at her own house. She was fundamentally unimaginative and, even though she often seemed more harried there than anywhere else, she rated her home's attractions highly. It was like her to insist on giving him a dinner he didn't want, but which she could not understand him not wanting. Birthdays in Lucy's world were always celebrated, never forgotten: there must be cake and candles and cards and presents; time must be marked, order preserved, traditions upheld.

As the taxi passed through the Blackwall Tunnel, speeding them below the Thames into south London, Strike recognised that the act of bringing Nina with him to the family party was a declaration of non-conformity. In spite of the conventional bottle of wine held on her lap, she was highly strung, happy to take risks and chances. She lived alone and talked books not babies; she was not, in short, Lucy's kind of woman.

Nearly an hour after he had left Denmark Street, with his wallet fifty pounds lighter, Strike helped Nina out into the dark chill of Lucy's street and led her down a path beneath the large magnolia tree that dominated the front garden. Before ringing the doorbell Strike said, with some reluctance:

'I should probably tell you: this is a birthday dinner. For me.'

'Oh, you should have said! Happy—'

'It isn't today,' said Strike. 'No big deal.'

And he rang the doorbell.

Strike's brother-in-law, Greg, let them inside. A lot of arm slapping followed, as well as an exaggerated show of pleasure at the sight of Nina. This emotion was conspicuous by its absence in Lucy, who bustled down the hall holding a spatula like a sword and wearing an apron over her party dress.

'*You didn't say you were bringing someone!*' she hissed in Strike's ear as he bent to kiss her cheek. Lucy was short, blonde and round-faced; nobody ever guessed that they were related. She was the result of another of their mother's liaisons with a well-known musician. Rick was a rhythm guitarist who, unlike Strike's father, maintained an amicable relationship with his offspring.

'I thought you asked me to bring a guest,' Strike muttered to his sister as Greg ushered Nina into the sitting room.

'I asked *whether you were going to*,' said Lucy angrily. 'Oh God – I'll have to go and set an extra – and *poor Marguerite*—'

'Who's Marguerite?' asked Strike, but Lucy was already hurrying off towards the dining room, spatula aloft, leaving her guest of honour alone in the hall. With a sigh, Strike followed Greg and Nina into the sitting room.

'Surprise!' said a fair-haired man with a receding hairline, getting up from the sofa at which his bespectacled wife was beaming at Strike.

'Christ almighty,' said Strike, advancing to shake the outstretched hand with genuine pleasure. Nick and Ilsa were two of his oldest friends and they were the only place where the two halves of his early life intersected: London and Cornwall, happily married.

'No one told me you were going to be here!'

'Yeah, well, that's the surprise, Oggy,' said Nick as Strike kissed Ilsa. 'D'you know Marguerite?'

'No,' said Strike, 'I don't.'

So this was why Lucy had wanted to check whether he was bringing anyone with him; this was the sort of woman she imagined him falling for, and living with for ever in a house with a magnolia tree in the front garden. Marguerite was dark, greasy skinned and morose-looking, wearing a shiny purple dress that appeared to have been bought when she was a little thinner. Strike was sure she was a divorcée. He was developing second sight on that subject.

'Hi,' she said, while thin Nina in her strappy black dress chatted with Greg; the short greeting contained a world of bitterness.

So seven of them sat down to dinner. Strike had not seen much of his civilian friends since he had been invalided out of the army. His voluntarily heavy workload had blurred the boundaries between weekday and weekend, but now he realised anew how much he liked Nick and Ilsa, and how infinitely preferable it would have been if the three of them had been alone somewhere, enjoying a curry.

'How do you know Cormoran?' Nina asked them avidly.

'I was at school with him in Cornwall,' said Ilsa, smiling at Strike across the table. 'On and off. Came and went, didn't you, Corm?'

And the story of Strike and Lucy's fragmented childhood was trotted out over the smoked salmon, their travels with their itinerant mother and their regular returns to St Mawes and the aunt and uncle who had acted as surrogate parents throughout their childhood and teens.

'And then Corm got taken to London by his mother again when he was, what, seventeen?' said Ilsa.

Strike could tell that Lucy was not enjoying the conversation: she hated talk about their unusual upbringing, their notorious mother.

'And he ended up at a good rough old comprehensive with me,' said Nick. 'Good times.'

'Nick was a useful bloke to know,' said Strike. 'Knows London like the back of his hand; his dad's a cabbie.'

'Are you a cabbie too?' Nina asked Nick, apparently exhilarated by the exoticism of Strike's friends.

'No,' said Nick cheerfully, 'I'm a gastroenterologist. Oggy and I had a joint eighteenth birthday party—'

'—and Corm invited his friend Dave and me up from St Mawes for it. First time I'd ever been to London, I was so excited—' said Ilsa.

'—and that's where we met,' finished Nick, grinning at his wife.

'And still no kids, all these years later?' asked Greg, smug father of three sons.

There was the tiniest pause. Strike knew that Nick and Ilsa had been trying for a child, without success, for several years.

'Not yet,' said Nick. 'What d'you do, Nina?'

The mention of Roper Chard brought some animation to Marguerite, who had been regarding Strike sullenly from the other end of the table, as though he were a tasty morsel placed remorselessly out of reach.

'Michael Fancourt's just moved to Roper Chard,' she stated. 'I saw it on his website this morning.'

'Blimey, that was only made public yesterday,' said Nina. The 'blimey' reminded Strike of the way Dominic Culpepper called waiters 'mate'; it was, he thought, for Nick's benefit, and perhaps to demonstrate to Strike that she too could mingle happily with the proletariat. (Charlotte, Strike's ex-fiancée, had never altered her vocabulary or accent, no matter where she found herself. Nor had she liked any of his friends.)

'Oh, I'm a big fan of Michael Fancourt's,' said Marguerite. '*House of Hollow*'s one of my favourite novels. I adore the Russians, and there's something about Fancourt that makes me think of Dostoevsky . . . '

Lucy had told her, Strike guessed, that he had been to Oxford, that he was clever. He wished Marguerite a thousand miles away and that Lucy understood him better.

'Fancourt can't write women,' said Nina dismissively. 'He tries but he can't do it. His women are all temper, tits and tampons.'

Nick had snorted into his wine at the sound of the unexpected word 'tits'; Strike laughed at Nick laughing; Ilsa said, giggling:

'You're thirty-six, both of you. For God's sake.'

'Well, I think he's marvellous,' repeated Marguerite, without the flicker of a smile. She had been deprived of a potential partner, one-legged and overweight though he might be; she was not going to give up Michael Fancourt. 'And incredibly attractive. Complicated and clever, I always fall for them,' she sighed in an aside to Lucy, clearly referring to past calamities.

'His head's too big for his body,' said Nina, cheerfully disowning her excitement of the previous evening at the sight of Fancourt, 'and he's phenomenally arrogant.'

'I've always thought it was so touching, what he did for that young American writer,' said Marguerite as Lucy cleared the starters away and motioned to Greg to help her in the kitchen.

'Finishing his novel for him – that young novelist who died of Aids, what was his—?'

'Joe North,' said Nina.

'Surprised you felt up to coming out tonight,' Nick said quietly to Strike. 'After what happened this afternoon.'

Nick was, regrettably, a Spurs fan.

Greg, who had returned carrying a joint of lamb and had overheard Nick's words, immediately seized on them.

'Must've stung, eh, Corm? When everyone thought they had it in the bag?'

'What's this?' asked Lucy like a schoolmistress calling the class to order as she set down dishes of potatoes and vegetables. 'Oh, not football, Greg, please.'

So Marguerite was left in possession of the conversational ball again.

'Yes, *House of Hollow* was inspired by the house his dead friend left to Fancourt, a place where they'd been happy when young. It's terribly touching. It's really a story of regret, loss, thwarted ambition—'

'Joe North left the house jointly to Michael Fancourt and Owen Quine, actually,' Nina corrected Marguerite firmly. 'And they *both* wrote novels inspired by it; Michael's won the Booker – and Owen's was panned by everyone,' Nina added in an aside to Strike.

'What happened to the house?' Strike asked Nina as Lucy passed him a plate of lamb.

'Oh, this was ages ago, it'll have been sold,' said Nina. 'They wouldn't want to co-own anything; they've hated each other for years. Ever since Elspeth Fancourt killed herself over that parody.'

'You don't know where the house is?'

'He's not *there*,' Nina half-whispered.

'Who's not where?' Lucy said, barely concealing her irritation. Her plans for Strike had been disrupted. She was never going to like Nina now.

'One of our writers has gone missing,' Nina told her. 'His wife asked Cormoran to find him.'

'Successful bloke?' asked Greg.

No doubt Greg was tired of his wife worrying volubly about her brilliant but impecunious brother, with his business barely breaking even in spite of his heavy workload, but the word 'successful', with everything it connoted when spoken by Greg, affected Strike like nettle rash.

'No,' he said, 'I don't think you'd call Quine successful.'

'Who's hired you, Corm? The publisher?' asked Lucy anxiously.

'His wife,' said Strike.

'She's going to be able to pay the bill, though, right?' asked Greg. 'No lame ducks, Corm, that's gotta be your number one rule of business.'

'Surprised you don't jot those pearls of wisdom down,' Nick told Strike under his breath as Lucy offered Marguerite more of anything on the table (compensation for not taking Strike home and getting to marry him and live two streets away with a shiny new coffee maker from Lucy-and-Greg).

After dinner they retired to the beige three-piece suite in the sitting room, where presents and cards were presented. Lucy and Greg had bought him a new watch, 'Because I know your last one got broken,' Lucy said. Touched that she had remembered, a swell of affection temporarily blotted out Strike's irritation that she had dragged him here tonight, and nagged him about his life choices, and married Greg . . . He removed the cheap but serviceable replacement he had bought himself and put Lucy's watch on instead: it was large and shiny with a metallic bracelet and looked like a duplicate of Greg's.

Nick and Ilsa had bought him 'that whisky you like': Arran Single Malt, it reminded him powerfully of Charlotte, with whom he had first tasted it, but any possibility of melancholy remembrance was chased away by the abrupt appearance in the doorway of three pyjama-ed figures, the tallest of whom asked:

'Is there cake yet?'

Strike had never wanted children (an attitude Lucy deplored) and barely knew his nephews, whom he saw infrequently. The eldest and youngest trailed their mother out of the room to fetch his birthday cake; the middle boy, however, made a beeline for Strike and held out a homemade card.

'That's you,' said Jack, pointing at the picture, 'getting your medal.'

'Have you got a medal?' asked Nina, smiling and wide-eyed.

'Thanks, Jack,' said Strike.

'I want to be a soldier,' said Jack.

'Your fault, Corm,' said Greg, with what Strike could not help feeling was a certain animus. 'Buying him soldier toys. Telling him about your gun.'

'Two guns,' Jack corrected his father. 'You had two guns,' he told Strike. 'But you had to give them back.'

'Good memory,' Strike told him. 'You'll go far.'

Lucy appeared with the homemade cake, blazing with thirty-six candles and decorated with what looked like hundreds of Smarties. As Greg turned out the light and everyone began to sing, Strike experienced an almost overwhelming desire to leave. He would ring a cab the instant he could escape the room; in the meantime, he hoisted a smile onto his face and blew out his candles, avoiding the gaze of Marguerite, who was smouldering at him with an unnerving lack of restraint from a nearby chair. It was not his fault that he had been made to play the decorated helpmeet of abandoned women by his well-meaning friends and family.

Strike called a cab from the downstairs bathroom and announced half an hour later, with a decent show of regret, that he and Nina would have to leave; he had to be up early the next day.

Out in the crowded and noisy hall, after Strike had neatly dodged being kissed on the mouth by Marguerite, while his nephews worked off their overexcitement and a late-night sugar rush, and Greg helped Nina officiously into her coat, Nick muttered to Strike:

'I didn't think you fancied little women.'

'I don't,' Strike returned quietly. 'She nicked something for me yesterday.'

'Yeah? Well, I'd show your gratitude by letting her go on top,' said Nick. 'You could squash her like a beetle.'

16

> … let not our supper be raw, for you shall have blood enough, your belly full.
>
> Thomas Dekker and Thomas Middleton, *The Honest Whore*

Strike knew immediately upon waking the following morning that he was not in his own bed. It was too comfortable, the sheets too smooth; the daylight stippling the covers fell from the wrong side of the room and the sound of the rain pattering against the window was muffled by drawn curtains. He pushed himself up into a sitting position, squinting around at Nina's bedroom, glimpsed only briefly by lamplight the previous evening, and caught sight of his own naked torso in a mirror opposite, thick dark chest hair making a black blot against the pale blue wall behind him.

Nina was absent, but he could smell coffee. As he had anticipated, she had been enthusiastic and energetic in bed, driving away the slight melancholy that had threatened to follow him from his birthday celebrations. Now, though, he wondered how quickly he would be able to extricate himself. To linger would be to raise expectations he was not prepared to meet.

His prosthetic leg was propped against the wall beside the bed. On the point of sliding himself out of bed to reach it he drew back, because the bedroom door opened and in walked Nina, fully dressed and damp-haired, with newspapers under her arm, two mugs of coffee in one hand and a plate of croissants in the other.

'I nipped out,' she said breathlessly. 'God, it's horrible out there. Feel my nose, I'm frozen.'

'You didn't have to do that,' he said, gesturing to the croissants.

'I'm starving and there's a fabulous bakery up the road. Look at this – *News of the World* – Dom's big exclusive!'

A photograph of the disgraced peer whose hidden accounts Strike had revealed to Culpepper filled the middle of the front page, flanked on three sides by pictures of two of his lovers and of the Cayman Island documents Strike had wrested from his PA. LORD PORKER OF PAYWELL screamed the headline. Strike took the paper from Nina and skim-read the story. Culpepper had kept his word: the heartbroken PA was not mentioned anywhere.

Nina was sitting beside Strike on the bed, reading along with him, emitting faintly amused comments: 'Oh God, how anyone could, look at him' and 'Oh wow, that's disgusting'.

'Won't do Culpepper any harm,' Strike said, closing the paper when both had finished. The date at the top of the front page caught his eye: 21 November. It was his ex-fiancée's birthday.

A small, painful tug under the solar plexus and a sudden gush of vivid, unwelcome memories . . . a year ago, almost to the hour, he had woken up beside Charlotte in Holland Park Avenue. He remembered her long black hair, wide hazel-green eyes, a body the like of which he would never see again, never be permitted to touch . . . They had been happy, that morning: the bed a life raft bobbing on the turbulent sea of their endlessly recurring troubles. He had presented her with a bracelet, the purchase of which had necessitated (though she did not know it) the taking out of a loan at horrifying rates of interest . . . and two days later, on his own birthday, she had given him an Italian suit, and they had gone out to dinner and actually fixed on a date when they would marry at last, sixteen years after they had first met . . .

But the naming of a day had marked a new and dreadful phase in their relationship, as though it had damaged the precarious tension in which they were used to living. Charlotte had become steadily more volatile, more capricious. Rows and scenes, broken china, accusations of his unfaithfulness (when it had been she, as he now believed, who had been secretly meeting the man to whom she was now engaged) . . . they had struggled on for nearly four months until, in a final, filthy explosion of recrimination and rage, everything had ended for good.

A rustle of cotton: Strike looked around, almost surprised to find himself still in Nina's bedroom. She was about to strip off her top, intending to get back into bed with him.

'I can't stay,' he told her, stretching across for his prosthesis again.

'Why not?' she asked with her arms folded across her front, gripping the hem of her shirt. 'Come on – it's Sunday!'

'I've got to work,' he lied. 'People need investigating on Sundays too.'

'Oh,' she said, trying to sound matter-of-fact but looking crestfallen.

He drank his coffee, keeping the conversation bright but

impersonal. She watched him strap his leg on and head for the bathroom, and when he returned to dress she was curled up in a chair, munching a croissant with a slightly forlorn air.

'You're sure you don't know where this house was? The one Quine and Fancourt inherited?' he asked her as he pulled on his trousers.

'What?' she said, confused. 'Oh – God, you're not going looking for that, are you? I told you, it'll have been sold years ago!'

'I might ask Quine's wife about it,' said Strike.

He told her that he would call her, but briskly, so that she might understand these to be empty words, a matter of form, and left her house with a feeling of faint gratitude, but no guilt.

The rain jabbed again at his face and hands as he walked down the unfamiliar street, heading for the Tube station. Christmassy fairy lights twinkled from the window of the bakery where Nina had just bought croissants. Strike's large hunched reflection slid across the rain-spotted surface, clutching in one cold fist the plastic carrier bag which Lucy had helpfully given him to carry his cards, his birthday whisky and the box of his shiny new watch.

His thoughts slid irresistibly back to Charlotte, thirty-six but looking twenty-five, celebrating her birthday with her new fiancé. Perhaps she had received diamonds, Strike thought; she had always said she didn't care for such things, but when they had argued the glitter of all he could not give her had sometimes been flung back hard in his face . . .

Successful bloke? Greg had asked of Owen Quine, by which he meant: 'Big car? Nice house? Fat bank balance?'

Strike passed the Beatles Coffee Shop with its jauntily positioned black-and-white heads of the Fab Four peering out at him, and entered the relative warmth of the station. He did not want to spend this rainy Sunday alone in his attic rooms in Denmark Street. He wanted to keep busy on the anniversary of Charlotte Campbell's birth.

Pausing to take out his mobile, he telephoned Leonora Quine.

'Hello?' she said brusquely.

'Hi, Leonora, it's Cormoran Strike here—'

'Have you found Owen?' she demanded.

'Afraid not. I'm calling because I've just heard that your husband was left a house by a friend.'

'What house?'

She sounded tired and irritable. He thought of the various moneyed husbands he had come up against professionally, men who hid bachelor apartments from their wives, and wondered whether he had just given away something that Quine had been keeping from his family.

'Isn't it true? Didn't a writer called Joe North leave a house jointly to—?'

'Oh, *that*,' she said. 'Talgarth Road, yeah. That was thirty-odd years ago, though. What d'you wanna know about that for?'

'It's been sold, has it?'

'No,' she said resentfully, 'because bloody Fancourt never let us. Out of spite, it is, because *he* never uses it. It just sits there, no use to anyone, mouldering away.'

Strike leaned back against the wall beside the ticket machines, his eyes fixed on a circular ceiling supported by a spider's web of struts. This, he told himself again, is what comes of taking on clients when you're wrecked. He should have asked if they owned any other properties. He should have checked.

'Has anyone gone to see whether your husband's there, Mrs Quine?'

She emitted a hoot of derision.

'He wouldn't go *there*!' she said, as though Strike were suggesting that her husband had hidden in Buckingham Palace. 'He hates it, he never goes near it! Anyway, I don't think it's got furniture or nothing.'

'Have you got a key?'

'I dunno. But Owen'd *never* go there! He hasn't been near it in years. It'd be an 'orrible place to stay, old and empty.'

'If you could have a look for the key—'

'I can't go tearing off to Talgarth Road, I've got Orlando!' she said, predictably. 'Anyway, I'm telling you, he wouldn't—'

'I'm offering to come over now,' said Strike, 'get the key from you, if you can find it, and go and check. Just to make sure we've looked everywhere.'

'Yeah, but – it's Sunday,' she said, sounding taken aback.

'I know it is. D'you think you could have a look for the key?'

'All right, then,' she said after a short pause. 'But,' with a last burst of spirit, 'he won't be there!'

Strike took the Tube, changing once, to Westbourne Park and then, collar turned up against the icy deluge, marched towards the address that Leonora had scribbled down for him at their first meeting.

It was another of those odd pockets of London where millionaires sat within a stone's throw of working-class families who had occupied their homes for forty years or more. The rain-washed scene presented an odd diorama: sleek new apartment blocks behind quiet nondescript terraces, the luxurious new and the comfortable old.

The Quines' family home was in Southern Row, a quiet

back street of small brick houses, a short walk from a white-washed pub called the Chilled Eskimo. Cold and wet, Strike squinted up at the sign overhead as he passed; it depicted a happy Inuit relaxing beside a fishing hole, his back to the rising sun.

The door of the Quines' house was a peeling sludge green. Everything about the frontage was dilapidated, including the gate hanging on by only one hinge. Strike thought of Quine's predilection for comfortable hotel rooms as he rang the door-bell and his opinion of the missing man fell a little further.

'You were quick,' was Leonora's gruff greeting on opening the door. 'Come in.'

He followed her down a dim, narrow hallway. To the left, a door stood ajar onto what was clearly Owen Quine's study. It looked untidy and dirty. Drawers hung open and an old electric typewriter sat skewed on the desk. Strike could picture Quine tearing pages from it in his rage at Elizabeth Tassel.

'Any luck with the key?' Strike asked Leonora as they entered the dark, stale-smelling kitchen at the end of the hall. The appliances all looked as though they were at least thirty years old. Strike had an idea that his Aunt Joan had owned the identical dark brown microwave back in the eighties.

'Well, I found *them*,' Leonora told him, gesturing towards half a dozen keys lying on the kitchen table. 'I dunno whether any of them's the right one.'

None of them was attached to a key ring and one of them looked too big to open anything but a church door.

'What number Talgarth Road?' Strike asked her.

'Hundred and seventy-nine.'

'When were you last there?'

'Me? I never been there,' she said with what seemed genuine indifference. 'I wasn't int'rested. Silly thing to do.'

'What was?'

'Leaving it to them.' In the face of Strike's politely enquiring face she said impatiently, 'That Joe North, leaving it to Owen and Michael Fancourt. He said it was for them to write in. They've never used it since. Useless.'

'And you've never been there?'

'No. They got it round the time I had Orlando. I wasn't int'rested,' she repeated.

'Orlando was born then?' Strike asked, surprised. He had been vaguely imagining Orlando as a hyperactive ten-year-old.

'In eighty-six, yeah,' said Leonora. 'But she's handicapped.'

'Oh,' said Strike. 'I see.'

'Upstairs sulking now, cos I had to tell her off,' said Leonora, in one of her bursts of expansiveness. 'She nicks things. She knows it's wrong but she keeps doing it. I caught her taking Edna-Next-Door's purse out of her bag when she come round yesterday. It wasn't cos of the money,' she said quickly, as though he had made an accusation. 'It's cos she liked the colour. Edna understands cos she knows her, but not everyone does. I tell her it's wrong. She knows it's wrong.'

'All right if I take these and try them, then?' Strike asked, scooping the keys into his hand.

'If y'want,' said Leonora, but she added defiantly, 'He won't be there.'

Strike pocketed his haul, turned down Leonora's afterthought offer of tea or coffee and returned to the cold rain.

He found himself limping again as he walked towards Westbourne Park Tube station, which would mean a short journey with minimal changes. He had not taken as much care as usual in attaching his prosthesis in his haste to get out of Nina's flat, nor had he been able to apply any of those soothing products that helped protect the skin beneath it.

Eight months previously (on the very day that he had later been stabbed in his upper arm) he had taken a bad fall down some stairs. The consultant who had examined it shortly afterwards had informed him that he had done additional, though probably reparable, damage to the medial ligaments in the knee joint of his amputated leg and advised ice, rest and further investigation. But Strike had not been able to afford rest and had not wished for further tests, so he had strapped up the knee and tried to remember to elevate his leg when sitting. The pain had mostly subsided but occasionally, when he had done a lot of walking, it began to throb and swell again.

The road along which Strike was trudging curved to the right. A tall, thin, hunched figure was walking behind him, its head bowed so that only the top of a black hood was visible.

Of course, the sensible thing to do would be to go home, now, and rest his knee. It was Sunday. There was no need for him to go marching all over London in the rain.

He won't be there, said Leonora in his head.

But the alternative was returning to Denmark Street, listening to the rain hammering against the badly fitting window beside his bed under the eaves, with photo albums full of Charlotte too close, in the boxes on the landing . . .

Better to move, to work, to think about other people's problems . . .

Blinking in the rain, he glanced up at the houses he was passing and glimpsed in his peripheral vision the figure following twenty yards behind him. Though the dark coat was shapeless,

Strike had the impression from the short, quick steps, that the figure was female.

Now Strike noticed something curious about the way she was walking, something unnatural. There was none of the self-preoccupation of the lone stroller on a cold wet day. Her head was not bowed in protection against the elements, nor was she maintaining a steady pace with the simple view of achieving a destination. She kept adjusting her speed in tiny but, to Strike, noticeable increments, and every few steps the hidden face beneath the hood presented itself to the chilly onslaught of the driving rain, then vanished again into shadow. She was keeping him in her sights.

What had Leonora said at their first meeting?

I think I've been followed. Tall, dark girl with round shoulders.

Strike experimented by speeding up and slowing down infinitesimally. The space between them remained constant; her hidden face flickered up and down more frequently, a pale pink blur, to check his position.

She was not experienced at following people. Strike, who was an expert, would have taken the opposite pavement, pretended to be talking on a mobile phone; concealed his focused and singular interest in the subject . . .

For his own amusement, he faked a sudden hesitation, as though he had been caught by a doubt as to the right direction. Caught off guard, the dark figure stopped dead, paralysed. Strike strolled on again and after a few seconds heard her footsteps echoing on the wet pavement behind him. She was too foolish even to realise that she had been rumbled.

Westbourne Park station came into sight a little way ahead: a long, low building of golden brick. He would confront her there, ask her the time, get a good look at her face.

Turning into the station, he drew quickly to the far side of the entrance, waiting for her, out of sight.

Some thirty seconds later he glimpsed the tall, dark figure jogging towards the entrance through the glittering rain, hands still in her pockets; she was frightened that she might have missed him, that he was already on a train.

He took a swift, confident step out into the doorway to face her – the false foot slipped on the wet tiled floor and skidded.

'*Fuck!*'

With an undignified descent into half-splits, he lost his footing and fell; in the long, slow-motion seconds before he reached the dirty wet floor, landing painfully on the bottle of whisky in his carrier bag, he saw her freeze in silhouette in the entrance, then vanish like a startled deer.

'Bollocks,' he gasped, lying on the sopping tiles while people at the ticket machines stared. He had twisted his leg again as he fell; it felt as though he might have torn a ligament; the knee that had been merely sore was now screaming in protest. Inwardly cursing imperfectly mopped floors and prosthetic ankles of rigid construction, Strike tried to get up. Nobody wanted to approach him. No doubt they thought he was drunk – Nick and Ilsa's whisky had now escaped the carrier bag and was rolling clunkily across the floor.

Finally a London Underground employee helped him to his feet, muttering about there being a sign warning of the wet floor; hadn't the gentleman seen it, wasn't it prominent enough? He handed Strike his whisky. Humiliated, Strike muttered a thank you and limped over to the ticket barriers, wanting only to escape the countless staring eyes.

Safely on a southbound train he stretched out his throbbing leg and probed his knee as best he could through his suit trousers. It felt tender and sore, exactly as it had after he had fallen down those stairs last spring. Furious, now, with the girl who had been following him, he tried to make sense of what had happened.

When had she joined him? Had she been watching the Quine place, seen him go inside? Might she (an unflattering possibility) have mistaken Strike for Owen Quine? Kathryn Kent had certainly done so, briefly, in the dark . . .

Strike got to his feet some minutes before changing at Hammersmith to better prepare himself for what might be a perilous descent. By the time he reached his destination of Barons Court, he was limping heavily and wishing that he had a stick. He made his way out of a ticket hall tiled in Victorian pea green, placing his feet with care on the floor covered in grimy wet prints. Too soon he had left the dry shelter of the small jewel of a station, with its art nouveau lettering and stone pediments, and proceeded in the relentless rain towards the rumbling dual carriageway that lay close by.

To his relief and gratitude, he realised that he had emerged on that very stretch of Talgarth Road where the house he sought stood.

Though London was full of these kinds of architectural anomalies, he had never seen buildings that jarred so obviously with their surroundings. The old houses sat in a distinctive row, dark red brick relics of a more confident and imaginative time, while traffic rumbled unforgivingly past them in both directions, for this was the main artery into London from the west.

They were ornate late-Victorian artists' studios, their lower windows leaded and latticed and oversized arched north-facing windows on their upper floors, like fragments of the vanished Crystal Palace. Wet, cold and sore though he was, Strike paused for a few seconds to look up at number 179, marvelling at its distinctive architecture and wondering how much the Quines would stand to make if Fancourt ever changed his mind and agreed to sell.

He heaved himself up the white front steps. The front door was sheltered from the rain by a brick canopy richly ornamented with carved stone swags, scrolls and badges. Strike brought out the keys one by one with cold, numb fingers.

The fourth one he tried slid home without protest and turned as though it had been doing so for years. One gentle click and the front door slid open. He crossed the threshold and closed the door behind him.

A shock, like a slap in the face, like a falling bucket of water. Strike fumbled with his coat collar, dragging it up over his mouth and nose to protect them. Where he should have smelled only dust and old wood, something sharp and chemical was overwhelming him, catching in his nose and throat.

He reached automatically for a switch on the wall beside him, producing a flood of light from two bare light bulbs hanging from the ceiling. The hallway, which was narrow and empty, was panelled in honey-coloured wood. Twisted columns of the same material supported an arch halfway along its length. At first glance it was serene, gracious, well-proportioned.

But with eyes narrowed Strike slowly took in the wide, burn-like stains on the original woodwork. A corrosive, acrid fluid – which was making the still, dusty air burn – had been splashed everywhere in what seemed to have been an act of wanton vandalism; it had stripped varnish from the aged floorboards, blasted the patina off the bare wood stairs ahead, even been thrown over the walls so that large patches of painted plaster were bleached and discoloured.

After a few seconds of breathing through his thick serge collar, it occurred to Strike that the place was too warm for an uninhabited house. The heating had been cranked up high, which made the fierce chemical smell waft more pungently than if it had been left to disperse in the chill of a winter's day.

Paper rustled under his feet. Looking down, he saw a smattering of takeaway menus and an envelope addressed TO THE OCCUPIER/ CARETAKER. He stooped and picked it up. It was a brief, angry handwritten note from the next-door neighbour, complaining about the smell.

Strike let the note fall back onto the doormat and moved forwards into the hall, observing the scars left on every surface where the chemical substance had been thrown. To his left was a door; he opened it. The room beyond was dark and empty; it had not been tarnished with the bleach-like substance. A dilapidated kitchen, also devoid of furnishings, was the only other room on the lower floor. The deluge of chemicals had not spared it; even a stale half loaf of bread on the sideboard had been doused.

Strike headed up the stairs. Somebody had climbed or descended them, pouring the vicious, corrosive substance from a capacious container; it had spattered everywhere, even onto the landing windowsill, where the paint had bubbled and split apart.

On the first floor, Strike came to a halt. Even through the thick wool of his overcoat he could smell something else, something that the pungent industrial chemical could not mask. Sweet, putrid, rancid: the stench of decaying flesh.

He did not try either of the closed doors on the first floor. Instead, with his birthday whisky swaying stupidly in its plastic bag, he followed slowly in the footsteps of the pourer of acid, up a second flight of stained stairs from which the varnish had been burned away, the carved banisters scorched bare of their waxy shine.

The stench of decay grew stronger with every step Strike took. It reminded him of the time they stuck long sticks into the ground in Bosnia and pulled them out to sniff the ends, the one fail-safe way of finding the mass graves. He pressed his collar more tightly to his mouth as he reached the top floor, to the studio where a Victorian artist had once worked in the unchanging northern light.

Strike did not hesitate on the threshold except for the seconds it took to tug his shirt sleeve down to cover his bare hand, so that he would make no mark on the wooden door as he pushed it open. Silence but for a faint squeak of hinges, and then the desultory buzzing of flies.

He had expected death, but not this.

A carcass: trussed, stinking and rotting, empty and gutted, lying on the floor instead of hanging from a metal hook where surely it belonged. But what looked like a slaughtered pig wore human clothing.

It lay beneath the high arched beams, bathed in light from that gigantic Romanesque window, and though it was a private house and the traffic sloshed still beyond the glass, Strike felt that he stood retching in a temple, witness to sacrificial slaughter, to an act of unholy desecration.

Seven plates and seven sets of cutlery had been set around the decomposing body as though it were a gigantic joint of meat. The torso had been slit from throat to pelvis and Strike was tall enough to see, even from the threshold, the gaping black cavity that had been left behind. The intestines were gone, as though they had been eaten. Fabric and flesh had been burned away all over the corpse, heightening the vile impression that it had been cooked and feasted upon. In places the burned, decomposing cadaver was shining, almost liquid in appearance. Four hissing radiators were hastening the decay.

The rotted face lay furthest away from him, near the window. Strike squinted at it without moving, trying not to breathe. A wisp of yellowing beard clung still to the chin and a single burned-out eye socket was just visible.

And now, with all his experience of death and mutilation, Strike had to fight down the urge to vomit in the almost suffocating mingled stenches of chemical and corpse. He shifted his carrier bag up his thick forearm, drew his mobile phone out of his pocket and took photographs of the scene from as many angles as he could manage without moving further into the room. Then he backed out of the studio, allowing the door to swing shut, which did nothing to mitigate the almost solid stink, and called 999.

Slowly and carefully, determined not to slip and fall even though he was desperate to regain fresh, clean, rain-washed air, Strike proceeded back down the tarnished stairs to wait for the police in the street.

17

Best while you have it use your breath,
There is no drinking after death.

John Fletcher, *The Bloody Brother*

It was not the first time that Strike had visited New Scotland Yard at the insistence of the Met. His previous interview had also concerned a corpse, and it occurred to the detective, as he sat waiting in an interrogation room many hours later, the pain in his knee less acute after several hours of enforced inaction, that he had had sex the previous evening then too.

Alone in a room hardly bigger than the average office's stationery cupboard, his thoughts stuck like flies to the rotting obscenity he had found in the artist's studio. The horror of it had not left him. In his professional capacity he had viewed bodies that had been dragged into positions intended to suggest suicide or accident; had examined corpses bearing horrific traces of attempts to disguise the cruelty to which they had been subjected before death; he had seen men, women and children maimed and dismembered; but what he had seen at 179 Talgarth Road was something entirely new. The malignity of what had been done there had been almost orgiastic, a carefully calibrated display of sadistic showmanship. Worst to contemplate was the order in which acid had been poured, the body disembowelled: had it been torture? Had Quine been alive or dead while his killer laid out place settings around him?

The huge vaulted room where Quine's body lay would now, no doubt, be swarming with men in full-body protective suits, gathering forensic evidence. Strike wished he were there with them. Inactivity after such a discovery was hateful to him. He burned with professional frustration. Shut out from the moment the police had arrived, he had been relegated to a mere blunderer who had stumbled onto the scene (and 'scene', he thought suddenly, was the right word in more ways than one: the body tied up and arranged in the light from that giant church-like window . . . a sacrifice to some demonic power . . . seven plates, seven sets of cutlery . . .)

The frosted glass window of the interrogation room blocked out everything beyond it but the colour of the sky, now black. He had been in this tiny room for a long time and still the police had not finished taking his statement. It was difficult to gauge how much of their desire to prolong the interview was genuine suspicion, how much animosity. It was right, of course, that the person who discovered a murder victim should be subjected to thorough questioning, because they often knew more than they were willing to tell, and not infrequently knew everything. However, in solving the Lula Landry case Strike might be said to have humiliated the Met, who had so confidently pronounced her death suicide. Strike did not think he was being paranoid in thinking that the attitude of the crop-haired female detective inspector who had just left the room contained a determination to make him sweat. Nor did he think that it had been strictly necessary for quite so many of her colleagues to look in on him, some of them lingering only to stare at him, others delivering snide remarks.

If they thought they were inconveniencing him, they were wrong. He had nowhere else to be and they had fed him quite a decent meal. If they had only let him smoke, he would have been quite comfortable. The woman who had been questioning him for an hour had told him he might go outside, accompanied, into the rain for a cigarette, but inertia and curiosity had kept him in his seat. His birthday whisky sat beside him in its carrier bag. He thought that if they kept him here much longer he might break it open. They had left him a plastic beaker of water.

The door behind him whispered over the dense grey carpet.

'Mystic Bob,' said a voice.

Richard Anstis of the Metropolitan Police and the Territorial Army entered the room grinning, his hair wet with rain, carrying a bundle of papers under his arm. One side of his face was heavily scarred, the skin beneath his right eye pulled taut. They had saved his sight at the field hospital in Kabul while Strike had lain unconscious, doctors working to preserve the knee of his severed leg.

'Anstis!' said Strike, taking the policeman's proffered hand. 'What the—?'

'Pulled rank, mate, I'm going to handle this one,' said Anstis, dropping into the seat lately vacated by the surly female detective. 'You're not popular round here, you know. Lucky for you, you've got Uncle Dickie on your side, vouching for you.'

He always said that Strike had saved his life, and perhaps it was true. They had been under fire on a yellow dirt road in Afghanistan. Strike himself was not sure what had made him sense the imminent explosion. The youth running from the roadside ahead with what looked like his younger brother could simply have been fleeing the gunfire. All he knew was that he had yelled at the driver of the Viking to brake, an injunction not followed – perhaps not heard – that he had reached forward, grabbed Anstis by the back of the shirt and hauled him one-handed into the back of the vehicle. Had Anstis remained where he was he would probably have suffered the fate of young Gary Topley, who had been sitting directly in front of Strike, and of whom they could find only the head and torso to bury.

'Need to run through this story one more time, mate,' said Anstis, spreading out in front of him the statement that he must have taken from the female officer.

'All right if I drink?' asked Strike wearily.

Under Anstis's amused gaze, Strike retrieved the Arran Single Malt from the carrier bag and added two fingers to the lukewarm water in his plastic cup.

'Right: you were hired by his wife to find the dead man . . . we're assuming the body's this writer, this—'

'Owen Quine, yeah,' supplied Strike, as Anstis squinted over his colleague's handwriting. 'His wife hired me six days ago.'

'And at that point he'd been missing—?'

'Ten days.'

'But she hadn't been to the police?'

'No. He did this regularly: dropped out of sight without telling anyone where he was, then coming home again. He liked taking off for hotels without his wife.'

'Why did she bring you in this time?'

'Things are difficult at home. There's a disabled daughter and money's short. He'd been away a bit longer than usual. She thought he'd gone off to a writer's retreat. She didn't know the name of the place, but I checked and he wasn't there.'

'Still don't see why she called you rather than us.'

'She says she called your lot in once before when he went

walkabout and he was angry about it. Apparently he'd been with a girlfriend.'

'I'll check that,' said Anstis, making a note. 'What made you go to that house?'

'I found out last night the Quines co-owned it.'

A slight pause.

'His wife hadn't mentioned it?'

'No,' said Strike. 'Her story is that he hated the place and never went near it. She gave the impression she'd half forgotten they even owned it—'

'Is that likely?' murmured Anstis, scratching his chin. 'If they're skint?'

'It's complicated,' said Strike. 'The other owner's Michael Fancourt—'

'I've heard of him.'

'—and she says he won't let them sell. There was bad blood between Fancourt and Quine.' Strike drank his whisky; it warmed throat and stomach. (Quine's stomach, his entire digestive tract, had been cut out. Where the hell was it?) 'Anyway, I went along at lunchtime and there he was – or most of him was.'

The whisky had made him crave a cigarette worse than ever.

'The body's a real fucking mess, from what I've heard,' said Anstis.

'Wanna see?'

Strike pulled his mobile phone from his pocket, brought up the photographs of the corpse and handed it across the desk.

'Holy shit,' said Anstis. After a minute of silent contemplation of the rotting corpse he asked, disgusted, 'What are those around him . . . plates?'

'Yep,' said Strike.

'That mean anything to you?'

'Nothing,' said Strike.

'Any idea when he was last seen alive?'

'The last time his wife saw him was the night of the fifth. He'd just had dinner with his agent, who'd told him he couldn't publish his latest book because he's libelled Christ knows how many people, including a couple of very litigious men.'

Anstis looked down at the notes left by DI Rawlins.

'You didn't tell Bridget that.'

'She didn't ask. We didn't strike up much of a rapport.'

'How long's this book been in the shops?'

'It isn't in the shops,' said Strike, adding more whisky to his beaker. 'It hasn't been published yet. I told you, he rowed with his agent because she told him he couldn't publish it.'

'Have you read it?'

'Most of it.'

'Did his wife give you a copy?'

'No, she says she's never read it.'

'She forgot she owned a second house and she doesn't read her own husband's books,' said Anstis without emphasis.

'Her story is that she reads them once they've got proper covers on,' said Strike. 'For what it's worth, I believe her.'

'Uh-huh,' said Anstis, who was now scribbling additions to Strike's statement. 'How did you get a copy of the manuscript?'

'I'd prefer not to say.'

'Could be a problem,' said Anstis, glancing up.

'Not for me,' said Strike.

'We might need to come back to that one, Bob.'

Strike shrugged, then asked:

'Has his wife been told?'

'Should have been by now, yeah.'

Strike had not called Leonora. The news that her husband was dead must be broken in person by somebody with the necessary training. He had done the job himself, many times, but he was out of practice; in any case, his allegiance this afternoon had been to the desecrated remains of Owen Quine, to stand watch over them until he had delivered them safely into the hands of the police.

He had not forgotten what Leonora would be going through while he was interrogated at Scotland Yard. He had imagined her opening the door to the police officer – or two of them, perhaps – the first thrill of alarm at the sight of the uniform; the hammer blow dealt to the heart by the calm, understanding, sympathetic invitation to retire indoors; the horror of the pronouncement (although they would not tell her, at least at first, about the thick purple ropes binding her husband, or the dark empty cavern that a murderer had made of his chest and belly; they would not say that his face had been burned away by acid or that somebody had laid out plates around him as though he were a giant roast . . . Strike remembered the platter of lamb that Lucy had handed around nearly twenty-four hours previously. He was not a squeamish man, but the smooth malt seemed to catch in his throat and he set down his beaker).

'How many people know what's in this book, d'you reckon?' asked Anstis slowly.

'No idea,' said Strike. 'Could be a lot by now. Quine's agent, Elizabeth Tassel – spelled like it sounds,' he added helpfully, as Anstis scribbled, 'sent it to Christian Fisher at Crossfire Publishing and he's a man who likes to gossip. Lawyers got involved to try and stop the talk.'

'More and more interesting,' muttered Anstis, writing fast. 'You want anything else to eat, Bob?'

'I want a smoke.'

'Won't be long,' promised Anstis. 'Who's he libelled?'

'The question is,' said Strike, flexing his sore leg, 'whether it's libel, or whether he's exposed the truth about people. But the characters I recognised were – give us a pen and paper,' he said, because it was quicker to write than to dictate. He said the names aloud as he jotted them down: 'Michael Fancourt, the writer; Daniel Chard, who's head of Quine's publisher; Kathryn Kent, Quine's girlfriend—'

'There's a girlfriend?'

'Yeah, they've been together over a year, apparently. I went to see her – Stafford Cripps House, part of Clement Attlee Court – and she claimed he wasn't at her flat and she hadn't seen him ... Liz Tassel, his agent; Jerry Waldegrave, his editor, and' – a fractional hesitation – 'his wife.'

'He's put his wife in there as well, has he?'

'Yeah,' said Strike, pushing the list over the desk to Anstis. 'But there are a load of other characters I wouldn't recognise. You've got a wide field if you're looking for someone he put in the book.'

'Have you still got the manuscript?'

'No.' Strike, expecting the question, lied easily. Let Anstis get a copy of his own, without Nina's fingerprints on it.

'Anything else you can think of that might be helpful?' Anstis asked, sitting up straight.

'Yeah,' said Strike. 'I don't think his wife did it.'

Anstis shot Strike a quizzical look not unmixed with warmth. Strike was godfather to the son who had been born to Anstis just two days before both of them had been blown out of the Viking. Strike had met Timothy Cormoran Anstis a handful of times and had not been impressed in his favour.

'OK, Bob, sign this for us and I can give you a lift home.'

Strike read through the statement carefully, took pleasure in correcting DI Rawlins's spelling in a few places, and signed.

His mobile rang as he and Anstis walked down the long corridor towards the lifts, Strike's knee protesting painfully.

'Cormoran Strike?'

'It's me, Leonora,' she said, sounding almost exactly as she usually did, except that her voice was perhaps a little less flat.

Strike gestured to Anstis that he was not ready to enter the lift and drew aside from the policeman, to a dark window beneath which traffic was winding in the endless rain.

'Have the police been to see you?' he asked her.

'Yeah. I'm with them now.'

'I'm very sorry, Leonora,' he said.

'You all right?' she asked gruffly.

'Me?' said Strike, surprised. 'I'm fine.'

'They ain't giving you a hard time? They said you was being interviewed. I said to 'em, "He only found Owen cos I asked him, what's he bin arrested for?"'

'They hadn't arrested me,' said Strike. 'Just needed a statement.'

'But they've kept you all this time.'

'How d'you know how long—?'

'I'm here,' she said. 'I'm downstairs in the lobby. I wanna see you, I made 'em bring me.'

Astonished, with the whisky sitting on his empty stomach, he said the first thing that occurred to him.

'Who's looking after Orlando?'

'Edna,' said Leonora, taking Strike's concern for her daughter as a matter of course. 'When are they gonna let you go?'

'I'm on my way out now,' he said.

'Who's that?' asked Anstis when Strike had rung off. 'Charlotte worrying about you?'

'Christ, no,' said Strike as they stepped together into the lift. He had completely forgotten that he had never told Anstis about the break-up. As a friend from the Met, Anstis was sealed off in a compartment on his own where gossip could not travel. 'That's over. Ended months ago.'

'Really? Tough break,' said Anstis, looking genuinely sorry as the lift began to move downwards. But Strike thought that some of Anstis's disappointment was for himself. He had been one of the friends most taken with Charlotte, with her extraordinary beauty and her dirty laugh. 'Bring Charlotte over' had been Anstis's frequent refrain when the two men had found themselves free of hospitals and the army, back in the city that was their home.

Strike felt an instinctive desire to shield Leonora from Anstis, but it was impossible. When the lift doors slid open there she was, thin and mousy, with her limp hair in combs, her old coat wrapped around her and an air of still wearing bedroom slippers even though her feet were clad in scuffed black shoes. She was flanked by the two uniformed officers, one female, who had evidently broken the news of Quine's death and then brought her here. Strike deduced from the guarded glances they gave Anstis that Leonora had given them reason to wonder; that her reaction to the news that her husband was dead had struck them as unusual.

Dry-faced and matter-of-fact, Leonora seemed relieved to see Strike.

'There you are,' she said. 'Why'd they keep you so long?'

Anstis looked at her curiously, but Strike did not introduce them.

'Shall we go over here?' he asked her, indicating a bench along the wall. As he limped off beside her he felt the three police officers draw together behind them.

'How are you?' he asked her, partly in the hope that she might exhibit some sign of distress, to assuage the curiosity of those watching.

'Dunno,' she said, dropping onto the plastic seat. 'I can't believe it. I never thought he'd go there, the silly sod. I s'pose some burglar got in and done it. He should've gone to a hotel like always, shouldn't he?'

They had not told her much, then. He thought that she was more shocked than she appeared, more than she knew herself. The act of coming to him seemed the disorientated action of somebody who did not know what else to do, except to turn to the person who was supposed to be helping her.

'Would you like me to take you home?' Strike asked her.

'I 'spect they'll give me a lift back,' she said, with the same sense of untroubled entitlement she had brought to the statement that Elizabeth Tassel would pay Strike's bill. 'I wanted to see you to check you was all right and I hadn't got you in trouble, and I wanted to ask you if you'll keep working for me.'

'Keep working for you?' Strike repeated.

For a split-second he wondered whether it was possible that she had not quite grasped what had happened, that she thought Quine was still out there somewhere to be found. Did her faint eccentricity of manner mask something more serious, some fundamental cognitive problem?

'They think I know something about it,' said Leonora. 'I can tell.'

Strike hesitated on the verge of saying 'I'm sure that's not true,' but it would have been a lie. He was only too aware that

Leonora, wife of a feckless, unfaithful husband, who had chosen not to contact the police and to allow ten days to elapse before making a show of looking for him, who had a key to the empty house where his body had been found and who would undoubtedly be able to take him by surprise, would be the first and most important suspect. Nevertheless, he asked:

'Why d'you think that?'

'I can tell,' she repeated. 'Way they were talking to me. And they've said they wanna look in our house, in his study.'

It was routine, but he could see how she would feel this to be intrusive and ominous.

'Does Orlando know what's happened?' he asked.

'I told her but I don't think she realises,' said Leonora, and for the first time he saw tears in her eyes. 'She says, "Like Mr Poop" – he was our cat that was run over – but I don't know if she understands, not really. You can't always tell with Orlando. I haven't told her someone killed him. Can't get my head around it.'

There was a short pause in which Strike hoped, irrelevantly, that he was not giving off whisky fumes.

'Will you keep working for me?' she asked him directly. 'You're better'n them, that's why I wanted you in the first place. Will you?'

'Yes,' he said.

'Cos I can tell they think I had something to do with it,' she repeated, standing up, 'way they was talking to me.'

She drew her coat more tightly around her.

'I'd better get back to Orlando. I'm glad you're all right.'

She shuffled off to her escort again. The female police officer looked taken aback to be treated like a taxi driver but after a glance at Anstis acceded to Leonora's request for a lift home.

'The hell was that about?' Anstis asked him after the two women had passed out of earshot.

'She was worried you'd arrested me.'

'Bit eccentric, isn't she?'

'Yeah, a bit.'

'You didn't tell her anything, did you?' asked Anstis.

'No,' said Strike, who resented the question. He knew better than to pass information about a crime scene to a suspect.

'You wanna be careful, Bob,' said Anstis awkwardly, as they passed through the revolving doors into the rainy night. 'Not to get under anyone's feet. It's murder now and you haven't got many friends round these parts, mate.'

'Popularity's overrated. Listen, I'll get a cab – no,' he said firmly, over Anstis's protestations, 'I need to smoke before I go anywhere. Thanks, Rich, for everything.'

They shook hands; Strike turned up his collar against the rain and with a wave of farewell limped off along the dark pavement. He was almost as glad to have shaken off Anstis as to take the first sweet pull on his cigarette.

18

> For this I find, where jealousy is fed,
> Horns in the mind are worse than on the head.
>
> Ben Jonson, *Every Man in His Humour*

Strike had completely forgotten that Robin had left the office in what he categorised as a sulk on Friday afternoon. He only knew that she was the one person he wanted to talk to about what had happened, and while he usually avoided telephoning her at weekends, the circumstances felt exceptional enough to justify a text. He sent it from the taxi he found after fifteen minutes tramping wet, cold streets in the dark.

Robin was curled up at home in an armchair with *Investigative Interviewing: Psychology and Practice*, a book she had bought online. Matthew was on the sofa, speaking on the landline to his mother in Yorkshire, who was feeling unwell again. He rolled his eyes whenever Robin reminded herself to look up and smile sympathetically at his exasperation.

When her mobile vibrated, Robin glanced at it irritably; she was trying to concentrate on *Investigative Interviewing*.

Found Quine murdered. C

She let out a mingled gasp and shriek that made Matthew start. The book slipped out of her lap and fell, disregarded, to the floor. Seizing the mobile, she ran with it to the bedroom.

Matthew talked to his mother for twenty minutes more, then went and listened at the closed bedroom door. He could hear Robin asking questions and being given what seemed to be long, involved answers. Something about the timbre of her voice convinced him that it was Strike on the line. His square jaw tightened.

When Robin finally emerged from the bedroom, shocked and awestruck, she told her fiancé that Strike had found the missing man he had been hunting, and that he had been murdered. Matthew's natural curiosity tugged him one way, but his dislike of Strike, and the fact that he had dared contact Robin on a Sunday evening, pulled him another.

'Well, I'm glad something's happened to interest you tonight,' he said. 'I know you're bored shitless by Mum's health.'

'You bloody hypocrite!' gasped Robin, winded by the injustice.

The row escalated with alarming speed. Strike's invitation to the wedding; Matthew's sneering attitude to Robin's job; what their life together was going to be; what each owed the other: Robin was horrified by how quickly the very fundamentals of their relationship were dragged out for examination and recrimination, but she did not back down. A familiar frustration and anger towards the men in her life had her in its grip – to Matthew, for failing to see why her job mattered to her so much; to Strike, for failing to recognise her potential.

(But he had called her when he had found the body . . . She had managed to slip in a question – 'Who else have you told?' – and he had answered, without any sign that he knew what it would mean to her, 'No one, only you.')

Meanwhile, Matthew was feeling extremely hard done by. He had noticed lately something that he knew he ought not to complain about, and which grated all the more for his feeling that he must lump it: before she worked for Strike, Robin had always been first to back down in a row, first to apologise, but her conciliatory nature seemed to have been warped by the stupid bloody job . . .

They only had one bedroom. Robin pulled spare blankets from on top of the wardrobe, grabbed clean clothes from inside it and announced her intention to sleep on the sofa. Sure that she would cave before long (the sofa was hard and uncomfortable) Matthew did not try to dissuade her.

But he had been wrong in expecting her to soften. When he woke the following morning it was to find an empty sofa and Robin gone. His anger increased exponentially. She had doubtless headed for work an hour earlier than usual, and his imagination – Matthew was not usually imaginative – showed him that big, ugly bastard opening the door of his flat, not the office below . . .

19

> . . . I to you will open
> The book of a black sin, deep printed in me.
> . . . my disease lies in my soul.
>
> Thomas Dekker, *The Noble Spanish Soldier*

Strike had set his alarm for an early hour, with the intention of securing some peaceful, uninterrupted time without clients or telephone. He rose at once, showered and breakfasted, took great care over the fastening of the prosthesis onto a definitely swollen knee and, forty-five minutes after waking, limped into his office with the unread portion of *Bombyx Mori* under his arm. A suspicion that he had not confided to Anstis was driving him to finish the book as a matter of urgency.

After making himself a mug of strong tea he sat down at Robin's desk, where the light was best, and began to read.

Having escaped the Cutter and entered the city that had been his destination, Bombyx decided to rid himself of the companions of his long journey, Succuba and the Tick. This he did by taking them to a brothel where both appeared satisfied to work. Bombyx departed alone in search of Vainglorious, a famous writer and the man whom he hoped would be his mentor.

Halfway along a dark alleyway, Bombyx was accosted by a

woman with long red hair and a demonic expression, who was taking a handful of dead rats home for supper. When she learned Bombyx's identity Harpy invited him to her house, which turned out to be a cave littered with animal skulls. Strike skim-read the sex, which took up four pages and involved Bombyx being strung up from the ceiling and whipped. Then, like the Tick, Harpy attempted to breast-feed from Bombyx, but in spite of being tied up he managed to beat her off. While his nipples leaked a dazzling supernatural light, Harpy wept and revealed her own breasts, from which leaked something dark brown and glutinous.

Strike scowled over this image. Not only was Quine's style starting to seem parodic, giving Strike a sense of sickened surfeit, the scene read like an explosion of malice, an eruption of pent-up sadism. Had Quine devoted months, perhaps years, of his life to the intention of causing as much pain and distress as possible? Was he sane? Could a man in such masterly control of his style, little though Strike liked it, be classified as mad?

He took a drink of tea, reassuringly hot and clean, and read on. Bombyx was on the point of leaving Harpy's house in disgust when another character burst in through her door: Epicoene, whom the sobbing Harpy introduced as her adopted daughter. A young girl, whose open robes revealed a penis, Epicoene insisted that she and Bombyx were twin souls, understanding, as they did, both the male and the female. She invited him to sample her hermaphrodite's body, but first to hear her sing. Apparently under the impression that she had a beautiful voice, she emitted barks like a seal until Bombyx ran from her with his ears covered.

Now Bombyx saw for the first time, high on a hill in the middle of the city, a castle of light. He climbed the steep streets towards it until hailed from a dark doorway by a male dwarf, who introduced himself as the writer Vainglorious. He had Fancourt's eyebrows, Fancourt's surly expression and sneering manner, and offered Bombyx a bed for the night, 'having heard of your great talent'.

To Bombyx's horror, a young woman was chained up inside the house, writing at a roll-top desk. Burning brands lay white hot in the fire, to which were attached phrases in twisted metal such as *pertinacious gudgeon* and *chrysostomatic intercourse*. Evidently expecting Bombyx to be amused, Vainglorious explained that he had set his young wife Effigy to write her own book, so that she would not bother him while he created his next masterpiece. Unfortunately, Vainglorious explained, Effigy had no talent, for which she must be punished. He removed one of the brands from the fire, at which Bombyx fled the house, pursued by Effigy's shrieks of pain.

Bombyx sped on towards the castle of light where he imagined he would find his refuge. Over the door was the name *Phallus Impudicus*, but nobody answered Bombyx's knock. He therefore skirted the castle, peering in through windows until he saw a naked bald man standing over the corpse of a golden boy whose body was covered in stab wounds, each of which emitted the same dazzling light that issued from Bombyx's own nipples. Phallus's erect penis appeared to be rotting.

'Hi.'

Strike started and looked up. Robin was standing there in her trench coat, her face pink, long red-gold hair loose, tousled and gilded in the early sunlight streaming through the window. Just then, Strike found her beautiful.

'Why are you so early?' he heard himself ask.

'Wanted to know what's going on.'

She stripped off her coat and Strike looked away, mentally castigating himself. Naturally she looked good, appearing unexpectedly when his mind had been full of the image of a naked bald man, displaying a diseased penis . . .

'D'you want another tea?'

'That'd be great, thanks,' he said without lifting his eyes from the manuscript. 'Give me five, I want to finish this . . .'

And with a feeling that he was diving again into contaminated water, he re-immersed himself in the grotesque world of *Bombyx Mori*.

As Bombyx stared through the window of the castle, transfixed by the horrible sight of Phallus Impudicus and the corpse, he found himself roughly seized by a crowd of hooded minions, dragged inside the castle and stripped naked in front of Phallus Impudicus. By this time, Bombyx's belly was enormous and he appeared ready to give birth. Phallus Impudicus gave ominous directions to his minions, which left the naive Bombyx convinced that he was to be the guest of honour at a feast.

Six of the characters that Strike had recognised – Succuba, the Tick, the Cutter, Harpy, Vainglorious and Impudicus – were now joined by Epicoene. The seven guests sat down at a large table on which stood a large jug, the contents of which were smoking, and a man-sized empty platter.

When Bombyx arrived in the hall, he found that there was no seat for him. The other guests rose, moved towards him with ropes and overpowered him. He was trussed up, placed on the platter and slit open. The mass that had been growing inside him was revealed to be a ball of supernatural light, which was ripped out and locked in a casket by Phallus Impudicus.

The contents of the smoking jug were revealed to be vitriol, which the seven attackers poured gleefully over the still-living, shrieking Bombyx. When at last he fell silent, they began to eat him.

The book ended with the guests filing out of the castle, discussing their memories of Bombyx without guilt, leaving behind them an empty hall, the still-smoking remains of the corpse on the table and the locked casket of light hanging, lamp-like, above him.

'Shit,' said Strike quietly.

He looked up. Robin had placed a fresh tea beside him without his noticing. She was perched on the sofa, waiting quietly for him to finish.

'It's all in here,' said Strike. 'What happened to Quine. It's here.'

'What d'you mean?'

'The hero of Quine's book dies exactly the way Quine died. Tied up, guts torn out, something acidic poured over him. In the book they eat him.'

Robin stared at him.

'The plates. Knives and forks . . . '

'Exactly,' said Strike.

Without thinking, he pulled his mobile out of his pocket and brought up the photos he had taken, then caught sight of her frightened expression.

'No,' he said, 'sorry, forgot you're not—'

'Give it to me,' she said.

What had he forgotten? That she was not trained or experienced, not a policewoman or a soldier? She wanted to live up to his momentary forgetfulness. She wanted to step up, to be more than she was.

'I want to see,' she lied.

He handed over the telephone with obvious misgivings.

Robin did not flinch, but as she stared at the open hole in the cadaver's chest and stomach her own insides seemed to shrink in horror. Raising her mug to her lips, she found that she did not want to drink. The worst was the angled close-up of the face, eaten away by whatever had been poured on it, blackened and with that burned-out eye socket . . .

The plates struck her as an obscenity. Strike had zoomed in on one of them; the place setting had been meticulously arranged.

'My God,' she said numbly, handing the phone back.

'Now read this,' said Strike, handing her the relevant pages.

She did so in silence. When she had finished, she looked up at him with eyes that seemed to have doubled in size.

'My *God*,' she said again.

Her mobile rang. She pulled it out of the handbag on the sofa beside her and looked at it. Matthew. Still furious at him, she pressed 'ignore'.

'How many people,' she asked Strike, 'd'you think have read this book?'

'Could be a lot of them by now. Fisher emailed bits of it all over town; between him and the lawyers' letters, it's become hot property.'

And a strange, random thought crossed Strike's mind as he spoke: that Quine could not have arranged better publicity if he had tried . . . but he could not have poured acid over himself while tied up, or cut out his own guts . . .

'It's been kept in a safe at Roper Chard that half the company seems to know the code for,' he went on. 'That's how I got hold of it.'

'But don't you think the killer's likely to be someone who's *in* the—?'

Robin's mobile rang again. She glanced down at it: Matthew. Again, she pressed 'ignore'.

'Not necessarily,' said Strike, answering her unfinished question. 'But the people he's written about are going to be high on the list when the police start interviewing. Of the characters I recognise, Leonora claims not to have read it, so does Kathryn Kent—'

'Do you believe them?' asked Robin.

'I believe Leonora. Not sure about Kathryn Kent. How did the line go? "To see thee tortur'd would give me pleasure"?'

'I can't believe a woman would have done that,' said Robin at once, glancing at Strike's mobile now lying on the desk between them.

'Did you never hear about the Australian woman who skinned her lover, decapitated him, cooked his head and buttocks and tried to serve him up to his kids?'

'You're not serious.'

'I'm totally serious. Look it up on the net. When women turn, they really turn,' said Strike.

'He was a big man . . . '

'If it was a woman he trusted? A woman he met for sex?'

'Who do we know for sure has read it?'

'Christian Fisher, Elizabeth Tassel's assistant Ralph, Tassel herself, Jerry Waldegrave, Daniel Chard – they're all characters, except Ralph and Fisher. Nina Lascelles—'

'Who are Waldegrave and Chard? Who's Nina Lascelles?'

'Quine's editor, the head of his publisher and the girl who helped me nick this,' said Strike, giving the manuscript a slap.

Robin's mobile rang for the third time.

'Sorry,' she said impatiently, and picked it up. 'Yes?'

'Robin.'

Matthew's voice sounded strangely congested. He never cried and he had never before shown himself particularly overcome by remorse at an argument.

'Yes?' she said, a little less sharply.

'Mum's had another stroke. She's – she's—'

An elevator drop in the pit of her stomach.

'Matt?'

He was crying.

'Matt?' she repeated urgently.

''S dead,' he said, like a little boy.

'I'm coming,' said Robin. 'Where are you? I'll come now.'

Strike was watching her face. He saw tidings of death there and hoped it was nobody she loved, neither of her parents, none of her brothers . . .

'All right,' she was saying, already on her feet. 'Stay there. I'm coming.

'It's Matt's mother,' she told Strike. 'She's died.'

It felt utterly unreal. She could not believe it.

'They were only talking on the phone last night,' she said. Remembering Matt's rolling eyes and the muffled voice she had just heard, she was overwhelmed with tenderness and sympathy. 'I'm so sorry but—'

'Go,' said Strike. 'Tell him I'm sorry, will you?'

'Yes,' said Robin, trying to fasten her handbag, her fingers grown clumsy in her agitation. She had known Mrs Cunliffe since primary school. She slung her raincoat over her arm. The glass door flashed and closed behind her.

Strike's eyes remained fixed for a few seconds on the place where Robin had vanished. Then he looked down at his watch. It was barely nine o'clock. The brunette divorcée whose emeralds lay in his safe was due at the office in just over half an hour.

He cleared and washed the mugs, then took out the necklace he had recovered, locked up the manuscript of *Bombyx Mori* in the safe instead, refilled the kettle and checked his emails.

They'll postpone the wedding.

He did not want to feel glad about it. Pulling out his mobile, he called Anstis, who answered almost at once.

'Bob?'

'Anstis, I don't know whether you've already got this, but there's something you should know. Quine's last novel describes his murder.'

'Say that again?'

Strike explained. It was clear from the brief silence after he had finished speaking that Anstis had not yet had the information.

'Bob, I need a copy of that manuscript. If I send someone over—?'

'Give me three quarters of an hour,' said Strike.

He was still photocopying when his brunette client arrived.

'Where's your secretary?' were her first words, turning to him with a coquettish show of surprise, as though she was sure he had arranged for them to be alone.

'Off sick. Diarrhoea and vomiting,' said Strike repressively. 'Shall we go through?'

20

Is Conscience a comrade for an old Soldier?

Francis Beaumont and John Fletcher, *The False One*

Late that evening Strike sat alone at his desk while the traffic rumbled through the rain outside, eating Singapore noodles with one hand and scribbling a list for himself with the other. The rest of the day's work over, he was free to turn his attention fully to the murder of Owen Quine and in his spiky, hard-to-read handwriting was jotting down those things that must be done next. Beside some of them he had jotted the letter A for Anstis, and if it had crossed Strike's mind that it might be considered arrogant or deluded of a private detective with no authority in the investigation to imagine he had the power to delegate tasks to the police officer in charge of the case, the thought did not trouble him.

Having worked with Anstis in Afghanistan, Strike did not have a particularly high opinion of the police officer's abilities. He thought Anstis competent but unimaginative, an efficient recogniser of patterns, a reliable pursuer of the obvious. Strike did not despise these traits – the obvious was usually the answer and the methodical ticking of boxes the way to prove it – but this murder was elaborate, strange, sadistic and grotesque, literary in inspiration and ruthless in execution. Was Anstis capable of comprehending the mind that had nurtured a plan of murder in the fetid soil of Quine's own imagination?

Strike's mobile rang, piercing in the silence. Only when he had put it to his ear and heard Leonora Quine did he realise that he had been hoping it would be Robin.

'How are you?' he asked.

'I've had the police here,' she said, cutting through the social niceties. 'They've been all through Owen's study. I didn't wanna, but Edna said I should let 'em. Can't we be left in peace after what just happened?'

'They've got grounds for a search,' said Strike. 'There might be something in Owen's study that'll give them a lead on his killer.'

'Like what?'

'I don't know,' said Strike patiently, 'but I think Edna's right. It was best to let them in.'

There was a silence.

'Are you still there?' he asked.

'Yeah,' she said, 'and now they've left it locked up so I can't get in it. And they wanna come back. I don't like them being here. Orlando don't like it. One of 'em,' she sounded outraged, 'asked if I wanted to move out of the house for a bit. I said, "No, I bloody don't." Orlando's never stayed anywhere else, she couldn't deal with it. I'm not going anywhere.'

'The police haven't said they want to question you, have they?'

'No,' she said. 'Only asked if they can go in the study.'

'Good. If they want to ask you questions—'

'I should get a lawyer, yeah. That's what Edna said.'

'Would it be all right if I come and see you tomorrow morning?' he asked.

'Yeah.' She sounded glad. 'Come round ten, I need to go shopping first thing. Couldn't get out all day. I didn't wanna leave them in the house without me here.'

Strike hung up, reflecting again that Leonora's manner was unlikely to be standing her in good stead with the police. Would Anstis see, as Strike did, that Leonora's slight obtuseness, her failure to produce what others felt was appropriate behaviour, her stubborn refusal to look at what she did not wish to look at – arguably the very qualities that had enabled her to endure the ordeal of living with Quine – would have made it impossible for her to kill him? Or would her oddities, her refusal to show normal grief reactions because of an innate though perhaps unwise honesty, cause the suspicion already lying in Anstis's mundane mind to swell, obliterating other possibilities?

There was an intensity, almost a feverishness, about the way Strike returned to his scribbling, left hand still shovelling food into his mouth. Thoughts came fluently, cogently: jotting down the questions he wanted answered, locations he wanted cased, the trails he wanted followed. It was a plan of action for himself and a means of nudging Anstis in the right direction, of helping open his eyes to the fact that it was not *always* the wife when a husband was killed, even if the man had been feckless, unreliable and unfaithful.

At last Strike cast his pen down, finished the noodles in two large mouthfuls and cleared his desk. His notes he put into the cardboard folder with Owen Quine's name on the spine, having first crossed out 'Missing Person' and substituted the word 'Murder'. He turned off the lights and was on the point of locking the glass door when he thought of something and returned to Robin's computer.

And there it was, on the BBC website. Not headline news,

of course, because whatever Quine might have thought, he had not been a very famous man. It came three stories below the main news that the EU had agreed a bailout for the Irish Republic.

> The body of a man believed to be writer Owen Quine, 58, has been found in a house in Talgarth Road, London. Police have launched a murder inquiry following the discovery, which was made yesterday by a family friend.

There was no photograph of Quine in his Tyrolean cloak, nor were there details of the horrors to which the body had been subjected. But it was early days; there was time.

Upstairs in his flat, some of Strike's energy deserted him. He dropped onto his bed and rubbed his eyes wearily, then fell backwards and lay there, fully dressed, his prosthesis still attached. Thoughts he had managed to keep at bay now pressed in upon him . . .

Why had he not alerted the police to the fact that Quine had been missing for nearly two weeks? Why had he not suspected that Quine might be dead? He had had answers to these questions when DI Rawlins had put them to him, reasonable answers, sane answers, but he found it much more difficult to satisfy himself.

He did not need to take out his phone to see Quine's body. The vision of that bound, decaying corpse seemed imprinted on his retinas. How much cunning, how much hatred, how much perversity had it taken to turn Quine's literary excrescence into reality? What kind of human being could bring themselves to slit a man open and pour acid over him, to gut him and lay plates around his empty corpse?

Strike could not rid himself of the unreasonable conviction that he ought somehow to have smelled the scene from afar, like the carrion bird he had trained to be. How had he – with his once-notorious instinct for the strange, the dangerous, the suspicious – not realised that the noisy, self-dramatising, self-publicising Quine had been gone too long, that he was too silent?

Because the silly bastard kept crying wolf . . . and because I'm knackered.

He rolled over, heaved himself off the bed and headed for the bathroom, but his thoughts kept scurrying back to the body: the gaping hole in the torso, the burned-out eye sockets. The killer had moved around that monstrosity while it was still bleeding, when Quine's screams had perhaps barely stopped echoing through the great vaulted space, and gently straightened forks . . . and there was another question for his list: what, if anything, had the neighbours heard of Quine's final moments?

Strike got into bed at last, covered his eyes with a large, hairy forearm and listened to his own thoughts, which were gabbling at him like a workaholic twin who would not pipe down. Forensics had already had more than twenty-four hours. They would have formed opinions, even if all tests were not yet in. He must call Anstis, find out what they were saying . . .

Enough, he told his tired, hyperactive brain. *Enough*.

And by the same power of will that in the army had enabled him to fall instantly asleep on bare concrete, on rocky ground, on lumpy camp beds that squeaked rusty complaints about his bulk whenever he moved, he slid smoothly into sleep like a warship sliding out on dark water.

21

Is he then dead?
What, dead at last, quite, quite for ever dead?

William Congreve, *The Mourning Bride*

At a quarter to nine the next morning Strike made his way slowly down the metal stairs, asking himself, not for the first time, why he did not do something about getting the birdcage lift fixed. His knee was still sore and puffy after his fall, so he was allowing over an hour to get to Ladbroke Grove, because he could not afford to keep taking taxis.

A gust of icy air stung his face as he opened the door, then everything went white as a flash went off inches from his eyes. He blinked – the outlines of three men danced in front of him – he threw up his hand against another volley of flashes.

'Why didn't you inform the police that Owen Quine was missing, Mr Strike?'

'Did you know he was dead, Mr Strike?'

For a split-second he considered retreat, slamming the door on them, but that meant being trapped and having to face them later.

'No comment,' he said coolly and walked into them, refusing to alter his course by a hair's breadth, so that they were forced to step out of his path, two asking questions and one running backwards, snapping and snapping. The girl who so often joined Strike for smoking breaks in the doorway of the guitar shop was gaping at the scene through the window.

'Why didn't you tell anyone he'd been missing for more than a fortnight, Mr Strike?'

'Why didn't you notify the police?'

Strike strode in silence, his hands in his pockets and his expression grim. They scurried along beside him, trying to make him talk, a pair of razor-beaked seagulls dive-bombing a fishing trawler.

'Trying to show them up again, Mr Strike?'

'Get one over on the police?'

'Publicity good for business, Mr Strike?'

He had boxed in the army. In his imagination he wheeled around and delivered a left hook to the floating rib area, so that the little shit crumpled . . .

'Taxi!' he shouted.

Flash, flash, flash went the camera as he got into it; thankfully the lights ahead turned green, the taxi moved smoothly away from the kerb and they gave up running after a few steps.

Fuckers, Strike thought, glancing over his shoulder as the taxi rounded a corner. Some bastard at the Met must have tipped them off that he had found the body. It would not have been Anstis, who had held back the information from the official statement, but one of the embittered bastards who had not forgiven him for Lula Landry.

'You famous?' asked the cabbie, staring at him in the rear-view mirror.

'No,' said Strike shortly. 'Drop me at Oxford Circus, will you?'

Disgruntled at such a short fare, the cabbie muttered under his breath.

Strike took out his mobile and texted Robin again.

2 journalists outside door when I left. Say you work for Crowdy.

Then he called Anstis.

'Bob.'

'I've just been doorstepped. They know I found the body.'

'How?'

'You're asking me?'

A pause.

'It was always going to come out, Bob, but I didn't give it to them.'

'Yeah, I saw the "family friend" line. They're trying to make out I didn't tell you lot because I wanted the publicity.'

'Mate, I never—'

'Be good to have that rebutted by an official source, Rich. Mud sticks and I've got a livelihood to make here.'

'I'll get it done,' promised Anstis. 'Listen, why don't you come over for dinner tonight? Forensics have got back with their first thoughts; be good to talk it over.'

'Yeah, great,' said Strike as the taxi approached Oxford Circus. 'What time?'

He remained standing on the Tube train, because sitting meant having to get up again and that put more strain on his sore knee. As he was going through Royal Oak he felt his mobile buzz and saw two texts, the first from his sister Lucy.

Many Happy Returns, Stick! Xxx

He had completely forgotten that today was his birthday. He opened the second text.

Hi Cormoran, thanks for warning about journos, just met them, they're still hanging round the outside door. See you later. Rx

Grateful that the day was temporarily dry, Strike reached the Quine house just before ten. It looked just as dingy and depressing in weak sunlight as it had the last time he had visited, but with a difference: there was a police officer standing in front of it. He was a tall young copper with a pugnacious-looking chin and when he saw Strike walking towards him with the ghost of a limp, his eyebrows contracted.

'Can I ask who you are, sir?'

'Yeah, I expect so,' said Strike, walking past him and ringing the doorbell. Anstis's dinner invitation notwithstanding, he was not feeling sympathetic to the police just now. 'Should be just about within your capabilities.'

The door opened and Strike found himself face to face with a tall, gangling girl with sallow skin, a mop of curly light brown hair, a wide mouth and an ingenuous expression. Her eyes, which were a clear, pale green, were large and set far apart. She was wearing what was either a long sweatshirt or a short dress that ended above bony knees and fluffy pink socks, and she was cradling a large plush orang-utan to her flat chest. The toy ape had Velcro attachments on its paws and was hanging around her neck.

'Hullo,' she said. She swayed very gently, side to side, putting weight first on one foot, then on the other.

'Hello,' said Strike. 'Are you Orlan—?'

'Can I have your name, please, sir?' asked the young policeman loudly.

'Yeah, all right – if I can ask why you're standing outside this house,' said Strike with a smile.

'There's been press interest,' said the young policeman.

'A man came,' said Orlando, 'and with a camera and Mum said—'

'Orlando!' called Leonora from inside the house. 'What are you doing?'

She came stumping down the hall behind her daughter, gaunt and white-faced in an ancient navy blue dress with its hem hanging down.

'Oh,' she said, 'it's you. Come in.'

As he stepped over the threshold, Strike smiled at the policeman, who glared back.

'What's your name?' Orlando asked Strike as the front door closed behind them.

'Cormoran,' he said.

'That's a funny name.'

'Yeah, it is,' said Strike and something made him add, 'I was named after a giant.'

'That's funny,' said Orlando, swaying.

'Go in,' said Leonora curtly, pointing Strike towards the kitchen. 'I need the loo. Be with you in a mo.'

Strike proceeded down the narrow hallway. The door of the study was closed and, he suspected, still locked.

On reaching the kitchen he discovered to his surprise that he was not the only visitor. Jerry Waldegrave, the editor from Roper Chard, was sitting at the kitchen table, clutching a bunch of flowers in sombre purples and blues, his pale face anxious. A second bunch of flowers, still in its cellophane, protruded from a sink half filled with dirty crockery. Supermarket bags of food sat unpacked on the sides.

'Hi,' said Waldegrave, scrambling to his feet and blinking earnestly at Strike through his horn-rimmed glasses. Evidently he did not recognise the detective from their previous meeting on the dark roof garden because he asked, as he held out his hand, 'Are you family?'

'Family friend,' said Strike as they shook hands.

'Terrible thing,' said Waldegrave. 'Had to come and see if I could do anything. She's been in the bathroom ever since I arrived.'

'Right,' said Strike.

Waldegrave resumed his seat. Orlando edged crabwise into the dark kitchen, cuddling her furry orang-utan. A very long minute passed while Orlando, clearly the most at ease, unabashedly stared at both of them.

'You've got nice hair,' she announced at last to Jerry Waldegrave. 'It's like a hairstack.'

'I suppose it is,' said Waldegrave and he smiled at her. She edged out again.

Another brief silence followed, during which Waldegrave fidgeted with the flowers, his eyes darting around the kitchen.

'Can't believe it,' he said at last.

They heard the loud flushing of a toilet upstairs, a thumping on the stairs, and Leonora returned with Orlando at her heels.

'Sorry,' she said to the two men. 'I'm a bit upset.'

It was obvious that she was referring to her stomach.

'Look, Leonora,' said Jerry Waldegrave in an agony of awkwardness, getting to his feet, 'I don't want to intrude when you've got your friend here—'

'Him? He's not a friend, he's a detective,' said Leonora.

'Sorry?'

Strike remembered that Waldegrave was deaf in one ear.

'He's called a name like a giant,' said Orlando.

'He's a detective,' said Leonora loudly, over her daughter.

'Oh,' said Waldegrave, taken aback. 'I didn't – why—?'

'Cos I need one,' said Leonora shortly. 'The police think I done it to Owen.'

There was a silence. Waldegrave's discomfort was palpable.

'My daddy died,' Orlando informed the room. Her gaze was direct and eager, seeking a reaction. Strike, who felt that something was required of one of them, said:

'I know. It's very sad.'

'Edna said it was sad,' replied Orlando, as though she had hoped for something more original, and she slid out of the room again.

'Sit down,' Leonora invited the two men. 'They for me?' she added, indicating the flowers in Waldegrave's hand.

'Yes,' he said, fumbling a little as he handed them over but remaining on his feet. 'Look, Leonora, I don't want to take up any of your time just now, you must be so busy with – with arrangements and—'

'They won't let me have his body,' said Leonora with devastating honesty, 'so I can't make no arrangements yet.'

'Oh, and there's a card,' said Waldegrave desperately, feeling in his pockets. 'Here . . . well, if there's anything we can do, Leonora, anything—'

'Can't see what anyone can do,' said Leonora shortly, taking the envelope he proffered. She sat down at the table where Strike had already pulled up a chair, glad to take the weight off his leg.

'Well, I think I'll be off, leave you to it,' said Waldegrave.

'Listen, Leonora, I hate to ask at a time like this, but *Bombyx Mori* . . . have you got a copy here?'

'No,' she said. 'Owen took it with him.'

'I'm so sorry, but it would help us if . . . could I have a look and see if any of it's been left behind?'

She peered up at him through those huge, outdated glasses.

'Police've taken anything he left,' she said. 'They went through the study like a dose of salts yesterday. Locked it up and taken the key – I can't even go in there myself now.'

'Oh, well, if the police need . . . no,' said Waldegrave, 'fair enough. No, I'll see myself out, don't get up.'

He walked up the hall and they heard the front door close behind him.

'Dunno why he came,' said Leonora sullenly. 'Make him feel like he's done something nice, I suppose.'

She opened the card he had given her. There was a watercolour of violets on the front. Inside were many signatures.

'Being all nice now, because they feel guilty,' said Leonora, throwing the card down on the Formica-topped table.

'Guilty?'

'They never appreciated him. You got to market books,' she said, surprisingly. 'You got to promote 'em. It's up to the publishers to give 'em a push. They wouldn't never get him on TV or anything like he needed.'

Strike guessed that these were complaints she had learned from her husband.

'Leonora,' he said, taking out his notebook. 'Is it all right if I ask you a couple of questions?'

'I s'pose. I don't know nothing, though.'

'Have you heard from anyone who spoke to Owen or saw him after he left here on the fifth?'

She shook her head.

'No friends, no family?'

'No one,' she said. 'D'you want a cup of tea?'

'Yeah, that'd be great,' said Strike, who did not much fancy anything made in this grubby kitchen, but wanted to keep her talking.

'How well d'you know the people at Owen's publisher?' he asked over the noisy filling of the kettle.

She shrugged.

'Hardly at all. Met that Jerry when Owen done a book signing once.'

'You're not friendly with anyone at Roper Chard?'

'No. Why would I be? It was Owen worked with them, not me.'

'And you haven't read *Bombyx Mori*, have you?' Strike asked her casually.

'I've told you that already. I don't like reading 'em till they're published. Why's everyone keep asking me that?' she said, looking up from the plastic bag in which she had been rummaging for biscuits.

'What was the matter with the body?' she demanded suddenly. 'What happened to him? They won't tell me. They took his toothbrush for DNA to identify him. Why won't they let me see him?'

He had dealt with this question before, from other wives, from distraught parents. He fell back, as so often before, on partial truth.

'He'd been lying there for a while,' he said.

'How long?'

'They don't know yet.'

'How was it done?'

'I don't think they know that exactly, yet.'

'But they must . . . '

She fell silent as Orlando shuffled back into the room, clutching not just her plush orang-utan but also a sheaf of brightly coloured drawings.

'Where's Jerry gone?'

'Back to work,' said Leonora.

'He's got nice hair. I don't like your hair,' she told Strike. 'It's fuzzy.'

'I don't like it much, either,' he said.

'He don't want to look at pictures now, Dodo,' said her mother impatiently, but Orlando ignored her mother and spread her paintings out on the table for Strike to see.

'I did them.'

They were recognisably flowers, fish and birds. A child's menu could be read through the back of one of them.

'They're very good,' said Strike. 'Leonora, d'you know if the police found any bits of *Bombyx Mori* yesterday, when they searched the study?'

'Yeah,' she said, dropping teabags into chipped mugs. 'Two old typewriter ribbons; they'd fallen down the back of the desk. They come out and ask me where the rest of 'em were; I said, he took 'em when he went.'

'I like Daddy's study,' announced Orlando, 'because he gives me paper for drawing.'

'It's a tip, that study,' said Leonora, switching the kettle on. 'Took 'em ages to look through everything.'

'Auntie Liz went in there,' said Orlando.

'When?' asked Leonora, glaring at her daughter with two mugs in her hands.

'When she came and you were in the loo,' said Orlando. 'She walked into Daddy's study. I seen her.'

'She don't have no right to go in there,' said Leonora. 'Was she poking around?'

'No,' said Orlando. 'She just walked in and then she walked out and she saw me an' she was crying.'

'Yeah,' said Leonora with a satisfied air. 'She was tearful with me an' all. Another one feeling guilty.'

'When did she come over?' Strike asked Leonora.

'First thing Monday,' said Leonora. 'Wanted to see if she could help. Help! She's done enough.'

Strike's tea was so weak and milky it looked as though it had never known a teabag; his preference was for a brew the colour of creosote. As he took a polite, token sip, he remembered Elizabeth Tassel's avowed wish that Quine had died when her Dobermann bit him.

'I like her lipstick,' announced Orlando.

'You like everyone's everything today,' said Leonora vaguely, sitting back down with her own mug of weak tea. 'I asked her why she done it, why she told Owen he couldn't publish his book, and upset him like that.'

'And what did she say?' asked Strike.

'That he's gone and put a load of real people in it,' said Leonora. 'I dunno why they're so upset about that. He always does it.' She sipped her tea. 'He's put me in loads of 'em.'

Strike thought of Succuba, the 'well-worn whore', and found himself despising Owen Quine.

'I wanted to ask you about Talgarth Road.'

'I don't know why he went there,' she said immediately. 'He hated it. He wanted to sell it for years but that Fancourt wouldn't.'

'Yeah, I've been wondering about that.'

Orlando had slid onto the chair beside him, one bare leg twisted underneath her as she added vibrantly coloured fins to a picture of a large fish with a pack of crayons she appeared to have pulled from thin air.

'How come Michael Fancourt's been able to block the sale all these years?'

'It's something to do with how it was left to 'em by that bloke Joe. Something about how it was to be used. I dunno. You'd have to ask Liz, she knows all about it.'

'When was the last time Owen was there, do you know?'

'Years ago,' she said. 'I dunno. Years.'

'I want more paper to draw,' Orlando announced.

'I haven't got any more,' said Leonora. 'It's all in Daddy's study. Use the back of this.'

She seized a circular from the cluttered work surface and pushed it across the table to Orlando, but her daughter shoved it away and left the kitchen at a languid walk, the orang-utan swinging from her neck. Almost at once they heard her trying to force the door of the study.

'Orlando, *no*!' barked Leonora, jumping up and hurrying into the hall. Strike took advantage of her absence to lean back and pour away most of his milky tea into the sink; it spattered down the bouquet clinging traitorously to the cellophane.

'*No*, Dodo. You can't do that. *No.* We're not allowed – *we're not allowed, get off it—*'

A high-pitched wail and then a loud thudding proclaimed Orlando's flight upstairs. Leonora reappeared in the kitchen with a flushed face.

'I'll be paying for that all day now,' she said. 'She's unsettled. Don't like the police here.'

She yawned nervously.

'Have you slept?' Strike asked.

'Not much. Cos I keep thinking, *Who?* Who'd do it to him? He upsets people, I know that,' she said distractedly, 'but that's just how he is. Temperamental. He gets angry over little things. He's always been like that, he don't mean anything by it. Who'd kill him for that?

'Michael Fancourt must still have a key to the house,' she went on, twisting her fingers together as she jumped subject. 'I thought that last night when I couldn't sleep. I know Michael Fancourt don't like him, but that's ages ago. Anyway, Owen never did that thing Michael said he did. He never wrote it. But Michael Fancourt wouldn't kill Owen.' She looked up at Strike with clear eyes as innocent as her daughter's. 'He's rich, isn't he? Famous . . . he wouldn't.'

Strike had always marvelled at the strange sanctity conferred upon celebrities by the public, even while the newspapers denigrated, hunted or hounded them. No matter how many famous people were convicted of rape or murder, still the belief persisted, almost pagan in its intensity: not *him*. It couldn't be *him*. He's *famous*.

'And that bloody Chard,' burst out Leonora, 'sending Owen threatening letters. Owen never liked him. And then he signs the card and says if there's anything he can do . . . where's that card?'

The card with the picture of violets had vanished from the table.

'She's got it,' said Leonora, flushing angrily. 'She's taken it.' And so loudly that it made Strike jump she bellowed 'DODO!' at the ceiling.

It was the irrational anger of a person in the first raw stages of grief and, like her upset stomach, revealed just how she was suffering beneath the surly surface.

'DODO!' shouted Leonora again. 'What have I told you about taking things that don't belong—?'

Orlando reappeared with startling suddenness in the kitchen, still cuddling her orang-utan. She must have crept back down without them hearing, as quiet as a cat.

'You took my card!' said Leonora angrily. 'What have I told you about taking things that don't belong to you? Where is it?'

'I like the flowers,' said Orlando, producing the glossy but now crumpled card, which her mother snatched from her.

'It's *mine*,' she told her daughter. 'See,' she went on, addressing Strike and pointing to the longest handwritten message, which was in precise copperplate: '"Do let me know if there is anything you need. Daniel Chard." Bloody hypocrite.'

'Daddy didn't like Dannulchar,' said Orlando. 'He told me.'

'He's a bloody hypocrite, I know that,' said Leonora, who was squinting at the other signatures.

'He give me a paintbrush,' said Orlando, 'after he touched me.'

There was a short, pregnant silence. Leonora looked up at her. Strike had frozen with his mug halfway to his lips.

'What?'

'I didn't like him touching me.'

'What are you talking about? Who touched you?'

'At Daddy's work.'

'Don't talk so silly,' said her mother.

'When Daddy took me and I saw—'

'He took her in a month ago or more, because I had a doctor's appointment,' Leonora told Strike, flustered, on edge. 'I don't know what she's on about.'

'. . . and I saw the pictures for books that they put on, all coloured,' said Orlando, 'an' Dannulchar did touch—'

'You don't even know who Daniel Chard is,' said Leonora.

'He's got no hair,' said Orlando. 'And after Daddy took me to see the lady an' I gave her my best picture. She had nice hair.'

'What lady? What are you talking—?'

'When Dannulchar touched me,' said Orlando loudly. 'He touched me and I shouted and after he gave me a paintbrush.'

'You don't want to go round saying things like that,' said Leonora and her strained voice cracked. 'Aren't we in enough— Don't be stupid, Orlando.'

Orlando grew very red in the face. Glaring at her mother, she left the kitchen. This time she slammed the door hard behind her; it did not close, but bounced open again. Strike heard her stamping up the stairs; after a few steps she started shrieking incomprehensibly.

'Now she's upset,' said Leonora dully, and tears toppled out of her pale eyes. Strike reached over to the ragged kitchen roll on the side, ripped some off and pressed it into her hand. She cried silently, her thin shoulders shaking, and Strike sat in silence, drinking the dregs of his horrible tea.

'Met Owen in a pub,' she mumbled unexpectedly, pushing up her glasses and blotting her wet face. 'He was there for the festival. Hay-on-Wye. I'd never heard of him, but I could tell he was someone, way he was dressed and talking.'

And a faint glow of hero worship, almost extinguished by years of neglect and unhappiness, of putting up with his airs and tantrums, of trying to pay the bills and care for their daughter in this shabby little house, flickered again behind her tired eyes. Perhaps it had rekindled because her hero, like all the best heroes, was dead; perhaps it would burn for ever now, like an eternal flame, and she would forget the worst and cherish the idea of him she had once loved . . . as long as she did not read his final manuscript, and his vile depiction of her . . .

'Leonora, I wanted to ask you something else,' Strike said gently, 'and then I'll be off. Have you had any more dog excrement through your letter box in the last week?'

'In the last week?' she repeated thickly, still dabbing her eyes. 'Yeah. Tuesday we did, I think. Or Wednesday, was it? But yeah. One more time.'

'And have you seen the woman you thought was following you?'

She shook her head, blowing her nose.

'Maybe I imagined it, I dunno . . .'

'And are you all right for money?'

'Yeah,' she said, blotting her eyes. 'Owen had life insurance. I made him take it out, cos of Orlando. So we'll be all right. Edna's offered to lend me till it comes through.'

'Then I'll be off,' said Strike, pushing himself back to his feet.

She trailed him up the dingy hall, still sniffing, and before the door had closed behind him he heard her calling:

'Dodo! Dodo, come down, I didn't mean it!'

The young policeman outside stood partially blocking Strike's path. He looked angry.

'I know who you are,' he said. His mobile phone was still clutched in his hand. 'You're Cormoran Strike.'

'No flies on you, are there?' said Strike. 'Out of the way now, sonny, some of us have got proper work to do.'

22

... what murderer, hell-hound, devil can this be?

Ben Jonson, *Epicoene, or The Silent Woman*

Forgetting that getting up was the difficult part when his knee was sore, Strike dropped into a corner seat on the Tube train and rang Robin.

'Hi,' he said, 'have those journalists gone?'

'No, they're still hanging round outside. You're on the news, did you know?'

'I saw the BBC website. I rang Anstis and asked him to help play down the stuff about me. Has he?'

He heard her fingers tapping on the keyboard.

'Yeah, he's quoted: "DI Richard Anstis has confirmed rumours that the body was found by private investigator Cormoran Strike, who made news earlier this year when he—"'

'Never mind that bit.'

'"Mr Strike was employed by the family to find Mr Quine, who often went away without informing anyone of his whereabouts. Mr Strike is not under suspicion and police are satisfied with his account of the discovery of the body."'

'Good old Dickie,' said Strike. 'This morning they were implying I conceal bodies to drum up business. Surprised the press are this interested in a dead fifty-eight-year-old has-been. It's not as though they know how grisly the killing was yet.'

'It isn't Quine who's got them interested,' Robin told him. 'It's you.'

The thought gave Strike no pleasure. He did not want his face in the papers or on the television. The photographs of him that had appeared in the wake of the Lula Landry case had been small (room had been required for pictures of the stunning model, preferably partially clothed); his dark, surly features did not reproduce well in smudgy newsprint and he had managed to avoid a full-face picture as he entered court to give evidence against Landry's killer. They had dredged up old photographs of him in uniform, but these had been years old, when he had been several stone lighter. Nobody had recognised him on appearance alone since his brief burst of fame and he had no wish to further endanger his anonymity.

'I don't want to run into a bunch of hacks. Not,' he added wryly, as his knee throbbed, 'that I could run if you paid me. Could you meet me—'

His favourite local was the Tottenham, but he did not want to expose it to the possibility of future press incursions.

'—in the Cambridge in about forty minutes?'

'No problem,' she said.

Only after he had hung up did it occur to Strike, first, that he ought to have asked after the bereaved Matthew, and second, that he ought to have asked her to bring his crutches.

The nineteenth-century pub stood on Cambridge Circus. Strike found Robin upstairs on a leather banquette among brass chandeliers and gilt-framed mirrors.

'Are you all right?' she asked in concern as he limped towards her.

'Forgot I didn't tell you,' he said, lowering himself gingerly into the chair opposite her with a groan. 'I knackered my knee again on Sunday, trying to catch a woman who was following me.'

'What woman?'

'She tailed me from Quine's house to the Tube station, where I fell over like a tit and she took off. She matches the description of a woman Leonora says has been hanging around since Quine disappeared. I could really use a drink.'

'I'll get it,' said Robin, 'as it's your birthday. And I got you a present.'

She lifted onto the table a small basket covered in cellophane, adorned with ribbon and containing Cornish food and drink: beer, cider, sweets and mustard. He felt ridiculously touched.

'You didn't have to do that . . .'

But she was already out of earshot, at the bar. When she returned, carrying a glass of wine and a pint of London Pride, he said, 'Thanks very much.'

'You're welcome. So do you think this strange woman's been watching Leonora's house?'

Strike took a long, welcome pull on his pint.

'And possibly putting dog shit through her front door, yeah,' said Strike. 'I can't see what she had to gain from following me, though, unless she thought I was going to lead her to Quine.'

He winced as he raised the damaged leg onto a stool under the table.

'I'm supposed to be doing surveillance on Brocklehurst and Burnett's husband this week. Great bloody time to knacker my leg.'

'I could follow them for you.'

The excited offer was out of Robin's mouth before she knew it, but Strike gave no evidence of having heard her.

'How's Matthew doing?'

'Not great,' said Robin. She could not decide whether Strike had registered her suggestion or not. 'He's gone home to be with his dad and sister.'

'Masham, isn't it?'

'Yes.' She hesitated, then said: 'We're going to have to postpone the wedding.'

'Sorry.'

She shrugged.

'We couldn't do it so soon . . . it's been a horrible shock for the family.'

'Did you get on well with Matthew's mother?' Strike asked.

'Yes, of course. She was . . . '

But in fact, Mrs Cunliffe had always been difficult; a hypochondriac, or so Robin had thought. She had been feeling guilty about that in the last twenty-four hours.

'. . . lovely,' said Robin. 'So how's poor Mrs Quine doing?'

Strike described his visit to Leonora, including the brief appearance of Jerry Waldegrave and his impressions of Orlando.

'What exactly's wrong with her?' Robin asked.

'Learning difficulties they call it, don't they?'

He paused, remembering Orlando's ingenuous smile, her cuddly orang-utan.

'She said something strange while I was there and it seemed to be news to her mother. She told us she went into work with her father once, and that the head of Quine's publisher touched her. Name of Daniel Chard.'

He saw reflected in Robin's face the unacknowledged fear that the words had conjured back in the dingy kitchen.

'How, touched her?'

'She wasn't specific. She said, "He touched me" and "I don't like being touched". And that he gave her a paintbrush after he'd done it. It might not be that,' said Strike in response to Robin's loaded silence, her tense expression. 'He might've accidentally knocked into her and given her something to placate her. She kept going off on one while I was there, shrieking because she didn't get what she wanted or her mum had a go at her.'

Hungry, he tore open the cellophane on Robin's gift, pulled out a chocolate bar and unwrapped it while Robin sat in thoughtful silence.

'Thing is,' said Strike, breaking the silence, 'Quine implied in *Bombyx Mori* that Chard's gay. I think that's what he's saying, anyway.'

'Hmm,' said Robin, unimpressed. 'And do you believe everything Quine wrote in that book?'

'Well, judging by the fact that he set lawyers on Quine, it upset Chard,' said Strike, breaking off a large chunk of chocolate and putting it in his mouth. 'Mind you,' he continued thickly, 'the Chard in *Bombyx Mori*'s a murderer, possibly a rapist and his knob's falling off, so the gay stuff might not have been what got his goat.'

'It's a constant theme in Quine's work, sexual duality,' said Robin and Strike stared at her, chewing, his brows raised. 'I nipped into Foyles on the way to work and bought a copy of *Hobart's Sin*,' she explained. 'It's all about a hermaphrodite.'

Strike swallowed.

'He must've had a thing about them; there's one in *Bombyx Mori* too,' he said, examining the cardboard covering of his chocolate bar. 'This was made in Mullion. That's down the coast from where I grew up . . . How's *Hobart's Sin* – any good?'

'I wouldn't be fussed about reading past the first few pages if its author hadn't just been murdered,' admitted Robin.

'Probably do wonders for his sales, getting bumped off.'

'My point is,' Robin pressed on doggedly, 'that you can't necessarily trust Quine when it comes to other people's sex lives, because his characters all seem to sleep with anyone and anything. I looked him up on Wikipedia. One of the key features of his books is how characters keep swapping their gender or sexual orientation.'

'*Bombyx Mori*'s like that,' grunted Strike, helping himself to more chocolate. 'This is good, want a bit?'

'I'm supposed to be on a diet,' said Robin sadly. 'For the wedding.'

Strike did not think she needed to lose any weight at all, but said nothing as she took a piece.

'I've been thinking,' said Robin diffidently, 'about the killer.'

'Always keen to hear from the psychologist. Go on.'

'I'm *not* a psychologist,' she half laughed.

She had dropped out of her psychology degree. Strike had never pressed her for an explanation, nor had she ever volunteered one. It was something they had in common, dropping out of university. He had left when his mother had died of a mysterious overdose and, perhaps because of this, he had always assumed that something traumatic had made Robin leave too.

'I've just been wondering why they tied his murder so obviously to the book. On the surface it looks like a deliberate act of revenge and malice, to show the world that Quine got what he deserved for writing it.'

'Looks like that,' agreed Strike, who was still hungry; he

reached over to a neighbouring table and plucked a menu off it. 'I'm going to have steak and chips, want something?'

Robin chose a salad at random and then, to spare Strike's knee, went up to the bar to give their order.

'But on the other hand,' Robin continued, sitting back down, 'copy-catting the last scene of the book could have seemed like a good way of concealing a different motive, couldn't it?'

She was forcing herself to speak matter-of-factly, as though they were discussing an abstract problem, but Robin had not been able to forget the pictures of Quine's body: the dark cavern of the gouged-out torso, the burned-out crevices where once had been mouth and eyes. If she thought about what had been done to Quine too much, she knew that she might not be able to eat her lunch, or that she might somehow betray her horror to Strike, who was watching her with a disconcertingly shrewd expression in his dark eyes.

'It's all right to admit what happened to him makes you want to puke,' he said through a mouthful of chocolate.

'It doesn't,' she lied automatically. Then, 'Well, obviously – I mean, it was horrific—'

'Yeah, it was.'

If he had been back with his SIB colleagues he would have been making jokes about it by now. Strike could remember many afternoons laden with pitch-black humour: it was the only way to get through certain investigations. Robin, however, was not yet ready for professionally callous self-defence and her attempt at dispassionate discussion of a man whose guts had been torn out proved it.

'Motive's a bitch, Robin. Nine times out of ten you only find out *why* when you've found out *who*. It's means and opportunity we want. Personally,' he took a gulp of beer, 'I think we might be looking for someone with medical knowledge.'

'Medical—?'

'Or anatomical. It didn't look amateur, what they did to Quine. They could've hacked him to bits, trying to remove the intestines, but I couldn't see any false starts: one clean, confident incision.'

'Yes,' said Robin, struggling to maintain her objective, clinical manner. 'That's true.'

'Unless we're dealing with some literary maniac who just got hold of a good textbook,' mused Strike. 'Seems a stretch, but you don't know . . . If he was tied up and drugged and they had enough nerve, they might've been able to treat it like a biology lesson . . .'

Robin could not restrain herself.

'I know you always say motive's for lawyers,' she said a little desperately (Strike had repeated this maxim many times since she had come to work for him), 'but humour me for a moment. The killer must have felt that to murder Quine in the same way as the book was worth it for some reason that outweighed the obvious disadvantages—'

'Which were?'

'Well,' said Robin, 'the logistical difficulties of making it such an – an *elaborate* killing, and the fact that the pool of suspects would be confined to people who've read the book—'

'Or heard about it in detail,' said Strike, 'and you say "confined", but I'm not sure we're looking at a small number of people. Christian Fisher made it his business to spread the contents of the book as far and as wide as he could. Roper Chard's copy of the manuscript was in a safe to which half the company seems to have had access.'

'But . . .' said Robin.

She broke off as a sullen barman came over to dump cutlery and paper napkins on their table.

'But,' she resumed when he had sloped away, 'Quine can't have been killed that recently, can he? I mean, I'm no expert . . .'

'Nor am I,' said Strike, polishing off the last of the chocolate and contemplating the peanut brittle with less enthusiasm, 'but I know what you mean. That body looked as though it had been there at least a week.'

'Plus,' said Robin, 'there must have been a time lag between the murderer reading *Bombyx Mori* and actually killing Quine. There was a lot to organise. They had to get ropes and acid and crockery into an uninhabited house . . .'

'And unless they already knew he was planning to go to Talgarth Road, they had to track Quine down,' said Strike, deciding against the peanut brittle because his steak and chips were approaching, 'or lure him there.'

The barman set down Strike's plate and Robin's bowl of salad, greeted their thanks with an indifferent grunt and retreated.

'So when you factor in the planning and practicalities, it doesn't seem possible that the killer can have read the book any later than two or three days after Quine went missing,' said Strike, loading up his fork. 'Trouble is, the further back we set the moment when the killer started plotting Quine's murder, the worse it looks for my client. All Leonora had to do was walk a few steps up her hall; the manuscript was hers for the reading as soon as Quine finished it. Come to think of it, he could've told her how he was planning to end it months ago.'

Robin ate her salad without tasting it.

'And does Leonora Quine seem . . . ' she began tentatively.

'Like the kind of woman who'd disembowel her husband? No, but the police fancy her and if you're looking for motive, she's lousy with it. He was a crap husband: unreliable, adulterous and he liked depicting her in disgusting ways in his books.'

'*You* don't think she did it, do you?'

'No,' Strike said, 'but we're going to need a lot more than my opinion to keep her out of jail.'

Robin took their empty glasses back to the bar for refills without asking; Strike felt very fond of her as she set another pint in front of him.

'We've also got to look at the possibility that somebody got the wind up that Quine was going to self-publish over the internet,' said Strike, shovelling chips into his mouth, 'a threat he allegedly made to a packed restaurant. That might constitute a motive for killing Quine, under the right conditions.'

'You mean,' said Robin slowly, 'if the killer recognised something in the manuscript that they didn't want to get a wider audience?'

'Exactly. The book's pretty cryptic in parts. What if Quine had found out something serious about somebody and put a veiled reference in the book?'

'Well, that would make sense,' said Robin slowly, 'because I keep thinking, *Why kill him?* The fact is, nearly all of these people had more effective means of dealing with the problem of a libellous book, didn't they? They could have told Quine they wouldn't represent it or publish it, or they could have threatened him with legal action, like this Chard man. His death's going to make the situation much worse for anyone who's a character in the book, isn't it? There's already much more publicity than there would have been otherwise.'

'Agreed,' said Strike. 'But you're assuming the killer's thinking rationally.'

'This wasn't a crime of passion,' retorted Robin. 'They planned it. They really thought it through. They must have been ready for the consequences.'

'True again,' said Strike, eating chips.

'I've been having a bit of a look at *Bombyx Mori* this morning.'

'After you got bored with *Hobart's Sin*?'

'Yes . . . well, it was there in the safe and . . . '

'Read the whole thing, the more the merrier,' said Strike. 'How far did you get?'

'I skipped around,' said Robin. 'I read the bit about Succuba and the Tick. It's spiteful, but it doesn't feel as though there's anything . . . well . . . *hidden* there. He's basically accusing both his wife and his agent of being parasites on him, isn't he?'

Strike nodded.

'But later on, when you get to Epi – Epi – how do you say it?'

'Epicoene? The hermaphrodite?'

'Is that a real person, do you think? What's with the singing? It doesn't feel as though it's really *singing* he's talking about, does it?'

'And why does his girlfriend Harpy live in a cave full of rats? Symbolism, or something else?'

'And the bloodstained bag over the Cutter's shoulder,' said Robin, 'and the dwarf he tries to drown . . . '

'And the brands in the fire at Vainglorious's house,' said Strike, but she looked puzzled. 'You haven't got that far? But Jerry Waldegrave explained that to a bunch of us at the Roper Chard party. It's about Michael Fancourt and his first—'

Strike's mobile rang. He pulled it out and saw Dominic Culpepper's name. With a small sigh, he answered.

'Strike?'

'Speaking.'

'What the fuck's going on?'

Strike did not waste time pretending not to know what Culpepper was talking about.

'Can't discuss it, Culpepper. Could prejudice the police case.'

'Fuck that – we've got a copper talking to us already. He says this Quine's been slaughtered exactly the way a bloke's killed in his latest book.'

'Yeah? And how much are you paying the stupid bastard to shoot his mouth off and screw up the case?'

'Bloody hell, Strike, you get mixed up in a murder like this and you don't even think of ringing me?'

'I don't know what you think our relationship is about, mate,' said Strike, 'but as far as I'm concerned, I do jobs for you and you pay me. That's it.'

'I put you in touch with Nina so you could get in that publisher's party.'

'The least you could do after I handed you a load of extra stuff you'd never asked for on Parker,' said Strike, spearing stray chips with his free hand. 'I could've withheld that and shopped it all round the tabloids.'

'If you want paying—'

'No, I don't want paying, dickhead,' said Strike irritably, as Robin turned her attention tactfully to the BBC website on her own phone. 'I'm not going to help screw up a murder investigation by dragging in the *News of the World*.'

'I could get you ten grand if you throw in a personal interview.'

'Bye, Cul—'

'Wait! Just tell me which book it is – the one where he describes the murder.'

Strike pretended to hesitate.

'*The Brothers Balls* . . . *Balzac*,' he said.

Smirking, he cut the call and reached for the menu to examine the puddings. Hopefully Culpepper would spend a long afternoon wading through tortured syntax and palpated scrotums.

'Anything new?' Strike asked as Robin looked up from her phone.

'Not unless you count the *Daily Mail* saying that family friends thought Pippa Middleton would make a better marriage than Kate.'

Strike frowned at her.

'I was just looking at random things while you were on the phone,' said Robin, a little defensively.

'No,' said Strike, 'not that. I've just remembered – Pippa2011.'

'I don't—' said Robin, confused, and still thinking of Pippa Middleton.

'Pippa2011 – on Kathryn Kent's blog. She claimed to have heard a bit of *Bombyx Mori*.'

Robin gasped and set to work on her mobile.

'It's here!' she said, a few minutes later. '"What would you say if I told you he'd read it to me"! And that was . . .' Robin scrolled upwards, 'on October the twenty-first. October the twenty-first! She might've known the ending before Quine even disappeared.'

'That's right,' said Strike. 'I'm having apple crumble, want anything?'

When Robin had returned from placing yet another order at the bar, Strike said:

'Anstis has asked me to dinner tonight. Says he's got some preliminary stuff in from forensics.'

'Does he know it's your birthday?' asked Robin.

'Christ, no,' said Strike, and he sounded so revolted by the idea that Robin laughed.

'Why would that be bad?'

'I've already had one birthday dinner,' said Strike darkly. 'Best present I could get from Anstis would be a time of death. The earlier they set it, the smaller the number of likely suspects: the ones who got their hands on the manuscript early. Unfortunately, that includes Leonora, but you've got this mysterious Pippa, Christian Fisher—'

'Why Fisher?'

'Means and opportunity, Robin: he had early access, he's got to go on the list. Then there's Elizabeth Tassel's assistant Ralph, Elizabeth Tassel herself and Jerry Waldegrave. Daniel Chard presumably saw it shortly after Waldegrave. Kathryn Kent denies reading it, but I'm taking that with a barrel of salt. And then there's Michael Fancourt.'

Robin looked up, startled.

'How can he—?'

Strike's mobile rang again; it was Nina Lascelles. He hesitated, but the reflection that her cousin might have told her he had just spoken to Strike persuaded him to take the call.

'Hi,' he said.

'Hi, Famous Person,' she said. He heard an edge, inexpertly covered by breathy high spirits. 'I've been too scared to call you in case you're being inundated with press calls and groupies and things.'

'Not so much,' said Strike. 'How're things at Roper Chard?'

'Insane. Nobody's doing any work; it's all we can talk about. Was it really, honestly murder?'

'Looks like it.'

'God, I can't believe it . . . I don't suppose you can tell me anything, though?' she asked, barely suppressing the interrogative note.

'The police won't want details getting out at this stage.'

'It was to do with the book, wasn't it?' she said. '*Bombyx Mori*.'

'I couldn't say.'

'And Daniel Chard's broken his leg.'

'Sorry?' he said, thrown by the non sequitur.

'Just so many odd things happening,' she said. She sounded keyed up, overwrought. 'Jerry's all over the place. Daniel rang him up from Devon just now and was yelling at him again – half the office heard because Jerry put him on speakerphone by accident and then couldn't find the button to turn him off. He can't leave his weekend house because of his broken leg. Daniel, I mean.'

'Why was he yelling at Waldegrave?'

'Security on *Bombyx*,' she said. 'The police have got a full copy of the manuscript from somewhere and Daniel's *not* happy about it.

'Anyway,' she said, 'I just thought I'd ring and say congrats – I suppose you congratulate a detective when they find a body, or don't you? Call me when you're not so busy.'

She rang off before he could say anything else.

'Nina Lascelles,' he said as the waiter reappeared with his apple crumble and a coffee for Robin. 'The girl—'

'Who stole the manuscript for you,' said Robin.

'Your memory would've been wasted in HR,' said Strike, picking up his spoon.

'Are you serious about Michael Fancourt?' she asked quietly.

'Course,' said Strike. 'Daniel Chard must've told him what Quine had done – he wouldn't have wanted Fancourt to hear it from anyone else, would he? Fancourt's a major acquisition for them. No, I think we've got to assume that Fancourt knew, early on, what was in—'

Now Robin's mobile rang.

'Hi,' said Matthew.

'Hi, how are you?' she asked anxiously.

'Not great.'

Somewhere in the background, someone turned up the music: '*First day that I saw you, thought you were beautiful . . .*'

'Where are you?' asked Matthew sharply.

'Oh . . . in a pub,' said Robin.

Suddenly the air seemed full of pub noises; clinking glasses, raucous laughter from the bar.

'It's Cormoran's birthday,' she said anxiously. (After all, Matthew and his colleagues went to the pub on each other's birthdays . . .)

'That's nice,' said Matthew, sounding furious. 'I'll call you later.'

'Matt, no – wait—'

Mouth full of apple crumble, Strike watched out of the corner of his eye as she got up and moved away to the bar without explanation, evidently trying to redial Matthew. The accountant was unhappy that his fiancée had gone out to lunch, that she was not sitting shiva for his mother.

Robin redialled and redialled. She got through at last. Strike finished both his crumble and his third pint and realised that he needed the bathroom.

His knee, which had not troubled him much while he ate, drank and talked to Robin, complained violently when he stood. By the time he got back to his seat he was sweating a little with the pain. Judging by the expression on her face, Robin was still trying to placate Matthew. When at last she hung up and rejoined him, he returned a short answer to whether or not he was all right.

'You know, I could follow the Brocklehurst girl for you,' she offered again, 'if your leg's too—?'

'No,' snapped Strike.

He felt sore, angry with himself, irritated by Matthew and suddenly a bit nauseous. He ought not to have eaten the chocolate before having steak, chips, crumble and three pints.

'I need you to go back to the office and type up Gunfrey's last invoice. And text me if those bloody journalists are still around, because I'll go straight from here to Anstis's, if they are.

'We really need to be thinking about taking someone else on,' he added under his breath.

Robin's expression hardened.

'I'll go and get typing, then,' she said. She snatched up her coat and bag and left. Strike caught a glimpse of her angry expression, but an irrational vexation prevented him from calling her back.

23

> For my part, I do not think she hath a soul so black
> To act a deed so bloody.
>
> John Webster, *The White Devil*

An afternoon in the pub with his leg propped up had not much reduced the swelling in Strike's knee. After buying painkillers and a cheap bottle of red on the way to the Tube, he set out for Greenwich where Anstis lived with his wife Helen, commonly known as Helly. The journey to their house in Ashburnham Grove took him over an hour due to a delay on the Central line; he stood the whole way, keeping his weight on his left leg, regretting anew the hundred pounds he had spent on taxis to and from Lucy's house.

By the time he got off the Docklands Light Railway spots of rain were again peppering his face. He turned up his collar and limped away into the darkness for what should have been a five-minute walk, but which took him nearly fifteen.

Only as he turned the corner into the neat terraced street with its well-tended front gardens did it occur to Strike that he ought, perhaps, to have brought a gift for his godson. He felt as little enthusiasm for the social part of the evening ahead as he felt eager to discuss with Anstis the forensic information.

Strike did not like Anstis's wife. Her nosiness was barely concealed beneath a sometimes cloying warmth; it emerged from time to time like a flick knife flashing suddenly from beneath a fur coat. She gushed gratitude and solicitousness every time Strike swam into her orbit, but he could tell that she itched for details of his chequered past, for information about his rock star father, his dead, drug-taking mother, and he could well imagine that she would yearn for details of his break-up with Charlotte, whom she had always treated with an effusiveness that failed to mask dislike and suspicion.

At the party following the christening of Timothy Cormoran Anstis – which had been postponed until he was eighteen months old, because his father and his godfather had to be airlifted out of Afghanistan and discharged from their respective hospitals – Helly had insisted on making a tearful, tipsy speech about how Strike had saved her baby's daddy's life, and how much it meant to her to have him agree to be Timmy's guardian angel, too. Strike, who had not been able to think of any valid reason to refuse being the boy's godfather, had stared at the tablecloth while Helly spoke, careful not to meet Charlotte's eye in case she made him laugh. She had been wearing – he remembered it vividly – his favourite peacock blue wrap-over dress, which had clung to every inch of her perfect figure. Having a woman that beautiful on his arm, even while he was still on crutches, had acted as a counterweight to the half a leg still not yet fit for a prosthesis. It had transformed him from the Man With Only One Foot to the man who had managed – miraculously, as he knew nearly every man who came into contact with her must think – to snag a fiancée so stunning that men stopped talking in mid-sentence when she entered the room.

'Cormy, darling,' crooned Helly when she opened the door. 'Look at you, all famous . . . we thought you'd forgotten us.'

Nobody else ever called him Cormy. He had never bothered to tell her he disliked it.

She treated him, without encouragement, to a tender hug that he knew was intended to suggest pity and regret for his single status. The house was warm and brightly lit after the hostile winter night outside and he was glad to see, as he extricated himself from Helly, Anstis stride into view, holding a pint of Doom Bar as a welcoming gift.

'Ritchie, let him get inside. Honestly . . . '

But Strike had accepted the pint and taken several grateful mouthfuls before he bothered to take off his coat.

Strike's three-and-a-half-year-old godson burst into the hall, making shrill engine noises. He was very like his mother, whose features, small and pretty though they were, were oddly bunched up in the middle of her face. Timothy sported Superman pyjamas and was swiping at the walls with a plastic lightsaber.

'Oh, Timmy, darling, *don't*, our lovely new paintwork . . . He wanted to stay up and see his Uncle Cormoran. We tell him about you all the time,' said Helly.

Strike contemplated the small figure without enthusiasm, detecting very little reciprocal interest from his godson. Timothy was the only child Strike knew whose birthday he had a hope of remembering, not that this had ever led Strike to buy him a present. The boy had been born two days before the Viking had exploded on that dusty road in Afghanistan, taking with it Strike's lower right leg and part of Anstis's face.

Strike had never confided in anyone how, during long hours in his hospital bed, he had wondered why it had been Anstis he had grabbed and pulled towards the back of the vehicle. He had gone over it in his mind: the strange presentiment, amounting almost to certainty, that they were about to explode, and the reaching out and seizing of Anstis, when he could equally have grabbed Sergeant Gary Topley.

Was it because Anstis had spent most of the previous day Skyping Helen within earshot of Strike, looking at the newborn son he might otherwise never have met? Was that why Strike's hand had reached without hesitation for the older man, the Territorial Army policeman, and not Red Cap Topley, engaged but childless? Strike did not know. He was not sentimental about children and he disliked the wife he had saved from widowhood. He knew himself to be merely one among millions of soldiers, dead and living, whose split-second actions, prompted by instinct as much as training, had forever altered other men's fates.

'Do you want to read Tim his bedtime story, Cormy? We've got a new book, haven't we, Timmy?'

Strike could think of little he wanted to do less, especially if it involved the hyperactive boy sitting on his lap and perhaps kicking his right knee.

Anstis led the way into the open-plan kitchen and dining area. The walls were cream, the floorboards bare, a long wooden table stood near French windows at the end of the room, surrounded by chairs upholstered in black. Strike had the vague idea that they had been a different colour when he had last been here, with Charlotte. Helly bustled in behind them and thrust a highly coloured picture book into Strike's hands. He had no choice but to sit down on a dining-room chair, with his godson placed firmly beside him, and to read the story of *Kyla the Kangaroo Who Loved to Bounce* which was (as he would not usually have noticed) published by Roper Chard. Timothy did not appear remotely interested in Kyla's antics and played with his lightsaber throughout.

'Bedtime Timmy, give Cormy a kiss,' Helly told her son, who, with Strike's silent blessing, merely wriggled off his chair and ran out of the kitchen yelling protests. Helly followed. Mother and son's raised voices grew muffled as they thumped upstairs.

'He'll wake Tilly,' predicted Anstis and, sure enough, when Helly reappeared it was with a howling one-year-old in her arms, whom she thrust at her husband before turning to the oven.

Strike sat stolidly at the kitchen table, growing steadily hungrier, and feeling profoundly grateful that he did not have children. It took nearly three quarters of an hour for the Anstises to persuade Tilly back into her bed. At last the casserole reached the table and, with it, another pint of Doom Bar. Strike could have relaxed but for the sense that Helly Anstis was now gearing up for the attack.

'I was so, so sorry to hear about you and Charlotte,' she told him.

His mouth was full, so he mimed vague appreciation of her sympathy.

'Ritchie!' she said playfully as her husband made to pour her a glass of wine. 'I don't think so! We're expecting again,' she told Strike proudly, one hand on her stomach.

He swallowed.

'Congratulations,' he said, staggered that they looked so pleased at the prospect of another Timothy or Tilly.

Right on cue, their son reappeared and announced that he was hungry. To Strike's disappointment, it was Anstis who left the table to deal with him, leaving Helly staring beadily at Strike over a forkful of *boeuf bourguignon*.

'So she's getting married on the fourth. I can't even *imagine* what that feels like for you.'

'Who's getting married?' Strike asked.

Helly looked amazed.

'Charlotte,' she said.

Dimly, down the stairs, came the sound of his godson wailing.

'Charlotte's getting married on the fourth of December,' said Helly, and with her realisation that she was the first to give him the news came a look of burgeoning excitement; but then something in Strike's expression seemed to unnerve her.

'I . . . I heard,' she said, dropping her gaze to her plate as Anstis returned.

'Little bugger,' he said. 'I've told him I'll smack his bum for him if he gets out of bed again.'

'He's just excited,' said Helly, who still seemed flustered by the anger she had sensed in Strike, 'because Cormy's here.'

The casserole had turned to rubber and polystyrene in Strike's mouth. How could Helly Anstis know when Charlotte was getting married? The Anstises hardly moved in the same circles as her or her future husband, who (as Strike despised himself for remembering) was the son of the Fourteenth Viscount of Croy. What did Helly Anstis know about the world of private gentlemen's clubs, of Savile Row tailoring and coked-up supermodels of which the Hon. Jago Ross had been a habitué all his trust-funded life? She knew no more than Strike himself. Charlotte, to whom it was native territory, had joined Strike in a social no-man's-land when they had been together, a place where neither was comfortable with the other's social set, where two utterly disparate norms collided and everything became a struggle for common ground.

Timothy was back in the kitchen, crying hard. Both his parents stood up this time and jointly moved him back towards his bedroom while Strike, hardly aware that they had gone, was left to disappear into a fug of memories.

Charlotte had been volatile to the point that one of her stepfathers had once tried to have her committed. She lied as other women breathed; she was damaged to her core. The longest consecutive period that she and Strike had ever managed together was two years, yet as often as their trust in each other had splintered they had been drawn back together, each time (so it seemed to Strike) more fragile than they had been before, but with the longing for each other strengthening. For sixteen years Charlotte had defied the disbelief and disdain of her family and friends to return, over and over again, to a large, illegitimate and latterly disabled soldier. Strike would have advised any friend to leave and not look back, but he had come to see her like a virus in his blood that he doubted he would ever eradicate; the best he could hope for was to control its symptoms. The final breach had come eight months previously, just before he had become newsworthy through the Landry case. She had finally told an unforgivable lie, he had left her for good and she had retreated into a world where men still went grouse shooting and women had tiaras in the family vault; a world she had told him she despised (although it looked as though that had been a lie too . . .).

The Anstises returned, minus Timothy but with a sobbing and hiccupping Tilly.

'Bet you're glad you haven't got any, aren't you?' said Helly gaily, sitting back down at the table with Tilly on her lap. Strike grinned humourlessly and did not contradict her.

There had been a baby: or more accurately the ghost, the promise of a baby and then, supposedly, the death of a baby. Charlotte had told him that she was pregnant, refused to consult a doctor, changed her mind about dates, then announced that all was over without a shred of proof that it had ever been real. It was a lie most men would have found impossible to forgive and for Strike it had been, as surely she must have known, the lie to end all lies and the death of that tiny amount of trust that had survived years of her mythomania.

Marrying on the fourth of December, in eleven days' time . . . how could Helly Anstis know?

He was perversely grateful, now, for the whining and tantrums of the two children, which effectively disrupted conversation all through a pudding of rhubarb flan and custard. Anstis's suggestion that they take fresh beers into his study to go over the forensic report was the best Strike had heard all day. They left a slightly sulky Helly, who clearly felt that she had not had her money's worth out of Strike, to manage the now very sleepy Tilly and the unnervingly wide-awake Timothy, who had reappeared to announce that he had spilled his drinking water all over his bed.

Anstis's study was a small, book-lined room off the hall. He offered Strike the computer chair and sat on an old futon. The curtains were not drawn; Strike could see a misty rain falling like dust motes in the light of an orange street lamp.

'Forensics say it's as hard a job as they've ever had,' Anstis began, and Strike's attention was immediately all his. 'All this is unofficial, mind, we haven't got everything in yet.'

'Have they been able to tell what actually killed him?'

'Blow to the head,' said Anstis. 'The back of his skull's been stoved in. It might not've been instantaneous, but the brain trauma alone would've killed him. They can't be sure he was dead when he was carved open, but he was almost certainly unconscious.'

'Small mercies. Any idea whether he was tied up before or after he was knocked out?'

'There's some argument about that. There's a patch of skin under the ropes on one of his wrists that's bruised, which they think indicates he was tied up before he was killed, but we've no indication whether he was still conscious when the ropes were put on him. The problem is, all that bloody acid everywhere's taken away any marks on the floor that might've shown a struggle, or the body being dragged. He was a big, heavy guy—'

'Easier to handle if he was trussed up,' agreed Strike, thinking of short, thin Leonora, 'but it'd be good to know the angle he was hit at.'

'From just above,' said Anstis, 'but as we don't know whether he was hit standing, sitting or kneeling . . . '

'I think we can be sure he was killed in that room,' said Strike, following his own train of thought. 'I can't see anyone being strong enough to carry a body that heavy up those stairs.'

'The consensus is that he died more or less on the spot where the body was found. That's where the greatest concentration of the acid is.'

'D'you know what kind of acid it was?'

'Oh, didn't I say? Hydrochloric.'

Strike struggled to remember something of his chemistry lessons. 'Don't they use that to galvanise steel?'

'Among other things. It's as caustic a substance as you can legally buy and it's used in a load of industrial processes.

Heavy-duty cleaning agent as well. One weird thing about it is, it occurs naturally in humans. In our gastric acid.'

Strike sipped his beer, considering.

'In the book, they pour vitriol on him.'

'Vitriol's sulphuric acid, and hydrochloric acid derives from it. Seriously corrosive to human tissue – as you saw.'

'Where the hell did the killer get that amount of the stuff?'

'Believe it or not, it looks like it was already in the house.'

'Why the hell—?'

'Still haven't found anyone who can tell us. There were empty gallon containers on the kitchen floor, and dusty containers of the same description in a cupboard under the stairs, full of the stuff and unopened. They came from an industrial chemicals company in Birmingham. There were marks on the empty ones that looked as though they'd been made by gloved hands.'

'Very interesting,' said Strike, scratching his chin.

'We're still trying to check when and how they were bought.'

'What about the blunt object that bashed his head in?'

'There's an old-fashioned doorstop in the studio – solid iron and shaped like one, with a handle: almost certainly that. It fits with the impression in his skull. That's had hydrochloric acid poured all over it like nearly everything else.'

'How's time of death looking?'

'Yeah, well, that's the tricky bit. The entomologist won't commit himself, says the condition of the corpse throws out all the usual calculations. The fumes from the hydrochloric acid alone would've kept insects away for a while, so you can't date the death from infestation. No self-respecting blowfly wants to lay eggs in acid. We had a maggot or two on bits of the body that weren't doused in the stuff, but the usual infestation didn't occur.

'Meanwhile, the heating in the house had been cranked right up, so the body might've rotted a bit faster than it would ordinarily have done in this weather. But the hydrochloric acid would've tended to mess with normal decomposition. Parts of him are burned to the bone.

'The deciding factor would have been the guts, last meal and so on, but they'd been lifted clean out of the body. Looks like they left with the killer,' said Anstis. 'I've never heard of that being done before, have you? Pounds of raw intestine taken away.'

'No,' said Strike, 'it's a new one on me.'

'Bottom line: forensics are refusing to commit themselves to a time frame except to say he's been dead at least ten days. But I had a private word with Underhill, who's the best of them, and he told me off the record that he thinks Quine's been dead a good two weeks. He reckons, though, even when they've got everything in the evidence'll still be equivocal enough to give defending counsel a lot to play with.'

'What about pharmacology?' asked Strike, his thoughts circling back to Quine's bulk, the difficulty of handling a body that big.

'Well, he might've been drugged,' agreed Anstis. 'We haven't had blood results back yet and we're analysing the contents of the bottles in the kitchen as well. But' – he finished his beer and set down the glass with a flourish – 'there's another way he could've made things easy for a killer. Quine liked being tied up – sex games.'

'How d'you know that?'

'The girlfriend,' said Anstis. 'Kathryn Kent.'

'You've already talked to her, have you?'

'Yep,' said Anstis. 'We found a taxi driver who picked up Quine at nine o'clock on the fifth, a couple of streets away from his house, and dropped him in Lillie Road.'

'Right by Stafford Cripps House,' said Strike. 'So he went straight from Leonora to the girlfriend?'

'Well, no, he didn't. Kent was away, staying with her dying sister, and we've got corroboration – she spent the night at the hospice. She says she hasn't seen him for a month, but was surprisingly forthcoming on their sex life.'

'Did you ask for details?'

'I got the impression she thought we knew more than we did. They came pouring out without much prodding.'

'Suggestive,' said Strike. 'She told me she'd never read *Bombyx Mori*—'

'She told us that too.'

'—but her character ties up and assaults the hero in the book. Maybe she wanted it on record that she ties people up for sex, not torture or murder. What about the copy of the manuscript Leonora says he took away with him? All the notes and the old typewriter ribbons? Did you find them?'

'Nope,' said Anstis. 'Until we find out whether he stayed somewhere else before he went to Talgarth Road, we're going to assume the killer took them. The place was empty except for a bit of food and drink in the kitchen and a camping mattress and sleeping bag in one of the bedrooms. It looks like Quine was dossing down there. Hydrochloric acid's been poured around that room too, all over Quine's bed.'

'No fingerprints? Footprints? Unexplained hair, mud?'

'Nothing. We've still got people working on the place, but the acid's obliterated everything in its path. Our people are wearing masks just so the fumes don't rip their throats out.'

'Anyone apart from this taxi driver admitted to seeing Quine since he disappeared?'

'Nobody's seen him entering Talgarth Road but we've got a neighbour at number 183 who swears she saw Quine *leave* it at one in the morning. Early hours of the sixth. The neighbour was letting herself in after a bonfire-night party.'

'It was dark and she was two doors down, so what she actually saw was . . . ?'

'Silhouette of a tall figure in a cloak, carrying a holdall.'

'A holdall,' repeated Strike.

'Yep,' said Anstis.

'Did the cloaked figure get into a car?'

'No, it walked out of sight, but obviously a car could have been parked round the corner.'

'Anyone else?'

'I've got an old geezer in Putney swearing he saw Quine on the eighth. Rang his local police station and described him accurately.'

'What was Quine doing?'

'Buying books in the Bridlington Bookshop, where the bloke works.'

'How convincing a witness is he?'

'Well, he's old, but he claims he can remember what Quine bought and the physical description's good. And we've got another woman who lives in the flats across the road from the crime scene who reckons she passed Michael Fancourt walking past the house, also on the morning of the eighth. You know, that author with the big head? Famous one?'

'Yeah, I do,' said Strike slowly.

'Witness claims she looked back at him over her shoulder and stared, because she recognised him.'

'He was just walking past?'

'So she claims.'

'Anybody checked that with Fancourt yet?'

'He's in Germany, but he's said he's happy to cooperate with us when he gets back. Agent bending over backwards to be helpful.'

'Any other suspicious activity around Talgarth Road? Camera footage?'

'The only camera's at the wrong angle for the house, it watches traffic – but I'm saving the best till last. We've got a different neighbour – other side, four doors down – who swears he saw a fat woman in a burqa letting herself in on the afternoon of the fourth, carrying a plastic bag from a halal takeaway. He says he noticed because the house had been empty so long. He claims she was there for an hour, then left.'

'He's sure she was in Quine's house?'

'So he says.'

'And she had a key?'

'That's his story.'

'A burqa,' repeated Strike. 'Bloody hell.'

'I wouldn't swear his eyesight's great; he's got very thick lenses in his glasses. He told me he didn't know of any Muslims living in the street, so it had caught his attention.'

'So we've got two alleged sightings of Quine since he walked out on his wife: early hours of the sixth, and on the eighth, in Putney.'

'Yeah,' said Anstis, 'but I wouldn't pin too much hope on either of them, Bob.'

'You think he died the night he left,' said Strike, more statement than question, and Anstis nodded.

'Underhill thinks so.'

'No sign of the knife?'

'Nothing. The only knife in the kitchen was a very blunt, everyday one. Definitely not up to the job.'

'Who do we know had a key to the place?'

'Your client,' said Anstis, 'obviously. Quine himself must've had one. Fancourt's got two, he's already told us that by phone. The Quines lent one to his agent when she was organising some repairs for them; she says she gave it back. A next-door neighbour's got a key so he can let himself in if anything goes wrong with the place.'

'Didn't he go in once the stink got bad?'

'One side *did* put a note through the door complaining about the smell, but the key holder left for two months in New Zealand a fortnight ago. We've spoken to him by phone. Last time he was in the house was in about May, when he took delivery of a couple of packages while some workmen were in and put them in the hall. Mrs Quine's vague about who else might have been lent a key over the years.

'She's an odd woman, Mrs Quine,' Anstis went on smoothly, 'isn't she?'

'Haven't thought about it,' lied Strike.

'You know the neighbours heard her chasing him, the night he disappeared?'

'I didn't know.'

'Yeah. She ran out of the house after him, screaming. The neighbours all say' – Anstis was watching Strike closely – 'that she yelled "I know where you're off to, Owen!"'

'Well, she thought she did know,' Strike said with a shrug. 'She thought he was going to the writer's retreat Christian Fisher told him about. Bigley Hall.'

'She's refusing to move out of the house.'

'She's got a mentally handicapped daughter who's never slept anywhere else. Can you imagine Leonora overpowering Quine?'

'No,' said Anstis, 'but we know it turned him on to be tied up, and I doubt they were married for thirty-odd years without her knowing that.'

'You think they had a row, then she tracked him down and suggested a bit of bondage?'

Anstis gave the suggestion of a small, token laugh, then said:

'It doesn't look great for her, Bob. Angry wife with the key to the house, early access to the manuscript, plenty of motive if she knew about the mistress, especially if there was any question of Quine leaving her and the daughter for Kent. Only her word for it that "I know where you're going" meant this writer's retreat and not the house on Talgarth Road.'

'Sounds convincing when you put it like that,' Strike said.

'But you don't think so.'

'She's my client,' said Strike. 'I'm being paid to think of alternatives.'

'Has she told you where she used to work?' asked Anstis, with the air of a man about to play his trump card. 'Back in Hay-on-Wye, before they were married?'

'Go on,' said Strike, not without a degree of apprehension.

'In her uncle's butcher's shop,' said Anstis.

Outside the study door Strike heard Timothy Cormoran Anstis thudding down the stairs again, screaming his head off at some fresh disappointment. For the first time in their unsatisfactory acquaintance, Strike felt a real empathy for the boy.

24

> All well bred persons lie – Besides, you are a woman; you must never speak what you think . . .
>
> William Congreve, *Love for Love*

Strike's dreams that night, fuelled by a day's consumption of Doom Bar, by talk of blood, acid and blowflies, were strange and ugly.

Charlotte was getting married and he, Strike, was running to an eerie Gothic cathedral, running on two whole, functioning legs, because he knew that she had just given birth to his child and he needed to see it, to save it. There she was, in the vast, dark empty space, alone at the altar, struggling into a blood red gown, and somewhere out of sight, perhaps in a cold vestry, lay his baby, naked, helpless and abandoned.

'Where is it?' he asked.

'You're not seeing it. You didn't want it. Anyway, there's something wrong with it,' she said.

He was afraid of what he would see if he went to find the baby. Her bridegroom was nowhere to be seen but she was ready for the wedding, in a thick scarlet veil.

'Leave it, it's horrible,' she said coldly, pushing past him, walking alone away from the altar, back up the aisle towards the distant doorway. 'You'd only touch it,' she shouted over her shoulder. 'I don't want you *touching* it. You'll see it eventually. It'll have to be announced,' she added in a vanishing voice, as she became a sliver of scarlet dancing in the light of the open doors, 'in the papers . . . '

He was suddenly awake in the morning gloom, his mouth dry and his knee throbbing ominously in spite of a night's rest.

Winter had slid in the night like a glacier over London. A hard frost had iced the outside of his attic window and the temperature inside his rooms, with their ill-fitting windows and doors and the total lack of insulation under the roof, had plummeted.

Strike got up and reached for a sweater lying on the end of his bed. When he came to fix on his prosthesis, he found that his knee was exceptionally swollen after the journey to and from Greenwich. The shower water took longer than usual to heat up; he cranked up the thermostat, fearing burst pipes and frozen gutters, sub-zero living quarters and an expensive plumber. After drying himself off, he unearthed his old sports bandages from the box on the landing to strap up his knee.

He knew, now, as clearly as though he had spent the night puzzling it out, how Helly Anstis knew Charlotte's wedding plans. He had been stupid not to think of it before. His subconscious had known.

Once clean, dressed and breakfasted he headed downstairs. Glancing out of the window behind his desk, he noted that the knifelike cold was keeping away the little cluster of journalists who had waited in vain for his return the previous day. Sleet pattered on the windows as he moved back to the outer office and Robin's computer. Here, in the search engine, he typed: *charlotte campbell hon jago ross wedding*.

Pitiless and prompt came the results.

Tatler, December 2010: Cover girl Charlotte Campbell on her wedding to the future Viscount of Croy . . .

'*Tatler*,' said Strike aloud in the office.

He only knew of the magazine's existence because its society pages were full of Charlotte's friends. She had bought it, sometimes, to read ostentatiously in front of him, commenting on men she had once slept with, or whose stately homes she had partied in.

And now she was the Christmas cover girl.

Even strapped up, his knee complained at having to support him down the metal stairs and out into the sleet. There was an early morning queue at the counter of the newsagents. Calmly he scanned the shelves of magazines: soap stars on the cheap ones and film stars on the expensive; December issues almost sold out, even though they were still in November. Emma Watson in white on the cover of *Vogue* ('The Super Star Issue'), Rihanna in pink on *Marie Claire* ('The Glamour Issue') and on the cover of *Tatler* . . .

Pale, perfect skin, black hair blown away from high cheekbones and wide hazel-green eyes, flecked like a russet apple. Two huge diamonds dangling from her ears and a third on the hand lying lightly against her face. A dull, blunt hammer blow to the heart, absorbed without the slightest external sign. He took the magazine, the last on the shelf, paid for it and returned to Denmark Street.

It was twenty to nine. He shut himself in his office, sat down at his desk and laid the magazine down in front of him.

IN–CROY–ABLE! Former Wild Child turned future Viscountess, Charlotte Campbell.

The strapline ran across Charlotte's swanlike neck.

It was the first time he had looked at her since she had clawed his face in this very office and run from him, straight into the arms of the Honourable Jago Ross. He supposed that they must airbrush all their pictures. Her skin could not be this flawless, the whites of her eyes this pure, but they had not exaggerated anything else, not the exquisite bone structure, nor (he was sure) the size of the diamond on her finger.

Slowly he turned to the contents page and then to the article within. A double-page picture of Charlotte, very thin in a glittering silver floor-length dress, standing in the middle of a long gallery lined with tapestries; beside her, leaning on a card table and looking like a dissolute arctic fox, was Jago Ross. More photographs over the page: Charlotte sitting on an ancient four-poster, laughing with her head thrown back, the white column of her neck rising from a sheer cream blouse; Charlotte and Jago in jeans and wellington boots, walking hand in hand over the parkland in front of their future home with two Jack Russells at their heels; Charlotte windswept on the castle keep, looking over a shoulder draped in the Viscount's tartan.

Doubtless Helly Anstis had considered it four pounds ten well spent.

On 4 December this year, the seventeenth-century chapel at the Castle of Croy (NEVER 'Croy Castle' – it annoys the family) will be dusted off for its first wedding in over a century. Charlotte Campbell, breathtakingly beautiful daughter of 1960s It Girl Tula Clermont and academic and broadcaster Anthony Campbell, will marry the Hon Jago Ross, heir to the castle and to his father's titles, principal of which is Viscount of Croy.

The future Viscountess is a not altogether uncontroversial addition to the Rosses of Croy, but Jago laughs at the idea that anyone in his family could be less than delighted to welcome the former wild child into his old and rather grand Scottish family.

'Actually, my mother always hoped we'd marry,' he says. 'We were boyfriend and girlfriend at Oxford but I suppose we were just too young ... found each other again in London ... both just out of relationships ...'

Were you? thought Strike. *Were you both just out of relationships? Or were you fucking her at the same time I was, so that she didn't know which of us had fathered the baby she was worried she might be carrying? Changing the dates to cover every eventuality, keeping her options open ...*

... made headlines in her youth when she went missing from Bedales for seven days, causing a national search ... admitted to rehab at the age of 25 ...

'Old news, move on, nothing to see,' says Charlotte brightly. 'Look, I had a lot of fun in my youth, but it's time to settle down and honestly, I can't wait.'

Fun, was it? Strike asked her stunning picture. *Fun, standing on that roof and threatening to jump? Fun, calling me from that psychiatric hospital and begging me to get you out?*

Ross, fresh from a very messy divorce that has kept the gossip columns busy ... 'I wish we could have settled it without the lawyers,' he sighs ... 'I can't wait to be a step-mummy!' trills Charlotte ...

('If I have to spend one more evening with the Anstises' bratty kids, Corm, I swear to God I'll brain one of them.' And, in Lucy's suburban back garden, watching Strike's nephews playing football, 'Why are these children such *shits*?' The expression on Lucy's round face when she overheard it . . .)

His own name, leaping off the page.

> . . . including a surprising fling with Jonny Rokeby's eldest son Cormoran Strike, who made headlines last year . . .

. . . a surprising fling with Jonny Rokeby's eldest son . . .

. . . Jonny Rokeby's eldest . . .

He closed the magazine with a sudden, reflexive movement and slid it into his bin.

Sixteen years, on and off. Sixteen years of the torture, the madness and occasional ecstasy. And then – after all those times she had left him, throwing herself into the arms of other men as other women cast themselves onto railway tracks – he had walked out. In doing so, he had crossed an unforgivable Rubicon, for it had always been understood that he should stand rock-like, to be left and returned to, never flinching, never giving up. But on that night when he had confronted her with the tangle of lies she had told about the baby in her belly and she had become hysterical and furious, the mountain had moved at last: out of the door, with an ashtray flung after it.

His black eye had barely healed when she had announced her engagement to Ross. Three weeks it had taken her, because she knew only one way to respond to pain: to wound the transgressor as deeply as possible, with no thought for the consequences to herself. And he knew in his bones, no matter how arrogant his friends might tell him he was being, that the

Tatler pictures, the dismissal of their relationship in the terms that would hurt him most (he could hear her spelling it out for the society mag: 'he's *Jonny Rokeby's* son'); the Castle of Fucking Croy . . . all of it, *all* of it, was done with a view to hurting him, wanting him to watch and to see, to regret and to pity. She had known what Ross was; she had told Strike about the poorly disguised alcoholism and violence, passed through the blue-blooded network of gossip that had kept her informed through the years. She had laughed about her lucky escape. Laughed.

Self-immolation in a ball gown. *Watch me burn, Bluey*. The wedding was in ten days' time and if he had ever been sure of anything in his life, it was that if he called Charlotte right now and said 'Run away with me,' even after their filthy scenes, the hateful things she had called him, the lies and the mess and the several tons of baggage under which their relationship had finally splintered, she would say yes. Running away was her life's blood and he had been her favourite destination, freedom and safety combined; she had said it to him over and over again after fights that would have killed them both if emotional wounds could bleed: 'I need you. You're my everything, you know that. You're the only place I've ever felt safe, Bluey . . . '

He heard the glass door on to the landing open and close, the familiar sounds of Robin arriving at work, removing her coat, filling the kettle.

Work had always been his salvation. Charlotte had hated the way he could switch, from crazy, violent scenes, from her tears and her pleas and her threats, to immerse himself totally in a case. She had never managed to stop him putting on his uniform, never prevented his return to work, never succeeded in forcing him away from an investigation. She deplored his focus, his allegiance to the army, his ability to shut her out, seeing it as a betrayal, as abandonment.

Now, on this cold winter's morning, sitting in his office with her picture in the bin beside him, Strike found himself craving orders, a case abroad, an enforced sojourn on another continent. He did not want to trail after unfaithful husbands and girlfriends, or insert himself into the petty disputes of shoddy businessmen. Only one subject had ever matched Charlotte for the fascination it exercised over him: unnatural death.

'Morning,' he said, limping into the outer office, where Robin was making two mugs of tea. 'We'll have to be quick with these. We're going out.'

'Where?' asked Robin in surprise.

The sleet was sliding wetly down their windows. She could still feel how it had burned her face as she hurried over the slippery pavements, desperate to get inside.

'Got stuff to do on the Quine case.'

It was a lie. The police had all the power; what could he do that they were not doing better? And yet he knew in his gut that Anstis lacked the nose for the strange and the warped that would be needed to find this killer.

'You've got Caroline Ingles at ten.'

'Shit. Well, I'll put her off. Thing is, forensics reckon Quine died very soon after he disappeared.'

He took a mouthful of hot, strong tea. He seemed more purposeful, more energised than she had seen him for a while.

'That puts the spotlight right back on the people who had early access to the manuscript. I want to find out where they all live, and whether they live alone. Then we're going to recce their houses. Find out how hard it would've been to get in and out carrying a bag of guts. Whether they might have places they could bury or burn evidence.'

It was not much, but it was all he could do today, and he was desperate to do something.

'You're coming,' he added. 'You're always good at this stuff.'

'What, being your Watson?' she said, apparently indifferent. The anger she had carried with her out of the Cambridge the previous day had not quite burned out. 'We could find out about their houses online. Look at them on Google Earth.'

'Yeah, good thinking,' rejoined Strike. 'Why case locations when you could just look at out-of-date photos?'

Stung, she said:

'I'm more than happy—'

'Good. I'll cancel Ingles. You get online and find out addresses for Christian Fisher, Elizabeth Tassel, Daniel Chard, Jerry Waldegrave and Michael Fancourt. We'll nip along to Clem Attlee Court and have another look from the point of view of hiding evidence; from what I saw in the dark there were a lot of bins and bushes . . . Oh, and call the Bridlington Bookshop in Putney. We can have a word with the old bloke who claims he met Quine there on the eighth.'

He strode back into his office and Robin sat down at her computer. The scarf she had just hung up was dripping icily onto the floor, but she did not care. The memory of Quine's mutilated body continued to haunt her, yet she was possessed of an urge (concealed from Matthew like a dirty secret) to find out more, to find out everything.

What infuriated her was that Strike, who of all people should have understood, could not see in her what so obviously burned in him.

25

Thus 'tis when a man will be ignorantly officious,
do services, and not know his why . . .

Ben Jonson, *Epicoene, or The Silent Woman*

They left the office in a sudden flurry of feathery snowflakes, Robin with the various addresses she had taken from an online directory on her mobile phone. Strike wanted to revisit Talgarth Road first, so Robin told him the results of her directory searches while standing in a Tube carriage that, at the tail end of the rush hour, was full but not packed. The smell of wet wool, grime and Gore-Tex filled their nostrils as they talked, holding the same pole as three miserable-looking Italian backpackers.

'The old man who works in the bookshop's on holiday,' she told Strike. 'Back next Monday.'

'All right, we'll leave him till then. What about our suspects?'

She raised an eyebrow at the word, but said:

'Christian Fisher lives in Camden with a woman of thirty-two – a girlfriend, do you think?'

'Probably,' agreed Strike. 'That's inconvenient . . . our killer needed peace and solitude to dispose of bloodstained clothing – not to mention a good stone's worth of human intestine. I'm looking for somewhere you can get in and out of without being seen.'

'Well, I looked at pictures of the place on Google Street View,' said Robin with a certain defiance. 'The flat's got a common entrance with three others.'

'And it's miles away from Talgarth Road.'

'But you don't *really* think Christian Fisher did it, do you?' asked Robin.

'Strains credulity a bit,' Strike admitted. 'He barely knew Quine – he's not in the book – can't see it.'

They alighted at Holborn, where Robin tactfully slowed her pace to Strike's, not commenting on his limp or the way he was using his upper body to propel himself along.

'What about Elizabeth Tassel?' he asked as he walked.

'Fulham Palace Road, alone.'

'Good,' said Strike. 'We'll go and have a look at that, see if she's got any freshly dug flower beds.'

'Won't the police be doing this?' Robin asked.

Strike frowned. He was perfectly aware that he was a jackal slinking on the periphery of the case, hoping the lions might leave a scrap on a minor bone.

'Maybe,' he said, 'maybe not. Anstis thinks Leonora did it and he doesn't change his mind easily; I know, I worked with him on a case in Afghanistan. Speaking of Leonora,' he added casually, 'Anstis has found out she used to work in a butcher's.'

'Oh bugger,' said Robin.

Strike grinned. At times of tension, her Yorkshire accent became more pronounced: he had heard '*boo*gger'.

They got onto a much emptier Piccadilly line train to Barons Court; relieved, Strike fell into a seat.

'Jerry Waldegrave lives with his wife, right?' he asked Robin.

'Yes, if she's called Fenella. In Hazlitt Road, Kensington. A Joanna Waldegrave lives in the basement—'

'Their daughter,' said Strike. 'Budding novelist, she was at the Roper Chard party. And Daniel Chard?'

'Sussex Street, Pimlico, with a couple called Nenita and Manny Ramos—'

'Sound like servants.'

'—and he's got a property in Devon as well: Tithebarn House.'

'Which is presumably where he's currently laid up with his broken leg.'

'And Fancourt's ex-directory,' she finished, 'but there's loads of biographical stuff about him online. He owns an Elizabethan place just outside Chew Magna called Endsor Court.'

'Chew Magna?'

'It's in Somerset. He lives there with his third wife.'

'Bit far to go today,' said Strike regretfully. 'No bachelor pad near Talgarth Road where he could stash guts in the freezer?'

'Not that I could find.'

'So where was he staying when he went to stare at the crime scene? Or had he come up for the day for a spot of nostalgia?'

'If it really was him.'

'Yeah, if it was him . . . and there's Kathryn Kent too. Well, we know where she lives and we know it's alone. Quine got dropped off in her vicinity on the night of the fifth, Anstis says, but she was away. Maybe Quine had forgotten she was at her sister's,' Strike mused, 'and maybe when he found out she wasn't home he went to Talgarth Road instead? She could have come back from the hospice to meet him there. We'll have a look round her place second.'

As they moved west Strike told Robin about the different

witnesses who claimed to have seen a woman in a burqa entering the building on the fourth of November and Quine himself leaving the building in the early hours of the sixth.

'But one or both of them could be mistaken or lying,' he concluded.

'A woman in a burqa. You don't think,' said Robin tentatively, 'the neighbour might be a mad Islamophobe?'

Working for Strike had opened her eyes to the array and intensity of phobias and grudges she had never realised burned in the public's breast. The tide of publicity surrounding the solving of the Landry case had washed onto Robin's desk a number of letters that had alternately disturbed and amused her.

There had been the man who had begged Strike to turn his clearly considerable talents to an investigation of the stranglehold of 'international Jewry' on the world banking system, a service for which he regretted he would not be able to pay but for which he did not doubt that Strike would receive worldwide acclaim. A young woman had written a twelve-page letter from a secure psychiatric unit, begging Strike to help her prove that everybody in her family had been spirited away and replaced with identical impostors. An anonymous writer of unknown gender had demanded that Strike help them expose a national campaign of satanic abuse which they knew to be operating through the offices of the Citizens Advice Bureau.

'They could be loons,' Strike agreed. 'Nutters love murder. It does something to them. People have to listen to them, for a start.'

A young woman wearing a hijab was watching them talk from an opposite seat. She had large, sweet, liquid-brown eyes.

'Assuming somebody really did enter the house on the fourth, I've got to say a burqa's a bloody good way of getting in and out without being recognised. Can you think of another way of totally concealing your face and body that wouldn't make people challenge you?'

'And they were carrying a halal takeaway?'

'Allegedly. Was his last meal halal? Is that why the killer removed the guts?'

'And this woman—'

'Could've been a man . . . '

'—was seen leaving the house an hour later?'

'That's what Anstis said.'

'So they weren't lying in wait for Quine?'

'No, but they could have been laying in plates,' said Strike and Robin winced.

The young woman in the hijab got off at Gloucester Road.

'I doubt there'd be closed-circuit cameras in a bookshop,' sighed Robin. She had become quite preoccupied with CCTV since the Landry case.

'I'd've thought Anstis would have mentioned it,' agreed Strike.

They emerged at Barons Court into another squall of snow. Squinting against the feathery flakes they proceeded, under Strike's direction, up to Talgarth Road. He was feeling the need for a stick ever more strongly. On his release from hospital, Charlotte had given him an elegant antique Malacca cane that she claimed had belonged to a great-grandfather. The handsome old stick had been too short for Strike, causing him to list to the right as he walked. When she had packaged up his things to remove from her flat, the cane had not been among them.

It was clear, as they approached the house, that the forensics team was still busy in number 179. The entrance was taped up and a single police officer, arms folded tightly against the cold, stood guard outside. She turned her head as they approached. Her eyes fixed on Strike and narrowed.

'Mr Strike,' she said sharply.

A male plain-clothes officer with ginger hair who had been standing in the doorway talking to somebody just inside whipped around, caught sight of Strike and descended the slippery steps at speed.

'Morning,' said Strike brazenly. Robin was torn between admiration for his cheek and trepidation; she had an innate respect for the law.

'What are you doing back here, Mr Strike?' asked the ginger-haired man suavely. His eyes wandered over Robin in a way that she found vaguely offensive. 'You can't come in.'

'Pity,' said Strike. 'We'll just have to peruse the perimeter, then.'

Ignoring the pair of officers watching his every move, Strike limped past them to number 183 and proceeded through the gates and up the front steps. Robin could think of nothing to do but follow him; she did it self-consciously, aware of the eyes on her back.

'What are we doing?' she muttered as they reached the shelter of the brick canopy and were hidden from the staring police. The house seemed empty, but she was a little worried that someone might be about to open the front door.

'Gauging whether the woman who lives here could've seen a cloaked figure carrying a holdall leaving 179 at two in the morning,' said Strike. 'And you know what? I think she could, unless that street lamp's out. OK, let's try the other side.

'Parky, isn't it?' Strike said to the frowning constable and her companion as he and Robin walked back past them. 'Four doors down, Anstis said,' he added quietly to Robin. 'So that'll be 171 . . . '

Again, Strike marched up the front steps, Robin walking foolishly after him.

'You know, I was wondering whether he could've mistaken the house, but 177's got that red plastic dustbin in front. Burqa would've walked up the steps right behind it, which would've made it easy to tell—'

The front door opened.

'Can I help you?' said a well-spoken man in thick-lensed glasses.

As Strike began to apologise for coming to the wrong house, the ginger-haired officer shouted something incomprehensible from the pavement outside 179. When nobody responded, he climbed over the plastic tape blocking entrance to the property and began to jog towards them.

'That man,' he shouted absurdly, pointing at Strike, 'is not a policeman!'

'He didn't say he was,' replied the spectacled man in meek surprise.

'Well, I think we're done here,' Strike told Robin.

'Aren't you worried,' Robin asked him as they walked back towards the Tube station, a little amused but mostly eager to leave the scene, 'what your friend Anstis is going to say about you skulking around the crime scene like this?'

'Doubt he'll be happy,' Strike said, looking around for CCTV cameras, 'but keeping Anstis happy isn't in my job description.'

'It was decent of him to share the forensic stuff with you,' Robin said.

'He did that to try and warn me off the case. He thinks everything points to Leonora. Trouble is, at the moment, everything does.'

The road was packed with traffic, which was watched by a single camera as far as Strike could see, but there were many side roads leading off it down which a person wearing Owen Quine's Tyrolean cloak, or a burqa, might slide out of sight without anyone being the wiser as to their identity.

Strike bought two takeaway coffees in the Metro Café that stood in the station building, then they passed back through the pea-green ticket hall and set off for West Brompton.

'What you've got to remember,' said Strike as they stood at Earl's Court waiting to change trains, Robin noticing how Strike kept all his weight on his good leg, 'is that Quine disappeared on the fifth. Bonfire night.'

'God, of course!' said Robin.

'Flashes and bangs,' said Strike, gulping coffee fast so as to empty his cup before they had to get on; he did not trust himself to balance coffee and himself on the wet, icy floors. 'Rockets going off in every direction, drawing everyone's attention. No big surprise that nobody saw a figure in a cloak entering the building that night.'

'You mean Quine?'

'Not necessarily.'

Robin pondered this for a while.

'Do you think the man in the bookshop's lying about Quine going in there on the eighth?'

'I don't know,' said Strike. 'Too early to say, isn't it?'

But that, he realised, was what he believed. The sudden activity around a deserted house on the fourth and fifth was strongly suggestive.

'Funny, the things people notice,' said Robin as they climbed the red-and-green stairs at West Brompton, Strike now grimacing every time he put down his right leg. 'Memory's an odd thing, isn't—'

Strike's knee suddenly felt red hot and he slumped against the railings along the bridge over the tracks. A suited man behind him swore impatiently at finding a sudden, sizeable impediment in his path and Robin walked on a few paces, still talking, before realising that Strike was no longer beside her. She hurried back to find him pale, sweating and obliging commuters to take a detour around him as he stood slumped against the railings.

'Felt something go,' he said through gritted teeth, 'in my knee. Shit . . . *shit*!'

'We'll get a taxi.'

'Never get one in this weather.'

'Then let's get back on the train and go back to the office.'

'No, I want—'

He had never felt his dearth of resources more keenly than at this moment, standing on the iron lattice bridge beneath the arched glass ceiling where snow was settling. In the old days there had always been a car for him to drive. He could have summoned witnesses to him. He had been Special Investigation Branch, in charge, in control.

'If you want to do this, we need a taxi,' Robin said firmly. 'It's a long walk up Lillie Road from here. Haven't—'

She hesitated. They never mentioned Strike's disability except obliquely.

'Haven't you got a stick or something?'

'Wish I had,' he said through numb lips. What was the point in pretending? He was dreading having to walk even to the end of the bridge.

'We can get one,' said Robin. 'Chemists sometimes sell them. We'll find one.'

And then, after another momentary hesitation, she said:

'Lean on me.'

'I'm too heavy.'

'To balance. Use me like a stick. Do it,' she said firmly.

He put his arm around her shoulders and they made their way slowly over the bridge and paused beside the exit. The snow had temporarily passed, but the cold was, if anything, worse than it had been.

'Why aren't there seats anywhere?' asked Robin, glaring around.

'Welcome to my world,' said Strike, who had withdrawn his arm from around her shoulders the instant they had stopped.

'What d'you think's happened?' Robin asked, looking down at his right leg.

'I dunno. It was all puffed up this morning. I probably shouldn't have put the prosthesis on, but I hate using crutches.'

'Well, you can't go traipsing up Lillie Road in the snow like this. We'll get a cab and you can go back to the office—'

'No. I want to do something,' he said angrily. 'Anstis is convinced it's Leonora. It isn't.'

Everything was pared down to the essential when you were in this degree of pain.

'All right,' said Robin. 'We'll split up and you can go in a cab. OK? *OK?*' she said insistently.

'All right,' he said, defeated. 'You go up to Clem Attlee Court.'

'What am I looking for?'

'Cameras. Hiding places for clothing and intestines. Kent can't have kept them in her flat if she took them; they'd stink. Take pictures on your phone – anything that seems useful . . . '

It seemed pathetically little to him as he said it, but he had to do something. For some reason, he kept remembering Orlando, with her wide, vacant smile and her cuddly orang-utan.

'And then?' asked Robin.

'Sussex Street,' said Strike after a few seconds' thought. 'Same thing. And then give me a ring and we'll meet up. You'd better give me the numbers of Tassel's and Waldegrave's houses.'

She gave him a piece of paper.

'I'll get you a taxi.'

Before he could thank her she had marched away onto the cold street.

26

I must look to my footing:
In such slippery ice-pavements men had need
To be frost-nail'd well, they may break their
necks else . . .

John Webster, *The Duchess of Malfi*

It was fortunate that Strike still had the five hundred pounds in cash in his wallet that had been given him to cut up a teenage boy. He told the taxi driver to take him to Fulham Palace Road, home of Elizabeth Tassel, took note of the route as he travelled and would have arrived at her house in a mere four minutes had he not spotted a Boots. He asked the driver to pull up and wait, and re-emerged from the chemists shortly afterwards, walking much more easily with the aid of an adjustable stick.

He estimated that a fit woman might make the journey on foot in less than half an hour. Elizabeth Tassel lived further from the murder scene than Kathryn Kent but Strike, who knew the area reasonably well, was sure that she could have made her way through most residential backstreets while avoiding the attention of cameras, and that she might have avoided detection even with a car.

Her home looked drab and dingy on this bleak winter's day.

Another red brick Victorian house, but with none of the grandeur or whimsy of Talgarth Road, it stood on a corner, fronted by a dank garden overshadowed by overgrown laburnum bushes. Sleet fell again as Strike stood peering over the garden gate, trying to keep his cigarette alight by cupping it in his hand. There were gardens front and back, both well shielded from the public view by the dark bushes quivering with the weight of the icy downpour. The upper windows of the house looked out over the Fulham Palace Road Cemetery, a depressing view one month from midwinter, with bare trees reaching bony arms silhouetted into a white sky, old tombstones marching into the distance.

Could he imagine Elizabeth Tassel in her smart black suit, with her scarlet lipstick and her undisguised fury at Owen Quine, returning here under cover of darkness, stained with blood and acid, carrying a bag full of intestines?

The cold was nipping viciously at Strike's neck and fingers. He ground out the stub of his cigarette and asked the taxi driver, who had watched with curiosity tinged with suspicion as he scrutinised Elizabeth Tassel's house, to take him to Hazlitt Road in Kensington. Slumped in the back seat he gulped down painkillers with a bottle of water that he had bought in Boots.

The cab was stuffy and smelled of stale tobacco, ingrained dirt and ancient leather. The windscreen wipers swished like muffled metronomes, rhythmically clearing the blurry view of broad, busy Hammersmith Road, where small office blocks and short rows of terraced houses sat side by side. Strike looked out at Nazareth House Care Home: more red brick, church-like and serene, but with security gates and a lodge keeping a firm separation between those cared for and those who were not.

Blythe House came into view through the misty windows, a

grand palace-like structure with white cupolas, looking like a large pinkish cake in the grey sleet. Strike had a vague notion that it was used as a store for one of the big museums these days. The taxi turned right into Hazlitt Road.

'What number?' asked the driver.

'I'll get out here,' said Strike, who did not wish to descend directly in front of the house, and had not forgotten that he still had to pay back the money he was squandering. Leaning heavily on the stick and grateful for its rubber-coated end, which gripped the slippery pavement well, he paid the driver and walked along the street to take a closer look at the Waldegrave residence.

These were real townhouses, four storeys high including the basements, golden brick with classical white pediments, carved wreaths beneath the upper windows and wrought-iron balustrades. Most of them had been converted into flats. There were no front gardens, only steps descending to the basements.

A faintly ramshackle flavour had permeated the street, a gentle middle-class dottiness that expressed itself in the random collections of pot plants on one balcony, a bicycle on another and, on a third, limp, wet and possibly soon-to-be-frozen washing forgotten in the sleet.

The house that Waldegrave shared with his wife was one of the very few that had not been converted into flats. As he stared up at it, Strike wondered how much a top editor earned and remembered Nina's statement that Waldegrave's wife 'came from money'. The Waldegraves' first-floor balcony (he had to cross the street to see it clearly) sported two sodden deckchairs printed with the covers of old Penguin paperbacks, flanking a tiny iron table of the kind found in Parisian bistros.

He lit another cigarette and re-crossed the road to peer down at the basement flat where Waldegrave's daughter lived, considering as he did so whether Quine might have discussed the contents of *Bombyx Mori* with his editor before delivering the manuscript. Could he have confided to Waldegrave how he envisaged the final scene of *Bombyx Mori*? And could that amiable man in horn-rimmed glasses have nodded enthusiastically and helped hone the scene in all its ludicrous gore, knowing that he would one day enact it?

There were black bin bags heaped around the front door of the basement flat. It looked as though Joanna Waldegrave had been having a comprehensive clear-out. Strike turned his back and contemplated the fifty windows, at a conservative estimate, that overlooked the Waldegrave family's two front doors. Waldegrave would have had to have been very lucky not to be seen coming and going out of this heavily overlooked house.

But the trouble was, Strike reflected gloomily, that even if Jerry Waldegrave had been spotted sneaking into his house at two in the morning with a suspicious, bulging bag under his arm, a jury might take some persuading that Owen Quine had not been alive and well at the time. There was too much doubt about the time of death. The murderer had now had as long as nineteen days in which to dispose of evidence, a long and useful period.

Where could Owen Quine's guts have gone? What, Strike asked himself, did you do with pounds and pounds of freshly severed human intestine and stomach? Bury them? Dump them in a river? Throw them in a communal bin? They would surely not burn well . . .

The front door of the Waldegraves' house opened and a woman with black hair and heavy frown lines walked down the three front steps. She was wearing a short scarlet coat and looked angry.

'I've been watching you out of the window,' she called to Strike as she approached and he recognised Waldegrave's wife, Fenella. 'What do you think you're doing? Why are you so interested in my house?'

'I'm waiting for the agent,' Strike lied at once, showing no sign of embarrassment. 'This is the basement flat for rent, right?'

'Oh,' she said, taken aback. 'No – that's three down,' she said, pointing.

He could tell that she teetered on the verge of an apology but decided not to bother. Instead she clattered past him on patent stilettos ill suited to the snowy conditions towards a Volvo parked a short way away. Her black hair revealed grey roots and their brief proximity had brought with it a whiff of bad breath stained with alcohol. Mindful that she could see him in her rear-view mirror, he hobbled in the direction she had indicated, waited until she had pulled away – very narrowly missing the Citroën in front of her – then walked carefully to the end of the road and down a side street, where he was able to peer over a wall into a long row of small private back gardens.

There was nothing of note in the Waldegraves' except an old shed. The lawn was scuffed and scrubby and a set of rustic furniture sat sadly at its far end with a look of having been abandoned long ago. Staring at the untidy plot, Strike reflected gloomily on the possibility of lock-ups, allotments and garages he might not know about.

With an inward groan at the thought of the long, cold, wet walk ahead, he debated his options. He was nearest to Kensington Olympia, but it only opened the District line he needed at weekends. As an overground station, Hammersmith would be easier to navigate than Baron's Court, so he decided on the longer journey.

He had just passed into Blythe Road, wincing with every step on his right leg, when his mobile rang: Anstis.

'What are you playing at, Bob?'

'Meaning?' asked Strike, limping along, a stabbing in his knee.

'You've been hanging around the crime scene.'

'Went back for a look. Public right of way. Nothing actionable.'

'You were trying to interview a neighbour—'

'He wasn't supposed to open his front door,' said Strike. 'I didn't say a word about Quine.'

'Look, Strike—'

The detective noticed the reversion to his actual name without regret. He had never been fond of the nickname Anstis had given him.

'I told you, you've got to keep out of our way.'

'Can't, Anstis,' said Strike matter-of-factly. 'I've got a client—'

'Forget your client,' said Anstis. 'She's looking more and more like a killer with every bit of information we get. My advice is, cut your losses because you're making yourself a lot of enemies. I warned you—'

'You did,' said Strike. 'You couldn't have been clearer. Nobody's going to be able to blame you, Anstis.'

'I'm not warning you off because I'm trying to cover my arse,' snapped Anstis.

Strike kept walking in silence, the mobile pressed awkwardly to his ear. After a short pause Anstis said:

'We've got the pharmacological report back. Small amount of blood alcohol, nothing else.'

'OK.'

'And we're sending dogs out to Mucking Marshes this

afternoon. Trying to keep ahead of the weather. They say there's heavy snow on the way.'

Mucking Marshes, Strike knew, was the UK's biggest landfill site; it serviced London, the municipal and commercial waste of which was floated down the Thames in ugly barges.

'You think the guts were dumped in a dustbin, do you?'

'A skip. There's a house renovation going on round the corner from Talgarth Road; they had two parked out front until the eighth. In this cold the guts might not have attracted flies. We've checked and that's where everything the builders take away ends up: Mucking Marshes.'

'Well, good luck with that,' said Strike.

'I'm trying to save you time and energy, mate.'

'Yeah. Very grateful.'

And after insincere thanks for Anstis's hospitality of the previous evening Strike rang off. He then paused, leaning against a wall, the better to dial a new number. A tiny Asian woman with a pushchair, whom he had not heard walking behind him, had to swerve to avoid him, but unlike the man on the West Brompton bridge she did not swear at him. The walking stick, like a burqa, conferred protective status; she gave him a small smile as she passed.

Leonora Quine answered within three rings.

'Bloody police are back,' was her greeting.

'What do they want?'

'They're asking to look all over the house and garden now,' she said. 'Do I have to let 'em?'

Strike hesitated.

'I think it's sensible to let them do whatever they want. Listen, Leonora,' he felt no compunction about reverting to a military peremptoriness, 'have you got a lawyer?'

'No, why? I ain't under arrest. Not yet.'

'I think you need one.'

There was a pause.

'D'you know any good ones?' she asked.

'Yes,' said Strike. 'Call Ilsa Herbert. I'll send you her number now.'

'Orlando don't like the police poking—'

'I'm going to text you this number, and I want you to call Ilsa immediately. All right? *Immediately.*'

'All right,' she said grumpily.

He rang off, found his old school friend's number on his mobile and sent it to Leonora. He then called Ilsa and explained, with apologies, what he had just done.

'I don't know why you're saying sorry,' she said cheerfully. 'We love people who are in trouble with the police, it's our bread and butter.'

'She might qualify for legal aid.'

'Hardly anyone does these days,' said Ilsa. 'Let's just hope she's poor enough.'

Strike's hands were numb and he was very hungry. He slid the mobile back into his coat pocket and limped on to Hammersmith Road. There on the opposite pavement was a snug-looking pub, black painted, the round metal sign depicting a galleon in full sail. He headed straight for it, noting how much more patient waiting drivers were when you were using a stick.

Two pubs in two days . . . but the weather was bad and his knee excruciating; Strike could not muster any guilt. The Albion's interior was as cosy as its exterior suggested. Long and narrow, an open fire burned at the far end; there was an upper gallery with a balustrade and much polished wood. Beneath a black iron spiral staircase to the first floor were two amps and a microphone stand. Black-and-white photographs of celebrated musicians were hung along one cream wall.

The seats by the fire were taken. Strike bought himself a pint, picked up a bar menu and headed to the tall table surrounded by barstools next to the window onto the street. As he sat down he noticed, sandwiched between pictures of Duke Ellington and Robert Plant, his own long-haired father, sweaty post-performance, apparently sharing a joke with the bass player whom he had once, according to Strike's mother, tried to strangle.

('Jonny was never good on speed,' Leda had confided to her uncomprehending nine-year-old son.)

His mobile rang again. With his eyes on his father's picture, he answered.

'Hi,' said Robin. 'I'm back at the office. Where are you?'

'The Albion on Hammersmith Road.'

'You've had an odd call. I found the message when I got back.'

'Go on.'

'It's Daniel Chard,' said Robin. 'He wants to meet you.'

Frowning, Strike turned his eyes away from his father's leather jumpsuit to gaze down the pub at the flickering fire. 'Daniel Chard wants to meet me? How does Daniel Chard even know I exist?'

'For God's sake, you found the body! It's been all over the news.'

'Oh yeah – there's that. Did he say why?'

'He says he's got a proposition.'

A vivid mental image of a naked, bald man with an erect, suppurating penis flashed in Strike's mind like a projector slide and was instantly dismissed.

'I thought he was holed up in Devon because he'd broken his leg.'

'He is. He wonders whether you'd mind travelling down to see him.'

'Oh, does he?'

Strike pondered the suggestion, thinking of his workload, the meetings he had during the rest of the week. Finally, he said:

'I could do it Friday if I put off Burnett. What the hell does he want? I'll need to hire a car. An automatic,' he added, his leg throbbing painfully under the table. 'Could you do that for me?'

'No problem,' said Robin. He could hear her scribbling.

'I've got a lot to tell you,' he said. 'D'you want to join me for lunch? They've got a decent menu. Shouldn't take you more than twenty minutes if you grab a cab.'

'Two days running? We can't keep getting taxis and buying lunch out,' said Robin, even though she sounded pleased at the idea.

'That's OK. Burnett loves spending her ex's money. I'll charge it to her account.'

Strike hung up, decided on a steak and ale pie and limped to the bar to order.

When he resumed his seat his eyes drifted absently back to his father in skin-tight leathers, with his hair plastered around his narrow, laughing face.

The Wife knows about me and pretends not to . . . she won't let him go even if it's the best thing for everyone . . .

I know where you're off to, Owen!

Strike's gaze slid along the row of black-and-white megastars on the wall facing him.

Am I deluded? he asked John Lennon silently, who looked down at him through round glasses, sardonic, pinch-nosed.

Why did he not believe, even in the face of what he had to admit were suggestive signs to the contrary, that Leonora had murdered her husband? Why did he remain convinced that she had come to his office not as a cover but because she was genuinely angry that Quine had run away like a sulky child? He would have sworn on oath that it had never crossed her mind that her husband might be dead . . . Lost in thought, he had finished his pint before he knew it.

'Hi,' said Robin.

'That was quick!' said Strike, surprised to see her.

'Not really,' said Robin. 'Traffic's quite heavy. Shall I order?'

Male heads turned to look at her as she walked to the bar, but Strike did not notice. He was still thinking about Leonora Quine, thin, plain, greying, hunted.

When Robin returned with another pint for Strike and a tomato juice for herself she showed him the photographs that she had taken on her phone that morning of Daniel Chard's town residence. It was a white stucco villa complete with balustrade, its gleaming black front door flanked by columns.

'It's got an odd little courtyard, sheltered from the street,' said Robin, showing Strike a picture. Shrubs stood in big-bellied Grecian urns. 'I suppose Chard could have dumped the guts into one of those,' she said flippantly. 'Pulled out the tree and buried them in the earth.'

'Can't imagine Chard doing anything so energetic or dirty, but that's the way to keep thinking,' said Strike, remembering the publisher's immaculate suit and flamboyant tie. 'How about Clem Attlee Court – as full of hiding places as I remember?'

'Loads of them,' said Robin, showing him a fresh set of pictures. 'Communal bins, bushes, all sorts. The only thing is, I just can't imagine being able to do it unseen, or that somebody wouldn't notice them fairly quickly. There are people around all the time and everywhere you go you're being overlooked by about a hundred windows. You might manage it in the middle of the night, but there are cameras too.

'But I did notice something else. Well . . . it's just an idea.'

'Go on.'

'There's a medical centre right in front of the building. Might they not sometimes dispose of—'

'Human waste!' said Strike, lowering his pint. 'Bloody hell, that's a thought.'

'Should I get onto it, then?' asked Robin, trying to conceal the pleasure and pride she felt at Strike's look of admiration. 'Try and find out how and when—?'

'Definitely!' said Strike. 'That's a much better lead than Anstis's. He thinks,' he explained, answering her look of enquiry, 'the guts were dumped in a skip close by Talgarth Road, that the killer just carried them round the corner and chucked them in.'

'Well, they could have,' began Robin, but Strike frowned exactly the way Matthew did if ever she mentioned an idea or a belief of Strike's.

'This killing was planned to the hilt. We're not dealing with a murderer who'd just have dumped a holdall full of human guts round the corner from the corpse.'

They sat in silence while Robin reflected wryly that Strike's dislike of Anstis's theories might be due to innate competitiveness more than any objective evaluation. Robin knew something about male pride; quite apart from Matthew, she had three brothers.

'So what were Elizabeth Tassel's and Jerry Waldegrave's places like?'

Strike told her about Waldegrave's wife thinking he had been watching her house.

'Very shirty about it.'

'Odd,' said Robin. 'If I saw somebody staring at our place I wouldn't leap to the conclusion that they were – you know – *watching* it.'

'She's a drinker like her husband,' said Strike. 'I could smell it on her. Meanwhile, Elizabeth Tassel's place is as good a murderer's hideout as I've ever seen.'

'What d'you mean?' asked Robin, half amused, half apprehensive.

'Very private, barely overlooked.'

'Well, I still don't think—'

'—it's a woman. You said.'

Strike drank his beer in silence for a minute or two, considering a course of action that he knew would irritate Anstis more than any other. He had no right to interrogate suspects. He had been told to keep out of the way of the police.

Picking up his mobile, he contemplated it for a moment, then called Roper Chard and asked to speak to Jerry Waldegrave.

'Anstis told you not to get under their feet!' Robin said, alarmed.

'Yeah,' said Strike, the line silent in his ear, 'advice he's just repeated, but I haven't told you half what's been going on. Tell you in—'

'Hello?' said Jerry Waldegrave on the end of the line.

'Mr Waldegrave,' said Strike and introduced himself, though he had already given his name to Waldegrave's assistant. 'We met briefly yesterday morning, at Mrs Quine's.'

'Yes, of course,' said Waldegrave. He sounded politely puzzled.

'As I think Mrs Quine told you, she's hired me because she's worried that the police suspect her.'

'I'm sure that can't be true,' said Waldegrave at once.

'That they suspect her, or that she killed her husband?'

'Well – both,' said Waldegrave.

'Wives usually come in for close scrutiny when a husband dies,' said Strike.

'I'm sure they do, but I can't . . . well, I can't believe any of it, actually,' said Waldegrave. 'The whole thing's incredible and horrible.'

'Yeah,' said Strike. 'I was wondering whether we could meet so I could ask you a few questions? I'm happy,' said the detective, with a glance at Robin, 'to come to your house – after work – whatever suits.'

Waldegrave did not answer immediately.

'Naturally I'll do anything to help Leonora, but what do you imagine I can tell you?'

'I'm interested in *Bombyx Mori*,' said Strike. 'Mr Quine put a lot of unflattering portraits in the book.'

'Yeah,' said Waldegrave. 'He did.'

Strike wondered whether Waldegrave had been interviewed by the police yet; whether he had already been asked to explain the contents of bloody sacks, the symbolism of a drowned dwarf.

'All right,' said Waldegrave. 'I don't mind meeting you. My diary's quite full this week. Could you make . . . let's see . . . lunch on Monday?'

'Great,' said Strike, reflecting sourly that this would mean him footing the bill, and that he would have preferred to see inside Waldegrave's house. 'Where?'

'I'd rather stick close to the office; I've got a full afternoon. Would you mind Simpson's-in-the-Strand?'

Strike thought it an odd choice but agreed, his eyes on Robin's. 'One o'clock? I'll get my secretary to book it. See you then.'

'He's going to meet you?' said Robin as soon as Strike had hung up.

'Yeah,' said Strike. 'Fishy.'

She shook her head, half laughing.

'He didn't seem particularly keen, from all I could hear. And don't you think the fact that he's agreed to meet at all looks like he's got a clear conscience?'

'No,' said Strike. 'I've told you this before; plenty of people hang around the likes of me to gauge how the investigation's going. They can't leave well enough alone, they feel compelled to keep explaining themselves.

'Need a pee . . . hang on . . . got more to tell you . . .'

Robin sipped her tomato juice while Strike hobbled away using the new stick.

Another flurry of snow passed the window, swiftly dispersing. Robin looked up at the black-and-white photographs opposite and recognised, with a slight shock, Jonny Rokeby, Strike's father. Other than the fact that both were over six feet tall, they did not resemble each other in the slightest; it had taken a DNA test to prove paternity. Strike was listed as one of the rock star's progeny on Rokeby's Wikipedia entry. They had met, so Strike had told Robin, twice. After staring for a while at Rokeby's very tight and revealing leather trousers, Robin forced herself to gaze out of the window again, afraid of Strike catching her staring at his father's groin.

Their food arrived as Strike returned to the table.

'The police are searching the whole of Leonora's house now,' Strike announced, picking up his knife and fork.

'Why?' asked Robin, fork suspended in mid-air.

'Why d'you think? Looking for bloody clothing. Checking the garden for freshly dug holes full of her husband's innards. I've put her on to a lawyer. They haven't got enough to arrest her yet, but they're determined to find something.'

'You genuinely don't think she did it?'

'No, I don't.'

Strike had cleared his plate before he spoke again.

'I'd love to talk to Fancourt. I want to know why he joined Roper Chard when Quine was there and he was supposed to hate him. They'd have been bound to meet.'

'You think Fancourt killed Quine so he wouldn't have to meet him at office parties?'

'Good one,' said Strike wryly.

He drained his pint glass, picked up his mobile yet again, dialled Directory Enquiries and shortly afterwards was put through to the Elizabeth Tassel Literary Agency.

Her assistant, Ralph, answered. When Strike gave his name, the young man sounded both fearful and excited.

'Oh, I don't know . . . I'll ask. Putting you on hold.'

But he appeared to be less than adept with the telephone system, because after a loud click the line remained open. Strike could hear a distant Ralph informing his boss that Strike was on the telephone and her loud, impatient retort.

'What the bloody hell does he want now?'

'He didn't say.'

Heavy footsteps, the sound of the receiver being snatched off the desk.

'Hello?'

'Elizabeth,' said Strike pleasantly. 'It's me, Cormoran Strike.'

'Yes, Ralph's just told me. What is it?'

'I was wondering if we could meet. I'm still working for Leonora Quine. She's convinced that the police suspect her of her husband's murder.'

'And what do you want to talk to me for? *I* can't tell you whether she did or not.'

Strike could imagine the shocked faces of Ralph and Sally, listening in the smelly old office.

'I've got a few more questions about Quine.'

'Oh, for God's sake,' growled Elizabeth. 'Well, I suppose I could do lunch tomorrow if it suits. Otherwise I'm busy until—'

'Tomorrow would be great,' said Strike. 'But it doesn't have to be lunch, I could—?'

'Lunch suits me.'

'Great,' said Strike at once.

'Pescatori, Charlotte Street,' she said. 'Twelve thirty unless you hear differently.'

She rang off.

'They love their bloody lunches, book people,' Strike said. 'Is it too much of a stretch to think they don't want me at home in case I spot Quine's guts in the freezer?'

Robin's smile faded.

'You know, you could lose a friend over this,' she said, pulling on her coat. 'Ringing people up and asking to question them.'

Strike grunted.

'Don't you care?' she asked, as they left the warmth for biting cold, snowflakes burning their faces.

'I've got plenty more friends,' said Strike, truthfully, without bombast.

'We should have a beer every lunchtime,' he added, leaning heavily on his stick as they headed off towards the Tube, their heads bowed against the white blur. 'Breaks up the working day.'

Robin, who had adjusted her stride to his, smiled. She had enjoyed today more than almost any since she had started work for Strike, but Matthew, still in Yorkshire, helping plan his mother's funeral, must not know about the second trip to a pub in two days.

27

> That I should trust a man, whom I had known betray his friend!
>
> William Congreve, *The Double-Dealer*

An immense carpet of snow was rolling down over Britain. The morning news showed the north-east of England already buried in powdery whiteness, cars stranded like so many hapless sheep, headlamps feebly glinting. London waited its turn beneath an increasingly ominous sky and Strike, glancing at the weather map on his TV as he dressed, wondered whether his drive to Devon the next day would be possible, whether the M5 would even be navigable. Determined though he was to meet the incapacitated Daniel Chard, whose invitation struck him as highly peculiar, he dreaded driving even an automatic with his leg in this condition.

The dogs would still be out on Mucking Marshes. He imagined them as he attached the prosthesis, his knee puffier and more painful than ever; their sensitive, quivering noses probing the freshest patches of landfill under these threatening gunmetal clouds, beneath circling seagulls. They might already have started, given the limited daylight, dragging their handlers through the frozen garbage, searching for Owen Quine's guts.

Strike had worked alongside sniffer dogs. Their wriggling rumps and wagging tails always added an incongruously cheerful note to searches.

He was disconcerted by how painful it was to walk downstairs. Of course, in an ideal world he would have spent the previous day with an ice pack pressed to the end of his stump, his leg elevated, not tramping all over London because he needed to stop himself thinking about Charlotte and her wedding, soon to take place in the restored chapel of the Castle of Croy . . . not Croy Castle, *because it annoys the fucking family*. Nine days to go . . .

The telephone rang on Robin's desk as he unlocked the glass door. Wincing, he hurried to get it. The suspicious lover and boss of Miss Brocklehurst wished to inform Strike that his PA was at home in his bed with a bad cold, so he was not to be charged for surveillance until she was up and about again. Strike had barely replaced the receiver when it rang again. Another client, Caroline Ingles, announced in a voice throbbing with emotion that she and her errant husband had reconciled. Strike was offering insincere congratulations when Robin arrived, pink-faced with cold.

'It's getting worse out there,' she said when he had hung up. 'Who was that?'

'Caroline Ingles. She's made up with Rupert.'

'*What?*' said Robin, stunned. 'After all those lap-dancers?'

'They're going to work on their marriage for the sake of the kids.'

Robin made a little snort of disbelief.

'Snow looks bad up in Yorkshire,' Strike commented. 'If you want to take tomorrow off and leave early—?'

'No,' said Robin, 'I've booked myself on the Friday-night

sleeper, I should be fine. If we've lost Ingles, I could call one of the waiting-list clients—?'

'Not yet,' said Strike, slumping down on the sofa and unable to stop his hand sliding to his swollen knee as it protested painfully.

'Is it still sore?' Robin asked diffidently, pretending she had not seen him wince.

'Yeah,' said Strike. 'But that's not why I don't want to take on another client,' he added sharply.

'I know,' said Robin, who had her back to him, switching on the kettle. 'You want to concentrate on the Quine case.'

Strike was not sure whether her tone was reproachful.

'She'll pay me,' he said shortly. 'Quine had life insurance, she made him take it out. So there's money there now.'

Robin heard his defensiveness and did not like it. Strike was making the assumption that her priority was money. Hadn't she proved that it was not when she had turned down much better paid jobs to work for him? Hadn't he noticed the willingness with which she was trying to help him prove that Leonora Quine had not killed her husband?

She set a mug of tea, a glass of water and paracetamol down beside him.

'Thanks,' he said, through gritted teeth, irritated by the painkillers even though he intended to take a double dose.

'I'll book a taxi to take you to Pescatori at twelve, shall I?'

'It's only round the corner,' he said.

'You know, there's pride, and then there's stupidity,' said Robin, with one of the first flashes of real temper he had ever seen in her.

'Fine,' he said, eyebrows raised. 'I'll take a bloody taxi.'

And in truth, he was glad of it three hours later as he

limped, leaning heavily on the cheap stick, which was now warping from his weight, to the taxi waiting at the end of Denmark Street. He knew now that he ought not to have put on the prosthesis at all. Getting out of the cab a few minutes later in Charlotte Street was tricky, the taxi driver impatient. Strike reached the noisy warmth of Pescatori with relief.

Elizabeth was not yet there but had booked under her name. Strike was shown to a table for two beside a pebble-set and whitewashed wall. Rustic wooden beams crisscrossed the ceiling; a rowing boat was suspended over the bar. Across the opposite wall were jaunty orange leather booths. From force of habit, Strike ordered a pint, enjoying the light, bright Mediterranean charm of his surroundings, watching the snow drifting past the windows.

The agent arrived not long afterwards. He tried to stand as she approached the table but fell back down again quickly. Elizabeth did not seem to notice.

She looked as though she had lost weight since he had last seen her; the well-cut black suit, the scarlet lipstick and the steel-grey bob did not lend her dash today, but looked like a badly chosen disguise. Her face was yellowish and seemed to sag.

'How are you?' he asked.

'How do you think I am?' she croaked rudely. 'What?' she snapped at a hovering waiter. 'Oh. Water. Still.'

She picked up her menu with an air of having given away too much and Strike could tell that any expression of pity or concern would be unwelcome.

'Just soup,' she told the waiter when he returned for their order.

'I appreciate you seeing me again,' Strike said when the waiter had departed.

'Well, God knows Leonora needs all the help she can get,' said Elizabeth.

'Why do you say that?'

Elizabeth narrowed her eyes at him.

'Don't pretend to be stupid. She told me she insisted on being brought to Scotland Yard to see you, right after she got the news about Owen.'

'Yeah, she did.'

'And how did she think that would look? The police probably expected her to collapse in a heap and all sh-she wants to do is see her detective friend.'

She suppressed a cough with difficulty.

'I don't think Leonora gives any thought to the impression she makes on other people,' said Strike.

'N-no, well, you're right there. She's never been the brightest.'

Strike wondered what impression Elizabeth Tassel thought she made on the world; whether she realised how little she was liked. She allowed the cough that she had been trying to suppress free expression and he waited for the loud, seal-like barks to pass before asking:

'You think she should have faked some grief?'

'I don't say it's fake,' snapped Elizabeth. 'I'm sure she is upset in her own limited way. I'm just saying it wouldn't hurt to play the grieving widow a bit more. It's what people expect.'

'I suppose you've talked to the police?'

'Of course. We've been through the row in the River Café, over and over the reason I didn't read the damn book properly. And they wanted to know my movements after I last saw Owen. Specifically, the three days after I saw him.'

She glared interrogatively at Strike, whose expression remained impassive.

'I take it they think he died within three days of our argument?'

'I've no idea,' lied Strike. 'What did you tell them about your movements?'

'That I went straight home after Owen stormed out on me, got up at six next morning, took a taxi to Paddington and went to stay with Dorcus.'

'One of your writers, I think you said?'

'Yes, Dorcus Pengelly, she—'

Elizabeth noticed Strike's small grin and, for the first time in their acquaintance, her face relaxed into a fleeting smile.

'It's her real name, if you can believe it, not a pseudonym. She writes pornography dressed up as historical romance. Owen was very sniffy about her books, but he'd have killed for her sales. They go,' said Elizabeth, 'like hot cakes.'

'When did you get back from Dorcus's?'

'Late Monday afternoon. It was supposed to be a nice long weekend, but *nice*,' said Elizabeth tensely, 'thanks to *Bombyx Mori*, it was *not*.

'I live alone,' she continued. 'I can't *prove* I went home, that I didn't murder Owen as soon as I got back to London. I certainly *felt* like doing it . . .'

She drank more water and continued:

'The police were mostly interested in the book. They seem to think it's given a lot of people a motive.'

It was her first overt attempt to get information out of him.

'It looked like a lot of people at first,' said Strike, 'but if they've got the time of death right and Quine died within three days of your row in the River Café, the number of suspects will be fairly limited.'

'How so?' asked Elizabeth sharply, and he was reminded of one of his most scathing tutors at Oxford, who used this two-word question like a giant needle to puncture ill-founded theorising.

'Can't give you that information, I'm afraid,' Strike replied pleasantly. 'Mustn't prejudice the police case.'

Her pallid skin, across the small table, was large-pored and coarse-grained, the olive-dark eyes watchful.

'They asked me,' she said, 'to whom I had shown the manuscript during the few days I had it before sending it to Jerry and Christian – answer: nobody. And they asked me with whom Owen discusses his manuscripts while he's writing them. I don't know why that was,' she said, her black eyes still fixed on Strike's. 'Do they think somebody egged him on?'

'I don't know,' Strike lied again. '*Does* he discuss the books he's working on?'

'He might have confided bits in Jerry Waldegrave. He barely deigned to tell me his titles.'

'Really? He never asked your advice? Did you say you'd studied English at Oxford—?'

'I took a first,' she said angrily, 'but that counted for less than nothing with Owen, who incidentally was thrown off his course at Loughborough or some such place, and never got a degree at all. Yes, and Michael once kindly told Owen that I'd been "lamentably derivative" as a writer back when we were students, and Owen never forgot it.' The memory of the old slight had given a purple tinge to her yellowish skin. 'Owen shared Michael's prejudice about women in literature. Neither of them minded women *praising* their work, of c-course—' She coughed into her napkin and emerged red-faced and angry. 'Owen was a bigger glutton for praise than any author I've ever met, and they are most of them insatiable.'

Their food arrived: tomato and basil soup for Elizabeth and cod and chips for Strike.

'You told me when we last met,' said Strike, having swallowed his first large mouthful, 'that there came a point when you had to choose between Fancourt and Quine. Why *did* you choose Quine?'

She was blowing on a spoonful of soup and seemed to give her answer serious consideration before speaking.

'I felt – at that time – that he was more sinned against than sinning.'

'Did this have something to do with the parody somebody wrote of Fancourt's wife's novel?'

'"Somebody" didn't write it,' she said quietly. 'Owen did.'

'Do you know that for sure?'

'He showed it to me before he sent it to the magazine. I'm afraid,' Elizabeth met Strike's gaze with cold defiance, 'it made me laugh. It was painfully accurate and very funny. Owen was always a good literary mimic.'

'But then Fancourt's wife killed herself.'

'Which was a tragedy, of course,' said Elizabeth, without noticeable emotion, 'although nobody could have reasonably expected it. Frankly, anybody who's going to kill themselves because of a bad review has no business writing a novel in the first place. But naturally enough, Michael was livid with Owen and I think the more so because Owen got cold feet and denied authorship once he heard about Elspeth's suicide. It was, perhaps, a surprisingly cowardly attitude for a man who liked to be thought of as fearless and lawless.

'Michael wanted me to drop Owen as a client. I refused. Michael hasn't spoken to me since.'

'Was Quine making more money for you than Fancourt at the time?' Strike asked.

'Good God, no,' she said. 'It wasn't to my *pecuniary* advantage to stick with Owen.'

'Then why—?'

'I've just told you,' she said impatiently. 'I believe in freedom of speech, up to and including upsetting people. Anyway, days after Elspeth killed herself, Leonora gave birth to premature twins. Something went badly wrong at the birth; the boy died and Orlando is . . . I take it you've met her by now?'

As he nodded, Strike's dream of the other night came back to him suddenly: the baby that Charlotte had given birth to, but that she would not let him see . . .

'Brain damaged,' Elizabeth went on. 'So Owen was going through his own personal tragedy at the time, and unlike Michael, he hadn't b-brought any of it on h-himself—'

Coughing again, she caught Strike's look of faint surprise and made an impatient staying gesture with her hand, indicating that she would explain when the fit had passed. Finally, after another sip of water, she croaked:

'Michael only encouraged Elspeth to write to keep her out of his hair while he worked. They had nothing in common. He married her because he's terminally touchy about being lower middle class. She was an earl's daughter who thought marrying Michael would mean non-stop literary parties and sparkling, intellectual chat. She didn't realise she'd be alone most of the time while Michael worked. She was,' said Elizabeth with disdain, 'a woman of few resources.

'But she got excited at the idea of being a writer. Have you any idea,' said the agent harshly, 'how many people think they can write? You cannot imagine the crap I am sent, day in, day out. Elspeth's novel would have been rejected out of hand under normal circumstances, it was so pretentious and silly, but they weren't normal circumstances. Having encouraged her to produce the damn thing, Michael didn't have the balls to tell her it was awful. He gave it to his publisher and they took it to keep Michael happy. It had been out a week when the parody appeared.'

'Quine implies in *Bombyx Mori* that Fancourt really wrote the parody,' said Strike.

'I know he does – and *I* wouldn't want to provoke Michael Fancourt,' she added in an apparent aside that begged to be heard.

'What do you mean?'

There was a short pause in which he could almost see Elizabeth deciding what to tell him.

'I met Michael,' she said slowly, 'in a tutorial group studying Jacobean revenge tragedies. Let's just say it was his natural milieu. He adores those writers; their sadism and their lust for vengeance . . . rape and cannibalism, poisoned skeletons dressed up as women . . . sadistic retribution is Michael's obsession.'

She glanced up at Strike, who was watching her.

'What?' she said curtly.

When, he wondered, were the details of Quine's murder going to explode across the newspapers? The dam must already be straining, with Culpepper on the case.

'Did Fancourt take sadistic retribution when you chose Quine over him?'

She looked down at the bowl of red liquid and pushed it abruptly away from her.

'We were close friends, very close, but he's never said a word to me from the day that I refused to sack Owen. He did his best to warn other writers away from my agency, said I was a woman of no honour or principle.

'But I hold one principle sacred and he knew it,' she said firmly. 'Owen hadn't done anything, in writing that parody, that Michael hadn't done a hundred times to other writers. Of course I regretted the aftermath deeply, but it was one of the times – the few times – when I felt that Owen was morally in the clear.'

'Must've hurt, though,' Strike said. 'You'd known Fancourt longer than Quine.'

'We've been enemies longer than we've been friends, now.'

It was not, Strike noted, a proper answer.

'You mustn't think . . . Owen wasn't always – he wasn't *all* bad,' Elizabeth said restlessly. 'You know, he was obsessed with virility, in life and in his work. Sometimes it was a metaphor for creative genius, but at other times it's seen as the bar to artistic fulfilment. The plot of *Hobart's Sin* turns on Hobart, who's both male and female, having to choose between parenthood and abandoning his aspirations as a writer: aborting his baby, or abandoning his brainchild.

'But when it came to fatherhood in real life – you understand, Orlando wasn't . . . you wouldn't have chosen your child to . . . to . . . but he loved her and she loved him.'

'Except for the times he walked out on the family to consort with mistresses or fritter away money in hotel rooms,' suggested Strike.

'All right, he wouldn't have won Father of the Year,' snapped Elizabeth, 'but there was love there.'

A silence fell over the table and Strike decided not to break it. He was sure that Elizabeth Tassel had agreed to this meeting, as she had requested the last, for reasons of her own and he was keen to hear them. He therefore ate his fish and waited.

'The police have asked me,' she said finally, when his plate was almost clear, 'whether Owen was blackmailing me in some way.'

'Really?' said Strike.

The restaurant clattered and chattered around them, and outside the snow fell thicker than ever. Here again was the familiar phenomenon of which he had spoken to Robin: the suspect who wished to re-explain, worried that they had not made a good enough job of it on their first attempt.

'They've taken note of the large dollops of money passing from my account to Owen's over the years,' said Elizabeth.

Strike said nothing; her ready payment of Quine's hotel bills had struck him as out of character in their previous meeting.

'What do they think anyone could blackmail me for?' she asked him with a twist to her scarlet mouth. 'My professional life has been scrupulously honest. I have no private life to speak of. I'm the very definition of a blameless spinster, aren't I?'

Strike, who judged it impossible to answer such a question, however rhetorical, without giving offence, said nothing.

'It started when Orlando was born,' Elizabeth said. 'Owen had managed to get through all the money he'd ever made and Leonora was in intensive care for two weeks after the birth, and Michael Fancourt was screaming to anybody who'd listen that Owen had murdered his wife.

'Owen was a pariah. Neither he nor Leonora had any family. I lent him money, as a friend, to get baby things. Then I advanced him money for a mortgage on a bigger house. Then there was money for specialists to look at Orlando when it was clear that she wasn't developing quite as she should, and therapists to help her. Before I knew it, I was the family's personal bank. Every time royalties came in Owen would make a big fuss about repaying me, and sometimes I'd get a few thousand back.

'At heart,' said the agent, the words tumbling out of her, 'Owen was an overgrown child, which could make him unbearable or charming. Irresponsible, impulsive, egotistical, amazingly lacking in conscience, but he could also be fun, enthusiastic and engaging. There was a pathos, a funny fragility about him, however badly he behaved, that made people feel protective. Jerry Waldegrave felt it. Women felt it. *I* felt it. And the truth is that I kept on hoping, even believing, that one day he'd produce another *Hobart's Sin*. There was always something, in every bloody awful book he's written, something that meant you couldn't completely write him off.'

A waiter came over to take away their plates. Elizabeth waved away his solicitous enquiry as to whether there had been something wrong with her soup and asked for a coffee. Strike accepted the offer of the dessert menu.

'Orlando's sweet, though,' Elizabeth added gruffly. 'Orlando's very sweet.'

'Yeah ... she seemed to think,' said Strike, watching her closely, 'that she saw you going into Quine's study the other day, while Leonora was in the bathroom.'

He did not think that she had expected the question, nor did she seem to like it.

'She saw that, did she?'

She sipped water, hesitated, then said:

'I'd challenge anyone depicted in *Bombyx Mori*, given the chance of seeing what other nasty jottings Owen might have left lying around, not to take the opportunity of having a look.'

'Did you find anything?'

'No,' she said, 'because the place was a tip. I could see immediately that it would take far too long to search and,' she raised her chin defiantly, 'to be absolutely frank, I didn't want to leave fingerprints. So I left as quickly as I walked in. It was the – possibly ignoble – impulse of a moment.'

She seemed to have said everything she had come to say. Strike ordered an apple and strawberry crumble and took the initiative.

'Daniel Chard wants to see me,' he told her. Her olive-dark eyes widened in surprise.

'Why?'

'I don't know. Unless the snow's too bad, I'm going down to visit him in Devon tomorrow. I'd like to know, before I meet him, why he's portrayed as the murderer of a young blond man in *Bombyx Mori*.'

'I'm not providing a key to that filthy book for you,' retorted Elizabeth with a return of all her former aggression and suspicion. 'No. Not doing it.'

'That's a shame,' said Strike, 'because people are talking.'

'Am I likely to compound my own egregious mistake in sending the damn thing out into the world by gossiping about it?'

'I'm discreet,' Strike assured her. 'Nobody needs to know where I got my information.'

But she merely glared at him, cold and impassive.

'What about Kathryn Kent?'

'What about her?'

'Why is the cave of her lair in *Bombyx Mori* full of rat skulls?'

Elizabeth said nothing.

'I know Kathryn Kent's Harpy, I've met her,' said Strike

patiently. 'All you're doing by explaining is saving me some time. I suppose you want to find out who killed Quine?'

'So bloody transparent,' she said witheringly. 'Does that usually work on people?'

'Yeah,' he said matter-of-factly, 'it does.'

She frowned, then said abruptly and not altogether to his surprise:

'Well, after all, I don't owe Kathryn Kent any loyalty. If you must know, Owen was making a fairly crude reference to the fact that she works at an animal-testing facility. They do disgusting things there to rats, dogs and monkeys. I heard all about it at one of the parties Owen brought her to. There she was, falling out of her dress and trying to impress me,' said Elizabeth, with contempt. 'I've seen her work. She makes Dorcus Pengelly look like Iris Murdoch. Typical of the dross – the dross—'

Strike managed several mouthfuls of his crumble while she coughed hard into her napkin.

'—the *dross* the internet has given us,' she finished, her eyes watering. 'And almost worse, she seemed to expect me to be on her side against the scruffy students who'd attacked their laboratories. I'm a vet's daughter: I grew up with animals and I like them much better than I like people. I found Kathryn Kent a horrible person.'

'Any idea who Harpy's daughter Epicoene's supposed to be?' asked Strike.

'No,' said Elizabeth.

'Or the dwarf in the Cutter's bag?'

'I'm not explaining any more of the wretched book!'

'Do you know if Quine knew a woman called Pippa?'

'I never met a Pippa. But he taught creative writing courses;

middle-aged women trying to find their *raison d'être*. That's where he picked up Kathryn Kent.'

She sipped her coffee and glanced at her watch.

'What can you tell me about Joe North?' Strike asked.

She glanced at him suspiciously.

'Why?'

'Curious,' said Strike.

He did not know why she chose to answer; perhaps because North was long dead, or because of that streak of sentimentality he had first divined back in her cluttered office.

'He was from California,' she said. 'He'd come over to London to find his English roots. He was gay, a few years younger than Michael, Owen and me, and writing a very frank first novel about the life he'd led in San Francisco.

'Michael introduced him to me. Michael thought his stuff was first class, and it was, but he wasn't a fast writer. He was partying hard, and also, which none of us knew for a couple of years, he was HIV-positive and not looking after himself. There came a point when he developed full-blown Aids.' Elizabeth cleared her throat. 'Well, you'll remember how much hysteria there was about HIV when it first emerged.'

Strike was inured to people thinking that he was at least ten years older than he was. In fact, he had heard from his mother (never one to guard her tongue in deference to a child's sensibilities) about the killer disease that was stalking those who fucked freely and shared needles.

'Joe fell apart physically and all the people who'd wanted to know him when he was promising, clever and beautiful melted away, except – to do them credit—' said Elizabeth grudgingly, 'Michael and Owen. They rallied round Joe, but he died with his novel unfinished.

'Michael was ill and couldn't go to Joe's funeral, but Owen was a pall bearer. In gratitude for the way they'd looked after him, Joe left the pair of them that rather lovely house, where they'd once partied and sat up all night discussing books. I was there for a few of those evenings. They were . . . happy times,' said Elizabeth.

'How much did they use the house after North died?'

'I can't answer for Michael, but I'd doubt he's been there since he fell out with Owen, which was not long after Joe's funeral,' said Elizabeth with a shrug. 'Owen never went there because he was terrified of running into Michael. The terms of Joe's will were peculiar: I think they call it a restrictive covenant. Joe stipulated that the house was to be preserved as an artists' refuge. That's how Michael's managed to block the sale all these years; the Quines have never managed to find another artist, or artists, to sell to. A sculptor rented it for a while, but that didn't work out. Of course, Michael's always been as picky as possible about tenants to stop Owen benefiting financially, and he can afford lawyers to enforce his whims.'

'What happened to North's unfinished book?' asked Strike.

'Oh, Michael abandoned work on his own novel and finished Joe's posthumously. It's called *Towards the Mark* and Harold Weaver published it: it's a cult classic, never been out of print.'

She checked her watch again.

'I need to go,' she said. 'I've got a meeting at two thirty. My coat, please,' she called to a passing waiter.

'Somebody told me,' said Strike, who remembered perfectly well that it had been Anstis, 'that you supervised work on Talgarth Road a while back?'

'Yes,' she said indifferently, 'just one more of the unusual jobs Quine's agent ended up doing for him. It was a matter of coordinating repairs, putting in workmen. I sent Michael a bill for half and he paid up through his lawyers.'

'You had a key?'

'Which I passed to the foreman,' she said coldly, 'then returned to the Quines.'

'You didn't go and see the work yourself?'

'Of course I did; I needed to check it had been done. I think I visited twice.'

'Was hydrochloric acid used in any of the renovation, do you know?'

'The police asked me about hydrochloric acid,' she said. 'Why?'

'I can't say.'

She glowered. He doubted that people often refused Elizabeth Tassel information.

'Well, I can only tell you what I told the police: it was probably left there by Todd Harkness.'

'Who?'

'The sculptor I told you about who rented the studio space. Owen found him and Fancourt's lawyers couldn't find a reason to object. What nobody realised was that Harkness worked mainly in rusted metal and used some very corrosive chemicals. He did a lot of damage in the studio before being asked to leave. Fancourt's side did *that* clean-up operation and sent *us* the bill.'

The waiter had brought her coat, to which a few dog hairs clung. Strike could hear a faint whistle from her labouring chest as she stood up. With a peremptory shake of the hand, Elizabeth Tassel left.

Strike took another taxi back to the office with the vague intention of being conciliatory to Robin; somehow they had rubbed each other up the wrong way that morning and he was not quite sure how it had happened. However, by the time he had finally reached the outer office he was sweating with the pain in his knee and Robin's first words drove all thought of propitiation from his mind.

'The car hire company just called. They haven't got an automatic, but they can give you—'

'It's got to be an automatic!' snapped Strike, dropping onto the sofa in an eruption of leathery flatulence that irritated him still further. 'I can't bloody drive a manual in this state! Have you rung—?'

'Of course I've tried other places,' said Robin coldly. 'I've tried everywhere. Nobody can give you an automatic tomorrow. The weather forecast's atrocious, anyway. I think you'd do better to—'

'I'm going to interview Chard,' said Strike.

Pain and fear were making him angry: fear that he would have to give up the prosthesis and resort to crutches again, his trouser leg pinned up, staring eyes, pity. He hated hard plastic chairs in disinfected corridors; hated his voluminous notes being unearthed and pored over, murmurs about changes to his prosthesis, advice from calm medical men to rest, to mollycoddle his leg as though it were a sick child he had to carry everywhere with him. In his dreams he was not one-legged; in his dreams he was whole.

Chard's invitation had been an unlooked-for gift; he intended to seize it. There were many things he wanted to ask Quine's publisher. The invitation itself was glaringly strange. He wanted to hear Chard's reason for dragging him to Devon.

'Did you hear me?' asked Robin.

'What?'

'I said, "I could drive you."'

'No, you can't,' said Strike ungraciously.

'Why not?'

'You've got to be in Yorkshire.'

'I've got to be at King's Cross tomorrow night at eleven.'

'The snow's going to be terrible.'

'We'll set out early. Or,' said Robin with a shrug, 'you can cancel Chard. But the forecast for next week's awful too.'

It was difficult to reverse from ingratitude to the opposite with Robin's steely grey-blue eyes upon him.

'All right,' he said stiffly. 'Thanks.'

'Then I need to go and pick up the car,' said Robin.

'Right,' said Strike through gritted teeth.

Owen Quine had not thought women had any place in literature: he, Strike, had a secret prejudice, too – but what choice did he have, with his knee screaming for mercy and no automatic car for hire?

28

> . . . that (of all other) was the most fatal and dangerous exploit that ever I was ranged in, since I first bore arms before the face of the enemy . . .
>
> Ben Jonson, *Every Man in His Humour*

At five o'clock the following morning, a muffled and gloved Robin boarded one of the first Tube trains of the day, her hair glistening with snowflakes, a small backpack over her shoulder and carrying a weekend bag into which she had packed the black dress, coat and shoes that she would need for Mrs Cunliffe's funeral. She did not dare count on getting back home after the round trip to Devon, but intended to go straight to King's Cross once she had returned the car to the hire company.

Sitting on the almost empty train she consulted her own feelings about the day ahead and found them mixed. Excitement was her dominant emotion, because she was convinced that Strike had some excellent reason for interviewing Chard that could not wait. Robin had learned to trust her boss's judgement and his hunches; it was one of the things that so irritated Matthew.

Matthew . . . Robin's black-gloved fingers tightened on the handle of the bag beside her. She kept lying to Matthew. Robin was a truthful person and never, in the nine years that they had been together, had she lied, or not until recently. Some had been lies of omission. Matthew had asked her on the telephone on Wednesday night what she had done at work that day and she had given him a brief and heavily edited version of her activities, omitting her trip with Strike to the house where Quine had been murdered, lunch at the Albion and, of course, the walk across the bridge at West Brompton station with Strike's heavy arm over her shoulder.

But there had been outright lies too. Just last night he had asked her, like Strike, whether she oughtn't take the day off, get an earlier train.

'I tried,' she had said, the lie sliding easily from her lips before she considered it. 'They're all full. It's the weather, isn't it? I suppose people are taking the train instead of risking it in their cars. I'll just have to stick with the sleeper.'

What else could I say? thought Robin as the dark windows reflected her own tense face back at her. *He'd have gone ballistic.*

The truth was that she wanted to go to Devon; she wanted to help Strike; she wanted to get out from behind her computer, however much quiet satisfaction her competent administration of the business gave her, and investigate. Was that wrong? Matthew thought so. It wasn't what he'd counted on. He had wanted her to go with the advertising agency, into human resources, at nearly twice the salary. London was so expensive. Matthew wanted a bigger flat. He was, she supposed, carrying her . . .

Then there was Strike. A familiar frustration, a tight knot in her stomach: *we'll have to get someone else in.* Constant mentions of this prospective partner, who was assuming mythical substance in Robin's mind: a short-haired, shrew-faced woman like the police officer who had stood guard outside the crime scene in Talgarth Road. She would be competent and trained in all the ways that Robin was not, and unencumbered (for the very first time, in this half empty, brightly lit Tube carriage, with the world dark outside and her ears full of rumble and clatter, she said it openly to herself) by a fiancé like Matthew.

But Matthew was the axis of her life, the fixed centre. She loved him; she had always loved him. He had stuck with her through the worst time in her life, when many young men would have left. She wanted to marry him and she was going to marry him. It was just that they had never had fundamental disagreements before, never. Something about her job, her decision to stay with Strike, about Strike himself, had introduced a rogue element into their relationship, something threatening and new . . .

The Toyota Land Cruiser that Robin had hired had been parked overnight in the Q-Park in Chinatown, one of the nearest car parks to Denmark Street, where there was no parking at all. Slipping and sliding in her flattest smart shoes, the weekend bag swinging from her right hand, Robin hurried through the darkness to the multi-storey, refusing to think any more about Matthew, or what he would think or say if he could see her, heading off for six hours alone in the car with Strike. After placing her bag in the boot, Robin sat back in the driver's seat, set up the sat nav, adjusted the heating and left the engine running to warm up the icy interior.

Strike was a little late, which was unlike him. Robin whiled away the wait by acquainting herself fully with the controls. She loved cars, had always loved driving. By the age of ten she had been able to drive the tractor on her uncle's farm as long as someone helped her release the handbrake. Unlike Matthew, she had passed her test the first time. She had learned not to tease him about this.

Movement glimpsed in her rear-view mirror made her look up. A dark-suited Strike was making his way laboriously towards the car on crutches, his right trouser leg pinned up.

Robin felt a sick, swooping feeling in the pit of her stomach – not because of the amputated leg, which she had seen before, and in much more troubling circumstances, but because it was the first time that she had known Strike forsake the prosthesis in public.

She got out of the car, then wished she hadn't when she caught his scowl.

'Good thinking, getting a four-by-four,' he said, silently warning her not to talk about his leg.

'Yeah, I thought we'd better in this weather,' said Robin.

He moved around to the passenger seat. Robin knew she must not offer help; she could feel an exclusion zone around him as though he were telepathically rejecting all offers of assistance or sympathy, but she was worried that he would not be able to get inside unaided. Strike threw his crutches onto the back seat and stood for a moment precariously balanced; then, with a show of upper body strength that she had never seen before, pulled himself smoothly into the car.

Robin jumped back in hastily, closed her door, put her seatbelt on and reversed out of the parking space. Strike's pre-emptive rejection of her concern sat like a wall between them and to her sympathy was added a twist of resentment that he would not let her in to that tiny degree. When had she ever fussed over him or tried to mother him? The most she had ever done was pass him paracetamol . . .

Strike knew himself to be unreasonable, but the awareness

merely increased his irritation. On waking it had been obvious that to try to force the prosthesis onto his leg, when the knee was hot, swollen and extremely painful, would be an act of idiocy. He had been forced to descend the metal stairs on his backside, like a small child. Traversing Charing Cross Road on ice and crutches had earned him the stares of those few early-morning pedestrians who were braving the sub-zero darkness. He had never wanted to return to this state but here he was, all because of a temporary forgetfulness that he was not, like the dream Strike, whole.

At least, Strike noted with relief, Robin could drive. His sister, Lucy, was distractible and unreliable behind the wheel. Charlotte had always driven her Lexus in a manner that caused Strike physical pain: speeding through red lights, turning up one-way streets, smoking and chatting on her mobile, narrowly missing cyclists and the opening doors of parked cars . . . Ever since the Viking had blown up around him on that yellow dirt road, Strike had found it difficult to be driven by anyone except a professional.

After a long silence, Robin said:

'There's coffee in the backpack.'

'What?'

'In the backpack – a flask. I didn't think we should stop unless we really have to. And there are biscuits.'

The windscreen wipers were carving their way through flecks of snow.

'You're a bloody marvel,' said Strike, his reserve crumbling. He had not had breakfast: trying and failing to attach his false leg, finding a pin for his suit trousers, digging out his crutches and getting himself downstairs had taken twice the time he had allowed. And in spite of herself, Robin gave a small smile.

Strike poured himself coffee and ate several bits of shortbread, his appreciation of Robin's deft handling of the strange car increasing as his hunger decreased.

'What does Matthew drive?' he asked as they sped over the Boston Manor viaduct.

'Nothing,' said Robin. 'We haven't got a car in London.'

'Yeah, no need,' said Strike, privately reflecting that if he ever gave Robin the salary she deserved they might be able to afford one.

'So what are you planning to ask Daniel Chard?' Robin asked.

'Plenty,' said Strike, brushing crumbs off his dark jacket. 'First off, whether he'd fallen out with Quine and, if so, what about. I can't fathom why Quine – total dickhead though he clearly was – decided to attack the man who had his livelihood in his hands and who had the money to sue him into oblivion.'

Strike munched shortbread for a while, swallowed, then added:

'Unless Jerry Waldegrave's right and Quine was having a genuine breakdown when he wrote it and lashed out at anyone he thought he could blame for his lousy sales.'

Robin, who had finished reading *Bombyx Mori* while Strike had been having lunch with Elizabeth Tassel the previous day, said:

'Isn't the writing too coherent for somebody having a breakdown?'

'The syntax might be sound, but I don't think you'd find many people who'd disagree that the content's bloody insane.'

'His other writing's very like it.'

'None of his other stuff's as crazy as *Bombyx Mori*,' said Strike. '*Hobart's Sin* and *The Balzac Brothers* both had plots.'

'This has got a plot.'

'Has it? Or is Bombyx's little walking tour just a convenient way of stringing together a load of attacks on different people?'

The snow fell thick and fast as they passed the exit to Heathrow, talking about the novel's various grotesqueries, laughing a little over its ludicrous jumps of logic, its absurdities. The trees on either side of the motorway looked as though they had been dusted with tons of icing sugar.

'Maybe Quine was born four hundred years too late,' said Strike, still eating shortbread. 'Elizabeth Tassel told me there's a Jacobean revenge play featuring a poisoned skeleton disguised as a woman. Presumably someone shags it and dies. Not a million miles away from Phallus Impudicus getting ready to—'

'Don't,' said Robin, with a half laugh and a shudder.

But Strike had not broken off because of her protest, or because of any sense of repugnance. Something had flickered deep in his subconscious as he spoke. Somebody had told him . . . someone had said . . . but the memory was gone in a flash of tantalising silver, like a minnow vanishing in pondweed.

'A poisoned skeleton,' Strike muttered, trying to capture the elusive memory, but it was gone.

'And I finished *Hobart's Sin* last night as well,' said Robin, overtaking a dawdling Prius.

'You're a sucker for punishment,' said Strike, reaching for a sixth biscuit. 'I didn't think you were enjoying it.'

'I wasn't, and it didn't improve. It's all about—'

'A hermaphrodite who's pregnant and gets an abortion because a kid would interfere with his literary ambitions,' said Strike.

'You've read it!'

'No, Elizabeth Tassel told me.'

'There's a bloody sack in it,' said Robin.

Strike looked sideways at her pale profile, serious as she watched the road ahead, her eyes flicking to the rear-view mirror.

'What's inside?'

'The aborted baby,' said Robin. 'It's horrible.'

Strike digested this information as they passed the turning to Maidenhead.

'Strange,' he said at last.

'Grotesque,' said Robin.

'No, it's strange,' insisted Strike. 'Quine was repeating himself. That's the second thing from *Hobart's Sin* he put in *Bombyx Mori*. Two hermaphrodites, two bloody sacks. Why?'

'Well,' said Robin, 'they aren't *exactly* the same. In *Bombyx Mori* the bloody sack doesn't belong to the hermaphrodite and it hasn't got an aborted baby in it . . . maybe he'd reached the end of his invention,' she said. 'Maybe *Bombyx Mori* was like a – a final bonfire of all his ideas.'

'The funeral pyre for his career is what it was.'

Strike sat deep in thought while the scenery beyond the window became steadily more rural. Breaks in the trees showed wide fields of snow, white upon white beneath a pearly grey sky, and still the snow came thick and fast at the car.

'You know,' Strike said at last, 'I think there are two alternatives here. Either Quine genuinely was having a breakdown, had lost touch with what he was doing and believed *Bombyx Mori* was a masterpiece – or he meant to cause as much trouble as possible, and the duplications are there for a reason.'

'What reason?'

'It's a key,' said Strike. 'By cross-referencing his other books, he was helping people understand what he was getting at in

Bombyx Mori. He was trying to tell without being had up for libel.'

Robin did not take her eyes off the snowy motorway, but inclined her face towards him, frowning.

'You think it was all totally deliberate? You think he wanted to cause all this trouble?'

'When you stop and think about it,' said Strike, 'it's not a bad business plan for an egotistical, thick-skinned man who's hardly selling any books. Kick off as much trouble as you can, get the book gossiped about all over London, threats of legal action, loads of people upset, veiled revelations about a famous writer ... and then disappear where the writs can't find you and, before anyone can stop you, put it out as an ebook.'

'But he was furious when Elizabeth Tassel told him she wouldn't publish it.'

'Was he?' said Strike thoughtfully, 'Or was he faking? Did he keep badgering her to read it because he was getting ready to stage a nice big public row? He sounds like a massive exhibitionist. Perhaps it was all part of his promotional plan. He didn't think Roper Chard got his books enough publicity – I had that from Leonora.'

'So you think he'd already planned to storm out of the restaurant when he met Elizabeth Tassel?'

'Could be,' said Strike.

'And to go to Talgarth Road?'

'Maybe.'

The sun had risen fully now, so that the frosted treetops sparkled.

'And he got what he wanted, didn't he?' said Strike, squinting as a thousand specks of ice glittered over the windscreen. 'Couldn't have arranged better publicity for his book if he'd tried. Just a pity he didn't live to see himself on the BBC news.

'Oh, bollocks,' he added under his breath.

'What's the matter?'

'I've finished all the biscuits . . . sorry,' said Strike, contrite.

'That's all right,' Robin said, amused. 'I had breakfast.'

'I didn't,' Strike confided.

His antipathy to discussing his leg had been dissolved by warm coffee, by their discussion and by her practical thoughts for his comfort.

'Couldn't get the bloody prosthesis on. My knee's swollen to hell: I'm going to have to see someone. Took me ages to get sorted.'

She had guessed as much, but appreciated the confidence.

They passed a golf course, its flags protruding from acres of soft whiteness, and water-filled gravel pits now sheets of burnished pewter in the winter light. As they approached Swindon Strike's phone rang. Checking the number (he half expected a repeat call from Nina Lascelles) he saw that it was Ilsa, his old schoolfriend. He also saw, with misgivings, that he had missed a call from Leonora Quine at six thirty, when he must have been struggling down Charing Cross Road on his crutches.

'Ilsa, hi. What's going on?'

'Quite a lot, actually,' she said. She sounded tinny and distant; he could tell that she was in her car.

'Did Leonora Quine call you on Wednesday?'

'Yep, we met that afternoon,' she said. 'And I've just spoken to her again. She told me she tried to speak to you this morning and couldn't get you.'

'Yeah, I had an early start, must've missed her.'

'I've got her permission to tell—'

'What's happened?'

'They've taken her in for questioning. I'm on my way to the station now.'

'Shit,' said Strike. '*Shit.* What have they got?'

'She told me they found photographs in her and Quine's bedroom. Apparently he liked being tied up and he liked being photographed once restrained,' said Ilsa with mordant matter-of-factness. 'She told me all this as though she was talking about the gardening.'

He could hear faint sounds of heavy traffic back in central London. Here on the motorway the loudest sounds were the swish of the windscreen wipers, the steady purr of the powerful engine and the occasional whoosh of the reckless, overtaking in the swirling snow.

'You'd think she'd have the sense to get rid of the pictures,' said Strike.

'I'll pretend I didn't hear that suggestion about destroying evidence,' said Ilsa mock-sternly.

'Those pictures aren't bloody evidence,' said Strike. 'Christ almighty, *of course* they had a kinky sex life, those two – how else was Leonora going to keep hold of a man like Quine? Anstis's mind's too clean, that's the problem; he thinks everything except the missionary position is evidence of bloody criminal tendencies.'

'What do you know about the investigating officer's sexual habits?' Ilsa asked, amused.

'He's the bloke I pulled to the back of the vehicle in Afghanistan,' muttered Strike.

'*Oh,*' said Ilsa.

'And he's determined to fit up Leonora. If that's all they've got, dirty photos—'

'It isn't. Did you know the Quines have got a lock-up?'

Strike listened, tense, suddenly worried. Could he have been wrong, completely wrong—?

'Well, did you?' asked Ilsa.

'What've they found?' asked Strike, no longer flippant. 'Not the guts?'

'*What* did you just say? It sounded like "not the guts"!'

'What've they found?' Strike corrected himself.

'I don't know, but I expect I'll find out when I get there.'

'She's not under arrest?'

'Just in for questioning, but they're sure it's her, I can tell, and I don't think she realises how serious things are getting. When she rang me, all she could talk about was her daughter being left with the neighbour, her daughter being upset—'

'The daughter's twenty-four and she's got learning difficulties.'

'Oh,' said Ilsa. 'Sad . . . Listen, I'm nearly there, I'll have to go.'

'Keep me posted.'

'Don't expect anything soon. I've got a feeling we're going to be a while.'

'*Shit*,' Strike said again as he hung up.

'What's happened?'

An enormous tanker had pulled out of the slow lane to overtake a Honda Civic with a Baby On Board sign in its rear window. Strike watched its gargantuan silver bullet of a body swaying at speed on the icy road and noted with unspoken approval that Robin slowed down, leaving more braking room.

'The police have taken Leonora in for questioning.'

Robin gasped.

'They've found photos of Quine tied up in their bedroom and something else in a lock-up, but Ilsa doesn't know what—'

It had happened to Strike before. The instantaneous shift from calm to calamity. The slowing of time. Every sense suddenly wire-taut and screaming.

The tanker was jack-knifing.

He heard himself bellow 'BRAKE!' because that was what he had done last time to try to stave off death—

But Robin slammed her foot on the accelerator. The car roared forward. There was no room to pass. The lorry hit the icy road on its side and spun; the Civic hit it, flipped over and skidded on its roof towards the side of the road; a Golf and a Mercedes had slammed into each other and were locked together, speeding towards the truck of the tanker—

They were hurtling towards the ditch at the side of the road. Robin missed the overturned Civic by an inch. Strike grabbed hold of the door handle as the Land Cruiser hit the rough ground at speed – they were going to plough into the ditch and maybe overturn – the tail end of the tanker was swinging lethally towards them, but they were travelling so fast that she missed that by a whisker – a massive jolt, Strike's head hit the roof of the car, and they had swerved back onto the icy tarmac on the other side of the pile-up, unscathed.

'Holy fucking—'

She was braking at last, in total control, pulling up on the hard shoulder, and her face was as white as the snow spattering the windscreen.

'There was a kid in that Civic.'

And before he could say another word she had gone, slamming the door behind her.

He leaned over the back of his seat, trying to grab his crutches. Never had he felt his disability more acutely. He had just managed to pull the crutches into the seat with him when he heard sirens. Squinting through the snowy rear window, he spotted the distant flicker of blue light. The police were there already. He was a one-legged liability. He threw the crutches back down, swearing.

Robin returned to the car ten minutes later.

'It's OK,' she panted. 'The little boy's all right, he was in a car seat. The lorry driver's covered in blood but he's conscious—'

'Are you OK?'

She was trembling a little, but smiled at the question.

'Yeah, I'm fine. I was just scared I was going to see a dead child.'

'Right then,' said Strike, taking a deep breath. 'Where the *fuck* did you learn to drive like that?'

'Oh, I did a couple of advanced driving courses,' said Robin with a shrug, pushing her wet hair out of her eyes.

Strike stared at her.

'When was this?'

'Not long after I dropped out of university. I was . . . I was going through a bad time and I wasn't going out much. It was my dad's idea. I've always loved cars.

'It was just something to do,' she said, putting on her seatbelt and turning on the ignition. 'Sometimes when I'm home, I go up to the farm to practise. My uncle's got a field he lets me drive in.'

Strike was still staring at her.

'Are you sure you don't want to wait a bit before we—?'

'No, I've given them my name and address. We should get going.'

She shifted gear and pulled smoothly out onto the motorway. Strike could not look away from her calm profile; her eyes were again fixed on the road, her hands confident and relaxed on the wheel.

'I've seen worse steering than that from defensive drivers in the army,' he told her. 'The ones who drive generals, who're trained to make a getaway under fire.' He glanced back at the tangle of overturned vehicles now blocking the road. 'I still don't know how you got us out of that.'

The near-crash had not brought Robin close to tears, but at these words of praise and appreciation she suddenly thought she might cry, let herself down. With a great effort of will she compressed her emotion into a little laugh and said:

'You realise that if I'd braked, we'd have skidded right into the tanker?'

'Yeah,' said Strike, and he laughed too. 'Dunno why I said that,' he lied.

29

> There is a path vpon your left hand side,
> That leadeth from a guiltie conscience
> Vnto a forrest of distrust and feare,–
>
> Thomas Kyd, *The Spanish Tragedie*

In spite of their near-crash, Strike and Robin entered the Devonshire town of Tiverton shortly after twelve. Robin followed the sat nav's instructions past quiet country houses topped with thick layers of glittering white, over a neat little bridge spanning a river the colour of flint and past a sixteenth-century church of unexpected grandeur to the far side of the town, where a pair of electric gates were discreetly set back from the road.

A handsome young Filipino man wearing what appeared to be deck shoes and an over-large coat was attempting to prise these open manually. When he caught sight of the Land Cruiser he mimed to Robin to wind down her window.

'Frozen,' he told her succinctly. 'Wait a moment, please.'

They sat for five minutes until at last he had succeeded in unfreezing the gates and had dug a clearing in the steadily falling snow to allow the gates to swing open.

'Do you want a lift back to the house?' Robin asked him.

He climbed into the back seat beside Strike's crutches.

'You friends of Mr Chard?'

'He's expecting us,' said Strike evasively.

Up a long and winding private driveway they went, the Land Cruiser making easy work of the heaped, crunchy overnight fall. The shiny dark green leaves of the rhododendrons lining the path had refused to bear their load of snow, so that the approach was all black and white: walls of dense foliage crowding in on the pale, powdery drive. Tiny spots of light had started popping in front of Robin's eyes. It had been a very long time since breakfast and, of course, Strike had eaten all the biscuits.

Her feeling of seasickness and a slight sense of unreality persisted as she got down out of the Toyota and looked up at Tithebarn House, which stood beside a dark patch of wood that pressed close to one side of the house. The massive oblong structure in front of them had been converted by an adventurous architect: half of the roof had been replaced by sheet glass; the other seemed to be covered in solar panels. Looking up at the place where the structure became transparent and skeletal against the bright, light grey sky made Robin feel even giddier. It reminded her of the ghastly picture on Strike's phone, the vaulted space of glass and light in which Quine's mutilated body had lain.

'Are you all right?' said Strike, concerned. She looked very pale.

'Fine,' said Robin, who wanted to maintain her heroic status in his eyes. Taking deep lungfuls of the frosty air, she followed Strike, surprisingly nimble on his crutches, up the gravel path towards the entrance. Their young passenger had disappeared without another word to them.

Daniel Chard opened the front door himself. He was wearing

a mandarin-collared, smock-like shirt in chartreuse silk and loose linen trousers. Like Strike, he was on crutches, his left foot and calf encased in a thick surgical boot and strapping. Chard looked down at Strike's dangling, empty trouser leg and for several painful seconds did not seem able to look away.

'And you thought you had problems,' said Strike, holding out his hand.

The small joke fell flat. Chard did not smile. The aura of awkwardness, of otherness, that had surrounded him at his firm's party clung to him still. He shook Strike's hand without looking him in the eye and his welcoming words were:

'I've been expecting you to cancel all morning.'

'No, we made it,' said Strike unnecessarily. 'This is my assistant, Robin, who's driven me down. I hope—'

'No, she can't sit outside in the snow,' said Chard, though without noticeable warmth. 'Come in.'

He backed away on his crutches to let them move over the threshold onto highly polished floorboards the colour of honey.

'Would you mind removing your shoes?'

A stocky, middle-aged Filipina woman with her black hair in a bun emerged from a pair of swing doors set into the brick wall on their right. She was clothed entirely in black and holding two white linen bags into which Strike and Robin were evidently expected to put their footwear. Robin handed hers over; it made her feel strangely vulnerable to feel the boards beneath her soles. Strike merely stood there on his single foot.

'Oh,' said Chard, staring again. 'No, I suppose . . . Mr Strike had better keep his shoe on, Nenita.'

The woman retired wordlessly into the kitchen.

Somehow, the interior of Tithebarn House increased Robin's unpleasant sensation of vertigo. No walls divided its vast interior.

The first floor, which was reached by a steel and glass spiral staircase, was suspended on thick metal cables from the high ceiling. Chard's huge double bed, which seemed to be of black leather, was visible, high above them, with what looked like a huge crucifix of barbed wire hanging over it on the brick wall. Robin dropped her gaze hastily, feeling sicker than ever.

Most of the furniture on the lower level comprised cubes of white or black leather. Vertical steel radiators were interspersed with artfully simple bookshelves of more wood and metal. The dominant feature of the under-furnished room was a life-size white marble sculpture of an angel, perched on a rock and partially dissected to expose half of her skull, a portion of her guts and a slice of the bone in her leg. Her breast, Robin saw, unable to tear her eyes away, was revealed as a mound of fat globules sitting on a circle of muscle that resembled the gills of a mushroom.

Ludicrous to feel sick when the dissected body was made of cold, pure stone, mere insentient albescence, nothing like the rotting carcass preserved on Strike's mobile . . . *don't think about that* . . . she ought to have made Strike leave at least one biscuit . . . sweat had broken out on her upper lip, her scalp . . .

'You all right, Robin?' asked Strike sharply. She knew she must have changed colour from the look on the two men's faces, and to her fear that she might pass out was added embarrassment that she was being a liability to Strike.

'Sorry,' she said through numb lips. 'Long journey . . . if I could have a glass of water . . . '

'Er – very well,' said Chard, as though water were in short supply. 'Nenita?'

The woman in black reappeared.

'The young lady needs a glass of water,' said Chard.

Nenita gestured to Robin to follow her. Robin heard the publisher's crutches making a gentle *thump, thump* behind her on the wooden floor as she entered the kitchen. She had a brief impression of steel surfaces and whitewashed walls, and the young man to whom she had given a lift prodding at a large saucepan, then found herself sitting on a low stool.

Robin had assumed that Chard had followed to see that she was all right, but as Nenita pressed a cold glass into her hand she heard him speak somewhere above her.

'Thanks for fixing the gates, Manny.'

The young man did not reply. Robin heard the clunk of Chard's crutches recede and the swinging of the kitchen doors.

'That's my fault,' Strike told Chard, when the publisher rejoined him. He felt truly guilty. 'I ate all the food she brought for the journey.'

'Nenita can give her something,' said Chard. 'Shall we sit down?'

Strike followed him past the marble angel, which was reflected mistily in the warm wood below, and they headed on their four crutches to the end of the room, where a black iron wood-burner made a pool of welcome warmth.

'Great place,' said Strike, lowering himself onto one of the larger cubes of black leather and laying his crutches beside him. The compliment was insincere; his preference was for utilitarian comfort and Chard's house seemed to him to be all surface and show.

'Yes, I worked closely with the architects,' said Chard, with a small flicker of enthusiasm. 'There's a studio' – he pointed through another discreet pair of doors – 'and a pool.'

He too sat down, stretching out the leg that ended in the thick, strapped boot in front of him.

'How did it happen?' Strike asked, nodding towards the broken leg.

Chard pointed with the end of his crutch at the metal and glass spiral staircase.

'Painful,' said Strike, eyeing the drop.

'The crack echoed all through the space,' said Chard, with an odd relish. 'I hadn't realised one can actually *hear* it happening.

'Would you like a tea or coffee?'

'Tea would be great.'

Strike saw Chard place his uninjured foot on a small brass plate beside his seat. Slight pressure, and Manny emerged again from the kitchen.

'Tea, please, Manny,' said Chard with a warmth conspicuously absent in his usual manner. The young man disappeared again, sullen as ever.

'Is that St Michael's Mount?' Strike asked, pointing to a small picture hanging near the wood-burner. It was a naive painting on what seemed to be board.

'An Alfred Wallis,' said Chard, with another minor glow of enthusiasm. 'The simplicity of the forms . . . primitive and naive. My father knew him. Wallis only took up painting seriously in his seventies. You know Cornwall?'

'I grew up there,' said Strike.

But Chard was more interested in talking about Alfred Wallis. He mentioned again that the artist had only found his true *métier* late in life and embarked on an exposition of the artist's works. Strike's total lack of interest in the subject went unnoticed. Chard was not fond of eye contact. The publisher's eyes slid from the painting to spots around the large brick interior, seeming to glance at Strike only incidentally.

'You're just back from New York, aren't you?' asked Strike when Chard drew breath.

'A three-day conference, yes,' said Chard and the flare of enthusiasm faded. He gave the impression of repeating stock phrases as he said, 'Challenging times. The arrival of electronic reading devices has been a game-changer. Do you read?' he asked Strike, point-blank.

'Sometimes,' said Strike. There was a battered James Ellroy in his flat that he had been intending to finish for four weeks, but most nights he was too tired to focus. His favourite book lay in one of the unpacked boxes of possessions on the landing; it was twenty years old and he had not opened it for a long time.

'We need readers,' muttered Daniel Chard. 'More readers. Fewer writers.'

Strike suppressed the urge to retort, *Well, you've got rid of one of them, at least.*

Manny reappeared bearing a clear perspex tray on legs, which he set down in front of his employer. Chard leaned forward to pour the tea into tall white porcelain mugs. His leather furniture, Strike noted, did not emit the irritating sounds his own office sofa did, but then, it had probably cost ten times as much. The backs of Chard's hands were as raw and painful-looking as they had been at the company party, and in the clear overhead lighting set into the underside of the hanging first floor he looked older than he had at a distance; sixty, perhaps, yet the dark, deep-set eyes, the hawkish nose and the thin mouth were handsome still in their severity.

'He's forgotten the milk,' said Chard, scrutinising the tray. 'Do you take milk?'

'Yeah,' said Strike.

Chard sighed, but instead of pressing the brass plate on the floor he struggled back onto his one sound foot and his crutches, and swung off towards the kitchen, leaving Strike staring thoughtfully after him.

Those who worked with him found Daniel Chard peculiar, although Nina had described him as shrewd. His uncontrolled rages about *Bombyx Mori* had sounded to Strike like the reaction of an over-sensitive man of questionable judgement. He remembered the slight sense of embarrassment emanating from the crowd as Chard mumbled his speech at the anniversary party. An odd man, hard to read . . .

Strike's eyes drifted upwards. Snow was falling gently onto the clear roof high above the marble angel. The glass must be heated in some way, to prevent the snow settling, Strike concluded. And the memory of Quine, eviscerated and trussed, burned and rotting beneath a great vaulted window returned to him. Like Robin, he suddenly found the high glass ceiling of Tithebarn House unpleasantly reminiscent.

Chard re-emerged from the kitchen and swung back across the floor on his crutches, a small jug of milk held precariously in his hand.

'You'll be wondering why I asked you to come here,' said Chard finally, when he had sat back down and each of them held his tea at last. Strike arranged his features to look receptive.

'I need somebody I can trust,' said Chard without waiting for Strike's answer. 'Someone outside the company.'

One darting glance at Strike and he fixed his eyes safely on his Alfred Wallis again.

'I think,' said Chard, 'I may be the only person who's realised that Owen Quine did not work alone. He had an accomplice.'

'An accomplice?' Strike repeated at last, as Chard seemed to expect a response.

'Yes,' said Chard fervently. 'Oh yes. You see, the style of *Bombyx Mori* is Owen's, but somebody else was in on it. Someone helped him.'

Chard's sallow skin had flushed. He gripped and fondled the handle of one of the crutches beside him.

'The police will be interested, I think, if this can be proven?' said Chard, managing to look Strike full in the face. 'If Owen was murdered because of what was written in *Bombyx Mori*, wouldn't an accomplice be culpable?'

'Culpable?' repeated Strike. 'You think this accomplice persuaded Quine to insert material in the book in the hope that a third party would retaliate murderously?'

'I . . . well, I'm not sure,' said Chard, frowning. 'He might not have expected that to happen, precisely – but he certainly intended to wreak havoc.'

His knuckles were whitening as they tightened on the handle of his crutch.

'What makes you think Quine had help?' asked Strike.

'Owen couldn't have known some of the things that are insinuated in *Bombyx Mori* unless he'd been fed information,' said Chard, now staring at the side of his stone angel.

'I think the police's main interest in an accomplice,' said Strike slowly, 'would be because he or she might have a lead on the killer.'

It was the truth, but it was also a way of reminding Chard that a man had died in grotesque circumstances. The identity of the murderer did not seem of pressing interest to Chard.

'Do you think so?' asked Chard with a faint frown.

'Yeah,' said Strike, 'I do. And they'd be interested in an accomplice if they were able to shed light on some of the more oblique passages in the book. One of the theories the police are bound to be following is that someone killed Quine to stop him revealing something that he had hinted at in *Bombyx Mori*.'

Daniel Chard was staring at Strike with an arrested expression.

'Yes. I hadn't . . . Yes.'

To Strike's surprise, the publisher pulled himself up on his crutches and began to move a few paces backwards and forwards, swinging on his crutches in a parodic version of those first tentative physiotherapy exercises Strike had been given, years previously, at Selly Oak Hospital. Strike saw now that he was a fit man, that biceps rippled beneath the silk sleeves.

'The killer, then—' Chard began, and then 'What?' he snapped suddenly, staring over Strike's shoulder.

Robin had re-emerged from the kitchen, a much healthier colour.

'I'm sorry,' she said, pausing, unnerved.

'This is confidential,' said Chard. 'No, I'm sorry. Could you return to the kitchen, please?'

'I – all right,' said Robin, taken aback and, Strike could tell, offended. She threw him a look, expecting him to say something, but he was silent.

When the swing doors had closed behind Robin, Chard said angrily:

'Now I've lost my train of thought. Entirely lost—'

'You were saying something about the killer.'

'Yes. Yes,' said Chard manically, resuming his backwards and forwards motion, swinging on his crutches. 'The killer, then, if they knew about the accomplice, might want to target him too? And perhaps that's occurred to him,' said Chard, more to himself than to Strike, his eyes on his expensive floorboards. 'Perhaps that accounts . . . Yes.'

The small window in the wall nearest Strike showed only the dark face of the wood close by the house; white flecks falling dreamily against the black.

'Disloyalty,' said Chard suddenly, 'cuts at me like nothing else.'

He stopped his agitated thumping up and down and turned to face the detective.

'If,' he said, 'I told you who I suspect to have helped Owen, and asked you to bring me proof, would you feel obliged to pass that information to the police?'

It was a delicate question, thought Strike, running a hand absently over his chin, imperfectly shaved in the haste of leaving that morning.

'If you're asking me to establish the truth of your suspicions . . . ' said Strike slowly.

'Yes,' said Chard. 'Yes, I am. I would like to be sure.'

'Then no, I don't think I'd need to tell the police what I'm up to. But if I uncovered the fact that there was an accomplice and it looked like they might have killed Quine – or knew who had done it – I'd obviously consider myself duty bound to inform the police.'

Chard lowered himself back onto one of the large leather cubes, dropping his crutches with a clatter on the floor.

'Damn,' he said, his displeasure echoing off the many hard surfaces around them as he leaned over to check that he had not dented the varnished wood.

'You know I've also been engaged by Quine's wife to try and find out who killed him?' Strike asked.

'I had heard something of the sort,' said Chard, still examining his teak floorboards for damage. 'That won't interfere with this line of enquiry, though?'

His self-absorption was remarkable, Strike thought. He

remembered Chard's copperplate writing on the card with the painting of violets: *Do let me know if there is anything you need.* Perhaps his secretary had dictated it to him.

'Would you like to tell me who the alleged collaborator is?' asked Strike.

'This is extremely painful,' mumbled Chard, his eyes flitting from Alfred Wallis to the stone angel and up to the spiral stairs.

Strike said nothing.

'It's Jerry Waldegrave,' said Chard, glancing at Strike and away again. 'And I'll tell you why I suspect – how I know.

'His behaviour has been strange for weeks. I first noticed it when he telephoned me about *Bombyx Mori*, to tell me what Quine had done. There was no embarrassment, no apology.'

'Would you have expected Waldegrave to apologise for something Quine had written?'

The question seemed to surprise Chard.

'Well – Owen was one of Jerry's authors, so yes, I would have expected some regret that Owen had depicted me in that – in that way.'

And Strike's unruly imagination again showed him the naked Phallus Impudicus standing over the body of a dead young man emitting supernatural light.

'Are you and Waldegrave on bad terms?' he asked.

'I've shown Jerry Waldegrave a lot of forbearance, a considerable forbearance,' said Chard, ignoring the direct question. 'I kept him on full pay while he went to a treatment facility a year ago. Perhaps he feels hard done by,' said Chard, 'but I've been on his side, yes, on occasions when many another man, a more prudent man, might have remained neutral. Jerry's personal misfortunes are not of my making. There is resentment. Yes, I would say that there is definite resentment, however unjustified.'

'Resentment about what?' asked Strike.

'Jerry isn't fond of Michael Fancourt,' mumbled Chard, his eyes on the flames in the wood-burner. 'Michael had a – a flirtation, a long time ago, with Fenella, Jerry's wife. And as it happens, I actually *warned Michael off*, because of my friendship with Jerry. Yes!' said Chard, nodding, deeply impressed by the memory of his own actions. 'I told Michael it was unkind and unwise, even in his state of . . . because Michael had lost his first wife, you see, not very long before.

'Michael didn't appreciate my unsolicited advice. He took offence; he took off for a different publisher. The board was very unhappy,' said Chard. 'It's taken us twenty-odd years to lure Michael back.

'But after all this time,' Chard said, his bald pate merely one more reflective surface among the glass, polished wood and steel, 'Jerry can hardly expect his personal animosities to govern company policy. Ever since Michael agreed to come back to Roper Chard, Jerry has made it his business to – to undermine me, subtly, in a hundred little ways.

'What I believe happened is this,' said Chard, glancing from time to time at Strike, as though to gauge his reaction. 'Jerry took Owen into his confidence about Michael's deal, which we were trying to keep under wraps. Owen had, of course, been an enemy of Fancourt's for a quarter of a century. Owen and Jerry decided to concoct this . . . this dreadful book, in which Michael and I are subjected to – to disgusting calumnies as a way of drawing attention away from Michael's arrival and as an act of revenge on both of us, on the company, on anyone else they cared to denigrate.

'And, most tellingly,' said Chard, his voice echoing now through the empty space, 'after I told Jerry, explicitly, to make sure the manuscript was locked safely away he allowed it to be read widely by anyone who cared to do so, and having made sure it's being gossiped about all over London, he resigns and leaves me looking—'

'When did Waldegrave resign?' asked Strike.

'The day before yesterday,' said Chard, before plunging on: 'and he was extremely reluctant to join me in legal action against Quine. That in itself shows—'

'Perhaps he thought bringing in lawyers would draw more attention to the book?' Strike suggested. 'Waldegrave's in *Bombyx Mori* himself, isn't he?'

'*That!*' said Chard and sniggered. It was the first sign of humour Strike had seen in him and the effect was unpleasant. 'You don't want to take everything at face value, Mr Strike. Owen never knew about *that*.'

'About what?'

'The Cutter character is Jerry's own work – I realised it on a third reading,' said Chard. 'Very, very clever: it looks like an attack on Jerry himself, but it's really a way of causing Fenella pain. They are still married, you see, but very unhappily. *Very* unhappily.

'Yes, I saw it all, on re-reading,' said Chard. The spotlights in the hanging ceiling made rippled reflections on his skull as he nodded. 'Owen didn't write the Cutter. He barely knows Fenella. He didn't know about that old business.'

'So what exactly are the bloody sack and the dwarf supposed to—?'

'Get it out of Jerry,' said Chard. 'Make him tell you. Why should I help him spread slander around?'

'I've been wondering,' Strike said, obediently dropping that line of enquiry, 'why Michael Fancourt agreed to come to

Roper Chard when Quine was working for you, given that they were on such bad terms?'

There was a short pause.

'We were under no legal obligation to publish Owen's next book,' said Chard. 'We had a first-look option. That was all.'

'So you think Jerry Waldegrave told Quine that he was about to be dropped, to keep Fancourt happy?'

'Yes,' said Chard, staring at his own fingernails. 'I do. Also, I had offended Owen the last time I saw him, so the news that I might be about to drop him no doubt swept away any last vestige of loyalty he might once have felt towards me, because I took him on when every other publisher in Britain had given up on—'

'How did you offend him?'

'Oh, it was when he last came into the office. He brought his daughter with him.'

'Orlando?'

'Named, he told me, for the eponymous protagonist of the novel by Virginia Woolf.' Chard hesitated, his eyes flickering to Strike and then back to his nails. 'She's – not quite right, his daughter.'

'Really?' said Strike. 'In what way?'

'Mentally,' mumbled Chard. 'I was visiting the art department when they came in. Owen told me he was showing her around – something he had no business doing, but Owen always made himself at home . . . great sense of entitlement and self-importance, always . . .

'His daughter grabbed at a mock-up cover – grubby hands – I seized her wrist to stop her ruining it—' He mimed the action in mid-air; with the remembrance of this act of near desecration came a look of distaste. 'It was instinctive, you know, a desire to protect the image, but it upset her very much. There was a scene. Very embarrassing and uncomfortable,' mumbled Chard, who seemed to suffer again in retrospect. 'She became almost hysterical. Owen was furious. That, no doubt, was my crime. That, and bringing Michael Fancourt back to Roper Chard.'

'Who,' Strike asked, 'would you think had most reason to be upset at their depiction in *Bombyx Mori*?'

'I really don't know,' said Chard. After a short pause he said, 'Well, I doubt Elizabeth Tassel was delighted to see herself portrayed as parasitic, after all the years of shepherding Owen out of parties to stop him making a drunken fool of himself, but I'm afraid,' said Chard coldly, 'I haven't got much sympathy for Elizabeth. She allowed that book to go out unread. Criminal carelessness.'

'Did you contact Fancourt after you'd read the manuscript?' asked Strike.

'He had to know what Quine had done,' said Chard. 'Better by far that he heard it from me. He was just home from receiving the Prix Prévost in Paris. I did not make that call with relish.'

'How did he react?'

'Michael's resilient,' muttered Chard. 'He told me not to worry, said that Owen had done himself more harm than he had done us. Michael rather enjoys his enmities. He was perfectly calm.'

'Did you tell him what Quine had said, or implied, about him in the book?'

'Of course,' said Chard. 'I couldn't let him hear it from anyone else.'

'And he didn't seem upset?'

'He said, "The last word will be mine, Daniel. The last word will be mine."'

'What did you understand by that?'

'Oh, well, Michael's a famous assassin,' said Chard, with a small smile. 'He can flay anyone alive in five well chosen – when I say "assassin",' said Chard, suddenly and comically anxious, 'naturally, I'm talking in literary—'

'Of course,' Strike reassured him. 'Did you ask Fancourt to join you in legal action against Quine?'

'Michael despises the courts as a means of redress in such matters.'

'You knew the late Joseph North, didn't you?' asked Strike conversationally.

The muscles in Chard's face tightened: a mask beneath the darkening skin.

'A very – that was a very long time ago.'

'North was a friend of Quine's, wasn't he?'

'I turned down Joe North's novel,' said Chard. His thin mouth was working. '*That's all I did.* Half a dozen other publishers did the same. It was a mistake, commercially speaking. It had some success, posthumously. Of course,' he added dismissively, 'I think Michael largely rewrote it.'

'Quine resented you turning his friend's book down?'

'Yes, he did. He made a lot of noise about it.'

'But he came to Roper Chard anyway?'

'There was nothing personal in my turning down Joe North's book,' said Chard, with heightened colour. 'Owen came to understand that, eventually.'

There was another uncomfortable pause.

'So . . . when you're hired to find a – a criminal of this type,' said Chard, changing subject with palpable effort, 'do you work with the police on that, or—?'

'Oh yeah,' said Strike, with a wry remembrance of the

animosity he had recently encountered from the force, but delighted that Chard had played so conveniently into his hands. 'I've got great contacts at the Met. *Your* movements don't seem to be giving them any cause for concern,' he said, with faint emphasis on the personal pronoun.

The provocative, slippery phrasing had its full effect.

'The police have looked into *my* movements?'

Chard spoke like a frightened boy, unable to muster even a pretence of self-protective sangfroid.

'Well, you know, everyone depicted in *Bombyx Mori* was bound to come in for scrutiny from the police,' said Strike casually, sipping his tea, 'and everything you people did after the fifth, when Quine walked out on his wife, taking the book with him, will be of interest to them.'

And to Strike's great satisfaction, Chard began at once to review his own movements aloud, apparently for his own reassurance.

'Well, I didn't know anything about the book at all until the seventh,' he said, staring at his bound-up foot again. 'I was down here when Jerry called me ... I headed straight back up to London – Manny drove me. I spent the night at home, Manny and Nenita can confirm that ... on the Monday I met with my lawyers at the office, talked to Jerry ... I was at a dinner party that night – close friends in Notting Hill – and again Manny drove me home ... I turned in early on Tuesday because on Wednesday morning I was going to New York. I was there until the thirteenth ... home all day the fourteenth ... on the fifteenth ... '

Chard's mumbling deteriorated into silence. Perhaps he had realised that there was not the slightest need for him to explain himself to Strike. The darting look he gave the detective was suddenly cagey. Chard had wanted to buy an ally; Strike could tell that he had suddenly awoken to the double-edged nature of such a relationship. Strike was not worried. He had gained more from the interview than he had expected; to be unhired now would cost him only money.

Manny came padding back across the floor.

'You want lunch?' he asked Chard curtly.

'In five minutes,' Chard said, with a smile. 'I must say goodbye to Mr Strike first.'

Manny stalked away on rubber-soled shoes.

'He's sulking,' Chard told Strike, with an uncomfortable half-laugh. 'They don't like it down here. They prefer London.'

He retrieved his crutches from the floor and pushed himself back up into a standing position. Strike, with more effort, imitated him.

'And how is – er – Mrs Quine?' Chard said, with an air of belatedly ticking off the proprieties as they swung, like strange three-legged animals, back towards the front door. 'Big redheaded woman, yes?'

'No,' said Strike. 'Thin. Greying hair.'

'Oh,' said Chard, without much interest. 'I met someone else.'

Strike paused beside the swing doors that led to the kitchen. Chard halted too, looking aggrieved.

'I'm afraid I need to get on, Mr Strike—'

'So do I,' said Strike pleasantly, 'but I don't think my assistant would thank me for leaving her behind.'

Chard had evidently forgotten the existence of Robin, whom he had so peremptorily dismissed.

'Oh, yes, of course – Manny! Nenita!'

'She's in the bathroom,' said the stocky woman, emerging from the kitchen holding the linen bag containing Robin's shoes.

The wait passed in a faintly uncomfortable silence. At last Robin appeared, her expression stony, and slipped her feet back into her shoes.

The cold air bit their warm faces as the front door swung open while Strike shook hands with Chard. Robin moved directly to the car and climbed into the driver's seat without speaking to anyone.

Manny reappeared in his thick coat.

'I'll come down with you,' he told Strike. 'To check the gates.'

'They can buzz the house if they're stuck, Manny,' said Chard, but the young man paid no attention, clambering into the car as before.

The three of them rode in silence back down the black-and-white drive, through the falling snow. Manny pressed the remote control he had brought with him and the gates slid open without difficulty.

'Thanks,' said Strike, turning to look at him in the back seat. ''Fraid you've got a cold walk back.'

Manny sniffed, got out of the car and slammed the door. Robin had just shifted into first gear when Manny appeared at Strike's window. She applied the brake.

'Yeah?' said Strike, winding the window down.

'I didn't push him,' said Manny fiercely.

'Sorry?'

'Down the stairs,' said Manny. 'I didn't push him. He's lying.'

Strike and Robin stared at him.

'You believe me?'

'Yeah,' said Strike.

'OK then,' said Manny, nodding at them. 'OK.'

He turned and walked, slipping a little in his rubber-soled shoes, back up to the house.

30

> . . . as an earnest of friendship and confidence, I'll acquaint you with a design that I have. To tell truth, and speak openly one to another . . .
>
> William Congreve, *Love for Love*

At Strike's insistence, they stopped for lunch at the Burger King at Tiverton Services.

'You need to eat something before we go up the road.'

Robin accompanied him inside with barely a word, making no reference even to Manny's recent, startling assertion. Her cold and slightly martyred air did not entirely surprise Strike, but he was impatient with it. She queued for their burgers, because he could not manage both tray and crutches, and when she had set down the loaded tray at the small Formica table he said, trying to defuse the tension:

'Look, I know you expected me to tell Chard off for treating you like staff.'

'I didn't,' Robin contradicted him automatically. (Hearing him say it aloud made her feel petulant, childish.)

'Have it your own way,' said Strike with an irritable shrug, taking a large bite of his first burger.

They ate in disgruntled silence for a minute or two, until Robin's innate honesty reasserted itself.

'All right, I did, a bit,' she said.

Mellowed by greasy food and touched by her admission, Strike said:

'I was getting good stuff out of him, Robin. You don't start picking arguments with interviewees when they're in full flow.'

'Sorry for my amateurishness,' she said, stung all over again.

'Oh, for Christ's sake,' he said. 'Who's calling you—?'

'What were you intending, when you took me on?' she demanded suddenly, letting her unwrapped burger fall back onto the tray.

The latent resentment of weeks had suddenly burst its bounds. She did not care what she heard; she wanted the truth. Was she a typist and a receptionist, or was she something more? Had she stayed with Strike, and helped him climb out of penury, merely to be shunted aside like domestic staff?

'Intending?' repeated Strike, staring at her. 'What d'you mean, intend—?'

'I thought you meant me to be – I thought I was going to get some – some training,' said Robin, pink-cheeked and unnaturally bright-eyed. 'You've mentioned it a couple of times, but then lately you've been talking about getting someone else in. I took a pay cut,' she said tremulously. 'I turned down better-paid jobs. I thought you meant me to be—'

Her anger, so long suppressed, was bringing her to the verge of tears, but she was determined not to give in to them. The fictional partner whom she had been imagining for Strike would never cry; not that no-nonsense ex-policewoman, tough and unemotional through every crisis . . .

'I thought you meant me to be – I didn't think I was just going to answer the phone.'

'You don't just answer the phone,' said Strike, who had just finished his first burger and was watching her struggle with her anger from beneath his heavy brows. 'You've been casing murder suspects' houses with me this week. You just saved both our lives on the motorway.'

But Robin was not to be deflected.

'What were you expecting me to do when you kept me on?'

'I don't know that I had any particular plan,' Strike said slowly and untruthfully. 'I didn't know you were this serious about the job – looking for training—'

'*How could I not be serious?*' demanded Robin loudly.

A family of four in the corner of the tiny restaurant was staring at them. Robin paid them no attention. She was suddenly livid. The long cold journey, Strike eating all the food, his surprise that she could drive properly, her relegation to the kitchen with Chard's servants and now this—

'You give me half – *half* – what that human resources job would have paid! Why do you think I stayed? I helped you. I helped you solve the Lula Landry—'

'OK,' said Strike, holding up a large, hairy-backed hand. 'OK, here it is. But don't blame me if you don't like what you're about to hear.'

She stared at him, flushed, straight-backed on her plastic chair, her food untouched.

'I *did* take you on thinking I could train you up. I didn't have any money for courses, but I thought you could learn on the job until I could afford it.'

Refusing to feel mollified until she heard what was coming next, Robin said nothing.

'You've got a lot of aptitude for the job,' said Strike, 'but you're getting married to someone who hates you doing it.'

Robin opened her mouth and closed it again. A sensation of

having been unexpectedly winded had robbed her of the power of speech.

'You leave on the dot every day—'

'I do not!' said Robin, furious. 'In case you hadn't noticed, I turned down a day off to be here now, driving you all the way to Devon—'

'Because he's away,' said Strike. 'Because he won't know.'

The feeling of having been winded intensified. How could Strike know that she had lied to Matthew, if not in fact, then by omission?

'Even if that – whether that's true or not,' she said unsteadily, 'it's up to me what I do with my – it's not up to Matthew what career I have.'

'I was with Charlotte sixteen years, on and off,' said Strike, picking up his second burger. 'Mostly off. She hated my job. It's what kept breaking us up – one of the things that kept breaking us up,' he corrected himself, scrupulously honest. 'She couldn't understand a vocation. Some people can't; at best, work's about status and pay cheques for them, it hasn't got value in itself.'

He began unwrapping the burger while Robin glared at him.

'I need a partner who can share the long hours,' said Strike. 'Someone who's OK with weekend work. I don't blame Matthew for worrying about you—'

'He doesn't.'

The words were out of her mouth before Robin could consider them. In her blanket desire to refute everything that Strike was saying she had let an unpalatable truth escape her. The fact was that Matthew had very little imagination. He had not seen Strike covered in blood after the killer of Lula Landry had stabbed him. Even her description of Owen Quine lying trussed and disembowelled seemed to have been blurred for him by the thick miasma of jealousy through which he heard everything connected to Strike. His antipathy for her job owed nothing to protectiveness and she had never admitted as much to herself before.

'It can be dangerous, what I do,' said Strike through another huge bite of burger, as though he had not heard her.

'I've been useful to you,' said Robin, her voice thicker than his, though her mouth was empty.

'I know you have. I wouldn't be where I am now if I hadn't had you,' said Strike. 'Nobody was ever more grateful than me for a temping agency's mistake. You've been incredible, I couldn't have – don't bloody cry, that family's gawping enough already.'

'I don't give a monkey's,' said Robin into a handful of paper napkins and Strike laughed.

'If it's what you want,' he told the top of her red-gold head, 'you can go on a surveillance course when I've got the money. But if you're my partner-in-training, there'll be times that I'm going to have to ask you to do stuff that Matthew might not like. That's all I'm saying. You're the one who's going to have to work it out.'

'And I will,' said Robin, fighting to contain the urge to bawl. 'That's what I want. That's why I stayed.'

'Then cheer the fuck up and eat your burger.'

Robin found it hard to eat with the huge lump in her throat. She felt shaken but elated. She had not been mistaken: Strike had seen in her what he possessed himself. They were not people who worked merely for the pay cheque . . .

'So, tell me about Daniel Chard,' she said.

He did so while the nosy family of four gathered up their

things and left, still throwing covert glances at the couple they could not quite work out (had it been a lovers' tiff? A family row? How had it been so speedily resolved?).

'Paranoid, bit eccentric, self-obsessed,' concluded Strike five minutes later, 'but there might be something in it. Jerry Waldegrave could've collaborated with Quine. On the other hand, he might've resigned because he'd had enough of Chard, who I don't think would be an easy bloke to work for.

'D'you want a coffee?'

Robin glanced at her watch. The snow was still falling; she feared delays on the motorway that would prevent her catching the train to Yorkshire, but after their conversation she was determined to demonstrate her commitment to the job, so she agreed to one. In any case, there were things she wished to say to Strike while she was still sitting opposite him. It would not be nearly as satisfying to tell him while in the driver's seat, where she could not watch his reaction.

'I found out a bit about Chard myself,' she said when she had returned with two cups and an apple pie for Strike.

'Servants' gossip?'

'No,' said Robin. 'They barely said a word to me while I was in the kitchen. They both seemed in foul moods.'

'According to Chard, they don't like it in Devon. Prefer London. Are they brother and sister?'

'Mother and son, I think,' said Robin. 'He called her Mamu.

'Anyway, I asked to go to the bathroom and the staff loo's just next to an artist's studio. Daniel Chard knows a lot about anatomy,' said Robin. 'There are prints of Leonardo da Vinci's anatomical drawings all over the walls and an anatomical model in one corner. Creepy – wax. And on the easel,' she said, 'was a very detailed drawing of Manny the Manservant. Lying on the ground, in the nude.'

Strike put down his coffee.

'Those are very interesting pieces of information,' he said slowly.

'I thought you'd like them,' said Robin, with a demure smile.

'Shines an interesting side-light on Manny's assurance that he didn't push his boss down the stairs.'

'They really didn't like you being there,' said Robin, 'but that might have been my fault. I said you were a private detective, but Nenita – her English isn't as good as Manny's – didn't understand, so I said you were a kind of policeman.'

'Leading them to assume that Chard had invited me over to complain about Manny's violence towards him.'

'Did Chard mention it?'

'Not a word,' said Strike. 'Much more concerned about Waldegrave's alleged treachery.'

After visits to the bathroom they returned to the cold, where they had to screw up their eyes against oncoming snow as they traversed the car park. A light frosting had already settled over the top of the Toyota.

'You're going to make it to King's Cross, right?' said Strike, checking his watch.

'Unless we hit trouble on the motorway,' said Robin, surreptitiously touching the wood trim on the door's interior.

They had just reached the M4, where there were weather warnings on every sign and where the speed limit had been reduced to sixty, when Strike's mobile rang.

'Ilsa? What's going on?'

'Hi, Corm. Well, it could be worse. They haven't arrested her, but that was some intense questioning.'

Strike turned the mobile onto speakerphone for Robin's benefit and together they listened, similar frowns of concentration on their faces as the car moved through a vortex of swirling snow, rushing the windscreen.

'They definitely think it's her,' said Ilsa.

'Based on what?'

'Opportunity,' said Ilsa, 'and her manner. She really doesn't help herself. Very grumpy at being questioned and kept talking about you, which put their backs up. She said you'll find out who really did it.'

'Bloody hell,' said Strike, exasperated. 'And what was in the lock-up?'

'Oh yeah, that. It was a burned, bloodstained rag in among a pile of junk.'

'Big effing deal,' said Strike. 'Could've been there years.'

'Forensics will find out, but I agree, it's not much to go on seeing as they haven't even found the guts yet.'

'You know about the guts?'

'Everyone knows about the guts now, Corm. It's been on the news.'

Strike and Robin exchanged fleeting looks.

'When?'

'Lunchtime. I think the police knew it was about to break and brought her in to see if they could squeeze anything out of her before it all became common knowledge.'

'It's one of their lot who's leaked it,' said Strike angrily.

'That's a big accusation.'

'I had it from the journalist who was paying the copper to talk.'

'Know some interesting people, don't you?'

'Comes with the territory. Thanks for letting me know, Ilsa.'

'No problem. Try and keep her out of jail, Corm. I quite like her.'

'Who is that?' Robin asked as Ilsa hung up.

'Old school friend from Cornwall; lawyer. She married one of my London mates,' said Strike. 'I put Leonora onto her because – shit.'

They had rounded a bend to find a huge tailback ahead of them. Robin applied the brake and they drew up behind a Peugeot.

'*Shit*,' repeated Strike, with a glance at Robin's set profile.

'Another accident,' said Robin. 'I can see flashing lights.'

Her imagination showed her Matthew's face if she had to telephone him and say that she was not coming, that she had missed the sleeper. His mother's funeral . . . *who misses a funeral*? She should have been there already, at Matt's father's house, helping with arrangements, taking some of the strain. Her weekend bag ought already to have been sitting in her old bedroom at home, her funeral clothes pressed and hanging in her old wardrobe, everything ready for the short walk to the church the following morning. They were burying Mrs Cunliffe, her future mother-in-law, but she had chosen to drive off into the snow with Strike, and now they were gridlocked, two hundred miles from the church where Matthew's mother would be laid to rest.

He'll never forgive me. He'll never forgive me if I miss the funeral because I did this . . .

Why did she have to have been presented with such a choice, today of all days? Why did the weather have to be so bad? Robin's stomach churned with anxiety and the traffic did not move.

Strike said nothing, but turned on the radio. The sound of

Take That filled the car, singing about there being progress now, where once there was none. The music grated on Robin's nerves, but she said nothing.

The line of traffic moved forward a few feet.

Oh, please God, let me get to King's Cross on time, prayed Robin inside her head.

For three quarters of an hour they crawled through the snow, the afternoon light fading fast around them. What had seemed a vast ocean of time until the departure of the night train was starting to feel to Robin like a rapidly draining pool in which she might shortly be sitting alone, marooned.

Now they could see the crash ahead of them; the police, the lights, a mangled Polo.

'You'll make it,' said Strike, speaking for the first time since he had turned on the radio as they waited their turn to be waved forwards by the traffic cop. 'It'll be tight, but you'll make it.'

Robin did not answer. She knew it was all her fault, not his: he had offered her the day off. It was she who had been insistent on coming with him to Devon, she who had lied to Matthew about the availability of train seats today. She ought to have stood all the way from London to Harrogate rather than miss Mrs Cunliffe's funeral. Strike had been with Charlotte sixteen years, on and off, and the job had broken them. She did not want to lose Matthew. Why had she done this; why had she offered to drive Strike?

The traffic was dense and slow. By five o'clock they were travelling in thick rush-hour traffic outside Reading and crawled to a halt again. Strike turned up the news when it came on the radio. Robin tried to care what they would say about Quine's murder, but her heart was in Yorkshire now, as though it had leapfrogged the traffic and all the implacable, snowy miles between her and home.

'Police have confirmed today that murdered author Owen Quine, whose body was discovered six days ago in a house in Barons Court, London, was murdered in the same way as the hero of his last, unpublished book. No arrest has yet been made in the case.

'Detective Inspector Richard Anstis, who is in charge of the investigation, spoke to reporters earlier this afternoon.'

Anstis, Strike noted, sounded stilted and tense. This was not the way he would have chosen to release the information.

'We're interested in hearing from everyone who had access to the manuscript of Mr Quine's last novel—'

'Can you tell us exactly how Mr Quine was killed, Detective Inspector?' asked an eager male voice.

'We're waiting for a full forensic report,' said Anstis, and he was cut across by a female reporter.

'Can you confirm that parts of Mr Quine's body were removed by the killer?'

'Part of Mr Quine's intestines were taken away from the scene,' said Anstis. 'We're pursuing several leads, but we would appeal to the public for any information. This was an appalling crime and we believe the perpetrator to be extremely dangerous.'

'Not again,' said Robin desperately and Strike looked up to see a wall of red lights ahead. 'Not another accident . . . '

Strike slapped off the radio, unwound his window and stuck his head out into the whirling snow.

'No,' he shouted to her. 'Someone stuck at the side of the road . . . in a drift . . . we'll be moving again in a minute,' he reassured her.

But it took another forty minutes for them to clear the obstruction. All three lanes were packed and they resumed their journey at little more than a crawl.

'I'm not going to make it,' said Robin, her mouth dry, as they finally reached the edge of London. It was twenty past ten.

'You are,' said Strike. 'Turn that bloody thing off,' he said, thumping the sat nav into silence, '*and don't take that exit*—'

'But I've got to drop you—'

'Forget me, you don't need to drop me – next left—'

'I can't go down there, it's one way!'

'Left!' he bellowed, tugging the wheel.

'Don't do that, it's danger—'

'D'you want to miss this bloody funeral? Put your foot down! First right—'

'Where are we?'

'I know what I'm doing,' said Strike, squinting through the snow. 'Straight on . . . my mate Nick's dad's a cabbie, he taught me some stuff – right again – ignore the bloody No Entry sign, who's coming out of there on a night like this? Straight on and left at the lights!'

'I can't just leave you at King's Cross!' she said, obeying his instructions blindly. 'You can't drive it, what are you going to do with it?'

'Sod the car, I'll think of something – up here, take the second right—'

At five to eleven the towers of St Pancras appeared to Robin like a vision of heaven through the snow.

'Pull over, get out and run,' said Strike. 'Call me if you make it. I'll be here if you don't.'

'*Thank you.*'

And she had gone, sprinting over the snow with her weekend

bag dangling from her hand. Strike watched her vanish into the darkness, imagined her skidding a little on the slippery floor of the station, not falling, looking wildly around for the platform . . . She had left the car, on his instructions, at the kerb on a double line. If she made the train he was stranded in a hire car he couldn't drive and which would certainly be towed.

The golden hands on the St Pancras clock moved inexorably towards eleven o'clock. Strike saw the train doors slamming shut in his mind's eye, Robin sprinting up the platform, red-gold hair flying . . .

One minute past. He fixed his eyes on the station entrance and waited.

She did not reappear. Still he waited. Five minutes past. Six minutes past.

His mobile rang.

'Did you make it?'

'By the skin of my teeth . . . it was just about to leave . . . Cormoran, thank you, thank you so much . . . '

'No problem,' he said, looking around at the dark icy ground, the deepening snow. 'Have a good journey. I'd better sort myself out. Good luck for tomorrow.'

'*Thank you!*' she called as he hung up.

He had owed her, Strike thought, reaching for his crutches, but that did not make the prospect of a journey across snowy London on one leg, or a hefty fine for abandoning a hire car in the middle of town, much more appealing.

31

Danger, the spur of all great minds.

George Chapman, *The Revenge of Bussy d'Ambois*

Daniel Chard would not have liked the tiny rented attic flat in Denmark Street, Strike thought, unless he could have found primitive charm in the lines of the old toaster or desk lamp, but there was much to say for it if you happened to be a man with one leg. His knee was still not ready to accept a prosthesis on Saturday morning, but surfaces were within grabbing reach; distances could be covered in short hops; there was food in the fridge, hot water and cigarettes. Strike felt a genuine fondness for the place today, with the window steamy with condensation and blurry snow visible on the sill beyond.

After breakfast he lay on his bed, smoking, a mug of dark brown tea beside him on the box that served as a bedside table, glowering not with bad temper but concentration.

Six days and nothing.

No sign of the intestines that had vanished from Quine's body, nor of any forensic evidence that would have pegged the potential killer (for he knew that a rogue hair or print would surely have prevented yesterday's fruitless interrogation of Leonora). No appeals for further sightings of the concealed figure who had entered the building shortly before Quine had died (did the police think it a figment of the thick-lensed neighbour's imagination?). No murder weapon, no incriminating footage of unexpected visitors to Talgarth Road, no suspicious ramblers noticing freshly turned earth, no mound of rotting guts revealed, wrapped in a black burqa, no sign of Quine's holdall containing his notes for *Bombyx Mori*. Nothing.

Six days. He had caught killers in six hours, though admittedly those had been slapdash crimes of rage and desperation, where fountains of clues had gushed with the blood and the panicking or incompetent culprits had splattered everyone in their vicinity with their lies.

Quine's killing was different, stranger and more sinister.

As Strike raised his mug to his lips he saw the body again as clearly as though he had viewed the photograph on his mobile. It was a theatre piece, a stage set.

In spite of his strictures to Robin, Strike could not help asking himself: why had it been done? Revenge? Madness? Concealment (of what?)? Forensic evidence obliterated by the hydrochloric acid, time of death obscured, entrance and departure of the crime scene achieved without detection. *Planned meticulously. Every detail thought out. Six days and not a single lead* . . . Strike did not believe Anstis's claim to have several. Of course, his old friend was no longer sharing information, not after the tense warnings to Strike to butt out, to keep away.

Strike brushed ash absently off the front of his old sweater and lit a fresh cigarette from the stub of his old one.

We believe the perpetrator to be extremely dangerous, Anstis had said to the reporters, a statement, in Strike's view, that was both painfully obvious and strangely misleading.

And a memory came to him: the memory of the great adventure of Dave Polworth's eighteenth birthday.

Polworth was Strike's very oldest friend; they had known each other since nursery. Through childhood and adolescence Strike had moved away from Cornwall regularly and then returned, the friendship picking up again wherever Strike's mother and her whims had last interrupted it.

Dave had an uncle who had left for Australia in his teens and was now a multi-millionaire. He had invited his nephew to come and stay for his eighteenth birthday, and to bring a mate.

Across the world the two teenagers had flown; it had been the best adventure of their young lives. They had stayed in Uncle Kevin's massive beachside house, all glass and shining wood, with a bar in the sitting room; diamond sea spray in a blinding sun and enormous pink prawns on a barbecue skewer; the accents, the beer, more beer, the sort of butterscotch-limbed blondes you never saw in Cornwall and then, on Dave's actual birthday, the shark.

'They're only dangerous if they're provoked,' said Uncle Kevin, who liked his scuba diving. 'No touching, lads, all right? No arsing around.'

But for Dave Polworth, who loved the sea, who surfed, fished and sailed at home, arsing around was a way of life.

A killer born, with its flat dead eyes and its ranks of stiletto teeth, but Strike had witnessed the blacktip's lazy indifference as they swam over it, awed by its sleek beauty. It would have been content to glide away through the azure gloom, he knew that, but Dave was determined to touch.

He had the scar still: the shark had torn away a tidy chunk of his forearm and he had only partial feeling in his right thumb. It had not affected his ability to do his job: Dave was a civil engineer in Bristol now, and they called him 'Chum' in the Victory Inn where he and Strike still met to drink Doom Bar on their visits home. Stubborn, reckless, a thrillseeker to his core, Polworth still scuba-dived in his free time, though he left the basking sharks of the Atlantic well alone.

There was a fine crack on the ceiling over Strike's bed. He did not think he had ever noticed it before. His eyes followed it as he remembered the shadow on a seabed and a sudden cloud of black blood; the thrashing of Dave's body in a silent scream.

The killer of Owen Quine was like that blacktip, he thought. There were no frenzied, indiscriminate predators among the suspects in this case. None of them had a known history of violence. There was not, as so often when bodies turned up, a trail of past misdemeanours leading to the door of a suspect, no bloodstained past dragging behind any of them like a bag of offal for hungry hounds. This killer was a rarer, stranger beast: the one who concealed their true nature until sufficiently disturbed. Owen Quine, like Dave Polworth, had recklessly taunted a murderer-in-waiting and unleashed horror upon himself.

Strike had heard the glib assertion many times, that everyone had it in them to kill, but he knew this to be a lie. There were undoubtedly those to whom killing was easy and pleasurable: he had met a few such. Millions had been successfully trained to end others' lives; he, Strike, was one of them. Humans killed opportunistically, for advantage and in defence, discovering in themselves the capacity for bloodshed when no alternative seemed possible; but there were also people who had drawn up short, even under the most intense pressure, unable to press their advantage, to seize the opportunity, to break the final and greatest taboo.

Strike did not underestimate what it had taken to bind, batter and slice open Owen Quine. The person who had done it had achieved their goal without detection, successfully disposed of the evidence and appeared not to be exhibiting sufficient distress or guilt to alert anyone. All of this argued a dangerous personality, a *highly* dangerous personality – if disturbed. While they believed themselves to be undetected and unsuspected, there was no danger to anybody around them. But if touched again . . . touched, perhaps, in the place where Owen Quine had managed to touch them . . .

'Fuck,' murmured Strike, dropping his cigarette hastily into the ashtray beside him; it had burned down to his fingers without him noticing.

So what was he to do next? If the trail away from the crime was practically non-existent, Strike thought, he must pursue the trail *towards* the crime. If the aftermath of Quine's death was unnaturally devoid of clues, it was time to look at his last few days of life.

Strike picked up his mobile and sighed deeply, looking at it. Was there, he asked himself, any other way of getting at the first piece of information he sought? He ran through his extensive list of acquaintances in his head, discarding options as quickly as they occurred. Finally, and without much enthusiasm, he concluded that his original choice was most likely to bring him the goods: his half-brother Alexander.

They shared a famous father, but had never lived under the same roof. Al was nine years younger than Strike and was Jonny Rokeby's legitimate son, which meant that there was virtually no point of coincidence in their lives. Al had been privately educated in Switzerland and he might be anywhere right now: in Rokeby's LA residence; on a rapper's yacht; even a white Australian beach, for Rokeby's third wife was from Sydney.

And yet of his half-siblings on his father's side, Al had shown himself more willing than any of the others to forge a relationship with his older brother. Strike remembered Al visiting him in hospital after his leg had been blown off; an awkward encounter, but touching in retrospect.

Al had brought with him to Selly Oak an offer from Rokeby that could have been made by mail: financial help in starting Strike's detective business. Al had announced the offer with pride, considering it evidence of his father's altruism. Strike had been sure that it was no such thing. He suspected that Rokeby or his advisers had been nervous about the one-legged, decorated veteran selling his story. The offer of a gift was supposed to stop his mouth.

Strike had turned down his father's largesse and then been refused by every single bank to which he applied for a loan. He had called Al back with immense reluctance, refusing to take the money as a gift, turning down a proffered meeting with his father but asking whether he could have a loan. This had evidently caused offence. Rokeby's lawyer had subsequently pursued Strike for his monthly payments with all the zeal of the most rapacious bank.

Had Strike not chosen to keep Robin on his payroll, the loan would already have been cleared. He was determined to repay it before Christmas, determined not to be beholden to Jonny Rokeby, which was why he had taken on a workload that had lately seen him working eight or nine hours, seven days a week. None of this made the prospect of calling his younger brother for a favour any more comfortable. Strike could understand Al's loyalty to a father whom he clearly loved, but any mention between them of Rokeby was necessarily charged.

Al's number rang several times and finally went to voicemail. As relieved as he was disappointed, Strike left a brief message asking Al to call him and hung up.

Lighting his third cigarette since breakfast, Strike reverted to his contemplation of the crack in the ceiling. The trail towards the crime . . . so much depended on when the killer had seen the manuscript, had recognised its potential as a blueprint for murder . . .

And, once again, he flicked through the suspects as though they were a hand of cards he had been dealt, examining their potentialities.

Elizabeth Tassel, who made no secret of the rage and pain *Bombyx Mori* had caused her. Kathryn Kent, who claimed not to have read it at all. The still unknown Pippa2011, to whom Quine had read parts of the book back in October. Jerry Waldegrave, who had had the manuscript on the fifth, but might, if Chard was to be believed, have known what was in there way before. Daniel Chard, who claimed that he had not seen it until the seventh, and Michael Fancourt, who had heard about the book from Chard. Yes, there were sundry others, peeking and peering and giggling at the most salacious parts of the book, emailed all over London by Christian Fisher, but Strike found it very hard to work up even the vaguest of cases against Fisher, young Ralph in Tassel's office, or Nina Lascelles, none of whom were featured in *Bombyx Mori* nor had really known Quine.

He needed, Strike thought, to get closer, close enough to ruffle the people whose lives had already been mocked and distorted by Owen Quine. With only a little more enthusiasm than he had brought to the task of calling Al, he scrolled through his contact list and called Nina Lascelles.

It was a brief call. She was delighted. Of course he could come over tonight. She'd cook.

Strike could think of no other way to probe for further details of Jerry Waldegrave's private life or for Michael Fancourt's reputation as a literary assassin, but he did not look forward to the painful process of reattaching his prosthesis, not to mention the effort it would require to detach himself again, tomorrow morning, from Nina Lascelles's hopeful clutches. However, he had Arsenal versus Aston Villa to watch before he needed to leave; painkillers, cigarettes, bacon and bread.

Preoccupied with his own comfort, a mixture of football and murder on his mind, it did not occur to Strike to glance down into the snowy street where shoppers, undeterred by the freezing weather, were gliding in and out of the music stores, the instrument makers and the cafés. Had he done so, he might have seen the willowy, hooded figure in the black coat leaning against the wall between numbers six and eight, staring up at his flat. Good though his eyesight was, however, he would have been unlikely to spot the Stanley knife being turned rhythmically between long, fine fingers.

32

Rise my good angel,
Whose holy tunes beat from me that evil spirit
Which jogs mine elbow . . .

Thomas Dekker, *The Noble Spanish Soldier*

Even with snow chains on its tyres the old family Land Rover driven by Robin's mother had had a hard job of it between York station and Masham. The wipers made fan-shaped windows, swiftly obliterated, onto roads familiar to Robin since childhood, now transformed by the worst winter she had seen in many years. The snow was relentless and the journey, which should have taken an hour, lasted nearly three. There had been moments when Robin had thought she might yet miss the funeral. At least she had been able to speak to Matthew on her mobile, explaining that she was close. He had told her that several others were still miles away, that he was afraid his aunt from Cambridge might not make it at all.

At home Robin had dodged the slobbering welcome of their old chocolate Labrador and hurtled upstairs to her room, pulling on the black dress and coat without bothering to iron them, laddering her first pair of tights in her haste, then running back downstairs to the hall where her parents and brothers were waiting for her.

They walked together through the swirling snow beneath black umbrellas, up the gentle hill Robin had climbed every day of her primary school years and across the wide square that was the ancient heart of her tiny home town, their backs to the giant chimney of the local brewery. The Saturday market had been cancelled. Deep channels had been made in the snow by those few brave souls who had crossed the square that morning, footprints converging near the church where Robin could see a crowd of black-coated mourners. The roofs of the pale gold Georgian houses lining the square wore mantels of bright, frozen icing, and still the snow kept coming. A rising sea of white was steadily burying the large square tombstones in the cemetery.

Robin shivered as the family edged towards the doors of St Mary the Virgin, past the remnant of a ninth-century round-shafted cross that had a curiously pagan appearance, and then, at last, she saw Matthew, standing in the porch with his father and sister, pale and heart-stoppingly handsome in his black suit. As Robin watched, trying to catch his eye over the queue, a young woman reached up and embraced him. Robin recognised Sarah Shadlock, Matthew's old friend from university. Her greeting was a little more lascivious, perhaps, than was appropriate in the circumstances, but Robin's guilt about having come within ten seconds of missing the overnight train, about not having seen Matthew in nearly a week, made her feel she had no right to resent it.

'Robin,' he said urgently when he saw her and he forgot to shake three people's hands as he held out his arms to her. As they hugged she felt tears prickle beneath her eyelids. This was real life, after all, Matthew and home . . .

'Go and sit at the front,' he told her and she obeyed, leaving her family at the back of the church to sit in the front pew with Matthew's brother-in-law, who was dandling his baby daughter on his knee and greeted Robin with a morose nod.

It was a beautiful old church and Robin knew it well from the Christmas, Easter and harvest services she had attended all her life with her primary school and family. Her eyes travelled slowly from familiar object to familiar object. High above her over the chancel arch was a painting by Sir Joshua Reynolds (or, at the very least, the *school* of Joshua Reynolds) and she fixed upon it, trying to compose her mind. A misty, mystical image, the boy-angel contemplating the distant vision of a cross emitting golden rays ... Who had really done it, she wondered, Reynolds or some studio acolyte? And then she felt guilty that she was indulging her perennial curiosity instead of feeling sad about Mrs Cunliffe ...

She had thought that she would be marrying here in a few weeks' time. Her wedding dress was hanging ready in the spare room's wardrobe, but instead, here was Mrs Cunliffe's coffin coming up the aisle, shining black with silver handles, Owen Quine still in the morgue ... no shiny coffin for his disembowelled body yet, rotted and burned ...

Don't think about that, she told herself sternly as Matthew sat down beside her, the length of his leg warm against hers.

The last twenty-four hours had been so packed with incident that it was hard for Robin to believe she was here, at home. She and Strike might have been in hospital, they had come close to slamming head first into that overturned lorry ... the driver covered in blood ... Mrs Cunliffe was probably unscathed in her silk-lined box ... *Don't think about that ...*

It was as though her eyes were being stripped of a comfortable soft focus. Maybe seeing things like bound and disembowelled bodies did something to you, changed the way you saw the world.

She knelt a little late for prayer, the cross-stitched hassock rough beneath her freezing knees. *Poor Mrs Cunliffe* . . . except that Matthew's mother had never much liked her. *Be kind*, Robin implored herself, even though it was true. Mrs Cunliffe had not liked the idea of Matthew being tied to the same girlfriend for so long. She had mentioned, within Robin's hearing, how good it was for young men to play the field, sow their wild oats ... The way in which Robin had left university had tainted her, she knew, in Mrs Cunliffe's eyes.

The statue of Sir Marmaduke Wyvill was facing Robin from mere feet away. As she stood for the hymn he seemed to be staring at her in his Jacobean dress, life-sized and horizontal on his marble shelf, propped up on his elbow to face the congregation. His wife lay beneath him in an identical pose. They were oddly real in their irreverent poses, cushions beneath their elbows to keep their marble bones comfortable, and above them, in the spandrels, allegorical figures of death and mortality. *Till death do us part* . . . and her thoughts drifted again: she and Matthew, tied together for ever until they died ... *no, not tied* ... *don't think tied* ... *What's wrong with you?* She was exhausted. The train had been overheated and jerky. She had woken on the hour, afraid that it would get stuck in the snow.

Matthew reached for her hand and squeezed her fingers.

The burial took place as quickly as decency allowed, the snow falling thick around them. There was no lingering at the graveside; Robin was not the only one perceptibly shivering.

Everyone went back to the Cunliffes' big brick house and

milled around in the welcome warmth. Mr Cunliffe, who was always a little louder than the occasion warranted, kept filling glasses and greeting people as though it were a party.

'I've missed you,' Matthew said. 'It's been horrible without you.'

'Me too,' said Robin. 'I wish I could have been here.'

Lying again.

'Auntie Sue's staying tonight,' said Matthew. 'I thought I could maybe come over to your place, be good to get away for a bit. It's been full on this week . . . '

'Great, yes,' said Robin, squeezing his hand, grateful that she would not have to stay at the Cunliffes'. She found Matthew's sister hard work and Mr Cunliffe overbearing.

But you could have put up with it for a night, she told herself sternly. It felt like an undeserved escape.

And so they returned to the Ellacotts' house, a short walk from the square. Matthew liked her family; he was glad to change out of his suit into jeans, to help her mother lay the kitchen table for dinner. Mrs Ellacott, an ample woman with Robin's red-gold hair tucked up in an untidy bun, treated him with gentle kindness; she was a woman of many interests and enthusiasms, currently doing an Open University degree in English Literature.

'How're the studies going, Linda?' Matthew asked as he lifted the heavy casserole dish out of the oven for her.

'We're doing Webster, *The Duchess of Malfi*: "And I am grown mad with 't."'

'Difficult, is it?' asked Matthew.

'That's a quotation, love. Oh,' she dropped the serving spoons onto the side with a clatter, 'that reminds me – I bet I've missed it—'

She crossed the kitchen and snatched up a copy of the *Radio Times*, always present in their house.

'No, it's on at nine. There's an interview with Michael Fancourt I want to watch.'

'Michael Fancourt?' said Robin, looking round. 'Why?'

'He's very influenced by all those Revenge Tragedians,' said her mother. 'I'm hoping he'll explain the appeal.'

'Seen this?' said Robin's youngest brother, Jonathan, fresh back from the corner shop with the extra milk requested by his mother. 'It's on the front page, Rob. That writer with his guts ripped out—'

'Jon!' said Mrs Ellacott sharply.

Robin knew that her mother was not reprimanding her son out of any suspicion that Matthew would not appreciate mention of her job, but because of a more general aversion to discussing sudden death in the aftermath of the burial.

'What?' said Jonathan, oblivious to the proprieties, shoving the *Daily Express* under Robin's nose.

Quine had made the front page now that the press knew what had been done to him.

HORROR AUTHOR WROTE OWN MURDER.

Horror author, Robin thought, *he was hardly that . . . but it makes a good headline.*

'Is your boss gonna solve it, d'you reckon?' Jonathan asked her, thumbing through the paper. 'Show up the Met again?'

She began to read the account over Jonathan's shoulder, but caught Matthew's eye and moved away.

A buzzing issued from Robin's handbag, discarded in a sagging chair in the corner of the flagged kitchen, as they ate their meal of stew and baked potatoes. She ignored it. Only when they had finished eating and Matthew was dutifully helping her mother clear the table did Robin wander to her bag to check her messages. To her great surprise she saw a missed call from Strike. With a surreptitious glance at Matthew, who was busily stacking plates in the dishwasher, she called voicemail while the others chatted.

You have one new message. Received today at seven twenty p.m.

The crackle of an open line, but no speech.

Then a thud. A yell in the distance from Strike:

'No you don't, you fucking—'

A bellow of pain.

Silence. The crackle of the open line. Indeterminate crunching, dragging sounds. Loud panting, a scraping noise, the line dead.

Robin stood aghast, the phone pressed against her ear.

'What's the matter?' asked her father, glasses halfway down his nose as he paused on the way to the dresser, knives and forks in his hand.

'I think – I think my boss has – has had an accident—'

She pressed Strike's number with shaking fingers. The call went straight to voicemail. Matthew was standing in the middle of the kitchen watching her, his displeasure undisguised.

33

Hard fate when women are compell'd to woo!

Thomas Dekker and Thomas Middleton,
The Honest Whore

Strike did not hear Robin calling because, unbeknownst to him, his mobile had been knocked onto silent when it had hit the ground fifteen minutes previously. Nor was he aware that his thumb had hit Robin's number as the phone slipped through his fingers.

He had only just left his building when it happened. The door onto the street had swung shut behind him and he had had two seconds, with his mobile in his hand (waiting for a ring-back from the cab he had reluctantly ordered) when the tall figure in the black coat had come running at him through the darkness. A blur of pale skin beneath a hood and a scarf, her arm outstretched, inexpert but determined, with the knife pointing directly at him in a wavering clutch.

Bracing himself to meet her he had almost slipped again but, slamming his hand to the door, he steadied himself and the mobile fell. Shocked and furious with her, whoever she was, for the damage her pursuit had already done to his knee he bellowed – she checked for a split-second, then came at him once more.

As he swung his stick at the hand in which he had already seen the Stanley knife his knee twisted again. He let out a roar of pain and she leapt back, as though she had stabbed him without knowing it, and then, for the second time, she had panicked and taken flight, sprinting away through the snow leaving a furious and frustrated Strike unable to give chase, and with no choice but to scrabble around in the snow for his phone.

Fuck this leg!

When Robin called him he was sitting in a crawling taxi, sweating with pain. It was small consolation that the tiny triangular blade he had seen glinting in his pursuer's hand had not pierced him. His knee, to which he had felt obliged to fit the prosthesis before setting out for Nina's, was excruciating once more and he was burning with rage at his inability to give chase to his mad stalker. He had never hit a woman, never knowingly hurt one, but the sight of the knife coming at him through the dark had rendered such scruples void. To the consternation of the taxi driver, who was watching his large, furious-looking passenger in the rear-view mirror, Strike kept twisting in his seat in case he saw her walking along the busy Saturday-night pavements, round-shouldered in her black coat, her knife concealed in her pocket.

The cab was gliding beneath the Christmas lights of Oxford Street, large, fragile parcels of silver wrapped with golden bows, and Strike fought his ruffled temper as they travelled, feeling no pleasure at the thought of his imminent dinner date. Again and again Robin called him, but he could not feel the mobile vibrating because it was deep in his coat pocket, which lay beside him on the seat.

'Hi,' said Nina with a forced smile when she opened the door to her flat half an hour after the agreed time.

'Sorry I'm late,' said Strike, limping over the threshold. 'I had an accident leaving the house. My leg.'

He had not brought her anything, he realised, standing there in his overcoat. He should have brought wine or chocolates and he felt her notice it as her big eyes roved over him; she had good manners herself and he felt, suddenly, a little shabby.

'And I've forgotten the wine I bought you,' he lied. 'This is crap. Chuck me out.'

As she laughed, though unwillingly, Strike felt the phone vibrate in his pocket and automatically pulled it out.

Robin. He could not think why she wanted him on a Saturday.

'Sorry,' he told Nina, 'gotta take this – urgent, it's my assistant—'

Her smile slipped. She turned and walked out of the hall, leaving him there in his coat.

'Robin?'

'Are you all right? What happened?'

'How did you—?'

'I've got a voicemail that sounds like a recording of you being attacked!'

'Christ, did I call you? Must've been when I dropped the phone. Yeah, that's exactly what it was—'

Five minutes later, having told Robin what had happened, he hung up his coat and followed his nose to the sitting room, where Nina had laid a table for two. The room was lamp-lit; she had tidied, put fresh flowers around the place. A strong smell of burnt garlic hung in the air.

'Sorry,' he repeated as she returned carrying a dish. 'Wish I had a nine-to-five job sometimes.'

'Help yourself to wine,' she said coolly.

The situation was deeply familiar. How often had he sat opposite a woman who was irritated by his lateness, his divided attention, his casualness? But here, at least, it was being played out in a minor key. If he had been late for dinner with Charlotte and taken a call from another woman as soon as he had arrived he might have expected a face full of wine and flying crockery. That thought made him feel more kindly towards Nina.

'Detectives make shit dates,' he told her as he sat down.

'I wouldn't say "shit",' she replied, softening. 'I don't suppose it's the sort of job you can leave behind.'

She was watching him with her huge mouse-like eyes.

'I had a nightmare about you last night,' she said.

'Getting off to a flying start, aren't we?' said Strike, and she laughed.

'Well, not really about you. We were together looking for Owen Quine's intestinal tract.'

She took a big swig of wine, gazing at him.

'Did we find it?' Strike asked, trying to keep things light.

'Yes.'

'Where? I'll take any leads at this point.'

'In Jerry Waldegrave's bottom desk drawer,' said Nina and he thought he saw her repress a shudder. 'It was horrible, actually. Blood and guts when I opened it . . . and you hit Jerry. It woke me up, it was so real.'

She drank more wine, not touching her food. Strike, who had already taken several hearty mouthfuls (far too much garlic, but he was hungry), felt he was being insufficiently sympathetic. He swallowed hastily and said:

'Sounds creepy.'

'It's because of what was on the news yesterday,' she said, watching him. 'Nobody realised, nobody knew he'd – he'd been killed like that. Like *Bombyx Mori*. You didn't tell me,' she said, and a whiff of accusation reached him through the garlic fumes.

'I couldn't,' said Strike. 'It's up to the police to release that kind of information.'

'It's on the front page of the *Daily Express* today. He'd have liked that, Owen. Being a headline. But I wish I hadn't read it,' she said, with a furtive look at him.

He had met these qualms before. Some people recoiled once they realised what he had seen, or done, or touched. It was as though he carried the smell of death on him. There were always women who were attracted by the soldier, the policeman: they experienced a vicarious thrill, a voluptuous appreciation at the violence a man might have seen or perpetrated. Other women were repelled. Nina, he suspected, had been one of the former, but now that the reality of cruelty, sadism and sickness had been forced on her she was discovering that she might, after all, belong in the second camp.

'It wasn't fun at work yesterday,' she said. 'Not after we heard that. Everyone was . . . It's just, if he was killed that way, if the killer copied the book . . . It limits the possible suspects, doesn't it? Nobody's laughing about *Bombyx Mori* any more, I can tell you that. It's like one of Michael Fancourt's old plots, back when the critics said he was too grisly . . . And Jerry's resigned.'

'I heard.'

'I don't know why,' she said restlessly. 'He's been at Roper Chard ages. He's not being himself at all. Angry all the time, and he's usually so lovely. And he's drinking again. A lot.'

She was still not eating.

'Was he close to Quine?' Strike asked.

'I think he was closer than he thought he was,' said Nina slowly. 'They'd worked together quite a long time. Owen drove him mad – Owen drove everyone mad – but Jerry's really upset, I can tell.'

'I can't imagine Quine enjoying being edited.'

'I think he was tricky sometimes,' said Nina, 'but Jerry won't hear a word against Owen now. He's obsessed by his breakdown theory. You heard him at the party, he thinks Owen was mentally ill and *Bombyx Mori* wasn't really his fault. And he's still *raging* against Elizabeth Tassel for letting the book out. She came in the other day to talk about one of her other authors—'

'Dorcus Pengelly?' Strike asked, and Nina gave a little gasp of laughter.

'You don't read that crap! Heaving bosoms and shipwrecks?'

'The name stuck in my mind,' said Strike, grinning. 'Go on about Waldegrave.'

'He saw Liz coming and slammed his office door as she walked past. You've seen it, it's glass and he nearly broke it. Really unnecessary and obvious, it made everyone jump out of their skins. She looks ghastly,' added Nina. 'Liz Tassel. Awful. If she'd been on form, she'd have stormed into Jerry's office and told him not to be so bloody rude—'

'Would she?'

'Are you crazy? Liz Tassel's temper is legendary.'

Nina glanced at her watch.

'Michael Fancourt's being interviewed on the telly this evening; I'm recording it,' she said, re-filling both their glasses. She still had not touched her food.

'Wouldn't mind watching that,' said Strike.

She threw him an oddly calculating look and Strike guessed that she was trying to assess how much his presence was due to a desire to pick her brains, how much designs on her slim, boyish body.

His mobile rang again. For several seconds he weighed the offence he might cause if he answered it, versus the possibility that it might herald something more useful than Nina's opinions about Jerry Waldegrave.

'Sorry,' he said and pulled it out of his pocket. It was his brother, Al.

'Corm!' said the voice over a noisy line. 'Great to hear from you, bruv!'

'Hi,' said Strike repressively. 'How are you?'

'Great! I'm in New York, only just got your message. What d'you need?'

He knew that Strike would only call if he wanted something, but unlike Nina, Al did not seem to resent the fact.

'Wondering if you fancied dinner this Friday,' said Strike, 'but if you're in New York—'

'I'm coming back Wednesday, that'd be cool. Want me to book somewhere?'

'Yeah,' said Strike. 'It's got to be the River Café.'

'I'll get on it,' said Al without asking why: perhaps he assumed that Strike merely had a yen for good Italian. 'Text you the time, yeah? Look forward to it!'

Strike hung up, the first syllable of an apology already on his lips, but Nina had left for the kitchen. The atmosphere had undoubtedly curdled.

34

O Lord! what have I said? my unlucky tongue!

William Congreve, *Love for Love*

'Love is a mirage,' said Michael Fancourt on the television screen. 'A mirage, a chimera, a delusion.'

Robin was sitting between Matthew and her mother on the faded, sagging sofa. The chocolate Labrador lay on the floor in front of the fire, his tail thumping lazily on the rug in his sleep. Robin felt drowsy after two nights of very little sleep and days of unexpected stresses and emotion, but she was trying hard to concentrate on Michael Fancourt. Beside her Mrs Ellacott, who had expressed the optimistic hope that Fancourt might let drop some bons mots that would help with her essay on Webster, had a notebook and pen on her lap.

'Surely,' began the interviewer, but Fancourt talked over him.

'We don't love each other; we love the *idea* we have of each other. Very few humans understand this or can bear to contemplate it. They have blind faith in their own powers of creation. All love, ultimately, is self-love.'

Mr Ellacott was asleep, his head back in the armchair closest to the fire and the dog. Gently he snored, with his spectacles halfway down his nose. All three of Robin's brothers had slid discreetly from the house. It was Saturday night and their mates were waiting in the Bay Horse on the square. Jon had come home from university for the funeral but did not feel he owed it to his sister's fiancé to forgo a few pints of Black Sheep with his brothers, sitting at the dimpled copper tables by the open fire.

Robin suspected that Matthew had wanted to join them but that he had felt it would be unseemly. Now he was stuck watching a literary programme he would never have tolerated at home. He would have turned over without asking her, taking it for granted that she could not possibly be interested in what this sour-looking, sententious man was saying. It was not easy to like Michael Fancourt, thought Robin. The curve of both his lip and his eyebrows implied an ingrained sense of superiority. The presenter, who was well known, seemed a little nervous.

'And that is the theme of your new—?'

'One of the themes, yes. Rather than castigating himself for his foolishness when the hero realises that he has simply imagined his wife into being, he seeks to punish the flesh-and-blood woman whom he believes has duped him. His desire for revenge drives the plot.'

'Aha,' said Robin's mother softly, picking up her pen.

'Many of us – most, perhaps,' said the interviewer, 'consider love a purifying ideal, a source of selflessness rather than—'

'A self-justifying lie,' said Fancourt. 'We are mammals who need sex, need companionship, who seek the protective enclave of the family for reasons of survival and reproduction. We select a so-called loved one for the most primitive reasons – my hero's preference for a pear-shaped woman is self-explanatory, I think. The loved one laughs or smells like the parent who gave one youthful succour and all else is projected, all else is invented—'

'Friendship—' began the interviewer a little desperately.

'If I could have brought myself to have sex with any of my male friends, I would have had a happier and more productive life,' said Fancourt. 'Unfortunately, I'm programmed to desire the female form, however fruitlessly. And so I tell myself that one woman is more fascinating, more attuned to my needs and desires, than another. I am a complex, highly evolved and imaginative creature who feels compelled to justify a choice made on the crudest grounds. This is the truth that we've buried under a thousand years of courtly bullshit.'

Robin wondered what on earth Fancourt's wife (for she seemed to remember that he was married) would make of this interview. Beside her, Mrs Ellacott had written a few words on her notepad.

'He's not talking about revenge,' Robin muttered.

Her mother showed her the notepad. She had written: What a shit he is. Robin giggled.

Beside her, Matthew leaned over to the *Daily Express* that Jonathan had left abandoned on a chair. He turned past the front three pages, where Strike's name appeared several times in the text alongside Owen Quine's, and began to read a piece on how a high street chain of stores had banned Cliff Richard's Christmas songs.

'You've been criticised,' said the interviewer bravely, 'for your depiction of women, most particularly—'

'I can hear the critics' cockroach-like scurrying for their pens as we speak,' said Fancourt, his lip curling in what passed for a smile. 'I can think of little that interests me less than what critics say about me or my work.'

Matthew turned a page of the paper. Robin glanced sideways

at a picture of an overturned tanker, an upside-down Honda Civic and a mangled Mercedes.

'That's the crash we were nearly in!'

'What?' said Matthew.

She had said it without thinking. Robin's brain froze.

'That happened on the M4,' Matthew said, half laughing at her for thinking she could have been involved, that she could not recognise a motorway when she saw one.

'Oh – oh yes,' said Robin, pretending to peer more closely at the text beneath the picture.

But he was frowning now, catching up.

'*Were* you nearly in a car crash yesterday?'

He was speaking quietly, trying not to disturb Mrs Ellacott, who was following Fancourt's interview. Hesitation was fatal. Choose.

'Yes, I was. I didn't want to worry you.'

He stared at her. On Robin's other side she could feel her mother making more notes.

'This one?' he said, pointing at the picture, and she nodded. 'Why were you on the M4?'

'I had to drive Cormoran to an interview.'

'I'm thinking of women,' said the interviewer, 'your views on women—'

'Where the hell was the interview?'

'Devon,' said Robin.

'*Devon?*'

'He's buggered his leg again. He couldn't have got there by himself.'

'You drove him to *Devon*?'

'Yes, Matt, I drove him to—'

'So that's why you didn't come up yesterday? So you could—'

'Matt, of course not.'

He flung down the paper, pulled himself up and strode from the room.

Robin felt sick. She looked around at the door, which he had not slammed, but closed firmly enough to make her father stir and mutter in his sleep and the Labrador wake up.

'Leave him,' advised her mother, her eyes still on the screen.

Robin swung round, desperate.

'Cormoran had to get to Devon and he couldn't drive with only one leg—'

'There's no need to defend yourself to *me*,' said Mrs Ellacott.

'But now he thinks I lied about not being able to get home yesterday.'

'*Did* you?' her mother asked, her eyes still fixed beadily upon Michael Fancourt. 'Get *down*, Rowntree, I can't see over you.'

'Well, I could've come if I'd got a first-class ticket,' Robin admitted as the Labrador yawned, stretched and resettled himself on the hearthrug. 'But I'd already paid for the sleeper.'

'Matt's always going on about how much more money you would have made if you'd taken that HR job,' said her mother, her eyes on the TV screen. 'I'd have thought he'd appreciate you saving the pennies. Now shush, I want to hear about revenge.'

The interviewer was trying to formulate a question.

'But where women are concerned, you haven't always – contemporary *mores*, so-called political correctness – I'm thinking particularly of your assertion that female writers—'

'This *again*?' said Fancourt, slapping his knees with his hands (the interviewer perceptibly jumped). 'I said that the greatest female writers, with almost no exceptions, have been childless. A fact. And I have said that women generally, by virtue of their desire to mother, are incapable of the necessarily single-minded focus anyone must bring to the creation of literature, *true* literature. I don't retract a word. That is a *fact*.'

Robin was twisting her engagement ring on her finger, torn between her desire to follow Matt and persuade him she had done nothing wrong and anger that any such persuasion should be required. The demands of *his* job came first, always; she had never known him apologise for late hours, for jobs that took him to the far side of London and brought him home at eight o'clock at night . . .

'I was going to say,' the interviewer hurried on, with an ingratiating smile, 'that this book might give those critics pause. I thought the central female character was treated with great understanding, with real empathy. Of course' – he glanced down at his notes and up again; Robin could feel his nerves – 'parallels are bound to be drawn – in dealing with the suicide of a young woman, I expect you're braced – you must be expecting—'

'That stupid people will assume that I have written an autobiographical account of my first wife's suicide?'

'Well, it's bound to be seen as – it's bound to raise questions—'

'Then let me say this,' said Fancourt, and paused.

They were sitting in front of a long window looking out onto a sunny, windswept lawn. Robin wondered fleetingly when the programme had been filmed – before the snows had come, clearly – but Matthew dominated her thoughts. She ought to go and find him, yet somehow she remained on the sofa.

'When Eff – Ellie died,' began Fancourt, 'when she died—'

The close-up felt painfully intrusive. The tiny lines at the corners of his eyes deepened as he closed them; a square hand flew to conceal his face.

Michael Fancourt appeared to be crying.

'So much for love being a mirage and a chimera,' sighed Mrs Ellacott as she tossed down her pen. 'This is no good. I wanted blood and guts, Michael. *Blood and guts.*'

Unable to stand inaction any longer, Robin got up and headed for the sitting-room door. These were not normal circumstances. Matthew's mother had been buried that day. It behoved her to apologise, to make amends.

35

We are all liable to mistakes, sir; if you own it to be so, there needs no farther apology.

William Congreve, *The Old Bachelor*

The Sunday broadsheets next day strove to find a dignified balance between an objective assessment of Owen Quine's life and work and the macabre, Gothic nature of his death.

'A minor literary figure, occasionally interesting, tipping latterly into self-parody, eclipsed by his contemporaries but continuing to blaze his own outmoded trail,' said the *Sunday Times* in a front-page column that led to a promise of much more excitement within: *A sadist's blueprint: see pages 10–11* and, beside a thumbnail photograph of Kenneth Halliwell: *Books and Bookmen: literary killers p. 3 Culture.*

'Rumours about the unpublished book that allegedly inspired his murder are now spreading beyond London's literary circles,' the *Observer* assured its readers. 'Were it not for the dictates of good taste, Roper Chard would have an instant bestseller on its hands.'

KINKY WRITER DISEMBOWELLED IN SEX GAME, declared the *Sunday People*.

Strike had bought every paper on his way home from Nina

Lascelles's, difficult though it was to manage them all and his stick over snowy pavements. It occurred to him as he struggled towards Denmark Street that he was unwisely encumbered, should his would-be assailant of the previous evening reappear, but she was nowhere to be seen.

Later that evening he worked his way through the news stories while eating chips, lying on his bed with his prosthetic leg mercifully removed once more.

Viewing the facts through the press's distorting lens was stimulating to his imagination. At last, having finished Culpepper's piece in the *News of the World* ('Sources close to the story confirm that Quine liked to be tied up by his wife, who denies that she knew the kinky writer had gone to stay in their second home') Strike slid the papers off his bed, reached for the notebook he kept by his bed and scribbled himself a list of reminders for the following day. He did not add Anstis's initial to any of the tasks or questions, but *bookshop man* and *MF when filmed?* were both followed by a capital *R*. He then texted Robin, reminding her to keep her eyes peeled for a tall woman in a black coat the following morning and not to enter Denmark Street if she was there.

Robin saw nobody answering that description on her short journey from the Tube and arrived at the office at nine o'clock next morning to find Strike sitting at her desk and using her computer.

'Morning. No nutters outside?'

'No one,' said Robin, hanging up her coat.

'How's Matthew?'

'Fine,' lied Robin.

The aftermath of their row about her decision to drive Strike to Devon clung to her like fumes. The argument had simmered and erupted repeatedly all through their car journey back to Clapham; her eyes were still puffy from crying and lack of sleep.

'Tough for him,' muttered Strike, still frowning at the monitor. 'His mother's funeral.'

'Mm,' said Robin, moving to fill the kettle and feeling annoyed that Strike chose to empathise with Matthew today, exactly when she would have welcomed an assurance that he was an unreasonable prick.

'What are you looking at?' she asked, setting a mug of tea at Strike's elbow, for which he gave her muttered thanks.

'Trying to find out when Michael Fancourt's interview was filmed,' he said. 'He was on telly on Saturday night.'

'I watched that,' said Robin.

'Me too,' said Strike.

'Arrogant prat,' said Robin, sitting down on the mock-leather sofa, which for some reason did not emit farting noises when she did it. Perhaps, Strike thought, it was his weight.

'Notice anything funny when he was talking about his late wife?' Strike asked.

'The crocodile tears were a bit much,' said Robin, 'seeing how he'd just been explaining how love's an illusion and all that rubbish.'

Strike glanced at her again. She had the kind of fair, delicate complexion that suffered from excess emotion; the swollen eyes told their own story. Some of her animosity towards Michael Fancourt, he guessed, might be displaced from another and perhaps more deserving target.

'Thought he was faking, did you?' Strike asked. 'Me too.'

He glanced at his watch.

'I've got Caroline Ingles arriving in half an hour.'

'I thought she and her husband had reconciled?'

'Old news. She wants to see me, something about a text she found on his phone over the weekend. So,' said Strike, heaving himself up from the desk, 'I need you to keep trying to find out when that interview was filmed, while I go and look over the case notes so I look like I can remember what the hell she's on about. Then I've got lunch with Quine's editor.'

'And I've got some news about what the doctor's surgery outside Kathryn Kent's flat does with medical waste,' said Robin.

'Go on,' said Strike.

'A specialist company collects it every Tuesday. I contacted them,' said Robin and Strike could tell by her sigh that the line of enquiry was about to fizzle out, 'and they didn't notice anything odd or unusual about the bags they collected the Tuesday after the murder. I suppose,' she said, 'it was a bit unrealistic, thinking they wouldn't notice a bag of human intestines. They told me it's usually just swabs and needles, and they're all sealed up in special bags.'

'Had to check it out, though,' said Strike bracingly. 'That's good detective work – cross off all the possibilities. Anyway, there's something else I need doing, if you can face the snow.'

'I'd love to get out,' said Robin, brightening at once. 'What is it?'

'That man in the bookshop in Putney who reckons he saw Quine on the eighth,' said Strike. 'He should be back off his holidays.'

'No problem,' said Robin.

She had not had an opportunity over the weekend to discuss with Matthew the fact that Strike wished to give her investigative training. It would have been the wrong time before the funeral, and after their row on Saturday night would have seemed provocative, even inflammatory. Today she yearned to get out onto the streets, to investigate, to probe, and to go home and tell Matthew matter-of-factly what she had done. He wanted honesty, she would give him honesty.

Caroline Ingles, who was a worn-out blonde, spent over an hour in Strike's office that morning. When finally she had departed, looking tear-stained but determined, Robin had news for Strike.

'That interview with Fancourt was filmed on the seventh of November,' she said. 'I phoned the BBC. Took ages, but got there in the end.'

'The seventh,' repeated Strike. 'That was a Sunday. Where was it filmed?'

'A film crew went down to his house in Chew Magna,' said Robin. 'What did you notice on the interview that's making you this interested?'

'Watch it again,' said Strike. 'See if you can get it on YouTube. Surprised you didn't spot it at the time.'

Stung, she remembered Matthew beside her, interrogating her about the crash on the M4.

'I'm going to change for Simpson's,' said Strike. 'We'll lock up and leave together, shall we?'

They parted forty minutes later at the Tube, Robin heading for the Bridlington Bookshop in Putney, Strike for the restaurant on the Strand, to which he intended to walk.

'Spent way too much on taxis lately,' he told Robin gruffly, unwilling to tell her how much it had cost him to take care of the Toyota Land Cruiser with which he had been stranded on Friday night. 'Plenty of time.'

She watched him for a few seconds as he walked away from her, leaning heavily on his stick and limping badly. An observant childhood spent in the company of three brothers had given Robin an unusual and accurate insight into the frequently contrary reaction of males to female concern, but she wondered how much longer Strike could force his knee to support him before he found himself incapacitated for longer than a few days.

It was almost lunchtime and the two women opposite Robin on the train to Waterloo were chatting loudly, carrier bags full of Christmas shopping between their knees. The floor of the Tube was wet and dirty and the air full, again, of damp cloth and stale bodies. Robin spent most of her journey trying without success to view clips of Michael Fancourt's interview on her mobile phone.

The Bridlington Bookshop stood on a main road in Putney, its old-fashioned paned windows crammed from top to bottom with a mixture of new and second-hand books, all stacked horizontally. A bell tinkled as Robin crossed the threshold into a pleasant, mildewed atmosphere. A couple of ladders stood propped against shelves crammed with more horizontally piled books reaching all the way to the ceiling. Hanging bulbs lit the space, dangling so low that Strike would have banged his head.

'Good morning!' said an elderly gentleman in an over-large tweed jacket, emerging with almost audible creaks from an office with a dimpled glass door. As he approached, Robin caught a strong whiff of body odour.

She had already planned her simple line of enquiry and asked at once whether he had any Owen Quine in stock.

'Ah! Ah!' he said knowingly. 'I needn't ask, I think, why the sudden interest!'

A self-important man in the common fashion of the unworldly and cloistered, he embarked without invitation into a lecture on Quine's style and declining readability as he led her into the depths of the shop. He appeared convinced, after two seconds' acquaintance, that Robin could only be asking for a copy of one of Quine's books because he had recently been murdered. While this was of course the truth, it irritated Robin.

'Have you got *The Balzac Brothers*?' she asked.

'You know better than to ask for *Bombyx Mori*, then,' he said, shifting a ladder with doddery hands. 'Three young journalists I've had in here, asking for it.'

'Why are journalists coming here?' asked Robin innocently as he began to climb the ladder, revealing an inch of mustard-coloured sock above his old brogues.

'Mr Quine shopped here shortly before he died,' said the old man, now peering at spines some six feet above Robin. '*Balzac Brothers*, *Balzac Brothers* . . . should be here . . . dear, dear, I'm sure I've got a copy . . .'

'He actually came in here, to your shop?' asked Robin.

'Oh yes. I recognised him instantly. I was a great admirer of Joseph North and they once appeared on the same bill at the Hay Festival.'

He was coming down the ladder now, feet trembling with every step. Robin was scared he might fall.

'I'll check the computer,' he said, breathing heavily. 'I'm sure I've got a *Balzac Brothers* here.'

Robin followed him, reflecting that if the last time the old man had set eyes on Owen Quine had been in the mid-eighties, his reliability in identifying the writer again might be questionable.

'I don't suppose you could miss him,' she said. 'I've seen pictures of him. Very distinctive-looking in his Tyrolean cloak.'

'His eyes are different colours,' said the old man, now gazing at the monitor of an early Macintosh Classic that must, Robin thought, be twenty years old: beige, boxy, big chunky keys like cubes of toffee. 'You see it close up. One hazel, one blue. I think the policeman was impressed by my powers of observation and recall. I was in intelligence during the war.'

He turned upon her with a self-satisfied smile.

'I was right, we *do* have a copy – second hand. This way.'

He shuffled towards an untidy bin full of books.

'That's a very important bit of information for the police,' said Robin, following him.

'Yes, indeed,' he said complacently. 'Time of death. Yes, I could assure them that he was alive, still, on the eighth.'

'I don't suppose you could remember what he came in here for,' said Robin with a small laugh. 'I'd love to know what he read.'

'Oh yes, I remember,' said her companion at once. 'He bought three novels: Jonathan Franzen's *Freedom*, Joshua Ferris's *The Unnamed* and . . . and I forget the third . . . told me he was going away for a break and wanted reading matter. We discussed the digital phenomenon – he more tolerant of reading devices than I . . . *somewhere* in here,' he muttered, raking in the bin. Robin joined the search half-heartedly.

'The eighth,' she repeated. 'How could you be so sure it was the eighth?'

For the days, she thought, must blend quite seamlessly into each other in this dim atmosphere of mildew.

'It was a Monday,' he said. 'A pleasant interlude, discussing Joseph North, of whom he had very fond memories.'

Robin was still none the wiser as to why he believed this particular Monday to have been the eighth, but before she could enquire further he had pulled an ancient paperback from the depths of the bin with a triumphant cry.

'There we are. There we are. I *knew* I had it.'

'I can never remember dates,' Robin lied as they returned to the till with their trophy. 'I don't suppose you've got any Joseph North, while I'm here?'

'There was only one,' said the old man. '*Towards the Mark*. Now, I know we've got that, one of my personal favourites . . . '

And he headed, once more, for the ladder.

'I confuse days all the time,' Robin soldiered on bravely as the mustard-coloured socks were revealed again.

'Many people do,' he said smugly, 'but I am an adept at reconstructive deduction, ha ha. I remembered that it was a Monday, because always on a Monday I buy fresh milk and I had just returned from doing so when Mr Quine arrived at the shop.'

She waited while he scanned the shelves above her head.

'I explained to the police that I was able to date the particular Monday precisely because that evening I went to my friend Charles's house, as I do most Mondays, but I distinctly remembered telling him about Owen Quine arriving in my bookshop *and* discussing the five Anglican bishops who had defected to Rome that day. Charles is a lay preacher in the Anglican Church. He felt it deeply.'

'I see,' said Robin, who was making a mental note to check the date of such a defection. The old man had found North's book and was slowly descending the ladder.

'Yes, and I remember,' he said, with a spurt of enthusiasm, 'Charles showed me some remarkable pictures of a sinkhole that appeared overnight in Schmalkalden, Germany. I was stationed near Schmalkalden during the war. Yes . . . that evening, I remember, my friend interrupted me telling him about Quine visiting the shop – his interest in writers is negligible – "Weren't you in Schmalkalden?" he said' – the frail, knobbly hands were busy at the till now – 'and he told me a huge crater had appeared . . . extraordinary pictures in the paper next day . . .

'Memory is a wonderful thing,' he said complacently, handing Robin a brown paper bag containing her two books and receiving her ten-pound note in exchange.

'I remember that sinkhole,' said Robin, which was another lie. She took her mobile out of her pocket and pressed a few buttons while he conscientiously counted change. 'Yes, here it is . . . Schmalkalden . . . how amazing, that huge hole appearing out of nowhere.

'But that happened,' she said, looking up at him, 'on the first of November, not the eighth.'

He blinked.

'No, it was the eighth,' he said, with all the conviction a profound dislike of being mistaken could muster.

'But see here,' said Robin, showing him the tiny screen; he pushed his glasses up his forehead to stare at it. 'You definitely remember discussing Owen Quine's visit and the sinkhole in the same conversation?'

'Some mistake,' he muttered, and whether he referred to the *Guardian* website, himself or Robin was unclear. He thrust her phone back at her.

'You don't remem—?'

'Is that all?' he said loudly, flustered. 'Then good day to you, good day.'

And Robin, recognising the stubbornness of an offended old egoist, took her leave to the tinkling of the bell.

36

> Mr Scandal, I shall be very glad to confer with you about these things which he has uttered – his sayings are very mysterious and hieroglyphical.
>
> William Congreve, *Love for Love*

Strike had thought that Simpson's-in-the-Strand was an odd place for Jerry Waldegrave to want to meet for lunch and his curiosity increased as he approached the imposing stone façade, with its revolving wooden doors, its brass plaques and hanging lantern. Chess motifs decorated the tiled surround of the entrance. He had never set foot there, aged London institution though it was. He had assumed it to be the home of well-heeled businessmen and out-of-towners treating themselves.

Yet Strike felt at home as soon as he set foot inside the lobby. Once an eighteenth-century gentleman's chess club, Simpson's spoke to Strike in an old and familiar language, of hierarchy, order and stately decorum. Here were the dark, sludgy clubland colours that men choose without reference to their womenfolk: thick marble columns and solid leather armchairs that would support a drunken dandy and, glimpsed beyond double doors, past the coat-check girl, a restaurant full of dark wood panelling.

He might have been back in one of the sergeants' messes he had frequented during his military career. All that was needed to make the place feel truly familiar were regimental colours and a portrait of the Queen.

Solid wood-backed chairs, snowy tablecloths, silver salvers on which enormous joints of beef reposed; as Strike sat down at a table for two beside the wall he found himself wondering what Robin would make of the place, whether she would be amused or irritated by its ostentatious traditionalism.

He had been seated for ten minutes before Waldegrave appeared, peering myopically around the dining room. Strike raised a hand and Waldegrave made his way with a shambling walk towards their table.

'Hello, hello. Nice to see you again.'

His light brown hair was as messy as ever and his crumpled jacket had a smear of toothpaste on the lapel. A faint gust of vinous fumes reached Strike across the small table.

'Good of you to see me,' said Strike.

'Not at all. Want to help. Hope you don't mind coming here. I chose it,' said Waldegrave, 'because we won't run into anyone I know. My father brought me here once, years ago. Don't think they've changed a thing.'

Waldegrave's round eyes, framed by his horn-rimmed glasses, travelled over the heavily moulded plasterwork at the top of the dark wood panelling. It was stained ochre, as though tarnished by long years of cigarette smoke.

'Get enough of your co-workers during office hours, do you?' Strike asked.

'Nothing wrong with them,' said Jerry Waldegrave, pushing his glasses up his nose and waving at a waiter, 'but the atmosphere's poisonous just now. Glass of red, please,' he told the young man who had answered his wave. 'I don't care, anything.'

But the waiter, on whose front a small knight chess piece was embroidered, answered repressively:

'I'll send over the wine waiter, sir,' and retreated.

'See the clock over the doors as you come in here?' Waldegrave asked Strike, pushing his glasses up his nose again. 'They say it stopped when the first woman came in here in 1984. Little in-joke. And on the menu, it says "bill of fare". They wouldn't use "menu", you see, because it was French. My father loved that stuff. I'd just got into Oxford, that's why he brought me here. He hated foreign food.'

Strike could feel Waldegrave's nervousness. He was used to having that effect on people. Now was not the moment to ask whether Waldegrave had helped Quine write the blueprint for his murder.

'What did you do at Oxford?'

'English,' said Waldegrave with a sigh. 'My father was putting a brave face on it; he wanted me to do medicine.'

The fingers of Waldegrave's right hand played an arpeggio on the tablecloth.

'Things tense at the office, are they?' asked Strike.

'You could say that,' replied Waldegrave, looking around again for the wine waiter. 'It's sinking in, now we know how Owen was killed. People erasing emails like idiots, pretending they never looked at the book, don't know how it ends. It's not so funny now.'

'Was it funny before?' asked Strike.

'Well . . . yeah, it was, when people thought Owen had just done a runner. People love seeing the powerful ridiculed, don't they? They aren't popular men, either of them, Fancourt and Chard.'

The wine waiter arrived and handed the list to Waldegrave.

'I'll get a bottle, shall I?' said Waldegrave, scanning it. 'I take it this is on you?'

'Yeah,' said Strike, not without trepidation.

Waldegrave ordered a bottle of Château Lezongars, which Strike saw with profound misgiving cost nearly fifty quid, though there were bottles on the list that cost nearly two hundred.

'So,' said Waldegrave with sudden bravado, as the wine waiter retreated, 'any leads yet? Know who did it?'

'Not yet,' said Strike.

An uncomfortable beat followed. Waldegrave pushed his glasses up his sweaty nose.

'Sorry,' he muttered. 'Crass – defence mechanism. It's – I can't believe it. I can't believe it happened.'

'No one ever can,' said Strike.

On a rush of confidence, Waldegrave said:

'I can't shake this mad bloody idea that Owen did it to himself. That he staged it.'

'Really?' said Strike, watching Waldegrave closely.

'I know he can't have done, I know that.' The editor's hands were playing a deft scale on the edge of the table now. 'It's so – so *theatrical*, how he was – how he was killed. So – so grotesque. And . . . the awful thing . . . best publicity any author ever got his book. God, Owen loved publicity. Poor Owen. He once told me – this isn't a joke – he once told me in all seriousness that he liked to get his girlfriend to interview him. Said it clarified his thought processes. I said, "What do you use as a mic?", taking the mickey, you know, and you know what the silly sod said? "Biros mostly. Whatever's around."'

Waldegrave burst into panting chuckles that sounded very like sobs.

'Poor bastard,' he said. 'Poor silly bastard. Lost it completely at the end, didn't he? Well, I hope Elizabeth Tassel's happy. Winding him up.'

Their original waiter returned with a notebook.

'What are you having?' the editor asked Strike, focusing short-sightedly on his bill of fare.

'The beef,' said Strike, who had had time to watch it being carved from the silver salver on a trolley that circulated the tables. He had not had Yorkshire pudding in years; not, in fact, since the last time he had gone back to St Mawes to see his aunt and uncle.

Waldegrave ordered Dover sole, then craned his neck again to see whether the wine waiter was returning. When he caught sight of the man approaching with the bottle he noticeably relaxed, sinking more comfortably into his chair. His glass filled, he drank several mouthfuls before sighing like a man who had received urgent medical treatment.

'You were saying Elizabeth Tassel wound Quine up,' Strike said.

'Eh?' said Waldegrave, cupping his right hand around his ear.

Strike remembered his one-sided deafness. The restaurant was indeed filling up, becoming noisier. He repeated his question more loudly.

'Oh yeah,' said Waldegrave. 'Yeah, about Fancourt. The pair of them liked brooding on the wrongs Fancourt did them.'

'What wrongs?' asked Strike, and Waldegrave swigged more wine.

'Fancourt's been badmouthing them both for years.' Waldegrave scratched his chest absent-mindedly through his creased shirt and drank more wine. 'Owen, because of that parody of his dead wife's novel; Liz, because she stuck by Owen – mind you, nobody's ever blamed Fancourt for leaving Liz Tassel. The woman's a bitch. Down to about two clients now. Twisted. Probably spends her evenings working out how much she lost: fifteen per cent of Fancourt's royalties is big money. Booker dinners, film premieres . . . instead she gets Quine interviewing himself with a biro and burnt sausages in Dorcus Pengelly's back garden.'

'How do you know there were burnt sausages?' asked Strike.

'Dorcus told me,' said Waldegrave, who had already finished his first glass of wine and was pouring a second. 'She wanted to know why Liz wasn't at the firm's anniversary party. When I told her about *Bombyx Mori*, Dorcus assured me Liz was a lovely woman. *Lovely.* Couldn't have known what was in Owen's book. Never have hurt anyone's feelings – wouldn't hurt a bloody fly – ha!'

'You disagree?'

'Bloody right I disagree. I've met people who got their start in Liz Tassel's office. They talk like kidnap victims who've been ransomed. Bully. Scary temper.'

'You think she put Quine up to writing the book?'

'Well, not directly,' said Waldegrave. 'But you take a deluded writer who was convinced he wasn't a bestseller because people were jealous of him or not doing their jobs right and lock him in with Liz, who's always angry, bitter as sin, banging on about Fancourt doing them both down, and is it a surprise he gets wound up to fever pitch?

'She couldn't even be bothered to read his book properly. If he hadn't died, I'd say she got what she deserved. Silly mad bastard didn't just do over Fancourt, did he? Went after her as well, ha ha! Went after bloody Daniel, went after me, went after ev'ryone. *Ev'ryone.*'

In the manner of other alcoholics Strike had known, Jerry Waldegrave had crossed the line into drunkenness with two glasses of wine. His movements were suddenly clumsier, his manner more flamboyant.

'D'you think Elizabeth Tassel egged Quine on to attack Fancourt?'

'Not a doubt of it,' said Waldegrave. 'Not a doubt.'

'But when I met her, Elizabeth Tassel said that what Quine wrote about Fancourt was a lie,' Strike told Waldegrave.

'Eh?' said Waldegrave again, cupping his ear.

'She told me,' said Strike loudly, 'that what Quine writes in *Bombyx Mori* about Fancourt is false. That Fancourt didn't write the parody that made his wife kill herself – that Quine wrote it.'

'I'm not talking about *that*,' said Waldegrave, shaking his head as though Strike were being obtuse. 'I don't mean – forget it. Forget it.'

He was more than halfway down the bottle already; the alcohol had induced a degree of confidence. Strike held back, knowing that to push would only induce the granite stubbornness of the drunk. Better to let him drift where he wanted to go, keeping one light hand on the tiller.

'Owen liked me,' Waldegrave told Strike. 'Oh yeah. I knew how to handle him. Stoke that man's vanity and you could get him to do anything you wanted. Half an hour's praise before you asked him to change anything in a manuscript. 'Nother half hour's praise before you asked him to make another change. Only way.

'He didn't really wanna hurt me. Wasn't thinking straight,

silly bastard. Wanted to get back on the telly. Thought ev'ryone was against him. Didn't realise he was playing with fire. Mentally ill.'

Waldegrave slumped in his seat and the back of his head collided with that of a large overdressed woman sitting behind him. 'Sorry! Sorry!'

While she glared over her shoulder he pulled in his chair, causing the cutlery to rattle on the tablecloth.

'So what,' Strike asked, 'was the Cutter all about?'

'Huh?' said Waldegrave.

This time, Strike felt sure that the cupped ear was a pose.

'The Cutter—'

'Cutter: editor – obvious,' said Waldegrave.

'And the bloody sack and the dwarf you try and drown?'

'Symbolic,' said Waldegrave, with an airy wave of the hand that nearly upset his wine glass. 'Some idea of his I stifled, some bit of lovingly crafted prose I wanted to kill off. Hurt his feelings.'

Strike, who had heard a thousand rehearsed answers, found the response too pat, too fluent, too fast.

'Just that?'

'Well,' said Waldegrave, with a gasp of a laugh, 'I've never drowned a dwarf, if that's what you're implying.'

Drunks were always tricky interviewees. Back in the SIB, intoxicated suspects or witnesses had been a rarity. He remembered the alcoholic major whose twelve-year-old daughter had disclosed sexual abuse at her school in Germany. When Strike had arrived at the family house the major had taken a swing at him with a broken bottle. Strike had laid him out. But here in the civilian world, with the wine waiter hovering, this drunken, mild-mannered editor could choose to walk away and there would be nothing Strike could do about it. He could only hope for a chance to double back to the subject of the Cutter, to keep Waldegrave in his seat, to keep him talking.

The trolley now wended its stately way to Strike's side. A rib of Scottish beef was carved with ceremony while Waldegrave was presented with Dover sole.

No taxis for three months, Strike told himself sternly, salivating as his plate was heaped with Yorkshire puddings, potatoes and parsnips. The trolley trundled away again. Waldegrave, who was now two-thirds of the way down his bottle of wine, contemplated his fish as though he was not quite sure how it had ended up in front of him, and put a small potato in his mouth with his fingers.

'Did Quine discuss what he was writing with you, before he handed in his manuscripts?' asked Strike.

'Never,' said Waldegrave. 'The only thing he ever told me about *Bombyx Mori* was that the silkworm was a metaphor for the writer, who has to go through agonies to get at the good stuff. That was it.'

'He never asked for your advice or input?'

'No, no, Owen always thought he knew best.'

'Is that usual?'

'Writers vary,' said Waldegrave. 'But Owen was always up the secretive end of the scale. He liked the big reveal, you know. Appealed to his sense of drama.'

'Police will have asked you about your movements after you got the book, I suppose,' said Strike casually.

'Yeah, been through all that,' said Waldegrave indifferently. He was attempting, without much success, to prise spines out of the Dover sole he had recklessly asked to be left on the bone. 'Got the manuscript on Friday, didn't look at it until the Sunday—'

'You were meant to be away, weren't you?'

'Paris,' said Waldegrave. 'Anniversary weekend. Di'n't happen.'

'Something came up?'

Waldegrave emptied the last of the wine into his glass. Several drops of the dark liquid fell onto the white tablecloth and spread.

'Had a row, a bloody awful row, on the way to Heathrow. Turned round, went back home.'

'Rough,' said Strike.

'On the rocks for years,' said Waldegrave, abandoning his unequal struggle with the sole and throwing down his knife and fork with a clatter that made nearby diners look round. 'JoJo's grown up. No point any more. Splitting up.'

'I'm sorry to hear that,' said Strike.

Waldegrave shrugged lugubriously and took more wine. The lenses of his horn-rimmed glasses were covered in fingerprints and his shirt collar was grubby and frayed. He had the look, thought Strike, who was experienced in such matters, of a man who has slept in his clothes.

'You went straight home after the row, did you?'

''S a big house. No need to see each other if we don't want to.'

The drops of wine were spreading like crimson blossoms on the snowy tablecloth.

'Black spot, that's what this reminds me of,' said Waldegrave. '*Treasure Island*, y'know . . . black spot. Suspicion on everyone who read that bloody book. Ev'ryone looking sideways at ev'ry-one else. Ev'ryone who knows the ending's suspect. Police in my bloody office, ev'ryone staring . . .

'I read it on Sunday,' he said, lurching back to Strike's

question, ''n I told Liz Tassel what I thought of her – and life went on. Owen not answering his phone. Thought he was probably having a breakdown – had my own bloody problems. Daniel Chard going berserk . . .

'Fuck him. Resigned. Had enough. Accusations. No more. Being bloody bawled out in front of the whole office. No more.'

'Accusations?' asked Strike.

His interview technique was starting to feel like the dexterous flicking of Subbuteo football figures; the wobbling interviewee directed by the right, light touch. (Strike had had an Arsenal set in the seventies; he had played Dave Polworth's custom-painted Plymouth Argyles, both boys lying belly-down on Dave's mum's hearthrug.)

'Dan thinks I gossiped about him to Owen. Bloody idiot. Thinks the world doesn't know . . . been gossip for years. Didn't have to tell Owen. Ev'ryone knows.'

'That Chard's gay?'

'Gay, who cares . . . repressed. Not sure Dan even *knows* he's gay. But he likes pretty young men, likes painting 'em in the nude. Common knowledge.'

'Did he offer to paint you?' asked Strike.

'Christ, no,' said Waldegrave. 'Joe North told me, years ago. Ah!'

He had caught the wine waiter's eye.

''Nother glass of this, please.'

Strike was only grateful he had not asked for a bottle.

'I'm sorry, sir, we don't do that by the—'

'Anything, then. Red. Anything.

'Years ago, this was,' Waldegrave went on, picking up where he had left off. 'Dan wanted Joe to pose for him; Joe told him to piss off. Common knowledge, f'years.'

He leaned back, ramming the large woman behind him again, who unfortunately was now eating soup. Strike watched her angry dining companion summon a passing waiter to complain. The waiter bent down to Waldegrave and said apologetically, yet with firmness:

'Would you mind pulling in your chair, sir? The lady behind you—'

'Sorry, sorry.'

Waldegrave tugged himself nearer Strike, placed his elbows on the table, pushed his tangled hair out of his eyes and said loudly:

'Head up his bloody arse.'

'Who?' asked Strike, finishing with regret the best meal he had had in a long time.

'Dan. Handed the bloody company on a plate . . . rolling in it all his life . . . let him live in the country and paint his houseboy if that's what he wants . . . had enough of it. Start my own . . . start my own bloody company.'

Waldegrave's mobile phone rang. It took him a while to locate it. He peered over his glasses at the caller's number before answering.

'What's up, JoJo?'

Busy though the restaurant was, Strike heard the response: shrill, distant screaming down the line. Waldegrave looked horrified.

'JoJo? Are you—?'

But then the doughy, amiable face became tauter than Strike could have believed. Veins stood out on Waldegrave's neck and his mouth stretched in an ugly snarl.

'Fuck you!' he said, and his voice carried loudly to all the surrounding tables so that fifty heads jerked upwards, conversations stalled. '*Do not call me on JoJo's number!* No, you drunken fucking – you heard me – I drink because I'm fucking married to *you*, that's why!'

The overweight woman behind Waldegrave looked around, outraged. Waiters were glaring; one had so far forgotten himself as to have paused with a Yorkshire pudding halfway to a Japanese businessman's plate. The decorous gentleman's club had doubtless seen other drunken brawls, but they could not fail to shock among the dark wood panels, the glass chandeliers and the bills of fare, where everything was stolidly British, calm and staid.

'Well, *whose fucking fault's that*?' shouted Waldegrave.

He staggered to his feet, ramming his unfortunate neighbour yet again, but this time there was no remonstrance from her companion. The restaurant had fallen silent. Waldegrave was weaving his way out of it, a bottle and a third to the bad, swearing into his mobile, and Strike, stranded at the table, was amused to find in himself some of the disapproval felt in the mess for the man who cannot hold his drink.

'Bill, please,' said Strike to the nearest gaping waiter. He was disappointed that he had not gotten to sample the spotted dick, which he had noted on the bill of fare, but he must catch Waldegrave if he could.

While the diners muttered and watched him out of the corners of their eyes, Strike paid, pulled himself up from the table and, leaning on his stick, followed in Waldegrave's ungainly footsteps. From the outraged expression of the maître d' and the sound of Waldegrave still yelling just outside the door, Strike suspected that Waldegrave had taken some persuasion to leave the premises.

He found the editor propped up against the cold wall to the

left of the doors. Snow was falling thickly all around them; the pavements were crunchy with it, passers-by muffled to the ears. The backdrop of solid grandeur removed, Waldegrave no longer looked like a vaguely scruffy academic. Drunk, grubby and crumpled, swearing into a phone disguised by his large hand, he might have been a mentally ill down-and-out.

'*. . . not my fucking fault, you stupid bitch!* Did I write the fucking thing? Did I? . . . You'd better fucking talk to her then, hadn't you? . . . If you don't, I will . . . Don't you threaten me, you ugly fucking slut . . . if you'd kept your legs closed . . . *you fucking heard me—*'

Waldegrave saw Strike. He stood gaping for a few seconds then cut the call. The mobile slipped through his fumbling fingers and landed on the snowy pavement.

'Bollocks,' said Jerry Waldegrave.

The wolf had turned back into the sheep. He groped with bare fingers for the phone in the slush around his feet and his glasses fell off. Strike picked them up for him.

'Thanks. Thanks. Sorry about that. Sorry . . . '

Strike saw tears on Waldegrave's puffy cheeks as the editor rammed his glasses back on. Stuffing the cracked phone into his pocket, he turned an expression of despair upon the detective.

''S ruined my fucking life,' he said. 'That book. 'N I thought Owen . . . one thing he held sacred. Father daughter. One thing . . . '

With another dismissive gesture, Waldegrave turned and walked away, weaving badly, thoroughly drunk. He had had, the detective guessed, at least a bottle before they met. There was no point following him.

Watching Waldegrave disappear into the swirling snow, past the Christmas shoppers scrambling, laden, along the slushy pavements, Strike remembered a hand closing ungently on an upper arm, a stern man's voice, an angrier young woman's. '*Mummy's made a beeline, why don't you grab* her?'

Turning up his coat collar Strike thought he knew, now, what the meaning was: of a dwarf in a bloody bag, of the horns under the Cutter's cap and, cruellest of all, the attempted drowning.

37

> ... when I am provok'd to fury, I cannot incorporate with patience and reason.
>
> William Congreve, *The Double-Dealer*

Strike set out for his office beneath a sky of dirty silver, his feet moving with difficulty through the rapidly accumulating snow, which was still falling fast. Though he had touched nothing but water, he felt a little drunk on good rich food, which gave him the false sense of well-being that Waldegrave had probably passed some time mid-morning, drinking in his office. The walk between Simpson's-in-the-Strand and his draughty little office on Denmark Street would take a fit and unimpaired adult perhaps a quarter of an hour. Strike's knee remained sore and overworked, but he had just spent more than his entire week's food budget on a single meal. Lighting a cigarette, he limped away through the knife-sharp cold, head bowed against the snow, wondering what Robin had found out at the Bridlington Bookshop.

As he walked past the fluted columns of the Lyceum Theatre, Strike pondered the fact that Daniel Chard was convinced that Jerry Waldegrave had helped Quine write his book, whereas Waldegrave thought that Elizabeth Tassel had played upon his sense of grievance until it had erupted into print. Were these, he wondered, simple cases of displaced anger? Having been baulked of the true culprit by Quine's gruesome death, were Chard and Waldegrave seeking living scapegoats on whom to vent their frustrated fury? Or were they right to detect, in *Bombyx Mori*, a foreign influence?

The scarlet façade of the Coach and Horses in Wellington Street constituted a powerful temptation as he approached it, the stick doing heavy duty now, and his knee complaining: warmth, beer and a comfortable chair . . . but a third lunchtime visit to the pub in a week . . . not a habit he ought to develop . . . Jerry Waldegrave was an object lesson in where such behaviour might lead . . .

He could not resist an envious glance through the window as he passed, towards lights gleaming on brass beer pumps and convivial men with slacker consciences than his own—

He saw her out of the corner of his eye. Tall and stooping in her black coat, hands in her pockets, scurrying along the slushy pavements behind him: his stalker and would-be attacker of Saturday night.

Strike's pace did not falter, nor did he turn to look at her. He was not playing games this time; there would be no stopping to test her amateurish stalking style, no letting her know that he had spotted her. On he walked without looking over his shoulder, and only a man or woman similarly expert in counter-surveillance would have noticed his casual glances into helpfully positioned windows and reflective brass door plates; only they could have spotted the hyper-alertness disguised as inattentiveness.

Most killers were slapdash amateurs; that was how they were caught. To persist after their encounter on Saturday night argued high-calibre recklessness and it was on this that Strike was counting as he continued up Wellington Street, outwardly oblivious to the woman following him with a knife in her pocket. As he crossed Russell Street she had dodged out of sight, faking entrance to the Marquess of Anglesey, but soon reappeared, dodging in and out of the square pillars of an office block and lurking in a doorway to allow him to pull ahead.

Strike could barely feel his knee now. He had become six foot three of highly concentrated potential. This time she had no advantage; she would not be taking him by surprise. If she had a plan at all, he guessed that it was to profit from any available opportunity. It was up to him to present her with an opportunity she dare not let pass, and to make sure she did not succeed.

Past the Royal Opera House with its classical portico, its columns and statues; in Endell Street she entered an old red telephone box, gathering her nerve, no doubt, double-checking that he was not aware of her. Strike walked on, his pace unchanging, his eyes on the street ahead. She took confidence and emerged again onto the crowded pavement, following him through harried passers-by with carrier bags swinging from their hands, drawing closer to him as the street narrowed, flitting in and out of doorways.

As he drew nearer to the office he made his decision, turning left off Denmark Street into Flitcroft Street, which led to Denmark Place, where a dark passage, plastered with flyers for bands, led back to his office.

Would she dare?

As he entered the alleyway, his footsteps echoing a little off the dank walls, he slowed imperceptibly. Then he heard her coming – running at him.

Wheeling around on his sound left leg he flung out his walking stick – there was a shriek of pain as her arm met it – the Stanley knife was knocked out of her hand, hit the stone wall, rebounded and narrowly missed Strike's eye – he had her now in a ferocious grip that made her scream.

He was afraid that some hero would come to her aid, but no one appeared, and now speed was essential – she was stronger than he had expected and struggling ferociously, trying to kick him in the balls and claw his face. With a further economical twist of his body he had her in a headlock, her feet skidding and scrambling on the damp alley floor.

As she writhed in his arms, trying to bite him, he stooped to pick up the knife, pulling her down with him so that she almost lost her footing, then, abandoning the walking stick, which he could not carry while managing her, he dragged her out onto Denmark Street.

He was fast, and she so winded by the struggle that she had no breath to yell. The short cold street was empty of shoppers and no passers-by on Charing Cross Road noticed anything amiss as he forced her the short distance to the black street door.

'Need in, Robin! Quickly!' he shouted on the intercom, slamming his way through the outer door as soon as Robin had buzzed it open. Up the metal steps he dragged her, his right knee now protesting violently, and she started shrieking, the screams echoing around the stairwell. Strike saw movement behind the glass door of the dour and eccentric graphic designer who worked in the office beneath his.

'Just messing around!' he bellowed at the door, heaving his pursuer upstairs.

'Cormoran? What's – oh my *God*!' said Robin, staring down

from the landing. 'You can't – what are you playing at? Let her go!'

'She's just – tried – to bloody – knife me again,' panted Strike, and with a gigantic final effort he forced his pursuer over the threshold. 'Lock the door!' he shouted at Robin, who had hurried in behind them and obeyed.

Strike threw the woman onto the mock-leather sofa. The hood fell back to reveal a long pale face with large brown eyes and thick dark wavy hair that fell to her shoulders. Her fingers terminated in pointed crimson nails. She looked barely twenty.

'You bastard! *You bastard!*'

She tried to get up, but Strike was standing over her looking murderous, so she thought better of it, slumping back onto the sofa and massaging her white neck, which bore dark pink scratch marks where he had seized her.

'Want to tell me why you're trying to knife me?' Strike asked.

'Fuck you!'

'That's original,' said Strike. 'Robin, call the police—'

'Noooo!' howled the woman in black like a baying dog. 'He hurt me,' she gasped to Robin, tugging down her top with abandoned wretchedness to reveal the marks on the strong white neck. 'He dragged me, he pulled me—'

Robin looked to Strike, her hand on the receiver.

'Why have you been following me?' Strike said, panting as he stood over her, his tone threatening.

She cowered into the squeaking cushions yet Robin, whose fingers had not left the phone, detected a note of relish in the woman's fear, a whisper of voluptuousness in the way she twisted away from him.

'Last chance,' growled Strike. '*Why—?*'

'What's happening up there?' came a querulous enquiry from the landing below.

Robin's eyes met Strike's. She hurried to the door, unlocked it and slid out onto the landing while Strike stood guard over his captive, his jaw set and one fist clenched. He saw the idea of screaming for help pass behind the big dark eyes, purple-shadowed like pansies, and fade away. Shaking, she began to cry, but her teeth were bared and he thought there was more rage than misery in her tears.

'All OK, Mr Crowdy,' Robin called. 'Just messing around. Sorry we were so loud.'

Robin returned to the office and locked the door behind her again. The woman was rigid on the sofa, tears tumbling down her face, her talon-like nails gripping the edge of the seat.

'Fuck this,' Strike said. 'You don't want to talk – I'm calling the police.'

Apparently she believed him. He had taken barely two steps towards the phone when she sobbed:

'I wanted to stop you.'

'Stop me doing what?' said Strike.

'Like you don't know!'

'Don't play fucking games with me!' Strike shouted, bending towards her with two large fists clenched. He could feel his damaged knee only too acutely now. It was her fault he had taken the fall that had damaged the ligaments all over again.

'Cormoran,' said Robin firmly, sliding between them and forcing him to take a pace backwards. 'Listen,' she told the girl. 'Listen to me. Tell him why you're doing this and maybe he won't call—'

'You've gotta be fucking joking,' said Strike. 'Twice she's tried to stab—'

'—maybe he won't call the police,' said Robin loudly, undeterred.

The woman jumped up and tried to make a break for it towards the door.

'No you don't,' said Strike, hobbling fast around Robin, catching his assailant round the waist and throwing her none too gently back onto the sofa. '*Who are you?*'

'You've hurt me now!' she shouted. 'You've really hurt me – my ribs – I'll get you for assault, you bastard—'

'I'll call you Pippa, then, shall I?' said Strike.

A shuddering gasp and a malevolent stare.

'You – you – fuck—'

'Yeah, yeah, fuck me,' said Strike irritably. '*Your name.*'

Her chest was heaving under the heavy overcoat.

'How will you know if I'm telling the truth, even if I tell you?' she panted, with a further show of defiance.

'I'll keep you here till I've checked,' said Strike.

'Kidnap!' she shouted, her voice as rough and loud as a docker's.

'Citizen's arrest,' said Strike. 'You tried to fucking knife me. Now, for the last bloody time—'

'Pippa Midgley,' she spat.

'Finally. Have you got ID?'

With another mutinous obscenity she slid a hand into her pocket and drew out a bus pass, which she threw to him.

'This says Phillip Midgley.'

'No shit.'

Watching the implication hit Strike, Robin felt a sudden urge, in spite of the tension in the room, to laugh.

'Epicoene,' said Pippa Midgley furiously. 'Didn't you get it? Too subtle for you, *dickhead*?'

Strike looked up at her. The Adam's apple on her scratched, marked throat was still prominent. She had buried her hands in her pockets again.

'I'll be Pippa on all my documents next year,' she said.

'Pippa,' Strike repeated. 'You're the author of "I'll turn the handle on the fucking rack for you", are you?'

'*Oh*,' said Robin, on a long drawn-out sigh of comprehension.

'*Oooooh*, you're so *clever*, Mr Butch,' said Pippa in spiteful imitation.

'D'you know Kathryn Kent personally, or are you just cyber-friends?'

'Why? Is knowing Kath Kent a crime now?'

'How did you know Owen Quine?'

'I don't want to talk about that bastard,' she said, her chest heaving. 'What he's done to me . . . what he's done . . . pretending . . . he lied . . . lying fucking bastard . . .'

Fresh tears splattered down her cheeks and she dissolved into hysterics. Her scarlet-tipped hands clawed at her hair, her feet drummed on the floor, she rocked backwards and forwards, wailing. Strike watched her with distaste and after thirty seconds said:

'Will you *shut the fuck*—'

But Robin quelled him with a glance, tore a handful of tissues out of the box on her desk and pushed them into Pippa's hand.

'T-t-ta—'

'Would you like a tea or coffee, Pippa?' asked Robin kindly.

'Co . . . fee . . . pl . . .'

'She's just tried to bloody knife me, Robin!'

'Well, she didn't manage it, did she?' commented Robin, busy with the kettle.

'Ineptitude,' said Strike incredulously, 'is no fucking defence under the law!'

He rounded on Pippa again, who had followed this exchange with her mouth agape.

'Why have you been following me? What are you trying to stop me doing? And I'm warning you – just because Robin here's buying the sob stuff—'

'You're working for *her*!' yelled Pippa. 'That twisted bitch, his widow! She's got his money now, hasn't she – we know what you've been hired to do, we're not fucking stupid!'

'Who's "we"?' demanded Strike, but Pippa's dark eyes slid again towards the door. 'I swear to God,' said Strike, whose much-tried knee was now throbbing in a way that made him want to grind his teeth, 'if you go for that door one more fucking time I'm calling the police and I'll testify and be glad to watch you go down for attempted murder. And it won't be fun for you inside, Pippa,' he added. 'Not pre-op.'

'Cormoran!' said Robin sharply.

'Stating facts,' said Strike.

Pippa had shrunk back onto the sofa and was staring at Strike in unfeigned terror.

'Coffee,' said Robin firmly, emerging from behind the desk and pressing the mug into one of the long-taloned hands. 'Just tell him what all this is about, for God's sake, Pippa. *Tell him*.'

Unstable and aggressive though Pippa seemed, Robin could not help pitying the girl, who appeared to have given almost no thought to the possible consequences of lunging at a private detective with a blade. Robin could only assume that she possessed in extreme form the trait that afflicted her own younger brother Martin, who was notorious in their family for the lack of foresight and love of danger that had resulted in more trips to casualty than the rest of his siblings combined.

'We know she hired you to frame us,' croaked Pippa.

'Who,' growled Strike, 'is "*she*" and who is "*us*"?'

'Leonora Quine!' said Pippa. 'We know what she's like and we know what she's capable of! She hates us, me and Kath, she'd do anything to get us. She murdered Owen and she's trying to pin it on us! You can look like that all you want!' she shouted at Strike, whose heavy eyebrows had risen halfway to his thick hairline. 'She's a crazy bitch, she's jealous as hell – she couldn't stand him seeing us and now she's got you poking around trying to get stuff to use against us!'

'I don't know whether you believe this paranoid bollocks—'

'We know what's going on!' shouted Pippa.

'*Shut up.* Nobody except the killer knew Quine was dead when you started stalking me. You followed me the day I found the body and I know you were following Leonora for a week before that. Why?' And when she did not answer, he repeated: 'Last chance: why did you follow me from Leonora's?'

'I thought you might lead me to where he was,' said Pippa.

'Why did you want to know where he was?'

'So I could fucking kill him!' yelled Pippa, and Robin was confirmed in her impression that Pippa shared Martin's almost total lack of self-preservation.

'And why did you want to kill him?' asked Strike, as though she had said nothing out of the ordinary.

'Because of what he did to us in that horrible fucking book! You know – you've read it – Epicoene – that bastard, that bastard—'

'Bloody calm down! So you'd read *Bombyx Mori* by then?'

'Yeah, of course I had—'

'And that's when you started putting shit through Quine's letter box?'

'Shit for a shit!' she shouted.

'Witty. When did you read the book?'

'Kath read the bits about us on the phone and then I went round and—'

'When did she read you the bits on the phone?'

'W-when she came home and found it lying on her doormat. Whole manuscript. She could hardly get the door open. He'd fed it through her door with a note,' said Pippa Midgley. 'She showed me.'

'What did the note say?'

'It said "Payback time for both of us. Hope you're happy! Owen."'

'"Payback time for both of us"?' repeated Strike, frowning. 'D'you know what that meant?'

'Kath wouldn't tell me but I know she understood. She was d-devastated,' said Pippa, her chest heaving. 'She's a – she's a wonderful person. You don't know her. She's been like a m-mother to me. We met on his writing course and we were like – we became like—' She caught up her breath and whimpered: 'He was a bastard. He lied to us about what he was writing, he lied about – about everything—'

She began to cry again, wailing and sobbing, and Robin, worried about Mr Crowdy, said gently:

'Pippa, just tell us what he lied about. Cormoran only wants the truth, he's not trying to frame anyone . . .'

She did not know whether Pippa had heard or believed her; perhaps she simply wanted to relieve her overwrought feelings, but she took a great shuddering breath and out spilled a torrent of words:

'He said I was like his second daughter, he *said* that to me; I told him *everything*, he knew my mum threw me out and *everything*. And I showed him m-m-my book about my life and he w-was so k-kind and interested and he said he'd help me get it p-published and he t-told us both, me and Kath, that we were in his n-new novel and he said I w-was a "b-beautiful lost soul" – *that's what he said to me*,' gasped Pippa, her mobile mouth working, 'and he p-pretended to read a bit out to me one day, over the phone, and it was – it was lovely and then I r-read it and he'd – he'd written *that* . . . Kath was in b-bits . . . the cave . . . Harpy and Epicoene . . . '

'So Kathryn came home and found it all over the doormat, did she?' said Strike. 'Came home from where – work?'

'From s-sitting in the hospice with her dying sister.'

'And that was *when*?' said Strike for the third time.

'Who cares when it—?'

'*I fucking care!*'

'Was it the ninth?' Robin asked. She had brought up Kathryn Kent's blog on her computer, the screen angled away from the sofa where Pippa was sitting. 'Could it have been Tuesday the ninth, Pippa? The Tuesday after bonfire night?'

'It was . . . yeah, I think it was!' said Pippa, apparently awestruck by Robin's lucky guess. 'Yeah, Kath went away on bonfire night because Angela was so ill—'

'How d'you know it was bonfire night?' Strike asked.

'Because Owen told Kath he c-couldn't see her that night, because he had to do fireworks with his daughter,' said Pippa. 'And Kath was really upset, because he was supposed to be leaving! He'd promised her, he'd promised at *long bloody last* he'd leave his bitch of a wife, and then he says he's got to play sparklers with the reta—'

She drew up short, but Strike finished for her.

'With the retard?'

'It's just a joke,' muttered Pippa, shamefaced, showing more regret about her use of the word than she had about trying to stab Strike. 'Just between me and Kath: his daughter was always the excuse why Owen couldn't leave and be with Kath . . . '

'What did Kathryn do that night, instead of seeing Quine?' asked Strike.

'I went over to hers. Then she got the call that her sister Angela was a lot worse and she left. Angela had cancer. It had gone everywhere.'

'Where was Angela?'

'In the hospice in Clapham.'

'How did Kathryn get there?'

'Why's that matter?'

'Just answer the bloody question, will you?'

'I don't know – Tube, I s'pose. And she stayed with Angela for three days, sleeping on a mattress on the floor by her bed because they thought Angela was going to die any moment, but Angela kept hanging on so Kath had to go home for clean clothes and that's when she found the manuscript all over the doormat.'

'Why are you sure she came home on the Tuesday?' Robin asked and Strike, who had been about to ask the same thing, looked at her in surprise. He did not know about the old man in the bookshop and the German sinkhole.

'Because on Tuesday nights I work on a helpline,' said Pippa, 'and I was there when Kath called me in f-floods, because she'd put the manuscript in order, and read what he'd written about us—'

'Well, this is all very interesting,' said Strike, 'because Kathryn Kent told the police that she'd never read *Bombyx Mori*.'

Pippa's horrified expression might, under other circumstances, have been amusing.

'*You fucking tricked me!*'

'Yeah, you're a really tough nut to crack,' said Strike. 'Don't even *think* about it,' he added, standing over her as she tried to get up.

'He was a – a shit!' shouted Pippa seething with impotent rage. 'He was a user! Pretending to be interested in our work and using us all along, that l-lying b-bastard . . . I thought he understood what my life's been about – we used to talk for hours about it and he encouraged me with my life story – he t-told me he was going to help me get a publishing deal—'

Strike felt a sudden weariness wash over him. What was this mania to appear in print?

'—and he was just trying to keep me sweet, telling him all my most private thoughts and feelings, and Kath – what he did to Kath – you *don't understand* – I'm glad his bitch wife killed him! If she hadn't—'

'Why,' demanded Strike, 'd'you keep saying his wife killed Quine?'

'Because Kath's got proof!'

A short pause.

'What proof?' asked Strike.

'Wouldn't you like to know!' shouted Pippa with a cackle of hysterical laughter. 'Never you mind!'

'If she's got proof, why hasn't she taken it to the police?'

'Out of compassion!' shouted Pippa. 'Something *you* wouldn't—'

'Why,' came a plaintive voice from outside the glass door, 'is there still all this *shouting*?'

'Oh bloody hell,' said Strike as the fuzzy outline of Mr Crowdy from downstairs pressed close to the glass.

Robin moved to unlock the door.

'Very sorry, Mr Crow—'

Pippa was off the sofa in an instant. Strike made a grab for her but his knee buckled agonisingly as he lunged. Knocking Mr Crowdy aside she was gone, clattering down the stairs.

'Leave her!' Strike said to Robin, who looked braced to give chase. 'Least I've got her knife.'

'Knife?' yelped Mr Crowdy and it took them fifteen minutes to persuade him not to contact the landlord (for the publicity following the Lula Landry case had unnerved the graphic designer, who lived in dread that another murderer might come seeking Strike and perhaps wander by mistake into the wrong office).

'Jesus H. Christ,' said Strike when they had at last persuaded Crowdy to leave. He slumped down on the sofa; Robin took her computer chair and they looked at each other for a few seconds before starting to laugh.

'Decent good cop, bad cop routine we had going there,' said Strike.

'I wasn't faking,' said Robin, 'I really did feel a bit sorry for her.'

'I noticed. What about me, getting attacked?'

'Did she *really* want to stab you, or was it play-acting?' asked Robin sceptically.

'She might've liked the idea of it more than the reality,' acknowledged Strike. 'Trouble is, you're just as dead if you're knifed by a self-dramatising twat as by a professional. And what she thought she'd gain by stabbing me—'

'Mother love,' said Robin quietly.

Strike stared at her.

'Her own mother's disowned her,' said Robin, 'and she's going through a really traumatic time, I expect, taking hormones and God knows what else she's got to do before she has the operation. She thought she had a new family, didn't she? She thought Quine and Kathryn Kent were her new parents. She told us Quine said she was a second daughter to him and he put her in the book as Kathryn Kent's daughter. But in *Bombyx Mori* he revealed her to the world as half male, half female. He also suggested that, beneath all the filial affection, she wanted to sleep with him.

'Her new father,' said Robin, 'had let her down very badly. But her new mother was still good and loving, and she'd been betrayed as well, so Pippa set out to get even for both of them.'

She could not stop herself grinning at Strike's look of stunned admiration.

'Why the hell did you give up that psychology degree?'

'Long story,' said Robin, looking away towards the computer monitor. 'She's not very old . . . twenty, d'you think?'

'Looked about that,' agreed Strike. 'Pity we never got round to asking her about her movements in the days after Quine disappeared.'

'She didn't do it,' said Robin with certainty, looking back at him.

'Yeah, you're probably right,' sighed Strike, 'if only because shoving dog shit through his letter box might've felt a bit anticlimactic after carving out his guts.'

'And she doesn't seem very strong on planning or efficiency, does she?'

'An understatement,' he agreed.

'Are you going to call the police about her?'

'I don't know. Maybe. But shit,' he said, thumping himself on the forehead, 'we didn't even find out why she was bloody singing in the book!'

'I think I might know,' said Robin after a short burst of typing and reading the results on her computer monitor. 'Singing to soften the voice . . . vocal exercises for transgendered people.'

'Was that all?' asked Strike in disbelief.

'What are you saying – that she was wrong to take offence?' said Robin. 'Come on – he was jeering at something really personal in a public—'

'That's not what I meant,' said Strike.

He frowned out of the window, thinking. The snow was falling thick and fast.

After a while he said:

'What happened at the Bridlington Bookshop?'

'God, yes, I nearly forgot!'

She told him all about the assistant and his confusion between the first and the eighth of November.

'Stupid old sod,' said Strike.

'That's a bit mean,' said Robin.

'Cocky, wasn't he? Mondays are always the same, goes to his friend Charles every Monday . . . '

'But how do we know whether it was the Anglican bishop night or the sinkhole night?'

'You say he claims Charles interrupted him with the sinkhole story while he was telling him about Quine coming into the shop?'

'That's what he said.'

'Then it's odds on Quine was in the shop on the first, not the eighth. He remembers those two bits of information as connected. Silly bugger's got confused. He *wanted* to have seen

Quine after he'd disappeared, he wanted to be able to help establish time of death, so he was subconsciously looking for reasons to think it was the Monday in the time frame for the murder, not an irrelevant Monday a whole week before anyone was interested in Quine's movements.'

'There's still something odd, though, isn't there, about what he claims Quine said to him?' asked Robin.

'Yeah, there is,' said Strike. 'Buying reading matter because he was going away for a break . . . so he was already planning to go away, four days before he rowed with Elizabeth Tassel? Was he already planning to go to Talgarth Road, after all those years he was supposed to have hated and avoided the place?'

'Are you going to tell Anstis about this?' Robin asked.

Strike gave a wry snort of laughter.

'No, I'm not going to tell Anstis. We've got no real proof Quine was in there on the first instead of the eighth. Anyway, Anstis and I aren't on the best terms just now.'

There was another long pause, and then Strike startled Robin by saying:

'I've got to talk to Michael Fancourt.'

'Why?' she asked.

'A lot of reasons,' said Strike. 'Things Waldegrave said to me over lunch. Can you get on to his agent or whatever contact you can find for him?'

'Yes,' said Robin, making a note for herself. 'You know, I watched that interview back just now and I still couldn't—'

'Look at it again,' said Strike. 'Pay attention. *Think.*'

He lapsed into silence again, glaring now at the ceiling. Not wishing to break his train of thought, Robin merely set to work on the computer to discover who represented Michael Fancourt.

Finally Strike spoke over the tapping of her keyboard.

'What does Kathryn Kent think she's got on Leonora?'

'Maybe nothing,' said Robin, concentrating on the results she had uncovered.

'And she's withholding it "out of compassion" . . .'

Robin said nothing. She was perusing the website of Fancourt's literary agency for a contact number.

'Let's hope that was just more hysterical bullshit,' said Strike.

But he was worried.

38

That in so little paper
Should lie th' undoing . . .

John Webster, *The White Devil*

Miss Brocklehurst, the possibly unfaithful PA, was still claiming to be incapacitated by her cold. Her lover, Strike's client, found this excessive and the detective was inclined to agree with him. Seven o'clock the following morning found Strike stationed in a shadowy recess opposite Miss Brocklehurst's Battersea flat, wrapped up in coat, scarf and gloves, yawning widely as the cold penetrated his extremities and enjoying the second of three Egg McMuffins he had picked up from McDonald's on his way.

There had been a severe weather warning for the whole of the south-east. Thick dark blue snow already lay over the entire street and the first tentative flakes of the day were drifting down from a starless sky as he waited, moving his toes from time to time to check that he could still feel them. One by one the occupants left for work, slipping and sliding off towards the station or clambering into cars whose exhausts sounded particularly loud in the muffled quiet. Three Christmas trees sparkled at Strike from living-room windows, though December would only start the following day, tangerine, emerald and neon blue lights winking garishly as he leaned against the wall, his eyes on the windows of Miss Brocklehurst's flat, laying bets with himself as to whether she would leave the house at all in this weather. His knee was still killing him, but the snow had slowed the rest of the world to a pace that matched his own. He had never seen Miss Brocklehurst in heels lower than four inches. In these conditions, she might well be more incapacitated than he was.

In the last week the search for Quine's killer had started to eclipse all his other cases, but it was important to keep up with them unless he wanted to lose business. Miss Brocklehurst's lover was a rich man who was likely to put plenty more jobs Strike's way if he liked the detective's work. The businessman had a predilection for youthful blondes, a succession of whom (as he had freely confessed to Strike at their first meeting) had taken large amounts of money and sundry expensive gifts from him only to leave or betray him. As he showed no sign of developing better judgement of character, Strike anticipated many more lucrative hours spent tailing future Miss Brocklehursts. Perhaps it was the betrayal that thrilled his client, reflected Strike, his breath rising in clouds through the icy air; he had known other such men. It was a taste that found its fullest expression in those who became infatuated with hookers.

At ten to nine the curtains gave a small twitch. Faster than might have been expected from his attitude of casual relaxation, Strike raised the night-vision camera he had been concealing at his side.

Miss Brocklehurst stood briefly exposed to the dim snowy street in bra and pants, though her cosmetically enhanced breasts had no need of support. Behind her in the darkness of the bedroom walked a paunchy, bare-chested man who briefly cupped one breast, earning himself a giggled reproof. Both turned away into the bedroom.

Strike lowered his camera and checked his handiwork. The most incriminating image he had managed to capture showed the clear outline of a man's hand and arm, Miss Brocklehurst's face half turned in a laugh, but her embracer's face was in shadow. Strike suspected that he might be about to leave for work, so he stowed the camera in an inside pocket, ready to give slow and cumbersome chase, and set to work on his third McMuffin.

Sure enough, at five to nine Miss Brocklehurst's front door opened and the lover emerged; he resembled her boss in nothing except age and a moneyed appearance. A sleek leather messenger bag was slung diagonally across his chest, large enough for a clean shirt and a toothbrush. Strike had seen these so frequently of late that he had come to think of them as Adulterer's Overnight Bags. The couple enjoyed a French kiss on the doorstep curtailed by the icy cold and the fact that Miss Brocklehurst was wearing less than two ounces of fabric. Then she retreated indoors and Paunchy set off towards Clapham Junction, already speaking on his mobile phone, doubtless explaining that he would be late due to the snow. Strike allowed him twenty yards' head start then emerged from his hiding place, leaning on the stick that Robin had kindly retrieved from Denmark Place the preceding afternoon.

It was easy surveillance, as Paunchy was oblivious to anything but his telephone conversation. They walked down the gentle incline of Lavender Hill together, twenty yards apart, the snow falling steadily again. Paunchy slipped several times in his handmade shoes. When they reached the station it was easy for Strike to follow him, still gabbling, into the same carriage and, under pretext of reading texts, to take pictures of him on his own mobile.

As he did so, a genuine text arrived from Robin.

Michael Fancourt's agent just called me back – MF says he'd be delighted to meet you! He's in Germany but will be back on 6th. Suggests Groucho Club whatever time suits? Rx

It was quite extraordinary, Strike thought, as the train rattled into Waterloo, how much the people who had read *Bombyx Mori* wanted to talk to him. When before had suspects jumped so eagerly at the chance to sit face to face with a detective? And what did famous Michael Fancourt hope to gain from an interview with the private detective who had found Owen Quine's body?

Strike got out of the train behind Paunchy, following him through the crowds across the wet, slippery tiles of Waterloo station, beneath the ceiling of cream girders and glass that reminded Strike of Tithebarn House. Out again into the cold, with Paunchy still oblivious and gabbling into his mobile, Strike followed him along slushy, treacherous pavements edged with clods of mucky snow, between square office blocks comprised of glass and concrete, in and out of the swarm of financial workers bustling along, ant-like, in their drab coats, until at last Paunchy turned into the car park of one of the biggest office blocks and headed for what was obviously his own car. Apparently he had felt it wiser to leave the BMW at the office than to park outside Miss Brocklehurst's flat. As Strike watched, lurking behind a convenient Range Rover, he felt the mobile in his pocket vibrate but ignored it, unwilling to draw attention to himself. Paunchy had a named parking space. After collecting a few items from his boot he headed into the building, leaving Strike free to amble over to the wall where the directors' names were written and take a photograph of Paunchy's full name and title for his client's better information.

Strike then headed back to the office. Once on the Tube he examined his phone and saw that his missed call was from his oldest friend, the shark-mangled Dave Polworth.

Polworth had the ancient habit of calling Strike 'Diddy'. Most people assumed this was an ironic reference to his size (all through primary school, Strike had been the biggest boy of the year and usually of the year above), but in fact it derived from the endless comings and goings from school that were due to his mother's peripatetic lifestyle. These had once, long ago, resulted in a small, shrill Dave Polworth telling Strike he was like a didicoy, the Cornish word for gypsy.

Strike returned the call as soon as he got off the Tube and they were still talking twenty minutes later when he entered his office. Robin looked up and began to speak, but seeing that Strike was on the phone merely smiled and turned back to her monitor.

'Coming home for Christmas?' Polworth asked Strike as he moved through to the inner office and closed his door.

'Maybe,' said Strike.

'Few pints in the Victory?' Polworth urged him. 'Shag Gwenifer Arscott again?'

'I never,' said Strike (it was a joke of long standing), 'shagged Gwenifer Arscott.'

'Well, have another bash, Diddy, you might strike gold this time. Time someone took her cherry. And speaking of girls neither of us ever shagged . . .'

The conversation degenerated into a series of salacious and very funny vignettes from Polworth about the antics of the mutual friends they had both left behind in St Mawes. Strike was laughing so much he ignored the 'call waiting' signal and did not bother to check who it was.

'Haven't got back with Milady Berserko, have you, boy?' Dave asked, this being the name he usually used for Charlotte.

'Nope,' said Strike. 'She's getting married in . . . four days,' he calculated.

'Yeah, well, you be on the watch, Diddy, for signs of her galloping back over the horizon. Wouldn't be surprised if she bolts. Breathe a sigh of relief if it comes off, mate.'

'Yeah,' said Strike. 'Right.'

'That's a deal then, yeah?' said Polworth. 'Home for Christmas? Beers in the Victory?'

'Yeah, why not,' said Strike.

After a few more ribald exchanges Dave returned to his work and Strike, still grinning, checked his phone and saw that he had missed a call from Leonora Quine.

He wandered back into the outer office while dialling his voicemail.

'I've watched Michael Fancourt's documentary again,' said Robin excitedly, 'and I've realised what you—'

Strike raised a hand to quiet her as Leonora's ordinarily deadpan voice spoke in his ear, sounding agitated and disorientated.

'Cormoran, I've been bloody arrested. I don't know why – nobody's telling me nothing – they've got me at the station. They're waiting for a lawyer or something. I dunno what to do – Orlando's with Edna, I don't – anyway, that's where I am . . .'

A few seconds of silence and the message ended.

'Shit!' said Strike, so loudly that Robin jumped. 'SHIT!'

'What's the matter?'

'They've arrested Leonora – why's she calling me, not Ilsa? *Shit . . .*'

He punched in Ilsa Herbert's number and waited.

'Hi Corm—'

'They've arrested Leonora Quine.'

'What?' cried Ilsa. '*Why?* Not that bloody old rag in the lock-up?'

'They might have something else.'

(Kath's got proof . . .)

'Where is she, Corm?'

'Police station . . . it'll be Kilburn, that's nearest.'

'Christ almighty, why didn't she call me?'

'Fuck knows. She said something about them finding her a lawyer—'

'Nobody's contacted me – God above, doesn't she *think*? Why didn't she give them my name? I'm going now, Corm, I'll dump this lot on someone else. I'm owed a favour . . .'

He could hear a series of thunks, distant voices, Ilsa's rapid footsteps.

'Call me when you know what's going on,' he said.

'It might be a while.'

'I don't care. Call me.'

She hung up. Strike turned to face Robin, who looked appalled.

'Oh no,' she breathed.

'I'm calling Anstis,' said Strike, jabbing again at his phone.

But his old friend was in no mood to dispense favours.

'I warned you, Bob, I warned you this was coming. She did it, mate.'

'What've you got?' Strike demanded.

'Can't tell you that, Bob, sorry.'

'Did you get it from Kathryn Kent?'

'Can't say, mate.'

Barely deigning to return Anstis's conventional good wishes, Strike hung up.

'Dickhead!' he said. 'Bloody *dickhead*!'

Leonora was now in a place where he could not reach her. Strike was worried about how her grudging manner and the animosity to the police would appear to interlocutors. He could almost hear her complaining that Orlando was alone, demanding to know when she would be able to return to her daughter, indignant that the police had meddled with the daily grind of her miserable existence. He was afraid of her lack of self-preservation; he wanted Ilsa there, fast, before Leonora uttered innocently self-incriminating comments about her husband's general neglect and his girlfriends, before she could state again her almost incredible and suspicious claim that she knew nothing about her husband's books before they had proper covers on, before she attempted to explain why she had temporarily forgotten that they owned a second house where her husband's remains had lain decaying for weeks.

Five o'clock in the afternoon came and went without news from Ilsa. Looking out at the darkening sky and the snow, Strike insisted Robin go home.

'But you'll ring me when you hear?' she begged him, pulling on her coat and wrapping a thick woollen scarf around her neck.

'Yeah, of course,' said Strike.

But not until six thirty did Ilsa call him back.

'Couldn't be worse,' were her first words. She sounded tired and stressed. 'They've got proof of purchase, on the Quines' joint credit card, of protective overalls, wellington boots, gloves and ropes. They were bought online and paid for with their Visa. Oh – and a burqa.'

'You're fucking kidding me.'

'I'm not. I know you think she's innocent—'

'Yeah, I do,' said Strike, conveying a clear warning not to bother trying to persuade him otherwise.

'All right,' said Ilsa wearily, 'have it your own way, but I'll tell you this: she's not helping herself. She's being aggressive as hell, insisting Quine must have bought the stuff himself. A burqa, for God's sake . . . The ropes bought on the card are identical to the ones that were found tying the corpse. They asked her why Quine would want a burqa or plastic overalls of a strength to resist chemical spills, and all she said was: "I don't bloody know, do I?" Every other sentence, she kept asking when she could go home to her daughter; she just doesn't get it. The stuff was bought six months ago and sent to Talgarth Road – it couldn't look more premeditated unless they'd found a plan in her handwriting. She's denying she knew how Quine was going to end his book, but your guy Anstis—'

'There in person, was he?'

'Yeah, doing the interrogation. He kept asking whether she really expected them to believe that Quine never talked about what he was writing. Then she says, "I don't pay much attention." "So he *does* talk about his plots?" On and on it went, trying to wear her down, and in the end she says, "Well, he said something about the silkworm being boiled." That was all Anstis needed to be convinced she's been lying all along and she knew the whole plot. Oh, and they've found disturbed earth in their back garden.'

'And I'll lay you odds they'll find a dead cat called Mr Poop,' snarled Strike.

'That won't stop Anstis,' predicted Ilsa. 'He's absolutely sure it's her, Corm. They've got the right to keep her until eleven a.m. tomorrow and I'm sure they're going to charge her.'

'They haven't got enough,' said Strike fiercely. 'Where's the DNA evidence? Where are the witnesses?'

'That's the problem, Corm, there aren't any and that credit card bill's pretty damning. Look, I'm on your side,' said Ilsa patiently. 'You want my honest opinion? Anstis is taking a punt, hoping it's going to work out. I think he's feeling the pressure from all the press interest. And to be frank, he's feeling agitated about you slinking around the case and wants to take the initiative.'

Strike groaned.

'Where did they get a six-month-old Visa bill? Has it taken them this long to go through the stuff they took out of his study?'

'No,' said Ilsa. 'It's on the back of one of his daughter's pictures. Apparently the daughter gave it to a friend of his months ago, and this friend went to the police with it early this morning, claiming they'd only just looked at the back and realised what was on there. What did you just say?'

'Nothing,' Strike sighed.

'It sounded like "Tashkent".'

'Not that far off. I'll let you go, Ilsa . . . thanks for everything.'

Strike sat for a few seconds in frustrated silence.

'Bollocks,' he said softly to his dark office.

He knew how this had happened. Pippa Midgley, in her paranoia and her hysteria, convinced that Strike had been hired by Leonora to pin the murder on somebody else, had run from his office straight to Kathryn Kent. Pippa had confessed that she had blown Kathryn's pretence never to have read *Bombyx Mori* and urged her to use the evidence she had against Leonora. And so Kathryn Kent had ripped down her lover's daughter's picture (Strike imagined it stuck, with a magnet, to the fridge) and hurried off to the police station.

'*Bollocks*,' he repeated, more loudly, and dialled Robin's number.

39

I am so well acquainted with despair,
I know not how to hope . . .

Thomas Dekker and Thomas Middleton,
The Honest Whore

As her lawyer had predicted, Leonora Quine was charged with the murder of her husband at eleven o'clock the following morning. Alerted by phone, Strike and Robin watched the news spread online where, minute by minute, the story proliferated like multiplying bacteria. By half past eleven the *Sun* website had a full article on Leonora headed ROSE WEST LOOKALIKE WHO TRAINED AT THE BUTCHER'S.

The journalists had been busily collecting evidence of Quine's poor record as a husband. His frequent disappearances were linked to liaisons with other women, the sexual themes of his work dissected and embellished. Kathryn Kent had been located, doorstepped, photographed and categorised as 'Quine's curvy red-headed mistress, a writer of erotic fiction'.

Shortly before midday, Ilsa called Strike again.

'She's going to be up in court tomorrow.'

'Where?'

'Wood Green, eleven o'clock. Straight from there to Holloway, I expect.'

Strike had once lived with his mother and Lucy in a house a mere three minutes away from the closed women's prison that served north London.

'I want to see her.'

'You can try, but I can't imagine the police will want you near her and I've got to tell you, Corm, as her lawyer, it might not look—'

'Ilsa, I'm the only chance she's got now.'

'Thanks for the vote of confidence,' she said drily.

'You know what I mean.'

He heard her sigh.

'I'm thinking of you too. Do you really want to put the police's backs—?'

'How is she?' interrupted Strike.

'Not good,' said Ilsa. 'The separation from Orlando's killing her.'

The afternoon was punctuated with calls from journalists and people who had known Quine, both groups equally desperate for inside information. Elizabeth Tassel's voice was so deep and rough on the phone that Robin thought her a man.

'Where's Orlando?' the agent demanded of Strike when he came to the phone, as though he had been delegated charge of all members of the Quine family. 'Who's got her?'

'She's with a neighbour, I think,' he said, listening to her wheeze down the line.

'My God, what a mess,' rasped the agent. 'Leonora ... the worm turning after all these years ... it's incredible ... '

Nina Lascelles's reaction was, not altogether to Strike's surprise, poorly disguised relief. Murder had receded to its rightful place on the hazy edge of the possible. Its shadow no longer touched her; the killer was nobody she knew.

'His wife *does* look a bit like Rose West, doesn't she?' she asked Strike on the phone and he knew that she was staring at the *Sun*'s website. 'Except with long hair.'

She seemed to be commiserating with him. He had not solved the case. The police had beaten him to it.

'Listen, I'm having a few people over on Friday, fancy coming?'

'Can't, sorry,' said Strike. 'I'm having dinner with my brother.'

He could tell that she thought he was lying. There had been an almost imperceptible hesitation before he had said 'my brother', which might well have suggested a pause for rapid thought. Strike could not remember ever describing Al as his brother before. He rarely discussed his half-siblings on his father's side.

Before she left the office that evening Robin set a mug of tea in front of him as he sat poring over the Quine file. She could almost feel the anger that Strike was doing his best to hide, and suspected that it was directed at himself quite as much as at Anstis.

'It's not over,' she said, winding her scarf around her neck as she prepared to depart. 'We'll prove it wasn't her.'

She had once before used the plural pronoun when Strike's faith in himself had been at a low ebb. He appreciated the moral support, but a feeling of impotence was swamping his thought processes. Strike hated paddling on the periphery of the case, forced to watch as others dived for clues, leads and information.

He sat up late with the Quine file that night, reviewing the notes he had made of interviews, examining again the photographs he had printed off his phone. The mangled body of Owen Quine seemed to signal to him in the silence as corpses often did, exhaling mute appeals for justice and pity. Sometimes the murdered carried messages from their killers like signs forced into their stiff dead hands. Strike stared for a long time at the burned and gaping chest cavity, the ropes tight around ankles and wrists, the carcass trussed and gutted like a turkey, but try as he might, he could glean nothing from the pictures that he did not already know. Eventually he turned off all the lights and headed upstairs to bed.

It was a bittersweet relief to have to spend Thursday morning at the offices of his brunette client's exorbitantly expensive divorce lawyers in Lincoln's Inn Fields. Strike was glad to have something to while away time that could not be spent investigating Quine's murder, but he still felt that he had been lured to the meeting under false pretences. The flirtatious divorcée had given him to understand that her lawyer wanted to hear from Strike in person how he had collected the copious evidence of her husband's duplicity. He sat beside her at a highly polished mahogany table with room for twelve while she referred constantly to 'what Cormoran managed to find out' and 'as Cormoran witnessed, didn't you?', occasionally touching his wrist. It did not take Strike long to deduce from her suave lawyer's barely concealed irritation that it had not been his idea to have Strike in attendance. Nevertheless, as might have been expected when the hourly fee ran to over five hundred pounds, he showed no disposition to hurry matters along.

On a trip to the bathroom Strike checked his phone and saw, in tiny thumbnail pictures, Leonora being led in and out of Wood Green Crown Court. She had been charged and driven away in a police van. There had been plenty of press photographers but no members of the public baying for her blood; she was not supposed to have murdered anyone that the public much cared about.

A text from Robin arrived just as he was about to re-enter the conference room:

Could get you in to see Leonora at 6 this evening?

Great, he texted back.

'I thought,' said his flirtatious client, once he had sat back down, 'that Cormoran might be rather impressive on the witness stand.'

Strike had already shown her lawyer the meticulous notes and photographs he had compiled, detailing Mr Burnett's every covert transaction, the attempted sale of the apartment and the palming of the emerald necklace included. To Mrs Burnett's evident disappointment, neither man saw any reason for Strike to attend court in person given the quality of his records. Indeed, the lawyer could barely conceal his resentment of the reliance she seemed to place upon the detective. No doubt he thought this wealthy divorcée's discreet caresses and batted eyelashes might be better directed towards him, in his bespoke pinstripe suit, with his distinguished salt-and-pepper hair, instead of a man who looked like a limping prize fighter.

Relieved to quit the rarefied atmosphere, Strike caught the Tube back to his office, glad to take off his suit in his flat, happy to think that he would soon be rid of that particular case and in possession of the fat cheque that had been the only reason he had taken it. He was free now to focus on that thin, grey-haired fifty-year-old woman in Holloway who was touted as WRITER'S MOUSY WIFE EXPERT WITH CLEAVER on page two of the *Evening Standard* he had picked up on the journey.

'Was her lawyer happy?' Robin asked when he reappeared in the office.

'Reasonably,' said Strike, staring at the miniature tinsel Christmas tree she had placed on her tidy desk. It was decorated with tiny baubles and LED lights.

'Why?' he asked succinctly.

'Christmas,' said Robin, with a faint grin but without apology. 'I was going to put it up yesterday, but after Leonora was charged I didn't feel very festive. Anyway, I've got you an appointment to see her at six. You'll need to take photo ID—'

'Good work, thanks.'

'—and I got you sandwiches and I thought you might like to see this,' she said. 'Michael Fancourt's given an interview about Quine.'

She passed him a pack of cheese and pickle sandwiches and a copy of *The Times*, folded to the correct page. Strike lowered himself onto the farting leather sofa and ate while reading the article, which was adorned with a split photograph. On the left-hand side was a picture of Fancourt standing in front of an Elizabethan country house. Photographed from below, his head looked less out of proportion than usual. On the right-hand side was Quine, eccentric and wild-eyed in his feather-trimmed trilby, addressing a sparse audience in what seemed to be a small marquee.

The writer of the piece made much of the fact that Fancourt and Quine had once known each other well, had even been considered equivalent talents.

Few now remember Quine's breakout work, *Hobart's Sin*, although Fancourt touts it still as a fine example of what he calls Quine's magical-brutalism. For all Fancourt's reputation of a man who nurses his grudges, he brings a surprising generosity to our discussion of Quine's oeuvre.

'Always interesting and often underrated,' he says. 'I suspect that he will be treated more kindly by future critics than our contemporaries.'

This unexpected generosity is the more surprising when one considers that 25 years ago Fancourt's first wife, Elspeth Kerr, killed herself after reading a cruel parody of her first novel. The spoof was widely attributed to Fancourt's close friend and fellow literary rebel: the late Owen Quine.

'One mellows almost without realising it – a compensation of age, because anger is exhausting. I unburdened myself of many of the feelings about Ellie's death in my last novel, which should not be read as autobiographical, although . . .'

Strike skimmed the next two paragraphs, which appeared to be promoting Fancourt's next book, and resumed reading at the point where the word 'violence' jumped out at him.

It is difficult to reconcile the tweed-jacketed Fancourt in front of me with the one-time self-described literary punk who drew both plaudits and criticism for the inventive and gratuitous violence of his early work.

'If Mr Graham Greene was correct,' wrote critic Harvey Bird of Fancourt's first novel, 'and the writer needs a chip of ice in his heart, then Michael Fancourt surely has what it takes in abundance. Reading the rape scene in *Bellafront* one starts to imagine that this young man's innards must be glacial. In fact, there are two ways of looking at *Bellafront*, which is undoubtedly accomplished and original. The first possibility is that Mr Fancourt has written an unusually mature first novel, in which he has resisted the neophyte tendency to insert himself into the (anti-)heroic role. We may wince at its grotesqueries or its morality, but nobody could deny the power or artistry of the prose. The second, more disturbing, possibility is that Mr Fancourt does not possess much of an organ in which to place a chip of ice and his singularly inhuman tale corresponds to his own inner landscape. Time – and further work – will tell.'

Fancourt hailed originally from Slough, the only son of an unwed nurse. His mother still lives in the house in which he grew up.

'She's happy there,' he says. 'She has an enviable capacity for enjoying the familiar.'

His own home is a long way from a terraced house in Slough. Our conversation takes place in a long drawing room crammed with Meissen knick-knacks and Aubusson rugs, its windows overlooking the extensive grounds of Endsor Court.

'This is all my wife's choice,' says Fancourt dismissively. 'My taste in art is very different and confined to the grounds.' A large trench to the side of the building is being prepared for the concrete foundation to support a sculpture in rusted metal representing the Fury Tisiphone, which he describes with a laugh as an 'impulse buy … the avenger of murder, you know … a very powerful piece. My wife loathes it.'

And somehow we find ourselves back where the interview began: at the macabre fate of Owen Quine.

'I haven't yet processed Owen's murder,' says Fancourt quietly. 'Like most writers, I tend to find out what I feel on a subject by writing about it. It is how we interpret the world, how we make sense of it.'

Does this mean that we can expect a fictionalised account of Quine's killing?

'I can hear the accusations of bad taste and exploitation already,' smiles Fancourt. 'I dare say the themes of lost friendship, of a last chance to talk, to explain and make amends may make an appearance in due course, but Owen's murder has already been treated fictionally – by himself.'

He is one of the few to have read the notorious manuscript that appears to have formed the blueprint of the murder.

'I read it the very day that Quine's body was discovered. My publisher was very keen for me to see it – I'm portrayed in it, you see.' He seems genuinely indifferent about his inclusion, however insulting the portrait may have been. 'I wasn't interested in calling in lawyers. I deplore censorship.'

What did he think of the book, in literary terms?

'It's what Nabokov called a maniac's masterpiece,' he replies, smiling. 'There may be a case for publishing it in due course, who knows?'

He can't, surely, be serious?

'But why shouldn't it be published?' demands Fancourt. 'Art is supposed to provoke: by that standard alone, *Bombyx Mori* has more than fulfilled its remit. Yes, why not?' asks the literary punk, ensconced in his Elizabethan manor.

'With an introduction by Michael Fancourt?' I suggest.

'Stranger things have happened,' replies Michael Fancourt, with a grin. 'Much stranger.'

'Christ almighty,' muttered Strike, throwing *The Times* back onto Robin's desk and narrowly missing the Christmas tree.

'Did you see he only claims to have read *Bombyx Mori* the day you found Quine?'

'Yeah,' said Strike.

'He's lying,' said Robin.

'We *think* he's lying,' Strike corrected her.

Holding fast to his resolution not to waste any more money on taxis, but with the snow still falling, Strike took the number 29 bus through the darkening afternoon. It ran north, taking Strike on a twenty-minute journey through recently gritted roads. A haggard woman got on at Hampstead Road, accompanied by a small, grizzling boy. Some sixth sense told Strike that the three of them were headed in the same direction and, sure enough, both he and the woman stood to get out in Camden Road, alongside the bare flank of HMP Holloway.

'You're gonna see Mummy,' she told her charge, whom Strike guessed to be her grandson, though she looked around forty.

Surrounded by bare-limbed trees and grass verges covered in thick snow, the jail might have been a redbrick university faculty but for authoritarian signs in government-issue blue and white, and the sixteen-foot-high doors set into the wall so that prison vans might pass. Strike joined the trickle of visitors, several of them with children who strained to make marks in the untouched snow heaped beside the paths. The line shuffled together past the terracotta walls with their cement frets, past the hanging baskets now balls of snow in the freezing December air. The majority of his fellow visitors were women; Strike was unique among the men not merely for his size but for the fact that he did not look as though life had pummelled him into a quiescent stupor. A heavily tattooed youth in sagging jeans walking ahead of him staggered a little with every step. Strike had seen neurological damage back in Selly Oak, but guessed that this kind had not been sustained under mortar fire.

The stout female prison officer whose job it was to check IDs examined his driver's licence, then stared up at him.

'I know who you are,' she said, with a piercing look.

Strike wondered whether Anstis had asked to be tipped off if he went to see Leonora. It seemed probable.

He had arrived deliberately early, so as not to waste a minute of his allotted time with his client. This foresight permitted him a coffee in the visitors' centre, which was run by a children's charity. The room was bright and almost cheerful, and many of the kids greeted the trucks and teddies as old friends. Strike's haggard companion from the bus watched, gaunt and impassive, as the boy with her played with an Action Man around Strike's large feet, treating him like a massive piece of sculpture (*Tisiphone, the avenger of murder . . .*).

He was called through to the visitors' hall at six on the dot. Footsteps echoed off the shiny floors. The walls were of concrete blocks but bright murals painted by the prisoners did their best to soften the cavernous space, which echoed with the clang of metal and keys and the murmur of talk. The plastic seats were fixed either side of a small, low central table, similarly immovable, so as to minimise contact between prisoner and visitor, and prevent the passing of contraband. A toddler wailed. Warders stood around the walls, watching. Strike, who had only ever dealt with male prisoners, felt a repugnance for the place unusual in him. The kids staring at gaunt mothers, the subtle signs of mental illness in the fiddling and twitching of bitten fingers, drowsy, over-medicated women curled in their plastic seats were quite unlike the male detention facilities with which he was familiar.

Leonora sat waiting, tiny and fragile, pathetically glad to see him. She was wearing her own clothes, a loose sweatshirt and trousers in which she looked shrunken.

'Orlando's been in,' she said. Her eyes were bright red; he could tell that she had been crying for a long time. 'Didn't want to leave me. They dragged her out. Wouldn't let me calm her down.'

Where she would have shown defiance and anger he could hear the beginnings of institutionalised hopelessness. Forty-eight hours had taught her that she had lost all control and power.

'Leonora, we need to talk about that credit card statement.'

'I never had that card,' she said, her white lips trembling. 'Owen always kept it, I never had it except sometimes if I needed to go to the supermarket. He always gave me cash.'

Strike remembered that she had come to him in the first place because money was running out.

'I left all our finances up to Owen, that's how he liked it, but he was careless, he never used to check his bills nor his bank statements, used to just sling 'em in his office. I used to say to him, "You wanna check those, someone could be diddling you," but he never cared. He'd give anything to Orlando to draw on, that's why it had her picture—'

'Never mind the picture. Somebody other than you or Owen must have had access to that credit card. We're going to run through a few people, OK?'

'All right,' she mumbled, cowed.

'Elizabeth Tassel supervised work on the house in Talgarth Road, right? How was that paid for? Did she have a copy of your credit card?'

'No,' said Leonora.

'Are you sure?'

'Yeah, I'm sure, cos we offered it to her and she said it was easier just to take it out of Owen's next royalties cos he was due some any time. He sells well in Finland, I dunno why, but they like his—'

'You can't think of *any* time where Elizabeth Tassel did something for the house and had the Visa card?'

'No,' she said, shaking her head, 'never.'

'OK,' said Strike, 'can you remember – and take your time – any occasion when Owen paid for something with his credit card at Roper Chard?'

And to his astonishment she said, 'Not at Roper Chard exactly, but yeah.

'They were all there. I was there, too. It was . . . I dunno . . . two years ago? Maybe less . . . a big dinner for publishers, it was, at the Dorchester. They put me and Owen at a table with all the junior people. Daniel Chard and Jerry Waldegrave were nowhere near us. Anyway, there was a silent auction, you know, when you write down your bid for—'

'Yeah, I know how they work,' said Strike, trying to contain his impatience.

'It was for some writers' charity, when they try and get writers outta prison. And Owen bid on a weekend in this country house hotel and he won it and he had to give his credit card details at the dinner. Some of the young girls from the publishers were there all tarted up, taking payment. He gave the girl his card. I remember that because he was pissed,' she said, with a shadow of her former sullenness, 'an' he paid eight hundred quid for it. Showin' off. Tryin' to make out he earned money like the others.'

'He handed his credit card over to a girl from the publishers,' repeated Strike. 'Did she take the details at the table or—?'

'She couldn't make her little machine work,' said Leonora. 'She took it away and brought it back.'

'Anyone else there you recognised?'

'Michael Fancourt was there with his publisher,' she said, 'on the other side of the room. That was before he moved to Roper Chard.'

'Did he and Owen speak?'

'Not likely,' she said.

'Right, what about—?' he said, and hesitated. They had never before acknowledged the existence of Kathryn Kent.

'His girlfriend coulda got at it any time, couldn't she?' said Leonora, as though she had read his mind.

'You knew about her?' he asked, matter-of-fact.

'Police said something,' replied Leonora, her expression bleak. 'There's always been someone. Way he was. Picking them up at his writing classes. I used to give him right tellings-off. When they said he was – when they said he was – he was tied up—'

She had started to cry again.

'I knew it must've been a woman what done it. He liked that. Got him going.'

'You didn't know about Kathryn Kent before the police mentioned her?'

'I saw her name on a text on his phone one time but he said it was nothing. Said she was just one of his students. Like he always said. Told me he'd never leave us, me and Orlando.'

She wiped her eyes under her outdated glasses with the back of a thin, trembling hand.

'But you never saw Kathryn Kent until she came to the door to say that her sister had died?'

'Was that her, was it?' asked Leonora, sniffing and dabbing at her eyes with her cuff. 'Fat, i'n't she? Well, she could've got his credit card details any time, couldn't she? Taken it out of his wallet while he was sleeping.'

It was going to be difficult to find and question Kathryn Kent, Strike knew. He was sure she would have absconded from her flat to avoid the attentions of the press.

'The things the murderer bought on the card,' he said, changing tack, 'were ordered online. You haven't got a computer at home, have you?'

'Owen never liked 'em, he preferred his old type—'

'Have you ever ordered shopping over the internet?'

'Yeah,' she replied, and his heart sank a little. He had been hoping that Leonora might be that almost mythical beast: a computer virgin.

'Where did you do that?'

'Edna's, she let me borrow hers to order Orlando an art set for her birthday so I didn't have to go into town,' said Leonora.

Doubtless the police would soon be confiscating and ripping apart the kind-hearted Edna's computer.

A woman with a shaved head and a tattooed lip at the next table began shouting at a warder, who had warned her to stay in her seat. Leonora cowered away from the prisoner as she erupted into obscenities and the officer approached.

'Leonora, there's one last thing,' said Strike loudly, as the shouting at the next table reached a crescendo. 'Did Owen say anything to you about meaning to go away, to take a break, before he walked out on the fifth?'

'No,' she said, ''F course not.'

The prisoner at the next table had been persuaded to quieten down. Her visitor, a woman similarly tattooed and only slightly less aggressive-looking, gave the prison officer the finger as she walked away.

'You can't think of anything Owen said or did that might've suggested he was planning to go away for a while?' Strike persisted as Leonora watched their neighbours with anxious, owl-like eyes.

'What?' she said distractedly. 'No – he never tells – told me – always just went . . . If he knew he was going, why wouldn't he say goodbye?'

She began to cry, one thin hand over her mouth.

'What's going to happen to Dodo if they keep me in prison?' she asked him through her sobs. 'Edna can't have her for ever. She can't handle her. She went an' left Cheeky Monkey behind an' Dodo had done some pictures for me,' and after a disconcerted moment or two Strike decided that she must be talking about the plush orang-utan that Orlando had been cradling on his visit to their house. 'If they make me stay here—'

'I'm going to get you out,' said Strike with more confidence than he felt; but what harm would it do to give her something to hold on to, something to get her through the next twenty-four hours?

Their time was up. He left the hall without looking back, wondering what it was about Leonora, faded and grumpy, fifty years old with a brain-damaged daughter and a hopeless life, that had inspired in him this fierce determination, this fury . . .

Because she didn't do it, came the simple answer. *Because she's innocent*.

In the last eight months a stream of clients had pushed open the engraved glass door bearing his name and the reasons they had sought him had been uncannily similar. They had come because they wanted a spy, a weapon, a means of redressing some balance in their favour or of divesting themselves of inconvenient connections. They came because they sought an advantage, because they felt they were owed retribution or compensation. Because overwhelmingly, they wanted more money.

But Leonora had come to him because she wanted her husband to come home. It had been a simple wish born of weariness and of love, if not for the errant Quine then for the daughter who missed him. For the purity of her desire, Strike felt he owed her the best he could give.

The cold air outside the prison tasted different. It had been a long time since Strike had been in an environment where following orders was the backbone of daily life. He could feel his freedom as he walked, leaning heavily on the stick, back towards the bus stop.

At the back of the bus, three drunken young women wearing headbands from which reindeer antlers protruded were singing:

'They say it's unrealistic,
But I believe in you Saint Nick . . .'

Bloody Christmas, thought Strike, thinking irritably of the presents he would be expected to buy for his nephews and godchildren, none of whose ages he could ever remember.

The bus groaned on through the slush and the snow. Lights of every colour gleamed blurrily at Strike through the steamed-up bus window. Scowling, with his mind on injustice and murder, he effortlessly and silently repelled anyone who might have considered sitting in the seat beside him.

40

> Be glad thou art unnam'd; 'tis not worth the owning.
>
> Francis Beaumont and John Fletcher, *The False One*

Sleet, rain and snow pelted the office windows in turn the following day. Miss Brocklehurst's boss turned up at the office around midday to view confirmation of her infidelity. Shortly after Strike had bidden him farewell, Caroline Ingles arrived. She was harried, on her way to pick up her children from school, but determined to give Strike the card for the newly opened Golden Lace Gentleman's Club and Bar that she had found in her husband's wallet. Mr Ingles's promise to stay well away from lap-dancers, call girls and strippers had been a requirement of their reconciliation. Strike agreed to stake out Golden Lace to see whether Mr Ingles had again succumbed to temptation. By the time Caroline Ingles had left, Strike was very ready for the pack of sandwiches waiting for him on Robin's desk, but he had taken barely a mouthful when his phone rang.

Aware that their professional relationship was coming to a close, his brunette client was throwing caution to the winds and inviting Strike out to dinner. Strike thought he could see Robin smiling as she ate her sandwich, determinedly facing her monitor. He tried to decline with politeness, at first pleading his heavy workload and finally telling her that he was in a relationship.

'You never told me that,' she said, suddenly cold.

'I like to keep my private and professional lives separate,' he said.

She hung up halfway through his polite farewell.

'Maybe you should have gone out with her,' said Robin innocently. 'Just to make sure she'll pay her bill.'

'She'll bloody pay,' growled Strike, making up for lost time by cramming half a sandwich into his mouth. The phone buzzed. He groaned and looked down to see who had texted him.

His stomach contracted.

'Leonora?' asked Robin, who had seen his face fall.

Strike shook his head, his mouth full of sandwich.

The message comprised three words:

It was yours.

He had not changed his number since he had split up with Charlotte. Too much hassle, when a hundred professional contacts had it. This was the first time she had used it in eight months.

Strike remembered Dave Polworth's warning:

You be on the watch, Diddy, for signs of her galloping back over the horizon. Wouldn't be surprised if she bolts.

Today was the third, he reminded himself. She was supposed to be getting married tomorrow.

For the first time since he had owned a mobile phone, Strike wished it had the facility to reveal a caller's location. Had she sent this from the Castle of Fucking Croy, in an interlude between checking the canapés and the flowers in the chapel? Or was she standing on the corner of Denmark Street, watching his office like Pippa Midgley? Running away from a grand, well-publicised wedding like this would be Charlotte's crowning achievement, the very apex of her career of mayhem and disruption.

Strike put the mobile back into his pocket and started on his second sandwich. Deducing that she was not about to discover what had made Strike's expression turn stony, Robin screwed up her empty crisp packet, dropped it in the bin and said:

'You're meeting your brother tonight, aren't you?'

'What?'

'Aren't you meeting your brother—?'

'Oh yeah,' said Strike. 'Yeah.'

'At the River Café?'

'Yeah.'

It was yours.

'Why?' asked Robin.

Mine. The hell it was. If it even existed.

'What?' said Strike, vaguely aware that Robin had asked him something.

'Are you OK?'

'Yeah, I'm fine,' he said, pulling himself together. 'What did you ask me?'

'Why are you going to the River Café?'

'Oh. Well,' said Strike, reaching for his own packet of crisps, 'it's a long shot, but I want to speak to anyone who witnessed Quine and Tassel's row. I'm trying to get a handle on whether he staged it, whether he was planning his disappearance all along.'

'You're hoping to find a member of staff who was there that night?' said Robin, clearly dubious.

'Which is why I'm taking Al,' said Strike. 'He knows every waiter in every smart restaurant in London. All my father's kids do.'

When he had finished lunch he took a coffee into his office and closed the door. Sleet was again spattering his window. He could not resist glancing down into the frozen street, half-expecting (hoping?) to see her there, long black hair whipping around her perfect, pale face, staring up at him, imploring him with her flecked green-hazel eyes . . . but there was nobody in the street except strangers swaddled against the relentless weather.

He was crazy on every count. She was in Scotland and it was much, much better so.

Later, when Robin had gone home, he put on the Italian suit that Charlotte had bought him over a year ago, when they had dined at this very restaurant to celebrate his thirty-fifth birthday. After pulling on his overcoat he locked his flat door and set out for the Tube in the sub-zero cold, still leaning on his stick.

Christmas assailed him from every window he passed; spangled lights, mounds of new objects, of toys and gadgets, fake snow on glass and sundry pre-Christmas sale signs adding a mournful note in the depths of the recession. More pre-Christmas revellers on the Friday-night Tube: girls in ludicrously tiny glittering dresses risking hypothermia for a fumble with the boy from Packaging. Strike felt weary and low.

The walk from Hammersmith was longer than he had remembered. As he proceeded down Fulham Palace Road he realised how close he was to Elizabeth Tassel's house. Presumably she had suggested the restaurant, a long way from the Quines' place in Ladbroke Grove, precisely because of its convenience to her.

After ten minutes Strike turned right and headed through the darkness towards Thames Wharf, through empty echoing streets, his breath rising in a smoky cloud. The riverside garden that in summer would be full of diners at white table-clothed chairs was buried under thick snow. The Thames glinted darkly beyond the pale carpet, iron-cold and menacing. Strike turned into the converted brick storage facility and was at once subsumed in light, warmth and noise.

There, just inside the door, leaning against the bar with his elbow on its shiny steel surface, was Al, deep in friendly conversation with the barman.

He was barely five foot ten, which was short for one of Rokeby's children, and carrying a little too much weight. His mouse-brown hair was slicked back; he had his mother's narrow jaw but he had inherited the weak divergent squint that added an attractive strangeness to Rokeby's handsome face and marked Al inescapably as his father's son.

Catching sight of Strike, Al let out a roar of welcome, bounced forwards and hugged him. Strike barely responded, being hampered by his stick and the coat he was trying to remove. Al fell back, looking sheepish.

'How are you, bruv?'

In spite of the comic Anglicism, his accent was a strange mid-Atlantic hybrid that testified to years spent between Europe and America.

'Not bad,' said Strike, 'you?'

'Yeah, not bad,' echoed Al. 'Not bad. Could be worse.'

He gave a kind of exaggerated Gallic shrug. Al had been educated at Le Rosey, the international boarding school in

Switzerland, and his body language still bore traces of the Continental manners he had met there. Something else underlay the response, however, something that Strike felt every time they met: Al's guilt, his defensiveness, a preparedness to meet accusations of having had a soft and easy life compared to his older brother.

'What're you having?' Al asked. 'Beer? Fancy a Peroni?'

They sat side by side at the crammed bar, facing glass shelves of bottles, waiting for their table. Looking down the long, packed restaurant, with its industrial steel ceiling in stylised waves, its cerulean carpet and the wood-burning oven at the end like a giant beehive, Strike spotted a celebrated sculptor, a famous female architect and at least one well-known actor.

'Heard about you and Charlotte,' Al said. 'Shame.'

Strike wondered whether Al knew somebody who knew her. He ran with a jet-set crowd that might well stretch to the future Viscount of Croy.

'Yeah, well,' said Strike with a shrug. 'For the best.'

(He and Charlotte had sat here, in this wonderful restaurant by the river, and enjoyed their very last happy evening together. It had taken four months for the relationship to unravel and implode, four months of exhausting aggression and misery . . . *it was yours*.)

A good-looking young woman whom Al greeted by name showed them to their table; an equally attractive young man handed them menus. Strike waited for Al to order wine and for the staff to depart before explaining why they were there.

'Four weeks ago tonight,' he told Al, 'a writer called Owen Quine had a row with his agent in here. By all accounts the whole restaurant saw it. He stormed out and shortly afterwards – probably within days and maybe even that night—'

'—he was murdered,' said Al, who had listened to Strike with his mouth open. 'I saw it in the paper. You found the body.'

His tone conveyed a yearning for details that Strike chose to ignore.

'There might be nothing to find out here, but I—'

'His wife did it, though,' said Al, puzzled. 'They've got her.'

'His wife didn't do it,' said Strike, turning his attention to the paper menu. He had noticed before now that Al, who had grown up surrounded by innumerable inaccurate press stories about his father and his family, never seemed to extend his healthy mistrust of British journalism to any other topic.

(It had had two campuses, Al's school: lessons by Lake Geneva in the summer months and then up to Gstaad for the winter; afternoons spent skiing and skating. Al had grown up breathing exorbitantly priced mountain air, cushioned by the companionship of other celebrity children. The distant snarling of the tabloids had been a mere background murmur in his life . . . this, at least, was how Strike interpreted the little that Al had told him of his youth.)

'The wife didn't do it?' said Al when Strike looked up again.

'No.'

'Whoa. You gonna pull another Lula Landry?' asked Al, with a wide grin that added charm to his off-kilter stare.

'That's the idea,' said Strike.

'You want me to sound out the staff?' asked Al.

'Exactly,' said Strike.

He was amused and touched by how delighted Al seemed to be at being given the chance to render him service.

'No problem. No problem. Try and get someone decent for you. Where's Loulou gone? She's a smart cookie.'

After they had ordered, Al strolled to the bathroom to see

whether he could spot the smart Loulou. Strike sat alone, drinking Tignanello ordered by Al, watching the white-coated chefs working in the open kitchen. They were young, skilled and efficient. Flames darted, knives flickered, heavy iron pans moved hither and thither.

He's not stupid, Strike thought of his brother, watching Al meander back towards the table, leading a dark girl in a white apron. *He's just . . .*

'This is Loulou,' said Al, sitting back down. 'She was here that night.'

'You remember the argument?' Strike asked her, focusing at once on the girl who was too busy to sit but stood smiling vaguely at him.

'Oh yeah,' she said. 'It was really loud. Brought the place to a standstill.'

'Can you remember what the man looked like?' Strike said, keen to establish that she had witnessed the right row.

'Fat bloke wearing a hat, yeah,' she said. 'Yelling at a woman with grey hair. Yeah, they had a real bust-up. Sorry, I'm going to have to—'

And she was gone, to take another table's order.

'We'll grab her on the way back,' Al reassured Strike. 'Eddie sends his best, by the way. Wishes he could've been here.'

'How's he doing?' asked Strike, feigning interest. Where Al had shown himself keen to forge a friendship, his younger brother, Eddie, seemed indifferent. He was twenty-four and the lead singer in his own band. Strike had never listened to any of their music.

'He's great,' said Al.

Silence fell between them. Their starters arrived and they ate without talking. Strike knew that Al had achieved excellent grades in his International Baccalaureate. One evening in a military tent in Afghanistan, Strike had seen a photograph online of eighteen-year-old Al in a cream blazer with a crest on the pocket, long hair swept sideways and gleaming gold in the bright Geneva sun. Rokeby had had his arm around Al, beaming with paternal pride. The picture had been newsworthy because Rokeby had never been photographed in a suit and tie before.

'Hello, Al,' said a familiar voice.

And, to Strike's astonishment, there stood Daniel Chard on crutches, his bald head reflecting the subtle spots shining from the industrial waves above them. Wearing a dark red open-necked shirt and a grey suit, the publisher looked stylish among this more bohemian crowd.

'Oh,' said Al, and Strike could tell that he was struggling to place Chard, 'er – hi—'

'Dan Chard,' said the publisher. 'We met when I was speaking to your father about his autobiography?'

'Oh – oh yeah!' said Al, standing up and shaking hands. 'This is my brother Cormoran.'

If Strike had been surprised to see Chard approach Al, it was nothing to the shock that registered on Chard's face at the sight of Strike.

'Your – your brother?'

'Half-brother,' said Strike, inwardly amused by Chard's evident bewilderment. How could the hireling detective be related to the playboy prince?

The effort it had cost Chard to approach the son of a potentially lucrative subject seemed to have left him with nothing to spare for a three-way awkward silence.

'Leg feeling better?' Strike asked.

'Oh, yes,' said Chard. 'Much. Well, I'll . . . I'll leave you to your dinner.'

He moved away, swinging deftly between tables, and resumed his seat where Strike could no longer watch him. Strike and Al sat back down, Strike reflecting on how very small London was once you reached a certain altitude; once you had left behind those who could not easily secure tables at the best restaurants and clubs.

'Couldn't remember who he was,' said Al with a sheepish grin.

'He's thinking of writing his autobiography, is he?' Strike asked.

He never referred to Rokeby as Dad, but tried to remember not to call him Rokeby in front of Al.

'Yeah,' said Al. 'They're offering him big money. I dunno whether he's going to go with that bloke or one of the others. It'll probably be ghosted.'

Strike wondered fleetingly how Rokeby might treat his eldest son's accidental conception and disputed birth in such a book. Perhaps, he thought, Rokeby would skip any mention of it. That would certainly be Strike's preference.

'He'd still like to meet you, you know,' said Al, with an air of having screwed himself up to say it. 'He's really proud . . . he read everything about the Landry case.'

'Yeah?' said Strike, looking around the restaurant for Loulou, the waitress who remembered Quine.

'Yeah,' said Al.

'So what did he do, interview publishers?' Strike asked. He thought of Kathryn Kent, of Quine himself, the one unable to find a publisher, the other dropped; and the ageing rock star able to take his pick.

'Yeah, kind of,' said Al. 'I dunno if he's going to do it or not. I think that Chard guy was recommended to him.'

'Who by?'

'Michael Fancourt,' said Al, wiping his plate of risotto clean with a piece of bread.

'Rokeby knows Fancourt?' asked Strike, forgetting his resolution.

'Yeah,' said Al, with a slight frown; then: 'Let's face it, Dad knows everyone.'

It reminded Strike of the way Elizabeth Tassel had said 'I thought everyone knew' why she no longer represented Fancourt, but there was a difference. To Al, 'everyone' meant the 'someones': the rich, the famous, the influential. The poor saps who bought his father's music were nobodies, just as Strike had been nobody until he had burst into prominence for catching a killer.

'When did Fancourt recommend Roper Chard to – when did he recommend Chard?' asked Strike.

'Dunno – few months ago?' said Al vaguely. 'He told Dad he'd just moved there himself. Half a million advance.'

'Nice,' said Strike.

'Told Dad to watch the news, that there'd be a buzz about the place once he moved.'

Loulou the waitress had moved back into view. Al hailed her again; she approached with a harried expression.

'Give me ten,' she said, 'and I'll be able to talk. Just give me ten.'

While Strike finished his pork, Al asked about his work. Strike was surprised by the genuineness of Al's interest.

'D'you miss the army?' Al asked.

'Sometimes,' admitted Strike. 'What are you up to these days?'

He felt a vague guilt at not having asked already. Now that he came to think about it, he was not clear how, or whether, Al had ever earned his living.

'Might be going into business with a friend,' said Al.

Not working, then, thought Strike.

'Bespoke services . . . leisure opportunities,' muttered Al.

'Great,' said Strike.

'Will be if it comes to anything,' said Al.

A pause. Strike looked around for Loulou, the whole point of being here, but she was out of sight, busy as Al had probably never been busy in his life.

'You've got credibility, at least,' said Al.

'Hmn?' said Strike.

'Made it on your own, haven't you?' said Al.

'What?'

Strike realised that there was a one-sided crisis happening at the table. Al was looking at him with a mixture of mingled defiance and envy.

'Yeah, well,' said Strike, shrugging his large shoulders.

He could not think of any more meaningful response that would not sound superior or aggrieved, nor did he wish to encourage Al in what seemed to be an attempt to have a more personal conversation than they had ever managed.

'You're the only one of us who doesn't use it,' said Al. 'Don't suppose it would've helped in the army, anyway, would it?'

Futile to pretend not to know what 'it' was.

'S'pose not,' said Strike (and indeed, on the rare occasions that his parentage had attracted the attention of fellow soldiers he had met nothing but incredulity, especially given how little he looked like Rokeby).

But he thought wryly of his flat on this ice-cold winter night:

two and a half cluttered rooms, ill-fitting windowpanes. Al would be spending tonight in Mayfair, in their father's staffed house. It might be salutary to show his brother the reality of independence before he romanticised it too much . . .

'S'pose you think this is self-pitying bloody whinging?' demanded Al.

Strike had seen Al's graduation photograph online a bare hour after interviewing an inconsolable nineteen-year-old private who had accidentally shot his best friend in the chest and neck with a machine gun.

'Everyone's entitled to whinge,' said Strike.

Al looked as though he might take offence, then, reluctantly, grinned.

Loulou was suddenly beside them, clutching a glass of water and deftly removing her apron with one hand before she sat down with them.

'OK, I've got five minutes,' she said to Strike without preamble. 'Al says you want to know about that jerk of a writer?'

'Yeah,' said Strike, focusing at once. 'What makes you say he was a jerk?'

'He loved it,' she said, sipping her water.

'Loved—?'

'Causing a scene. He was yelling and swearing, but it was for show, you could tell. He wanted everyone to hear him, he wanted an audience. He wasn't a good actor.'

'Can you remember what he said?' asked Strike, pulling out a notebook. Al was watching excitedly.

'There was loads of it. He called the woman a bitch, said she'd lied to him, that he'd put the book out himself and screw her. But he was enjoying himself,' she said. 'It was fake fury.'

'And what about Eliz – the woman?'

'Oh, she was bloody furious,' said Loulou cheerfully. '*She* wasn't pretending. The more he ponced about waving his arms and shouting at her, the redder she got – shaking with anger, she could hardly contain herself. She said something about "roping in that stupid bloody woman" and I think it was around then that he stormed out, parking her with the bill, everyone staring at her – she looked mortified. I felt awful for her.'

'Did she try and follow him?'

'No, she paid and then went into the loo for a bit. I wondered whether she was crying, actually. Then she left.'

'That's very helpful,' said Strike. 'You can't remember anything else they said to each other?'

'Yeah,' said Loulou calmly, 'he shouted, "All because of Fancourt and his limp fucking dick."'

Strike and Al stared at her.

'"All because of Fancourt and his limp fucking dick"?' repeated Strike.

'Yeah,' said Loulou. 'That was the bit that made the restaurant go quiet—'

'You can see why it would,' commented Al, with a snigger.

'She tried to shout him down, she was absolutely incensed, but he wasn't having any of it. He was loving the attention. Lapping it up.

'Look, I've got to get going,' said Loulou, 'sorry.' She stood up and re-tied her apron. 'See you, Al.'

She did not know Strike's name, but smiled at him as she bustled away again.

Daniel Chard was leaving; his bald head had reappeared over the crowd, accompanied by a group of similarly aged and elegant people, all of them walking out together, talking, nodding to each other. Strike watched them go with his mind elsewhere. He did not notice the removal of his empty plate.

All because of Fancourt and his limp fucking dick . . .

Odd.

I can't shake this mad bloody idea that Owen did it to himself. That he staged it . . .

'You all right, bruv?' asked Al.

A note with a kiss: *Payback time for both of us . . .*

'Yeah,' said Strike.

Load of gore and arcane symbolism . . . stoke that man's vanity and you could get him to do anything you wanted . . . two hermaphrodites, two bloody bags . . . A beautiful lost soul, that's what he said to me . . . the silkworm was a metaphor for the writer, who has to go through agonies to get at the good stuff . . .

Like the turning lid that finds its thread, a multitude of disconnected facts revolved in Strike's mind and slid suddenly into place, incontrovertibly correct, unassailably right. He turned his theory around and around: it was perfect, snug and solid.

The problem was that he could not yet see how to prove it.

41

Think'st thou my thoughts are lunacies of love?
No, they are brands firèd in Pluto's forge . . .

Robert Greene, *Orlando Furioso*

Strike rose early next morning after a night of broken sleep, tired, frustrated and edgy. He checked his phone for messages before showering and after dressing, then went downstairs into his empty office, irritated that Robin was not there on a Saturday and feeling the absence, unreasonably, as a mark of her lack of commitment. She would have been a useful sounding board this morning; he would have liked company after his revelation of the previous evening. He considered phoning her, but it would be infinitely more satisfying to tell her face to face rather than doing it over the telephone, particularly if Matthew were listening in.

Strike made himself tea but let it grow cold while he pored over the Quine file.

The sense of his impotence ballooned in the silence. He kept checking his mobile.

He wanted to do something, but he was completely stymied by lack of official status, having no authority to make searches of private property or to enforce the cooperation of witnesses.

There was nothing he could do until his interview with Michael Fancourt on Monday, unless . . . Ought he to call Anstis and lay his theory before him? Strike frowned, running thick fingers through his dense hair, imagining Anstis's patronising response. There was literally not a shred of evidence. All was conjecture – *but I'm right*, thought Strike with easy arrogance, *and he's screwed up*. Anstis had neither the wit nor the imagination to appreciate a theory that explained every oddity in the killing, but which would seem to him incredible compared to the easy solution, riddled with inconsistencies and unanswered questions though the case against Leonora was.

Explain, Strike demanded of an imaginary Anstis, *why a woman smart enough to spirit away his guts without trace would have been dumb enough to order ropes and a burqa on her own credit card. Explain why a mother with no relatives, whose sole preoccupation in life is the well-being of her daughter, would risk a life sentence. Explain why, after years of accommodating Quine's infidelity and sexual quirks to keep their family together, she suddenly decided to kill him?*

But to the last question Anstis might just have a reasonable answer: that Quine had been on the verge of leaving his wife for Kathryn Kent. The author's life had been well insured: perhaps Leonora would have decided that financial security as a widow would be preferable to an uncertain hand-to-mouth existence while her feckless ex squandered money on his second wife. A jury would buy that version of events, especially if Kathryn Kent took the stand and confirmed that Quine had promised to marry her.

Strike was afraid that he had blown his chance with Kathryn Kent, turning up unexpectedly on her doorstep as he had – in retrospect a clumsy, inept move. He had scared her, looming out of the darkness on her balcony, making it only too easy for Pippa Midgley to paint him as Leonora's sinister stooge. He ought to have proceeded with finesse, eased himself into her confidence the way he had done with Lord Parker's PA, so that he could extract confessions like teeth under the influence of concerned sympathy, instead of jack-booting to her door like a bailiff.

He checked his mobile again. No messages. He glanced at his watch. It was barely half past nine. Against his will, he felt his attention tugging to be free of the place where he wanted and needed it – on Quine's killer, and the things that must be done to secure an arrest – to the seventeenth-century chapel in the Castle of Croy . . .

She would be getting dressed, no doubt in a bridal gown costing thousands. He could imagine her naked in front of the mirror, painting her face. He had watched her do it a hundred times; wielding the make-up brushes in front of dressing-table mirrors, hotel mirrors, so acutely aware of her own desirability that she almost attained unselfconsciousness.

Was Charlotte checking her phone as the minutes slipped by, now that the short walk up the aisle was so close, now that it felt like the walk along a gangplank? Was she still waiting, hoping, for a response from Strike to her three-word message of yesterday?

And if he sent an answer now . . . what would it take to make her turn her back on the wedding dress (he could imagine it hanging like a ghost in the corner of her room) and pull on her jeans, throw a few things in a holdall and slip out of a back door? Into a car, her foot flat to the floor, heading back south to the man who had always meant escape . . .

'Fuck this,' Strike muttered.

He stood up, shoved the mobile in his pocket, threw back the last of his cold tea and pulled on his overcoat. Keeping busy was the only answer: action had always been his drug of choice.

Sure though he was that Kathryn Kent would have decamped to a friend's now that the press had found her, and notwithstanding the fact that he regretted turning up unannounced on her doorstep, he returned to Clem Attlee Court only to have his suspicions confirmed. Nobody answered the door, the lights were off and all seemed silent within.

An icy wind blew along the brick balcony. As Strike moved away, the angry-looking woman from next door appeared, this time eager to talk.

'She's gawn away. You press, are you?'

'Yeah,' said Strike, because he could tell the neighbour was excited at the idea and because he did not want Kent to know that he had been back.

'The things your lot've written,' she said with poorly disguised glee. 'The things you've said about her! No, she's gawn.'

'Any idea when she'll be back?'

'Nah,' said the neighbour with regret. Her pink scalp was visible through the sparse, tightly permed grey hair. 'I could call ya,' she suggested. 'If she shows up again.'

'That'd be very helpful,' said Strike.

His name had been in the papers a little too recently to hand over one of his cards. He tore out a page of his notebook, wrote his number out for her and handed it over with a twenty-pound note.

'Cheers,' she said, businesslike. 'See ya.'

He passed a cat on his way back downstairs, the same one, he was sure, at which Kathryn Kent had taken a kick. It watched him with wary but superior eyes as he passed. The gang of youths he had met previously had gone; too cold today if your warmest item of clothing was a sweatshirt.

Limping through the slippery grey snow required physical effort, which helped distract his busy mind, making moot the question of whether he was moving from suspect to suspect on Leonora's behalf, or Charlotte's. Let the latter continue towards the prison of her own choosing: he would not call, he would not text.

When he reached the Tube, he pulled out his phone and telephoned Jerry Waldegrave. He was sure that the editor had information that Strike needed, that he had not known he needed before his moment of revelation in the River Café, but Waldegrave did not pick up. Strike was not surprised. Waldegrave had a failing marriage, a moribund career and a daughter to worry about; why take a detective's calls too? Why complicate your life when it did not need complicating, when you had a choice?

The cold, the ringing of unanswered phones, silent flats with locked doors: he could do nothing else today. Strike bought a newspaper and went to the Tottenham, sitting himself beneath one of the voluptuous women painted by a Victorian set-designer, cavorting with flora in their flimsy draperies. Today Strike felt strangely as though he was in a waiting room, whiling away the hours. Memories like shrapnel, for ever embedded, infected by what had come later . . . words of love and undying devotion, times of sublime happiness, lies upon lies upon lies . . . his attention kept sliding away from the stories he was reading.

His sister Lucy had once said to him in exasperation, 'Why do you put up with it? Why? Just because she's beautiful?'

And he had answered: 'It helps.'

She had expected him to say 'no', of course. Though they

spent so much time trying to make themselves beautiful, you were not supposed to admit to women that beauty mattered. Charlotte *was* beautiful, the most beautiful woman he had ever seen, and he had never rid himself of a sense of wonder at her looks, nor of the gratitude they inspired, nor of pride by association.

Love, Michael Fancourt had said, *is a delusion.*

Strike turned the page on a picture of the Chancellor of the Exchequer's sulky face without seeing it. Had he imagined things in Charlotte that had never been there? Had he invented virtues for her, to add lustre to her staggering looks? He had been nineteen when they met. It seemed incredibly young to Strike now, as he sat in this pub carrying a good two stone of excess weight, missing half a leg.

Perhaps he *had* created a Charlotte in her own image who had never existed outside his own besotted mind, but what of it? He had loved the real Charlotte too, the woman who had stripped herself bare in front of him, demanding whether he could still love her if she did *this*, if she confessed to *this*, if she treated him like *this* . . . until finally she had found his limit and beauty, rage and tears had been insufficient to hold him, and she had fled into the arms of another man.

And maybe that's love, he thought, siding in his mind with Michael Fancourt against an invisible and censorious Robin, who for some reason seemed to be sitting in judgement on him as he sat drinking Doom Bar and pretending to read about the worst winter on record. *You and Matthew* . . . Strike could see it even if she could not: the condition of being with Matthew was not to be herself.

Where was the couple that saw each other clearly? In the endless parade of suburban conformity that seemed to be Lucy and Greg's marriage? In the tedious variations on betrayal and disillusionment that brought a never-ending stream of clients to his door? In the wilfully blind allegiance of Leonora Quine to a man whose every fault had been excused because 'he's a writer', or the hero worship that Kathryn Kent and Pippa Midgley had brought to the same fool, trussed like a turkey and disembowelled?

Strike was depressing himself. He was halfway down his third pint. As he wondered whether he was going to have a fourth, his mobile buzzed on the table where he had laid it, face down.

He drank his beer slowly while the pub filled up around him, looking at his phone, taking bets against himself. *Outside the chapel, giving me one last chance to stop it? Or she's done it and wants to let me know?*

He drank the last of his beer before flipping the mobile over.

Congratulate me. Mrs Jago Ross.

Strike stared at the words for a few seconds, then slid the phone into his pocket, got up, folded the newspaper under his arm and set off home.

As he walked with the aid of his stick back to Denmark Street he remembered words from his favourite book, unread for a very long time, buried at the bottom of the box of belongings on his landing.

> *. . . difficile est longum subito deponere amoren,*
> *difficile est, uerum hoc qua lubet efficias . . .*
> . . . it is hard to throw off long-established love:
> Hard, but this you must manage somehow . . .

The restlessness that had consumed him all day had gone. He felt hungry and in need of relaxation. Arsenal were playing Fulham at three; there was just time to cook himself a late lunch before kick-off.

And after that, he thought, he might go round to see Nina Lascelles. Tonight was not a night he fancied spending alone.

42

MATHEO: . . . an odd toy.
GIULIANO: Ay, to mock an ape withal.

Ben Jonson, *Every Man in His Humour*

Robin arrived at work on Monday morning feeling tired and vaguely battle-weary, but proud of herself.

She and Matthew had spent most of the weekend discussing her job. In some ways (strange to think this, after nine years together) it had been the deepest and most serious conversation that they had ever had. Why had she not admitted for so long that her secret interest in investigative work had long pre-dated meeting Cormoran Strike? Matthew had seemed stunned when she had finally confessed to him that she had had an ambition to work in some form of criminal investigation since her early teens.

'I'd have thought it would've been the last thing . . .' Matthew had mumbled, tailing off but referring obliquely, as Robin knew, to the reason she had dropped out of university.

'I just never knew how to say it to you,' she told him. 'I thought you'd laugh. So it wasn't Cormoran making me stay, or anything to do with him as a – as a person' (she had been on the verge of saying 'as a man', but saved herself just in time). 'It was me. It's what I want to do. I love it. And now he says he'll train me, Matt, and that's what I always wanted.'

The discussion had gone on all through Sunday, the disconcerted Matthew shifting slowly, like a boulder.

'How much weekend work?' he had asked her suspiciously.

'I don't know; when it's needed. Matt, I love the job, don't you understand? I don't want to pretend any more. I just want to do it, and I'd like your support.'

In the end he had put his arms around her and agreed. She had tried not to feel grateful that his mother had just died, making him, she could not help thinking, just a little more amenable to persuasion than he might usually have been.

Robin had been looking forward to telling Strike about this mature development in her relationship but he was not in the office when she arrived. Lying on the desk beside her tiny tinsel tree was a short note in his distinctive, hard-to-read handwriting:

> No milk, gone out for breakfast, then to Hamleys, want to beat crowds. PS Know who killed Quine.

Robin gasped. Seizing the phone, she called Strike's mobile, only to hear the engaged signal.

Hamleys would not open until ten but Robin did not think she could bear to wait that long. Again and again she pressed redial while she opened and sorted the post, but Strike was still on the other call. She opened emails, the phone clamped to one ear; half an hour passed, then an hour, and still the engaged tone emanated from Strike's number. She began to feel irritated, suspecting that it was a deliberate ploy to keep her in suspense.

At half past ten a soft ping from the computer announced the arrival of an email from an unfamiliar sender called

Clodia2@live.com, who had sent nothing but an attachment labelled *FYI*.

Robin clicked on it automatically, still listening to the engaged tone. A large black-and-white picture swelled to fill her computer monitor.

The backdrop was stark; an overcast sky and the exterior of an old stone building. Everyone in the picture was out of focus except the bride, who had turned to look directly at the camera. She was wearing a long, plain, slim-fitting white gown with a floor-length veil held in place by a thin diamond band. Her black hair was flying like the folds of tulle in what looked like a stiff breeze. One hand was clasped in that of a blurred figure in a morning suit who appeared to be laughing, but her expression was unlike any bride's that Robin had ever seen. She looked broken, bereft, haunted. Her eyes staring straight into Robin's as though they alone were friends, as though Robin were the only one who might understand.

Robin lowered the mobile she had been listening to and stared at the picture. She had seen that extraordinarily beautiful face before. They had spoken once, on the telephone: Robin remembered a low, attractively husky voice. This was Charlotte, Strike's ex-fiancée, the woman she had once seen running from this very building.

She was *so* beautiful. Robin felt strangely humbled by the other woman's looks, and awed by her profound sadness. Sixteen years, on and off, with Strike – Strike, with his pube-like hair, his boxer's profile and his half a leg . . . not that those things mattered, Robin told herself, staring transfixed at this incomparably stunning, sad bride . . .

The door opened. Strike was suddenly there beside her, two carrier bags of toys in his hands, and Robin, who had not heard him coming up the stairs, jumped as though she had been caught pilfering from the petty cash.

'Morning,' he said.

She reached hastily for the computer mouse, trying to close down the picture before he could see it, but her scramble to cover up what she was viewing drew his eyes irresistibly to the screen. Robin froze, shamefaced.

'She sent it a few minutes ago, I didn't know what it was when I opened it. I'm . . . sorry.'

Strike stared at the picture for a few seconds then turned away, setting the bags of toys down on the floor by her desk.

'Just delete it,' he said. He sounded neither sad nor angry, but firm.

Robin hesitated, then closed the file, deleted the email and emptied the trash folder.

'Cheers,' he said, straightening up, and by his manner informed her that there would be no discussion of Charlotte's wedding picture. 'I've got about thirty missed calls from you on my phone.'

'Well, what do you expect?' said Robin with spirit. 'Your note – you said—'

'I had to take a call from my aunt,' said Strike. 'An hour and ten minutes on the medical complaints of everyone in St Mawes, all because I told her I'm going home for Christmas.'

He laughed at the sight of her barely contained frustration.

'All right, but we've got to be quick. I've just realised there's something we could do this morning before I meet Fancourt.'

Still wearing his coat he sat down on the leather sofa and talked for ten solid minutes, laying his theory before her in detail.

When he had finished there was a long silence. The misty,

mystical image of the boy-angel in her local church floated into Robin's mind as she stared at Strike in near total disbelief.

'Which bit's causing you problems?' asked Strike kindly.

'Er . . .' said Robin.

'We already agreed that Quine's disappearance might not've been spontaneous, right?' Strike asked her. 'If you add together the mattress at Talgarth Road – convenient, in a house that hasn't been used in twenty-five years – and the fact that a week before he vanished Quine told that bloke in the bookshop he was going away and bought himself reading material – and the waitress at the River Café saying Quine wasn't really angry when he was shouting at Tassel, that he was enjoying himself – I think we can hypothesise a staged disappearance.'

'OK,' she said. This part of Strike's theory seemed the least outlandish to her. She did not know where to begin in telling him how implausible she found the rest of it, but the urge to pick holes made her say, 'Wouldn't he have told Leonora what he was planning, though?'

'Course not. She can't act to save her life; he *wanted* her worried, so she'd be convincing when she went round telling everyone he'd disappeared. Maybe she'd involve the police. Make a fuss with the publisher. Start the panic.'

'But that had never worked,' said Robin. 'He was always flouncing off and nobody cared – surely even he must have realised that he wasn't going to get massive publicity just for running away and hiding in his old house.'

'Ah, but this time he was leaving behind him a book he thought was going to be the talk of literary London, wasn't he? He'd drawn as much attention to it as he could by rowing with his agent in the middle of a packed restaurant, and making a public threat to self-publish. He goes home, stages the grand walkout in front of Leonora and slips off to Talgarth Road. Later that evening he lets in his accomplice without a second thought, convinced that they're in it together.'

After a long pause Robin said bravely (because she was not used to challenging Strike's conclusions, which she had never known to be wrong):

'But you haven't got a single bit of evidence that there *was* an accomplice, let alone . . . I mean . . . it's all . . . opinion.'

He began to reiterate points he had already made, but she held up her hand to stop him.

'I heard all that the first time, but . . . you're extrapolating from things people have said. There's no – no *physical* evidence at all.'

'Of course there is,' said Strike. '*Bombyx Mori*.'

'That's not—'

'It's the single biggest piece of evidence we've got.'

'You're the one,' said Robin, 'who's always telling me: *means and opportunity*. You're the one who's always saying motive doesn't—'

'I haven't said a word about motive,' Strike reminded her. 'As it happens, I'm not sure what the motive was, although I've got a few ideas. And if you want more physical evidence, you can come and help me get it right now.'

She looked at him suspiciously. In all the time she had worked for him he had never asked her to collect a physical clue.

'I want you to come and help me talk to Orlando Quine,' he said, pushing himself back off the sofa. 'I don't want to do it on my own, she's . . . well, she's tricky. Doesn't like my hair. She's in Ladbroke Grove with the next-door neighbour, so we'd better get a move on.'

'This is the daughter with learning difficulties?' Robin asked, puzzled.

'Yeah,' said Strike. 'She's got this monkey, plush thing, hangs round her neck. I've just seen a pile of them in Hamleys – they're really pyjama cases. Cheeky Monkeys, they call them.'

Robin was staring at him as though fearful for his sanity.

'When I met her she had it round her neck and she kept producing things out of nowhere – pictures, crayons and a card she sneaked off the kitchen table. I've just realised she was pulling it all out of the pyjama case. She nicks things from people,' Strike went on, 'and she was in and out of her father's study all the time when he was alive. He used to give her paper to draw on.'

'You're hoping she's carrying around a clue to her father's killer inside her pyjama case?'

'No, but I think there's reasonable chance that she picked up a bit of *Bombyx Mori* while she was skulking around in Quine's office, or that he gave her the back of an early draft to draw on. I'm looking for scraps of paper with notes on them, a discarded couple of paragraphs, anything. Look, I know it's a long shot,' said Strike, correctly reading her expression, 'but we can't get into Quine's study, the police have already been through everything in there and come up with nothing and I'm betting the notebooks and drafts Quine took away with him have been destroyed. Cheeky Monkey's the last place I can think of to look, and,' he checked his watch, 'we haven't got much time if we're going to Ladbroke Grove and back before I meet Fancourt.

'Which reminds me . . .'

He left the office. Robin heard him heading upstairs and thought he must be going to his flat, but then the sounds of rummaging told her that he was searching the boxes of his possessions on the landing. When he returned, he was holding a box of latex gloves that he had clearly filched before leaving the SIB for good, and a clear plastic evidence bag of exactly the size that airlines provided to hold toiletries.

'There's another crucial bit of physical evidence I'd like to get,' he said, taking out a pair of gloves and handing them to an uncomprehending Robin. 'I thought you could have a bash at getting hold of it while I'm with Fancourt this afternoon.'

In a few succinct words he explained what he wanted her to get, and why.

Not altogether to Strike's surprise, a stunned silence followed his instructions.

'You're joking,' said Robin faintly.

'I'm not.'

She raised one hand unconsciously to her mouth.

'It won't be dangerous,' Strike reassured her.

'That's not what's worrying me. Cormoran, that's – that's *horrific.* You – are you really serious?'

'If you'd seen Leonora Quine in Holloway last week, you wouldn't ask that,' said Strike darkly. 'We're going to have to be bloody clever to get her out of there.'

Clever? thought Robin, still fazed as she stood with the limp gloves dangling from her hand. His suggestions for the day's activities seemed wild, bizarre and, in the case of the last, disgusting.

'Look,' he said, suddenly serious. 'I don't know what to tell you except I can feel it. *I can smell it, Robin.* Someone deranged, bloody dangerous but efficient lurking behind all this. They got that idiot Quine exactly where they wanted him by playing on his narcissism, and I'm not the only one who thinks so either.'

Strike threw Robin her coat and she put it on; he was tucking evidence bags into his inside pocket.

'People keep telling me there was someone else involved: Chard says it's Waldegrave, Waldegrave says it's Tassel, Pippa Midgley's too stupid to interpret what's staring her in the face and Christian Fisher – well, he's got more perspective, not being in the book,' said Strike. 'He put his finger on it without realising it.'

Robin, who was struggling to keep up with Strike's thought processes and sceptical of those parts she could understand, followed him down the metal staircase and out into the cold.

'This murder,' said Strike, lighting a cigarette as they walked down Denmark Street together, 'was months if not years in the planning. Work of genius, when you think about it, but it's over-elaborate and that's going to be its downfall. You can't plot murder like a novel. There are always loose ends in real life.'

Strike could tell that he was not convincing Robin, but he was not worried. He had worked with disbelieving subordinates before. Together they descended into the Tube and onto a Central line train.

'What did you get for your nephews?' Robin asked after a long silence.

'Camouflage gear and fake guns,' said Strike, whose choice had been entirely motivated by the desire to aggravate his brother-in-law, 'and I got Timothy Anstis a bloody big drum. They'll enjoy that at five o'clock on Christmas morning.'

In spite of her preoccupation, Robin snorted with laughter.

The quiet row of houses from which Owen Quine had fled a month previously was, like the rest of London, covered in snow, pristine and pale on the roofs and grubby grey underfoot. The happy Inuit smiled down from his pub sign like the presiding deity of the wintry street as they passed beneath him.

A different policeman stood outside the Quine residence now and a white van was parked at the kerb with its doors open.

'Digging for guts in the garden,' Strike muttered to Robin as they drew nearer and spotted spades lying on the van floor. 'They didn't have any luck at Mucking Marshes and they're not going to have any luck in Leonora's flower beds either.'

'So *you* say,' replied Robin *sotto voce*, a little intimidated by the staring policeman, who was quite handsome.

'So *you're* going to help me prove this afternoon,' replied Strike under his breath. 'Morning,' he called to the watchful constable, who did not respond.

Strike seemed energised by his crazy theory, but if by any remote chance he was right, Robin thought, the killing had grotesque features even beyond that carved-out corpse . . .

They headed up the front path of the house beside the Quines', bringing them within feet of the watchful PC. Strike rang the bell, and after a short wait the door opened revealing a short, anxious-looking woman in her early sixties who was wearing a housecoat and wool-trimmed slippers.

'Are you Edna?' Strike asked.

'Yes,' she said timidly, looking up at him.

When Strike introduced himself and Robin Edna's furrowed brow relaxed, to be replaced by a look of pathetic relief.

'Oh, it's *you*, I've heard all about *you*. You're helping Leonora, you're going to get her out, aren't you?'

Robin felt horribly aware of the handsome PC, listening to all of it, feet away.

'Come in, come in,' said Edna, backing out of their way and beckoning them enthusiastically inside.

'Mrs – I'm sorry, I don't know your surname,' began Strike, wiping his feet on the doormat (her house was warm, clean and much cosier than the Quines', though identical in layout).

'Call me Edna,' she said, beaming at him.

'Edna, thank you – you know, you ought to ask to see ID before you let anyone into your house.'

'Oh, but,' said Edna, flustered, 'Leonora told me all about you . . .'

Strike insisted, nevertheless, on showing her his driving licence before following her down the hall into a blue-and-white kitchen much brighter than Leonora's.

'She's upstairs,' said Edna when Strike explained that they had come to see Orlando. 'She's not having a good day. Do you want coffee?'

As she flitted around fetching cups she talked non-stop in the pent-up fashion of the stressed and lonely.

'Don't get me wrong, I don't mind having her, poor lamb, but . . .' She looked hopelessly between Strike and Robin then blurted out, 'But how long for? They've no family, you see. There was a social worker round yesterday, checking on her; she said if I couldn't keep her she'd have to go in a home or something; I said, you can't do that to Orlando, they've never been apart, her and her mum, no, she can stay with me, but . . .'

Edna glanced at the ceiling.

'She's very unsettled just now, very upset. Just wants her mum to come home and what can I say to her? I can't tell her the truth, can I? And there they are next door, digging up the whole garden, they've gone and dug up Mr Poop . . .'

'Dead cat,' Strike muttered under his breath to Robin as tears bubbled behind Edna's spectacles and bounced down her round cheeks.

'Poor lamb,' she said again.

When she had given Strike and Robin their coffees Edna went upstairs to fetch Orlando. It took ten minutes for her to persuade the girl to come downstairs, but Strike was glad to see Cheeky Monkey clutched in her arms when she appeared, today dressed in a grubby tracksuit and wearing a sullen expression.

'He's called like a giant,' she announced to the kitchen at large when she saw Strike.

'I am,' said Strike, nodding. 'Well remembered.'

Orlando slid into the chair that Edna pulled out for her, holding her orang-utan tightly in her arms.

'I'm Robin,' said Robin, smiling at her.

'Like a bird,' said Orlando at once. 'Dodo's a bird.'

'It's what her mum and dad called her,' explained Edna.

'We're both birds,' said Robin.

Orlando gazed at her, then got up and walked out of the kitchen without speaking.

Edna sighed deeply.

'She takes upset over anything. You never know what she's—'

But Orlando had returned with crayons and a spiral-bound drawing pad that Strike was sure had been bought by Edna to try to keep her happy. Orlando sat down at the kitchen table and smiled at Robin, a sweet, open smile that made Robin feel unaccountably sad.

'I'm going to draw you a robin,' she announced.

'I'd *love* that,' said Robin.

Orlando set to work with her tongue between her teeth. Robin said nothing, but watched the picture develop. Feeling that Robin had already forged a better rapport with Orlando than he had managed, Strike ate a chocolate biscuit offered by Edna and made small talk about the snow.

Eventually Orlando finished her picture, tore it out of the pad and pushed it across to Robin.

'It's beautiful,' said Robin, beaming at her. 'I wish I could draw a dodo, but I can't draw at all.' This, Strike knew, was a lie. Robin drew very well; he had seen her doodles. 'I've got to give you something, though.'

She rummaged in her bag, watched eagerly by Orlando, and eventually pulled out a small round make-up mirror decorated on the back with a stylised pink bird.

'There,' said Robin. 'Look. That's a flamingo. Another bird. You can keep that.'

Orlando took her gift with parted lips, staring at it.

'Say thank you to the lady,' prompted Edna.

'Thank you,' said Orlando and she slid the mirror inside the pyjama case.

'Is he a bag?' asked Robin with bright interest.

'My monkey,' said Orlando, clutching the orang-utan closer. 'My daddy give him to me. My daddy died.'

'I'm sorry to hear that,' said Robin quietly, wishing that the image of Quine's body had not slid instantly into her mind, his torso as hollow as a pyjama case . . .

Strike surreptitiously checked his watch. The appointment with Fancourt was drawing ever closer. Robin sipped some coffee and asked:

'Do you keep things in your monkey?'

'I like your hair,' said Orlando. 'It's shiny and yellow.'

'Thank you,' said Robin. 'Have you got any other pictures in there?'

Orlando nodded.

'C'n I have a biscuit?' she asked Edna.

'Can I see your other pictures?' Robin asked as Orlando munched.

And after a brief pause for consideration, Orlando opened up her orang-utan.

A sheaf of crumpled pictures came out, on an assortment of different sized and coloured papers. Neither Strike nor Robin turned them over at first, but made admiring comments as Orlando spread them out across the table, Robin asking questions about the bright starfish and the dancing angels that Orlando had drawn in crayon and felt tip. Basking in their appreciation, Orlando dug deeper into her pyjama case for her working materials. Up came a used typewriter cartridge, oblong and grey, with a thin strip tape carrying the reversed words it had printed. Strike resisted the urge to palm it immediately as it disappeared beneath a tin of coloured pencils and a box of mints, but kept his eye on it as Orlando laid out a picture of a butterfly through which could be seen traces of untidy adult writing on the back.

Encouraged by Robin, Orlando now brought out more: a sheet of stickers, a postcard of the Mendip Hills, a round fridge magnet that read *Careful! You may end up in my novel!* Last of all she showed them three images on better-quality paper: two proof book illustrations and a mocked-up book cover.

'My daddy gave me them from his work,' Orlando said. 'Dannulchar *touched* me when I wanted it,' she said, pointing at a brightly coloured picture that Strike recognised: Kyla the Kangaroo Who Loved to Bounce. Orlando had added a hat and handbag to Kyla and coloured in the line drawing of a princess talking to a frog with neon felt tips.

Delighted to see Orlando so chatty, Edna made more coffee.

Conscious of the time, but aware of the need not to provoke a row and a protective grab of all her treasures, Robin and Strike chatted as they picked up and examined each of the pieces of paper on the table. Whenever she thought something might be helpful, Robin slid it sideways to Strike.

There was a list of scribbled names on the back of the butterfly picture:

> Sam Breville. Eddie Boyne? Edward Baskinville? Stephen Brook?

The postcard of the Mendip Hills had been sent in July and carried a brief message:

> Weather great, hotel disappointing, hope the book's going well! V xx

Other than that, there was no trace of handwriting. A few of Orlando's pictures were familiar to Strike from his last visit. One had been drawn on the reverse of a child's restaurant menu, another on the Quines' gas bill.

'Well, we'd better head off,' said Strike, draining his coffee cup with a decent show of regret. Almost absent-mindedly he continued to hold the cover image for Dorcus Pengelly's *Upon the Wicked Rocks*. A bedraggled woman lay supine on the stony sands of a steep cliff-enclosed cove, with the shadow of a man falling across her midriff. Orlando had drawn thickly lined black fish in the seething blue water. The used typewriter cassette lay beneath the image, nudged there by Strike.

'I don't want you to go,' Orlando told Robin, suddenly tense and tearful.

'It's been lovely, hasn't it?' said Robin. 'I'm sure we'll see each other again. You'll keep your flamingo mirror, won't you, and I've got my robin picture—'

But Orlando had begun to wail and stamp. She did not want another goodbye. Under cover of the escalating furore Strike wrapped the typewriter cassette smoothly in the cover illustration for *Upon the Wicked Rocks* and slid it into his pocket, unmarked by his fingerprints.

They reached the street five minutes later, Robin a little shaken because Orlando had wailed and tried to grab her as she headed down the hall. Edna had had to physically restrain Orlando from following them.

'Poor girl,' said Robin under her breath, so that the staring PC could not hear them. 'Oh God, that was dreadful.'

'Useful, though,' said Strike.

'You got that typewriter ribbon?'

'Yep,' said Strike, glancing over his shoulder to check that the PC was out of sight before taking out the cassette, still wrapped in Dorcus's cover, and tipping it into a plastic evidence bag. 'And a bit more than that.'

'You did?' said Robin, surprised.

'Possible lead,' said Strike, 'might be nothing.'

He glanced again at his watch and sped up, wincing as his knee throbbed in protest.

'I'm going to have to get a move on if I'm not going to be late for Fancourt.'

As they sat on the crowded Tube train carrying them back to central London twenty minutes later, Strike said:

'You're clear about what you're doing this afternoon?'

'Completely clear,' said Robin, but with a note of reservation.

'I know it's not a fun job—'

'That's not what's bothering me.'

'And like I say, it shouldn't be dangerous,' he said, preparing to stand as they approached Tottenham Court Road. 'But . . . '

Something made him reconsider, a slight frown between his heavy eyebrows.

'Your hair,' he said.

'What's wrong with it?' said Robin, raising her hand self-consciously.

'It's memorable,' said Strike. 'Haven't got a hat, have you?'

'I – I could buy one,' said Robin, feeling oddly flustered.

'Charge it to petty cash,' he told her. 'Can't hurt to be careful.'

43

Hoy-day, what a sweep of vanity comes this way!

William Shakespeare, *Timon of Athens*

Strike walked up crowded Oxford Street, past snatches of canned carols and seasonal pop songs, and turned left into the quieter, narrower Dean Street. There were no shops here, just block-like buildings packed together with their different faces, white, red and dun, opening into offices, bars, pubs or bistro-type restaurants. Strike paused to allow boxes of wine to pass from delivery van to catering entrance: Christmas was a more subtle affair here in Soho, where the arts world, the advertisers and publishers congregated, and nowhere more so than at the Groucho Club.

A grey building, almost nondescript, with its black-framed windows and small topiaries sitting behind plain, convex balustrades. Its cachet lay not in its exterior but in the fact that relatively few were allowed within the members-only club for the creative arts. Strike limped over the threshold and found himself in a small hall area, where a girl behind a counter said pleasantly:

'Can I help you?'

'I'm here to meet Michael Fancourt.'

'Oh yes – you're Mr Strick?'

'That's me,' said Strike.

He was directed through a long bar room with leather seats packed with lunchtime drinkers and up the stairs. As he climbed Strike reflected, not for the first time, that his Special Investigation Branch training had not envisaged him conducting interviews without official sanction or authority, on a suspect's own territory, where his interviewee had the right to terminate the encounter without reason or apology. The SIB required its officers to organise their questioning in a template of *people, places, things* . . . Strike never lost sight of the effective, rigorous methodology, but these days it was essential to disguise the fact that he was filing facts in mental boxes. Different techniques were required when interviewing those who thought they were doing you a favour.

He saw his quarry immediately he stepped into a second wooden-floored bar, where sofas in primary colours were set along the wall beneath paintings by modern artists. Fancourt was sitting slantwise on a bright red couch, one arm along its back, a leg a little raised in an exaggerated pose of ease. A Damien Hirst spot painting hung right behind his over-large head, like a neon halo.

The writer had a thick thatch of greying dark hair, his features were heavy and the lines beside his generous mouth deep. He smiled as Strike approached. It was not, perhaps, the smile he would have given someone he considered an equal (impossible not to think in those terms, given the studied affectation of ease, the habitually sour expression), but a gesture to one whom he wished to be gracious.

'Mr Strike.'

Perhaps he considered standing up to shake hands, but Strike's height and bulk often dissuaded smaller men from leaving their seats. They shook hands across the small wooden table. Unwillingly, but left with no choice unless he wanted to sit on the sofa with Fancourt – a far too cosy situation, particularly with the author's arm lying along the back of it – Strike sat down on a solid round pouffe that was unsuited both to his size and his sore knee.

Beside them was a shaven-headed ex-soap star who had recently played a soldier in a BBC drama. He was talking loudly about himself to two other men. Fancourt and Strike ordered drinks, but declined menus. Strike was relieved that Fancourt was not hungry. He could not afford to buy anyone else lunch.

'How long've you been a member of this place?' he asked Fancourt, when the waiter had left.

'Since it opened. I was an early investor,' said Fancourt. 'Only club I've ever needed. I stay overnight here if I need to. There are rooms upstairs.'

Fancourt fixed Strike with a consciously intense stare.

'I've been looking forward to meeting you. The hero of my next novel is a veteran of the so-called war on terror and its military corollaries. I'd like to pick your brains once we've got Owen Quine out of the way.'

Strike happened to know a little about the tools available to the famous when they wished to manipulate. Lucy's guitarist father, Rick, was less famous than either Strike's father or Fancourt, but still celebrated enough to cause a middle-aged woman to gasp and tremble at the sight of him queuing for ice creams in St Mawes – 'ohmigod – *what are you doing here?*' Rick had once confided in the adolescent Strike that the one sure way to get a woman into bed was to tell her you were writing a song about her. Michael Fancourt's pronouncement that he was interested in capturing something of Strike in his next novel felt like a variation on the same theme. He had clearly not appreciated that seeing himself in print was neither a novelty to Strike, nor something he had ever chased. With an unenthusiastic nod to acknowledge Fancourt's request, Strike took out a notebook.

'D'you mind if I use this? Helps me remember what I want to ask you.'

'Feel free,' said Fancourt, looking amused. He tossed aside the copy of the *Guardian* that he had been reading. Strike saw the picture of a wizened but distinguished-looking old man who was vaguely familiar even upside-down. The caption read: *Pinkelman at Ninety*.

'Dear old Pinks,' said Fancourt, noticing the direction of Strike's gaze. 'We're giving him a little party at the Chelsea Arts Club next week.'

'Yeah?' said Strike, hunting for a pen.

'He knew my uncle. They did their national service together,' said Fancourt. 'When I wrote my first novel, *Bellafront* – I was fresh out of Oxford – my poor old Unc, trying to be helpful, sent a copy to Pinkelman, who was the only writer he'd ever met.'

He spoke in measured phrases, as though some invisible third party were taking down every word in shorthand. The story sounded pre-rehearsed, as though he had told it many times, and perhaps he had; he was an oft-interviewed man.

'Pinkelman – at that time author of the seminal *Bunty's Big Adventure* series – didn't understand a word I'd written,' Fancourt went on, 'but to please my uncle he forwarded it to Chard Books, where it landed, most fortuitously, on the desk of the only person in the place who *could* understand it.'

'Stroke of luck,' said Strike.

The waiter returned with wine for Fancourt and a glass of water for Strike.

'So,' said the detective, 'were you returning a favour when you introduced Pinkelman to your agent?'

'I was,' said Fancourt, and his nod held the hint of patronage of a teacher glad to note that one of his pupils had been paying attention. 'In those days Pinks was with some agent who kept "forgetting" to hand on his royalties. Whatever you say about Elizabeth Tassel, she's honest – in business terms, she's honest,' Fancourt amended, sipping his wine.

'She'll be at Pinkelman's party too, won't she?' said Strike, watching Fancourt for his reaction. 'She still represents him, doesn't she?'

'It doesn't matter to me if Liz is there. Does she imagine that I'm still burning with malice towards her?' asked Fancourt, with his sour smile. 'I don't think I give Liz Tassel a thought from one year's end to the next.'

'Why *did* she refuse to ditch Quine when you asked her to?' asked Strike.

Strike did not see why he should not deploy the direct attack to a man who had announced an ulterior motive for meeting within seconds of their first encounter.

'It was never a question of me asking her to drop Quine,' said Fancourt, still in measured cadences for the benefit of that invisible amanuensis. 'I explained that I could not remain at her agency while he was there, and left.'

'I see,' said Strike, who was well used to the splitting of hairs. 'Why d'you think she let you leave? You were the bigger fish, weren't you?'

'I think it's fair to say that I was a barracuda compared to

Quine's stickleback,' said Fancourt with a smirk, 'but, you see, Liz and Quine were sleeping together.'

'Really? I didn't know that,' said Strike, clicking out the nib of his pen.

'Liz arrived at Oxford,' said Fancourt, 'this strapping great girl who'd been helping her father castrate bulls and the like on sundry northern farms, *desperate* to get laid, and nobody fancied the job much. She had a thing for me, a *very* big thing – we were tutorial partners, juicy Jacobean intrigue calculated to get a girl going – but I never felt altruistic enough to relieve her of her virginity. We remained friends,' said Fancourt, 'and when she started her agency I introduced her to Quine, who notoriously preferred to plumb the bottom of the barrel, sexually speaking. The inevitable occurred.'

'Very interesting,' said Strike. 'Is this common knowledge?'

'I doubt it,' said Fancourt. 'Quine was already married to his – well, his murderess, I suppose we have to call her now, don't we?' he said thoughtfully. 'I'd imagine "murderess" trumps "wife" when defining a close relationship? And Liz would have threatened him with dire consequences if he'd been his usual indiscreet self about her bedroom antics, on the wild off-chance that I might yet be persuaded to sleep with her.'

Was this blind vanity, Strike wondered, a matter of fact, or a mixture of both?

'She used to look at me with those big cow eyes, waiting, hoping . . . ' said Fancourt, a cruel twist to his mouth. 'After Ellie died she realised that I wasn't going to oblige her even when grief-stricken. I'd imagine she was unable to bear the thought of decades of future celibacy, so she stood by her man.'

'Did you ever speak to Quine again after you left the agency?' Strike asked.

'For the first few years after Ellie died he'd scuttle out of any bar I entered,' said Fancourt. 'Eventually he got brave enough to remain in the same restaurant, throwing me nervous looks. No, I don't think we ever spoke to each other again,' said Fancourt, as though the matter were of little interest. 'You were injured in Afghanistan, I think?'

'Yeah,' said Strike.

It might work on women, Strike reflected, the calculated intensity of the gaze. Perhaps Owen Quine had fixed Kathryn Kent and Pippa Midgley with the identical hungry, vampiric stare when he told them he would be putting them into *Bombyx Mori* . . . and they had been thrilled to think of part of themselves, their lives, forever encased in the amber of a writer's prose . . .

'How did it happen?' asked Fancourt, his eyes on Strike's legs.

'IED,' said Strike. 'What about Talgarth Road? You and Quine were co-owners of the house. Didn't you ever need to communicate about the place? Did you ever run into each other there?'

'Never.'

'Haven't you been there to check on it? You've owned it – what—?'

'Twenty, twenty-five years, something like that,' said Fancourt indifferently. 'No, I haven't been inside since Joe died.'

'I suppose the police have asked you about the woman who thinks she saw you outside on the eighth of November?'

'Yes,' said Fancourt shortly. 'She was mistaken.'

Beside them, the actor was still in full and loud flow.

'. . . thought I'd bloody had it, couldn't see where the fuck I was supposed to be running, sand in my bloody eyes . . .'

'So you haven't been in the house since eighty-six?'

'No,' said Fancourt impatiently. 'Neither Owen nor I wanted it in the first place.'

'Why not?'

'Because our friend Joe died there in exceptionally squalid circumstances. He hated hospitals, refused medication. By the time he fell unconscious the place was in a disgusting state and he, who had been the living embodiment of Apollo, was reduced to a sack of bones, his skin . . . it was a grisly end,' said Fancourt, 'made worse by Daniel Ch—'

Fancourt's expression hardened. He made an odd chewing motion as though literally eating unspoken words. Strike waited.

'He's an interesting man, Dan Chard,' said Fancourt, with a palpable effort at reversing out of a cul-de-sac into which he had driven himself. 'I thought Owen's treatment of him in *Bombyx Mori* was the biggest missed opportunity of all – though future scholars are hardly going to look to *Bombyx Mori* for subtlety of characterisation, are they?' he added with a short laugh.

'How would you have written Daniel Chard?' Strike asked and Fancourt seemed surprised by the question. After a moment's consideration he said:

'Dan's the most *unfulfilled* man I've ever met. He works in a field where he's competent but unhappy. He craves the bodies of young men but can bring himself to do no more than draw them. He's full of inhibitions and self-disgust, which explains his unwise and hysterical response to Owen's caricature of him. Dan was dominated by a monstrous socialite mother who wanted her pathologically shy son to take over the family business. I think,' said Fancourt, 'I'd have been able to make something interesting of all that.'

'Why did Chard turn down North's book?' Strike asked.

Fancourt made the chewing motion again, then said:

'I like Daniel Chard, you know.'

'I had the impression that there had been a grudge at some point,' said Strike.

'What gave you that idea?'

'You said that you "certainly didn't expect to find yourself" back at Roper Chard when you spoke at their anniversary party.'

'You were there?' said Fancourt sharply and when Strike nodded he said: 'Why?'

'I was looking for Quine,' said Strike. 'His wife had hired me to find him.'

'But, as we now know, she knew exactly where he was.'

'No,' said Strike, 'I don't think she did.'

'You *genuinely* believe that?' asked Fancourt, his large head tilted to one side.

'Yeah, I do,' said Strike.

Fancourt raised his eyebrows, considering Strike intently as though he were a curiosity in a cabinet.

'So you didn't hold it against Chard that he turned down North's book?' Strike asked, returning to the main point.

After a brief pause Fancourt said:

'Well, yes, I did hold it against him. Exactly why Dan changed his mind about publishing it only Dan could tell you, but I think it was because there was a smattering of press around Joe's condition, drumming up middle-England disgust about the unrepentant book he was about to publish, and Dan, who had not realised that Joe now had full-blown Aids, panicked. He didn't want to be associated with bathhouses and Aids, so he told Joe he didn't want the book after all. It was an act of great cowardice and Owen and I—'

Another pause. How long had it been since Fancourt had bracketed himself and Quine together in amity?

'Owen and I believed that it killed Joe. He could hardly hold a pen, he was virtually blind, but he was trying desperately to finish the book before he died. We felt that was all that was keeping him alive. Then Chard's letter arrived cancelling their contract; Joe stopped work and within forty-eight hours he was dead.'

'There are similarities,' said Strike, 'with what happened to your first wife.'

'They weren't the same thing at all,' said Fancourt flatly.

'Why not?'

'Joe's was an infinitely better book.'

Yet another pause, this time much longer.

'That's considering the matter,' said Fancourt, 'from a purely literary perspective. Naturally, there are other ways of looking at it.'

He finished his glass of wine and raised a hand to indicate to the barman that he wanted another. The actor beside them, who had barely drawn breath, was still talking.

'. . . said, "Screw authenticity, what d'you want me to do, saw my own bloody arm off?"'

'It must have been a very difficult time for you,' said Strike.

'Yes,' said Fancourt waspishly. 'Yes, I think we can call it "difficult".'

'You lost a good friend and a wife within – what – months of each other?'

'A few months, yes.'

'You were writing all through that time?'

'Yes,' said Fancourt, with an angry, condescending laugh, 'I was writing *all through that time*. It's my profession. Would anyone ask you whether you were *still in the army* while you were having private difficulties?'

'I doubt it,' said Strike, without rancour. 'What were you writing?'

'It was never published. I abandoned the book I was working on so that I could finish Joe's.'

The waiter set a second glass in front of Fancourt and departed.

'Did North's book need much doing to it?'

'Hardly anything,' said Fancourt. 'He was a brilliant writer. I tidied up a few rough bits and polished the ending. He'd left notes about how he wanted it done. Then I took it to Jerry Waldegrave, who was with Roper.'

Strike remembered what Chard had said about Fancourt's over-closeness to Waldegrave's wife and proceeded with some caution.

'Had you worked with Waldegrave before?'

'I've never worked with him on my own stuff, but I knew of him by reputation as a gifted editor and I knew that he'd liked Joe. We collaborated on *Towards the Mark*.'

'He did a good job on it, did he?'

Fancourt's flash of bad temper had gone. If anything, he looked entertained by Strike's line of questioning.

'Yes,' he said, taking a sip of wine, 'very good.'

'But you didn't want to work with him now you've moved to Roper Chard?'

'Not particularly,' said Fancourt, still smiling. 'He drinks a lot these days.'

'Why d'you think Quine put Waldegrave in *Bombyx Mori*?'

'How can I possibly know that?'

'Waldegrave seems to have been good to Quine. It's hard to see why Quine felt the need to attack him.'

'Is it?' asked Fancourt, eyeing Strike closely.

'Everyone I talk to seems to have a different angle on the Cutter character in *Bombyx Mori*.'

'Really?'

'Most people seem outraged that Quine attacked Waldegrave at all. They can't see what Waldegrave did to deserve it. Daniel Chard thinks the Cutter shows that Quine had a collaborator,' said Strike.

'Who the hell does he think would have collaborated with Quine on *Bombyx Mori*?' asked Fancourt, with a short laugh.

'He's got ideas,' said Strike. 'Meanwhile Waldegrave thinks the Cutter's really an attack on you.'

'But I'm Vainglorious,' said Fancourt with a smile. 'Everyone knows that.'

'Why would Waldegrave think that the Cutter is about you?'

'You'll need to ask Jerry Waldegrave,' said Fancourt, still smiling. 'But I've got a funny feeling you think you know, Mr Strike. And I'll tell you this: Quine was quite, quite wrong – as he really should have known.'

Impasse.

'So in all these years, you've never managed to sell Talgarth Road?'

'It's been very difficult to find a buyer who satisfies the terms of Joe's will. It was a quixotic gesture of Joe's. He was a romantic, an idealist.

'I set down my feelings about all of this – the legacy, the burden, the poignancy of his bequest – in *House of Hollow*,' said Fancourt, much like a lecturer recommending additional reading. 'Owen had his say – such as it was –' added Fancourt, with the ghost of a smirk, 'in *The Balzac Brothers*.'

'*The Balzac Brothers* was about the house in Talgarth Road, was it?' asked Strike, who had not gleaned that impression during the fifty pages he had read.

'It was set there. Really it's about our relationship, the three of us,' said Fancourt. 'Joe dead in the corner and Owen and I trying to follow in his footsteps, make sense of his death. It was set in the studio where I think – from what I've read – you found Quine's body?'

Strike said nothing, but continued to take notes.

'The critic Harvey Bird called *The Balzac Brothers* "wincingly, jaw-droppingly, sphincter-clenchingly awful".'

'I just remember a lot of fiddling with balls,' said Strike and Fancourt gave a sudden, unforced girlish titter.

'You've read it, have you? Oh yes, Owen was obsessed with his balls.'

The actor beside them had paused for breath at last. Fancourt's words rang in the temporary silence. Strike grinned as the actor and his two dining companions stared at Fancourt, who treated them to his sour smile. The three men began talking hurriedly again.

'He had a real *idée fixe*,' said Fancourt, turning back to Strike. 'Picasso-esque, you know, his testicles the source of his creative power. He was obsessed in both his life and his work with machismo, virility, fertility. Some might say it was an odd fixation for a man who liked to be tied up and dominated, but I see it as a natural consequence . . . the yin and yang of Quine's sexual persona. You'll have noticed the names he gave us in the book?'

'Vas and Varicocele,' said Strike and he noted again that slight surprise in Fancourt that a man who looked like Strike read books, or paid attention to their contents.

'Vas – Quine – the duct that carries sperm from balls to

penis – the healthy, potent, creative force. Varicocele – a painful enlargement of a vein in the testicle, sometimes leading to infertility. A typically crass Quine-esque allusion to the fact that I contracted mumps shortly after Joe died and in fact was too unwell to go to the funeral, but also to the fact that – as you've pointed out – I was writing under difficult circumstances around that time.'

'You were still friends at this point?' Strike clarified.

'When he started the book we were still – in theory – friends,' said Fancourt, with a grim smile. 'But writers are a savage breed, Mr Strike. If you want life-long friendship and selfless camaraderie, join the army and learn to kill. If you want a lifetime of temporary alliances with peers who will glory in your every failure, write novels.'

Strike smiled. Fancourt said with detached pleasure:

'*The Balzac Brothers* received some of the worst reviews I've ever read.'

'Did you review it?'

'No,' said Fancourt.

'You were married to your first wife at this point?' Strike asked.

'That's right,' said Fancourt. The flicker of his expression was like the shiver of an animal's flank when a fly touches it.

'I'm just trying to get the chronology right – you lost her shortly after North died?'

'Euphemisms for death are so interesting, aren't they?' said Fancourt lightly. 'I didn't "lose" her. On the contrary, I tripped over her in the dark, dead in our kitchen with her head in the oven.'

'I'm sorry,' said Strike formally.

'Yes, well . . .'

Fancourt called for another drink. Strike could tell that a delicate point had been reached, where a flow of information might either be tapped, or run forever dry.

'Did you ever talk to Quine about the parody that caused your wife's suicide?'

'I've already told you, I never talked to him again about anything after Ellie died,' said Fancourt calmly. 'So, no.'

'You were sure he wrote it, though?'

'Without question. Like a lot of writers without much to say, Quine was actually a good literary mimic. I remember him spoofing some of Joe's stuff and it was quite funny. He wasn't going to jeer *publicly* at Joe, of course, it did him too much good hanging around with the pair of us.'

'Did anyone admit to seeing the parody before publication?'

'Nobody said as much to me, but it would have been surprising if they had, wouldn't it, given what it caused? Liz Tassel denied to my face that Owen had shown it to her, but I heard on the grapevine that she'd read it pre-publication. I'm sure she encouraged him to publish. Liz was insanely jealous of Ellie.'

There was a pause, then Fancourt said with an assumption of lightness:

'Hard to remember these days that there was a time when you had to wait for the ink and paper reviews to see your work excoriated. With the invention of the internet, any subliterate cretin can be Michiko Kakutani.'

'Quine always denied writing it, didn't he?' Strike asked.

'Yes he did, gutless bastard that he was,' said Fancourt, apparently unconscious of any lack of taste. 'Like a lot of *soi-disant* mavericks, Quine was an envious, terminally competitive creature who craved adulation. He was terrified that he was going to be ostracised after Ellie died. Of course,' said Fancourt, with unmistakable pleasure, 'it happened anyway. Owen had benefited from a lot of reflected glory, being part of a triumvirate with Joe and me. When Joe died and I cut him adrift, he was seen for what he was: a man with a dirty imagination and an interesting style who had barely an idea that wasn't pornographic. Some authors,' said Fancourt, 'have only one good book in them. That was Owen. He shot his bolt – an expression he would have approved of – with *Hobart's Sin*. Everything after that was pointless rehashes.'

'Didn't you say you thought *Bombyx Mori* was "a maniac's masterpiece"?'

'You read that, did you?' said Fancourt, with vaguely flattered surprise. 'Well, so it is, a true literary curiosity. I never denied that Owen could write, you know, it was just that he was never able to dredge up anything profound or interesting to write about. It's a surprisingly common phenomenon. But with *Bombyx Mori* he found his subject at last, didn't he? Everybody hates me, everyone's against me, I'm a genius and nobody can see it. The result is grotesque and comic, it reeks of bitterness and self-pity, but it has an undeniable fascination. And the language,' said Fancourt, with the most enthusiasm he had so far brought to the discussion, 'is admirable. Some passages are among the best things he ever wrote.'

'This is all very useful,' said Strike.

Fancourt seemed amused.

'How?'

'I've got a feeling that *Bombyx Mori*'s central to this case.'

'"Case"?' repeated Fancourt, smiling. There was a short pause. 'Are you *seriously* telling me that you still think the killer of Owen Quine is at large?'

'Yeah, I think so,' said Strike.

'Then,' said Fancourt, smiling still more broadly, 'wouldn't it be more useful to analyse the writings of the killer rather than the victim?'

'Maybe,' said Strike, 'but we don't know whether the killer writes.'

'Oh, nearly everyone does these days,' said Fancourt. 'The whole world's writing novels, but nobody's reading them.'

'I'm sure people would read *Bombyx Mori*, especially if you did an introduction,' said Strike.

'I think you're right,' said Fancourt, smiling more broadly.

'When exactly did you read the book for the first time?'

'It would have been . . . let me see . . .'

Fancourt appeared to do a mental calculation.

'Not until the, ah, middle of the week after Quine delivered it,' said Fancourt. 'Dan Chard called me, told me that Quine was trying to suggest that I had written the parody of Ellie's book, and tried to persuade me to join him in legal action against Quine. I refused.'

'Did Chard read any of it out to you?'

'No,' said Fancourt, smiling again. 'Frightened he might lose his star acquisition, you see. No, he simply outlined the allegation that Quine had made and offered me the services of his lawyers.'

'When was this telephone call?'

'On the evening of the . . . seventh, it must have been,' said Fancourt. 'The Sunday night.'

'The same day you filmed an interview about your new novel,' said Strike.

'You're very well-informed,' said Fancourt, his eyes narrowing.

'I watched the programme.'

'You know,' said Fancourt, with a needle-prick of malice,

'you don't have the appearance of a man who enjoys arts programmes.'

'I never said I enjoyed them,' said Strike and was unsurprised to note that Fancourt appeared to enjoy his retort. 'But I did notice that you misspoke when you said your first wife's name on camera.'

Fancourt said nothing, but merely watched Strike over his wine glass.

'You said "Eff" then corrected yourself, and said "Ellie",' said Strike.

'Well, as you say – I misspoke. It can happen to the most articulate of us.'

'In *Bombyx Mori*, your late wife—'

'—is called "Effigy".'

'Which is a coincidence,' said Strike.

'Obviously,' said Fancourt.

'Because you couldn't yet have known that Quine had called her "Effigy" on the seventh.'

'Obviously not.'

'Quine's mistress got a copy of the manuscript fed through her letter box right after he disappeared,' said Strike. 'You didn't get sent an early copy, by any chance?'

The ensuing pause became over-long. Strike felt the fragile thread that he had managed to spin between them snap. It did not matter. He had saved this question for last.

'No,' said Fancourt. 'I didn't.'

He pulled out his wallet. His declared intention of picking Strike's brains for a character in his next novel seemed, not at all to Strike's regret, forgotten. Strike pulled out some cash, but Fancourt held up a hand and said, with unmistakable offensiveness:

'No, no, allow me. Your press coverage makes much of the fact that you have known better times. In fact, it puts me in mind of Ben Jonson: "I am a poor gentleman, a soldier; one that, in the better state of my fortunes, scorned so mean a refuge".'

'Really?' said Strike pleasantly, returning his cash to his pocket. 'I'm put more in mind of

sicine subrepsti mi, atque intestina pururens
ei misero eripuisti omnia nostra bona?
Eripuisti, eheu, nostrae crudele uenenum
Uitae, eheu nostrae pestis amicitiae.'

He looked unsmilingly upon Fancourt's astonishment. The writer rallied quickly.

'Ovid?'

'Catullus,' said Strike, heaving himself off the low pouffe with the aid of the table. 'Translates roughly:

So that's how you crept up on me, an acid eating away
My guts, stole from me everything I most treasure?
Yes, alas, stole: grim poison in my blood
The plague, alas, of the friendship we once had.

'Well, I expect we'll see each other around,' said Strike pleasantly.

He limped off towards the stairs, Fancourt's eyes upon his back.

44

All his allies and friends rush into troops
Like raging torrents.

Thomas Dekker, *The Noble Spanish Soldier*

Strike sat for a long time on the sofa in his kitchen-sitting room that night, barely hearing the rumble of the traffic on Charing Cross Road and the occasional muffled shouts of more early Christmas party-goers. He had removed his prosthesis; it was comfortable sitting there in his boxers, the end of his injured leg free of pressure, the throbbing of his knee deadened by another double dose of painkillers. Unfinished pasta congealed on the plate beside him on the sofa, the sky beyond his small window achieved the dark blue velvet depth of true night, and Strike did not move, though wide awake.

It felt like a very long time since he had seen the picture of Charlotte in her wedding dress. He had not given her another thought all day. Was this the start of true healing? She had married Jago Ross and he was alone, mulling the complexities of an elaborate murder in the dim light of his chilly attic flat. Perhaps each of them was, at last, where they really belonged.

On the table in front of him in the clear plastic evidence bag, still half wrapped in the photocopied cover of *Upon the Wicked*

Rocks, sat the dark grey typewriter cassette that he had taken from Orlando. He had been staring at it for what seemed like half an hour at least, feeling like a child on Christmas morning confronted by a mysterious, inviting package, the largest under the tree. And yet he ought not to look, or touch, lest he interfere with whatever forensic evidence might be gleaned from the tape. Any suspicion of tampering . . .

He checked his watch. He had promised himself not to make the call until half past nine. There were children to be wrestled into bed, a wife to placate after another long day on the job. Strike wanted time to explain fully . . .

But his patience had limits. Getting up with some difficulty, he took the keys to his office and moved laboriously downstairs, clutching the handrail, hopping and occasionally sitting down. Ten minutes later he re-entered his flat and returned to the still-warm spot on the sofa carrying his penknife and wearing another pair of the latex gloves he had earlier given to Robin.

He lifted the typewriter tape and the crumpled cover illustration gingerly out of the evidence bag and set the cassette, still resting on the paper, on the rickety Formica-topped table. Barely breathing, he pulled out the toothpick attachment from his knife and inserted it delicately behind the two inches of fragile tape that were exposed. By dint of careful manipulation he managed to pull out a little more. Reversed words were revealed, the letters back to front.

YOB EIDDE WENK I THGUOHT DAH I DN

His sudden rush of adrenalin was expressed only in Strike's quiet sigh of satisfaction. He deftly tightened the tape again, using the knife's screwdriver attachment in the cog at the top of the cassette, the whole untouched by his hands, then, still wearing the latex gloves, slipped it back into the evidence bag. He checked his watch again. Unable to wait any longer, he picked up his mobile and called Dave Polworth.

'Bad time?' he asked when his old friend answered.

'No,' said Polworth, sounding curious. 'What's up, Diddy?'

'Need a favour, Chum. A big one.'

The engineer, over a hundred miles away in his sitting room in Bristol, listened without interrupting while the detective explained what it was he wanted done. When finally he had finished, there was a pause.

'I know it's a big ask,' Strike said, listening anxiously to the line crackling. 'Dunno if it'll even be possible in this weather.'

'Course it will,' said Polworth. 'I'd have to see when I could do it, though, Diddy. Got two days off coming up . . . not sure Penny's going to be keen . . . '

'Yeah, I thought that might be a problem,' said Strike, 'I know it'd be dangerous.'

'Don't insult me, I've done worse than this,' said Polworth. 'Nah, she wanted me to take her and her mother Christmas shopping . . . but fuck it, Diddy, did you say this is life or death?'

'Close,' said Strike, closing his eyes and grinning. 'Life and liberty.'

'And no Christmas shopping, boy, which suits old Chum. Consider it done, and I'll give you a ring if I've got anything, all right?'

'Stay safe, mate.'

'Piss off.'

Strike dropped the mobile beside him on the sofa and rubbed his face in his hands, still grinning. He might just have told Polworth to do something even crazier and more pointless than grabbing a passing shark, but Polworth was a man who enjoyed danger, and the time had come for desperate measures.

The last thing Strike did before turning out the light was to re-read the notes of his conversation with Fancourt and to underline, so heavily that he sliced through the page, the word 'Cutter'.

45

Didst thou not mark the jest of the silkworm?

John Webster, *The White Devil*

Both the family home and Talgarth Road continued to be combed for forensic evidence. Leonora remained in Holloway. It had become a waiting game.

Strike was used to standing for hours in the cold, watching darkened windows, following faceless strangers; to unanswered phones and doors, blank faces, clueless bystanders; to enforced, frustrating inaction. What was different and distracting on this occasion was the small whine of anxiety that formed a backdrop to everything he did.

You had to maintain a distance, but there were always people who got to you, injustices that bit. Leonora in prison, white-faced and weeping, her daughter confused, vulnerable and bereft of both parents. Robin had pinned up Orlando's picture over her desk, so that a merry red-bellied bird gazed down upon the detective and his assistant as they busied themselves with other cases, reminding them that a curly-haired girl in Ladbroke Grove was still waiting for her mother to come home.

Robin, at least, had a meaningful job to do, although she felt that she was letting Strike down. She had returned to the office two days running with nothing to show for her efforts, her evidence bag empty. The detective had warned her to err on the side of caution, to bail at the least sign that she might have been noticed or remembered. He did not like to be explicit about how recognisable he thought her, even with her red-gold hair piled under a beanie hat. She was very good-looking.

'I'm not sure I need to be quite so cautious,' she said, having followed his instructions to the letter.

'Let's remember what we're dealing with here, Robin,' he snapped, anxiety continuing to whine in his gut. 'Quine didn't rip out his own guts.'

Some of his fears were strangely amorphous. Naturally he worried that the killer would yet escape, that there were great, gaping holes in the fragile cobweb of a case he was building, a case that just now was built largely out of his own reconstructive imaginings, that needed physical evidence to anchor it down lest the police and defence counsel blew it clean away. But he had other worries.

Much as he had disliked the Mystic Bob tag with which Anstis had saddled him, Strike had a sense of approaching danger now, almost as strongly as when he had known, without question, that the Viking was about to blow up around him. Intuition, they called it, but Strike knew it to be the reading of subtle signs, the subconscious joining of dots. A clear picture of the killer was emerging out of the mass of disconnected evidence, and the image was stark and terrifying: a case of obsession, of violent rage, of a calculating, brilliant but profoundly disturbed mind.

The longer he hung around, refusing to let go, the closer he circled, the more targeted his questioning, the greater the chance that the killer might wake up to the threat he posed.

Strike had confidence in his own ability to detect and repel attack, but he could not contemplate with equanimity the solutions that might occur to a diseased mind that had shown itself fond of Byzantine cruelty.

The days of Polworth's leave came and went without tangible results.

'Don't give up now, Diddy,' he told Strike over the phone. Characteristically, the fruitlessness of his endeavours seemed to have stimulated rather than discouraged Polworth. 'I'm going to pull a sickie Monday. I'll have another bash.'

'I can't ask you to do that,' muttered Strike, frustrated. 'The drive—'

'I'm offering, you ungrateful peg-legged bastard.'

'Penny'll kill you. What about her Christmas shopping?'

'What about my chance to show up the Met?' said Polworth, who disliked the capital and its inhabitants on long-held principle.

'You're a mate, Chum,' said Strike.

When he had hung up, he saw Robin's grin.

'What's funny?'

'"Chum",' she said. It sounded so public school, so unlike Strike.

'It's not what you think,' said Strike. He was halfway through the story of Dave Polworth and the shark when his mobile rang again: an unknown number. He picked up.

'Is that Cameron – er – Strike?'

'Speaking.'

'It's Jude Graham 'ere. Kath Kent's neighbour. She's back,' said the female voice happily.

'That's good news,' said Strike, with a thumbs-up to Robin.

'Yeah, she got back this morning. Got a friend staying with

'er. I asked 'er where she'd been, but she wouldn't say,' said the neighbour.

Strike remembered that Jude Graham thought him a journalist.

'Is the friend male or female?'

'Female,' she answered regretfully. 'Tall skinny dark girl, she's always hanging around Kath.'

'That's very helpful, Ms Graham,' said Strike. 'I'll – er – put something through your door later for your trouble.'

'Great,' said the neighbour happily. 'Cheers.'

She rang off.

'Kath Kent's back at home,' Strike told Robin. 'Sounds like she's got Pippa Midgley staying with her.'

'Oh,' said Robin, trying not to smile. 'I, er, suppose you're regretting you put her in a headlock now?'

Strike grinned ruefully.

'They're not going to talk to me,' he said.

'No,' Robin agreed. 'I don't think they will.'

'Suits them fine, Leonora in the clink.'

'If you told them your whole theory, they might cooperate,' suggested Robin.

Strike stroked his chin, looking at Robin without seeing her.

'I can't,' he said finally. 'If it leaks out that I'm sniffing up that tree, I'll be lucky not to get a knife in the back one dark night.'

'Are you serious?'

'Robin,' said Strike, mildly exasperated, 'Quine was tied up and disembowelled.'

He sat down on the arm of the sofa, which squeaked less than the cushions but groaned under his weight, and said:

'Pippa Midgley liked you.'

'I'll do it,' said Robin at once.

'Not alone,' he said, 'but maybe you could get me in? How about this evening?'

'Of course!' she said, elated.

Hadn't she and Matthew established new rules? This was the first time she had tested him, but she went to the telephone with confidence. His reaction when she told him that she did not know when she would be home that night could not have been called enthusiastic, but he accepted the news without demur.

So, at seven o'clock that evening, having discussed at length the tactics that they were about to employ, Strike and Robin proceeded separately through the icy night, ten minutes apart with Robin in the lead, to Stafford Cripps House.

A gang of youths stood again in the concrete forecourt of the block and they did not permit Robin to pass with the wary respect they had accorded Strike two weeks previously. One of them danced backwards ahead of her as she approached the inner stairs, inviting her to party, telling her she was beautiful, laughing derisively at her silence, while his mates jeered behind her in the darkness, discussing her rear view. As they entered the concrete stairwell her taunter's jeers echoed strangely. She thought he might be seventeen at most.

'I need to go upstairs,' she said firmly as he slouched across the stairwell for his mates' amusement, but sweat had prickled on her scalp. *He's a kid*, she told herself. *And Strike's right behind you.* The thought gave her courage. 'Get out of the way, please,' she said.

He hesitated, dropped a sneering comment about her figure, and moved. She half expected him to grab her as she passed but he loped back to his mates, all of them calling filthy names after her as she climbed the stairs and emerged with relief, without being followed, on to the balcony leading to Kath Kent's flat.

The lights inside were on. Robin paused for a second, gathering herself, then rang the doorbell.

After some seconds the door opened a cautious six inches and there stood a middle-aged woman with a long tangle of red hair.

'Kathryn?'

'Yeah?' said the woman suspiciously.

'I've got some very important information for you,' said Robin. 'You need to hear this.'

('Don't say "I need to talk to you",' Strike had coached her, 'or "I've got some questions". You frame it so that it sounds like it's to her advantage. Get as far as you can without telling her who you are; make it sound urgent, make her worry she's going to miss something if she lets you go. You want to be inside before she can think it through. Use her name. Make a personal connection. Keep talking.')

'What?' demanded Kathryn Kent.

'Can I come in?' asked Robin. 'It's very cold out here.'

'Who are you?'

'You need to hear this, Kathryn.'

'Who—?'

'Kath?' said someone behind her.

'Are you a journalist?'

'I'm a friend,' Robin improvised, her toes over the threshold. 'I want to help you, Kathryn.'

'Hey—'

A familiar long pale face and large brown eyes appeared beside Kath's.

'It's her I told you about!' said Pippa. 'She works with him—'

'Pippa,' said Robin, making eye contact with the tall girl,

'you know I'm on your side – there's something I need to tell you both, it's urgent—'

Her foot was two thirds of the way across the threshold. Robin put every ounce of earnest persuasiveness that she could muster into her expression as she looked into Pippa's panicked eyes.

'Pippa, I wouldn't have come if I didn't think it was really important—'

'Let her in,' Pippa told Kathryn. She sounded scared.

The hall was cramped and seemed full of hanging coats. Kathryn led Robin into a small, lamp-lit sitting room with plain magnolia-painted walls. Brown curtains hung at the windows, the fabric so thin that the lights of buildings opposite and distant, passing cars shone through them. A slightly grubby orange throw covered the old sofa, which sat on a rug patterned with swirling abstract shapes, and the remains of a Chinese takeaway sat on the cheap pine coffee table. In the corner was a rickety computer table bearing a laptop. The two women, Robin saw, with a pang of something like remorse, had been decorating a small fake Christmas tree together. A string of lights lay on the floor and there were a number of decorations on the only armchair. One of them was a china disc reading *Future Famous Writer!*

'What d'you want?' demanded Kathryn Kent, her arms folded.

She was glaring at Robin through small, fierce eyes.

'May I sit down?' said Robin and she did so without waiting for Kathryn's answer. ('Make yourself at home as much as you can without being rude, make it harder for her to dislodge you,' Strike had said.)

'What d'you want?' Kathryn Kent repeated.

Pippa stood in front of the windows, staring at Robin, who

saw that she was fiddling with a tree ornament: a mouse dressed as Santa.

'You know that Leonora Quine's been arrested for murder?' said Robin.

'Of course I do. I'm the one,' Kathryn pointed at her own ample chest, 'who found the Visa bill with the ropes, the burqa and the overalls on it.'

'Yes,' said Robin, 'I know that.'

'Ropes and a burqa!' ejaculated Kathryn Kent. 'Got more than he bargained for, didn't he? All those years thinking she was just some dowdy little . . . boring little – little *cow* – and look what she did to him!'

'Yes,' said Robin, 'I know it looks that way.'

'What d'you mean, "looks that"—?'

'Kathryn, I've come here to warn you: they don't think she did it.'

('No specifics. Don't mention the police explicitly if you can avoid it, don't commit to a checkable story, keep it vague,' Strike had told her.)

'What d'you mean?' repeated Kathryn sharply. 'The police don't—?'

'And you had access to his card, more opportunities to copy it—'

Kathryn looked wildly from Robin to Pippa, who was clutching the Santa-mouse, white-faced.

'But Strike doesn't think you did it,' said Robin.

'Who?' said Kathryn. She appeared too confused, too panicked, to think straight.

'Her boss,' stage-whispered Pippa.

'Him!' said Kathryn, rounding on Robin again. 'He's working for *Leonora*!'

'He doesn't think you did it,' repeated Robin, 'even with the credit card bill – the fact you even had it. I mean, it looks odd, but he's sure you had it by acci—'

'She gave it me!' said Kathryn Kent, flinging out her arms, gesticulating furiously. 'His daughter – she gave it me, I never even looked on the back for weeks, never thought to. I was being *nice*, taking her crappy bloody picture and acting like it was good – I was being *nice*!'

'I understand that,' said Robin. 'We believe you, Kathryn, I promise. Strike wants to find the real killer, he's not like the police.' ('Insinuate, don't state.') '*He's* not interested in just grabbing the next woman Quine might've – you know—'

The words *let tie him up* hung in the air, unspoken.

Pippa was easier to read than Kathryn. Credulous and easily panicked, she looked at Kathryn, who seemed furious.

'Maybe I don't care who killed him!' Kathryn snarled through clenched teeth.

'But you surely don't want to be arrest—?'

'I've only got your word for it they're interested in me! There's been nothing on the news!'

'Well . . . there wouldn't be, would there?' said Robin gently. 'The police don't hold press conferences to announce that they think they might have the wrong pers—'

'Who had the credit card? *Her.*'

'Quine usually had it himself,' said Robin, 'and his wife's not the only person who had access.'

'How d'you know what the police are thinking any more than I do?'

'Strike's got good contacts at the Met,' said Robin calmly. 'He was in Afghanistan with the investigating officer, Richard Anstis.'

The name of the man who had interrogated her seemed to carry weight with Kathryn. She glanced at Pippa again.

'Why're you telling me this?' Kathryn demanded.

'Because we don't want to see another innocent woman arrested,' said Robin, 'because we think the police are wasting time sniffing around the wrong people and because,' ('throw in a bit of self-interest once you've baited the hook, it keeps things plausible') 'obviously,' said Robin, with a show of awkwardness, 'it would do Cormoran a lot of good if he was the one who got the real killer. Again,' she added.

'Yeah,' said Kathryn, nodding vehemently, 'that's it, isn't it? He wants the publicity.'

No woman who had been with Owen Quine for two years was going to believe that publicity wasn't an unqualified boon.

'Look, we just wanted to warn you how they're thinking,' said Robin, 'and to ask for your help. But obviously, if you don't want . . . '

Robin made to stand.

('Once you've laid it out for her, act like you can take it or leave it. You're there when she starts chasing you.')

'I've told the police everything I know,' said Kathryn, who appeared disconcerted now that Robin, who was taller than her, had stood up again. 'I haven't got anything else to say.'

'Well, we're not sure they were asking the right questions,' said Robin, sinking back onto the sofa. 'You're a writer,' she said, turning suddenly off the piste that Strike had prepared for her, her eyes on the laptop in the corner. 'You notice things. You understood him and his work better than anyone else.'

The unexpected swerve into flattery caused whatever words of fury Kathryn had been about to fling at Robin (her mouth had been open, ready to deliver them) to die in her throat.

'So?' Kathryn said. Her aggression felt a little fake now. 'What d'you want to know?'

'Will you let Strike come and hear what you've got to say? He won't if you don't want him to,' Robin assured her (an offer unsanctioned by her boss). 'He respects your right to refuse.' (Strike had made no such declaration.) 'But he'd like to hear it in your own words.'

'I don't know that I've got anything useful to say,' said Kathryn, folding her arms again, but she could not disguise a ring of gratified vanity.

'I know it's a big ask,' said Robin, 'but if you help us get the real killer, Kathryn, you'll be in the papers for the *right* reasons.'

The promise of it settled gently over the sitting room – Kathryn interviewed by eager and now admiring journalists, asking about her work, perhaps: *Tell me about* Melina's Sacrifice . . .

Kathryn glanced sideways at Pippa, who said:

'That bastard *kidnapped* me!'

'You tried to attack him, Pip,' said Kathryn. She turned a little anxiously to Robin. '*I* never told her to do that. She was – after we saw what he'd written in the book – we were both . . . and we thought *he* – your boss – had been hired to fit us up.'

'I understand,' lied Robin, who found the reasoning tortuous and paranoid, but perhaps that was what spending time with Owen Quine did to a person.

'She got carried away and didn't think,' said Kathryn, with a look of mingled affection and reproof at her protégée. 'Pip's got temper issues.'

'Understandable,' said Robin hypocritically. 'May I call Cormoran – Strike, I mean? Ask him to meet us here?'

She had already slipped her mobile out of her pocket and glanced down at it. Strike had texted her:

On balcony. Bloody freezing.

She texted back:

Wait 5.

In fact, she needed only three minutes. Softened by Robin's earnestness and air of understanding, and by the encouragement of the alarmed Pippa to let Strike in and find out the worst, when he finally knocked Kathryn proceeded to the front door with something close to alacrity.

The room seemed much smaller with his arrival. Next to Kathryn, Strike appeared huge and almost unnecessarily male; when she had swept it clear of Christmas ornaments, he dwarfed the only armchair. Pippa retreated to the end of the sofa and perched on the arm, throwing Strike looks composed of defiance and terror.

'D'you want a drink of something?' Kathryn threw at Strike in his heavy overcoat, with his size fourteen feet planted squarely on her swirly rug.

'Cup of tea would be great,' he said.

She left for the tiny kitchen. Finding herself alone with Strike and Robin, Pippa panicked and scuttled after her.

'You've done bloody well,' Strike murmured to Robin, 'if they're offering tea.'

'She's *very* proud of being a writer,' Robin breathed back, 'which means she could understand him in ways that other people . . .'

But Pippa had returned with a box of cheap biscuits and Strike and Robin fell silent at once. Pippa resumed her seat at the end of the sofa, casting Strike frightened sidelong glances that had, as when she had cowered in their office, a whiff of theatrical enjoyment about them.

'This is very good of you, Kathryn,' said Strike, when she had set a tray of tea on the table. One of the mugs, Robin saw, read *Keep Clam and Proofread*.

'We'll see,' retorted Kent, her arms folded as she glared at him from a height.

'Kath, sit,' coaxed Pippa, and Kathryn sat reluctantly down between Pippa and Robin on the sofa.

Strike's first priority was to nurse the tenuous trust that Robin had managed to foster; the direct attack had no place here. He therefore embarked on a speech echoing Robin's, implying that the authorities were having second thoughts about Leonora's arrest and that they were reviewing the current evidence, avoiding direct mention of the police yet implying with every word that the Met was now turning its attention to Kathryn Kent. As he spoke a siren echoed in the distance. Strike added assurances that he personally felt sure that Kent was completely in the clear, but that he saw her as a resource the police had failed to understand or utilise properly.

'Yeah, well, you could be right there,' she said. She had not so much blossomed under his soothing words as unclenched. Picking up the *Keep Clam* mug she said with a show of disdain, 'All they wanted to know about was our sex life.'

The way Anstis had told it, Strike remembered, Kathryn had volunteered a lot of information on the subject without being put under undue pressure.

'I'm not interested in your sex life,' said Strike. 'It's obvious he wasn't – to be blunt – getting what he wanted at home.'

'Hadn't slept with her in years,' said Kathryn. Remembering the photographs in Leonora's bedroom of Quine tied up, Robin dropped her gaze to the surface of her tea. 'They had nothing in common. He couldn't talk to her about his work, she wasn't interested, didn't give a damn. He told us – didn't he?' – she looked up at Pippa, perched on the arm of the sofa beside her – 'she never even read his books properly. He wanted someone to connect to on that level. He could really talk to me about literature.'

'And me,' said Pippa, launching at once into a speech: 'He was interested in identity politics, you know, and he talked to me for hours about what it was like for me being born, basically, in the wrong—'

'Yeah, he told me it was a relief to be able to talk to someone who actually understood his work,' said Kathryn loudly, drowning Pippa out.

'I thought so,' said Strike, nodding. 'And the police didn't bother asking you about any of this, I take it?'

'Well, they asked where we met and I told them: on his creative writing course,' said Kathryn. 'It was just gradual, you know, he was interested in my writing . . . '

'. . . in our writing . . . ' said Pippa quietly.

Kathryn talked at length, Strike nodding with every appearance of interest at the gradual progression of the teacher–student relationship to something much warmer, Pippa tagging along, it seemed, and leaving Quine and Kathryn only at the bedroom door.

'I write fantasy with a twist,' said Kathryn and Strike was surprised and a little amused that she had begun to talk like Fancourt: in rehearsed phrases, in sound-bites. He wondered fleetingly how many people who sat alone for hours as they scribbled their stories practised talking about their work during their coffee breaks and he remembered what Waldegrave had told him about Quine, that he had freely admitted to role-playing interviews with a biro. 'It's fantasy slash erotica really, but quite literary. And that's the thing about traditional publishing, you know, they don't want to take a chance on something that hasn't been seen before, it's all about what fits their sales categories, and if you're blending several genres, if you're creating something entirely new, they're afraid to take a chance ... I know that *Liz Tassel*,' Kathryn spoke the name as though it were a medical complaint, 'told Owen my work was too *niche*. But that's the great thing about indie publishing, the freedom—'

'Yeah,' said Pippa, clearly desperate to put in her two pennys' worth, 'that's true, for genre fiction I think indie can be the way to go—'

'Except I'm not really genre,' said Kathryn, with a slight frown, 'that's my point—'

'—but Owen felt that for my memoir I'd do better going the traditional route,' said Pippa. 'You know, he had a real interest in gender identity and he was fascinated with what I'd been through. I introduced him to a couple of other transgendered people and he promised to talk to his editor about me, because he thought, with the right promotion, you know, and with a story that's never really been told—'

'Owen loved *Melina's Sacrifice*, he couldn't wait to read on. He was practically ripping it out of my hand every time I finished a chapter,' said Kathryn loudly, 'and he told me—'

She stopped abruptly in mid-flow. Pippa's evident irritation at being interrupted faded ludicrously from her face. Both of them, Robin could tell, had suddenly remembered that all the time Quine had been showering them with effusive encouragement, interest and praise, the characters of Harpy and Epicoene had been taking obscene shape on an old electric typewriter hidden from their eager gazes.

'So he talked to you about his own work?' Strike asked.

'A bit,' said Kathryn Kent in a flat voice.

'How long was he working on *Bombyx Mori*, do you know?'

'Most of the time I knew him,' she said.

'What did he say about it?'

There was a pause. Kathryn and Pippa looked at each other.

'I've already told him,' Pippa told Kathryn, with a significant glance at Strike, 'that he told us it was going to be different.'

'Yeah,' said Kathryn heavily. She folded her arms. 'He didn't tell us it was going to be like that.'

Like that . . . Strike remembered the brown, glutinous substance that had leaked from Harpy's breasts. It had been, for him, one of the most revolting images in the book. Kathryn's sister, he remembered, had died of breast cancer.

'Did he say what it was going to be like?' Strike asked.

'He lied,' said Kathryn simply. 'He said it was going to be the writer's journey or something but he made out . . . he told us we were going to be . . .'

'"Beautiful lost souls,"' said Pippa, on whom the phrase seemed to have impressed itself.

'Yeah,' said Kathryn heavily.

'Did he ever read any of it to you, Kathryn?'

'No,' she said. 'He said he wanted it to be a – a—'

'Oh, *Kath*,' said Pippa tragically. Kathryn had buried her face in her hands.

'Here,' said Robin kindly, delving into her handbag for tissues.

'No,' said Kathryn roughly, pushing herself off the sofa and disappearing into the kitchen. She came back with a handful of kitchen roll.

'He said,' she repeated, 'he wanted it to be a surprise. That bastard,' she said, sitting back down. '*Bastard.*'

She dabbed at her eyes and shook her head, the long mane of red hair swaying, while Pippa rubbed her back.

'Pippa told me,' said Strike, 'that Quine put a copy of the manuscript through your door.'

'Yeah,' said Kathryn.

It was clear that Pippa had already confessed to this indiscretion.

'Jude next door saw him doing it. She's a nosy bitch, always keeping tabs on me.'

Strike, who had just put an additional twenty through the nosy neighbour's letter box as a thank-you for keeping him informed of Kathryn's movements, asked:

'When?'

'Early hours of the sixth,' said Kathryn.

Strike could almost feel Robin's tension and excitement.

'Were the lights outside your front door working then?'

'Them? They've been out for months.'

'Did she speak to Quine?'

'No, just peered out the window. It was two in the morning or something, she wasn't going to go outside in her nightie. But she'd seen him come and go loads of times. She knew what he l-looked like,' said Kathryn on a sob, 'in his s-stupid cloak and hat.'

'Pippa said there was a note,' said Strike.

'Yeah – "Payback time for both of us",' said Kathryn.

'Have you still got it?'

'I burned it,' said Kathryn.

'Was it addressed to you? "Dear Kathryn"?'

'No,' she said, 'just the message and a bloody kiss. *Bastard!*' she sobbed.

'Shall I go and get us some real drink?' volunteered Robin surprisingly.

'There's some in the kitchen,' said Kathryn, her reply muffled by application of the kitchen roll to her mouth and cheeks. 'Pip, you get it.'

'You were sure the note was from him?' asked Strike as Pippa sped off in pursuit of alcohol.

'Yeah, it was his handwriting, I'd know it anywhere,' said Kathryn.

'What did you understand by it?'

'I dunno,' said Kathryn weakly, wiping her overflowing eyes. 'Payback for me because he had a go at his wife? And payback for him on everyone ... even me. Gutless bastard,' she said, unconsciously echoing Michael Fancourt. 'He could've told me he didn't want ... if he wanted to end it ... why do that? *Why?* And it wasn't just me ... Pip ... making out he cared, talking to her about her life ... she's had an awful time ... I mean, her memoir's not great literature or anything, but—'

Pippa returned carrying clinking glasses and a bottle of brandy, and Kathryn fell silent.

'We were saving this for the Christmas pudding,' said Pippa, deftly uncorking the cognac. 'There you go, Kath.'

Kathryn took a large brandy and swigged it down in one. It seemed to have the desired effect. With a sniff, she straightened her back. Robin accepted a small measure. Strike declined.

'When did you read the manuscript?' he asked Kathryn, who was already helping herself to more brandy.

'Same day I found it, on the ninth, when I got home to grab some more clothes. I'd been staying with Angela at the hospice, see . . . he hadn't picked up any of my calls since bonfire night, not one, and I'd told him Angela was really bad, I'd left messages. Then I came home and found the manuscript all over the floor. I thought, Is that why he's not picking up, he wants me to read this first? I took it back to the hospice with me and read it there, while I was sitting by Angela.'

Robin could only imagine how it would have felt to read her lover's depiction of her while she sat beside her dying sister's bed.

'I called Pip – didn't I?' said Kathryn; Pippa nodded, '—and told her what he'd done. I kept calling him, but he *still* wouldn't pick up. Well, after Angela had died I thought, Screw it. I'm coming to find *you*.' The brandy had given colour to Kathryn's wan cheeks. 'I went to their house but when I saw her – his wife – I could tell she was telling the truth. He wasn't there. So I told her to tell him Angela was dead. He'd met Angela,' said Kathryn, her face crumpling again. Pippa set down her own glass and put her arms around Kathryn's shaking shoulders, 'I thought he'd realise at least what he'd done to me when I was losing . . . when I'd lost . . . '

For over a minute there were no sounds in the room but Kathryn's sobs and the distant yells of the youths in the courtyard below.

'I'm sorry,' said Strike formally.

'It must have been awful for you,' said Robin.

A fragile sense of comradeship bound the four of them now. They could agree on one thing, at least; that Owen Quine had behaved very badly.

'It's your powers of textual analysis I'm really here for,' Strike told Kathryn when she had again dried her eyes, now swollen to slits in her face.

'What d'you mean?' she asked, but Robin heard gratified pride behind the curtness.

'I don't understand some of what Quine wrote in *Bombyx Mori*.'

'It isn't hard,' she said, and again she unknowingly echoed Fancourt: 'It won't win prizes for subtlety, will it?'

'I don't know,' said Strike. 'There's one very intriguing character.'

'Vainglorious?' she said.

Naturally, he thought, she would jump to that conclusion. Fancourt was famous.

'I was thinking of the Cutter.'

'I don't want to talk about that,' she said, with a sharpness that took Robin aback. Kathryn glanced at Pippa and Robin recognised the mutual glow, poorly disguised, of a shared secret.

'He pretended to be better than that,' said Kathryn. 'He pretended there were some things that were sacred. Then he went and . . .'

'Nobody seems to want to interpret the Cutter for me,' said Strike.

'That's because some of us have some decency,' said Kathryn.

Strike caught Robin's eye. He was urging her to take over.

'Jerry Waldegrave's already told Cormoran that he's the Cutter,' she said tentatively.

'I like Jerry Waldegrave,' said Kathryn defiantly.

'You met him?' asked Robin.

'Owen took me to a party, Christmas before last,' she said. 'Waldegrave was there. Sweet man. He'd had a few,' she said.

'Drinking even then, was he?' interjected Strike.

It was a mistake; he had encouraged Robin to take over because he guessed that she seemed less frightening. His interruption made Kathryn clam up.

'Anyone else interesting at the party?' Robin asked, sipping her brandy.

'Michael Fancourt was there,' said Kathryn at once. 'People say he's arrogant, but I thought he was charming.'

'Oh – did you speak to him?'

'Owen wanted me to stay well away,' she said, 'but I went to the Ladies and on the way back I just told him how much I'd loved *House of Hollow*. Owen wouldn't have liked that,' she said with pathetic satisfaction. 'Always going on about Fancourt being overrated, but *I* think he's marvellous. Anyway, we talked for a while and then someone pulled him away, but yes,' she repeated defiantly, as though the shade of Owen Quine were in the room and could hear her praising his rival, 'he was charming to *me*. Wished me luck with my writing,' she said, sipping her brandy.

'Did you tell him you were Owen's girlfriend?' asked Robin.

'Yes,' said Kathryn, with a twist to her smile, 'and he laughed and said, "You have my commiserations." It didn't bother him. He didn't care about Owen any more, I could tell. No, I think he's a nice man and a marvellous writer. People are envious, aren't they, when you're successful?'

She poured herself more brandy. She was holding it remarkably well. Other than the flush it had brought to her face, there was no sign of tipsiness at all.

'And you liked Jerry Waldegrave,' said Robin, almost absentmindedly.

'Oh, he's lovely,' said Kathryn, on a roll now, praising anyone that Quine might have attacked. 'Lovely man. He was very, *very* drunk, though. He was in a side room and people were steering clear, you know. That bitch Tassel told us to leave him to it, that he was talking gibberish.'

'Why do you call her a bitch?' asked Robin.

'Snobby old cow,' said Kathryn. 'Way she spoke to me, to everyone. But I know what it was: she was upset because Michael Fancourt was there. I said to her – Owen had gone off to see if Jerry was all right, he wasn't going to leave him passed out in a chair, whatever that old bitch said – I told her: "I've just been talking to Fancourt, he was charming." She didn't like that,' said Kathryn with satisfaction. 'Didn't like the idea of him being charming to me when he hates her. Owen told me she used to be in love with Fancourt and he wouldn't give her the time of day.'

She relished the gossip, however old. For that night, at least, she had been an insider.

'She left soon after I told her that,' said Kathryn with satisfaction. 'Horrible woman.'

'Michael Fancourt told me,' said Strike, and the eyes of Kathryn and Pippa were instantly riveted on him, eager to hear what the famous writer might have said, 'that Owen Quine and Elizabeth Tassel once had an affair.'

One moment of stupefied silence and then Kathryn Kent burst out laughing. It was unquestionably genuine: raucous, almost joyful, shrieks filled the room.

'Owen and *Elizabeth Tassel*?'

'That's what he said.'

Pippa beamed at the sight and sound of Kathryn Kent's exuberant, unexpected mirth. She rolled against the back of the sofa, trying to catch her breath; brandy slopped onto her trousers as she shook with what seemed entirely genuine amusement. Pippa caught the hysteria from her and began to laugh too.

'Never,' panted Kathryn, 'in . . . a . . . *million* . . . years . . .'

'This would have been a long time ago,' said Strike, but her long red mane shook as she continued to roar with unfeigned laughter.

'Owen and Liz . . . never. Never, ever . . . you don't understand,' she said, now dabbing at eyes wet with mirth. 'He thought she was *awful*. He would've told me . . . Owen talked about everyone he'd slept with, he wasn't a *gentleman* like that, was he, Pip? I'd have known if they'd ever . . . I don't know *where* Michael Fancourt got that from. *Never*,' said Kathryn Kent, with unforced merriment and total conviction.

The laughter had loosened her up.

'But you don't know what the Cutter really meant?' Robin asked her, setting her empty brandy glass down on the pine coffee table with the finality of a guest about to take their leave.

'I never said I didn't know,' said Kathryn, still out of breath from her protracted laughter. 'I *do* know. It was just awful, to do it to Jerry. Such a bloody hypocrite . . . Owen tells me not to mention it to anyone and then he goes and puts it in *Bombyx Mori* . . .'

Robin did not need Strike's look to tell her to remain silent and let Kathryn's brandy-fuelled good humour, her enjoyment of their undivided attention and the reflected glory of knowing sensitive secrets about literary figures do their work.

'All right,' she said. 'All right, here it is . . .

'Owen told me as we were leaving. Jerry was very drunk that night and you know his marriage is on the rocks, has been for years . . . he and Fenella had had a really terrible row the night before the party and she'd told him that their daughter might not be his. That she might be . . .'

Strike knew what was coming.

'... Fancourt's,' said Kathryn, after a suitably dramatic pause. 'The dwarf with the big head, the baby she thought of aborting because she didn't know whose it was, d'you see? The Cutter with his cuckold's horns ...

'And Owen told me to keep my mouth shut. "It's not funny," he said, "Jerry loves his daughter, only good thing he's got in his life." But he talked about it all the way home. On and on about Fancourt and how much he'd hate finding out he had a daughter, because Fancourt never wanted kids ... All that bullshit about protecting Jerry! Anything to get at Michael Fancourt. *Anything*.'

46

> Leander strived; the waves about him wound,
> And pulled him to the bottom, where the ground
> Was strewed with pearl . . .
>
> Christopher Marlowe, *Hero and Leander*

Grateful for the effect of cheap brandy and to Robin's particular combination of clear-headedness and warmth, Strike parted from her with many thanks half an hour later. Robin travelled home to Matthew in a glow of gratification and excitement, looking more kindly on Strike's theory as to the killer of Owen Quine than she had done before. This was partly because nothing that Kathryn Kent had said had contradicted it, but mainly because she felt particularly warm towards her boss after the shared interrogation.

Strike returned to his attic rooms in a less elevated frame of mind. He had drunk nothing but tea and believed more strongly than ever in his theory, but all the proof he could offer was a single typewriter cassette: it would not be enough to overturn the police case against Leonora.

There were hard frosts overnight on Saturday and Sunday, but during the daytime glimmers of sunshine pierced the cloud blanket. Rain turned some of the accumulated snow in the gutters to sliding slush. Strike brooded alone between his rooms and his office, ignoring a call from Nina Lascelles and turning down an invitation to dinner at Nick and Ilsa's, pleading paperwork but actually preferring solitude without pressure to discuss the Quine case.

He knew that he was acting as though he were held to a professional standard that had ceased to apply when he had left the Special Investigation Branch. Though legally free to gossip to whomever he pleased about his suspicions, he continued to treat them as confidential. This was partly longstanding habit, but mainly because (much as others might jeer) he took extremely seriously the possibility that the killer might hear what he was thinking and doing. In Strike's opinion, the safest way of ensuring that secret information did not leak was not to tell anybody about it.

On Monday he was visited again by the boss and boyfriend of the faithless Miss Brocklehurst, whose masochism now extended to a wish to know whether she had, as he strongly suspected, a third lover hidden away somewhere. Strike listened with half his mind on the activities of Dave Polworth, who was starting to feel like his last hope. Robin's endeavours remained fruitless, in spite of the hours she was spending pursuing the evidence he had asked her to find.

At half past six that evening, as he sat in his flat watching the forecast, which predicted a return of arctic weather by the end of the week, his phone rang.

'Guess what, Diddy?' said Polworth down a crackling line.

'You're kidding me,' said Strike, his chest suddenly tight with anticipation.

'Got the lot, mate.'

'Holy shit,' breathed Strike.

It had been his own theory, but he felt as astonished as if Polworth had done it all unaided.

'Bagged up here, waiting for you.'

'I'll send someone for it first thing tomorrow—'

'And I'm gonna go home and have a nice hot bath,' said Polworth.

'Chum, you're a bloody—'

'I know I am. We'll talk about my credit later. I'm fucking freezing, Diddy, I'm going home.'

Strike called Robin with the news. Her elation matched his own.

'Right, tomorrow!' she said, full of determination. 'Tomorrow I'm going to get it, I'm going to make sure—'

'Don't go getting careless,' Strike talked over her. 'It's not a competition.'

He barely slept that night.

Robin made no appearance at the office until one in the afternoon, but the instant he heard the glass door bang and heard her calling him, he knew.

'You haven't—?'

'Yes,' she said breathlessly.

She thought he was going to hug her, which would be crossing a line he had never even approached before, but the lunge she had thought might be meant for her was really for the mobile on his desk.

'I'm calling Anstis. We've done it, Robin.'

'Cormoran, I think—' Robin started to say, but he did not hear her. He had hurried back into his office and closed the door behind him.

Robin lowered herself into her computer chair, feeling

uneasy. Strike's muffled voice rose and fell beyond the door. She got up restlessly to visit the bathroom, where she washed her hands and stared into the cracked and spotted mirror over the sink, observing the inconveniently bright gold of her hair. Returning to the office, she sat down, could not settle to anything, noticed that she had not switched on her tiny tinsel Christmas tree, did so, and waited, absent-mindedly biting her thumbnail, something she had not done for years.

Twenty minutes later, his jaw set and his expression ugly, Strike emerged from the office.

'Stupid fucking dickhead!' were his first words.

'No!' gasped Robin.

'He's having none of it,' said Strike, too wound up to sit, but limping up and down the enclosed space. 'He's had that bloody rag in the lock-up analysed and it's got Quine's blood on it – big effing deal, could've cut himself months ago. He's so in love with his own effing theory—'

'Did you say to him, if he just gets a warrant—?'

'*DICKHEAD!*' roared Strike, punching the metal filing cabinet so that it reverberated and Robin jumped.

'But he can't deny – once forensics are done—'

'That's the bleeding point, Robin!' he said, rounding on her. 'Unless he searches *before* he gets forensics done, there might be nothing there to find!'

'But did you tell him about the typewriter?'

'If the simple fact that it's *there* doesn't hit the prick between the eyes—'

She ventured no more suggestions but watched him walk up and down, brow furrowed, too intimidated to tell him, now, what was worrying her.

'Fuck it,' growled Strike on his sixth walk back to her desk.

'Shock and awe. No choice. Al,' he muttered, pulling out his mobile again, 'and Nick.'

'Who's Nick?' asked Robin, desperately trying to keep up.

'He's married to Leonora's lawyer,' said Strike, punching buttons on his phone. 'Old mate . . . he's a gastroenterologist . . . '

He retreated again to his office and slammed the door.

For want of anything else to do, Robin filled the kettle, her heart hammering, and made them both tea. The mugs cooled, untouched, while she waited.

When Strike emerged fifteen minutes later, he seemed calmer.

'All right,' he said, seizing his tea and taking a gulp. 'I've got a plan and I'm going to need you. Are you up for it?'

'Of course!' said Robin.

He gave her a concise outline of what he wanted to do. It was ambitious and would require a healthy dose of luck.

'Well?' Strike asked her finally.

'No problem,' said Robin.

'We might not need you.'

'No,' said Robin.

'On the other hand, you could be key.'

'Yes,' said Robin.

'Sure that's all right?' Strike asked, watching her closely.

'No problem at all,' said Robin. 'I want to do it, I really do – it's just,' she hesitated, 'I think he—'

'What?' said Strike sharply.

'I think I'd better have a practice,' said Robin.

'Oh,' said Strike, eyeing her. 'Yeah, fair enough. Got until Thursday, I think. I'll check the date now . . . '

He disappeared for the third time into his inner office. Robin returned to her computer chair.

She desperately wanted to play her part in the capture of Owen Quine's killer, but what she had been about to say, before Strike's sharp response panicked her out of it, was: 'I think he might have seen me.'

47

Ha, ha, ha, thou entanglest thyself in thine own work like a silkworm.

John Webster, *The White Devil*

By the light of the old-fashioned street lamp the cartoonish murals covering the front of the Chelsea Arts Club were strangely eerie. Circus freaks had been painted on the rainbow-stippled walls of a long low line of ordinarily white houses knocked into one: a four-legged blonde girl, an elephant eating its keeper, an etiolated contortionist in prison stripes whose head appeared to be disappearing up his own anus. The club stood in a leafy, sleepy and genteel street, quiet with the snow that had returned with a vengeance, falling fast and mounting over roofs and pavements as though the brief respite in the arctic winter had never been. All through Thursday the blizzard had grown thicker and now, viewed through a rippling lamp-lit curtain of icy flakes, the old club in its fresh pastel colours appeared strangely insubstantial, pasteboard scenery, a *trompe l'œil* marquee.

Strike was standing in a shadowy alley off Old Church Street, watching as one by one they arrived for their small party. He saw the aged Pinkelman helped from his taxi by a stone-faced

Jerry Waldegrave, while Daniel Chard stood in a fur hat on his crutches, nodding and smiling an awkward welcome. Elizabeth Tassel drew up alone in a cab, fumbling for her fare and shivering in the cold. Lastly, in a car with a driver, came Michael Fancourt. He took his time getting out of the car, straightening his coat before proceeding up the steps to the front door.

The detective, on whose dense curly hair the snow was falling thickly, pulled out his mobile and rang his half-brother.

'Hey,' said Al, who sounded excited. 'They're all in the dining room.'

'How many?'

''Bout a dozen of them.'

'Coming in now.'

Strike limped across the street with the aid of his stick. They let him in at once when he gave his name and explained that he was here as Duncan Gilfedder's guest.

Al and Gilfedder, a celebrity photographer whom Strike was meeting for the first time, stood a short way inside the entrance. Gilfedder seemed confused as to who Strike was, or why he, a member of this eccentric and charming club, had been asked by his acquaintance Al to invite a guest whom he did not know.

'My brother,' said Al, introducing them. He sounded proud.

'Oh,' said Gilfedder blankly. He wore the same type of glasses as Christian Fisher and his lank hair was cut in a straggly shoulder-length bob. 'I thought your brother was younger.'

'That's Eddie,' said Al. 'This is Cormoran. Ex-army. He's a detective now.'

'Oh,' said Gilfedder, looking even more bemused.

'Thanks for this,' Strike said, addressing both men equally. 'Get you another drink?'

The club was so noisy and packed it was hard to see much of

it except glimpses of squashy sofas and a crackling log fire. The walls of the low-ceilinged bar were liberally covered in prints, paintings and photographs; it had the feeling of a country house, cosy and a little scruffy. As the tallest man in the room, Strike could see over the crowd's heads towards the windows at the rear of the club. Beyond lay a large garden lit by exterior lights so that it was illuminated in patches. A thick, pristine layer of snow, pure and smooth as royal icing, lay over verdant shrubbery and the stone sculptures lurking in the undergrowth.

Strike reached the bar and ordered wine for his companions, glancing as he did so into the dining room.

Those eating filled several long wooden tables. There was the Roper Chard party, with a pair of French windows beside them, the garden icy white and ghostly behind the glass. A dozen people, some of whom Strike did not recognise, had gathered to honour the ninety-year-old Pinkelman, who was sitting at the head of the table. Whoever had been in charge of the *placement*, Strike saw, had sat Elizabeth Tassel and Michael Fancourt well apart. Fancourt was talking loudly into Pinkelman's ear, Chard opposite him. Elizabeth Tassel was sitting next to Jerry Waldegrave. Neither was speaking to the other.

Strike passed glasses of wine to Al and Gilfedder, then returned to the bar to fetch a whisky for himself, deliberately maintaining a clear view of the Roper Chard party.

'Why,' said a voice, clear as a bell but somewhere below him, 'are *you* here?'

Nina Lascelles was standing at his elbow in the same strappy black dress she had worn to his birthday dinner. No trace of her former giggly flirtatiousness remained. She looked accusatory.

'Hi,' said Strike, surprised. 'I didn't expect to see you here.'

'Nor I you,' she said.

He had not returned any of her calls for over a week, not since the night he had slept with her to rid himself of thoughts of Charlotte on her wedding day.

'So you know Pinkelman,' said Strike, trying for small talk in the face of what he could tell was animosity.

'I'm taking over some of Jerry's authors now he's leaving. Pinks is one of them.'

'Congratulations,' said Strike. Still, she did not smile. 'Waldegrave still came to the party, though?'

'Pinks is fond of Jerry. Why,' she repeated, 'are *you* here?'

'Doing what I was hired to do,' said Strike. 'Trying to find out who killed Owen Quine.'

She rolled her eyes, clearly feeling that he was pushing his persistence past a joke.

'How did you get in here? It's members only.'

'I've got a contact,' said Strike.

'You didn't think of using me again, then?' she asked.

He did not much like the reflection of himself he saw in her large mouse-like eyes. There was no denying that he had used her repeatedly. It had become cheap, shameful, and she deserved better.

'I thought that might be getting old,' said Strike.

'Yeah,' said Nina. 'You thought right.'

She turned from him and walked back to the table, filling the last vacant seat, between two employees whom he did not know.

Strike was in Jerry Waldegrave's direct line of vision. Waldegrave caught sight of him and Strike saw the editor's eyes widen behind his horn-rimmed glasses. Alerted by Waldegrave's transfixed stare, Chard twisted in his seat and he, too, clearly recognised Strike.

'How's it going?' asked Al excitedly at Strike's elbow.

'Great,' said Strike. 'Where's that Gilsomething gone?'

'Downed his drink and left. Doesn't know what the hell we're up to,' said Al.

Al did not know why they were here either. Strike had told him nothing except that he needed entry to the Chelsea Arts Club tonight and that he might need a lift. Al's bright red Alfa Romeo Spider sat parked a little down the road. It had been agony on Strike's knee to get in and out of the low-slung vehicle.

As he had intended, half the Roper Chard table now seemed acutely aware of his presence. Strike was positioned so that he could see them reflected clearly in the dark French windows. Two Elizabeth Tassels were glaring at him over their menus, two Ninas were determinedly ignoring him and two shiny-pated Chards summoned a waiter each and muttered in their ears.

'Is that the bald bloke we saw in the River Café?' asked Al.

'Yeah,' said Strike, grinning as the solid waiter separated from his reflected wraith and made his way towards them. 'I think we're about to be asked whether we've got the right to be in here.'

'Very sorry, sir,' began the waiter in a mutter as he reached Strike, 'but could I ask—?'

'Al Rokeby – my brother and I are here with Duncan Gilfedder,' said Al pleasantly before Strike could respond. Al's tone expressed surprise that they had been challenged at all. He was a charming and privileged young man who was welcome everywhere, whose credentials were impeccable and whose casual roping of Strike into the family pen conferred upon him that same sense of easy entitlement. Jonny Rokeby's eyes looked out of Al's narrow face. The waiter muttered hasty apologies and retreated.

'Are you just trying to put the wind up them?' asked Al, staring over at the publisher's table.

'Can't hurt,' said Strike with a smile, sipping his whisky as he watched Daniel Chard deliver what was clearly a stilted speech in Pinkelman's honour. A card and present were brought out from under the table. For every look and smile they gave the old writer, there was a nervous glance towards the large, dark man staring at them from the bar. Michael Fancourt alone had not looked around. Either he remained in ignorance of the detective's presence, or was untroubled by it.

When starters had been put in front of them all, Jerry Waldegrave got to his feet and moved out from the table towards the bar. Nina and Elizabeth's eyes followed him. On Waldegrave's way to the bathroom he merely nodded at Strike, but on the way back, he paused.

'Surprised to see you here.'

'Yeah?' said Strike.

'Yeah,' said Waldegrave. 'You're, er . . . making people feel uncomfortable.'

'Nothing I can do about that,' said Strike.

'You could try not staring us out.'

'This is my brother, Al,' said Strike, ignoring the request.

Al beamed and held out a hand, which Waldegrave shook, seeming nonplussed.

'You're annoying Daniel,' Waldegrave told Strike, looking directly into the detective's eyes.

'That's a shame,' said Strike.

The editor rumpled his untidy hair.

'Well, if that's your attitude.'

'Surprised you care how Daniel Chard feels.'

'I don't particularly,' said Waldegrave, 'but he can make life unpleasant for other people when he's in a bad mood. I'd like tonight to go well for Pinkelman. I can't understand why you're here.'

'Wanted to make a delivery,' said Strike.

He pulled a blank white envelope out from an inside pocket.

'What is this?'

'It's for you,' said Strike.

Waldegrave took it, looking utterly confused.

'Something you should think about,' said Strike, moving closer to the bemused editor in the noisy bar. 'Fancourt had mumps, you know, before his wife died.'

'What?' said Waldegrave, bewildered.

'Never had kids. Pretty sure he's infertile. Thought you might be interested.'

Waldegrave stared at him, opened his mouth, found nothing to say, then walked away, still clutching the white envelope.

'What was that?' Al asked Strike, agog.

'Plan A,' said Strike. 'We'll see.'

Waldegrave sat back down at the Roper Chard table. Mirrored in the black window beside him, he opened the envelope Strike had given him. Puzzled, he pulled out a second envelope. There was a scribbled name on this one.

The editor looked up at Strike, who raised his eyebrows.

Jerry Waldegrave hesitated, then turned to Elizabeth Tassel and passed her the envelope. She read what was written on it, frowning. Her eyes flew to Strike's. He smiled and toasted her with his glass.

She seemed uncertain as to what to do for a moment; then she nudged the girl beside her and passed the envelope on.

It travelled up the table and across it, into the hands of Michael Fancourt.

'There we are,' said Strike. 'Al, I'm going into the garden for a fag. Stay here and keep your phone on.'

'They don't allow mobiles—'

But Al caught sight of Strike's expression and amended hastily:

'Will do.'

48

> Does the silkworm expend her yellow labours
> For thee? For thee does she undo herself?
>
> Thomas Middleton, *The Revenger's Tragedy*

The garden was deserted and bitterly cold. Strike sank up to his ankles in snow, unable to feel the cold seeping through his right trouser leg. All the smokers who would ordinarily have congregated on the smooth lawns had chosen the street instead. He ploughed a solitary trench through the frozen whiteness, surrounded by silent beauty, coming to a halt beside a small round pond that had become a disc of thick grey ice. A plump bronze cupid sat in the middle on an oversized clam shell. It wore a wig of snow and pointed its bow and arrow, not anywhere that it might hit a human being, but straight up at the dark heavens.

Strike lit a cigarette and turned back to look at the blazing windows of the club. The diners and waiters looked like paper cutouts moving against a lit screen.

If Strike knew his man, he would come. Wasn't this an irresistible situation to a writer, to the compulsive spinner of experience into words, to a lover of the macabre and the strange?

And sure enough, after a few minutes Strike heard a door open, a snatch of conversation and music hastily muffled, then the sound of deadened footsteps.

'Mr Strike?'

Fancourt's head looked particularly large in the darkness.

'Would it not be easier to go on to the street?'

'I'd rather do this in the garden,' said Strike.

'I see.'

Fancourt sounded vaguely amused, as though he intended, at least in the short term, to humour Strike. The detective suspected that it appealed to the writer's sense of theatre that he should be the one summoned from the table of anxious people to talk to the man who was making them all so nervous.

'What's this about?' asked Fancourt.

'Value your opinion,' said Strike. 'Question of critical analysis of *Bombyx Mori*.'

'Again?' said Fancourt.

His good humour was cooling with his feet. He pulled his coat more closely around him and said, the snow falling thick and fast:

'I've said everything I want to say about that book.'

'One of the first things I was told about *Bombyx Mori*,' said Strike, 'was that it was reminiscent of your early work. Gore and arcane symbolism, I think were the words used.'

'So?' said Fancourt, hands in his pockets.

'So, the more I've talked to people who knew Quine, the clearer it's become that the book that everyone's read bears only a vague resemblance to the one he claimed to be writing.'

Fancourt's breath rose in a cloud before him, obscuring the little that Strike could see of his heavy features.

'I've even met a girl who says she heard part of the book that doesn't appear in the final manuscript.'

'Writers cut,' said Fancourt, shuffling his feet, his shoulders hunched up around his ears. 'Owen would have done well to cut a great deal more. Several novels, in fact.'

'There are also all the duplications from his earlier work,' said Strike. 'Two hermaphrodites. Two bloody bags. All that gratuitous sex.'

'He was a man of limited imagination, Mr Strike.'

'He left behind a scribbled note with what looks like a bunch of possible character names on it. One of those names appears on a used typewriter cassette that came out of his study before the police sealed it off, but it's nowhere in the finished manuscript.'

'So he changed his mind,' said Fancourt irritably.

'It's an everyday name, not symbolic or archetypal like the names in the finished manuscript,' said Strike.

His eyes becoming accustomed to the darkness, Strike saw a look of faint curiosity on Fancourt's heavy-featured face.

'A restaurant full of people witnessed what I think is going to turn out to be Quine's last meal and his final public performance,' Strike went on. 'A credible witness says that Quine shouted for the whole restaurant to hear that one of the reasons Tassel was too cowardly to represent the book was "Fancourt's limp dick".'

He doubted that he and Fancourt were clearly visible to the jittery people at the publisher's table. Their figures would blend with the trees and statuary, but the determined or desperate might still be able to make out their location by the tiny luminous eye of Strike's glowing cigarette: a marksman's bead.

'Thing is, there's nothing in *Bombyx Mori* about your dick,' continued Strike. 'There's nothing in there about Quine's mistress and his young transgendered friend being "beautiful lost souls", which is how he told them he was going to describe them. And you don't pour acid on silkworms; you boil them to get their cocoons.'

'*So?*' repeated Fancourt.

'So I've been forced to the conclusion,' said Strike, 'that the *Bombyx Mori* everyone's read is a different book to the *Bombyx Mori* Owen Quine wrote.'

Fancourt stopped shuffling his feet. Momentarily frozen, he appeared to give Strike's words serious consideration.

'I – no,' he said, almost, it seemed, to himself. 'Quine wrote that book. It's his style.'

'It's funny you should say that, because everyone else who had a decent ear for Quine's particular style seems to detect a foreign voice in the book. Daniel Chard thought it was Waldegrave. Waldegrave thought it was Elizabeth Tassel. And Christian Fisher heard *you*.'

Fancourt shrugged with his usual easy arrogance.

'Quine was trying to imitate a better writer.'

'Don't you think the way he treats his living models is strangely uneven?'

Fancourt, accepting the cigarette Strike offered him and a light, now listened in silence and with interest.

'He says his wife and agent were parasites on him,' Strike said. 'Unpleasant, but the sort of accusation anyone could throw at the people who might be said to live off his earnings. He implies his mistress isn't fond of animals and throws in something that could either be a veiled reference to her producing crap books or a pretty sick allusion to breast cancer. His transgendered friend gets off with a jibe about vocal exercises – and that's after she claimed she showed him the life story she was writing and shared all her deepest secrets. He accuses Chard of effectively killing Joe North, and makes a crass suggestion of what Chard really wanted to do to him. And there's the accusation that you were responsible for your first wife's death.

'All of which is either in the public domain, public gossip or an easy accusation to sling.'

'Which isn't to say it wasn't hurtful,' said Fancourt quietly.

'Agreed,' said Strike. 'It gave plenty of people reason to be pissed off at him. But the only real revelation in the book is the insinuation that you fathered Joanna Waldegrave.'

'I told you – as good as told you – last time we met,' said Fancourt, sounding tense, 'that that accusation is not only false but impossible. I am infertile, as Quine—'

'—as Quine should have known,' agreed Strike, 'because you and he were still ostensibly on good terms when you had mumps and he'd already made a jibe about it in *The Balzac Brothers*. And that makes the accusation contained in the Cutter even stranger, doesn't it? As though it was written by someone who didn't know that you were infertile. Didn't any of this occur to you when you read the book?'

The snow fell thickly on the two men's hair, on their shoulders.

'I didn't think Owen cared whether any of it was true or not,' said Fancourt slowly, exhaling smoke. 'Mud sticks. He was just flinging a lot around. I thought he was looking to cause as much trouble as possible.'

'D'you think that's why he sent you an early copy of the manuscript?' When Fancourt did not respond, Strike went on: 'It's easily checkable, you know. Courier – postal service – there'll be a record. You might as well tell me.'

A lengthy pause.

'All right,' said Fancourt, at last.

'When did you get it?'

'The morning of the sixth.'

'What did you do with it?'

'Burned it,' said Fancourt shortly, exactly like Kathryn Kent. 'I could see what he was doing: trying to provoke a public row, maximise publicity. The last resort of a failure – I was not going to humour him.'

Another snatch of the interior revelry reached them as the door to the garden opened and closed again. Uncertain footsteps, winding through the snow, and then a large shadow looming out of the darkness.

'What,' croaked Elizabeth Tassel, who was wrapped in a heavy coat with a fur collar, 'is going on out here?'

The moment he heard her voice Fancourt made to move back inside. Strike wondered when was the last time they had come face to face in anything less than a crowd of hundreds.

'Wait a minute, will you?' Strike asked the writer.

Fancourt hesitated. Tassel addressed Strike in her deep, croaky voice.

'Pinks is missing Michael.'

'Something you'd know all about,' said Strike.

The snow whispered down upon leaves and onto the frozen pond where the cupid sat, pointing his arrow skywards.

'You thought Elizabeth's writing "lamentably derivative", isn't that right?' Strike asked Fancourt. 'You both studied Jacobean revenge tragedies, which accounts for the similarities in your styles. But you're a very good imitator of other people's writing, I think,' Strike told Tassel.

He had known that she would come if he took Fancourt

away, known that she would be frightened of what he was telling the writer out in the dark. She stood perfectly still as snow landed in her fur collar, on her iron-grey hair. Strike could just make out the contours of her face by the faint light of the club's distant windows. The intensity and emptiness of her gaze were remarkable. She had the dead, blank eyes of a shark.

'You took off Elspeth Fancourt's style to perfection, for instance.'

Fancourt's mouth fell quietly open. For a few seconds the only sound other than the whispering snow was the barely audible whistle emanating from Elizabeth Tassel's lungs.

'I thought from the start that Quine must've had some hold on you,' said Strike. 'You never seemed like the kind of woman who'd let herself be turned into a private bank and skivvy, who'd choose to keep Quine and let Fancourt go. All that bull about freedom of expression . . . *you* wrote the parody of Elspeth Fancourt's book that made her kill herself. All these years, there's only been your word for it that Owen showed you the piece he'd written. It was the other way round.'

There was silence except for the rustle of snow on snow and that faint, eerie sound emanating from Elizabeth Tassel's chest. Fancourt was looking from the agent to the detective, open-mouthed.

'The police suspected that Quine was blackmailing you,' Strike said, 'but you fobbed them off with a touching story about lending him money for Orlando. You've been paying Owen off for more than a quarter of a century, haven't you?'

He was trying to goad her into speech, but she said nothing, continuing to stare at him out of the dark empty eyes like holes in her plain, pale face.

'How did you describe yourself to me when we had lunch?'

Strike asked her. '"The very definition of a blameless spinster"? Found an outlet for your frustrations, though, didn't you, Elizabeth?'

The mad, blank eyes swivelled suddenly towards Fancourt, who had shifted where he stood.

'Did it feel good, raping and killing your way through everyone you knew, Elizabeth? One big explosion of malice and obscenity, revenging yourself on everyone, painting yourself as the unacclaimed genius, taking sideswipes at everyone with a more successful love life, a more satisfying—'

A soft voice spoke in the darkness, and for a second Strike did not know where it was coming from. It was strange, unfamiliar, high-pitched and sickly: the voice a madwoman might imagine to express innocence, kindliness.

'No, Mr Strike,' she whispered, like a mother telling a sleepy child not to sit up, not to struggle. 'You poor silly man. You poor thing.'

She forced a laugh that left her chest heaving, her lungs whistling.

'He was badly hurt in Afghanistan,' she said to Fancourt in that eerie, crooning voice. 'I think he's shell-shocked. Brain damaged, just like little Orlando. He needs help, poor Mr Strike.'

Her lungs whistled as she breathed faster.

'Should've bought a mask, Elizabeth, shouldn't you?' Strike asked.

He thought he saw the eyes darken and enlarge, her pupils dilating with the adrenalin coursing through her. The large, mannish hands had curled into claws.

'Thought you had it all worked out, didn't you? Ropes, disguise, protective clothing to protect yourself against the acid –

but you didn't realise you'd get tissue damage just from inhaling the fumes.'

The cold air was exacerbating her breathlessness. In her panic, she sounded sexually excited.

'I think,' said Strike, with calculated cruelty, 'it's driven you literally mad, Elizabeth, hasn't it? Better hope the jury buys that anyway, eh? What a waste of a life. Your business down the toilet, no man, no children . . . Tell me, was there ever an abortive coupling between the two of you?' asked Strike bluntly, watching their profiles. 'This "limp dick" business . . . sounds to me like Quine might've fictionalised it in the real *Bombyx Mori*.'

With their backs to the light he could not see their expressions, but their body language had given him his answer: the instantaneous swing away from each other to face him had expressed the ghost of a united front.

'When was this?' Strike asked, watching the dark outline that was Elizabeth. 'After Elspeth died? But then you moved on to Fenella Waldegrave, eh, Michael? No trouble keeping it up there, I take it?'

Elizabeth emitted a small gasp. It was as though he had hit her.

'For Christ's sake,' growled Fancourt. He was angry with Strike now. Strike ignored the implicit reproach. He was still working on Elizabeth, goading her, while her whistling lungs struggled for oxygen in the falling snow.

'Must've really pissed you off when Quine got carried away and started shouting about the contents of the real *Bombyx Mori* in the River Café, did it, Elizabeth? After you'd warned him not to breathe a word about the contents?'

'Insane. You're insane,' she whispered, with a forced smile

beneath the shark eyes, her big yellow teeth glinting. 'The war didn't just cripple you—'

'Nice,' said Strike appreciatively. 'There's the bullying bitch everyone's told me you are—'

'You hobble around London trying to get in the papers,' she panted. 'You're just like poor Owen, just like him . . . how he loved the papers, didn't he, Michael?' She turned to appeal to Fancourt. 'Didn't Owen adore publicity? Running off like a little boy playing hide-and-seek . . . '

'You encouraged Quine to go and hide in Talgarth Road,' said Strike. 'That was all your idea.'

'I won't listen to any more,' she whispered and her lungs were whistling as she gasped the winter air and she raised her voice: '*I'm not listening, Mr Strike, I'm not listening. Nobody's listening to you, you poor silly man . . .*'

'You told me Quine was a glutton for praise,' said Strike, raising his voice over the high-pitched chant with which she was trying to drown out his words. 'I think he told you his whole prospective plot for *Bombyx Mori* months ago and I think Michael here was in there in some form – nothing as crude as Vainglorious, but mocked for not getting it up, perhaps? "Payback time for both of you", eh?'

And as he had expected, she gave a little gasp at that and stopped her frantic chanting.

'You told Quine that *Bombyx Mori* sounded brilliant, that it would be the best thing he'd ever done, that it was going to be a massive success, but that he ought to keep the contents very, very quiet in case of legal action, and to make a bigger splash when it was unveiled. And all the time you were writing your own version. You had plenty of time on your hands to get it right, didn't you, Elizabeth? Twenty-six years of empty evenings, you could have written plenty of books by now, with your first from Oxford ... but what would you write about? You haven't exactly lived a full life, have you?'

Naked rage flickered across her face. Her fingers flexed, but she controlled herself. Strike wanted her to crack, wanted her to give in, but the shark's eyes seemed to be waiting for him to show weakness, for an opening.

'You crafted a novel out of a murder plan. The removal of the guts and the covering of the corpse in acid weren't symbolic, they were designed to screw forensics – but everyone bought it as literature.

'And you got that stupid, egotistical bastard to collude in planning his own death. You told him you had a great idea for maximising his publicity and his profits: the pair of you would stage a very public row – you saying the book was too contentious to put out there – and he'd disappear. You'd circulate rumours about the book's contents and finally, when Quine allowed himself to be found, you'd secure him a big fat deal.'

She was shaking her head, her lungs audibly labouring, but her dead eyes did not leave his face.

'He delivered the book. You delayed a few days, until bonfire night, to make sure you had lots of nice diversionary noise, then you sent out copies of the fake *Bombyx* to Fisher – the better to get the book talked about – to Waldegrave and to Michael here. You faked your public row, then you followed Quine to Talgarth Road—'

'No,' said Fancourt, apparently unable to help himself.

'Yes,' said Strike, pitiless. 'Quine didn't realise he had anything to fear from Elizabeth – not from his co-conspirator in the comeback of the century. I think he'd almost forgotten by then that what he'd been doing to you for years was blackmail, hadn't he?' he asked Tassel. 'He'd just developed the habit of asking you for money and being given it. I doubt you ever even talked about the parody any more, the thing that ruined your life . . .

'And you know what I think happened once he let you in, Elizabeth?'

Against his will, Strike remembered the scene: the great vaulted window, the body centred there as though for a grisly still life.

'I think you got that poor naive, narcissistic sod to pose for a publicity photograph. Was he kneeling down? Did the hero in the real book plead, or pray? Or did he get tied up like *your* Bombyx? He'd have liked that, wouldn't he, Quine, posing in ropes? It would've made it nice and easy to move behind him and smash his head in with the metal doorstop, wouldn't it? Under cover of the neighbourhood fireworks, you knocked Quine out, tied him up, sliced him open and—'

Fancourt let out a strangled moan of horror, but Tassel spoke again, crooning at him in a travesty of consolation:

'You ought to see someone, Mr Strike. *Poor* Mr Strike,' and to his surprise she reached out to lay one of her big hands on his snow-covered shoulder. Remembering what those hands had done, Strike stepped back instinctively and her arm fell heavily back to her side, hanging there, the fingers clenching reflexively.

'You filled a holdall with Owen's guts and the real manuscript,' said the detective. She had moved so close that he could again smell the combination of perfume and stale cigarettes. 'Then you put on Quine's own cloak and hat and left. Off you went, to feed a fourth copy of the fake *Bombyx Mori* through Kathryn Kent's letter box, to maximise suspects and incriminate another woman who was getting what you never got – sex. Companionship. At least one friend.'

She feigned laughter again but this time the sound was manic. Her fingers were still flexing and unflexing.

'You and Owen would have got on so well,' she whispered. 'Wouldn't he, Michael? Wouldn't he have got on marvellously with Owen? Sick fantasists . . . people will laugh at you, Mr Strike.' She was panting harder than ever, those dead, blank eyes staring out of her fixed white face. 'A poor cripple trying to recreate the sensation of success, chasing your famous fath—'

'Have you got proof of any of this?' Fancourt demanded in the swirling snow, his voice harsh with the desire not to believe. This was no ink-and-paper tragedy, no greasepaint death scene. Here beside him stood the living friend of his student years and whatever life had subsequently done to them, the idea that the big, ungainly, besotted girl whom he had known at Oxford could have turned into a woman capable of grotesque murder was almost unbearable.

'Yeah, I've got proof,' said Strike quietly. 'I've got a second electric typewriter, the exact model of Quine's, wrapped up in a black burqa and hydrochloric-stained overalls and weighted with stones. An amateur diver I happen to know pulled it out of the sea just a few days ago. It was lying beneath some notorious cliffs at Gwithian: Hell's Mouth, a place featured on Dorcus Pengelly's book cover. I expect she showed it to you when you visited, didn't she, Elizabeth? Did you walk back there alone with your mobile, telling her you needed to find better reception?'

She let out a ghastly low moan, like the sound of a man who has been punched in the stomach. For a second nobody moved, then Tassel turned clumsily and began running and stumbling away from them, back towards the club. A bright yellow rectangle of light shivered then disappeared as the door opened and closed.

'But,' said Fancourt, taking a few steps and looking back at Strike a little wildly, 'you can't – you've got to stop her!'

'Couldn't catch her if I wanted to,' said Strike, throwing the butt of his cigarette down into the snow. 'Dodgy knee.'

'She could do anything—'

'Off to kill herself, probably,' agreed Strike, pulling out his mobile.

The writer stared at him.

'You – you cold-blooded bastard!'

'You're not the first to say it,' said Strike, pressing keys on his phone. 'Ready?' he said into it. 'We're off.'

49

Dangers, like stars, in dark attempts best shine.

Thomas Dekker, *The Noble Spanish Soldier*

Out past the smokers at the front of the club the large woman came, blindly, slipping a little in the snow. She began to run up the dark street, her fur-collared coat flapping behind her.

A taxi, its 'For Hire' light on, slid out of a side road and she hailed it, flapping her arms madly. The cab slid to a halt, its headlamps making two cones of light whose trajectory was cut by the thickly falling snow.

'Fulham Palace Road,' said the harsh, deep voice, breaking with sobs.

They pulled slowly away from the kerb. The cab was old, the glass partition scratched and a little stained by years of its owner's smoking. Elizabeth Tassel was visible in the rear-view mirror as the street light slid over her, sobbing silently into her large hands, shaking all over.

The driver did not ask what was the matter but looked beyond the fare to the street behind, where the shrinking figures of two men could be seen, hurrying across the snowy road to a red sports car in the distance.

The taxi turned left at the end of the road and still Elizabeth

Tassel cried into her hands. The driver's thick woollen hat was itchy, grateful though she had been for it during the long hours of waiting. On up the King's Road the taxi sped, over thick powdery snow that resisted tyres' attempts to squash it to slush, the blizzard swirling remorselessly, rendering the roads increasingly lethal.

'You're going the wrong way.'

'There's a diversion,' lied Robin. 'Because of the snow.'

She met Elizabeth's eyes briefly in the mirror. The agent looked over her shoulder. The red Alfa Romeo was too far behind to see. She stared wildly around at the passing buildings. Robin could hear the eerie whistling from her chest.

'We're going in the opposite direction.'

'I'm going to turn in a minute,' said Robin.

She did not see Elizabeth Tassel try the door, but heard it. They were all locked.

'You can let me out here,' she said loudly. 'Let me out, I say!'

'You won't get another cab in this weather,' said Robin.

They had counted on Tassel being too distraught to notice where they were going for a little while longer. The cab was barely at Sloane Square. There was over a mile to go to New Scotland Yard. Robin's eyes flickered again to her rear-view mirror. The Alfa Romeo was a tiny red dot in the distance.

Elizabeth had undone her seatbelt.

'Stop this cab!' she shouted. 'Stop it and let me out!'

'I can't stop here,' said Robin, much more calmly than she felt, because the agent had left her seat and her large hands were scrabbling at the partition. 'I'm going to have to ask you to sit down, madam—'

The screen slid open. Elizabeth's hand seized Robin's hat and a handful of hair, her head almost side by side with Robin's, her expression venomous. Robin's hair fell into her eyes in sweaty strands.

'Get off me!'

'Who are you?' screeched Tassel, shaking Robin's head with the fistful of hair in her hand. 'Ralph said he saw a blonde going through the bin – *who are you?*'

'Let go!' shouted Robin, as Tassel's other hand grabbed her neck.

Two hundred yards behind them, Strike roared at Al:

'Put your fucking foot down, there's something wrong, look at it—'

The taxi ahead was careering all over the road.

'It's always been shit in ice,' moaned Al as the Alfa skidded a little and the taxi took the corner into Sloane Square at speed and disappeared from view.

Tassel was halfway into the front of the taxi, screaming from her ripped throat – Robin was trying to beat her back one-handed while maintaining a grip on the wheel – she could not see where she was going for hair and snow and now both Tassel's hands were at her throat, squeezing – Robin tried to find the brake, but as the taxi leapt forwards realised she had hit the accelerator – she could not breathe – taking both hands off the wheel she tried to prise away the agent's tightening grip – screams from pedestrians, a huge jolt and then the ear-splitting crunch of glass, of metal on concrete and the searing pain of the seatbelt against her as the taxi crashed, but she was sinking, everything going black—

'Fuck the car, leave it, we've got to get in there!' Strike bellowed at Al over the wail of a shop alarm and the screams of the scattered bystanders. Al brought the Alfa to an untidy skidding halt in the middle of the road a hundred yards from where the taxi had smashed its way into a plate glass window. Al jumped out as Strike struggled to stand. A group of passers-by, some of them Christmas party-goers in black tie who had sprinted out of the way as the taxi mounted the kerb, watched, stunned, as Al ran, slipping and almost falling, over the snow towards the crash.

The rear door of the cab opened. Elizabeth Tassel flung herself from the back seat and began to run.

'Al, get her!' Strike bellowed, still struggling through the snow. 'Get her, Al!'

Le Rosey had a superb rugby team. Al was used to taking orders. A short sprint and he had taken her down in a perfect tackle. She hit the snowy street with a hard bang over the screamed protests of many women watching and he pinned her there, struggling and swearing, repelling every attempt of chivalrous men to help his victim.

Strike was immune to all of it: he seemed to be running in slow motion, trying not to fall, staggering towards the ominously silent and still cab. Distracted by Al and his struggling, swearing captive, nobody had a thought to spare for the driver of the taxi.

'Robin . . .'

She was slumped sideways, still held to her seat by the belt. There was blood on her face, but when he said her name she responded with a muddled groan.

'Thank fuck . . . thank fuck . . .'

Police sirens were already filling the square. They wailed over the shop alarm, the mounting protests of the shocked Londoners, and Strike, undoing Robin's seatbelt, pushing her gently back into the cab as she attempted to get out, said:

'Stay there.'

'She knew we weren't going to her house,' mumbled Robin. 'Knew straight away I was going the wrong way.'

'Doesn't matter,' panted Strike. 'You've brought Scotland Yard to us.'

Diamond-bright lights were twinkling from the bare trees around the square. Snow poured down upon the gathering crowd, the taxi protruding from the broken window and the sports car parked untidily in the middle of the road as the police cars came to a halt, their flashing blue lights sparkling on the glittering glass-strewn ground, their sirens lost in the wail of the shop alarm.

As his half-brother tried to shout an explanation as to why he was lying on top of a sixty-year-old woman, the relieved, exhausted detective slumped down beside his partner in the cab and found himself – against his will and against the dictates of good taste – laughing.

One week later

50

CYNTHIA: How say you, Endymion, all this was for love?

ENDYMION: I say, madam, then the gods send me a woman's hate.

John Lyly, *Endymion: or, the Man in the Moon*

Strike had never visited Robin and Matthew's flat in Ealing before. His insistence that Robin take time off work to recover from mild concussion and attempted strangulation had not gone down well.

'Robin,' he had told her patiently over the phone, 'I've had to shut up the office anyway. Press crawling all over Denmark Street . . . I'm staying at Nick and Ilsa's.'

But he could not disappear to Cornwall without seeing her. When she opened her front door he was glad to see that the bruising on her neck and forehead had already faded to a faint yellow and blue.

'How're you feeling?' he asked, wiping his feet on the doormat.

'Great!' she said.

The place was small but cheerful and it smelled of her perfume, which he had never noticed much before. Perhaps a week without smelling it had made him more sensitive to it. She led him through to the sitting room, which was painted magnolia like Kathryn Kent's and where he was interested to note the copy of *Investigative Interviewing: Psychology and Practice* lying cover upwards on a chair. A small Christmas tree stood in the corner, the decorations white and silver like the trees in Sloane Square that had formed the background of press photographs of the crashed taxi.

'Matthew got over it yet?' asked Strike, sinking down into the sofa.

'I can't say he's the happiest I've ever seen him,' she replied, grinning. 'Tea?'

She knew how he liked it: the colour of creosote.

'Christmas present,' he told her when she returned with the tray, and handed her a nondescript white envelope. Robin opened it curiously and pulled out a stapled sheaf of printed material.

'Surveillance course in January,' said Strike. 'So next time you pull a bag of dog shit out of a bin no one notices you doing it.'

She laughed, delighted.

'Thank you. *Thank you!*'

'Most women would've expected flowers.'

'I'm not most women.'

'Yeah, I've noticed that,' said Strike, taking a chocolate biscuit.

'Have they analysed it yet?' she asked. 'The dog poo?'

'Yep. Full of human guts. She'd been defrosting them bit by bit. They found traces in the Dobermann's bowl and the rest in her freezer.'

'Oh God,' said Robin, the smile sliding off her face.

'Criminal genius,' said Strike. 'Sneaking into Quine's study and planting two of her own used typewriter ribbons behind the desk . . . Anstis has condescended to have them tested now; there's none of Quine's DNA on them. He never touched them – ergo, he never typed what's on there.'

'Anstis is still talking to you, is he?'

'Just. Hard for him to cut me off. I saved his life.'

'I can see how that would make things awkward,' Robin agreed. 'So they're buying your whole theory now?'

'Open and shut case now they know what they're looking for. She bought the duplicate typewriter nearly two years ago. Ordered the burqa and the ropes on Quine's card and got them sent to the house while the workmen were in. Loads of opportunity to get at his Visa over the years. Coat hanging up in the office while he went for a slash . . . sneak out his wallet while he was asleep, pissed, when she drove him home from parties.

'She knew him well enough to know he was slapdash on checking things like bills. She'd had access to the key to Talgarth Road – easy to copy. She'd been all over the house, knew the hydrochloric acid was there.

'Brilliant, but over-elaborate,' said Strike, sipping his dark brown tea. 'She's on suicide watch, apparently. But you haven't heard the most mental bit.'

'There's more?' said Robin apprehensively.

Much as she had looked forward to seeing Strike, she still felt a little fragile after the events of a week ago. She straightened her back and faced him squarely, braced.

'She kept the bloody book.'

Robin frowned at him.

'What do you—?'

'It was in the freezer with the guts. Bloodstained because she'd carried it away in the bag with the guts. The real manuscript. The *Bombyx Mori* that Quine wrote.'

'But – why on earth—?'

'God only knows. Fancourt says—'

'You've seen him?'

'Briefly. He's decided he knew it was Elizabeth all along. I'll lay you odds what his next novel's going to be about. Anyway, he says she wouldn't have been able to bring herself to destroy an original manuscript.'

'For God's sake – she had no problem destroying its author!'

'Yeah, but this was *literature*, Robin,' said Strike, grinning. 'And get this: Roper Chard are very keen to publish the real thing. Fancourt's going to write the introduction.'

'You *are* kidding?'

'Nope. Quine's going to have a bestseller at last. Don't look like that,' said Strike bracingly as she shook her head in disbelief. 'Plenty to celebrate. Leonora and Orlando will be rolling in money once *Bombyx Mori* hits the bookshelves.

'That reminds me, got something else for you.'

He slid his hand into the inside pocket of the coat lying beside him on the sofa and handed her a rolled-up drawing that he had been keeping safe there. Robin unfurled it and smiled, her eyes filling with tears. Two curly haired angels danced together beneath the carefully pencilled legend To Robin love from Dodo.

'How are they?'

'Great,' said Strike.

He had visited the house in Southern Row at Leonora's invitation. She and Orlando had met him hand in hand at the door, Cheeky Monkey dangling around Orlando's neck as usual.

'Where's Robin?' Orlando demanded. 'I wanted Robin to be here. I drew her a picture.'

'The lady had an accident,' Leonora reminded her daughter,

backing away into the hall to let Strike in, keeping a tight hold on Orlando's hand as though frightened that someone might separate them again. 'I told you, Dodo, the lady did a very brave thing and she had a crash in a car.'

'Auntie Liz was *bad*,' Orlando told Strike, walking backwards down the hall, still hand in hand with her mother but staring at Strike all the way with those limpid green eyes. 'She was the one who made my daddy die.'

'Yes, I – er – I know,' Strike replied, with that familiar feeling of inadequacy that Orlando always seemed to induce in him.

He had found Edna from next door sitting at the kitchen table.

'Oh, you were clever,' she told him over and again. 'Wasn't it *dreadful*, though? How's your poor partner? *Wasn't* it terrible, though?'

'Bless them,' said Robin after he had described this scene in some detail. She spread Orlando's picture out on the coffee table between them, beside the details of the surveillance course, where she could admire them both. 'And how's Al?'

'Beside himself with bloody excitement,' said Strike gloomily. 'We've given him a false impression of the thrill of working life.'

'I liked him,' said Robin, smiling.

'Yeah, well, you were concussed,' said Strike. 'And Polworth's bloody ecstatic to have shown up the Met.'

'You've got some very interesting friends,' said Robin. 'How much are you going to have to pay to repair Nick's dad's taxi?'

'Haven't got the bill in yet,' he sighed. 'I suppose,' he added, several biscuits later, with his eyes on his present to Robin, 'I'm going to have to get another temp in while you're off learning surveillance.'

'Yeah, I suppose you will,' agreed Robin, and after a slight hesitation she added, 'I hope she's rubbish.'

Strike laughed as he got to his feet, picking up his coat.

'I wouldn't worry. Lightning doesn't strike twice.'

'Doesn't anyone ever call you that, among all your many nicknames?' she wondered as they walked back through to the hall.

'Call me what?'

'"Lightning" Strike?'

'Is that likely?' he asked, indicating his leg. 'Well, merry Christmas, partner.'

The idea of a hug hovered briefly in the air, but she held out her hand with mock blokeyness, and he shook it.

'Have a great time in Cornwall.'

'And you in Masham.'

On the point of relinquishing her hand, he gave it a quick twist. He had kissed the back of it before she knew what had happened. Then, with a grin and a wave, he was gone.

Acknowledgements

Writing as Robert Galbraith has been pure joy and the following people have all helped make it so. My heartfelt thanks go to:

SOBE, Deeby and the Back Door Man, because I'd never have got as far without you. Let's plan a heist next.

David Shelley, my incomparable editor, stalwart support and fellow INFJ. Thank you for being brilliant at your job, for taking seriously all the things that matter and for finding everything else as funny as I do.

My agent, Neil Blair, who cheerfully agreed to help me achieve my ambition of becoming a first-time author. You are truly one in a million.

Everyone at Little, Brown who worked so hard and enthusiastically on Robert's first novel without having a clue who he was. My special gratitude to the audiobook team, who took Robert to number one before he was unmasked.

Lorna and Steve Barnes, who enabled me to drink in The Bay Horse, examine the tomb of Sir Marmaduke Wyvill and find out that Robin's hometown is pronounced 'Mass-um' not 'Mash-em', saving me much future embarrassment.

Fiddy Henderson, Christine Collingwood, Fiona Shapcott, Angela Milne, Alison Kelly and Simon Brown, without whose hard work I would not have had time to write *The Silkworm*, or indeed anything else.

Mark Hutchinson, Nicky Stonehill and Rebecca Salt, who can take a great deal of credit for the fact that I still have some marbles left.

My family, especially Neil, for much more than I can express in a few lines, but in this case for being so supportive of bloody murder.

READ
THE FIRST NOVEL FEATURING CORMORAN STRIKE

‘Reminds me why I fell in love with crime fiction in the first place’
Val McDermid

‘A scintillating novel’
The Times

When a troubled model falls to her death from a snow-covered Mayfair balcony, it is assumed that she has committed suicide. However, her brother has his doubts, and calls in private investigator Cormoran Strike to look into the case.

Strike is a war veteran – wounded both physically and psychologically – and his life is in disarray. The case gives him a financial lifeline, but it comes at a personal cost: the more he delves into the young model's complex world, the darker things get – and the closer he gets to terrible danger . . .

A gripping, elegant mystery steeped in the atmosphere of London – from the hushed streets of Mayfair to the backstreet pubs of the East End to the bustle of Soho – *The Cuckoo's Calling* introduces Cormoran Strike in the acclaimed first crime novel by Robert Galbraith – J.K. Rowling's pseudonym.

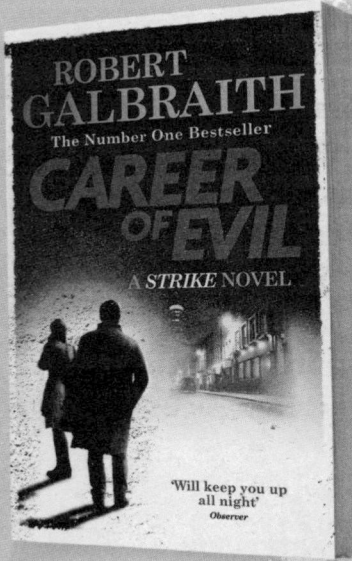

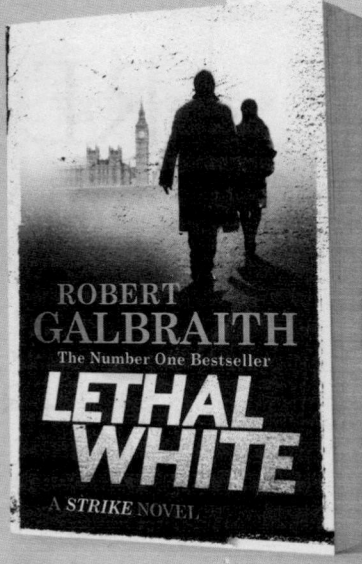

Praise for *The Cuckoo's Calling*

'A sharply contemporary novel full of old-fashioned virtues ... wonderfully fresh and funny'
Jake Kerridge, *Daily Telegraph*

'The most engaging British detective to emerge so far this year ... it marks the start of a fine crime career'
Daily Mail

'Rowling's descriptions of contemporary London are excellent'
Mail on Sunday

'A brilliant depiction of London life ... at heart it's an engrossing and well-crafted whodunnit. Unsurprisingly excellent'
Sunday Mirror

'An accomplished piece that thoroughly deserves its retrospective success'
Financial Times

'In a rare feat, Galbraith combines a complex and compelling sleuth and an equally well-formed and unlikely assistant with a baffling crime ... Readers will hope to see a lot more of this memorable sleuthing team'
Publishers Weekly

'Laden with plenty of twists and distractions, this debut ensures that readers will be puzzled and totally engrossed for quite a spell'
Library Journal

'Utterly compelling ... a team made in heaven'
Saga Magazine

'Instantly absorbing ...Kate Atkinson's fans will appreciate his reliance on deduction and observation along with Galbraith's skilled storytelling'
Booklist

By Robert Galbraith

The Cuckoo's Calling

The Silkworm

Career of Evil

Lethal White

Troubled Blood

The Cuckoo's Calling

Robert Galbraith

SPHERE

First published in Great Britain in 2013 by Sphere
Paperback edition published in 2014 by Sphere
This reissue published in 2018 by Sphere

35

A CIP catalogue record for this book is available from the British Library.

ISBN 978-0-7515-4925-6

Typeset in Bembo by M Rules
Printed and bound in Great Britain by
Clays Ltd, Elcograf S.p.A.

Papers used by Sphere are from well-managed forests and other responsible sources.

Sphere
An imprint of
Little, Brown Book Group
Carmelite House
50 Victoria Embankment
London EC4Y 0DZ

An Hachette UK Company
www.hachette.co.uk

www.littlebrown.co.uk

To the real Deeby
with many thanks

Why were you born when the snow was falling?
You should have come to the cuckoo's calling,
Or when grapes are green in the cluster,
Or, at least, when lithe swallows muster
        For their far off flying
        From summer dying.

Why did you die when the lambs were cropping?
You should have died at the apples' dropping,
When the grasshopper comes to trouble,
And the wheat-fields are sodden stubble,
        And all winds go sighing
        For sweet things dying.

Christina G. Rossetti, 'A Dirge'

Prologue

Is demum miser est, cuius nobilitas miserias nobilitat.

Unhappy is he whose fame makes his misfortunes famous.

Lucius Accius, *Telephus*

The buzz in the street was like the humming of flies. Photographers stood massed behind barriers patrolled by police, their long-snouted cameras poised, their breath rising like steam. Snow fell steadily on to hats and shoulders; gloved fingers wiped lenses clear. From time to time there came outbreaks of desultory clicking, as the watchers filled the waiting time by snapping the white canvas tent in the middle of the road, the entrance to the tall red-brick apartment block behind it, and the balcony on the top floor from which the body had fallen.

Behind the tightly packed paparazzi stood white vans with enormous satellite dishes on the roofs, and journalists talking, some in foreign languages, while soundmen in headphones hovered. Between recordings, the reporters stamped their feet and warmed their hands on hot beakers of coffee from the teeming café a few streets away. To fill the time, the woolly-hatted cameramen filmed the backs of the photographers, the balcony, the tent concealing the body, then repositioned themselves for wide shots that encompassed the chaos that had exploded inside the sedate and snowy Mayfair street, with its lines of glossy black doors framed by white stone porticos and flanked by topiary shrubs. The entrance to number 18 was bounded with tape. Police officials, some of them white-clothed forensic experts, could be glimpsed in the hallway beyond.

The television stations had already had the news for several hours. Members of the public were crowding at either end of the road, held at bay by more police; some had come, on purpose, to look, others had paused on their way to work. Many held mobile telephones aloft to take pictures before moving on. One young man, not knowing which was the crucial balcony, photographed each of them in turn, even though the middle one was packed with a row of shrubs, three neat, leafy orbs, which barely left room for a human being.

A group of young girls had brought flowers, and were filmed handing them to the police, who as yet had not decided on a place for them, but laid them self-consciously in the back of the police van, aware of camera lenses following their every move.

The correspondents sent by twenty-four-hour news channels kept up a steady stream of comment and speculation around the few sensational facts they knew.

'... from her penthouse apartment at around two o'clock this morning. Police were alerted by the building's security guard ...'

'... no sign yet that they are moving the body, which has led some to speculate ...'

'... no word on whether she was alone when she fell ...'

'... teams have entered the building and will be conducting a thorough search.'

A chilly light filled the interior of the tent. Two men were crouching beside the body, ready to move it, at last, into a body bag. Her head had bled a little into the snow. The face was crushed and swollen, one eye reduced to a pucker, the other showing as a sliver of dull white between distended lids. When the sequinned top she wore glittered in slight changes of light, it gave a disquieting impression of movement, as though she breathed again, or was tensing muscles, ready to rise. The snow fell with soft fingertip plunks on the canvas overhead.

'Where's the bloody ambulance?'

Detective Inspector Roy Carver's temper was mounting. A paunchy man with a face the colour of corned beef, whose shirts were usually ringed with sweat around the armpits, his short supply of patience had been exhausted hours ago. He had been here nearly as long as the corpse; his feet were so cold that he could no longer feel them, and he was light-headed with hunger.

'Ambulance is two minutes away,' said Detective Sergeant Eric Wardle, unintentionally answering his superior's question as he entered the tent with his mobile pressed to his ear. 'Just been organising a space for it.'

Carver grunted. His bad temper was exacerbated by the conviction that Wardle was excited by the presence of the photographers. Boyishly good-looking, with thick, wavy brown hair now frosted with snow, Wardle had, in Carver's opinion, dawdled on their few forays outside the tent.

'At least that lot'll shift once the body's gone,' said Wardle, still looking out at the photographers.

'They won't go while we're still treating the place like a fucking murder scene,' snapped Carver.

Wardle did not answer the unspoken challenge. Carver exploded anyway.

'The poor cow jumped. There was no one else there. Your so-called witness was coked out of her—'

'It's coming,' said Wardle, and to Carver's disgust, he slipped back out of the tent, to wait for the ambulance in full sight of the cameras.

*

The story forced news of politics, wars and disasters aside, and every version of it sparkled with pictures of the dead woman's flawless face, her lithe and sculpted body. Within hours, the few known facts had spread like a virus to millions: the public row with the famous boyfriend, the journey home alone, the overheard screaming and the final, fatal fall . . .

The boyfriend fled into a rehab facility, but the police remained inscrutable; those who had been with her on the evening before her death were hounded; thousands of columns of newsprint were filled, and hours of television news, and the woman who swore she had overheard a second argument moments before the body fell became briefly famous too, and was awarded smaller-sized photographs beside the images of the beautiful dead girl.

But then, to an almost audible groan of disappointment, the witness was proven to have lied, and *she* retreated into rehab, and the famous prime suspect emerged, as the man and the lady in a weather-house who can never be outside at the same time.

So it was suicide after all, and after a moment's stunned hiatus, the story gained a weak second wind. They wrote that she was unbalanced, unstable, unsuited to the superstardom her wildness and her beauty had snared; that she had moved among an immoral moneyed class that had corrupted her; that the decadence of her new life had unhinged an already fragile personality. She became a morality tale stiff with Schadenfreude, and so many columnists made allusion to Icarus that *Private Eye* ran a special column.

And then, at last, the frenzy wore itself into staleness, and even the journalists had nothing left to say, but that too much had been said already.

Three Months Later

Part One

Nam in omni adversitate fortunae
infelicissimum est genus infortunii, fuisse
felicem.

For in every ill-turn of fortune
the most unhappy sort of unfortunate man
is the one who has been happy.

Boethius, *De Consolatione Philosophiae*

1

Though Robin Ellacott's twenty-five years of life had seen their moments of drama and incident, she had never before woken up in the certain knowledge that she would remember the coming day for as long as she lived.

Shortly after midnight, her long-term boyfriend, Matthew, had proposed to her under the statue of Eros in the middle of Piccadilly Circus. In the giddy relief following her acceptance, he confessed that he had been planning to pop the question in the Thai restaurant where they just had eaten dinner, but that he had reckoned without the silent couple beside them, who had eavesdropped on their entire conversation. He had therefore suggested a walk through the darkening streets, in spite of Robin's protests that they both needed to be up early, and finally inspiration had seized him, and he had led her, bewildered, to the steps of the statue. There, flinging discretion to the chilly wind (in a most un-Matthew-like way), he had proposed, on one knee, in front of three down-and-outs huddled on the steps, sharing what looked like a bottle of meths.

It had been, in Robin's view, the most perfect proposal, ever, in the history of matrimony. He had even had a ring in his pocket, which she was now wearing; a sapphire with two diamonds, it fitted perfectly, and all the way into town she kept staring at it on her hand as it rested on her lap. She and Matthew had a story to tell now, a funny family story, the kind you told your children, in which his planning (she loved that he had planned it) went awry, and turned into something spontaneous. She loved the tramps, and the moon, and Matthew, panicky and flustered, on one knee; she loved Eros, and dirty old Piccadilly, and the black cab they had taken home to Clapham. She was, in fact, not far off loving the whole of London, which she had not so far warmed to, during the month she had lived there. Even the pale and pugnacious commuters squashed into the Tube carriage around her were gilded by the radiance of the ring, and as she emerged into the chilly March daylight at Tottenham Court Road underground station, she stroked the underside of the platinum band with her thumb, and experienced an explosion of happiness at the thought that she might buy some bridal magazines at lunchtime.

Male eyes lingered on her as she picked her way through the roadworks at the top of Oxford Street, consulting a piece of paper in her right hand. Robin was, by any standards, a pretty girl; tall and curvaceous, with long strawberry-blonde hair that rippled as she strode briskly along, the chill air adding colour to her pale cheeks. This was the first day of a week-long secretarial assignment. She had been temping ever since coming to live with Matthew in London, though not for much longer; she had what she termed 'proper' interviews lined up now.

The most challenging part of these uninspiring piecemeal jobs was often finding the offices. London, after the small town in Yorkshire she had left, felt vast, complex and impenetrable. Matthew had told her not to walk around with her nose in an *A–Z*, which would make her look like a tourist and render her vulnerable; she therefore relied, as often as not, on poorly hand-drawn maps that somebody at the temping agency had made for her. She was not convinced that this made her look more like a native-born Londoner.

The metal barricades and the blue plastic Corimec walls surrounding the roadworks made it much harder to see where she ought to be going, because they obscured half the landmarks drawn on the paper in her hand. She crossed the torn-up road in front of a towering office block, labelled 'Centre Point' on her map, which resembled a gigantic concrete waffle with its dense grid of uniform square windows, and made her way in the rough direction of Denmark Street.

She found it almost accidentally, following a narrow alleyway called Denmark Place out into a short street full of colourful shopfronts: windows full of guitars, keyboards and every kind of musical ephemera. Red and white barricades surrounded another open hole in the road, and workmen in fluorescent jackets greeted her with early-morning wolf-whistles, which Robin pretended not to hear.

She consulted her watch. Having allowed her usual margin of time for getting lost, she was a quarter of an hour early. The nondescript black-painted doorway of the office she sought stood to the left of the 12 Bar Café; the name of the occupant of the office was written on a scrappy piece of lined paper Sellotaped beside the buzzer for the second floor. On an ordinary day, without the brand-new ring glittering upon her finger, she might have found this off-putting; today, however, the dirty paper and the peeling paint on the door were, like the tramps from last night, mere picturesque details on the backdrop of her grand romance. She checked her watch again (the sapphire glittered and her heart leapt; she would watch that stone glitter all the rest of her life), then decided, in a burst of euphoria, to go up early and show herself keen for a job that did not matter in the slightest.

She had just reached for the bell when the black door flew open from the inside, and a woman burst out on to the street. For one strangely static second the two of them looked directly into each other's eyes, as each braced to withstand a collision. Robin's senses were unusually receptive on this enchanted morning; the split-second view of that white face made such an impression on her that she thought, moments later, when they had managed to dodge each other, missing contact by a centimetre, after the dark woman had hurried off down the street, around the corner and out of sight, that she could have drawn her perfectly from memory. It was not merely the extraordinary beauty of the face that had impressed itself on her memory, but the other's expression: livid, yet strangely exhilarated.

Robin caught the door before it closed on the dingy stairwell. An old-fashioned metal staircase spiralled up around an equally antiquated birdcage lift. Concentrating on keeping her high heels from catching in the metalwork stairs, she proceeded to the first landing, passing a door carrying a laminated and framed poster saying *Crowdy Graphics*, and continued climbing. It was only when she reached the glass door on the floor above that Robin realised, for the first time, what kind of business she had been sent to assist. Nobody at the agency had said. The name on the paper beside the outside buzzer was engraved on the glass panel: *C. B. Strike*, and, underneath it, the words *Private Detective.*

Robin stood quite still, with her mouth slightly open, experiencing a moment of wonder that nobody who knew her could have understood. She had never confided in a solitary human being (even Matthew) her lifelong, secret, childish ambition. For this to happen today, of all days! It felt like a wink from God (and this too she somehow connected with the magic of the day; with Matthew, and the ring; even though, properly considered, they had no connection at all).

Savouring the moment, she approached the engraved door very slowly. She stretched out her left hand (sapphire dark, now, in this dim light) towards the handle; but before she had touched it, the glass door too flew open.

This time, there was no near-miss. Sixteen unseeing stone of dishevelled male slammed into her; Robin was knocked off her feet and catapulted backwards, handbag flying, arms windmilling, towards the void beyond the lethal staircase.

2

Strike absorbed the impact, heard the high-pitched scream and reacted instinctively: throwing out a long arm, he seized a fistful of cloth and flesh; a second shriek of pain echoed around the stone walls and then, with a wrench and a tussle, he had succeeded in dragging the girl back on to firm ground. Her shrieks were still echoing off the walls, and he realised that he himself had bellowed, 'Jesus Christ!'

The girl was doubled up in pain against the office door, whimpering. Judging by the lopsided way she was hunched, with one hand buried deep under the lapel of her coat, Strike deduced that he had saved her by grabbing a substantial part of her left breast. A thick, wavy curtain of bright blonde hair hid most of the girl's blushing face, but Strike could see tears of pain leaking out of one uncovered eye.

'Fuck – sorry!' His loud voice reverberated around the stairwell. 'I didn't see you – didn't expect anyone to be there . . . '

From under their feet, the strange and solitary graphic designer who inhabited the office below yelled, 'What's happening up there?' and a second later, a muffled complaint from above indicated that the manager of the bar downstairs, who slept in an attic flat over Strike's office, had also been disturbed – perhaps woken – by the noise.

'Come in here . . . '

Strike pushed open the door with his fingertips, so as to have no accidental contact with her while she stood huddled against it, and ushered her into the office.

'Is everything all right?' called the graphic designer querulously.

Strike slammed the office door behind him.

'I'm OK,' lied Robin, in a quavering voice, still hunched over with her hand on her chest, her back to him. After a second or two, she straightened up and turned around, her face scarlet and her eyes still wet.

Her accidental assailant was massive; his height, his general hairiness, coupled with a gently expanding belly, suggested a grizzly bear. One of his eyes was puffy and bruised, the skin just below the eyebrow cut. Congealing blood sat in raised white-edged nail tracks on his left cheek and the right side of his thick neck, revealed by the crumpled open collar of his shirt.

'Are you M-Mr Strike?'

'Yeah.'

'I–I'm the temp.'

'The what?'

'The temp. From Temporary Solutions?'

The name of the agency did not wipe the incredulous look from his battered face. They stared at each other, unnerved and antagonistic.

Just like Robin, Cormoran Strike knew that he would forever remember the last twelve hours as an epoch-changing night in his life. Now, it seemed, the Fates had sent an emissary in a neat beige trench coat, to taunt him with the fact that his life was bubbling towards catastrophe. There was not supposed to be a temp. He had intended his dismissal of Robin's predecessor to end his contract.

'How long have they sent you for?'

'A-a week to begin with,' said Robin, who had never been greeted with such a lack of enthusiasm.

Strike made a rapid mental calculation. A week at the agency's exorbitant rate would drive his overdraft yet further into the region of irreparable; it might even be the final straw his main creditor kept implying he was waiting for.

''Scuse me a moment.'

He left the room via the glass door, and turned immediately right, into a tiny dank toilet. Here he bolted the door, and stared into the cracked, spotted mirror over the sink.

The reflection staring back at him was not handsome. Strike had the high, bulging forehead, broad nose and thick brows of a young Beethoven who had taken to boxing, an impression only heightened by the swelling and blackening eye. His thick curly hair, springy as carpet, had ensured that his many youthful nicknames had included 'Pubehead'. He looked older than his thirty-five years.

Ramming the plug into the hole, he filled the cracked and grubby sink with cold water, took a deep breath and completely submerged his throbbing head. Displaced water slopped over his shoes, but he ignored it for the relief of ten seconds of icy, blind stillness.

Disparate images of the previous night flickered through his mind: emptying three drawers of possessions into a kitbag while Charlotte screamed at him; the ashtray catching him on the brow-bone as he looked back at her from the door; the journey on foot across the dark city to his office, where he had slept for an hour or two in his desk chair. Then the final, filthy scene, after Charlotte had tracked him down in the early hours, to plunge in those last few *banderillas* she had failed to implant before he had left her flat; his resolution to let her go when, after clawing his face, she had run out of the door; and then that moment of madness when he had plunged after her – a pursuit ended as quickly as it had begun, with the unwitting intervention of this heedless, superfluous girl, whom he had been forced to save, and then placate.

He emerged from the cold water with a gasp and a grunt, his face and head pleasantly numb and tingling. With the cardboard-textured towel that hung on the back of the door he rubbed himself dry and stared again at his grim reflection. The scratches, washed clean of blood, looked like nothing more than the impressions of a crumpled pillow. Charlotte would have reached the underground by now. One of the insane thoughts that had propelled him after her had been fear that she would throw herself on the tracks. Once, after a particularly vicious row in their mid-twenties, she had climbed on to a rooftop, where she had swayed drunkenly, vowing to jump. Perhaps he ought to be glad that the Temporary Solution had forced him to abandon the chase. There could be no going back from the scene in the early hours of this morning. This time, it had to be over.

Tugging his sodden collar away from his neck, Strike pulled back the rusty bolt and headed out of the toilet and back through the glass door.

A pneumatic drill had started up in the street outside. Robin was standing in front of the desk with her back to the door; she whipped her hand back out of the front of her coat as he re-entered the room, and he knew that she had been massaging her breast again.

'Is – are you all right?' Strike asked, carefully not looking at the site of the injury.

'I'm fine. Listen, if you don't need me, I'll go,' said Robin with dignity.

'No – no, not at all,' said a voice issuing from Strike's mouth, though he listened to it with disgust. 'A week – yeah, that'll be fine. Er – the post's here . . . ' He scooped it from the doormat as he spoke and scattered it on the bare desk in front of her, a propitiatory offering. 'Yeah, if you could open that, answer the phone, generally sort of tidy up – computer password's Hatherill23, I'll write it down . . . ' This he did, under her wary, doubtful gaze. 'There you go – I'll be in here.'

He strode into the inner office, closed the door carefully behind him and then stood quite still, gazing at the kitbag under the bare desk. It contained everything he owned, for he doubted that he would ever see again the nine tenths of his possessions he had left at Charlotte's. They would probably be gone by lunchtime; set on fire, dumped in the street, slashed and crushed, doused in bleach. The drill hammered relentlessly in the street below.

And now the impossibility of paying off his mountainous debts, the appalling consequences that would attend the imminent failure of this business, the looming, unknown but inevitably horrible sequel to his leaving Charlotte; in Strike's exhaustion, the misery of it all seemed to rear up in front of him in a kind of kaleidoscope of horror.

Hardly aware that he had moved, he found himself back in the chair in which he had spent the latter part of the night. From the other side of the insubstantial partition wall came muffled sounds of movement. The Temporary Solution was no doubt starting up the computer, and would shortly discover that he had not received a single work-related email in three weeks. Then, at his own request, she would start opening all his final demands. Exhausted, sore and hungry, Strike slid face down on to the desk again, muffling his eyes and ears in his encircling arms, so that he did not have to listen while his humiliation was laid bare next door by a stranger.

3

Five minutes later there was a knock on the door and Strike, who had been on the verge of sleep, jerked upright in his chair.

'Sorry?'

His subconscious had become entangled with Charlotte again; it was a surprise to see the strange girl enter the room. She had taken off her coat to reveal a snugly, even seductively fitting cream sweater. Strike addressed her hairline.

'Yeah?'

'There's a client here for you. Shall I show him in?'

'There's a what?'

'A client, Mr Strike.'

He looked at her for several seconds, trying to process the information.

'Right, OK – no, give me a couple of minutes, please, Sandra, and then show him in.'

She withdrew without comment.

Strike wasted barely a second on asking himself why he had called her Sandra, before leaping to his feet and setting about looking and smelling less like a man who had slept in his clothes. Diving under his desk into his kitbag, he seized a tube of toothpaste, and squeezed three inches into his open mouth; then he noticed that his tie was soaked in water from the sink, and that his shirt front was spattered with flecks of blood, so he ripped both off, buttons pinging off the walls and filing cabinet, dragged a clean though heavily creased shirt out of the kitbag instead and pulled it on, thick fingers fumbling. After stuffing the kitbag out of sight behind his empty filing cabinet, he hastily reseated himself and checked the inner corners of his eyes for debris, all the while wondering whether this so-called client was the real thing, and whether he would be prepared to pay actual money for detective services. Strike had come to realise, over the course of an eighteen-month spiral into financial ruin, that neither of these things could be taken for granted. He was still chasing two clients for full payment of their bills; a third had refused to disburse a penny, because Strike's findings had not been to his taste, and given that he was sliding ever deeper into debt, and that a rent review of the area was threatening his tenancy of the central London office that he had been so pleased to secure, Strike was in no position to involve a lawyer. Rougher, cruder methods of debt collection had become a staple of his recent fantasies; it would have given him much pleasure to watch the smuggest of his defaulters cowering in the shadow of a baseball bat.

The door opened again; Strike hastily removed his index finger from his nostril and sat up straight, trying to look bright and alert in his chair.

'Mr Strike, this is Mr Bristow.'

The prospective client followed Robin into the room. The immediate impression was favourable. The stranger might be distinctly rabbity in appearance, with a short upper lip that failed to conceal large front teeth; his colouring was sandy, and his eyes, judging by the thickness of his glasses, myopic; but his dark grey suit was beautifully tailored, and the shining ice-blue tie, the watch and the shoes all looked expensive.

The snowy smoothness of the stranger's shirt made Strike doubly conscious of the thousand or so creases in his own clothes. He stood up to give Bristow the full benefit of his six feet three inches, held out a hairy-backed hand and attempted to counter his visitor's sartorial superiority by projecting the air of a man too busy to worry about laundry.

'Cormoran Strike; how d'you do.'

'John Bristow,' said the other, shaking hands. His voice was pleasant, cultivated and uncertain. His gaze lingered on Strike's swollen eye.

'Could I offer you gentlemen some tea or coffee?' asked Robin.

Bristow asked for a small black coffee, but Strike did not answer; he had just caught sight of a heavy-browed young woman in a frumpy tweed suit, who was sitting on the thread-bare sofa beside the door of the outer office. It beggared belief that two potential clients could have arrived at the same moment. Surely he had not been sent a second temp?

'And you, Mr Strike?' asked Robin.

'What? Oh – black coffee, two sugars, please, Sandra,' he said, before he could stop himself. He saw her mouth twist as she closed the door behind her, and only then did he remember that he did not have any coffee, sugar or, indeed, cups.

Sitting down at Strike's invitation, Bristow looked round the tatty office in what Strike was afraid was disappointment. The prospective client seemed nervous in the guilty way that Strike had come to associate with suspicious husbands, yet a faint air of authority clung to him, conveyed mainly by the obvious expense of his suit. Strike wondered how Bristow had found him. It was hard to get word-of-mouth business when your only client (as she regularly sobbed down the telephone) had no friends.

'What can I do for you, Mr Bristow?' he asked, back in his own chair.

'It's – um – actually, I wonder whether I could just check . . . I think we've met before.'

'Really?'

'You wouldn't remember me, it was years and years ago . . . but I think you were friends with my brother Charlie. Charlie Bristow? He died – in an accident – when he was nine.'

'Bloody hell,' said Strike. 'Charlie . . . yeah, I remember.'

And, indeed, he remembered perfectly. Charlie Bristow had been one of many friends Strike had collected during a complicated, peripatetic childhood. A magnetic, wild and reckless boy, pack leader of the coolest gang at Strike's new school in London, Charlie had taken one look at the enormous new boy with the thick Cornish accent, and appointed him his best friend and lieutenant. Two giddy months of bosom friendship and bad behaviour had followed. Strike, who had always been fascinated by the smooth workings of other children's homes, with their sane, well-ordered families, and the bedrooms they were allowed to keep for years and years, retained a vivid memory of Charlie's house, which had been large and luxurious. There had been a long sunlit lawn, a tree house, and iced lemon squash served by Charlie's mother.

And then had come the unprecedented horror of the first day back at school after Easter break, when their form teacher had told them that Charlie would never return, that he was dead, that he had ridden his bike over the edge of a quarry, while holidaying in Wales. She had been a mean old bitch, that teacher, and she had not been able to resist telling the class that Charlie, who as they would remember *often disobeyed grown-ups*, had been *expressly forbidden* to ride anywhere near the quarry, but that he had done so anyway, *perhaps showing off* – but she had been forced to stop there, because two little girls in the front row were sobbing.

From that day onwards, Strike had seen the face of a laughing blond boy fragmenting every time he looked at, or imagined, a quarry. He would not have been surprised if every member of Charlie Bristow's old class had been left with the same lingering fear of the great dark pit, the sheer drop and the unforgiving stone.

'Yeah, I remember Charlie,' he said.

Bristow's Adam's apple bobbed a little.

'Yes. Well it's your name, you see. I remember so clearly Charlie talking about you, on holiday, in the days before he died; "my friend Strike", "Cormoran Strike". It's unusual, isn't it? Where does "Strike" come from, do you know? I've never met it anywhere else.'

Bristow was not the first person Strike had known who would snatch at any procrastinatory subject – the weather, the congestion charge, their preferences in hot drinks – to postpone discussion of what had brought them to his office.

'I've been told it's something to do with corn,' he said, 'measuring corn.'

'Really, is it? Nothing to do with hitting, or walkouts, ha ha . . . no . . . Well you see, when I was looking for someone to help me with this business, and I saw your name in the book,' Bristow's knee began jiggling up and down, 'you can perhaps imagine how it – well, it felt like – like a sign. A sign from Charlie. Saying I was right.'

His Adam's apple bobbed as he swallowed.

'OK,' said Strike cautiously, hoping that he had not been mistaken for a medium.

'It's my sister, you see,' said Bristow.

'Right. Is she in some kind of trouble?'

'She's dead.'

Strike just stopped himself saying, 'What, her too?'

'I'm sorry,' he said carefully.

Bristow acknowledged the condolence with a jerky inclination of the head.

'I – this isn't easy. Firstly, you should know that my sister is – was – Lula Landry.'

Hope, so briefly re-erected at the news that he might have a client, fell slowly forwards like a granite tombstone and landed with an agonising blow in Strike's gut. The man sitting opposite him was delusional, if not actually unhinged. It was an impossibility akin to two identical snowflakes that this whey-faced, leporine man could have sprung from the same genetic pool as the bronze-skinned, colt-limbed, diamond-cut beauty that had been Lula Landry.

'My parents adopted her,' said Bristow meekly, as though he knew what Strike was thinking. 'We were all adopted.'

'Uh huh,' said Strike. He had an exceptionally accurate memory; thinking back to that huge, cool, well-ordered house, and the blazing acres of garden, he remembered a languid blonde mother presiding at the picnic table, the distant booming voice of an intimidating father; a surly older brother picking at the fruit cake, Charlie himself making his mother laugh as he clowned; but no little girl.

'You wouldn't have met Lula,' Bristow went on, again as though Strike had spoken his thoughts aloud. 'My parents didn't adopt her until after Charlie had died. She was four years old when she came to us; she'd been in care for a couple of years. I was nearly fifteen. I can still remember standing at the front door and watching my father carrying her up the drive. She was wearing a little red knitted hat. My mother's still got it.'

And suddenly, shockingly, John Bristow burst into tears. He

sobbed into his hands, hunch-shouldered, quaking, while tears and snot slid through the cracks in his fingers. Every time he seemed to have himself under some kind of control, more sobs burst forth.

'I'm sorry – sorry – Jesus . . . '

Panting and hiccoughing, he dabbed beneath his glasses with a wadded handkerchief, trying to regain control.

The office door opened and Robin backed in, carrying a tray. Bristow turned his face away, his shoulders heaving and shaking. Through the open door Strike caught another glimpse of the besuited woman in the outer office; she was now scowling at him from over the top of a copy of the *Daily Express.*

Robin laid out two cups, a milk jug, a sugar bowl and a plate of chocolate biscuits, none of which Strike had ever seen before, smiled in perfunctory fashion at his thanks and made to leave.

'Hang on a moment, Sandra,' said Strike. 'Could you . . . ?'

He took a piece of paper from his desk and slid it on to his knee. While Bristow made soft gulping noises, Strike wrote, very swiftly and as legibly as he could manage:

Please google Lula Landry and find out whether she was adopted, and if so, by whom. Do not discuss what you are doing with the woman outside (what is she doing here?). Write down the answers to questions above and bring them to me here, without saying what you've found.

He handed the piece of paper to Robin, who took it wordlessly and left the room.

'Sorry – I'm so sorry,' Bristow gasped, when the door had closed. 'This is – I'm not usually – I've been back at work, seeing clients . . . ' He took several deep breaths. With his pink eyes the resemblance to an albino rabbit was heightened. His right knee was still jiggling up and down.

'It's just been a dreadful time,' he whispered, taking deep breaths. 'Lula . . . and my mother's dying . . .'

Strike's mouth was watering at the sight of the chocolate biscuits, because he had eaten nothing for what felt like days; but he felt it would strike an unsympathetic note to start snacking while Bristow jiggled and sniffed and mopped his eyes. The pneumatic drill was still hammering like a machine gun down in the street.

'She's given up completely since Lula died. It's broken her. Her cancer was supposed to be in remission, but it's come back, and they say there's nothing more they can do. I mean, this is the second time. She had a sort of breakdown after Charlie. My father thought another child would make it better. They'd always wanted a girl. It wasn't easy for them to be approved, but Lula was mixed race, and harder to place, so,' he finished, on a strangled sob, 'they managed to get her.

'She was always b-beautiful. She was d-discovered in Oxford Street, out shopping with my mother. Taken on by Athena. It's one of the most prestigious agencies. She was modelling f-full time by seventeen. By the time she died, she was worth around ten million. I don't know why I'm telling you all this. You probably know it all. Everyone knew – thought they knew – all about Lula.'

He picked up his cup clumsily; his hands were trembling so much that coffee slopped over the edge on to his sharply pressed suit trousers.

'What exactly is it that you would like me to do for you?' Strike asked.

Bristow replaced the cup shakily on the desk, then gripped his hands together tightly.

'They say my sister killed herself. I don't believe it.'

Strike remembered the television pictures: the black body bag on a stretcher, flickering in a storm of camera flashes as it was loaded into an ambulance, the photographers clustering around as it started to move, holding up their cameras to the dark windows, white lights bouncing off the black glass. He knew more about the death of Lula Landry than he had ever meant or wanted to know; the same would be true of virtually any sentient being in Britain. Bombarded with the story, you grew interested against your will, and before you knew it, you were so well informed, so opinionated about the facts of the case, you would have been unfit to sit on a jury.

'There was an inquest, wasn't there?'

'Yes, but the detective in charge of the case was convinced from the outset that it was suicide, purely because Lula was on lithium. The things he overlooked – they've even spotted some of them on the internet.'

Bristow jabbed a nonsensical finger at Strike's bare desktop, where a computer might have been expected to stand.

A perfunctory knock and the door opened; Robin strode in, handed Strike a folded note and withdrew.

'Sorry, d'you mind?' said Strike. 'I've been waiting for this message.'

He unfolded the note against his knee, so that Bristow could not see through the back, and read:

Lula Landry was adopted by Sir Alec and Lady Yvette Bristow when she was four. She grew up as Lula Bristow but took her mother's maiden name when she started modelling. She has an older brother called John, who is a lawyer. The girl waiting outside is Mr Bristow's girlfriend and a secretary at his firm.

They work for Landry, May, Patterson, the firm started by Lula and John's maternal grandfather. The photograph of John Bristow on LMP's home page is identical to the man you're talking to.

Strike crumpled the note and dropped it into the waste-paper basket at his feet. He was staggered. John Bristow was not a fantasist; and he, Strike, appeared to have been sent a temp with more initiative, and better punctuation, than any he had ever met.

'Sorry, go on,' he said to Bristow. 'You were saying – about the inquest?'

'Yeah,' said Bristow, dabbing the end of his nose with the wet handkerchief. 'Well, I'm not denying that Lula had problems. She put Mum through hell, as a matter of fact. It started around the same time our father died – you probably know all this, God knows there was enough about it in the press . . . but she was expelled from school for dabbling in drugs; she ran off to London, Mum found her living rough with addicts; the drugs exacerbated the mental problems; she absconded from a treatment centre – there were endless scenes and dramas. In the end, though, they realised she had bipolar disorder and put her on the right medication, and ever since then, as long as she was taking her tablets, she was fine; you'd never have known there was anything wrong with her. Even the coroner accepted that she *had* been taking her medication, the autopsy proved it.

'But the police and the coroner couldn't see past the girl who had a history of poor mental health. They insisted that she was depressed, but I can tell you myself that Lula wasn't depressed at all. I saw her on the morning before she died, and she was absolutely fine. Things were going very well for her, particularly career-wise. She'd just signed a contract that would have brought in five million over two years; she asked me to look over it for her, and it was a bloody good deal. The designer was a great friend of hers, Somé, I expect you've heard of him? And she was booked solid for months; there was a shoot in Morocco coming up, and she loved the travelling. So you see, there was no reason whatsoever for her to take her own life.'

Strike nodded politely, inwardly unimpressed. Suicides, in his experience, were perfectly capable of feigning an interest in a future they had no intention of inhabiting. Landry's rosy, golden-hued morning mood might easily have turned dark and hopeless in the day and half a night that had preceded her death; he had known it happen. He remembered the lieutenant in the King's Royal Rifle Corps, who had risen in the night after his own birthday party, of which, by all accounts, he had been the life and soul. He had penned his family a note, telling them to call the police and not go into the garage. The body had been found hanging from the garage ceiling by his fifteen-year-old son, who had not noticed the note as he hurried through the kitchen on the way to fetch his bicycle.

'That's not all,' said Bristow. 'There's evidence, hard evidence. Tansy Bestigui's, for a start.'

'She was the neighbour who said she heard an argument upstairs?'

'Exactly! She heard a man shouting up there, right before Lula went over the balcony! The police rubbished her evidence, purely because – well, she'd taken cocaine. But that doesn't mean she didn't know what she'd heard. Tansy maintains to this day that Lula was arguing with a man seconds before she fell. I know, because I've discussed it with her very recently. Our firm is handling her divorce. I'm sure I'd be able to persuade her to talk to you.

'And then,' said Bristow, watching Strike anxiously, trying to gauge his reaction, 'there was the CCTV footage. A man walking towards Kentigern Gardens about twenty minutes before Lula fell, and then footage of the same man running hell for leather away from Kentigern Gardens after she'd been killed. They never found out who he was; never managed to trace him.'

With a kind of furtive eagerness, Bristow now drew from an inside pocket of his jacket a slightly crumpled clean envelope and held it out.

'I've written it all down. The timings and everything. It's all in here. You'll see how it fits together.'

The appearance of the envelope did nothing to increase Strike's confidence in Bristow's judgement. He had been handed such things before: the scribbled fruits of lonely and misguided obsessions; one-track maunderings on pet theories; complex timetables twisted to fit fantastic contingencies. The lawyer's left eyelid was flickering, one of his knees was jerking up and down and the fingers proffering the envelope were trembling.

For a few seconds Strike weighed these signs of strain against Bristow's undoubtedly hand-made shoes, and the Vacheron Constantin watch revealed on his pale wrist when he gesticulated. This was a man who could and would pay; perhaps long enough to enable Strike to clear one instalment of the loan that was the most pressing of his debts. With a sigh, and an inner scowl at his own conscience, Strike said:

'Mr Bristow—'

'Call me John.'

'John . . . I'm going to be honest with you. I don't think it would be right to take your money.'

Red blotches blossomed on Bristow's pale neck, and on the undistinguished face, as he continued to hold out the envelope.

'What do you mean, it wouldn't be right?'

'Your sister's death was probably as thoroughly investigated as anything can be. Millions of people, and media from all over the world, were following the police's every move. They would have been twice as thorough as usual. Suicide is a difficult thing to have to accept—'

'I don't accept it. I'll never accept it. She didn't kill herself. Someone pushed her over that balcony.'

The drill outside stopped suddenly, so that Bristow's voice rang loudly through the room; and his hair-trigger fury was that of a meek man pushed to his absolute limit.

'I see. I get it. You're another one, are you? Another fucking armchair psychologist? Charlie's dead, my father's dead, Lula's dead and my mother's dying – I've lost everyone, and I need a bereavement counsellor, not a detective. D'you think I haven't heard it about a hundred fucking times before?'

Bristow stood up, impressive for all his rabbity teeth and blotchy skin.

'I'm a pretty rich man, Strike. Sorry to be crass about it, but there you are. My father left me a sizeable trust fund. I've looked into the going rate for this kind of thing, and I would have been happy to pay you double.'

A double fee. Strike's conscience, once firm and inelastic, had been weakened by repeated blows of fate; this was the knock-out punch. His baser self was already gambolling off into the realms of happy speculation: a month's work would give him enough to pay off the temp and some of the rent arrears; two months, the more pressing debts . . . three months, a chunk of the overdraft gone . . . four months . . .

But John Bristow was speaking over his shoulder as he moved towards the door, clutching and crumpling the envelope that Strike had refused to take.

'I wanted it to be you because of Charlie, but I found out a bit about you, I'm not a complete bloody idiot. Special investigation branch, military police, wasn't it? Decorated as well. I can't say I was impressed by your offices,' Bristow was almost shouting now, and Strike was aware that the muffled female voices in the outer office had fallen silent, 'but apparently I was wrong, and you can afford to turn down work. Fine! Bloody forget it. I'm sure I'll find somebody else to do the job. Sorry to have troubled you!'

4

The men's conversation had been carrying, with increasing clarity, through the flimsy dividing wall for a couple of minutes; now, in the sudden silence following the cessation of the drill, Bristow's words were plainly audible.

Purely for her own amusement, in the high spirits of this happy day, Robin had been trying to act convincingly the part of Strike's regular secretary, and not to give away to Bristow's girlfriend that she had only been working for a private detective for half an hour. She concealed as best she could any sign of surprise or excitement at the outbreak of shouting, but she was instinctively on Bristow's side, whatever the cause of the conflict. Strike's job and his black eye had a certain beaten-up glamour, but his attitude towards her was deplorable, and her left breast was still sore.

Bristow's girlfriend had been staring at the closed door ever since the men's voices had first become audible over the noise of the drill. Thick-set and very dark, with a limp bob and what might have been a monobrow if she had not plucked it, she looked naturally cross. Robin had often noticed how couples tended to be of roughly equivalent personal attractiveness, though of course factors such as money often seemed to secure a partner of significantly better looks than oneself. Robin found it endearing that Bristow, who on the evidence of his smart suit and his prestigious firm could have set his sights on somebody much prettier, had chosen this girl, who she assumed was warmer and kinder than her appearance suggested.

'Are you sure you wouldn't like a coffee, Alison?' she asked.

The girl looked around as though surprised at being spoken to, as though she had forgotten that Robin was there.

'No thanks,' she said, in a deep voice that was surprisingly melodious. 'I knew he'd get upset,' she added, with an odd kind of satisfaction. 'I've tried to talk him out of doing this, but he wouldn't listen. Sounds like this so-called detective is turning him down. Good for him.'

Robin's surprise must have shown, because Alison went on, with a trace of impatience:

'It'd be better for John if he'd just accept the facts. She killed herself. The rest of the family have come to terms with it, I don't know why he can't.'

There was no point pretending that she did not know what the woman was talking about. Everyone knew what had happened to Lula Landry. Robin could remember exactly where she had been when she had heard that the model had dived to her death on a sub-zero night in January: standing at the sink in the kitchen of her parents' house. The news had come over the radio, and she had emitted a little cry of surprise, and run out of the kitchen in her nightshirt to tell Matthew, who was staying for the weekend. How could the death of someone you had never met affect you so? Robin had greatly admired Lula Landry's looks. She did not much like her own milkmaid's colouring: the model had been dark, luminous, fine-boned and fierce.

'It hasn't been very long since she died.'

'Three months,' said Alison, shaking out her *Daily Express*. 'Is he any good, this man?'

Robin had noticed Alison's contemptuous expression as she took in the dilapidated condition, and undeniable grubbiness, of the little waiting room, and she had just seen, online, the pristine, palatial office where the other woman worked. Her answer was therefore prompted by self-respect rather than any desire to protect Strike.

'Oh yes,' she replied coolly. 'He's one of the best.'

She slit open a pink, kitten-embellished envelope with the air of a woman who daily dealt with exigencies much more complex and intriguing than Alison could possibly imagine.

Meanwhile, Strike and Bristow were facing each other across the inner room, the one furious, the other trying to find a way to reverse his position without jettisoning his self-respect.

'All I want, Strike,' said Bristow hoarsely, the colour high in his thin face, 'is *justice*.'

He might have struck a divine tuning fork; the word rang through the shabby office, calling forth an inaudible but plangent note in Strike's breast. Bristow had located the pilot light Strike shielded when everything else had been blown to ashes. He stood in desperate need of money, but Bristow had given him another, better reason to jettison his scruples.

'OK. I understand. I mean it, John; I understand. Come back and sit down. If you still want my help, I'd like to give it.'

Bristow glared at him. There was no noise in the office but the distant shouts of the workmen below.

'Would you like your – er, wife, is she? – to come in?'

'No,' said Bristow, still tense, with his hand on the doorknob. 'Alison doesn't think I ought to be doing this. I don't know why she wanted to come along, actually. Probably hoping you'd turn me down.'

'Please – sit down. Let's go over this properly.'

Bristow hesitated, then moved back towards his abandoned chair.

His self-restraint crumbling at last, Strike took a chocolate biscuit and crammed it, whole, into his mouth; he took an unused notepad from his desk drawer, flicked it open, reached for a pen and managed to swallow the biscuit in the time it took Bristow to resume his seat.

'Shall I take that?' he suggested, pointing to the envelope Bristow was still clutching.

The lawyer handed it over as though unsure he could trust Strike with it. Strike, who did not wish to peruse the contents in front of Bristow, put it aside with a small pat, which was intended to show that it was now a valued component of the investigation, and readied his pen.

'John, if you could give me a brief outline of what happened on the day your sister died, it would be very helpful.'

By nature methodical and thorough, Strike had been trained to investigate to a high and rigorous standard. First, allow the witness to tell their story in their own way: the untrammelled flow often revealed details, apparent inconsequentialities, that would later prove invaluable nuggets of evidence. Once the first gush of impression and recollection had been harvested, then it was time to solicit and arrange facts rigorously and precisely: *people, places, property . . .*

'Oh,' said Bristow, who seemed, after all his vehemence, unsure where to start, 'I don't really . . . let's see . . . '

'When was the last time you saw her?' Strike prompted.

'That would have been – yes, the morning before she died. We . . . we had an argument, as a matter of fact, though thank God we made it up.'

'What time was this?'

'It was early. Before nine, I was on my way in to the office. Perhaps a quarter to nine?'

'And what did you argue about?'

'Oh, about her boyfriend, Evan Duffield. They'd just got back together again. The family had thought it was over and we'd been so pleased. He's a horrible person, an addict and a chronic self-publicist; about the worst influence on Lula you could imagine.

'I might have been a bit heavy-handed, I – I see that now. I was eleven years older than Lula. I felt protective of her, you know. Perhaps I was bossy at times. She was always telling me that I didn't understand.'

'Understand what?'

'Well . . . anything. She had lots of issues. Issues with being adopted. Issues with being black in a white family. She used to say I had it easy . . . I don't know. Perhaps she was right.'

He blinked rapidly behind his glasses. 'The row was really the continuation of a row we'd had on the telephone the night before. I just couldn't believe she'd been so stupid as to go back to Duffield. The relief we all felt when they split up . . . I mean, given her own history with drugs, hooking up with an addict . . . ' He drew breath. 'She didn't want to hear it. She never did. She was furious with me. She'd actually given instructions to the security man at the flats not to let me past the front desk next morning, but – well, Wilson waved me through anyway.'

Humiliating, thought Strike, to have to rely on the pity of doormen.

'I wouldn't have gone up,' said Bristow miserably, blotches of colour dappling his thin neck again, 'but I had the contract with Somé to give back to her; she'd asked me to look over it and she needed to sign it . . . She could be quite blasé about things like that. Anyway, she wasn't too happy that they'd let me upstairs, and we rowed again, but it burned itself out quite quickly. She calmed down.

'So then I told her that Mum would appreciate a visit. Mum had just got out of hospital, you see. She'd had a hysterectomy. Lula said she might pop in and see her later, at her flat, but that she couldn't be sure. She had things on.'

Bristow took a deep breath; his right knee started jiggling up and down again and his knobble-knuckled hands washed each other in dumb show.

'I don't want you to think badly of her. People thought her selfish, but she'd been the youngest in the family and rather indulged, and then she was ill and, naturally, the centre of attention, and then she was plunged into this extraordinary life where things, people, revolved around her, and she was pursued everywhere by the paparazzi. It wasn't a normal existence.'

'No,' said Strike.

'So, anyway, I told Lula how groggy and sore Mum was feeling, and she said she might look in on her later. I left; I nipped into my office to get some files from Alison, because I wanted to work from Mum's flat that day and keep her company. I next saw Lula at Mum's, mid-morning. She sat with Mum for a while in the bedroom until my uncle arrived to visit, and then nipped into the study where I was working, to say goodbye. She hugged me before she . . . '

Bristow's voice cracked, and he stared down into his lap.

'More coffee?' Strike suggested. Bristow shook his bowed head. To give him a moment to pull himself together, Strike picked up the tray and headed for the outer office.

Bristow's girlfriend looked up from her newspaper, scowling, when Strike appeared. 'Aren't you finished?' she asked.

'Evidently not,' said Strike, with no attempt at a smile. She glared at him while he addressed Robin.

'Could I get another cup of coffee, er . . . ?'

Robin stood up and took the tray from him in silence.

'John needs to be back in the office at half past ten,' Alison informed Strike, in a slightly louder voice. 'We'll need to be off in ten minutes at the most.'

'I'll bear that in mind,' Strike assured her blandly, before returning to the inner office, where Bristow was sitting as though in prayer, his head bowed over his clasped hands.

'I'm sorry,' he muttered, as Strike sat back down. 'It's still difficult talking about it.'

'No problem,' said Strike, picking up his notebook again. 'So Lula came to see your mother? What time was that?'

'Elevenish. It all came out at the inquest, what she did after that. She got her driver to take her to some boutique that she liked, and then she went back to her flat. She had an appointment at home with a make-up artist she knew, and her friend Ciara Porter joined her there. You'll have seen Ciara Porter, she's a model. Very blonde. They were photographed together as angels, you probably saw it: naked except for handbags and wings. Somé used the picture in his advertising campaign after Lula died. People said it was tasteless.

'So Lula and Ciara spent the afternoon together at Lula's flat, and then they left to go out to dinner, where they met up with Duffield and some other people. The whole group went on to Uzi, the nightclub, and they were there until past midnight.

'Then Duffield and Lula argued. Lots of people saw it happen. He manhandled her a bit, tried to make her stay, but she left the club alone. Everyone thought he'd done it, afterwards, but he turned out to have a cast-iron alibi.'

'Cleared on the evidence of his drug dealer, wasn't he?' asked Strike, still writing.

'Yes, exactly. So – so Lula arrived back at her flat around twenty past one. She was photographed going inside. You probably remember that picture. It was everywhere afterwards.'

Strike remembered: one of the world's most photographed women, head bowed, shoulders hunched, eyes heavy and arms folded tightly around her torso, twisting her face away from the photographers. Once the verdict of suicide had been clearly established, it had taken on a macabre aspect: the rich and beautiful young woman, less than an hour from her death, attempting to conceal her wretchedness from the lenses she had courted, and which had so adored her.

'Were there usually photographers outside her door?'

'Yes, especially if they knew she was with Duffield, or they wanted to get a shot of her coming home drunk. But they weren't only there for her that night. An American rapper was supposed to be arriving to stay in the same building that evening; Deeby Macc's his name. His record company had rented the apartment beneath hers. In the event he never stayed there, because with the police all over the building it was easier for him to go to a hotel. But the photographers who had chased Lula's car when she left Uzi joined the ones who were waiting for Macc outside the flats, so that made quite a crowd of them around the entrance of the building, though they all drifted away not long after she'd gone inside. Somehow they got a tip-off that Macc wouldn't be there for hours.

'It was a bitterly cold night. Snowing. Below freezing. So the street was empty when she fell.'

Bristow blinked and took another sip of cold coffee, and

Strike thought about the paparazzi who had left before Lula Landry fell from her balcony. Imagine, he thought, what a shot of Landry diving to her death would have gone for; enough to retire on, perhaps.

'John, your girlfriend says you need to be somewhere at half past ten.'

'What?'

Bristow seemed to return to himself. He checked the expensive watch and gasped.

'Good God, I had no idea I'd been here so long. What – what happens now?' he asked, looking slightly bewildered. 'You'll read my notes?'

'Yeah, of course,' Strike assured him, 'and I'll call you in a couple of days when I've done some preliminary work. I expect I'll have a lot more questions then.'

'All right,' said Bristow, getting dazedly to his feet. 'Here – take my card. And how would you like me to pay?'

'A month's fee in advance will be great,' said Strike. Quashing feeble stirrings of shame, and remembering that Bristow himself had offered a double fee, he named an exorbitant amount, and to his delight Bristow did not quibble, nor ask whether he accepted credit cards nor even promise to drop the money in later, but drew out a real chequebook and a pen.

'If, say, a quarter of it could be in cash,' Strike added, chancing his luck; and was staggered for the second time that morning when Bristow said, 'I did wonder whether you'd prefer . . . ' and counted out a pile of fifties in addition to the cheque.

They emerged into the outer office at the very moment that Robin was about to enter with Strike's fresh coffee. Bristow's girlfriend stood up when the door opened, and folded her newspaper with the air of one who had been kept waiting too long. She was almost as tall as Bristow, large-framed, with a surly expression and big, mannish hands.

'So you've agreed to do it, have you?' she asked Strike. He had the impression that she thought he was taking advantage of her rich boyfriend. Very possibly she was right.

'Yes, John's hired me,' he replied.

'Oh well,' she said, ungraciously. 'You're pleased, I expect, John.'

The lawyer smiled at her, and she sighed and patted his arm, like a tolerant but slightly exasperated mother to a child. John Bristow raised his hand in a salute, then followed his girlfriend out of the room, and their footsteps clanged away down the metal stairs.

5

Strike turned to Robin, who had sat back down at the computer. His coffee was sitting beside the piles of neatly sorted mail lined up on the desk beside her.

'Thanks,' he said, taking a sip, 'and for the note. Why are you a temp?'

'What d'you mean?' she asked, looking suspicious.

'You can spell and punctuate. You catch on quick. You show initiative – where did the cups and the tray come from? The coffee and biscuits?'

'I borrowed them all from Mr Crowdy. I told him we'd return them by lunchtime.'

'Mr who?'

'Mr Crowdy, the man downstairs. The graphic designer.'

'And he just let you have them?'

'Yes,' she said, a little defensively. 'I thought, having offered the client coffee, we ought to provide it.'

Her use of the plural pronoun was like a gentle pat to his morale.

'Well, that was efficiency way beyond anything Temporary Solutions has sent here before, take it from me. Sorry I kept calling you Sandra; she was the last girl. What's your real name?'

'Robin.'

'Robin,' he repeated. 'That'll be easy to remember.'

He had some notion of making a jocular allusion to Batman

and his dependable sidekick, but the feeble jest died on his lips as her face turned brilliantly pink. Too late, he realised that the most unfortunate construction could be put on his innocent words. Robin swung the swivel chair back towards the computer monitor, so that all Strike could see was an edge of a flaming cheek. In one frozen moment of mutual mortification, the room seemed to have shrunk to the size of a telephone kiosk.

'I'm going to nip out for a bit,' said Strike, putting down his virtually untouched coffee and moving crabwise towards the door, taking down the overcoat hanging beside it. 'If anyone calls . . .'

'Mr Strike – before you go, I think you ought to see this.'

Still flushed, Robin took, from on top of the pile of opened letters beside her computer, a sheet of bright pink writing paper and a matching envelope, both of which she had put into a clear plastic pocket. Strike noticed her engagement ring as she held the things up.

'It's a death threat,' she said.

'Oh yeah,' said Strike. 'Nothing to worry about. They come in about once a week.'

'But—'

'It's a disgruntled ex-client. Bit unhinged. He thinks he's throwing me off the scent by using that paper.'

'Surely, though – shouldn't the police see it?'

'Give them a laugh, you mean?'

'It isn't funny, it's a death threat!' she said, and Strike realised why she had placed it, with its envelope, in the plastic pocket. He was mildly touched.

'Just file it with the others,' he said, pointing towards the filing cabinets in the corner. 'If he was going to kill me he'd have made his move before now. You'll find six months' worth of letters in there somewhere. Will you be all right to hold the fort for a bit while I'm out?'

'I'll cope,' she said, and he was amused by the sour note in her voice, and her obvious disappointment that nobody was going to fingerprint the be-kittened death threat.

'If you need me, my mobile number's on the cards in the top drawer.'

'Fine,' she said, looking at neither the drawer nor him.

'If you want to go out for lunch, feel free. There's a spare key in the desk somewhere.'

'OK.'

'See you later, then.'

He paused just outside the glass door, on the threshold of the tiny dank bathroom. The pressure in his guts was becoming painful, but he felt that her efficiency, and her impersonal concern for his safety, entitled her to some consideration. Resolving to wait until he reached the pub, Strike headed down the stairs.

Out in the street, he lit a cigarette, turned left and proceeded past the closed 12 Bar Café, up the narrow walkway of Denmark Place past a window full of multicoloured guitars, and walls covered in fluttering fliers, away from the relentless pounding of the pneumatic drill. Skirting the rubble and wreckage of the street at the foot of Centre Point, he marched past a gigantic gold statue of Freddie Mercury stood over the entrance of the Dominion Theatre across the road, head bowed, one fist raised in the air, like some pagan god of chaos.

The ornate Victorian face of the Tottenham pub rose up behind the rubble and roadworks, and Strike, pleasurably aware of the large amount of cash in his pocket, pushed his way through its doors, into a serene Victorian atmosphere of gleaming scrolled dark wood and brass fittings. Its frosted glass half-partitions, its aged leather banquettes, its bar mirrors covered in gilt, cherubs and horns of plenty spoke of a confident and ordered world that was in satisfying contrast to the ruined street. Strike ordered a pint of Doom Bar and took it to the back of the almost deserted pub, where he placed his glass on a high circular table, under the garish glass cupola in the ceiling, and headed straight into the Gents, which smelled strongly of piss.

Ten minutes later, and feeling considerably more comfortable, Strike was a third of the way into his pint, which was deepening the anaesthetic effect of his exhaustion. The Cornish beer tasted of home, peace and long-gone security. There was a large and blurry painting of a Victorian maiden, dancing with roses in her hands, directly opposite him. Frolicking coyly as she gazed at him through a shower of petals, her enormous breasts draped in white, she was as unlike a real woman as the table on which his pint rested, or the obese man with the ponytail who was working the pumps at the bar.

And now Strike's thoughts swarmed back to Charlotte, who was indubitably real; beautiful, dangerous as a cornered vixen, clever, sometimes funny, and, in the words of Strike's very oldest friend, 'fucked to the core'. Was it over, really over, this time? Cocooned in his tiredness, Strike recalled the scenes of last night and this morning. Finally she had done something he could not forgive, and the pain would, no doubt, be excruciating once the anaesthetic wore off: but in the meantime, there were certain practicalities to be faced. It had been Charlotte's flat that they had been living in; her stylish, expensive maisonette in Holland

Park Avenue, which meant that he was, as of two o'clock that morning, voluntarily homeless.

('Bluey, just move in with me. For God's sake, you know it makes sense. You can save money while you're building up the business, and I can look after you. You shouldn't be on your own while you're recuperating. Bluey, don't be silly . . .

Nobody would ever call him Bluey again. Bluey was dead.)

It was the first time in their long and turbulent relationship that he had walked out. Three times previously it had been Charlotte who had called a halt. There had been an unspoken awareness between them, always, that if ever he left, if ever he decided he had had enough, the parting would be of an entirely different order to all those she had instigated, none of which, painful and messy though they had been, had ever felt definitive.

Charlotte would not rest until she had hurt him as badly as she could in retaliation. This morning's scene, when she had tracked him to his office, had doubtless been a mere foretaste of what would unfold in the months, even years, to come. He had never known anyone with such an appetite for revenge.

Strike limped to the bar, secured a second pint and returned to the table for further gloomy reflection. Walking out on Charlotte had left him on the brink of true destitution. He was so deeply in debt that all that stood between him and a sleeping bag in a doorway was John Bristow. Indeed, if Gillespie called in the loan that had formed the down payment on Strike's office, Strike would have no alternative but to sleep rough.

('I'm just calling to check how things are going, Mr Strike, because this month's instalment still hasn't arrived . . . Can we expect it within the next few days?')

And finally (since he had started looking at the inadequacies of his life, why not make a comprehensive survey?) there was his recent weight gain; a full stone and a half, so that he not only felt fat and unfit, but was putting unnecessary additional strain on the prosthetic lower leg he was now resting on the brass bar beneath the table. Strike was developing the shadow of a limp purely because the additional load was causing some chafing. The long walk across London in the small hours, kitbag over his shoulder, had not helped. Knowing that he was heading into penury, he had been determined to travel there in the cheapest fashion.

He returned to the bar to buy a third pint. Back at his table beneath the cupola, he drew out his mobile phone and called a friend in the Metropolitan Police whose friendship, though of only a few years' duration, had been forged under exceptional conditions.

Just as Charlotte was the only person to call him 'Bluey', so Detective Inspector Richard Anstis was the only person to call Strike 'Mystic Bob', which name he bellowed at the sound of his friend's voice.

'Looking for a favour,' Strike told Anstis.

'Name it.'

'Who handled the Lula Landry case?'

While Anstis searched out their numbers, he asked after Strike's business, right leg and fiancée. Strike lied about the status of all three.

'Glad to hear it,' said Anstis cheerfully. 'OK, here's Wardle's number. He's all right; loves himself, but you'll be better off with him than Carver; he's a cunt. I can put in a word with Wardle. I'll ring him right now for you, if you like.'

Strike tweaked a tourist leaflet from a wooden display on the wall, and copied down Wardle's number in the space beside a picture of the Horse Guards.

'When're you coming over?' Anstis asked. 'Bring Charlotte one night.'

'Yeah, that'd be great. I'll give you a ring; got a lot on just now.'

After hanging up, Strike sat in deep thought for a while, then called an acquaintance much older than Anstis, whose life path had run in a roughly opposite direction.

'Calling in a favour, mate,' said Strike. 'Need some information.'

'On what?'

'You tell me. I need something I can use for leverage with a copper.'

The conversation ran to twenty-five minutes, and involved many pauses, which grew longer and more pregnant until finally Strike was given an approximate address and two names, which he also copied down beside the Horse Guards, and a warning, which he did not write down, but took in the spirit in which he knew it was intended. The conversation ended on a friendly note, and Strike, now yawning widely, dialled Wardle's number, which was answered almost immediately by a loud, curt voice.

'Wardle.'

'Yeah, hello. My name's Cormoran Strike, and—'

'You're what?'

'Cormoran Strike,' said Strike, 'is my name.'

'Oh yeah,' said Wardle. 'Anstis just rang. You're the private dick? Anstis said you were interested in talking about Lula Landry?'

'Yeah, I am,' said Strike again, suppressing another yawn as he examined the painted panels on the ceiling; bacchanalian revels that became, as he looked, a feast of fairies: *Midsummer Night's*

Dream, a man with a donkey's head. 'But what I'd really like is the file.'

Wardle laughed.

'You didn't save *my* fucking life, mate.'

'Got some information you might be interested in. Thought we could do an exchange.'

There was a short pause.

'I take it you don't want to do this exchange over the phone?'

'That's right,' said Strike. 'Is there anywhere you like to have a pint after a hard day's work?'

Having jotted down the name of a pub near Scotland Yard, and agreed that a week today (failing any nearer date) would suit him too, Strike rang off.

It had not always been thus. A couple of years ago, he had been able to command the compliance of witnesses and suspects; he had been like Wardle, a man whose time had more value than most of those with whom he consorted, and who could choose when, where and how long interviews would be. Like Wardle, he had needed no uniform; he had been constantly cloaked in officialdom and prestige. Now, he was a limping man in a creased shirt, trading on old acquaintances, trying to do deals with policemen who would once have been glad to take his calls.

'Arsehole,' said Strike aloud, into his echoing glass. The third pint had slid down so easily that there was barely an inch left.

His mobile rang; glancing at the screen, he saw his office number. No doubt Robin was trying to tell him that Peter Gillespie was after money. He let her go straight to voicemail, drained his glass and left.

The street was bright and cold, the pavement damp, and the puddles intermittently silver as clouds scudded across the sun.

Strike lit another cigarette outside the front door, and stood smoking it in the doorway of the Tottenham, watching the workmen as they moved around the pit in the road. Cigarette finished, he ambled off down Oxford Street to kill time until the Temporary Solution had left, and he could sleep in peace.

6

Robin had waited ten minutes, to make sure that Strike was not about to come back, before making several delightful telephone calls from her mobile phone. The news of her engagement was received by her friends with either squeals of excitement or envious comments, which gave Robin equal pleasure. At lunchtime, she awarded herself an hour off, bought three bridal magazines and a packet of replacement biscuits (which put the petty cash box, a labelled shortbread tin, into her debt to the tune of forty-two pence), and returned to the empty office, where she spent a happy forty minutes examining bouquets and bridal gowns, and tingling all over with excitement.

When her self-appointed lunch hour was over, Robin washed and returned Mr Crowdy's cups and tray, and his biscuits. Noting how eagerly he attempted to detain her in conversation on her second appearance, his eyes wandering distractedly from her mouth to her breasts, she resolved to avoid him for the rest of the week.

Still Strike did not return. For want of anything else to do, Robin neatened the contents of her desk drawers, disposing of what she recognised as the accumulated waste of other temporaries: two squares of dusty milk chocolate, a bald emery board and many pieces of paper carrying anonymous telephone numbers and doodles. There was a box of old-fashioned metal acro clips, which she had never come across before, and a considerable number of small, blank blue notebooks, which, though unmarked, had an air of officialdom. Robin, experienced in the world of offices, had the feeling that they might have been pinched from an institutional store cupboard.

The office telephone rang occasionally. Her new boss seemed to be a person of many names. One man asked for 'Oggy'; another for 'Monkey Boy'; while a dry, clipped voice asked that 'Mr Strike' return Mr Peter Gillespie's call as soon as possible. On each occasion, Robin contacted Strike's mobile phone, and reached only his voicemail. She therefore left verbal messages, wrote down each caller's name and number on a Post-it note, took it into Strike's office and stuck it neatly on his desk.

The pneumatic drill rumbled on and on outside. Around two o'clock, the ceiling began to creak as the occupant of the flat overhead became more active; otherwise, Robin might have been alone in the whole building. Gradually solitude, coupled with the feeling of pure delight that threatened to burst her ribcage every time her eyes fell on the ring on her left hand, emboldened her. She began to clean and tidy the tiny room under her interim control.

In spite of its general shabbiness, and an overlying grubbiness, Robin soon discovered a firm organisational structure that pleased her own neat and orderly nature. The brown card folders (oddly old-fashioned, in these days of neon plastic) lined up on the shelves behind her desk were arranged in date order, each with a handwritten serial number on the spine. She opened one of them, and saw that the acro clips had been used to secure loose leaves of paper into each file. Much of the material inside was in a deceptive, difficult-to-read hand. Perhaps this was how the police worked; perhaps Strike was an ex-policeman.

Robin discovered the stack of pink death threats to which Strike had alluded in the middle drawer of the filing cabinet, beside a slim sheaf of confidentiality agreements. She took one of these out and read it: a simple form, requesting that the signatory refrain from discussing, outside hours, any of the names or information they might be privy to during their working day. Robin pondered for a moment, then carefully signed and dated one of the documents, carried it through to Strike's inner office, and placed it on his desk, so that he might add his name on the dotted line supplied. Taking this one-sided vow of secrecy gave back to her some of the mystique, even glamour, that she had imagined lay beyond the engraved glass door, before it had flown open and Strike had nearly bowled her down the stairwell.

It was after placing the form on Strike's desk that she spotted the kitbag stuffed away in a corner behind the filing cabinet. The edge of his dirty shirt, an alarm clock and a soap bag peeked from between the open teeth of the bag's zip. Robin closed the door between inner and outer offices as though she had accidentally witnessed something embarrassing and private. She added together the dark-haired beauty fleeing the building that morning, Strike's various injuries and what seemed, in retrospect, to have been a slightly delayed, but determined, pursuit. In her new and joyful condition of betrothal, Robin was disposed to feel desperately sorry for anyone with a less fortunate love life than her own – if desperate pity could describe the exquisite pleasure she actually felt at the thought of her own comparative paradise.

At five o'clock, and in the continuing absence of her temporary boss, Robin decided that she was free to go home. She hummed to herself as she filled in her own time sheet, bursting into song as she buttoned up her trench coat; then she locked the office door, slid the spare key back through the letter box and proceeded, with some caution, back down the metal stairs, towards Matthew and home.

7

Strike had spent the early afternoon at the University of London Union building, where, by dint of walking determinedly past reception with a slight scowl on his face, he had gained the showers without being challenged or asked for his student card. He had then eaten a stale ham roll and a bar of chocolate in the café. After that he had wandered, blank-eyed in his tiredness, smoking between the cheap shops he visited to buy, with Bristow's cash, the few necessities he needed now that bed and board were gone. Early evening found him holed up in an Italian restaurant, several large boxes propped up at the back, beside the bar, and spinning out his beer until he had half forgotten why he was killing time.

It was nearly eight before he returned to the office. This was the hour when he found London most lovable; the working day over, her pub windows were warm and jewel-like, her streets thrummed with life, and the indefatigable permanence of her aged buildings, softened by the street lights, became strangely reassuring. We have seen plenty like you, they seemed to murmur soothingly, as he limped along Oxford Street carrying a boxed-up camp bed. Seven and a half million hearts were beating in close proximity in this heaving old city, and many, after all, would be aching far worse than his. Walking wearily past closing shops, while the heavens turned indigo above him, Strike found solace in vastness and anonymity.

It was some feat to force the camp bed up the metal stairwell to the second floor, and by the time he reached the entrance bearing his name the pain in the end of his right leg was excruciating. He leaned for a moment, bearing all his weight on his left foot, panting against the glass door, watching it mist.

'You fat cunt,' he said aloud. 'You knackered old dinosaur.'

Wiping the sweat off his forehead, he unlocked the door, and heaved his various purchases over the threshold. In the inner office he pushed his desk aside and set up the bed, unrolled the sleeping bag, and filled his cheap kettle at the sink outside the glass door.

His dinner was still in a Pot Noodle, which he had chosen because it reminded him of the fare he used to carry in his ration pack: some deep-rooted association between quickly heated and rehydrated food and makeshift dwelling places had made him reach automatically for the thing. When the kettle had boiled, he added the water to the tub, and ate the rehydrated pasta with a plastic fork he had taken from the ULU café, sitting in his office chair, looking down into the almost deserted street, the traffic rumbling past in the twilight at the end of the road, and listening to the determined thud of a bass from two floors below, in the 12 Bar Café.

He had slept in worse places. There had been the stone floor of a multi-storey car park in Angola, and the bombed-out metal factory where they had erected tents, and woken coughing up black soot in the mornings; and, worst of all, the dank dormitory of the commune in Norfolk to which his mother had dragged him and one of his half-sisters when they were eight and six respectively. He remembered the comfortless ease of hospital beds in which he had lain for months, and various squats (also with his mother), and the freezing woods in which he had camped on army exercises. However basic and uninviting the camp bed looked lying under the one naked light bulb, it was luxurious compared with all of them.

The act of shopping for what he needed, and of setting up the bare necessities for himself, had lulled Strike back into the familiar soldierly state of doing what needed to be done, without question or complaint. He disposed of the Pot Noodle tub, turned on the lamp and sat himself down at the desk where Robin had spent most of the day.

As he assembled the raw components of a new file – the hardback folder, the blank paper and an acro clip; the notebook in which he had recorded Bristow's interview; the pamphlet from the Tottenham; Bristow's card – he noticed the new tidiness of the drawers, the lack of dust on the computer monitor, the absence of empty cups and debris, and a faint smell of Pledge. Mildly intrigued, he opened the petty cash tin, and saw there, in Robin's neat, rounded writing, the note that he owed her forty-two pence for chocolate biscuits. Strike pulled forty of the pounds Bristow had given him from his wallet and deposited them in the tin; then, as an afterthought, counted out forty-two pence in coins and laid it on top.

Next, with one of the biros Robin had assembled neatly in the top drawer, Strike began to write, fluently and rapidly, beginning with the date. The notes of Bristow's interview he tore out and attached separately to the file; the actions he had taken thus far, including calls to Anstis and to Wardle, were noted, their numbers preserved (but the details of his other friend, the provider of useful names and addresses, were not put on file).

Finally Strike gave his new case a serial number, which he wrote, along with the legend *Sudden Death, Lula Landry*, on the spine, before stowing the file in its place at the far right of the shelf.

Now, at last, he opened the envelope which, according to Bristow, contained those vital clues that police had missed. The lawyer's handwriting, neat and fluid, sloped backwards in densely written lines. As Bristow had promised, the contents dealt mostly with the actions of a man whom he called 'the Runner'.

The Runner was a tall black man, whose face was concealed by a scarf and who appeared on the footage of a camera on a late-night bus which ran from Islington towards the West End. He had boarded this bus around fifty minutes before Lula Landry died. He was next seen on CCTV footage taken in Mayfair, walking in the direction of Landry's house, at 1.39 a.m. He had paused on camera and appeared to consult a piece of paper (*poss an address or directions?* Bristow had added helpfully in his notes) before walking out of sight.

Footage taken from the same CCTV camera shortly after showed the Runner sprinting back past the camera at 2.12 and out of sight. *Second black man also running – poss lookout? Disturbed in car theft? Car alarm went off around the corner at this time*, Bristow had written.

Finally there was CCTV footage of *a black man closely resembling the Runner* walking along a road close to Gray's Inn Square, several miles away, later in the morning of Landry's death. *Face still concealed*, Bristow had written.

Strike paused to rub his eyes, wincing because he had forgotten that one of them was bruised. He was now in that light-headed, twitchy state that signified true exhaustion. With a long, grunting sigh he considered Bristow's notes, with one hairy fist holding a pen ready to make his own annotations.

Bristow might interpret the law with dispassion and objectivity in the office that had provided him with his smart engraved business card, but the contents of this envelope merely confirmed Strike's view that his client's personal life was dominated by an unjustifiable obsession. Whatever the origin of Bristow's preoccupation with the Runner – whether because he nursed a secret fear of that urban bogeyman, the criminal black male, or for some other, deeper, more personal reason – it was unthinkable that the police had not investigated the Runner, and his (possibly lookout, possibly car thief) companion, and certain that they had had good reason for excluding him from suspicion.

Yawning widely, Strike turned to the second page of Bristow's notes.

> At 1.45, Derrick Wilson, the security guard on duty at the desk overnight, felt unwell and went into the back bathroom, where he remained for approximately a quarter of an hour. For fifteen minutes prior to Lula's death, therefore, the lobby of her building was deserted and anybody could have entered and exited without being seen. Wilson only came out of the bathroom after Lula fell, when he heard Tansy Bestigui screaming.
>
> This window of opportunity tallies exactly with the time the Runner would have reached 18 Kentigern Gardens if he passed the security camera on the junction of Alderbrook and Bellamy Roads at 1.39.

'And how,' murmured Strike, massaging his forehead, 'did he see through the front door, to know the guard was in the bog?'

I have spoken to Derrick Wilson, who is happy to be interviewed.

And I bet you've paid him to do it, Strike thought, noting the security guard's telephone number beneath these concluding words.

He laid down the pen with which he had been intending to add his own notes, and clipped Bristow's jottings into the file. Then he turned off the desk lamp and limped out to pee in the toilet on the landing. After brushing his teeth over the cracked basin, he locked the glass door, set his alarm clock and undressed.

By the neon glow of the street lamp outside, Strike undid the straps of his prosthetic, easing it from the aching stump, removing the gel liner that had become an inadequate cushion against pain. He laid the false leg beside his recharging mobile phone, manoeuvred himself into his sleeping bag and lay with his hands behind his head, staring up at the ceiling. Now, as he had feared, the leaden fatigue of the body was not enough to still the misfiring mind. The old infection was active again; tormenting him, dragging at him.

What would she be doing now?

Yesterday evening, in a parallel universe, he had lived in a beautiful apartment in a most desirable part of London, with a woman who made every man who laid eyes on her treat Strike with a kind of incredulous envy.

'Why don't you just move in with me? Oh, for God's sake, Bluey, doesn't it make sense? Why not?'

He had known, from the very first, that it was a mistake. They had tried it before, and each time it had been more calamitous than the last.

'We're engaged, for God's sake, why won't you live with me?'

She had said things that were supposed to be proofs that, in the process of almost losing him for ever, she had been as irrevocably changed as he had, with his one and a half legs.

'I don't need a ring. Don't be ridiculous, Bluey. You need all your money for the new business.'

He closed his eyes. There could be no going back from this morning. She had lied once too often, about something too serious. But he went over it all again, like a sum he had long since solved, afraid he had made some elementary mistake. Painstakingly he added together the constantly shifting dates, the refusal to check with chemist or doctor, the fury with which she had countered any request for clarification, and then the sudden announcement that it was over, with never a shred of proof that it had been real. Along with every other suspicious circumstance, there was his hard-won knowledge of her mythomania, her need to provoke, to taunt, to test.

'Don't you dare fucking *investigate* me. Don't you dare treat me like some drugged-up *squaddie*. I am not a fucking case to be solved; you're supposed to love me and you won't take my word even on *this* . . .'

But the lies she told were woven into the fabric of her being, her life; so that to live with her and love her was to become slowly enmeshed by them, to wrestle her for the truth, to struggle to maintain a foothold on reality. How could it have happened, that he, who from his most extreme youth had needed to investigate, to know for sure, to winkle the truth out of the smallest conundrums, could have fallen in love so hard, and for so long, with a girl who spun lies as easily as other women breathed?

'It's over,' he told himself. 'It had to happen.'

But he had not wanted to tell Anstis, and he could not face telling anyone else, not yet. There were friends all over London who would welcome him eagerly to their homes, who would throw open their guest rooms and their fridges, eager to condole and to help. The price of all of those comfortable beds and home-cooked meals, however, would be to sit at kitchen tables, once the clean-pyjamaed children were in bed, and relive the filthy final battle with Charlotte, submitting to the outraged sympathy and pity of his friends' girlfriends and wives. To this he preferred grim solitude, a Pot Noodle and a sleeping bag.

He could still feel the missing foot, ripped from his leg two and a half years before. It was there, under the sleeping bag; he could flex the vanished toes if he wanted to. Exhausted as Strike was, it took a while for him to fall asleep, and when he did, Charlotte wove in and out of every dream, gorgeous, vituperative and haunted.

Part Two

Non ignara mali miseris succurrere disco.

No stranger to trouble myself, I am learning to care for the unhappy.

Virgil, *Aeneid*, Book 1

1

'"With all the gallons of newsprint and hours of televised talk that have been poured forth on the subject of Lula Landry's death, rarely has the question been asked: *why do we care?*

'"She was beautiful, of course, and beautiful girls have been helping to shift newspapers ever since Dana Gibson cross-hatched lazy-lidded sirens for the *New Yorker*.

'"She was black, too, or rather, a delicious shade of *café au lait*, and this, we were constantly told, represented progression within an industry concerned merely with surfaces. (I am dubious: could it not be that, this season, *café au lait* was the 'in' shade? Have we seen a sudden influx of black women into the industry in Landry's wake? Have our notions of female beauty been revolutionised by her success? Are black Barbies now outselling white?)

'"The family and friends of the flesh-and-blood Landry will be distraught, of course, and have my profound sympathy. We, however, the reading, watching public, have no personal grief to justify our excesses. Young women die, every day, in 'tragic' (which is to say, unnatural) circumstances: in car crashes, from overdoses, and, occasionally, because they attempted to starve themselves into conformity with the body shape sported by Landry and her ilk. Do we spare any of these dead girls more than a passing thought, as we turn the page, and obscure their ordinary faces?"'

Robin paused to take a sip of coffee and clear her throat.

'So far, so sanctimonious,' muttered Strike.

He was sitting at the end of Robin's desk, pasting photographs into an open folder, numbering each one, and writing a description of the subject of each in an index at the back. Robin continued where she had left off, reading from her computer monitor.

'"Our disproportionate interest, even grief, bears examination. Right up until the moment that Landry took her fatal dive, it is a fair bet that tens of thousands of women would have changed places with her. Sobbing young girls laid flowers beneath the balcony of Landry's £4.5 million penthouse flat after her crushed body was cleared away. Has even one aspiring model been deterred in her pursuit of tabloid fame by the rise and brutal fall of Lula Landry?"'

'Get on with it,' said Strike. 'Her, not you,' he added hastily. 'It's a woman writing, right?'

'Yes, a Melanie Telford,' said Robin, scrolling back to the top of the screen to reveal the head shot of a jowly middle-aged blonde. 'Do you want me to skip the rest?'

'No, no, keep going.'

Robin cleared her throat once more and continued.

'"The answer, surely, is no." That's the bit about aspiring models being deterred.'

'Yeah, got that.'

'Right, well . . . "A hundred years after Emmeline Pankhurst, a generation of pubescent females seeks nothing better than to be reduced to the status of a cut-out paper doll, a flat avatar whose fictionalised adventures mask such disturbance and distress that she threw herself from a third-storey window. Appearance is all: the designer Guy Somé was quick to inform the press that she jumped wearing one of his dresses, which sold out in the twenty-four hours after her death. What better advert could there be than that Lula Landry chose to meet her maker in Somé?

'"No, it is not the young woman whose loss we bemoan, for she was no more real to most of us than the Gibson girls who dripped from Dana's pen. What we mourn is the physical image flickering across a multitude of red-tops and celeb mags; an image that sold us clothes and handbags and a notion of celebrity that, in her demise, proved to be empty and transient as a soap bubble. What we actually miss, were we honest enough to admit it, are the entertaining antics of that paper-thin good-time girl, whose strip-cartoon existence of drug abuse, riotous living, fancy clothes and dangerous on-off boyfriend we can no longer enjoy.

'"Landry's funeral was covered as lavishly as any celebrity wedding in the tawdry magazines who feed on the famous, and whose publishers will surely mourn her demise longer than most. We were permitted glimpses of various celebrities in tears, but her family were given the tiniest picture of all; they were a surprisingly unphotogenic lot, you see.

'"Yet the account of one mourner genuinely touched me. In response to the enquiry of a man who she may not have realised was a reporter, she revealed that she had met Landry at a treatment facility, and that they had become friends. She had taken her place in a rear pew to say farewell, and slipped as quietly away again. She has not sold her story, unlike so many others who consorted with Landry in life. It may tell us something touching about the real Lula Landry, that she inspired genuine affection in an ordinary girl. As for the rest of us—"'

'Doesn't she give this ordinary girl from the treatment facility a name?' interrupted Strike.

Robin scanned the story silently.

'No.'

Strike scratched his imperfectly shaven chin.

'Bristow didn't mention any friend from a treatment facility.'

'D'you think she could be important?' asked Robin eagerly, turning in her swivel chair to look at him.

'It could be interesting to talk to someone who knew Landry from therapy, instead of nightclubs.'

Strike had only asked Robin to look up Landry's connections on the internet because he had nothing else for her to do. She had already telephoned Derrick Wilson, the security guard, and arranged a meeting with Strike on Friday morning at the Phoenix Café in Brixton. The day's post had comprised two circulars and a final demand; there had been no calls, and she had already organised everything in the office that could be alphabetised, stacked or arranged according to type and colour.

Inspired by her Google proficiency of the previous day, therefore, he had set her this fairly pointless task. For the past hour or so she had been reading out odd snippets and articles about Landry and her associates, while Strike put into order a stack of receipts, telephone bills and photographs relating to his only other current case.

'Shall I see whether I can find out more about that girl, then?' asked Robin.

'Yeah,' said Strike absently, examining a photograph of a stocky, balding man in a suit and a very ripe-looking redhead in tight jeans. The besuited man was Mr Geoffrey Hook; the redhead, however, bore no resemblance to Mrs Hook, who, prior to Bristow's arrival in his office, had been Strike's only client. Strike stuck the photograph into Mrs Hook's file and labelled it No. 12, while Robin turned back to the computer.

For a few moments there was silence, except for the flick of photographs and the tapping of Robin's short nails against the keys. The door into the inner office behind Strike was closed to conceal the camp bed and other signs of habitation, and the air was heavy with the scent of artificial limes, due to Strike's liberal use of cheap air-freshener before Robin had arrived. Lest she perceive any tinge of sexual interest in his decision to sit at the other end of her desk, he had pretended to notice her engagement ring for the first time before sitting down, then made polite, studiously impersonal conversation about her fiancé for five minutes. He learned that he was a newly qualified accountant called Matthew; that it was to live with Matthew that Robin had moved to London from Yorkshire the previous month, and that the temping was a stopgap measure before finding a permanent job.

'D'you think she could be in one of these pictures?' Robin asked, after a while. 'The girl from the treatment centre?'

She had brought up a screen full of identically sized photographs, each showing one or more people dressed in dark clothes, all heading from left to right, making for the funeral. Crash barriers and the blurred faces of a crowd formed the backdrop to each picture.

Most striking of all was the picture of a very tall, pale girl with golden hair drawn back into a ponytail, on whose head was perched a confection of black net and feathers. Strike recognised her, because everyone knew who she was: Ciara Porter, the model with whom Lula had spent much of her last day on earth; the friend with whom Landry had been photographed for one of the most famous shots of her career. Porter looked beautiful and sombre as she walked towards Lula's funeral service. She seemed to have attended alone, because there was no disembodied hand supporting her thin arm or resting on her long back.

Next to Porter's picture was that of a couple captioned *Film producer Freddie Bestigui and wife Tansy*. Bestigui was built like a bull, with short legs, a broad barrel chest and a thick neck. His hair was grey and brush-cut; his face a crumpled mass of folds, bags and moles, out of which his fleshy nose protruded like a tumour. Nevertheless, he cut an imposing figure in his expensive black overcoat, with his skeletal young wife on his arm. Almost nothing could be discerned of Tansy's true appearance, behind the upturned fur of her coat collar and the enormous round sunglasses.

Last in this top row of photographs was *Guy Somé, fashion designer*. He was a thin black man who was wearing a midnight-blue frock coat of exaggerated cut. His face was bowed and his expression indiscernible, due to the way the light fell on his dark head, though three large diamond earrings in the lobe facing the camera had caught the flashes and glittered like stars. Like Porter, he appeared to have arrived unaccompanied, although a small group of mourners, unworthy of their own legends, had been captured within the frame of his picture.

Strike drew his chair nearer to the screen, though still keeping more than an arm's length between himself and Robin. One of the unidentified faces, half severed by the edge of the picture, was John Bristow, recognisable by the short upper lip and the hamsterish teeth. He had his arm around a stricken-looking older woman with white hair; her face was gaunt and ghastly, the nakedness of her grief touching. Behind this pair was a tall, haughty-looking man who gave the impression of deploring the surroundings in which he found himself.

'I can't see anyone who might be this ordinary girl,' said Robin, moving the screen down to scrutinise more pictures of famous and beautiful people looking sad and serious. 'Oh, look . . . Evan Duffield.'

He was dressed in a black T-shirt, black jeans and a military-style black overcoat. His hair, too, was black; his face all sharp planes and hollows; icy blue eyes stared directly into the camera lens. Though taller than both of them, he looked fragile compared to the companions flanking him: a large man in a suit and an anxious-looking older woman, whose mouth was open and who was making a gesture as though to clear a path ahead of them. The threesome reminded Strike of parents steering a sick child away from a party. Strike noticed that, in spite of Duffield's air of disorientation and distress, he had made a good job of applying his eyeliner.

'Look at those flowers!'

Duffield slid up into the top of the screen and vanished: Robin had paused on the photograph of an enormous wreath in the shape of what Strike took, initially, to be a heart, before realising it represented two curved angel wings, composed of white roses. An inset photograph showed a close-up of the attached card.

'"Rest in peace, Angel Lula. Deeby Macc",' Robin read aloud.

'Deeby Macc? The rapper? So they knew each other, did they?'

'No, I don't think so; but there was that whole thing about him renting a flat in her building; she'd been mentioned in a couple of his songs, hadn't she? The press were all excited about him staying there . . . '

'You're well informed on the subject.'

'Oh, you know, just magazines,' said Robin vaguely, scrolling back through the funeral photographs.

'What kind of name is "Deeby"?' Strike wondered aloud.

'It comes from his initials. It's "D. B." really,' she enunciated clearly. 'His real name's Daryl Brandon Macdonald.'

'A rap fan, are you?'

'No,' said Robin, still intent on the screen. 'I just remember things like that.'

She clicked off the images she was perusing and began tapping away on the keyboard again. Strike returned to his photographs. The next showed Mr Geoffrey Hook kissing his ginger-haired companion, hand palpating one large, canvas-covered buttock, outside Ealing Broadway Tube station.

'Here's a bit of film on YouTube, look,' said Robin. 'Deeby Macc talking about Lula after she died.'

'Let's see it,' said Strike, rolling his chair forwards a couple of feet and then, on second thoughts, back one.

The grainy little video, three inches by four, jerked into life. A large black man wearing some kind of hooded top with a fist picked out in studs on the chest sat in a black leather chair, facing an unseen interviewer. His hair was closely shaven and he wore sunglasses.

'. . . Lula Landry's suicide?' said the interviewer, who was English.

'That was fucked-up, man, that was fucked-up,' replied Deeby, running his hand over his smooth head. His voice was soft, deep and hoarse, with the very faintest trace of a lisp. 'That's what they do to success: they hunt you down, they tear you down. That's what envy does, my friend. The mother-fuckin' press chased her out that window. Let her rest in peace,

I say. She's getting peace right now.'

'Pretty shocking welcome to London for you,' said the interviewer, 'with her, y'know, like, falling past your window?'

Deeby Macc did not answer at once. He sat very still, staring at the interviewer through his opaque lenses. Then he said:

'I wasn't there, or you got someone who says I was?'

The interviewer's yelp of nervous, hastily stifled laughter jarred.

'God, no, not at all – not . . . '

Deeby turned his head and addressed someone standing off-camera.

'Think I oughta've brought my lawyers?'

The interviewer brayed with sycophantic laughter. Deeby looked back at him, still unsmiling.

'Deeby Macc,' said the breathless interviewer, 'thank you very much for your time.'

An outstretched white hand slid forwards on to the screen; Deeby raised his own in a fist. The white hand reconstituted itself, and they bumped knuckles. Somebody off-screen laughed derisively. The video ended.

'"The motherfuckin' press chased her out that window",' Strike repeated, rolling his chair back to its original position. 'Interesting point of view.'

He felt his mobile phone vibrate in his trouser pocket, and drew it out. The sight of Charlotte's name attached to a new text caused a surge of adrenalin through his body, as though he had just sighted a crouching beast of prey.

I will be out on Friday morning between 9 and 12 if you want to collect your things.

'What?' He had the impression that Robin had just spoken.

'I said, there's a horrible piece here about her birth mother.'

'OK. Read it out.'

He slid his mobile back into his pocket. As he bent his large head again over Mrs Hook's file, his thoughts seemed to reverberate as though a gong had been struck inside his skull.

Charlotte was behaving with sinister reasonableness; feigning adult calm. She had taken their endlessly elaborate duel to a new level, never before reached or tested: 'Now let's do it like grown-ups.' Perhaps a knife would plunge between his shoulder blades as he walked through the front door of her flat; perhaps he would walk into the bedroom to discover her corpse, wrists slit, lying in a puddle of congealing blood in front of the fireplace.

Robin's voice was like the background drone of a vacuum cleaner. With an effort, he refocused his attention.

'"... sold the romantic story of her liaison with a young black man to as many tabloid journalists as were prepared to pay. There is nothing romantic, however, about Marlene Higson's story as it is remembered by her old neighbours.

'" 'She was turning tricks,' says Vivian Cranfield, who lived in the flat above Higson's at the time she fell pregnant with Landry. 'There were men coming in and out of her place every hour of the day and night. She never knew who that baby's father was, it could have been any of them. She never wanted the baby. I can still remember her out in the hall, crying, on her own, while her mum was busy with a punter. Tiny little thing in her nappy, hardly walking ... someone must have called Social Services, and not before time. Best thing that ever happened to that girl, getting adopted.'

'"The truth will, no doubt, shock Landry, who has talked at

length in the press about her reunion with her long-lost birth mother . . ." – this was written,' explained Robin, 'before Lula died.'

'Yeah,' said Strike, closing the folder abruptly. 'D'you fancy a walk?'

2

The cameras looked like malevolent shoeboxes atop their pole, each with a single blank, black eye. They pointed in opposite directions, staring the length of Alderbrook Road, which bustled with pedestrians and traffic. Both pavements were crammed with shops, bars and cafés. Double-deckers rumbled up and down bus lanes.

'This is where Bristow's Runner was caught on film,' observed Strike, turning his back on Alderbrook Road to look up the much quieter Bellamy Road, which led, lined with tall and palatial houses, into the residential heart of Mayfair. 'He passed here twelve minutes after she fell . . . this'd be the quickest route from Kentigern Gardens. Night buses run here. Best bet to pick up a taxi. Not that that'd be a smart move if you'd just murdered a woman.'

He buried himself again in an extremely battered *A–Z*. Strike did not seem worried that anyone might mistake him for a tourist. No doubt, thought Robin, it would not matter if they did, given his size.

Robin had been asked to do several things, in the course of her brief temping career, that were outside the terms of a secretarial contract, and had therefore been a little unnerved by Strike's suggestion of a walk. She was pleased, however, to acquit Strike of any flirtatious intent. The long walk to this spot had been conducted in almost total silence, Strike apparently deep in thought, and occasionally consulting his map.

Upon their arrival in Alderbrook Road, however, he had said:

'If you spot anything, or you think of anything I haven't, tell me, won't you?'

This was rather thrilling: Robin prided herself on her observational powers; they were one reason she had secretly cherished the childhood ambition that the large man beside her was living. She looked intelligently up and down the street, and tried to visualise what someone might have been up to, on a snowy night, in sub-zero temperatures, at two in the morning.

'This way,' said Strike, however, before any insights could occur to her, and they walked off, side by side, along Bellamy Road. It curved gently to the left and continued for some sixty houses, which were almost identical, with their glossy black doors, their short railings either side of clean white steps and their topiary-filled tubs. Here and there were marble lions and brass plaques, giving names and professional credentials; chandeliers glinted from upper windows, and one door stood open to reveal a chequerboard floor, oil paintings in gold frames and a Georgian staircase.

As he walked, Strike pondered some of the information that Robin had managed to find on the internet that morning. As Strike had suspected, Bristow had not been honest when he asserted that the police had made no effort to trace the Runner and his sidekick. Buried in voluminous and rabid press coverage that survived online were appeals for the men to come forward, but they seemed to have yielded no results.

Unlike Bristow, Strike did not find any of this suggestive of police incompetence, or of a plausible murder suspect left uninvestigated. The sudden sounding of a car alarm around the time that the two men had fled the area suggested a good reason for their reluctance to talk to the police. Moreover, Strike did not know whether Bristow was familiar with the varying quality of CCTV footage, but he himself had extensive experience of frustrating blurry black-and-white images from which it was impossible to glean a true likeness.

Strike had also noticed that Bristow had said not a word in person, or in his notes, about the DNA evidence gathered from inside his sister's flat. He strongly suspected, from the fact that the police had been happy to exclude the Runner and his friend from further inquiries, that no trace of foreign DNA had been found there. However, Strike knew that the truly deluded would happily discount such trivialities as DNA evidence, citing contamination, or conspiracy. They saw what they wanted to see, blind to inconvenient, implacable truth.

But the Google searches of the morning had suggested a possible explanation for Bristow's fixation on the Runner. His sister had been researching her biological roots, and had managed to trace her birth mother, who sounded, even when allowance was made for press sensationalism, an unsavoury character. Doubtless revelations such as those that Robin had found online would have been unpleasant not just for Landry, but for her whole adoptive family. Was it part of Bristow's instability (for Strike could not pretend to himself that his client gave the impression of a well-balanced man) that he believed Lula, so fortunate in some ways, had tempted fate? That she had stirred up trouble in trying to plumb the secrets of her origins; that she had woken a demon that had reached out of the distant past, and killed her? Was that why a black man in her vicinity so disturbed him?

Deeper and deeper into the enclave of the wealthy Strike and Robin walked, until they arrived at the corner of Kentigern Gardens. Like Bellamy Road, it projected an aura of intimidating, self-contained prosperity. The houses here were high Victorian, red brick with stone dressings and heavy pedimented windows on four floors, with their own small stone balconies. White marble porticos framed each entrance, and three white steps led from the pavement to more glossy black front doors. Everything was expensively well maintained, clean and regimented. There were only a few cars parked here; a small sign declared that permits were needed for the privilege.

No longer set apart by police tape and massing journalists, number 18 had faded back into graceful conformity with its neighbours.

'The balcony she fell from was on the top floor,' said Strike, 'about forty feet up, I'd say.'

He contemplated the handsome frontage. The balconies on the top three floors, Robin saw, were shallow, with barely standing room between the balustrade and the long windows.

'The thing is,' Strike told Robin, while he squinted at the balcony high above them, 'pushing someone from that height wouldn't guarantee death.'

'Oh – but surely?' protested Robin, contemplating the awful drop between top balcony and hard road.

'You'd be surprised. I spent a month in a bed next to a Welsh bloke who got blown off a building about that height. Smashed his legs and pelvis, lot of internal bleeding, but he's still with us.'

Robin glanced at Strike, wondering why he had been in bed for a month; but the detective was oblivious, now scowling at the front door.

'Keypad,' he muttered, noting the metal square inset with buttons, 'and a camera over the door. Bristow didn't mention a camera. Could be new.'

He stood for a few minutes testing theories against the

intimidating red-brick face of these fantastically expensive fortresses. Why had Lula Landry chosen to live here in the first place? Sedate, traditional, stuffy, Kentigern Gardens was surely the natural domain of a different kind of rich: Russian and Arab oligarchs; corporate giants splitting their time between town and their country estates; wealthy spinsters, slowly decaying amidst their art collections. He found it a strange choice of abode for a girl of twenty-three, who ran, according to every story Robin had read out that morning, with a hip, creative crowd, whose celebrated sense of style owed more to the street than the salon.

'It looks very well protected, doesn't it?' said Robin.

'Yeah, it does. And that's without the crowd of paparazzi who were standing guard over it that night.'

Strike leaned back against the black railings of number 23, staring at number 18. The windows of Landry's former residence were taller than those on the lower floors, and its balcony, unlike the other two, had not been decorated with topiary shrubs. Strike slipped a packet of cigarettes out of his pocket and offered Robin one; she shook her head, surprised, because she had not seen him smoke in the office. Having lit up and inhaled deeply, he said, with his eyes on the front door:

'Bristow thinks someone got in and out that night, undetected.'

Robin, who had already decided that the building was impenetrable, thought that Strike was about to pour scorn on the theory, but she was wrong.

'If they did,' said Strike, eyes still on the door, 'it was planned, and planned well. Nobody could've got past photographers, a keypad, a security guard and a closed inner door, and out again, on luck alone. Thing is,' he scratched his chin, 'that degree of premeditation doesn't fit with such a slapdash murder.'

Robin found the choice of adjective callous.

'Pushing someone over a balcony's a spur-of-the-moment thing,' said Strike, as though he had felt her inner wince. 'Hot blood. Blind temper.'

He found Robin's company satisfactory and restful, not only because she was hanging off his every word, and had not troubled to break his silences, but because that little sapphire ring on her third finger was like a neat full stop: this far, and no further. It suited him perfectly. He was free to show off, in a very mild way, which was one of the few pleasures remaining to him.

'But what if the killer was already inside?'

'That's a lot more plausible,' said Strike, and Robin felt very pleased with herself. 'And if a killer was already in there, we've got the choice between the security guard himself, one or both of the Bestiguis, or some unknown person who was hiding in the building without anyone's knowledge. If it was either of the Bestiguis, or Wilson, there's no getting-in-and-out problem; all they had to do was return to the places they were supposed to be. There was still the risk she could have survived, injured, to tell the tale, but a hot-blooded, unpremeditated crime makes a lot more sense if one of them did it. A row and a blind shove.'

Strike smoked his cigarette and continued to scrutinise the front of the building, in particular the gap between the windows on the first floor and those on the third. He was thinking primarily about Freddie Bestigui, the film producer. According to what Robin had found on the internet, Bestigui had been in bed asleep when Lula Landry toppled over the balcony two floors above. The fact that it was Bestigui's own wife who had sounded the alarm, and insisted that the killer was still upstairs while her husband stood beside her, implied that she, at least, did not think him guilty. Nevertheless, Freddie Bestigui had been the man in closest proximity to the dead girl at the time of her death. Laymen, in Strike's experience, were obsessed with motive: opportunity topped the professional's list.

Unwittingly confirming her civilian status, Robin said:

'But why would someone pick the middle of the night to have an argument with her? Nothing ever came out about her not getting on with her neighbours, did it? And Tansy Bestigui definitely couldn't have done it, could she? Why would she run downstairs and tell the security guard if she'd just pushed Lula over the balcony?'

Strike did not answer directly; he seemed to be following his own train of thought, and after a moment or two replied:

'Bristow's fixated on the quarter of an hour after his sister went inside, after the photographers had left and the security guard had abandoned the desk because he was ill. That meant the lobby became briefly navigable – but how was anyone outside the building supposed to know that Wilson had left his post? The front door's not made of glass.'

'Plus,' interjected Robin intelligently, 'they'd have needed to know the key code to open the front door.'

'People get slack. Unless the security people change it regularly, loads of undesirables could have known that code. Let's have a look down here.'

They walked in silence right to the end of Kentigern Gardens, where they found a narrow alleyway which ran, at a slightly oblique angle, along the rear of Landry's block of houses. Strike was amused to note that the alley was called Serf's Way. Wide enough to allow a single car to pass, it had plentiful lighting and was devoid of hiding places, with long, high, smooth walls on either side of the cobbled passageway. They came in due course to a pair of large, electrically operated garage doors, with an enormous *PRIVATE* sign affixed to the wall beside them, which guarded the entrance to the underground cache of parking spaces for the Kentigern Gardeners.

When he judged that they were roughly level with the back of number 18, Strike made a leap, caught hold of the top of the wall and heaved himself up to look into a long row of small, carefully manicured gardens. Between each patch of smooth and well-tended lawn and the house to which it belonged was a shadowy stairwell to basement level. Anyone wishing to climb the rear of the house would, in Strike's opinion, require ladders, or a partner to belay him, and some sturdy ropes.

He let himself slide back down the wall, emitting a stifled grunt of pain as he landed on the prosthetic leg.

'It's nothing,' he said, when Robin made a concerned noise; she had noticed the vestige of a limp, and wondered whether he had sprained an ankle.

The chafing on the end of the stump was not helped by hobbling off over the cobbles. It was much harder, given the rigid construction of his false ankle, to navigate uneven surfaces. Strike asked himself ruefully whether he had really needed to hoist himself up on the wall at all. Robin might be a pretty girl, but she could not hold a candle to the woman he had just left.

3

'And you're *sure* he's a detective, are you? Because anyone can do that. Anyone can google people.'

Matthew was irritable after a long day, a disgruntled client and an unsatisfactory encounter with his new boss. He did not appreciate what struck him as naive and misplaced admiration for another man on the part of his fiancée.

'*He* wasn't googling people,' said Robin. '*I* was the one doing the googling, while he was working on another case.'

'Well I don't like the sound of the set-up. He's sleeping in his office, Robin; don't you think there's something a bit fishy there?'

'I told you, I think he's just split up with his partner.'

'Yeah, I'll bet he has,' said Matthew.

Robin dropped his plate down on top of her own and stalked off into the kitchen. She was angry at Matthew, and vaguely annoyed with Strike, too. She had enjoyed tracking Lula Landry's acquaintance across cyberspace that day; but seeing it retrospectively through Matthew's eyes, it seemed to her that Strike had given her a pointless, time-filling job.

'Look, I'm not *saying* anything,' Matthew said, from the kitchen doorway. 'I just think he sounds weird. And what's with the little afternoon walks?'

'It wasn't a *little afternoon walk*, Matt. We went to see the scene of the – we went to see the place where the client thinks something happened.'

'Robin, there's no need to make such a bloody mystery about it,' Matthew laughed.

'I've signed a confidentiality agreement,' she snapped over her shoulder. 'I can't tell you about the case.'

'*The case.*'

He gave another short, scoffing laugh.

Robin strode around the tiny kitchen, putting away ingredients, slamming cupboard doors. After a while, watching her figure as she moved around, Matthew came to feel that he might have been unreasonable. He came up behind her as she was scraping the leftovers into the bin, put his arms around her, buried his face in her neck and cupped and stroked the breast that bore the bruises Strike had accidentally inflicted, and which had irrevocably coloured Matthew's view of the man. He murmured conciliatory phrases into Robin's honey-coloured hair; but she pulled away from him to put the plates into the sink.

Robin felt as though her own worth had been impugned. Strike had seemed interested in the things she had found online. Strike expressed gratitude for her efficiency and initiative.

'How many proper interviews have you got next week?' Matthew asked, as she turned on the cold tap.

'Three,' she shouted over the noise of the gushing water, scrubbing the top plate aggressively.

She waited until he had walked away into the sitting room before turning off the tap. There was, she noticed, a fragment of frozen pea caught in the setting of her engagement ring.

4

Strike arrived at Charlotte's flat at half past nine on Friday morning. This gave her, he reasoned, half an hour to be well clear of the place before he entered it, assuming that she really was intending to leave, rather than lie in wait for him. The grand and gracious white buildings that lined the wide street; the plane trees; the butcher's shop that might have been stuck in the 1950s; the cafés bustling with the upper middle classes; the sleek restaurants; they had always felt slightly unreal and stagey to Strike. Perhaps he had always known, deep down, that he would not stay, that he did not belong.

Until the moment he unlocked the front door, he expected her to be there; yet as soon as he stepped over the threshold, he knew that the place was empty. The silence had that slack quality that speaks only of the indifference of uninhabited rooms, and his footsteps sounded alien and overloud as he made his way down the hall.

Four cardboard boxes stood in the middle of the sitting room, open for him to inspect. Here were his cheap and serviceable belongings, heaped together, like jumble-sale objects. He lifted a few things up to check the deeper levels, but nothing seemed to have been smashed, ripped or covered in paint. Other people his age had houses and washing machines, cars and television sets, furniture and gardens and mountain bikes and lawnmowers: he had four boxes of crap, and a set of matchless memories.

The silent room in which he stood spoke of a confident good taste, with its antique rug and its pale flesh-pink walls; its fine dark-wood furniture and its overflowing bookcases. The only change he spotted since Sunday night stood on the glass end table beside the sofa. On Sunday night there had been a picture of himself and Charlotte, laughing on the beach at St Mawes. Now a black-and-white studio portrait of Charlotte's dead father smiled benignly at Strike from the same silver picture frame.

Over the mantelpiece hung a portrait of an eighteen-year-old Charlotte, in oils. It showed the face of a Florentine angel in a cloud of long dark hair. Hers was the kind of family that commissioned painters to immortalise its young: a background utterly alien to Strike, and one he had come to know like a dangerous foreign country. From Charlotte he had learned that the kind of money he had never known could coexist with unhappiness and savagery. Her family, for all their gracious manners, their suavity and flair, their erudition and occasional flamboyance, was even madder and stranger than his own. That had been a powerful link between them, when first he and Charlotte had come together.

A strange stray thought came to him now, as he looked up at that portrait: that this was the reason it had been painted, so that one day, its large hazel-green eyes would watch him leave. Had Charlotte known what it would feel like, to prowl the empty flat under the eyes of her stunning eighteen-year-old self? Had she realised that the painting would do her work better than her physical presence?

He turned away, striding through the other rooms, but she had left nothing for him to do. Every trace of him, from his tooth floss to his army boots, had been taken and deposited in the boxes. He studied the bedroom with particular attention, and the room looked back at him, with its dark floorboards, white curtains and delicate dressing table, calm and composed. The bed, like the portrait, seemed a living, breathing presence. *Remember what happened here, and what can never happen again.*

He carried the four boxes one by one out on to the doorstep, on the last trip coming face to face with the smirking next-door neighbour, who was locking his own front door. He wore rugby shirts with the collars turned up, and always brayed with panting laughter at Charlotte's lightest witticisms.

'Having a clear-out?' he asked.

Strike shut Charlotte's door firmly on him.

He slid the door keys off his key ring in front of the hall mirror, and laid them carefully on the half-moon table, next to the bowl of potpourri. Strike's face in the glass was creviced and dirty-looking; his right eye still puffy; yellow and mauve. A voice from seventeen years before came to him in the silence: 'How the fuck did a pube-headed trog like you ever pull *that*, Strike?' And it seemed incredible that he ever had, as he stood there in the hall he would never see again.

One last moment of madness, the space between heartbeats, like the one that had sent him hurtling after her five days previously: he would stay here, after all, waiting for her to return; then cupping her perfect face in his hands and saying 'Let's try again.'

But they had already tried, again and again and again, and always, when the first crashing wave of mutual longing subsided, the ugly wreck of the past lay revealed again, its shadow lying darkly over everything they tried to rebuild.

He closed the front door behind him for the last time. The braying neighbour had vanished. Strike lifted the four boxes down the steps on to the pavement, and waited to hail a black cab.

5

Strike had told Robin that he would be late into the office on her last morning. He had given her the spare key, and told her to let herself in.

She had been very slightly hurt by his casual use of the word 'last'. It told her that however well they had got along, albeit in a guarded and professional way; however much more organised his office was, and how much cleaner the horrible washroom outside the glass door; however much better the bell downstairs looked, without that scrappy piece of paper taped beneath it, but a neatly typed name in the clear plastic holder (it had taken her half an hour, and cost her two broken nails, to prise the cover off); however efficient she had been at taking messages, however intelligently she had discussed the almost certainly nonexistent killer of Lula Landry, Strike had been counting down the days until he could get rid of her.

That he could not afford a temporary secretary was perfectly obvious. He had only two clients; he seemed (as Matthew kept mentioning, as though sleeping in an office was a mark of terrible depravity) to be homeless; Robin saw, of course, that from Strike's point of view it made no sense to keep her on. But she was not looking forward to Monday. There would be a strange new office (Temporary Solutions had already telephoned through the address); a neat, bright, bustling place, no doubt, full of gossipy women as most of these offices were, all engaged in activities that meant less than nothing to her. Robin might not believe in a murderer; she knew that Strike did not believe either; but the process of proving one nonexistent fascinated her.

Robin had found the whole week more exciting than she would ever have confessed to Matthew. All of it, even calling Freddie Bestigui's production company, BestFilms, twice a day, and receiving repeated refusals to her requests to be put through to the film producer, had given her a sense of importance she had rarely experienced during her working life. Robin was fascinated by the interior workings of other people's minds: she had been halfway through a psychology degree when an unforeseen incident had finished her university career.

Half past ten, and Strike had still not returned to the office, but a large woman wearing a nervous smile, an orange coat and a purple knitted beret *had* arrived. This was Mrs Hook, a name familiar to Robin because it was that of Strike's only other client. Robin installed Mrs Hook on the sagging sofa beside her own desk, and fetched her a cup of tea. (Acting on Robin's awkward description of the lascivious Mr Crowdy downstairs, Strike had bought cheap cups and a box of their own tea bags.)

'I know I'm early,' said Mrs Hook, for the third time, taking ineffectual little sips of boiling tea. 'I haven't seen you before, are you new?'

'I'm temporary,' said Robin.

'As I expect you've guessed, it's my husband,' said Mrs Hook, not listening. 'I suppose you see women like me all the time, don't you? Wanting to know the worst. I dithered for ages and ages. But it's best to know, isn't it? Best to know. I thought Cormoran would be here. Is he out on another case?'

'That's right,' said Robin, who suspected that Strike was actually doing something related to his mysterious personal life;

there had been a caginess about him as he had told her he would be late.

'Do you know who his father is?' asked Mrs Hook.

'No, I don't,' said Robin, thinking that they were talking about the poor woman's husband.

'Jonny Rokeby,' said Mrs Hook, with a kind of dramatic relish.

'Jonny Roke—'

Robin caught her breath, realising simultaneously that Mrs Hook meant Strike, and that Strike's massive frame was looming up outside the glass door. She could see that he was carrying something very large.

'Just one moment, Mrs Hook,' she said.

'What?' asked Strike, peering around the edge of the cardboard box, as Robin darted out of the glass door and closed it behind her.

'Mrs Hook's here,' she whispered.

'Oh, for fuck's sake. She's an hour early.'

'I know. I thought you might want to, um, organise your office a bit before you take her in there.'

Strike eased the cardboard box on to the metal floor.

'I've got to bring these in off the street,' he said.

'I'll help,' offered Robin.

'No, you go and make polite conversation. She's taking a pottery class and she thinks her husband's sleeping with his accountant.'

Strike limped off down the stairs, leaving the box beside the glass door.

Jonny Rokeby; could it be true?

'He's on his way, just coming,' Robin told Mrs Hook brightly, resettling herself at her desk. 'Mr Strike told me you do pottery. I've always wanted to try . . . '

For five minutes, Robin barely listened to the exploits of the pottery class, and the sweetly understanding young man who taught them. Then the glass door opened and Strike entered, unencumbered by boxes and smiling politely at Mrs Hook, who jumped up to greet him.

'Oh, Cormoran, your eye!' she said. 'Has somebody punched you?'

'No,' said Strike. 'If you'll give me a moment, Mrs Hook, I'll get out your file.'

'I know I'm early, Cormoran, and I'm awfully sorry . . . I couldn't sleep at all last night . . . '

'Let me take your cup, Mrs Hook,' said Robin, and she successfully distracted the client from glimpsing, in the seconds it took Strike to slip through the inner door, the camp bed, the sleeping bag and the kettle.

A few minutes later, Strike re-emerged on a waft of artificial limes, and Mrs Hook vanished, with a terrified look at Robin, into his office. The door closed behind them.

Robin sat down at her desk again. She had already opened the morning's post. She swung side to side on her swivel chair; then she moved to the computer and casually brought up Wikipedia. Then, with a disengaged air, as though she was unaware of what her fingers were up to, she typed in the two names: *Rokeby Strike.*

The entry appeared at once, headed by a black-and-white photograph of an instantly recognisable man, famous for four decades. He had a narrow Harlequin's face and wild eyes, which were easy to caricature, the left one slightly off-kilter due to a weak divergent squint; his mouth was wide open, sweat pouring down his face, hair flying as he bellowed into a microphone.

Jonathan Leonard 'Jonny' Rokeby, b. August 1st 1948, is the lead singer of 70s rock band The Deadbeats, member of the Rock and Roll Hall of Fame, multi-Grammy award winner . . .

Strike looked nothing like him; the only slight resemblance was in the inequality of the eyes, which in Strike was, after all, a transient condition.

Down the entry Robin scrolled:

. . . multi-platinum album Hold It Back in 1975. A record-breaking tour of America was interrupted by a drugs bust in LA and the arrest of new guitarist David Carr, with whom . . .

until she reached **Personal Life**:

Rokeby has been married three times: to art-school girlfriend Shirley Mullens (1969–1973), with whom he has one daughter, Maimie; to model, actress and human rights activist Carla Astolfi (1975–1979), with whom he has two daughters, television presenter Gabriella Rokeby and jewellery designer Daniella Rokeby, and (1981–present) to film producer Jenny Graham, with whom he has two sons, Edward and Al. Rokeby also has a daughter, Prudence Donleavy, from his relationship with the actress Lindsey Fanthrope, and a son, Cormoran, with 1970s supergroupie Leda Strike.

A piercing scream rose in the inner office behind Robin. She jumped to her feet, her chair skittering away from her on its wheels. The scream became louder and shriller. Robin ran across the office to pull open the inner door.

Mrs Hook, divested of orange coat and purple beret, and

wearing what looked like a flowery pottery smock over jeans, had thrown herself on Strike's chest and was punching it, all the while making a noise like a boiling kettle. On and on the one-note scream went, until it seemed that she must draw breath or suffocate.

'Mrs Hook!' cried Robin, and she seized the woman's flabby upper arms from behind, attempting to relieve Strike of the responsibility of fending her off. Mrs Hook, however, was much more powerful than she looked; though she paused to breathe, she continued to punch Strike until, having no choice, he caught both her wrists and held them in mid-air.

At this, Mrs Hook twisted free of his loose grip and flung herself on Robin instead, howling like a dog.

Patting the sobbing woman on the back, Robin manoeuvred her, by minuscule increments, back into the outer office.

'It's all right, Mrs Hook, it's all right,' she said soothingly, lowering her into the sofa. 'Let me get you a cup of tea. It's all right.'

'I'm very sorry, Mrs Hook,' said Strike formally, from the doorway into his office. 'It's never easy to get news like this.'

'I th-thought it was Valerie,' whimpered Mrs Hook, her dishevelled head in her hands, rocking backwards and forwards on the groaning sofa. 'I th-thought it was Valerie, n-not my own – n-not my own *sister*.'

'I'll get tea!' whispered Robin, appalled.

She was almost out of the door with the kettle when she remembered that she had left Jonny Rokeby's life story up on the computer monitor. It would look too odd to dart back to switch it off in the middle of this crisis, so she hurried out of the room, hoping that Strike would be too busy with Mrs Hook to notice.

It took a further forty minutes for Mrs Hook to drink her second cup of tea and sob her way through half the toilet roll Robin had liberated from the bathroom on the landing. At last she left, clutching the folder full of incriminating photographs, and the index detailing the time and place of their creation, her breast heaving, still mopping her eyes.

Strike waited until she was clear of the end of the street, then went out, humming cheerfully, to buy sandwiches for himself and Robin, which they enjoyed together at her desk. It was the friendliest gesture that he had made during their week together, and Robin was sure that this was because he knew that he would soon be free of her.

'You know I'm going out this afternoon to interview Derrick Wilson?' he asked.

'The security guard who had diarrhoea,' said Robin. 'Yes.'

'You'll be gone when I get back, so I'll sign your time sheet before I go. And listen, thanks for . . .'

Strike nodded at the now empty sofa.

'Oh, no problem. Poor woman.'

'Yeah. She's got the goods on him anyway. And,' he continued, 'thanks for everything you've done this week.'

'It's my job,' said Robin lightly.

'If I could afford a secretary . . . but I expect you'll end up pulling down a serious salary as some fat cat's PA.'

Robin felt obscurely offended.

'That's not the kind of job I want,' she said.

There was a slightly strained silence.

Strike was undergoing a small internal struggle. The prospect of Robin's desk being empty next week was a gloomy one; he found her company pleasantly undemanding, and her efficiency refreshing; but it would surely be pathetic, not to mention profligate, to pay for companionship, as though he were some rich, sickly Victorian magnate? Temporary Solutions were rapacious in their demand for commission; Robin was a luxury he could not afford. The fact that she had not questioned him about his father (for Strike had noticed Jonny Rokeby's Wikipedia entry on the computer monitor) had impressed him further in her favour, for this showed unusual restraint, and was a standard by which he often judged new acquaintances. But it could make no difference to the cold practicalities of the situation: she had to go.

And yet he was close to feeling about her as he had felt towards a grass snake that he had succeeded in trapping in Trevaylor Woods when he was eleven, and about which he had had a long, pleading argument with his Auntie Joan: '*Please* let me keep it ... *please* ...'

'I'd better get going,' he said, after he had signed her time sheet, and thrown his sandwich wrappers and his empty water bottle into the bin underneath her desk. 'Thanks for everything, Robin. Good luck with the job hunt.'

He took down his overcoat, and left through the glass door.

At the top of the stairs, on the precise spot where he had both nearly killed and then saved her, he came to a halt. Instinct was clawing at him like an importuning dog.

The glass door banged open behind him and he turned. Robin was pink in the face.

'Look,' she said. 'We could come to a private arrangement. We could cut out Temporary Solutions, and you could pay me directly.'

He hesitated.

'They don't like that, temping agencies. You'll be drummed out of the service.'

'It doesn't matter. I've got three interviews for permanent jobs next week. If you'd be OK about me taking time off to go to them—'

'Yeah, no problem,' he said, before he could stop himself.

'Well then, I could stay for another week or two.'

A pause. Sense entered into a short, violent skirmish with instinct and inclination, and was overwhelmed.

'Yeah . . . all right. Well, in that case, will you try Freddie Bestigui again?'

'Yes, of course,' said Robin, masking her glee under a show of calm efficiency.

'I'll see you Monday afternoon, then.'

It was the first grin he had ever dared give her. He supposed he ought to be annoyed with himself, and yet Strike stepped out into the cool early afternoon with no feeling of regret, but rather a curious sense of renewed optimism.

6

Strike had once tried to count the number of schools he had attended in his youth, and had reached the figure of seventeen with the suspicion that he had forgotten a couple. He did not include the brief period of supposed home schooling which had taken place during the two months he had lived with his mother and half-sister in a squat in Atlantic Road in Brixton. His mother's then boyfriend, a white Rastafarian musician who had rechristened himself Shumba, felt that the school system reinforced patriarchal and materialistic values with which his common-law stepchildren ought not to be tainted. The principal lesson that Strike had learned during his two months of home-based education was that cannabis, even if administered spiritually, could render the taker both dull and paranoid.

He took an unnecessary detour through Brixton Market on the way to the café where he was meeting Derrick Wilson. The fishy smell of the covered arcades; the colourful open faces of the supermarkets, teeming with unfamiliar fruit and vegetables from Africa and the West Indies; the halal butchers and the hairdressers, with large pictures of ornate braids and curls, and rows and rows of white polystyrene heads bearing wigs in the windows: all of it took Strike back twenty-six years, to the months he had spent wandering the Brixton streets with Lucy, his young half-sister, while his mother and Shumba lay dozily on dirty cushions back at the squat, vaguely discussing the important spiritual concepts in which the children ought to be instructed.

Seven-year-old Lucy had yearned for hair like the West Indian girls. On the long drive back to St Mawes that had terminated their Brixton life, she had expressed a fervent desire for beaded braids from the back seat of Uncle Ted and Aunt Joan's Morris Minor. Strike remembered Aunt Joan's calm agreement that the style was very pretty, a frown line between her eyebrows reflected in the rear-view mirror. Joan had tried, with diminishing success through the years, not to disparage their mother in front of the children. Strike had never discovered how Uncle Ted had found out where they were living; all he knew was that he and Lucy had let themselves into the squat one afternoon to find their mother's enormous brother standing in the middle of the room, threatening Shumba with a bloody nose. Within two days, he and Lucy were back in St Mawes, at the primary school they attended intermittently for years, taking up with old friends as though they had not left, and swiftly losing the accents they had adopted for camouflage, wherever Leda had last taken them.

He had not needed the directions Derrick Wilson had given Robin, because he knew the Phoenix Café on Coldharbour Lane of old. Occasionally Shumba and his mother had taken them there: a tiny, brown-painted, shed-like place where you could (if not a vegetarian, like Shumba and his mother) eat large and delicious cooked breakfasts, with eggs and bacon piled high, and mugs of tea the colour of teak. It was almost exactly as he remembered: cosy, snug and dingy, its mirrored walls reflecting tables of mock-wood Formica, stained floor tiles of dark red and white, and a tapioca-coloured ceiling covered in moulded wallpaper. The squat middle-aged waitress had short straightened hair and dangling orange plastic earrings; she moved aside to let Strike past the counter.

A heavily built West Indian man was sitting alone at one table, reading a copy of the *Sun*, under a plastic clock that bore the legend *Pukka Pies*.

'Derrick?'

'Yeah . . . you Strike?'

Strike shook Wilson's big, dry hand, and sat down. He estimated Wilson to be almost as tall as himself when standing. Muscle as well as fat swelled the sleeves of the security guard's sweatshirt; his hair was close-cropped and he was clean-shaven, with fine almond-shaped eyes. Strike ordered pie and mash off the scrawled menu board on the back wall, pleased to reflect that he could charge the £4.75 to expenses.

'Yeah, the pie 'n' mash is good here,' said Wilson.

A faint Caribbean lilt lifted his London accent. His voice was deep, calm and measured. Strike thought that he would be a reassuring presence in a security guard's uniform.

'Thanks for meeting me, I appreciate it. John Bristow's not happy with the results of the inquest on his sister. He's hired me to take another look at the evidence.'

'Yeah,' said Wilson, 'I know.'

'How much did he give you to talk to me?' Strike asked casually.

Wilson blinked, then gave a slightly guilty, deep-throated chuckle.

'Pony,' he said. 'But if it makes the man feel better, yuh know? It won't change nuthin'. She killed huhself. But ask your questions. I don't mind.'

He closed the *Sun*. The front page bore a picture of Gordon Brown looking baggy-eyed and exhausted.

'You'll have gone over everything with the police,' said Strike, opening his notebook and setting it down beside his plate, 'but it would be good to hear, first hand, what happened that night.'

'Yeah, no problem. An' Kieran Kolovas-Jones might be comin',' Wilson added.

He seemed to expect Strike to know who this was.

'Who?' asked Strike.

'Kieran Kolovas-Jones. He was Lula's regular driver. He wants to talk to you too.'

'OK, great,' said Strike. 'When will he be here?'

'I dunno. He's on a job. He'll come if he can.'

The waitress put a mug of tea in front of Strike, who thanked her and clicked out the nib of his pen. Before he could ask anything, Wilson said:

'You're ex-milit'ry, Mister Bristow said.'

'Yeah,' said Strike.

'Mi nephew's in Afghanistan,' said Wilson, sipping his tea. 'Helmand Province.'

'What regiment?'

'Signals,' said Wilson.

'How long's he been out there?'

'Four month. His mother's not sleeping,' said Wilson. 'How come you left?'

'Got my leg blown off,' said Strike, with an honesty that was not habitual.

It was only part of the truth, but the easiest part to communicate to a stranger. He could have stayed; they had been keen to keep him; but the loss of his calf and foot had merely precipitated a decision he had felt stealing towards him in the past couple of years. He knew that his personal tipping point was drawing nearer; that moment by which, unless he left, he would find it too onerous to go, to readjust to civilian life. The army shaped you, almost imperceptibly, with the years; wore you into a surface conformity that made it easier to be swept along by the tidal force of military life. Strike had never become entirely submerged, and had chosen to go before that happened. Even so, he remembered the SIB with a fondness that was unaffected by the loss of half a limb. He would have been glad to remember Charlotte with the same uncomplicated affection.

Wilson acknowledged Strike's explanation with a slow nod of the head.

'Tough,' he said, in his deep voice.

'I got off light compared with some.'

'Yeah. Guy in mi nephew's platoon got blown up two weeks ago.'

Wilson sipped his tea.

'How did you get on with Lula Landry?' Strike asked, pen poised. 'Did you see a lot of her?'

'Just in and out past the desk. She always said hullo and please and thank you, which is more'n a whole lotta these rich fuckers manage,' said Wilson laconically. 'Longest chat we ever had was about Jamaica. She was thinking of doing a job over there; asking me where tuh stay, what's it like. And I got her autograph for mi nephew, Jason, for his birthday. Got her to sign a card, sent it outta Afghanistan. Just three weeks before she died. She asked after Jason by name every time I saw her after that, and I liked the girl for that, y'know? I been knocking around the security game forra long time. There's people who'd expect you to take a bullet for them and they don't bother rememb'ring yuh name. Yeah, she was all right.'

Strike's pie and mash arrived, steaming hot. The two men accorded it a moment's respectful silence as they contemplated the heaped plate. Mouth watering, Strike picked up his knife and fork and said:

'Can you talk me through what happened the night Lula died? She went out, what time?'

The security guard scratched his forearm thoughtfully, pushing up the sleeve of his sweatshirt; Strike saw tattoos there, crosses and initials.

'Musta bin just gone seven that evening. She was with her friend Ciara Porter. I remember, as they were going out the door, Mr Bestigui come in. I remember that, because he said something to Lula. I didn't hear what it was. She didn't like it, though. I could tell by the look on her face.'

'What kind of look?'

'Offended,' said Wilson, the answer ready. 'So then I seen the two of them on the monitor, Lula and Porter, getting in their car. We gotta camera over the door, see. It's linked to a monitor on the desk, so we can see who's buzzing to get in.'

'Does it record footage? Can I see a tape?'

Wilson shook his head.

'Mr Bestigui didn't want nothing like that on the door. No recording devices. He was the first to buy a flat, before they were all finished, so he had input into the arrangements.'

'The camera's just a high-tech peephole, then?'

Wilson nodded. There was a fine scar running from just beneath his left eye to the middle of his cheekbone.

'Yeah. So I seen the girls get into their car. Kieran, guy who's coming to meet us here, wasn't driving her that night. He was supposedta be picking up Deeby Macc.'

'Who was her chauffeur that night?'

'Guy called Mick, from Execars. She'd had him before. I seen all the photographers crowdin' round the car as it pulled away. They'd been sniffin' around all week, because they knew she was back with Evan Duffield.'

'What did Bestigui do, once Lula and Ciara had left?'

'He collected his post from me and went up the stairs to his flat.'

Strike was putting down his fork with every mouthful, to make notes.

'Anyone go in or out after that?'

'Yeah, the caterers – they'd been up at the Bestiguis' because they were having guests that night. An American couple arrived just after eight and went up to Flat One, and nobody come in or out till they left again, near midnight. Didn't see no one else till Lula come home, round half past one.

'I heard the paps shouting her name outside. Big crowd by that time. A bunch of them had followed her from the night-club, and there was a load waiting there already, looking out for Deeby Macc. He was supposedta be getting there round half twelve. Lula pressed the bell and I buzzed her in.'

'She didn't punch the code into the keypad?'

'Not with them all around her; she wanted to get in quick. They were yelling, pressing in on her.'

'Couldn't she have gone in through the underground car park and avoided them?'

'Yeah, she did that sometimes when Kieran was with her, 'cause she'd given him a control for the electric doors to the garage. But Mick didn't have one, so it had to be the front.

'I said good morning, and I asked about the snow, 'cause she had some in her hair; she was shivering, wearin' a skimpy little dress. She said it was way below freezing, something like that.

Then she said, "I wish they'd fuck off. Are they gonna stay there all night?" 'Bout the paps. I told her they were still waiting for Deeby Macc; he was late. She looked pissed off. Then she got in the lift and went up to her flat.'

'She looked pissed off?'

'Yeah, really pissed off.'

'Suicidal pissed off?'

'No,' said Wilson. 'Angry pissed off.'

'Then what happened?'

'Then,' said Wilson, 'I had to go into the back room. My guts were starting to feel really bad. I needed the bathroom. Urgent, yuh know. I'd caught what Robson had. He was off sick with his belly. I was away maybe fifteen minutes. No choice. Never had the shits like it.

'I was still in the can when the bawling started. No,' he corrected himself, 'first thing I heard was a bang. Big bang in the distance. I realised later, that must've been the body – Lula, I mean – falling.

'*Then* the bawlin' started, getting louder, coming down the stairs. So I pull up my pants and go running out into the lobby, and there's Mrs Bestigui, shaking and screaming and acting like one mad bitch in her underwear. She says Lula's dead, that she's been pushed off her balcony by a man in her flat.

'I tell her to stay where she is and I run out the front door. And there she was. Lyin' in the middle of the road, face down in the snow.'

Wilson swigged his tea, and continued to cradle the mug in his large hand as he said:

'Half her head was caved in. Blood in the snow. I could tell her neck was broken. And there was – yeah.'

The sweet and unmistakable smell of human brains seemed

to fill Strike's nostrils. He had smelled it many times. You never forgot.

'I ran back inside,' resumed Wilson. 'Both the Bestiguis were in the lobby; he was tryin' to get her back upstairs, inna some clothes, and she was still bawling. I told them to call the police and to keep an eye on the lift, in case he tried to come down that way.

'I grabbed the master key out the back room and I ran upstairs. No one on the stairwell. I unlocked the door of Lula's flat—'

'Didn't you think of taking anything with you, to defend yourself?' Strike interrupted. 'If you thought there was someone in there? Someone who'd just killed a woman?'

There was a long pause, the longest so far.

'Didn't think I'd need nothing,' said Wilson. 'Thought I could take him, no problem.'

'Take who?'

'Duffield,' said Wilson quietly. 'I thought Duffield was up there.'

'Why?'

'I thought he musta come in while I was in the bathroom. He knew the key code. I thought he musta gone upstairs and she'd let him in. I'd heard them rowing before. I'd heard him angry. Yeah. I thought he'd pushed her.

'But when I got up to the flat, it was empty. I looked in every room and there was no one there. I opened the wardrobes, even, but nothing.

'The windows in the lounge was wide open. It was below freezing that night. I didn't close them, I didn't touch nothing. I come out and pressed the button on the lift. The doors opened straight away; it was still at her floor. It was empty.

'I ran back downstairs. The Bestiguis were in their flat when I passed their door; I could hear them; she was still bawling and he was still shouting at her. I didn't know whether they'd called the police yet. I grabbed my mobile off the security desk and I went back out the front door, back to Lula, because – well, I didn't like to leave her lying there alone. I was gonna call the police from the street, make sure they were coming. But I heard the siren before I'd even pressed nine. They were there quick.'

'One of the Bestiguis had called them, had they?'

'Yeah. He had. Two uniformed coppers in a panda car.'

'OK,' said Strike. 'I want to be clear on this one point: you believed Mrs Bestigui when she said she'd heard a man up in the top flat?'

'Oh yeah,' said Wilson.

'Why?'

Wilson frowned slightly, thinking, his eyes on the street over Strike's right shoulder.

'She hadn't given you any details at this point, had she?' Strike asked. 'Nothing about what she'd been doing when she heard this man? Nothing to explain why she was awake at two in the morning?'

'No,' said Wilson. 'She never gave me no explanation like that. It was the way she was acting, y'know. Hysterical. Shaking like a wet dog. She kept saying "There's a man up there, he threw her over." She was proper scared.

'But there was nobody there; I can swear that to you on the lives of mi kids. The flat was empty, the lift was empty, the stairwell was empty. If he was there, where did he go?'

'The police came,' Strike said, returning mentally to the dark, snowy street, and the broken corpse. 'What happened then?'

'When Mrs Bestigui saw the police car out her window, she

came straight back down in her dressing gown, with her husband running after her; she come out into the street, into the snow, and starts bawling at them that there's a murderer in the building.

'Lights are going on all over the place now. Faces at windows. Half the street's woken up. People coming out on to the pavements.

'One of the coppers stayed with the body, calling for back-up on his radio, while the other one went with us – me and the Bestiguis – back inside. He told them to go back in their flat and wait, and then he got me to show him the building. We went up to the top floor again; I opened up Lula's door, showed him the flat, the open window. He checked the place over. I showed him the lift, still on her floor. We went back down the stairs. He asked about the middle flat, so I opened it up with the master key.

'It was dark, and the alarm went off when we went in. Before I could find the light switch or get to the alarm pad, the copper walked straight into the table in the middle of the hall and knocked over this massive vase of roses. Smashed and went everywhere, glass an' water an' flowers all over the floor. That caused a loada trouble, later . . .

'We checked the place. Empty, all the cupboards, every room. The windows were closed and bolted. We went back to the lobby.

'Plain-clothes police had arrived by this time. They wanted keys to the basement gym, the pool and the car park. One of 'em went off to take a statement from Mrs Bestigui, another one was out front, calling for more back-up, because there are more neighbours coming out in the street now, and half of them are talking on the phone while they're standing there, and some of them are taking pictures. The uniformed coppers are trying to make them go back into their houses. It's snowing, really heavy snow . . .

'They got a tent up over the body when forensics arrived. The press arrived round the same time. The police taped off half the street, blocked it off with their cars.'

Strike had cleaned his plate. He shoved it aside, ordered fresh mugs of tea for both of them and took up his pen again.

'How many people work at number eighteen?'

'There's three guards – me, Colin McLeod an' Ian Robson. We work in shifts, someone always on duty, round the clock. I shoulda been off that night, but Robson called me roundabout four in the afternoon, said he had this stomach bug, felt really bad with it. So I said I'd stay on, work through the next shift. He'd swapped with me the previous month so I could sort out a bit of fambly business. I owed him.

'So it shouldn'ta been me there,' said Wilson, and for a moment he sat in silence, contemplating the way things should have been.

'The other guards got on OK with Lula, did they?'

'Yeah, they'd tell yuh same as me. Nice girl.'

'Anyone else work there?'

'We gotta couple of Polish cleaners. They both got bad English. You won't get much outta them.'

Wilson's testimony, Strike thought, as he scribbled into one of the SIB notebooks he had filched on one of his last visits to Aldershot, was of an unusually high quality: concise, precise and observant. Very few people answered the question they had been posed; even fewer knew how to organise their thoughts so that no follow-up questions were needed to prise information out of them. Strike was used to playing archaeologist among the ruins of people's traumatised memories; he had made himself the confidant of thugs; he had bullied the terrified, baited the dangerous and laid traps for the cunning. None of these skills were required with Wilson, who seemed almost wasted on a pointless trawl through John Bristow's paranoia.

Nevertheless, Strike had an incurable habit of thoroughness. It would no more have occurred to him to skimp on the interview than to spend the day lying in his underpants on his camp bed, smoking. Both by inclination and by training, because he owed himself respect quite as much as the client, he proceeded with the meticulousness for which, in the army, he had been both feted and detested.

'Can we back up briefly and go through the day preceding her death? What time did you arrive for work?'

'Nine, same as always. Took over from Colin.'

'Do you keep a log of who goes in and out of the building?'

'Yeah, we sign everyone in and out, 'cept residents. There's a book at the desk.'

'Can you remember who went in and out that day?'

Wilson hesitated.

'John Bristow came to see his sister early that morning, didn't he?' prompted Strike. 'But she'd told you not to let him up?'

'He's told you that, has he?' asked Wilson, looking faintly relieved. 'Yeah, she did. But I felt sorry for the man, y'know? He had a contrac' to give back to her; he was worried about it, so I let him go up.'

'Had anyone else come into the building that you know of?'

'Yeah, Lechsinka was already there. She's one of the cleaners. She always arrives at seven; she was mopping the stairwell when I got in. Nobody else came until the guy from the security comp'ny, to service the alarms. We get it done every six months. He musta come around nine forty; something like that.'

'Was this someone you knew, the man from the security firm?'

'No, he was a new guy. Very young. They always send someone diff'rent. Missus Bestigui and Lula were still at home, so I let him into the middle flat, and showed him where the control panel was an' got him started. Lula went out while I was still in there, showin' the guy the fuse box an' the panic buttons.'

'You saw her go out, did you?'

'Yeah, she passed the open door.'

'Did she say hello?'

'No.'

'You said she usually did?'

'I don't think she noticed me. She looked like she was in a hurry. She was going to see her sick mother.'

'How d'you know, if she didn't speak to you?'

'Inquest,' said Wilson succinctly. 'After I'd shown the security guy where everything was, I went back downstairs, an' after Missus Bestigui went out, I let him into their flat to check that system too. He didn't need me tuh stay with him there; the positions of the fuse boxes and panic buttons are the same in all the flats.'

'Where was Mr Bestigui?'

'He'd already left for work. Eight he leaves, every day.'

Three men in hard hats and fluorescent yellow jackets entered the café and sat at a neighbouring table, newspapers under their arms, work boots clogged with filth.

'How long would you say you were away from the desk each time you were with the security guy?'

'Mebbe five minutes in the middle flat,' said Wilson. 'A minute each for the others.'

'When did the security guy leave?'

'Late morning. I can't remember exactly.'

'But you're sure he left?'

'Oh yeah.'

'Anyone else visit?'

'There was a few deliveries, but it was quiet compared to how the rest of the week had been.'

'Earlier in the week had been busy, had it?'

'Yeah, we'd had a lot of coming and going, because of Deeby Macc arriving from LA. People from the production company were in and out of Flat Two, checking the place was set up for him, filling up the fridge and that.'

'Can you remember what deliveries there were that day?'

'Packages for Macc an' Lula. An' roses – I helped the guy up with them, because they come in a massive,' Wilson placed his large hands apart to show the size, 'a huh-*uge* vase, and we set 'em up on a table in the hallway of Flat Two. That's the roses that got smashed.'

'You said that caused trouble; what did you mean?'

'Mister Bestigui had sent them to Deeby Macc an' when he heard they'd been ruined he was pissed off. Shoutin' like a maniac.'

'When was this?'

'While the police were there. When they were trying to interview his wife.'

'A woman had just fallen to her death past his front windows, and he was upset that someone had wrecked his flowers?'

'Yeah,' said Wilson, with a slight shrug. 'He's like that.'

'Does he know Deeby Macc?'

Wilson shrugged again.

'Did this rapper ever come to the flat?'

Wilson shook his head.

'After we had all this trouble, he went to a hotel.'

'How long were you away from the desk when you helped put the roses in Flat Two?'

'Mebbe five minutes; ten at most. After that, I was on the desk all day.'

'You mentioned packages for Macc and Lula.'

'Yeah, from some designer, but I gave them to Lechsinka to put in the flats. It was clothes for him an' handbags for her.'

'And as far as you're aware, everyone who went in that day went out again?'

'Oh yeah,' said Wilson. 'All logged in the book at the front desk.'

'How often is the code on the external keypad changed?'

'It's been changed since she died, because half the Met knew it by the time they were finished,' said Wilson. 'But it din change the three months Lula lived there.'

'D'you mind telling me what it was?'

'Nineteen sixty-six,' said Wilson.

'"They think it's all over"?'

'Yeah,' said Wilson. 'McLeod was always bellyaching about it. Wanted it changed.'

'How many people d'you think knew the door code before Lula died?'

'Not that many.'

'Delivery men? Postmen? Bloke who reads the gas meter?'

'People like that are always buzzed in by us, from the desk. The residents don't normally use the keypad, because we can see them on camera, so we open the door for them. The keypad's only there in case there's no one on the desk; sometimes we'd be in the back room, or helping with something upstairs.'

'And the flats all have individual keys?'

'Yeah, and individual alarm systems.'

'Was Lula's set?'

'No.'

'What about the pool and the gym? Are they alarmed?'

'Jus' keys. Everyone who lives in the building gets a set of pool and gym keys along with their flat keys. And one key to the door leading to the underground car park. That door's got an alarm on it.'

'Was it set?'

'Dunno, I wasn't there when they checked that one. It shoulda been. The guy from the security firm had checked all the alarms that morning.'

'Were all these doors locked that night?'

Wilson hesitated.

'Not all of them. The door to the pool was open.'

'Had anyone used it that day, do you know?'

'I can't remember anyone using it.'

'So how long had it been open?'

'I dunno. Colin was on the previous night. He shoulda checked it.'

'OK,' said Strike. 'You said you thought the man Mrs Bestigui had heard was Duffield, because you'd heard them arguing previously. When was that?'

'Not long before they split, 'bout two months before she died. She'd thrown him out of her flat and he was hammerin' on the door and kicking it, trying to break it down, calling her filthy names. I went upstairs to get him out.'

'Did you use force?'

'Didn't need to. When he saw me coming he picked up his stuff – she'd thrown his jacket and his shoes out after him – and just walked out past me. He was stoned,' said Wilson. 'Glassy eyes, y'know. Sweating. Filthy T-shirt with crap all down it. I never knew what the fuck she saw in him.

'And here's Kieran,' he added, his tone lightening. 'Lula's driver.'

7

A man in his mid-twenties was edging his way into the tiny café. He was short, slight and extravagantly good-looking.

'Hey, Derrick,' he said, and the driver and security guard exchanged a dap greeting, gripping each other's hands and bumping knuckles, before Kolovas-Jones took his seat beside Wilson.

A masterpiece produced by an indecipherable cocktail of races, Kolovas-Jones's skin was an olive-bronze, his cheekbones chiselled, his nose slightly aquiline, his black-lashed eyes a dark hazel, his straight hair slicked back off his face. His startling looks were thrown into relief by the conservative shirt and tie he wore, and his smile was consciously modest, as though he sought to disarm other men, and pre-empt their resentment.

'Where'sa car?' asked Derrick.

'Electric Lane.' Kolovas-Jones pointed with his thumb over his shoulder. 'I got maybe twenty minutes. Gotta be back at the West End by four. Howya doing?' he added, holding out his hand to Strike, who shook it. 'Kieran Kolovas-Jones. You're . . . ?'

'Cormoran Strike. Derrick says you've got—'

'Yeah, yeah,' said Kolovas-Jones. 'I dunno whether it matters, probably not, but the police didn't give a shit. I just wanna know I've told someone, right? I'm not saying it wasn't suicide, you understand,' he added. 'I'm just saying I'd like this thing cleared up. Coffee, please, love,' he added to the middle-aged waitress, who remained impassive, impervious to his charm.

'What's worrying you?' Strike asked.

'I always drove her, right?' said Kolovas-Jones, launching into his story in a way that told Strike he had rehearsed it. 'She always asked for me.'

'Did she have a contract with your company?'

'Yeah. Well . . . '

'It's run through the front desk,' said Derrick. 'One of the services provided. If anyone wants a car, we call Execars, Kieran's company.'

'Yeah, but she always asked for me,' Kolovas-Jones reiterated firmly.

'You got on with her, did you?'

'Yeah, we got on good,' said Kolovas-Jones. 'We'd got – you know – I'm not saying close – well, close, yeah, kinda. We were friendly; the relationship had gone beyond driver and client, right?'

'Yeah? How far beyond?'

'Nah, nothing like that,' said Kolovas-Jones, with a grin. 'Nothing like that.'

But Strike saw that the driver was not at all displeased that the idea had been mooted, that it had been thought plausible.

'I'd been driving her for a year. We talked a lot, y'know. Had a lot in common. Similar backgrounds, y'know?'

'In what way?'

'Mixed race,' said Kolovas-Jones. 'And things were a bit dysfunctional in my family, right, so I knew where she was coming from. She didn't know that many people like her, not once she got famous. Not to talk to properly.'

'Being mixed race was an issue for her, was it?'

'Growing up black in a white family, what d'you think?'

'And you had a similar childhood?'

'Me father's half West Indian, half Welsh; me mother's half Scouse, half Greek. Lula usedta say she envied me,' he said, sitting up a little straighter. 'She said, "You know where you come from, even if it is bloody everywhere." And on my birthday, right,' he added, as though he had not yet sufficiently impressed upon Strike something which he felt was important, 'she give me this Guy Somé jacket that was worth, like, nine hundred quid.'

Evidently expected to show a reaction, Strike nodded, wondering whether Kolovas-Jones had come along simply to tell somebody how close he had been to Lula Landry. Satisfied, the driver went on:

'So, right, the day she died – day before, I should say – I drove her to her mum's in the morning, right? And she was not happy. She never liked going to see her mother.'

'Why not?'

'Because that woman's fucking weird,' said Kolovas-Jones. 'I drove them both out for a day, once, I think it was the mother's birthday. She's fucking creepy, Lady Yvette. *Darling, my darling* to Lula, every other word. She used to hang off her. Just fucking strange and possessive and over the top, right?

'Anyway, that day, right, her mum had just got out of hospital, so that wasn't gonna be fun, was it? Lula wasn't looking forward to seeing her. She was uptight like I hadn't seen her before.

'And then I told her I couldn't drive her that night, because I was booked for Deeby Macc, and she wasn't happy about that, neither.'

'Why not?'

''Cause she liked me driving her, didn't she?' said Kolovas-Jones, as though Strike was being obtuse. 'I used to help her out with the paps and stuff, do a bit of bodyguard stuff to get her in and out of places.'

By the merest flicker of his facial muscles, Wilson managed to convey what he thought of the suggestion that Kolovas-Jones was bodyguard material.

'Couldn't you have swapped with another driver, and driven her instead of Macc?'

'I coulda, but I didn't want to,' Kolovas-Jones confessed. 'I'm a big Deeby fan. Wanted to meet him. That's what Lula was pissed off about. Anyway,' he hurried on, 'I took her to her mum's, and waited, and then, this is the bit I wanted to tell you about, right?

'She come out of her mother's place and she was strange. Not like I'd ever seen her, right? Quiet, really quiet. Like she was in shock or something. Then she asked me for a pen, and she started scribbling something on a bit of blue paper. Wasn't talking to me. Wasn't saying anything. Just writing.

'So, I drove her to Vashti, 'cause she was supposedta be meeting her friend there for lunch, right—'

'What's Vashti? What friend?'

'Vashti – it's this shop – boutique, they call it. There's a café in it. Trendy place. And the friend was . . . ' Kolovas-Jones clicked his fingers repeatedly, frowning. 'She was that friend she'd made when she was in hospital for her mental problems. What was her fucking name? I used to drive the two of them around. Christ . . . Ruby? Roxy? Raquelle? Something like that. She was living at the St Elmo hostel in Hammersmith. She was homeless.

'Anyway, Lula goes into the shop, right, and she'd told me on the way to her mother's she was gonna have lunch there, right, but she's only in there a quarter of an hour or something, then she comes out alone and tells me to drive her home. So that was a bit fucking strange, right? And Raquelle, or whatever her name is – it'll come back to me – wasn't with her. We usedta give Raquelle a lift home normally, when they'd been out together. And the blue piece of paper was gone. And Lula never said a word to me all the way back home.'

'Did you mention this blue paper to the police?'

'Yeah. They didn't think it was worth shit,' said Kolovas-Jones. 'Said it was probably a shopping list.'

'Can you remember what it looked like?'

'It was just blue. Like airmail paper.'

He looked down at his watch.

'I gotta go in ten.'

'So that was the last time you ever saw Lula?'

'Yeah, it was.'

He picked at the corner of a fingernail.

'What was your first thought, when you heard she was dead?'

'I dunno,' said Kolovas-Jones, chewing at the hangnail he had been picking. 'I was fucking shocked. You don't expect that, do you? Not when you've just seen someone hours before. The press were all saying it was Duffield, because they'd had a row in that nightclub and stuff. I thought it might've been him, to tell you the truth. Bastard.'

'You knew him, did you?'

'I drove them a coupla times,' said Kolovas-Jones. A flaring of his nostrils, a tightness around the lines of his mouth, together suggested a bad smell.

'What did you think of him?'

'I thought he was a talentless tosser.' With unexpected virtuosity, he suddenly adopted a flat, drawling voice: '*Are we gonna need him later, Lules? He'd better wait, yeah?*' said Kolovas-Jones, crackling with temper. 'Never once spoke to me directly. Ignorant, sponging piece of shit.'

Derrick said, sotto voce, 'Kieran's an actor.'

'Just bit parts,' said Kolovas-Jones. 'So far.'

And he digressed into a brief exposition of the television dramas in which he had appeared, exhibiting, in Strike's estimation, a marked desire to be considered more than he felt himself to be; to become endowed, in fact, with that unpredictable, dangerous and transformative quality: fame. To have had it so often in the back of his car and not yet to have caught it from his passengers must (thought Strike) have been tantalising and, perhaps, infuriating.

'Kieran auditioned for Freddie Bestigui,' said Wilson. 'Didn't you?'

'Yeah,' said Kolovas-Jones, with a lack of enthusiasm that told the outcome plainly.

'How did that come about?' asked Strike.

'Usual way,' said Kolovas-Jones, with a hint of hauteur. 'Through my agent.'

'Nothing came of it?'

'They decided to go in another direction,' said Kolovas-Jones. 'They wrote out the part.'

'OK, so you picked up Deeby Macc from, where – Heathrow? – that night?'

'Terminal Five, yeah,' said Kolovas-Jones, apparently brought back to a sense of mundane reality, and glancing at his watch. 'Listen, I'd better get going.'

'All right if I walk you back to the car?' asked Strike.

Wilson showed himself happy to go along too; Strike paid the bill for all three of them and they left. Out on the pavement, Strike offered both his companions cigarettes; Wilson declined, Kolovas-Jones accepted.

A silver Mercedes was parked a short distance away, around the corner in Electric Lane.

'Where did you take Deeby when he arrived?' Strike asked Kolovas-Jones, as they approached the car.

'He wanted a club, so I took him to Barrack.'

'What time did you get him there?'

'I dunno . . . half eleven? Quarter to twelve? He was wired. Didn't want to sleep, he said.'

'Why Barrack?'

'Friday night at Barrack's best hip-hop night in London,' said Kolovas-Jones, on a slight laugh, as though this was common knowledge. 'And he musta liked it, 'cause it was gone three by the time he came out again.'

'So did you drive him to Kentigern Gardens and find the police there, or . . . ?'

'I'd already heard on the car radio what had happened,' said Kolovas-Jones. 'I told Deeby when he got back to the car. His entourage all started making phone calls, waking up people at the record company, trying to make other arrangements. They got him a suite at Claridge's; I drove him there. I didn't get home till gone five. Switched on the news and watched it all on Sky. Fucking unbelievable.'

'I've been wondering who let the paparazzi staking out number eighteen know that Deeby wasn't going to be there for hours. Someone tipped them off; that's why they'd left the street before Lula fell.'

'Yeah? I dunno,' said Kolovas-Jones.

He increased his pace very slightly, reaching the car ahead of the other two and unlocking it.

'Didn't Macc have a load of luggage with him? Was it in the car with you?'

'Nah, it'd all been sent ahead by the record company days before. He got off the plane with just a carry-on bag – and about ten security people.'

'So you weren't the only car sent for him?'

'There were four cars – but Deeby himself was with me.'

'Where did you wait for him, while he was in the nightclub?'

'I just parked the car and waited,' said Kolovas-Jones. 'Just off Glasshouse Street.'

'With the other three cars? Were you all together?'

'You don't find four parking spaces side by side in the middle of London, mate,' said Kolovas-Jones. 'I dunno where the others were parked.'

Still holding the driver's door open, he glanced at Wilson, then back at Strike.

'How's any of this matter?' he demanded.

'I'm just interested,' said Strike, 'in how it works, when you're with a client.'

'It's fucking tedious,' said Kolovas-Jones, with a sudden flash of irritation, 'that's what it is. Driving's mostly waiting around.'

'Have you still got the control for the doors to the underground garage that Lula gave you?' Strike asked.

'What?' said Kolovas-Jones, although Strike would have taken an oath that the driver had heard him. The flicker of animosity was undisguised now, and it seemed to extend not only to Strike, but also to Wilson, who had listened without comment since noting aloud that Kolovas-Jones was an actor.

'Have you still got—'

'Yeah, I've still got it. I still drive Mr Bestigui, don't I?' said Kolovas-Jones. 'Right, I gotta go. See ya, Derrick.'

He threw his half-smoked cigarette into the road and got into the car.

'If you remember anything else,' said Strike, 'like the name of the friend Lula was meeting in Vashti, will you give me a call?'

He handed Kolovas-Jones a card. The driver, already pulling on his seat belt, took it without looking at it.

'I'm gonna be late.'

Wilson raised his hand in farewell. Kolovas-Jones slammed the car door, revved the engine and reversed out of the parking space, scowling.

'He's a bit of a star-fucker,' said Wilson, as the car pulled away. It was a kind of apology for the younger man. 'He loved drivin' her. He tries to drive all the famous ones. He's been hoping Bestigui'll cast him in something for two years. He was well pissed off when he didn't get that part.'

'What was it?'

'Drug dealer. Some film.'

They walked off together in the direction of Brixton underground station, past a gaggle of black schoolgirls in uniforms with blue plaid skirts. One girl's long beaded hair made Strike think, again, of his sister, Lucy.

'Bestigui's still living at number eighteen, is he?' asked Strike.

'Oh yeah,' said Wilson.

'What about the other two flats?'

'There's a Ukrainian commodities broker and his wife renting Flat Two now. Got a Russian interested in Three, but he hasn't made an offer yet.'

'Is there any chance,' asked Strike, as they were momentarily impeded by a tiny hooded, bearded man like an Old Testament prophet, who stopped in front of them and slowly stuck out his tongue, 'that I could come and have a look inside some time?'

'Yeah, all right,' said Wilson after a pause in which his gaze slid furtively over Strike's lower legs. 'Buzz mi. But it'll have to be when Bestigui's out, y'understand. He's one quarrelsome man, and I need my job.'

8

The knowledge that he would be sharing his office again on Monday added piquancy to Strike's weekend solitude, rendering it less irksome, more valuable. The camp bed could stay out; the door between inner and outer offices could remain open; he was able to attend to bodily functions without fear of causing offence. Sick of the smell of artificial limes, he managed to force open the painted-shut window behind his desk, which allowed a cold, clean breeze to wipe the fusty corners of the two small rooms. Avoiding every CD, every track, that transported him back to those excruciating, exhilarating periods he had shared with Charlotte, he selected Tom Waits to play loudly on the small CD player he had thought he would never see again, and which he had found at the bottom of one of the boxes he had brought from Charlotte's. He busied himself setting up his portable television, with its paltry indoor aerial; he loaded his worn clothes into a black bin bag and walked to a launderette half a mile away; back at the office, he hung up his shirts and underwear on a rope he slung across one side of the inner office, then watched the three o'clock match between Arsenal and Spurs.

Through all these mundane acts, he felt as though he was accompanied by the spectre that had haunted him during his months in hospital. It lurked in the corners of his shabby office; he could hear it whispering to him whenever his attention on the task in hand grew slack. It urged him to consider how far he had fallen; his age; his penury; his shattered love life; his homelessness. *Thirty-five*, it whispered, *and nothing to show for all your years of graft except a few cardboard boxes and a massive debt.* The spectre directed his eyes to cans of beer in the supermarket, where he bought more Pot Noodles; it mocked him as he ironed shirts on the floor. As the day wore on, it jeered at him for his self-imposed habit of smoking outside in the street, as though he were still in the army, as though this petty self-discipline could impose form and order on the amorphous, disastrous present. He began to smoke at his desk, with the butts mounting in a cheap tin ashtray he had swiped, long ago, from a bar in Germany.

But he had a job, he kept reminding himself; a paid job. Arsenal beat Spurs, and Strike was cheered; he turned off the television and, defying the spectre, moved straight to his desk and resumed work.

At liberty, now, to collect and collate evidence in whatever way he chose, Strike continued to conform to the protocols of the Criminal Procedure and Investigation Act. The fact that he believed himself to be hunting a figment of John Bristow's disturbed imagination made no difference to the thoroughness and accuracy with which he now wrote up the notes he had made during his interviews with Bristow, Wilson and Kolovas-Jones.

Lucy telephoned him at six in the evening, while he was hard at work. Though his sister was younger than Strike by two years, she seemed to feel herself older. Weighed down, young, by a mortgage, a stolid husband, three children and an onerous job, Lucy seemed to crave responsibility, as though she could never have enough anchors. Strike had always suspected that she wanted to prove to herself and the world that she was nothing like their fly-by-night mother, who had dragged the two of them all over the country, from school to school, house to squat to camp, in pursuit of the next enthusiasm or man. Lucy was the only one of his eight half-siblings with whom Strike had shared a childhood; he was fonder of her than of almost anyone else in his life, and yet their interactions were often unsatisfactory, laden with familiar anxieties and arguments. Lucy could not disguise the fact that her brother worried and disappointed her. In consequence, Strike was less inclined to be honest with her about his present situation than he would have been with many a friend.

'Yeah, it's going great,' he told her, smoking at the open window, watching people drift in and out of the shops below. 'Business has doubled lately.'

'Where are you? I can hear traffic.'

'At the office. I've got paperwork to do.'

'On Saturday? How does Charlotte feel about that?'

'She's away; she's gone to visit her mother.'

'How are things going between you?'

'Great,' he said.

'Are you sure?'

'Yeah, I'm sure. How's Greg?'

She gave him a brief precis of her husband's workload, then returned to the attack.

'Is Gillespie still on your back for repayment?'

'No.'

'Because you know what, Stick' – the childhood nickname boded ill: she was trying to soften him up – 'I've been looking into this, and you could apply to the British Legion for—'

'Fucking hell, Lucy,' he said, before he could stop himself.

'What?'

The hurt and indignation in her voice were only too familiar: he closed his eyes.

'I don't need help from the British Legion, Luce, all right?'

'There's no need to be so *proud* . . . '

'How are the boys?'

'They're fine. Look, Stick, I just think it's outrageous that Rokeby's getting his lawyer to hassle you, when he's never given you a penny in his life. He ought to have made it a gift, seeing what you've been through and how much he's—'

'Business is good. I'm going to pay off the loan,' said Strike. A teenaged couple on the corner of the street were having an argument.

'Are you *sure* everything's all right between you and Charlotte? Why's she visiting her mother? I thought they hated each other?'

'They're getting on better these days,' he said, as the teenage girl gesticulated wildly, stamped her foot and walked away.

'Have you bought her a ring yet?' asked Lucy.

'I thought you wanted me to get Gillespie off my back?'

'Is she all right about not having a ring?'

'She's been great about it,' said Strike. 'She says she doesn't want one; she wants me to put all my money into the business.'

'Really?' said Lucy. She always seemed to think that she made a good job of dissimulating her deep dislike of Charlotte. 'Are you going to come to Jack's birthday party?'

'When is it?'

'I sent you an invitation over a week ago, Stick!'

He wondered whether Charlotte had slipped it into one of the boxes he had left unpacked on the landing, not having room for all his possessions in the office.

'Yeah, I'll be there,' he said; there was little he wanted to do less.

The call terminated, he returned to his computer and

continued work. His notes from the Wilson and Kolovas-Jones interviews were soon completed, but a sense of frustration persisted. This was the first case that he had taken since leaving the army that required more than surveillance work, and it might have been designed to remind him daily that he had been stripped of all power and authority. Film producer Freddie Bestigui, the man who had been in closest proximity to Lula Landry at the time of her death, remained unreachable behind his faceless minions, and, in spite of John Bristow's confident assertion that he would be able to persuade her to talk to Strike, there was not yet a secured interview with Tansy Bestigui.

With a faint sense of impotence, and with almost as much contempt for the occupation as Robin's fiancé felt for it, Strike fought off his lowering sense of gloom by resorting to more internet searches connected with the case. He found Kieran Kolovas-Jones online: the driver had been telling the truth about the episode of *The Bill* in which he had had two lines (Gang Member Two ... Kieran Kolovas-Jones). He had a theatrical agent, too, whose website featured a small photograph of Kieran, and a short list of credits including walk-on parts in *EastEnders* and *Casualty*. Kieran's photograph on the Execars home page was much larger. Here, he stood alone in a peaked hat and uniform, looking like a film star, evidently the handsomest driver on their books.

Evening shaded into night beyond the windows; while Tom Waits growled and moaned from the portable CD player in the corner, Strike chased the shadow of Lula Landry across cyberspace, occasionally adding to the notes he had already taken while speaking to Bristow, Wilson and Kolovas-Jones.

He could find no Facebook page for Landry, nor did she ever seem to have joined Twitter. Her refusal to feed her fans' ravenous appetite for personal information seemed to have inspired others to fill the void. There were countless websites dedicated to the reproduction of her pictures, and to obsessive commentary on her life. If half of the information here was factual, Bristow had given Strike but a partial and sanitised version of his sister's drive towards self-destruction, a tendency which seemed to have revealed itself first in early adolescence, when her adoptive father, Sir Alec Bristow, a genial-looking bearded man who had founded his own electronics company, Albris, had dropped dead of a heart attack. Lula had subsequently run away from two schools, and been expelled from a third, all of them expensive private establishments. She had slit her own wrist and been found in a pool of blood by a dormitory friend; she had lived rough, and been tracked to a squat by the police. A fan site called LulaMyInspirationForeva.com, run by a person of unknown sex, asserted that the model had briefly supported herself, during this time, as a prostitute.

Then had come sectioning under the Mental Health Act, the secure ward for young people with severe illnesses, and a diagnosis of bipolar disorder. Barely a year later, while shopping in a clothing store on Oxford Street with her mother, there had come the fairy-tale approach from a scout for a modelling agency.

Landry's early photographs showed a sixteen-year-old with the face of Nefertiti, who managed to project to the lens an extraordinary combination of worldliness and vulnerability, with long thin legs like a giraffe's and a jagged scar running down the inside of her left arm that fashion editors seemed to have found an interesting adjunct to her spectacular face, for it was sometimes given prominence in photographs. Lula's extreme beauty was on the very edge of absurdity, and the charm for which she was celebrated (in both newspaper obituaries and hysterical blogs) sat alongside a reputation for sudden outbursts of temper and a dangerously short fuse. Press and public seemed to have both loved her, and loved loathing her. One female journalist found her 'strangely sweet, possessed of an unexpected naiveté'; another, 'at bottom, a calculating little diva, shrewd and tough'.

At nine o'clock Strike walked to Chinatown and bought himself a meal; then he returned to the office, swapped Tom Waits for Elbow, and searched out online accounts of Evan Duffield, the man who, by common consent, even that of Bristow, had not killed his girlfriend.

Until Kieran Kolovas-Jones had displayed professional jealousy, Strike could not have said why Duffield was famous. He now discovered that Duffield had been elevated from obscurity by his participation in a critically acclaimed independent film, in which he had played a character indistinguishable from himself: a heroin-addicted musician stealing to support his habit.

Duffield's band had released a well-reviewed album on the back of their lead singer's new-found fame, and split up in considerable acrimony around the time that he had met Lula. Like his girlfriend, Duffield was extraordinarily photogenic, even in the unretouched long-lens photographs of him sloping along a street in filthy clothes, even in those shots (and there were several) where he was lunging in fury at photographers. The conjunction of these two damaged and beautiful people seemed to have supercharged the fascination with both; each reflecting more interest on to the other, which rebounded on themselves; it was a kind of perpetual motion.

The death of his girlfriend had fixed Duffield more securely than ever in that firmament of the idolised, the vilified, the deified. A certain darkness, a fatalism, hung around him; both his most fervent admirers and his detractors seemed to take pleasure in the idea that he had one booted foot in the afterworld already; that there was an inevitability about his descent into despair and oblivion. He seemed to make a veritable parade of his frailties, and Strike lingered for some minutes over another of those tiny, jerky YouTube videos, in which Duffield, patently stoned, talked on and on, in the voice Kolovas-Jones had so accurately parodied, about dying being no more than checking out of the party, and making a confused case for there being little need to cry if you had to leave early.

On the night that Lula had died, according to a multitude of sources, Duffield had left the nightclub shortly after his girlfriend, wearing – and Strike found it hard to see this as anything other than deliberate showmanship – a wolf's mask. His account of what he had got up to for the rest of the night might not have satisfied online conspiracy theorists, but the police seemed to have been convinced that he had had nothing to do with subsequent events at Kentigern Gardens.

Strike followed the speculative train of his own thoughts over the rough terrain of news sites and blogs. Here and there he stumbled upon pockets of feverish speculation, of theories about Landry's death that mentioned clues the police had failed to follow up, and which seemed to have fed Bristow's own conviction that there had been a murderer. LulaMyInspirationForeva had a long list of Unanswered Questions, which included, at number five, '*Who called off the paps before she fell?*'; at number nine, '*Why did the men with the covered faces runnin away from her flat at 2 a.m. never come forward? Where are they and who wer they?*'; and at number thirteen, '*Why was luLa wearing a different outfit to the one she came home in when she fell off the balcony?*'

Midnight found Strike drinking a can of lager and reading about the posthumous controversy that Bristow had mentioned, of which he had been vaguely aware while it unfolded, without being very interested. A furore had sprung up, a week after the inquest had returned a verdict of suicide, around the advertising shot for the wares of designer Guy Somé. It featured two models posing in a dirty alleyway, naked except for strategically placed handbags, scarves and jewels. Landry was perched on a dustbin, Ciara Porter sprawled on the ground. Both wore huge curving angel's wings: Porter's a swan-like white; Landry's a greenish black fading to glossy bronze.

Strike stared at the picture for minutes, trying to analyse precisely why the dead girl's face drew the eye so irresistibly, how she managed to dominate the picture. Somehow she made the incongruity, the staginess of it, believable; she really did look as though she had been slung from heaven because she was too venal, because she so coveted the accessories she was clutching to herself. Ciara Porter, in all her alabaster beauty, became nothing but a counterpoint; in her pallor and her passivity, she looked like a statue.

The designer, Guy Somé, had drawn much criticism upon himself, some of it vicious, for choosing to use the picture. Many people felt that he was capitalising on Landry's recent death, and sneered at the professions of deep affection for Landry that Somé's spokesman made on his behalf. LulaMyInspirationForeva, however, asserted that Lula would have wanted the picture to be used; that she and Guy Somé had been bosom friends: *Lula loved guy like a brother and would want him to pay this final tribute to her work and her beauty. This is an iconic shot that will live forever and will continue to keep Lula alive in the memories of we who loved her.*

Strike drank the last of his lager and contemplated the final four words of this sentence. He had never been able to understand the assumption of intimacy fans felt with those they had never met. People had sometimes referred to his father as 'Old Jonny' in his presence, beaming, as if they were talking about a mutual friend, repeating well-worn press stories and anecdotes as though they had been personally involved. A man in a pub in Trescothick had once said to Strike: 'Fuck, I know your old man better than you do!' because he was able to name the session musician who had played on the Deadbeats' biggest album, and whose tooth Rokeby had famously broken when he slapped the end of his saxophone in anger.

It was one in the morning. Strike had become almost deaf to the constant muffled thuds of the bass guitar from two floors below, and to the occasional creaks and hisses from the attic flat above, where the bar manager enjoyed luxuries like showers and home-cooked food. Tired, but not yet ready to climb into his sleeping bag, he managed to discover Guy Somé's approximate address by further perusal of the internet, and noted the close proximity of Charles Street to Kentigern Gardens. Then he typed in the web address www.arrse.co.uk, like a man turning automatically into his local after a long shift at work.

He had not visited the Army Rumour Service site since Charlotte had found him, months previously, browsing it on computer, and had reacted the way other women might had they found their partners viewing online porn. There had been a row, generated by what she took to be his hankering for his old life and his dissatisfaction with the new.

Here was the army mindset in its every particular, written in the language he too could speak fluently. Here were the acronyms he had known by heart; the jokes impenetrable to outsiders; every concern of service life, from the father whose son was being bullied at his school in Cyprus, to retrospective abuse of the Prime Minister's performance at the Chilcot Inquiry. Strike wandered from post to post, occasionally snorting in amusement, yet aware all the time that he was lowering his resistance to the spectre he could feel, now, breathing on the back of his neck.

This had been his world and he had been happy there. For all the inconveniences and hardships of military life, for all that he had emerged from the army minus half his leg, he did not regret a day of the time he had spent serving. And yet, he had not been of these people, even while among them. He had been a monkey, and then a suit, feared and disliked about equally by the average squaddie.

If ever the SIB talk to you, you should say 'No comment, I want a lawyer.' Alternatively, a simple 'Thank you for noticing me' will suffice.

Strike gave a final grunt of laughter, and then, abruptly, shut down the site and turned off the computer. He was so tired that the removal of his prosthesis took twice the time it usually did.

9

On Sunday morning, which was fine, Strike headed back to the ULU to shower. Once again, by consciously filling out his own bulk and allowing his features to slide, as they did naturally, into a scowl, he made himself sufficiently intimidating to repel challenges as he marched, eyes down, past the desk. He hung around the changing rooms, waiting for a quiet moment so that he would not have to shower in full view of any of the changing students, for the sight of his false leg was a distinguishing feature he did not want to impress on anybody's memory.

Clean and shaven, he caught the Tube to Hammersmith Broadway, enjoying the tentative sunshine gleaming through the glass-covered shopping precinct through which he emerged on to the street. The distant shops on King Street were heaving with people; it might have been a Saturday. This was a bustling and essentially soulless commercial centre, and yet Strike knew it to be a bare ten minutes' walk to a sleepy, countrified stretch of the Thames embankment.

While he walked, traffic rumbling past him, he remembered Sundays in Cornwall in his childhood, when everything closed down except the church and the beach. Sunday had had a particular flavour in those days; an echoing, whispering quiet, the gentle chink of china and the smell of gravy, the TV as dull as the empty high street, and the relentless rush of the waves on the beach when he and Lucy had run down on to the shingle, forced back on to primitive resources.

His mother had once said to him: 'If Joan's right, and I end up in hell, it'll be eternal Sunday in bloody St Mawes.'

Strike, who was heading away from the commercial centre towards the Thames, phoned his client as he walked.

'John Bristow?'

'Yeah, sorry to disturb you at the weekend, John . . . '

'Cormoran?' said Bristow, immediately friendly. 'Not a problem, not a problem at all! How did it go with Wilson?'

'Very good, very useful, thanks. I wanted to know whether you can help me find a friend of Lula's. It's a girl she met in therapy. Her Christian name begins with an R – something like Rachel or Raquelle – and she was living at the St Elmo hostel in Hammersmith when Lula died. Does that ring any bells?'

There was a moment's silence. When Bristow spoke again, the disappointment in his voice verged on annoyance.

'What do you want to speak to *her* for? Tansy's quite clear that the voice she heard from upstairs was male.'

'I'm not interested in this girl as a suspect, but as a witness. Lula had an appointment to meet her at a shop, Vashti, right after she saw you at your mother's flat.'

'Yeah, I know; that came out at the inquest. I mean – well, of course, you know your job, but – I don't really see how she would know anything about what happened that night. Listen – wait a moment, Cormoran . . . I'm at my mother's and there are other people here . . . need to find a quieter spot . . . '

Strike heard the sounds of movement, a murmured 'Excuse me', and Bristow came back on the line.

'Sorry, I didn't want to say all this in front of the nurse. Actually, I thought, when you rang, you might be someone else calling up to talk to me about Duffield. Everybody I know has rung to tell me.'

'Tell you what?'

'You obviously don't read the *News of the World*. It's all there, complete with pictures: Duffield turned up to visit my mother yesterday, out of the blue. Photographers outside the house; it caused a lot of inconvenience and upset with the neighbours. I was out with Alison, or I'd never have let him in.'

'What did he want?'

'Good question. Tony, my uncle, thinks it was money – but Tony usually thinks people are after money; anyway, I've got power of attorney, so there was nothing doing there. God knows why he came. The one small mercy is that Mum doesn't seem to have realised who he is. She's on immensely strong painkillers.'

'How did the press find out he was coming?'

'That,' said Bristow, 'is an excellent question. Tony thinks he phoned them himself.'

'How is your mother?'

'Poorly, very poorly. They say she could hang on for weeks, or – or it could happen at any moment.'

'I'm sorry to hear that,' said Strike. He raised his voice as he passed underneath a flyover, across which traffic was moving noisily. 'Well, if you do happen to remember the name of Lula's Vashti friend . . . '

'I'm afraid I still don't really understand why you're so interested in her.'

'Lula made this girl travel all the way from Hammersmith to Notting Hill, spent fifteen minutes with her and then walked out. Why didn't she stay? Why meet for such a short space of time? Did they argue? Anything out of the ordinary that happens around a sudden death could be relevant.'

'I see,' said Bristow hesitantly. 'But . . . well, that sort of behaviour wasn't really out of the ordinary for Lula. I did tell you that she could be a bit . . . a bit selfish. It would be like her to think that a token appearance would keep the girl happy. She often had these brief enthusiasms for people, you know, and then dropped them.'

His disappointment at Strike's chosen line of inquiry was so evident that the detective felt it might be politic to slip in a little covert justification of the immense fee his client was paying.

'The other reason I was calling was to let you know that tomorrow evening I'm meeting one of the CID officers who covered the case. Eric Wardle. I'm hoping to get hold of the police file.'

'Fantastic!' Bristow sounded impressed. 'That's quick work!'

'Yeah, well, I've got good contacts in the Met.'

'Then you'll be able to get some answers about the Runner! You've read my notes?'

'Yeah, very useful,' said Strike.

'And I'm trying to fix up a lunch with Tansy Bestigui this week, so you can meet her and hear her testimony first hand. I'll ring your secretary, shall I?'

'Great.'

There was this to be said for having an underworked secretary he could not afford, Strike thought, once he had rung off: it gave a professional impression.

St Elmo's Hostel for the Homeless turned out to be situated right behind the noisy concrete flyover. A plain, ill-proportioned and contemporaneous cousin of Lula's Mayfair house, red brick with humbler, grubby white facings; no stone steps, no garden, no elegant neighbours, but a chipped door opening directly on to the street, peeling paint on the window ledges and a forlorn air. The utilitarian modern world had encroached until it sat huddled and miserable, out of synch with its surroundings, the flyover a mere twenty yards away, so that the upper windows looked directly out upon the concrete barriers and the endlessly passing cars. An unmistakably institutional flavour was given by the large silver buzzer and speaker beside the door, and the unapologetically ugly black camera, with its dangling wires, that hung from the lintel in a wire cage.

An emaciated young girl with a sore at the corner of her mouth stood smoking outside the front door, wearing a dirty man's jumper that swamped her. She was leaning up against the wall, staring blankly towards the commercial centre barely five minutes' walk away, and when Strike pressed the buzzer for admission to the hostel, she gave him a look of deep calculation, apparently assessing his potentialities.

A small, fusty, grimy-floored lobby with shabby wooden panelling lay just inside the door. Two locked glass-panelled doors stood to left and right, affording him glimpses of a bare hall and a depressed-looking side room with a table full of leaflets, an old dartboard and a wall liberally peppered with holes. Straight ahead was a kiosk-like front desk, protected by another metal grille.

A gum-chewing woman behind the desk was reading a newspaper. She seemed suspicious and ill-disposed when Strike asked whether he could speak to a girl whose name was something like Rachel, and who had been a friend of Lula Landry's.

'You a journalist?'

'No, I'm not; I'm a friend of a friend.'

'Should know her name, then, shouldn't you?'

'Rachel? Raquelle? Something like that.'

A balding man strode into the kiosk behind the suspicious woman.

'I'm a private detective,' said Strike, raising his voice, and the bald man looked around, interested. 'Here's my card. I've been hired by Lula Landry's brother, and I need to talk to—'

'Oh, you looking for Rochelle?' asked the bald man, approaching the grille. 'She's not here, pal. She left.'

His colleague, evincing some irritation at his willingness to talk to Strike, ceded her place at the counter and vanished from sight.

'When was this?'

'It'd be weeks now. Coupla months, even.'

'Any idea where she went?'

'No idea, mate. Probably sleeping rough again. She's come and gone a good few times. She's a difficult character. Mental health problems. Carrianne might know something though, hang on. Carrianne! Hey! Carrianne!'

The bloodless young girl with the scabbed lip came in out of the sunshine, her eyes narrowed.

'Wha'?'

'Rochelle, have you seen her?'

'Why would I wanna see that fuckin' bitch?'

'So you haven't seen her?' asked the bald man.

'No. Gorra fag?'

Strike gave her one; she put it behind her ear.

'She's still round 'ere somewhere. Janine said she seen 'er,' said Carrianne. 'Rochelle reckoned she'd gorra flat or some't. Lying fuckin' bitch. An' Lula Landry left her ev'rything. *Not.* Whadd'ya want Rochelle for?' she asked Strike, and it was clear that she was wondering whether there was money in it, and whether she might do instead.

'Just to ask some questions.'

'Warrabout?'

'Lula Landry.'

'Oh,' said Carrianne, and her card-counting eyes flickered. 'They weren't such big fuckin' mates. You don't wanna believe everything Rochelle says, the lying bitch.'

'What did she lie about?' asked Strike.

'Fuckin' everything. I reckon she stole half the stuff she pretended Landry bought 'er.'

'Come on, Carrianne,' said the bald man gently. 'They *were* friends,' he told Strike. 'Landry used to come and pick her up in her car. It caused,' he said, with a glance at Carrianne, 'a bit of tension.'

'Not from me it fuckin' didn't,' snapped Carrianne. 'I thought Landry was a fuckin' jumped-up bitch. She weren't even that good-lookin'.'

'Rochelle told me she's got an aunt in Kilburn,' said the bald man.

'She dun gerron with 'er, though,' said the girl.

'Have you got a name or an address for the aunt?' asked Strike, but both shook their heads. 'What's Rochelle's surname?'

'I don't know; do you, Carrianne? We often know people just by their Christian names,' he told Strike.

There was little more to be gleaned from them. Rochelle had last stayed at the hostel more than two months previously. The bald man knew that she had attended an outpatients' clinic at St Thomas's for a while, though he had no idea whether she still went.

'She's had psychotic episodes. She's on a lot of medication.'

'She didn't give a shit when Lula died,' said Carrianne, suddenly. 'She didn't give a flying fuck.'

Both men looked at her. She shrugged, as one who has simply expressed an unpalatable truth.

'Listen, if Rochelle turns up again, will you give her my details and ask her to call me?'

Strike gave both of them cards, which they examined with interest. While their attention was thus engaged, he deftly twitched the gum-chewing woman's *News of the World* out of the small opening at the bottom of the grille and stowed it under his arm. He then bade them both a cheerful goodbye, and left.

It was a warm spring afternoon. Strike strode on down towards Hammersmith Bridge, its pale sage-green paint and ornate gilding picturesque in the sun. A single swan bobbed along the Thames beside the far bank. The offices and shops seemed a hundred miles away. Turning right, he headed along the walkway beside the river wall and a line of low, riverside terraced buildings, some balconied or draped in wisteria.

Strike bought himself a pint in the Blue Anchor, and sat outside at a wooden bench with his face to the water and his back to the royal-blue and white frontage. Lighting a cigarette, he turned to page four of the paper, where a colour photograph of Evan Duffield (head bowed, large bunch of white flowers in his hand, black coat flapping behind him) was surmounted by the headline: DUFFIELD'S DEATHBED VISIT TO LULA MOTHER.

The story was anodyne, really nothing more than an extended caption to the picture. The eyeliner and the flapping greatcoat, the slightly haunted, spaced-out expression, recalled Duffield's appearance as he had headed towards his late girlfriend's funeral. He was described, in the few lines of type below, as 'troubled actor-musician Evan Duffield'.

Strike's mobile vibrated in his pocket and he pulled it out. He had received a text message from an unfamiliar number.

News of the World page four Evan Duffield. Robin.

He grinned at the small screen before slipping the phone back in his pocket. The sun was warm on his head and shoulders. Seagulls cawed, wheeling overhead, and Strike, happily aware that he was due nowhere, and expected by no one, settled to read the paper from cover to cover on the sunny bench.

10

Robin stood swaying with the rest of the tightly packed commuters on a northbound Bakerloo Tube train, everyone wearing the tense and doleful expressions appropriate to a Monday morning. She felt the phone in her coat pocket buzz, and extricated it with difficulty, her elbow pressing unpleasantly into some unspecified flabby portion of a suited, bad-breathed man beside her. When she saw that the message was from Strike, she felt momentarily excited, nearly as excited as she had been to see Duffield in the paper yesterday. Then she scrolled down, and read:

Out. Key behind cistern of toilet. Strike.

She did not force the phone back into her pocket, but continued to clutch it as the train rattled on through dark tunnels, and she tried not to breathe in the flabby man's halitosis. She was disgruntled. The previous day, she and Matthew had eaten lunch, in company with two university friends of Matthew's, at his favourite gastropub, the Windmill on the Common. When Robin had spotted the picture of Evan Duffield in an open copy of the *News of the World* at a nearby table, she had made a breathless excuse, right in the middle of one of Matthew's stories, and hurried outside to text Strike.

Matthew had said, later, that she had shown bad manners,

and even worse not to explain what she was up to, in favour of maintaining that ludicrous air of mystery.

Robin gripped the handstrap tightly, and as the train slowed, and her heavy neighbour leaned into her, she felt both a little foolish, and resentful towards the two men, most particularly the detective, who was evidently uninterested in the unusual movements of Lula Landry's ex-boyfriend.

By the time she had marched through the usual chaos and debris to Denmark Street, extracted the key from behind the cistern as instructed, and been snubbed yet again by a superior-sounding girl in Freddie Bestigui's office, Robin was in a thoroughly bad temper.

Though he did not know it, Strike was, at that very moment, passing the scene of the most romantic moments of Robin's life. The steps below the statue of Eros were swarming with Italian teenagers this morning, as Strike went by on the St James's side, heading for Glasshouse Street.

The entrance to Barrack, the nightclub which had so pleased Deeby Macc that he had remained there for hours, fresh off the plane from Los Angeles, was only a short walk from Piccadilly Circus. The façade looked as if it was made out of industrial concrete, and the name was picked out in shining black letters, vertically placed. The club extended up over four floors. As Strike had expected, its doorway was surmounted by CCTV cameras, whose range, he thought, would cover most of the street. He walked around the building, noting the fire exits, and making for himself a rough sketch of the area.

After a second long internet session the previous evening, Strike felt that he had a thorough grasp of the subject of Deeby Macc's publicly declared interest in Lula Landry. The rapper had mentioned the model in the lyrics of three tracks, on two separate albums; he had also spoken about her in interviews as his ideal woman and soulmate. It was difficult to gauge how seriously Macc intended to be taken when he made these comments; allowance had to be made, in all the print interviews Strike had read, firstly for the rapper's sense of humour, which was both dry and sly, and secondly for the awe tinged with fear every interviewer seemed to feel when confronted with him.

An ex-gang member who had been imprisoned for gun and drug offences in his native Los Angeles, Macc was now a multimillionaire, with a number of lucrative businesses aside from his recording career. There was no doubt that the press had become 'excited', to use Robin's word, when news had leaked out that Macc's record company had rented him the apartment below Lula's. There had been much rabid speculation as to what might happen when Deeby Macc found himself a floor away from his supposed dream woman, and how this incendiary new element might affect the volatile relationship between Landry and Duffield. These non-stories had all been peppered with undoubtedly spurious comments from friends of both – 'He's already called her and asked her to dinner', 'She's preparing a small party for him in her flat when he hits London'. Such speculation had almost eclipsed the flurry of outraged comment from sundry columnists that the twice-convicted Macc, whose music (they said) glorified his criminal past, was entering the country at all.

When he had decided that the streets surrounding Barrack had no more to tell him, Strike continued on foot, making notes of yellow lines in the vicinity, of Friday-night parking restrictions and of those establishments nearby that also had their own security cameras. His notes complete, he felt that he had earned a cup of tea and a bacon roll on expenses, both of which he enjoyed in a small café, while reading an abandoned copy of the *Daily Mail*.

His mobile rang as he was starting his second cup of tea, halfway through a gleeful account of the Prime Minister's gaffe in calling an elderly female voter 'bigoted' without realising that his microphone was still turned on.

A week ago, Strike had allowed his unwanted temp's calls to go to voicemail. Today, he picked up.

'Hi, Robin, how're you?'

'Fine. I'm just calling to give you your messages.'

'Fire away,' said Strike, as he drew out a pen.

'Alison Cresswell's just called – John Bristow's secretary – to say she's booked a table at Cipriani at one o'clock tomorrow, so that he can introduce you to Tansy Bestigui.'

'Great.'

'I've tried Freddie Bestigui's production company again. They're getting irritated. They say he's in LA. I've left another request for him to call you.'

'Good.'

'And Peter Gillespie's telephoned again.'

'Uh huh,' said Strike.

'He says it's urgent, and could you please get back to him as soon as possible.'

Strike considered asking her to call Gillespie back and tell him to go and fuck himself.

'Yeah, will do. Listen, could you text me the address of the nightclub Uzi?'

'Right.'

'And try and find a number for a bloke called Guy Somé? He's a designer.'

'It's pronounced "Ghee",' said Robin.

'What?'

'His Christian name. It's pronounced the French way: "Ghee".'

'Oh, right. Well, could you try and find a contact number for him?'

'Fine,' said Robin.

'Ask him if he'd be prepared to talk to me. Leave a message saying who I am, and who's hired me.'

'Fine.'

It was borne in on Strike that Robin's tone was frosty. After a second or two, he thought he might know why.

'By the way, thanks for that text you sent yesterday,' he said. 'Sorry I didn't get back to you; it would have looked strange if I'd started texting, where I was. But if you could call Nigel Clements, Duffield's agent, and ask for an appointment, that would be great too.'

Her animosity fell away at once, as he had meant it to; her voice was many degrees warmer when she spoke again; verging, in fact, on excited.

'But Duffield can't have had anything to do with it, can he? He had a cast-iron alibi!'

'Yeah, well, we'll see about that,' said Strike, deliberately ominous. 'And listen, Robin, if another death threat comes in – they usually arrive on Mondays . . . '

'Yes?' she said eagerly.

'File it,' said Strike.

He could not be sure – it seemed unlikely; she struck him as so prim – but he thought he heard her mutter, 'Sod you, then,' as she hung up.

Strike spent the rest of the day engaged in tedious but

necessary spadework. When Robin had texted him the address, he visited his second nightclub of the day, this time in South Kensington. The contrast with Barrack was extreme; Uzi's discreet entrance might have been to a smart private house. There were security cameras over its doors, too. Strike then took a bus to Charles Street, where he was fairly sure Guy Somé lived, and walked what he guessed to be the most direct route between the designer's address and the house where Landry had died.

His leg was aching badly again by late afternoon, and he stopped for a rest and more sandwiches before setting out for the Feathers, near Scotland Yard, and his appointment with Eric Wardle.

It was another Victorian pub, this time with enormous windows reaching almost from floor to ceiling, looking out on to a great grey 1920s building decorated with statues by Jacob Epstein. The nearest of these sat over the doors, and stared down through the pub windows; a fierce seated deity was being embraced by his infant son, whose body was weirdly twisted back on itself, to show his genitalia. Time had eroded all shock value.

Inside the Feathers, machines were clinking and jingling and flashing primary-coloured lights; the wall-mounted plasma TVs, surrounded with padded leather, were showing West Bromwich Albion versus Chelsea with the sound off, while Amy Winehouse throbbed and moaned from hidden speakers. The names of ales were painted on the cream wall above the long bar, which faced a wide dark-wood staircase with curving steps and shining brass handrails, leading up to the first floor.

Strike had to wait to be served, giving him time to look around. The place was full of men, most of whom had military-short hair; but a trio of girls with tangerine tans stood around a high table, throwing back their over-straightened peroxide hair, in their tiny, tight spangled dresses, shifting their weight unnecessarily on their teetering heels. They were pretending not to know that the only solitary drinker, a handsome, boyish man in a leather jacket, who was sitting on a high bar seat beside the nearby window, was examining them, point by point, with a practised eye. Strike bought himself a pint of Doom Bar and approached their appraiser.

'Cormoran Strike,' he said, reaching Wardle's table. Wardle had the kind of hair Strike envied in other men; nobody would ever have called Wardle 'pubehead'.

'Yeah, I thought it might be you,' said the policeman, shaking hands. 'Anstis said you were a big bloke.'

Strike pulled up a bar stool, and Wardle said, without preamble:

'What've you got for me, then?'

'There was a fatal stabbing just off Ealing Broadway last month. Guy called Liam Yates? Police informant, wasn't he?'

'Yeah, he got a knife in the neck. But we know who did it,' said Wardle, with a patronising laugh. 'Half the crooks in London know. If that's your information—'

'Don't know where he is, though, do you?'

With a quick glance at the determinedly unconscious girls, Wardle slid a notebook out of his pocket.

'Go on.'

'There's a girl who works in Betbusters on the Hackney Road called Shona Holland. She lives in a rented flat two streets away from the bookie's. She's got an unwelcome house guest at the moment called Brett Fearney, who used to beat up her sister. Apparently he's not the sort of bloke you refuse a favour.'

'Got the full address?' asked Wardle, who was scribbling hard.

'I've just given you the name of the tenant and half the postcode. How about trying a bit of detective work?'

'And where did you say you got this?' asked Wardle, still jotting rapidly with the notebook balanced under the table on his knee.

'I didn't,' replied Strike equably, sipping his beer.

'Got some interesting friends, haven't you?'

'Very. Now, in a spirit of fair exchange . . . '

Wardle, replacing his notebook in his pocket, laughed.

'What you've just given me might be a crock of shit.'

'It isn't. Play fair, Wardle.'

The policeman eyed Strike for a moment, apparently torn between amusement and suspicion.

'What are you after, then?'

'I told you on the phone: bit of inside information on Lula Landry.'

'Don't you read the papers?'

'Inside information, I said. My client thinks there was foul play.'

Wardle's expression hardened.

'Hooked up with a tabloid, have we?'

'No,' said Strike. 'Her brother.'

'John Bristow?'

Wardle took a long pull on his pint, his eyes on the upper thighs of the nearest girl, his wedding ring reflecting red lights from the pinball machine.

'Is he still fixated on the CCTV footage?'

'He mentioned it,' admitted Strike.

'We tried to trace them,' said Wardle, 'those two black guys. We put out an appeal. Neither of them turned up. No big surprise –

a car alarm went off just about the time they would have been passing it – or trying to get into it. Maserati. Very tasty.'

'Reckon they were nicking cars, do you?'

'I don't say they went there specifically to nick cars; they might have spotted an opportunity, seeing it parked there – what kind of tosser leaves a Maserati parked on the street? But it was nearly two in the morning, the temperature was below zero, and I can't think of many innocent reasons why two men would choose to meet at that time, in a Mayfair street where neither of them, as far as we could find out, lived.'

'No idea where they came from, or where they went afterwards?'

'We're pretty sure the one Bristow's obsessed with, the one who was walking towards her flat just before she fell, got off the number thirty-eight bus in Wilton Street at a quarter past eleven. There's no saying what he did before he passed the camera at the end of Bellamy Road an hour and a half later. He tanked back past it about ten minutes after Landry jumped, sprinted up Bellamy Road and most probably turned right down Weldon Street. There's some footage of a guy more or less meeting his description – tall, black, hoodie, scarf round the face – caught on Theobalds Road about twenty minutes later.'

'He made good time if he got to Theobalds Road in twenty minutes,' commented Strike. 'That's out towards Clerkenwell, isn't it? Must be two, two and a half miles. And the pavements were frozen.'

'Yeah, well, it might not've been him. The footage was shit. Bristow thought it was very suspicious that he had his face covered, but it was minus ten that night, and I was wearing a balaclava to work myself. Anyway, whether he was in Theobalds

Road or not, nobody ever came forward to say they'd recognised him.'

'And the other one?'

'Sprinted off down Halliwell Street, about two hundred yards down; no idea where he went after that.'

'Or when he entered the area?'

'Could've come from anywhere. We haven't got any other footage of him.'

'Aren't there supposed to be ten thousand CCTV cameras in London?'

'They aren't everywhere yet. Cameras aren't the answer to our problems, unless they're maintained and monitored. The one in Garriman Street was out, and there aren't any in Meadowfield Road or Hartley Street. You're like everyone else, Strike; you want your civil liberties when you've told the missus you're at the office and you're at a lap-dancing club, but you want twenty-four-hour surveillance on your house when someone's trying to force your bathroom window open. Can't have it both ways.'

'I'm not after it either way,' said Strike. 'I'm just asking what you know about Runner Two.'

'Muffled up to the eyeballs, like his mate; all you could see were his hands. If I'd been him, and had a guilty conscience about the Maserati, I'd have holed up in a bar and exited with a bunch of other people; there's a place called Bojo's off Halliwell Street he could've gone and mingled with the punters. We checked,' Wardle said, forestalling Strike's question. 'Nobody recognised him from the footage.'

They drank for a moment in silence.

'Even if we'd found them,' said Wardle, setting down his glass, 'the most we could've got from them is an eyewitness account of her jumping. There wasn't any unexplained DNA in her flat. Nobody had been in that place who shouldn't have been in there.'

'It isn't just the CCTV footage that's giving Bristow ideas,' said Strike. 'He's been seeing a bit of Tansy Bestigui.'

'Don't talk to me about Tansy fucking Bestigui,' said Wardle irritably.

'I'm going to have to mention her, because my client reckons she's telling the truth.'

'Still at it, is she? Still hasn't given it up? I'll tell you about Mrs Bestigui, shall I?'

'Go on,' said Strike, one hand wrapped around the beer at his chest.

'Carver and I got to the scene about twenty, twenty-five minutes after Landry hit the road. Uniformed police were already there. Tansy Bestigui was still going strong with the hysterics when we saw her, gibbering and shaking and screaming that there was a murderer in the building.

'Her story was that she got up out of bed around two and went for a pee in the bathroom; she heard shouting from two flats above and saw Landry's body fall past the window.

'Now, the windows in those flats are triple-glazed or something. They're designed to keep the heat and the air conditioning in, and the noise of the hoi polloi out. By the time we were interviewing her, the street below was full of panda cars and neighbours, but you'd never have known it from up there except for the flashing blue lights. We could've been inside a fucking pyramid for all the noise that got inside that place.

'So I said to her, "Are you sure you heard shouting, Mrs Bestigui? Because this flat seems to be pretty much soundproofed."

'She wouldn't back down. Swore she'd heard every word. According to her, Landry screamed something like "You're too late," and a man's voice said, "You're a fucking liar." Auditory hallucinations, they call them,' said Wardle. 'You start hearing things when you snort so much coke your brains start dribbling out of your nose.'

He took another long pull on his pint.

'Anyway, we proved beyond doubt she couldn't have heard it. The Bestiguis moved into a friend's house the next day to get away from the press, so we put a few blokes in their flat, and a guy up on Landry's balcony, shouting his head off. The lot on the first floor couldn't hear a word he was saying, and they were stone-cold sober, and making an effort.

'But while we were proving she was talking shit, Mrs Bestigui was phoning half of London to tell them she was the sole witness to the murder of Lula Landry. The press were already on to it, because some of the neighbours had heard her screaming about an intruder. Papers had tried and convicted Evan Duffield before we even got back to Mrs Bestigui.

'We put it to her that we'd now proven she couldn't have heard what she said she'd heard. Well, she wasn't ready to admit it had all been in her own head. She'd got a lot riding on it now, with the press swarming outside her front door like she was Lula Landry reborn. So she came back with "Oh, didn't I say? I opened them. Yeah, I opened the windows for a breath of fresh air."'

Wardle gave a scathing laugh.

'Sub-zero outside, and snowing.'

'And she was in her underwear, right?'

'Looking like a rake with two plastic tangerines tied to it,' said Wardle, and the simile came out so easily that Strike was sure he was far from the first to have heard it. 'We went ahead and double-checked the new story; we dusted for prints, and right enough, she hadn't opened the windows. No prints on the latches or anywhere else; the cleaner had done them the morning before Landry died, and hadn't been in since. As the windows were locked and bolted when we arrived, there's only one conclusion to be drawn, isn't there? Mrs Tansy Bestigui is a fucking liar.'

Wardle drained his glass.

'Have another one,' said Strike, and he headed for the bar without waiting for an answer.

He noticed Wardle's curious gaze roaming over his lower legs as he returned to the table. Under different circumstances, he might have banged the prosthesis hard against the table leg, and said 'It's this one.' Instead, he set down two fresh pints and some pork scratchings, which to his irritation were served in a small white ramekin, and continued where they had left off.

'Tansy Bestigui definitely witnessed Landry falling past the window, though, didn't she? Because Wilson reckons he heard the body fall right before Mrs Bestigui started screaming.'

'Maybe she saw it, but she wasn't having a pee. She was doing a couple of lines of charlie in the bathroom. We found it there, cut and ready for her.'

'Left some, had she?'

'Yeah. Presumably the body falling past the window put her off.'

'The window's visible from the bathroom?'

'Yeah. Well, just.'

'You got there pretty quickly, didn't you?'

'Uniformed lot were there in about eight minutes, and

Carver and I were there in about twenty.' Wardle lifted his glass, as though to toast the force's efficiency.

'I've spoken to Wilson, the security guard,' said Strike.

'Yeah? He didn't do bad,' said Wardle, with a trace of condescension. 'It wasn't his fault he had the runs. But he didn't touch anything, and he did a proper search right after she'd jumped. Yeah, he did all right.'

'He and his colleagues were a bit lazy on the door codes.'

'People always are. Too many pin numbers and passwords to remember. Know the feeling.'

'Bristow's interested in the possibilities of the quarter of an hour when Wilson was in the bog.'

'We were, too, for about five minutes, before we'd satisfied ourselves that Mrs Bestigui was a publicity-mad cokehead.'

'Wilson mentioned that the pool was unlocked.'

'Can he explain how a murderer got into the pool area, or back to it, without walking right past him? A fucking *pool*,' said Wardle, 'nearly as big as the one I've got at my gym, and all for the use of three fucking people. A *gym* on the ground floor behind the security desk. Underground fucking parking. Flats done up with marble and shit like . . . like a fucking five-star hotel.'

The policeman sat shaking his head very slowly over the unequal distribution of wealth.

'Different world,' he said.

'I'm interested in the middle flat,' said Strike.

'Deeby Macc's?' said Wardle, and Strike was surprised to see a grin of genuine warmth spread across the policeman's face. 'What about it?'

'Did you go in there?'

'I had a look, but Bryant had already searched it. Empty. Windows bolted, alarm set and working properly.'

'Is Bryant the one who knocked into the table and smashed a big floral arrangement?'

Wardle snorted.

'Heard about that, did you? Mr Bestigui wasn't too chuffed about it. Oh yeah. Two hundred white roses in a crystal vase the size of a dustbin. Apparently he'd read that Macc asks for white roses in his rider. His *rider*,' Wardle said, as though Strike's silence implied an ignorance of what the term meant. 'Stuff they ask for in their dressing rooms. I'd've thought *you'd* know about this stuff.'

Strike ignored the insinuation. He had hoped for better from Anstis.

'Ever find out why Bestigui wanted Macc to have roses?'

'Just schmoozing, isn't it? Probably wanted to put Macc in a film. He was fucked off to the back teeth when he heard Bryant had ruined them. Yelling the place down when he found out.'

'Anyone find it strange that he was upset about a bunch of flowers, when his neighbour's lying in the street with her head smashed in?'

'He's one obnoxious fucker, Bestigui,' said Wardle, with feeling. 'Used to people jumping to attention when he speaks. He tried treating all of us like staff, till he realised that wasn't clever.

'But the shouting wasn't really about the flowers. He was trying to drown out his wife, give her a chance to pull herself together. He kept forcing his way in between her and anyone who wanted to question her. Big guy as well, old Freddie.'

'What was he worried about?'

'That the longer she bawled and shook like a frozen whippet, the more bloody obvious it became that she'd been doing coke. He must've known it was lying around somewhere in the flat. He can't have been delighted to have the Met come bursting in.

So he tried to distract everyone with a tantrum about his five-hundred-quid floral arrangement.

'I read somewhere that he's divorcing her. I'm not surprised. He's used to the press tiptoeing around him, because he's such a litigious bastard; he can't have enjoyed all the attention he got after Tansy shot her mouth off. The press made hay while they could. Rehashed old stories about him throwing plates at underlings. Punches in meetings. They say he paid his last wife a massive lump sum to stop her talking about his sex life in court. He's pretty well known as a prize shit.'

'You didn't fancy him as a suspect?'

'Oh, we fancied him a lot; he was on the spot and he's got a rep for violence. It never looked likely, though. If his wife knew that he'd done it, or that he'd been out of the flat at the moment Landry fell, I'm betting she'd have told us so: she was out of control when we got there. But she said he'd been in bed, and the bedclothes were disarranged and looked slept in.

'Plus, if he'd managed to sneak out of the flat without her realising it, and gone up to Landry's place, we're left with the problem of how he got past Wilson. He can't have taken the lift, so he'd have passed Wilson in the stairwell, coming down.'

'So the timings rule him out?'

Wardle hesitated.

'Well, it's just possible. *Just*, assuming Bestigui can move a damn sight faster than most men of his age and weight, and that he started running the moment he pushed her over. But there's still the fact that we didn't find his DNA anywhere in the flat, the question of how he got out of the flat without his wife knowing he'd gone, and the small matter of why Landry would have let him in. All her friends agreed she didn't like him.

Anyway,' Wardle finished the dregs of his pint, 'Bestigui's the kind of man who'd hire a killer if he wanted someone taken care of. He wouldn't sully his own hands.'

'Another one?'

Wardle checked his watch.

'My shout,' he said, and he ambled up to the bar. The three young women standing around the high table fell silent, watching him greedily. Wardle threw them a smirk as he walked back past with his drinks, and they glanced over at him as he resumed the bar stool beside Strike.

'How d'you think Wilson shapes up as a possible killer?' Strike asked the policeman.

'Badly,' said Wardle. 'He couldn't have got up and down quickly enough to meet Tansy Bestigui on the ground floor. Mind you, his CV's a crock of shit. He was employed on the basis of being ex-police, and he was never in the force.'

'Interesting. Where was he?'

'He's been knocking around the security world for years. He admitted he'd lied to get his first job, about ten years ago, and he'd just kept it on his CV.'

'He seems to have liked Landry.'

'Yeah. He's older than he looks,' said Wardle, inconsequentially. 'He's a grandfather. They don't show age like us, do they, Afro-Caribbeans? I wouldn't've put him as any older than you.' Strike wondered idly how old Wardle thought he was.

'You got forensics to check out her flat?'

'Oh yeah,' said Wardle, 'but that was purely because the higher-ups wanted to put the thing beyond reasonable doubt. We knew within the first twenty-four hours it had to be suicide. We went the extra mile, though, with the whole fucking world watching.'

He spoke with poorly disguised pride.

'The cleaner had been through the whole place that morning – sexy Polish girl, crap English, but bloody thorough with a duster – so the day's prints stood out good and clear. Nothing unusual.'

'Wilson's prints were in there, presumably, because he searched the place after she fell?'

'Yeah, but nowhere suspicious.'

'So as far as you're concerned, there were only three people in the whole building when she fell. Deeby Macc should have been there, but . . .'

'. . . he went straight from the airport to a nightclub, yeah,' said Wardle. Again, a broad and apparently involuntary grin illuminated his face. 'I interviewed Deeby at Claridge's the day after she died. Massive bloke. Like you,' he said, with a glance at Strike's bulky torso, 'only fit.' Strike took the hit without demur. 'Proper ex-gangster. He's been in and out of the nick in LA. He nearly didn't get a visa to get into the UK.

'He had an entourage with him,' said Wardle. 'All hanging around the room, rings on every finger, tattoos on their necks. He was the biggest, though. One scary fucker Deeby'd be, if you met him down an alleyway. Politer than Bestigui by ten fucking miles. Asked me how the hell I could do my job without a gun.'

The policeman was beaming. Strike could not help drawing the conclusion that Eric Wardle, CID, was, in this case, as starstruck as Kieran Kolovas-Jones.

'Wasn't a long interview, seeing as he'd only just got off a plane and never set foot inside Kentigern Gardens. Routine. I got him to sign his latest CD for me at the end,' Wardle added, as though he could not help himself. 'That brought the house down, he loved it. The missus wanted to put it on eBay, but I'm keeping . . . '

Wardle stopped talking with an air of having given away a little more than he had intended. Amused, Strike helped himself to a handful of pork scratchings.

'What about Evan Duffield?'

'Him,' said Wardle. The stardust that had sparkled over the policeman's account of Deeby Macc was gone; the policeman was scowling. 'Little junkie shit. He pissed us around from start to finish. He went straight into rehab the day after she died.'

'I saw. Where?'

'Priory, where else? Fucking rest cure.'

'So when did you interview him?'

'Next day, but we had to find him first; his people were being as obstructive as possible. Same story as Bestigui, wasn't it? They didn't want us to know what he'd really been doing. My missus,' said Wardle, scowling even harder, 'thinks he's sexy. You married?'

'No,' said Strike.

'Anstis told me you left the army to get married to some woman who looks like a supermodel.'

'What was Duffield's story, once you got to him?'

'They'd had a big bust-up in the club, Uzi. Plenty of witnesses to that. She left, and his story was that he followed her, about five minutes later, wearing this fucking wolf mask. It covers the whole head. Lifelike, hairy thing. He told us he'd got it from a fashion shoot.'

Wardle's expression was eloquent of contempt.

'He liked putting this thing on to get in and out of places, to piss off the paparazzi. So, after Landry left Uzi, he got in his car – he had a driver outside, waiting for him – and went to

Kentigern Gardens. Driver confirmed all that. Yeah, all right,' Wardle corrected himself impatiently, 'he confirmed that he drove a man in a wolf's head, who he assumed was Duffield as he was of Duffield's height and build, and wearing what looked like Duffield's clothes, and speaking in Duffield's voice, to Kentigern Gardens.'

'But he didn't take the wolf head off on the journey?'

'It's only about fifteen minutes to her flat from Uzi. No, he didn't take it off. He's a childish little prick.

'So then, by Duffield's own account, he saw the paps outside her flat and decided not to go in after all. He told the driver to take him off to Soho, where he let him out. Duffield walked round the corner to his dealer's flat in d'Arblay Street, where he shot up.'

'Still wearing the wolf's head?'

'No, he took it off there,' said Wardle. 'The dealer, name of Whycliff, is an ex-public schoolboy with a habit way worse than Duffield's. He gave a full statement agreeing that Duffield had come round at about half past two. It was only the pair of them there, and yeah, I'd take long odds that Whycliff would lie for Duffield, but a woman on the ground floor heard the doorbell ring and says she saw Duffield on the stair.

'Anyway, Duffield left Whycliff's around four, with the bloody wolf's head back on, and rambled off towards the place where he thought his car and driver were waiting; except that the driver was gone. The driver claimed a misunderstanding. He thought Duffield was an arsehole; he made that clear when we took his statement. Duffield wasn't paying him; the car was on Landry's account.

'So then Duffield, who's got no money on him, walks all the way to Ciara Porter's place in Notting Hill. We found a few people who'd seen a man wearing a wolf's head strolling along relevant streets, and there's footage of him cadging a free box of matches from a woman in an all-night garage.'

'Can you make out his face?'

'No, because he only shoved the wolf head up to speak to her, and all you can see is its snout. She said it was Duffield, though.

'He got to Porter's around half four. She let him sleep on the sofa, and about an hour later she got the news about Landry being dead, and woke him up to tell him. Cue histrionics and rehab.'

'You checked for a suicide note?' asked Strike.

'Yeah. There was nothing in the flat, nothing on her laptop, but that wasn't a surprise. She did it on the spur of the moment, didn't she? She was bipolar, she'd just argued with that little tosser and it pushed her over – well, you know what I mean.'

Wardle checked his watch, and drained the last of his pint.

'I'm gonna have to go. The wife'll be pissed off, I told her I'd only be half an hour.'

The over-tanned girls had left without either man noticing. Out on the pavement, both lit up cigarettes.

'I hate this fucking smoking ban,' said Wardle, zipping his leather jacket up to the neck.

'Have we got a deal, then?' asked Strike.

Cigarette between his lips, Wardle pulled on a pair of gloves.

'I dunno about that.'

'C'mon, Wardle,' said Strike, handing the policeman a card, which Wardle accepted as though it were a joke item. 'I've given you Brett Fearney.'

Wardle laughed outright.

'Not yet you haven't.'

He slipped Strike's card into a pocket, inhaled, blew smoke skywards, then shot the larger man a look compounded of curiosity and appraisal.

'Yeah, all right. If we get Fearney, you can have the file.'

11

'Evan Duffield's agent says his client isn't taking any further calls or giving any interviews about Lula Landry,' said Robin next morning. 'I did make it clear that you're not a journalist, but he was adamant. And the people in Guy Somé's office are ruder than Freddie Bestigui's. You'd think I was trying to get an audience with the Pope.'

'OK,' said Strike. 'I'll see whether I can get at him through Bristow.'

It was the first time that Robin had seen Strike in a suit. He looked, she thought, like a rugby player en route to an international: large, conventionally smart in his dark jacket and subdued tie. He was on his knees, searching through one of the cardboard boxes he had brought from Charlotte's flat. Robin was averting her gaze from his boxed-up possessions. They were still avoiding any mention of the fact that Strike was living in his office.

'Aha,' he said, finally locating, from amid a pile of his mail, a bright blue envelope: the invitation to his nephew's party. 'Bollocks,' he added, on opening it.

'What's the matter?'

'It doesn't say how old he is,' said Strike. 'My nephew.'

Robin was curious about Strike's relations with his family. As she had never been officially informed, however, that Strike had numerous half-brothers and sisters, a famous father and a mildly infamous mother, she bit back all questions and continued to open the day's paltry mail.

Strike got up off the floor, replaced the cardboard box in a corner of the inner office and returned to Robin.

'What's that?' he asked, seeing a sheet of photocopied newsprint on the desk.

'I kept it for you,' she said diffidently. 'You said you were glad you'd seen that story about Evan Duffield . . . I thought you might be interested in this, if you haven't already seen it.'

It was a neatly clipped article about film producer Freddie Bestigui, taken from the previous day's *Evening Standard*.

'Excellent; I'll read that on the way to lunch with his wife.'

'Soon to be ex,' said Robin. 'It's all in that article. He's not very lucky in love, Mr Bestigui.'

'From what Wardle told me, he's not a very lovable man,' said Strike.

'How did you get that policeman to talk to you?' Robin said, unable to hold back her curiosity on this point. She was desperate to learn more about the process and progress of the investigation.

'We've got a mutual friend,' said Strike. 'Bloke I knew in Afghanistan; Met officer in the TA.'

'You were in Afghanistan?'

'Yeah.' Strike was pulling on his overcoat, the folded article on Freddie Bestigui and the invitation to Jack's party between his teeth.

'What were you doing in Afghanistan?'

'Investigating a Killed In Action,' said Strike. 'Military police.'

'Oh,' said Robin.

Military police did not tally with Matthew's impression of a charlatan, or a waster.

'Why did you leave?'

'Injured,' said Strike.

He had described that injury to Wilson in the starkest of terms, but he was wary of being equally frank with Robin. He could imagine her shocked expression, and he stood in no need of her sympathy.

'Don't forget to call Peter Gillespie,' Robin reminded him, as he headed out of the door.

Strike read the photocopied article as he rode the Tube to Bond Street. Freddie Bestigui had inherited his first fortune from a father who had made a great deal of money in haulage; he had made his second by producing highly commercial films that serious critics treated with derision. The producer was currently going to court to refute claims, by two newspapers, that he had behaved with gross impropriety towards a young female employee, whose silence he had subsequently bought. The accusations, carefully hedged around with many 'alleged's and 'reported's, included aggressive sexual advances and a degree of physical bullying. They had been made 'by a source close to the alleged victim', the girl herself having refused either to press charges or to speak to the press. The fact that Freddie was currently divorcing his latest wife, Tansy, was mentioned in the concluding paragraph, which ended with a reminder that the unhappy couple had been in the building on the night that Lula Landry took her own life. The reader was left with the odd impression that the Bestiguis' mutual unhappiness might have influenced Landry in her decision to jump.

Strike had never moved in the kinds of circles that dined at Cipriani. It was only as he walked up Davies Street, the sun warm on his back and imparting a ruddy glow to the red-brick building ahead, that he thought how odd it would be, yet not unlikely, if he ran into one of his half-siblings there. Restaurants like Cipriani were part of the regular lives of Strike's father's legitimate children. He had last heard from three of them while in Selly Oak Hospital, undergoing physiotherapy. Gabi and Danni had jointly sent flowers; Al had visited once, laughing too loudly and scared of looking at the lower end of the bed. Afterwards, Charlotte had imitated Al braying and wincing. She was a good mimic. Nobody ever expected a girl that beautiful to be funny, yet she was.

The interior of the restaurant had an art deco feeling, the bar and chairs of mellow polished wood, with pale yellow tablecloths on the circular tables and white-jacketed, bow-tied waiters and waitresses. Strike spotted his client immediately among the clattering, jabbering diners, sitting at a table set for four and talking, to Strike's surprise, to two women instead of one, both with long, glossy brown hair. Bristow's rabbity face was full of the desire to please, or perhaps placate.

The lawyer jumped up to greet Strike when he saw him, and introduced Tansy Bestigui, who held out a thin, cool hand, but did not smile, and her sister, Ursula May, who did not hold out a hand at all. While the preliminaries of ordering drinks and handing around menus were navigated, Bristow nervous and over-talkative throughout, the sisters subjected Strike to the kind of brazenly critical stares that only people of a certain class feel entitled to give.

They were both as pristine and polished as life-size dolls recently removed from their cellophane boxes; rich-girl thin, almost hipless in their tight jeans, with tanned faces that had a waxy sheen especially noticeable on their foreheads, their long, gleaming dark manes with centre partings, the ends trimmed with spirit-level exactitude.

When Strike finally chose to look up from his menu, Tansy said, without preamble:

'Are you really' (she pronounced it 'rarely') 'Jonny Rokeby's son?'

'So the DNA test said,' he replied.

She seemed uncertain whether he was being funny or rude. Her dark eyes were fractionally too close together, and the Botox and fillers could not smooth away the petulance in her expression.

'Listen, I've just been telling John,' she said curtly. 'I'm not going public again, OK? I'm perfectly happy to tell you what I heard, because I'd love you to prove I was right, but you mustn't tell anyone I've talked to you.'

The unbuttoned neck of her thin silk shirt revealed an expanse of butterscotch skin stretched over her bony sternum, giving an unattractively knobbly effect; yet two full, firm breasts jutted from her narrow ribcage, as though they had been borrowed for the day from a fuller-figured friend. 'We could have met somewhere more discreet,' commented Strike.

'No, it's fine, because nobody here will know who you are. You don't look anything like your father, do you? I met him at Elton's last summer. Freddie knows him. D'you see much of Jonny?'

'I've met him twice,' said Strike.

'Oh,' said Tansy.

The monosyllable contained equal parts of surprise and disdain.

Charlotte had had friends like this; sleek-haired, expensively educated and clothed, all of them appalled by her strange yen for the enormous, battered-looking Strike. He had come up against them for years, by phone and in person, with their clipped vowels and their stockbroker husbands, and the brittle toughness Charlotte had never been able to fake.

'I don't think she should be talking to you at all,' said Ursula abruptly. Her tone and expression would have been appropriate had Strike been a waiter who had just thrown aside his apron and joined them, uninvited, at the table. 'I think you're making a big mistake, Tanz.'

Bristow said: 'Ursula, Tansy simply—'

'It's up to me what I do,' Tansy snapped at her sister, as though Bristow had not spoken, as though his chair was empty. 'I'm only going to say what I heard, that's all. It's all off the record; John's agreed to that.'

Evidently she too viewed Strike as domestic class. He was irked not only by their tone, but also by the fact that Bristow was giving witnesses assurances without his say-so. How could Tansy's evidence, which could have come from nobody but her, be kept off the record?

For a few moments all four of them ran their eyes over the culinary options in silence. Ursula was the first to put down her menu. She had already finished a glass of wine. She helped herself to another, and glanced restlessly around the restaurant, her eyes lingering for a second on a blonde minor royal, before passing on.

'This place used to be full of the most fabulous people, even at lunchtime. Cyprian only ever wants to go to bloody Wiltons, with all the other stiffs in suits . . .'

'Is Cyprian your husband, Mrs May?' asked Strike.

He guessed that it would needle her if he crossed what she evidently saw as an invisible line between them; she did not think that sitting at a table with her gave him a right to her conversation. She scowled, and Bristow rushed to fill the uncomfortable pause.

'Yes, Ursula's married to Cyprian May, one of our senior partners.'

'So I'm getting the family discount on my divorce,' said Tansy, with a slightly bitter smile.

'And her ex will go absolutely ballistic if she starts dragging the press back into their lives,' Ursula said, her dark eyes boring into Strike's. 'They're trying to thrash out a settlement. It could seriously prejudice her alimony if that all kicks off again. So you'd better be discreet.'

With a bland smile, Strike turned to Tansy:

'You had a connection with Lula Landry, then, Mrs Bestigui? Your brother-in-law works with John?'

'It never came up,' she said, looking bored.

The waiter returned to take their orders. When he had left, Strike took out his notebook and pen.

'What are you doing with those?' demanded Tansy, in a sudden panic. 'I don't want anything written down! John?' she appealed to Bristow, who turned to Strike with a flustered and apologetic expression.

'D'you think you could just listen, Cormoran, and, ah, skip the note-taking?'

'No problem,' said Strike easily, removing his mobile phone from his pocket and replacing the notebook and pen. 'Mrs Bestigui—'

'You can call me Tansy,' she said, as though this concession made up for her objections to the notebook.

'Thanks very much,' said Strike, with the merest trace of irony. 'How well did you know Lula?'

'Oh, hardly at all. She was only there for three months. It was just "Hi" and "Nice day". She wasn't interested in us, we weren't nearly hip enough for her. It was a bore, to be honest, having her there. Paps outside the front door all the time. I had to put on make-up even to go to the gym.'

'Isn't there a gym in the building?' asked Strike.

'I do Pilates with Lindsey Parr,' said Tansy, irritably. 'You sound like Freddie; he was always complaining that I didn't use the facilities at the flat.'

'And how well did Freddie know Lula?'

'Hardly at all, but that wasn't for lack of trying. He had some idea about luring her into acting; he kept trying to invite her downstairs. She never came, though. And he followed her to Dickie Carbury's house, the weekend before she died, while I was away with Ursula.'

'I didn't know that,' said Bristow, looking startled.

Strike noticed Ursula's quick smirk at her sister. He had the impression that she had been looking for an exchange of complicit glances, but Tansy did not oblige.

'I didn't know until later,' Tansy told Bristow. 'Yah, Freddie cadged an invitation from Dickie; there was a whole group of them there: Lula, Evan Duffield, Ciara Porter, all that tabloidy, druggie, trendy gang. Freddie must have stuck out like a sore thumb. I know he's not much older than Dickie, but he looks ancient,' she added spitefully.

'What did your husband tell you about the weekend?'

'Nothing. I only found out he'd been there weeks later, because Dickie let it slip. I'm sure Freddie went to try and make up to Lula, though.'

'Do you mean,' asked Strike, 'that he was interested in Lula sexually, or . . . ?'

'Oh yah, I'm sure he was; he's always liked dark girls better than blondes. What he really loves, though, is getting a bit of celebrity meat into his films. He drives directors mad, trying to crowbar in celebrities, to get a bit of extra press. I'll bet he was hoping to get her signed up for a film, and I wouldn't be at all surprised,' Tansy added, with unexpected shrewdness, 'if he had something planned around her and Deeby Macc. Imagine the press, with the fuss there was already about the two of them. Freddie's got a genius for that stuff. He loves publicity for his films as much as he hates it for himself.'

'Does he know Deeby Macc?'

'Not unless they've met since we separated. He hadn't met Macc before Lula died. God, he was thrilled that Macc was coming to stay in the building; he started talking about casting him the moment he heard.'

'Casting him as what?'

'I don't know,' she said irritably. 'Anything. Macc's got a huge following; Freddie wasn't going to pass that chance up. He'd probably have had a part written specially for him if he'd been interested. Oh, he would have been all over him. Telling him all about his pretend black grandmother.' Tansy's voice was contemptuous. 'That's what he always does when he meets famous black people: tells them he's a quarter Malay. Yeah, *whatever*, Freddie.'

'Isn't he a quarter Malay?' asked Strike.

She gave a snide little laugh.

'I don't know; I never met any of Freddie's grandparents, did I? He's about a hundred years old. I know he'll say anything if he thinks there's money in it.'

'Did anything ever come of these plans to get Lula and Macc into his films, as far as you're aware?'

'Well, I'm sure Lula was flattered to be asked; most of these model girls are dying to prove they can do something other than stare into a camera, but she never signed up to anything, did she, John?'

'Not as far as I know,' said Bristow. 'Although . . . but that was something different,' he mumbled, turning blotchily pink again. He hesitated, then, responding to Strike's interrogative gaze, he said:

'Mr Bestigui visited my mother a couple of weeks ago, out of the blue. She's exceptionally poorly, and . . . well, I wouldn't want to . . . '

His glance at Tansy was uncomfortable.

'Say what you like, I don't care,' she said, with what seemed like genuine indifference.

Bristow made the strange jutting and sucking movement that temporarily hid the hamsterish teeth.

'Well, he wanted to talk to my mother about a film of Lula's life. He, ah, framed his visit as something considerate and sensitive. Asking for her family's blessing, official sanction, you know. Lula dead barely three months . . . Mum was distressed beyond measure. Unfortunately, I was not there when he called,' said Bristow, and his tone implied that he was generally to be found standing guard over his mother. 'I wish, in a way, I had been. I wish I'd heard him out. I mean, if he's got researchers working on Lula's life story, much as I deplore the idea, he might know something, mightn't he?'

'What kind of thing?' asked Strike.

'I don't know. Something about her early life, perhaps? Before she came to us?'

The waiter arrived to place starters in front of them all. Strike waited until he had gone, and then asked Bristow:

'Have you tried to speak to Mr Bestigui yourself, and find out whether he knew anything about Lula that the family didn't?'

'That's just what's so difficult,' said Bristow. 'When Tony – my uncle – heard what had happened, he contacted Mr Bestigui to protest about him badgering my mother, and from what I've heard, there was a very heated argument. I don't think Mr Bestigui would welcome further contact from the family. Of course, the situation's further complicated by the fact that Tansy is using our firm for the divorce. I mean, there's nothing in that – we're one of the top family law firms, and with Ursula being married to Cyprian, naturally she would come to us . . . But I'm sure it won't have made Mr Bestigui feel any more kindly towards us.'

Though he had kept his gaze on the lawyer all the time that Bristow was talking, Strike's peripheral vision was excellent. Ursula had thrown another tiny smirk in her sister's direction. He wondered what was amusing her. Doubtless her improved mood was not hindered by the fact that she was now on her fourth glass of wine.

Strike finished his starter and turned to Tansy, who was pushing her virtually untouched food around her plate.

'How long had you and your husband been at number eighteen before Lula moved in?'

'About a year.'

'Was there anyone in the middle flat when she arrived?'

'Yah,' said Tansy. 'There was an American couple there with their little boy for six months, but they went back to the States not long after she arrived. After that, the property company couldn't get anyone interested at all. The recession, you know? They cost an arm and a leg, those flats. So it was empty until the record company rented it for Deeby Macc.'

Both she and Ursula were distracted by the sight of a woman passing the table in what, to Strike, appeared to be a crocheted coat of lurid design.

'That's a Daumier-Cross coat,' said Ursula, her eyes slightly narrowed over her wine glass. 'There's a waiting list of, like, six months . . . '

'It's Pansy Marks-Dillon,' said Tansy. 'Easy to be on the best-dressed list if your husband's got fifty mill. Freddie's the cheapest rich man in the world; I had to hide new stuff from him, or pretend it was fake. He could be such a bore sometimes.'

'You always look wonderful,' said Bristow, pink in the face.

'You're sweet,' said Tansy Bestigui in a bored voice.

The waiter arrived to clear away their plates.

'What were you saying?' she asked Strike. 'Oh, yah, the flats. Deeby Macc coming . . . except he didn't. Freddie was furious he never got there, because he'd put roses in his flat. Freddie is such a cheap bastard.'

'How well do you know Derrick Wilson?' Strike asked.

She blinked.

'Well – he's the security guard; I don't know him, do I? He seemed all right. Freddie always said he was the best of the bunch.'

'Really? Why was that?'

She shrugged.

'I don't know, you'd have to ask Freddie. And good luck with that,' she added, with a little laugh. 'Freddie'll talk to you when hell freezes over.'

'Tansy,' said Bristow, leaning in a little, 'why don't you just tell Cormoran what you actually heard that night?'

Strike would have preferred Bristow not to intervene.

'Well,' said Tansy. 'It was getting on for two in the morning, and I wanted a drink of water.'

Her tone was flat and expressionless. Strike noticed that, even in this small beginning, she had altered the story she had told the police.

'So I went to the bathroom to get one, and as I was heading back across the sitting room, towards the bedroom, I heard shouting. She – Lula – was saying, "It's too late, I've already done it," and then a man said, "You're a lying fucking bitch," and then – and then he threw her over. I actually saw her fall.'

And Tansy made a tiny jerky movement with her hands that Strike understood to indicate flailing.

Bristow set down his glass, looking nauseated. Their main courses arrived. Ursula drank more wine. Neither Tansy nor Bristow touched their food. Strike picked up his fork and began to eat, trying not to look as though he was enjoying his *puntarelle* with anchovies.

'I screamed,' whispered Tansy. 'I couldn't stop screaming. I ran out of the flat, past Freddie, and downstairs. I just wanted to tell security that there was a man up there, so they could get him.

'Wilson came dashing out of the room behind the desk. I told him what had happened and he went straight out on to the street to see her, instead of running upstairs. Bloody fool. If only he'd gone upstairs first, he might have caught him! Then Freddie came down after me, and started trying to make me go back to our flat, because I wasn't dressed.

'Then Wilson came back, and told us she was dead, and told Freddie to call the police. Freddie virtually dragged me back upstairs – I was completely hysterical – and he dialled 999 from our sitting room. And then the police came. And nobody believed a single word I said.'

She sipped her wine again, set down the glass and said quietly:

'If Freddie knew I was talking to you, he'd go ape.'

'But you're quite sure, aren't you, Tansy,' Bristow interjected, 'that you heard a man up there?'

'Yah, of course I am,' said Tansy. 'I've just said, haven't I? There was definitely someone there.'

Bristow's mobile rang.

'Excuse me,' he muttered. 'Alison . . . yes?' he said, picking up.

Strike could hear the secretary's deep voice, without being able to make out the words.

'Excuse me just a moment,' Bristow said, looking harried, and he left the table.

A look of malicious amusement appeared on both sisters' smooth, polished faces. They glanced at each other again; then, somewhat to his surprise, Ursula asked Strike:

'Have you met Alison?'

'Briefly.'

'You know they're together?'

'Yes.'

'It's a bit pathetic, actually,' said Tansy. 'She's with John, but she's actually obsessed with Tony. Have you met Tony?'

'No,' said Strike.

'He's one of the senior partners. John's uncle, you know?'

'Yes.'

'Very attractive. He wouldn't go for Alison in a million years. I suppose she's settled for John as consolation prize.'

The thought of Alison's doomed infatuation seemed to afford the sisters great satisfaction.

'This is all common gossip at the office, is it?' asked Strike.

'Oh, yah,' said Ursula, with relish. 'Cyprian says she's absolutely embarrassing. Like a puppy dog around Tony.'

Her antipathy towards Strike seemed to have evaporated. He was not surprised; he had met the phenomenon many times. People liked to talk; there were very few exceptions; the question was how you made them do it. Some, and Ursula was evidently one of them, were amenable to alcohol; others liked a spotlight; and then there were those who merely needed proximity to another conscious human being. A subsection of humanity would become loquacious only on one favourite subject: it might be their own innocence, or somebody else's guilt; it might be their collection of pre-war biscuit tins; or it might, as in the case of Ursula May, be the hopeless passion of a plain secretary.

Ursula was watching Bristow through the window; he was standing on the pavement, talking hard into his mobile as he paced up and down. Her tongue properly loosened now, she said:

'I bet I know what that's about. Conway Oates's executors are making a fuss about how the firm handled his affairs. He was the American financier, you know? Cyprian and Tony are in a real bait about it, making John fly around trying to smooth things over. John always gets the shitty end of the stick.'

Her tone was more scathing than sympathetic.

Bristow returned to the table, looking flustered.

'Sorry, sorry, Alison just wanted to give me some messages,' he said.

The waiter came to collect their plates. Strike was the only one who had cleared his. When the waiter was out of earshot, Strike said:

'Tansy, the police disregarded your evidence because they didn't think you could have heard what you claimed to have heard.'

'Well they were wrong, weren't they?' she snapped, her good humour gone in a trice. 'I did hear it.'

'Through a closed window?'

'It was open,' she said, meeting none of her companions' eyes. 'It was stuffy, I opened one of the windows on the way to get water.'

Strike was sure that pressing her on the point would only lead to her refusing to answer any other questions.

'They also allege that you'd taken cocaine.'

Tansy made a little noise of impatience, a soft 'cuh'.

'Look,' she said, 'I had some earlier, during dinner, OK, and they found it in the bathroom when they looked around the flat. The fucking *boredom* of the Dunnes. Anyone would have done a couple of lines to get through Benjy Dunne's bloody anecdotes. But I didn't imagine that voice upstairs. A man was there, and he killed her. *He killed her*,' repeated Tansy, glaring at Strike.

'And where do you think he went afterwards?'

'I don't know, do I? That's what John's paying you to find out. He sneaked out somehow. Maybe he climbed out the back window. Maybe he hid in the lift. Maybe he went out through the car park downstairs. I don't bloody know how he got out, I just know he was there.'

'We believe you,' interjected Bristow anxiously. 'We believe you, Tansy. Cormoran needs to ask these questions to – to get a clear picture of how it all happened.'

'The police did everything they could to discredit me,' said Tansy, disregarding Bristow and addressing Strike. 'They got there too late, and he'd already gone, so of course they covered it up. No one who hasn't been through what I went through with the press can understand what it was like. It was absolute bloody hell. I went into the clinic just to get away from it all. I can't believe it's legal, what the press are allowed to do in this country; and all for telling the truth, that's the bloody joke. I should've kept my mouth shut, shouldn't I? I would have, if I'd known what was coming.'

She twisted her loose diamond ring around her finger.

'Freddie was asleep in bed when Lula fell, wasn't he?' Strike asked Tansy.

'Yah, that's right,' she said.

Her hand slid up to her face and she smoothed nonexistent strands of hair off her forehead. The waiter returned with menus again, and Strike was forced to hold back his questions until they had ordered. He was the only one to ask for pudding; all the rest had coffee.

'When did Freddie get out of bed?' he asked Tansy, when the waiter had left.

'What do you mean?'

'You say he was in bed when Lula fell; when did he get up?'

'When he heard me screaming,' she said, as though this was obvious. 'I woke him up, didn't I?'

'He must have moved quickly.'

'Why?'

'You said: "I ran out of the flat, past Freddie, and downstairs." So he was already in the room before you ran out to tell Derrick what had happened?'

A missed beat.

'That's right,' she said, smoothing her immaculate hair again, shielding her face.

'So he went from fast asleep in bed, to awake and in the sitting room, within seconds? Because you started screaming and running pretty much instantaneously, from what you said?'

Another infinitesimal pause.

'Yah,' she said. 'Well – I don't know. I think I screamed – I screamed while I was frozen on the spot – for a moment, maybe – I was just so shocked – and Freddie came running out of the bedroom, and then I ran past him.'

'Did you stop to tell him what you'd seen?'

'I can't remember.'

Bristow looked as though he was about to stage one of his untimely interventions again. Strike held up a hand to forestall him; but Tansy plunged off on another tack, eager, he guessed, to leave the subject of her husband.

'I've thought and thought about how the killer got in, and I'm sure he must have followed her inside when she came in that morning, because of Derrick Wilson leaving his desk and being in the bathroom. I thought Wilson ought to have been bloody sacked for it, actually. If you ask me, he was having a sneaky sleep in the back room. I don't know how the killer would have known the key code, but I'm sure that's when he must have got in.'

'Do you think you'd be able to recognise the man's voice again? The one you heard shouting?'

'I doubt it,' she said. 'It was just a man's voice. It could have been anyone. There was nothing unusual about it. I mean, afterwards I thought, *Was it Duffield?*' she said, gazing at him intently, 'because I'd heard Duffield shouting upstairs, once before, from the top landing. Wilson had to throw him out; Duffield was trying to kick in Lula's door. I never understood what a girl with her looks was doing with someone like Duffield,' she added in parenthesis.

'Some women say he's sexy,' agreed Ursula, emptying the wine bottle into her glass, 'but I can't see the appeal. He's just skanky and horrible.'

'It's not even,' said Tansy, twisting the loose diamond ring again, 'as though he's got money.'

'But you don't think it was his voice you heard that night?'

'Well, like I say, it could have been,' she said impatiently, with a small shrug of her thin shoulders. 'He's got an alibi, though, hasn't he? Loads of people said he was nowhere near Kentigern Gardens the night Lula was killed. He spent part of it at Ciara Porter's, didn't he? Bitch,' Tansy added, with a small, tight smile. 'Sleeping with her best friend's boyfriend.'

'Were they sleeping together?' asked Strike.

'Oh, what do *you* think?' laughed Ursula, as though the question was too naive for words. 'I know Ciara Porter, she modelled in this charity fashion show I was involved in setting up. She's such an airhead and such a slut.'

The coffees had arrived, along with Strike's sticky toffee pudding.

'I'm sorry, John, but Lula didn't have very good taste in friends,' said Tansy, sipping her espresso. 'There was Ciara, and then there was that Bryony Radford. Not that she was a friend, exactly, but I wouldn't trust her as far as I could throw her.'

'Who's Bryony?' asked Strike disingenuously, for he remembered who she was.

'Make-up artist. Charges a fortune, and such a bloody bitch,' said Ursula. 'I used her once, before one of the Gorbachev Foundation balls, and afterwards she told ev—'

Ursula stopped abruptly, lowered her glass and picked up her coffee instead. Strike, who despite its undoubted irrelevance to the matter in hand was quite interested to know what Bryony had told everyone, began to speak, but Tansy talked loudly over him.

'Oh, and there was that ghastly girl Lula used to bring around to the flat, too, John, remember?'

She appealed to Bristow again, but he looked blank.

'You know, that ghastly – that rarely awful – coloured girl she sometimes dragged back. A kind of hobo person. I mean . . . she literally smelled. When she'd been in the lift . . . you could smell it. And she took her into the pool, too. I didn't think blacks could swim?'

Bristow was blinking rapidly, pink in the face.

'God knows what Lula was doing with her,' said Tansy. 'Oh, you must remember, John. She was fat. Scruffy. Looked a bit subnormal.'

'I don't . . . ' mumbled Bristow.

'Are you talking about Rochelle?' asked Strike.

'Oh, yah, I think that was her name. She was at the funeral, anyway,' said Tansy. 'I noticed her. She was sitting right at the back.

'Now, you will remember, won't you,' she turned the full force of her dark eyes upon Strike, 'that this is all entirely off the record. I mean, I cannot afford for Freddie to find out I'm talking to you. I'm not going to go through all that shit with the press again. Bill, please,' she barked at the waiter.

When it arrived, she passed it without comment to Bristow.

As the sisters were preparing to leave, shaking their glossy brown hair back over their shoulders and pulling on expensive jackets, the door of the restaurant opened and a tall, thin, besuited man of around sixty entered, looked around and headed straight for their table. Silver-haired and distinguished-looking, impeccably dressed, there was a certain chilliness about his pale blue eyes. His walk was brisk and purposeful.

'This is a surprise,' he said smoothly, stopping in the space between the two women's chairs. None of the other three had seen the man coming, and all bar Strike displayed equal parts of shock and something more than displeasure at the sight of him. For a fraction of a second, Tansy and Ursula froze, Ursula in the act of pulling sunglasses out of her bag.

Tansy recovered first.

'Cyprian,' she said, offering her face for his kiss. 'Yes, what a lovely surprise!'

'I thought you were going shopping, Ursula dear?' he said, his eyes on his wife as he gave Tansy a conventional peck on each cheek.

'We stopped for lunch, Cyps,' she replied, but her colour was heightened, and Strike sensed an ill-defined nastiness in the air.

The older man's pale eyes moved deliberately over Strike and came to rest on Bristow.

'I thought Tony was handling your divorce, Tansy?' he asked.

'He is,' said Tansy. 'This isn't a business lunch, Cyps. Purely social.'

He gave a wintry smile.

'Let me escort you out, then, m'dears,' he said.

With a cursory farewell to Bristow, and no word whatsoever for Strike, the two sisters permitted themselves to be shepherded out of the restaurant by Ursula's husband. When the door had swung shut behind the threesome, Strike asked Bristow:

'What was that about?'

'That was Cyprian,' said Bristow. He seemed agitated as he fumbled with his credit card and the bill. 'Cyprian May. Ursula's husband. Senior partner at the firm. He won't like Tansy talking to you. I wonder how he knew where we were. Probably got it out of Alison.'

'Why won't he like her talking to me?'

'Tansy's his sister-in-law,' said Bristow, putting on his overcoat. 'He won't want her to make a fool of herself – as he'll see it – all over again. I'll probably get a real bollocking for persuading her to meet you. I expect he's phoning my uncle right now, to complain about me.'

Bristow's hands, Strike noticed, were trembling.

The lawyer left in a taxi ordered by the maître d'. Strike headed away from Cipriani on foot, loosening his tie as he walked, and lost so deeply in thought that he was only jerked out of his reverie by a loud horn blast from a car he had not seen speeding towards him as he crossed Grosvenor Street.

With this salutary reminder that his safety would otherwise be in jeopardy, Strike headed for a patch of pale wall belonging to the Elizabeth Arden Red Door Spa, leaned up against it out of the pedestrian flow, lit up and pulled out his mobile phone. After some listening and fast-forwarding, he managed to locate that part of Tansy's recorded testimony that dealt with those moments immediately preceding Lula Landry's fall past her window.

. . . towards the bedroom, I heard shouting. She – Lula – was saying, 'It's too late, I've already done it,' and then a man said, 'You're a lying fucking bitch,' and then – and then he threw her over. I actually saw her fall.

He could just make out the tiny chink of Bristow's glass hitting the table top. Strike rewound again and listened.

. . . saying, 'It's too late, I've already done it,' and then a man said, 'You're a lying fucking bitch,' and then – and then he threw her over. I actually saw her fall.

He recalled Tansy's imitation of Landry's flailing arms, and the horror on her frozen face as she did it. Slipping his mobile back into his pocket, he took out his notebook and began to make notes for himself.

Strike had met countless liars; he could smell them; and he knew perfectly well that Tansy was of their number. She could not have heard what she claimed to have heard from her flat; the police had therefore deduced that she could not have heard it at all. Against Strike's expectation, however, in spite of the fact that every piece of evidence he had heard until this moment suggested that Lula Landry had committed suicide, he found himself convinced that Tansy Bestigui really believed that she had overheard an argument before Landry fell. That was the only part of her story that rang with authenticity, an authenticity that shone a garish light on the fakery with which she garnished it.

Strike pushed himself off the wall and began to walk east along Grosvenor Street, paying slightly more attention to traffic, but inwardly recalling Tansy's expression, her tone, her mannerisms, as she spoke of Lula Landry's final moments.

Why would she tell the truth on the essential point, but surround it with easily disproven falsehoods? Why would she lie about what she had been doing when she heard shouting from Landry's flat? Strike remembered Adler: 'A lie would have no sense unless the truth were felt as dangerous.' Tansy had come along today to make a last attempt to find someone who would believe her, and yet swallow the lies in which she insisted on swaddling her evidence.

He walked fast, barely conscious of the twinges from his right knee. At last he realised that he had walked all along Maddox Street and emerged on Regent Street. The red awnings of Hamleys Toy Shop fluttered a little in the distance, and Strike remembered that he had intended to buy a birthday present for his nephew's forthcoming birthday on the way back to the office.

The multicoloured, squeaking, flashing maelstrom into which he walked registered on him only vaguely. Blindly he moved from floor to floor, untroubled by the shrieks, the whirring of airborne toy helicopters, the oinks of mechanical pigs moving across his distracted path. Finally, after twenty minutes or so, he came to rest near the HM Forces dolls. Here he stood, quite still, gazing at the ranks of miniature marines and paratroopers but barely seeing them; deaf to the whispers of parents trying to manoeuvre their sons around him, too intimidated to ask the strange, huge, staring man to move.

Part Three

Forsan et haec olim meminisse iuvabit.

Maybe one day it will be cheering even to remember these things.

Virgil, *Aeneid*, Book 1

1

It started to rain on Wednesday. London weather; dank and grey, through which the old city presented a stolid front: pale faces under black umbrellas, the eternal smell of damp clothing, the steady pattering on Strike's office window in the night.

The rain in Cornwall had a different quality, when it came: Strike remembered how it had lashed like whips against the panes of Aunt Joan and Uncle Ted's spare room, during those months in the neat little house that smelled of flowers and baking, while he had attended the village school in St Mawes. Such memories swam to the forefront of his mind whenever he was about to see Lucy.

Raindrops were still dancing exuberantly on the windowsills on Friday afternoon, while at opposite ends of her desk, Robin wrapped Jack's new paratrooper doll, and Strike wrote her a cheque to the amount of a week's work, minus the commission of Temporary Solutions. Robin was about to attend the third of that week's 'proper' interviews, and was looking neat and groomed in her black suit, with her bright gold hair pinned back in a chignon.

'There you are,' they both said simultaneously, as Robin pushed across the desk a perfect parcel patterned with small spaceships, and Strike held out the cheque.

'Cheers,' said Strike, taking the present. 'I can't wrap.'

'I hope he likes it,' she replied, tucking the cheque away in her black handbag.

'Yeah. And good luck with the interview. D'you want the job?'

'Well, it's quite a good one. Human resources in a media consultancy in the West End,' she said, sounding unenthusiastic. 'Enjoy the party. I'll see you Monday.'

The self-imposed penance of walking down into Denmark Street to smoke became even more irksome in the ceaseless rain. Strike stood, minimally shielded beneath the overhang of his office entrance, and asked himself when he was going to kick the habit and set to work to restore the fitness that had slipped away along with his solvency and his domestic comfort. His mobile rang while he stood there.

'Thought you might like to know your tip-off's paid dividends,' said Eric Wardle, who sounded triumphant. Strike could hear engine noise and the sound of men talking in the background.

'Quick work,' commented Strike.

'Yeah, well, we don't hang around.'

'Does this mean I'm going to get what I was after?'

'That's what I'm calling about. It's a bit late today, but I'll bike it over Monday.'

'Sooner rather than later suits me. I can hang on here at the office.'

Wardle laughed a little offensively.

'You get paid by the hour, don't you? I'd've thought it suited you to string it out a bit.'

'Tonight would be better. If you can get it here this evening, I'll make sure you're the first to know if my old mate drops any more tip-offs.'

In the slight pause that followed, Strike heard one of the men in the car with Wardle say:

'. . . *Fearney's fucking face* . . .'

'Yeah, all right,' said Wardle. 'I'll get it over later. Might not be till seven. Will you still be there?'

'I'll make sure I am,' Strike replied.

The file arrived three hours later, while he was eating fish and chips out of a small polystyrene tray in his lap and watching the London evening news on his portable television. The courier buzzed the outer door and Strike signed for a bulky package sent from Scotland Yard. Once unwrapped, a thick grey folder full of photocopied material was disclosed. Strike took it back to Robin's desk, and began the lengthy process of digesting the contents.

Here were statements from those who had seen Lula Landry during the final evening of her life; a report on the DNA evidence lifted from her flat; photocopied pages of the visitors' book compiled by security at number 18, Kentigern Gardens; details of the medication Lula had been prescribed to control bipolar disorder; the autopsy report; medical records for the previous year; mobile phone and landline records; and a precis of the findings on the model's laptop. There was also a DVD, on which Wardle had scribbled CCTV 2 Runners.

The DVD drive on Strike's second-hand computer had not worked since he acquired it; he therefore slipped the disc into the pocket of the overcoat hanging by the glass door, and resumed his contemplation of the printed material contained within the ring-binder, his notebook open beside him.

Night descended outside the office, and a pool of golden light fell from the desk lamp on to each page as Strike methodically read the documents that had added up to a conclusion of suicide. Here, amid the statements shorn of superfluity, minutely detailed timings, the copied labels from the bottles of drugs found in Landry's bathroom cabinet, Strike tracked the truth he had sensed behind Tansy Bestigui's lies.

The autopsy indicated that Lula had been killed on impact with the road, and that she had died from a broken neck and internal bleeding. There was a certain amount of bruising to the upper arms. She had fallen wearing only one shoe. The photographs of the corpse confirmed LulaMyInspirationForeva's assertion that Landry had changed her clothes on coming home from the nightclub. Instead of the dress in which she had been photographed entering her building, the corpse wore a sequinned top and trousers.

Strike turned to the shifting statements that Tansy had given to the police; the first simply claiming a trip to the bathroom from the bedroom; the second adding the opening of her sitting-room window. Freddie, she said, had been in bed throughout. The police had found half a line of cocaine on the flat marble rim of the bath, and a small plastic bag of the drug hidden inside a box of Tampax in the cabinet above the sink.

Freddie's statement confirmed that he had been asleep when Landry fell, and that he had been woken by his wife's screams; he said that he had hurried into the sitting room in time to see Tansy run past him in her underwear. The vase of roses he had sent to Macc, and which a clumsy policeman had smashed, were intended, he admitted, as a gesture of welcome and introduction; yes, he would have been glad to strike up an acquaintance with the rapper, and yes, it had crossed his mind that Macc might be perfect in a thriller now in development. His shock at Landry's death had undoubtedly made him overreact to the ruin of his floral gift. He had initially believed his wife when she said she had overheard the argument upstairs; he had subsequently come, reluctantly, to accept the police view that Tansy's account was indicative of cocaine consumption. Her drug habit had placed great strain on the marriage, and he had admitted to the police that he was aware that his wife habitually used the stimulant, though he had not known that she had a supply in the flat that night.

Bestigui further stated that he and Landry had never visited each other's flats, and that their simultaneous stay at Dickie Carbury's (which the police appeared to have heard about on a subsequent occasion, for Freddie had been reinterviewed after the initial statement) had barely advanced their acquaintance. 'She associated mainly with the younger guests, while I spent most of the weekend with Dickie, who is a contemporary of mine.' Bestigui's statement presented the unassailable front of a rock face without crampons.

After reading the police account of events inside the Bestiguis' flat, Strike added several sentences to his own notes. He was interested in the half a line of cocaine on the side of the bath, and even more interested in the few seconds after Tansy had seen the flailing figure of Lula Landry fall past the window. Much would depend, of course, on the layout of the Bestiguis' apartment (there was no map or diagram of it in the folder), but Strike was bothered by one consistent aspect of Tansy's shifting stories: she insisted throughout that her husband had been in bed, asleep, when Landry fell. He remembered the way she had shielded her face, by pretending to push back her hair, as he pressed her on the point. All in all, and notwithstanding the police view, Strike considered the precise location of both Bestiguis at the moment Lula Landry fell off her balcony to be far from proven.

He resumed his systematic perusal of the file. Evan Duffield's statement conformed in most respects to Wardle's second-hand tale. He admitted to having attempted to prevent his girlfriend leaving Uzi by seizing her by the upper arms. She had broken free and left; he had followed her shortly afterwards. There was a one-sentence mention of the wolf mask, couched in the unemotional language of the policeman who had interviewed him: 'I am accustomed to wearing a wolf's-head mask when I wish to avoid the attentions of photographers.' A brief statement from the driver who had taken Duffield from Uzi confirmed Duffield's account of visiting Kentigern Gardens and moving on to d'Arblay Street, where he had dropped his passenger and left. The antipathy Wardle claimed the driver had felt towards Duffield was not conveyed in the bald factual account prepared for his signature by the police.

There were a couple of other statements supporting Duffield's: one from a woman who claimed to have seen him climbing the stairs to his dealer's, one from the dealer, Whycliff, himself. Strike recalled Wardle's expressed opinion that Whycliff would lie for Duffield. The woman downstairs could have been cut in on any payment. The rest of the witnesses who claimed to have seen Duffield roaming the streets of London could only honestly say that they had seen a man in a wolf mask.

Strike lit a cigarette and read through Duffield's statement again. He was a man with a violent temper, who had admitted to attempting to force Lula to remain in the club. The bruising to the upper arms of the body was almost certainly his work. If, however, he had taken heroin with Whycliff, Strike knew that the odds of him being in a fit state to infiltrate number 18, Kentigern Gardens, or to work himself into a murderous rage, were negligible. Strike was familiar with the behaviour of heroin addicts; he had met plenty at the last squat his mother had lived in. The drug rendered its slaves passive and docile; the absolute antithesis of shouting, violent alcoholics, or twitchy, paranoid coke-users. Strike had known every kind of substance-abuser, both inside the army and out. The glorification of Duffield's habit by the media disgusted him. There was no glamour in heroin. Strike's mother had died on a filthy mattress in the corner of the room, and nobody had realised she was dead for six hours.

He got up, crossed the room and wrenched open the dark, rain-spattered window, so that the thud of the bass from the 12 Bar Café became louder than ever. Still smoking, he looked out at Charing Cross Road, glittering with car lights and puddles, where Friday-night revellers were striding and lurching past the end of Denmark Street, umbrellas wobbling, laughter ringing above the traffic. When, Strike wondered, would he next enjoy a pint on a Friday with friends? The notion seemed to belong to a different universe, a life left behind. The strange limbo in which he was living, with Robin his only real human contact, could not last, but he was still not ready to resume a proper social life. He had lost the army, and Charlotte and half a leg; he felt a need to become thoroughly accustomed to the man he had become, before he felt ready to expose himself to other people's surprise and pity. The bright orange cigarette stub flew down into the dark street and was extinguished in the watery gutter; Strike pushed down the window, returned to his desk and pulled the file firmly back towards him.

Derrick Wilson's statement told him nothing he did not already know. There was no mention in the file of Kieran Kolovas-Jones, or of his mysterious blue piece of paper. Strike turned next, with some interest, to the statements of the two women with whom Lula had spent her final afternoon, Ciara Porter and Bryony Radford.

The make-up artist remembered Lula as cheerful and excited about Deeby Macc's imminent arrival. Porter, however, stated that Landry 'had not been herself', that she had seemed 'low and anxious', and had refused to discuss what was upsetting her. Porter's statement added an intriguing detail that nobody had yet told Strike. The model asserted that Landry had made specific mention, that afternoon, of an intention to leave 'everything' to her brother. No context was given; but the impression left was of a girl in a clearly morbid frame of mind.

Strike wondered why his client had not mentioned that his sister had declared her intention of leaving him everything. Of course, Bristow already had a trust fund. Perhaps the possible acquisition of further vast sums of money did not seem as noteworthy to him as it would to Strike, who had never inherited a penny.

Yawning, Strike lit another cigarette to keep himself awake, and began to read the statement of Lula's mother. By Lady Yvette Bristow's own account, she had been drowsy and unwell in the aftermath of her operation; but she insisted that her daughter had been 'perfectly happy' when she came to visit that morning, and had evinced nothing but concern for her mother's condition and prospects of recovery. Perhaps the blunt, unnuanced prose of the recording officer was to blame, but Strike took from Lady Bristow's recollections the impression of a determined denial. She alone suggested that Lula's death had been an accident, that she had somehow slipped over the balcony without meaning to; it had been, said Lady Bristow, an icy night.

Strike skim-read Bristow's statement, which tallied in all respects with the account he had given Strike in person, and proceeded to that of Tony Landry, John and Lula's uncle. He had visited Yvette Bristow at the same time as Lula on the day before the latter's death, and asserted that his niece had seemed 'normal'. Landry had then driven to Oxford, where he had attended a conference on international developments in family law, staying overnight in the Malmaison Hotel. His account of his whereabouts was followed by some incomprehensible comments about telephone calls. Strike turned, for elucidation, to the annotated copies of phone records.

Lula had barely used her landline in the week prior to her death, and not at all on the day before she died. From her mobile, however, she had made no fewer than sixty-six calls on her last day of life. The first, at 9.15 in the morning, had been to Evan Duffield; the second, at 9.35, to Ciara Porter. There followed a gap of hours, in which she had spoken to nobody on the mobile, and then, at 1.21, she had begun a positive frenzy of telephoning two numbers, almost alternately. One of these was Duffield's; the other belonged, according to the crabbed scribble beside the number's first appearance, to Tony Landry. Again and again she had telephoned these two men. Here and there were gaps of twenty minutes or so, during which she made no calls; then she would begin telephoning again, doubtless hitting 'redial'. All of this frenetic calling, Strike deduced, must have taken place once she was back in her flat with Bryony Radford and Ciara Porter, though neither of the two women's statements made mention of repeated telephoning.

Strike turned back to Tony Landry's statement, which cast no light on the reason his niece had been so anxious to contact him. He had turned off the sound on his mobile while at the conference, he said, and had not realised until much later that his niece had called him repeatedly that afternoon. He had no idea why she had done so and had not called her back, giving as his reason that by the time he realised that she had been trying to reach him, she had stopped calling, and he had guessed, correctly as it turned out, that she would be in a nightclub somewhere.

Strike was now yawning every few minutes; he considered making himself coffee, but could not muster the energy. Wanting his bed, but driven on by habit to complete the job in hand, he turned to the copies of security logbook pages showing the entrances and exits of visitors to number 18 on the day preceding Lula Landry's death. A careful perusal of signatures and initials revealed that Wilson had not been as meticulous in his record-keeping as his employers might have hoped. As Wilson had already told Strike, the movements of the building's residents were not recorded in the book; so the comings and goings of Landry and the Bestiguis were missing. The first entry Wilson had made was for the postman, at 9.10; next, at 9.22, came *Florist delivery Flat 2*; finally, at 9.50, *Securibell*. No time of departure was marked for the alarm checker.

Otherwise it had been (as Wilson had said) a quiet day. Ciara Porter had arrived at 12.50; Bryony Radford at 1.20. While Radford's departure was recorded with her own signature at 4.40, Wilson had added the entrance of caterers to the Bestiguis' flat at 7, Ciara's exit with Lula at 7.15 and the departure of the caterers at 9.15.

It frustrated Strike that the only page that the police had photocopied was the day before Landry's death, because he had hoped that he might find the surname of the elusive Rochelle somewhere in the entrance log's pages.

It was nearly midnight when Strike turned his attention to the police report on the contents of Landry's laptop. They appeared to have been searching, principally, for emails indicating suicidal mood or intent, and in this respect they had been unsuccessful. Strike scanned the emails Landry had sent and received in the last two weeks of her life.

It was strange, but nevertheless true, that the countless photographs of her otherworldly beauty had made it harder rather than easier for Strike to believe that Landry had ever really existed. The ubiquity of her features had made them seem abstract, generic, even if the face itself had been uniquely beautiful.

Now, however, out of these dry black marks on paper, out of erratically spelled messages littered with in-jokes and nicknames, the wraith of the dead girl rose before him in the dark office. Her emails gave him what the multitude of photographs had not: a realisation in the gut, rather than the brain, that a real, living, laughing and crying human being had been smashed to death on that snowy London street. He had hoped to spot the flickering shadow of a murderer as he turned the file's pages, but instead it was the ghost of Lula herself who emerged, gazing up at him, as victims of violent crimes sometimes did, through the detritus of their interrupted lives.

He saw, now, why John Bristow insisted that his sister had had no thought of death. The girl who had typed out these words emerged as a warm-hearted friend, sociable, impulsive, busy and glad to be so; enthusiastic about her job, excited, as Bristow had said, about the prospect of a trip to Morocco.

Most of the emails had been sent to the designer Guy Somé. They held nothing of interest except a tone of cheery confidentiality, and, once, a mention of her most incongruous friendship:

Geegee, will you pleeeeeze make Rochelle something for her birthday, please please? I'll pay. Something nice (don't be horrible). For Feb 21st? Pleezy please. Love ya. Cuckoo.

Strike remembered the assertion of LulaMyInspirationForeva that Lula had loved Guy Somé 'like a brother'. His statement to the police was the shortest in the file. He had been in Japan for a week and had arrived home on the night of her death. Strike knew that Somé lived within easy walking distance of Kentigern Gardens, but the police appeared to have been satisfied with his assertion that, once home, he had simply gone to bed. Strike had already noted the fact that anyone walking from Charles Street would have approached Kentigern Gardens from the opposite direction to the CCTV camera on Alderbrook Road.

Strike closed the file at last. As he moved laboriously through his office, undressing, removing the prosthesis and unfolding the camp bed, he thought of nothing but his own exhaustion. He fell asleep quickly, lulled by the sounds of humming traffic, the pattering rain and the deathless breath of the city.

2

A large magnolia tree stood in the front garden of Lucy's house in Bromley. Later in the spring it would cover the front lawn in what looked like crumpled tissues; now, in April, it was a frothy cloud of white, its petals waxy as coconut shavings. Strike had only visited this house a few times, because he preferred to meet Lucy away from her home, where she always seemed most harried, and to avoid encounters with his brother-in-law, for whom his feelings were on the cooler side of tepid.

Helium-filled balloons, tied to the gate, bobbled in the light breeze. As Strike walked down the steeply sloping front path to the door, the package Robin had wrapped under his arm, he told himself that it would soon be over.

'Where's Charlotte?' demanded Lucy, short, blonde and round-faced, immediately upon opening the front door.

More big golden foil balloons, this time in the shape of the number seven, filled the hall behind her. Screams that might have denoted excitement or pain were issuing from some unseen region of the house, disturbing the suburban peace.

'She had to go back to Ayr for the weekend,' lied Strike.

'Why?' asked Lucy, standing back to let him in.

'Another crisis with her sister. Where's Jack?'

'They're all through here. Thank God it's stopped raining, or we'd have had to have them in the house,' said Lucy, leading him out into the back garden.

They found his three nephews tearing around the large back lawn with twenty assorted boys and girls in party clothes, who were shrieking their way through some game that involved running to various cricket stumps on which pictures of pieces of fruit had been taped. Parent helpers stood around in the weak sunlight, drinking wine out of plastic cups, while Lucy's husband, Greg, manned an iPod standing in a dock on a trestle table. Lucy handed Strike a lager, then dashed away from him almost immediately, to pick up the youngest of her three sons, who had fallen hard and was bawling with gusto.

Strike had never wanted children; it was one of the things on which he and Charlotte had always agreed, and it had been one of the reasons other relationships over the years had foundered. Lucy deplored his attitude, and the reasons he gave for it; she was always miffed when he stated life aims that differed from hers, as though he were attacking her decisions and choices.

'All right, there, Corm?' said Greg, who had handed over the control of the music to another father. Strike's brother-in-law was a quantity surveyor, who never seemed quite sure what tone to take with Strike, and usually settled for a combination of chippiness and aggression that Strike found irksome. 'Where's that gorgeous Charlotte? Not split up again, have you? Ha ha ha. I can't keep track.'

One of the little girls had been pushed over: Greg hurried off to help one of the other mothers deal with more tears and grass stains. The game roared on in chaos. At last, a winner was declared; there were more tears from the runner-up, who had to be placated with a consolation prize from the black bin bag sitting beside the hydrangeas. A second round of the same game was then announced.

'Hi there!' said a middle-aged matron, sidling up to Strike. 'You must be Lucy's brother!'

'Yeah,' he said.

'We heard all about your poor leg,' she said, staring down at his shoes. 'Lucy kept us all posted. Gosh, you wouldn't even know, would you? I couldn't even see you limping when you arrived. Isn't it amazing what they can do these days? I expect you can run faster now than you could before!'

Perhaps she imagined that he had a single carbon-fibre prosthetic blade under his trousers, like a Paralympian. He sipped his lager, and forced a humourless smile.

'Is it true?' she asked, ogling him, her face suddenly full of naked curiosity. 'Are you really Jonny Rokeby's son?'

Some thread of patience, which Strike had not realised was strained to breaking point, snapped.

'Fucked if I know,' he said. 'Why don't you call him and ask?'

She looked stunned. After a few seconds, she walked away from him in silence. He saw her talking to another woman, who glanced towards Strike. Another child fell over, crashing its head on to the cricket stump decorated with a giant strawberry, and emitting an ear-splitting shriek. With all attention focused on the fresh casualty, Strike slipped back inside the house.

The front room was blandly comfortable, with a beige three-piece suite, an Impressionist print over the mantelpiece and framed photographs of his three nephews in their bottle-green school uniform displayed on shelves. Strike closed the door carefully on the noise from the garden, took from his pocket the DVD Wardle had sent, inserted it into the player and turned on the TV.

There was a photograph on top of the set, taken at Lucy's thirtieth birthday party. Lucy's father, Rick, was there with his second wife. Strike stood at the back, where he had been placed in every group photograph since he was five years old. He had been in possession of two legs then. Tracey, fellow SIB officer and the girl whom Lucy had hoped her brother would marry, was standing next to him. Tracey had subsequently married one of their mutual friends, and had recently given birth to a daughter. Strike had meant to send flowers, but had never got round to it.

He dropped his gaze to the screen, and pressed 'play'.

The grainy black-and-white footage began immediately. A white street, thick blobs of snow drifting past the eye of the camera. The 180° view showed the intersection of Bellamy and Alderbrook Roads.

A man walked, alone, into view, from the right side of the screen; tall, his hands deep in his pockets, swathed in layers, a hood over his head. His face looked strange in the black-and-white footage; it tricked the eye; Strike thought that he was looking at a stark white lower face and a dark blindfold, before reason told him that he was in fact looking at a dark upper face, and a white scarf tied over the nose, mouth and chin. There was some kind of mark, perhaps a blurry logo, on his jacket; otherwise his clothing was unidentifiable.

As the walker approached the camera, he bowed his head and appeared to consult something he drew out of his pocket. Seconds later, he turned up Bellamy Road and disappeared out of range of the camera. The digital clock in the lower right-hand portion of the screen registered 01:39.

The film jumped. Here again was the blurred view of the same intersection, apparently deserted, the same heavy flakes of snow obscuring the view, but now the clock in the lower corner read 02:12.

The two runners burst into view. The one in front was recognisable as the man who had walked out of range with his white scarf over his mouth; long-legged and powerful, he ran, his arms pumping, straight back down Alderbrook Road. The second man was smaller, slighter, hooded and hatted; Strike noticed the dark fists, clenched as he pelted along behind the first, losing ground to the taller man all the way. Under a street lamp, a design on the back of his sweatshirt was briefly illuminated; halfway along Alderbrook Road he veered suddenly left and up a side street.

Strike replayed the few seconds' footage again, and then again. He saw no sign of communication between the two runners; no sign that they had called to each other, or even looked for each other, as they sprinted away from the camera. It seemed to have been every man for himself.

He replayed the footage for a fourth time, and froze it, after several attempts, at the second when the design on the back of the slower man's sweatshirt had been illuminated. Squinting at the screen, he edged closer to the blurry picture. After a minute's prolonged staring, he was almost sure that the first word ended in 'ck', but the second, which he thought began with a 'J', was indecipherable.

He pressed 'play' and let the film run on, trying to make out which street the second man had taken. Three times Strike watched him split away from his companion, and although its name was unreadable onscreen, he knew, from what Wardle had said, that it must be Halliwell Street.

The police had thought that the fact that the first man had picked up a friend off-camera diminished his plausibility as a killer. This was assuming that the two were, indeed, friends. Strike had to concede that the fact that they had been caught on film together, in such weather, and at such an hour, acting in an almost identical fashion, suggested complicity.

Allowing the footage to run on, he watched as it cut, in almost startling fashion, to the interior of a bus. A girl got on; filmed from a position above the driver, her face was foreshortened and heavily shadowed, though her blonde ponytail was distinctive. The man who followed her on to the bus bore, as far as it was possible to see, a strong resemblance to the one who had later walked up Bellamy Road towards Kentigern Gardens. He was tall and hooded, with a white scarf over his face, the upper part lost in shadow. All that was clear was the logo on his chest, a stylised GS.

The film jerked to show Theobalds Road. If the individual walking fast along it was the same person who had got on the bus, he had removed his white scarf, although his build and walk were strongly reminiscent. This time, Strike thought that the man was making a conscious effort to keep his head bowed.

The film ended in a blank black screen. Strike sat looking at it, deep in thought. When he recalled himself to his surroundings, it was a slight surprise to find them multicoloured and sunlit.

He took his mobile out of his pocket and called John Bristow, but reached only voicemail. He left a message telling Bristow that he had now viewed the CCTV footage and read the police file; that there were a few more things he would like to ask, and would it be possible to meet Bristow sometime during the following week.

He then called Derrick Wilson, whose telephone likewise went to voicemail, to which he reiterated his request to come and view the interior of 18 Kentigern Gardens.

Strike had just hung up when the sitting-room door opened,

and his middle nephew, Jack, sidled in. He looked flushed and overwrought.

'I heard you talking,' Jack said. He closed the door just as carefully as his uncle had done.

'Aren't you supposed to be in the garden, Jack?'

'I've been for a pee,' said his nephew. 'Uncle Cormoran, did you bring me a present?'

Strike, who had not relinquished the wrapped parcel since arriving, handed it over and watched as Robin's careful handiwork was destroyed by small, eager fingers.

'*Cool*,' said Jack happily. 'A *soldier*.'

'That's right,' said Strike.

'He's got a gun an' *dev'rything*.'

'Yeah, he has.'

'Did you have a gun when you were a soldier?' asked Jack, turning over the box to look at the picture of its contents.

'I had two,' said Strike.

'Have you still got them?'

'No, I had to give them back.'

'Shame,' said Jack, matter-of-factly.

'Aren't you supposed to be playing?' asked Strike, as renewed shrieks erupted from the garden.

'I don't wanna,' said Jack. 'Can I take him out?'

'Yeah, all right,' said Strike.

While Jack ripped feverishly at the box, Strike slipped Wardle's DVD out of the player and pocketed it. Then he helped Jack to free the plastic paratrooper from the restraints holding him to the cardboard insert, and to fix his gun into his hand.

Lucy found them both sitting there ten minutes later. Jack was making his soldier fire around the back of the sofa and Strike was pretending to have taken a bullet to the stomach.

'For God's sake, Corm, it's his party, he's supposed to be playing with the others! Jack, I *told* you you weren't allowed to open any presents yet – pick it up – no, it'll have to stay in here – *no*, Jack, you can play with it later – it's nearly time for tea anyway . . . '

Flustered and irritable, Lucy ushered her reluctant son back out of the room with a dark backwards look at her brother. When Lucy's lips were pursed she bore a strong resemblance to their Aunt Joan, who was no blood relation to either of them.

The fleeting similarity engendered in Strike an uncharacteristic spirit of cooperation. He behaved, in Lucy's terms, well throughout the rest of the party, devoting himself in the main to defusing brewing arguments between various overexcited children, then barricading himself behind a trestle table covered in jelly and ice cream, thus avoiding the intrusive interest of the prowling mothers.

3

Strike was woken early on Sunday morning by the ringing of his mobile, which was recharging on the floor beside his camp bed. The caller was Bristow. He sounded strained.

'I got your message yesterday, but Mum's in a bad way and we haven't got a nurse for this afternoon. Alison's going to come over and keep me company. I could meet you tomorrow, in my lunch hour, if you're free? Have there been any developments?' he added hopefully.

'Some,' said Strike cautiously. 'Listen, where's your sister's laptop?'

'It's here in Mum's flat. Why?'

'How would you feel about me having a look at it?'

'Fine,' said Bristow. 'I'll bring it along tomorrow, shall I?'

Strike agreed that this would be a good idea. When Bristow had given him the name and address of his favourite place to eat near his office, and hung up, Strike reached for his cigarettes, and lay for a while smoking and contemplating the pattern made on the ceiling by the sun through the blind slats, savouring the silence and the solitude, the absence of children screaming, of Lucy's attempts to question him over the raucous yells of her youngest. Feeling almost kindly towards his peaceful office, he stubbed out the cigarette, got up and prepared to take his usual shower at ULU.

He finally reached Derrick Wilson, after several more attempts, late on Sunday evening.

'You can't come this week,' said Wilson. 'Mister Bestigui's round a lot at the moment. I gotta think about mi job, you understand me. I'll call you if there's a good time, all right?'

Strike heard a distant buzzer.

'Are you at work now?' called Strike, before Wilson could hang up.

He heard the security guard say, away from the receiver:

'(Just sign the book, mate.) What?' he added loudly, to Strike.

'If you're there now, could you check the logbook for the name of a friend who used to visit Lula sometimes?'

'What friend?' asked Wilson. '(Yeah, see yuh.)'

'The girl Kieran talked about; the friend from rehab. Rochelle. I want her surname.'

'Oh, her, yeah,' said Wilson. 'Yeah, I'll take a look an' I'll buzz y—'

'Could you have a quick look now?'

He heard Wilson sigh.

'Yeah, all right. Wait there.'

Indistinct sounds of movement, clunks and scrapings, then the flick of turning pages. While Strike waited, he contemplated various items of clothing designed by Guy Somé, which were arrayed on his computer screen.

'Yeah, she's here,' said Wilson's voice in his ear. 'Her name's Rochelle . . . I can' read . . . looks like Onifade.'

'Can you spell it?'

Wilson did so, and Strike wrote it down.

'When's the last time she was there, Derrick?'

'Back in early November,' said Wilson. '(Yeah, good evenin'.) I gotta go now.'

He put the receiver down on Strike's thanks, and the detective returned to his can of Tennent's and his contemplation of modern daywear, as envisaged by Guy Somé, in particular a hooded zip-up jacket with a stylised GS in gold on the upper left-hand side. The logo was much in evidence on all the ready-to-wear clothing in the menswear section of the designer's website. Strike was not entirely clear on the definition of 'ready-to-wear'; it seemed a statement of the obvious, though whatever else the phrase might connote, it meant 'cheaper'. The second section of the site, named simply 'Guy Somé', contained clothing that routinely ran into thousands of pounds. Despite Robin's best endeavours, the designer of these maroon suits, these narrow knitted ties, these minidresses embroidered with mirror fragments, these leather fedoras, was continuing to turn a corporate deaf ear to all requests for an interview concerning the death of his favourite model.

4

You think i wont fucking hurt you but your wrong you cunt I am comming for you I fucking trusted you and you did this to me. I am going to pull your fucking dick off and stuff it down yor throat They will find you chocking on your own dick When ive finish with you your own mother wont no you i am going to fucking kill you Strike you peice of shit

'It's a nice day out there.'

'Will you please read this? Please?'

It was Monday morning, and Strike had just returned from a smoke in the sunny street and a chat with the girl from the record shop opposite. Robin's hair was loose again; she obviously had no more interviews today. This deduction, and the effects of sunlight after rain, combined to lift Strike's spirits. Robin, however, looked strained, standing behind her desk and holding out a pink piece of paper embellished with the usual kittens.

'Still at it, is he?'

Strike took the letter and read it through, grinning.

'I don't understand why you aren't going to the police,' said Robin. 'The things he's saying he wants to do to you . . .'

'Just file it,' said Strike dismissively, tossing the letter down and rifling through the rest of the paltry pile of mail.

'Yes, well, that's not all,' said Robin, clearly annoyed by his attitude. 'Temporary Solutions have just called.'

'Yeah? What did they want?'

'They asked for me,' said Robin. 'They obviously suspect I'm still here.'

'And what did you say?'

'I pretended to be somebody else.'

'Quick thinking. Who?'

'I said my name was Annabel.'

'When asked to come up with a fake name on the spot, people usually choose one beginning with "A", did you know that?'

'But what if they send somebody to check?'

'Well?'

'It's you they'll try and get money from, not me! They'll try and make you pay a recruitment fee!'

He smiled at her genuine anxiety that he would have to pay money he could not afford. He had been intending to ask her to telephone the office of Freddie Bestigui again, and to begin a search through online telephone directories for Rochelle Onifade's Kilburn-based aunt. Instead he said:

'OK, we'll vacate the premises. I was going to check out a place called Vashti this morning, before I meet Bristow. Maybe it'd look more natural if we both went.'

'Vashti? The boutique?' said Robin, at once.

'Yeah. You know it, do you?'

It was Robin's turn to smile. She had read about it in magazines: it epitomised London glamour to her; a place where fashion editors found items of fabulous clothing to show their readers, pieces that would have cost Robin six months' salary.

'I know of it,' she said.

He took down her trench coat and handed it to her.

'We'll pretend you're my sister, Annabel. You can be helping me pick out a present for my wife.'

'What's the death-threat man's problem?' asked Robin, as they sat side by side on the Tube. 'Who is he?'

She had suppressed her curiosity about Jonny Rokeby, and about the dark beauty who had fled Strike's building on her first day at work, and the camp bed they never mentioned; but she was surely entitled to ask questions about the death threats. It was she, after all, who had so far slit open three pink envelopes, and read the unpleasant and violent outpourings scrawled between gambolling kittens. Strike never even looked at them.

'He's called Brian Mathers,' said Strike. 'He came to see me last June because he thought his wife was sleeping around. He wanted her followed, so I put her under surveillance for a month. Very ordinary woman: plain, frumpy, bad perm; worked in the accounts department of a big carpet warehouse. Spent her weekdays in a poky little office with three female colleagues, went to bingo every Thursday, did the weekly shop on Fridays at Tesco, and on Saturdays went to the local Rotary Club with her husband.'

'When did he think she was sleeping around?' asked Robin.

Their pale reflections were swaying in the opaque black window; drained of colour in the harsh overhead light, Robin looked older, yet ethereal, and Strike craggier, uglier.

'Thursday nights.'

'And was she?'

'No, she really was going to bingo with her friend Maggie, but all four Thursdays that I watched her, she made herself deliberately late home. She drove around a little bit after she'd left Maggie. One night she went into a pub and had a tomato juice on her own, sitting in a corner looking timid. Another night she waited in her car at the end of their street for forty-five minutes before driving around the corner.'

'Why?' asked Robin, as the train rattled loudly through a lengthy tunnel.

'Well that's the question, isn't it? Proving something? Trying to get him worked up? Taunting him? Punishing him? Trying to inject a bit of excitement into their dull marriage? Every Thursday, just a bit of unexplained time.

'He's a twitchy bugger, and he'd swallowed the bait all right. It was driving him mad. He was sure she was meeting a lover once a week, that her friend Maggie was covering for her. He'd tried following her himself, but he was convinced that she went to bingo on those occasions because she knew he was watching.'

'So you told him the truth?'

'Yeah, I did. He didn't believe me. He got very worked up and started shouting and screaming about everyone being in a conspiracy against him. Refused to pay my bill.

'I was worried he was going to end up doing her an injury, which was where I made my big mistake. I phoned her and told her he'd paid me to watch her, that I knew what she was doing, and that her husband was heading for breaking point. For her own sake, she ought to be careful how far she pushed him. She didn't say a word, just hung up on me.

'Well, he was checking her mobile regularly. He saw my number, and drew the obvious conclusion.'

'That you'd told her he was having her watched?'

'No, that I had been seduced by her charms and was her new lover.'

Robin clapped her hands over her mouth. Strike laughed.

'Are your clients usually a bit mad?' asked Robin, when she had freed her mouth again.

'He is, but they're usually just stressed.'

'I was thinking about John Bristow,' Robin said hesitantly.

'His girlfriend thinks he's deluded. And you thought he might be a bit . . . you know . . . didn't you?' she asked. 'We heard,' she added, a little shamefacedly, 'through the door. The bit about "armchair psychologists".'

'Right,' said Strike. 'Well . . . I might have changed my mind.'

'What do you mean?' asked Robin, her clear grey-blue eyes wide. The train was jolting to a halt; figures were flashing past the windows, becoming less blurred with every second. 'Do you – are you saying he's not – that he might be right – that there really was a . . . ?'

'This is our stop.'

The white-painted boutique they sought stood on some of the most expensive acreage in London, in Conduit Street, close to the junction with New Bond Street. To Strike, its colourful windows displayed a multitudinous mess of life's unnecessities. Here were beaded cushions and scented candles in silver pots; slivers of artistically draped chiffon; gaudy kaftans worn by faceless mannequins; bulky handbags of an ostentatious ugliness; all spread against a pop-art backdrop, in a gaudy celebration of consumerism he found irritating to retina and spirit. He could imagine Tansy Bestigui and Ursula May in here, examining price tags with expert eyes, selecting four-figure bags of alligator skin with a pleasureless determination to get their money's worth out of their loveless marriages.

Beside him, Robin too was staring at the window display, but only dimly registering what she was looking at. A job offer had been made to her that morning, by telephone, while Strike was smoking downstairs, just before Temporary Solutions had called. Every time she contemplated the offer, which she would have to accept or decline within the next two days, she felt a jab of some intense emotion to the stomach that she was trying to persuade herself was pleasure, but increasingly suspected was dread.

She ought to take it. There was much in its favour. It paid exactly what she and Matthew had agreed she ought to aim for. The offices were smart and well placed for the West End. She and Matthew would be able to lunch together. The employment market was sluggish. She should be delighted.

'How did the interview go on Friday?' asked Strike, squinting at a sequinned coat he found obscenely unattractive.

'Quite well, I think,' said Robin vaguely.

She recalled the excitement she had felt mere moments ago when Strike had hinted that there might, after all, have been a killer. Was he serious? Robin noted that he was now staring hard at this massive assemblage of fripperies as though they might be able to tell him something important, and this was surely (for a moment she saw with Matthew's eyes, and thought in Matthew's voice) a pose adopted for effect, or show. Matthew kept hinting that Strike was somehow a fake. He seemed to feel that being a private detective was a far-fetched job, like astronaut or lion tamer; that real people did not do such things.

Robin reflected that if she took the human resources job, she might never know (unless she saw it, one day, on the news) how this investigation turned out. To prove, to solve, to catch, to protect: these were things worth doing; important and fascinating. Robin knew that Matthew thought her somehow childish and naive for feeling this way, but she could not help herself.

Strike had turned his back on Vashti, and was looking at something in New Bond Street. His gaze, Robin saw, was fixed on the red letter box standing outside Russell and Bromley, its dark rectangular mouth leering at them across the road.

'OK, let's go,' said Strike, turning back to her. 'Don't forget, you're my sister and we're shopping for my wife.'

'But what are we trying to find out?'

'What Lula Landry and her friend Rochelle Onifade got up to in there, on the day before Landry died. They met here, for fifteen minutes, then parted. I'm not hopeful; it's three months ago, and they might not have noticed anything. Worth a try, though.'

The ground floor of Vashti was devoted to clothing; a sign pointing up the wooden stairs indicated that a café and 'lifestyle' were housed above. A few women were browsing the shining steel clothes racks; all of them thin and tanned, with long, clean, freshly blow-dried hair. The assistants were an eclectic bunch; their clothing eccentric, their hairstyles outré. One of them was wearing a tutu and fishnets; she was arranging a display of hats.

To Strike's surprise, Robin marched boldly over to this girl.

'Hi,' she said brightly. 'There's a fabulous sequinned coat in your middle window. I wonder whether I could try it on?'

The assistant had a mass of fluffy white hair the texture of candy floss, gaudily painted eyes and no eyebrows.

'Yeah, no probs,' she said.

As it turned out, however, she had lied: retrieving the coat from the window was distinctly problematic. It needed to be taken off the mannequin that was wearing it, and disentangled from its electronic tag; ten minutes later, the coat had still not emerged, and the original assistant had called two of her colleagues into the window display to help her. Robin, meanwhile, was drifting around without talking to Strike, picking out an assortment of dresses and belts. By the time the sequinned coat was carried out from the window, all three assistants involved in its retrieval seemed somehow invested in its future, and all accompanied Robin towards the changing room, one volunteering to help her carry the pile of extras she had chosen, the other two bearing the coat.

The curtained changing rooms consisted of ironwork frames draped with thick cream silk, like tents. As he positioned himself close enough to listen to what went on inside, Strike felt that he was only now starting to appreciate the full range of his temporary secretary's talents.

Robin had taken over ten thousand pounds' worth of goods into the changing room with her, of which the sequinned coat cost half. She would never have had the nerve to do this under normal circumstances, but something had got into her this morning: recklessness and bravado; she was proving something to herself, to Matthew, and even to Strike. The three assistants fussed around her, hanging up dresses and smoothing out the heavy folds of the coat, and Robin felt no shame that she could not have afforded even the cheapest of the belts now draped over the arm of the redhead with tattoos up both arms, and that none of the girls would ever receive the commission for which they were, undoubtedly, vying. She even allowed the assistant with pink hair to go and find a gold jacket she assured Robin would suit her admirably, and go wonderfully well with the green dress she had picked out.

Robin was taller than any of the shop girls, and when she had swapped her trench coat for the sequinned one, they cooed and gasped.

'I must show my brother,' she told them, after surveying her reflection with a critical eye. 'It isn't for me, you see, it's for his wife.'

And she strode back out through the changing-room curtains with the three assistants hovering behind her. The rich girls over by the clothing rack all turned to stare at Robin through narrow eyes as she asked boldly:

'What do you think?'

Strike had to admit that the coat he had thought so vile looked better on Robin than on the mannequin. She twirled on the spot for him, and the thing glittered like a lizard's skin.

'It's all right,' he said, masculinely cautious, and the assistants smiled indulgently. 'Yeah, it's quite nice. How much is it?'

'Not that much, by your standards,' said Robin, with an arch look at her handmaidens. 'Sandra would love this, though,' she said firmly to Strike, who, caught off guard, grinned. 'And it *is* her fortieth.'

'She could wear it with anything,' the candy-flossed girl assured Strike eagerly. 'So versatile.'

'OK, I'll try that Cavalli dress,' said Robin blithely, turning back to the changing room.

'Sandra told me to come with him,' she told the three assistants, as they helped her out of the coat, and unzipped the dress to which she had pointed. 'To make sure he doesn't make another stupid mistake. He bought her the world's ugliest earrings for her thirtieth; they cost an arm and a leg and she's never had them out of the safe.'

Robin did not know where the invention was coming from; she felt inspired. Stepping out of her jumper and skirt, she began to wriggle into a clinging poison-green dress. Sandra was becoming real to her as she talked: a little spoiled, somewhat bored, confiding in her sister-in-law over wine that her brother (a banker, Robin thought, though Strike did not really look like her idea of a banker) had no taste at all.

'So she said to me, take him to Vashti and get him to crack open his wallet. Oh yes, this is nice.'

It was more than nice. Robin stared at her own reflection; she had never worn anything so beautiful in her life. The green dress was magically constructed to shrink her waist to nothingness, to carve her figure into flowing curves, to elongate her pale neck. She was a serpentine goddess in glittering viridian, and the assistants were all murmuring and gasping their appreciation.

'How much?' Robin asked the redhead.

'Two thousand eight hundred and ninety-nine,' said the girl.

'Nothing to him,' said Robin airily, striding out through the curtains to show Strike, whom they found examining a pile of gloves on a circular table.

His only comment on the green dress was 'Yeah.' He had barely looked at her.

'Well, maybe it's not Sandra's colour,' said Robin, with a sudden feeling of embarrassment; Strike was not, after all, her brother or her boyfriend; she had perhaps taken invention too far, parading in front of him in a skintight dress. She retreated into the changing room.

Stripped again to bra and pants she said:

'The last time Sandra was here, Lula Landry was in your café. Sandra said she was gorgeous in the flesh. Even better than in pictures.'

'Oh yeah, she was,' agreed the pink-haired girl, who was clutching to her chest the gold jacket she had fetched. 'She used to be in here all the time, we used to see her every week. Do you want to try this?'

'She was in here the day before she died,' said the candy-floss-haired girl, helping Robin to wriggle into the gold jacket. 'In this changing room, actually in this one.'

'Really?' said Robin.

'It's not going to close over the bust, but it looks great open,' said the redhead.

'No, that's no good, Sandra's a bit bigger than me, if anything,' said Robin, ruthlessly sacrificing her fictional sister-in-law's figure. 'I'll try that black dress. Did you say Lula Landry was here actually the day before she died?'

'Oh yeah,' said the girl with pink hair. 'We had trouble with her and one of our girls. Mel gave her the sack for it, didn't you, Mel? I can't remember her name now … she was Australian …'

'And she had it coming,' said the tattooed redhead, who was holding up a black dress with lace inserts. 'She was always pestering the famous customers. She barged in here on Lula without so much as a by-your-leave. I heard her do it, I was in the cubicle next door.'

'She – followed – Lula – in here?' gasped Robin as she was inched into the black dress by the combined efforts of the three assistants. 'When she was changing?'

'Well – Lula was on the phone – but that's hardly the point, is it?' asked red-haired Mel. 'She marched in here with a random outfit Lula hadn't even asked for, just so she could ask Lula if she could get her a job as a make-up artist.'

Robin twitched the tight black dress straight and braced herself for the raising of the zip. It was oppressive enough to be crammed in here with three girls eager for commission. Now she wondered what it would feel like to be pestered for a job while she stood semi-dressed behind a flimsy curtain.

'She was on the phone when the girl interrupted her, did you say?'

'Yeah,' said Mel and then, with a certain defensiveness, 'I couldn't help overhearing, I was in the next booth collecting stuff another client had left. They're only silk, these curtains.'

'I'll bet she wasn't too pleased being interrupted if she was talking on the—'

''Course she wasn't,' said Mel, and she imitated the model's outraged voice: "I didn't ask for that, what are you doing in here?"'

The pink-haired girl heaved the zip skyward and Robin's ribcage was slowly compressed by a hidden boned corset. Strike, who had moved as close as he dared to the silk curtains in the hope that the contents of one of Lula's telephone calls were about to be revealed, was disconcerted to hear Robin's next question emerge as a groan.

'What happened then?'

'Talk about brazen!' said Mel indignantly, and in an Australian accent quite as bad as Robin's she said: '"Oh, I just thought you'd look so lovely in this, Lula, and by the way, I'm trying to break into the make-up game, can I give you my details? Blah, blah, blah.'

'What a cheek!' gasped Robin, now acutely uncomfortable in a lace and leather straitjacket. Two thirds of her breasts were squashed flat by the straining material, while the upper slopes overflowed the neckline. 'No, I – I definitely don't think Sandra would like this … I might try the coat again … I bet Lula told the girl where to get off, did she?'

'Well, no, actually, because – Lula was in a bit of a state when she— no, she took her details just to get rid of her. I do *love* that coat on you, I really do,' said Mel, reverting suddenly to a more professional, less gossipy tone.

Robin suspected that Mel saw her own shameless eavesdropping as justified if it had exposed the unprofessionalism of a colleague. To relate the contents of Lula's telephone conversation prior to the interruption might paint her as no less intrusive and rather more underhand than her brazen subordinate.

Robin wriggled out of the black dress, trying to think of a way to melt Mel's new reserve. The girl with the candy-floss hair came unexpectedly to her aid.

'I always said you should've gone to the police, Mel.'

'I didn't hear anything that mattered,' said Mel quickly. 'I couldn't help overhearing her,' she told Robin, helping her back into the sequinned coat. 'She wasn't exactly keeping her voice down—'

'And these curtains aren't thick,' agreed Robin sycophantically. 'You'd think she'd have more sense.'

'Exactly, with the press all over her all the time – and anyway, it wouldn't have made any difference. He wasn't there, was he? That was proven.'

Robin turned slowly this way and that, watching the play of light on the exorbitantly priced coat.

'You mean Evan Duffield?' she asked absently.

'I still think Mel should've gone to the police,' said the candy-floss haired girl. 'I said that at the time.'

'He never went to her flat!' said Mel. The desire to justify herself had loosened her tongue. 'No, all it was – he must've been saying he had something on and he didn't want to see her, because she was going, "Come after, then, I'll wait up, it don't matter. I probably won't be home till one anyway. Please come, please." Like, begging him. Anyway, she had her friend in the cubicle with her. Her friend heard everything, so she would've told the police, wouldn't she?'

Absently smoothing the iridescent surface of the coat she could never afford, Robin asked almost as an afterthought:

'And it was definitely Evan Duffield she was talking to, was it?'

'Of course it was,' said Mel, as though Robin had insulted her intelligence. 'Who else would she've been asking round to her place in the early hours? She sounded desperate to see him.'

'God, his eyes,' said the girl with the candy-floss hair. 'He is so gorgeous. And massive charisma in person. He came in here with her once. God, he's sexy.'

Five minutes later, having agreed with Strike in front of the assistants that the sequinned coat was the best of the bunch, they decided (with the assistants' agreement) that she ought to bring Sandra in to have a look at it the following day before they committed themselves. Strike reserved the five-thousand-pound coat under the name of Andrew Atkinson, gave an invented mobile phone number and left the boutique with Robin in a shower of friendly good wishes, as though they had already spent the money.

They walked fifty yards in silence, and Strike had lit up a cigarette before he said:

'Very, very impressive.'

Robin glowed with pride.

5

Strike and Robin parted at Bond Street station. Robin took the underground back to the office to call BestFilms, look through online telephone directories for Rochelle Onifade's aunt, and evade Temporary Solutions ('Keep the door locked' was Strike's advice).

Strike bought himself a newspaper and caught the underground to Knightsbridge, then walked, having plenty of time to spare, to the Serpentine Bar and Kitchen, which Bristow had chosen for their lunch appointment.

The trip took him across Hyde Park, down leafy walkways and across the sandy bridle path of Rotten Row. He had jotted down the bare bones of the girl called Mel's evidence on the Tube, and now, in the sun-dappled greenery, his mind drifted, lingering on the memory of Robin as she had looked in the clinging green dress.

He had disconcerted her by his reaction, he knew that; but there had been a weird intimacy about the moment, and intimacy was precisely what he wanted least at the moment, most especially with Robin, bright, professional and considerate as she was. He enjoyed her company and he appreciated the way that she respected his privacy, keeping her curiosity in check. God knew, thought Strike, moving over to avoid a cyclist, he had come across that particular quality rarely enough in life, particularly from women. Yet the fact that he would, quite soon, be free of Robin was an inextricable part of his enjoyment of her presence; the fact that she was going to move on imposed, like her engagement ring, a happy boundary. He liked Robin; he was grateful to her; he was even (after this morning) impressed by her; but, having normal sight and an unimpaired libido, he was also reminded every day she bent over the computer monitor that she was a very sexy girl. Not beautiful; nothing like Charlotte; but attractive, nonetheless. That fact had never been so crudely presented to him as when she walked out of the changing room in the clinging green dress, and in consequence he had literally averted his eyes. He acquitted her of any deliberate provocation, but he was realistic, all the same, about the precarious balance that must be maintained for his own sanity. She was the only human with whom he was in regular contact, and he did not underestimate his current susceptibility; he had also gathered, from certain evasions and hesitations, that her fiancé disliked the fact that she had left the temping agency for this ad hoc agreement. It was safest all round not to let the burgeoning friendship become too warm; best not to admire openly the sight of her figure draped in jersey.

Strike had never been to the Serpentine Bar and Kitchen. It was set on the boating lake, a striking building that was more like a futuristic pagoda than anything he had ever seen. The thick white roof, looking like a giant book that had been placed down on its open pages, was supported by concertinaed glass. A huge weeping willow caressed the side of the restaurant and brushed the water's surface.

Though it was a cool, breezy day, the view over the lake was splendid in the sunlight. Strike chose an outdoor table right beside the water, ordered a pint of Doom Bar and read his paper.

Bristow was already ten minutes late when a tall, well-made, expensively suited man with foxy colouring stopped beside Strike's table.

'Mr Strike?'

In his late fifties, with a full head of hair, a firm jaw and pronounced cheekbones, he looked like an almost-famous actor hired to play a rich businessman in a mini-series. Strike, whose visual memory was highly trained, recognised him immediately from the photographs that Robin had found online as the tall man who had looked as though he deplored his surroundings at Lula Landry's funeral.

'Tony Landry. John and Lula's uncle. May I sit down?'

His smile was perhaps the most perfect example of an insincere social grimace that Strike had ever witnessed; a mere baring of even white teeth. Landry eased himself out of his overcoat, draped it over the back of the seat opposite Strike and sat.

'John's delayed at the office,' he said. The breeze ruffled his hair, showing how it had receded at the temples. 'He asked Alison to call you and let you know. I happened to be passing her desk at the time, so I thought I'd come and deliver the message in person. It gives me an opportunity to have a private word with you. I've been expecting you to contact me; I know you're working your way slowly through all my niece's contacts.'

He slid a pair of steel-rimmed glasses out of his top pocket, put them on and took a moment to consult the menu. Strike drank some beer and waited.

'I hear you've been speaking to Mrs Bestigui?' said Landry, setting down the menu, taking off his glasses again and reinserting them into his suit pocket.

'That's right,' said Strike.

'Yes. Well, Tansy is undoubtedly well intentioned, but she is doing herself no favours at all by repeating a story the police have proven, conclusively, could not have been true. No favours at all,' repeated Landry portentously. 'And so I have told John. His first duty ought to be to the firm's client, and what is in her best interests.

'I will have the ham hock terrine,' he added to a passing waitress, 'and a still water. Bottled. Well,' he continued, 'it's probably best to be direct, Mr Strike.

'For many reasons, all of them good ones, I am not in favour of raking over the circumstances of Lula's death. I don't expect you to agree with me. You make money by digging through the seamy circumstances of family tragedies.'

He flashed his aggressive, humourless smile again.

'I'm not entirely unsympathetic. We all have our livings to make, and no doubt there are plenty of people who would say my profession is just as parasitic as yours. It might be helpful to both of us, though, if I lay certain facts in front of you, facts I doubt John has chosen to disclose.'

'Before we get into that,' said Strike, 'what exactly is keeping John at the office? If he isn't going to make it, I'll arrange an alternative appointment with him; I've got other people to see this afternoon. Is he still trying to sort out this Conway Oates business?'

He knew only what Ursula had told him, that Conway Oates had been an American financier, but this mention of the firm's dead client had the desired effect. Landry's pomposity, his desire to control the encounter, his comfortable air of superiority, vanished entirely, leaving him clothed in nothing but temper and shock.

'John hasn't – can he really have been so . . . ? That is strictly confidential business of the firm!'

'It wasn't John,' said Strike. 'Mrs Ursula May mentioned that there's been a bit of trouble around Mr Oates's estate.'

Clearly thrown, Landry spluttered, 'I am very surprised – I wouldn't have expected Ursula – Mrs May . . . '

'So will John be along at all? Or have you given him something that will keep him busy all through lunch?'

He enjoyed watching Landry wrestle his own temper, trying to regain control of himself and the encounter.

'John will be here shortly,' he said finally. 'I hoped, as I said, to be able to lay certain facts in front of you, in private.'

'Right, well, in that case, I'll need these,' said Strike, removing a notebook and pen from his pocket.

Landry looked quite as put out by the sight of these objects as Tansy had.

'There's no need to take notes,' he said. 'What I'm about to say has no bearing – or at least, no direct bearing – on Lula's death. That is,' he added pedantically, 'it will add nothing to any theory other than that of suicide.'

'All the same,' said Strike, 'I like to have my aide-memoire.'

Landry looked as though he would like to protest, but thought better of it.

'Very well, then. Firstly, you should know that my nephew John was deeply affected by his adopted sister's death.'

'Understandable,' commented Strike, tilting the notebook so that the lawyer could not read it, and writing the words *deeply affected*, purely to annoy Landry.

'Yes, naturally. And while I would never go so far as to suggest that a private detective refuse a client on the basis that they are under strain, or depressed – as I said, we all have our livings to make – in this case . . . '

'You think it's all in his head?'

'That's not how I'd have phrased it, but bluntly, yes. John has already suffered more sudden bereavements than many people experience in a lifetime. You probably weren't aware that he's already lost a brother . . . '

'Yeah, I knew. Charlie was an old schoolmate of mine. That's why John hired me.'

Landry contemplated Strike with what seemed to be surprise and disfavour.

'You were at Blakeyfield Prep?'

'Briefly. Before my mother realised she couldn't afford the fees.'

'I see. I did not know that. Even so, perhaps you're not fully aware . . . John has always been – let's use my sister's expression for it – highly strung. His parents had to bring in psychologists after Charlie died, you know. I don't claim to be a mental health expert, but it seems to me that Lula's passing has, finally, tipped him over the . . . '

'Unfortunate choice of phrase, but I see what you mean,' said Strike, writing Bristow off rocker. 'How exactly has John been tipped over the edge?'

'Well, many would say that instigating this reinvestigation is irrational and pointless,' said Landry.

Strike kept his pen poised over the notepad. For a moment, Landry's jaws moved as though he was chewing; then he said forcefully:

'Lula was a manic depressive who jumped out of the window after a row with her junkie boyfriend. There is no mystery. It was goddamn awful for all of us, especially her poor bloody mother, but those are the unsavoury facts. I'm forced to the conclusion that John is having some kind of breakdown, and, if you don't mind me speaking frankly . . . '

'Feel free.'

'. . . your collusion is perpetuating his unhealthy refusal to accept the truth.'

'Which is that Lula killed herself?'

'A view that is shared by the police, the pathologist and the coroner. John, for reasons that are obscure to me, is determined to prove murder. How he thinks that will make any of us feel any better, I could not tell you.'

'Well,' said Strike, 'people close to suicides often feel guilty. They think, however unreasonably, that they might have done more to help. A murder verdict would exonerate the family of any blame, wouldn't it?'

'None of us has anything to feel guilty about,' said Landry, his tone steely. 'Lula received the very best medical care from her early teens, and every material advantage her adoptive family could give her. "Spoiled rotten" might be the phrase best suited to describe my adopted niece, Mr Strike. Her mother would have literally died for her, and scant repayment she ever received.'

'You thought Lula ungrateful, did you?'

'There's no need to bloody write that down. Or are those notes destined for some tawdry rag?'

Strike was interested in how completely Landry had jettisoned the suavity he had brought to the table. The waitress arrived with Landry's food. He did not thank her, but glared at Strike until she had passed on. Then he said:

'You're poking around where you can only do harm. I was stunned, frankly, when I found out what John was up to. Stunned.'

'Hadn't he expressed doubts about the suicide theory to you?'

'He'd expressed shock, naturally, like all of us, but I certainly don't recall any suggestion of murder.'

'Are you close to your nephew, Mr Landry?'

'What has that got to do with anything?'

'It might explain why he didn't tell you what he was thinking.'

'John and I have a perfectly amicable working relationship.'

'"Working relationship"?'

'Yes, Mr Strike: we work together. Do we live in each other's pockets outside the office? No. But we are both involved in caring for my sister – Lady Bristow, John's mother, who is now a terminal case. Our out-of-hours conversations usually concern Yvette.'

'John strikes me as a dutiful son.'

'Yvette's all he has left now, and the fact that she's dying isn't helping his mental condition either.'

'She's hardly all he's got left. There's Alison, isn't there?'

'I am not aware that that is a very serious relationship.'

'Perhaps one of John's motives, in employing me, is a desire to give his mother the truth before she dies?'

'The truth won't help Yvette. Nobody enjoys accepting that they have reaped what they have sown.'

Strike said nothing. As he had expected, the lawyer could not resist the temptation to clarify, and after a moment he continued:

'Yvette has always been morbidly maternal. She adores babies.' He spoke as though this was faintly disgusting, a kind of perversion. 'She would have been one of those embarrassing women who have twenty children if she could have found a man of sufficient virility. Thank God Alec was sterile – or hasn't John mentioned that?'

'He told me Sir Alec Bristow wasn't his natural father, if that's what you mean.'

If Landry was disappointed not to be first with the information, he rallied at once.

'Yvette and Alec adopted the two boys, but she had no idea how to manage them. She is, quite simply, an atrocious mother. No control, no discipline; complete overindulgence and a point-blank refusal to see what is under her nose. I don't say it was all down to her parenting – who knows what the genetic influences were – but John was whiny, histrionic and clingy and Charlie was completely delinquent, with the result—'

Landry stopped talking abruptly, patches of colour high in his cheeks.

'With the result that he rode over the edge of a quarry?' Strike suggested.

He had said it to watch Landry's reaction, and was not disappointed. He had the impression of a tunnel contracting, a distant door closing: a shutting down.

'Not to put too fine a point on it, yes. And it was a bit late, then, for Yvette to start screaming and clawing at Alec, and passing out cold on the floor. If she'd had an iota of control, the boy wouldn't have set out expressly to defy her. I was there,' said Landry, stonily. 'On a weekend visit. Easter Sunday. I had been for a walk down to the village, and I came back to find them all looking for him. I headed straight for the quarry. I knew, you see. It was the place he'd been forbidden to go – so there he was.'

'You found the body, did you?'

'Yes, I did.'

'That must have been highly distressing.'

'Yes,' said Landry, his lips barely moving. 'It was.'

'And it was after Charlie died, wasn't it, that your sister and Sir Alec adopted Lula?'

'Which was probably the single most stupid thing Alec Bristow ever agreed to,' said Landry. 'Yvette had already proven herself a disastrous mother; was she likely to be any more successful while in a state of abandoned grief? Of course, she'd always wanted a daughter, a baby to dress in pink, and Alec thought it would make her happy. He always gave Yvette anything she wanted. He was besotted with her from the moment she joined his typing pool, and he was an unvarnished East Ender. Yvette has always had a predilection for a bit of rough.'

Strike wondered what the real source of Landry's anger could be.

'You don't get along with your sister, Mr Landry?' asked Strike.

'We get along perfectly well; it is simply that I am not blind to what Yvette is, Mr Strike, nor how much of her misfortune is her own damn fault.'

'Was it difficult for them to get approved for another adoption after Charlie died?' asked Strike.

'I dare say it would have been, if Alec hadn't been a multi-millionaire,' snorted Landry. 'I know the authorities were concerned about Yvette's mental health, and they were both a bit long in the tooth by then. It's a great pity that they weren't turned down. But Alec was a man of infinite resourcefulness and he had all sorts of strange contacts from his barrow-boy days. I don't know the details, but I'd be prepared to bet money changed hands somewhere. Even so, he couldn't manage a Caucasian. He brought another child of completely unknown provenance into the family, to be raised by a depressed and hysterical woman of no judgement. It was hardly a surprise to me that the result was catastrophic. Lula was as unstable as John and as wild as Charlie, and Yvette had just as little idea how to manage her.'

Scribbling away for Landry's benefit, Strike wondered whether his belief in genetic predetermination accounted for some of Bristow's preoccupation with Lula's black relatives. Doubtless Bristow had been privy to his uncle's views through the years; children absorbed the views of their relatives at some deep, visceral level. He, Strike, had known in his bones, long before the words had ever been said in front of him, that his mother was not like other mothers, that there was (if he believed in the unspoken code that bound the rest of the adults around him) something shameful about her.

'You saw Lula the day she died, I think?' Strike said.

Landry's eyelashes were so fair they looked silver.

'Excuse me?'

'Yeah . . . ' Strike flicked back through his notebook ostentatiously, coming to a halt at an entirely blank page. '. . . you met her at your sister's flat, didn't you? When Lula called in to see Lady Bristow?'

'Who told you that? John?'

'It's all in the police file. Isn't it true?'

'Yes, it's perfectly true, but I can't see how it's relevant to anything we've been discussing.'

'I'm sorry; when you arrived, you said you'd been expecting to hear from me. I got the impression you were happy to answer questions.'

Landry had the air of a man who has found himself unexpectedly snookered.

'I have nothing to add to the statement I gave to the police,' he said at last.

'Which is,' said Strike, leafing backwards through blank pages, 'that you dropped in to visit your sister that morning, where you met your niece, and that you then drove to Oxford to attend a conference on international developments in family law?'

Landry was chewing on air again.

'That's correct,' he said.

'What time would you say you arrived at your sister's flat?'

'It must have been about ten,' said Landry, after a short pause.

'And you stayed how long?'

'Half an hour, perhaps. Maybe longer. I really can't remember.'

'And you drove directly from there to the conference in Oxford?'

Over Landry's shoulder, Strike saw John Bristow questioning a waitress; he appeared out of breath and a little dishevelled, as though he had been running. A rectangular leather case dangled from his hand. He glanced around, panting slightly, and when he spotted the back of Landry's head, Strike thought that he looked frightened.

6

'John,' said Strike, as his client approached them.

'Hi, Cormoran.'

Landry did not look at his nephew, but picked up his knife and fork and took a first bite of his terrine. Strike moved around the table to make room for Bristow to sit down opposite his uncle.

'Have you spoken to Reuben?' Landry asked Bristow coldly, once he had finished his mouthful of terrine.

'Yes. I've said I'll go over this afternoon and take him through all the deposits and drawings.'

'I've just been asking your uncle about the morning before Lula died, John. About when he visited your mother's flat,' said Strike.

Bristow glanced at Landry.

'I'm interested in what was said and done there,' Strike continued, 'because, according to the chauffeur who drove her back from her mother's flat, Lula seemed distressed.'

'Of course she was distressed,' snapped Landry. 'Her mother had cancer.'

'The operation she'd just had was supposed to have cured her, wasn't it?'

'Yvette had just had a hysterectomy. She was in pain. I don't doubt Lula was disturbed at seeing her mother in that condition.'

'Did you talk much to Lula, when you saw her?'

A minuscule hesitation.

'Just chit-chat.'

'And you two, did you speak to each other?'

Bristow and Landry did not look at each other. A longer pause, of a few seconds, before Bristow said:

'I was working in the home office. I heard Tony come in, heard him speaking to Mum and Lula.'

'You didn't look in to say hello?' Strike asked Landry.

Landry considered him through slightly boiled-looking eyes, pale between the light lashes.

'You know, nobody here is obliged to answer your questions, Mr Strike,' said Landry.

'Of course not,' agreed Strike, and he made a small and incomprehensible note in his pad. Bristow was looking at his uncle. Landry seemed to reconsider.

'I could see through the open door of the home study that John was hard at work, and I didn't want to disturb him. I sat with Yvette in her room for a while, but she was groggy from the painkillers, so I left her with Lula. I knew,' said Landry, with the faintest undertone of spite, 'that there was nobody Yvette would prefer to Lula.'

'Lula's telephone records show that she called your mobile phone repeatedly after she left Lady Bristow's flat, Mr Landry.'

Landry flushed.

'Did you speak to her on the phone?'

'No. I had my mobile switched to silent; I was late for the conference.'

'They vibrate, though, don't they?'

He wondered what it would take to make Landry leave. He was sure that the lawyer was close.

'I glanced at my phone, saw it was Lula and decided it could wait,' he said shortly.

'You didn't call her back?'

'No.'

'Didn't she leave any kind of message, to tell you what she wanted to talk about?'

'No.'

'That seems odd, doesn't it? You'd just seen her at her mother's, and you say nothing very important passed between you; yet she spent much of the rest of the afternoon trying to contact you. Doesn't that seem as though she might have had something urgent to say to you? Or that she wanted to continue a conversation you'd been having at the flat?'

'Lula was the kind of girl who would call somebody thirty times in a row, on the flimsiest pretext. She was spoiled. She expected people to jump to attention at the sight of her name.'

Strike glanced at Bristow.

'She was – sometimes – a bit like that,' her brother muttered.

'Do you think your sister was upset purely because your mother was weak from her operation, John?' Strike asked Bristow. 'Her driver, Kieran Kolovas-Jones, is emphatic that she came away from the flat in a dramatically altered mood.'

Before Bristow could answer, Landry, abandoning his food, stood up and began to put on his overcoat.

'Is Kolovas-Jones that strange-looking coloured boy?' he asked, looking down at Strike and Bristow. 'The one who wanted Lula to get him modelling and acting work?'

'He's an actor, yeah,' said Strike.

'Yes. On Yvette's birthday, the last before she became ill, I had a problem with my car. Lula and that man called by to give me a lift to the birthday dinner. Kolovas-Jones spent most of the journey badgering Lula to use her influence with Freddie Bestigui to get him an audition. Quite an *encroaching* young man. Very familiar in his manner. Of course,' he added, 'the less I knew about my adopted niece's love life, the better, as far as I was concerned.'

Landry threw a ten-pound note down on the table.

'I'll expect you back at the office soon, John.'

He stood in clear expectation of a response, but Bristow was not paying attention. He was staring, wide-eyed, at the picture on the news story that Strike had been reading when Landry arrived; it showed a young black soldier in the uniform of the 2nd Battalion The Royal Regiment of Fusiliers.

'What? Yes. I'll be straight back,' he told his uncle distractedly, who was looking at him coldly. 'Sorry,' Bristow added to Strike, as Landry walked away. 'It's just that Wilson – Derrick Wilson, you know, the security guard – he's got a nephew out in Afghanistan. For a moment, God forbid ... but it's not him. Wrong name. Dreadful, this war, isn't it? And is it worth this loss of life?'

Strike shifted the weight off his prosthesis – the trudge across the park had not helped the soreness in his leg – and made a non-committal noise.

'Let's walk back,' said Bristow, when they had finished eating. 'I fancy some fresh air.'

Bristow chose the most direct route, which involved navigating stretches of lawn that Strike would not have chosen to walk, on his own, because it demanded much more energy than tarmac. As they passed the memorial fountain to Diana, Princess of Wales, whispering, tinkling and gushing along its long channel of Cornish granite, Bristow suddenly announced, as though Strike had asked:

'Tony's never liked me much. He preferred Charlie. People said that Charlie looked like Tony did, when he was a boy.'

'I can't say he spoke about Charlie with much fondness before you arrived, and he doesn't seem to have had much time for Lula, either.'

'Didn't he give you his views on heredity?'

'By implication.'

'No, well, he's not usually shy about them. It made an extra bond between Lula and me, the fact that Uncle Tony considered us a pair of sow's ears. It was worse for Lula; at least my biological parents must have been white. Tony's not what you'd call unprejudiced. We had a Pakistani trainee last year; she was one of the best we've ever had, but Tony drove her out.'

'What made you go and work with him?'

'They made me a good offer. It's the family firm; my grandfather started it, not that that was an inducement. No one wants to be accused of nepotism. But it's one of the top family law firms in London, and it made my mother happy to think I was following in her father's footsteps. Did he have a go at my father?'

'Not really. He hinted that Sir Alec might have greased some palms to get Lula.'

'Really?' Bristow sounded surprised. 'I don't think that's true. Lula was in care. I'm sure the usual procedures were followed.'

There was a short silence, after which Bristow said, a little timidly:

'You, ah, don't look very much like *your* father.'

It was the first time that he had acknowledged openly that he might have been sidetracked on to Wikipedia while researching private detectives.

'No,' agreed Strike. 'I'm the spitting image of my Uncle Ted.'

'I gather that you and your father aren't – ah – I mean, you don't use his name?'

Strike did not resent the curiosity from a man whose family background was almost as unconventional and casualty-strewn as his own.

'I've never used it,' he said. 'I'm the extramarital accident that cost Jonny a wife and several million pounds in alimony. We're not close.'

'I admire you,' said Bristow, 'for making your own way. For not relying on him.' And when Strike did not answer, he added anxiously, 'I hope you didn't mind me telling Tansy who your father is? It – it helped get her to talk to you. She's impressed by famous people.'

'All's fair in securing a witness statement,' said Strike. 'You say that Lula didn't like Tony, and yet she took his name professionally?'

'Oh no, she chose Landry because it was Mum's maiden name; nothing to do with Tony. Mum was thrilled. I think there was another model called Bristow. Lula liked to stand out.'

They wove their way through passing cyclists, bench-picnickers, dog walkers and roller-skaters, Strike trying to disguise the increasing unevenness in his step.

'I don't think Tony's ever really loved anyone in his life, you know,' said Bristow suddenly, as they stood aside to allow a helmeted child, wobbling along on a skateboard, to pass. 'Whereas my mother's a very loving person. She loved all three of her children very much, and I sometimes think Tony didn't like it. I don't know why. It's something in his nature.

'There was a breach between him and my parents after Charlie died. I wasn't supposed to know what was said, but I heard enough. He as good as told Mum that Charlie's accident was her fault, that Charlie had been out of control. My father threw Tony out of the house. Mum and Tony were only really reconciled after Dad died.'

To Strike's relief, they had reached Exhibition Road, and his limp became less perceptible.

'Do you think there was ever anything between Lula and Kieran Kolovas-Jones?' he asked, as they crossed the street.

'No, that's just Tony leaping to the most unsavoury conclusion he can think of. He always thought the worst when it came to Lula. Oh, I'm sure Kieran would have been only too eager, but Lula was smitten by Duffield – more's the pity.'

They walked on down Kensington Road, with the leafy park to their left, and then into the white-stuccoed territory of ambassadors' houses and royal colleges.

'Why do you think your uncle didn't come and say hello to you, when he called at your mother's the day she got out of hospital?'

Bristow looked intensely uncomfortable.

'Had there been a disagreement between you?'

'Not . . . not exactly,' said Bristow. 'We were in the middle of a very stressful time at work. I – ought not to say. Client confidentiality.'

'Was this to do with the estate of Conway Oates?'

'How do you know that?' asked Bristow sharply. 'Did Ursula tell you?'

'She mentioned something.'

'Christ almighty. No discretion. *None.*'

'Your uncle found it hard to believe that Mrs May could have been indiscreet.'

'I'll bet he did,' said Bristow, with a scornful laugh. 'It's – well, I'm sure I can trust you. It's the kind of thing a firm like ours is touchy about, because with the kind of clients we attract – high net worth – any hint of financial impropriety is death. Conway Oates held a sizeable client account with us. All the money's present and correct; but his heirs are a greedy bunch and they're claiming it was mismanaged. Considering how volatile the market's been, and how incoherent Conway's instructions became towards the end, they should be grateful there's anything left. Tony's irritable about the whole business and . . . well, he's a man who likes to spread the blame around. There have been scenes. I've copped my share of criticism. I usually do, with Tony.'

Strike could tell, by the almost perceptible heaviness that seemed to be descending upon Bristow as he walked, that they were approaching his offices.

'I'm having difficulty contacting a couple of useful witnesses, John. Is there any chance you'd be able to put me in touch with Guy Somé? His people don't seem keen on letting anyone near him.'

'I can try. I'll call him this afternoon. He adored Lula; he ought to want to help.'

'And there's Lula's birth mother, too.'

'Oh yes,' sighed Bristow. 'I've got her details somewhere. She's a dreadful woman.'

'Have you met her?'

'No, I'm going on what Lula told me, and everything that was in the papers. Lula was determined to find out where she came from, and I think Duffield was encouraging her – I strongly suspect him of leaking the story to the press, though she always denied that . . . Anyway, she managed to track her down, this Higson woman, who told her that her father was an African student. I don't know whether that was true or not. It was certainly what Lula wanted to hear. Her imagination ran wild: I think she had visions of herself being the long-lost daughter of a high-ranking politician, or a tribal princess.'

'But she never traced her father?'

'I don't know, but,' said Bristow, displaying his usual enthusiasm for any line of inquiry that might explain the black man caught on film near her flat, 'I'd have been the last person she'd have told if she did.'

'Why?'

'Because we'd had some pretty nasty rows about the whole business. My mother had just been diagnosed with uterine cancer when Lula went searching for Marlene Higson. I told Lula that she could hardly have chosen a more insensitive moment to start tracing her roots, but she – well, frankly, she had tunnel vision where her own whims were concerned. We loved each other,' said Bristow, running a weary hand over his face, 'but the age difference got in the way. I'm sure she tried to look for her father, though, because that was what she wanted more than anything: to find her black roots, to find that sense of identity.'

'Was she still in contact with Marlene Higson when she died?'

'Intermittently. I had the feeling that Lula was trying to cut the connection. Higson's a ghastly person; shamelessly mercenary. She sold her story to anyone who would pay, which, unfortunately, was a lot of people. My mother was devastated by the whole business.'

'There are a couple of other things I wanted to ask you.'

The lawyer slowed down willingly.

'When you visited Lula at her flat that morning, to return her contract with Somé, did you happen to see anyone who looked like they might have been from a security firm? There to check the alarms?'

'Like a repairman?'

'Or an electrician. Maybe in overalls?'

When Bristow screwed up his face in thought, his rabbity teeth protruded more than ever.

'I can't remember . . . let me think . . . As I passed the flat on the second floor, yes . . . there was a man in there fiddling with something on the wall . . . Would that have been him?'

'Probably. What did he look like?'

'Well, he had his back to me. I couldn't see.'

'Was Wilson with him?'

Bristow came to a halt on the pavement, looking a little bewildered. Three suited men and women bustled past, some carrying files.

'I think,' he said haltingly, 'I think both of them were there, with their backs to me, when I walked back downstairs. Why do you ask? How can that matter?'

'It might not,' said Strike. 'But can you remember anything at all? Hair or skin colour, maybe?'

Looking even more perplexed, Bristow said:

'I'm afraid I didn't really register. I suppose . . . ' He screwed up his face again in concentration. 'I remember he was wearing blue. I mean, if pressed, I'd say he was white. But I couldn't swear to it.'

'I doubt you'll have to,' said Strike, 'but that's still a help.'

He pulled out his notebook to remind himself of the questions he had wanted to put to Bristow.

'Oh, yeah. According to her witness statement to the police, Ciara Porter said that Lula had told her she wanted to leave everything to you.'

'Oh,' said Bristow unenthusiastically. 'That.'

He began to amble along again, and Strike moved with him.

'One of the detectives in charge of the case told me that Ciara had said that. A Detective Inspector Carver. He was convinced from the first that it was suicide and he appeared to think that this supposed talk with Ciara demonstrated Lula's intent to take her own life. It seemed a strange line of reasoning to me. Do suicides bother with wills?'

'You think Ciara Porter's inventing, then?'

'Not inventing,' said Bristow. 'Exaggerating, maybe. I think it's much more likely that Lula said something nice about me, because we'd just made up after our row, and Ciara, in hindsight, assuming that Lula was already contemplating suicide, turned whatever it was into a bequest. She's quite a – a fluffy sort of girl.'

'A search was made for a will, wasn't it?'

'Oh yeah, the police looked very thoroughly. We – the family – didn't think Lula had ever made one; her lawyers didn't know of one, but naturally a search was made. Nothing was found, and they looked everywhere.'

'Just supposing for a moment that Ciara Porter isn't misremembering what your sister said, though . . .'

'But Lula would never have left everything solely to me. Never.'

'Why not?'

'Because that would have explicitly cut out our mother, which would have been immensely hurtful,' said Bristow earnestly. 'It isn't the money – Dad left Mum very well off – it's more the message that Lula would have been sending, cutting her out like that. Wills can cause all kinds of hurt. I've seen it happen countless times.'

'Has your mother made a will?' Strike asked.

Bristow looked startled.

'I – yes, I believe so.'

'May I ask who her legatees are?'

'I haven't seen it,' said Bristow, a little stiffly. 'How is this . . . ?'

'It's all relevant, John. Ten million quid is a hell of a lot of money.'

Bristow seemed to be trying to decide whether or not Strike was being insensitive, or offensive. Finally he said:

'Given that there is no other family, I would imagine that Tony and I are the main beneficiaries. Possibly one or two charities will be remembered; my mother has always been generous to charities. However, as I'm sure you'll understand,' pink blotches were rising again up Bristow's thin neck, 'I am in no hurry to find out my mother's last wishes, given what must happen before they are acted upon.'

'Of course not,' said Strike.

They had reached Bristow's office, an austere eight-storey building entered by a dark archway. Bristow stopped beside the entrance and faced Strike.

'Do you still think I'm deluded?' he asked, as a pair of dark-suited women swept up past them.

'No,' said Strike, honestly enough. 'No, I don't.'

Bristow's undistinguished countenance brightened a little.

'I'll be in touch about Somé and Marlene Higson. Oh – and I nearly forgot. Lula's laptop. I've charged it for you, but it's password-protected. The police people found out the password, and they told my mother, but she can't remember what it was, and I never knew. Perhaps it was in the police file?' he added hopefully.

'Not as far as I can remember,' said Strike, 'but that shouldn't be too much of a problem. Where has this been since Lula died?'

'In police custody, and since then, at my mother's. Nearly all Lula's things are lying around at Mum's. She hasn't worked herself up to making decisions about them.'

Bristow handed Strike the case and bid him farewell; then, with a small bracing movement of his shoulders, he headed up the steps and disappeared through the doors of the family firm.

7

The friction between the end of Strike's amputated leg and the prosthesis was becoming more painful with every step as he headed towards Kensington Gore. Sweating a little in his heavy overcoat, while a weak sun made the park shimmer in the distance, Strike asked himself whether the strange suspicion that had him in its grip was anything more than a shadow moving in the depths of a muddy pool: a trick of the light, an illusory effect of the wind-ruffled surface. Had these minute flurries of black silt been flicked up by a slimy tail, or were they nothing but meaningless gusts of algae-fed gas? Could there be something lurking, disguised, buried in the mud, for which other nets had trawled in vain?

Heading for Kensington Tube station, he passed the Queen's Gate into Hyde Park; ornate, rust-red and embellished with royal insignia. Incurably observant, he noted the sculpture of the doe and fawn on one pillar and the stag on the other. Humans often assumed symmetry and equality where none existed. The same, yet profoundly different . . . Lula Landry's laptop banged harder and harder into his leg as his limp worsened.

In his sore, stymied and frustrated state, there was a dull inevitability about Robin's announcement, when he finally reached the office at ten to five, that she was still unable to penetrate past the telephone receptionist of Freddie Bestigui's production company; and that she had had no success in finding anyone of the name Onifade with a British Telecom number in the Kilburn area.

'Of course, if she's Rochelle's aunt, she could have a different surname, couldn't she?' Robin pointed out, as she buttoned her coat and prepared to leave.

Strike agreed to it wearily. He had dropped on to the sagging sofa the moment he had come through the office door, something that Robin had never seen him do before. His face was pinched.

'Are you all right?'

'Fine. Any sign of Temporary Solutions this afternoon?'

'No,' said Robin, pulling her belt tight. 'Perhaps they believed me when I said I was Annabel? I did try and sound Australian.'

He grinned. Robin closed the interim report she had been reading while she waited for Strike to return, set it neatly back on its shelf, bade Strike goodnight and left him sitting there, the laptop lying beside him on the threadbare cushions.

When the sound of Robin's footsteps was no longer audible, Strike stretched a long arm sideways to lock the glass door; then broke his own weekday ban on smoking in the office. Jamming the lit cigarette between his teeth, he pulled up his trouser leg and unlaced the strap holding the prosthesis to his thigh. Then he unrolled the gel liner from the stump of his leg and examined the end of his amputated tibia.

He was supposed to examine the skin surface for irritation every day. Now he saw that the scar tissue was inflamed and over-warm. There had been various creams and powders back in the bathroom cabinet at Charlotte's dedicated to the care of this patch of skin, subject as it was these days to forces for which it had not been designed. Perhaps she had thrown the corn powder and Oilatum into one of the still unpacked boxes? But he could not muster the energy to go and find out, nor did he want to refit the prosthesis just yet; and so he sat smoking on the sofa with the lower trouser leg hanging empty towards the floor, lost in thought.

His mind drifted. He thought about families, and names, and about the ways in which his and John Bristow's childhoods, outwardly so different, had been similar. There were ghostly figures in Strike's family history, too: his mother's first husband, for instance, of whom she had rarely spoken, except to say that she had hated being married from the first. Aunt Joan, whose memory had always been sharpest where Leda's had been most vague, said that the eighteen-year-old Leda had run out on her husband after only two weeks; that her sole motivation in marrying Strike Snr (who, according to Aunt Joan, had arrived in St Mawes with the fair) had been a new dress, and a change of name. Certainly, Leda had remained more faithful to her unusual married moniker than to any man. She had passed it to her son, who had never met its original owner, long gone before his unconnected birth.

Strike smoked, lost in thought, until the daylight in his office began to soften and dim. Then, at last, he struggled up on his one foot and, using the doorknob and the dado rail on the wall beyond the glass door to steady himself, hopped out to examine the boxes still stacked on the landing outside his office. At the bottom of one of them he found those dermatological products designed to assuage the burning and prickling in the end of his stump, and set to work to try and repair the damage first done by the long walk across London with his kitbag over his shoulder.

It was lighter now than it had been at eight o'clock two weeks ago; still daylight when Strike was seated, for the second time in ten days, in Wong Kei, the tall, white-fronted Chinese restaurant with a window view of an arcade centre called Play to Win. It had been extremely painful to reattach the prosthetic leg, and still more to walk down Charing Cross Road on it, but he had disdained the use of the grey metal sticks he had also found in the box, relics of his release from Selly Oak Hospital.

While Strike ate Singapore noodles one-handed, he examined Lula Landry's laptop, which lay open on the table, beside his beer. The dark pink computer casing was patterned with cherry blossom. It did not occur to Strike that he presented an incongruous appearance to the world as he hunched, large and hairy, over the prettified, pink and palpably feminine device, but the sight had drawn smirks from two of the black-T-shirted waiters.

'How's tricks, Federico?' asked a pallid, straggly-haired young man at half past eight. The newcomer, who dropped into the seat opposite Strike, wore jeans, a psychedelic T-shirt, Converse sneakers, and a leather bag slung diagonally across his chest.

'Been worse,' grunted Strike. 'How're you? Want a drink?'

'Yeah, I'll have a lager.'

Strike ordered the drink for his guest, whom he was accustomed, for long-forgotten reasons, to call Spanner. Spanner had a first-class degree in computer science, and was much better paid than his clothing suggested.

'I'm not that hungry, I had a burger after work,' Spanner said, looking down the menu. 'I could do a soup. Wonton soup, please,' he added to the waiter. 'Interesting choice of laptop, Fed.'

'It's not mine,' said Strike.

'It's the job, is it?'

'Yeah.'

Strike slid the computer around to face Spanner, who surveyed the device with the mixture of interest and disparagement characteristic of those to whom technology is no necessary evil, but the stuff of life.

'Junk,' said Spanner cheerfully. 'Where've you been hiding yourself, Fed? People've been worried.'

'Nice of them,' said Strike, through a mouthful of noodles. 'No need, though.'

'I was round Nick and Ilsa's coupla nights ago and you were the only topic of conversation. They were saying you've gone underground. Oh, cheers,' he said, as his soup arrived. 'Yeah, they've been ringing your flat and they keep getting the answering machine. Ilsa reckons it's woman trouble.'

It now occurred to Strike that the best way to inform his friends of his ruptured engagement might be through the medium of the unconcerned Spanner. The younger brother of one of Strike's old friends, Spanner was largely ignorant of, and indifferent to, the long and tortured history of Strike and Charlotte. Given that it was face-to-face sympathy and post-mortems that Strike wanted to avoid, and that he had no intention of pretending for ever that he and Charlotte had not split up, he agreed that Ilsa had correctly divined his main trouble, and that it would be better if his friends avoided calling Charlotte's flat henceforth.

'Bummer,' said Spanner, and then, with the incuriosity towards human pain versus technological challenges that was characteristic of him, he pointed a spatulate fingertip at the Dell and asked: 'What d'you want doing with this, then?'

'The police have already had a look at it,' said Strike, lowering his voice even though he and Spanner were the only people nearby not speaking Cantonese, 'but I want a second opinion.'

'Police've got good techie people. I doubt I'm gonna find anything they haven't.'

'They might not have been looking for the right stuff,' said Strike, 'and they might not've realised what it meant even if they found it. They seemed mostly interested in her recent emails, and I've already seen them.'

'What am I looking for, then?'

'All activity on or leading up to the eighth of January. The most recent internet searches, stuff like that. I haven't got the password, and I'd rather not go back to the police and ask unless I have to.'

'Shouldn't be a problem,' said Spanner. He was not writing these instructions down, but typing them on to his mobile phone; Spanner was ten years younger than Strike, and he rarely wielded a pen by choice. 'Who's it belong to, anyway?'

When Strike told him, Spanner said:

'The model? Whoa.'

But Spanner's interest in human beings, even when dead or famous, was still secondary to his fondness for rare comics, technological innovation and bands of which Strike had never heard. After eating several spoonfuls of soup, Spanner broke the silence to enquire brightly how much Strike was planning to pay him for the work.

When Spanner had left with the pink laptop under his arm, Strike limped back to his office. He washed the end of his right leg carefully that night and then applied cream to the irritated and inflamed scar tissue. For the first time in many months, he took painkillers before easing himself into his sleeping bag. Lying there waiting for the raw ache to deaden, he wondered whether he ought to make an appointment to see the consultant in rehabilitation medicine under whose care he was supposed to fall. The symptoms of choke syndrome, the nemesis of amputees, had been described to him repeatedly: suppurating skin and swelling. He was wondering whether he might be showing the early signs, but he dreaded the prospect of returning to corridors stinking of disinfectant; of doctors with their detached interest in this one small mutilated portion of his body; of further minute adjustments to the prosthesis necessitating still more visits to that white-coated, confined world he had hoped he had left for ever. He feared advice to rest the leg, to desist from normal ambulation; a forced return to crutches, the stares of passers-by at his pinned-up trouser leg and the shrill enquiries of small children.

His mobile, charging as usual on the floor beside the camp bed, made the buzzing noise that announced the arrival of a text. Glad for any minor distraction from his throbbing leg, Strike groped in the dark and picked up the telephone from the floor.

Please could you give me a quick call when convenient?
Charlotte

Strike did not believe in clairvoyance or psychic ability, yet his immediate irrational thought was that Charlotte had somehow sensed what he had just told Spanner; that he had twitched the taut, invisible rope still binding them, by placing their break-up on an official footing.

He stared at the message as though it was her face, as though he could read her expression on the tiny grey screen.

Please. (I know you don't have to: I'm asking you to, nicely.) *A quick call.* (I have a legitimate reason for desiring speech with you, so we can do it swiftly and easily; no rows.) *When convenient.*

(I do you the courtesy of assuming that you have a busy life without me.)

Or, perhaps: *Please.* (To refuse is to be a bastard, Strike, and you've hurt me enough.) *A quick call.* (I know you're expecting a scene; well, don't worry, that last one, when you were such an unbelievable shit, has finished me with you for ever.) *When convenient.* (Because, let's be honest, I always had to slot in around the army and every other damn thing that came first.)

Was it convenient now? he asked himself, lying in pain that the pills had yet to touch. He glanced at the time: ten past eleven. She was clearly still awake.

He put the mobile back on the floor beside him, where it lay silently charging, and raised a large hairy arm over his eyes, blotting out even the strips of light on the ceiling cast by the street lamps through the window slats. Against his will, he saw Charlotte the way that he had laid eyes on her for the first time in his life, as she sat alone on a windowsill at a student party in Oxford. He had never seen anything so beautiful in his life, and nor, judging by the sideways flickering of countless male eyes, the overloud laughter and voices, the angling of extravagant gestures towards her silent figure, had any of the rest of them.

Gazing across the room, the nineteen-year-old Strike had been visited by precisely the same urge that had come over him as a child whenever snow had fallen overnight in Aunt Joan and Uncle Ted's garden. He wanted his footsteps to be the first to make deep, dark holes in that tantalisingly smooth surface: he wanted to disturb and disrupt it.

'You're pissed,' warned his friend, when Strike announced his intention to go and talk to her.

Strike agreed, downed the dregs of his seventh pint and

strode purposefully over to the window ledge where she sat. He was vaguely aware of people nearby watching, primed, perhaps, for laughter, because he was massive, and looked like a boxing Beethoven, and had curry sauce all down his T-shirt.

She looked up at him when he reached her, with big eyes, and long dark hair, and soft, pale cleavage revealed by the gaping shirt.

Strike's strange, nomadic childhood, with its constant uprootings and graftings on to motley groups of children and teenagers, had forged in him an advanced set of social skills; he knew how to fit in, to make people laugh, to render himself acceptable to almost anyone. That night, his tongue had become numb and rubbery. He seemed to remember swaying slightly.

'Did you want something?' she asked.

'Yeah,' he said. He pulled his T-shirt away from his torso and showed her the curry sauce. 'What d'you reckon's the best way to get this out?'

Against her will (he saw her trying to fight it), she giggled.

Some time later, an Adonis called the Honourable Jago Ross, known to Strike by sight and reputation, swung into the room with a posse of equally well-bred friends, and discovered Strike and Charlotte sitting side by side on the windowsill, deep in conversation.

'You're in the wrong fucking room, Char, darling,' Ross had said, staking out his rights by the caressing arrogance of his tone. 'Ritchie's party's upstairs.'

'I'm not coming,' she said, turning a smiling face upon him. 'I've got to go and help Cormoran soak his T-shirt.'

Thus had she publicly dumped her Old Harrovian boyfriend for Cormoran Strike. It had been the most glorious moment of Strike's nineteen years: he had publicly carried off Helen of Troy right under Menelaus's nose, and in his shock and delight he had not questioned the miracle, but simply accepted it.

Only later had he realised that what had seemed like chance, or fate, had been entirely engineered by her. She had admitted it to him months later: that she had, to punish Ross for some transgression, deliberately entered the wrong room, and waited for a man, any man, to approach her; that he, Strike, had been a mere instrument to torture Ross; that she had slept with him in the early hours of the following morning in a spirit of vengefulness and rage that he had mistaken for passion.

There, in that first night, had been everything that had subsequently broken them apart and pulled them back together: her self-destructiveness, her recklessness, her determination to hurt; her unwilling but genuine attraction to Strike, and her secure place of retreat in the cloistered world in which she had grown up, whose values she simultaneously despised and espoused. Thus had begun the relationship that had led to Strike lying here on his camp bed fifteen years later, racked with more than physical pain, and wishing that he could rid himself of her memory.

8

When Robin arrived next morning, it was, for the second time, to a locked glass door. She let herself in with the spare key that Strike had now entrusted to her, approached the closed inner door and stood silent, listening. After a few seconds, she heard the faintly muffled but unmistakable sound of deep snoring.

This presented her with a delicate problem, because of their tacit agreement not to mention Strike's camp bed, or any of the other signs of habitation lying around the place. On the other hand, Robin had something of an urgent nature to communicate to her temporary boss. She hesitated, considering her options. The easiest route would be to try and wake Strike by clattering around the outer office, thereby giving him time to organise himself and the inner room, but that might take too long: her news would not keep. Robin therefore took a deep breath and rapped on the door.

Strike woke instantly. For one disorientated moment he lay there, registering the reproachful daylight pouring through the window. Then he remembered setting down the mobile phone after reading Charlotte's text, and knew that he had forgotten to set the alarm.

'Don't come in!' he bellowed.

'Would you like a cup of tea?' Robin called through the door.

'Yeah – yeah, that'd be great. I'll come out there for it,' Strike added loudly, wishing, for the first time, that he had fitted a lock on the inner door. His false foot and calf was standing propped against the wall, and he was wearing nothing but boxer shorts.

Robin hurried away to fill the kettle, and Strike fought his way out of his sleeping bag. He dressed at speed, making a clumsy job of putting on the prosthesis, folding the camp bed into its corner, pushing the desk back into place. Ten minutes after she had knocked on the door, he limped into the outer office smelling strongly of deodorant, to find Robin at her desk, looking very excited about something.

'Your tea,' she said, indicating a steaming mug.

'Great, thanks. Just give me a moment,' he said, and he left to pee in the bathroom on the landing. As he zipped up his fly, he caught sight of himself in the mirror, crumpled-looking and unshaven. Not for the first time, he consoled himself that his hair looked the same whether brushed or unbrushed.

'I've got news,' said Robin, when he had re-entered the office through the glass door and, with reiterated thanks, picked up his mug of tea.

'Yeah?'

'I've found Rochelle Onifade.'

He lowered the mug.

'You're kidding. How the hell . . . ?'

'I saw in the file that she was supposed to attend an outpatient clinic at St Thomas's,' said Robin excitedly, flushed and talking fast, 'so I rang up the hospital yesterday evening, pretending to be her, and I said I'd forgotten the time of my appointment, and they told me it's at ten thirty on Thursday morning. You've got,' she glanced at her computer monitor, 'fifty-five minutes.'

Why had he not thought to tell her to do this?

'You genius, you bloody genius . . . '

He had slopped hot tea over his hand, and put the mug down on her desk.

'D'you know exactly . . . ?'

'It's in the psychiatric unit round the back of the main building,' said Robin, exhilarated. 'See, you go in off Grantley Road, there's a second car park . . . '

She had turned the monitor towards him to show him the map of St Thomas's. He checked his wrist, but his watch was still in the inner room.

'You'll have time if you leave now,' Robin urged him.

'Yeah – I'll get my stuff.'

Strike hurried to fetch his watch, wallet, cigarettes and phone. He was almost through the glass door, cramming his wallet into his back pocket, when Robin said:

'Er – Cormoran . . . '

She had never called him by his first name before. Strike assumed that this accounted for her slight air of bashfulness; then he realised that she was pointing meaningfully at his navel. Looking down, he saw that he had done up the buttons on his shirt wrongly, and was exposing a patch of belly so hairy that it resembled black coconut matting.

'Oh – right – cheers . . . '

Robin turned her attention politely to her monitor while he undid and refastened the buttons.

'See you later.'

'Yeah, 'bye,' she said, smiling at him as he departed at speed; but within seconds he was back, panting slightly.

'Robin, I need you to check something.'

She already had the pen in her hand, waiting.

'There was a legal conference in Oxford on the seventh of January. Lula Landry's uncle Tony attended it. International family law. Anything you can find out. Specifically about him being there.'

'Right,' said Robin, scribbling.

'Cheers. You're a genius.'

And he was gone, with uneven steps, down the metal stairs.

Though she hummed to herself as she settled down at her desk, a little of Robin's cheerfulness drained away as she drank her tea. She had half hoped that Strike would invite her along to meet Rochelle Onifade, whose shadow she had hunted for two weeks.

Rush hour past, the crowds on the Tube had thinned. Strike was pleased, because the end of his stump was still smarting, to find a seat with ease. He had bought himself a pack of Extra Strong Mints at the station kiosk before boarding his train, and was now sucking four simultaneously, trying to conceal the fact that he had not had time to clean his teeth. His toothbrush and toothpaste were hidden inside his kitbag, even though it would have been much more convenient to leave them on the chipped sink in the bathroom. Catching sight of himself again, in the darkened train window, with his heavy stubble and his generally unkempt appearance, he asked himself why, when it was perfectly obvious that Robin knew he slept there, he maintained the fiction that he had some other home.

Strike's memory and map sense were more than adequate to the task of locating the entrance to the psychiatric unit at St Thomas's, and he proceeded there without mishap, arriving at shortly after ten. He spent five minutes checking that the automatic double doors were the only entrance on Grantley Road, before positioning himself on a stone wall in the car park, some twenty yards away from the entrance, giving him a clear view of everyone entering and leaving.

Knowing only that the girl he sought was probably homeless, and certainly black, he had thought through his strategy for finding her on the Tube, and concluded that there was really only one option open to him. At twenty past ten, therefore, when he saw a tall, thin black girl walking briskly towards the entrance, he called out (even though she looked too well-groomed, too neatly dressed):

'Rochelle!'

She glanced up to see who had shouted, but kept walking without any sign that the name had a personal application, and disappeared into the building. Next came a couple, both white; then a group of people of assorted ages and races whom Strike guessed to be hospital workers; but on the mere off-chance he called again:

'Rochelle!'

Some of them glanced at him, but returned immediately to their conversations. Consoling himself that frequenters of this entrance were probably used to a degree of eccentricity in those they met in its vicinity, Strike lit a cigarette and waited.

Half past ten passed, and no black girl went through the doors. Either she had missed her appointment, or she had used a different entrance. A feather-light breeze tickled the back of his neck as he sat smoking, watching, waiting. The hospital building was enormous, a vast concrete box with rectangular windows; there were surely numerous entrances on every side.

Strike straightened his injured leg, which was still sore, and considered, again, the possibility that he would have to return to see his consultant. He found even this degree of proximity to a hospital slightly depressing. His stomach rumbled. He had passed a McDonald's on the way here. If he had not found her by midday, he would go and eat there.

Twice more he shouted 'Rochelle!' at black women who entered and exited the building, and both times they glanced back, purely to see who had shouted, in one case giving him a look of disdain.

Then, just after eleven, a short, stocky black girl emerged from the hospital with a slightly awkward, rocking, side-to-side gait. He knew quite well that he had not missed her going in, not only because of her distinctive walk, but because she wore a very noticeable short coat of magenta-coloured fake fur, which flattered neither her height nor her breadth.

'Rochelle!'

The girl stopped, turned and stared around, scowling, looking for the person who had called her name. Strike limped towards her, and she glared at him with an understandable mistrust.

'Rochelle? Rochelle Onifade? Hi. My name's Cormoran Strike. Can I have a word?'

'I always come in Redbourne Street entrance,' she told him five minutes later, after he had given a garbled and fictitious account of the way he had found her. 'I come out this way 'cause I was gonna go to McDonald's.'

So that was where they went. Strike bought two coffees and two large cookies, and carried them to the window table where Rochelle was waiting, curious and suspicious.

She was uncompromisingly plain. Her greasy skin, which was the colour of burned earth, was covered in acne pustules and pits; her small eyes were deep-set and her teeth were crooked and rather yellow. The chemically straightened hair showed four inches of black roots, then six inches of harsh, coppery wire-red. Her tight, too-short jeans, her shiny grey handbag and her bright white trainers looked cheap. However, the squashy fake-fur jacket, garish and unflattering though Strike found it, was of a different quality altogether: fully lined, as he saw when she took it off, with a patterned silk, and bearing the label not (as he had expected, remembering Lula Landry's email to the designer) of Guy Somé, but of an Italian of whom even Strike had heard.

'You sure you inna journalist?' she asked, in her low, husky voice.

Strike had already spent some time outside the hospital trying to establish his bona fides in this respect.

'No, I'm not a journalist. Like I said, I know Lula's brother.'

'You a friend of his?'

'Yeah. Well, not exactly a friend. He's hired me. I'm a private detective.'

She was instantly, openly scared.

'Whaddayuhwanna talk to me for?'

'There's nothing to worry about . . . '

'Whyd'yuhwanna talk to me, though?'

'It's nothing bad. John isn't sure that Lula committed suicide, that's all.'

He guessed that the only thing keeping her in the seat was her terror of the construction he might put on instant flight. Her fear was out of all proportion to his manner or words.

'There's nothing to worry about,' he assured her again. 'John wants me to take another look at the circumstances, that's—'

'Does 'e say I've got something to do wiv 'er dying?'

'No, of course not. I'm just hoping you might be able to tell me about her state of mind, what she got up to in the lead-up to her death. You saw her regularly, didn't you? I thought you might be able to tell me what was going on in her life.'

Rochelle made as though to speak, then changed her mind and attempted to drink her scalding coffee instead.

'So, what – 'er brother's trying to make out she never killed 'erself? What, like she was pushed out the window?'

'He thinks it's possible.'

She seemed to be trying to fathom something, to work it out in her head.

'I don't 'ave to talk to you. You ain't real police.'

'Yeah, that's true. But wouldn't you like to help find out what—'

'She jumped,' declared Rochelle Onifade firmly.

'What makes you so sure?' asked Strike.

'I jus' know.'

'It seems to have come as a shock to nearly everyone else she knew.'

'She wuz depressed. Yeah, she wuz on stuff for it. Like me. Sometimes it jus' takes you over. It's an illness,' she said, although she made the words sound like 'it's uh nillness'.

Nillness, thought Strike, for a second distracted. He had slept badly. *Nillness*, that was where Luna Landry had gone, and where all of them, he and Rochelle included, were headed. Sometimes illness turned slowly to nillness, as was happening to Bristow's mother . . . sometimes nillness rose to meet you out of nowhere, like a concrete road slamming your skull apart.

He was sure that if he took out his notebook, she would clam up, or leave. He therefore continued to ask questions as casually as he could manage, asking her how she had come to attend the clinic, how she had first met Lula.

Still immensely suspicious, she gave monosyllabic answers at first, but slowly, gradually, she became more forthcoming. Her own history was pitiful. Early abuse, care, severe mental illness, foster homes and violent outbursts culminating, at sixteen, in homelessness. She had secured proper treatment as the indirect result of being hit by a car. Hospitalised when her bizarre behaviour had made treating her physical wounds nearly impossible, a psychiatrist had at last been called in. She was on drugs now, which, when she took them, greatly eased her symptoms. Strike found it pathetic, and touching, that the outpatient clinic where she had met Lula Landry seemed to have become, for Rochelle, the highlight of her week. She spoke with some affection of the young psychiatrist who ran the group.

'So that's where you met Lula?'

'Di'n't her brother tell ya?'

'He was vague on the details.'

'Yeah, she come to our group. She wuz referred.'

'And you got talking?'

'Yeah.'

'You became friends?'

'Yeah.'

'You visited her at home? Swam in the pool?'

'Why shou'n't I?'

'No reason. I'm only asking.'

She thawed very slightly.

'I don't like swimming. I don't like water over m'face. I went in the jacuzzi. And we went shoppin' an' stuff.'

'Did she ever talk to you about her neighbours; the other people in her building?'

'Them Bestiguis? A bit. She din' like them. That woman's a bitch,' said Rochelle, with sudden savagery.

'What makes you say that?'

'Have you met 'er? She look at me like I wuz dirt.'

'What did Lula think of her?'

'She din' like 'er neither, nor her husband. He's a creep.'

'In what way?'

'He jus' is,' said Rochelle, impatiently; but then, when Strike did not speak, she went on. 'He wuz always tryin' ter get her downstairs when his wife wuz out.'

'Did Lula ever go?'

'No fuckin' chance,' said Rochelle.

'You and Lula talked to each other a lot, I suppose, did you?'

'Yeah, we did, at f— Yeah, we did.'

She looked out of the window. A sudden shower of rain had caught passers-by unawares. Transparent ellipses peppered the glass beside them.

'At first?' said Strike. 'Did you talk less as time went on?'

'I'm gonna have to go soon,' said Rochelle, grandly. 'I got things to do.'

'People like Lula,' said Strike, feeling his way, 'can be spoiled. Treat people badly. They're used to getting their own—'

'I ain't no one's servant,' said Rochelle fiercely.

'Maybe that's why she liked you? Maybe she saw you as someone more equal – not a hanger-on?'

'Yeah, igzactly,' said Rochelle, mollified. 'I weren't impressed by her.'

'You can see why she'd want you as a friend, someone more down-to-earth . . .'

'Yeah.'

'. . . and you had your illness in common, didn't you? So you understood her on a level most people wouldn't.'

'And I'm black,' said Rochelle, 'and she wuz wanting to feel proper black.'

'Did she talk to you about that?'

'Yeah, 'course,' said Rochelle. 'She wuz wanting to find out where she come from, where she belong.'

'Did she talk to you about trying to find the black side of her family?'

'Yeah, of course. And she . . . yeah.'

She had braked almost visibly.

'Did she ever find anyone? Her father?'

'No. She never found 'im. No fuckin' chance.'

'Really?'

'Yeah, *really.*'

She began eating fast. Strike was afraid that she would leave the moment she had finished.

'Was Lula depressed when you met her at Vashti, the day before she died?'

'Yeah, she wuz.'

'Did she tell you why?'

'There don't 'ave to be a reason why. It's uh nillness.'

'But she told you she was feeling bad, did she?'

'Yeah,' she said, after a fractional hesitation.

'You were supposed to be having lunch together, weren't you?' he asked. 'Kieran told me that he drove her to meet you. You know Kieran, right? Kieran Kolovas-Jones?'

Her expression softened; the corners of her mouth lifted.

'Yeah, I know Kieran. Yeah, she come to meet me at Vashti.'

'But she didn't stop for lunch?'

'No. She wuz in a hurry,' said Rochelle.

She bowed her head to drink more coffee, concealing her face.

'Why didn't she just ring you? You've got a phone, have you?'

'Yeah, I gotta phone,' she snapped, bristling, and drew from the fur jacket a basic-looking Nokia, stuck all over with gaudy pink crystals.

'So why d'you think she didn't call to say she couldn't see you?'

Rochelle glowered at him.

'Because she didn't like using the phone, because of them listenin' in.'

'Journalists?'

'Yeah.'

She had almost finished her cookie.

'Journalists wouldn't have been very interested in her saying that she wasn't coming to Vashti, though, would they?'

'I dunno.'

'Didn't you think it was odd, at the time, that she drove all the way to tell you she couldn't stay for lunch?'

'Yeah. No,' said Rochelle. And then, with a sudden burst of fluency:

'When ya gotta driver it don't matter, does it? You jus' go wherever you want, don't cost you nothing extra, you just get them to take you, don't ya? She was passing, so she come in to tell me she wasn't gonna stop because she 'ad to get 'ome to see fucking Ciara Porter.'

Rochelle looked as though she regretted the traitorous 'fucking' as soon as it was out, and pursed her lips together as though to ensure no more swear words escaped her.

'And that was all she did, was it? She came into the shop, said "I can't stop, I've got to get home and see Ciara" and left?'

'Yeah. More uh less,' said Rochelle.

'Kieran says they usually gave you a lift home after you'd been out together.'

'Yeah,' she said. 'Well. She wuz too busy that day, weren' she?'

Rochelle did a poor job of masking her resentment.

'Talk me through what happened in the shop. Did either of you try anything on?'

'Yeah,' said Rochelle, after a pause. 'She did.' Another hesitation. 'Long Alexander McQueen dress. He killed hiself and all,' she added, in a distant voice.

'Did you go into the changing room with her?'

'Yeah.'

'What happened in the changing room?' prompted Strike.

'Some silly Aussie cow come shoving in, askin' to do Lula's make-up or sumthin',' said Rochelle. 'Stepped on my effing foot, never mind me.'

Strike heard the bone-deep bitterness of the perennially overlooked, of the pushed aside.

'Yeah, I heard about that. The girl got sacked for it afterwards.'

'Good,' said Rochelle.

'Lula was pretty nice to her, though, wasn't she?' asked Strike. 'Didn't she take her details?'

'That wasn't—' began Rochelle, but she stopped short. 'It was only to get rid of her.'

'What was Lula doing when the girl walked in?'

Her eyes reminded him of those of a bull he had once come face to face with as a small boy: deep-set, deceptively stoic, unfathomable.

'Trying on the dress.'

'I heard she was on the phone.'

'Oh. Well, yeah. She mighta bin.'

'Who was she on the phone to?'

'I dunno.'

She drank, obscuring her face again with the paper cup.

'Was it Evan Duffield?'

'It mighta bin.'

'Can you remember what she said?'

'No.'

'One of the shop assistants overheard her, while she was on the phone. She seemed to be making an appointment to meet someone at her flat much later. In the early hours of the morning, the girl thought.'

'Yeah?'

'So that doesn't seem like it could have been Duffield, does it, seeing as she already had an arrangement to meet him at Uzi?'

'Know a lot, don't you?' she said.

'Everyone knows they met at Uzi that night,' said Strike. 'It was in all the papers.'

The dilating or contracting of Rochelle's pupils would be almost impossible to see, because of the virtually black irises surrounding them.

'Yeah, I s'pose,' she conceded.

'Was it Deeby Macc?'

'No!' She yelped it on a laugh. 'She din' know his number.'

'Famous people can nearly always get each other's numbers,' said Strike.

Rochelle's expression clouded. She glanced down at the blank screen on her gaudy pink mobile.

'I don' think she had his,' she said.

'But you heard her trying to make an arrangement to meet someone in the small hours?'

'No,' said Rochelle, avoiding his eyes, swilling the dregs of her coffee around the paper cup. 'I can' remember nuthin' like that.'

'You understand how important this could be?' said Strike, careful to keep his tone unthreatening. 'If Lula made an arrangement to meet someone at the time she died? The police never knew about this, did they? You never told them?'

'I gotta go,' she said, throwing down the last morsel of cookie, grabbing the strap of her cheap handbag and glaring at him.

Strike said:

'It's nearly lunchtime. Can I buy you anything else?'

'No.'

But she did not move. He wondered how poor she was, whether she ate regularly or not. There was something about her, beneath the surliness, that he found touching: a fierce pride, a vulnerability.

'Yeah, all right then,' she said, dropping her handbag and slumping back on to the hard chair. 'I'll have a Big Mac.'

He was afraid she might leave while he was at the counter, but when he returned with two trays, she was still there; she even thanked him grudgingly.

Strike tried a different tack.

'You know Kieran quite well, do you?' he asked, pursuing the glow that had illuminated her at the mention of his name.

'Yeah,' she said, self-consciously. 'I met him a lot with 'er. 'E wuz always driving 'er.'

'He says that Lula was writing something in the back of the car, before she arrived at Vashti. Did she show you, or give you, anything she'd written?'

'No,' she said. She crammed fries into her mouth and then said, 'I ain't seen nuthin like that. Why, what was it?'

'I don't know.'

'Maybe it were a shopping list or something?'

'Yeah, that's what the police thought. You're sure you didn't notice her carrying a bit of paper, a letter, an envelope?'

'Yeah, I'm sure.'

'Where did she write down the Australian girl's details?'

'She didn't write 'em. The girl did. Back of a till thing.'

'A receipt?'

'Yeah,' said Rochelle. 'Kieran know you're meeting me?'

'Yeah, I told him you were on my list. He told me you used to live at St Elmo's.'

This seemed to please her.

'Where are you living now?'

'What's it to you?' she demanded, suddenly fierce.

'It's nothing to me. I'm just making polite conversation.'

This drew a small snort from Rochelle.

'I got my own place in Hammersmith now.'

She chewed for a while and then, for the first time, proffered unsolicited information.

'We usedta listen to Deeby Macc in his car. Me, Kieran and Lula.'

And she began to rap:

No hydroquinone, black to the backbone,
Takin' Deeby lightly, better buy an early tombstone,
I'm drivin' my Ferrari – fuck Johari – got my head on straight
Nothin' talks like money talks – I'm shoutin' at ya, Mister Jake.

She looked proud, as though she had put him firmly in his place, with no retort possible.

'Tha's from "Hydroquinone",' she said. 'On *Jake On My Jack*.'

'What's hydroquinone?' Strike asked.

'Skin light'ner. We usedta rap that with the car windows down,' said Rochelle. A warm, reminiscent smile lit her face out of plainness.

'Lula was looking forward to meeting Deeby Macc, then, was she?'

'Yeah, she wuz,' said Rochelle. 'She knew 'e liked 'er, she wuz pleased with herself about that. Kieran wuz proper excited an' all, he kep' askin' Lula to introduce him. He wanted to meet Deeby.'

Her smile faded; she picked morosely at her burger, then said:

'Is that all you wanna know, then? 'Cause I gotta go.'

She began wolfing the remnants of her meal, cramming food into her mouth.

'Lula must have taken you to a lot of places, did she?'

'Yeah,' said Rochelle, her mouth full of burger.

'Did you go to Uzi with her?'

'Yeah. Once.'

She swallowed, and began to talk about the other places she had seen during the early phase of her friendship with Lula, which (in spite of Rochelle's determined attempts to repudiate any suggestion that she had been dazzled by the lifestyle of a multimillionairess) had all the romance of a fairy tale. Lula had snatched Rochelle away from the bleak world of her hostel and group therapy and swept her, once a week, into a whirl of expensive fun. Strike noted how very little Rochelle had told him about Lula the person, as opposed to Lula the holder of the magic plastic cards that bought handbags, jackets and jewellery, and the necessary means by which Kieran appeared regularly, like a genie, to whisk Rochelle away from her hostel. She described, in loving detail, the presents Lula had bought her, shops to which Lula had taken her, restaurants and bars to which they had gone together, places lined with celebrities. None of these, however, seemed to have impressed Rochelle in the slightest; for every name she mentioned there was a deprecating remark:

''E wuz a dick.' 'She's plastic all over.' 'They ain't nuthing special.'

'Did you meet Evan Duffield?' Strike asked.

''Im.' The monosyllable was heavy with contempt. ''E's a twat.'

'Is he?'

'Yeah, 'e is. Ask Kieran.'

She gave the impression that she and Kieran stood together, sane, dispassionate observers of the idiots populating Lula's world.

'In what way was he a twat?'

''E treated 'er like shit.'

'Like how?'

'Sold stories,' said Rochelle, reaching for the last of her fries. 'One time she tested ev'ryone. Told us all a diff'rent story to see which ones got in the papers. I wuz the only one who kep' their mouf shut, ev'ryone else blabbed.'

'Who'd she test?'

'Ciara Porter. 'Im, Duffield. That Guy Summy,' Rochelle pronounced his first name to rhyme with 'die', 'but then she reckoned it wasn't 'im. Made excuses for 'im. But 'e used 'er as much as anyone.'

'In what way?'

'He di'n't want 'er to work for anyone else. Wanted 'er to do it all for 'is company, get 'im all the publicity.'

'So, after she'd found out she could trust you . . .'

'Yeah, then she bought me the phone.'

There was a missed beat.

'So she cud get in touch wiv me whenever she wanted.'

She swept the sparkling pink Nokia suddenly off the table and stuffed it deep into the pocket of her squashy pink coat.

'I suppose you've had to take over the charges yourself now?' Strike asked.

He thought that she was going to tell him to mind his own business, but instead she said:

''Er family 'asn't noticed they're still payin' for it.'

And this thought seemed to give her a slightly malicious pleasure.

'Did Lula buy you that jacket?' Strike asked.

'No,' she snapped, furiously defensive. 'I got this myself, I'm working now.'

'Really? Where are you working?'

'Whut's it to you?' she demanded again.

'I'm showing polite interest.'

A tiny, brief smile touched the wide mouth, and she relented again.

'I'm doing afternoons in a shop up the road from my new place.'

'Are you in another hostel?'

'No,' she said, and he sensed again the digging in, the refusal to go further that he would push at his peril. He changed tack.

'It must have been a shock to you when Lula died, was it?'

'Yeah. It wuz,' she said, thoughtlessly; then, realising what she had said, she backtracked. 'I knew she wuz depressed, but you never 'spect people tuh do that.'

'So you wouldn't say she was suicidal when you saw her that day?'

'I dunno. I never saw 'er for long enough, did I?'

'Where were you when you heard she'd died?'

'I wuz in the hostel. Loadsa people knew I knew her. Janine woke me up and told me.'

'And your immediate thought was that it was suicide?'

'Yeah. An' I gotta go now. I gotta go.'

She had made up her mind and he could see that he was not going to be able to stop her. After wriggling back into the ludicrous fur jacket, she hoisted her handbag on to her shoulder.

'Say hullo to Kieran for me.'

'Yeah, I will.'

'See yuh.'

She waddled out of the restaurant without a backward glance.

Strike watched her walk past the window, her head down, her brows knitted, until she passed out of sight. It had stopped raining. Idly he pulled her tray towards him and finished her last few fries.

Then he stood up so abruptly that the baseball-capped girl who had been approaching his table to clear and wipe it jumped back a step with a little cry of surprise. Strike hurried out of the McDonald's and off up Grantley Road.

Rochelle was standing on the corner, clearly visible in her furry magenta coat, part of a knot of people waiting for the lights to change at a pedestrian crossing. She was gabbling into the pink jewelled Nokia. Strike caught up with her, insinuating himself into the group behind her, making of his bulk a weapon, so that people moved aside to avoid him.

'... wanted to know who she was arrangin' to meet that night ... yeah, an'—'

Rochelle turned her head, watching traffic, and realised that Strike was right behind her. Removing the mobile from her ear, she jabbed at a button, cutting the call.

'What?' she asked him aggressively.

'Who were you calling then?'

'Mind yer own fuckin' business!' she said furiously. The waiting pedestrians stared. 'Are you followin' me?'

'Yeah,' said Strike. 'Listen.'

The lights changed; they were the only two not to start off over the road, and were jostled by the passing walkers.

'Will you give me your mobile number?'

The implacable bull's eyes looked back at him, unreadable, bland, secretive.

'Wha' for?'

'Kieran asked me to get it,' he lied. 'I forgot. He thinks you left a pair of sunglasses in his car.'

He did not think she was convinced, but after a moment she dictated a number, which he wrote down on the back of one of his own cards.

'That all?' she asked aggressively, and she proceeded across the road as far as an island, where the lights changed again. Strike limped after her. She looked both angry and perturbed by his continuing presence.

'*What?*'

'I think you know something you're not telling me, Rochelle.'

She glared at him.

'Take this,' said Strike, pulling a second card out of his overcoat pocket. 'If you think of anything you'd like to tell me, call, all right? Call that mobile number.'

She did not answer.

'If Lula was murdered,' said Strike, while the cars whooshed by them, and rain glittered in the gutters at their feet, 'and you know something, you could be in danger from the killer too.'

This evoked a tiny, complacent, scathing smile. Rochelle did not think she was in danger. She thought she was safe.

The green man had appeared. Rochelle gave a toss of her dry, wiry hair and moved away across the road, ordinary, squat and plain, still clutching her mobile in one hand and Strike's card in the other. Strike stood alone on the island, watching her with a feeling of impotence and unease. She might never have sold her story to the newspapers, but he could not believe that she had bought that designer jacket, ugly though he found it, from the proceeds of a job in a shop.

9

The junction of Tottenham Court and Charing Cross Roads was still a scene of devastation, with wide gashes in the road, white hardboard tunnels and hard-hatted builders. Strike traversed the narrow walkways barricaded by metal fences, past the rumbling diggers full of rubble, bellowing workmen and more drills, smoking as he walked.

He felt weary and sore; very conscious of the pain in his leg, of his unwashed body, of the greasy food lying heavily in his stomach. On impulse, he took a detour right up Sutton Row, away from the clatter and grind of the roadworks, and called Rochelle. It went to voicemail, but it was her husky voice that answered: she had not given him a fake number. He left no message; he had already said everything he could think of saying; and yet he was worried. He half wished he had followed her, covertly, to find out where she was living.

Back on Charing Cross Road, limping on to the office through the temporary shadow of the pedestrian tunnel, he remembered the way that Robin had woken him up that morning: the tactful knock, the cup of tea, the studied avoidance of the subject of the camp bed. He ought not to have let it happen. There were other routes to intimacy than admiring a woman's figure in a tight dress. He did not want to explain why he was sleeping at work; he dreaded personal questions. And he had let a situation arise in which she had called him

Cormoran and told him to do up his buttons. He ought never to have overslept.

As he climbed the metal stairs, past the closed door of Crowdy Graphics, Strike resolved to treat Robin with a slightly cooler edge of authority for the rest of the day, to counterbalance that glimpse of hairy belly.

The decision was no sooner made than he heard high-pitched laughter, and two female voices talking at the same time, issuing from his own office.

Strike froze, listening, panicking. He had not returned Charlotte's call. He tried to make out her tone and inflection; it would be like her to come in person and overwhelm his temp with charm, to make of his ally a friend, to saturate his own staff with Charlotte's version of the truth. The two voices melded in laughter again, and he could not tell whose they were.

'Hi, Stick,' said a cheery voice as he pushed open the glass door.

His sister, Lucy, was sitting on the sagging sofa, with her hands around a mug of coffee, bags from Marks and Spencer and John Lewis heaped all around her.

Strike's first surge of relief that she was not Charlotte was nevertheless tainted with a lesser dread of what she and Robin had been talking about, and how much each of them now knew about his private life. As he returned Lucy's hug, he noticed that Robin had, again, closed the inner door on the camp bed and kitbag.

'Robin says you've been out detecting.' Lucy seemed in high spirits, as she so often was when she was out alone, unencumbered by Greg and the boys.

'Yeah, we do that sometimes, detectives,' said Strike. 'Been shopping?'

'Yes, Sherlock, I have.'

'D'you want to go out for a coffee?'

'I've already got one, Stick,' she said, holding up the mug. 'You're not very sharp today. Are you limping a bit?'

'Not that I've noticed.'

'Have you seen Mr Chakrabati recently?'

'Fairly recently,' lied Strike.

'If it's all right,' said Robin, who was putting on her trench coat, 'I'll take lunch, Mr Strike. I haven't had any yet.'

The resolution of moments ago, to treat her with professional *froideur*, now seemed not only unnecessary but unkind. She had more tact than any woman he had ever met.

'That's fine, Robin, yeah,' he said.

'Nice to meet you, Lucy,' Robin said, and with a wave she disappeared, closing the glass door behind her.

'I really like her,' said Lucy enthusiastically, as Robin's footsteps clanged away. 'She's great. You should try and get her to stay on permanently.'

'Yeah, she's good,' said Strike. 'What were you two having such a laugh about?'

'Oh, her fiancé – he sounds a bit like Greg. Robin says you've got an important case on. It's all right. She was very discreet. She says it's a suspicious suicide. That can't be very nice.'

She gave him a meaningful look he chose not to understand.

'It's not the first time. I had a couple of those in the army, too.'

But he doubted that Lucy was listening. She had taken a deep breath. He knew what was coming.

'Stick, have you and Charlotte split up?'

Better get it over with.

'Yeah, we have.'

'*Stick!*'

'It's fine, Luce. I'm fine.'

But her good humour had been obliterated in a great gush of fury and disappointment. Strike waited patiently, exhausted and sore, while she raged: she had known all along, known that Charlotte would do it all over again; she had lured him away from Tracey, and from his fantastic army career, rendered him as insecure as possible, persuaded him to move in, only to dump him—

'I ended it, Luce,' he said, 'and Tracey and I were over before . . . ' but he might as well have commanded lava to flow backwards: why hadn't he realised that Charlotte would never change, that she had only returned to him for the drama of the situation, attracted by his injury and his medal? The bitch had played the ministering angel and then got bored; she was dangerous and wicked; measuring her own worth in the havoc she caused, glorying in the pain she inflicted . . .

'I left her, it was my choice . . . '

'Where have you been living? When did this happen? That absolute bloody *bitch* – no, I'm sorry, Stick, I'm not going to pretend any more – all the years and years of *shit* she's put you through – oh God, Stick, why didn't you marry Tracey?'

'Luce, let's not do this, please.'

He moved aside some of her John Lewis bags, full, he saw, of small pants and socks for her sons, and sat down heavily on the sofa. He knew he looked grubby and scruffy. Lucy seemed on the verge of tears; her day out in town was ruined.

'I suppose you haven't told me because you knew I'd do this?' she said at last, gulping.

'It might've been a consideration.'

'All right, I'm sorry,' she said furiously, her eyes shining with tears. 'But that *bitch*, Stick. Oh God, tell me you're never going to go back to her. Please just tell me that.'

'I'm not going back to her.'

'Where are you staying – Nick and Ilsa's?'

'No. I've got a little place in Hammersmith' (the first place that occurred to him, associated, now, with homelessness). 'Bedsit.'

'Oh *Stick* . . . come and stay with us!'

He had a fleeting vision of the all-blue spare room, and Greg's forced smile.

'Luce, I'm happy where I am. I just want to get on with work and be on my own for a bit.'

It took him another half-hour to shift her out of his office. She felt guilty that she had lost her temper; apologised, then attempted to justify herself, which triggered another diatribe about Charlotte. When she finally decided to leave, he helped her downstairs with her bags, successfully distracting her from the boxes full of his possessions that still stood on the landing, and finally depositing her into a black cab at the end of Denmark Street.

Her round, mascara-streaked face looked back at him out of the rear window. He forced a grin and a wave before lighting another cigarette, and reflecting that Lucy's idea of sympathy compared unfavourably with some of the interrogation techniques they had used at Guantanamo.

10

Robin had fallen into the habit of buying Strike a pack of sandwiches with her own, if he happened to be in the office over lunchtime, and reimbursing herself from petty cash.

Today, however, she did not hurry back. She had noticed, though Lucy had seemed oblivious, how unhappy Strike had been to find them in conversation. His expression, when he had entered the office, had been every bit as grim as the first time they had met.

Robin hoped that she had not said anything to Lucy that Strike would not like. Lucy had not exactly pried, but she had asked questions to which it was difficult to know the answer.

'Have you met Charlotte yet?'

Robin guessed that this was the stunning ex-wife or girlfriend whose exit she had witnessed on her first morning. Near-collision hardly constituted a meeting, however, so she answered:

'No, I haven't.'

'Funny.' Lucy had given a disingenuous little smile. 'I'd have thought she'd have wanted to meet you.'

For some reason, Robin had felt prompted to reply:

'I'm only temporary.'

'Still,' said Lucy, who seemed to understand the answer better than Robin did herself.

It was only now, wandering up and down the aisle of crisps

without really concentrating on them, that the implications of what Lucy had said slid into place. Robin supposed that Lucy might have meant to flatter her, except that the mere possibility of Strike making any kind of pass was extremely distasteful to her.

('Matt, honestly, if you saw him ... he's enormous and he's got a face like some beaten-up boxer. He is not remotely attractive, I'm sure he's over forty, and ... ' she had cast around for more aspersions to cast upon Strike's appearance, 'he's got that sort of pubey hair.'

Matthew had only really become reconciled to her continuing employment with Strike now that Robin had accepted the media consultancy job.)

Robin selected two bags of salt and vinegar crisps at random, and headed towards the cash desk. She had not yet told Strike that she would be leaving in two and a half weeks' time.

Lucy had moved from the subject of Charlotte only to interrogate Robin on the amount of business coming through the shabby little office. Robin had been as vague as she dared, intuiting that if Lucy did not know how bad Strike's finances were, it was because he did not want her to know. Hoping that he would be pleased for his sister to think that business was good, she mentioned that his latest client was wealthy.

'Divorce case, is it?' asked Lucy.

'No,' said Robin, 'it's a ... well, I've signed a confidentiality agreement ... he's been asked to reinvestigate a suicide.'

'Oh God, that won't be fun for Cormoran,' said Lucy, with a strange note in her voice.

Robin looked confused.

'Hasn't he told you? Mind you, people usually know without telling. Our mother was a famous – groupie, they call it, don't they?' Lucy's smile was suddenly forced, and her tone, though she was striving for detachment and unconcern, had become brittle. 'It's all on the internet. Everything is these days, isn't it? She died of an overdose and they said it was suicide, but Stick always thought her ex-husband did it. Nothing was ever proven. Stick was furious. It was all very sordid and horrible, anyway. Perhaps that's why the client chose Stick – I take it the suicide was an overdose?'

Robin did not reply, but it did not matter; Lucy went on without pausing for an answer:

'That's when Stick dropped out of university and joined the military police. The family was very disappointed. He's really bright, you know; nobody in our family had ever been to Oxford; but he just packed up and left and joined the army. And it seemed to suit him; he did really well there. I think it's a shame he left, to be honest. He could have stayed, even with, you know, his leg . . .'

Robin did not betray, by so much as a flicker of her eyelid, that she did not know.

Lucy sipped her tea.

'So whereabouts in Yorkshire are you from?'

The conversation had flowed pleasantly after that, right up until the moment that Strike had walked in on them laughing at Robin's description of Matthew's last excursion into DIY.

But Robin, heading back to the office with sandwiches and crisps, felt even sorrier for Strike than she had done before. His marriage – or, if they had not been married, his live-in relationship – had failed; he was sleeping in his office; he had been injured in the war, and now she discovered that his mother had died in dubious and squalid circumstances.

She did not pretend to herself that this compassion was

untinged with curiosity. She already knew that she would certainly, at some point in the near future, try and find the online particulars of Leda Strike's death. At the same time, she felt guilty that she had been given another glimpse of a part of Strike she had not been meant to see, like that patch of virtually furry belly he had accidentally exposed that morning. She knew him to be a proud and self-sufficient man; these were the things she liked and admired about him, even if the way these qualities expressed themselves – the camp bed, the boxed possessions on the landing, the empty Pot Noodle tubs in the bin – aroused the derision of such as Matthew, who assumed that anyone living in uncomfortable circumstances must have been profligate or feckless.

Robin was not sure whether or not she imagined the slightly charged atmosphere in the office when she returned. Strike was sitting in front of her computer monitor, tapping away at the keyboard, and while he thanked her for the sandwiches, he did not (as was usual) turn away from work for ten minutes for a chat about the Landry case.

'I need this for a couple of minutes; will you be OK on the sofa?' he asked her, continuing to type.

Robin wondered whether Lucy had told Strike what they had discussed. She hoped not. Then she felt resentful for feeling guilty; after all, she had done nothing wrong. Her aggravation put a temporary stop on her great desire to know whether he had found Rochelle Onifade.

'Aha,' said Strike.

He had found, on the Italian designer's website, the magenta fake-fur coat that Rochelle had been wearing that morning. It had become available for purchase only within the last two weeks, and it cost fifteen hundred pounds.

Robin waited for Strike to explain the exclamation, but he did not.

'Did you find her?' she asked, at last, when finally Strike turned from the computer to unwrap the sandwiches.

He told her about their encounter, but all the enthusiasm and gratitude of that morning, when he had called her 'genius' over and again, was absent. Robin's tone, as she gave him the results of her own telephone enquiries, was, therefore, similarly cool.

'I called the Law Society about the conference in Oxford on January the seventh,' she said. 'Tony Landry attended. I pretended to be somebody he'd met there, who'd mislaid his card.'

He did not seem particularly interested in the information he had requested, nor did he compliment her on her initiative. The conversation petered out in mutual dissatisfaction.

The confrontation with Lucy had exhausted Strike; he wanted to be alone. He also suspected that Lucy might have told Robin about Leda. His sister deplored the fact that their mother had lived and died in conditions of mild notoriety, yet in certain moods she seemed to be seized with a paradoxical desire to discuss it all, especially with strangers. Perhaps it was a kind of safety valve, because of the tight lid she kept on her past with her suburban friends, or perhaps she was trying to carry the fight into the enemy's territory, so anxious about what they might already know about her that she tried to forestall prurient interest before it could start. But he had never wanted Robin to know about his mother, or about his leg, or about Charlotte, or any of the other painful subjects which Lucy insisted on probing whenever she came close enough.

In his tiredness, and his bad mood, Strike extended to Robin, unfairly, his blanket irritation at women, who did not seem able just to leave a man in peace. He thought he might take his notes to the Tottenham this afternoon, where he would be able to sit and think without interruptions, and without being badgered for explanations.

Robin felt the atmospheric change keenly. Taking her cue from the silently munching Strike, she brushed herself free of crumbs, then gave him the morning's messages in a brisk and impersonal tone.

'John Bristow called with a mobile number for Marlene Higson. He's also got through to Guy Somé, who could meet you at ten o'clock on Thursday morning at his studio in Blunkett Street, if that suits. It's out in Chiswick, near Strand-on-the-Green.'

'Great. Thanks.'

They said very little else to each other that day. Strike spent the greater part of the afternoon at the pub, returning only at ten to five. The awkwardness between them persisted, and for the first time, he was quite pleased to see Robin leave.

Part Four

Optimumque est, ut volgo dixere, aliena insania frui.

And the best plan is, as the popular saying was, to profit by the folly of others.

Pliny the Elder, *Historia Naturalis*

1

Strike visited ULU early to shower, and dressed with unusual care, on the morning of his visit to the studio of Guy Somé. He knew, from his perusal of the designer's website, that Somé advocated the purchase and wear of such items as chaps in degraded leather, ties of metal mesh and black-brimmed headbands that seemed to have been made by cutting the tops out of old bowlers. With a faint feeling of defiance, Strike put on the conventional, comfortable dark blue suit he had worn to Cipriani.

The studio he sought had been a disused nineteenth-century warehouse, which stood on the north bank of the Thames. The glittering river dazzled his eyes as he tried to find the entrance, which was not clearly marked; nothing on the outside proclaimed the use to which the building was being put.

At last he discovered a discreet, unmarked bell, and the door was opened electronically from within. The stark but airy hallway was chilly with air conditioning. A jingling and clacking noise preceded the entrance into the hall of a girl with tomato-red hair, dressed in head-to-toe black and wearing many silver bangles.

'Oh,' she said, seeing Strike.

'I've got an appointment with Mr Somé at ten,' he told her. 'Cormoran Strike.'

'Oh,' she said again. 'OK.'

She disappeared the same way she had come. Strike used the

wait to call the mobile telephone number of Rochelle Onifade, as he had been doing ten times a day since he had met her. There was no response.

Another minute passed, and then a small black man was suddenly crossing the floor towards Strike, catlike and silent on rubber soles. He walked with an exaggerated swing of his hips, his upper body quite still except for a little counterbalancing sway of the shoulders, his arms almost rigid.

Guy Somé was nearly a foot shorter than Strike and had perhaps a hundredth of his body fat. The front of the designer's tight black T-shirt was decorated with hundreds of tiny silver studs which formed an apparently three-dimensional image of Elvis's face, as though his chest were a Pin Art toy. The eye was further confused by the fact that a well-defined six-pack moved underneath the tight Lycra. Somé's snug grey jeans bore a faint dark pinstripe, and his trainers seemed to be made out of black suede and patent leather.

His face contrasted strangely with his taut, lean body, for it abounded in exaggerated curves: the eyes exophthalmic so that they appeared fishlike, looking out of the sides of his head. The cheeks were round, shining apples and the full-lipped mouth was a wide oval: his small head was almost perfectly spherical. Somé looked as though he had been carved out of soft ebony by a master hand that had grown bored with its own expertise, and started to veer towards the grotesque.

He held out a hand with a slight crook of the wrist.

'Yeah, I can see a bit of Jonny,' he said, looking up into Strike's face; his voice was camp and faintly cockney. 'Much *butcher*, though.'

Strike shook hands. There was surprising strength in the fingers. The red-haired girl came jingling back.

'I'll be busy for an hour, Trudie, no calls,' Somé told her. 'Bring us some tea and bicks, darling.'

He executed a dancer's turn, beckoning to Strike to follow him.

Down a whitewashed corridor they passed an open door, and a flat-faced middle-aged oriental woman stared back at Strike through the gauzy film of gold stuff she was throwing over a dummy; the room around her was as brilliantly lit as a surgical theatre, but full of workbenches, cramped and cluttered with bolts of fabric, the walls a collage of fluttering sketches, photographs and notes. A tiny blonde woman, dressed in what appeared to Strike to be a giant black tubular bandage, opened a door and crossed the corridor in front of them; she gave him precisely the same cold, blank stare as the red-haired Trudie. Strike felt abnormally huge and hairy; a woolly mammoth attempting to blend in amongst capuchin monkeys.

He followed the strutting designer to the end of the corridor and up a spiral staircase of steel and rubber, at the top of which was a large white rectangular office space. Floor-to-ceiling windows all along the right-hand side showed a stunning view of the Thames and the south bank. The rest of the whitewashed walls were hung with photographs. What arrested Strike's attention was an enormous twelve-foot-tall blow-up of the infamous 'Fallen Angels' on the wall opposite Somé's desk. On closer inspection, however, he realised that it was not the shot with which the world was familiar. In this version, Lula had thrown back her head in laughter: the strong column of her throat rose vertically out of the long hair, which had become disarranged in her amusement, so that a single dark nipple protruded. Ciara Porter was looking up at Lula, the beginnings of laughter on her own face, but slower to get the joke: the viewer's attention was drawn, as in the more famous version of the picture, immediately to Lula.

She was represented elsewhere; everywhere. There on the left, among a group of models all wearing transparent shifts in rainbow colours; further along, in profile, with gold leaf on her lips and eyelids. Had she learned how to compose her face into its most photogenic arrangement, to project emotion so beautifully? Or had she simply been a pellucid surface through which her feelings naturally shone?

'Park your arse anywhere,' said Somé, dropping into a seat behind a dark wood and steel desk covered in sketches; Strike pulled up a chair composed of a single length of contorted perspex. There was a T-shirt lying on the desk, which carried a picture of Princess Diana as a garish Mexican Madonna, glittering with bits of glass and beads, and complete with a flaming scarlet heart of shining satin, on which an embroidered crown was perched lopsided.

'You like?' said Somé, noticing the direction of Strike's gaze.

'Oh yeah,' lied Strike.

'Sold out nearly everywhere; bad-taste letters from Catholics; Joe Mancura wore one on *Jools Holland*. I'm thinking of doing William as Christ on a long-sleeve for winter. Or Harry, do you think, with an AK47 to hide his cock?'

Strike smiled vaguely. Somé crossed his legs with a little more flourish than was strictly necessary and said, with startling bravado:

'So, the Accountant thinks Cuckoo might've been killed? I always called Lula "Cuckoo",' he added, unnecessarily.

'Yeah. John Bristow's a lawyer, though.'

'I know he is, but Cuckoo and I always called him the Accountant. Well, I did, and Cuckoo sometimes joined in, if she was feeling wicked. He was forever nosing into her percentages and trying to wring every last cent out of everyone. I suppose he's paying you the detective equivalent of the minimum wage?'

'He's paying me a double wage, actually.'

'Oh. Well he's probably a bit more generous now he's got Cuckoo's money to play with.'

Somé chewed on a fingernail, and Strike was reminded of Kieran Kolovas-Jones; the designer and driver were similar in build, too, small but well proportioned.

'All right, I'm being a bitch,' said Somé, taking his nail out of his mouth. 'I never liked John Bristow. He was always on Cuckoo's case about something. Get a life. Get out of the *closet*. Have you heard him rhapsodising about his mummy? Have you met his *girlfriend*? Talk about a beard: I think she's got one.'

He rattled out the words in one nervy, spiteful stream, pausing to open a hidden drawer in the desk, from which he took out a packet of menthol cigarettes. Strike had already noticed that Somé's nails were bitten to their quicks.

'Her family was the whole reason she was so fucked up. I used to tell her, "Drop them, sweetie, move on." But she wouldn't. That was Cuckoo for you, always flogging a dead horse.'

He offered Strike one of the pure white cigarettes, which the detective declined, before lighting one with an engraved Zippo. As he flipped the lid of the lighter shut, Somé said:

'I wish *I'd* thought of calling in a private detective. It never occurred to me. I'm glad someone's done it. I just cannot believe she committed suicide. My therapist says that's denial. I'm having therapy twice a week, not that it makes any fucking difference. I'd be snaffling Valium like Lady Bristow if I could still design when I'm on it, but I tried it the week after Cuckoo died and I was like a zombie. I suppose it got me through the funeral.'

Jingling and rattling from the spiral staircase announced the reappearance of Trudie, who emerged through the floor in jerky stages. She laid upon the desk a black lacquered tray, on which stood two silver filigree Russian tea glasses, in each of which was a pale green steaming concoction with wilted leaves floating in it. There was also a plate of wafer-thin biscuits that looked as though they might be made of charcoal. Strike remembered his pie and mash and his mahogany-coloured tea at the Phoenix with nostalgia.

'Thanks, Trudie. And get me an ashtray, darling.'

The girl hesitated, clearly on the verge of protesting.

'Just *do* it,' snarled Somé. 'I'm the fucking boss, I'll burn the building down if I want to. Pull the fucking batteries out of the fire alarms. But get the ashtray *first*.

'The alarm went off last week, and set off all the sprinklers downstairs,' Somé explained to Strike. 'So now the backers don't want anyone smoking in the building. They can stick that one right up their tight little bumholes.'

He inhaled deeply, then exhaled through his nostrils.

'Don't you ask questions? Or do you just sit there looking scary until someone blurts out a confession?'

'We can do questions,' said Strike, pulling out his notebook and pen. 'You were abroad when Lula died, weren't you?'

'I'd just got back, a couple of hours before.' Somé's fingers twitched a little on the cigarette. 'I'd been in Tokyo, hardly any sleep for eight days. Touched down at Heathrow at about ten thirty with *the* most fucking appalling jet lag. I can't sleep on planes. I wanna be awake if I'm going to crash.'

'How did you get home from the airport?'

'Cab. Elsa had fucked up my car booking. There should've been a driver there to meet me.'

'Who's Elsa?'

'The girl I sacked for fucking up my car booking. It was the last thing I fucking wanted, to have to find a cab at that time of night.'

'Do you live alone?'

'No. By midnight I was tucked up in bed with Viktor and Rolf. My cats,' he added with a flicker of a grin. 'I took an Ambien, slept for a few hours, then woke up at five in the morning. I switched on Sky News from the bed, and there was a man in a horrible sheepskin hat, standing in the snow in Cuckoo's street, saying she was dead. The ticker-tape across the bottom of the screen was saying it too.'

Somé inhaled heavily on the cigarette, and white smoke curled out of his mouth with his next words.

'I nearly fucking died. I thought I was still asleep, or that I'd woken up in the wrong fucking *dimension* or something . . . I started calling everyone . . . Ciara, Bryony . . . all their phones were engaged. And all the time I was watching the screen, thinking they'd flash up something saying there had been a mistake, that it wasn't her. I kept praying it was the bag lady. Rochelle.'

He paused, as though he expected some comment from Strike. The latter, who had been making notes as Somé spoke, asked, still writing:

'You know Rochelle, do you?'

'Yeah. Cuckoo brought her in here once. In it for all she could get.'

'What makes you say that?'

'She hated Cuckoo. Jealous as fuck; I could see it, even if Cuckoo couldn't. She was in it for the freebies, she didn't give a monkey's whether Cuckoo lived or died. Lucky for her, as it turned out . . .

'So, the longer I watched the news, I knew there wasn't a mistake. I fell a-fucking-part.'

His fingers trembled a little on the snow-white stick he was sucking.

'They said that a neighbour had overheard an argument; so of course I thought it was Duffield. I thought Duffield had knocked her through the window. I was all set to tell the pigs what a cunt he is; I was ready to stand in the dock and testify to the fucker's character. And if this ash falls off my cigarette,' he continued in precisely the same tone, 'I will fire that little bitch.'

As though she had heard him, Trudie's rapid footfalls grew louder and louder until she emerged again into the room, breathing heavily and clutching a heavy glass ashtray.

'*Thank* you,' said Somé, with a pointed inflection, as she placed it in front of him and scurried back downstairs.

'Why did you think it was Duffield?' asked Strike, once he judged Trudie to be safely out of earshot.

'Who else would Cuckoo have let in at two in the morning?'

'How well do you know him?'

'Well enough, little piss ant that he is.' Somé picked up his mint tea. 'Why do women do it? Cuckoo, too . . . she wasn't stupid – actually, she was razor-sharp – so what did she see in Evan Duffield? I'll tell you,' he said, without pausing for an answer. 'It's that wounded-poet crap, that soul-pain shit, that too-much-of-a-tortured-genius-to-wash bollocks. Brush your teeth, you little bastard. You're not fucking Byron.'

He slammed his glass down and cupped his right elbow in his

left hand, steadying his forearm and continuing to draw heavily on the cigarette.

'No man would put up with the likes of Duffield. Only women. Maternal instinct gone warped, if you ask me.'

'You think he had it in him to kill her, do you?'

'Of course I do,' said Somé dismissively. 'Of course he has. All of us have got it in us, somewhere, to kill, so why would Duffield be any exception? He's got the mentality of a vicious twelve-year-old. I can imagine him in one of his rages, having a tantrum and then just—'

With his cigarette-free hand he made a violent shoving movement.

'I saw him shouting at her once. At my after-show party, last year. I got in between them; I told him to have a go at me instead. I might be a little poof,' Somé said, the round-cheeked face set, 'but I'd back myself against that drugged-up fuck any day. He was a tit at the funeral, too.'

'Really?'

'Yeah. Lurching around, off his face. No fucking respect. I was full of tranks myself or I'd've told him what I thought of him. Pretending to be devastated, hypocritical little shit.'

'You never thought it was suicide?'

Somé's strange, bulging eyes bored into Strike.

'Never. Duffield says he was at his dealer's, disguised as a wolf. What kind of fucking alibi is that? I hope you're checking him out. I hope you're not dazzled by his fucking celebrity, like the police.'

Strike remembered Wardle's comments on Duffield.

'I don't think they found Duffield dazzling.'

'They've got more taste than I credited them with, then,' said Somé.

'Why are you so sure it wasn't suicide? Lula had had mental health problems, hadn't she?'

'Yeah, but we had a pact, like Marilyn Monroe and Montgomery Clift. We'd sworn that if either of us was thinking seriously of killing themselves, we'd call the other. She would've called me.'

'When did you last hear from her?'

'She phoned me on the Wednesday, while I was still in Tokyo,' said Somé. 'Silly cow always forgot it was eight hours ahead; I had my phone on mute at two in the morning, so I didn't pick up; but she left a message, and she was *not* suicidal. Listen to this.'

He reached into his desk drawer again, pressed several buttons, then held the mobile out to Strike.

And Lula Landry spoke close and real, slightly raw and throaty, in Strike's ear, in deliberately affected mockney.

'Aw wight, darlin'? Got something to tell you, I'm not sure whether you're going to like it but it's a biggie, and I'm so fucking happy I've gotta tell someone, so ring me when you can, OK, can't wait, mwah mwah.'

Strike handed back the phone.

'Did you call her back? Did you find out what the big news was?'

'No.' Somé ground out his cigarette and reached immediately for another one. 'The Japs had me in back-to-back meetings; every time I thought of calling her, the time difference was in the way. Anyway . . . to tell you the truth, I thought I knew what she was going to say, and I wasn't any too fucking pleased about it. I thought she was pregnant.'

Somé nodded several times with the fresh cigarette clutched between his teeth; then he removed it to say:

'Yeah, I thought she'd gone and got herself knocked up.'

'By Duffield?'

'I hoped to fuck not. I didn't know at the time that they'd got back together. She wouldn't have dared hook up with him if I'd been in the country; no, she waited till I was in Japan, the sneaky little bitch. She knew I hated him, and she cared what I thought. We were like family, Cuckoo and me.'

'Why did you think she might be pregnant?'

'It was the way she sounded. You've heard it – she was so excited . . . I had this feeling. It was the kind of thing Cuckoo would've done, and she'd have expected me to be as pleased as she was, and fuck her career, fuck *me*, counting on her to launch my brand-new accessories line . . .'

'Was this the five-million-pound contract her brother told me about?'

'Yeah, and I'll bet the Accountant pushed her to hold out for as much as she could get, too,' said Somé, with another flash of temper. 'It wasn't like Cuckoo to try and wring every last penny out of me. She knew it was going to be fabulous, and would take her to a whole new level if she fronted it. It shouldn't have been all about the money. Everyone associated her with my stuff; her big break came on a shoot for *Vogue* when she wore my Jagged dress. Cuckoo loved my clothes, she loved *me*, but people get to a certain level, and everyone's telling them they're worth more, and they forget who put them there, and suddenly it's all about the bottom line.'

'You must've thought she was worth it, to commit to a five-million-pound contract?'

'Yeah, well, I'd pretty much designed the range *for* her, so having to shoot around a fucking pregnancy wouldn't have been funny. And I could just imagine Cuckoo going silly afterwards, throwing it all in, not wanting to leave the fucking baby. She was the type; always looking for people to love, for a surrogate family. Those Bristows fucked her up good. They only adopted her as a toy for Yvette, who is the scariest bitch in the world.'

'In what way?'

'Possessive. Morbid. Didn't want to let Cuckoo out of her sight in case she died, like the kid she'd been bought to replace. Lady Bristow used to come to all the shows, getting under everyone's feet, till she got too ill. And there was an uncle, who treated Cuckoo like scum until she started pulling in big money. He got a bit more respectful then. They all know the value of a buck, the Bristows.'

'They're a wealthy family, aren't they?'

'Alec Bristow didn't leave *that* much, not relatively speaking. Not compared to proper money. Not like *your* old man. How come,' said Somé, swerving suddenly off the conversational track, 'Jonny Rokeby's son's working as a private dick?'

'Because that's his job,' said Strike. 'Go on about the Bristows.'

Somé did not appear to resent being bossed around; if anything, he seemed to relish it, possibly because it was such an unusual experience.

'I just remember Cuckoo telling me that most of what Alec Bristow left was in shares in his old company, and Albris has gone down the pan in the recession. It's hardly fucking Apple. Cuckoo had out-earned the whole fucking lot of them before she was twenty.'

'Was that picture,' said Strike, indicating the enormous 'Fallen Angels' image on the wall behind him, 'part of the five-million-pound campaign?'

'Yeah,' said Somé. 'Those four bags were the start of it. She's holding "Cashile" there; I gave them all African names, for her. She was fixated on Africa. That whorish real mother she unearthed had told her her father was African, so Cuckoo had gone mad on it; talking about studying there, doing voluntary work . . . never mind that the old slapper had probably been sleeping with about fifty Yardies. African,' said Guy Somé, grinding out his cigarette stub in the glass ashtray, 'my Aunt Fanny. The bitch just told Cuckoo what she wanted to hear.'

'And you decided to go ahead and use the picture for the campaign, even though Lula had just . . . ?'

'It was meant as a fucking *tribute*.' Somé spoke loudly over him. 'She'd never looked more beautiful. It was supposed to be a fucking tribute to her, to *us*. She was my muse. If the bastards couldn't understand that, fuck 'em, that's all. The press in this country are lower than scum. Judging everyone by their fucking selves.'

'The day before she died, some handbags were sent to Lula . . . '

'Yeah, they were mine. I sent her one of each of those,' said Somé, indicating the picture with the end of a new cigarette, 'and I sent Deeby Macc some clothes by the same courier.'

'Had he ordered them, or . . . ?'

'Freebies, dear,' drawled Somé. 'Just good business. Couple of customised hoodies and some accessories. Celebrity endorsements never hurt.'

'Did he ever wear the stuff?'

'I don't know,' said Somé in a more subdued tone. 'I had other things to worry about the next day.'

'I've seen YouTube footage of him wearing a hoodie with studs on it, like that,' said Strike, pointing at Somé's chest. 'Making a fist.'

'Yeah, that was one of them. Someone must've sent the stuff on to him. One had a fist, one had a handgun, and some of his lyrics on the backs.'

'Did Lula talk to you about Deeby Macc coming to stay in the flat downstairs?'

'Oh yeah. She wasn't *nearly* excited enough. I kept saying to her, babes, if he'd written three tracks about me I'd be waiting behind the front door *naked* when he got in.' Somé blew smoke in two long streams from his nostrils, looking sideways at Strike. 'I like 'em big and rough,' he said. 'But Cuckoo didn't. Well, look what she hooked up with. I kept telling her, you're the one making all this fucking song-and-dance about your roots; find yourself a nice black boy and settle down. Deeby would've been fucking perfect; why not?

'Last season's show, I had her walking down the catwalk to Deeby's "Butterface Girl". "Bitch you ain't all that, get a mirror that don' fool ya, Give it up an' tone it down, girl, 'cause you ain't no fuckin' Lula." Duffield hated it.'

Somé smoked for a moment in silence, his eyes on the wall of photographs. Strike asked:

'Where do you live? Around here?' though he knew the answer.

'No, I'm in Charles Street, in Kensington,' said Somé. 'Moved there last year. It's a long fucking way from Hackney, I can tell you, but it was getting silly, I had to leave. Too much hassle. I grew up in Hackney,' he explained, 'back when I was plain old Kevin Owusu. I changed my name when I left home. Like you.'

'I was never Rokeby,' said Strike, flicking over a page in his notebook. 'My parents weren't married.'

'We all know that, dear,' said Somé, with another flash of

malice. 'I dressed your old man for a *Rolling Stone* shoot last year: skinny suit and broken bowler. D'you see him much?'

'No,' said Strike.

'No, well, you'd make him look fucking old, wouldn't you?' said Somé, with a cackle. He fidgeted in his seat, lit yet another cigarette, clamped it between his lips and squinted at Strike through billows of menthol smoke.

'Why are we talking about me, anyway? Do people usually start telling you their life stories when you get out that notebook?'

'Sometimes.'

'Don't you want your tea? I don't blame you. I don't know why I drink this shit. My old dad would have a coronary if he asked for a cup of tea and got this.'

'Is your family still in Hackney?'

'I haven't checked,' said Somé. 'We don't talk. I practise what I preach, see?'

'Why do you think Lula changed her name?'

'Because she hated her fucking family, same as me. She didn't want to be associated with them any more.'

'Why choose the same name as her Uncle Tony, then?'

'He's not famous. It made a good name. Deeby couldn't have written "Double L U B Mine" if she'd been Lula Bristow, could he?'

'Charles Street isn't too far from Kentigern Gardens, is it?'

'About a twenty-minute walk. I wanted Cuckoo to move in with me when she said she couldn't stand her old place any more, but she wouldn't; she chose that fucking five-star prison instead, just to get away from the press. They drove her into that place. They bear responsibility.'

Strike remembered Deeby Macc: *The motherfuckin' press chased her out that window.*

'She took me to see it. *Mayfair*, full of rich Russians and Arabs and bastards like Freddie Bestigui. I said to her, sweetie, you can't live here; marble everywhere, marble isn't chic in our climate . . . it's like living in your own *tomb* . . .'

He faltered, then went on:

'She'd been through this head-fuck for a few months. There'd been a stalker who was hand-delivering letters through her front door at three in the morning; she kept getting woken up by the letter box going. The things he said he wanted to do to her, it scared her. Then she split up with Duffield, and she had the paps round the front of her house all the bloody time. Then she finds out they're hacking all her calls. And *then* she had to go and find that bitch of a mother. It was all getting too much. She wanted to be away from it all, to feel secure. I *told* her to move in with me, but instead she went and bought that fucking mausoleum.

'She took it because it felt like a fortress with the round-the-clock security. She thought she'd be safe from everyone, that nobody would be able to get at her.

'But she hated it from the word go. I knew she would. She was cut off from everything she liked. Cuckoo loved colour and noise. She liked being on the street, she liked walking, being free.

'One of the reasons the police said it wasn't murder was the open windows. She'd opened them herself; it was only her prints on the handles. But I know why she opened them. She always opened the windows, even when it was freezing cold, because she couldn't stand the silence. She liked being able to hear London.'

Somé's voice had lost all its slyness and sarcasm. He cleared his throat and went on:

'She was trying to connect with something real; we used to

talk about it all the time. It was our big thing. That's what made her get involved with bloody Rochelle. It was a case of "there but for the grace of God". Cuckoo thought that's what she'd have been, if she hadn't been beautiful; if the Bristows hadn't taken her in as a little plaything for Yvette.'

'Tell me about this stalker.'

'Mental case. He thought they were married or something. He was given a restraining order and compulsory psychiatric treatment.'

'Any idea where he is now?'

'I think he was deported back to Liverpool,' said Somé. 'But the police checked him out; they told me he was in a secure ward up there the night she died.'

'Do you know the Bestiguis?'

'Only what Lula told me, that he was sleazy and she's a walking waxwork. I don't need to know her. I know her type. Rich girls spending their ugly husbands' money. They come to my shows. They want to be my friend. Gimme an honest hooker any day.'

'Freddie Bestigui was at the same country-house weekend as Lula, a week before she died.'

'Yeah, I heard. He had a hard-on for her,' said Somé dismissively. 'She knew it, as well; it wasn't exactly a unique experience in her life, you know. He never got further than trying to get in the same lift, though, from what she told me.'

'You never spoke to her after their weekend at Dickie Carbury's, did you?'

'No. Did he do something then? You don't suspect Bestigui, do you?'

Somé sat up in his seat, staring.

'Fuck ... Freddie Bestigui? Well, he's a shit, I know that. This little girl I know . . . well, friend of a friend . . . she was working for his production company, and he tried to fucking rape her. No, I am not exaggerating,' said Somé. 'Literally. Rape. Got her a bit drunk after work and had her on the floor; some assistant had forgotten his mobile and came back for it, and walked in on them. Bestigui paid them both off. Everyone was telling her to press charges, but she took the money and ran. They say he used to discipline his second wife in some pretty fucking kinky ways; that's why she walked away with three mill; she threatened him with the press. But Cuckoo would never have let Freddie Bestigui into her flat at two in the morning. Like I say, she wasn't a stupid girl.'

'What do you know about Derrick Wilson?'

'Who's he?'

'The security guard who was on duty the night she died.'

'Nothing.'

'He's a big guy, with a Jamaican accent.'

'This might shock you, but not all the black people in London know each other.'

'I wondered whether you'd ever spoken to him, or heard Lula talk about him.'

'No, we had more interesting things to talk about than the security guard.'

'Does the same apply to her driver, Kieran Kolovas-Jones?'

'Oh, I know who Kolovas-Jones is,' said Somé, with a slight smirk. 'Striking little poses whenever he thought I might be looking out of the window. He's about five fucking feet too short to model.'

'Did Lula ever talk about him?'

'No, why would she?' asked Somé restlessly. 'He was her driver.'

'He's told me they were quite close. He mentioned that she'd given him a jacket you designed. Worth nine hundred quid.'

'Big fucking deal,' said Somé, with easy contempt. 'My proper stuff goes for upwards of three grand a coat. I slap the logo on shell suits and they sell like crazy, so it'd be silly not to.'

'Yeah, I was going to ask you about that,' said Strike. 'Your – ready-to-wear line, is it?'

Somé looked amused.

'That's right. That's the stuff that isn't made-to-measure, see? You buy it straight off the rack.'

'Right. How widely is that stuff sold?'

'It's everywhere. When were you last in a clothes shop?' asked Somé, his wicked bulging eyes roving over Strike's dark blue jacket. 'What is that, anyway, your demob suit?'

'When you say "everywhere" . . . '

'Smart department stores, boutiques, online,' rattled off Somé. 'Why?'

'One of two men caught on CCTV running away from Lula's area that night was wearing a jacket with your logo on it.'

Somé twitched his head very slightly, a gesture of repudiation and irritation.

'Him and a million other people.'

'Didn't you see—?'

'I didn't look at any of that shit,' said Somé fiercely. 'All the – all the coverage. I didn't want to read about it, I didn't want to think about it. I told them to keep it away from me,' he said, gesturing towards the stairs and his staff. 'All I knew was that she was dead and Duffield was behaving like someone with something to hide. That's all I knew. That was enough.'

'OK. Still on the subject of clothes, in the last picture of Lula, the one where she was walking into the building, she seemed to be wearing a dress and a coat . . .'

'Yeah, she was wearing Maribelle and Faye,' said Somé. 'The dress was called Maribelle—'

'Yeah, got it,' said Strike. 'But when she died, she was wearing something different.'

This seemed to surprise Somé.

'Was she?'

'Yeah. In the police pictures of the body—'

But Somé threw up his arm in an involuntary gesture of refutation, of self-protection, then got to his feet, breathing hard, and walked to the photograph wall, where Lula stared out of several pictures, smiling, wistful or serene. When the designer turned to face Strike again, the strange bulging eyes were wet.

'Fucking hell,' he said, in a low voice. 'Don't talk about her like that. "The body." Fucking hell. You're a cold-blooded bastard, aren't you? No fucking wonder old Jonny's not keen on you.'

'I wasn't trying to upset you,' said Strike calmly. 'I only want to know whether you can think of any reason she'd have changed her clothes when she got home. When she fell, she was wearing trousers and a sequinned top.'

'How the fuck should I know why she changed?' asked Somé, wildly. 'Maybe she was cold. Maybe she was— This is fucking ridiculous. How could I know that?'

'I'm only asking,' said Strike. 'I read somewhere that you'd told the press she died in one of your dresses.'

'That wasn't me, I never announced it. Some tabloid bitch rang the office and asked for the name of that dress. One of the seamstresses told her, and they called her my spokesman. Making out I'd tried to get publicity out of it, the cunts. Fucking hell.'

'D'you think you could put me in touch with Ciara Porter and Bryony Radford?'

Somé seemed off-balance, confused.

'What? Yeah . . . '

But he had begun to cry in earnest; not like Bristow, with wild gulps and sobs, but silently, with tears sliding down his smooth dark cheeks and on to his T-shirt. He swallowed and closed his eyes, turned his back on Strike, rested his forehead against the wall and trembled.

Strike waited in silence until Somé had wiped his face several times and turned again towards him. He made no mention of his tears, but walked back to his chair, sat down and lit a cigarette. After two or three deep drags, he said in a practical and unemotional voice:

'If she changed her clothes, it was because she was expecting someone. Cuckoo always dressed the part. She must've been waiting for someone.'

'Well that's what I thought,' said Strike. 'But I'm no expert on women and their clothes.'

'No,' said Somé, with a ghost of his malicious smile, 'you don't look it. You want to speak to Ciara and Bryony?'

'It'd help.'

'They're both doing a shoot for me on Wednesday: One Arlington Place in Islington. If you come along fivish, they'd be free to talk to you.'

'That's good of you, thanks.'

'It isn't good of me,' said Somé quietly. 'I want to know what happened. When are you speaking to Duffield?'

'As soon as I can get hold of him.'

'He thinks he's got away with it, the little shit. She must've changed because she knew he was coming, mustn't she? Even though they'd rowed, she knew he'd follow her. But he'll never talk to you.'

'He'll talk to me,' said Strike easily, as he put away his notebook and checked his watch. 'I've taken up a lot of your time. Thanks again.'

As Somé led Strike back down the spiral stairs and along the white-walled corridor, some of his swagger returned to him. By the time they shook hands in the cool tiled lobby, no trace of distress remained on show.

'Lose some weight,' he told Strike, as a parting shot, 'and I'll send you something XXL.'

As the warehouse door swung closed behind Strike, he heard Somé call to the tomato-haired girl at the desk: 'I know what you're thinking, Trudie. You're imagining him taking you roughly from behind, aren't you? Aren't you, darling? Big rough *soldier boy*,' and Trudie's squeal of shocked laughter.

2

Charlotte's acceptance of Strike's silence was unprecedented. There had been no further calls or texts; she was maintaining the pretence that their last, filthy, volcanic row had changed her irrevocably, stripped away her love and purged her of fury. Strike, however, knew Charlotte as intimately as a germ that had lingered in his blood for fifteen years; knew that her only response to pain was to wound the offender as deeply as possible, no matter what the cost to herself. What would happen if he refused her an audience, and kept refusing? It was the only strategy he had never tried, and all he had left.

Every now and then, when Strike's resistance was low (late at night, alone on his camp bed) the infection would erupt again: regret and longing would spike, and he saw her at close quarters, beautiful, naked, breathing words of love; or weeping quietly, telling him that she knew she was rotten, ruined, impossible, but that he was the best and truest thing she had ever known. Then, the fact that he was a few pressed buttons away from speaking to her seemed too fragile a barricade against temptation, and he sometimes pulled himself back out of his sleeping bag and hopped in the darkness to Robin's abandoned desk, switching on the lamp and poring, even for hours, over the case report. Once or twice he placed early-morning calls to Rochelle Onifade's mobile, but she never answered.

On Thursday morning, Strike returned to the wall outside St

Thomas's, and waited for three hours in the hope of seeing Rochelle again, but she did not turn up. He had Robin call the hospital, but this time they refused to comment on Rochelle's non-attendance, and resisted all attempts at getting an address for her.

On Friday morning, Strike returned from an outing to Starbucks to find Spanner sitting not on the sofa beside Robin's desk, but on the desk itself. He had an unlit roll-up in his mouth, and was leaning over her, apparently being more amusing than Strike had ever found him, because Robin was laughing in the slightly grudging manner of a woman who is entertained, but who wishes, nevertheless, to make it clear that the goal is well defended.

'Morning, Spanner,' said Strike, but the faintly repressive quality of his greeting did nothing to moderate either the computer specialist's ardent body language or his broad smile.

'All right, Fed? Brought your Dell back for you.'

'Great. Double decaff latte,' Strike told Robin, setting the drink down beside her. 'No charge,' he added, as she reached for her purse.

She was touchingly averse to charging minor luxuries to petty cash. Robin made no objection in front of their guest, but thanked Strike, and turned again to her work, which involved a small clockwise swivel of her desk chair, away from the two men.

The flare of a match turned Strike's attention from his own double espresso to his guest.

'This is a non-smoking office, Spanner.'

'What? You smoke like a fucking chimney.'

'Not in here I don't. Follow me.'

Strike led Spanner into his own office and closed the door firmly behind him.

'She's engaged,' he said, taking his usual seat.

'Wasting my powder, am I? Ah well. Put in a word for me if the engagement goes down the pan; she's just my type.'

'I don't think you're hers.'

Spanner grinned knowingly.

'Already queuing, are you?'

'No,' said Strike. 'I just know her fiancé's a rugby-playing accountant. Clean-cut, square-jawed Yorkshireman.'

He had formed a surprisingly clear mental image of Matthew, though he had never seen a photograph.

'You never know; she might fancy rebounding on to something a bit edgier,' said Spanner, swinging Lula Landry's laptop on to the desk and sitting down opposite Strike. He was wearing a slightly tatty sweatshirt and Jesus sandals on bare feet; it was the warmest day of the year so far. 'I've had a good look at this piece of crap. How much technical detail do you want?'

'None; but I need to know that you could explain it clearly in court.'

Spanner looked, for the first time, truly intrigued.

'You serious?'

'Very. Would you be able to prove to a defending counsel that you know your stuff?'

''Course I could.'

'Then just give me the important bits.'

Spanner hesitated for a moment, trying to read Strike's expression. Finally he began:

'Password's Agyeman, and it was reset five days before she died.'

'Spell it?'

Spanner did so, adding, to Strike's surprise: 'It's a surname. Ghanaian. She bookmarked the homepage of SOAS – School of Oriental and African Studies – and it was on there. Look here.'

As he spoke, Spanner's nimble fingers were clacking keyboard keys; he had brought up the home page he described, bordered with bright green, with sections on the school, news, staff, students, library and so on.

'When she died, though, it looked like this.'

And with another outburst of clicking, he retrieved an almost identical page, featuring, as the rapidly darting cursor soon revealed, a link to the obituary of one Professor J. P. Agyeman, Emeritus Professor of African Politics.

'She saved this version of the page,' said Spanner. 'And her internet history shows she'd browsed Amazon for his books in the month before she died. She was looking at a lot of books on African history and politics round then.'

'Any evidence she applied to SOAS?'

'Not on here.'

'Anything else of interest?'

'Well, the only other thing I noticed was that a big photo file was deleted off it on the seventeenth of March.'

'How d'you know that?'

'There's software that'll help you recover even stuff people think's gone from the hard drive,' said Spanner. 'How d'you think they keep catching all those paedos?'

'Did you get it back?'

'Yeah. I've put it on here.' He handed Strike a memory stick. 'I didn't think you'd want me to put it back on.'

'No – so the photographs were . . . ?'

'Nothing fancy. Just deleted. Like I say, your average punter doesn't realise you've got to work a damn sight harder than pressing "delete" if you really want to hide something.'

'Seventeenth of March,' said Strike.

'Yeah. St Patrick's Day.'

'Ten weeks after she died.'

'Could've been the police,' suggested Spanner.

'It wasn't the police,' said Strike.

After Spanner had left, he hurried into the outer office and displaced Robin, so that he could view the photographs that had been removed from the laptop. He could feel Robin's anticipation as he explained to her what Spanner had done and opened up the file on the memory stick.

Robin was afraid, for a fraction of a second, as the first photograph bloomed onscreen, that they were about to see something horrible; evidence of criminality or perversion. She had only heard about the concealment of pictures online in the context of dreadful abuse cases. After several minutes, however, Strike voiced her own feelings.

'Just social snaps.'

He did not sound as disappointed as Robin felt, and she was a little ashamed of herself; had she wanted to see something awful? Strike scrolled down, through pictures of groups of giggling girls, fellow models, the occasional celebrity. There were several pictures of Lula with Evan Duffield, a few of them clearly taken by one or other of the pair themselves, holding the camera at arm's length, both of them apparently stoned or drunk. Somé made several appearances; Lula looked more formal, more subdued, by his side. There were many of Ciara Porter and Lula hugging in bars, dancing in clubs and giggling on a sofa in somebody's crowded flat.

'That's Rochelle,' said Strike suddenly, pointing to a sullen little face glimpsed under Ciara's armpit in a group shot. Kieran Kolovas-Jones had been roped into this picture; he stood at the end, beaming.

'Do me a favour,' said Strike, when he had finished trawling through all two hundred and twelve pictures. 'Go through these for me, and try and at least identify the famous people, so we can make a start on finding out who might have wanted the photos off her laptop.'

'But there's nothing incriminating here at all,' said Robin.

'There must be,' said Strike.

He returned to his inner office, where he placed calls to John Bristow (in a meeting, and not to be disturbed; 'Please get him to call me as soon as you can'), to Eric Wardle (voicemail: 'I've got a question about Lula Landry's laptop') and to Rochelle Onifade (on the off-chance; no answer; no chance of leaving a message: 'Voicemail full'.)

'I'm still having no luck with Mr Bestigui,' Robin told Strike, when he emerged from his inner office to find her performing searches related to an unidentified brunette posing with Lula on a beach. 'I phoned again this morning, but he just won't call me back. I've tried everything; I've pretended to be all sorts of people, I've said it's urgent – what's funny?'

'I was just wondering why none of these people who keep interviewing you have offered you a job,' said Strike.

'Oh,' said Robin, blushing faintly. 'They have. All of them. I've accepted the human resources one.'

'Oh. Right,' said Strike. 'You didn't say. Congratulations.'

'Sorry, I thought I'd told you,' lied Robin.

'So you'll be leaving . . . when?'

'Two weeks.'

'Ah. I expect Matthew's pleased, is he?'

'Yes,' she said, slightly taken aback, 'he is.'

It was almost as if Strike knew how little Matthew liked her working for him; but that was impossible; she had been careful not to give the slightest hint of the tensions at home.

The telephone rang, and Robin answered it.

'Cormoran Strike's office? . . . Yes, who's speaking, please? . . . It's Derrick Wilson,' she told him, passing over the receiver.

'Derrick, hi.'

'Mister Bestigui's gone away for a coupla days,' said Wilson's voice. 'If you wanna come an' look at the building . . . '

'I'll be there in half an hour,' said Strike.

He was on his feet, checking his pockets for wallet and keys, when he became aware of Robin's slight air of dejection, though she was continuing to pore over the unincriminating photographs.

'D'you want to come?'

'Yes!' she said gleefully, seizing her handbag and closing down her computer.

3

The heavy black-painted front door of number 18, Kentigern Gardens, opened on to a marbled lobby. Directly opposite the entrance was a handsome built-in mahogany desk, to the right of which was the staircase, which turned immediately out of sight (marble steps, with a brass and wood handrail); the entrance to the lift, with its burnished gold doors, and a solid dark-wood door set into the white-painted wall. On a white cubic display unit in the corner between this and the front doors was a vast display of deep pink oriental lilies in tall tubular vases, their scent heavy on the warm air. The left-hand wall was mirrored, doubling the apparent size of the space, reflecting the staring Strike and Robin, the lift doors and the modern chandelier hung in cubes of crystal overhead, and lengthening the security desk to a vast stretch of polished wood.

Strike remembered Wardle: 'Flats done up with marble and shit like . . . like a fucking five-star hotel.' Beside him, Robin was trying not to look impressed. This, then, was how multi-millionaires lived. She and Matthew occupied the lower floor of a semi-detached house in Clapham; its sitting room was the same size as that designated for the off-duty guards, which Wilson showed them first. There was just enough room for a table and two chairs; a wall-mounted box contained all the master keys, and another door led into a tiny toilet cubicle.

Wilson was wearing a black uniform that was constabular in design, with its brass buttons, black tie and white shirt.

'Monitors,' he pointed out to Strike as they emerged from the back room and paused behind the desk, where a row of four small black-and-white screens was hidden from guests. One showed footage from the camera over the front door, affording a circumscribed view of the street; another displayed a similarly deserted view of an underground car park; a third the empty back garden of number 18, which comprised lawn, some fancy planting and the high back wall Strike had hoisted himself up on; and the fourth the interior of the stationary lift. In addition to the monitors, there were two control panels for the communal alarms and those for the doors into the pool and car park, and two telephones, one attached to an outside line, the other connected only to the three flats.

'That,' said Wilson, indicating the solid wooden door, 'goes to the gym, the pool an' the car park,' and at Strike's request he led them through it.

The gym was small, but mirrored like the lobby, so that it appeared twice as big. It had one window, facing the street, and contained a treadmill, rowing and step machines and a set of weights.

A second mahogany door led to a narrow marble stair, lit by cubic wall lights, which took them on to a small lower landing, where a plain painted door led to the underground car park. Wilson opened it with two keys, a Chubb and a Yale, then flicked a switch. The floodlit area was almost as long as the street itself, full of millions of pounds' worth of Ferrari, Audi, Bentley, Jaguar and BMW. At twenty-foot intervals along the back wall were doors like the one through which they had just come: inner entrances to each of the houses of Kentigern Gardens.

The electric garage doors leading from Serf's Way were close by number 18, outlined by silvery daylight.

Robin wondered what the silent men beside her were thinking. Was Wilson used to the extraordinary lives of the people who lived here; used to underground car parks and swimming pools and Ferraris? And was Strike thinking (as she was) that this long row of doors represented possibilities she had not once considered: chances of secret, hidden scurrying between neighbours, and of hiding and departing in as many ways as there were houses in the street? But then she noticed the numerous black snouts pointing from regular spots on the shadowy upper walls, feeding footage back to countless monitors. Was it possible that none of them had been watched that night?

'OK,' said Strike, and Wilson led them back onto the marble staircase, and locked up the car park door behind them.

Down another short flight of stairs, the smell of chlorine became stronger with every step, until Wilson opened a door at the bottom and they were assailed by a wave of warm, damp, chemically laden air.

'This is the door that wasn't locked that night?' Strike asked Wilson, who nodded as he pressed another switch, and light blazed.

They had walked on to the broad marble rim of the pool, which was shielded by a thick plastic cover. The opposite wall was, again, mirrored; Robin saw the three of them standing there, incongruous in full dress against a mural of tropical plants and fluttering butterflies that extended up over the ceiling. The pool was around fifteen metres long, and at the far end was a hexagonal jacuzzi, beyond which were three changing cubicles, fronted by lockable doors.

'No cameras here?' asked Strike, looking around, and Wilson shook his head.

Robin could feel sweat prickling on the back of her neck and under her arms. It was oppressive in the pool area, and she was pleased to climb the stairs ahead of the two men, back to the lobby, which in comparison was pleasant and airy. A petite young blonde had appeared in their absence, wearing a pink overall, jeans and a T-shirt, and carrying a plastic bucket full of cleaning implements.

'Derrick,' she said in heavily accented English, when the security guard emerged from downstairs. 'I neet key for two.'

'This is Lechsinka,' said Wilson. 'The cleaner.'

She favoured Robin and Strike with a small, sweet smile. Wilson moved around behind the mahogany desk and handed her a key from beneath it, and Lechsinka then ascended the stairs, her bucket swinging, her tightly bejeaned backside swelling and swaying seductively. Strike, conscious of Robin's sideways glance, withdrew his gaze from it reluctantly.

Strike and Robin followed Wilson upstairs to Flat 1, which he opened up with a master key. The door on to the stairwell, Strike noted, had an old-fashioned peephole.

'Mister Bestigui's place,' announced Wilson, stifling the alarm by entering the code on a pad to the right of the door. 'Lechsinka's already bin in this morning.'

Strike could smell polish and see the track marks of a vacuum cleaner on the white carpet of the hallway, with its brass wall lights and its five immaculate white doors. He noticed the discreet alarm keypad on the right wall, at right angles to a painting in which dreamy goats and peasants floated over a blue-toned village. Tall vases of orchids stood on a black japanned table beneath the Chagall.

'Where's Bestigui?' Strike asked Wilson.

'LA,' said the security guard. 'Back in two days.'

The light, bright sitting room had three tall windows, each of them with a shallow stone balcony beyond; its walls were Wedgwood blue and nearly everything else was white. All was pristine, elegant and beautifully proportioned. Here, too, there was a single superb painting: macabre, surreal, with a spear-bearing man masked as a blackbird, arm in arm with a grey-toned headless female torso.

It was from this room that Tansy Bestigui maintained she had heard a screaming match two floors above. Strike moved up close to the long windows, noting the modern catches, the thickness of the panes, the complete lack of noise from the street, though his ear was barely half an inch from the cold glass. The balcony beyond was narrow, and filled with potted shrubs trimmed into pointed cones.

Strike moved off towards the bedroom. Robin remained in the sitting room, turning slowly where she stood, taking in the chandelier of Venetian glass, the muted rug in shades of pale blue and pink, the enormous plasma TV, the modern glass and iron dining table and silk-cushioned iron chairs; the small silver *objets d'art* on glass side tables and on the white marble mantelpiece. She thought, a little sadly, of the IKEA sofa of which she had, until now, felt so proud; then she remembered Strike's camp bed in the office with a twinge of shame. Catching Wilson's eye, she said, unconsciously echoing Eric Wardle:

'It's a different world, isn't it?'

'Yeah,' he said. 'You couldn't have kids in here.'

'No,' said Robin, who had not considered the place from that point of view.

Her employer strode out of the bedroom, evidently absorbed

in establishing some point to his own satisfaction, and disappeared into the hall.

Strike was, in fact, proving to himself that the logical route from the Bestiguis' bedroom to their bathroom was through the hall, bypassing the sitting room altogether. Furthermore, it was his belief that the only place in the flat from which Tansy could conceivably have witnessed the fatal fall of Lula Landry – and realised what she was seeing – was from the sitting room. In spite of Eric Wardle's assertion to the contrary, nobody standing in the bathroom could have had more than a partial view of the window past which Landry had fallen: insufficient, at night, to be sure that whatever had fallen was a human, let alone to identify which human it had been.

Strike returned to the bedroom. Now that he was in solitary possession of the marital home, Bestigui was sleeping on the side nearest the door and the hall, judging by the clutter of pills, glasses and books piled on that bedside table. Strike wondered whether this had been the case while he cohabited with his wife.

A large walk-in wardrobe with mirrored doors led off the bedroom. It was full of Italian suits and shirts from Turnbull & Asser. Two shallow subdivided drawers were devoted entirely to cufflinks in gold and platinum. There was a safe behind a false panel at the back of the shoe racks.

'I think that's everything in here,' Strike told Wilson, rejoining the other two in the sitting room.

Wilson set the alarm when they left the flat.

'You know all the codes for the different flats?'

'Yeah,' said Wilson. 'Gotta, in case they go off.'

They climbed the stairs to the second floor. The staircase turned so tightly around the lift shaft that it was a succession of blind corners. The door to Flat 2 was identical to that of Flat 1, except that it was standing ajar. They could hear the growl of Lechsinka's vacuum cleaner from inside.

'We got Mister an' Missus Kolchak in here now,' said Wilson. 'Ukrainian.'

The hallway was identical in shape to that of number 1, with many of the same features, including the alarm keypad on the wall at right angles to the front door; but it was tiled instead of carpeted. A large gilt mirror faced the entrance instead of a painting, and two fragile, spindly wooden tables on either side of it bore ornate Tiffany lamps.

'Were Bestigui's roses on something like that?' asked Strike.

'On one that's jus' like 'em, yeah,' said Wilson. 'It's back in the lounge now.'

'And you put it here, in the middle of the hall, with the roses on it?'

'Yeah, Bestigui wanted Macc to see 'em soon as he walked in, but there was plenty of room to walk around 'em, you can see that. No need to knock 'em over. But he was young, the copper,' said Wilson tolerantly.

'Where are the panic buttons you told me about?' Strike asked.

'Round here,' said Wilson, leading him out of the hall and into the bedroom. 'There's one by the bed, and there's another one in the sitting room.'

'Have all the flats got these?'

'Yeah.'

The relative positions of the bedrooms, sitting room, kitchen and bathroom were identical to those of Flat 1. Many of the finishings were similar, down to the mirrored doors in the walk-in wardrobe, which Strike went to check. While he was opening doors and surveying the thousands of pounds' worth of women's dresses and coats, Lechsinka emerged from the bedroom with a belt, two ties and several polythene-covered dresses, fresh from the dry-cleaner's, over her arm.

'Hi,' said Strike.

'Hello,' she said, moving to a door behind him and pulling out a tie rack. 'Excuse, please.'

He stood aside. She was short and very pretty in a pert, girlish way, with a rather flat face, a snub nose and Slavic eyes. She hung up the ties neatly while he watched her.

'I'm a detective,' he said. Then he remembered that Eric Wardle had described her English as 'crap'.

'Like a policeman?' he ventured.

'Ah. Police.'

'You were here, weren't you, the day before Lula Landry died?'

It took a few tries to convey exactly what he meant. When she grasped the point, however, she showed no objection to answering questions, as long as she could continue putting the clothes away as she talked.

'I always clean stair first,' she said. 'Miz Landry is talking very loud at her brudder; he shouting that she gives boyfriend too much moneys, and she very bad with him.

'I clean number two, empty. Is clean already. Quick.'

'Were Derrick and the man from the security firm there while you were cleaning?'

'Derrick and . . . ?'

'The repairman? The alarm man?'

'Yes, alarm man and Derrick, yes.'

Strike could hear Robin and Wilson talking in the hall, where he had left them.

'Do you set the alarms again after you've cleaned?'

'Put alarm? Yes,' she said. 'One nine six six, same as door, Derrick tells me.'

'He told you the number before he left with the alarm man?'

Again, it took a few tries to get the point across, and when she grasped it, she seemed impatient.

'Yes, I already say this. One nine six six.'

'So you set the alarm after you'd finished cleaning in here?'

'Put alarm, yes.'

'And the alarm man, what did he look like?'

'Alarm man? Look?' She frowned attractively, her small nose wrinkling, and shrugged. 'I not see he's face. But blue – all blue . . . ' she added, and with the hand not holding polythened dresses, she made a sweeping gesture down her body.

'Overall?' he suggested, but she met the word with blank incomprehension. 'OK, where did you clean after that?'

'Number one,' said Lechsinka, returning to her task of hanging up the clothes, moving around him to find the correct rails. 'Clean big windows. Miz Bestigui talking on telephone. Angry. Upset. She say she no want to lie no more.'

'She didn't want to *lie*?' repeated Strike.

Lechsinka nodded, standing on tiptoes to hang up a floor-length gown.

'You heard her say,' he repeated clearly, 'on the phone, that she didn't want to lie any more?'

Lechsinka nodded again, her face blank, innocent.

'Then she see me and she shout "Go away, go away!"'

'Really?'

Lechsinka nodded and continued to put away clothes.

'Where was Mr Bestigui?'

'Not there.'

'Do you know who she was speaking to? On the phone?'

'No.' But then, a little slyly, she said, 'Woman.'

'A woman? How do you know?'

'Shouting, shouting on telephone. I can hear woman.'

'It was a row? An argument? They were yelling at each other? Loud, yeah?'

Strike could hear himself lapsing into the absurd, overdeliberate language of the linguistically challenged Englishman. Lechsinka nodded again as she pulled open drawers in search of the place for the belt, the only item now remaining in her arms. When at last she had coiled it up and put it away, she straightened and walked away from him, into the bedroom. He followed.

While she made the bed and neatened the bedside tables, he established that she had cleaned Lula Landry's flat last that day, after the model had left to visit her mother. She had noticed nothing out of the ordinary, nor had she spotted any blue writing paper, whether written on or blank. Guy Somé's handbags, and the various items for Deeby Macc, had been delivered to the security desk by the time she had finished, and the last thing she had done at work that day had been to take the designer's gifts up to Lula's and Macc's respective flats.

'And you set the alarms again after putting the things in there?'

'I put alarms, yes.'

'Lula's?'

'Yes.'

'And one nine six six in Flat Two?'

'Yes.'

'Can you remember what you put away in Deeby Macc's flat?'

She had to mime some of the items, but she managed to convey that she remembered two tops, a belt, a hat, some gloves and (she made a fiddling mime around her wrists) cufflinks.

After stowing these things in the open shelving area of the walk-in wardrobe, so that Macc could not miss them, she had reset the alarm and gone home.

Strike thanked her very much, and lingered just long enough to admire once more her tightly denimed backside as she straightened the duvet, before rejoining Robin and Wilson in the hall.

As they proceeded up the third flight of stairs, Strike checked Lechsinka's story with Wilson, who agreed that he had instructed the repairman to set the alarm to 1966, like the front door.

'I jus' chose a number that'd be easy for Lechsinka to remember, because of the front door. Macc coulda reset it to somethin' different if he'd wanted.'

'Can you remember what the repairman looked like? You said he was new?'

'Really young guy. Hair to here.'

Wilson indicated the base of his neck.

'White?'

'Yeah, white. Didn't even look like he was shaving yet.'

They had reached the front door of Flat Three, once the home of Lula Landry. Robin felt a frisson of something – fear, excitement – as Wilson opened the third smoothly painted white front door, with its glassy bullet-sized peephole.

The top flat was architecturally different from the other two: smaller and airier. It had been recently decorated throughout in shades of cream and brown. Guy Somé had told Strike that the flat's famous previous inhabitant loved colour; but it was now as impersonal as any upmarket hotel room. Strike led the way in silence to the sitting room.

The carpet here was not lush and woollen as in Bestigui's flat, but made of rough sand-coloured jute. Strike ran his heel across it; it made no mark or track.

'Was the floor like this when Lula lived here?' he asked Wilson.

'Yeah. She chose it. It was nearly new, so they left it.'

Instead of the regularly spaced long windows of the lower flats, each with three separate small balconies, the penthouse flat boasted a single pair of double doors leading on to one wide balcony. Strike unlocked and opened these doors and stepped outside. Robin did not like watching him do it; after a glance at Wilson's impassive face, she turned and stared at the cushions and the black-and-white prints, trying not to think about what had happened here three months previously.

Strike was looking down into the street, and Robin might have been surprised to know that his thoughts were not as clinical or dispassionate as she supposed.

He was visualising someone who had lost control completely; someone running at Landry as she stood, fine-boned and beautiful, in the outfit she had thrown on to meet a much-anticipated guest; a killer lost in rage, half dragging, half pushing her, and finally, with the brute strength of a highly motivated maniac, throwing her. The seconds it took her to fall through the air towards the concrete, smothered in its deceptively soft covering of snow, must have seemed to last an eternity. She had flailed, trying to find handholds in the merciless empty air; and then, without time to make amends, to explain, to bequeath or to apologise, without any of the luxuries permitted those who are given notice of their impending demise, she had broken on the road.

The dead could only speak through the mouths of those left

behind, and through the signs they left scattered behind them. Strike had felt the living woman behind the words she had written to friends; he had heard her voice on a telephone held to his ear; but now, looking down on the last thing she had ever seen in her life, he felt strangely close to her. The truth was coming slowly into focus out of the mass of disconnected detail. What he lacked was proof.

His mobile phone rang as he stood there. John Bristow's name and number were displayed; he took the call.

'Hi, John, thanks for getting back to me.'

'No problem. Any news?' asked the lawyer.

'Maybe. I've had an expert look at Lula's laptop, and he found out a file of photographs had been deleted from it after Lula died. Do you know anything about that?'

His words were met by complete silence. The only reason Strike knew that they had not been cut off was that he could hear a small amount of background noise at Bristow's end.

At last the lawyer said, in an altered voice:

'They were taken off *after* Lula died?'

'That's what the expert says.'

Strike watched a car roll slowly down the street below, and pause halfway along. A woman got out, swathed in fur.

'I – I'm sorry,' Bristow said, sounding thoroughly shaken. 'I'm just – just shocked. Perhaps the police removed this file?'

'When did you get the laptop back from them?'

'Oh . . . sometime in February, I suppose, early February.'

'This file was removed on March the seventeenth.'

'But – but this just doesn't make sense. Nobody knew the password.'

'Well, evidently somebody did. You said the police told your mother what it was.'

'My mother certainly wouldn't have removed—'

'I'm not suggesting she did. Is there any chance she could have left the laptop open, and running? Or that she gave somebody else the password?'

He thought that Bristow must be in his office. He could hear faint voices in the background, and, distantly, a woman laughing.

'I suppose that's possible,' said Bristow slowly. 'But who would have removed photographs? Unless . . . but God, that's horrible . . .'

'What is?'

'You don't think one of the nurses could have taken the pictures? To sell to a newspaper? But that's a dreadful thought . . . a nurse . . .'

'All the expert knows is that they were deleted; there's no evidence that they were copied and stolen. But as you say – anything's possible.'

'But who else – I mean, naturally I hate to think it could be a nurse, but who else *could* it be? The laptop's been at my mother's ever since the police gave it back.'

'John, are you aware of every visitor your mother's had in the last three months?'

'I think so. I mean, obviously, I can't be sure . . .'

'No. Well, there's the difficulty.'

'But why – why would anyone do this?'

'I can think of a few reasons. It would be a big help if you could ask your mother about this, though, John. Whether she had the laptop running in mid-March. Whether any of her visitors expressed an interest in it.'

'I – I'll try.' Bristow sounded very stressed, almost tearful. 'She's very, very weak now.'

'I'm sorry,' said Strike, formally. 'I'll be in touch shortly. 'Bye.'

He stepped back from the balcony and closed the doors, then turned to Wilson.

'Derrick, can you show me how you searched this place? What order you looked in the rooms that night?'

Wilson thought for a moment, then said:

'I come in here first. Looked around, seen the doors open. Didn't touch 'em. Then,' he indicated that they should follow him, 'I looked in here . . .'

Robin, following in the two men's wake, noticed a subtle change in the way that Strike was talking to the security man. He was asking simple, deft questions, focusing on what Wilson had felt, touched, seen and heard at each step of his way through the flat.

Under Strike's guidance, Wilson's body language started to change. He began to enact the way he had held the door jambs, leaning into rooms, casting a rapid look around. When he crossed to the only bedroom, he did it at a slow-motion run, responding to the spotlight of Strike's undivided attention; he dropped to his knees to demonstrate how he had looked under the bed, and at Strike's prompting remembered that a dress had lain crumpled beneath his legs; he led them, face set with concentration, to the bathroom, and showed them how he had swivelled to check behind the door before sprinting (he almost mimed it, arms moving exaggeratedly as he walked) back to the front door.

'And then,' said Strike, opening it and gesturing Wilson through, 'you came out . . .'

'I came out,' agreed Wilson, in his bass voice, 'an' I jabbed the lift button.'

He pretended to do it, and feigned pushing open the doors in his anxiety to see what was inside.

'Nothing – so I started running back down again.'

'What could you hear now?' Strike asked, following him; neither of them were paying any attention to Robin, who closed the flat door behind her.

'Very distant – the Bestiguis yelling – and I turn round this corner and—'

Wilson stopped dead on the stair. Strike, who seemed to have anticipated something like this, stopped too; Robin careered straight into him, with a flustered apology that he cut off with a raised hand, as though, she thought, Wilson was in a trance.

'And I slipped,' said Wilson. He sounded shocked. 'I forgot that. I slipped. Here. Backwards. Sat down hard. There was water. Here. Drops. Here.'

He was pointing at the stairs.

'Drops of water,' repeated Strike.

'Yeah.'

'Not snow.'

'No.'

'Not wet footprints.'

'Drops. Big drops. Here. Mi foot skidded and I slipped. And I just got up and kept running.'

'Did you tell the police about the drops of water?'

'No. I forgot. Till now. I forgot.'

Something that had bothered Strike all along had at last been made clear. He let out a great satisfied sigh and grinned. The other two stared.

4

The weekend stretched ahead, warm and empty. Strike sat at his open window again, smoking and watching the hordes of shoppers passing along Denmark Street, the case report open on his lap, the police file on the desk, making a list for himself of points still to be clarified, and sifting the morass of information he had collected.

For a while he contemplated a photograph of the front of number 18 as it had been on the morning after Lula died. There was a small, but to Strike significant, difference between the frontage as it had been then, and as it was now. From time to time he moved to the computer; once to find out the agent who represented Deeby Macc; then to look at the share price for Albris. His notebook lay open beside him at a page full of truncated sentences and questions, all in his dense, spiky handwriting. When his mobile rang, he raised it to his ear without checking who was on the other end.

'Ah, Mr Strike,' said Peter Gillespie's voice. 'How nice of you to pick up.'

'Oh, hello, Peter,' said Strike. 'Got you working weekends now, has he?'

'Some of us have no option but to work at weekends. You haven't returned any of my weekday phone calls.'

'I've been busy. Working.'

'I see. Does that mean we can expect a repayment soon?'

'I expect so.'

'You *expect* so?'

'Yeah,' said Strike. 'I should be in a position to give you something in the next few weeks.'

'Mr Strike, your attitude astounds me. You undertook to repay Mr Rokeby monthly, and you are now in arrears to the tune of—'

'I can't pay you what I haven't got. If you hold tight, I should be able to give you all of it back. Maybe even in a oner.'

'I'm afraid that simply isn't good enough. Unless you bring these repayments up to date—'

'Gillespie,' said Strike, his eyes on the bright sky beyond the window, 'we both know old Jonny isn't going to sue his one-legged war-hero son for repayment of a loan that wouldn't keep his butler in fucking bath salts. I'll give him back his money, with interest, within the next couple of months, and he can stick it up his arse and set fire to it, if he likes. Tell him that, from me, and now get off my fucking back.'

Strike hung up, interested to note that he had not really lost his temper at all, but still felt mildly cheerful.

He worked on, in what he had come to think of as Robin's chair, late into the night. The last thing he did before turning in was to underline, three times, the words 'Malmaison Hotel, Oxford' and to circle in heavy ink the name 'J. P. Agyeman'.

The country was lumbering towards election day. Strike turned in early on Sunday and watched the day's gaffes, counterclaims and promises being tabulated on his portable TV. There was an air of joylessness in every news report he watched. The national debt was so huge that it was difficult to comprehend. Cuts were coming, whoever won; deep, painful cuts; and sometimes, with their weasel words, the party leaders reminded

Strike of the surgeons who had told him cautiously that he might experience a degree of discomfort; they who would never personally feel the pain that was about to be inflicted.

On Monday morning Strike set out for a rendezvous in Canning Town, where he was to meet Marlene Higson, Lula Landry's biological mother. The arrangement of this interview had been fraught with difficulty. Bristow's secretary, Alison, had telephoned Robin with Marlene Higson's number, and Strike had called her personally. Though clearly disappointed that the stranger on the phone was not a journalist, she had initially expressed herself willing to meet Strike. She had then called the office back, twice: firstly to ask Robin whether the detective would pay her expenses to travel into the centre of town, to which a negative answer was given; next, in high dudgeon, to cancel the meeting. A second call from Strike had secured a tentative agreement to meet in her local pub; then an irritable voicemail message cancelled once more.

Strike had then telephoned her for a third time, and told her that he believed his investigation to be in its final phase, after which evidence would be laid to the police, resulting, he had no doubt, in a further explosion of publicity. Now that he came to think about it, he said, if she was unable to help, it might be just as well for her to be protected from another deluge of press inquiry. Marlene Higson had immediately clamoured for her right to tell everything she knew, and Strike condescended to meet her, as she had already suggested, in the beer garden of the Ordnance Arms on Monday morning.

He took the train out to Canning Town station. It was overlooked by Canary Wharf, whose sleek, futuristic buildings resembled a series of gleaming metal blocks on the horizon; their size, like that of the national debt, impossible to gauge from such a distance. But a few minutes' walk later, he was as far from the shining, suited corporate world as it was possible to be. Crammed up alongside dockside developments where many of those financiers lived in neat designer pods, Canning Town exhaled poverty and deprivation. Strike knew it of old, because it had once been home to the old friend who had given him Brett Fearney's location. Down Barking Road he walked, his back to Canary Wharf, past a building with a sign that advertised 'kills 4 Communities', at which he frowned for a moment before realising that somebody had swiped the 'S'.

The Ordnance Arms sat beside the English Pawnbroking Company Ltd. It was a large, low-slung, off-white-painted pub. The interior was no-nonsense and utilitarian, with a selection of wooden clocks on a terracotta-coloured wall and a lividly patterned piece of red carpet the only gesture to anything as frivolous as decoration. Otherwise, there were two large pool tables, a long and accessible bar and plenty of empty space for milling drinkers. Just now, at eleven in the morning, it was empty except for one little old man in the corner and a cheery serving girl, who addressed her only customer as 'Joey' and gave Strike directions through the back.

The beer garden turned out to be the grimmest of concrete back yards, containing bins and a solitary wooden table, at which a woman was sitting on a white plastic chair, with her fat legs crossed and her cigarette held at right angles to her cheek. There was barbed wire on top of the high wall, and a plastic bag had caught in it and was rustling in the breeze. Beyond the wall there rose a vast block of flats, yellow-painted and with evidence of squalor bulging over many of the balconies.

'Mrs Higson?'

'Call me Marlene, love.'

She looked him up and down, with a slack smile and a knowing gaze. She was wearing a pink Lycra vest top under a zip-up grey hoodie, and leggings that ended inches above her bare grey-white ankles. There were grubby flip-flops on her feet and many gold rings on her fingers; her yellow hair, with its inches of greying brown root, was pulled back into a dirty towelling scrunchie.

'Can I get you a drink?'

'I'll have a pint of Carling, if you twist my arm.'

The way she bent her body towards him, the way she pushed straw-like strands of hair out of her pouchy eyes, even the way she held her cigarette; all were grotesquely coquettish. Perhaps she knew no other way of relating to anything male. Strike found her simultaneously pathetic and repulsive.

'Shock?' said Marlene Higson, after Strike had bought them both beer, and joined her at the table. 'You can say that again, when I'd gave 'er up for lost. It near broke my 'eart when she wen', but I fort I was giving 'er a better life. I wouldna 'ad the strenf to do it uvverwise. Fort I was giving 'er all the fings I never 'ad. I grew up poor, proper poor. We 'ad nothing. Nothing.'

She looked away from him, drawing hard on her Rothman's; when her mouth puckered into hard little lines around the cigarette, it looked like a cat's anus.

'And Dez, me boyfriend, see, wasn't too keen – you know, with 'er being coloured, it were obvious she weren't 'is. They go darker, see; when she were born, she looked white. But I still never woulda given 'er up if I 'adn't seen a chance for 'er to get a better life, and I fort, she won't miss me, she's too young. I've gave 'er a good start, and mebbe, when she's older, she'll come and find me. And me dream come true,' she added, with a ghastly show of pathos. 'She come'n' found me.

'I'll tell you somefing reely strange, right,' she said, without drawing breath. 'A man friend of mine says to me, just a week before I got the call from 'er, "You know 'oo you look like?" he says. I says, "Dahn be ser silly," but he says, "Straight up. Across the eyes, and the shape of the eyebrows, y'know?"'

She looked hopefully at Strike, who could not bring himself to respond. It seemed impossible that the face of Nefertiti could have sprung from this grey and purple mess.

'You can see it in photos of me when I were younger,' she said, with a hint of pique. 'Point is, I fort I was giving her a better life, and then they went an' give her to those bastards, pardon my language. If I'd'a known, I'd of kept 'er, and I told 'er that. That made 'er cry. I'd of kept her and never let 'er go.

'Oh yeah. She talked to me. It all poured out. She got on all right wiv the father, with S'Ralec. He sounded all right. The mother's a right mad bitch, though. Oh yeah. Pills. Poppin' pills. Fackin' rich bitches takin' pills f' their fackin' nerves. Lula could talk to me, see. Well, it's a bond, innit. You can' break it, blood.

'She was scared what that bitch'd do, if she found out Lula was lookin' for 'er real mum. She was proper worried about what the cow was gonna do when the press found out about me, but there you are, when yore famous like she was, they find out ev'rythin', don' they? Oh, the lies they tell, though. Some o' the things they said abaht me, I'm still thinkin' o' suin'.

'What was I sayin'? 'Er mother, yeah. I says to Lula, "Why worry, love, sounds to me like you're better off wivout 'er anyway. Let 'er be pissed off if she don' want us to see each uvver." But she was a good girl, Lula, an' she kep' visitin' 'er, outta duty.

'Anyway, she 'ad 'er own life, she was free to do what she wanted, weren' she? She 'ad Evan, a man of 'er own. I told 'er I disapproved, mind,' said Marlene Higson, with a pantomime of strictness. 'Oh yeah. Drugs, I've seen too many go that way. But I 'ave to admit, 'e's a sweet boy underneath. I 'ave to admit that. He di'n't have nothin' to do wiv it. I can tell ya that.'

'Met him, did you?'

'No, but she called 'im once while she was with me and I 'eard them on the phone togevver, and they were a lovely couple. No, I got nuthin' bad to say about Evan. 'E 'ad nuthin' to do with it, that's proved. No, I've got nuthin' bad to say about 'im. As long as 'e'd of gone clean, 'e'd of 'ad my blessing. I said to 'er, "Bring 'im along, see wevver I approve," but she never. 'E was always busy. 'E's a lovely-lookin' boy, under all that 'air,' said Marlene. 'You can see it in all 'is photos.'

'Did she talk to you about her neighbours?'

'Oh, that Fred Beastigwee? Yeah, she told me all about 'im, offerin' 'er parts hin 'is films. I said to 'er, why not? It might be a larf. Even if she 'adn't liked it, it woulda bin, what, another 'arf mill in the bank?'

Her bloodshot eyes squinted at nothing; she seemed momentarily mesmerised, lost in contemplation of sums so vast and dazzling that they were beyond her ken, like an image of infinity. Merely to speak of them was to taste the power of money, to roll dreams of wealth around her mouth.

'Did you ever hear her talk about Guy Somé?'

'Oh yeah, she liked Gee, 'e was good to 'er. Person'lly, I prefer more classic things. It's not my kinda style.'

The shocking-pink Lycra, tight on the rolls of fat spilling over the waistband of her leggings, rippled as she leaned forward to tap her cigarette delicately into the ashtray.

'"'E's like a brother to me," she sez, an' I sez, never mind pretend brothers, why don't we try an' find my boys togevver? But she weren't int'rested.'

'Your boys?'

'Me sons, me ovver kids. Yeah, I 'ad two more after 'er: one wiv Dez, an' then later there wuz another one. Social Services took 'em off me, but I sez to 'er, wiv your money we could find 'em, gimme a bit, not much, I dunno, coupla grand, an' I'll try an' get someone to find 'em, keep it quiet from the press, I'll 'andle it, I'll keep you out of it. But she weren' interested,' repeated Marlene.

'Do you know where your sons are?'

'They took 'em as babies, I dunno where they are now. I was havin' problems. I ain't gonna lie to ya, I've had a bloody hard life.'

And she told him, at length, about her hard life. It was a sordid story littered with violent men, with addiction and ignorance, neglect and poverty, and an animal instinct for survival that jettisoned babies in its wake, for they demanded skills that Marlene had never developed.

'So you don't know where your two sons are now?' Strike repeated, twenty minutes later.

'No, how the fuck could I?' said Marlene, who had talked herself into bitterness. 'She weren' int'rested anyway. She already had a white brother, di'n't she? She wuz after black family. That's what she reely wanted.'

'Did she ask you about her father?'

'Yeah, an' I told 'er ev'rything I knew. 'E was an African student. Lived upstairs from me, jus' along the road 'ere, Barking Road, wiv two others. There's the bookie's downstairs now. Very good-looking boy. 'Elped me with me shopping a couple of times.'

To hear Marlene Higson tell it, the courtship had proceeded with an almost Victorian respectability; she and the African student seemed barely to have progressed past handshakes during the first months of their acquaintance.

'And then, 'cos 'e'd 'elped me all them times, one day I asked 'im in, y'know, jus' as a thank-you, really. I'm not a prejudiced person. Ev'ryone's the same to me. Fancy a cuppa, I sez, that were all. And then,' said Marlene, harsh reality clanging down amidst the vague impressions of teacups and doilies, 'I finds out I'm expecting.'

'Did you tell him?'

'Oh yeah, an' 'e was full of 'ow 'e was gonna 'elp, an' shoulder 'is respons'bilities, an' make sure I wuz all right. An' then it was the college 'olidays. 'E said 'e was coming back,' said Marlene, contemptuously. 'Then 'e ran a mile. Don't they all? And what was I gonna do, run off to Africa to find 'im?

'It was no skin off my nose, anyway. I wasn't breaking me 'eart; I was seeing Dez by then. 'E didn't mind the baby. I moved in with Dez not long after Joe left.'

'Joe?'

'That was his name. Joe.'

She said it with conviction, but perhaps, thought Strike, that was because she had repeated the lie so often that the story had become easy, automatic.

'What was his surname?'

'I can' fuckin' remember. You're like her. It was twenny-odd years ago. Mumumba,' said Marlene Higson, unabashed. 'Or something like that.'

'Could it have been Agyeman?'

'No.'

'Owusu?'

'I toldya,' she said aggressively, 'it were Mumumba or something.'

'Not Macdonald? Or Wilson?'

'You takin' the piss? Macdonald? Wilson? From Africa?'

Strike concluded that her relationship with the African had never progressed to the exchange of surnames.

'And he was a student, you said? Where was he studying?'

'College,' said Marlene.

'Which one, can you remember?'

'I don't bloody know. All right if I cadge a ciggie?' she added, in a slightly more conciliatory tone.

'Yeah, help yourself.'

She lit her cigarette with her own plastic lighter, puffed enthusiastically, then said, mellowed by the free tobacco:

'It mighta bin somethin' to do with a museum. Attached, like.'

'Attached to a museum?'

'Yeah, 'cause I remember 'im sayin' "Ay sometimes visit the museum in my free ahrs."' Her imitation made the African student sound like an upper-class Englishman. She was smirking, as though this choice of recreation was absurd, ludicrous.

'Can you remember which museum it was that he visited?'

'The – the Museum of England or summit,' she said; and then, irritably, 'You're like her. How the fuck am I s'posedta remember after all this time?'

'And you never saw him again after he went home?'

'Nope,' she said. 'I wasn't expecting to.' She drank lager. 'He's probably dead,' she said.

'Why do you say that?'

'Africa, innit?' she said. 'He coulda bin shot, couldn't 'e? Or starved. Anythin'. Y'know what it's like out there.'

Strike did know. He remembered the teeming streets of Nairobi; the aerial view of Angola's rainforest, mist hanging over the treetops, and the sudden breathtaking beauty, as the chopper turned, of a waterfall in the lush green mountainside; and the Masai woman, baby at her breast, sitting on a box while Strike questioned her painstakingly about alleged rape, and Tracey manned the video camera beside him.

'D'you know whether Lula tried to find her father?'

'Yeah, she tried,' said Marlene dismissively.

'How?'

'She looked up college records,' said Marlene.

'But if you couldn't remember where he went . . . '

'I dunno, she thought she'd found the place or summit, but she couldn't find 'im, no. Mebbe I wasn' remembrin' his name right, I dunno. She used to go on an' fuckin' on; what did 'e look like, where was 'e studyin'. I said to 'er, he was tall an' skinny an' you wanna be grateful you got my ears, not 'is, 'cause there wouldna bin no fuckin' modellin' career if you'd got them fucking elephant lugs.'

'Did Lula ever talk to you about her friends?'

'Oh, yeah. There was that little black bitch, Raquelle, or whatever she called 'erself. Leechin' all she could outta Lula. Oh, she did herself all right. Fuckin' clothes an' jewell'ry an' I-dunno-what-the-fuck else. I sez to Lula once, "I wouldn' mind a new coat." But I wasn' pushy, see. That Raquelle din' mind askin'.'

She sniffed, and drained her glass.

'Did you ever meet Rochelle?'

'That was 'er name, was it? Yeah, once. She come along in a fuckin' car with a driver to pick Lula up from seein' me. Like Lady Muck out the back window, sneerin' at me. She'll be missin' all of that now, I 'spect. In it for all she could get.

'An' there was that Ciara Porter,' Marlene ploughed on, with, if possible, even greater spite, 'sleepin' with Lula's boyfriend the night she fuckin' died. Nasty fuckin' bitch.'

'Do you know Ciara Porter?'

'I seen it in the fuckin' papers. 'E wen' off to 'er place, di'n't 'e, Evan? After he rowed with Lula. Went to Ciara. Fuckin' bitch.'

It became clear, as Marlene talked on, that Lula had kept her natural mother firmly segregated from her friends, and that, with the exception of a brief glimpse of Rochelle, Marlene's opinions and deductions about Lula's social set were based entirely on the press reports she had greedily consumed.

Strike fetched more drinks, and listened to Marlene describe the horror and shock she had experienced on hearing (from the neighbour who had run in with the news, early in the morning of the 8th) that her daughter had fallen to her death from her balcony. Careful questioning revealed that Lula had not seen Marlene for two months before she died. Strike then listened to a diatribe about the treatment she had received from Lula's adoptive family, following the model's death.

'They di'n't want me around, 'specially that fuckin' uncle. 'Ave ya met 'im, 'ave ya? Fuckin' Tony Landry? I contacted 'im abou' the funeral an' all I got was threats. Oh yeah. Fuckin' threats. I said to 'im, "I'm 'er mother. I gotta right to be there." An' he tole me I wasn't 'er mother, that mad bitch was 'er mother, *Lady* Bristow. Funny, I says, 'cause I remember pushing 'er outta *my* fanny. Sorry for my crudity, but there you are. An' he said I was causing distress, talkin' to the press. They come an' found *me*,' she told Strike furiously, and she jabbed her finger at the block of flats overlooking them. 'Press come an' foun' *me*. 'Course I tole my side o' the fuckin' story. 'Course I did.

'Well, I didn't wanna scene, not at a funeral, I didn't wanna ruin things, but I wasn't gonna be kept away. I went an' sat in the back. I seen fuckin' Rochelle there, givin' me looks like I wuz dirt. But nobody stopped me in the end.

'They got what they wanted, that fuckin' family. I di'n' get nothin'. Nothin'. Tha's not what Lula woulda wanted, I know that for a fact. She woulda wanted me to 'ave something. Not,' said Marlene, with an assumption of dignity, 'that I cared abou' the money. It weren' about the money for me. Nuthin' was gonna replace my daughter, not ten, not twenny mill.

'Mind you, she'd of bin livid if she'd known I didn't get nuthin',' she went on. 'All that money goin' begging; people can't believe it when I tell 'em that I got nuthin'. Struggling to make the rent, and me own daughter lef' millions. But there you are. That's how the rich stay rich, ain't it? They didn' need it, but they didn' mind a bit more. I dunno how that Landry sleeps at night, but that's 'is business.'

'Did Lula ever tell you she was going to leave you anything? Did she mention having made a will?'

Marlene seemed suddenly alert to a whiff of hope.

'Oh yeah, she said she'd look aft'r me, yeah. Yeah, she tole me she'd see me all right. D'you think I shoulda tole someone that? Mentioned it, like?'

'I don't think it would have made any difference, unless she made a will and left you something in it,' said Strike.

Her face fell back into its sullen expression.

'They prob'ly fuckin' destroyed it, them bastards. They coulda done. That's the sort of people they are. I wouldn't put nuthin' past that uncle.'

5

'I'm so sorry he hasn't got back to you,' Robin told the caller, seven miles away in the office. 'Mr Strike's incredibly busy at the moment. Let me take your name and number, and I'll make sure he phones you this afternoon.'

'Oh, there's no need for that,' said the woman. She had a pleasant, cultivated voice with a faint suspicion of hoarseness, as though her laugh would be sexy and bold. 'I don't really need to speak to him. Could you just give him a message for me? I wanted to warn him, that's all. God, this is . . . it's a bit embarrassing; it isn't the way I'd have chosen . . . Well, anyway. Could you please just tell him that Charlotte Campbell called, and that I'm engaged to Jago Ross? I didn't want him to hear about it from anyone else, or read about it. Jago's parents have gone and put it in the bloody *Times*. Mortifying.'

'Oh. All right,' said Robin, her mind suddenly paralysed like her pen.

'Thanks very much – Robin, did you say? Thanks. 'Bye.'

Charlotte rang off first. Robin replaced the receiver in slow motion, feeling acutely anxious. She did not want to deliver this news. She might be only the messenger, but she would feel as though she were delivering an assault on Strike's determination to keep his private life under wraps, on his firm avoidance of the subject of the boxes of possessions, the camp bed, the detritus of his evening meals in the bins every morning.

Robin pondered her options. She could forget to relay the message, and simply tell him to call Charlotte and get her to do her own dirty work (as Robin put it to herself). What, though, if Strike refused to call, and somebody else told him about the engagement? Robin had no means of knowing whether Strike and his ex (girlfriend? fiancée? wife?) had legions of mutual friends. If she and Matthew ever split up, if he became engaged to another woman (it gave her a twisting feeling in her chest to even think of it), all her closest friends and family would feel involved, and would undoubtedly stampede to tell her; she would, she supposed, prefer to be forewarned in as low-key and private a way as possible.

When she heard Strike ascending the stair nearly an hour later, apparently talking on his mobile and in good spirits, Robin experienced a sharp stab of panic to the stomach as though she were about to sit an exam. When he pushed open the glass door, and she saw that he was not holding a mobile at all, but rapping under his breath, she felt even worse.

'Fuck yo' meds and fuck Johari,' muttered Strike, who was holding a boxed electric fan in his arms. 'Afternoon.'

'Hello.'

'Thought we could use this. It's stuffy in here.'

'Yes, that would be good.'

'Just heard Deeby Macc playing in the shop,' Strike informed her, setting down the fan in a corner and peeling off his jacket. "Something something and Ferrari, Fuck yo' meds and fuck Johari." Wonder who Johari was. Some rapper he was having a feud with, d'you think?'

'No,' said Robin, wishing that he was not so cheerful. 'It's a psychological term. The Johari window. It's all to do with how well we know ourselves, and how well other people know us.'

Strike paused in the act of hanging up his jacket and stared at her.

'You didn't get that out of *Heat* magazine.'

'No. I was doing psychology at university. I dropped out.'

She felt, obscurely, that it might somehow even the playing field to tell him about one of her own personal failures, before delivering the bad news.

'You dropped out of university?' He seemed uncharacteristically interested. 'That's a coincidence. I did, too. So why "fuck Johari"?'

'Deeby Macc had therapy in prison. He became interested and did a lot of reading on psychology. I got that bit out of the papers,' she added.

'You're a mine of useful information.'

She experienced another elevator-drop in the pit of her stomach.

'There was a call, when you were out. From a Charlotte Campbell.'

He looked up quickly, frowning.

'She asked me to give you a message, which was,' Robin's gaze slid sideways, to hover momentarily on Strike's ear, 'that she's engaged to Jago Ross.'

Her eyes were drawn, irresistibly, back to his face, and she felt a horrible chill.

One of the earliest and most vivid memories of Robin's childhood was of the day that the family dog had been put down. She herself had been too young to understand what her father was saying; she took the continuing existence of Bruno, her oldest brother's beloved Labrador, for granted. Confused by her parents' solemnity, she had turned to Stephen for a clue as to how to react, and all security had crumbled, for she had seen, for the first time in her short life, happiness and comfort drain out of his small and merry face, and his lips whiten as his mouth fell open. She had heard oblivion howling in the silence that preceded his awful scream of anguish, and then she had cried, inconsolably, not for Bruno, but for the terrifying grief of her brother.

Strike did not speak immediately. Then he said, with palpable difficulty:

'Right. Thanks.'

He walked into the inner office, and closed the door.

Robin sat back down at her desk, feeling like an executioner. She could not settle to anything. She considered knocking on the door again, and offering a cup of tea, but decided against. For five minutes she restlessly reorganised the items on her desk, glancing regularly at the closed inner door, until it opened again, and she jumped, and pretended to be busy at the keyboard.

'Robin, I'm just going to nip out,' he said.

'OK.'

'If I'm not back at five, you can lock up.'

'Yes, of course.'

'See you tomorrow.'

He took down his jacket, and left with a purposeful tread that did not deceive her.

The roadworks were spreading like a lesion; every day there was an extension of the mayhem, and of the temporary structures to protect pedestrians and enable them to pick their way through the devastation. Strike noticed none of it. He walked automatically over trembling wooden boards to the Tottenham, the place he associated with escape and refuge.

Like the Ordnance Arms, it was empty but for one other drinker; an old man just inside the door. Strike bought a pint of

Doom Bar and sat down on one of the low red leather seats against the wall, almost beneath the sentimental Victorian maid who scattered rosebuds, sweet and silly and simple. He drank as though his beer was medicine, without pleasure, intent on the result.

Jago Ross. She must have been in touch with him, seeing him, while they were still living together. Even Charlotte, with all her mesmeric power over men, her astonishing sure-handed skill, could not have moved from reacquaintance to engagement in three weeks. She had been meeting Ross on the sly, while swearing undying love to Strike.

This put a very different light on the bombshell she had dropped on him a month before the end, and the refusal to show him proof, and the shifting dates, and the sudden conclusion of it all.

Jago Ross had been married once already. He had kids; Charlotte had heard on the grapevine that he was drinking hard. She had laughed with Strike about her lucky escape of so many years before; she had expressed pity for his wife.

Strike bought a second pint, and then a third. He wanted to drown the impulses, crackling like electrical charges, to go and find her, to bellow, to rampage, to break Jago Ross's jaw.

He had not eaten at the Ordnance Arms, nor since, and it had been a long time since he had consumed so much alcohol in one sitting. It took him barely an hour of steady, solitary, determined beer consumption to become properly drunk.

Initially, when the slim, pale figure appeared at his table, he told it thickly that it had the wrong man and the wrong table.

'No I haven't,' said Robin firmly. 'I'm just going to get myself a drink too, all right?'

She left him staring hazily at her handbag, which she had placed on the stool. It was comfortingly familiar, brown, a little shabby. She usually hung it up on a coat peg in the office. He gave it a friendly smile, and drank to it.

Up at the bar, the barman, who was young and timid-looking, said to Robin: 'I think he's had enough.'

'That's hardly my fault,' she retorted.

She had looked for Strike in the Intrepid Fox, which was nearest to the office, in Molly Moggs, the Spice of Life and the Cambridge. The Tottenham had been the last pub she was planning to try.

'Whassamatter?' Strike asked her, when she sat down.

'Nothing's the matter,' said Robin, sipping her half-lager. 'I just wanted to make sure you're OK.'

'Yez'm fine,' said Strike, and then, with an effort at clarity, 'I yam fine.'

'Good.'

'Jus' celebratin' my fiancée zengagement,' he said, raising his eleventh pint in an unsteady toast. 'She shou' never've left'm. Never,' he said, loudly and clearly, 'have. Left. The Hon'ble. Jago Ross. Who is'n outstanding *cunt*.'

He virtually shouted the last word. There were more people in the pub than when Strike had arrived, and most of them seemed to have heard him. They had been casting him wary looks even before he shouted. The scale of him, with his drooping eyelids and his bellicose expression, had ensured a small no-go zone around him; people skirted his table on the way to the bathrooms as though it was three times the size.

'Shall we take a walk?' Robin suggested. 'Get something to eat?'

'D'you know what?' he said, leaning forwards with his elbows on the table, almost knocking over his pint. 'D'you know what, Robin?'

'What?' she said, holding his beer steady. She was suddenly possessed of a strong desire to giggle. Many of their fellow drinkers were watching them.

'Y're a very nice girl,' said Strike. 'Y'are. Y're a very nice p'son. I've noticed,' he said, nodding solemnly. 'Yes. 'Ve noticed that.'

'Thank you,' she said, smiling, trying not to laugh.

He sat back in his seat, closed his eyes and said:

'Sorry. 'M'pissed.'

'Yes.'

'Don' do it much these days.'

'No.'

'Haven' eat'n anything.'

'Shall we go and get something to eat, then?'

'Yeah, we c'do,' he said, with his eyes still shut. 'She tol' me she was pregnant.'

'Oh,' said Robin, sadly.

'Yeah. Tol' me. An' then sh'said it was gone. Can't've been mine. Nev' added up.'

Robin said nothing. She did not want him to remember that she had heard this. He opened his eyes.

'She left 'im for me, an' now she's left 'im . . . no, she's lef' me fr'im . . . '

'I'm sorry.'

'. . . lef' me fr'im. Don' be sorry. Y're a nice person.'

He pulled cigarettes out of his pocket, and inserted one between his lips.

'You can't smoke in here,' she reminded him gently, but the barman, who seemed to have been waiting for a cue, came hurrying over towards them now, looking tense.

'You need to go outside to do that,' he told Strike loudly.

Strike peered up at the boy, bleary-eyed, surprised.

'It's all right,' Robin told the barman, gathering up her handbag. 'Come on, Cormoran.'

He stood, massive, ungainly, swaying, unfolding himself out of the cramped space behind the table and glaring at the barman, whom Robin could not blame for taking a step backwards.

'There'z no need,' Strike told him, 't'shout. No need. Fuckin' rude.'

'OK, Cormoran, let's go,' said Robin, standing back to give him space to pass.

'Juz a moment, Robin,' said Strike, one large hand held aloft. 'Juz a moment.'

'Oh God,' said Robin quietly.

''V'you ever done any boxing?' Strike asked the barman, who looked terrified.

'Cormoran, let's go.'

'I wuzza boxer. 'Narmy, mate.'

Over at the bar, some wisecracker murmured, 'I could've been a contender.'

'Let's go, Cormoran,' said Robin. She took his arm, and to her great relief and surprise he came along meekly. It reminded her of leading the enormous Clydesdale her uncle had kept on his farm.

Out in the fresh air Strike leaned back against one of the Tottenham's windows and tried, fruitlessly, to light his cigarette; Robin had to work the lighter for him in the end.

'What you need is food,' she told him, as he smoked with his eyes closed, listing slightly so that she was afraid he would fall over. 'Sober you up.'

'I don' wanna sober up,' Strike muttered. He overbalanced and only saved himself from falling with several rapid sidesteps.

'Come on,' she said, and she guided him across the wooden bridge spanning the gulf in the road, where the clattering machines and builders had at last fallen silent and departed for the night.

'Robin, didjer know I wuzza boxer?'

'No, I didn't know that,' she said.

She had meant to take him back to the office and give him food there, but he came to a halt at the kebab shop at the end of Denmark Street and had lurched through the door before she could stop him. Sitting outside on the pavement at the only table, they ate kebabs, and he told her about his boxing career in the army, digressing occasionally to remind her what a nice person she was. She managed to persuade him to keep his voice down. The full effect of all the alcohol he had consumed was still making itself felt, and food seemed to be doing little to help. When he went off to the bathroom, he took such a long time that she began to worry that he had passed out.

Checking her watch, she saw that it was now ten past seven. She called Matthew, and told him she was dealing with an urgent situation at the office. He did not sound pleased.

Strike wound his way back on to the street, bouncing off the door frame as he emerged. He planted himself firmly against the window and tried to light another cigarette.

'R'bin,' he said, giving up and gazing down at her. 'R'bin, d'you know wadda *kairos* mo . . . ' He hiccoughed. 'Mo . . . moment is?'

'A *kairos* moment?' she repeated, hoping against hope it was not something sexual, something that she would not be able to forget afterwards, especially as the kebab shop owner was listening in and smirking behind them. 'No, I don't. Shall we go back to the office?'

'You don't know whadditis?' he asked, peering at her.

'No.'

''SGreek,' he told her. '*Kairos. Kairos* moment. An' it means,' and from somewhere in his soused brain he dredged up words of surprising clarity, 'the telling moment. The special moment. The supreme moment.'

Oh please, thought Robin, *please don't tell me we're having one.*

'An' d'you know what ours was, R'bin, mine an' Charlotte's?' he said, staring into the middle distance, his unlit cigarette hanging from his hand. 'It was when she walk'd into the ward – I was in hosp'tal f'long time an' I hadn' seen her f'two years – no warning – an' I saw her in the door an' ev'ryone turned an' saw her too, an' she walked down the ward an' she never said a word an,' he paused to draw breath, and hiccoughed again, 'an' she kissed me aft' two years, an' we were back together. Nobody talkin'. Fuckin' beautiful. Mos' beaut'ful woman I've 'ver seen. Bes' moment of the whole fuckin' – 'fmy whole fuckin' life, prob'bly. I'm sorry, R'bin,' he added, 'f'r sayin' "fuckin'". Sorry 'bout that.'

Robin felt equally inclined to laughter and tears, though she did not know why she should feel so sad.

'Shall I light that cigarette for you?'

'Y're a great person, Robin, y'know that?'

Near the turning into Denmark Street he stopped dead, still swaying like a tree in the wind, and told her loudly that Charlotte did not love Jago Ross; it was all a game, a game to hurt him, Strike, as badly as she could.

Outside the black door to the office he halted again, holding up both hands to stop her following him upstairs.

'Y'gotta go home now, R'bin.'

'Let me just make sure you get upstairs OK.'

'No. No. 'M fine now. An' I might chunder. 'M legless. An',' said Strike, 'you don' get that fuckin' tired old fuckin' joke. Or do you? Know most of it now. Did I tell you?'

'I don't know what you mean.'

'Ne'r mind, R'bin. You go home now. I gotta be sick.'

'Are you sure . . . ?'

''M sorry I kep' sayin' fuck – swearin'. Y're a nice pers'n, R'bin. G'bye now.'

She looked back at him when she reached Charing Cross Road. He was walking with the awful, clumsy deliberation of the very drunk towards the dingy entrance to Denmark Place, there, no doubt, to vomit in the dark alleyway, before staggering upstairs to his camp bed and kettle.

6

There was no clear moment of moving from sleep to consciousness. At first he was lying face down in a dreamscape of broken metal, rubble and screams, bloodied and unable to speak; then he was lying on his stomach, doused in sweat, his face pressed into the camp bed, his head a throbbing ball of pain and his open mouth dry and rank. The sun pouring in at the unblinded windows scoured his retinas even with his eyelids closed: raw red, with capillaries spread like fine black nets over tiny, taunting, popping lights.

He was fully clothed, his prosthesis still attached, lying on top of his sleeping bag as though he had fallen there. Stabbing memories, like glass shards through his temple: persuading the barman that another pint was a good idea. Robin, across the table, smiling at him. Could he really have eaten a kebab in the state he was in? At some point he remembered wrestling his fly, desperate to piss but unable to extract the end of shirt caught in his zip. He slid a hand underneath himself – even this slight movement made him want to groan or vomit – and found, to his vague relief, that the zip was closed.

Slowly, like a man balancing some fragile package on his shoulders, Strike moved himself into a sitting position and squinted around the brightly lit room with no idea what time it could be, or indeed what day it was.

The door between inner and outer offices was closed, and he

could not hear any movement on the other side. Perhaps his temp had left for good. Then he saw a white oblong lying on the floor, just inside the door, pushed under the gap at the bottom. Strike moved gingerly on to his hands and knees, and retrieved what he soon saw was a note from Robin.

Dear Cormoran (he supposed there was no going back to 'Mr Strike' now),

I read your list of points to investigate further at the front of the file. I thought I might be able to follow up the first two (Agyeman and the Malmaison Hotel). I will be on my mobile if you would rather I came back to the office.

I have set an alarm just outside your door for 2 p.m., so that you have enough time to get ready for your 5 p.m. appointment at 1 Arlington Place, to interview Ciara Porter and Bryony Radford.

There is water, paracetamol and Alka-Seltzer on the desk outside.

Robin

PS Please don't be embarrassed about last night. You didn't say or do anything you should regret.

He sat quite still on his camp bed for five minutes, holding the note, wondering whether he was about to throw up, but enjoying the warm sunshine on his back.

Four paracetamol and a glass of Alka-Seltzer, which almost decided the vomiting question for him, were followed by fifteen minutes in the dingy toilet, with results offensive to both nose and ear; but he was sustained throughout by a feeling of profound gratitude for Robin's absence. Back in the outer office, he drank two more bottles of water and turned off the alarm, which had set his throbbing brains rattling in his skull. After some deliberation, he chose a set of clean clothes, took shower gel, deodorant, razor, shaving cream and towel out of the kitbag, pulled a pair of swimming trunks out of the bottom of one of the cardboard boxes on the landing, extracted the pair of grey metal crutches from another, then limped down the metal stair with a sports bag over his shoulder and the crutches in his other hand.

He bought himself a family-sized bar of Dairy Milk on the way to Malet Street. Bernie Coleman, an acquaintance in the Army Medical Corps, had once explained to Strike how the majority of the symptoms associated with a crashing hangover were due to dehydration and hypoglycaemia, which were the inevitable results of prolonged vomiting. Strike munched his way through the chocolate, crutches jammed under his arm and every step jarring his head, which still felt as though it was being compressed by tight wires.

But the laughing god of drunkenness had not yet forsaken him. Agreeably detached from reality and from his fellow human beings, he walked down the steps to the ULU pool with an unfeigned sense of entitlement, and as usual nobody challenged him, not even the only other occupant of the changing room, who, after one glance of arrested interest at the prosthesis Strike was unstrapping, kept his eyes politely averted. His false leg stuffed into a locker along with yesterday's clothes, and leaving the door open due to lack of change, Strike moved towards the shower on crutches, his belly spilling over the top of his trunks.

He noted, as he soaped himself, that the chocolate and paracetamol were beginning to take the edge off his nausea and pain.

Now, for the first time, he walked out to the large pool. There were only two students in here, both in the fast lane and wearing goggles, oblivious to everything but their own prowess. Strike proceeded to the far side, set the crutches down carefully beside the steps and slid into the slow lane.

He was more unfit than he had ever been in his life. Ungainly and lopsided, he kept swimming into the side of the pool, but the cool, clean water was soothing to body and spirit. Panting, he completed a single length and rested there, his thick arms spread along the side of the pool, sharing the responsibility for his heavy body with the caressing water and gazing up at the high white ceiling.

Little waves, outrunners sent by the young athletes on the other side of the pool, tickled his chest. The terrible pain in his head was receding into the distance; a fiery red light viewed through mist. The chlorine was sharp and clinical in his nostrils, but it no longer made him want to be sick. Deliberately, like a man ripping off a bandage on a congealing wound, Strike turned his attention to the thing he had attempted to drown in alcohol.

Jago Ross; in every respect the antithesis of Strike: handsome in the manner of an Aryan prince, possessor of a trust fund, born to fulfil a preordained place in his family and the world; a man with all the confidence twelve generations of well-documented lineage can give. He had quit a succession of high-flying jobs, developed a persistent drinking problem, and was vicious in the manner of an overbred, badly disciplined animal.

Charlotte and Ross belonged to that tight, interconnected network of public-schooled blue-bloods who all knew each other's families, connected through generations of interbreeding and old school ties. While the water lapped his thickly hairy chest, Strike seemed to see himself, Charlotte and Ross at a great distance, from the wrong end of a telescope, so that the arc of their story became clear: it mirrored Charlotte's restless day-to-day behaviour, that craving for heightened emotion that expressed itself most typically in destructiveness. She had secured Jago Ross as a prize when eighteen, the most extreme example she could find of his type and the very epitome of eligibility, as her parents had seen it. Perhaps that had been too easy, and certainly too expected, because she had then dumped him for Strike, who, for all his brains, was anathema to Charlotte's family; an uncategorisable mongrel. What was left, after all these years, to a woman who craved emotional storms, but to leave Strike again and again, until at last the only way to leave with real éclat was to move full circle, back to the place where he had found her?

Strike allowed his aching body to float in the water. The racing students were still thrashing their way up and down the fast lane.

Strike knew Charlotte. She was waiting for him to rescue her. It was the final, cruellest test.

He did not swim back down the pool, but hopped sideways through the water, using his arms to grip the long side of the pool as he had done during physiotherapy in the hospital.

The second shower was more pleasurable than the first; he made the water as hot as he could stand, lathered himself all over, then turned the dial to cold to rinse himself.

The prosthesis reattached, he shaved over a sink with a towel tied around his waist, then dressed with unusual care. He had never worn the most expensive suit and shirt that he owned. They had been gifts from Charlotte on his last birthday: raiment suitable for her fiancé; he remembered her beaming at him as he stared at his unfamiliarly well-styled self in a full-length mirror. The suit and shirt had hung in their carry case ever since, because he and Charlotte had not gone out much after last November; because his birthday had been the last truly happy day they had spent together. Soon afterwards, the relationship had begun to stagger back into the old familiar grievances, into the same mire in which it had foundered before, but which, this time, they had sworn to avoid.

He might have incinerated the suit. Instead, in a spirit of defiance, he chose to wear it, to strip it of its associations and render it mere pieces of cloth. The tailoring of the jacket made him look slimmer and fitter. He left the white shirt open at the throat.

Strike had had a reputation, in the army, for being able to bounce back from excessive alcohol consumption with unusual speed. The man staring at him out of the small mirror was pale, with purple shadows under his eyes, yet in the sharp Italian suit he looked better than he had done in weeks. His black eye had vanished at last, and his scratches had healed.

A cautiously light meal, copious amounts of water, another evacuatory trip to the restaurant bathroom, more painkillers; then, at five o'clock, a prompt arrival at number 1, Arlington Place.

The door was answered, after his second knock, by a cross-looking woman in black-framed glasses and a short grey bob. She let him in with an appearance of reluctance, then walked briskly away across a stone-floored hall which incorporated a magnificent staircase with a wrought-iron banister, calling 'Guy! Somebody Strike?'

There were rooms on both sides of the hall. To the left, a small knot of people, all of whom seemed to be dressed in black, were staring in the direction of some powerful light source that Strike could not see, but which illuminated their rapt faces.

Somé appeared, striding through this door into the hall. He too was wearing glasses, which made him look older; his jeans were baggy and ripped and his white T-shirt was emblazoned with an eye that appeared to be weeping glittering blood, which on closer examination proved to be red sequins.

'You'll have to wait,' he said curtly. 'Bryony's busy and Ciara's going to be hours. You can park yourself in there if you want,' he pointed towards the right-hand room, where the edge of a tray-laden table was visible, 'or you can stand around and watch like these useless fuckers,' he went on, suddenly raising his voice and glaring at the huddle of elegant young men and women who were staring towards the light source. They dispersed at once, without protest, some of them crossing the hall into the room opposite.

'Better suit, by the way,' Somé added, with a flash of his old archness. He marched back into the room from which he had come.

Strike followed the designer, and took up the space vacated by the roughly dispatched onlookers. The room was long and almost bare, but its ornate cornices, pale blank walls and curtainless windows gave it an atmosphere of mournful grandeur. A further group of people, including a long-haired male photographer bent over his camera, stood between Strike and the scene at the far end of the room, which was dazzlingly illuminated by a series of arc lights and light screens. Here was an artful arrangement of tattered old chairs, one on its side, and three models. They were a breed apart, with faces and bodies in rare proportions that fell precisely between the categories of strange and impressive. Fine-boned and recklessly slim, they had been chosen, Strike assumed, for the dramatic contrast in their colouring and features. Sitting like Christine Keeler on a back-to-front chair, long legs splayed in spray-on white leggings, but apparently naked from the waist up, was a black girl as dark-skinned as Somé himself, with an Afro and slanting, seductive eyes. Standing over her in a white vest decorated in chains, which just covered her pubis, was a Eurasian beauty with flat black hair cut into an asymmetric fringe. To one side, leaning alone and sideways on the back of another chair, was Ciara Porter; alabaster fair, with long baby-blonde hair, wearing a white semi-transparent jumpsuit through which her pale, pointed nipples were clearly visible.

The make-up artist, almost as tall and thin as the models, was bending over the black girl, pressing a pad into the sides of her nose. The three models waited silently in position, still as portraits, all three faces blank and empty, waiting to be called to attention. The other people in the room (the photographer appeared to have two assistants; Somé, now biting his fingernails on the sidelines, was accompanied by the cross-looking woman in glasses) all spoke in low mutters, as though frightened of disturbing some delicate equilibrium.

At last the make-up artist joined Somé, who talked inaudibly and rapidly to her, gesticulating; she stepped back into the bright light and, without speaking to the model, ruffled and rearranged Ciara Porter's long mane of hair; Ciara showed no sign that she knew she was being touched, but waited in patient silence. Bryony retreated into the shadows once more, and asked Somé something; he responded with a shrug and gave her some inaudible instruction that had her look around until her eyes rested on Strike.

They met at the foot of the magnificent staircase.

'Hi,' she whispered. 'Let's go through here.'

She led him across the hall into the opposite room, which was slightly smaller than the first, and dominated by the large table covered with buffet-style food. Several long, wheeled clothing racks, jammed with sequinned, ruffled and feathered creations arranged according to colour, stood in front of a marble fireplace. The displaced onlookers, all of them in their twenties, were gathered in here; talking quietly, picking in desultory fashion at the half-empty platters of mozzarella and Parma ham and talking into, or playing with, their phones. Several of them subjected Strike to appraising looks as he followed Bryony into a small back room which had been turned into a makeshift make-up station.

Two tables with big portable mirrors stood in front of the large single window, which looked out on to a spruce garden. The black plastic boxes standing around reminded Strike of those his Uncle Ted had taken fly-fishing, except that Bryony's drawers were crammed with coloured powders and paints; tubes and brushes lay lined up on towels spread across the table tops.

'Hi,' she said, in a normal voice. '*God*. Talk about cutting the tension with a knife, eh? Guy's always a perfectionist, but this is his first proper shoot since Lula died, so he's, you know, *seriously* uptight.'

She had dark, choppy hair; her skin was sallow, her features, though large, were attractive. She was wearing tight jeans on long, slightly bandy legs, a black vest, several fine gold chains around her neck, rings on her fingers and thumbs, and also what looked like black leather ballet shoes. This kind of footwear always had a slightly anaphrodisiac effect on Strike, because it reminded him of the fold-up slippers his Aunt Joan used to carry in her handbag, and therefore of bunions and corns.

Strike began to explain what he wanted from her, but she cut him off.

'Guy's told me everything. Want a ciggie? We can smoke in here if we open this.'

So saying, she wrenched open the door that led directly on to a paved area of the garden.

She made a small space on one of the cluttered make-up tables and perched herself on it; Strike took one of the vacated chairs and drew out his notebook.

'OK, fire away,' she said, and then, without giving him time to speak, 'I've been thinking about that afternoon non-stop ever since, actually. So, so sad.'

'Did you know Lula well?' asked Strike.

'Yeah, pretty well. I'd done her make-up for a couple of shoots, made her up for the Rainforest Benefit. When I told her I can thread eyebrows . . .'

'You can what?'

'Thread eyebrows. It's like plucking, but with threads?'

Strike could not imagine how this worked.

'Right . . .'

'. . . she asked me to do them for her at home. The paps were all over her, *all* the time, even if she was going to the salon. It was insane. So I helped her out.'

She had a habit of tossing back her head to flick her overlong fringe out of her eyes, and a slightly breathy manner. Now she threw her hair over to one side, raked it with her fingers and peered at him through her fringe.

'I got there about three. She and Ciara were all excited about Deeby Macc arriving. Girlie gossip, you know. I'd *never* have guessed what was coming. *Never.*'

'Lula was excited, was she?'

'Oh God, yeah, what d'you think? How would you feel if someone had written songs about . . . Well,' she said, with a breathy little laugh, 'maybe it's a girl thing. He's *so* charismatic. Ciara and I were having a laugh about it while I did Lula's eyebrows. Then Ciara asked me to do her nails. I ended up making them both up, as well, so I was there for, must've been three hours. Yeah, I left about six.'

'So you'd describe Lula's mood as excited, would you?'

'Yeah. Well, you know, she was a bit distracted; she kept checking her phone; it was lying in her lap while I was doing her eyebrows. I knew what that meant: Evan was messing her around again.'

'Did she say that?'

'No, but I knew she was really pissed off at him. Why do you think she said that to Ciara about her brother? About leaving him everything?'

This seemed a stretch to Strike.

'Did you hear her say that too?'

'What? No, but I heard *about* it. I mean, afterwards. Ciara told us all. I think I was in the loo when she actually said it. Anyway, I totally believe it. Totally.'

'Why's that?'

She looked confused.

'Well – she really loved her brother, didn't she? God, that was always obvious. He was probably the only person she could really rely on. Months before, around the time she and Evan split up the first time, I was making her up for the Stella show, and she was telling everyone her brother was really pissing her off, going on and on about what a freeloader Evan was. And you know, Evan was jacking her around again, that last afternoon, so she was thinking that James – is it James? – had had him right all along. She always knew he had her interests at heart, even if he was a bit bossy sometimes. This is a really, really exploitative business, you know. Everyone's got an agenda.'

'Who do you think had an agenda for Lula?'

'Oh my God, *everyone*,' said Bryony, making a wide sweeping gesture with her cigarette-holding hand, which encompassed all of the inhabited rooms outside. 'She was the *hottest* model out there, *everyone* wanted a piece of her. I mean, Guy—' But Bryony broke off. 'Well, Guy's a businessman, but he did *adore* her; he wanted her to go and live with him after that stalker business. He's still not right about her dying. I heard he tried to contact her through some spiritualist. Margo Leiter told me. He's still devastated, he can barely hear her name without crying. *Anyway*,' said Bryony, 'that's all I know. I never dreamed that afternoon would be the last time I saw her. I mean, *my God*.'

'Did she talk about Duffield at all, while you were – er – threading her eyebrows?'

'No,' said Bryony, 'but she wouldn't, would she, if he was really hacking her off?'

'So as far as you can remember, she mainly spoke about Deeby Macc?'

'Well . . . it was more Ciara and me talking about him.'

'But you think she was excited to meet him?'

'God, yeah, of course.'

'Tell me, did you see a blue piece of paper with Lula's handwriting on it when you were in the flat?'

Bryony shook her hair over her face again, and combed it with her fingers.

'What? No. No, I didn't see anything like that. Why, what was it?'

'I don't know,' said Strike. 'That's what I'd like to find out.'

'No, I didn't see it. Blue, did you say? No.'

'Did you see any paper at all with her writing on it?'

'No, I can't remember any papers. No.' She shook her hair out of her face. 'I mean, something like that could've been lying around, but I wouldn't have necessarily noticed it.'

The room was dingy. Perhaps he only imagined that she had changed colour, but he had not invented the way she twisted her right foot up on to her knee and examined the sole of the leather ballet slipper for something that was not there.

'Lula's driver, Kieran Kolovas-Jones . . . '

'Oh, that really, really cute guy?' said Bryony. 'We used to tease her about Kieran; he had such a gigantic crush on her. I think Ciara uses him now sometimes.' Bryony gave a meaningful little giggle. 'She's got a *bit* of a rep as a good-time girl, Ciara. I mean, you can't help liking her, but . . . '

'Kolovas-Jones says that Lula was writing something on blue paper in the back of his car, when she left her mother's that day . . . '

'Have you talked to Lula's mother yet? She's a bit weird.'

'. . . and I'd like to find out what it was.'

Bryony flicked her cigarette stub out of the open door and shifted restlessly on the desk.

'It could have been anything.' He waited for the inevitable suggestion, and was not disappointed. 'A shopping list or something.'

'Yeah, it could've been; but if, for the sake of argument, it was a suicide note . . . '

'But it wasn't – I mean, that's silly – how could it've been? Who'd write a suicide note that far in advance, and then get their face done and go out dancing? That doesn't make any sense at all!'

'It doesn't seem likely, I agree, but it would be good to find out what it was.'

'Maybe it had nothing to do with her dying. Why couldn't it have been a letter to Evan or something, telling him how hacked off she was?'

'She doesn't seem to have become hacked off with him until later that day. Anyway, why would she write a letter, when she had his telephone number and was going to see him that night?'

'I don't know,' said Bryony restlessly. 'I'm just saying, it could've been something that doesn't make any difference.'

'And you're quite sure you didn't see it?'

'Yes, I'm quite sure,' she said, her colour definitely heightened. 'I was there to do a job, not go snooping around her stuff. Is that everything, then?'

'Yeah, I think that's all I've got to ask about that afternoon,' said Strike, 'but you might be able to help me with something else. Do you know Tansy Bestigui?'

'No,' said Bryony. 'Only her sister, Ursula. She's hired me a couple of times for big parties. She's awful.'

'In what way?'

'Just one of those spoiled rich women – well,' said Bryony, with a twist to her mouth, 'she isn't *nearly* as rich as she'd like to be. Both those Chillingham sisters went for old men with bags of money; wealth-seeking missiles, the pair of them. Ursula thought she'd hit the jackpot when she married Cyprian May, but he hasn't got *nearly* enough for her. She's knocking forty now; the opportunities aren't there the way they used to be. I suppose that's why she hasn't been able to trade up.'

Then, evidently feeling that her tone needed some explanation, she continued:

'I'm sorry, but she accused me of listening to her bloody

voicemail messages.' The make-up artist folded her arms across her chest, glaring at Strike. 'I mean, *please.* She chucked me her mobile and told me to call her a cab, without so much as a bloody please or thank you. I'm dyslexic. I hit the wrong button and the next thing I know, she's screaming her bloody head off at me.'

'Why do you think she was so upset?'

'Because I heard a man she wasn't married to telling her he was lying in a hotel room fantasising about going down on her, I expect,' said Bryony, coolly.

'So she might be trading up after all?' asked Strike.

'*That's* not up,' said Bryony; but then she added hastily, 'I mean, pretty tacky message. Anyway, listen, I've got to get back out there, or Guy will be going ballistic.'

He let her go. After she had left, he made two more pages of notes. Bryony Radford had shown herself a highly unreliable witness, suggestible and mendacious, but she had told him much more than she knew.

7

The shoot lasted for another three hours. Strike waited in the garden, smoking and consuming more bottled water, while dusk fell. From time to time he wandered back into the building to check on progress, which seemed immensely slow. Occasionally he glimpsed or heard Somé, whose temper seemed frayed, barking instructions at the photographer or one of the black-clad minions who flitted between clothes racks. Finally, at nearly nine o'clock, after Strike had consumed a few slices of the pizza that had been ordered by the morose and exhausted stylist's assistant, Ciara Porter descended the stairs where she had been posing with her two colleagues, and joined Strike in the make-up room, which Bryony was busy stripping bare.

Ciara was still wearing the stiff silver minidress in which she had posed for the last pictures. Attenuated and angular, with milk-white skin, hair almost as fair, and pale blue eyes set very wide apart, she stretched out her endless legs, in platform shoes that were tied with long silver threads up her calves, and lit a Marlboro Light.

'God, I can't *believe* you're Rokers' son!' she said breathlessly, her chrysoberyl eyes and full lips both wide. 'Just *beyond* weird! I know him; he invited Looly and me to the Greatest Hits launch last year! And I know your brothers, Al and Eddie! They *told* me they had a big brother in the army! God. *Mad.* Is that you done, Bryony?' Ciara added pointedly.

The make-up artist seemed to be making a laborious business of gathering up the tools of her trade. Now she sped up perceptibly, while Ciara smoked and watched her in silence.

'Yep, that's me,' said Bryony brightly at last, hoisting a heavy box over her shoulder and picking up more cases in each hand. 'See you, Ciara. Goodbye,' she added to Strike, and left.

'She is *so* bloody nosy, and *such* a gossip,' Ciara told Strike. She threw back her long white hair, rearranged her coltish legs and asked:

'D'you see a lot of Al and Eddie?'

'No,' said Strike.

'And your *mum*,' she said, unfazed, blowing smoke out of the corner of her mouth. 'I mean, she's just, like, a *legend*. You know how Baz Carmichael did a whole collection two seasons back called "Supergroupie", and it was like, Bebe Buell and your mum were the *whole* inspiration? Maxi skirts and buttonless shirts and boots?'

'I didn't,' said Strike.

'Oh, it was, like – you know that great quote about Ossie Clark dresses, how men liked them because they could just, like, open them up really easily and fuck the girls? That's, like, your mum's whole *era*.'

She shook her hair out of her eyes again and gazed at him, not with the chilling and offensive appraisal of Tansy Bestigui, but in what seemed to be frank and open wonder. It was difficult for him to decide whether she was sincere, or performing her own character; her beauty got in the way, like a thick cobweb through which it was difficult to see her clearly.

'So, if you don't mind, I'd like to ask you about Lula.'

'God, yeah. Yeah. No, I really want to help. When I heard someone was investigating it, I was, like, well, *good. At last.*'

'Really?'

'God, yeah. The whole thing was *so* fucking shocking. I just couldn't believe it. She's still on my phone, look at this.'

She rummaged in an enormous handbag, finally retrieving a white iPhone. Scrolling down the contact list, she leaned into him, showing him the name 'Looly'. Her perfume was sweet and peppery.

'I keep expecting her to *call* me,' said Ciara, momentarily subdued, slipping the phone back into her bag. 'I can't delete her; I keep *going* to do it, and then just, like, *bottling* it, you know?'

She raised herself restlessly, twisted one of the long legs underneath her, sat back down and smoked in silence for a few seconds.

'You were with her most of her last day, weren't you?' Strike asked.

'*Don't* fucking remind me,' said Ciara, closing her eyes. 'I've only been over it, like, a *million* times. Trying to get my head around how you can go from, like, completely bloody happy to *dead* in, like, *hours.*'

'She was completely happy?'

'God, happier than I'd *ever* seen her, that last week. We got back from a job in Antigua for *Vogue*, and she and Evan got back together and they had the commitment ceremony; it was all *fantastic* for her, she was on cloud *nine.*'

'You were at this commitment ceremony?'

'Oh yeah,' said Ciara, dropping her cigarette end into a can of Coke, where it was extinguished with a small hiss. 'God, it was *beyond* romantic. Evan just, like, *sprang* it on her at Dickie Carbury's house. You know Dickie Carbury, the restaurateur? He's got this *fabulous* place in the Cotswolds, and we were all there for the weekend, and Evan had bought them both matching bangles from Fergus Keane, *gorgeous*, oxidised silver. He *forced* us all down to the lake after dinner in the freezing cold and the snow, and then he recited this *poem* he'd written to her, and put the bangle on her wrist. Looly was laughing her head off, but then she just, like, recited a poem she knew back to him. Walt Whitman. It was,' said Ciara, with an air of sudden seriousness, 'honestly, like, *so* impressive, just to have the perfect poem to say, just like *that*. People think models are dumb, you know.' She threw her hair back again and offered Strike a cigarette before taking another herself. 'I get *so bored* of telling people I've got a deferred place to read English at Cambridge.'

'Have you?' asked Strike, unable to suppress the surprise in his voice.

'Yeah,' she said, blowing out smoke prettily, 'but, you know, the modelling's going so well, I'm going to give it another year. It's opening doors, you know?'

'So this commitment ceremony was when – a week before Lula died?'

'Yeah,' said Ciara, 'the Saturday before.'

'And it was just an exchange of poems and bangles. No vows, no officiant?'

'No, it wasn't *legally binding* or anything, it was just, like, this lovely, this perfect *moment*. Well, except for Freddie Bestigui, he was being a bit of a pain. But at least,' Ciara drew hard on her cigarette, 'his bloody wife wasn't there.'

'Tansy?'

'Tansy Chillingham, yeah. She's a bitch. It's *so* not a surprise they're divorcing; they led, like, *totally* separate lives, you never saw them out together.

'To tell you the truth, Freddie wasn't *too* bad that weekend, seeing what a nasty rep he's got. He was just a bore, the way he kept trying to suck up to Looly, but he wasn't *awful* like they say he can be. I heard a story about this, like, *totally* naive girl he promised a bit part in a film . . . Well, I don't know whether it was true.' Ciara squinted for a moment at the end of her cigarette. 'She never reported it, anyway.'

'You said Freddie was being a pain; in what way?'

'Oh God, he kept, like, *cornering* Looly and going on about how great she'd be on screen, and like, what a *great* bloke her dad was.'

'Sir Alec?'

'Yeah, Sir Alec, of course. Oh my God,' said Ciara, wide-eyed, 'if he'd known her *real* father, Looly would've, like, flipped out *completely*! That would have been, like, the dream of her life! No, he just said he'd known Sir Alec years and years ago, and they came from, like, the same East End *manor* or something, so he should be considered, like, her godfather or something. I think he was trying to be funny, but *not*. Anyway, *everyone* could tell he was just trying to work out how to get her into a film. He was a jerk about the commitment ceremony; he kept shouting "I'll give away the bride." He was pissed; he drank like crazy all through dinner. Dickie had to shut him up. Then after the ceremony, we all had champagne back at the house and Freddie had, like, another two bottles on top of everything he'd already put away. He kept yelling at Looly that she'd make such a great actress, but she didn't care. She just ignored him. She was cuddled up with Evan on the sofa, just, like . . . '

And suddenly, tears were sparkling in Ciara's kohled eyes, and she squashed them out of sight with the flat palms of her pretty white hands.

'. . . *crazy* in love. She was so fucking happy, I'd never seen her happier.'

'You met Freddie Bestigui again, didn't you, on the evening

before Lula died? Didn't the two of you pass him in the lobby, on your way out?'

'Yeah,' said Ciara, still dabbing at her eyes. 'How did you know that?'

'Wilson, the security guard. He thought Bestigui said something to Lula that she didn't like.'

'Yeah. He's right. I'd forgotten about that. Freddie said something about Deeby Macc, about Looly being excited about him coming, how he really wanted to get them on film together. I can't remember exactly what it was, but he made it sound dirty, you know?'

'Did Lula know that Bestigui and her adoptive father had been friends?'

'She told me it was the first she'd ever heard of it. She always stayed out of Freddie's way at the flats. She didn't like Tansy.'

'Why not?'

'Oh, Looly wasn't interested in that whole, like, whose husband's got the biggest fucking *yacht* crap, she didn't want to get into their crowd. She was *so* much better than that. *So* not like the Chillingham girls.'

'OK,' said Strike, 'can you talk me through the afternoon and evening you were with her?'

Ciara dropped her second fag end into the Coke can, with another little spitting fizz, and immediately lit another.

'Yeah. OK, let me think. Well, I met her at her place in the afternoon. Bryony came over to do her eyebrows and ended up giving us both manicures. We just had, like, a girlie afternoon together.'

'How did she seem?'

'She was . . . ' Ciara hesitated. 'Well, she wasn't *quite* as happy as she'd been that week. But not suicidal, I mean, *no way*.'

'Her driver, Kieran, thought she seemed strange when she left her mother's house in Chelsea.'

'Oh God, yeah, well why wouldn't she be? Her mum had *cancer*, didn't she?'

'Did Lula discuss her mother, when she saw you?'

'No, not really. I mean, she said she'd just been sitting with her, because she was a bit, you know, pulled down after her op, but nobody thought then that Lady Bristow was going to *die*. The op was supposed to *cure* her, wasn't it?'

'Did Lula mention any other reason that she was feeling less happy than she had been?'

'No,' said Ciara, slowly shaking her head, the white-blonde hair tumbling around her face. She raked it back again and took a deep drag on her cigarette. 'She *did* seem a bit down, a bit distracted, but I just put it down to having seen her mum. They had a weird relationship. Lady Bristow was, like, *really* overprotective and possessive. Looly found it, you know, a bit claustrophobic.'

'Did you notice Lula telephoning anyone while she was with you?'

'No,' said Ciara, after a thoughtful pause. 'I remember her *checking* her phone a lot, but she didn't speak to anyone, as far as I can remember. If she was phoning anyone, she was doing it on the quiet. She was in and out of the room a bit. I don't know.'

'Bryony thought she seemed excited about Deeby Macc.'

'Oh, for God's sake,' said Ciara impatiently. 'It was everyone else who was excited about Deeby Macc – Guy and Bryony and – well, even I was, a bit,' she said, with endearing honesty. 'But Looly wasn't that fussed. She was in love with Evan. You can't believe everything Bryony says.'

'Did Lula have a piece of paper with her, that you can remember? A bit of blue paper, which she'd written on?'

'No,' said Ciara again. 'Why? What was it?'

'I don't know yet,' said Strike, and Ciara looked suddenly thunderstruck.

'God – you're not telling me she left a *note*? Oh my *God*. How fucking mad would that be? But – no! That would mean she'd have, like, already decided she was going to do it.'

'Maybe it was something else,' said Strike. 'You mentioned at the inquest that Lula expressed an intention to leave everything to her brother, didn't you?'

'Yeah, that's right,' said Ciara earnestly, nodding. 'Yeah, what happened was, Guy had sent Looly these *fabby* handbags from the new range. I *knew* he wouldn't have sent me any, even though *I* was in the advert too. Anyway, I unwrapped the white one, Cashile, you know, and it was just, like, *beautiful*; he does these detachable silk linings and he'd had it custom-printed for her with this amazing African print. So I said, "Looly, will you leave me this one?" just as a joke. And she said, like, *really* seriously, "I'm leaving everything to my brother, but I'm sure he'd let you have anything you want."'

Strike was watching and listening for any sign that she was lying or exaggerating, but the words came easily and, to all appearances, frankly.

'That was a strange thing to say, wasn't it?' he asked.

'Yeah, I s'pose,' said Ciara, shaking the hair back off her face again. 'But Looly was like that; she could go a bit dark and *dramatic* sometimes. Guy used to say, "Less of the cuckoo, Cuckoo." Anyway,' Ciara sighed, 'she didn't take the hint about the Cashile bag. I was hoping she'd just give it to me; I mean, she had *four*.'

'Would you say you were close to Lula?'

'Oh God, yeah, *super*-close, she told me *everything*.'

'A couple of people have mentioned that she didn't trust too easily. That she was scared of confidences turning up in the press. I've been told that she tested people to see whether she could trust them.'

'Oh yeah, she did get a bit, like, *paranoid* after her real mum started selling stories about her. She actually asked me,' said Ciara, with an airy wave of her cigarette, 'whether I'd told anyone she was back with Evan. I mean, *come on*. There was *no way* she was going to keep that quiet. *Everyone* was talking about it. I said to her, "Looly, the only thing worse than being talked about is not being talked about." That's Oscar Wilde,' she added, kindly. 'But Looly didn't like that side of being famous.'

'Guy Somé thinks that Lula wouldn't have got back with Duffield if he hadn't been out of the country.'

Ciara glanced towards the door, and dropped her voice.

'Guy *would* say that. He was just, like, *super*-protective of Looly. He adored her; he really loved her. He thought Evan was bad for her, but *honestly*, he doesn't know the real Evan. Evan's, like, *totally* fucked up, but he's a good person. He went to see Lady Bristow not long ago, and I said to him, "*Why*, Evan, what on *earth* did you put yourself through that for?" Because, you know, her family hated him. And d'you know what he said? "I just wanna speak to somebody who cares as much as I do that she's gone." I mean, how sad is that?'

Strike cleared his throat.

'The press have *totally* got it in for Evan, it's just *so* unfair, he can't do anything right.'

'Duffield came to your place, didn't he, the night she died?'

'God, yeah, and there you are!' said Ciara indignantly. 'They made out we were, like, *shagging* or something! He had no money, and his driver had disappeared, so he just, like, *hiked* across London so he could crash at mine. He slept on the sofa. So we were together when we heard the news.'

She raised her cigarette to her full mouth and drew deeply on it, her eyes on the floor.

'It was terrible. You can't imagine. Terrible. Evan was . . . oh my God. And then,' she said, in a voice barely louder than a whisper, 'they were all saying it was *him*. After Tansy Chillingham said she'd heard a row. The press just went crazy. It was awful.'

She looked up at Strike, holding her hair off her face. The harsh overhead light merely illuminated her perfect bone structure.

'You haven't met Evan, have you?'

'No.'

'D'you want to? You could come with me now. He said he was going along to Uzi tonight.'

'That'd be great.'

'Fabby. Hang on.'

She jumped up and called through the open door:

'Guy, sweetie, can I wear this tonight? Go on. To Uzi?'

Somé entered the small room. He looked exhausted behind his glasses.

'All right. Make sure you're photographed. Wreck it and I'll sue your skinny white arse.'

'I'm not going to wreck it. I'm taking Cormoran to meet Evan.'

She stuffed her cigarettes away into her enormous bag, which appeared to hold her day clothes too, and hoisted it over her shoulder. In her heels, she was within an inch of the detective's height. Somé looked up at Strike, his eyes narrowed.

'Make sure you give the little shit a hard time.'

'Guy!' said Ciara, pouting. 'Don't be horrible.'

'And watch yourself, Master Rokeby,' Somé added, with his usual edge of spite. 'Ciara's a terrible slut, aren't you, dear? And she's like me. She likes them big.'

'*Guy!*' said Ciara, in mock horror. 'Come on, Cormoran. I've got a driver outside.'

8

Strike, forewarned, was nowhere near as surprised to see Kieran Kolovas-Jones as the driver was to see him. Kolovas-Jones was holding open the left-hand passenger door, faintly lit by the car's interior light, but Strike spotted his momentary change of expression when he laid eyes on Ciara's companion.

'Evening,' said Strike, moving around the car to open his own door and get in beside Ciara.

'Kieran, you've met Cormoran, haven't you?' said Ciara, buckling herself in. Her dress had ridden up to the very top of her long legs. Strike could not be absolutely certain that she was wearing anything beneath it. She had certainly been braless in the white jumpsuit.

'Hi, Kieran,' said Strike.

The driver nodded at Strike in the rear-view mirror, but did not speak. He had assumed a strictly professional demeanour that Strike doubted was habitual in the absence of detectives.

The car pulled away from the kerb. Ciara started rummaging again in her bag; she removed a perfume spray and squirted herself liberally in a wide circle around her face and shoulders; then dabbed lip gloss over her lips, talking all the while.

'What am I going to need? Money. Cormoran, could you be a total darling and keep this in your pocket? I'm not going to take this massive thing in.' She handed him a crumpled wad of twenties. 'You're a sweetheart. Oh, and I'll need my phone. Have you got a pocket for my phone? *God*, this bag's a mess.'

She dropped it on the car floor.

'When you said that it would have been the dream of Lula's life to find her real father . . . '

'Oh God, it *would* have been. She used to talk about that *all the time*. She got really excited when that bitch – her birth mother – told her he was African. Guy always said that was bullshit, but he hated the woman.'

'He met Marlene Higson, did he?'

'Oh no, he just hated the whole, like, *idea* of her. He could see how excited Looly got, and he just wanted to *protect* her from being disappointed.'

So much protection, Strike thought, as the car turned a corner in the dark. Had Lula been that fragile? The back of Kolovas-Jones's head was rigid, correct; his eyes flickering more often than was necessary to rest upon Strike's face.

'And then Looly thought she had a lead on him – her real father – but that went completely cold on her. Dead end. Yeah, it was so sad. She really thought she'd found him and then it all just fell through her fingers.'

'What lead was this?'

'It was something about where the college was. Something her mother said. Looly thought she'd found the place it must have been, and she went to look at the records, or something, with this funny friend of hers called . . . '

'Rochelle?' suggested Strike. The Mercedes was now purring up Oxford Street.

'Yeah, Rochelle, that's right. Looly met her in rehab or something, poor little thing. Looly was, like, *unbelievably* sweet to her. Used to take her shopping and stuff. Anyway, they never found him, or it was the wrong place, or something. I can't remember.'

'Was she looking for a man called Agyeman?'

'I don't think she ever told me the name.'

'Or Owusu?'

Ciara turned her beautiful light eyes upon him in astonishment.

'That's *Guy's* real name!'

'I know.'

'Oh my God,' Ciara giggled. '*Guy's* dad never went to college. He was a *bus driver.* He used to beat Guy up for sketching dresses all the time. That's why Guy changed his name.'

The car was slowing down. The long queue, four people wide, stretching along the block, led to a discreet entrance that might have been to a private house. A gaggle of dark figures was gathered around a white-pillared doorway.

'Paps,' said Kolovas-Jones, speaking for the first time. 'Careful how you get out of the car, Ciara.'

He slid out of the driver's seat and walked around to the left-hand back door; but the paparazzi were already running; ominous, darkly clad men, raising their long-nosed cameras as they closed in.

Ciara and Strike emerged into flashes like gunfire; Strike's retinas were in sudden, dazzling whiteout; he ducked his head, his hand closed instinctively around Ciara Porter's slender upper arm, and he steered her ahead of him through the black oblong that represented sanctuary, as the doors opened magically to admit them. The queuing hordes were shouting, protesting at their easy entry, yelping with excitement; and then the flashes stopped, and they were inside, where there was an industrial roar of noises, and a loud insistent bass line.

'*Wow*, you've got a great sense of direction,' said Ciara. 'I usually, like, ricochet off the bouncers and they have to push me in.'

Streaks and blazes of purple and yellow light were still burned across Strike's field of vision. He dropped her arm. She was so pale that she looked almost luminous in the gloom. Then they were jostled further inside the club by the entry of another dozen people behind them.

'C'mon,' said Ciara, and she slipped a soft, long-fingered hand inside his and tugged him along behind her.

Faces turned as they walked through the packed crowd, both of them taller by far than the majority of clubbers. Strike could see what looked like long glass fish tanks set into the walls, containing what seemed to be great floating blobs of wax, reminding him of his mother's old lava lamps. There were long black leather banquettes along the walls, and, further in, nearer the dance floor, booths. It was hard to tell how big the club was, because of judiciously placed mirrors; at one point, Strike caught a glimpse of himself, head-on, looking like a sharply dressed heavy behind the silvery sylph that was Ciara. The music pounded through every part of him, vibrating through his head and body; the crowd on the dance floor was so dense that it seemed miraculous that they were managing even to stamp and sway.

They had reached a padded doorway, guarded by a bald bouncer who grinned at Ciara, revealing two gold teeth, and pushed open the concealed entrance.

They entered a quieter, though hardly less crowded bar area that was evidently reserved for the famous and their friends. Strike noticed a miniskirted television presenter, a soap actor, a comedian primarily famous for his sexual appetite; and then, in a distant corner, Evan Duffield.

He was wearing a skull-patterned scarf wound around his neck and skin-tight black jeans, sitting at the join of two black leather banquettes with arms stretched at right angles along the backs of the benches on either side, where his companions, mostly women, were crammed. His dark shoulder-length hair had been dyed blonde; he was pallid and bony-faced, and the smudges around his bright turquoise eyes were dark purple.

The group containing Duffield was emanating an almost magnetic force over the room. Strike saw it in the sneaking sidelong glances other occupants were shooting them; in the respectful space left around them, a wider orbit than anybody else had been granted. Duffield and his cohorts' apparent unselfconsciousness was, Strike recognised, nothing but expert artifice; they had, all of them, the hyper-alertness of the prey animal combined with the casual arrogance of predators. In the inverted food chain of fame, it was the big beasts who were stalked and hunted; they were receiving their due.

Duffield was talking to a sexy brunette. Her lips were parted as she listened, almost ludicrously immersed in him. As Ciara and Strike drew nearer, Strike saw Duffield glance away from the brunette for a fraction of a second, making, Strike thought, a lightning-fast recce of the bar, taking the measure of the room's attention, and of other possibilities it might offer.

'Ciara!' he yelled hoarsely.

The brunette looked deflated as Duffield jumped nimbly to his feet; thin and yet well muscled, he slid out from behind the table to embrace Ciara, who was eight inches taller than he in her platform shoes; she dropped Strike's hand to return the hug. The whole bar seemed, for a few shining moments, to be watching; then they remembered themselves, and returned to their chat and their cocktails.

'Evan, this is Cormoran Strike,' said Ciara. She moved her mouth close to Duffield's ear and Strike saw rather than heard her say, 'He's Jonny Rokeby's son!'

'All right, mate?' asked Duffield, holding out a hand, which Strike shook.

Like other inveterate womanisers Strike had encountered, Duffield's voice and mannerisms were slightly camp. Perhaps such men became feminised by prolonged immersion in women's company, or perhaps it was a way of disarming their quarry. Duffield indicated with a flutter of the hand that the others should move along the bench to make room for Ciara; the brunette looked crestfallen. Strike was left to find himself a low stool, drag it alongside the table and ask Ciara what she wanted to drink.

'Oooh, get me a Boozy-Uzi,' she said, 'and use my money, sweetie.'

Her cocktail smelled strongly of Pernod. Strike bought himself water, and returned to the table. Ciara and Duffield were now almost nose to nose, talking; but when Strike set down the drinks, Duffield looked around.

'So what d'you do, Cormoran? Music biz?'

'No,' said Strike. 'I'm a detective.'

'No shit,' said Duffield. 'Who'm I supposed to have killed this time?'

The group around him permitted themselves wry, or nervous, smiles, but Ciara said:

'Don't joke, Evan.'

'I'm not joking, Ciara. You'll notice when I am, because it'll be fucking funny.'

The brunette giggled.

'I said I'm *not* joking,' snapped Duffield.

The brunette looked as though she had been slapped. The rest of the group seemed imperceptibly to withdraw, even in the cramped space; they began their own conversation, temporarily excluding Ciara, Strike and Duffield.

'Evan, not nice,' said Ciara, but her reproach seemed to caress rather than sting, and Strike noticed that the glance she threw the brunette held no pity.

Duffield drummed his fingers on the edge of the table.

'So, what kind of a detective are you, Cormoran?'

'A private one.'

'Evan, darling, Cormoran's been hired by Looly's brother . . .'

But Duffield had apparently spotted someone or something of interest up at the bar, for he leapt to his feet and disappeared into the crowd there.

'He's always a bit ADHD,' said Ciara apologetically. 'Plus, he's still really, really fucked up about Looly. He *is*,' she insisted, half cross, half amused, as Strike raised his eyebrows and looked pointedly in the direction of the voluptuous brunette, who was now cradling an empty mojito glass and looking morose. 'You've got something on your smart jacket,' Ciara added, and she leaned forwards to brush off what Strike thought were pizza crumbs. He caught a strong whiff of her sweet, spicy perfume. The silver material of her dress was so stiff that it gaped, like armour, away from her body, affording him an unhampered view of small white breasts and pointed shell-pink nipples.

'What's that perfume you're wearing?'

She thrust a wrist under his nose.

'It's Guy's new one,' she said. 'It's called Éprise – it's French for "smitten", you know?'

'Yeah,' he said.

Duffield had returned, holding another drink, cleaving his

way back through the crowd, whose faces revolved after him, tugged by his aura. His legs in their tight jeans were like black pipe cleaners, and with his darkly smudged eyes he looked like a Pierrot gone bad.

'Evan, babes,' said Ciara, when Duffield had reseated himself, 'Cormoran's investigating—'

'He heard you the first time,' Strike interrupted her. 'There's no need.'

He thought that the actor had heard that, too. Duffield drank his drink quickly, and tossed a few comments into the group beside them. Ciara sipped her cocktail, then nudged Duffield.

'How's the film going, sweetie?'

'Great. Well. Suicidal drug dealer. It's not a stretch, y'know.'

Everyone smiled, except Duffield himself. He drummed his fingers on the table, his legs jerking in time.

'Bored now,' he announced.

He was squinting towards the door, and the group was watching him, openly yearning, Strike thought, to be scooped up and taken along.

Duffield looked from Ciara to Strike.

'Wanna come back to mine?'

'Fabby,' squeaked Ciara, and with a feline glance of triumph at the brunette, she downed her drink in one.

Just outside the VIP area, two drunk girls ran at Duffield; one of them pulled up her top and begged him to sign her breasts.

'Don't be dirty, love,' said Duffield, pushing past her. 'You gotta car, Cici?' he yelled over his shoulder, as he ploughed his way through the crowds, ignoring shouts and pointing fingers.

'Yes, sweetie,' she shouted. 'I'll call him. Cormoran, darling, have you got my phone?'

Strike wondered what the paparazzi outside would make of

Ciara and Duffield leaving the club together. She was shouting into her iPhone. They reached the entrance; Ciara said, 'Wait – he's going to text when he's right outside.'

Both she and Duffield looked slightly nervy; watchful, self-aware, like competitors waiting to enter a stadium. Then Ciara's phone gave a little buzz.

'OK, he's there,' she said.

Strike stood back to let her and Duffield out first, then walked rapidly to the front passenger seat as Duffield ran around the back of the car in the blinding popping lights, to screams from the queue, and threw himself into the back seat with Ciara, whom Kolovas-Jones had helped inside. Strike slammed the front passenger door, forcing the two men who had leaned in to take shot after shot of Duffield and Ciara to jump backwards out of the way.

Kolovas-Jones seemed to take an unconscionable amount of time to return to the car; Strike felt as though the Mercedes's interior was a test tube, simultaneously enclosed and exposed as more and more flashes fired. Lenses were pressed to the windows and windscreen; unfriendly faces floated in the darkness, and black figures darted back and forth in front of the stationary car. Beyond the explosions of light, the shadowy crowd-queue surged, curious and excited.

'Put your foot down, for fuck's sake!' Strike growled at Kolovas-Jones, who revved the engine. The paparazzi blocking the road moved backwards, still taking pictures.

'Bye-bye, you cunts,' said Evan Duffield from the back seat as the car pulled away from the kerb.

But the photographers ran alongside the vehicle, flashes erupting on either side; and Strike's whole body was bathed in sweat: he was suddenly back on a yellow dirt road in the juddering Viking, with a sound like firecrackers popping in the Afghanistan air; he had glimpsed a youth running away from the road ahead, dragging a small boy. Without conscious thought he had bellowed '*Brake!*' lunged forwards and seized Anstis, a new father of two days' standing, who was sitting right behind the driver; the last thing he remembered was Anstis's shouted protest, and the low metallic boom of him hitting the back doors, before the Viking disintegrated with an ear-splitting bang, and the world became a hazy blur of pain and terror.

The Mercedes had rounded the corner on to an almost deserted road; Strike realised that he had been holding himself so tensely that his remaining calf muscles were sore. In the wing mirror he could see two motorbikes, each being ridden pillion, following them. Princess Diana and the Parisian underpass; the ambulance bearing Lula Landry's body, with cameras held high to the darkened glass as it passed; both careered through his thoughts as the car sped through the dark streets.

Duffield lit a cigarette. Out of the corner of his eye, Strike saw Kolovas-Jones scowl at his passenger in the rear-view mirror, though he made no protest. After a moment or two, Ciara began whispering to Duffield. Strike thought he heard his own name.

Five minutes later, they turned another corner and saw, ahead of them, another small crowd of black-clad photographers, who began flashing and running towards the car the moment it appeared. The motorbikes were pulling up right behind them; Strike saw the four men running to catch the moment when the car doors opened. Adrenalin erupted: Strike imagined himself exploding out of the car, punching, sending expensive cameras crashing on to concrete as their holders crumpled. And as if he had read Strike's mind, Duffield said, with his hand poised on the door handle:

'Knock their fucking lights out, Cormoran, you're built for it.'

The open doors, the night air and more maddening flashes; bull-like, Strike walked fast with his big head bowed, his eyes on Ciara's tottering heels, refusing to be blinded. Up three steps they ran, Strike at the rear; and it was he who slammed the front door of the building in the faces of the photographers.

Strike felt himself momentarily allied with the other two by the experience of being hunted. The tiny, dimly lit lobby felt safe and friendly. The paparazzi were still yelling to each other on the other side of the door, and their terse shouts recalled soldiers recceing a building. Duffield was fiddling at an inner door, trying a succession of keys in the lock.

'I've only been here a couple of weeks,' he explained, finally opening it with a barging shoulder. Once over the threshold, he wriggled out of his tight jacket, threw it on to the floor by the door and then led the way, his narrow hips swinging in only slightly less exaggerated fashion than Guy Somé's, down a short corridor into a sitting room, where he switched on lamps.

The spare, elegant grey and black decor had been overlaid by clutter and stank of cigarette smoke, cannabis and alcohol fumes. Strike was reminded vividly of his childhood.

'Need a slash,' announced Duffield, and called over his shoulder as he disappeared, with a directive jab of the thumb, 'Drinks are in the kitchen, Cici.'

She threw a smile at Strike, then left through the door Duffield had indicated.

Strike glanced around the room, which looked as though it had been left, by parents of impeccable taste, in the care of a teenager. Every surface was covered in debris, much of it in the form of scribbled notes. Three guitars stood propped against the walls. A cluttered glass coffee table was surrounded by black-and-white seats, angled towards an enormous plasma TV. Bits of debris had overflowed from the coffee table on to the black fur rug below. Beyond the long windows, with their gauzy grey curtains, Strike could make out the shapes of the photographers still prowling beneath the street light.

Duffield had returned, tugging up his fly. On finding himself alone with Strike, he gave a nervous giggle.

'Make yourself at home, big fella. Hey, I know your old man, actually.'

'Yeah?' said Strike, sitting down in one of the squashy ponyskin cube-shaped armchairs.

'Yeah. Met him a couple of times,' said Duffield. 'Cool dude.'

He picked up a guitar, began to pick out a twiddling tune on it, thought better of it and put the instrument back against the wall.

Ciara returned, carrying a bottle of wine and three glasses.

'Couldn't you get a cleaner, dearie?' she asked Duffield reprovingly.

'They give up,' said Duffield. He vaulted over the back of a chair and landed with his legs sprawled over the side. 'No fucking stamina.'

Strike pushed aside the mess on the coffee table so that Ciara could set down the bottle and glasses.

'I thought you'd moved in with Mo Innes,' she said, pouring out wine.

'Yeah, that didn't work out,' said Duffield, raking through the detritus on the table for cigarettes. 'Ol' Freddie's rented me this place just for a month, while I'm going out to Pinewood. He wants to keep me away from me old *haunts*.'

His grubby fingers passed over a string of what seemed to be rosary beads; numerous empty cigarette packets with bits of card torn out of them; three lighters, one of them an engraved Zippo; Rizla papers; tangled leads unattached to appliances; a pack of cards; a sordid stained handkerchief; sundry crumpled pieces of grubby paper; a music magazine featuring a picture of Duffield in moody black and white on the cover; opened and unopened mail; a pair of crumpled black leather gloves; a quantity of loose change and, in a clean china ashtray on the edge of the debris, a single cufflink in the form of a tiny silver gun. At last he unearthed a soft packet of Gitanes from under the sofa; lit up, blew a long jet of smoke at the ceiling, then addressed Ciara, who had placed herself on the sofa at right angles to the two men, sipping her wine.

'They'll say we're fucking each other, again, Ci,' he said, pointing out of the window at the prowling shadows of the waiting photographers.

'And what'll they say Cormoran's here for?' asked Ciara, with a sidelong glance at Strike. 'A threesome?'

'Security,' said Duffield, appraising Strike through narrowed eyes. 'He looks like a boxer. Or a cage fighter. Don't you want a proper drink, Cormoran?'

'No, thanks,' said Strike.

'What's that, AA or being on duty?'

'Duty.'

Duffield raised his eyebrows and sniggered. He seemed nervous, shooting Strike darting looks, drumming his fingers on the glass table. When Ciara asked him whether he had visited Lady Bristow again, he seemed relieved to be offered a subject.

'Fuck, no. Once was enough. It was fucking horrible. Poor bitch. On her fucking deathbed.'

'It was *beyond* nice of you to go, though, Evan.'

Strike knew that she was trying to show Duffield off in his best light.

'Do you know Lula's mother well?' he asked Duffield.

'No. I only met her once before Lu died. She didn't approve of me. None of Lu's family approved of me. I dunno,' he fidgeted, 'I just wanted to talk to someone who really gives a shit that she's dead.'

'Evan!' Ciara pouted. '*I* care she's dead, excuse me!'

'Yeah, well . . . '

With one of his oddly feminine, fluid movements, Duffield curled up in the chair so that he was almost foetal, and sucked hard on his cigarette. On a table behind his head, illuminated by a cone of lamplight, was a large, stagey photograph of him with Lula Landry, clearly taken from a fashion shoot. They were mock-wrestling against a backdrop of fake trees; she was wearing a floor-length red dress, and he was in a slim black suit, with a hairy wolf's mask pushed up on top of his forehead.

'I wonder what *my* mum would say if I carked it? My parents've got an injunction out against me,' Duffield informed Strike. 'Well, it was mainly my fucking father. Because I nicked their telly a couple of years ago. D'you know what?' he added, craning his neck to look at Ciara, 'I've been clean five weeks, two days.'

'That's so fabulous, baby! That's fantastic!'

'Yeah,' he said. He swivelled upright again. 'Aren't you gonna ask me any questions?' he demanded of Strike. 'I thought you were investigating Lu's *murder*?'

The bravado was undermined by the tremor in his fingers. His knees began bouncing up and down, just like John Bristow's.

'D'you think it was murder?' Strike asked.

'No.' Duffield dragged on his cigarette. 'Yeah. Maybe. I dunno. Murder makes more sense than fucking suicide, anyway.

Because she wouldn'ta gone without leaving me a note. I keep waiting for a note to turn up, y'know, and then I'll know it's real. It don't feel real. I can't even remember the funeral. I was out of my fucking head. I took so much stuff I couldn't fucking walk. I think, if I could just remember the funeral, it'd be easier to get my head round.'

He jammed his cigarette between his lips and began drumming with his fingers on the edge of the glass table. After a while, apparently discomforted by Strike's silent observation, he demanded:

'Ask me something, then. Who's hired you, anyway?'

'Lula's brother John.'

Duffield stopped drumming.

'That money-grabbing, poker-arsed wanker?'

'Money-grabbing?'

'He was fucking *obsessed* with how she spent her fucking money, like it was any of his fucking business. Rich people always think everyone else is a fucking freeloader, have you noticed that? Her whole frigging family thought I was gold-digging, and after a bit,' he raised a finger to his temple and made a boring motion, 'it went in, it planted doubts, y'know?'

He snatched one of the Zippos from the table and began flicking at it, trying to make it ignite. Strike watched tiny blue sparks erupt and die as Duffield talked.

'I expect he thought she'd be better off with some rich fucking accountant, like him.'

'He's a lawyer.'

'Whatever. What's the difference, it's all about helping rich people keep their mitts on as much money as they can, innit? He's got his fucking trust fund from Daddy, what skin is it off his nose what his sister did with her own money?'

'What was it that he objected to her buying, specifically?'

'Shit for me. The whole fucking family was the same; they didn't mind if she chucked it their way, keep it in the fucking family, that was OK. Lu knew they were a mercenary load of fuckers, but, like I say, it still left its fucking mark. Planted ideas in her head.'

He threw the dead Zippo back on to the table, drew his knees up to his chest and glared at Strike with his disconcerting turquoise eyes.

'So he still thinks I did it, does he? Your client?'

'No, I don't think he does,' said Strike.

'He's changed his narrow fuckwitted mind, then, because I heard he was going round telling everyone it was me, before they ruled it as suicide. Only, I've got a cast-iron fucking alibi, so fuck him. Fuck. Them. All.'

Restless and nervy, he got to his feet, added wine to his almost untouched glass, then lit another cigarette.

'What can you tell me about the day Lula died?' Strike asked.

'The night, you mean.'

'The day leading up to it might be quite important too. There are a few things I'd like to clear up.'

'Yeah? Go on, then.'

Duffield dropped back down into the chair, and pulled his knees up to his chest again.

'Lula called you repeatedly between around midday and six in the evening, but you didn't answer your phone.'

'No,' said Duffield. He began picking, childishly, at a small hole in the knee of his jeans. 'Well, I was busy. I was working. On a song. Didn't want to stem the flow. The old inspiration.'

'So you didn't know she was calling you?'

'Well, yeah. I saw her number coming up.' He rubbed his

nose, stretched his legs out on to the glass table, folded his arms and said, 'I felt like teaching her a little lesson. Let her wonder what I was up to.'

'Why did you think she needed a lesson?'

'That fucking rapper. I wanted her to move in with me while he was staying in her building. "Don't be silly, don't you trust me?"' His imitation of Lula's voice and expression was disingenuously girlish. 'I said to her, "Don't *you* be fucking silly. Show me I got nothing to worry about, and come and stay with me." But she wouldn't. So then I thought, two can play at that fucking game, darling. Let's see how you like it. So I got Ellie Carreira over to my place, and we did a bit of writing together, and then I brought Ellie along to Uzi with me. Lu couldn't fucking complain. Just business. Just song-writing. Just friends, like her and that rapper-gangster.'

'I didn't think she'd ever met Deeby Macc.'

'She hadn't, but he'd made his intentions pretty fucking public, hadn't he? Have you heard that song he wrote? She was creaming her panties over it.'

'"Bitch you ain't all that . . ."' Ciara began to quote obligingly, but a filthy look from Duffield silenced her.

'Did she leave you voicemail messages?'

'Yeah, a couple. "Evan, will you call me, please. It's urgent. I don't want to say it on the phone." It was always fucking urgent when she wanted to find out what I was up to. She knew I was pissed off. She was worried I might've called Ellie. She had a real hang-up about Ellie, because she knew we'd fucked.'

'She said it was urgent, and that she didn't want to say it on the phone?'

'Yeah, but that was just to try and make me call. One of her little games. She could be fucking jealous, Lu. And pretty fucking manipulative.'

'Can you think why she'd be calling her uncle repeatedly that day as well?'

'What uncle?'

'His name's Tony Landry; he's another lawyer.'

'*Him?* She wouldn't be calling *him*, she fucking hated him worse than her brother.'

'She called him, repeatedly, over the same period that she was calling you. Leaving more or less the same message.'

Duffield raked his unshaven chin with dirty nails, staring at Strike.

'I dunno what that was about. Her mum, maybe. Old Lady B going into hospital or something.'

'You don't think something might have happened that morning which she thought was either relevant to or of interest to both you and her uncle?'

'There isn't any subject that could interest me and her fucking uncle at the same time,' said Duffield. 'I've met him. Share prices and shit are all he'd be interested in.'

'Maybe it was something about her, something personal?'

'If it was, she wouldn't call that fucker. They didn't like each other.'

'What makes you say that?'

'She felt about him like I feel about my fucking father. Neither of them thought we were worth shit.'

'Did she talk to you about that?'

'Oh, yeah. He thought her mental problems were just attention-seeking, bad behaviour. Put on. Burden on her mother. He got a bit smarmier when she started making money, but she didn't forget.'

'And she didn't tell you why she'd been calling you, once she got to Uzi?'

'Nope,' said Duffield. He lit another cigarette. 'She was fucked off from the moment she arrived, because Ellie was there. Didn't like that at all. In a right fucking mood, wasn't she?'

For the first time he appealed to Ciara, who nodded sadly.

'She didn't really talk to me,' said Duffield. 'She was mostly talking to you, wasn't she?'

'Yes,' said Ciara. 'And she didn't tell me there was anything, like, *upsetting* her or anything.'

'A couple of people have told me her phone was hacked . . .' began Strike; Duffield talked over him.

'Oh yeah, they were listening in on our messages for fucking weeks. They knew everywhere we were meeting and everything. Fucking bastards. We changed our phone numbers when we found out what was going on and we were fucking careful what messages we left after that.'

'So you wouldn't be surprised, if Lula had had something important or upsetting to tell you, that she didn't want to be explicit over the phone?'

'Yeah, but if it was that fucking important, she woulda told me at the club.'

'But she didn't?'

'No, like I say, she never spoke to me all night.' A muscle was jumping in Duffield's chiselled jaw. 'She kept checking the time on her fucking phone. I knew what she was doing; trying to wind me up. Showing me she couldn't wait to get home and meet fucking Deeby Macc. She waited until Ellie went off to the bog; then got up, came over to tell me she was leaving, and said I could have my bangle back; the one I gave her when we had our commitment ceremony. She chucked it down on the table in front of me, with everyone fucking gawping. So I picked it up and said, "Anyone fancy this, it's going spare?" and she fucked off.'

He did not speak as though Lula had died three months previously, but as though it had all happened the day before, and there was still a possibility of reconciliation.

'You tried to restrain her, though, right?' asked Strike.

Duffield's eyes narrowed.

'Restrain her?'

'You grabbed her arms, according to witnesses.'

'Did I? I can't remember.'

'But she pulled free, and you stayed behind, is that right?'

'I waited ten minutes, because I wasn't gonna give her the satisfaction of chasing her in front of all those people, and then I left the club and got my driver to take me to Kentigern Gardens.'

'Wearing the wolf mask,' said Strike.

'Yeah, to stop those fucking scumbags,' he nodded towards the window, 'selling pictures of me looking wasted or pissed off. They hate it when you cover your face. Depriving them of making their fucking parasitic living. One of them tried to pull Wolfie off me, but I held on. I got in the car and gave 'em a few pictures of the Wolf giving them the finger, out the back window. Got to the corner of Kentigern Gardens and there were more paps everywhere. I knew she must've got in already.'

'Did you know the key code?'

'Nineteen sixty-six, yeah. But I knew she'd've told security not to let me up. I wasn't gonna walk in in front of all of them and then get chucked out on me arse five minutes later. I tried to phone her from the car, but she wouldn't pick up.

I thought she'd probably gone downstairs to welcome Deeby fucking Macc to London. So I went off to see a man about pain relief.'

He ground out his cigarette on a loose playing card on the edge of the table and began hunting for more tobacco. Strike, who wanted to oil the flow of conversation, offered him one of his own.

'Oh, cheers. Cheers. Yeah. Well, I got the driver to drop me off and I went to visit my friend, who has since given the police a full statement *to that effect*, as Uncle Tony might say. Then I wandered around a bit, and there's camera footage in that station to prove that, and then about, I dunno . . . threeish? Fourish?'

'Half past four,' said Ciara.

'Yeah, I went to crash at Ciara's.'

Duffield sucked on the cigarette, watching the tip burn, then, exhaling, said cheerfully:

'So my arse is covered, is it not?'

Strike did not find his satisfaction likeable.

'And when did you find out that Lula was dead?'

Duffield drew his legs up to his chest again.

'Ciara woke me up and told me. I couldn't – I was fucking – yeah, well. Fucking hell.'

He put his arms over the top of his head and stared at the ceiling.

'I couldn't fucking . . . I couldn't believe it. Couldn't fucking believe it.'

And as Strike watched, he thought he saw realisation wash over Duffield that the girl of whom he spoke so flippantly, and who he had, by his own account, provoked, taunted and loved, was really and definitely never coming back; that she had been smashed into pulp on snow-covered asphalt, and that she and their relationship were now beyond the possibility of repair. For a moment, staring at the blank white ceiling, Duffield's face became grotesque as he appeared to grin from ear to ear; it was a grimace of pain, of the exertion necessary to beat back tears. His arms slipped down, and he buried his face in them, his forehead on his knees.

'Oh, *sweetie*,' said Ciara, putting her wine down on the table with a clunk, and reaching forward to place a hand on his bony knee.

'This has fucked me up proper,' said Duffield thickly from behind his arms. 'This has fucked me up good. I wanted to marry her. I fucking loved her, I did. Fuck, I don't wanna talk about it any more.'

He jumped up and left the room, sniffing ostentatiously and wiping his nose on his sleeve.

'Didn't I *tell* you?' Ciara whispered to Strike. 'He's a *mess*.'

'Oh, I don't know. He seems to have cleaned up his act. Off heroin for a month.'

'I *know*, and I don't want him to fall off the wagon.'

'This is a lot gentler than he would have had from the police. This is polite.'

'You've got an awful look on your face, though. Really, like, *stern* and as if you don't believe a word he's saying.'

'D'you think he's going to come back?'

'Yes, of course he is. *Please* be a bit nicer . . .'

She sat quickly back in her seat as Duffield walked back in; he was grim-faced and his camp strut was very slightly subdued. He flung himself into the chair he had previously occupied and said to Strike:

'I'm out of fags. Can I have another one of yours?'

Reluctantly, because he was down to three, Strike handed it across, lit it for him, then said:

'All right to keep talking?'

'About Lula? You can talk, if you want. I dunno what else I can tell you. I ain't got any more information.'

'Why did you split up? The first time, I mean; I'm clear on why she ditched you in Uzi.'

Out of the corner of his eye, he saw Ciara make an indignant little gesture; apparently this did not qualify as 'nicer'.

'What the fuck's that got to do with anything?'

'It's all relevant,' said Strike. 'It all gives a picture of what was going on in her life. It all helps explain why she might've killed herself.'

'I thought you were looking for a murderer?'

'I'm looking for the truth. So why *did* you break up, the first time?'

'Fuck, how's this fucking important?' exploded Duffield. His temper, as Strike had expected, was violent and short-fused. 'What, are you trying to make out it's my fault she fucking jumped off a balcony? How can us splitting up the first time have anything to do with it, knucklehead? That was two fucking months before she died. Fuck, I could call meself a detective and ask a lot of fuckass questions. Bet it pays all right, dunnit, if you can find some fuckwit rich client?'

'Evan, don't,' said Ciara, distressed. 'You said you wanted to help . . .'

'Yeah, I wanna help, but how's this fucking fair?'

'No problem, if you don't want to answer,' said Strike. 'You're under no obligation here.'

'I ain't got nothing to hide, it's just fucking personal stuff, innit? We split up,' he shouted, 'because of drugs, and her family and her friends putting down poison about me, and because she didn't trust nobody because of the fucking press, all right? Because of all the *pressure*.'

And Duffield made his hands into trembling claws and pressed them, like earphones, over his ears, making a compressing movement.

'Pressure, fucking *pressure*, that's why we split up.'

'You were taking a lot of drugs at the time, were you?'

'Yeah.'

'And Lula didn't like it?'

'Well, people round her were telling her she didn't like it, you know?'

'Like who?'

'Like her family, like fucking Guy Somé. That little pansy *twat*.'

'When you say that she didn't trust anybody because of the press, what do you mean by that?'

'Fuck, innit obvious? Don't you know all this, from your old man?'

'I know jack shit about my father,' said Strike coolly.

'Well, they were tapping her fucking *phone*, man, and that gives you a weird fucking *feeling*; haven't you got any imagination? She started getting paranoid about people selling stuff on her. Trying to work out what she'd said on the phone, and what she hadn't, and who mighta given stuff to the papers and that. It fucked with her head.'

'Was she accusing *you* of selling stories?'

'No,' snapped Duffield, and then, just as vehemently, 'Yeah, sometimes. *How did they know we were coming here, how did they know I said that to you, yadda yadda yadda* . . . I said to her, it's all part and fucking parcel of fame, innit, but she thought she could have her cake and eat it.'

'But you didn't ever sell stories about her to the press?'

He heard Ciara's hissing intake of breath.

'No I fucking didn't,' said Duffield quietly, holding Strike's gaze without blinking. 'No I fucking did not. All right?'

'And you split up for how long?'

'Two months, give or take.'

'But you got back together, what, a week before she died?'

'Yeah. At Mo Innes's party.'

'And you had this commitment ceremony forty-eight hours later? At Carbury's house in the Cotswolds?'

'Yeah.'

'And who knew that was going to happen?'

'It was a spontaneous thing. I bought the bangles and we just did it. It was beautiful, man.'

'It really was,' echoed Ciara sadly.

'So, for the press to have found out so quickly, someone who was there must have told them?'

'Yeah, I s'pose so.'

'Because your phones weren't being tapped then, were they? You'd changed your numbers.'

'I don't fucking know if they were being tapped. Ask the shits at the rags who do it.'

'Did she talk to you at all about trying to trace her father?'

'He was dead . . . what, you mean the real one? Yeah, she was interested, but it was no go, wannit? Her mother didn't know who he was.'

'She never told you whether she'd managed to find out anything about him?'

'She tried, but she didn't get anywhere, so she decided that she was gonna to do a course in African studies. That was gonna be Daddy, the whole fucking continent of Africa. Fucking Somé was behind that, shit-stirring as usual.'

'In what way?'

'Anything that took her away from me was good. Anything that bracketed them together. He was one possessive bastard where she was concerned. He was in love with her. I know he's a poof,' Duffield added impatiently, as Ciara began to protest, 'but he's not the first one I've known who's gone funny over a girlfriend. He'll fuck anything, man-wise, but he didn't want to let her out of his sight. He threw hissy fits if she didn't see him, he didn't like her working for anyone else.

'He hates my fucking guts. Right back atcha, you little shit. Egging Lu on with Deeby Macc. He'd've got a real kick out of her fucking him. Doing me over. Hearing all the fucking details. Getting her to introduce him, get his fucking clothes photographed on a gangster. He's no fucking fool, Somé. He used her for his business all the time. Tried to get her cheap and for free, and she was dumb enough to let him.'

'Did Somé give you these?' asked Strike, pointing at the black leather gloves on the coffee table. He had recognised the tiny gold GS logo on the cuff.

'You what?'

Duffield leaned over and hooked one of the gloves on to an index finger; he dangled it in front of his eyes, examining it.

'Fuck, you're right. They're going in the bin, then,' and he threw the glove into a corner; it hit the abandoned guitar, which let out a hollow, echoing chord. 'I kept them from that shoot,' said Duffield, pointing at the black-and-white magazine cover. 'Somé wouldn't give me the steam off his piss. Have you got another fag?'

'I'm all out,' lied Strike. 'Are you going to tell me why you invited me home, Evan?'

There was a long silence. Duffield glared at Strike, who intuited that the actor knew he was lying about having no cigarettes. Ciara was gazing at him too, her lips slightly parted, the epitome of beautiful bewilderment.

'What makes you think I've got anything to tell you?' sneered Duffield.

'I don't think you asked me back here for the pleasure of my company.'

'I dunno,' said Duffield, with a distinct overtone of malice. 'Maybe I hoped you were a laugh, like your old man?'

'Evan,' snapped Ciara.

'OK, if you haven't got anything to tell me . . . ' said Strike, and he pushed himself up out of the armchair. To his slight surprise, and Duffield's evident displeasure, Ciara set her empty wine glass down and began to unfold her long legs, preparatory to standing.

'All right,' said Duffield sharply. 'There's one thing.'

Strike sank back into his chair. Ciara thrust one of her own cigarettes at Duffield, who took it with muttered thanks, then she too sat down, watching Strike.

'Go on,' said the latter, while Duffield fiddled with his lighter.

'All right. I dunno whether it matters,' said the actor. 'But I don't want you to say where you got the information.'

'I can't guarantee that,' said Strike.

Duffield scowled, his knees jumping up and down, smoking with his eyes on the floor. Out of the corner of his eye, Strike saw Ciara open her mouth to speak, and forestalled her, one hand in the air.

'Well,' said Duffield, 'two days ago I was having lunch with Freddie Bestigui. He left his BlackBerry on the table when he went up to the bar.' Duffield puffed and jiggled. 'I don't wanna be fired,' he said, glaring at Strike. 'I need this fucking job.'

'Go on,' said Strike.

'He got an email. I saw Lula's name. I read it.'

'OK.'

'It was from his wife. It said something like, "I know we're supposed to be talking through lawyers, but unless you can do better than £1.5 million, I will tell everyone exactly where I was when Lula Landry died, and exactly how I got there, because I'm sick of taking shit for you. This is not an empty threat. I'm starting to think I should tell the police anyway." Or something like that,' said Duffield.

Dimly, through the curtained window, came the sound of a couple of the paparazzi outside laughing together.

'That's very useful information,' Strike told Duffield. 'Thank you.'

'I don't want Bestigui to know it was me who told you.'

'I don't think your name'll need to come into it,' said Strike, standing up again. 'Thanks for the water.'

'Hang on, sweetie, I'm coming,' said Ciara, her phone pressed to her ear. 'Kieran? We're coming out now, Cormoran and me. Right now. Bye-bye, Evan darling.'

She bent over and kissed him on both cheeks, while Duffield, halfway out of his chair, looked disconcerted.

'You can crash here if you—'

'No, sweetie, I've got a job tomorrow afternoon; need my beauty sleep,' she said.

More flashes blinded Strike as he stepped outside; but the paparazzi seemed confused this time. As he helped Ciara down the steps, and followed her into the back of the car, one of them shouted at Strike: 'Who the fuck are you?'

Strike slammed the door, grinning. Kolovas-Jones was back in the driver's seat; they were pulling away from the kerb, and this time they were not pursued.

After a block or so of silence, Kolovas-Jones looked in the rear-view mirror and asked Ciara:

'Home?'

'I suppose so. Kieran, will you turn on the radio? I fancy a bit of music,' she said. 'Louder than that, sweetie. Oh, I love this.'

'Telephone' by Lady Gaga filled the car.

She turned to Strike as the orange glow of street lights swept across her extraordinary face. Her breath smelled of alcohol, her skin of that sweet, peppery perfume.

'Don't you want to ask me anything else?'

'You know what?' said Strike. 'I do. Why would you have a detachable lining in a handbag?'

She stared at him for several seconds, then let out a great giggle, slumping sideways into his shoulder, nudging him. Lithe and slight, she continued to rest against him as she said:

'You *are* funny.'

'But why would you?'

'Well, it just makes the bag more, like, individual; you can customise them, you see; you can buy a couple of linings and swap them over; you can pull them out and use them as scarves; they're beautiful. Silk with gorgeous patterns. The zip edging is very rock-and-roll.'

'Interesting,' said Strike, as her upper leg moved to rest lightly along his own, and she gave a second, deep-throated giggle.

Call all you want, but there's no one home, sang Lady Gaga.

The music masked their conversation, but Kolovas-Jones's eyes were moving with unnecessary regularity from road ahead to rear-view mirror. After another minute, Ciara said:

'Guy's right, I do like them big. You're very *butch*. And, like, *stern*. It's sexy.'

A block later she whispered:

'Where do you live?' while rubbing her silky cheek against his, like a cat.

'I sleep on a camp bed in my office.'

She giggled again. She was definitely a little drunk.

'Are you serious?'

'Yeah.'

'We'll go to mine, then, shall we?'

Her tongue was cool and sweet and tasted of Pernod.

'Have you slept with my father?' he managed to say, between the pressings of her full lips on to his.

'No . . . *God*, no . . . ' A little giggle. 'He dyes his hair . . . it's, like, *purple* close up . . . I used to call him the rocking prune . . . '

And then, ten minutes later, a lucid voice in his mind urging him not to let desire lead on to humiliation, he surfaced for air to mutter:

'I've only got one leg.'

'Don't be silly . . . '

'I'm not being silly . . . it got blown off in Afghanistan.'

'Poor baby . . . ' she whispered. 'I'll rub it better.'

'Yeah – that's not my leg . . . It's helping, though . . . '

9

Robin ran up the clanging metal stairs in the same low heels that she had worn the previous day. Twenty-four hours ago, unable to dislodge the word 'gumshoe' from her mind, she had selected her frumpiest footwear for a day's walking; today, excited by what she had achieved in the old black shoes, they had taken on the glamour of Cinderella's glass slippers. Hardly able to wait to tell Strike everything she had found out, she had almost run to Denmark Street through the sunlit rubble. She was confident that any lingering awkwardness after Strike's drunken escapades of two nights previously would be utterly eclipsed by their mutual excitement about her dazzling solo discoveries of the previous day.

But when she reached the second landing, she pulled up short. For the third time, the glass door was locked, and the office beyond it unlit and silent.

She let herself in and made a swift survey of the evidence. The door to the inner office stood open. Strike's camp bed was folded neatly away. There was no sign of an evening meal in the bin. The computer monitor was dark, the kettle cold. Robin was forced to conclude that Strike had not (as she phrased it to herself) spent the night at home.

She hung up her coat, then took from her handbag a small notebook, turned on the computer and, after a few minutes' hopeful but fruitless wait, began to type up a precis of what she had found out the day before. She had barely slept for the excitement of telling Strike everything in person. Typing it all out was a bitter anticlimax. Where was he?

As her fingers flew over the keyboard, an answer she did not much like presented itself for her consideration. Devastated as he had been at the news of his ex's engagement, was it not likely that he had gone to beg her not to marry this other man? Hadn't he shouted to the whole of Charing Cross Road that Charlotte did not love Jago Ross? Perhaps, after all, it was true; perhaps Charlotte had thrown herself into Strike's arms, and they were now reconciled, lying asleep, entwined, in the house or flat from which he had been ejected four weeks ago. Robin remembered Lucy's oblique enquiries and insinuations about Charlotte, and suspected that any such reunion would not bode well for her job security. *Not that it matters*, she reminded herself, typing furiously, and with uncharacteristic inaccuracy. *You're leaving in a week's time.* The reflection made her feel even more agitated.

Alternatively, of course, Strike had gone to Charlotte and she had turned him away. In that case, the matter of his current whereabouts became a matter of more pressing, less personal concern. What if he had gone out, unchecked and unprotected, hell-bent on intoxication again? Robin's busy fingers slowed and stopped, mid-sentence. She swivelled on her computer chair to look at the silent office telephone.

She might well be the only person who knew that Cormoran Strike was not where he was supposed to be. Perhaps she ought to call him on his mobile? And if he did not pick up? How many hours ought she to let elapse before contacting the police? The idea of ringing Matthew at his office and asking his advice came to her, only to be swatted away.

She and Matthew had rowed when Robin arrived home, very late, after walking a drunken Strike back to the office from the Tottenham. Matthew had told her yet again that she was naive, impressionable and a sucker for a hard-luck story; that Strike was after a secretary on the cheap, and using emotional blackmail to achieve his ends; that there was probably no Charlotte at all, that it was all an extravagant ploy to engage Robin's sympathy and services. Then Robin had lost her temper, and told Matthew that if anybody was blackmailing her it was he, with his constant harping on the money she ought to be bringing in, and his insinuation that she was not pulling her weight. Hadn't he noticed that she was enjoying working for Strike; hadn't it crossed his insensitive, obtuse *accountant's* mind that she might be dreading the tedious bloody job in human resources? Matthew had been aghast, and then (though reserving the right to deplore Strike's behaviour) apologetic; but Robin, usually conciliatory and amiable, had remained aloof and angry. The truce effected the following morning had prickled with antagonism, mainly Robin's.

Now, in the silence, watching the telephone, some of her anger at Matthew spilled over on to Strike. Where was he? What was he doing? Why was he acting up to Matthew's accusations of irresponsibility? She was here, holding the fort, and he was presumably off chasing his ex-fiancée, and never mind their business . . .

. . . *his* business . . .

Footsteps on the stairwell: Robin thought she recognised the very slight unevenness in Strike's tread. She waited, glaring towards the stairs, until she was sure that the footfalls were proceeding beyond the first landing; then she turned her chair resolutely back to face the monitor and began pounding at the keys again, while her heart raced.

'Morning.'

'Hi.'

She accorded Strike a fleeting glance while continuing to type. He looked tired, unshaven and unnaturally well dressed. She was instantly confirmed in her view that he had attempted a reconciliation with Charlotte; by the looks of it, successfully. The next two sentences were pockmarked with typos.

'How're things?' asked Strike, noting Robin's clench-jawed profile, her cold demeanour.

'Fine,' said Robin.

She now intended to lay her perfectly typed report in front of him, and then, with icy calm, discuss the arrangements for her departure. She might suggest that he hire another temp this week, so that she could instruct her replacement in the day-to-day management of the office before she left.

Strike, whose run of appalling luck had been broken in fabulous style just a few hours previously, and who was feeling as close to buoyant as he had been for many months, had been looking forward to seeing his secretary. He had no intention of regaling her with an account of his night's activities (or at least, not those that had done so much to restore his battered ego), for he was instinctively close-lipped about such matters, and he was hoping to shore up as much as remained of the boundaries that had been splintered by his copious consumption of Doom Bar. He had, however, been planning an eloquent speech of apology for his excesses of two nights before, an avowal of gratitude, and an exposition of all the interesting conclusions he had drawn from yesterday's interviews.

'Fancy a cup of tea?'

'No thanks.'

He looked at his watch.

'I'm only eleven minutes late.'

'It's up to you when you arrive. I mean,' she attempted to backtrack, for her tone had been too obviously hostile, 'it's none of my business what you – when you get here.'

From having mentally rehearsed a number of soothing and magnanimous responses to Strike's imagined apologies for his drunken behaviour of forty-eight hours previously, she now felt that his attitude was distastefully free of shame or remorse.

Strike busied himself with kettle and cups, and a few minutes later set down a mug of steaming tea beside her.

'I said I didn't—'

'Could you leave that important document for a minute while I say something to you?'

She saved the report with several thumps of the keys and turned to face him, her arms folded across her chest. Strike sat down on the old sofa.

'I wanted to say sorry about the night before last.'

'There's no need,' she said, in a small, tight voice.

'Yeah, there is. I can't remember much of what I did. I hope I wasn't obnoxious.'

'You weren't.'

'You probably got the gist. My ex-fiancée's just got engaged to an old boyfriend. It took her three weeks after we split to get another ring on her finger. That's just a figure of speech; I never actually bought her a ring; I never had the money.'

Robin gathered, from his tone, that there had been no reconciliation; but in that case, where had he spent the night? She unfolded her arms and unthinkingly picked up her tea.

'It wasn't your responsibility to come and find me like that, but you probably stopped me collapsing in a gutter or punching someone, so thanks very much.'

'No problem,' said Robin.

'And thanks for the Alka-Seltzer,' said Strike.

'Did it help?' asked Robin, stiffly.

'I nearly puked all over this,' said Strike, dealing the sagging sofa a gentle punch with his fist, 'but once it kicked in, it helped a lot.'

Robin laughed, and Strike remembered, for the first time, the note she had pushed under the door while he slept, and the excuse she had given for her tactful absence.

'Right, well, I've been looking forward to hearing how you got on yesterday,' he lied. 'Don't keep me in suspense.'

Robin expanded like a water blossom.

'I was just typing it up . . . '

'Let's have it verbally, and you can put it into the file later,' said Strike, with the mental reservation that it would be easy to remove if useless.

'OK,' said Robin, both excited and nervous. 'Well, like I said in my note, I saw that you wanted to look into Professor Agyeman, and the Malmaison Hotel in Oxford.'

Strike nodded, grateful for the reminder, because he had not been able to remember the details of the note, read once in the depths of his blinding hangover.

'So,' said Robin, a little breathlessly, 'first of all I went along to Russell Square, to SOAS; the School of Oriental and African Studies. That's what your notes meant, isn't it?' she added. 'I checked a map: it's walking distance from the British Museum. Isn't that what all those scribbles meant?'

Strike nodded again.

'Well, I went in there and pretended I was writing a dissertation on African politics, and I wanted some information on Professor Agyeman. I ended up speaking to this really helpful secretary in the politics department, who'd actually worked for him, and she gave me loads of information on him, including a bibliography and a brief biography. He studied at SOAS as an undergraduate.'

'He did?'

'Yes,' said Robin. 'And I got a picture.'

From inside the notebook she pulled out a photocopy, and passed it across to Strike.

He saw a black man with a long, high-cheekboned face; close-cropped greying hair and beard and gold-rimmed glasses supported by overlarge ears. He stared at it for several long moments, and when at last he spoke, he said:

'Christ.'

Robin waited, elated.

'*Christ*,' said Strike again. 'When did he die?'

'Five years ago. The secretary got upset talking about it. She said he was so clever, and the nicest, kindest man. A committed Christian.'

'Any family?'

'Yes. He left a widow and a son.'

'A son,' repeated Strike.

'Yes,' said Robin. 'He's in the army.'

'In the army,' said Strike, her deep and doleful echo. 'Don't tell me.'

'He's in Afghanistan.'

Strike got up and started pacing up and down, the picture of Professor Josiah Agyeman in his hand.

'Didn't get a regiment, did you? Not that it matters. I can find out,' he said.

'I did ask,' said Robin, consulting her notes, 'but I don't really understand – is there a regiment called the Sappers or some—'

'Royal Engineers,' said Strike. 'I can check up on all that.'

He stopped beside Robin's desk, and stared again at the face of Professor Josiah Agyeman.

'He was from Ghana originally,' she said. 'But the family lived in Clerkenwell until he died.'

Strike handed her back the picture.

'Don't lose that. You've done bloody well, Robin.'

'That's not all,' she said, flushed, excited and trying to keep from smiling. 'I took the train out to Oxford in the afternoon, to the Malmaison. Do you know, they've made a hotel out of an old prison?'

'Really?' said Strike, sinking back on to the sofa.

'Yes. It's quite nice, actually. Well, anyway, I thought I'd pretend to be Alison and check whether Tony Landry had left something there or something . . .'

Strike sipped his tea, thinking that it was highly implausible that a secretary would be dispatched in person for such an enquiry three months after the event.

'Anyway, that was a mistake.'

'Really?' he said, his tone carefully neutral.

'Yes, because Alison actually did go to the Malmaison on the seventh, to try and find Tony Landry. It was incredibly embarrassing, because one of the girls on reception had been there that day, and she remembered her.'

Strike lowered his mug.

'Now that,' he said, 'is very interesting indeed.'

'I know,' said Robin excitedly. 'So then I had to think really fast.'

'Did you tell them your name was Annabel?'

'No,' she said, on a half-laugh. 'I said, well, OK then, I'll tell the truth, I'm his girlfriend. And I cried a bit.'

'You cried?'

'It wasn't actually that hard,' said Robin, with an air of surprise. 'I got right into character. I said I thought he was having an affair.'

'*Not* with Alison? If they've seen her, they wouldn't believe that . . .'

'No, but I said I didn't think he'd really been at the hotel at all . . . Anyway, I made a bit of a scene and the girl who'd spoken to Alison took me aside and tried to calm me down; she said they couldn't give out information about people without a good reason, they had a policy, blah blah . . . you know. But just to stop me crying, in the end she told me that he had checked in on the evening of the sixth, and checked out on the morning of the eighth. He made a fuss about being given the wrong newspaper while he was checking out, that's why she remembered. So he was *definitely* there. I even asked her a bit, you know, hysterically, how she knew it was him, and she described him to a T. I know what he looks like,' she added, before Strike could ask. 'I checked before I left; his picture's on the Landry, May, Patterson website.'

'You're brilliant,' said Strike, 'and this is all bloody fishy. What did she tell you about Alison?'

'That she arrived and asked to see him, but he wasn't there. They confirmed that he was staying with them, though. And then she left.'

'Very odd. She should have known he was at the conference; why didn't she go there first?'

'I don't know.'

'Did this helpful hotel employee say she'd seen him at any times other than check-in and check-out?'

'No,' said Robin. 'But we know he went to the conference, don't we? I checked that, remember?'

'We know he signed in, and probably picked up a name tag. And then he drove back to Chelsea to see his sister, Lady Bristow. Why?'

'Well . . . she was ill.'

'Was she? She'd just had an operation that was supposed to cure her.'

'A hysterectomy,' said Robin. 'I don't imagine you'd feel wonderful after that.'

'So we've got a man who doesn't like his sister very much – I've had that from his own lips – who believes she's just had a life-saving operation and knows she's got two of her children in attendance. Why the urgency to see her?'

'Well,' said Robin, with less certainty, 'I suppose . . . she'd just got out of hospital . . . '

'Which he presumably knew was going to happen before he drove off to Oxford. So why not stay in town, visit her if he felt that strongly about it, and then head out to the afternoon session of the conference? Why drive fifty-odd miles, stay overnight in this plush prison, go to the conference, sign in and then double back to town?'

'Maybe he got a call saying she was feeling bad, something like that? Maybe John Bristow rang him and asked him to come?'

'Bristow's never mentioned asking his uncle to drop in. I'd say they were on bad terms at the time. They're both shifty about that visit of Landry's. Neither of them likes talking about it.'

Strike stood up and began to walk up and down, limping slightly, barely noticing the pain in his leg.

'No,' he said, 'Bristow asking his sister, who by all accounts was the apple of his mother's eye, to drop by – that makes sense. Asking his mother's brother, who was out of town and by no means her biggest fan, to make a massive detour to see her . . . that doesn't smell right. And now we find out that Alison went looking for Landry at his hotel in Oxford. It was a work day. Was she checking up on him on her own account, or did someone send her?'

The telephone rang. Robin picked up the receiver. To Strike's surprise, she immediately affected a very stilted Australian accent.

'Oy'm sorry, shiz not here . . . Naoh . . . Naoh . . . I dunnaoh where she iz . . . Naoh . . . My nem's Annabel . . . '

Strike laughed quietly. Robin threw him a look of mock anguish. After nearly a minute of strangled Australian, she hung up.

'Temporary Solutions,' she said.

'I'm getting through a lot of Annabels. That one sounded more South African than Australian.'

'Now I want to hear what happened to you yesterday,' said Robin, unable to conceal her impatience any longer. 'Did you meet Bryony Radford and Ciara Porter?'

Strike told her everything that had happened, omitting only the aftermath of his excursion to Evan Duffield's flat. He placed particular emphasis on Bryony Radford's insistence that it was dyslexia that had caused her to listen to Ursula May's voicemail messages; on Ciara Porter's continuing assertion that Lula had told her she would leave everything to her brother; on Evan Duffield's annoyance that Lula had kept checking the time while she was in Uzi; and on the threatening email that Tansy Bestigui had sent her estranged husband.

'So where *was* Tansy?' asked Robin, who had listened to every word of Strike's story with gratifying attention. 'If we can just find out . . . '

'Oh, I'm pretty sure I know where she was,' said Strike. 'It's getting her to admit it, when it might blow her chances of a multimillion-pound settlement from Freddie, that's going to be the difficult bit. You'll be able to work it out too, if you just look through the police photographs again.'

'But . . .'

'Have a look at the pictures of the front of the building on the morning Lula died, and then think about how it was when we saw it. It'll be good for your detective training.'

Robin experienced a great surge of excitement and happiness, immediately tempered by a cold pang of regret, because she would soon be leaving for human resources.

'I need to change,' said Strike, standing up. 'Please will you try Freddie Bestigui again for me?'

He disappeared into the inner room, closed the door behind him and swapped his lucky suit (as he thought he might henceforth call it) for an old and comfortable shirt, and a roomier pair of trousers. When he passed Robin's desk on the way to the bathroom, she was on the telephone, wearing that expression of disinterested attentiveness that betokens a person on hold. Strike cleaned his teeth in the cracked basin, reflecting on how much easier life with Robin would be, now that he had tacitly admitted that he lived in the office, and returned to find her off the telephone and looking exasperated.

'I don't think they're even bothering to take my messages now,' she told Strike. 'They say he's out at Pinewood Studios and can't be disturbed.'

'Ah well, at least we know he's back in the country,' said Strike.

He took the interim report out of the filing cabinet, sank back down on the sofa and began to add his notes of yesterday's conversations, in silence. Robin watched out of the corner of her eye, fascinated by the meticulousness with which Strike tabulated his findings, making a precise record of how, where and from whom he had gained each piece of information.

'I suppose,' she asked, after a long stretch of silence, during which she had divided her time between covert observation of Strike at work, and examination of a photograph of the front of number 18, Kentigern Gardens on Google Earth, 'you have to be very careful, in case you forget anything?'

'It's not only that,' said Strike, still writing, and not looking up. 'You don't want to give defending counsel any footholds.'

He spoke so calmly, so reasonably that Robin considered the implication of his words for several moments, in case she could have misunderstood.

'You mean . . . in general?' she said at last. 'On principle?'

'No,' said Strike, continuing his report. 'I mean that I specifically do not want to allow the defending counsel in the trial of the person who killed Lula Landry to get off because he was able to show that I can't keep records properly, thereby calling into question my reliability as a witness.'

Strike was showing off again, and he knew it; but he could not help himself. He was, as he put it to himself, on a roll. Some might have questioned the taste of finding amusement in the midst of a murder inquiry, but he had found humour in darker places.

'Couldn't nip out for some sandwiches, Robin, could you?' he added, just so that he could glance up at her satisfyingly astonished expression.

He finished his notes during her absence, and was just about to call an old colleague in Germany when Robin burst back in, holding two packs of sandwiches and a newspaper.

'Your picture's on the front of the *Standard*,' she panted.

'What?'

It was a photograph of Ciara following Duffield into his flat. Ciara looked stunning; for half a second Strike was transported back to half past two that morning, when she had lain, white and naked, beneath him, that long silky hair spread on the pillow like a mermaid's as she whispered and moaned.

Strike refocused: he was half cropped out of the picture; one arm raised to keep the paparazzi at bay.

'That's all right,' he told Robin with a shrug, handing her back the paper. 'They think I was the minder.'

'It says,' said Robin, turning to the inside page, 'that she left Duffield's with her security guard at two.'

'There you go, then.'

Robin stared at him. His account of the night had terminated with himself, Duffield and Ciara at Duffield's flat. She had been so interested in the various pieces of evidence he had laid out before her, she had forgotten to wonder where he had slept. She had assumed that he had left the model and the actor together.

He had arrived at the office still wearing the clothes in the photograph.

She turned away, reading the story on page two. The clear implication of the piece was that Ciara and Duffield had enjoyed an amorous encounter while the supposed minder waited in the hall.

'Is she stunning-looking in person?' asked Robin with an unconvincing casualness as she folded the *Standard*.

'Yeah, she is,' said Strike, and he wondered whether it was his imagination that the three syllables sounded like a boast. 'D'you want cheese and pickle, or egg mayonnaise?'

Robin made her selection at random and returned to her

desk chair to eat. Her new hypothesis about Strike's overnight whereabouts had eclipsed even her excitement over the progress of the case. It was going to be difficult to reconcile her view of him as a blighted romantic with the fact that he had just (it seemed incredible, and yet she had heard his pathetic attempt to conceal his pride) slept with a supermodel.

The telephone rang again. Strike, whose mouth was full of bread and cheese, raised a hand to forestall Robin, swallowed, and answered it himself.

'Cormoran Strike.'

'Strike, it's Wardle.'

'Hi, Wardle; how's it going?'

'Not so good, actually. We've just fished a body out of the Thames with your card on it. Wondered what you could tell us about it.'

10

It was the first taxi that Strike had felt justified in taking since the day he had moved his belongings out of Charlotte's flat. He watched the charges mount with detachment, as the cab rolled towards Wapping. The taxi driver was determined to tell him why Gordon Brown was a fucking disgrace. Strike sat in silence for the entire trip.

This would not be the first morgue Strike had visited, and far from the first corpse he had viewed. He had become almost immune to the despoliation of gunshot wounds; bodies ripped, torn and shattered, innards revealed like the contents of a butcher's shop, shining and bloody. Strike had never been squeamish; even the most mutilated corpses, cold and white in their freezer drawers, became sanitised and standardised to a man with his job. It was the bodies he had seen in the raw, unprocessed and unprotected by officialdom and procedure, that rose again and crawled through his dreams. His mother in the funeral parlour, in her favourite floor-length bell-sleeved dress, gaunt yet young, with no needle marks on view. Sergeant Gary Topley lying in the blood-spattered dust of that Afghanistan road, his face unscathed, but with no body below the upper ribs. As Strike had lain in the hot dirt, he had tried not to look at Gary's empty face, afraid to glance down and see how much of his own body was missing . . . but he had slid so swiftly into the maw of oblivion that he did not find out until he woke up in the field hospital . . .

An Impressionist print hung on the bare brick walls of the small anteroom to the morgue. Strike fixed his gaze on it, wondering where he had seen it before, and finally remembering that it hung over the mantelpiece at Lucy and Greg's.

'Mr Strike?' said the grey-haired mortician, peering around the inner door, in white coat and latex gloves. 'Come on in.'

They were almost always cheerful, pleasant men, these curators of corpses. Strike followed the mortician into the chilly glare of the large, windowless inner room, with its great steel freezer doors all along the right-hand wall. The gently sloping tiled floor ran down to a central drain; the lights were dazzling. Every noise echoed off the hard and shiny surfaces, so that it sounded as though a small group of men was marching into the room.

A metal trolley stood ready in front of one of the freezer doors, and beside it were the two CID officers, Wardle and Carver. The former greeted Strike with a nod and a muttered greeting; the latter, paunchy and mottle-faced, with suit shoulders covered in dandruff, merely grunted.

The mortician wrenched down the thick metal arm on the freezer door. The tops of three anonymous heads were revealed, stacked one above the other, each draped in a white sheet worn limp and fine through repeated washings. The mortician checked the tag pinned to the cloth covering the central head; it bore no name, only the previous day's scribbled date. He slid the body out smoothly on its long-runnered tray and deposited it efficiently on to the waiting trolley. Strike noticed Carver's jaw working as he stepped back, giving the mortician room to wheel the trolley clear of the freezer door. With a clunk and a slam, the remaining corpses vanished from view.

'We won't bother with a viewing room, seeing as we're the only ones here,' said the mortician briskly. 'Light's best in the middle,' he added, positioning the trolley just beside the drain, and pulling back the sheet.

The body of Rochelle Onifade was revealed, bloated and distended, her face forever wiped of suspicion, replaced by a kind of empty wonder. Strike had known, from Wardle's brief description on the telephone, whom he would see when the sheet was revealed, but the awful vulnerability of the dead struck him anew as he looked down on the body, far smaller than it had been when she had sat opposite him, consuming fries and concealing information.

Strike told them her name, spelling it so that both the mortician and Wardle could transcribe it accurately on to clipboard and notebook respectively; he also gave the only address he had ever known for her: St Elmo's Hostel for the Homeless, in Hammersmith.

'Who found her?'

'River police hooked her out late last night,' said Carver, speaking for the first time. His voice, with its south London accent, held a definite undertone of animosity. 'Bodies usually take about three weeks to rise to the surface, eh?' he added, directing the comment, more statement than question, at the mortician, who gave a tiny, cautious cough.

'That's the accepted average, but I wouldn't be surprised if it turns out to be less in this case. There are certain indications . . . '

'Yeah, well, we'll get all that from the pathologist,' said Carver, dismissively.

'It can't have been three weeks,' said Strike, and the mortician gave him a tiny smile of solidarity.

'Why not?' demanded Carver.

'Because I bought her a burger and chips two weeks ago yesterday.'

'Ah,' said the mortician, nodding at Strike across the body. 'I was going to say that a lot of carbohydrates taken prior to death can affect the body's buoyancy. There's a degree of bloating . . . '

'That's when you gave her your card, is it?' Wardle asked Strike.

'Yeah. I'm surprised it was still legible.'

'It was stuck in with her Oyster card, in a plastic cover inside her back jeans pocket. The plastic protected it.'

'What was she wearing?'

'Big pink fake-fur coat. Like a skinned Muppet. Jeans and trainers.'

'That's what she was wearing when I bought her the burger.'

'In that case, the contents of the stomach should give an accurate—' began the mortician.

'D'you know if she's got any next of kin?' Carver demanded of Strike.

'There's an aunt in Kilburn. I don't know her name.'

Slivers of glistening eyeball showed through Rochelle's almost closed lids; they had the characteristic brightness of the drowned. There were traces of bloody foam in the creases around her nostrils.

'How are her hands?' Strike asked the mortician, because Rochelle was uncovered only to the chest.

'Never mind her hands,' snapped Carver. 'We're done here, thanks,' he told the mortician loudly, his voice reverberating around the room; and then, to Strike: 'We want a word with you. Car's outside.'

He was helping police with their inquiries. Strike remembered hearing the phrase on the news when he had been a small boy, obsessed by every aspect of police work. His mother had always blamed this strange early preoccupation on her brother,

Ted, ex-Red Cap and fount of (to Strike) thrilling stories of travel, mystery and adventure. *Helping police with their inquiries*: as a five-year-old, Strike had imagined a noble and disinterested citizen volunteering to give up his time and energy to assist the police, who issued him with magnifying glass and truncheon and allowed him to operate under a cloak of glamorous anonymity.

This was the reality: a small interrogation room, with a cup of machine-made coffee given to him by Wardle, whose attitude towards Strike was devoid of the animosity that crackled from Carver's every open pore, but free of every trace of former friendliness. Strike suspected that Wardle's superior did not know the full extent of their previous interactions.

A small black tray on the scratched desk held seventeen pence in change, a single Yale key and a plastic-covered bus pass; Strike's card was discoloured and crinkled but still legible.

'What about her bag?' Strike asked Carver, who was sitting across the desk, while Wardle leaned up against the filing cabinet in the corner. 'Grey. Cheap and plastic-looking. That hasn't turned up, has it?'

'She probably left it in her squat, or wherever the fuck she lived,' said Carver. 'Suicides don't usually pack a bag to jump.'

'I don't think she jumped,' said Strike.

'Oh don't you, now?'

'I wanted to see her hands. She hated water over her face, she told me so. When people have struggled in the water, the position of their hands—'

'Well, it's nice to get your expert opinion,' said Carver, with sledgehammer irony. 'I know who you are, Mr Strike.'

He leaned back in his chair, placing his hands behind his head, revealing dried patches of sweat on the underarms of his shirt. The sharp, sour, oniony smell of BO wafted across the desk.

'He's ex-SIB,' threw in Wardle, from beside the filing cabinet.

'I know that,' barked Carver, raising wiry eyebrows flecked with scurf. 'I've heard from Anstis all about the fucking leg and the life-saving medal. Quite the colourful CV.'

Carver removed his hands from behind his head, leaned forwards and laced his fingers together on the desk instead. His corned-beef complexion and the purple bags under his hard eyes were not flattered by the strip lighting.

'I know who your old man is and all.'

Strike scratched his unshaven chin, waiting.

'Like to be as rich and famous as Daddy, would you? Is that what all this is about?'

Carver had the bright blue, bloodshot eyes that Strike had always (since meeting a major in the Paras with just such eyes, who was subsequently cashiered for serious bodily harm) associated with a choleric, violent nature.

'Rochelle didn't jump. Nor did Lula Landry.'

'Bollocks,' shouted Carver. 'You're speaking to the two men who *proved* Landry jumped. We went through every bit of fucking evidence with a fine-toothed fucking comb. I know what you're up to. You're milking that poor sod Bristow for all you can get. Why are you fucking smiling at me?'

'I'm thinking what a tit you're going to look when this interview gets reported in the press.'

'Don't you dare fucking threaten me with the press, dickhead.'

Carver's blunt, wide face was clenched; his glaring blue eyes vivid in the purple-red face.

'You're in a heap of trouble here, pal, and a famous dad, a

peg-leg and a good war aren't going to get you out of it. How do we know you didn't scare the poor bitch into fucking jumping? Mentally ill, wasn't she? How do we know you didn't make her think she'd done something wrong? You were the last person to see her alive, pal. I wouldn't like to be sitting where you are now.'

'Rochelle crossed Grantley Road and walked away from me, as alive as you are. You'll find someone who saw her after she left me. Nobody's going to forget that coat.'

Wardle pushed himself off the filing cabinets, dragged a hard plastic chair over to the desk and sat down.

'Let's have it, then,' he told Strike. 'Your theory.'

'She was blackmailing Lula Landry's killer.'

'Piss off,' snapped Carver, and Wardle snorted in slightly stagey amusement.

'The day before she died,' said Strike, 'Landry met Rochelle for fifteen minutes in that shop. She dragged Rochelle straight into a changing cubicle, where she made a telephone call begging somebody to meet her at her flat in the early hours of the following morning. That call was overheard by an assistant at the shop; she was in the next cubicle; they're separated by a curtain. Girl called Mel, red hair and tattoos.'

'People will spout any amount of shit when there's a celebrity involved,' said Carver.

'If Landry phoned anyone from that cubicle,' said Wardle, 'it was Duffield, or her uncle. Her phone records show they were the only people she called, all afternoon.'

'Why did she want Rochelle there when she made the call?' asked Strike. 'Why drag her friend into the cubicle with her?'

'Women do that stuff,' said Carver. 'They piss in herds, too.'

'Use your fucking intelligence: she was making the call on

Rochelle's phone,' said Strike, exasperated. 'She'd tested everyone she knew to try and see who was talking to the press about her. Rochelle was the only one who kept her mouth shut. She established that the girl was trustworthy, bought her a mobile, registered it in Rochelle's name but took care of all the charges. She'd had her own phone hacked, hadn't she? She was getting paranoid about people listening in and reporting on her, so she bought a Nokia and registered it to somebody else, to give herself a totally secure means of communication when she wanted it.

'I grant you, that doesn't necessarily rule out her uncle, or Duffield, because calling them on the alternative number might have been a signal they'd organised between them. Alternatively, she was using Rochelle's number to speak to somebody else; someone she didn't want the press to know about. I've got Rochelle's mobile number. Find out what network she was with and you'll be able to check all this. The unit itself is a crystal-covered pink Nokia, but you won't find that.'

'Yeah, because it's at the bottom of the Thames,' said Wardle.

'Course it isn't,' said Strike. 'The killer's got it. He'll have got it off her before he threw her into the river.'

'Fuck off!' jeered Carver, and Wardle, who had seemed interested against his better judgement, shook his head.

'Why did Landry want Rochelle there when she made the call?' Strike repeated. 'Why not make it from the car? Why, when Rochelle was homeless, and virtually destitute, did she never sell her story on Landry? They'd have given her a great wad for it. Why didn't she cash in, once Landry was dead, and couldn't be hurt?'

'Decency?' suggested Wardle.

'Yeah, that's one possibility,' said Strike. 'The other's that she was making enough by blackmailing the killer.'

'*Boll-ocks*,' moaned Carver.

'Yeah? That Muppet coat she was pulled up wearing cost one and a half grand.'

A tiny pause.

'Landry probably gave it to her,' said Wardle.

'If she did, she managed to buy her something that wasn't in the shops back in January.'

'Landry was a model, she had inside contacts – fuck this shit,' snapped Carver, as though he had irritated himself.

'Why,' said Strike, leaning forwards on his arms into the miasma of body odour that surrounded Carver, 'did Lula Landry make a detour to that shop for fifteen minutes?'

'She was in a hurry.'

'Why go at all?'

'She didn't want to let the girl down.'

'She got Rochelle to come right across town – this penniless, homeless girl, the girl she usually gave a lift home afterwards, in her chauffeur-driven car – dragged her into a cubicle, and then walked out fifteen minutes later, leaving her to make her own way home.'

'She was a spoiled bitch.'

'If she was, why turn up at all? Because it was worth it, for some purpose of her own. And if she wasn't a spoiled bitch, she must have been in some kind of emotional state that made her act out of character. There's a living witness to the fact that Lula begged somebody, over the phone, to come and see her, at her flat, sometime after one in the morning. There's also that piece of blue paper she had before she went into Vashti, and which nobody's admitting to having seen since. What did she do with it? Why was she writing in the back of the car, before she saw Rochelle?'

'It could've been—' said Wardle.

'It wasn't a fucking shopping list,' groaned Strike, thumping the desk, 'and nobody writes a suicide note eight hours in advance, and then goes dancing. She was writing a bloody *will*, don't you get it? She took it into Vashti to get Rochelle to witness it and I think she tricked a pushy Aussie shop assistant into witnessing it as well—'

'Bollocks!' said Carver, yet again, but Strike ignored him, addressing Wardle.

'. . . which fits with her telling Ciara Porter that she was going to leave everything to her brother, doesn't it? She'd just made it legal. It was on her mind.'

'Why suddenly make a will?'

Strike hesitated and sat back. Carver leered at him.

'Imagination run out?'

Strike let out his breath in a long sigh. An uncomfortable night of alcohol-sodden unconsciousness; last night's pleasurable excesses; half a cheese and pickle sandwich in twelve hours: he felt hollowed-out, exhausted.

'If I had hard evidence, I'd have brought it to you.'

'The odds of people close to a suicide killing themselves go right up, did you know that? This Raquelle was a depressive. She has a bad day, remembers the way out her mate took, and does a copycat jump. Which leads us right back to *you*, pal, persecuting people and pushing them . . . '

'. . . over the edge, yeah,' said Strike. 'People keep saying that. Very poor fucking taste, in the circumstances. What about Tansy Bestigui's evidence?'

'How many times, Strike? We proved she couldn't have heard it,' Wardle said. 'We proved it beyond doubt.'

'No you didn't,' said Strike – finally, when he least expected it, losing his temper. 'You based your whole case on one almighty fuck-up. If you'd taken Tansy Bestigui seriously, if you'd broken her down and got her to tell you the whole fucking truth, Rochelle Onifade would still be alive.'

Pulsating with rage, Carver kept Strike there for another hour. His last act of contempt was to tell Wardle to make sure he saw 'Rokeby Junior' firmly off the premises.

Wardle walked Strike to the front door, not speaking.

'I need you to do something,' said Strike, halting at the exit, beyond which they could see the darkening sky.

'You've had enough from me already, mate,' said Wardle, with a wry smile. 'I'm gonna be dealing with that,' he jerked his thumb over his shoulder, towards Carver and his temper, 'for days because of you. I told you it was suicide.'

'Wardle, unless someone brings the fucker in, there are two more people in danger of being knocked off.'

'Strike . . .'

'What if I bring you proof that Tansy Bestigui wasn't in her flat at all when Lula fell? That she was somewhere she could have heard everything?'

Wardle looked up towards the ceiling, and closed his eyes momentarily.

'If you've got proof . . .'

'I haven't, but I will have in the next couple of days.'

Two men walked past them, talking, laughing. Wardle shook his head, looking exasperated, and yet he did not turn away.

'If you want something from the police, call Anstis. He's the one who owes you.'

'Anstis can't do this for me. I need you to call Deeby Macc.'

'What the fuck?'

'You heard me. He's not going to take my calls, is he? But

he'll speak to you; you've got the authority, and it sounds as though he liked you.'

'You're telling me Deeby Macc knows where Tansy Bestigui was when Lula Landry died?'

'No, of course he bloody doesn't, he was in Barrack. I want to know what clothes he got sent on from Kentigern Gardens to Claridge's. Specifically, what stuff he got from Guy Somé.'

Strike did not pronounce the name *Ghee* for Wardle.

'You want . . . why?'

'Because one of the runners on that CCTV footage was wearing one of Deeby's sweatshirts.'

Wardle's expression, arrested for a moment, relapsed into exasperation.

'You see that stuff everywhere,' he said after a moment or two. 'That GS stuff. Shell suits. Trackies.'

'This was a customised hoodie, there was only one of them in the world. Call Deeby, and ask him what he got from Somé. That's all I need. Whose side d'you want to be on if it turns out I'm right, Wardle?'

'Don't threaten me, Strike . . . '

'I'm not threatening you. I'm thinking about a multiple murderer who's walking around out there planning the next one – but if it's the papers you're worried about, I don't think they're going to go too easy on anyone who clung to the suicide theory once another body surfaced. Call Deeby Macc, Wardle, before someone else gets killed.'

11

'No,' said Strike forcefully, on the telephone that evening. 'This is getting dangerous. Surveillance doesn't fall within the scope of secretarial duties.'

'Nor did visiting the Malmaison Hotel in Oxford, or SOAS,' Robin pointed out, 'but you were happy enough that I did both of them.'

'You're not following anyone, Robin. I doubt Matthew would be very happy about it, either.'

It was funny, Robin thought, sitting in her dressing gown on her bed, with the phone pressed to her ear, how Strike had retained the name of her fiancé, without ever having met him. In her experience, men did not usually bother to log that kind of information. Matthew frequently forgot people's names, even that of his newborn niece; but she supposed that Strike must have been trained to recall such details.

'I don't need Matthew's permission,' she said. 'Anyway, it wouldn't be dangerous; you don't think *Ursula May*'s killed anyone . . .'

(There was an inaudible '*do* you?' at the end of the sentence.)

'No, but I don't want anyone to hear I'm taking an interest in her movements. It might make the killer nervous, and I don't want anyone else thrown from a height.'

Robin could hear her own heart thumping through the thin material of her dressing gown. She knew that he would not tell her who he thought the killer was; she was even a little frightened of knowing, notwithstanding the fact that she could think of nothing else.

It was she who had called Strike. Hours had passed since she had received a text saying that he had been compelled to go with the police to Scotland Yard, and asking her to lock up the office behind her at five. Robin had been worried.

'Call him, then, if it's going to keep you awake,' Matthew had said; not quite snapping, not quite indicating that he was, without knowing any of the details, firmly on the side of the police.

'Listen, I want you to do something for me,' said Strike. 'Call John Bristow first thing tomorrow and tell him about Rochelle.'

'All right,' said Robin, with her eyes on the large stuffed elephant Matthew had given her on their first Valentine's Day together, eight years previously. The present-giver himself was watching *Newsnight* in the sitting room. 'What are you going to be doing?'

'I'm going to be on my way to Pinewood Studios for a few words with Freddie Bestigui.'

'How?' said Robin. 'They won't let you near him.'

'Yeah, they will,' said Strike.

After Robin had hung up, Strike sat motionless for a while in his dark office. The thought of the semi-digested McDonald's meal lying inside Rochelle's bloated corpse had not prevented him consuming two Big Macs, a large box of fries and a McFlurry on the way back from Scotland Yard. Gassy noises from his stomach were now mingling with the muffled thuds of the bass from the 12 Bar Café, which Strike barely noticed these days; the sound might have been his own pulse.

Ciara Porter's messy, girlish flat, her wide, groaning mouth, the long white legs wrapped tightly around his back, belonged to a life lived long ago. All his thoughts, now, were for squat and graceless Rochelle Onifade. He remembered her talking fast into her phone, not five minutes after she had left him, dressed in exactly the same clothes she had been wearing when they pulled her out of the river.

He was sure he knew what had happened. Rochelle had called the killer to say that she had just lunched with a private detective; a meeting had been arranged over her glittering pink phone; that night, after a meal or a drink, they had sauntered through the dark towards the river. He thought of Hammersmith Bridge, sage green and gold, in the area where she claimed to have a new flat: a famous suicide spot, with its low sides, and the fast-flowing Thames below. She could not swim. Night-time: two lovers play-fighting, a car sweeps by, a scream and a splash. Would anyone have seen?

Not if the killer had iron-clad nerves and a liberal dash of luck; and this was a murderer who had already demonstrated plenty of the former, and an unnerving, reckless reliance on the latter. Defending counsel would undoubtedly argue diminished responsibility, because of the vainglorious overreaching that made Strike's quarry unique in his experience; and perhaps, he thought, there was some pathology there, some categorisable madness, but he was not much interested in the psychology. Like John Bristow, he wanted justice.

In the darkness of his office, his thoughts veered suddenly and unhelpfully back in time, to the most personal death of all; the one that Lucy assumed, quite wrongly, haunted Strike's every investigation, coloured every case; the killing that had fractured his and Lucy's lives into two epochs, so that everything in their memory was cleaved clearly into that which had happened before their mother died, and that which had happened afterwards. Lucy thought he had run away to join the RMP because of Leda's death; that he had been driven to it by his unsatisfied belief in his stepfather's guilt; that every corpse he saw in the course of his professional life must recall their mother to his mind; that every killer he met must seem to be an echo of their stepfather; that he was driven to investigate other deaths in an eternal act of personal exculpation.

But Strike had aspired to this career long before the last needle had entered Leda's body; long before he had understood that his mother (and every other human) was mortal, and that killings were more than puzzles to be solved. It was Lucy who never forgot, who lived in a swarm of memories like coffin flies; who projected on to any and all unnatural deaths the conflicting emotions aroused in her by their mother's untimely demise.

Tonight, however, he found himself doing the very thing that Lucy was sure must be habitual: he was remembering Leda and connecting her to this case. *Leda Strike, supergroupie.* It was how they always captioned her in the most famous photograph of all, and the only one that featured his parents together. There she was, in black and white, with her heart-shaped face, her shining dark hair and her marmoset eyes; and there, separated from each other by an art dealer, an aristocratic playboy (one since dead by his own hand, the other of AIDS) and Carla Astolfi, his father's second wife, was Jonny Rokeby himself, androgynous and wild: hair nearly as long as Leda's. Martini glasses and cigarettes, smoke curling out of the model's mouth, but his mother more stylish than any of them.

Everyone but Strike had seemed to view Leda's death as the

deplorable but unsurprising result of a life lived perilously, beyond societal norms. Even those who had known her best and longest were satisfied that she herself had administered the overdose they found in her body. His mother, by almost unanimous consent, had walked too close to the unsavoury edges of life, and it was only to be expected that she would one day topple out of sight and fall to her death, stiff and cold, on a filthy-sheeted bed.

Why she had done it, nobody could quite explain, not even Uncle Ted (silent and shattered, leaning against the kitchen sink) or Aunt Joan (red-eyed but angry at her little kitchen table, with her arms around nineteen-year-old Lucy, who was sobbing into Joan's shoulder). An overdose had simply seemed consistent with the trend of Leda's life; with the squats and the musicians and the wild parties; with the squalor of her final relationship and home; with the constant presence of drugs in her vicinity; with her reckless quest for thrills and highs. Strike alone had asked whether anyone had known his mother had taken to shooting up; he alone had seen a distinction between her predilection for cannabis and a sudden liking for heroin; he alone had unanswered questions and saw suspicious circumstances. But he had been a student of twenty, and nobody had listened.

After the trial and the conviction, Strike had packed up and left everything behind: the short-lived burst of press, Aunt Joan's desperate disappointment at the end of his Oxford career, Charlotte, bereft and incensed by his disappearance and already sleeping with someone new, Lucy's screams and scenes. With the sole support of Uncle Ted, he had vanished into the army, and refound there the life he had been taught by Leda: constant uprootings, self-reliance and the endless appeal of the new.

Tonight, though, he could not help seeing his mother as a spiritual sister to the beautiful, needy and depressive girl who had broken apart on a frozen road, and to the plain, homeless outsider now lying in the chilly morgue. Leda, Lula and Rochelle had not been women like Lucy, or his Aunt Joan; they had not taken every reasonable precaution against violence or chance; they had not tethered themselves to life with mortgages and voluntary work, safe husbands and clean-faced dependants: their deaths, therefore, were not classed as 'tragic', in the same way as those of staid and respectable housewives.

How easy it was to capitalise on a person's own bent for self-destruction; how simple to nudge them into non-being, then to stand back and shrug and agree that it had been the inevitable result of a chaotic, catastrophic life.

Nearly all the physical evidence of Lula's murder had long since been wiped away, trodden under foot or covered by thickly falling snow; the most persuasive clue Strike had was, after all, that grainy black-and-white footage of two men running away from the scene: a piece of evidence given a cursory check and tossed aside by the police, who were convinced that nobody could have entered the building, that Landry had committed suicide, and that the film showed nothing more than a pair of larcenous loiterers with intent.

Strike roused himself and looked at his watch. It was half past ten, but he was sure the man to whom he wished to speak would be awake. He flicked on his desk lamp, took up his mobile and dialled, this time, a number in Germany.

'Oggy,' bellowed the tinny voice on the other end of the phone. 'How the fuck are you?'

'Need a favour, mate.'

And Strike asked Lieutenant Graham Hardacre to give him

all the information he could find on one Agyeman of the Royal Engineers, Christian name and rank unknown, but with particular reference to the dates of his tours of duty in Afghanistan.

12

It was only the second car he had driven since his leg had been blown off. He had tried driving Charlotte's Lexus, but today, trying not to feel in any way emasculated, he had hired an automatic Honda Civic.

The journey to Iver Heath took under an hour. Entrance into Pinewood Studios was effected by a combination of fast talk, intimidation and the flashing of genuine, though outdated, official documentation; the security guard, initially impassive, was rocked by Strike's air of easy confidence, by the words 'Special Investigation Branch', by the pass bearing his photograph.

'Have you got an appointment?' he asked Strike, feet above him in the box beside the electric barrier, his hand covering the telephone receiver.

'No.'

'What's it about?'

'Mr Evan Duffield,' said Strike, and he saw the security guard scowl as he turned away and muttered into the receiver.

After a minute or so, Strike was given directions and waved through. He followed a gently winding road around the outskirts of the studio building, reflecting again on the convenient uses to which some people's reputations for chaos and self-destruction could be put.

He parked a few rows behind a chauffeured Mercedes occupying a space with a sign in it reading: PRODUCER FREDDIE BESTIGUI, made his unhurried exit from the car while Bestigui's driver watched him in the rear-view mirror, and proceeded through a glass door that led to a nondescript, institutional set of stairs. A young man was jogging down them, looking like a slightly tidier version of Spanner.

'Where can I find Mr Freddie Bestigui?' Strike asked him.

'Second floor, first office on the right.'

He was as ugly as his pictures, bull-necked and pockmarked, sitting behind a desk on the far side of a glass partition wall, scowling at his computer monitor. The outer office was busy and cluttered, full of attractive young women at desks; film posters were tacked to pillars and photographs of pets were pinned up beside filming schedules. The pretty girl nearest the door, who was wearing a switchboard microphone in front of her mouth, looked up at Strike and said:

'Hello, can I help you?'

'I'm here to see Mr Bestigui. Not to worry, I'll see myself in.'

He was inside Bestigui's office before she could respond.

Bestigui looked up, his eyes tiny between pouches of flesh, black moles sprinkled over the swarthy skin.

'Who are you?'

He was already pushing himself up, thick-fingered hands clutching the edge of his desk.

'I'm Cormoran Strike. I'm a private detective, I've been hired . . .'

'*Elena!*' Bestigui knocked his coffee over; it was spreading across the polished wood, into all his papers. 'Get the fuck out! Out! OUT!'

'. . . by Lula Landry's brother, John Bristow—'

'*ELENA!*'

The pretty, thin girl wearing the headset ran inside and stood fluttering beside Strike, terrified.

'Call security, you dozy little bitch!'

She ran outside. Bestigui, who was five feet six inches at the most, had pushed his way out from behind his desk now; as unafraid of the enormous Strike as a pit bull whose yard has been invaded by a Rottweiler. Elena had left the door open; the inhabitants of the outer office were staring in, frightened, mesmerised.

'I've been trying to get hold of you for a few weeks, Mr Bestigui . . . '

'You are in a shitload of trouble, my friend,' said Bestigui, advancing with a set jaw, his thick shoulders braced.

'. . . to talk about the night Lula Landry died.'

Two men in white shirts and carrying walkie-talkies were running along the glass wall to Strike's right; young, fit, tense-looking.

'Get him out of here!' Bestigui roared, pointing at Strike, as the two guards bounced off each other in the doorway, then forced their way inside.

'Specifically,' said Strike, 'about the whereabouts of your wife, Tansy, when Lula fell . . . '

'Get him out of here and call the fucking police! How did he get in here?'

'. . . because I've been shown some photographs that make sense of your wife's testimony. Get your hands off me,' Strike added to the younger of the guards now tugging his upper arm, 'or I'll knock you through that window.'

The security guard did not let go, but looked towards Bestigui for instructions.

The producer's bright dark eyes were fixed intently on Strike. He clenched and relaxed his thug's hands. After several long seconds he said:

'You're full of shit.'

But he did not instruct the waiting guards to drag Strike from his room.

'The photographer was standing on the pavement opposite your house in the early hours of the eighth of January. The guy who took the pictures doesn't realise what he's got. If you don't want to discuss it, fine; police or press, I don't care. It'll come to the same thing in the end.'

Strike took a few steps towards the door; the guards, each of whom was still holding him by the arm, were caught by surprise, and momentarily forced into the absurd position of holding him back.

'Get out,' Bestigui said abruptly to his minions. 'I'll let you know if I need you. Close the door behind you.'

They left. When the door had closed, Bestigui said:

'All right, whatever your fucking name is, you can have five minutes.'

Strike sat down, uninvited, in one of the black leather chairs facing Bestigui's desk, while the producer returned to his seat behind it, subjecting Strike to a hard, cold glare that was quite unlike the one Strike had received from Bestigui's estranged wife; this was the intense scrutiny of a professional gambler. Bestigui reached for a packet of cigarillos, pulled a black glass ashtray towards himself and lit up with a gold lighter.

'All right, let's hear what these alleged photographs show,' he said, squinting through clouds of pungent smoke, the picture of a film mafioso.

'The silhouette,' said Strike, 'of a woman crouching on the

balcony outside your sitting-room windows. She looks naked, but as you and I know, she was in her underwear.'

Bestigui puffed hard for a few seconds, then removed the cigarillo and said:

'Bullshit. You couldn't see that from the street. Solid stone bottom of the balcony; from that angle you wouldn't see anything. You're taking a punt.'

'The lights were on in your sitting room. You can see her outline through the gaps in the stone. There was room then, of course, because the shrubs weren't there, were they? People can't resist fiddling with the scene afterwards, even when they've got away with it,' Strike added, conversationally. 'You were trying to pretend that there was never any room for anyone to squat on that balcony, weren't you? But you can't go back and Photoshop reality. Your wife was perfectly positioned to hear what happened up on the third-floor balcony just before Lula Landry died.

'Here's what I think happened,' Strike went on, while Bestigui continued to squint through the smoke rising from his cigarillo. 'You and your wife had a row while she was undressing for bed. Perhaps you found her stash in the bathroom, or you interrupted her doing a couple of lines. So you decided an appropriate punishment would be to shut her outside on the sub-zero balcony.

'People might ask how a street full of paps didn't notice a part-naked woman being shoved out on a balcony over their heads, but the snow was falling very thickly, and they'll have been stamping their feet trying to keep the circulation going, and their attention was focused on the ends of the street, while they were waiting for Lula and Deeby Macc. And Tansy didn't make any noise, did she? She ducked down and hid; she didn't want to show herself, half naked, in front of thirty photographers. You might even have shoved her out there at the same time that Lula's car came round the corner. Nobody would have been looking at your windows if Lula Landry had just appeared in a skimpy little dress.'

'You're full of shit,' said Bestigui. 'You haven't got any photographs.'

'I never said I had them. I said I'd been shown them.'

Bestigui took the cigarillo from his lips, changed his mind about talking, and replaced it. Strike allowed several moments to elapse, but when it became clear that Bestigui was not going to avail himself of the opportunity to speak, he continued:

'Tansy must've started hammering on the window immediately after Landry fell past her. You weren't expecting your wife to start screaming and banging on the glass, were you? Understandably averse to anyone witnessing your bit of domestic abuse, you opened up. She ran straight past you, screaming her head off, out of the flat, and downstairs to Derrick Wilson.

'At which point you looked down over the balustrade and saw Lula Landry lying dead in the street below.'

Bestigui puffed smoke slowly, without taking his eyes off Strike's face.

'What you did next might seem quite incriminating to a jury. You didn't dial 999. You didn't run after your half-frozen, hysterical wife. You didn't even – which the jury might find more understandable – run and flush away the coke you knew was lying in open view in the bathroom.

'No, what you did next, before following your wife or calling the police, was to wipe that window clean. There'd be no prints to show that Tansy had placed her hands on the outside of the glass, would there? Your priority was to make sure that nobody could prove you had shoved your wife out on to a balcony in a temperature of minus ten. What with your unsavoury reputation for assault and abuse, and the possibility of a lawsuit from a young employee in the air, you weren't going to hand the press or a prosecutor any additional evidence, were you?

'Once you'd satisfied yourself that you'd removed any trace of her prints from the glass, you ran downstairs and compelled her to return to your flat. In the short time available to you before the police arrived, you bullied her into agreeing not to admit where she'd been when the body fell. I don't know what you promised her, or threatened her with; but whatever it was, it worked.

'You still didn't feel completely safe, though, because she was so shocked and distressed you thought she might blurt out the whole story. So you tried to distract the police by ranting about the flowers that had been knocked over in Deeby Macc's flat, hoping Tansy would pull herself together and stick to the deal.

'Well she has, hasn't she? God knows how much it's cost you, but she's let herself be dragged through the dirt in the press; she's put up with being called a coke-addled fantasist; she's stuck to her cock-and-bull story about hearing Landry and the murderer argue, through two floors, and soundproofed glass.

'Once she realises there's photographic proof of where she was, though,' said Strike, 'I think she'll be glad to come clean. Your wife might think she loves money more than anything in the world, but her conscience is troubling her. I'm confident she'll crack pretty fast.'

Bestigui had smoked his cigarillo down to its last few

millimetres. Slowly he ground it out in the black glass ashtray. Long seconds passed, and the noise in the outside office filtered through the glass wall beside them: voices, the ringing of a telephone.

Bestigui stood up and lowered Roman blinds of canvas down over the glass partition, so that none of the nervy girls in the office beyond could see in. He sat back down and ran thick fingers thoughtfully over the crumpled terrain of his lower face, glancing at Strike and away again, towards the blank cream canvas he had created. Strike could almost see options occurring to the producer, as though he was riffling a deck of cards.

'The curtains were drawn,' Bestigui said finally. 'There wasn't enough light coming out of the windows to make out a woman hiding on the balcony. Tansy's not going to change her story.'

'I wouldn't bet on that,' said Strike, stretching out his legs; the prosthesis was still uncomfortable. 'When I put it to her that the legal term for what the pair of you have done is "conspiring to pervert the course of justice", and that a belated show of conscience might keep her out of the nick; when I add in the public sympathy she's bound to get as the victim of domestic abuse, and the amount of money she's likely to be offered for exclusive rights to her story; when she realises she's going to get her say in court, and that she'll be believed, and that she'll be able to bring about the conviction of the man she heard murdering her neighbour – Mr Bestigui, I don't think even you've got enough money to keep her quiet.'

The coarse skin around Bestigui's mouth flickered. He picked up his packet of cigarillos but did not extract one. There was a long silence during which he turned the packet between his fingers, round and round.

At last he said:

'I'm admitting nothing. Get out.'

Strike did not move.

'I know you're keen to phone your lawyer,' he said, 'but I think you're overlooking the silver lining here.'

'I've had enough of you. I said, get out.'

'However unpleasant it's going to be, having to admit to what happened that night, it's still preferable to becoming the prime suspect in a murder case. It's going to be about the lesser of evils from here on in. If you cough to what really happened, you're putting yourself in the clear for the actual murder.'

He had Bestigui's attention now.

'You couldn't have done it,' said Strike, 'because if you'd been the one who threw Landry off the balcony two floors above, you wouldn't have been able to let Tansy back inside within seconds of the body falling. I think you shut your wife outside, headed off into the bedroom, got into bed, got comfy – the police said the bed looked disarranged and slept in – and kept an eye on the clock. I don't think you wanted to fall asleep. If you'd left her too long on that balcony, you'd have been up for manslaughter. No wonder Wilson said she was shaking like a whippet. Probably in the early stages of hypothermia.'

Another silence, except for Bestigui's fat fingers drumming lightly on the edge of the desk. Strike took out his notebook.

'Are you ready to answer a few questions now?'

'Fuck you!'

The producer was suddenly consumed by the rage he had so far suppressed, his jaw jutting and his shoulders hunched, level with his ears. Strike could imagine him looking thus as he bore down on his emaciated, coked-up wife, hands outstretched.

'You're in the shit here,' said Strike calmly, 'but it's entirely up to you how deep you sink. You can deny everything, battle it out with your wife in the court and the papers, end up in jail for perjury and obstructing the police. Or you can start cooperating, right now, and earn Lula's family's gratitude and good will. That'd go a long way to demonstrating remorse, and it'll help when it comes to pleas for clemency. If your information helps catch Lula's killer, I can't see you getting much worse than a reprimand from the bench. It's going to be the police who'll get the real going-over from the public and the press.'

Bestigui was breathing noisily, but seemed to be pondering Strike's words. At last he snarled:

'There wasn't any fucking killer. Wilson never found anyone up there. Landry jumped,' he said, with a small, dismissive jerk of his head. 'She was a fucked-up little druggie, like my fucking wife.'

'There was a killer,' said Strike simply, 'and you helped him get away with it.'

Something in Strike's expression stifled Bestigui's clear urge to jeer. His eyes were slits of onyx as he mulled over what Strike had said.

'I've heard you were keen to put Lula in a film?'

Bestigui seemed disconcerted by the change of subject.

'It was just an idea,' he muttered. 'She was a flake but she was fucking gorgeous.'

'You fancied getting her and Deeby Macc into a film together?'

'Licence to print money, those two together.'

'What about this film you've been thinking of making since she died – what do they call it, a biopic? I hear Tony Landry wasn't happy about it?'

To Strike's surprise, a satyr's grin impressed itself on Bestigui's pouchy face.

'Who told you that?'

'Isn't it true?'

For the first time, Bestigui seemed to feel he had the upper hand in the conversation.

'No, it's not true. Anthony Landry has given me a pretty broad hint that once Lady Bristow's dead, he'll be happy to talk about it.'

'He wasn't angry, then, when he called you to talk about it?'

'As long as it's tastefully handled, yadda yadda . . .'

'D'you know Tony Landry well?'

'I know of him.'

'In what context?'

Bestigui scratched his chin, smiling to himself.

'He's your wife's divorce lawyer, of course.'

'For now he is,' said Bestigui.

'You think she's going to sack him?'

'She might have to,' said Bestigui, and the smile became a self-satisfied leer. 'Conflict of interest. We'll see.'

Strike glanced down at his notebook, considering, with the gifted poker player's dispassionate calculation of the odds, how much risk there was in pushing this line of questioning to the limit, on no proof.

'Do I take it,' he said, looking back up, 'that you've told Landry you know he's sleeping with his business partner's wife?'

One moment's stunned surprise, and then Bestigui laughed out loud, a boorish, aggressive blast of glee.

'Know that, do you?'

'How did *you* find out?'

'I hired one of your lot. I thought Tansy was doing the dirty, but it turned out she was giving alibis to her bloody sister, while Ursula was having it away with Tony Landry. It'll be a shitload of fun to watch the Mays divorcing. High-powered lawyers on both sides. Old family firm broken up. Cyprian May's not as limp as he looks. He represented my second wife. I'm going to have a fucking blast watching that one play out. Watching the lawyers screw each other for a change.'

'That's a nice bit of leverage you've got with your wife's divorce lawyer, then?'

Bestigui smiled nastily through the smoke.

'Neither of them know I know yet. I've been waiting for a good moment to tell them.'

But Bestigui seemed to remember, suddenly, that Tansy might now be in possession of an even more powerful weapon in their divorce battle, and the smile faded from his crumpled face, leaving it bitter.

'One last thing,' said Strike. 'The night that Lula died: after you'd followed your wife down into the lobby, and brought her back upstairs, did you hear anything outside the flat?'

'I thought your whole fucking point is that you can't hear anything inside my flat with the windows closed?' snapped Bestigui.

'I'm not talking about outside in the street; I'm talking about outside your front door. Tansy might've been making too much noise to hear anything, but I'm wondering whether, when the pair of you were in your own hall – perhaps you stayed there, trying to calm her down, once you'd got her inside? – you heard any movement on the other side of the door? Or was Tansy screaming too much?'

'She was making a fuck of a lot of noise,' said Bestigui. 'I didn't hear anything.'

'Nothing at all?'

'Nothing suspicious. Just Wilson, running past the door.'

'Wilson.'

'Yeah.'

'When was this?'

'When you're talking about. When we'd got back inside our flat.'

'Immediately after you'd shut the door?'

'Yeah.'

'But Wilson had already run upstairs while you were still in the lobby, hadn't he?'

'Yeah.'

The crevices in Bestigui's forehead and around his mouth deepened.

'So when you got to your flat on the first floor, Wilson must've been out of sight and earshot already?'

'Yeah . . . '

'But you heard footsteps on the stairs, immediately after closing your front door?'

Bestigui did not answer. Strike could see him putting it all together in his own mind for the very first time.

'I heard . . . yeah . . . footsteps. Running past. On the stairs.'

'Yes,' said Strike. 'And could you make out whether there was one set, or two?'

Bestigui frowned, his eyes unfocused, looking beyond the detective into the treacherous past. 'There was . . . one. So I thought it was Wilson. But it couldn't . . . Wilson was still up on the third floor, searching her flat . . . because I heard him coming down again, afterwards . . . after I'd called the police, I heard him go running past the door . . .

'I forgot that,' said Bestigui, and for a fraction of a second he seemed almost vulnerable. 'I forgot. There was a lot going on. Tansy screaming.'

'And, of course, you were thinking about your own skin,' said Strike briskly, inserting notepad and pen back in his pocket and hoisting himself out of the leather chair. 'Well, I won't keep you; you'll be wanting to call your lawyer. You've been very helpful. I expect we'll see each other again in court.'

13

Eric Wardle called Strike the following day.

'I phoned Deeby,' he said curtly.

'And?' said Strike, motioning to Robin to pass him pen and paper. They had been sitting together at her desk, enjoying tea and biscuits while discussing the latest death threat from Brian Mathers, in which he promised, not for the first time, to slit open Strike's guts and piss on his entrails.

'He got sent a customised hoodie by Somé. Handgun in studs on the front and a couple of lines of Deeby's own lyrics on the back.'

'Just the one?'

'Yeah.'

'What else?' asked Strike.

'He remembers a belt, a beanie hat and a pair of cufflinks.'

'No gloves?'

Wardle paused, perhaps checking his notes.

'No, he didn't mention gloves.'

'Well, that clears that up,' said Strike.

Wardle said nothing at all. Strike waited for the policeman to either hang up or impart more information.

'The inquest is on Thursday,' said Wardle abruptly. 'On Rochelle Onifade.'

'Right,' said Strike.

'You don't sound that interested.'

'I'm not.'

'I thought you were sure it was murder?'

'I am, but the inquest won't prove that one way or the other. Any idea when her funeral's going to be?'

'No,' said Wardle irritably. 'What does that matter?'

'I thought I might go.'

'What for?'

'She had an aunt, remember?' said Strike.

Wardle rang off in what Strike suspected was disgust.

Bristow called Strike later that morning with the time and place of Rochelle's funeral.

'Alison managed to find out all the details,' he told the detective on the telephone. 'She's super-efficient.'

'Clearly,' said Strike.

'I'm going to come. To represent Lula. I ought to have helped Rochelle.'

'I think it was always going to end this way, John. Are you bringing Alison?'

'She says she wants to come,' said Bristow, though he sounded less than enamoured of the idea.

'I'll see you there, then. I'm hoping to speak to Rochelle's aunt, if she turns up.'

When Strike told Robin that Bristow's girlfriend had discovered the time and place of the funeral, she appeared put out. She herself had been trying to find out the details at Strike's request, and seemed to feel that Alison had put one over on her.

'I didn't realise you were this competitive,' said Strike, amused. 'Not to worry. Maybe she had some kind of head-start on you.'

'Like what?'

But Strike was looking at her speculatively.

'What?' repeated Robin, a little defensively.

'I want you to come with me to the funeral.'

'Oh,' said Robin. 'OK. Why?'

She expected Strike to reply that it would look more natural for them to turn up as a couple, just as it had seemed more natural for him to visit Vashti with a woman in tow. Instead he said:

'There's something I want you to do for me there.'

Once he had explained, clearly and concisely, what it was that he wanted her to do, Robin looked utterly bewildered.

'But why?'

'I can't say.'

'Why not?'

'I'd rather not say that, either.'

Robin no longer saw Strike through Matthew's eyes; no longer wondered whether he was faking, or showing off, or pretending to be cleverer than he was. She did him the credit, now, of discounting the possibility that he was being deliberately mysterious. All the same, she repeated, as though she must have heard him wrongly:

'*Brian Mathers.*'

'Yeah.'

'The Death Threat Man.'

'Yeah.'

'But,' said Robin, 'what on earth can he have to do with Lula Landry's death?'

'Nothing,' said Strike, honestly enough. 'Yet.'

The north London crematorium where Rochelle's funeral was held three days later was chilly, anonymous and depressing. Everything was smoothly nondenominational; from the darkwood pews and blank walls, carefully devoid of any religious device; to the abstract stained-glass window, a mosaic of little jewel-bright squares. Sitting on hard wood, while a whiny-voiced minister called Rochelle 'Roselle' and the fine rain speckled the gaudy patchwork window above him, Strike understood the appeal of gilded cherubs and plaster saints, of gargoyles and Old Testament angels, of gem-set golden crucifixes; anything that might give an aura of majesty and grandeur, a firm promise of an afterlife, or retrospective worth to a life like Rochelle's. The dead girl had had her glimpse of earthly paradise: littered with designer goods, and celebrities to sneer at, and handsome drivers to joke with, and the yearning for it had brought her to this: seven mourners, and a minister who did not know her name.

There was a tawdry impersonality about the whole affair; a feeling of faint embarrassment; a painful avoidance of the facts of Rochelle's life. Nobody seemed to feel that they had the right to sit in the front row. Even the obese black woman wearing thick-lensed glasses and a knitted hat, who Strike assumed was Rochelle's aunt, had chosen to sit three benches from the front of the crematorium, keeping her distance from the cheap coffin. The balding worker whom Strike had met at the homeless hostel had come, in an open shirt and a leather jacket; behind him was a fresh-faced, neatly suited young Asian man who Strike thought might turn out to be the psychiatrist who had run Rochelle's outpatient group.

Strike, in his old navy suit, and Robin, in the black skirt and jacket she wore to interviews, sat at the very back. Across the aisle were Bristow, miserable and pale, and Alison, whose damp double-breasted black raincoat glistened a little in the cold light.

Cheap red curtains opened, the coffin slid out of sight, and the drowned girl was consumed by fire. The silent mourners exchanged pained, awkward smiles at the back of the crematorium; hovering, trying not to add unseemly haste of departure to the other inadequacies of the service. Rochelle's aunt, who projected an aura of eccentricity that bordered on instability, introduced herself as Winifred, then announced loudly, with an accusatory undertone:

'Dere's sandwiches in the pub. I thought dere would be more people.'

She led the way outside, as if brooking no opposition, up the street to the Red Lion, the six other mourners following in her wake, heads bowed slightly against the rain.

The promised sandwiches sat, dry and unappetising, on a metal foil tray covered in cling film, on a small table in the corner of the dingy pub. At some point on the walk to the Red Lion Aunt Winifred had realised who John Bristow was, and she now took overpowering possession of him, pinning him up against the bar, gabbling at him without pause. Bristow responded whenever she allowed him to get a word in edgewise, but the looks he cast towards Strike, who was talking to Rochelle's psychiatrist, became more frequent and desperate as the minutes passed.

The psychiatrist parried all Strike's attempts to engage him in conversation about the outpatients' group he had run, finally countering a question about disclosures Rochelle might have made with a polite but firm reminder about patient confidentiality.

'Were you surprised that she killed herself?'

'No, not really. She was a very troubled girl, you know, and Lula Landry's death was a great shock to her.'

Shortly afterwards he issued a general farewell and left.

Robin, who had been trying to make conversation with a

monosyllabic Alison at a small table beside the window, gave up and headed for the Ladies.

Strike ambled across the small lounge and sat down in Robin's abandoned seat. Alison threw him an unfriendly look, then resumed her contemplation of Bristow, who was still being harangued by Rochelle's aunt. Alison had not unbuttoned her rain-flecked coat. A small glass of what looked like port stood on the table in front of her, and a slightly scornful smile played around her mouth, as though she found her surroundings ramshackle and inadequate. Strike was still trying to think of a good opener when she said unexpectedly:

'John was supposed to be at a meeting with Conway Oates's executors this morning. He's left Tony to meet them on his own. Tony's absolutely furious.'

Her tone implied that Strike was in some way responsible for this, and that he deserved to know what trouble he had caused. She took a sip of port. Her hair hung limply to her shoulders and her big hands dwarfed the glass. In spite of a plainness that would have made wallflowers of other women, she radiated a great sense of self-importance.

'You don't think it was a nice gesture for John to come to the funeral?' asked Strike.

Alison gave a scathing little 'huh', a token laugh.

'It's not as though he *knew* this girl.'

'Why did *you* come along, then?'

'Tony wanted me to.'

Strike noted the pleasurable self-consciousness with which she pronounced her boss's name.

'Why?'

'To keep an eye on John.'

'Tony thinks John needs watching, does he?'

She did not answer.

'They share you, John and Tony, don't they?'

'What?' she said sharply.

He was glad to have discomposed her.

'They share your services? As a secretary?'

'Oh – oh, no. I work for Tony and Cyprian; I'm the senior partners' secretary.'

'Ah. I wonder why I thought you were John's too?'

'I work on a completely different level,' said Alison. 'John uses the typing pool. I have nothing to do with him at work.'

'Yet romance blossomed across secretarial rank and floors?'

She met his facetiousness with more disdainful silence. She seemed to see Strike as intrinsically offensive, somebody undeserving of manners, beyond the pale.

The hostel worker stood alone in a corner, helping himself to sandwiches, palpably killing time until he could decently leave. Robin emerged from the Ladies, and was instantly suborned by Bristow, who seemed eager for assistance in coping with Aunt Winifred.

'So, how long have you and John been together?' asked Strike.

'A few months.'

'You got together before Lula died, did you?'

'He asked me out not long afterwards,' she said.

'He must have been in a pretty bad way, was he?'

'He was a complete mess.'

She did not sound sympathetic, but slightly contemptuous.

'Had he been flirting for a while?'

He expected her to refuse to answer; but he was wrong. Though she tried to pretend otherwise, there was unmistakable self-satisfaction and pride in her answer.

'He came upstairs to see Tony. Tony was busy, so John came to wait in my office. He started talking about his sister, and he got emotional. I gave him tissues, and he ended up asking me out to dinner.'

In spite of what seemed to be lukewarm feelings for Bristow, he thought that she was proud of his overtures; they were a kind of trophy. Strike wondered whether Alison had ever, before desperate John Bristow came along, been asked out to dinner. It had been the collision of two people with an unhealthy need: *I gave him tissues, and he asked me out to dinner.*

The hostel worker was buttoning up his jacket. Catching Strike's eye, he gave a farewell wave, and departed without speaking to anyone.

'So how does the big boss feel about his secretary dating his nephew?'

'It's not up to Tony what I do in my private life,' she said.

'True enough,' said Strike. 'Anyway, he can't talk about mixing business with pleasure, can he? Sleeping with Cyprian May's wife as he is.'

Momentarily fooled by his casual tone, Alison opened her mouth to respond; then the meaning of his words hit her, and her self-assurance shattered.

'That's not true!' she said fiercely, her face burning. 'Who said that to you? It's a lie. It's a *complete* lie. It's not true. It isn't.'

He heard a terrified child behind the woman's protest.

'Really? Why did Cyprian May send you to Oxford to find Tony on the seventh of January then?'

'That – it was only – he'd forgotten to get Tony to sign some documents, that's all.'

'And he didn't use a fax machine or a courier because . . . ?'

'They were sensitive documents.'

'Alison,' said Strike, enjoying her agitation, 'we both know that's balls. Cyprian thought Tony had sloped off somewhere with Ursula for the day, didn't he?'

'He didn't! He hadn't!'

Up at the bar, Aunt Winifred was waving her arms, windmill-like, at Bristow and Robin, who were wearing frozen smiles.

'You found him in Oxford, did you?'

'No, because—'

'What time did you get there?'

'About eleven, but he'd—'

'Cyprian must've sent you out the moment you got to work, did he?'

'The documents were urgent.'

'But you didn't find Tony at his hotel or in the conference centre?'

'I missed him,' she said, in furious desperation, 'because he'd gone back to London to visit Lady Bristow.'

'Ah,' said Strike. 'Right. Bit odd that he didn't let you or Cyprian know that he was going back to London, isn't it?'

'No,' she said, with a valiant attempt at regaining her vanished superiority. 'He was contactable. He was still on his mobile. It didn't matter.'

'Did you call his mobile?'

She did not answer.

'Did you call it, and not get an answer?'

She sipped her port in simmering silence.

'In fairness, it would break the mood, taking a call from your secretary while you're on the job.'

He thought that she would find this offensive, and was not disappointed.

'You're disgusting. You're really disgusting,' she said thickly, her cheeks a dull dark red with the prudishness she tried to disguise under a show of superiority.

'Do you live alone?' he asked her.

'What's that got to do with anything?' she asked, completely off-balance now.

'Just wondered. So you don't see anything odd in Tony booking into an Oxford hotel for the night, driving back to London the following morning, then returning to Oxford again, in time to check out of his hotel the next day?'

'He went back to Oxford so that he could attend the conference in the afternoon,' she said doggedly.

'Oh, really? Did you hang around and meet him there?'

'He was there,' she said evasively.

'You've got proof, have you?'

She said nothing.

'Tell me,' said Strike, 'would you rather think that Tony was in bed with Ursula May all day, or having some kind of confrontation with his niece?'

Over at the bar, Aunt Winifred was straightening her knitted hat and retying her belt. She seemed to be preparing to leave.

For several seconds Alison fought herself, and then, with an air of unleashing something long suppressed, she said in a ferocious whisper:

'They aren't having an affair. I *know* they aren't. It wouldn't happen. Ursula only cares about money; it's all that matters to her, and Tony's got less than Cyprian. Ursula wouldn't want Tony. She wouldn't.'

'Oh, you never know. Physical passion might have overpowered her mercenary tendencies,' said Strike, watching Alison closely. 'It can happen. It's hard for another man to judge, but he's not bad-looking, Tony, is he?'

He saw the rawness of her pain, her fury, and her voice was choked as she said:

'Tony's right – you're taking advantage – in it for all you can get – John's gone funny – Lula *jumped*. She *jumped*. She was always unbalanced. John's like his mother, he's hysterical, he imagines things. Lula took drugs, she was one of those sort of people, out of control, always causing trouble and trying to get attention. Spoilt. Throwing money around. She could have anything she liked, anyone she wanted, but nothing was enough for her.'

'I didn't realise you knew her.'

'I – Tony's told me about her.'

'He really didn't like her, did he?'

'He just saw her for what she was. She was no good. Some women,' she said, her chest heaving beneath the shapeless raincoat, 'aren't.'

A chill breeze cut through the musty air of the lounge as the door swung shut behind Rochelle's aunt. Bristow and Robin kept smiling weakly until the door had closed completely, then exchanged looks of relief.

The barman had disappeared. Only four of them were left in the little lounge now. Strike became aware, for the first time, of the eighties ballad playing in the background: Jennifer Rush, 'The Power of Love'. Bristow and Robin approached their table.

'I thought you wanted to speak to Rochelle's aunt?' asked Bristow, looking aggrieved, as though he had been through an ordeal for nothing.

'Not enough to chase after her,' replied Strike cheerfully. 'You can fill me in.'

Strike could tell, by the expressions on Robin's and Bristow's faces, that both thought this attitude strangely lackadaisical. Alison was fumbling for something in her bag, her own face hidden.

The rain had stopped, the pavements were slippery and the sky was gloomy, threatening a fresh downpour. The two women walked ahead in silence, while Bristow earnestly related to Strike all that he could remember of Aunt Winifred's conversation. Strike, however, was not listening. He was watching the backs of the two women, both in black – almost, to the careless observer, alike, interchangeable. He remembered the sculptures on either side of the Queen's Gate; not identical at all, in spite of the assumptions made by lazy eyes; one male, one female, the same species, yes, but profoundly different.

When he saw Robin and Alison come to a halt beside a BMW he assumed must be Bristow's, he too slowed up, and cut across Bristow's rambling recital of Rochelle's stormy relations with her family.

'John, I need to check something with you.'

'Fire away.'

'You say you heard your uncle come into your mother's flat on the morning before Lula died?'

'Yep, that's right.'

'Are you absolutely sure that the man you heard was Tony?'

'Yes, of course.'

'You didn't see him, though?'

'I . . . ' Bristow's rabbity face was suddenly puzzled. '. . . no, I – I don't think I actually saw him. But I heard him let himself in. I heard his voice from the hall.'

'You don't think that, perhaps, because you were expecting Tony, you assumed it *was* Tony?'

Another pause.

Then, in a changed voice:

'Are you saying Tony wasn't there?'

'I just want to know how certain you are that he was.'

'Well ... until this moment, I was completely certain. Nobody else has got a key to my mother's flat. It couldn't have been anyone *except* Tony.'

'So you heard someone let themselves into the flat. You heard a male voice. Was he talking to your mother, or to Lula?'

'Er . . . ' Bristow's large front teeth were much in evidence as he pondered the question. 'I heard him come in. I think I heard him speaking to Lula . . . '

'And you heard him leave?'

'Yes. I heard him walk down the hall. I heard the door close.'

'When Lula said goodbye to you, did she make any mention of Tony having just been there?'

More silence. Bristow raised a hand to his mouth, thinking.

'I – she hugged me, that's all I . . . Yes, I think she said she'd spoken to Tony. Or did she? Did I assume she'd spoken to him, because I thought . . . ? But if it wasn't my uncle, who was it?'

Strike waited. Bristow stared at the pavement, thinking.

'But it must have been him. Lula must have seen whoever it was, and not thought their presence remarkable, and who else could that have been, except Tony? Who else would have had a key?'

'How many keys are there?'

'Four. Three spares.'

'That's a lot.'

'Well, Lula and Tony and I all had one. Mum liked us all to be able to let ourselves in and out, especially while she's been ill.'

'And all these keys are present and accounted for, are they?'

'Yes – well, I think so. I assume Lula's came back to my

mother with all her other things. Tony's still got his, I've got mine, and my mother's . . . I expect it's somewhere in the flat.'

'So you aren't aware of any key that's been lost?'

'No.'

'And none of you has ever lent your key to anyone?'

'My God, why would we do that?'

'I keep remembering how that file of photographs was removed from Lula's laptop while it was in your mother's flat. If there's another key floating around . . . '

'There can't be,' said Bristow. 'This is . . . I . . . why are you saying Tony wasn't there? He must have been. He says he saw me through the door.'

'You went into the office on the way back from Lula's, right?'

'Yes.'

'To get files?'

'Yes. I just ran in and grabbed them. I was quick.'

'So you were back at your mother's house . . . ?'

'It can't have been later than ten.'

'And the man who came in, when did he arrive?'

'Maybe . . . maybe half an hour afterwards? I can't honestly remember. I wasn't watching the clock. But why would Tony say he was there if he wasn't?'

'Well, if he knew you'd been working at home, he could easily say that he came in, and didn't want to disturb you, and just walked down the hall to speak to your mother. She, presumably, confirmed his presence to the police?'

'I suppose so. Yes, I think so.'

'But you're not sure?'

'I don't think we've ever discussed it. Mum was groggy and in pain; she slept a lot that day. And then the next morning we had the news about Lula . . . '

'But you've never thought it was strange that Tony didn't come into the study and speak to you?'

'It wasn't strange at all,' said Bristow. 'He was in a foul temper about the Conway Oates business. I'd have been more surprised if he had been chatty.'

'John, I don't want to alarm you, but I think that both you and your mother could be in danger.'

Bristow's little bleat of nervous laughter sounded thin and unconvincing. Strike could see Alison standing fifty yards away, her arms folded, ignoring Robin, watching the two men.

'You – you can't be serious?' said Bristow.

'I'm very serious.'

'But . . . does . . . Cormoran, are you saying you know who killed Lula?'

'Yeah, I think I do – but I still need to speak to your mother before we wrap this up.'

Bristow looked as though he wished he could drink the contents of Strike's mind. His myopic eyes scanned every inch of Strike's face, his expression half afraid, half imploring.

'I must be there,' he said. 'She's very weak.'

'Of course. How about tomorrow morning?'

'Tony will be livid if I take off any more time during work hours.'

Strike waited.

'All right,' said Bristow. 'All right. Ten thirty tomorrow.'

14

The following morning was fresh and bright. Strike took the underground to genteel and leafy Chelsea. This was a part of London that he barely knew, for Leda had never, even in her most spendthrift phases, managed to secure a toehold in the vicinity of the Royal Chelsea Hospital, pale and gracious in the spring sun.

Franklin Row was an attractive street of more red brick; here were plane trees, and a great grassy space bordered with railings, in which a throng of primary school children were playing games in pale blue Aertex tops and navy blue shorts, watched by tracksuited teachers. Their happy cries punctuated the sedate quiet otherwise disturbed only by birdsong; no cars passed as Strike strolled down the pavement towards the house of Lady Yvette Bristow, his hands in his pockets.

The wall beside the partly glass door, set at the top of four white stone steps, bore an old-fashioned Bakelite panel of door-bells. Strike checked to see that Lady Yvette Bristow's name was clearly marked beside Flat E, then retreated to the pavement and stood waiting in the gentle warmth of the day, looking up and down the street.

Ten thirty arrived, but John Bristow did not. The square remained deserted, but for the twenty small children running between hoops and coloured cones beyond the railings.

At ten forty-five, Strike's mobile vibrated in his pocket. The text was from Robin:

Alison has just called to say that JB is unavoidably detained. He does not want you to speak to his mother without him present.

Strike immediately texted Bristow:

How long are you likely to be detained? Any chance of doing this later today?

He had barely sent the message when the phone began to ring.

'Yeah, hello?' said Strike.

'Oggy?' came Graham Hardacre's tinny voice, all the way from Germany. 'I've got the stuff on Agyeman.'

'Your timing's uncanny.' Strike pulled out his notebook. 'Go on.'

'He's Lieutenant Jonah Francis Agyeman, Royal Engineers. Aged twenty-one, unmarried, last tour of duty started eleventh of January. He's back in June. Next of kin, a mother. No siblings, no kids.'

Strike scribbled it all down in his notebook, with the mobile phone held between jaw and shoulder.

'I owe you one, Hardy,' he said, putting the notebook away. 'Haven't got a picture, have you?'

'I could email you one.'

Strike gave Hardacre the office email address, and, after routine enquiries about each other's lives, and mutual expressions of goodwill, terminated the call.

It was five to eleven. Strike waited, phone in hand, in the peaceful, leafy square, while the gambolling children played with their hoops and their beanbags, and a tiny silver plane drew a thick white line across the periwinkle sky. At last, with a small chirrup clearly audible in the quiet street, Bristow's texted reply arrived:

No chance today. I've been forced to go out to Rye. Maybe tomorrow?

Strike sighed.

'Sorry, John,' he muttered, and he climbed the steps and rang Lady Bristow's doorbell.

The entrance hall, quiet, spacious and sunny, nevertheless had a faintly depressing air of communality that a bucket-shaped vase of dried flowers and a dull green carpet and pale yellow walls, probably chosen for their inoffensiveness, could not dissipate. As at Kentigern Gardens, there was a lift, this one with wooden doors. Strike chose to walk upstairs. The building had a faint shabbiness that in no way diminished its quiet aura of wealth.

The door of the top flat was opened by the smiling West Indian Macmillan nurse who had buzzed him through the front door.

'You're not Mister Bristow,' she said brightly.

'No, I'm Cormoran Strike. John's on his way.'

She let him in. Lady Bristow's hallway was pleasantly cluttered, papered in faded red and covered in watercolours in old gilt frames; an umbrella stand was full of walking sticks, and coats hung on a row of pegs. Strike glanced right, and saw a sliver of the study at the end of the corridor: a heavy wooden desk and a swivel chair with its back to the door.

'Will you wait in the sitting room while I check whether Lady Bristow is ready to see you?'

'Yeah, of course.'

He walked through the door she indicated into a charming room with primrose walls, lined with bookcases bearing photographs. An old-fashioned dial telephone sat on an end table beside a comfortable chintz-covered sofa. Strike checked that the nurse was out of sight before slipping the receiver off the hook and repositioning it, unobtrusively skewed on its rests.

Close by the bay window on a *bonheur du jour* stood a large photograph, framed in silver, showing the wedding of Sir and Lady Alec Bristow. The groom looked much older than his wife, a rotund, beaming, bearded man; the bride was thin, blonde and pretty in an insipid way. Ostensibly admiring the photograph, Strike stood with his back to the door, and slid open a little drawer in the delicate cherrywood desk. Inside was a supply of fine pale blue writing paper and matching envelopes. He slid the drawer shut again.

'Mister Strike? You can come through.'

Back through the red-papered hall, a short passage, and into a large bedroom, where the dominant colours were duck-egg blue and white, and everywhere gave an impression of elegance and taste. Two doors on the left, both ajar, led to a small en-suite bathroom, and what seemed to be a large walk-in wardrobe. The furniture was delicate and Frenchified; the props of serious illness – the drip on its metal stand, the bedpan lying clean and shiny on a chest of drawers, with an array of medications – were glaring impostors.

The dying woman wore a thick ivory-coloured bed jacket and reclined, dwarfed by her carved wooden bed, on many white pillows. No trace of Lady Bristow's youthful prettiness remained. The raw bones of the skeleton were clearly delineated now, beneath fine skin that was shiny and flaking. Her eyes were sunken, filmy and dim, and her wispy hair, fine as a baby's, was grey against large expanses of pink scalp. Her emaciated arms lay limp on top of the covers, a catheter protruded. Her death was an almost palpable presence in the room, as though it stood waiting patiently, politely, behind the curtains.

A faint smell of lime blossom pervaded the atmosphere, but did not entirely eclipse that of disinfectant and bodily decay; smells that recalled, to Strike, the hospital where he had lain helpless for months. A second large bay window had been raised a few inches, so that the warm fresh air and the distant cries of the sports-playing children could enter the room. The view was of the topmost branches of the leafy sunlit plane trees.

'Are you the detective?'

Her voice was thin and cracked, her words slightly slurred. Strike, who had wondered whether Bristow had told her the truth about his profession, was glad that she knew.

'Yes, I'm Cormoran Strike.'

'Where's John?'

'He's been held up at the office.'

'Again,' she murmured, and then: 'Tony works him very hard. It isn't fair.' She peered at him, blurrily, and indicated a small painted chair with one slightly raised finger. 'Do sit down.'

There were chalky white lines around her faded irises. As he sat, Strike noticed two more silver-framed photographs standing on the bedside table. With something akin to an electric shock, he found himself looking into the eyes of ten-year-old Charlie Bristow, chubby-faced, with his slightly mullety haircut: frozen for ever in the eighties, his school shirt with its long pointed collar, and the huge knot in his tie. He looked just as he had when he had waved goodbye to his best friend, Cormoran Strike, expecting to meet each other again after Easter.

Beside Charlie's photograph was a smaller one, of an exquisite little girl with long black ringlets and big brown eyes, in a navy blue school uniform: Lula Landry, aged no more than six.

'Mary,' said Lady Bristow, without raising her voice, and the nurse bustled over. 'Could you get Mr Strike . . . coffee? Tea?' she asked him, and he was transported back two and a half decades, to Charlie Bristow's sunlit garden, and the gracious blonde mother, and the iced lemonade.

'A coffee would be great, thank you very much.'

'I do apologise for not making it myself,' said Lady Bristow, as the nurse departed, with heavy footfalls, 'but as you can see, I am entirely dependent, now, on the kindness of strangers. Like poor Blanche Dubois.'

She closed her eyes for a moment, as though to concentrate better on some internal pain. He wondered how heavily medicated she was. Beneath the gracious manner, he divined the faintest whiff of something bitter in her words, much as the lime blossom failed to cover the smell of decay, and he wondered at it, considering that Bristow spent most of his time dancing attendance on her.

'Why isn't John here?' asked Lady Bristow again, with her eyes still shut.

'He's been held up at the office,' repeated Strike.

'Oh, yes. Yes, you said.'

'Lady Bristow, I'd like to ask you a few questions, and I apologise in advance if they seem over-personal, or distressing.'

'When you have been through what I have,' she said quietly, 'nothing much can hurt you any more. Do call me Yvette.'

'Thank you. Do you mind if I take notes?'

'No, not at all,' she said, and she watched him take out his pen and notebook with a dim show of interest.

'I'd like to start, if you don't mind, with how Lula came into your family. Did you know anything about her background when you adopted her?'

She looked the very picture of helplessness and passivity lying there with her limp arms on the covers.

'No,' she said. 'I didn't know anything. Alec might have known, but if he did, he never told me.'

'What makes you think your husband knew something?'

'Alec always went into things as deeply as he could,' she said, with a faint, reminiscent smile. 'He was a very successful businessman, you know.'

'But he never told you anything about Lula's first family?'

'Oh no, he wouldn't have done that.' She seemed to find this a strange suggestion. 'I wanted her to be mine, just mine, you see. Alec would have wanted to protect me, if he knew anything. I could not have borne the idea that somebody out there might come and claim her one day. I had already lost Charlie, and I wanted a daughter so badly; the idea of losing her, too . . . '

The nurse returned bearing a tray with two cups on it and a plate of chocolate bourbons.

'One coffee,' she said cheerfully, placing it beside Strike on the nearer of the bedside tables, 'and one camomile tea.'

She bustled out again. Lady Bristow closed her eyes. Strike took a gulp of black coffee and said:

'Lula went looking for her biological parents in the year before she died, didn't she?'

'That's right,' said Lady Bristow, with her eyes still closed. 'I had just been diagnosed with cancer.'

There was a pause, in which Strike put down his coffee cup with a soft chink, and the distant cheers of the small children in the square outside floated through the open window.

'John and Tony were very, very angry with her,' said Lady Bristow. 'They didn't think she ought to have started trying to find her biological mother, when I was so very ill. The tumour was already advanced when they found it. I had to go straight on to chemotherapy. John was very good; he drove me back and forth to the hospital, and came to stay with me during the worst bits, and even Tony rallied round, but all Lula seemed to care about . . .' She sighed, and opened her faded eyes, seeking Strike's face. 'Tony always said that she was very spoiled. I dare say it was my fault. I had lost Charlie, you see; I couldn't do enough for her.'

'Do you know how much Lula managed to find out about her birth family?'

'No, I don't, I'm afraid. I think she knew how much it upset me. She didn't tell me a great deal. I know that she found the mother, of course, because there was all the dreadful publicity. She was exactly what Tony had predicted. She hadn't ever wanted Lula. An awful, awful woman,' whispered Lady Bristow. 'But Lula kept seeing her. I was having chemotherapy all through that time. I lost my hair . . .'

Her voice trailed away. Strike felt, as perhaps she meant him to, like a brute as he pressed on:

'What about her biological father? Did she ever tell you she'd found out anything about him?'

'No,' said Lady Bristow weakly. 'I didn't ask. I had the impression that she had given up on the whole business once she found that horrible mother. I didn't want to discuss it, any of it. It was too distressing. I think she realised that.'

'She didn't mention her biological father the last time you saw her?' Strike pressed on.

'Oh no,' she said, in her soft voice. 'No. That was not a very long visit, you know. She told me, the moment she arrived, I remember, that she could not stay long. She had to meet her friend Ciara Porter.'

Her sense of ill-usage wafted gently towards him like the smell of the bedridden she exuded: a little fusty, a little overripe. Something about her recalled Rochelle; although they were as different as two women could be, both gave off the resentment of those who feel short-changed and neglected.

'Can you remember what you and Lula talked about that day?'

'Well, I had been given so many painkillers, you understand. I had had a very serious operation. I can't remember every detail.'

'But you remember Lula coming to see you?' asked Strike.

'Oh yes,' she said. 'She woke me up, I had been sleeping.'

'Can you remember what you talked about?'

'My operation, of course,' she said, with just a touch of asperity. 'And then, a little bit, about her big brother.'

'Her big . . . ?'

'Charlie,' said Lady Bristow, pitifully. 'I told her about the day he died. I had never really talked to her about it before. The worst, the very worst day of my life.'

Strike could imagine her, prostrate and a little groggy, but no less resentful for all that, holding her unwilling daughter there at her side by talking about her pain, and her dead son.

'How could I have known that that would be the last time I would ever see her?' breathed Lady Bristow. 'I didn't realise that I was about to lose a second child.'

Her bloodshot eyes filled. She blinked, and two fat tears fell down on to her hollow cheeks.

'Could you please look in that drawer,' she whispered,

pointing a withered finger at the bedside table, 'and get me out my pills?'

Strike slid it open and saw many white boxes inside, of varying types and with various labels upon them.

'Which . . . ?'

'It doesn't matter. They're all the same,' she said.

He took one out; it was clearly labelled Valium. She had enough in there to overdose ten times.

'If you could pop a couple out for me?' she said. 'I'll take them with some tea, if it's cool enough.'

He handed her her pills and the cup; her hands trembled; he had to support the saucer and he thought, inappropriately, of a priest offering communion.

'Thank you,' she murmured, relaxing back on to her pillows as he replaced her tea on the table, and fixing him with her plaintive eyes. 'Didn't John tell me you knew Charlie?'

'Yes, I did,' said Strike. 'I've never forgotten him.'

'No, of course not. He was a most lovable child. Everyone always said so. The sweetest boy, the very sweetest I have ever known. I miss him every single day.'

Outside the window, the children shrieked, and the plane trees rustled, and Strike thought of how the room would have looked on a winter morning months ago, when the trees must have been bare-limbed, when Lula Landry had sat where he was sitting, with her beautiful eyes perhaps fixed on the picture of dead Charlie while her groggy mother told the horrible story.

'I had never really talked to Lula about it before. The boys had gone out on their bikes. We heard John screaming, and then Tony shouting, shouting . . . '

Strike's pen had not made contact with paper yet. He watched the dying woman's face as she talked.

'Alec wouldn't let me look, wouldn't let me anywhere near the quarry. When he told me what had happened, I fainted. I thought I would die. I wanted to die. I could not understand how God could have let it happen.

'But since then, I've come to think that perhaps I have deserved all of it,' said Lady Bristow distantly, her eyes fixed on the ceiling. 'I've wondered whether I'm being punished. Because I loved them too much. I spoiled them. I couldn't say no. Charlie, John and Lula. I think it must be punishment, because otherwise it would be too unspeakably cruel, wouldn't it? To make me go through it again, and again, and again.'

Strike had no answer to give. She invited pity, but he found he could not pity her even as much as, perhaps, she deserved. She lay dying, wrapped in invisible robes of martyrdom, presenting her helplessness and passivity to him like adornments, and his dominant feeling was distaste.

'I wanted Lula so much,' said Lady Bristow, 'but I don't think she ever . . . She was a darling little thing. So beautiful. I would have done anything for that girl. But she didn't love me the way Charlie and John loved me. Maybe it was too late. Maybe we got her too late.

'John was jealous when she first came to us. He had been devastated about Charlie . . . but they ended up being very close friends. Very close.'

A tiny frown crumpled the paper-fine skin of her forehead.

'So Tony was quite wrong.'

'What was he wrong about?' asked Strike quietly.

Her fingers twitched upon the covers. She swallowed.

'Tony didn't think we should have adopted Lula.'

'Why not?' asked Strike.

'Tony never liked any of my children,' said Yvette Bristow.

'My brother is a very hard man. Very cold. He said dreadful things after Charlie died. Alec hit him. It wasn't true. It wasn't true – what Tony said.'

Her milky gaze slid to Strike's face, and he thought he glimpsed the woman she must have been when she still had her looks: a little clingy, a little childish, prettily dependent, an ultra-feminine creature, protected and petted by Sir Alec, who strove to satisfy her every whim and wish.

'What did Tony say?'

'Horrible things about John and Charlie. Awful things. I don't,' she said weakly, 'want to repeat them. And then he phoned Alec, when he heard that we were adopting a little girl, and told him we ought not to do it. Alec was furious,' she whispered. 'He forbade Tony our house.'

'Did you tell Lula about all this when she visited that day?' asked Strike. 'About Tony, and the things he said after Charlie died; and when you adopted her?'

She seemed to sense a reproach.

'I can't remember exactly what I said to her. I had just had a very serious operation. I was a little drowsy from all the drugs. I can't remember precisely what I said now . . .'

And then, with an abrupt change of subject:

'That boy reminded me of Charlie. Lula's boyfriend. The very handsome boy. What is his name?'

'Evan Duffield?'

'That's right. He came to see me a little while ago, you know. Quite recently. I don't know exactly . . . I lose track of time. They give me so many drugs now. But he came to see me. It was so sweet of him. He wanted to talk about Lula.'

Strike remembered Bristow's assertion that his mother had not known who Duffield was, and he wondered whether Lady

Bristow had played this little game with her son; making herself out to be more confused than she really was, to stimulate his protective instincts.

'Charlie would have been handsome like that, if he'd lived. He might have been a singer, or an actor. He loved performing, do you remember? I felt very sorry for that boy Evan. He cried here, with me. He told me that he thought she was meeting another man.'

'What other man was that?'

'The singer,' said Lady Bristow vaguely. 'The singer who'd written songs about her. When you are young, and beautiful, you can be very cruel. I felt very sorry for him. He told me he felt guilty. I told him he had nothing to feel guilty about.'

'Why did he say he felt guilty?'

'For not following her into her apartment. For not being there, to stop her dying.'

'If we could just go back for a moment, Yvette, to the day before Lula's death?'

She looked reproachful.

'I'm afraid I can't remember anything else. I've told you everything I remember. I was just out of hospital. I was not myself. They'd given me so many drugs, for the pain.'

'I understand that. I just wanted to know whether you remember your brother, Tony, visiting you that day?'

There was a pause, and Strike saw something harden in the weak face.

'No, I don't remember Tony coming,' said Lady Bristow at last. 'I know he says he was here, but I don't remember him coming. Maybe I was asleep.'

'He claims to have been here when Lula was visiting,' said Strike.

Lady Bristow gave the smallest shrug of her fragile shoulders.

'Maybe he was here,' she said, 'but I don't remember it.' And then, her voice rising, 'My brother's being much nicer to me now he knows that I'm dying. He visits a lot now. Always putting down poison about John, of course. He's always done that. But John has always been very good to me. He has done things for me while I've been ill . . . things no son should have to do. It would have been more appropriate for Lula . . . but she was a spoiled girl. I loved her, but she could be selfish. Very selfish.'

'So on that last day, the last time you saw Lula—' said Strike, returning doggedly to the main point, but Lady Bristow cut across him.

'After she left, I was very upset,' she said. 'Very upset indeed. Talking about Charlie always does that to me. She could see how distressed I was, but she still left to meet her friend. I had to take pills, and I slept. No, I never saw Tony; I didn't see anyone else. He might say he was here, but I don't remember anything until John woke me up with a supper tray. John was cross. He told me off.'

'Why was that?'

'He thinks I take too many pills,' said Lady Bristow, like a little girl. 'I know he wants the best for me, poor John, but he doesn't realise . . . he couldn't . . . I've had so much pain in my life. He sat with me for a long time that night. We talked about Charlie. We talked into the early hours of the morning. And while we were talking,' she said, dropping her voice to a whisper, 'at the very time we were talking, Lula fell . . . she fell off the balcony.

'So it was John who had to break the news to me, the next morning. The police had arrived on the doorstep, at the crack of dawn. He came into the bedroom to tell me and . . .'

She swallowed, and shook her head, limp, barely alive.

'That's why the cancer came back, I know it. People can only bear so much pain.'

Her voice was becoming more slurred. He wondered how much Valium she had already taken, as she closed her eyes drowsily.

'Yvette, would it be all right if I used your bathroom?' he asked.

She assented with a sleepy nod.

Strike got up, and moved quickly, and surprisingly quietly for a man of his bulk, into the walk-in wardrobe.

The space was lined with mahogany doors that reached to the ceiling. Strike opened one of the doors and glanced inside, at overstuffed railings of dresses and coats, with a shelf of bags and hats above, breathing in the musty smell of old shoes and fabric which, in spite of the evident costliness of the contents, evoked an old charity shop. Silently he opened and closed door after door, until, on the fourth attempt, he saw a cluster of clearly brand-new handbags, each of a different colour, that had been squeezed on to the high shelf.

He took down the blue one, shop-new and shiny. Here was the GS logo, and the silk lining that was zipped into the bag. He ran his fingers around it, into every corner, then replaced it deftly on the shelf.

He selected the white bag next: the lining was patterned with a stylised African print. Again he ran his fingers all around the interior. Then he unzipped the lining.

It came out, just as Ciara had described, like a metal-edged scarf, exposing the rough interior of the white leather. Nothing was visible inside until he looked more closely, and then he saw the line of pale blue running down the side of the stiff rectangular cloth-covered board holding the base of the bag in shape.

He lifted up the board and saw, beneath it, a folded piece of pale blue paper, scribbled all over in an untidy hand.

Strike replaced the bag swiftly on the shelf with the lining bundled inside, and took from an inside pocket of his jacket a clear plastic bag, into which he inserted the pale blue paper, shaken open but unread. He closed the mahogany door and continued to open others. Behind the penultimate door was a safe, operated by a digital keypad.

Strike took a second plastic bag from inside his jacket, slid it over his hand and began to press keys, but before he had completed his trial, he heard movement outside. Hastily thrusting the crumpled bag back into a pocket, he closed the wardrobe door as quietly as possible and walked back into the bedroom, to find the Macmillan nurse bending over Yvette Bristow. She looked around when she heard him.

'Wrong door,' said Strike. 'I thought it was the bathroom.'

He went into the small en-suite, and here, with the door closed, before flushing the toilet and turning on the taps for the nurse's benefit, he read the last will and testament of Lula Landry, scribbled on her mother's writing paper and witnessed by two women. First came the childlike signature of Rochelle Onifade and her address: St Elmo's Hostel, Hammersmith. Below was the unfamiliar name of Mia Thompson, who had given as her contact address a house in Adelaide. A deep fold just above Mia Thompson's signature told Strike that she had almost certainly not seen what she was signing. The fact that she had given Lula contact details in Australia suggested that she had known her days at Vashti, and in London, were numbered, knowledge that had perhaps emboldened her to burst into Lula Landry's changing room and ask for assistance with a new career.

Yvette Bristow was still lying with her eyes closed when he returned to the bedroom.

'She's asleep,' said the nurse, gently. 'She does this a lot.'

'Yes,' said Strike, the blood pounding in his ears. 'Please tell her I said goodbye, when she wakes up. I'm going to have to leave now.'

They walked together down the comfortable passageway.

'Lady Bristow seems very ill,' Strike commented.

'Oh yes, she is,' said the nurse. 'She could die any time now. She's very poorly.'

'I think I might have left my . . . ' said Strike vaguely, wandering left into the yellow sitting room he had first visited, leaning over the sofa to block the nurse's view and carefully replacing the telephone receiver he had taken off the hook.

'Yes, here it is,' he said, pretending to palm something small and put it in his pocket. 'Well, thanks very much for the coffee.'

With his hand on the door, he turned to look at her.

'Her Valium addiction's as bad as ever, then?' he said.

Unsuspicious, trusting, the nurse smiled a tolerant smile.

'Yes, it is, but it can't hurt her now. Mind you,' she said, 'I'd give those doctors a piece of my mind. She's had three of them giving her prescriptions for years, from the labels on the boxes.'

'Very unprofessional,' said Strike. 'Thanks again for the coffee. Goodbye.'

He jogged down the stairs, his mobile already out of his pocket, so exhilarated that he did not concentrate on where he was going, so that he took a corner on the stair and let out a bellow of pain as the prosthetic foot slipped on the edge; his knee twisted and he fell, hard and heavy, down six stairs, landing in a heap at the bottom with an excruciating, fiery pain in both the joint and the end of his stump, as though it was freshly severed, as though the scar tissue was still healing.

'Fuck. *Fuck!*'

'Are you all right?' shouted the Macmillan nurse, gazing down at him over the banisters, her face comically inverted.

'I'm fine – fine!' he shouted back. 'Slipped! Don't worry! *Fuck, fuck, fuck,*' he moaned under his breath, as he pulled himself back to his feet on the newel post, scared to put his full weight on the prosthesis.

He limped downstairs, leaning on the banisters as much as possible; half hopped across the lobby floor and hung on the heavy front door as he manoeuvred himself out on to the front steps.

The sporting children were receding in a distant crocodile, pale and navy blue, winding their way back to their school and lunch. Strike stood leaning against warm brick, cursing himself fluently and wondering what damage he had done. The pain was excruciating, and the skin that had already been irritated felt as though it had been torn; it burned beneath the gel pad that was supposed to protect it, and the idea of walking all the way to the underground was miserably unappealing.

He sat down on the top step and phoned a taxi, after which he made a further series of calls, firstly to Robin, then to Wardle, then to the offices of Landry, May, Patterson.

The black cab swung around the corner. For the very first time, it occurred to Strike how like miniature hearses they were, these stately black vehicles, as he hoisted himself upright and limped, in escalating pain, down to the pavement.

Part Five

Felix qui potuit rerum cognoscere causas.

Lucky is he who has been able to understand the causes of things.

Virgil, *Georgics*, Book 2

1

'I'd have thought,' said Eric Wardle slowly, looking down at the will in its plastic pocket, 'you'd have wanted to show this to your client first.'

'I would, but he's in Rye,' said Strike, 'and this is urgent. I've told you, I'm trying to prevent two more murders. We're dealing with a maniac here, Wardle.'

He was sweating with pain. Even as he sat here, in the sunlit window of the Feathers, urging the policeman to action, Strike was wondering whether he might have dislocated his knee or fractured the small amount of tibia left to him in the fall down Yvette Bristow's stairwell. He had not wanted to start fiddling with his leg in the taxi, which was now waiting for him at the kerb outside. The meter was eating steadily away at the advance Bristow had paid him, of which he would never receive another instalment, for today would see an arrest, if only Wardle would rouse himself.

'I grant you, this might show motive . . .'

'Might?' repeated Strike. 'Might? Ten million might constitute a motive? For fuck's—'

'. . . but I need evidence that'll stand up in court, and you haven't brought me any of that.'

'I've just told you where you can find it! Have I been wrong yet? I told you it was a fucking will, and there,' Strike jabbed the plastic sleeve, 'it fucking is. Get a warrant!'

Wardle rubbed the side of his handsome face as though he had toothache, frowning at the will.

'Jesus Christ,' said Strike, 'how many more times? Tansy Bestigui was on the balcony, she heard Landry say "I've already done it" . . .'

'You put yourself on very thin ice there, mate,' said Wardle. 'Defence makes mincemeat of lying to suspects. When Bestigui finds out there aren't any photos, he's going to deny everything.'

'Let him. She won't. She's ripe to tell anyway. But if you're too much of a pussy to do anything about this, Wardle,' said Strike, who could feel cold sweat on his back and a fiery pain in what remained of his right leg, 'and anyone else who was close to Landry turns up dead, I'm gonna go straight to the fucking press. I'll tell them I gave you every bit of information I had, and that you had every fucking chance to bring this killer in. I'll make up my fee in selling the rights to my story, and you can pass that message on to Carver for me.

'Here,' he said, pushing across the table a piece of torn paper, on which he had scribbled several six-figure numbers. 'Try them first. Now get a fucking warrant.'

He pushed the will across the table to Wardle and slid off the high bar stool. The walk from the pub to the taxi was agony. The more pressure he put on his right leg, the more excruciating the pain became.

Robin had been calling Strike every ten minutes since one o'clock, but he had not picked up. She rang again as he was climbing, with enormous difficulty, up the metal stairs towards the office, heaving himself up with the use of his arms. She heard his ringtone echoing up the stairwell, and hurried out on to the top landing.

'There you are! I've been calling and calling, there's been loads . . . What's the matter, are you all right?'

'I'm fine,' he lied.

'No you're . . . What's happened to you?'

She hastened down the stairs towards him. He was white, and sweaty, and looked, in Robin's opinion, as though he might be sick.

'Have you been drinking?'

'No I haven't been bloody drinking!' he snapped. 'I've – sorry, Robin. In a bit of pain here. I just need to sit down.'

'What's happened? Let me . . .'

'I've got it. No problem. I can manage.'

Slowly he pulled himself to the top landing and limped very heavily to the old sofa. When he dropped his weight into it, Robin thought she heard something deep in the structure crack, and noted, *We'll need a new one*, and then, *But I'm leaving*.

'What happened?' she asked.

'I fell down some stairs,' said Strike, panting a little, still wearing his coat. 'Like a complete tit.'

'What stairs? What happened?'

From the depths of his agony he grinned at her expression, which was part horrified, part excited.

'I wasn't wrestling anyone, Robin. I just slipped.'

'Oh, I see. You're a bit – you look a bit pale. You don't think you could have done something serious, do you? I could get a cab – maybe you should see a doctor.'

'No need for that. Have we still got any of those painkillers lying around?'

She brought him water and paracetamol. He took them, then stretched out his legs, flinched and asked:

'What's been going on here? Did Graham Hardacre send you a picture?'

'Yes,' she said, hurrying to her computer monitor. 'Here.'

With a shunt of her mouse and a click, the picture of Lieutenant Jonah Agyeman filled the monitor.

In silence, they contemplated the face of a young man whose irrefutable handsomeness was not diminished by the overlarge ears he had inherited from his father. The scarlet, black and gold uniform suited him. His grin was slightly lopsided, his cheekbones high, his jaw square and his skin dark with an undertone of red, like freshly brewed tea. He conveyed the careless charm that Lula Landry had had too; the indefinable quality that made the viewer linger over her image.

'He looks like her,' said Robin in a hushed voice.

'Yeah, he does. Anything else been going on?'

Robin seemed to snap back to attention.

'Oh God, yes . . . John Bristow called half an hour ago, to say he couldn't get hold of you, and Tony Landry's called three times.'

'I thought he might. What did he say?'

'He was absolutely – well, the first time, he asked to speak to you, and when I said you weren't here, he hung up before I could give him your mobile number. The second time, he told me you had to call him straight away, but slammed down the phone before I could tell him you still weren't back. But the third time, he was just – well – he was incredibly angry. Screaming at me.'

'He'd better not have been offensive,' said Strike, scowling.

'He wasn't really. Well, not to me – it was all about you.'

'What did he say?'

'He didn't make a lot of sense, but he called John Bristow a "stupid prick", and then he was bawling something about Alison walking out, which he seemed to think had something to do with you, because he was yelling about suing you, and defamation, and all kinds of things.'

'Alison's left her job?'

'Yes.'

'Did he say where she – no, of course he didn't, why would he know?' he finished, more to himself than to Robin.

He looked down at his wrist. His cheap watch seemed to have hit something when he had fallen downstairs, because it had stopped at a quarter to one.

'What's the time?'

'Ten to five.'

'Already?'

'Yes. Do you need anything? I can hang around a bit.'

'No, I want you out of here.'

His tone was such that instead of going to fetch her coat and handbag, Robin remained exactly where she was.

'What are you expecting to happen?'

Strike was busy fiddling with his leg, just below the knee.

'Nothing. You've just worked a lot of overtime lately. I'll bet Matthew will be glad to see you back early for once.'

There was no adjusting the prosthesis through his trouser leg.

'Please, Robin, go,' he said, looking up.

She hesitated, then went to fetch her trench coat and bag.

'Thanks,' he said. 'See you tomorrow.'

She left. He waited for the sound of her footsteps on the stairs before rolling up his trouser leg, but heard nothing. The glass door opened, and she reappeared.

'You're expecting someone to come,' she said, clutching the edge of the door. 'Aren't you?'

'Maybe,' said Strike, 'but it doesn't matter.'

He mustered a smile at her tight, anxious expression.

'Don't worry about me.' When her expression did not change, he added: 'I boxed a bit, in the army, you know.'

Robin half laughed.

'Yes, you mentioned that.'

'Did I?'

'Repeatedly. That night you . . . you know.'

'Oh. Right. Well, it's true.'

'But who are you . . . ?'

'Matthew wouldn't thank me for telling you. Go home, Robin, I'll see you tomorrow.'

And this time, albeit reluctantly, she left. He waited until he heard the door on to Denmark Street bang shut, then rolled up his trouser leg, detached the prosthesis and examined his swollen knee, and the end of his leg, which was inflamed and bruised. He wondered exactly what he had done to himself, but there was no time to take the problem to an expert tonight.

He half wished, now, that he had asked Robin to fetch him something to eat before she left. Clumsily, hopping from spot to spot, holding on to the desk, the top of the filing cabinet and the arm of the sofa to balance, he managed to make himself a cup of tea. He drank it sitting in Robin's chair, and ate half a packet of digestives, spending most of the time in contemplation of the face of Jonah Agyeman. The paracetamol had barely touched the pain in his leg.

When he had finished all the biscuits, he checked his mobile. There were many missed calls from Robin, and two from John Bristow.

Of the three people who Strike thought might present themselves at his office this evening, it was Bristow he hoped would make it there first. If the police wanted concrete evidence of murder, his client alone (though he might not realise it) could provide it. If either Tony Landry or Alison Cresswell turned up at his offices, *I'll just have to* . . . then Strike snorted a little in his empty office, because the expression that had occurred to him was 'think on my feet'.

But six o'clock came, and then half past, and nobody rang the bell. Strike rubbed more cream into the end of his leg, and reattached the prosthesis, which was agony. He limped through into the inner office, emitting grunts of pain, slumped down in his chair and, giving up, took the false leg off again and slid down, to lay his head on his arms, intending to do no more than rest his tired eyes.

2

Footsteps on the metal stairs. Strike sat bolt upright, not knowing whether he had been asleep five minutes or fifty. Somebody rapped on the glass door.

'Come in, it's open!' he shouted, and checked that the unattached prosthesis was covered by his trouser leg.

To Strike's immense relief, it was John Bristow who entered the room, blinking through his thick-lensed glasses and looking agitated.

'Hi, John. Come and sit down.'

But Bristow strode towards him, blotchy-faced, as full of rage as he had been the day that Strike had refused to take the case, and gripped the back of the offered chair instead.

'I told you,' he said, the colour waxing and waning in his thin face as he pointed a bony finger at Strike, 'I told you *quite clearly* that I didn't want you to see my mother without me present!'

'I know you did, John, but—'

'She's *unbelievably* upset. I don't know what you said to her, but I've had her crying and sobbing down the phone to me this afternoon!'

'I'm sorry to hear that; she didn't seem to mind my questions when—'

'She's in a dreadful state!' shouted Bristow, his buck teeth glinting. 'How *dared* you go and see her without me? How *dared* you?'

'Because, John, as I told you after Rochelle's funeral, I think we're dealing with a murderer who might kill again,' said Strike. 'The situation's dangerous, and I want an end to it.'

'*You* want an end to it? How do you think *I* feel?' shouted Bristow, and his voice cracked and became a falsetto. 'Do you have any idea of how much damage you've done? My mother's devastated, and now my girlfriend seems to have vanished into thin air, which Tony is blaming on you! What have you done to Alison? Where is she?'

'I don't know. Have you tried calling her?'

'She's not picking up. What the hell's been going on? I've been on a wild goose chase all day, and I come back—'

'Wild goose chase?' repeated Strike, surreptitiously shifting his leg to keep the prosthesis upright.

Bristow threw himself into the seat opposite, breathing hard and squinting at Strike in the bright evening sun streaming in through the window behind him.

'Somebody,' he said furiously, 'called my secretary up this morning, purporting to be a very important client of ours in Rye, who was requesting an urgent meeting. I travelled all the way there to find that he's out of the country, and nobody had called me at all. Would you mind,' he added, raising a hand to shield his eyes, 'pulling down that blind? I can't see a thing.'

Strike tugged the cord, and the blind fell with a clatter, casting them both into a cool, faintly striped gloom.

'That's a very strange story,' said Strike. 'It's almost as though somebody wanted to lure you away from town.'

Bristow did not reply. He was glaring at Strike, his chest heaving.

'I've had enough,' he said abruptly. 'I'm terminating this investigation. You can keep all the money I've given you. I've got to think of my mother.'

Strike slid his mobile out of his pocket, pressed a couple of buttons and laid it on his lap.

'Don't you even want to know what I found today in your mother's wardrobe?'

'You went – *you went inside my mother's wardrobe*?'

'Yeah. I wanted to have a look inside those brand-new handbags Lula got, the day she died.'

Bristow began to stutter:

'You – you . . . '

'The bags have got detachable linings. Bizarre idea, isn't it? Hidden under the lining of the white bag was a will, handwritten by Lula on your mother's blue notepaper, and witnessed by Rochelle Onifade. I've given it to the police.'

Bristow's mouth fell open. For several seconds he seemed unable to speak. Finally he whispered:

'But . . . what did it say?'

'That she was leaving everything, her entire estate, to her brother, Lieutenant Jonah Agyeman of the Royal Engineers.'

'Jonah . . . who?'

'Go and look on the computer monitor outside. You'll find a picture there.'

Bristow got up and moved like a sleepwalker towards the computer in the next room. Strike watched the screen illuminate as Bristow shifted the mouse. Agyeman's handsome face shone out of the monitor, with his sardonic smile, pristine in his dress uniform.

'Oh my God,' said Bristow.

He returned to Strike and lowered himself back into the chair, gaping at the detective.

'I – I can't believe it.'

'That's the man who was on the CCTV footage,' said Strike,

'running away from the scene the night that Lula died. He was staying in Clerkenwell with his widowed mother while he was on leave. That's why he was hotfooting it along Theobalds Road twenty minutes later. He was heading home.'

Bristow drew breath in a loud gasp.

'They all said I was deluded,' he almost shouted. 'But I wasn't bloody deluded at all!'

'No, John, you weren't deluded,' said Strike. 'Not deluded. More like bat-shit insane.'

Through the shaded window came the sounds of London, alive at all hours, rumbling and growling, part man, part machine. There was no noise inside the room but Bristow's ragged breathing.

'Excuse me?' he said, ludicrously polite. 'What did you call me?'

Strike smiled.

'I said you're bat-shit insane. You killed your sister, got away with it, and then asked me to reinvestigate her death.'

'You – you cannot be serious.'

'Oh yeah, I can. It's been obvious to me from the start that the person who benefits most from Lula's death is you, John. Ten million quid, once your mother gives up the ghost. Not to be sniffed at, is it? Especially as I don't think you've got much more than your salary, however much you bang on about your trust fund. Albris shares are hardly worth the paper they're written on these days, are they?'

Bristow gaped at him for several long moments; then, sitting up a little straighter, he glanced at the camp bed propped in the corner.

'Coming from a virtual down-and-out who sleeps in his office, I find that a laughable assertion.' Bristow's voice was calm and derisory, but his breathing was abnormally fast.

'I know you've got much more money than I have,' said Strike. 'But, as you rightly point out, that's not saying much. And I will say for myself that I haven't yet stooped to embezzling from clients. How much of Conway Oates's money did you steal before Tony realised what you were up to?'

'Oh, I'm an embezzler too, am I?' said Bristow, with an artificial laugh.

'Yeah, I think so,' said Strike. 'Not that it matters to me. I don't care whether you killed Lula because you needed to replace the money you'd nicked, or because you wanted her millions, or because you hated her guts. The jury will want to know, though. They're always suckers for motive.'

Bristow's knee had begun jiggling up and down again.

'You're unhinged,' he said, with another forced laugh. 'You've found a will in which she leaves everything not to me, but to *that man.*' He pointed towards the outer room, where he had viewed Jonah's picture. 'You tell me that it was that same man who was walking towards Lula's flat, on camera, the night she fell to her death, and who was seen sprinting back past the camera ten minutes later. And yet you accuse me. *Me.*'

'John, you knew before you ever came to see me that it was Jonah on that CCTV footage. Rochelle told you. She was there in Vashti when Lula called Jonah and arranged to meet him that night, and she witnessed a will leaving him everything. She came to you, told you everything and started blackmailing you. She wanted money for a flat and some expensive clothes, and in return she promised to keep her mouth shut about the fact that you weren't Lula's heir.

'Rochelle didn't realise you were the killer. She thought Jonah pushed Lula out of the window. And she was bitter enough, after seeing a will in which she didn't feature, and being dumped in that shop on the last day of Lula's life, not to care about the killer walking free as long as she got the money.'

'This is utter rubbish. You're out of your mind.'

'You put every obstacle you could in the way of me finding Rochelle,' Strike went on, as though he had not heard Bristow. 'You pretended you didn't know her name, or where she lived; you acted incredulous that I thought she might be useful to the inquiry and you took photos off Lula's laptop so that I couldn't see what she looked like. True, she could have pointed me directly to the man you were trying to frame for murder, but on the other hand, she knew that there was a will that would deprive you of your inheritance, and your number one objective was to keep that will quiet while you tried to find and destroy it. Bit of a joke, really, it being in your mother's wardrobe all along.

'But even if you'd destroyed it, John, what then? For all you knew, Jonah himself knew that he was Lula's heir. And there was another witness to the fact that there was a will, though you didn't know it: Bryony Radford, the make-up artist.'

Strike saw Bristow's tongue flick around his mouth, moistening his lips. He could feel the lawyer's fear.

'Bryony doesn't want to admit that she went snooping through Lula's things, but she saw that will at Lula's place, before Lula had time to hide it. Bryony's dyslexic, though. She thought "Jonah" said "John". She tied that in with Ciara saying that Lula was leaving her brother everything, and concluded that she needn't tell anybody what she'd read on the sly, because you were getting the money anyway. You've had the luck of the devil at times, John.

'But I can see how – to a twisted mind like yours – the best solution to your predicament was to fit Jonah up for murder. If he was doing life, it wouldn't matter whether or not the will ever surfaced – or whether he, or anyone else, knew about it – because the money would come to you in any case.'

'Ridiculous,' said Bristow breathlessly. 'You ought to give up detecting and try fantasy writing, Strike. You haven't got a shred of proof for anything you're saying—'

'Yes I have.' Strike cut across him, and Bristow stopped talking immediately, his pallor visible through the gloom. 'The CCTV footage.'

'That footage shows Jonah Agyeman running from the scene of the killing, as you've just acknowledged!'

'There was another man caught on camera.'

'So he had an accomplice – a lookout.'

'I wonder what defending counsel will say is wrong with you, John?' asked Strike softly. 'Narcissism? Some kind of God complex? You think you're completely untouchable, don't you, a genius who makes the rest of us look like chimps? The second man running from the scene wasn't Jonah's accomplice, or his lookout, or a car thief. He wasn't even black. He was a white man in black gloves. He was you.'

'No,' said Bristow. The one word throbbed with panic; but then, with an almost visible effort, he hitched a contemptuous smile back on to his face. 'How can it be me? I was in Chelsea with my mother. She told you so. Tony saw me there. I was in Chelsea.'

'Your mother is a Valium-addicted invalid who was asleep most of that day. You didn't get back to Chelsea until after you'd killed Lula. I think you went into your mother's room in the small hours, reset her clock and then woke her up, pretending it was dinner time. You think you're a criminal genius, John, but that's been done a million times before, though rarely with such an easy mark. Your mother hardly knows what day it is, the amount of opiates she's got in her system.'

'I was in Chelsea all day,' repeated Bristow, his knee jiggling up and down. 'All day, except for when I nipped into the office for files.'

'You took a hoodie and gloves out of the flat beneath Lula's. You're wearing them in the CCTV footage,' said Strike, ignoring the interruption, 'and that was a big mistake. That hoodie was unique. There was only one of them in the world; it had been customised for Deeby Macc by Guy Somé. It could only have come out of the flat beneath Lula's, so we know that's where you'd been.'

'You have absolutely no proof,' said Bristow. 'I am waiting for proof.'

'Of course you are,' said Strike, simply. 'An innocent man wouldn't be sitting here listening to me. He'd have stormed out by now. But don't worry. I've got proof.'

'You can't have,' said Bristow hoarsely.

'Motive, means and opportunity, John. You had the lot.

'Let's start at the beginning. You don't deny that you went to Lula's first thing in the morning . . .'

'No, of course not.'

'. . . because people saw you there. But I don't think Lula ever gave you the contract with Somé that you used to get upstairs to see her. I think you'd swiped that at some point previously. Wilson waved you up, and minutes later you were having a shouting match with Lula on her doorstep. You couldn't pretend that didn't happen, because the cleaner overheard it. Fortunately for you, Lechsinka's English is so bad that she confirmed your version of the row: that you were furious that Lula had reunited with her free-loading druggie boyfriend.

'But I think that row was really about Lula's refusal to give you money. All her sharper friends have told me you had quite the reputation for coveting her fortune, but you must have been particularly desperate for a handout that day, to force your way in and start shouting like that. Had Tony noticed a lack of funds in Conway Oates's account? Did you need to replace it urgently?'

'Baseless speculation,' said Bristow, his knee still jerking up and down.

'We'll see whether it's baseless or not once we get to court,' said Strike.

'I've never denied that Lula and I argued.'

'After she refused to hand over a cheque, and slammed the door in your face, you went back down the stairs, and there was the door to Flat Two standing open. Wilson and the alarm repairman were busy looking at the keypad, and Lechsinka was somewhere in there by then – maybe hoovering, because that would have helped mask the noise of you creeping into the hall behind the two men.

'It wasn't that much of a risk, really. If they'd turned and seen you, you could have pretended you'd come in to thank Wilson for letting you up. You crossed the hall while they were busy with the alarm fuse box, and you hid somewhere in that big flat. There's loads of space. Empty cupboards. Under the bed.'

Bristow was shaking his head in silent denial. Strike continued in the same matter-of-fact tone:

'You must have heard Wilson telling Lechsinka to set the alarm to 1966. Finally, Lechsinka, Wilson and the Securibell guy left, and you had sole possession of the flat. Unfortunately for you, however, Lula had now left the building, so you couldn't go back upstairs and try and bully her into coughing up.'

'Total fantasy,' said the lawyer. 'I never set foot in Flat Two in my life. I left Lula's and went in to the office to pick up files—'

'From Alison, isn't that what you said, the first time we went through your movements that day?' asked Strike.

Patches of pink blossomed again up Bristow's stringy neck. After a small hesitation, he cleared his throat and said:

'I don't remember whether – I just know that I was very quick; I wanted to get back to my mother.'

'What effect do you think it's going to have in court, John, when Alison takes the stand and tells the jury how you asked her to lie for you? You played the devastated bereaved brother in front of her, and then asked her out to dinner, and the poor bitch was so delighted to have a chance to look like a desirable female in front of Tony that she agreed. A couple of dates later, you persuaded her to say she saw you at the office on the morning before Lula died. She thought you were just over-anxious and paranoid, didn't she? She believed that you already had a cast-iron alibi from her adored Tony, later in the day. She didn't think it mattered if she told a little white lie to calm you down.

'But Alison wasn't there that day, John, to give you any files. Cyprian sent her off to Oxford the moment she got to work, to look for Tony. You became a bit nervous, after Rochelle's funeral, when you realised I knew all about that, didn't you?'

'Alison isn't very bright,' said Bristow slowly, his hands washing themselves in dumb show, and his knee jiggling up and down. 'She must have confused the days. She clearly misunderstood me. I never asked her to say she saw me at the office. It's her word against mine. Maybe she's trying to revenge herself on me, because we've split up.'

Strike laughed.

'Oh, you're definitely dumped, John. After my assistant rang you this morning to lure you to Rye—'

'*Your assistant?*'

'Yeah, of course; I didn't want you around while I searched your mother's flat, did I? Alison helped us out with the name of the client. I rang her, you see, and told her everything, including the fact that I've got proof that Tony's sleeping with Ursula May, and that you're about to be arrested for murder. That seemed to convince her that she ought to look for a new boyfriend and a new job. I hope she's gone to her mother's place in Sussex – that's what I told her to do. You've been keeping Alison close because you thought she was your fail-safe alibi, and because she's a conduit to knowing what Tony, whom you fear, is thinking. But lately, I've been getting worried that she might outlive her usefulness to you, and fall off something high.'

Bristow tried for another scathing laugh, but the sound was artificial and hollow.

'So it turns out that nobody saw you nip into your office for files that morning,' continued Strike. 'You were still hiding out in the middle flat at number eighteen, Kentigern Gardens.'

'I wasn't there. I was in Chelsea, at my mother's,' said Bristow.

'I don't think you were planning to murder Lula at that point,' Strike continued regardless. 'You probably just had some idea of waylaying her again when she came back. Nobody was expecting you at the office that day, because you were supposed to be working from home, to keep your sick mother company. There was a full fridge and you knew how to get in and out without setting off the alarm. You had a clear view of the street, so if Deeby Macc and entourage were to appear, you had plenty of time to get out of there, and walk downstairs with some cock-and-bull story about having been waiting for your sister at her place. The only remote risk was the possibility of deliveries into the flat; but that massive vase of roses arrived without anyone noticing you hiding in there, didn't it?

'I expect the idea of the murder started to germinate then, all those hours you were alone, in all that luxury. Did you start to imagine how wonderful it would be if Lula, who you were sure was intestate, died? You must've known your sick mother would be a much softer touch, especially once you were her only remaining child. And that in itself must have felt great, John, didn't it? The idea of being the only child, at long last? And never losing out again to a better-looking, more lovable sibling?'

Even in the thickening gloom, he could see Bristow's jutting teeth, and the intense stare of the weak eyes.

'No matter how much you've fawned over your mother, and played the devoted son, you've never come first with her, have you? She always loved Charlie most, didn't she? Everyone did, even Uncle Tony. And the moment Charlie had gone, when you might have expected to be the centre of attention at last, what happens? Lula arrives, and everyone starts worrying about Lula, looking after Lula, adoring Lula. Your mother hasn't even got a picture of you by her deathbed. Just Charlie and Lula. Just the two she loved.'

'Fuck you,' snarled Bristow. 'Fuck you, Strike. What do you know about anything, with your whore of a mother? What was it she died of, the clap?'

'Nice,' said Strike, appreciatively. 'I was going to ask you whether you looked into my personal life when you were trying to find some patsy to manipulate. I bet you thought I'd be particularly sympathetic to poor bereaved John Bristow, didn't you, what with my own mother having died young, in suspicious circumstances? You thought you'd be able to play me like a fucking violin . . .

'But never mind, John. If your defence team can't find a personality disorder for you, I expect they'll argue that your upbringing's to blame. Unloved. Neglected. Overshadowed. Always felt hard done by, haven't you? I noticed it the first day I met you, when you burst into those moving tears at the memory of Lula being carried up the drive into your home, into your life. Your parents hadn't even taken you with them to get her, had they? They left you at home like a pet dog, the son who wasn't enough for them once Charlie had died; the son who was about to come a poor second all over again.'

'I don't have to listen to this,' whispered Bristow.

'You're free to leave,' said Strike, watching the place where he could no longer make out eyes in the deepening shadows behind Bristow's glasses. 'Why not leave?'

But the lawyer merely sat there, one knee still jiggling up and down, his hands sliding over each other, waiting to hear Strike's proof.

'Was it easier the second time?' the detective asked quietly. 'Was it easier killing Lula than killing Charlie?'

He saw the pale teeth, bared as Bristow opened his mouth, but no sound came out.

'Tony knows you did it, doesn't he? All that bullshit about the hard, cruel things he said after Charlie died. Tony was there; he saw you cycling away from the place where you'd pushed Charlie over. Did you dare him to ride close to the edge? I knew Charlie: he couldn't resist a dare. Tony saw Charlie dead at the bottom of that quarry, and he told your parents that he thought you'd done it, didn't he? That's why your father hit him. That's why your mother fainted. That's why Tony was thrown out of the house after Charlie died: not because Tony said that your mother had raised delinquents, but because he told her she was raising a psychopath.'

'This is— No,' croaked Bristow. 'No!'

'But Tony couldn't face a family scandal. He kept quiet. Panicked a bit when he heard they were adopting a little girl, though, didn't he? He called them and tried to stop it happening. He was right to be worried, wasn't he? I think you've always been a bit scared of Tony. What a fucking irony that he backed himself into a corner where he had to give you an alibi for Lula's murder.'

Bristow said nothing at all. He was breathing very fast.

'Tony needed to pretend he was somewhere, anywhere, other than shacked up in a hotel with Cyprian May's wife that day, so he said he doubled back to London to go and visit his sick sister. Then he realised that both you and Lula were supposed to have been there at the same time.

'His niece was dead, so she couldn't contradict him; but he had no choice but to pretend he saw you through the study door, and didn't talk to you. And you backed him up. Both of you, lying through your teeth, wondering what the other one was up to, but too scared to question each other. I think Tony kept telling himself he'd wait until your mother died before he confronted you. Perhaps that's how he kept his conscience quiet. But he's still been worried enough to ask Alison to keep an eye on you. And meanwhile, you've been feeding me that bullshit about Lula hugging you, and the touching reconciliation before she returned home.'

'I was there,' said Bristow, in a rasping whisper. 'I was in my mother's flat. If Tony wasn't there, that's his affair. You can't prove I wasn't.'

'I'm not in the business of proving negatives, John. All I'm saying is, you've now lost every alibi except your Valium-addled mother.

'But for the sake of argument, let's assume that while Lula's visiting your groggy mother, and Tony's off fucking Ursula in a hotel somewhere, you're still hiding out in Flat Two, and starting to think out a much more daring solution to your cash-flow problem. You wait. At some point you put on the black leather gloves that have been left in the wardrobe for Deeby, as a precaution against fingerprints. That looks fishy. Almost as though you're starting to contemplate violence.

'Finally, in the early afternoon, Lula comes back home, but unfortunately for you – as you no doubt saw through the peephole of the flat – she's with friends.

'And now,' said Strike, his voice hardening, 'I think the case against you starts to become serious. A defence of manslaughter – it was an accident, we tussled a bit and she fell over the balcony – might have held water if you hadn't stayed downstairs all that time, while you knew she had visitors. A man with nothing worse on his mind than bullying his sister into giving him a large cheque might, just might, wait until she was alone again; but you'd already tried that and it hadn't worked. So why not go up there when she was, perhaps, in a better mood, and have a go with the restraining presence of her friends in the next room? Maybe she'd have given you something just to get rid of you?'

Strike could almost feel the waves of fear and hatred emanating from the figure fading into the shadows across the desk.

'But instead,' he said, 'you waited. You waited all that evening, having watched her leave the building. You must have been pretty tightly wound by then. You'd had time to formulate a rough plan. You'd been watching the street; you knew exactly who was in the building, and who wasn't; you'd worked out that there might just be a means of getting clean away, without anyone being the wiser. And let's not forget – you'd killed before. That makes a difference.'

Bristow made a sharp movement, little more than a jerk; Strike tensed, but Bristow remained stationary, and Strike was acutely aware of the unattached prosthesis merely resting against his leg.

'You were watching out of the window and you saw Lula come home alone, but the paparazzi were still out there. You must have despaired at that point, did you?

'But then, miraculously, as though the universe really did want nothing more than to help John Bristow get what he wanted, they all left. I'm pretty sure that Lula's regular driver tipped them off. He's a man who's keen to forge good contacts with the press.

'So now the street's empty. The moment has arrived. You pulled on Deeby's hoodie. Big mistake. But you must admit, with all the lucky breaks you got that night, something had to go wrong.

'And then – and I'm going to give you full marks for this, because it puzzled me for a long time – you took a few of those white roses out of their vase, didn't you? You wiped the ends dry – not quite as thoroughly as you should have done, but pretty well – and you carried them out of Flat Two, leaving the door ajar again, and climbed the stairs to your sister's flat.

'You didn't notice that you'd left a few little drops of water from the roses, by the way. Wilson slipped on them, later.

'You got up to Lula's flat, and you knocked. When she looked through the peephole, what did she see? White roses.

She'd been standing on her balcony, with the windows wide open, watching and waiting for her long-lost brother to come down the street, but somehow he seems to have got in without her seeing him! In her excitement, she throws open the door – and you're in.'

Bristow was completely still. Even his knee had stopped jiggling.

'And you killed her, just the same way you killed Charlie, just the same way you later killed Rochelle: you pushed her, hard and fast – maybe you lifted her – but she was caught by surprise, wasn't she, just like the others?

'You were yelling at her for not giving you money, for depriving you, just as you've always been deprived, haven't you, John, of your portion of parental love.

'She yelled at you that you wouldn't get a penny, even if you killed her. As you fought, and you forced her across her sitting room towards that balcony and the drop, she told you she had another brother, a real brother, and that he was on his way, and that she'd made a will in his favour.

'"It's too late, I've already done it!" she screamed. And you called her a lying fucking bitch, and you threw her down into the street to her death.'

Bristow was barely breathing.

'I think you must have dropped the roses at her front door. You ran back out, picked them up, sprinted down the stairs and back into Flat Two, where you rammed them back into their vase. Fuck me, you were lucky. That vase got smashed accidentally by a copper, and those roses were the one clue to show that someone had been in that flat; you can't have replaced them the way the florist had arranged them, not when you knew you had minutes to get clear of that building.

'The next bit took nerve. I doubt you expected anyone to raise the alarm straight away, but Tansy Bestigui had been on the balcony below you. You heard her screaming, and realised you had even less time to get out of there than you'd been counting on. Wilson ran out to the street to check Lula, and then, waiting at the door, staring through the peephole, you saw him run upstairs to the top floor.

'You reset the alarm, let yourself out of the flat and edge down the stairwell. The Bestiguis are bellowing at each other in their own flat. You run downstairs – heard by Freddie Bestigui, though he had other preoccupations at the time – the lobby's empty – you run through it and out on to the street, where it's snowing thick and fast.

'And you ran, didn't you; hoodie up, face covered, gloved hands pumping. And at the end of the street, you saw another man running, running for his life, away from the corner where he'd just seen his sister fall to her death. You didn't know each other. I don't think you had a thought to spare for who he was, not then. You ran as fast as you could, in Deeby Macc's borrowed clothes, past the CCTV camera that caught you both on film, and off down Halliwell Street, where your luck caught up with you again, and there were no more cameras.

'I expect you chucked the hoodie and the gloves in a bin and grabbed a taxi, did you? The police never bothered looking for a suited white man who was out and about that night. You went home to your mother's, you made food for her, you changed the time on her clock and you woke her up. She's still convinced that the two of you were talking about Charlie – nice touch, John – at the precise moment that Lula plunged to her death.

'You got away with it, John. You could have afforded to keep paying Rochelle for life. With your luck, Jonah Agyeman might even have died in Afghanistan; you've been getting your hopes up every time you've seen a picture of a black soldier in the paper, haven't you? But you didn't want to trust to luck. You're a twisted, arrogant fucker, and you thought you could arrange things better.'

There was a long silence.

'No proof,' said Bristow, at last. It was so dark in the office now that he was barely more than a silhouette to Strike. 'No proof at all.'

'I'm afraid you're wrong there,' said Strike. 'The police should have got a warrant by now.'

'For what?' asked Bristow, and he finally felt confident enough to laugh. 'To search the bins of London for a hoodie that you say was thrown away three months ago?'

'No, to look in your mother's safe, of course.'

Strike was wondering whether he could raise the blind quickly enough. He was a long way from a light switch, and the office was very dark, but he did not want to take his eyes off Bristow's shadowy figure. He was sure that this triple murderer would not have come unprepared.

'I've given them a few combinations to try,' Strike went on. 'If they don't work, I suppose they'll have to call in an expert to open it. But if I were a betting man, I'd put my money on 030483.'

A rustle, the blur of a pale hand, and Bristow lunged. The knife point grazed Strike's chest as he slammed Bristow sideways; the lawyer slid off the desk, rolled over and attacked again, and this time Strike fell over backwards in his chair, with Bristow on top of him, trapped between the wall and the desk.

Strike had one of Bristow's wrists, but he couldn't see where the knife was: all was darkness, and he threw a punch that hit Bristow hard under the chin, knocking his head back and sending his glasses flying; Strike punched again, and Bristow hit the wall; Strike tried to sit up, with Bristow's lower body pinning his agonising half-leg to the ground, and the knife struck him hard in the upper arm: he felt it pierce the flesh, and the flow of warm blood, and the white-hot stinging pain.

He saw Bristow raise his arm in dim silhouette against the faint window; forcing himself up against the lawyer's weight, he deflected the second knife blow, and with an almighty effort managed to throw the lawyer off, and the prosthesis slid out of his trouser leg as he tried to pin Bristow down, with his hot blood spattering over everything, and no knowledge of where the knife was now.

The desk was knocked over by Strike's wrestling weight, and then, as he knelt with his good knee on Bristow's thin chest, groping with his good hand to find the knife, light split his retinas in two, and a woman was screaming.

Dazzled, Strike glimpsed the knife rising to his stomach; he seized the prosthetic leg beside him and brought it down like a club on Bristow's face, once, twice—

'Stop! Cormoran, STOP! YOU'RE GOING TO KILL HIM!'

Strike rolled off Bristow, who was no longer moving, dropped the prosthetic leg and lay on his back, clutching his bleeding arm beside the overturned desk.

'I thought,' he panted, unable to see Robin, 'I told you to go home?'

But she was already on the telephone.

'Police and ambulance!'

'And get a taxi,' Strike croaked from the floor, his throat dry from so much talking. 'I'm not travelling to hospital with this piece of shit.'

He stretched out an arm and retrieved the mobile that lay several feet away. The face was smashed, but it was still recording.

Epilogue

Nihil est ab omni
Parte beatum.

Nothing is an unmixed
blessing.

Horace, *Odes*, Book 2

Ten Days Later

The British Army requires of its soldiers a subjugation of individual needs and ties that is almost incomprehensible to the civilian mind. It recognises virtually no claims higher than its own; and the unpredictable crises of human life – births and deaths, weddings, divorces and illness – generally cause no more deviation to the military's plans than pebbles pinging on the underbelly of a tank. Nevertheless, there are exceptional circumstances, and it was due to one such circumstance that Lieutenant Jonah Agyeman's second tour of duty in Afghanistan was cut short.

His presence in Britain was urgently required by the Metropolitan Police, and while the army does not generally rate the claims of the Met higher than its own, in this case it was prepared to be helpful. The circumstances surrounding the death of Agyeman's sister were garnering international attention, and a media storm around a hitherto obscure Sapper was deemed unhelpful both to the individual and the army he served. And so Jonah was put on a plane back to Britain, where the army did its impressive best to shield him from the ravenous press.

It was assumed by considerable numbers of the news-reading public that Lieutenant Agyeman would be delighted, firstly to be home from combat, and secondly to have returned to the prospect of wealth beyond his wildest imaginings.

Mia Thompson had already been tracked by the press to her parents' house in Adelaide, where she had confirmed in a blaze of publicity that she had had no idea what she was signing that day in the changing room. The will, in consequence, was invalid. Nevertheless, it seemed certain that Lula's last wishes would be honoured by her family. The dying Yvette Bristow was of the same opinion as the news-reading public: if anyone was to inherit a fortune it ought to be the young soldier, not the uncle who was now known to have concealed crucial evidence in his niece's murder and to be a philanderer to boot. Jonah, in short, would shortly be in possession of the ten million pounds for which his sister had been murdered.

However much the public might assume this prospect to gladden the young Sapper's heart, the soldier whom Cormoran Strike met in the Tottenham pub one lunchtime, ten days after the arrest of his sister's killer, was almost truculent, and seemed still to be in a state of shock.

The two men had, for different periods of time, lived the same life, and risked the same death. It was a bond that no civilian could understand, and for half an hour they talked about nothing but the army.

'You were a Suit, yeah?' Agyeman said. 'Trust a Suit to fuck up my whole life.'

Strike smiled. He saw no ingratitude in Agyeman, even though the stitches in his arm pulled painfully every time he raised his pint.

'My mother wants me to come out,' said the soldier. 'She keeps saying, that'll be one good thing to come out of this mess.'

It was the first, oblique reference to the reason they were here, and that Jonah was not where he belonged, with his regiment, in the life he had chosen.

Then, quite suddenly, he began to talk, as though he had been waiting for Strike for months.

'She never knew my dad had another kid. He never told her.

He was never even sure that Marlene woman was telling the truth about being pregnant. Right before he died, when he knew he had days left, he told me. "Don't upset your mother," he said. "I'm telling you this because I'm dying, and I don't know whether you've got a half-brother or sister out there." He said the mother had been white, and that she'd disappeared. She might have aborted it. Fuck me. If you'd known my dad. Never missed a Sunday at church. Took communion on his deathbed. I'd never expected anything like that, never.

'I was never even going to say anything to her about Dad and this woman. But then, out of the blue, I get this phone call. Thank Christ I was there, on leave. Only, Lula,' he said her name tentatively, as though he was not sure whether he had the right to it, 'said she'd've hung up if it'd been my mum. She said she didn't want to hurt anyone. She sounded all right.'

'I think she was,' said Strike.

'Yeah . . . but fuck me, it was weird. Would you believe it if some supermodel called you up and told you she was your sister?'

Strike thought of his own bizarre family history.

'Probably,' he said.

'Yeah, well, I suppose. Why would she lie? That's what I thought, anyway. So I gave her my mobile number and we talked a few times, when she could hook up with her friend Rochelle. She had it all figured out, so the press wouldn't find out. Suited me. I didn't want my mother upset.'

Agyeman had pulled out a packet of Lambert and Butler cigarettes and was turning the box nervously in his fingers. They would have been bought cheap, Strike thought, with a small pang of remembrance, at the NAAFI.

'So she phones me up the day before it – it happened,' Jonah continued, 'and she was begging me to come over. I'd already told her I couldn't meet her that leave. Man, the situation was doing my head in. My sister the supermodel. Mum was worried about me leaving for Helmand. I couldn't spring it on her, that Dad had had another kid. Not then. So I told Lula I couldn't see her.

'She begged me to meet her before I left. She sounded upset. I said maybe I could get out later, you know, after Mum was in bed. I'd tell her I was going out for a quick drink with a mate or something. She told me to come really late, like at half one.

'So,' said Jonah, scratching the back of his neck uncomfortably, 'I went. I was on the corner of her road . . . and I saw it happen.'

He wiped his hand across his mouth.

'I ran. I just ran. I didn't know what the hell to think. I didn't want to be there, I didn't want to have to explain anything to anyone. I knew she'd had mental problems, and I remembered how upset she'd been on the phone, and I thought, did she lure me here to see her jump?

'I couldn't sleep. I was glad to leave, to tell you the truth. To get away from all the fucking news coverage.'

The pub buzzed around them, crowded with lunchtime customers.

'I think the reason she wanted to meet you so badly was because of what her mother had just told her,' Strike said. 'Lady Bristow had taken a lot of Valium. I'm guessing she wanted to make the girl feel too bad to leave her, so she told Lula what Tony had said about John all those years before: that he pushed his younger brother Charlie into that quarry, and killed him.

'That's why Lula was in such a state when she left her mother's flat, and that's why she kept trying to call her uncle and find out whether there was any truth in the story. And I think she was desperate to see you, because she wanted someone, anyone, she could love and trust. Her mother was difficult and dying, she hated her uncle, and she'd just been told her adoptive brother was a killer. She must have been desperate. And I think she was scared. The day before she died, Bristow had tried to force her to give him money. She must have been wondering what he'd do next.'

The pub clattered and rang with talk and clinking glasses, but Jonah's voice sounded clearly over all of it.

'I'm glad you broke the bastard's jaw.'

'And his nose,' said Strike cheerfully. 'It's lucky he'd stuck a knife in me, or I might not have got off with "reasonable force".'

'He came armed,' said Jonah thoughtfully.

''Course he did,' said Strike. 'I'd had my secretary tip him off, at Rochelle's funeral, that I was getting death threats from a nutter who wanted to slit me open. That planted the seed in his head. He thought, if it came to it, he'd try and pass off my death as the work of poor old Brian Mathers. Then, presumably, he'd have gone home, doctored his mother's clock and tried to pull the same trick all over again. He's not sane. Which isn't to say he's not a clever fucker.'

There seemed little more to say. As they left the pub, Agyeman, who had bought the drinks with nervous insistence, made what might have been a tentative offer of money to Strike, whose impecunious existence had padded out much of the media coverage. Strike cut the offer short, but he was not offended. He could see that the young Sapper was struggling to deal with the idea of his enormous new wealth; that he was buckling under the responsibility of it, the demands it made, the appeals it attracted, the decisions it entailed; that he was much more overawed than glad. There was also, of course, the horrible and ever-present knowledge of how his millions had come to him. Strike guessed that Jonah Agyeman's thoughts were flitting wildly between his comrades back in Afghanistan, visions of sports cars and of his half-sister lying dead in the snow. Who was more conscious than the soldier of capricious fortune, of the random roll of the dice?

'He won't get off, will he?' asked Agyeman suddenly, as they were about to part.

'No, of course not,' said Strike. 'The papers haven't got it yet, but the police found Rochelle's mobile phone in his mother's safe. He didn't dare get rid of it. He'd reset the code of the safe so that no one could get in but him: 030483. Easter Sunday, nineteen eighty-three: the day he killed my mate Charlie.'

It was Robin's last day. Strike had invited her to come with him to meet Jonah Agyeman, whom she had done so much to find, but she had refused. Strike had the feeling that she was deliberately withdrawing from the case, from the work, from him. He had an appointment at the Amputee Centre at Queen Mary's Hospital that afternoon; she would be gone by the time he returned from Roehampton. Matthew was taking her to Yorkshire for the weekend.

As Strike limped back to the office through the continuing chaos of the building work, he wondered whether he would ever see his temporary secretary again after today, and doubted it. Not so very long ago, the impermanence of their arrangement had been the only thing that reconciled him to her presence, but now he knew that he would miss her. She had come with him in the taxi to the hospital, and wrapped her trench coat around his bleeding arm.

The explosion of publicity around Bristow's arrest had done

Strike's business no harm at all. He might even genuinely need a secretary before long; and indeed, as he made his way painfully up the stairs to his office, he heard Robin's voice on the telephone.

'. . . an appointment for Tuesday, I'm afraid, because Mr Strike's busy all day Monday . . . Yes . . . absolutely. . . I'll put you down for eleven o'clock, then. Yes. Thank you. Goodbye.'

She swung around on her swivel chair as Strike entered.

'What was Jonah like?' she demanded.

'Nice guy,' said Strike, lowering himself into the collapsed sofa. 'Situation's doing his head in. But the alternative was Bristow winding up with ten mill, so he'll have to cope.'

'Three prospective clients phoned while you were out,' she said, 'but I'm a bit worried about that last one. He could be another journalist. He was much more interested in discussing you than his own problem.'

There had been quite a few such calls. The press had seized with glee upon a story that had angles aplenty, and everything they loved best. Strike himself had featured heavily in the coverage. The photograph they had used most, and he was glad of it, was ten years old and had been taken while he was still a Red Cap; but they had also dug out the picture of the rock star, his wife and the supergroupie.

There had been plenty written about police incompetence; Carver had been snapped hurrying down the street, his jacket flying, the sweat patches just visible on his shirt; but Wardle, handsome Wardle, who had helped Strike bring Bristow in, had so far been treated with indulgence, especially by female journalists. Mostly, however, the news media had feasted all over again on the corpse of Lula Landry; every version of the story sparkling with pictures of the dead model's flawless face, and her lithe and sculpted body.

Robin was talking; Strike had not been listening, his attention diverted by the throbbing in his arm and leg.

'... a note of all the files and your diary. Because you'll need someone, now, you know; you're not going to be able to take care of all this on your own.'

'No,' he agreed, struggling to his feet; he had intended to do this later, at the moment of her departure, but now was as good a moment as any, and it made an excuse to leave the sofa, which was extremely uncomfortable. 'Listen, Robin, I haven't ever said a proper thank-you ...'

'Yes you have,' she said hurriedly. 'In the cab on the way to the hospital – and anyway, there's no need. I've enjoyed it. I've loved it, actually.'

He was hobbling away into the inner office, and did not hear the catch in her voice. The present was hidden at the bottom of his kitbag. It was very badly wrapped.

'Here,' he said. 'This is for you. I couldn't have done it without you.'

'Oh,' said Robin, on a strangled note, and Strike was both touched and faintly alarmed to see tears spill down her cheeks. 'You didn't have to ...'

'Open it at home,' he said, but too late; the package was literally coming apart in her hands. Something slithered, poison-green, out of the split in the paper, on to the desk in front of her. She gasped.

'You ... oh my God, Cormoran ...'

She held up the dress she had tried on, and loved, in Vashti, and stared at him over the top of it, pink-faced, her eyes sparkling.

'You can't afford this!'

'Yeah, I can,' he said, leaning back against the partition wall, because it was marginally more comfortable than sitting on the sofa. 'Work's rolling in now. You've been incredible. Your new place is lucky to get you.'

She was frantically mopping her eyes with the sleeves of her shirt. A sob and some incomprehensible words escaped her. She reached blindly for the tissues that she had bought from petty cash, in anticipation of more clients like Mrs Hook, blew her nose, wiped her eyes and said, with the green dress lying limp and forgotten across her lap:

'I don't want to go!'

'I can't afford you, Robin,' he said flatly.

It was not that he had not thought about it; the night before, he had lain awake on the camp bed, running calculations through his mind, trying to come up with an offer that might not seem insulting beside the salary offered by the media consultancy. It was not possible. He could no longer defer payment on the largest of his loans; he was facing an increase in rent and he needed to find somewhere to live other than his office. While his short-term prospects were immeasurably improved, the outlook remained uncertain.

'I wouldn't expect you to match what they'd give me,' Robin said thickly.

'I couldn't come close,' said Strike.

(But she knew the state of Strike's finances almost as well as he did and had already guessed at the most she could expect. The previous evening, when Matthew had found her in tears at the prospect of leaving, she had told him her estimate of Strike's best offer.

'But he hasn't offered you anything at all,' Matthew had said. 'Has he?'

'No, but if he did . . .'

'Well, it would be up to you,' Matthew had said stiffly. 'It'd be your choice. You'd have to decide.'

She knew that Matthew did not want her to stay. He had sat for hours in Casualty while they stitched Strike up, waiting to take Robin home. He had told her, rather formally, that she had done very well, showing such initiative, but he had been distant and faintly disapproving ever since, especially when their friends clamoured for the inside details on everything that had appeared in the press.

But surely Matthew would like Strike, if only he met him? And Matthew himself had said that it was up to her what she did . . .)

Robin drew herself up a little, blew her nose again and told Strike, with calmness slightly undermined by a small hiccough, the figure for which she would be happy to stay.

It took Strike a few seconds to respond. He could just afford to pay what she had suggested; it was within five hundred pounds of what he himself had calculated that he could manage. She was, whichever way you looked at it, an asset that it would be impossible to replace at the price. There was only one tiny fly in the ointment . . .

'I could manage that,' he said. 'Yeah. I could pay you that.'

The telephone rang. Beaming at him, she answered it, and the delight in her voice was such that it sounded as though she had been eagerly anticipating the call for days.

'Oh, hullo, Mr Gillespie! How are you? Mr Strike's just sent you a cheque, I put it in the post myself this morning . . . All the arrears, yes, and a little bit more . . . Oh no, Mr Strike's adamant he wants to pay off the loan . . . Well, that's very kind of Mr Rokeby, but Mr Strike would rather pay. He's hopeful he'll be able to clear the full amount within the next few months . . . '

An hour later, as Strike sat on a hard plastic chair at the Amputee Centre, his injured leg stretched in front of him, he reflected that if he had known that Robin was going to stay, he would not have bought her the green dress. The gift would not, he was sure, find favour with Matthew, especially once he had seen her in it, and heard that she had previously modelled it for Strike.

With a sigh, he reached for a copy of *Private Eye* lying on the table beside him. When the consultant first called him, Strike did not respond; he was immersed in the page headed 'LandryBalls', crammed with examples of journalistic excess relating to the case that he and Robin had solved. So many columnists had mentioned Cain and Abel that the magazine had run a special feature.

'Mr Strick?' shouted the consultant, for the second time. 'Mr Cameron Strick?'

He looked up, grinning.

'Strike,' he said clearly. 'My name's Cormoran Strike.'

'Oh, I do apologise . . . this way . . . '

As Strike limped after the doctor, a phrase floated up out of his subconscious, a phrase he had read long before he had seen his first dead body, or marvelled at a waterfall in an African mountainside, or watched the face of a killer collapsing as he realised he was caught.

I am become a name.

'On to the table, please, and take off the prosthesis.'

Where had it come from, that phrase? Strike lay back on the table and frowned up at the ceiling, ignoring the consultant now bending over the remainder of his leg, muttering as he stared and gently prodded.

It took minutes to dredge up the lines Strike had learned so long ago.

I cannot rest from travel: I will drink
Life to the lees; all times I have enjoy'd
Greatly, have suffer'd greatly, both with those
That loved me, and alone; on shore and when
Thro' scudding drifts the rainy Hyades
Vext the dim sea: I am become a name . . .